THE RAJ QUARTET

Now dramatised as

The Jewel in the Crown

Paul Scott was born in north London in 1920. During the Second World War he held a commission in the Indian army, after which he worked for several years in publishing and for a literary agency. His first novel, *Johnnie Sahib*, was published in 1952, followed by thirteen others, of which the best known are the 'Raj Quartet': *The Jewel in the Crown* (1966), *The Day of the Scorpion* (1968), *The Towers of Silence* (1971) and *A Division of the Spoils* (1975). His last novel, *Staying On* (1977), won the Booker Prize. He died in 1978.

PAUL SCOTT

THE RAJ QUARTET

Now dramatised as

The Jewel in the Crown

incorporating:
The Jewel in the Crown
The Day of the Scorpion
The Towers of Silence
A Division of the Spoils

Mandarin

Published in the United Kingdom in 1997 by
Mandarin Paperbacks

3 5 7 9 10 8 6 4 2

The Jewel in the Crown first published in Britain 1966
Copyright © Paul Scott 1966
The Day of the Scorpion first published in Britain 1968
Copyright © Paul Scott 1968
The Towers of Silence first published in Britain 1971
Copyright © Paul Scott 1971
A Division of the Spoils first published in Britain 1975
Copyright © Paul Scott 1975

Mandarin Paperbacks
Random House UK Limited
20 Vauxhall Bridge Road, London SW1V 2SA

Random House Australia (Pty) Limited
20 Alfred Street, Milsons Point, Sydney
New South Wales 2061, Australia

Random House New Zealand Limited
18 Poland Road, Glenfield, Auckland 10, New Zealand

Random House South Africa (Pty) Limited
Endulini, 5a Jubilee Road, Parktown 2193, South Africa

Random House UK Limited Reg. No. 954009

A CIP catalogue record for this book
is available from the British Library

Papers used by Random House UK Limited
are natural, recyclable products made from wood grown in
sustainable forests. The manufacturing processes conform to
the environmental regulations of the country of origin

Printed and bound in the United Kingdom by
Cox & Wyman Ltd, Reading, Berkshire

ISBN 0 7493 3685 4

CONTENTS

The Jewel
in the Crown

To
Dorothy Ganapathy
with love

Part One

MISS CRANE

Imagine, then, a flat landscape, dark for the moment, but even so conveying to a girl running in the still deeper shadow cast by the wall of the Bibighar Gardens an idea of immensity, of distance, such as years before Miss Crane had been conscious of standing where a lane ended and cultivation began: a different landscape but also in the alluvial plain between the mountains of the north and the plateau of the south.

It is a landscape which a few hours ago, between the rainfall and the short twilight, extracted colour from the spectrum of the setting sun and dyed every one of its own surfaces that could absorb light: the ochre walls of the houses in the old town (which are stained too with their bloody past and uneasy present); the moving water of the river and the still water of the tanks; the shiny stubble, the ploughed earth, of distant fields; the metal of the grand trunk road. In this landscape trees are sparse, except among the white bungalows of the civil lines. On the horizon there is a violet smudge of hill country.

This is the story of a rape, of the events that led up to it and followed it and of the place in which it happened. There are the action, the people, and the place; all of which are interrelated but in their totality incommunicable in isolation from the moral continuum of human affairs.

In the Bibighar Gardens case there were several arrests and an investigation. There was no trial in the judicial sense. Since then people have said there was a trial of sorts going on. In fact, such people say, the affair that began on the evening of August 9th, 1942, in Mayapore, ended with the spectacle of two nations in violent opposition, not for the first time nor as yet for the last because they were then still locked in an imperial embrace of such long standing and subtlety it was no longer possible for them to know whether they hated or loved one another, or what it was that held them together and seemed to have confused the image of their separate destinies.

*

In 1942, which was the year the Japanese defeated the British army in Burma and Mr Gandhi began preaching sedition in India, the English then

3

living in the civil and military cantonment of Mayapore had to admit that the future did not look propitious. They had faced bad times before, though, and felt that they could face them again, that now they knew where they stood and there could be no more heart-searching for quite a while yet about the rights and wrongs of their colonial-imperialist policy and administration.

As they were fond of putting it at the club, it was a question of first things first, and when they heard that Miss Crane, the supervisor of the district's Protestant mission schools, had taken Mr Gandhi's picture down from the walls of her study and no longer entertained Indian ladies to tea but young English soldiers instead, they were grateful to her as well as amused. In peace time opinions could be as diverse and cranky as you wished. In war you had to close the ranks; and if it was to be a question of sides Miss Crane seemed to have shown at last which she was really on.

What few people knew was that the Indian ladies themselves had taken the initiative over the question of tea on Tuesdays at Edwina Crane's bungalow. Miss Crane suspected that it was the ladies' husbands who had dissuaded them from making the weekly appearance, not only because Mr Gandhi's picture had gone but in case such visits could have been thought of, in this explosive year, as a buttering-up of the *raj*. What hurt her most was that none of the ladies had bothered to discuss their reasons with her. They had one by one or two by two just stopped coming and made feeble excuses when she met any of them in the bazaar or on her way to the mission schoolrooms.

She was sorry about the ladies whom she had always encouraged to be frank with her, but not at all sorry about Mr Gandhi's portrait. The ladies had an excuse. Mr Gandhi did not. She believed he was behaving abominably. She felt, in fact, let down. For years she had laughed at Europeans who said that he was not to be trusted, but now Mr Gandhi had extended what looked like an open invitation to the Japanese to come and help him rid India of the British – and if he thought that they would be the better masters then she could only assume he was out of his senses or, which was worse, revealing that his philosophy of non-violence had a dark side that added up to total invalidation of its every aspect. The Japanese, apparently, were to do his violence for him.

Reacting from her newly found distrust of the Mahatma and her disappointment in the behaviour of the ladies (the kind of disappointment she had actually become no stranger to) she wondered whether her life might not have been spent better among her own people, persuading them to appreciate the qualities of Indians, instead of among Indians, attempting to prove that at least one Englishwoman admired and respected them. She had to admit that a searching analysis of her work would show that in the main the people she had got on with best of all were those of mixed blood; which seemed, perhaps, to emphasise the fact that she was neither one thing nor the other herself – a teacher without real qualifications, a missionary worker who did not believe in God. She had never been wholly

4

accepted by Indians and had tended to reject the generality of the English. In this there was a certain irony. The Indians, she thought, might have taken her more seriously if she had not been a representative of the kind of organisation they were glad enough to make use of but of which old suspicions died hard. By the same token, if she had not worked for the mission she would, she believed, never have acquired an admiration for the Indians through love and respect for their children, nor been led to such sharp criticism of her own race, in whose apparently neglectful and indifferent care the future of those children and the present well-being of their parents were held. She had never been slow to voice her criticism. And this, possibly, had been a mistake. The English always took such criticism so personally.

However, Miss Crane was of a generation that abided by (even if it did not wholly believe in) certain simple rules for positive action. It was, she told herself, never too late to mend, or try to mend. Thinking of the young British soldiers who were in Mayapore in ever-increasing numbers, and remembering that most of them looked fresh out from home, she wrote to the Station Staff Officer, had an interview with him, and arranged to entertain a party of up to a dozen at a time at tea every Wednesday afternoon from five o'clock until six-thirty. The SSO thanked her for her generosity and said he wished more people realised what it meant to an English lad to be in a home again, if only for an hour or two. For all their flag-wagging the ladies of the cantonment tended to have a prejudice against the British Other Rank. The SSO did not say this but the implication was there. Miss Crane guessed from his speech and manner that he had risen from the ranks himself. He said he hoped she would not have cause to regret her invitation. Young soldiers, although mostly maligned, were indeed apt to be clumsy and noisy. She had only to ring him up if things proved too much for her or if she had anything to complain about. She smiled and reminded him that the life she led had never been sheltered and she had often heard herself referred to in Mayapore as a tough old bird.

The soldiers who came to Miss Crane's bungalow for tea spoke with cockney accents but they were not clumsy. With one exception, a boy called Barrett, they handled the bone china with big-fisted dexterity. They were not too shy and not over noisy. The parties always ended on a gratifyingly free and easy note. Afterwards, she stood on the front verandah and waved them down the path that led through her pretty, well-kept garden. Outside the gate they lit cigarettes and went back to barracks in a comradely bunch making some clatter with their boots on the hard surface of the road. Having helped her old Indian servant Joseph to clear away, Miss Crane then retired to her room to read reports and deal with letters from the headquarters of the mission, and – since the soldiers' tea was on a Wednesday and Thursday was her day to visit and stay overnight at the school in Dibrapur, seventy-five miles away – prepare her Gladstone bag for the journey and look out a tin of boiled sweets as a gift for the Dibrapur

5

children. While she did these things she also found time to think about the soldiers.

There was one particular boy who came regularly of whom she was very fond. His name was Clancy. He was what middle-class people of her own generation would have called one of nature's gentlemen. It was Clancy who sat down last and stood up first, Clancy who saw to it that she had a piece of her own fruit cake and that she did not go sugarless for want of the passing back up the table of the bowl. He always asked how she was, and gave the most lucid answers to her inquiries about their training and sports and communal life in the barracks. And whereas the others called her Mum, or Ma'am, Clancy called her Miss Crane. She was herself meticulous in the business of getting to know their names and dignifying them with the prefix Mister. She knew that private soldiers hated to be called by their surnames alone if the person talking to them was a woman. But although she never omitted to say Mister Clancy when addressing him, it was as Clancy that she thought of him. It was a nice name, and his friends called him that, or Clance.

Clancy, she was glad to notice, was liked by his comrades. His attentiveness to her wasn't resented, or laughed at. He seemed to be a natural leader. He commanded respect. He was good-looking and fitted his uniform of khaki shirt and shorts better than the other boys. Only his accent, and his hands – with torn finger-nails, never quite clean of vestiges of oil and grease from handling rifles and guns – marked him as an ordinary member of the herd.

Sometimes, when they had gone and she worked on her files and thought about them, she was sad. Some of those boys, Clancy more easily than the others because he was bound to get a position of responsibility, might be killed. She was also sad, but in a different way, when the thought passed through her head, as it couldn't help doing, that probably they all laughed at her on the quiet and talked about her when she wasn't there to hear as the old maid who served up char and wads.

She was, as mission headquarters knew, an intelligent and perceptive woman whose understanding, common sense and organising ability, more than made up for what in a woman connected with a Christian mission were of doubtful value: her agnosticism, for instance, and her fundamentally anti-British, because pro-Indian, sympathies.

*

Edwina Crane had lived in India for thirty-five of her fifty-seven years. She was born in London in 1885 of moderately well-to-do middle-class parents; her mother died early and she spent her youth and young womanhood looking after her lost lonely father, a schoolmaster who became fond of the bottle and his own company so that gradually the few friends they had drifted away along with the pupils who attended his private school. He died in an Edwardian summer when she was twenty-one, leaving her

6

penniless and fit for nothing, she felt, except the job of paid companion or housekeeper. The scent of lime trees in fading flower stayed with her afterwards as the smell of death. She thought she was lucky when the first job she got was as governess to a spoiled little boy who called her Storky and tried to shock her once with a precocious show of sexuality in the night-nursery.

She was not shocked. In the later stages of her father's illness she had had to deal with his incontinence, and before that with his drunken outbursts in which he had not been above telling her those facts of life she had not already learned or ridiculing her for her long nose and plain looks and slender hopes of marriage. Sober, he was always ashamed, but too uncourageous to tell her so. She understood this, and because of it learned to value courage in others and try hard, not always successfully, to show it herself. In some ways her father was like a child to her. When he was dead she wept, then dried her eyes and sold most of the few remaining possessions to pay for a decent funeral, having refused financial help from the rich uncle who had kept away during her father's lifetime and moral support from the poor cousins who reappeared at his death.

So the little boy did not shock her. Neither did he enchant her. Living alone with her father she had tended to believe that he and she were of a kind apart, singled out to support a special cross compounded of genteel poverty and drunkenness, but the wealthy and temperate household in which she had now come to live seemed unhappy too, and this had the effect of making the world she knew look tragically small just at the moment when it might have been opening up. It was the desire she had to find a place in an unknown world that would come at her as new and fresh and, if not joyful, then at least adventurous and worthwhile, that made her apply for a post as travelling nurse-companion to a lady making the passage back to India with two young children. The lady, who had a pale face and looked delicate, but turned out resilient, explained that if proved satisfactory, the person who obtained the post could stay on in India after they arrived, with a view to acting as governess. If unsatisfactory, such a person would easily find a similar job with a family taking the passage home, failing which her passage home would be paid. The lady seemed to take a fancy to her and so Miss Crane was employed.

The voyage was pleasant because Mrs Nesbitt-Smith treated her like a member of the family, and the children, a blue-eyed girl and a blue-eyed boy, both said they loved her and wanted her to live with them for ever. When they reached Bombay, Major Nesbitt-Smith met them and treated her like one of the family too; but Miss Crane could not help noticing from then on that the major's wife gradually withdrew, and by the time they reached the husband's station in the Punjab was treating her not exactly like a servant but like a poor relation with whom the family had somehow got saddled and so for the present made use of. It was Miss Crane's first experience of social snobbery abroad, which was never the same as snobbery at home because it was complicated by the demands, sometimes conflicting, of white solidarity and white supremacy. Her employers felt a duty to accord her a recognition they would have withheld from the highest-born Indian, at the same time a compulsion to place her on one of the lowest rungs of the ladder of their own self-contained society – lower outside the household than in, where, of course, she stood in a position far superior to that of any native servant. Miss Crane disapproved of this preoccupation with the question of who was who and why. It went against the increasingly liberal grain of her strengthening conscience. It also seemed to make life very difficult. She thought that Mrs Nesbitt-Smith was sometimes hard put to it to know what expression to wear when talking to her and decided that the confusion she must often have been in accounted for the frequent look of concern, almost of pain, at having to speak at all.

She was with the Nesbitt-Smiths for three years. She had a strong constitution which meant she was seldom ill even in that difficult climate. She was fond of the children and reacted to the politeness of the servants by overcoming the shyness she had been used to feel at home. There was, as well, India, which at first had seemed strange, even frightening, but presently full of compensations that she found difficult to name but felt in her heart. She had few friends and still felt isolated from people as individuals, but she was aware now of a sense of community. That sense sprang, she knew, from the seldom-voiced but always insistent, even when mute, clan-gathering call to solidarity that was part of the social pattern she had noted early on and disapproved of. She still disapproved of it but was honest enough to recognise it as having always been a bleak but real enough source of comfort and protection. There was a lot to fear in India, and it was good to feel safe, to know that indifferently as Mrs Nesbitt-Smith might sometimes treat her, Mrs Nesbitt-Smith and her like would always rally round if she found herself in any kind of danger from outside the charmed circle of privilege on whose periphery she spent her days. She knew that the India she found full of compensations was only the white man's India. But it was an India of a kind, and that at least was a beginning.

At this stage she fell in love, not with the young assistant chaplain to the station who sometimes conducted the services at the local Protestant church (which would have been a possible match, indeed was one that in her good moods Mrs Nesbitt-Smith chaffed her about and smilingly pushed her towards) but hopelessly and secretly with a Lieutenant Orme who was as handsome as Apollo, as kind, gentle and gay with her as any hero in a romantic novel, as ignorant or unheeding of her regard as his good looks so well enabled him to be in a station remarkable that year for the number of pretty well-placed girls of whom he could have his pick: hopelessly in love, because she had no chance; secretly, because she found she did not blush or act awkwardly in his presence, and Mrs Nesbitt-Smith, even had she bothered to observe the reactions of her children's governess to a man so splendidly equipped, in every sense, as Lieutenant Orme, would not have been able to tell that Miss Crane had longings in directions which were, by tradition, totally closed to her. That she neither blushed nor acted awkwardly puzzled Miss Crane. Her heart beat when he stood close by and perhaps there came a slight dryness into her mouth, but her feelings, she decided, must have been too intense, too adult, for her to act like the fluttering stupid girls who knew nothing of the world's reality.

When Lieutenant Orme was posted away, still uncommitted and with his usual glittering luck, as ADC to a general, to the frenzied disappointment of up to twenty pretty girls, as many plain ones and all their mothers, no one, Miss Crane believed, could have suspected the extent to which his departure darkened her own life. Only the children, her two most intimate human contacts, noticed that her manner changed. They gazed at her through those still remarkably blue but now older and calculating upper middle-class eyes and said, 'What's wrong, Miss Crane? Have you got a pain, Miss Crane?' and danced round her singing, 'Old Crane's got a pain,' so that she lost her temper, slapped them and sent them away screaming through shadow and sunlight to be comforted by the old ayah of whom, she knew, they had become fonder.

Before the next hot weather began Major Nesbitt-Smith's regiment was ordered home. 'I and the children will be going on ahead,' she overheard Mrs Nesbitt-Smith say to a friend, 'and of course Crane will be coming with us.' Speaking of her to others Mrs Nesbitt-Smith usually referred to her as Crane, but as Miss Crane to her face and the children, and, in rare moments of warmth and gratitude, as Edwina, as when for instance she lay in her darkened punkah-cooled room with Miss Crane kneeling by her bedside soothing with cologne one of her raging headaches.

For many days after the news of the regiment's impending return to England, Miss Crane went about her duties with no particular thoughts in her head because she had firmly put Lieutenant Orme out of them some time ago and nothing had come to take his place. 'And he,' she said to herself presently, 'was a fancy, a mere illusion that never stood a chance of becoming real for me. Now that I've banished the illusion from my thoughts I can see them for what they are, what they have always been, empty, starved, waiting to be filled. How will they be filled at home, in England? By care of the children as they grow, and become old, beyond me? By substituting different children for these and a different Mrs Nesbitt-Smith for this one? Households that are not the same household and yet the same? And so on, year after year, as Crane, Miss Crane, and sometimes, increasingly rarely, until no more, Edwina?'

In the evenings between five o'clock – when the children had had their tea and became the temporary sole charge of the ayah for play and bath – and seven o'clock when she supervised their supper before going in to dine alone or, if circumstances permitted, with the family, Miss Crane was free. Mostly she spent those two short hours in her room, having her own bath, resting, reading, writing an occasional letter to another of her kind who had exchanged this station for another or gone back to England. But now she began to feel restless and took to putting on her boots and – parasol opened and protectively raised – walking down the lane of the civil lines in which the Nesbitt-Smiths' bungalow stood. The lane was shaded by trees that thinned out gradually as the bungalows gave way to open cultivated fields. Sometimes she walked in the opposite direction, towards the cantonment bazaar beyond which lay the railway station and the native town which she had entered only on one occasion – with a group of laughing ladies and timid companions in carriages, stoutly accompanied by gentlemen – to inspect a Hindu temple which had frightened her, as the native town had frightened her with its narrow dirty streets, its disgusting poverty, its raucous dissonant music, its verminous dogs, its starving, mutilated beggars, its fat white sacred Brahmini bulls and its ragged population of men and women who looked so resentful in comparison with the servants and other officiating natives of the cantonment.

On the day that she found herself questioning the prospect of a future that was, as it were, an image seen in a series of mirrors that reflected it until it became too small for the eye to see – a diminishing row of children and Nesbitt-Smiths and Edwina Cranes – the walk she went on at five was the one that brought her out to the open spaces where the road led on into the far distance. Reaching this point, she stopped, afraid to go farther. The sun was still hot, still high enough to make her narrow her eyes as she gazed from under the brim of her hat and the cotton canopy of the parasol, towards the horizon of the flat, wide, immense Punjabi plain. It seemed impossible, she thought, that the world continued beyond that far-away boundary, that somewhere it changed its nature, erupted into hills and forests and ranges of mountains whose crests were white with eternal snows where rivers had their source. It seemed impossible too that beyond the plains there could be an ocean where those rivers had their end. She felt dwarfed, famished in the spirit, pressed down by a tremendous weight of land, and of air and incomprehensible space that even the flapping, wheeling crows had difficulty keeping up in. And she thought for a moment that she was being touched by the heavy finger of a god; not the familiar uplifting all-forgiving God she went through the motions of praying to, but one neither benign nor malign, neither creating nor destroying, sleeping nor waking, but existing, and leaning his weight upon the world.

Acknowledging that women such as herself tended to turn to if not actually to seek sanctuary in religion, she walked on the following evening in the other direction and when she came to the Protestant church she turned into the compound and went up the broad gravel path, past the hummocky graves marked by the headstones of those who had died far from home, but who in their resting place, had they woken, might have been comforted by the English look of the church and its yard and the green trees planted there. The side door of the church was on the latch. She went in and sat in a pew at the back, stared at the altar and gazed at the darkening east window of stained glass which she saw every Sunday in the company of the Nesbitt-Smiths.

The god of this church was a kind, familiar, comfortable god. She had him in her heart but not in her soul. She believed in him as a comforter but not as a redeemer. He was very much the god of a community, not of the dark-skinned community that struggled for life under the weight of the Punjabi sky but of the privileged pale-faced community of which she was a marginal member. She wondered whether she would be Crane to Him, or Miss Crane, or Edwina. If she thought of Him as the Son she would, she presumed, be Edwina, but to God in His wrath, undoubtedly Crane.

'Miss Crane?'

Startled by the voice she looked over her shoulder. It was the senior chaplain, an elderly man with a sharp pink nose and a fringe of distinguishing white hair surrounding his gnomic head. His name was Grant, which caused restrained smiles during services when he intoned prayers that began Grant, O Lord, we beseech Thee. She smiled now, although she was embarrassed being found by him there, betraying herself as a woman in need almost certainly not of rest but of reassurance. A plain somewhat horse-faced woman in her middle twenties, alone in an empty Protestant church, on a day when no service was due, was somehow already labelled. In later years, Miss Crane came to look upon that moment as the one that produced in her the certainty of her own spinsterhood.

'You are resting from your labours,' Mr Grant said in his melodious congregational voice, and added, more directly, when she had nodded and looked down at her lap, 'Can I be of any help, child?' so that without warning she wanted to weep because child was what her father had often called her in his sober, loving moments. However, she did not weep. She had not wept since her father's death and although there would come a time when she did once more it had not arrived yet. Speaking in a voice whose steadiness encouraged her, she said, 'I'm thinking of staying on,' and, seeing the chaplain's perplexity, the way he glanced round the church as if something had begun to go on there which nobody had bothered to forewarn him of but which Miss Crane knew about and thought worth staying for, she explained, 'I mean in India, when the Nesbitt-Smiths go home.'

The chaplain said, 'I see,' and frowned, perhaps because she had called them the Nesbitt-Smiths. 'It should not be difficult, Miss Crane. Colonel and Mrs Ingleby, for instance, strike me as worth approaching. I know you are well thought of. Major and Mrs Nesbitt-Smith have always spoken highly.'

The future looked dark, a blank featureless territory with, in its centre, a pinprick of light that seemed to be all that was left of Edwina Crane.

'I think I should like,' she said, giving expression to a thought that had never properly been a thought until now, 'to train for the Mission.'

He sat down next to her and together they watched the east window.

'Not,' she went on, 'no, not to carry the Word. I am not a truly religious woman.' She glanced at him. He was still watching the window. He did not seem to be particularly upset by her confession. 'But there are schools, aren't there?' she said. 'I meant train to teach at the mission schools.'

'Ah yes, I see, to teach not our own children but those of our dark brethren in Christ?'

She nodded. She found herself short of breath. He turned to look at her fully, and asked her, 'Have you seen the school here?'

Yes, she had seen the school, close to the railway station, but – 'Only from the outside,' she told him.

'Have you ever talked to Miss Williams?'

'Who is Miss Williams?'

'The teacher. But then you would be unlikely to know her. She is a lady of mixed blood. Would you like to visit the school?'

'Very much.'

The chaplain nodded and presently, after the appearance of having thought more deeply, said, 'Then I will arrange it, and if you are of the same mind I will write to the superintendent in Lahore, not that there is anything much for you to judge by in Miss Williams's little school.' He shook his head. 'No, Miss Crane. This isn't an area where we've had much success, although more than the Catholics and the Baptists. There are of course a great number of schools throughout the country, of various denominations, all committed to educating what I suppose we must call the heathen. In this matter the Church and the missions have always led the way. The government has been, shall we say, slow to see the advantages. So, perhaps, have the Indians. The school here, for instance. A handful of children at the best of times. At the times of the festivals none. I mean, of course, the Hindu and Moslem festivals. The children come, you see, mainly for the chappattis, and in the last riots the school was set fire to, but that was before your time.'

*

The mission school was not the one she had had in mind which was close to the railway, the Joseph Wainwright Christian School, a substantial building, a privately endowed school for Eurasian children, the sons and daughters of soldiers, railway officials and junior civil servants whose blood had been mixed with that of the native population. The mission school was on the outskirts of the native town itself, a poor, small, rectangular building with a roof of corrugated iron in a walled compound bare of grass, with nothing to identify it apart from the cross roughly painted on the yellow stucco above the door. She was too ashamed to admit her mistake to Mr Grant, who had brought her in a tonga, and now handed her down and led her through the opening in the wall where once, before the last riots, there might have been a gate.

To come with him at midday she had had to obtain permission from Mrs Nesbitt-Smith and explain her reason for wanting leave of absence from the task of teaching the young Nesbitt-Smiths. Mrs Nesbitt-Smith had stared at her as if she were mad and exclaimed, 'Good heavens, Crane! What on earth has possessed you?' And then added, with what looked like genuine concern, which was touching and therefore far more upsetting than the outburst, 'You'd be with blacks and half-castes, cut off from your own kind. And besides, Edwina, we're all very fond of you.'

She was undoubtedly acting like a fool, far from sure even that she was acting on an impulse she had interpreted correctly. To begin with, to have confused the Eurasian school with the mission school proved how ignorant she was of what was there under her own nose, proved how little was really known by people such as herself about the life of the town they were supposed to have a duty to, a duty whose proper execution earned them the privileges they enjoyed. If she had not even known where this particular mission school was, what, she wondered, could she hope to contribute to other mission schools or deserve to gain from them?

The door of the school was open. There was a sound of children singing. When they reached the door the singing stopped. Mr Grant said that Miss Williams was expecting them and then stood aside. She crossed the threshold directly into the schoolroom. The woman on the dais said, 'Stand up, children,' and motioned with her arms at the pupils who were seated on several rows of benches, facing her. They stood up. A phrase written in block capitals on the blackboard drew Miss Crane's attention. Welcome Miss Crane Mem. At another sign from the teacher the children chanted it slowly. 'Welcome, Miss Crane Mem.' Trying to say, 'Thank you', she found her tongue and the roof of her mouth dry. The visit on which she had set out in the role of a suppliant for employment was looked upon here as the visit of an inquisitive memsahib. She was terrified of the obligation this put her under and of the stuffy whitewashed room, the rows of children and the smell of burning cowpats that was coming through the open door and windows from the back of the compound where no doubt the God-sent chappattis were being cooked. And she was afraid of Miss Williams, who wore a grey cotton blouse, long brown skirt and black button boots, and was younger than she and sallow-complexioned in the way that some of the most insufferable of the European women were who had spent a lifetime in the country; only in Miss Williams's case the sallowness denoted a half-Indian origin, the kind of origin for which Miss Crane had been taught to feel a certain horror.

Miss Williams left the dais on which there were the teacher's desk and only one chair. Invited, Miss Crane sat, and the chaplain stood next to her. He had said, 'Miss Crane, this is Miss Williams,' but had not said, 'Miss Williams, this is Miss Crane,' and as Miss Crane sat down she attempted to smile at the girl to apologise for an omission not her own, but her lips were as parched as her mouth, and she was conscious, then, of an expression growing on her face similar to that which she had seen so often on Mrs Nesbitt-Smith's. It became etched more deeply when at last she submitted to the duty to look at the children, found herself the lone, inarticulate object of their curiosity and awe, perhaps their fear. The simple dress she had put on, her best in order to look her best – white muslin with a frilled hem but no other decoration beyond the mother-of-pearl buttons down the pleated choker; and the hat, a straw boater perched squarely upon her piled up hair; the folded parasol of white cotton with a pink lining, a gift from Mrs Nesbitt-Smith last Christmas – now seemed to envelop her, to encumber her with all the pompous frippery of a class to which she did not belong.

At Miss Williams's command a little girl, barefoot and dressed in a shapeless covering that looked like sacking, but whose pigtail was decked with flowers for the occasion, came forward with a nosegay, curtsied and held the nosegay up. Miss Crane took it. Again she tried to say 'Thank You', but her words must have been unintelligible because the little girl had to look at Miss Williams for confirmation that the ritual of presentation was over. Neither seeing nor smelling the flowers, Miss Crane held them to her nose, and when she looked up again the little girl was back in her place, standing with the other little girls in the front row.

'I think,' Mr Grant said, 'that the children may sit down again, don't you, Miss Crane? Then presently they can either sing the song or say the poem I'm sure Miss Williams here has been rehearsing hard all morning.'

For a moment Miss Crane stared helplessly at the flowers in her lap, aware that Miss Williams and Mr Grant were both watching her, both waiting for her. She nodded her head, ashamed because in the first public duty of her life she was failing.

Sitting down when Miss Williams told them to, the children were silent. Miss Crane thought that they had sensed her discomfort and had interpreted it as displeasure or boredom. She forced herself to look at Miss Williams and say, 'I should love to hear the song,' then remembered Mr Grant had said poem or song, and added, 'or the poem. Or both. Please let them do what they have rehearsed.'

Miss Williams turned to the class and said in her slow, curiously accented English, 'Now children, what shall we sing? Shall we sing the song about There is a Friend?' and then, 'Achchha,' a word Miss Crane knew well enough, but which was followed by rapid words in Hindustani she could not catch because they sped by too quickly. I can't, she thought, even speak the language properly, so how can I hope to teach?

Once more the children got to their feet. Miss Williams beat time in the air, slowly, and sang the first line of the hymn which otherwise Miss Crane might not easily have recognised; and then paused, beat again and set them all singing, unevenly, shyly, and in voices still unused to the odd, flat, foreign scale.

'There's a Friend for little children
  Above the bright blue sky,
A Friend Who never changes,
  Whose love will never die;
Our earthly friends may fail us,
  And change with changing years,

14

This Friend is always worthy,
Of that dear Name He bears.

There's a rest for little children,
Above the bright blue sky,
Who love the Blessèd Saviour
And to the Father cry;
A rest from every turmoil,
From sin and sorrow free,
Where every little pilgrim
Shall rest eternally.'

As they sang Miss Crane looked at them. They were a ragged little band. As a child the hymn had been one of her favourites and if it had been sung as English children sang it, with a piano or organ accompaniment, as it used to be sung in her father's shabby school, she might have been borne down by an intensity of feeling, or regret and sadness for a lost world, a lost comfort, a lost magic. But she was not borne down, nor uplifted. She felt an incongruity, a curious resistance to the idea of subverting these children from worship of their own gods to worship of one she herself had sung to when young but now had no strong faith in. But she had, too, a sudden passionate regard for them. Hungry, poor, deprived, hopelessly at a disadvantage, they yet conveyed to her an overwhelming impression of somewhere – and it could only be there, in the Black Town – being loved. But love, as their parents knew, was not enough. Hunger and poverty could never be reduced by love alone. There were, to begin with, free chappattis.

And it came to Miss Crane then that the only excuse she or anyone of her kind had to be there, alone, sitting on a chair, holding a nosegay, being sung to, the object of the awe of uninstructed children, was if they sat there conscious of a duty to promote the cause of human dignity and happiness. And then she was no longer really ashamed of her dress, or deeply afraid of the schoolhouse or of the smell of burning cowpats. The cowpats were all that there was for fuel, the schoolhouse was small and stuffy because there was not enough money spent, not enough available, to make it large and airy, and her dress was only a symbol of the status she enjoyed and the obligations she had not to look afraid, not to be afraid, to acquire a personal grace, a personal dignity, as much as she could of either, as much as was in her power, so that she could be a living proof of there being, somewhere in the world, hope of betterment.

When the singing was sung and she had said, in halting Hindustani, 'Thank you. It was very good,' she asked Miss Williams whether she could stay while they had their chappattis and perhaps watch some of their games, and then, if Miss Williams had time to answer, ask one or two questions about the kind of work a teacher was required to do.

And so Miss Crane set out on the long and lonely, difficult and sometimes dangerous road that led her, many years later, to Mayapore, where she was superintendent of the district's Protestant mission schools.

Although she had taken Mr Gandhi's portrait down, there was one picture, much longer in her possession, which she kept hanging on the wall above the desk in her combined bedroom and study. She had had it since 1914, the fifth year of her service in the mission, the year in which she left the school in Muzzafirabad, where she had assisted a Mr Cleghorn, to take over on her own account the school in Ranpur.

The picture had been a gift, a parting token of esteem. The head of the mission himself had presided over the gathering at which the presentation was made, although it was Mr Cleghorn who handed the gift over while the children clapped and cheered. In the drawer of her desk she still had the inscribed plate that had been fixed to the frame. The plate was of gilt, now discoloured, and the lettering of the inscription was black, faded, but still legible. It said: 'Presented to Edwina Lavinia Crane, in recognition of her courage, by the staff and pupils of the School of the Church of England Mission, Muzzafirabad, NWFP.'

Before she reached Ranpur she removed the plate because she was embarrassed by the word courage. All she had done was to stand on the threshold of the schoolhouse, into which she had already herded the children, and deny entry – in fluent Urdu, using expressions she could hardly have repeated to her superiors – to a detachment of half-hearted rioters. At least, she had assumed they were half-hearted, although later, only an hour later, they or more determined colleagues sacked and burned the Catholic mission house down the road, attacked the police station and set off for the civil lines where the military dispersed them by shooting one of the ringleaders and firing the rest of their volleys into the air. For four days the town lived under martial law and when peace was restored Miss Crane found herself disagreeably in the public eye. The District Magistrate called on her, accompanied by the District Superintendent of Police, and thanked her. She felt it imperative to say that she was by no means certain she had done the right thing, that she wondered, in fact, whether it wouldn't have been better to have let the rioters in to burn whatever it was they wanted to get rid of, the prayer books or the crucifix. She had refused to let them and so they had gone away angrier than ever, and burned the Catholics to the ground and caused a great deal of trouble.

When Mr Cleghorn returned from leave, anxious for news of what he had only heard as rumour, she decided to apply for a transfer so that she could get on with her job without constant reminders of what she thought of as her false position. She told Mr Cleghorn that it was quite impossible to teach children who, facing her, saw her as a cardboard heroine and no doubt had, each of them, only one eye on the blackboard because the other was fixed on the doorway, expectant of some further disturbance they wanted her to quell. Mr Cleghorn said that he would be sorry to see her go, but that he quite understood and that if she really meant what she said he would write personally to mission headquarters to explain matters.

16

When the instructions for her transfer came she discovered that she had been promoted by being put in sole charge of the school at Ranpur. Before she left there was a tea, and then the presentation of the picture – a larger, more handsomely framed copy of the picture on the wall behind her desk in the Muzzafirabad schoolroom, a semi-historical, semi-allegorical picture entitled *The Jewel in Her Crown*, which showed the old Queen (whose image the children now no doubt confused with the person of Miss Crane) surrounded by representative figures of her Indian Empire: princes, landowners, merchants, money-lenders, sepoys, farmers, servants, children, mothers, and remarkably clean and tidy beggars. The Queen was sitting on a golden throne, under a crimson canopy, attended by her temporal and spiritual aides: soldiers, statesmen and clergy. The canopied throne was apparently in the open air because there were palm trees and a sky showing a radiant sun bursting out of bulgy clouds such as, in India, heralded the wet monsoon. Above the clouds flew the prayerful figures of the angels who were the benevolent spectators of the scene below. Among the statesmen who stood behind the throne one was painted in the likeness of Mr Disraeli holding up a parchment map of India to which he pointed with obvious pride but tactful humility. An Indian prince, attended by native servants, was approaching the throne bearing a velvet cushion on which he offered a large and sparkling gem. The children in the school thought that this gem was the jewel referred to in the title. Miss Crane had been bound to explain that the gem was simply representative of tribute, and that the jewel of the title was India herself, which had been transferred from the rule of the British East India Company to the rule of the British crown in 1858, the year after the Mutiny when the sepoys in the service of the Company (that first set foot in India in the seventeenth century) had risen in rebellion, and attempts had been made to declare an old moghul prince king in Delhi, and that the picture had been painted after 1877, the year in which Victoria was persuaded by Mr Disraeli to adopt the title Empress of India.

The Jewel in Her Crown was a picture about which Miss Crane had very mixed feelings. The copy that already hung on the classroom wall in Muzzafirabad when she first went there as assistant to Mr Cleghorn she found useful when teaching the English language to a class of Muslim and Hindu children. This is the Queen. That is her crown. The sky there is blue. Here there are clouds in the sky. The uniform of the sahib is scarlet. Mr Cleghorn, an ordained member of the Church and an enthusiastic amateur scholar of archaeology and anthropology, and much concerned with the impending, never-got-down-to composition of a monograph on local topography and social customs, had devoted most of his time to work for the Church and for the older boys in the middle school. He did this at the expense of the junior school, as he was aware. When Miss Crane was sent to him from Lahore in response to his requests for more permanent help in that field of his responsibility he had been fascinated to notice the practical use she made of a picture which, to him, had never been more than something hanging on the wall to brighten things up.

He was fond of remarking on it, whenever he found her in class with half a dozen wide-eyed children gathered round her, looking from her to the picture as she took them through its various aspects, step by step. 'Ah, the picture again, Miss Crane,' he would say, 'admirable, admirable. I should never have thought of it. To teach English and at the same time love of the English.'

She knew what he meant by love of the English. He meant love of their justice, love of their benevolence, love – anyway – of their good intentions. As often as she was irritated by his simplicity, she was touched by it. He was a good man: tireless, inquisitive, charitable. Mohammedanism and Hinduism, which still frightened her in their outward manifestations, merely amused him: as a grown man might be amused by the grim, colourful but harmless games of children. If there were times when she thought him heedless of the misery of men, she could not help knowing that in his own way he never forgot the glory of God. Mr Cleghorn's view was that God was best served, best glorified, by the training and exercise of the intellect. Physically timid – as she knew him to be from his fear of dogs, his mortal terror, once, of a snake which the watchman had to be sent for to despatch, his twitching cheeks and trembling hands when they were met on one or two occasions on the outskirts of villages by delegations of men who looked fierce but were actually friendly – he was morally courageous, and for this she admired him.

He fought long and hard for any money he thought the mission could afford and he could spend well. He had an ear and an eye for injustice and had been known to plead successfully with the District Magistrate for suspension of sentences or quashing of convictions in cases he believed deserved it. Mr Cleghorn – the District Magistrate used to say – was wasted in the Church and should have gone into the Civil.

He showed most determination, however, in promoting the education of boys of the middle-class – Anglo-Indians, Hindus, Muslims, Sikhs. If they had above average intelligence they were all one to him, all 'children whom the Lord has blessed with brains and sensibilities'. His work here was chiefly that of detecting just where a youth's talents lay and in persuading him and his parents to set a course in that direction. 'Look at young Shankar Ram,' he might say to Miss Crane, who had but the vaguest notion which Shankar Ram he referred to, 'he says he wants to be a civil servant. They all want to be civil servants. What chance has he got, though, beyond the post office and telegraphs? He should be an engineer. It may not be in his blood, but it is in his heart and mind.' And so he would set about depressingly often without success looking for ways, for means, for opportunities to send young Shankar Ram out into the great world beyond Muzzafirabad to build bridges. In this, Miss Crane used to think, Mr Cleghorn looked remarkably unlike any ordinary man of God, for the Shankar Ram in question, ninety-nine times out of a hundred, turned out

18

to be as far away from conversion to Christianity as the women of India were from social emancipation. And over the question of women, British or Indian, Mr Cleghorn was infuriatingly conservative. Women's interests were his blind spot. 'Your sex is made, alas,' he said once, 'and yet not alas, no, Heaven be praised, your sex is made, Miss Crane, for marriage or for God,' and in the one intimate moment there ever was between them, took her hand and patted it, as if to comfort her for the fact that the first, the temporal of these blessings, was certainly denied her.

Sometimes Miss Crane wanted to point to the picture on the wall which showed the old Queen resplendent on her throne and say to him, 'Well there, anyway, was a woman of affairs,' but never did, and was touched when she unwrapped the presentation parcel and saw an even gaudier copy of the enigmatic picture; touched because she knew that Mr Cleghorn, deeply considering the parting gift she might most value, had characteristically hit upon the one she could have done without.

But a couple of days later, as he saw her into the Ladies' First-Class compartment of a train, while young Joseph, a poor boy who had worked in the mission kitchens but had asked to serve and was coming with her, was seeing to the luggage, Mr Cleghorn handed her his own personal gift which, unwrapped as the train moved out into the bleak frontier landscape, turned out to be a copy of a book called *Fabian Essays in Socialism*, edited by Mr George Bernard Shaw. It was inscribed to 'My friend and colleague, Edwina Crane,' signed, 'Arthur St John Cleghorn', and dated July 12th, 1914.

This book she still had, in the bookcase in her room in Mayapore.

*

When she paused in the work she was doing at her desk, as she felt entitled to do at her age, which was one for contemplation as well as action, she would sometimes glance at the picture and find her attention fixed on it. After all these years it had acquired a faint power to move her with the sense of time past, of glory departed, even although she knew there had never been glory there to begin with. The India of the picture had never existed outside its gilt frame, and the emotions the picture was meant to conjure up were not much more than smugly pious. And yet now, as always, there was a feeling somewhere in it of shadowy dignity.

It still stirred thoughts in her that she found difficult to analyse. She had devoted her life, in a practical and unimportant way, to trying to prove that fear was evil because it promoted prejudice, that courage was good because it was a sign of selflessness, that ignorance was bad because fear sprang from it, that knowledge was good because the more you knew of the world's complexity the more clearly you saw the insignificance of the part you played. It was, possibly, Miss Crane felt, this concept of personal insignificance which, lying like the dark shadows of the rain clouds behind the gaudy colours of the picture of the Queen and her subjects, informed them with a graver splendour. There was, for Miss Crane, in the attitude of

19

the old Queen on her throne, something ironically reminiscent of the way she herself had sat years ago on a dais, dressed in white muslin; and the message that she was always trying to read into this stylised representation of tribute and matriarchal care was one that conveyed the spirit of dignity without pomp, such as a mother, her own mother, had conveyed to her as a child, and the importance of courageously accepting duties and obligations, not for self-aggrandizement, but in self-denial, in order to promote a wider happiness and well-being, in order to rid the world of the very evils the picture took no account of: poverty, disease, misery, ignorance and injustice.

And it was because (turning late, but perhaps not too late, to her own countrymen) she saw in a young man called Private Clancy, beneath the youthful brash male urge to thrust himself into prominence (and she was not blind to that aspect of his behaviour) a spark of tenderness, an instinct for self-denial that made him see to it that she had a slice of cake and sweetened tea, and, perhaps (she admitted it) because he reminded her physically in his plebeian way of the privileged and handsome Lieutenant Orme (who was killed in the First World War and won a posthumous VC) that she thought of Clancy more often than she thought of his more plodding comrades. The tenderness, she guessed, was wafer-thin, but it was there, she believed; there, for instance, in his cheery attitude to Joseph with whom he cracked good-natured jokes in soldier's Urdu that set the old servant grinning and looking forward to the soldiers' visits; there in his friendship with the boy called Barrett who was clumsy, dull, ugly and unintelligent. In fact it was his friendship with Barrett, as much as his special politeness to her and attitude to Joseph, and the way he and Barrett never missed coming to tea, that caused her to consider what she really meant, in Clancy's case, by tenderness; caused her, indeed, consciously to use that word in her thoughts about him. She knew that boys like Clancy often made friends of those whose physical and mental attributes would show their own superior ones to the best advantage. She knew that in choosing Barrett as what she understood was called a mucker, Clancy was simply conforming to an elementary rule of psychological behaviour. But whereas in the normal way Barrett would have been used by a boy like Clancy as a butt, frequently mocked, defended only if others tried to mock him, she felt that Clancy never used Barrett to such a purpose. While Clancy was present the others never mocked him. Poor Barrett was a primitive. In that spry company he could have stood out like a scarecrow in a field of cocky young green wheat. For Miss Crane, for a while, he did, but then she noticed that for the others he did not, or no longer did, and she thought that this was because over a period, through Clancy's influence, Barrett had been accepted as one of them, that with Clancy's help Barrett had developed facets of his personality that they recognised as those of the norm, and, through Clancy's insistence, no longer noticed facets they must at first have thought foreign.

It was Barrett who – when the rains came and tea had to be indoors, and she gave the soldiers the run of the bungalow and even remembered to provide ashtrays and cigarettes and invite them to smoke rather than spend an hour and a half in an agony of deprivation whose relief she had originally noticed but not easily understood in the way they all lighted up directly they got to the gate on the first leg of the journey home – Barrett who first commented on the picture of the old Queen on her canopied throne, commented on in his dull-ox way, simply by going up to and staring at it, Clancy who spoke for both of them by joining Barrett and then saying, 'It's what they call an allegorical picture, isn't it, Miss Crane?' using the word with a kind of pride in his hard-won education that she found endearing and a bit shattering, because, watching Barrett looking at the picture, she had been on the point of saying, 'It's really an allegory, Mr Barrett,' but had not, remembering that Barrett would not begin to know what an allegory was.

'Yes, it is an allegory,' she said.

'It's a nice old picture,' Clancy said. 'A very nice old picture. Things were different those days, weren't they, Miss Crane?'

She asked him what he meant. He said, 'Well, I mean, sort of simpler, sort of cut and dried.'

For a while Miss Crane considered this, then said, 'More people thought they were. But they weren't really. You could almost say things are simpler now. After all these years there can't be any doubt. India *must* be independent. When the war's over, we've *got* to give her up.'

'Oh,' Clancy said, looking at the picture still, and not at her. 'I really meant about God and that, and people believing. I don't know much about the other thing, except a bit what Congress is and old Gandhi says, and if you ask me, Miss Crane, he's barmy.'

'Barmy's right,' Barrett said dutifully.

Miss Crane smiled.

'I used to have his picture up too. Over there. You can see where it was.'

They turned to look where she pointed: the upright oblong patch of paler distemper, all that was left to Miss Crane of the Mahatma's spectacled, smiling image, the image of a man she had put her faith in which she had now transferred to Mr Nehru and Mr Rajagopalachari who obviously understood the different degrees of tyranny men could exercise and, if there had to be a preference, probably preferred to live a while longer with the imperial degree in order not only to avoid submitting to but to resist the totalitarian. Looking at Clancy and Barrett and imagining in their place a couple of indoctrinated storm-troopers or ancestor-worshippers whose hope of heaven lay in death in battle, she knew which she herself preferred. There was in this choice, she realised, a residual grain of that old instinct to stay within the harbour of the charmed circle, an understanding of the magic of kind safeguarding kind and of the reliance she could place in a boy, for instance, such as Clancy, should poor old Joseph suddenly go berserk and come into the room armed and mad and dangerous to pay her back for imaginary wrongs, or real wrongs she had not personally done him but had done representatively because she was of her race and of her colour, and he could not in his simple rage any longer distinguish between individual and crowd.

But there was as well in her choice, she believed, an intellectual as well as emotional weight tipping the scales in favour of lads like Clancy who, ignorant as they might be of the source and direction of its flow, were borne nevertheless on the surface of waters native to them, waters she had come to think of as constituting the moral drift of history; waters of a river that had to toss aside logs thrown into it by prejudice or carry them with it towards the still invisible because still far-distant sea of perfect harmony where the debris would become water-logged and rotten, finally disintegrate, or be lost, like a matchstick in a majestic ocean. Clancy, after all, was not simply Clancy or Clance, but the son of his father and of his father's fathers, and so long as they stayed at home the English – for all their hypocrisy, or even because of it – had always done as much as any other European race to undam the flow; as much, perhaps a fraction more, because of their isolation, their unique position in the European land-mass, a position that hampered their physical invasion but not the subtler invasion of their minds by the humane concepts of classical and Renaissance Europe that rose into the air and flew like migratory birds to wherever they were perennially welcome.

It was, Miss Crane believed, this ability of Clancy's to hear the faint rumble, which was all that was audible to him of the combined thunder of centuries of flight, that enabled him to say, partly in sorrow, partly in pride – life patently being better for his own kind now than then – 'Things were different those days, sort of simpler, sort of cut and dried.' He felt, however unconsciously, the burden of the freedom to think, to act, worship or not worship, according to his beliefs; the *weight* left on the world by each act of liberation; and if in his relative innocence he read a religious instead of a social message into the picture that provoked his comment, well, Miss Crane told herself, it came to the same thing in the end. God, after all, was no more than a symbol, the supreme symbol of authority here on earth; and Clancy was beginning to understand that the exercise of authority was not an easy business, especially if those who exercised it no longer felt they had heaven on their side.

*

That year the rains were late. They reached Mayapore towards the end of June. The young soldiers suffered from the extreme heat that preceded them, welcomed the first downpours, but by the end of the second week of July were complaining about the damp and the humidity.

Miss Crane had become used to ignoring the weather. In the dry she wore wide-brimmed hats, cotton or woollen dresses and sensible shoes; in the wet, blouses and gaberdine skirts, gumboots when necessary, with a lightweight burberry cape and an oilskin-covered sola topee. For transport in and around Mayapore she rode a ramshackle-looking but sturdy Raleigh bicycle; the car – a ten-year old Ford – was kept for longer runs. In the past the Ford had taken her as far as Calcutta, but she no longer trusted it for that. On the few occasions – once or twice a year – that she needed to go to Calcutta she now went by train, and she went alone because Joseph, aged fifty in a land whose native expectation of life was still less than forty years, felt too old to accompany her. He fretted if away from Mayapore, and pretended that he did not trust the chaukidar to guard the bungalow from thieves. Joseph shopped, did the cooking, looked after the stores and supervised the sweeper, a twelve-year-old girl from the bazaar. In the hot weather he slept on the verandah; in the cold and in the wet, on a camp-bed in the storeroom. He still went regularly to church, on Sunday evenings, and borrowed her bicycle for that purpose. The church – that of the mission, not the church of St Mary in the civil lines – was situated not far from Miss Crane's bungalow, close to the Mandir Gate bridge, one of the two bridges that spanned the river-bed that divided the civil lines from the native town.

On the native town side of the Mandir Gate bridge was to be found the Tirupati temple within whose precincts was a shrine that sheltered the recumbent figure of the sleeping Vishnu. Between the Mandir Gate bridge, on the civil lines side, and the second bridge, the Bibighar bridge, lived the Eurasian community, close at hand to the depots, godowns and offices of the railway station. The railway followed the course of the river-bed. The tracks crossed the roads that led to the bridges. At the bridgeheads on the civil lines side, consequently, there were level-crossings whose gates, when closed to let railway traffic through, sealed both bridges off, making a barrier between the European and the native populations. When the gates of the level-crossings were shut, road traffic coming from the town to the civil lines became congested on the bridges. Miss Crane, returning on her bicycle from the native town, was sometimes held up in such congestions, hemmed in by other cyclists and by pedestrians, clerks going back to work at District Headquarters after lunch in their homes, servants returning to the civil bungalows after shopping in the bazaar for vegetables; tailors on their way to measure a sahib or a sahib's lady who preferred the work and the prices of the bazaar tailors to those of the cantonment tailor, Darwaza Chand; pedlars with boxes on their heads, farmers driving their buffalo carts back to villages in the plains north of the cantonment, women and children going begging or scavenging; and, occasionally, car-borne Europeans, a bank official or businessman, the District Superintendent of Police, the Station Commander, English and Indian Army officers in yellow-painted fifteen-hundred-weight trucks. Sometimes on these journeys she would see and nod to, but never speak to, the white woman – said to be mad – who dressed like a nun, kept a refuge for the sick and the dying and was called Sister Ludmila by the Indians.

Miss Crane used the Mandir Gate bridge into the native town in order to go from her bungalow to the Chillianwallah Bazaar school, a journey that took her past the church of the mission and the principal mission school, over the bridge, past the Tirupati temple, through narrow dirty streets of open shop fronts, past the gateway of the Chillianwallah bazaar itself where fish, meat and vegetables were sold, and into an even narrower street, a dark alleyway between old, crumbling houses, down whose centre ran an open water-duct. The alley was a cul-de-sac. At its closed-in head were the high wall and arched gateway of the bazaar school. The gateway opened into a narrow mud compound where the children played. Stunted banana trees gave a little shade in the early mornings and late afternoons. The mud was reddish brown, baked hard by the sun and pressed flat by the pupils' bare feet. Even in the wet monsoon an afternoon's sunshine would dry and harden it to its old concrete consistency.

The Chillianwallah Bazaar schoolhouse was a two-storey building with steps up to a verandah with shuttered balconied windows above the verandah roof. At least seventy years old, the house had been the property of Mr Chillianwallah, a Parsee who left Bombay and made a fortune in Mayapore out of government building contracts in the 1890s. Mr Chillianwallah had built the barracks in the civil lines, the church of St Mary, the bungalow presently lived in by the Deputy Commissioner, and – in a philanthropic fit – the bazaar in the native town. Still in the throes of that fit he presented the house in the alley to the church of St Mary, and until the mission built a more substantial schoolhouse in the civil lines, opposite the mission church, the house in the alley had been its only foothold on the shaky ladder of conversion. For several years after the building of the larger mission school in the civil lines in 1906, the Chillianwallah house and compound had been used by the mission as a place of refuge for the old and sick and dying but as the civil lines school became filled to overflowing with the children of Eurasians, and the numbers of Indian children attending fell away, the mission reopened the house in the alley for lessons in the hope of regaining the foothold they had virtually lost, and the old and sick and dying had some thirty years to wait for the coming of Sister Ludmila.

The Chillianwallah Bazaar school was now the second of Miss Crane's responsibilities in Mayapore District. Her third was in Dibrapur, near the coalmines; her first the larger school in the civil lines, opposite the mission church, where in co-operation with a succession of English teachers whose qualifications to teach were more apparent than her own and whose religious convictions put hers to shame, she supervised the work of the Anglo-Indian class mistresses and taught mathematics and English to the older Eurasian and Indian Christian girls. From this school most of the pupils passed into the Government Higher School whose foundation in 1920 had done much to undermine the mission's influence.

The teacher at the Chillianwallah Bazaar school, whose pupils were all Indian, was a middle-aged, tall, thin, dark-skinned Madrassi Christian, Mr F. Narayan: the F for Francis, after St Francis of Assisi. In his spare time, of which he had a great deal, and to augment his income, of which he had

24

little, Mr Narayan wrote what he called Topics for the local English language weekly newspaper, *The Mayapore Gazette*. In addition, his services were available as a letter-writer, and these were services used by both his Hindu and Muslim neighbours. He could converse fluently in Urdu and Hindi and the local vernacular, and wrote an excellent Urdu and Hindi script, as well as his native Tamil and acquired Roman–English. In Europe, Miss Crane thought, a man of his accomplishments might have gone a long way – in the commercial rather than the pedagogic field. She suspected him, because Joseph had hinted at it, of selling contraceptives to Christian and progressive Hindu families. She did not disapprove, but was amused because Mr Narayan himself had an ever-pregnant wife, and a large, noisy, undisciplined family of boys and girls.

His wife Mary Narayan, as dark-skinned as himself, was a girl he brought back one year from leave in Madras. He said she was a Christian too, but Miss Crane doubted it, never having seen her go to church but instead, on more than one occasion, entering and leaving the Tirupati temple. He said she was now twenty-five, which Miss Crane doubted as well. She wouldn't have been surprised if Mrs Narayan had only been thirteen or fourteen at the time Francis Narayan married her.

Mr and Mrs Narayan lived in the upstairs rooms of the Chillianwallah Bazaar school. Their children, three girls and two boys to date (apart from the one still suckling whose sex she had somehow never made a note of) sat on the front benches in the schoolroom and were, Miss Crane had begun to notice, virtually the only regular attendants. On Sunday mornings, Mr Narayan and his two eldest children – one boy, John Krishna, and a girl, Kamala Magdalene – left the house in the Chillianwallah Bazaar in a cycle-tonga driven by a convert called Peter Paul Akbar Hossain, precariously negotiated the water-duct down the cul-de-sac, crossed the Mandir Gate bridge, and attended the service at the mission church where Mr Narayan also assisted with the collection. His wife, he said, had to stay at home to look after the younger children. Miss Crane took this information, too, with a pinch of salt. She wondered whether it might be interesting to stand outside the Tirupati temple on a Sunday morning to see whether Mrs Narayan's absence from the mission church was due to the stronger call of Lord Venkataswara, the god of the temple whose image was taken from the sanctuary once a year and carried down to the banks of the river to bless all those from whom he received the prescribed sacrifice.

But on Sunday mornings Miss Crane was otherwise engaged. She went to the service at St Mary's, cycling there rain or shine along the tidy, tree-lined, geometrically laid out roads of the cantonment, holding an umbrella up if the weather was inclement. Miss Crane's umbrella was a cantonment joke. In the rains, reaching the side door, parking the Raleigh, she worked the canopy vigorously up and down to shake the drops from it. This flapping bat-wing noise was audible to those in the pews closest to the door, the pews on the lectern side of the church, whose English occupants smiled at the unmistakable sounds of Miss Crane's arrival, much as years

25

before other people in another church had smiled when Mr Grant offered up his prayers.

The other congregational joke about Miss Crane was over her tendency to fall asleep during the sermon, which she did with great discretion, maintaining a ramrod back and squared shoulders, so that only her closed eyes gave the game away, and even her closed eyes seemed, initially, no more than a likely sign of her preoccupation with images conjured by the chaplain's words which, for a moment, she thought of having a closer personal look at. Her eyes closed, then opened; presently closed again, only to open again. The third time that the lids snapped shut – abruptly, never slowly or heavily – they usually stayed shut; and Miss Crane was then away; and only a slight backward jerk of her head when the chaplain said Now God the Father God the Son and the congregation exhaled a corporate sigh of relief, proved that she hadn't heard a word and that the eyes she now just as abruptly opened had been closed in sleep.

Her violent shaking of the umbrella – not unlike the sound of alighting angry angels – and her firm fast sleep during the service, her reputation for outspokenness, her seeming imperviousness to the little drops of conde-scension falling from those who, in the way these things were reckoned, were above her in social station – all these had contributed to the idea the Mayapore English had of her as a woman whose work for the missionaries had broadened rather than narrowed her. There was certainly nothing sanctimonious about Edwina Crane. The somewhat grudging personal regard she was held in was increased by her refusal to be browbeaten on the women's committees she sat on. Since the war began the English ladies of Mayapore had not been slow to recognise the need and answer the call for committees: knitting-bee committees, troops entertainment committees, social welfare committees, Guides recruitment committees, War Week committees, committees to direct the voluntary work done in the hospital and the Greenlawns nursing home and by the ladies who had in mind the welfare of the children of Indian mothers working on the road extension and proposed airstrip out at Banyaganj and in the British–Indian Electrical factory. Called in originally to help with the Guides recruitment by Mrs White, the wife of the Deputy Commissioner, she was now a member of the social welfare, the voluntary hospital workers and the Indian mothers committees and if among themselves the ladies spoke of her in tones that would have suggested to a stranger that Miss Crane was only a mission school teacher and as many rungs below them as it was socially possible to be and still be recognised, they themselves collectively understood that actual denigration was not intended, and individually respected her even if they thought her 'cranky about the natives'.

It was the wife of the Deputy Commissioner who was responsible for creating an image of Miss Crane which the ladies of Mayapore had now come to regard as definitive of her. 'Edwina Crane,' Mrs White said, 'has obviously missed her vocation. Instead of wasting her time in the missions and thumping the old tub about the iniquities of the British Raj and the intolerable burdens borne by what her church calls our dark brethren, she should have been headmistress of a good school for girls, back in the old home counties.'

Until the war Miss Crane had not gone out much in European society. Occasional dinners with the chaplain and his wife (it was the chaplain who was responsible for calling the station's attention to Miss Crane's tendency to sleep during his sermons), an annual invitation to the Deputy Commissioner's garden party and once a year to his bungalow during the cold months when his wife 'dined the station' – these had been the main events on her white social calendar, indeed still were, but her work on the committees had widened the circle of English women who were ready to stop and talk to her in the cantonment bazaar or invite her to coffee or tea, and the particular dinner at the Deputy Commissioner's to which Miss Crane now went was the one to which higher ranking English were invited, and eminent Indians such as Lady Chatterjee, widow of Sir Nello Chatterjee who had founded the Mayapore Technical College.

For these full-dress occasions, Miss Crane wore her brown silk: a dinner gown that revealed the sallow-skinned cushion of flesh below her now prominent collar-bones. She decorated the dress with a posy of artificial flowers, cut and shaped out of purple and crimson velvet. The dress had half sleeves. She wore elbow-length gloves of brown lisle silk so cut at the wrists that the hands of the gloves could be removed to reveal her own bony brown hands. Her greying hair, for these occasions, would be combed more loosely above her forehead and gathered into a coil that hung a fraction lower than usual at the back of her neck. Her fingers, unadorned, were short-nailed, thin but supple. From her, as her table-companions knew, came a scent of geranium and mothballs, the former of which grew fainter as the evening progressed, and the latter stronger, until both were lost for them in the euphoria of wine and brandy.

On her wrist before and after dinner, and on her lap during it, she carried a home-made sachet handbag of brown satin lined with crimson silk. The brown satin did not quite match, nor did it complement, the brown of her dress. In the bag which could be drawn open and shut on brown silk cords was a silver powder compact – which was the source of the geranium smell – a plain lawn handkerchief, the ignition key of the Ford, a few soiled rupee notes, her diary of engagements, a silver pencil with a red silk tassel, and a green bottle of smelling salts. At the DC's dinners Miss Crane drank everything she was offered: sherry, white burgundy, claret and brandy, and always smelled the salts before setting off home in the car, to clear her head, which Mrs White had been relieved to find was a strong enough one for her not to fear the possibility of Miss Crane being overcome and letting the side down.

Reaching home, driving the Ford into the corrugated iron garage beside the bungalow, she would be met by old Joseph and scolded for being late. In the house she drank the milk that he had warmed and re-warmed, ate the biscuits he had put out on a doily-covered plate, took the aspirin he said

27

she needed, and retired, answering his 'God bless you, madam' with her own 'Goodnight', entered her room and slowly, tiredly, got rid of the long skirted encumbrance which in the morning Joseph would air and put back in the chest where she kept her few bits of finery and spare linen; put it there proudly because his mistress was a Mem in spite of the bicycle, the topee and the gumboots and her work which took her into the stinking alleys of the heathen, native town.

*

By this summer of 1942 Miss Crane had been in Mayapore for seven years, and during them she had seen many Europeans come and go. The Deputy Commissioner and his wife, Mr and Mrs White, had been there only four years, since 1938, the year that the previous DC, an irritable widower called Stead, had retired, nursing a grievance that he had never been promoted Divisional Commissioner or sent to the Secretariat. The Assistant Commissioner and his wife, Mr and Mrs Poulson, had come to Mayapore shortly afterwards. The Poulsons were friends of the Whites; in fact White had especially asked for Poulson to be sent to Mayapore. Ronald Merrick, the District Superintendent of Police, was a bachelor, a young man sometimes over-anxious, it was said, to excel in his duties, quarrelsome at the club, but sought after by the unmarried girls. He had been in the town only two years. Only the District and Sessions Judge, who together with the DC and the Superintendent of Police formed the triumvirate of civil authority in the District, had been in Mayapore as long as Miss Crane, but he was an Indian. His name was Menen and Miss Crane had never met him to talk to. Menen was a friend of Lady Chatterjee who lived on the Bibighar bridge side of the civil lines in the old MacGregor House, so called because rebuilt by a Scotsman of that name on the foundations of the house built by a prince in the days when Mayapore was a Native State. The raja had been deposed in 1814 and the state annexed by the East India Company, absorbed into the province of whose score of districts it now ranked as second in size and importance.

Although Lady Chatterjee was the leader of Indian society in Mayapore, Miss Crane scarcely knew her. She met her at the Deputy Commissioner's but had never been to the MacGregor House which, it was said, was the one place where English and Indians came together as equals, or at least without too much caution on the part of the Indians or too much embarrassment on the part of the English. Miss Crane did not actually regret never going to the MacGregor House. She thought Lady Chatterjee overwesternised, a bit of a snob, socially and intellectually; amusing enough to listen to at the DC's dinner-table but not in the drawing-room afterwards, when the women were alone for a while and Lady Chatterjee asked questions of them which Miss Crane thought were calculated to expose them as lacking in social background at home or cosmopolitan experience abroad, finally lapsing into dignified silence and letting the

English small-talk get under way without attempting to contribute to it, content to wait for the men to rejoin them when she would again have the opportunity of sparkling and making everybody laugh. The English women found Lady Chatterjee easier-going if they had the men with them. They were all, Miss Crane concluded, rather afraid of her. And Lady Chatterjee, Miss Crane thought, was – although not afraid of them – certainly on her guard, as stuffy in her own way as the English women. For Miss Crane she seemed to have no feelings whatsoever; a disinterest that might have been due to her discovery by direct questioning at the first dinner they attended together that Miss Crane had no degree, in fact no qualifications to teach other than the rough and ready training she had received years ago in Lahore after leaving the service of the Nesbitt-Smiths. On the other hand, Lady Chatterjee's indifference was equally probably due to a disapproval of missions and missionaries and of anyone connected with them. Westernised though she was, Lady Chatterjee was of Rajput stock, a Hindu of the old ruling-warrior caste. Short, thin, with greying hair cut in European style, seated upright on the edge of a sofa, with the free end of her saree tight-wound round her shoulders, and her remarkably dark eyes glittering at you, her beaky Rajput nose and pale skin proclaiming both authority and breeding, she looked every inch a woman whom only the course of history had denied the opportunity of fully exercising the power she was born to.

Widowed some years earlier by the death of a husband who had been older than she and by whom she had had no children, an Indian who was knighted for his services to the Crown and his philanthropy to his own countrymen, Lady Chatterjee, so far as Miss Crane was concerned, now seemed to be continuing what must have been Sir Nello's policy of getting the best out of both worlds. She thought this in rather bad taste. Friends in the old days of Sir Henry Manners and his wife who, for a time, had been Governor and Governor's lady of the province, Lady Chatterjee still went annually to Rawalpindi or Kashmir to stay with Lady Manners, now a widow like herself; and a Manners girl, Daphne, a niece of Sir Henry, rather plain, big-boned and as yet unmarried, was working in the hospital at Mayapore for the war effort and living in the MacGregor House as Lady Chatterjee's guest. It was, no doubt, Lady Chatterjee's standing with distinguished English people like old Lady Manners as much as the position she enjoyed in Mayapore as Sir Nello's widow and as member of the board of Governors of the Technical College, member of the committee of the purdah hospital in the native town, that caused her to be treated with such outward consideration by the leaders of the English colony. With the DC and his wife she was on Christian name terms. (She had not been with Stead, their predecessor in office.) She was always welcome at the DC's bungalow. She played bridge there and Mrs White played bridge at the MacGregor House. But whatever from the Whites' point of view in this cordiality ranked as part of their duty to be seen as well as felt to be the representatives of a government that had at heart the well-being of all the people living in the district, Indian or British, there certainly seemed to be from all accounts a genuine sympathy and understanding between them and Sir Nello's widow.

But – and this was what interested Miss Crane – at the MacGregor House, said to be equally welcome were Indians: barristers, teachers, doctors, lawyers, municipal officers, higher civil servants, among whom were men of the local Congress Party sub-committee, and men not of that committee but known for the possibly even greater vehemence of their anti-British views.

How often such men found themselves at the MacGregor House face to face with the liberal English, Miss Crane did not know; neither did she know whether Lady Chatterjee would hope by such confrontations to dampen their anti-British ardour or inspire even more radical feelings in the hearts of the liberal English. All she knew was that from her own point of view Lady Chatterjee appeared to lack the true liberal instinct herself. She admitted, though, that behind her lack of empathy for Lady Chatterjee there were probably the particular kinds of blindness and deafness that followed social rebuff. Admitting this, she also admitted a more fundamental truth.

And that truth was that after virtually a lifetime of service in the mission schools she was lonely. Since the death of old Miss de Silva who had been the teacher in Dibrapur, there was not a man or a woman in Mayapore, in India, anywhere, British or Indian, she could point to as a friend of the sort to whom she could have talked long and intimately. When, in the May of 1942, Mr Gandhi demanded that the British should leave India – leave her, he said, 'to God, or to anarchy,' which meant leaving her to the Japanese – and she took down his portrait and her Indian ladies stopped coming to tea, she saw that the bungalow would not be particularly empty without them because they had not looked on her as a person, but only as a woman who represented something they felt ought to be represented. She also saw that she herself had looked on the teas not as friendly but as meaningful gatherings. There was no one else in Mayapore to drop by, nowhere in Mayapore she could casually drop by at herself. Such acts of dropping by as were undertaken by herself or others were for reasons other than human intimacy. Now the soldiers came in place of the ladies, on a different day, Wednesday and not Tuesday (as though to keep Tuesdays free in case the ladies underwent a change of heart). And in the case of the soldiers there had probably been a notice put up in the Regimental Institute: 'Personnel wishing to avail themselves of an invitation to tea on Wednesday afternoons at the home of Miss E. Crane, superintendent of the Church of England Mission Schools (Mayapore District) should give their names to their Unit Welfare Officer.'

Sometimes she wondered to what extent her decision to entertain the soldiers had been due to an instinct finally to find refuge in that old privileged circle that surrounded and protected the white community. Her social and political beliefs were, she could not help realising, by the standards of the present day, somehow old-fashioned, over-simplified. Lacking a real education she had matured slowly and had, she supposed, grasped hold of the ideas of a generation previous to her own as if they were mint-new. Events had gone ahead of her, taking with them younger people who were, in their opinions, in advance of her. She understood, it seemed, little of practical present-day politics. This comparative ignorance defined the gulf that separated her not only from the younger liberal English people such as she met at the Deputy Commissioner's and whom she found it difficult to talk to, but from Lady Chatterjee who, lending half an ear to what she might have to say about Indian independence and the sacred duty of the British to grant it, conveyed at once an impression of having heard it all too long ago for it to be worth hearing again.

'I am,' Miss Crane told herself, 'a relic of the past,' mentally crossed out 'of the past' as a redundant clause, and looked up at the picture of the old Queen, stared at it waiting for it to reveal something simple but irrefutable that perhaps the MacGregor House set had lost sight of. What seemed to her so extraordinary was that although her own ladies had stopped coming to tea the parties at the MacGregor House continued. The English community apparently saw nothing wrong in this even though they knew they now had their backs to a wall that the Indians seemed set on removing, brick by brick. It was, they said, the duty of people like the DC and his wife to keep their ears to the ground, and where better to do that than at the MacGregor House? It was rumoured, for instance, that on instructions from Government the DC had already prepared a list of Congress party members in the Mayapore district who would have to be arrested under the Defence of India Rules if Congress voted in favour of Mr Gandhi's civil disobedience resolution, a resolution under which the British would be called upon to leave India on pain of finding the realm impossible to defend, their armies on the Assam–Burma frontier impossible to feed, clothe, arm or support; impossible, for the simple reason that there would be no one who was willing to operate the railways, the posts and telegraphs, the docks, the depots, the factories, the mines, the banks, the offices, or any of the administrative and productive services of a nation they had exploited for over two hundred years and, by failing to defend Burma, brought to the point of having to succumb to yet another set of imperialistic warmongers.

Miss Crane feared such an uprising. For her the only hope for the country she loved lay in the coming together at last of its population and its rulers as equal partners in a war to the death against totalitarianism. If Congress had not resigned from the provincial ministries in 1939 in a fit of pique because the Viceroy without going through the motions of consulting them had declared war in the name of the King-Emperor on India's behalf, and if Mr Gandhi had not had a brainstorm and seized the moment of Britain's greatest misfortune to press home his demands for political freedom, if things had been left to Mr Nehru who obviously found Gandhi an embarrassment and to Mr Rajagopalachari (who had headed the provincial ministry in Madras and had wanted to arm and train the entire nation to fight the Japanese) then at this moment, Miss Crane believed, an Indian cabinet would have been in control in Delhi, Lord Linlithgow would have been Governor-General of a virtually independent dominion and all the things that she had hoped and prayed for to happen in India would have happened, and the war would be under process of firm and thoughtful prosecution.

Sometimes Miss Crane woke up in the night and lay sleepless, listening to the rain, and was alarmed, conscious of dangers that were growing and which people were preparing to face but not to understand, so that virtually they were not facing them at all. We only understand, she said, the way to meet them, or, sometimes, the way to avert them.

But on this occasion they were not averted.

*

In the first week of August Miss Crane caught one of her rare colds. She had never believed in running risks with her health. She telephoned to the school in Dibrapur to say that she would not be coming on the Thursday but would come on the following Saturday. Then she went home and put herself to bed and sweated the chill out. By the weekend she felt perfectly fit again. And so on the morning of the 8th of August – on the day on which Congress were to vote on Mr Gandhi's resolution – Miss Crane set off in her Ford the seventy-odd miles to Dibrapur.

The school in Dibrapur, the third of Miss Crane's responsibilities in Mayapore District, was situated in comparative isolation, on the road midway between the village of Kotali and the town of Dibrapur itself. Dibrapur lay on the southern border of the Mayapore District. There was no church, no European population. The Dibrapur mines, so-called, were now administered from Aligarh in the adjoining district of the province.

Most of the children who attended the school came from Kotali. They had only three miles to walk. If they went to the school run by the District Board in a neighbouring village the distance was four miles. The mission schoolhouse had been built in its isolated position years ago so that it could serve the surrounding villages as well as Dibrapur. Since the expansion of the Government's own educational programme and the setting up of primary schools by District Boards the mission school had not lost many pupils for the simple reason that it had never attracted many. The Kotali children came because it was nearer and a few children still came from Dibrapur because at the mission school the English language was taught. The Dibrapur children were usually the sons – very occasionally the daughters – of shopkeepers, men who fancied their male offspring's chances as government contractors or petty civil servants and who knew that the gift of conversing fluently in English was therefore invaluable. And so, from Dibrapur, up to half a dozen boys and two or three girls would tramp the three miles every day to the school of the mission, carrying with them, like the children from Kotali, their food-tins and their canvas bags. In the school of the mission there were no chappattis; only instruction, good intentions and medicine for upset stomachs.

Having stood now for nearly thirty years the Dibrapur schoolhouse was in constant need of some kind of repair, and, in the summer of 1942, certainly a coat of whitewash that it would have to wait for until the end of the rains. What it most urgently needed was attention to the roof and during this summer Miss Crane's thoughts in connexion with the school had been almost exclusively concerned with the estimates periodically obtained by Mr Chaudhuri, the teacher, and the Allocation, which in crude terms meant the money available. So far Mr Chaudhuri had failed to obtain an estimate from any local builder that came within sight of balancing what had to be spent with what there was to spend. He did not seem to have much of a head for business or talent for bargaining. 'We need,' Miss Crane had been thinking, 'another five hundred rupees. We need, in fact, more; not only a repair to the roof, but a new roof, in fact practically a new school.' Sometimes she could not help wondering whether they also needed a new teacher-in-charge, but always put the thought out of her head as uncharitable, as one sparked off by personal prejudice. The fact that for one reason or another she and Mr Chaudhuri had never hit it off should not, she realised, blind her to his remarkable qualities as a teacher.

Mr Chaudhuri had held the Dibrapur appointment for not quite a year. His predecessor, old Miss de Silva, a Eurasian woman from Goa, had been dead for just a bit longer. With Mary de Silva's death Miss Crane had lost the last person in the world who called her Edwina. On her first visit to Dibrapur as superintendent, seven years ago, the older woman – fat, white-haired, ponderous, and with a voice as dark and forthcoming as her extraordinary popping black eyes – had said, 'You got the job *I* wanted. My name's Mary de Silva. My mother was as black as your hat.'

'Mine's Edwina Crane,' Miss Crane said, shaking the pudgy, man-strong hand, 'I didn't *know* you wanted the job, and my mother's been dead for longer than I care to remember.'

'Well in that case I'll call you Edwina, if you don't mind. I'm too old to bow and scrape to a *new* superintendent. And also if you don't mind we'll start by talking about the bloody roof.'

So they had talked about the roof, and the walls, and the tube-well that wanted resinking in another place, and then about the children, and Mary de Silva's intention to send, by hook or crook, a boy called Balarachama Rao to the Government Higher School in Mayapore. 'His parents won't hear of it. But *I'll* hear of it. Where do *you* stand, Edwina Crane?'

'In matters of this sort, Mary de Silva,' she replied, 'I stand to do what the teachers on the spot advise me should be done.'

'Then find a decent lodging in Mayapore for Master Balarachama. That's the snag. He's got no place to live if he's admitted. The parents say they've no relatives there. Which is nonsense. Indians have relatives *every*where. I

33

ought to know.' Her skin was no sallower than little Miss Williams's had been.

Miss Crane found lodgings in Mayapore for Balarachama and spent a month, which is to say most of her time in four weekly visits to Dibrapur, persuading his parents to let him go. When she had at last succeeded Mary de Silva said, 'I'm not going to thank you. It was your duty. And it was mine. But come back now and help me break into the bottle of rum I've been saving since Christmas.' So she went back with Mary de Silva to the bungalow the Chaudhuris now lived in, half a mile down the road from the school, and drank rum, heard the story of Mary de Silva's life and told her own. There had been many other occasions of drinking rum and lime in Mary de Silva's living-room, discreetly, but in enough quantity for tongues to be loosened and for Miss Crane to feel that here, in Dibrapur, with Mary de Silva, she had come home again after a lifetime travelling. For six years she went weekly to Dibrapur, and stayed the night with Mary de Silva. 'It's not necessary you know,' Miss de Silva said, 'but it's nice. The last superintendent only came once a month and never stayed the night. That was nice too.'

At the end of the six years, when the roof of the school had been repaired once and needed repairing again, and the new tube-well had been sunk, the walls patched and painted twice, there came the day she reached the schoolhouse and found it closed, and, driving on to Mary de Silva's bungalow, found the old teacher in bed, lying quietly, temporarily deserted by the servant who had gone down to Dibrapur to fetch the doctor. Miss de Silva was mumbling to herself. When she had finished what she had to say, and nodded, her eyes focused on Miss Crane. She smiled and said, 'Well, Edwina. I'm for it. You might see to the roof again,' then closed her eyes and died as if someone had simply disconnected a battery.

After seeing Mary de Silva's body safely and quickly transported to Mayapore and buried in the churchyard of St Mary, Miss Crane put the task of finding a temporary teacher into the hands of Mr Narayan to give him something to do, and went back to Dibrapur to reopen the school and keep it going until the temporary arrived. She also wrote to the headquarters of the mission to report Miss de Silva's death and the steps she had taken to keep the school going until a permanent appointment was made. She recommended a Miss Smithers, with whom she had worked in Bihar. She did not get Miss Smithers. She got first of all a cousin of Mr Narayan who drank, and then, from Calcutta, Mr D. R. Chaudhuri, BA, BSc – qualifications which not only astonished her but made her suspicious. Mission headquarters had been rather astounded too, so she gathered from their letter, but not suspicious. Mr Chaudhuri did not profess to be a Christian, they told her, on the other hand he did not profess any other religion. He had resigned from an appointment in a Government training college and had asked the mission to employ him in the humblest teaching capacity. They had offered him several posts, all of which he declined until, suddenly, the post in Dibrapur fell vacant, and this, from their description, had appealed to him as 'the right kind of beginning'. 'He will be wasted in Dibrapur, of course, and is unlikely to be with you for long,' they wrote, in confidence. 'He will be accompanied by his wife, so perhaps you would arrange to see that the late Miss de Silva's bungalow is made ready for them. We understand he has private but limited means. You will find Mr Chaudhuri a reserved young man and, by and large, unwilling to discuss the reasons for his decision to abandon a more distinguished academic career. We have, however, satisfied ourselves from interviews with Mr Chaudhuri and inquiries outside, that his wish to teach young children in the villages arises from a genuine sympathy for the depressed classes of his own race and a genuine belief that educated men like himself should more often be prepared to sacrifice their private interests in the interest of the country as a whole. It appears, too, that he feels his work in this direction should be with schools such as our own, not because of the religious basis of our teaching but because he has a low opinion of the local government primary schools and thinks of them as staffed by teachers to whom politics are more important than any educational consideration.'

In spite of this promising situation there had been between herself and Mr Chaudhuri right from the beginning what Miss Crane thought of as an almost classical reserve – classical in the sense that she felt they each suspected the other of hypocrisy, of unrevealed motives, of hiding under the thinnest of liberal skins deeply conservative natures, so that all conversations they had that were not strictly to do with the affairs of the school seemed to be either double-edged or meaningless.

For weeks Miss Crane fought against her own reserve. She did not minimise her grief for and memories of Miss de Silva when it came to analysing the possible causes of it. Knowing that Mr Chaudhuri had been told she visited Miss de Silva once a week, she visited him once a week too and stayed overnight in old Miss de Silva's bungalow, now unrecognisable as the same place, furnished as it was by Mr and Mrs Chaudhuri in the westernised-Indian style. She did this in case he should misunderstand her not doing it; at the same time she was aware that he might have taken her visits as a sign of her not trusting in his competence. She continued the visits in the hope that eventually she would feel at home there once more.

Tall, wiry, and square-shouldered, Mr Chaudhuri had the fine-boned face of a Bengali, was handsome in a way Miss Crane recognised but did not personally consider handsome. With every feature and plane of his face sharp and prominent and in itself indicative of strength, the whole face, for her, still suggested weakness – and yet not weakness, because even weakness required to be conveyed as a special expression, and Mr Chaudhuri's face was capable of conveying only two: blank indifference or petulant annoyance. His smile, she saw, would have been pleasant if it had ever got up into his eyes as well.

His English was excellent, typically Indian in its inflexions and rhythms, but fluent as spoken and crisply correct when written. He also taught it very well. He made Mr Narayan, by comparison, look and sound like a bazaar comedian. And yet, with Mr Narayan, Miss Crane found conversation easy and direct. Not so with Mr Chaudhuri. There had been a period in her career when, highly sensitive herself to the sensitivity of Indians who knew the English language, even some of its subtlest nuances, but seldom if ever the rough and tumble of its everyday idiom, she had inured herself to the temptation to say things like, Don't be silly; or, Nonsense. For some years now, though, she had not bothered to put a curb on her tongue, and wished she never had. When you chose your words the spontaneity went out of the things you wanted to say. She had learned to hate the feeling it gave her of unnaturalness. If she had always been as outspoken as she was now, she thought, then even if she had made enemies she might also have made friends. By developing self-confidence in the manner of her speech earlier in her career she believed she might have developed an inner confidence as well, the kind that communicated itself to people of another race as evidence of sincerity, trustworthiness. Too late for that, the outspokenness, she knew, often looked to Indians like the workaday thoughtless rudeness of any Englishwoman. Only English-women themselves admired it, although with men like Mr Narayan she could conduct a slanging match and feel no bones were broken. With Mr Chaudhuri she found herself reverting to the soft phrase, the cautious sentiment, and then spoiling whatever effect this had had by letting slip words that came more easily to her. She had said Nonsense! to him early on in their association and had seen at once that her tenuous hold on his willingness to co-operate was temporarily lost. From this unfortunate set-back they had never made much advance. If Mrs Chaudhuri had been a more sophisticated woman Miss Crane felt she might have made progress with Mr Chaudhuri through intimate contact with his wife, but apart from a High School education and her years spent at the feet of a music teacher, Mrs Chaudhuri was uninstructed in the ways of the sophisticated world and had a remarkably old-fashioned notion of the role of a wife.

*

Before Miss Crane set out in the Ford for Dibrapur on the morning of the 8th of August Joseph tried to dissuade her from going. He said there would be trouble. He had heard rumours.

She said, 'We are always hearing rumours. Does that stop you from doing your work? Of course not. I have work in Dibrapur. So to Dibrapur I must go.'

He offered to come with her.

'And who will look after the house, then?' she asked. 'No, Joseph, for both of us it is business as usual.'

It was business as usual all the way to Dibrapur, which she reached at four o'clock in the afternoon, having stopped on the way to eat her sandwiches and drink coffee from the flask. In the villages there were people who shouted Quit India! and others who asked for baksheesh.

Driving slowly to avoid hitting cows and buffalo, dogs, hens and children, she smiled and waved at the people whatever they shouted.

In Kotali, the last village before the schoolhouse, she stopped the car and spoke to some of the mothers whose children went to Mr Chaudhuri for lessons. The mothers said nothing about trouble. She did not mention it herself. They would know better than she what was to be expected. Kotali looked very peaceful. Leaving the village behind she met the children making their way home, carrying their food-tins and canvas bags. Their average age was eight. She stopped the car again and distributed some of the boiled sweets.

Reaching the schoolhouse she drove into the compound. Here there were trees and shade. She found Mr Chaudhuri tidying up the schoolroom. 'Is there any news?' she asked, rather hoping that if trouble were coming and this were to be an eleventh hour it would be made productive of something more than politeness.

'News?' he replied. 'What sort of news, Miss Crane?'

'Of the Congress vote.'

'Oh, that,' he said. 'No, I have not listened.'

In the room of the schoolhouse that served as an office there was a radio. Sometimes Mr Chaudhuri used the radio as a medium of instruction. She turned it on now. There was music. She switched off. It was European music. The only music she ever listened to when with the Chaudhuris was Indian classical music.

'Perhaps, however,' he said, 'there is news of the roof?'

'No, there isn't. I've checked through all the estimates again and there's not one that's low enough. Can't you find someone to do it cheaper?'

'I have tried all who are willing to do it at all. If we wait much longer even the low estimates will go up. And these people cannot work for nothing.'

She was about to say, Well, that's not what I'm asking, I'm not asking them to do it for nothing. She would have said that to Mr Narayan. She held back from saying it to Mr Chaudhuri. Instead she said, 'No. Well, come on. I'd like a cup of tea.' And even that sounded brusque.

Mr Chaudhuri closed the school, padlocked the door, and joined her in the Ford. At his bungalow tea was not ready. He did not apologise; but while she was resting on her bed, waiting to be called, she heard him taking his wife to task for not ordering things better. When tea was ready it was served on the verandah. Mrs Chaudhuri did not join them. She moved between kitchen and verandah, carrying things with her own hands, smiling but saying little, and when there seemed to be nothing more that they wanted stood in the shadow of the doorway, pretending not to be there, but watching her husband for the slightest indication from him that something had been forgotten, or was wrong, or needed to be replenished.

'It is *this*,' Miss Crane often told herself, 'this awful feudal attitude to his wife that makes it difficult for me to like him.'

But it was not that. In the evenings Mrs Chaudhuri sometimes sang to them. Directly she was seated cross-legged on the rush mat, gently

37

supporting the onion-shaped tamboura, she became a different woman; self-assured, holding her bony body gracefully erect, not unlike the way Lady Chatterjee held hers when sitting on a sofa at the DC's. After Mrs Chaudhuri had sung a couple of songs Mr Chaudhuri would say, almost under his breath, 'It is enough,' and then Mrs Chaudhuri would rise, take up the tamboura and disappear into an inner room. And Miss Crane knew that Mr and Mrs Chaudhuri loved one another, that Mr Chaudhuri was not a tyrant, that the woman herself preferred the old ways to the new because for her the old ways were a discipline and a tradition, a means of acquiring and maintaining peace of mind and inner stillness.

On this night, the night of August the 8th, which Miss Crane felt in her bones was a special night, one of crisis, she longed to make Mr Chaudhuri talk, to find the key to his reticence, a way of breaking down his reserve. It would have been easier for her if he had been as old-fashioned in his manners as his wife, because then their association would have been of an altogether different kind. But he was not. He was westernised. He wore European clothes at the school and, at least when she was staying with them, at home. They ate at a table, seated on hardwood chairs and talked about art and music and the affairs of the school, but never politics. There was a cloth on the table, there were knives and forks to eat with, and ordinary china plates. At dinner Mrs Chaudhuri sat with them, although she took almost no part in the conversation and ate practically nothing. A woman servant waited on them, the same woman who did the cooking. Miss Crane would have felt more comfortable if the woman had been an untouchable because that would have proved, in the Chaudhuris, emancipation from the rigidity of caste. But the woman was a Brahmin.

They had coffee in the room that overlooked the verandah, in which she and Miss de Silva had sat on old cane chairs, but where they now sat on low divans with their feet on Kashmiri rugs. Miss de Silva had been content with an oil lamp; Mr Chaudhuri had rigged up an electric light that ran from a generator in the compound. They sat in the unflattering light of one naked electric bulb around which moths and insects danced their nightly ritual of primitive desire for what might burn their wings. At this point, between the eating and the singing, Mrs Chaudhuri always left them, presumably to help or supervise the woman in the kitchen.

Tonight Miss Crane drank the bitter coffee, more conscious than ever of the unsympathetic silence that always fell directly she and Mr Chaudhuri were alone. She longed to know the news but accepted in its place as proof that in one respect at least the night was normal: the croaking – beyond the verandah – of the frogs who had come out in their invisible battalions after the evening rains.

She wanted to say: Mr Chaudhuri, what honestly is the school to you? but did not. To say that to a man was to question a course which, to judge by his actions, he had set his mind, even his heart on.

'You are a fool, Edwina Crane,' she told herself later as she undressed, preparing for bed. 'You have lost another opportunity, because hearts are no longer set on anything and minds function as the bowels decide, and Mr Chaudhuri would talk if you knew the questions to ask and the way to ask them. But he is of that younger generation of men and women who have seen what I have seen, understood what I understand, but see and understand other things as well.'

*

And so she slept, and woke at four, as if aware that at such an hour people of her colour might have cause to be wakeful, on their guard. For at this hour the old man in spectacles was also woken and taken, and the Deputy Commissioner in Mayapore was woken, and warned, and told to set in motion those plans whose object was to prevent, to deter. And in the morning, having slept again only fitfully, Miss Crane was also woken and told by Mr Chaudhuri that on the day before in Bombay the Congress had voted in favour of the working committee's resolution, that the Mahatma was arrested, that the entire working committee were arrested, that this no doubt was the signal for arrests all over the country. At nine she walked to the school with Chaudhuri to take the Sunday morning Bible class and found that only the children from Kotali had arrived. So she sent him on his bicycle into Dibrapur. He returned shortly before eleven and told her that the shops were closing in the town, that the police were out in force, that the rumour was that three of the municipal officers had been arrested by order of the District Superintendent of Police in Mayapore and taken to Aligarh, that crowds were collecting and threatening to attack the post office and the police station.

*

'Then I'll ring Mayapore and find out what is happening there,' Miss Crane said.

She put down the reports she had been co-ordinating. There was a telephone in Mr Chaudhuri's bungalow.

'You can't,' he told her. 'I have already tried. The lines have probably been cut.'

'I see. Well then. One of us must take the children back to Kotali, rather than risk anything happening to them here. So I'd better do that and be getting on my way. You had better go back to look after Mrs Chaudhuri, and perhaps keep an eye on the school if you can manage it.'

Mr Chaudhuri looked round the shabby little room and then at Miss Crane.

'There is nothing to safeguard here,' he said, 'except the children. Take them in the car and I will come with you on my bicycle. If there are bad people on the road you will be safer if I am also seen.'

'Oh, I shall be safe enough. What about your wife?'

'You are the only English person here,' he said. 'My wife will be all right.

39

They may well come here after they have finished with the post office and the police station, or whatever it is they have in mind. They may come from either direction. So we will both go with the children to Kotali.'

Miss Crane looked round the room too. The schoolhouse had always reminded her of the one she visited years ago with Mr Grant. Mr Chaudhuri was right. There wasn't much in the building worth saving, except the building itself, and even the worth of that was doubtful. She doubted, too, that either of them, in present circumstances, could stand in the doorway and successfully deny entry to an angry crowd. She glanced at Chaudhuri, remembering Muzzafirabad where she had been alone.

'You seem pessimistic,' she said.

'I have seen the people and heard the talk.'

'You're sure about the telephone?'

'Yes, I am sure.'

For a moment they looked at each other straight, and Miss Crane thought: This is the way it happens when there is real trouble – the little seed of doubt, of faint distrust, of suspicion that the truth is not actually being told. If the phone is cut, then it is cut. If it is not cut perhaps Mr Chaudhuri has picked it up, got no immediate answer and jumped to conclusions. Or it may not be cut and Mr Chaudhuri may know that it is not but tells me it is because he wants me to set off on the road to Kotali.

'Very well, Mr Chaudhuri,' she said. 'I think you are right. We'll cram the kids into the Ford somehow and you can come along on your bike.'

He said, 'One thing I hope you understand. I am not afraid to stay here. If you wish the building to be protected I will stay and chance my arm.'

'If they find it empty they may leave it alone,' she said.

'It is as I was thinking.'

She nodded, and stood up, collecting the reports, putting them tidily together, edge to edge. Chaudhuri waited. She said, 'Tell me your honest opinion. Is it serious this time?'

'It is serious.'

They always know, she thought, and then: This is how it happens too, to call them 'they' as though they are different.

'All right then, Mr Chaudhuri. Perhaps you'd collect the children together.'

He nodded, went to the door and out to the courtyard at the back where the children were playing.

She put the reports into her brief-case and then remembered that her gladstone bag, although already packed for the journey home, was still at Mr Chaudhuri's bungalow. She went out, called to him above the yelling of the children to whom he had just broken the news that school was over.

'My bag,' she shouted. 'It's at the bungalow. I'll pop down and get it and say goodbye to your wife.'

'I have sent my wife to the house of a friend,' Mr Chaudhuri shouted back. 'And your bag is in the car. I brought it with me.'

'Thanks,' she said, and went back into the office for the brief-case. She switched on the radio. Again there was only music, from All-India Radio, English music for the forces. She left the radio on while she closed the straps of the brief-case. The radio was a life-line of sorts. I am calm, she thought, automatically calm, as in 1914, and 1919, and 1930, other times. Over thirty-five years I have become used to sudden alarms. But I am also afraid. In such circumstances I am always a bit afraid. And I am ashamed, and am always ashamed, because of my suspicions – this time first over the telephone, and now over the gladstone bag.

'Mr Chaudhuri,' she called, going to the doorway. 'When they're ready bring them round to the front and I'll get the car started.'

And in my voice, she said to herself, there – always there – the note of authority, the special note of *us* talking to *them*, which perhaps passes unnoticed when what we talk about is the small change of everyday routine but at times of stress always sounds like taking charge. But then, she thought, we are, we are in charge. Because we have an obligation and a responsibility. In this present instance her main responsibility lay seventy miles away in Mayapore. Things were always worse in the towns.

When she brought the car from its shelter at the side of the schoolhouse, Mr D. R. Chaudhuri, BA, BSc, was standing waiting, with the children of the poor and the sometimes hungry gathered round him, playing their games.

*

In times of civil disturbance news or rumours of riots in the towns attracted from the villages men whose main preoccupation was the prospect of loot. This is what Mr Chaudhuri had in mind when he spoke of bad people on the road between Dibrapur and Kotali, and Miss Crane knew that in leaving Dibrapur behind they were probably running into trouble as well as away from it.

There was also the question, for her, of continuing on from Kotali the seventy-odd miles through village after village to Mayapore. In this southern part of the district the land was slightly undulating, but still open, with cultivation on both sides of a good metalled road, and few trees. At least on most parts of the road you would be able to see trouble coming from a distance. From experience Miss Crane knew what to look out for: in the dry weather, when the dirt strips on either side of the metal were powdered to the consistency of ground chalk, the cloud of dust which as it got nearer revealed men strung out across the road; in the wet, the same men, but more suddenly, without the earlier warning of the dust they raised, so that at first glimpse you could already make out that some were carrying staves. Starting from one village, three or four men in the course of several miles could become a score. A car, coming at speed, showing no signs of stopping, could scatter them at the last moment, but still be vulnerable to the stones they might pick up at the car's approach. Miss Crane had, once in her life, in the troubles of 1919, run such a gauntlet, but

41

the car she was in that time was driven by a determined young European policeman who had come to rescue her from an outlying schoolhouse where, as her superintendent back at headquarters had suspected, she was virtually a prisoner.

'Whether I could do the same as the young policeman,' she thought, 'blowing the horn and driving like mad, will depend on the size of the crowd.' Mr Chaudhuri could not drive. She did not know whether to be glad or sorry.

The size of the crowd depended on three things: the nature of the disturbance in the town which dictated the likely quantity of loot to be expected; the general temper of the surrounding villages and the number of men in each of them who had time and inclination to take the opportunity of filling their pockets; and finally the degree of control that the village headmen and rural police were able to exercise.

Each village had its watchman or chaukidar, a paid servant of the Government, and the villages were organised in groups under police detachments. A gang reaching a village where the police post was effectively manned, might then be dispersed. At a post where the police decided to look the other way or judged from the temper of the crowd that it was wiser to lock themselves in, the crowd passed by; and grew.

Reaching the village of Kotali with the cargo of laughing children, Mr Chaudhuri still pedalling some distance behind, Miss Crane was met by the chaukidar and the headman and several men and women who had been on the point of setting out to bring the children back from school. The chief constable in charge of the police post in Garhwar, the next village along the road, had sent a message to say that he could no longer get through on the telephone to sub-divisional police headquarters in Dibrapur, that he assumed trouble had broken out following the news of Mr Gandhi's arrest, and that the people of Kotali should therefore be on their guard to protect their property and their lives from dacoits and rioters.

The people of Kotali were, the headman said, very angry with the chief constable in Garhwar. They said he must have been warned at least the day before to expect trouble, and had not bothered to tell them. If they had been told they would not have let the children go to school that morning. The mothers thanked Miss Crane for returning them safely and offered her some tea, which she drank by the roadside, sitting on the chair they brought out and put under a tree. They gave Mr Chaudhuri tea as well.

'I shall pray for rain,' she told him, smiling. 'There's nothing like a good downpour to cool people off. If it's wet they'll stay at home.'

Mr Chaudhuri said nothing. He finished his tea and walked away and spoke for some time to the chaukidar and the headman. When he came back Miss Crane was finishing her second cup. She was hungry but had refused the offer of food.

'You must stay here, Miss Crane,' Mr Chaudhuri told her. 'In this village everyone is your friend because of the children. It is dangerous to drive to Mayapore.'

She shook her head, put the cup down on the tray a young girl stood holding in readiness. 'No,' she said, 'I have to be getting on.'

'They will look after you. The headman invites you to stay in his home.'

'It's very kind of him and I truly appreciate it, but I must try to get back.'

'Then stay for just an hour or two only. I will go back to Dibrapur. Who knows but that it is all a storm in a teapot? If it is then you can stay one more night in the bungalow and go to Mayapore tomorrow. The telephone will probably be working again by then.'

'And if it isn't all a storm in a teapot?'

'Then you shouldn't go to Mayapore at all. You should stay here where everyone is your friend.'

'I've got friends in Mayapore too. And Mr Chaudhuri, I also have responsibilities. I know you mean it kindly but I do really have to be getting on.'

'You have had nothing to eat.'

'I'm not hungry.'

'I will get you something to eat.'

'I don't think I *could* eat. You see this sort of thing always makes me feel a bit sick.' It wasn't true. This sort of thing always made her ravenously hungry. But if she stayed for the food, she thought, her determination to be on her way might weaken.

Mr Chaudhuri raised his arms slightly, a gesture of surrender. 'Then I am coming with you,' he said, 'we had better go now,' and turned away, ignoring her reply of, 'Don't be silly, it's quite unnecessary,' went to speak again to the chaukidar and the headman. Two or three of the children gathered round her. To please her they recited 'One, Two, Buckle my Shoe'. She laughed and said that it was well done. Mr Chaudhuri was walking up the road to the headman's house. He glanced back and indicated he would not be very long. A mother came with a plate covered by a napkin. Beneath it there were piping hot chappattis. More tea was offered. Another woman brought a bowl of dal, and a spoon. She waved the spoon aside and began to eat, breaking off bits of chappatti and scooping the dal up with them. The sweat was forming on her forehead. It was so hot and humid. While she ate the people stood watching. I hate it, she thought, I have always hated it, this being watched, like something in a zoo, seated on a chair, under a tree, by the roadside.

'You see,' she said to Mr Chaudhuri when he came back, 'they've forced it on me.'

'It is for kindness,' he said, as if giving her a lesson she had never learned properly, 'and for hospitality.'

'Well, I know that,' she couldn't help replying. 'But help me out with the chappattis. There are far more here than I can cope with.'

'No,' he said, 'they are for you. Try to finish them. Do not give offence. I also will eat. They are preparing. Then we will go to Mayapore.'

'What about Mrs Chaudhuri?' she asked.

43

'She is safe with her friend. They will send someone from here to tell her where I have gone.'

After a moment, looking up, catching his watchful eye, she said, 'Thank you, Mr Chaudhuri,' and then, after a bit of difficulty, 'I should have been afraid alone.'

*

In the next village, Garhwar, the police were waiting, squatting by the roadside in the shade of a banyan tree. Near the tree there was a whitewashed Hindu shrine. The priest in charge of the shrine sat half-naked on the hard-mud verandah of his hut, watching them. The police were armed with sticks. Seeing the car approach, the head constable got up from his haunches and flagged them to a stop. It was his duty to warn her, he told Miss Crane in Urdu, having saluted her and glanced at Mr Chaudhuri, that it was dangerous to proceed. He had been instructed to stand by and to expect trouble.

'When were you so instructed?' Miss Crane asked, also in Urdu.

He had been instructed early that morning to stand by, and yesterday to be prepared for trouble.

'You should have sent a message at once to Kotali,' she said.

He had sent a message to Kotali. He had done so on his own initiative. He had not been instructed to send any message but only to stand by and be prepared for trouble.

'You should have sent a message yesterday, but it's no matter,' Miss Crane said. Perhaps he would be good enough to tell her if he had any information about what was happening in Mayapore and between Garhwar and Mayapore.

'I have no information,' he said. 'The telephone line to Dibrapur is now out of order.'

'You mean cut?'

It was possible that it was cut. Also possible that it was just out of order. It was because he had been warned to stand by and to expect trouble and because immediately afterwards he found the telephone out of order that he had sent messages to Kotali and to the other villages in his jurisdiction. He had sent the messages by ordinary men and women from Garhwar as he could not afford to send any of his men in case trouble came suddenly. He had done everything possible. There was not much he could do with a handful of men if real trouble came. There were many bad people in the villages. His life and the lives of his men were in danger. Perhaps the memsahib would tell the sub-inspector sahib in Tanpur that Head Constable Akbar Ali in Garhwar was standing by as instructed but was without means of communication.

'Shall we reach Tanpur safely then, do you think?' Miss Crane asked.

He did not know, but the police in the Tanpur division of the district, under whose jurisdiction the Dibrapur sub-division came, were all men of character and determination. He thought it possible that she would reach Tanpur, but it was his duty to warn her that it was dangerous to proceed, and of course he could not answer for the division beyond Tanpur, where there were many villages full of bad people who might be converging on Tanpur, and perhaps on Mayapore, if Mayapore was in a state of civil disturbance. But Sub-Inspector Govindas Lal Sahib in Tanpur would no doubt be in a better position to advise her about that.

They reached Tanpur at two o'clock. Tanpur was a small town, dirty, poor, and smelling of ordure. The police who were out in force, patrolling the main street, consisted of six men and the assistant sub-inspector. But there was no sign of Sub-Inspector Govindas Lal who, his assistant said, had been trying to make contact with the District Superintendent Sahib's headquarters in Mayapore and had gone out an hour ago in a truck with one constable and three linesmen from the posts and telegraphs to find out where the wires were cut between Tanpur and Mayapore. The lines were also cut between Tanpur and Dibrapur, but the line to Mayapore was the most vital. Mr Chaudhuri told the assistant sub-inspector that the police post in Garhwar was also cut off, but that they had seen no lines down between there and Tanpur itself, or indeed any lines down all the way from the schoolhouse in Dibrapur. The assistant sub-inspector explained that to telephone from Garhwar to Tanpur or from Tanpur to Garhwar the call had to go through the Dibrapur exchange, and that it looked as though the lines must have been cut close to the Dibrapur exchange or even that the Dibrapur posts and telegraphs had been destroyed.

'Is it safe to proceed?' Mr Chaudhuri asked.

'Who can say?' the man replied. 'If no harm has come to the sub-inspector sahib, then you will find him on the road ahead.' In Tanpur itself there had been crowds collecting in the morning but the sub-inspector sahib had persuaded them to disperse. He had put it about that the military were on their way from Mayapore to maintain order. The shops were still closed, which was contrary to regulations, but the people were staying in their homes and the last instructions from Mayapore, early that morning, were to the effect that crowds should be persuaded to disperse if possible, but not provoked. The shopkeepers could have been forced to open their shops, but if people were not to be provoked it was better to let them stay shut. So far, then, all was quiet, but if the sub-inspector sahib did not return soon he did not know how long this state of affairs would continue. 'But we are pulling on all right,' he said to Miss Crane, suddenly, in English.

'We'll see the sub-inspector and tell him.'

But they did not see the sub-inspector. Five miles beyond Tanpur they found what looked like his truck, upside down on the roadside where it had been overturned in the place where it must have been parked, next to a telegraph pole. If the truck belonged to the sub-inspector then he had found where the wires were cut, but not been given time to repair them. They lay tangled and coiled in the ditch at the side of the road.

'We must go back,' Mr Chaudhuri said. 'They have abducted Sub-Inspector Govindas Lal.'

'And the linesmen,' Miss Crane pointed out.

'Perhaps it was the linesmen who abducted him. The posts and telegraphs people are sometimes very bolshie.'

'But there were only three linesmen. And the sub-inspector had a man with him and was probably armed. There must have been other men.'

'Which is why we should turn back, Miss Crane.'

The sky was clouded over, but there was still no rain. 'It's ridiculous,' she said. 'Yesterday I drove along this road and everything was as quiet as the grave and safe as houses. Now suddenly there are cut telegraph wires, upturned trucks and vanished sub-inspectors of police. It is really very *silly*.' She laughed. 'No, Mr Chaudhuri, if you like I'll take you back to Tanpur, but I shall press on afterwards to Mayapore because I've just seen the *funny* side. But if I take you back to Tanpur the people will know we've gone back for a good reason, and then it will come out about the sub-inspector. And the assistant sub-inspector will probably panic and the funny side might stop being funny.'

Mr Chaudhuri was silent for a while. Presently he sighed and said, 'I don't follow your reasoning, Miss Crane. It is an example no doubt of British phlegm. You are mad. And I am mad to let you go, let alone go with you. All I ask is that if we see a crowd of people on the road, you put your foot hard on the accelerator.'

She turned her head and again they looked at each other straight. She had stopped smiling, not because she was annoyed with him for calling her mad or had already stopped seeing the funny side, but because she felt there was between them an unexpected mutual confidence, confidence of the kind that could spring up between two strangers who found themselves thrown together quite fortuitously in difficult circumstances that might turn out to be either frightening or amusing.

And for Miss Crane there was something else besides, a feeling she had often had before, a feeling in the bones of her shoulders and in the base of her skull that she was about to go over the hump thirty-five years of effort and willingness had never really got her over; the hump, however high or low it was, which, however hard you tried, still lay in the path of thoughts you sent flowing out to a man or woman whose skin was a different colour from your own. Were it only the size of a pebble, the hump was always there, disrupting the purity of that flow, the purity of the thoughts.

'Yes, I will try,' she said, 'try to put my foot down and keep it there,' and then wished that there were words she could use that would convey to him the regard she held him in at that moment, a regard deeper, harder than that she had felt for the ragged singing children years ago; deeper, harder, because her regard for the children had sprung partly from her pity for them – and for Mr Chaudhuri she had no pity; only respect and the kind of affection that came from the confidence one human being could feel in another, however little had been felt before.

'Then,' Mr Chaudhuri said, 'let us proceed.' His lips looked very dry. He was afraid, and so was she, but now perhaps they both saw the comic side, and she did not have to say anything special to him just because his skin was brown or because she had never understood him. After all, he had never fully understood her either. She set the car in motion again and after a while she began to sing. Presently to her surprise and pleasure he joined in. It was the song she always liked the children to learn. All over India, she thought, there were brown and off-white children and adults who could sing the song or, at least, remember it if they ever heard it again and, perhaps, remember it in connexion with Miss Crane Mem. She sang it now, not sentimentally, but with joy, not piously, but boldly, almost as though it were a jolly march. When they had sung it right through once, they began again.

> 'There's a *Friend* for little *chil*dren
>   Ab*ove* the bright blue *sky*,
> A *Friend* Who never *changes*,
>   Whose *love* will never *die*;
> De *da*, de da, de *da*, *dum*
>   And *change* with changing *years*,
> This *Friend* is always *worthy*—'

Ahead of them the rioters were spread out across the road.

*

'I can't,' she said, as the car got nearer.

'You must,' he said. 'Blow the horn, keep blowing it and press the accelerator, *press*.'

He leaned out of the window to show his dark Bengali face, and waved his arm in a motion demanding right of way. 'Faster,' he shouted at her. 'Faster, you're slowing down, keep pressing and blowing.'

'I shall kill someone,' she shouted back. 'I can't. I can't. Why don't they move away?'

'Let them be killed. Faster. And blow!'

For a moment, closing on the crowd, she thought she and Mr Chaudhuri had won, that the men were moving to give way, but then they cohered again into a solid mass. They must have seen her white face. A man in front began to wave his arms, commanding them to stop.

'Keep going!' Mr Chaudhuri shouted. 'Close your eyes if you must but keep going!'

She tightened her mouth preparing to obey, but failed. She couldn't drive into a mass of living creatures. 'I'm sorry,' she cried, and began to press on the brake pedal. She stopped the car some twenty yards from the man who was waving his arms, but kept the engine running. 'They weren't going to move, they'd have died. I'm sorry.'

'Don't speak,' Mr Chaudhuri said. 'Now leave it to me. Don't speak.' He put a hand on her wrist. 'Trust me,' he said. 'I know you never have, but trust me now. Do whatever I say. *Whatever* I say.'

She nodded. 'I trust you. I'll do what you say.' In her physical panic there was a kind of exhilaration as though she were drunk on the Deputy Commissioner's brandy. 'But don't run risks. I'm not worth risks. I'm old and it's all gone and I've failed.' She laughed. The men were approaching, swaggering. 'After all, it's me they want,' she said. 'Not you. So that's it. If this is where it ends for me, let it end.'

'Please, Miss Crane,' he said, 'don't be ridiculous.'

The car was surrounded now. She found it difficult to distinguish face from face. They all looked the same, they all smelt the same: of liquor and garlic and sweat-soaked cotton cloth. Most were dressed in white homespun shirts and dhotis. Some wore the white Congress cap. They were chanting the words that the whole of India, it seemed to her, had been chanting since early in the spring. *Quit India! Quit India!* Mr Chaudhuri was talking to the leader. The leader was asking what he was doing riding in a car with an Englishwoman. Mr Chaudhuri was not answering his questions but trying to shout him down, trying to tell him that Miss Crane was an old friend of India, that only that morning she had saved the lives of many Indian children from drunken power-mad policemen and was on her way to a secret meeting of the Congress Committee in Mayapore whose confidence she enjoyed and whose efforts to overthrow the English she wholeheartedly endorsed.

The leader said he did not believe Mr Chaudhuri. Mr Chaudhuri was a traitor. No self-respecting Indian male would ride with a dried-up virgin memsahib who needed to feel the strength of a man inside her before she could even look like a woman, and what would Mr Chaudhuri do if they decided to take the memsahib out of the car and show her what women were for and what men could do? Not, the leader said, spitting on to the bonnet of the Ford, that he would waste his strength and manhood on such a dried-up old bag of bones. 'She speaks Hindi,' Mr Chaudhuri said, 'and hears these insults. Are you not ashamed to speak so of a *guru*, a teacher, as great a *guru* as Mrs Annie Besant, and a follower of the Mahatma? Great evil will come to you and your seed if you so much as lay a finger on her.'

'Then we will lay one on you, brother,' the leader said, and dragged open the door, whose lock Miss Crane had failed, month after month, to have repaired. 'Go,' Mr Chaudhuri said, as he was taken out. 'Go now. It's all right. No harm will come to me.'

'Pigs!' she cried in Urdu, trying to hold on to Mr Chaudhuri's arm, using the words she had used years ago, in Muzzafirabad. 'Sons of pigs, cow-eaters, impotent idolaters, fornicators, abhorred of the Lord Shiva ...'

'Go!' shrieked Mr Chaudhuri, from outside the car, kicking the door shut, his arms held by four men, 'or do you only take orders from white men? Do you only keep promises you make to your own kind?'

'No!' she shouted back. 'No, no! I don't!' and, pressing the accelerator, released the brake, nearly stalling the engine so that the car jerked, paused, and jerked again, throwing the laughing men away from the bonnet, and then it leapt away so that they had to jump out of its path. A couple of hundred yards further on she stopped and looked back. Three of the men were chasing after the car. Behind them Mr Chaudhuri was being pushed from one man to the other. A stick was brought down heavily on his shoulders. She shouted, 'No! No! Mr Chaudhuri!' and opened the door, climbed out. The three men held their arms out, laughing, and called, 'Ah, memsahib, memsahib,' and came towards her. Remembering, she reached into the car and found the starting handle, stood in the road, threatening them with it. They laughed louder and struck postures of mock defence and defiance, jumped about grinning, like performing monkeys. Mr Chaudhuri had his head covered by his hands. The sticks were coming down, thwack, thwack. Then he was on his knees, and then out of sight, surrounded by the men who were beating him. Miss Crane cried out, 'Devils! Devils!' and began to move towards the three men, still waving the starting handle. They moved back, pretending to be alarmed. The youngest of them reached into his dhoti as if about to expose himself, shouted something at her. Suddenly they turned and ran back to their leader who had called out to them. The other rioters were standing over Mr Chaudhuri who lay unmoving in the middle of the road. A couple of them were going through his pockets. The leader was now pointing at the car. Five or six men left the group surrounding Mr Chaudhuri and came towards Miss Crane. Instinctively she backed, but held her ground next to the car. Reaching her they pushed her aside, roughly, angrily, as if ashamed they had not yet summoned up the courage to disobey their leader and attack her. Bending to the task they got their weight under the running-board and the mudguards and began to heave rhythmically, until of a sudden the car turned over. From this display of strength one of them, anyway, got courage. Turning from the car he came at Miss Crane, raised his hand and hit her across the face, once, twice, then pushed her back towards the ditch and, using both arms, tumbled her down the three-foot embankment. Falling, she lost consciousness. When she came to and had collected her senses and strength she scrambled up the bank on her hands and knees and found the Ford burning and the rioters in the distance.

Limping, she walked to where Mr Chaudhuri still lay. Reaching him she knelt and said, 'Mr Chaudhuri,' but could not touch him because of his bloody face and open eyes and the awful thing that had happened to the side of his head. 'No,' she said, 'no, it isn't true. Oh God. Oh God, forgive me. Oh God, forgive us all,' and then covered her face and wept, which she had not done for years, and continued weeping for some time.

She dried her eyes by wiping them on the sleeve of her blouse, once, twice, three times. She felt the first heavy drops of rain. Her raincape had been in the back of the car. She said, in anguish, 'But there's nothing to cover him with, nothing, nothing,' and stood up, crouched, got hold of his feet and dragged him to the side of the road.

'I can't help it,' she said, as if to him, when he lay bloody and limp and inhuman in the place she had dragged him to. 'There's nothing I can do, nothing, nothing,' and turned away and began to walk with long unsteady strides through the rain, past the blazing car, towards Mayapore. As she walked she kept saying, 'Nothing I can do. Nothing. Nothing.'

A hundred yards past the car she stopped. 'But there is,' she said, and turned and walked back until she reached Mr Chaudhuri's body. She sat down in the mud at the side of the road, close to him, reached out and took his hand.

'It's taken me a long time,' she said, meaning not only Mr Chaudhuri, 'I'm sorry it was too late.'

*

As Mr Poulson said afterwards, the troubles in Mayapore began for him with the sight of old Miss Crane sitting in the pouring rain by the roadside holding the hand of a dead Indian. On that day, the day of the arrests of members of the Congress sub-committees in the district, Mayapore itself had been quiet. The uprising got off to a slow start. Only Dibrapur and the outlying districts appeared to have jumped the gun. Mr Poulson set off from Mayapore in the afternoon, in a car, accompanied by one of Mr Merrick's inspectors of police, and a truck-load of constables, to investigate rumours of trouble in the sub-divisions that couldn't be contacted by telephone, and although when he reached the village of Candgarh he found the sub-inspector of police from Tanpur, one constable and three linesmen from posts and telegraphs, locked in the police post, it was not until he proceeded along the road to Tanpur and found first of all Miss Crane's burnt-out car and then Miss Crane herself that he really began to take the troubles seriously.

The troubles which Mr Poulson and several others began by not taking seriously took until the end of August to put down. Everyone in Mayapore at that time would have a different story to tell, although there were stories of which each individual had common knowledge. There was, to begin with, the story of Miss Crane, although that was almost immediately lost sight of following the rape of the English girl in the Bibighar Gardens on the night of August the 9th, at an hour when Miss Crane was lying in the first delirium of pneumonia in a bed in the Mayapore General Hospital. Later, when Miss Crane found it impossible to identify any of the men arrested that day in Tanpur, for a short while she came again into prominence. People wondered whether she was genuinely at a loss to recognise her own attackers and Mr Chaudhuri's murderers, or whether she was being obstinate, over-zealous in the business of being fair at all costs to the bloody blacks.

But the Bibighar Gardens affair was not lost sight of. It seemed to the European population to be the key to the whole situation they presently found themselves in, the sharpest warning of the most obvious danger to all of them, but most especially to the women. Afterwards it was never clear whether the steps taken by the authorities following the rape of the English girl in the Bibighar Gardens sparked off worse riots than had been planned or whether the riots would have taken place in any case. There were some who said one thing and some the other. Those who held that there would have been little or no rioting if it hadn't been for the rape and the steps taken to avenge it believed that the men the Deputy Commissioner had ordered to be arrested on the morning of the 9th August were the right ones to have arrested, and that the action taken in regard to the Bibighar Gardens affair had caused worse disorders than the civil disobedience that was stopped by the arrests. Those who held that there would have been disorders in any event and that the Bibighar Gardens affair was purely symptomatic of general treachery said that the members of the local Congress committees whom Mr White had no alternative but to arrest were simply figureheads, and that the real ringleaders of the intended rebellion had been under cover in places like Tanpur and Dibrapur. But at the time, there was no distinguishing cause from effect and the events of the following three weeks were of the kind that could only be dealt with as and when they arose.

It was not until the first week of September, the first week of quiet, that Miss Crane returned from hospital to her bungalow, and another fortnight was to pass before she felt strong enough to attempt to take up the reins again. It was therefore some six or seven weeks after the beginning of the uprisings in Mayapore district and some three or four weeks after their end, that on a Tuesday afternoon Miss Crane once more opened her home to soldiers from the barracks.

They would be, she knew, changed in some respects from the boys they were before the riots began. In hospital, and since, she had closed her mind to stories of the troubles, but she knew that the military had been called out in aid of the civil power, that for three or four days Mr White was said to have lost his head and handed Mayapore over to the control of the local Brigade Commander. She had heard Indians say, although she had tried not to listen, that in those few days of Brigadier Reid, things had been almost as bad as in the days of General Dyer in Amritsar in 1919. There had not been any indiscriminate shooting of unarmed civilians, but there had been, apart from controlled shootings and consequent deaths, the forcible feeding with beef – if the story were to be believed – of six Hindu youths who were suspected or guilty of the rape in the Bibighar Gardens. There had been no public whippings, as in General Dyer's day, when youths were clapped to a triangle in the open street and flogged simply as suspects in an attack on an Englishwoman, but there were rumours that the youths who had been forcibly fed with beef had also been whipped and had now disappeared into the anonymous mass of those imprisoned with or without trial.

In the native town itself, as Mr Francis Narayan repeatedly told her, there had been many charges by mounted police, and firing by the military to disperse crowds and punish looters and fire-raisers. In the district as a whole, as in many other provinces of India, there had been widespread disruption of railways, posts, telegraphs, looting of warehouses, shops, houses and Government grain and seed stores (which the people would be sorry for next year, Mr Narayan pointed out, if the crops failed). Police posts had been attacked, policemen murdered. In one sub-division of the district, so it was rumoured, the Indian magistrate had run the Congress flag up over his courthouse, released prisoners from custody, fined liberals and moderates, illicitly collected revenues and hidden away money that should have been paid into the treasury. Miss Crane suspected that the story was apocryphal, but there did seem to be evidence that one of Mr White's Indian subordinates was in disgrace and, since order was restored, had spent an hour weeping at the Deputy Commissioner's bungalow.

She was, in fact, too old a hand to believe everything told her as incontrovertible truth, and too old a hand not to know that her simple soldiers who had found themselves fresh out from England, suddenly acting in aid of the civil power to reduce rebellion in a colonial empire they knew little about but must now think badly of (remembering home and the blitz and their comrades dead on the plains around Mandalay), would find it difficult to make sense of what had happened, and why it had happened, and why, now that it was over, the English and the Indians had apparently patched their quarrel and come together once more in a compulsive harmony.

There was in that word compulsive, she knew, the idea of a key to the situation, the idea of there being somewhere in this curious centuries-long association a kind of love with hate on the obverse side, as on a coin. But Miss Crane found herself now too tired, too easily weighed down by the sheer pressure of the climate and the land and the hordes of brown faces and the sprinkling of stiff-lipped white ones, to channel any of her remaining pneumonia-sapped energy into solving moral and dialectical problems. But she wished that in the days when she had had the energy, days which had ended abruptly on the road from Tanpur, she had taken one of the soldiers aside – and she was thinking of Clancy – and said:

'For years, since the eighteenth century, and in each century since, we have said at home, in England, in Whitehall, that the day would come when our rule in India will end, not bloodily, but in peace, in – so we made it seem – a perfect gesture of equality and friendship and love. For years, for nearly a century, the books that Indians have read have been the books of our English radicals, our English liberals. There has been, you see, a seed. A seed planted in the Indian imagination and in the English imagination. Out of it was to come something sane and grave, full of dignity, full of thoughtfulness and kindness and peace and wisdom. For all these qualities are in us, in you, and in me, in old Joseph and Mr Narayan and Mr White and I suppose in Brigadier Reid. And they were there, too, in Mr Chaudhuri. For years we have been promising and for years finding means of putting the fulfilment of the promise off until the promise stopped

52

looking like a promise and started looking only like a sinister prevarication, even to me, let alone to Indians who think and feel and know the same as me. And the tragedy is that between us there is this little matter of the colour of the skin, which gets in the way of our seeing through each other's failings and seeing into each other's hearts. Because if we saw through *them*, into *them*, then we should know. And what we should know is that the promise is a promise and will be fulfilled.'

But she had never said this to anyone, even to Clancy. And the day came when Clancy reappeared, coming in force with his mates who had heard that the old maid had had a bad time and been brave and nearly died, and they were anxious to make her laugh and feel happy, so that she would forget her troubles and know that she was among friends, stout lads who had been through it a bit themselves, and who were grateful to her for the small thing she did for them that reminded them of home and safety.

But throughout that tea-time, not one of them, not even Clancy, so much as looked at old Joseph, so when they had gone and she had helped Joseph clear away but found no words to heal the wound to the old man's pride and self-respect, she left him to finish and, going into her room, took down the picture of the old Queen and locked it away, in the chest, against the time when there might, remotely, be an occasion to put it back up again.

Part Two

THE MACGREGOR HOUSE

Dooliya le aō
re morē babul ke kaharwa.
Chali hoon sajan ba ke des.

(O my father's servants, bring my palanquin.
I am going to the land of my husband)

(A morning raga.)
Translation by Dipali Nag

Next, there is the image of a garden: not the Bibighar garden but the garden of the MacGregor House: intense sunlight, deep and complex shadows. The range of green is extraordinary, palest lime, bitter emerald, mid-tones, neutral tints. The textures of the leaves are many and varied; they communicate themselves through sight to imaginary touch, exciting the finger-tips: leaves coming into the tenderest flesh, superbly in their prime, crisping to old age; all this at the same season because here there is no autumn. In the shadows there are dark blue veils, the indigo dreams of plants fallen asleep, and odours of sweet and necessary decay, numerous places layered with the cast-off fruit of other years softened into compost, feeding the living roots that lie under the garden massively, in hungry immobility.

From the house there is the sound of a young girl singing. She sings a raga, the song of the young bride saying goodbye to her parents, before setting out on the journey to her new home far away. There are ragas for morning and evening. This one is for morning. The dew is not yet off the ground. The garden is still cool. A blue-black crow with a red-yellow beak swoops from the roof of the house looking for its breakfast. Where the sunlight strikes the lawn the dew is a scattering of crystals.

Surrounding the lawn there are bushes of bougainvillaea; white and red. Some of the bushes are hybrids and have branches that bear sprays of both colours. Elsewhere there are jasmine and beds of dark-red canna lilies. The house stands in the middle of the garden, protected from the outside world by close-formed battalions of trees: neem, pipul, gol mohur, tamarind, casuarina and banyan; it goes back to the late eighteenth century and was

54

built by a prince who conceived a passion for a singer of classical music. To build a house and install a woman in it is an expensive way to beg her favours. It was said that he came to visit her morning and evening, and that she sang to him, the same songs perhaps that the girl is singing now, and that he became enamoured finally only of her voice and was content to listen while she instructed the pupils he permitted her to receive. Scheherazade told stories to postpone the hour of her execution. The singer sang to guard her honour. When the singer died the prince grieved. People said he died of a broken heart. The house was deserted, closed. Like the state it decayed, fell into ruin. The prince's son succeeded to the *gaddi*. He despised his father for his futile attachment to the singer. He would let no one live there. He built another house nearby, the Bibighar, where he kept his courtesans. He was a voluptuary. He emptied the treasury. His people starved. An Englishman at his court was poisoned and so the new prince was deposed, imprisoned, his state annexed, and his people were glad of it until time lay over the memory of the old bad but not the badness of the present. The decayed house of the singer was rebuilt by a red-faced Scottish nabob called MacGregor who feared God and favoured Muslims, and was afraid of temples. The story goes that he burnt the Bibighar to the ground because he said it had been an abomination. He died at the hands of mutinous sepoys.

His young wife is the first ghost. She comes dressed in the fashion of the times and stands on the verandah, swaying to and fro, as if nursing her dead baby, but her arms are empty. There is blood on her torn bodice. Her name is Janet MacGregor. A Muslim servant called Akbar Hossain died defending her.

MacGregor rebuilt the singer's house more than a hundred years ago on the decayed princely foundations, with money got, it was rumoured, from bribes. Foursquare, there is a flagged inner courtyard; on the outer aspect, verandahs with rounded arches shading the upper as well as the ground floor rooms. The brickwork is stuccoed and painted cream that always dries yellow. Stone steps lead from the gravel driveway to the front entrance. In the arches of the verandahs green chicks can be lowered or rolled up according to the season and the time of day. On the upper verandah there is a balustrade, but not on the lower whose level is three feet from the ground. Ranged along the ground, in front of it, there are clay pots filled with shrubs and flowers, and climbing plants that have embraced the pillars of the arches. An old man with a grizzled head, dressed in a white vest and khaki shorts that expose the knobs and sinews of his rheumatic legs, tends the plants and the flowers. This is Bhalu. His black skin is burnt purple. His bare toes cling to the gravel and are as horny as the shell of a tortoise.

It was on the stone steps leading to the verandah that the girl stumbled at the end of her headlong flight in the dark from the Bibighar Gardens; stumbled, fell, and crawled on her hands and knees the rest of the way to safety and into the history of a troubled period.

*

Yes, I remember Miss Crane, old Lady Chatterjee says. Long ago as it is, I still regret having thought of her at the time as a mediocre person but I only ever met her at Connie and Robin White's, and only at those awful dull dinners poor Connie had to give as Mrs Deputy C when she needed Miss Crane as an extra woman to make up her table and balance the bachelors. Miss Crane wasn't my cup of tea. With one or two exceptions such as Connie White and Ethel Manners the European women never were and those who come out to India now don't seem to be anybody's except their husbands' and not always then. They're mostly lumps. In those days they were nearly all harpies. I used to think Miss Crane would have been a harpy if she'd got married and had a position to keep up. As it was, she was a lump with a harpy exterior, the kind of person who had nothing much to say but gave the impression of thinking a lot, which is all right in a man but distasteful in a woman. There aren't many women in positions of real authority and so it seems to me the rest of us have a duty to speak our minds. It's the only way the world can judge us unless we are among the fortunate few who are allowed to express themselves through action. Otherwise we have to rely on our tongues. I'm thinking of talk in mixed company. Woman-chatter has never greatly appealed to me because the minds that are spoken between the withdrawal from the dining-room and the return of the gents usually prove to be empty and you might as well give yourself a rest and think of something bleak and cool like snow.

I wrote Miss Crane off as mediocre because although she chatted quite pleasantly and intelligently over coffee she was mostly mumchance at the dinner table. Oh, not mumchance *tout court*. No. She never struck me as shy, although she was probably afraid of me. Her silence was of the ominous kind, which is where the idea of harpy came in because nothing was more ominous than the silence of a European harpy. But true harpy silence is always accompanied by a sly look or a vulgar little grimace from one harpy to another. There was nothing of that kind of harpy about Miss Crane. And then, over coffee, which is the time real harpies bare their talons, she showed herself, as I have said, surprisingly capable of *chat*, chat of an ingenuous nature, and this suggested lumpishness and made me think of her as another woolly liberal, a poor woman who had struggled hard against odds, even injustice, or plain bad luck, and had had to latch on to something both soothing to the mind and enlivening to the physique, like struggling through the monsoon on that dotty bicycle of hers to check that all the children were learning to be unselfish and public-spirited and keeping clean and reasonably well-fed in the process.

There was that typical silliness of a picture of Mr Gandhi that she took down or was said to have taken down because she decided the old boy was being naughty whereas of course he was simply being astute. The English have always revered saints but hated them to be shrewd. English people who thought Gandhi a saint were identifying themselves with the thousands or millions of Indians who said he *was*, but saintliness to an Indian means quite a different thing than it means to an Englishman. An English person automatically thinks of a saint as someone who is going to be martyred, a man whose logic isn't going to work in a final show-down with the severely practical world, a man in fact who is a saint *per se*. Apart from occasional temptations (for which they prescribe hair-shirts) they expect these saints of theirs to be so *un*earthbound that they have one foot in heaven already. And of course by heaven they mean the opposite of earth. They divide the material from the spiritual with their usual passion for tidiness and for people being orderly and knowing their place. On the other hand, to the Hindu there can't be this distinction. For him the material world is illusory and Heaven a name for personal oblivion. Personally I have always found the material world far from illusory and have never welcomed as pleasurable the idea of mindless embodiment in a dull corporate state of total peace, which is how you could describe the Hindu concept of God. The point is, though, that on this difficult journey from illusion to oblivion *anything* counts as practical, because everything is speculative. Well, but to come back to Mr Gandhi, the Hindus called him a saint because for thirty years he was the most *active* Hindu on the scene, which may sound like a paradox to European ears but after all, given our bodies, to travel from illusion to oblivion requires tremendous mental and physical stamina – and, if you are anxious to shorten the journey for others, a notable degree of leadership and a high content of hypnotic persuasion in oratory. But as for Western religious *mores*, well, to get from the practical world of affairs to an impractical heaven requires nothing but an act we're all capable of, dying I mean, although disappointment in the event undoubtedly follows. Irreligious as I am I can't help being contemptuous of the laziness of western religions, and I can't help criticising myself for not being even a bad Hindu. But at least I don't make the kind of mistake Miss Crane made. If Mr Gandhi thought of his material acts as largely illusory, as private steps taken in public towards his own desirable personal merging with the absolute, I really do as a practical woman have to admire his shrewdness, his perfect timing in putting the cat among the pigeons.

But for Miss Crane, poor woman, pigeons were vulnerable creatures and cats soft little beasts, and both had lessons to learn. I found out a lot about her when all that awful business was over, in fact I tried to make up for my previous bad judgment, but by then she was difficult to get to know, and in the event there wasn't much time. Rather late in the day I invited her here, but she never came. So I called on her once or twice. Her virtues were still less obvious to me than her failings. She still gave me the impression she thought pigeons were to be taught the benefits of giving themselves up and cats the advantages of restraint. Both benefits and advantages were spiritual and therefore for her divisible from the material kind – which to me, passionately committed to what goes on around me, is a nullification of nature. I am not a Hindu but I *am* an Indian. I don't *like* violence but I believe in its inevitability. It is so *positive*. I hate negation. I sit here in the MacGregor House in a positive state of old age, bashing off here and there and everywhere whenever the mingy old government gives me a P form, and it doesn't worry me in the least that in the new India I seem already to be an anachronism, a woman who remembers everything too well quite to make her mark as a person worth listening to today. You could say that the same thing has happened to Mr Nehru for whom I have always had a fondness because he has omitted to be a saint. I still have a fondness for him because the only thing about him currently discussed with any sort of lively passion is the question of who is to succeed him. I suppose we are still waiting for the Mahatma because the previous one disappointed and surprised us by becoming a saint and martyr in the western sense when that silly boy shot him. I'm sure there's a lesson in that for us. If the old man were alive today I believe he'd dot us all one on the head with his spinning-wheel and point out that if we go on as we are we shall end up believing in saints the way you English do and so lose the chance of ever having one again in our public life. I have a feeling that when it was written into our constitution that we should be a secular state we finally put the lid on our Indian-ness, and admitted the *legality* of our long years of living in sin with the English. Our so-called independence *was* rather like a shot-gun wedding. The only Indians who don't realise that we are now really westerners are our peasants. I suppose they'll cotton on to it one day, and then they'll want to be westerners too, like practically everyone else in the East and Far East.

*

She sits, then, an old Rajput lady, wound in a dark silk saree whose glittering threads catch the light, with her white hair cut short, waved, tinted with the blue of dust from an enamelled Rajputana sky, much as years before she sat erect on the edge of a sofa and frightened Edwina Crane into the realisation that to work to, and put her trust in, the formula of a few simple charitable ideas was not enough.

*

But Miss Crane (the old lady goes on), if you are really interested in her, well let me explain why in the end I changed my opinion of her. She was not mediocre. She showed courage and that's the most difficult thing in the world for any human being to show and the one I respect most, especially physical courage. I usually suspect cant in all the chat that goes on about moral courage. Moral courage smells of refusal. The physical sort is like an invitation, and I find that open. I find it appealing. And in any case, you know, physical courage is not without morality. We speak of moral courage as if it's on a higher human plane, but physical courage is usually informed by moral courage too, and often couldn't be expressed without it. Perhaps you could say the same the other way round. Perhaps these notions of courage are western notions, divisible in the usual western way that says black is black, and white is white, and right is the opposite of wrong.

What an old mess I'm in with my Rajput blood, my off-white skin, my oriental curiosity, my liking for the ways of your occidental civilisation, and my funny old tongue that is only properly at home in English. At my age I smoke too many cigarettes and drink too much black-market whisky. I adore the Gothic monstrosities of the old public buildings of Bombay and the temple by the sea at Mahabalipuram. I think Corbusier did an interesting job at Chandigarh and the Taj Mahal brings a stupid lump into my throat. Did you ever see what they call the floating palace at Udaipur? Or the long vista from the Arc du Carrousel through the Place de la Concorde the whole length of the Champs Elysées at night with the traffic clustered at the Etoile? Or the city of London deserted on a Sunday morning when the sun is shining in October? The Malayan archipelago from the air? The toe of Italy from 40,000 feet up in a Comet? New York by night from the Beekman Tower, the first sight of Manhattan from the deck of a liner coming up the Hudson late in the afternoon? An old woman drawing water from a well in a village in Andhra Pradesh, or my great-niece Parvati playing the tamboura and singing a morning or evening raga? Well, of course you've seen *her*. But have you understood yet who she is?

These are not divisible, are they, these sights and people I've listed except, I suppose, in the minds of the people who encounter them and decide their meaning. Oh dear, I'm as bad as you, as any of us. Even when I'm not looking for a meaning one springs naturally to my mind. Do you think it is a disease?

Have the other half and then we'll bash off in and have dinner.

*

In the MacGregor House there is a room where the late Sir Nello Chatterjee deposited souvenirs of a life-time's magpie habit of picking up whatever caught his eye that might be reckoned a curiosity. He obviously engaged in a love affair with cuckoo clocks and cheap brightly coloured leatherwork, mostly orange, of the kind bought from bumboats at the Red Sea side of the Suez Canal. Perhaps the leatherwork celebrated a boyish delight not so much in the pouffes, purses and handbags, as in the lucky dip of baskets and ropes by which they were raised for inspection from the bobbing coracle-bazaars to the austere rock-firm height of the deck of an ironclad ocean-going steamer. He can seldom have resisted the temptation to possess the risen prize, or the obverse temptation to feel the feathery weight of the basket going down empty, weighted only by the coins or notes which were his response to and interpretation of the bargaining gestures of the fezzed nightgowned figure precariously astride below.

The pouffes and purses are scattered round this room in the MacGregor

House, curiously dry and lifeless, like seaweed taken from its element, but also capable of bringing to the nose of a knowledgeable traveller the recollected smell of oil and water, of the faint stagnation that seems to surround a big ship directly it stops moving. India also seems to be at anchor. The cuckoo clocks are silent, ornate artificial bowers gathering dust, harbouring behind their shutters a score or more of startled birds who are probably hysterical from long incarceration and imminent expectation of winding and release. In Sir Nello's day the visitor to the room was entertained by the simultaneous cacophonous display of each bird's jack-in-a-box emergence, a sight Lady Chatterjee says she remembers as putting her in mind of a fantasy she suffered after visiting the morgue in Paris with an amorous medical student. Normally kept embalmed in their own disuse by her orders even when Sir Nello was alive, they have remained so, permanently, since his death. The visitor is discouraged from asking a command performance; instead, invited to admire the stuffed tiger prowling in a nightmare of immobility on a wooden plinth, the glassed ivory replica of the Albert Memorial that plays 'Home Sweet Home' on a mechanical dulcimer, shells and stones from the Connecticut shore, a bronze miniature of the Eiffel Tower, little medallions from the kiosks in the Notre Dame Cathedral that are cold with the blessing of the commercial piety they evoke. There are paper lanterns that were carried away from a restaurant in Singapore in exchange for the payment of Sir Nello's grasping admiration and substantial appetite, the mangy boots of some Mongolian merchant encountered in Darjeeling after a journey over the Himalaya and engaged in Sir Nello's brand of thrusting acquisitive conversation. There are no weapons, no illuminated Moghul manuscripts or ancient jewellery, no Brobdingnagian trappings purloined from a flattered and impecunious prince's elephant stables: nothing of value except in the terms one eccentric might use of another eccentric's relics. There is, for instance, under glass, the old briar pipe that long ago was filled and tamped by the broad but increasingly shaky finger of Sir Henry Manners, one-time Governor of the province in which the town of Mayapore played, in 1942, its peculiar historic role, but Manners was gone ten years before that, carried temporarily away by retirement to Kashmir and then off permanently by the claret and the sunshine which he loved, and a disease which even now is curable only in Paris, Athens and Mexico and of which he knew nothing until it ate through the walls of his intestines and attacked his liver, which the doctors described as a cancerous invasion. And Sir Nello has been dead almost as many years, of a simple heart failure. They had been friends and their wives had been friends and, as widows, remained so right up until Lady Manners's death in 1948.

Of an admirable quartet – admirable because they overcame that little obstacle of the colour of the skin – only Lili Chatterjee survives to recall directly the placid as well as the desperate occasions. Of the other actors Reid has gone, and the girl, and young Kumar into oblivion, probably changing his name once more. The Whites and the Poulsons and young Ronald Merrick seem to be lost, temporarily at least, in the anonymity of time or other occupations. Miss Crane set fire to herself. They are the chance victims of the hazards of a colonial ambition. Museums, though, arrest history in its turbulent progress. So – the MacGregor House.

*

'When I first saw Daphne,' Lady Chatterjee said, referring to the girl, old Lady Manners's niece, 'she struck me as, well, good-natured but inept. She was big and rather clumsy. She was always dropping things.'

The MacGregor House still echoes faintly to the tinkling of shattered glass that can't be traced to present accident or blamed on any servant. Both Lili Chatterjee and her great-niece Parvati tread lightly and the servants go barefoot: so how account for the occasional sound of stoutly shod feet mounting the stairs or crossing the tiled floor of the main hall except by admitting Miss Manners's continuing presence? Through the insistent weeping of the summer rains there would be, one imagines, a singing of songs other than the ragas, in a voice not Parvati's, and the songs would be too recent to be attributable to Janet MacGregor. In any case Janet was a girl who can be imagined as given more to silence than sound, even at the end with the blood on her bodice and death approaching. Was the blood that of her baby or her husband? Perhaps it was her own. History doesn't record the answer or even pose the question. Janet MacGregor is a private ghost, an invisible marginal note on the title deeds of the MacGregor House that passed from European to Indian ownership when Sir Nello bought it in the early nineteen-thirties to mark the occasion of his return to the province and district of his birth. Lili Chatterjee was his second wife, fifteen years his junior. He had no children from either, which accounted possibly for the cuckoo clocks. And Nello was Lili's second husband. Her first was a Rajput prince who broke his neck at polo. She had no children by this athletic heir to a sedentary throne. And this, perhaps, followed by her similarly unproductive life with Nello accounts for her air of unencumbered wisdom, her capacity for free comment and advice. Widow first of a prince she was also the daughter of one. Her education began in Geneva and ended in Paris. For her second husband, reduced as she had been by academic training and worldly experience from a state of privilege to one of common-sense, she chose a man who had a talent for making money as well as for spending it. There were – perhaps still are although she does not mention them – blood relations who never spoke to her again for marrying out of the Rajput into the Vaisya caste. Sir Nello's father had only been a pleader in the courts of law.

And Nello's grandfather (she says) and his grandfather's fathers were only prosperous merchants and small landowners. Nello used to have some old family property still, out near Tanpur, but it all went a long time ago. I think Nello gave some away to the peasants. He told me he had, but it

61

may just have been a yarn, he may have got the idea from Tolstoy. He adored *Resurrection*. And he was very impressionable and eager to act out what he was impressed by. We Indians often are. Nello was a terrific mimic. He did Henry Manners at a party once and the Governor heard about it. So next time they met – Nello used to be called in quite often in an advisory capacity over questions of industrialisation in the province – next time they met Henry said, Well come on, Chatterjee, let's see it. And the point about Nello is that he couldn't resist doing the man right in front of him. He liked an audience that could judge him by the highest standards. That's how they became friends and why Henry gave him that old briar pipe you've seen in the glass case. Henry said he thought Nello's imitation would be even better if he had a real pipe in his mouth and not just an imaginary one. Of course, it wasn't better, but Nello pretended it was, and that's very Indian too, to pretend rather than give offence. Nello didn't even like the feel of the pipe in his mouth. He never smoked. Or drank. In fact on the quiet he was a bit of a glutton for self-denial, which is probably why he made a lot of money. And he was half-serious about religion. He said to me once, 'Lili, what would you say if I became *sannyasi*?' You know what that means? It means when a man chucks everything up, leaves his home and family and bashes off with a staff and a begging-bowl. So I said, 'Well, Nello, I'd bash off with you.' So that put paid to that.

It's the fourth stage, you know, *sannyasa*, the fourth and last, on earth anyway. I mean in the Hindu code of how you should live your life. The first stage is training and discipline and celibacy, the next is raising a family and establishing a household. In the third stage – I suppose you'd call it middle-age, what you English call a man's prime, but really a time when your children are beginning to find you a bit of a bore and think their ideas best – in the third stage you prepare to loosen the bonds. You make sure your children are married off and provided for, and you bless your grandchildren and try not to stand in anybody's way. Then you reach the fourth. You bash off into the forest before you become a doddering old burden, and try to make up for lost time in the business of earning religious merit, which of course you can earn all your life but earn best near the end when you give up your worldly possessions, reject the world's claims and try to forget Self. Of course, the English are always aghast at the idea of *sannyasa*. They think it's awful, opting out of your responsibilities like that and then expecting to live off the charity of strangers. I always point out to them that they have their *sannyasis* too: all those poor old people nobody wants who get sent to Twilight Homes. You must admit the Hindus are practical. You needn't bother your head about the religious side. It's like the cow in that respect. The cow became holy and beef unclean to stop the peasants eating it when they were hungry. If they ate their cows there'd be no milk, no bullocks to pull the carts to take stuff to the market or to help plough the fields or draw the water or turn the grindstone. Well, everybody knows that. But it's the same with *sannyasa*. We persuade old people to bash off and make one less mouth to feed by making them think it's a way of acquiring merit. And we make sure they're fed and not left to starve by persuading people who can afford it to believe they acquire merit too every time they give a wandering *sannyasi* a copper or a few grains of rice. We do have our own special brand of social security, you see. And we've had it far longer than anyone else. And nobody pays taxes for it.

Women can also become *sannyasi*. Shall *I*, do you think? Is the MacGregor House becoming my ashram? These days I'm much alone as you can guess from my talking your head off like this. But I was really thinking of Miss Crane. You say her name was Edwina. That's something I didn't know. I find it rather difficult to get used to. I should have thought of her more as Mildred. Anyway, to me she has always been Crane, Miss Crane. A bird with long legs and elongated neck trying to flap its way out of danger, too slowly, you know, like in slow motion at the movies. On one of those three or four occasions I went to see her after the trouble, when people were saying she was already round the bend, I tried to get her to tell me why she'd resigned from the mission. There weren't any pictures on the walls. But there were these two blank spaces where you could see pictures had been. Well, I knew about one blank space, but not the other. I said, 'I see you're beginning to pack.' Mr Gandhi had gone, as I knew, but I was curious to know what the other picture had been. A picture of Mr Nehru? The founder of the mission? The Light of the World?

But all she said was, 'No, I shan't need to pack,' so I guessed the mission johnnies had given her permission to stay on in the bungalow. You must visit it. It's still there. I went past it the other day on my way to the Purdah Hospital. I'm still on the committee, still making a nuisance of myself. Look out they say, here comes old Chatters. I bash off there the second Tuesday of every month and usually go the Bibighar bridge way but they're resurfacing the road and you get stuck for ages in the traffic, so this time we went by the Mandir Gate bridge, and Shafi took the wrong turning, stupid fellow. So there we were, not going past the old mission church but Miss Crane's bungalow. I haven't been down that road for years. It seems to be full of banias who've moved in from the bazaar. There was this big gross fellow on Miss Crane's little verandah picking his toes and listening to his transistor, and I think there were a couple of goats eating what there was of the grass and half a dozen children playing tag. She had such a pretty garden, too. Horticulture was the only subject we seemed to have in common. I told her she must come and see the garden here when she felt up to it, but she never did. The garden here at the MacGregor House is the same as it was then, so you can imagine it in those days. Bhalu grows the same flowers in the same beds year after year. He's always been an orderly type of man. Daphne used to pick the marigolds for the table, but she did tend to trample the edges of the beds and she'd only been with me a few days before Bhalu came and begged me to stop young memsahib trying to help him. Because he *grew* the flowers he thought he should be allowed to cut them. I told him the young memsahib liked flowers and wanted to help and although she was always smiling had had a lot of unhappiness and had lost all her family except her Auntie Ethel, so we had to be patient, but perhaps try to get her interested in ferns and evergreens which always grow wild in the shrubbery and made much *chic*-er decorations than marigolds. Now it's Parvati who picks the marigolds. But she's as light as a feather and old Bhalu's only too glad to have extra time to snooze and dream he's back in the army, looking after Colonel James Sahib's garden. I haven't the faintest idea who Colonel James was, but as Bhalu gets older the colonel gets more and more VIP in his imagination, and now it seems the colonel can't have been anything less than personal aide to the Viceroy. It used to be a status symbol for an Indian family to hire a servant who'd worked for the old-style British. It still is, but that kind of servant is getting so old now, and useless, that it's better to get someone from the bazaar and train them up. Bhalu used to refer to Nello as the Chota Sahib. Indians were always called that by servants who'd worked for *your* people, to distinguish them from British burra Sahibs. Burra means big, and chota means small. But you must know that too. Nello always laughed, but I think it hurt him a bit, knowing his head gardener called him a chota sahib.

I wish Daphne had known Nello, but of course he died several years before she came to stay with me. They had the same sense of fun. In a big girl that kind of thing is more noticeable, isn't it? Or do I mean that big girls are jollier than ordinary size ones? But tiny girls are often jolly too, aren't they? I mean tiny English girls. Indian girls are mostly tiny. Look at Parvati now. If they're big they're awfully earnest and sometimes violent. They seem to act as if they have a special position to keep up. If they're taller than their husbands the situation becomes fraught. I was an inch shorter than Nello and five inches shorter than my first husband Ranji.

I'm trying to remember how tall Miss Crane was. Taller than I of course, but medium English height probably. The neck and the legs and the nose are all I vividly remember. I mostly saw her sitting down or sitting up. Dinner at Connie White's, and then when I visited her at the British General Hospital and at her bungalow after she'd been discharged but still wasn't well enough to get up. She received me the first time I went to her bungalow lying on a charpoy on the verandah. It was difficult seeing her in the British hospital. The English friends I had who were ill usually went to the Greenlawns nursing home and had private rooms they couldn't afford. If I wanted to visit there I could always fix it with Doctor Mayhew. And if anyone was in the general hospital they always seemed to have a room in the private wing and all I had to do then was ring Ian Macintosh who was the Civil Surgeon and ask him to tell someone to warn the sister-in-charge. But Miss Crane was in the public wing in a ward with three or four other beds and Ian was out of station the day I decided to go. I'd never been in at the main reception before. The girl there – she was Anglo-Indian, but as white as a European – said I couldn't see Miss Crane, and when I insisted she kept me waiting in the hall and only pretended to have sent a message to the ward sister. What she had done was send a warning up to her. It was rather silly because Daphne had been doing voluntary work at the hospital and she *lived* with me, but because I was an Indian I wasn't really allowed in, anyway, not welcome. There wasn't actually a rule about it, just an unwritten one. I could have gone to the military wing because there were Indian King's commissioned officers on the station. That meant I could have visited say Lieutenant Shashardri or his wife, but the civil wing was sacrosanct. When Mrs Menen who was the wife of the District and Sessions Judge was ill she had a room in the nursing home, which Ian Macintosh always insisted should be multi-racial, provided people could pay for a room there. Although even then there was an unwritten rule that an Indian patient had to be of a certain type to get a bed. It didn't matter much and never caused any trouble because if an Indian was rich enough to afford it but not the right type his wife anyway was almost bound to be the kind of woman who wouldn't dream of going anywhere but the Purdah Hospital.

Anyway, there I was, the day I went to visit Miss Crane, sat down in the hall, hoping I looked as if I hadn't the slightest idea that anything was wrong, and after a bit all these lumpy QAs and harpy VADs started popping into reception on some excuse or other but actually to see if the rumour were true, that an Indian woman had had the brass to present herself at the desk and expect to be allowed up into the wards. I felt like something in a zoo, but then we often did in those days. I would probably have been sitting there still if Bruce Mayhew who had a consultant appointment there hadn't come whirling in and stopped dead and said, 'Hello, Lili, what on earth are you doing sitting *there*?' I told him I'd come to visit Miss Crane and that the girl at reception was trying to get hold of the ward-sister for me. I didn't want to get the receptionist into trouble, but of course Bruce knew what was happening. He said there was no need to bother the ward-sister and that he was going up there himself and would take me. When we got into the room where Miss Crane was he stayed with us long enough to make it clear to the other English women in the ward that I was *somebody*. Not that it made any difference. When Bruce went out one of them rang the bell. Ordinarily a nurse would have answered it, but the ward-sister came in herself. I know Bruce spoke to her on his way out because he told me so afterwards. He went specially to her cubby-hole and apologised for taking a visitor in to see Miss Crane without her permission. He didn't say who I was because he knew it wasn't necessary. I mean he knew she had been told an Indian woman had been trying to get in, and that she had intentionally locked herself in her cubby-hole so that she couldn't be 'found'. Anyway, in she stalked a few minutes after Bruce had gone and only a few seconds after this woman had rung the bell. She stopped in her tracks as if amazed to see anyone there. She said, 'What are you doing here, don't you know visitors aren't allowed at this time of day?' I told her Doctor Mayhew had given me permission because no one had been able to find her. Oh, *I* am in charge of this ward, not Doctor Mayhew, she said, please leave at once. Was it you who rang the bell, Miss Crane? As if Miss

Crane had rung to get me thrown out. And before Miss Crane could say anything, this woman who'd actually rung piped up, No, it was me who rang, my rest is being disturbed. She sounded like the wife of a foreman from the British-Indian Electrical. Cockney, overlaid with a year or two of listening to how the wives of the directors spoke. I'm sorry. That's awfully snob of me, isn't it, but I was upset and angry not only because of what was happening, but also because I saw I'd probably put myself in the wrong over the question of official visiting hours. But Daphne had always said nobody took any notice of them and just wandered about at almost any old time. And there *were* other people going in to visit patients. It was my bad luck that there was nobody visiting any of these other women in Miss Crane's ward just then. And what was so awfully unfair was the fact that poor old Miss Crane had only had two visitors the whole time she'd been there – the chaplain and Mr Poulson who really only saw her officially. The poor man didn't have time for more than that. It was he who rescued her, you remember. After she'd come through the pneumonia he had to ask her a lot of questions about the men who had killed Mr Chaudhuri. He didn't *have* to do that, it was really Ronald Merrick's job, but Mr Poulson and Mr White knew Miss Crane had to be treated gently and they knew Merrick wasn't a gentle sort of man. And Miss Crane hadn't been helpful with her answers. She wasn't popular any longer in the hospital. People thought she was holding something back so that an Indian killer would go free. When I visited her she'd been in the hospital three weeks and had only just been taken out of a side ward into this room with the lumps and harpies. Bruce Mayhew had told me on the way up that he appreciated my coming to see her. She had almost no white friends. For a day or two at the beginning she'd been thought a lot of in the hospital because she'd come through a bad time in the first riots. They would have liked her to be a heroine of the kind that breathed fire and got a few rioters swinging on the end of a rope. But she didn't breathe fire, and although in the end they got some of the men who'd led the mob and killed Mr Chaudhuri, that was due to the tenacity of the sub-inspector in Tanpur, and people thought justice would have been done quicker if Miss Crane had helped with proper descriptions. I suppose it didn't help her, my going to see her, and certainly didn't help me, my going to see *her*, although there was nothing much that would have helped *me* in the circumstances. The few white friends she had were the kind who hadn't the time to go and see her, and her Indian friends weren't the kind who'd have dared even to try. Some of the soldiers from the barracks clubbed together and sent her flowers and there were a few gifts from poor Indians like Mr Narayan who taught at the Chillianwallah school. Probably more gifts of that kind than ever reached her. The hospital staff wouldn't even have to look at the card to tell whether flowers came from an Indian or a European. I expect a lot were thrown away, so that she never had the chance of knowing how much the Indians liked her, not just for not giving evidence that wasn't absolutely in line with what she remembered, but for herself. I know Connie White and Mavis Poulson always *meant* to go and see her in hospital, but things were in such a frightful state, almost a state of siege, they never had the proper opportunity. It must have made her feel loved by no one. And about my own visit, you must bear in mind that Indians were hardly popular among the whites just then, and then of course, there was the other business, too. They all knew I was the woman in whose house Daphne was staying. It's what I told myself when I'd got over the anger and annoyance of being thrown out by that harpy sister.

What made being thrown out more or less bearable was the fact that Miss Crane didn't seem to care whether I stayed or went, so the situation resolved itself. The sister stood over the bed and I got up and Miss Crane said, 'Thank you for visiting me, Lady Chatterjee.' But the way she said it made it sound as if I were too late, or she were too late, or as if nothing that happened now could alter the way she saw things. A couple of days later Bruce rang me and said any time I wanted to visit Miss Crane I only had to appear at the reception desk. He'd kicked up an awful fuss apparently. He said the hospital staff simply hadn't realised who I was. I said, Oh Bruce, of course they realised. If I'd been just Mrs Chatterjee the whole thing would have been a joke to them, something they could score over and then forget. But being Lady Chatterjee, the widow of a man knighted by their own King, that made it awfully serious, something they really had to take a stand over, quite apart from the personal jealousy they might feel not being Knights' ladies themselves. After all, practically every Indian who had them gave up his title and honours about this time and returned his decorations to the Viceroy for forwarding to King George or whatever, and that was thought frightful. If it wasn't thought frightful it was thought only right, because the Europeans always looked on Indian titles as a bit of a joke. If Nello had been alive I expect he'd have reverted to plain Mister along with the rest of them. These days a lot of people still use their titles even though they're not recognised by Government but in *those* days people used to say to me, Why don't you drop the Lady? Nello would have dropped the Sir. So I said I can't choose a course of action for a husband who's dead. If I drop the Lady I'm really dishonouring *him*, just for my own peace of mind. Anyway, he *deserved* his title.

There were people in Mayapore who said I only kept up with Lady Manners for snob reasons, *Indian* snob reasons, like calling an English person by his Christian name. They said the same when I had Daphne come to live here at the MacGregor House. She was Henry Manners's brother's daughter. Connie White told me people tried to snub Daphne in places like the Gymkhana, snub her by pretending not to know where Daphne was staying so that they could smirk or look shocked when she said the MacGregor House. She didn't go to the club much – at least not at first – because I wasn't allowed in there, even as a guest. The Deputy Commissioner himself couldn't have got me past the door. Even the Viceroy couldn't. She only went to show friendly to the girls she worked with at the hospital, but then Ronald Merrick tried to set his cap at her and began to take her out and around and she was at the club with him several times. That was another bad mark against her. Mr Merrick was just about the most eligible bachelor on the station. He was quite good-looking, if a man with a permanent sneer in his eyes can ever be called that, but the main thing about him was his position as District Superintendent of Police. All the unmarried girls who didn't mind too much that he had no 'family' to speak of had hopes of hooking him. He'd never taken much notice of them so they didn't take very kindly to Daphne for apparently getting hold of him without so much as a finger raised. Neither Robin White nor Jack Poulson liked him much, but they said he was good at his job. Judge Menen couldn't stand him, but never said so in so many words. I had him round at the MacGregor House because I'd been on good terms with his predecessor, a rather older man called Angus MacGilvray. I thought Mr Merrick would be annoyed if he didn't even get an invitation, but I was surprised when he accepted it. He only came, though, because it was here he had the opportunity to meet Indians socially. You could see his mind working away, storing up little things that were said, so that he could go home and make a note on the confidential files that were kept so that whenever there was any civil trouble the most influential congress wallahs and anyone who ranked as dangerous could be locked up right away. I guessed he cottoned on to Daphne because he saw it as a duty to be on terms with someone who might let slip things that were going on here that were kept from him when he visited. He saw the MacGregor House as a sort of Cliveden, a hot-bed of Indian intrigue, a forcing-house for English reds – which of course would be the opposite of Cliveden-ish, but you know what I mean. But I was wrong, I think. His reasons for cottoning on to Daphne were much more complicated than that. By the time I realised how complicated, it was too late.

I often wish I could have that time all over again, but knowing what I know now. Not just for Daphne's sake, but for Miss Crane's sake. I think I could have stopped Miss Crane from becoming *sannyasi* in that especially horrible way. It's all right to give everything up as long as you realise just what it is you've *had*. Poor Miss Crane didn't. That last time I saw her at the bungalow, when she was sitting in her room and I noticed the two blank spaces on the walls, she said, 'Lady Chatterjee, why do you come to see me?' And all I could think of to say was, 'To see if you want anything.' Well, I ask you, what was the good of that? Can you imagine a woman of Miss Crane's temperament admitting that she needed help? What should I have said, do you think? Said instead of what I did say? Well, if she were there now, and not that fat fellow picking his toes and listening to film music on his little radio, I think I'd say, 'Because neither of us must give up, and I can see you're about to.'

I must get my times sorted out. I work it out that I paid her *three* visits, not four. The first time in the hospital, and then on the occasion when she was still laid up but at home and I found her resting on the verandah with that old servant of hers hovering about, watching from the doorway to make sure she wasn't upset, and then a few weeks later when I'd heard about her resignation which came as a surprise to everybody. After my first visit to the bungalow I thought I should keep away for a while, but then people told me she'd had her soldiers to tea again. So I thought, Now's the time. Now we can get to know each other. But I didn't go right then. I had so much to do. I didn't go until I heard about her resignation and that people were saying she must have gone a bit bats. I called one afternoon. The servant was on the verandah, which of course was perfectly normal, but I realised he was on guard. He said Miss Crane was very busy and couldn't see anyone and I was about to go when she called out, Who is it? and he went inside, then came out again and said I could go in. She was in her bedroom, sitting in an armchair. She didn't get up and didn't ask me to sit down, but I sat all the same and it was then she said, Lady Chatterjee, why do you come to see me? I thought for a moment, and then came out with this silly remark, To see if you want anything. It's kind of you, she said, but there's nothing I want. I said, I hear you've resigned from the mission. She simply nodded her head. I looked round the room, as you do, don't you, when you're with someone in a room you've just heard they're going away from. And I saw those two blank spaces on the walls, one of which must have been made by Gandhi and the other by someone else. So I made this remark about packing already. Oh, I shan't need to pack, she said, and then after a bit, while I was trying to work out why, she *smiled*, but to herself, not to me, so I thought, Well, it's true. She's nuts. It was because I thought, Oh, she's nuts, that I didn't ask what she meant, didn't say, The mission johnnies are going to *give* you the bungalow then? I didn't ask because it seemed so unlikely and I thought her answer would only add to the feeling I had that she was off her head, and I didn't feel up to coping with the embarrassment of having it proved. So I left it at that, she wouldn't need to pack. Poor Miss Crane. I ought to have followed up, I ought to have said, Why? Not that she'd have come right out with the real answer. The awful thing is it was in my mind afterwards that it may have been only then, when we were sitting there talking about not needing to pack, that she really understood why she wasn't going to pack, saw why there wouldn't be any need. That smile, you see, coming some while after she'd said, Oh I shan't pack, I shan't be packing, I shan't need to. Then she changed the subject. She asked how Daphne was. How is Miss Manners? Like that, in that tone of voice, of someone asking about a *colleague*, as if between them they represented something, which I suppose they did. She didn't know young Kumar. If she'd known about Hari Kumar I expect she'd have said, How is Miss Manners? in the same tone as before but added, Is it true what I hear, what I hear about what they've done to young Mr Kumar?

*

Dinner is the only meal Parvati has with the family, such as the family is: that is to say, Lili Chatterjee and young Parvati, the two of them. When there are no guests there is this picture to be had of them sharing one end of the long polished dining-room table, with two places laid close together, the old woman and the young girl, talking in English because even now that is the language of Indian society, in the way that half a century ago French was the language of polite Russians.

The man who serves them is quite young, too young to have been more than a small lad about the house at the time Miss Manners lived there, and actually he was not even that. He is a recent acquisition. He is from the south, a cousin of some kind of Bhalu, the old gardener. It amuses Lady Chatterjee that although it was on Bhalu's recommendation that Ram Dass, whom she calls Ramu, got the job of houseboy he has since had little to do with the gardener because Bhalu's position is so inferior to his own. He will not even admit a family connection. Sometimes from the servants' quarters behind the house you can hear them quarrelling. The cook despises them both. He has cooked for a maharanee in his time. There is a girl sweeper called Sushila. Lady Chatterjee turns a blind eye to evidence that the Muslim driver, the handsome grinning Shafi, sleeps with Sushila. It is difficult to get enough servants and their wage demands get higher every year. Some of the rooms in the MacGregor House are shut up.

With all the chicks lowered the house is dark and cool even at midday. The ceilings are very high. In such rooms human thought is in the same danger as an escaped canary would be, wheeling up and up, round and round, fluttering in areas of shadow and in crevices you can imagine untouched by any human hand since the house was rebuilt by MacGregor. In these rooms, at night, even the artificial illumination of lamps and brackets fails to reach the remoter angles and areas that would lie far beyond the reach of a man standing on the shoulders of another. It is best to depend upon a humdrum eye-level for impressions; the strain on the neck otherwise is no less acute than the strain on the senses then of other years impinging on the present. There is in any case always a lulling feeling of immediacy in these ground-floor rooms, the present lying as it does in the lower levels, like the mist of a young day in ancient hollows. It is in going upstairs that the feeling of mounting into the past first comes and ever afterwards persists, no matter how many times the routine journey is undertaken. Bedrooms, after all, are more specifically the repositories of their old occupants' intimate sensations than the public rooms below.

Collecting a key from some arcane source or other – a guest never penetrates the barrier from behind which the control and ordering of the household is directed – Lady Chatterjee goes up the broad uncarpeted polished wood staircase that curves from the black and white tiled hall to the complex of landings and corridors and opens the mahogany, brass-knobbed door of the room where Miss Manners slept and which she still calls Daphne's room. It smells musty, as unused as the late Sir Nello's museum of schoolboy curios which suitably enough lies directly below it, with a view to the garden when the chicks are raised and a continuing view through the gaps between the bushiness of the shorter trees to the plains that surround Mayapore and the smudge of hills on the horizon. There is the spire of St Mary's church, a mile or two distant, still standing, still as irrelevant to its background as any architecture, Anglo or Indian, seems to be in this strangely unfinished landscape that makes the monotonous chanting of the crows which are never at rest sound like the cries of creatures only partially evolved, not yet born, but sharpened already by desires the world will eventually recognise as hunger.

In the desk there are two of the letters Miss Manners wrote to her aunt which Lady Manners afterwards gave to Lili Chatterjee, perhaps not wanting them herself, or the recollections they stirred; and these, possibly, reveal similar hungers and contrasting desires: uncoordinated, irrelevant. She must have written them – unless she wrote them at night when the crows fitfully slept, impatient of morning – to the same accompaniment they are read to all this time after. The letters, read to the accompaniment of this continuing unchanging sound, are curiously dead, strangely inarticulate. Why pretend otherwise? They do not resurrect the writer. They are merely themselves; like the photograph of Miss Manners which is signed with a calligraphic flourish by one Subhas Chand who used to take portraits of those people on the station who wanted a record for friends and relatives of what Mayapore had done to them. Subhas Chand, Lady Chatterjee says, had a booth in the shop of the chemist, Dr Gulab Singh Sahib. And Clancy was pictured there, in full-face, as his handsome pushing self in spotless khaki drill, and in matey combination with the rustic Barrett, staring out at the world from a background (again irrelevant) of draped velvet and gothic fern (maidenhair in a brass bowl on a romantic revival monumental column around which graveyard ivy is invisible but naggingly present to the impressionable eye).

The pictures of Clancy lie irrelevant too, like gifts kept from a Christmas cracker, among the rest of Miss Crane's unclaimed personal effects which have somehow been preserved at Mission Headquarters in Calcutta; mouldering relics not of Miss Crane alone but also of sustained Christian honesty, and of the disinterested shrugs of distant Crane cousins, offspring of those poor ones who on her father's death turned up for the funeral in the mild hope of benefit and then departed, putting her out of mind and of temptation's reach of their own slender pockets in case the brave funeral face and declarations of self-sufficiency turned out to be untrustworthy. Having already seen in Calcutta pictures of Clancy, the Subhas Chand technique and signature, the quality of the matt-surfaced sepia paper he used for his prints (small cabinet size), all strike harmonious echoes of recognition when the picture of Miss Manners, memorially enclosed in a silver-plated frame, is first lifted from its place on the dressing-table which she sat at combing her apparently curly short-cut sepia hair.

You can't from this (Lady Chatterjee says, rubbing at a speck of tarnish on the frame) get a real idea of her personality. I think looking at pictures of people you don't or didn't know but only know about is intensely

71

unsatisfactory. Of course, it's fascinating to see for the first time a portrait of someone like that, someone whose name was at one time on a lot of people's lips, as they say. You're probably feeling that now, but once the initial curiosity has been satisfied there's a sense of anti-climax, isn't there? Or perhaps even of no climax at all because you can't be absolutely sure the picture is anything like a good likeness or even that it's a picture of the right person? Do you know, I sometimes take a second look at pictures of myself and Nello – that one downstairs taken at the garden party in Simla for instance, where we're sandwiched between Lord Willingdon and the Aga Khan, and I think: Is that really Nello? Did I really look like that? Did I ever smile in quite such a smug way? Almost coy-smug, glancing at something that has caught my eye but isn't in the picture. Since I can't even guess what it could have been that caught my eye, let alone remember what it was, I begin to wonder whether the woman in the picture (who anyway doesn't *feel* like me) isn't an impersonator, and the plump chap with her a man who isn't Nello but is taking Nello off almost as successfully as Nello used to take off Henry Manners. Willingdon and the Aga Khan look all right, but then when you meet and chat to blokes as high up as that you tend to look at them in only two dimensions, which is the way the camera looks at them too, so the photographic result is bound to seem authentic.

Daphne had this picture taken by Subhas Chand two or three months after she came to stay here. It wasn't her idea. Lady Manners wrote me and said: Tell Daphne I'd like a picture of her for my birthday but not to bother to frame it because I've got trunks full of frames from Henry's old Rogues' Gallery. It's what she and Henry called their collection of photographs. The Rogues' Gallery. Everything from old daguerreotypes of Henry's pa with his foot on a dead buffalo to groups taken at some beano with all the princes except one scowling at the camera because Henry's handsome aide had got the protocol wrong and stood a chap with a nine-gun salute closer to the Governor than a chap with eleven guns. And then there were all the snaps given to Henry and Henry's pa by servants – timid old boys pretending to look like tribesmen, all white whiskers and lopsided turbans. Henry never threw a single snap away. They all got framed and went with him wherever they were posted. When he died, Ethel had them packed up and put into trunks. I often wonder who this old silver frame originally had in it. I inherited it complete with Daphne's picture along with the two letters. I think if Daphne had given me a copy too, at the time she bashed off to Subhas Chand to have her picture taken for her Aunt Ethel's birthday, I think if I'd always had it, I'd see it as far more like Daphne than I do. But it came afterwards. It came here into this house, into this bedroom, when Daphne wasn't alive to come back in herself. I expect I resented it. It's always struck me as not quite belonging. It's Daphne all right – she had that kind of hopeful smile – perhaps she'd nearly knocked over one of old Subhas Chand's spotlights just before she sat down, and was still thinking: There I go again, just like me, catch me in a china shop,

Auntie. It's a sweet smile though, isn't it? And that's come through. But photographers like Subhas Chand always make people's skin look like wax. There's not the tiniest crack in it anywhere, and around the eyes where there ought to be cracks, lines anyway, it's all been smoothed out by touching up and the real Daphne simply isn't looking out of them.

She had a habit of blinking whenever she began to speak, as if she couldn't get out the first word or two with her eyes open. And often she shut her eyes at the end of what she was saying. When she shut her eyes this little smile you see in the photograph used to come on automatically, as if her eyelids and lips were working off the same set of nerves. And it *was* nervousness that made her do it. I used to think of it as affectation. I met her for the first time when I went up to Pindi to spend Christmas with Ethel Manners. It was Daphne's first Christmas in India and Ethel wanted to cheer her up. I'd expected to find someone mopey, instead there she was, blinking at me and chatting at me. I sensed the affectation before I pinpointed the mannerism, before I *noticed* the blinking, but once I'd separated the cause from the effect I realized that what I called affectation was nothing more complicated than straightforward shyness. The eye-shutting and the smiling were to give herself confidence in company. Once she got used to you the mannerism disappeared. But it came back at once if a stranger came into the room. People instinctively liked her, though, and she never gave in to her shyness, she never seemed at a loss for a word.

What old Subhas Chand hasn't been able to disguise, at least from me, is that this is the portrait of a girl who was more comfortable in specs. She had to wear them to read or to write letters. According to the oculists, she really needed them all the time but her aunt discouraged her and said specs were a lot of nonsense for young people. What she meant was that specs just weren't attractive, especially on a girl. I discouraged her too, not because I thought specs could be unattractive, but because I knew you could cure bad sight by exercises, splashing the eyes with cold water, looking alternately from short to long distances, looking up from concentrated work like writing a letter or reading a book and focusing on some fixed object in the room several feet away. But Auntie, she used to say, she got into the habit of calling me Auntie, I can't *see* into long distances, I can't even see short distances properly. She used to stand at the window there, putting her specs on and taking them off. Eventually she made out where the hills are. She wanted so much to see everything there was to see. India was what we used to call a thing with her. She'd always wanted to come out. She was born in the Punjab but didn't remember any of it because her mother couldn't stand the climate and her father resigned from his service and went home into private practice when Daphne was still almost a baby. He was IMS. Years younger than his brother Henry. I don't think he minded leaving India at the time. He obviously chose to be a doctor instead of an administrator so that he wouldn't have to compete with clever brother Henry all his life. By all accounts his wife, Daphne's mother, was a tartar. She had to have everything her own way and she was a frightful snob. India obviously didn't suit her as the wife of a junior man in the IMS. Law and medicine are the two things we Indians have always shone at so I expect George – Daphne's dad – had too many Indian colleagues for Mrs George's liking. She wanted him to be what today you people call a Top Person, with rooms in Harley Street and masses of top hospital appointments. But when he was in a fair way to getting what she wanted she changed her tack and saw herself as a leader of county society, so then there was the flat in town and the house in Wiltshire and poor George working himself to death bashing off from one place to the other. You can tell the effect it had on him from something Daphne said to me. She said, 'Poor daddy always regretted leaving India, didn't he? I wish he were here with me now to see it all again.' There were times when I thought she worked doubly hard at knowing India simply to make up to her father for what he had missed and probably admitted regretting having given up just to please her mother. And like all those apparently frail women who can't stand the Indian climate Daphne's ma turned out as strong as an ox. At least until she got cancer. And in my opinion that is a disease of the strong rather than of the weak.

*

Picture her then: Daphne Manners, a big girl (to borrow a none too definite image from Lady Chatterjee) leaning on the balcony outside her bedroom window, gazing with concentration (as one might gaze for two people, one being absent, once deprived, since dead, and now regretted) at a landscape calculated to inspire in the most sympathetic western heart a degree of cultural shock. There is (even from this vantage point above a garden whose blooms will pleasurably convey scent if you bend close enough to them) a pervading redolence, wafting in from the silent, heat-stricken trembling plains; from the vast panorama of fields, from the river, from the complex of human dwellings (with here and there, spiky or bulbous, a church, a mosque, a temple), from the streets and lanes and the sequestered white bungalows, the private houses, the public buildings, the station, from the rear quarters of the MacGregor House. A smell. Could it be of ordure?

After a few months the newcomer will cease to notice it. Ubiquitous, it translates itself from repellent through almost attractive because familiar stages into an essence distilled by an empirically committed mind, so that an old hand, temporarily bereft of it, nostalgically remembering it in some less malodorous place, will describe it to himself as the sub-continental equivalent of acrid wood-smoke at the end of a burnished copper autumn. But let the old hand's bereavement be of comparatively short duration: European leave, a rarified, muscular effort above the Himalayan snow lines. Let it not be, for instance, an eighteen-year absence ended by chance and luck and the lepidopteristic intention to pin down the truth about Miss Crane, Miss Manners and young Kumar, and the events that seemed first to flutter and then to shatter Mayapore but actually seem to have left it untouched, massively in continuing brick-and-mortar possession of itself (if not of the landscape feebly invaded by its architectural, artisan formation). No, let it not be long, let it be short so that on renewed association the returning traveller will cry, possessively, even gratefully: Ah, India! Otherwise, after eighteen years and a too swift transition by Comet through the increasingly disturbing ambience of Beirut and Bahrein (the warmth correspondingly mounting, bringing the smell out like the warmth of a woman's skin releasing the hidden but astonishing formula of an unusual perfume) the nose – unused, but imagining itself prepared – will flex its nostrils against the grave revelation of the car or taxi drive from Bombay's Santa Cruz airport, along a road that leads through fields where the source of the wafting smell may be tracked to the squatting early morning figures of male labourers casting their pellets upon the earth, there to lie, and harden, and encrust, and disintegrate, and lift in the currents of air into the generality of the prevailing winds.

Taking possession of the room to help, as Lady Chatterjee says, in the business of getting to know the surroundings that was Daphne's, left alone there, moving across the broad acres of uncarpeted floor, between the mosquito-net-shrouded bed and the door that leads into the private bathroom, one might – by attempting the journey from one island of Kashmir rug to another, not wetting one's feet in the striated sea of dark stained boards – play a variation of that old childhood game of not stepping on the cracks between paving stones and wonder if Daphne had time for similar absurdities. The bathroom is long and narrow. Green glazed tiles act on the walls from floor to shoulder height as shadowy mirrors of the room's contents and of its headless occupant. Perhaps Daphne, with her uncertain sight, was unaware of this and strode oblivious of truncated duplication by reflection from the door to the porcelain pedestal whose cistern, high up, is activated by one's pulling like a bell ringer on a long chain whose pot handgrip, moulded to the shape of the palm, emphasises the luxuriousness of a comparatively rare machine. The porcelain tub is as big as an artificial lake, empty at this moment as if drained for an annual scraping. Its webbed claw feet are those of some dead, amphibious monster sentenced to support it like Atlas supporting the world. The immense brass taps suggest twin flows of piped-out water of ship's pump velocity, but only the cold tap works; the hot – when the stiff faucet is finally budged – produces a hollow rasping echo and a skitter of rust flakes. But the cold is warm enough. The bathroom is airless. There is no fan and only one window high up above the lavatory pedestal. At the opposite end of the bathroom – fifteen paces on bare feet across lukewarm mosaic that is slightly uneven and impresses the soles with the not unpleasant sensation of walking over the atrophied honeycomb of some long forgotten species of giant bee – there is an old-fashioned marble-topped washstand with an ormolu mirror on the wall above it, plain white china soap-dishes and a white jug on the slab; beneath the stand a slop-bowl with a lid and a wicker-bound handle. Here too is the towel-rack, a miniature gymnastic contraption of parallel mahogany bars and upright poles, hung with immense fluffy towels and huckabacks in a diminishing range of sizes, each embroidered in blue with the initials LC.

Returning to the other end, literally ascending the throne which is mounted on a broad dais anciently carpeted in the deep blue red of mouldy cherries, the splendour of the paper-holder fixes the attention. Here are lions, gilt-maned, gilt-faced, each holding in its gilt jaws an end of the bracket which supports the roll of buff, wood-chip austerity paper. The jaw of the nearer lion (and presumably that of its mate on the other side) adequately receives the ball of the little finger. Its head is as large as a clenched fist, so large that its cheek rests almost upon the cheek of its gilded counterpart. The effect is of two big cats grinning over the simple duty they have to hold, in readiness, something that is required for a cat-like but, because of the paper, ridiculous human function.

Lying in the bath, the eyes engage the single 75-watt bulb in a shade the shape of a pantomime Aladdin's hat, and attempt to see, above, the distant shadowy ceiling. A brass jug, dented from falls on to the mosaic floor, rests on the wooden rack that lies athwart the tub. The scoop. One remembers and, having soaped, stands and scoops and pours and scoops again and so, closing the eyes against the contrary evidence of the sex, attempts a re-enactment of Miss Manners refreshing herself after a hard day on the wards of the Mayapore hospital.

*

(To Lady Manners)

The MacGregor House,
MacGregor Road,
Mayapore, I.
26th February, 1942

Dear Auntie Ethel,

Please forgive me for not having written sooner. I hope you got Lili's telegram saying we'd arrived here safely. I'm sure you did. I can hardly believe it's a week since we said goodbye to you in Rawalpindi. It was sweet of you to let me come. The days have flown and looking back on them there scarcely seem to have been enough of them for us to have packed in everything we've done. I've just come back from my *second* day on the wards in the hospital which will show you no time has been wasted!

After Lahore the journey down was very interesting, much nicer than the one I did alone last year from Bombay to Pindi, which rather scared me because it was all so new and strange. I suppose I enjoyed this one because I've learned some of the ropes and anyway had Lili with me. She really *is* extraordinary, isn't she? Those awful English women in the carriage got out the next morning in Lahore. They were utterly beastly and never said a civil word to either of us. And those mounds of luggage they had that took up more than half the space! They hogged the little wc cubicle for over an hour after the train pulled out, and then sat up for ages drinking and smoking and talking as if neither of us was there while Lili and I were trying to get to sleep. (We had the upper and lower berth on one side of the carriage and they had the upper and lower on the other side.) I was so fagged I didn't wake up until the train had stopped at Lahore and there was all the fuss of them getting out. There was a chap to meet them, the husband of the one with her brains tied up in a scarf, I think. He came into the carriage at one point to look for something the one with the scarf was complaining had either been lost or *stolen*. They'd been out on the platform for some time while the coolies collected the luggage and he came in prepared to be rude. The poor chap looked awfully embarrassed when he saw *me*. They'd only complained to him about Lili, I expect. I was sitting up on the top bunk keeping an eye on *our* bags, with my hair all over the place. Lili had been up and dressed since five (so she told me afterwards) and was sitting there below me looking marvellous and cool as a cucumber, reading a book and pretending to be quite unaware of what was going on. Anyway he begged our pardon and thrashed about for a time, and the coolies thrashed about, searching under the seat and everywhere that didn't make it look too pointed that these women had suggested *we* might have pinched whatever it was one of them had lost. Then one of them called through the doorway, 'It's all right, Reggie, luckily it's been found.' I liked that 'luckily'! Reggie was as red as a beetroot by now and went out with his tail between his legs, and I think there was a row when he got back on the platform. The last thing we heard was the harpy saying very loudly, 'I don't care. The whole thing is a disgrace. I don't know what the country's coming to. After all first class *is* first class.' That word of Lili's is awfully apt, isn't it? Harpy.

It was marvellous from then on though. We had the whole compartment to ourselves and a lovely breakfast brought in. You know, until now I never did quite believe that story you told me about the time Sir Nello was turned out of a first class compartment by a couple of box-wallah Englishmen. It seemed to me that if the railways allow an Indian to make a first class booking then no one should be able to stop them using what they've paid for. I think if you hadn't been at Pindi station to see us off, though, there'd have been trouble with these two women about Lili and me actually getting in. Me only because I was with Lili. Was that why you got into the carriage first and condescended to them in that marvellous nineteenth-century way, before they had a chance of seeing her and realising they were going to have to travel with an Indian woman?

When I remember how awful it is travelling at home in the blackout, with no heating in the trains, just a dim blue light, and the stations in darkness, people jam-packed in the corridors as well as in the compartments, but on the whole everyone helping everyone else and trying to be cheerful, I get really angry about the kind of thing that happens over here. Honestly, Auntie, a lot of the white people in India don't know they're born. Of course I never travelled first class at home, and there was sometimes bad feeling among the non-commissioned boys in the services when they were packed like sardines and the pinkest young subaltern fresh out of Octu travelled in comparative comfort, but that's service life. *This* is to do with civilians. Well, I mustn't go on about it.

It's much warmer here in Mayapore than Pindi. I only need a sheet at night and it won't be long before I have to have a fan going all the time. Lili's given me a marvellous room all to myself, and a super bathroom (although the seat's a bit wonky on the wc! and there's an inhibiting paper-holder guarded by lions). The MacGregor House is fascinating. I have to keep reminding myself that you never actually visited it because Uncle Henry had retired and left the province before Nello bought the place. But of course you remember Mayapore itself, although Lili says there have been lots of changes since then. The Technical College, for instance, the one Nello built and endowed and got his knighthood for, and the new buildings put up by the British-Indian Electrical. They're building an aerodrome out at Banyaganj which the English people say has ruined the duckshooting! How Hitler would laugh! (There are some lakes out there which Lili says were a favourite European picnic spot.) A couple of evenings ago we went to dinner with the Deputy Commissioner and his wife, Robin and Constance White, who said they met you and Uncle Henry years ago, but didn't think you'd remember them because they were very junior. Mr White was under a Mr Cranston at the time, and they said you'd remember *him* all right if only because of the occasion when he was in camp, touring his district, and you and Uncle Henry, who were also touring, called in unexpectedly and found him bathing in a pool. Apparently you both stood on the bank talking for ages and he stood there doing his best to answer sensibly and be polite, standing very straight as if at attention, up to his waist in rather muddy water, and not daring to move because he had no bathing-drawers on. He thought afterwards that you and Uncle Henry *knew*, and were just keeping him in that awkward situation for the fun of it. I promised Mr White I'd mention this when I wrote to you, and ask if you really did know, because he's always wondered. It seems Mr Cranston never was certain. But it is one of the funny stories about the Governor and his Lady that went around for years and years – as you can judge, since it came up only the other night here in Mayapore, after all that time.

I liked Mr White, and his wife, although like all pukka mems *she* is a bit frightening at first. (I used to be frightened of *you*.) But they both seem to admire and respect Lili. It was a very private and friendly sort of party, with just two other men to balance Lili and myself at the table – Mr Macintosh the Civil Surgeon, who is a widower and another old friend of Lili's, and Judge Menen. He's married, but his wife is in the local nursing home at the moment. I liked the judge. He has a wonderful sense of humour, or so I realised later in the evening. At first I thought him a bit snooty and critical, and put it down to an inferiority complex about being the only male Indian present. He's much older than Mr White, but then of course it takes an

Indian longer to rise to a position of authority, doesn't it? Anyway, after a bit I saw that he was pulling my leg in a way I'd have cottoned on to at once if he'd been English. It reminded me of when I first met Lili. Those dry amusing things she sometimes comes out with. If she were English, you'd laugh at once, but because she's not, then until you get to know her you think (as I used to think) What is she getting at? What's behind that remark? How am I supposed to reply or react without giving offence or appearing to have taken offence?

From what Lili tells me a lot of the English here are rather critical of the DC. They think of him as a man who does more than is absolutely necessary to show friendly to the Indians. They say he'll find himself taken advantage of, eventually. They talk about the 'good old days' of his predecessor, a Mr Stead, who kept 'a firm hand' and made it quite clear in the district 'who was boss'. This kind of attitude has been brought home to me in the two days I've worked at the hospital and I realise how lucky I've been so far, living with you, and not getting mixed up with average English people. Matron, a marvellous woman who's been out here for years and knows the score, said one particularly interesting thing when she interviewed me. The interview was fixed up by Lili through the Civil Surgeon who is medical overlord of everything that goes on in the district – but you know that! Matron said, 'You have three sponsors, Mr Macintosh, myself, and your own surname which is one people in this area remember as distinguished even if at the time there were a lot who disagreed with your uncle's progressive policies. If you're wise you'll trade on all three but avoid too obvious an association with the fourth.' Well, I knew what she meant by 'the fourth' and I must say I got my hackles up, and said, 'My *real* sponsor is Lady Chatterjee.' She said, 'I know. It's mainly why I'm taking you on. Even voluntary workers have to pass my personal test of worthiness. But this is a *British* general hospital, and I am its matron, and have long ago learned the lesson I had to learn if I were ever to do my job properly, and that lesson was to understand the necessity of excluding as extraneous any considerations other than those of the patients' well-being and the staff's efficiency' (she talks like that, rather officially, as if she has learned a speech). 'There's a lot' (she went on) 'that you may instinctively dislike about the atmosphere in which you'll be working. I don't ask you to learn to like it. I only ask, indeed demand, that your work won't be affected *by* the atmosphere.' 'Perhaps the atmosphere should be changed,' I said. At that moment, you know, I couldn't have cared less whether I was allowed to work at the hospital or not. After all, I wasn't going to be *paid*. She said, quick as a flash, 'I'm sure it should. I hope one day it will. If you'd prefer to delay working here until it does, and let someone else do the rewarding job of making sick people as comfortable as you can you only have to tell me. I shall quite understand. Although I'm sure that when you were driving an ambulance at home in the Blitz you never stopped to worry about what the wounded people you were taking to hospital felt about life or what their prejudices were. I imagine you were more concerned to try and stop them dying.' Well of course it was true, what she said. I stared at her through these awful glasses I have to wear if I'm to feel absolutely confident and I wished I was driving an ambulance still. I did get a kind of kick out of it, even if I was terrified a lot of the time. 1940. How long ago it seems! Only eighteen months, but an age and a world away, as they say. Here the war has only just begun – and sometimes I'm not sure a lot of people realise that it has. Back home it seemed in a curious way to be already over, or to be settled down to go on for centuries. In Mayapore I think more than ever of poor Daddy and poor David. The war that killed them has only just caught up with Mayapore. At times it's like waiting for them to be killed all over again, at other times like thinking of people who lived and died on another planet. I'm glad Mummy went before it all started. I can't, as most of the English here do, blame the Indians for resisting the idea of war, a war they have no proper say in. After all I've seen the real thing, in a minor civilian way, but most of the people who lay down the law here about beating the Jap and the Hun (those *awful* old-fashioned expressions that seem to give *them* heart but always depress *me*) haven't even heard a rifle fired in anger. British India is still living in the nineteenth century. To them Hitler is only a *joke*, because 'he was a house-painter and still looks like one even in uniform'. Three cheers for the Cavalry. Up the Navy! Sorry! I guess I've had one too many of Auntie Lili's gimlets. I've got to get the old glad rags on soon, because we're having a party to which no less a person than the District Superintendent of Police is coming. Lili says he's a bachelor. I hope a dedicated one! I can't bear the type of man who tries not to look as if he's noticed I'm not really attractive. Remember Mr Swinson?!! Auntie dear, I love you and think often of you and of us together in Pindi. I long really to be going up to Srinagar with you in May, but Auntie Lili seems determined to keep me here, and of course I'm now committed to the hospital. And I am seeing more of India this way. There are a couple of other local voluntary bodies like me in the civilian wing, but the rulers of the roost are the official VADs and the QAs. You should see the airs some of the QAs give themselves. At home they'd simply be ordinary ward nurses, or staff nurses at most. Here they rank as sisters. Neither they nor the voluntary bods are supposed to do anything menial. That's all left to the poor little Anglo-Indian girls. Today, for the war effort, I rolled miles of bandages – I mean rolling bandages is *clean*. But I stood on my feet to do it, and they're killing me! Well, the boy has just come in to draw my bath. More presently. I'm loving it but finding it strange all over again, as I did when I came out last year. Mayapore is a bit off-putting in a way dear old Pindi isn't. Is it something to do with the fact that that part of the world is predominantly Muslim, and here it is Hindu? Please look after yourself and think often of your loving niece.

Daphne.

*

Dear Auntie Ethel,

Many thanks for your letter and news of the goings on in Srinagar. Glad you got the photograph safely and in time for your birthday, but gladder still that you liked the dress length. The photograph seemed to me so awful that I had to send something else as well to make up for it, and then wondered choosing that colour whether I hadn't made everything worse! Not much clothes sense, I'm afraid, although I did feel that particular piece would suit you. Relieved you think so too! Hope old Hussein doesn't make a mess of it. Actually he's a better tailor than the man we have here. Lili and I had an iced cake in honour of your birthday, and a few people in to share it who stayed on afterwards for drinks (which I felt you would approve of!).

The rains have really set in now down here after a late start that set everyone in Mayapore hoarding foodstuffs in case of famine. I mean everyone in Mayapore who could afford it. Jack Poulson says it's the curse of India, the way the middle-class and well-to-do Indians swoop into the stores the moment a crisis even threatens. But that's apparently nothing to the corruption that goes on in higher circles where bulk foodstuffs are handled.

The grass at the front of the house is unbelievably green. I adore the rains. But how damp everything gets. The boy cleans *all* my shoes, every day, just to stop them from going mouldy. I've bought myself a huge cape and a sort of sou'wester, not that I've had much need of either because I mostly get a lift to and from the hospital in Mr Merrick's car which he sends round with a police driver (a very militant Muslim who tells us all the Hindus have concealed weapons in their houses to chop off the heads of English and Mohammedans alike). If it's a petrol-less day (how we all complain about *that*) Mr Merrick sends his official truck, ostensibly on urgent duty (transferring prisoners from the jail to the courthouse). I find it a bit embarrassing and have told him several times that I can quite easily go on my bicycle on *any* day, or anyway get a tonga, but he insists that with all this Congress-inspired anti-British feeling boiling up again, and the MacGregor House being isolated on the outskirts of the cantonment, it's really his duty to see I don't come to any harm.

I like him better than I used to. I can't close my eyes to the fact that he's been kind and considerate. It's his manner that's against him (and something behind his manner, naturally). And of course a District Superintendent of Police *is* a bit off-putting. But now that I've got used to him – and got over something that I think I must tell you – I quite enjoy the times he takes me out. Except when he adopts an official tone, as on a night or so ago when he warned me against what he called my association with Mr Kumar, which he said had set people talking, not English people only but Indians as well. I'm afraid I laughed and thoughtlessly said, Oh stop acting like a policeman all the time. Which I realized at once was the last thing one ought ever to say to him because he takes his job very seriously and is proud of having got where he is and is determined to shine at the job and not to care who dislikes him for doing it properly.

I feel I must tell you, *but please keep it to yourself*, I've told nobody, not even Aunt Lili. About a month ago he invited me to his bungalow for dinner. He'd gone to a lot of trouble. It was the best English-style meal I've had in India (except that time when you had the Swinsons and they made such a fuss beforehand about hating Indian food). Another point in his favour from my point of view was that his houseboy is obviously devoted to him, and took pleasure in arranging everything properly for his sahib's candle-lit dinner for two. The excuse for the dinner, if there had to be an excuse, was for me to hear some of his records afterwards. You remember I told you at the time about the show put on by the military at the end of April, complete with band and parade? And about meeting Brigadier Reid who said he met us in Pindi? And how I went to the show with a couple of the girls from the hospital and on to the club afterwards with some young army officers? Ronald Merrick looked in at the club later that evening (he had had a lot to do, controlling the crowds, etc). Well we were all saying complimentary things about the music and the marching – it *was* rather striking – and I must have been more full of it than the others. Anyway Ronald turned to me and said, 'Oh, you like military bands? So do I.' Apparently he had piles of records. He said I must hear them some time.

So this was the occasion. I don't like them all that much! Not well enough to want to listen to records, so whenever he raised the subject afterwards I sort of put it off. Actually I'd almost forgotten about the records when he finally asked me to dinner. I said yes before I knew what I was doing, and when he said: 'Good, and afterwards you can hear some of those records I've been promising to play,' I thought Oh Lord! What have I let myself in for! In the event it wasn't too bad (the music I mean). We'd been around quite a bit together and there was tons to talk about. By now the music was just a part of a pleasant evening. I'd been to his bungalow before, but only with other people for a Sunday morning beer party, but seeing it empty I realised how comfortable and pleasant it was. He doesn't smoke, or drink much, so I suppose his money goes further than that of men in similar positions who do. The bungalow is mainly PWD furnished, of course, but he has several rather glamorous things of his own. To begin with there was this super radiogram (on which he played a couple of Sousa marches). Then he had very nice tableware, and a marvellous Persian rug that he said he'd bought in an auction in Calcutta. His taste in pictures though was what really struck me. He's so very conventional in his behaviour you'd expect something nondescript on his walls. It's true there were pig-sticking and polo pictures in the dining-room and a David Wright cutie in his bedroom (he showed me round the whole bungalow but in such a sweet way that there wasn't anything awkward about the bedroom, as there might have been with another man) but in the living-room there was nothing on the walls except these two rather good reproductions of those Henry Moore drawings of people huddled in the underground during the Blitz, which I find difficult to look at, but do admire. He seemed touchingly pleased when I said, 'Oh, Henry Moore! What a surprising man you are!' One other thing that struck me – in the closet (the one used by guests just off the hall) he'd had the boy put out scented soap (Coty Chypre) and a little pink hand towel which was obviously brand new. I had the feeling it had been bought especially for the occasion. (The soap in his own bathroom was Lifebuoy, so don't jump to the wrong conclusion!)

There was another surprise too. After he'd played a couple of these Sousa marches he put on another record and said, 'I like this kind of thing, too,' and what do you think it was? The *Clair de Lune* movement from Debussy's *Suite Bergamasque*, played by Walter Gieseking. It was one of my brother David's favourites. When it began I thought: Whenever did I tell Ronald that David loved this? Then knew I never had. It was extraordinary. All that awful blaring (but sometimes stirring) Sousa and then this tender moonlit music that actually I could hardly bear to listen to, but loved all the same, although it seemed such an unusual thing for a policeman to like as well.

While it was playing the boy brought in the coffee – *Turkish*. There was a choice of brandy or liqueurs (curaçao or *crème de menthe*, very dull). All the bottles were unopened – fresh from the store, just for me. I expect if I ever dine there again the brandy will be at the same level we left it. While we were drinking it he asked me a lot of questions about my family, about how David was killed, and about daddy, and then about me, and what I thought about life and all that sort of thing, but in a chatty, sympathetic way that made me open up. (He must be a wizard at interrogation! That's not fair. But you know what I mean.) Gradually I realised he had begun to talk about himself. And I was thinking: People don't like you much, but you're fundamentally *kind* and that's why you and I have always got on surprisingly well. He said he came of 'a very ordinary family' and that although his father had done well enough, he was still only a grammar school boy and his grandparents had been 'pretty humble sort of people'. He had worked hard and done all right so far in the Indian Police which he thought of as an essential if not especially attractive service, and his main regret was that being in it he wasn't allowed to join up. His other regret was that he'd never really had any 'youth' or met 'the right sort of girl' for him. He was often 'pretty lonely'. He knew he hadn't much to offer. He realised his background and mine were 'rather different'. Our friendship meant a lot to him.

Then he dried up. I just didn't know what to say, because I didn't know if I'd understood or misunderstood what he was driving at. We sort of stared at each other for a while. Then he said, 'I'm only asking whether after you've had time to think about it you'd consider the possibility of becoming engaged to me.'

Do you know, Auntie, that's the only proposal I've ever had? I'm sure by the time you were my age you'd had dozens. Does every girl find the first one oddly moving? I suppose it depends on the man. But if he's, you know, all right, decent enough, you can't *not* be touched, can you, whatever you *feel* about him as a person? I don't think my feelings for Ronald Merrick could ever be described as more than passingly affectionate. He's fair-haired and youngish and has blue eyes and is really awfully good-looking but there was and still is (perhaps more so than ever) a distinct reservation (from my point of view) that must be something to do with what I feel as the lack of *real* candour between him and whoever he's dealing with. I never feel quite *natural* when I'm with him, but can never be sure whether that is my fault or his. But when he came out with this request (you can hardly call it a proposal, can you?) I wanted very much to have been able to make things *all right* for him and say 'Yes'. Do men know how vulnerable they look when they slough off that tough, not-caring skin they mostly seem to wear when there are more than two people in a room? Far more vulnerable than women, when *they* let their hair down.

What made it so extraordinary was that he never so much as touched my hand. At the time, this *not* touching added to my wish not to hurt him. Later, thinking about it, it added to the sense I had of the coldness surrounding the occasion. We were sitting at opposite ends of the sofa. Perhaps I ought to have taken my specs out and put them on! Looking back on it I can't really recall whether I felt that what had been said was a shock or not. It seemed to be a shock, anyway a surprise, but in retrospect the whole evening was *obviously* leading up to it, so I can't think why I should have been surprised, or even believe that I was. There must have been lots of things said before he came out with it that I inwardly took notice of. At some stage or other I decided that physically, in spite of his looks, he repelled me, but I think that came later, and was only momentary, when I'd established for both of us the fact that although I didn't want to hurt him I had never thought and never would think of him in the way he seemed to want me to. The feeling of faint repulsion probably came through because of the sense I had of relief, of having got out of a difficult situation and retreated *into myself* in a way that left no room for others whoever they might be. I was now more concerned about the possible effect of my 'refusal'. Honestly, I'm sure that all I said was 'Thank you, Ronald – but –' but that was enough. You know how people talk about faces 'closing up'? I think 'close-down' is nearer to it, because close up suggests a sort of *constriction*, a *change*, whereas what actually happens is that the face remains exactly the same but all the lights go out. Like a house where the people have gone away. If you knock at the door now there won't be any answer.

We had some more Sousa and presently he drove me home and we talked quite easily about nothing. When we got to the MacGregor House I asked him whether he'd like to come in for a nightcap. He said no, but escorted me up the steps to the verandah. When we shook hands he hung on to mine for a moment and said, 'Some ideas take some getting used to,' from which I gathered he hadn't yet given up, but it was a different man who said it. The District Superintendent of Police, the Ronald Merrick I don't care for. The same one who later – only a few days ago – annoyed me by warning me about my 'association with young Kumar'.

One of the servants was waiting on the verandah. I thanked Ronald for the evening, and then said goodnight to them both. I heard the car drive away and the servant beginning to lock up as I went upstairs. I knew Aunt Lili had planned an early night for once, so I didn't go to her room. The house was very quiet. It's the first time I've ever been conscious of the fact that it's supposed to be haunted. It didn't feel haunted in the eerie sense. Just big and empty and somehow desolate and occupied in the wrong way. What am I trying to tell you? Not that I felt frightened. But that I suddenly wanted to be with *you*.

I never told you, but there was a time – my second month in India last year – when if someone had offered me a passage home I'd have accepted like a shot. Goodness knows I loved being with you. But during that second month, perhaps not the whole month but two or three weeks of it, I had what I can only describe now as a permanent sinking heart. I hated everything, hated it because I was afraid of it. It was all so alien. I could hardly bear to leave the bungalow. I started to have awful dreams, not *about* anything, just dreams of faces. They used to come up out of nowhere, normal looking at first but then distorting and exploding, leaving a blank space for others to come up and take their place. They weren't the faces of people I knew. They were people I invented in alarming detail – alarming because it didn't seem possible to imagine faces so exactly. I suppose I was obsessed by the idea of being surrounded by strangers and had to have them even in my dreams. I never told you but I think that day on the verandah with the durzi you guessed what I was going through. I remember the way you looked at me when I lost my temper and snatched away that blouse he was doing his best to copy. You know, if I'd been living with the Swinsons that would probably have been the point of no return for me. I'd have been assimilated from then on into that inbred little cultural circle of English women – men, too, but particularly women – abroad in a colony.

I suppose it's only natural that wherever we go we should need the presence of someone known and dependable and proven. If there's no someone there has to be some *thing*. In Pindi during those particular weeks I became ridiculously attached to my luggage, my clothes, as if they were the only things I could trust. Even you, you see, seemed to have failed me. You knew everybody, everything, and I felt cut off from you because *I* didn't, however much you took me out and about. And you took the dirt and poverty and squalor in your stride, as if it didn't exist, although I knew that's not what you actually felt about it. But this is why I snatched the blouse from Hussein. I couldn't bear to see him holding it up, examining it, *touching it with his black fingers*. I *hated* myself for feeling that, but couldn't stop feeling it, so I shouted at him. When I went to my room I sat down and wanted to burst into tears and be rescued and taken home, home. I've never felt so badly the fact that I no longer have a home in England, with Mummy gone, and Daddy, and David.

Much the same thing happened to me the second week I was here at the MacGregor House, and my initial curiosity in my surroundings had been satisfied. But in Mayapore 'home' had become the bungalow in Pindi, and you. I hope none of this showed in my letters and worried you. I'm over it now. I love it all. But for a while I hated Mayapore. I asked myself what on earth had I done, coming to this awful place? I even suspected Aunt Lili of having me here only because I was English and it was a feather in her cap to have a white person staying in her house. (Isn't that disgraceful?) And I even thought back on that train journey and found myself less critical of those two beastly women. After all, I thought, how were they to have known that Lili wouldn't do something that *revolted* them? And in the hospital I realised how much easier it was to talk to another English woman, even if you disagreed with everything she said. People of the same nationality use a kind of shorthand in conversation, don't they? You spend less effort to express more, and you've got so used to the effortlessness that anything that needs effort is physically and mentally tiring, and you get short-tempered, and then tireder and more short-tempered from trying not to let the temper show.

I think this is why *I failed to keep my resolution never to go to the club. I made that resolution originally because it was impossible for Lili Chatterjee ever to go with me.* I have never liked the club, but it amuses me – it is so self-conscious about its exclusiveness and yet so vulgar. Someone is always drunk, the talk is mostly scurrilous, and yet its members somehow preserve, goodness knows how, an outward air of rectitude, almost as though there were inviolable *rules* for heartless gossip and insufferable behaviour. It was a week or two before I realised that because I lived at the MacGregor House most of the women I met at the club disliked me and a lot of the men were embarrassed by me. Not to have noticed the dislike straight away shows the extent of the relief I must have felt at first *simply to be there among my own kind.*

Mummy once said to me, 'You seem to like *everybody*. It's unnatural. It's also unfortunate. You're going to waste so much time before you've worked out who the people are *it's worth your while to know*.' I used to think she meant worth while in the ambitious sense. Now I wonder whether she meant worth my while in the sense of the interests of *my privacy and peace of mind and sense of security*. But either way she would be wrong, wouldn't she? I'm sure this longing for security and peace is wrong and that we should extend our patience time and time again almost right up to its breaking point, put ourselves out on a limb, dare other people to saw the limb off, whoever they are, black or white.

But it isn't easy, is it? The night I came home from my evening with Ronald Merrick I thought, as I was climbing the stairs, that at the top I was in for something unpleasant and I wanted to turn and run and get back to *him* of all people. I actually stood still, half-way up, and looked down into the hall and there was this servant, a boy called Raju, staring up at me. Oh heavens, he was only making sure he didn't turn out the light before I got up on to the landing, only doing his job, but I said to myself: What are *you* staring at? I was in my long green dress, the one you like that shows my awful shoulders. I felt – well, you know what I felt. He was too far away for me to see his expression. He was just a brown blob in white shirt and trousers, and then in the place where his face was one of my imaginary faces came, that of someone I'd never seen before. I called out, 'Goodnight, Raju,' and heard him say, 'Goodnight, madam' (he's a South Indian Christian so he says 'madam'), and then I continued up the stairs and when I got on to the landing I think I expected to see our resident ghost, Janet MacGregor. But there wasn't anything. I've not seen her *yet*. I felt relieved, but also cheated.

One day I must tell you about Hari Kumar. So far in my letters to you he's really just a name, isn't he? And I must tell you about a curious woman called Sister Ludmila who wears nun's clothing and collects dead bodies. I wish you were here so that I could talk to you any old time. The gong's just gone for dinner. It's raining frogs and the lizards are playing hide and seek on the wall and making that peculiar chopping noise. Tonight Lili and I are dining alone and afterwards I expect we'll play mahjong. Tomorrow I hope to visit the local Hindu temple with Mr Kumar.

Love, Daphne.

*

I wish you could have been here in the rains (Lady Chatterjee says) and then you would have seen it how Daphne loved it best. But I understand. You have to travel about and the wet season wouldn't have been the best time to do so. The garden is already beginning to look dry and tired and brown. I love every season, though. And I especially love it at night like this. I always sit on the front verandah because you don't get the smell of the river – which I never notice, but know that English guests do – and anyway you can see down the drive, which is nice, remembering the people who used to come up it, and anticipating those who might come up it now, and you can just make out the beds of canna lilies when we have the verandah light on like this. When there's a moon it's best with the light off, but when I give my party for you we'll have all the lights on, including those in the garden itself. I'd put them on for you now, for you to see the effect, but we're asked to conserve things as much as possible because of the war with China, and I suppose that includes conserving electricity.

Let me go on, then, about Miss Crane. She was an old school English liberal in the sense I grew to understand the term, someone who as likely as not had no gift for broad friendships. In Miss Crane's case I think it went further than this. I think she had no gift for friendship of any kind. She loved India and all Indians but no particular Indian. She hated British policies, and so she disliked all Britons unless they turned out to be adherents to the same rules she abided by. I suppose what I'm saying is that she made friendships in her head most of the time and seldom in her heart. To punish someone whose conduct didn't coincide with her preconceived notions of what he stood for she took his picture down. How ineffectual a gesture that was. But how revealing, how symptomatic of her weakness. As a gesture it lacked even the pathetic absurdity of turning the portrait of the black sheep of the family to the wall. At least in that gesture there was – and would be still if anyone ever did it nowadays – a flesh and blood anger, something positive. But she had courage. The Miss Cranes of the world often do, and I think at the end the reason for her madness was that she also had the courage to see the truth if not to live with it, see how all her good works and noble thoughts had been going on in a vacuum. I have a theory that she saw clearly but too late how she had never dirtied her hands, never got grubby for the sake of the cause she'd always believed she held dear, and that this explains why Mr Poulson found her like that, sitting in the rain by the roadside, holding the hand of that dead schoolteacher, Mr Chaudhuri.

Daphne, though, Daphne was different. Wouldn't you say? You've read those two letters now? Don't bother to make copies. Take them with you. Let me have them back one day when you've finished with them. I know them almost by heart. I only wish I'd known about them at the time. Yes, I wish it, but ask myself, Well how would it have helped if I had known, what could I have done if I'd seen them? She had to make her own marvellous mistakes. I say marvellous. *She* didn't ever shrink from getting grubby. She flung herself into everything with zest. The more afraid she was of something the more determined she was not to shrink from experiencing it. She had us all by the ears finally. We were all afraid for her, even *of* her, but more of what she seemed to have unlocked, like Pandora who bashed off to the attic and prised the lid of the box open.

Is this why I always sit here, on the front verandah? Those are the steps, you know. Well of course you do. You keep on looking at them, and looking down the drive, almost expecting to see someone who has run all the way in darkness from the Bibighar. On that night I was in the hall with Mr Merrick, just there by the entrance to the living-room. We couldn't see the steps from there. His car was parked away from the steps, in shadow. Afterwards, thinking about that, I wondered if he had left it so that it wasn't at once obvious to the outside world that he was here, actually at the MacGregor House when the whole of British Mayapore was seething with rumours about the riots in the sub-divisions, and rumours about Miss Crane who was already in hospital.

He said as soon as he came in, 'Are you all right, Lady Chatterjee?' which amused me really, because for the first time since we'd known each other he seemed to be treating me as one of you, as if I were Lady Green or Brown or Smith, living alone in a house only just on the fringe of safety. I gave him a drink, he said he hadn't much time, but drank it willingly enough, which I thought unusual, because he was an abstemious sort of man. I remember thinking: When you are worried, when you are concerned, when your face is alive, you're really quite good-looking. I said, 'I expect you've come to see Daphne, but she's at the club,' and he said, 'Yes, they said at the hospital she'd gone straight on to the club, but she isn't there.' 'Oh, isn't she?' I said, and I got worried too, but tried not to show it, so I said, 'But I'm sure she's all right.'

And then he asked outright, 'Is she with Hari Kumar?' I said, 'No, I don't think so.' I hadn't thought she was with Kumar. I'd even had the impression the association Mr Merrick warned her against had ended. I didn't know he'd warned her against it. I didn't know Mr Merrick had proposed to her. She'd kept all that from me. But she hadn't been able to keep from me the feelings she'd had for Kumar, nor the fact that she hadn't seen him for at least a week, in fact more like three weeks. So when Mr Merrick said, 'Is she with Kumar?' I replied, quite truthfully, 'No, I don't think so.' And then I wondered. But I said nothing. One did not voluntarily mention Kumar's name to Mr Merrick. He said, 'Well, at this time of night where can she be?' I said, 'Oh probably with friends,' and I went to the phone and rang several places where she might have been. It took ages. The telephone lines in Mayapore were blocked with official calls. Mr Merrick kept going to the verandah and coming back again each time I'd finished a call. 'She'll be in soon,' I said, 'come and have another drink,' and again, to my surprise, he said he would. He was in uniform still. He looked awfully tired.

'Is it serious?' I asked him. 'It seems to be,' he said, and then blurted out, 'What a damned mess,' and looked as if he was about to beg my pardon for swearing. 'Some of the people you know,' he said, 'are locked up.' I nodded. I knew which ones. I didn't want to talk about them. 'But here I am,' he said, 'having a drink with you. Do you mind?' I laughed and told him not a bit, unless when he'd finished his peg he was going to haul me off to jail in a black maria as a suspected secret revolutionary. He smiled but said nothing, and I thought: Oh, am I in for it? Then he came out with this special thing, 'I asked her to marry me. Did she tell you?' It was a shock. I told him, no, and realised for the first time how awfully dangerous the whole situation was. 'Is Miss Crane all right?' I asked. I didn't want to talk to him about Daphne, or Hari Kumar. Or about where they might be. Mr Merrick had always disliked young Kumar and I have to confess that my own feelings towards him were mixed. It always seemed to me that he had too big a chip on his shoulder. And he was in some trouble once. Mr Merrick had had him in for questioning. At that time I didn't know the boy from Adam, but a friend – Anna Klaus of the Purdah Hospital – once rang me and said the police had arrested this boy for apparently no good reason. So, well, you know me. I asked Judge Menen about it. So far as I could see it all turned out to be a storm in a teacup and he hadn't really been arrested at all but only taken in for questioning. It turned out that my old friend Vassi knew him. That's Mr Srinivasan, who still lives here, and whom you must meet. Anyhow I asked young Kumar round one evening because my curiosity had been aroused and that's how he came into my life, or rather into Daphne's life. He was brought up in England. His father had had tremendous plans for him, but the plans collapsed when the father died a bankrupt and poor Hari was sent home here to Mayapore, only of course it wasn't home to him. He was two years old when his father took him to England, and eighteen when he came back. He spoke like an English boy. Acted like one. Thought like one. They say that when he first reached India he was spelling his name the way his father had spelled it. Coomer. Harry Coomer. But probably his aunt stopped that. She was the closest relative he had and I think in her own rather orthodox Hindu way she was very good to him, but that meant not disciplining him enough, letting him waste his time which also meant letting him have time to brood about his bad luck. It worried me a bit, the way Daphne seemed to take to him, worried me because I couldn't be sure whether he felt quite the same way about her. She knew I had these reservations. So did young Kumar. Perhaps I should have come right out with it. But I didn't. And I think I must blame myself for any note of furtiveness that crept into what Mr Merrick called the association between Kumar and Daphne. And when Mr Merrick was here that night and said that he had asked Daphne to marry him and I realised how dangerous things could be, I remembered that in the morning she had seemed especially happy – not especially happy for the Daphne I knew, but especially happy for the Daphne who had been mooning about for days and hardly going out anywhere except to the club and pretending in her typical way that nothing was wrong, and there suddenly seemed to be no doubt at all that she *was* with Kumar, that she had been happy because they'd agreed to meet again. No doubt in my mind, nor I think in Mr Merrick's. And believing I knew for sure that she was with Kumar I also believed I knew where and made the mistake of thinking that if *I* knew Mr Merrick might also guess, and go there and find them together, which I did not want. In fact it struck me that the less said the better, because the place where I guessed they were was also the place where Mr Merrick had first met young Kumar and taken him in for questioning, and so the whole situation had come full-circle and I felt that some kind of disaster was inevitable. So I made us both stop talking about Daphne and asked about poor old Miss Crane who had been taken to hospital. I said, 'Is she all right?' and he said yes, so far as he knew, and then looked at his watch and got up and asked if he might use the phone to talk to his headquarters. Before he got to it the phone rang. It was the Deputy Commissioner. Mr Merrick had told his people where he'd be. I remember Mr Merrick answering it and telling Robin White he'd personally checked all his patrols, that the town itself was quiet for the moment because nearly all the shops in the bazaar had closed and the people seemed to be staying indoors, almost as if there was an official curfew. Then he said, 'No, I'm here because Miss Manners is missing.' He made it sound as if I'd *reported* her missing, and it seemed to be such a ridiculous word to use, but at the same time true. He spoke a bit longer then handed the phone to me and said Robin would like a word with me and would I forgive him if he didn't wait but got off straight away. Robin said, 'Lili, what's this about Daphne?' I said I didn't really know, that I thought she had gone straight to the club from the hospital, but Mr Merrick said she wasn't there, so now I supposed I was worried too. I said, 'Are things bad, Robin?' and he said, 'Well, Lili, we don't know. Would you like to come and stay the night with us?' I laughed and asked, 'Why? Are people moving into the funk holes?'

There was a plan as you probably know to move English women and children into places like the club, Smith's hotel and the DC's bungalow if the threatened uprising really got going, and finally into the old barracks if things got as bad as in the Mutiny which some of the Jonahs said they would. Robin had had to work the plan out with Brigadier Reid, but this was the first time I'd ever heard him talk seriously about it. He said, 'No, not yet, but one or two of the women whose husbands are out of station have gone into the club.' 'Well,' I said, 'that's one place I can't go, isn't it, Robin?' He told me afterwards he hadn't quite known how to take that, he'd never heard me say anything bitter. But I didn't mean it to sound bitter. It just slipped out. It was just a case of my automatically stating my position. He said, 'Well, give me a ring, when Daphne gets back. Perhaps you'd ring in half an hour in any event?' I said I would. When I came away from the phone Mr Merrick's car was gone. It was nearly nine o'clock. Daphne had always rung if anything came up at the last moment that meant she couldn't get back at her usual time. I thought, well perhaps she's tried to ring, but simply hasn't been able to get through. But I didn't really believe it. I had only one clear picture in my mind and that was of Daphne and young Kumar, and of the place they used to call the Sanctuary. It was a place I had personally never been to, which was absurd of me. I had a horror of it, I suppose, in spite of what Anna Klaus used to say, and a horror of the woman who ran it, who called herself Sister Ludmila and collected people she found dying in the streets. Daphne was awfully impressed with Sister Ludmila. Anyway, I went round the back to see what the servants were up to, because I suddenly noticed none of them was about. They'd been very glum all day. There was no one in the kitchen, nobody attending to the dinner. I went to the kitchen door and shouted across the compound and after a bit Raju appeared. He said cook wasn't feeling well. I said, 'You mean he's drunk. Tell him dinner at nine-thirty or you'll all be looking for a job, including you. *Your* business is at the front of the house, Raju.'

I went back to the living-room and poured myself a peg, and then I heard Raju at the front. I thought: He's drunk too *and* incapable, the stupid boy's fallen flat on his face by the sound of it. So I went out to scold him. It wasn't Raju. I couldn't take it in at first. She was on her hands and knees. She'd fallen and hurt herself on the steps, but only fallen because she was already hurt and exhausted from running. She looked up and said, 'Oh, Auntie.' She was still in her khaki hospital uniform. It was torn and muddy and she had blood on her face. Even when she said, 'Oh, Auntie,' I couldn't take it in that it was Daphne.

The lights are on in the garden of the MacGregor House, in honour of the stranger. The shrubs, artificially illuminated by the manipulation of a battery of switches on the wall of the verandah, looking strikingly theatrical. There is no breeze but the stillness of the leaves and branches is unnatural. As well as these areas of radiance the switches have turned on great inky pools of darkness. Sometimes the men and women you talk to, moving from group to group on the lawn, present themselves in silhouette; although the turn of a head may reveal a glint in a liquidly transparent eye and the movement of an arm the skeletal structure of a hand holding a glass that contains light and liquid in equal measure. In the darkness too, strangely static and as strangely suddenly galvanised, are the fireflies of the ends of cigarettes.

The people in the garden are the inheritors. Somewhere, farther away in time than in distance, the fire that consumed Edwina Crane spurts unnoticed, licks and catches hold. In this illuminated darkness one might notice this extra brilliance and hear, against the chat and buzz of casual night-party conversation, the ominous crackle of wood.

There was a shed in the compound behind Miss Crane's bungalow. In true English fashion she kept gardening instruments there. How typical of her to choose (on a windlessday when the first post-monsoon heats had dried the wood out and prepared it for a creaking season of contraction and pre-cool-weather warmth) a site where a conflagration would not threaten the bungalow itself. She locked herself in and soaked the walls with paraffin and set them alight and died, one hopes, in the few seconds it took for the violently heated air to scorch the breath out of her lungs.

The story goes that for this act of becoming *suttee* (which Lady Chatterjee describes as *sannyasa* without the travelling) she dressed for the first time in her life in a white saree, the saree for her adopted country, the whiteness for widowhood and mourning. And there is a tale that Joseph, returning empty-handed from some wild-goose errand she had sent him on, fell on his knees in the compound and cried to the smouldering pyre, 'Oh, Madam, Madam,' just as, several weeks before, Miss Manners, falling on her knees, had looked up and said, 'Oh, Auntie.'

In such a fashion human beings call for explanations of the things that happen to them and in such a way scenes and characters are set for exploration, like toys set out by kneeling children intent on pursuing their grim but necessary games.

Part Three

SISTER LUDMILA

Her origins were obscure. Some said she was related to the Romanovs; others that she had been a Hungarian peasant, a Russian spy, a German adventuress, a run-away French novice. But all this was conjecture. What was clear, at least to the Mayapore Europeans, was that saintly as she might now appear she had no business calling herself Sister. The Catholic and Protestant churches withheld their recognition, but accepted her existence because she had long ago won the battle of the Habit by declaring to the irate Roman priest who turned up to cast out this particular abomination that the clothes she wore were of her own design, that although a genuine religious had superior status and a larger stake in life eternal, she could not possibly have any exclusive claim to modesty or special vulnerability to heat-stroke: hence the long light gown of thin grey cotton (unadorned either by cross or penitential cord, and tied at the waist by an ordinary leather belt obtainable in any bazaar) and the wide winged cap of white starched linen that sheltered her neck and shoulders from the sun and could be seen on the darkest night.

'But you call yourself Sister Ludmila,' the priest said.

'No. It is the Indians who call me that. If you object take your objections to them. There is anyway a saying, God is not mocked.'

In those days (in 1942), on every Wednesday morning, Sister Ludmila set out on foot from the cluster of old buildings where she fed the hungry, ministered to the sick, and cleansed and comforted those who for want of her nightly scavenging would have died in the street.

She carried a locked leather bag that was attached to her belt by a chain. Behind her walked a stalwart Indian youth armed with a stick. It was seldom the same boy for more than a month or two. Mr Govindas, the manager of the Mayapore branch of the Imperial Bank of India in the cantonment, which was the place she was bound for on these Wednesday outings, said to her once, 'Sister Ludmila, where does that boy come from?' 'From heaven, I suppose.' 'And the boy who accompanied you last month? From heaven also?' 'No,' Sister Ludmila said, 'he came from jail and has recently gone back in.' 'It is what I am warning you of,' Mr Govindas pointed out, 'the danger of trusting a boy simply because he looks strong enough to protect you.'

Sister Ludmila merely smiled and handed over her cheque made out to cash.

Week by week she came to Mr Govindas for two hundred rupees. The cheques were drawn upon the Imperial Bank of India in Bombay. The Imperial Bank has long since become the State Bank and Mr Govindas long since retired. His memory remains sharp, though. Since she never paid money in and was known by Mr Govindas to pay all her trade accounts by cheque as well, he could only assume that either her fortune was large or her account credited regularly from elsewhere. The long-standing instruction from the Bombay branch authorising the cashing facilities at Mayapore described her as Mrs Ludmila Smith and the cheques were signed accordingly. By pumping a friend in Bombay, Mr Govindas eventually discovered that the money came from the treasury of a small princely state and might be reckoned as some sort of pension because Mrs Ludmila Smith's husband, said to be an engineer, had died while on the ruler's pay-roll. She took the two hundred rupees as follows: fifty rupees in notes of Rs. 5 denomination, one hundred rupees in notes of Rs. 1, and fifty rupees in small change. Mr Govidas estimated that most of the small change and a fair proportion of the one-rupee notes were distributed to the poor and that the rest went on wages for her assistants and casual purchases in the market. He knew that her meat, grain and vegetables were supplied on monthly account by local contractors, and that medicines were bought from Dr Gulab Singh Sahib's pharmacy at a trade discount of $12\frac{1}{2}$% plus 5% for monthly settlement. He knew that Sister Ludmila drank only one glass of orange juice a day and ate one meal of rice or pulses in the evening, with curds to follow, except on Fridays when she had a modest curry of vegetables and, on Christian festivals, fish. The rest of the food was consumed by her assistants and in meals for the hungry. He knew many such things about her. He sometimes thought that if he were to write down all the things he knew or heard about her he would fill up several pages of the bank's foolscap. But knowing all this he still believed that he knew nothing of importance. In this belief, in Mayapore, in 1942, Mr Govindas was not alone.

Her age, for instance. Well – how old was she? Under the nunnish pleats and folds and fly-away wings of starched linen her face described by some as inscrutable lived perpetually in an aseptic, reverent light. Her hands were those of a women who had always directed the work of others. Time had barely touched them. A single ring, a gold band, adorned her wedding finger. Her throat was protected by a high-necked starched white linen bib that also covered her breast and shoulders. Her eyes were dark and deep set, and there was an impression of prominent cheekbones – proof perhaps of Magyar blood. Her voice, also dark and deep, matched the eyes. She spoke fluent but rather staccato English and a vile bazaar Hindi. Mr Govindas had heard English people say that her English accent was Germanic. It was also said that she possessed a French as well as a British passport. At a guess, it was assumed she was about fifty years old, give or take five years.

Having collected the two hundred rupees and deposited them in the leather bag that was chained to her waist, Sister Ludmila bade Mr Govindas good-day, thanked him for escorting her personally from his inner sanctum to the door, and set out on the journey home, attended by her young man of the moment who had spent the ten minutes or so that it took her to cash her cheque sitting on his hunkers in the street outside, gossiping with anyone who also happened to be waiting or idling his time away. Such talk as went on between the bodyguard and his chance companions was usually vulgar. The other men would want to know whether the crazy white woman had yet invited him to share her bed or when exactly it was that he planned to run off with the cash she hired him to protect. The ribaldry was good-natured, but behind it there might always have been detected a note of black uncertainty. To a man in health, her business seemed too closely connected with death for comfort.

*

From the Mayapore branch of the Imperial Bank which was situated in the arcaded Victoria road, the main shopping centre of the European canton-ment, Sister Ludmila's journey back to the sanctuary took her through the Eurasian quarter, past the church of the mission, over the level crossing for which, like Miss Crane – to whom she had nodded but never spoken – she sometimes had to wait to be opened before she could continue across the crowded Mandir Gate bridge. Once over the river, outside the Tirupati temple, she paused and distributed money to the beggars and to the leper who sat cross-legged, displaying the pink patches of a diseased trunk and holding up lopped tree-branch arms. On this side of the river the sun seemed to strike more fiercely and indiscriminately as though the smells of poverty and dirt would be wasted in shade. Colour was robbed of the advantage of its singularity, its surprise. At ground level, the spectrum contracted into ranges of exhausted greys and yellows. Even the scarlet flower in a woman's braided hair, lacking its temperate complementary green, was scorched to an insipid brown. Here, the white starched cap of Sister Ludmila looked like some prehistoric bird miraculously risen, floating, bobbing and bucking, visible from afar.

Beyond the temple the road forks into two narrower roads. At the apex a holy tree shelters a shrine, ruminant cows, old men, and women with their fingers held to their nostrils. At the head of the road that forks to the right towards the jail the Majestic Cinema announces an epic from the Ramayana (now, as then). The left-hand fork is narrower, darker, and leads past open-fronted shops to the Chillianwallah Bazaar. Down this road Sister Ludmila, all that time ago, proceeded with the boy behind her and a dozen children running by her side and to her front, each hopeful of an anna. She walked upright, the locked bag in her folded arms, and ignored the cries of the shopkeepers inviting her to buy pān, cloth, soda-water, melons or jasmine. At the end of the lane she turned left and entered the

Chillianwallah Bazaar through the open archway in the high concrete wall that surrounds it.

In the middle of the walled area there are fish and meat markets – large open-sided godowns floored in concrete and roofed with sloping sheets of corrugated iron supported by concrete pillars. In the open, ranged along the enclosing walls, women have set out their rainbow vegetables and spices on mats, and sit among them holding their idle scales like so many huddled figures of unblindfolded and so sharp-eyed mercantile justice. From one of them Sister Ludmila bought green chillis and then marched on until she reached the exit on the other side of the walled square. Here, before passing through the exit, she turned aside and mounted a flight of rickety wooden steps to an open doorway on the upper floor of a building – a warehouse, obviously – whose side, at this point, forms part of the bazaar wall. Across the face of the building a sign in blue characters on a faded white background announces 'Romesh Chand Gupa Sen, Contractors'. Her bodyguard waited at the foot of the steps and smoked a bidi, squatting on his hunkers again, impatient of this unaccustomed interruption in the journey home. After ten minutes Sister Ludmila came out of the doorway and down the steps and led the way out of the bazaar, through another complex of lanes and alleys of old Muslim houses with shuttered windows above and closed doors at street level; until, abruptly, the houses gave way to open ground that was (still is) scattered with the huts and shacks of the untouchables. Beyond the huts there is a stagnant water-tank on whose farther bank are laid out to dry the long coloured sarees and murky rags belonging to the black-skinned, braceleted, bare-legged women who stand thigh-high in the water, washing themselves and their clothes. There are three trees but otherwise the land looks waste and desolate. Crows screech, flap and wheel aloft making for the river which is not visible from where Sister Ludmila walked, but can be smelt, and sensed – for behind a rise in the ground the land seems to fall away, then reappear more distantly. On the opposite bank are the godowns and installations belonging to the railway. The lane Sister Ludmila took lies roughly parallel to the winding course of the river and leads to a gateless opening in a broken-down wall that surrounds a compound. Within the compound there are three squat single-storey buildings, relics of the early nineteenth century, once derelict but patched up, distempered white, calm, silent, stark, functional, and accompanied (these days) by a fourth building of modern design. This was the Sanctuary, since re-named.

*

Sister Ludmila? Sister? (A pause.) I have forgotten. No, I remember. Put on the garments of modesty, He said. So I obeyed. The priest who came was very angry. I turned him away. When the priest had gone I asked God whether I had done wisely. Wisely and well, He said. And laughed. He likes a good joke. If God is never happy what chance of happiness is there for us?

Such long dolorous faces that we pull. Never a smile when we say our prayers. How can one bear the thought of Eternity if in Heaven it is not permitted to laugh? Or come to that, permitted to weep? Is not our capacity to laugh and cry the measure of our humanity? No matter. It is not for this you have come. I have not thanked you. So I do so now. These days there are few visitors, and those that there are I cannot see. After they have gone He describes them to me. I'm sorry about your eyes, He said, but there's nothing I can do unless you want a miracle. No, I said, no miracle, thank You. I shall get used to it and I expect You will help me. Anyway, when you've lived a long time and can hardly hobble about on sticks but spend most of the day in bed your eyes aren't much use. It would need three miracles, one for the eyes, one for the legs and one to take twenty years off my age. Three miracles for one old woman! What a waste! Besides, I said, miracles are to convince the unconvinced. What do You take me for? An unbeliever?

It will be interesting, after you have gone, to find out who you are and what you look like. I mean from His point of view. It is almost a relief no longer to have sight of my own. I feel closer now to God. These days it is amusing to have the day described to me first by one of the helpers here and afterwards by Him. It is raining, they say; Sister, can you not hear the rain on the roof? Today has been hot and dry, He tells me after they have gone and I have said my prayers to summon Him. My prayers always bring Him. However busy He is, He finds time to drop by before I go to sleep. He talks mostly of the old times. Today in the heat and dryness you went to the bank, He says, surely you remember? Surely you remember your relief when Mr Govindas accepted your cheque and gave it to the clerk and the clerk came back with the two hundred rupees? And remember thanking Me? Thank God! you said in a voice only I could hear, the money has not been stopped; and remembered the old days in Europe and your mother saying, The money has been stopped, am I a woman to starve, am I not destined for splendour? I loved my mother. I thought her beautiful. When she was in luck she gave money to the Sisters. They are clothed like that, she said, in answer to my question, because those are the garments of modesty which God has bid them put on.

One day the Sisters passed by. Sister, my mother said to one of them, here is something for your box. But they continued. My mother called after them. She had recently had a special stroke of luck. I remember her telling me, This week I had a special stroke of luck. She bought gloves and good red meat. She would have given money to the Sisters, but they passed by. She cried out after them: Are we not all creatures of chance? Is one coin more tainted than another?

You understand …? Yes, you understand. This I am telling you about was in Brussels. I remember there was a fine apartment and then a poor one. We shall go back soon to St Petersburg, my mother used to say, but at other times she said we would go back to Berlin, and at others to Paris. Where then, I wondered, did we really live, where did we belong? There was about our lives a temporary feeling. Even a child of six could sense it. Since then I have always felt it. I am six years older than the century. It was 1900. I remember my mother saying, Today is the first day of the new century. It was an exciting moment. We had gloves and warm coats and stout shoes. The magic of Christmas was still in the streets. On everyone's face I could see a look of satisfaction at the thought of the new century beginning. My mother said: This will be our lucky year. Oh, the warmth of our gloved hands together! Our cosy reflection in the windows of the shops, my mother leaning down to whisper a promise or a fancy to me, her gloved finger on the pane, pointing out a box of crystallised fruits lying in a nest of lace-edged paper. A gentleman with a fur collar to his coat raised his hat to us. My mother bowed. We walked on through the crowded street. There was a park, and a frozen lake, and roast chestnuts sold at a stall. Perhaps that was another winter, another place. All the lovely things that happened to me as a child I seem to gather up and press together and remember as occurring on that first day of our lucky new century; our lucky new year after a warm, well-fed Christmas when a gentleman who smoked a cigar gave me a doll with flaxen hair and bright blue eyes. The things that happened that were not lovely I remember as happening on the day the sisters refused to take my mother's charity. I was a bit older then, I think. Surely it was the time of the poor apartment? With the money that the Sisters had refused my mother bought me barley sugar and sugared almonds. I watched her give the tainted coins to the shop assistant and take the bags in exchange. She held the bags for me in one of her gloved hands. I was afraid of the sweets because they were bought with money the Sisters had refused and this was the same as with money refused by God because I thought the Sisters were in direct communication with Him. Why are they dressed like that? That is the question I had asked. And my mother said they were dressed like that because God had bid them put on the garments of modesty. Whatever the Sisters did had the stamp of God's special authority on it. I did not fully know the meaning of tainted, but if the money given for the sweets was tainted then the sweets had become tainted and my mother's gloves had become tainted. The glove on my own hand held in hers would also be tainted, and the taintedness would seep through the soft leather into my palm. But the worst thing was the feeling that God did not want anything to do with us. The Sisters were His special instruments. He had used them to turn His back on us.

Ah, but then suddenly I saw the truth! How could I have been so blind? How angry He would be with them for refusing the money my mother had offered! I was not sure what modesty was, but if there had been a time when He had been forced to bid the Sisters wear its garments, had not this been a mark more of their punishment than their grace? Were they not also the garments of penance? What had they done to be made to wear those special clothes? What more dreadful clothes would He bid them put on now, as further punishment? They had refused money. The money was to help people God said should be helped, the poor, the hungry. And how poor, how hungry such people must be if they were poorer than us, and hungry all the time! And the Sisters, walking the streets in garments that betrayed some earlier shame, had condemned those poor to even greater poverty and sharper hunger. Would He now put some red ugly mark on their foreheads, so that the poor could get out of their way when they saw them coming? Or make them dress in the kind of clothes they'd not dare show themselves in for fear of being laughed at or having stones thrown at them? I clung to my mother's hand. I said, 'Mother, what will He do to them?' She stared at me, not understanding, so I repeated, 'What will He do? What will God do to the Sisters this time?' She said nothing, but started walking again, holding my hand tightly. We went past a beggar woman. I hung back. We must give her some of the barley sugar, I said. My mother laughed. She gave me a coin instead. I put it in the old woman's dirty hand. She said God bless you. I was afraid, but we had good shoes and gloves and warm coats and God's blessing, and had made up to Him for what the Sisters had done wrong. The fire would be burning in the grate at home and there were the barley sugars and sugared almonds still to be eaten. I said to my mother, 'Is *this* our lucky year?' For the first time I felt that I knew what she meant by luck. It was a warmth in the heart. Without realising it you found that you were smiling and could not remember what had made you smile. Often on my mother's lips I had seen this kind of smile.

*

The Sanctuary? Yes, it has changed. Now it is for orphan children. There is a new building and a governing body of charitable Indians. There are few who remember that old name, The Sanctuary. By God's grace I am permitted to stay, to live out my life in this room. Sometimes the children come to the window and stare through it, half-afraid of me, half-amused by the old woman they see here confined to her bed. I hear their whispers, and can picture the way their hands come up suddenly to cover their mouths to stifle a laugh. I hear when one of the helpers calls them, and then the scampering of their little bare feet and then farther away their shouts which tell me they have already forgotten the sight they have just found so enthralling, so funny. There is one of them, a little girl who brings me the sweet-sour smelling marigolds whose stalks and leaves are slightly sticky to the touch. Her parents died of hunger in Tanpur. She does not remember them. I tell her stories from the Ramayana and from Hans Andersen and feel the way her eyes stay fixed and full of wonder, seeing beyond me into the world of legend and fantasy, the reality behind the illusion. What a blessing to the old is blindness. I thank God for it now. There was a time when I wept, for I have always loved to look upon the world, although I dried my eyes and would not bother Him with it, but smiled at Him and said Good Luck! when He came into the room to say He was sorry. Good luck, I said, the world You made is a wonderful place. What ever is Heaven like? Why, Sister Ludmila, He said, the same as here. He has got into the habit of calling me that for old time's sake and perhaps for His own. Am I forgiven? I asked. For what? He wanted to know. For calling myself Sister, for allowing them to call me Sister, for putting on the garments of modesty? What is this nonsense? He asked. Look, imagine that today is Wednesday. It has been hot and dry and Mr Govindas has honoured your cheque. Why should you think Mr Govindas would honour it and I refer it to drawer? He is, you know, a considerable Man of the world.

But you have not come to talk about this. Forgive me. Allow, though, a blind old woman an observation. Your voice is that of a man to whom the word Bibighar is not an end in itself or descriptive of a case that can be opened as at such and such an hour and closed on such and such a day. Permit me, too, a further observation? That given the material evidence there is also in you an understanding that a specific historical event has no definite beginning, no satisfactory end? It is as if time were telescoped? Is that the right word? As if time were telescoped and space dovetailed? As if Bibighar almost had not happened yet, and yet has happened, so that at once past, present and future are contained in your cupped palm. The route you came, the gateway you entered, the buildings you saw here in the Sanctuary – they are to me in spite of the new fourth building, the same route I took, the same buildings I returned to when I brought the limp body of young Mr Coomer back to the Sanctuary. Coomer. Harry Coomer. Sometimes it was spelled Kumar. And Harry was spelled Hari. He was a black-haired deep brown boy, a creature of the dark. Handsome. Such sinews. I saw him without his shirt, washing at the pump. The old pump. It is gone. Can you picture it where it was, under the foundations of the new building that I know from people's descriptions of it looks like a fantasy of Corbusier?

—but in the old days, before Corbusier, only the pump – and young Kumar washing there, the morning after we had found him lying as if dead in the waste ground near the river and carried him home on the stretcher. We always took the stretcher with us on those nightly missions. When we got him back Mr de Souza examined him. And laughed. 'This one is drunk, Sister,' he said. 'All the years I have worked for you I have said to myself: one night we shall lay upon the stretcher and carry home the useless carcase of a drunken man.' De Souza. He is a new name to you? He came from Goa. There was Portuguese blood in him somewhere, but a long way back. In Goa every other family is called de Souza. He was dark, darker by a shade or two than young Kumar. You prefer me to pronounce it Kumar. And why not? To hear him speak you might think him Coomer. But to see him, well, Coomer was impossible. And the name of course was rightly Kumar. He told me once that he had become invisible to white people. But I saw white women, how they watched him on the sly. He was handsome in the western way, in spite of his dark skin.

It was so with the policeman. The policeman saw him too. I always suspected the policeman. Blond, also good-looking, also he had sinews, his arms were red and covered with fine blond hairs, and his eyes were blue, the pale blue of a child's doll; he looked right but he did not smell right. To me, who had been about in the world, he smelt all wrong. 'And who is that?' he said. 'Also one of your helpers? The boy there? The boy washing at the pump?' This was the morning the policeman came to the Sanctuary; six months before the affair in the Bibighar. They were looking for a man they wanted. Do not ask me to remember who the man was or what he was supposed to have done. Published a seditious libel, incited workers to strike or riot, resisted arrest, escaped from confinement. I don't know. The British Raj could do anything. The province was back under the rule of the British Governor because the Congress ministry had resigned. The Viceroy had declared war. So the Congress said, No, we do not declare war, and had gone from the ministry. Anything that offended was an offence. A man could be imprisoned without trial. It was even punishable for shopkeepers to close their shops at an unappointed time. To hear of these things, to read of them, to consider them now, an element of disbelief enters. At the time this was not so. Never it is so.

And so there he was, Merrick, the policeman, with his hairy red arms and china blue eyes, watching young Kumar at the pump in the way later I saw Kumar watched on other occasions. I did not fully appreciate. Even if I had fully appreciated what could I have done? Foreseen? Intervened? So ordained things that the affair in the Bibighar six months later would not have occurred?

For me Bibighar began on the night we found young Kumar on the waste ground near the river, lying as if dead. Some distance off were the huts and hovels of the outcastes, but it was late and no lights were showing. It was by chance that we found him as we came back from the nightly scouring of the bazaar by way of the Tirupati temple and the river bank, a journey that brought us by the other side of the tank where the untouchable women wash their clothes, as you will have seen on your way here. You can picture us as we always went, Mr de Souza in front with the torch, then myself and a boy behind with a folded stretcher over his shoulder and a stout stick in his free hand. Only once ever were we attacked, but they ran off when the boy threw the stick down and made for them, whirling the rolled stretcher over his head as if it weighed nothing. But that was a good boy. After a month the kind of boy I needed to take most of the weight of the stretcher would become bored, and when such a boy became bored his mind would usually turn to mischief. I never promised these boys more than four or five weeks' work. Towards the end of them I would begin to keep my eyes open for another lad wandering in the bazaar, sturdy and fresh from his village or some outlying district, a lad looking for work in a place where he believed fortunes were going for the asking. Sometimes such a boy would come to me, being told that there was easy money to be made with the mad white woman who prowled the streets at night looking for the dead and dying. Sometimes the previous boy would be jealous of the new boy and make up bad things about him, but usually the old one was glad enough to

101

be off, with a bonus in his pocket and a chit addressed to whom it might concern extolling his honesty and willingness. Seeing the soldiers in the barracks some of the boys enlisted, others became officers' servants, one went to jail, and another to the provincial capital to become a police constable. The police were often at the Sanctuary. The boy who joined them had seen and admired the uniform and the air of authority. In the villages the police are local men. They do not have the same glamour for a boy as the police here in town. Some of these boys sent letters to tell me how they were getting on. Always I was touched by such letters because the boys were all illiterate and had paid good money to a scribe to send me a few lines. Only once did such a boy come back to the Sanctuary to beg.

We walked in darkness. 'Over there,' I called to Mr de Souza, 'flash your torch, there, in the ditch.' My eyes were sharper than anyone's in those days. I knew every inch of the way, where a hump should be, or a shadow, and where there should be neither. There are images that stay vividly in your mind, even after many years; images coupled with the feeling that at the same time came to you. Sometimes you can know that such an image has been selected to stay with you for ever out of the hundreds you every day encounter. Ah, you think, I shall remember this. But no. That is not quite correct. You do not think that. It is a sensation, not a thought, a sensation like a change in temperature for which there is no accounting and only some time afterwards, forgetting the sensation, do you think, I expect I shall always remember that. So it was, you see, that first night of young Kumar. In the light of the torch, his face; the two of us down in the ditch, kneeling. Above us, the stretcher boy with the rolled stretcher aslant his shoulder, a young giant, dark against the stars. I must have glanced up and asked him to get the stretcher ready. The smell of the river was very strong. On a still night, when the earth has cooled, the water continues warm and the smell near the banks is powerful. When there is a wind the smell reaches the Sanctuary. The river flows downstream from the temple past the place appointed for the outcastes. In entering the river for any reason at this point the outcastes will not pollute the water the caste Hindus bathe in, but this is to reckon without the pollution from other towns upstream of Mayapore. In the waste ground where we knelt, in the ditch, the smell of the river mixes with the smell of night-soil. At dawn, here, the untouchables empty their bowels. Without the blessing of God upon you it is a terrible place to be. Poor Kumar. Lying there. Such a place of human degradation. India is a place where men died, still die, in the open, for want of succour, for want of shelter, for want of respect for the dignity of death.

Who is it, Mr de Souza? I asked. It was the standard question. He knew many people. It was the first step in the drill of identification. Sometimes he knew. Sometimes I knew. Sometimes the stretcher-boy knew. For instance, a man known to be starving or dying of a disease, a man who would not go to hospital or come voluntarily to the Sanctuary, a man whose family were dead or lost or scattered, who had no hope of the world but only of a happier reincarnation or of an eternity of oblivion. But we usually knew where such men were to be found – such women too – and there would come the night when they could be lifted on to the stretcher, beyond protest, beyond defeat, and carried to the Sanctuary. For a fee the Brahmin priests would see to it that after they were dead they were suitably disposed of. The Hindus took their dead from us, the Mohammedans theirs, the State theirs. The State's dead were those we found dying, who were not identified. Such dead were taken to the morgue and if unclaimed after three days delivered to the students in the hospitals. Every morning at the Sanctuary there would be women whose husbands, sons, and sometimes I suppose lovers, had not come home the night before. And often, too, the police. But all this was none of my business. I left that side of things to Mr de Souza. My business was with the dying, not the dead. For the dead I could do nothing. For the dying, the little neither I nor the sisters had been able to do for my mother: a clean bed, a hand to hold, a word through layers of unconsciousness to reach and warm the cold diminishing centre of the departing soul.

'Who is it?' I asked Mr de Souza. He was a man of heart and a man of talent, a lapsed Catholic, who took nothing from the Sanctuary except his bed and board and clothing. 'I don't know,' he said. He turned young Kumar over then, to see if there were wounds on his back. We had found him lying partly on his side, which is not usually the position of a drunken man. Someone, you see, had been ahead of us, and had been through the pockets, whoever it was from the huts who must have seen him staggering along the river bank and had now returned home, possessing the wallet, turned out the lamps and feigned sleep. From the huts there was wakefulness, unnatural silence.

And we turned young Kumar back again, shining the torch on to his face again. And this is what I remember. This is the image. The face unchanged even after the body had been turned once, twice. The eyes shut, the black hair curling over the forehead which even in that state of his insensibility seemed to be furrowed by anger. Oh, such determination to reject! It was an expression you often saw on the faces of young Indians in those days. But in Kumar the expression had unusual strength. We got him on to the stretcher. I led the way back here to the Sanctuary. It was into this room where I lie and you sit that we brought him. It used to be Mr de Souza's office. I had a room in the next building where the clinic used to be, which is now the children's sick bay. And here in this room Mr de Souza, bending over young Kumar, suddenly laughed. 'This one is drunk, Sister!' he said. 'It is what I have been waiting for all the time I have worked for you. To find that only we have carried home the useless carcase of a drunken man.'

'This one,' I said, 'is only a boy. To be so drunk he must also be unhappy. Let him lie.'

And so he lay. Before I went to sleep I prayed for him. Each night into sleep I took with me the memory of the face of one of the rescued and it almost pleased me that for once it was the face of a young man who was neither dying nor suffering from injury. We went, you know, into places where the police did not care to because they were afraid of being attacked, which is why sometimes we brought home hurt and wounded. When we did this we sent the police a message. Sometimes they came here on their own initiative, as they did on the morning after we brought young Kumar back. But never before had the District Superintendent come himself. If he had come the day before, the day after, there might never have been Bibighar. You might then have been able to say Bibighar to me now and I would have nothing stronger than an impression of ruins and a garden. But he came that day, Merrick, in short sleeves showing his red arms and with a clarity in his blue eyes, a determination to miss nothing, a madness, an intention to find evidence. Ah, but of what? 'I want to see,' he said, 'the woman who calls herself Sister Ludmila.'

And Mr de Souza replied, 'It is we who call her that.' Mr de Souza was afraid of nobody. I was through there, in the little room next door where now they hoard the clothing for the children, the books and stationery and games and rubber balls and cricket bats, but where in those days we kept special medicines from Dr Gulab Singh Sahib's, under lock and key, and the safe for the money I collected each week from the Mayapore branch of the Imperial Bank, a safe for which Mr de Souza also had a key. He slept here, where I am lying, with his desk there, where you are sitting, and the table there by the window the children stand at, under the light-bulb that at night no longer glares at me. That was where we put the stretcher when we came in. Sometimes we made more than one journey. He was standing there, Merrick, early on this Wednesday morning. I was opening the safe to get out the bag and the cheque book, and through the open doorway I heard him say this: 'I want to see the woman who calls herself Sister Ludmila.'

'It is we who call her that,' Mr de Souza said. 'Right now she is busy. Can I be of help?' And Merrick said, 'Who are *you*?' And de Souza smiled, I could hear the smile in his voice. 'I am nobody. Hardly worthy of your consideration.' In what they call a police transcript those words might look servile. To me they sounded defiant. So I came out and said, 'It is all right, Mr de Souza,' and saw Merrick there, carrying a little cane, dressed in shorts and a short-sleeved shirt, and a Sam Browne belt with a holster and a pistol in the holster, and his china blue eyes taking us all in. 'Mrs Ludmila Smith?' he said. I bowed. He said, 'My name is Merrick. I am the District Superintendent of Police.' Which already I knew, having seen him on horseback commanding the police who were controlling the crowds at the times of festivals, and driving in his truck over the Mandir Gate bridge. He had with him Rajendra Singh, the local sub-inspector who took bribes and stole watches from the men he arrested. Rajendra Singh had such a wrist-watch on. It was a finer watch than the one on Mr Merrick's wrist, but less serviceable perhaps. The Indians always had a tendency towards the tawdry, the English towards the apparently straightforward, the workable. But there was nothing straightforward about Mr Merrick. He worked the wrong way, like a watch that wound up backwards, so that at midday, for those who knew, he showed midnight. Perhaps no one could have cheated destiny by so arranging things that Kumar and Merrick never met. But I am sorry that it was here, although that was probably destined too, written on the walls when I first came here and saw the tumble-down buildings and recognised that they would serve my purpose.

'In what way can I assist you?' I asked him, and with a gesture I dismissed Mr de Souza, because I knew this would please Merrick. But also it confirmed that it was I who was in command. In my white cap, my garments of modesty. To match Merrick's uniform. One does not live in the world of affairs for nothing. One learns the rules, the unwritten laws, the little by-ways of the labyrinth of protocol. I offered Mr Merrick Mr de Souza's chair, but he preferred to remain standing. He said he wished to conduct a search. Again, with a gesture, I gave assent or at least indicated awareness that to resist such a thing was not worth the trouble, indeed that the search itself was the only troublesome thing, that it was he, Merrick, who was putting himself out, using up his time. I did not even ask him what or whom the search was for. There are so many things that one could say in such circumstances. With less experience of official interference I might have said all of them. And he was sharp. He looked at me and showed me with his eyes alone that he had instinctively divined the reasons for my unprotesting acquiescence. He guessed that I had nothing to hide that I knew of, but also guessed that I was a woman whose luck had often been better than her judgment but might not always be.

'Then where shall we begin?' he said. I told him wherever he wished. When we got outside I saw his truck at the gate of the compound and a constable posted there, and then, after he had been through the first two buildings and we were walking towards the third building, I remember the sight of young Kumar, without his shirt, bending his head under the pump. He straightened up. We were a hundred yards away from him. He looked round. And Merrick stood still. And gazed at him. 'And who is that?' he asked, 'also one of your helpers?' Over this distance he stared at Kumar. I called Mr de Souza who was following us. 'He spent the night with us,' I told Mr Merrick. 'Mr de Souza perhaps knows his name.' You understand, at this point I had not yet spoken to Kumar, but that morning had been told by de Souza only that the boy was all right but suffering from hangover and uncommunicative and not especially grateful for being brought to the Sanctuary, and had so far withheld his name. I thought that perhaps while Mr Merrick was conducting his search de Souza might have gone to the boy and said, Look, the police are here, who are you? and been told.

'Mr de Souza,' I said, 'the boy who spent the night with us –?' And de Souza said casually, 'As you see he is all right now and making ready to go.' 'I'm afraid no one can go until I say so,' Merrick said, not to me but to the sub-inspector, avoiding cleverly, you see, a direct engagement. 'Are we then all under arrest?' I asked, but laughed, and indicated that arrested or not I wished to conduct him to the third building. He smiled and said that they were looking for someone, as no doubt I had guessed, and then walked

105

on with me and Mr de Souza, leaving the sub-inspector behind. Some sign from Merrick had made the sub-inspector stay put, to keep an eye on Kumar. When we reached the third building Merrick stopped on the verandah steps and turned round. I did so too. The boy had resumed his washing under the pump. The sub-inspector stood where we had left him, his legs apart and hands behind his back. I looked at Merrick. He also was watching the boy. They formed a triangle, Merrick, Kumar, Rajendra Singh – each equidistant apart. There was this kind of pattern, this kind of dangerous geometrical arrangement of personalities. 'This building where we are now,' he said, but not looking at me, still looking at Kumar, 'is what is known as the death house?' I laughed. I said I believed that sometimes people who had never been to the Sanctuary called it that. 'Are there any dead this morning?' he asked. 'No, not this morning. Not for several days.' 'Homeless?' 'No, I do not house the homeless.' 'The hungry?' 'Those who are hungry know the days when there is rice. Today is not such a day.' 'The sick?' 'The clinic receives only in the evening. Only people who cannot afford to lose a morning or a day's work come to our clinic.' 'And your medical qualifications?' 'Mr de Souza is in charge of the clinic. He gave up paid work as a lay practitioner to work with me for nothing. The health authorities of the municipal board sometimes come to see us. They approve of what they find. As District Superintendent of Police you must know most of these things.' 'And the dying?' 'We have the voluntary services of Dr Krishnamurti, and also of Dr Anna Klaus of the Purdah Hospital. You can of course also inspect my title to the land and buildings.'

'It is a curious arrangement,' Mr Merrick said.

'It is a curious country.'

We went on into the third building. We had six beds in one room and four in another. In the year of the famine they were always occupied. Similarly in the year of the cholera. Now there was no widespread famine, no present outbreak of cholera. But scarcely a week went by that two or three of the beds were not in use. On this morning, however, they were all empty. The white sheets gleamed. He said nothing but seemed astonished. Such cleanliness. Such comfort. What? For the dying? The starved unwashed dying? Such a waste! Go into the bazaar and look around and in a few hours you would find occupants for each of the beds – occupants who would benefit, get well. The world has a vested interest in those capable of being made well. At one moment he turned as if to say something, but thought better. The Sanctuary was outside his comprehension. He had not yet worked it out that in this so efficiently organised civilisation there was only one service left that was open to me to give, the service that in a country like India there was no official time or energy left over for. The service that a woman such as myself could supply out of unwanted, unearned, undeserved rupees. For in this life, living, there is no dignity except perhaps in laughter. At least when the world has done its worst for a man, and a man his worst for the world, let him savour dignity then. Let him go out in cleanliness and such peace as cleanliness and comfort can give him. Which is little enough.

Perhaps in his bones, in his soul, Merrick was conscious of the meaning of the room he stood in, in his shorts and short-sleeved shirt and belt and holster. He looked at the polished floor and then with a sort of childish rudeness at my hands. Yes, they have always been soft and white. 'Who does the work?' he asked. 'Anyone,' I said, 'who needs to earn a few rupees.' Why should I do the work myself when I had unearned undeserved rupees that would help fill the cooking pot of one of the untouchable women you saw on your way here, washing in the stagnant tank? 'Where are these helpers today?' he said. I led him out into the compound behind the building where the helpers' quarters were. Perhaps there he saw it too, the distinction between the place of the living and the place of the dead: the smoky cookhouse, the mud and thatch and the men and women who earned rupees and lived in what among the living passed as cleanliness but in comparison with the rooms for the dying was dirt. He made them come out of their quarters, and stand in the compound, and then entered those hovels, going alone and coming out empty-handed, having found no one in hiding.

He pointed at the people with his cane. 'These are your regular helpers?' he asked, and I told him that in the Sanctuary nobody was regular, that I hired and fired without compunction, wishing to spread whatever benefit it was in my power to give. 'Is Mr de Souza also irregular?' he asked. 'No,' I replied, 'because the Sanctuary is as much his as mine. He sees the point of it. These people are only interested in the rupees.'

'In life,' he said, 'rupees are a great consideration,' and continued to smile. But the smile of a man wearing a belt and holster is always a special smile. It was in the great war when I first noticed that an armed man smiles in a way that keeps you out of his thoughts. And this is how it was with Merrick. When he had satisfied himself that the death house had no secrets he said, 'Then there is just your night visitor,' and went back to the front verandah, to that dangerous geometrical situation, pausing at the head of the steps, glancing to where the sub-inspector still stood, and then at Kumar who was still standing by the pump, buttoning up his shirt. Smiling, Mr Merrick I mean, smiling and standing there. He said, 'Thank you, Sister Ludmila. I need take up no more of your time,' and saluted me by bringing the tip of his cane into touch with the peak of his cap, and ignored Mr de Souza who was waiting behind us, and walked down the steps. And when he began to walk the sub-inspector was also set in motion. And they converged, in this way, on young Kumar who also continued, standing, buttoning his shirt, doing up the cuffs. Waiting. Having seen, but making no attempt to avoid. Without moving I spoke quietly to Mr de Souza. 'Who is the boy?' 'His name is Coomer.' 'Coomer?' 'In fact, Kumar. A nephew by marriage, I believe, of Romesh Chand Gupta Sen.' 'Oh,' I said, and remembered having heard something. But where? When? 'Why Coomer?' I asked. 'Ah, why?' Mr de Souza said. 'It would be interesting, if not best, to go down.' So we went down, following a few yards behind Mr Merrick, so that we heard the first words, the first words in the affair that led to Bibighar. As we approached. Merrick. A clear voice. As if speaking to a servant. That tone. That language. The Englishman's Urdu. *Tumara nām kya hai?* What's your name? Using the familiar *tum* instead of the polite form. And Kumar. Looking surprised. Pretending a surprise not felt but giving himself up to its demands. Because it was a public place.

'What?' he said. And spoke for the first time in my hearing. *In perfect English. Better accented than Merrick's.* 'I'm afraid I don't speak Indian.' That face. Dark. And handsome. Even in the western way, handsome, far handsomer than Merrick. And then Sub-Inspector Rajendra Singh began to shout in Hindi, telling him not to be insolent, that the Sahib asking him questions was the District Superintendent of Police and he had better jump to it and answer properly when spoken to. When he had finished Kumar looked back at Merrick and asked, 'Didn't this man understand? It's no use talking Indian at me.' 'Sister Ludmila,' Merrick said, but still staring at young Kumar, 'is there a room where we can question this man?' 'Question? Why question?' Kumar asked. 'Mr Kumar,' I said, 'these are the police. They are looking for someone. It is their duty to question anyone they find here for whom I cannot vouch. We brought you here last night because we found you lying in a ditch and thought you were ill or hurt, but you were only drunk. Now, what is so terrible in that? Except hangover.' I was trying to smooth over, you see, to make laughter or at least smiling of a different kind than Mr Merrick's. 'Come,' I said, 'come to the office,' and made to lead the way but already the Bibighar affair had gone too far. In those few seconds it had begun and could not be stopped because of what Mr Merrick was and what young Kumar was. Oh, if they had never met! If young Kumar had never been drunk, or been brought back; if there had never been that night-procession – the four of us, myself leading with the torch, Mr de Souza and the boy bearing the stretcher, and Kumar on it, but now recovered, standing there by the pump in the compound, facing Merrick.

'Is that your name: Ku*mar*?' Merrick asked, and Kumar replied 'No, but it will do.' And Merrick, smiling again, said, 'I see. And your address?'

And Kumar stared from Merrick to me, still pretending surprise, and said, 'What is all this? Can anyone just barge in, then?'

'Come,' I said. 'To the office. And don't be silly.'

'I think,' Mr Merrick said to me, 'we won't waste any more of your time. Thank you for your co-operation.' And signed to Rajendra Singh who stepped forward and made to take the boy by the arm but was brushed aside. Not with a violent motion, more with a shrug away to avoid distasteful contact. At this moment perhaps Merrick could have stopped it. But did not. Rajendra Singh was not a man to be shrugged off if Mr Merrick was there to back him up. And he was bigger than Kumar. He hit him across the cheek with the back of his hand. A soft, glancing blow, done to insult as much as to sting. I was angry. I shouted, 'That will be enough of that.' It stopped them. It saved Kumar from the fatal act of retaliation. I said, 'This is my property. In it I will not tolerate such behaviour.' That sub-inspector – he was a coward. Now he was afraid that he had gone too far. When he struck Kumar he had also taken hold of his arm, but let it go. 'And you,' I said to Kumar, 'stop being silly. They are the police. Answer their questions. If you have nothing to hide you have nothing to fear. Come,' and again I made as if to lead them to the office. But Merrick, no, he was not going to take the smooth way out. He had already chosen the twisted, tragic way. He said, 'We seem to have got beyond the stage when a talk in your office would have been a satisfactory preliminary. I am taking him into custody.'

'On what charge?' Kumar said.

'On no charge. My truck's waiting. Now, collect your baggage.'

'But I have a charge,' Kumar said.

'Then make it at the *kotwali*.'

'A charge of assault by this fellow with the beard.'

'Obstructing or resisting the police is also an offence,' Mr Merrick said and turned to me. 'Sister Ludmila. Has this man any possessions to be returned to him?' I looked at Kumar. His hand went to his hip pocket. Only now had he thought to look for his wallet. I said to him, 'We found nothing. We turn out pockets, you understand, for the purpose of identification.' Kumar stayed silent. Perhaps, I thought, he thinks it is we who have robbed him. Not until his hand went like that to his hip pocket was I certain that he had been robbed as he lay drunk the night before, out there in the fields, near the river bank. But in any case a lesser man would have cried out, 'My wallet!' or 'It's gone! My money! Everything!' drawing, attempting to draw a red herring. Ah, a lesser man would have cried out like that, if not to create a diversion, then in the little agony of sudden loss that always, to an Indian, in those days anyway, looked like the end of his constricted little world. And Kumar was an Indian. But had not cried out. Instead, let his hand fall away, and said to Merrick, 'No, I have nothing. Except one thing.'

'And that?' Merrick inquired, still smiling as if already knowing.

'A statement. I come with you under protest.'

And all the time in those accents so much more English even than Merrick's. And in Merrick's book, this counted against him. For in Merrick's voice there was a different tone, a tone regulated by care and ambition rather than by upbringing. It was an enigma! Fascinating! Especially to me, a foreigner who had known an Englishman more of Merrick's type than Kumar's, and had heard this Englishman often rail against the sharp clipped-spoken accents of privilege and power. And here, in spite of the reversal implied by the colours of the skin, the old resentments were still at work, still further complicating the conflict. Kumar walked of his own accord towards the gateway and the waiting truck. But Merrick showed no sign of concern because he had the sub-inspector to trot after the prisoner. Another Indian. In this way mating black with black, and, again, touching his cap with the tip of his cane and thanking me for my services, keeping me talking, while I watched, at increasing distance, the affair between Kumar and the sub-inspector which was one of catching up, then push, and pull, and finally of what looked from where I stood like a violent meeting between Rajendra Singh, Kumar, a constable and the back of the truck with Kumar pushed, shoved, perhaps punched into the back of it, so that he fell inside rather than climbed. And the constable going in after him. And then the sub-inspector waiting, for Merrick. 'Why do you let them treat him like that?' I asked. I was not surprised. Only pained. For these were violent, difficult times. But Merrick had already turned and was on his way to the truck and pretended not to hear. When he reached the truck he talked to the sub-inspector and then the sub-inspector got into the back too. Well, so it went. Such things happened every day. And at this time, you understand, I had no way of telling what Kumar was suspected of, let alone of judging what he might have been guilty of. Only I had seen the darkness in him, and the darkness in the white man, in Merrick. Two such darknesses in opposition can create a blinding light. Against such a light ordinary mortals must hide their eyes.

*

It is good of you to come again so soon. Have you yet seen Bibighar? The ruins of the house, and the garden gone wild in the way most Indians like gardens to be? They tell me it has not changed, that sometimes even now Indian families have picnics there, and children play. The Europeans seldom went, except to look and sneer and be reminded of that other Bibighar in Cawnpore. And at night it was always deserted. People said it was haunted and not a good place then, even for lovers. It was built by a prince and destroyed by an Englishman. I'm sorry. You are right to correct me. A Scotsman. Forgive me for momentarily forgetting. Such nice distinctions.

Bibighar. It means the house of women. There he kept his courtesans. The prince I mean. You have seen the Purdah Hospital here in the town, in the old black town as it used to be called? Beyond Chillianwallah? Surrounded now by houses? And changed. But it was a palace in the days when Mayapore was the seat of a native ruler and the only foothold the English had was one cut out by trade, need, avarice, a concern to open the world God had given them, like an oyster suspected of a pearl. Here all the pearls were black. Rare. Oh, infinitely desirable. But it must have taken courage as well as greed to harvest them. Go into the old palace now, the Purdah Hospital, and look at what remains of the old building, the narrow gallery of tiny airless rooms, the kind of room these English merchants had to enter to strike bargains, and there is an impression – from the size of the rooms – of cruelty, of something pitiless. And it must have been like this in the Bibighar. We cannot know for sure because only the foundations are left and there never was an artist's impression of the place as it was before the Scotsman destroyed it. The Bibighar bridge was a later construction, and so to visit his women the prince must have gone either by the Mandir Gate bridge or by palanquin and boat, and so must his father in order to visit the singer in the house that he also had built on that side of the river, the house the Scotsman rebuilt and renamed after himself. Indeed yes, the house where you are staying. Before the Scotsman rebuilt and renamed it, was the MacGregor House also a warren of tiny rooms and low, dark galleries? Or was the singer given unaccustomed space, room for her voice to spread, her soul to expand?

Go to the Purdah Hospital. Lady Chatterjee will take you. Ask to go to the room at the top of the old tower. From there you can see over the roofs of the black town across the river and make out the roof of the MacGregor House. I wonder how often the prince who loved the singer climbed the steps of the tower to look at it? And I wonder whether his son also climbed the tower to look across the river at the Bibighar? From the Bibighar also it must have been possible in those days to see the house of the singer. They are only one mile distant. Not far, but far enough for a girl running at night.

In those days, when Mayapore was a kingdom, on that side of the river there were no other buildings, and so those two houses were marks on the landscape, monuments to love, the love of the father for the singer and the love of the son for the courtesans, the son who despised his father for an attachment which, so the story goes, was never consummated. Day by day I think the son climbed the tower of the palace or to the highest room in the Bibighar to survey that other house, the singer's house, to glory in its decay, and said to himself, *Such is the fate of love never made manifest.* And night after night caroused in the Bibighar, his private brothel, aware of the ruin that grew stone by mouldering stone one mile distant. Now it is the Bibighar that is nothing and the singer's house that still stands, the one destroyed and the other rebuilt, in each case by this man, this MacGregor.

Let me explain something. In 1942, the year of Bibighar, I am in Mayapore more than seven years and knew little of Bibighar, little of MacGregor. This was the case with most people. Bibighar. MacGregor. These were just names to us. Take the road, we might say, over the Bibighar bridge, past the Bibighar gardens, and then turn into the MacGregor road and follow it along until you reach the MacGregor House which stands at the junction of MacGregor and Curzon roads, and Curzon road will lead you straight to the Victoria road and the cantonment bazaar.

This would have been the quickest way to the bank – it is only a short distance from here to the Bibighar bridge. But usually I went the other way, through the Chillianwallah Bazaar and past the Tirupati temple. The real life of Mayapore is on the Mandir Gate bridge side. I would go over the bridge and past the church of the mission and the girls' school, through the Eurasian quarter, Station road, Railway cuttings, Hastings avenue, and into Victoria road from that side.

But then, after that day in August nineteen forty-two, the names Bibighar and MacGregor became special ones. They passed into our language with new meanings. What is this Bibighar? we asked. Who was MacGregor? we wanted to know. And then there seemed to be no scarcity of people able to tell us. Take MacGregor. It was said of him that he feared God, favoured mosques and Muslims and was afraid of temples, and burnt the Bibighar because it was an abomination, burnt it and then knocked down what was left, leaving only the foundations, the gardens and the surrounding wall. It was also said that he did this following the poisoning of an Englishman at the prince's court, an event which was used as an excuse for the annexation of the state by the British government, the old East India Company. But MacGregor did not burn the Bibighar so soon. The first record of MacGregor in Mayapore was in 1853, just four years before the Mutiny, but nearly thirty years after the annexation. In 1853 Mayapore was not the headquarters of the district. MacGregor was not an official. He was a private merchant, of the kind who began to flourish after the old East India Company ceased to trade but continued to govern. He made his money out of spices, grain, cloth and bribes. His old factory and warehouse stood where the railway depot now stands and there is still a siding there that bears his name, the MacGregor siding. The railway did not come to Mayapore until ten years after he died, so obviously his influence was still felt, his memory fresh. You can picture his laden wagons setting off along the road that became the Grand Trunk road, and picture Mayapore at that time, before the railway. Still on that side of the river there were not many buildings, no barracks, no civil lines. There was, I think, a chapel where St Mary's is, and a Circuit House where the Court house stands. The District Officer lived in Dibrapur then. He would have stayed in the Circuit house when he came to Mayapore to hear petitions, settle cases, collect revenues. I wonder how many times he had to listen to subtle complaints which when he boiled them down he was able to see as complaints about MacGregor? I think of MacGregor as red-faced, his cheeks devasted by ruptured veins, virtual ruler of Mayapore, snapping his fingers at authority, terrorising clerks, merchants, landowners, district officers and junior civilians alike; corrupt, violent – and yet in a few years lifting Mayapore out of the apathy it sank into after the annexation that should have transformed it from an old feudal backwater into a flourishing modern community, safe and happy under the rule of the Raj. I think he was the kind of man the merchants and landowners he dealt with would understand. It is said that he spoke the language of the greased palm, and this language is international. I think they would always know where they stood with MacGregor. But not with the austere, incorruptible, so perfect, so English District Officer.

You see how these facts about MacGregor do not fit the story that he burned the Bibighar because it was an abomination? But then this was the European version of the tale. Perhaps, also, it is the story he told his wife, whom he married and brought to Mayapore only after he had established his fortune and rebuilt the singer's house and called it by his own name. By that time he had already burned Bibighar, not, according to the Indian

112

version, because it was an abomination in his eye and the eye of the Lord, an abomination even twenty or thirty years after its last occupation, but because he fell in love with an Indian girl and lost her to a boy whose skin was the same colour as her own. There are two versions of the Indian account of the burning of Bibighar. The first is that he discovered the girl and her lover met in the Bibighar, and that he then destroyed it in a fit of jealous rage. The second is that he told the girl she would have to leave the MacGregor House and live in the Bibighar. He took her there and showed her the repairs he had made to it and the furnishings and clothes he had bought for her comfort and enjoyment. When she asked him why she must leave the MacGregor House he said: Because I am going to Calcutta to bring back an English wife. So that night she stole away with her true lover. When he found that she had gone he ordered the Bibighar to be burned to the ground, and then utterly obliterated.

And these stories ring truer, don't they? Truer than the tale that he burned Bibighar because it was an abomination. Poor MacGregor! I think of him only as a man of violent passions, and of emotions lacking any subtlety. If he had not burned the Bibighar like a child destroying a toy it had been told it mustn't play with, I wonder – would he have survived the Mutiny? The rebellious sepoys murdered their officers in Dibrapur and then roamed the countryside, eventually setting out for Mayapore with some idea of reaching Delhi, or of joining up with larger detachments of mutineers. It doesn't seem to be known where MacGregor was killed, perhaps on the steps of his house or with the Muslim servant Akbar Hossain whose body was found at the gate. History was left the impression that nothing could have saved MacGregor because the sepoys knew he had burned the Bibighar and it was rumoured that his Indian mistress and her lover died in the fire. One wonders – did Janet know these tales? Was she happy with MacGregor or was her life in Mayapore a constant torment? Is it only for her dead child that her ghost comes looking? Or to warn people with white skins that the MacGregor House is not a good place for them to be?

It is curious. But there has always been this special connection between the house of the singer and the house of the courtesans. Between the MacGregor House and the Bibighar. It is as though across the mile that separates them there have flowed the dark currents of a human conflict, even after Bibighar was destroyed, a current whose direction might be traced by following the route taken by the girl running in darkness from one to the other. A current. The flow of an invisible river. No bridge was ever thrown across it and stood. You understand what I am telling you? That MacGregor and Bibighar are the place of the white and the place of the black? To get from one to the other you could not cross by a bridge but had to take your courage in your hands and enter the flood and let yourself be taken with it, lead where it may. This is a courage Miss Manners had.

I think at first she was not in love with Kumar. Physically attracted, yes, and that is always a powerful compulsion. But I saw other white women, the way they looked at him. Well, they found it easy enough to resist temptation because they saw him as if he stood on the wrong side of water in which even to dabble their fingers would have filled them with horror. Perhaps there were times when the girl felt the horror of it too, but resisted such a feeling because she knew it to be contradictory of what she first felt when she saw him. And then she rejected the notion of horror entirely, realising that it was no good waiting for a bridge to be built, but a question of entering the flood, and meeting *there*, letting the current take them both. It is as if she said to herself: Well, life is not just a business of standing on dry land and occasionally getting your feet wet. It is merely an illusion that some of us stand on one bank and some on the opposite. So long as we stand like that we are not living at all, but dreaming. So jump, jump in, and let the shock wake us up. Even if we drown, at least for a moment or two before we die we shall be awake and alive.

She came several times to the Sanctuary. With him. With Kumar. She had said to him one day (at least I suppose she had said to him): Do you know anything about this woman, this woman who calls herself Sister Ludmila? Echoing something Mr Merrick had said to her. Or Lady Chatterjee. And young Kumar probably smiled and told her that he did; even that once I had found him and taken him for dead and carried him back drunk on a stretcher to the Sanctuary. Unless he kept that quiet. I think he did. But they came. And looked at everything. Walking hand in hand. Which had become natural for her but not I think for him. I mean he seemed to be aware of the effect such a gesture might have on those who observed it. But she seemed unaware. She came also several times by herself. She brought fruit and her willing hands. She had it in mind to help. Once she offered money. Her mother had died the year before the war and her father and brother had both been killed in it. She had a small inheritance, but all her aunt's money, Lady Manners's money, was to come to her when the old lady died. I said, No, I have no need of money, unless it is stopped. If it is ever stopped, I said, then I will ask you. She said, Then how else can I help? And I asked her why she wanted to. Surely, I said, there are countless other good causes you could support? I remember how she looked at me then. When she was alone with me she often wore spectacles. I do not think *he* ever saw her wearing them. Not wearing them for him was a vanity. She said, 'I have not been thinking in terms of good causes.' I acknowledged with a smile, but did not fully understand. Later I understood. I think, yes, later I understood. She did not divide conduct into parts. She was attempting always a wholeness. When there is wholeness there are no causes. Only there is living. The contribution of the whole of one's life, the whole of one's resources, to the world at large. This, like the courage to leap, is a wholeness I never had.

You know of course the image of the dancing Siva? He of the two legs and four arms, dancing, leaping within a circle of cosmic fire, with one foot raised and the other planted on the body of ignorance and evil to keep it in its place? You can see it there, behind you on my wall, carved in wood, my

Siva dancing. The dance of creation, preservation and destruction. A complete cycle. A wholeness. It is a difficult concept. One must respond to it in the heart, not the intellect. She also looked at my little wooden Siva. Peering at it. Putting on her glasses. She was a big girl. Taller than I. With that northern bigness of bone. I would not call her pretty. But there was grace in her. And joy. In spite of a certain clumsiness. She was prone to minor accidents. She smashed once a box containing bottles of medicine. On several occasions they met here. She and young Kumar. She came from her work at the hospital and while she waited helped with the evening clinic. Once he was late. We left the clinic and waited in my room until he came. I felt that he had intended not to come but changed his mind. So I left them together. And on that other evening, the night of Bibighar, he did not come at all. When it was dusk she went away alone. I saw her to the gate. She took the road to the Bibighar bridge, going on her bicycle. I begged her to be careful. The town was still quiet, but the surrounding countryside was not. It was the day, you remember, the day of the first outbreaks in Dibrapur and Tanpur. In the hospital that day she had seen the woman from the mission who had been found holding the hand of the dead man. She came direct from seeing her, from the hospital to the Sanctuary, to meet young Kumar surely. But he never came. We sat in my room and she told me about the woman from the mission who was ill with pneumonia because she had sat out like that, in the roadway, in the rain, holding the dead man's hand. Crane. Her name was Crane. Miss Crane. It was raining also while we sat and talked, waiting for Kumar who never arrived, but at sunset the rain stopped and the sun came out. I remember the light of it on Miss Manners's face. She looked very tired. As the light began to go she said she must be getting home. And went on her bicycle. By way of Bibighar. The same bicycle. I mean the same that was found in the ditch in the Chillianwallah Bagh near the house of Mrs Gupta Sen, where Hari Kumar lived. By Merrick. Found by Merrick. So it was said. But if Hari was one of the men who raped her why would he steal her bicycle and leave it like that, close to his home, as evidence?

And you see, when she left, wheeling her bicycle from the gate, turning to wave and then mounting and going into the twilight, I felt that she was going beyond my help, and remembered young Kumar driven only a few months before in the back of Merrick's truck, going alone to a place where he also would be beyond reach of help. On that day when Merrick had driven away, taking young Kumar to be questioned, I said to Mr de Souza, Kumar? Kumar? The nephew of Romesh Chand Gupta Sen? This is what you think? And then went with him back to the office to finish the business Mr Merrick had interrupted me in, getting ready, it being a Wednesday, to go to the bank, saying a prayer to God that on my arrival Mr Govindas would not look embarrassed and take me on one side and say: 'Sister Ludmila, this week there is no money, we have heard from Bombay cancelling your facilities.'

But when I got to the bank, leaving the boy to wait outside, Mr Govindas came out of his inner room and smiled as usual and took me in, to sit and talk, while they cashed my cheque for two hundred rupees. 'Sister Ludmila,' he said, 'that boy outside. Where did he come from?' It was a joke between us. So I said, 'Why, from heaven I suppose.' 'And the previous boy? Also he came from heaven?' 'Well no,' I said, 'he came from jail and has recently gone back in.' 'It is what I am warning you against. Not to trust a boy simply because he looks strong enough to protect you.'

But of course I knew this. I knew that after a week or two such a boy would become bored and that when this happened his mind would turn to mischief. The boy on that particular day, already he was bored. When I got back outside with the two hundred rupees and the locked bag chained to my waist he was gossiping with people who had nothing better to do and was reluctant to leave them. But. He followed. He knew his duty. And so back we went, through the Eurasian quarter, past the church of the mission, and over the Mandir Gate bridge to the Tirupati temple. I have never been into the temple. The god of the temple is Lord Venkataswara who is a manifestation of Vishnu. And in the courtyard of the temple there is a shrine and an image of Vishnu asleep. It was of the image of the sleeping Vishnu that we talked, Miss Manners and I, that evening of Bibighar. Kumar had taken her there about two or three weeks before. Although he believed in nothing like that. But she wished to see the temple. His uncle had arranged it with the Brahmin priest. And so they had gone together and now she talked of it, to me who had never been. The rain stopped and the sun came out. It lighted her face, her tiredness, her own wish to sleep. I was able to visualise what she told me because of her tired face and because I had seen an image of the sleeping Vishnu in the temple at a place called Mahabalipuram, a temple by the sea, in the south, not far from Madras. Also there is in the south, you know, a very famous temple called Tirupati. High on a hill. The temple here in Mayapore takes its name from it. It is said that originally the people of Mayapore came from the south, that a Maharajah of Mayapore married a South Indian girl and built the temple to honour her and to honour the god she worshipped. Since then there has been so much assimilation it is impossible to divide and detect.

But in Mayapore there is the Tirupati temple. Mandir means temple. It is a word from the north. And so you have the meeting of south and north. The Tirupati temple, the Mandir Gate. In ancient days the town was walled. At night the gates were closed. The Mandir Gate then opened on the Mandir Gate steps. Coming from the north you would have had to cross the river by boat and climb the steps to the Mandir Gate. Later they built the Mandir Gate bridge. The steps remained but became simply the steps you see that lead up to the Tirupati temple. There were other gates to the south. There was never a Bibighar gate. The wall had gone, I think, before the Bibighar was built. The Bibighar bridge was built after MacGregor's day. What a mixture! MacGregor, Bibighar, Mandir and Tirupati.

Leaving the bank that day with the boy following, armed with his stick, I passed through the Eurasian quarters, and went past the church of the mission where the Eurasians worshipped. A little Church of England in miniature. And waited at the level crossing because it was closed to allow a train to pass. And eventually moved, going with the crowd over the Mandir Gate bridge, and paused on the other side, to distribute some money to the beggars and to the leper who always sat there, with his limbs cut back like those of a bush that had to be pruned in order to ensure the bloom. And then, taking the left fork from the holy tree, past the open shop-fronts, turning a deaf ear to the offers of pan, cloth, soda water, melons and jasmine, and through by the open archway in the wall surrounding the Chillianwallah Bazaar, stopping to buy chillis which Mr de Souza had a liking for, and going then to the other side of the market square, past the loud meat and the stinking fish and the hunched figures of the market women with their scales lying idle like sleeping metal reptiles and up the stairway to the offices of Romesh Chand Gupta Sen, whose dead brother's widow, Mrs Gupta Sen, lived in one of those concrete houses built on the Chillianwallah reclamation, in the Chillianwallah Bagh.

'Arrested!' he said. The uncle-by-marriage. Romesh Chand. 'That boy,' he said, 'that boy will be the death of me. Who does he think he is? Why cannot he learn the ways of honour and obedience, the ways befitting a young Indian?' And called, ringing a little brass bell as though the office were a temple, so that I understood better young Kumar's disobedience, remembering from that morning the voice, the Englishness, and those northern sinews, that handsomeness. Do you understand? How it was alien, this background, this warren of little dirty rooms above the warehouses of the contractor? To him. Alien to him, to Kumar? Who spoke English with what you call a public school accent? Who had been taken to England by his father when he was too young to remember the place he was born in, and lived there, lived in England, until he was eighteen years old? But whose uncle back in India was a bania, sitting at a desk wearing the achkan, the highnecked coat, and with clerks under him, squatting in little partitioned cells, among grubby papers, one even holding paper money in his toes? For a time, after his father's death and his return to India, young Kumar was made to work there. But had rebelled and now did some work for the *Mayapore Gazette*. So much I gathered. I did not ask questions. Simply I went there to tell the uncle of Mr Merrick's action. So that steps could be taken. What steps I did not know. But he rang the little bell for his head clerk and sent him away with a chit, a note to a lawyer to come at once. There was no telephone in that place. One could tell that Romesh Chand was a man who did not believe in telephones, in the necessity for telephones, or in acting in any way that could be counted 'modern' or foreign. But who believed in his own power, his own importance. He asked how it was that his nephew came to be at the Sanctuary. I did not tell the whole truth. I said only that he had stayed the night there, that in the morning the police had come looking for a man they wanted and had taken Kumar away for questioning because he was the only stranger there. 'It is kind of you to take trouble to inform me,' he said. I said it was no trouble and came away. But all day I did not get young Kumar out of my mind. That afternoon I sent Mr de Souza into the bazaar to find out what he could and went myself to the purdah hospital to speak to Anna Klaus, the doctor from Berlin who came to India to escape from Hitler and who was my good friend. After she had heard my opinion of the kind of boy young Kumar was, she telephoned Lady Chatterjee who was on the hospital committee. And said after she had telephoned, 'Well, that is all I can do. Lady Chatterjee will speak to Judge Menen or the Deputy Commissioner. Perhaps. And your Mr Merrick will find himself asked questions. Which is all right as far as it goes. But it depends, doesn't it, depends on your young Mr Kumar, on what he has done? Or on what he is suspected of having done? If it is anything remotely subversive they can lock him up without a by-your-leave.' Which I knew. And came back here, and found Mr de Souza ahead of me. 'It is all right,' he said, 'the police only kept him a couple of hours. When the lawyer sent by Romesh Chand arrived at the police station they had already let him go.' I asked de Souza how he knew this. He said he had spoken to Romesh Chand's head clerk who was not supposed to have known what was going on but had found out by gossiping to the lawyer's clerk. So, Mr de Souza said, it is all right, and we can forget Mr Kumar. Yes, I said. It is all right. Dr Klaus, also she came that evening. And I told her. She said, 'Well, that's all right then. That's all over.' And again I said yes. But did not think so. When we went out that night with the stretcher I could not get it out of my mind that it was not all right and not all over. I asked myself, Did I then do wrong? To warn Romesh Chand? To get Dr Klaus to arrange it that important people would ask questions? Young Kumar was questioned and then allowed to go. And after he had gone his uncle's lawyer arrived. Merrick probably knew this but took no notice. An Indian lawyer was nothing. But later that day, when perhaps so far as Merrick was concerned the case of young Kumar had been settled and forgotten, he would have been rung by the Judge or Deputy Commissioner, or by someone ringing on the Deputy Commissioner's or the Judge's instructions and asked: Who is this boy Kumar you've got at one of the kotwalis for questioning? And Merrick would have said, He's not there any longer, why do you ask? And whoever it was who was ringing would say, Well, that's probably a good thing. We have been asked what's happening. Your young suspect seems to have a lot of influential friends.

To be asked after by people in authority could undo all the good Kumar might have done for himself by answering questions properly once he got to the police station, would count against him in Merrick's book – in Merrick's books, where Kumar had already gone down as a boy who spoke better English than he, and would now go down as a boy who had friends who were able to speak to Judge Menen or the Deputy Commissioner, just as if he were a white boy, and not a black boy. And had stared arrogantly and said, Didn't this fellow understand it's no good talking Indian to me?

And later, yes, later, walked in public, here in the Sanctuary in view of anyone who cared to watch, hand in hand with the white girl, Miss Manners. And perhaps walked like that elsewhere, where Merrick would hear about it, or see it. I did not know until too late that Merrick also knew Miss Manners. All Europeans all knew each other, but theirs, Merrick's and Miss Manners's, was a special way of knowing, it seemed. And that night of Bibighar I understood that it was this special way. Merrick came when it was dark. In his truck. Alone. He said, 'I believe you know a girl called Daphne Manners? I have just come from the MacGregor House. She isn't home yet. Have you seen her?' 'Yes,' I said. 'She was here. But left just before it got dark.' I did not think there was any personal interest in his inquiry. There was trouble in the district. And he was a policeman. I thought only of the girl. Of what could have happened to her. I assumed, you see, that Lady Chatterjee had rung the police because Miss Manners had not reached home.

He said, 'Why was she here?' I told him she sometimes came to help at the clinic. He seemed surprised and said, 'I didn't know that. I knew she came here once because she talked about it. How often does she come?' 'Very rarely,' I said. For suddenly I was cautious. And then he asked, did she come alone, had she been alone tonight, did I know where she had planned to go when she left at dusk? Yes, alone, I said, alone tonight, and home so far as I knew, back to the MacGregor House. By which route? 'Well, from here,' I said, 'it's quicker by the Bibighar. Didn't you come that way from the MacGregor House?' It seemed that he hadn't, that from the MacGregor House he had driven first to the kotwali on the Mandir Gate bridge side, and then remembered she had once talked to him of a visit to the Sanctuary and drove here from that direction. 'So you probably missed her,' I said, and Merrick replied, 'But you say she left at dusk. I was at the MacGregor House more than an hour after dusk and until nearly nine o'clock and she hadn't got back.'

And then because I was worried for her and momentarily forgot about Merrick and Kumar, I said what I had not intended to say, said what could not help putting the name Kumar into his mind. I said, 'Perhaps she called at Mrs Gupta Sen's.' Seeing his face I wished that I had not said it. It was as if in mentioning Mrs Gupta Sen I had actually pronounced the name Kumar. He said, 'I see.' Behind his eyes there was a smile. And everything fitted into place, fitted back into that dangerous geometrical position I had had warning of, with Merrick and Kumar as two points of a triangle, with the third point made this time not by Rajendra Singh but by Miss Manners. I had that sensation which sometimes comes to us all, of returning to a situation that had already been resolved on some previous occasion, of being again committed to a tragic course of action, having learned nothing from the other time or those other times when Merrick and I may have stood like this, here in this room where I am bedridden and you ask your questions, with the name Kumar in our minds and the name of a girl who was missing and who had to be found. The revelation that Merrick was concerned as more than a policeman and my own betrayal of the boy, of

Kumar, through talking of the house in Chillianwallah Bagh, talking of Mrs Gupta Sen's – these were the springs that had to be touched each time our lives completed one revolution and again reached the point where Merrick and I stood in the room. And each time the springs *were* touched, touched as surely as night follows day, touched before they could be recognised for what they were. I should have known that Merrick knew the girl. It was stupid of me. It was the price I paid for devoting myself to the interests of the dying instead of the living. I should not have assumed that just because she was a friend of Hari Kumar she could not also be a friend of Mr Merrick. If I had not been stupid then we might have escaped from the cycle of inevitability and Merrick would not have left, as he did, already convinced that Kumar alone could solve the mystery of the girl's disappearance.

But I had not known that Merrick knew the girl or that in his own curious way he was fond of her. But I guessed it then, after I had said, 'Perhaps she called in at Mrs Gupta Sen's,' and saw the excitement behind his otherwise blank but revealing china blue eyes. For he had long ago chosen Hari Kumar, chosen him as a victim, having stood and watched him washing at the pump, and afterwards taken him away for questioning, to observe more closely the darkness that attracted the darkness in himself. A different darkness, but still a darkness. On Kumar's part a darkness of the soul. On Merrick's a darkness of the mind and heart and flesh. And again, but in an unnatural context, the attraction of white to black, the attraction of an opposite, of someone this time who had perhaps never even leapt into the depths of his own private compulsion, let alone into those of life or of the world at large, but had stood high and dry on the sterile banks, thicketed around with his own secrecy and also with the prejudice he had learned because he was one of the white men in control of a black man's country.

Merrick had known for a long time about Miss Manners and Kumar. I realise that therefore Kumar was already in his mind as someone who might know where she was. But there is something that perhaps you do not know yet. Something I partly gathered when she came that night of Bibighar, the night when Kumar did not arrive, something I learned more fully of on a later occasion, when she came to say goodbye because she was going up north to stay with her aunt, Lady Manners, until it was all over. She was pregnant. She made no secret of it. For a time we spoke of ordinary unimportant things. I was greatly struck by her calmness. I remember thinking, It is the calmness of a beautiful woman. And yet she was not beautiful, as you know, as everyone you have spoken to will have told you, as you have seen for yourself from her photograph. At one point we both fell silent. It was not the silence of people who have run out of things to say. It was the silence of people who felt understanding and affection, who were only uncertain just how much at that moment the friendship should be presumed upon. It was I who made the decision. To speak of Kumar. I said, 'Do you know where he is?' meaning where he was imprisoned. I did not need actually to pronounce his name. She looked at me and the expression on her face told me two things, that she did not know but hoped, just for a second or two before the hope faded, that I did. She shook her head. She had asked. But nobody in authority would tell her. She had also called at the house in Chillianwallah Bagh, hoping that his aunt might know. But Mrs Gupta Sen would not so much as come out of her room to speak to her. More than this, I think, for the moment she had not dared to do in case she did him harm. He had been arrested, that night of Bibighar, with some other boys. Earlier that day, you remember, several people had been taken into custody for political reasons. It was said they had been put into closed railway carriages and taken away, no one knew where. It was also said that the arrests of five or six boys on the night of the Bibighar affair had caused the riots in the town. But the riots no doubt were already planned. Perhaps the riots were worse because of the rumours of the terrible things that were happening to the boys arrested after Bibighar. Or perhaps they seemed to be worse because among the English there was this belief that after Bibighar none of their women was safe. They said that it was because of Bibighar that the Deputy Commissioner was persuaded to see the situation as one that was out of hand and called in the military before it was actually necessary. Perhaps the truth of these things will never be known. Before Miss Manners came to say goodbye to me it had occurred to me that perhaps it weighed on her mind that unwittingly she had been at the very centre of all those troubles. But when she came she had this look of calmness, of concentration, the look, I think, of all women who for the first time are with child and find that the world around them has become relatively unimportant. I put my hand on hers and said, 'You *will* go through? Go through to the end?' She said, 'Why do you ask?' and smiled, so that I knew she would go through. I said, 'Have they tried to dissuade you?' She nodded. Yes, they had tried. She said, 'They make it sound awfully simple. Like a duty.'

But of course it was not simple at all. For them, perhaps, yes it would be simple. An obligation even. To get rid. To abort. To tear the disgusting embryo out of the womb and throw it to the pi-dogs. That's what I heard a woman say. A white woman. Is it true, she asked another – 'Is it true that that Manners girl is pregnant and has gone to Kashmir to *have* the baby?' They were in Gulab Singh's pharmacy buying cosmetics. Things were back to normal by then. And being told that it seemed to be true, she said, 'Well, what are we to make of that? That she *enjoyed* it?' Poor Miss Manners. How short a time it took for her to become 'that Manners girl'. Perhaps before Bibighar she had also sometimes been called this. But immediately after Bibighar her name was spoken by Europeans with the reverence they might have used to speak of saints and marytrs. But now. That Manners girl. And that ugly comment – 'Perhaps she enjoyed it.' And then the woman smiled and said in a loud voice, 'Personally, if it had happened to me, I would have had a public abortion outside their bloody temple and thrown the filthy muck to the pi-dogs. Or made them stuff it down their priests' throats.' And continued selecting powders and lotions for her white skin and succeeded, as that kind of woman always did, still does, in talking to the man who was serving her without once looking at him or letting her hands come within touching distance of his. One of the women, perhaps, that I had seen months before watching young Kumar when he accompanied me to the pharmacy, having met me on the way and stopped and talked for a while and offered to carry back to the Sanctuary the medicines I was going to buy, offered because that day I had no boy with me. Young Kumar and I had become friends. At least I felt that he was mine and I was his in spite of the fact that there was still an idea in his head that he had no friends at all. When he came out of the pharmacy he said, 'As you saw, I've become invisible to white people.' Perhaps he had not noticed the way the white women eyed him. Perhaps only he had noticed the way they pushed past him, or turned their backs, or called to the assistant he was already speaking to. He hated going into the cantonment shops for this reason. And yet I know for him there must have been a terrible longing to go into them, to become again part of them, because of their Englishness, because England was the only world he knew, and he hated the black town on this side of the river as much as any white man fresh out from England would hate it. Hated it more, because for him the black town was the place where he had to live, not the place he occasionally had to pass through with his handkerchief held to his nose on the way back across the bridge to the civil lines and the world of the club where white people gathered.

But Kumar is another story, isn't he? One that you must come to. I will tell you a name that might help you, that possibly no one heard of but myself, or has long ago forgotten. Colin. Colin Lindsey. Kumar told me about Colin when I saw him drunk on a second occasion. It was because of Colin Lindsey that he was drunk that first time, that night we found him and brought him back to the Sanctuary. In England Colin Lindsey was Hari Kumar's closest friend. They went to the same school. Colin tried to get his parents to look after Hari when Hari's father died and Hari was forced to come back to India. When he was not quite eighteen. With that Englishness. That English voice, that English manner, and English name, Harry Coomer. Speaking no Indian language. An Englishman with a black skin who in Mayapore became what he called invisible to white people.

But not invisible to the women in the pharmacy. Or to Miss Manners. Or to Merrick. And I was telling you something. About Merrick and what he already knew of the association between the girl and Kumar. I said to her, this day that she came to say goodbye, 'Miss Manners, I have a confession. It has been a lot on my conscience.' And told her how Merrick had come to the Sanctuary on the night of the Bibighar. How at this time I did not know that she and Merrick knew each other more than in the way one white person might know another on a civil and military station. But realised now that his interest was not only that of a policeman who had been told a white girl was missing. And then forgot, in my concern for what might have happened to her, that it was dangerous to mention the name Kumar to him, realised too late that it was especially dangerous to mention Kumar even obliquely in any connection with herself. And had said, 'Perhaps she called in at Mrs Gupta Sen's.'

'Why does it worry you,' she wanted to know, 'why is it on your conscience? I know Mr Merrick came here and that when he left he went to Hari's house.' I said: But later he went back. He left here and went to the house in Chillianwallah Bagh and asked for Hari and was told he was not at home. And then drove back to the MacGregor House. And found you had returned. In that state. And at once gathered patrols and surrounded the whole Bibighar area, and arrested the first five boys he found in that vicinity. *And went back to the house in Chillianwallah Bagh.* And went upstairs with constables and found Hari. With marks on his face, they say, bathing them, attempting to reduce evidence. And outside in the ditch, your bicycle.

Yes, she said. This is true. How did you know?

From Mr de Souza, I said. He has many friends and finds out a lot of things. Some are true, some are just rumours. This obviously is true. And it is on my conscience. That if I had not mentioned the house in Chillianwallah Bagh Mr Merrick would not have gone looking for Hari Kumar. Because *you* said nothing. We all of us know that *you* said nothing. That you said you did not see who it was who attacked you. We know that you have never implicated anyone. We know this from what Lady Chatterjee has said. I know it from Anna Klaus. We know that you even refused to attempt to identify the other boys who were arrested because you insisted you had never seen them properly in the dark. There is indeed one question in my mind. If Mr Merrick had not gone back to the MacGregor House and found you, like that, would you have let it be known, at all, what had happened?

After a moment or two she said: 'Why should I keep it secret? A crime has been committed. There were five or six men. Four of them assaulted me. What are you trying to say to me? That you too think Hari was involved?'

No, I said. No, not that. Only I am trying to unburden. To ask you to help me to unburden. There is, you see, this other thing I remember. On that evening of Bibighar, when you came to the Sanctuary to wait for Kumar. While you waited you told me about the visit to the temple. As you talked I had an impression. An impression that you had not seen him since then. Had not seen him for two weeks or more. That on the day of the visit to the temple there had been some disagreement between you. A quarrel. That it disappointed but did not surprise you that by dusk he still had not come to the Sanctuary to meet you and you had to leave on your own. As you left, I had the idea that you would call at his house before going home. To see him. To put right between you whatever had gone wrong. Which was why when Merrick was questioning me I said that you might have gone to the house in Chillianwallah Bagh. And this made him think at once of Kumar, because he knew where Kumar lived. He would have remembered it clearly from the day he took him away to the police station for questioning. I was not able to put all this into words to myself at the time, at the time Merrick was standing here in this room on the night of Bibighar. But the words were there, waiting to come. And came later, when I heard that Kumar was among the boys arrested, Kumar among those who had been taken away, and then I remembered how Merrick's expression changed because I said that you might have gone to Mrs Gupta Sen's. And he looked round the room. As if he could tell that you and Kumar had been in the room on other occasions, had waited for each other here, that on this evening you had also been waiting for Kumar. As if at last he had discovered one of the places where you and Kumar met. I saw how important the discovery was to him, and that he was not just a policeman making inquiries about a missing girl. I had sensed this a moment or two before, when he seemed surprised to hear that you sometimes came to help at the clinic. It was the surprise of a man who felt he had a right to know all about your movements. Am I right?

Yes, she said. He seemed to think he had a right.

And he knew about you and Kumar?

Everybody on that side of the river knew, she said. Mr Merrick warned me against the association.

And after this warning, I said, perhaps it was that you and Kumar had the quarrel, when you visited the temple? And did not see each other again? So that Mr Merrick thought you had taken his warning to heart?

Yes, she said. I suppose that is the way it happened. The way it might have looked to him.

So then, you see, she could not unburden me. Of blame, of guilt, of treacherously saying to Merrick: Perhaps she has called in at Mrs Gupta Sen's? Of being instrumental in reviving in him the exciting suspicion that Miss Manners and young Kumar still met in secret, here in the Sanctuary. Of opening up for him a way of *punishing* Kumar whom he had already chosen, chosen as a victim. For Merrick was a man unable to love. Only he was able to punish. In my heart I feel this is true. It was Kumar whom Merrick wanted. Not Miss Manners. And it was probably her association with Kumar that first caused Merrick to look in her direction. This is the way I see it. And there is another thing I see.

This.

That young Kumar was in the Bibighar that night. Or on some other night. Because the child she bore was surely Kumar's child? Why else should she look, carrying it, like a woman in a state of grace? Why else should she refuse to get rid, refuse to abort, to throw the disgusting embryo to the mongrels? Why else? Unless having leapt she accepted the logic of her action, and all its consequences? Including the assault in darkness by a gang of ruffians. And believed that from such an assault she carried India in her belly? But would this fit the picture I had of her as she sat here, calm, concentrated, already nursing the child in her imagination, feeling that so long as she had the child she had not entirely lost her lover?

There was one question I longed to put to her. Partly I did not because I felt I knew the truth and partly I did not because I believed it was a question she would refuse to answer. For Kumar's sake. There are ways, aren't there, in which one person can enjoin another to her own silence? And she had surrounded herself, and Kumar's memory, with this kind of silence. They hated her for it. The Europeans. Just as they criticised that woman from the mission – Miss Crane – criticised her for being unable to describe the men who murdered the teacher. But in the case of Daphne Manners the situation was worse, because for a time, after the rape, she was for them an innocent white girl savaged and outraged by black barbarians and it was only gradually that they realised they were going to be denied public revenge. Because she would not identify either. Because at one point she was reported as saying that for all she knew they could have been British soldiers with their faces blacked like commandos. Because she asked if the boys arrested were all Hindus and on being told they were said that something must be wrong because at least one of the men who raped her was circumcised which meant he was probably a Muslim. She said she knew he was circumcised and would tell them why she knew if they really wanted her to. She said this in front of witnesses at the private hearing they held at the MacGregor House. The hearing was held because the whites were lusting for a trial. But what kind of trial could they have when it looked as if the victim herself would stand up in court and cast suspicion even on their own soldiers? And openly discuss such immodest details as a man's circumcision? So they got no trial. But what need did they have of a trial? The boys they arrested did not have to be found guilty of anything, but simply locked up and sent away, God knew where, with countless others. And with them, Kumar.

And then of course they turned on her. Oh, not publicly. Not to her face. Among each other. It would not have done for the Indians to know what they were thinking. But for the first time you would hear the English asking each other the questions Indians had been asking all the time. What was she doing at night in the Bibighar Gardens anyway? Obviously she had gone into the gardens voluntarily because nothing had ever been said about her being dragged off her bicycle as she rode past. And if she had been dragged off the bicycle wouldn't she have seen at least one of the boys who dragged her off? Wasn't there a street lamp on the roadside opposite the Bibighar? And wasn't there, not a hundred yards away, at the head of the Bibighar bridge, the level crossing and the hut where the gatekeeper lived with his family, all of whom are said to have sworn they had seen and heard nothing until Mr Merrick's patrols stormed in and lined them all up for questioning?

I will tell you the story that was finally told, that was finally accepted by all the gossips of British Mayapore as the unpalatable truth. You do not have to look far for its source of origin. No farther I think than to Mr

Merrick. She had gone, they said, to Bibighar because Kumar had asked her to. Anyone could see the kind of boy Kumar was. The worst type of educated black. Vain, arrogant, puffed-up. Only by consorting with a white woman could his vanity be satisfied. And only a plain girl like Daphne Manners could ever have been inveigled into such an association. So confident did he become she would do anything he asked that he sometimes had the nerve to keep away from her for days, even weeks, at a time, the nerve to arrange a meeting and not turn up, to quarrel publicly with her, to humiliate her. And would then allow her the pleasure of being with him again for an hour or two. And all the time planning the biggest humiliation of all, which coincided, in all likelihood not by chance, with the time chosen by those Indians who thought to show the English who was master. For days before the planned uprising he kept away from her, working her to a fever pitch of desire for him, then sent her a message to meet him in the Bibighar. She flew to the rendezvous and found not only Kumar but a gang of toughs who then one by one systematically raped her. It was her shame and humiliation that made her keep silent. What English girl would want to admit the truth of a thing like that? But young Kumar was not as clever as he thought. That kind of so-called educated Indian never was. So arrogant and stupid had he become that he stole her bicycle and hadn't the common sense to leave it even a short distance from his own house. Perhaps he thought it didn't matter because by morning he expected the British would all be fighting for their lives. For one other thing was certain. A vain boy like that, for all his so-called English ways, was almost certainly playing a treacherous part in the uprising. Ah no, waste no pity on young Kumar. Whatever he got while in the hands of the police he deserved. And waste no pity on her either. She also got what she deserved.

This is what the English said. I spoke of it to Anna Klaus. Anna was fond of Miss Manners. It was Anna Klaus who treated her after the assault. I did not ask her the truth of the other rumour that went round. That Anna Klaus had told the Deputy Commissioner that in her opinion Miss Manners, before the assault, had not been *intacta*. For what could this prove either way about the affair of Bibighar? No doubt the Deputy Commissioner had his reasons for feeling he had to ask Dr Klaus the question. If he asked it. There was, you see, after everything was over, and the English had re-established their control, there was for a while, before other subjects of gossip took it out of their minds, a desire in Mayapore to destroy Miss Manners, her reputation and her memory.

And perhaps they would have succeeded. Except for this one fact. That Mayapore is an Indian town. And after a while when tempers had cooled and the English had forgotten the twenty-one-day wonder of the affair in the Bibighar, the Indians still remembered it. They did not understand it. Perhaps because of the punishments people said had been exacted they would have preferred to forget it too. But out of it, out of all its mysteries, to them there seemed to be at least one thing that emerged, perhaps not clearly, but insistently, like an ache in an old wound that had healed itself. That Daphne Manners had loved them. And had not betrayed them, even when it seemed that they had betrayed her. Few Indians doubted that she had indeed been raped by men of their own race. Only they did not believe that among the boys arrested there was even one of those responsible. And this, they felt, was a belief they held with her. A cross, if you like, that they shared with her. And so, after the event, honoured her for the things she was reported to have said which shocked them at the time as much as they shocked the English. And particularly they remembered how she had said: For all I know they could have been British soldiers with their faces blacked.

Well! What courage it took to say that! In those days! When the cantonment was full of white soldiers and the Japanese were hammering at the gates down there in Burma, and the British were prone to describe as treachery anything that could not be called patriotic. And you must remember that. That these were special days. That tempers were very short because consciences were shorn. What sort of white Imperial power was it that could be chased out of Malaya and up through Burma by an army of yellow men? It was a question the Indians asked openly. The British only asked it in the unaccustomed stillness of their own hearts. And prayed for time, stability and loyalty, which are not things usually to be reaped without first being sown.

Perhaps, though, your prayers were granted. Because you are a curious people. In the main very conscious, as you walk in the sun, of the length or shortness of the shadows that you cast.

Part Four

AN EVENING AT THE CLUB

The Mayapore district of the province is still administered in five sub-divisions as it was in the days of the British. It covers an area of 2,346 square miles. In 1942 the population was one and a quarter million. It stands now, in 1964, at one and a half million, 160,000 of whom live in the town of Mayapore and some 20,000 in the suburb of Banyaganj where the airport is. From the airport there is a daily Viscount service to Calcutta and a twice-weekly Fokker Friendship service to Agra for the Delhi connection. The area in the vicinity of the airport has become the centre of a light industrial factory development. Between Banyaganj and Mayapore there are to be found the modern labour-saving, whitewashed, concrete homes of the new British colony, and then, closer to town still, the old British–Indian Electrical factory, newly extended but still controlled by British capital. From the British–Indian Electrical the traveller who knew Mayapore in the old days and came in by air would find himself on more familiar ground as he passed, in succession, the red-brick Mayapore Technical College which was founded and endowed by Sir Nello Chatterjee, and the cream-stucco Government Higher School. Just beyond the school the railway comes in on the left with the bend of the river and from here the road – the Grand Trunk road – leads directly into the old cantonment and civil lines.

*

Going from the cantonment bazaar which is still the fashionable shopping centre of Mayapore, along the Mahatma Gandhi road, once styled Victoria road, the traveller will pass the main police barracks on his left and then, on his right, the Court house and the adjacent cluster of buildings, well shaded by trees, that comprised, still comprise, the headquarters of the district administration. Close by, but only to be glimpsed through the gateway in a high stucco wall, similarly shaded, is the bungalow once known as the chummery where three or four of Mr White's unmarried sub-divisional officers – usually Indians of the uncovenanted provincial civil service – used to live when not on tour in their own allotted areas of the district. Beyond the chummery, on both sides of the road, there are other bungalows whose style and look of spaciousness mark them also as relics of the British days, the biggest being that in which Mr Poulson, assistant commissioner and joint magistrate, lived with Mrs Poulson. Almost opposite the Poulsons' old place is the bungalow of the District Superintendent of Police. A quarter of a mile farther on, the Mahatma Gandhi road meets the south-eastern angle of the large square open space known as the *maidan*, whose velvety short-cropped grass is green during and after the rains but brown at this season. If you continue in a northerly direction, along Hospital road, you come eventually to the Mayapore General Hospital and the Greenlawns nursing home. If you turn left, that is to say west, and travel along Club road you arrive eventually at the Gymkhana. Both the club and hospital buildings can be seen distantly from the T-junction of the old Victoria, Hospital and Club roads. And it is along Club road, facing the *maiden*, that the bungalow of the Deputy Commissioner is still to be found, in walled, arboreal seclusion.

At half-past six in the evening the sun has set behind and starkly silhouetted the trees that shelter the club buildings on the western side of the *maidan*. The sky above the *maidan*, colourless during the day, as if the heat had burnt out its pigment, now undergoes a remarkable transformation. The blue is revealed at last but in tones already invaded by the yellowing refraction of the sun so that it is awash with an astonishing, luminous green that darkens to violet in the east where night has already fallen and reddens in the west where it is yet to come. There are some scattered trees on the edge of the *maidan*, the homes of the wheeling sore-throated crows which Lady Chatterjee says were once referred to by an American woman as 'those durn birds'. Certainly, in India, they are ubiquitous. Driving slowly down Club road with Lady Chatterjee, in a grey Ambassador that belongs to a lawyer called Srinivasan whom one has not met but is about to, one might indulge in the fancy of a projection from the provable now to the hallowed then, between which the one sure animated connection is provided by the crows, the familiar spirits of dead white sahibs and living black inheritors alike. At this hour the *maidan* is well populated by an Indian middle class that enjoys the comparative cool of the evening. There are even women and young girls. They stroll or squat and talk, and children play games. But the overall impression is of the whiteness of men's clothes and caps and of boys' shirts, a whiteness which, like the brown of the grass, has been touched by the evening light to a pink as subtle as that of that extraordinary bird, the flamingo. There is a hush, a sense emanating from those taking the air of their – well, yes, a sense of their what? Of their self-consciousness at having overstepped some ancient, invisible mark? Or is this a sense conveyed only to an Englishman, as a result of his residual awareness of a racial privilege now officially extinct, so that, borne clubwards at the invitation of a Brahmin lawyer, on a Saturday evening, driven by a Muslim chauffeur in the company of a Rajput lady, through the quickly fading light that holds lovely old Mayapore suspended between the day and the dark, bereft of responsibility and therefore of any sense of dignity other than that which he may be able to muster in himself, as himself, he may feel himself similarly suspended, caught up by his own people's history and the thrust of a current that simply would not wait for them wholly to comprehend its force, and he may then sentimentally recall, in passing, that the *maidan* was once sacrosanct to the Civil and Military, and respond, fleetingly, to the tug of a vague generalised regret that the *maidan* no longer looks as it did once, when at this time of day it was empty of all but a few late riders cantering homeward.

Not that the *maidan* did not find itself in those days – on certain occasions – even more densely populated than it is this evening. The British held their annual gymkhana here, and their Flower Show, and it was the scene of displays such as that put on by the military complete with band in aid of War Week, which Daphne Manners attended with other girls from the Mayapore General Hospital and several young officers from the military lines, which, like St Mary's Church, are to be seen on the far side of the *maidan*. The flower show is still held, Lady Chatterjee says; indeed until five years ago she exhibited in it herself; but the roses that used to be grown by English women who felt far from home and had infrequent hopes of European leave are no longer what they were and most of the space in the marquees is taken up with flowering shrubs and giant vegetables. The gymkhana, too, is still an annual event because Mayapore is still a military station, one – that is to say – with a certain formal respect for tradition. Cricket week draws the biggest crowds, bigger even than in the old days, but then any event on the *maidan* now is bound to be more crowded, because although the British gymkhanas, flower shows and cricket weeks were also attended by Indians, that attendance was regulated by invitation or by the cost of the ticket, and the *maidan* was then enclosed by an outer picket of stakes and rope and an inner picket of poles and hessian (except in the case of the cricket when the hessian had to be dispensed with in the practical as well as aesthetic interests of the game) – pickets which effectively conveyed to the casual passer-by the fact that something private was going on. Nowadays there are no pickets other than those – as at the gymkhana, for instance – whose purpose is to separate the spectators from the participants, and there are influential Indians in Mayapore, the heirs to civic pride, who feel that it is a mistake to leave the *maidan* thus open to invasion by any Tom, Dick and Harry. Last year's gymkhana [Lady Chatterjee explains] was ruined by the people who wandered about on those parts of the *maidan* where the gymkhana was not being held but got mixed up with the people who had paid for seats and even invaded the refreshment tents in the belief that they were open to all. So great was the confusion that the club secretary, a Mr Mitra, offered to resign, but was dissuaded from such a drastic course of action when his committee voted by a narrow margin to reinstate the old system of double enclosure in future. As for the cricket, well, on two occasions in the past five years, the players walked off in protest at the rowdyism going on among the free-for-all spectators, and the last time this happened the spectators invaded the

130

field in retaliation to protest against the players' high-handedness. There followed a pitched battle which the police had to break up with *lathi* charges just as they had in the days when the battle going on was of a more serious nature.

From problems such as these the British living in Mayapore today naturally remain aloof – so far as one can gather from Lady Chatterjee (who, when questioned on such delicate matters, has a habit of sitting still and upright, answering briefly and then changing the subject). It is rare (or so one deduces from her reluctance to swear that it is not) to see any member of the English colony at a public event on the *maidan*. They do not exhibit at the flower show. They do not compete at the gymkhana. They do not play cricket there. There would seem to be an unwritten law among them that the *maidan* is no longer any concern of theirs, no longer even to be spoken of except as a short cut to describing something mutually recognisable as alien. Indeed, you might ask one of them (for instance the English woman who sits with another in the lounge-bar of the Gymkhana club, turning over the pages of a none-too-recent issue of the *Sunday Times* Magazine – today's fashionable equivalent of *The Tatler or The Onlooker*) whether she went to the flower show last month and be met with a look of total incomprehension, have the question patted back like a grubby little ball that has lost its bounce, be asked, in return, as if one had spoken in a foreign language she has been trained in but shown and felt no special aptitude or liking for: 'Flower show?' and to explain, to say then, 'Why yes – the flower show on the *maidan*,' will call nothing forth other than an upward twitch of the eyebrows and a downward twitch of the mouth, which, after all, is voluble enough as an indication that one has suggested something ridiculous.

Apart from this Englishwoman and her companion there are several other English people in the lounge. But Lady Chatterjee is the only Indian and she has only sat where she is sitting (bringing her guest with her) because the first person met, as the club was entered and found not yet to house Mr Srinivasan, was an Englishman called Terry who had been playing tennis and greeted her gaily, with a reproach that she came to the club too seldom and must have a drink while she waited for her official host and so had led her and her house-guest to the table where the two English ladies already sat and then gone off to shower and change, leaving Lady Chatterjee wrapped in her sari, the stranger in his ignorance, and the table in awkward silence punctuated only by Lady Chatterjee's attempts at explanations to the guest of his surroundings and his attempts to engage Terry's waiting ladies in a small talk that grows large and pregnant with *lacunae*, for want of simple politeness.

A question arises in one's mind about the extent to which the club has changed since Daphne Manners's day. The servants still wear white turbans beribboned to match the wide sashes that nip in the waists of their knee-length white coats. White trousers flap baggily above their bare brown feet, and stir old memories of padding docile service. Perhaps in the decor of this particular lounge-bar, change of an ephemeral nature may be seen: the formica-topped counter instead of the old wood that needed polishing, glazed chintz curtains decorated with spiral abstractions instead of cabbage roses, and chairs whose severe Scandinavian welcome brings the old cushioned-wicker comfort gratefully back to the mind.

But it would be foolish to suppose that such contemporaneity is a manifestation of anything especially significant, or to jump to the conclusion that the obvious preference shown for this room by the handful of English members present proves, in itself, their subconscious determination to identify themselves only with what is progressive and therefore superior. This lounge-bar, giving on to a verandah from which the tennis can be watched, was always the favourite of the Mayapore ladies, and for the moment at any rate the only ladies in the club, apart from Lady Chatterjee, are English. If Indian ladies on the whole are still happier at home, who but they are to blame for the look the room has of being reserved for Europeans?

But then, why are there no Indian men in the room either? And why are some of the Englishmen not sitting with their own women in the lounge-bar but standing in the other room where drinks are served, talking to Indian men? And why do they manage to convey (even at a distance, in the glimpse you have of them between square pillars across the passage and through wide open doors to the old smoking-room) a sense of almost old-maidish decorum, of physical fastidiousness unnatural to men when in the company of their own sex? Why, whenever one of them breaks away, crosses the passage and enters the lounge bar to rejoin his lady, is there presently a rather too noisy laugh from him and a shrug and secret little smile from her? Why does he now exude the aggressive, conscious masculinity that seemed to be held in abeyance in the smoking-room?

The arrival in the lounge-bar of a grey-haired, pale-brown man of some sixty-odd years puts only a temporary stop to such private speculations. Mr Srinivasan is of medium height, thin, punctilious in manner. His skin has a high polish. He is immaculately turned out. The light-weight suit, the collar and tie, point another interesting difference. The inheritors come properly dressed but the Englishmen expose thick bare necks and beefy arms. Mr Srinivasan makes a formal old-fashioned apology for being late, for having failed to arrive first and greet his guests. He also makes a joke (once current among the English) about Mayapore time which it seems is still generally reckoned to be half-an-hour in arrear of Indian Standard. One gets up to shake his hand, and meets the mild but penetrating gaze that reveals a readiness to withstand the subtlest insult that an experience-sharpened sensibility is capable of detecting. Lady Chatterjee who addresses him as Vassi, says, 'You know Terry Grigson's wife, of course?' and Srinivasan bows in the direction of the English woman who, still protectively immersed in the shallow enchantment of the *Sunday Times* Magazine achieves a token emergence by a slight lift of the head (which would be a look at Mr Srinivasan if the eyelids did not simultaneously lower) and by a movement of the lips (that might be 'Good Evening' if they actually opened more than a gummy fraction). Her companion, also introduced, nods, and being younger and less inhibited perhaps by ancient distinctions looks as if she might be drawn into the general conversation, but Mrs Grigson, with a perfect sense of timing, turns the *Sunday Times* Magazine towards her and points out some extraordinary detail of Coventry Cathedral so that they are then both lost in the illustrated complexities of modern Anglo-Saxon art; and the uncharitable thought occurs that, for the English, art has anyway always had its timely, occupational value.

And it could occur to you, too, that Mr Srinivasan is not at ease in the lounge-bar, that if he had only managed to conduct his affairs in accordance with Indian Standard instead of Mayapore time he would have been waiting at the entrance when his second best car, the Ambassador, drove up and deposited its passengers, and would then have taken them into the old smoking-room, not had to leave them to the jovial Terry Grigson whose wife finds nothing to laugh about but with whom Mr Srinivasan and his guests are momentarily stuck, for politeness' sake, at least until Terry comes back from the showers and changing-room—

—as he does, beaming and raw-faced, in a creased bush shirt and floppy creased grey trousers, but not before Mr Srinivasan with a thin, almost tubercular finger, has summoned a bearer and asked everybody what they are drinking and sent the bearer off to collect it, having been answered even by Mrs Grigson, and by her companion who taking her cue from Mrs Grigson also said, 'Nothing for me, thank you.' Terry comes back between the sending away of the bearer with the curtailed order and his return with a tray of three lonely gins and tonics, by which time Terry has also been asked by Mr Srinivasan what he will drink, thanked him, and said, 'I'll go a beer.' When the gins and tonics arrive and Srinivasan says to the bearer, 'And a beer for Mr Grigson,' Mrs Grigson pushes her empty glass at Terry and says, 'Order me another of these, Terry, will you?' which he does, with a brief, almost private gesture at the bearer. The other woman, lacking Mrs Grigson's nerve for studied insult, would go drinkless did Terry not say, while Srinivasan talks to Lili Chatterjee, 'What about you, Betty?' which enables her to shrug, grimace, and say, 'Well, I suppose I might as well.' Since no money passes and no bills are yet presented for signing, one wonders who in fact will pay for them, but trusts – because Grigson looks almost self-consciously trustworthy – that he will see to it afterwards that Mr Srinivasan's bar account is not debited with a charge it seems his wife and her friend would rather die than have an Indian settle.

And now, perhaps abiding by yet another unwritten rule, perhaps having even received some secret, clan-gathering sign, a dumpy Englishwoman at an adjacent table leans across and asks Mrs Grigson a question which causes Mrs Grigson to incline her angular body by a degree or two and with this inclination fractionally shift the position of her chair, so that by a narrow but perceptible margin she succeeds in dissociating herself from those with whom she actually shares a table. It is difficult to hear what it is that so arouses her interest, because Lili Chatterjee, Mr Srinivasan and (to his lone, team-captain's credit) Mr Grigson are also talking with animation, and the stranger can only observe and make possibly erroneous deductions: possibly erroneous but not probably. There is nothing so inwardly clear as social rebuff – a rebuff which in this case is also directed at the stranger because he has arrived with one Indian as the guest of another.

And in the momentary hiatus of not knowing exactly what it is that anyone is talking about, one may observe Terry Grigson's off-handsome face and see that old familiar expression of strain, of deep-seated reservation that qualifies the smile and points up the diplomatic purpose; a purpose which, given a bit more time, may not prevail against the persistence of his sulky segregationist wife. And this, perhaps, is a pity, considering all the chat that goes on at home about the importance of trade and exports and of making a good impression abroad.

'Well no,' Terry Grigson says, in answer to Mr Srinivasan's for-form's-sake inquiry whether he and his wife will join the trio of Srinivasan, Lili Chatterjee and her house-guest for dinner at the club, 'It's very kind of you, but we're going on to Roger's farewell and have to get back and change.'

The Roger referred to is, one gathers, the retiring managing director of British–Indian Electrical. Almost every month one more member of this transient European population ups stakes, retires, returns to England or moves on to another station. For each farewell, however, there is a housewarming, or a party to mark the occasion of a wife's arrival to join her husband in the place where for the next year or two he will earn his living. Whatever that living actually is – with the British–Indian Electrical, with one of the other industrial developments, or teaching something abstruse at the Mayapore Technical College, it will be earned by someone considered superiorly equipped to manage, guide, execute or instruct. He will be a member of that new race of Sahibs. He will be, in whatsoever field, an Expert.

'There is actually a most interesting but undoubtedly apocryphal story about the status of English experts in India nowadays,' Mr Srinivasan says in his rather high-pitched but melodious lawyer's voice when the party in the lounge bar has been broken up by the quick-downing by Terry Grigson of his beer and by the ladies of their gin-fizzes, and their departure to change into clothes that will be more suitable for the purpose of bidding Roger God-speed. Upon that departure Mr Srinivasan has led Lady Chatterjee and the stranger across the lounge, through the pillared passage and the open doors into the comfortable old smoking-room that has club chairs, potted palms, fly-blown hunting prints and – in spite of the spicy curry-smells wafted in from the adjacent dining-room by the action of the leisurely turning ceiling fans – an air somehow evocative of warmed-up gravy and cold mutton. In here, only one Englishman now remains. He glances at Mr Srinivasan's party – but retains the pale mask of his anonymity, a mask that he seems to wear as a defence against the young, presumably inexpert Indians who form the group of which he is the restrained, withheld, interrogated, talked-at centre. It is because one asks Mr Srinivasan who this white man is, and because Mr Srinivasan says he does not know but supposes he is a 'visiting expert' that the interesting but perhaps apocryphal story is told.

'There was,' Mr Srinivasan says, 'this Englishman who was due to go home. An ordinary tourist actually. He fell into conversation with a Hindu businessman who for months had been trying to get a loan from Government in order to expand his factory. A friend had told the businessman, "But it is impossible for you to get a loan from Government because you are not employing any English technical adviser." So the businessman asked himself: "Where can I get such an adviser and how much will it cost me seeing that he would expect two or three years' guaranteed contract at minimum?" Then he met this English tourist who had no rupees left. And the Hindu gentleman said, "Sir, I think you are interested in earning rupees five thousand?" The English tourist agreed straight away. "Then all you will do, sir," the Hindu gentleman said, "is to postpone departure for two weeks while I write to certain people in New Delhi." Then he telegraphed Government saying, "What about loan? Here already I am at the expense of employing technical expert from England and there is no answer coming from you." To which at once he received a telegraph reply to the effect that his factory would be inspected by representatives of Government on such and such a day. So he went back to the English tourist and gave him five thousand rupees and said, "Please be at my factory on Monday, are you by any chance knowing anything about radio components?" To which the English tourist replied, "No, unfortunately, only I am knowing about ancient monuments." "No matter," the Hindu gentleman said, "on Monday whenever I jog your elbow simply be saying – 'This is how it is done in Birmingham.'" So on Monday there was this most impressive meeting in the executive suite of the factory between the Hindu businessman who knew all about radio component manufacture, the English tourist who knew nothing and the representatives of Government who also knew nothing. Before lunch they went round the premises and sometimes one of the officials of Government asked the Englishman, "What is happening here?" and the Hindu gentleman jogged the Englishman's elbow, and the Englishman who was a man of honour, a man to be depended upon to keep his word said, "This is how we do it in Birmingham." And after a convivial lunch the Government representatives flew back to Delhi and the English tourist booked his flight home first class by BOAC and within a week the Hindu businessman was in receipt of a substantial Government loan with a message of goodwill from Prime Minister Nehru himself.'

And one notes, marginally, that the new wave of satire has also broken on the Indian shore and sent minor flood-streams into the interior, as far as Mayapore.

Mr Srinivasan is the oldest man in the smoking-room.

'Yes, of course,' he says, speaking of the younger men – the Indians, 'they are all businessmen. No sensible young man in India today goes into civil administration or into politics. These fellows are all budding executives.'

Several of the budding executives wear bush shirts, but the shirts are beautifully laundered. Their watch-straps are of gold-plated expanding metal. One of them comes over and asks Lady Chatterjee how she is. He declines Srinivasan's invitation to have a drink and says he must be dashing off to keep a date. He is a bold, vigorous-looking boy. His name is Surendranath. When he has gone Mr Srinivasan says, 'There is a case in point. His father is old ICS on the judicial side. But young Surendranath is an electrical engineer, or rather a boy with a degree in electrical engineering who is working as personal assistant to the Indian assistant sales director of British–Indian Electrical. He took his degree in Calcutta and studied sales techniques in England, which is a reversal of the old order when the degree would have been taken in London and the sales technique either ignored or left to be picked up as one went blundering along from one shaky stage of prestige and influence to another. He is commercially astute and a very advanced young man in everything except his private life, that is to say his forthcoming marriage, which he has been quite happy to leave his parents to arrange, because he trusts to their judgment in such relatively minor matters.

'The thin, studious-looking boy is also a case in point. His name is Desai. His father was interned with me in 1942 because we were both leading members of the local Congress party sub-committee. His father told me last year when we chanced to meet in New Delhi that young Desai said to him once, "Just because you were in jail you think this entitles you to believe you know everything?" They were quarrelling about Mr Nehru whom this mild-looking young man had called a megalomaniac who had already outlived his usefulness by 1948 but gone on living disastrously in the past and dragging India back to conditions worse than in the days of the British because he knew nothing of world economic structure and pressures. My old friend Desai was secretary to the minister for education and social services in the provincial Congress Ministry that took office in 1937, and resigned in 1939. Before becoming secretary to the Minister he was in the uncovenanted provincial civil service and a lawyer like myself. But his son, this young man over there, is a potential expert on centrifugal pumps and says that people like us are to blame for India's industrial and agricultural backwardness because instead of learning everything we could about really important things we spent our time playing at politics with an imperial power any fool could have told us would beat us at that particular game with both hands tied. Such accusations are a salutary experience to old men like me who at the time thought they were doing rather well.

'Also you will have noticed, I think, that there are no old men in this room except for myself. Where are my old companions in political crime? Lili, please do not put on your inscrutable Rajput princess face. You know the answer. Dead, gone, retired, or hidden in our burrows grinding the mills of the administration exceeding slow but not always exceeding fine. You might find one or two of us at the other club. Didn't you know about the other club? Oh well, that is an interesting story. We sit with the lady whose husband was one of the founder members.'

'Nello put up money but rarely went,' Lady Chatterjee says.

'Also he chose the name, isn't it?'

Sometimes one could suspect Mr Srinivasan of deliberate self-parody.

Lady Chatterjee explains, 'They wanted to call it the MHC. All Nello did was get them to drop the H.'

'So MHC became MC, which stands simply for Mayapore Club. The H would have made it the Mayapore Hindu Club. No matter. An English wag anyway dubbed it the Indian Club which I believe is an instrument for body-building. Also it was known among Indian wits as the Mayapore Chatterjee Club, or MCC for short. But whatever you called it it was always the *wrong* club. Of course it was originally meant to be an English-type club for Indians who were clubbable, but it was not for nothing that the H for Hindu was suggested. It became a place where the word Hindu was actually more important than the word Club. And Hindu did not mean Congress. No, no. Please be aware of the distinction. In this case Hindu meant Hindu Mahasabha. Hindu nationalism. Hindu narrowness. It meant rich banias with little education, landowners who spoke worse English than the youngest English sub-divisional officer his eager but halting Hindi. It meant sitting without shoes and with your feet curled up on the chair, eating only horrible vegetarian dishes and drinking disgusting fruit juice. Mayapore, you understand, is not Bombay, and consequently the Mayapore club was not like the Willingdon club which was founded by your viceroy Lord Willingdon in a fit of rage because the Indian guests he invited – in ignorance – to a private banquet at the Royal Yacht Club were turned away from the doors in their Rolls-Royces before he cottoned on to what was happening. Ah well, perhaps dear old Nello imagined in Mayapore a little Willingdon? But what happened? One by one the type of Indian who would have loved the club because it was the nearest he was then able to get to enjoying the fruits of what he had been educated up by your people to see as just one but an important aspect of civilised life – one by one this type of Indian stopped going to the Mayapore and with each abstention the feet of the bania were more firmly established under the table – or rather, upon the seat of his chair –

'I think they are ready in the dining-room.'

*

'The point is, you see,' Mr Srinivasan says, having apologised for the absence of beef, the omnipresence of mutton, 'that these old men, my peers, my old companions in crime and adversity, those who aren't dead, those who are still living in Mayapore, now find themselves somehow less conspicuous at the Mayapore club than at the Gymkhana. Just look at the young faces that surround us. So many of these boys are telling us that we cannot expect to dine out for ever on stories of how we fought and got rid of the British, that some of us never dine out at all, except with each other, like old soldiers mulling over their long-ago battles. And when it comes to spending a few hours at a club, most of us – although not I – choose the company of men who rest on laurels of a different kind, men with whom it is easier to identify than it is with the members here because here everyone is go-ahead and critical of our past. I mean, for instance, that it is easier for us to identify with men like Mr Romesh Chand Gupta Sen, now a venerable gentleman of nearly eighty years and still going every morning to his office above his warehouse in the Chillianwallah Bazaar. To the chagrin of his sons and grandsons, I should add. And on one evening a week to the Mayapore club to discuss business prospects with men who were not interested in politics then, and now are interested neither in technical experts nor in theories of industrial expansion, but instead interested as they always were simply in making money and being good Hindus.'

*

There have been prawn cocktails. Now the curried mutton arrives. The chief steward comes to oversee its serving, but breaks off from this duty to walk over and greet a party of English, two of the men and two of the women who were in the lounge-bar. The steward indicates the table he has reserved for them, but they ignore him and select another more to their liking. Both the men are still wearing shorts. Their legs are bare to the ankles. The women have plump, mottled arms, and wear sleeveless cotton shifts. Without the knitted cardigans you feel they would put on at home of an evening over these summer dresses they have a peeled, boiled look. They are young. They sit together – opposite their husbands – an act of involuntary segregation that by now is probably becoming familiar to the Indians as they get used to a new race of sahibs and memsahibs from Stevenage and Luton but may still puzzle them when they recollect how critical the old-style British were of the Indian habit of keeping men and women so well separated that a mixed party was almost more than an English host and hostess could bear to contemplate.

The dining-room, like the smoking-room, has probably changed little since Daphne Manners's time. It is a square room, with a black and white tiled floor, and walls panelled in oak to shoulder height, and whitewashed above. Three square pillars, similarly panelled to the same height, support the ceiling at apparently random but presumably strategic points. There are something like a score of tables, some round, some rectangular, each with its white starched cloth, its electro-plated cutlery and condiment

138

tray, its mitred napkins, its slim chromium flower vase holding a couple of asters, its glass jug filled with water and protected by a weighted muslin cover. There is a large Tudor-style fireplace whose black cavity is partly hidden by a framed tapestry screen. Above the fireplace there is a portrait of Mr Nehru looking serene in a perplexed sort of way. One can assume that when Daphne Manners dined here the frame contained a coloured likeness of George VI wearing a similar expression. Four fans are suspended from the ceiling on slender tubes that whip unsteadily with the movement of the turning blades. There are two arched exits, one leading into the smoking-room and the other into the main hall. There is also a third exit but that only leads into the kitchens. Against the wall, close to the kitchen exit, stands a monumental oak sideboard or dumb-waiter. On its top tier there are spare napkins, knives, forks and spoons, water-jugs, and on the lower tier, baskets of bread, bowls of fruit, bottles of sauce and spare cruets. Light is provided by stubby candle-style wall-brackets and a couple of wooden chandeliers with parchment shades, and during daytime by the windows that look on to the porticoed verandah at the front of the club, windows whose curtains are now pulled back and are open to let in the night air.

Well: it can be pictured all those years ago, especially on a Saturday evening, with a band thumping in the lounge-bar from which the old wicker tables and chairs have been cleared, and the dining-room rearranged to provide for a cold buffet supper. In the flagged yard at the back that fringes the tennis courts there are coloured lights slung in the trees, and couples used to sit out there to cool off between dances, waiting for the next foxtrot or quickstep. Some swam in the little floodlit pool that lies behind the changing- and shower-rooms, the pool which, tonight, is in darkness, in need of scraping (Mr Srinivasan says as he conducts his guests on a tour of inspection after the ice-cream that followed the curried mutton), and is seldom used because it is open to all and neither race seems particularly to fancy the idea of using it when it can't be guaranteed that the person last using it was clean. There is a story that two or three years ago an Englishman emptied all the chamber pots from the ablution cubicles into it.

*

'But I was telling you earlier on,' Mr Srinivasan says, leading the way back through the now deserted lounge-bar to the smoking-room – which has filled up and even sports a few ladies in sarees who are, one gathers, military wives – 'I was telling you about the kind of man whom old fellows like myself who were reared on briefs and files and nurtured on politics now find it easier to fit in with than we find it here at the Gymkhana.'

Mr Srinivasan raises his finger and a bearer appears and takes an order for coffee and brandy.

'And I mentioned Romesh Chand Gupta Sen,' he continues. 'He is a case in point. With Romesh Chand it has always been a question of business first and politics last. Well, not even last. Nowhere. He has made three fortunes, the first during the old peace-time days, the second during the war and the third since independence. None of his sons was allowed to continue education beyond Government Higher School. I asked him why this was. He said, "To succeed in life it is necessary to read a little, to write less, to be able to calculate a simple multiplication and to develop a sharp eye for the main chance." He married a girl who could not even write her name. She could not run a household either, but his mother trained her up to that, which is what Hindu mothers are for. When his younger brother married a girl called Shalini Kumar, Romesh prophesied no good coming of the union, because she came of a family who allowed education even if they did not wholly believe in it, and as a result Shalini's brother went to live in England and Shalini herself could write beautifully in English. She was widowed at an early age. You may find this difficult to believe, but on her husband's death the women of Romesh Chand's family did their best to persuade her to defy the law and become *suttee*. Of course she refused. What woman in her right mind wants to burn alive on her husband's funeral pyre? Also she refused to leave her dead husband's house in Chillianwallah Bagh. I tell you this because it is perhaps relevant to your interest?

'It was Romesh Chand who insisted that that Anglicised nephew of hers, Hari Kumar, should be brought back from England when her brother, Hari's father, died and left him homeless and penniless. Actually we suspected Hari's father of committing suicide when he realised he'd come to the end of a series of foolish speculations. Be that as it may, when Mrs Gupta Sen heard the news of her brother's death she went to Romesh and asked him for money that would enable Hari to stay in Berkshire to finish at his public school and go on to a university. This would be, what? 1938. She had almost no means of her own. She lived as a widow, alone in the house in Chillianwallah Bagh, mainly on her brother-in-law Romesh's charity. It was because she had always wanted a son, a child of her own, that she fell in with Romesh's counter-proposal that Hari should be brought home to live with her and learn how to be a good Hindu. To bring about this satisfactory state of affairs Romesh said he would even be willing to pay Hari's passage and increase Mrs Gupta Sen's monthly allowance. She had lived a long time alone, you know, seldom leaving the house. Almost she had become a good Hindu herself.

'She lived with great simplicity. Young Hari must have had a shock. From the outside the house in Chillianwallah Bagh looked modern. I suppose it still does. What I believe you used to call suntrap. All the houses on the Chillianwallah Bagh reclamation and development were put up in the late 'twenties. It was waste ground before then, and was called Chillianwallah Bagh because the land belonged to the estate of a Parsee called Chillianwallah. The Parsees have also always concentrated on business but they are much more westernised, hardly Indians at all. The land was bought from the Chillianwallah heirs by a syndicate of Mayapore businessmen headed by old Romesh Chand, who would never have lived in the sort of modern European-style house that was to be put up there, but saw nothing new-fangled in the anticipated profits. In fact it was to make sure of the amenities for development, such as lighting and water and drainage, and a Government grant-in-aid, that he saw to it his otherwise unsatisfactory younger brother – the one who married Shalini Kumar – got a seat on the Municipal Board. So, in time, up went these concrete suntrap-style monstrosities – suntrap only in the style because with so much sun about it's necessary to keep it out, not trap it, to have very small windows, you see, unless you have wide old-fashioned verandahs. And into one of them, into number twelve, Romesh's brother moved with his wife Shalini, the same house young Hari came to live in nearly ten years later and must have been shocked by, because inside they are dark and airless, with small rooms and steep stairs and no interior plan and Indian-style bathrooms. And in number twelve there was almost no furniture because although Mrs Gupta Sen's husband had bought a lot to go with the house, Romesh paid for it with a loan, and had since sold most of it to pay himself back. The house itself also belonged to him on mortgage. I know these things because I was what in England you would call the family lawyer.

'Yes, you are right. Lili bet me you'd cotton on. Indeed yes. It was I. I was the lawyer Romesh Chand sent for that morning Sister Ludmila went to his office and told him Hari Kumar had been taken away by the police. They thought he was arrested. This, of course, was about six months before my own arrest. It never bothered Romesh that I was politically committed. He understood the uses of politics in the same way that he understood the law of diminishing returns. After I had gone to the police station and found that Hari was already released I went back to my office, sent my clerk with a message to Romesh, and then went on to the house in Chillianwallah Bagh, to find out what it had all been about.

'Hari would not come down from his room to see me. But Mrs Gupta Sen and I were good friends. We always spoke in English. With Romesh I had to talk in Hindi. She said, "Tell Romesh everything was a mistake. There is nothing for him to go to botheration over." I asked her whether it was true, what the police had told me, that Hari had been drunk and taken by that mad woman to what she called her sanctuary. I had not known him ever to drink heavily. He was a great worry to his family but he had always seemed to be sober in his habits. She did not know whether he had been drunk. She said, "But I know that his life here, and therefore mine, is becoming unbearable."'

'Young Hari Kumar, you know, was typical of the kind of boy Nello had in mind when he financed and founded the Mayapore club. But by Hari's time it was already choc-a-bloc with the banias looking like squatting Buddhas contemplating the mysteries of profit and loss. And of course there were no women. It wasn't intended to be a club for men only but that is what it had become and has remained. Which is one of the reasons why I

141

am the exception to the rule, a staunch Gymkhana supporter! The lady over there is the wife of Colonel Varma. She is delightful. You must meet her. General and Mrs Mukerji aren't here tonight, but that is because no doubt they are invited to Roger's number one farewell. Next Saturday will be number two farewell and even I am invited to that.'

'So am I,' Lady Chatterjee says. 'I was supposed to go to number one with the other governors of the Technical Coll, but said I couldn't, so I'm at number two as well.'

'Then we will go together? Good. Meanwhile you, my dear fellow, have noticed, I expect, that all the English have now left the club?'

'To go to Roger's?'

'Oh, no. Of your fellow-countrymen who were here this evening only Mr and Mrs Grigson and the lady who was with Mrs Grigson will be at number one party. The Grigsons are senior. The other English you saw were junior. They will go to number two. Roger refers to them as foremen. In fact Roger has been known to call the Gymkhana the Foreman's Club. It was one of the gentlemen of the type Roger refers to as foremen who emptied the chamber pots into the swimming pool. After he had emptied them one of his friends had the idea of making a little Diwali, a parody of our festival of lights. So they got hold of some candles and stuck them into the pots and lighted them and set them afloat. A few of our Indian members who were present complained to the secretary, and one of our youngest and strongest members even complained directly to the gentlemen who were having such an enjoyable time at our expense. But they threatened to throw him into the pool, and used language that I cannot repeat. As an innocent bystander I found the whole situation most interesting. It was an example of the kind of club horseplay we had heard of at second or third hand and a person like myself couldn't help but remember student rags from his college days. This particular demonstration was hardly a student rag, however. Of course they were drunk, but *in vino veritas*. They were acting without inhibition. Forgive me, Lili, you find the subject disagreeable. Let us have Colonel Varma and his wife to join us.'

The colonel is a tall wiry man and his wife a neat wiry woman who seems to wear traditional Indian costume more for its theatrical effect than for comfort or from conviction. The tough little shell of skin-thin masculinity that used to harden the outward appearance of the British military wives also encloses Mrs Varma. What terror she must strike in the tender heart of every newly commissioned subaltern! Her wit is sharp, probably as capable of wounding as her husband's ceremonial sword. Tonight he is in mufti. They are going to the pictures, the ten o'clock performance; the English pictures at the Eros, not the Indian pictures at the Majestic. For a while the talk is of Paris, because the film is about Paris – the film itself is said to be rotten but the photography interesting – and then the Varmas say goodbye; Mr Srinivasan's party breaks up and Lili goes to powder her nose.

'While we wait for Lili,' he says, 'let me show you something—' and

leads the way into the black and white tiled hall where between two
mounted buffalo heads there is a closed mahogany door with brass finger-
plates and a brass knob. The mounted heads and the door all bear
inscriptions: the latter on enamel and the former on ivory. The first buffalo
was presented by Major W.A. Tyrrell-Smith in 1915, and the second by Mr
Brian Lloyd in 1925. The enamel plate on the door bears the single word:
Secretary.

Mr. Srinivasan knocks and getting no answer opens the door and
switches on the light and so reveals a small office with an old roll-top desk
and an air of desuetude. 'As the first Indian secretary of the Gymkhana,
from 1947 to 1950 actually, I have a certain right of entry,' he says and goes
to a bookcase in which a few musty volumes mark the stages of the club's
administrative history. Among them are books bound like ledgers and
blocked on the spine in gilt with the words 'Members' Book', and in black
with the numerals denoting the years covered.

'You would be interested in this,' he says, and takes down the book
imprinted '1939–1945'.

The pages are feint-ruled horizontally in blue and vertically in red to
provide columns for the date, the member's name and the name of his
guest.

'If you look through the pages you will see the signatures of one or two
Indian members. But they were of course all officers who held the King-
Emperor's commission. By and large such gentlemen found it only
comfortable to play tennis here and then go back to their quarters. The
committee were in rather a quandary when King's commissioned Indian
officers first began to turn up in Mayapore. It was always accepted that any
officer on the station should automatically become a member. Indeed it
was compulsory for him to pay his subscription whether he ever entered
the place or not. And you could not keep him out if he was an Indian
because that would have been to insult the King's uniform. There was talk
in the 'thirties of founding another club and reserving the Gymkhana for
senior officers, which would have made it unlikely that any Indian officer
on station would have been eligible. But the money simply wasn't
available. In any case the Indian officers more or less solved the problem
themselves by limiting their visits to appearances on the tennis courts.
One was never known to swim in the pool, seldom to enter the bar, never
to dine. There were plenty of face-saving excuses that both sides could
make. The Indian could pretend to be teetotal and to be reluctant to come
to the club and not share fully in its real life. The English would accept this
as a polite, really very gentlemanly way of not directly referring to the fact
that his pay was lower than that of his white fellow-officer and that
therefore he could not afford to stand what I believe is still called his
whack. If he was married the situation was easier still. The English always
assumed that Indian women found it distasteful to be publicly in mixed
company and so there was a tacit understanding that a married Indian

143

officer would appear even less frequently than his bachelor colleagues, because he preferred to stay in quarters with his wife.

'And really there was remarkably little bad feeling about all this kind of thing on either side. An Indian who sought and obtained a commission knew what problems he was likely to encounter. Usually it was enough for him to know that he couldn't actually be blackballed at the Gymkhana merely because he was Indian, and enough for the English members to know that he was unlikely to put in any prolonged or embarrassing appearance. And of course British commanding officers could always be relied upon to iron out any difficulties that arose in individual cases. It wasn't until the war began and the station began to fill up not only with a larger number of Indian King's commissioned officers but also with English officers holding emergency commissions that the committee actually had to meet and pass a *rule*. But then happily, you see, a realistic analysis of the situation provided its own solution. In the first place the influx of officers into the station obviously meant a severe strain on the club's facilities. In the second place the new officers were not only holders of temporary commissions but tended to be temporary in themselves, I mean liable to posting at almost any time. And of course among them there were likely to be men called up from all walks of civilian life, men of the type who, well, wouldn't be at home in the atmosphere of the club. And so for once the committee found themselves thinking of ways of keeping out some of their own countrymen as well as Indians. We, who were not eligible, watched all this from the sidelines with great interest. The rule the committee passed was a splendid English compromise. It was to the effect that for the duration of the war special arrangements would need to be made to extend club hospitality to as many officers on station as possible. To do this the compulsory subscription was waived in the case of all but regular officers and two new types of membership were introduced. Officers with temporary or emergency commissions could enjoy either what was called Special Membership, which involved paying the subscription and was meant of course to attract well-brought-up officers who could be assumed to know how to behave, or Privileged Temporary Membership which entitled the privileged temporary member to use the club's facilities on certain specific days of the week but which could be withdrawn without notice. Outwardly the no notice provision was meant to advertise the committee's thoughtful recognition of the temporary nature of war-time postings to the station. What it really meant was that an emergency officer who misbehaved once could be barred from entry thenceforth. The privileged temporary member had to pay his bills on the spot. He also had to pay a cover charge if he used the dining-room and what was called a Club Maintenance Subscription if he used the pool or the tennis courts. He was allowed to bring only one "approved" guest at any one time, for whom he paid an extra cover charge. Approved was officially held to mean approved by the committee but it also meant approved by the man's commanding officer who no doubt made it clear to these young innocents who were in uniform for a specific and limited purpose what kind of guest would be admitted. Officially it was said to be an insurance against a young man bringing the wrong sort of *woman*. Unofficially it meant bringing no Anglo-Indian or Indian woman, and no Anglo-Indian or Indian man unless that man was himself a King's commissioned officer. In any case, the expense of an evening at the club was usually reckoned to have been raised to the level that no war-time temporary officer would be able to afford more than once a month unless he was well-off. This was the period during which Smith's Hotel really flourished. So did the station restaurant, and of course the Mayapore Indian club enjoyed unaccustomed affluence. The Chinese restaurant in the cantonment bazaar made a fortune and you had to book a seat at the Eros Cinema two or three days in advance. As for the old Gymkhana club, well, it had its unhappy experiences, but by and large managed to maintain its air of all-white social superiority.

'The curious anomaly was, though, that even in those expansive days which the die-hards used to refer to as the thin end of the wedge, Indian officers of the civil service, even of the covenanted civil service, were not admitted as guests let alone as members. Which meant that the District and Sessions Judge, dear old Menen, such a distinguished fellow, couldn't enter, even if brought by the Deputy Commissioner. There was no written rule about it. It was simply an unwritten rule rigorously applied by the committee and if you take Menen as a leading example, never challenged by those who were excluded.

'Here in this book, though, you will see that as far back as May the twenty-second, 1939, the Deputy Commissioner, Mr Robin White, had the temerity to bring *to* and the luck to succeed in bringing *in* no less than three Indians who did not hold the King Emperor's commission – the provincial Minister for Education and Social Services, the Minister's secretary – my old friend Desai – and myself. That is Mr White's own handwriting, of course. Perhaps you can judge character from handwriting? Well, but all this is a long story. We must leave it for tonight. Lili will be looking for us.'

Before the book is closed, though, a flick through the pages relating to 1942 reveals familiar names. The rule of the club has always been that a member signs his name on his first visit and then again on those occasions when he brings a guest. Brigadier Reid's almost illegible signature appears on a date in April; Robin White's on one or two occasions as host to men Mr Srinivasan identifies variously as members of the Secretariat, Revenue Settlement Officers, the Divisional Commissioner, and – once – the Governor and his lady. And there too on several occasions is a curiously rounded and childlike signature easily read as that of Mr Ronald Merrick, the District Superintendent of Police, and, in the same hand, the name of his guest, Miss Daphne Manners.

And on a date in February 1942 a Captain Colin Lindsey signed in, presumably on his first appearance as a temporary privileged member of the Gymkhana Club of Mayapore. Captain Lindsey's signature is steady and sober, unlike the signature that does not actually accompany it, but which one can see, by its side, in the imagination: the signature of his old friend Harry Coomer who round about this time was found drunk by Sister Ludmila in the waste ground where the city's untouchables lived in poverty and squalor.

*

At night the old cantonment area, the area north of the river, still conveys an idea of space that has only just begun to succumb to the invasion of brick and mortar, the civilising theories of necessary but discreet colonial urbanisation. From the now dark and deserted *maidan*, across which the uninterrupted currents of warm – even voluptuous – air build up an impetus that comes upon the cheek as a faintly perceptible breath of enervating rather than refreshing wind, there issues a darkness of the soul, a certain heaviness that enters the heart and brings to life a sadness such as might grow in, weigh down (year by year until the burden becomes at once intolerable and dear) the body of someone who has become accustomed to but has never quite accepted the purpose or conditions of his exile, and who sees, in the existence of this otherwise meaningless space so curiously and yet so poetically named *maidan*, the evidence of the care and thought of those who preceded him, of their concern for what they remembered as somehow typical of home; the silence and darkness that blessed an enduring acre of unenclosed common which, if nothing else, at least illustrated of its own accord the changing temper of the seasons. With here a house. And there a steeple. And everywhere the sky. Bland blue. Or on the march with armoured clouds. Or grey, to match the grey stone of a Norman church. Or dark: an upturned black steel receptacle for scattered magnetic sparks of light or, depending on the extroverted or introverted mood, an amazing cyclorama lit only by the twinkling nocturnal points of a precise but incalculable geometry.

And there is, at night, a strengthening of that special smell: a dry, nostril-smarting mixture of dust from the ground and of smoke from dung-fires: a smell that takes some getting used to but which, given time, will become inseparably part of whatever notion the traveller, the exile, the old hand, may have of India as a land of primitive, perhaps even tragic beauty. It is a smell which seems to have no visible source. It is not only the smell of habitation. It is the smell, perhaps, of centuries of the land's experience of its people. It is to be smelt out there on the broad plains as well as here in the town. And because it is also the smell of the plains, to smell it – perhaps a degree or two stronger – as the car turns a corner and passes a roadside stall lighted by a naphtha lamp, only deepens the sense of pervasiveness, of ubiquity, of vastness, of immensity, of endless, endless acres of earth and stone lying beyond the area of the lamp's light.

This is the bigger car, the Studebaker. This is the long way home:

northwards along the western boundary of the *maidan*, with the old Smith's Hotel on the left, built in the Swiss chalet style and dimly lit as befits an institution that has years behind it but isn't finished yet. This is Church road. It leads to St Mary's and to the military lines. It is the road that old Miss Crane cycled along, every Sunday, rain or shine, and it cannot have changed much, although the banyan trees that shade it during the day and clasp branches overhead to make a theatrically lit green tunnel at night, must have sunk a few more roots during the last twenty years. Church road is an extension of the Mandir Gate Bridge road and at this hour the car is slowed by the plodding processions of carts drawn by white humped oxen lumbering homeward, back to the villages on the plains to the north of Mayapore. The bells on their necks can be heard through the open windows of the Studebaker – dulled by but insistent on the hot wind created by mechanical movement. The carts return empty of produce. The produce has been sold in the Chillianwallah bazaar. Now they are more lightly loaded with private purchases and the farmers' children, most of whom lie huddled, asleep, although a few sit upright staring with the fixity of waking dreams into the headlights.

For a moment, as the Studebaker half-circles the roundabout and takes the right-hand road along the northern edge of the *maidan*, the spire of St Mary's may carry the stranger into a waking dream of his own; so English it is. So perfect. It must, surely, be very like the church in a district of the Punjab which Miss Crane entered all those years ago, looking for an image of herself that would not diminish her. The same grey stone. The same safe comfortable look of housing the spirit of England's personal protector. But few English now attend the services. This has become the church of the Anglo-Indian community. The minister is the Reverend A. M. Ghosh. Is there, perhaps, a congregational joke about his holiness?

Close by St Mary's and its churchyard is the minister's house. Like the church it is, tonight, in darkness. A few bungalows lie back on the left, continuing the line of building from St Mary's corner to the beginning of the military lines opposite the *maidan*. From the air, by day, these are revealed as a geometrical complex of roads and clusters of old and new buildings: the red, tree-shaded Victorian barracks lying closest to the road the Studebaker travels on; the newer low concrete blocks farther back. But from the road, at night, the impression is of space, infrequent habitation marked by lonely points of light. It is not until farther on that the large palladian-style mansion of the old artillery mess comes into view, and the first jawans are seen: two soldiers on guard duty at a white pole barrier that denies free entry by a left-hand turn into the dark. The old artillery mess is now the area headquarters. In 1942 it was the headquarters of the brigade commanded by Brigadier Reid. Once past it, the sense of space diminishes. Tree-backed stucco walls, and side-roads lit by infrequent street-lamps, mark the neat suburban area of the senior officers' bungalows. And then, ahead, is the main block of the ocean-liner-lit Mayapore General Hospital. The Studebaker turns right, into Hospital road, the road that runs along the eastern edge of the *maidan* and leads back to the T-junction of Hospital road, Club road and Mahatma Gandhi road – once Victoria road – the principal highway of the civil lines.

'Let us,' Mr Srinivasan says, 'extend the tour a little more. It is not very late,' and directs the driver to go on down past the chummery, the Court house, and the police barracks, into the cantonment bazaar and then to turn right again following the route that Sister Ludmila used to take, to and from the Imperial (now the State) Bank of India, through the narrower roads where the Eurasians lived in small bungalows backing on to the installations of the railway and out again, with a left turn, into the Mandir Gate Bridge road, past the main mission school and the church of the mission (both of which still flourish) to the level crossing where the car is halted to wait for the mail train that comes from the west and is due at any moment.

Beyond the level crossing lies the bridge and beyond the bridge the black town, still well-lit and lively. The steps leading up from the river to the Tirupati temple are floodlit by a neon standard. There are men walking up and down them, coming from, going into the temple precincts by the river gate. From here the river smell lying upon the warm air enters the open windows of the stationary car.

'They always close the level crossing gates,' Mr Srinivasan complains, 'at the precise moment the train is officially scheduled, even if they know jolly well it is half an hour late. Let me fill in the time by telling you the story of how Robin White took the Minister for Education and me and my old friend Desai to the club in May 1939.

*

'We were all at the DC's bungalow and at six in the evening after three hard hours of conference, Robbie said to us, "How about a drink at the club?" Naturally we thought he meant the Mayapore, but then he said, "The Gymkhana." We were astonished. The Minister begged to be excused. Perhaps he thought it was a joke. But Mr White would not hear of it. He said, "It is all arranged, the car is outside. Just come for an hour." So off we went. It was the first time I had entered, the first time any Indian civilian had entered. Also it was the last because Mr White was stopped by the committee from repeating his social indiscretion. But on the night when we arrived, you should have seen the porter's face when he opened the car door and saw us! Robbie said to the porter, "Hossain, tell the secretary I am here with the Minister for Education, and his party." It was quite a moment! We walked, Desai and I, slowly in the wake of Mr White and the Minister, slowly because Robbie was obviously giving the porter time to run in and find the secretary. On the verandah we all stopped and although it was nearly dark Robbie made great play of standing there and pointing out the amenities of the club's grounds, in fact he kept us there until he judged that the secretary had been found and warned. By now, you understand, it was clear to me that the visit had not been arranged at all, only considered as a possibility. The Deputy Commissioner had waited with typical British restraint to see what kind of a man the Minister for Education was before committing himself to the risky enterprise of taking him to the club. But it was all right. The Minister had turned out to be Wellington and Balliol, and to share with Mr Deputy Commissioner a love of Shakespeare, Mr Dryden and the novelist Henry James, as well as a concern for the Government Higher School and the schools run by the District Boards. Also they enjoyed a disagreement about Mr Rudyard Kipling whom Mr White thought poorly of but the Minister, anticipating Mr T. S. Eliot, thought well of. It is always necessary to have a mutual irritant, it's the best way of testing the toughness of individual fibre.

'And so the secretary came out. A man called Taylor, an ex-ranker of the Cavalry who had achieved gentleman's status by being commissioned Lieutenant Quartermaster and official club status because what he didn't know about organising the annual gymkhana could have been written on the face of a threepenny bit. I saw him coming from his office into the hall. Robbie White had a great talent for seeing through the back of his head. He turned round and called out, 'Oh, hello, Taylor, we have the honour of entertaining representatives of our provincial government. Allow me, Minister, to introduce you to our most important member, the Secretary, Lieutenant Taylor.' Which left poor Taylor in an impossible position, because although he hated Indians he adored Deputy Commissioners and being thought important. Which Robbie knew. Robbie was a senior member of the committee but he had been clever enough to hold his fire for months, until the proper opportunity arose. I mean the opportunity to bring as guests whom it was not socially inadmissible to describe as honourable. Even a provincial minister of state, after all, is a minister of state, and however much the run-of-the-mill English colonial might object to his colour, it couldn't be denied that the Minister had been appointed as the result of a democratic election, an election held with the full approval and authority of the King-Emperor's Governor-General. And all in accordance with the *official* English policy to promote their Indian Empire by easy stages to self-governing dominion status.

'All the same, Robbie White was sticking his neck out. A club was a club, a private institution no outsider could enter, even as a guest of the Deputy Commissioner unless a club official allowed it. Remember Lord Willingdon and the Royal Yacht Club fiasco in Bombay! But Robin knew his man. The secretary looked sick, but he was afraid to make a scene. He tried to lead us into the little ante-room along the corridor from here, but Robbie knew he had got us in now, so he stalked straight into the smoking-room and totally ignored the silence that fell like a stone.

'My dear fellow, shall I ever forget my embarrassment? The more acute, you know, because it was an embarrassment aggravated by a pride I cannot properly describe. There was I, a just-on-middle-aged man who had thought never to enter this sacred edifice. Do you know what struck me

most about it? Its old-fashioned shabbiness. I can't think what I had
expected. But it was a shock. Let me qualify that. By shock I mean the sort
of shock you describe as one of recognition. I suppose that by keeping us
out the English had led us too easily to imagine the club as a place where
their worst side would be reflected in some awful insidious way. But the
opposite was the case. And the opposite was what one recognised and what
one saw at once one should have really expected. Perhaps you will
understand this better if I describe Robin White to you as I remember him.
He was quite a young man, still in his thirties, very tall, and with one of
those narrow English faces which used to appal us when we saw them for
the first time because they seemed to be incapable of expressing any
emotion. And we wondered: Is it that this man is very clever and
potentially well-disposed, or is it that he is a fool? If he is a fool is he a
useful fool or a dangerous fool? How much does he know? What on earth is
he thinking? When he smiles is he smiling at one of our jokes or at a joke of
his own? Is it distaste for us that makes him put up his chilly little barrier,
or is it shyness? Almost it was more comfortable to deal with the other
type of English face, the extrovert face, even though we knew that the
chances of it remaining open and friendly for more than six months were
remote. At least in that sort of face there was no mystery to solve. The
stages of its transformation were not only clear to see but also predictable.
But with this narrow, introverted face, it took a long time to feel at ease.
Often a man with a face like this would appear and disappear without our
ever knowing the truth about him. Sometimes we heard no more of him.
At other times we heard he had succeeded to some important position, and
then at least we realised that he had been no fool, although his subsequent
reputation might also prove that he had been no friend either.

'For instance, with Stead, Robin White's predecessor, we all knew what
we were up against. There were members of the local Congress sub-
committee who preferred Stead's regime because Stead was almost a
caricature of the traditional choleric Collector. We always said that he
punished the district to avenge himself for what he considered unfair
treatment by his own superiors in the service. If he had not been
approaching retiring age in 1937 our first provincial minister for internal
affairs would have tried to get him promoted to the relatively harmless
position of Divisional Commissioner and pressed the claims of an Indian
to succeed him. In which case we should not have had Robin White. We
could have done worse, but not, I think, any better. This was my personal
view. It was not shared by us all. Some of us, as I said, preferred Stead
because he gave our committee so many reasons to complain to Congress
in Delhi where questions would be asked in the so-called central
legislative assembly, and so many reasons for the District and Municipal
Boards to complain to the provincial ministry. There were too many of us
who preferred gnawing at the bone of short-term contention to pursuing a
long-term policy that could lead from co-operation to autonomy.

'Stead, you know, was a Muslim lover, if lover is the right word to describe a man who basically thought all Indians inferior. He made no secret of his preference, and this only added fuel to that ridiculous communal fire. Two of his sub-divisional officers were Muslims. When the Congress Ministry came into power he transferred one of these Muslims from an outside area to Mayapore itself, which meant that this man was really acting as assistant commissioner and joint magistrate in the town. Unfortunately this Muslim Syed Ahmed was of the militant kind. All Muslim offenders either got off lightly in his court or were acquitted. Hindus were dealt with very severely. In retaliation the Hindu-dominated District Board decided that in the village schools all the Muslim children had to sing Congress songs and salute the Congress flag. Communal differences have always tended to snowball. There were riots in Tanpur, which was in the jurisdiction of the second of Stead's Muslim sub-divisional officers, a man called Mohammed Khan. Our committee complained to the ministry that Mohammed Khan and Syed Ahmed were both inciting the Muslim community to create disorders. The ministries had no jurisdiction over the civil service but in certain circumstances pressure could be brought to bear, especially if you could make out a good case. Stead was eventually directed by the Divisional Commissioner to transfer Syed Ahmed to Tanpur. Mohammed Khan was posted to another district and Stead found himself with a young English assistant commissioner called Tupton, who was posted here from another district. It didn't make much difference because this fellow Tupton also thought Muslims manlier than Hindus, so Stead was laughing up his sleeve – until he was retired and we got Robin White. And it didn't take Robin long to cross swords with Tupton and arrange for him to be replaced by a man of his own choice, young John Poulson.

'In fact, I can tell you, it was the way he got rid of Tupton and brought in Poulson that first made us see that behind that not unfriendly but curiously expressionless face there was more than met the eye. To begin with, his getting rid of Tupton made it clear that there was an understanding of what constituted an unneccessary irritant. When it became clear also that he was not moving in a reverse direction, away from the Muslims towards the Hindus, but making a point of showing friendliness to both, we saw that he was strictly the fair-minded type. There was also a statesmanlike air about him. He requested, in the most diplomatic terms, that the District and Municipal Boards should reconsider the rule they had laid down about the compulsory salutation of the Congress flag in the primary schools. I recall the words in one part of his letter. "The Congress, I appreciate, inspires the allegiance not only of a majority of Hindus but of quite a large number of Muslims. I submit however that although Congress is fundamentally an Indian national party and that it is correct to lead Indian children towards a patriotic sense of national duty by ritual observances, it is perhaps unwise to leave an impression on their minds of the kind of exclusion the Congress itself is rightly at pains to eradicate."

'Well, you see, he had us by the hip, or at least had by the hip those of us who appreciated the subtlety of the English language. As a member of the sub-committee – and he had had the foresight to send us a copy of his letter to the District and Municipal Boards – as a member of the sub-committee who considered his submission I argued for an hour over the significance of the words "impression" and "exclusion".

'Perhaps to you Congress is synonymous with Hindu. To us – originally – it was always the All-India Congress – founded, incidentally, by an Englishman. But since there have always been more Hindus than Muslims in India, it has also always gone without saying that its membership is and was predominantly Hindu. This did not in itself make it a party of Hindu policy. Unfortunately, there is always an unmapped area of dangerous fallibility between a policy and its pursuit. Do you not agree? Well, surely as an Englishman, a member of a race that once ruled us, you must agree? Was there not an unmapped area of dangerous fallibility between your liberal Whitehall policies for India and their pursuit here on the spot? What had Mr Stead to do with official English policy without irrevocably violating it by his personal passions and prejudices? Do you not agree that the Mr Steads of your world kicked and swore against every directive from Parliament and Whitehall that seemed to them to be reprehensible? As reprehensible as it would be for the garrison of a beleaguered fort to wave the white flag when plenty of ammunition was still to hand? Did not such people always feel themselves to be the quantity left out of the official equation, the unofficial but very active repository of the old sterling qualities they thought the politicians had lost sight of or never had? Don't you agree, my dear fellow, that those of your compatriots whom you have observed this evening, by and large, are still in the grip of some traumatic process that persuades them to ignore the directives of your government at home to export or die? Don't you think that we should get on better with the Russians and the Americans?

'Well, so it was, you understand, with members of the Congress. Perhaps even in a greater degree because the official Congress policy wavered between the extremes of that curious unworldly man and our sophisticated Kashmiri Pandit who realised always and perhaps still realises that half a cake is better than no cake at all.

'So why should you expect the Congress to abide by rules no one else ever abided by? In countless places like Mayapore it became narrowly exclusive. In the same way that Stead became narrowly impenetrable, and your compatriots in the lounge-bar have become narrowly insular, needing the money they earn, the money we are quite prepared to pay them, but affecting to despise the people they earn it from.

'Forgive me. Lili is signalling me to shut up. But I am an old man. I am entitled, am I not, to say what I think? – and of course to stray from the point. I was telling of the Deputy Commissioner's letter and the perfect English flexibility of that sentence: "It is perhaps unwise to leave an impression on their minds of the kind of exclusion Congress itself is rightly at pains to eradicate."

152

'He was not only calling us to reaffirm the official party line which held Congress to be a body representative of all India, but pointing out very subtly what in our hearts we knew, that many of our local activities were contrary to the party line, if you judged the party line on its highest originating level, especially when those activities were directed at children. "It is perhaps unwise to leave an impression on their minds." This made us think of the kind of minds we left an impression on. The minds of children. Once we had to face the fact that we were acting as adults who knew the rough and tumble of everyday party politics, but acting in a world of children who didn't, also we had to face the fact that these children for a long time now had equated Congress with Hinduism and the singing of Congress songs and the salutation of the Congress flag as an act of defiance not only of the British Raj but of Muslim national aspirations. Because it was we, their elders, who had simplified the issues in this convenient way.

'Unfortunately my arguments in favour of supporting the Deputy Commissioner's submission, my arguments in favour of dropping the morning ritual in our district schools, were defeated by a five to two majority. And I was deputed, as a disciplinary exercise, to draft the committee's reply to Mr White. I remember only one sentence because the rest of my draft was torn to shreds, and this sentence alone remained as mine. Let me repeat it. It makes almost no sense out of context, but the interesting thing is that the Deputy Commissioner recognised its authorship. When he next met me he quoted it: "The salutation of the Indian National Congress flag should not be susceptible of any narrow, communal interpretation." He said: "I quite agree, Mr Srinivasan. At least, on one point your committee answered my letter." From that moment we were friends, which is why when he heard that I was lunching with Mr Desai and the Minister for Education he invited me to accompany them when they went to his bungalow to discuss the extension of primary education in his district. By then, as you probably realise, our provincial ministries had got over their teething troubles. But of course it was already 1939, although none of us could have guessed on that evening he took us to the club that by the end of the year the Ministry would have resigned over the ridiculous point of order raised on the Viceroy's declaration of war on Germany. Or guessed that we should then get thrown back on to the old personal autocratic rule of British Governors with a nominated council. That evening when we went to the Gymkhana it seemed as if the whole world was opening up to us.

'But this is the point I am tortuously trying to make. It was not until I came into the club with Desai and the Minister and Mr White that I really understood what it was that men like Robin White stood for, stood for against all narrow opposition. I do not mean opposition in Whitehall. But opposition here. On the spot. In Mayapore. I saw then how well he *fitted* the club. How well the club fitted him. Like him, it had no expression that you could easily analyse. It was shabby and comfortable. But rather awe-inspiring – I suppose because the English as a ruling class attached so much importance to it. And yet the majority of the people who were there – well, you felt that no matter how well they thought they were made for the club the club wasn't really made for them. In the club, in the smoking-room to be exact, for the first time I saw the face behind the face of Robin White. It seemed to go awfully well with the shabby leather chairs that looked forbidding but turned out to be amazingly comfortable to sit on. And Robin, you know, *looked* at the servants when he spoke to them. You could see him receiving a brief but clear impression of them as men. He did not feel superior to them, only more responsible for them. It was his sense of responsibility that enabled him to accept his privileged position with dignity. That is always the kind of attitude that makes for confidence. In one dazzling moment – forgive the dramatic adjective – in one dazzling moment I really felt I understood what it was the English always imagined lay but only rarely succeeded in showing *did* lie behind all the flummery of their power and influence. And that is why I have always loved the club since then –'

'Even now –?'

'Oh well – I love it for what it was and even now it is really no different if you know what you are looking for. One always saw and sees through pretence. It is only that now that their responsibility has gone there is no longer any need for the average English person to pretend. And you have as well this very interesting situation in which emptying chamber pots into the pool can also be interpreted as a gesture of *your own* one-time under-privileged people against the kind of social forces that no longer work but used to keep them in their place. I mean, well, please forgive me, so many of your present-day experts are not what members of the club of twenty years ago would have called gentlemen, are they? They are what the English ladies of Mayapore would have called BOR types? British Other Rank? Well, you know, you send a chap like that to Mayapore today to teach us how to run one of those complicated bits of machinery and of course he is treated as a member of a superior race but I do not feel that he generally has much of a feeling of *responsibility* to teach, merely a need to earn a living in relatively pleasant surroundings and a feeling that what he finds so simple other people also should find simple, so that he is likely to become impatient. We cotton on very quickly to the superficial aspects of machinery, but not to its inner logic. This is what young men like Surendranath and Desai mean when they say we wasted time playing at politics. Anyway our shortcomings give the expert a feeling of consider-able superiority and he also gets a bit of a kick, of which perhaps he is also slightly ashamed, to be automatically entitled to be a member of the Gymkhana. He laughs at what the Gymkhana used to represent – that old-fashioned upper-class English stuffiness and pretence – which is why I suppose he comes dressed in shorts and short-sleeved shirts and uses vulgar expressions. He knows almost nothing about British–Indian his-tory, so writes off everything that seems to be connected with it as an example of old type British snobbery. Which means also that in a way he writes *us* off too. And of course underneath all this there is this other thing, his natural distrust of us, his natural dislike of black people, the dislike he may think he hasn't got but soon finds he has when he's been out here a while, the distrust and dislike he shares with those old predecessors of his, but has the rude courage to express in physical action, like emptying chamber pots into the swimming pool. There is as well a more subtle complication. In his heart he also shares with that old ruling-class of English he affects to despise a desire to be looked-up to abroad, and shares with them also the sense of deprivation because he has not been able to inherit the Empire he always saw as a purely ruling-class institution. If you said any of this to him openly he genuinely would not understand, and would deny what of it he did understand. But we understand it. To us it is very clear. But clearest of all now that there is no official policy of foreign government or mystique of foreign leadership that calls for pretence in public and private life, is the fact that behind all that pretence there was a fear and dislike between us that was rooted in the question of the colour of the skin. Even when we most loved, there was the fear, and when there was only the fear and no love there was the dislike. In this odd love-hate affair we always came off worst because you see – the world being what it was, what it is – *we* recognised and still recognise only too clearly that you were, that you are, far ahead of us in the practical uses of practical knowledge and we still equate fair skin with superior intelligence. Even equate it with beauty. The sun is too strong here. It darkens us and saps us. Paleness is synonymous with worldly success, because paleness is the mark of intellectual, not physical endeavour, and worldly success is seldom achieved with the muscles. Well – here already is the train.'

And presently, with a mechanical precision recognisable as one not wrought by local invention but by foreign instruction, the gates of the level crossing swing back and leave the road open to the bridge and the temple and the black town. The Studebaker (also a foreign importation, sold by its American owner for a handsome profit to a Brahmin friend of Mr Srinivasan's in Calcutta) glides forward and there below is the sweep of the river, glittering with the artificial jewels of the night's illumination. Obstructing the traffic that has been waiting to move in the opposite direction, from the black town to the civil lines (the old descriptive usages die hard), is another but shorter procession of carts drawn by white, humpbacked oxen. Their round eyes glint red in the headlights.

'Stop!' Mr Srinivasan cries suddenly. 'Would you like to see the temple? It is not too late? Oh no, come, Lili – let us show at least one thing tonight that is truly *Indian*,' and directs the Muslim driver to park wherever he can find a place.

At the bridgehead on the black-town side, with the Tirupati temple on the left, the road broadens into a square whose other end is marked by the holy tree and wayside shrine. On the right, almost opposite the temple, is the Majestic Cinema where the epic from the Ramayana is showing to packed houses. Beyond the square – it may be remembered – the road forks to the right in the direction of the jail and to the left to the Chillianwallah Bazaar. The square is lighted by a single standard close to the holy tree, but it is not dark because the shops are open-fronted and not yet shuttered, still open for custom, and lit by unshaded electric bulbs or glaring pressure lamps that hurt the eye to look at. Somewhere nearby – yes, from the coffee-house – there is the amplified sound of recorded music, a popular song of a celluloid civilisation – a girl's voice, nasal, thin, accompanied by strings, brass and percussion. There are a cow or two, parked cycle-rickshaws, many people, and several beggar women who converge upon the Studebaker, carrying sleeping children aslant their bangled arms. Their eyes and the rings in their nostrils capture, lose, and recapture, shards of splintered light.

They reach the car and surround it, accompanying it, half-running, half-walking. When it stops their hands come through the open windows. It is necessary, in the end, for Mr Srinivasan to threaten them with the police. They retreat, but only far enough to allow the passengers to alight. The driver stays with the car and he is left in peace, but the party that now makes its way back towards the temple is followed by the most persistent of the women. Sometimes, making a way through the crowd, you think they have given up. A hand lightly touching your sleeve and then tugging it proves otherwise. To look straight into her eyes would be fatal. In India the head too often has to be turned away. 'You must not give them anything,' Mr Srinivasan says. An observer of the scene would notice that since leaving the car the beggar women have concentrated on the more vulnerable flank of the trio walking towards the temple: the white man. The observer would perhaps notice too that the woman who makes her dumb appeal through that gesture, that brief contact with the white man's sleeve, and who now keeps her voice down to a whisper and limits her vocabulary of begging to one urgently repeated word, 'Sahib, Sahib,' is the last to admit defeat, walking with the visitors almost to the entrance of the temple.

'I'm afraid,' Mr Srinivasan says, 'that you will have to take off your shoes. If you like you could keep your socks on.'

Socks? Ah, well, risk all!

The open gateway is fairly narrow, but it is deep because the gate is at the base of the tall stone tower that mounts in diminishing tiers of sculpted figures, the details of which cannot be seen at night. Inside the passage through the tower a temple servant squats by an oil-lamp, surrounded by chappals and shoes. With chalk he makes a mark on the soles and gives Mr Srinivasan a slip of paper. The stone floor of the passage is warm to the bare feet and rather gritty. The descent into the main courtyard of the temple is by a shallow flight of four steps. The feet come into contact with sand. There are people walking, people praying and people sitting on the ground who seem to be gossiping. The illumination is dim. In the centre of the courtyard is the square building of the inner sanctuary, with steps leading up, and carved pillars supporting an ornamental roof. Around the walls of the courtyard there are other sanctuaries. Some are in darkness; others are lit to show that the god or goddess is awake. The figures, often no bigger than dolls, are painted and garlanded. A bell is rung in the main sanctuary: by a devotee of Lord Venkataswara warning the god that he seeks admittance. Slowly the trio of visitors walks round the courtyard until the entrance into Lord Venkataswara's sanctuary is revealed. A man with a shaved head, bare chest, and the string of the sacred thread looped over his light brown shoulder stands near a pillar. He is one of the priests of the temple. The black-skinned, loin-clothed devotee stands at the open doors of the sanctuary in an attitude of prayer – both arms raised above his head, the palms together. The short length of rope attached to the tongue of the iron bell that is suspended from the roof still moves. It is possible to get only a glimpse of the inner sanctum: a gleam of gold, silver and ebony, in the heart of the stone. There is a bitter-sweet smell in the air. The sand beneath the feet varies from grit to velvet softness. Through the river entrance comes the smell of the water.

There are trees in the courtyard. In the day they afford some shade. Behind the main sanctuary is the sanctuary of the sleeping Vishnu. The stone of the sanctuary floor is rubbed black and shiny. Inside, in the dim light of the oil-lamps set in the walls the carved recumbent god sleeps through an eternity of what look like pleasant dreams. He is longer than a lying man would be. He is part of his own stone pallet, carved into it, out of it, inseparable from it. He is smooth and naked, with square shoulders and full lips that curve at the corners into a smile. The eyelids are shut but seem always to be on the point of fluttering voluptuously open. Once this imminent awakening has made its impression, the stiff limbs begin to suggest a hidden flexibility as though, at least, the god may be expected to ease the cramp of long sleep out of them. The delicately carved but powerful hand would then drop from the stone pillow and fall aslant the breast. And then perhaps the full lips would part and he would speak one word, speaking it softly, as in a dream, but revealing a secret that would enable whatever mortal man or woman happened to be there to learn the secret of power on earth and peace beyond it.

'I am sorry we cannot take you into the holy of holies,' Mr Srinivasan says, 'although I might swing it if I can convince the priest that you are a Buddhist. But perhaps some other time. Lili is looking tired.'

Not only tired but, oddly, out of place.

'These days,' Srinivasan explains, as shoes are found, socks retrieved from pockets and a coin given to the shoe-minder, 'the temples are all controlled by Government. In fact you could really say the priests have become civil servants. They are paid salaries, and collect fees according to official scales. It cuts down a lot on all that extortion that used to go on. This is one of the things we old congressmen insisted on ... that India should be a secular democratic state, not a priest-ridden autocracy.'

Before the car is reached, the same beggar-women encroach. Settled and safe in the Studebaker, Srinivasan says, 'Well, we are holy now, I suppose. It is in order to be charitable,' and throws some coins out of the window. The women scrabble for them in the dust, and the car, free of them, moves forward, taking the left fork from the square, where Sister Ludmila walked with her leather handbag chained to her waist. The lane is narrow, and harshly lit, and crowded. The bonnet of the Studebaker is like the prow of a boat, ploughing through a busy waterway. The chauffeur drives on the clutch and the horn. At the end of the lane, where it opens on to the walled square of the Chillianwallah Bazaar market the town is suddenly dark and dead. The market is closed. The houses are shuttered. Only a few lights show. The headlamps create dense angular shadows. The smell off the river comes through the narrow openings between deserted buildings.

Turning a corner there is a glimpse of the old palace, the Purdah Hospital: a high wall, an iron gateway in it, foliage inside the grounds, a light showing behind the leaves. A dog with white and yellow markings crosses the road in front of the car. The sky ahead expands, displaying its stars in counter-attraction to the goods that were for sale in the shops. Somewhere, to the left, is the place once known as the Sanctuary and to the right the Chillianwallah Bagh reclamation.

'She died years ago, they say,' Mr Srinivasan explains, speaking of Mrs Gupta Sen who had been Shalini Kumar before her marriage. The car enters an area of well laid out but unmetalled badly lit roads, along which the suntrap houses of the rich merchants cluster in walled compounds, a few showing lights behind barred windows. Here there are the black, feathery silhouettes of coconut palms, leaning tall and drunken between the gaps in the houses. The car turns twice. But each road, each collection of dwellings, looks the same. Number twelve is an anonymous dark bulk. A grandson of Romesh Chand lives there for a few months in the year in the cold weather. The car, on Srinivasan's order, stops outside the iron, padlocked gate. There is nothing to feel except the night warmth and nothing to see except the shadows in the compound, and the culvert that leads from the road to the gate across the monsoon ditch in the bordering grass where the bicycle was found.

And young Kumar? Where is he now? Srinivasan shrugs. Dead perhaps. Upon Kumar's arrest after the rape in the Bibighar Romesh Chand disowned him. Perhaps, also, young Kumar disowned his family. Well, it is a vast country. Easy to get lost in. And again the sense of immensity (of weight and flatness, and absence of orientating features) blankets the mind with an idea of scope so limitless that it is deadening. Here, on the ground, nothing is likely, everything possible. Only from the air can one trace what looks like a pattern, a design, an abortive, human intention. The Studebaker noses forward, lost, at bay, but committed to automatic progression, out on to the Chillianwallah Bagh Extension road, which to the south leads to the now non-existent southern gate of the old walled town, and to the north of the Bibighar bridge.

The bridge has a low, stone parapet and is arched, as if perpetually tensed against the ache of rheumatism from having its supports so long in water. And so, down, to its northerly head, having led the traveller back across the invisible water (which in these less well-lit reaches does not glitter) to the second level-crossing: having led across the eternal back to the transitory, from the waters that have their source in the snows of far-off mountain ranges to the parallel lines of steel that carry the trains eastward to the unimaginable coast.

And here is the hut of the level-crossing keeper lit these days by a neon standard. The well-sprung car bounces luxuriously over the uneven surface of the wooden boards that have been set between the rails. It is not difficult to imagine the sensation of cycling over the crossing, with the light system showing green and, coming from the left, the smoky metallic railway smell that is the same anywhere in the world, and was certainly no different twenty-two years ago, so that it is possible to breathe in sharply and think: This is what she smelt as she cycled back from Sister Ludmila's Sanctuary.

But ahead, there is a change. The road is being re-surfaced. One remembers Lili Chatterjee having mentioned it. There are now warning lamps and mounds of chipped stone and x-shaped trestle ends that support long barricading poles: a familiar manifestation of public works-in-progress. The work in progress sends the car over to the right-hand side of the road, a few feet closer to the wall of the Bibighar Gardens.

An ordinary wall, such as you would find anywhere in India, a little higher than a man, stuccoed, greying, peeling. Old. With trees behind it screening an interior. As the car goes by nothing is said, but the silence is commentary enough.

Bibighar.

After a time even the most tragic name acquires a kind of beauty.

From here the car follows the route taken by the girl who ran in the darkness. Yes. This is what she must have felt: beyond the darkness of the buildings and the habitation, the space, the limitless territory. Through such ordinary ways, such unspectacular, unlit avenues. And all the time the curious smell – not of the railway now, but of the land – which perhaps she had learned to accept or not to notice, if not to love, to need.

Part Five

YOUNG KUMAR

When Hari Kumar's father died of an overdose of sleeping pills in Edinburgh and the lawyers told him that there wasn't even enough money to pay in full what was owed to Mr and Mrs Carter who ran the house in Berkshire he rang the Lindseys and asked them what they thought he should do. Although the lawyers insisted that he could put the notion right out of his head he had an old-fashioned idea that he was responsible for his father's debts, if in fact there were debts. The Lindseys found it as difficult to believe the lawyers' tale of bankruptcy as he did himself. They said he must come over to Didbury right away and stay with them. He was not to worry, because Mr Lindsey would see the lawyers and get proper sense out of them.

His father's death occurred in the middle of the Easter holidays of 1938, a few weeks before Hari's eighteenth birthday. The Lindseys were in Paris when it happened. If they had been at home Hari would probably have been with them and certainly have had their support at the funeral. He spent most of his vacations with the Lindseys. Their son Colin was his oldest friend. He had been with them up until the day before they were due to entrain for Paris. If his father had not written from Edinburgh and warned him that he was coming down to Sidcot and wanted to discuss plans for the future, he would have gone to Paris too, relying as usual on his father's agreement *in absentia*. Instead the letter had come and he had gone home and found his father not arrived and the housekeeper and her husband, Mr and Mrs Carter, in a disagreeable mood. He hadn't been expected and the Carters said they knew nothing of his father's plans to leave Edinburgh. He did not care very much for the Carters. In Sidcot the staff seldom stayed long. The Carters had been in residence for a couple of years, which was something of a record. He could not remember how many different housekeepers and handyman-gardeners his father had employed. In the old days, before he went to prep school and then on to Chillingborough, there had been a succession of disagreeable governesses and tutors as well as of domestic servants, some of whom made it plain that they preferred to work for white gentlemen. The house had never been to him what, since he had got to know the Lindseys, he had learned to think of us as a home. He saw his father three or four times a year and seldom for longer than a week at a time. He did not remember his mother. He understood that she had died in India when he was born. He did not remember India either.

The reason he found it difficult to believe what the lawyers told him was that there had always seemed to be plenty of money. When he was old enough to appreciate the difference in degrees of affluence he realised that the house in Sidcot was substantial, bigger and more expensively furnished than the Lindseys'; and as well as the house in Sidcot there was a succession of flats in London which his father moved into and out of, in accordance with some principle Hari did not understand and took no interest in beyond what was necessary to record accurately the change of address and telephone number, so that his letters should not go astray and he could be sure of going to the right place if his father rang the school and suggested lunch in town on Hari's way home at the end of term. On such occasions he usually took Colin with him. And Colin once said, looking round the sumptuous but unwelcoming flat, 'Your father must be stinking rich.' And Hari shrugged and replied, 'I suppose he is.'

This was probably the moment when he began consciously to be critical of his father who spoke English with that appalling sing-song accent, spelled the family name Coomer, and told people to call him David because Duleep was such a mouthful. Duleep had chosen the name Hari for his only surviving child and only son (the son for whom he had prayed and longed and whose life had now been planned down to the last detail) because Hari was so easily pronounced and was really only distinguishable in the spelling from the diminutive of Saxon Harold, who had been King of the English before the Normans came.

*

The story is that Duleep Kumar, against the wishes and with only the reluctant permission of his parents, went to England to study for the law, just about the time that Miss Crane left the service of the Nesbitt-Smiths and entered the fuller service of the mission, about the time, too, that there died, in a penury as great if not as spectacular as Duleep's, the mother of a young girl who then entered an orphanage and in later years called herself Sister Ludmila.

The Kumars were landowners in a district of the United Provinces. They were rich by Indian standards and loyal to a foreign crown that seemed ready to respect the laws of property. There were many Kumars, but as a youth Duleep began to notice that no matter how much they were looked up to by people whose skin was the same colour as their own, the callowest white-skinned boy doing his first year in the covenanted civil service could snub them by keeping them waiting on the verandah of the sacred little bungalow from whose punkah-cooled rooms was wafted an air of effortless superiority. Power, Duleep felt, lay not in money but in this magical combination of knowledge, manner, and race. His father – one of those frequently kept waiting – disagreed. 'In the end,' he said, 'it is money that counts. What is a snub? What is an insult? Nothing. It costs nothing to give and nothing to receive. Hurt pride is quickly nursed back to health in the warmth of a well-lined pocket. That young man who keeps me waiting is a fool. He refuses gifts because he has been taught that any gift from an Indian is a bribe. At home he would not be so careful. But in forty years he will be poor, living on his pension in his own cold climate.'

'But in those forty years,' Duleep pointed out, 'he will have wielded power.'

'What is this power?' his father asked. 'He will have settled a few land disputes, seen to the maintenance of public works, extended a road, built a drain, collected revenues on behalf of Government, fined a few thousand men, whipped a score and sent a couple of hundred to jail. But you will be a comparatively rich man. Your power will be material, visible to your eyes when you look at the land you own. Your trouble will be a single one – the slight inconvenience of being kept waiting by one of this young man's successors who will also refuse gifts and in his turn wield what you call power and die rich in nothing except his colonial recollections.'

Duleep laughed. He laughed at his father's wry humour. But mostly he laughed because he knew otherwise. When his father died the land so proudly possessed would be divided by his children, and later by his children's children, and then by his children's children's children, and in the end there would be nothing and the power would have dwindled away field by field, village by village. And a young man would still sit in the sacred bungalow, making himself ready to listen with an agreeable but non-committal expression to tales of distress and poverty and injustice, thinking all the time of his own career, planning to follow his predecessors one step at a time up the ladder to a desk in the Secretariat, or a seat on the Governor-General's Council, or to a place on the bench of the High Court of Justice.

Duleep Kumar was the youngest of a family of four boys and three girls. Perhaps a family of seven children was counted auspicious, for after his birth (in 1888) it seemed for several years that his parents were satisfied and intended no further addition. He was the baby, the last-born son. It could have been that his brothers and sisters grew up to be jealous of the attention and affection lavished on him. Certainly in later years, in the matter of his own son Hari's welfare, no interest was shown by and no help forthcoming from those of Duleep's elders who survived him. In the long run, things might have worked out better if there had been no surviving Kumar at all to take an interest; but there was Shalini, the little girl Duleep's mother bore when he was in his eleventh year. The evidence points to a special bond between the last-born son and the last-born daughter, one that in all likelihood originated in Duleep's sense of isolation from his older brothers and sisters, when the first flush of his parents' spoiling had worn thin, and caused him even at that early age to cast a critical eye upon the world around him and a restless one towards the world beyond. Of the four brothers only Duleep completed the course at the Government Higher School and went on to the Government College. His family thought that to study at the college was a waste of time, so they opposed the plan, but finally gave in. In later years he was fond of quoting figures from the provincial census taken round about this time, that showed a male population of twenty-four and a half million and a female population of twenty-three million. Of the males one and a half million were literate; of the females less than fifty-six thousand, a figure which did not include his three elder sisters. His father and brothers were literate in the vernacular, semi-literate in English. It was because as a youth Duleep had acquired a good knowledge of the language of the administrators that he began to accompany his father on visits to petition the sub-divisional officer, and had the first intimations of the secrets hidden behind the bland face of the white authority. There grew in him a triple determination – to break away from a landlocked family tradition, to become a man who instead of requesting favours, granted them, and to save Shalini from the ignorance and domestic tyranny not only his other sisters but his two elder brothers' wives seemed to accept uncomplainingly as all that women could hope for from the human experience. When Shalini was three years old he began to teach her her letters in Hindi. When she was five she could read in English.

Duleep was now sixteen years old. The Government College to which he had gained admittance was at the other end of the earth: a hundred miles away. His mother wept at his going. His brothers scoffed. His elder sisters and sisters-in-law looked at him as if he were setting out on some shameful errand. His father did not understand, but gave him his blessing the night before his departure and in the morning accompanied him to the railway station in a doolie drawn by bullocks.

And perhaps that is when what could be called the tragedy of Duleep Kumar began. He was a boy whose passion for achievement was always just that much greater than his ability to achieve. And it was a passion that had become used to the constant irritants of home. Far removed from there, in the company of boys of diverse backgrounds but similar ambitions, the original sense of frustration upon which these passions had thrived began to diminish. Here, everyone was in the same boat, but as the BA course progressed he became uncomfortably aware of the process that separated the quick-witted from the plodders. For the first time in his life he found himself having to admit that other boys, if not actually cleverer, could certainly be quicker. Analysing this he came readily to an explanation. The quick boys, surely, all came from progressive homes where English was spoken all the time. On the college teaching staff there was a preponderance of Englishmen. At the Government Higher School, most of the instruction, although in English, had been in the hands of Indians. He had always understood exactly what the Indian teachers were saying, and he had often felt that what they were saying he could have said better. But now he sat through lectures increasingly at a loss to follow not the words so much as the thinking behind the words. And he did not dare to ask questions. Nobody asked questions. They listened attentively. They filled exercise books with meticulous notes of what they thought had been said. To ask questions was to admit ignorance. In a competitive world like this such an admission would probably have been fatal.

He was, however, discovering a new irritant: the frustrations not of a hidebound orthodox Indian family, but of the English language itself. Listening to his fellow students he was amazed that they seemed unable to comprehend the difference between the way they spoke and the way the Englishmen spoke. It was not only a question of pronunciation or idiom. He was too young to be able to formulate the problem. But he was aware of having come close to the heart of another important secret. To uncover it might lead to an understanding of what in the sub-divisional officer looked like simple arrogance and in the English teachers intellectual contempt.

There came a time when he was able to say to his son Hari: 'It is not only that if *you* answer the phone a stranger on the other end would think he was speaking to an English boy of the upper classes. It is that you *are* that boy in your mind and behaviour. Conversely when I was your age, it was not only that I spoke English with an even stronger *babu* accent than I speak it now, but that everything I said, because everything I thought, was in conscious mimicry of the people who rule us. We did not necessarily admit this, but that is what was always in their minds when they listened to us. It amused them mostly. Sometimes it irritated them. It still does. Never they could listen to us and forget that we were a subject, inferior people. The more idiomatic we tried to be the more naïve our thinking seemed, because we were thinking in a foreign language that we had never properly considered in relation to our own. Hindi, you see, is spare and beautiful. In it we can think thoughts that have the merit of simplicity and truth. And between each other convey these thoughts in correspondingly spare, simple, truthful images. English is not spare. But it is beautiful. It cannot be called truthful because its subtleties are infinite. It is the language of a people who have probably earned their reputation for perfidy and hypocrisy because their language itself is so flexible, so often light-headed with statements which appear to mean one thing one year and quite a different thing the next. At least, this is so when it is written, and the English have usually confided their noblest aspirations and intentions to paper. Written, it looks like a way of gaining time and winning confidence. But when it is spoken, English is rarely beautiful. Like Hindi it is spare then, but crueller. We learned our English from books, and the English, knowing that books are one thing and life another, simply laughed at us. Still laugh at us. They laughed at me, you know, in that Indian college I went to before I came over here that first disastrous time to study law. At the college I learned the importance of obtaining a deep understanding of the language, a real familiarity with it, spoken and written. But of course I got it mostly all from books. A chapter of Macaulay was so much easier to understand, and certainly more exciting, than a sentence spoken by Mr Croft who taught us history. In the end I was even trying to speak Macaulayesque prose. Later I found out that any tortuous path to a simple hypothesis was known among the English staff as a Kumarism. And it was later still before I really understood that a Kumarism was not something admirable but something rather silly. But I think this notoriety helped me to scrape through. I was a long way down the list. But it was a triumph by my standards.'

And it was in the glow of this triumph that, aged nineteen, he returned home, not for the first time since going to the station in the doolie – naturally enough there had been the vacations – but for the first time as a young man of proven worth, and of ambitions that now pointed to the necessity of making the passage across the black water, to England, to sit for the examinations of the Indian Civil Service, which in those days was the only place where the examinations could be taken: a rule which effectively restricted the number of Indians able to compete.

He found his parents less jubilant over his academic success than they were concerned about his failure to fulfil a primary function: to be married, to increase, to ensure at least one son who could officiate eventually in his funeral rites and see him on the way, with honour, to another world.

The girl they had in mind, whose name was Kamala and whose horoscope, according to the astrologers, was in an auspicious confluence with his own, was already fifteen; in fact, they said, nearly sixteen.

'Kamala!' he shouted. 'Who, what, is Kamala?' and would not even listen to the answer.

The Kumar home was a rambling rural agglomeration of low buildings built around a central courtyard, walled within a large compound, on the outskirts of the principal village within their holding, a distance of five miles from the town where the English sub-divisional officer had his headquarters. Five miles by buffalo cart to the nearest outpost of civilisation, Duleep thought. Ah! What a prison! He played with Shalini and in intervals of playing retaught her the lessons he was pleased to find she had not forgotten in the three months that had gone since he last saw her. Between them now there was an adoration; she, in his eyes, such a sweet-tempered pretty and intelligent child, and he, in hers, a handsome, godlike but miraculously earthbound and playful brother whose wisdom knew no end, and kindness no inexplicable boundaries of sudden silence or bad temper; no temper anyway when they were together. But she heard his shouting at her brothers, quarrelling with her father. Once too, when he thought he was alone, she heard him weeping; and gathered flowers to charm away his unhappiness so that he should smile again, and tell her tales of Rama, the god-king.

In the end he decided to strike a bargain with his parents. He would agree in principle to the marriage with the girl Kamala. But there could be no question of actual marriage until he had completed his studies in England and sat for the examinations. He would submit only to a formal betrothal.

And how long, his father wanted to know, would he be away in England? Two or three years, perhaps. His father shook his head. By then Kamala would be eighteen or nineteen and still living with her parents. Did Duleep want his wife to be a laughing-stock before ever she came to his bed? And had he thought of the cost of going to England to study? Where did he think so much money was coming from? Duleep was prepared for this objection. He would sign away to his elder brothers whatever proportion of his inheritance might be reckoned to equal the cost of his studies abroad.

'There are only so many maunds to a sack, and you cannot give up what has not yet come to you,' his father pointed out. 'Besides which your inheritance is what makes you an attractive proposition to your future parents-in-law.'

'My education, my career, mean nothing to them?' Duleep asked.

His father shook his head. 'What you call your career has not yet begun. Perhaps you have overlooked the advantage of the dowry your wife would bring to this household? With such advantage money might be found to send you to England. But you would have to marry first. You are nineteen already. And all your brothers were married before their nineteenth year. Your future wife will soon be sixteen. By that age all your elder sisters were already married. I have had to find three dowries already. I am not a man with a bottomless pocket. And in a few years there will be yet another dowry to find for Shalini.'

Family affairs were the one thing there was always time for. The negotiations with his father extended over many days. Towards the end of them Duleep went to him and said, 'Very well. I will marry Kamala. But then immediately I will go to England.'

For these interviews they met in the room his father had, these past few years, set aside for meditation – an act which might have warned them all of what was to come later. In this room there was no furniture. They sat on rush mats on the tiled floor. On the whitewashed walls there was no decoration other than a highly coloured lithograph of the God of Fortune, Ganesha, in a little rosewood frame, and, on the sill of the small unglazed barred window, a pewter jug that usually held a handful of marigolds or frangipani.

'I do not wish you,' his father said now, raising a new objection, 'to enter the administration. If you are not content to look after your property then I suggest that you become a lawyer. For this you can study, I believe, in Calcutta.'

'What have you got against the administration?' Duleep asked.

'It is the administration of a foreign government. I should feel shame for my son to serve it. Better he should oppose the administration in the courts to help his own people.'

'Shame?' Duleep said. 'But you do not feel shame to be kept waiting on the verandah of the little burra-sahib. You have said yourself: What is an insult? What is hurt pride?'

'I should feel shame,' old Kumar said, 'if the little burra-sahib were my own son.'

It was a subtle point. It took a day or two for Duleep to swallow it, to judge the actuality of his father's sudden antipathy towards the Raj which, if it was not sudden, had always been kept well concealed.

'All right,' Duleep told him a few days later. 'I have thought about it. I will become a lawyer. Perhaps a barrister. But for this I must study in England.'

'And first you will marry the girl Kamala?'

'Yes, Father. First I will marry Kamala.'

*

Of his close family only his mother and an aunt had seen Kamala Prasad, his future wife. To do so they had paid a visit to the Prasads' home. Pleased with what they saw and with what was known about her upbringing, they reported back to Duleep's father. Reassured by the astrologers and satisfied with the proposed dowry, all that remained from the Kumars' point of view – granted Duleep's obedient submission to their wishes – was to seal the arrangement with a formal betrothal and then to fix the date of the wedding.

Kamala Prasad lived some twenty miles away. For the betrothal ceremony only male Prasads made the journey to the Kumars' house: the prospective bride's father and uncles, and two of her married brothers. They brought sweets and small gifts of money, but came in the main to satisfy themselves that the house Kamala would live in was up to the standard they had been led to expect. Duleep, who had watched his brothers perform the same duties, bowed to his future father-in-law and then knelt to touch his feet in a gesture of humility. The father-in-law marked Duleep's forehead with the tilak – the sign of auspiciousness. For a while the guests sat in formal conversation, took some refreshment and then went back to the station on the first stage of their journey home. The ceremony left little impression on him; it had seemed rather pointless, but for Shalini, with Duleep as the centre of attraction, it had been magical. 'On your wedding day, will you wear a sword and ride a horse, just like a king?' she asked.

'Well, I suppose so,' he said, and laughed, and privately thought: What a farce! His main interest lay in the arrangements he had begun to make with the advice and help of the principal of the Government College to go to England in September for the opening of what, fascinatingly, was called the Michaelmas term.

The betrothal ceremony took place in January, and then almost immediately there was difficulty over fixing the date of the wedding. The astrologers said that the ideal time fell in the second week of March. Kumar suggested the first week in September. The boat on which he had booked his passage through an agent in Bombay left in the second week. The astrologers shook their heads. If the wedding could not be managed in the second week of March it would need to be postponed until the fourth week of October.

167

'It is all nonsense,' Duleep insisted. 'All they mean is that by April the weather will be too hot and from June until October likely to be too wet.' He had no intention of spending nearly six months as a married man before setting out for England. In fact he had no intention of sleeping with a barely sixteen-year-old girl, however pretty, however nubile. He would go through the ceremony. He would even spend one night or two with her so that she would not be disgraced. But he would not make love to her. He would kiss her and be kind to her, and tell her that when he returned from England as a young man qualified in an honourable profession it would be time enough for her to take on the duties of a wife and the burdens of motherhood. He almost hoped that she would turn out to be unattractive.

Sometimes he woke in the middle of the night and thought that every step he had taken since leaving the college had been the wrong one. He had given up his plan to enter the administration. He had submitted to the demands of his parents to marry. He had undertaken to study for a profession his heart had not been set on. All he had succeeded in hanging on to was his determination to go to England. When he woke in the mornings the prospect of England was enough to enable him to enter the new day bright and cheerful, and he could not help responding to the warmth of parental approbation that had settled about him. He heard his father say once to an old friend, 'After his marriage, of course, Duleepji is to continue his studies in England,' as if that had been his father's wish, not his own, and he judged that paternal pride could grow like good seed in the most unlikely ground so long as that ground were first soaked with the sweat of filial duty. But, in the darkness of half-sleep and half-waking, he would search without success for a practical interpretation of that single, challenging word, England; for an interpretation that would ease him, bring comfort that extended beyond his general desire to his particular purpose. Power – in the sense he understood it – seemed to have been potentially lessened by his all too easy, equivocal agreement to enter the services of the law where power was interpreted, perhaps challenged, but never directly exercised. In myself, he thought, there is possibly a fatal flaw, the dark root of the plant of compromise that never bears any blossom that isn't rank-smelling; and turned over, to sleep again, his hand upon the firm breast of the submissive, loving girl who now always followed him into his dreams.

He had his way. The astrologers discovered an unexpected conjunction of fortunate stars. The marriage was arranged to take place in the first week of September. 'You see, Shalini,' he told his little sister, 'it was all nonsense, as I said,' but stopped himself from adding, 'Like the Kumars, the Prasads carry the burden of too many daughters and are only too anxious to have Kamala off their hands, even at the tail-end of the wet monsoon.' Looking at Shalini he found himself assessing the burden that she, in her ninth year, already represented in terms of the complicated sum of her necessary dowry and her parents' desire that she should be happy, and suitably matched, transferred to a household that would bring honour to them and good fortune to her, be given to a husband who would bless her with kindness and whom she would find it possible to feel affection for and be dutiful to, and so give satisfaction to him and to his family, and to herself and to hers.

'I hope,' he told himself, thinking of his own future wife, 'that I can find it in my heart not to hate her.'

The first list of guests on the groom's side which his father prepared ran to nearly three hundred names. After negotiations with the Prasad family the list was cut to just below two hundred. There would be twice that number on the bride's side. To the bride's family the cost would be crippling. In the middle of August the Prasads began to gather. The Kumars also gathered. They came from the Punjab, from Madras, from Bengal, from Lucknow and the home province, and from Bombay, from as far off as Rawalpindi. Duleep was the last of old Kumar's sons. There would only be one other marriage in this particular generation: Shalini's. The house was full. The guest house that had been erected outside the compound for the weddings of Duleep's sisters was also full.

The journey to Delali was made early in the morning of the day of the wedding. Miraculously the rains had ended early, which was counted a good omen. In Kamala's home the first ceremonies had been going on for two days. Three coaches of the train to Delali were reserved for the groom's party. A delegation of Prasads was at Delali station to meet them. Duleep and his family were taken to the house of a brother of the bride's father. And there Duleep was dressed in the style of a warrior king, in tight white trousers, embroidered coat, sword, cloak and sequined turban upon which was placed a tinsel crown from which garlands of roses and jasmine hung, half shadowing his face, filling his nostrils with their sweet narcotic scent. As evening came he was led out to the caparisoned horse on which he mounted, with his best man, a young cousin, behind him in the saddle. The procession to the bride's house began at half-past six. It was accompanied by men with lanterns, drums, trumpets and fireworks. The evening was loud with the noise and explosion of their progression. It gave him a headache. The procession was followed by the people of Delali who wanted to see for themselves what kind of a husband old Prasad's youngest daughter had managed to get hold of. They shouted good-natured insults and Duleep's champions replied in kind.

Dismounting at the entrance to the bride's house, he was led through the compound to the married women's courtyard, sat down, and put through the first of his ordeals.

'So next week you are going to England,' one of the women said. 'Do you tire so quickly that you need to run away?'

'Oh no,' Duleep replied, entering into the spirit of the testing, 'but a young husband is wiser to accept the truth of the saying: Moderation in all things.'

'Perhaps the bride will have different ideas,' another woman said.

'The pot of honey,' Duleep said, 'tastes better after a long abstinence.'

'What if the honey should go sour?' an even bolder woman asked.

'To a faithful tooth even the sourest honey tastes sweet.'

The women laughed and hid their faces. Duleep was a man. The news was quickly carried to the bride who had sat for hours in her inner chamber, after her ritual purifying bathe, attended by the women whose job it was to clothe her in her red robes and heavy jewellery, put henna on her hands and feet and kohl on her eyes.

'As handsome as a prince,' they said, 'and bold with it. Ah, what eyes! But also gentle. Assuredly yes, you are fortunate. Such husbands do not grow on trees. He will be worth the waiting for, after the initial taste.'

The second ordeal was the ceremony itself which was due to begin at the auspicious hour of half an hour before midnight, in the main courtyard, and would go on for hours, in accordance with the Vedic rites. He sat next to his bride, facing the sacred fire on the other side of which the pandit sat. She was heavily veiled and kept her head bowed. Duleep dared not look at her. But he had the impression of her scent and smallness and temporary magnificence. The veil over her head was tied to the pommel of his sword which, in the olden days, he would have had to use to cut off the branch of a tree to show his vigour. Already they were united, indissolubly, throughout life and perhaps beyond it. And he had not yet seen her face. She had not yet looked at his. If she saw anything of him at all it could be no more than his gold, embroidered slippers and tight-trousered legs. Unless she had peeped. He did not think she had. The pandit was intoning mantras. Incense was thrown on the flames of the fire. Duleep and Kamala walked round the fire with Duleep leading, and then again, reversing the order, with Kamala ahead. She received rice into her cupped hands, and poured it into his, and he threw it into the flames. Together they walked the seven auspicious steps, and then the pandit recited their names and the names of their forbears, and Kamala was led away and he would not be close to her again until the night after the next when she would be led by his own mother into his room at home. But already it was morning. Tomorrow, then, Kamala would travel to Duleep's house, in clothes brought to her as gifts from the Kumars.

Duleep slept late, got up and broke his fast and inspected the dowry that was on show on trestle tables under awnings, in case a miserable, unexpected rain ruined the proceedings. There were clothes for himself and the bride, jewellery, small coffers of silver coins and one hundred rupee notes, family ceremonial costume, plate, household utensils, and, in a box, title deeds to land. He went to bed early, astonished by so much personal wealth, the cost to a girl's father of a husband for her, and in the morning was dressed again in his king's raiment, encumbered by his velvet sheathed sword and mounted on the caparisoned horse to lead the doolie procession to the railway station. The small figure of his still-veiled wife, dressed in scarlet, heavily jewelled, was supported by her father and mother out to the palanquin. He fancied that the moment before she entered she faltered and wept and was only persuaded to enter by some comforting, courage-giving words of her mother.

When the doolie curtains were closed the bearers took up the weight, and the women who followed the palanquin began to sing the song of the bride, the morning raga, the song of the young girl who leaves her childhood home for the home of her husband.

> *Dooliya la aō*
> *re morē babul ke kaharwa.*
> *Chali hoon sajan ba ke des.*

*

On the outskirts of their own village which they reached in procession from the railway station towards evening, they were met by what looked like the whole population. The married women approached the doolie (a doolie provided by the Kumars to replace the doolie left behind with the Prasads at Delali) opened the curtains and inspected the bride. From the way they looked at him afterwards he assumed that they had found no major fault. Of the family only Shalini had been left behind. She ran from the compound and clung to the bridle of his horse which, like the new doolie, had been waiting at the station.

'Duleep, Duleep,' she cried, 'oh, how beautiful you are. Why did you marry her? Why didn't you wait for me?' And walked proudly, possessively, leading the horse into the compound. But came later, long after she should have been in bed, to the room in which he prepared himself and said, 'I am sorry, Duleep.'

'Why sorry?' he asked, taking her on to his knee. She encircled her arms around his neck.

'Because,' she said, 'because I have seen her.'

'Then why should you be sorry?' he asked, his heart beating so loudly he could hardly bear the pain and uncertainty of it.

'Because she is like a princess,' Shalini told him. 'Did you fight for her? Did you slay evil spirits and rescue her? Did you, Duleepji? Did you? Did you?'

'I suppose I did,' he said, and kissed her, and sent her away, and then waited in the room into which Kamala would presently be led by his mother and given into his care.

*

The trouble was, he told Hari years later, that when he unveiled Kamala, and saw her, he fell in love with her. Perhaps this was true and accounted for the fact that his career in England reading for the law was a failure from the start. His final return, defeated, was hard to bear because no word of reproach was spoken by his father for the wasted years, the wasted money. Returning to India, he laboured under the weight of many burdens: the

171

burden of knowing that his mind was incapable of adjusting itself to the pace set by better men, and the burden of knowing that time and again, in England, allowances had been made for him because he was an Indian who had travelled a long way, at considerable cost, and had so obviously set his heart on lifting himself by his bootstraps from the state of underprivilege into which he had been born. And then there was the burden of knowing that he could not blame his parents for the fact that in England he had often been cold, miserable and shy, and not infrequently dismayed by the dirt, squalor and poverty, the sight of barefoot children, ragged beggars, drunken women, and evidence of cruelty to animals and humans: sins which in India only Indians were supposed to be capable of committing or guilty of allowing. He could blame his parents for forcing him into a premature marriage that disrupted the involved pattern of his scholarly pretensions, but he could not blame them for this dismay, nor could he blame them for the constant proof he had that among the English, at home with them, he was a foreigner. He was invariably treated with kindness, even with respect, but always with reserve; the kind of reserve that went hand in hand with best – and therefore uneasy – behaviour. He found himself longing for the rough and tumble of life at home. To learn the secret of the Englishness of the English he realised that you had to grow up among them. For him, it was too late. But it was not too late for his son. He never anticipated successors in the plural. One son was enough. One son would succeed where he had failed, so long as he had advantages Duleep himself had never enjoyed.

The trouble was, Duleep thought, that India had made its mark on him and no subsequent experience would ever erase it. Beneath the thin layers of anglicisation was a thickness of Indianness that the arranged marriage had only confirmed and strengthened. 'And for an *Indian* Indian,' he told Hari, 'there simply isn't any future in an *Anglo*-Indian world.' Of one thing Duleep was certain: the English, for all their protestations to the contrary, were going to hold on to their Empire well beyond his own lifetime and far into if not beyond Hari's as well. If he had a theory at all about the eventual departure of the English it was that they were waiting for Indian boys who would be as English, if not more English, than they were themselves, so that handing over the reins of power they would feel no wrench greater than a man might feel when giving into the care of an adopted son a business built up from nothing over a period of alternating fortune and disaster.

To Duleep, Indian independence was as simple as that, a question of evolution rather than of politics, of which he knew nothing. He believed in the intellectual superiority of the English. Manifestly it was not with physical strength that they ruled an empire. They ruled it because they were armed with weapons of civil intelligence that made the comparable Indian armoury look primitive by comparison. As witness to that was the example of the pale-skinned boy who sat on the verandah of the sub-divisional officer's bungalow. And no one had ever made *him* marry a

172

sixteen-year-old girl. It did not matter to this boy, fundamentally, whether he went to the grave with male or female issue or without. He had never been distracted from his duty or ambition by the overwhelming physical sensation of finding, in front of him, a girl who had been thrust into the room by his own mother, a girl who when unveiled had filled him with the simple impulse to possess, to forget, to cast out the spirits of discipline and learning and celibacy, and enter, in full vigour, into the second stage of life which was attended by spirits of an altogether different nature.

'The fact that I fell in love with your mother,' he told Hari, 'proved one thing, which in itself proved many others. It proved my Indianness. It wasn't just a case of there being here opportunity for a young man to satisfy his sexuality in the terms you would understand it. What young man anyway could resist that excitement, of removing the veil and not being disappointed in what he saw, and of knowing that the girl who stood so meekly in front of him was his to do as he liked with? No, it wasn't as simple as that. At that moment, you see, I automatically entered the second stage of life according to the Hindu code. I became husband and householder. In my heart, then, my ambitions were all for my family, my as yet non-existent family of sons and daughters. Do you see that? Do you understand this strong psychological undertow? Oh, well, yes, naturally I would have pleasure, physical pleasure. But where else should this pleasure lead except to happiness and fulfilment for my own flesh and blood? Certainly it should not have been followed by another long period of celibacy, of learning and education. I was now, in an instant, already past that stage. In the Hindu code I was no longer a student but a man, with a man's responsibilities, a man's sources of delight, which are not the same as a boy's and not the same as a student's. And yet, in the eyes of the western world, which I took passage to, I was still a boy, still a student. In that old lower middle-class English saying: I was living a lie. Isn't it?'

In such a way Duleep Kumar excused his failure, if failure it was in fact, but tortured himself with it because he was not reproached by his father or mother. Perhaps he was reproached by his wife, Kamala, who had also entered the second stage, having herself been entered, torn open, and then abandoned and left with recollections of her extraordinary and painful translation from child to woman, living at some seasons of the year with her own parents, at other seasons with Duleep's; and greeting him on his return with a humility that had gone a bit sour, so that Duleep felt it, and decided that if you looked at the situation squarely he had managed to get for himself the worst of both worlds. After all, he brought back no crock of gold, no princely raiment, no means to free her from the tyranny of a matriarchal household which his absence in England had probably given her expectations of. If she had no proper notion of the ambition that attended his departure she had, certainly, an understanding of the failure that attended his return.

'I went away,' Duleep said, 'a feared but adored Hindu husband. I returned as a half-man – unclean by traditional Hindu standards and custom because I had crossed the black water. But I had crossed it to no obvious advantage. To purify myself I was persuaded to consume the five products of the cow. Which includes the cow's dung and urine. Although not, of course, its flesh.'

In England he had never admitted to people that he was married. He was ashamed to. For a month or so he had anticipated and feared news of Kamala's pregnancy. His relief was relative to his disappointment. He could not have borne the distraction of knowing he was to be a father, but only with a sense of the reflection on his virility was he able to enjoy the freedom of finding he was not. He longed to receive letters, but their arrival filled him with frustration, even despair. His father wrote in Hindi, and addressed the envelopes in English in block capitals such as you would find figured by children in a kindergarten. Each letter was a sermon, a formal communication from father to son. The few letters he received from Kamala were as naïve as those of a child, the result of hours of labour and instruction. He knew that his own letters had to be read aloud to her. Only his letters to and from Shalini were pleasurable.

Restored to his wife, still unqualified even for the career he had not set his heart on, he set about the business of instructing her in lettering. She submitted ungraciously. She did not want to learn more than she already knew. She thought it a waste of time, an affront to her status as a married woman. Her sisters-in-law poked fun at her if they saw her with books. 'It is only because Shalini is cleverer than you that you act in this stupid way,' he said, when she pretended to have forgotten the lesson he had taught her the day before.

The old rambling house was a hive of inactivity. The women quarrelled among themselves. His mother's voice, raised above all in pitch and authority, brought only a brooding truce. His father spent hours alone in meditation. His brothers idled the days away, gambling and cock-fighting. For a time Duleep himself fell into a similar state of inertia. He need never lift a finger. He need do no work. He played with Shalini, now aged nearly twelve. We are waiting, he told himself, for our father to die. And then we shall have the pleasure of squabbling among ourselves over the inheritance. We shall squabble for three or four years and by then my brother's children will be old enough to marry and the money so carefully hoarded will begin to be squandered, land will be sold and divided and my prophecy will come true.

He had toyed with the idea of continuing his studies in India, and then with the notion that he could apply for a post in the uncovenanted provincial civil service. He had also thought to take his wife away and set up house on his own, but he did not want to leave Shalini behind. Her parents would not let her go to school. He tried to get hold of a teacher from the Zenana Mission, an organisation that sent teachers into orthodox Indian homes to instruct the women privately, but the Mission lost interest when it was learned that only one young girl would attend the lessons. For a couple of years or more, he realised, Shalini's education

174

would be his own responsibility. And by now Kamala was pregnant and he began to make plans for his son's future: a future which at times seemed very unlikely to take the shape he wanted it to. He could not imagine Kamala being persuaded to cross the black water. He could not imagine her living in England. In any case, he knew he would be ashamed of her. In England she would be a laughing-stock. Here it was he who was the laughing-stock. The problem looked insoluble. His son would grow up with precisely the same disadvantages he suffered from himself. He could have blamed himself for marrying such a girl. Or he could have blamed his parents for forcing him to marry her. He could have blamed India, and the Hindu tradition. It was easier to blame Kamala. Already she had become shrill and demanding. They quarrelled frequently. He was no longer in love with her. Occasionally he felt sorry for her.

Their first child, a daughter, survived two days. A year later, in 1914, in the first year of England's war with Germany, there was a second daughter; and she survived for a year. A third child, another daughter, was stillborn in 1916. Poor Kamala seemed to be incapable of bearing a healthy baby, let alone a son. Deprived in this way too, their quarrels became bitter. He discovered that she blamed him for her failure. To bear a strong son was her duty. She was determined to do it. 'But how can I do my duty alone?' she asked. 'It is *you*. All your years studying books have sapped your manhood.' Furious, he left the house, taking some money, intending never to return. He had a vague idea that he would join the army; but remembered Shalini and went home when the last of his money had been spent. He returned penniless and disgraced. In the month that he had been away Shalini had become betrothed to one Prakash Gupta Sen. The Gupta Sens were previously connected by marriage with the Lucknow branch of the Kumar family.

Shalini complained to him – not about her betrothal but about his absence during the ceremonial formalities. 'Why did you stay away, Duleepji?' she wanted to know. 'If you had been here you could have gone with my father and my brothers to Mayapore. And if you had gone you could have told me truly what kind of boy this Prakash is. *They* say he is intelligent and good-looking. Why cannot I know what *you* think? I could have believed you.'

'Is that all you can say? Is that all it means to you? What he looks like?'

But already she had become a woman.

'What else can it mean, Duleepji? Besides, I am fifteen. One cannot stay a child for ever.'

Shalini's marriage took place almost a year later – in 1917. Again the house was full. Duleep was astonished at the calm way she accepted the situation and even blossomed in the warmth of the formal flattery always accorded to a bride. When he saw young Prakash Gupta Sen he was horrified. Fat, vain, pompous, lecherous. In a few years this would be proved. Duleep avoided Shalini. 'My nerve has gone,' he told himself. 'Why don't I make a scene? Why do I let this terrible thing go forward?' And knew the answer. 'Because already I am defeated. The future holds nothing for me. I am only half anglicised. The stronger half is still Indian. It pleases me to think the future holds nothing for anyone else either.'

On the night of Shalini's wedding he slept with his wife again. She wept. They both wept. And exchanged undertakings that in future they would be kind, forgiving and understanding. On the morning of Shalini's ritual departure he watched from the gateway. She entered the palanquin without hesitation.

And Duleep saw one thing at last: that in helping her to open her mind and broaden her horizons he had taught her the lesson he himself had never learned: the value of moral as well as physical courage. He only saw her on two subsequent occasions: the first during the week she spent after her marriage in her parental home, with Prakash, and the second five years later when on the eve of his departure for England with his two-year-old son Hari, he visited her in Mayapore during the festival of *Rakhi-Bandan*, bringing her gifts of clothing and receiving from her a bracelet made of elephant hair: the festival during which brothers and sisters reaffirm the bond between them and exchange vows of duty and affection. By this time his wife Kamala had been dead for two years and poor Shalini was still childless. Her husband, Duleep knew, spent most of his time with prostitutes. He died some years later of a seizure in the house of his favourite.

'Imagine,' Shalini wrote to her brother at that time, 'Prakash's sisters actually suggested I should become suttee to honour such a man and acquire merit for myself!'

And Duleep replied from Sidcot, 'Leave Mayapore, and come to us in England.'

'No,' she wrote back. 'My duty – such as it is – is here. I feel, Duleepji, that we shall never see each other again. Don't you feel the same? We Indians are very fatalistic! Thank you for sending me books. They are my greatest pleasure. Also for the photograph of Hari. What a handsome boy he is! I think of him as my English nephew. Perhaps one day, if ever he comes to India, I shall meet him if he can bear to visit his old Indian aunt. Think of it – I shan't see thirty again! Duleepji – I am so pleased for you. In the picture of Hari I see again my kind brother on whose knee I used to sit. Well. Enough of this nonsense.'

*

These were all stories that Duleep eventually told to Hari. In turn, when Hari's father was dead, in the few weeks of English boyhood that were left to him, Hari told them to Colin Lindsey. He thought of them as stories which had no bearing on his own life – even then, with his passage to India booked, and paid for by the aunt with the peculiar name, Shalini.

There was one other story. This too he told Colin. It seemed incredible to both of them; not because they couldn't imagine it happening, but because neither of them could think of it as happening in Harry Coomer's family.

It went like this: that two weeks after Shalini's ritual return to her parents' home, and one week after her final departure to Mayapore with her husband, her father announced his intention to divest himself of all his worldly goods, to depart from his family and his responsibilities, and wander the countryside: become, eventually, *sannyasi*.

'I have done my duty,' he said. 'It is necessary to recognise that it is finished. It is necessary not to become a burden. Now my duty is to God.'

His family were shocked. Duleep pleaded with him but his resolve was unshaken. 'When are you leaving us, then?' Duleep asked.

'I shall go in six months' time. It will take until then to order my affairs. The inheritance will be divided equally among the four of you. The house will belong to your elder brother. Your mother must be allowed to live here for as long as she wishes, but your elder brother and his wife will become heads of the household. All will be done as it would be done if I were dead.'

Duleep shouted, 'You call this good? You call it holy? To leave our mother? To bury yourself alive in *nothing*? To beg your bread when you are rich enough to feed a hundred starving beggars?'

'Rich?' his father asked. 'What is rich? Today I have riches. With one stroke of a pen on a document I can rid myself of what you call my riches. But what stroke of a pen on what kind of document will ensure my release from the burden of another lifespan after this? Such a release can only be hoped for, only earned by renouncing all earthly bonds.'

Duleep said, 'Ah well, yes! How fine! In what way could you be ashamed now to find your son a little burra sahib? What difference could it make to you now, what I was or where I was? Is it for this that I gave in to you? Is it to see you shrug me off and walk away from me and my brothers and our mother that I obeyed you?'

'While there is duty there must be obedience. My duty to you is over. Your obedience to me is no longer necessary. You have different obligations now. And I have a duty of still another kind.'

'It is monstrous!' Duleep shouted. 'Monstrous and cruel and selfish! You have ruined my life. I have sacrificed myself for nothing.'

As he had found earlier it was easier to blame anyone than to blame himself, but he regretted the attack. He suffered greatly at the recollection of it. He tried to speak about it to his mother, but these days she went about her daily tasks dumb and unapproachable. When the time drew near for his father to go he went to him and begged his forgiveness.

'You were always my favourite son,' old Kumar admitted. 'That was a sin, to feel more warmly towards one than to the others. Better you should have had no ambition. Better you should have been like your brothers. I could not help but exert authority more strongly over the only son who ever seemed ready to defy it. And I was ashamed of my preference. My exertion of authority perhaps went beyond the bounds of reason. A father does not ask his son to forgive him. It is only open to him to bless him and to commit to this son's care that good woman, your mother.'

'No,' Duleep said, weeping. 'That duty is not for me. That is for your eldest son. Don't burden me with that.'

'A burden will fall upon the heart most ready to accept it,' old Kumar said, and then knelt and touched his youngest son's feet, to humble himself.

Even in the business of becoming *sannyasi* old Kumar seemed determined upon the severest shock to his pride. He underwent no rituals. He did not put on the long gown. On the morning of his departure he appeared in the compound dressed only in a loin cloth, carrying a staff and a begging-bowl. Into the bowl his stony-faced wife placed a handful of rice. And then he walked through the gateway and into the road, away from the village.

For a while they followed him, some distance behind. He did not look back. When Duleep and his brothers gave up following him their mother continued. They watched but said nothing to each other, waiting for their mother who, after a while, sat down on the roadside and stayed there until Duleep joined her, urged her to her feet and supported her back to the house.

'You must not give in to sorrow,' she told him later, lying on her bed in a darkened room from which she had ordered the servants to remove every article of comfort and luxury. 'It is the will of God.'

*

Thereafter his mother lived the life of a widow. She gave her household keys into the care of her eldest daughter-in-law and moved into a room at the back of the house that overlooked the servants' quarters. She cooked her own food and ate it in solitude. She never left the compound. After a while her sons and daughters-in-law accepted the situation as inevitable. By such behaviour, they said, she was acquiring merit. They seemed content, then, to forget her. Alone, Duleep went every day to her room and sat with her for a while and watched while she spun khadi. To communicate at all he had to say things that needed no answer or ask simple questions which she could respond to with a nod or shake of the head.

In this way he brought her news: of the end of England's war with Germany, of business affairs he had begun to take an interest in, of his wife Kamala's latest pregnancy, of the birth of yet another stillborn child, a girl. Once he brought news, a rumour, that his father had been recognised but not spoken to by one of the Lucknow Kumars who had been travelling in Bihar and had seen him on the platform of a railway station with his begging-bowl. His mother did not even pause in her spinning. In 1919 he told her something of the troubles in the Punjab, but did not mention the massacre of unarmed Indian civilians by British-commanded Gurkha troops in Amritsar. In this same year he brought the news that Kamala was again with child, and in 1920, a few weeks after the festival of Holi, the news that he had a son. By now the old lady had taken to muttering while she spun. He could not be sure that she ever heard what he said. She did not look at him when he told her about Hari, nor two days later when he told her that Kamala was dead; that now he had a strong healthy son but no wife. She did not look at him either when he began to laugh. He laughed because he could not weep; for Kamala, or for his son, or his father or old mad mother. 'She made it, you see, Mother,' he shouted at her hysterically in English. 'She knew her duty all right. My God, yes! She knew her duty and did it in the end. It didn't matter that it cost her her life. We all know our duty, don't we? Just like I know mine. At last I've got a son and I have a duty to him, but I've also got you, and Father charged me with a duty to you as well.'

It was a duty that took another eighteen months to discharge. One morning he went to his mother's room and found the spinning-wheel abandoned and the old woman on her bed. When he spoke to her she opened her eyes and looked at him and said:

'Your father is dead, Duleepji.' Her voice was hoarse and cracked through long disuse. 'I saw it in a dream. Is the fire kindled yet?'

'The fire, Mother?'

'Yes, son. The fire must be kindled.'

She slept.

In the evening she woke and asked him again, 'Son, is the fire kindled?'

'They are making it ready.'

'Wake me when they have finished.'

She slept again, until morning, and then opened her eyes and asked him, 'Do the flames leap high, Duleepji?'

'Yes, Mother,' he said. 'The fire is kindling.'

'Then it is time,' she said. And smiled, and closed her eyes, and told him: 'I am not afraid,' and did not wake again.

*

It was in the October of 1921 that his mother died. A year later, when he had sold his property to his brothers and paid a visit to his sister Shalini, in Mayapore, he took his son to Bombay and there embarked for England. When he sailed he was comparatively well-off and during the course of the next sixteen years he managed from time to time to increase his capital and income with fortunate investments and lucky enterprises. Perhaps it was true that he had in him what he once referred to as a fatal flaw, although if there was a flaw like this it was not one that led to compromise, as he had thought. He had compromised, certainly, in his youth, but had stood by his duty in early manhood. The flaw was perhaps more likely to be found in the quality of his passion. There may have been impurities in it from the beginning, or the impurities may have entered with the frustrations that, in another man, could so easily have diluted the passion

179

but in him roused and strengthened it to the point where the passion alone guided his thoughts and actions, and centred them all on Hari.

A stranger could look at the life, times and character of Duleep Kumar – or Coomer as he became – and see a man and a career and a background which in themselves, separately or in combination, made no sense. The only sense they made lay in Hari: Hari's health, Hari's happiness, Hari's prospects, power for Hari in a world where boys like Hari normally expected none; these were the notches on the rule Duleep used to measure his own success or failure: and these were what he looked for as the end results of any enterprise he embarked upon.

When Colin Lindsey's father kept his promise to see the lawyers, to try and make some sense out of the apparently absurd report that Duleep Kumar had died a bankrupt, the senior partner of that firm said to him:

'In his own country, Coomer would probably have made a fortune and kept it. He told me once that as a boy he'd only wanted to be a civil servant or a lawyer, and had never once thought of becoming a businessman. The curious thing is that he really had a flair for financial manipulation. I mean a flair in the European sense. It was the most English thing about him when you boiled it down. In his own country he might have knocked spots off the average businessman out there. He saw things in a broad light, not a narrow one. At least, I should say he always began every enterprise seeing it that way, but then narrowed it all down to a question of making money as fast as possible for that son of his so that he could become something he isn't. What a pity! In the last year or two when his affairs began to go down hill, I was always warning him, trying to head him off from foolish speculation. And I suppose this is where – well, blood, background, that sort of thing, finally begin to tell. He got frightened. In the end he went right off his head, to judge from the mess he's left behind. And of course couldn't face it. I don't think he committed suicide because he couldn't face the consequences but because he couldn't face what he knew those consequences would mean for that boy of his. Back home to India, in other words, with his tail between his legs. Coomer, you know, might have found himself in pretty serious trouble. I've said nothing to the son on that score. It's probably best that he shouldn't get to know. But there's one aspect of the business that the bank says looks like a clear case of forgery.'

Mr Lindsey was shocked.

The lawyer, seeing his expression, said, 'You can be thankful you haven't invested in any of Coomer's businesses.'

'I never had that sort of money,' Lindsey replied. 'And actually I scarcely knew him. We were sorry for the boy, that's all. As a matter of fact, it's a surprise to me to hear you say his father was so devoted to him. So far as we could see the opposite was true. I suppose we're a pretty soft-hearted family. My own son included. He asked Harry to spend a summer holiday with us some years ago when he found out that he was going to be on his own. It's been like that ever since.'

The lawyer said, 'But you see, Mr Lindsey, keeping himself out of

Harry's light was Coomer's way of devoting himself to his son's best interests. I don't mean that he deliberately tried to give people the impression his son was neglected so that they'd invite him to their homes and he'd grow up knowing what English people were really like. He kept out of Harry's way because he knew that if Harry grew up as he wanted him to there'd come a time when Harry would be ashamed of him. For instance, there was the question of Coomer's accent. It seemed pretty good to me, but of course it *was* an Indian accent. He certainly didn't want Harry to learn anything from it. He didn't want Harry to learn anything from him at all. He told me so. He said he looked forward to the day when he'd see Harry didn't care much for his company. He didn't want the boy to be ashamed of him but too dutiful to show it. All he wanted for Harry was the best English education and background that money could buy.'

And not only money, Lindsey thought. The bitter seed had been sown. It was probably this as much as anything that finally dispelled whatever doubts he may have felt about the reasonableness of his rejection of his son Colin's impossible story-book proposal that Harry should come to live with them permanently if it could possibly be arranged – this – even more than the shock to his well-bred system of learning that young Coomer's father had put someone else's name to a document – this: that young Coomer's lonely situation had not been the result of neglect but of a deliberate policy that had a special and not particularly upright end in view – entrance into a society that stood beyond his father's natural reach to gain for him wholly on his own resources.

Now Lindsey remembered – or rather allowed to make the journey from the back of his mind to the front of it – the comments passed by friends whose judgments he trusted except when they clashed with his liberal beliefs (which were perched, somewhat shakily, on the sturdy shoulders of his natural clannish instincts). He could not actually recall the words of these comments, but he certainly recalled the ideas which lay behind them: that in India, so long as you kept them occupied, the natives could be counted on very often to act in the common interest; that the real Indian, the man most to be trusted, was likely to be your servant, the man who earned the salt he ate under your roof, and next to him the simple peasant who hated the bloodsuckers of his own race, cared nothing for politics, but cared instead, like a sensible fellow, about the weather, the state of the crops, and fair play; respected impartiality, and represented the majority of this simple nation that was otherwise being spoiled by too close a contact with the sophisticated ideas of modern western society. The last man you could trust, these people said (and damn it all, they knew, because they had been there or were related to people who had been there) was the westernised Indian, because he was not really an Indian at all. The only exceptions to this rule were to be found among the maharajahs, people like that, who had been born into the cosmopolitan ranks of those whose job was to exercise authority and were interested in preserving the old social *status quo.*

181

There had been a time when his son Colin had thought Harry's father was a maharajah, or rajah, or anyway, a rich landowner of the kind who stood next to maharajahs in importance. Over the years the impression had gradually been adjusted (sometimes by these same friends who said that Hari's father was probably the son of a petty zamindar, whatever a zamindar was). But had the initial impression ever been adjusted to anything like the truth? Had the whole thing been a sham? Lindsey hated to think so. But thought so now, and returned home from his altruistic visit to the lawyers feeling that by and large he and his own son had been put upon, led by the nose into an unsavoury affair because they had been too willing to believe the best about people and discount the worst, ignored the warnings of those who had watched the Lindsey adoption of Harry Coomer with expressions sometimes too clearly indicative of their belief that no good could be expected to come of it.

At dinner that night, listening to his fair and good-looking son talking to black-haired, brown-faced Harry, he was surprised to find himself thinking: 'But how extraordinary! If you close your eyes and listen, you can't tell the difference. And they seem to talk on exactly the same wave-length as well.'

But his eyes were no longer to be closed. He took Harry on one side and said to him, 'I'm sorry, old chap. There's nothing I can do. The lawyers have convinced me of that.'

Harry nodded. He looked disappointed. But he said, 'Well, thanks anyway. I mean for trying,' and smiled and then waited as if for the arm Lindsey was normally in the habit of laying fondly on the boy's shoulders.

Tonight Lindsey found himself unable to make that affectionate gesture.

*

His sharpest memories were of piles of leaves, wet and chill to the touch, as if in early morning after a late October frost. To Hari, England was sweet cold and crisp clean pungent scent; air that moved, crowding hollows and sweeping hilltops; not stagnant, heavy, a conducting medium for stench. And England was the park and pasture-land behind the house in Sidcot, the gables of the house, the leaded diamond-pane windows, and the benevolent wistaria.

Waking in the middle of the night on the narrow string-bed in his room at Number 12 Chillianwallah Bagh he beat at the mosquitoes, fisted his ears against the sawing of the frogs and the chopping squawk of the lizards in heat on the walls and ceiling. He entered the mornings from tossing dreams of home and slipped at once into the waking nightmare, his repugnance for everything the alien country offered: the screeching crows outside and the fat amber-coloured cockroaches that lumbered heavy-backed but light-headed with waving feathery antennae from the bedroom to an adjoining bathroom where there was no bath – instead, a tap, a bucket, a copper scoop, a cemented floor to stand on and a slimy runnel for taking the dirty water out through a hole in the wall from which it fell and spattered the caked mud of the compound; draining him layer by layer of his Englishness, draining him too of his hope of discovering that he had imagined everything from the day when the letter came from his father asking him to meet him in Sidcot to talk about the future. This future? There had never been such a meeting so perhaps there wasn't this future. His father had never arrived, never left Edinburgh, but died in his hotel bedroom.

Sometimes when a letter reached him from Colin Lindsey he looked at the writing on the envelope as if to confirm to some inner, more foolishly expectant and hopeful spirit than his own that the letter was not one from his father telling him that everything was a mistake. He longed for letters from England, but when they arrived and he tore them open and read them through, first quickly and then a second time slowly, he found that the day had darkened in a way that set him brooding upon some act of violence that was motiveless; aimless, except to the extent that it was calculated to transport him miraculously back to his native air, his native heath, and people whose behaviour did not revolt him. In such moods he never replied to a letter. He waited until the acutest pain of receiving it was over, and, in a day or two, made a first attempt at an answer that would not expose him as a coward; for that would never do; it would be foreign to the scale of values he knew he must hang on to if he were to see the nightmare through to its unimaginable, unforeseeable, but presumably logical end.

In this way Colin Lindsey never had the opportunity of guessing the weight of the burden of exile his friend struggled under. In one letter, he wrote to Harry: 'I'm glad you seem to be settling down. I'm reading quite a lot about India to try and get a clearer picture of you in it. Sounds terrific. Wish I could come out. Have you stuck any good pig lately? If you do, don't leave the carcase in front of a mosque, or the devotees of the Prophet will have you by the knackers. Advice from an old hand! We drew the match with Wardens last Saturday. We miss that Coomer touch – those elegant sweeps to his noble leg and those slow snazzy off-breaks. Funny to think that your cricket will be starting just about the time the school here begins its football season. Not that I shall be seeing the football this year. Has it been decided yet what you are going to do? I'm definitely leaving at the end of this summer term. Dad says he'll stump up for a crammer if I want to matriculate (some hopes) but I've decided to accept my uncle's offer to go into the London office of that petroleum company he's something to do with.'

To this, after several days, Hari replied, 'The idea always was, you remember, that I'd swot for the ICS exams after leaving Chillingborough and sit for them in London, then come out here and learn the ropes. These days you can sit for the exams over here as well, but I don't think I'll be doing that. My aunt's old brother-in-law runs some kind of business in Mayapore and I gather the idea is that I should go into it. But first I'm supposed to learn the language. Although my uncle-in-law thinks my own language could be useful he says it's not much good to him if I can't understand a word of what 90% of the people I'd be dealing with were talking about. It's raining cats and dogs here these days. Sometimes it gives over and the sun comes out and the whole place steams. But the rain goes on, I'm told, until September, and then it begins to cool down, but only for a few weeks. It starts getting hot again pretty soon in the new year, and by April and May I gather you can't even sweat. I'm down with gippy-tum, and can only face eating fruit, although I wake up thinking of bacon and eggs. Please give my love to your mother and father, and remember me to Connolly and Jarvis, and of course to old Toad-in-the-hole.'

Sealing such a letter once he was tempted to tear it up and write another that would give Colin some idea of what it had meant to find himself living on the wrong side of the river in a town like Mayapore. Then he would have said: 'There is nothing that isn't ugly. Houses, town, river, landscape. All of them are reduced to sordid uniform squalor by the people who live in them. If there's an exception to this, you'd no doubt find it on the other side of the river, in what are called the civil lines. And perhaps you'd eventually get used to it, even enjoy it, because the civil lines are where *you*'d be; that would be *your* retreat. But I am here in the Chillianwallah Bagh. It's what they call modern. You're somebody by their standards if you live in one of these stifling concrete monstrosities. The whole place stinks of drains, though. In my room – if you can call it a room: with unglazed barred windows it looks more like a cell – there's a bed (a wooden frame with a string mesh), a chair, a table which Aunt Shalini has covered with a ghastly piece of purple cloth embroidered in silver thread, a wardrobe called an almirah with a door that doesn't work. My trunk and suitcases are mildewed. There's a fan in the middle of the ceiling. More often than not it stops working during the night and you wake up suffocating. My aunt and I live alone. We have four servants. They live in the compound at the back. They speak no English. When I'm in a room downstairs they watch me from doorways and through windows because I'm the nephew from 'Bilaiti'. My aunt, I suppose, is a good woman. She's not forty yet, but looks more than fifty. We don't understand each other. She tries to understand me harder than I can bother to try to understand her. But at least she is bearable. I detest the others. From their point of view I'm unclean. They want me to drink cow-piss to purify myself of the stain of living abroad, crossing the forbidden water. Purify! I have seen men and women defaecate in the open, in some wasteland near the river. At night the smell of the river comes into my bedroom. In my bathroom, in one corner, there is a hole in the floor and two sole-shaped ledges to put your feet on before you squat. There are always flies in the bathroom. And cockroaches. You get used to them, but only by debasing your own civilised instincts. At first they fill you with horror. Even terror. It is purgatory, at first, to empty the bowels.

'But the house is a haven of peace and cleanliness compared with what's outside and what goes on out there. We get our milk straight from a cow. Aunt Shalini boils it, thank God. The milkman comes in the morning and milks his cow outside the house, near a telegraph pole. To this pole he ties a dead, stuffed calf which the cow nuzzles. This keeps her in milk. The calf was starved to death because the cow's milk was taken by the milkman to sell to good Hindus. Since I knew that, I take only lemon or lime in my tea when Aunt Shalini can get them from the bazaar. I've only been to the bazaar once. That was during the first week I was here, towards the end of May. The temperature was 110 degrees. I hadn't yet taken in what was happening to me. I went to the bazaar with Aunt Shalini because I wanted to be decent to her and she seemed keen for me to go. What was it? Some kind of nightmare? The leper, for instance, who hung about at the entrance to the bazaar and whom nobody seemed to take any special notice of. Was he real? Yes, he was real enough. What was left of his hand came close to my sleeve. Aunt Shalini put a coin into his bowl. She knows about lepers. They are part of her daily experience. And when she put the coin into his bowl I remembered that story my father told me, which I told you, and neither of us quite believed about the way my grandfather was said to have left his home and gone begging to acquire merit and become part of the Absolute. Well – did he end up as a leper too? Or did he just find himself communing with God?

'All those stories that my father told me; at the time they seemed to be simply stories. A bit romantic even. To get the full flavour of them you have to imagine them taking place here, or somewhere like it, somewhere even more primitive. I look at Aunt Shalini and try to see her as that young kid who was married off at all that cost to the fellow who died of syphilis or something. Died in a brothel, anyway. I wish Father hadn't told me about that. I find myself watching her at table, hoping she won't touch anything but the outer rim of the plate. Poor Aunt Shalini! She asks me questions about England, the kind of question you can't answer because at home it never gets asked.

'Home. It still slips out. But this is home, isn't it, Colin? I mean I shan't wake up tomorrow at Chillingborough or Sidcot, or in what we always called "my" room at Didbury? I shall wake up here, and the first thing I'll be conscious of will be the sound of the crows. I shall wake up at seven and the household will have been up and about for at least an hour. There'll be a smell from the compound of something being cooked in ghi. My stomach will turn over at the thought of breakfast. I'll hear the servants shouting at each other. In India everybody shouts. There'll be a pedlar or beggar at the gate out front. And he'll be shouting. Or there may be the man who screams. When I first heard him I thought he was a madman who'd got loose. But he is a madman who has never been locked up. His madness is thought of as a sign that God has personally noticed him. He is therefore holier than any of the so-called sane people. Perhaps underneath this idea that he's holy is the other idea that insane is the only sensible thing for an Indian to be, and what they all wish they were.

185

'The sun will probably be out in the morning. It hurts the eyes to look out of the window. There's no gradation of light. Just flat hard glare and sudden shadow as a cloud passes. Later it will rain. If the rain falls heavily enough you won't be able to hear the people shouting. But after a bit the sound of the rain sends you barmy too. Since coming here I've started smoking. The cigarettes are always damp though. About eleven o'clock an old man called Pandit Babu Sahib arrives, ostensibly to teach me Hindi. My aunt pays for the lessons. The pandit has a dirty turban and a grey beard. He smells of garlic. It sickens me to catch his breath. The lessons are a farce because he speaks no English I recognise. Sometimes he doesn't turn up at all, or turns up an hour late. They have no conception of time. To me they are still "they".

'You ask me what I'm going to do. I don't know. I'm at the mercy of my aunt's in-laws for the moment. There are some Kumars still in Lucknow, apparently, and a brother of Aunt Shalini's and his wife in the old Kumar house in the United Provinces. But they want nothing to do with me. Aunt Shalini wrote to them when she got the news of Father's death. They weren't interested. Father cut himself off from everyone but Aunt Shalini. He sold his land to his brothers before emigrating to England. This brother of his who's still alive is afraid – so Aunt Shalini thinks – that I plan to claim back part of the property. She suggests going to a lawyer to see if the original sale was in order. In this she's like every other Indian. If they can get involved in a long and crippling lawsuit they seem to be happy. But I want nothing to do with that sort of thing. So I'm dependent on her and her brother-in-law, Romesh Chand Gupta Sen, until I can earn a living. But what decent living can I earn without some kind of recognised qualification? Aunt Shalini would let me go to one of the Indian colleges, but it's not for her to say, because Romesh Chand controls the purse-strings. (After all, the Gupta Sens *own* her.) There's a Technical College here that was founded by a rich Indian called Chatterjee. Sometimes I think I might try and get in there and work for an engineering degree or diploma or whatever it is a place like that hands out.

'Do you know the worst thing? Well, not the worst, but the thing that makes me feel really up against it? Neither Aunt Shalini nor Romesh Chand, nor any of their friends and relatives, know any English people, at least not socially, or any who matter. Aunt Shalini doesn't know any because she doesn't have any social life. The others make it a point of principle not even to try to mix. This is a tight, closed, pseudo-orthodox Hindu society. I'm beginning to see just what it was that my father rebelled against. If they knew a few English I don't think it would be long before some kind of special interest was taken in my future. My five years at Chillingborough can't mean nothing, and there must be all kinds of scholarships and grants I could be put on to. But Aunt Shalini knows nothing about them, and seems afraid to raise the subject with anyone, and the Gupta Sens clearly don't want to know. Romesh Chand says I'll be useful to him in his business. I've seen his offices. I think I'd go mad if I had to work there. The main office is over a warehouse that overlooks the Chillianwallah Bazaar, and there's a sub-office at the railway sidings. He's a grain and fresh vegetable contractor to the military station on the other side of the river. He's also a grain dealer on his own account. And Aunt Shalini says he's got his fingers in a lot of other enterprises. He owns most of the Chillianwallah Bagh property. This is the India you won't read about in your pig-sticking books. This is the acquisitive middle-class merchant India of money under the floorboards, and wheat and rice hoarded up until there is a famine somewhere and you can off-load it at a handsome profit, even if most of it has gone bad. Then you sell it to the Government and bribe the government agent not to notice that it's full of weevils. Or you can sell it to the Government while it's still in good condition and there's no famine and the Government can let it go bad – unless of course it's stolen from their warehouses and bought up cheap and stored until a government official can be bribed to buy it all over again. Aunt Shalini tells me about such things. She is very naïve. She tells me things like this to make me laugh. She does not realise that she is talking about the people I'm supposed to feel kindred affection for, men like her husband, for instance, the late Prakash Gupta Sen. Somehow I must fight my way out of this impossible situation. But fight my way to where?'

*

Indeed, to where? It was not a question Colin could have helped him to answer because Hari never asked it of anyone but himself, and it was several months before he put it even to himself so directly, in such unequivocal terms. He had not asked himself the question before because he could not accept the situation as a real one. In that situation there was a powerful element of fantasy, sometimes laughable, mostly not; but a fantasy that was always inimical to the idea of a future stemming directly from it. In terms of a future, first the fantasy had to be destroyed. Something projected from the real world outside had to hit and shatter it. During this period he hung on to his Englishness as if it were some kind of protective armour, hung on to it with a passionate conviction the equal of that which his father had once had that to live in England was probably enough in itself to transform life. And because he now felt that his Englishness was the one and only precious gift his father had given him he liked to forget that he had once been critical of him and year by year more ashamed of him. He fell into the habit of saying to himself whenever a new horror was revealed to him: 'This is what my father hated and drove himself mad trying to ensure I'd never be touched by.' Madness was the only way he could explain his father's 'suicide'. And he was old enough, too, to guess that loneliness had heightened the degree of insanity. If Duleep Kumar had not been lonely perhaps he might have found the courage to face up to the financial disaster which the lawyers had succeeded in convincing his son of but never in explaining to that son's satisfaction. In Mayapore, Hari saw that disaster as the work of the same malign spirit that now made his own life miserable.

Through most of his first experience of the rains he was chronically and depressingly off-colour. Whatever he ate turned his bowels to water. In such circumstances a human being goes short on courage. His indisposition and his distaste for what lay outside Number 12 Chillianwallah Bagh kept him confined to the house for days at a time. He slept through the humid afternoons as if drugged and grew to fear the moment when his Aunt Shalini would want his company, or suggest a walk because the rains had let up and the evening was what she called cool. They would go, then, towards the stinking river, along the Chillianwallah Bagh Extension road to the Bibighar bridge, but turn back there as if what lay on the other side was prohibited, or, if not actually prohibited, undesirable. In all that time from May until the middle of September he did not cross over into the civil lines. At first he did not cross because there was no call to; but later he did not cross because the other side of the river became synonymous with freedom and the time did not strike him as ripe to test it. He did not want to tempt the malign spirit.

He crossed the river in the third week of September, in 1938, when the rains had gone and his illness was over and he could no longer find any excuse not to go through the motions of pleasing his uncle, Romesh Chand Gupta Sen; when, in fact, he had decided to please his uncle as much as was in his power, because he had talked to his uncle's lawyer, a man called Srinivasan, and now had hopes of persuading the uncle to send him to the Mayapore Technical College, or to the college in the provincial capital.

'I will become,' he told himself, 'exactly what my father wanted me to become, and like this pay the malign spirit out. I'll become an Indian the English will welcome and recognise.'

His father's death had raised the question of moral indebtedness.

*

He went with some documents Romesh Chand told him were needed by a Mr Nair, the chief clerk at the warehouse near the railway sidings. He travelled by cycle-rickshaw. Few of the clothes he had brought from England were of any use to him. His aunt had helped to fit him out with shirts and trousers run up by the bazaar tailor. The trousers he wore today were white and wide-bottomed. With them he wore a white short-sleeved shirt, and carried a buff-coloured sola topee. Only his shoes were English; and those were hand-made and very expensive. One of Aunt Shalini's servants had polished them by now to a brilliance he himself had never achieved.

The traffic was held up on the Mandir Gate bridge. Immediately in front of the rickshaw, obstructing the view, was an open lorry loaded with sacks of grain. A sweating, half-naked coolie sat on top of the sacks smoking a bidi. Abreast of the rickshaw was another; behind, a bus. The rickshaw had come to a halt opposite the temple. There were beggars squatting in the roadway near the temple gate. He looked away in case he should recognise the leper. He heard the clanking of the train on the opposite bank but could not see it because of the lorry. Five minutes after he heard the train the traffic began to move. The bridge had a parapet of whitened stone. He had a brief impression of water and openness, and banks curving away in muddy inlets and promontories, and then the three wheels of the rickshaw were juddering over the wooden planks of the level crossing and he was translated into this other half of the world.

His disappointment was as keen as his anticipation had been. The road from the Mandir Gate bridge to the railway station was lined with buildings that reminded him of those on the Chillianwallah Bagh Extension road: but before the rickshaw boy took a turn to the right, ringing his bell and shouting a warning to an old man who was chasing a berserk water-buffalo, he saw a vista of trees and a hint, beyond the trees, of space and air. When the rickshaw boy drew up in the forecourt of the station goods-yard, which looked like all goods-yards, graceless and functional, he told him to wait. The boy seemed to object, but young Kumar could not understand what he said, and walked away without paying, the one sure way he knew of keeping him there. He entered the godown that bore across its front the sign *Romesh Chand Gupta Sen and Co., Contractors*. Inside there was the nutty fibrous smell of all such places. It was dark and comparatively cool. Labourers were carrying sacks of grain from a stack out into the sunlit siding on the other side of the warehouse and loading them into a goods wagon. The air was full of floating dust and chaff. Set into the wall closest to him was an open door and a bank of windows that overlooked the vast cavern of the godown. This was the office. It was lit by naked electric light-bulbs. He entered. The head clerk was not there. Two or three young men in dhotis and shirts of home-spun cotton sat at trestle tables writing in ledgers. They remained seated. In his uncle's office over the warehouse in the Chillianwallah Bazaar the young clerks stood up whenever he went into their musty ill-lit rooms. That embarrassed him. All the same, suspecting that these clerks at the railway godown knew who he was, he could not help noticing the difference in their behaviour and momentarily feeling diminished by it. He asked where the chief clerk was. The man he spoke to replied fluently enough, answering English for English, but in a manner that was obviously intended to be offensive.

'Then I'll leave these papers with you,' Kumar said, and put them on the desk. The young man picked them up and threw them into a wire basket.

'They are marked urgent, by the way,' Kumar pointed out.

'Then why do you leave them with me? Why don't you take them with you and look for Mr Nair in the station master's office?'

'Because that's your job, not mine,' Kumar said, and turned as if to walk out.

'These documents are entrusted to you, not to me.'

They stared at each other.

Kumar said, 'If you're not competent to deal with them by all means let them lie in your little wire basket. I'm only a delivery boy.'

When he was at the door the other man called, 'I say, Coomer.'

He turned, annoyed to have it proved that the other man did know who he was.

'If your uncle wants to know whom you gave these papers to, tell him – Moti Lal.'

It was a name he expected to forget but in fact had cause to remember.

When he got outside the warehouse the rickshaw boy had turned nasty. He wanted to be paid off. Kumar climbed in and told him to go to the cantonment bazaar. He had worked out how to say it in Hindi. When the boy shook his head Kumar repeated the order but raised his voice. The boy took hold of the handlebars and wheeled the rickshaw around, ran with it for a few paces and jumped on to the saddle. Kumar had to shout at him again when he began to turn back along the way they had come. They had another argument. Kumar guessed the reason for the boy's objections. He did not want to take an Indian passenger so far. An Indian passenger seldom paid more than the minimum fare.

Eventually the boy submitted to his bad luck and turned towards the cantonment, and then Kumar found himself travelling along wide avenues of well-spaced bungalows. Here there was shade and a sense of mid-morning hush such as fell at home, between breakfast and lunch during the holidays at Didbury. The road was metalled but the pathways were kutcha. In the sudden quietness he could hear the rhythmic click of the pedals. He lit a cigarette because the odour of the leather cushions and the smell of the boy's stale sweat were now more noticeable.

The boy made a series of left and right hand turns and Kumar wondered whether he was being taken out of his way deliberately, but then – where the road they were now travelling on met another at a T-junction – he could see a section of arcaded shops, and one with a sign over it: Dr Gulab Singh Sahib (P) Ltd: Pharmacy. They had reached the Victoria road. He told the boy to turn left and indicated with a curt flick of the hand, whenever the boy looked over his shoulder to suggest that now was the time to stop, that the journey should continue. He wanted to see beyond the canton-ment bazaar. He wanted to go as far as the place he knew was called the *maidan*.

There were English women in the arcades of the Victoria road. How pale they looked. Their cars were parked in the shade along one side of the bazaar. There was this shade to be had because at ten-thirty in the morning the sun was casting shadows. There were also horse tongas. The tonga-carts were painted in gay colours, and the horses' bridles were decorated with silver medallions and red and yellow plumes. Some of the English women were wearing slacks. Briefly he had an impression that these made them look ugly, but this was an impression that did not survive the warmth of the feeling he had that here at last he was again in the company

190

of people he understood. He looked from one side of the road to the other: here was a shop called Darwaza Chand, Civil and Military Tailor; here the Imperial Bank of India; there the offices of the *Mayapore Gazette* which it interested him to see because Aunt Shalini had made a point of ordering the *Gazette* especially for him so that he could read the local news in English. The shops in the cantonment all advertised in the *Gazette*. The names were familiar to him. He wished that he had a lot of money so that he could tell the rickshaw boy to stop at the Imperial Bank, go in and cash a cheque, and then stroll across the road to Darwaza Chand and order some decent suits and shirts. He wished, as well, that he had the courage to go into the English Coffee House, drink a cup or two and smoke a cigarette and chat to the two pretty young white girls who were just now entering. And he would have liked to tap the rickshaw boy on his bony back, get out at the Mayapore Sports Emporium and test the weight and spring of the English willow cricket bats that were for sale there, at a price. The sight of the bats in the window made him long to open his shoulders and punish a loose ball. After he had selected a bat he would go across the road to the Yellow Dragon Chinese Restaurant and eat some decent food; and, in the evening, pay a visit to the Eros Cinema where at 7.30 and 10.30 that evening they were showing a film he had seen months ago with the Lindseys at the Carlton in the Haymarket. He would have liked the Lindseys to be here in Mayapore to see it with him again. Going past the cinema – a building with a white stuccoed facceade and a steel mesh concertina gate closing the dark cavern of the open foyer, and set well back in a sanded forecourt – he felt the pain of his exile more sharply than ever.

He told the boy to go in the direction of the *maidan*. The cinema was the last building in the cantonment bazaar – or the first, depending which way you came. Beyond it there was a section of tree-shaded road with low walls on either side and, on the other side of the walls, the huts and godowns of the Public Works Department. The rickshaw boy got up some speed on this stretch, negotiated the crossroads formed by the Victoria and Grand Trunk roads and rode on past the Court house, the Police barracks, the District Headquarters, the chummery, the District Superintendent's bungalow and the bungalow which the Poulsons were to take over in 1939.

In this way Hari Kumar reached the *maidan*. He told the rickshaw boy to stop. The vast space was almost empty. There were two riders – white children mounted on ponies. Their syces ran behind. The crows were wheeling and croaking, but to Hari they no longer looked predatory. There was peace. And Hari thought: Yes, it is beautiful. In the distance, on the other side of the *maidan*, he could see the spire of St Mary's. He got down from the rickshaw and stood in the shade of the trees and watched and listened. Half-closing his eyes he could almost imagine himself on the common near Didbury. The rains had left their green mark on the turf, but he did not know this because he had never seen the *maidan* before; he had never seen it in May when the grass was burnt to ochre.

He wanted to mount and ride and feel the air moving against his face.

Could one hire a pony from somewhere? He turned to the rickshaw boy. It was impossible to ask. He did not know the right words. Perhaps he did not need to know, or need to ask because he could guess the answer. The *maidan* was the preserve of the *sahiblog*. But he felt, all the same, that he would only have to speak to one of them to be recognised, to be admitted. He got back into the rickshaw and told the boy to go back to the cantonment bazaar. He would buy a few things at Dr Gulab Singh's pharmacy; some Odol toothpaste and some Pears' soap. Surreptitiously, he felt in his wallet. He had a five-rupee note and four one-rupee notes. About fifteen shillings. The rickshaw boy would ask for three but really be content with two.

On the return journey he became aware that there were very few cycle rickshaws on the road. There were cars, cycles and horse-tongas. In the cycle-rickshaws the passengers were always Indians. In one rickshaw the passenger had his sandalled feet up on a wooden crate of live chickens. He felt the shame that rubbed off on to him because he travelled by rickshaw, so marking himself as out of his own black-town element because the cycle-rickshaws all came from the other side of the river.

When they reached Gulab Singh's he told the boy to stop, and got down, mounted the double kerb and entered the shadowy arcade. In Gulab Singh's window there were brand goods so familiar, so Anglo-Saxon, he felt like shouting for joy. Or in despair. He could not tell which. He entered. The shop was dark and cool, set out with long rectangular glass cases on table-legs, as in a museum. It smelt faintly of pepper and richly of unguents. At one end there was a counter. There were several English women walking round, each attended by an Indian assistant. There was a man as well, who looked a bit like Mr Lindsey. The Englishman's clothes showed his own up for what they were. Babu clothes. Bazaar stuff. The English were talking to each other. He could hear every word they said if he paid attention. The man who looked like Mr Lindsey was saying: 'Why hasn't it come? You said Tuesday and today is Tuesday. I might just as well have ordered it myself. Well, give me the other thing and send the rest up jolly sharp.'

Kumar stood at the counter and waited for the assistant to finish serving the Englishman. The Englishman glanced at him and then turned his attention back to what the assistant was doing: wrapping an unidentifiable cardboard carton.

'Right,' the Englishman said, taking the package. 'I'll expect the other things by six this evening.'

When the Englishman had gone Kumar said, 'Have you got some Pears' soap?'

The assistant, a man several years older than himself, waggled his head from side to side, and went away. Kumar could not be sure that he had understood. Another assistant came through the doorway marked *Dispensary*, but he was carrying a package which he took over to a woman who was studying the articles for sale in one of the glass cases. At the other side of the shop there was a photographic booth. Kumar waited. When he next saw his own assistant the man was opening another of the glass cases for a group of white women.

Kumar moved away from the unattended counter and took up a position from which he judged he would be able to catch the assistant's eye. He was right. He did. But the assistant's expression was that of someone who did not remember ever having been spoken to about Pears' soap. Kumar wished that the assistant's new customers had been men. He could have interrupted their conversation, then, without putting himself in the wrong. Instead, he found himself in the ignominious role of watcher on the sidelines, in a situation another man was taking advantage of: hiding, as Kumar put it to himself, behind the skirts of a group of women. He looked around and saw the man who had come from the dispensary going back there. He said to him, 'I asked someone if you had any Pears' soap.'

The man stopped: perhaps because Kumar's voice automatically arrested him with its sahib-inflections. Momentarily he seemed to be at a loss, assessing the evidence of his eyes and the evidence of his ears. 'Pears'?' he said at last. 'Oh yes, we have Pears'. Who is it for?'

It was a question Kumar had not expected, and one he did not immediately understand. But then did. Who did this fellow think he was? Some *babu* shopping for his master?

'Well, it's for me, naturally,' he said.

'One dozen or two dozen?'

Kumar's mouth was dry.

'One bar,' he said, trying to be dignified about it.

'We only sell it by the dozen,' the man explained, 'but you could get it in the bazaar, I expect,' and then added something in Hindi, which Kumar did not understand.

He said, 'I'm sorry. I don't speak Hindi. What are you trying to say?'

And was conscious, now, that because he was annoyed he had raised his voice, and other people in the shop were watching and listening. He caught the eye of one of the Englishwomen. Slowly she turned away with a smile he could only attach two words to: bitter, contemptuous.

'I was saying,' the man replied, 'that if you are only wanting one bar of Pears' soap you will find it cheaper in the Chillianwallah Bazaar because there they are taking no notice of regulated retail prices.'

'Thank you,' Kumar said, 'you have been most helpful,' and walked out.

*

The room in the Chillianwallah Bazaar office where Kumar worked was larger than the rest. He shared it with other English-speaking clerks. They were afraid of him because of his manner and his family connection with their employer. Proud of their own fluency in what passed among them for English – a language not generally in use at Romesh Chand's warehouse – they resented his intrusion but in a perverse way were flattered by the sense of further elevation his presence gave them. They were boys who, if they could help it, never spoke their mother tongue, and so looked down on the men in the small, airless partitioned cells, old clerks who conducted their business and correspondence in the vernacular. By arriving in their own midst Kumar had confirmed their superiority but threatened their security. In front of him they no longer dared to criticise Romesh Chand, or the head clerks, in case one of Kumar's jobs was to act as a family spy. And even when they felt reassured that it was not they could not help wondering which of them might lose his job to the Anglicised boy who knew nothing about the business but had the manner of a burra sahib. Their conduct towards him was a compound of suspicion, awe, envy and servility.

They sickened him. He thought them spineless, worse than a bunch of girls, giggling one day and sulking the next. He found it difficult to follow what they were saying. They ran all their words one into the other. They sang their sentences. Their pronunciation was peculiar. At first he tried to understand them, but then saw the danger of trying too hard. He wondered how long a man could work among them and not fall into the same habits of speech, not acquire the alien habits of thought that controlled the speech. At night, alone in his bedroom, he sometimes talked aloud to himself, trying to detect changes of tone, accent and resonance in order to correct them. To maintain the Englishness of his voice and habits became increasingly important to him. Even after the disastrous visit to Gulab Singh's pharmacy it remained important. He remembered what his father had said: 'If you answer the telephone people think it is an Englishman speaking.' There were no telephones at his uncle's office. There was no telephone at Number 12 Chillianwallah Bagh. Even if there had been telephones there would have been no Englishman to ring or to be rung by. But this absence of Englishness in his exterior public life he saw as a logical projection of the fantasy that informed his private inner one.

It was at this period, after the visit to the pharmacy, that the notion of having become invisible to white people first entered his head, although it took some time for the notion to be formulated quite in this way. When he had become used to crossing the river from the bazaar to the railway warehouse and used to the way English people seemed to look right through him if their eyes chanced to meet his own, the concept of invisibility fell readily enough into its place, but still more time was needed for that concept to produce its natural corollary in his mind: that his father had succeeded in making him nothing, nothing in the black town, nothing in the cantonment, nothing even in England because in England he was now no more than a memory, a familiar but possibly unreal signature at the end of meaningless letters to Colin Lindsey; meaningless because, as the months went by, the letters deviated further and further from the truth. The letters became, in fact, exercises by young Kumar to keep his Englishness in trim. He knew this. He knew his letters were unsatisfactory. He recognised the signs of growing-away that could be read in Colin's replies. But the association with Colin continued to be precious to him. Colin's signature at the bottom of a letter was the proof he needed that his English experience had not been imagined.

*

Where does one draw the line under the story of Hari Kumar, Harry Coomer: the story of him prior to Bibighar?

Sister Ludmila said that for her Bibighar began on the morning Merrick took Kumar away in his police truck; so at least Kumar has to be brought to that point, brought anyway to the moment when, in the dark, his body was turned over by Mr de Souza and his face lit by the torch. Such darkness, Sister Ludmila said; the kind of expression which was familiar to her on the faces of young Indians, but was, in Hari's case, especially significant.

And where does one go for the evidence of the story of Kumar prior to Bibighar? Well, there is the lawyer Srinivasan. There is Sister Ludmila. There is no longer Shalini Gupta Sen; no Gupta Sen who knows, or will admit to knowing. There are other witnesses: and, specifically, there is that certain signature in the Members' Book of the Mayapore Gymkhana Club. There is also the signature of Harry Coomer in the Members' Book for 1939 of the Mayapore Indian Club. The Mayapore Chatterjee Club. The MCC. The other club. The wrong one. And this is to be found in a ledger somewhat similar to those used at the right club, under a date in May 1939, which oddly enough roughly coincides with the day the Deputy Commissioner challenged a tradition and made a forced entry at the Gymkhana.

'I put young Kumar up for the Indian Club' (Srinivasan said) 'because it was something I felt he needed. We only met a few times. I'm afraid he didn't like me. He distrusted me because I was his uncle Romesh's lawyer. Apart from that English manner of his which I found overbearing I quite liked him as a person, if not as a type. If we'd got on better, if he'd trusted me, perhaps I should have been able to do something for him, taken him to Lili Chatterjee's for instance and got him into a few mixed English and Indian parties. But by the time he got into what used to be called the MacGregor House set it was too late. He'd already got on the wrong side of the policeman, Merrick, and been taken in for questioning. The evening in 1939 I took him to the Indian Club wasn't a success. The banias were there, with their feet on the chairs. He hated it. I don't think he ever went again, and a few weeks later he left his uncle's office. He'd got wind of the marriage the Gupta Sens were thinking of arranging for him, and he'd given up hope of getting his uncle to agree to his going to the Technical College. I can tell you this, that if it hadn't been for his Aunt Shalini he'd have been in a bad way when he walked out of Romesh Chand's office. The old man was ready to wash his hands of him. I remember how she begged and pleaded with Romesh to continue the allowance he paid her. Well, he kept it going but cut it down. She pinched and scraped and went without things herself to give Hari something for his pocket; and of course she fed and housed and clothed him. I told her that as long as she did that she was stopping him from standing on his own feet. He was already nineteen. A man by our standards. But she wouldn't hear any criticism of him. And don't get the wrong impression. He didn't just sit back. I remember for instance that he applied for a job at the British–Indian Electrical. He had two or three interviews and for a time it looked as if he'd got in. Naturally they were interested. His English public school education didn't count for nothing. It didn't matter to them that he had no qualifications. They could have taught him what he needed to know, and trained him up on the administrative side. But he fell foul of one of the Englishmen there, so Shalini Gupta Sen told me. It wasn't difficult to guess why. In those days, you know, the commercial people were always looked down upon as the lowest form of Anglo-Indian life. Even schoolmasters ranked higher in the colonial social scale. The man Hari fell foul of probably spoke English with a Midlands accent, and resented the fact that an Indian spoke it like a managing director.

'After the British–Indian Electrical debacle I tried to get Romesh to understand that the boy's talents were being wasted. But let me confess. It wasn't a problem I spent any sleepless nights over. You want me to be frank. And frankly I did not much care for the kind of Indian Duleep Kumar had turned his son into. Please remember that in those days I was only in my forties, also that my main interest was in politics. And I did not respond to Hari Kumar as a political animal. His father had taught him no doubt that Indian politics were all a nonsense, all window-dressing. Hari did not take them seriously. He had no real knowledge of them, no conception for instance of the step forward that provincial power had meant to the Congress. He scarcely realised that the province he lived in had once been ruled directly by a British Governor and a nominated council. He took democracy for granted. He had no experience of autocracy. Politically he was an innocent. Most Englishmen were. In those days I had no time for such people. Today, of course, I am a political innocent myself. It is the fate that awaits us all, all of us anyway who ever had strong views about political affairs when we were younger. Particularly it awaits those of us who paid for our views with imprisonment. Prison left its disagreeable mark. It made us attach too much importance to the things that led us to it.'

*

When Hari left his uncle's employment he also told Pandit Baba Sahib he no longer wanted Hindi lessons. He did this to save his aunt from spending money uselessly. He had picked up enough Hindi to give orders, picked up in fact what the average Englishman in India thought worth while bothering with. His series of interviews with the British–Indian Electrical Company took place in the early part of the rainy season of 1939. His rejection was a blow, even though he had expected it after his final interview. For the first time he wrote a letter to Colin that gave young Lindsey – or should have given him – a clearer idea of what Hari Kumar was up against.

'There was a strong likelihood of being sent back home to learn the technical ropes,' he told his friend in Didbury. 'First in Birmingham and then in the London office of the parent company. Things went swimmingly at the first interview with a pleasant chap called Knight who was at Wardens from 1925 to 1930. He played in the Chillingborough–Wardens match of 1929, when apparently they beat us by twenty-two runs. We didn't talk about the job at all, really, although it was Knight who mentioned London and Birmingham and got my hopes up. It sounded like the answer to a prayer, one that had been here on my doorstep all these months. I told him the whole thing, about father, etc. He seemed pretty sympathetic. The next interview was with the managing director, and that was stickier – probably because, as Knight had let slip, he was grammar-school with a university veneer. But even so, I still thought it was going well, even when he poured a bit of cold water on the idea of sending me home for training. He said there was a sort of understanding with the Technical College here to look primarily among their graduates for young Indians who had executive prospects, but that they were also working on a scheme with the college for extra-mural courses for their own "promising men", something to do with part-time training in the firm and part-time education at the college. If I got some kind of diploma from the college then it might be possible to send me home for more intensive instruction. He made rather heavy weather of my not having matriculated and said, "Of course, Coomer, at your age most young Indians have a BA or a BSc." I felt like saying, "Well, of a sort," but didn't, because I guessed anyway that he appreciated the difference between a BSc Mayapore and a man who'd been at Chillingborough on the classical side. Anyway, the second interview ended on an optimistic note. I saw Knight again for a few minutes afterwards and he said that in the month since he and I had had a chat he'd written to someone at the London office who'd been in touch with old Toad-in-the-hole, and that I'd been given a good reference.

'I had to wait another two weeks for interview number three which both Knight and the managing director had warned me about, but given me the impression was not much more than a formality, an interview with a fellow they called the Technical Training Manager, a fellow called Stubbs, who is best described as a loud-mouthed —. He began right away by shoving a little cylinder at me, across his enormous desk, and asking me to tell him what it was and what it was used for. When I said I didn't know but that it looked like a sort of valve he smirked and said, "Where are you from, laddie? Straight down from the tree?" Then he picked up a printed sheet and read out a list of questions. Long before he got to the end I said, "I've already told Mr Knight I know nothing about electricity." He took no notice. Probably I shouldn't have mentioned Mr Knight. He went on until he'd asked me the last question and I'd said, "I don't know," for the last time. Then he glared and said, "You some sort of comedian or something? Are you deliberately wasting my time?" I told him that was for him to decide. He leaned back in his swivel chair, and we stared at each other for what seemed ages. Then he said, "There's only you and me in this room, Coomer or whatever your name is. Let me tell you this. I don't like bolshie black laddies on my side of the business." I got up and walked out. Which is what he wanted me to do and what I couldn't avoid doing unless I wanted to crawl.

'So now you know what I am, Colin, a bolshie black laddie. (Remember that bastard Parrott, in our first year at Chillingborough?) I'm a bolshie black laddie because I know how to construe Tacitus but haven't any idea what that fellow Stubbs was talking about. And that wasn't the end of it. I had a letter from Knight about three days later asking me to go and see him. He told me that for the moment there weren't any vacancies. He was quite a different fellow. Puzzled and embarrassed, doing the right thing by an old Chillingburian, but underneath it all bloody unfriendly. Stubbs must have spun them all a yarn. And because Stubbs was a white man they felt they had to believe him. After all, for the job I was applying for, there were probably a score of BAs and BScs, failed or otherwise, who would be willing to jump when Stubbs said jump.

'The one thing that puzzled me was why it was Stubbs who was allowed to call the tune? Why him? Surely Knight knew what kind of a man he was? But he never so much as hinted he'd like to hear my side of what happened. He never referred to my interview with Stubbs at all. In fact when I came away I wondered why he'd bothered to call me in. He could have given me the brush-off by letter. Later I realised he probably wanted to have another look at me – sort of through Stubbs's eyes, bearing in mind whatever it was Stubbs had told them. And then I guessed that at this second interview with Knight I couldn't have made much of an impression, although it was hardly my fault because as soon as I sat down in front of him I could tell it was no go, and I was damned disappointed. Trying not to show it probably made me look as if I didn't care a damn. But I cared like hell, Colin. After a while the conversation just dried up because he had nothing more to tell me and I had nothing I could say except something like Please, sir, give me a chance. Perhaps he was waiting for me to say "sir". I don't think I ever said "sir" at the first interview, but if I didn't he hadn't noticed. But since he'd talked to Stubbs he was probably on the look-out for that sort of thing. Anyway, he suddenly stopped looking at me, so I got to my feet and said thank you. He said he'd keep a note about me in case something turned up, and stood up too, but stayed behind his desk, and didn't offer to shake hands. I think he had it in mind to give me some kind of tip about remembering that this wasn't Chillingborough and that I should start learning how to behave in front of white men. Anyway that was the feeling in the room. There was that desk between us. For me to be in his office at all had suddenly become a privilege. A privilege I ought to know how to respect. I don't remember coming away – only finding myself outside the main gate of the factory, and getting on my bike and riding back along the Grand Trunk road, over the Bibighar bridge, back to my side of the river.'

*

For a while after what Srinivasan called the British–Indian Electrical debacle, Hari did nothing. He regretted writing that letter to Lindsey, regretted it more and more as week after week went by and he got no reply. Other things fell into place in his mind: Mr Lindsey's attitude to him towards the end of his last few weeks in England, which he had always attributed to the man's embarrassment at having been unable to do anything constructive for him financially; the experience on the boat, in which, once past Suez, the English people who had spoken to him freely enough from Southampton onwards began to congregate in exclusive little groups so that for the last few days of the voyage the only Englishmen he managed to talk to were those making the passage for the first time. He had shared a cabin with two other boys, Indian students returning home. He had not got on very well with them because he discovered that he had nothing in common with them. They asked his opinion on subjects he had never given a thought to. They were students of political economy and intended to become university teachers. He had thought them incredibly dull and rather old-maidish. It seemed that he shocked them by sleeping in the nude and dressing and undressing in the cabin instead of in the lavatory cubicle.

And so Hari came, one painful step at a time, to the realisation that his father's plans for him had been based upon an illusion. In India an Indian and an Englishman could never meet on equal terms. It was not how a man thought, spoke and behaved that counted. Perhaps this had been true in England as well and the Lindseys had been exceptions to the general rule. He did not blame his father. His anger was directed against the English for fostering the illusion his father had laboured under. If he had felt more liking for his fellow-countrymen he might at this stage have sided with them, sought an occasion for paying the English out. But he did not care for any Indian he had met and what he knew or read of their methods of resisting English domination struck him as childish and inept. In any case *they* did not trust him. Neither, it seemed, did the English. He recognised that to the outside world he had become nothing. But he did not feel in himself that he was nothing. Even if he were quite alone in the world he could not be nothing. And he was not quite alone. There was still Colin, at home, and Aunt Shalini in Mayapore. The affection he had for her, grudging at first, when he first recognised it as affection, had become genuine enough. In her self-effacement he saw evidence of a concern for his welfare which was just as acute – perhaps more acute than Mrs Lindsey's which had been so effusively, openly and warmly expressed. He could not help knowing that in her odd, retiring way his Aunt Shalini was fond of him. The trouble was that her fondness could not reach him or encourage him outside the ingrown little world which was the only one she knew, one that stifled him and often horrified him. It was difficult for him to enter it even briefly to show her that he returned fondness for fondness. To enter it he had to protect himself from it by nursing his contempt and showing his dislike. He could not help it if often she believed the contempt and dislike were meant for her. When she gave him money he could not thank her properly. It was Gupta Sen money. Perhaps she understood his dislike of such money and the way his dislike grew in proportion to his increasing need; or perhaps he had hurt her by the curt words with which he acknowledged it. She took to putting the money in an envelope and leaving it on his bedroom table. It touched him that in writing his name on the envelope she always spelled it Harry.

It touched him too that she seemed to consider him as head of the household, head in the Hindu family sense because he was a man; potentially a breadwinner, husband and father; procreator. He could not imagine himself becoming a married man. Indian girls did not attract him. The English girls he saw in the cantonment seemed to move inside the folds of some invisible purdah that made their bodies look unreal, asexual. His lusts centred upon an anthropomorphous being whose sex was obvious from the formation of the thighs and swollen breasts but whose colour was ambivalent; dumb, sightless and unmoving beneath his own body which at night, under waking or sleeping stress, sometimes penetrated the emptiness and drained itself of the dead weight of its fierce but undirected impulse.

*

Four weeks after the final meeting with Knight, Hari applied for another job. He had spent the intervening time trying to work out the logic of a situation which he now accepted as real and not illusory. That precious gift from his father, his Englishness, was clearly, in many respects, a liability, but he still regarded it fundamentally as an asset. It was the only thing that gave him distinction. He was strong, healthy, and not bad-looking, but so were countless other young men. Where he scored over them was in his command of the English language. Logic pointed to a deliberate exploitation of this advantage. It occurred to him that he might well earn money by setting up as a private tutor and coaching boys who wanted to improve their speech; but such a life did not appeal to him. He doubted that it would be active enough or that he would have the patience it needed, let alone the skill. The other possibility, perhaps the only other one, was much more interesting.

Having read the *Mayapore Gazette* now for over a year he saw where his qualifications might gain him a natural foothold. Owned by an Indian, edited by an Indian, it was also obviously written and sub-edited by Indians. Its leaders and general articles were of a fairly high standard, but its reports of local events were often unintentionally funny. Hari imagined that the paper's reputed popularity among the Mayapore English was due to the fact that it gave them something to laugh at, as well as an opportunity to see their names in print on the social and sporting pages. For an Indian-owned newspaper it was shrewdly non-committal. It left political alignment to the local vernacular newspapers, of which there were several, and to an English language paper called *The Mayapore Hindu*, which some of the official English read as a duty and others bought in order to compare its reports with the Calcutta *Statesman* and *The Times of India*, but which most of them ignored. It had been suppressed on more than one occasion.

Once Hari had decided to apply for a job with the *Mayapore Gazette* he spent several days copying out particularly bad examples of syntax and idiom from old issues, and then rewriting them. When he was satisfied that he could do the work he had in mind to persuade the editor to give him, he wrote and asked for an interview. He drafted the letter several times until he was satisfied that he had stripped it to its essentials. According to the headings at the top of the leader column on the middle page of the *Gazette* the editor's name was B. V. Laxminarayan. He told Mr Laxminarayan that he was looking for a job. He told him his age, and gave brief details of his education. He said that to save him the trouble of replying he would ring Mr Laxminarayan in two or three days to find out whether he could see him. He hesitated, but in the end decided, to add that Mr Knight of the British–Indian Electrical Company would probably be prepared to pass on the references that had been obtained from the headmaster of Chillingborough. He signed the letter 'Hari Kumar' and marked the envelope 'Personal' to reduce the odds on its being opened and destroyed by some employee who was concerned for the safety of his own position. He had not worked in the office of his uncle for nothing. He doubted that Mr Laxminarayan would know Knight, or know him well enough to ring him, or – if he was wrong in either of these two suppositions – that Knight would have the nerve to tell an Indian any story other than that there had been several interviews but no vacancy. Also he relied on Knight's conception of what it was gentlemanly to say as one prospective employer to another about a young man who had played cricket against his old school.

Hari was right in the second of his suppositions. Laxminarayan knew Knight, but not well enough to ring him unless he wanted confirmation of a story about the British–Indian Electrical Company's activities. In any case he would not have rung him about Kumar's letter. Laxminarayan did not like Mr Knight, whom he described to himself as a two-faced professional charmer whose liberal inclinations had long ago been suffocated by his mortal fear of the social consequences of sticking his neck out. 'Knight,' he told Hari later, 'can now only be thought of as a pawn.' He had these harsh things to say about Knight in order not to have to think them about himself.

Laxminarayan was interested in the letter signed by Hari Kumar, but when he replied, 'By all means ring, although I have no immediate vacancy,' he had no intention of employing him. In fact he had been told by the absentee proprietor, Madhu Lal, who lived in Calcutta, to reduce the overheads and produce a more rational percentage of net profit to total investment. His own private view was that the *Gazette's* circulation would be increased if the paper could be seen to commit itself to the cause of Indian nationalism. He knew that the *Gazette* was anathema to the members of the local Congress sub-committee, and that it was a bit of a joke to the English. He believed that he could sell it even more widely among the English if he could get up their blood pressure. The bulk of its present readership – self-consciously westernised Indians and snob English – would not be lost, because they were sheep by definition. But he reckoned that over a twelve-month period he could add five or ten thousand copies to the weekly circulation if Madhu Lal ever allowed him to make the paper a repository of informed and controversial local and national opinion – non-Hindu, non-Muslim, non-British, but Indian in the best sense.

Laxminarayan conscientiously believed in his paper. Believing in it was a way of continuing to believe in himself and frank criticism of its shortcomings was a more rewarding occupation than criticism of his own. He had found a way of substituting positive thought for negative action; which perhaps was just as well. He was too deeply committed to the compromise of early middle age to be able to rekindle – in a practical, sensible way – the rebellious spark of his youth. Certainly it was just as well from Hari's point of view. When Laxminarayan first met him it took no more than a few minutes of conversation for the smothered demon in the older man to kick out, to attempt – impotently – to take control of his judgment. The demon disliked Kumar: the manner, the voice, the way the fellow sat, with his head up, his legs crossed, one black hand resting on the other side of the desk – an embryo black sahib, talking with a sahib's assurance, the kind of assurance that conveyed itself as superiority subtly restrained in the interests of the immediate protocol. The demon only stopped kicking because Laxminarayan's internal flanks were inured to the pain of the demon's spurs and because he saw, in Kumar, a potential asset, an asset in terms of the type of periodical Mr Madhu Lal wanted the *Gazette* to be. And when Kumar handed him some papers, written proof of his talents as a sub-editor – paragraphs and columns that he recognised as extracts from old issues now transformed into the simple, clear, standard English that in times of stress even eluded the overworked editor, he knew that he would offer Kumar a job and probably get rid of one of the boys who worried him but for whom he cared most, one of the boys who had little talent but a lot of heart and would in all likelihood turn out eventually to be an embarrassment.

*

Laxminarayan. These days he lives in a bungalow that once belonged to a Eurasian family who left Mayapore in 1947 – a bungalow in the Curzon

202

road. He is now an old man. He is writing a history of the origins of Indian nationalism that will probably never be finished, let alone published: his apologia for many years of personal compromise. He recognises that the policy of Madhu Lal paid off because the *Mayapore Gazette* has enjoyed an uninterrupted existence. Left to him, to Laxminarayan, it might have been done to death in 1942, in which year *The Mayapore Hindu* was suppressed for the third or fourth time. But he is amused, now, at the *Gazette's* Hindu-National basis – its air of having always supported the causes it has become locally popular to promote. Its new owner is a Brahmin refugee from Pakistan. Its new editor is the owner's cousin. With regard to politics at the centre it gives most space to the speeches and activities of Mr Morarji Desai. It plans, next year, to publish itself in a simultaneous Hindi edition, as a first step towards dispensing entirely with English. This, more than anything, saddens Mr Laxminarayan who throughout his life has had what he calls a love–hate relationship with the English language. It is the language in which he learned to think his revolutionary thoughts, and the language which so readily lent itself to the business of making the cautious middle-way he took look and sound like common sense instead of like a case of cold feet.

'What am I now?' (he would ask you, if you went to see him at his home where he is surrounded by grandchildren whose high-pitched voices seem to come from every room and from the sunlit garden which – as the English would say – has been let go). 'Well, I will tell you. I am an old man who has lived through one of the greatest upheavals of modern history – the first, and I think the most passionate, of a whole series of upheavals, rebellions against the rule of the white man which have now become so common-place they are almost boring. And I came through it without a scratch. A veritable Vicar of Bray, you understand. Retired now on pension. Honorary life member of the Mayapore Club where good Hindus forgather. Young journalists come to see me when they hear that I steered the *Gazette* through those stormy pre-independence waters and say, 'Sir, please tell us what it was really like in the days of the British.' Just like your own young people may occasionally say, What was it really like during Hitler and Mussolini? The old colonial British have become a myth, you see. Our young men meet the new Englishmen and say to themselves, 'What was all the fuss about? These fellows don't look like monsters and they seem only to be interested in the things we are interested in. They are not interested in the past and neither are we except to the extent that we wonder what the fuss was about and aren't sure that our own government is doing any better, or even that it is a government that represents us. It seems more to be the government of an uneasy marriage between old orthodoxy and old revolutionaries, and such people have nothing to say to us that we want to hear.'

'I gave Kumar a job and later got rid of a fellow called Vidyasagar who was arrested in 1942 with several other members of the staff of *The Mayapore*

Hindu, and was then put in prison. I was asked to take some steps in that disagreeable business young Kumar was involved in at the time of Bibighar. I'm afraid I refused. No one asked me to use my good offices in the cause of poor Vidyasagar who was given fifteen strokes for an infringement of prison regulations. Not that there was anything I could have done for either of them. But it stuck in my throat that when both of these boys were arrested, for different reasons, only Kumar had people to speak for him, people to ring me up and say, 'Can't you get Hari out of jail? You were his employer. Can't you do something for him? Can't *you* prove he was nowhere in the vicinity of the Bibighar?' People like Lady Chatterjee. And that fellow Knight at the British–Indian Electrical whose conscience probably bothered him. Even the assistant commissioner, Mr Poulson, sent for me and asked me questions about what Hari Kumar's political affiliations really were. I said, 'Mr Poulson, he is like myself. He has none. He is a lickspittle of the Raj.' I was angry. I did not see why I should raise a finger to help him. If the British couldn't see for themselves that he was innocent, who was I to intervene? He was more British than they were.'

A week after Hari got his job on the *Mayapore Gazette* he received a letter from Colin Lindsey. It was dated towards the end of July 1939. Colin apologised for not having written for so long. 'A few months ago I joined the Territorial Army and your own last letter reached me in training camp,' he explained. 'We were pretty busy. If there's a war – and the odds are there will be – I shall put in for a commission; otherwise I get a kick out of just being an acting unpaid lance-corporal. (They made me up in camp, this summer.) I expect you'll be thinking of the army too, won't you, Harry? I mean if anything happens. I'm told the Indian army is quite an outfit, and no longer officered only by the British. Maybe we'll meet up in some dugout or other, like *Journey's End*! Sorry you had such an unpleasant experience at that factory or whatever it was. I can't understand why your aunt's in-laws wouldn't stump up to see you through the ICS. Dad tells me a friend of his says Indians can become High Court Judges even, so the ICS seems to be the thing. That or the army. I recommend the latter. It's a great life. And honestly, Harry, you'd make a first-rate platoon commander – which is what I want to be if the war ever gets going. Then you could waggle a couple of fingers at that fellow Stubbs who was obviously other rank material only. Like me, at the moment! I've got a feeling that by the time you get this I shall be in France. Why the hell does it always have to be France? The feeling in my own unit is that the Jerrys ought to come straight over here. Then we could really show them a thing or two. Major Crowe, our CO, reckons that with all that guns-and-butter stuff the poor blighters are half-starved anyway and haven't got the strength to shoulder a rifle, let alone manhandle their artillery. Dear old Harry! Wish you were here. Then we could be in it together. For my money it's the only thing to be in, these days. The fond parents send their love.'

*

'One time he spoke to me of a letter from that boy Lindsey' (Sister Ludmila said). 'Why did he treat me as a mother-confessor? This I never earned. He spoke in that way he had, of believing in nothing, which was not natural to him, but was what he had acquired. 'Sister,' he said, 'what would you have done if you had received a letter from an old friend that showed you suddenly you were speaking different languages?' I do not remember what I replied. Unless I said, 'There is only God's language.' Meaning, you understand, the truth – that this language matters and no other. He did not hold himself entirely free of blame for what happened because when he wrote he did not tell Lindsey what was in his heart. Perhaps he did not tell him because he could not. Did not tell him because he did not know himself.'

*

From the *Mayapore Gazette* Hari received sixty rupees a month, the equivalent of just over four pounds. He gave half to his Aunt Shalini because Uncle Romesh Chand reduced her allowance on the day Hari began work for Mr Laxminarayan. The sixty rupees were paid to Hari as a sub-editor. If Laxminarayan published any of Hari's original reports he was to pay him at the rate of one anna a line. For sixteen lines, then, Hari would earn a rupee.

All this he told Colin when he replied to young Lindsey's letter. He was looking, perhaps, for a way of showing Lindsey that in Mayapore the threat of German ambitions seemed very far away, and Lindsey's curiously pre-1914 heroics strikingly out of tune with what Hari felt about his own immediate obligations and clearly recollected as the contempt for war which he and Colin had shared, or at least professed to share. Something had happened to Colin. It puzzled Hari to know what. There had been a time when they agreed that it might be necessary to pursue a line of conscientious objection to what they called compulsory physical violence in the interests of a nation's political and economic aims. Now, here was Colin talking nostalgically about *Journey's End*. Did the wearing of a uniform so corrupt a man? And what, anyway, in Colin's case had led him voluntarily to put one on? Colin had once said that patriotism, like religious fervour, was a perversion of the human instinct for survival. Chillingborough was a forcing house of administrators, not of soldiers. To an administrator a soldier represented the last-ditch defence of a policy: one to which, on the whole, it was shameful to retreat.

'I'm glad,' Hari wrote, 'that you're finding life in the TA not too wearing –'

That English subtlety! It struck him even as he wrote the words that they could be read either as manly understatement or bitchy criticism.

'– and I suppose if things come to a head India will be in the war too. Which will mean me.'

He sat and thought for a moment. He did not feel that it would mean him at all.

'It's difficult to apply a theory when faced with a situation that calls for some kind of positive reaction,' he continued. 'I suppose you've been faced with one in much the way that I have.'

He remembered the time when Mr Lindsey had described Adolf Hitler as a bloody housepainter, and later as a man who, 'anyway, got things done'. He also remembered that during Munich, which had coincided with his own act of appeasement of Uncle Romesh Chand, Colin had written him a letter which expressed relief that Mr Chamberlain's common sense had averted hostilities. To Hari in Mayapore, Munich had meant nothing. He judged retrospectively that to the Mayapore English, blanketed as they were in the colonial warmth of their racial indestructibility, it had meant nothing either. He did not doubt, though, that the tone of Colin's latest letter was an accurate reflection of a mood now shared by the English as a whole, at home and abroad. He tried to enter it himself, but could not. The inspiration for it was not to be found in the Chillianwallah Bagh, nor was it to be found in the cantonment, in the magistrates' courts, in the sessions and appeal court of the District Judge, or even on the *maidan*, places with which Hari had become increasingly familiar as a result of his job on the *Gazette*. It was not to be found in them because he entered such places as an Indian. He entered by permission, not by right. He did not care for what he saw. He did not care for what he felt – the envy of the English and their institutions that came to fill the vacuum left by the loss of his own English identity. He found it depressingly easy to imagine Colin in the place of the young Englishman who sat as a magistrate – not precisely with the power of life or death (because his judicial powers were restricted) – but with the power to send a man who was old enough to be his father to jail for a year; depressingly easy because in this young man Colin himself could be seen, if only symbolically, in an unpleasant light. On the other hand, he could not imagine himself presiding in the place of the Indian magistrate who appeared one day in the place of the Englishman, and conducted his court with no less acidity or assurance. For the first time Hari found himself asking: What is an Indian doing sitting there, fining that man, jailing this woman, sending this case up to the court of sessions? He felt an unexpected resistance to the idea of an Indian doing an Englishman's work. When he paused to consider this resistance he realised that he had responded as a member of a subject race. The thought alarmed him.

*

'Such a fuss,' he wrote to Colin two months later (when, far away in Europe, the war had already begun) about the resignation of those provincial ministries which had been dominated by the Congress. 'Of course you can see both points of view. The Viceroy had to declare war on India's behalf because he's the King-Emperor's representative, and the

206

Germans now rank as the King's enemies. But since for some time now the British policy towards India has been to treat her as an embryo Dominion that only needs time to become self-governing, the Viceroy might at least have gone through the motions of consulting Indian leaders. Some people say that under the 1935 Act he was actually committed to consultation, but even if he wasn't how much more effective it would have been if the declaration could have been made with a simultaneous Indian statement of intention to co-operate freely. And one can understand why with all this talk going on about British War Aims the Indians feel one of them should be independence for India immediately the war is over. Failure to state that as a definite aim, with a definite date, has led a lot of Indians to believe that independence should be insisted on *now*. They say that only a free country fights with a will. And they fear a repetition after the war of all the prevarication that's been going on these last ten years or more. But I think they're a lot to blame for the delay themselves. The Congress says it represents all-India, but it doesn't. All this disagreement among themselves about who represents what just plays into the hands of the kind of English who don't want to give India up – the kind of people my father always assumed would get their way. On the whole I think he was probably right. For instance, now that the Congress ministries have all resigned most of the provinces are back under old-style rule of a Governor and a council, which seems to me the very sort of thing a sensible party would have wanted to avoid because it puts them back years politically. But then I have never been and probably never will be able to make sense of Indian politics. As for the effect of the war on the English here, so far as I can see there hasn't been any. Frankly, it's something that seems to be taking place in almost another world – if you can say that it's taking place anywhere. To judge from the news nothing much is happening, is it? The English here say that Hitler now realises he's bitten off more than he can chew and will end up by being a sensible chap and coming to some arrangement with France and Britain. Some Indians say that their own leaders, Nehru especially, have been warning the West for years about the threat Hitler has always represented.'

Apart from a short letter from Colin which was written over the Christmas of 1939, a Christmas which Colin had spent at home, after completing a course of training as an officer cadet, Hari heard nothing for nearly a year. A note from Mr Lindsey in the spring of 1940 informed him that Colin was 'somewhere in France' and that Hari's last letter had been forwarded to him. He said that the best thing for Hari to do in future would be to write to Colin at Didbury so that the letters could be sent on to wherever he happened to be.

Hari could not help remembering the attitude Colin's father had taken in 1938, an attitude he had begun to see during the past two years as proof that the man had stopped trusting him. 'What will he do with my letters?' he asked himself. 'Read them? Censor them? Not forward them if I say anything he thinks might upset Colin, or if I say something he doesn't personally like?' The shadow of Mr Lindsey fell across the notepaper whenever he wrote. Here was a further disruption to the even flow of thoughts going out to his old friend. The belief that he and Colin were growing further and further apart as a result not only of circumstances but also of the intervention of the powerful force of the malign spirit that had driven his father to death and himself into exile, now took hold of him, but the letter he eventually received from Colin in the August of 1940 seemed to show that between them nothing had fundamentally changed. The structure of a friendship is seldom submitted to analysis until it comes under pressure; and when Hari attempted an analysis of his friendship with Colin he found it healthily straightforward. It was an attraction of like for like that had long ago outgrown whatever initial morbid or childish curiosity there had been in the colours of the skin and the magic of the genes. Colin's letter turned back the years. Here was the authentic voice of his friend Lindsey. Reading between the lines Hari understood that Colin had not had an easy passage. This pegged them level again. The letter gave him little general information. Young Lindsey had been at Dunkirk, and since then 'in hospital for a bit, not because I was badly hurt but because it took rather a long time to get the proper treatment and dressings, and things went bad on me, but are all right now.' The letter was written from home on a spell of leave between leaving hospital and returning to his unit.

'It was a bloody shambles if you ask me. It amuses me when I hear Dad say to people his son was at Dunkirk, as if that was something to be proud of. My lasting reaction is one of anger, but undirected anger because no one person or even group of persons could be held responsible more than any other person or any other group. I suppose it was our old friend Nemesis catching up with us at last. I lost one good friend. I went to see his sister the other day. Ridiculous how one gets involved in these trite melodramatic situations. We both hated it. When I got back from hospital Dad gave me a couple of letters from you that he'd saved up. We had a bit of a row about that. I was worried what you'd have been thinking, not getting any answers. At first he said he hadn't wanted to bother me, and that you'd understand anyway that I was otherwise engaged. Then he admitted he'd read them and thought them full of a lot of "hot-headed" political stuff. Hari, I only tell you this so that if you ever write letters to me care of home again you can bear in mind that they might be read. He's promised not to do that ever again, and sees that it was wrong, but he's got some funny notions in his head nowadays. I don't want to hurt the old boy but in lots of ways he seems like a stranger to me. And that's a cliché situation too, isn't it? So cliché that I almost distrust my reactions to it. But there are so many things he says and does that get on my nerves. He keeps a *Times* wall map, and sticks pins in it like a general. The pin that's stuck in Dunkirk has a little paper union jack on it. I have an idea it represents me. Write and tell me some sensible things.'

Sensible things? On the day Hari received this letter he had been in the District Court listening to the appeal against conviction of a man accused and found guilty in the magistrate's court at Tanpur of stealing another man's cow and selling it to a man who had given it away as part of his daughter's dowry. The accused man said that the cow had become his property because its owner refused to stop it wandering on to his land and it had fed constantly free of cost and consumed fodder in excess of its market value. The appeal was based on the grounds that the Tanpur magistrate had not admitted the evidence of two witnesses who would swear to the fact that the convicted man had given the original owner repeated warnings of his intention to sell. Judge Menen dismissed the appeal and Hari then left the court because the next and last case was an appeal against imprisonment under section 188 of the Indian Penal Code, and Hari's editor never published reports of such controversial matters.

'Sensible things?' Hari wrote back to Colin. 'I suppose that in wartime especially you can reckon it sensible if not actually fair to imprison a man for speaking his mind. But this is not a purely wartime measure. It is a long-standing one provided for in a section of the criminal procedure code. Section 144 enables the civil authority to decide for itself that such and such a man is a potential local threat to public peace, and thus to *order* him to stay quiet on pain of arrest and imprisonment. If he disobeys the order he gets prosecuted and punished under section 188. I believe he can appeal as far as the provincial High Court if he has a mind to. I was at the District and Sessions Court on the day your letter came. I left the court just before the Judge (an Indian) heard such an appeal, so I know nothing of the actual proceedings. But I saw the prisoner on my way out, waiting with two constables, and recognised him as a fellow called Moti Lal. He recognised me too and said, "Hello, Coomer," and was then hustled in through the door prisoners enter the court by. The last time I saw this man he was working as a clerk at my uncle's depot at the railway sidings. I made inquiries when I got back to the office. It seems my uncle sacked him a few months ago, ostensibly for inefficiency. But I guess from what my editor told me that the real reason was that my uncle heard from someone that Moti Lal was mixed up with what you could call the underground side of the Congress Party. I asked my uncle's lawyer, a Brahmin called Srinivasan, what Moti Lal had actually been arrested for. It seems he was always "inciting" workers and students to strike or to riot and had disobeyed an order prohibiting him from giving a speech at a meeting of senior students at the Technical College. He was also suspected of being the leader of a group of young men who were printing and distributing seditious literature, but no evidence was found. Anyway, he got six months. And his appeal was dismissed. An ex-colleague on the *Gazette* – a fellow called Vidyasagar who now works for a radical newspaper called *The Mayapore Hindu* told me about it when I met him in court yesterday.

'Vidyasagar is a pleasant chap whom I rather like but have a bad conscience about. The first few weeks I worked on the *Gazette* the editor sent me round with him practically everywhere, and then sacked him. Vidya took it well. He said he guessed what was in the editor's mind when he was detailed to show me the ropes. He said, "I don't hold it against you, Kumar, because you don't know anything." He chips me a bit whenever we happen to meet and says that given time I might learn to be a good Indian.

'But I'm not sure I know what a good Indian *is*. Is he the fellow who joins the army (because it is a family tradition to join the army), or the fellow who is rich enough and ambitious enough to contribute money to Government War Funds, or is he the rebellious fellow who gets arrested like Moti Lal? Or is the good Indian the Mahatma, whom everyone here calls Gandhiji, and who last month, after Hitler had shown Europe what his army was made of, praised the French for surrendering and wrote to the British cabinet asking them to adopt 'a nobler and braver way of fighting', and let the Axis powers walk into Britain. The nobler and braver way means following his prescribed method of non-violent non-co-operation. That sounds like a 'good Indian'. But then there is Nehru, who obviously thinks this attitude is crazy. He seems to want to fight Hitler. He says England's difficulties aren't India's opportunity. But then he adds that India can't, because of that, be stopped from continuing her own struggle for freedom. Perhaps then, the good Indian is that ex-Congress fellow Subhas Chandra Bose who makes freedom the first priority and is now in Berlin, toadying to Hitler, and broadcasting to us telling us to break our chains. Or is he Mr Jinnah who has at last simplified the communal problem by demanding a separate state for Muslims if the Hindu-dominated Congress succeeds in getting rid of the British? Or is he one of the Indian princes who has a treaty with the British Crown that respects his sovereign rights and who doesn't intend to lose them simply because a lot of radical Indian politicians obtain control of British India? This is actually a bigger problem than I ever guessed, because the princes rule almost one-third of the whole of India's territory. And then again, should we forget all these sophisticated aspects of the problem of who is or is not a good Indian and see him as the simple peasant who is only interested in ridding himself of the burden of the local money lender and becoming entitled to the whole of whatever it is he grows? And where do the English stand in all this?

'The answer is that I don't really know because out here I don't rank as one. I never meet them, except superficially in my capacity as a member of the press at the kind of public social functions that would make *you* in beleaguered rationed England scream with rage or laughter. And then, if I speak to them, they stare at me in amazement because I talk like them. If one of them (one of the men – never one of the women) asks me how I learned to speak English so well, and I tell him, he looks astonished, almost hurt, as if I was pulling a fast one and expecting him to believe it.

'One of the things I gather they can't stand at the moment is the way the Americans (who aren't even in the war yet – if ever) are trying to butt in and force them to make concessions to the Indians whom of course the British look upon as their own private property. The British are cock-a-hoop that Churchill has taken over because he's the one Englishman who has always spoken out against any measure of liberal reform in the administration of the Indian Empire. His recent attempt following the defeat of the British Expeditionary Force in France to lull Indian ambitions with more vague promises of having a greater say in the running of their own country (which seems not to amount to much more than adding a few safe or acceptable Indians to the Viceroy's council) only makes the radical Indians laugh. They remember (so my editor tells me) all the promises that were made in the Great War – a war which Congress went all out to help to prosecute believing that the Crown was worth standing by because afterwards the Crown would reward them by recognising their claims to a measure of self-government. These were promises that were never fulfilled. Instead even sterner measures were taken to put down agitation and the whole sorry business of Great War promises ended in 1919 with the spectacle of the massacre in the Jallianwallah Bagh at Amritsar, when that chap General Dyer fired on a crowd of unarmed civilians who had no way of escaping and died in hundreds. The appearance of Churchill as head of the British war cabinet (greeted by the English here with such joy) has depressed the Indians. I expect they are being emotional about it. I'd no idea Churchill's name stank to this extent. They call him the arch-imperialist. Curious how what seems right for England should be the very thing that seems wrong for the part of the Empire that Disraeli once called the brightest jewel in her crown. Liberal Indians, of course, say that Churchill has always been a realist – even an opportunist – and will be astute enough to change coat once again and make liberal concessions. As proof of this they point to the fact that members of the socialist opposition have been brought into the cabinet to give the British Government a look of national solidarity.

'But I wonder about the outcome. I think there's no doubt that in the last twenty years – whether intentionally or not – the English *have* succeeded in dividing and ruling, and the kind of conversation I hear at these social functions I attend – Guides recruitment, Jumble Sales, mixed cricket matches (usually rained off and ending with a bun-fight in a series of tents invisibly marked Europeans Only and Other Races) – makes me realise the extent to which the English now seem to depend upon the divisions in Indian political opinion perpetuating their own rule at least until after the war, if not for some time beyond it. They are saying openly that it is 'no good leaving the bloody country because there's no Indian party represen-tative enough to hand it over to". They prefer Muslims to Hindus (because of the closer affinity that exists between God and Allah than exists between God and the Brahma), are constitutionally predisposed to Indian princes, emotionally affected by the thought of untouchables, and mad keen about the peasants who look upon any Raj as God. What they dislike is a black reflection of their own white radicalism which centuries ago led to the Magna Carta. They hate to remember that within Europe they were ever in arms against the feudal *status quo*, because being in arms against it out here is so very much *bad form*. They look upon India as a place that

211

they came to and took over when it was disorganised, and therefore think that they can't be blamed for the fact that it is disorganised now.

'But isn't two hundred years long enough to unify? They accept credit for all the improvements they've made. But can you claim credit for one without accepting blame for the other? Who, for instance, five years ago, had ever heard of the concept of Pakistan – the separate Muslim state? I can't believe that Pakistan will ever become a reality, but if it does it will be because the English prevaricated long enough to allow a favoured religious minority to seize a political opportunity.

'How this must puzzle you – that such an apparently domestic problem should take precedence in our minds over what has just happened in Europe. The English – since they are at war – call the recognition of that precedence sedition. The Americans look upon the resulting conflict as a storm in an English teacup which the English would be wise to pacify if they're to go on drinking tea at four o'clock every afternoon (which they only did after they opened up the East commercially). But of course the Americans see the closest threat to their security as coming from the Pacific side of their continent. Naturally they want a strong and unified India, so that if their potential enemies (the Japanese) ever get tough, those enemies will have to guard their back door as well as their front door.

'Working on this paper has forced me to look at the world and try and make sense out of it. But after I've looked at it I still ask myself where I stand in relation to it and that is what puzzles me to know. Can you understand that, Colin? At the moment there seems to be no one country that I owe an undivided duty to. Perhaps this is really the pattern of the future. I don't know whether that encourages me or alarms me. If there's no country, what else is left but the anthropological distinction of colour? That would be a terrible conflict because the scores that there are to settle at this level are desperate. I'm not sure, though, that the conflict isn't one that the human race deserves to undergo.'

*

So there were no 'sensible things' that Hari was able to tell Colin, but perhaps it was enough for each of them that over such a distance, of time as well as space, they still found it possible to make contact. There was a saying among young Indians that friendships made with white men seldom stood the strain of separation and never the acuter strain of reunion on the Indian's native soil.

'What would you do,' he asked Sister Ludmila, 'if you had a letter from an old friend that showed you were suddenly speaking different languages?' Perhaps it is odd that Kumar should have remembered this earlier *Journey's End* letter of Lindsey's, remembered it well enough to have it on his mind when he asked this question, as if the later one which Colin wrote after his baptism of fire asking him to tell him some sensible things was of less importance than the letter written in the nostalgic neo-patriotic mood

212

Hari had been puzzled by. But then the unexpected side of a man's personality is more memorable than the proof he may appear to give from time to time that he is unchanged, unchangeable. The image of Lindsey as someone who spoke a new language had made its mark on Kumar, so that later he was able to say to Sister Ludmila:

'I should have challenged him then. I should have told him what it had really been like for me in Mayapore. I should have said, "We've both changed, perhaps we no longer have anything in common. It's probably as ridiculous to believe that if I came back to Didbury now we should be at ease with each other as to believe that if you came out to Mayapore you would want even to be *seen* associating with me." Yes, I should have said that. I didn't say it because I didn't want to think it. We continued to exchange letters whose sole purpose was to reassure ourselves that there had been a time when we'd been immune to all pressures except those of innocence.

'When Colin came to India in 1941 and wrote to me from Meerut, I felt a sort of wild exhilaration. But it only lasted a very short while. I was resigned to what I knew must happen. If he had come straight to Mayapore there might have been a chance for us. But Meerut was a long way off. It seemed unlikely that he would ever be posted to a station close enough to Mayapore to make a meeting possible. And every week that went by could only add to the width of the gulf he'd realise there was between a man of his colour and a man of mine who had no official position, who was simply an Indian who worked for his living and lived in a native town. He would feel it widen to the point where he realised there was no bridging it at all, because the wish to bridge it had also gone. I remembered my own revulsion, my horror of the dirt and squalor and stink, and knew that Colin would feel a similar revulsion. But in his case there would be somewhere to escape to. There would be places to go and things to do that would provide a refuge. He would learn to need the refuge and then to accept it as one he had a duty to maintain, to protect against attack, to see in the end as the real India – the club, the mess, the bungalow, the English flowers in the garden, the clean, uniformed servants, the facilities for recreation, priority of service in shops and post-offices and banks, and trains; all the things that stem from the need to protect your sanity and end up bolstering your ego and feeding your prejudices.

'And then even if Colin had been strong-willed enough to resist these physical and spiritual temptations and to come to Mayapore to seek me out, where could we have met and talked for longer than an hour or two? Since the war began the black town has been out of bounds even to officers unless they are on official duty of some kind. I could not go to the Gymkhana. And what would *he* have made of the other club when it's hateful even to me? If we had met at Smith's Hotel there could have been an embarrassing scene. The Anglo-Indian proprietor doesn't like it if undistinguished Indians turn up there. At the Chinese Restaurant officers are supposed to use only the upstairs dining-room, and no Indian is allowed above the ground floor unless he holds the King's commission. We could have gone to the pictures but he would have disliked sitting in the seats I would be allowed to sit in. There is the English Coffee House, but it is not called the English Coffee House for nothing. If he were stationed in Mayapore perhaps we could meet for an hour or two in his quarters. Or perhaps he could get permission to cross the bridge and visit me in the Chillianwallah Bagh. I considered all these possibilities because they had to be thought out. And of course I saw that the one constant factor was not so much the place of meeting but the determination to meet. And what friendship can survive in circumstances like that?

'From Meerut he moved to Ambala, and then to somewhere near Lahore. In his first letter he said that on the map Meerut didn't look too far away from Mayapore. In his second he said he wondered if he would ever be close enough to make a meeting possible. In his third he did not mention the possibility of a meeting at all. And then I guessed that it had happened, in just three months. He had seen what he would only be able to call *my* India. And had been horrified. Even afraid. How could he know that I had been also horrified, also afraid? How could he know that for three years I had hoped, longed to be rescued, and had confused the idea of rescue with the idea of my Englishness and with the idea of my friendship with an Englishman? How could he know any of this? In one respect I was more English than he. As an Englishman he could admit his horror if not his fear. As an Anglicised Indian, the last thing I ever dared to do in my letters to *him* was admit either, for fear of being labelled "hysterical". And so I saw the awful thing that had happened – that looking at what he would have to call *my* India, the suspicion that I had returned to my natural element had been confirmed.

'Well, I say I saw it, then; but did I? Didn't I still make excuses for Colin and excuses for myself? When there was no letter from Lahore, didn't I say, "It's all right, he's not a civilian who has nothing to do but wake up, eat, go to work and come back home to see what the postman has brought." And then when the war came close, when the Japanese bombed Pearl Harbor, invaded Siam and Malaya and Burma and even fluttered the English dovecots in Mayapore, didn't I say to myself, "Well, poor old Colin is in the thick of it again?" And even suffer pangs of conscience that I hadn't been man enough to stand by something that was sure at least, my English upbringing, and join the army, fight for the people I had once felt kinship to, even if out here they obviously didn't feel kin to me? And didn't I see what a damned useless mess I'd made of my life since 1938, sulking as badly as those poor clerks I despised, making no new friends, repaying Aunt Shalini's kindness and affection with nothing that she would understand as love or even thanks?

'And then I saw them. English soldiers in the cantonment, with that familiar regimental name on their shoulder tabs. In the January of 1942. Familiar from the letters from Colin, first from Meerut, and then Ambala, and then from near Lahore. Captain C. Lindsey, then the name and number of the unit, followed by the address, and ending with the words India Command.'

*

'It was,' Sister Ludmila said, 'the second occasion I saw him drunk that he talked so, about Colin. I told you there had been such an occasion. After he had been to the temple, with her, with the girl. This is when he told me these things. He had never told her. I said to her, that time she came to the Sanctuary to say goodbye, "Do you know of the man Lindsey?" and she thought for a while and then said, "No, tell me."

'But I said, "It's not important." It wasn't important by then. To you perhaps it is important. So long after. "I saw him," young Kumar told me, "or at least I thought I saw him, coming out of the Imperial Bank, getting into an army truck that had the same insignia on its tailboard that those British soldiers wore on their sleeves." But he was not sure. And even then made excuses for him. Already at this time, you see, with the war suddenly brought to our doorstep by the Japanese, India had changed. There was this air of military rush and secrecy – and on the day he thought he saw Colin he went home expecting a letter saying, "Look, I'm stationed near Mayapore and sometimes come into the cantonment. Where can we meet?" But there was never such a letter. So as the days went by he thought, "No, the man I saw was not Colin. Colin could not come near Mayapore and send me no word at all. India could not have done that to him. Not that. How could India do that to anybody, let alone to Colin?"

'Can you imagine this? The feeling every day of Kumar's that if the post did not bring a letter then there would be a chance encounter somewhere in that area north of the river? Every day he cycled from the Chillianwallah Bagh to the office of the *Mayapore Gazette*, and on some days left the office and cycled to an event that he was required to report on. And this was another thing, another thing he told me. How even as a reporter he was invisible to white people. He would go to this event, that event. The gymkhana, the flower show, the Guides display, the Higher School Sports, the Technical College graduation, the Technical College cricket, the hospital fête. He knew nearly every important English civilian by sight and name and every distinguished Indian by sight and name, but they did not know him, for there was at these functions, you understand, what you call press officer or steward, and he, only, would be available to young Kumar, and sometimes not even him, because at an important function Mr Laxminarayan would also be in attendance. On this occasion, I mean the second occasion of his drunkenness he said, " – oh, there was a time when I thought I would make a name for myself. People would read the *Gazette* and say, What good English! How splendid! Who is this young Kumar? But they do not even know my name. At most I am 'the *Gazette* boy'. My name is never printed. No one really knows that I exist. I am a vaguely familiar face. But – I had it coming. He uses me. Laxminarayan. Sometimes he

215

keeps me chained to the desk turning *babu* English into decent English. Sometimes he sends me out. But he keeps me as an anonymous cog in his anonymous machine. Once I heard an Englishman say to him, 'I say, Laxminarayan, what's happening to the *Gazette*? Apart from Topics by 'Stroller' it isn't funny any more.' My editor only laughed. He did not explain why it isn't funny. He punishes me, you see, for Vidyasagar, for everything, for his own shortcomings."'

*

'It was at such a function,' Sister Ludmila said, 'that he saw this Lindsey for the second time. Saw and knew, beyond a doubt, standing not far away, close enough not to mistake the features, the expression, the mannerisms, the way of holding the body – whatever it was that had impressed itself indelibly on Kumar's mind as authentic Lindsey. What occasion? I forget. But remember it was February, the end of February. And that he mentioned the *maidan*. I have even still, this recollection, not my own but Kumar's. From Kumar I have inherited it. And feel almost as if I had been there. Am there. Towards evening. In Kumar's body. A dark face in the crowd. Has it been cricket? This I would not know. Cricket I do not understand. But I understand how towards evening on the *maidan* the races came uncertainly together in a brief intermingling pattern which from above, to God you understand, looked less informal than it looked from the ground because from above you would be able to see the white current and the dark current; as from a cliff, the sea, separating itself stream from stream and drift from drift, but amounting in God's Eyes to no more than total water.

'And he sees Lindsey. Ah well, as boys, what secrets of mind and body did they share? He told me of autumn in England. This too I see and feel. And am aware of young Kumar and young Lindsey as boys, running home across chill fields to come and toast their hands at a warm grate, just as I remember the blessing of gloves in a cold winter, and the way the breath could transform a window and fill the heart with a different kind of warmth. Ah, such safety. Such microcosmic power. To translate, to reduce, to cause to vanish with the breath alone the sugary fruits in their nest of lace-edged paper. To know that they are there, and yet not there. This is a magic of the soul. But it was a magic Kumar could not conjure, on the *maidan*, that hot evening, to make Lindsey disappear. Lindsey looked at him, and then away, without recognition, not understanding that in those *babu* clothes, under the bazaar topee, there was one black face he ought to have seen as being different from the rest.'

*

I am invisible, Kumar said, not only to white people because they are white and I am black but invisible to my white friend because he can no longer distinguish me in a crowd. He thinks – yes, this is what Lindsey thinks: 'They all look alike.' He makes me disappear. I am nothing. It is not his fault. He is right. I am nothing, nothing, nothing. I am the son of my father whose own father left home with a begging-bowl in his hand and a cloth round his loins, having blessed his children and committed their mother to their care. For a while she followed him and then sat by the roadside and returned home to live out her days in her private fantasy.

So I go from the *maidan*, in my bazaar trousers, my bazaar shirt, my Anglo-Indian topee, knowing that I am unrecognisable because I am nothing and would not be welcome if I were recognised. And meet, also coming away, Vidyasagar. He also is nothing. I do not remember the rest. There was clarity up to a point. Drinking cheap liquor in an airless room in a house in a back street on our own side of the river. And Vidyasagar laughing and telling the others that soon I would become a good Indian because the liquor was bootleg and we drank it at Government's expense. The others were young men like Vidya, dressed as Vidya was dressed, in shirts and trousers, like mine. But I remember helping them to destroy my topee because it was the badge of all government toadies. I remember too that they kept refilling my glass. They wanted me to be drunk. Partly it was malice, partly fun. In that poky little room there was desperation as well as fervour.

*

Sister Ludmila said: 'He found out later that they took him back to the Chillianwallah Bagh, right to the gates of his house, so that he would not be robbed, or picked up by the police, and then left him, thinking he went inside, but he wandered out on to the road again, going back towards the river and into the waste ground. And must have stumbled and fallen down into the ditch and there become unconscious and had his wallet stolen by someone who had seen him and followed him.

'"Who is it?" I asked Mr de Souza. "I don't know," he said, and turned him over to see if there were wounds on his back, and then turned him again, shining the torch on his face. And this is what I remember, of Bibighar beginning. The eyes shut, the black hair curling over the forehead. Ah! Such darkness! Such determination to reject.

'We got him on to the stretcher then, and carried him here to the Sanctuary. "This one is drunk, sister," Mr de Souza said. "We have carried home only a drunken man." "To be so drunk and so young," I said, "he must also be unhappy. Let him lie." And so he lay. And before I went to sleep I prayed for him.'

Part Six

CIVIL AND MILITARY

I

Military

*Edited Extracts from the unpublished memoirs of Brigadier A. V.
Reid, DSO, MC: 'A Simple Life.'*

Late in the March of 1942 when we were still in Rawalpindi and hard on
the heels of the news that our only son Alan was missing in Burma, I
received orders to go to Mayapore and assume command of the infantry
brigade then still in process of formation in that area. The news of this
appointment was given to me on the phone by General 'Tubby' Carter. I
was to leave at once and Tubby knew I should want a little time to break
the news to Meg who was still unfit and would be unable to accompany
me. I did not welcome the idea of leaving her on her own at a moment
when we were heavy of heart hoping for further news of Alan and yet
dreading what that news might be. After talking to Tubby I went straight
round to the nursing home and told Meg of the task that had been
entrusted to me.

She knew that in ordinary circumstances I would welcome the opportunity of getting back to a real job of soldiering. It had begun to look as if I
would spend the rest of the war with my feet under a desk, and with our son
also in uniform I suppose we had almost come to terms with this prospect
and had accepted the fact that age and experience must eventually make
way for youthful eagerness. But now, with Alan's fate uncertain, it seemed
as if some understanding deity had stepped in to redress the balance and
had called on me to play a part which – if the news of Alan was the worst
there could be when it came – would at least give me the satisfaction of
knowing I might strike an active blow at the enemy in return.

Meg reacted to the news as she had always done at times of crisis and
difficulty – with no sign of any thought for herself. Seeing how ill and pale
she looked I wished that it had been in my power to call Alan into the
room, fit and well, his usual cheery self, and so bring the roses back to her
cheeks. I am thankful that she was spared the news that he died working on
the infamous Burma–Siam railway, news which for me darkened the days

of our Victory, but I am grateful that she lived long enough to share with me the hope that was revived when we first heard that he was a prisoner-of-war and not dead, as we had feared. When I said goodbye to her on the eve of my departure for Mayapore there was also the burden of realising that these were dark days for our country. There was a tough job ahead.

I arrived in Mayapore on April 3rd (1942) and immediately set about the first phase of my task, that of welding the (—th) Indian Infantry Brigade into a well-trained fighting machine which I could lead confidently into the field to play its part in a theatre of war where the Jap had temporarily proved himself master. The task was not going to be an easy one. The majority of the troops were green, and the surrounding countryside, suitable enough for run-of-the-mill training, very dissimilar from the ground we should eventually be required to contest.

I had been in Mayapore many years before. I remembered it as a delightful station with some lakes out at a place called Banyaganj where there was excellent duck-shooting to be had. The old artillery mess was a fine example of 19th Century Anglo-Indian architecture, with a lovely view on to the *maidan*. It tended to get uncomfortably warm from March onwards but one could usually get away, down to Mussoorie or up to Darjeeling. It was not too far by train from Calcutta either, so one had plenty of opportunity to relax if one's duties allowed.

I did not have any illusions about relaxation now. Obviously there was a difference between a station as it once appeared to a young subaltern who had recently met the girl he was seriously thinking of asking to marry him, and the station, the same though it was, to which he returned nearly thirty years later as a senior officer at a moment when his country's fortunes were at a low ebb, and the country to which he had dedicated his life which represented the very cornerstone of the Empire had achieved considerable measures of self-government and stood virtually on the threshold of independence, an independence that had been postponed, for the moment, in the interests of the free world as a whole.

I went to Mayapore with every confidence in the troops, and with a fervent prayer that I should not personally be found wanting. I had been glad to hear from Tubby that there was a station commander on tap who would relieve the brigade staff of the general military administration of the district, and also to hear that the collector – called in this 'non-regulation' province a deputy commissioner – was a youngish fellow who was well thought of by Europeans and Indians alike. As senior military officer in the district, however, I knew I should be responsible in the last resort for the civil peace, and for the well-being of both soldiers and civilians, and the last thing I wanted was to become involved in the kind of situation that would distract me from my main job and give rise to the employment of troops on tasks that might have been avoided with a little forethought.

In view of the increasing unrest in India at this time, one of the first things I did after reaching Mayapore was to see the Deputy Commissioner, whose name was White, in order to listen to what he had to say about the state of his district and to tell him frankly that a lot of time and energy might be saved later if we agreed to show a firm hand at the first sign of trouble. I had already decided to bring the Brigade's British battalion – the (—th) Berkshires – into Mayapore and to move the 4/5 Pankot Rifles out of Mayapore, where I had found them, to the vicinity of Banyaganj where the Berkshires had been situated. My reasons were twofold. The British troops were newly out from home and I judged from my first inspection of them that they were far from happy in the rather primitive quarters which were all Banyaganj had to offer. There was an airfield in process of construction nearby (which I noted had denuded the lakes of duck), and scarcely a mile separated the far from salubrious coolie encampment from the battalion. More huts were being built but a lot of the men were under canvas and in April that was no joke. Conscious of the problem involved in appearing to make a distinction I nevertheless felt that Johnny Jawan would be less uncomfortable in Banyaganj than was Tommy Atkins. Also, in moving the Berkshires into the Mayapore barracks there was in my mind the belief that their presence in the cantonment might act as an extra deterrent to civil unrest, which at all costs I wished to avoid. I had, in any case, determined to use British soldiers in the first instance in the event of military aid being requested by the civil power.

In bringing the Berkshires into Mayapore I was also not unaware of the good effect this would have on our own people there – men and women doing difficult jobs at a time of special crisis. It was with this in mind too that I ordered an Army or War Week – complete with a military band – for the end of April, which was held on the *maidan* and was counted a great success. I feel that without immodesty (because the idea was mine but the fulfilment of it lies to the credit of those who organised or took part in it) I can claim that the excitement and 'lift' which the War Week gave to Mayapore distracted attention from the fact that the Cabinet Mission which Sir Winston – then Mr Churchill – had sent to Delhi, to seek an end to the deadlock between the British Government and those Indian politicians who claimed to represent the Indian people and were demanding even further measures of self-government, had failed to come to any kind of reasonable understanding. This was the mission known as the Cripps Mission, after its leader, Sir Stafford Cripps, the socialist minister who eventually became Chancellor of the Exchequer when, after the war, our island race paid its peculiar tribute to the architect of our victory by ousting him from office. It was after the failure of the Cripps Mission in April 1942 that Mr Gandhi launched his famous Quit India campaign, which of course looked to us like an invitation to the Emperor of Japan to walk in and take over the reins of government!

Unfortunately I found White – the Deputy Commissioner – not wholly alive to the situation I believed might face us if Indian leaders were allowed to continue to speak out against the war effort and rouse the masses to adopt a policy of what Mr Gandhi called non-violent non-co-operation, a policy that could bring the country to a standstill. White seemed to be convinced that when the Indian National Congress talked about non-violent non-co-operation they really meant non-violent. He obviously had more faith than I in the ability of a demonstrating crowd to resist the hysteria that can turn it in a moment into a howling mob intent on taking revenge for some imaginary act of brutality perpetrated by the police or the military. He did not, in fact, appear to anticipate demonstrations of any magnitude, unless they were organised purely for the purpose of offering *satyagraha*, in defiance of the Defence of India Rules, so that the authorities would be bound to arrest the demonstrators and have their prisons filled to overflowing. My first meeting with White took place before Mr Gandhi had launched his Quit India campaign, but at a time when it was clear that the Cabinet Mission headed by Cripps was failing to reach agreement about the way in which Indian leaders could be identified more closely with the affairs of the nation. White still seemed to hope that at the last moment a working arrangement would be made. I had no such expectations. Right from the beginning of the war with Germany relations between ourselves and the Indians had steadily deteriorated. At the outset of that war Congress members of the central assembly had walked out to protest the sending abroad of Indian troops to the Middle East and Singapore and the Congress ministries in the provinces had resigned because the Viceroy had declared war without consulting them! Whatever our faults in the past, I as a simple soldier with only rudimentary political views could not help feeling that the sincere efforts we made in the years before the war to hand over more power to the Indians themselves had revealed nothing so clearly as the fact that they had not achieved the political maturity that would have made the task of granting them self-government easy. The act of 1935 which envisaged a federal government at the centre, representative of all walks of Indian life, and elected states governments in the provinces, seemed to a man like myself (who had everything to lose and nothing to gain by Indian independence) a statesman-like, indeed noble concept, one that Britain could have been proud of as a fitting end to a glorious chapter in her imperial history. Unfortunately it led only to a scramble for power and the central federal government scheme came to nothing. One could not help feeling that the heartrending cries for freedom sounded hollow in retrospect as one watched the scramble and listened to the squabbles that broke out between Hindus, Muslims, Sikhs, Princes and others. The Congress, for instance, openly admitted that they took provincial office in 1937 to prove that the federal scheme was unworkable at the centre and that they alone represented India. Unfortunately, this belief of theirs, that they were the democratic majority, seemed to be borne out on paper at least by their sweeping victory in the elections that were held prior to their taking provincial office. Be that as it may, one would have thought that two years of provincial power, with little or no interference from the Governors, who retained a watching brief on behalf of the central government and the Crown, would have moulded statesmen, but the resignations after the declaration of war – which left the Governors with no alternative but to assume personal control – struck most of my fellow countrymen whose thoughts now lay principally with the safety of our homeland and the fight against tyranny, as proof that nothing had been learned at all of political responsibility, and that we could therefore no longer count on 'leading' Indians to take a broad view of the real things that were at stake in the free world.

I think it is true to say that we came to this realisation with reluctance, and that it was a measure of our continuing hope for Indian freedom and of our readiness to extend our patience right up to its breaking point that even in our darkest hour – the defeat of our arms in South-East Asia – we opened the bowling once again on Mr Churchill's initiative and tried hard to find a way of giving the Indians a fair crack of the whip, which was more than Hitler would have done and more than we knew could be expected of the Jap. It was clear to us, however, that chaps like Gandhi had got on to our scent and were in full cry, heedless of the ravenous yellow pack that was on to *them*, indeed on to all of us. On April 6th a few bombs fell on Madras. Even that did not seem to bring the Indians to their senses, in fact they blamed us more than they blamed the enemy! Inspired by Mr Gandhi they had got hold of the idea that there was no quarrel between India and Japan and that if the British absconded the Japanese wouldn't attack her. A little later, it is true, Mr Gandhi very kindly suggested that the British army could stay in India and use it as a base from which to fight the Japanese, and that in ports like Bombay and Calcutta he could promise there wouldn't be any riots to disrupt the flow of arms and war material! – providing of course that we had otherwise left the country to be ruled by himself and his colleagues! What he thought the strategic difference was between ceasing to govern but continuing to use India as a base was not easy to tell if you looked at the situation from the point of view of the Japanese High Command! It was clear to most of us that at last his peculiar theories were being shown up for what they were: the impractical dreams of a man who believed that everyone was – or should be – as simple and innocent as himself. There were times, of course, when we found it difficult to put even this well-meaning construction on his speeches and writings.

When I looked out on to the *maidan* from the window of my room in the old artillery mess in Mayapore, or drove round the cantonment, I could not help but feel proud of the years of British rule. Even in these turbulent times the charm of the cantonment helped one to bear in mind the calm, wise and enduring things. One had only to cross the river into the native town to see that in our cantonments and civil lines we had set an example for others to follow and laid down a design for civilised life that the Indians would one day inherit. It seemed odd to think that in the battle that lay ahead to stop all this from falling into the hands of the Japanese the Indians were not on our side.

I remembered vividly the hours spent as a young man, exercising Rajah on the Mayapore *maidan*, and practising polo shots with Nigel Orme, who was ADC to General Grahame and won a posthumous VC at Passchendaele. Rajah, as readers may recall from an earlier chapter, was the first polo pony I owned, and Nigel Orme, although senior to me in rank and service, one of the best and truest friends I ever had. It looked to me as if fate had called me back to the place where I first got the 'feel' of India and first realised that whatever success or failure was in store for me in the profession I had chosen, there would always be a sense of one-ness with the country and a feeling of identification with our aspirations for it. I remembered Meg as she had been in my thoughts then, all those years ago, so calm, so collected, kind and generous, ever ready with a smile – to me the most beautiful girl in the world. And I thought of our son, Alan, and of our daughter Caroline – safe now from Nazi or Japanese frightfulness, thank heaven, with her Aunt Cissie in Toronto. These three were truly my hostages to fortune and our fine boy seemed already to have been taken from us in part payment. More than anything else in the world I wished for victory to our arms, health and happiness for Meg, and to be reunited with her and darling Caroline and young Alan. I do not think that any of us older serving soldiers can be blamed if, at the time, we felt bitter that the country which had benefited in so many ways from British rule appeared determined to hinder our efforts to save it from invasion at a time when we could least spare the strength. Pondering these matters on the level at which they affected me personally I couldn't help wishing that I could be left to concentrate on my main task and leave the politicians to 'muddle through' in their own mysterious ways. But I knew that this could not be. The brigade was my responsibility, but so was the safety of our women and children and the peace of the district as a whole. Those of us who were in contact with 'places higher up' knew that it was thought we must be prepared to face the gravest danger from within the camp as well as from outside it; from the enemy in the tent as well as from the enemy at the gate; and that it was not beyond the bounds of possibility that the Congress planned the kind of open rebellion that could snowball into a campaign of terror and bloodshed and civil war such as we had not seen in India since the days of the Mutiny. As events proved later our anxieties on this score were only too well-founded. Before the summer was out the country was in the grip of rebellion and in Mayapore the commotions got off to the worst kind of start. It was in this pleasant old district that two dastardly attacks on Englishwomen were made, within a few hours of each other; the first upon an elderly mission teacher, Miss Crane, and the second on a young woman, Daphne Manners, who was criminally assaulted in a place called the Bibighar Gardens.

Although on first acquaintance Mr Deputy Commissioner White and I did not, as they say nowadays, hit it off, I came presently to admire his tenacity. For me his physical courage was never in doubt, and I judged, correctly as it turned out, that he would never allow any personal reservations he might have about official government policy to sway him in his dutiful application of it in his own district. As a case in point, when I asked him rather bluntly what he would do if he had orders to arrest leaders of the local sub-committee of the Congress party (I knew that District Officers had been warned to keep special note of those of them whose prompt imprisonment might halt the tide of rebellion), he replied, quite simply, 'Well, arrest them of course,' but then added, 'even though I know that that is the very worst thing we can do.'

I asked him why he felt this. He said, 'Because the kind of men I would have to arrest are those who honestly believe in non-violence and have the power to move the crowd to self-sacrifice rather than to attack. Put such fellows in clink and you leave the crowd to a different kind of leader altogether.'

I could not agree, but recognised the sincerity of White's convictions. Of course to me, mass *satyagraha* was almost as harmful as open revolt. Naturally I asked him what he knew of or proposed to do about the kind of leader who might take the place of the Congressmen he had such faith in. He said, 'Oh well, that's like looking for needles in haystacks. A few are known. You can arrest those. But the others go free, and among them probably the most efficient because they've been efficient enough not to become known. You could spend your life working up a secret file and still miss the key chaps because Congress doesn't know them and you don't know them. They're nothing to do with Congress at all. They're young or middle-aged fellows with bees in their bonnets who think Congress the lickspittle of the Raj. Well, who has a life to spend detecting that kind of needle in this kind of haystack? Isn't it better to leave the fellows who have nothing to gain by violence free to control the crowd and direct it in true *satyagraha*?'

I told him that what he said probably made sense, so long as you could trust originally in the concept of non-violence, which I personally thought a lot of eye-wash. Pressed further, White admitted that he left what he called 'the needles in the haystack' to his District Superintendent of Police, a man called Merrick, whom I had met on a previous occasion and instinctively liked.

Although White's attitude left me in some uncertainty about the degree of determination to be expected from the civil power in the event of trouble in this district, I was confident that the police could be counted on to act swiftly and efficiently if need be.

White's thinking was wholly 'modern', typical of the new-style administration of the Thirties that had to take into account every half-baked notion that was relevant to the workable solution of a problem. The judge was an Indian called Menen, an old-school Indian I was glad to notice, but somewhat self-contained in true judicial style. Of the triumvirate only young Merrick, the District Superintendent of Police, seemed to me to have seized happily upon the greater freedom of action that the war and the Congress provincial resignations had given to district rule.

I had a special meeting with Merrick and told him that I relied upon him to use his discretion, particularly in regard to what the Deputy Commissioner had called 'the needles in the haystack'. I put it to him bluntly that I had a brigade to command and train for use against the enemy at the gate and not, if I could help it, for use against the enemy in the camp. I told him I would appreciate it if he stuck his neck out occasionally. I had not mistaken my man. He was young enough still to respond to simple issues with the right mixture of probity and keenness. I could not help but admire him, too, for his outspokenness. He was a man who came from what he called 'a very ordinary middle-class background'. The Indian Police had been the one job he felt he could do. I knew what he meant, and liked him for his total lack of pretence. Police duties are always disagreeable, but they have to be carried out. Now that we were at war with the Axis Powers he regretted the circumstances that had led him to undertake service in a field that precluded him from wearing a different uniform. He asked me, in fact, what chance there was of strings being pulled to release him so that he could join up 'even as a private'. Thinking of Alan – whom physically he somewhat resembled – I appreciated his patriotic scale of values, but was unable to give him any hope of a transfer. In any case, I realised that in the present situation he was more valuable to his country as head of the local police than he would be as an untrained junior officer, let alone as a private soldier. He promised to comply with my request to keep me informed, *sub rosa*, of the temper of the district as he gauged it to be.

Having seen and talked to White and to Merrick I felt that I had done as much as could be done for the moment to buy time in which to concentrate on my job without too often casting a glance in the direction of a local threat to our security. In any case the arrival of my third battalion, the —th Ranpurs, gave me plenty to do. Originally I had been promised a battalion of Sikhs, but one from my old regiment was, needless to say, an even greater boost to my morale! Bringing one company of the Ranpurs into the Mayapore barracks (and so relieving the Berkshires of some of their station guard duties) I sent their remaining companies and the battalion headquarters into the area of Marpuri, northwest of Mayapore, an area I had already selected as the best of two likely sites chosen by my brigade staff. Now that my command was complete I could really get down to work!

*

The Berkshires were settling down well. The move from Banyaganj into the cantonment had certainly done the trick. The old barracks near the artillery mess were spacious and cool, and the men enjoyed the unaccustomed luxury of being able to avail themselves within reason of the ministrations of the native servants attached to the barracks, many of whom were the sons of men who had looked after an earlier generation of Tommies. They were now also closer on hand to the home entertainments so readily laid on by our ladies. It was, incidentally, many years since there had actually been a gunner regiment stationed in Mayapore, but the artillery mess had been famous in its day and naturally the name had stuck. In recent years Mayapore had been the home of an NCOs' school and the cool weather station of the Pankots. Since the war began it had turned itself virtually into a brigade staging point. Unfortunately, from the point of view of my brigade staff, the colonel-commandant of the NCOs' school who had also acted as station commander was on sick leave upon my arrival – a leave that turned out to be permanent because the school was transferred to the Punjab – so I inherited on paper at least the station commander's role. The Station Staff Officer (whom I managed to retain) had to do most of the work that would normally have rested on the station commander's shoulders, but he was an old ranker and a hard and dedicated worker.

I had elected to live in the artillery mess itself rather than move into the accommodation that was available to me, not only because my poor Meg was unable to join me and establish a household, which she had done so often before, in so many different parts of India, but because I felt I wanted to be on constant call and in a position to keep my staff on its toes. The rooms I occupied in the mess in the old guest suite which overlooked the *maidan*, were spacious but simple. There in the little sitting-room that I had turned into a private office, I could find a retreat from the press of routine to think out the best solutions to the many problems that confronted me. But it was in this room, towards the end of June, when the rains had just begun, that Tubby Carter rang me with the news that Alan was reported a prisoner-of-war. Somehow one had always gone on hoping that he would reach India safely with one of the parties of our troops and civilians who had struggled back against great odds and in conditions of great privation to be restored to those who most sorely missed them. I asked Tubby if he would break the news to Meg. And here Tubby proved himself once again a good and true friend who, although my senior in rank, was always ready to use his seniority for the welfare of an old comrade-in-arms. He ordered me to Rawalpindi so that I could break the news to her myself. In less than thirty-two hours of Tubby's telephone call I was at Meg's bedside.

Neither Meg nor I had any illusions about what it meant to be a captive of the Japanese, but we found solace in the knowledge that Alan was alive and – if we knew our son – probably kicking. Speaking of him to her, I felt the relief it was to do so knowing that at least it was in order to think of him in the present rather than the past tense. That evening Tubby came to the nursing home with a bottle of champagne. In ordinary circumstances it might have seemed wrong to drink champagne at a time when our son was probably suffering hardship, but Tubby put things into perspective by raising his glass and inviting us to drink to Alan's safe return. I was proud of Meg when she raised her glass too and said simply, 'To Alan,' and smiled as if he were there in the room and the occasion of the toast a happy one. In the few long weeks that we had been separated she seemed to have gone down hill alarmingly. She had lost more weight and her eyes no longer sparkled. I realised suddenly that Tubby had not ordered me back to Rawalpindi only to break the news of Alan's capture to her but so that I could face up to the graver news that eventually I would have to bear.

When we had said goodnight to Meg, Tubby took me in to Colonel 'Billy' Aitken's office and left me there. Billy said, 'I'm afraid there's no doubt. Meg's got cancer.' We had known Billy for years. In civilian life he could have risen to the top of his profession and become a rich man, but as he had so often said, he preferred to give his time to looking after those of his countrymen – and women – who lived ordinary lives doing often dull and unrewarding jobs abroad, than to prescribing sugar-pills for 'fashionable' but hysterical women in Harley Street. I asked him, 'How long?' For a moment we looked at each other. He guessed I would prefer to know the truth. He said, 'Perhaps six months. Perhaps three. Perhaps less. We shall operate, but the end will be the same.' He left me alone for a bit, for which I was grateful. I found it hard to believe that in just a few minutes I had to adjust myself to accept that darling Meg was to be taken from me by a fate even crueller than that which had taken Alan. Alan at least had had the satisfaction of getting in a blow or two. I think I realised as I sat there alone in Billy Aitken's office that I should never see Alan again either.

Billy and Tubby came back together and took me to Billy's quarters. Tubby asked me whether I wanted to relinquish my command and come back to 'Pindi. He hinted that there was a job going that was mine for the asking and would carry a major-general's hat. I asked him not to press me for an answer until I had had time to think it over. A room had been reserved for me at the club. They drove me back there and I made an effort to sleep so that I could wake up and make my decision in a clearer state of mind. In the morning I asked Billy the most important thing, which I had forgotten to ask the previous evening: whether Meg knew how ill she was. He said he had not told her but he was sure she was in no doubt. I said, 'Billy, *don't* tell her.' He knew then what my decision was, to go back to my brigade and to go back as soon as possible, so that neither Meg nor I would have to pretend for longer than we could manage. I knew this was my duty. I knew, too, that this was what Meg would want for us both. One cannot adopt a way of life without accepting every one of its responsibilities. It was hard to accept them at this moment, but I was sustained in the belief that Meg would understand and find strength herself in my decision. In spite of this, our parting was far from easy. I thought afterwards on the 'plane to Calcutta on which Tubby had wangled me a seat that it would have been easier if she had asked me not to go back to Mayapore. There seemed to be between us a terrible burden of things we had never said to each other. Before I left, Tubby assured me that he would send for me to be with Meg at the end, but this did not prove to be possible. I shall not write her name again. Goodbye dear Meg, cherished wife and mother of my children. God willing, we shall be reunited in a happier place.

I had laid it down that at the commencement of the wet monsoon our training should continue so far as possible without interruption. I had managed through constant pressure in the appropriate quarters to get the last company of the Pankots in Banyaganj out of tents into huts before the rains began. The Ranpurs in Marpuri were less fortunate, but if they tended to be damp in one respect the same could not be said of their spirits!

In July our field training began to get under way and I was heartened by the keenness with which all ranks responded to the challenge of getting out on to the ground, even when the 'enemy' was only imaginary. My brigade major, young Ewart Mackay, proved worth his weight in gold. A regular, his enthusiasm was infectious. It spread throughout the Brigade Headquarters staff. Cheerful, efficient and an all-round sportsman (he shone particularly at tennis) he was also a dedicated soldier and could be a stern disciplinarian. Later in the war he commanded with valour and distinction the 2nd Muzzafirabad Guides, his old regiment. His pretty wife, Christine (the elder daughter of General 'Sporran' Robertson) was with him at Mayapore and fulfilled the role of hostess with charm and grace. Christine and Ewart gave me 'open house' at the delightful bungalow they occupied in Fort Road, and it was Christine who organised the little dinner parties which, in other circumstances, would have been another and still dearer woman's task to arrange.

Heartened as I was on the two occasions in July when we took the brigade 'out' to test its mobility and degree of cohesion, I was still unable to lose sight of the role it played as a local force for order. In taking it out the fact was not lost on me that the resulting display of military strength (more impressive to those not in the know than to those who were!) could not but make an impression on the population who were being increasingly subjected to Congress anti-war propaganda. One of the most despicable aspects of that propaganda was the tale put about that in the retreat from Burma and Malaya the authorities had shown indifference to the welfare of Indian troops and the native population. To anyone such as myself who knew the affection the English officer felt for his sepoys and native NCOs, the imaginary picture painted by Congress of Indian soldiers left behind without leaders to be captured or killed, or of groups of leaderless native troops and panicky villagers being pushed off roads, railways and ferries to give priority to 'fleeing whites' was laughable.

It was in the middle of July that my divisional (and area) commander told me that local civil authorities had received secret orders from provincial governors to combat in every possible way the poison of the insidious and lying propaganda of the Indian National Congress. This was the occasion when I sought yet a further discussion with the Deputy Commissioner.

From my point of view White was very much the unknown quantity. I was confident in the police and sure of the loyalty of our own Indian troops. Every man of the Berkshires had been trained in the drill of duties in aid of

228

the civil power, and at the first sign of disturbances patrols and riot squads were ready to go into action. Although these young English boys (many of them civilians themselves little more than a year ago, and with only a very sketchy idea of the problems of administering Imperial possessions abroad) found the drill of 'duties in aid' rather farcical, not to say puzzling when they recalled those of their countrymen who had already laid down their lives to protect India from both Nazi and Japanese tyranny, they very quickly adjusted themselves to accepting the role they might have to play as one more job to be done. When I gave this battalion of 'modern' young English lads an address on the subject of military aid to the civil authorities I began by quoting those immortal lines of the soldier's poet Rudyard Kipling:

'—it's Tommy this, an' Tommy that, an'
   "Tommy, fall be'ind,"
But it's "Please to walk in front, sir," when
   there's trouble in the wind—'

And I suppose a psychologist would say that I couldn't have chosen a better way of putting the situation to them!

One could say that the basic thinking behind the military drill for suppression of civil disturbance is as simple as this: that failing the retreat of the crowd in the face of an armed might even greater than that of the police, the life of one ringleader, forfeited, equals the saving of many other lives. There have been times in our history when this simple equation has not looked, on the ground, as simple as it looks in the textbooks. I am thinking here, of course, of the *cause célèbre* of General Dyer in Amritsar in 1919, who found himself in a position not unlike that which I myself had to anticipate in 1942.

In 1919, as in 1942, the country was seething with unrest, and all the signs indicated open rebellion on a scale equal to that of the Mutiny in 1857. Ordered to Amritsar, Dyer came to a conclusion which the historians – fortified by the hindsight historians are fortunate enough to be able to bring to their aid – have described as fatal: the conclusion that in Amritsar there was to be found the very centre of an imminent armed revolt that could well lead to the destruction of our people and our property and the end of our Imperial rule. Learning that a crowd intended to forgather at a certain hour in a large but enclosed plot of ground called the Jallianwallah Bagh, Dyer prohibited the meeting by written and verbal proclamation in accordance with the rules laid down. This proclamation was defied and his warnings ignored. He took personal command of the troops he sent to disperse it. His on-the-spot orders to disperse also having been defied, he then ordered the troops to fire. The Jallianwallah Bagh, from a military point of view, was a death-trap, and many civilians died, including women and children.

Ever since the Dyer affair, which was seized upon by 'reformers' as a stick to beat us with, the army had naturally become supersensitive to the issues involved, and we were now in the unhappy position of finding ourselves in what practically amounted to a strait-jacket.

In the first place, unless the civil authority had collapsed or was otherwise non-operational – when it would be a question of proclaiming martial law – the military was powerless to intervene unless called upon, in writing, by the civil power, usually the senior civilian in the area. Such a request for aid was, in a sense, really only a call to stand by.

For example:

To: O. C. Troops

I have come to the conclusion that the Civil Authorities are unable to control the situation and that the assistance of the military has become necessary. I accordingly request such assistance.

Place:
Date: Time: Signature:
                                 Appointment.

Imagine now that having received such a request I had a platoon of infantry standing by. The civil authority might then ask me to give support at a point where trouble was imminent or had already broken out. Let us say, for instance (to choose one of the many incidents that occurred in Mayapore in August 1942) that a threatening crowd had gathered outside the main Hindu temple in the square upon which, having crossed the river by the main Mandir Gate bridge, there debouched the road that led from the civil lines.

The platoon of the Berkshires which had hastened by truck from District Headquarters, debussed some two hundred yards from the crowd who were crossing the bridge and hastily formed up on the road in a hollow square (there being shops and buildings on either side of the road whose roof tops or windows represented a threat to the flanks and the rear). In the centre of the hollow square thus formed by the sections of the platoon were to be found the following personnel:

> Platoon commander
> Representative of the Police
> Magistrate
> Bugler
> Bannermen
> Medical orderly
> Platoon Sergeant
> Signals orderly
> Diarist

The meaning of the word 'aid' comes into clearer perspective when you remember that apart from the platoon commander there was also a magistrate present. In the affair of the crowd crossing the Mandir Gate bridge the magistrate in question was a Mr Poulson, who was senior assistant to the Deputy Commissioner.

In the case we are considering, there were three distinct phases of operation. The first being what we might call the Testing phase, the second that of Decision and the third that of the Action which logically followed the decision.

Testing consisted first in the ordering by the platoon commander to the bugler to sound off, thus calling the attention of the crowd to the existence of a legally constituted force of opposition. The warning note having been given, the first of the bannermen raised the banner on which orders in English and the vernacular were inscribed. These were orders to disperse. Sometimes the raising of such a banner was enough to make a crowd obey. After the raising of the first banner a second note on the bugle was sounded and then, if the platoon commander considered that the situation warranted it, the second banner was raised. Upon this was inscribed again in English and the vernacular a clear warning that unless the crowd dispersed force would be resorted to. Since the crowd was usually making a pretty frightful din on its own account one could not rely on verbal warnings being heard: hence, the banners.

It was at the moment when the second banner giving warning of intention to fire was raised that both the platoon commander and the magistrate found themselves in the relative no-man's-land of having to make a decision which the text-books necessarily left to the man on the spot.

Fortunately, in the case of the first Mandir Gate bridge riot, the attending magistrate, Mr Poulson, did not hesitate to give the platoon commander the signed chit requesting him to open fire once it was seen that the crowd had no intention of falling back or dispersing. By the time all the necessary drill had been completed only a few yards separated the front of the mob from the forward file of riflemen, and brickbats were being thrown. From the town, on the other side of the river, a pall of smoke showed where an act of arson had already been perpetrated. (This was the kotwali, or police station, near the temple.) At the same time, unnoticed by the troops on the Mandir Gate Bridge road, a detachment from the crowd was making for the railway station along the tracks from the level crossing where the police had failed to hold them, and yet another platoon of the Berkshires was hastening to that area from District Headquarters to reinforce the police (commanded at that point by Mr Merrick, their District Superintendent).

Meanwhile, to return to our platoon on the Mandir Gate Bridge road: as so often happened the mob had pushed old women to the front to inhibit the soldiers. It was the platoon commander's job to select as targets one or two of the men in the crowd, who, by their actions, he judged to be its leaders. There are occasions when only one of the soldiers, a man who has distinguished himself as a marksman, is issued with live ammunition, but the disturbances in Mayapore had gone far beyond the stage when such an

231

insurance against a high casualty rate was considered wise. Nevertheless, in this present instance, the subaltern in charge now spoke individually to each man of the forward file, gave two of them specific targets and told the others to fire over the heads of the crowd when he gave his order to fire. It required considerable self-discipline and composure to go patiently through such motions while under attack, but badly bruised on the shoulder by a stone as he was the subaltern did so. He had to remember not to call any man by his name in case he was overheard by someone in the crowd which would lead to the man being identified! In the resulting volley both the marksmen found their targets and the crowd faltered, but only for as long as it took for new leaders to come forward and urge them in the Mahatma's current phrase 'to do or die'. This time the subaltern had no alternative but to order a second volley in which two civilians were killed and five wounded, including, as chance would have it, one woman. Seizing the initiative, the platoon commander ordered the detachment to advance and continue firing, but over the heads of the now retreating mob. The wounded woman was the first to be given attention by the medical orderly. The wound was found to be superficial because, no doubt, the soldier whose bullet had hit her had been sighting upon a man who had moved at the crucial moment.

Present at these proceedings there was one man, usually a member of the battalion or brigade intelligence section, whose duty was that of 'diarist'; that is to say, he was required to observe and make notes for later inclusion in the war diary of the unit or formation. This was a dispassionate factual report which did not take into account the thought processes leading to particular decisions which the subaltern's own report would do. The magistrate would also be required to submit a report on the incident to the civil authority. The representative from the police (an inspector or sub-inspector) would do likewise to his superior officer. In this way a number of reports on the same incident would be available if required by any court set up to investigate charges of brutality or excessive use of force. I must emphasise, however, that it was not always possible to fulfil, to the letter, all of the drill laid down for the employment of troops in these duties. As perhaps even the least imaginative of readers may judge, there could arise situations in which any one or even several of the 'required' personnel were not available, and only the need for instant action undeniably present!

*

In going into the above details I am conscious not only of digressing but of having moved my story, such as it is, forward to the point where the reader has found himself in the midst of action without knowing the stages that led to it. So I go back now to the day in July when I had a further meeting with Mr White, the Deputy Commissioner who, I knew, had recently received orders to combat the anti-war propaganda of the Indian National

Congress, and whose attitude I felt it necessary to re-assess and, if necessary, confide to my divisional commander who, as area commander also, had virtually the entire province in his military jurisdiction.

I found White somewhat changed in regard to his appreciation of the situation. I personally had little doubt but that some kind of confrontation was inevitable, and was heartened to some extent to realise that the Deputy Commissioner also now seemed to believe that the situation had probably gone beyond the point where it could be retrieved. He was, however, still convinced that the 'disturbances', when they came, would be of a 'non-violent' nature, unless the leaders of the Congress were put away, in which case, he said, he felt unable to answer for the civil peace. I pounced on this and asked him point-blank, 'In the event of such arrests then, you would think it advisable to ask us to stand by?' He said at once that I had 'taken him up too literally'. He was in an uneasy frame of mind and I saw that there was no sense in pressing him, much as I should have liked to come away with a clear understanding. With regard to the Congress propaganda, he said he had talked to the editors of the various local newspapers and given warnings to those whose recent tendency had been to support the 'anti-war' line. This seemed to be satisfactory. I asked him to be good enough to bear in mind as often as he could the situation from my point of view – which was that of a man who was interested in the conditions obtaining in Mayapore first of all as they did or did not affect my training programme and then as they affected our people.

It was at this meeting that White said something that has stayed in my mind ever since as an indication of the true sense of vocation our finest colonial administrators have always felt. 'Brigadier,' he said, 'please bear one thing in mind yourself if my attitude gives you any cause to feel dissatisfied. If your assistance is asked for I know I can rely on it and upon its effectiveness. To you, afterwards, it will have been an unpleasant task effectively carried out and will therefore rank in your scale of values as one of your successes. To me, in my scale, to have called you in at all could never rank as anything but one of my personal failures.' I protested that *personal* failure was putting rather too strong a point on it but he smiled and shook his head. Most of the men whom he had had to mark down for arrest if orders came from government were his personal friends.

Then he said, 'But don't be alarmed, Brigadier. I am also a realist. I use the word "failure" but I'm not a fellow to wallow in it.'

With this I had to be content, and on the whole was, because as I have said before I had come to respect White for the sense of responsibility that after several meetings I could not help but get an impression of from his very demeanour, which was reserved, somewhat 'intellectual', but very down-to-earth and practical in terms of action. White was fairly typical, I realise, of the new race of District Officers who reached maturity just at the moment when our Indian Empire was due to come of age and receive 'the key of the door' from our government at home – perhaps prematurely, but as a token of our patience and goodwill and historical undertakings.

After the failure of the Cripps Mission and the subsequent opening of Mr Gandhi's Quit India campaign, I recollect that the main question in the minds of most Englishmen was whether or no Mr Gandhi would succeed in carrying the Indian National Congress (certainly the strongest political force in India) to the point where they would collectively identify themselves with his curious doctrine and so give it the force and impetus of an organised, nationwide movement. I have never been a close follower of the ups and downs of politicians, but I was aware that Mr Gandhi had been 'in' and 'out' of Congress, sometimes pursuing a personal policy that the Congress endorsed and sometimes one that they did not. Mr Nehru, who was the actual leader of the Congress, had for some time been considered by us as a more sensible middle-of-the-way fellow who knew the international language of politicians and could possibly be counted on to see sense. A lot of his life recently had been spent in jail, but as I recollect it he had been freed in order to take part in the negotiations with the cabinet mission and was still at large and very much a force to be reckoned with. It was clear to us that he found Mr Gandhi an embarrassment and for a time our hopes rested upon his more practical and statesmanlike attitude winning the day.

Perhaps at this stage I should rehearse exactly what we knew was at stake and what we felt the opposition amounted to. In the first place we had our backs to the wall in the Far East and had not yet been able to regain the initiative and/or end the stalemate in Europe and North Africa. At any moment we expected the Jap to commence operations against the eastern bulwark of India. A Japanese victory in India would have been disastrous. Lose India and the British land contribution to what had become a global war would virtually be confined to the islands of our homeland itself, and to the action in North Africa, and the main weight of resistance to totalitarianism thrown on to the Americas. We regarded India as a place it would be madness (as Mr Gandhi begged us) to make 'an orderly retreat from'! Apart from the strategic necessity of holding India there was of course also the question of her wealth and resources.

So much for what was at stake. As for the opposition, this amounted in the first instance to demands (inspired by Gandhi) that we leave India 'to God or to anarchy' or alternatively were challenged to hold it against a massive campaign of 'non-violent non-co-operation', which meant in effect that the native population would go on strike and in no way assist us to maintain the country as a going concern from which we could train, equip, supply and launch an army to chuck the Jap out of the Eastern archipelago!

Surely, we thought, men like Nehru would resist such a suicidal design?

At the beginning of August it looked like a foregone conclusion that Nehru had, as we say, sold the pass for reasons best known to himself. He had not found in himself the political strength to resist the Mahatma at this moment. Everything now depended upon the vote of the All-India Congress Committee on Mr Gandhi's Quit India resolution. This was made on August the 8th. Historians since have attempted to prove that the passing of the resolution was no more sinister than words on paper and that Mr Gandhi hadn't even outlined in his own mind the precise course that consolidated non-violent non-co-operation was to take. My own belief was and remains that the non-violent non-co-operation movement was planned down almost to fine detail by underground members of the Congress acting on instructions from those who wished to look publicly like that famous trio of monkeys, 'hearing no evil, speaking no evil, seeing no evil'.

How else can I account for the violence in my own district that erupted on the very day following the passing of the Quit India resolution and the dawn arrests of members of the Congress party? A violence which immediately involved a European woman, Miss Crane, the mission teacher, and on the same night was directed at the defenceless person of a young English girl, the niece of a man famous in the province some years before as governor; a girl who was violently attacked and outraged by a gang of hooligans in the area known as the Bibighar Gardens? These two incidents were portents of the greatest danger to our people, and coming hard on each other's heels as they did, I could only come to one conclusion, that the safety of English people, particularly of our women, was in grave peril.

*

As it so happened I was out at Marpuri with the Ranpurs when I received a message early in the evening of August the 9th from my staff-captain to the effect that there had been civil commotion in two outlying subdivisions of the district, Dibrapur and Tanpur, and that a detachment of police from Mayapore, accompanied by Mr Poulson, the assistant commissioner, had driven out in that direction during the late afternoon and rescued a police patrol and a group of telegraph linesmen from the police post at a village called Candgarh where they had been imprisoned by rioters. Proceeding along the road towards Tanpur, Mr Poulson had encountered first a burnt-out car and some distance farther on the English mission teacher guarding the body of a dead Indian, one of her subordinates in the mission schools, who had been battered to death by, presumably, the same roaming mob. As Mr Poulson told me later, it was the sight of the mission teacher sitting on the roadside in the pouring rain that led him to believe that the troubles in Mayapore were to be of a greater degree than either he or Mr White had anticipated. I had spent the night at Marpuri with the Ranpurs, and did not know either of the Congress Vote or of the arrests of Congress leaders until my staff captain telephoned me about mid-morning on the 9th. He had had a signal from Division, and had also been informed by the Deputy Commissioner that a number of local congressmen in the district had now been detained as planned. During this first telephone call my staff captain told me everything was quiet and that the Deputy Commissioner had said there was no cause at present for alarm. I had therefore resolved to stay at Marpuri to watch the battalion exercise. But receiving the further communication from my staff captain about the incident near Tanpur, early in the evening, I resolved to return forthwith and ordered him to meet me at the Deputy Commissioner's bungalow.

I reached the Deputy Commissioner's bungalow in Mayapore at about nine o'clock. There was now further trouble in the offing. Mr White had recently had the news that this young English girl, Miss Manners, was 'missing'. Merrick, the head of the police, was out looking for her. White told me that following the rumours of violence out at Tanpur and the attack on the mission teacher several of the English women who lived in the civil lines had moved into the Gymkhana club – one of the sites previously selected as a collection point in the event of serious threat to lives and property. Taking White on one side I asked him whether he didn't think it wise for us to give a combined display of strength – joint patrols of police and military – either that night or first thing in the morning. He said he did not think so because the town itself was quiet. Most of the shops in the bazaar had shut down. This was against regulations but he felt it better to allow the population to remain indoors and not to provoke them. I questioned him about the mob violence in Dibrapur and Tanpur. He said he believed it was the result of a 'spontaneous reaction' to the news of the arrests, on the part of men who had the time and inclination to make a bit of trouble. Meanwhile communications with Tanpur and Dibrapur had been restored and the police there had reported that they were again in control of their subdivisions. Several men had been arrested in Tanpur, among them, it was thought, one or two of those who had attacked the mission teacher and murdered her Indian companion. The teacher herself was in the Mayapore General Hospital suffering from shock and exposure.

Later, just as I was leaving, young Poulson came in. He had toured the cantonment as far as the Mandir Gate bridge, crossed the bridge and driven down Jail Road to the prison to supervise the transfer of the jailed Congressmen to the railway station where he had seen them safely stowed away in a special carriage and sent off on the journey to a destination that was to be kept secret. I had a few words with Poulson who was obviously less sanguine than his chief about the immediate future. He was pretty concerned for his wife, because she was pregnant. They already had one little girl, and she was with them in Mayapore. The Whites' two children, twin boys, had gone back to school in England the year before the war began. One knew that Mrs White must feel the separation rather badly in the present circumstances, but she was a tireless and forthright woman – rather more commanding in 'presence' than her husband who was very much the 'thinker'. She never showed any sign of self-pity at the prospect of not seeing her sons again until the war was won, but I knew how much this must weigh on her mind.

I had hoped, as well, to see Merrick, but he was out searching for the missing girl – Miss Manners – who lived with a Lady Chatterjee, in one of the old houses near the Bibighar Gardens. Lady Chatterjee had been a friend of Sir Henry and Lady Manners when Sir Henry was Governor of the province. Sir Henry was dead, but I had known Lady Manners slightly in Rawalpindi and recollected that I had met the Manners girl on some occasion or other both in 'Pindi and in Mayapore. She had been in 'Pindi with her aunt and since coming to Mayapore to stay with Lady Chatterjee had been doing voluntary work at the Mayapore General Hospital. She had rather shocked the ladies of the cantonment by her attachment to a young Indian. I remembered Christine Mackay, the wife of my brigade major, saying something about it. On the whole, since coming to Mayapore, I had been too occupied to pay much attention to cantonment gossip, but realising who it was who was 'missing' I could not help feeling a serious premonition of trouble.

Asking White to keep me informed I then returned to my own quarters and put a call through to the Area Commander. I was heartened to hear from him that, as a whole, the province – indeed the country in general – seemed settled and quiet. The Congress committees had been banned by Government and many members of them detained under the Defence of India Rules as a precautionary measure. The General said he felt that the arrests had nipped the Congress revolt nicely in the bud and that we could now concentrate on our job of training and equipping our forces. I told him of the things that had occurred that day in my own sphere of command but he said they sounded to him like isolated incidents that had gone off at half-cock because the men who were supposed to have been behind them were now safely under lock and key. I went to bed in a relatively easy frame of mind and slept soundly, realising how tired I was as a result of my twenty-four-hour visit to the Ranpurs.

My orderly woke me at seven, as I had instructed him, and told me that the District Superintendent of Police was waiting to see me. Guessing that something was up I gave orders for him to be brought to my room at once. Arriving a few minutes later he apologised for coming so early and for intruding on my privacy. Spick and span as he was I judged from his look of fatigue and strain that he had been up all night. I said, 'Well, Merrick, what's the grief this morning?'

He told me that the missing girl, Miss Manners, had been attacked in the Bibighar Gardens the previous night and raped by a gang of ruffians. Fortunately he had called at Lady Chatterjee's home for the second time that evening only a few minutes after the poor girl had herself returned after running all the way in a state of considerable distress through deserted, ill-lit roads. Merrick had at once driven to his headquarters and collected a squad and rushed to the Bibighar area. He had found five men, not far away, drinking home-distilled liquor in a hut on the other side of the Bibighar bridge. He at once arrested them (the distillation and drinking of such liquor was in any case illegal) and was then fortunate enough to find Miss Manners's bicycle, which had been stolen by one of the culprits, in a ditch outside a house in the Chillianwallah Bagh. Entering the house he discovered that there lived in it the Indian youth with whom Miss Manners had been associated. This youth, whose name as I recollect it was Kumar, had cuts and abrasions on his face. Merrick immediately arrested him and then secured all six fellows in the cells at his headquarters.

I congratulated him on his prompt action but asked him why he had come personally to see me at this early hour. He said there were several reasons. First, he wished to be sure that I had the earliest possible notification of the 'incident' of which he took the most serious view. Secondly, he wanted to know whether he had my permission to transfer the detained men to the guard room of the Berkshires if he judged that it would be wise to move them to a place of greater security. Thirdly, he wished to put it to me that in his opinion the Deputy Commissioner was seriously misjudging the gravity of the situation, a situation which in a few hours had seen violent attacks on *two* English women, and the murder of an Indian attached to a Christian mission. He then reminded me that earlier in the summer I had asked him to 'stick his neck out' if he thought it necessary.

I could not help but ask him in what way he felt he was sticking it out now. He said he was convinced that the men he had arrested last night were those who had assaulted Miss Manners but that it might be difficult to prove. I said, 'Well, the poor girl can probably identify them,' but he doubted it. He had asked if she knew any of the men responsible but she said she didn't because it had all been 'done in darkness' and she had not seen them clearly enough to be able to identify them. Since one of the fellows arrested was the man she had been associating with, Merrick believed that for the moment at any rate she was not telling the truth, but he hoped she would do so when she came out of her shock and realised who her real friends were. Meanwhile he had the fellows under lock and key and had spent most of the night interrogating them. They still protested their complete innocence in the matter, but he was convinced of their guilt, particularly in the case of the man Kumar, who obviously stole her bicycle and who was caught in the act of bathing his face to reduce or remove the evidence of cuts and bruises received when the girl fought back before being overpowered.

I asked Merrick if it was known how Miss Manners had come to be at the Bibighar. He said he was afraid it looked to him as if she had gone to meet Kumar there, an aspect of the case that he hoped could be glossed over for the girl's sake. He had met her himself on several occasions and counted himself as one of her friends, enough of a friend anyway to have warned her not long ago that her association with the Indian was one she would be well advised to end. But she seemed to be completely under Kumar's spell. Kumar, Merrick said, had once been taken in for questioning by the police when they were searching the town for a prisoner who had escaped from jail. During questioning it transpired that Kumar knew the escaped man, whose name was Moti Lal, but there was no evidence at that time that their acquaintance was more than superficial. Although 'westernised',

Merrick considered Kumar to be a pretty unsavoury character, aware of his attraction for women and not above latching on to a white woman for the pleasure of humiliating her in subtle ways. He worked on a local newspaper, and gave no obvious trouble, but was known to have consorted with young men suspected of anarchistic or revolutionary activities – young men of the type of the other five arrested. Several of these men had been seen with Kumar on other occasions and they were all men on whose activities the police had been keeping an eye. Merrick's opinion was that Kumar and these five had plotted together to take advantage of Kumar's association with Miss Manners. Going to the Bibighar that night, expecting to find only Kumar, she found not only Kumar but five others – men who then set on her in the most cowardly and despicable way.

I was deeply shocked by this sorry tale and agreed with Merrick that the less said about her attachment to one of the suspected men the better, especially if things came to the head of a public trial. Meanwhile, I agreed, he seemed to have sufficient grounds to hold the men in custody on suspicion of this crime alone, which I thought was fortunate because once the story got round that an English girl had been outraged there wasn't a white man or woman in the country who wouldn't rejoice that the suspects were already apprehended. The effect on the Indian population of knowing that this kind of thing couldn't be got away with would also be exemplary.

Merrick said he was glad to feel that I approved of his actions. He believed that the events of the previous day were simply a prelude to a violence which, if becoming no worse, would certainly become more widespread and would take all our combined efforts to resist. He had heard of my suggestion to White that both police and military patrols should be seen to be on the alert today and regretted that this proposal had been turned down.

I invited Merrick to have breakfast with me but he declined and said he must be getting back to work. Before he went I told him that if circumstances warranted it one or all of the six prisoners could be moved into the greater security of the Berkshires' guard room, providing that the police supplied their own guards and the Berkshires were absolved of direct responsibility for them. Merrick obviously feared an attack on his own jail by a 'do or die' crowd bent on releasing the men arrested for the rape. He had no doubt that by this morning the whole town knew of the incident. In India it was almost impossible to keep anything secret. Rumours began with the whispered gossip of native servants and spread quickly to the rest of the population. But a crowd attracted by the idea of rescuing their 'heroes' would have to show a lot of determination to try to penetrate the Berkshires' lines because this would mean a direct attack on a military installation – and on the whole this was something Indian mobs usually avoided. Much as I sometimes found it irksome not to take immediate control of this explosive situation – which an attack on the military would have entitled me to do without signed permission of the civil authority –

the last thing I wanted was to become involved at this level, which is why I qualified my permission to move the prisoners into military lines with the phrase 'if circumstances warranted it'. But I certainly endorsed Merrick's opinion that the six prisoners must be held under maximum security. Their forcible release to go free and boast of their attack on an English-woman was at all costs to be avoided.

After breakfast I rang the Deputy Commissioner and told him that I had spoken to Merrick, and that Merrick had told me about the attack on Miss Manners. I again offered to co-operate with military patrols as a precautionary propaganda measure, but he said the district was quiet and that he was trying hard to maintain an atmosphere of normality. Most District Headquarters availed themselves of the services of what I suppose we must call spies or informers. White's informers reported to him that the population was more puzzled than angry, uncertain what their arrested Congress leaders really expected of them. To provoke them now was, he was sure, the very last thing a sensible man should do. Fortunately, for the present anyway, Muslim and Hindu communities were living together on terms of amity and although in a sense this could be counted a bad sign – since it suggested an alliance against the English – in another sense it was a good thing, because there was little or no danger of a communal situation developing that would snowball into something worse.

As usual, when I spoke to the Deputy Commissioner I was impressed by his calm and balanced thinking. I asked what he felt about the attack on Miss Manners and whether he didn't see it as a prelude to attacks on Europeans in general. He said it might well have been an isolated incident, such as that at Tanpur, the work of hooligans, men who had probably come in to Mayapore from one of the outlying villages expecting to find it in the grip of civil disturbance, only to be disappointed and therefore capable of taking it out on the first defenceless person they happened to see. I said the impression I got from Merrick was that the culprits were not villagers but young anarchists who lived in Mayapore. To this he did not immediately reply, so I asked him whether he thought the men arrested were not the real culprits. He said he had to keep an open mind on the subject and that a lot depended on the girl's own evidence once she was fit enough to give it. He thought Merrick might have made a mistake, but could not criticise him for his prompt action, at least not in the light of what Merrick himself had told him of the circumstances attending the arrests.

Having spoken to the Deputy Commissioner I then called my own staff together, told them of the situation as seen (a) by Merrick and (b) by Mr White, and finally (c) as seen by myself, that is to say one that was potentially grave but at present under the control of those whose duty it was to control it. In other words, for us, I said, it was 'business as usual', and I ordered my staff car for ten o'clock so that I could pay an unexpected visit to the Pankots out at Banyaganj. Taking me on one side when the others had gone, Ewart Mackay told me that he and his wife had already heard about the attack on Miss Manners and his wife's private view was that it was something the poor girl had been heading for, although naturally Christine and he were shocked and grieved. The point was, though, that Christine Mackay felt I should know that she did not see the attack on Miss Manners as evidence that European women generally were in danger. She had asked if the man Kumar had been involved and Ewart said she would be more than glad to hear that he had actually been arrested.

In other words, from this private source, I had confirmation of the reasonableness of young Merrick's personal suspicions but also of the Deputy Commissioner's broader impersonal attitude. I therefore set off for Banyaganj fairly confident that there was at least a breathing space for us to concentrate on more important things. In Banyaganj itself work was proceeding on the construction of the airfield. My heart went out to those poor and simple labourers, men and women, who needed every anna they could earn and did not lightly drop their tools and their baskets of stones at anyone's beck and call. I could not help thinking that if every one of the women working so hard in the heat and humidity of that August morning, with her ragged saree torn and mud-spattered, had taken the Mahatma at his word, and gone home to spin cotton she would have been hard put to it to feed her children – children for whose welfare, and hers, a committee of our own women had been set up and was actually represented that morning by young Mavis Poulson and the wife of the Station Staff Officer, who were doing their best to attend single-handed to the screaming wants of Hindu and Muslim babies of both sexes and to pregnant mothers who had collapsed under the weight of the baskets. Fortunately there were some stout-looking lads from the RAF in the vicinity so I felt that Mrs Poulson and Mrs Brown wouldn't come to much harm, and continued my journey to the headquarters of the Pankots. I spent a pleasant day there, watching their battle drill.

This was indeed the calm before the storm! I returned to Mayapore at about 5 pm and gave Mrs Poulson and Mrs Brown a lift, to save them the discomfort of the journey back to the cantonment in the RAF bus. Mrs Poulson also seemed to share Christine Mackay's view of the fate that had overtaken Miss Manners. Mrs Poulson said that the whole business must be extremely distasteful to Lady Chatterjee who probably felt a special degree of responsibility for what had happened, not only because Miss Manners was her house guest but because she herself was an Indian. I asked Mrs Poulson what she knew of the man Kumar and she said at once, hearing from me that he had been arrested, 'Well, you've got the right man. A trouble-maker if ever I saw one.' She thought that if poor Miss Manners had not been such an 'innocent' about India this distressing business would never have arisen, and she added how extraordinary and yet how logical it was that the two Europeans who had so far suffered injury in the present troubles were both women, and both women of radical, pro-Indian views. Mrs Brown, I noticed, was less positive on the subject, but I put this down to shyness. Her husband, as readers may remember, had risen from the ranks. I made a special point of trying to bring her into the conversation. I had a great respect for her husband's capabilities as Station Staff Officer. I am sure, however, that she felt much the same way as did Mrs Poulson, that is to say that they both thought the girl had been unwise but of course were dismayed by her fate and determined to stand by her. I was touched by this as yet further proof of our solidarity. Armed thus, one can face any crisis.

I dropped Mrs Brown in the cantonment bazaar where she had some shopping to do and took Mrs Poulson back to her bungalow. Declining her kind offer to come in and have a drink I left her to her task of supervising the putting to bed of her little daughter whose name, I think, was Anne, and ordered the driver to return to brigade headquarters. The rain had let up again and the late afternoon sun had come out. The *maidan* looked peaceful and I was reminded of those far-off days when I was a young man without a care in the world. That evening after dinner I wrote some personal letters and retired early to work on a field-training scheme that my staff had drafted for my consideration. Reading it through, and finding little to criticise, I felt a glow of confidence. If only the scheme had been more than a scheme! The Japanese would not have been resting so peacefully in their beds that night!

This was, however, to be the last comfortable night's sleep I was to enjoy myself for many days.

*

In the personal diary which I kept at this time the space allotted to the following day – August 11th – is blank, but there is a brief note on August 12th headed 2 a.m. which reads, 'A moment's respite after a day of widespread riots throughout the district. I received at 20.00 hours (Aug 11) a request for aid from the deputy commissioner. Cold comfort for our forces in Assam and Burma to know that those whose role is to supply and eventually reinforce them are being hindered in this way.'

Looking back to that day in August which marked the beginning of disturbances throughout most of the country, and remembering – as hour by hour reports of commotions, riots, arson and sabotage began to come in – the sense that grew of what we had feared and tried to stop finally facing us I cannot but be puzzled by the opinion still held in some quarters that the uprising was indeed a spontaneous expression of the country's anger at the imprisonment of their leaders. In my opinion, final proof to the contrary, if any is needed, lies in the words spoken by the Mahatma to his followers at the time of his arrest, 'Do or die.' Nothing, I feel, could be plainer than that. I did not hear of those words until the 11th, on which day the crowds that collected and attacked police stations, telegraph offices, and sabotaged stretches of railway line, were crying them as their motto.

Again the immediate seat of disturbances was in Tanpur and Dibrapur, and the police in those areas were sorely pressed. During the afternoon of the 11th the police in Mayapore, directed by mounted officers, were fully occupied in dispersing and redispersing the crowds that attempted to collect. Several constables were injured. A score of men were arrested and taken to jail. In a village just south of Mayapore an Indian sub-divisional officer of the uncovenanted civil service was attacked and held prisoner in the police post and was not rescued until the following day when our own patrols scoured the area. The Congress flag was run up in the village, and also over the court house in Dibrapur – a town that was cut off for several days. The post-office in Dibrapur, which had been attacked on the 9th of August (the day of the attack on the mission school teacher) was this time destroyed by fire. Until our troops retrieved the situation on the 17th August Dibrapur – 70-odd miles away from Mayapore – was in the hands of the mob. In fact one of the mob's leaders declared himself Deputy Commissioner and district headquarters to have been transferred from Mayapore to Dibrapur! The sub-divisional officer who was legally and constitutionally in charge of that sub-division (again an Indian) was at first imprisoned but then released and installed in the court house as 'District and Sessions Judge'. He later claimed that he was forced to co-operate with the self-appointed Deputy Commissioner and that he had hidden most of the money from the local treasury to save it from falling into the rioters' hands. Restoration of the money and his previous good record probably saved him from paying the penalty of his apparent defection to the side of the rioters. There were, unfortunately, several cases spread throughout the country where magistrates and even senior Indian district officers complied with the orders of the mob leaders, and considerable sums of Government's money was stolen. In some areas the new self-appointed officials 'fined' townsmen and villagers and put the money into their own pockets along with revenues they had collected 'on behalf of free India'. There was not, I think, any instance of an English civil servant being coerced in this way, and there was, thank God, virtually no loss of European life. The one instance I remember was the murder of two Air Force officers (not in our own district) by a mob who – imagining them to be the pilots of an aircraft that had recently taken part in a punitive raid on a mutinous village nearby – immediately set on them in this foul way and tore them to pieces.

But to go back to the 11th, and to Mayapore itself: the District Superintendent of Police showed, throughout that day, considerable tactical ability. It was impossible for Merrick to have men everywhere they were needed, but there were three main danger areas – the area of the Chillianwallah Bagh Extension road which led from the south of the town directly to the Bibighar bridge, the 'square' opposite the Tirupati temple leading to the Mandir Gate bridge and the road leading west to the jail (the jail on the black town side of the river, not the cells at Police Headquarters in the civil lines where the six men suspected of the rape were being held). It was anticipated that there would be two main objectives of attack – the jail and the civil lines.

The day had begun normally enough until the police in the city reported that 'hartal' was being observed. At 8 a.m. however (an hour that more or less coincided with the renewed uprising in Dibrapur) a crowd was found to be collecting on the Chillianwallah Bagh Extension road. This was dispersed by 9.30 a.m. but at once there was evidence that the dispersal had only led to the collection of another crowd in the vicinity of Jail road. Fortunately, Merrick had anticipated the moves that might be made in the event of any organised defiance of the agents of law and order and had already ordered his forces to deploy. There were several skirmishes. The post office on Jail road was threatened but secured. Meanwhile reports had begun to come in of 'isolated' acts of violence and sabotage in the district's outlying areas. At 1200 hours the sub-inspector of police in charge of the kotwali near the Tirupati temple received an 'ultimatum' to join the forces of 'free India' and co-operate in the 'release of the six martyrs of the Bibighar Gardens'. This ultimatum was delivered to him in the form of a printed pamphlet! The attempt to identify the rebellion in Mayapore with the Bibighar Gardens affair as though it were simply a crusade to release men whom the population thought wrongfully imprisoned was, I thought, not only a cunning move but proof of the existence of underground leaders of considerable intelligence. With this Merrick agreed. At first sight of the pamphlet he had at once raided the offices of an English language newspaper called *The Mayapore Hindu* and found a press there that suggested that not only newspapers were printed on those premises but that they were also equipped to print in the vernacular. The type from which the pamphlet had been set up in English and Hindi had already been 'distributed' but Merrick felt justified in arresting every member of the staff actually on the premises and in destroying the press from which pamphlets of the kind distributed could have been run off.

This operation had been completed by 1300 hours, only 60 minutes after the delivery of the pamphlet to the kotwali in the temple square, which said a lot for Merrick's capacity for prompt action, as well as for his intelligence or 'spy' system. He told me that afternoon when I visited District Headquarters where the Deputy Commissioner and his staff were gathered in force, that one of the men on *The Mayapore Hindu* whom he had arrested was a close friend of the man Kumar, the principal suspect in the Manners case. He felt that it was very likely now that by interrogating this fellow (the note in my diary gives his name as Vidyasagar) Kumar's duplicity would be proved.

I confess that I felt sickened to realise the extent to which some of these so-called educated young Indians would go to defy and attack the people who had given them the opportunity to make something of themselves. I was also concerned about the capacity they had for violence in the sacred name of *satyagraha*. I said as much to Merrick who then reminded me that, in his job, he had to deal almost every day with fellows of this kind. If he sometimes 'bent the rules' and paid them back in their own coin, he believed that the end justified the means. He said he was almost 'off his head' at the thought that a decent girl like Daphne Manners, with every advantage civilised life had to offer, should have been taken in by a fellow like Kumar who had had the benefit of an English public school education. I was astonished to have this information about Kumar's background and felt that my own sense of values had been pretty well knocked for six.

Merrick described Gandhi on this occasion (when we drank a hasty cup of tea together) as a 'crazy old man' who had completely lost touch with the people he thought he still led, and so was the dupe of his own 'dreams and crazy illusions', and had no idea how much he was laughed at by the kind of young men, he, Merrick, had to keep in order.

That afternoon at district headquarters I found the Deputy Commissioner calm and decisive in his reactions to the reports that were coming in. I told him that I was prepared to order the provost in charge of the military police to assist in the transfer of the six prisoners to the Berkshires' lines. This took White by surprise because apparently Merrick had not discussed such a possibility with him. He said he had no intention of aggravating racial feeling by placing six men suspected of raping an English woman under the noses of English soldiers. I grew rather heated at what I thought to be an unwarranted criticism of my men's capacity for self-restraint. He then assured me he had not meant any such thing, but simply that the job of guarding such prisoners could only be extremely distasteful and therefore bad for the morale of the Berkshires who, if called out in aid, would need to exercise a high degree of level temper and self-discipline. It was bad enough, he said, that the news of the attack on Miss Manners had become current. He did not wish to have the Berkshires 'reminded hourly by the suspects' presence in their midst of an affair that can only excite strong basic emotions'.

On this subject we did not see eye to eye, and broke off conversation somewhat tartly. At eight o'clock that evening I received the expected request for aid, at once ordered what we had come to call the riot squad to report to district headquarters and the rest of the Berkshires to stand by, and drove to White's bungalow to which he had now returned and where I found him in conference with Judge Menen and members of his staff. Judge Menen looked as imperturbable as ever. I could not help wondering whether under that grave, judicial exterior lurked a heart that beat in unison with his countrymen's hopes for 'freedom'.

Since 4 p.m. it had apparently become clear to White that the available police were in insufficient strength to continue their task of discouraging the collection of crowds, particularly as a detachment of the city police had been sent to reinforce the police in Tanpur and attempt to re-establish contact with Dibrapur, thereby reducing their strength in Mayapore. Anticipating from the temper of the town's population that determined efforts might be made the following day to penetrate the civil lines, and getting some impression of the scale and nature of the revolt from his staff's collation of the day's reports from his own and other districts and provinces, the Deputy Commissioner decided, round about 7.30 p.m., to ask for military support. Reaching him at about 8.15 I was thanked for our prompt response. He said he still hoped that on the morrow it would not prove necessary to request the full weight of our strength. We agreed to keep the platoon of the Berkshires at District Headquarters on immediate call and to send some troops overnight to Dibrapur in the company of a magistrate and a police officer to see what was going on there and to try for pacification and reduction. Wishing to keep the Berkshires intact, I decided that the platoon going to Dibrapur should come from the Ranpurs at Marpuri. They were well placed to cross the river at a point some six miles west of Mayapore and to approach Dibrapur by a flank road from which they might catch the rebels in Dibrapur by surprise. I gave the orders at once by telephone to the duty officer at Marpuri.

I decided to be present myself at the rendezvous between the Ranpurs and the two representatives of the civil power and left with the latter in my staff car at 2200 hours. Making contact with the Ranpurs I then led the party to the bridge at a village called Tanipuram where we found the local police on their toes. The sub-inspector in charge reported that at dusk men had been seen approaching the bridge who had gone away at the sight of his men patrolling. The village had been quiet all day in spite of the rumours of Mayapore town being in a state of turmoil. Leaving the Ranpurs to proceed in the direction of Dibrapur I then drove back to the place of rendezvous – the railway halt that served the surrounding villages. I telephoned through to Mayapore and managed to get connected to District Headquarters. I left a message that the Ranpurs were safely on their way, and then – feeling I had done as much as was possible that night – was driven home. By now we were in the early hours of the morning of the 12th and a steady rain was falling which I felt would do much to dampen the ardour of any potential night-raiders!

*

In the morning, after only three hours or so sleep, my signals officer woke me with a message from the platoon of Ranpurs who had been on their way to Dibrapur that they had been held up on the road about ten miles from Dibrapur by a roadblock in the shape of a felled tree. No obstacle to the men, it was of course one to the transport. The tree had been removed with some difficulty because of the rain which was still falling and the slippery state of the road and kutcha edges. The subaltern in charge of the platoon, a young Indian, had proposed to send two sections ahead on foot to the next village one mile distant but the accompanying magistrate and the police officer had insisted on the party remaining intact while the obstruction was dealt with. If the subaltern had not been persuaded against his better judgment it is possible that the destruction of the bridge beyond the village – a bridge across a tributary of the main river flowing through Mayapore – might have been stopped. The bridge was blown some twenty minutes after they had begun work on clearing the roadblock. They heard the sound of the explosion. Reaching the village (which was deserted of all but a few

246

old men and women) the subaltern had again got on to brigade signals and reported that the road to Dibrapur had now been rendered impassable for transport. He requested further orders.

This was the situation I was immediately faced with on the morning of the 12th. A glance at the map quickly confirmed that there was no alternative route to Dibrapur that did not involve a retracing of steps almost as far north as the bridge at Tanipuram, and the alternative route from there was little better than a good-weather track, from the point of view of mechanical transport. The bridge at Tanipuram only had to be blown now and I realised I had temporarily lost the use of two 3-ton lorries, a 15-cwt truck and valuable wireless equipment!

Fortunately my Brigade Intelligence Officer, a somewhat reserved but extremely able young man called Davidson, had already seen the danger and anticipated my orders for the police to be requested to make immediate contact with their post at the bridge at Tanipuram to check the situation there and give warning to be on the look-out for saboteurs. I rang the Deputy Commissioner and told him that I stood to lose valuable transport and equipment unless I had carte-blanche to secure the road. I told him why, and added that it seemed clear that the rebels in Dibrapur were led by pretty skilled men and that Dibrapur had obviously been chosen as the strong point for the rebellion in this district.

White gave the situation a moment or two's thought and then said that on the whole he agreed with me and gave me carte-blanche to command the road while the Ranpurs were 'withdrawn'. I told him that I had not necessarily been contemplating withdrawal, but instead the securing of the road during whatever period was required to re-bridge the river at the scene of demolition. We were sadly short of the necessary equipment, but even if it were several hours before the Ranpurs could proceed it was surely better late than never!

His answer amazed me. He said, 'No, I request withdrawal but agree to your commanding the road until your men are back this side of Tanipuram. I'll confirm that in writing at once.'

I asked him, 'And what if the bridge has gone at Tanipuram?'

He said, 'That will call for another appreciation, but speaking off the cuff it would look to me as if you had lost immediate use of three trucks and a wireless.' He then rang off. I dressed hurriedly and had breakfast, determined that if news came in that the bridge at Tanipuram had also gone I would order the Ranpurs to make their weight felt in that area, magistrate or no magistrate. But I was relieved, presently, to have a call from police headquarters to tell me that Tanipuram reported the bridge still standing and no sign of trouble.

I had decided not to withdraw the Ranpurs until the promised written request to that effect had come in from the Deputy Commissioner. I received this request by 0800 hours and at once told Ewart to order the transport and men to come back.

I then discussed the situation at Dibrapur with Davidson, my IO, who said he imagined that the view of the Deputy Commissioner was that if Dibrapur *were* the centre of the rebellion in the district, it could be left to stew in its own juice for a while, because the rebels had no 'troops' as such, and Mayapore was of greater importance. He thought that the Deputy Commissioner had decided that the pacification of his district should spread outwards from Mayapore.

Of all my staff, I suppose Davidson had achieved the greatest degree of frankness with me (except for Ewart who was by way of being a personal friend). When I first assumed command, the IO had been a young fellow called Lindsey, whom I took an immediate shine to. He had seen action in France with the ill-fated British Expeditionary Force. His association with the Berkshires dated back to his Territorial Army days before the war. He had come out to India with the new battalion as a company commander. On reaching India he had been sent for training in Intelligence duties, on completion of which, having expressed a wish to serve in a formation which included a unit of his old regiment, he was at once put in charge of our Brigade Intelligence Section. Early in April, a week after my arrival in Mayapore, he received posting orders to a G 3(I) appointment at Division. I made some fuss but Ewart persuaded me not to hinder the transfer. In his opinion, since coming to Mayapore, Lindsey had shown signs of restlessness and uncertainty and Ewart suspected that he had spoken to a friend on the divisional staff about getting a move. Lindsey's successor, Davidson, did not strike me as a particularly good substitute at first and we crossed swords on several occasions. Of Jewish origin, he had a layer of sensitivity that I did not at once comprehend.

After talking to Davidson, I decided to visit White. I drove first to his bungalow, and being told by Mrs White that he was touring the cantonment and the city, but expected to be back by ten o'clock, I decided to wait. I discussed the situation with her and found her own attitude shrewdly balanced between my own and her husband's. She said, 'Robin has always tried to see at least one year ahead. He knows that the people who oppose us now are the same we are going to have to live with and feel responsible for afterwards.' I said, 'Yes, providing the Japanese don't take over.' She said, 'I know. It's what I personally feel. But then I'm thinking of the twins and of never seeing them again. Robin thinks of that too, but knows that to think it isn't what he is paid for.'

I saw at once that between Mr and Mrs White there was the same fine sense of partnership which I had been blessed with in my own life.

When White returned, accompanied by young Jack Poulson, he at once apologised for any annoyance he might have given me earlier that morning about the Ranpurs and the bridge. I asked him whether I was right in thinking he had decided Dibrapur could be left to stew for a day or two in the hope that the successful reduction of unrest in Mayapore would leave it isolated and open to pacification. He seemed surprised, and thought for a moment, and then said, 'Yes, I suppose in military terms that is a way of putting it.'

I asked him what the civil terms were and he said at once, 'The saving of life and protection of property.' I asked him whether he therefore felt that the military were not to be trusted. He said, 'Your fellows are armed. My fellows have a few delaying weapons like explosives but otherwise their bare hands and their passions.'

I was surprised at his description of the rebels as 'his fellows', until I realised that just as I took my share of responsibility seriously so White took his, and I was aware of the curious enmity, as well as the amity, that could grow between two men of the same background, simply because the spheres of their responsibility differed. And yet, I thought, in the end, the result we both hoped for was the same.

The news that morning on the civil side was that the employees of the British–Indian Electrical Company were out on strike and that students of the Government Higher School and the Mayapore Technical College planned mass *satyagraha* that afternoon in a march across the Bibighar bridge and along the Grand Trunk road to the airfield at Banyaganj where work had also come to a stop following acts of intimidation against the men and women who had at first resisted the Congress call to cease work.

White intensely disliked action against students, whose volatile natures were unpredictable. They might be content to march in an orderly fashion and allow a number of their fellows to be arrested and then disperse, satisfied to have embarrassed the authorities and identified themselves with Congress ideals. But the slightest 'wind from another direction', as White put it, could lead them to throw themselves unarmed on the police or the military in a movement of mass hysteria that could only lead to a tragic loss of life. He asked, therefore, that his police be reinforced by troops and that the officer commanding them be asked to control the actions of the police as well as those of his own men. The police, White said, were inclined to be 'tough' with students. White then put it to me that the ease with which his informants had got hold of the details of these plans only led him to see the students' demonstration as a move to tempt our forces to concentrate mainly on the Bibighar bridge and the area of the colleges. He expected another attack, across the Mandir Gate bridge, by men and women of the ordinary population and one on the jail, and believed that these would coincide with the movement of the students.

I could not but admire his cool and, as I thought, sensible appraisal. I suggested that this morning might be a good time for a drumbeat proclamation by the civil and military authorities through the main areas of the city forbidding gatherings. He had considered this and now considered it again. Finally he said, 'No, it comes under my heading of provocation and reminds me too readily of the prelude to the massacre in Amritsar. It may also remind *them*. They don't need the proclamation because they know what is allowed and what isn't.'

I think that from this conversation – begun in an atmosphere of coolness almost amounting to distrust – I learned more about the workings of the civilian mind than I had ever done in a comparable time during my service in the country. I came away with a deep and abiding impression of the Deputy Commissioner's total involvement with the welfare of the people as a whole, irrespective of race or creed or colour. He must have had many doubts as to the various courses of action to be taken, but I think he had to solve them all with, in mind, what his wife had called the realisation that these were the people we were going to have to live in peace with when the troubles were over. In the aftermath of the troubles in Mayapore I believe that he was criticised for having 'lost his head'. If this is true, I should like to put the record straight. White 'went it alone' for as long as he was able, and I, in the few days in which circumstances made his task almost impossible, tried to make the best of a bad job. I should also put on record my opinion that White would have 'worked himself into the ground' before admitting he was beaten if, on the evening of August 12th, he had not received direct orders from his Commissioner (who was situated two hundred miles away from him!) and who, in turn, acted on the instructions of the provincial governor, to employ 'to the utmost' the military forces available to him. I had a similar notification from my divisional and area commander. By the night of the 12th, the province, viewed as a whole, was certainly in a state of such violent unrest that without difficulty it could be called a state of rebellion – one which our immediate superiors could only view with the gravest doubts for the immediate future.

That meeting on the morning of the 12th was virtually the last between White and myself that has left any clear impression on my mind. I have already described on an earlier page – as an example of the drill of military aid to the civil power – the action that afternoon on the Mandir Gate Bridge road when, as White had anticipated, believing the authorities fully occupied in reducing the student demonstration, the mob attempted penetration of the civil lines from the temple square, set fire to the *kotwali* in the vicinity of the temple and deployed towards the railway station. Simultaneously to the action this side of the Mandir Gate bridge the police were desperately defending the jail. Two of them died and the mob in that quarter succeeded in breaking into the prison and releasing a number of prisoners before a force of the Berkshires, who were rushed to the spot, were able to regain the initiative.

As readers may recall from my earlier detailed description of the action on the Mandir Gate Bridge road, the troops 'in aid' followed up the advantage they had gained in breaking up the mob in confusion with their firing, by pressing forward. In this way, the main body of the retreating rioters was pushed back across the bridge, although small groups managed to escape along some of the side roads.

Halting on the civil lines side of the bridge, the platoon commander asked the magistrate, Mr Poulson, whether he should remain there or cross the bridge and enter the city to command the temple square where already he could see new 'leaders' exhorting the fleeing crowd to stand and form up again. Poulson, intent upon keeping the force of law and order intact according to the drill book, requested the Berkshire subaltern to remain at the bridgehead. Firing could now be heard from the direction of the railway station and Poulson assumed correctly that in crossing the bridge originally the crowd had split into two, with one body advancing along the Mandir Gate Bridge road and the other infiltrating along the tracks towards the railway station. He told the subaltern that if the troops crossed over into the square they might find themselves caught between the mob that was trying to re-form in the town and the mob retreating from the firing at the railway station. As it was, when men and women fleeing from the railway station came into view they found the Berkshires holding the bridge – their one line of retreat.

Unfortunately, in spite of Mr Poulson's prompt request and the subaltern's equally prompt response – to 'open a way' across the bridge for these unarmed fleeing civilians – the civilians panicked at the sight of the troops and misinterpreted as hostile the movements of the platoon, which were actually made to give them way. Those at the front of the crowd tried to fall back and were trampled underfoot. Many scrambled down the banks of the river and attempted to swim across, and I'm afraid a number of men and women were drowned. This incident was the cause of great misunderstanding. We were accused by the Indians, later, of deliberately setting a trap and of showing no mercy towards those who were caught in it. Attempts were made to bring evidence that the troops at the bridge had fired into the mob, thereby causing many of them to throw themselves into the river. So far as I could gather this 'evidence' rested entirely on the fact that several of those who were drowned were found to have bullet wounds when the bodies were recovered. These wounds can only have been incurred in the action at the railway station, when non-compliance with the orders to disperse, and attacks on the troops with stones and brickbats, had led to a volley from the troops. As I think I have mentioned, the police at the railway station were commanded by Merrick, the District Superintendent. He showed great energy and determination and recklessness for his own safety. Mounted, he continually pressed forward to scatter the crowd and stop it forming a united front. Only when he was forced to retreat did he give orders to his few armed police, and permission to the troops, to fire.

It was a bitter afternoon, the climax coming when news reached us at District Headquarters that the jail had been attacked and forced. By now a heavy rain was falling. Between five and six o'clock a storm raged overhead as if reflecting the one which raged on the ground. It was in these inclement conditions that yet another force of Berkshires (which I myself accompanied, along with the Deputy Commissioner) were rushed across the bridge in open transports, and closed in on the jail. The rain and the alarm spread by the news of the failure of the riots in the civil lines had reduced the size of the crowds on Jail road, and no doubt the spectacle of several lorry-loads of armed troops and the speed with which I had ordered them to proceed shook the determination of the men and women still in this area. Nevertheless the area in the immediate vicinity of the jail had to

251

be cleared by debussing the troops and firing repeated volleys over the heads of the crowd. Once we were in control of the area of access to the jail itself, the picket-gate in the huge old wooden doors of the prison had to be forced with pickaxes. The insurgents had locked themselves in. They had also broken into the armoury, but fortunately their familiarity with such weapons as they found turned out to be practically nil, otherwise our men might have found themselves forcing an entrance under serious fire. Even as it was, one of our soldiers was wounded when, led by their platoon commander, the Berkshires entered the jail courtyard.

Their failure to hold the jail was the final blow to the rebels' hopes that day, and as was usually the case when reverses of this nature were suffered, anger turned inwards. On the night of the 12th/13th when it could not clearly be said who had the upper hand in terms of civil control, factions of the mob took time off from harrying us to settle old scores between each other. There was looting and arson in the city, but it was directed this time against native shops and houses, and even against persons. A dead body found in the morning could so easily be claimed as that of a 'martyr in the cause of freedom' who had been beaten to death by the police or the military! There were also a few incidents in the cantonment where small groups of men who had escaped along side roads and found places of hiding, emerged after dark and caused slight damage along the railway line. That night, too, a fire broke out in one of the depots on the railway sidings.

By now, the Deputy Commissioner had received the instructions from his superiors to contest the rebellion in his district with the full weight of the forces available to him, and I had been informed of this development by my area commander. My own 'private' instructions were that if in the next few hours I deemed that the civil authority was no longer operational, I had discretion to assume full command and declare martial law. However, from what I had seen that afternoon, I believed that between us White and I could restore order so long as we agreed that the situation had deteriorated to below the point at which either of us could be held responsible for a text-book reply to every incident. I had told my area commander this, and added that my greatest concern was with the situation in Dibrapur which, after the day's experiences in Mayapore, I took an increasingly serious view of.

I had a short meeting with White late that night. This was one of the several meetings which I have no really detailed recollection of, because they were now all taking place hurriedly and in an atmosphere of urgency, but I do recall his strained face and his immediate question on seeing me, 'Well, you're taking over, I suppose?' I said, 'Do you request that?' He shook his head, but agreed to my sending, on the morrow, a force to Dibrapur by the direct road south from Mayapore. But the area commander phoned me again that night from his headquarters and asked me to approach Dibrapur from the north-west on foot from the demolished bridge which, meanwhile, was to be repaired as quickly as possible by the engineers so that normal communications could be re-established along the road as soon as Dibrapur was pacified.

The Ranpurs were held up constantly along that short ten-mile stretch of road beyond the bridge by road blocks and home-made 'land-mines' from which they suffered several casualties. In this way, my belief that Dibrapur had been chosen as the stronghold of a planned uprising was upheld and it was not until the morning of the 17th that I was able to report to the Deputy Commissioner that the town was once again in the hands of legally constituted forces. To assist the Ranpurs I had to send a company of the Pankots along the direct route southwards through Tanpur, and by and large the operation assumed something of the nature of a full-dress military attack. I declared martial law in Dibrapur on the night of the 13th when the Ranpurs first entered the town. For three days they were engaged in restoring law and order. On the 17th an officer on the Deputy Commissioner's staff again took control on behalf of the civil authority, and those of our agents who had appeared to co-operate with the rebels (the Indian sub-divisional officer, a magistrate, and several constables) were brought back to Mayapore to be dealt with in the first instance by the Deputy Commissioner. This was the occasion when the sub-divisional officer, by restoring money he said he had hidden to stop it falling into the rebels' hand, was not proceeded against.

In the interim, throughout the district the rebellion had passed through increasingly violent stages of appearing virtually uncontrollable to a state when we could feel that the impetus that had set it in motion had been successfully counteracted. In any physical conflict the initial driving power needed to take active steps always seems to provide one with one's sharpest memories. Discipline and drill then take over and come into their own, proving their worth, but providing the individual with no especially memorable recollections. But I do recall that on the 14th of August, another serious attempt to penetrate the civil lines was made in the names of the 'Martyrs of the Bibighar and the Mandir Gate Bridge'.

One could not help but be moved on this occasion by the spectacle of crowds in which so many women, young and old, exposed themselves to the threat of wounds or even death. One detected in the attempts made on the 14th a closer adherence to the Mahatma's principles of non-violence. It was as if, overnight, these simple townspeople had become disenchanted with leaders who had encouraged them to grab any weapon ready to hand and to believe that the police and the soldiers could be overcome by such means. Now they came in a spirit of unarmed defiance, carrying banners which exhorted us to Quit India and deliver to them the 'innocent victims' of the Bibighar Gardens. The crowd that attempted to cross the Bibighar bridge was composed largely of women and children and so touching was the sight of them that our men were reluctant to fire, even although while the women were to the fore, the orders were to fire over their heads. I noticed a soldier of the Berkshires break ranks to comfort a little girl who was running up and down looking for her mother, one of the many women, no doubt, who had prostrated themselves on the road so that the soldiers would have to step over them when pressing forward to clear the bridge.

There is little doubt that the affair of the assault on Miss Manners in the Bibighar Gardens gave the population a 'popular' rallying cry, but I never took seriously the arguments which were put forward to prove that it was the action taken by the police to 'avenge' the rape that caused the riots in the town. The stories that the six arrested men had been brutally treated were, I am sure, quite without foundation, although once again I would add a reminder that the police, apart from the most senior officers, such as the District Superintendent, were themselves Indians, and there have been – it must be admitted – occasions in our history when white officials have been unfairly blamed for the actions of their native subordinates whom 'by the book' it was their responsibility to control. I doubt that even the Indians, however, took seriously the tale that was told about one or several of the arrested men (all Hindus) being 'forced to eat beef'. It is true that in the police you would find a fairly high proportion of Muslims, but if the populace had really thought the beef-feeding story was true, that would have given rise at once to a rumour that Muslim members of the police were responsible and hence to the kind of communal disturbance we were fortunate to be spared at this juncture. Such tales, in relation to the Bibighar affair, were no doubt the result of gossip after the event, when peace had been restored. Certainly no tales of this kind came to my notice at the time, and when they did there seemed to me to be no point in investigating them, which in any case it would not have been my job to do.

Unfortunately, as I think it to have been, the seriousness of the uprising in Mayapore which took all of us every ounce of our energy to combat, denied the authorities the proper chance to pursue and extend the evidence against the men who had been arrested for the rape, and the inability of the girl herself to offer evidence leading to identification left the case in a judicially unsatisfactory state. There was never cause to remove the suspects to the greater security of the Berkshires' lines, but, if they were truly guilty (and my mind remained open on that score) they must have counted themselves lucky to be disposed of in the way they were. The most that could be done, relying upon the evidence of their past activities and associations, was to deal with them under the Defence of India Rules and accordingly this was done. As for the attack upon the mission teacher and the murder of her Indian subordinate, here again a failure quickly to identify any of the men arrested that day in Tanpur as those responsible, led possibly to a corresponding failure of justice, although eventually one or two men suffered the supreme penalty.

According to official statements published later, the number of occasions throughout the country on which the police and/or military had to fire upon the populace totalled over 500. Over 60,000 people were arrested, over 1,000 killed and over 3,000 severely injured. Indian authorities dispute these figures in regard to the numbers killed and put the figure even as high as 40,000! In the case of my own troops the figures were as follows: Number of incidents in which firing was resorted to: 23 (12 of these having been in Dibrapur). Number of people estimated as killed as the result of firing: 12. Number of people estimated as wounded as a result of firing: 53. I think these figures are proof of the restraint our men showed. I do not have figures relating to those arrested, because this was the task of the police. Nor do I have the figures of those in the district who were punished, for instance by whipping, a subject on which the Indians have always been tender-minded. The damage done in the towns and outlying areas of the district was severe and it was several weeks before order had been completely restored in the sense that a civil authority would minimally recognise as 'order' – that is to say, an uninterrupted system of communication, full and open access by road and rail from one point to the other, and local communities wholly in the control of the police and under the jurisdiction of legally appointed magistrates. As White said, it was, finally, the people themselves who suffered from the disruption to their normal peaceful way of life. It is said, for instance, that the Bengal famine of 1943 might have been averted or, if not averted, at least alleviated had the 'rebellion' never taken place. There were many cases of thoughtless destruction of shops and warehouses and food stores.

I am conscious that I have written perhaps over-lengthily of what in terms of my life as a whole was an affair neither of long duration nor of special significance from a military point of view. Perhaps the deep and lasting impression it has made on me can be related to the fact that it came at a time when I was facing the kind of personal loss it is still difficult to speak of. There were moments – as I went about these daily tasks – when I felt that my life, simple as it had been, had unkindly already distributed the whole of its rewards to me; and, seeing the strength and unity of the tide that seemed to be flowing against us, I could not help asking myself the questions: In what way are we at fault? In what way have I personally failed?

It was on the 18th of August, the day after I had been able to report to the Deputy Commissioner that Dibrapur was at last restored to his authority, and that my officers – by now scattered in many different areas of the district – believed that the worst of the insurrection was over – that a telegram reached me from Tubby Carter, ordering me to come at once to Rawalpindi. The telegram had been delayed because of the troubles, even although it originated in military channels. I knew, of course, that by 'ordering' me he was simply advising me of the necessity of returning. I spoke at once on the telephone to the area commander and he gave me leave to travel immediately by any means I was able. It was already evening. I left the brigade in the capable hands of young Ewart Mackay and the CO of the Pankots, and travelled all through the night to Calcutta in my staff car, not trusting to the railway, and, I admit, wearing a loaded pistol in my holster. I was accompanied by my batman as well as the driver. My batman was a Hindu, but the driver was a Muslim. I thought how salutary a lesson it was to those who talked so readily of 'differences' that in that car there could be found – travelling in perfect amity – a representative of each of the three main 'powers' in India – Hindu, Muslim and Christian. The journey itself, however, seemed endless. In the dark, with all these troubles freshly behind me I pondered the immensity, the strange compelling beauty of India.

Even now, that night remains in my mind as totally unreal. I did not reach Calcutta until well into the morning of the 19th, although the driver – sensing that something was personally wrong for me – drove recklessly. Armed too, I think he would have helped to sell our lives dearly had we been attacked. I went at once, on reaching Cal, to my old friend Wing Commander 'Pug' Jarvis, who had been warned by Tubby and had expected my arrival the previous morning. It was nearly midnight before the RAF plane he had got me on to took off from Dum Dum. Fortunately it was going direct to Chaklala, with only a short delay in Delhi. In the early morning of the 20th I was met by Tubby at Chaklala. He drove me direct to his bungalow and then to the resting place which she had come to just the day before, too soon for me to be present, which was an alleviation of my grief I had sorely hoped to be granted.

I returned to Mayapore in the second week of September, but about two weeks after my return I received orders to take command of a brigade which was already in the field, east of the Brahmaputra, preparing to face the real enemy. Of this brigade, and our preparations for action against the Japanese, I will write in another chapter. But in this welcome translation to a more immediately active role, I detected the understanding hand of my old friend in Rawalpindi, who knew that for me only one kind of duty was now possible

II

The Civil

An edited transcript of written and spoken comments
by Robin White, CIE (Ex-ICS)

(1) I was interested in what you sent me of the late Brigadier Reid's unpublished memoirs describing his relationship with the civil authority in Mayapore in 1942. I didn't keep a diary, as Reid appears to have done, and it is a long time since I thought much about any of the events in question, but I am sure that from a military point of view his account is a viable enough reconstruction of what happened. From the civil point of view there are of course some inaccuracies, or anyway gaps in the narrative or alternative interpretations, that would need attention if a more general and impersonal picture were required to emerge.

I doubt, however, that there is much I myself can contribute all this time after. I have not been in India since 1948 and have long since lost touch with both old friends and old memories. I can confirm that Ronald Merrick did indeed succeed in obtaining his release from the Indian Police, but I was not concerned in any way with this and knew of no official reason why the authorities should have agreed, in his case, to let him go. He was commissioned into an Indian regiment, I think, and was wounded in Burma in either 1944 or 1945. As I recollect it he was killed during the communal riots that attended partition in 1947.

I was interested to hear of your recent visit to Mayapore and glad to learn that Lili Chatterjee is still living in the MacGregor House, a name I had quite forgotten – although I remember the house itself. I am glad, too, to hear that Srinivasan is still alive and remembers our association. I never saw him again after the morning when I had to order him and other members of the local Congress party sub-committee to be taken in custody. I knew little of the 'Sanctuary' run by Sister Ludmila, which I'd also forgotten about, but I'm pleased to hear that now, as *The Manners Memorial Home for Indian Boys and Girls*, it perpetuates the name of a family which was once highly thought of in the province. You do not say in what way the Home was founded. Presumably on money left either by Miss Manners or her aunt, Lady Manners. Is it known, by the way, what happened to the child, if it survived?

I return Brigadier Reid's manuscript with many thanks. I was touched by several passages in it. Neither my wife nor I knew of the illness of Mrs Reid until we saw a notice of her death a few days after he was summoned back to Rawalpindi. We knew that his son was a prisoner-of-war, of course. It was something I bore constantly in mind in my dealings with him. I'm sorry to realise that the son also died. There were many occasions when Reid annoyed me (obviously he felt the same about me) and others when I respected him, but on the whole he was never quite my sort of person. We rather got the impression that his posting to the command of a brigade in the field was a move on the part of the military authorities to disembarrass Mayapore of a man whose reputation, after the troubles, was thought to have become locally over-controversial. I'm glad to feel that Reid was not given this impression himself. Since you did not send me the subsequent chapters of his book, I don't know what he had to say about his eventual return to a desk job. I believe he never did attain his objective of a 'confrontation with the true enemy'. For a time, naturally, I followed what I could of his fortunes with some interest. But, as I say, this is all a long time ago and my own career in India came to an end not many years after.

I am sorry that I cannot be more helpful.

*

(2) I have had a letter from Lili Chatterjee, and gather it is from you that she got my address. She tells me that at the end of your stay in Mayapore this year, she delivered into your hands, as well as two letters, a journal written by Miss Manners during the time she lived with her aunt in Kashmir, awaiting the birth of the child. Lili Chatterjee tells me that for some time she kept the existence of the journal secret from you, and that she would

not have handed it over unless she had finally made up her mind that your interest in what you call the Bibighar Gardens affair was genuine. I gather that she received the journal from Lady Manners several years after the events it describes, and that Lady Manners, herself then approaching death, felt that of all the people in the world whom she knew Lili Chatterjee alone should take possession of it. Lili tells me that the journal makes it clear exactly what happened.

I gather that your concern with this affair arose from a reading of Brigadier Reid's unpublished book, which came into your hands as a result of your known interest in this period of British–Indian history. Lili tells me that you have been to some trouble to trace persons who would be in a position either to describe from personal experience, or to comment on, on the basis of informed personal opinion, the events of those years in Mayapore. I gather for instance that in an attempt to 'reconstruct' the story of Miss Crane, the Mission School superintendent, you visited, among other places, the headquarters of the organisation to which she had belonged, and browsed among her unclaimed relics. I met Miss Crane once or twice, and my wife knew her quite well in connection with local committee work. I also met Miss Manners on a number of occasions, but I'm afraid I knew almost nothing of the man Kumar. I met him only casually, twice at most. Jack Poulson would have been able to tell you more about him because after the arrests I gave Poulson the job of conducting the various inquiries. Unfortunately I can't help you to trace Poulson. He emigrated to New Zealand, I believe, and I have not heard of him for many years. However, Lili tells me that you have traced and talked to a friend of Kumar's in England, a man called Lindsey – the same Lindsey, perhaps, who according to Reid's account applied for a transfer from the Brigade Intelligence staff in Mayapore? My recollection is that Kumar was originally sent to the jail in the provincial capital, but if as you say his aunt left Mayapore years ago and not even his old uncle or Srinivasan have heard of him since then, it looks as though upon his release he began an entirely new life somewhere in India or, perhaps, in Pakistan.

In view of what Lili Chatterjee has told me I am willing – subject to a prior understanding that my memory cannot be absolutely relied upon – to have a talk.

*

(3) Thank you for having given me the opportunity before we meet to read a copy of the short extract from Daphne Manners's journal in which she describes what actually happened in the Bibighar, and the letter she wrote to her aunt about Merrick's 'proposal'. Thank you too for letting me see what you call the deposition of the man Vidyasagar. I did not know this man at all, and at this distance his name means nothing to me. I do remember Laxminarayan and the newspaper. I was interested to hear that Laxminarayan is still living in Mayapore, and I'm glad he was able to put

you in touch with Vidyasagar before you left India. Miss Manners was obviously telling the truth (I mean, writing the truth, in her journal) and if Vidyasagar's 'deposition' is also true – and there seems small reason to doubt it since there could hardly be much point in his lying at this stage – then I can only express a deep sense of shock. One's own responsibility isn't shrugged off lightly. I feel perhaps that I should balance any adverse picture by explaining the ways in which I thought Merrick a responsible and hard-working officer. However, I gather from what you say that on the basis of the various documents – Reid's memoirs, Miss Manners's journal and letters, and Sister Ludmila's recollections, not to mention Vidyasagar's deposition – you have pretty well made your mind up about the central characters in the affair and particularly about the kind of man Merrick was, and that my own contribution to your investigations should be confined to more general matters. A reading of these documents – which I now return – has certainly had much of the effect on me that you suggested it might. I find myself remembering things I have not thought of for years, and so perhaps, after all, I can be of some help.

*

(4) *Verbal Transcript*

Areas of dangerous fallibility between a policy and its pursuit? Yes, that sounds like Srinivasan. Is it this sort of dangerous area you want to try and map? Not only? I see. Very well, let's concentrate on the association between Reid and myself. But you'll have to ask the questions.

Well, I made one or two notes about inaccuracies in Reid's account, but what struck me finally was that quite apart from Reid's simple soldier attitude which antagonised me again just as much on paper as when we met face to face, he had somehow managed to make everything that happened look logical in his own terms, and I remembered more and more clearly the feeling I myself had in those days of not being able to rehearse the sequence of events that had led to a situation that seemed to be logical in itself but jolly well wasn't.

Every time Reid came into my office with that look on his face of being ready and eager to straighten us all out I felt like a man who had been playing a fish that might turn out to be either a minnow or a whale, and Reid's entrance, or even a telephone call from him, or from one of the officers on his staff, was just like someone suddenly tapping me on the elbow in midstream and telling me, quite inaccurately, what I was doing wrong. He had a genius for smothering any but your bluntest instincts, which is why I once lost my temper and told him rather rudely to leave me alone. He didn't bring that out in his book, but I'm not sure that this particular omission couldn't be traced to the fact that he had a hide like a rhinocerous and my show of temper had as much effect on him as the bite of a gnat. I know that his book gives an impression of a not insensitive man, but he was sensitive, broadly, only to major issues and *grand* emotions. In his daily contact with other human beings he did tend to bear pretty much the proportional weight of a sledgehammer to a pin.

When I first met Reid I saw him as a man it was going to take a lot of patience and energy to restrain. As so often happened when a man was taken from behind a desk, he had formed an opinion about what he was always calling his task or his role – as if it were pretty well cut and dried and took precedence over anyone else's, and I thought that having formed his opinion of his task he was also determined to carry it out *in toto*, however irrelevant some of its aspects turned out to be. I remember saying to my wife that if the Indians didn't start a rebellion Reid would be forced to invent one just so that by suppressing it he would feel he'd done his whole duty. She told me I'd better treat him gently because, as we all knew by then, his son was missing in Burma. I think I hoped as much as he did that the poor boy would turn up, and was even more concerned than he by the news that young Reid was a prisoner-of-war in the hands of the Japanese.

You could say that my association with Reid was fairly typical of the conflict between the civil and the military, so perhaps I was no less guilty of conforming to a generalised pattern of behaviour than he was.

No, you're quite right to correct me. I don't mean at all that the Civil were always progressive and the Military reactionary. I've fallen into my own trap, haven't I? Let me put it right. The drama Reid and I played out was that of the conflict between Englishmen who liked and admired Indians and believed them capable of self-government, and Englishmen who disliked or feared or despised them, or, just as bad, were indifferent to them as individuals, thought them extraneous to the business of living and working over there, except in their capacity as servants or soldiers or as dots on the landscape. On the whole civil officers were much better informed about Indian affairs than their opposite numbers in the military. In the later stages of our administration it would have been rare to find in the civil a man of Reid's political simplicity.

Put my finger on the main weakness of Reid's analysis of the political situation in India from the beginning of the 'thirties –? No, because analysis is the wrong word. He had an attitude, that was all. We all had an attitude but his struck me as pretty childish. It was emotional and non-analytical. But I was always taught that politics were people, and a lot of Englishmen thought as Reid thought and felt as he felt, which was why even when he was getting my goat most with his talk of Indians and Englishmen having to sink their differences in order to beat the Jap I recognised the *force* of his attitude. After all the Japanese were practically hammering at the door, and even though what Reid meant by Indians and English sinking differences was the Indians doing all the sinking, calling a halt to their political demands and the English maintaining the *status quo* and sinking nothing – one couldn't help admitting that the situation was very similar to the one a quarrelsome household would face if they looked out of the window and saw burglars trying to get in, or a gang of hooligans preparing to burn the house down. The head of the house would immediately feel obliged to take a lead and stand no nonsense from inside.

But straightforward as that situation might look – just a question of ceasing to squabble and presenting a united front to repel Japanese boarders – its straightforwardness depends on the nature of the squabbling in the house, doesn't it? On the whole I dislike analogies, but let's pursue this one a bit further. Let's imagine that the people in the house are a pretty mixed bunch, and that those who have the least say in how things are run are those the house belonged to originally. The present self-appointed owner has been saying for years that eventually, when he is satisfied that they've learned how to keep the roof repaired, the foundations secure and the whole in good order, he'll get out and give them the house back, because that is his job in life: to teach others how to make something of themselves and their property. He's been saying this long enough to believe it himself but ruling the household with a sufficiently confusing mixture of encouraging words and repressive measures to have created a feeling among his 'family' that by and large he's kidding, and that the only language he understands is the language *he* uses – a combination of physical and moral pressure. He's also said he'll leave – but stayed put – long enough to create factions below stairs among the people who hope to inherit or rather get the house back. He hasn't necessarily intended to create these factions, but their existence does seem to suit his book. Deny people something they want, over a longish period, and they naturally start disagreeing about precisely what it is they *do* want. So he likes nothing better than to give private interviews to deputations from these separate factions and to use the arguments of minority factions as moral levers to weaken the demands put forward by the majority faction. He's got into the habit of locking up over-vociferous members of all factions in the basement and only letting them out when they go on hunger strike like Gandhi used to.

We were in India for what we could get out of it. No one any longer denies that, but I think there are two main aspects of the British–Indian affair which we prefer to forget or ignore. The first was that we were originally *able* to exploit India because the first confrontation – to use Reid's cant word – was that of an old, tired civilisation that was running down under the Moghuls and a comparatively new energetic civilisation that had been on the up-grade ever since the Tudors. English people tend to think of India as a Victorian acquisition, but it was originally really an Elizabethan one. And you only have to consider the difference between the Elizabethans and the Victorians to get an idea of the changes that took place in our attitude to our prize and therefore of the second aspect of the affair which we forget or ignore – the confusion surrounding the moral issue. The moral issue is bound to arise eventually and grow, and finally appear to take precedence in any long-standing connection between human beings, especially if their status is unequal. The *onus* of moral leadership falls naturally on the people who rank as superior, but just as a people over-endowed with power can explain that power away as God-given and start talking about morality and the special need to uplift the poor and ignorant – the people they have power *over* – so can a people who have had too long an experience of what today is called underprivilege pass the buck to *their* god. At almost precisely the same time that the English were developing their theories of the White Man's burden to help them bear the weight of its responsibility, the Hindus and the Muslims were taking a long hard look at *their* religions, not to explain their servitude but to help them to end it. A lot of nonsense has been talked, you know, about the communal problem in India as if we waited in vain throughout the centuries of our influence for the Hindus and Muslims to settle their differences, but the communal problem never really became a problem until Hindu and Muslim revivalists and reformers got to work in the nineteenth century, in much the same way our own did, to see what comfort and support and ways forward could be found in these old philosophies. I think the English, however unconsciously and unintentionally, created the division between Muslim India and Hindu India. More recently in Kenya we shrieked accusations of barbarism at the Kikuyu for their Mau Mau rebellion, but hit a man in the face long enough and he turns for help to his racial memory and tribal gods. The Hindus turned to theirs, the Muslims to theirs. It wasn't from *social* awareness that Gandhi identified himself with the outcastes of the Hindu religion. Untouchability was foreign to original Hinduism and in this attempted return by a subject people to the source of their religious inspiration it was bound to happen that untouchability should be chosen as the intended victim of a revival, and non-violence re-emerge as a main tenet of its revitalisation. The Muslims' investigation of their religion was more dangerous, because Mohammed preached Holy War against the infidel. I think the English were perversely attracted to the idea of that danger. I always found it interesting that on the whole most English people were happier consorting with Muslims than with Hindus, but then fundamentally we've always been a bit embarrassed by the 'weakness' of Christianity. We saw the same weakness in Hinduism, but a sort of Eastern version of muscular Christianity in the religion of Allah.

In those days I was intensely *puzzled* by Gandhi. On the whole I distrust great men. I think one should. I certainly distrusted Gandhi – but not in the way Reid, for instance, distrusted him. I distrusted Gandhi because I couldn't see how a man who wielded such power and influence could remain uninhibited by it, and always make the right decisions for the right reasons. And yet I always felt his appeal to my conscience behind even my severest doubts about his intentions.

There's one story about Gandhi that I didn't know at the time, and it's particularly interested me since. Perhaps you know it too?

Yes. That's it. Do you think it relevant? It strikes me as fundamental to an understanding of the man. I mean to be declared outcaste by his community merely because he expressed an intention as a young man to go to England to study law! And did you know this, that the leaders of his community declared in advance that any fellow going to see him off or wishing him good luck would be punished with a fine. Something like a rupee each. And think how long he was abroad between first departure and return. Nearly a quarter of a century altogether. I wonder what he thought of India when he eventually got back to it after all those years in England and all those years in South Africa? Do you think his heart sank? Even though he returned a hero because of what he had done for the Indians in South Africa where he first initiated *satyagraha*. I mean India is far from what Brigadier Reid called salubrious. Perhaps Gandhi took one look at it and thought, Good God, is this what I've been longing to return to? I mention this because presently we come to the important question of *doubt* in public life.

I suppose it's also relevant that he returned to India just at the time when friendly co-operation between the British and the Indians was reaching the peak of its last notable phase, early in the First World War. If I remember correctly he sailed from South Africa to England in the summer of 1914 and got there just about the time we declared war on Germany. He told Indian students in London that England's predicament was not India's opportunity – a healthy opinion which Nehru borrowed twenty-five years later – and all through the Great War, in India, he was in favour of the recruitment of young Indians to the services. By and large India really went all out to help and not hinder us in that war. There was a strong smell of freedom for them in the air, and of self-government or measures of self-government which they could earn by helping to fight Britain's enemies, which they seemed happy to do anyway. It was in 1917, wasn't it, that we actually declared specifically that the goal for India was Dominion status? I think Gandhi got back to India early in 1915, and rather crossed swords – as Reid would have said – with people like Annie Besant. But even as early as this he proved himself to be something of an enigma. In his first public speech he said he was ashamed to have to speak in English in order to be understood by a largely Indian audience. Most Indian leaders prided themselves on their English. He criticised a prince who had just referred to India's poverty, and sarcastically pointed out the splendour of the surroundings – they were laying the foundation stone of a new University. Benares? Yes, the Hindu University in Benares. Then he said there was a lot of work to be done before India could think of self-government. That was one in the eye for the politically self-satisfied! At the same time he pointed at Government detectives in the crowd and asked why Indians were so distrusted. That was a snub to the Raj. He referred to the young Indian anarchists and said he was also an anarchist, but not one who believed in violence, although without violence he admitted the anarchists wouldn't have managed to get the decision to partition Bengal reversed. What a mixture of ideas this seemed to be! Mrs Besant tried to interrupt but the audience of students asked him to continue. The fellow in charge of the meeting told him to explain himself more clearly and he said what he wanted to do was to get rid of the awful suspicion that surrounded every move made in India. He wanted love and trust, and freedom to say what was in the heart without fear of the consequences. Most of the people on the platform left – I suppose they felt compromised or outraged or just publicly embarrassed – so he stopped speaking and afterwards the British stepped in. The police ordered him out of the city.

It must have been as it would be at a political meeting here, or in a television interview, if a well-known man actually got up or faced the camera and said exactly what was in his mind, without worrying how many times he seemed to contradict himself, and certainly without thinking of his own reputation, in a genuinely creative attempt to break through the sense of *pre-arranged* emotions and reactions that automatically accompanies any general gathering of people. In India that sense of pre-arrangement was always particularly strong because the Indians are normally the politest men and women in the world, which is probably why at a pinch they can be among the most hysterical and blood-thirsty. I suppose the widespread use of a foreign language has exaggerated their natural politeness. I've often wondered whether things wouldn't have gone infinitely better for us if all our civil servants had been compelled to acquire complete fluency both in Hindi and in the main language of their province and forced to conduct every phase of government in that language. Gandhi was right, of course, it was shameful that in talking to university students he had to speak a foreign language. The reason he had to speak it wasn't only because all the young men there had achieved their present status by learning and reading in English, but because it was probably the only language they *all* shared in common. We did nothing really to integrate communities, except by building railways between one and the other to carry their wealth more quickly into our own pockets.

Gandhi, you know, always struck me as the only man in public life anywhere in the world who had a highly developed instinct and capacity for thinking aloud – and this was an instinct and a capacity that seldom got smothered by other instincts. I'm sure it led eventually to the chap being completely misunderstood. People in public life are supposed to project what today we call an image, and ideally the image has to be constant. Gandhi's never was. The phases he went through just in the years 1939 to 1942 were inconstant enough for history to have labelled him as sufficiently politically confused to rank either as a band-wagoner or a half-baked pain in the neck. But I think what he was actually doing was trying to bring into the open the element of *doubt* about ideas and attitudes which we all undergo but prefer to keep quiet about.

And don't you think that can be partially traced back to the depression he must have felt way back in the nineteenth century at being able to leave his homeland only as an outcaste? Don't you think that the element of doubt entered very strongly at that moment as well as on his return? 'Am I doing the right thing?' he must have asked himself. After all he was only nineteen or so. To go to England and study for the law was something he could only do by being publicly rejected by his caste-community. Caste probably had a truly religious significance for him in those days. Going to England was significant only in terms of his worldly ambition. No man is without ambition, but perhaps few men have been forced to doubt the power for good that ambition represents as much as Gandhi was forced to do. I felt in the end that he was working out a personal salvation in public all the time. And of course the kind of doubt a man has of himself, of his actions, of his thinking, plays a prominent but invariably secret part in the actual events of the day. It was right to bring it into the open for once. He was never afraid to say openly that he'd changed his mind or been wrong, or that he was thinking about a problem and would only express his views after he'd worked out some kind of solution.

What would have happened, I wonder, if I had publicly represented my doubts about the wisdom of imprisoning Congress leaders in August 1942? God knows. I can't have been the only district officer who felt that it was the last thing it was wise to do or the only one to write long confidential memoranda on the subject to his commissioner. But I didn't have the nerve to stand up in the open and rehearse in public the pros and cons of doing what I was instructed to do.

I sometimes wish that on August the 9th I'd gone to the temple square beyond the Mandir Gate bridge with a megaphone, called out to the people there and said, 'Look, Government tells me to imprison X Y and Z because the Indian National Congress has endorsed the Mahatma's resolution calling on us to Quit India and leave her to God, or to anarchy, in other words, so far as we are concerned, to the Japanese. But if I imprison these men, who will lead you? Will you be glad to be rid of them? Or will you feel lost? Congress talks about non-violent non-co-operation, but what does that mean? How won't you co-operate? How will you withhold co-operation without defending yourselves against us when we try to *force* you to co-operate? We'll try to force you because we believe we're fighting for our lives. When you defend yourselves how will you do so without violence? If I threw down this megaphone and struck one of your young men on the face, what would you do? What would he do? If he does nothing and I strike him again, what then? What if I then do it again and again, until his face is bloody? Until he is dead? Will you just stand by and watch? The Mahatma says so, it seems, but do *you* say so?'

But of course I never did go to the temple square with a megaphone. Doubts and all I locked up X Y and Z. And I think it was wrong. The men who ordered me to lock them up had probably had similar doubts before initiating the policy, but once it was laid on none of us was left with any official alternative but to carry it out.

I suppose true anarchy in public life is inaction arising out of the element of doubt as opposed to action following the element of decision. And of course between the doubt, the decision, the action and the consequences, I suppose you find what Srinivasan calls the areas of dangerous fallibility. Well, that's not a shattering discovery. We all know it. But Gandhi had the *courage* to operate openly on the ground of the dangerous areas, didn't he? Is that what you're getting at? Wise as we can be after the event, no one at the time pointed out that this was what he was doing. If he stepped too noticeably out of the acceptable line he was locked up, but released when it was thought his talents would be more valuable politically on a free rein.

What is clear to me beyond *any* doubt is that we turned him fundamentally into a power harmful to our policies when we resorted to the repressive measures of the Rowlatt Act, immediately after the Great War at a time when he and all Indians had every reason to expect a major advance towards self-government as a reward for co-operating so freely in the war with Germany. Were we mad? Or plain stupid? Or merely perfidious? Or terrified? Or just common-or-garden cocky after victory, thick-skinned and determined to give away nothing? What in hell was the good of declaring Dominion status as our aim for India in 1917 and not much more than a year later instituting trial without jury for political crimes and powers of detention at provincial level under the Defence of India Rules, ostensibly to deal with so-called anarchists but in practice to make any expression of free-will and free opinion technically punishable? What kind of a 'dominion' was that?

Well, you remember the result: riots, and then General Dyer at Amritsar and a return to distrust and fear and suspicion, and Gandhi emerging as the Mahatma, the one man who might provide an answer – but now it was going to be an Indian answer, not a British one. I'm sorry. I still get hot under the collar when I think about 1919. And I'm still deeply ashamed, after all these years.

No, I was too young at the time. I went out to India as a young civilian as we called ourselves in 1921. I had hardly a thought in my head. I'd done my swotting and passed the exams, and read all the the myth and legend. I wanted nothing better in those days than to get out into my first sub-division under the old pipul tree, puffing at a pipe and fancying myself no end as a promising administrator who would straighten out young and old and be remembered as White Sahib, become a legend myself and still be talked about fifty years after I'd gone as the fellow who brought peace and prosperity to the villages.

But of course I had to face reality at once. I simply wasn't cut out for paternalism. My superiors were the last of that breed. I disliked my first district officer. He probably didn't deserve it. But I hated India – the real India behind the pipe-puffing myth. I hated the loneliness, and the dirt, the smell, the conscious air of superiority that one couldn't get through the day without putting on like a sort of protective purdah. I hated Indians because they were the most immediately available target and couldn't hit back except in subtle ways that made me hate them even more.

And then one day, I remember it clearly, I was touring the district with the land settlement officer, going from village to village. On horseback, old style. I was fed to the teeth with village accountants who cringed and tahsildars who presumed and cringed all in the same breath, and I was critical of the settlement officer who obviously felt and acted like God going for a casual stroll, giving with the right hand and taking with the left. Then something went wrong with the camp *bandobast*. We were bogged down in some god-forsaken village and had to spend the night in a mud-hut. I was ready to cry from frustration and from my own sense of inadequacy. The settlement officer was drinking toddy with the village elders still playing at Christ and the Apostles, and I was alone in the hut. My bowels were in a terrible state and I couldn't face anything, let alone toddy. I was lying on a charpoy, without a mosquito net, and suddenly saw this middle-aged Indian woman standing in the doorway watching me. When our eyes met she made *namaste* and then disappeared for a moment, and came back with a bowl of curds and a spoon.

I was on my dignity at once, and waved her away, but she came to the bedside and spooned up a helping of the curds and held it out and made me eat, just as if I were her nephew or son and needed building up. She said nothing and I couldn't even look at her – only at her black hands and the white curds. Afterwards I fell asleep and when I woke up I felt better and wondered whether I hadn't dreamed it all, until I saw the bowl of unfinished curds covered with a cloth, on a brass tray by the bedside and a flower on the tray next to the bowl. It was morning then, and the settlement officer was snoring in the other bed. I felt that I had been given back my humanity, by a nondescript middle-aged Indian woman. I felt that the curds and the flowers were for affection, not tribute, affection big enough to include a dash of well-meant motherly criticism, the suggestion that my indisposition could be overcome easily enough once I'd learned I had no real enemies. I remember standing in the open doorway and breathing in deeply; and getting it: the scent behind the smell. They had brass pots of hot water ready for my bathe. Before the bathe I was sat down on an old wooden chair and shaved by the *nai*, the barber, without soap, just his fingers and warm water and a cut-throat. He scraped the razor all over my face and forehead, even over the eyelids. I held my breath, waiting for the cut that would blind me. But it was all gentle and efficient, a kind of early morning *puja*, and afterwards my face felt newly made and I went to the bathing enclosure and scooped water out of the brass pots of hot water that stood waiting. Brooke had the right word for it. The benison of hot water. Later I looked among the women but couldn't tell which of them had come into the hut the night before and fed me as she would have fed her own son. There was another flower on the pommel of my saddle. It embarrassed me. But I loved it too. I looked at the settlement officer. He had no flower and hadn't noticed mine. As we rode away I looked back, and waved. The people made no move in reply, but I felt it coming from them – the good wish, the challenge to do well by them and by myself. I've never forgotten that. I expect that afterwards the bowl and spoon I'd eaten from had to be thrown away.

No. One did tend to spend the whole of one's career in the same province, but that village was not in the district where I eventually became Deputy Commissioner. Why? Did you think it lay close to Dibrapur?

*

(5) Thank you for sending me the edited transcript of the recording of our interview. I see you have ironed out a lot of the inconsistencies and repetitions but haven't been able to disguise the way that I kept leading away from the point. You were obviously right to end the interview when we got round finally to the business of Dibrapur, which probably needs more careful discussion than it would have got just then.

I don't know about Mary Tudor and Calais as you put it, but I certainly *remember* Dibrapur. There was terrible poverty there, the kind you would get in any region where an old source of wealth has retreated farther and farther. In the nineteenth century it was the headquarters of the district. I don't recall exactly when it was that they began to mine the coal, but gradually these particular veins were worked out and the adjoining district inherited the wealth and prosperity. Labour was still drawn from Dibrapur, but in decreasing quantities.

In any depressed area, anywhere in the world, you can assume that emotions and attitudes will be exaggerated. In one respect Reid was right and some kind of organised force *was* at work in Dibrapur, but how much was due to planning and how much to intelligent seizing of opportunity never was clear. Where he was wrong, I'm sure, was in attributing the force to an underground force of *Congress,* and I think Vidyasagar's deposition bears this out, and where I was right, I suspect, was in believing that *any* force of Indian national life could have been controlled by the Congress. The majority of Indians (excluding wild young men like Vidyasagar) have always respected authority – how else could we have ruled millions with a few thousand? Congress was the shadow authority. If we had not banned the Congress committees and imprisoned their leaders at the centre and in most of the provinces, I'm convinced that there would have been no rebellion of the kind that occurred. Gandhi, you know, didn't expect to be arrested this time. Politically, 'Quit India' was a sort of kite he flew. Morally, it was an appeal like a cry in the dark. But even if in places like Dibrapur there had been rebellion I am equally convinced that to contain it I would only have had to appeal to a man like Srinivassan for instance to go there and talk to the people and exhort them to non-violent non-co-operative methods. Strikes, hartal, that sort of thing. I honestly believe that the Indian is emotionally predisposed against violence. That would explain the hysteria that usually marks his surrender to it. He then goes beyond all ordinary bounds, like someone gone mad because he's destroying his own faith as well. We on the other hand are emotionally disposed *towards* violence, and have to work hard at keeping ourselves in order. Which is why at the beginning of our wars we've always experienced a feeling of relief and said things like, 'Now we know where we stand.' The other thing to remember about Indians, Hindus anyway, is that their religion teaches them that man, as man, is an illusion. I don't say that any more of them believe that than Christians believe Christ was the son of God or was talking practical sense when he said we should turn the other cheek. But just as the Christian ideal works on our Christian conscience while we're engaged in battering each other to death, or blowing each other up, so that we know that to do so is wrong, so I think when the Indians start battering each other they feel in the backs of their minds that the battering isn't quite real. I think this partly explains why unarmed mobs were always ready to face our troops and police. They themselves weren't real, the troops weren't real, the bullets were never fired and people didn't die except in a world that was an illusion itself. I agree that this doesn't explain why in such a non-existent world it was thought worth while opposing the troops in the first place.

But of course for me the people in the Dibrapur sub-division *were* real. They were bad farmers and poor shopkeepers. It wasn't their fault. The heyday of the coal-mines was pre-Great War, but that heyday denuded part of the land permanently and led to unploughed fields, and the splitting up of families. There were several villages in that area where there were practically no young men. They'd all gone to the mining areas in the adjacent district. You know the sort of thing that happens as well as I do. We made special efforts there – I remember talking to Miss Crane about them once, because she had one of her schools near Dibrapur – but there was a lot of apathy as well as a lot of resentment. The young Indian I had out there in his own sub-divisional headquarters was an extremely intelligent and capable man. It was the toughest sub-division in the district. He had a lot of problems but also a lot of *nous.* The fellow who appointed himself deputy commissioner was one of the local tahsildars who was also a local landowner. My own man had always had a lot of trouble with him. In his account Reid leaves a slight doubt in the reader's mind about the Indian sub-divisional officer's actual behaviour during the troubles. I know at the time people were going around saying that when it was all over the chap broke down in my office and spent hours crying and asking to be let off. No such thing. We talked the situation out quite unemotionally, and I was satisfied that short of sacrificing his life – which I wouldn't have expected any sane man to do – the sub-divisional officer had made the best of a bad job, managed to restrain the self-appointed deputy commissioner quite a bit, in spite of the fact that as so-called Judge he was more or less kept prisoner. And he certainly saved a sizeable sum of money for the treasury. I expect the rumour about him crying arose from the fact that when we shook hands and parted there *were* tears in his eyes, and people probably noticed them as he left my bungalow. I hadn't been kind to him, just fair, I hope, but Indians have never been ashamed of responding to fairness in a way an Englishman would be ashamed to.

But that is jumping ahead. I know there was a failure in our intelligence system to pinpoint in advance the men who emerged as local leaders in

Dibrapur and succeeded in cutting the town off for several days. I suppose I did use the expression 'needles in a haystack' when talking about such people to Reid, but I don't actually remember doing so. The police in the Dibrapur sub-division were – perhaps not unexpectedly in view of the toughness of their job – of a lower morale than elsewhere. Some ran away, and one or two constables took over and sided with the rebels. As you will have gathered, everything happened pretty quickly and our police – never numerous – were scattered very thinly in proportion to the area and the size of the population. I agreed to Reid sending troops on the night of the 11th in the hope that their prompt appearance at that particular moment would be as inhibiting as the appearance of troops usually was. Reid rather underplays the attempts made that day by the civil authority to get into Dibrapur with police and magistrates, and says nothing about the road blocks on the *main* road. There were no blown bridges on the main road, but there was a series of felled trees that denied the road to the full use of transport, and the police found that the nearer they got to Dibrapur the less helpful the villagers were in helping them to clear the road. On the night in question the message I had had from Tanpur was to the effect that one truckload of police had 'disappeared'. It turned out later that they were locked up in the *kotwali* in one of the villages near Dibrapur. All the wires were down, of course, between Dibrapur and Tanpur.

The news of the blown bridge on Reid's flank road was certainly a poser, but I couldn't help being rather amused because he had made the use of the flank road sound so professional and clever, and suddenly there he was in danger of losing two 3-ton lorries and a 15-cwt truck and his wireless. And he was mad as hell. I hope that my amusement didn't sway my decision. I requested the withdrawal of the troops on that road because I felt that if the rebels had the initiative and the means to blow a bridge (a fairly harmless occupation in itself, just a matter of destroying a ton or so of brick and mortar!) a meeting of the rebels and troops whose tempers had shortened might result in the very kind of bloody affair I wanted to avoid. I know that my decision is open to question, but I made it, and stand by it, and I think it was right. If there had not then been pressure from above to use troops to the full I should certainly have left Dibrapur to stew even longer than I did. That intelligence officer, Davidson, was right when he suggested to Reid that my idea was for pacification to spread outwards from Mayapore. But Reid was jumping on hot bricks. I don't offer this as an excuse, although perhaps I do offer it as a contributory factor to any decision of mine that I still have doubts about. When you have a man like Reid constantly at your elbow you do tend to lose your concentration. I think I would have withstood his nagging if the provincial civil authority hadn't begun to press too. It is difficult actually to recall the real sense of urgency that arose in a few hours when reports were coming in pointing to an uprising that was getting out of hand. Anyway there was the pressure from Reid, the pressure from provincial headquarters, and the pressure of my own doubts. So I let Reid have his way about Dibrapur. His little battle there was by no means uncontrolled. I have no complaints or accusations on that score. But I don't think it was accompanied by any *special* restraint, and I still believe, as I believed then, that the deaths of men, women and children in Dibrapur could have been avoided if the town had been allowed to 'stew' until the people themselves were of the temper (and it never took long for them to regain it) to make its *realignment* (and that is the proper word) just part of the day's routine.

Perhaps it was unfair that the action of his troops in Dibrapur (of which he does not give us the benefit of any detailed description in his book) should have been the main cause of the reputation Reid had afterwards for being over-controversial in the district 'during the current phase of pacification'. (The official jargon for 'let's all be friends again'.) My commissioner asked me to comment on Reid, confidentially. Complaints against any of us, civil or military, very quickly reached a high level as you know. I gave it as my opinion that Reid had at no time exceeded his duty and had been, throughout, a constant reassurance to me in the execution of my own. I added that, left to ourselves, and not ordered to make the fullest use of the means available, the force actually used might have been less and the result the same, or even better. I didn't see why Reid should carry the can back for people who had panicked at provincial headquarters. I don't think this comment of mine pleased anyone from the commissioner upwards. For a time I expected to be moved myself, but the luck or ill-luck of the game fixed on Reid – unless it were really true that his posting could be put down to the influence of friends of his who thought that following the death of his wife he would be happier if employed in a more active role. It is so easy – particularly when looking for a chosen scapegoat of an action you have taken part in – to hit upon a particular incident as proof that a scapegoat has been found when, in fact, the authorities have simply shrugged their shoulders, and a purely personal consideration has then stepped in and established the expected pattern of offence and punishment.

*

(6) Thank you for your reply to my written comments on the transcription of our interview. Yes, I do dislike the element of 'Yes, you did. No, I didn't' that all too readily rises to the surface. Reid had his attitudes and opinions and I had mine. One can't go on for ever justifying one's own and refuting someone else's with any kind of passion – but I'm sorry that the points I've been making notes of in the past few days in answer to specific statements in Reid's book don't come up now except extraneously. May I take one of them, though, and kill any idea Reid might have left that Menen, the District and Sessions Judge, was predisposed towards the rebels? Menen was predisposed towards nothing except the due process of the law which he had no special faith in, God knows, but certainly recognised his sworn duty to. I'm also slightly worried about any impression that could be left of

my having either been in collusion with Merrick over – or turned a blind eye to – the treatment of the Bibighar suspects. I feel I should be allowed to say something about this if you are going to publish Vidyasagar's deposition. Vidyasagar ranks as a self-confessed lawbreaker so that's neither here nor there.

In his deposition he is noticeably unforthcoming about the names of his associates. So to what extent we can rely on his statement that Hari Kumar was not one of his fellow-conspirators, neither of us can judge accurately. The picture we get from Miss Manners's journal (or rather from that short section of it which you have allowed me to see) is not in itself *evidence* of Kumar's non-complicity in the kind of activities Vidyasagar engaged in, and it's quite possible, reading the deposition, to imagine that Vidyasagar gave Merrick cause *genuinely* to disbelieve him during his interrogation. What worries me is that people should think I at any time, then or afterwards, knew about Merrick's treatment of the men suspected of the *rape*. He admitted to me that he had 'bent the rules' when dealing with the suspects – in order to frighten them and get them to tell the truth, for example threatened them with caning, and in one case had even had one boy 'prepared as if for punishment' – I think his expression was. He *volunteered* this information to me on the morning following the arrests, and when Menen approached me later and said rumours were going round that the boys had been whipped I was able to say how I thought such a rumour had arisen, and that I'd already warned Merrick to 'stop playing about'. More serious, in my opinion, was the second rumour, that they had been forced to eat beef. Merrick said he'd look into it, and he told me later that it was quite untrue, but might have been caused by a mistake made in the cells when one of the Muslim constables who was guarding them had his own meal sent in. Reid was quite right when he said that the job of suppressing the riots distracted our full attention from the boys suspected of rape and made it finally impossible to find any concrete evidence against them in connection with the assault. Menen did pursue the business of the rumours of caning and beef-eating. I gave him permission to have the boys themselves questioned on the matter. He told me that the lawyer whom he sent to talk to them reported that none of the boys, including Kumar, complained of having been either whipped or forced to eat beef. And none of them ever said anything about it to Jack Poulson, who had the job of examining them when we were preparing the political case against them. But all this time after I'm uncomfortably aware of having failed to investigate the rumours more fully. It seems pretty clear that they were ill-treated. However, I don't think that there was actually a miscarriage of justice. Merrick was obviously acting in the heat of the moment, believing them guilty of attacking a girl he was fond of. It didn't take long for us to realise that a charge of rape simply wouldn't stick, but the evidence available about their political activities was sufficient for us to feel justified in seeing whether they couldn't be dealt with under the Defence of India Rules. The case was referred to the Divisional Commissioner, and actually as high as the Governor. I've forgotten the details of the evidence, but it was pretty conclusive. So I still feel that the five boys first arrested were guilty of the kind of offences the rules were meant to cover. Only Kumar remains a conundrum to me. If he was treated as badly as Vidyasagar's 'informant' said, why didn't he speak out when Menen's lawyer talked to him? Why didn't he complain to Jack Poulson during the official examination? One can appreciate the silence of the other boys if what Vidyasagar says about police threats is true. But Kumar had already suffered – and presumably could prove it, and he was of a different calibre from the other boys surely? Perhaps the parts of Miss Manners's journal which you haven't shown me throw some light on this problem?

I suppose it is his silence on this subject that you have in mind when you say in your note to me that 'Kumar was a man who felt in the end he had lost everything, even his Englishness, and could then only meet every situation – even the most painful – in silence, in the hope that out of it he would dredge back up some self-respect'.

I quite see, from what you've told me about your 'reconstruction' of Hari Kumar's life, and from what I have read in Daphne Manners's journal, that Kumar might indeed have reacted in this way, but if Vidyasagar's informant was speaking the truth when he said that on the night of his arrest Kumar was caned on Merrick's instructions 'until he groaned' I should still have thought Kumar would have seized the opportunity to make charges when Menen's lawyer interviewed him and asked him point-blank whether it was true. To complain of having been unjustifiably and savagely beaten in the course of interrogation would not itself have been a betrayal of Miss Manners's request to Kumar to 'say nothing'. I mean, isn't there a limit to the stiffness of *any* upper lip?

But then I expect my objections to your conclusions are really based on my inner unwillingness to accept the unsupported evidence of Merrick's behaviour – or to admit my own failure to suspect it at the time. I have no comment to make on the figure you quote from 'official' sources that, excluding the United Provinces, there were 958 sentences of whipping after the insurrection, except to say that this was a legal punishment for people caught taking part in riots. If Kumar had been arrested during a riot he might well have been caned. I suppose what you are getting at is that this kind of punishment was 'in the air' and that Merrick seized an opportunity, bent the rules, and got away with it.

Having said all this I'll now confine myself, as you request, to the larger issue – although before finally leaving behind the question of 'Yes, I did. No, you didn't', I would point out – perhaps unnecessarily – that one should not confuse the uncertainty that surrounds actions and events with the 'areas of dangerous fallibility' that lie *between* doubts, decisions and actions. Taking as an example the question of the forcible feeding – it either happened or did not happen. In attempting to map the 'dangerous area' we are not concerned with *facts* the truth of which, however unascertainable now, *was known to somebody at the time*?

I have thought hard about the true 'dangerous area' and must admit, somewhat reluctantly, that I can't grasp the issues firmly enough to come up with anything remotely resembling a premise from which you could work. I find myself too readily back-tracking into the old condition of statement and refutation and counter-statement. For instance, taking Reid's jejune account of the 1935 scheme for Federation – and his comment, 'It led only to a scramble for power', which leaves the unknowledgeable reader with the impression that we had made a handsome offer and then had to sit back and watch in dismay while the Indians proved themselves too immature either to understand the issues or to grasp their opportunity – all I can really turn my mind to are the alternative readings that show why, as *statesmen*, the Indians rejected Federation, and how the whole federal scheme and proposal could be seen in the light of our having offered the Indians a constitution that would only have prolonged, perhaps even perpetuated, our power and influence, if only as Imperial Arbitrators.

Similarly – again taking Reid's comments as a kind of basic 'norm' – one could write at length demolishing his casual inference that the Cripps Mission of 1942 failed because of Indian intransigence, or counter-state – equally casually and briefly and inaccurately – that this was a typical Churchillian move, made to dress the window and make friends and influence people abroad after the defeat in Asia, but which amounted in itself to no more than a grudging repetition of old promises and even older reservations.

And that's not what we're after, is it? Even though one is so tempted to cut away at the foundations of Brigadier Reid's apparently unshakeable foursquare little edifice of simple cause and simple effect in order to redress the balance and present the obverse, and just as inaccurate, picture of a tyrannical and imperialistic power grinding the faces of its coloured subjects in the dust.

In fact we are not at all after the blow-by-blow account of the politics that led to the action. Actually any one man would be incapable of giving such an account – if he confined himself to the blows. There were so many blows he would spend more than his lifetime recording them. To make the preparation of any account a reasonable task he would have to adopt an attitude towards the available material. The action of such an attitude is rather like that of a sieve. Only what is relevant to the attitude gets through. The rest gets thrown away. The real relevance and truth of what gets through the mesh then depends on the relevance and truth of the attitude, doesn't it? If one agrees with that one is at once back on the ground of personal preference – even prejudice – which may or may not have anything to do with 'truth', so-called.

Anyway, let me imagine (as you helpfully suggested in your note) that I am about to embark on a history of the British–Indian relationship. I would have to adopt an attitude to the mass of material confronting me. What would it be?

I think it would be as simple – childlike almost – as this: I would take as my premise that the Indians wanted to be free, and that we also wished this, but that they had wanted to be free for just that much longer than we had felt or agreed that they should be; that given this situation the conflict arose partly as a result of the lack of synchronisation of the timing of the two wishes, but also because this, in time, developed into a lack of synchronisation of the wishes themselves. Being human, the longer the Indians were denied freedom the more they wanted to be free on their own terms, and the more they wanted to be free on their own terms the more we – also being human – insisted that they must initially acquire freedom on ours. The longer this conflict continued, the more abstruse the terms of likely agreement became on either side. It was then a question of the greater morality outlasting and outweighing the lesser. Which was why, of course, in the end the Indians won.

Having put it in those simple words (and they form a mesh you could sift an enormous lot of detailed evidence through), I am reminded of what you said during our interview about 'the moral drift of history', and see how perhaps the impetus behind that drift stems in the main from our consciences, and that the dangerous area is the *natural* place for our consciences to work in, with or without us, usually without. The trouble is that the word dangerous always suggests something slightly sinister, as though there were an unbreakable connection at source between 'danger' and 'wrong'. 'Danger' does have this connotation, but I suppose it doesn't if we remember we only use the word to convey our fear of the personal consequences, the danger we'd be in ourselves if we followed our consciences all the time.

I remember that during our talk you referred to the 'beat' and the 'pause' and I think described these as the unrecorded moments of history. I wish I could relate this theory to a particular event in my life and see how I came out on the right side rather than the wrong, or that I could relate it to an event in Reid's. But even in attempting to relate it, I'm back again in the world of describable events. And when I attempt to relate the theory to all the events in the lives of all the people who were connected with the action – however directly or remotely – my mind simply won't take in the complex of emotions and ambitions and reactions that led, say, to any one of the single actions that was part of the general describable pattern. Perhaps though, the mind can respond to a sense of a cumulative, impersonal justice? The kind of justice whose importance lies not only in the course apparently and overwhelmingly taken, but in its exposure of the dangers that still lie ahead, threatening to divert the drift once more?

*

III

(Appendix to 'Civil and Military')

A Deposition by S. V. Vidyasagar

In my sixteenth year I was plucked in the matriculation and left the Mayapore Government Higher School with the reproaches of my parents and no prospects to a career. For nearly twelve months I was living a life of shame and wickedness, going with loose women and impairing my health. So bad did I become that my father turned me out of the house. My mother secretly gave me rupees one hundred which she had saved from the household expenses over many months. I regret that even this token of affection and motherly trust I squandered on drink and fornication. For many weeks I was at death's door in my squalid surroundings but upon recovery I was still only taking notice of girls and liquor. Many times I was praying for guidance and self-discipline, but only I had to see a pretty girl and at once I was following her and making immoral suggestions in front of everybody, so that my reputation was badly compromised and no decent person would come close to me, unless they were boys of my own kind whose parents were having nothing to do with them or not knowing that they were acting in this way until their neighbours or friends pointed it out.

In this manner I became seventeen and now, revolted by my way of life and resolving upon both moral and physical improvement, I went back to my father's house and begged forgiveness. My mother and sister wept at my return but my father was stern with me and called me to account for my past wickedness. I said that I could account for it only as a madness and that now I was trusting to recovery by God's grace and my own determination. Seeing me so sorrowful and humble of mien my father opened his arms to me once more. Beginning thus a new and upright life I took employment as a clerk with my father's assistance and recommendation and paid the whole of my monthly emolument to my mother, taking from her only a few annas for daily expenditure. At this time also I was bitterly regretting the irresponsibility and bad behaviour that had led me to well-deserved failure in the Higher School. At night I would read in my room burning the midnight oil until my mother begged me to be taking more care of my health and not running the risk of falling asleep in the office and losing my job.

So, determined not to be giving my parents any more trouble I drew up a chart which I pinned to the wall above my bed, allotting so much of my leisure hours to study, so much to sleep and so much to healthy exercise. On fine evenings I would stroll out to the Chillianwallah Bagh extension to look at the fine houses of our well-off neighbours and wander by the river bank. There I saw and caught the eyes of many girls but always I drew back before the temptation to speak to them or follow them proved too much to be difficult. I avoided those parts of the town where I might fall in with my erstwhile companions, especially the street in which many prostitutes lived and whose glances from an upper room could be the ruination of any innocent and upright young man chancing to be in the vicinity.

I was now firmly set upon a course of life both bodily healthy and spiritually uplifting and even upon these walks I would take a book with me and sit down by the river bank to study, casting but few looks at the black braids and silken sarees of the girls nearby. In this way, I happened to fall in with Mr Francis Narayan, who was teacher at the Christian mission school in Chillianwallah Bazaar and a well-known figure in Mayapore, always riding his bicycle to and fro and speaking at random. Falling into conversation with him I found myself telling him of my earlier bad life and reformed character and my hopes for the future. Learning that I was working as a humble clerk and sadly regretting my failure in the matriculation he said he would bear me in mind for any suitable post he heard about. But expecting nothing to come of this friendly meeting I continued to apply myself daily to my tasks and programme of self-improvement and further education. Now I began to feel somewhat of impatience and to cast covetous glances upon the books in the Mayapore Book Depot in the road near the Tirupati temple which I passed daily on my way home in the evenings. My father was head clerk to a contractor and the office in which I worked was belonging to a friend of my father's employer, a merchant with two marriageable daughters. One day I stopped as usual at the Mayapore Book Depot to browse among the many volumes. Under pretext merely of examining, I was reading chapter by chapter a book about 1917 Declaration of Self-Government. I had become interested in political affairs. Dearly I wished to possess this volume but its price was beyond my means although I knew that my mother would give me the requisite money were I but to ask her. As I stood that evening reading the next chapter, I saw that I was unwatched for the moment by the owner and his assistant and without conscious thought I went out with the book under my arm. Elated and yet afraid of being followed and apprehended as a common thief I wandered without due care and found myself in my old district. A voice called out to me and looking in that direction I saw one of my old friends, a young man senior to the rest of us who had talked and mixed with us but not accompanied us on our bouts of drinking and other bad things. His name was Moti Lal. Seeing the book under my arm he took hold of it and looked at the title and said, 'So you are becoming grown-up at last.' He invited me to have coffee in the shop where he had been sitting and I agreed. He asked me what I had been doing all these many months, so I told him. He also was a clerk, in the warehouse of Romesh Chand Gupta Sen. I asked him whether he had seen any of our other old friends but he said they had also become respectable like me.

On this occasion suddenly I was seeing that my old life was not so disreputable as my conscience was telling me. It was wicked no doubt to drink so much bad liquor and to go with immoral women without due discrimination, but now I saw that we had been doing such things because

277

our energies were in need of special outlet. Fortified by this discovery I walked back to the Mayapore Book Depot, restored the stolen book to its rightful owner and said that I had taken it away in a fit of absent-mindedness. After this he allowed me to sit many hours in the back of the shop studying new volumes that had come in from Calcutta and Bombay.

I was in my eighteenth year when Mr Narayan, the mission teacher, called at my home and said that the editor of the *Mayapore Gazette* was looking for an energetic young man with good English who would act as office boy and apprentice journalist. Mr Narayan confided in me that it was he who wrote the articles known as *Topics*, by 'Stroller', for the *Gazette*, which he did in order to augment his emoluments as a teacher. My father was against the idea that I should leave my present employment. He pointed out that in due course, so long as I attended carefully to my duties, I had prospects of becoming head clerk and even of marrying one of my employer's daughters if I showed application and diligence. In the past few months my father had become in very much poor health. Every day he would walk to his office, never even one minute late, but working frequently far beyond the appointed hour of closing and returning home to face my mother's complaints that his supper was spoiled. Since adopting a more manly attitude towards my own life I had learned respect for my father where before only there had been criticism. Also I was affectionate towards him because of his no doubt love for me. I did not want to displease him but also I wished to apply for the job Mr Narayan had already put in my way by speaking to the editor about me. Eventually my father gave his consent for me to apply to 'The Gazette'. I feared greatly his death – which took place six months later – and I did not want to displease him in the twilight of his life or think of him leaving this world without a son to officiate at his funeral rites. Therefore I feared my own temper and resulting quarrel and being turned out again. But I thank God who moved him to give in to my wishes. In due course I became an employee of the *Mayapore Gazette*.

After my father's death I became 'head of the household' and had to arrange the marriage of my only surviving sister, who was then sixteen. These family obligations took up a great deal of my time in 1937/8. My mother and I were now living alone together. She was also always persuading me to become married. In those days I was somewhat innocent in these respects. I feared that my experiences with immoral women would make it dangerous for me to be a husband and father, even though I had not – by God's will – suffered any lasting disease. Also I was dedicating my life, after my father's death, to politics and to my work as a 'rising' journalist.

My duties now took me daily into the cantonment where the offices of the *Gazette* were situated and I was becoming familiar with the life on that side of the river. As a student also I had been going daily over the river to the Government Higher School but now as 'apprentice journalist' to Mr Laxminarayan I was learning things I was not bothering about or knowing before. For instance I became familiar with the administration of law and order, and of the social life of the English.

In this way as a young Indian of no consequence I suffered many social indignities and became bitter, remembering the care with which my father had needed to account for every penny and had feared to be absent from his profession even for one day. I became friendly with several young fellows of my age, and also again with Moti Lal, and we would talk far into the night about all this kind of thing often in my own home while my mother was sleeping. But it was not until Mr Laxminarayan employed in my stead Hari Kumar, the nephew of the rich merchant, Romesh Chand Gupta Sen in whose employment also was Moti Lal at one time, and I took up new employment with *Mayapore Hindu*, that I became involved with groups of young men who felt as I was feeling, leaderless in a world where their fathers were afraid to lose a day's work and even Indian politicians were living on a different plane from us. We decided to be on the alert to seize any opportunity that would bring the day of our liberation nearer.

By this time the English were at war with Germany and the Congress ministries had resigned and only we could imagine that once again our country would be forced to bear a disproportionate share of the cost of a war which was not of our seeking and from which we did not expect any reward but instead only promises coming to nothing. In those days we had to be careful to avoid arrest unless of course one of us decided to seek arrest deliberately by open infringement of regulations. Also we had to be careful when choosing our friends or casual acquaintances. Many innocent-seeming fellows were police spies and one or two of my friends were arrested as a result of information given to the authorities by people of that kind who were sometimes only interested in settling old scores and would make up tales to persuade the police to arrest one of us and put us out of harm's way. Moti Lal also was arrested, for defying order under section 144 prohibiting him from speaking at a meeting of students. He was sent to prison but succeeded in escaping.

When the Japanese invaded Burma and defeated the English we felt that at last our freedom was in sight. Neither I nor my friends were afraid of Japanese. We knew that we would be able to make trouble for the Japanese also if they invaded India and treated us badly like the British. Many of our soldiers who were left behind by their British officers and captured in Burma and Malaya were given their freedom by the Japanese and formed 'Indian National Army' under Subhas Chandra Bose. If the Japanese had won the war our comrades in the Indian National Army would have been recognised everywhere as heroes, but instead many of them were severely punished by the British when the war was over and our 'national leaders' stood by and did nothing to save them.

In those days we were knowing that only young men who were ready to give life and take life could ever make India a 'great power'. We did not understand the ramblings and wanderings of our leaders. Unfortunately it was difficult for us to form anything but small groups. We told each other that if once the people rose against their oppressors we young men would be able to link up with each other and give an example of bravery and determination that would infect all.

279

This was the position at the time of the rebellion in 1942. With several other young men I had prepared myself for any kind of sacrifice. After my arrest I was interrogated for hours to give information about 'underground system', but if there was any such system I was not knowing of it, only I knew boys like myself who were ready to take the foremost place in facing the enemy. On the very day of my arrest, August 11, I and several fellows were planning to join and exhort the crowds who would be forming up later that day to march on the civil lines. News of such plans spread quickly from one end of town to the other. A crowd had tried to form up that morning on Chillianwallah Bagh Extension road but had been dispersed by the police who seemed to crop up everywhere at a moment's notice. I and my fellows were not among this crowd because at that hour we were engaged in printing pamphlets to distribute among the people exhorting them to help to release the boys unjustly accused of attacking an English woman. We delivered one such pamphlet to the police post near the Tirupati temple by wrapping it round a stone and throwing it through open window so that the one amongst us chosen for this dangerous task would have the chance of getting away without being seen. Having done this we then dispersed going each to our separate homes or places of employment. Only one hour later the District Superintendent of Police and many constables descended upon the offices of *Mayapore Hindu* where I was working. I and other staff-members present were immediately arrested because the police found an old hand-press in a back room that they said had been used for printing seditious literature.

This was not true and only I among those arrested was guilty of such an act to my knowledge, but I denied it. With those arrested was the editor, who told the police that I had been absent from work that morning and that his hand-press had been used only for innocent advertising purposes. I did not know about what the editor had said until later, because we were kept separately, but eventually I learned that they had all been released, although *Mayapore Hindu* was suppressed and the offices closed by order. Still I said nothing, because I hoped to keep secret the true whereabouts of the printing press and the names of my accomplices. I was removed from the kotwali to cells in police headquarters in the civil lines where the boys who had been arrested near the Bibighar two days before were being held, but I did not see any of them. I was kept in a cell secluded from others and then, after interrogation, taken to the prison in Jail road. I was in the Jail road prison when the people attacked it and overcame the guards and police at the gate and forced their way in. Several prisoners were released but unfortunately for me this act of liberation occurred in a different 'block' and soon afterwards the soldiers attacked the jail and our short-lived hopes of freedom were over. In this action many innocent people lost their lives which the authorities tried to disguise giving very low figures for killed and wounded.

I had been taken from the kotwali to the cells in the civil lines in the late afternoon of the 11th, and was interrogated there personally by the District

Superintendent of Police. He was very clever with his questions but I had determined on complete silence. I knew that I would be locked up in any case, because I saw that he had a file about my suspected activities. He knew the names of many of my friends and even casual acquaintances and I wondered what spy had been in our midst. He kept asking me about Moti Lal. Also about Kumar and the other boys who had been arrested after the 'attack' on the English woman. It was no good denying that I knew Moti Lal and most of these boys because the Superintendent even had a note of dates and places where some of us had been seen together, or been known to have been together, beginning with a night in February when a few of us were drinking and Hari Kumar became too drunk so that we took him home only to hear later that he had wandered out again and been arrested and questioned. Two of the other boys arrested for the 'rape' were among those who were present on that occasion in February, and I could not help wondering whether after he was questioned Hari Kumar had agreed to spy on us and it was him we had to thank for our present predicament. Later I was ashamed to have had such thoughts, but I must be honest and mention that for a time I was suspicious.

None of the boys arrested for the 'rape' had been my accomplices in any of my own illegal activities, but the Superintendent also had 'on file' the names of three of the boys who were my accomplices and had been with me that morning at the secret press which we had taken over after Moti Lal's arrest. This press was in the house of one of the prostitutes. The police often visited this house themselves but were too alternatively engaged to notice anything of evidence that secret literature was also printed there.

When the Superintendent mentioned the names of some of the boys I had been with that morning I said (as it had been agreed between us if any of us were arrested) that we had not seen each other for two or three days. I admitted nothing to the Superintendent. I said that on that morning I had not felt well and so had gone to work late and in any case had been worried for my safety with all the troubles going on in the city.

After leaving the house where our secret printing press was, with the pamphlets which I had 'run off' and which my colleagues were now going to distribute, I had taken precaution of going to my home and telling my mother to say that I had been unwell and had not left home until now. My mother was very afraid, because this was proof that I was doing things against the authorities, but she said she would tell this story if she was asked. It was the first time I had kept away from my office duties to do this kind of work, which is why I took such a precaution. When the Superintendent asked me where I had been that morning I knew that the editor or one of my fellow staff members on *Mayapore Hindu* had mentioned my absence, but I told him about not having been well, and he looked annoyed and I could see that already he had had my mother questioned. I prayed that my real accomplices had all managed to tell satisfactory stories if they had been questioned also.

281

I was much afraid at this interrogation because of what we had heard about the horrible treatment of the boys arrested for the attack on the English woman. It was because of what we had heard that I and my accomplices hastened to print the pamphlet and distribute it during the day. The information about the dreadful behaviour of the police towards these boys came to us from someone who had spoken to one of the orderlies in the police headquarters who said that all the boys had been beaten senseless and then revived and forced to eat beef to be made to confess. But we believed they were not guilty and suspected that the story of the attack on the English woman was much exaggerated or even a fabrication because the boy 'Kumar' had been friendly with her and the English people therefore hated him. I knew nothing about Kumar's movements on the night in question but a friend of the other boys who were arrested said that except for Kumar they had merely been drinking home-distilled liquor in an old hut and knew nothing about the 'attack' until the police broke in and arrested them. This friend also had been drinking but came away a few moments before the arrests which he saw from a place of hiding. He thought that the level-crossing keeper at the Bibighar bridge had given them away because the keeper knew that they used the old hut to drink home-distilled liquor in and sometimes joined them and made them give him a drink to keep quiet about this illegal activity. I know that this is true about the hut and the drinking because I also sometimes went there. It was not the same place in which we drank on the night that Hari Kumar was with us and became intoxicated. To drink such stuff we had to find different locations to put the police off the scent. If we wanted a drink we could not afford proper liquor which is why we drank this bad stuff.

During my interrogation the Superintendent said, 'Isn't it true that you are a close friend of Kumar and that on the night of the 9th of August you and Kumar and your other friends were drinking in the hut near the Bibighar bridge and that then you left them because they were beginning to talk badly about going into the cantonment to find a woman?'

I saw that he was offering me a chance to ingratiate myself and bear false witness, and so much fearful as I was of being beaten, I said no it was not true, only it was true that I knew Hari Kumar and some of the boys he named, but on the night of the 9th August I was working late at offices of *Mayapore Hindu* 'subbing' the reports of outbreaks that had taken place during the day in Dibrapur and Tanpur, and that my editor would no doubt testify to this. I was speaking truth and the Superintendent was angry because he knew I was speaking it. He said, 'You'll regret your lying before I've done with you.' He then left me alone in the room. I looked round for ways of escape but there was not even a window through which I might attempt to regain my longed-for freedom. The room was lighted by one electric bulb. There was a table and a chair at which the policeman had been sitting and the stool on which I was sitting. In one corner there was an iron trestle.

When I realised that there was no escape I prayed for strength to endure my torture without giving away the names of my accomplices. I thought that in a moment they would come for me and that the Superintendent Sahib was even now ordering them to prepare things. But he came back alone and sat down at the desk again and started to ask all the same questions. I do not know how long all this went on. I was hungry and thirsty. After some time he left the room again without succeeding in hearing any different thing from me and two constables came in and took me into a truck and drove me to the jail in Jail road. On the way I hoped to be rescued by our people, but the truck drove very fast and there was no incident. I was in this jail for a week and was then taken to Court and charged with printing and publishing seditious literature. A police spy gave evidence of seeing me throw the pamphlet into the kotwali, which was not true, but I could not prove it. Also the illegal press had been found, no doubt also as result of spying, and all my accomplices apprehended. I was sentenced to two years rigorous imprisonment. To serve my sentence I was sent to the jail near Dibrapur and locked at first into a filthy cell. I believed that the Superintendent in Mayapore had given orders for me to be especially harshly treated. At first I could not eat the disgusting food they gave me, hungry though I was. One day I quite lost my reason and threw the plate on the floor. The next day I was taken out of my cell and told that for infringing prison regulations I was to receive fifteen strokes of the cane. They took me at once into a small room and there I saw the same kind of iron trestle I had seen in the room where the Superintendent had questioned me. They showed me the cane they were going to use. It was about four feet long and half an inch thick. They stripped me of all my clothes, bent me over the trestle and tied my wrists and ankles and carried out 'the sentence'. Towards the end I could no longer support my suffering and fainted away.

I was sent later to another prison. I was allowed no communication with anyone, not even my family. They told me one day that my mother was dead. I wept and begged of God to be forgiven for the suffering I had caused her, in this freedom-work I had felt I had to do. I did not resent any of my punishment because I was guilty of all the 'crimes' I was punished for. I did not think of them as being crimes and therefore my punishment was not punishment but part of the sacrifice I was called upon to make.

It was towards the end of my imprisonment that one of the boys who had been accused of the attack on the English woman was brought also into this prison from another jail. These boys had all been kept in separate prisons because the authorities had wished to keep them apart no doubt so that two of them should not confirm the story of their unjust punishment to fellow prisoners. When I saw this boy I cried out in amazement because I had thought they were all tried and condemned long ago. In prison I had heard once that they were hanged. But this boy told me there had never been any evidence against them. He thought it had been all a 'put-up job', and that there was probably no rape in the Bibighar at all. Finally the

283

authorities had locked them all up as undesirables, all being known or suspected of indulging in subversive activities. We were not able to speak often to each other and he seemed too much afraid to talk about the rumours I had heard of torture and defilement.

When I was released from prison, my own home was no longer available. I had frequently to report to the police. My old employer Mr Laxminarayan found lodging for me and gave me some work so that I could keep body and soul together. I was in poor health and weighed only 97 pounds and was much troubled with coughing. In time I was able to regain some of my health and strength.

Of the boys arrested after the attack in the Bibighar only one of them I ever saw again who came back to live in Mayapore. This was the boy who came to the prison where I was. Hearing he was back in his home I visited him and asked him, 'Why were you afraid to speak much to me?' Even still he was reluctant to tell. He had suffered much and was afraid of the police who, he said, were always watching him. Still in those days the British were in power and had won the war and we wondered somewhat hopelessly about the future even though people kept saying that this time the British were really getting ready to quit.

This boy was speaking to me one evening in Mayapore, towards the end of 1946, and suddenly he said, 'I will tell you.' He spoke for a long time. He said that on the night of Bibighar when he and the other four who were still drinking in the hut were arrested they were taken at once to Police headquarters and locked in a cell. At this time only they knew that they had been caught drinking illegal liquor and were laughing and joking. Then they saw Hari Kumar brought in. His face was cut and bruised. They thought that this had been done by the police. One of them called out, 'Hello, Hari', but Kumar was not taking any notice. After that, except for my informant, none of the boys saw Kumar again. My informant was telling me all this in confidence, so I prefer to respect that and not divulge his name. These days all these things are forgotten and we are living different lives. Our young men today are not taking any interest in such matters. So I will call my friend 'Sharma' which is not his name nor the name of any of the other boys. Sharma was a fine, strong fellow, who like me had been 'a great one for the ladies' as a youth but had also somewhat reformed. He and his companions, other than Kumar, were locked in one cell, and taken out one by one. As one by one they went and did not come back, those remaining were no longer laughing and joking. They had also headache from too much drinking and were very much thirsty. Finally only Sharma was left. When his turn came he was taken downstairs by two constables and told to strip. When he was standing there naked one of the constables knocked at a door at the far end of the room and opened it and the District Superintendent came in. 'Sharma' was greatly humiliated to be forced to stand there so immodestly, especially in front of a white man. The constables now held Sharma's arms behind him and then the Superintendent – who carried a little stick – came over and held the stick out and lifted the exposed private parts and stared at them for some seconds. Sharma did not understand why this embarrassment should be done on him. He said, 'Why are you doing this, Superintendent Sahib?' The policeman said nothing. After inspecting the clothing which Sharma had been made to take off – also using the little stick to turn the clothing over and look at it – the policeman left the room. Later, of course, Sharma realised that the policeman was looking for evidence of rape practised upon a lady who had bled. When the Superintendent had gone the constables told Sharma to put on his underdrawers, but they did not give him back any of his other clothes. He was now taken out of the room by another door where he found his drinking companions in a cell, also wearing nothing but their underdrawers. Kumar was not with them. They tried to joke again, asking why the Sahib was so interested in certain parts of their bodies, but they were not feeling like laughing in this instance. Then one by one they were again taken away, and did not come back. When Sharma's turn came – and he was again the last – he was taken into the room where he had been stripped, and found the Superintendent sitting behind a desk. I think this was the same room in which Superintendent Sahib questioned me two evenings later. Sharma was not given a stool to sit on, however. He was made to stand in front of the desk. Then he was questioned. He did not understand the questions because he was thinking only of being charged with drinking home-distilled toddy. But suddenly the Superintendent said, 'How did you know she would be in the Bibighar Gardens?' and he began to see what might be behind all this rigmarole because of the word 'she' and the humiliation recently practised on him. But still he did not know what the policeman was trying to find out, until the policeman said, 'I'm inquiring into the attack and criminal assault on the English girl this evening, the girl who thought your friend Kumar was also a friend of hers.' Then there were many questions, such as, 'When did Kumar suggest all you fellows going together? Was she there when you arrived? How long did you wait for her? Who was the first man to assault her? You were led by Kumar, weren't you? If it hadn't been for Kumar you would never have thought of going to the Bibighar, would you? Were you just the fellow who was told to keep watch and never had the chance to enjoy her? Why should you suffer for the others if you just kept watch? How many times did you enjoy her, then? How many times did Kumar enjoy her? Why are you afraid? A fellow who has enjoyed drinking a lot of liquor starts thinking also about enjoying a woman, doesn't he? Why do you blame yourself for a perfectly natural thing? You shouldn't have drunk the liquor, but you did, and look what's happened. Why don't you be a man and admit that you drank too much and felt passionate? You're no weakling. You're a fine healthy fellow. Why be ashamed to admit your natural desires? If I drink too much liquor I also feel these things quite badly. There's no sign of blood on you or on your underclothes. She wasn't a virgin, was she? And you were the first fellow because you were the most passionate and couldn't wait. Isn't that it? Or perhaps you've been careful to wash? Or change your underclothes? Knowing what you have done was wrong? Knowing you would have to suffer if you were caught? Well, you are caught and have to suffer. Be a man and admit you deserve punishment. If you admit you deserve punishment you'll be let off lightly because I understand this kind of thing. And she wasn't a virgin, was she? She went with anyone who was able to satisfy her. And liked brown-skinned fellows. That's what young Hari Kumar told you, isn't it? Isn't it?'

This you see is what Sharma so much remembered. How the policeman finally kept saying, Isn't it? Isn't it? and banging his stick on the desk, because losing his temper at Sharma's all the time saying he knew nothing of what the Superintendent Sahib was talking about.

Then the policeman threw the stick on the desk and said, 'I see there's only one way to break *you*,' and he called out to the constables who took Sharma into the next room and through a door into another room. This room was even more dimly lit but he saw Kumar, naked, fastened over one of the iron trestles. In this position also I know it is difficult to breathe. Sharma said he did not know how long Kumar had been fastened in this way, but he said he could hear the sound of Kumar trying to breathe. He did not know at first that it was Kumar. Only he could see the blood on his buttocks. But then the policeman, the Superintendent, came in and said, 'Kumar, here's a friend of yours come to hear you confess. Just say "Yes, I was the man who organised the rape" and you'll be released from this contraption and won't be beaten any more.' Sharma said that Kumar only made 'a sort of sound' so the Superintendent Sahib gave an order and a constable came forward with a cane and gave Kumar several strokes. Sharma shouted out to Kumar that he knew nothing and had said nothing. He also shouted, 'Why are you treating this fellow so?' He said the constables then continued to beat Kumar until he groaned. Sharma could not look at this terrible punishment. After a while he was taken away and locked alone in a cell. Ten minutes or so later he was taken back into the room where Kumar had been. The trestle was now unoccupied. He was fastened to it after they had taken off his underdrawers. He said they then put what felt like a wet cloth on his buttocks and gave him nine strokes. He said the pain was so awful that he could not understand how Kumar had borne so much of it. They put the wet cloth over him so that his skin should not be cut and leave permanent marks. When they had finished he was taken back to the cell. Later he was put into another cell where his companions were. Kumar was not with them. He told them what had been done to him and to Kumar. The others had not been beaten but were afraid their turn was coming. The youngest of them began to weep. They did not at all understand what was happening. By now it was early morning. The Superintendent came down to the cell, with two constables. The constables were ordered to show the others what even nine strokes of the cane over a wet cloth could do to the buttocks. They held Sharma down and uncovered him. Then the Superintendent said that if any one of them so much as hinted at any time, to any person, during their 'forthcoming interrogation, trial and punishment' that any one of them had been 'hurt' or harshly treated, they would all suffer even more severely the punishment Sharma could describe to them both from personal experience and from having seen another man undergo it.

Half an hour later some food was brought in. They were hungry and tired and frightened. They began to eat. After a few mouthfuls also they vomited. The 'mutton' in the curry was beef. The two Muslim jailors who were standing watching them laughed and told them that now they were outcastes and even God had turned his face from them.

Part Seven

THE BIBIGHAR GARDENS

Daphne Manners (Journal addressed to Lady Manners) Kashmir, April 1943

I am sorry, Auntie, for all the trouble and embarrassment I've caused you. I began to apologise once before, when Aunt Lili brought me back to Rawalpindi, last October, but you wouldn't listen. So I apologise now, not for my behaviour but for the effect it's had on you who did nothing to deserve our exile. But I want to thank you, too, for your loving care of me, for voluntarily taking on the responsibility of looking after me, and for never once making me feel that this was a burden, although I know it must have been, and is as bad here where you see hardly anyone as it was in Pindi where so many of your old friends made themselves scarce. I sometimes try to put myself in your shoes and work out what it must be like to be the aunt of 'that Manners girl'. I know that's how people speak of me and think of me, and that it rubs off on to you. And all the marvellous things you and Uncle Henry did to make things seem right in India, for English people, are forgotten. This is really what I mean when I say I'm sorry. Sorry for giving people who criticised you and Uncle Henry the last word, for seeming to prove to them that everything you and he stood for was wrong.

The awful thing is that if you ever read this I shan't be here to smile and make the apology look human and immediate. If I get through to the other side of what I have to face we shall probably continue in the state we live in at the moment, of talking about as few subjects as possible that can remind either of us of the real reason why we are here. You won't in that case read this because I only write it as an insurance against permanent silence. I write it because I have premonitions of not getting through and I should hate to kick the bucket knowing I'd made no attempt to set the record straight and break the silence we both seem to have agreed is okay for the living, if not for the dead. Sorry about the morbid note! I don't feel morbid, just prepared. Perhaps I've felt like that all along, ever since the doctor in London told me to take it easy and stop driving ambulances in the blackout. Possibly the suspicion that I had to cram as much of my life as I could into as short a time as possible accounts for things I've done that people settled into the comfortable groove of three score and ten would reckon hasty and ill-advised.

288

If I'm right, and my premonitions aren't just morbid fancies, it would be odd, wouldn't it, how someone who looks so strong and healthy could be really just a mess of physiological sums added up wrong! After Mother died I used to be afraid of getting cancer. I've since been afraid of a tumour on the brain, to account for my poor sight and occasional headaches. All these sophisticated diseases also afflict Indian peasants but *they* are just statistics in the records of the birth and death rates and life expectancy charts. I often wish that I could feel and think myself equally anonymous, stricken (if I must be stricken) by God, and not by something the doctors know all about and can account and prepare you for.

But let me say this; medically I feel there is only one thing really 'wrong' with me, and that this may only be wrong for me because I'm not very efficiently put together. Like the doctor in Pindi, Dr Krishnamurti talks about a Caesarian. I've said that I don't want that. Maybe I'm just pigheaded, but you've no idea how important it is to me to try to do this thing properly. I don't want to be cut open, to have the child torn out like that. I want to bear it. I want to give it life, not have its life or my life or both our lives saved for us by clever doctors. I want to try my best to end with a good conscience what I began with one. I think Dr Krishnamurti almost understands this. He looks at me in such an odd way. And this is another thing I am so thankful to you for, that you've never even thought of distinguishing between an English and an Indian doctor, let alone resisted my consulting an Indian. Long ago (well, it seems long ago but can't have been much more than a year) I wrote to you from Mayapore saying how glad I was that I'd had the fortune to be with someone like you instead of like the Swinsons (whom I always remember as 'my first colonials'. And what a shock they were to me!) If I'd been their niece then even if they hadn't packed me off somewhere out of the way they'd never have allowed anyone but a white doctor to come near me. But perhaps if I'd been a niece of the Swinsons I'd have run a mile rather than see Dr Krishnamurti anyway. Or would never have got into what the Swinsons no doubt call 'this mess'.

Oddly enough there was a Dr Krishnamurti in Mayapore, a colleague of Dr Anna Klaus. I asked our Dr Krishnamurti whether he was any relation of the one in Mayapore and he said he expected so, if you traced the family far enough back. I told him that I was glad his name was Krishnamurti, because it was a link with Mayapore. He looked embarrassed and surprised. I'm not sure that he wasn't shocked, my saying that name, Mayapore, so casually. He's got over the embarrassment of having to touch me, but not the embarrassment of what it seems I represent to Indians as well as to British. This thing – whatever it is – that I represent has now passed from the purely notional to the acutely physical phase. In Pindi I saw how even the few people who came to see us – or rather came to see you in spite of me – couldn't keep their eyes off my waist-line. Now of course the distortion caused by the unknown child (unknown, unwanted, unloved it seems by anyone but me) is the most immediately obvious thing about me. If I went down into the bazaar, and didn't confine myself to the house and garden, I'd feel it necessary to go with a little bell, like a leper, so that people could go indoors and stay clear until I'd passed! If I'd been assaulted by men of my own race I would have been an object of pity. Religiously-minded people would probably have admired me as well for refusing to abort. But they weren't men of my own race. And so even the Indians in Pindi used to avert their eyes when I went into the cantonment, as if they were afraid some awful punishment would pass from me to them.

Even you, Auntie, seem to keep your eyes level with mine these days.

*

Of course, I wasn't a virgin. Anna Klaus told me later that she had been asked and had given her answer. She wanted me to know that the question had come up and been dealt with. She didn't press me for any comment. I didn't make any. But I tell you, Auntie, to set the record straight. My first lover was a friend of my brother David. My second a man I met in London during the time I was driving the ambulances. Two lovers – but, you see, *not* lovers. We made love but weren't in love, although for a time I thought I was in love with the first man.

It is only Hari I have ever loved. Almost more than anything else in the world I long to talk about him to you, even if it were only to say, 'Oh yes, Hari said something like that,' or 'I saw that one time when I was with Hari.' Just to speak his name to another person, to bring him back into the ordinary world of my life. But I can't. I know that your face would go blank, and this is something I couldn't bear, to have him shut out like that, by you. He has been shut out enough. If I cry – and I sometimes do – it's because I know that I have shut him out as well. Is it true, I wonder, that you know where he is? I often think you know, that so many of the people I count as friends know, but won't tell me. I don't blame you, though. Your silence is for what you believe is my good, and mine has been for what I think is Hari's. God knows there have been affairs between people of Hari's colour and people of mine before, and even marriages, and children, and blessings as well as unhappiness. But this was one affair that somehow never stood a chance. I've given up hope of ever seeing him again.

This is why, especially, the child I bear is important to me. Even though I can't be positive it is his. But I think so, I believe so. If it isn't, it is still a child. Its skin may be as dark as Hari's or almost as pale as mine, or somewhere in between. But whatever colour – he, or she, is part of my flesh and blood; my own typically ham-fisted offering to the future!

*

A day or two since I wrote anything in this book. I write at night, mostly, huddled in your sheepskin, close to the dying log fire. It is a land of such marvellous contrasts. Tonight, in Mayapore, the heat will be awful. One

290

would sit under the fan, with all the windows open, but if I went to the little lattice window here and peeped through the cretonne curtains I would see the snow on the mountains. And yet in a few weeks the valley will be filled with people on leave. They will swim in the lakes and throng the river in their shikaras. Shall we move into Srinagar then, Auntie, and live on one of the houseboats and fill it with flowers and have our fortunes told?

*

Marigolds. How Bhalu hated it when I usurped his position and went gathering them early in the morning to put in a vase for Lili's breakfast tray! I was in Bhalu's bad books for trampling one of his flower beds and cutting marigolds the day Hari first came to the MacGregor House. Since I've never talked to you about Hari I don't know how much Auntie Lili told you. But soon after I went down to Mayapore with her she was asked by someone, Anna Klaus in fact, whether she knew a Mr Kumar, or Coomer as it was sometimes spelt, and if in any case she could ask Judge Menen what Mr Kumar had done to deserve being hustled away by the police, hit by a sub-inspector in the presence of witnesses and taken in 'for questioning'. Lili didn't tell me much about any of this but I gathered that she was taking some sort of interest in a young Indian who was in trouble simply for answering back, or something like that. Her not telling me much was all part of that attitude of hers we both know so well. Like at Lahore, on our way down to Mayapore, when she sat in our compartment cool as a cucumber pretending that nothing was going on while all the time those two Englishwomen were really accusing her of having pinched a piece of their beastly luggage. As you know, Auntie, it's difficult ever to get Lili to talk about the things Indians have to put up with, but that doesn't mean she doesn't feel badly about them, or that if she can help someone who's in trouble, as Hari was, she'll just sit back and do nothing.

In fact I never heard the full story of Hari's 'arrest' until Hari told me himself, long afterwards, one evening when we'd gone together to the Tirupati temple. *I didn't even know until then that the man who'd actually taken him in for questioning was Ronald Merrick.* I felt badly about that. I felt that everyone had deliberately kept it from me, Aunt Lili, Anna Klaus, Judge Menen, even Sister Ludmila – especially Sister Ludmila because it seemed it had all happened in the Sanctuary, in front of her. I felt badly because I had been out with Ronald as well as Hari, and it looked as if all the people I liked and trusted had simply sat back and watched and waited to see what might happen. Since then I've realised that it wasn't really like that. It was only like I think it always has been in India for people of either race who try to live together outside their own enclosed little circles. Inside those circles the gossip never stops and everybody knows everybody else's business. But outside them it's as if the ground is so uncertain that to stand on it is enough. Yesterday's misunderstandings or injustices are best forgotten. You learn from them but keep what has been learned to yourself, hoping others have also learned. The important thing is to keep the ground occupied, and once you start talking about anything except *today* you're adding to the danger that's always there, of people turning tail and scurrying back to the safe little place where they know they can talk their heads off because in there they all have to pretend to think alike.

But when I found out from Hari that it was Ronald Merrick who had taken him into custody and questioned him, and had stood by and watched a sub-inspector hit him, I felt I'd been made a laughing-stock. I'd always assumed that Ronald was much too high and mighty to have been involved personally in such a local little matter as the arrest and questioning of a 'suspect'. I was angry with Ronald for warning me about my association with Hari (as he had done only a few days before the visit to the temple) without bothering to mention that he had *personally* arrested and questioned him. I was angry with everyone, but most of all I suppose angry with myself. But what I said to Hari that night made him think I was only angry with him, and even accusing him of deceit, which is supposed to be a typically Indian failing so far as the average stolid good old no-nonsense Englishwoman is concerned. I suppose my reaction struck Hari as typical too, typical of the roughshod-riding English mem. After we parted I meant to have it out with Aunt Lili when she got back, but she was late and I went to bed. I sat up for ages, thinking of the times Ronald Merrick had been at the MacGregor House, and the times Hari had been (but never on the same occasion). I worked it out that the evening Ronald came to dinner, after I'd come to stay with Lili (I remember mentioning in my first letter to you from Mayapore that the District Superintendent of Police was coming that evening and that I had to change into my glad rags) must have been only a day or two after Lili had been rung by Anna Klaus and asked to speak to Judge Menen about 'Mr Kumar or Coomer', because I know that happened in the first few days of my stay at the MacGregor House. Perhaps if I'd been more settled I'd have asked more questions about Hari, who he was, and what had happened to him. But I didn't. On the night Lili had Ronald there to dinner, with several other guests, she must have known that *he* had been responsible for taking Hari into custody and probably knew he had stood by while Hari was struck by the sub-inspector. But she never said anything to him about it, either then or later, so far as I could tell. Neither did she say anything to Hari on the few later occasions he came to the house, at least not in front of me.

I wondered why. And why she had never told me the whole story. But wondering this I realised that no one who knew the story had *ever* said anything to me. I only knew that after Hari's first visit Lili had become reserved about him. I sensed her lack of real liking for him. And this had made me hesitant about telling her much about what Ronald came to call 'my association with Mr Kumar'. I saw the *extent* of the silence that had surrounded this association, and how I had automatically contributed to it. I'd also kept quiet – to everyone but you – about Ronald's 'proposal', and this was the same *kind* of silence.

This is when I knew that I really loved Hari, and wanted him near me all the time, and also when I began to be afraid for him. There seemed to have been a conspiracy among everyone I knew at all well to say nothing, but wait, almost as if holding their breath, perhaps wanting me to like Hari, for himself, simply as a man, but scared of the consequences and also of the other thing, that I was attracted to the idea of doing something unconventional for the hell of it, which of course would have hurt him more than me. But it was a conspiracy that seemed to be rooted in love as well as fear. I felt as if they saw my affair with Hari as the logical but terrifying end of the attempt they had all made to break out of their separate little groups and learn how to live together – terrifying because even they couldn't face with equanimity the breaking of the most fundamental law of all – that although a white man could make love to a black girl, the black man and white girl association was still taboo.

And then all my determination to have things out with Lili in the morning was undermined. Partly because there was nothing really to 'have out', partly because I was afraid. I couldn't see myself talking to Lili about any of this, because to talk would have been to introduce aspects of my 'association' *that had nothing to do with what I felt for Hari*. But thinking of what I felt for him, and looking in the mirror as I got ready for bed, I thought, Well – but does he love me? What *am* I? Just a big-boned girl with a white skin whose mother justifiably accused her of awkwardness, and whose father and brother were kind as the men of a family are always kind to a daughter or sister who is a good sport but not much else.

Sorry, Auntie. Not making a bid for *your* kindness. Just stating the truth, and explaining the awful doubts I had, the suspicion that perhaps what people said was true, that a coloured man who goes with a white girl only does so for special reasons.

*

When I first met him I thought him horribly prickly. He was supposed to come with his Aunt Shalini, but he came alone and was ill at ease. Later Aunt Lili said she wasn't surprised he'd come alone, because his Aunt Shalini was probably one of those embarrassingly shy little Indian women who either never went anywhere or cast a blight on any place they *did*. I'd virtually forgotten whatever Lili had told me about 'Mr Kumar'. It was some time in March and she'd decided to have a small cocktail party. When she made out her list she said, 'And we'll ask young Mr Kumar and see what he looks like.' I said, 'Which Mr Kumar?' and she said, 'Oh, you remember. The young man I was asked to speak to Judge Menen about because he got arrested by mistake.' Then she said, 'But don't for goodness' sake say anything to him about *that*.' Well, you know me! I've always tended to put my foot in it by coming out with things bald-faced. I used to be much worse, because I was so dreadfully shy and conscious of being clumsy, and the only thing I could think to do not to look awkward was to chat at people and say the first thing that came into my head, which more often than not turned out to be the wrong thing.

I've forgotten who most of the people were who came that time for cocktails. There was Dr Anna Klaus, I know, because that was the first time I'd met her, although I'd seen her talking to Dr Mayhew when she came to the Mayapore General for some consultation or other. And Matron was there. And Vassi (the lawyer, Mr Srinivasan, who was a friend of Lili's and also of Hari's aunt and 'uncle'). Hari's editor on the *Mayapore Gazette*, Mr Laxminarayan, was also supposed to be there but didn't turn up, probably because he found out Hari had been invited and he didn't feel the protocol would be right if he and a junior member of the staff were at the same function! At least that's what Hari said later. I know the Whites looked in for half an hour, and there were some teachers from the Higher School and the Technical College.

He was late turning up. He hadn't wanted to come, but had decided to face it. He was ashamed of his clothes. He didn't know any of us except Vassi and they didn't like each other much. When I say he didn't know any of us I'm wrong. He knew quite a lot of people by sight, because as a reporter on the *Gazette* it was his job to. He let slip to Aunt Lili that they had met before and that she had once answered a question he put to her when she won second prize for her roses at the flower show. I was standing next to her when he let on about that. He made it sound as if she ought to have remembered talking to him. She pretended to, but from the way she pretended I could tell that she disliked being *made* to pretend, which she only did because she thought he was hurt not to be recognised. And he saw through her pretence too. And at once became what I call prickly.

I put my foot in it too. When he spoke he sounded just like an Englishman. So I blurted out, 'Wherever did you learn to speak English as well as you do?' He just looked at me and said, 'England.' So of course I bashed on in a panic, expressing astonishment and interest, falling over myself to be friendly, but only succeeding in being inquisitive. Then Lili took me away and made me talk to some other people and the next time I saw him he was standing more or less alone, on the edge of a group of the teachers. So I went up to him and said, 'Let me show you the garden.' It was getting dusk and we were already *in* the garden, so it was a frightfully stupid thing to say. But it was this time of speaking to him that I really noticed how good-looking he was. And tall. So many of the Indian men I talked to I topped by an inch or two, which was something that usually added to my hysteria at a party where I was feeling shy and awkward.

But he let me show him the garden. Which is why I remember I'd been in trouble with Bhalu that morning. I showed him the flower bed I'd trampled on getting at the marigolds. I asked him whether he'd had a nice garden when he lived in England and he said he supposed it had been all right but that he'd never taken much notice of it. Then I said, 'Do you miss it all, though?' and he said at once, 'Not any more,' and sort of moved away and said it was time for him to go. So we walked back and re-joined the party which was breaking up. He said goodbye to Lili and thanked her rather brusquely and then just nodded goodbye to me. And I remember afterwards, when he'd gone, and one or two people stayed for dinner, all Indians, how forcibly it struck me that except for the colour of his skin he wasn't Indian at all – in the sense I understood it.

When everyone had gone and Lili and I were having a nightcap she said, 'Well, what were you able to make of young Mr Coomer?'

I said, 'I think he's a terribly sad man.' It was the first thing that came into my mind, and yet I didn't seem to have thought of it like that until then. And Lili said nothing except something like, 'Let's have the other half and then bash off to bed.'

*

I'm glad that I'm writing all this down, because even if you never read it it's helping me to understand things better. I think I've been blaming Lili for taking against Hari. No, let me be honest. I don't think I've been blaming her, I know I have. And I think I've been wrong. Reliving that first meeting with him I see how Lili, who was responsible for me to you, probably watched the way we left the party to inspect the garden, and didn't misinterpret but responded to the little warning bell that she must have learned, during her life, never to ignore. Remembering all the wonderful things about Lili, I *must* be wrong to think that she could ever really have harboured resentment of Hari for the critical attitude he adopted towards her in those few insignificant moments when they first met at her party. And Lili, after all, is a woman too. She can't have been totally unmoved by Hari's physical presence. Nor unconcerned, when she saw us going off together (only for ten minutes!), about me, and how *I* might be moved by it.

I used to think the fact that she seemed to 'drop' him after that first well-meaning attempt to gather him into what was called the MacGregor House set was due to nothing more than her annoyance at his prickliness, or anyway to the stuffiness she can sometimes astonish you with if people don't behave in exactly the way she personally considers 'good form'. And knowing that she had put herself out to help him when he was a total stranger to her I thought she was annoyed that he hadn't shown the faintest sign of gratitude, and hadn't even said – as he was so capable of saying because the language and the idiom and the inflexions were natural to him – 'Thank you for the party, *and for everything*', when he said goodbye.

Perhaps this apparent brashness contributed to her reservations about Hari, but I am sure, now, that if he and I had simply smiled distantly at each other and passed each other by, the first thing she would have said, when the party was over, would have been something like, 'Poor Mr Kumar needs bringing out. We need to knock that chip off his shoulder. After all, it's not really his fault that it's there.' But she had seen that the chip on Hari's shoulder was insignificant compared with the possible danger that lay ahead for me, for him, if that clumsy but innocent walk in the garden developed into the kind of familiarity which Lili, as a woman of the world, saw at once as not unlikely.

*

Was it now that my dreams came back? Do you remember, Auntie? Those dreams I wrote to you about once? The dreams I had when I first came to India, and which I had again after I'd left Pindi and gone to Mayapore? The dreams of *faces*, the faces of strangers? Dreamed, imagined, constructed out of nothing, but with an exactness that was frightening because they were so real? The faces of strangers I had to take with me even into dreams because I felt that I was surrounded by strangers when I was awake?

The first two weeks or so in Mayapore, when everything was new to me and I was getting to know my surroundings, I didn't have those dreams. But as I told you in that letter, there was a period when the newness had worn off, when I hated everything because I was afraid of it. I think the cocktail party marked the beginning of this. I wanted to pack my bags and go back to Pindi – which interested me because when I was suffering this kind of homesickness in Pindi I wanted to pack my bags and go back to England. And just as I think you guessed something of what I was going through, so I believe did Lili. But how much of my restlessness – which I tried so hard to disguise – did she put down to my thinking about Mr Kumar? How much, indeed, *was* due to my thinking about him?

It was at this time that I broke my vow, never to go to the club because Lili couldn't go with me. The girls I worked with at the Mayapore General were always on at me to go with them. And it was so easy to talk to them. I used to feel the relief of leaving the MacGregor House and cycling to the hospital and when I got there not caring what I said or how I said it, and being able to flop into a chair and complain about the heat – using all the little tricks of expression and gesture that you know will be understood, and which don't have to be thought about. The luxury, the case, of being utterly natural. Giving back as good as you got if someone was edgy or bitchy. Being edgy and bitchy yourself. Letting it rip, like a safety valve.

So I started going with some of them to the club for a drink on my way home. They were usually picked up by young officers from the barracks, round about 5.30. There wasn't any serious attachment going. Just boys and girls getting together in their off-duty and maybe sleeping somewhere if it could be fixed. We used to drive to the club in tongas, or in army trucks if the boys could 'swing the transport' as they called it. Then we'd congregate in the lounge-bar or the smoking-room, or on the terrace. Or there was a games room, where they had a portable and a lot of old dance records, Victor Sylvester, Henry Hall, and some new ones, Dinah Shore, Vera Lynn, and the Inkspots. Usually round about 6.30 I'd slip away and get a tonga home. I felt horribly guilty about going to the club because I'd told

Lili I jolly well wouldn't. She'd always said, 'Don't be silly, of course you must go.' And I owned up at once, the moment I'd been, although on the way back that first time I was thinking up all kinds of excuses for being late. Once I'd owned up it made going again that much simpler, though. I felt less and less guilty and more and more at home in the club. Several times I stayed to dinner there, and only rang Aunt Lili at the last moment.

And then one day one of the boys who was a bit drunk and who'd insisted on coming with me to the phone said, 'She's not really your aunt, is she?' I said, 'No. Why?' And he said, 'Well, you don't look as if you've got a touch of the tar brush. I've had a bet on it.' And all kinds of little things fitted into place – oh, less in connection with what the boys and girls had said, but over the sort of things some of the civilian women had said, or rather *not* said. The way they'd looked when I said 'The MacGregor House' when they asked me where I was staying. The way some of the civilian men had chipped in and asked questions about you and Uncle Henry, as if (as I realised now) to test it out that I really was a niece of a one-time Governor and not some by-blow of Lili Chatterjee's family.

But there is this, too, Auntie – I think this kind of thing would have run off me like water off a duck's back if all the time, underneath the easy pleasure of being with the boys and girls, there hadn't been a sort of creeping boredom, like a paralysis. Basically I hated the way that after a few drinks everything people said was loaded with a kind of juvenile smutty innuendo. After a while I began to see that the ease of companionship wasn't really ease at all, because once you had got to know each other, and had then had to admit that none of you really had much in common except what circumstance had forced on you, the companionship seemed forced itself. We were all imprisoned in it, and probably all hated it, but daren't let go of it. I got so that I would just sit there listening to the things that were said, thinking, 'No, this is wrong. And I haven't got this time to waste. I haven't this time to spare.'

It was the evening I went to the club after the visit to the War Week Exhibition on the *maidan* that I first *admitted* this to myself. Was it just coincidence that I'd seen Hari again that afternoon, for the first time since the party? I suppose not. The two things were connected – the second meeting with Hari and my looking round the club and listening and saying to myself 'I haven't this time to waste'. And of course that other man was at the club too. Ronald Merrick I mean. Perhaps this wasn't coincidence either.

•

I went to the War Week Exhibition on the Saturday afternoon, at about four o'clock, with three or four girls from the hospital and two or three young subalterns from the Berkshires. We went to watch the parade and the military band which was the week's grand finale. There were the finals of the boxing, too, and the wrestling. The boxing was nearly all between

English boys, but the wrestling was between Indians from one of the Indian regiments. One of the girls said, 'Oh no, I couldn't bear to watch *that*,' so we went to the boxing and watched these young soldiers dab at each other and make each other's noses bleed. Then we went into the tea-tent. The parade was scheduled for 5.30. I've never seen anything like that tea-tent. Flowers everywhere. Long trestle-tables covered with dazzling white cloths. Silver-plated urns. Iced cakes, cream cakes, jellies, trifles. One of the boys we were with whistled and said that 'some wog contractor was putting on a show and making a packet'. And of course this was probably true, and at once cancelled out the thought that only the English were having a beano, although it didn't cancel out the picture you had of people at home scuttling off to the shops with their dismal little ration books. And it didn't cancel out the thought of all the people who weren't allowed in the tent, not because they couldn't afford the price of the tea-ticket, but because this was the tent for 'Officers and Guests' only. There were a few Indian women there, the wives of Indian officers. But the mass of faces was white – except behind the tables where the servants were running up and down trying to serve everyone at once. And 'Officers' was really only a polite way of saying 'Europeans' because there were plenty of civilians and their wives there too, but only white civilians, like the Deputy Commissioner, and several men I recognised from Lili's parties as teachers or executives from the British–Indian Electrical.

The DC was standing talking to the Brigade Commander and as we passed them Mr White said, 'Hello, Miss Manners. You know Brigadier Reid, I think.' Why was I so pleased? Because at once the boys I was with sort of stood to attention and the girls looked as if butter wouldn't melt in their mouths. Apparently the Brigadier was previously stationed in Pindi and had met us once or twice at parties, but we only vaguely remembered one another. He asked after you and then the DC said, 'How's Lili?' and I said 'Fine' and felt that somehow I was vindicated and no longer ranked in our little group as the odd girl who lived with 'that Indian woman'. Because even if she was 'that Indian woman' the Deputy Commissioner called her Lili. And yet afterwards I was annoyed, too, because the DC hadn't said, 'Where's Lili?' He knew, without even having to think about it, that she was unlikely to be in the tent and therefore probably wouldn't be on the *maidan* at all because she wouldn't go to 'the other tent'.

Anyway, I introduced the boys and girls, which rather made their day, but also helped to make mine later, when we were on our way across the *maidan* to the parade and I saw Hari and went up to him and talked to him for about five minutes while the others waited where I'd left them, and were prepared to wait because they couldn't be sure who Hari might be if I was on chatting terms with the DC and the Brig. When I got back to them one of the subalterns said, 'Who was that?' so I just said, 'Oh, a boy who was at Chillingborough,' as if I had known him then and he had been a friend of my brother or some other male relation. Which shut them up, because none of them had been to anywhere as good. I was quite shameless. About being so snobbish, I mean. Because this was *their* weapon, not mine. I mean it was their weapon, then, in Mayapore, even if it wasn't at home. I enjoyed the brief sensation I had of turning their world momentarily upside down.

*

Hari was at the War Week Exhibition for the *Gazette*. I didn't recognise him at first – partly because I don't see people very well without my glasses, but mainly because he looked different. It took me several meetings before I realised that since the cocktail party he'd spent money on new clothes – narrower, better fitting trousers (and not 'babu' white). In spite of his awkwardness at that party, I think that after it he had expected more invitations, and spent money he couldn't afford so that he wouldn't feel so out of place. At one of our later meetings I said, 'But I'm sure you used to smoke. You had a cigarette at the party.' He admitted this but said he'd given it up. Even then I didn't immediately connect the new clothes and the money saved from giving up smoking, or see what these things meant in terms of the hopes Lili's invitation had raised for him.

He'd spent all his life in England, or anyway from the age of two when his father sold all his land in the UP and went to live there. His mother had died when he was born, and once they were in England his father cut himself off from everyone except this one sister, Hari's Aunt Shalini who had been married off at sixteen to a Gupta Sen, the brother of a rich Mayapore bania. In England Hari's father made a lot of money, but then lost it, and died and left Hari penniless and homeless. And so there he was, just in his last year at Chillingborough, quite alone. His Aunt Shalini borrowed money from her well-off brother-in-law to pay Hari's passage back to India. He worked for a time in the uncle's office in the bazaar, but eventually got this job on the newspaper, because of his knowledge of English. Aunt Lili told me a bit of this (she got it from Vassi) but for ages I assumed that because his aunt's brother-in-law was rich money was no problem to him, and I thought his working on a newspaper was from choice, not necessity. It took some time as well for me to understand that all the plans he and his father had had for him had come to nothing, because his 'Uncle' Romesh wouldn't spend a penny on further education, but set him to work, and his Aunt Shalini had virtually no money of her own. And then, of course, it took some time for the penny to drop that Hari's Englishness meant nothing in India, because he lived with his aunt in one of the houses in the Chillianwallah Bagh – which was on the wrong side of the river.

When I went up to him on the *maidan* that day I said, 'It's Mr Kumar, isn't it?' which the white people nearby obviously took note of. I misjudged the reason for his silence and the reluctant way he shook hands. I said, 'I'm Daphne Manners, we met at Lili Chatterjee's,' and he said, yes, he remembered, and asked how we both were. We chatted on like that for a while, with me doing most of the chatting and feeling more and more like the squire's daughter condescending to the son of one of her father's tenants, because that's how he seemed to *want* to make me feel. I wondered why. I broke off finally, saying, 'Come along any evening. It's open house,' for which he thanked me with that expression that meant he wouldn't dream of coming along unless specially asked and perhaps not even then because he took the invitation as a meaningless form of politeness.

So off I went and rejoined the gang and sat for an hour watching the parade and listening to the band. And in the club that evening I stayed on for dinner and we talked about the marching and the drill. All the boys were awfully proud of themselves because of the boxing and the regimental precision of the Berkshires. You could sense flags flying everywhere. When Ronald Merrick turned up he came straight over to me, which wasn't at all usual. Since the dinner party at Aunt Lili's, when we didn't particularly hit it off, we'd only exchanged a few words and had the odd drink or two for form's sake if we bumped into each other at the club. He always seemed busy and unrelaxed, and happiest in the smoking-room talking to other men and getting into arguments. He had a bit of a reputation for being on the quarrelsome side, and apart from a number of unmarried girls who chased him people didn't like him much. But this evening he came straight over to me and said, 'Did you enjoy the parade? I saw you on the *maidan*.' He sat and had drinks with us, and then came out with this semi-invitation to me to come along one evening and listen to his Sousa records, which the other girls chipped me about when he'd gone, coming out with that old joke about etchings, and never trusting a policeman. One of them said, 'Daphne's obviously got what it takes for Mr Merrick. I've been trying to land *that* fish for ages.' One of the boys made a joke about what she meant by 'takes', so the subject was back to normal. Being a Saturday there was a dance on too, and the usual horseplay at the swimming pool. And out on the terrace you didn't only *sense* the flags waving, you could see them. Scores of little flags strung among the fairy lights. There was an atmosphere of 'We'll show them'. The boy I was dancing with said that War Week had given the bloody Indians something to think about. Then he began to get amorous and I had to fight him off. I left him and went into the ladies and sat on the seat and listened to the scurrilous chat going on on the other side of the door and thought, No, it's wrong, wrong. And later, back in the lounge-bar, deafened by the thumping band, I thought, 'I haven't this time to waste. I haven't this time to spare.'

I felt as if the club were an ocean-going liner, like the *Titanic*, with all the lights blazing and the bands playing, heading into the dark, with no one on the bridge.

*

Auntie, promise me one thing, that if the child survives but you can't bear to have it near you, you'll try to see that the money I leave is used to give it some kind of decent start in life? I look around, trying to think where the child might go if it lives and I don't. I don't presume on your affection for me to extend to what is only half my flesh and blood, and half that of someone unknown to you – perhaps someone unknown to me, someone disreputable. I have got myself used to the idea that you won't want it under your roof, in fact, please don't worry on that score. It's inevitable that a child so badly *mis*conceived should suffer a bit for *my* faults. In any case, let's be frank, you probably won't live for as long as the child would need you to if he first came to a fully conscious, recollective existence while under your roof. I think of Lili. But wonder, too. Perhaps as the child grows, some likeness to Hari will become apparent. I so much hope so. Because that will be my vindication. I have nightmares of the child growing up to resemble no one, black-skinned, beyond redemption, a creature of the dark, a tiny living mirror of that awful night. And yet, even so, it will be a child. A god-given creature, if there is a god, and even if there isn't, deserving of that portion of our blessing we can spare.

I suppose the child – if I'm not here to nurture him – will have to go into a home. Couldn't it be as well my home in a way? There is that woman whom they call Sister Ludmila. I asked her once whether she needed money. She said not, but promised to tell me if she ever did. Perhaps as she gets older (and I don't know how old she is) she will spare a thought for the new-born as well as for the dying. It's a logical progression.

By 'decent start in life', I don't mean background or education, but much simpler things like warmth, comfort, enough to eat, and kindness and affection. Oh, all the things squandered on me.

If it is a boy, please name him Harry, or Hari if his skin is dark enough to *honour* that kind of spelling. If a girl – I don't know. I haven't made up my mind. I haven't thought of 'it' as a girl. But if she is please *don't* call her Daphne. That's the girl who ran from Apollo, and was changed into a laurel bush! With me it's been the other way round, hasn't it? Rooted clumsily in the earth, thinking I'm running free, chasing the sun-god. When I was in my teens Mother once said, 'Oh, for goodness' sake stop *gallumping*!' which puzzled and then hurt me because being tall I had an idea that I was a sort of graceful Diana type – long-legged and slender, taut as a bow, flitting through the forest! Poor Mother! She had a frightful talent for pouring cold water on people. It was David who taught me to see that she did this because she never knew from one minute to the next what it was she really wanted, so she felt that things were always going wrong around her, and had to hit out at the nearest likely culprit, usually Daddy, but often me. She adored David, though, which is probably why he saw through her more easily than Daddy and I did and was able to explain her to me. She never had her defences up for *him*. I suppose it was because even after years of living comfortably in England she still talked about India as if she had only just escaped from it a minute ago that I grew to feel sorry for it, and then to love it and want it for its own sake, as well as for Daddy's. When I was old enough to understand them he used to show me snaps and photographs and tell me what I thought were wonderful tales of the 'land where I was born', so that when I first came back out here I was always looking for the India I thought I knew because I had seen it in my imagination, like a kind of mirage, shimmering on the horizon, with hot, scented breezes blowing in from far-away hills ...

*

It's funny how in spite of what you know about the rains before you come to India you think of it as endlessly dry and scorched, one vast Moghul desert, with walled, scattered towns where all the buildings are shaped like mosques, with arches of fretted stone. Occasionally from the window of a train – the one I went up to Pindi on when I first came out – there are glimpses of the country you've imagined. I'm glad I came before and not in the middle of the rains. It's best to undergo the exhaustion of that heat, the heat of April and May that brings out the scarlet flowers of the gol mohurs, the 'flames of the forest' (such a dead, dry, lifeless-looking tree before the blossoms burst) the better to know the joy of the wild storms and lashing rains of the first downpours that turn everything green. That is *my* India. The India of the rains.

*

There's another name besides Hari's that we never mention. Bibighar. So although you were in Mayapore once, and may have visited the gardens, I don't know whether you have a picture of them in your mind or not. There it is all greenness. Even in the hottest months, before the rains, there is a feeling of greenness, a bit faded and tired, but still green – wild and overgrown, a walled enclosure of trees and undergrowth, with pathways and sudden open spaces where a hundred years ago there were probably formal gardens and fountains. You can still see the foundations of the old house, the Bibighar itself. In one part of them there is a mosaic floor with steps up to it as if it was once the entrance. They've built pillars round the mosaic since and roofed it over, to make it into a sort of shelter or pavilion. Men from the Public Works come once or twice a year and cut back the shrubbery and creepers. At the back of the grounds the wall is crumbled and broken and gives on to waste ground. At the front of the garden there is an open archway on to the road but no gate. So the garden is never closed. But few people go in. Children think it is haunted. Brave boys and girls play there in the morning, and in the dry weather well-off Indians sometimes picnic. But mostly it's deserted. The house was built by a prince, so Lili told me, and destroyed by that man MacGregor, whose house is named after him, and whose wife Janet is supposed to haunt the verandah, nursing her dead baby. It was Lili who first took me into the Bibighar. Hari had heard something about it, but had never seen it, or realised that the long wall on the Bibighar Bridge road was the wall surrounding it, and had never been in it until I took him there one day. There were children playing the first time I visited it with Lili but they ran off when they saw us. I expect they thought we were daylight Bibighar ghosts. And afterwards I never saw anyone there at all.

*

Hari and I got into the habit of going to the Bibighar, and sitting there in the pavilion, because it was the one place in Mayapore where we could be together and be utterly natural with each other. And even then there was the feeling that we were having to hide ourselves away from the inquisitive, the amused, and the disapproving. Going in there, through the archway, or standing up and getting ready to go back into the cantonment – those were the moments when this feeling of being about to hide or about to come out of hiding to face things was strongest. And even while we were there, there was often a feeling of preparedness, in case someone came in and saw us together, even though we were doing nothing but sitting side by side on the edge of the mosaic 'platform' with our feet dangling, like two kids sitting on a wall. But at least we could be pretty sure no white man or woman would come into the gardens. They never did. The gardens always seemed to have a purely Indian connection, just as the *maidan* really had a purely English one.

Perhaps you say: But if you wanted to be with Hari, and he wanted to be with you, that was no crime, surely, and there were tons of places you could have gone and been happy together? Well, but where? The MacGregor House? His house in the Chillianwallah Bagh? Yes. But where else? Auntie, where else? Where else that people wouldn't have stared and made us self-conscious, armed us in preparation to withstand an insult or a vulgar scene? The club was out. There was the other club, what they call the Indian Club, but Hari wouldn't take me there because there *I* would have been stared at by what he called the banias with their feet on the chairs. The English coffee shop was out. The Chinese Restaurant was out – after one visit when he was stopped from following me upstairs. I'd been there before with an English officer – and automatically, without thinking, began to go up. So we had to sit downstairs while I was subjected to the stage whisper comments of the people going to the room above, and the curious, uncomfortable stares of the British non-commissioned soldiers who shared the downstairs room with us. Even the poor little fleapit cinema in the cantonment was out because I wouldn't have had the nerve to try to take Hari into the sacrosanct little 'balcony' and he wouldn't have made me sit on a wooden form in the pit. Neither would he take me to the Indian cinema opposite the Tirupati temple, although I asked him to. He said, 'What, and sit through four hours of the *Ramayana*, holding our noses, getting fleas and sweating our guts out?'

Auntie, in Mayapore there wasn't anywhere we could be alone together

303

in public that didn't involve some kind of special forethought or preparation. We spent a few evenings at the MacGregor House while Auntie Lili was out playing bridge, and a couple of evenings with his sweet little Aunt Shalini, but a friendship between two human beings can't be limited in this way, can it? You can't not be affected by the fact that it's a friendship you're both having to work hard at.

*

And of course it was a friendship I began in a conscious frame of mind. Naturally, as I'd known he wouldn't, he never just dropped in to open house. I told Lili I'd met him on the *maidan* and invited him to come any time. In retrospect her reaction strikes me as that of someone who was subconsciously pleased, but afraid of the consequences for me, or, if not afraid, full of reservations. She told me more about him. Perhaps she was trying to warn me, but she only succeeded in adding fuel to my reforming zeal. She must have told me about his having been to Chillingborough before I met him on the *maidan*, because I'm sure he never mentioned Chillingborough at the party. But otherwise I've forgotten exactly how and when I fitted him together in my mind. All I know, what I admit to, is this – that I was conscious at the meeting on the *maidan* of doing a good deed. The thought revolts me now. I can't bear to remember that I ever condescended, even unintentionally, to the man I fell in love with.

When a couple of weeks had gone by and he still hadn't dropped in I wrote him a note. I got his address from Aunt Lili who had it in her book. As you know I've always been hopeless at bridge, and Lili was going round to the Whites to make up a four with Judge Menen whose wife was in the Greenlawns Nursing Home. Which left me alone on a Saturday evening. After the flag-wagging of War Week I didn't want to go to the club. I didn't know what I wanted to do. I thought of Hari. I'd been thinking of him a lot. It was Saturday morning. I wrote him a note and sent it by one of the servants to the Chillianwallah Bagh. The servant came back and said that Kumar Sahib hadn't been in but that he'd left the note. So I didn't know whether Hari would come that evening or not, which made Lili's silent criticism worse, and my determination to have everything ready stronger. I told cook to prepare dinner for two, chicken pulao, with piles and piles of saffron rice and onion pickles and mounds of lovely hot chappattis, and lots of iced beer, and what I called Mango-Melba to follow. I checked the cocktail cabinet and sent the boy to the liquor store for more Carew's gin. Then I went down to the cantonment myself, to the Sports Emporium, and bought a batch of records that had just come in, and a box of needles because Lili wasn't very good about changing them and used the same ones over and over and mixed the old ones with the new. We had a Decca portable she'd bought the last time she was in Cal. And when I got back I sent Bhalu crazy the way I bashed round the garden gathering armfuls of flowers! I felt a bit like Cho Cho San getting ready for Pinkerton! Lili went off to the Whites about six-thirty while I was still in the bath. She came into the bedroom and called out, 'Daphne, I'm bashing off now and will be back about midnight, I expect. Have a good time.' I cried out, 'Oh, I will. Give my love all round.' And then she said, 'I hope he has the good manners to turn up,' so I shouted back, 'Of course he will. He'd have sent a note by now if he hadn't been going to.' Poor Lili. She really thought he wasn't going to. So did I. I dressed in that awful electric blue dress that turns muddy green in the artificial light, but I felt I didn't care what I looked like. I knew I could never look anything but myself. And there was joy in not caring for once, but just being myself.

And he came, bang on the dot of 7.30, in a horse tonga. To get a horse tonga he must have gone to the station, because on the other side of the river you can usually only get cycle tongas. Or perhaps he had come from the cantonment bazaar, from Darwaza Chand's shop, and had waited there while they finished making the new shirt that made him smell of fresh, unlaundered cotton.

*

I'd cheated a bit in my note by not making it really clear I'd be alone. For all I knew he was the sort of Indian boy who'd think it wrong to dine alone with a woman, or if *he* didn't mind, that his aunt would refuse to let him come if she knew Lili was going to be out. I could see he was on tenterhooks at first, waiting for Lili to appear. We were on the verandah, and Raju was serving the drinks. It must have been on this occasion that he refused a cigarette and admitted he'd given it up. Not smoking made him more on tenterhooks, and suddenly I was on them too because I saw what a trap I'd laid for myself. He'd probably think Lili had gone out to avoid him because she disapproved of the idea of his coming to a meal, or, just as bad, that I'd asked him round secretly on a night she was going out because I knew she would disapprove. So before the situation got out of hand I told him the truth, that Saturday was one of Lili's bridge nights, and I hated bridge and had wanted a quiet dinner with someone I could talk to about home, but had cheated when writing my note in case he or his aunt thought it odd for a girl to invite a boy round on an evening when she was going to be by herself.

He seemed puzzled at first. It must have been about four years since an English person had spoken to him in the way that in England he'd have been used to and thought nothing of. I hated even being conscious of this fact, but I was, so there's no use in pretending otherwise.

Even on that first evening we were having to work at a basis for ordinary human exchange, although it was probably the only evening we met without feeling an immediate sense of pressure and disapproval from outside. Within a minute or two of realising Lili was out I could see him beginning to relax, beginning to forget himself and start looking at and considering me. We had about three gin fizzes and then went in and ate, sitting close together at one end of the table. I'd worked it out before that although it would have been nice for me if I could have just told Raju to bring the food in and leave me to serve it, it would be better for Hari's morale if we were *both* waited on hand and foot. Raju of course tried to cut Hari down to size a bit by addressing him in Hindi, but soon gave up when he realised Hari spoke it really no better than I did! And I was glad to see how he also relaxed at the table, once we'd made a joke about his inability to speak the language, and tackled the grub! Like me. We both waded in like a couple of kids. At Lili's parties I'd noticed how the Indian men sort of held back, as if it was faintly indelicate to eat hearty in mixed company. I kept sending Raju out to bring more hot chappattis which Hari ended up by scoffing without noticing how many he'd had. Later, when I had a similar dinner at his Aunt Shalini's I realised that there was a difference between our food and theirs, and understood better why Hari ate as if he'd not had a square meal for weeks. I've never been able to stand anything cooked in ghi, which affects my bileduct immediately and there was ghi in some of the dishes Mrs Gupta Sen gave us.

But that is going on too far ahead. After we'd done right by the grub, we sort of collapsed in the drawing-room and then Raju brought in the brandy and coffee, and Hari did the honours at the gramophone. All through dinner we'd talked and talked about 'home'. We were almost exactly the same age, so remembered the same things in relation to the same phases of our lives, I mean like seeing the *R 101* blundering overhead. Aeroplanes and Jim Mollison and Amy Johnson, Amelia Earhart lost in the Timor Sea; films like *Rain* and *Mata Hari*. And things like cricket and Jack Hobbs, Wimbledon and Bunny Austin and Betty Nuttall, motor racing and Sir Malcolm Campbell, Arsenal and Alec James, the proms at the poor old bombed Queen's Hall – although Hari had never been there because he had no real taste for music apart from jazz and swing.

When he first started putting the records on you could see how much pleasure they gave him, but also how they suddenly brought back his uncertainty. After he'd played two and put on a third, a Victor Sylvester, he got his courage up and said, 'I've almost forgotten how and was never much good anyway, but would you like to dance?' I said I was once described as an elephant with clogs on myself, but perhaps together we'd sort each other out, so we stood up and held hands and backs. At first he held me too far away for it to work properly, and we were both watching each other's feet all the time and apologising and taking it awfully seriously, and when the record ended I think he expected me to sit down or suggest going on to the verandah, not only because it hadn't worked but because he thought I might have agreed to dance with him in order not to make it look too obvious that I felt it would be distasteful to be held by an Indian. But I asked him to find a particular record 'In the Mood', which, as you probably *don't* know, is quick and easy, an absolute natural, and waited for him, forced him to dance again, and this time we looked over each other's shoulders and not at our feet, and danced closer, and felt each other slipping into a sort of natural rhythm.

*

If you ever read this I shan't be around to feel diminished by your criticism. I can kid myself that I'm reliving it for no one except the one person who knows how far short of perfect re-enactment an account like this must fall. Perhaps as well as being an insurance against permanent silence it is a consolation prize to me, to give me a chance to have him with me again in a way that is more solid than unfettered recollection, but still insubstantial. But second best is better than third – the third best of random thoughts unpinned down. Oh, I could conjure him now, just with this scratchy old pen, in a form that might satisfy you better, but do more or less than justice to what he actually was. I could do this if I ignored the uncertainty I felt, the clumsiness we both shared; do it if I pretended that from the moment we held each other we felt the uncomplicated magic of straightforward physical attraction. But it was never uncomplicated. Unless you could say that the opposing complications cancelled each other out – on his side the complication of realising that the possession of a white girl could be a way of bolstering his ego, and on mine the complication of the curious almost titillating *fear* of his colour. How else account for the fact that in dancing the second time we stared (I think fixedly) over each other's shoulders, as if afraid to look directly into each other's eyes?

We didn't dance a third time, but in sitting out now there was no sense of physical rebuff as there would have been if I'd refused to dance at all or sat down after that first awkward impersonal shuffle. Our separation, our sitting, he in his chair and I in mine, was a mutual drawing-back from dangerous ground – a drawing-back from the danger to ourselves but also from the danger to the other, because neither of us could be certain that the other fully saw the danger or understood the part that might be played by the *attraction to danger* in what we felt for each other.

And that is how Lili found us when she got back, sitting companionably at the end of an evening we had both obviously enjoyed because we were still talking easily, with our tensions so well concealed we couldn't even be certain that it was tension the other one shared.

He stayed for no more than ten minutes after she got back; and yet during that time, while she talked to him, I could see his armour going back on layer by layer, and Lili change from faintly frosty to friendly back to frosty again – as if at one moment before he was fully re-armed she had seen the kind of vulnerable spot in him she was afraid of and so put up her own shutters, not to lock him out but to try – by putting them up – to lock me in, to keep us apart for everybody's sake.

One is not sensitive usually to the effect people have on one another unless one of them happens to be someone you love. In this case, I suppose, already I loved them both.

War Week was towards the end of April, so the evening Hari came to dinner at the MacGregor House must have been in the early part of May. One or two of the girls from the hospital went up that month to places like Darjeeling for a spot of leave. It was terribly hot in Mayapore. The moon was that curious lopsided shape which I think you told me is caused by dust particles in the atmosphere. There wasn't much leave going because of all the political crises that kept boiling up, simmering down and boiling up again. Matron said I could have a couple of weeks off and I think Lili would have liked to get away into the hills for a bit, but we were pretty short-staffed at the hospital and I didn't feel I was entitled to leave so soon after starting work. I suggested to Lili that she should go by herself and leave me to cope, but she wouldn't hear of it. So we sweated it out, as practically everybody else from the Deputy Commissioner downwards was doing. It became too hot, really, to have parties – a few times out to dinner, and a few times having people in to dinner, that was about the sum total.

The day after Hari's visit he sent me a note, thanking me formally for the evening, and a few days later I got an invitation from Mrs Gupta Sen to have dinner at her house in the Chillianwallah Bagh the following Saturday. Lili had one too, but she said it was only for form's sake, and that anyway she was playing bridge again, so couldn't go. After I'd accepted I got another note, this time from Hari, saying that as the house was difficult to find (all the numbers were haywire and the Chillianwallah Bagh was really a system of roads, not just one road) he would call for me in a tonga at about 7.15, if that was all right. He said he hoped I wouldn't find the evening too dull, there was no gramophone or anything like that. I asked Lili if she thought this was a hint that he'd like it if I took ours along, with a few records, but she said that wouldn't do at all, you couldn't take a thing like a gramophone because not only might Mrs Gupta Sen think it wrong to have such a thing in the house (especially when the records were all European music, which probably hurt her ears) but she would more likely than not look upon it as an insult, a criticism of the kind of hospitality she had to offer. So I took Lili at her word, and I think she was right.

His Aunt Shalini was sweet, and spoke very good English. She said Hari's father taught her when she was a little girl and that she loved having Hari living with her because now she'd been able to pick it up again and improve her accent. She showed me some snaps of Hari taken in England, which her brother, Hari's father Duleep, had sent her from time to time. There were several taken in the garden, showing the house they lived in in Berkshire, which looked to me like a small mansion. Then there were later pictures of Hari, with some English friends, whose name was Lindsey.

I'd been pretty nervous, anticipating this visit to the Chillianwallah Bagh, and it didn't help when Hari was late picking me up and I was sitting alone on the verandah of the MacGregor waiting for him to arrive. Lili had already gone off to bridge. She'd warned me to have at least a couple of drinks before Hari arrived in case Mrs Gupta Sen was teetotal, and I got a bit squiffy, drinking more than I needed because of the extra twenty minutes or so that I had to wait. He was awfully embarrassed about being late, which I think he thought I'd see as a typical Indian failing. He said he'd had difficulty getting a tonga because they had all seemed to be out ferrying people to the first house of the flicks. I was relieved when we got into the tonga and I saw the shapes of a wrapped bottle of gin and a bottle of lime or lemon in a little canvas bag on the seat. It was as good as dark by the time we got across the Bibighar bridge – actually it was as we went past the Bibighar wall that I asked Hari what he thought of the gardens. We had a bit of a laugh when it turned out he didn't even know properly what they were or that they were there. I said, 'I've only been in Mayapore a few months and you've been here for four years, and I know it better than you. But then that's like living in London and never going to the Tower.'

We turned off the Chillianwallah Bagh Extension road. The streets were badly lit and there was an awful smell from the river. I wondered what on earth I'd let myself in for, and I must confess my heart sank. It rose again a bit when I saw the type of house in the district we'd driven in to – cheek by jowl, but modern-looking and civilised, all squares and angles. I was amused the way Hari had to keep telling the driver things like 'Dahne ki taraf aur ek dam sidhe ki rasta' just like me, muddling through in pidgin Hindi. I chipped him about it and gradually he relaxed.

But then when we had stopped at his house he became unrelaxed again because one of the servants had closed the gate. He shouted out but no one came and the tonga-wallah didn't seem prepared to get out and open it himself. So Hari climbed down and opened it. It was only a few paces between the gate and the open area in front of the porch, which was lit by an unshaded electric light bulb, and we could have walked it, which might have been better because the tonga-wallah started making trouble about the tiny space he had to turn round in, which was something I had to leave Hari to deal with. Because his Hindi was as bad as mine I understood what was going on, and how he had to bribe the fellow to come back at 'gyarah baje' and refused to pay him meanwhile.

Suddenly I was fed up with the awful position Hari was being put in by a bloody-minded tonga-wallah, and was about to say 'Oh, tell the stupid man I'd rather walk home than put him to any bother,' but stopped myself in time, because that would have been taking charge and would have made matters worse, so instead when Hari had got his way and the man had reluctantly agreed to come back at eleven, I said, 'What a fuss they make,' as if I was personally used to it, which he probably knew I wasn't, and which made it look as if I was acting like a Mem, slumming. Sort of amused, at Hari's expense. Knowing what I'd done I wanted to get back into the tonga and go home, and have an enormous drink.

Instead we went indoors, encased in a sort of gloom, a sort of trembling expectancy of disaster, or if not disaster then awful boredom and discomfort, and unease. Thank heaven for Aunt Shalini, who came into the little hall like a miniature Rajput princess, beautifully and almost undetectably made-up, wearing a pale lilac saree, perfectly simple and plain, just cotton, but looking marvellous and cool. She shook hands, which made my feeble self-conscious efforts at *namaste* look silly. She said, 'Come in and have a drink,' and led us into the living-room, small but beautifully bare and uncluttered, with a rug or two, a divan and one tiny but very comfortable wicker chair which she made me sit in while, as she said, Hari 'did the honours' at the drinks table – a Benares brass tray on a carved ebony mother-of-pearl inlaid stand, on which there were exactly three glasses and the bottles Hari had taken out of the canvas bag as surreptitiously as he could. While she was talking to me I saw the physical likeness between herself and Hari, although of course she was tiny. In front of her I felt a bit of a gawk, big, clumsy, dressed unsuitably and showing far too much bare skin. Hari was wearing a grey cotton suit, but he had to take the jacket off presently because the fans were only working at half power.

When we'd had just one drink – and by this time I felt I really needed two – she said, 'Shall we go in?' and stood up and led the way next door to a small box-like dining-room. She called out to the boy to switch the fans on, and then we began to eat.

She'd taken so much trouble with the table, to make me feel at home. There was a bowl of water in the centre with frangipani blooms floating in it. And handwoven lace mats at the three places. She described every dish, but I've forgotten most of the names, and some of them I found difficult. When the main dish came on – Chicken tandoori – she said to Hari, 'Haven't we any iced beer?' and he got up and went away for a while and came back with the beer in bottles, followed by a servant with glasses and a tray. She said, 'Haven't we a jug, Hari?' So he sent the servant back for a jug, then went out himself again with the bottles. The boy brought the beer back decanted in a jug. The rest of the servants were watching from doorways and through the barred-window openings into the adjoining rooms. Aunt Shalini drank nothing, not even water, so Hari and I had the beer between us. My glass was an old tumbler with the Roman 'key' design, and his was smaller and thicker. He was conscious, overly-conscious, of the insignificant ways in which the table fell short of what he had once been used to and thought I would consider essential – but towards the end of the meal, when I had been watching him without realising I did so, he caught my eye, and I think he saw then that whatever I noticed as 'faults' had only added to my feeling of being 'at home', and to my feeling for him and his aunt as people honouring me, expressing some kind of groping hope that one day our different *usages* would mean nothing, mean as little as they meant that evening to me.

After dinner was the time she showed me the snaps. I was longing for a cigarette but didn't dare open my bag. Suddenly she said, 'Hari, haven't we any Virginia cigarettes for Miss Manners?' How sensitive she was to every change of mood in her guests! How tolerant of any taste she personally found *dis*tasteful – like the smoking and the drinking. And I think Hari was surprised too at the tremendous ability she had to entertain an English girl – her first English guest ever, so I discovered. What I admired Hari for was the way he didn't *press* things like drink and cigarettes, but left his aunt in control, in her own house, which an insensitive blustering boy intent on proving his Englishness probably wouldn't have done. The other nice thing he did was to have a cigarette too, so that I shouldn't feel I was the only messy person in the room, but I noticed how he just let it burn away without smoking it properly. He was afraid to get the taste for it again.

The only thing that went a bit wrong was over the business of going to the wc! When we got up from the dinner-table Hari made himself scarce for a while. I think he'd told Aunt Shalini to be sure to give me the opportunity to go, but that she didn't quite have the nerve to say anything to me when the time came. The next time I went to the house she had got over this embarrassment, but on this particular evening I think Hari's realisation that I hadn't 'been' rather cast a blight on his evening. Round about 10.30 it began to cast a blight on mine too. I began to wonder whether they even *had* a wc of the kind they felt I could be invited to use. Actually it turned out that there was a downstairs as well as whatever there might have been upstairs. No seat, but she'd thoughtfully put a chamber pot on a little stool which I didn't dare use, and there was a bowl and a jug of water, on a table that looked as if it didn't always belong there, and some soap and towels and a hand mirror. I went in there after we heard the tonga-wallah come back and Hari went out to speak to him. I stood up and said, 'May I powder my nose?' So she took me into the passage near the kitchens and opened the door and switched on the light and said, 'Please, anytime you come, here it is.' There were a couple of cockroaches running up and down, but I didn't care. Lili shrieks blue murder if she so much as glimpses one, but although when I first got to India I was horrified to find them sharing places like bathrooms and wc's I no longer care.

When I said goodbye to Aunt Shalini I wanted to stoop down and kiss her, but didn't in case that offended her. Hari insisted on coming back in the tonga with me, but wouldn't come in for a nightcap. I think he was trying to avoid doing anything that would create an atmosphere of *Well, that's all over, now we can relax.* So after he'd driven off in the tonga I sat on the verandah and had a long cool drink of nimbo and waited for Lili to come home.

*

The next day I sent one of the boys round to Aunt Shalini's with an enormous bunch of flowers I'd raided the garden for, and a note of thanks. Bhalu was very cross with me, so I gave him ten chips and asked him not to complain to Madam and get me in trouble, which made him grin, the old rascal. After that he had me wound round his little finger. Perhaps he was wound round mine too, and we were partners in crime – crime because Lili paid all the servants extra when she had anyone staying in the house and it was understood guests weren't to tip them. He never complained again to Lili about my cutting flowers, but round about the first of each month when he'd been paid his wages he used to stand about saluting and grinning, until I gave him a few chips. He bought a new pair of chappals with the first lot of money I gave him, and looked very smart, but oddly more tortoiselike than ever, with his khaki shorts and knobbly black bare legs and these enormous army-style sandals, clopping about on the gravel. You could tell he preferred bare feet, but the chappals represented status. He was once a gardener to a Colonel James in Madras, and Colonel James's household has been Bhalu's standard of pukka life ever since, even though I think he knows the garden of the MacGregor House is far superior to any other garden he's ever worked in, which may be why he has to feel the whole of it belongs to him, and that he's tending it to the honour and glory of James Sahib rather than of Lili.

*

I'm gossiping, aren't I, Auntie? Putting off the moment when I have to write about the thing you really want to know. But yet, not gossiping, because you can't isolate the good and happy things from the bad and unhappy ones. And you see for me there was a growing sense of joy, whatever there was for the people who watched and waited.

It was now that Mayapore seemed to change for me. It was no longer just the house, the road to the cantonment bazaar, the road to the hospital, the hospital, the *maidan*, the club. It extended to the other side of the river and, because of that, in all directions, across that enormous flat plain that I used to stand staring at from the balcony of my room, putting on my glasses and taking them off, doing what Lili called my eye exercises. I felt that Mayapore had got bigger, and so had made me smaller, had sort of split my life into three parts. There was my life in the hospital, which also included the club and the boys and girls and all the good-time stuff that wasn't really good-time at all, just the easiest, the least exacting, so long as you ignored the fact that it was only the easiest for the least admirable part of your nature. There was my life at the MacGregor House, where I lived with Lili and mixed with Indians and English, the kind who made an effort to work together. But this mixing was just as self-conscious as the segregation. At the club you stood on *loud*, committed ground. At the MacGregor House it was silent and determinedly neutral. With Hari I began to feel that here at last was ground wholly personal to me, where I might learn to talk in my own tone of voice. Perhaps this is why I felt Mayapore had got bigger but made me smaller, because my association with Hari – the one thing that was beginning to make me feel like a person again – was hedged about, restricted, pressed in on until only by making yourself tiny could you squeeze into it and stand, imprisoned but free, diminished by everything

312

that loomed from outside, *but not diminished from the inside*, and that was the point, that's why I speak of joy.

Sometimes, knowing the effort it cost to squeeze into this restricted, dangerous little space, I was afraid, as I was that evening Ronald Merrick 'proposed' to me and brought me back to the MacGregor House, and I wanted to run back down the stairs and call out to Ronald, and was afraid of seeing the ghost of Janet MacGregor. This occasion, the occasion of his proposal after our dinner and my coming back to the MacGregor and being afraid, was in the middle of June. The rains were late. We were all exhausted, physically and mentally. That probably also accounts for my fear that night. That, and the feeling I had that Ronald represented something I didn't fully understand, but probably ought to trust. There's an awful weight still on my mind about Ronald. I feel that just as you and the others may know where Hari is, so there are things about Ronald that no one is prepared to discuss in front of me. I think about him a lot. He is like a dark shadow, just on the edge of my life.

Auntie, did he hurt Hari in some special horrible way? I think he did. But no one would say, at least would not say to me. And I didn't dare question anyone too closely. I was equally a party to the conspiracy to keep me a prisoner in the MacGregor House after that night in the Bibighar. I only left it twice, once to visit Aunt Shalini, who wouldn't see me, and then on the day before Lili took me up to 'Pindi and I went to the Sanctuary to say goodbye to Sister Ludmila. Ronald Merrick was on Sister Ludmila's conscience too. It seems she hadn't realised that he and I knew each other more than casually, hadn't realised that I might not know that it was Ronald who took Hari in for questioning that day he found him at the Sanctuary. But by then I was afraid to probe too deeply. I trusted no one. Only to my silence. And to Hari's. But I remembered how after the Bibighar on the one occasion we came briefly face to face Ronald would not look at me straight, the time the Assistant Commissioner came with Judge Menen and a young English sub-divisional officer and held a sort of 'inquiry' at which Ronald gave evidence and I made everybody uneasy, perhaps angry, with my answers to their questions.

Before I tell you what actually happened in the Bibighar, I must say something about Ronald, and something about Sister Ludmila. I think Ronald first took real notice of me that day on the *maidan*, when I went to the War Week Exhibition, took notice of me because he saw me go up to Hari and talk to him, as a lot of English people did. If he already had his eye on Hari, as some sort of potential subversive type (nothing could have been farther from the truth, but Ronald had his job to do) he probably looked at my going up to him like that, as a policeman would, but also as an Englishman who didn't want an English girl getting mixed up with the 'wrong' type of Indian. I mean that would account for the fact that when he saw me in the club that evening he came straight up to me and said, 'Did you enjoy the parade? I saw you on the *maidan*,' when usually we only nodded, or occasionally had a drink if circumstances made it awkward for him not to offer me one.

He probably had an idea that it would be kind to head me off, but also – because he was a policeman – wasn't above looking at me as a possible source of information about Hari: Do you remember my saying in a letter that with Ronald I never felt there was any real candour between him and the person he was dealing with? He took his job so seriously, and I think he felt he had to prove his worth all the time, so that nothing came naturally to him, nothing came spontaneously, or easily or *happily*.

I wonder just *how* much, once he'd made the move of showing friendly to me, wanting to head me off for my own good, he was genuinely and quite unexpectedly attracted to me as a person? Certainly from then on he began to pay attention. And although I didn't appreciate it at the time I see now that he became my new contact with the sort of world the club represented, the flag-wagging little world – but through him it wore a subtler mark – the Henry Moores, the Debussy. The one constant in my life was Lili and the MacGregor House, the variants were Hari on his side and Ronald on his. Those two seemed so far apart I don't think I ever referred to one in front of the other. But they weren't far apart at all. Which was why I was so angry, felt such a fool, when I discovered the truth, that they'd been – what? enemies – since that day in the Sanctuary, when Hari was struck and dragged away, and Sister Ludmila had watched it all happening.

*

She dressed like one of those sisters of mercy with huge white flyaway linen caps. I'd seen her once or twice in the cantonment bazaar, walking in front of a boy who was armed with a stick, holding a leather bag that she kept chained to the belt round her waist. I was with a girl from the hospital and I said, 'Whoever's that?' She said, 'That's the mad Russian woman who collects dead bodies and isn't a nun at all, but just dresses like one.' I was only passingly interested, not only because India has its fair share of eccentrics of both colours but also because it was during that period of unhappiness, of dislike for everything around me. A few weeks later I saw her again and mentioned her to Lili who said, 'She doesn't do any harm, and Anna Klaus helps her sometimes, and likes her, but she makes me shiver, bashing off collecting people she finds dying.'

Aunt Lili hates anything grisly or sordid, doesn't she? She told me that once as a young girl, the first time she went to Bombay and saw the slums, she cried. I think well-off privileged Indians like Lili have a sort of deep-rooted guilt that they bury under layers of what looks like indifference, because there's so little they can individually do to lessen the horror and the poverty. They subscribe to charities and do voluntary work but must feel it's like trying to dam up a river with a handful of twigs. And with Lili I think there's also a horror of death. She told me about going to the morgue in Paris with a medical student and how afterwards she had nightmares of all the corpses rising up and falling back and rising up again, which is why she hated Nello to show off his cuckoo clocks in the museum room at the MacGregor House! The room where he put Uncle Henry's old briar pipe in a glass case – the one Uncle Henry gave him to improve his imitations.

I took Hari into the museum room once, round about the beginning of the time when we knew that we both liked being together and so had to face the fact that there was almost no place we could be, except at his house or at Lili's. The Bibighar came a bit later. The time I took him in to the museum room we were joking about everything, but there was this sense already of cheating, of having to cheat and hide, buy time, buy privacy – paying for them with blows to our joint pride. I thought as I looked round the room, 'Well, Hari and I are exhibits too. We could stand here on a little plinth, with a card saying *Types of Opposites. Indo-British, circa 1942. Do not Touch.*' Then all the people who stared at us in the cantonment, but looked away directly we looked at them, could come and stare to their hearts' content. I think it was in Hari's mind too. We never went into the museum room again. I said, 'Come on, Hari – it's mouldy and dead,' and held my hand out without thinking, then realised that except for dancing, casual contact like getting in and out of a tonga, we had never touched each other, even as friends, let alone as man and woman. I nearly withdrew my hand, because the longer I held it out and he hesitated to take it, the more loaded with significance the gesture became. It hadn't been meant as significant – just natural, warm and companionable. He took it finally. And then I wanted him to kiss me. To kiss me would have been the only way of making the hand-holding right. Holding hands and not kissing seemed wrong because it was incomplete. It wouldn't have been incomplete if he'd taken my hand the moment I'd held it out. When we got out of the room he let go. I felt deserted, caught out, left alone to face something, like once at school when I admitted to some silly trivial thing several of us had done and found I was the only girl to own up, which made me look a fool, not a heroine. It was this sort of thing with Hari – these repeated experiences of finding myself emotionally out on a limb – that added up and made me feel sometimes – as I suppose I did climbing the staircase that night after Ronald Merrick's proposal – 'It's probably all wrong my association with Hari Kumar' – I mean made me feel it *before* Ronald put it into so many words. And added up in that other unfinished sum that posed the question, 'Well, what does he really feel for me? A big-boned white girl with not much to be said in her favour.'

*

And then there were the rains. They came fresh and clean, wild, indiscriminate. And changed the garden, Mayapore, the whole landscape. That awful foreboding colourlessness was washed out of the sky. I'd wake at night, shivering because the temperature had fallen, and listen to the lashing on the trees, the wonderful rumbling and banging of the thunder, and watch the way the whole room was lit as if from an explosion, with the furniture throwing sudden flamboyant shadows, black dancing shapes petrified in the middle of a complicated movement – a bit of secret night-time devilry that they returned to the moment the unexpected light went out, only to be caught and held still in it again a few moments later.

I was at the Chillianwallah Bagh on the last night of the dry. For two nights there had been sheet lightning and distant thunder. It was towards the end of June, about a week, perhaps less, after my dinner with Ronald Merrick when he had said, on the steps of the MacGregor House, 'Some ideas take some getting used to.' Sitting with Hari and Aunt Shalini this time I saw how unreal my life had become because there didn't seem to be any kind of future in front of me that I wanted and could have. *Why?* Holding one hand out, groping, and the other out backwards, linked to the security of what was known and expected. Straining like that. Pretending the ground between was occupied, when all the time it wasn't.

The tonga came at eleven and on the way home we suddenly saw her, lit by the sheet lightning – the wide white wings of the cap, a man ahead of her, and one behind carrying what looked like a pole, but was a rolled-up stretcher. I'd said – not wanting the evening to end – 'Let's drive back through the bazaar and past the temple,' and he'd agreed, and then I suffered pangs of conscience at the thought of the extra rupees the boy would want; because now I'd fitted Hari into place, and knew he hadn't any spare rupees to throw away. On the other hand I wouldn't have dared offer him even an anna. That time we went to the Chinese Restaurant I said quite without thinking, 'Let's go Dutch on a chop suey,' and his face closed down, the way Ronald Merrick's did when I rejected his proposal. The Chinese Restaurant was a far from happy experience, what with the insult it seemed I'd offered Hari suggesting Dutch and then the insult to us both when the proprietor stopped him from following me upstairs.

I said, 'That's the mad Russian woman who collects dead bodies, isn't it?' She was going away from us, turning up a side street. Hari said she wasn't mad and he didn't think she was Russian. He said, 'We call her Sister Ludmila.' He'd once written a piece for the *Gazette* about the Sanctuary, but his editor had refused to publish it because of the implication that the British were responsible for letting people die in the streets. So he'd altered the article, because that wasn't what he'd meant. He'd altered it to show that *nobody* cared, not even the people who were dying, nobody except Sister Ludmila. But the editor still wouldn't publish it. He said Sister Ludmila was a joke. I asked Hari if I could visit the Sanctuary. He said he'd take me there if I really wanted to see it, but that I mustn't be upset if she treated me like some kind of inquisitive snooper. She kept herself very much to herself and was only really interested in people who were dying and had no bed to die in, although she also ran an evening clinic that people could go to who couldn't afford to take time off from work to go to the day-time clinics, and she doled out free rice on certain days of the week, to children and mothers mostly. I asked him how he had got to know her and he simply said, 'By chance.'

*

She had an image of the Siva dancing in a circle of cosmic fire, carved in wood, and a framed biblical text: 'He that soweth little shall reap little, and he that soweth plenteously shall reap plenteously. Let every man do according as he is disposed in his heart, not grudging, or of necessity; for God loveth a cheerful giver.' There seemed to be a connection between the Christian text and the Hindu image, because *this* Siva was smiling. And the way the god's limbs are thrust out and jaunty-looking gives the image a feeling of happiness, doesn't it? The only immobile thing is the right foot (even the right leg is bent at the knee and springy-looking). The right foot is the one that presses down on the crouching figure of the little demon, which is why that foot has to be firm and unmoving. The left leg is kicking up, the first pair of arms are gesturing cautiously but invitingly, and the second pair are holding the circle of flame, holding it away but also keeping it burning. And of course the god is winged, which gives the whole image an airy flying feeling that makes you think you could leap into the dark with him and come to no harm.

These were the only bits of decoration in her whitewashed 'cell' – the Siva and the text. At our last meeting she gave the text to me, because she said she knew it by heart anyway. But I've always been too embarrassed to show it to you and I don't think I deserved to be given it anyway. It's in my big suitcase, the one with the straps round it.

What an extraordinary woman she was. When evening comes I think of her preparing to set out on that nightly expedition into the alleys and dark cul-de-sacs, and into the waste land between the temple and the Bibighar bridge. I got into the habit of going there about once a week straight from the hospital – to help with the evening clinic, not just because it was another place Hari and I could meet. I once asked her whether I could go with her at night on her missions. She laughed and said, 'No, that is only for people who have nothing else to offer.' I thought she meant I could offer money, but she said she had enough, more than enough, although promised that if ever she didn't and I still wanted to help I could.

We took to each other. Perhaps I liked her originally because she was fond of Hari and saw nothing wrong in our being there together. She used to let us sit in the office, or in her room. When it was dark he and I would cycle back to the MacGregor House, but he didn't often come in on those occasions. The days I knew I'd be going to the Sanctuary I went to the hospital on my bicycle and left early to avoid the car or van that Mr Merrick was always sending round for me. The same in the evenings, after work. I'd leave a message for the driver that I'd either gone or was working late. Sometimes, though, I'd let myself be driven back to the MacGregor, and then go on to the Sanctuary by cycle. I didn't want the hospital to know

I helped at Sister Ludmila's clinic. It wasn't often that I did, but I guessed it was against the hospital rules or something. I saw Anna Klaus there one evening and said, 'Don't split on me!' She laughed and said people probably knew anyway because in a town like Mayapore it was almost impossible to keep anything a secret.

But not all the people who would have liked to know did. I mean people on our side of the river, people like Ronald Merrick. I kept it from Ronald because this was the part of my life I shared willingly with no one. Ronald was part of another life. Lili yet another. I didn't know I'd divided my life up into these watertight compartments, I mean I didn't consciously know. Subconsciously, yes, and I was aware of the subterfuge involved, but not aware of it in a way that ever allowed me in those days to use the word subterfuge – at least not until the evening when I went to the temple with Hari, and found out about Ronald's part in his arrest, and felt everyone had cheated, and then realised I'd been cheating just as badly myself, and became afraid, recognised that I'd really been afraid all along, afraid like everybody else of going out on a limb in case somebody sawed it off – which was ironic, wasn't it, because I used to kid myself that's what we all ought to do, kid myself it was what I was doing. But if I was out on a limb I had one arm securely round the tree-trunk.

I suppose I thought that everything I did was an adventure of some sort. An evening at the MacGregor House with Lili and a few 'mixed' friends, an evening at the club with Ronald or the girls and boys, an hour or two at Sister Ludmila's clinic, a walk with Hari on a Sunday morning to the Bibighar. Well, they were adventures, weren't they? because each of these things was done – unintentionally but for all practical purposes – in defiance of the others. I was breaking every rule there was. The funny thing is that people couldn't be absolutely certain which rule I was breaking in what way at what time because they were so hedged about with their own particular rule they could only follow me far enough to see that I'd broken it and gone away, and become temporarily invisible, so that when I came back, when I returned to their own fold they didn't know enough about what I'd been doing and where I'd been to make real charges against me, other than the general one of being – what? Unstable? Asking for trouble? Unaligned? Bad enough of course, but people do like to be able to define other people's instability and non-alignment, and if they can't their own fear of what you might come to represent forces them to make another bid for your allegiance.

To be rejected – which I suppose is one of the easiest ways of making your mark, you have to come *right out* with something they see as directly and forcefully opposed to what they think they believe in. To be accepted you have to be seen and heard to appear to stand for what they think they believe in. To be neither one thing nor the other is probably unforgivable.

But, Auntie, it was awfully difficult for me. I did genuinely *like* several of the girls and boys I mixed with at the club. I genuinely liked Ronald, when he was the closest he could ever get to being easy and natural with me. I even liked him when he was difficult and 'official' because I thought I knew why he acted like that. And I loved Lili, even at her most standoffish, when that old Rajput princess blood showed through and she sort of gathered up the hem of her cloak. Saree, I mean! I liked the *fun* of the English before it became self-conscious and vulgar and violent, and I liked the simple almost childish fun of the Indians, and their seriousness, before it became prissy and prickly and imitative of European sulks. With Hari I can't connect a word such as 'like', because my liking was hopelessly encumbered with the physical effect he had on me, which turned liking into love but didn't leave me insensitive to his pigheadedness and prickliness. All of which makes me sound on paper like a paragon of virtuous broad-mindedness, until you remember the horrible mess I made of everything.

*

I hate the impression we automatically get of things and places and people that make us say, for instance, 'This is Indian. This is British.' When I first saw the Bibighar I thought: How Indian! Not Indian as I'd have thought of a place as Indian before I came out, but Indian as it struck me then. But when you say something like that, in circumstances like that, I think you're responding to the attraction of a place which you see as alien on the surface but underneath as proof of something general and universal. I wish I could get hold of the right words to say just what I mean. The Taj Mahal is 'typically Indian', isn't it? Picture-book Moghul stuff. But what makes you give out to it emotionally is the feeling of a man's worship of his wife, which is neither Indian nor un-Indian, but a general human emotion, expressed in this case in an 'Indian' way. This is what I got from the Bibighar. It was a place in which you sensed something having gone badly wrong at one time that hadn't yet been put right but could be if only you knew how. That's the sort of thing you could imagine about any place, but imagining it there, feeling that it was still alive, I said, 'How Indian,' because it was the first place in Mayapore that hit me in this way, and the surprise of being hit made me think I'd come across something typical when all the time it was typical of no place, but only of human acts and desires that leave their mark in the most unexpected and sometimes chilling way.

Usually it was a Sunday morning place, but one day Hari and I sheltered there from the rain, dashing in from the road in the late afternoon, on our bikes, and running up the steps that divided one level of old lawn from another, to the 'pavilion', the roofed-over mosaic. We stood under it and I had a cigarette. We'd been on our way to tea at Aunt Shalini's. It was a Saturday. I had a half-day off from the hospital and after lunch I'd cycled to the cantonment bazaar to see if those awful photographs I'd had taken for your birthday were ready at Gulab Singh's where that little man Subhas Chand had a booth. I saw Hari coming out of the *Gazette* offices and called

out to him. I said, 'Come and help me choose my picture for Auntie Ethel,
then if they're any good you can have one.' So we went to Subhas Chand
and looked at the proofs. I said, 'Oh, Lord,' but Hari said they were all
pretty good and helped me choose the one to make up cabinet size for you.
Afterwards I made him come to Darwaza Chand's with me while I chose
that dress length. There were hardly any people shopping at that time.
Those who were stared at us in the usual unpleasant manner. When I
looked at my watch and saw it was already four o'clock I invited him back
to the MacGregor House for tea, but he said, 'No, come to see Aunt
Shalini.' I'd not been to his house since the night before the rains set in. I
told him I'd like to but I'd better change first. He said, 'Why? Unless you
want to tell Lady Chatterjee where you're going.' But it was her purdah
hospital committee afternoon, and there wasn't any need to tell Raju, so
we set off. We went the Bibighar bridge side. He hated taking me over by
the Mandir Gate bridge because that way we had to go through the bazaar.
And that's how we were caught, cycling past the Bibighar. Down it came,
as it does, and we dashed in there, expecting it to dry up in twenty minutes
or so. But it went on and on, and blew up a storm.

I told him the sort of thing I felt about the Bibighar. It was odd, sitting
there on the mosaic floor, having to shout to make ourselves heard, then
relapsing into silence until the noise outside got less. I asked him to have
his picture taken too, but he said he made a rotten photograph. I said,
'Don't be silly. What about those Aunt Shalini showed me?' He said he
'was younger then'! I asked him whether he still heard from those English
friends of his, the Lindseys, but he shrugged the question away. He'd
always been prickly about them when Aunt Shalini mentioned them. I
thought they'd given up writing to him and he felt badly about it, but from
something Sister Ludmila asked me the last time I saw her I got the feeling
there was more to it than that, something to do with the boy, the Lindsey
son, whom Aunt Shalini always described as Hari's greatest friend 'at
home'.

Anyway, we were marooned there in the Bibighar and it began to get
dark. We'd missed having tea, and I knew I had to be back by seven to
change for dinner, because Aunt Lili was having Judge Menen and his wife
in, to celebrate Mrs Menen coming out of hospital. I was shivering a bit,
and I thought I'd caught a chill. I wanted him to warm me. An English boy
would have snuggled up, I suppose, but there we were, with at least a foot
or two between us. I got edgy. I wanted to take his hand and hold it to my
face.

*

When we came away, that evening we sheltered from the rains, it felt just
as if we had had a quarrel, a lovers' quarrel. But we weren't lovers and
there'd been no quarrel. And again I thought: It's wrong, wrong because it
doesn't *work*. He saw me home, and although the next day was Sunday

neither of us mentioned any arrangement to meet. I was back at the MacGregor a few minutes before Aunt Lili and was soaking in a bath when I heard her calling to Raju on the landing. It was like hearing a homely sound after a long absence. I didn't see Hari again for over a week. I spent an evening or two at the club, once with Ronald and once with the boys and girls, and the rest of my evenings with Lili. But all the time I was thinking of Hari, wanting to see him but not doing anything about it. It was like sitting on a beach as a kid, watching the sea, wanting to go in but not having the courage. Yes – you promise yourself – when this cloud has gone by and the sun comes out then I'll go in. And the cloud goes by and the sun is warm and comforting, and the sea looks chilly.

I told myself the trouble was we'd run out of places to go where the risk of being stared at, the risk of creating a situation, could be minimised. In the club I was definitely getting the cold shoulder from the women. It was this thrashing about for ideas for new places that made me think of the Tirupati temple.

I asked Aunt Lili if English people were ever allowed in. She said she had no idea but imagined none had ever asked, because Mayapore wasn't a tourist town and the temple wasn't famous, but she'd have a word with one of the teachers at the Higher School or Technical College because if an Englishman had been in it would most likely have been a teacher or someone interested in art and culture. She wasn't sure about an English girl being allowed, though. I told her not to bother, because I would ask Hari. She said, 'Yes, you could do that I suppose,' and looked as if she was about to question the whole business of Hari, so I started talking about my day in the hospital to head her off. I wrote a note to Hari just saying, 'I'd love to see inside the Tirupati temple. Could we go together one day? Preferably at night because it always looks more exciting after dark.'

A day or two later he rang up from the *Gazette* office. They hadn't a telephone at Aunt Shalini's. He caught me a few moments before I was due to start out for the hospital and told me that if I really wanted to go he'd ask his uncle. His uncle was the kind of man who paid a lot of money to the priests in the hopes of buying the merit he didn't have time to acquire in any other way. At least that's how Hari put it. I said I really did want to go and that if he'd arrange it for the Saturday evening we could have a quiet dinner together at the MacGregor first, and then come back and play the gramophone. He sounded a bit cool. I had an idea I'd done the wrong thing asking him to take me to a *temple*. But we fixed it on a to-be-confirmed basis for the following Saturday when I knew Lili was playing bridge. Neither of us said anything about meeting meanwhile, although I thought he might turn up on the Tuesday evening at the Sanctuary. He didn't though, and I still hadn't heard from him by the Friday evening.

But I'd seen Ronald at the club, and stayed on to dinner with him. He drove me back to the MacGregor and on the way there he asked me to have dinner with him on the Saturday. I said I couldn't because I was hoping to visit the temple. When he stopped the car at the house there was no one on the porch, no sign of Raju, but he didn't get out to open the door for me. Instead he said, 'Who's taking you? Mr Kumar?' After I'd admitted it he was quiet for a bit, but then came out with what he said he'd been meaning to say for some time, that people were talking about my going out and about with an Indian, which was always tricky, but more tricky these days, especially when the man in question 'hadn't got a very good reputation' and 'tried to make capital out of the fact that he'd lived for a while in England', a fact which he seemed to think 'made him English'.

Then Ronald said, 'You know what I feel for you. It's because I feel it that I haven't said anything to you before. But it's my duty to warn you against this association with Mr Kumar.'

That's when I laughed and said, 'Oh, stop acting like a policeman.'

He said, 'Well, it's partly a police matter. He was under suspicion at one time, and still is, but of course you must know all about that.'

I told him I knew nothing about it at all, and wasn't interested because I'd met Hari at a party at the MacGregor and if Lili thought him the kind of man she could invite to her house that was good enough for me. I said I'd be grateful if people would stop telling me who could be my friends and who not, and that I personally didn't care *what* colour people were, and it was obviously only Hari's colour, the fact that he was an Indian, that got people's goat.

Ronald said, 'That's the oldest trick in the game, to say colour doesn't matter. It does matter. It's basic. It matters like hell.'

I started getting out of the car. He tried to stop me, and took my hand. He said, 'I've put it badly. But I can't help it. The whole idea revolts me.'

I don't know why I was sorry for him. Perhaps because of his honesty. It was like a child's. The kind of self-centred honesty a child shows. We call it innocence. But it is ignorance and cruelty as well. I said, 'It's all right, Ronald. I understand.'

He let go of me as if my arm had scalded him. I shut the door and said, 'Thanks for the meal and for bringing me home,' but it seemed to be the wrong thing to say. There simply wasn't a right thing to say. He drove off and I went into the house.

*

On Friday evening Hari sent round a chit saying that it was fixed for us to visit the temple the following evening, between 9.30 and 10.30, so I sent the boy back with an answer asking him to come to dinner at 7.30 for 8.

Came Saturday, he arrived promptly, as if to make up for past mistakes. He came in a cycle tonga, which explained the promptness but was probably also meant to point the difference between his life and mine. Somehow that difference became the theme of the evening. He was deliberately trying to put me off. I'm sure of that. For instance, he'd started smoking again, cheap Indian cigarettes – not bidis, but smelly and cumulatively unpleasant. I tried one but hated it, so we ended up smoking our own. He'd also brought a couple of records which he said were a present to me. I wanted to play them right away but he said, no, we'd wait until we got back from the temple, and looked at his watch. It was only 7.45 but he suggested that we ought to start eating. I said, 'Don't you want the other half?' He said he didn't but would wait while I did, which meant he didn't want to, so I told Raju to tell cook we'd eat right away, and we went into the dining-room. When we got in there he complained that the fans were going too fast. I told Raju to turn them to half speed. It got very hot. When the food came in he ignored the forks and began scoffing up mouthfuls with pieces of chappatti. I followed suit. He called out to Raju, 'Boy, bring water', and I began to giggle because it reminded me of the time you and I sat next to that rich Indian family in Delhi and how shocked I was at the apparently rude way the man talked to the waiter, 'Boy, bring this. Boy, bring that', but you pointed out that it was an exact English translation of the pukka sahib's 'Bearer, pani lao.' I thought Hari was having a game, taking off rich Indians of the English-speaking middle class, and wondered if he'd been drinking before he came. Our fingers and mouths were in a bit of a mess by the time we'd finished. Raju – who noticed what was happening even if he didn't understand it – brought in napkins and bowls of warm water, and we washed. I half expected Hari to belch and ask for a toothpick. In its way it was a perfect imitation. Normally he smiled at Raju but apart from his 'Boy, do so and so' he treated him as if he weren't in the room. And I began to wonder whether the Indians had got this habit from the English, or the English from the Indians, or whether the whole thing dated back to some time when servants were treated like dirt everywhere and the habit had only been kept up in the Empire by Sahibs and Memsahibs and modern Indians wanting to be smart.

The other thing Hari was doing, of course, was acting like an Indian male of that kind, very polite on the surface but underneath selfish and aggressive, ordering the arrangements to his own but not necessarily anyone else's liking – the curtailment of the pre-dinner drinks, the early start on the meal – and now the equally early start going to the temple which ended up by being a late start because at the last moment he said perhaps we'd better listen to the records he'd bought so that we could get into the mood – a curious kind of hark-back to that dance record, which made me suddenly wary, conscious that the mood Hari was in was less comic than bitter.

And even over the playing of the gramophone he made us go through a typical sort of modern Indian farce. Raju was told to bring the gramophone out, but was shoved aside when it came to winding the damn' thing up, and sent to look for the needles which were in the compartment of the gramophone where they were meant to be, all the time. Hari deliberately scratched the first record by being clumsy with it and then pretended not to notice the awful clack clack every time the needle jumped over the dent in the groove. And he had chosen Indian music, something terribly difficult, an evening raga that went on and on. What he didn't reckon with was the fact that I instinctively loved it. When he saw that I did, he changed the record before it was finished, and put on one that excited and moved me even more. The odd thing was I could see it really made *him* savagely irritated and seeing that, the idea that he had been having a joke with me just wouldn't hold water any longer. I felt lost, because I realised he had been trying in his own way to put me off, as Ronald and everyone wanted, and that he was sufficiently fond of me personally to believe that what he hated – the music, and eating with your fingers – I would hate too. His discovery that I didn't hate it, but loved it or didn't mind it, was another gulf between us, one for which there was no accounting, because I was white and he was black, and my liking for what he hated or had never had the patience or inclination to learn to like, to get back to, made even his blackness look spurious, like that of someone made up to act a part.

He let the second record play to the end, and then *I* took charge and said, 'We'd better go', and called out to Raju to bring my scarf. I had an idea I'd need to cover my head to go into the temple. Hari had brought an umbrella in case it rained while we weren't under cover. On the way to the temple in the cycle tonga we said almost nothing. I'd not been in a cycle tonga before. To shift the weight of two people the poor boy had to stand out of the saddle and lean his whole strength on each pedal alternately. But I liked it better than the horse tongas, because we faced the way we were going. To travel in a horse tonga, facing backwards (which I suppose one does to avoid the smell if the horse breaks wind) always gives me a feeling of trying to hang back, of not wanting things to disappear. With the cycle tonga there was the opposite feeling, of facing the road ahead, of knowing it better and not being scared when you had to get out.

*

At the temple entrance there was a man waiting for us, a temple servant who spoke a bit of English. We took our shoes off in the archway of the main gate, and Hari paid some money over that his uncle had given him. I couldn't see how much it was but guessed from the attention we got that it was probably quite a lot, more than Hari had ever been given by his uncle before.

Well, you've been in temples. Isn't it odd how even with all that noise outside, to go in is like entering somewhere quite cut off – not a place of quiet – but cut off, reserved for a human activity that doesn't need *other* human activity to make it function itself. Churches are quiet in this way, but then they are usually quiet because they are empty. The temple wasn't quiet. It wasn't empty. But it was cut off. Once through the archway you walked into the *idea* of being alone. I was glad to have Hari with me, because my *skin* was afraid, although I wasn't afraid *inside* the skin. I was astonished by the sight of men and women just squatting around, under the trees in the courtyard, squatting in that wholly Indian peasant way, self-supported on the haunches, with arms stretched out and balanced on the bent knees, and the bottom not quite touching the earth. Gossiping. At first I was critical of this, until I remembered that the shrine in the centre of the courtyard was the real temple, and outside it was like the outside of a church where our Sunday morning congregations gather and chat after the service.

Around the walls of the courtyard there were the shrines of various aspects of the Hindu gods. Some awake and lit, some asleep and dark. In those doll-like figures there's a look of what puritans call the tawdriness of Roman Catholicism, isn't there? The dolls seemed to reflect that, but knowingly, as if pointing a moral – the absurdity of the need which the poor and ignorant have for images. Hari said, 'The guide wants to know if we'd like to make *puja* to the Lord Venkataswara.'

The holy of holies! I was excited. I hadn't expected to be allowed in there, and I was very conscious of the uniqueness of being allowed. Every so often one was startled by the ringing of a bell at the entrance to the central shrine. There were men and women waiting. Our guide forced his way through to take us in ahead of them. I hated that. He spoke to a priest who was standing watching us. Then he came and said something long and involved to Hari. I was surprised that Hari seemed to understand. When he replied to the man's question I realised Hari had learned more of the language than he was prepared to let on and only here, in the temple, couldn't keep up the pretence. He turned to me and said, 'I have to ring the bell to warn the god that we're here. When I've done so, look as if you're praying. Goodness knows what we're in for.'

I put my scarf on my head. The priest was watching us all the time. The bell was hung on a chain from the roof of the shrine at the head of the steps. I could see the inside now, a narrow passage leading to a brightly lit grotto, and the idol with a black face and gilt robes and silver ornaments. Hari reached up and pulled the rope that moved the tongue of the bell, then put his hands together. I followed suit and closed my eyes and waited until I heard him say, 'We go in now.'

He led the way. There were ordinary tubular steel bars in the passage, forming a barricade. We took up position round them with several other people – rather as at a communion rail, except that we stood and didn't kneel, and the bars formed a rectangle, with us on the outside and a space on the inside for the priest to come down from the little grotto. He was standing by the grotto while we were sorting ourselves out, and then came with a gilt cup. We held our hands out, as for the Host, and he poured what looked like water into them. He went to the Indians first, to make sure we'd know what to do. We raised the liquid to our lips. It was sweet-sour tasting, and stung a bit. Perhaps because our lips were dry. After we'd carried our hands to our lips we had to pass them over our heads, rather like making a sign of the cross. Then the priest came back with a golden cap – a sort of basin, and held it over our heads, and intoned prayers for each of us. He also had a gilt tray and when he'd finished with the cap he put it back on the tray. Round the tray there were little mounds of coloured powder and some petals. He stuck his finger in the powder and marked our foreheads. The petals turned out to be a small string of roses, and he gave them to me, putting them round my neck. It seemed to be all over in a second or two. On the way out Hari put some more money on a tray held by another priest at the door.

I felt nothing while I was doing *puja*. But when I came out my lips were still stinging and I could smell the sweet-sourness everywhere. I had a suspicion that we'd drunk cow urine. People were staring at us. I felt protected from their hostility, if it was hostility and not just curiosity, protected by the mark on my forehead and the little string of red rose petals. I still have the petals, Auntie. They are in a white paper bag, with Sister Ludmila's text, in the suitcase. Dry and brown now. The faintest wind would blow them into fragments.

There was one other thing to do, something to see, an image of the sleeping Vishnu. Lord Venkataswara, the god of the temple, is a manifestation of Vishnu, although the black, silver and gold image looked to me far from that of a preserver. The sleeping Vishnu had a grotto to himself, behind the main shrine. The grotto was built into the outer wall. You had to go into it and then turn a corner before you found the god asleep on his stone bed. Only three or four people could get in at once. Inside it was cool. The place was lit by oil lamps and the god was quite a shock. One had expected something small, miniature, like the rest: instead, this bigger than lifesize reclining figure that overpowered you with a sense of greater strength in sleep than in wakefulness. And such good dreams he was dreaming! Dreams that made him smile.

I could have stood and watched him for ages, but Hari nudged me and whispered that there were other people waiting to come in. We had to force our way through them, back into the courtyard. We went to the other gateway, the one that looked out on to the steps leading down to the river. After *puja* one should bathe, but there was only one man doing so at that moment. We could just make him out, standing in the water up to his waist. His head was shaved. Nearby there was a shed and platform where the temple barbers worked, and where devotees gave their hair to the god.

Hari said, 'Shall we go and get our shoes?' He had had enough. Perhaps I had too, because I wasn't part of its outwardness at all. I felt like a trespasser. So we went back through the courtyard and collected our shoes. More money passed. I suppose it all goes into the pockets of the priests. At the gateway we were besieged by beggars. Our tonga boy was waiting for us and saw us before we saw him, and came pressing forward, ringing his bell and shouting, afraid that one of the other tonga boys would slip in and take us away. We were back in the din and the dirt. There was music from a coffee shop over the road. With my shoes back on, my feet felt gritty. Deliberately I'd not worn stockings.

*

When we got back to the MacGregor House we sat on the verandah. I asked Hari to send the tonga boy round to the back to get some food. He didn't look more than seventeen or so – a cheerful, pleasant boy who obviously felt that with this long evening hire his luck was in. Alone for a moment I went round the back and called Raju, and asked him to bring the boy to me. He appeared from nowhere, as if he'd been expecting me. I gave him ten chips. A fortune. But he deserved it. And it was part of my *puja*. I think Raju disapproved. Perhaps he extracted a precentage, or gave the boy short commons or no commons at all. In the end one can't bear it any more – the indifference of one Indian for another – and doesn't want to know what goes on.

It came on to rain, which drove us in from the verandah. Hari's earlier mood had gone. He looked exhausted, as if he had failed – not just at whatever he had set out to achieve that evening but at everything he'd set his heart on. I wanted to have it out with him, but it was difficult to know how to begin. And when we began it started off all wrong because I said, 'You've been trying to put me off, haven't you?'

He pretended not to understand and said, 'Put off? What do you mean, put off?' Which frustrated me so that I said, as if I were in a temper, 'Oh, put off, put me off, put me off *you*, like everybody else has tried.'

He asked who 'everybody else' was.

I said, 'Well, everybody. People like Mr Merrick for instance. He thinks you're a bad bet.'

Hari said, 'Well, he should know, I suppose.'

I told him that was a ridiculous thing to say because only he knew what kind of bet he was. He said, 'What's all this talk about anyway? What does it mean, bet? Good bet, bad bet? What am I supposed to be, a racehorse or something? Some kind of stock or share people keep an eye on to see if it's worth investing in?'

I'd not seen him angry before. He'd not seen me angry either. We lost our tempers, which is why I don't remember just what it was we said that led me to accuse him of criticising a man he'd probably never met, and then to the realisation that we'd been talking at cross purposes because no one had ever told me it was Ronald who took him into custody and stood by and watched him hit by one of his subordinates. I remember saying something like, 'You mean it was Ronald himself?' and I can still see the surprise on his face when the penny dropped at last and he knew I really hadn't known.

If only I'd contained my anger then. Well, I tried, because I wasn't angry with him but with Ronald, other people, myself as much as anybody. I said, 'Where did it happen, then?' and again he looked astonished. He said, 'Well, in the Sanctuary of course.' That was another blow. I asked him to tell me about it.

He'd been drunk. He wouldn't say why. He'd wandered out as drunk as a coot and collapsed in a ditch in that awful waste ground near the river and been picked up by Sister Ludmila and her helpers who thought he'd been attacked or was ill, or dying, until they got him back to the Sanctuary. He

327

slept it off there, and in the morning Ronald came to the Sanctuary with some policemen, looking for a man who'd escaped from a jail and was thought to have come back to Mayapore because that was where the escaped man used to live. He wasn't there, but Hari was. Well, you can imagine it, I expect, imagine how Hari would react to being browbeaten by a man like Ronald. The sub-inspector accompanying Ronald hit Hari in the face for not answering 'smartly', and in the end he was hustled away and punched and kicked when he got into the back of the truck.

One trouble was that he knew the man the police were looking for. This came out while Ronald questioned him in front of the sub-inspector at the kotwali. But he'd only known him as a clerk in his uncle's warehouse. Another trouble was that Hari deliberately made a point of confusing the police about his name. Coomer. Kumar. He said 'either would do'. Finally Ronald sent the sub-inspector out of the room and talked to Hari alone, or tried to talk to him, which was probably difficult because Hari had taken a dislike to him. I don't know why Hari got drunk. Perhaps from an accumulation of blows that had finally made him feel he cared for nothing and believed in nothing. He told me he was convinced he was going to be locked up anyway, so didn't watch his tongue. I think from the way he told me all this he was trying to help find excuses for Ronald that he couldn't find himself. Ronald asked him why he'd got drunk, and where. Hari wouldn't say where because he thought – and said – that where was none of Ronald's business – but gladly explained why. He explained it by saying he'd got drunk because he hated the whole damned stinking country, the people who lived in it and the people who ran it. He even said, 'And that goes for you too, Merrick.' He knew Merrick's name because he'd often been in the courts as a reporter. He said Merrick only smiled when he said 'and that goes for you too', and then told him he could go, and even apologised – sarcastically of course – for having 'inconvenienced him'. When he got back home he discovered Sister Ludmila had scared up some influential people to ask questions about his 'arrest' but this only amused him, if amused is the right word to use when he was really feeling bitter. He said it had amused him when eventually Lili invited him to a party, and also amused him to see Merrick watching the way I went up to him that day on the *maidan*. I didn't know Ronald had seen that, but it fitted in. Hari thought I had always known the whole story, and was only condescending to him when I broke away from the white officers and white nurses to throw a crumb of comfort to him.

I said, 'So it's amused you whenever we've been out together?'

He said, 'Yes, you could put it that way. If you want to. But you've been very kind, and I'm grateful.'

I said, 'I didn't mean anything as kindness,' and stood up. He stood up too. He would only have had to touch me, for the stupidity to have ended then, but he didn't. He was afraid to. He was too conscious of the weight that would have made touching a gesture of defiance of the rule Ronald had described a few evenings before as 'basic', and he didn't have that kind of courage, and so I was deprived of my own. The defiance had to come from him first, to make it human, to make it right.

I said, 'Goodnight, Hari.' Oh, even in that goodnight there was a way left open to him that 'goodbye' would have closed. But I mustn't blame him. He had good reasons to be afraid. I rehearsed them to myself upstairs in my room, sitting, waiting, determining to have things out with Lili. When I heard the cycle tonga go down the drive my determination began to go with it, and then I was worried, worried for him, because he was a man who would find it awfully difficult to hide, and I believed that was what he wanted to do. To hide. To disappear into a sea of brown faces.

That word Ronald Merrick used was the right one – association. Hari and I could be enemies, or strangers to each other, or lovers, but never friends because such a friendship was put to the test too often to survive. We were constantly having to ask the question, Is it worth it? Constantly having to examine our motives for wanting to be together. On my side the motive was physical attraction. I didn't have enough self-confidence to assure myself that Hari felt the same for me. But this didn't change what I felt. I was in love with him. I wanted him near me. I told myself I didn't care what people said. I didn't care what he'd done, or what people like Ronald Merrick thought he'd done or was capable of doing. I wanted to protect him from danger. If it helped him not to be seen with me any longer I was prepared to let him go, to let him hide. But because I was in love I kidded myself there was a time limit to 'any longer', a magic formula that took the sting out of the decision I made to let the next move come from him.

When Lili asked me next morning about the visit to the temple I chatted away as if nothing had happened. Several times I was on the point of saying, 'Did you know it was Ronald who arrested Hari?' But I didn't want to hear her say yes. I didn't want to pave the way to a discussion that might have forced Lili to confess for instance that she had since had doubts about Hari and regretted her haste in rushing to the defence of a man she didn't know but had since learned more of that made her feel Ronald had been right to suspect him and done nothing he need be ashamed of when he took Hari in for questioning.

I knew that Lili would be the first to realise something had happened between Hari and myself if the days went by without any word from him or meeting between us. I was aware of helping him by keeping quiet, aware of distracting attention from him, but not aware then of the truth of what I was actually doing – indulging my unfulfilled passion for him by weaving a protective web round him which even excluded me. I didn't feel that it excluded me. Later I did.

I went about my job, my ordinary life. No letter from him. To avoid having to answer Lili's questions, if she decided to ask them, I took to going almost every evening to the club. And people noticed it. I was glad they did. If I was at the club obviously I wasn't out with Hari. The first time I saw Ronald there he came up to me and said, 'Did you enjoy the temple?' I shrugged and said, 'Oh, it was all right. A bit of a racket, though. You can't say boo without it costing money.' He smiled. I couldn't tell whether he was pleased or puzzled. I wondered whether he saw through my casual pretence, but then decided that even if he saw through it he wouldn't see what lay behind it. I hated him that night. Hated him and smiled at him. Played the game. And again felt how easy it was, how simple. To act at conforming. Because all the time there was nothing to conform with, except an idea, a charade played round a phrase: white superiority.

And all the time wanting Hari. Seeing him in my imagination looking over the shoulder of every pink male face and seeing in every pink male face the strain of pretending that the world was this small. Hateful. Ingrown. About to explode like powder compressed ready for firing.

I thought that the whole bloody affair of *us* in India had reached flash point. It was bound to because it was based on a violation. Perhaps at one time there was a moral as well as a physical force at work. But the moral thing had gone sour. Has gone sour. Our faces reflect the sourness. The women look worse than the men because consciousness of physical superiority is unnatural to us. A white man in India can feel physically superior without unsexing himself. But what happens to a woman if she tells herself that ninety-nine per cent of the men she sees are not men at all, but creatures of an inferior species whose colour is their main distinguishing mark? What happens when you unsex a nation, treat it like a nation of eunuchs? Because that's what we've done, isn't it?

God knows what happens. What will happen. The whole thing seems to go from bad to worse, year after year. There's dishonesty on both sides because the moral issue has gone sour on them as well as on us. We're back to basics, the basic issue of who jumps and who says jump. Call it by any fancy name you like, even 'the greatest experiment of colonial government and civilising influence since pre-Christian Rome', to quote our old friend Mr Swinson. It's become a vulgar scramble for power on their part and an equally vulgar smug hanging on on ours. And the greater their scramble the greater our smugness. You can't hide that any longer because the moral issue, if it ever really existed at all, is dead. It's our fault it's dead because it was our responsibility to widen it, but we narrowed it down and narrowed it down by never suiting actions to words. We never suited them because out here, where they *needed* to be suited and to be seen to be suited, that old primitive savage instinct to attack and destroy what we didn't understand because it looked different and was different always got the upper hand. And God knows how many centuries you have to go back to trace to its source their apparent fear of skins paler than their own. God help us if they ever lose that fear. Perhaps fear is the wrong word. In India anyway. It is such a primitive emotion and their civilisation is so old. So perhaps I should say God help us if ever they substitute fear for tiredness. But tiredness is the wrong word too. Perhaps we haven't got a word for what they feel. Perhaps it's hidden in that stone carving of Vishnu sleeping, looking as if he might wake at any minute and take them to oblivion in a crack of happy thunder.

Was this the difference between my own emotions and Hari's? That he could wait and I couldn't? In the end I couldn't bear the silence, the inaction, the separation, the artificiality of my position. I wrote to him. I had no talent for self-denial. It's an Anglo-Saxon failing, I suppose. Constantly we want proof, here and now, proof of our existence, of the mark we've made, the sort of mark we can wear round our necks, to label us, to make sure we're never lost in that awful dark jungle of anonymity.

But in my impatience there was Anglo-Saxon planning, forethought, an acceptance that time went through certain fixed exercises that the clock and the calendar had been invented to define. The farther away from the equator you get the more sensitive you become to the rhythm of light and dark, the way it expands and contracts and organises the seasons, so that time itself develops a specific characteristic that alerts you to its absurd but meticulous demands. If I'd been an Indian girl perhaps I'd have said in my note to Hari: Tonight, please. Instead I gave three or four days' notice. Three or four. I forget which, which shows how unimportant the actual number was, how unimportant as well the actual day suggested – although I remember which. As everybody probably does. August the ninth. In my note I said I was sorry for any misunderstanding, and that I wanted to talk to him. I said I'd go to the Sanctuary on that evening and hoped to meet him there.

I got no reply, but when the day came I felt happy, almost lightheaded. At breakfast time the telephone rang. I thought it was Hari and rushed to answer before Raju could get there. It wasn't Hari. It was little Mrs Srinivasan wanting to speak to Lili. I sent Raju up to Lili's bedroom to tell her to pick up the extension. When I went up to say goodbye to her Lili said, 'They've arrested Vassi.'

Well, you know all that side of things. We'd been prepared for it but it was a shock when it actually happened. When I got to the hospital the girls were acting as if they'd been personally responsible for saving the day by locking up the Mahatma and his colleagues and Congressmen all over the country. A year earlier most of them wouldn't even have known what Congress was. The atmosphere in the hospital that morning was like that in the club at the end of War Week. One of them said, 'Have you noticed the orderlies? They've got their tails between their legs all right.' Once this had been pointed out the girls seemed to go out of their way to find new methods of humiliating them. And there was a subtle change in their attitude to me, as if they were trying to make me feel that I'd been backing the wrong horse for months.

It wasn't until the afternoon that they began to get scared. First there was the rumour of rioting in the sub-divisions, then the confirmation that the assistant commissioner had gone out with police patrols to find out why contact couldn't be made with a place called Tanpur. It came on to rain. And about a quarter to five, when I was getting ready to go off duty, there was a flap because Mr Poulson had brought in the mission teacher, Miss Crane. At first we thought she'd been raped, but I got the true story from Mr Poulson. I saw him as I was going to Matron's office. Miss Crane had been attacked on her way home from Dibrapur, and had her car burnt out, and had seen one of her teachers – an Indian – murdered. She was suffering from shock and exposure. She'd sat on the roadside guarding the murdered man's body. As I'd met Miss Crane once at the Deputy Commissioner's bungalow I got permission from Matron to go in and see her. But she was already wandering and didn't recognise me. I thought she was for it. She kept saying, 'I'm sorry. Sorry it's too late,' mumbling about there having been too many chappattis for her to eat alone, and asking why I hadn't shared them, why had I gone hungry? I held her hand and tried to make contact with her but all she would do for a while was keep repeating, 'I'm sorry it's too late.' But suddenly she said, 'Mine's Edwina Crane and my mother's been dead for longer than I care to remember,' and then went off into a delirium about mending the roof and there being nothing she could do. 'Nothing,' she said, over and over. 'There's nothing I can do.'

*

It was raining when I left the hospital.* There was no sign of Ronald's driver or of the truck. He would have been busy that evening anyway. But I had my bicycle and my rain cape and sou'wester. I'd told Lili that I'd be calling in at the club and I'd also promised to see the girls there, but looking in on Miss Crane had made me late and so I cycled direct to the Sanctuary, down Hospital road, Victoria road, and over the river by way of the Bibighar bridge. Perhaps the rain as well as the rumours was keeping nearly everyone indoors, because I saw few people. I got to the Sanctuary at about 5.45. The rain was letting up a bit then.

I've never described the Sanctuary to you, have I? You turn off the Chillianwallah Bagh Extension road along a track that skirts the waste ground near the river where the poorest untouchables live in horrible squalid huts. Then you come to a walled compound in which there are three old buildings that date back to the early nineteenth century. One is the office, the other the clinic and Sister Ludmila's 'cell' and the third and largest the place where she tends the sick and dying. There must be nearly an acre of ground enclosed by those walls. The place looks derelict and you can smell the river most of the time. But inside the buildings everything is clean and neat, scrubbed and whitewashed.

She has one principal assistant, a middle-aged Goanese called de Souza, and several men and women whom she hires at random. I've always wondered where her money comes from.

Hari wasn't there. I went to the office first and saw Mr de Souza. He said Sister Ludmila was in her room, and that no one had turned up so far for the evening clinic, probably because of the rumours of trouble. I went across to

---

* Section of Journal shown to Robin White begins here.

the clinic and knocked at her door. I'd not seen her since the week of the visit to the temple. She knew Hari and I had been planning to go there. She asked me to come in and tell her about it.

The rain stopped and in about ten minutes or so the sun came out, as if often does, at the end of an afternoon's wet, but of course it was already setting. She said, 'Will Hari be coming?' I told her I wasn't sure. And then she asked me about the temple. She herself had never been inside it. I described our *puja* to the Lord Venkataswara and the image of the sleeping Vishnu. I wanted to ask her about the night she found Hari lying drunk in a ditch in the waste-land outside the Sanctuary, but didn't. As the minutes went by and he still did not come I thought, 'It's all going, going away before I've touched any of it or understood any of it.' I watched the wooden carving of the Dancing Siva. It seemed to move. There came a point when I couldn't watch it any longer because it was draining me of my own mobility. I felt I was becoming lost in it.

I turned to her. She always sat very upright, on a hard wooden chair, with her hands folded on her lap, showing her wedding ring. I never saw her without her cap so I don't know whether she'd shorn her hair. On other occasions when I'd been in her room its bareness and simplicity had always conveyed an idea to me of its safety, but this evening I thought, 'No, it's her safety, not the room's.' I felt this going away from me too. There was so much I wanted to know about her, but I'd only once asked her a personal question. She spoke English very well, but with a strong accent. I'd asked her where she'd learned it and she said, 'From my husband. His name was Smith.' One heard many different tales about her – for instance that she had run away from a convent as a young novice and wore the nunnish clothing in the hope of being forgiven. I don't think this was true. I think there was no tale about her that was true. Only her charity was true. For me it always outweighed my curiosity. When you spoke to her there wasn't any mystery. In herself she was all the explanation I felt she needed. And that is rare, isn't it? To be explained by yourself, by what you are and what you do, and not by what you've done, or were, or by what people think you might be or might become.

I stayed for an hour, until it was dusk. I told myself that Hari was probably working late, but I knew this didn't explain his silence. I wondered whether he had been arrested again but decided that was unlikely. The arrests that had been made were of prominent members of the local Congress, like Vasi. I thought of calling in at Aunt Shalini's but when I got out on the Chillianwallah Bagh Extension road I changed my mind and turned in the direction of the Bibighar bridge. It was almost dark. Thinking it might rain again I'd put my cape and sou'wester back on instead of strapping them to the carrier, and it was warm and clammy. I crossed the bridge and the level crossing. When I got to the street lamp opposite the Bibighar I stopped and took the cape off, and put it over the handlebars. It was stopping like this that made me wheel the bike across the road to look in through the gate of the Bibighar. When I stopped I'd had a strong impression of Hari in the Bibighar, sitting in the pavilion alone, not expecting me, but thinking of me, wondering whether I would turn up.

I went through the open gateway and along the path to the place where we always left our cycles – a place where we could lean them against the wall but keep an eye on them from the pavilion. When I got to this place there was no cycle. I looked across in the direction of the pavilion. At first there was nothing, but then I saw the glow of a cigarette being drawn on. I suppose the distance between the path by the wall and the pavilion is about a hundred yards. You can walk it straight by going up over what was once the lawn and the series of little steps. That's why we usually left our cycles against the wall, to save lugging them up the steps. The other way to the pavilion is by the path that skirts the grounds. I wasn't sure whether it was Hari in the pavilion and so I went up by the path.

When I got round to the side of the pavilion I could see the man standing on the mosaic platform. I said, 'Hari, is that you?' He said, 'Yes.' I turned the lamp off and left the cycle against a tree and then went up to the pavilion. When I got there I found I'd brought the cape with me.

I said, 'Didn't you get my note?' But it was a silly thing to ask. He didn't answer. I felt for a cigarette and realised I'd run out. I asked him for one of his. He gave it to me. It made me cough, so I threw it away. I sat down on the mosaic. The roof overhangs the edge and the mosaic is always dry. There was no need for the cape. I put it on the ground nearby. With so many trees around it sounds as if it's raining long after it has stopped. The water drips from the roof as well as from the leaves. Eventually he sat down too and lit another cigarette. I said, 'Let me try one of those again.' He opened the packet and held it out. I took a cigarette. Then I took hold of his hand, the one in which he held his own cigarette, and lit mine from his. I smoked without inhaling. After a while he said, 'What were you trying to prove? That you don't mind our touching?'

I said, 'I thought we'd got beyond that.'

'No,' he said, 'we can never get beyond it.'

I said, 'But we have. I have. It was never an obstacle anyway. At least not for me.'

He asked why I'd come to the Bibighar. I told him I'd waited for an hour at the Sanctuary, that I'd looked in on my way past because I thought he might be there.

After a while he said, 'You oughtn't to be out alone tonight. I'll see you home. Throw that disgusting thing away.'

He waited, then leaned towards me and held my wrist and took the cigarette and threw it into the garden. I couldn't bear it, having him so near, knowing I was about to lose him. That catching hold of my wrist was like the impatient gesture of a lover. For him it was like that too. I willed him not to let go. There was an instant when I was afraid, perhaps because he wanted me to be. But then we were kissing. His shirt had rucked up because he was wearing it loose over his waistband and my hand was touching his bare back, and then we were both lost. There was nothing gentle in the way he took me. I felt myself lifted on to the mosaic. He tore at my underclothes and pressed down on me with all his strength. But this was not me and Hari. Entering me he made me cry out. And then it was us.

*

They came when we lay half-asleep listening to the croaking of the frogs, his hand covering one breast, my own in his black hair, moving to trace the miracle of his black ear.

Five or six men. Suddenly. Climbing on to the platform. My nightmare faces. But not faces. Black shapes in white cotton clothing; stinking, ragged clothing. Converging on Hari, pulling him away. And then darkness. And a familiar smell. But hot and suffocating. Covering my head. As I began to struggle I could think of nothing but the thing that covered my head. I knew it, but did not know it because it was smothering me. And then there was a moment – the moment, I suppose, when the man holding me down and covering me with this suffocating but familiar thing, lifted his weight away – a moment when I forgot the covering and felt only my exposed nakedness. He must have lifted his weight away when the others had finished dealing with Hari and came to help. There was pressure on my knees and ankles and then my wrists – a moment of terrible openness and vulnerability and then the first experience of that awful animal thrusting, the motion of love without one saving split-second of affection.

*

I no longer dream of faces. In bad dreams now I'm usually blind. This kind of dream begins with the image of Siva. I see him only with my sense of recollection. Suddenly he leaves his circle of cosmic fire and covers me, imprisons my arms and legs in darkness. Surreptitiously, I grow an extra arm to fight him or embrace him, but he always has an arm to spare to pin me down, a new lingam growing to replace the one that's spent. This dream ends when I'm no longer blind and see the expression on his face which is one of absolution and invitation. I wake then, remembering how after they had gone I found myself holding my raincape, breathing, aware of the blessing of there being air with which to fill my lungs, and thinking, 'It was mine, my own cape that I use to keep the rain off, mine all the time, part of my life.' I clung to the cape. I held it to my body, covering myself. I thought I was alone. I had this idea that Hari had gone with them because he had been one of them.

But then I saw him, the shape of him, lying as I was lying, on the mosaic. They had bound his hands and mouth and ankles with strips of cloth, torn for all I knew from their own clothing, and then placed him where he would have had to close his eyes if he didn't want to see what was happening.

I crawled like a kid across the mosaic and struggled with the knots,

335

struggled because they were tight and difficult and because I was also trying to cover myself with the cape. I untied the gag round his mouth first, in case he was finding it difficult to breathe, and then the strips of rag round his ankles, and then the one round his wrists. And as I untied him he continued to lie as they had left him, so that presently I gathered him in my arms because I couldn't bear it. I couldn't bear the sound of him crying.

*

He cried for shame, I suppose, and for what had happened to me that he'd been powerless to stop. He said something that I was too dazed to catch but thinking back on it it always comes to me as an inarticulate begging for forgiveness.

I was suddenly very cold. He felt me shivering. Now *he* held *me*, and for a time we clung to each other like two children frightened of the dark. But I couldn't stop shivering. He moved the cape until it was round my shoulders and then covered me at the front. He got up and searched for things that belonged to me. I felt them in his hands and took them from him. He said, 'Put your arms round my neck.' I did so. He lifted me and carried me over to the steps and down them one at a time. I thought of all the steps between the pavilion and the gate, and then of the bicycle. I thought he was going to carry me across the garden, but he turned on to the path. When he went past the place where I'd left the bicycle I said, 'No, it's here somewhere.' He didn't understand. I said, 'My bicycle.' He put me down but continued to hold me. He said he couldn't see it, that the men must have stolen it or hidden it. He said he'd come back in the morning to look for it. I asked him about his own bicycle. He'd left it in the bazaar to be repaired. He'd not had it all day. He picked me up again and carried me down the path. I felt myself becoming a dead weight in his arms. I asked him to put me down. He did so but then lifted me again. While we were in the garden I let him do this. If I'd asked him to carry me all the way to the MacGregor House I think he'd have managed it somehow. But when we got to the gateway and he put me down again – as if to catch his breath – the world outside the garden came back into focus. On the other side of the gate there was the beginning of what another white girl would have thought of as safety. It was safety of a kind for me too. But not for him. When he moved to pick me up again I pushed him away – as you'd push away a child who was reaching out to touch something that would burn it or scald it. Seeing the gateway I imagined him carrying me through it, into the light, into the cantonment.

I said, 'No. I've got to go home alone. We've not been together. I've not seen you.'

He tried to take hold of my arm. I moved away from him. I said, 'No. Let me go. You've not been near me. You don't know anything. You know nothing. Say nothing.' He wouldn't listen. He caught me, tried to hold me close, but I struggled. I was in a panic, thinking of what they'd do to him.

No one would believe me. He said, 'I've got to be with you. I love you. Please let me be with you.'

If he hadn't said that perhaps I'd have given in. The thought that he was right and I was wrong and that the only way to have faced it was with the truth is one of the things I have to puzzle over now and carry with me – a burden as heavy if less obvious than the child. And you may wonder why when he said he loved me my determination to resist didn't come abruptly to an end. But love isn't like that, is it? It wasn't for me. It bewildered me. It sent me from panic to worse panic, because of what they might do to him if he said to *them*, 'I love her. We love each other.'

I beat at him, not to escape myself but to make *him* escape. I was trying to beat sense and reason and cunning into him. I kept saying, 'We've never seen each other. You've been at home. You say nothing. You know nothing. Promise me.'

I was free and began to run without waiting to hear him promise. At the gate he caught me and tried to hold me back. Again I asked him to let me go, *please* to let me go, to say nothing, to know nothing, *for my sake* if that was the only way he could say nothing and know nothing for his own. For an instant I held him close – it was the last time I touched him – and then I broke free again and was out of the gateway and running; running into and out of the light of the street lamp opposite, running into the dark and grateful for the dark, going without any understanding of direction. I stopped and leaned against a wall. I wanted to turn back. I wanted to admit that I couldn't face it alone. And I wanted him to know that I thought I'd done it all wrong. He wouldn't know what I felt, what I meant. I was in pain. I was exhausted. And frightened. Too frightened to turn back.

I said, 'There's nothing I can do, nothing, nothing,' and wondered where I'd heard those words before, and began to run again, through those awful ill-lit deserted roads that should have been leading me home but were leading me nowhere I recognised; into safety that wasn't safety because beyond it there were the plains and the openness that made it seem that if I ran long enough I would run clear off the rim of the world.*

*

It seemed so simple at the time to say, 'Hari wasn't there,' and to feel, just by saying it, that I put him out of harm's reach. It's all too easy now to think that his only real protection was the truth, however disagreeable it would have been for us to tell it, to have it told, however threatening and dangerous the truth would have been for him. Well, if he had been an Englishman – that young subaltern who began to paw me at the War Week dance, for instance – the truth would have worked and it would never have occurred to us to tell anything else, I suppose. When people realised what he and I had been doing in the Bibighar they would have stood by us while they tried to see justice done, and then when it had been done or when

* End of section of Journal shown to Robin White.

they'd pursued every possible line to an end short of justice because the men couldn't be caught turned round and made it clear that it was now our duty, mine in particular, to make ourselves scarce.

But it wasn't an Englishman. And of course there are people who would say that it would never have happened if it had been, and I expect they would be right because he and I would never have had to go to the Bibighar to be alone, we would never have been there after dark. He would have seduced me in the back of a truck in the car park of the Gymkhana club, or in the place behind the changing-rooms of the swimming-pool, or in a room in one of the chummeries, or even in my bedroom at the MacGregor on a night Lili was out playing bridge. And there are people who would say that even if this subaltern and I had made love in the pavilion in the Bibighar we would never have been attacked by a gang of Indian hooligans. Which is probably right too, although their reasons for saying so wouldn't be strictly correct. They'd invest the subaltern with some sort of superman quality that enabled him to make short work of a gang of bloody wogs, whereas, in fact, the gang of bloody wogs would have been made short work of by their own fear of white people. Miss Crane was hit a few times, but it was the Indian teacher with her who was murdered. They assaulted me because they had watched an Indian making love to me. The taboo was broken for them.

I think Hari understood this. I think this is what he saw and was ashamed of and asked to be forgiven for. All that I saw was the danger to him as a black man carrying me through a gateway that opened on to the world of white people.

I look for similes, for something that explains it more clearly, but find nothing, because there *is* nothing. It is itself; an Indian carrying an English girl he has made love to and been forced to watch being assaulted – carrying her back to where she would be safe. It is its own simile. It says all that needs to be said, doesn't it? If you extend it, if you think of him carrying me all the way to the MacGregor House, giving me into Aunt Lili's care, ringing for the doctor, ringing for the police, answering questions, and being treated as a man who'd rescued me, the absurdity, the implausibility become almost unbearable. Directly you get to the point where Hari, taken on one side by Ronald for instance, has to say, 'Yes, we were making love,' the nod of understanding that *must* come from Ronald *won't*, unless you blanch Hari's skin, blanch it until it looks not just like that of a white man but like that of a white man too shaken for another white man not to feel sorry for, however much he may reproach him.

And that is why I fought him, why I beat at him, why I said, 'We've not seen each other. You know nothing.'

So easy to say. 'I've not seen Hari. I've not seen Hari since we visited the temple.' That's what I told Lili when I was lying on the sofa in the living-room. She had understood at last what was wrong and had asked, 'Was it Hari?' And out it came, perhaps too glibly, but incontrovertible. 'No. No. I've not seen Hari. I've not seen him since we visited the temple.'

'Who was it, then?' she asked. I couldn't look at her. I said, 'I don't know. Five or six men. I didn't see. It was dark. They covered my head.'

Then if you didn't see them, how can you be sure one of them wasn't Hari Kumar? That was a question that had to be answered, wasn't it? She didn't ask it. Instead she said, 'Where?' and I said, 'The Bibighar,' and again there was a question. What was I doing in the Bibighar? It wasn't asked. Not then. Not by Lili. But the trap was beginning to close. It had been closing ever since I got back and stumbled and fell on the steps of the verandah.

I hurt my knee badly. I think I passed out for a few seconds. When I came to, and was trying to get up, Lili was there staring at me as if she didn't recognise me. I remember her saying the name Raju. I suppose she called him to help or he'd come out with her. The next thing I remember is being in the living-room and being given a glass of brandy. Raju and Bhalu must have carried me in. I remember Bhalu standing on the rug without his chappals. His bare feet. And Raju's bare feet. Black hands. And black faces. After I'd drunk the brandy Lili asked them to carry memsahib upstairs. When they came towards me I couldn't bear it and began to cry out and tell her to send them away. It was then that Lili knew what had happened. When I opened my eyes again she and I were alone and I was ashamed to look at her. She said then, 'Was it Hari?' and I gave her the answer I'd rehearsed.

And I'm still ashamed of the way I cried out when Bhalu and Raju came towards me. I cried out because they were black. I'm ashamed because this proved that in spite of loving Hari I'd not exorcised that stupid primitive fear. I'd made Hari an exception. I don't mean that I loved him in spite of his blackness. His blackness was inseparable from his physical attraction. I think I mean that in loving him and in being physically attracted to him I'd invested his blackness with a special significance or purpose, taken it out of its natural context instead of identifying myself with it *in* its context. There was an element here of self-satisfaction and special pleading and extra pride in love because of the personal and social barrier I thought my love had helped me to surmount. It had not surmounted it at all. No, that is not quite true. It had partly surmounted it. Enough for me to be ashamed then, as well as now, and to ask Lili to call Raju and Bhalu back and help me upstairs. I thanked them and tried to show them that I was sorry. In the morning, on my tray, there were flowers from the garden, which Lili said Bhalu had cut for me.

*

Before they helped me upstairs Raju had rung Dr Klaus. On our way up to my room Lili said, 'Anna's coming. It's all right, Daphne. Anna's coming.' Lili waited with me in my room. We heard a car or truck drive up and Lili said, 'That will be her.' A few moments later there was a knock on the bedroom door and Lili called out, 'Come in, Anna.' I didn't want to see even Anna, so I turned my head away when the door opened. I heard Lili say, 'No, no, you mustn't come in.' She got up and went outside and closed the door. When she came back she told me it was Ronald, that he had been at the house before, looking for me. I said, 'It's very kind of him, but I'm back now, so tell him it's all right.' Lili said, 'But you see, my dear, it isn't, is it?' And then she began to question me again, to get the answers to questions Ronald had asked. In the Bibighar, but when? How many men? What kind of men? Did I recognise any? Would I recognise any? How did I get back?

She left me for a few minutes. I heard her talking to Ronald in the passage. When she came back she said nothing but sat on the bed and held my hand. Like that we heard Ronald drive away. He was driving very fast. Without looking at her I said, 'You told him it wasn't Hari, didn't you?'

She said she had, so I knew Ronald had asked. The way they'd both jumped to the conclusion that Hari was involved only strengthened my resolve to lie my head off.

It was then just a matter of waiting for Anna. I was glad when she got there, glad to be treated like a sort of specimen, clinically, unemotionally. When she'd finished I asked her to tell Lili to get one of the boys to run a bath. I had an idea that if only I could lie in warm water for an hour I might begin to feel clean. She pretended to agree, but she'd given me a strong sedative. I remember the sound of running water, and passing into a half-sleep, imagining that the running water was pouring rain. She ran the water only to lull me. When I woke it was morning. She was still at the bedside. I said, 'Have you been here all night?' She hadn't of course, but had called in first thing. I always liked Anna, but until that morning I'd also been a bit afraid of her, as one is of people whose experiences haven't been happy. One hesitates to question them. I never asked Anna about Germany. Now there was no need. We had found something in common. Which is why we were able to smile at each other, distantly, just for a moment or two, as if the connection between us was only just discernible.

*

I've told the truth, Auntie, as well as I know how. I'm sorry I wasn't able to tell it before. I hate lies. But I think I would tell them again. Nothing that happened after the Bibighar proves to me now that I was wrong to fight for Hari by denying I'd seen him. I know in my bones that he suffered. I know that he is being punished. But I mustn't believe that he is being punished more badly because of my lies than he would have been by the truth.

When I think of the contortions people went through in an attempt to prove I was lying and in an attempt to implicate him I tremble at the thought of what could have happened to him if just once, by a slip of the tongue, I'd admitted that we were in the Bibighar together.

But this doesn't help me to bear the knowledge that those other boys are unjustly punished. How can people be punished when they are innocent? I know that they went to prison in the end for reasons said to be unconnected with the assault. I hang on to that, in the hope that it is true. But if it hadn't been for the assault I think they'd be free today. They must have been the wrong men. I know I said I didn't see the men, and this was true. But I had an impression of them, of their clothes, their smell, a sense of them as men, not boys. They were hooligans from some village who had come into Mayapore for the hell of it. From what people said the boys who were arrested didn't sound like hooligans at all.

I didn't hear about the arrests until late the following day. Anna and Lili knew already. Ronald had come back the previous night and told them he'd got 'the men responsible under lock and key'. They said nothing to me at the time because I was asleep by then and nothing in the morning because one of the men was Hari. About half-past twelve Lili came in with Anna. She said, 'Jack Poulson has to talk to you, but he can talk in front of Anna.' I asked her to stay too, but she said it would be best for Anna and Jack to be alone with me. When Jack Poulson came in he looked like a Christian martyr who'd just refused to disown God for the last time. I was embarrassed by him and he was embarrassed by me. Anna stood by the open door on to the balcony and Jack stood close to her until I told him to sit down. He apologised for having to ask questions and explained that Mr White had given him the job of 'dealing with the evidence' since it was not merely a police matter but one that involved the station as a whole.

I had had time to think, time to worry about the questions Lili hadn't asked the previous night, but which I'd seen as ones that would have to be answered. What was I doing in the Bibighar? How did I know that Hari wasn't there if I didn't see the men who attacked me? I realised that the only way I could get through an interrogation without involving Hari was to relive the whole thing in my mind as it would have happened, as it would have had to be, if Hari hadn't been in the Bibighar with me.

My story was this: that after seeing Miss Crane I'd left the hospital and gone to the Sanctuary. I made a point of asking Jack Poulson not to say too much about the Sanctuary – if he could help it – because I went there to assist at the clinic and was sure this was a breach of hospital regulations even for a voluntary unpaid nursing officer. He smiled, as I'd intended he should. But then he stopped smiling and by his silence forced me to go on, unaided, to the difficult part of the story.

I left the Sanctuary about dusk. It had seemed clear that no one would come to the clinic because of the rumours of trouble. The whole town was unnaturally quiet. The people had imposed their own curfew. But far from frightening me it lulled me into a false sense of security. For once I felt I had Mayapore completely to myself. I cycled to the Chillianwallah Bagh Extension road and then over the Bibighar bridge and the level crossing.

At this point Jack Poulson said, 'Did you see anyone near the crossing?'

I thought about that. (I still hadn't been told about the arrests.) So far we were still dealing with fact, with truth, but I had to judge the extent to which I could allow myself to tell it. I saw nothing dangerous in the truth so far, so I tried to conjure an accurate picture of crossing the bridge and the railway lines. I said, 'No. There was no one about. The light showed green at the crossing – and I seem to remember lights and voices coming from the keeper's hut. When I say voices I mean a child crying. A feeling of some kind of domestic crisis that was taking up everyone's attention. Anyway, I cycled on. When I got to the street lamp opposite the Bibighar I stopped and got off.'

After waiting for a moment Jack said, 'Why?'

I said, 'I stopped originally to take off my cape. I'd put it on when I left Sister Ludmila's because I thought it was going to rain again, but it hadn't done, and you know what it's like wearing a rain cape for no reason.'

Jack nodded and then asked if I'd actually stopped *under* the streetlamp. I thought: That means somebody saw me, either that or they're trying to establish that someone could have seen me. I wasn't bothered because I was still telling the truth. But I was wary, and I was glad that the half-lie I was about to tell was closer to the truth than the story I'd first thought of and rejected – that I stopped by the Bibighar to put my cape *on* because I thought it was going to rain, or because it had come on to rain and I'd decided to shelter for a while in the Bibighar. I rejected that story because it hadn't been about to rain, and didn't rain, and anyone could have proved that it didn't.

So I said, yes, I'd stopped under the streetlamp and taken my cape off. And my rain-hat. I'd put my hat in the pocket of the cape and put the cape over the handlebars.

Mr Poulson said, 'What do you mean when you say *originally* you stopped to take off your cape?'

This was the first real danger point. Again I was glad I'd rejected the idea of a melodramatic attack by unknown assailants who overpowered me and dragged me into the Bibighar. I said, 'You'll think it awfully silly, or if not silly then foolish or careless.' Now that I was actually telling the lie I congratulated myself. In an odd way the lie was so much in character. Typical of that silly blundering *gallumping* girl Daphne Manners. I looked Jack Poulson straight in the eye and came out with it. 'The cantonment was so quiet and deserted I wondered whether I'd see the ghosts.'

'The ghosts?' he asked. He was trying to look official but only succeeded in looking as inquisitive as I was pretending to have been, the night before. I said, 'Yes, the ghosts of the Bibighar. I'd never been there in the dark' – that was dangerous, but it passed – 'and I remembered having heard that the place was supposed to be haunted. So I sort of said, Up the Army, Steady the Buffs, and crossed the road and went in. You can always get in because there's no gate. I thought it was a bit of a lark and that when I got back I'd be able to say to Lili, "Well, I've laid those Bibighar ghosts. Bring on Janet MacGregor." I wheeled my bike up the pathway to the pavilion, then parked it, turned the lamp off, and went up on to the mosaic platform.'

But Mr Poulson had never been in the Bibighar. He went later to inspect the scene, but for the moment I had to tell him what the mosaic platform was before he was in the picture. 'Anyway,' I said, 'I sat on the platform and had a cigarette' – (that slipped out and was also dangerous because if any cigarette ends had survived the night's rains they'd not be English ones) – 'and waited for the ghosts to show up. I was saying things to myself like, Come on, ghosts, let's be having you, and then began to think about Miss Crane, and wonder whether I hadn't been an awful fool. I suppose it *was* mad of me, sitting there, last night of all nights. But I didn't take what had happened in outlying parts of the district seriously, did you? I suppose they were watching me. I didn't hear anything – except the dripping and the croaking – I mean the dripping from the leaves and the roof and the croaking of the frogs. The men came rather suddenly. Almost from nowhere.'

Mr Poulson reassumed his Christian martyr face. He said, 'And you didn't see them?' Which was the other warning note. I said, 'Well, for an instant perhaps. But it was all so quick. I didn't have any warning. One moment I was alone and the next surrounded.'

Of course this was the part of the story Jack Poulson wanted to know about but found so acutely embarrassing he could hardly look at me while I told it. He kept glancing at Anna, for moral support, and at the time I wondered why she just stood there, obviously listening but staring at the garden, detaching herself from the interrogation, turning herself into an impersonal lump that would only spring into action and become Anna Klaus again if her patient's voice betrayed signs of distress.

Jack Poulson said, 'I'm sorry to have to press these questions. But is there anything you remember about these men, or about any one of them, anything that will help you to identify them?'

I played for time. I said, 'I don't think so. I mean they all look alike, don't they? Especially in the dark,' and was conscious of having said something that could be thought indelicate, as well as out of character. He asked me how they were dressed. I had a pretty clear recollection of white cotton clothing – you know, dhotis and high-necked shirts, peasant dress, dirty and smelly. But the warning bells rang again. I saw *the danger to Hari if the men were ever caught.* I think that if I were taken to the Bibighar, at night, and confronted with those men, I would know them. You can recognise people again, even when you think there's been nothing to identify them by, even if there's been only a second or two to get an impression you can hardly believe is an impression, or at least not one worth describing or trying to describe. I was afraid of *being* confronted, afraid of finding myself having to say, 'Yes, these are the men,' because then they would plead provocation, they'd go on their knees and scream and beg for mercy and say that such a thing would never have occurred to them *if the white woman hadn't already been making love to an Indian.*

The trap was now fully sprung, Auntie, wasn't it? Once you've started lying there's no end to it. I'd lied myself into a position there was no escaping from except by way of the truth. I didn't dare tell the truth so the only thing I could do was to confuse and puzzle people and make them hate me – that, and stretch every nerve-end to keep Hari out of it by going on and on insisting that he was never there, making it so that they would never be able to accuse or bring to trial or punish the men who assaulted me because they knew that the principal witness would spike every gun they tried to bring into action.

But of course I was forgetting or anyway reckoning without the power they had to accuse and punish on suspicion alone. There was a moment when I nearly told the truth, because I saw the way things might go. I'm glad I didn't because then I think they would have proved somehow that Hari was technically guilty of rape, because he'd been there and made love to me and incited others to follow his example. At least my lying spared him being punished for rape. It also spared those innocent boys being punished for it too. I've never asked what the punishment for rape is. Hanging? Life imprisonment? People talked about swinging them on the end of a rope. Or firing them from the mouth of a cannon, which is what we did to mutineers in the nineteenth century.

So when Jack Poulson asked me how the men were dressed I said I wasn't sure, but then decided it was safer to tell the truth and say 'Like peasants' than to leave the impression of men dressed like Hari, in shirts and trousers.

Mr Poulson said, 'Are you sure?' which rather played into my hands because he said it as if my evidence was contradicting the story he'd been building up, or other people had built up for him, a picture with Hari at its centre. So I said, Yes, like peasants or labourers. And I added for good measure, 'They smelt like that, too.' Which was true. He said, 'Did any of them smell of drink?' I thought of the time Hari was found on the waste ground by Sister Ludmila. For the moment it looked safer to tell the truth again and say I didn't remember any special smell of drink.

Mr Poulson said, 'I'm sorry to have to subject you to this.' I told him it was all right, I knew it had to be done. For the first time in the interrogation we looked at each other for longer than a split second. He said, 'There's the important question of the bicycle. You say you left it on the path near the pavilion. Did you leave your cape on the handlebars?'

I couldn't immediately see the significance of this question. I assumed he knew that the cape had been used to cover my head because I'd told Lili and Anna. He'd got all this kind of detail from them. He never asked a single question about the assault itself. Poor fellow! I expect he'd rather have died than do so, magistrate though he was. But it was an English girl who'd been assaulted and his magisterial detachment just wouldn't hold out. I decided to tell the truth about the cape. I said, 'No, I'm pretty sure I took it with me on to the platform. In fact I did. I thought the mosaic might be damp, but it wasn't. So I didn't sit on the cape, I just kept it by me.'

He seemed to be satisfied with that, and later when the whole business of the bicycle and what had happened to it blew up in my face I realised what he'd been after. He was trying to establish at what stage 'they'd' found the bicycle. If I'd left the cape on the handlebars that would mean they'd known the bicycle was there before they attacked me, because they'd used the cape. If I hadn't left it on the handlebars it could mean they didn't find the bicycle until they were making off along the path. And this would suggest that they had gone along the path and not out through the broken wall at the back of the garden. There couldn't have been any footprints though, because the paths were all gravel, and anyway with the rains and the police bashing about in the dark all that kind of evidence would lead nowhere. His next question was, 'You say you were suddenly surrounded. Do you mean they closed in on you from all sides of the platform?'

And again, the warning bell. If I said, Yes, from all sides, the next question wouldn't be a question at all, but a statement impossible to refute: 'So you never got an impression of the man or men who came at you from behind?'

I realised it was going to be difficult to kill completely the idea of there having been at least one man I never saw, especially if he was a man who kept out of sight in case I recognised him. Hari, for instance. The pavilion is open on all sides. I could only minimise the danger. I said, 'Well, no, not from all sides. Originally I was sitting on the edge of the platform, then I threw my cigarette away and turned round – as you would, to get to your feet. They were coming at me from behind. I don't know – perhaps I'd heard a sound that made me decide to get out of the place. It *was* pretty creepy. When I turned round there were these two just standing upright after climbing on to the platform and the other three or four vaulting on to it.'

Did I call out? No – I was too surprised to call out. Did any of them say anything? I think one of them giggled.

Mr Poulson questioned the margin of error there might be in my statement about 'the other three or four'. Was it three, or was it four? Was the total number of men five or six? I said I couldn't remember. All I remembered was the awful sensation of being attacked swiftly by as many men as there were, five or six. Men of that kind, labourers, hooligans, stinking to high heaven. I said it was like being thrown into one of those disgusting third-class compartments on an Indian train. And that I didn't want to talk about it any more.

Anna came to life then. She turned round and said, 'Yes, I think it is enough, Mr Poulson,' in that very forthright German voice of hers. He got up at once, glad enough to be out of it, if only for a while. Anna saw him to the door. She came back for a moment to make sure I was all right, then left me alone. Lili brought up some fruit and curds for my lunch and after that I dozed until late afternoon. I woke and found Lili in the room and Raju just leaving it. He'd brought up tea.

When I'd had a cup Lili said, 'I think Mr Poulson should have told you. Some boys were arrested last night. One of them was Hari.'

My bicycle had been found in the ditch outside Hari's house in the Chillianwallah Bagh. I didn't believe it. It was such a monstrous *fatal* intervention. I said, 'But he wasn't there! It wasn't Hari!' She wanted to believe me. I tried not to panic. If some men had been arrested I thought they must be the ones responsible and that they would already have talked about the Indian who'd been making love to me there. I was going to have to deny this, deny it and go on denying it, and hope that Hari would keep his promise to say nothing, to know nothing. I felt that he had *given* me that promise when he let me go. I asked Lili when he'd been arrested and why, and who by. When I took it in that he'd been in custody ever since the night before and that Ronald was responsible, that Ronald had found the bicycle outside Hari's house, I said, 'He's lying, isn't he? He found the bicycle in the Bibighar and took it to Hari's house and planted it in the ditch.'

Lili was shocked because she knew it *could* be true, but she refused to believe it. She couldn't accept that an English official would stoop to that. But there are only three possible explanations for the bicycle and only one is likely. I left the bicycle by the path against a tree. It was very dark on the path. You'd easily miss seeing the bicycle if you didn't know just where it was and if you had no lamp. I think when Hari carried me down the path we'd gone past the place before I said, 'It's here somewhere,' and he put me down. He wasn't interested in the bicycle. He was only concerned to carry me home. I suppose he had some dim idea that if the bicycle were there he could put me on it and wheel me home. But the bicycle was a bad joke, just at that moment, wasn't it? He hardly bothered to look. I think the bicycle was still where I'd left it, and that when Ronald rushed to the Bibighar with his police patrol they found it almost at once and Ronald put it into the back of a truck and drove to Hari's house and dumped it in the ditch. I think he was the sort of officer who let his men have a lot of elbow room and in return could get them to plant evidence like this for him and say nothing. Remember the incident of the sub-inspector hitting Hari and getting away with it? There was nothing to connect Hari with the assault in the Bibighar except his known association with me and Ronald's jealousy and suspicion and prejudice. What else made him go to Hari's house? And why when he got there did he spend time searching for the bicycle? If it was in a ditch outside it would have had to be *searched* for, wouldn't it?

If the bicycle *was* in the ditch before Ronald got there I suppose it's possible that one of his men found it during the course of whatever drill they go through when they go to a place to pick up a suspect. But the impression I got before the so-called inquiry was that according to Ronald they only went into the house because they found the bicycle outside it, and that it was only then that Ronald realised that the house was Hari's. If this was the impression he gave people at first he can't have been thinking very clearly because he wouldn't have to give English people any reason for going to Hari's house. Apparently he'd been there once that night already. He was probably not thinking clearly because Lili had repeated to him what I'd told her – that Hari wasn't with me, that Hari wasn't responsible. He wanted Hari to be responsible. I think he had to change the emphasis when it came to making a proper report, had to say that he'd gone to Hari's house and *then* found the bicycle, not the other way round.

I give Ronald this much benefit of the doubt, that after he left the MacGregor House, knowing what had happened to me, he went to his headquarters, collected a patrol, rushed to the Bibighar, found nothing, and then searched the area in the vicinity, arrested those boys who were drinking hooch in a hut on the other side of the river, and then headed straight for the house in the Chillianwallah Bagh, where he found Hari with cuts on his face and where his police found the bicycle. He went to the Chillianwallah Bagh because he thought I was lying, knew I was lying, and because the boys he arrested in the hut on the other side of the bridge were known to be acquaintances of Hari's. But he went mainly because he hated Hari. He wanted to prove that Hari was guilty. And this leaves only the two other explanations for the bicycle. Either Hari went back for it after I'd left him, found it, rode it home, then realised the danger and shoved it into the ditch – which would mean he lost his head because if he *saw* the danger he wouldn't leave the bicycle outside his own house. Or one of the men who attacked me knew Hari, knew where he lived, stole the bicycle and left it outside Hari's house, guessing that the police would search near there – which means that whoever it was who knew Hari also knew that Hari and I were friends. And this leads, surely, to the proposition that such a man anticipated that we'd be in the Bibighar that night. But we didn't even anticipate that ourselves. The coincidence of there being one man or several men in the Bibighar that night who recognised Hari in the dark and thought fast enough to steal the bicycle and leave it outside his house is too much to swallow, isn't it? And who could such a man be? One of Lili's servants? One of Mrs Gupta Sen's? One who might have been able to read my note, in English, asking Hari to meet me on the night of August the 9th, *in the Sanctuary*? No, it won't wash. It won't even wash if you think – as I did for a while – of this unknown but very clever or very lucky man or boy being one of those stretcher-bearers Sister Ludmila used to hire, never for more than a few weeks because after that they got bored and 'their thoughts turned to mischief'. On the day I went to say goodbye to her I noticed that she had a new boy. She told me about the boys who wrote to her after they'd left, and how only one of them had ever come back to beg. And it did cross my mind that perhaps the one who came back to beg was the one who was with her and Mr de Souza the night they brought Hari in to the Sanctuary. Such a boy might have taken an interest in Hari, followed him around, got to know his movements, even watched us on those occasions we went to the Bibighar. But why? Such a boy, back in his village, might have talked about the Indian and the white girl, and led a gang of fellow hooligans into Mayapore, attracted by rumours of trouble and the idea of loot, and come to the Bibighar from the wasteground at the back to shelter for the night, and seen Hari there, and me, watched our love-making. The men who attacked us *had* been watching. That is certain. But the coincidence is too much to take. The men were hooligans. It was Ronald Merrick who planted the bicycle. I know it. I don't think Hari had many friends, but I don't think he had any enemies either, except for Ronald – none, anyway, who would go to the lengths that were gone to incriminate him.

If it wasn't Ronald, then it must have been Hari himself who took the bicycle, then panicked and left it outside his house. I don't think Hari panicked.

But I did. I told Lili to leave me alone. I wanted to think. It became quite clear. Ronald searched the Bibighar, found the bicycle, put it in the truck, then drove across the bridge, *towards Chillianwallah Bagh*, questioned the level-crossing keeper, found the boys who were 'friends' of Hari's, arrested them, drove on to Hari's house, planted the bike and then stormed into the house. And when Hari was arrested they probably searched his room. Had he destroyed my note asking him to meet me in the Sanctuary? The note was never mentioned so he must have done. This may have been the only thing he had time to do, if he hadn't thrown it away before. The photograph I gave him was mentioned. Ronald took it away, as 'evidence' – a copy of the same photograph that I sent you and which Hari helped me to choose from the proofs that day at Subhas Chand's. At the informal inquiry at the MacGregor House Mr Poulson said, 'Mr Kumar had your photograph in his bedroom. Was it one you gave him?' – you know – as if trying to establish that Hari was obsessed with me and had stolen the photograph to stare at at night, and as if giving me the opportunity to recant, to go on to their side, to get rid of my silly notions of loyalty and break down and admit that I'd been infatuated, that Hari had worked on my emotions in the most callous and calculating way, that it was a relief to tell the truth at last, that I had come to my senses and was no longer afraid of him, let alone infatuated, that he'd attacked and brutalised me and then submitted me to the base indignity of being raped by friends of his, and that then he'd tried to terrorise me with threats to my life if I gave him away, threats which he said would be all too easy to carry out because the British were about to be given the bum's rush. Oh, I know what was in their minds – perhaps against their personal judgment – but in their minds as the story they ought to believe because of what might be at stake. Of the trio who made up the board of private inquiry, or whatever it was officially called – Mr Poulson, a startled and embarrassed young English sub-divisional officer whose name I forget, and Judge Menen – only Judge Menen, who presided, maintained an air of utter detachment. It was a detachment that struck me as that of fatigue, fatigue amounting to hopelessness. But the fact that he was there heartened me, not only because he was an Indian but because I was sure he wouldn't have been there if there was any likelihood of the accused men coming in front of him in the District Court. I suppose if the inquiry had led to what the board by now had no hope of but the English community still wanted, the case would have gone up for trial in the Provincial High Court.

But I've gone a step too far ahead. I must go back for a moment to the evening of the 10th – when I sent Lili out of the room to give myself time to think because I was panicky about what might have been found that could incriminate Hari, and about who the other arrested men were, and what they might have said. Then I was overwhelmed by the typically blunt thoughtless English way I'd assumed everything would be all right for Hari if *I* said he was innocent. I'd run away from Hari, believing that just by putting distance between us I was helping him. But I saw him now standing where I'd left him, at the gate of the Bibighar. Auntie, what did he do? Go back to look for the bicycle, and remove it, thinking he was helping *me*? Or begin his journey home on foot? There was blood on my neck and face when I got back – so Anna told me. It must have come from Hari's face when we clung to each other. In the dark I didn't see how badly or how little those men had hurt him. I never asked. I never thought. He was bathing his face, apparently, when Ronald burst into his room. Of course they tried to prove he'd been hurt by me fighting back. But all I can think of now is the callous way I left him, to face up to everything alone, to say nothing, deny everything, because I'd told him to, but having to say nothing and deny everything with those scratches or abrasions on his face that he couldn't account for. When it came out at the inquiry that his face was cut I said, 'Why ask me about them? Ask Mr Kumar. I don't know. He wasn't there.' Mr Poulson said, 'He *was* asked. He wouldn't say,' and then changed the subject. Ronald was giving evidence at the time. I stared at him, but he refused to look at me. I said, 'Perhaps he had a scrap with the police. It wouldn't be the first time he was hit by a police officer.' It did no good. It was the wrong thing to say at that time in that place. It made them sympathise with Ronald rather than me. I didn't mind, though, because in any case I was beginning to hate myself. I hated myself because I realised Hari had taken me at my word and said nothing – quite literally nothing. Nothing. Nothing. Nothing. Said nothing in spite of evidence against him, which I hadn't reckoned with when I ran off and left him.

They hurt him, didn't they? Tortured him in some way? But he said nothing, nothing. When they arrested him he must have stood there – with the cuts on his face, my photograph in his room, my bicycle in the ditch outside, and said nothing. At one time during those days of question and answer Lili told me, 'He won't account for his movements. He denies having been in the Bibighar. He says he hasn't seen you since the night you both went to the temple. But he won't say where he was or what he was doing between leaving the office and getting home, some time after nine. He must have reached home about the time you did, Daphne.'

And of course these were the other things I hadn't reckoned with or known about: Ronald's first visit to the house in the Chillianwallah Bagh, his visit to the MacGregor House, his visit to the Sanctuary. When I left Hari at the Bibighar I suppose I assumed that all he had to do was to pretend to have been at home all evening, to persuade Aunt Shalini to swear he had been at home, if the question ever arose, or to make up another story, whatever he thought best, whatever he thought would work. But for Hari, no story worked. *I never gave him a chance to calm me down and say – as I would have let an Englishman say –* 'Look, for Pete's sake, if I haven't been here in the Bibighar, where in hell have I been? How do I account for this swollen lip, or black eye, or scratched cheek,' whatever it was.

I never gave him the chance because even in my panic there was this assumption of superiority, of privilege, of believing I knew what was best for both of us, because the colour of my skin automatically put me on the side of those who never told a lie. But we've got far beyond that stage of colonial simplicity. We've created a blundering judicial robot. We can't stop it working. It works for us even when we least want it to. We created it to prove how fair, how civilised we are. But it is a white robot and it can't distinguish between love and rape. It only understands physical connection and only understands it as a crime because it only exists to punish crime. It would have punished Hari for this, and if physical connection between the races is a crime he's been punished justly. One day someone may come along, cross a wire by mistake, or fix in a special circuit with the object of making it impartial and colour-blind, and then it will probably explode.

*

After Lili had told me about Hari's arrest and I'd thought for a bit I rang for Raju and told him I wanted Poulson Sahib sent for. I'd got over my panic. I was angry, even angry with Lili. I felt she'd let me down by allowing them to hold Hari in custody without doing a thing to stop it. She was very patient with me, but we were shut off from each other as we'd never been before. She said that if I really wanted to see Mr Poulson she'd ring him. I think she believed I was going to confess. She knew I'd been lying. But for her the truth would be as bad as the lies. She had brought Hari into the house, and he was an Indian. A fellow-countryman. For a day or two after the Bibighar, I felt like an interloper, one of her harpies who'd inexplicably become involved with the life of an Indian family, and had taken to sitting in her bedroom the better to keep what was left of her racial integrity intact.

Mr Poulson came after dinner. Lili brought him up. She asked whether I wanted her to stay. I said it might be better if Mr Poulson and I were alone. Directly she'd gone I said, 'Why didn't you tell me they arrested Hari Kumar last night?' Normally I liked him. Tonight I despised him, but then I was ready to despise everybody. He looked as if he wanted to fall through the floor. He said Hari had been arrested because the evidence seemed to add up that way, in spite of my 'belief' that he hadn't been involved. I said, 'What evidence? What evidence that can possibly contradict *my* evidence. You must all be mad if you think you can pin anything on Hari.'

350

He said that the evidence last night had pointed to Hari, and that it couldn't be ruled out that he was there, in spite of my belief that he wasn't.

I said it wasn't a question of belief. I asked him whether he really thought I wouldn't *know* if Hari had been among those who attacked me. That scared him. He was afraid of an intimate confession. When I realised this I thought I saw how to play the whole thing, play it by scaring them at the thought of what I might come out with, in court. I asked him about the other men. He pretended he didn't know anything about them. I smiled and said, 'I see Ronald is keeping it all very much to himself. But that's no wonder, is it? After all, it's pretty obvious he planted the bicycle.'

Lili had been shocked, but her shock was nothing to Jack Poulson's. He said, 'What on earth makes you say a thing like that?' I told him to ask Ronald. It seemed wiser to leave it at that, to leave Mr Poulson with something tricky to bite on. Before he went – and he went because 'in his view there was nothing it would be advantageous to pursue for the moment' – I said, 'Hari wasn't there. I doubt that any of the men you've arrested were there. It's the usual thing, isn't it? An English woman gets assaulted and at once everyone loses all sense of proportion. If Ronald or any of you think you're going to get away with punishing the first poor bloody Indians you've clapped hands on just to give the European community a field-day you've got another think coming. It'll never stand up in court because *I'll* stand up in court and say what I'm saying to you. Only I might be more explicit about a lot of things.'

He got up and mumbled something about being sorry and that everyone appreciated what a terrible time I'd had, that he was sure no one who was innocent could possibly be punished. I said, 'Then tell me this. Forget the *one* innocent man you've got locked up at the moment. Do the others fit my description of them at all?'

He said he didn't know. He hadn't seen them. But I wasn't letting him off so lightly. I was chancing my arm, but it seemed worth it. I said, 'Oh, come off it, Jack. You know all right. Even if you haven't seen them you must know who they are. Are they what I said? Smelly peasants? Dirty labourers? Or boys like Hari? The kind of boy Mr Merrick seems to have it in for?'

I'd hit the mark. But he still insisted he didn't know. He said he believed that one or two of them were known for or suspected of political activities of 'the anarchist type'. I pounced on that. I said, 'Oh, you mean educated boys? Not smelly peasants?'

He shook his head, not denying it but closing the way to further discussion.

*

Retrospectively, I'm sorry for the bad time I gave poor Jack Poulson. But it had to be done. I'm pretty sure he went away thinking, 'It won't stick. Not with those fellows Merrick's got locked up.' I don't know how much more he would say when he got back to the Deputy Commissioner's bungalow, which was almost certainly where he was headed. To Mr White probably all he needed to say was something like, 'Either she's lying, or Kumar is innocent, but if she's lying or continues to lie he ranks as innocent anyway because we'll never prove him guilty. The same goes for the others. Merrick's made a gaffe.'

Robin White detached himself from the affair, to the extent that he left Jack Poulson in charge of it up to the point where a final decision had to be made. If he'd been a man like his predecessor Mr Stead (whom men like Vassi loathed) God knows what would have happened. I suppose to Robin the assault on a silly English girl wasn't very important when he compared it with the other things he had to deal with. I don't know whether Mr Poulson ever said anything to Mr White about the bicycle and my accusation against Ronald. It wouldn't have been an easy thing for him to pass on. At the inquiry the bicycle was never mentioned, and the only time Hari was mentioned was when Ronald was giving evidence of arrest. He answered questions which Jack Poulson seemed to have worked out carefully in advance. In fact the evidence of the arrests struck me as ridiculous. Mr Poulson read out the names of the men arrested and simply asked Ronald where and at what time they'd been taken into custody, and what they had been doing. As I already knew from what Lili had told me, the other poor boys had been drinking hooch in a hut near the Bibighar bridge but at the inquiry the *unfairness* of it struck me all over again. According to Ronald, Hari was in his bedroom, 'washing his face on which there were cuts and abrasions'. I nearly interrupted and said, 'What about the bicycle?' but thought better of it. The bicycle not being mentioned was a good sign. I wondered if Jack Poulson had talked to Ronald in private and decided from the answers he got that he'd better keep the bicycle business quiet, not only for Ronald's sake, but for the sake of the Service, the flag and all that. But I did come out with the remark about the cuts on Hari's face when Jack Poulson asked me whether I recalled 'marking' any of the men who attacked me. I mean the remark about Hari probably having had a scrap with the police.

After the so-called evidence of arrests Ronald was dismissed and then they got down to the business of going over my statement again and asking questions, and I saw how the evidence of arrests was so thin that although it proved nothing it could also prove anything. Judge Menen had kept quiet – I mean he'd not asked me any questions so far, but towards the end he said, 'I must ask you why you refused the other day to attempt to identify the men held in custody,' which I had done, when the worst of the troubles in Mayapore were over and they wanted to push the case to a conclusion of some sort and get it over with. I said, 'I refused to attempt identification because they must be the wrong men. I shall say so in court, if necessary.'

Judge Menen said he understood why I should feel this in regard to 'the man Kumar' but the refusal to attempt identification of the other men might be interpreted as wilful obstruction by the principal witness and this might lead to the prosecution being able to prove its case in spite of that witness's evidence, because the wilful obstruction might be held as a sign of general unreliability.

I thought about this. Mr Poulson brightened up a bit. He didn't mind that Menen was an Indian and perhaps shouldn't speak to a white girl like that. It was the Law that spoke. He thought the clever old Judge had forced me into a corner by scaring me with a legal technicality, a reminder that even the principal witness couldn't obstruct the Crown in the pursuit of justice. But I thought I saw my way out. And I wasn't really convinced that Judge Menen was on particularly sure ground himself. I said, 'If my evidence is thought unreliable for that reason, does it become less unreliable if I go through the farce of looking at these men, with no intention whatsoever of saying I recognise them? You prefer me to go through that farce? You'd only have my word for it that I didn't recognise them. Simply looking at them isn't a test of reliability in itself, is it?'

Menen's poker face didn't alter. He said they would assume, continue to assume, that I was telling the truth, and reminded me that the whole inquiry was based on the assumption that I was telling the truth, that it was only the refusal to comply with the request to attempt identification which could raise the question of unreliability. He went on, 'In your statement you say you had a brief impression of the men who attacked you. You have described them as peasants or labourers. That being so, with such an impression in your mind, why do you refuse to co-operate in the important business of helping us, as best you can, to decide whether the men being held are held on sufficient grounds?'

Looking at him I thought: You know they're the wrong men too. You want me to go down to the jail and look at them and say, No, they aren't as I remember them at all. Either you want that, or you want me to make it *quite* plain, perhaps outrageously plain, that it's useless for anyone to expect to bring this case to court with these boys as defendants.

But I was still afraid of confronting them. I was sure they were the wrong boys, but I didn't know. I didn't want to face them. If they were the right boys there was a danger – only very slight, but still a danger – of their panicking at the sight of me and incriminating Hari. And if they were the right boys and I recognised them I didn't want to have to say, 'No, these aren't the men.' I wasn't sure I could trust myself to carry it off, even for Hari's sake. *I didn't want to tell that sort of lie.* There's a difference between trying to stop an injustice and obstructing justice.

I said, 'No, I won't co-operate. One of these men is innocent. If one innocent man is accused I'm not interested in the guilt or innocence of the others. I refuse absolutely to go anywhere near them. The men who raped me were peasants. The boys you've got locked up aren't, so they're almost certainly all innocent too. For one thing they're all Hindus, aren't they?'

Mr Poulson agreed that they were all Hindus.

I smiled. I'd prepared this one awfully well, I thought. I said, 'Then that's another thing. One of the men was a Muslim. He was circumcised. If you want to know how I know I'm quite prepared to tell you but otherwise prefer to leave it at that. One was a Muslim. They were all hooligans. Apart from that I can't tell you a thing. I can't tell you more than I have done. The impression I had of them was strong enough for me to know that I could say, "No, these aren't the men," but not strong enough for me to say, "Yes, these *are* the men." For all I knew they could have been British soldiers with their faces blacked. I don't imagine they were, but if by saying so I can convince you I know you've got at least one wrong man, well then I say so.'

Mr Poulson and the young man whose name I don't remember both looked profoundly shocked. Judge Menen stared at me and then said, 'Thank you, Miss Manners. We have no more questions. We are sorry to have had to subject you to this examination.'

He got to his feet and we all stood, just as if it was a courtroom and not the dining-room of the MacGregor House. But there the similarity ended. Instead of Judge Menen going out he stood still and made it clear that it was my privilege to leave first. When I got to the door Jack Poulson was ahead of me to open it. A purely automatic gesture, part of the Anglo-Indian machinery. But I could *smell* his shock. Bitter, as if he'd just eaten some aromatic quick-acting paralysing herb.

*

I went upstairs and poured myself a drink. I thought it was all over and that I'd won and Hari would be released in the next few hours, or the next day. I stood on the balcony as I'd done so often during the past two weeks. During the riots you could hear the shouting and the firing and the noise of trucks and lorries going from one part of the civil lines to the other. For a day or two there'd been policemen at the gate of the MacGregor House. They said the house might be attacked, but we'd been more worried about Anna Klaus than about ourselves. At one time she was practically a prisoner in the Purdah Hospital in the native town, and we didn't see her for a couple of days. Mrs White wanted Lili and me to move into the Deputy Commissioner's bungalow, but Lili wouldn't go. Neither would I. That's when the police guard appeared. The sight of the police guard made me feel like a prisoner too. Ronald never came near himself. He'd washed his hands of me. I felt that with a few exceptions the whole European community was ready to do that or had already done it. I didn't care. I got to the stage of believing that everything was coming to an end for us, I mean for white people. I didn't care about that either. One evening Lili told me the rioters had broken into the jail. I thought: That's how it will resolve itself. They'll free Hari. I didn't know he wasn't in that jail. But I thought: The Indians will take over. Perhaps they won't punish me. Perhaps Hari will come to the house. But I couldn't visualise it clearly enough. Nothing like that would happen. The soldiers were out and there was the sound of firing, and everything was only a question of time for *us*, hopeless for *them*. The robot was working.

But I was worried about Anna, and Sister Ludmila. They were the only white people I knew who lived or worked on that side of the river. Sister Ludmila told me later that she defied the curfew and went out every night with Mr de Souza and her stretcher bearer. There was plenty of work for them. The police turned them back once or twice but generally they managed to give them the slip. The 'death house', as people called it, was always occupied. And every morning the police went there, and the women whose husbands or sons hadn't come home.

I was worried for you, too, until Lili told me she'd got Robin White to send you a message through official channels that I was all right. They tried to keep my name out of reports that appeared in the national newspapers. Some hopes. Thank God we'd talked on the phone before my name was given away. Even so I was afraid you'd come down to Mayapore. I bless you for not doing, for understanding. If you'd come down I couldn't have borne it. I had to work it out alone. I bless Lili for understanding that too. At first I thought her detachment was due to disapproval, then that it was due to that curious Indian indifference to pain. But of course her 'indifference' was wholly 'European', wholly civilised, like yours, like my own. There are pains we feel, and pains we recognise in others, that are best left alone, not from callousness but from discretion. Anna's detachment was rather different. Hers also was European, but Jewish, self-protective as well as sensitive, as if she didn't want to be reminded of pain because to be reminded would transfer her sensitivity from my pain to what she remembered of her own. By keeping that amount of distance she was able to establish a friendship between us, trust, regard, the kind of regard that can spring up between strangers who sense each other's mettle. One shouldn't expect more. But affection comes from a different source, doesn't it? I'm thinking of the affection there is between you and me, which is not only an affection of the blood because there is the same kind of affection between myself and Lili. It's one that overcomes, that exists, but for which there isn't necessarily any accounting because trust doesn't enter into it at all, except to the extent that you trust because of the affection. You trust after you have learned to love.

I could never feel affectionate in that way towards Anna. Neither, I'm sure, could she towards me. But we were good and trusting, understanding friends. One develops an instinct for people. I wander on about this because when I stood on the balcony, drinking my well-deserved gin and lime-juice, I saw Ronald and Mr Poulson come out of the house and get into Ronald's truck. Judge Menen wasn't with them. He stayed behind to have a drink with Lili.

And I thought: How curious. Ronald and Jack Poulson are just *people* to me. I felt no real resentment, not even of Ronald, let alone of Jack who was obviously going off somewhere to chew the rag with Ronald. But I felt they were outside the circle of those people 'it was worth my while to know', as my mother put it once, probably meaning something else entirely. To me my own meaning was clear. I already *knew* them. They were predictable people, predictable because they worked for the robot. What the robot said they would also say, what the robot did they would do, and what the robot believed was what they believed because people like them had fed that belief into it. And they would always be right so long as the robot worked, because the robot was the standard of rightness.

There was no *originating passion* in them. Whatever they felt that was original would die the moment it came into conflict with what the robot was geared to feel. At the inquiry it needed Judge Menen to break through the robot's barrier – if break is the appropriate word to use to describe the actions of a man who made even getting out of a chair look like an exercise in studied and balanced movement. But he got through. At one moment he was sitting on *their* side, the robot side, and the next moment he was through. We were through together, he *brought* me through or joined me on the other side – whichever way you like to put it. So it seemed right, now, that he should have stayed behind to have a drink with Lili, and leave the robot boys to go off on their own and work out how to make it look as if the robot had brought the inquiry to some kind of a logical conclusion. They had to save the robot's face, as well as their own.

It was odd to find myself thinking this about Mr Poulson. Mr and Mrs White thought very highly of him. He was still pretty young, young enough to be cautious, which may sound silly, but isn't, because a young man has a living to earn, a family to support, a career to build. But it probably needs something like what came to be called the Bibighar Gardens affair to sort out the mechanical men from the men who are capable of throwing a spanner into the works. Which is another way of describing what I feel about Judge Menen. What is so interesting is that the spanner he threw into the works, the spanner that brought the inquiry to a stop was the right spanner. It must take years of experience and understanding to know which spanner to use, and the exact moment to use it. I think he knew so well, that in the end he handed the spanner to me just to give himself the additional satisfaction of letting me throw it in for him. He knew that the only way to bring the robot to a temporary halt was to go right to the heart of what had set it in motion – the little cog of judicial procedure which had been built into it in the fond hope that once it was engaged it would only stop when justice had been done. By going to the heart of the mechanism he exposed it for what it was and gave me the chance to bring it to a halt by imposing an impossible task on it – the task of *understanding* the justice of what it was doing, and of proving that its own justice was the equal or the superior of mine. But it was only a *temporary* halt.

Long before Judge Menen left I came in from the balcony and had my bath. I was finished and dressed for dinner before Lili came in and asked if I was all right, and if I would like to see Anna who had called on her way home from the Purdah Hospital. I said, 'Is Judge Menen still here?' She told me he'd gone about ten minutes ago. And had sent me his love. I'd never seen Lili *moved* before. I'd only seen her amused, or wry, or disapproving, or detached. I think it was Judge Menen who had moved her with whatever it was he said to her – or rather caused her to be moved directly she set eyes on me again after talking to him. I don't know what it was he had said. I never shall. That is typical of Lili. Typical of him too. And in a terribly English way Lili and I sort of got out of each other's light – put yards of space between us, but were together again.

I went down with her and greeted Anna. Lili asked her to stay to dinner. She said she would. For me it was like a sudden treat, a picnic plan confided to a child early on a golden summer morning. When Lili went out to tell Raju to tell cook it was dinner for three I gave Anna a freshener for her drink. She said, 'You look better. Please keep it up.'

And I said, 'I think I shall. I think we've won.' I said 'we' because Anna had stood by me all that time. I knew, before the inquiry, that she'd been asked that naked question: 'In your opinion was Miss Manners *intacta* before the assault?' And I knew what she had replied. When I said 'I think we've won', she raised her glass.

*

This was the last evening of happiness I had. After it I was optimistic but not happy. In the end even my optimism went. I needed Hari. I needed Lili too, and Anna, and you, but most of all I needed him. I'd built my own enclosed little circle, hadn't I? The one I'd feel safe in. A circle of safety in no-man's-land. Wherever we go, whatever we do, we seem to hedge ourselves about with this illusory protection. Hours went by. Days. More than a week. I never went out. When people came I escaped to my room. The MacGregor House was gradually filled again with vibrations whose source I had never pinned down before but now did and saw as inseparable from it: trust, compromise, something fundamentally exploratory and non-committal, as if the people in it were trying to *learn*, instead of teach – and so forgive rather than accuse. There is that old, disreputable saying, isn't there? 'When rape is inevitable, lie back and enjoy it.' *Well, there has been more than one rape.* I can't say, Auntie, that I lay back and enjoyed mine. But Lili was trying to lie back and enjoy what we've done to her country. I don't mean done in malice. Perhaps there was love. Oh, somewhere, in the past, and now, and in the future, love as there was between me and Hari. But the spoilers are always there, aren't they? The Swinsons. The bitches who travelled as far as Lahore. The Ronald Merricks. The silly little man who summed up his own silly little island-history when he whistled and said, 'some wog contractor is making a packet.'

Connie White came to see me one day. She brought Mavis Poulson with her. But she realised after ten minutes or so that she'd get nowhere because bringing edgy, virtuously pregnant Mavis had been a mistake. She sent her away. As the Deputy Commissioner's wife she could do such a thing with no more than the personal courage it took to make Mavis dislike her for a day or two. When we were alone she said, 'My husband doesn't know I'm here. I shan't tell him I've been. And I oughtn't to interfere, I know. But they've sent Hari Kumar away. They've put him and the other boys in prison.'

It wasn't a shock. I was prepared for it. Days of silence from Lili had prepared me for it. I didn't understand it but that wasn't the same as not believing it could happen. I asked what they were putting him in prison for. She made a gesture that defined the futility of both the question and the answer. She said, 'All the papers went to the Commissioner, and it's out of our hands now. But I wanted to know if there's anything you can tell *me* that you wouldn't tell Jack or Robin, or Lili.'

I said, 'What sort of thing, for heaven's sake?'

Again she made that gesture, whose meaning we both knew. She said probably only I could tell her what sort of thing. I thought it was a trap. I smiled at her. She said, 'Well, you know what men are. They always tell themselves they can't afford the luxury of real curiosity. I mean curiosity about people. Oh, I know they solve all kinds of complex problems that prove we're made of water and gas or something, and that the universe is still exploding and travelling outwards at umpteen million light years a second which I suppose is fascinating, but of no practical use to *us* when it comes to trying to keep the servants happy and stopping them from making off just as effectively at a rate measurable in miles an hour.'

I laughed. It was so absurd. Small talk. Chat. Jolly jokes. Bless her. This was her armoury. The key – the chink in the armour – was that word 'curiosity'. I knew what I was supposed to say. 'What are you curious about?' I laughed again. I expect she thought I was bats. They say poor old Miss Crane went round the bend. Lili went to see her once while I was still at the MacGregor. Perhaps twice. I don't remember. We didn't talk about it much. Miss Crane had taken all the pictures down from her walls or something, although she wasn't going anywhere. Later she committed suttee. You saw the report of it in *The Times of India*, I think. We both saw it. Neither of us mentioned it. Perhaps Lili wrote to you and told you more about it. Of course it's wrong to say 'committed' suttee. Suttee, or *sati* (is that the right way to spell it?) is a sort of state of wifely grace, isn't it? So you don't commit it. You enter into it. If you're a good Hindu widow you *become* suttee. Should I become it, Auntie? Is Hari dead? I suppose you could say we're hermits enough here to rank as *sannyasis* anyway. But no. I've not done with the world yet. I've still got at least one duty to perform.

And I knew I had a duty to perform for Connie White. After I'd stopped laughing I said, 'Well then, what are you curious about?'

You can't not pay for a joke. You've got to cough up the price put on it. She said, 'Well, it all seems to begin with a man called Moti Lal.'

I'd never heard of Moti Lal, but it turned out he was the man Ronald was looking for the first time he arrested Hari. Moti Lal was once employed by Hari's uncle. He was always haranguing groups of students and young men and labourers. When he started trying to organise the staff at the place

358

where he worked old Romesh Chand sacked him. He also got served with an order under section 144 of the Criminal Procedure Code. I think Ronald instigated that. It's the one that calls on you to abstain from an act likely to cause a disturbance in the district, isn't it? Anyway, like so many other people were doing, to keep the British embarrassed, he defied it, and was prosecuted under section 188 of the Penal Code and sentenced to six months. I remember all this jabberwocky because I latched on to it while Connie talked about it, hoping it would explain what could happen to Hari. It didn't, but I looked it up afterwards in the law books in Lili's library.

Moti Lal was sent to the jail in Aligarh. He escaped. And Ronald was looking for him when he called at the Sanctuary on the morning Hari was there with a hangover. I asked Connie what all this Moti Lal business had to do with an innocent man being sent to prison for a crime he didn't commit. She said, 'But that's the point. Hari Kumar isn't being sent to prison for the assault. He's being sent for political reasons. He knew Moti Lal.'

Again I laughed. I said, 'Hari knew Moti Lal. I know Hari. Why don't you send me to jail too? I suppose all those other boys knew Moti Lal as well?'

She said she wasn't really concerned about the other boys. There were police files on all of them. They'd all been examined by Jack Poulson. Both Jack and her husband believed that they were the kind of boys who, if they hadn't been taken into custody on the night of the Bibighar, would have been arrested within forty-eight hours for rioting or sabotage. Whatever one felt about the justice or injustice of it, they were 'fair game' in present circumstances, and safer out of the way.

I said, 'Fair game is the right description. You could hardly release them now, could you? They were arrested for the worst crime of all, and everybody knows it. And the same goes for Hari, doesn't it? Only it's even trickier for him. Because everybody knows we used to go out together.'

She agreed that it was trickier for Hari, or rather had been trickier when it was still uncertain whether he'd taken part in the assault. But none of the boys was being charged with assault. That case was still open. The police were still working on it. But it looked unlikely that they'd ever catch the men who were responsible, unless the men began to boast – either back in their villages, or wherever they came from, or in the jails. You couldn't rule out the possibility that the men who'd assaulted me were among those arrested during the subsequent rioting. The police only hoped they weren't among those killed. Connie didn't think they would be because men of 'that kind' weren't likely to have risked their lives defying the military. If they'd been arrested they'd have been with the men who got caught looting. If they were still free they could, of course, be anywhere, and probably the only thing to hope for was an informer, someone with a grudge against them who heard them boasting. The trouble was that in India you could never rely on evidence when it was come by in this way.

I don't know what Connie was trying to do. Relieve me of the anxiety that Hari might still be punished for the assault; put me on my guard, because she guessed the truth and therefore also guessed that I didn't want the men caught in case they incriminated Hari; catch me *off* my guard, hoping for a careless word that would undo all the good I'd so far done. Perhaps she was trying to do none of these things. When you've lied your head off you suspect nearly everyone of cunning and evasion and deceit. I expect she was just curious, as she said, exercising her woman's right to satisfy her curiosity now that the men had made everything irrevocable.

She said Moti Lal had never been caught. He'd gone 'underground'. The boys who'd been drinking hooch when they were arrested all swore they'd not seen Moti Lal since he was sent to prison. Jack Poulson thought they were lying. The trouble was that Hari Kumar had 'gradually emerged' during all these investigations and interrogations as 'a young man of whom the gravest suspicions had to be entertained' (which also sounded to me like something Jack Poulson must have said). The police had kept a file on him for several months. He'd been had in for questioning at the time they were looking for Moti Lal. He'd 'made a mystery over his name', and had at first given the wrong one – which in itself was a punishable offence, although Ronald Merrick hadn't proceeded against him because the offence in Hari's case was only technical. But Hari had gone on record as saying, 'I hate the whole stinking country, the people who live in it and the people who rule it.' He'd worked in the same firm as Moti Lal. He was a one-time colleague of a young anarchist called Vidyasagar who'd been arrested for distributing seditious literature and delivering a pamphlet to the police calling on them to assist the people to 'liberate the martyrs of the Bibighar Gardens'. At the time of his arrest, after the assault on me, his room had been searched. The police thought it curious that there were no letters in his room; no letters, except one – a letter from someone in England who wasn't identified because he'd only signed his Christian name, but it was clear he was in the forces, and had been at Dunkirk. He described Dunkirk as a shambles. He asked Hari to bear in mind that letters might be opened. His father had opened some of them while this boy was in France and hadn't forwarded them because they were full of 'hot-headed political stuff'. Nobody could understand why Hari had kept just this one letter out of all the letters he must have had from time to time from different people. Of course they didn't intend to pursue the business of who this rather 'bolshie' sounding English boy might be. It was enough that the letter more or less proved Hari was a bolshie himself. Without much difficulty a case had been made out to show that Hari Kumar – in spite of seeming to be such a quiet, uncommitted, well-educated young man – was a leading member of a group of dangerous fellows whose early arrest alone had deprived them of the opportunity to act openly against the war effort. The papers relating to Kumar and the other boys had been sent to the commissioner, and the commissioner had agreed with the decision Robin White had 'very reluctantly' come to: the decision that these boys should be imprisoned under the Defence of India Rules.

By the time Connie got to this point in her harangue I was laughing in the way you do when the alternative is to cry. I knew who the English boy must be. I said, 'But it's a farce! It's absurd! Hari can prove it's a ridiculous *monstrous* farce!'

She said, 'But my dear, that's what puzzles *me*. The other boys denied everything – everything except that they all know each other, which they hardly *could* deny. They shouted and wept and insisted that they were innocent of everything except drinking hooch. And we knew they were lying. But Hari was an altogether different matter. He was examined personally by Jack Poulson. But to every question he said nothing. He neither denied nor agreed. The only thing he ever said in his own defence was 'I wasn't at the Bibighar. I haven't seen Miss Manners since the night we visited the temple.' And of course he only said that when they were accusing him of assault. To all the other questions his only answer was, 'I have nothing to say.' It's unnatural. I mean to *me* it's unnatural. The men simply took his silence as a confession of guilt. I expect if I were a man I'd have done the same. But I'm a woman, like you. I think of Hari Kumar and listen to Jack talking to Mavis about him, and to my husband talking to old Menen, and I think, "It's wrong. A man doesn't say nothing, unless he's trying to put a noose round his own neck. He fights for his life and his freedom. He fights because he *is* a man."'

We were sitting on the verandah. Oh, everything was there – the wicker chairs, the table with the tea tray on it, the scent of the flowers, the scent of India, the air of certainty, of *perpetuity*; but, as well, the odd sense of none of it happening at all because it had begun wrong and continued wrong, and so was already ended, and was wrong even in its ending, because its ending, for me, was unreal and remote, and yet *total* in its envelopment, as if it had already turned itself into a beginning. Such constant hope we suffer from! I think the MacGregor House was built on such foundations. The steps up to the verandah where I'd stumbled and fallen were only a few feet away. I had never seen Janet MacGregor's ghost, but I felt that she must have seen mine.

Connie said, 'I expect it's frightfully silly of me, but you know if Hari Kumar had been an Englishman I could have understood his silence better, although even then it would have had to be a silence imposed on him by a woman.'

I began to laugh again. I laughed because I saw that this time there really was nothing I could do – for Connie, for myself, or for Hari, for anyone. My legs – bare from the knee down – were an anachronism, an outrage. To play the scene with anything like *style* I needed a long dress of white muslin, and a little straw boater on my head. I needed to be conscious of the dignity of the occasion. I needed to be able to say, 'But Harry is an Englishman,' and then to rise, put up my little parasol and detach myself from Constance White's company, so that she would *know* but say nothing because this was a world where men died in the open and women wept in private, and the Queen sat like a wise old lady on her throne and succeeded in that difficult feat of proving that there was a world where corruption also died for lack of stinking air.

Oh well, it was fine, wasn't it? Me sitting there in one chair and Connie White in another, showing acres of bare ill-looking flesh, sweating under the arms, and Hari sweating in a disgusting jailhouse, beyond the reach of either of us, wondering what he'd gained by acting like a white man should when a girl made him give a promise: a promise for his sake, yes, but for her own too. She wanted him. She wanted him to be around to make love to her again. It was marvellous. Marvellous because he was black. I wanted him and he was black so his blackness was part of what I wanted. Sitting there with Connie, laughing my head off, I hoped for one bitter, selfish moment that he suffered as much as I did, for putting his bloody acquired English pride above his compulsion to enter *me*. I wished him joy of his stupid sense of values. I thought: How typical! You tell an Indian to say nothing and he takes it literally.

Afterwards, of course, I knew he hadn't taken it literally. He'd interpreted it that way deliberately. To punish himself. To give him something new about himself that he could mock. When Connie had gone, no wit the wiser for her visit, but I suppose convinced I was unbalanced, Lili found me weeping in my room, because the comic mood had gone, the melodrama had exploded, not into tragedy but just into life and all the stupid cross-currents that tossed you indiscriminately from one thought to another but managed to keep you up. You can never drown. Never, never. Until you're dead. So why be so ridiculously afraid of the truth?

But with Lili sitting on my bed, wanting to comfort me but also wanting to chastise me for my absurdity, I was a child again. I wept and cried out, 'I want him, I want him. Bring him back to me, Auntie. Please help to bring him back.'

She said nothing. Like Hari. For them I suppose there *is* nothing to say. Nothing, that is, if they are intent on building instead of on destroying. Behind all the chatter and violence of India – what a deep, lingering silence. Siva dances in it. Vishnu sleeps in it. Even their music is silence. It's the only music I know that sounds conscious of *breaking* silence, of going back into it when it's finished, as if to prove that every man-made sound is an illusion.

What an odd concept of the world that is! We shall never understand it. They don't really understand it themselves, I suspect. Is it to try to understand it that Sister Ludmila wanders the streets collecting the bodies of the dead and the dying? Is it just a concept that could be traced to some long-forgotten overwhelming, primitive experience of pain and suffering? I ask because it struck me, a few weeks later, when I knew I was pregnant and I asked Lili to send for Anna Klaus, that Anna stood on the same edge of reality and illusion herself, because she'd been deprived and had suffered and continued to live. She's a great believer in anaesthetising the patient, a great giver of sedatives. I remember how she stood in my bedroom frowning her little professional frown as she sorted things out in her black bag. Such a wealth of compromise there is in a doctor's bag! She seemed to be a long way away from me, and yet to be taking me with her – millions of miles away down long glazed white-tiled tunnels, subterranean passages of human degradation that were saved from filthiness because we northerners have learned how to make suffering aseptic and non-contagious. At first I had a silly idea she was preparing something for me to take to get rid of the child. I said, 'What's that, what's that?' She said, 'What a fuss! It is only to give you a quiet night. Expectant mothers must be contemplative. Like nuns.'

So I lay there, letting her get on with it. But suddenly I said, 'What am I to do, Anna? I can't live without him.'

She didn't look at me. She was measuring the potion. She spoke to the medicine, not to me. After all, this was the one thing she could really trust, really believe in, really love. She said, 'This you must learn to do. To live without.'

She handed me the glass, and stood by, until I'd drunk every drop.

Appendix to Part 7

Letters from Lady Manners to Lady Chatterjee

Srinagar, 31 May '43

My Dear Lili,

I hope you've forgiven me for not accepting your offer to come up last month, and for the silence since then that has been broken only by my two telegrams. When I wired you a week ago I promised I would write. If you would like to, do come next month. I shall be on the houseboat.

I'm afraid there are going to be endless legal complications. Poor Daphne died intestate, so I think the money becomes subject to the statutory trusts, on the child's behalf, unless the part of it which Daphne inherited from her mother is claimed by Mrs George's nephews and nieces. Mrs George Manners had a married sister, someone Daphne used to refer to as Auntie Kate, who was killed in a road accident. The husband married again, but there were two or three children from the first marriage – cousins of Daphne's with whom she remembered playing as a child. I expect if Daphne had died intestate but without issue the cousins would have had some sort of claim. I'm not sure what the situation is when the child in question is illegitimate. It will all have to be gone into and dealt with by the lawyers in London – which is where all the money is held anyway. Daphne was very careful with her small inheritance. She never touched the principal but drew on the income through the banks over here. Anyway, I have asked Mr Docherty in 'Pindi to do whatever has to be done to start sorting things out – but it will take ages before we know what properly belongs to the child and even longer before we know how use can be made of it over here.

Meanwhile the responsibility for her is mine. When you come up, Lili, perhaps you will be able to say whether you think the child is Hari Kumar's. I have a special reason for wanting to know. Not a reason connected with any legal claim or criminal charge. There is no question of attempting to establish paternity. Mr Kumar is beyond either our incriminations or our help, *and that is how I want it left*. But in giving shelter and affection to the child for Daphne's sake – and for its own – I should be happier knowing to what extent one might do so in the belief that its parentage wasn't surrounded by doubt as well as tragedy. I know I don't need to tell you that I want your *opinion*, not your reassurance, and that if you don't feel able to give one I shouldn't want you to pretend, simply to set my mind at rest.

She is a sweet and pretty child. Her skin is going to be pale, but not nearly pale enough for her to pass as white. I'm glad. As she grows older she won't be driven by the temptation to wear a false face. At least that is one thing she'll be spared – the misery and humiliation experienced by so many Eurasian girls. I intend to bring her up as an Indian, which is one of the reasons I have called her Parvati. The other reason is that I believe this is a name Daphne would like. Parvati Manners. Later she may decide to change that surname.

She was reluctant to come into the world but having done so seems equally determined not to let go of it. Dr Krishnamurti has found a wet-nurse, a pretty young Kashmiri girl who has lost her own first-born and lavishes affection on Parvati. She'd make a perfect ayah but says she won't leave Srinagar. She's the wife of one of the boys who paddles the shikaras during the season and I've promised him employment as soon as I move down on to the lake. Perhaps I can persuade them both to come to 'Pindi in September. He looks a frightful rogue but they're a handsome pair and she keeps him in order. It's touching to watch them playing with Parvati as if she were their own. While she feeds the baby he stays nearby, on guard. He's partly fascinated, partly embarrassed by the process, but intensely proud of his wife's talent, and I suppose of the part he played in filling her breasts with the milk now given to someone else's child. And I suppose they both see the money she earns as a compensation for their own loss; a gift from Allah.

It would please Daphne to watch them too. She only saw the child for a second or so. She was in labour for forty-eight hours. You and I have never had children so perhaps we can be classed as almost as ignorant of the process as men are – I mean anyway men who aren't doctors. Dr Krishnamurti was wonderful. Poor Daphne, to look at her you'd have thought her big and strong enough to have babies by the dozen, but the pelvis was wrong, and the baby was the wrong way round. He wanted her to go into hospital and have it turned, but she refused. So he did the whole thing here, bringing up a couple of nurses and an anaesthetist and loads of equipment. That was two or three weeks before she was due. He told me he'd turned the baby but that at the drop of a hat it could turn back again into a position that would lead to a breech delivery. He said he'd advised her to stand no nonsense and opt for a Caesarian so that directly it started the whole thing could just be got on with. But she refused. She had some idea that it was her duty to push the child out of her womb as nature intended. Krishnamurti and I have always been frank with one another. It's sad to think all this awful business was what was needed to make us friends. At the beginning I told him what your Doctor Klaus confided to you, that Daphne's heart was irregular. After examining her he told me it was nothing to worry about in itself, although he agreed that it was probably this irregularity that led to the doctors in London warning her off driving ambulances. It's odd that she never mentioned it. Well, no, not odd. Typical. She always pretended it was her eyesight that caused her to be what she once referred to as 'dismissed the service'. The point is, though, that the heart condition wasn't a complication in childbirth, only what Krishnamurti called 'a slight additional debit on the balance sheet'.

At one moment during that awful forty-eight hours I thought she wanted the child to die, or failing that to die herself. Since then I've changed my mind. She only wanted to 'do it right'. The child did turn again. I suppose because it couldn't get out. Krishnamurti had had the foresight to bring all the equipment back here. He turned the bedroom into an operating theatre. Poor Daphne wasn't compos mentis enough to know what was going on. It was I who gave permission for the Caesarian.

So I have that on my conscience. She should have been in hospital. Krishnamurti took every care. But she died of peritonitis. For a couple of days afterwards I wouldn't even look at the child. I'd seen it cut out. Krishnamurti let me watch. I was dressed up like a nurse in theatre in a white gown, with a mask over my mouth and nostrils. I needed to see this side of life. I'd never have forgiven myself for being too faint-hearted to watch. When it began I thought I'd never stand it. It seemed obscene, like opening a can – which isn't obscene but is when the can is a human abdomen. But then when the can was open and I saw what they were lifting out I felt I was being born again myself. It was a miracle and it made you realise that no miracle is beautiful because it exists on a plane of experience where words like beauty have no meaning whatsoever.

It also meant absolutely nothing to me that the curious knotted little bundle of flesh that was lifted out of Daphne – (perhaps prised is a better word because with their long rubber gloves on they seemed to have to search for and encourage it to emerge) – was obviously *not* the same skin colour as its mother. The difference in colour was subtle, so subtle that were it not for one particular recollection I'd now be persuaded that the fact that the difference between them meant nothing was due to my failing to notice one at the time. But I did notice it. The particular recollection I have is of thinking, Yes – I see – the father *was* dark-skinned. But at the time this caused no emotional response. I noted it and then forgot it. I only remembered it when Daphne was dead and they tried to show me the child to take my mind off things. But that wasn't the reason I rejected it. I rejected it because in the state of mind I was in I blamed it for killing Daphne. If anything its Indian-ness was what first made me feel pity for it and start thinking of it as 'she'. I thought: Poor scrap – there's not a thing she can look forward to.

I told you Daphne saw her for a second or two – between one unconsciousness and another. The nurse held the child close to her. She tried to touch it but didn't have the strength. But she did smile. Which is why I really want you to see Parvati yourself and judge if there is any resemblance at all to Hari Kumar. I'm afraid I can't see Daphne in her – but perhaps you will. Relatives are usually the last to see a family likeness.

Affectionately,
Ethel.

*

My Dear Lili,   Rawalpindi, 5 Aug '47
I have decided to leave 'Pindi. I refuse to live in a place whose people at the stroke of a pen will be turned into enemies of India – the country my husband tried to serve – and you can count on it that 'enemy' isn't overstating the case. The creation of Pakistan is our crowning failure. I can't bear it. They should never have got rid of Wavell. Our only justification for two hundred years of power was unification. But we've divided one composite nation into two and everyone at home goes round saying what a swell the new Viceroy is for getting it all sorted out so quickly. Which of course is right. But he's a twentieth-century swell – and India's still living in the nineteenth century – which is where we're leaving her. In Delhi they've all been blinded by him. I mean the Indians have. What they don't realise is that he was only intended to be the glamorous dressing in the shop window – a window we've been trying to get up attractively ever since the war ended. Behind the window the shop is as nineteenth-century as ever – albeit *radical* nineteenth-century. The slogan is still insular. India's independence at any cost, not for India's sake, but for our own.

I'm going down to the Residency in Gopalakand to stay with an old friend of Henry's, Sir Robert Conway, who is adviser to the Maharajah. The maharajahs are being sacrificed too – mostly their own fault, but the people who wield the knife are really the old Fabians and crusty Trade Unionists in London, *not* the Congress. Perhaps we can meet in Gopalakand? Little Parvati sends her love to Auntie Lili – and so do I.

Affectionately,
Ethel.

*

My Dear Lili,

Can you possibly join me here? I'm at HH of Gopalakand's town palace, such as it is. I've been under the weather and there are a number of things I'd like to discuss. I also want to show you – and give you if you'll take them – certain items left by Daphne, writings of hers, etc., letters and a journal.

Under the terms of my new will I've made provision for Parvati and left money for the endowment of a children's home, thereby carrying out a wish expressed by Daphne. I've named you as one of the trustees and suggested that the home should be called The Manners Memorial Home for Indian Boys and Girls – which is a way of remembering my niece but avoiding the embarrassment that a name like The Daphne Manners Memorial Home might cause people who have long memories. I've suggested that the Home should be in Mayapore. One of the things we might discuss is the use of the site known as The Sanctuary. You told me last year that that woman's eyesight was failing. If it is possible and practicable to use the Sanctuary as a base for the home, one of the provisions of the endowment should be that Sister Ludmila is entitled to continue living there in grace and favour, as it were.

When you've read poor Daphne's journal – which I've kept to myself all these years, although I think you always suspected the existence of something of the sort – you'll understand better why my thoughts have run on these lines. The other thing we must discuss is Parvati's future. I don't want to sound morbid, but the time isn't far off when my death will leave her alone in the world. I am still of the opinion that nothing should be done to try and trace the man you and I are both certain is the father. Each time you see her you say she looks more like Hari than the time before. This is a comfort to me because I know you are telling the truth and not just reassuring me; but it doesn't persuade me that the poor boy should be tracked down and made to face evidence of his responsibility. I'm sure you agree. Without any difficulty I could have arranged for this to be done while he was in prison, and if he is still alive could still arrange it, I suppose, even though he must have been released two or three years ago. I think you are right to suspect that when his Aunt Shalini left Mayapore in 1944 she returned to her old home in the U P solely in order to set up some kind of household he'd have been able to return to when he came out – even if his sojourn there was not of long duration. Obviously someone knows the truth – probably that man Romesh Chand Gupta Sen. Your lawyer friend Srinivasan's assertion – when he came out of prison himself and asked after Mrs Gupta Sen – that Romesh Chand simply shrugged the question away and said she'd gone home to her village and that he'd broken off all connection with the Kumar family, probably amounts to no more than an attempt on the old man's part to disguise the fact that he knew what had happened but didn't care to say. My own belief is that when Hari was released he probably went to his Aunt Shalini's but then took himself off elsewhere, perhaps even changed his name. A boy imprisoned for the reasons he was ostensibly detained for would not lack friends in the new India. My guess is he wanted none of them. He might be dead – a chance victim of that awful savagery – that Hindu–Muslim bloodbath last year that marked the end of our unifying and civilising years of power and influence.

No, my dear. Leave poor Hari Kumar to work out his own salvation, if he's still alive to work it out and if there's a salvation of any kind for a boy like him. He is the left-over, the loose-end of our reign, the kind of person we created – I suppose with the best intentions. But for all Nehru's current emergence as a potential moral force in world affairs, I see *nothing* in India that will withstand the pressure of the legacy of the division we English have allowed her to impose on herself, and are morally responsible for. In allowing it we created a precedent for partition just at the moment when the opposite was needed, allowed it – again with the best intentions – as a result of tiredness, and failing moral and physical pretensions that just wouldn't stand the strain of looking into the future to see what abdication on India's terms instead of ours was going to mean. Perhaps finally we had no terms of our own because we weren't clever enough to formulate them in twentieth-century dress, and so the world is going to divide itself into isolated little pockets of dogma and mutual resistance, and the promise that always seemed to lie behind even the worst aspects of our colonialism will just evaporate into history as imperial mystique, foolish glorification of a severely practical and greedy policy.

Do you remember dear Nello with Henry's pipe in his mouth, pacing up and down, copying Henry, saying, in Henry's voice, 'Policy? Policy? To hell with policy! What are you thinking and feeling, dear chap? That's the point! Don't let's waste bloody time on second-rate notions of what is *likely*. Let's consider the damned unlikely and see where we go from there.' How I laughed at the time. Remembering it now I don't laugh any more. Such a marvellous opportunity *wasted*. I mean for us, by us. Indians feel it too, don't they? I mean, in spite of the proud chests and all the excitement of sitting down as free men at their own desks to work out a constitution. Won't that constitution be a sort of love-letter to the English – the kind an abandoned lover writes when the affair has ended in what passes at the time as civilised and dignified mutual recognition of incompatibility? In a world grown suddenly dull because the beloved, thank God, has gone, offering his killing and unpredictable and selfish affections elsewhere, you attempt to recapture, don't you, the moments of significant pleasure – which may not have been mutual at all, but anyway existed. But this recapture is always impossible. You settle for the second-rate, you settle for the lesson you appear to have learned and forget the lesson you hoped to learn and might have learned, and so learn nothing at all, because the second-rate is the world's common factor, and any damn fool people can teach it, any damn fool people can inherit it.

What terrifies me is the thought that gradually, when the splendours of civilised divorce and protestations of continuing as good friends are worked out, the real animus will emerge, the one both our people just managed to keep in check when there was reason to suppose that it was wrong, because it could lead neither rulers nor ruled anywhere. I mean of course the dislike and fear that exists between black and white. And this is a fifth-rate passion, appropriate only to a nation of vulgar shopkeepers and a nation of fat-bellied banias. I remember that time dear Nello mimicked Henry, the look of awful shock on the face of one of Henry's aides (an awfully well-bred chap, whose grandfather made a fortune out of bottling sauce or something – not that this was against him, but he'd somehow never risen above it) and the way, while I was still laughing, this aide turned to me and seemed as if he were about to say, 'Good heavens, Lady Manners! Do you allow *that* in Sir Henry's own drawing-room?' And all he meant was that Nello was brown-skinned and poor Henry was white, although actually he was grey and yellow and ill, and on his way to the grave. I suppose everything gets stripped down to *that*, in the end, because that is the last division of all, isn't it? The colour of the skin, I mean; not dying.

Well, you and I have always tried to keep open house. *You anyway, I suspect, will have to keep it open for a long time yet.* What this letter is really all about, Lili, is this: When I'm gone, will you give Parvati a roof?

My Love,
Ethel.

*

Imagine, then, a flat landscape, one that turns, upends, following in reverse the bends and twists of night flight 115, the Viscount service to Calcutta; a landscape that is dark but shows immediately below as a system of lights, clustering neatly round a central point with a few minor galaxies beyond its periphery – the flarepath of the airfield, the suburb of Banyaganj, divorced from the parent body because the link with Mayapore, the Grand Trunk Road, is unlit except by the occasional night traffic (miniature headlamps moving at what looks even from this height like excessive speed) and a relatively small and isolated constellation about midway, where the new English colony live on hand for the Technical College, the factories, and the airfield which they use as casually as a bus terminal. Apart from the stranger there is one other Englishman on flight 115 – the same man who at the club that evening occasionally looked across at Srinivasan's private party; perhaps less from curiosity than from a desire to obtain momentary relief from the business of concentrating on questions being put to him by talkative young men like Surendranath and Desai who were trying to make up for the time they think their fathers lost.

Similarly surrounded as he has been in the airport lounge, this other Englishman now sits in the almost empty airliner several seats away from the stranger. The other passengers are Indian businessmen. They, too, sit separately from each other, on their way to deals in West Bengal. When the illuminated sign on the bulkhead goes out (*Fasten seat belts. No smoking*) portfolios will be opened and papers studied. The flight is of such short duration; the respite granted as precious to a man as the time he spends in more intimate surroundings reading the morning newspapers to find out what happened yesterday and judge how it might affect what could happen today. One of them – the man who sat in the airport lounge with his feet curled up on the interior-sprung chair – wears the dhoti. There is not room on the aircraft seat for him to continue in similar comfort, for which the stranger is grateful, because who knows where those feet have been in the past twenty-four hours?

The aircraft seems to be having difficulty attaining height. From the oval shaped port the flarepath comes again into view, not much farther below than it was the last time of looking, and then the lights of Mayapore come back in focus, slightly blurred, which may be due to the condensation on the double glazing of the windows, but at least they conform to the pattern that is known and is now recognisable, because the watcher has had time to orientate himself.

One can even detect where the *maidan* lies: a dark space enclosed by evenly plotted points of illumination, Hospital road, Club road, Church road (a name unaltered in spite of Victoria having become Mahatma Gandhi), and Artillery road. The plane banks, nosing east, almost taking the course of the river that leads to Miss Crane's unimaginable coast. With this God's-eye view of the created world she never had to cope, which perhaps was a pity, because the topography she found so inhibiting from ground-level reveals itself from this height, and at this speed, as random and unplanned, with designs hacked into it by people who only worked things out as they went along.

The neon standard that lights the faithful from the Tirupati temple to the river and back again shows up relatively brightly, and plotting from this and the neon light above the keeper's hut at the level crossing at the northern head of the Bibighar bridge, the stranger (returning to Calcutta for a second inspection of mouldering missionary relics) is able to fix the approximate position of the Bibighar Gardens and the MacGregor House.

The Bibighar Gardens are dark (now, as then) – but from the MacGregor House there is the burst of light that Lili Chatterjee promised: all the lights turned on in the occupied rooms and all the floodlights in the garden; pale from here but suddenly unmistakable, so that foolishly one searches that distant area for signs of Lili herself, and imagines that she stands below the steps of the verandah with Parvati, staring up at the winking red, green and amber riding lights of the airborne commercial juggernaut.

*

This is the last image then – the MacGregor House – in which there are sounds of occupation other than those made by Lili and Parvati: of tinkling broken glass, of sensibly shod feet taking the rise from the black-and-white tiled hallway to the corridor above from which brass-knobbed mahogany doors lead into rooms that give their occupants the opportunity to view the reality for themselves and the dream for others, and to make up their own minds about the precise meaning of what lies beyond.

These sounds are ones that the casual visitor will today attribute to Parvati's presence, not to her mother's. But Parvati steps lightly and breaks nothing (except perhaps a young man's heart). She is another story, which is why her presence here is tentative, although this suits her, because of her shyness and the impression you get of her as a girl who has not yet met the world face to face, let alone subjected it to the force of her personality. To come upon her unexpectedly, to find her standing alone in a room of the MacGregor House or sitting in the shade in the garden counting the petals of a flower – to see her expression of intense but distant pleasure (distant because in spite of its intensity the source of it is obviously far away in some private world that trembles on the brink between her youthful illusions and her maturer judgment), to hear her early in the mornings and evenings practising her singing, to listen to the grave and studious application with which she attacks a difficult phrase, admits defeat with a low cry of exasperation, then re-attacks it, this is to leave the MacGregor House with an idea of Parvati as a girl admirably suited to her surroundings where there is always the promise of a story continuing instead of finishing, and of Lady Chatterjee as the repository of a tradition established for the sake of the future rather than of the past.

'Well, I don't know about that,' (Lady Chatterjee says, taking the stranger for one last look round the old place, accepting the support of his arm, shading her eyes from the late afternoon sun with her free hand – and Shafi already waiting to take him in good time to the airport). 'I mean, a repository sounds like a place for storing furniture when you bash off to some other station. I suppose an Englishman could say that the whole of India is that sort of place. You all went, but left so much behind that you couldn't carry with you wherever you were going, and these days those of you who come back can more often than not hardly bother to think about it, let alone ask for the key to go in and root about among all the old dust sheets to see that everything worth-while that you left is still there and isn't falling to pieces with dry rot.' She pauses and then asks, 'Has Parvati said goodbye to you properly?'

Yes, Parvati has said goodbye, and now runs down the steps from the verandah (late, because she tends to work on Mayapore time instead of Indian Standard), making her way to her evening lesson with her *guru* who has sung in London, New York and Paris, and these days receives for instruction only the most promising pupils – girls who have both the talent and the stamina for a course of training that lasts eight years. One day, perhaps, Parvati will also sing in those western capitals, and then become a *guru* herself, instructing a new generation of girls in the formal complexities of the songs her English mother once described as the only music in the world she knew that sounded conscious of breaking silence

and going back into it when it was finished. Before she goes out of sight –
running in a pale pink saree – she pauses and waves, and the stranger waves
back, wishing her well for the evening lesson. Twice a day she runs like
this, and in the intervals locks herself up for hours of rigorous practice.
Sometimes a young man appears, bearing the twin drums, the *tablas,* to
help her with the necessary percussion which otherwise she provides
herself with sharp little flicks of her supple fingers on the onion-shaped
tamboura. Her skin is the palest brown and in certain lights her long dark
hair reveals a redness more familiar in the north.

> Dooliya le aō re morē babul ke kaharwa.
> Chali hoon sajan ba ke des. Sangaki sakha
> saba bichchuda gayee hai apne ri apne ghar jaun.
>
> Oh, my father's servants, bring my palanquin.
> I am going to the land of my husband. All my
> companions are scattered. They have gone to
> different homes.
>
> (A morning raga.)
> Translation by Dipali Nag.

The Day
of the Scorpion

To
Fern and John
with deep affection and regard

PROLOGUE

The writer encountered a Muslim woman once in a narrow street of a predominantly Hindu town, in the quarter inhabited by money-lenders. The feeling he had was that she was coming in search of a loan. She wore the *burkha*, that unhygienic head-to-toe covering that turns a woman into a walking symbol of inefficient civic refuse collection and leaves you without even an impression of her eyes behind the slits she watches the gay world through, tempted but not tempting; a garment in all probability inflaming to her passions but chilling to her expectations of having them satisfied. Pity her for the titillation she must suffer.

After she had passed there was a smell of Chanel No. 5, which suggested that she needed money because she liked expensive things. Perhaps she had a rebellious spirit, or laboured under a confusion of ideas and intentions. On the other hand she may merely have been submissive to her husband, drenching herself for his private delight with a scent she did not realize was also one of public invitation – and passed that day through the street of the moneylenders only because it was a short cut to the mosque. It was a Friday, and it is written in the Koran: 'Believers, when the call is made for prayer on Friday, hasten to the remembrance of Allah and leave off all business. That would be best for you, if you but knew it. Then, when the prayers are ended, disperse and go in quest of Allah's bounty.' Perhaps, when the service was over, it was her intention to return by the way she had come.

If she was going to divine service then she was bound for the Great Mosque, which lies in the heart of the city. Its minaret is not the only minaret in Ranpur, but it is the tallest and the only one from which the call to prayer is made nowadays; the other mosques of Ranpur are no longer in use as houses of worship. Some of them have decayed, others less ruinous are used as storerooms by the municipality. There are still Muslims in Ranpur but the days are gone when the great festivals of the îd al-fitr and the îd al-Adzha could fill the mosques with thousands of the faithful from the city and the surrounding villages of the plain. The days are gone because thousands of the faithful are gone. Some of those that remain still mourn friends and relatives who chose Islam but never reached that land of promise, having died on the way, some of illness, many by violence.

375

Sometimes a train they travelled on would pass one coming out of Islam, laden with passengers who had neither chosen Islam nor been content to stay when they found themselves living there, in the houses they were born in. These people mourned too for what they had left behind and for friends and relatives who started on the journey with them but did not live to finish it. Some of the survivors settled in Ranpur which was, still is, a sprawling city, seat of the provincial government. There are temples and bathing places on the banks of the sacred river, with steps and burning ghats. Bridges connect the north to the south bank which is less densely populated than the north where lateral and tangential industrial development has broken the landscape with chimneys taller than any minaret. From the air this expansion outwards from the ancient nucleus falls into something like a pattern. From the ground no pattern can be seen (except to the east in the military precision with which the roads and installations of the cantonment were built by a people who are also gone) and the nucleus itself is a warren of narrow streets and chowks in which one may too easily get lost and, being lost, marvel that anyone could know of a short cut to the mosque or to anywhere, let alone find it. Here, you might think no experience would be long enough to acquire such knowledge, in fact that confusion seems to be almost deliberate, the result of recognition of a need to huddle together in order not to be destroyed by a land that seems at best indifferent, at worst malignly opposed, to human occupation.

To leave the narrow streets and crowded chowks behind and enter the area once distinguished by the title Civil Lines, an area of broad avenues and spacious bungalows in walled compounds which culminates in the palladian grandeur of Government House, the Secretariat and the Legislative Assembly; to continue, still in an easterly direction, past the maidan, the government college, the hospital and the film studios and enter the cantonment, which someone once described as Aldershot with trees planted to provide shade instead of cut down to make room, is to pass from one period of history to another and to feel that the people from the small and distant island of Britain who built and settled here were attempting to express in the architectural terms that struck them as suitable their sense of freedom at having space around them at last, a land with length and breadth to it that promised ideal conditions for concrete and abstract proof of their extraordinary talent for running things and making them work. And yet here too there is an atmosphere of circumspection, of unexpected limits having been reached and recognized, and quietly, sensibly settled for. Too late to reduce the scale and crowd everything together, each road and building has an air of being turned inwards on itself to withstand a siege.

If you look in places like Ranpur for evidence of things these island people left behind which were of value, you might choose any one or several of the public works and installations as visible proof of them: the roads and railways and telegraph for a modern system of communication, the High Court for a sophisticated code of civil and criminal law, the college for education to university standard, the State Legislature for democratic government, the Secretariat for a civil service made in the complex image of that in Whitehall; the clubs for a pattern of urbane and civilized behaviour, the messes and barracks for an ideal of military service to the mother country. These were bequeathed, undoubtedly; these and the language and the humpy graves in the English cemetery of St Luke's in the oldest part of the cantonment, many of whose headstones record an early death, a cutting-off before the prime or in the prime, with all that this suggests in the way of unfinished business.

But it is not these things which most impress the stranger on his journey into the civil lines, into the old city itself (where he becomes lost and notes the passage of a woman dressed in the *burkha* in the street of the moneylenders) and then back past the secretariat, the Legislative Assembly and Government House, and on into the old cantonment in a search for points of present contact with the reality of twenty years ago, the repercussions, for example, of the affair in the Bibighar Gardens. What impresses him is something for which there is no memorial but which all these things collectively bear witness to: the fact that here in Ranpur, and in places like Ranpur, the British came to the end of themselves as they were.

*

More than two hundred miles south-west of Ranpur but still inside the boundary of the province of which Ranpur is the principal city lies the town of Premanagar, and – some five miles farther, marking the site of an earlier town of that name – the Premanagar Fort.

Premanagar is most easily prounounced Premman'ugger. Old-style British used to call it Pre*mah*'n'gh, strongly accenting the second syllable and all but swallowing the third and fourth, which gave the Fort status of the kind enjoyed by a tent when it is called a marquee. Originally built by the Rajputs, the Fort was partially destroyed and patched up by the Moghuls who held it against the Mahrattas but lost it to the British. In the mid-nineteenth century it was for a time the seat of an English freebooting gentleman of doubtful origin called Turner who raised a company of mercenaries which he styled Turner's Horse. His men terrorized the countryside and were said to be devoted to their leader. Apart from his Horse Turner had six wives, and a modest fortune which he lost gambling in Calcutta trying to buy a seventh. He died in a skirmish which most historians of the Mutiny of 1857 overlook, probably because so far as one can see nothing led up to it and it led nowhere itself. And old daguerreotype reveals Turner as a man with side whiskers and fixed, pale-looking eyes that were probably blue. One suspects that he was murdered. His irregular cavalry either died with him or disappeared in search of further adventure, so no Turner's Horse lived on to perpetuate his memory. He was, it is said, a press-ganged sailor who deserted in Madras and sought his fortune up-country. But no matter. He is a body buried as it were in the foundations of that other ruined stronghold, the British Empire.

Real bodies were in fact buried in the foundations of the Premanagar Fort. It was a fashion of the times, but the parents of young men (and sometimes the young men's wives) who were bricked up alive to give a fort an auspicious start in life were handsomely rewarded. It is said, though, that the misfortunes of this particular fort were once traced to the fact that the treasurer at the court of the Rajput prince who built it – and bricked up a promising young man and his child wife – pocketed the bereaved family's pension for the five years it took the boy's father to pluck up the courage to go over the treasurer's head and hint at injustice. It is not known what then happened to the treasurer, or the complainant. And anyway it is all conjecture. It has the sound of a myth devised later to explain or anyway celebrate misadventure. The British – as usual – had the best of it. They inherited a partial ruin and preserved it with reverent determination as if awestruck at the thought of changing anything that might then be turned to their disadvantage. Until 1939 the Fort was a detention barracks, and a magnet for military schemes run by grey colonels who had forgotten that as rosy subalterns they had always found such exercises distracting to their sense of what one was in the world to do.

After 1939, the Fort became a prison – a place of civil instead of military detention. It comprised the foundations of the old outer wall, a broken-down despoiled Hindu temple in what had once been the precincts of the South Gate, a still stout inner wall, a pretty mosque, two wells, a flagpole, and a walled courtyard of red earth. Here, in the courtyard, between August 1942 and the date of his release, the Fort's most distinguished prisoner created a garden to pass the time. Traces of it still remain. Given better luck than Turner his memory might have been perpetuated by the habit, dear to Indians, of naming a place after its founder or its most illustrious inhabitant. But it is not known now as Kasim's Garden. Besides, it was only a patch.

Below the hill on which the redstone Fort rests in the massive immobility of its functional decline are other ruins, the site of excavations in 1926 by a team of Frenchmen whose leader became *persona non grata* with the Deputy Commissioner and the Provincial Governor when a complaint was lodged by an English lady, a Miss Frayle, that Professor Lebrun had made an improper suggestion to her while pointing out a recently uncovered frieze of Hindu erotica. The expedition departed for Pondicherry in amused, Gallic disgrace, collectively shrugging its shoulders; and the inquisitive English who subsequently took an archaeological interest in the diggings at Premanagar found the erotica disappointingly mild, so mild in fact that Miss Frayle's reputation suffered and she packed her bags and left for Persia.

Beyond the ruins is the plain, eroded by time, low rainfall, occasional floods and poor husbandry: a complex of old dry river-beds (nullahs) and scantily grassed hummocks over which herds of goats tinkled and still do, seeking the shade of infrequent trees and of bushes whose exhausted-looking leaves become yellowed by the dust blown up from the unmetalled strips on either side of the trunk road. This road stands out in the arid landscape, a hardened artery. The lifeblood of the country, traffic, flows along it thinly and irregularly. Even today you can stand on the roadside and hear nothing for an hour on end except sometimes the goatbells and the wind in the telegraph wires. The wind is hot. At midday the Fort's outline is distorted by the shifting, shimmering air. At a suitable distance it takes on the look of a mirage and at certain times of the year, when climatic conditions are right, actually produces one – a replica of itself, hovering above ground, sometimes upside down. English people, observing the apparition, used to find themselves thinking of Kipling or A. E. W. Mason, and looking forward to sundown, at which hour it was customary to refresh the body and relieve the spirit of the otherwise oppressive burdens of their duty.

Ranpur and the Fort at Premanagar are the first two images in the story to be told.

BOOK ONE

The Prisoners in the Fort

Part One

AN ARREST, 1942

I

Ex-chief Minister Mohammed Ali Kasim was arrested at his home in Ranpur at 5 a.m. on August 9th 1942 by a senior English police officer who arrived in a car, with a motor-cycle escort, two armed guards and a warrant for his detention under the Defence of India Rules. The officer waited for ten minutes on the wrong side of the locked iron gates while the chaukidar went off to rouse one of the servants who in turn roused another who roused Mr Kasim. By the time the officer gained the entrance hall Mr Kasim was standing there in his pyjamas.

'Good morning,' the ex-Chief Minister said. 'I'm sorry they've dragged you out of bed. Is that for me?'

'I'm afraid it is,' the officer replied. Mr Kasim glanced briefly at the warrant, asked the Englishman to step inside and promised not to be long. Mrs Kasim came out and offered him an early morning cup of tea which he felt he had to decline in the circumstances. She nodded, as if she quite understood, and then returned to help her husband get ready.

Ten minutes later Mr and Mrs Kasim came into the vestibule together.

'Where are you actually taking me?' Mr Kasim asked.

The officer hesitated. 'My orders are to drive to Government House. Beyond that I can't say.'

'Oh, well, that's just an initial formality. They'll hardly put me up there for the duration. I hope it's not going to be the Kandipat jail, though. It's so damp and depressing.' He turned to his wife, to embrace her, and the officer moved away and looked at one of the many portraits on the wall, a head and shoulders study of an elderly Indian wearing a number of rather splendid-looking decorations: the ex-Chief Minister's father, probably. He noted a likeness. The Kasims had always been rich and influential. The house was large and richly furnished, but had the spicy smell of Indian cooking and Indian perfumes which the Englishman always found disturbing, not quite civilized, or civilized in a way that suggested there was no distinction to be made between ancient and modern societies.

'I'm ready,' Mr Kasim said.

'Haven't you a bag?'

'Oh, that's here.' He pointed to a suitcase and a bedroll standing against the wall. 'I packed last night when I had news of the Congress Committee vote in Bombay. I thought it would save us time.'

The officer looked at the luggage and disguised his reaction – one of surprise and slight annoyance – by pursing his lips. Lists and arrangements for the detentions had been made secretly for some time, but the arrests, if they had to be made at all, were supposed to come as a surprise.

Saying nothing the officer stooped, picked up the suitcase and bedroll and carried them out to the waiting car where they were taken from him by one of the servants who had now all been alerted and stood around in the forecourt to see their master off to jail.

It was still dark. Mrs Kasim did not come out of the house. The Englishman waited until Mr Kasim was settled in the back seat of the car, gave a nod to the motor-cyclists and as they kicked their machines into life entered the car himself and closed the door. Now that the most embarrassing part of his job was done he would have liked a cigarette. He put his hand in his pocket. He would offer one to Mr Kasim to show him that he appreciated his co-operation. The last time he had arrested a member of Congress there had been a most objectionable scene: sarcasm, abuse and a lecture all the way to the jail about the iniquities of the *raj*. Mr Kasim was a model of restraint and good behaviour. But then he was a Muslim, and the Muslims were men of action, not words. You knew better where you stood with them and they knew when to bow with dignity to the inevitable. Remembering Mr Kasim was a Muslim, though, the officer realized he probably didn't smoke, and realizing that, he thought it would be better manners to deny himself as well.

*

'I'm sorry, Mr Kasim,' Sir George Malcolm said.

They were in the large lofty-ceilinged room where in 1937 Mr Kasim had presented himself to the preceding Governor and listened to formal and rather grudging words of invitation to form a ministry, and in the October of 1939 presented himself again to hand in his written resignation and the resignations of his colleagues. He had been in the room on many other occasions, but these were the two that came most significantly to mind.

'Please don't apologize,' he said. 'Are they arresting Gandhiji too?'

'Yes, so I understand.'

'And the Committee in Bombay?'

The Governor nodded, then said, 'Rather a broad sweep this time, as a matter of fact. Even chaps in your district sub-committees are going into the bag.'

Through one of the tall windows light was now showing. Kasim could just make out the distant bulk of the Secretariat. During his own ministry the lights had often burned there all night. A tale was told that on the occasion of his resignation the preceding Governor had waited until he was alone with his ADC and then said, 'Thank God, now for a bit of peace.' An

English wit in the Secretariat had commented, 'Well, why not? The war is nearly two months old,' and like the rest reverted to the habit of leaving the office at 4 p.m. to get in a game of tennis and a drink at the club before going home to dress for dinner.

The Governor said, 'I gather you packed last night. Did your colleagues do the same, d'you think?'

'Perhaps. I don't know. Should they have?'

'Most of them.'

'Are they in the building?'

'No. They're elsewhere.'

'In Kandipat?'

The Governor did not answer. Kasim did not expect him to. In a case of mass arrests like this the British would be absurdly secretive about the places where leading Congressmen were to be kept under lock and key.

'If they are in Kandipat or elsewhere, why have I been brought here?'

The Governor took off his spectacles, dangled them, then placed them on the blotter. His desk was untidy. In his predecessor's day it had always been unpleasantly immaculate.

'I wanted to have a talk,' he said.

'Before sending me to Kandipat?'

'I think not Kandipat. Don't you agree?'

Kasim smiled. 'Do I have a choice, then?'

'Possibly.' The Governor leaned back in his chair and put one arm over it. With his other hand he played with the spectacles. 'What a damn' silly thing, isn't it? What did your people expect us to do? Sit back and let you bring the country to a standstill? Did anyone in his right mind really expect us to be blackmailed into granting independence just like that in the middle of a world war, with the Japanese preening themselves on the Chindwin?'

'Does anyone in his right mind think that arresting us all from Gandhi down will help?'

'If it stops you from inciting the factory workers to strike, the railways to stop, the ports to close, the soldiers to lay down their arms. That's what you voted for in Bombay yesterday.'

'I did not vote, Governor-ji.'

'No, you did not vote because you resigned from the Congress Committee last year. On the other hand you haven't resigned from the Congress Party. There have been rumours that you were considering it.'

'They are unfounded.'

'Are they? Are they, truly?'

Kasim folded his hands.

'They are mostly the result of one-time wishful thinking on the part – for instance – of Mr Jinnah.'

The Governor laughed. 'Yes, I heard about that. Is *that* true? That Jinnah promised you a portfolio in Bengal or Sind if you'd go over to the League?'

'Let us just say that his interest was aroused by my resignation from the

All India Congress Committee. A certain gentleman was commissioned to ask what my further intentions might be. It is true that there were hints about a rosy ministerial future in one of the Muslim majority provinces, but nothing specific was promised.'

'And your reply?'

'Merely the truth. That I resigned from the committee in order to devote more time to my legal work and that in any case I was not an opportunist. Perhaps I should emphasize that I am not before we go further. You are thinking of offering me a loophole through which I could escape going to prison, I believe.'

'Not a loophole. But it would be an awful waste of your time and talent if you went to jail just when you were seriously considering resigning from Congress, wouldn't it?'

'I am not seriously considering it, Governor-ji. I am not considering it at all and have never considered it.'

'Will you consider it now?'

'Will you give me reasons why I should?'

The Governor sat forward, replaced his spectacles and picked up a pencil. 'Yes, Mr Kasim. I'll give you reasons, although as I see it they all point to one reason only – that you are no longer in sympathy with Congress policy. You haven't been in sympathy for a long time and grow intellectually and emotionally further and further away from Congress with every week that goes by. You were impatient with Congress when they won the provincial elections in 1937 but dithered about taking office. You were impatient with the face-saving formula which allowed them to pretend to take office just to show that the scheme for a federal central government wouldn't work. You were alarmed when you found yourself unable to form a provincial ministry which would have more accurately reflected the wishes of the electorate. The Congress majority in the province was slim enough to warrant a coalition. You wanted Nawaz Shah in your cabinet but none of your Congress colleagues would agree because he was a Muslim Leaguist. You were enough of a realist to bow to the inevitable, and a good enough party disciplinarian to make sure that on any major point of legislation in the Assembly your compromises were with the Muslim League and not the Hindu Mahasabah. You were criticized for that. People said scratch Kasim and you'll find one of Jinnah's men underneath. But you preferred to run the risk of that sort of criticism and to invite defeat in the Assembly than adjust your programme to ensure a comfortable majority of Congressites and Hindu rightwingers.' The Governor smiled. 'You see, I've done my homework. So let me continue. You knew what was going on in the districts, and knew that most of what the Muslims said was going on was gross exaggeration, but you recognized the dangers and were appalled at the evidence you had of what actual communal intimidation did exist. You saw that whatever the Congress professed to be, a national party, a secular party, a party dedicated to the ideal of independence and national unity, there were people in it who could never see it as anything but a Hindu dominated organization whose real motive was power for the Hindus and who were coming into the open now that they'd got power. That alarmed you too. Every instance that came to your notice of a Muslim being discriminated against, of an injustice against a Muslim, of violence done to a Muslim, of Muslim children being forced to salute the Congress flag or sing a Congress hymn in school, you saw not only as reprehensible in itself, whatever the provocation might have been, but as another nail in the coffin, another wedge driven between the two major communities. And something else alarmed you, the realization that you were a man not with one master but two, the electorate to whom you were responsible, and the Congress High Command. It alarmed you because the High Command itself wasn't administratively committed. It wasn't answerable to an electorate, but it controlled and directed you who were. So when Britain declared war on Germany and the Viceroy declared war on Germany and the Congress High Command objected to having war declared over its head and called on all Congress ministries to resign, you resigned. You resigned at the dictate of a political organization that had no electoral responsibility to the country, except in the provinces through men like yourself. You saw the constitutional absurdity of this, but you handed your resignation in, handed it in here in this room to my predecessor, and he was a man who welcomed it because he was a man of the old school who thought India ungovernable except by decree, a man who'd sat back and laughed up his sleeve for two and a half years as he watched the farce of a ministry trying to serve both its electorate and its political bosses, and who sat back now, breathed a sigh of relief and assumed Governor's control which I've inherited. And it wasn't just the constitutional absurdity that struck you, it was the political folly of resigning, of having to resign. Without power, politics are so much hot air, and power is what your party got rid of. You knew what would happen and have seen it happen. How many seats in the Legislative Assembly reserved for Muslims were won in 1937 by non-League Muslims? A tidy few including your own. How many would be won now if we had an election tomorrow? Any? Where would your slim Congress Party majority be with most of your non-aligned Muslims and even some of your Congress Muslims gone over to the League? Repeat that picture all over India and where is your party's proof of speaking for all India? Where is it, Mr Kasim? Where has it gone? You know the answer as well as I do. Up the spout. Down the creek. Sunk. Why? Because your party overlooked the fact that on the first assumption of political power the old battle was won and the new one begun. The old battle was for Indian independence and although you may not think so now, Indian independence became a foregone conclusion in 1937 when men like you became provincial ministers. Getting rid of us was still part of your programme but getting rid of us was no longer the battle. The real battle was to maintain and extend the area of your party's power. I've no patience with people, and they're chiefly my fellow-countrymen, who profess horror at what they

call the sorry spectacle of the Indians squabbling among themselves
because they're unable to agree about how the power they're going to
inherit should be divided. Of course you must disagree. Of course you
must squabble. It's a sign that you know you're no longer fighting for a
principle because you know the principle has been conceded. You're
fighting for political power over what has been conceded. It's logical. It's
essential. It's an inescapable human condition. When you all resigned the
power you'd got, in the belief that you were striking another blow for
India's independence, you weren't striking a blow for that at all. You were
striking a blow at your own existing and potential political power. You
were narrowing the area you could hope to exercise it in. It isn't so much
what you all did between 1937 and 1939 to make a lot of Muslims believe
the League had been right and that a Congress ruled India would mean a
Hindu India that has made eventual partition of this country almost
certainly inevitable, it's the fact that you relinquished power, and you
relinquished it because you didn't understand the importance of keeping
it. I say you, but I don't mean you, Mr Kasim. You well knew its
importance and the folly of giving it up, just as you well know the latest
folly your party has committed, the folly of not admitting the consequences of the first idiocy, of thinking you can put the clock back to 1939,
ignore Jinnah and pretend the real quarrel is still with Britain and that the
British are just playing that old game of dividing and ruling and hanging on
like grim death. You well know that when Cripps came out in April your
party had its last chance to retrieve its position. You well know that for the
first time in all the long melancholy history of conferences, working
parties and round table negotiations the Cripps Mission wasn't just *us*
going through the old motions of palming you off with as little as possible.
It was us again, but us under pressure from outside, from our allies, from
America in particular, and I think you understood the peculiar advantages
of negotiating with people under that sort of pressure. I think you
understood too that the Cripps proposals were the best you are going to get
while the war is on and that this was the last chance you had to contain
Jinnah. But what happens? Your party shies like a frightened horse from
the mere idea that any province or group of provinces should have the
power to secede from a post-war Indian constitution and set up a
constitution of its own. What does it mean, they ask? What but Pakistan?
But who even a few years ago had ever heard of Pakistan let alone thought
of it as practicable? Well, it's more than practicable now. It's damn' well
certain. It needn't have been if you'd agreed to the Cripps proposals, come
back into office, got on with the war and at the end of the war gone to a
country you'd helped lead to victory and independence and trusted in the
good sense of those people not to let their country be split down the
middle. Instead of which you walk out on Cripps, spend the whole summer
in cloud cuckoo land working up some absurd theory that if you make
India untenable for the British they'll leave and the Japanese won't walk in.
And while you're producing this ludicrous scheme you allow Jinnah to

continue to extend the area of his power because in the Muslim majority provinces Jinnah's men have remained in office. And now comes the crowning folly, a resolution that's as good as a call to nation-wide insurrection. And you don't agree with that either, do you, Mr Kasim? You know the British simply aren't going to forgive all this Quit India nonsense going on while they're trying to concentrate on turning the tables on the Japanese, not – mark you – just to save themselves and their country but you and your country. You know all this, Mr Kasim, but you're still a pillar of the Congress Party, one of its most famous favoured Muslims, good propaganda and apparently living proof of the truth of their claim that they're an all India party, the sort of man who's influential enough in this province for me not to think twice about locking you up as a potential inciter of riots and strikes, because your party, your party, Mr Kasim, yesterday committed high treason by conspiring to take steps calculated to aid and comfort the King-Emperor's enemies. And the one big question in my mind is why is it still your party, Mr Kasim? What official policy or policies has it adopted and pursued in the last three years that you have honestly felt to be either wise or expedient?'

'Perhaps none,' Kasim said.

'Exactly. And so, my dear Kasim, don't go into the wilderness with the rest of them this morning. However long it is, and my guess is it's for the duration, what a waste of your talent, what misplaced loyalty. Get out now. Write to Maulana Azad. Write this morning, write here and now. Send in your resignation. What more suitable moment? And the moment you write your resignation I tear up this stupid document authorizing your arrest. There's not a single act committed by you since you resigned office in 1939, not a speech, not a letter, not a pamphlet, not a thing said in public or overheard in private that warrants your being locked up. All that warrants it now is your continued allegiance to the Congress, your continued standing as a leading member of an organization we're outlawing.'

'I quite understand, Sir George.'

The Governor studied the expression on Kasim's face. Then he got up, walked to one of the long windows, looked out, and came back again, pacing slowly. Kasim waited, his hands still folded on his lap.

'I want you on my executive council,' the Governor said. 'If it were constitutionally possible for me to re-establish autonomy in this province I know whom I'd invite to head the administration. Short of that I want you *in*, I want to use your talents, Mr Kasim.'

'It is very kind of you, Sir George. I am immensely flattered.'

'But you refuse, don't you? You refuse to resign. You insist on going to jail. Forgive me, then. I hope you don't feel insulted. That wasn't my intention.'

Kasim made a gesture of dismissal. 'Please. I know this.'

The Governor sat down, took off his spectacles and played with them as before, but with both hands, leaning forward, with his elbows on the desk.

'Waste!' he exclaimed suddenly. 'Waste! Why, Mr Kasim? You agree with everything I've said, but you don't even ask for time to consider my suggestion. You reject it out of hand. Why?'

'Because you only offer me a job. I am looking for a country and I am not looking for it alone.'

'A country?'

'To disagree about the ways of looking for it is as natural as you say it is to squabble about how power will be divided when it is found. And as you say, I have disagreed many times about these ways, and people have many times expected me to resign and change my political allegiance. And if ways and means were all that mattered I expect Congress would have seen the back of me long ago. But these are not what matter, I believe. What matters is the idea to which the ways and means are directed. I have pursued this idea for a quarter of a century, and it is an idea which for all my party's faults I still find embodied in that party and only in that party, Governor-ji, nowhere else. Incidentally, I do not agree with you when you speak of Indian independence having become a foregone conclusion. Independence is not something you can divide into phases. It exists or does not exist. Certain steps might be taken to help bring it into existence, others can be taken that will hinder it doing so. But independence alone is not the idea I pursue, nor the idea which the party I belong to tries to pursue, no doubt making many errors and misjudgements in the process. The idea, you know, isn't simply to get rid of the British. It is to create a nation capable of getting rid of them and capable simultaneously of taking its place in the world as a nation, and we know that every internal division of our interests hinders the creation of such a nation. That is why we go on insisting that the Congress is an All India Congress. It is an All India Congress first, because you cannot detach from it the idea that it is right that it should be. Only second is it a political party, although one day that is what it must become. Meanwhile, Governor-ji, we try to do the job that your Government has always found it beneficial to leave undone, the job of unifying India, of making all Indians feel that they are, above all else, Indians. You think perhaps we do this to put up a strong front against the British. Partly only you would be right. Principally we do it for the sake of India when you are gone. And we are working mostly in the dark with only a small glimmer of light ahead, because we have never had that kind of India, we do not know what kind of India that will be. This is why I say we are looking for a country. I can look for it better in prison, I'm afraid, than from a seat on your Excellency's executive council.'

While Kasim was talking the Governor had searched for and found a folder from which he now took a paper. He handed it across the desk. Kasim unfolded his hands, took the paper, felt in his pocket for his spectacles.

'As you will see, Mr Kasim, that is a very short note which, if signed, will be your undertaking not to commit or cause to be committed any act whose effect is to disturb the peace or to hinder the defence of the realm.

The undertaking would be valid for a period of six months from the date of signature. As you'll also see there's a rider to the effect that the signatory would, if called upon, use his best endeavours to inhibit the effects of any such acts committed within the province by others. You'll notice the paper says nothing about resigning from Congress. But sign the paper and I'll still tear this other paper up.'

'Yes, I see,' Mr Kasim said. He put the note back on the Governor's desk and replaced his spectacles in their case. 'You are expecting trouble, then. You have realized the disadvantages of having to lock us up to stop us rousing what you call the mob. But the mob perhaps rouses itself. And it is uncontrolled. It wants to know what you've done with us. All kinds of undesirable elements emerge. You want me therefore to become a sort of *ex-officio* peacemaker, armed with soothing words and no integrity. As you say, the paper says nothing about resigning from Congress, but it need not do so, of course. If I signed it I would be expelled. To sign it is tantamount to resignation. I could not sign it. You didn't expect me to, but I suppose you thought it was worth a try. I'm afraid you must cope with the mob without me.'

'Well we can do that and will.' For a while the Governor was silent, watching Kasim. Then he said, 'You are in a curious position.'

'I do not see it as curious.'

'I was thinking of your private position. Of your elder son, for instance, who holds the King-Emperor's commission. He fought in Malaya, and now he's a prisoner of war of the Japanese. It has always puzzled me why you allowed him to join the army.'

'Allow? He was under no obligation to seek my approval. It was his wish. India must have an army as well as a government. He became an officer. I became a minister.'

'And you both served under the crown. Quite. But you no longer do. He does. No doubt you have heard rumours of the pressures being put on Indian prisoners, officers and men, to secure their release from prison camp by joining units that will fight side by side with the Japanese. News of your imprisonment might well be used by the enemy to add to those pressures in your son's case. He was an excellent officer, I believe. He would be useful to them. His loyalty as an officer might be subjected to severe strain if he hears that we have put his father in jail. In his present circumstances he cannot simply resign his commission as you resigned your ministerial appointment. That is the difference, isn't it?'

'I think it is a difference he will appreciate. Just as he will appreciate that I cannot let personal considerations affect my political judgement.'

'Yes,' the Governor said, 'I expect it is,' and stood up in a way that conveyed to Kasim that the interview was at an end. He stood up too. In the pit of his stomach he felt the old familiar hollowness. He did not want to go to prison.

The Governor held out his hand. Kasim took it.

'I'm afraid that for the time being at any rate your whereabouts aren't to be made known, and this restriction must unfortunately apply in the case of your family. They will write to you care of Government House, and your own letters will automatically come here. I hope, Mr Kasim, that occasionally you will think of writing personally to me.'

'Thank you. Am I to be allowed newspapers?'

'I shall give the necessary instructions.'

'Then I'll say goodbye.'

'Goodbye, Mr Kasim.'

Kasim bowed his head, hesitated, and then walked towards the double doors behind which, he knew, the young police officer to whom the senior man had handed him over, and two British military policemen, would be waiting. But just before he reached the doors he heard the Governor call his name, and turned. The Governor was still standing behind the desk. He made a gesture with both hands, indicating the desk, the papers on it.

'May I send you away with an interesting thought that has suddenly struck me?'

'What is that, your Excellency?'

'That one day this desk will probably be yours.'

Kasim smiled, looked round the room. The thought, just at that moment, was almost sickening. He said, 'Yes. You are probably right,' and, still smiling, turned and took the last few paces to his more immediate prison.

*

At dusk Mr Kasim was taken from the upstairs room where he had been kept all day and driven to the sidings of the railway station at Ranpur cantonment. Here he was transferred to a carriage of the kind used to transport troops, most of whose windows had been blocked by steel shutters. The young officer in charge of him was joined by another. An armed sentry stood guard at the only door of the carriage that was still in use. When approaching the carriage Kasim saw that it was uncoupled. There were other soldiers and police in the vicinity. When he entered the carriage he expected to find other occupants, friends, ex-colleagues; but he was alone. The two young officers talked to each other in low voices and mostly in monosyllables. He made up his bed on one of the wooden benches. A tray was brought in with his dinner: soup, chicken and vegetables, and rice pudding with jam – obviously chosen from the European style menu at the station restaurant. While he ate it one of the officers went for his own dinner. Half an hour later he returned and his companion went for his. Kasim's tray was taken by a British MP. Another armed sentry joined the first. At about nine o'clock the carriage was coupled to others, and the other officer returned from the restaurant. The two officers settled in the middle of the carriage leaving the guards at one end and Mr Kasim at the other. The train started. Kasim read. The officers continued to talk in low voices. They smoked cigarettes. Occasionally they shared a joke. A ten o'clock while the train was still moving slowly, uncertainly, picking its way across points and iron bridges, Mr Kasim gave the officers a start by rising suddenly and opening his suitcase. He sensed that they touched their holsters to make sure their revolvers were still there. From the suitcase he took out his prayer mat, then turned to them.

'I suppose neither of you can tell me which direction west is?' He smiled, was rewarded with vague, uncomprehending but not totally unfriendly negative replies, and then unrolled the mat on the floor, stood for a moment and composed himself in order to begin saying his Isha prayers in a peaceable frame of mind. He then performed in full the four Rak'ahs prescribed.

During the night he woke several times. The officers and the guards were taking it in turns to doze. He observed their faces: slack, remote in the dim pools of light from the overhead bulbs that had been left on. The light scarcely reached the end of the carriage where he lay and once, because he had moved and attracted the attention of the officer whose turn it was to keep watch, he returned the man's incurious, dispassionate, half-dreaming gaze for what seemed like an age before the man suddenly realized that Kasim's eyes were also open and looked away, stared down at his folded arms. When Kasim next awoke this man was asleep, his companion sitting forward, elbows resting on his knees, contemplating his clasped hands in one of which a cigarette was burning. Kasim raised his arm and looked at the luminous dial of his wrist-watch. Nearly five o'clock. The train was not moving but presumably wasn't at its destination. Distantly, through the silence, he heard the cry of jackals. He rose, aware of the sharp movement of the wakeful officer keeping a check on him. From his suitcase he took the waterproof bag, leather case, soap-box, towel and shaving kit that he had packed the night before last, and went into the cubicle. There was no lock on the door. A single bulb illuminated dirty green tiles and old, cracked porcelain. Iron bars were set in the window. Behind them was a pane of frosted glass. He showered and shaved, put back on the clothes he had travelled in. The train had begun to move again. The motion set the door swinging open and shut. When he came out both officers were awake. He nodded good-morning to them, returned his things to the suitcase, got out his prayer mat and performed the two Rak'ahs of the Fajr prayers. Making the last prostration he repeated to himself a passage from the Koran. Oh God, glory be to You who made Your servant go by night from the Sacred Mosque to the farther Mosque. Praise be to Allah who has never begotten a son, who has no partner in his Kingdom, who needs none to defend him from humiliation.

Kneeling he rolled the mat up again, returned it to the case and snapped the locks shut. He made up his bedroll and secured the straps. Then he sat on the hard slatted bench. The officers went in turn to the cubicle at the other end of the carriage. The sentry who squatted at the door rose and woke the sleeping sentry, and then lowered the window and looked out. The train came to a halt. Rain was drumming on the roof. Kasim wondered whether his wife was yet awake. He thought of his married daughter in the Punjab, of his son Ahmed in Mirat, and of his elder son Sayed who was God knew in what hell-hole of a prison camp.

The train was, almost imperceptibly, once more in motion. Both officers had completed their ablutions. Now the sentries took it in turns to go into the farther cubicle. The officers mumbled at each other. One of them looked at his watch and stretched, went to the open window. The first light must be beginning to show, Kasim thought. The officer stayed at the window for some time. The overhead bulbs went out. The carriage was permeated with a grey mistiness that brought with it the notion of early morning chill, and the faces of his guards were suddenly like those of strangers. The officer left the window and joined his companion. He must have made some sign. They began to adjust their belts. One reached for his cap. Kasim looked away, feeling the hollowness again. A few minutes later the train came to a halt. For a moment, because of the quietness, Kasim imagined they were held up by signals, but the silence was then broken by a voice speaking outside. Turning to look Kasim saw one of the officers at the window. He spoke to someone well below the level of the carriage. A moment later he opened the door and got down. His companion stayed in the carriage but stood at the open door. He lit a cigarette. One of the soldiers slung his rifle over his shoulder and studied the palm of his left hand as if he'd got a cut or a splinter. The carriage echoed metallically. It was being uncoupled. The rain had stopped falling. There was a whistle from up ahead. Kasim stood. The sentry stopped looking at his hand and the officer in the doorway glanced round, then back through the doorway again. He answered a voice from below and came away from the door. An officer with an armband round his sleeve hauled himself up into the carriage.

'Mr Mohammed Ali Kasim?' he inquired, as if making a formal identification.

'Yes.'

'This way, please.'

Kasim picked up his suitcase and bedroll. The others stood aside for him. At the doorway he looked down into the face of the officer whose eye he had held during the night. He said, 'I'd be grateful if you'd help me with my baggage.'

Standing below, near by, were two military policemen. The carriage was in a goods yard. A 15-cwt truck was parked at the shuttered entrance to a warehouse. Kasim smelt coal dust. The officer reached up and Kasim nudged the suitcase forward until he felt its weight taken. The bedroll followed. The officer set both down on the cinders. Kasim turned round to face inwards as he climbed down the narrow, perpendicular steps; then stood waiting. The officer with the armband came down. He indicated the luggage.

'This is all your luggage?'

'Yes.'

'Very well. My men will take you to the truck. Go with them, please.'

'May I be told where you are taking me?'

The officer with the armband hesitated.

'To the Fort,' he said abruptly.

'The Fort?'

Again the officer hesitated. Kasim thought he was surprised. 'You're in Premanagar,' he explained.

'Thank you. I didn't know.'

He glanced round. One railway siding looked like any other. He had not been in Premanagar since his tour of the province in 1938. He had never visited the Fort, but he had seen it from a distance. He had no clear visual recollection of it. Premanagar, he remembered, was not far from Mirat where his son Ahmed was. If they ever told his family where he was, and allowed him visitors, perhaps he would see Ahmed.

II

Major Tippit was a small man with very little hair. What was left of it was yellowy white. His face was lined and wrinkled. He had a high complexion. 'I'm a historian really,' he explained. 'I retired from the army in 1938, but they dug me out. It was decent of them to give me the Fort, wasn't it?'

Kasim agreed that it was.

'There's a lot of history in the Fort. I'm writing a monograph. Perhaps you'd like to read some of it and give me an opinion, one day when you have a moment.'

'I have a great number of moments.'

'I'm sorry I wasn't here when you arrived. Let us see, now, how long has it been?'

Major Tippit glanced at the papers on his desk but did not make any effort to find one in particular.

Kasim said, 'Nine days.'

'And you are comfortable?'

'I am comfortable.'

'Have you any complaints?'

'Several.'

'Oh yes. Lieutenant Moran Singh told me he'd made a note of them. It's here somewhere I expect. I'll look into them.'

'Can't you look into them now?'

Major Tippit had very pale blue eyes. He gazed out of them at Kasim as if he had reasons for not dealing with complaints but couldn't remember what they were. He clasped his bony little hands together on the desk – the kind of man, Kasim guessed, who, lacking skill, energy or resolution, would make up for them with a mindless, vegetable implacability. The unpleasant young Sikh, nominally under Major Tippit's command, would know exactly how far he could go, what would be allowed to him by way of license, and what disallowed.

'First of all,' Kasim said, 'is it really Government's intention to keep me in solitary confinement? I understand the Fort has a number of civil prisoners like myself. We are not criminals. We shall probably be here for some time. The others seem to mix quite freely. I can see them in the outer courtyard from the window of my room. But since coming here I've been kept isolated and have spoken to no one except my guards and Lieutenant Moran Singh. Is this state of affairs merely temporary or is it to continue?'

'Yes, I see.'

Kasim waited.

'I am sorry you feel like that. The old zenana house is extremely interesting. I must come over one day and point out some of its more remarkable features.'

'Some of my fellow-prisoners would be interested in it too.'

'Oh, I don't think so. If I may make bold, they are not of similar intellectual calibre. The other prisoners here are very much from the rank and file of your movement.' A look of almost intense disappointment came on to Major Tippit's face, as if he had only just realized what they were talking about. 'We were told several weeks ago that we might have to provide accommodation for a VIP detenu. Of course we immediately thought of Mr Gandhi or Mr Nehru. At first I believed we had nothing suitable. Amazing how you can overlook something that's right under your nose. I had become so used to sitting here and looking through the window and seeing the zenana house, so used to going over there and using it for my own private purposes – I did a great deal of reading and writing and studying there – that I came to think of it really as an extension of my office. Then of course it struck me how eminently suitable it was. In the heart of the citadel, and if I may say so, constantly under my eye. One has that kind of obligation if one takes one's duties seriously. I made the necessary arrangements at once. It was the last thing I did before going on leave. One has to be prepared. I knew I would miss using the little house. I always found it so conducive to meditation. I confess I was a little sad when I returned last night and Lieutenant Moran Singh said that the zenana house was now occupied. However, I was most interested when he told me who you were. A member of the ancient house of Kasim. The Fort was once within the territory administered by the Kasim who was a viceroy of the great Moghul. But you know that? Your kinsman, the present Nawab of Mirat, is directly descended from him. I thought last night how interesting it was that a Kasim should have come back to stay in Premanagar. And frankly I was rather relieved that the occupant of the zenana house was of the Faith. Tell me, are you a Sunni or a Shiah Muslim?'

'Major Tippit, you have not answered my complaint. My impression is that the officers who conducted me from Ranpur brought a letter to you from Sir George Malcolm. Is there anything in that letter that suggested I should be kept isolated?'

'A letter?'

'I think the one near your left elbow. I recognize the heading.'

Tippit looked down, picked the letter up, glanced at it.

'Oh yes. Lieutenant Moran Singh mentioned a letter. I have not read it yet.'

'Would you do so now?'

Tippit looked down again, stared at the letter. His eyes showed no movement of reading. After a while he replaced the letter near his left elbow.

'Well?' Kasim asked. 'Is there anything that suggests or orders solitary confinement?'

'No.'

'Is there anything about newspapers?'

'You have permission to read newspapers.'

'Good. But I have not been given any. That is my other complaint.'

'I will speak to Lieutenant Moran Singh about it.'

'I've spoken to Lieutenant Moran Singh about it several times. I've given him a list of the newspapers I want. I've also written to my wife asking her to send newspapers. That letter and several other letters are still here. They are on your desk.'

'I'll read them as soon as possible. You understand that they must be read?'

'I understand nothing of the sort. They will be read in Ranpur, either in the censorship office at the Secretariat or by a member of the Governor's staff. Sometimes by both. I have not so far written personally to the Governor as he requested me, but I shall be doing so presently. I should like to be able to make some comments to him on whatever the current situation is.'

Major Tippit glanced up – not, it seemed, recognizing a threat. He said, 'Things have been very distressing, haven't they?'

'Major Tippit, how can I tell how things have been? I have no radio, no newspapers, my guards tell me nothing, Lieutenant Moran Singh tells me nothing and does not even post my letters. No letters have been given to me either. By now I should think there would be several.'

'Such senseless violence. It is difficult to know where to apportion blame. And that poor girl, that unfortunate woman. It has incensed people. Looting, rioting, burning. Yes, yes. One expects. Deplores but expects. But these other things . . . I was delayed because the railways have been so uncertain. In Ranpur feeling is running high. In Mayapore the civil have handed over to the military. The whole country is seething. Will you have some tea?'

'No thank you.'

'It is ten o'clock. I always have tea at ten o'clock. A regular régime. While I'm away things get out of hand. It is five past ten.' He said this without looking at his watch. He made no effort to have tea brought in. Chapprassis were waiting on the bench outside, but he did not call one of them. He said, 'But they will be better now that I am back. Lieutenant Moran Singh has conducted everything with precision and now that I am back to say the word everything will fall into place. I'm afraid I cannot change the arrangements for your accommodation. Have you any other requests?'

'I should like further supplies of pen, paper and ink.'

'I will tell Lieutenant Moran Singh. He will arrange it with one of the clerks.'

'There are two habitable rooms in the zenana house, the one I have as a bedroom and the one I use as a study. I should like to share these rooms with one of your other prisoners.'

'Which one?'

'Any one. I don't know who you have got here.'

'As I said, rank and file. I cannot allow it. It is against my principles. I am surprised that you wish it. You are a man who has been in a position of authority. Well, well, that is a lonely business. I too am living alone in this fortress, Mr Kasim. I am glad you are here. We can talk together sometimes. I am interested in Islamic art and literature as well as in history. The early eighteenth-century Urdu poet, Gaffur, was also of your ancient family, so I understand. I have translated some of his verses into English. You might like to have a look at them.'

Kasim bowed his head.

'In one or two cases I believe I have managed to convey something of the splendour and simplicity of the original. You are well acquainted with the poems of Gaffur, Mr Kasim?'

'At one time, yes. As a boy. Since then other things have tended to occupy my mind. You said that the country is seething.'

'Looting. Arson. Sabotage. Policemen have been murdered. Track has been torn up. Magistrates imprisoned in their own jails, Congress flags run up. Troops called out. Inevitable loss of life. Waste. Violence. Terrible violence. To no purpose. It's being stamped out. It's best forgotten. I should not talk about it.'

'You said something about a girl.'

'She was raped. Another woman was attacked. An elderly woman. The Indian who was driving her to safety was murdered.'

'Were they Europeans?'

'English. The woman was a mission school teacher. The girl who was raped was of good family. They have arrested the men.'

'Was this in Ranpur?'

'No. In Mayapore. The military have taken over. Your people have done terrible things. I do not understand you, Mr Kasim. Over this we are in opposite camps. We are enemies. But I am a humane man.' Major Tippit paused. 'I'm a historian, really. The present does not interest me. The future even less. Only through art and contemplation of the past can man live with man. I hope you will be content. Think upon the Fort as a refuge from life's turmoils and disappointments.'

Kasim waited, then when he saw that for the moment Tippit had no more to say, he rose, thanked his jailer for the interview and said, 'I have your permission to return to my quarters?'

*

He walked alone across the space that separated the Fort commander's office and the zenana house, under the eyes of the chapprassis and the armed sentries who patrolled the colonnaded veranda of the old barracks. In the centre of the courtyard a neem tree provided some shade. Puddles in the red earth reflected the blue of the sky. Puffs of cloud too light to cast shadows moved quickly, driven by the prevailing south-west wind. By midday it would probably rain.

The courtyard was enclosed to the east by the barracks, to the north, west and south by high crenellated red brick walls with bastions built into the angles. In the west and south wall there were gateways closed by studded wooden doors. Close to the southern wall was the square pavilion where Major Tippit lived. Abutting on to the northern wall was the old zenana house, a two-storey construction of stone and brick with fretted wooden arches shading the upper and lower verandas. A wooden stairway gave access to the first floor. The rooms below were in use as storehouses. The dry smell of grain and sacking pervaded the place. Above, the veranda gave on to rooms all but two of which were ruinous. The farthest of these were boarded in. The two which were habitable were closest to the wooden staircase. Inside, they were lit by the open doors and by windows in the outer walls. These windows were blocked by fretted stone screens that gave the occupant views, through any one of their many apertures, of the outer courtyard and the inner and outer walls of the Fort. The courtyard where the zenana house stood had obviously been the women's. The barracks must have been servants' quarters. He could not see what lay behind the southern wall, other than the dome of the mosque, but from the outer windows of his rooms in the zenana he could see beyond the farther walls to the plain.

The walls of his two rooms were whitewashed. In one room there were a bed, a chair and a wardrobe; in the other a table, a chair and a calendar. The calendar was Kasim's own. He did not mark off the days. There seemed no point in doing so when the period of his imprisonment was not determined. 'I rise at six as usual, waking by habit,' he wrote now to his wife. 'They give me breakfast at eight. The two hours are spent bathing and dressing and reading. After breakfast I walk round the compound, unless it is raining, then write in my journal, and letters, until lunch. After lunch I doze for a while, then read until four, when they bring me some tea. After tea I walk again. After that I bathe. Then read. Then supper. Time of course hangs heavily. Today I expect letters at last. Please give my love to the children when you write to them. I am told there has been some unrest. I hope you are safe and unharmed by it. There must be a great deal for you to attend to. Do not write more often than you can well afford to. One thing I dislike is not being allowed to shave myself. They have taken my things away and send a barber every other day. Today is a bristly morning. I suppose they are afraid I might hurt myself with the razor. Even my little mirror is gone. I shall forget what I look like, no doubt. They have let me keep your and the children's photographs, because they are only covered with mica. I have the portraits on my desk. Pray remember every morning and night Ahmed Gaffur Ali Rashid. Our noble but eccentric ancestor! Looking at the photographs has reminded me of him.'

There was no such person as Ahmed Gaffur Ali Rashid. His wife would therefore see at once that this particular sentence contained the simple code message – an anagram – they had agreed upon to tell her where he was being held. He hoped the censors would not see it first. They would look for such codes in his first few letters to her. This was his fourth. He ran his hand over the stubble on his chin and then over his cheeks, wondering whether prison fare had made his face thinner.

*

So: Kasim's face. There was history in it; the history of Islam's holy wars and imperial expansions. He traced his genealogy back to a warrior-adventurer called Mir Ali who came from Turkey in the heyday of the Muslims' Indian empire just as years later young Britons came out in the heyday of their own. Mir Ali married a Hindu princess and they both adopted the new religion the great Moghul Akbar had devised in an attempt to establish a cornerstone on which to build the fabric of a dream, an India undivided by conflicting notions of God and the ways to worship God. Akbar wished his fellow-Muslims and the conquered Hindus to feel equal in one respect at least. But in the reign of Aurangzeb the Kasims re-embraced Islam. The empire was already running down but the Muslims still held the keys of the kingdom and under Aurangzeb the old proselytizing faith in Allah and his prophet was re-established as a buttress for the crumbling walls of state. A new wave of conversions, even among the proud Rajputs, showed that when belief is at odds with worldly ambition the former is the more likely to bow its head.

The reward for one of those Kasims who re-embraced Islam – the eldest grandson of Mir Ali – was the vice-regal appointment over a territory that stretched from Ranpur to Mirat. He was murdered by his son who had been one of his deputies. Internecine war, war against rebellious Hindu rulers and chieftains, war against the invaders from the west – the Mahrattas – marked the final years of the dying Moghul dynasty. The deputies of the great Moghul were carving out principalities and scrambling for power in the gathering darkness, unwittingly opening the gates that would let in the flood that was to swamp them: the flood of ubiquitous, restless foreign merchants whom they thought at first easy sources of income and personal riches, French, British, Portuguese merchants who came to trade but stayed on to secure their trade by taking possession of the source of wealth, the very land itself. The merchants fought each other too, and there is no honour among thieves. A self-appointed prince, leaning on one of the foreigners to help him subjugate a neighbouring pocket-kingdom, too often found he was subjugated himself, imprisoned, then released by the forces of a different foreigner, set up as their puppet and in the end manipulated out of existence. By the beginning of the nineteenth century, of all those principalities that had been carved out of the territory administered by Mir Ali's eldest grandson, only one remained, and this was the tiny state of Mirat whose ruler, also a Kasim, had by wit and good fortune failed to arouse the acquisitive instincts of the British, had helped them at the right time rather than for the right reasons, secured his jagir and their recognition of his claim to be called Nawab. And since there was now no princely neighbour near enough for the British to look upon the Nawab of Mirat as a threat to their own peaceful mercantile and administrative pursuits he was allowed to continue, to blossom as it were like a small and insignificant rose in the desert of dead Moghul ambitions.

All this was in Kasim's face: a face of the kind that could be celebrated in profile on a coin – a forehead sloping to a balding crown, a fleshy but handsomely proportioned nose which stood on guard with an equally fleshy but handsome chin over a mouth whose lips were by no means thin, but were firm-set, determined, not unsensual. Full-face there was a broadness of cheek and jowl and neck, suggestive of a thyroid condition. The black hair that fringed his temples and the back of his head was flecked with grey. These, the thickness and the baldness, conveyed a different idea of Kasim; of a Kasim bearing the marks not of proconsular dignity and autocratic power but instead the marks of centuries of experience of duller but not unworthy occupations. This was a middle-class Kasim, a Kasim – as indeed Mohammed Ali was – of the branch that traced its connection to Mir Ali through the younger son of that Turkish warrior and his Hindu bride, and this was a branch that had rooted itself more modestly but more deeply in the adopted country. It boasted no viceroy, no Nawab, no captain of armies. It had prospered in other ways, in trade and in the professions. It might be called the Ranpur branch, and it had provided India with merchants, imams, scholars, lawyers, officials, philosophers, mathematicians, doctors, and a poet – Gaffur Mohammed whose verses Major Tippit admired. It had provided her more recently with a member of the provincial Governor's council, Mohammed Ali Kasim's father whose portrait an arresting officer took a moment off from duty to study, and with the first chief minister of the province, Mohammed Ali himself, a man in whom perhaps could be detected yet another inheritance, Akbar's old dream of a united sub-continent. For this he had come to prison. For this he had incurred the displeasure of Mr Jinnah whose name was also Mohammed Ali, who now had visions of a separate Muslim state but whose forbears were converts from Hinduism and had not come from Turkey.

One month after his incarceration in the Fort at Premanagar Mohammed Ali Kasim (known to the newspapers usually as M.A.K. and to free and easy English as Mac) sought and obtained Major Tippit's permission to make a little garden in front of the zenana house. He also wrote his first letter to the Governor.

*

It took a little while (he wrote) for newspapers and letters to reach me, but presently I was inundated. Having caught up in quite a short while (since there was little else to occupy me) with the events (as reported) that followed the news of the nation-wide arrests, my immediate desire was to address you on the matter, because the newspapers invariably sought to establish that the rioting and disturbance only just now coming to an end were planned by Congress and indeed led by Congress in the shape of mysterious underground leaders people such as myself are thought to have chosen and briefed to carry out the job if we were arrested and couldn't carry it out ourselves. I recalled what I said during our interview about mobs that rouse themselves and, needing leaders, encourage the emergence of all kinds of undesirable elements. By and large I should say this is exactly what happened, although some of the incidents (in Dibrapur for example) show evidence of forethought. Those undesirable elements I mentioned do not of course come into existence overnight, but they are not underground elements of Congress. Neither can they be Communist-inspired, because the Indian Communists have become pro-war minded ever since Hitler invaded Russia, and would hardly do anything to disrupt the war effort against Fascism. They are inspired surely only by themselves, and are a danger to all of us.

There seems to be a general belief, however, that Congress had the wind taken out of its sails by the sudden arrest of so many of its leaders. The point is made that Mr Gandhi probably expected the Quit India resolution as it is now called to lead not to prison but to serious talks with the Viceroy. I am in agreement. (My own act of packing my bags directly I heard the resolution had been endorsed was the result of purely personal logic, and I confess I hoped it was an act I would look back on with that affectionate self-mockery we reserve for those of our fears which subsequent events show to have been groundless.) What I cannot see is how the two views can be reconciled. If the arrests came as a surprise (as I'm sure they did to most of us) surely the men who were arrested and surprised were not men who had planned for rebellion in their absence? Gandhi, you know, never said *how* the country was to be organized to withdraw from the war effort. As you know he has never been much of a chap for detail, and even those closest to him have often been puzzled to know exactly what it is he has in mind. People on your side who don't like him accuse him of deviousness and of course the general impression now is that his latest and most devious scheme has backfired. You yourself used the word blackmail, and the British in general have met the recent threats to their security in precisely the frame of mind of chosen victims of blackmail who refuse to be victimized. I hope that on reconsideration you will reject, if you haven't already done so, the blackmail theory. It's a theory that works two ways in any case. We could accuse the British of trying to blackmail us into putting everything into the war effort with false promises of independence when the war is won. You would answer that by saying they are not false, although you cannot prove that to us, and Churchill has made it clear that the rights and freedoms embodied in the Atlantic Charter do not apply to India so far as he is concerned. We, for our part, would answer your charge of blackmail by pointing out that the war is irrelevant to the situation because we are demanding nothing that we have not been demanding for years. The war perhaps has made us demand it with greater insistence and has strengthened your hand in not granting it yet, but it has not changed the nature of the demand, nor the nature of the resistance. It has merely added a different emotional factor and a new set of practical considerations; and on these our natures and our views widen our differences. What I hope you will be in agreement with me over is my belief that had we been allowed to continue at liberty the violent events of the past few weeks simply would not have occurred. You would have been faced with the far more onerous task of seeking a way round the deadlock created by a coordinated, peaceful, passive end to the co-operation of the Indian people in the war effort. This would have been the type of 'sabotage' Congress leaders, and Congress leaders only, could have directed. Perhaps it is Machiavellian of *me* to glimpse in Government's prompt arrests of leaders a Machiavellian intention: the intention of turning the onerous task into the simpler one of strong-arm tactics. It is easier to fire on rioters led by undesirable elements than to force resisting workers back into an arms factory, dockers back to the docks and engine-drivers back to the controls of their locomotives. And Government must have realized that the people of India would be incensed by the wholesale arrests and imprisonment of their leaders: incensed, at a loss, anxious to perform what their leaders wanted them to perform, but prey to anger, fear, and all the passions that lead to violence. I find it not at all difficult to accuse Government of deliberate provocation of the people of India: either that or of holding the insulting belief that the people of India are so spineless and apathetic that the disappearance from their midst of the men who have risen to positions of responsibility to them would at once leave them as malleable and directable as dull and unimportant clay.

That they are neither spineless nor apathetic has been proved all too well. I have read the accounts of the riots, burnings, lootings, acts of sabotage, acts of murder, the accounts of crowds of men, women and children attempting to oppose unarmed the will and strength of Government, and accounts of the firing upon these crowds by the police and the military, of deaths on both sides, of attempts to seize jails, derail trains, blow bridges, seize installations; accounts of what amounts to a full-scale but spontaneous insurrection – but with what a sad difference – for most of it has been conducted with the bare hands or with what the bare hands could pick up. There are Indians, I do not doubt, especially among those of us in prison (and our numbers have been considerably swelled since the morning of August 9th) who are proud of what the nation attempted. I cannot be one of them, for my chief reactions are anger and sorrow, and an emotion that I can't easily describe but which is probably due to a special sense of impotence, of powerlessness to do anything that will help to alter things in any way.

The reactions of sorrow and anger are by no means partisan. I feel them for and on behalf of people quite unknown to me, the young men for instance who are out here as soldiers, young Englishmen who as we all know have absolutely no idea about India except that it is a long way from home and full of strange, dark-skinned people. In many case soldiers like this have found themselves acting as you call it in aid of the civil power. Their principal feeling must have been one of bewilderment that changed swiftly to deep and burning resentment, because all they would under-stand was that the country they have come all this way to defend apparently didn't want them and was bent on getting rid of them. There was the terrible affair of the two Canadian Air Force officers who were literally torn to pieces by people from a village that had been bombed and who thought these men had flown the aeroplanes in question. Even if they were, the situation as I see and feel it is not changed. It is one that involves us all, as does the bombing, the entire scene and history of this lamentable business. In our own province I have been especially distressed by the two incidents involving English women, the attack on the Mission School Superintendent near Tanpur, and the rape of Miss Manners in the Bibighar Gardens in Mayapore. In this latter case I do indeed feel a personal involvement over and above any other. I knew, of course, Miss Manners's uncle, Sir Henry Manners, from the time in the early thirties when he governed the province and I sat by his invitation on several of the committees he set up in an attempt to break down some of the barriers between Government and people.

Manners was a Governor of great skill – tolerant, sympathetic, admir-able in every way. His term of office in Government House was one of hope for us, a bright spot on a rather gloomy horizon. What enemies he made were reactionary English and extremist Indians. Perhaps without the opportunity he gave me, to make whatever mark I did make on those committees, my own party would not have given me the greater opportunity that led to office. You will understand then the weight of my personal distress at the news of the criminal assault on the niece of a man like that. It is an incident that seems all too understandably to have added fuel to the fires of violence in Mayapore, and perhaps in the rest of the province. The first reports I read, which did not disclose Miss Manners's name – referring to her merely as a young Englishwoman, victim of sexual assault by six Indian youths who had all been promptly arrested – struck me possibly as exaggerations because the reports were hysterical in pitch, and of course I hoped that they were not true. But it seems they were, at least in regard to the fact that the girl *was* attacked, and criminally used; and the eventual disclosure of her name and her connection with the late Sir Henry Manners came as a considerable personal shock.

I have since, however, become puzzled and vaguely disturbed by what I can gather of the consequences of this affair, and the piece in the *Statesman* yesterday, referring to the rape of Miss Manners (although mercifully omitting her name again – a first step towards some sort of privacy for the poor creature) does bear out my own feelings that some quite extraordinary veil has been drawn over the whole unfortunate business, but a veil that does not satisfy the lawyer in me. I had been reading the papers daily in expectation of further news about the six men who according to the early reports were arrested. Now, according to the *Statesman*, it seems that these six men were not charged with rape. The *Statesman* refers to a very brief paragraph in the *Mayapore Gazette* of one week ago which gave the names of two or three men recently imprisoned under the Defence of India rules, without trial of course. According to the *Statesman*, these men were among the six originally arrested as suspects in the rape. Again, according to the *Statesman*, which has been ferreting about, *all* six have been imprisoned under the rule. Quite justifiably, the *Statesman* asks whether the original reports that 'the suspected culprits have been arrested, thanks to the prompt action of the local police under their District Superintendent, were the result of wishful thinking or confusion on the part of the reporter, or whether subsequent investigation showed them to be innocent. If they were innocent, then as the *Statesman* again properly asks, is it not curious that six men suspected of rape should all turn out to be men whose political activities earned them imprisonment as detenus? Clearly now, there is unlikely to be any arrest or trial in connection with the rape itself and one must assume the real culprits have gone free. The question raised by the *Statesman* comes to this: Have six men been arrested for rape, found to be innocent either because they are or for lack of evidence that would hold up in a court of law, but have been put away under this convenient act because someone still believes them to be guilty, or is determined to punish them for some reason or other? I doubt that anyone will provide the answer the *Statesman* seeks and presently – although the affair itself will be a long time fading from memory – the legal aspects will quickly be forgotten; as will the curious side issues that stay in my own mind from my reading of the reports and collection of casual data: for instance the apparent fact that one of the arrested men, a man called Kumar, was a friend of Miss Manners; and the fact that Miss Manners (if the *Statesman* has interpreted correctly) declined, according to gossip, to give evidence because the men arrested were not the kind she remembered as the type who attacked her.

I imagine that the details of this distressing affair – which has exacerbated racial feeling throughout the country – have had something of your personal attention, more particularly in view of the victim's family connections in India. I presume she is the daughter of a brother of Henry Manners. One of the reports gave her address in Mayapore as The MacGregor House, which I remember as the home of Sir Nello and Lady Chatterjee who were friends of Sir Henry and Lady Manners. I take it Miss Manners was staying with Lady Chatterjee but that otherwise she normally lives with her aunt whom I knew fairly well and who, I believe, still lives in Rawalpindi. I have written a brief letter to Lady Manners, which I enclose. I should be most grateful if you would forward it. I have left it unsealed so that you can quickly assure yourself that I have written nothing to her apart from words of sympathy and regret for the terrible thing that happened to her niece. I cannot, I realize, expect any particular comment from you on the points I have raised in this letter. I offer them as someone whose enforced position as a mere spectator has in no way diminished his sense of involvement, curiosity, and concern with justice.

*

'His Excellency thanks you for your letter' (one of Sir George's secretaries wrote a month later), 'and wishes me also to convey to you Lady Manners's thanks for your personal message which his Excellency communicated to her.'

Kasim looked up, Lieutenant Moran Singh who had brought the letter over to the zenana house still stood in the doorway, smiling.

'Such influential people you are knowing,' Moran Singh said. 'Letters from Government House and such-like.' He turned and went out. Presently Kasim heard him shouting at one of the sentries. Moran Singh had relatives in Ranpur. He had offered to convey private messages to Mrs Kasim through those relatives, for a consideration. He took bribes, he sold Government stores. He had said to Kasim, 'Major Tippit is mad,' and had hinted that – again for a consideration – he could persuade Tippit to allow Kasim to be visited regularly by selected fellow-prisoners. Moran Singh represented everything in India that Kasim loathed. He had declined these offers.

Kasim wrote in his journal: 'A reply from Government House, which makes it clear that the Governor's request that I write to him occasionally wasn't really the friendly gesture I believed it to be. It is apparently to be a one-sided correspondence. He wanted me to commit my thoughts to paper but won't commit his own. He wants to keep track of me. I am a specimen under observation. They must be his orders that keep me isolated from other prisoners. He thinks isolation will give me time and opportunity to re-assess my position. Underneath that liberal man to man exterior is the indomitable public servant. Perhaps he is waiting for me to crack under the strain. I could be out of Premanagar by Christmas if I wrote to him and said

I'd changed my mind and was willing to resign from Congress and accept nomination to his executive council. And God knows I might do useful work. But I must not be hard on him. They are only spiritual hardships I suffer here, and his policy in regard to me is dictated by good intentions and the determination to do everything he can to govern the province successfully and ease the condition of the people. The Governor buries himself neither in past nor future but in the present. It is an English trait. They will only see that there is no future for them in India when India no longer fits into the picture they have of themselves and of their current obligations. When that time comes they won't particularly care what happens to us. Sooner or later the Governor will find that I don't fit in to whatever picture he has of the current problems of this province. Perhaps I am already beginning to fade out of it. He would have written, I expect, if he had seen an immediate way in which I could be useful to him. One can't help admiring this barefaced attitude. We might learn something from it. There is too much emotion in our own public life. The English could never be accused of that. They lock us up, release us and lock us up again according to what suits them at the time, with a bland detachment that, fortunately or unfortunately, is matched by an equally bland acceptance on our part. They act collectively, and so can afford detachment. We react individually, which weakens us. We haven't yet acquired the collective instinct. The English send Kasim to prison. But it is Kasim who goes to prison. The prisoner in the zenana house is a man. But who is his jailer? The jailer is an idea. But in the prisoner the idea is embodied in a man. From his solitude the man reaches out to others. He writes to Sir George Malcolm. He writes to old Lady Manners. But he cannot reach them as people. They are protected from him by the collective instinct of their race. A reply comes, but it is not from them. It is from someone speaking for them. It has not been expedient for either of them to write. I understand in both cases why this should be. But to understand does not warm the heart.'

*

Several months later, the May of the following year, the prisoner in the zenana house saw two notices in the same issue of the *Times of India*. Under Births there was this entry: *Manners. On May 7th, at Srinagar. To Daphne, a daughter, Parvati.* And under Deaths, this: *Manners. On May 7th, at Srinagar; Daphne, daughter of the late Mr & Mrs George Manners, beloved niece of Ethel and the late Sir Henry Manners.*

There were times, Mr Kasim told himself, when he thought he would never understand the English. What curious brand of arrogance and insensitivity could lead an old lady to announce to the world the birth of an obviously half-caste child to the unmarried niece who, nine months before, had been raped by Indians in the Bibighar Gardens? 'It is as if,' he wrote in his journal, 'old Lady Manners were flinging an accusation into our faces, to make sure we know that this is an incident that cannot be forgotten and is one we have a continuing responsibility for. I do not remember her as the sort of woman who would make this kind of gesture; but of course the girl has died, presumably in childbirth. I suppose she is telling us that she will never forgive us for what a handful of our men did on that particular night. Or do these announcements mean that she has forgiven us now and taken the child, so tragically and violently conceived, to her heart, for India's sake? One cannot tell. The English have a saying, "He wears his heart on his sleeve," but this is something they never reveal except very occasionally to each other.'

Part Two

A HISTORY

I

'So it was with Henry, and so now with poor Daphne,' Lady Manners murmured. And handed her niece's diary to Suleiman to lock up in the black tin box as he had locked up some of her husband's private papers, years before, with an air of reverence or anyway forbearance; but he took Daphne's book as if it were nothing special, put it in the box – whose lid was open – and stood, waiting, not catching her eye, still wearing the old astrakhan cap he had complained of months before in 'Pindi and had had money off her to renew.

Well, he is jealous, she thought, and still resents being sent for, travelling alone and uncomfortably on the bus all that way from Pindi to Srinagar, just to order the household for the journey back in the same direction, a beast-of-burden who has no burden worthy of the years, the centuries, the everlastingness of his service. He is an old man. His hair has gone grey, like mine. Why has he never grown a beard? If he grows a beard I must watch for signs of it and be prepared for the morning he will come to me and say, Memsahib, let me go, I am an old man. Before I die I must see Mecca, and having seen it dye my beard red, come back and live out my remaining years in peace and honourable retirement with the blessing of Allah the Merciful.

So, too, I would go, but not to Mecca. Where then? And how? I do not know how or where. Nor who has mercy to spare.

And she looked out of the window on to the placid waters of the lake, and heard the crying of the child. She made a gesture and said a word, both meaning the same thing. *Khatam*. Finished. Suleiman closed the lid of the box, turned the key and handed it to her. His old brown fingers were still supple from a lifetime of manipulative care of her property, and Henry's property, which were his gods, his ikons, but to care for Daphne's was nothing to him. It was all gone. But what? Well it has gone, she thought, whatever it was. And took the key from him, and put it in her handbag, aware of the finality of the gesture without understanding why she should think of it as final. You were handsome once, she told Suleiman without speaking. You had one wife we knew about and two concubines you pretended were your wife's sisters. And were a rogue and a rake, and had children, God knows how many, by whom, nor where scattered. Now you are alone and I am alone, and we cannot speak of it even yet as a man and a woman might speak who share recollections. But if you were to die I should weep. And if I were to die you would cover your head and speak to no one for days. But here in the world where both of us live – poised between entrance and exit, or exit and entrance – we will maintain the relationship of mistress and servant, although we have grown far beyond it and use it simply as a shorthand to get through the day without trouble to one another.

Suleiman took hold of the box and carried it through into the passage that ran along the side of the houseboat – the side adjacent to the bank of the island to which the boat was moored – from her bedroom, with its single bed, past the empty guest bedroom with its two beds, and into the dining-room, up the two steps into the living-room beyond which was the veranda with its view on to the water and the opposite bank where the tongas waited, ready to transport the passengers from the shikaras to the square where the buses and motor-cars halted.

In the water immediately below the verandah there was a cluster of shikaras – one for the luggage, one for the passengers, and upwards of half a dozen laden with Kashmiri art: woodwork, shawls, carpets, flowers; and even a fortune teller – although it was only 7.30 in the September morning, and the mist through which a future might be seen to have substance had not yet cleared. But in the last half-hour before a departure there was always the possibility of a sale. From her room, Lady Manners heard the cries of the vendors offering inducements, bribes, to persuade Suleiman to go back in and bring her out to be tempted.

And today, she thought, I am going to be tempted. And followed Suleiman through to the veranda where he was standing, a thin, frail, stoop-shouldered man, in a moth-eaten fez and floppy pyjamas, with Henry's old Harris tweed jacket hanging on him to keep out the early morning September chill, showing his shirt-tail, blue against the baggy white trousers: and holding the box to his breast, like a reliquary, saying nothing, but watching the opposite shore, standing on guard over the piled luggage. Aware she had come, he spoke to the khansamar, ordered him to have the luggage stowed, and the khansamar beckoned to the man below who came scrambling. The vendors, seeing that departure was imminent, set up a new cry, making their appeal directly to her, holding up whatever it was they most wished her to be tempted by. She beckoned to the man who had sold her a shawl three years before, and had ever since been hopeful. She beckoned to him because of this, not because his shikara was closest (although it was, having been paddled into position early). He clambered, laden, across her own empty shikara and the luggage shikara, elbowing the men who were dealing with the luggage, reached the houseboat verandah and laid his bundle down, salaamed, untied the knot, opened and released a cascade of fine woven wool, with gold, silver and coloured embroidery. The khansamar had brought out a chair. She sat on it and watched the man – his skull-cap, and his touchingly dishonest eyes whenever he looked up to emphasize the truth of the lies he was telling her.

But Suleiman (she thought) stands detached from this foolery. Well, there was a time when he protected me from rogues, for he was our rogue, our beloved rogue, who never cheated us but knew rogues, being brought up with them; and their ways, being brought up in them; and saw lesser rogues off, and equal rogues, and bigger rogues. He taught me all I know about the ways of the bazaars and what he taught me is all that he knows too. He stands, holding the reliquary, and lets me get on with it as if I were a pupil old enough to know better, too old to be corrected. And does not look, but listens to the crying of the child.

And I choose this one, to warm my shoulders on a frosty night, for I am of an age that can grace a faint vulgarity, am I not? So much silver-thread, and too much scarlet silk. Shall I ever wear it? Perhaps that is doubtful. Or even this one? The green is a bit bilious, after such an early breakfast. Well, any of them? Am I too old, then, for this kind of gesture? For whose sake am I making it? My own? Henry's? Suleiman's? Daphne's? Or for Kashmir's because after all these years of arriving and departing I feel it in my bones that I am going this time never to return? Or is it an insurance? To buy believing it the last, to ensure that it is not? Perhaps I buy for the child, for Parvati, whose crying Suleiman listens to and will not speak of. Has Suleiman yet looked at the child?

She chose a shawl that could have offended no one. But when she had paid for it and gone back inside after repeating the word and the gesture: Khatam: she regretted buying something that would give her neither pleasure nor pain, and wondered at the marvel of losing an opportunity to make a gesture others and she herself could have described later as out of character. In the end, she saw, habit became a vice, and good taste an end in itself: nothing could ever come of it.

Fifteen minutes later the khansamar knocked at the door of her room where she sat alone staring through the little window at the lake, her old-fashioned veiled topee already on her head, gloves on her hands, repeating to herself, with no outward sign that she was doing so, the little prayer she always offered up at the beginning of a journey. The khansamar told her that all was ready. She rose, thanked him for his service, and went out. She had distributed tips the night before. The staff of the houseboat, and of the house she had lived in from the November of 1942 all through the hard winter to June when she had come down to the lake, were gathered on the forward veranda and on the sunroof. Fifteen of them all told: twelve from the boat, and three from the house. She stood for a moment. They watched her in silence. Then she said, 'Thank you,' and allowed the khansamar to help her down the steps into the shikara which had an embroidered canopy and a spring mattress – the kind of shikara Henry once said made him feel when with her like Anthony making himself at home with Cleopatra on her barge. At the foot of the mattress, the young ayah already sat, veiled for the journey from the valley she had never left before, nursing the child.

When Lady Manners was settled Suleiman stepped aboard and sat in the narrow prow, still holding the reliquary. Behind her the three boatmen raised their pointed, elongated, heart-shaped paddles and began to negotiate a passage between the clustered boats of the vendors. She turned to wave, but the outline of the houseboat had become infuriatingly unclear. She realized, too, that she had forgotten to look at the flowers in the vase by her bedside, to make sure they were quite dead; and thinking of those flowers thought as well of Daphne's rhetorical question, written down while the snows still held, when the summer that had somehow never been was yet to come:

'Shall we go down to the lake, then, Aunty, and live in a house-boat and fill it with flowers, and have our fortunes told?'

*

I am leaving in two days' time (she had written to her old friend Lili Chatterjee in Mayapore), and so ends, as they say, a chapter – the burden of which you know and have lightened, not only by your too short visit this summer but by your wise counsel, and by the opinion you were able to express, after seeing the child. When I am re-established in Pindi, at Christmas-time for instance, perhaps you would come up and pay me a visit? I do not expect to be much invited out. My own race hardly knows any longer what to make of me and the existence of the child under my roof no doubt ranks as something of a scandal, such a lively, vocal repository for memories of events my countrymen are pretending it is best to forget – or if not best to forget at least wise to consider over and adequately dealt with. I don't make my appeal to you, or invitation, from any sense the last few months may have given me of isolation, but from that other more important sense of contact with a friend who speaks my language and with whom, over Christmas, I should so dearly love to exchange gifts of conversation, plans and recollections.

Today we are moving the houseboat down the lake from the isolated position you thought so pretty to its winter berth, to shorten the distance for the luggage shikaras the day after tomorrow. Since you were here I acquired neighbours. They are now gone back to Pankot where they are stationed. Their boat has been moved away and this last few days I have been alone again, which on the whole I prefer. These people who came and moored near by were punctilious about sending cards across when they arrived. I had Aziz return the compliment. Result: an almost tangible air of embarrassment and curiosity emanating from their boat; cautious nods if we happened to cross one another's bows when out in the shikaras. But no visit, except towards the end of their stay, and that by one of them alone, one of the two daughters, when the rest of them were out enjoying themselves one afternoon. She saw me reading on the sun-deck as she went past alone in their shikara, and waved, then had the boatmen come in close and asked whether she could come on board for a few moments. I couldn't very well refuse, although I thought it a bit offhand after the days that had gone by without a word exchanged. She came straight to the point and said it was embarrassment really that had kept them away, not knowing what on earth they'd be able to say to me that wouldn't make it obvious they were all avoiding any mention of poor Daphne ('the awful business of your niece' she called it). But they were going back to their station soon and she said she didn't like the idea of leaving without speaking to me. I thought it a rather thin excuse but not an uncourageous thing to do. She said she often heard the baby crying and would very much like to see her. So I took her down into the cabin where little Parvati has her cot. The girl – her name is Sarah Layton – looked at her for quite a long time without saying anything. Parvati was asleep and the ayah was adopting her possessive, on guard attitude, which probably added to the girl's uneasiness. I think she'd expected the baby to have the kind of pale skin that makes the mixture of blood difficult to detect unless you're looking for it. Eventually she said, 'She's so tiny,' as if she had never seen a four-month-old baby before, then thanked me for letting her see her. I invited her to stay and have some tea under the awning on the sun-deck. She only hesitated for a moment. On our way out she caught sight of the trunks with Daphne's name on them and hesitated again. She puzzled me. Nice young English girls in India don't usually give an impression of bothering their heads with anything much apart from the question of which men in the immediate vicinity are taking the most notice of them. Of course, they do go broody every now and again, but Miss Layton's broodiness struck me as odd and intricate, not at all the result of simple self-absorption.

The name Layton had vaguely rung my bell at the time of the exchange of visiting cards and directly she mentioned Ranpur and Pankot I remembered it as a name quite well known there but couldn't recall ever having met one of them. Henry and I were there for the five years of his appointment as Governor but one's social life was fairly crowded. Over tea she told me that she and her sister and mother were sharing the houseboat with an aunt and an uncle. Her father, Colonel Layton, is a prisoner of war in Germany. He commanded the 1st Pankot Rifles in North Africa. He was in prison camp in Italy for a time but as we've advanced from the south a lot of the prisoners have been moved back, so our recent successes there haven't brought Colonel Layton's release and return any nearer. The revelation that her father was a prisoner of war went some way to explain her sudden visit and attempt at apology. In her father's absence she was probably trying to do what was right and thought that coming to see me made up for the rudeness of the rest of the family. They may have believed that story themselves about not wanting to intrude on my privacy, but of course underneath this apparent delicacy of feeling is the deep disapproval I meet everywhere now and am used to. Perhaps dismay is more accurate a description, dismay that I should have stood by and let Daphne bear a child whose father might be any one of half a dozen ruffians, dismay that instead

413

of bundling it off as unwanted to some orphanage when Daphne died bearing it, I take care of it, and have given it that name, Parvati Manners.

I asked Miss Layton whether she was enjoying her holiday. She said it was the first real one they'd had since the war began. Both girls have joined the WAC(I) and work in Area Headquarters at Pankot. They decided to come to Srinagar this year because the sister – the younger of the two – is to be married soon. I'd seen the usual crowd of young men visiting their houseboat so naturally I asked if the sister's fiancé was also in Srinagar. Apparently not. The engagement took place when he was stationed in Pankot, and originally the wedding was to have been there, towards Christmas of this year. But he was suddenly posted to Mirat and has written to say that the wedding must be brought forward and has to be in Mirat, the sooner the better, and the honeymoon can't be for longer than two or three days. Which means, of course, that he expects to be going back into the field (he was in one of the regiments whose remnants managed to get out of Burma in 1942). So the young bride will be a grass window almost directly she's married. This is why the Laytons have gone back to Pankot earlier than they planned. They'll be off to Mirat soon after they arrive and it seems they hope to stay in the palace guest house so the younger Layton girl is very excited. I told Sarah Layton she'd like Mirat, especially if they stayed there as guests of the Nawab, who entertained Henry and me when we were on tour in that area. Lending the guest house to service people who can't get accommodation in the cantonment is probably part of the Nawab's war effort. He must be getting on a bit, now, and so must his wazir, that extraordinary Russian *émigré* Count, Bronowsky, or whatever his name was, whom the Nawab brought back from Monte Carlo in the twenties, at the time of the scandal over the Nawab's relationship with a European woman. I told Miss Layton to look out for Bronowsky, and how all the English used to hate him until they realized what a good influence he was on the Nawab. She asked whether I had any idea what they ought to take as a present, if the Nawab let them stay in the guest house. Apparently they've been arguing and discussing it for days. I told her the Nawab was distantly related to ex-chief minister M. A. Kasim, and that the famous classic Urdu poet Gaffur was an eighteenth-century connection of both; and suggested that the most flattering gift might be a specially bound copy of Gaffur's poems. She was very pleased by the suggestion and said she'd tell her mother and aunt and try to get hold of a copy. I told her she could buy one in Srinagar and might even get it bound here, in a few days. Alternatively that there used to be a shop in Ranpur, in the bazaar, which did excellent leatherwork and gold-leaf blocking.

After we'd finished talking about the book she looked at me with the most extraordinary expression of envy that I've ever seen in a girl so young. She said, 'What a lot you know.' I laughed and said it was one of the few advantages of old age, to be a repository of bits and pieces of casual information that sometimes come in useful. But she said she didn't really mean that, she meant know as distinct from remember. She couldn't properly explain it and got up and said she mustn't take up any more of my time. I told her to come again, and she said she would if there were an opportunity. I took it she meant there probably wouldn't be and as it turned out I never saw her again, except to wave to. I didn't see their departure but after they'd gone one of the boys who'd been on their cookboat brought round a little bunch of flowers with a card 'With best wishes and many thanks from Sarah Layton'.

I have been thinking over what she said about knowing as distinct from remembering. Perhaps all it amounts to is that as we talked and I trotted out these little bits of information I gave the impression, common in elderly people, not only of having a long full life behind me that I could dip into more or less at random for the benefit of a younger listener, but also of being undisturbed by any doubts about the meaning and value of that life and the opinions I'd formed while leading it; although that suggests knowingness, and when she said, 'What a lot you know' she made it sound like a state of grace, one that she envied me in the mistaken belief that I was in it, while she was not and didn't understand how, things being as she finds them, one ever achieved it. It would be interesting to meet the rest of the family, who from their general appearance and conduct I would describe as typically army if I hadn't learned that people are never typical. But what I mean is that one could probably plot a graph of typical experience, attitude, behaviour and expectations of an army family in India and find it a rough but not inaccurate guide to that girl's background and the surrounding circumstances of her daily life. I was touched by the flowers – and by the fact that they have not lasted and will be dead by the time I leave and go down to Pindi.

*

Picture her then, an old lady dressed in a fawn tweed jacket and skirt, a high collar to a cream silk blouse that is buttoned with mother-of-pearl. No longer agile she scarcely welcomes the luxury of the embroidered mattress in the shikara which she finds it difficult to get down to and stretch out on; difficult but not yet impossible for someone trained to the custom of not inviting sympathy, or causing amusement, with evidence of weakness or infirmity; so that now, reclining safely, propped against the back rest, her topee-covered head turned at an angle of dignified farewell, one hand raised and the other seeking and finding some kind of old woman's reassurance from the pleats and buttons just below her throat, there is an air about her of faded Edwardian elegance, Victorian even, for Victorian women were great travellers when they bothered to travel at all; and the early morning mist swathed in the mountains and above the lake, the movement of the boat, the pointed paddles dipping and sweeping, the totem figure of Suleiman, the huddled permissive attitude of the Kashmiri girl nursing the child, all combine to make, as it were, a perpetual willow-pattern of the transient English experience of outlandish cultures.

415

If English people in India could be said to live in (in the sense of belonging to) any particular town, the Laytons lived in Ranpur and Pankot. Ranpur was the permament cool weather station of Colonel Layton's regiment, the 1st Pankot Rifles. Their hot weather station was in the hills of Pankot itself, a place to which the provincial government also moved during the summer. It was from the hills and valleys around Pankot that the regiment recruited its men: sturdy agriculturalists who had a martial tradition going back (it was said) to pre-Moghul times. Somewhere round about the sixteenth century the hill people turned their backs on the old hill gods, embraced Islam and intermarried with their country's Moghul conquerors. So far as the British were concerned they ranked as Muslims, although it might have been more accurate to describe them as polytheists. In the hill villages images of old local Hindu gods were still to be found. To these the women liked to make offerings – at sowing and harvest-times, when they were in love, when they were pregnant, after the birth of a son or the death of a husband. The men held aloof from such things, unless they were going a journey, when they made sure that a female relation left a bowl of curds and a chaplet of flowers at the local wayside shrine the day before.

The only mosque in the entire hill area was in Pankot itself. Many of the boys who made the trek from their village to Pankot to offer themselves as soldiers at the recruiting depot were unable to distinguish between the mosque, the Kali temple, and the Protestant and Catholic churches. They knew the names of Allah, and of their tribal gods, they accepted that Allah was all-knowing, all-seeing and all-merciful, more powerful than the gods of the hills; so powerful in fact that it was better not to involve him in everyday matters. When you died you would go to his abode. While you lived here on earth it was necessary to be honest, industrious and vigorous. If you lived a good life, did not drink or smoke, practised good husbandry, took wives, procreated, did not cheat or steal, kept your roof repaired, your family fed, then you would please Allah. To live such a life, however, it was necessary to please authority as well – to pay your taxes, to offer gifts of money to minor officials and of loyalty to senior ones, to propitiate the gods of the hills who, being less powerful than Allah, had both the time and the inclination to make things difficult for mortal man by withholding rain, sending too much, making the earth sour, turning male children into female children in your wife's womb, poisoning your blood with sickness, filling the air with bad vapours. Since Allah was all-knowing obviously he understood this. To feed and flatter the hill gods was something you did to help in the business of making your life pleasant for Allah to look upon. All the same such things were best left to the women, because women did not really understand about Allah: they did not need to. For a man it was different; Allah was a man: the perfect husbandman, the supreme warrior. He blessed ears of corn and strengthened your sword-arm. To die in battle, fighting his enemies, was the one sure way of going to Heaven. There were people living on the plains below the hills, and even in Pankot, who did not understand about Allah either. Such ignorance meant that their men were not much better than women. The white man, however, understood about Allah. In Pankot there were white men's mosques. There was also Recruiting Officer Sahib's *Daftar*, where a boy could go to become a sipahi, a soldier. The white man's enemies were also Allah's enemies. The white man called Allah God-Father, but he was the same Allah. They called the prophet Jesuschrist, not Mohammed; but then did not the same sky cover the whole world? In Pankot did it not cover the mosque, the Hindi temple, the two churches, the Governor's summer residence, Flagstaff House and Recruiting Officer Sahib's *Daftar*? To the boys coming in from the Pankot hills these places were all seats of mystery and authority. And of them all Recruiting Officer *Daftar* was the one they recognized as the most important in practical as well as mystical terms.

Not one of them made the journey from his hill or his valley to Pankot who was not forewarned of and rehearsed in the incalculable mysteries of the *Daftar* by an older male relation. To make the journey to the *Daftar* was the first test of manhood. To be rejected was thought by some to be a shame a boy could never recover from. In Pankot bazaar there were men – it was said – who begged or starved because they had been rejected and were afraid to go home. To be accepted was imperative if – having chanced one's arm – one were ever again to look another man in the eye. And so they came, year after year, with stern faces (that in a moment could crack into a grin, because the Pankot people were of a happy disposition), blanket over shoulder, bare-foot, each – inevitably – wearing or bearing some token of an earlier family connection with the Pankot Rifles – a pair of carefully mended khaki shorts, a row of medals, a chit from an uncle who had risen to the rank of Havildar or Jemadar and who begged the favour of offering his nephew in the service of the King-Emperor (whom they confused, vaguely, with the great Moghul and Allah) and gave, as reference, the name of an Englishman who more likely than not turned out to be retired, or dead, although not forgotten. The *Daftar* had a long memory.

*

The main recruiting season extended from the beginning of April until the end of September and coincided with the civil and military retreat from the plains to the hills which – in the old days – brought to Pankot not only the Governor, his administrators, their clerks and their files from Ranpur but detachments of the Pankot Rifles and the Ranpur Regiment from Ranpur.

From April to September Pankot lived a full social life. One met the same people as in Ranpur but in different, more delightful surroundings. Receptions at the Governor's summer residence (built in the Swiss Gothic style, with a preponderance of wood, instead of as in Ranpur in stone and stucco in Anglo-Indian palladian with a preponderance of colonnaded

417

veranda) were less magnificent but no less formal. The important clubs had Pankot duplicates (wood again, instead of stone) and there was the Pankot Club itself which subalterns and junior civilians preferred because there you met all the girls recently out from home who might turn out good for a lark.

Pankot was a place to let off steam in. It was thoroughly English. The air was crisp, the trees coniferous. India, real India, lay below. To the north – defining the meeting point of heaven and earth, distantly, was the impressive jagged line of the Himalaya (usually invisible behind cloud, but occasionally revealed, like the word of God). Summer in Pankot was hotter than summer in England, but the mornings and the nights were cool and the rains fell with nothing like the fury they fell with in the plains. Winter, during the hours between sun-up and sunset, was like an English spring.

As hill stations went Pankot ranked as one of the second class. It attracted almost no tourists and few leave-takers (who preferred Darjeeling, Naini Tal and Kashmir). There was a rail connection from Ranpur, narrow gauge and single track. The journey took eight hours up and six hours down. There was also a road which was used by the Indian bus and by the military who sent soldiers of the Pankot Rifles and the Ranpur Regiment up and down by lorry. In places road and rail converged, passed under or over one another or marched parallel. The ascent was slow. Embankments gave way to cuttings. Signs of habitation became fewer. The characters of villages changed. There were fewer water-buffalo, more white-humped cattle; many more goats. Rocky out-crops appeared; and then the road began to wind into the foothills, a dusty coil connecting the parched plain to the green-clad heights. Sound was muffled, amplified, thrown back – depending on the formation of hill-face, precipice, re-entry. There was a scent of timber.

Pankot was built upon three hills and their conjoint valley. The railway ended against a rocky face that the road found its way round, through a tunnel of trees, up, over the top and down into the enclosed vale – grassed acres scattered with hutments that bore the unmistakable signs of military occupation. Here, mists gathered in the evening and the early morning. Out of such mists, a mile ahead, emerged the Indo-Tyrolean architecture of the Pankot Bazaar – a V-shaped township of three-storey wooden buildings with fretted overhanging verandas above open-fronted shops where they sold embroidered shawls, beaten silver, filigree wooden boxes inlaid with brass lotus designs. There were Indian coffee shops, fortune-tellers, the local branch of the Imperial Bank of India, a garage, a bicycle shop, the Hindu Hotel, the Muslim Hotel. At the tip of the V the buses halted. Here there were ponies and tongas for hire, even a taxi or two. This was the favourite place of pedlars and itinerant Holy men and small boys in rags and moth-eaten fur caps who competed with each other to shine the visitors' shoes. There was a smell of petrol, horse manure, cattle dung, incense and sandalwood, of spicy food being cooked in the open over charcoal fires. The shop signs were in English and in the vernacular in both the Nagari and the Arabic scripts. Here, too, were the Kali temple and the mosque. In the centre of the square formed by the lower tip of the V, the temple and the mosque, stood a phallic stone monolith, erected in 1925, a memorial to the soldiers of the Pankot Rifles who had given their lives in the Great War. In November it received a wreath of poppies, offerings of ghi, buttermilk and flowers.

The arms of the V mounted quite steeply, reaching up into the hills behind the bazaar. The right-hand fork from War Memorial Square was the less steep, but it led finally to the majestic heights dominated by the Governor's summer residence. The left-hand fork led more abruptly to a lower area where rich Indians and minor princes owned chalet-style houses (a few of which had 'Mahal' in their names, to denote that they were palaces). This was an area the generality of the English had little knowledge of. To them Pankot was properly reached by taking the right-hand fork. Here were the clubs, the administrative quarters, the golf course, the bungalows and houses of seasonal occupation; most of them hidden by pines, marked by roadside posts at drive-entrances. And yet there was no feeling of enclosure. The road, at every turn, gave views. There were English people who said they were reminded of the Surrey hills near Caterham. Upon retirement from the civil or the military some of them came to Pankot – not to die (although they did – and were buried in the churchyard of St John's – C of E – or St Edward's – RC) but to enjoy their remaining years in a place that was peculiarly Indian but very much their own, and where servants were cheap, and English flowers could be grown (sometimes spectacularly) in the gardens, and life take on the serenity of fulfilment, of duty done without the depression of going home wondering what it had been done for.

It was in Pankot that Sarah Layton's childhood memories of India were chiefly centred. She and Susan were born there (in 1921 and 1922 respectively). Their christening was recorded in the parish register of St John's Church (Sarah in March, an Aries, and Susan in November, a Scorpio). The register also recorded the marriage in 1920 of their father John Frederick William Layton (Lieutenant, 1st Pankot Rifles, son of James William Layton, ICS) to their mother Mildred Rose Muir, daughter of Howard Campbell Muir – Lieut.-General (GS). Neither James William Layton nor General Muir was laid to rest in the churchyard of St John, Pankot, but there were headstones there that celebrated both names, those of General Muir's unmarried aunt and James Layton's great-aunt – the former dead of fever, aged nineteen, the latter in childbirth, aged twenty-three.

Sarah and Susan's father, John Layton, was in Pankot for the second time in his life in 1913. He was then nineteen years old, newly returned from Chillingborough and Sandhurst. His choice of a military instead of a civil career was his own but his choice of regiment had been dictated by a sense of family connection. To begin with, Pankot had lain within his civilian father's first district. Layton had no personal recollection of the place. He had spent one summer there with his parents as a child of three, when his father was working at the secretariat in Ranpur and went up to Pankot with the provincial government when it took its annual breather in the hills. Afterwards the Laytons went down to Mayapore where Mr James Layton had been appointed assistant commissioner and joint magistrate. A later appointment still, as acting deputy commissioner took the Laytons down to Dibrapur and when that job was finished young John Layton was eight and due to go home to England to school. His parents, taking their long leave, accompanied him. During school holidays he lived with his paternal grandfather in Surrey. His parents returned to India. Shortly after their return Mr James Layton was appointed Deputy Commissioner for the Pankot District. During his tour of office there he made a name for himself with the people of the hills. He had certain eccentricities which endeared him to them. He used to escape from his office and his staff and his wife and ride ten or twenty miles on his pony between sun-up and sunset to talk to the villagers.

In India, as a child, young John Layton was inclined to be sickly. He inherited his mother's constitution. Even in England his health gave some cause for anxiety. There had been a plan, indeed a promise, that in the long summer holiday of 1907 when he was thirteen he would spend a month in Pankot with his parents. His England-based grandfather advised against it and suggested that instead his parents should take long leave and come to England. Only Mrs Layton was able to make the journey.

Sick before she set out (the ill-effects of life in places like Mayapore and Dibrapur had become too deep-rooted for the healthier climate of Pankot to have made much difference) she was sick when she reached home. She was not the mother young Layton remembered. In later life he found it difficult to recall the conflicting emotions the sight of her actually aroused in him. As he said to his daughter Sarah (in a rare moment of confidence – rare but perhaps not unexpected because Sarah was her father's daughter while Susan was her mother's), 'I suppose I was disappointed. My mother looked old in the wrong sort of way. Well, I mean like someone on the stage made up for it. When she died it was like part of an act. I felt my real mother was still in Pankot, thousands of miles away, and this one was a feeble impostor – so when father married again and came back to England with his new wife Mabel in 1909 she was more real to me than my own mother had been. Why am I telling you this?'

*

Sarah's paternal grandmother, the first Mrs Layton, died in England of double pneumonia in 1907 after a bout of malarial fever six weeks after returning home to visit her son. Young Layton was then back at school, in his first term at Chillingborough. He went home to Surrey for the funeral and wrote a letter to his father in India saying he was sorry, and describing –

with his grandfather's help – the headstone that was going to be erected on his mother's grave.

His father's second wife was the widow of a major of the 1st Pankot Rifles who had died heroically on the North-West Frontier. Young Layton met her in the summer of 1909 when his father brought her home on long leave. He liked her. In a curious way she reminded him of his real mother – the one he'd had a picture of. She treated him as if he were already a man, which in a way he was, being fifteen, a promising classical scholar, not bad-looking and growing out of childish debility. He was still thin, but he had bones, and his voice had broken. He was startled by his resemblance to his father, and flattered when his stepmother mentioned it. He had his father's eyes, she said. She was well-fleshed, heavier than he, but she often made him offer her his arm and when he did so she leant on it. She made him feel gallant. She asked him to call her by her first name, Mabel – a name he had not liked but liked now.

To his father's eventual question, 'Well, John, what do you think of her?' he could only say in fullness of heart, 'Oh, she's topping,' and was amazed then when his father took his hand, as a woman might have done, and exerted a momentary pressure. They were lying on this occasion in his Surrey grandfather's orchard under an apple tree whose fruits were suspended in the branches – midway between their summer green sour and their rosy autumn ripe.

'What will it be, John,' his father asked presently, 'the administration or the army?'

'Oh, the army,' he said, thinking of his stepmother's first dead hero husband. 'The Pankot Rifles,' and then half sat up as if to apologize. His father lay back – eyes closed, smiling. 'I mean,' young Layton continued, 'if you agree, I'd like to, well, you know, not make capital out of your standing in the civil, but make a go of it on my own in something different. Do you mind?'

His father said, 'Not in the least,' then smiled more broadly and repeated: 'Not in the very least.'

*

When young Layton returned to India in 1913 his father was member for finance on the provincial governor's executive council. He and Mabel lived in a vast old bungalow in Ranpur. Layton stayed with them for a week and Mabel gave a dinner party for him at which he met the commanding officer of the 1st Pankot Rifles and the adjutant, and their wives. Before the guests arrived Mabel inspected him to make sure that the tailor in London had made his uniform correctly and that he was wearing it properly. It consisted of tight dark blue overalls that were strapped under the heels of wellington boots, a white shirt with a stiff narrow winged collar, a narrow black silk bow-tie, a black silk cummerbund, a waist-length jacket of dark green barathea frogged with black braid and clasped at the neck by a little silver chain. It was hot but not especially uncomfortable. He was proud to be wearing it and not put out when Mabel tapped his chest with her fan and said, 'Let it wear you, then you'll grow into it,' and kissed him and raised her arm in the way a woman did in those days to command the support of a man she approved of.

A week later he joined his regiment in Ranpur (the month was October) and a week after that went up to the Pankot Hills to the depot where he was initiated into the lore of recruitment, initial training, and transportation back to Ranpur of men returning from leave in their villages. In October and November boys still came down from the hills to Pankot to present themselves at the *Daftar*, often accompanied by an elder brother who had come up with his battalion in April from Ranpur and later gone on leave. The recruiting season was also the leave seasn. 2/Lieut. John Layton sometimes sat with the senior subaltern in the *Daftar*, learning the technique of selection and rejection. At others he watched the boys drilling under the depot Subahdar-major, or took command of the morning and evening parades. Apart from the subaltern appointed as Recruiting Officer Sahib there were two other British officers permanently at Pankot, the depot commander and his adjutant. Layton lived with the senior subaltern in a bungalow near the golf course. His military duties took up little time, but he had social duties. Social duties included calling (by leaving his card) on European officials and civilians (usually retired) and their wives, in order of seniority. Pankot was never empty but in the winter there was an air about the place of almost cosy relaxation. Wherever he went in Pankot he was known as James Layton's son and as Mabel's stepson. He did not mind having no special identity of his own. Life, in its fullest sense, was a question of service. He had an idea that his real mother, from ill-health rather than any other cause, had not fully understood this. In Pankot she also was remembered but as someone who hadn't been quite up to meeting the demands the country made on white people – certainly not up to meeting them in the way her successor, Mabel Layton, met them.

He was careful to take plenty of exercise. He rode and played tennis and at weekends went for long walks by himself; but solitariness, to Layton, was attractive only in prospect. He found the lonely hillpaths disturbing.

The house in which his father and Mabel lived during the summer was shut up. He looked forward to 1914 and hoped he would not have the bad luck to be left in Ranpur. He would have liked to spend at least one hot weather in Pankot while his father and Mabel were on station. By 1915 he would probably be on the North-West Frontier, because the 1st Pankots had not been there since 1907, the year Mabel's husband was killed and his own mother died in England. He also looked forward to the time – still further in the future because peace-time promotion was slow – when as senior subaltern he would live for a whole year in Pankot in charge of recruitment. Perhaps by then his father would have retired and come to live in Pankot permanently. Some people said that India was ruinous to familial devotion, because of the long periods when children were separated from their parents. Some people even tried the experiment of educating their children at special schools in India, but that didn't work very well. The children were marked, for life, as of the country. So far as young Layton was concerned, the years in England had only served to strengthen his devotion to his father, his stepmother, and the country they served.

*

In November he returned to Ranpur. He did not see Pankot again until the summer of 1919. In the hot weather of 1914 he was, as he had expected, left behind in Ranpur. By the time his parents came back from the hills war had been declared on Germany. In 1915 the 1st Pankots moved to Dehra Dun and then to Poona. There was some uncertainty about what role they were to play, and where, but eventually they were brigaded and sailed for Suez. They were in action in Mesopotamia. Subahdar Muzzafir Khan Bahadur was awarded a posthumous VC. The Colonel collected a DSO and two officers, one of them Layton, collected MCs. In 1918, somewhat depleted, they went to Palestine and in 1919 sailed back to India, where their return to Ranpur was temporarily held up because their arrival coincided with civil unrest in the Punjab, the consequence (according to the Indians) of the Rowlatt Acts which were intended to enable the Government of India (in spite of the 1917 declaration of Dominion status as its long-term political aim) to continue to exercise in peace-time certain war-time measures under the Defence of India Rules for the protection of the realm against subversion. These means included imprisonment of Indians without trial. According to the English the disturbances were simply a disagreeable sign of the times, proof that the war had ruined people's sense of values and let reds and radicals – white as well as black – get above themselves.

But the action of General Dyer in April in Amritsar in the Jallianwallah Bagh, where he personally led a detachment of Gurkhas who fired on an unarmed crowd of civilians who were defying his order not to hold a public meeting, killing several hundred and wounding upwards of a thousand, nipped the anticipated revolution nicely in the bud and in May the 1st Pankots left the staging camp where they had been halted and held in reserve, in case further troops were needed to act in aid of the civil power, and continued their journey home.

Pankot gave the regiment an official welcome – a full-dress military parade attended by the Governor and members of his council and by the General Officer commanding in Ranpur, Lieut.-General Muir. Subahdar Muzzafir Khan Bahadur's seven-year-old son and his widow (an unidentifiable figure dressed overall in a black *burkha* that made her look like an effigy) were presented to the Governor and the General (the widow through the medium of those officers' wives) and the son received his father's medal from the Governor. The officers who had been decorated stood on the saluting platform with the Governor and the General while the battalion marched past with fife and drum, followed by the 1st Ranpurs (second-in-command, Major A. V. Reid, DSO, MC) who had also seen service in the Middle East but had returned home sooner, and the scratch war-time Pankot battalions, soon to be disbanded. The rear was brought up, proudly, by the 4/5 Pankot Rifles who were destined to live on and go down to Maypore and make it their permanent cool weather station.

Young Layton, as was his due, stood with the other decorated officers on the saluting platform.

'I remember thinking,' he told Sarah, 'that there was something wrong, something that meant all this pomp wasn't what we wanted, and that something irretrievable had been lost. Innocence I suppose. Perhaps I felt this only because father was dead, the war had been a mess and I'd done nothing to deserve my MC, or because Mabel was crying. Well, it was all splendid enough, I suppose.'

*

Layton's father had died unexpectedly in 1917 after a short illness caused by an abscess on the liver – the end result of a long-standing amoebic infection which had never been properly diagnosed or treated.

He died in the Minto Hospital in Ranpur and was buried in the churchyard of St Luke's. If he had lived another year, Mabel said, he would have got his KCIE. Since his death Mabel had altered, her stepson thought. There had always been a hard streak in her. Without it her gaiety would have seemed shallow. Now the gaiety had gone and the hard streak emerged when it was least expected: in private rather than in public. She cried at the ceremonial parade. But when she took her stepson to St Luke's to show him his father's grave her behaviour was off-hand. She seemed to have lost the knack, or the will, to make people feel at home in her company.

A year later, after her stepson's marriage to Mildred Muir and after there had been a committee of inquiry into the massacre in the Jallianwallah Bagh, a report by the Indian National Congress, a debate in the House of Commons on the findings of the Army Council, and General Dyer had been retired on half-pay (disgraced, whereas twelve months before he had been hailed as the saviour of India and was still thought of as such by all right-thinking people), Mabel Layton surprised everybody by refusing to identify herself with the ladies of Pankot and Ranpur who busied themselves collecting money for the General Dyer fund. These ladies had misinterpreted the tears at the ceremonial parade and the stony face over tea and coffee for patriotism of the most exemplary kind, and were shocked when by refusing either to contribute or help to collect money that would keep the wolf from the old General's door she appeared in an entirely different light: widow of a soldier who had died for the empire, widow – for a second time – of a civilian whose work for the empire had killed him, stepmother of a young officer who had fought for his country gallantly, step-mother-in-law of the second daughter of General Muir, but who was, it seemed, nevertheless insensible to the true nature of what the men in her life (including her father, who had been an admiral) had stood or still stood for.

When the total sum collected for General Dyer was heard to have reached the substantial fee of £26,000 the ladies of Pankot and Ranpur felt vindicated, justified. But Mabel Layton's comment was 'Twenty-six thousand? Well, now, how many unarmed Indians died in the Jallianwallah Bagh? Two hundred? Three hundred? There seems to be some uncertainty, but let's say two hundred and sixty. That's one hundred pounds a piece. So we know the current price for a dead brown,' and sent a cheque for £100 to the fund the Indians were raising for the families of Jallianwallah victims. But only young Layton and the Indian to whom she entrusted the money knew this.

'I'm keeping it dark for your sake,' Mabel told him, but with an edge in her voice that made it sound as if she felt he had personally driven her to secrecy. 'People would misunderstand. They usually do. You have a career to think of. You can't have a stepmother who seems to be going native, which is the last thing I'd do. I hate the damned country now anyway. It's taken two husbands from me. To me it's not a question of choosing between poor old Dyer and the bloody browns. The choice was made for me when we took the country over and got the idea we did so for its own sake instead of ours. Dyer can look after himself, but according to the rules the browns can't because looking after them is what we get paid for. And if it's *really* necessary every so often to shoot some of them down like ninepins for their own good the least we can do is admit it, just say Hard Luck to the chap who shoots too many, and see to it that the women and children who lost their menfolk, or the children who lost their parents don't starve. There were kids who got shot too, weren't there, at Amritsar? What do we owe them?'

She paid the £100 to one Sir Ahmed Akbar Ali Kasim, a wealthy Ranpur Muslim, one of her late husband's Indian colleagues on the provincial governor's executive council, whose son Mohammed Ali had already shown brilliance in his chosen profession, the law, and was inspired that year of the Jallianwallah Bagh massacre to join the Congress Party whose aim in that same year and for the same bloody reasons and under M. K. Gandhi's leadership was reversed from independence by peaceful co-operation to independence as soon as possible by non co-operation.

'You are young,' Sir Ahmed Akbar told his son. 'Your heart is stronger than your head. When you are as old as I am you will not be so confused by these emotional issues. You think Jallianwallah was a new experience? You are wrong. You think the Indian Congress can ensure that it will be the last episode of this kind? You will be wrong again. You think Jallianwallah proves that the British are lying, talking freedom but acting tyrannically and dealing destruction? Again you are wrong. Jallianwallah could never have happened if the British who talk freedom were not sincere. It happened because they are sincere. They have frightened their opponents with their sincerity. I do not mean us. We are not their opponents. Their opponents, the ones who matter but who will matter less and less, are also British. They are men like General Dyer. Why do you call that man a monster? He believed God had charged him with a duty to save the empire. He believed this sincerely, just as he believed sincerely that in Amritsar there was to be found an invidious threat to that empire. Why do you repeat parrot-fashion that the English are hypocrites? With this you can never charge them. You can only charge them with sincerity and of being divided among themselves about what it is right to be sincere about. It is only an insincere people that can be accused of hyprocrisy. Sometimes I think we are the hypocrites because we have lived too long as a subject people to remember what sincerity means, or to know from one day to the next what we believe in.

'Look' (the old man said, and showed Mohammed Ali a slip of paper), 'do you know what this is? It is a cheque for the rupee equivalent of one hundred pounds made out in my name by an Englishwoman. In exchange for it I am charged to send my own draft to the fund for the Jallianwallah widows and orphans, and not to reveal the name of the donor. Perhaps you think this smells a bit of hypocrisy. To me it smells only of sincerity. It is a straw in the wind which proves to me that for a long time I have been correct in my forecast of which way the wind would blow.

'You look at the English people you meet. Some of them you like. Some you hate. Many you are indifferent to. But even the ones you like do not matter. The ones who matter you will never see – they are tucked away in England – and they are indifferent to us as individuals. You think these officials over here rule us? These viceroys, these governors, these commissioners and commanders-in-chief and brigadier-generals? Then you are wrong. We are ruled by people who do not even know where Ranpur is. But now they know where Jallianwallah Bagh is and what it is, and many of them do not like what they know. Those of them who *do* like what they know are the ones you hear about and hear from. Like the General at Amritsar they are frightened people and frightened people shriek the loudest and fire at random.

'Ah, well, they were Indians who actually died at Amritsar, but the Jallianwallah Bagh was also the scene of a suicide. There will be other such scenes. It takes a long time for a new nation to be born, and a long time for an old nation to die by its own hand. You will hasten nothing by failing to distinguish between the English who really rule us and the English who interpret and administer that rule. Haven't you yet understood that we are part and parcel of the Englishmen's own continual state of social and political evolvement and that to share the fruits we must share the labour and abide by the rules they abide by?'

'You mean,' Mohammed Ali said, 'submit to being shot down for protesting the freedom to speak our minds?'

426

'For this they have shot down their own people, and not so long ago. Out here we shall always be a step behind whatever progress the English make at home.'

Mohammed Ali smiled. 'No,' he said, 'we shall be several steps ahead.'

For a while the old man was silent, not because his son had stumped him. He was merely considering the violent landscape so casually mapped.

'Perhaps I am too old,' he said eventually. 'I can't see small print without my spectacles and even then I get a headache. I think the lady who donated this money also finds it difficult to read the small print. She is anyway only concerning herself with the capital letters of an ancient contract. In *your* contract is *everything* writ large, or is it that your eyesight is superhuman?'

*

John Layton was in his twenty-sixth year when he came back to India in 1919. In the last year of his service abroad he was acting adjutant of the battalion. On returning to Ranpur he relinquished the appointment to an officer of the 2nd Battalion who was senior to him. Temporarily he was without regimental employment. He was the natural choice for the role of Recruiting Officer Sahib. He went up to Pankot in May, with Mabel. They lived in the bungalow near the golf course that he had shared with the senior subaltern in the October and November of 1913.

Both Mabel and his father had talked of retiring to Pankot when the time came. They had had their eye on a place called Rose Cottage, inconveniently placed on the other side of the main hill dominated by the Governor's Summer Residence but to them the most attractive of the few privately owned houses and bungalows: attractive because of its garden, its views, and the fact that it was owned by an elderly widower who had been in tea in Assam and couldn't be expected to live much longer.

Layton's father had not been a rich man. What little he left Mabel inherited, but she had money of her own and money from her first husband who had died well-breeched in spite of having lived extravagantly. Since Mabel was childless he would eventually inherit everything. It would be useful. In peace-time an officer found it virtually impossible to live on his pay – he was not expected to – few attempted to however simple their tastes – he found it quite impossible to save. To serve the empire he needed money of his own. For the moment Layton had no worries on this score. Until his death his civilian father had paid sums of money into his account whenever he could afford them; and Layton suspected – surprised at the amount standing to his credit – that Mabel had contributed regular sums herself. Furthermore she declared her intention of handing over to him in full the principal she had inherited from his father, and the accumulated interest, directly he got married. Such funds together with what he had been able to save while on active service represented the kind of basic security without which a man of his kind would feel at a disadvantage

427

when it came to thinking of the future in terms of fatherhood and of a proper education for his children.

When his Surrey grandfather died – and the old boy surely couldn't go on much longer – he imagined he would inherit the Surrey property into the bargain. His own children might spend part of their childhood there, with their mother (whoever she might be) or their grandmother Mabel, or some relation of their mother's. The long-term plan looked sound. In his twenty-sixth year he felt it was time to be thinking of marriage.

III

The GOC Ranpur, Lieut-General Muir, had three daughters, Lydia, Mildred and Fenella. They were known as Lyddy, Millie and Fenny. 1919 was their first Indian season – the war had postponed it. It was Mildred to whom Layton was most attracted. Fenny was boisterous and silly. Lydia had been engaged to a naval officer at home who was lost in the Atlantic. She bore her loss rather bitterly and Layton distrusted the element of sympathy that would initially enter any relationship a man could have with her. With Millie he felt at ease, even when they were alone and ran out of things to say to one another.

Mrs Muir was an expert chaperone. Opportunities to be alone with any one of her daughters were neither too few nor too many. It was said that she kept a list of eligible men and that a sign of being on it was the sudden myopia that afflicted that regal eye when you danced out of the ballroom on to the terrace of Flagstaff House and sat one of her daughters down in a place where the artificial light from the crystal chandeliers just failed to illumine the stone flags and the balustrade, but (ideally) lit her eyes and caught some of the facets of the jewellery she was wearing.

He decided after several such meetings that he was in love with Mildred Muir and – which was more important – that she was attracted to him. Eventually he declared his love, proposed to her and having got her acceptance asked the general for an interview, addressed himself to the older man with painstaking old-fashioned formality which (Mildred later told her daughter Sarah) swept the old boy off his feet.

The engagement was announced in September. The May of 1920 was chosen as the ideal time for the marriage. Layton would then have finished his twelve-month tour as Recruiting Officer, and he would be due for long leave. He and Mildred would honeymoon in Kashmir and then take a trip home to England to visit his grandfather in Surrey.

Of these plans his stepmother Mabel seemed to approve although he could not actually get her to talk for long about them. In November he took her back to Ranpur. On his return from the war he had found her living at Smith's Hotel and to this place she returned now, refusing an invitation from General and Mrs Muir to stay at Flagstaff House. After a weekend with the Muirs Layton went back to Pankot alone and this time found that

428

solitude came easier to him. He rode and spent weekends walking in the hills. News of his progress on such occasions passed from village to village and wherever he went he found himself pressed to accept hospitality and knew that it would not do to refuse it. He was the only son of Layton Sahib and also the sahib who knew best how to tell the story of Subahdar Muzzafir Khan Bahadur's gallantry. Old and young men gathered round him in the evenings – and beyond the light cast by the flickering oil-lamps he was often aware of the veiled presence of listening women, and afterwards would sleep the sound sleep of satisfied appetite for food and drink and human correspondence that left in his mind an impression of the hill people's grave simplicity and cheerful dignity so that he thought 'Well, home is here,' and knew that for English people in India there was no home in the sense of brick and mortar, orchard and pasture, but that it was lodged mysteriously in the heart.

*

Late in the August of 1920, newly returned with his bride from England, he found Mabel still lodging at Smith's. They stayed with her there for a week before going on up to Pankot to join General and Mrs Muir and Fenny. Lydia had gone back to England with them after the Kashmir honeymoon and had stayed there, declaring that she would never go to India again. She never did. She took a job as secretary to a Bayswater physician, and later married him.

In October Mildred returned to the plains with her husband. Her first baby was due in the second half of March. By then it would be hot and she expressed a wish for the baby to be born in Pankot. There was a nursing home there, part of the hospital and convalescent home that was the Pankot extension of the general hospital in Ranpur. Still without regular regimental employment, Layton acted variously as his father-in-law's aide and as adjutant of the 1st Pankots, filling a leave vacancy. He sat on courts of inquiry and went on courses. In February 1921 he took Mildred up to Pankot. Mrs Muir accompanied them and so did Fenny. They stayed in the GOC's summer residence, a section of which was opened up for this unseasonable occupation. Five weeks later, on March 27th, Sarah was born.

Layton was only momentarily disappointed that his first child was a girl. She was a delicate rosy-cheeked image of Mildred and himself with none of that red ancient wrinkled look of the new-born baby. All that lacked to complete his happiness was a home of his own to bring her and her mother back to when they came out of the Pankot Nursing Home. They stayed throughout that summer in Flagstaff House. He wrote to Mabel asking her to join them, but she seemed to have no liking for the hills now and stayed in Ranpur. She did not see her stepson's first child until late in the following October, when the Laytons went down to Ranpur. They now had for the first time what could pass as a permanent home – permanent in the transient, military sense. The adjutant of the 1st Pankots had gone to the staff college in Quetta and Layton succeeded to the appointment. He moved his family into the bungalow that was to be their home for the next few years, No. 3 Kabul road, Ranpur: a stuccoed colonnaded structure, well shaded by trees in a large compound with adequate stabling and servants' quarters, and a lawn where Sarah and Susan (born in Pankot, in 1922) played – mainly under the eye of Dost Mohammed the head *mali* who knew the ways of snakes and scorpions so well that neither child ever saw a live snake and only one living scorpion in the moment when, encircled by a ring of fire created by Dost Mohammed, it arched its tail over its body and (so he said) stung itself to death.

*

Sarah remembered the scorpion (she watched what Dost Mohammed called its suicide with the detached curiosity of a child) and the garden at No. 3 Kabul road – the shadowy veranda, a dark retreat from the intensity of sunlight; the high-ceilinged bedroom which she shared with Susan, twin child-size beds under twin mosquito nets, and slatted doors which Mumtez, their old ayah, closed at night and guarded, making her bed up against them, sleeping across the threshold. Sarah remembered being woken in the early mornings by the hoarse screeching of the crows. She confused these memories of the old bungalow in Ranpur with other more clearly sustained memories of Pankot; but neither Ranpur nor Pankot struck her when she came back to them, a young woman, as having survived the years of her growing up in England in the way she herself survived them: to her eighteen-year-old eye, in the summer of 1939, their reality was only a marginally accurate reflection of the mind picture she had of them. There was too much space between the particular places she remembered – places which were strongholds of her childhood recollections – and the strongholds themselves had a prosaicness of brick and mortar that did not match the magical, misty but more vivid impression they had left on her when young, so that returning to them, Pankot and Ranpur – Ranpur particularly – seemed to have spread themselves too thin and yet too thick on the ground for comfort.

The sensation she had was one of insecurity which from day to day, and from moment to moment in any one day, could be cushioned by a notion of personal and family history. India to her was at once alien and familiar. The language came back slowly to her, in stops and starts. She was surprised by what she remembered of it, puzzled by what she seemed to have forgotten, but realized then that what she had ever learned of it was the shorthand of juvenile command and not the language of adult communication.

And yet (Sarah thought) over here in an odd and curious way we *are* children. I am aware, coming back, of entering a region of almost childish presumptions – as if everything we are surrounded by is the background for

430

a game. But Susan and I are somehow left out of the game, as if even now we are not old enough to be depended upon to know the rules and act accordingly. Before we are allowed to play we have to know the rules. Without them the game can be seen to be a game, and if it's seen to be a game someone will come along and tell us to put our toys away. And this of course is what is going to happen. This is what I feel, coming back here. And directly it happens all the magic of the game will evaporate, the Fort will be seen to have been made of paper, the soldiers of lead and tin, and I of wax or china or pot. And Mumtez will not lie across the threshold, keeping our long night safe from ogres. Mumtez is gone long ago anyway. Where? Mother scarcely remembers her, which means perhaps that she was in our service for no longer than a year. She remembers Dost Mohammed but not the day of the scorpion. Instead she remembers the day of the snake who neither I nor Susan remember – I suppose because mother and Dost Mohammed between them kept the day of the snake well away from us.

But older children forget the toys that have been put up into the attic; only the younger ones remember and then they too in their turn forget and play games as if they were not games at all but part of life. But it is all a business of cobwebs and old chests and long days indoors that find us thrown back on our own frail resources, because we are afraid to go outside and wet our feet and catch a chill. Pankot is such a place. Pankot is a retreat. So is Ranpur. Not the real Pankot, not the real Ranpur, but *our* Ranpur and Pankot. We see them as different from what they really are which is why when we come back to them we are aware of the long distances that separate one place of vivid recollection from another. In Ranpur we become aware of the immensity of the surrounding plain and in Pankot of the very small impression we have made on hills which when we are away from them we think of as safe, enclosed and friendly but which are in reality unfriendly, vast and dangerous. That is our first shock when we return. It's not something we like to see or think about, so after a time we don't see it and don't think about it.

*

The house in Pankot and the bungalow in Ranpur which their parents were living in during the summer and winter respectively when Sarah and Susan returned to India in 1939 were not places either of the girls remembered. To begin with each was larger than its predecessor because Layton had now assumed command of the 1st Pankots after a fairly humdrum but not unsuccessful career, which during their daughters' absence at home had taken him (and his wife) from Ranpur to Lahore, and Delhi, Peshawar and Quetta, but since houses and bungalows were built very much to the same pattern neither girl was particularly aware of what made these homes different from those they lived in as children.

Sarah and Susan came back to India accompanied by their Aunt Fenny and Uncle Arthur – Major and Mrs Grace who had been taking home leave in 1939 – the year Susan finished with school, and Sarah, who had finished with school one term before, had come to the end of the short secretarial course she had insisted on taking, determined anyway to be prepared to be of some use to someone, somewhere.

Aunt Fenny, the youngest of the Muir girls, had married Arthur Grace in 1924. Her marriage coincided with her father's retirement. It had surprised people at the time that Fenny took so long to make up her mind between the several officers who from time to time laid siege to her affections. And her choice, coming when it did, in – as it were – the last year of her Indian opportunity (General and Mrs Muir having decided to retire to England) and lighting upon Arthur Grace, left an idea in people's minds that she knew she had delayed too long. Arthur Grace was possibly the least eligible of the subalterns who wooed her, and the gossip was that at this last moment she panicked and said yes to his proposal merely because he happened to make it on a particular day, at a particular hour, when she was especially concerned about her future.

His career had not been successful; they had not managed to produce children, and Aunt Fenny had become year by year more and more unrecognizable as the pretty but shallow girl who had had a good time in Pankot in 1919 and 1920 – a bridesmaid who had caught her sister Mildred's bouquet when Mildred and John Layton were married in the church of St John in Pankot early one May morning, and who had been so solidly surrounded by interested young escorts at Pankot station later that day that she scarcely had time to wave her newly-married sister off on her honeymoon.

Youngest daughter, bridesmaid, a godmother to Susan and Sarah – these were the happy stages Fenny passed through before joining the company of honourable matrons as the wife of Arthur Grace. And then, in her turn, Sarah – being then but three years old – acted as a bridesmaid to Aunt Fenny; although of that she had really no recollection whatsoever beyond what was evidenced by the family iconography, a photograph in Aunt Lydia's house in London and the same photograph in her mother's album in India.

It showed the Layton and the Muir families gathered together in slightly self-conscious but handsome, well-dressed and orderly array around a younger Aunt Fenny and a thinner Uncle Arthur with Sarah standing there, a little to one side, in front of Aunt Fenny, holding a nosegay whose scent she almost thought she could reconjure (in isolation from the unrecollected even that caused her to be holding it) and by her side the image of a five-year-old boy in satin page-boy rig whom she could not reconjure at all but whose name, apparently, was Giles, and who was the son of her father's commanding officer.

Perhaps the group portrait was most notable for its inclusion of Mabel Layton who stood next to her first husband's old comrade-in-arms, by then the commanding officer of the 1st Pankots, Giles's father, with on her other side an elderly Indian civilian who was present at the wedding because of his connection with the Governor who was also there with his wife shoulder to shoulder with General and Mrs Muir. The photograph was taken in the gardens of Flagstaff House at Pankot and in the background there could be seen the wooden balustrades and the kindly wistaria. Mabel Layton wore a wide-brimmed hat that all but hid her face, except for a mouth – held midway between repose and a smile.

As a child in India Sarah was afraid of Aunty Mabel (as she insisted on being called). This may have had something to do with the fact that Aunty Mabel was not really her grandmother, but her father's stepmother, and stepmothers were never nice people in story books. She liked Aunty Mabel in England better than she had in India, perhaps because she herself had grown up a bit. Mabel came to England with Major and Mrs Layton in the summer of 1933 when Sarah was turned twelve: the year great-grandfather Layton in Surrey was dying at last at the age of ninety-four.

Although in that long period of exile in England as schoolgirls, she and Susan lived in London with Aunt Lydia, they usually spent several weeks of the summer holidays with their grand-grandfather. A casual observer might have thought that Susan was the old man's favourite child. It was Susan who sat on his knee to listen to his rather gruesome fairy-stories and his stories of their father's and grandfather's boyhoods in Surrey. Sarah did not mind this apparent favouritism. Between herself and her ancient relative there was a silent understanding that Susan needed looking after because she was the baby of the family. His stories either went over Susan's head or bored her, or frightened her. Towards the end of great-grandfather's life Susan decided that she was too old to sit on his knee although she enjoyed the preferential treatment his invitation – increasingly reluctantly accepted – always gave proof of.

Susan did not cry when great-grandfather Layton died; neither did Sarah but she felt they didn't cry for different reasons. He died towards the end of the summer of 1933, shortly before Sarah's and Susan's parents were due to go back to India with Aunty Mabel. Sarah believed Susan did not cry because Susan had never thought of her great-grandfather as a person, but as an old and rather smelly piece of furniture that had to be put up with in the summer and sometimes came to life in a way that was personally disagreeable to her but reassuring to her sense of self-importance and of everything in the house being at her disposal. In the summer of his death Susan had acquired other reassurances: her father's instead of her great-grandfather's knee, her mother's arms. It was the first reunion since the year of separation, 1930, when their mother, accompanied by Aunt Fenny, had brought the girls home to settle them at Aunt Lydia's and at school before rejoining their father in India; and Susan – in the few weeks before great-grandpa died – now tearfully seized the opportunity to tell her mother she hated everything in England. This puzzled Sarah. Sarah had stifled her own unhappiness in England because she didn't want it to rub off on to her sister who had seemed to take the uprooting and replanting (in what their parents always referred to as home – but which was as outlandish at first as Iceland would be to a Congo pigmy) as if nothing much had happened to her at all. The tears Susan now shed were counterfeit of those Sarah had kept in, and Sarah pondered the unfairness of it, the sudden inexplicable emergence of Susan as a little girl with a secretive side to her nature, who had not repaid Sarah for looking after her by trusting her enough to confide what was really going on in her mind but instead saved it all up to confide to her mother. From her state of puzzlement Sarah passed into one of distrust herself. Susan's outbust about the hatefulness of life in England, at Aunt Lydia's, at school, at great-grandpa's, was surely a pose, a bald-faced bid for the bulk of everyone's attention at a time when it should have been concentrated on great-grandpa who was dying, and it did not escape Sarah that she herself was being accused – although of what she wasn't quite sure. She felt out of things, cut off from her family by Susan's emotional claims on it and her implied criticism of the way she, Sarah, had tried in exile to represent it by looking after her sister as much like a grown-up person as she was capable of. And so when great-grandfather died, Sarah did not weep, because she felt – not necessarily understanding it – the final uselessness of giving way to an emotion: a life, well-spent, was over. It happened to everyone. It would happen to her mother and father, and to Aunty Mabel – to Aunty Mabel sooner than any of them, unless there were an accident or a war, or some special kind of Indian disaster such as cholera or unexpected illness. Susan, though, stayed dry-eyed – Sarah thought – because the death of anyone as old as great-grandpa was remote from her, relevant only to the extent it disrupted other people's concentration on matters she thought of as really important.

Susan did not want to go to the funeral. There was no difficulty about that. The difficulty that arose was over Sarah's resistance to the suggestion that she should not go either but stay behind and look after Susan.

'No, I want to go,' she told her mother – with whom, after the years of separation she had not yet established an easy relationship. 'Great-grandpa was very good to us. Mrs Bailey can look after Susan.' Mrs Bailey was the old housekeeper, who had been left three hundred pounds. 'In fact Susan can help her with the funeral meats.' Funeral meats was an expression Sarah had picked up in the last day or so from Mrs Bailey herself. She thought that as food it sounded unappetizing to eat and doleful to prepare and that it might do Susan good to be made to take a hand getting it ready. She hoped as well that the baking of funeral meats would get rid of the sweet odour in the house that reminded her of cut-flowers going bad in vases.

On the day of the funeral she shared a car to the parish church with Aunty Mabel and two of the elderly Layton relatives who had turned up earlier, had had to be met at the station and on the way to the church talked to Mabel about people Sarah did not know unless they were referred to as Mildred or John, which meant her parents. She did not cry at the service (no one did) nor later in the cemetery, standing by the amateur-looking grave that after a certain amount of necessary palaver received the coffin with great-grandpa in it; nor on the journey back. She cried later that night, in the dark, when Susan – who was not speaking to her – had gone to sleep. What made her cry was the thought that great-grandpa had put off dying until her father and mother and Aunty Mabel could get back home from India, but had not spun it out to put them in a position of having either to postpone their departure or leave England again still in a state of uncertainty. It seemed to be a thoughtful way of doing what the doctor had called 'going out'. No one's plans had been messed up. It struck her that he had deliberately stayed alive long enough to give them the satisfaction of believing they had made the last weeks of his life as jolly as they could be, confined to bed as he was, and then 'gone out' soon enough to give them time to do everything that had to be done, get over doing it, then pack their bags and catch the train and the boat their passages had been booked on months ago.

She cried at this evidence of consideration for others; and then at the thought that in some way she had failed Susan as an elder sister, because Susan obviously hadn't been as carefree as her behaviour had previously suggested, didn't feel enough consideration had been given to *her*. Sarah cried, too, because more than anything in the world at that moment she wanted to go back to India with her parents and Aunty Mabel and Susan. Without great-grandpa and the Surrey summer, England again looked to her like the alien land in which she and her sister had been sentenced to spend a number of years as part of the process of growing up. She felt grown-up enough now; quite ready, aged twelve, to tackle the business of helping her mother to look after father; quite ready to take Susan back, even alone, to the old bungalow in Ranpur where Mumtez guarded them against the dark and mysterious nights (for as such they now came at her). The knowledge that her parents no longer lived at No. 3 Kabul road, that Mumtez had long since gone, even been forgotten, that her mother and father were going back to a place called Lahore which was quite unknown to her, did not diminish the vividness of the picture she had of what a return to India would be like. She did not mind, either, that according to Aunt Lydia India was 'an unnatural place for a white woman'. In any case she did not believe it. Her mother was natural enough for anyone, and so was Aunty Mabel if you thought about it and didn't let it upset you when she averted her face when you went to kiss her (so that your lips merely brushed the soft part of her cheek near the earlobe). Aunty Mabel never let anyone get really close to her, but sometimes you found her looking at you, and felt the challenge of her interest in you; in what you were doing or thinking and in why you were doing and thinking it.

*

It was Mabel who told Sarah the truth about the scorpion; two days after great-grandfather's funeral (and Susan still not talking to her, so that she was alone in the orchard until Mabel, also walking alone, came upon her and said, 'Well, if you're doing nothing, take me for a walk').

They went through the orchard and through the gate in the iron rail fence that enclosed it from the meadow. This meadow sloped down to a brook and a spinney. There was a path, worn by custom. The meadow was let to a man who kept cows there. Susan was afraid to walk down to the spinney unless the cows were all bunched together at the far end of the field, but Sarah liked cows. In India they were sacred. In England they weren't, but they were warm and sweet-smelling. She liked the way they tore at the tough grass with their thick curled tongues. She wondered how they avoided pulling it up by its roots and what they thought about when they looked up from their tearing and munching, flicking their ears and striking their flanks with their fly-whisk tails, and watched you watching them. Sometimes they took no notice of you at all, but cropped their way with ragged herd instinct from one part of the meadow to another without pausing to look up as you passed near by. At other times they all held their heads up or turned them to watch you pass behind their rumps. Now, as Sarah walked with Aunty Mabel towards the spinney they were pulling up grass on either side of the path. She could smell their breath and thought Aunty Mabel hesitated to pass through their midst. 'They're quite docile,' Sarah said, and took Aunty Mabel's hand, partly to reassure her and partly because just here the track was ridged and rather difficult for an elderly lady to negotiate. 'They're not great-grandpa's,' she said, forgetting for the moment that nothing was great-grandpa's any longer. 'They belong to Mr Birtwhistle. He lets us watch them being milked sometimes.'

'Do you enjoy that?'

Sarah thought. 'No. But I'm interested in it. I mean enjoy is how I'd describe liking something artificial like a book or a game. But milking is to do with actual life, isn't it, so I like it but I don't enjoy it. Does that make sense?'

'Of a kind.'

When they reached the brook Sarah showed Aunty Mabel the stepping-stones which gave access to the opposite bank and the woodland. 'It used to be our private wood,' she explained, meaning her own and Susan's, and private in the sense of pretend. 'There's a fence on the other side of the spinney. The land on the other side of that belongs to Mr Birtwhistle but it's all right to go in so long as you keep to the edges. I mean it's all right for me and Susan. Or has been. I suppose everything will undergo changes now. It's probably our last summer. Daddy's going to let the house and might even sell it.' She stopped, realizing that she was talking to Aunty Mabel as if she were a stranger instead of a member of the family who probably knew far more about her father's plans than she did herself. And she kept forgetting that Aunty Mabel had visited great-grandfather years ago, long before the 1914–18 war, with grandfather Layton, to meet her stepson, Sarah's father, and so must know the brook and the stepping-stones, the spinney, and the neighbour's land on the other side, and that this might be the last summer of all that any Layton would come here.

'Shall you miss it?' Aunty Mabel asked.

'I expect so, although we only ever come in July and August. I probably wouldn't mind not coming if I knew I could and had simply gone somewhere else for a change. It will be knowing I can't come that will make it seem sad, as if a phase of my life has ended for ever.'

They stood looking at the brook. Sarah didn't sit on the bank because Aunty Mabel was much too old for that sort of thing. Near the water the earth was always damp. It was a hot day, but shady here. Aunty Mabel had a coat on though. She was cold in England. Three years ago Sarah had felt the cold too but had got used to it. She had dreams sometimes, in colour, like a film, of herself in sunshine in Pankot. The brook babbling over the stones reminded her of Pankot in miniature. But then everything in England was on a miniature scale. She thought this had an effect on the people who lived there always. In comparison with her mother and Aunt Fenny and Aunty Mabel, for instance, Aunt Lydia – although taller than any of them – seemed to Sarah to lack a dimension that the others didn't lack. Lacking this dimension was what Sarah supposed came of living on a tiny island. She felt this, but also felt she hadn't yet developed the reasoning power to work it out in terms that would adequately convey what she felt to other people. So she kept quiet about it and was conscious of Aunty Mabel keeping quiet about something too, and noted this down mentally as one of the things she'd not noticed before that distinguished her Indian family from her English family – distinguished her father, mother, Aunt Fenny and Aunty Mabel from Aunt Lydia, Uncle Frank (Aunt Lydia's physician husband) and poor old great-grandpa. Her English family kept quiet about nothing, but were always speaking their minds. Aunt Lydia sometimes presumed to speak other people's too. And all at once she saw the correspondence between (in particular) Aunty Mabel who never said very much at all and her sister, Susan, who said a lot, but hoarded important things up until someone came along (their parents for instance) whom she judged to be worth speaking her mind to.

Sarah did not understand this unexpected connection between her sister and Aunty Mabel but knew it was an Indian connection. The English who went to India were different from those who didn't. When they came back they felt like visitors. And the people they came back to felt that the connection between them had become too tenuous for comfort (tenuous was one of Sarah's favourite new words). There were areas of sensitivity neither side dared probe too deeply.

Sarah said, 'I think we'd better go back otherwise we'll be late for tea and make things difficult for Mrs Bailey.'

'If you think so,' Aunty Mabel said.

On their way to the house Sarah had what she secretly called one of her funny turns. All that happened in a funny turn (nobody ever noticed them because obviously there was nothing to see) was that everything went very far away, taking its sound with it. It was rather like looking through the wrong end of great-grandpa's field-glasses and at the same time getting the wireless tuned in badly. Sarah had decided that her funny turns were all to do with growing up. At any given moment (she imagined) her bones and flesh expanded a fraction beyond the capacity her blood had to pump itself into all the crevices it was supposed to get at, leaving her brain briefly deprived of nourishment and her eyes and ears in consequence fractionally just incapable of making an accurate recording of what was really going on. She had worked it out that there was no common factor to the turns. It wasn't a question of how cold or hot the weather was, or of how much or how little she had been exerting herself, or of how hungry or how overfull she was, or how she felt. She found the sensation very interesting, but if it happened while she was talking to somebody, she worried a bit about talking sensibly. When it happened now, as they went back into the orchard (Sarah taking care to shut the gate properly) she also worried about making sure that Aunty Mabel didn't fall on one of the hummocks in the rough grass. She was never certain of her own balance during a funny turn because balance depended on getting your sense of perspective and distance right.

So she took her time closing the gate, hoping that in a few seconds she would stop feeling like a giant in a tiny landscape, that Aunty Mabel would come back into her proper proportions, bringing the orchard with her. She said (in a voice that rang in her head but gave no impression of being loud enough for Aunty Mabel to hear), 'I think there's a stone in my sandal.' Sometimes it helped to bend down, because that sent the blood into the head where it was needed. She bent down. A little to one side of her feet there was a fallen apple. Her feet and the apple were tiny, far away. One of the things about a funny turn was that although you felt gigantic in relation to everything else any part of yourself that you looked at was small and far away too. When she had fumbled with her sandal she touched the apple, fascinated by her distant hand; picked the apple up, and was stung by the wasp that was searching its soft bruised underside. The pain was sharp. Her brain recorded the message accurately, but there was still a layer of insensitivity separating her recognition of the pain and her realization that the pain was happening to her. She heard herself cry out. She stood upright.

'What's wrong?' Aunty Mabel asked.

'I've been stung.'

She was all right then – the funny turn was finished. Her little finger hurt. Aunty Mabel took the stung hand and looked at the tiny red puncture – the originating centre of the swelling and inflammation that was already beginning to show.

'A wasp or a bee?'

'Oh, a wasp. It was having a go at the apple.'

'Have you been stung by a wasp before?'

'Yes, twice.'

'That's all right, then. We'll get back and put something on it.'

438

'Mrs Bailey recommends lemon juice.'

'That will do.'

'Why is it all right that I've been stung before?'

'Because some people are allergic.'

'Does that mean they could die?'

'Yes. But it's very rare.'

'I thought only snake bites and scorpion stings were fatal.'

'No. And not always they.'

They walked side by side through the orchard towards the lawn and the house. On a day like this tea would normally have been in the garden in the shade of the cedar. Not having tea in the garden was one of the family's concessions to the formal discipline of mourning, or a sign anyway of their respect for the feelings of people like Mrs Bailey. Sarah was glad that none of her family seemed to believe in God. She didn't really believe in God herself. She didn't like religious people; rather she did not like them directly they stopped being ordinary and started to be religious. Truly religious people, like nuns and monks and saints were a different matter. She thought of them as truly religious because they gave up their lives to it, and giving up your life to it struck her as the only thing to do if you believed in it. If you didn't believe in it the most you could do was to be charitable and try not to be selfish.

She was worried because Susan had never been stung either by a wasp or a bee. Susan led a charmed life. Aunt Lydia said Susan would always fall on her feet. Sarah could not remember Susan hurting herself badly – not badly enough to leave a scar. Susan did not remember the day of the scorpion, although she had knelt by Sarah's side, watching Dost Mohammed build a fire round it.

'Is it true,' Sarah asked Aunty Mabel as they crossed the empty sun-struck lawn, 'that scorpions kills themselves if you build a ring of fire round them so that they know they can't get out?'

'No.'

Sarah was not surprised, in spite of having once seen what looked like proof that they did.

Aunty Mabel said: 'Their skins are very sensitive to heat, which is why they live under stones and in holes and only come out a lot during the wet. If you build a ring of fire round them they're killed by the heat. They look as if they sting themselves to death because of the way they arch their tails over their bodies. But it's only a reflex action. They're attacking the fire, and get scorched to death by it.'

After a few moments Sarah said, 'Yes, I see,' and was sorry it wasn't true that they committed suicide, even though for some time now she had ceased to believe old Dost Mohammed's story and in the practical experiment he conducted in support of it. She admired intelligence and courage because she often felt herself to be lacking in both; and it had always seemed to her that the small black scorpion found in the servants' quarters at No. 3 Kabul road, Ranpur, had shown intelligence and courage of a high order; intelligence enough to know that it could never set about escaping without burning itself painfully to death, courage enough to make a voluntary end of it by inflicting on its own body the paralysing stab it knew would kill it. Sarah admired soldiers of ancient times who fell on their swords because they had lost a battle. She had a childhood nightmare of her father losing a battle one day and deciding to fall on his, or shoot himself, to avoid being captured.

Now that Aunty Mabel had confirmed what she already suspected about the death of the scorpion she was able to link one truth with the other: which was that the last thing she would want her father to do if he lost a battle was fall on his sword. It was an awfully impractical thing to do. And it would be impractical of the scorpion to kill itself. After all the fire might go out, or be doused by rain. It was more practical of the scorpion to attempt to survive by darting its venomous tail in the direction of what surrounded it and was rapidly killing it. Just as brave too. Perhaps braver. After all there was a saying: Never say die.

In the kitchen where Mrs Bailey was cutting cucumber sandwiches and watching the kettle Sarah had her hand seen to. After tea, which the family had in the drawing-room with all the windows open on to the flagged terrace that overlooked the garden, Susan sat in the window-seat reading one of her mother's magazines, and Sarah went upstairs to their bedroom. She sat in a window-seat too, which had a view across to Mr Birtwhistle's meadow. She had a pencil and an exercise book and drew a family tree, beginning with great-grandpa.

She had no idea why she drew the family tree but doing it made her feel better. It gave her a sense of belonging and of the extraordinary capacity families had for surviving and passing themselves on and handing things down. She extended the tree by mapping in what she described to herself as the Muir branch: giving her mother the two sisters Mrs Layton was entitled to (Aunt Fenny and Aunt Lydia, with their respective husbands, Uncle Arthur and Uncle Frank) and the parents they were entitled to, General and Mrs Muir. She and Susan were entitled to them too. They had Muir blood in their veins as well as Layton blood. At Christmas Aunt Lydia and Uncle Frank always took them up to Scotland where General and Mrs Muir lived in retirement. Sarah did not like Scotland. It was cold and craggy. Before her mother and father sailed back to India they were going up to Scotland too, but she and Susan weren't going with them. They were going back to Aunt Lydia's in Bayswater. Aunt Lydia and Uncle Frank had not come down for the funeral but had sent flowers. In her heart of hearts (as she put it to herself) she had never really taken to Aunt Lydia but had done her best not to show it because Susan didn't like Aunt Lydia much either and between them, Sarah felt, they could have made life miserable for themselves by exaggerating the things about Aunt Lydia they didn't like and were in mutual agreement about, and minimizing the things about her which they – Sarah anyway – did like.

When she analysed the pros and cons of Aunt Lydia she knew that it was

Aunt Lydia's dislike of India that stood in the way of her feeling affection for her. She took a red and blue pencil and drew a red ring round her Indian relatives on the family tree and a blue ring round her English relatives. Great-grandpa had a blue ring and so did Uncle Frank and Aunt Lydia (although Aunt Lydia had spent eighteen months in India after the war). There was a warming preponderance of red crayon on the tree.

'That is my heritage,' Sarah said, then noticed that so far she had put no ring at all round Aunty Mabel. She put down the red pencil to pick up the blue and then paused.

'Why ever was I going to do that?' she asked herself. And retrieved the red pencil, ringed Aunty Mabel firmly with that fiery colour; the one denoting the Indian connection.

*

Six years later in the July of 1939 she came across the exercise book among other relics of her childhood that had been packed in a leather trunk and stored in Aunt Lydia's glory-hole. She sorted the trunk out now to make sure that nothing was worth saving from the bonfire – an incinerator, actually, at the far end of the untended weedy walled enclosure that Aunt Lydia called a garden – worth saving from the holocaust into which her English years were being thrown and causing her a degree of pain at separation she had not expected.

She sorted the contents of the trunk on a day when Aunt Lydia was out shopping with Susan and Aunt Fenny who was back again with Uncle Arthur from India. Susan was buying clothes for the tropics. Sarah thought that buying clothes for the tropics in Kensington was a waste of time. But Susan had set her heart on a topee with a veil swathed round its crown and hanging over the brim at the back to give extra shade to the neck; and on white shirts and jodhpurs to complete the outfit. Wearing these she would look like the heroine in The Garden of Allah. She also wanted some dresses in silk and georgette (which would be sweaty). And a shooting stick. And anything else that caught her eye and further excited the image she had of herself as a young girl – dressed and ready for a romantic encounter in an outpost of empire – whose father was a lieutenant-colonel, recently appointed to the command of the first battalion of his old regiment, the Pankot Rifles, and destined, no doubt, if there were a war – which seemed likely – to become a brigadier and then a major-general.

Possibly, she thought, the difference between herself and Susan was that Susan was capable of absorbing things into her system without really thinking whether they were acceptable to her or not; whereas she herself absorbed nothing without first subjecting it to scrutiny. Perhaps this was wrong. Perhaps she tried too hard to work things out. She didn't relax. She didn't have a talent for just enjoying herself, which was a pity because she must miss a lot that Susan never missed.

Finding nothing worth saving from the trunk she took the contents in several batches and several armfuls down the two flights of stairs and down the half-flight into the semi-basement and the kitchen whose door gave access to the garden.

There, on a warm July evening scented by warmed brick, bruised grass and the fumes of traffic in the park and on the Bayswater road, she set fire to the relics of a youth she did not understand but felt had given a certain set to her bones, a toughness to her skin, and caused her now (half-shielding her cheeks from the heat of the fire in the incinerator) to stand watching the conflagration as it were in her own right as a person who now inherited the conflicting attitudes of the Laytons and the Muirs, and of Aunty Mabel, and of grand-grandpa who had 'gone out' on an August morning to the scent of cedars and stale flowers in vases, so that she had a vision of herself and her family as the thing she was burning, and of that thing, of that self, as an instrument of resistance and at the same time of acceptance. She could feel the heat on her bones, the heat on her skin. Within them remained the nub, the hard core of herself which the flames did not come near nor illuminate.

So I am really in darkness, she said, and this truly is the difference between myself and Susan who lives in a perpetual and recognizable light. The light that falls on Susan also falls on Aunt Fenny and Uncle Arthur. It falls, but in a way that makes different shadows, on Aunt Lydia and Uncle Frank. I do not know how it falls on Mother and Father – it is a long time since I have seen them – and I do not know who is in darkness except myself.

Two weeks later, accompanied by her sister Susan, her Aunt Fenny and her Uncle Arthur, Sarah Layton sailed back to India on the P & O.

Part Three

A WEDDING, 1943

I

Having handed young Kasim a glass of the forbidden whisky Count Bronowsky said, 'So Mrs Layton drinks, you say. Do you mean in secret?'

Ahmed, taking the glass, held it well away from his nose. He disliked the smell of alcohol. In the palace there wasn't a drop to be had except what his servant or he himself managed to smuggle into his room there. He smuggled it on principle and had trained himself to drink a certain amount every day. It disappointed him that regular tippling hadn't yet given him a real taste for it let alone made him a slave of habit. A serious drinker, and finally an alcoholic, struck him sometimes as the only thing really open to him to become in his own right.

'I don't know about in secret,' he said. 'But she begins first, finishes last and has two drinks to anybody else's one. Also I've noticed that her behaviour is erratic.'

Bronowsky limped from the liquor trolley to the larger of the two cane armchairs that had been placed on the veranda, with a view on to the dark garden. He sat, settled his lame left leg on the foot-stool, raised his glass and looked at Ahmed with his right eye. The left leg and the blind left eye – covered by a black patch whose elastic, pitched at an angle, was countersunk by long use in a ring round his narrow head – were said to be the result of getting half blown-up in pre-revolutionary St Petersburg by an anarchist while driving along Nevsky Prospect to the Winter Palace.

'In what way erratic?'

Ahmed sat in the other chair and watched the Count select and light one of the gold-tipped cigarettes that came in rainbow colours from a shop in Bombay.

'She is irritable one moment, almost friendly at another. The almost friendliness occurs when she has a glass in her hand.'

'Her husband is a prisoner of war in Germany, you said?'

'Yes.'

'Is she still attractive would you say?'

'Her hair is not grey. She frequently powders her nose.'

'Ah – Her sister, this Mrs Grace, she is also erratic?'

'No. She is perfectly predictable. You can depend on her to be rude at any time. And she does not trouble to lower her voice.'

'Dear boy, what have you overheard her saying about you?'

Ahmed smiled. 'It seems I am quite efficient for an Indian.'

'But it was a compliment.'

'I would also make a good *maître d'hôtel* if I didn't stink so abominably of garlic.'

'I doubt Mrs Grace would know a good *maître* from a bad one. The English seldom do. But she meant well. And you *do*.'

'Garlic strengthens the constitution. My father used to carry an onion in his pocket to ward off colds. But that was mere superstition. Eating garlic is scientific. Also garlic is stronger on the breath than the smell of whisky. So you see it has its religious and social uses too.'

From a quarter mile or so away the drumming resumed. A Hindu wedding feast. Ahmed kept time on the arm of the chair with the fingers of his free hand. During Ramadan such a noisy manifestation of Hindu gaiety could cause communal trouble. He almost welcomed the prospect.

Bronowsky eased and re-settled the stiff lame leg. 'Tell me about the two Miss Laytons. Are they more to your taste? The one who is to be married – begin with her.'

'What an inquisitive man you are!' Ahmed thought. He was not inquisitive himself. To him people were remote, people and things and the ideas they seemed to find electrifying. But he quite enjoyed these regular sessions with Bronowsky, partly because the old wazir had taken him up as if he were someone worth giving time to, but mostly because Bronowsky's endless curiosity about other people helped him to form opinions about them himself, to consider them with greater objectivity and interest than he felt when actually dealing with them. The exercise, he found, enabled him to peel off a layer or two of his own incuriosity. True, when the sessions were over, he usually felt those layers thickening up again and was likely to tell himself that Bronowsky encouraged him to call and chatter mainly because he preferred (or was suspected of preferring) above all other the company of young men. Nevertheless each session left a residual grain of involvement.

'Oh, Miss Layton,' he said, and conjured a picture of Susan Layton holding a length of white material up under her chin and hectic-coloured cheeks. 'People do things for her. She must have trained them to think she can't do them for herself. Every time she lifts a finger to do something on her own she makes it look like an attempt at the impossible. People come running. It's not just the wedding, I think. She has probably always been the centre of attraction.'

'Is she fond of this Captain Bingham?'

Ahmed thought. How could he judge? He did not really know what fond was. His father was fond of his mother. His brother had had been fond of the army. He himself was fond of chewing cloves of garlic. Bronowsky was fond of gossip. Fond seemed to be a combination of impulse, appetite and gratification. But even that didn't define it properly. He himself, for instance, had an impulse to make love to girls. He visited prostitutes. He had acquired a taste for sexual intercourse and had gratified it not infrequently. He was therefore, he supposed, fond of copulating as well as of eating garlic, but this was not what the world meant by fond or Count Bronowsky meant when he asked if the younger Miss Layton was fond of Captain Bingham. That kind of fond hinted at a capacity for denying yourself if self-denial was for the good of what you were fond of. He did not think Miss Layton had this capacity.

He said, 'No. I don't imagine she is really *fond* of Captain Bingham.'

'You mean it is merely a physical attraction?'

'On his part, yes. He is more attracted to her than she is to him.'

'How do you know?'

'I think, when he touches her, instead of being agitated she is irritated. Especially if she has her mind on the cut of a dress.'

'Embarrassment,' Bronowsky said. 'Obviously, what you saw was her reaction to a tender gesture made in front of others. The English are very shy of their sexuality. If you were a fly on the wall and saw Miss Layton and Captain Bingham together you might be surprised. Even shocked.'

Ahmed said nothing. He had been a fly on the wall; or rather an unnoticed figure rounding a corner of the guest-house veranda where Miss Layton stood, holding up the length of white material, reacting rather violently to Captain Bingham's two waist-embracing arms and saying, 'Oh, Teddie, for God's sake.' Which was interesting and quite contrary to Bronowsky's supposition, because in public Miss Susan Layton submitted to Captain Bingham's protective and possessive touch with equanimity, even with approval, in fact with an air of demanding it quite frequently as if it were due to her at regular intervals. And she was no less eager in such circumstances to give as well as receive a caress. Only when they were alone, apparently, did the exchange of caresses become distasteful. Fortunately for him he had not been seen on the occasion of the breaking away from Captain Bingham.

'What are you thinking?' Bronowsky asked.

Ahmed smiled, took another sip of the whisky, and said, 'Of being a fly on the wall.'

'Does the idea appeal?'

'Flies on walls sometimes get swatted.'

'Every occupation has its hazards. Tell me about the younger sister, the Miss Layton who isn't to be married.'

'But she isn't the younger.'

'Ah. That is always interesting. I imagine she isn't as pretty. But perhaps more serious-minded?'

'She asks a lot of questions.'

'Questions about what?'

'The administration in Mirat. Native customs. Local history.'

'Is she so very plain then?'

'I find all white girls unattractive. They look only half-finished. When they have fair hair they look even more unnatural.'

445

'She is fair, then?'

'Yes. And to an Englishman probably as attractive as her sister. And she is better-natured. Is that dangerous?'

'Why?'

'I understand it can be. This kind of English person invites our confidence. They ask questions, at first of a general nature, then of a more intimate kind. You think, well, he is interested, she wishes to be friends. But it is a trap. One wrong move, one hint of familiarity on your part, and snap. It shuts.'

'So says Professor Nair no doubt.'

'But don't you agree? I am asking you. I have no experience. It is what I've been told, not only by Professor Nair. Snap.'

'What are you really asking me? Whether you should be careful how you answer these fascinating intimate questions you anticipate Miss Layton asking you?'

'No. I am always careful. I was only asking your opinion of the belief generally held.'

'What belief?'

'That the friendly English are more dangerous than the rude ones.'

'Are you sure you mean English? Not white? Am I dangerous?'

'Oh, you are the most dangerous man in Mirat. Everybody says so. It goes without saying. One risks everything just talking to you. But then you are exceptional in every way, and I meant English, not white. If we had been subjugated by the Russians I would have said Russians. It isn't the whiteness that matters. It's the position of the English as rulers that makes their friendship dangerous. Dangerous on two counts. It weakens our resolve to defy them and it is against their own clan instincts. They are consciously or subconsciously aware of weakening their position by friendliness, so this friendliness always has to be on their own guarded terms. If we unwittingly think of it as mutual and go too far they are doubly incensed, first as individuals who feel they have been taken what they call advantage of, secondly as members of a class they fear they may have betrayed by their own thoughtless stupidity. Then, snap! They are indifferent to the effect of such a situation on us.'

'Is that what you believe?'

'It's what I am told. People are always warning us. It is well known. Fortunately, unlike my father I have never felt the urge to make friends with any Englishman, or Englishwoman. But it is interesting to observe them. It is interesting to come across one of the friendly ones, like the elder Miss Layton. It is like being a student of chemistry, knowing a formula, waiting to see it proved in a laboratory test.'

'Your glass is empty. Help yourself.'

Ahmed got up to do so. Bronowsky held his own glass out as Ahmed was passing him. Ahmed took it, but for a moment the older man retained his own hold on it.

'Have you kept your promise to me and written to your father?'

'No.'

'Why not?'

'The same reason as always. I begin writing and stop, there isn't anything to say, and even if there were every word would be read by someone else before the letter reached him. It is very off-putting. I write to my mother. She tells him what I am doing.'

'It isn't the same.'

Ahmed, in possession of Bronowsky's glass, went to the drinks trolley and poured generous measures of White Horse: two fingers for himself, three for Bronowsky. He filled both glasses almost to the brim with soda-water and came back to the chair where Bronowsky sat looking up with his good eye half shut as if measuring an effect. Ahmed offered him the replenished glass, but Bronowsky did not take it immediately.

'It isn't the same,' he repeated. 'Is it?'

'No, but he's used to the idea that I'm a disappointing sort of son.'

Bronowsky now grasped the base of the tumbler and when Ahmed felt it held securely he let go.

'You are more used to it than he is,' Bronowsky said. 'I think the idea that you're a disappointment to him has become your basic security. You'd feel lost without it. You know, dear boy, the most disturbing thing that happened to me when I was about your age was discovering that my father approved a particular step I proposed to take.'

'What step was that?'

'Marriage. The girl was my cousin, we weren't in love, but she would probably have made me a good wife and we always got on well enough together. I decided on marriage because I thought my father particularly disliked her. I anticipated the most vigorous opposition. Instead he embraced me. He almost wept. Really very alarming. I cooled off the idea at once. I felt some regret, of course. Perhaps I loved her after all. But I felt better directly I told him I'd changed my mind. He turned away without a word, but with his old comforting look of utter disdain. I felt secure again and never again felt insecure until he died. Then I had to earn his posthumous disapproval in a variety of ways, doing things I felt he would despise me for. Making liberal gestures rather popular at the time among intellectual landowners. Not gestures I had my heart in, but then you don't need your heart in good to do it. I did the right thing for the wrong reasons, which is what you are doing, efficiently carrying out the job you are paid for, even earning the approbation of the ungracious Mrs Grace. But you are carrying it out well because you think your father disapproved of your taking it and would be ashamed to know that a woman like Mrs Grace described you as a potentially first-rate hotel manager. You want him to be ashamed because his being ashamed of you is what you understand. You feel exactly the same about it as another boy might feel about his father being proud of him. Determined to keep it up. But the question you should ask yourself is whether he is ashamed. Has he ever been? Isn't it truer to say you grew up in a household where clear views were held on a number of questions that concern India, that you expected to inherit this clarity as you might inherit a share of the household goods and chattels and were startled to find you didn't. Startled is the wrong word. It was obviously a much slower process. But the upshot of it all was compensation for feelings of inadequacy, transference of your disappointment. You imagined the disappointment was your father's. But perhaps the truth was that he observed your struggles to take an interest with affection and compassion but didn't know how to help you. You didn't make things easier by withdrawing from him although what you were really doing was withdrawing from yourself. It's because you are fond of him that you don't write to him in prison.'

Ahmed smiled.

'You shouldn't be afraid of your emotions,' Bronowsky continued. 'In any case to be afraid of them is un-Indian. Now there's a danger for you if you like. You young men ought to watch out for it – losing your Indianness. It's a land of extremes, after all, it needs men with extremes of temperament. All this Western sophistication, plus the non-Western cult of non-violence, is utterly unnatural. One without the other might do but the combination of the two strikes me as disastrous. After all the sophistication of the West is only a veneer. Underneath it we are a violent people. But you Indians see no deeper than our surface. Add to that the non-violence cult and the result is emasculation.'

Ahmed grinned. Bronowsky said, 'Fornication can be a refuge as well as an entertainment. Your visits to the Chandi Chowk are no proof of your masculinity, dear boy.'

'Oh well, what am I to do? Raise an army to release the prisoners in the Fort at Premanagar?'

'You could do worse. In fact I can think of nothing more splendid. It interests me that it's the first thing that occurs to you. Such a passionate idea. How could the world fail to respond to it? It's what sons are for, to lead armies to deliver their fathers from fortresses. The British would lock you up for ever. They would laugh as well, of course, because projects obviously doomed to failure have their comical side, but they would laugh unmaliciously. They would respect you. On the other hand if you announced your intention to fast unto death if they didn't release your father they'd let you get on with it. They'd feed you forcibly. They'd be furious with you for attempting moral blackmail. I must say I'd sympathize with them. Non-violence is ridiculous. I'm not in favour of it. Can you stay to dinner?'

'No, I had a sudden invitation from Professor Nair.'

'What is he up to?'

'Nothing he tells me about.'

'Perhaps you don't listen hard enough. He's always up to something. Nawab Sahib expects to be kept informed. He will be back on Friday, incidentally.'

'Did you enjoy your visit to Gopalakand?'

'It was amusing. I left Nawab Sahib to enjoy himself a few days longer. He will be pleased with poems of Gaffur. Which of them thought of it?'

'I don't know.'

'Have they been into the palace?'

'I took them over the public rooms this morning. Will Nawab Sahib be going to the reception?'

'He will if I say so. I think I shall say so. What is arranged for tomorrow?'

'They are going shopping again. But in the morning before breakfast Miss Layton wants to ride.'

'Which Miss Layton?'

'The inquisitive one. Miss Sarah.'

'Alone?'

'I'm expected to ride with her I think.' Ahmed sipped his whisky. 'I shall keep a respectful few paces behind, naturally.'

'Do you think she has her mother's permission, or that of this Captain Bingham?'

'I didn't ask. I exist to carry out orders.'

'Don't be upset if you find you've got up early and had horses saddled for nothing. Her mother or Captain Bingham might veto her little jaunt if she's arranged it without mentioning it and they find out about it.'

'Oh, I shan't be upset.'

'Who else is there in the wedding party?'

'A Major Grace is arriving on Friday. He is the bride's uncle. Captain Bingham's friend sometimes visits – a Captain Merrick. He will be best man.'

'Merrick?'

'Yes. Do you know him?'

'I don't think so. Merrick. A vaguely familiar name. But in some other connection—? Well, you'd better be off if you're dining with Nair.'

Ahmed drained his glass and returned it to the trolley. 'Thanks for the drink,' he said, and stood for a moment looking down at Bronowsky, who never shook hands or exchanged formal greetings or farewells with people he looked upon as intimates. For a man of nearly seventy, Ahmed thought, he had worn very well. His face was unlined, his complexion pink. In the early years of his administration as chief minister in Mirat the anti-Bronowsky faction – said to have been headed by the late Begum – had nearly succeeded in poisoning him. His rows with the Nawab were almost legendary. They still occurred. But his influence over the Nawab was now thought to be complete.

Ahmed himself owed his position at the court to Bronowsky although it had taken some time for this to become clear to him. Originally he had thought it was the Nawab who had the notion of taking under his wing the unsatisfactory younger son of a distant but distinguished kinsman, a boy who had failed abysmally at college and showed no aptitude for any career of the kind open to a Kasim of the Ranpur branch: law, politics, the civil service. True, it was Bronowsky who had written the letters and even visited Ranpur but he appeared to do so in the capacity of agent, not principal, and gave no impression of himself caring one way or the other about the outcome of the Nawab's invitation. To Ahmed that invitation looked like one founded on charity rather than on interest and he believed it looked like that to his father, with whom discussion had been brief. His father was then still head of the provincial ministry, a busy man, and a worried man, almost entirely wrapped in the business of protesting the Viceroy's declaration of war on Germany without prior consultation with Indian leaders. By the time Ahmed reached Mirat his father, following Congress instructions, had resigned.

But, 'Well, *you* are safe,' the Nawab had said to Ahmed when they had news of M A K's arrest in 1942. 'You are under our protection. For this you must thank Count Bronowsky.' Why Bronowsky? Ahmed asked; and learned that it was the wazir's idea, not the Nawab's, that he should come to Mirat to learn something about the administration of a Native State. 'While you have been here,' the Nawab continued, 'you will have heard many adverse things about Bronowsky Sahib. It is not unknown for me to think and say adverse things about him myself. What you should know about him, however, is that his loyalty to the House of Kasim is without parallel even among Kasims, and that it is the future of the House he always thinks of.'

It was a loyalty Ahmed had not got the measure of, and he did not understand where he fitted in with whatever Bronowsky saw as the pattern of a scheme to promote the interests of Kasims. In the past year he had been aware of Bronowsky's appraisal; before that Bronowsky had scarcely taken any notice of him. His duties had been of an almost menial clerical kind, those of dogsbody to one official's secretary after another. The officials had grandiloquent titles. Ahmed had worked under the secretary to the Minister for Finance, under the secretary to the Minister for Education, under the secretary to the Minister for Public Works, under the secretary to the Minister for Health, under the chief clerk to the Attorney-General. Most of these ministers were related to the Nawab, two bore the name of Kasim. All were nominated by the Nawab and served as members of his Council of State.

The Council of State was Bronowsky's brain-child. In the twenty years of his administration he had transformed Mirat from a feudal autocracy where Ruler met ruled only at periodical durbars into a miniature semi-democratic state where the durbars still took place but where the machinery of government was brought out of the dark recesses of rooms and passages in the palace into, comparatively, the light of day.

He had separated the judiciary from the executive, reframed the criminal and civil legal codes, created the position of Chief Justice and during his chief ministership so far always succeeded in appointing to it a man from outside Mirat whose impartiality could be counted on – in one case an Englishman just retired from the bench of a provincial High Court of British India. Bronowsky had done all these things with a minimum of overt opposition because it was to do them that the Nawab brought him back from Monte Carlo in 1921. 'I must be a modern state,' the Nawab was reported saying. 'Make me modern.' What Bronowsky did by way of making the Nawab of Mirat modern was also the means by which he gradually cut the ground from under the feet of British officials of the Political Department who objected to the appointment of a 'bloody *émigré* Russian' as chief minister of a state with which, small it was, they had always had what they felt to be a special relationship. For all they knew Bronowsky was a red, a spy, a man who would cause trouble and feather his nest at the same time.

The Resident at Gopalakand who advised the Nawab of Mirat as well as the Maharajah of Gopalakand had protested the appointment of Bronowsky and the sacking of the Nawab's brother to make room for him. Before the present Nawab succeeded as Ruler the British had thought badly of him, had favoured the brother who struck them as altogether more amiable, a more malleable, more temperate man – not given as the heir apparent was given to wild and extravagant behaviour with money and women. The ruler in those days, the present Nawab's father, was anxious for nothing so much as to live in peace with the representatives of the paramount power. He listened attentively to their stern warnings about his elder son's sowing of wild oats, reacted as they intended he should react to hints that if the boy didn't mend his ways he would never be thought fit to rule Mirat – whereas the old Nawab's second son was a model of a young prince. Such a model son, succeeding, would certainly be confirmed by the King-Emperor's agents. In his case there would be no danger of an interregnum, no danger of Mirat's affairs coming under the direct control of the political department. The old man began to manœuvre for a position from which he could effectively disinherit his elder son in favour of the younger. The elder got wind of the plot, but it was luck that came to his rescue, luck in the shape of a proposal for marriage with the daughter of the ruler of a less ancient but far more powerful state with whom the British had an even closer relationship. The old Nawab was flattered. He attempted to arrange the alliance, but through the marriage of the girl to his younger son. The girl would have none of it. She had seen the man she wanted, through the zenana screen at a wedding celebration. The marriage took place as she wished. The old Nawab – and the British too – hoped that perhaps the marriage would see the end of the elder son's extravagances. It did not. He had only married the girl to secure his inheritance. The British, he knew, would never dare depose him now because to do so would outrage and insult the powerful father-in-law he had so fortunately acquired. When his father died he was confirmed in the succession. His Begum, headstrong as an unmarried girl became intolerable as his wife. He hated her. He hated the brother who had tried to steal his inheritance and who now, following the tradition, had become his chief minister – and a lickspittle of the British. The Nawab took mistresses, eventually a white woman. The scandal had begun. Out of the scandal Bronowsky emerged.

'Well, good night,' Ahmed said. Bronowsky said nothing, until Ahmed was at the bottom of the verandah steps, putting on his bicycle clips.

'Give my felicitations to Professor Nair,' he called. 'And be sure to mention the fact that you are going riding alone tomorrow with one of the Miss Laytons.'

'Why?'

'He will advise you more satisfactorily than I how to comport yourself, how to interpret accurately and safely her many little gestures and inflexions of voice which you might be in danger of misinterpreting. He will speak of such things as he speaks of all things – from the vast fund of his experience.'

Ahmed smiled, took his bicycle from the rack and prepared to mount.

'Oh and one other thing,' Bronowsky said, lowering his voice but enunciating carefully. 'Find out what you can about his visitor.'

'Has he got a visitor, then?'

'Yes. Two. A woman not identified and an elderly scholar by name of Pandit Baba Sahib. He comes from Mayapore. The question is, for what purpose?'

'Must there be a special one?'

'Professor Nair's visitors usually have a purpose, or if they don't have one when they arrive they have one when they go home.'

'Considering you only returned from Gopalakand today you're well informed.'

'I pay to be. And Pandit Baba is not unknown to us in Mirat. Have you had enough whisky to see you through an evening of fruit juice?'

'I think I shall manage.'

'Have a good time then, dear boy. And take care if you are tempted to come home by way of the Chandi Chowk.'

Ahmed waved, mounted and rode down the gravel drive of Bronowsky's bungalow to the gate which the watchman – already muffled in a shawl and armed with a stick – held open for him. Outside, he turned right, pedalled along the metalled road towards the city. To his left stretched the expanse of open ground which separated the City from the palace. Soft warm airs blew across it. The moon whose first appearance had ushered in the month of Ramadan was nearly full. It hung above the city, not giving much light, the shape and colour of an orange. It would wax and wane and become invisible. Its slender reappearance would announce the îd. During this month more than 1,300 years ago it was said that the Koran had been revealed by Allah to his Prophet. A good Muslim was supposed to fast from sunrise to sunset. Ahmed, remembering the whisky, stopped pedalling, stood astride and felt in his pocket for the clove of garlic. He popped it into his mouth and crunched, resumed his journey. The road was unlit, his cycle lamp out of order, but the night was luminous and he liked cycling in the dark. It could be a risky business and he preferred activities that had an element of danger in them, so long as the activities themselves were of a commonplace kind and only dangerous by virtue of some extraneous

452

circumstance. Riding a bicycle in the dark or a horse over rough country were one thing, deliberately courting danger was another. To Ahmed, the kind of danger that added spice to a situation was danger that came suddenly and unexpectedly; only so could it retain what he thought of as essential to it: spontaneity, or mystery, or both. He had once suggested to Professor Nair that his attitude to danger could be summed up by describing it as one that distinguished between the danger to a man who joined a riot and the danger to a man who found himself involved in one in the course of moving peaceably between point a and point b. Ahmed had experienced both kinds of danger as a student. It was the unexpected riot he enjoyed. 'One did not feel,' he told Nair, 'that one had to take sides, one merely hit out in one's own defence, and there wasn't any moral problem to puzzle out either before or after. I was knocked off my bicycle by one faction and subjected to rescue by the other. I dished out bloody noses indiscriminately and felt fine, and nobody noticed or thought to wonder whose side I was on, so when I'd finished having my fun I just rode away and left them all to it.'

Closer in to the city the road became overhung on one side by the trees in the grounds of the Hindu Boys' College, an institution which like the Council of State owed its existence to Count Bronowsky. Numerically in a minority, a mere twenty per cent of the population, the Muslims of Mirat had maintained a firm grip on the administration since the days of the Moghuls. Until Bronowsky's day few Hindus had held any public post of any importance. There were more mosques than temples, not because the rich Hindus of Mirat were unready to build temples but because permission to build was more often refused than granted. The same restrictions had been placed on the building and endowment of schools for Hindu boys and girls, who were generally thought to be too clever by half. For the Muslim children an Academy of Higher Education had been established in the late nineteenth century, but its record was poor; there was a saying that a boy left there with no qualifications except for reciting passages from the Koran, but that this alone was enough to pass him into the service of an official – particularly of a tax-collector. Until the foundation of the Hindu Boys' College in 1924, non-Muslims whose parents wanted them educated above middle-school standards had to compete for places in colleges outside Mirat, and having left Mirat the tendency was not to return but to seek employment in the service of the Government of India. Muslims, jealous guardians of their own entrenched position in the administration of the State, saw no harm in this draining of potential talent among the Hindus whose job, in their opinion, was trading and moneylending. But Bronowsky saw harm and persuaded the Nawab to see harm too, and to allocate a modest annual sum from the State's revenue for a college that would be open to the sons of rich or poor Hindus. The rest of the money was provided by prominent Hindu businessmen. The building that was erected reflected the combination of civic pride and sense of communal and personal grandiosity with which the money was contributed: red brick with white facings, Gothic windows and Gothic arches. Coconut palms were planted in the forecourt. From the beginning it had been a success.

*

'Is that you, Ahmed?' Professor Nair called as Ahmed – having passed the watchman at the gate of the college and walked his bicycle off the drive that led to the main building and on to a narrow path – came in sight of the Principal's bungalow. Nair stood at the head of the steps, silhouetted by the light from the open door. He was dressed in his white pyjamas.

'Yes, professor,' Ahmed called back. 'Am I late?'

'Oh no. At least only by a few minutes.'

'Count Sahib is back from Gopalakand. I had to call in. He sent his regards by the way.'

Ahmed put his cycle in the rack, climbed the steps and let his hands be taken in both of Nair's. The professor stood about a foot shorter than Ahmed.

'I have an important visitor,' he whispered. 'Do you mind taking off your shoes and socks? He's an awful stickler for orthodoxies. I'm afraid he won't eat with us.'

'Who is he?' Ahmed asked, bending to untie his shoe-laces.

'Pandit Baba Sahib of Mayapore. He is writing a commentary on the Bhagavad Gita. I don't mean right now. I mean it is his principal occupation. Please don't offer to shake hands, and don't sit where your shadow will fall on him. It's all rather nerve-racking. Frankly I came out to relax. I am longing for a cigarette but daren't smoke one in case he smells it. At times like this one's bad habits come home to roost. Had Count Sahib any interesting news?'

'None that he shared with me. May I keep my socks?'

'Oh by all means. The floors get so dirty. Come. Meet Panditji. Like me he is a great admirer of your father.'

The house smelt of incense, which was unusual. Pandit Baba Sahib had probably been in Mrs Nair's puja room. That was one of the rooms in Professor Nair's house that Ahmed had never entered. In fact he had only seen two rooms, the room where they sat and talked, which was entered from the right of the square hallway, and the room where they ate, which was entered from the left. An open door at the far end of the hall gave on to a courtyard, where Mrs Nair kept a tethered goat. Ahmed gathered that other rooms, such as the bedroom, bathroom and puja room were entered from this courtyard.

When he came into the living-room – Nair stepping aside and graciously waving him on – he saw that the chairs had been removed and cushions and rugs put down in their place. Pandit Baba Sahib was seated cross-legged on one cushion, resting his left elbow on a pile of three or four. He too was dressed in pyjamas. He had a grey beard and a grey turban. A pair of steel-rimmed spectacles with circular lenses were lodged half-way down his rather stubby nose.

'This is our young visitor,' Nair said. 'Son of our illustrious M A K. A young gentleman of many talents but currently Social Secretary to the Nawab Sahib.'

Panditji stared at Ahmed above the rims of his glasses. The whites of his eyes were yellow. He did not smile, he made no gesture of greeting. He simply stared. There was a certain kind of Hindu who inspired in Ahmed involuntary little twitches of distaste, the relics no doubt of the racial and religious animosity his own forbears had felt towards the forbears of men like Pandit Baba Sahib. It was no hardship to him to keep his distance or to stand where even his shadow could not reach the figure on the cushions who had made no attempt to acknowledge Nair's introduction and continued to stare up with an expression Ahmed would have thought genuinely disapproving had he not guessed it as probably an expression that Pandit Baba assumed automaticaly when meeting strangers, especially if the stranger was young. Ahmed gazed back, with Nair at his side still holding him by the elbow.

Presently Pandit Baba spoke. He had a high light voice. He spoke in Hindi.

'You do not look like your father.'

'Oh, you know him,' Ahmed said, but in English. 'Most people would agree with you. They say I take after my mother. Personally I never see any resemblance in myself to any member of my family.'

Pandit Baba frowned.

'Why do you answer me, and at such length, in a foreign language?'

'Because I speak Hindi rather badly.'

'You wish us to converse in Urdu?' Panditji asked, switching to it.

'I should prefer English, Pandit Sahib. It's the language we always speak at home. My mother is a Punjabi you see, and English was the only language she had in common with my father. Even in Urdu I express myself poorly.'

'Do you not feel shame to speak always in the language of a foreign power, the language of your father's jailers?' Pandit Baba asked – reverting to Hindi. At any moment Ahmed expected a bit of Bengali, a sentence or two in Tamil, perhaps a passage in Sanskrit. The Pandit was obviously proud of his facility. His refusal so far to speak in English did not mean he spoke it badly or was not proud of understanding and being able to speak it; but it was fashionable among Hindus of Baba's kind to decry it, to declare that once the British had been got rid of their language must go with them; although what would be put in its place it was difficult to tell. Even Pandit Baba Sahib would fare badly if he went out into some of the villages around Mirat and tried to understand what was said to him. He would need an interpreter, as most officials did. And the odds were the interpreter would interpret the local dialect in the language and idiom of the British.

'No,' Ahmed said. 'I'm not ashamed.'

'*Baitho,*' Professor Nair interrupted, and squatted on a cushion, motioning Ahmed to follow suit, which he did. His trousers made it an uncomfortable operation. Pandit Baba scrutinized him, this time through the lenses of his spectacles. The Pandit – Ahmed now saw – was sitting on a double thickness of cushions. His was a commanding position.

'I do not know your father in person, only I am admiring him from the distance,' he said suddenly, in English, 'and familiarizing myself to his photographs. It is a face after all much known in newspapers.'

Ahmed nodded. Pandit Baba, having spoken, subjected Ahmed to further scrunity. It was extraordinary, Ahmed thought, how men distinguished in one field – and he assumed that Pandit Baba Sahib was distinguished – seemed to claim for themselves wisdom in all spheres of human activity; wisdom and the right to make pronouncements which they expected you to listen to and learn from. The most amusing thing was to see a group of distinguished men together, with no one but each other to make pronouncements to. They were as suspicious of each other, then, as children. He had seen such gatherings in his father's house while – outside the compound walls – crowds waited in patient homage, or simple curiosity, for a sight of these extraordinary, benign and powerful faces, and he had observed the change that came over those faces when they parted company with each other and went out to meet the crowds. He thought that if Pandit Baba smiled now he would look like them, as they came from the house to the veranda, their games, sulks, quarrels temporarily suspended, and their suspicions making way for the feelings of relief and pleasure at re-entering a familiar world whose plaudits reaffirmed the huge capacity they believed they had, individually and collectively, to solve its problems, its mysteries and its injustices. Perhaps (Ahmed thought, still meeting Pandit Baba's apparently unwinking gaze) it was his early experience of distinguished men that had led him to feel that there was distance between himself and other people and their ideas. Gandhi had once given him an orange, Pandit Nehru had patted his head, and Maulana Azad had taken him on to his knee; but oranges, head-pats and knee-rides – as he realized even at the time – were not the objects of those visitations, and the visitations themselves although promising excitement always left the excitement on the other side of the wall where the crowds waited. 'Why do they wait?' he had asked his elder brother Sayed. 'Because they know we are saving India,' came the steady reply. As a boy Sayed had been a bit of a bore. 'Saving India from what?' Ahmed said. 'Well, from the British of course.' But in the morning, as he went to school, he noticed that the British were still there and looking quite unperturbed. When he got to school he found there weren't to be any lessons because the teachers and the older boys were on strike to protest the arrest the previous night of people who had been carried away with enthusiasm at the sight of the Mahatma visiting Ahmed's father, and – after seeing the Mahatma off at the station – had got out of hand and thrown brickbats at the police who were jostling them, hitting them with lathis and treading them under horse-hoof. Two days later his father was arrested too – for making the speech the Mahatma had asked him to make – and was in prison – that time – for six months.

'Speak what is in your mind,' Pandit Baba commanded. What insolence, Ahmed thought. There are two categories of things in my mind, he should say, the stuff people like you have fed into it and my own reactions to that stuff. The result is cancellation, so I have nothing in my mind.

'I was thinking of my father in prison,' he said. After a moment or two the miracle happened. The Pandit's lips lifted at the corners. He was bestowing a smile of sympathy and of elderly approval of a young man's filial regard. Ahmed considered its quality; it struck him as no less dishonest than the expression of disapproval. How could Pandit Baba be moved to feel either approval or disapproval when the person who was the object of it was a complete stranger to him? Well, it is this that puts me off (Ahmed told himself), this ease with which people feel emotions, or pretend to feel them.

'I meant,' he continued, 'the first time, when I was quite young, a schoolboy still.'

The smile did not disappear. A man like Panditji could mesmerize you into submission, hypnotize you into regarding him as a source of spiritual comfort. It was undoubtedly his intention to try, and when you knew a man's intentions you were even more in danger of being subjected to them because to be aware of an intention somehow increased its force. I shall destroy you, one man might say to another; and at once he would have a confederate, the man himself. Ideas seemed to have a life, a power of their own. Men became slaves to them. To challenge an idea as an alternative to accepting it was to be no less a slave to it. Neither to accept nor challenge it was the most difficult thing of all; perhaps impossible. The idea of Pandit Baba as a personification of wisdom, a fount of knowledge and self-knowledge, which was presumably the idea the Pandit had of himself and worked hard at conveying, was not to be got rid of by privately or even publicly asserting that the man was probably a self-opinionated and pompous fool who relied on his venerable age and appearance to command what respect his behaviour and ideas in themselves could not.

'Do not think of it as prison,' Pandit Baba said, going back to Hindi. 'It is those who call themselves jailers who are in prison, and perhaps all of us who are outside the walls. For what is outside in one sense is inside in another. In time we must break the walls down. This duty to break them down is *our* sentence of imprisonment. To break them down will be to free ourselves *and* our jailers. And we cannot sit back and wait for the orders of release. We must write the orders ourselves.' In English he added, in case Ahmed had misunderstood, 'I speak metaphorically.'

Ahmed nodded. In India nearly everybody spoke metaphorically except the English who spoke bluntly and could make their most transparent lies look honest as a consequence; whereas any truth contained in these metaphorical rigmaroles was so deviously presented that it looked devious itself.

'You had a pleasant journey from Mayapore, Panditji?' he asked, to see how Pandit Baba would react to such a barefaced attempt to change the subject. The Pandit reacted, after a few seconds, with a vague gesture of the arm that rested on the cushions and then opened his mouth as if to continue his parable.

Ahmed said hastily, 'And is this your first visit to Mirat?'

Professor Nair answered for Panditji. 'Oh no, not his first visit. Panditji was at one time living in Mirat.'

Ahmed glanced at Nair and noticed the minuscule gems of sweat encrusted on his bald domed head. It was quite cool in the room. A table-fan, set on the floor in one corner, moved its round whirring wire cage from side to side like a spectator at a slow-motion tennis match – more interested, Ahmed felt, in the conversation than he was.

'But for the last few years,' Nair was saying, but looking all the time at Pandit Baba as if the Pandit had become a museum-piece suddenly and Nair his curator, 'he has been in Mayapore.'

'Yes, I see,' Ahmed said, looking again at the Pandit – and the eyes, slightly enlarged by the spectacle lenses, that were still gazing at him. 'Then you were in Mayapore during the riots.'

'Which riots are you meaning?'

'The riots in August last year.'

Again Ahmed had to wait for a reply. Pandit Baba Sahib's sympathy had gone and his disapproval was undergoing a change. He now looked at Ahmed as if he felt he had been threatened with violence.

'You must be speaking of something that has escaped my notice,' he said at last. His heart had resumed the business of pumping cold blood. An old man like me, his expression now said, should not be put in danger of losing his temper. 'I am not remembering any riots in Mayapore in August last year.' He paused, continued. 'A riot – and since you are knowing English somewhat better than me, perhaps you will correct me or corroborate – a riot I believe according to English dictionary refers to the violent unlawful actions of unlawful assembly of people. In Mayapore and India in general only I remember spontaneous demonstrations of innocent and law-abiding people to protest against the unlawful imprisonment without trial of men such as your father, and in Mayapore, particularly, demonstrations against the unlawful arrest of innocent men accused of a crime none of them committed. If this what you are mistakenly calling riots, then – yes – I was in Mayapore at this time, when many people suffered the consequence of resisting unlawful acts by those supposed to be in lawful authority.'

Ahmed inclined his head, a movement he had found useful in the last few years, a movement suggestive of submission without verbal acknowledgement of it. He had discovered that this combination often forced people to move from attack to defence. They felt compelled to justify the victory which had just been ambiguously conceded to them.

'It is necessary all the time to have the truth of things clearly in the mind, you see,' Pandit Baba said, 'and to speak of them in truthful terms. Loose speech leads to loose thinking. When you speak of riots you are speaking as the English speak. You must speak like an Indian, and think like an Indian.' The corners of his lips lifted again. 'I know it is not always easy. But to take only easy ways is often to end up with difficulties.'

Ahmed nodded and wondered what reason Nair had for asking him at short notice on an evening when there was another guest, a guest Nair had failed to mention in the note of invitation sent round that morning but whose presence had not escaped the notice of Bronowsky, that was to say – of Bronowsky's spies. He wondered whether he would catch a glimpse of the woman Baba had brought with him, but doubted it. It was an all-male evening. He wouldn't even see Mrs Nair.

'Professor Nair tells me you are writing a commentary on the Bhagavad Gita. Does the work go well, Panditji?'

Again the gesture of the arm that rested on the cushion. Interpreting this, now, as a cue for Professor Nair to interrupt, Ahmed looked at their host. The sweat still shone on Nair's head. He still gazed at Pandit Baba. His smile had become fixed. He said nothing. He smiled, stared and perspired. Ahmed had the feeling that if Panditji got up and left the room it would take Nair several minutes to regain his normal composure – or lack of composure: he was a restless man, usually. Surely Panditji's presence in itself wasn't as nerve-racking as Nair's almost catatonic reaction to it seemed to suggest? Ahmed looked back at Panditji and found himself still under scrutiny.

'Your father, I believe, is in the Fort at Premanagar,' Pandit Baba said.

'So people say.'

'You have no comfirmation of this?'

'No.'

'You think he may be elsewhere?'

'Officially I have no information, Pandit Sahib. Unofficially it seems to be understood by people that he is, or was, in Premanagar.'

'But you are able to communicate. You write letters to him, and he writes back to you.'

'I usually communicate through my mother.'

'And the letters of course are directed through the prison authorities.'

'Of course.'

'And censored.'

'Naturally.'

'But occasionally you manage a more private kind of correspondence.'

For a while Ahmed did not answer. Eventually he said, 'I can't say whether my mother sometimes manages that. For myself the answer is no.'

'But before he went to jail, some kind of simple code was arranged, so that even a letter going through the authorities and the censor might contain some private or intimate information?'

Ahmed laughed, shook his head. Panditji raised his eyebrows.

'No such code was arranged?'

'No.'

'I am not an agent provocateur,' Panditji announced, and frowned. 'But let us talk of something else. Your father is in good health, I trust?'

'Yes, I believe so.'

'And your mother?'

'She is well, too.'

'Presumably she is not hopeful of being permitted to visit him.'

'No. She's resigned to everything. His being absent in prison is all a part of her experience of marriage.'

'You speak sadly or bitterly of that?'

Ahmed smiled. 'No. It is just the truth.'

Pandit Baba nodded. He said, 'It is perhaps more difficult for her – being of the Mohammedan faith – more difficult than for some other Congressmen's wives. Her family in the Punjab – they are perhaps more sympathetic to the policies of Mr Jinnah and the Muslim League than to those of the Congress?'

'That is correct,' Ahmed admitted.

'Since a long time, or since the political turncoating in the Punjab of Sir Sikander Hyat-Khan in 1937?'

'Perhaps, yes, since then.'

'This will no doubt be a sorrow to her, to have her husband imprisoned, to have no family member to turn to without feeling disloyal to that husband.'

'Actually I think my mother is angry sooner than sad.'

'What makes her angry?'

'Oh, quite a lot of things. For instance she loses her temper when she hears people describe father as a show-case Muslim.'

'Show-case? What is this?' I have not heard this expression.'

'It means Muslims whom the Congress chose for positions of power in order to prove to everybody that they're not a Hindu-riddled organization.'

'Ah. Yes. I see. Show-case. And so Muslims who follow Mr Jinnah and his Muslim League say that Mohammed Ali Kasim, a Congress man, is a show-case Muslim?'

'They do I suppose, but members of Congress say it as well. Members who are jealous and think such Muslims have unfair advantages because of their propaganda value.' Ahmed hesitated. 'There is of course some truth in that.'

'Truth is not divisible, Mr Kasim. There cannot be such a thing as some truth. You are meaning to say that in some cases it is true that a Muslim had unfair advantages over a Hindu in the Congress because the high command chose him for his propaganda value first and his talents second. This may or may not be true. But it cannot be a matter in which there is *some* truth.'

Ahmed again inclined his head.

460

'You are staying in Mirat for a week or two, Panditji?'

Pandit Baba smiled, the smile of a man willing to be sidetracked because for him all paths led eventually in the direction he intended to go. 'It will not be so long. I shall return quite soon to Mayapore, I believe.'

'Only a short holiday, then.'

'I am not taking holiday.'

'There are texts in the college library that Panditji wants to have a look at,' Professor Nair explained. He was still smiling, but in the last few seconds had wiped the sweat off his head with a folded handkerchief, had come out of the catatonic trance. 'It is to inspect these texts Panditji is honouring us with a stay,' he added, quite unnecessarily; and then, more informatively, 'but before he leaves I hope to persuade him to address our students.'

Pandit Baba closed his eyes, inclined his head modestly to the right and then to the left.

Ahmed said, 'If you live in Mayapore, Panditji, perhaps you knew that English girl, Miss Manners? One gathers her circle of friends in Mayapore wasn't exclusively English.'

'No, I did not know her personally.'

'She's dead now. She had a child. There was a notice in the newspapers.'

'It did not escape our attention, Mr Kasim.' Pandit Baba paused. 'You have some personal interest in this matter?'

'No, but it was talked about a lot at the time, and when anyone mentions Mayapore these days you automatically think of Miss Manners – and the rape in the Bibighar Gardens.'

'It is not established that there was rape. Only that there were arrests, and imprisonment without trial of suspects, imprisonment not for rape but for so-called political activities.'

'So-called?'

'So-called. How can one say definitely when nothing is made public, when there is such a convenient regulation as Defence of India Rule?'

'Do you mean that the whole affair was invented, never took place at all?'

'I did not mean this. Simply I was speaking of evidence. Clearly it was thought that rape had occurred.'

'I expect the girl thought so herself,' Ahmed could not resist saying.

'I agree that it is not an experience the victim could be in doubt about.'

'You think that perhaps *she* made it up?'

'I do not think anything, Mr Kasim. Only I am saying that to speak of the rape of Miss Manners in the Bibighar Gardens is to speak of an affair as if it had happened when it is not legally established as having happened. If you say there was rape I would not agree or disagree. Also I would not agree or disagree if you said no, there was no rape, the girl was hallucinated or lying and making up stories for one reason or another. Only I can agree if you state simply that it was generally accepted through reports and rumour that there was rape, that certain men were arrested as suspects, that

461

presently the British attempted to hush everything up, that no case was ever brought to court, that it was said the girl herself refused to identify those arrested, that in the end there was officially no rape and no punishment for rape.'

'Did you know any of the men who were arrested, Panditji?'

'Yes. I knew. They were boys of some education.'

'Did you know the one who was friendly with Miss Manners?'

After a moment Pandit Baba said, 'You are speaking of Hari Kumar.'

'I think that was his name. Did you know Kumar?'

Again a slight pause. 'Once when he first returned from England his aunt sought my assistance to teach him Hindi. Of all these boys I knew him best. He also could only speak properly English. He was not at all a good student. He had no wish to speak his native language. He employed himself on a local newspaper that was published in English. Always he was attempting to forget that he was an Indian, because he had lived in England since earliest childhood. His father took him there when he was two years old only. He went to English public school and had English friends. He did not understand why he could not have such friends here. His father died, you see, and he had no relative but his aunt in Mayapore. She paid for his passage and gave him a roof and was kind to him, being a widow with no children. But to him, she was a foreigner. All of us were foreigners to Hari Kumar. He knew only English people and English ways. Only he wanted these people and these ways. In Mayapore he could not have them. He was a most unfortunate young man. His case should be taken to heart.'

'But eventually he had one English friend, didn't he? I mean Miss Manners.'

'They were sometimes together. I do not know whether she was his friend.'

'People said they were friends and more.'

'I have no knowledge of this. I do not find it informative to take notice of idle gossip. They were sometimes together. This I can vouch for. People say she was unlike other English people. I do not know what they mean when they are saying that. English people are not mass-produced. They do not come off a factory line all looking, speaking, thinking, acting the same. Neither do we. But we are Indians and they are English. True intimacy is not possible. It is not even desirable. Only it is desirable that there should be peace between us, and this is not possible while the English retain possession of what belongs to us, because to get it back we must fight them. In fighting them we do not have to hate them. But also when we have got back from them what they have taken from us and are at peace with them this does not mean that we should love them. We can never be friends with the English, or they with us, but we need not be enemies. Men are not born equal, nor are they born brothers. The lion does not lie down with the tiger, or the crow nest with the swallow. The world is created in a diversity of phenomena and each phenomenon has its own diversity. Between mankind there may be common truth and justice and common wisdom to lead to amity. But between men there are divisions and love cannot be felt truly except by like and like. Between like and unlike there can only be tolerance, and absence of enmity – which is not at all the same thing as friendship. Perhaps the truth of this is most apparent to the Hindu who is born to understand and accept this concept of diversity.'

Ahmed waited a moment to make sure Pandit Baba had finished, then he said, 'A little while ago you said the people demonstrated against the arrest of Kumar and the others for a crime they hadn't committed, but how did they know they hadn't committed it?'

Pandit Baba smiled again.

'You are like your father in one way. You have perhaps some of his forensic skill. In a moment you plan to raise the question of riot again, you will say that it would be correct to describe the demonstrations as riots because the demonstrators had no means of knowing whether these boys were guilty or not at that time, and were only acting instinctively and therefore unlawfully, therefore riotously.'

'Isn't it a debatable point?'

'All points are debatable. But there are two things that must be taken into consideration. The first is that the demonstrations in Mayapore and the attacks on government installations were no different in main respect from similar demonstrations and attacks in other parts of the country, demonstrations against the arrest of Congress leaders – men such as your father. In Mayapore, however, there was additional weight and temper arising out of the arrests of these boys. But you see not out of the arrests as arrests but out of what quickly became known, that some of these boys were tortured and defiled by the police on the same night of their arrest in order to get them to confess. This knowledge came from the police headquarters itself, as did the knowledge that in spite of torture no confession was obtained. Some of these boys were whipped and they were forced to eat beef. They were Hindus, boys of some education. One was Kumar. We did not think it possible that such boys could set upon and rape an English girl. Also it was believed that all they had been doing was drinking illicit liquor in a hut on the other side of the river from the Bibighar Gardens. It was in the hut that they were arrested. Kumar was not with them but they were known to the police to be acquaintances of Kumar. It was to find Kumar that the police went to the hut. The police went to find Kumar because of his association with the girl who was reported to have been raped. The head of the police in Mayapore, the English District Superintendent, he also was associated with the girl. It was the District Superintendent who personally conducted the interrogations, who ordered the boys to be beaten and forced to eat beef. All night he was there, in the police headquarters, asking them questions. Meanwhile, if there was rape, the real culprits, hooligans no doubt, made good their escape. But District Superintendent was not interested in them. Only he was interested in punishing these boys, especially Kumar, because of Kumar's association with the white girl. District Superintendent was an evil man, Mr Kasim. His cruelty and perversions were known to his men and consequently to some of us. It was one of his own Muslim constables who next morning whispered the truth to people outside, because he was ashamed of what had been done. He spoke too of a bicycle which the police found in the Bibighar Gardens when they searched there at night. It belonged to the girl. He said that District Superintendent ordered the bicycle to be put in the police truck. Later when they had arrested the boys in the hut they drove to the house where Kumar was living. District Superintendent told them to take the bicycle out of the truck and leave it in the ditch outside this house. Then they went into the house and arrested Kumar, pretended to search the area and so 'found' the bicycle and said that Kumar had stolen it from the white girl after raping her. Some of the police were thinking this was a great joke. But the man who told of these things did not think it was funny. Later, people were saying he became frightened and denied what he had secretly told. Perhaps if there had been a trial for rape he would have been persuaded to tell the truth of these things. But there was in any case no trial. District Superintendent had been too clever. Even people like Judge Menen and the Deputy Commissioner became suspicious that the wrong boys had been arrested, and Judge Menen heard the rumours of torture and defilement. He had the boys questioned but they were too frightened to say anything, we understand. Except Kumar who was not saying anything at all to anybody, and did not even seem to want to save himself. But chiefly there was no trial because Miss Manners herself was saying the men arrested could not have had anything to do with it. So now District Superintendent produced evidence that all these boys were engaged in subversive activites and no doubt the English thought it was not possible to set them free in any event. So they were imprisoned without trial under Defence of India Rule, as your father and many others are imprisoned.'

'Surely it would be difficult to produce evidence of subversive activities, Panditji, unless it was actually there?'

'Not so difficult, Mr Kasim. But no doubt in all but one case these boys had done and said things that patriotic young Indians say and do, boys of some education, and of certain temperaments. The police had files on them as they had files on many such boys. In the other case, in Kumar's case, also they had a file because once he was taken into custody for refusing to answer questions and for making difficulties about giving his proper name. Unfortunately the police officer whose questions he refused to answer was this same Englishman, the District Superintendent. If Kumar had answered District Superintendent properly, if he had said "sir" and looked frightened and done some grovelling, District Superintendent would not have taken notice of him. But this was not Hari Kumar's way, who hated India, and wanted to be treated like an English boy, and spoke English and only English, and with what is called I understand Public School accent, and so was annoyed to be asked questions by District Superintendent who did not have such good education but expected to be

464

treated all the time like a Sahib because of his white face. But to think of Hari Kumar engaged in subversive activities with other young Indians is to those of us who know him, Mr Kasim, only laughable. He did not like India. He did not like Indians. Only he liked England and his memories of being in England and having English friends. He was not a boy who would plot with other young Indians to get rid of the English.'

'Is he still in prison?'

'They are all still in prison, but I think not together. He is in the Kandipat jail in Ranpur, a long way from Mayapore. For many months his aunt did not know which prison they had sent him to. Now at last she is permitted to write and to send him some food and some books. He thanks her for them but she cannot be sure that he is allowed to eat the food or read the books. I know these things because I am in her confidence. Poor lady. Her sufferings are most sad to see. She was very fond of her English nephew as she called him.'

Suddenly Pandit Baba looked at Professor Nair.

'You say nothing, my friend.'

'Oh, but I am listening with a great deal of interest. I did not know you were so closely concerned with this very interesting case.'

'Yes,' Pandit Baba said. 'It is interesting. You find this also? It is the kind of case – by which I mean the case of the arrest and punishment of six boys – the kind of case our young friend's father here would have loved to take charge of in the days when he was so illustriously practising the law and defending countrymen of his who were wrongfully accused.' He looked again at Ahmed. 'Unfortunately it is a case that can never be subjected to the searching eyes of the law. But this does not mean it should be forgotten. And it is not only in the courts that justice is done. You look hungry, Mr Kasim. Let me not keep you and Professor Nair any longer from your supper. I shall have retired before you finish, for I have some work to do, so allow me to say good night.'

Nair rose, and Ahmed – somewhat stiffly – followed suit, bowed to Panditji and followed Professor Nair out of the room and across the hall and into the dining-room. A servant who had been squatting in the doorway that led out to the compound got up, went out and shouted orders to the cook. Nair set the fan going and they sat at opposite ends of the table which was dressed Western-style.

'Do you mind vegetarian?' Professor Nair whispered. 'It's the smell of cooking you see. One has to think of everything.'

II

The horses had been behaving badly. Sarah wondered whether young Mr Kasim had deliberately chosen them for their iron mouths and vicious natures or whether it had been a question of taking the best of a bad bunch from the palace stables. Her own mount, for instance, had shied twice at its early morning shadow, missed its footing on some shale and having reached the promising openness of the comparatively flat turf in the middle of the waste ground separating the palace from the city, resolutely come to a halt, stretched its neck and cropped grass. Mr Kasim, who seemed to be having difficulty restraining his own mount from surging forward in a gallop for the city gates, grew nearly level but some feet away and held it there by what looked like main force. She noted the ridged muscle on his bare forearms. The brim of his topee darkened his face and hid his expression.

'Are you a Sunni or a Shiah, Mr Kasim?' Because of the distance between them she had raised her voice. She thought she sounded like a games mistress.

'A Shiah,' Ahmed said, and wrenched his horse's head to the left to stop it closing in on Sarah's.

'Is there a great deal of difference?'

'I beg your pardon?'

'Much difference?'

Pandering to his horse to make it feel it had got its way he led it round in a tight circle and brought it to stand again in its original position.

'Not really. The Shiahs dispute the rights of the three Khalifs who succeeded Mohammed. You could say it's a political division.'

'Who are the Shiahs for?'

'What?'

'Who do they say should have succeeded Mohammed?'

'Oh. A man called Ali. He was Mohammed's son-in-law. We mourn his death at the beginning of Muharram. The Mohammedan new year. But then the Sunnis often join in the mourning too.'

'Is the Nawab a Shiah Muslim?'

'Yes.'

'Are there any Sunnis in Mirat?'

'Yes, a few.'

'I think if you rode on a bit this damned thing would stop eating grass and at least pretend to do what I want it to.'

For answer Ahmed set his horse towards her and when he was near enough reached over, took the reins from her and jerked. The horse brought its head up.

'Keep him like that,' Ahmed suggested, holding the reins in short, so that the horse's neck looked painfully arched. She slid her left hand along the reins until her fist touched Ahmed's. She could smell the garlic on his breath. Perhaps he meant her to because he had heard what her Aunty Fenny said.

'Thanks.'

She set the horse at a walk. It jerked its head continually, trying to force her to lengthen the rein. Ahmed resumed his position, a few paces behind her on her left. Obviously he had no intention of making conversation; but was it shyness, dislike or indifference? At least, she felt, you could rely on him. He'd make no bones about disciplining the horse for her and, no longer dressed in a lounge suit but instead in short-sleeved shirt and jodhpurs, he looked like a man her future brother-in-law Teddie Bingham would describe as being 'useful in a scrap', than which for Teddie there was probably no higher praise of his own sex. Muslim men, after all, did have this quality. Sarah corrected herself: not Muslim men, but Indians who were descended like Mr Kasim from Middle Eastern stock: Arabs, Persians and Turks. They had retained the sturdiness of races whom extremes of heat and cold (she was thinking of deserts) had toughened.

England's climate had also toughened her people. Years ago Sarah had written an essay with the rather grandiloquent title: The Effect of Climate and Topography upon the Human Character. The idea, she remembered, had first come to her in the summer holiday of the year great-grandpa died and she had walked across Mr Birtwhistle's field encouraging Aunt Mabel not to be put off by the cows and then stood by the brook thinking how much like Pankot in miniature her surroundings were; the year when she was struck by the difference between her Indian family and her English family. 'England,' she had written when she was a couple of years older, 'although temperate climatically speaking, combines within a very limited geographical area a diversity of weather and natural features. Such conditions react upon the inhabitants to make them strong, active, energetic and self-sufficient. It is these qualities which they take abroad with them into their tropical and subtropical colonies, lands whose native populations are inclined because of things like heat and humidity to be less strong, less active, less energetic and more willing to be led, a fact which has enabled European races in general but the English in particular to gain and keep control of such territories. Upon the return of our colonial exiles to the land of their birth they are struck by the smallness of everything and by the fact that the self-sufficiency of their race, thus re-encountered, is really the result of the self-satisfaction of a people who have had comparatively little to contend with in the human struggle against nature.' She remembered the opening paragraph almost word for word and also remembered the red-pencil comment of the headmistress in the margin, 'An interesting essay and well developed so far as the question of climatic influences is concerned. I do not fully understand your reference to topography as an influence, however, and perhaps you fail to understand it yourself, as witness your failure to develop that aspect of your argument.'

'But I do understand it,' Sarah had assured herself, 'and it's all there, she just hasn't read it.' Reading it again, though, she thought that perhaps a bit of clarification would do no harm, then that it would be a definite improvement; finally that the headmistress was right and that clarification was essential, but in her mind first and only then on paper; and in her mind the clarification obstinately refused to come. She was stuck with that single recollection of a notion that had reached her out of the blue, that the place near the brook in the spinney beyond Mr Birtwhistle's fields

467

was like Pankot in miniature and that this somehow explained why her Indian family were not like her English family.

Over to the right of the waste ground there were a few trees and a road and facing the road a substantial bungalow behind grey stucco walls. 'Who lives there?' she asked Ahmed, holding the reins tight in one hand and pointing.

'That's Count Bronowsky's house.'

'Is he really a count?'

'Yes, I think so.'

'Dare we gallop?'

'If you'd like to.'

'Where to? To the city gates?'

'There's a nullah. We'll have to bear left and join the city gate road.'

'I don't mind nullahs.'

'It's too wide to jump.'

'Come on then.'

She dug in her heels. A moment she loved: the slight hesitation, the gathering of propulsive forces in the animal she sat astride, the first leap forward that always seemed to her like a leap into a world of unexplored delight which she could only cut a narrow channel through and which she would reach the farther end of too soon but not without experiencing on the way something of the light and mysterious pleasure that existed for creatures who broke free of their environment. Ahead she made out the broken line of the nullah and as the horse did not at once respond to movement of wrist and pressure of heel had a second or two of fear that had itself broken free into a curious region of stillness and excitement; and then the horse began veering left; a quick glance over her shoulder showed her Ahmed. She felt an extraordinary, exhilarating sense of the perfection of their common endeavour. Together they galloped along the line of the nullah and charged through the gap where the nullah petered out a few yards from the road. From here she could see the city gate, isolated relic of the city wall, and how the road led to it and had come diagonally across the waste ground from the palace. They passed through splashes of shade from the trees that lined the road, drew level with and passed a line of lumbering carts drawn by humped white oxen, and then a file of women with baskets on their heads. The air was salurated by the pale smell of centuries of dung-fire smoke. The city was close. Why, it looms, Sarah thought, I don't want it: and exerted pressure with her right heel and right wrist to bring the horse round in a fine galloping sweep. She sensed the animal's bloody-minded resistance. It seemed as if it would neither turn nor slow, but would charge mindlessly on and dash itself and her to pieces on the city of Mirat. But then she felt the slight change of rhythm and the neat little spasm of adjustment to the centre of gravity, and Mirat began to swing towards her left shoulder. She exerted pressure to slow the horse to a canter, and then to a trot. At this end of the waste ground there was a group of three banyan trees, two of them with a fine display of rooted branches.

She reined in beneath the youngest of the trees and looked round. Mr Kasim had reined in too, and waited exactly as before, a few paces behind her, to her left. Such precision! She smiled at him, pleased for both of them. The smile she got in return, though, was as distant as ever. Obviously he had not shared her pleasure; instead, probably, shared her moments of dismay, wondering what blame would be put on him if she fell and was injured. In his position Teddie would have felt obliged to say, Are you all right? or, You'd better go easy on that brute. And have got himself ready to complain to the head syce when they returned to the palace; all of which – Sarah realized – would spoil the morning for her by introducing the all-too-familiar note of criticism that day in day out acted in you and on you as part of a general awareness of being in charge, of having to be prepared to throw your weight about, so that really there was nothing you could enjoy for its own sake, nothing you could give yourself over to entirely.

She looked towards the town and said, 'It's funny, Mr Kasim, but I've not once heard the muezzin since I've been here, and yet there are all those minarets.'

'The wind's been in the wrong direction, I expect.'

'They do call then?'

'Oh yes. They call.'

'Five times a day?'

'Yes.'

'Will the îd al-fitr prayers be said in the mosques or out here?'

'Out here. Why?'

'I read somewhere that they're supposed to be held in the open air if possible.'

'You must have seen such meetings before, in open places?'

'No. I don't think so. I suppose because I've only been in places where they make them stay in the mosques in case of trouble. Or perhaps I've seen them but not known what was going on.'

'Last year the îd fell during the wet season. The prayers were indoors then.'

'Why is it preferred for them to be in the open?'

Mr Kasim paused, as if considering; but he might have been reluctant to answer so many questions about his religion. She, after all, was an infidel. When the answer came, though, it suggested mockery; mockery of her and of the beliefs of his own people.

'Because of the crowds, I expect. The idea is wholly practical.'

'You mean you have to cater for all the people who never go into a mosque normally?'

'Yes,' Ahmed said. And added, 'But I'm no kind of authority. The Imam at the Abu-Q'rim mosque would probably have a different explanation.'

'When exactly will the îd fall?'

'When the new moon is seen.'

'Supposing it's cloudy?'

'Then you calculate and usually make it thirty days instead of twenty-

469

nine or thirty after the beginning of Ramadan, to be on the safe side. But it won't be cloudy this year and of course the calculation is already made. In fact the Id is due about a week after your sister's wedding.'

'Is it? But how nice. That means everybody will be happy.' She turned. It was uncomfortable having to sit askew in the saddle just to talk to him. She set the horse at a walk and then at a trot. Everybody will be happy. Everybody will be happy. Distantly she could see the roof of the palace. The sun was already hot and the short-lived freshness of early morning already staling. She noted the first phase of that curious phenomenon of the Indian plain, the gradual disappearance of the horizon, as if the land were expanding, stretching itself, destroying the illusion that the mind, hand and eye could stake a claim to any part that bore a real relation to the whole. It is always retreating, Sarah told herself, always making off, getting farther and farther away and leaving people and what people have built stranded. Behind her, she knew, Mr Kasim rode at a constant watchful distance, but as the land expanded it left them in relation to the horizon getting closer and closer together. She felt that a god looking down would observe this shortening of distance and wonder what it was about his lesser creations that made them huddle together when they might have emulated giants, become giant riders on giant horses. Why – Sarah cried to herself – that's how I used to feel! That's how I felt on the day of the wasp. And tried now to induce the feeling again, but failed. Well, I am full-grown, she thought, and those were growing pains. Full grown. Full grown. She persuaded the horse into a canter and thought of the men she might have married and the children she might have had since becoming full-grown, and wondered whether there was really such a thing as love and if there were what subtle influences it might have on the purely animal response, some men, but not Teddie, had wakened in her. She wondered if Teddie had awakened Susan in that way, and Susan Teddie; and envied her not for being woken but for apparently being endowed with a nature that was ready to take all the rest on trust. My trouble is, she thought, I question everything, every assumption. I'm not content to let things be, to let things happen. If I don't change that I shall never be happy.

Again they moved left to avoid the nullah which on this side did not peter out but passed under the road, through a culvert. It was shallow, though, and the banks were easy. Sarah urged her horse down into it. The clay bottom was cracked, so quickly had the post-monsoon sun dried out whatever water settled here during the rains, but there was mud still in the shadow of the culvert. The ground bore the imprint of cattle, goat and horses' hooves.

'Do you come this way, Mr Kasim, I mean when you ride alone?' she called.

She did not hear his reply clearly. It might have been 'Sometimes'. She took the rise back out of the nullah. They were now close to the house Mr Kasim said was Count Bronowsky's: newish-looking Anglo-Indian palladian, she noted; isolated in an extensive walled garden, probably built for him, by him. That sort of man knew how to feather his nest: a foreigner, a European, in the service of a native prince, a throw-back to the days of the nabobs of the old trading companies – French, English and Portuguese. She did not think she would like old Count Bronowsky, although it was said he had done fine things. Fine things for himself too, she imagined, judging by the house. She could not imagine her father retiring to live in such a place, rather to a gabled villa in Purley, or a timbered cottage in Pankot if he chose to live the rest of his days in India. People like Teddie and Susan closed their eyes to the fact that her father's generation must be the last generation of English people who would have such a choice. War or no war, it was all coming to an end, and the end could not come neatly. There would be people who had to be victims of the fact that it could not. She herself was surely one of them, and perhaps Mr Kasim too.

Suddenly she wheeled the horse round in the same kind of tight circle Mr Kasim had described before they set off on their gallop. She caught him before he had time to hang back, and so confronted him in the act of reining in, but having done so she could not find an acceptable way of explaining her impulsive action, either to him or to herself. Curiously, though, in the moment before being embarrassed at finding herself at a loss, she thought that the world might be a more interesting and useful place to live in if there were more such empty gestures as the one she had apparently made. They were only empty in the sense that there was room in them for meaning to be poured. That kind of meaning wasn't found easily. It was better, then, to leave the gesture unaccompanied. To make words up just for the sake of saying something would be incongruous. So she closed her mouth and smiled, turned her horse's head and continued on at a walk, listening to the sound that never seemed to stop between sun-up and sundown, was taken for granted and seldom heard consciously at all: the sore-throated calling of the crows.

When they returned to the guest house she saw her future brother-in-law and his best man waiting on the terrace.

'Hello,' she called. 'What a nice surprise. Are you here for breakfast?'

*

The officer Susan Layton was to marry, Teddie Bingham, was the kind of man Mrs Layton would have preferred her husband to be on hand to approve of. She had complained to Sarah that it was bad enough having to write to Colonel Layton and tell him that his youngest daughter was getting married to a man he had never heard of, could not meet and might not like, without the additional worry of searching for the right sort of phrases to convey to him the idea that in his absence she had done everything necessary to be reassured about Captain Bingham's background and found nothing amiss. She did not want to worry him. God knew he had worries of his own. Letters to a prisoner of war had to be cheerful and soothing.

'All you need tell him,' Sarah pointed out, 'is the name of Teddie's regiment and that Susan and he love each other. That's all he'll need to know. And that's all there is to tell. After all, nothing is amiss, is it?'

'There's the question of his parents. It's easier if a man has parents. All there seems to be is an uncle in Shropshire, a father in the Muzzafirabad Guides who broke his neck hunting and a mother who married again, had an unhappy time and died in Mandalay. Your Aunt Mabel says she knew some Muzzy Guides people but doesn't remember a Bingham, which is neither here nor there because she only remembers what she wants to. But it means all we've got to go on is Dick Rankin's word and Teddie himself.'

General Rankin was the Area Commander. Teddie had come to the Area Headquarters in Pankot from the staff college in Quetta. It was not a good posting for an officer who had commanded a company of the Muzzafirabad Guides in Burma, acted as second-in-command of the depleted battalion during the retreat. From Quetta he might have had a G2 appointment, or at least a posting to the staff of an active division. He admitted this himself. He hoped and believed the posting to Pankot was only temporary. The one good thing about it, he added, was that it had brought him and Susan together.

Before Susan it had brought him Sarah. She and Susan, both mustered into the Women's Auxiliary Corps, worked as clerks at Area Headquarters which had stationed itself permanently in Pankot for the duration to avoid the confusion and pressures of the yearly move from Ranpur to the hills and back again. Corporal Sarah Layton was the first of the two Layton girls he noticed, and for a time it seemed that he would prove to be the exception to the rule which, according to interested observers in Pankot, made it almost inevitable that any man first taking an interest in Sarah Layton would presently cool off her and start paying attention to Susan, who admittedly was prettier, livelier, always to be counted on to do what Pankot people described as making things go. The result was that one was never sure which group of men Susan would next be seen as the sparkling centre of, only certain that from time to time, in these groups, there would turn up a man who, briefly, had been conspicuous as a companion of her quieter, elder sister. Once he had succumbed to Susan's more obvious attractions he became one of a crowd; one ceased to notice him and, as a consequence, did not mark his disappearance. Susan, it was assumed, took none of her men seriously. They came, direct or via Sarah, danced attendance, and were replaced.

When Teddie Bingham showed signs of being Susan-proof it was to Sarah rather than to himself that he drew attention. The ladies of Pankot discussed this interesting situation over bridge, committee-teas, behind the counter of the canteen of the Regimental Institute for British soldiers of non-commissioned rank, and behind the scenes at rehearsals for their amateur theatricals. It was, they agreed, time that Sarah Layton settled down. She was all of twenty-two. She was very presentable, quite pretty, and well behaved. Her background was excellent, in fact impeccable within the context of Anglo-India in general and Pankot in particular. She was practically born in Flagstaff House (the senior ladies reminded those less well-endowed with detailed knowledge of Pankot history), her mother was a Muir, her maternal grandfather had been G O C Ranpur; her paternal grandfather had a distinguished career in the Civil, she was related by his second marriage to old Mabel Layton, and her father – now a prisoner in Germany – had commanded the 1st Pankot Rifles in North Africa.

And, in herself, Sarah Layton was upright, honest, and, one imagined, a tower of strength to her mother. Mrs Layton, it had to be admitted, had not borne up under the strain of separation from her husband with the case and cheerfulness one had the right to expect of a senior military wife. One found her vagueness and general air of distraction difficult to deal with. It had become an aggravating duty, where once it had been a pleasure, to partner her at bridge, for instance. She was not alway meticulous about paying her losses, either. Fortunately, a hint to Sarah Layton was known to be effective. It was rumoured that native shopkeepers like Mohammed Hossain the tailor, and Jalal-ud-din, the general merchant, had taken to referring overdue accounts to Sarah as an insurance against painful accumulation. Honorary secretaries of ladies' committees on which Mrs Layton sat had become used to mentioning the dates and times of meetings to Sarah, because this seemed to be the best way of reducing the odds against Mrs Layton turning up. On top of all this, there was – how should one put it? – a tendency in Colonel Layton's lady towards over-indulgence with the bottle.

Sarah Layton, it was obvious, was the temporary rock on which the Layton household had come to rest, and it seemed unfair that her mother should be demonstrably more alert to the existence of her younger daughter. One could not exactly describe Mrs Layton's attitude to Susan as fond – one gave her credit for retaining, in public, a proper manner of emotional detachment from the affairs of her children – but if one assumed fondness behind the manner then Susan, clearly, was the favourite daughter – and seemed to know it. That she knew it was, perhaps, the one major flaw in the bright little crystal. The minor flaws – vanity and pertness – were probably marginal evidence of the existence of this major one. But one forgave her in any case. She could not help it if people were attracted to her. It would be unnatural of her to pretend this was not so and only a girl with a remarkable capacity for self-effacement would not take advantage of it.

All the same one was sorry for the comparatively – and it was only comparatively – less attractive sister. One had never doubted that eventually she would come across a man who, looking for more than a casual flirtation, would prefer the things she had to offer. What made the association between Teddie Bingham and Sarah Layton so especially interesting to the ladies of Pankot was the fact that Teddie, in their majority opinion, was really rather good-looking; that is he was if sandy reddish hair and pale eyelashes weren't on one's personal list of things in a man one found disagreeable. The qualification was made and accepted because one lady, a Mrs Fosdick, said she was allergic to men with red hair and that she always counted pale eyelashes a sign of weakness and untrustworthiness. Another lady, a Mrs Paynton, said nonsense, pale eyelashes denoted an exceptionally amorous nature, and if that is what Mrs Fosdick meant by weakness and untrustworthiness she was all for it. The ladies smiled. Their interest in Teddie Bingham thus aroused in regard to a specific point, they turned to a reconsideration of Sarah Layton and agreed that in life it was the quiet and unassuming people who in the end surprised one most. One had to remember, too, that both the Layton girls had come back out with, as it were, the dew of maidenhood still fresh on their young faces. Parents in India, reunited with their daughters, were well aware of the attendant dangers. On any station there were never enough young girls to go round. Even the plainest poor creature might expect attention from young men fired by climate and scarcity. The girls were fired by the climate too, and the sensation of power over herds of – as it were – panting young men could easily go to their heads. The first year was the one to watch out for. A girl needed her parents then. Wise parents stood by and let a girl enjoy the illusion of having her head in the first six months. One might expect anything up to six announcements that she had met the one man in the world for her. In the second six months one had to shorten the rein because this was the period when having found and discarded six Prince Charmings she could be expected to select as a seventh a man who had shown no interest in her at all, probably because he was already spoken for and had dropped out of the game of romantic musical chairs.

When the year was up and a girl had been through a complete cycle of seasons, it was time for her parents to take a hand. It was remarkable how docile the girls became, how easily they could now be led into the right sort of match. The second year was the year of engagements and marriages; the third year was devoted to maternity. With the first grandson or grand-daughter one could sit back with a sigh of relief that one's duty had been properly done.

The war had disrupted this ideal pattern. The Layton girls, for instance, were among the last girls to come out as members of what old Anglo-Indian wags used to call the fishing-fleet. These days one only got people like nurses. On the other hand the supply of men had become a torrent of all sorts where once it had been a steady dependable flow mostly of one sort only – the right. (Pankot, for instance, was full of the most extraordinary people.) One felt, as it were, besieged. Through the smoke and confusion one tried to maintain contact. One sought the reassurance that the old nucleus was still established at the centre. It was heartening to know that the elder Layton girl seemed to have chosen a man one could describe as pukka. He was a Muzzy Guide. His father had been a Muzzy Guide. If his association with Sarah Layton developed as one hoped, one could then say that Colonel Layton's departure from the bosom of his family long before the end of that first traditionally difficult year when a girl stood in need of the steadying hand of a father as well as of the guiding hand of a mother, had not had any real ill-effect. One might congratulate Sarah Layton on her own good sense.

In this way the ladies of Pankot, at bridge, at tea, behind the counter of the canteen of the Regimental Institute and in rehearsal breaks in their production of *The Housemaster*, discussed the various ramifications of Sarah's friendship with Teddie. They seemed to have set their hearts on an engagement. One could – they said – always do with a really good wedding, and with a Layton girl involved one could expect a reception at Flagstaff House, perhaps count on the General to give the bride away. Life had become a shade drabber each successive year of the war. One was lucky if the Governor and his Lady spent more than May and June in the summer residence. Last year, 1942, when all that turmoil was going on down in the plain, there had hardly been even the shadow of a season. As for home comforts, those too were rapidly becoming a thing of the past. The influx of troops, the establishment of training camps, the departure of one's own menfolk, had driven one out of one's rightful bungalows to pig in at Smith's Hotel, the club annexe, or, if one was luckier than other grass widows, into (in Pankot idiom) grace and favour bungalows such as Mrs Layton and her daughters occupied in the vicinity of the old Pankot Rifles depot, although that meant one spent a fortune in tonga fares just to go to the club for morning coffee. By rights, the station felt, Mrs Layton and her daughters should have been living in Rose Cottage. As it was there was insufficient room there because old Mabel Layton, who had bought the cottage some time in the thirties, shared the place and expenses with Miss Batchelor, a retired missionary (and a born spinster if ever there was one) and both of them seemed destined to live for ever. On the whole, though, one envied the retired people who had their own places, although some of them had been reduced to taking in paying-guests, and as they died off the military requisitioned their bungalows for use as nurses' hostels and chummery messes.

Meanwhile, one coped and made what one could of any occasion that might briefly bring back memories of what life in India had been like before the war. In the heat generated by their expectations of the wedding, warmth was felt for the Laytons as a family and a symbol. One forgave Mrs Layton her vagueness, her forgetfulness, her understandable little indulgences. After all, she was still an attractive woman. Better a few too many chota pegs than the possible alternative.

The news that Teddie Bingham and Sarah Layton were no longer to be seen in each other's company came as a sad disappointment. Hopes that they had merely had a tiff and that a reconciliation would spur them on to a mutual declaration of affection were dashed when Teddie turned up at a club dance as a member of a trio of officers escorting Susan. It was calculated that he had more than his fair share of dances with her, including the last waltz. It was noticed that Sarah was not at the dance at all. Mrs Paynton reported an encounter with Sarah in Jalal-ud-din's shop the morning after and having received – in response to her friendly inquiry after Captain Bingham's health – an evasive reply that was barely polite. As Mrs Paynton said, Sarah Layton had always been punctilious in her observance of the rules laid down for the exchange of pleasantries – although (and perhaps the others would agree with her?) when one came to think of it she had never seemed entirely relaxed. In the present circumstances one had to make allowances. On the other hand perhaps one ought to consider more closely what it was about a girl who consistently lost men to her younger sister. Young men being what they were, nine times out of ten their desertion of Sarah in favour of Susan could be explained readily enough. But Teddie Bingham, surely, had been the one extra time, and ten out of ten suggested there was more to it than Susan's good looks and jolly temperament proving too strong as competition.

'If you ask me,' young Mrs Smalley said – and hesitated because she was never asked and had not been asked now. But she had searched for just such an occasion to make her mark with this group of her elders and betters. So, flushed but determined, she contined – 'the trouble is she doesn't really take it seriously . . .'

After an appreciable pause Mrs Paynton inquired, 'Take what seriously?'

'Any of it,' Mrs Smalley said. 'Us. India. What we're here for. I mean in spite of everying. In spite of her – well, what she was brought up to. I mean although men never talk about it they feel it, don't they? I mean in a more direct way than even we do. I think they're more sensitive than women are to, well, people – people like Sarah Layton. I believe that after a while they get a horrible feeling she's laughing at them. At all of us. Oh – I'm sorry. Perhaps I ought not to have said that . . .'

There was silence. The ladies looked at one another. Poor Mrs Smalley wished the ground would open and swallow her. She – a Smalley (for what that was worth) had criticized a Layton, in public. And had talked about – *it*. One never talked about *it*. At least not in so direct a way.

Suddenly Mrs Paynton spoke. Mrs Smalley stared at her. She thought she might have misheard. But she had not.

'My dear,' Mrs Paynton had said. 'How extremely interesting.' Now she turned to the others. 'I'm not at all sure Lucy hasn't put her finger bang on the spot.'

Trembling, Lucy Smalley accepted a cigarette from Mrs Fosdick.

'It was last year I first felt it,' she said, having been persuaded to explain in greater detail what she meant when she said Sarah Layton didn't take 'any of it' seriously. 'I mean whenever we talked about all those dreadful things that were going on in places like Mayapore.' When she said 'we' she was speaking figuratively. She had rarely ventured a word herself. Because she had not, she had had more time to watch and listen. Whenever Sarah had been present with Mrs Layton, Mrs Smalley had taken special note of her because Sarah was the one woman in the group Mrs Smalley could treat as junior to herself. 'I thought perhaps she was a bit shy, so I always made a point of talking to her. It was never anything she said, but gradually I couldn't help feeling she was thinking a lot. I thought that sometimes she was bursting to come out with something, well, critical of us. Just as if she thought it was all our fault. And yet not, well, quite that. I mean I don't think she's a radical or anything. I think the best way I can describe it is to say that sometimes she looked at me as if I were, well, not a real person. I mean that's the reaction I had. She made me feel that everything we were saying was somehow a joke to her, the sort of joke she couldn't share.'

Again, the ladies exchanged glances. 'I think I know what you mean, Lucy,' Mrs Paynton said. 'And I think it's something like that, in the back of one's mind you know, that makes one feel even more strongly that it's time she settled down.'

The ladies agreed. Mrs Smalley was conscious that her moment of glory had passed its peak. The others, led by Mrs Paynton, now absorbed her suspicions of Sarah Layton, adapted them, and came to the conclusion that Miss Layton probably didn't mean to give people the impression of having unsound ideas and would be straightened out quickly enough if the right man came along. Perhaps Captain Bingham had been the wrong man. Things might be better for her when that little minx of a sister was married.

Three weeks later when Susan and Teddie took the station by surprise by announcing that they were to be married, Mrs Fosdick declared that a man who could woo one girl, switch his allegiance to her sister and end by marrying her was scarcely to be trusted to remain faithful for long, and that her opinion of the significance of pale eyelashes had therefore been vindicated. The other ladies said that Captain Bingham's choice, wavering though it might seem, was proof of there being something in the Layton girls that appealed to his deepest sensibility and that his final choice as between the two of them showed up even more clearly that the elder girl, although perhaps outwardly possessed of whatever it was that appealed in this way, was inwardly unsatisfactory in this other way that men sensed more quickly than women but which had at last been pinned down as unsoundness, if only of the incipient kind; and when it was noticed that Sarah Layton smiled at Teddie and Susan the idea the ladies might have had that she bore no grudge and took it all like a good soldier was edged out of their minds by this other idea – the faintly disagreeable one that she was smiling at them instead of with them.

All the same, they looked forward to the wedding. When Captain Bingham was posted quite suddenly as a G3 (Operations) to a new divisional headquarters stationed in Mirat, Mrs Fosdick said she wouldn't be in the least surprised if the whole thing now fell through and Susan, with so many other eligible men to choose from, decided she had made a mistake. The Laytons' departure for a late – last-fling-for-Susan – holiday in Srinagar strengthened her belief that Susan would soon find other fish to fry. The final surprise and disappointment came when the Laytons returned early from Kashmir and announced that the wedding, far from being either postponed or cancelled, had been hastened forward and would take place out of Pankot, in Mirat. One felt (the ladies said) that even taking into account the exigencies of war-time, and the fact that Captain Bingham was obviously soon returning to active service in the field, the Layton wedding had taken on a hole-in-the-corner air which it was somehow not easy to forgive.

'I'm not at all sure,' Mrs Paynton announced, 'that Mrs Layton should allow herself to be rushed like this. I get the impression she's really quite upset but is trying not to show it for the girl's sake. Apparently Susan is coming back to Pankot with them after the wedding because there'll only be a three-day honeymoon and after that Captain Bingham is off. You don't suppose . . .'

She did not say what was not supposed because she knew the other ladies must have supposed it already, as she had done, and rejected the supposition as too outlandish in relation to a Layton to be considered seriously for a moment – unless, perhaps, the Layton girl involved had happened to be Sarah. If Mrs Smalley was right and had put her finger on what was wrong with Sarah Layton, what was disturbing about her, then one could say that nothing was beyond the bounds of possibility.

*

Teddie Bingham's posting to Mirat and his discovery soon after arrival that if he wanted to get married his bride would have to come to him, be content with a seventy-two-hour honeymoon in the Nanoora Hills and prepared to kiss him goodbye as soon as it was over, were not the only events that threatened to disrupt the harmonious pattern of the wedding. Susan, somewhat to her family's surprise, shrugged these disappointments away and said that anyway being married in Mirat should be fun, especially if – as was suggested – they stayed beforehand at the palace guest house. They could go to Ranpur (she said), meet Aunt Fenny and Uncle Arthur (who was to give her away), and travel to Mirat as a party. So, provisionally, it was arranged, but soon after the return from the Kashmir holiday Major Grace informed them he could not get down to Mirat earlier than the Friday before the wedding. He had to attend a series of conferences and there was no getting out of this disagreeable duty. Mrs Layton said she did not much care for the idea of travelling down and staying for nearly a week in the guest house without a man to look after them. Again Susan brushed the objection aside. The guest house would be perfectly safe. According to Teddie the Nawab of Mirat had handed it over to the station commander for the duration, to provide extra accommodation for military visitors (and their families) and although it wasn't in the cantonment it was in the grounds of the palace and was guarded. 'That still leaves the train journey,' Mrs Layton pointed out. 'You're forgetting Teddie's best man,' Susan reminded her. One of Teddie's friends in Pankot was a man called Tony Bishop, another old Muzzy Guide wounded in Burma and presently acting as ADC to General Rankin. Tony had already agreed to support him at the wedding. It would be the simplest thing in the world to get General Rankin to give him special leave so that he could go down to Mirat with them.

So Mrs Layton spoke to General Rankin and got his promise to allow Captain Bishop to escort them. But one week before the party was due to leave Tony Bishop went down with jaundice. Mrs Layton visited him in the military wing of the Pankot General Hospital.

'It's no good,' she said, 'he'll be there for three weeks, so now there's no best man. But it's a blow. Of all Teddie's friends Tony Bishop strikes me as the most sensible.'

'Best men are two a penny,' Susan retorted, and went up to Area Headquarters where she put a call through to Teddie at his divisional Headquarters and spoke to him personally. 'He'll get someone in Mirat, probably the man he shares quarters with,' she said when she came back. The remarkable thing, Sarah realized, was that for once Susan had done something herself instead of getting someone to do it for her. Her mother said no more about being unaccompanied on the train. It had never been a serious objection. There were bound to be plenty of officers on their way to Mirat and Susan would only have to stand a few moments on the platform with her mother, Aunt Fenny and Sarah, before a gaggle of subalterns approached them and inquired if any help was needed. Which was precisely what happened.

*

There were two Mirats: the Mirat of palaces, mosques, minarets, and crowded bazaars, and the Mirat of open spaces, barracks, trees, and geometrically laid out roads with names like Wellesley, Gunnery and Mess. The two Mirats were separated by an expanse of water, random in shape, along one side of which ran the railway and the road connecting them. The water and the gardens south of it were the Izzat Bagh, so-called because the first Nawab declared that Kasims would rule in Mirat until the lake dried up: a fairly safe bet because it had never done so in living memory. But it was a boast, and boasts were always considered dangerous. Providence ought not to be tempted. A man could lose face simply as a result of tempting it. The inhabitants of the city anticipated the worst. Instead, so it was said, for two successive years after the Nawab's announcement the wet monsoon was abnormally heavy and prolonged. When, in the second year, the lake flooded its banks and destroyed the huts of the fishermen, drowning several, people took it as a sign of celestial approval of the reign of the house of Kasim whose honour – or izzat – had been so dramatically upheld. The lake was adopted as a symbol of the Nawab's power, of his fertility, of an assured succession reaching into the far distant future. The mullahs declared the lake blessed by Allah, and the Hindus – eighty per cent of the population – were prohibited from using it even during the festival of Divali. A mosque was erected on the southern shore and a new palace was built with gardens going down to the water. The court poet – Gaffur Mohammed – celebrated the establishment of the new palace and its garden in this verse:

> So you must accept, Gaffur,
> That your words are no more than the petals of a rose.
> They must fade, lose scent, and fall into obscurity.
> Only for a while can they perfume the garden
> Of the object of your praise. O, would they could grow,
> Lord of the Lake, eternally.

It was in these gardens that a guest house in the European Palladian style was built in the late nineteenth century, round about the time that a British military cantonment was established with the Nawab's approval in the area north of the lake.

*

There were two halts for Mirat: Mirat (City) and Mirat (Cantonment). The latter was the first arrived at if you travelled from Ranpur. The mail train was scheduled to reach Mirat (Cantonment) at 07.50 hours but was usually anything between half an hour and one hour later. Having deposited its passengers at Mirat (Cantonment) it took a half-hour rest and then chugged out, at a rate never exceeding 10 mph, negotiating points, junctions and level-crossings until it reached the long isolated embankment that separated the lake from the waste land that had once – before the coming of the cantonment – been characteristic of the northern environs of the city. The train crawled along the bleak strip of ground that raised the railway to one level and the trunk road to another, slightly lower, with a kind of reluctance, as if the engine-driver expected subsidence or, anyway, signals showing green that would flash red at the last moment, scarcely leaving him time to apply his brakes. Between the presiding power and the old glory there was, as it were, a sense of impending disaster.

Although the Laytons and Mrs Grace were to stay at the palace guest house it was at Mirat (Cantonment) they alighted, on Teddie Bingham's instructions. 'Make sure,' he had written to Mrs Layton, 'you don't get carried on into the city. Of course I'll be there to meet you, and even if I'm unable to I'll get someone to do so for me. But I thought it worth mentioning, just in case anything goes wrong, and remembering you're staying at the palace guest house you think you have to travel on into the city itself. No one ever does.'

'Things are looking up,' he said now above the din on the arrival platform. 'You're only twenty-five minutes behind schedule. I've got breakfast organized. I expect you're ready for it.' He pecked the cheek Mrs Layton offered, shook hands with Mrs Grace whom he had met only twice, held Sarah's hand for a prolonged few seconds as if the switch of his affections from her to her sister still needed some explanation, then turned and kissed and held on to pretty little Susan who had an air of being flushed and dishevelled in spite of the fact that not a hair was out of place and she had worked for half an hour on perfecting the pallor she had decided suited her as the wife-to-be of an officer who would soon be away to the war. It was on Teddie's cheeks a flush was actually visible, but he appeared brisk, fully in control of the problems posed by an arrival. The flush seemed to be one of pleasure combined with effort: the pleasure of seeing his future wife again and the effort he would always put into doing even the most ordinary things right, more especially when there were members of the opposite sex depending upon him for their comfort and safety. He had an Indian NCO in attendance whose khaki drill shirt and knee-length shorts stood out from his limbs and body in stiff, starched, knife-edged perfection. The man's pugree was an exotic affair of khaki cloth and diaphanous khaki muslin which gave his otherwise gravely held head a quirk of flirtatiousness and added a note of self-conscious gallantry to the way in which he stood by the open carriage and took charge of the mounds of luggage which the red-turbanned coolies were already fighting over.

'Don't worry about your things,' Teddie Bingham said. 'Noor Hussain's got the luggage *bando* taped,' and having thanked the officers in the adjacent compartment who had looked after Mrs Layton and her party on the journey from Ranpur and were now travelling on south, escorted the ladies through the crowd to the station restaurant, explaining that Noor Hussain would see the luggage safely stowed in a 15-cwt truck and taken to the guest house where they would find it waiting. For personal conveyance he had laid on a couple of taxis, and those too would be waiting directly breakfast was over.

Entering the restaurant behind her mother and Aunt Fenny, but ahead of Susan and Teddie who were obviously conscious of their duty as an engaged couple to stay close, Sarah concentrated on the smells coming from the kitchens. Whatever the day held in store breakfast was a meal she felt it was wise to give her undivided attention to. Once she was seated at the table, the orders given for cornflakes or porridge, egg and bacon, toast and marmalade, the first cup of tea or coffee drunk, and perhaps the first cigarette of the day lighted, she thought she would be able to view the sight of Susan and Teddie sitting together opposite her with more confidence in their future than she felt capable of drumming up at the moment.

There was (Sarah thought) something about Teddie Bingham that didn't wear well. He was not a man who grew on you. In this respect he was like the countless other young men to whom she had been mildly attracted and then lost interest in or lost to Susan with no hard feelings on either side. What was special about Teddie was the fact that Susan had agreed to marry him. Sarah could not understand why. She hoped, but did not believe, that they loved one another. She did not believe it because until they announced their engagement there seemed to have been nothing to distinguish him as a man apart, in the crowd of men round Susan.

'But then,' Sarah thought, 'we all have the same sort of history. Birth in India, of civil or military parents, school in England, holidays spent with aunts and uncles, then back to India.' It was a ritual. A dead hand lay on the whole enterprise. But still it continued: back and forth, the constant flow, girls like herself and Susan, and boys like Teddie Bingham: so many young white well-bred mares brought out to stud for the purpose of coupling with so many young white well-bred stallions, to ensure the inheritance and keep it pukka. At some date in the foreseeable future it would stop. At home you understood this, but something odd happened when you came back. You could not visualize it, then, ever stopping.

She looked across the table at Susan, at her mother, at Aunt Fenny, and remembered her Aunt Lydia saying that India was an unnatural place for a white woman. As a child she had not understood, but had understood since, and agreed with Aunt Lydia that it was. They did not transplant well. Temperate plants, in the hot-house they were brought on too quickly and faded fast, and the life they lived, when the heat had dried them out and left only the aggressive husk, was artificial. Among them, occasionally, you would find a freak in whom the sap still ran. She was thinking of her old Aunt Mabel in Pankot, and of the Manners girl's aunt in Srinagar who, in the midst of their conversation, had suddenly filled her with an alarming sense of her own inadequacy as a human being, so that on returning to her own houseboat she had sat in front of a mirror and stared at herself, wishing she were anything but what her outward appearance proved she was: an average girl whose ordinariness was like a sentence of life imprisonment.

'You are not going to tell us, I hope,' Aunt Fenny said to Teddy when she had taken her place, fussed about a stain on the tablecloth, studied the bill of fare, ordered porridge and poached eggs and returned her spectacles to their red leather pouch, 'that the wedding has to be even earlier, tomorrow for instance, because if so there'll be no one to give Susan away. Arthur simply can't get down until Friday.'

'No, don't worry, Mrs Grace, Saturday it is.'

'What about your best man, Teddie?' Mrs Layton asked.

'It's all fixed. I asked the chap I share quarters with if he'd stand in and he said he'd be glad to. Since then he's been bustling around making sure everything's all right at the guest house. He'll be along after breakfast to help us get sorted out. His name's Merrick. I hope you'll like him.'

'Merrick?' Aunt Fenny repeated. 'It doesn't ring a bell. What is he?'

'A gee-three-eye,' Teddie said, who took so many things literally.

Aunt Fenny turned to Mrs Layton. 'Millie, wasn't there a Merrick on General Rollings's staff in Lahore in thirty-one? It could be the same family.'

'Oh, I don't remember, Fenny. It's all so long ago.'

'Of course you remember. He married one of those awful Selby girls. No. I'm wrong . . .' Aunt Fenny paused. There was a family joke that Aunt Fenny kept the army List on her bedside table, and still referred to it whenever she gave a party and was in doubt about the seniority of one of her guests and consequently where to seat him and his wife. 'It wasn't Merrick. It was Mayrick. I don't know a Merrick. Is he an emergency officer?'

'He got an immediate commission, I gather,' Teddie explained. 'He was in the Indian Police.'

'Isn't that unusual?' Aunt Fenny wanted to know. 'Young Mr Creighton pulled every string there is to get out of the civil and into the army for the duration, but they wouldn't let him go. He told me he'd only heard of one instance of it being allowed and I think that was a case of the poor young man in question absolutely pining away at the prospect of not being in on the shooting and becoming quite useless at his work. Perhaps it was Mr Merrick. What is his first name?'

'Ronald.'

'Ronald Merrick. What rank?'

Teddie looked faintly surprised. 'Captain.'

'My dear boy, I gathered that when you said he was a G3 (I). I meant his rank in the police.'

'Oh, that. Superintendent or something, I think.'

'What district?'

'He did tell me. Now what was it? Is there a place called Sunder-something?'

'Sundernagar,' Aunt Fenny pronounced. 'A backward area. Relatively unimportant.' Captain Merrick thus disposed of she smiled blandly.

'Did you enjoy Kashmir?' Teddie asked.

'It was all right. The wrong end of the season and of course we had to cut it short.'

'I know. I'm sorry.'

'We had a vaguely unpleasant experience too. Millie wanted to move our boat up the lake to where she and John spent their honeymoon. There was only one other boat up there and it all seemed quite idyllic, if over-quiet and slightly inconvenient. Unfortunately our neighbour turned out to be someone on whom it was impossible to call. I'll give you three guesses.'

Teddie coloured up in anticipation of hearing something he'd rather not hear in front of Susan. Sarah glanced at her mother who was still reading the menu, apparently not listening. Only her mother knew about her visit to Lady Manners, and only for her mother's sake had Sarah said nothing to the others.

'I give up,' Teddie said.

'Old Lady Manners. And the child—'

'Oh, I see.' His blush deepened.

Mrs Layton put the menu down. 'What is the guest house like, Teddie?'

'I've only seen it from the outside, but the station commander says it's pretty comfortable. Ronald Merrick knows more about it than I do. He's been there a couple of times to check on the bando-bast. Incidentally, you'll have it all to yourselves. It's in the palace grounds and it's staffed by palace servants, but the Nawab's put it at the Station Commander's disposal for the duration, so it's really treated as cantonment territory and there's no need to stand on ceremony.'

'Shall we see the Nawab?' Susan asked.

Teddie assumed his playful expression. 'Why should you want to see the Nawab?'

'Because there was a scandal about him. He fell in love with a white woman and followed her all the way to the South of France.'

'Oh, did he? Who told you that?'

'I did, but I thought everybody knew,' Aunt Fenny said. 'The affair between between the Nawab of Mirat and Madame X or whatever they called her, was quite a *cause célèbre* in the early twenties. She was Russian or Polish and pretended to be of good family, but was probably a lady's maid. I don't know what originally brought her to India but she got her hooks into the Nawab, played him for what he was worth, cried off when he wanted her to marry him as his second wife and scooted back to Europe with the Nawab after her. They ended up somewhere like Nice or Monte Carlo. I remember there was a story about some jewellery which she claimed he'd given her – presumably for services rendered. He threatened legal action and they say this Count Bronowsky acted as go-between – so successfully that the Nawab brought him back and made him his prime minister.'

'Oh yes,' Teddie said. 'I've heard of Bronowsky. He's still around.'

'If he was really a Russian count I'll eat my hat but the Nawab's been under his thumb ever since and he's even dazzled the Political Department, according to Arthur. But then of course he had to, otherwise they'd have made the Nawab get rid of him years ago.'

'You haven't answered my question, Teddie,' Susan reminded him, 'but of course once Aunt Fenny starts it's difficult to get a word in edgeways.'

She smiled at Mrs Grace, but Sarah recognized the hectic little flush spreading over her powdered cheeks as a sign of the temper her sister seemed to find it hard to control whenever she felt even fleetingly neglected. Content, often, to sit and listen and think her thoughts, her most casual remarks or gestures demanded and usually received immediate reponses, from women as well as men. Sarah sometimes marvelled at the way Susan could suddenly divert a conversation by throwing into it a comment or a question, and at the way she could then just as suddenly retire from it and leave people disorientated. It was as if she periodically and deliberately sought to test the strength of the impact of her personality.

'I asked,' Susan said, turning back to Teddie, 'whether we shall see the Nawab.'

'I don't know. He's away at the moment but may be back at the weekend. Colonel and Mrs Hobhouse – that's the Station Commander and his wife – say we ought to invite him to the reception, but that it's not certain whether he'll come.'

'Why? Because the reception is to be at the club?'

'No. He's allowed in as a guest, you know. Because of Ramadan. I mean he'll be fasting between sun-up and sundown.'

'I'd like to have a Nawab at my wedding,' Susan said, 'especially one who used to be wicked. Besides, if we make a bit of a fuss of him he'll have to send a wedding present and it might turn out to be a tray of super rubies or a fabulous emerald, or a few spare ropes of pearls.'

Teddie smiled, and glanced affectionately down at her left hand, at the finger on which she wore his own modest cluster of engagement diamonds. She chose this moment to lean back in her chair, an indication that the others could again talk to each other.

Breakfast came to the table at last.

*

There were twelve tables in the station restaurant. Sarah counted them. Ten were occupied. The floor was patterned by black and white tiles. The ceiling was high; three four-bladed fans, suspended from it, revolved at half speed. The windows on the platform side were frosted to shut out the sight of trains, travellers and coolies. On one wall there was a portrait of the King-Emperor, George VI, and on another a pre-war poster of invitation to Agra to admire the stale image of the Taj Mahal. The bearers were dressed in white and had cummerbunds of green and black, white gloves and bare feet. At one table two Indian officers, Sikhs, sat together. A nursing officer of the QAIMNS was breakfasting with a captain of Ordnance, an Anglo-Indian girl with a subaltern of the Service Corps. The rest of the customers were British officers. Some had arrived on the 07.50. Others would be waiting for a departure.

And presumably (Sarah told herself) with the exception of the two Sikhs and the little Anglo-Indian girl, we all represent something. And looked at her own family, considering them for the moment as strangers to her, like the rest of the people eating English breakfasts in a flat and foreign landscape. There, she thought, watching Aunt Fenny, is a big-boned, well-fleshed woman. To look at her you'd say she has transplanted better than the thinner, sad-faced woman by her side, but her manner is a shade too self-assured, her voice a shade too loud, and when she stops speaking her mouth sets a shade too grimly, and the first impression that she has transplanted well is overridden by another, the impression that when she finds herself alone she will sit with a far-away look on her face, a look that would be gentle if it weren't for the mouth. However quietly or gently she moves or sits the mouth will stay fixed and grim so that all her thoughts and recollections will enter the room and surround her not with happiness but with regrets and accusations. Which means that even then you would not be able to feel sorry for her. The thinner, sad-faced woman is her sister. They have the same nose and a manner towards each other of intimacy that is neither casual nor closely affectionate and betrays a long but not

485

necessarily deep experience of each other. Their real intimacy was over long ago. It ended with childhood, and was quite likely an intimacy only one of them felt, most likely the sad thin one who uses her hands with a curious vagueness, as if certain gestures which are habit are no longer appropriate because the person they were habitually made to, to express contentment, affection, to establish contact, to claim loyalty, to offer it, is no longer close to her.

Well, she was cheating. Sarah realized. No one looking at her mother could know that about her from her gestures. Would they know the other thing? Would they, by looking at her, be able to tell that the vagueness, the air of slight distraction, was proof – as Sarah knew it was – that Mrs Layton was already, at 8.30 in the morning, beginning to work out how long it would be before she could decently have a drink? You are still attractive, Sarah thought, and you are only forty-five. It is three years since you were with him. And India is full of men. So don't think I don't understand about the bottle in the wardrobe, the flask in your handbag.

She turned to Teddie and Susan. For her, the lightly but firmly sketched portrait of compatibility and pre-marital pleasure in each other's company which they presented in public, carried no conviction. In Teddie, Sarah was conscious of there seeming to be nothing behind his intentions – touchingly good on the surface – that gave them either depth or reality. In Susan she had become aware of a curious aptitude for deliberate performance. Susan was playing Susan and Sarah could no longer get near her. The distance between them had the feeling of permanence because the part of Susan called for a pretty, brown-haired, blue-eyed, flush-cheeked girl who entered, almost feverishly, into the fun and responsibilities of a life Sarah herself believed mirthless and irresponsible. It was mirthless because it was irresponsible, and irresponsible because its notion of responsibility was the notion of a vanished age. The trouble was, she thought, that in India, for them, there was no private life; not in the deepest sense; in spite of their attempts at one. There was only a public life. She looked again at the faces in the restaurant – ordinary private faces that seemed constantly to be aware of the need to express something remote, beyond their capacity to imagine – martyrdom in the cause of a power and a responsibility they had not sought individually but had collectively inherited, and the stiffness of a refusal to be intimidated; group expressions arising from group psychology. And yet they were the faces of people whose private consciousness of self was the principal source of their vitality.

Once out of our natural environment (she thought) something in us dies. What? Our belief in ourselves as people who each have something special to contribute? What we shall leave behind is what we have done as a group and not what we could have done as individuals which means that it will be second-rate.

She lit a cigarette and listened to Teddie and Aunt Fenny talking about Lord Wavell who was to be the new Viceroy and Lord Louis Mountbatten who was to be Supreme Commander of the new South-East Asia

486

Command. Aunt Fenny was saying that it was a mistake to divest GHQ in India of its traditional military role. Teddie said Lord Wavell would make a good Viceroy because he was a soldier and people could trust him. New winds were blowing, but the dust they raised seemed to Sarah to be as stale as ever. Hot coffee was brought, the bearer sent with orders for morning papers: the *Times of India* for Mrs Layton, *The Civil and Military Gazette* for Aunt Fenny; nothing for Susan unless the new edition of *The Onlooker* was out; for Sarah the *Statesman* which Aunt Fenny disapproved of because although it was an English newspaper it was always criticizing Government or GHQ and was currently (she said) exaggerating the seriousness of the famine in Bengal, and blaming everybody for it except the Indian Merchants who had hoarded tons of rice and were waiting for the market price to rise to an even more astronomic figure. 'Besides,' she said, 'the Bengalis won't eat anything but rice. There are tons of wheat going begging but they'd rather die than change their damned diet.'

Sarah tapped ash carefully into the glass ashtray and felt put off by the sight of the stub of her previous one, marked red by her lipstick, a sign of her personal private life, her none-too-hopeful message in a bottle cast back up by an indifferent tide on an island on which she sometimes felt herself the only one alive who still wanted to be rescued.

*

They were confronted by a forbidding openness, of water and unabsorbed light, a sort of milky translucence that deadened the nerves of the eyeballs and conveyed the impression that here one would live perpetually with a slight headache.

'There's the palace now,' Captain Merrick said. Sarah heard from her mother a low exclamation that could have been one of admiration or of disappointment. For the moment she herself was blinded by the vast area of sky and water.

'You're looking in the wrong direction, Miss Layton.' His voice was close. He was leaning forward. She had an impression that his fingers had touched her very lightly on the shoulder. The voice was resonant. There was something in its tone that acted as an irritant, although not an unpleasant one. 'I'm not looking in any direction,' she said. She raised her left hand to shade her eyes. 'There's so much glare.'

'I was afraid you'd find that, sitting up front. I'll tell the fellow to stop, then we can change places.'

Sarah shook her head. 'No. I can see the palace now—' Distantly, a dusty-rose-coloured structure with little towers, and a white-domed mosque with one slim minaret on the edge of the lake, reflected in the water – and – among the trees, at the end of the lakeside road they travelled on, a small palladian-style greystone mansion. The guest house.

The lake was on their left. Fishermen were casting nets from long low boats. The nets fell on the water, rippling its glassy surface as if sudden areas of chill were causing patches of gooseflesh.

Again the voice in her ear.

'You see where the reeds begin? That's the boundary of the fishing rights. They're not allowed to work closer to the palace. It's a traditional family occupation, the rights are handed down from father to son. They're quite a proud sect. Muslims, of course.'

Her mother spoke. When Captain Merrick replied his voice was no longer just behind her. He had sat back. But the voice was still resonant. It was a good voice, but not public school. Aunt Fenny had already commented on that fact, in the ladies' room at the station restaurant. 'Of course,' she said, 'you can get some peculiar people in the police. I don't suppose Captain Merrick's family would bear close inspection. But he's quite the little gentleman, isn't he, and terribly efficient over detail. That's a sign of a humble origin, too. Did you hear him tell Teddie the luggage has already arrived at the guest house? That means he called there to make sure, before coming to collect us. How shall we go? You, Susan and Teddie in one taxi, me, Sarah and Captain Merrick in the other?' But Mrs Layton said, 'No, I'll go with Sarah and Captain Merrick. Then I'll feel less like a mother-in-law.' She retired into a cubicle. Susan and Aunt Fenny went out. Sarah waited, gazing at her ordinary face in the mirror, combing her hair which was the same colour her mother's had been before it began to fade and she took to using bleach; a dark blonde, difficult to curl, badly in need of the permanent wave she would have to undergo before the wedding. She hated her hair. She hated her chin and cheekbones. They were too prominent. She repaired her make-up without interest. She envied Susan for having the kind of face that powder and lipstick could alter. Through these her own face always came back at her with a kind of dull incorruptibility, authentic bony Layton, quite unlike the rounder, more gently moulded Muir face. Well, she thought, it would wear better. There was a toughness in the Layton face that weathered storms. Her great-grandfather had had it, her father had had it, and now she had it.

Mrs Layton came out of the cubicle. She had her handbag with her. Through the mirror Sarah saw her mother glance at her, then look away. Without speaking she came across to one of the hand-basins, set her bag down, washed her hands, touched her hair and adjusted her hat. Silences between them were not unusual. They were strange silences which Sarah found difficult to break once they had set in. She sometimes thought of them as silences her mother used to establish between them a closeness that had never existed before and which she thought it too late to establish now except in this exchange of sentences unspoken and of gestures unoffered. There were occasions – and this was one of them – when Sarah felt a surge of almost hysterical – because pent-up – affection for this vague distracted woman who was her mother. The old forthright manner with its edge of sharpness that demanded respect, loyalty, more than it demanded love, was gone. It seemed now that nothing at all was being demanded and nothing given, except whatever casual things they were that were asked and given by habit – and these silences, which seemed to express a need that went much deeper than mere reliance on Sarah to forget she had not been loved as much as Susan and to give the kind of help Susan never could have given.

*

Following her mother and Aunt Fenny out of the restaurant – but this time in the wake and not the van of Susan and Teddie because Teddie's best-man-to-be had gravitated as if by a force of nature to the role of escorting her, seeing that doors were kept open for her to pass through, that any remark she made would get a suitable response, and of making light and suitable conversation himself should she seem to be in need of cheering up – Sarah remembered how within a few weeks of her arrival in Pankot in 1939 she had decided that India affected Englishmen in two ways: it made them thin and pale or beefy and red. Her father and – potentially – her new escort belonged to the former category, Uncle Arthur and (potentially) Teddie Bingham to the latter. The thin pale Englishmen were reserved and mostly polite to other people, including Indians even when they didn't like them; the red beefy ones acquired loud voices and were given to displays of bad temper in public. Between these two types of opposites there seemed to be no shades of colour or grades of behaviour worth noting. The young men fell potentially into one or the other of these categories directly they set foot in Bombay or went out to their first station. Their pinkness, you saw then, judging by its texture in each individual case, would fade or deepen; their flesh, depending upon built-in things like bone structure and muscle tone, would shrink or thicken; their good nature, according to the amount of self-control needed to sustain it, would become fixed and frozen, or would explode dramatically under the pressure of the climate and their growing inability – Uncle Arthur was a case in point – to take any real pleasure in the company kept.

But one thing was shared in common by these two broadly distinguishable types of men: their attitude to English women. After a time Sarah had been able to analyse it. They approached you first (she decided) as if you were a member of a species that had to be protected, although from what was not exactly clear if you ruled out extinction: it seemed to be enough that the idea of collective responsibility for you should be demonstrated, without regard to any actual or likely threat to your welfare. In circumstances where no threat seemed to exist the behaviour of the men aroused your suspicion that perhaps it did after all but in a way men alone had the talent for understanding; and so you became aware of the need to be grateful to them for the constant proof they offered of being ready to defend you, if only from yourself.

This collective public approach also affected their personal, private approaches. When young men talked to her, danced or played tennis with her, invited her to go riding, to watch them play men's games, to go with them to a show, became amorous or fumbled with her unromantically in the dark of a veranda or a motor-car, she had the impression that they did so in a representative frame of mind. 'Well here I am, white, male and pure-bred English, and here you are pure-bred English, white and female, we ought to be doing something about it.' The potential red beefy types were usually more enthusiastic for doing something about it than the potential thin pale types, but however hot or cold the degree of enthusiasm was Sarah could never feel it as an enthusiasm for her, but instead as an enthusiasm for an ideal she was supposed to share and which the young man in question apparently assumed was a ready-made link, a reliable primary connection between them that might or might not be more intimately strengthened according to taste. The ideal was difficult to define and Sarah had thought she ought to define it before deciding whether she should reject it or uphold it. She certainly had no intention of casually accepting it and becoming thoughtlessly implicated in it, which is what she believed Susan had done.

In the station concourse Sarah said to Captain Merrick, 'Mother would like you to come with us. Teddie can take Susan and Aunt Fenny,' and got her mother into the back of the first taxi. She saw Teddie approaching and wondered whether her mother's objections were not so much to being made to feel like a mother-in-law as to Teddie himself. She said, 'I want to ride in front, Captain Merrick. You go in with Mother.'

The driver was an Indian civilian. He would probably smell. Captain Merrick hesitated, but both doors were open and she got in. Teddie joined them. 'Are you all right?' he asked Mrs Layton. She said she was and told him to look after Susan. A few moments later they were settled and the taxi moved away, out of the shade. The heat coming from the engine and the hot air blowing through the open window combined with the glare and the baked musty stench of the taxi-driver to smother Sarah in that blanketing numbness which, in India, was a defence against the transformation of the illusion of exhaustion into its reality. She half-closed her eyes. They were going down a wide street of arcaded shops – the cantonment bazaar. The jingling harness of horse-drawn tongas, bicycle bells, the sudden blare of Indian music from a radio as they passed a coffee-house were sounds which this morning rubbed the edge of a nerve already raw from the irritation of feeling that everything was going inexorably forward and leaving her behind, that she could not catch up, could not cope. The taxi turned from the bazaar into a wide avenue. Ahead, the centrepiece of a roundabout, was the inevitable statue of the great white queen, Victoria, in profile to them on the line of their approach to it, the head slightly bowed under the weight of the dumpling crown and an unspecified sorrow.

The road was now shaded by trees, lined by the grey-white walls of compounds behind which gardens and old bungalows of military family occupation were occasionally revealed in glimpses of deep shadowy verandas, patches of sun-struck lawns, beds of the ubiquitous crimson canna lilies. A scent of dew and strange blossom entered on the artificially created breeze and Sarah inclined her head, as if to a narcotic that might lift her spirits.

'We're coming to the church,' Captain Merrick said, and told the driver to slow down when they got to it so that the Memsahibs could see it better. His Urdu was fluent.

A greystone spire, Victorian Gothic; a churchyard, and leaning palm trees which always reminded Sarah of the India of old engravings. Behind their taxi the other taxi carrying Susan, Teddie and Aunt Fenny, also slowed. Mrs Layton did not remark on the church. Presently they regained their former speed.

'The chaplain's name is Fox, by the way,' Captain Merrick said, and then began to rehearse the next few days' programme. A small party at the club tonight to introduce them to the General who would be out of station for the wedding itself, and to the Station Commander and his wife. Dinner at the Station Commander's the following evening which the Chaplain would certainly attend. The G1 and his wife, the Station Commander and his wife, would have to be invited to the wedding. Teddie and Mrs Layton could work out between them who else among Teddie's fellow-officers and who else on the station should be invited. The club contractor was working on the basis of a small reception catering for between twenty and thirty people. Had Mrs Layton managed to get the cards printed in Ranpur? If not the printer Lal Chand who printed and published the *Mirat Courier* could produce them in twenty-four hours. The tailor Mrs Layton had mentioned in a letter to Teddie had been told to be at the guest house at midday to receive preliminary instructions. The steward in the guest house was under the control of the station staff officer, and would present the bill for meals and drinks at the end of their stay. Captain Merrick understood that these would be approximately at club prices. The rest of the guest house staff was supplied by the palace and there was no charge for accommodation, services or laundry other than personal laundry, all of which were to be accepted as part of the hospitality of the Nawab of Mirat to members of the services visiting the cantonment and unable to get accommodation in the club or the Swiss Hotel. The guest house was in the grounds of the palace, but there was a private way in and a separate compound. The private entrance, like the main entrance, was under armed guard, and there was a chaukidar. A palace motor-car would, Captain Merrick believed, be put at their disposal to help with things like shopping trips, and other motors from the palace garage would be lent for the wedding itself.

'I think that's about all, Mrs Layton, except that there's a young fellow who's distantly related to the Nawab and whose job it is to see that you have everything you need. He's an Indian, of course, a Muslim, and I think you'll like him. His name is Ahmed Kasim and he's a son of Mohammed

Ali Kasim, the Chief Minister in the provincial government of thirty-seven to thirty-nine.'

'MAK? But isn't he locked up?' Mrs Layton asked.

'Exactly, that's the point. I mean it's something I think necessary to remember when dealing with young Kasim. He's an attractive young fellow, well-educated, speaks first-rate English, not in the least the usual surly type of Westernized Indian who thinks he's a cut above everybody – and believe me I've had some experience with that sort—'

Mrs Layton said, 'Yes, I'm sure you have. Teddie tells us you were in the police. My sister is dying to hear how you managed to get out of that uniform into this. She knows a young man in the Civil who's tried everything but still hasn't managed to swing it. Were you ever in Ranpur?'

'Yes, some years ago, in a very junior capacity.'

'And before your army commission?'

'I was DSP Sundernagar.'

'Ah yes. We lived there once. Rather a remote district. Was there much trouble there last year?'

'No, very little. Fortunately. It helped me persuade the powers that be that I could be more usefully employed.'

Presently Mrs Layton said, 'You were telling us about Mr Kasim's son.'

'Yes, I was.' A further hesitation. 'I don't quite know how to put this. In Ranpur he'd present no problem, but this is native sovereign territory and as a representative of the palace young Kasim is entitled to – well, certain consideration. One can't just treat him as a sort of errand-boy. The State's barely more than the size of a pocket-handkerchief but it's run on very democratic lines and has a tradition of loyalty to the crown. One of the Nawab's sons is an officer in the Indian airforce and of course the Nawab handed his private army over to GHQ on the first day of the war. It was mustered into the Indian Army as the Mirat Artillery, and got captured by the Japs in Malaya. In other words, officially the military in Mirat take an extremely good view of the Nawab.'

'And of all his entourage, including Mr Kasim. Oh, we promise to be well behaved.'

Presently Captain Merrick said, 'I beg your pardon, Mrs Layton. I've put everything very clumsily. The point I intended to make was that friendly and co-operative though Kasim is on the surface, it's as well to treat him cautiously as well as considerately because it would be unnatural if he didn't resent us a bit.'

'We probably shan't have time to let it worry us, Captain Merrick.'

'No.'

And then, suddenly, they had left the avenue of trees behind and were driving alongside the lake. Dazzled, Sarah heard his voice: 'There's the palace now,' her mother's low exclamation and then his voice again, close to her ear. 'You're looking in the wrong direction, Miss Layton.'

*

492

Beyond the reeds the lake curved away and the road became splashed again by shade from old banyan trees. A high brick wall, topped by jagged bits of broken glass, had come in from the left. The taxi was slowing. Ahead, a culvert marked the private entrance to the guest house. There was nothing to be seen of it, nothing to see at all apart from the long straight road which eventually led – Captain Merrick said – through the waste ground into the old city of Mirat. There were walls on both sides of the road now. They turned in through an open gateway. A grey-bearded sepoy with a red turban and red sash round the waist of his khaki jacket came to attention. The taxi continued along a gravel drive that was flanked on either side by bushes of bougainvillaea and curved towards the left. The bushes thinned, there were patches of grass, and through trees a glimpse of rose-coloured stone.

'Do you know,' Mrs Layton said, 'it reminds me of the drive up to grandfather's old place.'

'But that was all laurel and rhododendrons,' Sarah pointed out, remembering – none too clearly – her great-grandfather's house which she had last seen the year of his death, as a child of twelve.

'The effect is the same.'

Sarah did not agree but did not say so, content anyway that her mother had settled momentarily into the kind of nostalgic mood that suggested the actual arrival would go well, although later that night there might be a hint of tearfulness at lonely bed-going – a whiteness under the rouge unfashionably applied low instead of high on the cheeks, an inner disintegration betrayed by a marginal relaxation of the muscles of the jaw and neck that produced a soft little pad of tender aging flesh under the courageous chin. Presently held high (as Sarah saw, looking over her shoulder) to receive a dab or two from the puff of a compact, there were, in its structure, the presentation to the world, signs of effort-in-achievement. Almost unconsciously bringing her hand up to stroke her own chin and neck in a gesture partly nervous and partly investigatory she marvelled at the havoc a few years would wreak on flesh so firm. There came a time when the face changed for ever, into its final mould. Hers had not done so, but her mother's had. Some faces then went all to bone, others went to slack, fallen, unoccupied folds and creases of skin. Her mother's would do that, and perhaps Susan's too, years hence. Her own would tauten. As an old woman she would probably have a disapproving but predatory look. Her mother would go on softening whereas she herself would harden exteriorly, become brittle interiorly. She would break into a thousand pieces, given the right blow. To kill her mother in old age would be a bloodier, more fleshy, less splintery affair. Her mother was protected already by incipient layers of blubber (like Aunt Fenny, but unlike Aunt Lydia). All the more credit to her therefore, Sarah thought, that she managed to convey a certain steeliness from within the softness.

Even at the most exasperating moments Sarah could feel, for her mother, a surge of love and deep affection that sprang goodness knew not from a long uninterrupted experience of her as a mother – the separation had been

493

too long for that – but rather from a sensation of being able to treat her as if she were a human being towards whom she had a duty that was scarcely filial at all: almost as if she were a stranger of a kind suddenly encountered. She felt such a surge now, but as usual was unable to express it because her mother was not even looking at her, but putting the compact away. Well, so it goes, Sarah thought. And so it went: the taxi moving slowly through a tunnel of alternating bars of sunlight and strips of shadow and then coming out abruptly into the gravelled forecourt where the NCO with the diaphanous pugree stood by the side of the parked fifteen hundredweight that had brought their luggage. They drove in under a shadowy porticoed entrance and drew up at the bottom of a shallow flight of steps. At the head of the steps two men were waiting. As Captain Merrick spoke they were joined by a third.

'The chap in the scarlet turban is Abdur Rahman. He's head bearer and belongs to the Nawab. The little fellow holding his topee is the steward, his name's Abraham – an Indian Christian. He's the SSO's chap. And yes – there's Mr Kasim.'

Sarah, looking up, saw Ahmed emerge from the dark interior.

*

'Was it wise?' she heard her Aunt Fenny asking, and recognized her mother's first-drink-of-the-day voice: 'Was what wise?'

'Letting her go riding alone with Mr Kasim.'

'I didn't let her as you call it. I didn't know.'

'Didn't know? You mean she just sneaked off?'

'Oh, Fenny, what's wrong with you? My daughters don't sneak off. They go. They don't have to ask permission. They're of age. They do what they like. One gets married. The other goes riding. How am I supposed to stop them? Why should I try?'

'You're becoming impossible to talk to sensibly. You know perfectly well why it's unwise for Sarah to ride alone with an Indian of that kind.'

'What kind?'

'Any kind, but especially Mr Kasim's kind.'

Sarah said, 'What of Mr Kasim's kind, Aunt Fenny?' and shaded her eyes from the glare of the lake that at midday always seemed to penetrate the shade of the deep porticoed terrace on which her mother and aunt were sitting, on chairs set back close to one of the open french windows which gave access to the terrace from the darkened sitting-room, and through which she had now stepped. She could not see the expressions on her aunt's or mother's face, and did not join them. She stood near them, gazing at the lake, letting that milky translucence work its illusion of detaching her from her familiar mooring in a world of shadow and floating her off into a sea of dangerous white-hot substance that was neither air nor water.

'I'm sorry,' Aunt Fenny said. 'I didn't know you were listening. I was saying I thought it unwise for you to ride alone with Mr Kasim.'

From the midst of that buoyant, dazzling opacity she said, 'Yes, I agree – it was unwise.' When they returned the syce had been waiting. He followed them round to the gravel forecourt below the terrace on which she presently stood and held her horse's head while she dismounted. Mr Kasim dismounted too. 'Come in and have some breakfast,' she suggested. He thanked her and said, 'Some other time perhaps,' asked her if there was anything special that either she or her family wanted to do, to see, or to have him bring or make arrangements for. 'No, I don't think so,' she said, 'thank you for taking me riding.' She wondered whether for some reason or other they should shake hands. He remounted, touched his topee with the tip of his crop and brought the horse's head round – all, as it were, in the same capable movement. As she came on to the terrace she listened to the sound of the hooves on the gravel.

'We shan't go riding again,' she said and lowered her head, turned, looked at Aunt Fenny and found the older woman's face set in that extraordinary mould that was the answer to the need to express something beyond the private emotional capacity to understand.

Sometimes she hated Aunt Fenny, mostly she was irritated by her. For the moment she felt inexplicably close to her and to her mother who had her eyes closed, one hand at rest on the arm of the wicker chair, the other clasping a half-empty glass of gin and lemon, apparently waiting for the day to come into its familiar focus as one totally indistinguishable from any other.

Well, they are my family, Sarah told herself. I love them. They are part of my safety and I suppose I'm part of theirs.

'What happened?' Aunt Fenny asked. Her voice, normally rich and well-risen, sounded flat and dry.

'Nothing happened. I meant it was unwise because it made us both self-conscious. It never occurred to me that it might. It wasn't until we actually set out that I realized it was the first time I'd been alone with an Indian who wasn't a servant. And there seemed to be nothing to talk about. He only spoke when spoken to and kept almost exactly the same number of paces behind me from start to finish.'

The stiffness had left Aunt Fenny's face but this softening only emphasized the lines that years of stiffening had left permanently on her, the private marks of public disapproval.

And what I remembered on the way back (Sarah thought, half-considering this face that was Aunt Fenny's but also that of an English woman in India) was the luggage in the little cabin, with that girl's name on it. She was never real to me until I saw the luggage. She was a name in a newspaper, someone they talked about in Pankot. She began to be real when I saw the luggage in the houseboat in Srinagar. The child must belong to the Indian they said she was in love with, otherwise why should that old lady keep it? But it might have been any half-caste baby. The luggage was different. It was inert. It belonged only to her. She was no longer alive to claim it, but this is what brought her to life for me. And this morning as I rode home, a few paces ahead of Mr Kasim, she was alive for me completely. She flared up out of my darkness as a white girl in love with an Indian. And then went out because – in that disguise – she is not part of what I comprehend.

'He is a perfectly pleasant young man,' Aunt Fenny said, 'and I understand his brother is an officer. But these days one simply can't tell what these young Indians are up to, let alone what they're thinking.'

'Perhaps they find the same difficulty in regard to us.'

'Yes, perhaps they do. But on the whole, my dear, we ought not to let that concern us. We have responsibilities that let us out of trying to see ourselves as they see us. In any case it would be a waste of time. To establish a relationship with Indians you can only afford to be yourself and let them like it or lump it.'

'Yes,' Sarah said. 'I suppose you're right. But out here are we ever really ourselves?'

III

There was, to begin with, the incident of the stone.

Apart from the black limousine travelling some seventy-five or hundred yards behind a wobbling bicycle ridden by an Indian carrying a raised umbrella as a protection against glare, there was no traffic on Gunnery Road; neither were there any visible pedestrians at the place where the incident occurred – the Victoria roundabout where a car coming down Gunnery Road and wishing to turn into Church Road had to slow down and describe a three-quarter circle round the monument. The driver of the limousine, an elderly man with a grey beard and wearing palace livery, having passed a file of peasant women with baskets on their heads going in the opposite direction, then began to concentrate on the cyclist and the possible obstacle he represented. He began to decelerate. Gunnery Road and the three other roads meeting at the roundabout were well shaded by big-branched thick-boled trees. The wobbling cyclist turned left. The way now seemed clear for the driver of the limousine to negotiate the roundabout, but encroaching age and several minor accidents had made him cautious, distrustful of what an apparently empty street might suddenly conjure in the shape of fast-driven vehicles.

The sound, when it came, did not immediately register. He allowed the limousine to continue to glide towards a point on the roundabout where he would be able to see what threatened from the left and how clear it was to the right. When the sound did register he braked, stared at the bonnet and the windscreen, then twisted round to confront the pane of glass dividing him from his passengers and, finding it unblemished, only then looked through it.

The passengers, both British officers, were thrust back hard, each into his separate corner. Their arms were still held in half-defensive attitudes.

496

They were looking from floor to window to floor and to the space between them on the seat: as one might look for some suspected poisonous presence – a snake for instance. The last thing the driver noticed was the shattered window on the nearside of the car – not the window in the door, which was lowered, but the fixed window that gave the passenger a clear view. It took the driver several seconds to realize that neither officer could have broken it, that something had been thrown. At this point both officers came to life, shouted something at him, each opened a door and jumped out. One word, one idea – half formed into the shape of an image actually seen – came into the driver's head. Bomb. He had heard of such things happening, but had no experience of them. He opened his own door, stumbled out and found himself climbing marble steps. He missed his footing, fell and lay motionless with his hands covering his head, waiting for the explosion.

After a while he sat up. Above him loomed the plinth on which the White Queen sat, hardened and sensitive, gazing up the length of Gunnery Road, which was still empty of traffic. The file of village women, now some four hundred yards away, continued their journey uninterruptedly. Turning he found both officers standing in the road a few feet from the car. They were looking towards and making gestures at the low grey stucco wall that marked the boundary of a compound. One of them had a handkerchief held to the left side of his face. They stopped looking at the wall and looked at him.

'Sahib,' he said to the one without the handkechief, after he had picked himself up, walked down the steps and approached them, 'I thought you jumped out because a bomb had been thrown.'

The officer did not smile. He had blue eyes. The driver was always fascinated by Sahibs with blue eyes. The eyes of the other Sahib were not so blue, hardly blue at all, but he had very pale eyelashes. There was blood on the handkerchief.

He followed the Sahibs back to the car and watched while they looked at the shattered window and into the back. He went round to the offside door and helped them to look. He did not know what he was looking for. An object of some kind. He found the object wedged in a corner under one of the tip-up seats. He picked it up. A stone. He said, 'Sahib, this is it.' He handed it to the Sahib with the blue eyes. The Sahib took and showed it to the other Sahib.

Presently the unwounded Sahib looked across at him and said, 'Did you see who threw this?'

'I saw no one, Sahib. Only the women with the baskets but we had gone many yards past them before it was thrown. The person who threw it must have hidden behind that tree, Sahib. There may have been such a man. I do not know. My mind was not on this kind of matter. There was a man on a bicycle in front of the car. He was not making signals. My mind was on this man on the bicycle. He is gone. He went to the left. I did not see any other man. I am sorry, Sahib. It is not an auspicious beginning.'

497

'You're damned right it isn't,' Teddie Bingham said. 'For God's sake, Ronnie, is there any blood on my uniform?'

'It'll sponge out. Let me have a look at that cut.'

Teddie took the handkerchief from his cheek. Blood oozed out of a jagged cut below the cheekbone. Captain Merrick clapped the handkerchief back on.

'It may need a stitch and there may be glass in it.'

'But, Christ, there isn't time.'

'You can't get married bleeding like a stuck pig. Come on. Get back in and mind you don't sit on a splinter or you'll really be in trouble. When we get to the church I'll root out the chaplain and use his phone to get a doctor. There may be time to ring through and warn Susan and Major Grace. It'll mean putting the ceremony back a few minutes.'

Before sitting Merrick inspected his own and Teddie's side of the seat for splinters, then told the driver to get on quickly to the church.

'The bloody bastard,' Teddie said. 'Whoever it was. Bugger him and bugger the Nawab. And bugger his bloody limousine.'

'Why?'

'Well, it's obvious, isn't it? A crest on the door as big as your arse. A bloody open invitation for some bolshie Nawab-hating blighter to heave a bloody great rock through the window.'

Merrick smiled, and was silent, contemplating the stone which he held balanced on the palm of his right hand.

*

Nawab Sahib was having the frayed end of his coat sleeve trimmed when Count Bronowsky told him there had been an incident involving one of the motor-cars on loan to the wedding party. The car, a 1926 Daimler, once the property of the late Begum, had been struck by a stone as it turned into Church Road at the Victoria roundabout. A window had been shattered and Captain Bingham cut on the cheek. The other occupant of the car, a Captain Merrick, was unhurt. He had telephoned the information through to Ahmed Kasim from the chaplain's house where Captain Bingham was receiving attention from a medical officer. The ceremony had been delayed for half an hour and the reception at the Gymkhana Club would now begin at 11.15 instead of at 10.45. There was therefore no need to hurry.

Nawab Sahib, who was standing patiently in the middle of the room – his left arm held out while his personal body-servant snipped stray bits of thread from his cuff – glanced at Bronowsky. The Count was dressed in a starched cream linen suit, cream silk shirt and dove-grey silk tie. He had his best ebony gold-topped cane to lean on. The Nawab then looked at young Ahmed who wore a grey linen jacket and trousers, noticeably less expensive but quite well cut and properly pressed.

The silent inspection over, the Nawab returned his attention to the make-and-mend operation on his own coat, and said,

'Has a substitute car been sent?'

'It was offered but declined. Captain Merrick insists the damaged one is perfectly serviceable.'

'Has the chief of police been informed?'

'Ahmed has telephoned him, your Highness.'

'Will he think to make contact with the military police in the cantonment? Or will he rush about in the city arresting every likely culprit?'

The questions, recognized by the Count as rhetorical, were left unanswered. Ali Baksh, the chief of police in Mirat, was currently under the cloud of the Nawab's unpredictable but cautious displeasure. Another reason for Bronowsky saying nothing was his understanding that the Nawab's composure was deceptive and so best left untampered with. Bronowsky had trained the Nawab to think of himself as a man who had to deny himself the luxury of violent criticism, even of expressing an opinion about anything except strictly personal matters, and who had a duty to the one million people he ruled never to leap to a conclusion or take any unconsidered action. But Bronowsky knew that although the Nawab had so far made no comment on the incident of the car his sense of outrage had been disturbed and fired.

Bronowsky smiled. Within sight of the end of his own reign he allowed himself the full pleasure of self-congratulation. Nawab Sahib had been transformed, step by painful step, from a tin-pot autocratic native prince of extravagant tastes and emotions into the kind of ruler-statesman whose air of informed detachment and benign loftiness was capable of leaving even the wiliest mind guessing and the coldest heart warmed briefly by curiosity; and wily minds and cold hearts were the combination Bronowsky found most common in English administrators. Nawab Sahib was Bronowsky's one and only creation, his lifetime's invention. He had fallen possessively in love with him and watched with compassion the struggle Nawab Sahib sometimes had to discipline himself to act and move – and think – in the ways Bronowsky had taught him.

Nawab Sahib removed his arm from the gentle support of the servant with the scissors and inspected the cuff. His private austerities were the last remarkable flowering of Bronowsky's design for a prince; remarkable because Bronowsky had not planned them. For Bronowsky, the austerities were to his design what the unexpected, seemingly inspired and unaccountable stroke of the brush could sometimes be to a painting, the stroke that seemed to have created the need for itself out of the combined resources of the canvas and the man who worked on it, and so was definitive of the process of creation itself and of the final element of mystery in any work of art.

The frayed cuff coats were not worn with the bombast of a rich miser, and it was difficult to say what emotion it was, precisely, that a man felt when he first noticed the spotless but threadbare cloth of the long-skirted high-necked coats, the clean but cheap and floppy trousers, the clean bare

499

feet in old patched sandals or polished down-at-heel shoes; but Bronowsky believed that a major part of that response was made up of respectful wariness, much the same – possibly – as one's response would normally be to the sight of a gentleman down on his luck, but without the measure of pity and contempt such a condition evoked. The Nawab was rich enough for any but the most exaggerated taste. He was surrounded by proofs of his public comfort and of his private generosity. His austerities were reserved wholly for himself. They appeared at once as the badge of his right to lead a personal, private life and as evidence of how spare such a life had to be when so much of his interest and energy was expended for the benefit of the people it was his inherited duty to protect and privilege to rule. And it was this – the duality of meaning to be read into the Nawab's appearance – and the fact that the appearance was not deliberately assumed, that excited in Bronowsky the special tenderness of the artist for his creation. The austerities had been gradual, so that neither Nawab Sahib nor Bronowsky had ever commented on them. Equally gradual, Bronowsky supposed, had been the growth of dandyism in himself. It was as though the love that existed between him and the Nawab had exerted an influence to make them opposites, but what pleased him more was the realization that when they were together the comparative splendour of his own plumage looked like that of a slightly more common species. People, observing them, would be less inclined to believe what they heard – that Bronowsky was the power behind the throne. In Bronowsky, pride in what he had made was stronger than personal vanity. It was part of his pride that Nawab Sahib alone should be credited with the talents and capabilities Bronowsky had worked hard to train him to acquire and exercise.

He believed that Nawab Sahib was quite unconscious of there being any particular meaning to read into his habit of wearing old and inexpensive clothes. The Nawab had said once as they were preparing to go out on a public occasion for which Bronowsky had arrived dressed in his uniform of Honorary Colonel, Mirat Artillery (a uniform he had designed himself and which incorporated certain decorative flourishes reminiscent of the uniform of the old Imperial Guard to which Bronowsky had never belonged): 'Sit low in the carriage, Dmitri. Otherwise how will they tell that it is not you who is Nawab?'

'Should I sit higher than a man can sit, your Highness,' Bronowsky said, 'they would still know I was but Bronowsky. A wazir must dress to do honour to the State and the Nawab Sahib is the State. His raiment is Mirat.'

The Nawab smiled: the same slow, grave smile that had been one of the persuasions the Russian felt to follow the small, lost, dark-skinned man of passion, sorrows and absurdities to his curious little kingdom in an alien land. And since the occasion of this particular courtly exchange Bronowsky had noticed how whenever he entered a room where the Nawab stood the Nawab said nothing until he had taken in at one short or prolonged glance – depending on the amount there was to scrutinize – the details of his wazir's dress and accessories. The ritual had become one he felt the Nawab depended on for reassurance. For some time Bronowsky had encouraged Ahmed also to take an interest in his clothes (or, anyway, to submit to directions and suggestions because interest in anything seemed to be something Ahmed was incapable of taking, unless visits to the Chandi Chowk could be counted as an interest as distinct from a compulsion).

That Ahmed should find increasing favour in the eyes of the Nawab was a continuing concern of Bronowsky's present policy, one of whose objects was the marriage of Ahmed to the Nawab's only daughter, Shiraz, whom the late Begum had brought up, out of spite, in a rigidly traditional manner, with the result that Shiraz, after her mother's death, would not come out of the seclusion she had been taught to regard as obligatory for a woman. Her mother had died just before Shiraz reached the age of puberty, and so she had never gone officially into purdah. The Nawab, urged by Bronowsky, had withheld his permission for that step to be taken; but the girl was so timid her father did not have the heart to follow Bronowsky's advice further and insist on her adopting the modern ways of the palace. She was now sixteen, virtually untutored, and proved to be tongue-tied in the presence of strangers on the few occasions Bronowsky had succeeded in persuading the Nawab to command her out of her self-made zenana to pay her respects to visitors Bronowsky considered important. She had been taught by her mother to regard the wazir as an ogre, a man who had her father in thrall and whose private life was so wicked as to be unspeakable; and it was only with patience that he had gradually succeeded in removing from her mind the idea that simply to look him in the eye was tantamount to gazing at the Devil. Mostly, denied the privacy of the veil, she kept her eyes downcast and fled to the security of her rooms at the first hint that she had done her duty.

The sad thing, Bronowsky thought, was that she was ravishingly pretty. He assumed – because neither the Nawab nor either of his two sons was handsome – that this prettiness, like the perverted desire to hide it, was a legacy from her mother. Bronowsky had never been permitted to see the Begum. She submitted him to long and unkind interrogation from behind a purdah-screen which left him no notion of her except what could be gathered from strong whiffs of expensive imported perfumes, the glint of rich silks and brocades through the tiny carved apertures, and the harshness of a high-pitched voice in which passion, cruelty and bitchiness were in roughly equal proportions. From such one-sided interviews Bronowsky would retreat confirmed in his hatred of women, raging impotently against the enormity of their abuse of the moral weapons God had mistakenly given them as armour against the poor savage male and his ridiculous codes of honour. Sometimes, looking at Shiraz – a dark red blush under the pale brown skin of her cheeks, her eyes downcast, the fabric of her saree shimmering not from reflections but from the trembling

501

underneath – Bronowsky wondered how much of her mother's temperament was concealed there and what it would take to release it and make some man's life – Ahmed's for instance – a misery. He comforted himself with the belief that the Begum, from all accounts, had always been a strong-willed woman and that what she had taught her daughter, once untaught, would release a temperament no more like the Begum's than the two sons' temperaments were like their father's.

Bronowsky thought little of either son. Both had eluded his influence. Mohsin, the elder, the future Nawab, product of the English tutors and public-school style college Bronowsky had agreed to early on as a sop to the Political Department, had acquired the pompousness of the English without the saving grace of their energy and without that curious tendency to iconoclasm which they called their sense of humour. He spent most of his time in Delhi, worthily and dully engaged in what he called his business interests, and as little as possible in Mirat, a place which his Westernized wife despised as socially backward. The younger, Abdur, similarly schooled, had acquired different English characteristics. He was a harmless young man who had graduated from an absorbing interest in cricket which he played badly to an equally absorbing interest in aeroplanes which he had not yet succeeded in learning to fly to the satisfaction of the Air Force.

Bronowsky admitted to himself that part of the reason for his letting the education and shaping of Mohsin and Abdur become the concern of others was to be found in the fact that neither of them had ever been well-favoured in appearance or manner. He thought, though, that it had been just as well. Their plainness and physical awkwardness had enabled him to concentrate the whole of his emotional impulse on the task of making a Nawab. A couple of handsome, active youths on hand could have caused his mind and will to wander in the bitter-sweet region mapped by his inclinations, explored by his imagination, but never – for many years – entered into. The discipline and self-denial involved in voluntary withdrawal from direct physical satisfaction of his needs had not been undergone only in order that he should never be guilty of corrupting another. He had come to recognize that the type of youth who attracted him was one whose attributes were wholly masculine and who therefore was attracted exclusively to women. The first sign that this was not necessarily so destroyed, for Bronowsky, the romantic fervour and loving admiration a young man could inspire in him, and left behind it only what he found grotesque. The man he could embrace was not the man for him. It had been as simple as that. The cessation of sexual activity had not been onerous. His affairs with men had been few: three in the twenty-one years between his nineteenth and fortieth birthdays. Physically there had been no women in his life.

Now, approaching seventy, he did not regret chances missed or opportunities wasted. He believed that if he had been born a woman he would have loved one man long, devotedly and faithfully. But having been born a man he did not now crave to have been blessed with normal appetites. He thought that anyway he had experienced to an extent few could claim the joy as well as the pain of loving unselfishly, from afar. He did not delude himself into supposing that his affection for Ahmed was the sentimental longing of an old bachelor for a son. He faced the truth. Ahmed was the latest manifestation of the unattainable, unattempted golden youth who came, sweetened the hour with his presence, and went unmolested into the arms of a deserving Diana, so that the whole world sang and the day was properly divided from the night. It amused him that this golden youth was brown, and touched him that in his old age the object of his undeclared and regulated passion should be someone his professional interest allowed a close connection with. It was as though the old Gods of the forest had rewarded him for his abstentions. He treated the reward with almost excessive care, conscious of the need to balance his emotional with his worldly judgement. Ahmed had become a feature of the policy he was formulating. It was a bonus that he filled so well Bronowsky's personal need: a bonus and a snare. It would never do to confuse the policy with the need or the need with the policy. And Bronowsky knew that if the interests of the need and the policy came into conflict for any reason, it was Ahmed who would be sacrificed because the policy, through all its shifts and changes to adapt to circumstances, was pre-determined by one thing that never altered: Bronowsky's devotion to his Prince.

*

'It is not auspicious,' the Nawab said. And sat down. 'A stone?'

'A stone, Sahib.'

'At one of the motor-cars?'

Bronowsky inclined his head. He motioned Ahmed to leave them. When Ahmed had gone the Nawab indicated a chair and said in the low voice Bronowsky automatically registered as a sign of special self-control, 'Please sit.' Bronowsky did so. He rested both hands on the gold knob of his cane. His white panama was on his lap. The Nawab sat with folded hands and crossed ankles, leaning his weight on his left elbow. The arms of the chair were carved with diminutive lion heads at the protruding tips. The room was dark from the closed shutters. A slanting column of sunlight, admitted by the gap between one set of shutters left partly open, fell just short of the Nawab's chair. The room was overfurnished. There was a preponderance of potted palms. Strangers coming to the palace were sometimes disturbed by a resemblance they could not quite give a name to. Only the elderly and well-travelled hit easily upon the explanation. The public rooms were furnished in the manner of a plush and gilt hotel of pre-Great War vintage on the Côte d'Azur. Only the dimensions of the rooms, the arched windows, the fretted stone screens, some of the mosaics and the

503

formal courtyard around which the main part of the palace was built remained Moghul in spirit and appearance.

'I'm afraid I do not understand this incident of the stone, Dmitri.'

'No,' Bronowsky agreed. 'It is a puzzle.'

'It is ten years since a stone was thrown.'

Bronowsky nodded.

The Nawab looked towards the window.

'It was thrown at the Begum.'

Bronowsky nodded. He remembered the occasion well. It had enlivened his convalescence from a bout of gastro-enteritis that laid him low for a week, an illness which his servants attributed to his having been given coffee and cakes during an interview in the Begum's apartment.

'From what young Kasim tells me,' the Count said, 'I believe it is one of the late Begum's motor-cars the stone was thrown at this morning.'

'Is that significant?'

'I should not think so – unless the culprit is a madman.'

'Do we understand correctly that he wasn't apprehended, and that there is no information about him at all?'

'That seems to be correct, Nawab Sahib.'

'Then it is unlikely that he will be caught.'

'Very unlikely.'

'One man alone is not usually responsible for such an incident. It is the kind of activity several people decide. Several decide. One acts. But this is relatively unimportant. What is important is to know why the stone was thrown.'

'May I suggest we put it another way, Sahib, and ask ourselves at whom, or even at what, the stone was thrown? If we can answer that the answer to the question why it was thrown probably follows.'

'Very well. At whom or at what was the stone thrown?'

'We know it was thrown at the car, but whether at the car or the occupants is the beginning of the puzzle. Let us assume it was thrown at the car. The car bears your Highness's crest. The symbolism would then be inescapable. Ergo – the stone was thrown at your Highness. The thrower may even have thought your Highness was riding in the car. But as you say, a stone has not been thrown for ten years and when it was thrown it was thrown at the Begum. Your Highness has never been subjected to any kind of personal or even symbolic attack. And it is Ramadan. A Muslim subject would not throw a stone during Ramadan. Your Highness's Hindu subjects are content. Those areas of the State of Mirat which suffered a poor crop are being assisted effectively by the Famine Relief Commission. Your Highness and I spent a week together in Gopalakand meeting the new Resident. I returned ahead, nothing untoward was reported to me when I returned. Your Highness was greeted on your own return last night at the station with the usual loyal address and popular demonstration. Ergo – let us assume from all this evidence that the stone was not thrown at the car but at the occupants.'

'Who are—?'

'Captain Bingham and Captain Merrick, both – so Ahmed tells me – staff officers in the divisional headquarters recently formed, temporarily stationed in Mirat, and due to leave in the middle of next week for special training prior to active duty in the field. In other words, officers without any military or administrative employment in the cantonment as such, detached from local affairs, virtually strangers to the population.'

'But British officers all the same, Count Sahib.'

'Quite so.'

'An anti-British demonstration—' The Nawab frowned. 'In which case, also an anti-palace demonstration. The wedding party are our guests.'

'We can't assume that the man who threw the stone at British officers riding in a limousine knew that they were on their way to a wedding, Sahib. Nor that the ladies in the wedding party have been staying at the guest house.'

'This nevertheless is the situation. The stone was thrown at our guests.'

'Beg pardon, Sahib. Captain Bingham is not a guest. He is the groom.'

'That is worse. It is a great mischief. They have given me a beautiful gift. We reply with a stone.'

'It happened in the cantonment, Sahib.'

'They are our guests wherever it happens. What am I to say to them when I meet them? That they have Mirat's hospitality but not Mirat's protection? I shall want a full report.'

'It will be as full as possible. Meanwhile your Highness can only express your regret. Your Highness might add that you are astonished and pained that such a thing should happen in Mirat, either in the cantonment or out of the cantonment.' Bronowsky paused. 'Even last August there were no anti-British demonstrations in Mirat. The prohibition of political demonstrations and meetings the previous July was extremely effective. Known agitators were made *persona non grata*. The police have been active in smelling out refugee-agitators from British India, and sending them back where they came from. The incident of the stone this morning is therefore a mystery.' Bronowsky glanced at his watch. 'If you are ready, Sahib, I think we should go. In the circumstances it would be a proper gesture to be at the reception early rather than late.'

*

A stone: such a little thing. But look at us – Sarah thought – it has transformed us. We have acquired dignity. At no other time do we move with such grace as we do now when we feel threatened by violence but untouched by its vulgarity. A stone thrown by an unknown Indian shatters the window of a car, a piece of flying glass cuts an Englishman on the cheek and at once we sense the sharing of a secret that sustains and extends us, and Teddie instead of looking slightly absurd getting married with lint and sticking plaster on his face looks pale and composed. The end of Teddie is not reached so easily after all. I was wrong when I thought he had nothing more to offer that he hadn't already given. He will always be ready to offer and willing to give himself in the cause of our solidarity.

And it was a special kind of solidarity, Sarah realized. It transcended mere clannishness because its whole was greater than all its parts together. It uplifted, it magnified. It added a rare gift to a life which sometimes seemed niggardly in its rewards, and left one inspired to attack the problems of that life with the grave simplicity proper to their fair and just solution. The hot-tempered words and extravagant actions that might have greeted the incident of the stone were sublimated in this surrender to collective moral force.

From her position behind Susan at the altar steps she observed the way Teddie stood, at attention, with a military rather than a religious deference to God. To her left, and a pace or two in front, stood Uncle Arthur who had just made the gesture of confirmation that it was he who gave Susan to Teddie. He was also at attention. He seemed to be staring up at the stained-glass window above the altar as if it might be through there that some light would fall to disperse the perpetual shadow of professional neglect it was understood by the family he suffered from and gamely plodded on in spite of. Glancing from Teddie to Uncle Arthur and back again Sarah thought: Why, what a curious thing a human being is; and was not surprised to hear Aunt Fenny sniff and to see that Susan was trembling as she put out her hand for Teddie to fit the ring on her finger. It is all over in such a short time, Sarah told herself, but in that short time everything about our lives changes for ever. We become something else, without necessarily having understood what we were before.

Teddie kissed his bride. Mercifully the cut had not been deep enough to need a stitch and the doctor had pronounced it free of splinters. Presumably it was not over-painful, but he cocked his head at an awkward angle, perhaps so as not to tickle Susan with any stray end of lint or sticking plaster. The kiss, Sarah noticed, was a firm one in spite of the angle at which contact was made. He did not wince; but breaking free smiled and touched the wound gingerly as if in a dumb show of apology for the inconvenience of it. It was the innocent gesture of a boy and the contrived one of a man with a sense of theatre who guessed that people were bound to wonder to what extent delayed shock or plain discomfort might impair the ardour of his performance, later, of private and more intimate duties.

Sarah stooped and gathered the folds of the bride's veil, followed the family into the vestry. The organist was playing a tune she thought was probably 'Perfect Love'. 'Hello, Mrs Bingham,' she said, and kissed Susan on one flushed happy cheek. 'I wanted to say it first.'

'I couldn't stop shivering,' Susan said. 'Did it show? I felt everybody could see.' She kissed her mother, and Aunt Fenny, and Uncle Arthur. 'It sounds funny,' she said at one point. 'Susan Bingham.'

'Oh, you'll get used to it,' Teddie said. 'Anyway you'd better.'

They signed the register.

Within half an hour of the incident of the stone two NCOs of the British Military Police had arrived on duty outside the church. Mounted on motor-cycles they led the bride and groom from the ceremony to the reception at the Gymkhana Club where they were to remain until the time came for them to escort the bridal car to the station. Their instructions were to keep an eye open for any further attempted act or demonstration of an anti-British nature – for as such for the moment, it was thought, the incident of the stone had to be treated.

The roar of the motor-bikes and the stand-no-nonsense demeanour of the men astride them seemed to release in the people who had attended the ceremony and now watched the departure of Teddie and Susan and presently made their way to their own waiting cars and taxis (and in one case a military truck, logged out as on civil duties), an animus of a subtly different nature from the one which had made them feel calm, remote and dignified. It entered and stirred them like the divine breath of a God who had bent his brow to call forth sterner angels.

The affair of the stone, first reacted to with a sense of shock, then treated as lamentable, regrettable, a challenge of the kind to which the only answer was to rally round and make the young couple feel that after all their day had not been ruined, was now seen as contemptible; mean, despicable, cowardly. Typical.

The scene of the crime, the Victoria roundabout, significantly marked by the presence of a police truck and three armed MPs, caused among the occupants of the cars as they passed by it on their way to the club some speculation about the exact spot from which the stone had been thrown and the likely escape-route of the demonstrator. Neither young Bingham nor his best man had apparently seen a thing. They had been looking at the memorial or intent on what they were saying to one another. The shock of the stone coming through the window, the fact that young Bingham was hurt and that the car took some time to pull up – according to the best man who had to explain things to the guests as they arrived as well as get the doctor, ring the police, and warn the bride and her uncle to hang on at the guest house for an extra half-hour; all of which he had done with an admirably cool head – were contributing factors to the ruffian having got away unseen.

It was probably the work of some fellow with a grudge, someone who had been dismissed for stealing from his master as likely as not – and who had heard about the wedding from a friend still employed in the cantonment and had hung about hoping for a chance to get his own back, not caring who it was he actually threw a stone at. If the culprit wasn't a fellow of that sort he was some clerk or student whose head was crammed with a lot of hot air about the iniquities of the *raj*: the kind who needed a kick up the backside or shipping out to Tokyo as a present to Hirohito or Subhas Chandras Bose. If he was that kind of fellow he was probably a member of a group at work outside the cantonment, in Mirat City, where the cantonment police had no jurisdiction.

Some of the princely states were jam-packed with political agitators who fled from the British provinces at the time of the mass Congress arrests, over a year ago, and even a small place like Mirat was known to have had its share. There was probably still a nucleus that had escaped the Mirat city police net. In any case the city police were probably corrupt. The princes were loyal to the crown because the crown protected their rights and privileges. A prince's subjects were often only loyal to him because they were terrified of the consequences of not being. At heart a lot of them shared the same aspirations as the Indian nationalists of British India, or had been persuaded by propaganda to believe they did. Perhaps the incident of the stone was a warning shot, a sign that dear old Mirat was suddenly going to explode. On the whole that might not be a bad thing. The Nawab would come running to the cantonment authorities for help and that would give the police the opportunity to root out the hidden subversive elements.

The danger of such elements lay in the contact they might have with Indian troops. That had always been the nightmare. It was the finest army in the world. Subvert it and it could turn and destroy its creators like a man swatting flies. With the war the dangers of subversion had increased. The army's ranks had been swelled with recruits whose loyalty to the salt they ate could not be counted on as part of the martial tradition of tribe or caste. And yet its loyalty seemed as sure as ever, which seemed in turn to prove that pride of service could inspire men of any race and any colour, given the opportunity. Such thoughts, spoken or left unspoken, led to the third and final change of mood. This was a mood in which it was felt that the stone had not found its mark but had rebounded from its impact with the impenetrable and unbreakable defences that always surrounded any inviolable truth. The stone changed nothing. Someone ought to pay for it but in the meantime it had to be treated as a joke; a joke in bad taste, certainly, but what else could be expected?

The two MPs who had escorted the bridal car greeted the guests on their arrival in the forecourt of the old Gymkhana Club by stopping each car and indicating where it should be parked. The MPs were brisk, cheerful and efficient, and the guests accepted their polite but firm directives with the friendly nods of people who, used to giving orders, enjoyed obeying them in circumstances they knew called for attention to the small details of security and discipline. From their cars they entered the club by steps unfamiliarly but pleasantly got up in red carpet. They went in twos and threes into the dim fan-cooled entrance hall of busts, mounted trophies and padding barefoot servants; through the ante-room, a lounge, and out through one of the open french windows on the terrace with its view on to an emerald-green lawn where a sprinkler was still at work.

*

Just as Captain Merrick returned to Sarah with a replenished glass of fruit-cup, the club secretary pressed through the adjacent group of people and said, 'Excuse me, Miss Layton. Have you seen your mother and uncle?'

'Mother was here a few minutes ago. I don't know where Uncle Arthur has got to.'

'I think they'd better be found.' He showed Sarah a card which she recognized as one of the wedding invitations. 'A servant just brought me this. One of the MPs sent it through. I'm afraid he's stopped the Nawab from coming in.'

'Stopped him? But why?'

'I suppose because he wasn't expecting an Indian to show up. I'll have to go out and start putting it right, but if your mother and uncle could be found and asked to come through I'd be grateful.'

'What's up?' a guest asked.

'The MPs have got the Nawab and his party stopped at the front door.'

'Good grief!' the guest said, laughed, and turned to pass the news on.

'I think I can probably find Major Grace,' Merrick said, '– if you'd scout round for your mother.'

'I'll try and keep him happy in the ante-room,' the secretary called.

Sarah made her way through the guests to the far end of the terrace. She found her mother listening to Mrs Hobhouse.

'Mother, the Nawab's arrived,' she said, interrupting a flow of reminiscences about the 1935 earthquake in Quetta.

'Oh, my dear,' Mrs Hobhouse said, 'Down tools. Fly. We *are* honoured. He only got back from Gopalakand last night. I'd better come with you. He's an old dear, but terribly hard going. Thank God for the red carpet. He'll probably think it's for him.'

'I'm afraid he won't,' Sarah said – taking the glass her mother seemed not to know she had in her hand and putting it on a near-by table. 'He's been refused entry.'

'Refused entry?' Mrs Layton repeated. 'I don't understand.'

Mrs Hobhouse grasped Sarah's elbow. 'My dear, whatever do you mean?'

'The MPs stopped him coming in. Captain Merrick's gone to find Uncle Arthur and the secretary wants us in the ante-room.'

She began to guide her mother back along the terrace. Mrs Hobhouse followed. 'But they can't have,' she said. 'I mean surely they were warned.' Suddenly she took Mrs Layton's other arm. 'Hold on. This is our job. Stay here with Sarah, and my husband and I will bring the old boy out. It's not right that either you or your brother-in-law should be placed in a position of having to apologize. If it really has happened it's club business or station business. Nothing to do with the wedding. Just stand here close to the door. Or better still go down on the lawn. I see Teddie and Susan are there. We'll bring the Nawab straight through and down. He'll feel it's a more conspicuous place anyway, better than hobnobbing in this crush.'

'I think Mrs Hobhouse is right, Mother. Come on.'

She led her mother down the stone steps into the glare. It was not unbearably hot. A light breeze had sprung up, was tangling Susan's veil. She stood in the middle of a group of Teddie's fellow officers, laughing. Sarah, catching sight of Captain Merrick leading Uncle Arthur along the terrace, called out and beckoned them down.

'I must say,' Uncle Arthur said when reaching them, 'this is turning out to be the most jinx-ridden affair I've ever been mixed up with, and that's saying something. Where's Fenny?'

'Shall I find her?' Captain Merrick asked.

'Well, that's easier said than done in this crush. I have a feeling there are more people drinking our drink and getting up their appetites for our food than were ever invited. Why couldn't they have set up a marquee or something? Separate the sheep from the goats. I'd swear half that gang on the terrace are just ordinary members of the club muscling in on the festivities. I've been having a word with the contractor's chap and warned him we're not going to pay a penny over the quotation. He's making a packet as it is. I say, cheer up, Mildred.'

'What?'

'You look half asleep.'

Mrs Layton stared at him, then said to Sarah, 'I'd better tell Susan and Teddie what's happened.'

'Aren't we going to the ante-room?' Captain Merrick asked Sarah, as her mother left her side and went over to the group of men clustered round the bride.

'Mrs Hobhouse thought it better if we stayed here and she and Colonel Hobhouse brought the Nawab down.'

'Good idea,' Major Grace said. 'Then we can pretend we know nothing about this snarl-up or whatever it is. I say, is this him now? Must be. How extraordinary. He looks like some downtrodden munshi.'

The chattering and laughter on the terrace did not lessen, but Sarah thought that abruptly it changed key. The Station Commander was walking slowly across the width of the terrace with a short little Indian, the top of whose truncated cone of a hat came level with Colonel Hobhouse's left epaulette – which in any case was lower than the right because the Colonel was bending slightly. The impression given by this sideways and downward inclination was one of deafness more than deference. Behind Colonel Hobhouse and the Nawab Mrs Hobhouse was similarly dwarfed by a tall thin man with an eye-patch.

'That must be Count Bronowsky,' Captain Merrick told Sarah, keeping his voice low. 'He's supposed to have been blown up by a bomb in St Petersburg but some unkind people say it's the result of peeping through keyholes. I'm told he's about seventy. He doesn't look it, does he?'

Behind Bronowsky and Mrs Hobhouse, the secretary walked with young Kasim.

At the head of the steps the Nawab paused, half turned with his left hand held in a gesture of command and invitation, and Ahmed detached himself from his position at the rear, came to the Nawab's side, made a firm elbow

510

upon which the Nawab now placed his hand. Slowly they descended the steps. Sarah saw the thin face of the old man with the eye-patch twitch, as if something had both pleased and amused him.

When they reached lawn level the Nawab removed his hand and Ahmed stood back to enable Mrs Hobhouse and the Count to precede him.

'Mrs Layton,' Colonel Hobhouse said, 'his Highness, Nawab Sir Ahmed Ali Guffur Kasim Bahadur.'

Mrs Layton nodded her head and murmured, 'How do you do. I'm so glad you were able to come.'

The Nawab returned the nod and waited.

'Nawab Sahib,' Colonel Hobhouse said, 'Mrs Layton wishes me to say on her behalf and on behalf of her family how deeply she has appreciated your many kindnesses in regard to the arrangements at the guest house.'

'Indeed, yes,' Mrs Layton murmured again.

The Nawab raised one hand, palm outwards. The lids fell over his eyes. The head jerked fractionally to one side.

The Station Commander hesitated, as if he had not been fed with a line and felt he could not now say what he had rehearsed and make sense. Sarah guessed his predicament. He had expected the Nawab or himself to make some reference to the incident of the stone, to express regret or make light of it. But the stone and the insult just given at the door cancelled each other out. Thanks had been offered for hospitality, been autocratically dismissed as quite unnecessary and without the formal expression of regret and reassurance that might have followed in regard to the stone there had emerged a silence which although short-lived was profound. Sarah, narrowing her eyes against the sunlight, was moved to a special intensity of feeling for the texture of the clothes she wore. The breeze was pressing the ankle-length skirt of her bridesmaid's gown against her legs. She had a fleeting image of them all as dolls dressed and positioned for a play that moved mechanically but uncertainly again and again to a point of climax, but then shifted its ground, avoiding a direct confrontation. Each shift was marked by just such a pause and the wonder perhaps was that the play continued. But the wind blew, nudging her through the creamy thinness of peach-coloured slipper satin and she and they were reanimated, prodded into speech and new positions. The Count Bronowsky, Chief Minister in Mirat. My daughter, Sarah. My brother-in-law, Major Grace. Captain Merrick. And this is my younger daughter, Susan, now Mrs Bingham.

Almost imperceptibly they had moved closer to the group that had surrounded Susan and which had now opened out leaving her exposed, vulnerable, tiny and tender in the ethereal whiteness of stiffened, wafting net and white brocade, several paces away from the spot where the Nawab's slow progress had finally come to a halt. For an instant Sarah thought that her mother would allow the presentation to end there – as if her duty were to show the Nawab no more than an image of the bride, an effigy set up to demonstrate the meaning and purpose of an alien rite. Her mother made a gesture, vague, evasive, but it – or some instinct of Susan's own – prompted the bride into motion, the totally unexpected motion – charming, unprecedented – of a curtsy. She sank into the billowy whiteness, bringing the effigy to life, and causing a hush among the watchers on the terrace. An Englishwoman did not curtsy to an Indian prince. But the hush was only one of astonishment and disapproval for the time it took for the watchers to feel what those closer to her felt almost instantaneously: a little shock-wave of enchantment: and when the Nawab was seen to take a hesitant step forward and then a firm one, and offer his hand, keeping it there until, rising, she put her own into it, the prettiness of the picture she made was enhanced by recognition of the fact that her impulsive action – so delightfully performed – had achieved what words and formal gestures could not – the re-establishment without loss of face of the essential *status quo*.

'Thank you for coming to my wedding,' Susan said, and Sarah – losing the drift of the Nawab's response, his involved but courteous good wishes for the health and happiness of bride and groom – considering still what Susan had just said, sensing something odd about it, turned her head and let her gaze come to rest on Count Bronowsky. By his side Mrs Hobhouse stood, silently watching – with a contented smile – the exchange of pleasantries between the Nawab and Susan and Teddie who by now had also been introduced. Bronowsky had a panama hat in the hand unencumbered by the ebony, gold-topped cane. She imagined what he would look like with it on and wondered whether he had worn it in the motor-car. Perhaps, under the hat, the pale pink skin would look like that of a high-caste Hindu. If he wore a cap such as the Nawab had on he might look very like a wealthy Muslim from the north – so subtle sometimes was the distinction between that kind of Indian and thin gaunt Europeans who had lived for years out East. Additionally shaded by the brim of a hat, travelling in a car with two Indians, the MPs could have assumed there was no white man in the small party arriving and expecting admittance.

She tried to assess the degree of humiliation Bronowsky would be capable of feeling. If he was really a count, the white Russian *émigré* who had been found by the Nawab in Monte Carlo and made use of as a go-between in the affair the Nawab was having, or had had and was trying to continue, with a European woman, and considering the fact that he had served for twenty years in a position that must have been even more testing than that of a British political adviser to an Indian ruler, then he had probably acquired a degree of immunity from attacks on his prestige and self-esteem.

But then, Sarah reminded herself, it was impossible to assume anything when it came to such matters. And often it was the thoughtless action, the unintentional insult, the casual attack which, catching you off guard, hurt most. Remembering the twitch of amusement when the Nawab made his imperious but frail, attractive gesture of command to be helped down the steps, Sarah was struck by the idea that perhaps the crooked fleeting smile was one of amusement at the Nawab's expense, an involuntary sign of underlying resentment of the fact that he, Bronowsky, should be subjected to the same humiliation as the Nawab, his master, but be denied the opportunity to get his own back so swiftly. 'One never knows,' Mr Hobhouse had said recently, 'what to make of the Count, but of course it's probably important to remember he's a dispossessed Russian and that the Nawab is not, after all, a little Tsarevich saved from a cellar in Ekaterinberg.'

Sarah wished she had seen how he reacted to the sight of Susan curtsying to the man who was not a little Tsarevich, or could see his expression now, as he waited his turn to be introduced. He stood, slightly stooped, his head inclined to catch whatever Mrs Hobhouse next said to him, but looking away half right, so that Sarah saw only his eye-patch profile. Was a black patch, on its own, expressive? Sarah thought that it was. Seen by itself, thus, it looked like the round bulging eye of a nocturnal creature abroad in sunlight, staring myopically, alerted by some unexpected but familiar sound of which it awaited a repetition in order to be certain of the accuracy of its judgement of the source: and Sarah, glancing in the direction indicated by the fixed intensity of the imaginarily luminous black patch, found that the source appeared to be Captain Merrick who, for the moment, stood alone, hands behind his back, unaware of the scrutiny he was under, taking a breather from the cumulatively exhausting duties of best man. Hatless, in full unflattering sunlight – the first time she was conscious of seeing Captain Merrick so – the years he could give Teddie showed. He was probably nearing thirty. In the company of Teddie and the young officers who surrounded Susan, he looked hardened, burnt by experiences distant from their own and placing him at distance now. He was not really Teddie's type. Chance alone – the sharing of quarters with Teddie and Captain Bishop's jaundice – had led to his presence at the wedding.

But the same could be said of all the other guests. And realizing that, Sarah understood what was odd about the thing Susan had said. The oddness was in that possessive phrase, 'my wedding'. She should have said 'our wedding' if the wedding had to be mentioned at all. She should not have said 'my wedding'. She should not have curtsied. She should not have been so composed, earlier, when she arrived promptly at the church at the postponed hour, and made no comment on the cause of the delay, walked slowly up the aisle on Uncle Arthur's arm and appeared not to see the damage to Teddie's cheek. Even in the vestry afterwards she had said nothing about the stone. She had said little about anything except to express concern that her shivering at the altar might have been too obvious and uncertainty about the suitability of the new name given her in exchange for the old one.

But she was guilty of all these acts and omissions, and 'my wedding' was – to Sarah – suddenly and touchingly significant, revealing as it did the extent to which Susan was conscious of the fact that no one else except Teddie seemed much concerned about it. Being married to Teddie was something she had set her heart on, presumably because in her mysterious self-sufficient way she was prepared to love him and be loved by him, but whatever the reason for the marriage the wedding was the one conclusive step she had to take to demonstrate in public the importance of what was happening to her. It was, on a much larger scale, like the gesture she made or sudden word she spoke which interrupted the flow of other people's thoughts and drew attention back to her existence. But the wedding, among strangers, in unfamiliar surroundings, already marred by the incident of the stone and the insult to the Nawab, was an affair that threatened to overwhelm her. She was fighting the threat with a single-minded determination, a tense, febrile assertion of her rights to her own illusion which Sarah, now that she understood, admired her for, loved her for, because she judged the amount of courage it took to close the eyes to the destructive counter-element of reality that entered any state of intended happiness.

She thought: That sort of courage is what distinguishes Susan from me, apart from her prettiness, and why men like Teddie have always finally preferred her company to mine. She creates an illusion of herself as the centre of a world without sadness and allows them entry. It is like when we are children. She is the little girl with the gift for making let's-pretend seem real; although when she was young it was the last talent I suspected in her. If she had it then she kept it secret, closely guarded. Now it has blossomed. One senses it in her as something tough and enduring but delicately poised, in constant need of fine adjustments so that it can contain or be contained, be shared, withheld, never diminished by exposure to ridicule.

The old protective instinct which she had thought atrophied by long disuse quickened and then lay still. All the outlets for it were overgrown and it understood it had woken to no purpose and must sleep again, become oblivious of its awakened hunger. Abruptly she moved away – taking the opportunity given by a general movement as the Count went forward to meet the bride and groom – and found herself facing Ahmed: a re-enactment in different dress and circumstances of the occasion on the waste ground when she rode at him, smiling and speechless, and he stared back, smiling less but just as silent: a meaningless situation then, equally meaningless now. They might have come from different planets. It was impossible to establish common ground; neither sense of duty nor personal compulsion would ever bridge the distance or shatter the glass from behind which they smiled and stared vacantly at one another like specimen products of alien cultures in display cabinets in a museum placed close together through an administrative oversight, or odd stroke of chance.

'He is very pleased with the book,' Ahmed announced suddenly.

'Oh yes. Gaffur. I'm glad.' She turned her head slightly, because of the garlic. It really was a revolting smell. The poems of Gaffur and the smell of garlic: a dark vision of an old lady under an awning on the sun-deck of a houseboat, and of trunks, musty, unclaimed, containing what was left of that girl: passed over Sarah's consciousness of her presence on a sunlit scene – inconsequential but positive – like vapours casting actual shadows.

'It was a bit of luck,' she said. The old lady knew so much: more than facts – the shape and substance and significance of an accumulation of detail that so often, in the mind, passed by, as a procession of irrelevancies.

'What was a bit of luck?'

The voice was not Ahmed's but that of Captain Merrick who had arrived at her side.

'The poems of Gaffur,' she replied, glancing up at Merrick. 'Just something we brought for the Nawab. Someone we met in Kashmir told us that Gaffur was a Kasim too, so we had a copy bound up, we wouldn't have known otherwise.'

'I don't even know about Gaffur. Is he famous?'

'Oh, not is, was.' She turned to Ahmed again. 'I mean in the sense of "was, not is", because he's dead. But he's still famous as a classic isn't he?'

Ahmed put his head on one side, letting the eyes close. He rarely made a typical Indian gesture. He held and used himself with the stiff composure of an Englishman. She had absorbed that fact unconsciously, was only conscious of it now when he responded with the gesture of the head, like any other Indian deflecting a compliment to himself or his country from its target.

'But something tells me,' she went on, 'you don't go in much for poetry. What did Gaffur write about? Deserts and roses, and moonlit gardens? Jugs of wine?'

Merrick laughed. 'That's Omar Khayyam.'

'Oh, no, just Persian,' she said. 'I mean they all wrote like that surely, Persian poets, Urdu poets. Was Gaffur an exception?'

'No, I think he wasn't,' Ahmed said. 'Roses and deserts and moonlit gardens pretty well fill the bill from what I remember.'

'Did you have to learn him as a boy?'

'Read is a more accurate word.' Ahmed hesitated, then added, 'I never learned anything my teachers thought important. In the end they gave me up.'

'I know what you mean,' Sarah said. 'It's how I feel about me, more or less, except that I think I'd say I never saw the importance of what I was taught and always felt I wanted to be taught quite different things – the sort of things no one thought of teaching. I was the kind of child who automatically asked why when I was told the cat sat on the mat. My teachers said I ought to curb a tendency to squander curiosity on the self-evident.'

'Then from their point of view, you're in the right place, Miss Layton. In India nothing is self-evident.'

She looked at him, puzzled. Ask him a question and he would answer, usually with that brevity which made asking a further question a grindingly self-conscious business. She did not remember him making

515

comments – of the kind that could remove verbal exchange from the level of an interrogation to that of a conversation – but in the last few moments he had made two, although the second had the familiar characteristic of those answers of his which seemed to kill a subject stone-dead, and left her suspended (she felt) like a vulture hovering over a carcass with no meat left on. She smiled, found herself tongue-tied, but hoped her silence would be interpreted as politeness and interest and would encourage him – if for once he was in the mood to talk – to continue. But it did not. He was not even looking at her now: instead at Captain Merrick, holding his head at an angle that disclosed an aggressive set of chin and jaw. He did not look angry but she wondered whether he was. He had been stopped at the door too, and had even less opportunity than Count Bronowsky to even up the score.

'Actually,' Captain Merrick said, 'that's something I feel bound to disagree with. I'd say things that are self-evident are common to all countries.' He was smiling and so now was Mr Kasim, but glancing from one to the other Sarah thought: No, you mustn't tangle with each other. She felt powerless to stop them. She saw Aunt Fenny hastening down the steps and moved to intercept her; but that was unnecessary. She was coming to them in any case.

'What's been going on?' she asked before she had quite reached them.

'Nothing's been going on, Aunt Fenny. The Nawab has arrived.'

'Well I know that. People up there are saying he had difficulty getting in.' She did not trouble to lower her voice. Aunt Fenny never did. She seemed not to have seen Mr Kasim standing almost next to her, but turned on him abruptly, thereby proving she had, and said, 'What a chapter of accidents!' and came back to Sarah, leaving her exclamation as it were – bouncing, to work its own way to a position of rest. 'I've been putting out Susan's going away things. I can't find the hat-box.'

A room in the annexe had been set aside for the bride's use. Sarah and Aunt Fenny had brought Susan's luggage with them. 'It must still be in the car,' Sarah said. 'I'll go and see.'

'No, I'm sure Captain Merrick won't mind—'

Seeing he was wanted he came closer.

'A hat-box. We think it's still in the car. The one Sarah and I came in.'

'I know where it's parked. I'll check. What should I do with the box, bring it to you or take it to the annexe?'

'If you'd bring it to me? Well, whatever you think. So long as it's found. God knows what we'll do if it's not there or been stolen. There wasn't a servant in sight at the annexe just now. Anyone could have walked in. I've nabbed a spare body and made him stand guard on peril of his life.'

Captain Merrick nodded and went. 'Come,' Aunt Fenny said. 'I must meet the Nawab.'

As Sarah followed Mrs Grace she carried with her an impression of Ahmed alone, disengaged; standing restricted in the centre of a world she would never enter, did not know and could not miss. How lucky we are, she thought. How very, very lucky.

'Nobody told us you was expecting any Indian gentleman, sir,' the MP explained as he accompanied Captain Merrick to the place where the bridal cars were parked.

'I realize that. It was very remiss of us.'

'We didn't think you allowed Indian gentlemen into the club, so the corporal and me, sir, we thought those three gentlemen was havin' a lark. I mean anyone could've got hold of one of those cards, sir, and written a fancy name on it.'

'You did your duty as you saw it, Sergeant, no one is blaming you.'

'All the same we dropped a right clanger, didn't we, sir? Especially seeing one of 'em was a white gentleman after all and another was his nibs.' The sergeant grinned. 'Captain Bates'll have my guts for garters.'

'Is he your officer?'

'That's right, sir. But no sweat. We live and learn. And I'll know the nabob next time, won't I?'

They stopped at the line of limousines. One of the drivers left the circle of men squatting under one of the old trees shading the lawn, but the sergeant ignored him, opened the doors and presently found the box on the floor under one of the tip-up seats. 'Here you are, sir, one hat-box, brides for the use of.'

'Thank you, Sergeant. Are you staying with us or expecting a relief?'

'Orders are to wait and escort the cars to the station, sir.'

'In that case there'll be something for you and the corporal to toast the bride and groom in. I'll lay it on and send one of the stewards out to take you round and show you where. But you'd better go one at a time.'

'Thank you, sir. That'll be very much appreciated.'

'Well even a copper has to eat.'

The sergeant grinned again, came to attention and saluted. Merrick, encumbered by the hat-box, and capless, sketched the idea of a salute in reply and made back towards the club entrance. As he reached the steps he paused, looked at the hat-box, and then instead of entering continued along the front until he reached the corner of the building where a path led off through a shrubbery marked by a directional finger on which the word Annexe was painted black on white. He returned a few minutes later, without the box, and walked along the side of the clubhouse, between a flower-bed and the tennis courts where an old man in shirt and dhoti and a youth in a ragged pair of khaki shorts were restoring the lime-wash markings. Merrick stopped, reached into his pocket for his cigarette case, selected one, lit it and began leisurely to smoke and watch, as if concerned about the straightness of the lines that were reappearing, brightly, on their faded predecessors. The youth was doing all the work. It was not arduous but the sun was hot and the gleam on his shoulders showed that he was sweating. He became conscious of the spectator, made a mistake in the marking. The old man spoke to him sharply. Merrick did not move. He

517

inhaled smoke slowly, deeply, continuing to watch until, growing tired of the scene, he threw the cigarette half-smoked into the flower-bed and continued along the path.

The lawn was now deserted. A single voice, a woman's raised in laughter, came from the almost equally deserted terrace. The wedding party had gone inside for the cold fork-lunch wedding breakfast and the ceremony of the cutting of the cake. Merrick looked at his watch. Ten minutes short of midday. He walked on the lawn, making for the steps, paused near them, stooped and picked up shreds of pink and white paper where someone had stood and brushed confetti from a dress or uniform. Straightening he saw himself watched by Count Bronowsky who had appeared at the head of the steps alone.

As Merrick joined him Bronowsky said: 'Ah, there you are, Captain Merrick. I suppose you have been undertaking yet another of the onerous duties of best man.'

'Just a small errand to recover a hat-box.'

'Well, you are a man for detail. I can see that. For instance, you share my compulsive instinct for tidiness. What was it, confetti?'

Merrick opened his hand.

'They say it's significant,' Bronowsky said, picking the scraps of paper from Merrick's palm and dropping them into the empty glass a guest had left on the balustrade. He picked the glass up too and placed it on a near-by table, for greater safety. While he did these things he continued to talk. 'I mean significant psychologically. Compulsively tidy people, one is told, are always wiping the slate clean, trying to give themselves what life denies all of us, a fresh start.' Having finished with the confetti and the glass he now looked at Merrick and, putting a hand on his shoulder, began to lead the way along the terrace towards the distant hum of conversation in the inner room where the bride and groom and guests had reassembled. 'You are married?' he asked casually.

'No—'

'Neither am I. Far better not. We'd drive our poor wives crazy, wouldn't we? Besides which, of course, there is this other thing about us – I mean about our tidiness. They say it's characteristic of someone who wishes to be the organizing centre of his own life and who has no gift for sharing.'

Bronowsky had stopped walking, but he retained his hold on Merrick's shoulder. The two men were of equal height.

'I am sorry,' Bronowsky went on. 'I am sorry about the incident this morning. You were not hit yourself?' He removed his hand but stood his ground, keeping Merrick waiting.

'No, apart from Captain Bingham's scratch the only damage was to the car.'

The Chief Minister remained where he was and did not answer. Merrick also kept still. Presently he said, 'Is there something you want, Count Bronowsky?'

'Yes. The answer to a question. But the question is impertinent. I hesitate, naturally—'

'Please don't.'

'Well. I have been wondering if you thought that perhaps the stone was thrown at you.'

'Oh? Why should you wonder that?'

'Mrs Grace tells me you were in the Indian Police.'

'That's quite true.' Merrick took out his cigarette case, opened and offered it to Bronowsky.

'No, thank you. I never smoke until evening.'

He watched while Merrick lit a cigarette then said, 'We shan't be missed for a bit, so let me tell you a little story. Years ago, when I was overhauling the administration in Mirat, I brought in a man who rather later in life than he felt he deserved had risen to be a judge of the High Court in Ranpur. I made him the State's Chief Justice, a grandiloquent title but with a salary to match. He retired in far greater comfort than would have been the case if he'd stayed in the ICS. He died peacefully in bed, but was once the victim of what the newspapers of my youth would have described as a murderous attack by a couple of ruffians who set on him in the dark as he walked from my house to his. I often warned him of the danger for a man in his position of walking alone, at night, in a usually deserted road. In fact for a time I made sure he was followed by a couple of my own stout lads. But he caught on to it and told me he would never visit me again if I treated him like that. So I withdrew the guards and then this thing happened. Two men whom he never got a proper look at jumped out at him. He was badly beaten.'

Merrick blew out smoke, and nodded his head.

'For a time,' Bronowsky continued, 'our police were completely at a loss because none of our known malcontents continued for long to be real suspects. The most likely ones had been arrested on suspicion of course, but protested their innocence vehemently – indeed with fortitude. In those days I had not yet succeeded in persuading the Mirat police to dispense with certain old-fashioned interrogatory methods. Anyway, for a time it looked as if the mystery of the attack on my highly prized Chief Justice would go unsolved, but then we had a stroke of luck. I was discussing the case with the poor fellow – who was still laid up and only just regaining his faculties – and he said, "You know, Bronowsky, I think I had a premonition about it." I asked him when and how. He thought for a bit and said he believed the premonition dated from a day about a week before the attack, when he was presiding over his court. It was a hot afternoon and the case before him was extremely complex. The people who had been admitted to the public seats were restless – fanning themselves with papers, whispering, that sort of thing, very distracting. He kept thinking, "In a minute I shall call them to order. In a minute I shall clear the court." But he somehow couldn't summon the necessary determination. He said, "I had an extraordinary sensation that something else" – and he didn't mean the case being heard – "– that something else had to be done first, done, or seen

through, attended to. I felt I was being not watched exactly but waited for."
After a while he stopped examining the faces of the pleaders and witnesses
and the face of the accused and looked across at the public benches.'

Bronowsky had been holding his panama hat in the same hand that held
the ebony cane. Now he took the hat in his free hand, hesitated, then
gestured with hat and cane, raising his arms slightly as though conjuring
an image of the courtroom and the judge's perplexity.

'Nothing extraordinary there, but after a while he noticed a young man
who was not fanning himself, was not whispering to his neighbours, but
leaning forward apparently absorbed. He found himself returning to meet
this man's gaze many times. I asked him if the face of the young man had
been familiar. Could it have been a man he had once sent to prison? He said
no, not familiar, not exactly familiar. He never forgot a face, especially the
face of a man he had sentenced. I asked him to think back carefully during
the next day or two, particularly about the more sensational cases he had
tried since coming to Mirat, because the young man might have been a
relative of someone he had sentenced to hang or to prison for life. When I
next saw him he said, "I've been thinking, as you told me, but not about
sensational cases, nor about cases I've dealt with in Mirat. I've been
considering the two cases I've never been able to shelve satisfactorily as
over and done with because of the element of doubt. They were cases
which *seemed* clear cut enough, but left me vaguely troubled. Both took
place a long time ago, one when I was a District and Sessions judge and the
other when I first became a judge of the High Court in Ranpur. In the
Ranpur case I had to send a man to the gallows. The young man who
watched me in court two weeks ago could easily have been his son. When
you sentence a man to death you never forget the expression on his face
while he listens to you. This was the same expression." I asked him to tell
me the dead man's name, and suggested we got the co-operation of the
police in Ranpur to find out whether the son or some other close relative
had been in Mirat two weeks ago.'

Bronowsky stopped, again made the gesture of half-raising his arms.

Merrick said, 'And so you caught the chap.'

'Oh, no. The Chief Justice wouldn't hear of it. Because of the element of
doubt that had stayed in his mind all those years. All the same I conducted
private inquiries and established to my own satisfaction that the hanged
man's son was in Mirat at the time of the attack. You see I was after the
accomplice. The result of my inquiries in that direction pointed to the
guilt of a young gentleman of Mirat of hitherto unblemished character, but
on whom the police were now able to keep an eye. Their vigilance was
rewarded later. You of course will understand the necessity of such
precautions. Professional criminals and openly organized political agitators are one thing. One can always cope with them. It is these others – the
dark young men of random destiny and private passions who present the
greater difficulty. For instance, the stone this morning – ostensibly thrown
at the Nawab Sahib's car. If it had happened in the city it could have

sparked off a communal riot. The Muslims might have blamed the Hindus and set fire to a Hindu shop. The Hindus might then have retaliated by slaughtering a pig outside the Abu-Q'rim mosque. The police would then have had to break up the fracas with lathi charges and hooligan elements would then have attacked the police station. All this for a stone, thrown at you perhaps, by one of those young men because in the past you carried out some duty with a vigour he thought cruelly unjust.'

Merrick laughed. 'I'll shoulder the responsibility if that helps to explain the damage to the Nawab's car to everyone's satisfaction. When I was a police officer I had enough brickbats chucked at me during riots and demonstrations to learn you can't dodge them all.'

'My dear Captain Merrick. You totally misunderstand the reason for my waylaying you like this—'

'Yes, well, I realize it isn't a chance meeting.'

'Quite so. I came to look for you. But not to ask you to shoulder responsibility. To seek your help in placing it.'

'What does that mean?'

'It means that directly Mrs Grace told me you had been in the Indian Police a number of apparently unrelated things fell into a pattern for me and even pointed to a likely source of inquiry. My interest isn't in you or the stone or the damage to Nawab Sahib's car. My interest is in Mirat.'

Merrick shrugged slightly and smiled. 'Well, don't worry. If I was the target you can rest assured that by this time next week the target will be in quite a different place, a long way from here.'

'But can you say the same of the man or youth who threw the stone, or of the people who put him up to it, of the people he discussed it with, whose help he had in plotting the time and place and day? I hardly have to tell you that such an incident was almost certainly planned, and planned in concert.'

'Perhaps, but it seems a lot of trouble to go to, I mean just to get a crack at an unimportant, comparatively junior police officer who's no longer even in the force.'

Bronowsky said nothing for a while. He transferred the hat back to the hand that rested on the ebony stick, then looked up.

'But you are not unimportant. Surely you are the Merrick who was district superintendent of police in Mayapore last year, at the time of the August riots and of the rape of the English girl, Daphne Manners, in the Bibighar Gardens?'

Merrick, arrested in the act of carrying the cigarette to his lips, now completed the movement. He inhaled and expelled then held the cigarette in a position suggestive of stubbing. Bronowsky pushed forward the ashtray on the table they stood next to and waited while Merrick, accepting the cue, carefully extinguished the tip, tapping and then pressing, then letting go and rubbing thumb and finger-tips to clear them of clinging particles.

He said, 'How do you arrive at that conclusion?'

'I deduce it. My deduction is correct? You are that officer?'

'I've no reason to deny it.'

'Nor to advertise it? Mrs Grace says you were DSP in Sundernagar, which I take it is the district you were transferred to after the Mayapore affair, and which you mention when anyone asks where you were before getting your commission. I imagine you are ready to talk about Sundernagar and other places, but prefer for personal reasons to gloss over Mayapore. If so I'm afraid I inadvertently let the cat out of the bag. I was telling Mrs Grace how much we appreciated your thoughtful action in ringing through to Ahmed and she said you were an excellent man for detail, probably as a result of your experience as a police officer. Well directly she mentioned that, certain bells – which for reasons I'll explain were very ready to ring – rang loud and clear, and I'm afraid I said almost at once, Merrick? Police? Surely that's the fellow who was DSP in Mayapore at the time of the Bibighar Gardens affair? I was so positive that it took me aback when she looked surprised and said she only knew about a place called Sundernagar. I'm afraid I insisted I was right, and she was obviously so intrigued I thought it fair to try and have a word with you before you go in.'

'Well, it's a bit of a nuisance, but it can't be helped. You'd better tell me about the little bells.'

'To begin with there was just the name, Merrick. It was vaguely familiar when Mr Kasim first mentioned it to me on Wednesday evening. But a young army officer called Merrick meant nothing to me. In fact I doubt whether the same young officer described by Mrs Grace as late of the Indian Police a moment ago would have meant anything either but for two other things that I was thinking about on the way here, wondering whether there could possibly be a connection between them. The incident of the stone, and a report I had from Mr Kasim on Thursday morning. Tell me, Captain Merrick, does the name Pandit Baba mean anything to you?'

Merrick did not answer immediately, but his expression was that of a man sorting out a number of images conjured by the name rather than that of someone taking time to search the dim reaches of an uncertain memory.

'As a matter of fact, it does.'

'Please tell me what.'

'He's one of those so-called venerable Hindu scholars who manages never to get caught inciting his eager young disciples to commit acts of violence against the Muslims, against the British, against anything the Pandit currently disapproves of.'

'But he does incite them?'

'I'm sure of it. In Mayapore I could never lay a finger on him though. Anything he did in public, like making a speech to college students, was all sweet reason and high-mindedness. He was quite capable of criticizing the Congress Party, too. I think the line he took was that they were poisoning Hinduism with politics, but he shunned publicity and discouraged any attempt to turn him into a renowned local figure. He was the perfect dedicated scholar. As far as I was concerned he was too good to be true. I also think he was a snake. A lot of the educated young Indians who got into trouble in Mayapore were under his influence at one time or another. We once arrested a chap for handing out seditious leaflets among workers in the British-Indian Electric factory. He said his pamphlet only repeated things Pandit Baba had discussed with a group of young men about ten days before. I thought I'd got him at last. We picked up some of the other boys, and then hauled in Baba Sahib. Within ten minutes the Pandit had them all grovelling and weeping and begging his forgiveness for misinterpreting his teaching. The one we'd arrested actually said he deserved to go to prison for his stupidity and unworthiness and the Pandit made a great show of being willing to go to prison in his stead as a penance for being such a poor *guru* that his innocent words could lead boys into trouble. Of course he knew he was as safe as houses. All the same he was more cautious afterwards.'

'Good. Thank you, Captain Merrick. Then you'll be interested to know that Pandit Baba is in Mirat at the moment. Mr Kasim was asked to meet him the other evening, ostensibly to enable Pandit Baba to be introduced to a son of M. A. Kasim, whom he professed to admire, which I doubt. But according to Mr Kasim, the Pandit spent most of the time talking about the Bibighar Gardens affair, with particular reference to the activities of the District Superintendent of Police, whom he can't have named, otherwise Ahmed would have hit on the connection at once. No doubt the omission was intentional. He knew Ahmed had already met you. I find Ahmed a useful extra pair of eyes and ears because of his objectivity. He tells me what happens more or less exactly as it happens and I then consider the implications. In this case I wasn't very sure what the implications were. To involve Ahmed in something? To pump him about something? Something to do with Ahmed's father? Perhaps, perhaps. But it made little sense. Neither did the stone-throwing. However, it all makes very good sense when the police officer whose reputation Pandit Baba was carefully tearing to shreds the other evening turns out to be one of the officers riding in the car that has a stone thrown at it. The venerable gentleman used to live in Mirat, incidentally. We felt very much the same about him as you did when you were in Mayapore. By we I mean the then chief of police and myself. He never actually became *persona non grata*, but things were going that way. I was glad when he made the decision for us, and went off to Mayapore.'

'And you believe he was behind the incident this morning.'

'Oh, I think so, don't you?'

Merrick turned, placed his hands on the balustrade and looked out across the dazzling garden. Bronowsky came to the balustrade as well but continued to support himself on the cane.

'Not that we should be able to prove it,' Bronowsky continued. 'I don't intend to try. The Pandit is playing a little game with me, I think. The opening move was his invitation to Ahmed. He knew every word would be reported back to me. He also knew that directly I realized he was back in Mirat I would set my spies on him. My spies tell me he didn't come to

Mirat alone but with a woman, who keeps in seclusion in the private rooms of Mrs Nair, who is the wife of the principal of the Hindu College, in whose bungalow Pandit Baba is staying. My spies also tell me that this morning between nine-forty-five and ten-forty-five, Pandit Sahib was scheduled to speak to the students of the college on the subject of his new study of the Bhagavad Gita. No doubt he did so, in full view of several hundred youths, standing on a dais, splendidly detached from anything so violent and vulgar as stone-throwing. Where my spies have been less successful is in getting the names of any of the young men with whom he has had private conversations. Perhaps he has had none. Perhaps it was all done before he actually reached Mirat. He is almost certainly in touch with very many people, throughout India.'

'Aren't you exaggerating a bit?'

'Oh, am I? Was the stone this morning then the first evidence you've had that you've been carefully tracked since leaving Mayapore?'

Bronowsky waited. Presently, as if reluctantly, Merrick said, 'Go on.'

'There was an incident in Sundernagar, perhaps? An anonymous letter referring to the fate of what, if I remember correctly, were called the innocent victims of the Bibighar Gardens? And in your first military establishment – another letter, or something even more direct to suggest there was some ill-wisher close at hand. For instance an inauspicious design drawn in chalk on the threshold of your quarters? Wherever you have been? Didn't it begin in Mayapore itself, and hasn't it continued, at intervals nicely calculated to make you believe that your last posting shook off whoever was intent on your discomfiture?'

Merrick allowed several seconds to elapse before replying.

'It's been much as you say. But it hasn't bothered me, and Mirat is their last opportunity. They can hardly go on persecuting me where I'm going unless some sepoy has been bribed to put a bullet through my head when nobody's looking.'

Bronowsky smiled. 'I don't think killing you is the idea, although I'm surprised they haven't thought of a more dramatic way of embarrassing you than throwing a stone. As you say, Mirat is their last opportunity for some time to come. The wedding would have been an excellent back-ground for something colourful. I understand, incidentally, that you're not a close friend of the groom. Did it pass through your mind that taking part in the wedding might bring your persecutors out into the open?'

Merrick said, 'No, it was the other way round. I agreed to be best man and then realized I was probably the worst possible choice. But it was too late to withdraw and I wouldn't have known how. All that business is something I prefer to forget. I'm sorry you've identified me.'

'My dear fellow, why? All I can say is that if I've correctly judged Mrs Grace's reactions to my quite unintentional disclosure, you are now an object not only of interest but of admiring curiosity. They will remember how at the time the DSP Mayapore was singled out by the English press for praise and congratulation. One recalls it all well enough, the newspaper reports and the gossip here in the club, on this very terrace. Well you can imagine. An English girl criminally assaulted by Indians, not just any English girl – if there could possibly be such a thing in India – but a connection of a one-time Governor in Ranpur who stayed at the palace in the thirties. Within – what was it, an hour or two – the police in Mayapore under their DSP had arrested the six culprits. Technically they were only suspects and not proven culprits but that hardly diminished the blaze of satisfaction at thoughts of revenge already afoot. It's all people talked about for days. Mirat has always had a floating population and we had people in from Mayapore who naturally enjoyed their reputations as experts on the rape and the riots, although these weren't really connected, were they? The rape was a local affair and the riots were on a national scale. Being a military and not a civil station, of course, the major focus of interest here was on that brigadier you had in Mayapore who took charge when the civil authorities decided they couldn't cope.'

'Brigadier Reid.'

'That's him. Reid. Most of the talk was of Reid but what it came down to in the majority view was that both the army and the police in Mayapore had acted with commendable vigour, whereas the civil had shilly-shallied. Well you know how people think these days – they say the civil has become so riddled with Indians that the old dependable type of English civilian has more or less died out and it's only the English army and police officer who can really handle an explosive situation. I remember a fellow sitting somewhere along there' – Bronowsky pointed to the far end of the terrace – 'one evening when I was having a drink with the Station Commander, not Hobhouse, his predecessor. There'd been a paragraph in the *Courier* about a farewell party in the Artillery Mess in Mayapore for Brigadier Reid, and, of course, the implication was that he'd got the sack. This fellow leaned across, pointed at the paragraph and said, "There you are. Reid saves the situation and then gets kicked out because he saved it his way, which probably means he killed twelve Indians where the Government thinks ten would have been enough. But the deputy commissioner who sat on his backside will probably get a plummy job in the Secretariat and a CIE." '

Merrick said, 'The Deputy Commissioner was a good enough man. And Reid didn't get the sack. He was given another brigade. It was a better job really. The brigade he had in Mayapore was only half-trained. The one he got was ready to go into the field. He's back at a desk now, though, so I've heard. Perhaps he didn't measure up. Perhaps he was a bit too old. His wife was dying when all that business was going on. We didn't know about that until afterwards.'

'Ah well, the truth is always one thing, but in a way it's the other thing, the gossip, that counts. It shows where people's hearts lie. Reid saving the situation and getting the sack is what they wanted to believe. Just as they wanted to believe that the fellow in charge of the police in Mayapore had arrested the right men in the Bibighar rape business. They blamed the civil for any excessive use of force the Brigadier was guilty of and they blamed the civil when it was gradually realized that the rape case was coming to nothing. Not even coming to court. They never thought of blaming the District Superintendent for arresting the wrong men because they were convinced they must have been the right men. And the people we got here from Mayapore during those few weeks following the rape took the line that it would have served the six suspects right if the rumours going round were true.'

'What rumours?'

'That the six boys were whipped and forced to eat beef to make them confess.'

'I see. That tale even reached Mirat, then?'

'Indeed it did.' Bronowsky paused. 'Was there any truth in it?'

'The beef business was a result of some minor confusion, I believe.'

'Confusion?'

'The jailers were Muslims and some food sent in for them was mistaken by an orderly for food sent in for the prisoners, who were all Hindus.'

'Ah, yes. A very reasonable explanation. And the whipping?'

'Judge Menen satisfied himself on that score by having the men examined.'

'Physically? Or merely by questioning?'

'I gathered questioning was all that was necessary. They all denied the rumour and swore they'd not been ill-treated.'

'You didn't examine them yourself?'

Merrick, who had answered most of Bronowsky's questions without facing him now did so. 'Why should I have? I'm the chap who was being accused of defiling and beating the prisoners.'

'Not actually accused, though? It was merely gossip, surely. Enough of it to cause the District Judge uneasiness?'

'Yes.'

'But not you?'

'No.'

'You ruled out the possibility of your subordinates having beaten the suspects?'

'I took personal charge of the interrogations. I knew everything that went on.'

'Except about the beef. You said there may have been confusion over the beef but you weren't present when the confusion arose?'

'I'm not in the witness-box.'

'Captain Merrick, I'm sorry. I don't mean to cross-examine you. But I have a natural curiosity. Would you satisfy it on one point? Were those men you arrested guilty of the rape?'

Merrick again looked across the balustrade, fixing his eyes, it seemed, on some intense but distant vision of incontrovertible truth.

'I think,' he said at last, 'that I shall believe they were until my dying day.'

After a while Bronowsky said, 'Our venerable pandit told Mr Kasim that he is acquainted with the aunt of one of your principal suspects, and was once engaged to try to teach him Hindi, the young man in question having lived most of his life in England.'

'Hari Kumar. That's quite correct. The aunt was a Mrs Gupta Sen.' He looked round at Bronowsky. 'Kumar wasn't just one of the principal suspects. He was *the* principal suspect. I believed then and believe now that he planned the whole thing. He'd been going out with Miss Manners for weeks, quite publicly. People were talking. In the end I warned her against that kind of association.'

'Oh, you knew her personally then?'

Merrick flushed. He took a fresh grip on the balustrade. 'Yes, I knew her very well.' He hesitated before continuing. 'Sometimes I blame myself for what happened to her because I think she partly took heed of my warning. She seemed to stop seeing him. She came more often to the club. She did voluntary work at the local hospital, and was living with an Indian woman. But that was all right, in its way. Lady Chatterjee was a very old friend of Miss Manners's aunt, Lady Manners. All the same, living with an Indian woman like that meant she came in contact with Indians socially. That was part of the trouble. But Kumar didn't run in those circles at all. He was nothing but a tin-pot reporter on the local gazette and gave himself airs because he'd been brought up expensively in England. I don't really know how she first met up with him, but I saw her go up to him once at one of those war week exhibitions that were all the rage last year, and it was obvious they already knew each other. I think he'd been once to the MacGregor House where she lived. But I knew him from the time I had to haul him in for questioning. We'd been making a search of a place called The Sanctuary where a mad old white woman used to take in the dying and starving. We were looking for a chap who'd escaped from prison, a fellow called Moti Lal who specialized in organizing subversive activities among well-educated youths. Needless to say he was an acquaintance of our venerable pandit. So was Kumar. Kumar was at The Sanctuary because that mad woman had found him drunk the night before. He needn't have been in any trouble the morning we found him but he chose to make a mystery out of his name. In England he'd been known as Harry Coomer. He thought he was too good to answer the questions of a mere district superintendent of police. I let him go because there was nothing to pin on him, but he went down on my list all right, and before long I'd connected him with most of our other suspected trouble-makers, including of course our venerable pandit. I didn't link the idea of a girl of Miss Manners's kind – well, any kind of decent English girl I suppose – getting mixed up with Master Kumar. In the end I warned her. And although she said it was really none of my business who she chose to be friends with I think she realized she wasn't doing herself any good. And I think she tried to end the association. Kumar wasn't going to stand for that. And she must still have been infatuated. The way I see it is that he bided his time, then sent her a message begging her to meet him again at the place they apparently often met, the Bibighar, and waited for her there with those friends of his. She denied having gone there to meet Kumar and made up a cock and bull story about passing the gardens that night and being curious to see if there really were ghosts there, as the Indians said. She and Kumar both swore they'd not seen each other for several weeks. She said she never saw the men who attacked her. Well, perhaps that was true. She said they came at her from behind, in the dark, and covered her head. Perhaps she simply wasn't prepared to believe Kumar could plan such a thing or be mixed up in it at all. In the end that infatuation of hers led to the whole damned thing going unpunished. When she found out we'd arrested Kumar she refused even to attempt to identify the other boys and started loading her evidence or threatening to load it, and if the thing had gone to trial she'd have turned it into a complete farce. I'd have been prepared to let her try but others weren't. She changed her story, only slightly, but just enough to turn the scales. She said she'd not seen the men because of the darkness and because they'd come upon her suddenly, but she had a clear impression of them as dirty, smelly hooligans of the kind who might have come in from one of the villages beacause of the news of the riots and disturbances that were just breaking out all over the province. She knew that the boys we had in custody were the last type you could describe as dirty and smelly. You can appreciate the visual impression there'd have been in court, with these six Indian youths in the dock in Western-style dress, most of them ex-students, and Miss Manners in the witness stand describing a gang of striking whooping bad-mashes. She might have changed her tune if she'd seen them all as I did the night I arrested them. Five of them half pissed in a derelict hut where they'd gone to celebrate on home-made hooch, and Kumar back home, actually bathing his face to try and clean up the marks she made on it, hitting out at her first attacker.'

'How did Kumar explain the marks?'

'Explain? Oh, Master Kumar never explained anything. He was above explanations. His speciality was dumb insolence. He refused to explain the marks. He refused to answer any question until he was back at my headquarters and was told what he was being charged with. His answer to that was that he hadn't seen Miss Manners since a night two or three weeks before when he'd gone to a local temple with her. What struck me as extraordinary really was that she said exactly the same thing. They were both so specific about their last meeting having been the visit to the temple it was as if they'd rehearsed it, or rather as if he'd terrified her or hypnotized her somehow into using just those words: I've not seen Hari Kumar since the night we visited the temple: while he for his part said: I've not seen Miss Manners since the night we visited the temple. I thought it didn't ring true, but everyone else thought it would sound pretty conclusive in court. I always hoped we could get it into court because on oath and in those sort of surroundings the terror and shame I think she was suffering might have been lifted. I'm sure she was under a kind of spell. I'll

528

never understand it. I can never get it out of my head either. The picture of her running home as she did, all alone along those badly lit streets. I expect you know she died nine months later, in child-birth?'

'Yes. As I recall it, her aunt inserted notices.'

'That was extraordinary too, wasn't it? Inserting notices. The death, yes. But the birth of an illegitimate half-caste kid whose father couldn't be identified?' Merrick raised his hands and let them fall again on to the balustrade.

'It shocks you?'

'Yes.' Merrick paused, as if considering the nature and depth of his reaction. 'It's like a direct challenge to everything sane and decent that we try to do out here.'

'It was a human life lost, and a human life beginning. Why not mark the occasion?'

'I'm sorry. I can't see it that way.'

'Most of your countrymen would agree with you,' Bronowsky said. 'I find it sad that in the end Miss Manners inspires more contempt than she does compassion, but I recognize that this is the way it has to be. You English all felt that she didn't want you, want any of you, and of course among exiles that is a serious breach of faith. It amounts to treachery, really. Poor lady. The Indians didn't want her either. There were those things that happened to Indian boys because of her. Happened or didn't happen. In any case they went to prison, and no one seriously believed their political affiliations or crimes or whatever it was that was used as an excuse to keep them under lock and key were of a kind to warrant detention. Even the English thought it a pretty transparent ruse to hold the suspects, a handy alternative to punishing the culprits. It was the kind of ruse that wouldn't have worked in more settled times. One forgets how highly charged the whole emotional and political atmosphere was. There were English here who talked as if a new Mutiny had broken out. Later, I remember, some of your more liberal-minded people had prickings of conscience. There was an article in the *Statesman*. I expect you saw it. It interested me but I looked in vain for any further developments. I thought, well that police officer was sticking his neck out but no one is going to cut it off. He's weathered the storm. I'm sorry to realize you didn't. Sundernagar was something of a backwater, wasn't it? Tell me, if you'd had a chance to serve in the police force of an Indian state such as Mirat, would you have been interested? Or would the army have exerted a stronger fascination? I know how much many of you young Englishmen in the civil and the police dislike the general policy of treating these as reserved occupations.'

'Would *you* have given me such a chance?'

'I don't know. Perhaps not. But I've never been inhibited, by any reservations. I might have about the consequences, in taking controversial action and making unpopular appointments, if that action or appointment attracts me strongly enough. My own appointment, after all, was monumentally controversial. Let me put it this way, rather. Were you not presently committed in quite a different direction, I should be interested to discuss such a possibility with you.'

'May I ask why?'

Bronowsky smiled. 'Because my instinct tells me you are something of an anachronism in this modern world of files, second-hand policies and disciplinary virtues. The Indian states are an anachronism too. The rubber-stamp administrator or executive is too advanced an animal for *us*, although ideally that is the likeness one looks for in the outward appearance. Detachment. Objectivity. Absolute incorruptibility – I don't mean in the venal sense of the word, or the word's opposite I suppose I should say. But a man can be – swerved – by his own passions, and to me incorruptibility always suggests a certain lack of concern. The concept of justice as a lady with a blindfold and a pair of scales someone else may lay a decisive finger on without her noticing has often struck me as question-able. It presupposes a readiness in those among whom she dispenses her gifts to keep their hands to themselves. You must agree that would be a perfect world and in such a world she would be a redundant figure. But we are dealing in imperfection. Keep the figure by all means, as a symbol of what might be achieved. Keep the illusion of detachment. Cultivate its manner. But admit it cannot be a controlling force without compromising itself. What is detachment, if it's without the power to make itself felt? Ah, that's the common factor – power! To exercise power in Mirat you need eyes in the back of your head as well as an unblinkered pair in front. And you need men around you who do not lack concern, who have enough concern to be in danger of it getting the better of them and leading them into error. God save us anyway from a world where there's no room for passionate mistakes.'

'You think I made one?'

'I think it's possible. For instance you haven't said what led you to the hut where the boys were celebrating, or to Kumar's house where you found him bathing his face. It strikes me as a significant omission. It suggests that your only reason for visiting Kumar so soon after you heard Miss Manners had been raped by a gang of unknown Indians was that Kumar had been associated with her in the past.'

'You think that reason insufficient?'

Bronowsky shook his head and looked down at his shoes, considering. 'This hut,' he said, 'where the other boys were found half-drunk. It was close to the Bibighar?'

'Just the other side of the river, in some waste ground.'

'And Kumar's house?'

'That was also on the other side of the river.'

'In roughly the same area as the hut?'

'No. But not far.'

'How soon after the rape, approximately, would you say you found the boys in the hut?'

'At the time I estimated it at approximately three-quarters of an hour.'

'Time enough for the five boys to get across the river to the hut and open a bottle.'

'Of course.'

'And get half drunk.'

Merrick paused. 'I used the expression loosely.'

'All the same it was the impression you had. That they were in liquor.'

'Yes.'

'And I suppose about ten minutes later you got to Kumar's house?'

'Yes.'

'So he had had at least three-quarters of an hour to get away from the Bibighar?'

'Yes.'

'And yet he was still bathing his face?'

'Yes.'

'Perhaps he hadn't gone straight home.'

'Perhaps.'

'He could have gone to the hut with the others and had a drink. Then one of them might have noticed the tell-tale marks in the light of whatever lamp they lit, and he thought it wiser to go home and clean up.'

'Very possibly.'

'There was a lamp?'

'Yes.'

'Did they say they'd seen Kumar that night?'

'They said they hadn't. Only two or three of them were friends of his so far as I knew. They insisted they'd spent the whole evening in the hut, alone.'

'Where might Kumar have gone if he hadn't gone straight home?'

'Anywhere. He might have waited in his own garden until he thought it safe to go in and upstairs.'

'Without being seen by his aunt, you mean?'

'His aunt, or a servant.'

'If he'd gone straight home how long would it have taken him?'

'About fifteen minutes. Twenty at most.'

'Walking?'

'Yes – walking.'

'Say ten or less if he'd had a bicycle?'

Again Merrick hesitated.

'Naturally.'

'I wonder about the business of bathing his face, you see. Working from the basis of the earliest moment he could have got home and into his room and started to clean himself up he would then have had a good half-hour before you arrived.'

'If he did go straight home then half an hour wasn't enough, was it? He was bathing his face. Do you really think I had insufficient reason for going to his home? The boys in the hut first, boys of Kumar's kind, two or three of them Kumar's friends, swilling hooch, laughing and joking. What more natural than that having started combing the area of the Bibighar and found them I should go straight to look for Kumar?'

'Well forgive me. That wasn't clear to me, the order and circumstances of arrest. All this is impertinent, I know, but perhaps not without interest to yourself, to talk about it again, with a stranger. And I am trying to get a picture. For instance, presumably you went immediately to the scene of the crime, the Bibighar, in case some of those fellows were still there and in any case to examine it. Now, if you stood in the Bibighar and said Yes, this is Kumar's work, would the route you then took to Kumar's house, presumably in a truck or jeep with some constables, would it have led you over the bridge and past the waste ground?'

'Yes.'

'So you saw the hut. I think earlier you used the word derelict. And perhaps we have established that there was a light showing *from* it?'

'Yes.'

'Well, is that the picture? That you saw the light, stopped the vehicle and rushed across the waste ground to the hut and found those boys?'

'Yes.'

'Well, wasn't there something strange about that? Didn't it strike you as odd? There you had a group of young men supposedly guilty of the most heinous crime of all, the rape of a white girl, getting on for perhaps an hour after they'd left her, but barely a few minutes away from the scene of the crime, in what sounds like a rather conspicuous place, a derelict hut in the middle of some waste ground, showing a light, laughing and joking and getting sozzled.'

'You find that inconsistent?'

'I do rather. It sounds to me more like the behaviour of boys who'd done what they insisted they'd done, and no more. Spent the whole evening in the hut, drinking illicit liquor, lighting a lamp when it got dark, just intoxicated enough to be careless about who saw it. The distillation and drinking of illegal hooch is not a very serious misdemeanour.'

Merrick smiled. 'You've drawn your picture out of context. You're forgetting what day it was and what had happened during the day. It was the ninth of August. On the eighth the Congress passed their Quit India resolution. On the morning of the ninth we arrested not only leading Congressmen but Congress members of sub-committees throughout India. Everything had come to the boil. In the afternoon in a place called Tanpur some police were abducted and an English mission teacher called Miss Crane was attacked by hoodlums. The fellow with her, an Indian, was murdered. We got Miss Crane back into the Mayapore hospital at above five o'clock. Nobody knew what would happen next. Shopkeepers put up their shutters and people stayed in their homes. I know the Congress has denied that there was any underground plan for rebellion. But I'd say later developments provided sufficient evidence of organized rebellion to make their denial look silly. Boys like the ones we arrested for the rape may not have been directly involved in that kind of organization, but that's what they wanted, that's what they had their hearts in, that's the kind of activity that appealed to them. They laugh at Gandhi, you know, all that crowd. All that passive resistance and non-violence nonsense is just a joke to them, just as it's a joke to the militant Hindu wing of the Congress and organizations like the Mahasabha and the RSSS. When you get down to the level of the educated fellow who thinks the world owes him a living in exchange for his matric or BA failed, the kind of chap who loathes the English who gave him the chance to rise above the gutters of the bazaar but is very happy to ape English manners and dress English style, then you're down at a level where nothing but anarchy reigns. When trouble comes decent people in the towns put up their shutters and close their doors. In the villages they harbour their cattle and guard their property and their lives. And out come the badmashes in the countryside, and the hooligans in the cities. But in the cities a lot of the hooligans can quote Shakespeare at you. When I went across the river that night I wasn't looking for people hiding in their homes, but foot-loose fellows like those in the hut. You see my interpretation of your picture of the fellows in the hut is quite different. What made them careless, showing a light, lounging around only a few minutes away from the Bibighar was an intoxication that only had a bit to do with the liquor. The rest was cockiness. They'd had a white woman. They thought the country was rising. Their day was dawning. They could see it quite clearly. The *raj* was on the run. The long knives were out. In a day or two the white man would be crawling, licking their shoes, and there'd be as many white women to rape or murder as they wanted.'

'And Kumar?'

'Kumar? Oh, Kumar! He was the worst of the lot. Have you heard of Chillingborough?'

'Chillingborough . . . yes. One of your big public schools at home?'

'Exactly. Well that's where Kumar was educated. To hear him speak, I mean if you looked away while he spoke, he sounded just like an English boy of that type. His mother died very early and his father took him to England when he was about two with the express intention of bringing him up not only to act and sound like the English, but to *be* English. The father was rich, but got involved in some sort of financial trouble, lost all his money and died leaving Kumar penniless. The aunt of his in Mayapore, a decent enough woman she was too, paid his passage back to India and tried to look after him. But nothing was good enough for him. He couldn't take what it involved, to be just another Westernized Indian boy in a place like Mayapore.'

'Poor Mr Kumar. It can't have been a happy experience.'

'Good Lord, you'd think a boy who'd had those advantages would have been man enough to face up to a set-back like that. I can't share your sympathy for him. But then I met him face to face. Kumar wasn't just a theory to me. I knew his type too well, and he was the type multiplied. To me it was quite clear what he was up to. He was out for revenge. Out to get his own back on us because in India he couldn't pretend to be English any longer. One of the executives in the British-Indian Electric factory told me he could have had a decent job there as sort of apprentice or trainee. But Mr Kumar refused to call the managing director sir, and was insolent to the man he'd have been working under. His aunt's brother-in-law was a merchant and contractor and for a time Kumar did some clerical work in the warehouse. That didn't suit him, but that's where he would have been first in contact with this chap I was telling you about who escaped from prison. Moti Lal. Moti Lal was a clerk in the same business.' Merrick suddenly slapped the balustrade. 'It's so damned obvious. Moti Lal. Pandit Baba. Going around with those boys who were drinking in the hut. Working as a journalist. And we found a letter in his room when we searched it. A letter from an English boy warning Kumar not to write bolshie things, because the boy's father had opened some of Kumar's letters and objected to his son getting such letters while he was still recovering from wounds got at Dunkirk. And he had a photograph in his room too. A photo of Miss Manners. Having a white woman running after him was the final perfect touch, from his point of view.'

Suddenly Merrick looked round at Bronowsky. He said, 'I didn't have to stand in the Bibighar and tell myself, yes, this is Kumar's work. I knew it was Kumar's work the moment I got to the MacGregor House and Lady Chatterjee told me Miss Manners had come back, in that state. I'd been at the house before. It wasn't the kind of night you allowed a white girl to be missing, and that's what it looked as if she was, missing. Sometimes I used to give her a lift home from the hospital. I was at the hospital that evening because of Miss Crane and when I left I looked for Miss Manners. They told me she'd gone to the club. Later I was at the club myself and inquired after her. I was told she'd not been in the club. I thought, so that's it, she's gone back to meeting Kumar. There was nothing I felt I could do about it, and with everything that was gong on I had my hands full. But later I went round to the MacGregor House, which was a pretty isolated place. I thought I'd make sure they were all right. I found Lady Chatterjee alone, Miss Manners hadn't been back, and she was worried. At least, she was worried when I told her Miss Manners hadn't been at the club. I had to go back to my headquarters. It must have been getting on for nine o'clock. On my way back to headquarters I remembered Miss Manners sometimes went over the river to that place called The Sanctuary. She helped Sister Ludmila with the clinic. So I wentd to The Sanctuary and found she had been there, but had left before dusk. It's not far from The Sanctuary to the house Kumar lived in. I thought the situation was serious enough to go and see if she'd arrived at Kumar's. She hadn't. And Kumar's aunt said Kumar wasn't at home either. Well that made it obvious to me. They were off somewhere together. I thought, well, God, she's welcome to him if that's what she wants, and drove back to the kotwali at the Mandir Gate. If I'd gone the other way, over the Bibighar bridge, I'd have come across her, running home along those dark streets. I'd probably have come across

Kumar as well, and those others. But I went to the kotwali. It was chance that made me decide to detour to the MacGregor House when I finally set off back for my headquarters. I got there ten or fifteen minutes after she'd returned, exhausted, in that awful condition. Lady Chatterjee had sent for the doctor, but not the police because Miss Manners hadn't explained her condition. But Lady Chatterjee suspected and I made her go up and get confirmation. The message I got back wasn't clear, but it was enough. Attack, criminal assault, five or six men, in the Bibighar Gardens. I had to drive back to get a police patrol, and order a comb. A good thirty minutes or more must have passed between her leaving the Bibighar and my arriving there. We were probably ten minutes beating through the gardens, and another five at the level-crossing hut, interrogating the keeper and searching the area. And all the time I knew I was wasting time. I knew where I ought to be looking. When I finally set off for Kumar's house I very nearly ignored that hut, in spite of the light showing that someone was there. I think what made me stop was partly a sort of automatic professional response, a realization that nothing could be overlooked, and partly a twinge of conscience, a recognition of the unfairness of leaping to a conclusion. But the sight of those boys, the revelation of what they were, who they were – well I had them out of there and into a truck and on the way back to my headquarters before they knew what had hit them. And I went on in my own truck, with three or four constables, to get Kumar. The aunt tried to stop us going upstairs. She was scared stiff. I knew I was right, then.' Merrick laughed. 'And do you know what he said, when we went into his room? Well, there he was, stripped to the waist, bending over a bowl, holding a flannel to his face. He looked up and said – "Who gave you permission to burst into my room, Merrick?" '

Bronowsky laughed, and presently Merrick replied with a sour grin, looked at his watch and moved from the balustrade.

'I shall have to go in I'm afraid.'

'We both must,' Bronowsky said. 'I'm sorry to have kept you so long, but sorrier that all we had to discuss needed to be compressed into what amounts to no more than a brief encounter. Perhaps in the not wholly unforeseeable future we may have the opportunity to resume. Anyway, if you are ever in Mirat again, or disposed to contemplate coming back, I hope you will let me know.'

They began to walk down the terrace. The sound of talk and laughter from the inner room had become louder in the last ten minutes or so. 'You could do with a drink, I expect,' Merrick said. 'I know I could.'

'I could but I must not. You'll find Nawab Sahib holding a glass of orange or lemon for politeness's sake, so I follow suit to keep him company. He takes Ramadan very seriously and as a matter of fact I think he enjoys the discipline of holding a glass and not so much as moistening his lips. Tonight he begins a special period of fast and prayer and cuts his intake almost to nothing, even after sundown. The îd is in ten days' time. I'm sorry you won't be here for it and that the charming Layton ladies will be gone too. Nawab Sahib would have liked to have you as guests to a meal in the palace.'

'He's been more than generous as it is—'

They turned in at the french windows. Several guests stood in the room they entered, presumably having come in there to avoid the crush in the room beyond, through whose open door the wedding party could now be seen.

Bronowsky paused and made Merrick do so too by holding his arm in a way which a stranger, had he been watching, might have interpreted as proof of intimacy and of knowledge and interests shared.

'Tell me,' the count said in a low voice so that Merrick automatically bent his head closer. 'Who is the outstandingly handsome young officer with the dark hair, talking to the girl in blue?'

Merrick glanced quickly round the room.

Oh that, he seemed about to say, *that is—*

But as if suddenly unsure of something – the name of a man, the colour of a dress, his questioner's intention, he looked back at Bronowsky and for a moment the question itself seemed to hang in the balance; and Bronowsky, observing the way the colour came and went on the ex-District Superintendent's cheeks, released his hold on his companion's arm and murmured:

'Well, it doesn't matter. Come, let's go in,' and led the way.

*

'He was in love with her,' Aunt Fenny said, beginning the job of unbuttoning Susan out of her wedding-gown while Mrs Layton folded the veil and Sarah laid out the going-away clothes on the bed in the little room in the annexe. 'A woman I met who'd been in Mayapore told me. She said it was well known at the time. The DSP definitely set his cap at Miss Manners, and everyone was surprised because they'd thought of him as a confirmed bachelor and all the unmarried girls who'd been trying to hook him wondered what he saw in her. I expect her background had a bit to do with it, but when a man like that decides to take the plunge he takes it terribly seriously. It must have been awful for him when she became infatuated with one of those dreadful Indian boys. I remember this woman saying he looked positively ill after Miss Manners had been assaulted and they were trying to make the charges stick. He must have been nearly out of his mind at the thought of those men getting away with it. No wonder he wangled his way out of the police and into the army and never mentions anything about having been in Mayapore. Count Bronowsky must have an extraordinary memory for names. Captain Merrick was obviously upset having it all come out like that. Did you see his face when he got back from fetching the hat-box?'

'Stop it, Aunt Fenny!' Susan shouted. 'Stop it! I'm trying, trying, *trying* to pretend that it's a nice day. I'm trying, *trying* to remember that I'm being

536

married to Teddie—' She jerked at the dress – not yet completely unbuttoned down the back – and pulled it away from her body, wrenched he arms out of the sleeves and pushed the unwieldy billowing damask down over her hips, breaking the thread of one of the buttons. Clothed now in only her brassiere, pants and suspender belt, she twisted round and kicked the discarded dress away from her feet. 'My dear child,' Aunt Fenny began – but Susan, flushed of face and white of body, snatched a sponge bag from the bed, said 'We've got fifteen minutes, Mummy,' and grabbing the neat little pile of fresh underclothes made for the bathroom.

'What have I done?' Aunt Fenny asked her sister.

'Nothing, Fenny. It's what you were saying, not what you were doing. The subject was hardly a suitable one in the circumstances, was it?'

'Oh dear. Yes, I do see. I am sorry. Poor pet. What are you looking for, Sarah?'

'One of the buttons came off.'

'I'll find it. Millie, you pack the dress away, and let Sarah get on with her own changing.' Fenny went down on her knees. 'I told him about our being moored close to Lady Manners's boat in Srinagar, but he never knew her. It was a bit of a relief because it slipped out, I mean about the houseboat business, and if he'd been a friend of old Lady M's it would have been rather embarrassing having to admit we'd not actually met her, he mightn't have understood how difficult it was for everybody. I was dying to hear something straight from the horse's mouth, but he was positively evasive when I suggested he come over to the guest house tomorrow or Monday and spend an evening with us. He said he might have to go to Calcutta. I mean go for good before Teddie and the rest of them leave next week. What a shame. He's been quite attentive to you, hasn't he, Sarah, pet?'

'Aunt Fenny, I just don't understand you.'

'Ah here it is. Millie, put it in your handbag for safety. Help me up, Sarah. What don't you understand?'

'You're still talking about that Manners business—'

'But Susan can't hear—'

'That's not what I mean. I mean you're quite prepared to gloat over the details, you're willing to sit Captain Merrick down, stick a glass in his hand and prise every last juicy bit of the story out of him, without any thought for his feelings at all. But when we had an opportunity to show friendly to the poor girl's aunt it was you who found the perfect excuse for keeping our distance. You said a visit would embarrass her.'

'Well, so it would,' Fenny said, turning to help Mrs Layton fold the dress into the suitcase. 'And if it hadn't embarrassed her it would certainly have embarrassed me. Everyone agrees that that woman's behaviour has been quite extraordinary.'

Sarah began to undress, contorting herself to get at the row of satin-covered buttons. She felt a tide of anger and frustration spread through her body.

'You could actually hear that revolting crying,' Fenny added. 'It was like

537

being next door to some awful Indian slum. It made one feel quite sick, the thought of an English woman living in it.'

'I was in it too,' Sarah said, and as she did so seemed to discover, through her finger-tips, the secret of undoing the dress, and to touch, as well, the spring of some deeper secret that had to do with the unlocking of her own precious individuality. She let the slipper-satin gown fall to her feet where it lay like an unwanted skin. 'I spent a whole hour in the slum, talking to the extraordinary woman and looking at the revolting baby. Of course it wasn't a slum and the baby wasn't revolting. But I'd agree about Lady Manners. She wasn't ordinary.'

'You went to see her?'

'Yes.'

'What for?'

'To apologize for us. Perhaps the rest was just curiosity, like yours, Aunt Fenny.'

She picked up the sloughed dress. It was a garment she would never wear again. Suddenly, the waste no longer offended her; she was glad – glad Susan had insisted on peach slipper-satin, had resisted her own puritan preference for a material that, with adaptations, could have served secondary long-term purposes.

'Did you know about this, Milly?' Aunt Fenny asked.

'Yes, I knew.'

'And approved?'

'I find it difficult to approve or disapprove of what I don't understand. Let's just say I knew you and Arthur would understand it even less. I told her not to mention it. But it doesn't matter now. May we forget it, please? May we just concentrate on getting Susan safely to the train?'

'You're absolutely right. I don't understand. Apologized for *us*? My dear child, sometimes you worry me. You worry us all. You worry us very much.'

'Yes, I know,' Sarah said, packing the bridesmaid's dress and satin shoes into tissue. 'I worry me too. Shall I put Susan's veil in my case? There's more room.'

Automatically Aunt Fenny handed the folded veil and tissue over. Fragile, even insubstantial, its packed bulk yet called for two hands to support it. Carefully, Sarah placed it in the suitcase on top of the other things: the veil, the most important of all the trappings of Susan's determined illusion, now done with, put away. She remembered the day spent in Aunt Lydia's glory-hole, the armfuls of stuff taken down into the Bayswater garden and burnt in the incinerator from whose heat she had stood back, shielding her face with a grubby hand and thinking of the perpetual light that seemed to shine upon the members of her family.

Perhaps, she thought, I am no longer in darkness, perhaps there is light and I have entered it. But she did not know what light exactly, nor what entering it would already have laid on her by way of obligations. But if it was light she wanted to share it. She looked at Aunt Fenny and at her mother, snapped the locks of the case shut as if completing, with a happy flourish, some special conjuring trick.

'But don't let's worry just now,' she said. 'It's not only Susan's day, it's ours too.'

*

And to end it, adding a third link to the chain forged by the throwing of the stone and the barring of the club doors to the Nawab, there was the curious incident of the woman in the white saree who appeared from out of the crowd on the platform of the cantonment station where the train for Nanoora was drawn up, and who seemed intent on joining the group seeing Teddie and Susan off, although she stayed a few paces behind them.

At first only the officers on the fringe of the group noticed her, and they thought nothing of her presence. But now from farther down the platform a warning whistle blew and as Captain Merrick came down from the compartment, leaving Mrs Layton and Sarah and Major and Mrs Grace to make their private family farewells to the departing couple, the group moved to give him room, spreading out, leaving a clear space, so that Merrick, turning, found the woman a few feet away, and coming closer.

The saree was only of cotton, but being white, suggestive of widowhood and mourning, the cheapness of the material could not be counted a sign of poverty. The thought that she might be a beggar did not enter the heads of any of the officers near by. She was not very dark skinned, and she looked clean, respectable. In fact the immediate impression everyone had, including Mrs Grace who now also left the compartment with her husband and Sarah, was that an unpleasant scene was about to take place, with the Indian woman claiming a seat in the first class.

But she seemeed to be a beggar after all. She had begun to speak, in Hindi, which the nearest of the officers got the drift of, and it was clear to others that Captain Merrick understood too because he answered her, also in Hindi. Help me, she had said, your Honour alone can help now. I beg you. Be merciful. To which Merrick replied: Please go away. There is nothing I can do for you.

She cried out, and fell to her knees – an alarming spectacle which, moving as it might have been on a stage to an audience already translated to a state of suspended disbelief, could only be a cause of embarrassment on a public platform. And the cry, the act of abasement, were not all. She pulled the saree from her head, revealing greying hair, reached out and grabbed poor Captain Merrick's feet and placed her forehead on the dirty ground, moaning and keening. It was impossible to touch her. One of the officers said, 'Jao! Jao!' and tried to help Merrick urge her away by pressing on her shoulder with his shin. She let go, but held her ground, scrabbled in the dirt and dust of the platform and symbolically smarmed her head with ash. She rocked and swayed, crying out the while inarticulately.

The extraordinary scene came to an abrupt end. An Indian railway official, the man who was checking reservations, emerged from a near-by compartment, saw what was happening and came at a run. He grabbed the woman roughly, pulled her to her feet, pushed her away, once, twice, as often as was necessary to press her back into the crowd of watching Indians, shouting angrily, threatening her with the police. Back among her own people she fell to her knees again, resumed her crying and gesturing, crazed by some grief that the bystanders could not understand or share, and which therefore seemed absurd to them. They watched her curiously, then parted as an elderly Indian with a grey beard and wearing steel-rimmed spectacles pushed his way through, approached her, spoke, raised her to her feet and led her away out of sight, down the platform.

'A madwoman,' the man in charge of reservations said. 'Please, no one is badly molested?'

That she was a madwoman seemed unquestionable, but to hear her so described by this particular man was like having official confirmation of the fact. It could be assumed that the woman was known: a poor, mad, harmless creature who pestered sahibs on railway platforms.

Teddie had his head thrust through an open window. A clean piece of sticking plaster adorned his cheek. 'What was all that?' he asked cheerfully. But he was not looking for an answer. There was another blast on the whistle. He turned back into the compartment.

'You'd better go, Mummy,' Susan said, and Mrs Layton broke away, pecked Teddie on the undamaged side of his face and allowed him to escort her to the doorway where Major Grace completed the task of handing her down. Teddie shut the door and Susan joined him at the open window.

'Somebody catch,' she shouted, and flung the tired little bouquet she had carried all morning into the air, but in Sarah's direction. She caught it and instinctively raised it to her nose to sniff the still sweet-smelling blooms. She looked up and found Susan watching her, waiting perhaps for some particular word or gesture but there was no word or gesture to find beyond a mouthing of the word 'Thanks'. All I can do as well, Sarah said silently, is wish you happiness.

And that seemed to be enough.

IV

Captain Merrick came to the guest house at the beginning of the short twilight. Sarah was alone on the terrace waiting, she explained, for the darkness to fall and the fireflies to come out. The rest of her family were still in their rooms.

'Haven't you slept this afternoon?' Merrick asked. She still wore the dress she'd changed into for the farewells at the station.

'Oh, I meant to rest but the place was too quiet. It's been such a hive of activity all week. So I wrote letters, well – one letter, to Father, about the wedding.' She looked at her watch. 'They'll be in Nanoora soon. Won't you ring for a drink?'

'If you'll have one too.'

'I may as well.'

Merrick went to the bell-push set in the wall near the french windows. He had changed out of best KD into a cotton bush shirt and slacks. After he'd rung he stood by the balustrade.

'The last place the light goes from is the lake,' Sarah said. 'But when it's really dark the lake's much darker than anything.'

'Water reflects the sky,' Merrick said, prosaically. He took out his cigarette case, came towards her. She shook her head.

'No, thanks. Not just now. But you do. It's part of the pleasure of this particular time of day. Smelling someone else's tobacco smoke.'

'You're very sensitive to atmosphere.'

'I suppose I am.' She thought for a moment. 'But not more than anyone else. Perhaps I think about it more.'

Abdur Rahman came out.

'What will you have, Ronald?' she asked, using his given name because for the first time it seemed natural to do so.

'Whisky if I may.'

'Whisky soda, Sahib *ke waste*, Abdur. *Burra peg hona chahie. Aur* Tom Collins *meri lie.*'

'Memsahib.'

When Abdur Rahman had gone Merrick said, 'You think I need a *burra peg* then?'

'I don't know about need. Deserve.'

'I used hardly to drink at all.'

He sat opposite her, lit his cigarette, then said, 'I'm off to Calcutta first thing in the morning, so I've really come to say goodbye to everybody.'

'Oh, I'm sorry.'

'The signal was in when we got back from the station. Three of us have to go, but it wasn't unexpected. The General warned us before he went himself. I think it means some change of location for the training and forming-up area. Perhaps things are on the move.'

Sarah said nothing for a while. The light, fading fast, perceptibly, had begun its tag-end of the day business of investing people you sat close to – Ronald Merrick in this case – with a curious extra density, a thickness and solidity that compensated for the darkening and fading of features, hands and clothes so that the person on whom darkness fell was not diminished but intensified. She thought of what he meant when he referred to things being on the move. Those things seemed to be so far away that they were almost unimaginable, and yet within a day or two he could be close to them and she could reach out and touch him now and he could carry the impression of her touch into areas of danger.

'Does it ever strike you,' she asked, 'how odd it is about war, I mean about the way it's concentrated in special places? And in between the places huge stretches of country, whole continents where life just goes on as usual?'

'Like here?'

She nodded. 'Like here.'

He said, after a while, 'I suppose the other curious thing is wanting to go to it. I needn't have.' He glanced at her. 'Will you write to me sometimes?'

She glanced back, ready to smile, taking it as a light-hearted, vaguely sentimental suggestion of the kind she could forgive him because he was, all said and done, a soldier; but she was aware, meeting his glance, of the request perhaps being as serious as it was unexpected.

'Yes, of course.'

'Thank you.'

He might have intended to add something but Abdur Rahman came out with the tray of drinks. Sarah took the cold glass, waiting until Merrick had said '*bus*' to the pouring soda water, then called 'Cheers'. The ice burned her lips, numbing them. This first moment of drinking chilled liquid always reminded her of the feeling in the lips as injections in the mouth wore off. She swallowed, closed her eyes and put her head back, making a faint exclamation of satisfaction she only partly felt.

Merrick said, 'I've enjoyed meeting you all, you know. It's been a long time since I was – with a family.' He sipped his whisky. 'I came to say goodbye but also with the hope of being able to apologize. I think I can to you. If you weren't alone I probably wouldn't think it opportune. It's not the sort of thing one can say to several people.'

Sarah had opened her eyes and turned her head, but he was looking doggedly in the direction of the lake.

'That stone someone chucked this morning was really thrown at me. I know it sounds childish and melodramatic but persecution of that kind has been going on ever since I left Mayapore. It's never bothered me but today all of you were involved. And that's what I want to apologize for, for two of the things that spoilt the day for Teddie and Susan, and all of you. The stone, and that unpleasant scene on the platform. I'm not sure I oughtn't to apologize for the insult to the Nawab too. I ought to have made sure those lads from the military police knew there were to be Indian guests. In any case they wouldn't have been on duty if the stone hadn't been thrown. I'm sorry. I was the worst best man Teddie could have chosen.'

'Oh, no!—'

'It's all to do with that Mayapore business.' He was looking at her now. 'You know about my connection with that?'

'Yes, I know.'

'I'm sorry – I mean for not saying who I really was and then being, well, faced with having to deny it and tell a lie or admit it and look as if I'd been telling one. It made me feel and look ridiculous, made it seem I'd something to hide or be ashamed of, but all I've wanted is to forget it, not have to answer questions about it in every new place I go to. I hope your

542

mother in particular understands that. She's had me under her roof. I'm not unconscious of the obligation that has put me under.'

Sarah resumed her watch on the lake. She felt vaguely ill-at-ease, conscious of those things about Ronald Merrick that Aunt Fenny put down as signs of a humble origin. Phrases like 'under her roof' and 'not unconscious of the obligation' had a stilted, self-advertising ring that she didn't altogether care for. It alarmed her to realize that she could respond, as automatically as Aunt Fenny, to the subtler promptings of the class-instinct. Why should I question his sincerity? she asked herself; realizing that this was what she was doing.

'We all understood,' she told him. 'I'd say it was the natural thing to do.'

'Thank you.'

'But I don't really understand about the stone and the woman on the station. Was she the mother of one of the boys that got arrested?'

Merrick smiled, took another drink.

'Well, you do understand, you see. It's all quite simple once you know who I am. But she wasn't the mother of one of the boys, she was his aunt. Although pretty much like a mother to him. It wasn't pleasant seeing her like that this morning. I remember her as respectable and dignified.' He drank again. 'I shan't forget it in a hurry. But of course I'm not supposed to. They want it to prey on my mind until I'm as convinced as they are that I made a terrible mistake, the kind of mistake I shan't be able to live with because it'll be impossible to correct it. But it's impossible now. They must know that. That poor woman was being used. She probably thought there's a chance I could work a miracle for her.'

Dim as a picture was Sarah comprehended vividly enough the essence of what it would convey if a whole light shone on it. She understood that he had carried a burden a long way, for a long time, had suddenly put it down and was intent on showing her – and himself – what it was before he shouldered it again and took it with him wherever he was going. Perhaps he hoped that showing it would lighten it, although – in the swiftly encroaching dark through which he was beginning to loom he looked capable of rejecting any claim that showing it might give a would-be sharer.

'Did you see that man who took her?' he asked. 'He's behind it. I heard he was in Mirat, and had a woman with him. He put her up to it, brought her all the way here from Mayapore, getting her hopes up that I could be moved by that kind of appeal, that I could do something. It's pretty cruel. He probably doesn't care a fig for her, or the boy, any of them. It's sheer pretence. The case is useful to him, that's all. It serves his purpose. But that's India for you. They're quite indifferent to one another's sufferings when it comes down to it, and we've become so lofty and detached, so starry-eyed about our own civilized values and about our own common-sense view prevailing that our policy has become one of indifference too. We don't rule this country any more. We preside over it, in accordance with a book of rules written by the people back home.'

'Yes,' Sarah said. 'Yes, I think that's true.'

Merrick drained his glass.

'When I was a youngster one of the first questions I asked the District Superintendent I worked my probationary period with was how much longer he thought we'd rule India. I was thinking of my future which was something I'd somehow never thought of as necessary when deciding to try for the Indian Police. But when I got out here it all seemed so unreal, like a play. I suddenly couldn't picture it as a thing I'd work at all my life. So I asked this extraordinary question, extraordinary I mean because it was absurd to be wondering about much more than learning the job I'd chosen and worked hard to get. He didn't think it extraordinary, though, and I've always remembered his reply. He said: "Don't bother your head about that, Merrick, because there's not a thing you can do. India will be ours until one day between questions and other business in the House of Commons the British people through their elected representatives will vote to get rid of it. The majority won't have the least idea what they're doing. Getting rid of India will be just one clause in a policy of reform dreamed up by intellectuals and implemented by the votes of mill-hands and post-office clerks, and if you think there's any connection between *their* India and the one you're going to help police you might as well go home now." '

He set his empty glass down.

'I've never accepted that,' he said. 'The fact, yes. But not the mentality that so often goes with it. Well, you know the sort of thing, I expect, although you don't really get it in the army because it's a tradition that you have your own self-contained community and a job to do that nobody outside thinks worth a button until the shooting begins. While there isn't any shooting you take it as all part of the game to be mucked about. You accept it philosophically. But in the civil and the police, in the business of daily administration of the country, there's the constant irritation of being strait-jacketed by policy from above. At the top the Government of India tries to fight the Secretary of State in Whitehall and at the bottom the district officer tries to fight the Government. But it's always a losing battle. You find yourself automatically implementing a policy you feel passionately is wrong and the only thing you can do short of resigning is detach yourself from the reality of the problem, from the human issues if you like. You become – a rubber stamp. That's the mentality I mean. It's something my first superintendent encouraged me to resist. Perhaps he was wrong. He was an officer of the old school. He'd seen what he called better times, times – he said – when you were master in your own bailiwick. I suppose I should have recognized that it was an older school, not mine, and that I live in a rubber-stamp age. And don't get the wrong impression, Miss Layton. I haven't been kicked out of the police. I applied for permission to transfer to the army at the beginning of the war. I pulled every string I knew, just like Mrs Grace's friend. It needed the Mayapore business, needed me to become what's known as a locally controversial figure, to persuade them to release me for the duration, but I had to plead pretty hard even then. I sometimes think that if I'd done something terribly wrong the rubber stamp would have endorsed it. That's its danger. It's a controlling force without the ability to judge. Once you're part of the rubber-stamp process yourself you could almost get away with murder. And that's wrong. Must be. You ought to be answerable for your actions, but you ought to be able to act, you ought to be involved. As an individual. As a person. As a fallible human being.'

'There are times,' Sarah said, 'when I think I don't know what a human being is.' Times – she told herself – when I look up and see that heaven is empty and that this is an age when all of us share the knowledge that it is and that there has never been a god nor any man made in that image. It is an intensely bleak discovery because it calls our bluff on everything. 'But I know what you mean,' she continued. 'It's easier for men. Being involved. No. That's a facile remark. It's not easy for any of us.' She looked at him. 'What was *she* like? the girl. The girl in the Mayapore business.'

'Rather like you,' he said, without hesitation, as if he had expected the question and knew in advance what his reply would be. 'Not physically. Well, she was taller.' He fingered the empty glass, slithered it to and fro, a few inches, on the table. 'I suppose a bit clumsy. She knocked things over. She made a joke of it. But she was very sensitive. She said she'd been gawky as a child. She still felt like that. Unco-ordinated. But I only saw her as – peculiarly graceful. Grave. Slow. Beautiful almost, because of that. The kind of girl you could talk to. Really talk to. Or just sit with. Our tastes were – much the same. In music. Pictures. That sort of thing. Our backgrounds were quite different, because mine is very ordinary, but Daphne didn't give a damn who your parents were or what school you went to.'

Sarah felt compelled to say it.

'Were you in love with her?'

He played with the glass a few seconds longer, then gave it up, stubbed his cigarette, studied the hand that had moved the glass, holding it stiffly with the fingers splayed, rubbing the back and the palm with the thumb and finger of his other hand.

'I don't know. I thought I was for a while. But if I was it wasn't at first sight. I'd met her several times and not thought of her that way. In fact my first impression of her was a bit unfavourable. I thought, Here we are, another of those English girls who come out here with bees in their bonnets about the rotten way we treat Indians. Give her time to find they're taking advantage of her and she'll get over it, she'll go the other way, be worse than any of us. In a year she won't have a good word to say for them. She was living with an Indian woman. You had to take that into account. Lady Chatterjee was one of those Westernized aristocratic Rajputs, an old friend of Daphne's aunt, and Daphne had come down with her from Pindi to see what she called something of the real India. I can't say I cottoned much to Lili Chatterjee. She belonged to that top layer of Indian society that mixes with our own top layer, but that's not real intimacy.

More like necessary mutual recognition of privilege and power. A banquet at Government House, a garden party at Viceregal Lodge. You'd find a lot of Lili Chatterjees there. You'd also find this particular one playing bridge in Mayapore with the Deputy Commissioner's wife. But not at the Mayapore club, not among ordinary English men and women when they were off duty. They pretend they don't care, the Lili Chatterjees I mean. Pretend they don't need to rub shoulders with the English middle-class in their cosy middle-class clubs and homes. But they resent it. Daphne resented it too. She wasn't able to draw the distinction. She didn't see why a line had to be drawn – has to be drawn. But it's essential, isn't it? You have to draw a line. Well, it's arbitrary. Nine times out of ten perhaps you draw it in the wrong place. But you need it there, you need to be able to say: There's the line. This side of it is right. That side is wrong. Then you have your moral term of reference. Then you can act. You can feel committed. You can be involved. Your life takes on something like a shape. It has form. Purpose as well, maybe. You know who you are when you wake up in the morning. Well sometimes you can rub the line out and draw it in a different place, bring it closer or push it farther out. But you need it there. It's like a blind man with a white stick needing the edge of the pavement. Poor Daphne tried to do without all that. I attempted to stop her – well, crossing the road. She didn't seem to know she was crossing it. I suppose that's when I first really looked at her, first considered her. And found out she wasn't just another of those English girls with bees in their bonnets. She was *this* girl. And it wasn't a bee. I don't know what it was. It was quite beyond me. But whatever it was it destroyed her.'

He cocked his head, considering her.

'I'm sorry, I said she was rather like you, didn't I, but I've mostly been describing the things that made her different. I'm not sure I can put my finger on what it was about you that reminded me of her.'

'Does that mean I don't any longer?' Self-conscious under his scrutiny she defended herself from it with the thought that he was an appalling man whom she didn't trust. He had a lively intelligence, perhaps less lively than its activity within the confines of a narrow mind made it seem; but she did not have to pay for the pleasure, of listening to a man – an Englishman in India – talking seriously, by liking him. She was interested in finding out why she reminded him of Miss Manners, but did not care whether the reason was flattering or the opposite of that.

'What I'm going to say,' he said, 'may sound impertinent.'

'No – I'm sure it won't.'

'Well – that first morning. When I'd joined you all in the station restaurant and you sat in front of the taxi next to the driver. I felt from your manner you were making the same sort of judgements of us that she did. And I thought – please forgive me – here's another one who doesn't see why a line must be drawn. But it was none of my business. And I was wrong anyway.'

'Why do you say that?'

'Because I can see the line's been drawn for you. You accept it. Do you remember in the taxi how I made rather heavy weather of young Kasim's position, and your mother very understandably thought I was speaking out of turn?'

'Yes, I remember that.'

'Talking about Kasim. It was a sort of Pavlovian response on my part. I'd met him and I think subconsciously he'd impressed me as a man of Hari Kumar's type.'

'Who is Hari Kumar?'

'The chief suspect in the Bibighar Gardens case. The man she was friendly with.'

'Yes, I see.'

'And yet not Kumar's type. Physically, yes, but finally Kasim bears no more resemblance to Kumar than you do to Miss Manners. But in the taxi I think there was a sort of fantasy in my mind of Hari and Daphne being about to come together again. I'm sorry – it sounds awful, but there it was. You sat there in the front seat, shading your eyes – and that was like her. She had a way of standing, peering at things a long way off, with just that gesture. And at the end of the journey, the guest house, and Ahmed there, well – waiting. On the other side of the line.'

For an instant Sarah held in her mind's eye an exact image of Ahmed as she had first seen him at the entrance to the guest house, emerging from the dim interior, and of herself still dazzled by the lake whose glare had become trapped inside her head, making it ache; and then this vision dissolved into another, of herself and Ahmed riding across the waste ground with constant distance between them except at those two moments, Ahmed's seizing of the reins, herself wheeling round suddenly to face him.

'That morning you went riding with him,' Ronald Merrick was saying, 'and Teddie and I turned up unexpectedly for breakfast. When we saw you coming back I thought, Well, that's it, I was right, it's all happening again. But then when you both got off your horses I realized it wasn't happening at all. You were friendly enough, but the barriers were up. The way you stood I could see you weren't sure how to leave him, I could see it crossing your mind: What do I do now, how do I get rid of him politely? You invited him in to breakfast, didn't you? Now if it had been Kumar he'd have accepted. But Mr Kasim knows where the line has to be drawn too. It was a relief to you both when he got back on and rode off. Am I right?'

Sarah felt he was right for the wrong reasons. She did not answer him immediately. He aggravated a grinding impatience in her which she knew she must discipline.

'I can't speak for Mr Kasim,' she began.

'Then for yourself,' he urged. 'It was a relief.'

'I wasn't under pressure.'

'We're always under that. Resisting it or pretending it's not there only adds to it.'

'What we are talking about, Ronald?' – she used his name again deliberately, as a little punishment for calling her Miss Layton after she had herself dispensed with that formality. 'The social pressure that keeps the ruled at arm's length from the rulers, or the biological pressure that makes a white girl think she mightn't like being touched by an Indian?'

Did he blush? She was not sure. The light was too far gone, absorbed, drained into the lake. He put up a hand and rubbed his forehead: a gentle action – a reflex, it seemed, of his mental registration of the need, now, to tread decisively but delicately on ground set with traps for the unwary.

'They are connected,' he said. 'If you visualize such a union, or if you consider its counterpart, the connection is quite clear. A white man, well, supposing I – or Teddie – I mean if one's tastes ran that way, to marry an Indian woman, or live with her. He would not be – what is the right word? Diminished? He wouldn't feel that. People would not really feel it of him, either. He has the dominant role, whatever the colour of his partner's skin. The Indians themselves have this prejudice about paleness. To them a fair skin denotes descent from the civilized Aryan invaders from the north, a black skin descent from the primitive aboriginals who were pushed into the jungles and hills, or fled south. There is this connotation paleness has of something more finely, more delicately adjusted. Well – superior. Capable of leading. Equipped mentally and physically to dominate. A dark-skinned man touching a white-skinned woman will always be conscious of the fact that he is – diminishing her. She would be conscious of it too.'

He relapsed into silence. Presently he said, 'I've said it all very badly. And I've broken one of the sacred rules, haven't I? One isn't supposed to talk about this kind of thing. One isn't supposed to talk about anything much.'

'I know,' she said. 'It's how we hide our prejudices and continue to live with them. Will you have the other half?'

'No, thank you. I ought to be going. I'm only half packed. Will you say goodbye and make my apologies to your family?'

Sarah glanced to her left. A light fell on the terrace from Aunt Fenny's and Uncle Arthur's room. A servant had wakened them. Her mother's room was dark.

'I expect Aunt Fenny will be out in a while.'

'I mustn't stay.'

He sat on for perhaps as long as half a minute, then rose.

'There's one,' he said. 'A firefly. The end of your vigil.'

But she did not see it. Standing, she thought of Teddie and Susan arrived already at the Nanoora Hills Hotel, observing the scene spread out below the balcony of their bridal room.

'The end of your vigil,' Merrick repeated, 'and the signal for me to depart.'

She smiled, went to the light-switch on the wall near the bell-push and flicked it on. Merrick, bathed in yellow light, lost that faded density. The sleeves of his bush shirt were still rolled up to the elbows. His arms were covered in fine blond hairs. Beneath the flesh on his cheeks the bone structure was emphasized by downward-pointing shadows. His eyes, his whole physical presence, struck her as those of a man chilled by an implacable desire to be approached, accepted. She felt reluctant to take the hand he slowly, consideringly held out as if uncertain that anyone would welcome contact.

'Well, goodbye,' she said, letting their hands meet. His felt warm and moist. The light had already attracted insects. They encircled the shade, distracting her. For politeness's sake she began to accompany him down the terrace but he said, 'No, please don't bother. Besides, you'll miss the next firefly.'

She watched him go – puzzled that by going he made her feel lonely. He did not look back. She returned her attention to the garden. After a while she heard the sound of the truck engine.

*

She paused in her walk below the terrace. The night air was India's only caress. She was among the fireflies now. One passed within a few feet, winking on and off. Since Ronald Merrick left she had bathed and changed, but still was the first out to begin the ritual of the evening at home – home being anywhere, any place there was – say – a veranda, a bit of a view and the padding slap of a barefoot servant answering a summons. Home, such as it was, was the passing of the hours themselves and only in sleep might one wander into the dangerous areas of one's exile (and perhaps, in one's thoughts, between one remark and another, one gesture and another). One carried the lares and penates, the family iconography, in one's head and in that sequestered region of the heart. Why we are like fireflies too, she told herself, travelling with our own built-in illumination; a myriad portable candles lighting windows against some lost wanderer's return.

She laughed, chasing one of the luminous pulsating bugs and then stopped, having remembered her father. 'I hope you are not lonely,' she said aloud. 'I hope you are well, I hope you are happy, I hope you will come back soon.' And turned back towards the terrace and was in time to see Aunt Fenny and Uncle Arthur come out and stand for a moment arrested by some unexpected thought, consideration, recollection. From this distance their exchange was all dumb show, and not much of it either. Two or more English together were very uninteresting to watch. Fenny left Uncle Arthur's side and went to her sister's room from which light showed behind the louvres of closed shutters. Fenny must have tapped. A vertical band of light appeared, widened, and Fenny went inside.

Alone, Uncle Arthur now sat in a wicker chair. Alone he relaxed. Alone he became almost communicative with himself. He shouted for the bearer, crossed his legs, jerked one rhythmically up and down, smoothed his balding head, scrubbed his moustache with the first joint of his left index finger, shifted his weight in the chair, drummed on the adjacent table with his right hand. Yawned. Eased his tie. Scratched his crotch. And hearing Abdur Rahman approach, stretched his neck back to speak to him. Perhaps he asked where she was because Abdur seemed to invite his glance to fall upon, to attempt to penetrate the darkness of the garden beyond the geometrical patterns of light falling upon gravel and grass.

Just then the vertical strip of light appeared again and widened and Aunt Fenny came out with Mrs Layton who brought her glass with her, and at once, so it seemed, a different pattern of the play was established and Uncle Arthur was on scene again, erect, sparing of movement. With the two women an element of grace entered. They sat, one on either side of Uncle Arthur who sank to his chair again, crossed his legs but kept the restless one still. Aunt Fenny was talking. The lone sound, the steady vibration of her voice reached Sarah, but not the words.

She began to walk towards them, conscious of coming at them from a great, a lonely distance away. She shivered a bit and the thought occurred that it was foolhardly to walk at night alone. She did not want to be alone. She remembered the sense she had had of being left behind when she saw that only one of the beds in her and Susan's room had been prepared for the night, mosquito net unrolled and draped, its counterpart left stiff and bunched above a smooth virgin counterpane.

'My family,' she told herself as she entered the geometrical pattern of light and the circle of safety. 'My family. My family. My family.'

BOOK TWO

Orders of Release

Part One

THE SITUATION

I

May 1944

The car took what she and her husband had called the Household Gate out of the grounds of Government House. Had it been called the Household Gate before her husband's term of office? She could not remember. She brought her hand up, seeking the reassurance of the pleated front of her blouse and the mother-of-pearl buttons.

The car was headed towards the city, but at the complex of roads that met at the Elphinstone Fountain the driver bore right, north, taking the road through the noisy, heavily trafficked commercial quarter. Behind the grandiose stone buildings of the offices and banks lay the labyrinth of the Koti Bazaar where she had shopped accompanied only by Suleiman, to the despair of Henry's *aides*. She glanced at the *aide* who accompanied her now and realized that she had already forgotten his name.

'You have a question, Lady Manners?'

How well trained he was. She nodded. 'I'm afraid I suddenly can't remember your name.'

'Rowan,' he said, without fuss.

'Rowan. It is a curious thing, memory. My husband had an astonishing one. Mine was only so-so. I used to try and bluff my way out of the awkward situations it seemed to lead me into, until I realized the situations weren't awkward at all, but the bluff was. The gate we left by, is it still called the Household Gate?'

'I've not heard it called that. H.E. calls it the side way. I think the official description is Curzon Gate because of the statue opposite.'

'But Government House was built before Curzon.'

'That's true. How about Little West?'

'It will do. But so will sideway. The next Governor will call it something else. It's a way of making ourselves feel at home in an institution. Shall you return to active duty, Captain Rowan?' Today he was wearing mufti but she recollected from their brief meeting the day before in the Governor's private office the ribbon of the Military Cross.

'No, I'm told not. But that's probably a good thing because I wasn't made in the mould of a good regimental officer.'

'Were you wounded?'

'Nothing so distinguished, I'm afraid. But I managed to contract a number of tropical things, one after the other.'

'What do you intend? A regular staff appointment?'

'No. I've applied to get back into the political department, which is what I always wanted. I was seconded before the war and served a probationary period, but then of course the army reclaimed me.'

'And you were in Burma?'

'Yes.'

They were through the commercial quarter, travelling along a tree-lined section of the Kandipat road with the railings of the Sir Ahmed Kasim Memorial Gardens on their right and on their left the houses of rich Indians, in spacious compounds. Most of the iron gates were padlocked, the occupants having retreated into the hills. An exception was number 8. She found herself uncertain which of the houses along this stretch of the Kandipat belonged to M.A.K. And another name was troubling her – the name of the girl with the look of envy who had sent a parting gift of flowers – a Pankot name.

She turned and said, 'Do you have the photograph, Captain Rowan?'

'H.E. gave me an envelope which he said you might ask for.'

'I'll have it now, if I may.'

He zipped open the leather document case on his knee, reached in and brought out a square buff envelope.

'Would you unseal it for me?'

She watched while he sought for an ungummed section of the flap. Having widened it he made a neat break with his finger. He handed the envelope to her. She had taken her reading-spectacles case from her handbag in readiness and now put the glasses on. From the envelope she withdrew a rectangular matt-surface print. There were two pictures on it, side by side; profile and full-face.

For a time she avoided the flat stare of the full-face, considered instead the side-view of it, the whorls of the neat, masculine ear, the black, apparently oily, neatly-cut hair. In the processing the skin had retained the two-level density of a dark face under artificial lighting, the impression that negative and positive were aligned, one on top of the other. So that is what he looked like, she thought, and stared at the full-face, at the oddly expressionless eyes whose whites conveyed an idea that they might be bloodshot. She closed her own eyes to consider, uninfluenced, a different but familiar image and, having conjured it exactly, reopened her eyes and felt a stab of recognition which in the next moment she did not trust. She replaced the photograph in the envelope, took off her spectacles. They had entered a semi-rural area of hovels. There was a smell of human and animal excrement. A naked ash-smeared Sadhu leaned against a parapet and watched them go past, his arms folded, his head tilted. She saw his mouth open and his neck muscles swell, but could not distinguish his shout above the shouting of little boys who ran alongside the car calling for baksheesh; keeping up with it because it was slowed by a farmer's cart ahead and a string of cyclists coming in the opposite direction. The light was opaque: one particle of dust to one particle of air. The temperature was in the hundreds.

She returned her spectacles case to her handbag. The envelope was too big to go in too. She gave it back to Captain Rowan.

'I shan't want it again.'

Rowan put the envelope back into his briefcase. He looked at his wrist-watch and then at her. Their glances met. 'We have about ten minutes, Lady Manners. Would you like me to go through the arrangements so that you know what to expect?'

Again she sought the reassurance of the pleats and buttons. She looked through the double thickness of glass at the necks of the driver and his companion.

'I've no doubt H.E. has arranged everything as I would wish.'

'Not without a certain element of awkwardness being involved. Awkwardness for you.'

'I couldn't expect otherwise.'

'Before we reach the Kandipat I shall pull the blinds down over the windows. The man sitting next to the driver has all the necessary documents to pass us through the gates. The car will stop twice. When it stops the second time we shall be inside the prison. We should be immediately next to a doorway that leads into a corridor and eventually to the jail superintendent's private quarters. We shall go to the end of the corridor and into a room marked "O". I shall leave you alone in room "O". There are a few details about room "O" but I can explain those at the time. There is only the one door. The man sitting next to the driver will be on duty in the corridor.'

'And I shall be alone in the room – throughout?'

'Yes.'

'I understand. I shall see and hear but not be seen or heard?'

'Yes. Afterwards it will take me about five minutes to rejoin you.'

'And I should wait in the room until you come for me?'

'If you would, Lady Manners.'

'Shall I be required to meet anyone at all?'

'No one.'

'Thank you.'

'When we leave, the car will have been reversed in the courtyard and will be parked ready. We shall then drive straight out and back to Government House.'

Again Rowan checked his watch. He leaned far back in his seat, canting his head to get a glimpse of the area they were approaching. He said, 'I think perhaps we should lower the blinds now. We're coming into Kandipat.'

He reached forward, pulled down one of the tip-up seats and transferred himself to it, stretched across to the little roller-blinds on her side of the car. Gradually the back of the car was filled with sub-aqueous light. She lost the sensation of forward movement. When he had completed the operation he resumed his seat next to her, resettled the document case on his lap. She raised her hands, feeling for the veil, groped round its prickly edge until she felt the smooth round knob of the hatpin. She pulled the hatpin out, jabbed it gently into the buff cord upholstery and coaxed the veil out of its folds, until it hung loose, shading the whole of her face and neck. Retrieving the pin she replaced it in the back of her hat.

'In case I forget – afterwards – Captain Rowan, thank you for what you have done, are doing, and have undertaken to do. Can I rely utterly on your discretion?'

'Of course.'

'I understood from H.E. that he chose you for a reason that would become clear to me. If he meant your courtesy and efficiency it has already done so. But whatever the reason he had in mind, I'm grateful. Forgive me for raising the question of discretion.' She smiled, then wondered whether he would see that she did, through the veil, in the dim museum-like light. He was not smiling. But her compliments had not embarrassed him. Well, she thought, you are a man who knows his worth, accepts its obligations with interest and its rewards with dignity, and I particularly thank God for you today.

*

She thanked God too for Captain Rowan not talking, for not attempting to disrupt her contemplation of the mystery of the inhumanity of man towards man that a prison was the repository of and which was entered consciously even when the actual entry was made blindly, so: stop and pause, start and move and stop finally. At some point, when the back of the car was overtaken by a violently sudden darkness the line dividing contemplation of the mystery from experience of it was crossed. A chill smell of masonry conjured the sensation of enclosure within walls sweating from a low but insistent fever – the fever of defeat and apprehension. The door on Captain Rowan's side of the car was opened. The cold damp smell of stone strengthened, came on a shaft of funnelled air with the implacable impact of an actual touching, so that Captain Rowan's hand, offering itself to hers, was a momentary shock, the flesh-touch of someone who had accompanied her into an area of distress. There were on either side of her glimmers of filtered light and, in front, steps and a narrow doorway that was open. She mounted the steps, grateful for his cupped hand at her elbow. The corridor was stone-flagged, stone-walled, lit by one naked bulb at its farther end where already she could make out the letter 'O' painted in white on a closed brown door. Reaching it she saw that the corridor turned at a right-angle towards flights of wooden stairs – up and down. After he had left her alone in Room O he would ascend or descend by one of those flights: descend, more likely.

He opened the door of Room O. A cold dry draught and a faint humming in the darkness, a subtle lethal scent as of chilled milk in frosted zinc containers – a scent that always caught her high up in the nostrils and made her conscious of the space between her eyes – distinguished the room at once as one whose atmosphere was regulated by an air conditioner. She thought: I shall catch a cold. Captain Rowan entered the room ahead of her and switched on the light – an act which registered in her mind as a consequence of particular rehearsal rather than of general familiarity.

The room was a square of bare whitewashed walls. It contained a table and a chair. On the table, which was covered by a piece of green baize, were a carafe of water with an inverted tumbler over its neck, an ashtray, a pad, two pencils, a table-lamp and a telephone. The chair had its back to the door. It stood close to and facing the farther wall. Into that part of the wall a grille was let in at eye-level for someone sitting in the chair. Above the grille was a smaller grille with a fine steel mesh. The table was set against the wall to the right of the chair.

Captain Rowan went to the table and switched on the lamp. It threw a small pool of light on to the white notepad.

'If you would sit, Lady Manners, I'll turn off the overhead light.'

She sat, lifted her veil. She could see nothing through the grille, but when the overhead light went off the grille was transformed into a faintly luminous rectangle. She felt Captain Rowan come close. He reached in front of her, manipulated a catch on the grille and opened it. Behind it was a pane of glass and behind the pane wide-spaced, downward-directed louvres of wood or metal. She found herself looking through the louvres into a room on a slightly lower level. There were a table, several chairs and a door in each of the three walls she could see. The table was covered in green baize. There were pads, pencils, two wafer carafes and – placed centrally – a telephone. Suspended above the table was a light. It was on and seemed to be powerful. There was no one in the room.

'Actually there's not much to explain,' Captain Rowan said. 'You can keep the table-lamp on without any light on this side of the window attracting attention from below. The light over the table down there is rather strong and the shade is adjusted so that the man sitting in the chair facing you tends to be a bit dazzled by it. I've tried it myself and I assure you that if you look up you simply can't see this grille let alone see anyone watching through it. But if the table-lamp here distracts you, just switch it off.'

'I think I should prefer it switched off.'

He pressed the button on the base of the lamp.

'Yes,' she said, 'now I feel less vulnerable.'

'Good. The microphone is in the telephone down there.' He switched the lamp on again. 'This is the speaker, above the grille. When I get down I shall ask whether you can hear. If you can, press the button that you'll find under the arm of the chair.'

She felt for it.

'Yes, I have it.'

'Would you press it now and watch the telephone downstairs?'

She did so. A green light on the instrument in the room on the other side of the grille came on in response to the pressure.

'That is also your line of communication. If the relay system breaks down all you need do is press the button. I will then pick up the telephone and say "Hello". Once the telephone is picked up there's a direct private connection between this room and that. All you need do is pick your own telephone up and tell me what's wrong. My reply may not seem relevant, naturally. But please don't hesitate to communicate if you think it necessary. The business can always be adjourned if you want to discuss any points with me.'

'Thank you, Captain Rowan.'

'Are you close enough to the grille?'

'Yes, and I shall put on my distance glasses.'

'Shall I turn the light off again?'

'If you would.'

Again the room darkened and the picture of the room below became brighter, clearer. She leaned forward.

'Then if everything is satisfactory, Lady Manners, I'll leave you.'

She nodded and said, 'Yes, please carry on with your own side of things.'

Presently she heard the door open. Light from the corridor came and went across the wall she faced. She fumbled for the clasp of her handbag, found it and opened a way for her hand into the familiar homely clutter. Without removing the case she opened it and took out her distance spectacles, put them on. Now she could appreciate the fuzzy quality of the baize, the contradictions of texture between the baize and the wood of the chair that would be the focus for her attention. There was a clock on the wall above the door behind the chair. It showed twenty minutes after ten.

Just before it showed twenty-five past the door below it opened and Captain Rowan entered. He put his briefcase on the table and sat in the chair the prisoner was to sit in and gazed at a point directly in front of him. His voice reached her rather metallically from the wall just above her head.

'The table is on a low dais and someone seated opposite sits slightly higher than the person in this chair. The head of the person in this chair is therefore raised a bit when he looks the other person in the eye. So.' Captain Rowan raised his head fractionally. 'You should now have a fuller face view. More chin and less forehead. If you have heard and understood please press the button twice.'

She did so. The green light on the telephone pulsed on and off, on and off.

'Good. Perhaps we should test the telephone connection.' He stood, leaned over and picked the receiver off the rest. She turned to her right, groped for her own instrument, found it, lifted the receiver and placed it against her ear. His voice was now in the instrument.

'Can you hear me?'

'Yes, thank you. It's working perfectly.'

'Shall we begin, then?'

'Please.'

'I'll wait until I hear you put your phone back.'

She replaced the receiver.

He looked up, narrowing his eyes against the bright light, put his own receiver down and said – his voice coming again through the speaker – 'I assure you no one can see the little window. I'm going outside for a moment. A clerk will come in. When I return I shall have an official from the Home and Law department of the Secretariat with me. The clerk and the official are both Indians. The clerk's duty is to make a shorthand transcript of the proceedings. The official from the Home and Law department is here because of the nature of the business which H.E. felt shouldn't be left entirely in the hands of someone on his private and personal staff.'

Rowan, while talking, had come round to the other side of the table and stood with his back to her. He took some papers from the briefcase. She saw him hesitate over the buff envelope which she had returned to his care.

He said, 'Although H.E. handed this envelope to me without explaining what was in it I gather it's a photograph of the man in question. I feel I ought to warn you that if so it was probably taken the year before last, sometime in August 1942. There are bound to be changes.' He put the envelope back in the briefcase. He looked round the table, then walked across to the door under the clock, opened it and went out.

She glanced at the clock. It showed about a quarter of a minute short of ten-thirty. The door on the left of the room opened. The clerk came in – a middle-aged Indian with a balding head and gold-rimmed spectacles. He wore a homespun cotton shirt and dhoti. His feet, sockless, were tucked into black leather shoes. He came down to a chair placed several feet to the left-rear of the table almost out of her sight, and sat. The sounds he made were clearly relayed. She could just make out his crossed legs and the shorthand notebook which he held ready on his knee. He made a few marks on it with his fountain pen, testing the nib and the flow of ink. Satisfied, he put the cap back on the pen and began to adjust the folds of his dhoti. It seemed an act of vanity, like that of a woman wearing a long-skirted dress making sure it hung gracefully. She particularly noted the action. The clerk was unaware of the presence of an invisible audience. He coughed, cleared his throat, began to tap the pen on the notebook; puk, puk, puk. She found herself fighting a tickle in her own throat and then remembered that no one could hear her if she coughed to clear it. She did so. The tapping continued uninterrupted: puk, puk, puk, puk.

Abruptly the door under the clock opened again – the tapping stopped and the clerk stood – and Captain Rowan entered followed by the official from the Secretariat – a lean elderly Indian wearing a grey chalk stripe suit and a pink tie. He carried a black document case. He cast an upward glance in the direction of the grille, then came and sat with Captain Rowan. Their backs were towards her. They sat with plenty of space between them. Midway, on the other side of the table, the empty chair faced her directly and her view of it was not obscured. The crackling of the papers the two men were leafing through was now the only sound.

'Shall we begin?' Captain Rowan asked suddenly.

The lean Indian's voice was soft and low-pitched.

'Oh yes. I am quite ready if you are.'

'Tell them we are ready, Babuji.'

The clerk went to the door in the right-hand wall, opened it and spoke to someone in Hindi, then closed the door again and went back to his chair.

For an instant Lady Manners closed her eyes. When she opened them the room still contained only the three men. Her hand tugged at the pleats and mother-of-pearl buttons and then lay inert. She breathed in and out slowly in an attempt to slow her heart-beat. The door opened again. She could not see who opened it because it opened on a side that would hide whoever entered until he was inside the room out of range of the door's arc. For a moment or so the door remained as it was at an angle of ninety degrees to the wall and no one came from behind it.

When he did he came hesitantly – a dark-skinned man dressed in loose-fitting grey trousers and a loose-fitting collarless grey jacket buttoned down the front. He wore chappals without socks. Having emerged beyond the range of the door he stopped and glanced at the occupants of the table and then at a man who was holding him by the right arm – to guide or restrain, or both; it wasn't easy to tell. The other man was in uniform – khaki shirt and shorts. He wore a pugree and carried a short baton. The hand on the arm suggested authority but also aid or comfort such as might be given in an unfamiliar situation to a man who normally gave no trouble, whose mind and body were disciplined to routine and were slow to respond to unusual demands.

The hand was on the arm for no longer than a few seconds. The guard let go, came to attention and dismissed, closing the door behind him. The man in the floppy collarless jacket and trousers stood alone.

'Sit down, please,' Captain Rowan said. He indicated the chair.

It was the same profile as in the photograph: the same neat, masculine ear. But not the same. The face of the man in the photograph had been held erect, was well fleshed; a dark, handsome face with hair that curled – a bit unruly on the forehead. This man's hair looked as though it had been cropped some months ago and had not grown out in its former fashion. Under the brown pigment of the face there was a pallor. The cheek was hollow. The head looked heavy, as if long stretches of time had been spent by the man, seated, legs apart, hands clasped between them, eyes cast down, considering the floor, the configuration of the stone. He moved towards the table, stood by the chair, still in profile.

'Baitho,' the official from the Home and Law department repeated.

The man extended his right hand, clutched the back of the chair and then with an awkward movement twisted round and sat, holding the back until the weight and position of his body forced him to release it. He gazed down at the table. His shoulders were hunched. It looked as if he might have his hands between his knees.

'*Kya, ham Hindi yah Angrezi men bolna karenge?*' Captain Rowan asked.

Briefly she had an impression from the man's glance at Rowan of eyes startlingly alert, in sockets which compared to those she recalled from the photograph were large and deeply shadowed. The man looked down again.

He said, '*Angrezi.*' The voice was notably clear.

'Very well. In English, then.'

Rowan opened a file.

'Your name is Kumar, your given name – Hari.'

'*Han.*'

'Son of the late Duleep Kumar of Didbury in the county of Berkshire, England.'

'*Han.*'

'At the time of your detention you were living at number 12 Chillian-wallah Bagh in Mayapore, a district of this province.'

'*Han.*'

'The occupier of the house in Chillianwallah Bagh being your aunt, Shalini Gupta Sen, *née* Kumar, widow of Prakash Gupta Sen.'

'*Han.*'

'You were taken into custody on August the ninth, nineteen forty-two by order of the District Superintendent of Police, in Mayapore, and detained for examination. On August the twenty-fourth as a result of that and subsequent examinations an order for your detention under Rule 26 of the Defence of India Rules was made and you were thereupon transferred in custody to the Kandipat jail, Kandipat, Ranpur, where you have remained in accordance with the terms of the order.'

'*Han.*'

'I understood you elected to speak in English. So far you have answered in Hindi. Do you therefore wish to have these proceedings conducted in Hindi and not English?'

Again Kumar looked up from the table, but this time his glance was not brief and only now was she convinced that the man in the room was the man in the photograph and the conviction did not come from the speaking of his name or his acknowledgement of it but from the sudden resemblance to the photograph that had become superimposed on his prison face, the prison structure of bone. The resemblance, she thought, must lie in the expression. He gazed at Captain Rowan in the way that he had gazed to order into the lens of a camera – as into a precision instrument that could do no more than the job it was designed for and could not penetrate beyond whatever line it was he had drawn and chosen to make his stand behind, the demarcation line between the public acceptance of humiliation and the defence of whatever sense he had of a private dignity.

'I beg your pardon,' he said – and she shut her eyes, to listen only to the

561

voice – 'it was a slip. I seldom have the opportunity of speaking English to anyone except myself.'

A pause.

'I understand,' another voice said above her head. She kept her eyes shut. The voices were those of two Englishmen talking. 'These proceedings,' the second of the two voices went on, 'are authorized by an order of the Governor in Council dated the fifteenth of May, nineteen hundred and forty-four and the purpose of the proceedings is to examine any facts relevant in your case to the detention order under the Defence of India Rule. You may if you wish decline to submit to the examination, in which case the proceedings will be terminated immediately. I am also instructed to advise you that the purpose of the proceedings is to examine and not to make a recommendation in regard to your detention. You should not assume that refusal or acceptance of the examination or the examination itself will have any bearing on the order for your detention or upon its eventual termination. On that understanding I now ask you whether you decline or submit to the examination.'

A pause.

'I submit to the examination on that undertaking.'

'Your submission is recorded. In the case of Kumar, Hari, son of the late Duleep Kumar, at present lodged in the Kandipat jail, Kandipat, Ranpur, under warrant dated August twenty-four, nineteen hundred and forty-two, Rule 26, Defence of India Rules, and in accordance with order dated fifteen May nineteen forty-four, of the Governor in Council, Government House, Ranpur, Captain Nigel Robert Alexander Rowan and Mr Vallabhai Ramaswamy Gopal examining. Examinee not under oath. Transcript of proceedings for submission on confidential file to His Excellency the Governor, copy on the confidential file to the Member for Home and Law, Executive Council.'

Again a pause. She opened her eyes. Kumar still sat with his shoulders hunched. He had returned to his contemplation of the table, as if in deference to a formal rigmarole that was no particular concern of his, but as the silence lengthened, was filled by nothing more enlivening to the ears than the sound of Captain Rowan adjusting and checking the papers in front of him, Kumar glanced up again to stare at his chief examiner and again she was struck by the alertness his eyes – and the clarity of his voice – were evidence of. She could not interpret it beyond that. Impossible to say whether he sensed danger or saw the examination as a source of hope. It could be either. It could be both. But whichever it was the alertness and the clarity betrayed the presence of the man inside the hunched submissive figure of the prisoner.

'Since a detention order under the Defence of India Rules is made without recourse to trial in the criminal courts,' Captain Rowan began, 'the documentary evidence in front of this examining board consists of summaries of evidence, statements and submissions by the civil authorities of the district in which you resided. In this instance, which involved five other men as well as yourself, the documents were submitted to the office of the Divisional Commissioner before the order for detention was made on you and these five other men. We are however only concerned with these documents as they relate to you. It is not within the terms of reference of this board to disclose the details of these documents to you, but it is upon them that we shall base our questions. I shall begin by reading to you a list of names. The question I ask in each case is – were you at the time of your detention personally acquainted with the man whose name I read out. I invite you to answer yes or no as the case may be, after each name. With the name I shall give a brief description – for example occupation – to reduce the risk of confusion. Is that understood?'

'Yes.'

'The first name is S. V. Vidyasagar, sub-editor employed on the *Mayapore Hindu*, originally employed as a reporter on the *Mayapore Gazette*. Were you acquainted with this man?'

'Yes.'

'Narayan Lal, employed as a clerk in the Mayapore Book Depot.'

'Yes.'

'Nirmal Bannerjee, unemployed, graduate in electrical engineering of the Mayapore Technical College, son of B. N. Bannerjee, a clerk in the offices of Dewas Chand Lal, Contractor.'

'Yes.'

'Bapu Ram, trainee at the British-Indian Electrical Company's factory, Mayapore.'

'Yes.'

'Moti Lal, last employed as a clerk at the warehouse of Romesh Chand Gupta Sen, contractor of Mayapore, sentenced to six months imprisonment in 1941 under section 188 of the Penal Code. Escaped from custody during February 1942, and according to this document not apprehended at the date of the document's origin.'

'Yes.'

'Puranmal Mehta, stenographer employed in the office of the Imperial Bank of India, Mayapore.'

'Yes.'

'Gopi Lal, unemployed, son of one Shankar Lal described as a hotel-keeper.'

'Yes.'

'Pandit B. N. V. Baba, of B-1, Chillianwallah Bazaar road, Mayapore, described as a teacher.'

'Yes.'

'I shall now divide those names into two groups. In the first we have two names – S. V. Vidyasagar and Pandit Baba. The questions I shall ask relate to the kind of acquaintanceship you had with these men. In the case of Pandit Baba the records at my disposal, those on your case file, give me no idea why at the time of your arrest you were asked what you knew of him. Perhaps that would be clear after a study of the case files of the other men arrested at the same time as yourself, but those case files are not available to this examining board because they aren't pertinent to this examination. I would stress the latter point to you. This board examines you wholly on the basis of the file pertaining to your own arrest and subsequent detention. In other words, you are examined by a board unprejudiced by anything that is recorded in the cases of the other men arrested. My first question, with regard to Pandit Baba, is therefore this: Would you tell the board why – in your opinion – you were asked what your relationship with him was? I would remind you that your reply to this question as recorded in the file was to the effect that you had nothing to say. In fact ninety-nine per cent of your recorded replies to questions were to that same effect. I hope the same situation isn't going to arise this morning. Will you then answer the question? Why should you have been asked if you knew this Pandit Baba? Have you any idea?'

There was an appreciable pause but when Kumar spoke any initial hesitancy he might have felt to answer questions was quite absent from the tone of voice.

'I believe he was thought to have a lot of influence over young Indians of the educated class.'

'Who thought this?'

'The civil authorities in Mayapore.'

'Including the police?'

'Yes. The police once had him in for questioning because one of his disciples got into trouble.'

'Disciples?'

'Young men who gathered round him to listen to him talk.'

'What sort of trouble had this particular follower got into?'

'I believe he'd published or distributed a political pamphlet, or made a speech. I forget which.'

'Were you one of Pandit Baba's followers?'

'No.'

'Did you know the man who got into trouble?'

'No.'

'Then who told you about this affair?'

'I heard it as a matter of course. I was employed on the *Mayapore Gazette*. In a newspaper office you hear quite a lot that never becomes common knowledge.'

'What happened to the man who published this pamphlet or made this speech?'

'He was sent to prison.'

'What was his name?'

'I forget.'

'What happened to the Pandit?'

'Nothing.'

'How well did you know Pandit Baba?'

'I knew him as a man my aunt hired to try to teach me an Indian language.' A pause. 'He smelt strongly of garlic.' A pause. 'He was very unpunctual.' A pause. 'The lessons weren't a success.'

'When was this?'

'In 1938.'

'He tried to teach you Hindustani?'

'Yes.'

'Until then you knew no Indian language at all?'

'None.'

A rustle of paper. Then Gopal's voice: 'I have several points in regard to the detenu's early background and I should like to raise them at this juncture.'

Rowan nodded. Gopal addressed Kumar direct:

'Your father took you to England when you were aged two, according to this document. You were born in the United Provinces. Your father was a landowner there. Have you an inheritance in the United Provinces?'

'No. My father sold his interest to his brothers before leaving for England.'

'Your father never taught you your native tongue?'

A pause.

'He was at pains to try to teach me nothing.'

'Why?'

'He wanted me brought up in an entirely English environment so far as that was possible. I had a governess, then a tutor. Then I went to a private school and on to Chillingborough. I didn't see much of him.'

'Why was he wanting this – did he tell you?'

'He wanted me to enter the Indian Civil Service, as an Indian, but with all the advantages of an Englishman.'

'What were those advantages, was he saying?'

'I think he thought of them as advantages of character, manner and attitude. And language.'

'Because he thought the English character, manner, attitude and language were superior to the Indian?'

'No. More viable in relation to the operation of the administration.'

'I am not fully understanding that reply.'

'It is an English administration, based on English ideas of government. He thought an Indian at a disadvantage unless he had been trained to identify himself completely with these ideas. He admired the administration as such. He thought it would be best continued by fully Anglicized Indians.'

'Did you share his ambition for you?'

'Yes.'

'Why?'

'I knew no other.'

'You wished to enter the Indian Civil Service and serve the administration?'

'Wish is the wrong word. It suggests the existence of an alternative

565

choice and a preference for one of them. In my case I was never aware of an alternative.'

'From this document,' Gopal went on, 'I see that your mother died soon after you were born. Did the loss of your mother contribute to your father's decision to leave India and establish himself as a businessman in England?'

'It made it easier for him to put his plan into practice.'

'It was some two years after your mother's death that he took you to England. Presumably it took a little time for him to make the necessary arrangements?'

'He had to wait until his own mother died.'

'She was ill?'

'No. He had promised his father to look after her.'

'Your grandfather was dead?'

'He'd left home.' A pause. 'He renounced his worldly goods and left home wearing a loin-cloth and carrying a begging bowl. He intended to become what is called *sannyasi*.' A pause. 'The family never saw him again, but my father kept his promise and stayed until his mother died.'

'I see. Had he always hoped to leave India and go to England?'

'If he had a son.'

'He had been in England before?'

'He studied law there before the First World War but failed the examinations. He had a business sense but no academic sense.'

'He was what we are calling Anglophile? He admired the English way of life?'

'He thought an intimate understanding of and a familiarity with it essential for anyone serving the administration.'

'What were his political views in regard to India?'

'We never discussed politics as such.'

'Was he in favour of constitutional development leading eventually to a form of independence or of more hasty means to that end?'

'The former I imagine. He said India would remain under British rule well beyond his lifetime and probably far into mine.'

'Would you then say that he was anxious that you should become the kind of Indian whom the British would be happy to see as one of their administrative successors?'

'Yes. In later years he talked much along those lines, whenever I saw him.'

'Was that also your ambition? To become that kind of Indian?'

'I had no recollection of India whatsoever. I didn't know what different kinds of Indian there might be. My upbringing was entirely English. There was probably little difference in my attitude to the prospect of coming to India when I was older and the attitude of the average English boy whose family intended he should have a career out here.'

'You had, then, no sense of coming home when eventually you came to India?'

'The sense I had was the exact opposite.'

'Were you perturbed by what you found?'

'Yes.'

'Perturbed by the condition of the people?'

'I was perturbed by my own condition.'

'You did not look around you and think – these are my people, this is my country, I must work to free them of the foreign yoke that weighs them down?'

'I wanted nothing more than to go home.'

'Home – to England?'

'Yes.'

'But later, perhaps, you were ashamed of this selfish attitude and began to listen to young men of your own age and kind, to be affected somewhat by their hot-headed but understandable talk and ambitions?'

'They might have been of my age. They weren't of my kind. I was a unique specimen.'

'Unique? Just because you had been brought up in England?'

'No. Because I came back to a family my father had cut himself off from – a middle-class, orthodox Hindu family.' A pause. 'My uncle-by-marriage tried to make me undergo a ritual purification to get rid of the stain of living abroad. The ritual included drinking cow-urine. It was a family that didn't believe in education, let alone Western-style education. Not a single member of the Kumar family or of the Gupta Sen family my aunt married into had ever entered the administration. They were middle-class Hindus of the merchant and petty landowning class. Against this background – yes, I was unique.'

Gopal said, 'Thank you, Mr Kumar. I have no further questions on this subject.'

Rowan nodded, glanced at his open file, then looked up at Kumar who slowly transferred his attention from Gopal. For a while the two men – whose voices sounded so alike – stared at each other.

'In England, you say, there was little difference between you and the average English boy who was being trained for a career out here. Why, then, were you so shocked by what you found? The average Englishman arriving in India isn't shocked at all. In fact, he's rather excited. How do you explain this difference?'

She saw Gopal look at Rowan, as if astounded that he should bother to ask such a question. She too wondered why he had. If Kumar's face had been capable of changing expression she imagined it would now reflect an astonishment the equal of Gopal's. Perhaps the time he took to reply reflected it. Eventually he said:

'The India I came to wasn't the one the Englishman comes to. Our paths began to diverge in the region of the Suez Canal. In the Red Sea my skin turned brown. In Bombay my white friends noticed it. In Mayapore I had no white friends because I had become invisible to them.'

'Invisible?'

'Invisible.'

Rowan looked down at his file.

'I see that your father died in Scotland early in 1938 and that you came out in May of that year and went to live with your father's sister, Mrs Shalini Gupta Sen, in Mayapore. Was she your only surviving relative?'

'She was the only relative my father kept in touch with.'

'Why?'

'He had personally supervised her education when she was a young girl. The Kumar women were all illiterate but he taught her to read and write English, and speak it. They remained very fond of each other. When she was about fifteen she was married to a man of more than thirty – Prakash Gupta Sen of Mayapore. He died before they had any children. She was always interested in her English nephew – which was the way she referred to me in letters to my father.'

'Your father's solicitors communicated with her and she agreed that you should live with her?'

'Yes. She borrowed the passage money from her brother-in-law.'

'The contractor, Romesh Chand Gupta Sen of Mayapore, whose office you worked in for a time?'

'For a time.'

'Was there no possible means of maintaining you in England to finish at your public school and then study for the ICS examinations as your father had wished?'

'The means perhaps, but they weren't offered. My father committed suicide. He'd had business failures. He tried to recoup but lost everything. That's why he killed himself. His English-style son existed only as long as the money lasted. He probably couldn't face telling me my English life had ended and my Indian life was beginning several years too soon.'

'Did you ever ask your relatives in Mayapore if they'd maintain you in England until you'd qualified?'

'The solicitor wrote to my Aunt Shalini, suggesting that.'

'I presume you had some friends in England whom you could have lived with?'

'It seemed like it – for a time.'

'The family of one of your friends at school perhaps?'

'Yes.'

Again the rustle of paper.

'In one of the reports on this file there's a reference to a letter which the police found in your room and took charge of. It was signed Colin and had a Berkshire address. Was Colin the boy whose family might have looked after you?'

'Yes.'

'But your aunt was unable to raise the money to keep you in England, until you'd qualified?'

'She had no money of her own. She was a childless widow whose husband died in debt to his brother. She depended on this brother of his for practically every penny.'

'We're speaking of Romesh Chand Gupta Sen, I take it?'

'Yes. He offered passage money, and offered her an allowance for taking me in. The solicitor said it was very generous. According to him I was probably only losing my last term at school. He said I could study for the ICS in India.'

'You still intended to enter the ICS then? You came out with that ambition unimpaired?'

'Yes.'

'You discussed it with your aunt, and her brother-in-law?'

'Yes. But it was made plain by Mr Gupta Sen that there was no money for any kind of further education. I was expected to start earning my living.'

'Which is when you started working in your uncle's warehouse?'

'Yes. In the office of his Chillianwallah Bazaar warehouse. I remember the leper.'

'The leper?'

'He stood at the gate of the bazaar.'

'Why do you remember this?'

'When I saw the leper I thought of my grandfather. I wondered whether he had become a leper too.'

'And it was during this period that you had Hindustani lessons from Pandit Baba?'

'Yes.'

'It must all have seemed very strange to you.'

'Very strange. Yes.'

'The next note on your file is that during the summer of 1939 you applied to be taken on as a trainee at the British–Indian Electrical factory. A trainee in what?'

'They had a scheme for training suitable young Indians for junior executive positions.'

'You failed to get taken on, I see. In fact the note says: "The applicant was turned down chiefly as a result of his sullen and unco-operative manner." Would that be a reasonable description of your attitude?'

'It would depend on who was describing it.'

'I infer from the note that the man who found you sullen and unco-operative was the manager in charge of technical training. An Englishman. What happened?'

'I'd already passed two interviews, with one of the directors and with the managing director. The interview with the technical training manager was supposed to be a formality but he insisted on asking me technical questions which I told him at the outset I wouldn't be able to answer. When he'd finished he insulted me.'

'How?'

'By suggesting that I was an ignorant savage.'

'Are those the words he used?'

'No. He said: Where are you from, laddie? Straight down off the tree?'

'What did you say to that?'

569

'Nothing.'

'And so the interview ended—'

'Not then. He said something else.'

'Well?'

'He said he didn't like bolshie black laddies on his side of the business.'

'How did you respond?'

'I got up and walked out.'

'Yes, I see.' Rowan turned a page of the file. 'The next note shows you as having taken employment as a sub-editor and reporter on an Indian-owned newspaper published locally in Mayapore in the English language. The *Mayapore Gazette*. I presume this went well because you were still employed there at the date of your arrest in 1942, some three years later. What led you to choose journalism as a profession?'

'I didn't think of it as journalism or of myself as a journalist. A few months living in Mayapore showed me I'd only one qualification to put to practical use. My native language. English. The *Gazette* was owned, edited and written entirely by Indians. The English it was printed in was often very funny. So far as I was concerned I worked on the *Gazette* as a corrector. I became an occasional reporter because I could earn four annas a line for anything I wrote which they published. In addition to my salary of sixty rupees a month.'

'Did your aunt and uncle-by-marriage approve of this job?'

'My aunt did. She used to buy the *Gazette* for me so that I could read about local affairs. She liked reading it too. She liked being able to talk English again. She was always very good to me. She did her best to make me comfortable and happy. It wasn't her fault that I was neither.'

'Your aunt approved but her brother-in-law didn't?'

'When I got the job at the *Gazette* he reduced my aunt's allowance.'

'Why?'

'He said I could contribute to my upkeep out of my salary. He gave me nothing when I worked in his office.'

'I now go back,' Rowan said, 'to the first group of names, which consists of two: Pandit Baba and S. V. Vidyasagar. It was in the *Mayapore Gazette* office that you met the second man, Vidyasagar?'

'Yes. It was Vidyasagar who showed me the ropes.'

'What kind of ropes?'

'Finding my way round the Civil lines. Where the District and Sessions court was, who the deputy commissioner was and where he lived. Which was police headquarters. Who to apply to for permission to attend and report on some social function on the *maidan*. Before I joined the *Gazette* there'd been no occasion for me to cross the river and enter the Civil lines and cantonment.'

'Your job on the *Gazette*, then, took you into what from your point of view were more pleasant surroundings, a happier environment altogether?'

'It was interesting to observe that environment.'

'You felt yourself no more than observer?'

'I was no more than an observer. Perhaps I was even less than that. But it was interesting. Observing all the things English people did to prove themselves they were still English. Interesting and instructive. It taught me to see the ridiculous side of my father's ambition. I realized he'd left an important factor out of his calculations about my future.'

'And what was that?'

'The fact that in India the English stop being unconsciously English and become consciously English. I had been unconsciously English too. But in India I could never become consciously English; only consciously Indian. Conscious of being something I'd no idea how to be.'

Again Rowan looked down and referred to his file.

'Vidyasagar is also described as a sub-editor on another Mayapore newspaper, the *Mayapore Hindu*. How long were you working together at the *Gazette*?'

'About three weeks.'

'Vidyasagar then left and joined the *Mayapore Hindu*?'

'He was sacked.'

'Do you know why?'

'When the editor of the *Gazette* took me on he did so with the intention of sacking Vidyasagar.'

'Did you know that?'

'No. But Vidyasagar did.'

Rowan hesitated. 'So there was cause there for some friction between you and Vidyasagar? Did he harbour any kind of grudge?'

'If he ever did he never showed it. When he was sacked he said he'd expected it and that it wasn't to worry me because he could easily get a job on the *Mayapore Hindu*. He always remained friendly.'

'Why did the editor of the *Mayapore Gazette* prefer you to Vidyasagar?'

'I wrote correct English. Vidyasagar had only been at the Government Higher School.'

'The editorial policy of the *Gazette* has always been pro-British, wouldn't you say? I mean in comparison with the *Mayapore Hindu* where Vidyasagar was subsequently employed. A note here mentions that the *Mayapore Hindu* had a history of closure by the civil authorities. In fact it was closed down for a time during the riots in August 1942. The *Mayapore Gazette* on the other hand has never been proscribed.'

'The *Gazette*'s policy was to print nothing that caused the authorities any misgivings. I don't know if that amounts to pro-Britishness.'

'I ask the question to find out if you think there'd be anything to be said for a view that as a young reporter and sub-editor your attitude to affairs in general was more in keeping with the paper's editorial policy than was the attitude of Vidyasagar, for example.'

'I had no comparable attitude. Vidyasagar was an ardent nationalist, like ninety-nine per cent of other young Indians of his age and class and education.'

571

'That's what I mean. The editor of the *Gazette* might have found such a young man an embarrassment. With you he felt on safer ground?'

'The editor never asked me if I had any political views or affiliations. He hired me because of my ability to transcribe copy into correct English.'

'Did you have any political views and affiliations when you joined the paper?'

'No.'

'I believe a great deal of the *Gazette* was taken up with reports of social and sporting functions organized by the English community in Mayapore.'

'Yes.'

'And you sometimes attended such functions in your capacity as a reporter?'

'In that capacity, yes.'

'You would be a more suitable representative of the *Gazette* at such a function than Vidyasagar – ? I mean from the editor's point of view.'

'Perhaps.'

'And from the point of view of the people attending the function?'

'From their point of view I would be no different from Vidyasagar.'

'Why?'

'We both had black faces.'

A pause.

'But as time went by you were able better than Vidyasagar to break down this rather artificial barrier. You got to know a few English people.'

'I got to know one.'

'You're referring to Miss Manners?'

'Yes.'

'During your interrogation, whenever you were asked to describe the circumstances in which you became acquainted with Miss Manners you always replied: I have nothing to say. The question was simple enough, surely?'

'It was also unnecessary. The person asking it knew those circumstances as well as I did.'

'This board does not. So I ask the same question. What were the circumstances in which you got to know Miss Manners?'

'I was invited to the house where she was staying.'

'Can you remember the date?'

'Either the end of February or the beginning of March, nineteen-forty-two.'

'I see. Then that would have been soon after an occasion in February 1942 when you were taken to the police station at the Mandir Gate bridge and asked questions about your identity and occupation?'

'The invitation was a consequence of that.'

'You mean you were invited to the house where Miss Manners was staying because you'd been questioned by the police?'

'My being questioned by the police made certain people in Mayapore aware of my existence, yes.'

'Please elucidate.'

'I was arrested in a place called The Sanctuary—'

'Arrested?'

'I was dragged into a police truck, taken to the police station, held, questioned and then released. It seemed to me like being arrested.'

'Very well. Continue—'

'The Sanctuary was run as a private charity for the sick and dying by a woman known as Sister Ludmila. After I was arrested – taken away – she got word to Romesh Chand Gupta Sen. He sent for his lawyer, a man called Srinivasan. Srinivasan was a friend of Lady Chatterjee who lived in the MacGregor House. Miss Manners was staying with her there. Sister Ludmila also mentioned my arrest to a German woman who was in charge of the Purdah Hospital. Doctor Klaus. Doctor Klaus was also a friend of Lady Chatterjee. By the time Mr Srinivasan got to the police station to ask why I had been taken there I'd been released. But Lady Chatterjee heard of the incident from Dr Klaus and asked Mr Srinivasan about me. So she became interested in my case.'

'Your case?'

'My personal history.'

'You mean she thought you sounded like a young man in need of some help?'

'I don't know. I assumed she was interested in what she was told about me by Srinivasan, otherwise she wouldn't have invited me to the MacGregor House to one of her mixed parties of British and Indian guests.'

'Lady Chatterjee has some influence in Mayapore?'

'She was the widow of the man who founded and endowed the Mayapore Technical College. That's what he was knighted for. She was a friend of Miss Manners's aunt, Lady Manners, the widow of an ex-Governor of this province. In Mayapore the British always accorded her respect.'

'To have her interested in you was an asset, would you say?'

'I imagine it could be.'

'When you accepted her invitation was it in your mind that Lady Chatterjee might help you?'

'I don't know.'

'It was an opportunity for you, surely, to meet influential Indians and English people socially?'

'It was an opportunity I was in two minds about grasping.'

'Why?'

'I'd been in Mayapore for nearly four years. It struck me as significant that it needed my arrest to open the door to that kind of opportunity.'

'Significant of what?'

'I wasn't sure. Perhaps it was to find the significance that I accepted and went along.'

'And did you find this significance?'

'Influential people are always anxious to exercise their influence. They enjoy helping lame dogs of the right kind. But they're also always very busy. Only lame dogs who have tripped up ever come much to their notice. By then, from the lame dog's point of view, it's usually too late. Lady Chatterjee was about three years too late. I'm not criticizing. It was simply so. Having me at the party wasn't a success.'

'Any particular reason?'

'Influential people like to be thanked. I didn't thank her. And it worried her when Miss Manners was so friendly to me.'

'There are two points there. What did you have to thank Lady Chatterjee for?'

'Nothing.'

'You mean nothing in your opinion. What in hers?'

'She asked Judge Menen to inquire why a fellow called Hari Kumar had been dragged into a police truck and carted off to answer stupid questions. I don't suppose it did me any good in Merrick's book.'

'District Superintendent Merrick of the Indian Police?'

'Yes. That Merrick.'

'And Miss Manners's friendliness towards you. You think it worried Lady Chatterjee. Why?'

'Miss Manners was in her care. She felt responsible for her to Lady Manners.'

'I quite understand that. I don't understand why Miss Manners's friendliness to you should worry her. Surely it was to make you feel that you had friends that she invited you to the party?'

'Miss Manners was a white girl. Her friendliness towards me was of a kind that embarrassed people to watch.'

Rowan hesitated. From her air-conditioned place of observation she thought she detected, in Rowan, a certain stiffening of the neck and shoulders. She felt it in her own.

'I'm not sure I understand,' he said. 'What are you suggesting?' He hesitated, then abruptly, coldly said, 'That Miss Manners threw herself at you?'

Kumar stared at Rowan. There was a muscular spasm low on one cheek.

'I'm suggesting that even someone like Lady Chatterjee was incapable of accepting immediately that a white girl could treat an Indian like a man. I found it difficult to accept it myself. For a time I thought she was making fun of me. She talked so readily. Without any kind of artificiality – or so it seemed. Just as if we'd been back home. Lady Chatterjee very naturally treated me with caution after that.'

'Why "very naturally"?'

'She probably thought I might take advantage of Miss Manners. That's the popular assumption, isn't it? That an Indian will always take advantage of an English person who is friendly.'

'It may be an assumption generally held among certain types of English who come into contact with certain types of Indian. I can't think why Lady Chatterjee should think you'd take advantage of Miss Manners unless you gave her cause.'

Kumar seemed lost momentarily in thought. He said, 'I may have done for all I know. My behaviour at that time left a lot to be desired.'

'In what direction?'

'I'd forgotten how to act in that kind of company. Or if I'd not forgotten, trying to act as I remembered I should act seemed – artificial. I said very little. I was socially ill-at-ease. Miss Manners told me later that I stood and stared at her. I wanted to say things but the right words wouldn't come. I was a bit suspicious. I wasn't shy. Suspicious, and then astonished – to be treated as an equal by a white person. The comparison between this and what I'd just experienced was so extraordinary.'

For a while none of the three men at the table spoke. Gopal suddenly opened his file again and said, 'With regard to that recent experience I have a question—'

'Is it in regard to what he calls his arrest?' Rowan asked.

'Yes—'

'I should like to go back a bit further and come to that in its turn.'

'By all means.'

Gopal rested again.

'You mentioned The Sanctuary,' Rowan began. 'You called it a place run as a private charity for the sick and the dying. I have a record here of the occasion when you were asked to go with the police to the kotwali after you'd refused to answer questions put to you by police officers who visited The Sanctuary and found you there. The record has a note to the effect that according to the person in charge of The Sanctuary – here called Mrs Ludmila Smith, not Sister Ludmila – you had been found the night before by her stretcher party, lying unconscious in some waste ground near the river. Imagining that you were ill or hurt they took you back to The Sanctuary – as was their habit whenever they found someone ill, starving or dying in the street. It turned out, however, that you were merely dead drunk. Is that correct?'

'Yes.'

'It was your habit to drink excessively?'

'I had never been drunk before. I was never drunk again.'

'When you were questioned by the police at the kotwali you were not at all co-operative. But you admitted you'd been drunk and that your main drinking companion of the night before had been Vidyasagar, and that the names of the others were Narayan Lal, Nirmal Bannerjee, Bapu Ram. You were uncertain about Puranmal Mehta – but said there was a fifth man there who might have been called Puranmal Mehta. Therefore three if not four of the men you got drunk with on that night in February were among the five other men who were arrested under suspicion of being implicated in the criminal assault on Miss Manners. The question I must ask you is – for what purpose had you and these other men, including Vidyasagar, gathered together on the occasion you got drunk?'

'There was no purpose behind the gathering together.'

'It was simply your habit every so often to foregather with these men?'

575

'No. It was the first time – and the last.'

'But you said some while ago that you always remained friendly with Vidyasagar.'

'I said he remained friendly with me.'

'You met quite often.'

'Our occupation brought us into frequent contact.'

'You would meet – as reporters – at some function or, say, in the law courts. Then perhaps, when you'd done your jobs, you'd go off together – as acquaintances?'

'No. We would meet as reporters. Once or twice he invited me to have coffee. I always refused.'

'Why?'

'I didn't want to become involved.'

'Involved how? Politically?'

'Not politically. Socially.' A pause. 'In those days I was at pains to preserve everything about me that was English.' A pause. 'I lived a ridiculous life, really. But I didn't see that. I thought of their life as ridiculous.'

'Vidyasagar's and his friends'?'

'Yes.'

'You despised them? Because they hadn't had your advantages?'

'No. I didn't despise them. But I thought them ludicrous, through no fault of their own.'

Gopal interrupted. 'In what way, ludicrous?'

'They were always laughing at the English. They pretended to hate them. But everything about their way of life was an aping of the English manner. The way they dressed, the style of slang, the things they'd learned.' A pause. ' "I say, Kumar old man, let's dash in for a cup of coffee." Perhaps it was exaggerated for my benefit. I was a bit of a joke to them. But it seemed ridiculous.'

'You say "they". You were – if only in a limited sense – acquainted with these other men as well as Vidyasagar?'

'I came to Mayapore in 1938. I met Vidyasagar in 1939. Obviously I saw something of them between then and August 1942. I knew them by sight, whether they were with Vidyasagar or alone. After the night I got drunk I knew most of them by name.'

'The night you got drunk was the beginning of a closer relationship?'

'You don't get drunk with men without establishing something more intimate in the way of relationship. But it was still distant. And shortly afterwards of course my life changed completely.'

'How?'

'I became friends with Miss Manners.'

'What hasn't been dealt with yet is the reason for your sudden switch in attitude to Vidyasagar and his friends. Until a night in February 1942 you say you found them ridiculous – to the extent that you would even refuse to have a cup of coffee with them if one of them asked you when he met

576

you in the street, or at some official function. But that night you join Vidyasagar and his friends not just for a cup of coffee but for a hard bout of drinking – which ended so far as you were concerned in waste ground near the river in a state of complete intoxication. What led to this sudden reversal of what we might call your policy in regard to men like Vidyasagar?'

'The realization that after all it was I who was ridiculous.'

'Please elucidate.'

'It is a private matter.'

'You could say that practically everything we are discussing is a private matter. I suggest that this is no more, no less private. If you find it difficult to talk about, to know where to begin for instance, suppose we begin by discussing the events of that night. How, for example, did you find yourself in the company of Vidyasagar?'

'We were both on the *maidan*.'

'As reporters?'

'Yes.'

'What was taking place on the *maidan*?'

'A cricket match.'

'Between which teams?'

'Teams from regiments stationed in the cantonment.'

'You were watching cricket with Vidyasagar?'

'No. We met as we were coming away.'

'He invited you to come and have a coffee?'

'He invited me to his home.'

'And you accepted?'

'Yes. I accepted.'

'Why?'

'There no longer seemed to be any point in refusing.'

Rowan said nothing for a while. 'Because your resistance was worn down at last or because something had happened to upset you?'

'I suppose it was a combination of the two.'

'Then what exactly was it that had happened to upset you?'

Kumar stared at the table.

'He was there.'

'Who was there?'

'Someone I used to know.'

'Someone you had known in England?'

Kumar nodded.

'Colin?'

Kumar nodded.

'Your old school friend? The boy whose parents might have given you a home after your father died?'

'Yes.'

'Why was this upsetting?'

No answer.

'You met and talked, and thought that he was less friendly than you remembered? Or did you only see him from a distance?'

'He was as close to me as I am to you.'

'Are you saying that he was close to you but didn't talk to you?'

'We neither of us spoke.'

'Are you sure it was this man, Colin?'

'Yes.'

'You knew he was in India?'

'He wrote to me when he first came out, in 1941. He wrote several times, from different places. He talked about coming to Mayapore. Later he talked about how unlikely it would be that he could travel so far. Later he didn't write at all.'

Gopal said, 'And what construction did you put on that?'

'I thought that he had gone on active service. I thought he was having a bad war. First Dunkirk, now perhaps the Middle East. But he came to Mayapore. I guessed he had come to Mayapore when I saw soldiers in the cantonment wearing the regimental flash.'

'The flash of the regiment you knew Colin was serving in?'

'Yes. When I started seeing the soldiers with the flashes I began to expect him any day. I mean expecting him to turn up at my house. Then I realized that probably wasn't possible, because my side of the river was out of bounds to soldiers stationed in the cantonment. So then I began expecting a letter asking where we could meet. There was never such a letter. So then I thought Colin hadn't come to Mayapore with his regiment.'

'Are you still sure that he did?'

'He was there, on the *maidan*, watching the cricket. I went up to him, to make sure. It was Colin. You don't forget the face of a man you grew up with.'

'Why didn't you speak to him?'

'He turned and looked at me.'

'Yes?'

'He didn't seem to recognize me. In India, you see, all Indians look alike to English people. It was the kindest construction I could put on it. Either that, or that he had been in India long enough now to understand that it would be hopeless for a British officer to have an Indian friend who lived on the wrong side of the river and had no official standing. But whichever it was the effect was the same. To Colin I was invisible.'

'I see. And that is why when you met Vidyasagar and he invited you home you accepted?'

'Yes. For all his faults – what I thought of as his faults – I realized he had a gift.'

'What sort of gift?'

'A gift for forgiveness.' Kumar looked up at Rowan. 'They still all laughed at my ridiculous English manner – at the absurdity of it in someone born an Indian, and still an Indian, incapable of being anything in India except an Indian – but their laughing at me was meant with kindness.

That's why I got drunk. They used to get hold of home-made hooch. One of them sometimes distilled it himself. That's the sort of stuff we drank that night. They were used to it, but I wasn't. I don't remember much after they'd helped me burn my topee—'

'Burn your topee?'

'The topee was a joke to them too. They said only Anglo-Indians and Government toadies and old-fashioned sahibs wore topees. So we burned mine. Then I suppose I passed out. When I met Vidyasagar later he told me they'd taken me all the way home to my house in Chillianwallah Bagh, so that I wouldn't get picked up by the police. But after they'd left me in the compound I must have wandered out again, on to that waste ground where Sister Ludmila found me.'

Rowan nodded. He now turned to Gopal.

'You have a point or two about Kumar's questioning by the police after he was found at The Sanctuary.'

'I think perhaps it has been taken care of. I had intended to question the examinee about his apparent reluctance to answer questions when he was taken to the kotwali. The reason for that reluctance now seems quite clear. Please continue the examination along whatever lines you decide.'

'Well, let's deal with that reluctance, nevertheless. When you were questioned at the kotwali you were not at all co-operative, according to the report on this file. You admitted that your main drinking companion of the night before had been Vidyasagar, though. Is that correct?'

'Admit is the wrong word. It suggests I'd felt I had something to hide and then changed my mind.'

'How would you describe your attitude to the police at the kotwali, then?'

'As that of someone responding quite naturally to a situation that involved him in unpleasantness without any explanation.'

'It was not clear to you why you were asked to accompany the police to the kotwali?'

'It wasn't clear to me why the District Superintendent had me forcibly taken from The Sanctuary, thrown into a truck, driven to the kotwali and then pushed into a room there.'

'Was he aware that force was used?'

'He watched it.'

'Isn't it true to say, though, that you brought it on yourself by being truculent when asked to identify yourself in The Sanctuary?'

'Perhaps. It wasn't easy that morning for me to identify myself.'

'What were you doing when first approached by the police officers who visited The Sanctuary?'

'Washing.'

'Where?'

'In the compound. Under a tap.'

'Getting rid of a thick head?'

'Yes.'

'Let me read from the report: "On being asked in Urdu what his name was Kumar affected not to understand any Indian language. Mrs Ludmila Smith then said – 'Mr Kumar, these are the police. They are looking for someone. It is their duty to question anyone they find here for whom I cannot personally vouch. I cannot personally vouch for you because all I know of you is that you were found by us last night unconscious from drink.' Kumar then made a gesture of defiance. The DSP addressed him directly as follows: 'Is that your name, then – Kumar?' To which Kumar replied, 'No, but it will do.' DSP then directed his sub-inspector to escort Kumar to the police truck. No evidence being found at The Sanctuary in regard to the escaped prisoner Moti Lal, DSP proceeded to the kotwali at the Mandir Gate bridge and formally questioned the man Kumar." Is that an accurate record of the events as you remember them?'

'Broadly. I don't remember a gesture of defiance unless I shrugged. And the report omits to mention that the sub-inspector raised his hand to hit me and would have done so if Sister Ludmila hadn't objected in the strongest terms to any violence being shown by anyone in her presence, on her private property.'

'Why did you say "No, but it will do" when DSP asked if your name was Kumar?'

'He pronounced it incorrectly. There was too much stress on the last syllable. And I was still in the habit of thinking of myself as Coomer, which is how we spelt the name at home. I mean, how we spelt it in England.'

'Weren't you being unnecessarily obtuse?'

'Not unnecessarily. Merrick spoke to me as if I were a lump of dirt. I wasn't in the mood for that. I had a hangover, to begin with.'

'At The Sanctuary, then, you admit you weren't in the mood – as you put it – to answer fairly and squarely questions put to you by the police in the course of their duty?'

'The course of their duty didn't automatically give them permission to treat me like a lump of dirt. In my view.'

'When you got to the kotwali, however, you became more co-operative?'

'I answered questions as soon as Merrick explained why he'd brought me in.'

'You mean the District Superintendent.'

'To me he was always Merrick. We came to have a special personal association.'

'What do you mean?'

'It will become clear if you ask enough questions about my various interrogations.'

'At the kotwali it was explained that the police were looking for an escaped prisoner – one Moti Lal – who had lived in Mayapore and was thought possibly to have come back and gone into hiding there. It so happened that although the DSP didn't know when he took you in for questioning that you knew this man, Moti Lal, you in fact did know him, and had to admit it when questioned.'

'Again admit seems to me to be the wrong word. I'd met Moti Lal because he was once employed by Romesh Chand Gupta Sen in the office of the warehouse in the railway sidings. I also knew Moti Lal had been sacked. Romesh Chand disliked his employees being politically active. He thought all their energies should be devoted to their work. I knew that sometime after he was sacked Moti Lal was sent to prison for subversive activities. I was in the District and Sessions court when he was brought up for his appeal. I didn't know he had escaped. And I didn't know the man at all – apart from what I've just told you.'

'Didn't you know that Moti Lal had been a very popular figure among young men like Vidyasagar?'

'One couldn't help knowing. One knew of Moti Lal's popularity just as one knew of Pandit Baba's.'

'We now come to more detailed consideration of the names in group two. In group one there were Pandit Baba and Vidyasagar. In group two there are six names. The first is Moti Lal, who at the time of your arrest under suspicion of criminal assault was still apparently unapprehended as an escaped prisoner. The five other men are Narayan Lal, Nirmal Bannerjee, Bapu Ram, Puranmal Mehta and Gopi Lal. According to police records these men were all intimates of Vidyasagar's. And according to your testimony at least three of them were your drinking companions with Vidyasagar on the occasion in February after the cricket match on the *maidan*. You would in fact agree that you had some kind of relationship with all the men in the two groups – however passing a relationship you may judge it to have been?'

'Yes.'

'With the exception of Pandit Baba, these were all young men whom you would describe, more or less, as ardent nationalists who looked forward to an early end to a British controlled administration?'

'They were all young men – Indians – therefore they would almost inevitably look forward to that.'

'After the night you drank with a certain number of them, would you say that you became more directly aware of their political desires and affiliations?'

'No.'

'Did you not in fact become privy to their political activities?'

'I never assumed that they ever did more than talk politics.'

'For what purpose then would you imagine they got together?'

'To drink bad liquor and exist for a while in a state of euphoria.'

'Are you aware that a couple of days after your arrest in August nineteen forty-two Vidyasagar was arrested in the act of distributing seditious pamphlets?'

'Yes. Merrick told me. He said Vidyasagar had confessed to acts of sedition and had implicated me as the leader of a plot to attack Miss Manners.'

'What was your reaction to that?'

'I didn't believe he had implicated me.'

'But you believed he had confessed to acts of sedition?'

'It didn't surprise me. The whole of Mayapore was by then engaged in such acts – or so one gathered.'

'You insist that neither before nor after the occasion when you drank home-made hooch with Vidyasagar and his friends were you involved in any way with their political activities.'

'Yes, I insist that.'

'But you saw quite a bit of them? I mean after the night you got drunk?'

'If anything I saw less.'

'How was that?'

'I've already said. I had become friendly with Miss Manners.'

'From a time towards the end of February or the beginning of March, until August, in nineteen forty-two, your social life became more or less exclusively involved with your friendship with Miss Manners.'

'It was the first time I'd had a social life. So it did not *become* exclusively involved with that.' A pause. 'And the date is wrong. It was from February or March until towards the end of July. At the time of my arrest on August 9th I had not seen Miss Manners since the night we went to the temple. About three weeks previously.'

'So you always insisted. But let us concentrate on these men, other than Moti Lal and Vidyasagar. And of course other than Pandit Baba. That leaves us with Narayan Lal, Nirmal Bannerjee, Bapu Ram, Puranmal Mehta and Gopi Lal. You say that you knew them as among Vidyasagar's friends but that if anything you saw less of them after the night you got drunk. I want you now to tell me about the last occasion you saw them. When was that?'

'I saw them last on the night of my arrest as a suspect in the criminal assault on Miss Manners.'

'In what circumstances?'

'They had also been arrested. I was taken through the room in which they were held.'

'Taken through a room at police headquarters?'

'Yes.'

'You were taken through the room as distinct from lodged in it?'

'I was in the room for about half a minute.'

'Did you speak to them?'

'No.'

'Did they speak to you?'

'One of them said, Hello, Hari.'

'You didn't reply?'

'No.'

'Why?'

'They were behind the bars of a cell in the room.'

'What was their demeanour?'

'They were laughing and joking.'

'And you were not?'

'No. I was not.'

'What happened then?'

'I was handed over by the two policemen who held me to two other policemen and taken to a room downstairs.'

'So you saw those five men in a cell on the night of August the ninth and recognized them all?'

'I recognized about three of them in the sense of being able to put a name to the face.'

'All the faces were familiar as men you knew but you didn't immediately recall all their names.'

'That is right.'

'You remembered all the names later?'

'No.'

'Please elucidate.'

'I was told the names.'

'By whom?'

'By District Superintendent Merrick.'

'Your memory is clear on that point, that District Superintendent Merrick told you the names of the men in the cell?'

'Yes.'

'He read out a list of names?'

'Yes.'

'And asked you whether you were acquainted with the men?'

'No.'

'No? What then?'

'He read out the list of names. Then he made a statement.'

'What was the statement?'

'He said: These men are all friends of yours and as you saw we have them under lock and key.'

'What did you say?'

'I said nothing.'

'Why?'

'It wasn't a question.'

'On reconsideration would you not agree with a statement to the effect that "when asked whether he knew the five other men in custody and with whom he had been confronted the prisoner refused to answer"?'

'No.'

'Would you not agree with the following statement? Upon being told dates and times and circumstances when he had been seen in the company of one or several of the other prisoners the prisoner Kumar refused any comment beyond the words: I have nothing to say.'

'Yes. I would agree with that.'

583

'Why did you have nothing to say?'

'I refused to comment on any statement because I didn't know what I was being charged with.'

'When did you ask what you were being charged with?'

'When I was taken into custody.'

'At number 12 Chillianwallah Bagh?'

'Yes.'

'Not at police headquarters?'

'I asked first in my room at 12 Chillianwallah Bagh. I asked again at police headquarters. I asked several times.'

'When were you first told?'

'After I'd been in custody for about an hour.'

Gopal suddenly interrupted. 'Please recollect carefully. Would it not be more accurate to say something to this effect': He glanced at his file and read out: 'At 22.45 hours the prisoner Kumar, having continually refused to answer questions relating to his activities that evening asked for what reason he had been taken into custody. Upon being told it was believed he could help the police with inquiries they were making into the criminal assault on an Englishwoman in the Bibighar Gardens earlier that evening he said: I have not seen Miss Manners since the night we visited the temple. On being asked why he named Miss Manners he refused to answer and showed signs of distress.'

'No,' Kumar said, 'it would not be more accurate.'

'In what way is that statement inaccurate in your view?' Gopal asked.

'I may have asked at 22.45 hours why I was taken into custody but it wouldn't have been for the first time. I asked several times. It was probably at 22.45 hours when the District Superintendent finally told me. But it didn't happen in the way it's written down there. He said he was making inquiries about an Englishwoman who was missing. His words were: "An Englishwoman, you know which one." He then made an obscene remark.'

'Let us be quite clear,' Gopal continued. 'According to you the investigating officer did not say "We believe you can help us with inquiries we're making into the criminal assault on an Englishwoman in the Bibighar Gardens" – to which you replied "I haven't seen Miss Manners since the night we visited the temple".'

'No. It wasn't like that. He made the obscene remark and followed it with another.'

'Are you saying it was from these remarks that you gathered who the Englishwoman was and what had happened to her?'

'I'm not saying what I gathered, only what was said to me.'

'Are you saying that what was said to you accounted for what is described as your distress?'

'I don't know what he meant by distress.'

Gopal said: 'Then how would *you* describe your demeanour at this stage of your interview at police headquarters?'

584

Kumar looked down at the table. Presently he said, 'I was shivering. It would have been noticeable.'

'Shivering?'

'The interview was in a private room in the basement. It was air-conditioned.'

'This room is air-conditioned. You are not shivering now, are you?'

'No.'

'Why were you shivering on that occasion?'

'I had no clothes on. I had had no clothes on for nearly an hour.'

'No clothes?' Gopal asked. 'You were asked questions by a police officer in a state of undress?'

She was observing the hollow-cheeked face intently. A tremor passed over it. It might have been a smile.

'The police officer who asked the questions was fully dressed,' Kumar said. 'But I was naked.'

'That is what I said,' Gopal snapped. 'Why were you naked?'

'I had been stripped. My clothes were piled on the table.'

'I meant for what purpose were you stripped?'

'Originally for inspection I believe.'

'A physical examination?'

'Inspection would be more accurate. There was no doctor present.'

'Gopal said, 'No doctor? Then who carried out the examination?'

'The District Superintendent.'

Gopal hesitated, then said, 'What kind of examination was it?'

'An inspection of my genitals. Doesn't it say so in the reports? He inspected my genitals for signs of blood.'

'Did he tell you that?'

'No. But it was obvious.'

'How?'

'When he'd finished he said: "So you've been intelligent enough to wash, we almost caught you at it, didn't we?" Later he said: "Well, she wasn't a virgin, was she, and you were the first to ram her?" So it was obvious the inquiry was about a woman who'd been assaulted.'

Captain Rowan interrupted: 'All this is, in a sense, irrelevant to the purpose of the inquiry. I should like to return to the main line of questioning,' but Gopal shook his head and said:

'All this is most important. It has a direct bearing on the detenu's statement that he was not immediately informed of the reason for being in custody and a direct bearing on the question of his distress as recorded. The impression I am getting here is that the physical examination and the references to other physical matters occurred before 22.45 hours. Hitherto the official suggestion has been that until then questions were asked in an ordinary line of interrogation and not answered and then at 22.45 hours the detenu was told the reason for the inquiries, appeared to incriminate himself by naming the woman and then showed signs of distress.'

'Perhaps,' Captain Rowan began, but she had pressed the button under the chair arm. The green light flicked on. Captain Rowan lifted his receiver as she lifted hers.

'Hello: Rowan here—'

'I have a question to ask – and something to say—'

'Oh, yes.'

'Does Mr Gopal know I'm listening? He glanced up at the grille when he came into the room.'

Rowan waited before replying, as if his caller had asked a longer question.

'The answer to that – the official answer – is no. But in that particular case I'm not sure. I'm in the middle of an examination. Is it urgent?'

'What I wanted to say is forget that I am here. You have your job to do. I don't want you to worry about trying to spare me from hearing unpleasant things.'

'Very well. I'll attend to it.'

'One other thing—'

'Yes?'

'Does Mr Kumar know that my niece is dead?'

'I'm not sure.'

'I should like to be sure.'

'Very well, and thank you. Goodbye.'

For a while after he put the telephone back on its rest no sound came through the speaker other than the slight rustle of paper. Then he spoke.

'Since we've had an interruption I think this is a suitable moment to break the examination off for five minutes.' He slapped the file shut. 'Babuji – tell the guard to hold the prisoner outside.'

The clerk got up and went to the door through which Kumar had entered, opened it and spoke to the guard. Kumar glanced round. His movements suggested that he had not clearly understood what Rowan said.

'We shall call you back,' Rowan told him. Kumar stood up.

'In about five minutes we shall continue the examination.'

It was extraordinary, she thought. When he stood he gave the appearance of a shambling man – one who might not be expected to think clearly or speak precisely. He ducked his head, then turned. The guard had appeared and now accompanied him out. The clerk also went out – closing the door behind him, leaving Rowan and Gopal alone.

Rowan said, 'Let's use these few minutes to consider really what our terms of reference are. If I may say so these questions about his interrogation by District Superintendent Merrick in regard to the criminal assault tend to lead away from the main point about his association with a group of fellows who were clearly politically committed and politically involved—'

'I'm sorry to disagree with you, Captain Rowan. Perhaps I have had less time than you to study the files of this curious case, and it is most unusual for a detenu to be examined, in fact I have never come across it before,

586

neither has my superior. I have assumed that since His Excellency personally ordered the examination some serious doubt has arisen about the order for detention. From my reading of the files – coupled with my recollections of the actual circumstances – I feel that the order rested entirely on the original suspicion this young man was under in regard to the criminal assault. For that reason I feel that the criminal assault aspect should now become the focus for our questions. It would have been useful if you had agreed to a previous consultation, but my clerk told me you were unable to find the time.'

'Well let me put it to you that the man was never charged with criminal assault although I agree the assault was the original cause of his arrest. He seems on the other hand to have been known to the police as a man to keep an eye on over anti-government activities of a seditious nature—'

'– on the frailest evidence, in my opinion—'

'Well, that's really what we're out to examine. I think the situation here is that at the *time* of his detention the circumstantial evidence of his implication in the assault was so strong that neither the Deputy Commissioner nor the Commissioner felt it reasonable to set him free—'

'– and used this ridiculous evidence of a connection with subversive elements as an excuse to imprison him without trial.'

'One has to consider the affair in the context of the time and circumstances. If the detention order was unjustly made we have the opportunity of seeing that now in clearer perspective. What we're not out to do is apportion blame among the several authorities who had the difficult job of investigating at the time. I am strongly against a line of questioning that can help the man to level accusations against particular officials. It will only confuse the issue from H.E.'s point of view. Kumar isn't under oath and the officials aren't here to answer. The man himself has never petitioned against the order and there's some cause to think he may have counted himself extremely lucky to get away with simple political detention.'

'Who has petitioned, then?'

'No one. No one can except the man in question.'

'Then why has H.E. suddenly ordered an examination?'

'I think chiefly as a result of private pleas – for instance by his relative – his aunt, Shalini Gupta Sen.'

'And perhaps by the late Miss Manners's aunt – Lady Manners? She, surely, must eventually have learned the truth?'

'That I wouldn't know,' Rowan said.

'I thought perhaps new evidence had come up and that the examination might be a preliminary to other proceedings.'

'Not to my knowledge.'

'Are the other five men to be examined?'

'I have no instructions. And their cases were different. They denied the criminal assault but never denied subversive political activity, even if they denied being engaged in such activities on the night in question which they said they'd spent drinking in a hut on some waste ground close to the Bibighar.'

'But Kumar did deny subversive activity—'

'According to the file his answer to every question was: "I have nothing to say".'

'It is somewhat different this morning, isn't it?'

'This morning he is not under suspicion of criminal assault. Which brings me back to the point. In my opinion the line of questioning should be confined as nearly as possible to facts bearing on the ostensible reasons for his *detention* – detention as distinct from arrest. The criminal assault is a dead file. The girl herself is dead. If she was intent on protecting him – for emotional reasons, as was thought at the time – we shall never know. A line of questioning that concentrates on facts relating to the assault and on the details of his arrest on suspicion of being guilty of rape can only be abortive, I believe.'

'I disagree. If there had been no rape he would never have been arrested. It is clear he was arrested only because he was known to consort with her. It has always been clear, Captain Rowan, if you will forgive my saying so, that Kumar was victimized by the British authorities in Mayapore for his association with a white girl. It is common knowledge.'

'Common knowledge isn't evidence. We must base our inquiries on the evidence in this file.'

'The evidence is worthless to a large extent, Captain Rowan. You have only to read it to see it is all too – what is the word you use?'

'Pat?'

'All too pat. Rigged. The girl knew what would happen. The record of her private examination before the District Judge and the Assistant Commissioner makes it perfectly clear that the case could never have come to trial with the six men who'd been arrested because one minute of her evidence in the witness-box would have killed the case for the prosecution stone dead. She remembered her attackers as men of the badmash-type – men who'd probably come in from the villages because of the rumours of riot and the prospect of loot.'

'Perhaps, but I think the prosecution might have built a lot on her *first* statement to the Assistant Commissioner, that it had been too dark to see who they were. It's clear to me that the case never came to trial for two reasons – firstly that the evidence against the arrested men was wholly circumstantial and secondly that the girl – presumably for emotional reasons – was obviously prepared – even to the extent of perjury – to explode the case in everyone's face if they attempted to bring it into court. As you will have read in the file, she even threatened to suggest her attackers could have been British soldiers with their faces blacked. It was never a serious suggestion but you can imagine what effect her making it, even as a joke, would have had on a jury. She could never have killed the case for the prosecution but with the chief witness working against the prosecution it's most likely that their case could have been proved.'

'And so the men would have gone free, Captain Rowan. The detention orders were made to ensure that never happened. The whole thing stank, Captain Rowan. You know it, I know it. H.E. knows it. That young man was as much a threat to the defence of India as I am. His only crime was to have been the friend of a white girl who got raped by a gang of hooligans or looters. What can we possibly turn up now that will shed any positive light at all on his political ideas and activities? The evidence on this file that attempts to point to political affiliations is laughable. I hardly see how one can even begin to frame viable questions from it. I will say frankly, Captain Rowan, that if we are to put this poor fellow through this examination we must give him every chance to tell us exactly what happened and not bother our heads about what it will look like on paper or what muck might be raked. I did not ask to be appointed one of his examiners, but since I am one I intend to examine and not be blinkered by any narrow interpretations of terms of reference that leave the record not worth the paper it's written on. Frankly I do not care anything about confusing H.E. with details about the assault. Once the examination is over we are both personally powerless to take any step or press for any step we think is justified. I shan't be surprised if the record simply goes on file and is conveniently forgotten and that poor fellow who may be having his hopes raised has them dashed again. But we are not powerless to pave the way for a justified step to be taken. Forgive me. I am perhaps overheated.'

As if by an association of ideas Gopal lifted the tumbler from one of the carafes and poured himself a glass of water. He sipped it delicately, then patted his lips with a folded handkerchief from his breast pocket.

'Very well, but if it's H.E.'s intention to review the detention order an examination that weighs heavily on the side of questions relating to the criminal assault may have a contrary effect. He may throw the record out as irrelevant. And of course you do realize that the examination might give grounds for renewed suspicion that the assault was an aspect of subversive activities plotted and executed by Kumar and others? You speak as if there was no evidence implicating Kumar in the rape. He was absent from home at the relevant time, never accounted for his movements and was bathing cuts and abrasions on his face when the police arrested him.'

'So the police record states. The first police report – the one signed by a sub-inspector – also mentioned that the girl's bicycle was found in the ditch outside Kumar's home. The second report, by the District Superintendent, dated one or two days later, states that this was an error and that the bicycle was found at the scene of the rape, in the Bibighar Gardens, and put in the back of the truck before the visit to Kumar's home. Which smells to me like an abortive attempt to plant evidence which the District Superintendent later realized wasn't going to wash. I personally have no faith whatsoever in the statements to the effect that Kumar was bathing his face when arrested. If Kumar's face was cut and bruised it was just as likely because the police hit him.'

'Then why didn't he say so? He was examined by the Assistant

589

Commissioner, and by a magistrate appointed by Judge Menen, as well as by the District Superintendent.'

'Who would have believed him? He had listened to innumerable criminal cases in the courts as a reporter for the *Mayapore Gazette* and knew what he was up against. He is an intelligent man – a product of your own English public schools.'

'I know. I went to the same one.'

Gopal stared at Rowan – as if suddenly suspicious.

'Oh? Does he recognize you then?'

'No. I was in my last term when he was in his first. But I remember him. He was the first Indian Chillingborough ever took, a bit of a showpiece. A few years later I watched him play cricket for the school against the old boys. He was very popular. I have a vague recollection of his friend Colin, too.' Rowan poured a glass of water also. 'It's one of the reasons H.E. chose me to make the examination. Until the other day I'd no idea the chief suspect in the Bibighar case was the fellow I knew as Harry Coomer. I wish I'd known years ago what he was having to face. There must have been several old Chillingburians out here who'd have been willing to help him.'

After a while Mr Gopal said, 'Do you think so, Captain Rowan? Willing, perhaps. Able – no. He is an English boy with a dark brown skin. The combination is hopeless.'

'Yes,' Rowan said after a while. 'Perhaps it is.'

II

'The examinee's last statement, please.'

The clerk flicked back one page of his notebook.

' "So it was obvious the inquiry was about a woman who'd been assaulted." '

'No – the whole of it.'

The clerk cleared his throat and recited in a monotone, ' "When he'd finished he said – So you've been intelligent enough to wash, we almost caught you at it, didn't we? Later he said: Well, she wasn't a virgin, was she, and you were the first to ram her? So it was obvious the inquiry was about a woman who'd been assaulted." '

'Thank you. Mr Gopal – you were making a point.'

'Yes. It is really a question of the order and time at which the detenu alleges certain things were done and certain things said.' Gopal now spoke directly to Kumar. 'I should like to go back to the moment when the police came to your house and took you into custody. According to the police report this was at approximately 21.40 hours. Is that correct?'

'I expect so.'

'I see – also from the report – that some three-quarters of an hour earlier the DSP called at your home to see if Miss Manners happened to be there. He spoke to your aunt. She said she had not seen Miss Manners for several

590

weeks. She said you had not yet returned from the newspaper office. Is that correct?'

'Yes.'

'Later when you came in she told you of DSP's visit and inquiry?'

'Yes.'

'At what time did you get home?'

'I didn't think to look.'

'Did your aunt not say something like, The DSP came here asking if Miss Manners was with us, because Lady Chatterjee has reported her missing?'

'She said the DSP had called wanting to speak to Miss Manners.'

'And you then asked how long ago?'

'Yes – I did. But she didn't reply.'

'Oh? Why was that?'

'Her attention was taken.'

'Taken by what?'

'She had noticed the state I was in.'

She sensed the little wave of Gopal's shock. Rowan's voice cut in, 'According to the police report that state was as follows: "An abrasion on his right cheek and a contusion on his left cheek, stains on shirt and trousers from contact with muddy ground or dirty floor." Is that an accurate report?'

'Yes.'

'Is it also correct,' Rowan continued, 'that when the police, led by District Superintendent Merrick, entered a room on the first floor of number 12 Chillianwallah Bagh, the shirt and trousers in which you'd come home were found discarded, that you were wearing a clean pair of trousers, no other garment, and were bathing your face in a bowl of water?'

'Yes.'

'After reaching home and speaking briefly to your aunt who told you DSP had called looking for Miss Manners you went upstairs, changed and began to wash.'

'Yes.'

'You were still washing when the police arrived, so you can't have been back home for longer than, say, ten minutes?'

'It would have been about that.'

'So if the police arrived at 21.40 you reached home about 21.30?'

'Yes.'

'According to the statement of Mr Laxminarayan, the editor of the *Mayapore Gazette*, you left the office of the *Gazette*, which was in the Victoria Road in the Civil lines, at approximately six-fifteen that evening.'

'Yes.'

'During interrogation, whenever you were asked to account for your movements between 6.15 and 9.40 p.m. your invariable reply was: "I have nothing to say." Do you have anything to say now?'

Kumar glanced down at the table. Gopal suddenly came to life. 'I have a point here,' he said. Rowan nodded. 'This contusion on the detenu's left cheek. There is a copy on this file of the medical report made out when the detenu was admitted to this prison. It was dated August 25th. It referred to traces of contusion still being visible on the face. Still visible, that is to say, after sixteen days. Unless further bruising was inflicted one might assume that the original blow or blows were therefore of considerable strength. Of course, it was never established what caused the contusion, but in the absence of any explanation by the detenu the impression the police reports seemed to leave was never counteracted. That impression was that the bruising was the result of blows by a woman defending herself from attack.' Gopal took out his handkerchief again, dabbled his lips. 'It is a point which a court of law might well have subjected to deeper considera-tion – the extent to which the contusion suffered could have been caused by a member of the female sex. I make the point in case it encourages the detenu to say what he was doing that led to his return home in the state described.'

'You have heard Mr Gopal's point. Are you prepared to comment on it?'

'I'm prepared to comment on it.'

Gopal nodded. 'Please do so.'

'It is a good point. I appreciate it being raised. I don't think it would have helped me in a court of law, if things had come to that.'

'Why?' Gopal wanted to know.

'Expert medical evidence would probably have held that a frightened woman can hit as hard as a man. But even if that had been expertly refuted the prosecution could have turned the point to my disadvantage.'

'How?'

'By suggesting that the men who assaulted Miss Manners fought among themselves.'

'Is that what happened?' Rowan asked casually.

Kumar stared at him. 'I have no idea.'

'Are you prepared to say where you were between 6.15 and 9.30 p.m. on the night in question?'

Kumar glanced at the table, then back at Rowan.

'No. I'm sorry. But I'm not.'

Rowan leaned back in his chair. Watching, she became aware – as though she sat at it herself – of the expanse of table-top that separated the interrogators from the interrogated. It was an area of suspicion that none of them apparently had the capacity to diminish – although Rowan was now attempting to do so.

'I find it difficult to understand,' he had begun. 'So far this morning you have been extremely co-operative. The impression you have made is of frankness and candour. Now suddenly you revert to that unhelpful attitude of "I have nothing to say" which nullified every attempt made at the time to allow you to state a case. I use the word unhelpful advisedly. It does not help us and it certainly doesn't help you. The purpose of this examination is to go over evidence which at the time seemed strong enough to warrant your detention. It may or may not be so that at the time other considerations – well let us call them suspicions – coloured the views of those whose responsibility it was, at a moment of acute crisis resulting from civil disorder, to weigh the evidence in regard to that detention. Such suspicions do not enter into what is being considered this morning. I hope that has become clear as the examination has gone forward. These suspicions do not enter into the question of what is being considered, but if the record suddenly disclosed a lack of candour that today might be called uncharacteristic you must see how that would allow room for suspicion once again to enter into the weighing of all the various considerations.'

'Yes,' Kumar said. 'I see that. But the suspicion is unavoidable. However hard you try to avoid questioning me about the criminal assault you'll find everything leads to it. And every time the question of the assault comes up the suspicion comes up too.'

'Well, need it? It's come up now, certainly. Perhaps it could be eradicated by your answering the question. I wonder if you realize how foolish your original refusal to answer was? I wonder if you realize how very close you were to being charged? Or if you realize the extent to which that charge – rather, I should say, the failure of the charge to be made – depended almost exclusively on Miss Manners's vigorous rebuttal of any suggestion that you were involved in any way whatever? If she had shown the slightest uncertainty, if she had – however reluctantly – admitted that in all fairness she could not actually swear you weren't among those who attacked her, in the dark, suddenly, then you would have been charged and tried. I put it to you, if you had been charged and tried, in court, been put on oath, would you in those circumstances have refused to answer this question?'

'I should have refused.'

'In court that refusal could have been fatal.'

'I know.'

'Have you truly and deeply considered the reasonableness of this attitude?'

'I have truly and deeply considered the attitude. I have considered it daily, since the night of August the ninth, nineteen forty-two. For one year, nine months and twelve days.'

'And you still find it reasonable?'

'I have never said it was reasonable. It has never been a question of reason. It isn't now.'

'A question of loyalty, perhaps?'

'It's not a word I much care for.'

'Care for it or not, it gets us a bit further? Can we go a bit further still and establish to what or to whom you felt you were being loyal by maintaining what looked to everyone else like an unreasonable silence?'

'I'm afraid we can't go further. At least, not in the same direction.'

Rowan leaned forward again, and referred to his file. Eventually he spoke. 'Only two things of interest to the police seem to have been found in your room. A photograph of Miss Manners and the letter from Colin. The photograph was self-explanatory. She had given it to you. The letter from

Colin is interesting though because – by your own evidence today – you had other letters from him. In fact I imagine that you heard quite often from him – at least until he came to India.'

'Yes.'

'I wondered why of all those letters you kept this particular one. It was an unfortunate choice because it was the one in which Colin told you two of your letters were opened by his father and not forwarded because his father thought them unsuitable reading for a young officer away on active service. The phrase "a lot of hot-headed political stuff" was the way he said his father described those letters. Why did you keep this particular letter from Colin?'

'It was the only one I ever had from him that really struck an authentic note. He went through various phases after he left school. But that one was from the man I remembered.'

'What sort of man was that?'

'The sort that found the liberal atmosphere of Chillingborough the right kind of atmosphere.'

'You would call Chillingborough a liberal institution?'

'It wasn't a flag-wagging place. It turned out more administrators than it did soldiers.'

She smiled and wondered if Rowan smiled too to be reminded so unexpectedly of his own words – 'I wasn't cast in the mould of a good regimental officer.'

'But for a time after leaving school,' Rowan said, 'your friend Colin became what you call a flag-wagger?'

'He was infected by the atmosphere of 1939, I think. He joined the Territorial Army, and wrote of nothing else.'

'The letter which you kept was one he wrote after he'd been wounded at Dunkirk, I gather?'

'Yes.'

'His baptism of fire had an effect on him which you approved of?'

'The effect of making him sound like the friend I knew.'

'And what was the hot-headed political stuff his father objected to in your letters?'

'It must have been mainly what I wrote about the pros and cons of Congress's resistance to the declaration of war, and their resignations from the provincial ministries.'

'And what were your views on that?'

'I think it was to find out if I had any that I wrote to Colin about the pros and cons.'

'You would write that kind of thing to Colin. Would you discuss it with Vidyasagar?'

'No.'

'In spite of the distance between you, Colin remained your closest friend, your confidant?'

'In my mind he did.'

594

'It was a way of maintaining contact with – what shall we call it – your inner sense of being English?'

'Yes.'

Rowan sat for a while without speaking. Then abruptly he said: 'Have we been discussing in any way the question you said we couldn't explore further in the same direction?'

'We've been discussing it.'

'But not exploring it further?'

'But not exploring it.'

'So we are back to the moment when you were found by the police bathing your face?'

'Yes.'

'With this vital period between 6.15 and 9.30 p.m. unaccounted for?'

'Yes.'

'If you had been with Miss Manners that evening, where would you have been likely to meet?'

'The most likely place would have been The Sanctuary.'

'Why?'

'Apart from caring for the sick and dying, Sister Ludmila ran a free evening clinic. Miss Manners helped fairly regularly in the clinic in her spare time from the Mayapore General Hospital.'

'You both found The Sanctuary a suitable place to meet?'

'We were both interested in the work Sister Ludmila did.'

'Is that the frankest reply you can give me?'

'No. Let's say that The Sanctuary was one of the few places in the whole of Mayapore where we could meet and talk and not attract abusive attention.'

'Abusive attention?'

'The attention paid by Europeans to the sight of a white girl in an Indian's company.'

'Apart from these meetings at The Sanctuary you also visited one another's houses?'

'Occasionally.'

'Where else did you spend time together?'

A pause.

'Sometimes, on a Sunday for instance, we went to the Bibighar Gardens.'

'I gather from the descriptions in the file that these Gardens consist of a comparatively small, wild, overgrown area – the site of the old garden surrounding a building once known as the Bibighar – a building no longer in existence but where an open-sided pavilion or shelter has been erected on part of the old foundations.'

'Yes. It was a quiet and pleasant place to talk.'

'During the daytime—'

'During daylight.'

'You never went there together except in daylight?'

'Never.'

'Because of the old stories about it being haunted?'

'Because it was hardly a suitable place to go to at night.'

'How many people knew that you used to go to the Bibighar?'

'No one, so far as I know.'

'You were always alone there?'

'We once frightened some children playing there. Indian children.'

'How?'

'They thought we were ghosts I expect.'

'Daylight ghosts?'

'Yes.'

'It was usually quite deserted even in daylight?'

'It was the place only Indians went to – but it was on the civil lines side of the river. I think Indians went there for picnics in the dry, cooler weather.'

'How many people other than Sister Ludmila and her staff knew you and Miss Manners used to meet at The Sanctuary?'

'Not many I think.'

'She mentioned The Sanctuary and her interest in it to District Superintendent Merrick, though?'

'She must have done.'

'Why must have done?'

'On the night she was missing he called there.'

'How do you know that?'

'He told me so himself – during my interrogation. He said he called at The Sanctuary because he remembered Miss Manners saying something about the place. I expect he made particular note of it because it was the same place he'd found me the previous February.'

'Did he tell you what he discovered when he called at The Sanctuary looking for Miss Manners?'

'He said Sister Ludmila admitted Miss Manners had been there but had left just as it got dark. So then he called at my house and spoke to my aunt.'

'Because Sister Ludmila told him that you and Miss Manners had often been at The Sanctuary together?'

'Perhaps. He would have called at my house anyway.'

'He was well acquainted with the fact that you and Miss Manners were friends?'

'Of course.'

'You have said that occasionally you visited Miss Manners at the MacGregor House. Did you ever meet Mr Merrick there?'

'No. She kept us well apart.'

'Kept you apart? Because of what had happened between you and Mr Merrick when he took you in for questioning that first time?'

'She didn't know until much later that Merrick had been personally involved in that. She kept us apart because she assumed in any case Mr Merrick wouldn't approve of our friendship.'

'I'm not sure why you use this expression – keeping apart.'

'He became a personal friend of Miss Manners too.'

'I see. You say became. You mean he became friendly with her after you and she had already established a friendly association.'

'Yes. He was on the *maidan* during the War Week Exhibition and saw her leave her English friends and come up and speak to me. Until then, so far as I know, he'd never taken any notice of her. After that he started inviting her out.'

'If his interview with you after your drinking bout left him under the strong impression that you were a man on whom the police should keep an eye – as seems to have been the case – it would follow, I think, that directly he saw you and Miss Manners were on friendly terms he would feel it his duty to try to protect her from what in his view was an undesirable association?'

'Yes, that could follow. It's a very reasonable explanation.'

'Did he in fact ever say anything to her about her association with you?'

'Yes.'

'She told you this?'

'Yes. It came up when I took her home after we'd visited the Tirupati temple.'

'She told you Mr Merrick disapproved of her going out with you?'

'She said Merrick's view was that I was a bad bet.'

'What was your reaction to that?'

'I said that Merrick should know if I was a bad bet or not.'

'Were you quarrelling?'

'Yes.'

'Why? Over something that happened at the temple?'

'Why do people who have grown fond of each other quarrel? I was in an over-sensitive mood. We both were. I realized what a ridiculous figure I made and what a lot of time she was wasting on me. She accused me of acting in a way calculated to put her off, which was true. That's when she told me Merrick said I was a bad bet. I told her he should know. I thought she always understood that Merrick was personally involved in that trouble I'd been in. It turned out she didn't. It made her feel she'd been made a fool of – unwittingly going out with Merrick as well as me. We parted on not very good terms.'

'But later you made it up?'

A pause.

'You're forgetting. We'd just come from the temple. I haven't seen Miss Manners since the night we visited the temple.'

'What night was that?'

'A Saturday. Three weeks before the night I was arrested under suspicion of assaulting her with five other men.'

Rowan leaned back again and turned to Gopal. 'I think we're now back to the question of the order and time at which he alleged certain things were done and certain things said. You were anxious to clarify that. Perhaps you would like to ask the questions.'

'Thank you.'

Gopal sipped water while reading a note on his file. Then he put the glass down, again dabbed his lips with the folded handkerchief. 'You were taken from 12 Chillianwallah Bagh at approximately 21.45, by truck to police headquarters in the Civil lines. You were held for perhaps a minute or less in a room where you saw five men whose faces you recognized even if you couldn't immediately recall all their names. You were then taken to a room downstairs. Up until this time, you allege, you were not told the reason for your removal from your home to police headquarters?'

'I wasn't told.'

'At 12 Chillianwallah Bagh the police entered the room and appre-hended you without saying anything?'

'Things were said, but not about the reason for the arrest.'

'What sort of things were said? Can you recall, for instance, the police officer's first words to you?'

'He didn't speak for a while.'

'What then did he do?'

'He stood and smiled at me.'

'Smiled?'

'I also noticed a nervous tic develop on his right cheek.'

'A smile and a nervous tic.'

'Then he pointed at the clothes lying on the floor and asked me if I'd just taken them off. I told him I had. He told me to put them on again. I asked him why. He said – Because you're coming with me. We're going to have another of our chats.'

'Did you obey immediately?'

'Not immediately. I asked him what we were going to have a chat about. He said I would find out. Then he asked if I would dress myself or prefer to be dressed forcibly. There were several constables with him, so I changed back into the clothes I'd taken off. Then I went downstairs with two constables holding my wrists behind my back. My aunt was being held in the living-room. I could hear her calling out to me. I wasn't allowed to see or speak to her. I was put into the back of a truck and driven to police headquarters.'

'Where you saw the five other men who had been arrested, one of whom said, "Hello, Hari" – a greeting which you did not return because unlike these other five you were not feeling like laughing and joking. When you saw these men, saw them behind bars – what conclusion did you reach?'

'Conclusion?'

'You saw they had been arrested, as you had been. What did you think they'd been arrested for?'

'I assumed they'd been caught drinking their home-made liquor.'

'Their demeanour was commensurate with that of boys who had broken a minor law and were still under the influence of liquor?'

'Yes.'

'And what was going through your mind about the possible causes of your own arrest?'

'I felt it could only have something to do with Miss Manners.'

'Why?'

'Because Merrick had been at my house earlier asking for her. People were very edgy that night. A European woman had been attacked out in a place called Tanpur while trying to protect an Indian teacher from her mission. The man had been murdered and she had been knocked about. Some of the country police had been locked in their own stations by roving mobs. Telegraph wires were down and people were talking about a new Mutiny. As you know, there'd been a lot of arrests early that morning from Gandhi all down the line. For instance Mr Srinivasan had been arrested – as a leading member of the Local Congress Party sub-committee. I knew I couldn't be arrested for any political reason, but it seemed likely I'd be the first to get arrested if the police thought something had happened to Miss Manners.'

'So really your arrest was not such a puzzle to you, you are saying?'

'I'm merely telling you what was passing through my mind. I'm answering the question. I'm telling you that and stating again that I was in custody for a long time before the District Superintendent actually accused me of criminal assault. Once he'd done that I realized from other things he'd said and asked me that the five men upstairs were supposed to have been my accomplices in that assault.'

'Very well. Let us come to the moment when you were taken downstairs. What was the first thing that happened?'

'I was ordered to strip.'

'Who gave the order?'

'The District Superintendent.'

'In this room there were yourself, the District Superintendent and two constables?'

'At this stage, yes.'

'When you were stripped the DSP then inspected you as you have previously described?'

'When I was stripped the two constables held me with my arms behind my back, in front of Merrick's desk. Merrick sat on the desk and poured himself a glass of whisky. Then he just sat and smiled at me until he'd drunk it. He took about five minutes to drink it. After that he stood up, carried out the inspection and said, "So you've been clever enough to wash, we nearly caught you at it, didn't we?" I asked him why I'd been brought in. He said I'd find out. He said we had plenty of time. He told me to relax because we had a lot to talk about. He then ordered the constables to manacle my wrists behind me. When they'd done that he sent them out of the room.' Kumar paused. 'Then he began to talk to me.'

'You mean, to question you?'

'No. It was talking mostly. Every so often he put in a question.'

'What you describe as talking mostly' – Gopal said – 'what kind of talking?'

'He talked about the history of the British in India. And about his own history. About his ideas. About his views of India's future and England's future. And his future. And mine.'

Gopal appeared to be nonplussed. He hesitated before saying, 'Why should he talk about such things? You are remembering accurately? The impression one has been getting is that District Superintendent exerted himself a great deal first to find Miss Manners and then to bring her attackers to book. Now you are saying he sat and talked to you about such irrelevancies.'

'They weren't irrelevancies to him.'

'You are saying that to talk to you about the history of the British in India was just as important at that moment to District Superintendent as to question you about your movements that evening?'

'Neither talking nor questioning was of paramount importance to him.'

'Not of paramount importance? What are you suggesting was?'

'The situation.'

Gopal looked at Rowan and asked, 'What is he talking about? I don't understand him.'

Kumar answered before Rowan had a chance to speak.

'It was a question of extracting everything possible from the situation while it lasted.'

'The situation?'

'Yes.'

'But *what* situation?'

'The situation of our being face to face, with everything finally in his favour.'

'Finally? You are suggesting he anticipated this face-to-face situation?'

'Yes. That almost goes without saying.'

'Are you claiming – are you claiming that he was a rival for the friendly attention of Miss Manners and had therefore looked forward to a situation which would place you – at disadvantage? Is this what you allege? You claim that an aspect to be considered is that of jealousy?'

Kumar hesitated. 'That would be an over-simplification. And there'd then be the question, jealousy of what kind, and jealousy of whom?'

'I cannot follow these arguments. Let us leave the matter of what you allege he talked about and consider the questions you allege he occasionally put in. Perhaps those will be easier to understand. Can you remember any of those questions?'

'Broadly.'

'Then say what you remember broadly.'

'They were such questions as: Those fellows up there admire you a lot, don't they? They'd do anything you say. Who marked your face? Why didn't you go to The Sanctuary tonight? Who's Colin? She wasn't a virgin, was she, and you were the first to ram her, weren't you?'

'Did you reply to any of those questions?'

'I told him if he wanted answers he first had to tell me why I'd been brought in.'

'And these questions were interpolated, you are saying, into his talk on other matters?'

'Yes.'

'For instance he would be talking about the future of the British in India and would suddenly say, Who is Colin?'

'Yes.'

'And always you replied as you have described?'

'Not always. Some of the questions I treated as rhetorical.'

'But you said, more than once, that you would only answer questions if he told you why you were in custody?'

'Yes.'

'Gradually, however, you suggest, you got a clear impression that you and the others upstairs were suspected of criminal assault on a lady?'

'Yes.'

'And did you at the same time suspect that this lady was Miss Manners?'

'Yes.'

'Did you not ask?'

'No.'

'You were a close friend of Miss Manners. You knew the police had been looking for her, you knew of the troubles in the district, you guessed a woman had been assaulted and realized that this woman might be your friend Miss Manners, but you did not say, "Has something happened to Miss Manners?"'

'No.'

'Why?'

'I realized that's what he was waiting for me to do. I think it was a basic aspect of the situation.'

'Let us forget what you call the situation.'

'It's impossible for me to forget the situation. It had a very special intensity.'

Rowan spoke, taking advantage of Gopal's hesitation.

'I think we should do better to leave any inner significance the situation may have had for both DSP and the prisoner and concentrate on the form and order of the interrogation. If there was an inner significance it might even become clear to us what it was if we confine ourselves rigorously to the outer forms.'

'It is what I have been trying to do,' Gopal said. He rustled his papers; eventually spoke again to Kumar.

'There came a point when according to your previous testimony DSP said that he was making inquiries about an Englishwoman who was missing, and added "You know which one", and followed this with what you call an obscene remark. What was that remark?'

'I prefer not to say.'

'What did you understand from it?'

'That he was definitely referring to Miss Manners and to the fact that she'd been assaulted by more than one man, all Indians.'

601

'And it was at this point that you said you hadn't seen Miss Manners since the time you visited the temple?'

'Yes.'

'In that case I'm afraid I must press you to repeat the obscene remark. I must press you because without it your refutation of the official statement – that you yourself were the first to mention Miss Manners – is incomplete.'

'I'm sorry. I still prefer not to say.'

'Why?'

'It was slanderous as well as obscene.'

Rowan said, 'I think we needn't press this—'

'Oh, but I think we must,' Gopal said. 'I do not understand what detenu is getting at when he talks of a situation, but there is here a situation of which we are getting a picture and it is important that the picture should be as complete in every detail as possible. The situation I speak of is one in which the detenu, under suspicion of rape, is kept standing naked for a very long time by the senior police officer of the district, who sits on his desk drinking whisky and conducting an interrogation with, if detenu is to be believed, a total disregard for detenu's dignity as a human being, and asking questions in a manner calculated to insult, outrage, and to provoke to make comments which are then recorded as incriminating evidence of detenu's knowledge of events he could not have known about if he was innocent only. And the picture of this situation is not easy to believe. It is necessary that detenu should be examined closely on it because it arises only out of what he has been saying. He cannot suddenly stop saying because it suits him.'

Again she sought the reassurance of the pleats and buttons of her blouse. Gopal was making statements which on the record would convey an impression of doubting Kumar, of disbelieving that a police officer would act as Kumar had said. But Gopal did not want to doubt or disbelieve. Underneath that apolitical, civil service, collaborative exterior pumped the old Anti-British fears, prejudices and superstitions. It came to her that Gopal disliked Kumar for the type of Indian Kumar was – which in every important way from Gopal's point of view was not an Indian way at all. It was not without pleasure that he assumed the hectoring tone, emerged suddenly, almost unexpectedly, as animated by a passion the record would show as one for a clinical sense of justice, the opposite of the real animus – a fastidious dislike of the white usurper on whose bandwagon he had a seat. Below her, yet another situation was in process. It fascinated, disturbed her, to have, suddenly, an insight into it. 'So I must press detenu,' Gopal was saying. It was the white man in Kumar he enjoyed attacking. But the objective was the revelation of the full outrage and unjust pressure Kumar the Indian had suffered.

'I am sorry,' Kumar said.

Gopal made an impatient gesture. How thin his fingers were, disapproving, permissive. They inspired her with dislike and pity: the twin responses to the odd combination of triumph and defeat the gesture implied.

Rowan took over.

'When – as you suggest – you understood from whatever it was you imply District Superintendent conveyed to you – that Miss Manners had been criminally assaulted and that you and the other men were under suspicion for that, you presumably made the statement as it appears in DSP's report. "I have not seen Miss Manners since the night we visited the temple." '

'Yes.'

'So the report is correct in that detail?'

'In that detail, yes.'

'And you are not inclined to dispute that this was at 22.45 hours?'

'No.'

'So a second detail of the report is correct.'

'Yes.'

'And you showed signs of distress, at this point, in that you were shivering, which makes the report accurate on three counts. I imagine, too, that you would not dispute the statement the report goes on to make that from that moment you reverted to the invariable reply to any question: "I have nothing to say." '

'I would not dispute that.'

'How long did your interrogation continue? How long were you in fact making this statement that you had nothing further to say?'

'I don't know.'

'Why not?'

'I lost track of things like time.'

'As long as an hour, two hours?'

'Perhaps.'

'Longer?'

'It could have been.'

'You were alone with the examining officer for two hours or more?'

'No. Other people came in after a bit.'

'The two constables?'

'Yes.'

'Anyone else?'

'One certainly. There may have been others.'

'Can't you remember?'

'I thought so. It seemed like it.'

'Are you saying you were confused? A bit giddy perhaps? And cold? Standing naked a long time in a cooled room?'

'I wasn't standing all the time.'

'You were allowed to sit?'

'No.'

Gopal re-entered the arena. 'I don't understand,' he said. 'You were not standing all the time but also you were not sitting. What were you doing? Lying down?'

'I was bent over a trestle.'

'Bent over a trestle?'

'Tied to it.' He hesitated, then added, 'For the persuasive phase of the interrogation.'

A pause.

Gopal said, 'Are you stating that you were physically ill-treated?'

'A cane was used.'

A rustle of paper. Captain Rowan's voice:

'Among the documents there is a copy of a report by a magistrate, Mr Iyenagar, who interviewed you at police headquarters on August 16th at the direction of the civil authorities. Do you recall that interview?'

'There were many interviews.'

'The one on August 16th was ordered by the civil authorities to inquire into rumours circulating in the bazaar of whipping and defilement of the prisoners held under suspicion of rape. Do you recall that now?'

'Yes, I recall it.'

'The report reads: *Iyenagar*: Have you any complaints to make about your treatment while in custody? *Kumar*: No. *Iyenagar*: If it were suggested that you had been subjected to physical violence of any kind, would there be any truth in that? *Kumar*: I have nothing to add to my first answer. *Iyenagar*: If it were suggested that you had been forced to eat any food which your religion made distasteful to you, would there be any truth in that suggestion? *Kumar*: I have no religious prejudices about food. *Iyenagar*: You understand that you have the opportunity here of making a complaint, if one is justified, which you need not fear making? *Kumar*: I have nothing more to say. *Iyenagar*: You have no complaint about your treatment from the moment of your arrest until now? *Kumar*: I have no complaint.'

Rowan looked up from his reading.

'Is that an accurate record of your interview with the magistrate?'

'Yes.'

'It is an accurate record, but you weren't telling the truth?'

'I was telling the truth.'

'You have just alleged that you were tied to a trestle and beaten with a cane.'

'Yes. I was.'

'Then why did you deny it when the magistrate asked you?'

'He asked if I had any complaint. I said I hadn't. I spoke the truth.'

'You had no complaint about being caned?'

'No.'

'Why?'

No answer.

Gopal said, 'Are you suggesting you were afraid of the consequences of complaining?'

'No.'

'What then?'

'It's difficult to explain now.'

'You did not complain, for reasons that now strike you as questionable?' Rowan asked.

'Not questionable.'

'What then?'

No answer.

'You are not on oath. The people you now complain about are not here to answer your accusations. Are you taking advantage of that?'

'No, and I am not complaining.'

Rowan's voice took on an edge. 'I see. You're merely stating facts. A bit late in the day, isn't it?'

'I don't know about late in the day—'

'Facts which you failed to state at the time for a reason you now find it difficult to give us.'

No answer.

'You say you were caned. How many times were you hit with this cane?' 'I don't know.

'Six times? Twelve times?'

No answer.

'More than twelve times?'

'I didn't count.'

'On what part of the body were you hit?'

'On the usual place for someone bent over.'

'The buttocks.'

'Yes.'

A rustle of paper.

'On your arrival in Kandipat you underwent the routine physical check. The documents are here. The examining doctor found you physically A1. Judging by this document it seems no marks were found that would have pointed to your having received a number of strokes with a cane on your buttocks. There is a note about traces of bruising on your face. The examination was made sixteen days after your arrest and first interrogation. The caning perhaps was not so severe as to cut the skin? Sixteen days is not a long time. Wouldn't you say that if your skin had been cut the marks would still have been visible?'

'They were visible.'

'The doctor saw them?'

'I don't know.

'You must answer more fully than that.'

'If he saw them he made no comment.'

'Nor any record. It is usual before the examination for a prisoner to be bathed. Were you so bathed?'

'Yes.'

'I understand such bathing is conducted under the eye of a prison officer. Was it so conducted?'

'Yes.'

'Did the prison officer comment on any marks there may have been on your buttocks?'

'No.'

'The marks were invisible to him too?'

'Indians of the lower class keep a pair of drawers on while bathing. I suppose it's because they're used to bathing in public. That's what happened when I was told to take a bath that day. I was told to keep my drawers on.'

Gopal said, 'It's a point I was about to make, Captain Rowan. And in the case of the physical examination it is doubtful that the doctor – who I see from the medical report was an Indian – would have asked for the drawers to be removed for longer than was necessary to examine the pubic region. Was that the case, Kumar?'

'There was also an examination of the anal passage.'

A pause.

Rowan said, 'What you're suggesting then is that the doctor was either incompetent and failed to see what was under his nose, or saw the marks and ignored them in his report.'

'I'm not making a suggestion.'

'Are these marks you say you had still visible to any degree?'

'No.'

'You were not hit severely enough for the marks to be permanent.'

'I was hit severely.'

'To the point where blood was drawn?'

'I think it was when they started to draw blood that they covered me with a wet cloth. Then they carried on.'

A pause.

Gopal said, 'Who were "they"?'

'I couldn't see. It must have been the constables. They tied me to the trestle anyway. They started when Merrick gave the order and stopped when he said so. When they stopped Merrick talked to me. When he stopped talking he gave the order and they started again. It went on like that.'

Gopal said, 'Until you lost consciousness?'

'I didn't lose consciousness.'

Rowan said, 'But you have no idea how many times you were hit?'

'It's difficult to breathe in that position. It's all you think of in the end.'

Rowan continued: 'You allege that when the investigating officer told the constables to stop he talked to you. You mean he questioned you?'

'It was more like talking.'

'What was he talking about this time?' Gopal asked acidly. 'Not surely about the history of the British in India?'

'He was talking to encourage me.'

'Encourage you? To confess?'

'That was part of it. Perhaps not the most important.'

'But important enough for us to concentrate on,' Gopal said. 'What did he say to encourage a confession?'

'He said Miss Manners had named me as one of the men, that she said she'd been stopped by me outside the Bibighar and attacked while I held her in conversation, then that she'd been dragged into the gardens and raped, first by me and then by my friends. He said he didn't believe her. He suggested I should tell him the real truth. He told me he knew the truth but wanted to hear it from me first.' A pause. 'I'm sorry. I've got confused. He said that before he had me tied to the trestle. But after they tied me to the trestle he said it again, only this time he left out the bit about wanting to hear the truth from me. He said he'd tell me what he knew to be the truth and all I had to do to stop being beaten was confirm it.'

'And what do you allege he told you?'

'He said she'd obviously asked us to meet her, egged us on, that then we'd given her more than she'd quite bargained for, and that she was now trying to have us punished for something we'd only been technically guilty of.' A pause. 'He made it sound very plausible. He left me to think about it. He seemed to be away for quite a long time. When he came back he had one of the other men with him. He told me one of my friends had come down to hear me confess. I don't know which of the men it was. I heard this man trying to tell me he knew nothing and had said nothing. They started hitting me again.' A pause. 'After that I think Merrick sent everyone out. I think we were alone. He spoke and acted even more obscenely.'

Rowan said, 'The word obscene is open to different interpretations. Your allegation of obscenity – the second you have made – is against an officer of the Indian Police and is damaging to the reputation of that officer. You must give examples of obscenity so that anyone reading the record of this examination may form his own conclusion whether the word is justified in the context of the allegation.'

Kumar had slowly transferred his gaze from Gopal to Rowan. He said, 'He asked me if I was enjoying it.'

'Enjoying it?'

'He said, "Aren't you enjoying it? Surely a randy fellow like you can do better than this?" '

'Is that all?'

'He said, "Aren't you enjoying it? Surely a randy fellow like you can do better than this? Surely a healthy fellow like you doesn't exhaust himself just by having it once?" ' A pause. 'He had his hand between my legs at the time.'

Gopal seemed to recoil. Rowan spoke sharply to the clerk. 'Strike that from the record. Delete anything that followed the detenu's statement "I think we were alone". When you've done that leave your notebook on this desk and wait outside until I recall you.'

When the clerk had obeyed and closed the door behind him Gopal moved as if to protest, but Rowan said to Kumar:

'Why are you making allegations of this kind?'

'I'm answering your questions.'

'Are you? Or are you lying?'

'I'm not lying.'

'I put it to you that you are, that you are telling a pack of lies, very carefully rehearsed over the past year or so for just such an occasion as this, or to cause trouble on your release. If such outrageous things were done to you – really done to you – you would have said so when examined by the magistrate specially appointed to question you on just this kind of point. I put it to you that you did not say so because they had not happened. I put it to you that you are basing this story on tales and rumours you've heard since being imprisoned, rumours that were investigated at the time and totally unsubstantiated. I put it to you that you have made these things up in the belief that they may protect you from the danger you'd still be in if the charge of rape were made even at this late stage. I put it to you that your entire testimony this morning has been compounded of omission, exaggeration and downright falsehood and that your detention is no more than you richly deserve. You have now an opportunity to retract. I advise you to think most carefully whether you should or should not take that opportunity.'

'I've nothing I wish to retract. I'm sorry. I seem to have misunderstood.'

'What do you mean, misunderstood? Misunderstood the questions?'

'Not the questions. The reason for asking them.'

'The reason was made clear at the beginning.'

'No, the form the questions would take was made clear. The reason for asking them was left for me to guess at. I made the wrong guess. Something has happened to her, hasn't it?'

'Do you mean to Miss Manners?'

'Yes.'

'Why do you ask that?'

'Because the guess I made was that perhaps she'd finally managed to persuade someone I'd done nothing to deserve being kept locked up. But this examination increasingly smells of uneasy consciences. Something's happened to her and I'm the loose end someone thought it would be a relief to tie neatly off. I'm sorry. When we began you were so fair-minded it would have hurt if I'd still been capable of feeling hurt. And it would have been nice if I'd been able to answer your questions truthfully without it becoming clear that I can't be neatly tied off and that nobody's conscience can be soothed down. But I answer them truthfully, as truthfully as I can, and you begin to see that I'm the least important factor and that without intending to you're asking questions about what I call the situation. That's why you're annoyed and accuse me of lying, because the situation threatens to be more than any conscience can cope with. What's happened to her? Is she dead?' A pause. 'I've sometimes felt it but never let myself think it. If she is, you should have said so. You should have said—'

'We assumed that you knew. You're not cut off completely from the outside world. You exchange letters with your aunt. You have newspapers, surely? You talk to fellow-prisoners – new arrivals, for instance.'

'My aunt's letters are heavily censored. In any case she would never refer to Miss Manners. She's never forgiven her. I think she found it easier to blame Miss Manners than anything or anyone else for what happened to me. And I'm in the special security block here. We're allowed books, but not newspapers. Once a week they circulate a foolscap page of war news, full of victories and pious platitudes. How and when did she die?'

'She died of peritonitis. About a year ago.'

'A year ago? Peritonitis?' A pause. ' – That's blood-poisoning, isn't it? Burst appendix, that sort of thing?'

'I gather the peritonitis was the result of a Caesarean operation undergone in far from ideal conditions.'

'A Caesarean? Yes. I see.' A pause. 'She married?'

'No. She didn't marry.'

'I see.'

'Do you still have nothing to retract?'

'Nothing.' A pause. 'Nothing.'

For a while after that he did not speak. He sat staring at Rowan. At first she did not detect it – there was no sound of it, no sign of it – except (and now she saw it) this curious unemotional expulsion from the deep-set eyes of rivulets that coursed down his cheeks: opaque in the glaring light like phosphorescent trails, a substance that released itself without disturbing the other mechanisms of his body. She shut her own eyes. She had had a sudden, astonishingly strong compulsion to touch him. No one had ever cried for Daphne, except herself; and this one person beside herself she could not reach. Between them there was a panel of thick glass and downwardly directed slats of wood or metal. The barrier that separated them was impenetrable. It was as if Hari Kumar were buried alive in a grave she could see down into but could not reach into or even speak to, establish a connection with of any kind.

She opened her eyes again. The twin rivulets gleamed on his prison cheeks, and then the image became blurred and she felt a corresponding wetness on her own – tears for Daphne that were also tears for him; for lovers who could never be described as star-crossed because they had had no stars. For them heaven had drawn an implacable band of dark across its constellations and the dark was lit by nothing except the trust they had had in each other not to tell the truth because the truth had seemed too dangerous to tell.

In her mind was the image of Suleiman with the box held to his breast in the manner of someone holding a reliquary. The truth was in the reliquary and in the mind that held the image of Suleiman and in the mind of the man in the room behind the glass panel: the truth and memory of their having been in the Bibighar that night, as lovers, moving to the motion of the joy of union; and of the terror of their separation and of how, afterwards, she had crawled on hands and knees across the floor of the pavilion and untied the strips of cotton cloth the spoilers had torn from their own ragged clothing and bound him with. For a while they held each other like children afraid of the dark, and then he picked her up and began to carry her away from the pavilion.

I look for similes (she had written – secretly, in the last stages of her pregnancy, her insurance against permanent silence) for something that explains it more clearly, but find nothing, because there is nothing. It is itself; an Indian carrying an English girl he has made love to and been forced to watch being assaulted – carrying her back to where *she* would be safe. It is its own simile. It says all that needs to be said, doesn't it? If you extend it – if you think of him carrying me all the way to the MacGregor House, giving me into Aunt Lili's care, ringing for the doctor, ringing for the police, answering questions, and being treated as a man who'd rescued me, the absurdity, the implausibility became almost unbearable. Directly you get to the point where Hari, taken on one side by Ronald Merrick for instance, has to say, 'Yes, we were making love,' the nod of understanding that *must* come from Ronald *won't*, unless you blanch Hari's skin, blanch it until it looks not just like that of a white man but like that of a white man too shaken for another white man not to feel sorry for, however much he may reproach him.

The image sharpened. She understood it in an exact depth and dimension as if she were Daphne and the man sitting in the chair down there were actually standing, waiting to pick her up again after a brief rest. He tried to take hold of my arm. I moved away from him. I said, 'No. Let me go. You've not been near me. You don't know anything. You know nothing. Say nothing.' He wouldn't listen to me. He caught me, tried to hold me close, but I struggled. I was in a panic, thinking of what they'd do to him. No one would believe me. He said, 'I've got to be with you. I love you. Please let me be with you.' I beat at him, not to escape myself but to make *him* escape. I was trying to beat sense and reason and cunning into him. I kept saying, 'We've not seen each other. You've been at home. You say nothing. You know nothing. Promise me.' I was free and began to run without waiting to hear him promise. At the gate he caught me and tried to hold me back. Again I asked him to let me go, please to let me go, to say nothing, to know nothing for my sake if that was the only way he could say nothing and know nothing for his own. For an instant I held him close – it was the last time I touched him – and then I broke free again and was out of the gateway, and running; running into and out of the light of the street lamp opposite, running into the dark and grateful for the dark, going without any understanding of direction. I stopped and leaned against a wall. I wanted to turn back. I wanted to admit that I couldn't face it alone. And I wanted him to know that I thought I'd done it all wrong. He wouldn't know what I felt, what I meant. I was in pain. I was exhausted. And frightened. Too frightened to turn back. I said, 'There's nothing I can do, nothing, nothing,' and wondered where I'd heard those words before, and began to run again, through those awful ill-lit deserted roads that should have been leading me home but were leading me nowhere I recognized; into safety that wasn't safety because beyond it there were the plains and the openness that made it seem that if I ran long enough I would run clear off the rim of the world.

Well – she had gone. Yes, eventually, she had gone clear off the rim of the world – then or later; keeping faith with a promise that was as well an imprisonment. For him it would have been then that she had gone. He must have watched her, perhaps he followed, perhaps followed her nearly all the way to the house and then felt for himself something of the terror she had felt for him, so that he too ran home and in the privacy of his room began to bathe his face because it was cut and bruised by the men who had come at them out of the dark; the unknown watchers, the unknown spoilers, the men for whom a taboo had been broken by watching Hari love her. He had said nothing, explained nothing. 'Say nothing,' she had begged. He had kept faith with that. They had both kept faith. She wondered whether he would see her death as releasing him from a promise made and almost absurdly kept. The promise had betrayed and imprisoned them both. Considering this she felt soiled as from an invasion of territory she had no title to.

'Do you want a few moments to compose yourself?' Rowan asked.

'I am composed. But you should have told me. You should have made it clear.'

'Are you saying that if you'd known Miss Manners was no longer alive your answers to some of our questions might have been different?'

'I answered the questions because I thought the examination was the result of some effort of hers. I answered the questions because I thought she wanted you to ask them. If I'd known she had nothing to do with it, and that it was only a case of bad consciences I wouldn't have answered the questions at all.'

'There was one important question you didn't answer.'

'I shall never answer it.'

'Did it strike you at the time that your refusal to answer questions was unhelpful not only to you but to those five other men who were suspected?'

'Yes, I had to consider that. It was part of the situation.'

'Do you know what happened to them?'

'I was told they were sent to detention.'

'Did you think that justified?'

'No.'

'You believed them innocent of anything, except perhaps illicit distilling and drinking?'

'On that night I'm sure they were innocent of anything else. I don't know how or why they were arrested but I know none of us would have been

611

arrested if it hadn't been for the assault. We were all punished for the assault, when it came to it. There was nothing I could do about that. Whether they deserved detention for political crimes, more or less than I do, I can't say. I wasn't able to let that enter into it.'

'Would it be in your power at all to remove the last shred of suspicion that they were implicated in the assault? It is accepted by this board that those suspicions were unavoidably part of the atmosphere in which your cases had to be examined when the question of detention under the Defence of India Rules came up. If you were being absolutely frank with us – for instance about your activities and movements on the night of the assault – would that frankness be helpful to those five men?'

'Are they still in prison?'

'Yes.'

'Are their cases also being reviewed?'

'That might depend a great deal on the result of the review of yours.'

'No,' Kumar said. 'You can't get rid of responsibility so easily. I think that is part of the situation too.'

The notion that Kumar could help five men who had never enjoyed Kumar's advantages seemed to interest Gopal.

'You are trying to cover everything with all this clever talk of a situation, but you are saying nothing about this situation. Time and again you leave an answer apparently complete but in fact it is only half-finished because of this so-called situation to which you relate it, and which you seem to want to mystify us with. What in fact was this situation?'

The rivulets were still visible. He did not seem to be aware of them and they now appeared to be motionless. She had an impression that they had ossified, that Rowan could have reached over and picked them away from Kumar's cheeks with his finger-nails, a piece at a time, and that each piece would fall with the light gyrating motion of something fragile, like an insect's wing.

'It was a situation of enactment.'

Gopal was impatient. 'Most situations are.'

'According to Merrick most situations are the consequence of one set of actions and the prelude to the next but negative in themselves.'

'These ideas of what you call the situation were DSP's not you own?'

'Yes. He wanted them to be clear to me. In fact from his point of view it was essential that they should be. Otherwise the enactment was incomplete.'

'And he made them clear?'

'Yes.'

'Perhaps,' Gopal suggested, 'you would be good enough to make them clear also to this board.'

'In a way that's impossible. The ideas, without the enactment, lose their significance. He said that if people would enact a situation they would understand its significance. He said history was a sum of situations whose significance was never seen until long afterwards because people had been

612

afraid to act them out. They couldn't face up to their responsibility for them. They preferred to think of the situations they found themselves in as part of a general drift of events they had no control over, which meant that they never really understood those situations, and so in a curious way the situations did become part of a general drift of events. He didn't think he could go so far as to say you could change the course of events by acting out situations you found yourself in, but that at least you'd understand better what that situation was and take what steps you could to stop things drifting in the wrong direction, or an unreal direction.'

'An interesting theory,' Rowan said. 'But is it relevant to the events you've been alleging took place?'

'You ask the question the wrong way round. You should ask how relevant the events were to the theory. The theory was exemplified in the enactment of the situation. The rape, the interrogation about the rape, were side issues. The real issue was the relationship between us.'

'What exactly does that mean?' Rowan asked.

'He said that up until then our relationship had only been symbolic. It had to become real.'

'What in fact did he mean by symbolic?'

'It was how he described it. He said for the moment we were mere symbols. He said we'd never understand each other if we were going to be content with that. It wasn't enough to say he was English and I was Indian, that he was a ruler and I was one of the ruled. We had to find out what that meant. He said people talked of an ideal relationship between his kind and my kind. They called it comradeship. But they never said anything about the contempt on his side and the fear on mine that was basic, and came before any comradely feeling. He said we had to find out about that too, we had to enact the situation as it really was, and in a way that would mean neither of us ever forgetting it or being tempted to pretend it didn't exist, or was something else.' A pause. 'All this was part of what he talked about before he put me through what he called the second phase of my degradation. Before he had me strapped to the trestle. The first phase was being kept standing without any clothes on. The third phase was his offer of charity. He gave me water. He bathed the lacerations. I couldn't refuse the water. I was grateful to him when he gave me the water. I remember thinking what a relief it was, having him treat me kindly, how nice it would be if I could earn his approval. It would have been nice to confess. I nearly did, because the confession he wanted was a confession of my dependence on him, my inferiority to him. He said the true corruption of the English is their pretence that they have no contempt for us, and our real degradation is our pretence of equality. He said if we could understand the truth there might be a chance for us. There might be some sense then in talking about his kind's obligations to my kind. The last phase could show the possibilities. He said I could forget the girl. What had happened to her was unimportant. So long as I understood how responsible I was for it. "That's what you've got to admit," he kept saying, "your responsibility for that girl getting rammed. If you were a hundred miles away you'd still be responsible." What happened in the Bibighar Gardens he saw as symbolic too, symptomatic of what he called the liberal corruption of both his kind and my kind. He accepted a share of responsibility for what happened, even though there was no common ground between himself and the kind of Englishman really responsible. The kind really responsible was the one who sat at home and kidded himself there was such a thing as the brotherhood of man or came out here and went on pretending there was. The permutations of English corruption in India were endless – affection for servants, for peasants, for soldiers, pretence at understanding the Indian intellectual or at sympathizing with nationalist aspirations, but all this affection and understanding was a corruption of what he called the calm purity of their contempt. It was a striking phrase, wasn't it? He accepted a share of responsibility for the rape in the Bibighar because even the English people who admitted to themselves that they had this contempt pretended among themselves that they didn't. They would always find some little niche to fit themselves into to prove they were part of the great liberal Christian display, even if it was only by repeating *ad nauseam* to each other that there wasn't a better fellow in the world than the blue-eyed Pathan, or the Punjabi farmer, or the fellow who blacks your boots. He called the English admiration for the martial and faithful servant class a mixture of perverted sexuality and feudal arrogance. What they were stirred or flattered by was an idea, an idea of bravery or loyalty exercised on their behalf. The man exercising bravery and loyalty was an inferior being and even when you congratulated him you had contempt for him. And at the other end of the scale when you thought about the kind of Englishmen who pretended to admire Indian intellectuals, pretended to sympathize with their national aspirations, if you were honest you had to admit that all they were admiring or sympathizing with was the black reflection of their own white ideals. Underneath the admiration and sympathy there was the contempt a people feel for a people who have learned things from them. The liberal intellectual Englishman was just as contemptuous of the Westernized educated Indian as the arrogant upper-class reactionary Englishman was of the fellow who blacks his boots and earns his praise.'

A pause.

'He said he was personally in a good position to see through all this pretence because his origins were humble. If he hadn't had brains he'd have ended up as a clerk in an office, working from nine to six. But he had brains. He'd got on. In India he'd got on far better than he could have done at home. In India he automatically became a Sahib. He hobnobbed on equal terms with people who would snub him at home and knew they would snub him. When he considered all the things that made him one of them in India – colonial solidarity, equality of position, the wearing of a uniform, service to king and country – he knew that these were fake. They didn't fool either him or the middle and upper class people he hobnobbed with. What they had in common was the contempt they all felt for the native race of the country they ruled. He could be in a room with a senior English official and a senior Indian official and he could catch the eye of the English official who at home would never give him a second thought, and between them there'd be a flash of compulsive understanding that the Indian was inferior to both of them, as a man. And then if the Indian left the room the understanding would subtly change. He was then the inferior man. He said you couldn't buck this issue, that relationships between people were based on contempt, not love, and that contempt was the prime human emotion because no human being was ever going to believe all human beings were born equal. If there was an emotion almost as strong as contempt it was envy. He said a man's personality existed at the point of equilibrium between the degree of his envy and the degree of his contempt. What would happen, he said, if he pretended that the situation was simply that of a just English police officer investigating a crime that had taken place and I pretended that I had no responsibility for it, and that there was such a thing as pure justice that would see me through, and if both of us recognized each other's claims to equal rights as human beings? Nothing would happen. Neither of us would learn a thing about our true selves. He said that the very existence of laws proved the contempt people had for each other.'

A pause.

'At one point he smeared his hand over my buttocks and showed me the blood on his palm. He said, "Look, it's the same colour as mine. Don't be fooled by that. People are. But prick an imbecile and he'll bleed crimson. So will a dog." Then he smeared his hand on my genitals. I was still on the trestle. After he'd had me taken from the trestle I was put in a small cell next door. It had a charpoy with a straw mattress. I heard them caning one of the others. Afterwards he came in alone with a bowl of water and a towel. My wrists and ankles were manacled to the legs of the charpoy. This was the third phase. I was still naked. He bathed the lacerations. Then he poured some water in a tin cup, pulled my head up by the hair and let the water come near my mouth.' A pause. 'I drank.' A pause. 'After I drank he told me I must say thank you, because he knew that if I were honest I'd admit I was grateful for the water. He said he knew it would be difficult to swallow my pride, but it had to be done. He would give me another drink of water. He would give it to me on the understanding that I was grateful for it, and would admit it. He pulled my head back again and put the cup close to my lips. Even while I was telling myself I'd never drink it and never say thank you I felt the water in my mouth. I heard myself swallow. He put the cup down and used both hands to turn my head to face him. He put his own head very close. We stared at each other.' A pause. 'After a bit I heard myself say it.'

A pause.

'That was one of the reasons why when they asked me if I had anything to complain about I said I hadn't. It was a way of making up to myself for thanking him for the water. After I'd said thank you he let go of my head. He smoothed my hair and patted my back. He said we both knew where things stood now. I could sleep now. There'd be no more questions for the present. I didn't have to confess tonight. The girl had incriminated me but it didn't matter. Tomorrow there would be questions. Tomorrow I could confess. When I woke up I'd be anxious to confess. My confession would show the girl up for a liar. I would be punished, but not for rape, because surely I could prove she'd agreed to the meeting, wanted the meeting? He would help me if I would confess to the truth. When I woke up I'd realize he was my one hope. I'd be grateful. I'd already thanked him for the water. That was enough for tonight. Now I could go to sleep. He rinsed the towel out and put it over my buttocks. Then he covered me with a blanket. I don't know how long I slept. I remember waking in the dark. My wrists and ankles felt as if they were still manacled to the charpoy. It was a shock to find they weren't. I had an impression of falling through space. I called out for help. The name I called was Merrick.'

A pause.

'Nobody answered. That gave me time to reason. The most humiliating discovery I made was that I'd believed what he said about Miss Manners incriminating me. I say had believed, but I was still believing it for minutes at a time, and then for another few minutes believing he was lying, then that he wasn't. Like that. Alternately. There can come a point, can't there, when the only attractive course of action for a man completely surrounded by others bent on his destruction is to help them destroy him, or do the job for them before they've quite mustered force for the final blow. It's attractive because it seems like the only way left to exercise his own free will. I made up my mind to confess to whatever he wanted. I thought, well anyway what's going to be destroyed? Nothing. An illusion of a human being, a ridiculous amalgam of my father's stupid ambition and my own equally stupid preferences and prejudices. A nonentity masquerading as a person of secret consequence, who thinks himself a bit too good for the world he's got to live in. He might as well be got rid of or, better still, get rid of himself, and who would feel there was any loss in that, except perhaps Aunt Shalini?'

A pause. She leaned back, closed her eyes, so that her understanding should come to her through only the unidentifying voice.

'But then, you see,' the voice said, 'the question arose – What did nonentity mean? And the answer was quite clear. It meant nothing because it was only a comparative – a way of comparing one person with another, and I wasn't to be compared, I was myself, and no one had any rights in regard to me. I was the only one with rights. I wasn't to be classified, compared, directed, dealt with. Nothing except people's laws had any claim on me and I hadn't broken any laws. If I had broken any it was the laws and not the people who operated them I had to answer to. There wasn't a single other person except myself I was answerable to for anything I did or said or thought. I wasn't to be categorized or defined by type, colour, race, capacity, intellect, condition, beliefs, instincts, manner or behaviour. Whatever kind of poor job I was in my own eyes I was Hari

Kumar – and the situation about Hari Kumar was that there was no one anywhere exactly like him. So who had the right to destroy me? *Who had the right as well as the means?* The answer was nobody. I wasn't sure that they even had the means. I decided that Merrick had lied and that far from incriminating me she probably didn't even know yet I'd been arrested. That's the moment when I knew I was sick of lying passively there in the dark. I managed to crawl out of bed and grope round the wall until I found the light-switch. It was pitch black and it took me quite a long time just to stand upright. When I had the light on I noticed he'd left the tin mug near my bed. There was still some water in it. I put the towel round my middle and walked up and down so as not to stiffen up again. The water was warm, the room was probably stifling, there wasn't a window, only a ventilator high up, but I was shivering. Even after I'd drunk the water I went on walking up and down, holding the tin mug. What I was doing reminded me of something but for a while I couldn't think what. Then I got it. Like my grandfather, going off to acquire merit. The loin-cloth and the begging-bowl. It was funny. Aunt Shalini's in-laws were always on at me about becoming a good Indian. This wasn't what they meant but I thought, well, here I am, a good Indian at last. Up until then whenever I thought of that story my father told me about his father leaving home, shrugging off his responsibilities it hadn't seemed possible that I was connected with a family where such a thing could happen. But walking up and down as I was, dressed in that towel, holding that cup, I understood the connection between his idea, and my idea that no one had any rights over me, that there wasn't anyone I was answerable to except myself. And I saw something else, something Merrick had overlooked. That the situation only existed on Merrick's terms if we both took part in it. The situation would cease to exist if I detached myself from it. He could ask his questions but there was no power on earth that said I had to answer them. He could try and probably succeed in making me answer them by using force, but it would be my weakness and not his strength that made me speak. So I came to a decision to go on saying nothing. I wouldn't answer his or anyone's questions except as it pleased me. I would never thank him again for a cup of water. I'd rely on no one, no one, for help of any kind. I don't know whether that made me a good Indian. But it seemed like a way of proving the existence of Hari Kumar, and standing by what he was.'

She opened her eyes and stared down into the room, was struck again by that extraordinary incongruity: the hunched submissiveness of the man's body, the alert and responsible intelligence of the man himself.

'Walking up and down with the tin mug – that's how Merrick found me when he came in. He looked as if he'd been home to bathe and change but not to sleep. He was very pale. I thought I saw the tic start up again on his cheek, but it was only for a second or two. I asked him what the time was. His response was automatic. He said it was six o'clock. Answering automatically like that showed him that our relationship had changed. He began to look puzzled. I walked up and down and every time I turned to

617

face him I saw this expression on his face, a sort of dawning mystification, and I thought, my God, the risks he's taken, he must have been very sure, he must have been absolutely convinced of my guilt. And he was still sure, still absolutely convinced, but he guessed or knew it had all begun to go wrong, and he couldn't work out why. I had a flash of admiration for him. He was totally unconcerned about what I could say or do that could get him into trouble. He said the constables would bring me something to eat and some fresh clothes to put on that had been collected from my home. They brought the food and clothes. Then they took me to a new cell, the one that turned out to be my home for a couple of weeks. I never saw anyone all that time except the two constables and Merrick, unless I was taken upstairs and examined by people like Iyenagar and the Assistant Commissioner. When Merrick examined me it was always in the room where the trestle was but there was never any physical violence. He questioned me every day, sometimes twice or three times, and I could tell that the conviction never left him. I was guilty. The day he told me Vidyasagar had been arrested he tried lying again, tried to make me believe Vidya had incriminated me by accusing me of trying to get him to take part in a plot to attack Miss Manners, but I had the impression that making me confess didn't interest him any more. Our last full session was the day after I'd been examined by Iyenagar. Merrick said he understood what I was doing. He called it pretending nothing had happened, wasn't happening and wouldn't happen. He said I was wrong, it had happened, was still happening and would go on happening and that he had more contempt for me than ever before. It wouldn't have done me any good to complain to the lawyer, but it disappointed him I hadn't had the guts to accuse him when I had the opportunity. He wouldn't bother to question me again. He admitted he'd lied about Miss Manners accusing me. He said she'd told a cock and bull story about going into the Bibighar Gardens because as she strode past she had a sudden idea that she might see the Bibighar ghosts if she went in. So she'd gone and sat in the pavilion and then been attacked by five or six men she hadn't got a proper look at. Then he said, "But it's not true. You were together in the Bibighar. You rammed her. You know it, she knows it, I know it. She's lying and you're lying. She's lying because she's ashamed and you're lying because you're afraid. You're so scared you're trying to convince yourself the whole business is an illusion, like some naked Hindu fakir pretending the world doesn't exist. What price Chillingborough now?" Then he got up and stood very close to me and reminded me step by step of all the things he'd done to me. He invited me to hit him. I think he really wanted me to.'

Kumar slowly looked down, as if to indicate that he had finished. After a while Rowan said, 'I shall call the clerk back in. Do you wish to make a statement to this effect?'

He shook his head, then raised it. For the first time a smile was fully recognizable. 'I've said it all. The clerk wasn't here to record it. That's part of the situation too, isn't it?'

She felt the first wave – scarcely more than a milky ripple – of an extraordinary tranquillity the nature of which she had no energy to determine; instead only the temptation to surrender to as a runner tired of the race would give in to the temptation to fall out of it. It will end, she told herself, in total and unforgivable disaster; *that* is the situation. As she continued to look down upon the tableau of Rowan, Gopal and Kumar – and the clerk who now re-entered, presumably as a result of the ring of a bell that Rowan had pressed – she felt that she was being vouchsafed a vision of the future they were all headed for. At its heart was the rumbling sound of martial music. It was a vision because the likeness of it would happen. In her own time it would happen. She would live to see what she had been committed to enshrined in the glittering reality of an actual deed, and the deed itself would be a vindication of a sort. But it would never happen in her heart where it had been enshrined this many a year. The tranquillity she felt was the first tranquillity of death. For her the race had ended in the Kandipat in this room with its secret sordid view on to another. The reality of the actual deed would be a monument to all that had been thought for the best. 'But it isn't the best we should remember,' she said, and shocked herself by speaking aloud, and clutched the folds and mother-of-pearl buttons in that habitual gesture. We must remember the worst because the worst is the lives we lead, the best is only our history, and between our history and our lives there is this vast dark plain where the rapt and patient shepherds drive their invisible flocks in expectation of God's forgiveness.

*

The room was empty. Only the light remained, the dim light, and the glaring light that shone on the empty chair. Kumar had gone with the rest. A hand had touched her shoulder. Looking round she was aware of Captain Rowan and of his voice repeating a question, 'Are you all right, Lady Manners?'

'Yes,' she said, and let him help her out of the chair. Standing she put her handbag on the table, took off her distance spectacles and returned them to the case. She thought how odd such human preparations for departure were. In the passage the weight of unconditioned air threatened to extinguish her. Her legs were shaky from the long inactivity of sitting. They went by stages through degrees of cold and heat: from the cool room to the close, warm corridor, out into the oven-scorched air and the furnace of the waiting motor-car. She sat with her eyes closed, felt the subsidence of the cushion as he lowered himself into the seat's opposite corner. Then the movement: the villainous shadow of the prison gateway. No pause this time. Sun-fish swam across her lowered lids. She raised them and was blinded by a spike of light that pierced the blinds as the motor-car turned at an angle into the sunlight and smell of Kandipat.

'He told the truth,' she announced with a suddenness that caused him to glance at her sharply.

'I'm glad you felt that,' he said. 'Sitting so close to him it was painfully apparent to me that he did.'

'You never mentioned to him that you remembered him at Chillingborough.'

'It seemed unnecessary. It could have struck a false note, too.'

She stayed silent for a moment or two then said, 'I expect you've realized *why* H.E. asked you to look into the files.'

'I've imagined he did so because you asked him to.'

'Then you're probably wondering two things. You're wondering why I should ask him and why I should wait a year after my niece's death before asking him. Is it safe now?'

'Safe?'

'To have the blinds raised. I feel I'm driving to my grave.'

Why, and so you are, a voice told her. She recognized it from other occasions. Old people talked to themselves. From a certain age. No. Always. Throughout life. But in old age the voice took on a detached ironical tone. Passion had this determination to outlive its prison of flesh and brittle bone. As it made arrangements to survive it grew away, like a child from its favourite parent, impatient for the moment of total severance and the long dark voyage of intimate self-discovery. And so you are, her voice said. Driving to your grave. The parting of our ways. A release for both of us. One to oblivion, one to eternal life so unintelligible to either of us it ranks as oblivion too. And already our commitment to each other is worked out and nearly over. Momentum will carry you through what motions are left to you to show your grasp of situations and responsibilities.

'The child,' she said. 'But even now I can't be sure. Only surer. She was so sure. To look at her towards the end you'd think, how astonishing! That combination of ungainly ordinariness and state of grace. One has to make do with approximations. Lies and approximations. When we say he spoke the truth we mean this. Everything becomes distorted. When the child cries its needs are so simple. When he cried he scarcely seemed to know it. Who will read the record?'

'H.E.'

'And the member for home and law?'

'He's an Englishman.'

'Why do you mention that?'

'Because it's pertinent. But Kumar will be released.'

'To what? In any case I don't want to know. I've had my amusement.'

'Amusement?'

'Isn't it all a charade? Over now. We go back into our corners and try to guess the word. Hari Kumar will have to guess it too. And Mr Merrick. Nothing can happen to Mr Merrick, can it? – everything in the file is the uncorroborated evidence of a prisoner. Nothing will touch him. That is part of the charade too.'

'It's safe now,' Rowan said. And began, one by one, to raise the blinds.

Part Two

A CHRISTENING

I

March–June 1944

The year had begun quietly, but the death in captivity of Mrs Gandhi and her husband's own illness and release, ostensibly on compassionate grounds, marked a time which seemed, in retrospect, to be one of dreams and auguries.

Early in March, when he came in from a tour of his subdivision, young Morland, an officer on the staff of the Deputy Commissioner for the Pankot district, reported a curious tale that was being circulated in the hills; the rumour of the birth to a woman whose husband had abandoned her of a child with two heads. The mother had not survived an hour and the child – a boy – died before the sun set on the first and only day of its life. Morland, suspecting that the death of a child with any considerable deformity might well have been assisted (although two heads had to be taken with a pinch of salt), had spent two weeks attempting to trace the rumour to its source, but had no luck. Everyone knew it had happened, but nobody was sure of the exact locality. Places were suggested, but going to them Morland was told: Not here, not here: and another village would be named, usually the one he had come from. The closer he tried to get to it the farther away the scene of the event became. But the effect on the people who discussed it with him was clear enough. Such things did not happen without a reason. It was a forewarning. But of what? Heads were shaken. Who could tell? On the journey home Morland noticed the constant freshness of the flowers placed on the little wayside shrines of the old tribal gods.

Having rid himself of the accumulated stains and strains of his tour, and taking his ease at the club, manipulating with excessive, youthful care that symbol of mature and contemplative manhood – a stubby briar – brick-red of face and bleached of head, Morland admitted he himself had come rather under the spell of the superstitious anxiety of the people of the hills and found his sleep disturbed by an odd sort of dream which, when he woke up, he never could remember anything of except that it seemed to have something to do with death by drowning. Morland always paused before he added, 'I don't know whether you know, but actually I swim like a fish.'

Within a week Morland was posted to the secretariat in Ranpur, his dream of death by drowning and the tale of the two-headed infant monster were all but forgotten, and Morland himself passed out of sight and mind (as he passes now into the limbo of only marginal images). But on March 18th, when the people of Pankot were startled by the news that the Japanese had crossed the Chindwin in force the day before, there were some who at once recollected the expectations of disaster Morland had brought with him from the remoter areas of the region. Five days later the Japanese crossed the frontier between Burma and Assam and stood on Indian soil, poised for the march on Delhi.

By the end of the month Imphal and Kohima and the whole of the British force in Manipur were isolated. Rumour ran that Imphal had fallen. In Delhi, the Member for Defence, Claude Auchinleck, assured the Assembly that it had not, that his information from the supreme commander, Mountbatten, was to the effect that it was still strongly held. In the Pankot club a wag said that Morland's tale of the monster with two heads was probably set going by natives who had heard about the separation of GHQ, Delhi, from its old responsibilities in the field; that all this streamlining and modernization was a lot of poppycock; and that the Japs would never have invaded India if the army in India hadn't been put in the way of its right hand not knowing what its left hand was doing. The joke was ill-received, not because the joker was necessarily thought to be talking nonsense but because, pretty clearly, it was no time for laughter. At Area Headquarters a picture was emerging on the map in General Rankin's office of total encirclement of the forces in Assam, and of the movements of formations from other parts of the front and from training areas in India in reinforcement. Rankin was heard to say, 'Well, this is it.'

Morland's dream was not the only one Pankot heard of. In Rose Cottage for instance, Miss Batchelor, the retired missionary teacher who lived with old Mabel Layton, also dreamed; and, unlike Morland who had been reticent, told everyone who cared to listen all the details that she could remember. She dreamed she woke and found Pankot empty. She walked down the hill from Rose Cottage and saw not a soul until she got to the club where one solitary tonga waited. Between the shafts there was a lame horse. Well, not really a horse. The more you looked at it the more obvious became its resemblance to an ass, a creature such as Our Lord sat astride of for the entry into Jerusalem.

'You'd better jump in,' the tonga wallah said, 'they're coming and everyone's gone on ahead to catch the train.' She hesitated to accept the invitation because this particular tonga wallah was a stranger to her and she didn't trust him. 'What are you waiting for, Barbie?' he said, and she saw that it was really Mr Maybrick – the retired tea planter who played the organ in the protestant church – but with his face stained and wearing native costume. So she jumped in and made room for herself among the piles of organ music, and off they bowled at a smart and pretty pace down the hill, past the golf course, where there were people playing, carrying coloured umbrellas. 'Those are the fifth-columnists,' Mr Maybrick

shouted at her. 'The golf course is the rendezvous.' It was known that the
Japanese had stealthily surrounded Pankot during the night. 'We must take
refuge, there's no time to catch the train,' she cried, trying to shout above
the noise and rushing of air caused by the tonga's swift passage. Mr
Maybrick was now driving four-in-hand. His whip whistled and cracked in
the air above the wild-maned heads of a team of galloping black horses. 'To
St John's! To St John's!' she shouted and was then at the reins herself and it
was her own short-cropped grey hair that was wild and flying. 'Alleluia!'
she called, 'Alleluia!' But the church had gone. 'You're just in time,' Mr
Maybrick said – in his ordinary clothes now, but wearing a clerical collar.
They were standing calmly, but sharing the knowledge that this was the
eleventh hour. They were in the compound of a little mission school. 'It's
really Muzzafirabad,' Miss Batchelor thought. Her old servant Francis was
tolling the bell. They could see hordes of Japanese crossing the golf course,
under cover of paper umbrellas. She turned to Mr Maybrick and said, 'We
must save a last bullet each,' but when they looked back to the golf course
the Japanese had gone and the children were coming to school, summoned
by the bell. 'Come along, children,' Barbie said, keeping her voice friendly
but authoritative. Francis said: 'The danger has not passed, memsahib.' But
she called to everyone, 'It's quite safe now.' They went into the schoolroom, but it was a church again and Mr Maybrick was playing the organ.
She sat in an empty pew to give thanks for their deliverance. 'And it was
extraordinary,' she said, whenever she told the dream, 'I've never felt so
much at peace. I think it was really a dream about poor Edwina Crane. I
went to Muzzafirabad just after she'd left. That was a long time ago – 1914
actually. They were tremendously proud of her there. She really *did* save
the mission from rioters, she just stood in the doorway, with all the
children safe inside, and told them to go away and not bother her. And they
obeyed. The children used to show me where she had stood, and I felt I'd
never live up to *their* special idea of a mission teacher. I think it was really
a dream to tell me that Edwina *is* at peace, in spite of that awful business of
her setting fire to herself, in 1942.'

*

And, presently, when Teddie was dead, a dream came to trouble Sarah. In
the dream they were saying goodbye to him and even he knew that he
would never come back. He had a look on his face that expressed the most
extraordinarily complete awareness of the place he was going to. The look
made him beautiful. They were all stunned by it and by the knowledge that
his presence was some kind of trick, because he was already gone. 'Of
course, Sarah, it'll be up to you really,' he said, just before he left them.
They had to fight their way through a group of Teddie's friends and avoid
the figure of the prostrated woman in the white saree, and after that Sarah
was running alone through a deserted street. When she got home her father
was waiting. 'I suppose you did your best,' he always seemed to say

although his lips never actually moved. In this dream she was intermittently being made love to by a man who never spoke to her. Who is that man? people asked her – her mother or father, or someone who happened to pass by. Oh, I don't know, she said. There was a superior kind of mystery about the man.

The dream had begun a few days after they had the news that Teddie was killed. The news was signalled from Comilla to Calcutta and from Calcutta to Area Headquarters in Pankot where it was intercepted by an alert signals corporal who knew Corporal Layton, and liked her for not being standoffish with non-commisioned men, and thought it best to have a word with someone else before the message went by dispatch-rider to the Pankot Rifles lines where all the Laytons' mail was sent. And so at 10.45 on an April morning Sarah was told by General Rankin that there was some bad news he thought it best to tell her privately so that she and her mother could work out how best to break it to her sister. She remembered the time, 10.45, because when General Rankin sat down he no longer obstructed her view of the clock behind his desk. He had made her sit directly she came in and did not sit himself until he had told her about Teddie and reassured himself that she was going to take it with reasonable composure. To one side of the clock there was the map with tell-tale clusters of flags around Imphal and Kohima. She thought of Teddie as permanently pinned, part of the map.

'Is your mother at home or will she be out shopping?' the General asked.

'They're both at Rose Cottage. I think there's bridge.'

The romantic period of Susan's pregnancy had ended. She was showing. Before long, she said, she would be showing very badly. The grace and favour bungalow stood virtually unprotected from the military gaze in the lines of the Pankot Rifles. She had complained for several weeks that it was like living in a barracks. Now she felt she was showing too much to spend the day happily at the club and had acquired a liking for resting on the veranda at the back of Aunt Mabel's, knitting and crocheting and gazing across the flower-filled garden to the Pankot hills, while her mother played bridge inside with Miss Batchelor and whoever else could be persuaded to forsake the club and the well-stocked bar, and gusty invasions of male company.

Hearing that Susan and her mother were at Rose Cottage the General nodded. Mrs Rankin had played there on two occasions recently and it was scarcely a week since a hint had been dropped to Sarah that her mother's losses were unpaid up. In the midst of this new catastrophe the little debt remained as a source of vague irritation and restraint between the Laytons and the Rankins, not to be forgotten but temporarily overlooked.

'You'd better go up there and get your mother on her own if you can,' Rankin said. 'I'll tell the transport people to provide you with a car, and I'll have a word with your section commander. Your mother may need you at home for a day or two I shouldn't wonder.' He paused. 'What a terrible, terrible thing.'

He went over to a cabinet, poured a small measure of brandy into a glass. 'Drink this. It's Hennessy three star, not country.'

She drank it down. She hated brandy. The smell reminded her of hospitals.

'Who looks after Susan?' Rankin asked, as if he too had been reminded. 'Beames or young Travers?'

'Dr Travers.'

'You may feel or your mother may feel he should be there when Susan is told. Meanwhile I'll ring my wife. We'll all do what we can.'

'Thank you,' she said and put the glass on his desk. 'I'd better go now.' She put the signal in her pocket. 'I think I ought to go by tonga. If I turn up in a car Susan may wonder and get alarmed before we're ready to say anything.'

'Would you like my wife to go with you? She'll be at the club. You could pick her up on your way.'

Ten rupees was what her mother owed. 'It's very kind of you,' she said, 'but it's not as if Mother and Susan are alone.'

'Wait a few minutes before you go. You've had a shock.'

'No, it's better like this. I mean better than just the telegram arriving.'

He saw her to the door. In the outer office the aide who had taken Captain Bishop's place opened the other door for her and accompanied her down the long arcaded veranda. He went with her all the way to the gravelled forecourt and out beyond the sentries who slapped the butts of their rifles. He hailed one of the tongas that stood lined up in the roadway. The sun was very hot, but the air was crisp; the famous Pankot air that always carried a promise of exhilaration and could be cold at night in winter so that fires were lit at four o'clock. Area Headquarters lay midway between the bazaar and the Governor's summer residence. Between these two were the golf course and the club. It was uphill, and the plumed horse took the slope at a nodding walk, jingling its bells and sometimes breaking wind. She remembered Barbie Batchelor's dream. She watched the road slipping by beneath her feet, her back to horse and driver and stable smell – a smell that was part of the smell of Pankot, the whole panorama of which was widening and deepening as the tonga gained height, disappearing as the road curved from the straight into the first of the bends on the hill on whose farther slope Rose Cottage lay with views to all the hills and valleys of the district her grandfather had ridden and her father had walked. Down on her left now was the golf course, come back into view, and, briefly visible, the bungalow where her father and Aunt Mabel lived after the First World War. More distantly she could see the familiar huts and old brick buildings of the Pankot Rifles depot, and the roof, among trees, of the grace and favour bungalow. Another bend in the road and the tonga, momentarily on the straight again, bowled past the flower-strewn embankment and then the open gateway of the club, giving a glimpse of white stucco columns and bright green lawns. Another turn and they were past the closed iron gates of the long driveway that corkscrewed up to the deserted summer residence. Climbing again now, slowly, past openings of private dwellings posted with familiar names: Millfoy, Rhoda, The Larches, Burleigh House, Sandy Lodge. At the top – Rose Cottage.

'Thairo,' she called, but the driver had already stopped. She got down, hidden from view by the high embankment. She wondered whether she should keep the tonga waiting, but decided not, gave him two rupees to save argument and turned into the steep little drive that was flanked by rockeries. Aunt Mabel was cutting roses, basket in arm, secateurs in hand, wearing old brogues, woollen stockings and a shapeless green tweed skirt. As a concession to the sun she had on a collarless sleeveless blouse, bright orange, that exposed her brown, old woman's mottled arms and neck. On her head there was a wide-brimmed pink cotton hat. These days you had to be careful not to come upon her too suddenly. The deafness that Sarah's mother thought of as assumed to match a mood had become more serious than that. But while Sarah was still several yards distant, her aunt turned. After a moment she put the secateurs in her basket and set it down on the grass, came to Sarah and took hold of her left arm, cocked her head to hear whatever it was Sarah had come at this unexpected time of day to say.

'Susan mustn't see me yet. Can you get Mother out here somehow?'

'What's wrong?'

'Teddie's been killed.'

Mabel's expression did not alter. After a moment she let go of Sarah's arm, then touched it again as a mark of reassurance, turned, picked up the basket and went inside. Sarah followed. The veranda at the front of Rose Cottage was narrow. It was cluttered with pots of flowering shrubs. The famous views were all at the back where the garden sloped to a wire fence, below which the land became precipitous. The cottage was one of the oldest in Pankot, built before the fashion came for building in a style more reminiscent of home. Stuccoed, whitewashed, with square columns on the verandas and high-ceilinged rooms inside, it was a piece of old Anglo-India, a bungalow with a large square entrance hall. The hall was panelled. Upon the polished wood Mabel's brass and copper shone. The bowls of flowers gave off a deep and dusty scent, and Sarah, standing in the doorway, half-closed her eyes and imagined the drone of bees on a summer's day at home in England, which she had thought of as Pankot in miniature. But England was far away and Pankot was miniature itself. Rose Cottage was not big enough to contain Susan's loss and the gestures of sorrow that presently must be made. They would be offered and the whole of Susan's loss and other people's sorrow would balloon and Pankot would not be able to contain it. She could not hear any voices. She turned away from the hall and stood on the veranda, amazed at the bright colours of flowers in the sunlight and the antics of a pair of butterflies whom Teddie's death had not affected. She waited for her mother to come out. At this time of day she would be in her first drinks of the day state: languid but mettlesome, neither to be loved nor criticized, and requiring an explanation she would not ask for in so many words and which Sarah in this case could not give.

She heard her mother's footsteps.

Mrs Layton was frowning, puzzled by and impatient of an interruption. The frown meant that Aunt Mabel had not said why Sarah had come. That Mabel had said nothing was too characteristic to be called unfair. Quickly Sarah began to formulate words. There's awfully bad news, Mother. But that wouldn't do at all. Bad news could be about her father. Shot while trying to escape. Killed by a disease made worse by malnutrition; or dead of lost hope or broken heart.

She said, 'Teddie's been killed,' and reached in her pocket, gave the crumpled signal form to her mother who took it, read it, went inside and sat on a hard hall chair and read it again. Mabel came out of the living-room followed by Barbie Batchelor, Mrs Fosdick and Mrs Paynton. They gathered round Mrs Layton. Becoming aware of them, Mrs Layton looked up from the telegram and said, 'Teddie's been killed.'

Sarah went past them into the living-room. Cigarette smoke still hung in the area of the abandoned bridge-table. Here again there were bowls and vases of flowers and deep overstuffed chairs, and a sofa dressed in flowered cretonne. At the far end the french windows were open on to the veranda. She could see the upholstered cane lounging chair and Susan's bare feet crossed at the ankles in an attitude that suggested deep repose of all the body. Her sister's drowsiness and fleshy calm made the veranda momentarily unapproachable. But she had assured herself no movement inside the house had penetrated that quiet, upset that delicate contemplation of a world without trouble.

She went back into the hall. They were talking in low voices. Her mother still sat. She had the fingers of one hand pressed lightly against her forehead. Miss Batchelor was leaning over her, supporting her back with an arm, but the support was unnecessary. Her mother's back was stiff. She caught Sarah's eye. And Sarah knew. It was she, Sarah, who must find a way of breaking the news to Susan, and the way she found would probably be clumsy, in which case Susan might forgive her but never forget.

She said to Aunt Mabel, 'I'm going out to try and tell Susan now. I think someone should ring Dr Travers in case she takes it badly.'

To make Aunt Mabel hear she spoke clearly. The others turned. She had sounded hard but reliable. Such a combination was understood. If no member of the Layton family had been up to it one of them would have taken charge in just that way. Without waiting for Aunt Mabel's reply she went back into the living-room, edged past the chairs round the bridge-table and stepped out on to the paved veranda. Susan was asleep. A faint perspiration was visible on her upper lip. Her swollen belly tautened the cotton smock and the skirt of the smock was rucked up above her bare knees. The rest of her looked too fragile for the burden of disfiguration, but in her sleep she was smiling. There was a faint upward lift to each corner of the moist closed lips.

Sarah could not wake her up and destroy such happiness. She sat on a near-by chair, watching her sister for the slightest sign that she was waking, and a ridiculous notion came to her that Susan should go on for ever dreaming and smiling and she go on sitting: in this silly uniform (she thought) with sleeves rolled up like a soldier's, but showing the white chevrons, and wearing sensible regulation shoes. One of her lisle stockings had a snag near the ankle. She wet a finger and applied it. It would do no good. It never did. The scent from the garden and from the ranges of hills where pine trees grew, oozing aromatic gums, came in waves with the faint breeze that here – even on the stillest day – could be felt on the cheek. Her father said that at eye level from the veranda of Rose Cottage the closest ground was five miles distant as the crow flew. He had worked it out with map and compass, sitting where she was sitting. That was the time he taught her to orientate a map with the lie of the land and take bearings to determine a six-point reference on the grid. He never taught Susan such things. But I am a grown woman, she told herself, not a leggy girl learning the tricks he would have taught the son he never had. In a letter at Christmas Colonel Layton said of Teddie, whose photograph they had sent, 'That son-in-law of mine looks all right. Not quite like seeing him in the flesh, but that will come, DV. Meanwhile I heartily approve and send my love to them both, and to you, Millie, and of course to Sarah.' Of course. Of course. She glanced back at Susan and saw under the book that lay open on the floor, pages down, a block of writing paper and the edge of an envelope that would contain the last letter Teddie wrote, the last she had received at least, to which she had not quite summoned the energy to reply, and so had put it by, to doze, and write later, beginning after lunch, and ending after tea, giving it then to Mabel's old servant Aziz to take down to the post.

She heard a faint sound and looked over her shoulder. Aunt Mabel was standing behind her, watching Susan too. She had never been able to tell what Aunt Mabel was thinking and now that true deafness was setting in even the old look of her sometimes watching you with inward curiosity about what you were thinking and why you were thinking it seldom appeared on the old but unwrinkled face. Her mother once said Mabel had no wrinkles because she cared for nothing and nobody, not even herself, and was never worried or concerned like an ordinary human being.

From the hall came the ring of the telephone. Mabel did not hear it. She moved to the balustrade and began to tend some of the flowers that were growing in pots and hanging baskets. Don't wake, Sarah told her sister. The telephone was promptly answered. She guessed the caller was Mrs Rankin. Mrs Rankin would be relieved that Mildred wasn't alone, but had Mrs Paynton and Mrs Fosdick to support her. In Mrs Rankin's book Mrs Paynton and Mrs Fosdick would count. And Sarah knew that she herself would count. While intending almost the opposite she was growing into a young pillar of the Anglo-Indian community. When they got back from the wedding she had been restless. It had been as if with Susan safely married her role of elder daughter had been taken from her. A married woman took precedence over a spinster. Sensing a release and a challenge she told herself: I must go to the war; and inquired about a transfer to the nursing services, which would take her as close to the war as a girl could get; closer than her clerking would ever take her. When she heard of it her mother made no comment; it was Mrs Rankin who took her aside and said, 'My dear, you mustn't think of it. It seems unfair because you're young, and want to do your bit, more than your bit if you can, but here's where it's going to be done. Have you thought of how much more your mother will need you if Susan has a baby?' And a week later Susan announced that this indeed was what she was going to do. Neither Sarah nor her mother ever said anything about the war Sarah could not go to, but between them now, in addition to the silences that hinted at need there were these new silences that were like a recollection of intended betrayal, silences of accusation, silences in which Sarah felt herself charged with having attempted to escape from her responsibilities, caring nothing for her mother, being jealous of her sister and forgetful of her father whose peace of mind depended on a certain picture of them holding a fort together. But these were charges she sometimes made against herself and needed no look in her mother's eye, no set of her mother's still lips, to remind her of.

She leaned back in the chair, turning her head to keep the silent watch: on Susan sleeping and smiling, and on Aunt Mabel taking dead heads off an azalea to give strength to buds not yet open. But that only worked with plants. The bud of Susan's belly wouldn't wax stronger with the cutting off of Teddie. Or would it? The image was grotesque but it had come and would not go away. It was merged with another, an image of a shapeless mindless hunger consuming Susan, consuming all of them, feeding on loss, on happiness and sorrow alike, rendering all human ambition exquisitely pointless because the hunger was enough itself.

Don't wake, she told Susan again, and closed her eyes to contribute to the persuasive arguments of the heat and scent and the siren whispers of the air. She opened them abruptly because Susan had stirred, shifted her legs and turned her head so that now she faced Sarah. After a while with eyes still closed she raised her right arm and made extra shade for her face with the crook of the elbow, then seemed to fall asleep again, but the weight of her own arm disturbed her, and her waking thoughts were more solemn than her sleeping ones. Unsmiling now she half lifted the lids of her eyes and observed Sarah through the fringes of her lashes and the shadow of her elbow. Sarah looked away. Presently she heard another movement – the sound perhaps of Susan lifting her arm to disperse the shadow, raising her head a bit to confirm the reality of Sarah's presence. A moment later Susan asked in a sleepy voice:

'Is it lunch-time already?'

Her eyes were shut again. She had moved her arm and made a pillow of both hands for her face.

'No. I've come back early.'

At the far end of the veranda Mabel stood watching, alerted by the movements Susan had made. She had kept an eye open. Sarah was grateful.

In spite of the marked withdrawal from other people, when a real pinch came – Sarah had always thought so – Mabel could be relied on. She was a point of reference. You could not embrace her but you could lean against her and if you ever did so perhaps you would find that she was a shelter too, because she stood firm, and cast a shadow.

'Why have you come back early?' Susan asked, long after Sarah thought she'd dozed off again. And then, 'Anyway, what is the time?' Susan had stopped wearing her watch. She had read somewhere that mothers-to-be shouldn't allow themselves to be distracted by artificial divisions of time. Sarah looked at her own wrist. Was it only thirty-five minutes?

'Eleven-twenty.'

She glanced back at Susan and watched the eyes open yet again. They conveyed a slight annoyance.

'Have you come on badly, or something?'

Sarah shook her head. Since Susan had stopped coming on herself she either pretended not to know when Sarah had a period or spoke of it as if it threatened to disrupt her own routine. So Sarah thought. But perhaps she had become self-conscious and read into Susan's manner what she felt about them herself: that hers were the menstrual flows of a virgin, sour little seepages such as Barbie Batchelor had presumably sustained for a good thirty years of her unreproductive life.

She said, 'No,' and then, seeing an opportunity, added, 'It's not that.' She found herself studying the snag in her stocking again, and automatically wetted her finger, dabbed it, found inspiration from the firm contact. 'Let's help Aunt Mabel with the flowers.' She had an idea that Susan ought to be standing, that it would be bad for her to be told what she had to be told, lying as she was.

She stood up. Susan watched her and then looked round and noticed her aunt standing at the balustrade, attending to the flowers and yet not attending to them.

'Why should we do that?' she asked, but fully awake now, returning her right arm to its crooked position above her head, looking at Aunt Mabel who, Sarah saw, remained still, resisting any temptation to dissociate herself from the situation that was arising.

'Come on,' Sarah said, 'you'll get as big as a house if you lie around all day. You ought to take much more exercise.'

'I am as big as a house, and I've done my exercise.'

'Well, I'm going to push the back of your chair up anyway. You always lie out on it much too flat.' She went round behind and heaved the levered back higher.

'Oh, Sarah, no. What on earth are you doing?'

'Sitting you up.' She readjusted the holding rod. Her arms were trembling. She came round to the front of the chair. 'I'd better lower the foot. Then you'll be almost respectable.' She knelt, and did as she had warned. When she had finished she continued kneeling. She said, 'Sorry. Have I made you awfully uncomfortable?'

Her sister was leaning forward, her hands clasped to the chair arms, her legs slightly apart with the smock ridden farther up from her knees. She was not displeased by the attention but puzzled by its suddenness and the absence of any immediately clear reason for it. Now she leant back, but kept her grip on the arms.

'What have they done, given you a day off?'

'Sort of.'

Susan waited.

'Well?'

Sarah reached for one of Susan's hands.

'Something's happened, which I have to tell you.'

The hand lay beneath hers, quite unresponsive.

'I don't know how to, but I've got to. I think I can only say it straight. It's about Teddie.'

She paused, deliberately, to let it sink in. When she believed that it had she went on:

'The signal came this morning and they stopped it being sent over because they knew I was on duty. The signal says – it says that Teddy's been killed. So that's what we have to start believing because there can't be any doubt. If there were any doubt it wouldn't say that, but it does, and I'm sorry, sorry.'

Now she took both of Susan's hands. But they were pulled away.

'No,' Susan said.

She stared down at Sarah.

'No.'

Mrs Fosdick came, and her mother, and Mrs Paynton, then Miss Batchelor. 'No,' she said, rejecting them all, jerking herself away from each touch of a hand on her arm or shoulder. 'No. No. No.'

She kicked out with one foot, as if kicking Sarah away. Sarah got up and the others closed in, filling the gap. They surrounded her completely. 'No,' Sarah heard her say again; but her voice was muffled now, as if she had covered her face.

Sarah went down the steps into the garden. At the end of the garden there was a place – a pergola dense with briar rose, and behind it a fir where there would be shade from the hot yellow light. As she went she heard a sound that made her stop: a drawn-out shriek, a desolate cry of anguish. When she reached the shade behind the pergola and under the fir she stood with her arms folded, and then sat and wondered whether Susan's cry had crossed the five measured miles to the other side of the valley, and wept – for what exactly she did not know – and it was over very quickly. She dried her eyes and did not want to be alone any longer. She got up, left the shade and reapproached the house with the sun heavy on her neck and heating her scalp. The situation was familiar. It had all happened before – people on a veranda and herself returning to join them. How many cycles had they lived through then, how many times had the news of Teddie's death been broken? How many times had Susan been taken indoors – almost dragged, stiffly resistant – in her mother's arms, while Mrs Fosdick and Mrs Paynton stood like silent supervisors of an ancient ritual concerning women's grief? Aunt Mabel had sat down, with the basket of dead heads on her lap.

'Are you all right, Aunty?' she asked, bending over her.

'Yes, thank you.'

'Can I get you anything?'

'No, thank you.'

'Let me take those.' She touched the handle of the basket but Aunt Mabel held on.

'Tell your mother she and Susan can have my room for the night if they would like that. I don't advise it, but Aziz can rig up extra beds and I can pig in with Barbie. You can have the little spare if they decide to stay.'

'Thanks, but I'll try and get them home.'

Mabel gazed up at her, then nodded. Sarah left her and joined Mrs Paynton and Mrs Fosdick who had gone into the sitting-room. There was no sound from anywhere in the house.

'They're in Barbie's room,' Mrs Paynton said, keeping her voice low. 'You mustn't be hurt, Sarah.'

'No,' said Mrs Fosdick. 'She didn't mean it, hitting out at you like that.'

'I wasn't hurt.'

A message had been left at Dr Travers's. Isobel Rankin had phoned and offered to look after Susan and her mother at Flagstaff House. Everyone would do everything they could. It was difficult to tell how Susan was taking it. She hadn't cried yet. But there had been that sound. Sarah guessed that the sound had shaken them. It wasn't the kind of sound a Layton made. The servants had heard it. The sound was shocking, Sarah thought, to everyone but her. They would have preferred her sister to cry, quietly, in the privacy of her room. Well there, in her mother's arms, she could have wept to her heart's content and earned their eager sympathy. God knew they weren't hard women; but there was something intemperate, savage, about a grief that went unaccompanied by a decent flow of tears. They all three stood in the room that Barbie Batchelor had made cosy with chintz and cretonne. Miss Batchelor came back. Her tall thin body, iron-grey short-cropped hair and unhealthy yellow face – a network of lines and wrinkles – suddenly struck Sarah as ridiculous. Missionary India had dried her out. There was nothing left of Barbie Batchelor.

'She's just sitting there,' Miss Batchelor said. 'She won't answer us and she won't lie down on the bed. I feel that if only she would lie down it would be all right.' She hesitated. 'It's not like Susan. Not like Susan at all. Poor Mildred can't get through to her, and one feels so useless. One feels so useless.'

Suprisingly Miss Batchelor herself burst into tears, and sat heavily in one of the cretonne-covered chairs. No one in Pankot had ever seen Barbie Batchelor cry. She had come a few years ago, in retirement from the Missions and in answer to the advertisement old Mabel Layton put in the

Ranpur papers for a single woman to share. Only once in her time in Pankot had she come into any sort of prominence, and that was at the time of the August riots down in the plains in 1942. She had cried: 'I know her!' when they read out the reports of the attack on the superintendent of the protestant mission schools in Mayapore, Edwina Crane, who, travelling from Dibrapur back to her headquarters, had seen her Indian companion murdered in front of her eyes and then been knocked senseless by the same mob and had her car burnt out; been found, later, holding the dead man's hand, sitting on the roadside in the pouring rain. 'I know her!' Miss Batchelor cried, and wrote, but had no reply, which was no surprise when eventually it was heard that Edwina Crane had gone very queer as the result of her terrible experience, and died by her own hand, setting fire to herself in a garden shed. 'Oh, poor Miss Crane,' Miss Batchelor was heard to say then. But she had not cried. 'I've always been useless, useless to everybody, how many of those little Indian children really loved God and came to Jesus?' Miss Batchelor said. They soothed her with murmurs of, 'Now don't be silly, how can you say that? There must be hundreds who are grateful to you.'

Sarah felt a suffocating claustrophobia, a tense need to destroy, and run, find air and light.

The claustrophobia was the beginning of the dream she was presently to have, where they were saying goodbye to Teddie, where she herself was running and being made love to by a man whose face she couldn't see and whom nobody seemed to know. He was there and then not there, then there again. He had a great, an insatiable, desire for her but it did not enslave her. He was a happy man and she was happy with him, not jealously possessive. He existed outside the area of claustrophobia, entered it and left it at random, without difficulty. He came to her because she could not go to him. A climax was never reached by either of them, but that did not spoil their pleasure. Disrupted as it was their loving had assurance. There was always the promise of a climax.

*

'She wants to go home,' young Travers said when he came out of Barbie Batchelor's room, where Susan was. He was not young, only younger than Beames, the civil surgeon to the station. 'And I think that's best, so I'll take her in the car with Mrs Layton.' She had refused a sedative. She had not lain down. She had hardly spoken. She did not speak in the car. When they reached home she went straight to her room. She lay on the bed then, while Sarah and her mother saw to the shutters and drew the curtains. She said, no, there was nothing she wanted, only for them to have their lunch and not bother with anything for her. She would be all right in a while.

The front compound of the grace and favour bungalow had a low wall and looked directly across the road to the back of the bleak Pankot Rifles mess, a rambling L-shaped structure, only partially concealed by trees. The

Layton dining-room and master-bedroom had views on to this. At the back there were two other bedrooms and the sitting-room and these had kinder views on to an attempted garden – a square of lawn, a wall. Behind the wall were the servants' quarters. The bedrooms – Susan's and Sarah's – were small. They interconnected. They shared a bathroom that was reached from the back veranda. The black labrador, Panther, who had been a puppy when the girls came out in 1939, had mourned the absence of Colonel Layton, then attached himself to Susan, and these days marked the veranda outside her bedroom as his special territory. He whimpered at her door and Sarah told Mahmud to take him to the kitchen compound and try to keep him there. She told Mahmud what had happened. Mahmud was not one of Sarah's childhood memories but he had been in her father's service for many years, almost ten. When he went, pulling the protesting Panther, she knew that the circumstances of the family's mourning were complete. Sorrow would fill the house and compound with a kind of formality and even the dog would quieten. She went to look for her mother and found her wandering aimlessly in her bedroom with a glass in her hand which, with a wholly uncharacteristic gesture, she abruptly tried to hide, covering it with the palm of her other hand. The telephone rang in the hall. Sarah went to answer it.

Returning, she said, 'It was the padre's wife. She wanted to come round now, but I put her off until this evening.'

Her mother must have emptied the glass and put it away, out of sight. 'I never cared much for Teddie, you know,' she said suddenly. She was sitting erect, almost on the edge of the old PWD armchair, rubbing one bare elbow. 'So I can't pretend to be bowled over exactly. And I don't think Susan ever really loved him. She was very secretive about the honeymoon. At least she was with me. Did she say anything to you?'

'No.' This direct approach disturbed and embarrassed her.

'I shouldn't think Teddie was very – experienced. Not that that's terribly important. Although it is if there's a lack of consideration too. And that's how he struck me, as likely to be inexperienced and inconsiderate. I'd always hoped that Muzzy Guide friend of his, Tony Bishop, would cut him out. But he never even tried. I don't think he cared for Teddie much either or Teddie's attitudes. The one thing they had in common was a regiment.'

'We'd better eat,' Sarah said.

'There's some cold chicken and salad. Tell Mahmud to get up a tray for her. She can't not eat.'

But she did not eat. The telephone kept ringing through lunch, and afterwards the chits began to arrive. Mahmud was sent to Jalal-ud-din's to stock up on tick with country gin and bottles of lemon and lime, and cashew nuts, for the expected invasion of callers. They began to arrive from five onwards: Isobel Rankin, Maisie Trehearne, the wife of Colonel Trehearne who commanded the Pankot Rifles Depot, the Adjutant, old Captain Coley, whose wife had not survived the Quetta earthquake and who himself had not risen since because his ambition did not survive either; Lucy Smalley, Mrs Beames, Carol and Christine Beames who worked at Area Headquarters with Sarah; Dicky Beauvais, deputizing for the most recent batch of Susan's pre-showing grass-widow gallants, young officers who came ostensibly to claim the company of the unmarried sister but had tended to end up fetching things for Susan.

They came, spoke in low tones, and went one by one or two by two. The last to come were Dr Travers and the Reverend Arthur Peplow with his wife Clarissa to both of whom Dr Travers had given a lift; and only the doctor and the chaplain entered Susan's room, Travers first, and then Peplow, after Travers came out and pronounced her well enough and wanting to have a word with him.

'She has asked for a Memorial Service,' Peplow told them ten minutes later, accepting a gimlet, 'and I think that very suitable. I shall be very happy to arrange it.'

'Not happy, darling,' said Mrs Peplow, who was always correcting his way of putting things.

'Of course not. Happy to be of use; the circumstances are sad enough. I think on Saturday week, so that I can announce it next Sunday at matins and evensong. If you agree, Mrs Layton.'

'If it's what Susan wants.'

And Susan wanted it. She only referred to it once, the day after, when she asked her mother to send for the durzi and tell him to bring bolts of whatever he had in grey – silk and chiffon. 'It's for the service,' she said. 'I shan't wear black. And grey will always come in.' She drew the design herself, basing it on one of her smocks which the durzi had already made up. She chose a silk for the smock foundation, a chiffon for the outer drapes which she had the durzi cut to hang full and loose; and in it she hardly showed at all, but stood in the shade of the veranda – while the tailor knelt with pins in mouth and chalk in hand – a white-faced grey-clad little ghost. For her veil she made over a circlet of blue velvet and pale blue velvet flowers and hung it with soft grey net. A grey suède handbag, gloves and shoes, were the only other expense – and these would come in too.

And she made an impression, yes, an impression, walking unsupported by but next to her mother, up the aisle of the church in which she had been christened, with Sarah coming along behind, in uniform. The whole station was represented, the pews were packed. In the days preceding the memorial service Pankot had become conscious of a need and of an occasion coming that would satisfy it. At its centre, Susan, veiled, revealed what that need was, moved them to an intensity of determination to fulfil it; to reaffirm. They lifted their voices high to sing, Lord, While Afar our Brothers Fight, Thy Church United Lifts Her Prayer; and lowered them to a grave and tender note of fervent understanding when they came to the third verse:

> For wives and mothers sore distress'd,
> For all who wait in silent fear,
> For homes bereaved which gave their best,

636

For hearts now desolate and drear
O God of Comfort, hear our cry,
And in the darkest hour draw nigh.

But the last two lines were sung in mounting passion because the verse stirred them to a sense of what was owed to people like the Laytons. In India hadn't the Laytons always given of their best? In those two young girls, the one sad in grey, the other brave in khaki, there ran the blood of Muirs and Laytons and there were those two names on headstones in the churchyard, stones so old now that the names could only be read with difficulty. A time would come – the congregation felt it, as it were a wind driving them before it so that they had to cling hard not to be scattered – when all their names and history would pass into that same dark.

After the hymn Mr Peplow read the 23rd Psalm and as he finished General Rankin went to the lectern and read from Corinthians: *Behold I show you a mystery, We shall not all sleep.* He read well until he reached the passage: O death where is thy sting? O grave where is thy Victory? when his voice became flat with self-consciousness. When he returned to his seat Mr Peplow said, very simply, 'Let us Pray.' They knelt and prayed for the deliverance from evil and the coming of the kingdom, for the whole state of Christ's church militant here on earth, for their sovereign George; and – after a pause – for the quiet repose of the soul of Edward Arthur David Bingham.

After the second lesson (*Man that is born of a woman hath but a short time to live*) which was read by Colonel Trehearne in his high, light, lilting voice, they rose to their feet again and sang 'Abide with Me', and it was remarked by those nearest to her that when they came to the opening lines of the last verse, *Hold Thou Thy Cross before my closing eyes; Shine through the gloom and point me to the skies*, Susan lowered her head and after the Amen sat down very quickly, with her head still bowed. She stayed like this throughout Mr Peplow's short address. He spoke of their sympathy for the young widow of a brave officer whom many of them had known, and remembered clearly for his cheerfulness, his kindly disposition. He had no doubt that Edward Bingham's was the kind of cheerfulness that adversity would not have diminished and it was this picture of him, young, smiling and in the prime of life that they must carry away with them. It would be a gallant soldier's best memorial.

He then spoke of the name Bingham, of the father who, like the son, had served in a famous regiment, and of the marriage only a short time ago of the younger Bingham into a family whose history of service to India went even further back. He did not need (he said) to speak at length about such things, for in this congregation the meaning of such service was fully understood and never had the meaning been clearer or the need to serve more pressing than now. This young officer had died, not in a foreign land, but on Indian soil, fighting off an enemy who had brought untold misery to the simple peoples of Burma and Malaya and would bring it to the Indians too if at what seemed like the eleventh hour we failed. But to fail, surely,

637

was not possible, and already the tide was turning. Perhaps this time next year we should see the forces of evil and destruction swept into the sea, Burma regained, Malaya relieved, and India safe from threat, free to turn again to the ways of peace. The victory would not be without cost, but men such as he whom they had prayed this morning in remembrance of would, he hoped, not have died in vain. They were troubled times they had lived through, were living through, and yet had to face, and it was not only for victory to their arms they had to pray but for God to grant wisdom to those in whose hands chiefly lay the future happiness and progress of the great sub-continent, with all its complex problems and manifold differences of caste and creed and race. He asked them to join him presently in a minute of silent prayer, for the repose of the gallant dead, for the safety of the soldiers of India and Britain fighting – even as they sat there – shoulder to shoulder on the eastern frontier, for the peace and blessing of God upon the bereaved, and for wisdom in the councils of the world.

He left the pulpit and when he sank to his knees in front of the altar the congregation followed suit in their pews, prayed their prayers and thought their thoughts. It was said that on the eastern frontier the soldiers of India and Britain fighting shoulder to shoulder had found among their enemy Indian soldiers once captured by the Japanese but now fighting for them. The thought was bitter. Somewhere at the back of the church a coin, got ready for the collection, dropped on the tiled floor, but it marked the silence even more heavily and in itself conveyed an assurance of anxious, charitable intention. Rising once more Mr Peplow announced the last hymn, No 437, 'For All the Saints, Who from their labours rest'. The collection was for the Red Cross. Four officers from area headquarters solemnly stalked the pews and were rewarded with the chink of coins and crackle of notes in the woven bags they offered on long wooden rods. As the congregation broke into the penultimate verse, 'But lo! there breaks a yet more glorious day', they delivered the collection to Mr Peplow, waited until he had raised it in humble offering and thanks, and then about-turned and regained their seats in time to join in:

> From earth's wide bounds, from ocean's farthest coast,
> Through gates of pearl streams in the countless host,
> Singing to Father, Son and Holy Ghost.
> Allelulia.

Once more they knelt, for the blessing, and rose to restrained chords from the invisible organ, played by Mr Maybrick, the retired tea planter; and waited while, accompanied by Mr Peplow, the Laytons left. After a decent interval, they began to crowd the aisles, their faces stiff with dignity, automatically taking or giving precedence, so that the Rankins were the first to arrive in the porch where Mr Peplow stood holding one of Susan's hands in both of his. He let her go so that Isobel Rankin could embrace her, which she did, lightly, making a token kiss of the air near one veiled cheek and murmuring, 'It was a beautiful service, I hope you felt that.' Susan murmured in return and put out her hand to take the one offered by General Rankin to whom she said, in a low but firm voice:

'Thank you for reading the lesson so clearly, and for everything.'

The General nodded, touched – Sarah saw – that Susan should think of thanking him at all. Presently the Rankins went, with subdued farewells, and others took their place. Dicky Beauvais touched Sarah's shoulder and said, 'I'll ring you later. Where'll you be?' She told him they were going on to lunch at Rose Cottage and only had to wait for Barbie Batchelor so that they could all go up together in the car General Rankin had lent them for the occasion. He touched his cap and went. Sarah was away from the porch now and shielded her eyes from the sun, and then Miss Batchelor was upon her, grinning but blowing her nose. The others emerged from the porch. Mr Peplow accompanied them down the gravel path that led in a curve through the hummocky graveyard – downward, because the church stood, among pine trees and cypress, on an eminence.

At Rose Cottage Susan went with Barbie into Barbie's room to change into the flowered smock and sandals that had been brought up by Mahmud earlier in the day. Barbie came out and told them Susan had asked for lunch on a tray. She would eat it out on the veranda.

'It's been such a strain for her,' Barbie said. 'I don't think she feels up to talking. I'll tell Aziz and then I think the form is for us all to go in and eat.'

They did so. There were curried eggs and rice. Afterwards Mabel and Barbie went to their rooms and her mother to the spare, for the ritual of sleep. Sarah went out on to the verandah. Susan had had her tray. She was resting on the same chair and in the same position Sarah had found her in ten days before. Sarah sat down, completing the pattern, presently turned her head and saw that Susan was watching her.

'What did Dicky Beauvais say?' she asked.

'Only that he'd ring.'

A pause.

'Is that what you're waiting for?'

Sarah looked away, towards the five-mile hill.

'No, Susan. I'm not waiting for anything.'

A pause.

'You're very lucky.'

'Why lucky?'

'Not to be waiting.' Susan's eyes were shut again. Gently, as if withdrawing into sleep, she turned her head into her folded hands.

At first Sarah did not notice the change in the rhythm of her sister's breathing; but then became conscious of it: conscious that the pauses between the rise and fall were unusually long, the rise and fall unnaturally abrupt. Sarah got up, went close, and understood what was happening. She reached out to touch Susan's head, but was afraid to. Close like this she could hear the suffocating attempts to deny the outlet for a pent-up misery. But what kind of misery? She could not tell. She thought: You have the courage of ten like me. And knelt, leaning on her hip, clasping one ankle, to

639

wait and try to convey to Susan that she was there if wanted. And after a while, still making that sound as if she were suffocating, Susan took one hand away from her face, groped for contact and held on, moving her head from side to side behind the hand that covered it, as if she would wear it down to the skull and Sarah's shoulder to the bone, to relieve her agony.

'There's no one here,' Sarah murmured. 'Let it come out.'

'I can't,' Susan said. Her voice was almost unrecognizable, a hoarse moan below the breath, but emphatic in its conviction. 'I can't. I've got to hang on.'

Sarah bent her head until her cheek rested on the tense knuckles.

'Yes,' she said. 'Yes, if you want.'

'Then it may be all right. I thought the service would help it all come back. But it didn't. It didn't, and I don't know how to face it without. I don't know how to face it.'

She pulled her hand away and flung herself round so that she was on her back, and lay like that, with her eyes shut, turning her head from side to side, pressing down on her swollen belly with both hands.

'At the service I prayed for the baby to die. I want him to die because I don't know how to face it alone. How can I face it with Teddie never never coming back? I didn't want the baby, but it pleased him so, and he wrote and wrote about it, and I could face it like that. But I can't face it alone. I can't bear it alone.'

'You won't be alone, Su—'

'But I am. I am alone.'

Abruptly she sat up, doubled herself over her folded arms and began to move her body in a tight rocking motion. 'Just like I was before, just as I've always been, just as if I'd never tried. But I did. I did try. I did try.'

'What did you try—?'

'You wouldn't understand. How could you? You're not like me. Whatever you do and wherever you go you'll always be yourself. But what am I? What am I? Why – there's nothing to me at all. Nothing. Nothing at all.'

Sarah sat quite still, watching that rocking motion, held by it, and by the revelation, what seemed to be the revelation, of what had lain behind the game that seemed to have ended, the game of Susan playing Susan. Susan nothing? Susan alone? She pondered the meaning of: Whatever you do and wherever you go you'll always be yourself: and recognized their truth. She was herself because her sense of self, her consciousness of individuality was tenacious, grindingly resistant to temptations to surrender it in exchange for a share in that collective illusion of a world morally untroubled, convinced of its capacity to find just solutions for every problem that confronted it, a world where everything was accepted as finally defined, a world that thought it knew what human beings were.

But it did not know what Susan was. In grey and on her knees; yes, it knew that Susan; and it knew Susan in white with the wind catching her veil, or standing at a carriage window flushed and smiling and taking a last sniff at a bunch of flowers before throwing them in that bride's gesture which proved a readiness to share her luck and fortune. It did not know her in a coloured smock, rocking to and fro, and had no answer to her cry that she was nothing.

It did not know her and had no answer and Sarah did not know her either – not as Susan – but with something of a shock recognized in the girl crouched on the chair a sibling whose pretty face and winning ways had been, after all, perhaps, only a fearful armour against the terrors of the night, a shield that was not visible to her but deluded others into believing her protected. What else had they been deluded by? By everything, perhaps, but most of all by the signs and portents of self-absorption, that apparent trick and talent for creating a world around her of which she was the organizing determinedly happy centre. It had not been that at all. There had been no secret garden, but only Susan crying to be let in and building the likeness of it for herself because she believed the secret garden was the place they all inhabited, and she could not bear the thought that she alone walked in a limbo of strange and melancholy desires.

Shifting her weight Sarah reached and put her arms round her sister.

'You do amount to something, and you're really not alone,' she said, and Susan turned into the embrace, with the weird sound of someone inwardly recognizing and inarticulately acknowledging refuge.

II

Several images converge. That woman in the *burkha*, glimpsed in Ranpur, making her way to the mosque through the street of the moneylenders: one merely chanced upon her and noted the smell of Chanel No 5; but – walking unhurriedly, in that enfolding garment – she defies her prosaic environment of time and place. She can be pictured years before, not in Ranpur but in Pankot, making her way along a section of the bazaar, like a ghost condemned to walk in a certain place, so many steps, presenting to the world a front, a proof of her existence, silently calling attention to herself; always appearing and disappearing in the same places, as though the route, as well as her presence, is significant.

There was such a woman in the dream Sarah had, but she was in widow's white, not purdah; and did not walk but remained prostrate. Yet, in the recurrence, in the uncertainty as to real intention, similarities existed. The whole of Sarah's dream was like the woman in the *burkha*. It came and went and stayed in her mind, so that sometimes, in daylight, awake, the visions of the dream would transpose themselves and she would find herself leaving Jalud-ud-din's and encountering, through the eyes of the woman who usually begged alms outside, this other woman, the one in white, lying in the dust, seeking for a mercy no one was capable of showing. For Sarah there came a time when the whole of that summer became inextricably entangled, as if, at this point, converging strands of circumstances met and intermingled, but did not cohere; and woven into them were the patterns of her dream, and Barbie's dream, and the tale from the hills that had sent young Morland in his sleep to an unexpected death by drowning. She found it difficult later to remember things in the order they happened. There was a sense in which they became interchangeable.

For instance: did she fancy she saw Lady Manners in the bazaar before the old lady strangely announced her presence in Pankot (strangely because having announced it she remained resolutely in a purdah of her own)? Or had Lady Manners re-entered her sleeping and waking consciousness before she had made her presence known, so that the glimpse Sarah thought she had of her, leaving Jalal-ud-din's in the company of a distinguished-looking Indian woman, seemed like some special manifestation rather than a visual confirmation of a presence that was the subject of common gossip? And what came first? Lady Manners or the letter that revived the other image of the stone thrown into the car taking poor Teddie and his best man to the wedding? And when, why, was it first suggested that Susan was dangerously withdrawn and the tale was resurrected of Poppy Browning's daughter who, bearing her first child three months after being told her husband had died in the Quetta earthquake, promptly smothered it?

The most logical sequence would be one in which the letter reviving the image of the stone came first, because this might be seen as having had an effect on Susan that set people talking about Poppy Browning's daughter and the business of the smothered child; and as having had the effect, as well, of reminding Pankot of the affair in the Bibighar Gardens in advance of Lady Manners's arrival, so that the arrival had the special poignancy Sarah seemed to remember as attaching to it.

*

There had been many letters: from all over India, from people who had seen Teddie's death gazetted or the notice in the *Times of India*. Most were addressed to Mrs Layton and she set about answering them with an industriousness that Sarah fancied was in part therapeutic, in part self-indulgent. All through the mornings, and on many an evening, Mrs Layton sat at the oak bureau in the grace and favour living-room, writing, writing. Page after page. There was apparently no end to the store of words, the flood of words. And she became more directly communicative. She discussed the letters with Sarah. She drank less.

There were also letters to originate: to Aunt Lydia in Bayswater, to Colonel Layton in Germany, to that uncle of Teddie's in Shropshire whom the marriage had relegated from his old status of next-of-kin and of whose nephew's death on active service it had therefore become Susan's or Mrs Layton's duty to inform him. The Shropshire uncle had promised a wedding present after the war; it seemed doubtful now that Susan would ever get it; he had not given an impression of a generous nature. There were letters to send to Aunt Fenny too – now left Delhi for Calcutta where Uncle Arthur had at last acquired a job [a strange-sounding kind] that carried the pip and crown of a Lieutenant-Colonelcy: the first to tell Fenny of Susan's loss and the second to put her off coming up, as she offered.

There were expected letters; one each for them from Tony Bishop who, but for the jaundice, would have been Teddie's best man, and who now worked in Bombay. There were unexpected letters, a formal note of condolence from the Nawab of Mirat to Susan and a less formal letter to Mrs Layton from Count Bronowsky who said that the Nawab was deeply affected to hear of the death in action of the husband of the charming girl to whom and to whose family he had had the privilege and pleasure of extending some small hospitality the previous year. He wanted the Laytons to know that they were welcome at any time, now or in the future, to stay as his guests again, at the palace, or in the summer palace in Nanoora. 'How kind,' Mrs Layton murmured, 'but quite out of the question,' and wrote to thank the Nawab and his wazir, and explained that Susan was awaiting the birth of her baby.

Susan detached herself from the business of the letters. She asked her mother and Sarah to open them, answer for her, and keep by any of those they thought she might look at later. She specified only one exception to this rule. And this was the letter for which they waited. It came [Sarah thought later, unable quite to recall the order of things] in a batch of mail on the Sunday of the week following the Memorial Service. The flimsy envelope, addressed to Susan, was franked by a field post office, and attested for the censor by an officer whose rank alone was legible.

'I think this is it,' Mrs Layton said. She handed the envelope to Sarah who was helping with lists and priorities. Susan was at the back, playing with Panther, throwing a ball from the veranda and waiting at the balustrade while he went to retrieve it. They could hear the scuttering sound of the dog's pads and claws as it hurled itself down the steps and, after an interval, hurled itself back up them again to drop the ball with a *puck* at Susan's feet, panting from the exertion, and with the pleasure of having a mistress who again took notice of him.

Sarah handed the envelope back. 'It must be.' She looked round, alerted to a change in the rhythm of the game by the dog's anxious whimper. Susan was standing by the open window, watching them.

'It's come, hasn't it?' she asked.

Mrs Layton held the envelope out. 'We think so. Here you are, darling. You'll want to take it away.'

Susan came over, took the letter and went back to the veranda. They heard Panther growl and Susan say to him, 'Oh, all right, just once more.' She must have thrown the ball then. The dog scuttered away. Mrs Layton opened another letter. 'It's from Agnes Ritchie in Lahore,' she told Sarah. 'Put her on B list.'

Sarah entered Agnes Ritchie's name in the B column of her list and when her mother gave her the letter put it with others in the B folder. Susan must have thrown the ball into the bushes of bougainvillaea. It was some time before they heard the dog return. Ball in mouth, it came into the living-room, looked round and went out again. They heard then, faintly, from the far end of the veranda, the scraping of its claws on the closed door of Susan's room. In a while this sound of insistence died away. Sarah got up and went outside. The labrador raised its head and glanced at her. The ball was held securely between its extended paws.

'Come on, Panther,' she said, 'I'll throw your ball for you.'

But the dog rested its head again and waited.

*

Mrs Rankin rang and spoke to Mrs Layton about the Red Cross aid committee meeting, Mrs Trehearne sent a chit about the British Other Ranks Hospital Welfare and Troops Entertainments committee. Dicky Beauvais came round and asked Sarah for tennis at five with supper and pictures to follow. Mahmud complained that the dhobi had failed to turn up and asked permission to go into the lines and if necessary into the bazaar to find him. Distantly they heard the bells of St John's announcing matins, and closer, the strains of the regimental band of the Pankot Rifles at practice in the grounds of the officers' mess. The crows swooped and squawked. It was an ordinary Sunday morning. But an hour after she had taken the letter Susan was still in her bedroom, secluded with her evidence of war.

'I've done enough,' Mrs Layton said. 'I'm going to wash my hair.' She gave Sarah the pile of envelopes, the result of the morning's spate, and went into her room, calling for Minnie, Mahmud's widowed niece who helped him run things by taking care of the intimate details of a household of women. The call for Minnie roused the dog. It went padding past the window, making for the source of this evidence of renewed activity. Sarah finished stamping the envelopes, went into the entrance hall and left them on the brass tray where Mahmud would find them on his return from his quest for the lost dhobi. She went into her own room. Minnie had made the bed, tied the laundry into a sheet and pinned Sarah's list to it. The connecting door into Susan's room was closed and she could not hear her sister moving.

She tapped, then opened the door. Susan was sitting on the bed with an album on her knee which Sarah recognized as the one containing the wedding photographs and press cuttings. The letter was on the bedside-table, propped between the table-lamp and a framed picture of Teddie – Susan's favourite because it showed him looking serious, with the mere ghost of a smile.

'Mother's washing her hair and I thought I'd do mine,' Sarah explained. 'You don't want the bathroom for ten minutes, do you?'

Susan shook her head.

'Was it a letter about Teddie?'

'Yes.' She put the album down, picked up the letter and began to read it but seemed to give up half-way. She offered the sheet of buff army paper to Sarah.

'Dear Mrs Bingham, Since it was with me that your husband worked most closely it is, I think, my duty – a very sad one – to offer you on behalf of his divisional commander and fellow officers, deep sympathy in the loss you have sustained by his death, of which you will by now have received official notification. He died as a result of wounds, having gone forward, under orders, with instructions to the commander of a subordinate formation then in contact with the enemy and under heavy pressure. With him at the time was Captain Merrick, whom you met in Mirat of course. Captain Merrick, although himself wounded – and at risk of his own life – rendered the utmost assistance to your husband, and stayed with him until the arrival of medical aid. Captain Merrick told the medical officer that your husband had not been conscious, and it may be some relief to you to know, therefore, that he did not suffer. Captain Merrick has now been evacuated to a base hospital and the Divisional Commander has been pleased to submit a report, in the form of a recommendation, in respect of Captain Merrick's action. Teddie – as most of us knew him here – ever cheerful and devoted to his task, is sadly missed by all of us. Those of us who met you, your mother and your sister, on the occasion of your wedding in Mirat, all send our special personal sympathies. Yours sincerely, Patrick Selby-Smith, Lt.-Colonel.'

Sarah returned the letter to its place by Teddie's portrait. Susan was going through the album again.

'I've never noticed it before,' she said, 'but there seems to be only one picture of him.'

'Of Colonel Selby-Smith?'

'No, of Captain Merrick. This is him, isn't it? It's really only half a face.'

Sarah sat on the bed next to her sister and studied the photograph. It was taken at the pillared entrance of the Mirat Gymkhana Club a moment or so before they left for the railway station. It showed Teddie with his plastered cheek turned from the camera and looking down at Susan who stood with her feet neatly together, in a tailored linen suit, wearing a little pill-box hat and holding the bouquet. Behind them on the steps, partly shadowed, were Aunt Fenny and her mother, Uncle Arthur and Colonel and Mrs Hobhouse. Behind these was the group of largely anonymous officers of whom she only recognized Ronald Merrick. Merrick was not looking into the camera but down on to Uncle Arthur's neck. In that little crowd of grinning young men he looked remote, humourless; but younger – she thought – than she remembered him looking in full light, under the sun. The camera and the shadows had smoothed out lines and not recorded the weathered texture of the skin. As a youth, at home, with his fair hair and blue eyes – she was sure they were blue – he must have seemed to those near to him comely and full of promise. 'She didn't care,' he had said, when talking that evening about Miss Manners, 'what your parents were or what

645

sort of school you went to.' He must have been conscious of them himself, though, and Sarah wondered about them, about the ambition that had driven him and the capacity that had enabled him to overcome what she supposed would count as disadvantages if you compared them with the advantages of a man like Teddie Bingham. She had never written to Captain Merrick, but then he had never written to her. Once – or was it twice? – he had sent his regards to them all through Teddie, perhaps more often than Teddie remembered to say. She wondered how literally he had taken what she recalled now as a promise to write sometimes. She had thought the request for letters part of the attempt he seemed to make to convey to others an idea that he was a man rather alone in the world, a man whose background and experience set him somewhat apart but gave him reserves of power to withstand what other men might feel as solitariness. She remembered how they had sat on the terrace the last time she saw him, waiting for the fireflies to come out, and how as the light faded Captain Merrick's body had resisted that diminishing effect, had intensified, thickened, impinged; and how she felt that if she had reached out and touched him then he could have carried the frail weight, the fleeting sensation, of her fingers on his arm or hand or shoulder into those areas of danger that co-existed with those of the impenetrable comfort that surrounded her, protected her, and barred her exit. He had appalled her, she had not trusted him, although why that was so she did not know clearly. He had stood under the light that lit his face and his need, and his implacable desire to be approached; and offered his hand. He still impinged; what he had done or tried to do for Teddie, did not seem to alter – except in a curious way to emphasize – her picture of him as a man obsessed by self-awareness; but the request for letters might have been genuine.

'Yes, that's Ronald Merrick,' she said. 'Are you sure it's the only one?' She turned the pages of the album. It struck her as disturbingly significant of some kind of failing in all of them that he should have been missed out of the main wedding groups, that none of them had noticed his absence at the time, nor remarked it later when the proofs were chosen and the enlargements made. 'Yes, I remember,' she said, turning back to the one photograph in which he was represented. 'Aunt Fenny couldn't find your hat-box and he went to look for it and then immediately he'd gone there was the fuss about getting the pictures taken while the Nawab was still in the garden.'

'I didn't even know my hat-box was lost,' Susan said, 'but I suppose you'd call that typical.'

'Perhaps he didn't want his picture taken.'

'Oh, everyone likes their picture taken.'

'He may have thought of it being in *The Onlooker* and people recognizing him as the policeman in the Manners case.'

Susan considered this. She smoothed the photograph with one finger as if feeling for an invisible pattern she thought must be there, in the grain of the paper. She said, suddenly, 'Teddie was terribly upset. About that I mean. I don't think he ever forgave him. But I must, musn't I? I mean I must write and thank him for trying to help Teddie. It's the right thing. Especially the right thing when he's not what Aunt Fenny calls one of us.' She smiled, as to herself, and continued smoothing the surface of the photograph. 'I think I envy him. Not being one of us. Because I don't know what we are, do you, Sarah?' She closed the album abruptly. 'The letter doesn't say which hospital or how badly wounded he is, but if it's a base hospital he must be pretty bad, mustn't he? If I enclose a letter for him when I write to Colonel Selby-Smith it would get sent back to wherever he is, wouldn't it?'

'Yes, that would be best.'

'I should write, shouldn't I?'

'It would be a kind thing to do.'

'Oh, not kind. I don't know kind. I don't know anything. I'm relying on you to say.' She was staring at the letter. 'I need help. I need help from someone like you, who knows.'

'Knows what?'

'What's right, and wrong.'

'Help with the letter?'

'Not just the letter. Everything.' She folded the letter and gave it to Sarah. 'Will you show it to Mother for me?'

'I will, but it would be nice if you showed it.'

'I know.' She was upright on the edge of the bed smoothing the counterpane now. 'But I'd rather not.'

'Why?'

'Mother didn't like Teddie. She didn't want me to marry him. She never said so, but it was obvious. She didn't really want me to marry anyone until Daddy comes back. She wants everything to be in abeyance, doesn't she? – because for her everything is. Everything – especially things about men and women. She didn't talk to me, you know.'

'Talk to you?'

'She made Aunt Fenny do it. Or anyway Aunt Fenny volunteered and Mother let her. I don't think that was right, do you?'

After a moment Sarah said, 'Was there anything you didn't know?'

'Oh, it isn't that. It was that Mother let Aunt Fenny. It made me feel she didn't care enough to make sure herself that I knew about the things I had to let Teddie do. She didn't want any of it to happen, so for her it wasn't happening. But at the time it just seemed to me to prove she didn't care, that nobody cared really.'

Sarah felt cold. Again she did not speak for a moment or two. Then she asked, 'Is that how you thought about it? That making love was just something you had to let Teddie do?'

Susan stopped the smoothing. 'I don't know. I didn't think about it much. All that was on the other side.'

'The other side? The other side of what?'

Sarah saw that her sister's cheeks had become flushed. She seemed, simultaneously, to become conscious of the warmth herself and brought her hands up and held them to her face. She no longer wore the engagement ring: only the plain gold band which had a thick old-fashioned look about it as if it might have been Teddie's mother's – the one relic of a life unhappily ended in Mandalay – although he had never said it was.

'I seem to have lost the knack,' Susan said.

'The knack of what?'

'Of hiding what I really feel. I'm out in the open. Like when you lift a stone and there's something underneath running in circles.'

'Oh, Susan.'

But she felt the truth, the pity of it, and was afraid. The wan hand of a casual premonition had stroked her neck.

Susan looked at her and, as if seeing the hand that Sarah only felt, at once covered her eyes and bowed her head. From under her palms her voice came muffled.

'I used to feel like a drawing that anyone who wanted to could come along and rub out.'

'That's nonsense.'

Susan uncovered her face and looked at Sarah, surveying – Sarah felt – her outline and density. She did not say: No one could ever rub you out. But such a judgement, held suddenly by Sarah of herself, briefly lit her sister's expression – calm, unenvious – without quietening the hectic flush that had reappeared after days of absence.

'No, it's not nonsense.' She looked down at her lap and her now folded hands. 'I felt it even when we were children in Ranpur and here, up in Pankot. I think it must have been something to do with the way Mummy and Daddy, everyone, were always talking about *home*, when we go home, when you go home. I knew "home" was where people lived and I had this idea that in spirit I must be already there and that this explained why in Ranpur and Pankot I was just a drawing people could rub out. But when we got home it wasn't any better. It was worse. I wasn't there either. I wanted to tell someone but there was only you I could talk to and when I looked at you I felt you'd never understand because you didn't look and never looked like someone people could rub out. Do you remember that awful summer? The summer they all came home and great-grandpa died? Well, I looked at them and felt no, they hadn't come home, that they could be rubbed out too and that perhaps I fitted in at last. So I longed to come out again, longed and longed for it. When we did come out we weren't kids any more. I wasn't frightened of India as I was as a kid. But everyone seemed real again and I knew I still didn't fit in because there wasn't anything to me, except my name and what I look like. It's all I had, it's all I have, and it amounts to nothing. But I knew I had to make do with it and I tried, I did try to make it amount to something.'

'I never knew you were frightened.'

'Oh yes. I think I was very frightened. I don't know why exactly. But I was always trying to get to the other side, the side where you and everyone else were, and weren't frightened. It was a sort of wall. Like the one there.' She nodded towards the closed window where Panther had tried to get in and Sarah glanced in that direction, saw that the wall she meant was the one at the end of the patch of garden that hid the servants' quarters. 'Was there a wall like that in the garden at Kabul road?'

'Yes.'

'Dividing the servants from us?'

'Yes.'

'I know I was frightened of the servants. No one else seemed to be. I suppose that was part of it. On the other side of the wall it was very frightening but only frightening to me and I expect I was ashamed and had this idea that if only I could get over I'd be like everyone else.'

'Is that what you wanted? To be like everyone else?'

'Oh, I think so. We do as children. I think that's what I wanted. Of course when we came out again I wasn't frightened any more, I thought of it more as wanting to make a life for myself that would add up just like everyone else's life seemed to add up. I mean everyone seemed so sure, so awfully sure, and I wasn't. I wasn't sure at all. I thought, if only I could make a life for myself, a life like theirs, a life everyone would recognize as a life, then no one could come along and rub me out, no one would try. Marrying Teddy was part of it, the best part, even though I didn't really love him.'

'I wondered,' Sarah said.

'Everybody wondered, didn't they? Well, that's the answer. I didn't. I thought I was in love a score of times, but knew I wasn't really, not inside where it's supposed to matter, and *that* frightened me too. It proved there wasn't anything inside, but I didn't want to go on being alone. I can remember it as clear as clear, the day I thought, why wait? Why wait for something that's never going to happen? I'm not equipped. Something's been left out. And I was always good at hiding what I felt, so I thought well, I'll get away with it and nobody will ever know. Whoever I marry will never know. And there was poor Teddie. He walked straight into it, didn't he? I married him because I quite liked him and I thought there probably wasn't much to him either. But I think there was. Yes, I think there was. He almost made me feel there might be something to me, in time. But he had a rotten honeymoon. Rotten.'

She turned, looked straight at Sarah and said:

'Not because I was scared or because he didn't *try* to make things different, but because I'd nothing to give him. That's why he was so pleased when I wrote and told him about the baby. He'd married a girl with nothing to her, but she'd given him something to make up for it. And having it to give him could have made *me* something, couldn't it? Who do I give the baby to now, Sarah? There isn't anybody. And I've nothing for it, except myself. And it's odd, awfully odd, but now when I think about what any of us could give it I can't see the answer.'

She hesitated, but held herself very still, and for a few seconds a half-formed picture came to trouble Sarah of Susan as a child holding herself like that, with the gritty surface of a faded red brick wall dark behind the halo of light on her hair; but the picture would not come more vividly or significantly to life and she could not say whether it was an Indian or an English memory.

'No,' Susan repeated. 'I try and try but I can't see the answer. I suppose the trouble is that people like us were finished years ago, and we know it, but pretend not to and go on as if we thought we still mattered.' Again she hesitated, then, looking full at Sarah again, asked, 'Why are we finished, Sarah? Why don't we matter?'

Because, Sarah thought, silently replying, we don't really believe in it any more. Not really believe. Not in the way I expect grandfather Layton believed – grandfather and those Muirs and Laytons at rest, at peace, fulfilled, sleeping under the hummocky graves, bone of India's bone; and our not believing seems like a betrayal of them, so we can't any longer look each other in the eye and feel good, feel that even the good things some of us might do have anything to them that will be worth remembering. So we hate each other, but daren't speak about it, and hate whatever lies nearest to hand, the country, the people in it, our own changing history that we are part of.

But she could not say this to Susan. Instead she asked, 'Why do you say *we*? *We* may be finished or not matter, or whatever it is. But you matter. I matter.' She wished she could believe it with the simple directness with which she said it. 'There's too much of it. Too much "we". Us. One of us. Oh I agree – one of us, I don't know what *we* are any longer, either. Stop thinking like that. You're a person, not a crowd.'

Again Susan studied her, calmly, but not – Sarah decided – unenviously, although the degree of heat generated by envy was slight, and said, 'How self-assured you are,' in a tone that reminded her – as a blow might remind – of that afternoon on the houseboat in Srinagar when she had looked at that old woman and heard herself say, 'What a lot you know.' What a lot you know. How self-assured you are. But I am not, not, not. Had *she* not been, that old fragile poised little lady, one of whose hands (she suddenly recalled) rested casually with faded Edwardian elegance on the little pearl buttons of a cream pleated blouse? Well, no, perhaps she had known nothing either, and been certain of nothing except that the years of belief were over and those of disbelief begun.

Sarah shook her head.

'I'm not self-assured at all. But I do know this – the baby matters too.' She meant, but did not say, that Susan had a duty to it. She did not want to use the word. There had been, still was, altogether too much talk of duty, almost none of love.

'Yes, I know,' Susan said. 'Everything must be done that can be. And if there's something I've been meaning to ask you. Mother said that if you do it, Aunty Mabel will agree.'

'If I do what?'

'Ask her. About the christening clothes.'

'What do I have to ask about the christening clothes?'

'Whether she'll lend them.'

'What christening clothes are those?'

'Yours. Mine got lost or something. But she still has yours. Barbie told me. She saw them in one of Aunty Mabel's presses when Aziz was doing it out.'

'How did Barbie know they were mine?'

'She asked Aunty Mabel. And that's what Aunty Mabel said. And Mother told me she remembered Aunty Mabel was given your christening gown because it was made up mostly of lace that had belonged to Aunty Mabel's first husband's mother, and of course Aunty Mabel never had any children so the lace wasn't used and she wanted it to be used for you.' Susan paused. 'I thought perhaps you knew. Hasn't Aunty Mabel ever taken it out and shown you and said, "Look, this is what you were christened in?" '

'No, never.'

'I thought perhaps it might have been a secret you had with her.'

'I never knew Aunty Mabel and I had any secrets. Wasn't the gown used for you too?'

'No. I had something modern, so Mummy said. And it got lost, or didn't last. Not like the lace. I'd like it if the baby could wear the gown you were christened in.'

'I'll ask Aunty Mabel. But it might be old and a bit smelly.'

'No. Barbie said it was beautiful. And that Aunty Mabel must have taken special care of it. There's something else I have to ask. I mean about the christening. Will you be godmother? Mother says Aunt Fenny will expect to be asked, but I don't want that.'

'I shouldn't make a very good one.' Sarah hesitated. 'I don't believe in it.'

To say this she had averted her eyes and in her mind was an image of Aunty Mabel kneeling by a press (as she had never seen her kneel) and holding (as she had never seen her hold) the mysterious gown, inspecting it for signs of age and wear as though it were a relic the god in whom Sarah did not believe had charged her to preserve against the revival of an almost forgotten rite. And glancing back at Susan she thought she saw the convulsive flicker of an ancient terror on the plumped-out but still pretty face.

'I know. But if anything happened to me you'd look after the baby, wouldn't you?'

'Nothing's going to happen to you.'

'But if it *did*.'

'Well, there are plenty of good orphanages.'

'Oh, Sarah – not even as a joke.'

'Then don't ask silly questions. Of course the baby would be looked after.'

'That's not what I'm saying, not what I'm asking. Looked after, looked after. I'm asking if *you'd* look after it, not just to say it would be looked after.'

'Something might happen to me too.'

It was unkind, she thought, the effect that embarrassment had. Of course she would look after the baby.

Susan turned her head, seemed to stare at Teddie's picture. She said, 'Yes, something might happen to you. It will. You'll get married. You'd want your own children. Not mine and Teddie's.'

'You'll get married too.'

'Oh no. Not just to give the child a father. Not again, like that, without really loving. And how can I learn that?'

'You'll love the baby.'

'Shall I?' Susan faced her again.

'When you've got the baby it will be all right, and after a while someone like Dicky Beauvais will ask you to marry him.'

'Not someone like Dicky Beauvais.'

She made it sound as if one phase of her life had ended.

'No, all right. But someone.'

'I shouldn't want to be taken pity on and that's what it would be I expect. Poor Teddie Bingham's widow, a child herself really, how will she manage?' Again she glanced at her dead husband's portrait, searching perhaps for something in his hallowed face that showed not pity but compassion for those he had, without meaning to, left behind to manage as they might.

'I think,' she said, 'that after all it would be better if you wrote to Captain Merrick for me. You could thank him so much more kindly, make him understand how much the Laytons are *beholden* to him for what he tried to do for Teddie. Whatever it was. Whatever it was.' She frowned, getting it seemed no clearer picture from the picture of Teddie of the unwanted gift he had made her of his death; and Sarah – catching the frown, considering the tone and rhythm of that repeated qualification, *whatever it was* – became aware of an element of doubt about the death that had entered for both of them.

'Well if you prefer it,' she said and then wondered: But what shall I say? and felt a little surge of resistance to the idea of saying anything, as though the act of writing would count as a surrender, proof that in the end he had succeeded in making her approach him – as herself, for herself, and as a Layton, for the Laytons.

'You could say I'm not fully recovered from the shock,' Susan went on, 'and tell him about the baby. Remind him, rather. He must have known about the baby. Teddie must have told them all about the baby. I expect they made one of those men's jokes about it. Ragged Teddie I mean, about him becoming a father. Perhaps he won't want reminding, but you'd better mention it, use it as one of the things that excuses me from writing to him myself. But I want him to know, I do not want him to know that I am beholden.'

It was a word that apparently fascinated her. Spoken, it created, almost, a cloistered air of peace, of withdrawal from the fierce currents of an angry shock-infested world; it did not lay balm to the little wound of doubt, but the wound nagged less. Beholden, beholden. It was transcendental, selfless, forgiving.

'Who knows,' Susan asked, turning to Sarah with that kind of expression on her face, 'perhaps he's lying somewhere, feeling it, feeling it badly, that he was bad luck for Teddie. Last time it was only a stone, this time I suppose it was a shell or bullets, but they were together again. I want to find out. I think I want to know. I think I want to know because I owe it to Teddie to know what happened, otherwise it's just like someone going out alone. But Captain Merrick will know, then he can tell me. Then Teddie may know I know. Do you think—' but she broke off and had to be prompted.

'Do I think what?'

'Do you think it would be nice if we asked Captain Merrick to be godfather?'

'No, I don't.'

'Why not?'

'I don't know. I just don't think it would be.'

'You mean perhaps he doesn't believe in it either. But he did perform a Christian act, didn't he, and it's that that counts, not going to church and making a fuss. It says in the letter, rendered the utmost assistance in spite of being wounded, rendered the utmost assistance and stayed with Teddie until the arrival of medical aid. He was trying to save Teddie's life. Not just for Teddie's sake, but for the baby's probably, and mine too. So I think we ought to ask, and not care what people like Aunt Fenny would think.'

'What would people like Aunt Fenny think?'

'They might think he wasn't suitable, a suitable sort of person.'

'Because he isn't one of us?'

'Yes.'

But, Sarah thought, remembering the night of the fireflies, in a way he is, is, is one of us; the dark side, the arcane side. But at once recollected the question she had asked herself on that occasion: Why should I question his sincerity?

Her resistance ebbed and yet still, as she said, 'Well I shouldn't worry about what Aunt Fenny might say' – thereby implying her approval of the way being opened to god-relationship with him – she felt the backlash of that strange dismay which the thought, the remembered impact, and the new notion of him as the dark side of their history filled her with; and he became at once inseparable from the image of the woman in white, of someone – anyone – who found it necessary to plead with him for an alleviation of suffering of which – if only unintentionally – he had been the cause.

'It can be done by proxy, can't it?' Susan was saying. 'If he agrees. He can be godfather without actually being at the christening.'

'Yes, I think so.'

'And it might help him to get better, to know we wanted him for that. Teddie said he used to be sorry for Captain Merrick before all that bother he caused at the wedding. He never got any letters, or almost never. I think that's as much the reason Teddie asked him to be best man as the fact that they shared quarters. Teddie was very upset about the stone. But he had a tender heart.'

'Well, and so have you.'

'Oh, no.' She looked down at her hands. 'I have no heart at all.' Again she looked up. 'Will you do that for me, Sarah, then? Write for me and find out where he is?'

'Yes, I'll do that.'

But there was no need for that particular letter. The day following there was a note from Captain Merrick himself; a note to Sarah, which Sarah showed to Susan. And when Susan had read it she cried out because she was convinced from certain signs and portents in the note that Captain Merrick no longer had the use of eyes or limbs.

*

143 British Military Hospital
AFPO 12
17 May 1944

Dear Miss Layton,

By now I expect you will have been told that Teddie was killed, just three weeks ago, but in case there has been some error or delay I've thought it wiser to write to you and not to Susan. Perhaps I would have done so in any case. I'm not very good at expressing myself on paper and would find it difficult to write a letter to her. You will find the right words to convey my feelings to her, I am certain, feelings of sympathy and, I suppose, helplessness in the face of what I know to her must be, for the moment, overwhelmingly sad circumstances. I am as you can see from the address and perhaps the handwriting which is that of one of the nursing sisters here, *hors de combat*, but my improvement is, I am told – and feel – steadily satisfactory. Perhaps someone from the formation has already told Susan this, but in case not – I must tell you that I was with Teddie at the time. That of the two of us it should have been I who came out of it strikes me as supremely illogical – for there was Teddie with everything to live for, and I – comparatively – with something less than that. It should have been the other way round that it happened. Yes, indeed it should.

I am to undergo some more surgery, not here but in Calcutta, so they tell me, and after that can look forward to a period of convalescence and then some sick leave by which time it will have been settled about the future. I should be grateful, of course, to have news, some assurance about your sister's state of mind and health, if you could spare a moment to drop me a line (care of this place – it would be forwarded – I go within a day or two possibly). That business lies a bit heavily. All sorts of things go through my mind. I wish I could speak of them more directly to you. Meanwhile my kind regards to you both, and to your mother. I hope you have had recent good news of your father. Sincerely yours, (for) Ronald Merrick (S.P., QAIMNS).

'You could go and see him,' Susan said. 'You could stay with Aunt Fenny and go and see him when they take him to Calcutta.'

'Aunt Fenny could do that.'

'No, not Aunt Fenny. You. He didn't like Aunt Fenny. He didn't like me either. But he liked you. And it's you he's written to. He wants to talk to you.'

After this Susan relapsed into silence. She sat most of that day on the veranda, staring at the red brick wall, while Panther lay beside her, guarding her from those invisible demons which dumb animals perceive as ever-present in human sorrow and abstraction. And long before it began to be said in Pankot that Susan Layton had become dangerously withdrawn (so that among those who remembered, the name and history of Poppy Browning's daughter began to be spoke of) the servants who lived behind that wall observed this fact for themselves and recalled the fateful augury of the monstrous birth high up in the remote hills. In secret places about the bungalow garden they disposed offerings of milk to quench the thirst, and flowers to appease with sweet perfumes the uncertain temper, of both good and evil spirits.

*

At the entrance to Flagstaff House there was a narrow open-fronted wooden hut, almost the duplicate of the sentry box that stood inside the gateway, but sheltering a book, not a man. The book was chained to the shelf on which it rested. A pencil, also chained, lay in the groove formed in the middle by the open leaves. Every evening a servant came down the drive, unchained the book, took it back to the house and left it on a table in the entrance hall. In the morning the book was returned to the hut. As well as the book there was a small wooden box with a slot cut in its lid, wide enough to take a visiting card. The box, too, was taken every evening into the house and returned next day. The book and the box were the means by which a visitor to or someone newly stationed in Pankot made an official call on the Area Commander. In the old days the call had been obligatory but nowadays a signature in the book or a card in the box was an indication of the presence in (or departure from) Pankot of someone to whom the old forms were still important or who knew them to be considered important to Flagstaff House and felt that to displease its incumbents was not a dignified thing to do.

It was in the book that Lady Manners announced her presence, one day towards the end of May – Lady Manners, or her ghost, or someone playing a joke, for no address was given beyond the bleak indication of permanent

655

residence, Rawalpindi; no one in Pankot had seen her or knew where she could be staying, and the sentries who had been on duty between 9 a.m. and 5 p.m. could not recall, with the degree of certainty Isobel Rankin hoped for when having them questioned by the steward, anyone reaching the gate on foot, by car, by tonga who had not entered but had gone to the book, signed and departed and who answered a description suited to the name, the rank, the whole condition which Mrs Rankin had in her mind as definitive of that unhappy woman.

Well, the servants would know, anyone's servants would know. But they did not, or pretended they did not, and so great an incidence of pretence was unlikely enough to confirm their denials. Where, then? Clearly not on the Pankot side of Pankot, the side, the real side, reached by taking that right-hand fork from the bazaar that led – gradually – to those majestic heights on which stood the summer residence which Lady Manners had once had the freedom of, all those years ago, longer than anyone now on station including old Mabel Layton, who had not bought Rose Cottage until a year in the thirties when the Manners régime was over, could remember; and which now – this season – once again stood empty. So, then, the other side, where English people never went. Certainly, yes, that would be like her, to come to Pankot and seclude herself among those who belonged to the other side. In Pankot these days there were several Indian officers, and some of them had wives (fragile, shy creatures whom Isobel Rankin took pains with) and they might know. But did not. It was a mystery. And why (if she were truly there and it was no joke, no spirit-mark – that signature) had she signed at all? And had she come alone, or with an entourage? Where was the child? Was the signature a form of apology, a first hesitant step back into the good opinion of her race? Or the opposite of that?

And it was strange, Pankot thought, or if not strange certainly not uninteresting, that two of the marginal actors in the comedy or tragedy of the Bibighar Gardens affair (and it depended on what mood you were in, which label seemed the more apt) should impinge simultaneously on the consciousness of sensible people who thought it would have been nicer to forget that it had ever happened: Lady Manners who had stood by and let her niece give birth and then taken the revoltingly conceived child to her bosom, and Captain Merrick who was said to have done his duty and had no thanks and now lay wounded as a result of some attempt – the actual details were not clear – to help poor Susan Bingham's husband, the day he was killed in action.

That story of the stone, which Mrs Layton had brought back from Mirat (referring to it casually, as if a stone were thrown at every wedding); the odd little circumstance of Teddie Bingham's scratch best man turning out to be who he was; and the revelation that Merrick had been sent to a backwater after the failure of the police to establish guilt in the Manners case, and then been allowed to enter the army: these burgeoned under the warmth of approbation felt for a man who had stayed with a dying brother officer,

656

until the stone itself became a symbol of martyrdom they all understood because they felt they shared it; and so, entering their consciousness, Merrick entered Pankot and was, for as long as interest in him lasted, part of the old hill station, at the still centre of its awareness of what was meant by the secret pass-phrase: one of us. One of us. And it did not matter that he was known, thought to be, not quite that by right. He had become it by example.

'Of course he was in love with her,' Barbie said – and it was through Barbie's more intimate knowledge and compulsive interpretation of things that were known casually to the Laytons that there filtered those elements of incidental intelligence which, even if their accuracy could not be proven, gave the facts the dark, ponderable glow of living issues. Yes, he had been in love with the Manners girl, but she had preferred that Indian, and she more than anyone else must have been to blame for the fact that he and his fellow-conspirators were never tried, never brought properly to book. She hadn't been able to stop them going to prison, but she had destroyed the case which had been built up so efficiently and swiftly by Mr Merrick. And obviously he had suffered for that, been made to pay for it, as men were made to pay. He had been sent to Sundernagar, just as though he was in disgrace. She had ruined his career. Well, she was dead, and one must not speak ill of the dead, and perhaps before she died she had regretted her infatuation. 'And I do not,' Barbie said, 'well, as a Christian how could I, feel as strongly as some about the child. We are all God's children. But that child has not been brought to God.' Old missionary zeal shone on her ruined parchment face, and there was a picture to be had by anyone present when she spoke like this, of Barbie storming down the hill to seek old Lady Manners out and fill her with so much dread of the Lord that she would go penitent with the child in her arms to Mr Peplow; although what he would do if she did had to remain in the shadow of a half conjecture, the child having no known father, a heathen name, Parvati (which Barbie remembered because that was the name of Siva's consort), and being dark-skinned into the bargain (so it was said), in witness of the original sin of its conception.

'No, I wouldn't,' Sarah said, parrying by direct denial Barbie's question whether she would recognize Lady Manners if she saw her. She wondered if her mother had let something be known after all, about her impulsive action in Srinagar.

'But last year you were so close, your mother said.'

'A hundred yards.'

'You must have had a glimpse?'

'Yes, a glimpse.'

It was evening. They moved in the garden among Aunt Mabel's roses, waiting her return from one of the solitary walks she took, stoutly shod; a deaf old woman climbing steep hills, in silence.

Suddenly Barbie said, 'Who is Gillian Waller?'

'I don't know. Why?'

'I thought she might be a relation. Mabel mentions her.'

'Without saying who she is?'

'I mean in her sleep.' Barbie looked embarrassed. 'I go in you know. To make sure. She's become forgetful. Of the light. Her book. She falls asleep with her spectacles on. One is so afraid of danger. Breakage. A splinter in the eye. And on cold nights in winter of insufficient warmth, sitting up asleep not properly covered.'

'You tuck her up.'

'She doesn't know, but you see I owe her. I'm grateful. And I'm a light sleeper myself. The slightest sound wakes me. Of course in the old days in remote parts one felt vigilance laid on one almost by God as a duty and it's become a habit. I sleep best between two and four. I don't need much and I like to be sure. About *her*. I anticipated a *lonely* retirement, you know, most of us do, in the missions. Well, she knew that. She'd seen some of us, growing old and keeping cheerful and doing it on our own. So. Well, that's it. And recently she's become very restless. And then this talking. Well, muttering. Gillian Waller. As if whoever that is, is on her mind. I'm afraid to ask. I hate to seem to pry. She's such a self-contained person. When I first came to Rose Cottage she terrified me. I've always been a great talker. Talk, talk. God is listening, Mr Cleghorn used to say when I caught him out *not*. He was Muzzafirabad, head of the mission there when I took over from Edwina Crane and worried so because they adored her, and I was older than she. It made me talk the more. Talk, Talk. It laps against her. I thought: she'll never stand it. And that made me talk harder. Waves and waves of my talking. Well, she's an edifice and I came to realize it didn't trouble her. She still likes to see me talk even if she can't catch all the words. Rock of ages. The sea pounds and pounds. There are people like that. She's one. Is Susan more cheerful?'

'Not cheerful, but holding on.'

'To what?' Barbie took Sarah's arm. 'To what?' And then, before Sarah could answer, asked, 'Who was Poppy Browning?'

'Poppy Browning? I don't know. Has Aunt Mabel talked about a Poppy Browning too?'

'No. It was gossip I overheard. Would you say that Susan is dangerously withdrawn?'

Sarah stopped, examined a red rose, bent her head to take its scent and again felt the touch of that casual premonition on the back of her neck, so that it seemed to her that she was arrested, suspended, between an uncertain future and a fading history that had something to do with bending her head like this to a bunch of sweet-smelling flowers: not those which Susan threw and she, Sarah, caught, but those there were evidence in an old photograph of her holding on the day of Aunt Fenny's wedding, while Aunty Mabel, half-shadowed by a wide-brimmed hat, stood: an edifice, rock of ages.

'We endure,' she told Barbie. 'We're built for it. In a strange way we're

658

built for it.' But was Susan? She faced Barbie. 'Is that what you overheard? People saying she's withdrawn?'

'Dangerously withdrawn. They stopped when they saw me. Mrs Fosdick, Mrs Paynton, Lucy Smalley. It was Lucy Smalley who was saying – "Yes, the last time I saw her I couldn't help but be reminded of Poppy Browning's daughter." Then they changed the subject.'

'Just talk then, Barbie, not serious concern. Otherwise they'd have roped you in. You're practically part of the family. You'd be the ideal person for someone really worried about Susan to have a word with.'

'Oh I wish,' Barbie said, holding Sarah's arm tight, then letting it go, abruptly, '– but I can't. Go with you. My old headquarters are in Calcutta, you know.'

*

Barbie's ministrations to Aunt Mabel were unobtrusive. She made herself scarce while Sarah followed Mabel along the rear veranda, holding the cradle-basket for the new crop of dead heads. The light had nearly gone. From inside Barbie touched the switch that turned on the globes on the veranda.

'When are you going then?' Mabel asked.

'Tomorrow.'

Mabel nodded, finished attending to the azalea.

'Where will you stay?'

'I rang Aunt Fenny. She'll put me up for a couple of nights.'

'I thought they lived in Delhi.'

'They moved to Calcutta in January.'

They went on to the next flower. Sarah said:

'I wanted to ask you something. Something special.' It was hard to speak up and still soften the blunt edges of a request. 'I wanted to ask you about an old christening gown.'

The capable old hands continued without pause, caressing, turning, searching, nipping; preserving the strength of the plant, coaxing it to vigour and ripe old age with the removal of those decayed relics of its former flowering. I am asking, Sarah thought, to take something like that from her, as well. And wondered if the same thought had occurred, shot home, a sharp wound swiftly healed by acceptance of its necessity – because without speaking Mabel suddenly turned and went inside, leaving Sarah alone there with the basket. There was silence inside the house but presently Barbie came to the french window and beckoned.

'She's in her room and wants you to go in.'

Sarah put the basket down by the chair that was Susan's favourite and followed Barbie through into the hall. The door of Mabel's room, which Sarah had seldom entered, stood open. She tapped, quite loudly. Mabel was on her knees by the open press at the foot of the bed, laying back folds of tissue paper – the same gestures, in exaggerated form, that she used to part foliage to expose the withered blooms on hidden stalks. She turned the last fold, wordlessly exposed the handiwork of a vanished generation. From a distance it was, as Sarah had predicted, yellowed, and perhaps close-to would be brittle-looking; but when she knelt and placed her hand between the lace and the fine lawn that lay beneath it the lace came alive against the pinkness of her skin.

'It's French,' Aunt Mabel said. 'If you like you can let Susan have it.'

'I didn't know about it,' Sarah replied. 'And it's for you to say.' She hesitated. 'It's exquisite.'

There were springs of lavender whose scent mixed with those of sandalwood. Around the hem of the lawn undergarment was a half-inch border of seed pearls. She marvelled at the industry gone into decoration that would not be noticed when the gown was worn. On that day, yes, that one day anyway, wearing this she had looked beautiful.

'My first husband's mother was French,' Mabel said. 'When we married he took me there, to see them. His mother's family. We sailed back to India from Marseilles. I never saw them again.'

'And they gave you the lace?'

'No, his mother gave me that in London. I never saw her again either. She was very handsome. He got his looks from her. And his courage. She was dying but we didn't know. She kept it from us. She saw he was happy.'

Sarah moved her hand under the lace. Astonishing. There was a motif of butterflies. They were alive, fluttering above her moving hand.

'It was an old château. Very old.'

'Where her family lived?'

'Yes. There was a tower.' A pause. 'She lived there. An old woman making lace. She was blind. She'd made lace all her life. I think she was a poor relation or an old retainer. I showed them this lace, this piece. His mother gave it to me – for a christening. And they said, It's Claudine's. Come and see her. Claudine made it, you can tell from the butterflies. So we climbed the tower and went into the room right at the top where she lived and worked. She ran her fingers over the lace, and put her hand under it like you're doing and said, "*Ah, oui, pauvre papillon. C'est un de mes prisonniers.*" And then something I didn't understand but which they told me meant her heart bled for the butterflies because they could never fly out of the prison of the lace and make love in the sunshine. She could feel the sunshine on her hands but her hands wove nothing but a prison for God's most delicate creatures.' A pause. 'I asked them to tell her that real butterflies might play in the sunshine but only lived for a day. It was rather silly and sentimental, but she smiled and nodded and took it as a compliment because she knew I was very young and didn't understand.'

Gently Sarah withdrew her hand. The butterflies were still. She thought of the christening to come and herself standing, perhaps by the side of Ronald Merrick, making vows in the name of a child swaddled in this lace, and knew that she did not want it used for such a purpose, for that occasion. She knew, but could not have explained.

'Please take it,' Mabel said. 'Anyway, I've meant that you should have it one day.'

Sarah began folding the tissue. She shook her head. 'I'm awfully grateful, but I think it should stay here.'

'No, take it,' Mabel repeated. She completed the folding of the gown into the tissue, lifted and held it so that, involuntarily, Sarah raised both hands to receive it. 'It's yours. It says so in my Will. But take it now. I've no use for it. Things shouldn't be kept if they can't be put to use.' She got slowly but quite steadily to her feet, leaving Sarah kneeling, holding the bulked-up tissue. Their glances met, and held. Then, as she turned her head and began to move away, Mabel said:

'You are very young too, but I expect you understand better than I did at your age.'

*

The tonga was still waiting and the driver was lighting his lamps. She told him to drive down to the bazaar, to Jalal-ud-din's. As well as the christening gown Mabel had given her two hundred rupees to help, she said, with her fare and expenses. 'But they've wangled a travel warrant for me,' Sarah had protested, 'and even given me a movement order to make it look as if I'm on official business.' General Rankin, no less than other right-thinking people in Pankot, approved of Sarah Layton's mission. 'Well, it will help with bills,' Mabel had said, 'I expect your mother owes some.'

Between Rose Cottage and the club there was no other traffic. In early June, before the coming of the summer rain, even the Pankot air lost its bite. The heat of the day lingered on into the dark. She longed for rain. Susan's baby would be born in the early weeks of the rain. The mornings would be misty and on days when there was no rain the hills would be vivid green. She sat in the back of the slow-going tonga, holding the parcel, and fancied she could feel the slight pulsation, the flickering of tiny white wings. She became aware of the quietness of the road, its look of desertion, and remembered Barbie's dream of her gallant ride to St John's and her own dream that began with Teddie, who knew where he was going and struck them dumb because of that.

But at the club entrance there were other tongas and from there down the long stretch to the bazaar, with the golf course on her right, and on her left the bungalows that skirted the foot of Central Hill, dominated by the churches of St John's and St Edward's, they passed others, and a military truck, a taxi or two, and presently there were the lights that marked the beginning of the bazaar.

She got down at the tonga stand, told the driver to wait because she wanted him to take her on down to the Pankot Rifles lines. The shops were open, some of them brightly lit so that the few street lamps were paled to nothing. But it was not an hour for civil shopping. Groups of British soldiers eyed her but let her pass without comment, knowing she was not for them. The corporal's chevrons on her sleeves could never trick them into believing otherwise. A white girl was an officer's girl, and probably an officer's daughter. A chokra trotted by her side, offering his services as a little beast of burden. He waited outside Gulab Singh Sahib's pharmacy while she went in and bought toothpaste and toothbrush to use in Calcutta and, as an afterthought, a bottle of toilet water to sweeten the journey. She paid what they owed and wondered where the line was drawn between necessity and luxury, the high cost of living and extravagance; and, outside, gave the three little parcels to the chokra but refused his offer to carry the parcel of tissue and lace.

'Jalal-ud-din's,' she told him and turned towards the store, walking down the arcaded frontage of Pankot's European-style shops; and saw her – the beggar woman who, for Sarah, had become interchangeable as a suppliant figure with the woman in the white saree. And afterwards, because she had concentrated on the figure of the beggar woman, recalled that embarrassing and distressing scene on Mirat station and Merrick's remote face, his muttered rejection of her plea in the same tongue the woman spoke in, she was unsure, as unsure as she was ashamed; unsure that the elderly white woman, half-hidden by a distinguished-looking middle-aged Indian woman, in the act of bending, climbing into a car through a door held open by an Indian driver, whose bulk almost immediately cut her off, was the woman from the houseboat; ashamed because the glimpse she had, the conviction that the woman was Lady Manners, caused her automatically to stop, half turn away, to avoid anything in the nature of a direct physical confrontation, as if – so – she might make up for an earlier impulsive action, eradicate it, rub it out, and identify herself with a collective conspiracy. She was ashamed to remember the way she stood, awkwardly poised, persuasively conveying in every exaggerated histrionic gesture and change of expression the portrait of a girl who feared she had left something behind at Gulab Singh Sahib's; so that the chokra, concerned, held up the three packages, inviting her to count. Then he pointed to the package she held herself, as though he thought some fit of absent-mindedness had caused her momentarily not to realize that she held it.

She smiled and nodded and faced towards Jalal-ud-din's again, the shame already warming her face; but there was no sign of the car. It had gone swiftly, silently, no doubt turning the corner of the inverted V to take the steep road into West Hill where people like the Laytons never went. She turned again, retraced her steps to the tonga stand and there gave the chokra his anna.

III

'Now tell me,' Aunt Fenny said, 'what have you really come for?'

The flat was air-conditioned. Perhaps that shadow of professional

662

neglect which Uncle Arthur had always seemed to work under had not lifted; but at least he appeared to have reached the point of contact with the earth of its dark rainbow, and found a crock of fairy gold: the flat, its high view far above the roofs of old aristocractic houses, the like of which he had never secured for his and Aunt Fenny's personal use; and a war-time sinecure which, so far as Sarah could make out, involved him in giving lectures of a para-military nature to young officers, on the structure of Indian military and civilian administration. He was, she gathered, seconded to a branch of welfare and education which had its eye on the capacity some of these young Englishmen might show for identifying themselves with the problems of a country with which the war alone had brought them in contact. Behind the lectures was a blandishment: Stay on, stay on. 'We give them a picture you know,' Colonel Grace said, 'of what it's really like in peace-time, eradicate some of those impressions they have, that we're a load of blimps, sitting on our fannies under punkahs and shouting Koi Hai.' To counteract all that they gave them the stuff. The real stuff. Sarah nodded, and the young men – three of those in question – smiled easily. According to Aunt Fenny the flat was usually fuller even than Sarah had found it of Uncle Arthur's 'chaps'. He had conceived it part of the duties of the department he headed to bring the chaps home, or have them call, in groups, swapping the scratch amenities of the temporary mess out at the place where the courses were held, for the more considerable ones of a genuine Anglo-Indian *pied-à-terre*, where they could imbibe, at breakfast, tiffin or dinner, those lessons that went deeper than any mere chat from a rostrum ever could. There had been no British intake into the ICS since the war began and the Indian army was dense with emergency officers of all kinds who had never thought of making a career of arms, least of all in India. Among them, surely, there were a few who would get the call, see the vision, understand the hard realities of imperial service and feel the urge to match themselves to them?

'They're mostly what Arthur calls in abeyance,' Fenny told Sarah as she showed her her room – a comfortable little white-walled box, as cold as a refrigerator, with the bulging grey Bengal monsoon sky – which Sarah had never seen in her life before – filling the hermetically sealed window. Overnight from Ranpur she had ridden into the June rain. It would not reach Pankot for a while yet. She felt, from this alone, that she had travelled into another world, so that it amazed her that it was ever possible to make the mistake of thinking of India as one country.

'What kind of abeyance?' (She was thinking of her mother.)

'Oh, you know, between postings, or getting better from jaundice, or just among the crowd that get stuck in depots and training establishments and apply for courses to stop themselves going barmy. We don't get many who are *born* slackers. At least Arthur doesn't bring them back here. Of course they're not usually quite our kind of people' – (Sarah nodded, again, gravely) – 'but then we're a bit of a dying species, aren't we, pet? And they're mostly nice cheerful chaps, and some of them *are* from good homes, and it's usually that kind who are seriously thinking of staying on after the war. Arthur's a great success with them – I think because he responds to them. He feels they genuinely want to know about India and what it's meant to the standard of life they enjoy back home and take so much for granted.'

'I expect you're a success with them too, Aunt Fenny.'

'Oh, I am! Do you know why? Because I'm happy. Isn't it gorgeous—?' She indicated not the room so much as the flat the room was a cold, rather remote, unlived-in part of. 'To be cool. Oh, to be cool.' There had been a time, surely, when Aunt Fenny had dismissed the more modern aspects of twentieth-century Anglo-Indian life as unwelcome signs of things going to the dogs. Sarah smiled. She herself preferred to be less cool, but it was nice to see Aunt Fenny enjoying something. This morning the lines of disapproval that fixed the mouth were like marks of an old illness, like smallpox, that had left no other trace. But it was at the moment Sarah was thinking this that Fenny stopped being happy about the flat and reverted to her older, probing, rather suspicious self.

'Now tell me, what have you really come for?'

Sarah told her. When she finished Aunt Fenny said, 'But, pet, couldn't I have done it for you and saved you all this trouble and expense?'

'They gave me a rail warrant.' She hesitated, observed Aunt Fenny's invisible hackles tremble with the effort she was making not to let them rise, and added, 'Susan has this idea he's lost a limb or his eyesight, and that if anyone goes to see him and then writes to her they might not tell her the truth, out of kindness.'

'But I could have seen him and then come up to Pankot.'

'That would have been expense and trouble for you and you could still have kept the facts from her out of kindness. I think she wanted it to be me because she believes she could see through it if I kept anything back.'

Aunt Fenny smiled, touched Sarah's arm.

'Do I detect six of one and half a dozen of another? I mean he took a bit of a shine to you in Mirat. Was it mutual?'

Sarah looked away, unable to take the opportunity to make Aunt Fenny feel less excluded from the question of Captain Merrick's bodily state of health. 'No, not at all. Anyway, I don't think he took a shine. I'm not really looking forward to it, but it seems to be important to Susan, and I'd like to get it over with as soon as possible. Do you think if I turned up this morning they'd let me see him?'

'You'll do no such thing. You'll tuck down here for the rest of the morning and catch up with some sleep. I'll ring the hospital and see what can be arranged for early evening or late afternoon, then you can have a relaxed day, see Mr Merrick at about five o'clock and come back here in time for drinks. Some of the boys are coming in for dinner. Do you really have to go back tomorrow?'

'Yes, I've booked my sleeper from Ranpur to Pankot for tomorrow night.'

'The old midnight special?'

'Yes.'

'So you'll have to be on the midday from Cal to get the connection? What about a reservation? It's not easy at such short notice.'

'Oh, I'll squeeze in. It's not difficult if you don't want a berth. Someone with a berth to Delhi will let me sit in. We get to Ranpur about nine in the evening, long before anyone wants to have their bed made up.'

'Yes, well, all the same I'll ask your uncle to pull some rank. He'll enjoy that. He's just like a boy about being able to say it's Colonel Grace speaking. But get your head down for now, pet. I can tell you didn't have a berth last night. Was it ghastly?'

'No, fun really. I sat up all night with some nurses who were on their way to Shillong.' And envied them, going to the war it seems I can never go to. We played cards and drank rather a lot of gin. And I listened while they discussed men in general and in particular the two officers who tried to get off with the two prettiest girls and had to be firmly ejected from the carriage when the train stopped at Benares. I fell asleep, near Dhanbad. The taste of the journey is still in my mouth.

She sat on the bed and at once knew how tired she was. Over-excited. Like a child. She was aware of Aunt Fenny stooping to unlace her shoes for her. She protested but it was done just the same. Weightless, her legs lifted easily on to the bed. Curtains were drawn. Comforted by all this evidence of family devotion and the softness of the pillow under her head, she fell asleep.

*

Before the taxi reached the Officers' wing of the military hospital the rain stopped. She arrived in bright sunshine and, mounting the steps to the pillared entrance, took off Aunt Fenny's heavy-duty macintosh. She had changed from uniform into mufti – a plain cotton dress whose lightness she was glad of in a humidity that was higher than she had ever experienced. After she had spoken to the English corporal at the desk and been asked to wait she sat and smoked, but the cigarette was damp. She dropped it, unfinished, into the sand-tray. The corporal answered the telephone, then spoke to a colleague whose uniform bore no chevrons. The private came across.

'Miss Layton for Captain Merrick?'

She nodded, followed him out of the reception hall into a corridor where there were lifts. The smell of ether-meth was settling on her stomach. She felt slightly faint. The private gave instructions to the Indian lift attendant then said to her, 'Sister Prior'll meet you at the top.' She thanked him, noticed – and was sorry for the embarrassment they must cause him – the septic spots on cheek and chin, vivid under the glare of the lift lights. He did not meet her glance. He smelt strongly of cheap hair oil. The attendant closed the mesh gates. Slowly they ascended. The letter from Ronald

Merrick had been signed by a nurse in the QAIMNS. But she could not remember the initials. Had it been P for Prior? No. It might have been P, but not for Prior because the letter had come from Comilla. There had been no letter from Calcutta.

The lift stopped and the attendant opened the gates. She thanked him and stepped on to the landing. The smell was stronger than ever. A window gave a view of trees and light to a table with flowers on it and chairs for waiting. But she was the only visitor. There was no sign of Sister Prior; the corridors left and right of the waiting-room were empty. Had the lift man let her out on the wrong floor? Or the boy with the pimples misheard the corporal? She went to the window and stared at the trees and the view between them and the vast *maidan* beyond which was the low-lying clutter of the city. A door shut somewhere along one of the corridors, and presently she heard the sound of a woman's footsteps. She turned, waited, and in a moment the woman entered the waiting-room area: a girl, rather, no older than herself, with dark hair rolled under a neat cap.

'Miss Layton? I'm Sister Prior.' She put out her hand, which Sarah took. The overall scrutiny she was under did not escape her. She wondered whether Sister Prior was the sort who would fall in love with a patient – in love with Merrick, for instance – and be jealously possessive of him. But she had scarcely had time.

'Am I upsetting regular visiting hours?' Sarah asked. Her hand had been let go of rather suddenly.

'That's all right. The message from your – uncle? Colonel—?'

'Colonel Grace.'

'Grace. Well, he said you'd come a long way.'

But Sister Prior made no move. They eyed each other levelly. The same height, Sarah thought, as well as the same age.

'I didn't quite get the relationship. You *are* a relative, aren't you?'

'No.'

'Well, I thought it was odd. I'd always understood he had none. I mean none at home let alone out here. But matron was under the impression from Colonel Grace there was a family connection.'

'I expect he mentioned my sister. Captain Merrick was best man at her wedding.' She paused, intending not to explain further, but found herself doing so. 'I'm really here on her behalf. We had a letter from him when he was in Comilla.'

'Yes, I see. I haven't told him you're coming. I thought I wouldn't in case you didn't turn up and he was disappointed. But I'll go and tell him now. If I just say Miss Layton will that be enough?'

'Enough, but a bit of a surprise. I live in Pankot.'

'Where?'

'It's a hill station north of Ranpur.'

'Oh. Yes, you have come a long way, haven't you? Is your sister in Calcutta, too?'

'She couldn't travel.'

'Isn't she well?'

'She's having a baby. It's due in three weeks.'

'I see. I hope you don't mind my asking all these questions. Ronald is rather a special case with us. He's been wonderfully brave. But we think terribly lonely. Do you know anything about his family?'

'No, nothing.'

'His record shows his next-of-kin as a cousin of some sort. Both his parents died before the war. I think it was a late marriage. I mean they were quite old. And he has no brothers and sisters, and then of course he's never married himself. And until we heard from Colonel Grace today we were under the impression he had no close friends. I mean the only letters he gets are the official sort. And since he's been here he's never asked me to write a personal letter to anyone, so I've been wondering, I mean how you knew where he was.'

'He wrote us from Comilla and said he was being transferred to Calcutta. Someone on General Rankin's staff at Pankot checked for us and got the hospital in Comilla to send us a signal where we could contact him. My sister's concerned rather specially. Captain Merrick was wounded at the same time her husband was killed.'

'Oh, I'm sorry. About her husband.'

Sister Prior had not once let her glance fall away. Sarah felt her own fixed by it. 'I'm sure he'll be glad to see you, and I do appreciate your coming such a very long way, but I hope you won't find it necessary to ask him too many questions on your sister's behalf. We try not to let them dwell too much on what happened.'

'I haven't come to ask questions. I've come mainly to tell him how grateful my sister is for what he tried to do to help her husband, in spite of being wounded himself. We don't know exactly what it was he did do, and I'm sure he won't talk about it even if I ask, but it was something that led the divisional commander to send in a recommendation.'

'A recommendation?'

'Yes.'

'You mean for a decoration?'

'Yes.'

'Does he know that?'

'Probably not.'

'I hope you won't mention it.'

'I won't mention it.'

'I suppose decorations serve some sort of purpose. I never see what, myself. But then I've seen too much of what earning them involves. I always think a thumping great cheque would fill the bill better. What can you do with a medal except stick it on their chests and leave them to stick it in a drawer? I expect that shocks you. With an uncle who's a colonel.'

'My father's a colonel too.' About to add: And it doesn't shock me: she changed her mind and said instead, 'I'll wait here while you break the news to Captain Merrick that I've called to see him.'

Sister Prior nodded. A smile – of distant irony – momentarily broadened her pretty lips. Sarah turned, embattled behind the barriers of her class and traditions because the girl had challenged her to stand up for them. Hearing Sister Prior's retreating footsteps she realized the opportunity to prepare herself for whatever it was she had to face in Ronald Merrick's room had gone. Perhaps in any case it would have been deliberately withheld. The sight might be shocking, and it might please Sister Prior to watch how she took it. She lit another of the damp cigarettes, gathered her things together: Aunt Fenny's macintosh, the box of fruit, the carton of two hundred Three Castles cigarettes packed in four round tins of fifty each. She wished to be ready to go with Sister Prior directly she returned. But the minutes ticked by. It was nearly five o'clock. Occasionally there were footsteps in the corridors, and the sound of doors opened and closed. Voices, once. And the rising clank and whisper of the lift. At five o'clock a dark-skinned Anglo-Indian nurse appeared, coming from the direction Sister Prior had taken.

'Miss Layton? Captain Merrick will see you now.'

She followed the girl down the corridor. Reaching a door numbered 27, which bore beneath a circular observation window a card in a metal frame in which was written in black ink, Captain R. Merrick, the girl tapped, opened and said, 'Miss Layton to see you, Captain Merrick,' and stood aside. Entering, Sarah halted abruptly, shocked to see him on his feet and coming towards her, aided by a stick, dragging the weight of one plastered leg – until, coming to her senses, she saw the man was not Merrick but a tall burly fellow who smiled and said, 'He's all yours. Ignore me. I was just visiting.' Automatically she smiled in return and looking beyond him saw Merrick in the bed by the window – or anyway a figure lying there, propped by pillows. A complex of bandage and gauze around the head, like a white helmet, left only the features and a narrow area of the cheeks exposed. The sheet that covered his body was laid over a semi-circular frame. She could see nothing of him except the small exposed area of the face and blue-pyjamaed chest and shoulders. His arms were under the arch of the sheet. His head was inclined a little to one side. He was looking at her. As she moved towards him she heard the door shut.

She said, 'Hello, Ronald,' and was then at the bedside. The down-draught from a fan whirling gently above held the sheet pressed against the frame. She could see the pattern of the mesh. She had an unpleasant idea that there was nothing beneath the frame, that what she could see was somehow all that was left of him, although she knew that was not possible. Embarrassed, she switched her glance quickly back to his face, determined to hold it there. He looked younger than she remembered, younger even than in that one and only photograph, as if pain had smoothed out his face and brought a glow of innocence to his complexion. She could not see his chin, but the upper lip was shaved. She wondered how he managed. And then remembered Sister Prior.

'I've brought some fruit and cigarettes. I hope that's all right. I remembered you smoked.' She put the packages on the bedside-table which was empty except for an invalid teapot from which she imagined he was given water. She glanced at him again as she did so, and saw him swallow. Perhaps he had difficulty with his voice. His eyes were closed now, but as she moved round to sit on the chair at the other side of the bed he opened them and watched her. Yes, they were blue. Extraordinarily blue. He swallowed again.

'I'm sorry,' he said, 'I thought Sister Prior was playing some kind of practical joke, or that I was funny in the head because she's not really the joking kind. How is Susan?'

'She's fine. She sent her love. And Mother of course. And Aunt Fenny. She and Uncle Arthur are in Calcutta now. She'll come and see you in a day or two. She asked me to be sure to find out if there's anything you need.'

'That's very kind of her. And kind of you. Are you in Calcutta long?'

'No, I go back tomorrow.'

'To Pankot?'

She nodded.

He said, 'Do smoke. There are some in the drawer.'

'Can I light one for you?'

'I'm afraid it involves more than that. I can't hold anything yet.'

She lit a cigarette from her own case, then – overcoming the reluctance she felt to do so – a mixture of embarrassment and faint revulsion – she stood, leaned forward and held the cigarette near his lips. He moved his head to help her place the tip in his mouth.

'I'm afraid they're very damp.'

He released the cigarette, let his head back on to the pillow and blew out slowly, without inhaling. After a moment's hesitation she inhaled from the cigarette herself. The sharing of the cigarette was an unexpected intimacy. For a while they smoked alternately.

'Your hands,' he said, 'smell so much nicer than Sister Prior's. She's a bit of a dragon.'

'A very pretty dragon.'

'You think so?'

'Don't you?'

'A man in hospital's no judge. All the nurses look pretty, but it's their hands and throats and elbows that count in the end. Sister Prior has very cold hands and red elbows. I'm not sure she hasn't got goitre too. The fact is she depresses me a bit. Sister Pawle in Comilla was much more like it. She's the one who wrote that letter for me. I was beginning to wonder whether it reached you. But this is miles better. Miles, miles better. And thanks for just turning up. You get used to taking the days as they come and it's better not to look forward to anything that isn't routine. But when you've gone I'll have something special to look back on, and count by, that I wasn't expecting.'

She held the cigarette for him but he shut his eyes briefly and thanked her, said he'd had enough. He couldn't actually stop smoking, but it did make him a bit dizzy. Sister Prior was slowly breaking him of the habit.

'What time do you go back tomorrow?' he asked.

'I ought to catch the midday train.'

'Then I shan't see you again.'

'I could come tomorrow morning. Would you like me to?'

His eyes were shut again.

'Oh, I should like it. But they wouldn't. They have other plans for me tomorrow. It's a good thing you turned up today.'

She waited for an explanation. When it seemed there wasn't to be one she asked him directly, 'Is it the surgery you mentioned in your letter?'

He nodded. He opened his eyes but didn't look at her. 'They were going to do it sooner. But I didn't travel as well as they expected. They made me feel like a bottle of wine when they said that. That I hadn't travelled well.'

'Did they fly you out?'

'Yes, it was fun. I've never flown in my life before, until all this. They flew me out of Imphal first, and then from Comilla. I've clocked up about three hours, I think. On my back though. It's an odd feeling flying on your back. You think of yourself as totally inulnerable. Well, you do taking off and in the air. Landing's a bit of a jolt. The chap who was in here when you arrived pranged on Dum-Dum a couple of weeks ago, coming in from Agartala. Extraordinary. The plane was a write-off, but he only bust a leg.'

She said after a while, 'Do you want to tell me about tomorrow, about what they're doing?'

He turned his head towards her, as if to study the depth of her interest.

'Oh, they'll poke about and come up with something and tell me afterwards. And don't be fooled. I look as weak as a kitten, I know, but I'm full of beans under this dopey exterior. Otherwise they wouldn't be doing it yet.'

'What time are they doing it?'

'Nine o'clock. Unless there's an emergency. I mean, not me. Someone else. I'm not a priority. Don't worry. I'm all right.'

'If I rang at about midday I expect they'd tell me how it went.'

'Yes, I'm sure they would.'

'Then I'll do that.'

'Thank you.' A pause. 'Teddie told me Susan was having a baby. He was very proud.'

'It's due next month. In about three weeks.'

He said, 'I expect she hopes it will be a boy.'

'I don't think she minds.'

Again he shut his eyes. 'What do you say?' he asked. 'She was such a happy girl. It's the happy people who are hardest hit when something like that happens. Teddie was a happy sort of man, too. They seemed made for each other. Well, I suppose that kind of happiness means there's a basic resilience, and that when she's got over the shock she'll come up smiling. Although—'

670

'Although what?'

'She struck me as happy in the way a little girl is. Perhaps that's a protection too. It interested me, the difference between you both.'

He brought the sentence to an abrupt end. She felt the full-stop. They had entered a zone of silence. For a moment she imagined he had fallen asleep, exhausted by the visit and unable to cope with the demands it made on him. Perhaps he was already under sedation, in preparation for whatever they were going to do to him in the morning. She felt a stirring of morbid curiosity, the beginning of a distasteful urge to draw the sheet away and observe the condition of his legs and abdomen, and arms from elbow downwards.

'I expect there are things you both want to know.'

She glanced up quickly.

'I hope my letter didn't worry you,' he added. 'Did you show it to Susan?'

'Yes, I did.' She hesitated. 'It did worry us a bit.'

'I'm sorry. Did anyone ever write to her from the division?'

'She had one the day before from Colonel Selby-Smith, so she knew you and Teddie had been together when it happened. He said you'd helped him. That's one of the reasons I'm here, to tell you how grateful she is. Well, all of us. And of course she's looking for reassurance, that you're all right, or going to be. The letter from Colonel Selby-Smith seemed to hint that what you tried to do to help Teddie made things worse for you. What worried us about your letter was that it had to be dictated.'

'Yes, I see.'

She waited, expecting an explanation, or a comment; the reassurance that she could take back to Susan. When it did not come it was, perversely, not concern for him – which might have filled her – but renewed reluctance to be drawn towards him which she felt; and this seemed to empty her. She thought, almost abruptly: He lacks a particular quality, the quality of candour; there is a point, an important point, at which it becomes difficult to deal with him. He isn't shut off. It isn't that. He's open, wide open, and he wants me to enter, to ask him about the legs I can't see, the forearms I can't see, the obscene mystery beneath the white helmet of bandages. But I won't. They, or their absence, their mystery – these I find appalling as well. It's unfair, perhaps unhuman of me. On the other hand, it can't be inhuman because I feel it, and I belong to the species, I'm a fully paid up member.

He had turned away, aware – possibly – that the purely physical equation of their eyes, meeting, lacked a value. When he began speaking she wondered whether the way in was being widened; salted, like the way in to a dangerous, derelict mine. She found herself exerting pressure on the ground with the soles of her feet and on her chair with the small of her back.

'I thought it might be something else that worried you,' he said, 'that thing I said about the business lying heavily and wanting to talk about it. Get it off my chest. As if I had some sort of confession to make.'

671

'Have you, Ronald?'

He turned again, stared at her. He smiled slightly.

'Well, we all have, I suppose. The fact is I feel responsible. Perhaps there's something about me that attracts disaster, not for myself, but for others. Do you think that's possible? That someone can be bad luck?'

'Perhaps.'

'I was the worst best man Teddie could have chosen. Remember me saying that? That night I came to say goodbye and found you watching fireflies?'

'Waiting for them. Yes, I do remember.'

'You denied I was the worst, but that didn't fool me. Teddie wasn't fooled either. When I saw him again he'd cooled off. I could see him putting distance between us. Oh, I'm sure there's something in it. You find you have – a victim. You haven't chosen him. But that's what he is. Afterwards he haunts you, just as if he were on your conscience. The irony is that you don't really have him there. You can question your conscience and come out with a clean bill. But he sticks, just the same. Teddie sticks. And that has a certain irony in it. I'm sorry. I'm making it worse. I mean, giving you more cause to worry, not less.'

'It was Susan who worried. But just about you and how you really are and how much of what is wrong is due to your staying and looking after Teddie.'

'Staying?'

'She was told you stayed with him until the arrival of medical aid.'

'I suppose that was one way of putting it, but there wasn't any alternative. Well, make that clear to her. We were both up the creek. The question is why? Whose creek?'

He closed his eyes again, and this time it occurred to her that closing them was deliberate, part of a total effect he was seeking to make. His voice was quite strong, it showed no real sign of fatigue.

'You see, I ask myself, continually ask myself, whatever fault it may have been of his, would it have happened if I hadn't been with him? And the answer is no. It wouldn't. It was the stone all over again. The stone that hit the car. Only this time it wasn't a stone. And of course it wasn't thrown at me. Everything about it was different, but the same. In effect.'

She said, 'You're imagining it. You ought to forget it and concentrate on getting better.'

He lay for a while, not speaking, not looking.

'No,' he said suddenly, so that she was almost startled. 'One doesn't get better by not facing it. Besides, I was fond of him. I may have envied him too. You know how it is. He had all the attributes, didn't he? The game. Playing it. I mean really believing that it was. Astonishing, because it's not a game, is it? Unless you play it, then I suppose that's what it becomes. I keep on telling myself that it was playing the game that killed him, so that his death becomes a kind of joke. Only I can't see it. To me it was just a mess that he wouldn't have got into without me.'

He turned again and watched her.

'I'm telling you, not Susan. I couldn't tell Susan. For her I'd play the game myself. But with you it isn't necessary, is it?'

'No, it's not necessary.'

'Anyway, you'd see through it. I lack the attributes. You notice things like that, but I feel you don't mind, that it doesn't matter to you that I'm not – not like Teddie. It mattered to Teddie. It made him over-meticulous about the rules. He was trying to point the difference between us. He never quite forgave me for what happened at the wedding. He didn't say much, but he made me feel – intended to make me feel – that I'd done something not quite – pukka – getting involved in that sort of thing, accepting the intimacy he offered when he asked me to be best man but failing to tell him just who he was inviting intimacy with. It was the sort of situation you couldn't actually say was wrong. All you could say was it wouldn't have happened if, for instance, I'd been a Muzzy Guide – wouldn't have happened then because a fellow-officer in the true sense of the word wouldn't have any – what? Areas of professional secrecy? He wasn't blaming me. He saw how reasonable it was for me not to go round saying, Look, I'm the police officer in the Manners case, and I get threatening anonymous notes, and any day someone might chuck a stone at me and involve me and whoever I'm with in an embarrassing police scene. Yes, he saw that. All the same he resented *being* involved. He saw it as an unnecessary vulgarity, one that marked the difference between my world and his. He recognized that these two worlds had to meet, I mean in war-time, but that didn't mean he had to like it or encourage the intimacy to continue. We had one brief talk after he'd got back from Nanoora and joined the General and the advance party in the training area we went to, and of course he said all the right things, that I had absolutely nothing to apologize for or explain; but after that he never mentioned Mirat to me again. When I say he told me about Susan having a baby, that isn't strictly true. He told someone else, and it came up in mess – as a cause for general congratulation. Well, you know. One makes a sort of joke about it. It was quite a night. We were pushing the boat out because the orders had just come from Corps to move the division down into the field. They were all a bit high. Which is partly why Teddie let it out, that he was going to be a father. And that was the night I really knew that he did resent having got mixed up socially with a chap who wasn't a Muzzy Guide or its equivalent. He was laughing at the things the others said to him. But when I congratulated him and asked him to give you and Susan my kind regards he became frigidly polite.'

'You're exaggerating. Teddie wasn't like that.' But she guessed that Teddie had been. 'Anyway, he sent on your kind regards.'

'Oh, but he would. He said "Yes of course. I'll do that." And that was his *word*. The frigidness and politeness were due to him turning it over in his mind first, whether he should agree or say "No, I think not if you don't mind, Merrick".'

'You make him sound terribly old-fashioned.'

'He was.' A pause. 'He believed in the old-fashioned virtues. The junior officers in a war-time divisional HQ are a pretty hybrid bunch. They divide, you know, into the amateurs and the professionals. But there's a paradox, because the professionals are invariably the temporary chaps like me. The amateurs are the permanent men like Teddie, who see it as a game. But even among *them* Teddie stood out as an anachronism. He had old-fashioned convictions. So did a lot of them. But in Teddie you felt he had the courage that was supposed to go with them. And when I look at it squarely, it was having that kind of courage that killed him. But he died an amateur. He should have had a horse.'

'The Muzzy Guides used to.'

'I know.'

Again he closed his eyes.

She said, 'What do you mean, he died an amateur?'

'I'll tell you, but I don't want you to tell Susan.'

'I can't promise not to.'

He smiled, but kept his eyes shut.

She said, 'She may prefer to know he died that way.'

'Yes,' he said presently. 'In its way it had a certain gallantry.' He paused, opened his eyes, glanced at her. 'You know about the Jiffs?'

'Jiffs?'

'They're what we call Indian soldiers who were once prisoners of the Japanese in Burma and Malaya, chaps who turned coat and formed themselves into army formations to help the enemy. There were a lot of them in that attempt the Japanese made to invade India through Imphal.'

'Yes, I've heard of them. Were there really a lot?'

'I'm afraid so. And officers like Teddie took it to heart. They couldn't believe Indian soldiers who'd eaten the king's salt and been proud to serve in the army generation after generation could be suborned like that, buy their way out of prison camp by turning coat, come armed hand in hand with the Japs to fight their own countrymen, fight the very officers who had trained them, cared for them and earned their respect. Well, you know. The regimental mystique. It goes deep. Teddie was always afraid of finding there were old Muzzy Guides among them. And of course that's what he did find. If Teddie had been the crying kind, I think he'd have cried. That would have been better, if he'd accepted the fact, had a good cry, then shrugged his shoulders and said, Well, that's life, once they were good soldiers, now they're traitors, shoot the lot.' Merrick hesitated. 'A lot *were* being shot. Our own soldiers despised them. They were a pretty poor bunch, badly led, badly equipped. And I suppose underneath the feeling artificially inspired by their propaganda – that they were the real patriots, fighting for India's independence – they were, deep down, bent with shame. The Japanese despised them too. They seldom used them in a truly combatant role and left them in the lurch time after time. Anyway, that's the picture we were getting, and we were also getting a picture of our own troops, Indian and British, killing them off rather than taking prisoners. That wasn't what we wanted. The whole thing of the Jiffs became rather my special pigeon in divisional intelligence. And I was trying to get a different picture. I wanted prisoners. Prisoners who would talk, talk about the whole thing, recruitment back in Malaya and Burma, inducements, pressures, promises. Which Indian officers had gone for the thing and which had only been sheep. When it came to the question of Indian King's commissioned officers who had joined the Jiffs, Teddie preserved a sort of tight-lipped silence. He made you feel an officer who turned traitor was probably best dead anyway, unmentionable, quite unspeakable. And perhaps not really a shock, because to him an educated Indian meant a political Indian. But the sepoys, NCOs and VCOs were a different matter. It's those he would have cried for. All those chaps whose fathers served before them, and had medals, and little chits from old commanding officers. Sometimes he said a lot of them probably joined so as to get back on their own side, and that in any major confrontation the Jiffs would come over and help kick the Japanese in the teeth. He became obsessed with the whole question. He seldom talked of anything else, to me anyway, because the Jiffs were my pigeon, and in a subtle way he used the Jiffs, his views on them, and mine, to point up the differences between us. Do you know what distinguishes the amateur?'

Sarah shook her head.

'The affection he has for his task, its end, its means and everyone who's involved with him in it. Most professional soldiers are amateurs. They love their men, their equipment, their regiments. In a special way they love their enemies too. It's common to most walks of life, isn't it? To fall in love with the means as well as the end of an occupation?'

'You think that's wrong?'

'Yes, I think it is. It's a confusion. It dilutes the purity of an act. It blinds you to the truth of a situation. It hedges everything about with a mystique. One should not be confused in this way.'

'Are you never confused, Ronald?'

'I am – frequently confused. But I do try to act, unemotionally. I do try for a certain professional detachment.'

'It's funny,' she said, 'I should have said you were actually quite an emotional person. Underneath. And that it sometimes runs you into trouble.'

He was watching her, but she detected nothing in his expression except – and this so suddenly that she felt she had observed it the moment that it fell on him – a curious serenity. 'Well, of course, you're right,' he said. 'I've certainly run into trouble in my time. It's one thing to try to act unemotionally and quite another thing to do so. No act is performed without a decision being made to perform it. I suppose emotion goes into a decision, especially into a major decision. My decision to get out of the police and into the army was an emotional one, wasn't it? Just like the one I made as a boy, to try to get into the Indian Police. But I don't think I was ever an amateur, either as a copper or a soldier. I had no affection for the job, in either case. But I did the job. I tried not to be confused. That was the difference between Teddie and me – the *real* difference, not the one that had to do with the fact that Teddie was a Muzzy Guide and I was, well, what I am – a boy from an elementary school who won a scholarship to a better one and found it difficult later not to be a bit ashamed of his parents, and very much ashamed of his grandparents. But any difference that Teddie saw in our attitudes, he'd always put down to the fact that I wasn't the same class. You can't disguise it, can you? It comes out in subtle ways, even when you've learned the things to say and how to say them. It comes out in not knowing the places or the people your kind of people know, it comes out in the lack of points of common contact. People like me carry around with them the vacuum of their own anonymous history, and there comes a moment when a fellow like Teddie looks at us and honestly believes we lack a vital gift as well, some sort of sense of inborn decency that's not our fault but makes us not quite trustworthy. I'm sorry. I'm not speaking ill of him. That's what he thought. And that's why he was killed. I'm only trying to make it clear, make this background clear. He was killed trying to show me how a thing should be done, because he didn't trust me to do it right. Well, it was his own fault – but remove me from the situation and it wouldn't have happened.'

'What situation?'

He closed his eyes and turned his head away. 'What situation? It was a simpler one than – another I remember. It began with a fellow called Mohammed Baksh. A Jiff. He was captured by a patrol from one of the companies of the British battalion of the Brigade that was probing forward on our right flank. Overnight things had become terribly confused and by morning the British battalion had found itself out on a limb. The advance of the Indian battalion on their left had been held up and it looked as if the British battalion might get cut off or have its flank turned. They were astride a road in hill country and we hadn't got a clear picture of the enemy's strength, or of where the major enemy attack was likely to come from. And this particular Brigadier was suffering from a bout of jitters, he was jumpy about losing his British battalion and wanted to pull them back, but the General had other ideas, of pushing another battalion forward astride the road and deploying both battalions to encircle whatever enemy units there were in the immediate vicinity. But he didn't want to issue the order without personal contact with the Brigadier. He decided to visit the Brigade and get things moving from there, unless he judged the Brigadier's on-the-spot appreciation had something to be said for it, or he thought him incapable of pressing forward immediately with the right sort of enthusiasm. He took Teddie with him. And at the last moment he turned to me and told me to go with them to make sure the Brigade Intelligence Officer had a complete picture of what we knew, and to assess on the spot anything he might be able to add that would be new to us.' A pause. 'We went in two jeeps. There were three in the General's. The General, Teddie, and the

Indian driver, two in mine, myself and my driver. Teddie drove the other jeep. He loved driving. A jeep particularly. And the driver liked sitting perched at the back, with a Sten gun. It was a lovely morning. Bright and crisp. During the day of course it got very hot. Have you ever been in Manipur?'

'No.'

'On the plain itself, around Imphal, it's like northern India up in the North-west Frontier, around Abbotabad; much the same view of hills and mountains. We were south of there, in the foothills. The road was pretty rough. Steep wooded banks one side, pretty long wooded drops the other – well, for much of its course. You flattened out every so often, when you went through a village. We reached the Brigade headquarters round about eight-thirty a.m. I wasn't in on the talk that went on between the Brigadier and General. I was with the Brigade Intelligence Officer and he'd just had the IO of the British battalion on the wireless, reporting that patrols had picked up this fellow Mohammed Baksh of the Jiffs. So far he hadn't given any information. They said he looked half-starved and had probably deserted several days before. I wasn't so sure. The picture I had was that most of the Jiffs looked pretty exhausted. They didn't have the stamina of the Japanese. The whole force had crossed the Chindwin and come through hill jungle. The Japanese are old hands at that. Advance first and worry about your lines of communications and supplies afterwards. That's their technique. It worked in Burma and Malaya, but it didn't work this time because we were ready for it. That's why the General wanted to push the other battalion forward. He guessed the Indian battalion on the left of the British was misinterpreting the strength of the opposition they'd met in the night. I realized it was important to know more about this Jiff fellow. If all that stood in the way of the British battalion was a Jiff formation, then the General could perform his containing operation easily.'

'Didn't the British battalion know what was in front of them?'

'No, they'd reached their objective, and the only reason for the pause was their discovery that their left flank was unprotected, because the Indian battalion hadn't kept pace. The Indians were stuck about two miles back, apparently contained by a Japanese force of at least battalion strength. But the General thought that if the Indian battalion was pinned down by the Japanese, so were the Japanese by the Indians, a sort of tactical stalemate, and since the British battalion was astride the road the initiative was still very much with the Brigade. The British battalion had sent patrols forward, of course, but found nothing except this stray Jiff and their patrols reported no apparent threat to their flank or rear. Down there, you know, it isn't country you can stand and get a view of. You have to probe it more or less yard by yard. But they had found the Jiff, and I wondered whether the fact that he hadn't given any information was because he spoke no English and the IO of the British battalion spoke hardly any Urdu. I asked the Brigade IO what was happening about Baksh. He said he'd asked the battalion to send him back but the answer had been, Come and get him, we can't spare either the transport or the men just to look after a Jiff.'

He stopped, said, 'I'm sorry. Would you help me drink from that contraption on the table?'

She rose, went round by the bed for the teapot and held it for him.

'Thanks.'

'Would you like to share another cigarette?'

'No, but you have one. I enjoy the smell.'

As she lit one she remembered having said much the same thing to him, the night of the fireflies.

'Just then,' he went on, 'the General and the Brigadier came out from their conference. I could see there had been a flaming row. The Brig was about ten years the senior man and was all for caution because men's lives were at stake, the lives of men he loved. The General on the other hand was all for modern ideas of dash, surprise, throwing away the book, using your equipment to its optimum limit, loving the whole impersonal power-game of move and counter-move.' A pause. 'They were both amateurs because they were both hot-headed. They were trying to make a lyric out of a situation that was merely prosaic. It only seemed problematical because we lacked information. But because it seemed problematical all this free emotional rein was given to the business of its solution. Well, there you are. If there are things you don't know, you call the gap in your knowledge a mystery and fill it in with a wholly emotional answer. That morning it struck me as supremely silly because, do you know, there wasn't a single sound of warfare anywhere. It was quite still. Sylvan almost – with the sunlight coming through the trees. A phrase came into my mind. The sweet indifference of man's enviroment to his problems. Pathetic fallacy or no, I really felt it, an indifference to us that amounted to contempt. The Brig had installed himself in an old bungalow, probably a traveller's resthouse. There was a village near by but the people had fled. The Brigade transport was harboured in a kind of glade – command truck, signals truck. Well, you can probably picture it, just like a Brigade command post on a field exercise. I was never able to get the picture of an exercise out of my mind, even when stuff was flying. There's something fundamentally childish about the arrangements for armed conflict. And there they were, the General and the Brigadier, both red in the face, and Teddie looking pink and embarrassed. They went over to the command truck. The IO was still with me. I told him that if I could get the General's permission I'd go and collect that Jiff myself, and see what I could get out of him. The IO was all for it, glad not to be bothered with such a minor detail. I went to the command truck and saw that something had just happened to put the General back in a good temper. The CO of the Indian battalion had been on the radio. They now realized they'd got the Japanese into a pocket and had decided that the Japanese force wasn't much more than company strength. It meant the Indians could mop the Japs up, complete their advance and make contact with the British battalion. The General asked me if there was anything new on my side, so I told him about the Jiff and that I'd like to go up and try and get him to talk and in any case bring him back. He said, "Yes, you do that, and make sure they understand the operational picture." '

Again he closed his eyes, and said nothing for a while, as if conjuring the image of that morning. But she knew, instinctively, what was coming. Something Teddie had said that marked the beginning of the fatal occasion.

'Of course the operational picture was Teddie's side, not mine, but there was nothing about this picture that a G.3 I. couldn't tell the battalion commander just as clearly as a G.3 Ops could. But Teddie said, "I'll do that, sir, I'll go with him." And the General was in a good enough mood to agree. If he'd thought about it clearly he would have said no. It was absurd, two divisional staff officers going off to a forward battalion to collect one miserable prisoner and to confirm verbally operational information that the CO would get over the radio anyway. But there we were, doing just that, as a result of the General's euphoria following the solution to his problem, but chiefly because of Teddie's obsession, his belief that I was not the man to deal with an Indian soldier who had turned coat. I didn't understand, I didn't have the touch or the sense of the traditions that were involved. Teddie thought he did. The Jiff was the only reason Teddie volunteered to go.

'But before we set off something else happened that gave him a better reason. I suppose we were about five minutes, checking with the Brigade IO, making sure of the location and route. We were about to leave when we were called back. I thought the General had changed his mind, but it wasn't that. Division had been on. The whole operational picture had changed. The division had been drawn into what amounted in military terms to a blind alley. On the map it was advancing roughly south-west to oppose a threat from that quarter, but the major threat was now seen to be south to south-east. In less difficult country it would just have been a question of swinging round in the hope of cutting the advancing force in two, but it's difficult to swing across the grain of hills like that. The reserve Brigade was the only one of the three not faced with that problem. But I won't bore you with tactics. It's enough for you to know there was a bit of a flap, and that this trip of Teddie's and mine was suddenly much more important to both the General and the Brigadier. The Brigadier was already on the radio to the CO of the British battalion, telling him to send a company back to support the Indians who were going in to clear this pocket of Japanese, make sure they didn't break through on to the road, but he wanted definite information about the Jiffs. He wanted to make sure there were no Jiff units waiting their chance to come in and command the road when our own troops swung away from it. He told the CO I was coming along, that the two of us were coming, one to help sort out the Jiff situation and relieve them of the prisoner and the other to put them in the picture as the General now saw it.

'So off we went, in my jeep, the two of us and the driver. There were only three miles to go. That company of the British battalion must have moved. We met them debussing and scattering into the hill on our left. When we got to the battalion we found the headquarters bivouacked just beyond a village, commanding the junction of the road and a track that led off down into a valley on the right. The junction had been their objective the previous night. They had a company in the jungle between the road and the track and another company in the jungle on the left of the road. The whole thing was terribly brisk and businesslike, that is it was until you realized that there were probably no enemy ahead. The CO was one of those cheery types with a wide moustache and a scarf in his neck – navy blue with white polka dots. We found him sitting on a shooting stick, drinking coffee. He had two spare mugs ready and got his batman filling them when he saw us coming. The complete host. At pains to appear quite unflappable.

'I let Teddie talk first. When he'd finished the CO just nodded, made one or two marks on his map and said, "Well, I could have told them that. There's nothing down the road, except perhaps some stray Jiffs and if they're all like the one we've got they're no problem." He sent for the IO then and told him to take me to the mule-lines where they had the Jiff under guard. Teddie began to follow but the CO called him back. The IO was a pleasant boy. He spoke French and German and had learned some Japanese, but he admitted his Urdu didn't extend much beyond what private soldiers who came out to India in the old days used to pick up in the barracks and bazaars. The only thing he'd got out of Mohammed Baksh was his name. He wasn't even sure whether Baksh had been an Indian prisoner of war or an Indian civilian in Malaya or Burma.

'But when I saw him I was pretty certain he'd been a soldier. He was squatting on his hunkers, under a tree, guarded by a young soldier on mule-lines picket, and directly he saw us coming he got to his feet and stood at attention, and stared straight ahead in that way old soldiers have, never quite meeting your eye unless you ask a personal question. He hadn't learned that as a civilian. He was a mess, though. Dirty, unshaven, undernourished. His uniform had nearly had it. I started firing questions at him. Name, age, what village he was born in, what year he had joined, what regiment, whether he had any relatives serving in the army, whether his parents were alive, and what his father was. All very quickly, not waiting for the answers, but asking him nothing about the Jiffs or the Japanese or how he'd been captured. I wanted to start him thinking about his home. He'd probably not seen it for two or three years, and coming back to Indian soil could have made him pretty homesick. Then I started asking the questions again, but this time waited for answers. The family questions first, the name of his village, what his father did, was his father still alive? He said he didn't know about his father and I could see the question had got him. It was then that Teddie appeared and that was the signal for Baksh to shut up like a clam, just when I thought I'd begun to break him.

'I decided to leave the personal things aside for a bit and started asking questions about the past few days. Teddie's Urdu wasn't all that hot. He kept asking me what I'd said, and putting in questions of his own, if Baksh had been in the Indian Army, what regiment, who'd been his old commanding officer. The chap got very confused and nervous, looking at Teddie, but not quite at Teddie, at one part of Teddie. It took me a while to get it. That he couldn't keep his eyes off Teddie's regimental flash. And then I realized what was eating him and said, Baksh, you're an old solider of this officer's regiment, aren't you? He stared at me and then sort of collapsed. Teddie rounded on me, wanted to know what I'd said, so I told him. I said Baksh had once been a Muzzy Guide. He said I was making it up, he didn't believe it. No sepoy of the Muzzy Guides would ever turn coat, he'd rather die. He said there'd been one battalion in Burma and one in Malaya, that he knew every man in the Burma battalion, which had been his own, and all the officers of the one in Malaya. If Baksh was a Muzzy Guide he'd have been in the Malaya battalion. He told me to ask him the name of the Commanding Officer. Well I did so, and Baksh just shook his head and for a moment I thought perhaps Teddie was right, but I kept on asking him and in the end he said, "Hostein Sahib, Hostein Sahib." I thought well, that proved it, Teddie *was* right. The Muzzy Guides wouldn't have an Indian CO. But Teddie said, "Hostein Sahib was what they called Colonel Hastings", and stared at me as if we'd uncovered something terribly sinister, so sinister it was unbelievable. He asked Baksh what happened to Hostein Sahib. The answer was that none of them had seen either Hastings or any of the other officers since the night the battalion, or what was left of it, went into the bag, south of Kuala Lumpur. The Indian soldiers and their British officers had been separated by their Japanese captors. There was a rumour that Hostein Sahib had been shot, then another that he was in a camp up-country, on the Siam border. The Indian officer who came to talk to them later, in Singapore, said Hostein Sahib and the other officers had had plans to get away by themselves to Sumatra and leave the sepoys and NCOs behind, but being captured by the Japanese had stopped it. None of the sepoys believed this, and for weeks they'd refused to listen to men like the Indian officer who came and went in a Japanese staff car and was on friendly terms with the Japanese camp commander.

'What he was trying to do was get them to join the Indian National Army. Baksh said he was a Sikh called Ranjit Singh. He told them he'd been captured up in Ipoh, that the British officers in his regiment had all tried to save their own skins and left him commanding a rearguard action. He'd been a lieutenant. Now he was a major. He used to visit them two or three times a week and tell them about the free Indian Government that was being formed and which it was the duty of every patriotic Indian soldier to support by joining the new Indian Army that would march to Delhi and drive the British out. He said the Japanese were not India's enemy, only enemies of the British. Why pine away in the prison camps which British cowardice and inefficiency had driven brave men into? The British had

681

always excused their imperialism by pointing out that their presence in India was a guarantee of freedom from invasion. But they hadn't kept the Japanese out of Burma and Malaya. The Japanese were freeing all Asia from the white man's yoke and self-respecting Indians couldn't just sit by and let another nation do their job for them.

'Baksh said that after several weeks other officers came, including a couple of Muslims who told them the whole of India was rising against the white imperialists and that men in the army back here were turning against their officers. I expect that would have been around August in forty-two. Some of Baksh's fellow-prisoners began to believe these tales and after a bit were taken out of camp and came back later in INA uniform, said how well they were treated and helped to recruit the rest. He said, "We were forced, Sahib – one man was tortured by an Indian officer because he refused to take the new oath. We didn't know what was true and what was not. We saw white sahibs working on the roads, like coolies. The world was turned upside down." '

Merrick paused.

'That was the kind of information I was after, I mean about the pressures and the officers responsible. There'll be a day of reckoning I suppose. God knows what will happen to all those chaps. The strength of the INA is three divisions. That's a lot of officers and a lot of men. A lot of sentences of death. Too many. It won't happen. I suppose we might hang Subhas Chandra Bose, who's at the head of the whole thing, but for the rest I expect it'll be a question of weeding out the hawks from the doves, tracking down those who've had their own men tortured. Baksh told me what they did to this chap who tried to stand out against them. It's too revolting to repeat.'

He closed his eyes, but when he continued his voice was still strong.

'I asked Baksh to describe what had led to his capture that morning and he told us that two days earlier the Japanese had ordered the officer commanding their unit to establish a listening post to keep watch on the track – the one that led down into the valley, and Baksh and two other men, both ex-Muzzafirabad Guides like himself – had been chosen. Their unit was in a village about three miles south of the junction and the listening post was established in the jungle about a mile ahead of the village in a place where they could look down and get a good view of quite a long stretch of the track. Patrols were to visit the listening post every two hours, but if they saw anything going on one of the three men was to go back and report. Baksh said it was a stupid arrangement, the kind of thing they found themselves doing because the Japanese seldom gave them a proper job. Anyway they spent the whole day watching the track and reporting to the patrols. They thought they'd be ordered back when it got dark, but when the last patrol reached them the leader said he hadn't had any orders to leave the post unmanned. He'd see about it when he got back and in any case send up a hot meal. They'd been on iron rations all day, with only water to drink. But nothing happened. They didn't dare desert the post or even have one man go back and see what was up because their officer, Lieutenant Karim, was always on at them about obeying orders to the letter and showing themselves the equal of the Japanese in endurance and discipline. Karim had been a Jemadar in one of the Punjabi regiments. He'd adopted the Japanese method of slapping soldiers when he was angry.

'So there they were, according to Baksh, stuck all night on the hillside. When it got light they expected the patrol to turn up, but it never did. They had no food left and only very little water. They drew lots for which of them would go back when the sun had been up a couple of hours, and Baksh was the unlucky one. He expected Karim would beat him up.

'When he got back to the village he found it deserted. The unit had gone. It didn't surprise him because the Japanese were always ordering them to move at a moment's notice, usually in the middle of the night. He said it didn't even surprise him that Lieutenant Karim had packed and gone without thinking of the three men at the listening post, and that the patrol leader who'd promised to send a hot meal had forgotten all about them. He said, "In the jungle our doubts returned, each man was only thinking of himself. There was no good spirit in us." Well, it sounded plausible, and Teddie believed it. So did the young IO. I wasn't wholly convinced. I kept an open mind, whether he was telling the truth or trying to cover up the fact that he was a deserter or a spy. He said he scouted around, filled the water bottles from the stream they'd been using, and found some tins of food carelessly left behind, then went back to the post. When they'd eaten they decided to go back to the village thinking by now someone must have noticed their absence and they'd be sent for. In the village they tried to work out which direction the unit had gone. They were afraid of the Japanese appearing and treating them as deserters, or of some of the villagers returning and taking revenge on them for things the Japanese had done. I asked him then how large the unit was. He said it was about half company strength, and had been detached from an INA battalion for special duties, but he didn't know what the special duties were because apart from advancing up the road behind a company of Japanese they hadn't done anything. I wasn't so sure about that either, but I asked him to go on with his story. He said he and the two others had begun to quarrel. One man wanted to go back to the listening post, another wanted to stay hidden in the village and Baksh wanted to scout back along the road in the direction they'd come from a couple of nights before. So they drew lots again, and Baksh won. They tracked back for a couple of miles, keeping to the jungle along the side of the road, and found nothing. He said it was as if God had waved his hand and caused all the soldiers of their own and the Japanese armies to disappear. They went back to the village and on to the listening post. The two others suggested they should go down into the valley. They were sure their unit must have been sent in that direction. Why else should the track leading down to the valley have been kept a watch on? Baksh said there was no point in sending troops into the valley. There was nothing there except the surrounding hills. The road and the high ground on the other side of it were the only features of military value.

They'd advanced along the road towards the village. In his opinion their troops had fanned out into the hills, not into the valley. He said they should cross the road and explore the hills, or stay where they were. In one case they'd at least be showing common sense and initiative, in the other obeying the last order received. If they went down into the valley they'd only be acting foolishly. They had a midday meal at the listening post and because they'd hardly slept at all the night before and were tired and hungry they decided to stay put and take it in turns, two men keeping watch and the other one sleeping. He said, "We had no strength left, Sahib, and no spirit. Through no fault of our own we had become deserters and were thinking and doing like that." It was agreed that at dusk they'd go back to the village. Baksh was the last to sleep. He said he woke when it was dark and found the others had gone. They had taken the rest of the food. He went to the village but knew they'd gone down into the valley and that they felt as he was feeling, that the end of the road had been reached and there was nothing for it now but capture by British or Indian troops. He slept in one of the deserted huts and woke during the night because of the sound of firing from the direction of the hill on the other side of the road. At least, he thought that was where it came from. It didn't sound close. When he woke again it was light. The firing had stopped but there were two British soldiers prodding him with their rifles. He was glad it was over. Now, he said, he would be shot, and knew he deserved death for being disloyal to the uniform of his father and fathers before him.' A pause. 'He broke down and wept and begged Teddie to shoot him then and there. That young IO was terribly embarrassed. Oddly enough Teddie wasn't. He held the man's shoulder and shook him a bit and said, "You're still a soldier. Act like one. You've done very wrong, but I am still your father and mother." The old formula. But Teddie meant it. He really meant it. In spite of what that man had done he felt it was his duty to do his best for him. And I suppose he felt compassion.'

'Did you?' Sarah asked. 'Did you feel that too, Ronald?'

'No. To me Baksh was merely a source of information. I had no feelings about the man himself. He'd made a choice. It hadn't worked out well. The law says he should be punished. Well, it happens all the time. You choose, you act, you pay or get paid. That's how I see it. Do you disapprove?'

'I can't, can I?' she said, then added, 'It's true after all. You pay or get paid. Although perhaps there are situations in which it's better for you to pay, more satisfying.' She thought: To the soul, whatever that is, more satisfying to the soul, if you know the choice was wrong. But what do I mean, *wrong*?

'Most people prefer to be paid. We're always looking for rewards. And Baksh got his. So did Teddie. It was a ridiculous scene in its way. It seemed to me to have nothing to do with the reality of what was actually happening. He knelt down and put his head on Teddie's boots, and that didn't embarrass Teddie either. I think it moved him. Very deeply. As if something he'd always believed in and put his trust in had been proved. He pulled Baksh to his feet, quite gently, and then they stared at each other. Measuring up. To each other, and to some standard of, well, what worked, what was possible about conduct. And Baksh gradually reassumed that old soldier look of not looking except into a middle-distance he wasn't even seeing. And Teddie nodded and said, "I remember Hostein Sahib, in Muzzafirabad. My name is Bingham, Bingham. Remember my name." It was a promise that didn't need explaining in so many words. They both understood that Teddie intended to do his best for him. The man felt he belonged again. You could see that. He might be court-martialled and shot, or imprisoned, but even in front of a firing-squad he would belong to the system that was executing him. I suppose it was months since he'd felt he belonged anywhere. It's extraordinary the lengths people will go to to convince themselves that they belong.'

He turned his head slightly and watched her, then said:

'Just then we heard firing on the hill. The Indians were going to clear that pocket of Japanese, with the company from the British battalion in support. The IO looked at his watch and asked me to question Baksh about the kind of arms this Jiff unit had and whether he thought it possible after all that they'd gone down into the valley and holed out there. The answer was that they had a mortar, a couple of machine guns. The rest carried rifles. They hadn't much spare ammunition. He looked back in the direction of the firing and then in the direction of the valley. I think we all got the same idea at once, that the Jiffs *had* gone into the valley and that they should have opposed the advance of the British battalion during the night or were supposed to harry the battalion once it was seen to have occupied the road junction. The firing on the hill might be their signal to attack. But a unit of only half-company strength was an absurdly small force. If Baksh hadn't lied about the strength, the Jiffs might have gone into the valley to join a Japanese force already holed out there. The IO said he'd better go and have a word with the old man, but before he'd gone more than a yard or so we heard the old man calling to him. I asked Baksh if he'd lied about the strength of the Jiff force. I suggested he'd lied from start to finish. He wouldn't answer me, but just looked dumbly at Teddie. Teddie said, "Leave the poor devil alone." But he asked a question himself. He asked the names of Baksh's two ex-Muzzy Guide companions from the listening post.' A pause. 'Aziz Khan and Fariqua Khan.' A pause. 'I expect I'll always remember them. The names. Not the men. We never saw the men.

'Presently I left Teddie to it and went to find the CO. There was the question of the valley, and who might be in it. If he intended to have a closer look I thought it worth staying for another half-hour. Not more. I'd done the job I came to do, so had Teddie. I knew we ought to be getting back to division and taking Baksh with us. I found the CO at the junction. Up along the road men were coming out of the jungle on either side. He told me he'd been ordered back about a mile and to leave a road block at the junction until the battalion from the reserve Brigade sent a company forward to man it. The little skirmish on the hill was nearly over and he

685

was to move on through the hills, south-east. That was in line with the revised picture we'd had from division. I asked what he thought about the possibility of there being Jiffs or Japanese in the valley. He said the company manning the road block could deal with them, if there were any. Then he said I'd better get moving. He meant we were in the way. We were. Well, you can imagine, a battalion suddenly on the move. I went back to the mule-lines to get Teddie and Baksh. But they weren't there. The mules were being loaded and led out and I couldn't tell which of the men had been on guard, but the one I spoke to said the IO and the Jiff and the other staff officer had gone down by what he called the short cut. I went back to where we'd left the jeep. It wasn't there either. Neither was the driver. It took me a couple of minutes to find the IO. He seemed surprised to see me. He said he thought I'd gone with Captain Bingham and the Jiff-type to see if the other two Jiffs were anywhere around. When we saw I'd no idea what he was talking about he told me how when he went back to the mule-lines, by the short cut, he found Teddie alone with Baksh. Teddie told him Baksh thought the other two ex-Muzzy Guides were in the valley and would be looking for an opportunity to give themselves up, especially to a Muzzy Guide officer. The IO had said, Well, we're pulling out, take a look if you must, it's all yours. When he asked where I was Teddie said I'd gone down to the road and that he'd pick me up there. Perhaps he intended to. I don't know. At the time I could only think he'd gone off his head and I'm afraid I said as much to the IO. I'm sorry. I think it counted against Teddie afterwards. The IO asked me if I thought the Jiff was trying something on. I said I didn't know, but I wanted him back.

'Sometimes, you know, I lie here and realize I'd probably be all in one piece still if that young IO had been pigheaded or scared of his CO, if he'd said, "Well, it's your funeral," and gone about his own business. But he was the eager-beaver type. He took me to a jeep parked off the road and told me to jump in, he'd take me down the track. The jeep belonged to the CO but he wouldn't be needing it, not where the battalion was going. He meant for the march into the hills. What transport the battalion had apart from the mules would go back to the Brigade pool. He called out to a sergeant to tell the CO there might be something going on down in the valley and he was going to take a look and in any case check that the company in the woods between the road and the track were pulling out in good order. Then we set off and turned into the track. Men were coming out on to it from the jungle and marching up it in single file. When we got round the first bend we saw Teddie about half a mile ahead. He was in the driver's seat, going quite slowly, and Baksh was in the back with the driver beside him. You couldn't tell at that distance how alert the driver was, or if he had Baksh well covered with his Sten gun. There was a shallow ravine on our right, with a ridge beyond it, but Teddie was at a point where the ravine came to an end and there was a neck of flattish ground between the track and the ridge, most of it jungle, but making a fairly easy connection between the ridge and the track. Farther on the ground obviously fell away quite steeply into the valley. When we saw Teddie stop the IO said, "I think he's only taking a quick look-see. He won't find them there, we've patrolled all that." All the same Teddie stopped and a second or so later we heard him, quite clearly. Calling to them. Aziz Khan. Fariqua Khan. Aziz Khan, Fariqua Khan. It was as if Teddie himself gave the signal. There was a single rifle shot and not more than a second or two later an explosion in the woods on our left and then another one bang on the track between us and Teddie's jeep, and then more or less continuously, one after the other in the wood. The company that had been located there and were still in there, moving out section by section, were being mortared from the ridge over on the right and there was more than one mortar, which meant Baksh had lied or there were some Japanese there too.

'I hand it to the young IO. The temptation was to get out of the jeep and dive for cover but he merely swore and started swinging round. The track was narrow, it needed a three-point turn. We were swung round with the wheels an inch or two from the ravine before I realized he meant to drive back up the hill. I remember shouting at him, "What are you doing? Didn't you see?" I don't think he had seen. He shouted back for me to hang on, but I jumped out and said I must get him. I don't think he understood what I was on about. He realized later but at the time he probably thought I didn't relish running the gauntlet back up the track, and was going to ground in the wood, or perhaps he wasn't thinking at all, just acting instinctively, getting back himself as quick as he could to where he was supposed to be and would be needed. The men who'd been marching up the track had scattered. I saw a couple of them leaning against the bank holding their faces. It was a sort of pandemonium. I registered it, but not as someone who had to do anything about it. I was thinking primarily of the other jeep and of what I'd seen in the first few seconds, between the rifle shot, the first mortar bomb explosion and the second one that fell slap on the track. I saw three things. I saw Teddie duck, or appear to duck. I saw the driver pitch over on top of him, as if he'd been hit. And I saw Baksh staring at them, then jumping clear and running on to that neck of flat ground. Then I couldn't see anything because of the explosion on the track itself.

'And I don't remember anything awfully clearly between jumping out of the IO's jeep and reaching Teddie's. I think I ran down the track until I reached the mortar-bomb crater and that the site of it acted as a warning signal. I must have gone up into the wood then and run the rest of the way under cover. I do seem to remember some difficult going, and falling, picking myself up again. I know it was a sudden shock to find the jeep was burning and that the driver was on the ground, not slumped over Teddie any longer, and that Teddie wasn't slumped forward but sideways. It wasn't at all how I'd last seen it. I realized another mortar bomb had fallen a few yards in front of the jeep and that the force of the explosion had hurled the driver off Teddie and also flung Teddie to one side. I don't know about the fire. I think the spare petrol cans had been hit and gone up. I don't really remember going up to the jeep, only being there, pulling Teddie out, trying to get a hold. I must have been hunched forward, protecting my face, reaching in and getting him by the waist or an arm. I don't remember being shot at, or know whether it was then, or when I got him out and dragged him into the wood, or when I had to go back and get the driver and drag him in too. I do remember there wasn't any sign of Baksh. They found him later. Dead of course. The other Jiffs must have shot him. They or the Japanese. It turned out there were Japanese as well.'

She thought: I don't know, I don't know, where that kind of courage comes from or why or what its purpose is, but I know it has a purpose. It's a kind of madness, a sublime insanity which even Ronald who's experienced it can't explain. He wanted to diminish Teddie for me but Teddie isn't diminished. He began to diminish himself, but now he isn't diminished either. For a moment they are both larger than life. Teddie calling stupidly for those men, and Ronald stupidly risking death to try and save him. And that's how I shall remember them. Without understanding why it makes them larger.

His eyes were shut again, had been for some moments, and that impediment in his throat was troubling him. He swallowed and said:

'I thought at first Teddie was dead too, but I'm afraid he wasn't, neither was the driver but the driver wasn't burnt. Teddie was.'

'But he was unconscious?'

'Not all the time.'

'Colonel Selby-Smith wrote that you said Teddie was unconscious and hadn't suffered.'

'Let Susan go on thinking that.' A pause. 'I got them both off the track and as far into the wood as I could manage. The driver's Sten gun was still in the jeep so I only had my revolver, and Teddie's of course, but I thought it was probably all up with the three of us anyway, either from another mortar bomb or from the bunch of Jiffs I expected any moment to come down from the ridge. I think it was becoming aware of that possibility that made me notice my left arm was numb, but I couldn't see any blood or any sign of having been hit. The arm and – other things – made it difficult to do anything about the field-dressings and I couldn't see where Teddie had been hit either. I had him on his back and didn't want to turn him over. It's odd, about – damage to people. I thought the driver was dying, that no one could be such a mess and survive. I thought it would be Teddie who might survive, although I hoped he wouldn't.' A pause. 'He would have been terrifly disfigured.'

She waited, then said:

'You don't need to tell me anything you don't like talking about, Ronald. I'd rather you didn't because I couldn't repeat it to Susan, and if I know it she'll see I'm keeping something back. And then she'll worry even more.' She hesitated. 'And you haven't told me anything about you, about what's wrong or what they've got to do to you.'

'Oh, nothing wrong they can't put right. I was burnt a bit. Shot up a bit. But in a few weeks I'll be back on my feet, which I suppose is something.'

She remembered the line from his letter: *There was Teddie with everything to live for and I – comparatively – with something less than that.* It no longer seemed like an affectation but a bare statement of the truth. She would have liked to get him to explain but felt the explanation was there, in front of her, and in her mind – secreted in all the dark corners of her recollections of her brief encounters with him, and with his reputation.

She said, 'Was it a long time before you got any help?'

'It seemed long. I think it was an hour. A bit more. But after a while I felt quite safe because I realized the Jiffs wouldn't expose themselves to our own direct fire by coming on to the track. They might try to cross it, and of course they'd come on to it if they thought they'd got the battalion pinned down, but somehow I assumed they'd do neither. It never struck me there might be larger forces coming up from the valley. There weren't, but I'm glad I didn't worry about it. I'm trying to make you see that staying there with Teddie and the driver wasn't the death-and-glory thing people might make out.' A pause. 'It was the snuggest place to be when you think of it. And there's this other thing. If all this is a confession of some sort, that is what it's about, what I see about it now, I mean when lying thinking, going back, analysing it. I want you to know. So that you understand the difference, the difference between Teddie and me, and why I say he died an amateur. He went down there for the *regiment.* I told you there was a touch of old-fashioned gallantry in it. All that paternalist business really meant something to him. *Man-bap.* I am your father and your mother. It would have been great if he'd gone down there and called as he did and if they'd come out, hanging their heads, and surrendered to him, trusting in the code, the old code. That's what he wanted. I don't mean there was anything vain or self-seeking about it. He wasn't doing it for himself or for them. He did it for the regiment. He risked everything for it, his own life, the driver's life, Baksh's life, his job. So much. So much it's incalculable. Who knows, his going down there might have looked to that bunch of Jiffs and Japs, who'd been clever enough to get so near without being seen, like the beginning of an advance into the valley. It could have triggered the whole thing off. But in any case he was putting the regiment above his job. If it had come off he could have become one of those people a regiment remembers, celebrates, as part of their legend. Teddie Bingham? By jove, yes but that was before your time. There were these poor misguided fellows from a Muzzy Guides battalion that got cut to pieces in Malaya back in '41–'42 and had gone into the bag and been forced to join a bunch of renegades we called Jiffs. A lot of them came up with the Japs when they crossed into Indian territory early in '44. Our own chaps shot them out of hand if they had the chance, and there weren't many prisoners until this Muzzy Guide gave himself up, a chap called Mohammed Baksh. Young Bingham was a divisional staff officer at the time, but once a Muzzy always a Muzzy. He'd gone forward with a message from the General to the CO of a battalion that was in danger of being cut off and saw Baksh. Well, directly Baksh saw him the fellow went to pieces, and begged young Bingham to shoot him for his act of treachery, but young Bingham made him stand like a man and talked to him as if he were his own erring son, made him feel he still belonged. "Are there any others with you?" Bingham asked and Baksh said yes, two, both from his old battalion, starved, wretched, hiding out, too afraid to surrender. Well, there was stuff flying but young Bingham never hesitated. "Come on," he said, "show me where," and off they went right into the thick of it and when they got near the place where Baksh had left the other two Bingham said, "What are their names?' Aziz Khan and Fariqua Khan. Brothers I think they were. So what does young Bingham do? He stands up straight where everyone could see him and pick him off and calls out to them, ordering them to return to duty as soldiers of the Muzzy Guides. And, by jove, in a couple of minutes out they came and back he marched them. He didn't even take their rifles away.'

Presently Merrick said:

'But of course it didn't come off and nobody will ever tell the tale like that. And anyway that kind of tale has had its day. Is that why it didn't come off?'

'There's your tale,' Sarah said.

'Oh no, mine was a professional action.' He looked at her and again she thought she detected in his expression that curious serenity. 'It's only amateurs who create legends. There's nothing memorable about doing a job. I said mine was a professional act. I didn't go to save Teddie. I went to get Mohammed Baksh. I want you to accept that, and the fact that when it came to it I didn't have the courage to go looking for him. I pulled Teddie out because I was afraid of what people would say if I left him to fry.' A pause. 'I don't mean that all this went consciously through my mind, but in retrospect I see no other interpretation.' A pause. 'Do you?'

Do I? (she asked herself). Yes, I see a man who was in love with those legends, that way of life, all those things that from a distance seemed to distinguish people like us from people of his own kind, people he knew better. I see a man still in love with them but who has chosen to live outside in the cold because he couldn't get in to warm his hands at this hearth with its dying fire. And it is strange because I long to exchange the creeping cold for a chill reality but feel in my bones that my kind of cold would not be his kind, just as the warmth I knew as a child was different from the warmth he always imagined. I don't understand the distinction he makes between what he calls amateur and what he calls professional, but feel it's a distinction he's made to heal a wound. After all, there are only people, tasks, myths and truth. And truth is a fire few of us get scorched by. Perhaps it's an imaginary flame, and can't be made by rubbing two sticks together.

She said, 'Some people would have been more afraid of pulling Teddie out than of what people would say if he'd been left there. And I don't think you risked your life just to get Mohammed Baksh.'

'No?'

'You went down there without thinking why you went, Ronald. I mean when the shooting had started. You saw they were in trouble and needed help. What you call the game only looks like a game to people who aren't in the team. I'm sorry but even if it's only as twelfth man you're a member of the team after all, aren't you?'

He smiled, turned his head so that he need not look at her. He said, 'You are, when it comes to it, very much the Colonel's daughter, I'm afraid.'

'I was born that way.'

She waited. He did not respond. Again she felt the pressure of his willing her to enter and explore the mysterious areas of his obsession. To counteract it she considered other mysteries, or anyway questions that remained unanswered: The outcome of the battle, whether it had ever been proven that Baksh had lied, and why; what other prisoners were taken and, more grotesquely, the circumstances of his vigil, with Teddie burnt but not unconscious all the time, and himself in some unexplained condition of numbness which perhaps wore off before the time was up.

'Did the driver come through?' she asked. He nodded. 'And Teddie – was Teddie aware of what you'd done?'

'I don't know. I don't think so. If you could use a word like expression in a case like that I'd say his was one of blank amazement. He never made a sound. I'm not sure he could see me. But his eyes moved. At one time I thought he'd gone, but his heart was still beating. I'm sorry. I shouldn't tell you things like that. Burning's a terrible thing. I was glad when they told me he'd had a bullet lodged in his back. I suppose the fire had cauterized the wound. At the time I thought he was only dying from burns.' He looked round at her again. 'Sitting with him reminded me of the last thing I did as DSP Mayapore, just before I was – transferred to Sundernagar. There was an English mission school superintendent living there who committed suicide. Suttee, as a matter of fact.'

'Oh – do you mean Miss Crane?'

'You knew her?'

'No, but the woman my aunt lives with was in the missions. She often talks about her. Edwina Crane.'

'That's her. Edwina Crane. A funny old bird. She'd been around for years but no one knew her at all well except I suppose the Indian children in the schools. If she had any friends they were Indians and half-castes. So it was ironic, because she was the first person from Mayapore to get hurt in the August riots. She was on her way back from a place called Dibrapur with an Indian teacher. A mob stopped them and murdered the teacher, beat her up and burned her car out. We had her in hospital the evening all that other business happened in the Bibighar. She'd been found sitting on the roadside in the pouring rain holding the dead Indian's hand. You couldn't get much out of her. She was half-delirious when I saw her and couldn't remember anything. When she got better I think she was already off her head. Melancholia. I heard she'd resigned from the mission and wasn't seeing anybody. Then she did this dramatic thing, dressed herself in Indian clothes, locked herself in a shed in her garden and burnt herself to death. A symbolic act, I suppose. She must have felt the India she knew had died, so like a good widow she made a funeral pyre. I had to go along there, poke about among her things, and question her old servant. There wasn't much to find, she hadn't left a note. But in a chest I turned up an old picture of Queen Victoria receiving tribute, a very stylized thing, with the old lady sitting on a throne under clouds and angels, and Indians of all kinds gathering round her like children. *Man-bap*. I am your father and mother. And in another place I found the little plate that had been taken off the frame. The picture must have been a gift in recognition of some special service years before. It went something like, To Edwina Crane, for her courage. The mission was in Muzzafirabad. Oh and it dated back years – I think before the First World War. But sitting there with Teddie made it all seem to connect, I mean connect what she had done all that time ago in Muzzafirabad and what he had just done, or tried to do. And then there was the other similarity – death by fire.'

He smiled at her. 'I think that made me feel – what you said. I mean for a moment there I was an amateur myself. I fell for it, really fell for it, the whole thing, the idea that there really was this possibility. Devotion. Sacrifice. Self-denial. A cause, an obligation. A code of conduct, a sort of final moral definition, I mean definition of us, what we're here for – people living among each other, in an environment some sort of God created. The whole impossible nonsensical dream.'

She waited. He had turned his head away again and when the silence continued unbroken the notion that he could have fallen asleep exhausted, nudged – but did not dislodge – the firmer belief she had that everything he said and did was rooted in acute awareness of himself as someone central to an occasion. And suddenly she had a vivid image of him on the platform of Mirat cantonment station, central to an earlier occasion that had been well marked by victims, although on that day, the day of the wedding, only the woman in the white saree had actually been present. But it was the significance of that lonely supplication that now struck her, for the first time, and recreated Bibighar in her mind as an occasion that continued, could not be ruled off as over, done with. Always, before, she had seen the white-clad figure as representative of an old misfortune that had left its mark; a sadness in a stranger's heart, an unknown and so unrecognizable grief; and it was only now, observing the faced-away figure of the man the woman had approached as if he were someone capable of granting an alleviation, that she understood the continuing nature of the misfortune, realized that the boy whom the woman pleaded for must, then at least, still have been paying a price, however far distant away in time had been the occasion of his fault, if there had ever been fault.

A new disturbing element of uncertainty stirred her. It caused her to press again with her feet on the floor and with the small of her back into the uncomfortable upright chair, so powerful was that sensation of not wishing to be drawn towards that central point of reference that was in

Merrick, that *was* Merrick. She felt deprived of speech and then saw that this was a protection. Briefly she was adjured to silence by an exquisite tautening of nerves that promised, if only they could snap, to leave her vividly possessed by an absolute, an exemplary, understanding of what had been only partially revealed to her by that incident on the station.

But the moment passed. She was still possessed merely by unanswered questions. What was new and disturbing apart from her realization that the boy had still been paying for his fault, was the shadow of permanent misfortune she saw as fallen on him with the girl's death. Had the girl before, or her aunt since, attempted to reduce the price he paid, might still be paying? Or had a net enclosed him, so subtly, irrevocably, that nothing they could try to do would help? And was Merrick alone responsible for that? Was it these victims, not Teddie, who now lay like a weight on that conscience of his which he said he could examine but give a clean bill to? Perhaps that was the way in to him, to become his victim and then to haunt his conscience. But if so, it seemed to her that it was an approach without access at the end. There was, for some reason, no way into him at all, and all the people whom he chose as victims lay scattered on his threshold.

She thought: You are, yes, our dark side, the arcane side. You reveal something that is sad about us, as if out here we had built a mansion without doors and windows, with no way in and no way out. All India lies on our doorstep and cannot enter to warm us or be warmed. We live in holes and crevices of the crumbling stone, no longer sheltered by the carapace of our history which is leaving us behind. And one day we shall lie exposed, in our tender skins. You, as well as us.

It was extraordinary how like each other they were, and at the same time rigidly divided by an antagonism she believed was mutual. She could not bear the thought of this man clinging through a god-relationship to the family she loved, honoured, felt a strange irritated anguish for. He would, through that relationship, attach himself like lichen to a wall, the crumbling stone of the blind house that was doomed to become a ruin. At least, she cried to herself, let it be as noble a ruin as it can; and then laughed at her absurd pride, the fastidious distaste of this Colonel's daughter for a man she had decided, for no clear reason, she could not trust. And there was this problem too: that she had given her word to Susan that she would ask him.

She opened her mouth, but could not say it. She spoke the first words that came into her head.

'Did you ever know old Lady Manners, as well as her niece?' And then remembered Aunt Fenny had already asked him that, the day of the wedding, and been told he didn't.

He turned his head towards her.

'No. Why?'

'I thought you might have. She's in Pankot.'

'Oh?' He waited. She did not explain. 'Is she well?'

'We don't know. None of us has actually seen her.' Did he look relieved? 'She signed the book at Flagstaff House.'

'Does she still have the child?'

'We don't know that either.'

'I see. Is Pankot such a large place, then?'

'She must be living on the west side. The Indian side. It's rather a mystery, why she signed the book.' She wondered what he would say if she told him now the story of what she had done in Srinagar. The white ward seemed full of shadows and echoes of departed voices. 'Incidentally,' she heard herself say, 'talking about children, before I go, I have a question from Susan,' and hesitated, struggling again with her reluctance and her sense of duty. 'She wonders whether you'd like to be one of the godfathers.' She knew her voice was flattened by a cold formality. The same lack of enthusiasm must show in her face. Guilt pricked her. She might just as well have left the duty unperformed as perform it so badly.

'How very kind of her,' he said. He glanced away as if to turn the possibility over in his mind. She wondered if he felt the dead weight that had descended, the weight of the right-thing, like a stone pressing them down, sapping their strength. With one simple remark he threw the weight off. 'But in all the circumstances it wouldn't be suitable, would it?' His glance returned, penetrating, implacable. She knew relief, felt only a small remorse. She was at a loss to understand what it was about him that so appalled her.

'Are you to be godmother?'

She nodded.

He smiled faintly. She noted for the first time what it was that was so unusual about the blueness of his eyes. It was a blueness she realized she associated with the eyes of dolls: a demanding but unseeing blue, incapable either of acceptance or rejection. If the pillows were taken away, if he were lain flat, would they close and be incapable of opening until with inquisitive fingers you swung the delicately balanced lids up for a glimpse of those little mirrors with their grave but startling illusion of response?

'Well,' he said, 'you don't believe in it either, do you? But tell her – tell her I was touched and very grateful.'

'Is your not believing in it the only reason?'

She was denied an answer. The door swung open. 'I'm sorry, Miss Layton,' Sister Prior said, advancing towards the bed – trim, capable and asexually attractive – 'I'm told your uncle's come to fetch you. I'm afraid I wasn't able to let him up. Fact is I'm going to turn you out. How are we?'

'We are well,' Merrick said.

'Are you sure my uncle's here? It wasn't arranged.'

'Quite sure. Unless there are two Colonel Graces.'

'I think there's only one. I'll say goodbye, then, Ronald. I expect Aunt Fenny will be round in a day or two. Is there anything speical you'd like her to bring you?'

'I don't think they're on the market.'

'What's that?'

'Nothing. Just my little joke. And thank you. Thank you for coming.'

'I'll ring tomorrow before I leave.'

'Well,' Sister Prior interrupted, 'tomorrow won't be at all a good day to ring us, will it, Captain Merrick?'

'No, Sister Prior. I suppose it won't.'

'The day after,' Sister Prior suggested.

'I shall be in Pankot the day after – I thought of ringing before I left.'

'Oh well, your uncle can keep in touch. I'm sorry to hustle you, but we have our little duties.'

Sarah laughed. Sister Prior in the ward, in front of her patient, was quite a different person from the one in the waiting-room. She did not like either, but preferred the bitterness to the professional coyness. She turned to Merrick.

'I'll write to you from Pankot.'

'Will you?'

The reply, meant – she believed – to shatter her, seemed to bounce off her. Never before had she been so conscious of the thickness of skin that was part of her inheritance. But consciousness of it at once began to thin it down. He had not meant, perhaps, to remind her of the earlier unkept promise, but had spoken involuntarily, out of genuine hope but lack of real expectation.

'Of course,' she said and then, determinedly, subtly stressing his Christian name because as yet he had not called her Sarah, she ended, 'Goodbye, Ronald.'

'Goodbye,' he said. For an instant there was a repetition of that difficulty with the throat. 'Goodbye,' he said again, and closed his eyes, as if he knew he had been played with long enough.

*

In the corridor Sister Prior said, 'He's marvellous, isn't he? You simply wouldn't know he's constantly in pain. He fights taking drugs. Is he a religious man?'

'Religious? No, I don't think so.'

'I ask because there are sects that think pain is something you have to bear. With Ronald we have to get up to all sorts of tricks. But the odd thing is him thinking he's not been drugged has the effect you'd expect if he actually wasn't.'

Sister Prior pressed the button to summon the lift. The Bengal sky beyond the window of the waiting-alcove was sodden with rain and cloud and evening. Below, waiting, was Uncle Arthur on whom fortune had smiled at last.

'Of course,' Sister Prior was saying – and this, surely, was a third persona? – the talkative, informed and uniformed bouncer? – 'it's all to the

695

good that he's not over-dependent. He'll come through tomorrow that much better.'

The lift arrived. Sister Prior waited while the attendant clanged back the gates. Entering, Sarah placed her hand so that the gates should not be shut and the descent begin, and it all be over without having come to its logical end.

'I'm sorry,' she said, 'but we know nothing and he wouldn't say.'

'Oh, I realized that. And you ought to know, oughtn't you? The left arm.'

'The left arm?'

'They took the hand off in Comilla. Tomorrow we have to take off from just above the elbow. Third degree burns and a bullet in the upper arm and one in the forearm. The right arm's a mess too, but we can save that. His face will be scarred for life but his hair will grow again, of course. He might even look human without the bandages.'

As if stung Sarah removed her hand from the gates and Sister Prior took her opportunity and slammed them shut. The lift lurched and began to go down. You bitch, she shouted silently. You bloody, bloody bitch. And wondered, presently (as the lift arrived and she smiled automatically in reply to fat old Uncle Arthur's brick-red grin behind the mesh – strayed like a Cheshire cat into the infirm and unstable world of suffering), whether she meant herself or Sister Prior.

IV

'We've gone in,' Uncle Arthur had said. 'We landed in Normandy this morning and established a beachhead. Your mother will be bucked, won't she? I'd lay odds on your father being home by Christmas. We thought we'd have a special drink to that.'

In the vestibule, watched by the sergeant and the orderly with pimples, he introduced her to the officer he had brought with him – one of the men, she imagined, who was to enjoy or suffer dinner with the course leader and his wife and whose evening was probably further disorientated by being asked to help collect the niece who had visited a patient in the military hospital.

'This is Major Clark. For some reason utterly escapes me I think he's sometimes known as Nobby. He was only a Captain a couple of months ago when he had to sit and suffer my interminable spouting. Decent of him to come back and visit us. My niece Sarah Layton. Be a good fellow and whistle the driver up.'

As Clark went out into the porticoed entrance she was aware of a broadness of back, a compactness of body, a physical wholeness. No burns, no bullets, no severance.

'How was young what's-his-name?'

'All right. Considering.'

'Good. Tell us all about it presently. I rang your aunt from the daftar. She

696

said to see if I could pick you up. She's wondering if she should ring your mother.'

'Why should she do that?'

'To make sure she's heard.'

'Heard what?'

'The good news. But she's bound to have. I say, are you all right?'

'Yes, thank you.' She smiled. Her face felt made of elastic.

'It's these places. The smell gets on your tummy. Come on, the gharry's here.'

The gharry was Uncle Arthur's staff car. Clark saw them into the back and sat himself next to the driver. As they turned into the road the rain fell. Lightning scarred the horizon.

'When are you off then?' Uncle Arthur inquired, raising his voice to be heard above the sluicing rain and the long, trundling, skittle-ball rolls of converging thunder. But it was Clark he'd spoken to.

'First thing in the morning.'

Clark sat with one arm along the back of the seat, his back wedged in the corner of the seat and the door, so that he could talk and be talked to, see and be seen. Vaguely she registered the voice, the intonation, the air of ease, the appraisal she was under. She looked out of the window, scarcely listened to their conversation. They came out into Chowringhee, a place of lights and bicycles and trams. The window was misting up. The city lights hastened the approaching dark. With the edge of her palm she cleared a view for herself and felt like a child intent on observing, from a position of safety and comfort, an alien and dangerous magic.

'Well, what d'you think of the second city of the Empire?' Uncle Arthur asked. 'It's her first visit,' he explained, not waiting for an answer, something she usually thought of as a failing in other people but as a virtue in him. His lack of curiosity had always made him easy to get on with. It was, she supposed, a wholly avuncular virtue, common to that species. She thought that in its unpossessive uninvolved affection there might be felt something of the granite-rock of always available love. Should she weep – and for a few seconds, alarmingly, she felt like doing so – he would be desperately embarrassed but inarticulately sound, a speechless comfort. 'You should have been here a couple of months ago. Major Clark would have shown you the ins and outs. Wouldn't you?'

'Would I, sir?'

'Well, dammit, Clark, you had a reputation. I doubt he ever got to bed before dawn. But no one would have guessed. Always looked as fresh as a daisy.'

She glanced at Uncle Arthur, realized he had already had a sundowner to celebrate that distant inaudible barrage of invasion, or had not quite recovered from a sumptuous lunch; and, catching Clark's eye, saw his judgement or knowledge corresponded with her own. There was, on his rather ugly face, an opacity, a semi-revelation of vanity and of amusement at someone else's expense which she did not understand and did not like.

She thought of herself as pinned by its calculated directness. And looked back at the streaming window, burning with a ludicrous little sense of injustice that he should exist, unmarked, to pass silent comments on Uncle Arthur who seemed to find him engaging and anyway gave him lifts and invitations, good counsel and reports presumably; carried him into the circle of her safety that rested for the moment in the existence of Aunt Fenny in Calcutta; and there, in Pankot, dark, silent and undisturbed by rain or rumours of war and amputation – in Susan and her mother – and far, far away, beyond the streaming window, in the still centre of her father's patience and yearning for release and a quiet passage through the night.

She had not recognized the road. The driver's turn into the forecourt of the apartments was unexpected. She felt the curious flattening of inquiring spirit the traveller suffers from, knowing himself without occupation or investment in the fortunes of a strange city. Sandwiched between Uncle Arthur and Major Clark (who, she noted, smelt of some aromatic substance, an aggressive exudation of his naked body beneath the thin cellular cotton of his khaki bush-shirt) she thought of the lift as taking her from one level of non-experience to another. It came to her that like Ronald Merrick she did not travel well, and then that she was whole and, unlike Susan, unbeholden. I do not, she thought, no I do not, give a damn. The Furies were riding across an uninhabited sky, to their own and no one else's destruction. The real world was a tame, repetitious place: one part of it, when you really looked, was much like another, a chemical accident, a mine of raw material for the creation of random artefacts to house and warm or satisfy the need for sensual pleasure or creature comfort. The lift was one such. It jerked to a stop.

'No, a drink first and a bath second,' she told Aunt Fenny who was abroad in the flat in housecoat, slippers and tidy chiffon turban, midway in her preparations for the evening: a revelation to Major Clark of intimate domestic detail which Sarah put down as a further sign that Aunt Fenny had entered the new age, in which old Flagstaff House values were shrewdly to be readjusted as an insurance against the extinction of those who had held them. Gimlet and cigarette in hand and for a moment alone, Sarah was conscious of belonging to a class engaged in small, continual acts whose purpose was survival through partial sharing in an evolution which, of all the family, only Aunt Lydia back in Bayswater had anticipated and closely witnessed the process of. It was a survival of exiles. Their enemy was light, not dark, the light of their own kind, of their own people at home from whom they had been too long cut off so that, returning there briefly, a deep and holy silence wrapped them and caused them to observe what was real as miniature. In India they had been betrayed by an illusion of topographical vastness into sins of pride that were foreign to their insular, pygmy natures. From the high window of this concrete monstrosity you could see the tragedy and the comic grandeur of tin-pot roofs, disguised at street level by those neo-classical façades which perversely illustrated the vanished age of reason. What reason? My history

(Sarah thought, drinking her sweet gimlet, then drawing on her bitter cigarette), my history, rendered down to a colonnaded front, an architectural perfection of form and balance in the set and size of a window, and to a smoky resentment in my blood, a foolish contrivance for happiness in my heart against the evidence that tells me I never have been happy and can't be while I live here. It's time we were gone. Gone. Every last wise, stupid, cruel, fond or foolish one of us.

She turned from contemplation of the rooftops, aroused by the sounds of more of Uncle Arthur's chaps arriving – among whom she sensed the presence of the next generation of her jailers. To avoid immediate confrontation she brushed past Major Clark who had been standing there as if about to speak and told Aunt Fenny – who was giving orders to the white-clad servant – that she'd finish her drink in the bath.

'I'll come in while you're dressing. I want to hear everything,' Fenny said. 'I've only got to slip into something and I'm ready. Have you anything pretty to wear? Iris Braithwaite from downstairs hopes to come, and perhaps Dora Pedley. They're always got up to kill. But the little party's for you, pet. Afterwards the boys will probably take you dancing or to the flicks, so do your best—' this last in almost a whisper, on the threshold of Sarah's room whose door she held open.

'Well I can't do more than my best, Aunt Fenny.'

'My dear, I'd forgotten. You look done up. Was it bad?'

'They're cutting off his arm.'

'Oh, no.'

The bath was already drawn. She rang the bell and, when he answered, gave her glass to the bearer and told him to bring it back refilled. She shivered in the bleak atmosphere of the air-conditioned room, gratefully entered the steam and humidity of the bathroom to undress in more familiar discomfort. Naked, she put on her shabby bathrobe and felt caressed, but stubborn in her refusal to succumb to a small passion for personal belongings. For a minute or so, back in the ice-box of the bedroom, she sat, smoked, combed out her hopeless hair and drank the second gimlet, smoothed cleansing cream on to her incorruptible Layton face. So uncomely was it (in her eyes) that a wave of pity for it released a succeeding wave of erotic desire to have it loved, it and all her body – untouched beneath the robe Barbie Batchelor had helped her choose the sensible material for. She went and lay in the bath, the tumbler on its edge, within reach, and wondered what else might be in reach.

No, I don't, she repeated, I don't give a damn. But knew she did. Even for Aziz Khan and Fariqua Khan for whose names she had already conjured faces, and – considering them now, their staring eyes and speechless open mouths (as if aghast at the injustice of no more than condign punishment) – she formulated questions: *Why really did Teddie interfere? What made him so anxious to be present when Ronald Merrick tried to get information out of captured Indian soldiers? Had he witnessed an earlier interrogation? Or was it merely, as Merrick seemed to suggest, because he had grown not* to trust him over anything? When the water had cooled below the point of comfort she got out, wrapped herself in one of Aunt Fenny's new-age towels – which was as big as a tent, as soft as down, fit only for a woman in love – and dried herself quickly as if to avoid contamination; but remained swathed for a few moments longer before substituting the shabby robe that had strayed with her from shabby Pankot.

The air-conditioning enveloped her as she passed from bathroom to bedroom. She felt like a clinical specimen captured and cosseted for some kind of experiment which Aunt Fenny, who knocked and entered, had already undergone and emerged from triumphantly, qualified to conduct on others.

'I've brought nothing long,' Sarah said. Fenny had on an emerald-green dinner gown.

'It doesn't matter. Mrs Braithwaite's just phoned to say Iris has gippy-tum and since they're over at the Pedleys it means Dora won't come either. So, pet, you'll be the only pebble on the beach. Now tell me about poor Mr Merrick.'

Sarah told her as much as it was necessary for her to know. When she had finished Fenny said, 'Why not stay a day or two longer? I mean if you could stand it. I'm sure it would cheer him up to see you again. He won't want to be bothered by me. Besides, I never know what to say to people in a bad way. I don't think I could. I've always been a terrible coward about illness. Arthur says that when he has only a cold even, I act as if I don't love him any more. I can't explain it but other people's physical troubles seem to strike me dumb. If you stay on a day or two and see him over the worst I promise I'll really put the red carpet out for him afterwards. I'm good at jollying people along.'

'Why?' Sarah exclaimed, pausing in the midst of applying foundation cream. 'Why should there be a red carpet? Why should we start getting involved at all?'

Aunt Fenny's face, reflected behind her own in the mirror, looked momentarily blank.

'Well, pet, you know the answer better than I do, I imagine. It's you who came all the way down here to see him.'

'For Susan.'

Fenny smiled. 'Only for Susan?'

'Yes.'

'Are you sure?'

'Yes, I'm sure. Why?'

'Well, he was awfully attentive in Mirat. I thought you might be a bit gone on him.'

'How could I be? He's not our class.'

The irony, she saw, was lost on Fenny.

'No. But he's made something of himself and that sort of thing doesn't matter like it used to, does it? I mean people say it's what a man does and is in himself that counts and I think that's true.'

700

'Am I really so unattractive, Aunty? A board-school boy with a brain and a gentlemanly veneer, and only one arm? Couldn't I do better than that?'

'Oh, Sarah.' Fenny flushed. 'Well, I was only thinking of you being happy. I thought you might be attracted to him and trying to hide your feelings because of what the rest of us might say. None of the things that are against him would matter to me if you did love him. I'd back you up, honestly, right to the hilt. So do you? Do you, pet?'

'As a matter of fact he appals me.' She finished her unrewarding work with the cosmetic, stared at her own face and at the reflection of poor Aunt Fenny's which now seemed as bereft as her own. 'And it would be wrong to run away with the idea that he liked Teddie, by the way.'

After a bit Fenny said, 'I shan't ask you why you say that. I'll just accept it. But I will ask you this. I've wanted to for ages. Were you in love with Teddie? Did it hurt to lose him to Susan?'

'No. I wasn't in love with Teddie either.' She got up from the stool and went to the white-painted fitted wardrobe, took out the dress she had brought as best. Its absurd nice-young-girl look touched nerves that caused alternate chills of irritation and desolation. Removing the robe and standing for a few seconds in her underwear, acutely self-conscious under Fenny's appraisal of her figure, she put the dress on, hastily but reluctantly, like some kind of outgrown but necessary disguise that fooled nobody any longer. She recalled, from somewhere, but did not immediately connect it to the day of the wedding, taking a dress off and feeling she had entered an area of light. Dealing deftly with the simple buttons and the hook and eye of the kind she always chose – on the large side because she had no patience and seldom any help – she said, 'You see, Aunt Fenny, I don't know what it means when people use that word. But thanks for worrying about me. Just don't, that's all. I've met men I'm attracted to and some of them have been attracted back. That's simple enough. But this other thing, love, love, that's never happened. If it has I never knew it, so it must be over-rated. It must be a bit of a sell.'

'Well,' Fenny said, more brightly, 'that's all right then, isn't it? You've got it all to come. One thing's absolutely certain. You won't be in love and not know it.'

'Did you know it, Aunt Fenny? Did you?'

Fenny's smile contracted, but did not disappear.

'Several times I thought I did, once I knew.'

'You were lucky, then.'

'No, pet. Not lucky. It wasn't Arthur.'

'I'm sorry.'

'No you must never be sorry. No, never. Ninety-nine per cent of life is compromise. It's part of the contract. I've been perfectly happy. I won't say content. Contentment's a different thing. I think I've reached the stage where I could honestly say if I didn't still think of myself as a young woman, well, I *am*, that I've had a good life. Nothing marvellous has ever happened to me, but nothing bad either. I don't suppose I've done a great deal of good anywhere but I hope no one could say I've ever done any real harm. When I pop off there won't be a thing you could put your finger on to prove, you know, that I'd done more than earn my keep. It's not much, but even that takes a bit of doing, and it's about the most the majority of us can expect of ourselves.'

'I know.'

'Well, smile for me to show that you do.'

Sarah smiled.

'And if you come here I'll tell you my secret.' Sarah went. She sat on the bed and suffered the warm weight of Aunt Fenny's well-nourished hand on her own chill bony arm. 'It's not a secret to your mother. Has she never told you?' Sarah shook her head. 'I'm not surprised. Families are funny things. They have far more secrets from each other than you'd think likely, don't they? We know a lot about our friends, but not much about our kith and kin.' She paused, but she was still smiling. She said, 'The secret is that I adored your father.'

'My father?'

'But adored him. Not from afar, either, but he only had eyes for Millie. He thought me silly and empty-headed, a terrible little flirt and never took me the least bit seriously. He still doesn't. If I said to him now, John, do you know I loved you madly, he'd think it was a joke because he never noticed then and has never noticed since. In fact only Millie noticed and even she's forgotten just *what* she noticed. So have I, in a way, you know, in the way you do when it's all so long ago. But you see, pet, even now, I mean but even now, perhaps especially now, because it's ages since I've seen him, if he walked into this room my heart would take a funny little turn. Just for a second. Then, bump, back to reality because there never was and couldn't be anything between us. If there had been, if he'd felt the same, well even if we'd never married I'd never be able to say as I do that nothing marvellous has ever happened to me, but he didn't, so it wasn't marvellous. But it *was* this thing you say you don't know about, and it's not just physical attraction. And if it ever happens to you, you mark my words, you'll jolly well know.'

Sarah, who had stared for a while at her own clasped hands, glanced up. She found it difficult to take her aunt as seriously as she probably deserved. Like Sarah's mother and father, Fenny belonged to a generation of men and women – the last one there might ever be – who seemed to have been warmed in their formative years by the virtues of self-assurance and moral certainty; what, she supposed, she used to think of as a perpetual light, one that shone (thinking of Aunt Lydia) on their radical as well as conservative notions of what one was in the world to do. And weren't these things illusion of a kind? And this love, which Fenny said was not just physical attraction, an illusion too? Sex she understood, and even a grand passion because that, presumably, was a compound of physical desire, envy, jealousy and possessiveness. But love of the kind Fenny had described, the kind she herself and no doubt Susan had grown up to believe in as right and acceptable, now seemed to her like one more standard of human behaviour that needed that same climate of self-assurance and moral certainty in which to flourish; like all the other flowers of modest, quiet perfection which Susan had imagined grew on the other side of the wall, in the secret garden.

'Susan—' she began.

'What about Susan, pet?' Then, like Uncle Arthur, without waiting: 'I was thinking of Susan, too, of when we saw her and Teddie off at the station on their way to Nanoora.'

'Were you? Why, Auntie?'

'Because of a similar occasion, when we saw your father and mother off on *their* honeymoon. I coped with it awfully well. Later there was a family joke about it. They said I was so busy being the centre of attraction for all the young officers who came down to wave them off that I hardly had time to wave to them myself. In Mirat I watched you so closely, pet, because it brought it all back to me. I knew something had made you unhappy and I wondered if you were feeling the same about Susan whisking Teddie away as I felt about Millie whisking John. You looked so sad.'

'I wasn't sad.'

'Truly?'

'Truly.'

'Then everything's all right, Now.' A squeeze of the arm. 'Finish making yourself look pretty and come in as soon as you can. And do think over what I said. I mean about staying for a bit, just so that you can enjoy yourself, and meet a few new faces. I'm sure General Rankin will turn a blind eye to a few days absence, and your mother can do without you very well. Just for once. Heaven knows when the baby comes you'll all be at sixes and sevens, so take advantage now, pet.' She hesitated. 'I know it's been difficult, for *many* reasons. In the old days coming out to India was a tremendous lark. All you've had is this dreary war and – what it's done to people.' People like my mother, you mean, Sarah thought. 'When your father gets home and realizes how much you've done to help your mother and Su, he'll be very proud of you, but awfully upset to know how little fun you've had.'

As if on cue the silence beyond the closed door was broken by a peal of men's laughter. Her aunt made a funny face. 'There you are,' she said. 'If you leave them too long they start telling each other horrid stories. Men simply aren't serious creatures at all, they make a joke of everything. I'd better go and keep them in order. What a shame Jimmy Clark's only here until tomorrow, he was one of Arthur's most promising chaps on the course and is such a nice man, but then he was at your father's old school. They're sending him down to do some special training in something rather hush-hush in Ceylon. He's only thirty but Arthur says he'll probably end up a lieutenant-colonel if the war goes on another year, which it probably won't. He got an emergency commission but we think he's the kind of man

703

who may want to stay on in the army either here or at home. Incidentally, he's been asking all about you.'

Fenny rose, gave Sarah what was meant as a reassuring pat. Sarah smiled up at her, feeling it incumbent on her to remain where she was, like a tense little chrysalis from which – in the ten or fifteen minutes of privacy that were left to her and encouraged by homilies and the dutiful desire to shake off all those dark and gloomy images of the world as a repository only of occasions and conditions of despair – she would emerge as the tough little butterfly of Aunt Fenny's affectionate imagination.

*

'No,' Aunt Fenny said, 'tonight the ladies will *not* withdraw. At least not for more than a few minutes. There are only two of us and frankly, Arthur, the walls in this flat are too thin for mutual comfort.' The chaps, cheered by cocktails, an Anglo-Indian curry, two bottles of South African hock and the expectation of brandy or liqueurs, laughed dutifully. There were six of them, including Jimmy Clark who sat on Sarah's right. On her left, at the head of the table, was her Uncle Arthur, deep in but chin above his cups. Opposite her, on Uncle Arthur's left, was a pale-faced young officer with a lick of hair who had begun the evening with what she had detected as intellectual reservations but who was now, long before its ending, apparently entranced and well on his way to what she knew men called being as pissed as a newt. Why a newt? She had kept newts one summer at Grandfather's, in a deep square blue Mackintosh's toffee tin and all she could recall was that the water turned sallow and the newts had died. Perhaps that was it. Sallowness, and death by drowning, like Mr Morland in his dream.

'We'll all withdraw and meet next door for coffee and what's-it. Have you boys decided how you'll finish up this evening? There's Ingrid Bergman and Gary Cooper at the New Empire.'

'Send not,' the pale young officer intoned, 'to ask for whom the bell tolls. It tolls for thee. I've seen it, it's rotten.'

'And unless you've booked there isn't a chance,' another man said.

'Well, Arthur and I are going on to the Purvises,' Fenny announced. 'We thought you young people might make up a party of your own. I'm sorry Iris and Dora couldn't come because then you might have preferred to stay here and dance to the gramophone. There's plenty to drink and bits to eat if you get peckish later, so do stay if you'd prefer to, or all go out somewhere. You can talk it over with coffee. It'll be in in just a few minutes.'

Catching Sarah's eye she nodded and rose. Noisily they followed suit. Major Clark helped Sarah with her chair.

In the living-room Fenny said, 'The thing is, pet, just to fall in with what they decide and not express a preference. Men much prefer the helpless happy type. My bet is they'll plump for the Grand Hotel. It's an officers' hostel these days and they feel at home there. They might mix in with another party. Don't be too put out or standoffish if you find yourself in a gang that includes chichis. Boys like these from home think we treat girls like that awfully badly, and perhaps we do. They laugh at them too, but feel sorry for them, and can't bear it when English girls turn up their noses. But you're not like that, pet, are you? You'll have a lovely time. It's quite a thing for them to *have* an English girl, and they'll adore just being seen there turning up with you. And, pet, there's safety in numbers. Well, listen to me. Birds and bees. I shan't start worrying about you until long after midnight. Jimmy Clark will look after you. He'll know exactly why I put him next to you.'

'Who are the Purvises?'

'Oh just some rather dreary civil types Arthur has to keep in with. They're having a bridge party – Indians, not cards – and want to muster forces for after dinner when it gets tense and embarrassing because everybody's said everything twice.'

'I've never been to a bridge party.'

'Think yourself lucky. It's part of the price you pay when you get posted to a place like this. Let's powder our noses and get moving with the coffee. Some of them *need* it.' She hesitated, apparently struck by a conscientious thought. 'Oh dear. Ought I to let you? I *am* responsible for you to your mother, aren't I?'

'I've been out with tipsy boys before.'

'But it's different here. Calcutta's not Pankot and some of them are tipsy already. Well, one of them is.'

'I don't think we need worry about him.'

Fenny stared at her. A slight flush came and went. 'Don't we? Heavens.' She smiled. 'What can you know about such things? Well, anyway. Come on. Powder noses and into the breach.'

*

The Purvises' bridge party was an official affair so Aunt Fenny and Uncle Arthur used the staff car. They dropped Sarah and Major Clark at the entrance to the Grand Hotel. A following taxi brought the five others. Between the departure of car and arrival of taxi, Clark – shooting away small boys and bent beggars – said, 'Be sure to tell me the moment you've had enough. It can get pretty rackety in here. It may not be quite up your street.'

'Oh, I don't know. Why not?'

'Well, I should say rather, it's not much up mine.'

'That didn't seem to be Uncle Arthur's impression earlier.'

'No.' She felt him glance down at her – not far down; he wasn't tall. She caught sight of the taxi that was bringing the others. 'It wouldn't be the first wrong one he's had. Let's go in. It's a hell of a long walk. They'll soon catch up.'

The long walk was through a shopping arcade. At the end of it was the reception hall. Near by a band thumped; a sound Susan once described as only a degree or so less fascinating than the sound of men *en masse*, waiting in the ante-room of a mess for you to arrive on ladies' night. Bands attracted Sarah too, but hearing this one prodded her alive to the fact that under a wakeful surface, articially stimulated by plenty to drink and too much chatter, she was exhausted. Was it only yesterday at this time that the train had left Ranpur? She smiled cheerfully at the other five, as they came up, and went in the midst of them through a lounge full of wicker chairs and tables, every one occupied, predominantly by men in uniform, and out on to a broad terrace where a band played to an almost empty floor, under a temporary rainy-season roof. In the dry, presumably, you could dance under the stars. Bearers moved tables together and arranged chairs. About to sit she felt herself held.

Clark said, 'I only dance where there's plenty of room and other people can see, so now's your chance.' He took her on to the floor. A quick-step. An over-familiar tune. Susan would know its name. For the first few moments she felt a pleasure at discovering he danced well and that she could follow. But after one and a half circuits of the floor the old problem arose. She had never been much good at talking and dancing together. The two duties seemed incompatible. She tried to recall what questions she had asked him at dinner. Not many. Dinner had centred mainly on conversation dominated by Uncle Arthur. She said the first thing that came into her head.

'Aunt Fenny tells me you were at Chillingborough.'

He nodded. They were not dancing close, but the realization that he never took his eyes off her was almost as inhibiting as that over-close proximity men occasionally attempted and sometimes embarrassingly established.

'It's Daddy's old school,' she said.

'I know. I hope he survived the experience.'

'Yes, I think so.' She did not know what else to say.

'Good, I survived it too.'

A turn or so.

'Have you been in India long?'

'Six months.'

She wondered whether to him that was a short or long time. 'Aunt Fenny said you were in the desert.'

'Mostly a euphemism for Cairo. But yes, I was for a time in what's called the desert.' A pause. 'Shall I ask the questions now and give you a rest?' She glanced up. His smile was remote. His skin, close to, had a coarseness of texture which she felt she ought to dislike, but didn't. 'How was your boy-friend?'

'My boy-friend?'

'The chap you took goodies to.'

But just then the band stopped on an up-beat and a clash of cymbals.

706

He shepherded her to the table. A bearer was unloading glasses and bottles from a tray. Only three of the five other men were sitting there.

'Isn't it on the early side for dropping out?' Clark asked. The one with a blond moustache said, 'No one's dropped out.' The others agreed. She thought: They don't like Clark: and recollected that he was a stranger to them. Perhaps they assumed from Clark's proprietary attitude that his earlier connection with Colonel and Mrs Grace was of a more intimate kind than their own and gave him rights in her which her aunt and uncle accorded formal recognition. It might not even be obvious to them that until today she and Clark had never met. She felt like saying something that would make the position clear, and was conscience-stricken by the fact that in spite of introductions she was uncertain of their names. To the blond moustached one who asked her what she would drink (Freddie? She would have to listen more closely) she said, 'Do you get kicked out if you only want coffee?' He said something about letting them try and coffee it was but what about having something with it, for instance a sticky green? To please him she agreed before the penny dropped that he meant *crème de menthe*. The order was given, the music started up and Freddie (or was he Tony? Why were men so often called by their diminutives?) said 'May I?' and was on his feet as if he had recognized his possible sole opportunity. She responded automatically and was in his arms, waltzing, before she admitted to herself that dancing with the blond-moustached man was the last thing she had wanted to do. She had noticed the heavy perspiration while sitting at the table. Mercifully he kept his distance, but his hands were wet. Susan said heavy sweat was the sign of a beer drinker which was why British Other Ranks perspired worse than officers.

'Mrs Grace told me you've come miles to visit someone at the BMH.'

'Well, just from Pankot.'

'Where's that?'

She told him.

'I was there myself last month. The BMH I mean, not Pankot. Nothing romantic though. Appendix. These days they give you a spinal. Interesting looking up at the ceiling and sort of half feeling it all going on.'

'It must have been awful.'

'Oh, I don't know. Interesting. Looking up at the ceiling.'

She felt for him. Obviously he found dancing and talking incompatible too. She came out with it. 'I've met so many people tonight I've got the names mixed up.'

'Leonard.'

'Mine's Sarah.'

'I know. Just now I nearly made an awful bloomer. At home I've got a Labrador dog called Sarah. Well, I mean she's a she-dog. I nearly said, like you do when you're thinking of something to say, "I've got a dog named after you." I stopped myself in time but then my mind went blank.' Their ankles made fleeting contact. 'Sorry.'

She smiled. 'Where's home?'

707

'Shropshire. I'm a Shropshire lad. There are poems about it, but I've never read them.'

'What are you, a farmer?'

'How did you guess?'

An image of Mr Birtwhistle's fields and Mr Birtwhistle's cows imposed itself behind Leonard's corn-stook hair and fiery, dripping face.

'I'm not really a farmer though. My father is.'

'It's a reserved occupation, isn't it?'

'Could be. But I'd only just gone in with him, and Dad's not so old. He's got Italian prisoners working for him. Says they're all right. I'm not missed. Well, not for that.'

'Will you go back to farming?'

'Expect so.' A pause. 'Your uncle makes India sound fascinating, though,' he added dutifully. They exchanged rather solemn glances. 'I suppose,' he said, 'you've lived here most of your life.'

'I went home to school. It works out about half and half.'

'Would you recommend it? Living in India?'

'Why, are you thinking about it?'

'Well, it sounds all right, responsible job, lots of servants. Your uncle says it will be years before the Indians can do without us entirely. Up in the Punjab I went round one of those experimental agricultural stations and I thought then there's a job I could do. A chap from England who knows a bit about farming looks at India generally and thinks he's back in the middle ages. I mean I don't know anything about politics or government or commerce, but I do know a bit about land. Some of the things you see make your hair stand on end. But then when I think of settling down here and getting married and having kids I don't think I'd like it much. I mean sending the kids back home wouldn't be my idea of having a family. Am I wrong?'

'I don't know.' She considered. 'I'd hate never to have been home. I'd feel I'd missed something important that I was entitled to, the thing that makes me English. You go back to claim an inheritance. Then if you have children of your own you send them back to claim theirs. It's part of the sacrifice parents have to make.'

'I couldn't make it. Even knowing that if I had a daughter, as well as a dog called Sarah, she might turn out like you if I did.'

She glanced up at him and felt his presence as a homely kindly man some girl other than herself would be fortunate to love and settle down with.

'But then,' he added, 'I don't think you're typical. Young memsahibs usually scare me to death.'

She laughed; but for the rest of the waltz they both seemed to find it difficult again to think of anything to say. As he led her back to the table he said, 'Are you really going back tomorrow?'

'I should.'

'You mean there's a chance not? That film at the New Empire isn't rotten. I could sit through it again any day. But perhaps you've seen it too?'

'Oh, in Pankot we never get anything new.'

'May I ring you then, in the morning? You'll know by then, won't you, what you've decided?'

'Yes.'

'Then I'll ring you. At ten o'clock.' He delivered her up to Major Clark. On her section of the table there was coffee and brandy. 'I hope you don't mind,' Clark said. 'I changed the order because I didn't think you looked like a girl who drank sticky green.' The chairs had been moved, too. She and Clark were now subtly isolated from the others. There were still two absentees. They arrived as the band started up again – the pale officer who had been tipsy and now looked paler than ever and the dark-haired boy whom she was pretty sure was Tony. As they approached the table Clark whispered to her, 'Let's dance again. I'll tell you why presently.'

A foxtrot. She hated foxtrots. She longed just to sit and drink her coffee, but went back on the floor. Clark said, 'That man's been sick. They ought to send him home.'

'He was all right at dinner.'

'Not really. And the air's hit him. I've suggested to the others he ought not to stay.'

She looked in the direction of the table. The man in question was supporting his head in his hands. Two of the others were leaning towards him. The dark-haired boy had his hand on his back. It looked as if they were encouraging him to call it a day and leave while the going was good, before she and Clark returned to the table. Leonard sat watching with his arms on the table, dissociating himself from the argument. There were now more dancers, the floor was quite crowded. Her view was cut off. Clark said, 'When this dance is finished would you do something for me?'

'What?'

'Go to the powder-room. I'll show you where it is. I'll come back for you in about ten minutes. It shouldn't take longer.'

'I don't mind him being a bit high.'

He looked down at her.

'I mind. So would you if he stayed. So would he tomorrow. He's not just high. He's over the edge. He'll end up crying probably. Don't you think so? Don't you think he's the crying type?'

'I don't know.'

'Well I assure you he is.' A pause. 'I'd be grateful if you'd do as I suggest.' He smiled. This time there was no trace of remoteness. She felt exposed to a sudden, inexplicable but encouraging warmth. Leaving go as the music ended, guided back through the doors between terrace and lounge, she was conscious of his body and of her own under its control and protection. Her elbow was held. 'This way.'

'Ten minutes,' he said a few paces from a door. 'I'll be here. If I'm not, go back in and give me another five. Don't stand outside, unless you don't mind being pestered by strangers.'

709

She stayed in the powder-room for a quarter of an hour. Two Anglo-Indian girls came in. Her presence seemed to inhibit them. They talked in low voices but she caught the lilt which, if their skins were light enough, helped girls like these to pass themselves off as natives of Cardiff and Swansea. She wondered what she would find to say to them if they joined the party. She stayed at the mirror until they had gone and then, coming out, found him waiting.

She said, 'I thought I'd give it the five extra minutes.'

'I'm afraid even ten was too many, so there's a change of plan.' He took her arm and led her into the lounge with the wicker chairs and tables and noisy men, and through into the arcade towards the street.

'What's happened?'

'I'll explain in a minute.'

Again he shooed boys and beggars. A taxi door was held open by one of the hotel bearers. She entered, understanding that he had sent the man to make sure of one.

The man's 'Salaam, Sahib,' marked the passing of baksheesh. Clark spoke to the driver but she did not hear what he said. He might have given Aunt Fenny's address. He joined her. The taxi moved.

'What did you mean, ten was too many?'

'Just that. He wouldn't budge. And the others were no particular help. I'm sorry.' He offered her a cigarette. Automatically, although not wanting it, she took one. 'It's a dreary place anyway. But then it's all most of them have. I'll show you something better. Unless you want to go home. It's only ten-thirty, though.'

After he had lit her cigarette she gazed through the window at a dark sea, the *maidan* side of Chowringhee.

'See those lights way across?' he asked. 'That's where I first met you.'

'Oh.' She looked. 'You're not really telling me the truth, are you?'

'I think so. Yes. That's the BMH.'

'I mean about why we've left the others.'

'I promised your aunt I'd see you came to no harm, Miss Layton.'

After a while she said, 'My name's Sarah,' and turned to look at him in the odd, distorting lights that flickered in and out of the cab. She thought: It's about now he'll make a pass. But he didn't. He simply stared back at her. She said, 'Where are we going?'

'Across the so-called bridge.'

'What does that mean?'

'You'll see.'

What she saw was that in the politest possible way she had been abducted, that he had never had any intention of sharing her with the others, would have found a way of ditching them even if the pale officer had been sober. It would have taken a bit longer but the end would have been the same. She supposed she should feel flattered as well as annoyed.

Perhaps that was what she felt, that or too tired to care much how she spent the rest of the evening.

As if he had followed her reasoning and wished to reassure her he said, 'I'll take you home if you'd prefer that,' but put his hand on hers in what she judged a pretence of consideration meant quite otherwise, meant in fact to have the effect it did, which was to leave her, when the touch was withdrawn, deprived of the source of a faint and therefore unsatisfactory physical response. 'The trouble is,' he said, 'if your aunt finds you there when she gets back she'll know the evening went wrong. That fellow doesn't deserve it but the less said about it all the better. Don't you agree? You and I are both leaving Cal tomorrow but they've got another week under your uncle's eye. I wouldn't want any of them to go back to their units with an adverse report, would you?'

'No.'

'I don't mean we should pretend the party never broke up or that you and I never went off somewhere else, but your aunt and uncle needn't be told why. If one of the others lets it out, that's their funeral. Now,' he ended, and touched her hand again, 'let's forget it and enjoy ourselves. This is the real Calcutta. I'm told this time last year these streets were littered with the corpses of people who came in to try and escape the famine. You have to hope the taxi doesn't conk out, they'd probably cut our throats and chuck us into the Hooghly.'

The taxi had increased speed. The road was ill-lit, a squalid urban area. Shrouded figures lay huddled under lean-to shelters and under arcades. Above, there were tenements. After a while the taxi took a road to the left, over a humped-back bridge. The darkness was now stabbed by the beams of the headlamps.

'All clear,' Clark said, 'we've passed the danger zone.'

The road became kuttcha. There were trees, then open spaces; clutches of houses came and went. 'All round here, in the old days, you'd find a lot of rich Indian merchants. But it's gone down. Don't let it depress you, though. We're not going slumming.'

They drove for another ten minutes, reached a crossroads marked by stalls and huts. Crossing another humped-back bridge the driver had to brake sharply to avoid a stray water-buffalo.

'That's India,' Clark commented. 'The internal combustion engine in confrontation with a creature evolved from the primeval slime.' Ahead there was a low stucco wall. They turned into it and through a gateway. She had an impression of a tall, rather narrow house, with many lighted windows. They drew up at an open doorway. When the engine died she heard the music of sitar, tablas and tamboura. He opened the door on his side, which was next the entrance, and helped her out.

'Walk right up and wait,' he said, 'I have to be persuasive.'

She climbed the few steps, smelling incense, but did not cross the threshold into the narrow hall in which she had a glimpse of curtained doorways guarded by a sleepy Buddha and agile Indian Gods cast in bronze.

711

She watched Clark bargaining with the driver, persuading him either to stay or return at a specified hour, and felt calm, which was odd, because standing made her realize that almost imperceptibly she was trembling, as if in the grip of a faint rigor. He came up the steps smiling vividly. 'Fixed,' he said, and harboured her in his right arm, leading her in. An Indian servant had come through one of the curtained doorways. Clark said, 'I've left a taxi-wallah out there, Billy. Try and see he doesn't get bored or go away, but don't give him anything stronger than beer.'

The man signified agreement. Clark led her through one set of curtains into a square room equipped like a bar. The music was coming from the room beyond.

'It's a free house,' he said, going behind a semicircular counter. 'So what'll you have, brandy? You never got to drink that other one, but this is better, Three Star. I'll make it long.' He popped a soda bottle, poured and came back out with two well-filled glasses. 'Cheers.' She answered by raising her glass. 'The house belongs to an Indian woman called Mira. While the music's on we just creep in and sit like mice.' Again he took her elbow, guided her through another curtained doorway into a room that surprised her by its length. Ceiling fans whirled sluggishly, wafting unfamiliar perfumes. A standard lamp at the far end illuminated a carpeted daïs on which the instrumentalists sat cross-legged. The rest of the room was unlit, but she clearly made out among the clutter of divans and couches men and women who sat with their faces towards the source of light. Clark took her on tiptoe to an unoccupied sofa against the wall just inside the doorway. A few feet in front of it a solitary Indian woman sat on cushions. She glanced round, seemed to smile, but returned her attention quickly to the music.

Sarah sat. Clark leant close to her and whispered, 'It's Pyari on the sitar.' She nodded, but only vaguely registered the name as one she might have heard mentioned as that of a famous man. She was never sure how much she liked Indian music or whether she agreed with the general opinion of the people she knew that it was a noise that showed more than anything else the hopelessness of attempting to understand the people who made it. She had an instinctive feeling, though, that even if it was not really what she understood as music it was being performed with great virtuosity. The sitar looked more capable of playing Pyari than he, an ordinary human being with only so many fingers, of playing it. His struggles were immense but must be paying off, judging by the extraordinary ripples of sound. The tablas were smacked with matching agility by a round little man with a bald copper-coloured head. In the background a statuesque woman produced a resonant whining accompaniment on the upright tamboura.

Sarah sipped her brandy and soda. An evening of Indian culture was the last thing she had expected a man like Clark to offer her, but she was hopeful that, unresponsive to it as she was, the music would go on for some time because when it stopped she would find herself out of place, not knowing what to say to the woman who reclined so elegantly on cushions.

She guessed that Indians like these laughed at English people like her. Again Clark leaned towards her and whispered, 'The woman on the couch down on the left in the spangled saree's a Maharanee, but she's suing for divorce. The elderly Englishman next to her had a distinguished career in the ICS. He's currently acting as her private legal adviser and escort while she's in Calcutta, but I don't imagine it goes further than that. That young white boy in mufti whose head he's fondling looks like an AB from a ship of His Majesty's Navy.'

Sarah glanced from the Maharanee to the man and stared, at first fascinated and then repelled by the hand that clutched, let go, and clutched again at the dark hair of a young man who sat at his feet uncomplaining. Clark whispered, 'It's one way for boys like that to see a few of the bright lights when they come ashore, and go back on board with a gold cigarette case like the officers have.'

The Maharanee turned, spoke to the retired civil servant, smiled and put her hand briefly on his free one, ignoring the boy and the older man's attentions to him. Sarah looked back at the musicians, and drank more brandy, felt hollow, embarrassed that in a roomful of Indians two Englishmen should so behave themselves. But the embarrassment was incoherent, less real than the curiosity which made not looking at them a conscious effort, a disciplinary exercise in tact that was also intended to display, for Clark's benefit, false proof of her inurement to all quirks of human taste and to evidence of their open satisfaction. She thought Clark had her under scrutiny. She resisted the impulse to find out, but a movement from him convinced her she had been right and that he was deliberately putting her through a test; but whether it was intended to confirm the presence of a physical aptitude or the absence of a moral quality, she did not know.

She decided to face it directly, and looked at him. He was, as she expected, now watching the musicians. His right arm rested on the back of the sofa. The hand – relaxed but too vigorously formed to look limp – hung a few inches away from her shoulder. His face, in profile, just touched by light, as it might be far back in the auditorium of a theatre with the play in progress, reflected the same quality of assertiveness and self-possession. She turned her head again, towards Pyari.

The music sounded as if it had reached a climax and would end abruptly; which it did. The applause was remarkably loud for such a thinly-scattered audience. She set her glass down and joined in, for politeness. The musicians abandoned their instruments and made *namaste*. Light entered the room at several points as servants rung curtains back and came in with trays.

The Indian woman on the cushions turned round.

'Jimmy, the movement control telephoned. The plane leaves for Colombo half an hour earlier than they originally told you.'

'Thanks, Mira. By the way, I've brought someone along to hear Pyari. Her name's Sarah.'

Sarah murmured hello. The Indian woman nodded, addressed Clark again almost immediately.

'Pyari's in good form, isn't he? They've asked him at Government House. Did you hear?'

'No? Will he go?'

'What do you think? He said he might send one of his third-year pupils because the people there wouldn't know the difference. But none of his pupils wanted to go either, even as a joke, unless he let them hide a bomb in the sitar. He said, "Why should we ruin a good instrument?" So that was that.'

Clark laughed, ignoring the fact that the joke was partly on Sarah. A bearer approached, offering *pan*. Sarah shook her head.

'You should,' he recommended, taking one and beginning to chew. 'It cleanses the blood. Haven't you ever eaten *pan*?'

'I did as a child.'

'Have another drink instead then.'

She surrendered her glass. She had emptied it, nervously. The Indian woman got gracefully to her feet and went farther down the room to talk to a man and woman who sat with their arms round each other.

'Mira's a stunner, isn't she?' Clark said.

'Yes. Beautiful.'

'She keeps a husband in drink and pays all his gambling debts and hotel bills, and his mistress's clothes and jewellery accounts.'

'Does she? Why?'

'Why not? She's so rich she can't count it. Anyway, she likes his mistress. They used to be lovers themselves, but she's mad about the Maharanee now, and as that's quite mutual everything in the garden's lovely. You can always tell. When Mira's crossed she shuts herself up in her rooms for days on end. But one way and other this party's been going on since the day before yesterday. So I gather. I only got in this morning. She's probably paying Pyari a thousand chips for the music, so why should he perform at Government House for nothing? Not that he would anyway. He's very anti-government because they've never done anything to encourage the arts. Most of his students confuse art with politics, so he makes political gestures every so often as part of his duties as a good *guru*, but he couldn't care less about politics himself. In fact' – he looked round the room – 'no one here could. Politics are for the poor and the bourgeois middle class. Most of these people have fortunes stashed away in banks in Lisbon and Zürich. The existence of well-to-do little neutral countries is a pointer to what global war is really all about, or haven't you noticed?'

The bearer returned with drinks.

'I expect you wonder how I got to know this place,' Clark continued. 'Mira has friends in Cairo. They wrote her when they knew I was coming to India. So whenever I come in to Calcutta this is my unofficial address, which explains why your Uncle Arthur had that odd idea I was always out on the tiles. I expect somebody reported to him my bed was never slept in. I

714

mean the one in the quaint monkish little quarters they gave me when I got myself sent on that course he runs. But as I was such a bright boy he obviously turned a blind eye.'

'Yes, I see.' She sipped the new, much stronger, brandy and soda, looked at him and asked, 'Has Mira got friends in Ceylon too?'

'We both have.'

'Then you'll be nice and comfortable.'

'It's one of my aims in life. Isn't it one of yours?'

She stared at her glass and, after a moment's hesitation, allowed the absurd truth to enter like a chill draught through all the ill-fitting doors of her inherited prejudices and superstitions. 'I suppose I've never given it much thought.'

'I guessed you hadn't.' He hesitated. 'But you're refreshingly honest. I thought I wasn't mistaken. That honour-of-the-regiment exterior is paper-thin, isn't it?'

Yes, she thought, pitifully thin; but its thinness was less pitiful than the fact that it was there and could be seen and was the only exterior, the only skin she had. She felt her hand taken, and this time held on to.

'I wonder why?' he asked. 'Didn't the second injection take?'

'The second injection of what?'

'India and the honour-of-the-regiment. It's usually fatal, surely? I mean isn't the first one bad enough? Growing up with all the other po-faced kids in a sort of ghastly non-stop performance of Where the Rainbow Ends? Then having to trot back for a time to a little island that's gone down because it's become full of vulgar money-grubbers and people without standards and all sorts of jacks-in-office trying to paint out the pink parts of the map?'

She smiled, but said, 'I suppose that's how it looks. It's only half the truth.'

'What's the other half?'

She moved her hand from under his. She hated simplifications, especially those to which her own ideas of the complex nature of reality might be reduced. He did not reclaim contact.

'Extraordinary, isn't it,' he said, 'that the people in this country who feel most like foreigners to each other are English people who've just arrived and the ones who have been here for several years. Last Christmas, after I left here, I was up in 'Pindi staying with a friend of a friend back home who's been out here for about ten years. And there they were, the man, the wife, and two of the po-faced kids, and right from the beginning we felt towards each other like I suppose those people do who suffer from that odd racial prejudice thing, as if in spite of our being the *same* colour and class, one of us was black, me, and the others white, them. We were tremendously polite but simply had nothing to say to each other. I felt I'd met a family who'd been preserved by some sort of perpetual Edwardian sunlight that got trapped between the Indian Ocean and the Arabian Sea round about the turn of the century. Of course, having gone straight there from

Mira's I was prepared to believe I'd struck something unusual. I hadn't, though, had I? It makes me want to say, Where have you all been? Come back. All is forgiven.'

She was still smiling. She said, 'Come back where? Forgiven by whom, and for what?'

But he was, after all, quite serious. 'I suppose one of the things you need to be forgiven for is deluding the Indians as well as yourselves into thinking that the values of 1911 are still current at home.'

'Why 1911?'

'Wasn't that the year of the Delhi Durbar? *Post*-Edwardian I grant you, but anything before 1900 would be a journalist's exaggeration and anything after 1914–18 quite irrelevant. And when I say deluding Indians I don't mean people of the kind you see in this room, I mean the kind who take you seriously, and that includes chaps like Gandhi and Nehru. Actually I hate the word Westernized, it's used so loosely. You could say Mira's Westernized, but she's modern West and that means a fair slice of modern East as well. Nehru and that lot, all the liberal-upper and bourgeois middle-class of India, they're one hundred per cent old-fashioned West. And it's all as dead as yesterday, isn't it? You ought to bury the body, or expose it to the vultures like the Parsees do. It didn't survive the Great War. It makes an awful smell. Of course there are still pockets of the stink at home, your kind of people go back to them and I was educated at one. Highly unsuccessfully. They went in a lot at Chillingborough for future colonial administrators, didn't they? They were even planning to have an Indian boy there – one who *wasn't* a Maharajah's son. He came round with his dad during my last term to have a look-see at one of the traditional founts of all liberal-imperial wisdom, and I thought, the poor little sod, he thinks this is where his future gets handed to him and unwrapped like a slab of chocolate. But he probably hadn't got a future.'

'Hadn't he?'

'As a tomb-attendant? I expect he's a sub-divisional officer now and wondering whether to stay in the executive or transfer to the judiciary. His deputy commissioner is more likely to be an Indian than an Englishman but the work he does and the attitudes that go with it will be the same as they were forty years ago when some pink-faced boy from Wiltshire sat under the same punkah and wrote many letters home to his mother.'

'What do you do for a living?'

'You mean in peace-time. The answer's the same in war or peace. I live.'

'On air?'

'No. I make money too.'

'At what?'

'At what? Do for a living? It's awfully unimportant, isn't it? Strip the guff from any job and what have you got? A way of making money. And please don't say, "Somebody has to run things." I know they do. Running things means making them pay. I run things to the extent I make things pay. To me a Viceroy is about as important or unimportant as a company secretary

716

who drafts the annual report for the shareholders to tell them what the board's been up to. Your board's made a lousy job of running things out here. The place is a goldmine, but it's stiff with unemployed BAs and people who die in the streets of hunger. That's a legacy from all those blue-eyed Bible thumpers and noble neo-classicists who came out here because they couldn't stand the commercial pace back home. You had a perfectly good thing going in that old merchant trading company who used to run things until the industrial revolution. What you wanted then was a bevy of steely-eyed brass founders and men of iron who'd have ground the faces of the Indian peasants in the dirt, sweated a few million to death and dragged India yelling into the nineteenth century. Instead of which you got the people who didn't like the smoke and the dark satanic mills because that sort of thing was vulgar, and after them you got the people who didn't like it because of the inhumanity that went with it. What you didn't get was the damned smoke. And that's the trouble. The Indian empire's been composed exclusively of English people who said No. Out here you've always had the negative side, the reactionaries and the counter-revolution-aries, but you've never had the bloody revolution. That's why an Indian urban dweller's life expectation is still thirty-five and why people die of starvation while the band plays at Government House, and Pyari plays the sitar at Mira's. Well, at home after the war we'll cut your empire adrift without the slightest compunction. It's a time-expired sore, a suppurating mess. From the point of view of people who really run things it's like a leg that you look at one morning and realize is too far gone in gangrene to be worth saving. Limping's better. It's going to be up to the Indians to grow a body from the limb. Of course most of them will make the mistake of thinking their independent body-politic is a whole, walking body. And at home we'll pretend we've fulfilled a moral obligation by giving it back to them. But that won't be the reason. We'll get rid of it because it doesn't pay and it's too late to make it pay. Give the war another year, the one in Europe anyway, and the one with Japan another year. Say summer 1946. You can expect a general election in England in the summer of 1946 at the latest, and the socialists will get in because the common soldier and the factory worker will put them in. Lopping off India is an article of faith with the socialists but when they see that keeping it doesn't pay they'll lop it double-quick. Who wants India's starving millions as one of what we'll all call our post-war problems?'

'Are you a socialist?'

'Good Lord, no. I'm what you'd call a low Tory, if you could call me anything at all.'

'Why are you so sure the socialists would win an election? Won't Mr Churchill's reputation count for anything?'

He laughed, and turned the question.

'Why do women always call him Mr Churchill? It makes him sound like a vicar who's been invited to judge the home-made calves-foot jelly. But the answer's yes, of course, his name *will* count. For everything patriotic, proud, victorious and time-expired. I don't suppose you've talked much to common British soldiers, have you? The fellows you refer to as BORs? You ought to. Ask them what they think of life out here, I mean the national service wallahs, not the regulars. Then you'll know. If there's one thing war shows the man in the street it's the difference between himself and the officer-caste. Back home it's obvious enough but on foreign service he feels it like a kick in the teeth. I'll tell you what your BOR in Deolali or your cockney motor mechanic with the Desert Rats or your Brummagem door-to-door salesman with Wingate in Burma thinks. He thinks, "All right, mate. Have it cushy whenever you can and be a Boy Scout while the shit flies. Get on winning the war your lot started. I'll even give you a cheer at the end. And when you've got the whole stinking mess sorted out, be a good lad and bugger off, out of my sight, out of my government and out of my bloody life. But for ever." And what goes for the officer-caste goes for Churchill. Your poor blighter of a BOR thinks it's all real, you see. He hears the popping of corks in the officers' tents and goes back to his mug of tea or stale NAAFI beer with murder in his heart knowing everything would be all right if he could guzzle brandy, or if the Colonel had to choke on a mug of tea with bromide in it to stop him feeling randy. He thinks his own lot ought to run things because there are more of his lot drinking tea with bromide in it than there are what he calls la-di-dah poofs swigging brandy and getting hot for women they won't know how to poke.'

With an effort Sarah kept her eyes coolly on a level with his. She understood that the test and his use of gutter-slang, were part of a process of seduction. He would use different methods with different women. The words he chose for her and the whole gravamen of his argument were calculated to expose her as someone for whom, primarily, he felt contempt. He wanted her on her mettle. Or in embarrassed confusion. Or weak and defeated. She was not sure which.

'Go on,' she said.

He laughed, again reached for her hand and grasped it hard. 'You're quite a girl, Sarah Layton.'

'No,' she said, 'I'm not quite a girl. I'm this one,' and was aware of having jerked him into unexpected recognition of her as a person and not a type. She told this from his heavy hand which became, for a second or two, uncharacteristically inert.

'He's on the ball in one sense, your BOR,' Clark continued. 'The brandy's real enough and so's the tea and bromide. His mistake comes in thinking the difference between them has some kind of moral significance and proves his rights as a human being have been infringed. But what he calls his rights as a human being start where his honest sensations stop, don't they? His honest sensations tell him to knock the Colonel down and pinch his brandy, but he's scared to do that and begins nursing a grievance and inventing a right, the right to a fair share. But when you cut out the moral claptrap your *fair* share of anything is what you're strong enough to grab.

Or would you prefer the word earn? In practice it comes to the same thing. Your fair share is what you take. Don't you agree?'

Did she? She felt as if the effort she had put into facing up to him had reduced her power of concentration, that somehow she had missed some of the words and that her sudden inability to answer exposed for both of them the real reason why she sat there, unprotesting. With a gesture half-affectionate, half-mocking, he moved his hand and placed the knuckles behind her ear, ruffling her hair. Understanding that it would amuse him to see her shrink from such contact, she deliberately – but slowly – changed the angle of her head and body to force disengagement. The hand moved away, only to rest again on her bare neck.

'You're very tense,' he said. 'Did your visit to the hospital upset you?'

'I expect so.'

'Is he a bit of a mess, then, this fellow you went to see?'

'They're amputating his arm.'

'Oh. Yes, that *is* bad, isn't it? But it explains one thing that puzzled me. The fact that you appeared to take such an instant dislike to me. It means you must have noticed me and that the dislike was merely a transference of the physical revulsion you felt for the poor blighter they're going to cut up. It's quite common. Amputation *is* revolting, but a woman especially won't accept that it is until she sees someone she likes the look of, then she thinks, "You're disgustingly whole, why have you got two arms, blast you?" Or legs, or whatever it is the chap she used to like hasn't got any longer.'

'But I didn't like him.'

'No?' The hand on her neck moved an inch or so. 'You came an awfully long way to see him then, but I'll accept that and I don't think it makes any difference. The revulsion was there. You took it out on me. Shall I tell you something?'

'What?'

'You're not so tense now.'

It was true. Her body had become capable of controlled and fluid movement: a new feeling that added to her confidence and for which she felt indebted to him in a way she could not explain, except by acknowledging that it flowed from his hand. His eyes and line of cheek, lit obliquely, gave his face – now fully turned towards her – an irony which she thought she understood.

'You're still a virgin, of course, aren't you?'

The shocking directness of the statement caused her to jerk her glance away. She felt that he had hit her. Presently, she said, as clearly and levelly as she could, 'Yes, I'm still a virgin-of-course,' and by doing so arrested the retreat of warmth. But she could not bring herself to face him. For a while she was conscious of his continued observation and of the way her body was becoming increasingly dependent on the support of his hand for whatever air it had of self-possession. When he removed his hand and placed it momentarily on hers before removing it entirely, it seemed to her

719

like a valedictory gesture, an acknowledgement of her as the person she had made him see behind the paper-thin exterior; the girl he had stalked, attacked, and tried to shock into a predictable herd-reaction. But when he took his hand away she felt he took that real self too and left her with nothing but her shell. She sat, coldly bereft, and then wondered if he had taken anything, had seen instead what she herself could not see, but began to have intimations of; that the shell was all there was because she had rejected all the things that had once filled it, and had not replaced them. One by one they had gone, the beliefs, affections and expectations of her childhood: but when? She stared across the room at the carpeted daïs where the unattended instruments lay and felt herself unattended too. Perhaps at her christening certain spectres had come like unbidden guests, spectres of that extinction-through-exile that awaited Muirs and Laytons and all their kind, and stolen away unseen, having cursed or blessed her with an awareness of their presence which would dog her footsteps and fill her mind, until, bit by bit, as she was bidden, she had cast out of herself all her inheritance and was left in possession – as it were of a relic – of a shell whose emptiness was the proof for future generations of where the fault had lain and why there could have been no other end, even for her. Perhaps especially not for her, because once – hunched on a window-seat – she had drawn her root and branch and ringed her Indian family proudly in red. Perhaps it had been a condition of the christening gift that what she discarded bit by bit should be discarded as proudly as it had once been put on, so that the possibility of looking for substitutes to ensure survival was excluded. If you went down you went down and the proudest way was not to go down fighting for eroded values but, simply, with them, however little you were responsible for them. Those values were your shell as well, what you were left with after you had rejected their substance. The shell was unalterable.

He said, 'I seem to have discovered the chink in your armour. But are you annoyed with me for asking, or because you have to admit you are? Or is it a bit of both? I can't believe it's that you're plain old-fashioned shocked or embarrassed. And you don't look like a girl who thinks a man should automatically assume the absence of a wedding ring on the hand of a well-brought-up young lady means she's saving it up for Mr Right. Or am I wrong?'

They were questions she could not answer except from a fund of outworn stock replies such as he would only receive with a gently derisive pretence of not having anticipated. The alternative was silence; which she chose.

'In any case,' he said, 'clearly I must apologize.'

The hand rested again on the back of her neck. The warmth flowed back in, revealing the one unchanging purpose to which she could be put, even as a shell. Her nipples hardened in simulation of giving suck, but she continued to stare at the daïs. There was sudden movement in the room. The man who played the tablas had come back in. A girl accompanied him.

'Mira *is* doing us proud,' he whispered, leaning close. 'It's Lakshmi Kripalani. She sings, in case you didn't know.'

She nodded, more in acknowledgement of his breath's faint palpations of her ear than of the words spoken. Mira was approaching. The Maharanee had also risen and was coming in her wake, but continued on towards the curtained doorway. Mira came to the sofa and leaned forward and spoke to her, excluding Clark.

'They'll be playing again soon. I'd better show you where you can freshen up.'

Clark removed his hand, relieved her of the unfinished glass of brandy.

'It's a good idea,' he said. 'They might go on for an hour. It depends on how inventive they're feeling. I'll keep this warm for you.'

Sarah got up with the half-formed intention of telling him that an hour was too long, that she should go home because they both had an early start to the day ahead; but she could not summon the determination. She followed Mira into the bar, through into the hall, then a passage, and up a staircase that turned twice. They came out on to a gallery whose barred windows were unshuttered and admitted the warm mulchy smell of the Bengal night. The gallery turned at right angles and continued along the length of the side of the house. Light came from naked bulbs fixed into sockets in the gallery roof. The Indians sometimes had a crude, uncluttered attitude towards electricity, Sarah thought. So often the bulb was accepted as a decoration in itself. Mira wore no chola under the dark saree. The elastic of a brassiere showed. At the end of the gallery she turned in at an open door. Sarah followed and paused – astonished at the room's opulence. A double bed, raised on a wide but shallow daïs and enclosed by a white mosquito net hung high and centrally so that the effect was of a regal canopy, was its main focus. The gossamer net shivered under the gentle changing pressures of air wafted by two revolving ceiling fans. The daïs was covered in white carpet and the bedcovers were of creamy white satin. The furniture was satin-walnut. Mira, still without speaking, had walked to a door, opened it and switched on a light.

'There's probably everything you want. If not, just ring and one of the girls will come.'

A fragrance, a chill; the bathroom was air-conditioned. It was larger than her bedroom at Pankot and marble-floored, with sheepskin rugs. Above the semi-sunken bath gilt faucets projected from marble green tiles. At one end of the bath pink frosted glass screened off the shower.

She looked at Mira, fearing her, chilled by her, but ready to praise what belonged to her. But Mira seemed quite indifferent and held the door open as if anxious to be gone. 'Thank you,' Sarah said, and went past her. The door was closed. The lavatory was in an adjoining cubicle. The cistern was the modern kind with a levered handle. It flushed quietly and immediately. In the pedestal wash-basin, piping hot water flowed. Back in the bathroom she sat on a luxurious stool with curved gilt claw legs and a padded green velvet seat. The legs of the marble-topped table matched the

721

legs of the stool. She studied herself in an immense mirror; a flattering one. Glancing at the array of bottles and sprays and jars she opened her handbag with misgivings about the quality of its contents but determined to use nothing that didn't belong to her, and then was held by a delayed reaction. Her eye had caught objects that struck her as incongruous. Among the scents, lotions and other items in a toilet battery of wholly feminine connection were two wood-backed bristle hair-brushes and a leather case. The zip was half undone. She reached out, zipped further, then completely, and lifted the cover, stared at the contents – four gold-plated containers and a matching safety razor.

She turned round, considered the bathroom, searching it for other clues to masculine occupation without much idea of what to look for, and noticed in one corner a bin with a padded seat that obviously lifted. She turned back to the mirror and went to work with powder from her compact, occasionally glancing at the bin's reflection. A dab of lipstick completed her repair operations. She shut her handbag. The click echoed. She sat for a while and felt in need of some show of kindness, such as Aunt Fenny had made, taking her shoes off, making her rest, and again remembered that she had not slept properly for two days; three, if she counted the night she last slept in Pankot, disturbed by a gift of lace, a meeting avoided, and expectation of new ground and a long journey. She looked at her watch. Eleven-thirty. Less than six hours since she had said Goodbye, Ronald, and got in return a goodbye that was not coupled with the blessing and absolution of her name.

Her name – she got up from the stool – her formidable, bony, yearning name – and walked to and opened the bin; stared down at the soiled expensive briefs, those meshes of mysterious and complex cellular imprisonment. She closed the lid, knowing that both bath and bedroom were tainted by his casual presence and the ludicrous talent he had for casual contemptuous excitation.

I am sensible now – she decided – after Pyari has played I shall go home, alone if necessary. She reached for door-handle and light-switch, intending to flick the one after opening the other, but when she opened the door a whole field of darkness faced her. She stood arrested by it and by the notion that darkness always contained dangers and presences.

Instinctively, but without conviction, she blamed Mira, who had apparently not even left the door open between bedroom and gallery. There would have been light enough then. Momentarily she was without a sense of direction. She felt along one wall, searching for another switch. Her elongated shadow probed the slant of bathroom light across the floor and up a blank wall. There was no switch. But she had her bearings. The five-mile hill, the five-mile door. Over there, she told herself; and was rewarded then by the suddenly visible pale strip of light making the boundary of bedroom and gallery. She walked towards it, and stopped.

'You're going the wrong way,' he said. 'I'm over here.'

His voice came from behind, from some intensely organized, centralized

722

point of reference. Turning towards it she was dazzled by the light from the decoy bathroom. The bed was darkly shadowed by one of the bathroom walls, which jutted into the room.

'You seem startled. Weren't you expecting me?'

'No.'

She turned and walked towards the slit of light, anticipated the driven-home look and the absent key. She jerked the handle. The absurdity of the handle's obedient but unfunctional mobility nullified her attempt to convey composure. Nothing looked sillier than trying to open a door the person watching you knew you knew was locked. She turned back, facing that equally absurd dark central point of reference.

'That's a pity,' he said. 'I thought you understood we had an appointment. Mira did, so you mustn't worry about our absence causing comment. Is it the dark that puts you off? I thought you'd prefer it. At first, anyway.'

'We have no appointment. Please turn the lights on and open the door.'

As she spoke she realized that her eyes had become more used to the dark areas beyond the shaft of light coming from the bathroom. There was a slow rhythmic movement and in the second before the restored bedside lamp reversed the negative image into a positive one she detected the stretched arm, sensed the manipulative action of his hand on the switch, and understood from the spare density of his form that he was naked.

He was seated on the edge of the bed, staring back at her across a still extended arm, caught and held in the ageless classic pose of a figure from some Renaissance ceiling. The shock he gave her was that of astonishment that in the flesh a man could look as he had been depicted for centuries in stone and paint. Lowering the arm he exposed a sculptured chest.

'Are you sure you want the door opened?'

'Yes.'

'The key's here on the table. I've also been thoughtful enough to bring our glasses. Have I miscalculated? I don't often, but it wouldn't be the first time. It's an occupational hazard of the male. You get a few more slaps in the face than you deserve, but you also get your screws, so you can't complain. Are you quite sure you don't want to lose that cherry?'

'Quite sure. I'll give you a minute to unlock the door.'

She moved, making for the bathroom. Casually, he got up and was there before her. She stood still. Naked, the earlier and only slight advantage he had in height was further diminished. In her high heels she eyed him almost levelly, but her manifest disadvantage in strength and weight was pressed home on her as if by an actual pressure of his limbs. She turned, sat on a padded satin-covered chair. Doing so disclosed to her the shameful fact that she was trembling. She faced him again, deliberately. She observed him dispassionately, from head to foot. Having quartered him she looked again to her front and said, 'I've seen you now, so may I go?'

'That wasn't the object of undressing. I turned the light off, remember? The only reason I'm like this is that making a pass at a girl and getting her

723

hot and then introducing the devastatingly practical note of pausing to take your clothes off always strikes me as highly comic. When a man wants a screw he ought not to beat about the bush. It's different for girls because their clothes can come off so gracefully. Have I really wasted my time?'

'Yes.'

'Well, that's an occupational hazard too.'

There was a pause. Presently he crossed her line of vision. When he reached the bed he felt under the mosquito net and drew something out. Blue material. His pyjama trousers. He put them on. The bunched tops of the trousers thickened his waist slightly. He lit a cigarette, then brought their glasses of brandy over. He put them on the floor, went back to the table for an ashtray, returned and sat on the floor himself, and gazed up at her.

'You're not really plain, are you? In fact you're quite pretty. And you've got thin shoulders. In the buff I expect your breasts look much more prominent.' He put his head on one side, considering her. 'But your hips are a shade too narrow. I bet you've got a hard little bottom. What I like best about you though is you never say anything too obvious. I know the dialogue that can go with this particular situation by heart and it gets pretty boring. So that's what I like best. Your not saying anything obvious and your Colonel's daughter's guts. It makes an unusual combination.' He drank, indicated her own glass. 'Drink up. It'll do you good. I never screw them when they're pissed so you're quite safe. I mean don't *not* drink because you think I'd take advantage if you had too much. But I don't suppose you ever have too much, do you? That's another point in your favour. Your aunt told me you have a thin time at home because your mother drinks. It's embarrassing, isn't it? My father drank a lot. He used to cry too. Does your mother cry? What she ought to do is give up drinking and find some young officer who'll screw her whenever she wants and bow out without making a fuss when the Colonel comes home. After all, that would be better for the Colonel, wouldn't it? To come home to a placid, loving woman, instead of a neurotic alcoholic who gets her screws out of bottles.'

'Like your father?'

'Yes, like him.'

'And what did *your* mother do for screws?'

'Oh, Mother was never hard up. She went in for handsome chauffeurs. When I was eighteen I put my foot down, though, and insisted that even if the chauffeurs went to bed with her they still had to call me either Master James, or Sir.'

'And did they?'

'Yes, but I expect it cost her an extra small fortune at the men's shops in Bond Street.' He smiled. 'Go on. You're doing very well. For one awful moment I thought you were going to say something like "Kindly leave my mother and father out of this." I hope you're not too cross with Aunt

Fenny, by the way. She was only trying to paint a little picture of you that would bring out my protective instincts. She said more than she intended, but that was my fault.'

'I realized that.'

'Do all your family view you with the same mixture of alarm and affection as she does?'

'Probably.'

'Why are you shivering?'

'Because I find it difficult to control myself.'

'And you feel you must? What do you find difficult to control? Your temper?'

'Yes.'

For the first time since coming to sit on the floor he freed her from her self-imposed obligation not to let her glance waver. He looked down at his glass and for a moment she escaped into the safe oblivion of private darkness. When she opened her eyes again he was watching her. She said, 'I'd be glad if you'd open the door now. If the taxi's still waiting I can go home without putting you to any trouble. If it's not I'm afraid you'll have to organize one. I don't know where we are.'

'Don't worry about the taxi. You're forgetting I promised Aunt Fenny you'd come to no harm.'

'She's my Aunt Fenny, not yours.'

The comfortable angle of his head and trunk, the casual, easy, disposition of his limbs created confusing images in her mind of strength and languor and confident patience. They were confusing because she herself felt she had come to the end of a tether.

He took his hand from his glass, stubbed his cigarette and rose. She anticipated a physical attack on her, but he did not make it. Instead he went back to the bedside table, picked up the key and returned. He resumed his former position on the floor, tossed the key two or three times like a coin, then placed it on the floor between them.

'*My* key for *your* Aunt Fenny,' he said. 'I pay the forfeit and keep Aunt Fenny. There's not much going on in her, but what goes on is tough as old boots. I like that. If she were five years younger and I were five years older we'd screw. She knows it. In that cosy closed-in little corner of her bird-brain mind where the real Aunt Fenny lives she knows it, just as she knows in the same cosy little corner that asking me to look after you was the most risky thing she could do if you wanted to hang on to that cherry of yours. Obviously what she really thinks is that you ought to get rid of it. Which means she thinks the same as I do, only with her the thought's subconscious. I'll tell you another thing. You're tougher than she is. Far tougher than you probably realize. With you the toughness goes an awfully long way in because you haven't got a bird-brain. It thinks. Potentially you're worth twenty Aunt Fennys. But the thinking and the toughness aren't worth a bag of peanuts if you lack joy. And that's what Aunt Fenny has that you haven't. Joy. Not much. She's too shallow to have much of anything, but I bet you she was a scorcher as a girl. I bet she went for joy first and let the thinking and toughness come later, and that means that in her late middle-age she still remembers how to get a kick out of life. It doesn't really matter which way round you do it, if you do it both ways. But why not do it both ways from the start? Isn't that sensible? Isn't the place already overcrowded with people who have thought for so long they've forgotten how to be happy, or with people who've spent so long trying to be happy they haven't had time to think, so end up not knowing what happiness is? For pete's sake, Sarah Layton, you don't know anything about joy at all, do you?'

'No,' she said. 'No, I don't,' and reached for the key and then, stupidly, lost sight of it because her eyes had responded – as if of their own accord – to a humiliation, an unidentifiable yearning, and a dim recollection of an empty gesture that had something to do with wrenching the reins of a horse and wheeling to confront imaginable but infinitely remote possibilities of profound contentment. She felt the metal of the key under her fingers and the flesh-shock of his hand on her knuckles.

'You're crying,' he said. 'Why? Because you really want me to make love to you? I couldn't promise that. Not love. You couldn't either, could you? Not with me. If you liked we could pretend that it was love but it wouldn't be honest and your honesty is part of what attracts me. You don't belong, do you? And the trouble is you know it, but I suppose while your father's away you feel you have to pretend you do belong, for his sake.'

'No,' she said. 'I do belong. That's what I know. That's the trouble. Please take your hand away.'

He did so. She grasped the key. It weighed nothing. What it would open was a prison of a kind.

'Wait,' he said. He got up, went to the far side of the bed. Through the net she saw blurred pictures of a stranger dressing. There was a superior kind of mystery about him. In her dream there had been no problems, no threat of violence. She had surrendered to him casually. The absence of a climax struck the one familiar note; that and an awareness of her father's unspeaking presence, his silent criticism of her failure to hold back for him the tide of changing circumstances, her failure to hold in trust days he had lost which belonged to him; days that must, to him, be an incalculably dear proportion of those few left in which the once perpetual-seeming light would shine on undisturbed by the brighter, honest, light whose heat would burn the old one to a shadow.

The stranger came from behind the net and stood for a moment watching her. Who is that man? people asked her in the dream. And her reply had always been, Oh, I don't know. She had never been convinced that she spoke the truth, but in any case now knew the answer. Who is that man? Why, one of us, one of the people we really are.

'Well,' he said, 'shall we go, Sarah Layton?' He came closer. 'If so you ought to bathe your eyes. My Aunt Fenny would think the worst had happened if she saw you now.'

She was holding the key in one hand and her handbag in the other. The blurred opaque image of his face cleared. Presently he bent forward, grasped the exposed end of the key and carefully took it from her. He held out his other hand and, when she did not move, reached further and touched the strap of the handbag, then grasped it. Her own grip loosened. She felt the smooth strip of leather slide from her fingers and watched him stand back, holding the two things she had surrendered and which he now seemed to be showing her, waiting for some kind of confirmation that she understood he had them. He transferred the key to the hand with which he held the handbag then stooped and picked up the ashtray and, with his free hand, their glasses, holding them from the insides, rim to rim, between thumb and fingers. He went to the bedside-table, placed the glasses and the ashtray by the lamp and, after a moment's hesitation, placed the handbag there as well. Still holding the key he went over to the door and inserted it in the lock but did not turn it. He came back and stood in front of her in further brief consideration and then went over to the bedside-table again and switched the lamp off so that the room was as it had been at the beginning of their encounter. The shaft of light from the bathroom stretched across the floor, separating them until he emerged from the shadow on the other side of it and crossed over on to her side, and squatted. He touched her right ankle, gently lifted and eased the shoe from her foot and then the shoe from the other foot, and placed the shoes neatly together on one side of the chair. The hand in which she had held the key was cupped and taken, and then the other, and both carried and held to his face, so that it seemed she had reached out and put her hands on his cheeks with a gesture of adoration. She closed her eyes, exploring the illusion of possession which such an adoration might create between two people and was then aware that her hands were no longer held except by the desire to explore. Her own head was taken. For a while they stayed so, enacting the tenderness of silent lovers, and then slowly bending her head she allowed him to deal with the old maid's hook and eye.

V

His hand was on her arm gentling her from sleep and in the second or two before she woke she knew the sweet relief of this evidence that she had only dreamt the scene in which Aunt Fenny told her Susan was in premature labour brought on by shock; and that the reality was this warm quiescence with which her body came back to life and consciousness, flesh to flesh with the body of the man who had penetrated it, liberated it, and was waking it again from profound rest so that it might enclose and be enclosed and go again, rapt, to the edge of feeling.

'I'm sorry,' the voice said. 'But we're nearly there.' A strange, unbeliev-able, soundless splintering; an extraordinary convolution of time and space. Her eyes opened and she saw the woman whose name was Mrs Roper. 'We're coming into Ranpur, Miss Layton. I'm sorry to disturb you.'

She pulled herself upright, understanding completely where she was and yet not understanding it at all, but she knew she was indebted to Mrs Roper and to Mrs Roper's friend, Mrs Perryman, and that this was because they had let her share the coupé and had even had the top bunk lowered so that she could rest properly. She knew from the lights in the ceiling, close to her head, that it was night, whereas it had been day when the bunk was lowered. Her uniform was crumpled.

'Can you manage, my dear?'

Mrs Roper's head scarcely came to the level of the bunk. The fans whisked the stray ends of her grey hair which was set in a way that suggested Mrs Roper remembered she was pretty as a girl. Mrs Roper's husband had been a Forestry Officer in Burma. He sent her back to India in 1941 and as she hadn't heard a word since the Japanese invasion she believed he was hiding out with one of the hill-tribes who had been their friends. Mrs Perryman's hair was brassy-blonde. Her husband had been in the medical service and died of cholera in 1939. She took in paying-guests, one of whom was Mrs Roper. They had been staying with Mrs Roper's brother's family on leave at Ootacamund and were on their way back to Simla, having returned by way of Calcutta to visit a friend of Mrs Perryman's whose husband was in jute. It was their first holiday since the beginning of the war, and they had saved for it, presumably. But they had not mentioned money.

Sarah knew all these things about them because they had talked incessantly from midday when the train left Howrah station until an hour after lunch. They had talked for kindly reasons because Uncle Arthur had taken them on one side to thank them for letting her share the coupé and to ask them to look after her because her great-Aunt, of whom she had been very fond, had died suddenly in Pankot and the shock had sent her sister into premature labour. She swung round on the bunk and was held by a reaction in her bloodstream, unexpected but familiar. Sound and sight became miniature, far away. From behind brass screens she heard Mrs Roper say, 'Now don't rush. I just thought you'd want plenty of time because we only stay in Ranpur ten minutes.'

With her foot she felt for the top of the nest of steps, far down in the distorted well of the coupé, and finding them, made the descent.

'You've had a nice long sleep. We nodded off too. Now don't bother about us. Is there anything we can do?'

'No thank you, Mrs Roper. I'm fine.'

'Leave the bunk. Directly we've had dinner Mrs Perryman and I are going to tuck down.'

In the cubicle she bathed her face in slow-running tepid water. There were specks of soot. The train was going over points, intersection after intersection. She steadied herself on the handgrip and confronted her mirror image. Did it show? Could anyone tell? That she had entered, like other women? Yes; to her it showed; vividly; more vividly than her anxiety for Susan, more strongly than the grief cushioned by disbelief that she felt for Aunty Mabel who walked in and out of her mind, condemned by a memory to go on performing the task to which so many hours of her last days had been stubbornly devoted; more strongly than the concern for her mother who had been alone to cope and for her father for whom Aunty Mabel was now an irretrievable part of a time she had been unable to hold back for him. She did not know why she should have wanted to hold it back. She did not even know she had tried to until she saw that it had gone. She had failed but she had entered. She had entered her body's grace.

Mrs Roper personally selected the coolie to carry Sarah's single suitcase. Thirty years of experience had given her an eye, she said; an eye for the kind of coolie an unaccompanied white girl could rely on not to intimidate her into paying him more than he deserved, and to make sure, in such a case as this, that the transfer from one train to another was smoothly accomplished.

'Shouldn't we find an escort for you?' Mrs Perryman asked. 'There must be at least one young officer on the platform we could whistle up.'

But Sarah was already at the open door of the carriage and there were nearly two hours to go before the train for Pankot left Ranpur. 'I'll go to the restaurant and then to the waiting-room if necessary. I'll be perfectly all right. Thank you for all your kindness.' She shook hands with them and stepped down. The platform was crowded. She saw bearers threading their way through with loaded trays, and called up to Mrs Roper that their meals were coming. Then she waved and followed the elderly coolie who had her suitcase on his head. Her childhood delight in travelling at night was still a potent force. She had always loved the noise, the risk, of railway stations. The journey to Calcutta was the first she had ever made alone. The case, hovering at eye level – and as bodies interposed themselves between her and its bearer looking as if it moved of its own accord without support – was a symbol of childhood's end. It struck her how curious an object a suitcase was. To it you consigned those few essential portable things that bore the invisible marks of your private possession of them; but the case itself was destined to live most of its useful life under the public gaze and in the hands of strangers.

At the door of the station restaurant the coolie halted. The turbanned head, which earned him an anna for all that it could carry at any one time, was set in a rigid thrust-up position that gave his eyes, under wrinkled, hooded lids, a preoccupied, anxious look. She changed her mind about going to the restaurant first. The Pankot train would be waiting at its special platform. She could look for her reservation and, if she were lucky, get the compartment opened and have a tray sent in. She gave the coolie instructions and once more followed him, to the end of the main platform, to the point where two subsidiary tracks came in to a bay, to sets of buffers, with a platform separating them. On one track there were three lit coaches, one of them painted blue and white, colours she had never seen before, and on the other the Pankot train, which she recognized because of the coaches: old-fashioned, squarer-cut, and with decorative flourishes in the woodwork. There were a few people on the platform, among them two Indian police, and a station official with a white topee. The Pankot train was in darkness. Some way along the platform under a lamp, a group of private soldiers were playing cards. Men off leave or on posting; perhaps both kinds. Tomorrow night they would be playing cards or writing home at the regimental institute and perhaps Mrs Fosdick or Mrs Paynton would be among the women who manned the tea-urns. She felt the first lick of a wave of nostalgia for the Pankot hills, but fought it down because upon its ripples grief could ride in. She spoke to the Indian in the white topee. No, the train was not ready yet. No, he did not have the key to unlock the compartments. But he went with her, looking with a torch for that strange advertisement of her name, noted and written on a piece of card by someone she would never see and placed in its metal bracket on the side of the carriage by someone she might see but never know.

Closer to the group of card-players this other card was found. A coupé. The discovery gave her childish pleasure, as did the fact that there was no name on the card but her own. Miss Layton. She would sleep undisturbed. She turned to the patient coolie and used the old old words of command. *Idhar thairo. Idhar thairo.* Stay here. Stay here. Dutifully he lowered the case and then squatted beside it as though it were a child he had carried far, out of some ancient servitude which he himself still had the habit of but hoped not to entrust with the other burden of the genes; and would not, for the genes of the case were hers, not his.

'What's the blue and white carriage?' she asked the man in the white topee.

'Oh, that is private. It belongs to a maharajah.'

'Which maharajah?'

'I do not know. There are so many.'

She thanked him for finding her compartment and walked back towards the restaurant, anticipating light and noise. This platform was sour and gloomy. Clark's words came back to her. 'A tomb-attendant?' Ahead of her a man was getting out of the blue and white carriage, a man in a white suit and panama hat. He had a stick and took the descent carefully. She noticed him because he might be the maharajah but quickly realized he could not be. The lamp on the platform revealed the fact that he was a European. He took out a cigarette case. He had got out of the carriage to smoke. Perhaps the maharajah was inside and did not like him smoking. He glanced at her, but concerned himself again with his cigarette, as if quite uninterested in her presence. He was oblivious of the fact that she had entered. Had entered. To him, perhaps, all women were assumed to have entered. Into their bodies' grace.

But beyond him she hesitated and turned. Her action caused him to look in her direction, with his one available eye. The other was the blind buffed eye of a nocturnal animal. She retraced her steps.

'Count Bronowsky?'

Already he had lifted his hat, but it was clear to her he did not recognize her, and for a moment she was afraid she had spoken to a man who looked like Bronowsky but was not. He said, 'Yes, I am Count Bronowsky.'

'I'm Sarah Layton. We stayed at the guest house last October when my sister was married.'

'Miss Layton? Well, forgive me. Why didn't I recognize you? But I know. It's the uniform. I see indeed it is you.' He held out his hand and, when she gave him hers, carried it with an old man's courtesy to his lips and held on to it. His accent, which she did not remember having remarked in Mirat struck her as comic, exaggerated. She had a sense of charade which probably emanated from him because she had had it on the morning of the wedding when he joined the group on the lawn of the Mirat Gymkhana club; a sense of charade, of puppet-show; of dolls manipulated to a point just short of climax.

'Nawab Sahib and I were so very distressed to hear of Captain Bingham's death,' he said. How clever still to remember Teddie's name; but then the old wazir could count a memory for names among his many – obviously many – talents. He had remembered Merrick's too.

'It was kind of you to write. Have you been staying in Ranpur?' She assumed that like herself he was on the point of departure.

'No, not staying.' He let her hand go. 'Have you?'

'I'm only changing trains. I've just got in from Calcutta.'

'That train is going to Pankot?'

'It is at midnight. I came along to make sure my booking was fixed. Now I'm going to have some supper.'

'In the restaurant?'

'Yes. It's still open.'

'And are you alone?' She nodded. 'My dear Miss Layton, I cannot allow it. We can do better for you than that. In the restaurant you will wait for twenty minutes for something badly cooked, I'm quite sure of it. And then you will not sleep a wink, and what dire consequences might ensue from entering such a place unaccompanied I do not know.' He took her arm, holding hat and stick and unlit cigarette in his other hand, and began to guide her to the steps of the Nawab's coach.

'But—'

'But I am inviting you. On behalf of Nawab Sahib, who is not here by the way. I invite you into more compatible surroundings. Besides, apart from my own pleasure there is that of a handsome young Englishman who is already bored by my company but too well bred to show it. Only his sense of duty persuades him to sit and listen to me as if every word I speak is of importance to him. And Ahmed will be here presently. You remember Ahmed? You rode horses together. Do you like champagne? Of course you like champagne. With perhaps some caviar. And some cold game pie. Or smoked ham with melon. When Nawib Sahib is not in the coach it is possible for me to indulge a taste for smoked ham. The champagne is from

731

my personal pre-war stock. I have been eking it out this past year but the Allied invasion of France encourages me to hope for fresh consignments before too long. You know the story of the true princess?'

'The one who needed twelve mattresses?'

'That is she. But even through twelve mattresses she felt the discomfort of one little pea from the pod. How can I let you suffer the discomfort of entering a public restaurant?'

'Well, I'm used to it. But thank you.'

The way in was like the entrance to a Pullman coach, but a thickness of carpet at once pointed a private superiority. The door that led into the main interior was closed and she waited until Bronowsky had negotiated the steps and joined her. His lameness, like his accent, was new to her. Perhaps it was only noticeable when he had something more agile to perform than walking. He opened the door on to a saloon of red and gold – a travelling throne-room such as she imagined the last Tsar Nicholas would have felt at home in. There were tables lit by crimson-shaded lamps, gilt chairs with crimson backs and seats, footstools, and salon sofas. At the far end an open doorway, hung with looped velvet curtains, gave a view of a dining-table set with a snowy white cloth and decked for a buffet.

As they went in the man Count Bronowsky had forewarned her of looked up from the document he was reading. Her arrival obviously surprised him and to get up he had first to secure the document to the briefcase on which he had been resting it, and uncross his legs. An army officer, he was wearing best KD.

'Allow me to introduce Captain Rowan,' Bronowsky said. 'This is Miss Layton whom I have just rescued from going alone to the restaurant. Nawab Sahib and I had the pleasure of her company at the Palace guest house last year on the occasion of her sister's marriage.'

Rowan nodded. Sarah thought she would not describe him as handsome. Her main impression of him was of a man, perhaps a little younger than Clark, who would be extremely difficult to get to know. There was something in the careful way in which he had overcome his surprise, temporarily withdrawn his interest from the document, and risen, still in possession of it and of the briefcase, that suggested a controlled expenditure of energy, a distrust of any kind of instant reaction, a firm belief in the importance of keeping reserves of whatever particular capacities he had. She judged that probably they were considerable.

A steward appeared in the doorway of the dining saloon. 'First,' Bronowsky said, 'champagne. We were going to wait for Ahmed, but only as a puritanical exercise in self-discipline. With champagne there should always be a sense of occasion, which you have kindly supplied. Come, sit. Do you smoke?' He offered her a silver box of pink cigarettes with gold tips. When they were settled he went on: 'I myself smoke only in the evenings, and then I'm afraid I smoke too many, but these are mild. My introduction to smoking was of a most unusual nature in that I was chastised by my father not *for* smoking but for showing an aversion for tobacco which he thought unmanly. All through one summer, when we were in the country, and I but sixteen, I was made to sit opposite him in his study at ten o'clock each morning and smoke a cigar under threat of a beating from my English tutor should I but turn a paler shade of pale. The fact that my tutor would not have hurt a fly and that I knew the threat no more than a threat, mere bombast, on the part of a man for whose moral cowardice I had the greatest contempt, did not diminish my valiant struggles to disguise my nausea. It became, you understand, a point of honour to smoke the disgusting thing to the bitter end and retire – apparently in good order. But my repugnance for cigar-tobacco has never left me. That winter, in St Petersburg, I took a perverse fancy for the gold-tipped cigarettes smoked by the lady who frequently visited us. I should perhaps explain that my mother died when I was ten. I would steal one of these cigarettes from this lady's handbag whenever I had the opportunity. She kept them in a tortoiseshell case. I remember the case quite clearly, the smooth feel of it in my fingers. And having stolen one I would smoke it after I had gone to bed delighting in the fact that I had stolen it from her and that, unwomanly as smoking was considered at that time, these particular cigarettes looked revoltingly effeminate. Hence my life-long habit – gold-tipped cigarettes, preferably pink, and after sunset. In such small ways we preserve the memories of our youth and remain to that extent forever young. What memories, Miss Layton – or I should say, what habits that will become memories do you think you will still celebrate when you are my age?'

'I don't know, but I'm sure there are some.'

'With girls perhaps it is different. They grow up and marry and have children of their own and everything from their own childhood is put by. Perhaps this is sad because much later what was put by as done with and forgotten may come back to plague them with an intense nostalgia. Their children grow up and go away and all the years a woman devotes to them are as if they have never been. Women are more courageous than men though. Perhaps they accept that their life's work, I mean in the biological sense, is very quickly over. But a man and his career, that is different. His career is the whole of his life. He can afford to introduce notes of absurdity. Perhaps he needs to. His body undergoes no biological change, his life is not divided in that way, nothing physically dramatic happens to him. He never carries his own creature inside him, the poor man has to make do with the one he was born as. Perhaps this explains why he cherishes the memory of its different stages of growth and hangs on to them, in the hope of seeing something whole.'

The champagne cork popped. They were all three silent witnesses of the ritual of pouring. The steward wore white gloves. He handed the glasses on a silver tray. Bronowsky said, 'Captain Rowan, I had not intended tonight to introduce a personal note, but there was a private reason for the champagne and Miss Layton's gift of her company prompts me to share my secret with you both. Today is my seventieth birthday, and I have a toast.' He grinned. 'As an Englishman you will probably appreciate it more than

Nawab Sahib would – who touchingly remembered the day and sent me a telegram this morning from Nanoora.' He raised his glass. ' "It is little I repair to the matches of the Southron folk, Though my own red roses there may blow; It is little I repair to the matches of the Southern folk, Though the red roses crest the caps, I know. For the field is full of shades as I near the shadowy coast, And a ghostly batsman plays to the bowling of a ghost, And I look through my tears on a soundless clapping host, As the run-stealers flicker to and fro, To and fro; O my Hornby and my Barlow long ago!" '

He raised his glass still higher, then lowered it and drank; and, when they followed suit (both – Sarah thought – rather put off their strokes by the unexpectedness of the occasion and the obscure, indeed incongruous, connection between the words and the man who spoke them) Bronowsky went on: 'The poem was explained to me by the charming boy from whom I learnt it in 1919, but I fear my own private interpretation is the one that remains with me. He was just eighteen and his parents had sent him from England to stay with a French family who were holidaying on the Italian Riviera. He learned, or was supposed to learn, French conversation from them. I, a poor Russian *émigré*, was hired to teach him the language's grammar and syntactical complexities, not I fear successfully because he fell madly in love with the Spanish maid of a neighbouring family. His other interest, his only other interest, was cricket. He came to me one day and said, Monsieur Bronowsky, please teach me a French poem. Well, I knew why. I had seen them together, holding hands and staring into each other's eyes, quite dumb, because the girl really only spoke her own language and what little French they might have exchanged quite deserted him the moment he was in her adorable presence. "But if she speaks only Spanish," I said to him, "what purpose will a French poem serve? Why not recite it to her in English?" He said he'd thought of that but he only knew one poem, which happened not to be suitable. I begged him to let me be the judge of that and made him recite it. I was extraordinarily moved and told him to repeat it to her in just the same manner, but perhaps a little slower and with slightly more expression. I also got him to write it down for me.'

'And was it successful?' Sarah asked. 'I mean with the Spanish maid?'

'Alas. He found her that same afternoon holding hands with a fisher-lad. He told me of this disaster when he came for his evening lesson. He was stunned, well, you could see it, but also well controlled, in the way of the English. He went home very soon after that in order, so he said, to get in some more cricket before the summer ended. You could tell he was quite finished with women. At least for a week or so.'

'What a sad story,' Sarah said.

'Isn't it? I'm delighted you see that it is sad as well as comic. And I've always thought how much that flirtatious young lady's memories were impoverished by the chance she missed to have her hand held and her ears simultaneously enchanted by a poem she would not have understood a word of but could hardly have failed to know was spoken from the heart.

You see he felt quite romantic about cricket, and so long as she didn't know what the poem was about, it was the perfect vehicle for him to express one passion through the medium of another. She would have heard the rhymes, and the slow alliterative and repetitive cadences which seem to be holding on to memories to stop them slipping too soon away. She would have heard the strange hard burr of a northern language, softly spoken, and so different from the loudly spoken languages of the south, which the sun seems to have melted so that they flow ever quickly onwards, with hardly a pause, like time itself. Above all, how could she not have detected the note of pride ringing through the lamentation! Oh, if I had been she, no doubt I would have positively swooned away.'

'Anyway,' Rowan said, 'congratulations. Your own journey south has been capped by conspicuous successes.'

'Ah,' Bronowsky exclaimed. 'I have understanding companions. Thank you. Steward. More champagne. Miss Leyton, what news of your father?'

'We haven't heard for some time, but we believe he's well.'

'And he'll be home soon, surely? And your mother and sister? Particularly your sister?'

'Yes, they're both well.' She would not intrude her anxiety. Or her grief.

'And what took you to Calcutta, alone?'

'My aunt lives there now.'

'Ah yes, I recall. Mrs Grace? And your uncle who gave your sister away? They are both in Calcutta? She nodded. 'And the officer who was best man, Captain Merrick, have you had news of him?'

She hesitated, again reluctant to introduce a sombre subject on the old man's birthday. In any case he was probably only being polite.

'He interested me considerably,' Bronowsky went on, as if prompting her. 'I thought him an unusual man.'

'Actually it was to visit him in the hospital that I went to Calcutta.'

'Really? What is wrong with him?'

'He was rather badly wounded at the same time Captain Bingham was killed. My sister was anxious to find out if there was anything we could do because she was told he'd tried to help Teddie. There's been a recommendation. I mean for a decoration.'

'Yes,' Bronowsky said after a moment's thought. 'Courage. He had physical courage. You could see that. I'm distressed to hear he was wounded. How badly?'

'He's lost an arm. He pulled Teddie out of a blazing truck while they were under fire.'

'Ah.' A pause. 'Yes. Which arm?'

'The left.'

A pause. 'Then that is something. I observed him picking up bits of confetti, also stubbing a cigarette. He was right-handed.' He turned to Rowan. 'You may remember the man we're speaking of. Merrick?'

'No. I don't think so.'

'I don't mean you would remember him personally. He went into the

735

army from the Indian Police. He figured rather prominently in that case involving an English girl, in Mayapore in 1942. The Bibighar.'

Rowan was drawing on his cigarette. He nodded. 'Oh yes. That case.'

'He was District Superintendent. In Mirat I had a long and interesting talk to him and found him still utterly convinced that the men he arrested were truly guilty. I myself and I suppose most people since have come to the conclusion they couldn't have been. It would have been understandable if Merrick had begun to waver in his opinion – unless you accept that he left the police temporarily under a cloud and he harboured a grudge. But he had tried for years to get into the army. He was a very ordinary man on the surface but underneath, I suspect, a man of unusual talents. Are those boys still in prison?'

'Which boys are those?'

'The ones arrested, not tried, but detained, as politicals.'

'I'm afraid I don't know, Count.'

'I hope they are not forgotten and just being left to rot. The provincial authorities have an obligation in this matter, surely.'

'I'm sure they are not just forgotten.'

'The Indians remember. Unfortunately not only Indians of the right sort. There is a venerable gentleman of Mayapore who last year visited Mirat and engaged in some tortuous processes of intimidation. The stone – Miss Layton, you recall the stone – was almost certainly thrown at the instigation of this slippery customer. He is one of those on whom we keep a watchful eye. I am told he has recently left Mayapore, but I am not told where he has gone, or why. Forgive me, it is an uncheerful subject, and Miss Layton must eat. We shan't wait for Ahmed. In any case he's probably only going to be interested in the champagne.'

Rowan looked at his watch and Bronowsky, who was rising, touched his arm. 'We shall be able to leave on the scheduled time. Ahmed will see to it. Come.' He led them to the dining saloon. Two stewards removed covers from the waiting dishes.

*

'I must go, I'm afraid,' Sarah said, putting down her coffee cup. Her watch showed twenty minutes to midnight and for some time now she had been nervously aware of mounting activity on the platform. Once she had parted the crimson velvet curtains that covered the window she sat near and had seen more soldiers, and officers directing them; Indian families with mounds of roped luggage, some of the women in purdah. The lights were on in the Pankot train but the view was too oblique for her to make out her patient coolie, who would still be waiting.

'Another five minutes,' Bronowsky pleaded. He had regaled them with more champagne and talk of pre-1914 Russia and post-1918 Europe, but for the last ten minutes she had been too conscious of the narrowing gap between the minute and hour hands of her wrist-watch to take in much of

736

what he said. She believed that Captain Rowan was similarly preoccupied, but disguising it better. Occasionally he glanced at her as if to say: I know how you feel, but don't worry.

'If I stay another five minutes I shall never want to go, and I've got my compartment to get unlocked.'

Bronowsky put down his glass. 'Then I mustn't be selfish. But Ahmed will be disappointed. He often talks about you.' They all three stood. He took her hand and kissed it. 'Thank you for my birthday present. You will return to Mirat? One day, very soon?'

'Yes. I should like to,' she said, and realized quite suddenly that she meant it, and knowing how unlikely it was that she would ever go again, felt a wrench at parting that was out of all proportion to the real loss or lack of expectation. She turned to Rowan.

'Goodbye, Captain Rowan.'

He took her hand, but not in farewell. 'I'll see you to your compartment,' he said, but Bronowsky intervened, insisted that this was a privilege he claimed for himself. She thought Rowan's face betrayed a momentary blankness, as if the refusal by Bronowsky of his offer to accompany her had made it necessary for him to dismiss from his mind some line of thought or plan of action he had wished to pursue; but since they had only just met and were unlikely ever to meet again, she knew she must be mistaken. But the impression remained, after they had said goodbye and while Bronowsky was handing her down on to the platform. Once down it vanished to the back of her mind, driven there by surprise.

'Why, they've cordoned us off,' she said.

'It saves us from being boarded and from constant explanations that we are not a public conveyance,' he said, and guided her inside the cordon of ropes that held the crowds away from the three coaches, to a point where a policeman was on duty. Originally there had been only two policemen. There were four or five now. The policeman let them through. She felt she would have understood the cordoning off and the presence of police if the Nawab had been travelling. But he was in Nanoora. She had assumed from some of the things said by Bronowsky and Rowan in the past hour and a half that Bronowsky was going to Nanoora too.

She glanced up the platform. They were level now with the front of the first of the three coaches which a locomotive was slowly approaching.

'There is our engine,' the Count said, pointing with his stick. He walked on her left, holding her left elbow. 'We are due to leave at half past midnight, so we must hope Ahmed isn't much longer delayed. If we fail to leave at twelve-thirty the railway people can't fit us in to their schedule again until two a.m. That is your coolie attracting our attention. Now, where is an inspector to unlock your compartment? The fellow over there in the white topee?' Bronowsky waved his stick. The coolie humped the suitcase and stood with that same upward-strained rigidity of neck and head.

It was the same kind of topee but a different man under it, and he had the key. He unlocked, entered and switched on lights and fans, and the coolie climbed up and deposited the bag, returned, touching his turban. She had two rupees ready but Bronowsky restrained her and gave the old man a folded note, which looked like five and must have been because after he salaamed he did not go away but waited near by as if accepting an obligation to see that the train carried her safely out of his hands and into those of God.

In the compartment adjacent to hers three young subalterns who looked like new postings from an OTS eyed her curiously, no doubt assuming that the elderly man with the eye-patch and ebony cane was her father, a sahib of the old school. No, she wanted to say to them, it's not as you think you see it. What you see is a trick, everything here is a trick. She turned to Bronowsky, feeling for questions.

'Have you a blanket and things like that?' he asked before she could speak.

'Yes they're in my case.'

'And you haven't left the key of the case behind in Calcutta?'

She laughed, looked in her handbag and reassured him. The question eluded her. 'Please don't stay, Count Bronowsky,' she said, and held her hand out. 'Thank you for a marvellous supper and for rescuing me from the restaurant. And – Happy Birthday.'

He took her hand, but was silent for a while, looking down at her through his one eye.

'How self-contained you are! I don't remember that when you were in Mirat. But of course we did not exchange many words and you were somewhat overshadowed by the occasion. A bride is always the centre of attraction. But Ahmed noticed you. He affects not to be susceptible to the charms of white ladies. But after you had gone I observed how on many mornings he rode across the waste-ground opposite my house and retraced exactly the course you had taken together, stopping under the same trees, cantering along the same stretch.' He smiled. 'I am confessing, aren't I? That I watched you from the window of my bedroom. I did, but not intentionally. I caught sight of you by chance, but was held by the spectacle. I was amused to see he was doing as he had warned, the night before, when he told me he was to take you riding. He said: Oh! I shall keep my distance, I shall keep my place. It was a joke, of course. Not a bitter one. He has great objectivity, perhaps too much. He is somewhat like an actor who knows every line in a play and plays his part to perfection but cannot light the character up from inside, so with him it is always a part. Well here is Ahmed Kasim, he says, committed to go riding with this English girl. What is expected, what does the world say? Yes, of course. Five paces behind. How amusing! Only he is perhaps less amused than he would have us think. You understand?'

'I understand, yes.'

'You understand what I am saying, but not why I am saying it. To tell you the truth I am not sure. It's probably the champagne. On the other hand, unlike the majority of people I am the opposite of tongue-tied by railway stations and scenes of departure. It must be due to a fear implanted in my mind years ago that even the simplest goodbye may turn out to be for ever and leave you with a feeling of remorse for big and little things you left unsaid. Not that you should ever say everything. Perhaps I am talking to stop you asking those questions you want to ask which I can't answer. I must beg forgiveness. I am only adding to the mystery. But mysteries are no bad thing, especially for the young. They warm the powers of perception and in themselves can be quite beautiful.'

A warning whistle blew. Bronowsky gripped her hand more firmly, reassuring her there was still time – far more for her than for him. 'But don't misinterpret. That picture you have in your mind now, of Ahmed retracing the course you took across the waste-ground. I did not intend a romantic allusion. I said he had great objectivity. He is a spectator, an observer, and when the need arises he can take a part, but not with his heart in it because he doesn't know what part he wants to play or, if he has an inkling, he doesn't see where it fits in. He's indifferent to all the passions that most arouse people in this country. I suppose with a family like his that's lived, breathed and thought nothing but politics it's not unnatural. But in India it's rare. And because it's rare he thinks of it as a disease peculiar to him. He said to me once: "My mother tells me to think hard about something my father once wrote to her – We are looking for a country. But when I think about it I can only make the comment that the country's here, and so am I, and shouldn't we stop squabbling over it and start living in it? What does it really matter who runs it, or who believes in Allah, or Christ, or the avatars of Hindu mythology, or who has a dark face and who has a light?"'

'Yes,' Sarah said, 'What does it matter?'

Bronowsky considered her, and for the first time she noticed how concentrated, how single-minded, a one-eyed man had to be, how deprived he was of the tragi-comic human right to laugh on one side of his face and cry on the other, like the king in the fairy tale. She felt pierced, as if by a singularity of purpose and intent. But that was a mystery too. Perhaps it was beautiful. She did not know. In a few minutes the chance to know would have gone, would have joined the sad jumble of all the other limited chances which (panic-stricken by the thought that the train would suddenly be gone without her), she felt everyone was given.

'He told me about his father's letter and his reactions to it some time *after* you rode together, after you had left Mirat.'

The whistle blew again.

'And you see, he had never spoken to me so frankly before. And I remembered those solitary rides he took, which I did – I must confess – see at first in a superficially romantic light. But now when I look at that picture of him over and over re-enacting that morning ride, I seem to see him trying to recapture something. Some moment he missed, or did not seize, and only understood later was significant.'

'Yes,' she said, 'there was a moment.'

'Tell me.'

'I can't. It wasn't clear. It was to do with the way he kept behind.'

'Something you said?'

'No. Didn't you see?'

'Beyond the mullah, when you galloped, you were outside my range. Two blurred specks. But coming back I thought you once had difficulty with your horse.'

'Not difficulty. I tricked him. I closed the gap. Just for a moment.'

'And then?'

'That was all. He waited for me to ride on.'

The third whistle. 'Thank you, Miss Layton,' he said. 'Now – you had better take your seat, but don't close the door. My steward has some extra luggage for you.' Looking behind she found the steward waiting with a small hamper held to his chest. 'Come.' He handed her up. She stood back and let the steward come in and place the hamper on the floor. When he left the compartment Bronowsky closed the door. She stood at the lowered window. 'There is some champagne,' he said, raising his voice, 'for a christening, which if my arithmetic is correct will take place in the quite near future. But there are also a few things for you to nibble if you get hungry. Shut the windows tight, lock the door and lower the blinds. And if you are in trouble knock loudly on the wall between you and the young officers next door who have been watching with very understandable interest. When next you write to Captain Merrick please remember me to him and tell him I recall our conversation. He will know what I mean.'

'Yes, I will. And thank you again.'

'Now. Please pander to an old man and an old Russian superstition. The circumstances are wrong but the gesture may overcome them. Just sit quietly for a moment, as one always should before setting out on a journey.'

She sat and exchanged smiles with him through the window. Presently the whistle sounded again – a sustained and urgent note. She got up. When she reached the window of the door the train was moving. Bronowsky stayed motionless – his panama hat held to his breast – but gliding away from her, becoming partially obscured by groups of people who slid past as if the platform were being pulled backwards by some strange law of lateral gravity. As the view of the station expanded she saw distantly the three coaches of the Nawab's private train, marooned under dwindling points of illumination. She thought, but could not be sure, that two figures were passing through the cordon, a man and a woman in purdah; but the glimpse was scarcely a glimpse; perhaps a brief hallucinatory image switched by her eye from one part of the platform to another.

When she had closed windows and meshes and lowered blinds, secured locks, it was twenty-four hours since she had entered her body's grace. She made up her bed with sheet and blanket, blew up her air pillow, but then sat, tracing the red and green tartan pattern of the pillow's cover with her right forefinger. Why red and green? Why tartan? She held the pillow to her, then lay down, letting it cushion her head.

Are you happy? he asked. I'm content. Then we're friends? Not friends. Enemies? No, not enemies – strangers still. Shall we make love again? She turned her head into the pillow, wanting him because she knew no other man. The pain of wanting was exquisite. She opened her mouth to receive an image of his but found only the warm flesh of her own hand that was not cunning or quick enough to hold back days or rescue a single firefly from all those that rode the night emitting signals of distress; the signal lights of souls gathering like migrant birds for a long journey because the home they knew had become inhospitable.

She dozed, woke, covered herself with the blanket as an insurance against the chill that would accompany their entry into the hills, but could not summon the resolution to turn off lights and fans. She dozed again, but sleep was held back by an instinct to keep watch on the night's dissembling progress. Ten minutes short of half past two. Going with him now, back into the danger zone. Are you sad? he asked. Just silent. Content and silent, he said, it's a good basis to build on, you will have a good life. And already up there in the hills (these hills) Aunty Mabel had gone, and been quickly buried, as was customary. And who knew whether hers had been a good life? I waited up, Aunt Fenny said, I waited up, pet, your mother rang. It was twenty-four minutes to three. At five it would be thirty-six hours since she had stood waiting for Sister Prior, and since Susan – lying on the veranda of Rose Cottage – had watched Aunty Mabel suddenly put down her basket on the rail between two of the azaleas, and sit, and die, as quietly as she had lived.

VI

At four Ahmed was woken by one of the stewards; and at half past, wearing a new dark grey tropical suit made up by Bronowsky's tailor, he went along the corridor and tapped at the door of his mother's compartment. She was lying fully dressed on her bunk. On the opposite bunk her maid snored with her back turned to the single light that lit his mother's head.

'Is it time?' Mrs Kasim asked, keeping her voice low.

'Yes, Mother. Don't get up.'

'Have you slept at all?'

'Yes. Is there anything I can get you?'

'No, Ahmed, nothing.'

'You shouldn't have stayed awake.'

She held on to his hand. 'It wasn't difficult. Stay with me until the train stops. But don't let talk. Poor Farina's exhausted.' He sat on the edge of the bunk. His mother nodded, closed her eyes. 'You look very smart,' she murmured, and gripped his hand more tightly, as if to thank him for taking trouble. Her hair was greyer than it had been even six months ago. He didn't know – had never known – what she really thought. She had always seemed content to echo his father's words. What have you got out of it, he wanted to ask, out of all this struggle and dedication and sacrifice? What have your compensations been? Are they so small that you notice a suit and get comfort from having me sit and say nothing?

After a while it began to worry him that perhaps the train was behind schedule, that he was committed to stay for a long time, uncomfortably perched; but there was now a change in the rhythm of the rapidly moving coach. His mother noticed it too. Deep – too deep – lines of concentration appeared on her forehead. Speed was being lost. Presently they had slowed to that tentative pace which always made Ahmed feel that a train had transformed itself from a mindless piece of careering machinery into a sentient intelligent creature, probing forward through a maze of obstacles.

His mother opened her eyes and leant up on one elbow. 'You had better go.'

He bent for her kiss.

'You've got the letter safely?'

'Yes, Mother, I've got it safely.' He patted his breast pocket.

She watched him until he pulled the door to between them. In the corridor he lit a cigarette. The dining-saloon still savoured of old festivity, too recent to have gone stale; but it seemed to belong to another time. A nodding steward jerked awake as Ahmed passed him. He found Bronowsky awake in the saloon, reading a small leather-bound book, smoking one of his pink cigarettes.

'I have been indulging several of my most private vices,' the Count said, 'wakefulness while the world dreams, the poetry of Pushkin and an unfinished bottle. There is still a glass left. Or would you prefer something stronger? Yes. Steward. Bring Kasim Sahib a large scotch and soda. Or no soda? No soda.'

'Is Captain Rowan up?'

'I hope so. He was woken at four-fifteen. I have kept watch as well. But that's a virtue. Has your mother slept?'

'No. she promises to.'

The scotch was brought. Ahmed took a generous gulp.

'Here,' Bronowsky said, reaching into his pocket. 'I have a present for you.' He offered a clove of garlic. 'Chew it before you reach the Circuit House.'

'Thanks.'

'Take care not to get close to Captain Rowan, though. He would be too polite to turn his head. He's expecting an appointment in the Political Department, he tells me. We talked for a while after you went to bed. I expect Sir George Malcolm has entrusted him with this present business mainly to help him get his hand in. He should do well. He has a talent for finding out what he wants to know without appearing to encourage conversation to rise above the level of casual chat, and for feigning indifference to the information when he gets it.'

'What did he want to know tonight?'

'He was fascinated by Merrick and the stone and Pandit Baba Sahib. His dismissal of Merrick's name as one that meant nothing to him was disingenuous. I'm too old a hand not to react when feigned indifference is set off by an aura of alertness. I sensed it when Miss Layton and I were talking and sensed it again when I told you in front of him about Merrick's loss of an arm. When we were alone he worked skilfully back to the subject. He began by asking me how and where I lost the sight of an eye. But of course I helped him. We are both professionals.'

'Are you warning me not to speak too freely to him? You know I never do that.' Ahmed smiled, and took another mouthful of the whisky. Had he really got a taste for it yet? He wasn't sure.

'I am giving you, possibly, an example of the discreet way in which the English set to work to re-establish a principle of justice, for their own peace of mind, while attempting to preserve the *status quo* resulting from the breaking of the principle. If Rowan knew of Merrick, which I firmly believe, his pretence otherwise suggests that the files on the six unfortunate detenus in the Manners case have quite recently been on His Excellency's desk. Which means that the detention orders are being reviewed, and possibly that poor Mr Merrick's reputation has suffered a set-back far more serious than the one that saw him packed off to a backwater by a department anxious to keep its mistakes from reaching the ears of more powerful departments which need to ensure that the principles of impartial justice are *seen* to be held sacrosanct. Assuming my interpretation is correct, do you understand Captain Rowan's interest in the recent history of the ex-District Superintendent in Mayapore?'

'No. It's too early in the morning, Count Sahib. And he'll be here in a minute.' The train was still at a crawl, single-mindedly solving the Chinese puzzle of steel links that unfairly confronted it.

'Sometimes, Ahmed, you are so deliberately obtuse that I could send you to bed for a week on bread and water.' The Count paused. 'The reason is – and you would do well to remember it – that Captain Rowan has recognized with the sure instinct of his race, that Mr Merrick's recent history is the key to the preservation of the *status quo*. It has probably already been decided that the six boys are unjustly detained and must be released. That is the principle of justice re-established. But how preserve the *status quo* when clearly a mistake was made by Merrick and compounded by superior authority? On paper your prime scapegoat is Merrick. But how unpleasant to have a scapegoat at all. Imagine the relief with which Captain Rowan will go back to Ranpur and initiate discreet inquiries – with the Governor's approval – into the truth of what he has heard tonight. A citation for bravery in the field and an amputated arm. What luck! It wipes the blot from the escutcheon and solves the problem of Mr Merrick's future civil or military employment. The boys go free, the files are closed, and all is – as they say – as it was before. The one thing the English fear is scandal, I mean private scandal. If Mr Merrick had ever been asked to account for his actions the outside world would never have heard of it.'

'You think he had actions to account for?'

'Undoubtedly.'

The train jerked to a halt. From somewhere beneath and a few feet behind, something clanked. Ahmed went to the window, parted the curtains and saw pools of diffused light on cinders, and under one of the standards that shed the light a limousine from the palace and an army truck. He pulled the curtain to, drained his glass and looked at Bronowsky.

'*Courage, mon ami*,' Bronowsky said, '*le diable est mort.*'

Ahmed repeated the words to himself, to translate them. He smiled. 'Is he?' he asked.

They waited for Rowan.

*

Eventually they were beyond the town. The windows of the limousine were lowered half-way. Sheet lightning spasmodically lit the night sky and the barren landscape.

'It's very close,' Rowan said. 'With any luck it'll be raining tomorrow.'

Ahmed agreed that with any luck it would, and mentally put up his guard. But where could a civilized exchange about the weather lead except to a mutual recognition that they had nothing to say that would destroy their all too ready-made images of each other? Rowan – the archetypal Englishman, unemphatic in speech and gesture but warmed inside no doubt by the belief that what he did would have its modest place in the margins of history; and himself, younger son of a veteran Congress Muslim, the son who failed and got packed off to kick his heels in one of the old princely states where he could embarrass no one; known to drink and to womanize, to be indifferent to politics, a potential wastrel and living proof of the continuing validity of the classic formula of misfortune that could afflict respected parents.

'Is there any point you think we ought to discuss before we arrive?' Rowan asked.

'No, everything is clear.' Clearer to him, he thought, than perhaps Rowan realized; although it would be wrong to make too firm an assumption on that score. He felt in his pocket for the clove of garlic and self-consciously carried it to his mouth. Rowan gave him a quick glance, as a guard would who had to bring a prisoner to a place of interrogation and keep alert for attempts at suicide. The car rode the unrepaired tarmac more evenly than the truck ahead in whose canvas-roofed interior two British military policemen sat stoic under the hypnosis of the twin sources of pursuing light.

Abruptly the gap between truck and limousine shortened.

'We're there, I think,' Rowan said. The truck turned across a culvert that separated the road from the eroded landscape. The limousine followed.

They were in a compound that had no walls. There were lights on in the Circuit House. Figures moved on the veranda. There were two other vehicles parked. Getting out of the limousine Ahmed surveyed the land beyond the compound, but the night was black and there was no view of the fort. He followed Rowan to the veranda. Rowan shook hands with an Englishman in civilian clothes and with one in the uniform of the civil police, but when he turned, wishing to make introductions, Ahmed said, 'I'll wait down there, if you don't mind,' and walked to a place where a chair and a table were set, and took up his position.

Presently Rowan joined him. 'Don't you wish to meet the Divisional Commissioner?'

'Not just now, unless it's essential.'

'Very well,' Rowan said, and left him.

Very well. It was one of the English phrases Ahmed had never understood. Rowan and the others would probably intepret his withdrawal and isolation as a sulky attempt to show them that after all he had a patriotic nature. They could not know that he isolated himself to preserve for as long as possible his sense of detachment from the issues of a situation not of his own devising.

And after a while there was a light, far off; gone as soon as seen; but his muscles had tensed, as though to force his body to leap up and stretch an arm to glean the light before it was extinguished. But he continued to sit still and it was a long time before the light reappeared, moving and unmistakable, a mile down the road and coming at speed.

He got up and stood by the veranda rail, then went to the head of the steps, ignoring Rowan whose shadow fell aslant the floor from the open doorway. He heard Rowan go back in and say something to the others. The approaching car slowed, turned in across the culvert. He was dazzled by the abrupt glare of the headlights and the lingering penumbra as they were doused. An officer got out of the front passenger seat and opened the near door at the back. Ahmed felt his way down the steps.

An old man emerged, grasped the young officer's arm and slowly straightened. Light from the veranda revealed sunken eyes wide open with the shock of transition to a strange environment. With his free hand the old man shaded them.

'Ahmed? Ahmed? Is that you?' The voice did not belong to the old man. It was his father's voice. The officer stood away and Ahmed felt his left arm taken in both the old man's hands.

'Ahmed?'

'Yes, Father.'

'Your mother, Ahmed. Your mother. What news of your mother?'

'She's well, you'll see her very soon.'

'They let the Mahatma out. Poor Kasturba was dead.'

'I know. But there's nothing like that.'

'Then God is good to me.' He clung to him. Ahmed felt him trembling. The officer turned his back.

'Come and sit,' Ahmed said.

Presently the old man released him and stood back, looking suspiciously towards the house. 'Who is there?'

'An officer on the Governor's staff and two others I don't know.'

'So many people? But there is a room where I can be alone?'

'We can talk on the veranda.'

'No. Please ask for a room. I must be alone for a few minutes, then we must talk. After that I will see them. Not before. Ask this officer to go and tell them.'

'I'll go myself. Wait here.'

The room he entered was barely furnished. Rowan and the others were standing round a deal table. He spoke to Rowan, ignoring the Commissioner and the policeman.

'My father asks for a room where he can be alone for a while.'

Rowan turned to the Commissioner. 'Is there another room, sir?'

'There's one at the end, where Mr Kasim was sitting. It's not locked.'

'Is it for devotional use?' Rowan asked, looking in Ahmed's direction.

'Apparently no one at the Fort bothered to reassure him my mother was neither ill nor dying. He's been expecting to hear the worst. So he's not yet ready to talk to anyone.'

'The Fort commander would have had the minimum instructions necessary, but I regret any worry he's been caused.' Again he spoke to the Commissioner. 'I think it would be better if we made this room available to Mr Kasim and wait in the other one ourselves. Is there a way to it other than along the veranda?'

The Commissioner mumbled and led them out through a back door. Ahmed waited until the sounds they made were no longer audible, then went back to his father. He found him sitting in the car. He helped him out and up the steps. Inside the room, in the glare of the light, the physical toll exacted by nearly two years in prison was fully revealed. The long-skirted high-necked coat that had once shown up a comfortable thickness of body, hung loosely. The flesh of the thickened jowls was fallen, the fringe of hair was wholly grey. The white cap of Congress seemed too big. The hawk-like nose had a hungry questing look.

'I'll leave this with you, Father.' He gave him the envelope which contained his mother's letter. 'It's from Mother. She wrote it a few hours ago.'

'Is she near by?'

'Not far. Let me know when you want me.'

For the first time since entering the room his father looked at him.

'No, I am all right. Stay here. We must talk. You are taller. And broader. How long has it been?'

'Nearly three years.'

'You have your full growth. You quite dwarf me. Quite dwarf me.'

The moment was over then. In the few seconds sitting in the car his father had recovered and put back up the barriers.

'They told me nothing until five o'clock yesterday, and then only to pack my things and get a few hours sleep. Am I free, or on my way to another jail?'

'You are free,' Ahmed said; but he had hesitated.

'On what conditions? Is there an amnesty? No – don't answer. Let me read your mother's letter. Sit down.' His father sat at the table. Ahmed chose a seat near the door, which was still open. The room was very warm. The fan was not working. Unhurriedly his father brought out his spectacle case and put the spectacles on. A slight tremor of the hands was the only sign that his composure was incomplete. The letter was very short but he lingered over it with the concentration Ahmed remembered as character-istic. Briefs, minutes, resolutions, correspondence: they had all been subjected to this slow searching analysis. Why does he take so long? Ahmed had once asked. His mother replied: He reads between the lines.

Kasim folded the letter and put it back in the envelope. He took his spectacles off, returned them to the case and the case to his pocket.

'Your mother says she hopes I will agree but that I'm not to be swayed by emotional or private considerations. You had better tell me what I'm being asked to agree to. All I gather otherwise is that she is on her way to Nanoora to stay with my kinsman, the Nawab, and that this could be the scene of our immediate reunion. I too am invited to Mirat?'

'Yes.'

'As a guest of the Nawab?'

'Yes. They call it – under his protection.'

'I see.' Kasim sat back. 'While in the sovereign state of Mirat I would be free to enjoy my rights as a private citizen, providing I did nothing to embarrass my host, which means nothing that incurs the displeasure of the Indian Government. Should I set foot outside the State on the other hand, and go back to Ranpur, then I should probably be arrested.'

'They haven't said so, Father.'

'They?'

'The Governor in Ranpur.'

'You've seen the Governor?'

'Not personally. Neither has Mother. But he sent representatives. One of them is here tonight.'

'On whose instigation did he send representatives? On the Viceroy's? From newspapers and letters received I gather Wavell is anxious to break the political deadlock of the past two years. Who else is being released into this kind of protection? Nehru?'

'The Viceroy knows, but the initiative's been with Malcolm. It's not a general arrangement.'

'I am the only Congressman of any importance being paroled?'

'Yes, Father. So far as I know, you're the only one.'

'Why?'

The question was snapped. In the past such a tone and such a whiplash of a word had entangled perjured witnesses and intimidated honest ones. There was no way round the truth.

'Because of my brother.'

A pause.

'There is news of Sayed, then?' Kasim asked calmly.

'Yes.'

'Of his death? He has died in prison camp?'

'No, Father. He's been captured.'

'I know he was captured. He was captured by the Japanese in Kuala Lumpur in 1942. It is a long time since we had any word.'

But the old man seemed suddenly older. 'We've had word now,' Ahmed said. His father might never forgive him for saying what he had to say. Sayed had always been the favourite son, the one in whom hope had been placed, whose life had not been a source of disappointment. It should have been Sayed who sat here. The old man would then not have looked so old. 'Sayed was captured a month ago in Manipur,' he went on. 'We don't know where he is except in a prison camp in India with some of the others. Directly the army knew who he was they told the civil authorities in Calcutta and those authorities told the authorities in Ranpur. Malcolm invited Mother to Government House, but didn't say why. She refused to go so he sent someone to the house. Then she wrote to me in Mirat. She said she'd suspected for some time that Sayed had joined the INA. About six months ago she had an anonymous letter delivered by hand, telling her Sayed sent his love and would see her soon. I think I know who might have sent it, but that doesn't matter. And previously one of Mother's friends told her they thought they'd recognized Sayed's voice on the Japanese radio.'

'The INA—?'

'The Indian National Army.'

'I know what the initials stand for. I was about to say – the INA? Sayed? The old man smiled. 'Captured in Manipur? Yes. Perhaps a man with this name, Lieutenant Sayed Kasim.'

'He was Major Kasim.'

'There you are then. Prisoners of war don't get promoted.'

'Major is his rank in the INA.'

'Rank? His *rank* in the INA? Is there such a thing? No. Sayed is not a major in the INA. He is Lieutenant Kasim and his regiment is the Ranpur Rifles. Why have you believed this ridiculous story? Someone has made a mistake, a ridiculous mistake, as a result of all this feeble propaganda which the British have rightly tried to scotch. Now they are believing it themselves, it seems. The Indian National Army? What can that be? A handful of madmen led by that other madman, Subhas Chandra Bose, who was never any good to Congress. He always had delusions of grandeur. First he escapes from India, then turns up in Berlin and then in Tokyo. He sets up an absurd paper government-in-exile and perhaps a few Indians living in Malaya put on a uniform and help him kowtow to the Japanese, fooling

748

themselves that if the Japanese ever defeat India they will allow Subhas to set up his paper-government in Delhi. But it is all wishful thinking and propaganda, there is no Indian National Army deserving of the name. If a Major Kasim was captured in Manipur he would be some unlucky fellow who foolishly accompanied the Japanese as an observer for Bose. He would not be Sayed. And Sayed would not be fighting and killing Indians. He would not be helping the Japanese to invade his own country.'

'There were thousands of Indians taken prisoner in Burma and Malaya. A lot of them felt they'd been deserted by their British officers. There were tales of a white road out and a black road out.'

'You are speaking up for them? You think your brother is one of them? You are calling your brother a traitor?' Kasim got up, Ahmed felt it obligatory to rise too. But they came no closer to one another. 'You forget that Sayed is an Indian officer. He holds, unless he is dead, the King-Emperor's commission. It was his choice. He was a good officer, the first Indian officer in his chosen regiment. It concerned me that he should choose to take a commission, but then I am a politician. He wished to be a soldier. I said to him once, Do you regret it? He only laughed. In the mess he said they were all equal, that there was only one standard and if you measured up to it you were accepted. To me it all seemed simple and naïve, but Sayed *was* naïve. He was naïve, he could never have made a success of politics, but he did not have it in him to be a traitor. In 1939 he said to me, "You are a minister of state, I am an officer in the Indian army. We are both necessary people.' He had no complaints, he encountered no difficulties. It was I who encountered difficulties because a son of mine had taken the King's commission. But I did not see them as difficulties. The world is full of fools who don't see an inch in front of their noses. What kind of independence will it be when we get it if we can't defend it? And how shall we be able to defend it if there aren't boys like Sayed willing to train and discipline themselves faithfully and steadfastly to inherit that side of our national responsibility? What are we living in, a jungle? When the British invited Indians to take the King's commission they were proving what my father called their sincerity. You do not hand your armed forces over to the command of men who will turn it against you. What kind of an army will it be if its officers think of their commissions as meaningless bits of paper? It is a contract, a contract. All of Muslim law is based on the sanctity of contract, of one man's word to another. You must be prepared to suffer and die for it. It is written. It is revealed. It is in our hearts. What are you telling me? That it is not in Sayed's? That he is not a man to keep his contract? That he is an opportunist? A cowardly scoundrel? Without a thought for his own honour or for mine, or his mother's, or for yours? Are you telling me this is the kind of India I have gone to prison for? If you are, you had better leave me here. I do not know that kind of India. I do not know that kind of man. He is not Sayed. He is not my son.'

'We've had a letter, Father. He's written to Mother.'

'A forgery.'

'He says you will help him.'

'Does he?'

'Eventually there'll be court-martials.'

'Will there?'

'In his letter he says he refused to join until they told him you'd been arrested.'

'Well?'

'He asked us to give you his love. He's sorry he failed.'

'Failed?'

'Failed to complete the march on Delhi.'

His father's mouth was working. 'The march on Delhi? What is that? Some city on the moon? Or do you march nowadays on your own capital? He thinks perhaps the Moghul empire still exists and has been ravaged by barbarians? And that I languish in some medieval dungeon, clanking my chains, crying out to my son to muster an army and ride to my rescue? God save me from such a deliverance. I would fear for my life. Such a son would strike me down. He would drag me from prison and have me trampled to death. I don't accept his love. I don't listen to his apology.'

The old man's voice had strengthened and risen to the pitch that had swayed juries, brought order to a noisy Legislative Assembly and sent ministers scuttling at midnight through the corridors of the Secretariat. Ahmed closed the door. The action calmed him and hardened his resolution. He could not escape involvement. He had to speak out.

'I've closed the door because it would be better if they don't hear. There *is* an Indian National Army and it isn't just a few madmen. It would suit the British very well if every Congressman said what you've just said. But do you think they will? A dozen Indian officers helping the Japanese would have no political significance. The British could shoot them for treachery and no one would need to raise a finger in protest. But hundreds of officers and thousands of men do have political significance. Whatever the members of your party feel individually, collectively you're going to have to stand by them, because the ordinary Indian won't see any difference between men like these who grabbed rifles and marched up through Burma with the Japanese and men who said the Indians had no quarrel with the Japanese and called on the whole country to sabotage the British war effort. Except that the young men who grabbed rifles and marched will look more heroic than the old men who went to jail and suffered nothing but personal inconvenience.'

'Then I had better go back and continue in that relatively comfortable state of personal inconvenience.'

'You can't go back, Father. They won't let you. I know Mother talks about hoping you'll agree, but she's got into the habit of thinking you have a choice, and knows you'd choose what you see as the honourable way. But the plain fact is they're chucking you out of the Fort. They pretend it's a compassionate release and men like the Governor may actually feel sorry for you. He obviously knew you well enough to guess you'd feel disgraced, and not proud, about Sayed. But if he knows you as well as that, the kindest thing would have been to keep you in prison, because being in prison is your one current public badge of honour, isn't it?'

'You have never thought so!' the old man cried. 'You have always been ashamed. Why? Do you think I have not been ashamed too? You think it is a matter of pride to look out of a window and know that this is as much as you will be allowed to see of the world? No! It is not a badge of honour, it is one of humiliation. But there are circumstances in which you weigh one humiliation against another, and choose. I have chosen many times before and I can choose again.'

Kasim sat. He took the white cap off and placed it on the table.

'No, Father. You can't choose. At least I don't think so.'

'You don't think so. We'll see. Let them take me forcibly to Mirat. But then let them stop me returning to Ranpur.'

'To do what? Something that will force them to arrest you again? What sort of thing will that be? They only arrested you last time because of your loyalty to the Congress. Wouldn't most of your time be spent persuading your friends and the wives of your colleagues who are still in prison that your release isn't a reward for making a deal with the Governor, or with Jinnah? When a man comes out of political detention and there's no amnesty to explain it his friends want to know why.'

'There is always the truth.'

'About Sayed? What will you do? Talk to your Congress friends as you've talked to me? Call Sayed a traitor? You might just as well write your letter of resignation now, and apply to Jinnah for membership of the League. Not that Jinnah would touch you with a barge-pole if you took that line with him. He'll have to call Sayed a patriot too, if he values his career as a future minister.'

Kasim looked up from contemplation of the cap. The sunken eyes glittered. 'To whom have you been talking? Obviously not your mother. To these representatives of Government? To my feeble-minded kinsman, the Nawab? To that European paederast, that *émigré* Wazir?'

'I've talked to all of them, but not about this.'

'No?'

Kasim looked again at the cap. 'Then I must apologize for having underestimated you. I had assumed your dissociation from the kind of affairs that have been the central concern of my life was a mask for your failure to understand them. But your assessment of my present position is shrewd, and I am indebted to you for bothering to open my eyes to it. Since one of my sons turns out to be a deserter and a traitor, it is some compensation to realize that the other one is not stupid, as I thought.'

Ahmed glanced down at the floor. He supposed he had invited it. It was only fair that his father should hurt him too. But when he looked up again he found his father's eyes closed and head bent forward. For a long time neither of them spoke. It was his father who broke the silence.

'I am sorry. You did not deserve that. Forgive me. And you have come all this way to meet me. In prison you forget that time doesn't stand still, that circumstances change and that without your knowing it you yourself are carried forward with them. It is a shock to come out and discover it. It is difficult to adjust. I must thank you for perhaps having saved me from too hastily making impractical or anachronistic gestures.'

He put his hands on the table, folded, attempting an illusion of unimpaired competence and capacity. But Ahmed guessed that the hands clasped one another to disguise evidence of a sudden and frightening lack of confidence.

'Presently,' the ex-chief minister said, 'you must call in these patient English officials, but there are a few points I wish to be clear on first. Was it the Governor or the Nawab who suggested I should be released from the Fort and sent to Mirat?'

'The Governor, through his representative. Mother asked me to find out if the Nawab would agree.'

'Then we need not concern ourselves with the Nawab's or his Wazir's motives, but only bear in mind what future political advantage they may see accruing from their generosity. Secondly. What reasons did the Governor give for making the suggestion?'

'None. At least, not in so many words, but the connection was clear enough, I suppose. The representative told Mother the news about Sayed and then said that the Governor had taken advice—'

'Advice?'

'The inference was that there had been a discussion with the Viceroy. The Governor said he'd be prepared to release you into the protection of anyone acceptable to both sides, and suggested the Nawab. He promised Mother that if she got the Nawab's approval the release would be arranged immediately.'

'But—?'

'There weren't any buts. Except for the condition of secrecy until the release had taken place. The Government will then report it as due to a concern for your health.'

'*My* health?'

'From their point of view it must be more acceptable that way round. I imagine they don't want an epidemic of Congress wives with fatal illnesses certified as authentic by Congress-minded doctors.'

'You miss the point that the Governor imagines it is also more acceptable from my point of view. He offers me an alibi that might stand me in good stead later on when my less fortunate colleagues are released.'

'No, Father. I hadn't missed that point.' He hesitated. 'There's one other thing, the Governor said that arrangements could be made for you to talk to Sayed.'

They stared at one another.

'And this is all?' Kasim asked suddenly, ignoring Ahmed's last remark. 'Nothing is said about the expected duration of my illness, nor about the conditions in which I am to live?'

'You'll have a private suite of rooms in the summer palace in Nanoora. We'll drive first to Mirat. The Nawab's private train will be waiting there for us. Mother is on it. So is Bronowsky. The Nawab's at the summer palace.'

'Which of course is heavily guarded.'

'Not heavily.'

'But where nevertheless I shall be incommunicado. I hope Bronowsky understands that Nanoora will suffer from a slight increase in the population in the form of inquisitive newspapermen anxious for every scrap of information they can pick up or invent about my state of health and mind?'

'He's going to issue bulletins. You won't be pestered.'

'You mean I shan't be allowed to be pestered. Well – my kinsman the Nawab of Mirat will be a more considerate jailer than Government, and in this matter you are right, I have no choice. But I am still their prisoner and this time your mother joins me. It is a sacrifice she will willingly make, but it is one I would have spared her. Do you understand that, Ahmed?'

'Yes, I think so.' He waited, but his father seemed to have no more to say. He was staring at the white cap again. 'Shall I go and tell them you're ready?' The old man nodded, but when Ahmed was about to open the door he was stopped by the sound of the voice continuing.

'What have you been trying to tell me?'

Ahmed turned round.

'That I should bow to the inevitable as I bow to this new humiliation? That I should prepare myself to play along with the crowd and so ensure my political future? Or that I should acknowledge defeat and retire from politics and grow onions to ward off the chills of old age? Have you ever tasted onions that flourish in the dry weather on mugs of shaving water begged from the prison barber on every second day? It is an interesting flavour. Perhaps it is only in the imagination that one tastes soap. But then the imagination of an ageing man is severely limited and prey to all kinds of quaint illusions and expectations.'

Kasim looked up. 'Unfortunately,' the old man said, 'we have only one life to live and we are granted only one notion of what makes it worth living. It isn't easy to write that notion off as mistaken or the life we live in pursuit of it as wasted.'

'I know.'

'Do you? You will. But not yet. You're young and your life is all before you.'

Yes, but what kind of life? Ahmed wondered. The life he lived now wasn't his own because he lived it in the dense shadows of his father's life and of the lives of men like him. He longed to grope his way out and cast a shadow of his own. The longing was so intense that his blood stirred. It was as if a voice inside him cried out: Rebel! Rebel!

But Rebel against what? In India only one kind of rebellion was possible, and that kind had become an old man's game. They had played it a long time and it wasn't over yet. The game and the men had grown old together and India had grown old with them.

'Well?' Kasim asked. 'What are you waiting for? Go and fetch them, or are you going to explain what you've been trying to tell me? Which of the two alternatives you think I should choose?'

Ahmed hesitated. The game had gone wrong but his father had always played it honourably. No doubt he would do so to the end. What was sad was the fact that his father was not looking for a country for himself but for his sons, and they could never inhabit it because a country was a state of mind and a man could properly exist only in his own. In his father's India, the India his father *was*, Ahmed felt himself an exile; but an exile from where he didn't know. His mind was not clear enough to penetrate the shadows of other men's beliefs which lay across it; and before these beliefs – so sure and positive, so vigorously upheld by words of challenge and acts of sacrifice – he felt stupidly unformed and incoherent. Perhaps it was a beginning of coherence for him to have understood the nature of his father's problem, and to have spoken out. But farther than that he could not go. Could not? Should not, rather. The problem was his father's, not his; and the hands the problem was in were safe enough. The old man would never compromise. Neither would he give up the fight. The sight of him sitting there, waiting to confront three men he thought of as his country's oppressors, moved Ahmed to despair and melancholy pride. The bizarre notion struck him that if only there were a mirror in the room he would take it down from the wall and put it on the table and say: 'There's the India you're eating out your heart looking for.' In the shape of his father's prison-diminished body, he felt for such an India an undemanding, a boundless love, and for an instant in his own heart and bones he understood his father's youthful longing and commitment and how it had never truly been fulfilled, and had never been corrupted, so that even in an old man's body it shone like something new and untried and full of promise.

But there was something missing; and knowing what it was and how he could cover up his silence and indecision and at the same time convey to his father something of what he felt he went to the table, picked up the white Congress cap and offered it.

'You've forgotten this,' he said. 'They pretend to laugh at it, but of course they're afraid of it really. If they see it on the table they might come to the wrong conclusion.'

His father stared at the cap, then bent his head. Ahmed put the cap on for him, gave it a jaunty tilt. His father's hands touched his, seeking to impose an adjustment. 'No, straight,' he said. 'And firm,' and muttered something which Ahmed only partly caught.

But outside, on the veranda, he caught the whole of it. The sky was lighter and the Fort stood immense and dark and implacable; mercilessly near. 'Straight and firm,' his father had said – 'like a crown of thorns.'

EPILOGUE

And after all it seemed that Susan had held somewhere in the back of her mind a memory of the day she once told Sarah she had forgotten: the day Dost Mohammed made a little circle of kerosene-soaked cotton-waste, set light to it and then opened a circular tin, shook it, and dropped the small black scorpion into the centre of the ring of fire. Poised, belligerent, the armoured insect moved stiffly, quickly – stabbing its arched tail, once, twice, three times. Sarah felt the heat on her face and drew back. When the flames died down the scorpion was still. Dost Mohammed touched it gingerly with a twig and then, getting no response, scooped the body into the tin.

'Is it whole?' Susan asked. For a while she had this strange idea that it couldn't be because it had been born nearly a month too soon. She received the child in her arms reluctantly, fearing that even at this stage one of them might destroy the other; or, failing this, that she would find some vestigial trace or growth which a few more weeks' gestation would have taken care of. What will you call him? people asked. 'I don't know,' she said. 'A name is so important. How can I choose an important thing like that entirely on my own?'

Susan had had a bad time. 'But,' Mrs Layton said, 'she was a brick.' And so it was generally agreed. A brick. Like her mother. Among those who knew the Laytons only one person withheld praise of the way in which Mildred Layton had coped in Sarah's absence and this was Barbie who maintained a tight-lipped, red-eyed silence, and made preparations for departure from a place of refuge that had not proved permanent. Perhaps it was to Mr Maybrick that she spoke confidentially and through Mr Maybrick that a story gained subterranean currency that Mildred Layton had ridden roughshod over her suggestion that Mabel had wanted to be buried in St Luke's cemetery in Ranpur, next to her second husband, and not in the cemetery of St John's. Had Mabel ever expressed such a preference? Perhaps she had, but only to Barbie, and there was nothing in the Will to confirm it. Even if there had been, who could blame Mildred for the hasty arrangements made to inter her stepmother-in-law's body in Pankot within twenty-four hours of the old woman's sudden death? What else could she have done, with Susan in labour brought on by the shock of witnessing that death, alone, on the veranda of Rose Cottage? The expense, the inconvenience (the sheer horror, if you liked) of packing the old woman with ice and transporting her to Ranpur would have been intolerable, and it was more important to help a new life into the world than to be certain that the remains of a spent one were buried in a place one had only an old maid's word had been the place desired by the departed.

And so Mabel Layton had gone to her last resting place in the late afternoon of the day following her death. There were mounds of flowers on the grave to make up for the thin scattering of people who managed to get away for the service. Mrs Layton's flurried presence was noted and respected. She would have been forgiven for not attending because Susan still lay in a room of the Pankot nursing home, as yet undelivered. Her mother had spent the night there and would return directly the funeral was over to spend another night, if need be. Was it, people wondered, a false alarm? It would be quite understandable, if so. It was a terrible thing for a young girl so far advanced in pregnancy to find herself sitting on a veranda with a dead woman. It would have been better if there had been some warning, if old Mabel had cried out or fallen or at least shown signs of being unwell; instead of which she had simply stopped tending the plants on the balustrade and sat down in a chair close to the one Susan was lying on, and given up the ghost. Well, she was an old woman and it was a good way to go; but not good for Susan who had only gradually become puzzled and then alarmed by the angle of the old woman's head. 'Are you awake, Aunty Mabel?' she asked, raising her voice because of the deafness. And, three hours later, when Rose Cottage was almost empty again of all the people Susan had sensibly and courageously helped to summon, her mother found her in the little spare, with her hands pressed to her abdomen and her eyes wide with terror and incomprehension.

'It can't have,' she said, when Dr Travers told her twenty minutes later that her labour seemed to have begun. 'It can't be. It isn't time. The baby isn't finished.' For thirty-three hours she lay in a room of the nursing home which Isobel Rankin had seen was made available – a lovely room, marked down on the official lists as exclusive to the wives of officers of senior field rank. And at five o'clock in the morning – as Sarah slept fitfully on the train from Ranpur, keeping watch on the night's progress (and Ahmed Kasim sat on the veranda of the Circuit House near Premanagar, keeping a different kind of watch) – Susan was delivered of a boy who looked absurdly, touchingly, like Teddie.

'It doesn't matter,' Susan said when Sarah told her Mr Merrick was grateful but felt he couldn't accept. 'I'm going to ask General Rankin, but there have to be two godfathers for a boy so you'd better ask Dicky. At least he's got two arms.' It was the only thing she ever said that showed how little or much she had taken in of Sarah's story about Teddie's death and Merrick's action and misfortune; but thereafter she began to show a tender devotion to the child which Dr Travers said was a sign of her having come through, of her confounding those Jeremiahs who once talked about her as being dangerously withdrawn like the daughter of a woman called Poppy Browning. Who said that? Mrs Layton demanded, not having heard the rumour but remembering Poppy Browning well enough from the old days in Lahore. Miss Batchelor had mentioned it, Dr Travers thought. 'That woman!' Mrs Layton cried; and another nail was driven into Barbie's coffin.

On the day before Barbie quit Rose Cottage for temporary sanctuary with the Peplows, Sarah found her wandering in the garden with Mabel's cradle-basket and Mabel's secateurs. 'I should have kept my mouth shut,' she said, 'I mean about St Luke's in Ranpur. But she *did* wish it. She *told* me. Quite clearly. Last year. I suggested we should go down to Ranpur to do some Christmas shopping but she said, Oh I shall never go back to Ranpur, at least not until I'm buried. I thought your mother knew all about it but was forgetting it in all the rush and confusion. But there you are. I've opened my mouth once too often. Rose Cottage is yours now, and it's not as if I expected to stay on or have longer than a week or two to make other arrangements if Mabel died before I did. What hurts is being misunderstood and leaving a place I've been happy in, under a cloud. I know it was unfair to you, my being here. If I hadn't been, there'd just have been room for you and Susan and your mother. I said so to Mabel. More than once. Oughtn't I to go, Mabel? I said. After all I'm not family, and they're not comfortable down there in the grace and favour. But she wouldn't hear of it. I don't know why. She lived a life of her own, didn't she? I never knew what she was thinking. It sometimes seemed to me she'd *found* herself, I mean her true self, and just wanted to be alone but have someone who would talk to her. Heaven knows I did that. Well, it's all over now. I've written to the Mission. I thought I might do some voluntary work. There are people starving and dying, aren't there? There must be something I can do, even if it's only laying out bodies. I shouldn't want paying. I've got my pension and the little annuity she'd left me. Not that I'm happy about that. Nor is your mother, I shouldn't wonder.'

'You mustn't think that, Barbie. You made Aunt Mabel's last years very pleasant. It's the only way she could repay you. And we've still got plenty. We're well off now.'

Barbie looked round the garden. Mabel's presence was like a scent. 'Shall you be happy here, all of you?'

'I don't know. I don't know at all, Barbie.'

'Will she marry Captain Beauvais?'

'Susan?'

'People think so. They say the child should have a father. I'd encourage it if I were you. If she doesn't marry again you'll never get away.' Suddenly Barbie flushed and grasped Sarah's arm. 'That's what you want, isn't it? To get away. But some people are made to live and others are made to help them. If you stay you'll end up like that, like me. Worse probably because all this' – she released Sarah's arm and made a broad gesture at the garden and the hills – 'it's coming to an end somehow, isn't it? Very soon.'

Abruptly Barbie left her and Sarah did not see her again until the morning of the christening when she sat alone in a pew near the altar while Sarah and Dicky, General and Mrs Rankin, and Sarah's mother, stood at the font and Mr Peplow received the new Edward Arthur David Bingham as a lively member of Holy Church. The baptism was hurried, almost furtive; and when it was over the Rankins went their way and the Laytons went theirs. There was no party but Dicky went back with Sarah and her mother to the grace and favour bungalow where the business of packing private possessions into crates for the move to Rose Cottage had been interrupted the day before. The child was placed in the care of Minnie who had been promoted to the position of ayah and had already notably proved her worth; but it was Sarah who dealt with the milk and the bottle and the rubber teat while Minnie watched, anxious to learn but so far unsuccessful in persuading the child to accept this substitute for his mother's breast.

In the afternoon Dicky drove Sarah to the nursing home – a week to the day and almost to the hour that he had driven Susan home from there with the child in her arms. He did not go in and Sarah told him she would get a tonga home. 'Shall I come and see you tonight?' he asked. She did not want him but thought it might be better, if only for her mother's sake, to have someone in the house to whom both of them could talk. 'Yes,' she said, 'come in time for drinks.'

'I do hope you find her better,' he said, 'Oh, I do hope so.' He turned away and Sarah went in. Twenty minutes later, escorted, she entered the room where Susan was, which was not a pretty room at all. There were bars at the window. Susan sat on an upright chair, hands folded on her lap, watching the gently falling rain and smiling. Another chair was placed near by and on this Sarah took up her position and waited until Susan slowly turned her head and looked at her.

'Hello, Su. I've come to see if there's anything you want.'

How pretty you look, Sarah thought. Pretty and happy. No, more than happy, profoundly content, totally withdrawn. You've found your way in. Why should that cause us pain and sorrow? Why should it hurt to think that you don't recognize me? Or only recognize me as someone belonging to a world that's become unreal to you and isn't to be compared with the one you've always imagined and imagine now, and smile at because you feel its protection all round you like a warmth?

Now you look back at the window, through the bars which you don't see. The little flush on your cheeks which used to look hectic no longer does so; it's a flush of pleasure and the smile is a smile of happiness, almost of beatitude. Why do we call it sickness? And pray for you to come back to us? When you come back you may remember what you did or tried to do, and why. And we are selfish enough to want you to remember and tell us because we're not people who will accept mysteries if we think there are explanations to be had.

But you scare us. We sense from the darkness in you the darkness in ourselves, a darkness and a death wish. Neither is admissible. We chase that illusion of perpetual light. But there's no such thing. What light there is, when it comes, comes harshly and unexpectedly and in it we look extraordinarily ugly and incapable.

She glanced round and spoke in a whisper to the young psychiatrist who stood waiting with Dr Travers. 'May I touch her?' The man nodded. Sarah had no faith in him; not because he was young – that was a good thing – but because his work was exclusively with men. She leaned forward.

'Susan? It's me – Sarah.'

But Susan did not look at her again and Sarah shrank from touching her. She did not want to intrude or disrupt the pattern of her sister's absorption. After a while she said, 'Goodbye, Susan. I'll see you again tomorrow,' but the words went unheeded or unheard and she rose and went with the doctors to the door. 'Can you keep her here?' she asked. Travers said they hoped so. The alternative – as Mrs Layton so much feared – was a place in Ranpur. But the patient was very quiet. It was probably only a passing phase. Travers said he could have sworn that a week ago her attitude to the child was normal; maternally loving and possessive.

It wasn't normal, Sarah wanted to say, but none of them had seen it; except Mahmoud's widowed niece, Minnie; and it had not been her place to say but only to watch and learn and be on her guard, and make offerings to the old tribal gods of the hills, which it seemed she and the other servants had got into a habit of doing, secretly, to ward off a rumoured evil of monstrous birth, and which she now continued to do because as far as Minnie was concerned the affliction which she had detected in the young memsahib's devotion to the child was of divine origin, as all madness was, a sign of God's special concern and interest.

Sarah waited until the rain stopped, then left the nursing home and took the first tonga in the line. 'To St John's,' she told the tonga-wallah. She did not want to be alone with her mother. When they reached the church she asked the man to wait and went into the churchyard, past the hummocky graves – old lichen-eaten crosses aslant in long wet grass. She took the path round the south side of the church, to the newer part of the cemetery and stood at Aunt Mabel's grave with its mounds of withered wreaths. Her own little posy, gathered from the garden of Rose Cottage after the funeral, was withered too. The ink had run on the cards, leaving ghostly traces of anonymous remembrances. *Ah, oui. Elle est une de Mes prisonnières.* That too had been a nail in poor Barbie's coffin because she had told Susan about the butterflies in the lace. Had she been listening or had Mabel repeated the story to her after Sarah had gone? No matter. 'Little prisoner, little prisoner. Shall I free you? Shall I free you?' Susan had said, touching the baby's cheek with her finger. But even that had passed them by as no more than a tender admonition.

Sarah left the graveside and on impulse went into the church through the south door which Mr Peplow always left open during the hours of daylight. She sat in a front pew and after a while had the curious feeling that she was not alone. Little prisoner, little prisoner, shall I free you? Is that what she had meant to do? And was it only yesterday that, finding herself alone with the servants in the grace and favour bungalow while Sarah was at the office and her mother at Rose Cottage measuring curtains, Susan had sent Mahmoud to the bazaar for blue ribbons and then sent Minnie after him to tell him white, not blue?

Uneasy, Sarah looked behind her but saw no one and turned back to her contemplation of the image of her sister's madness; but in the stillness she heard from outside the church the squeaking sound of a motor-car or taxi coming to a halt and then, after a second or two, the short note of summons on its horn; and presently, much closer, the unmistakable sound of footsteps on tiles, within the body of the church. She turned again. A woman in an old-fashioned veiled topee was coming down the aisle towards the altar, making for the south door; a woman who must have been there all the time on the darker side of the nave, and whom Sarah recognized. At the end of the aisle the woman genuflected, supporting herself with one hand on the end of the pew.

Why, what a lot you know, Sarah told her silently, what a lot, what a terrible, terrible lot. But now I know some of it too, and know that this kind of knowing isn't knowing but bowing my head, as you are bowing yours, under the weight of it.

The woman came towards her, one hand held to her breast clutching a cross that wasn't there except in the form of pleats and buttons. Level with her the woman hesitated. Sarah could make out little of the face through the veil, but smiled because she felt beholden, as Susan would have said. The woman said nothing but half raised a hand in a gesture that stopped short both of greeting and farewell, and then went out through the south door to the waiting transport. And when she had gone Sarah moved, stumbling over the hassocks, wanting to ask, to ask; but just what she didn't know. She hesitated too, and was lost. Outside, rounding the buttressed corner of the church she saw the old woman opening the lych-gate, began to run, and stopped. The rain was falling again; gentle rain. All the hills of Pankot were green and soft. She ran down the gravel pathway, past the graves of Muirs and Laytons, understanding that this was part of her dream, the running and the absence of an end to the journey. When she got to the road the car was gone.

Little prisoner, shall I free you? Divine intervention! Well, Minnie had understood and not gone beyond the gate in Mahmoud's wake, to change an order for blue ribbons, but crept cautiously back to the end of the veranda where she had been sorting bundles of laundry for the dhobi, and where Susan Mem was dressing the baby in the lace he was to wear on the morrow, talking to him in her strange guttural tongue.

Divine intervention; odd, alien custom. Which? How could Minnie know? All she could do was watch and wait. After a while the dressing was over. The mother hugged the child to her and then walked out into the bright sunshine of the rainfree afternoon, across the patch of grass towards the wall that hid the servants' quarters. There, for many days, Mahmoud had lit bonfires to destroy the accumulation of unwanted years. And there Susan placed the child on the grass, took the ready-to-hand tin of kerosene and sprinkled a wide circle around it. For a time Minnie stared, fascinated, believing herself a hidden witness of a secret initiation. But when Susan Mem set fire to the kerosene and the flames leapt, arcing their way round in a geometrical perfection, Minne snatched a sheet from the dhobi's bundle and ran, threw the sheet on to the flames, entered the circle and picked the child up and carried it to safety.

She stood some way off. Susan Mem had not moved. She knelt and watched the flames dying and did not appear to notice the trampled sheet or the fact that the child was no longer there. The grass was too wet for the flames to catch hold. Only the spirit burned, and left a scorched smouldering ring.

'Pankot Rifles Depot *ki taraf jao*,' Sarah told the tonga-wallah who snapped his whip and clicked his tongue. They bowled down the lane from St John's, from the eminence towards the valley. As they went past the nursing home which was set far back from the road in wooded grounds Sarah leant her head against the canopy and imagined herself Susan, leaning her head against the bars that separated her from the window pane. She closed her eyes as perhaps Susan was doing, even now, and after a while felt the quietness of her own happiness and grace welling up inside her; and smiled, ignoring the rain that seemed to be falling on her face.

The Towers
of Silence

To
Penny
With all my Love

Part One

THE UNKNOWN INDIAN

I

In September 1939, when the war had just begun, Miss Batchelor retired from her post as superintendent of the Protestant mission schools in the city of Ranpur.

Her elevation to superintendent had come towards the end of her career in the early part of 1938. At the time she knew it was a sop but tackled the job with her characteristic application to every trivial detail, which meant that her successor, a Miss Jolley, would have her work cut out untangling some of the confusion Miss Batchelor usually managed to leave behind, like clues to the direction taken by the cheery and indefatigable leader of a paper chase whose ultimate destination was not clear to anybody, including herself.

Miss Batchelor, christened Barbara (Barbie for short), knew she had many shortcomings, most of which were due to two besetting sins. She seldom stopped talking and was inclined to act without thinking. She had often prayed to be blessed with a more cautious and tranquil nature but had always done so by falling enthusiastically on her knees and speaking to God aloud, which may have accounted for the fact that these prayers were never answered. Her attempts to reform without intercession were also unsuccessful. When she held her tongue people asked rather anxiously about her health – not without cause because the stress of keeping quiet gave her headaches; and the headaches were not helped by the worry of work piling up if she put any of it off to think about it first. So in the end she was content to bear the burden of her own nature in the belief that God had known best what was right for her. Secretly she was rather proud of her voice. It carried.

Barbie was a believer in the good will and good sense of established authority. If the mission had told her that her furrow was not ploughed, that she was good for a few years yet, she would have squared her shoulders, spat on her palms and pressed on, grateful to be made use of. But the mission said no such thing and she outwardly accepted the situation with her usual bustling equanimity. Inwardly she accepted it with mingled relief and apprehension.

'I shall be glad to slow down,' she said. People smiled. They could not imagine Barbie except at top speed. In putting her out to grass the mission, which always looked after its own, would have provided her with temporary accommodation in Ranpur and helped to establish her eventually in Darjeeling or Naini Tal where they had twilight bungalows. They would have given her an assisted passage home, but the war made that difficult and in any case Barbie said she didn't want it. She had not been in England for thirty years.

It seemed that Barbie wanted nothing except her pension and her freedom to go where and do what she liked. She let it be known that she had plans. She said she did not intend to be idle in retirement. She would find a pied-à-terre and devote herself to some kind of voluntary work. She had saved. She was perfectly content, perfectly happy. She would always be available should the mission need her help or advice. They had only to ask and she would come, at the double.

The facts were that she had no plans and no clear idea where to go or what to do. She would have liked to be of use to someone or something but could not visualize whom or what. On the whole it did not matter much so long as being useful left her with a certain amount of time to devote to a personal problem.

Barbie had what her mother would have called a secret sorrow. She had been a fairly competent teacher, especially of small children, because they brought out her maternal instincts, and she had often been rewarded by proofs of her capacity to earn affection and esteem from pupils and their parents. But to Barbie the teaching of reading, writing and arithmetic had never been as important as the teaching of Christianity.

For almost as long as she could remember she had believed in God, in Christ the Redeemer and in the existence of Heaven. They were very real to her. The fate of unbelievers was equally real, particularly the fate of those who were unbelievers through no fault of their own. This was why when both her parents were dead she had given up her job at a Church school in South London, joined the mission and come to India.

To bring even one Hindu or Muslim child to God struck her as a very satisfactory thing to do and she imagined that in the mission it would be open to her to do this for scores, possibly hundreds. Once in India she was disappointed to find that all the emphasis was upon the mission's educational function, that the mission gates were ajar to let Indian children in to learn things that would be useful to them but not wide open in a way that encouraged teachers to go out and bring the children in, as into a fold.

Initially disturbed by this secular attitude and by the discipline imposed inside the mission to discourage its members from excessive displays of zeal, she soon accepted them as sensible measures taken by those who knew best and who were anxious to preserve and hold what had been won rather than risk losing it all in trying too hard to gain more. She discovered that the missions were not popular with the civil administration or with the military authorities and had not been since the mutiny of 1857, which people said started because the Indian sepoys believed they were to be forcibly converted, having first been polluted by the introduction of cartridges greased with pig fat. Moreover, the authorities, both civil and military, seemed to take considerable trouble to enable Hindus to go on being Hindus and Muslims to be Muslims by giving them every opportunity to practise their rites and hold their festivals and by giving official recognition to the communal differences between them.

'Well, one step at a time,' Barbie told herself and settled to the business of teaching Eurasian children whose parents were Christians already, the children of converts and the children of Hindu and Muslim parents who were anxious for their sons, and occasionally daughters, to get a good grounding in the English they had to know if they wanted to get on, but very few of whom would ever be baptized.

Over the years she became inured to this system. The Bishop Barnard schools, named after one of the founders of the mission to which she belonged, had expanded considerably between the wars and in the principal cities become distinguished and proud of an academic reputation that attracted Indian girls and boys whose parents were advanced enough to want to educate them to the standard required for entrance to government colleges and Indian universities. As reputation and supply of pupils increased so did the demand for teachers with the right kind of qualifications. Year by year the religious basis of instruction was chipped away and women like Barbie kept in junior posts or elevated to administrative positions in which neither their missionary ambitions (what was left of them) nor their lack of academic stature could do much harm. With the appointment of Barbie's successor, Miss Jolley, even that preserve of the old guard was infiltrated. Miss Jolley was young, she had letters after her name and her file disclosed her religion as non-conformist, not C of E which in Barbie's day had been a primary requirement.

But it was not in all this that Barbie's secret sorrow lay. It lay in the fact that in recent years she had felt her faith loosening its grip. She believed in God as firmly as ever but she no longer felt that He believed in her or listened to her. She felt cut off from Him as she would if she had spent her life doing something of which He disapproved. This puzzled her because she didn't think He could disapprove. He could be better pleased, but that was another matter entirely and one for which neither she nor the mission was exclusively responsible. One did what one could and it should not be necessary to be a saint or a martyr to feel His presence. She no longer felt it. She could not help blaming the mission just a bit for this and she thought there might be a chance of regaining the joyful sense of contact now that she was retiring. She would not hurt anyone by explaining this but her cheerful expression was not entirely due to her habit of keeping one; although that came into it too because she secretly feared a lonely old age.

*

767

The address in the advertisement for a single woman to share accommodation with another, which appeared in the *Ranpur Gazette* a week or two before Barbie's retirement, sounded attractive: Mrs Mabel Layton, Rose Cottage, Club Road, Pankot.

She had never been to Pankot. It was the hill station where most official Ranpur people spent the hot weather and to which a few of them eventually retired. Since Ranpur was the place in which she chanced to be when her career petered out the idea of retiring to Pankot herself appealed to her. She wrote to Mrs Layton at once, giving an account of herself, mentioning the sum she could afford and suggesting that if she took the short holiday she had been thinking of spending in Darjeeling – seeing old missionary acquaintances – in Pankot instead, they could meet and come to a decision.

She assumed that Mrs Layton was a widow and that the advertisement implied means as small as her own. The name of the house, seeming diminutive, rather bore that out. Barbie had long since lost the immediately tell-tale signs of a poverty-stricken lower-middle-class English background and could stand her own in any company as what, in her earlier life, had been called a gentlewoman, but she had remained a little fearful of women born in superior walks of life, especially if they had money to support their position.

Mabel Layton's reply was encouragingly simple and friendly.

'Dear Miss Batcherlor, I have had a number of answers to my advertisement but I imagine from your own that we could get on well together. Unless you have changed your mind, in which case please write and tell me, I shall do nothing further about the accommodation available until you have had a chance to see it. If you come to Pankot on holiday perhaps you would like to spend it here at Rose Cottage. Smith's Hotel – a tiny branch of the one you will know of in Ranpur – is rather crowded nowadays and a bit expensive. With regard to a permanent arrangement, should we decide to make one, the sum you say you can afford is ten rupees a month higher than I intended asking, and should expect. Rose Cottage is a very old bungalow, one of the oldest in Pankot. Its main attraction is the garden. It is a little inconveniently situated but after your long and arduous work in the missions I fancy you don't especially wish to be at the hub of things. If you decide to come up just write or telegraph the time of your arrival and I will get my old servant Aziz to meet you and help you with your bags. As you probably know the train leaves Ranpur daily at midnight and reaches Pankot about 8 a.m.'

The kindly tone of this letter offset Barbie's first impression on receiving it. The envelope was lined and the writing paper thick. The address and telephone number were printed; in fact engraved. A smoothing motion of Barbie's fingers confirmed this. She felt alarmed, uncertain that she could live up to such things. But having read the letter she felt only pleasure and gratitude. Out of a number of applicants Mabel Layton had selected her and was actually prepared to keep the vacancy open until she could go to Pankot and see Rose Cottage for herself. This meant, Barbie thought, that although Mabel Layton needed someone to help with expenses the need was not so desperate that she could not afford to wait for the right person. She seemed to be a woman who liked to keep up standards, in important matters such as her choice of friends and in minor ones like the kind of paper used when writing to them.

Barbie sat down to reply.

'Dear Mrs Layton, Thank you for your letter and for your very kind suggestion that I should spend my holiday at Rose Cottage. I accept most gratefully. I hand over officially to my successor here on September 30th. She is very capable and my duties are already negligible. Therefore I can plan to leave without delay. I should be able to come up on the train that reaches Pankot on the morning of October 2nd. As soon as I have made the booking I shall write to you again or telegraph. Meanwhile I can begin my packing at once. I hope you will not mind if I bring with me rather more luggage than might be expected of someone coming to Pankot on a vacation. Conditions here do not easily permit of other people's stuff lying around for long, so I am anxious to leave behind as little as I can even if it means bringing things with me which I do not actually need for a holiday and should have to bring back with me if we do not come to a permanent arrangement. Fortunately I have always travelled fairly light. A long experience of postings from one station to another has taught . . .'

At this point Barbie realized she had set off on a tack that could well have the effect of boring poor Mrs Layton to tears.

But her luggage was a priority. She had wanted to make this clear. The importance of luggage was often overlooked. Barbie had never overlooked it but since hearing officially from mission headquarters in Calcutta that her retirement 'need not be postponed' her luggage had been perhaps overmuch on her mind. At the end of her career the tide of affairs which had involved her was on the ebb, leaving her revealed. And what was revealed did not amount to a great deal, which meant that every bit counted. There was, to begin with, herself, but apart from herself there was only her luggage and of that there was little enough although rather a lot in comparison: bedroll, camp-equipment, clothes, linen, many unread books, papers, photograph albums, letters, mementoes of travel, presents from past pupils, a framed and very special picture, a few ornaments and one piece of furniture. This latter was a writing-table and was the only item that still remained from the stuff she had originally brought out from England. It had legs that folded in and so was portable. Someone once told her that it was late Georgian or early Victorian and had probably belonged to a general for use in writing orders and campaign dispatches under canvas. She was very fond of it, kept it polished and the tooled leather surface stuck down at the corner where it tended to come away. It rather annoyed her to see Miss Jolley using it as if it were mission property and not Barbie's private possession; but so far she had not felt quite up to warning her that when she went the table went with her.

Mrs Layton could not possibly be interested in such things but it was important to Barbie to establish their existence as inseparable from her own and therefore to be taken into account in any plan to welcome her in Pankot. The luggage by itself, with the exception of the table, was merely luggage she knew, but without it she did not seem to have a shadow.

However, commonsense prevailed. She crumpled the letter, began again, determined to put herself into the recipient's place as she had been taught by her earliest mission instructor in the field, and record no more than was necessary to convey the prosaic details of her acceptance of Mabel Layton's invitation and of her intended time of arrival.

This accomplished she sealed the letter and called Thomas Aquinas. Thomas Aquinas was not her personal servant. He went with the superintendent's bungalow. He tip-toed everywhere but banged doors so loudly that sometimes you jumped out of your skin. He also suffered from chronic catarrh and sniffed perpetually. He was called Thomas Aquinas because the Catholics had got him first. She gave him the letter and told him to post it at the Elphinstone Fountain post office and not in the collection box on the Koti Bazaar road which she thought untrustworthy. She did not want the letter delayed. She hoped, as she watched Thomas take it, that she had struck the right note in it.

'Always remember,' she had been told, 'that a letter never smiles. You may smile as you write it but the recipient will see nothing but the words.'

The time was 1914, the man Mr Cleghorn, the place Muzzafirabad. Mr Cleghorn was handing her back the draft of her request to mission headquarters for a special discount on another half-dozen *First Steps in Bible Reading*, a limp-bound book illustrated by line drawings which the children earned marks for colouring – good marks for delicate tints, poorer marks for bold ones. A little Hindu girl once gave Jesus a bright blue complexion because that was the colour of Krishna's face in the picture her parents had at home.

Barbie sighed, got up from the writing-table, opened the almirah and got out a suitcase. At Muzzafirabad she had succeeded a younger, brilliant, indeed heroic woman, and was conscious of her shortcomings even then. Among them was the tendency to make a ruling without first thinking out its consequences. After the Krishna episode she had taken away the blue crayons. And then the children had no way of colouring the sky.

II

When she arrived in Pankot at twelve minutes past 8 a.m. on October 2nd, Mrs Layton's old servant Aziz was waiting at the station looking from one alighting European woman and another to the snapshot she had sent with her second letter as insurance against not being recognized immediately and being left until only she and some strange old man occupied the platform and there could be little doubt that each was waiting for the other. She had wished to appear efficient and thoughtful. She had also always had a horror of being stranded. She had just managed to restrain herself from sending two different snapshots by separate posts, realizing in time that these might both irritate Mrs Layton and confuse the servant.

'Perhaps he would like to keep it,' she said when Mrs Layton offered the snapshot back, complimenting her on the foresight which had eased Aziz of some of the burden of his responsibility. 'He was so good with the bags and so helpful about the trunk.'

The trunk, a metal one, was full of relics of her work in the mission schools. It had been her intention to leave it and the writing-table in Ranpur and to send for them later, if she were staying in Pankot. Thomas Aquinas had misunderstood and had the trunk loaded on to the van which preceded Barbie to the station. When she got there the van had gone and trunk, suitcases and cardboard boxes were already crammed into the coupé which Thomas Aquinas stood guard over. She was less worried about arriving in Pankot with the trunk than about leaving the writing-table behind now unaccompanied. There and then she wrote a note to Miss Jolley telling her what had happened and confirming that she would send for the writing-table at the first opportunity. She gave the note to Thomas, with a further five rupees to add to the fifty she had already given him as parting baksheesh.

Mrs Layton's servant, Aziz, had two tongas waiting in the concourse of Pankot station. Seeing the trunk he declared it too heavy for a tonga, took charge of it and left it in the ticket office for delivery by some mysterious agency he assured her he could command. He loaded one tonga with Barbie and her small hand baggage and the other with her suitcase, bedroll, cardboard boxes of odds and ends, and himself. He sat in the passenger seat gripping on to this paraphernalia and indicated that his tonga would lead the way.

On the old two-wheeled horse tongas you rode with your back to horse and driver and watched the ground unravel beneath the footboard, back towards the place you had come from. Driving like this from the station, Barbie had an impression mainly of the rock face which brought the railway to a halt, then of a narrow metalled road with broad strips of kuttcha on either side, steep banks of rocky earth and overhanging trees. The road curved uphill, this way, that way. There was nothing much to see but after the plains the air at this altitude struck her as sweet and welcoming. In a while she felt the strain put on horse and tonga slacken, as if a crest had been reached. The tonga stopped. Twisting round to discover the reason she found the other tonga also halted and Aziz getting down.

'Memsahib,' he called, rather fiercely. 'Pankot.'

He spread one arm towards the panorama revealed on this side of the miniature mountain-pass. She got down to see it better and stood for quite a minute before saying aloud, 'Praise God!'

Down in Ranpur after the rains, in places where there were grass and trees, the green nature of these things re-asserted itself. Through so much of the year they showed dusty, parched and brown. But in the plains, after the wet, there was never any green like this. Here, all looked like rich and private pasture. Flocks of blackfaced sheep and long-haired goats, herded by sturdy skull-capped peasants, tinkled down a slope, making for the road down which the tongas would also go: a long straight road that led directly into the valley formed by three hills – on the crest of one of which Barbie was standing. The valley itself was under a thin blanket of morning mist. At its centre was a township: the bazaar, a triangular pattern of wooden buildings whose upper storeys, decorated in Indian hill-style with verandahs and ornamental roofs, were clearly visible above the vapour. Beyond the bazaar one hill rose to the left and another much more steeply to the right. She could tell it was to the right that the British had chosen to build. She could see the roofs of many bungalows and buildings, a golf-course and the spire of a church. On this side of the town she could make out the random pattern of army installations.

The crests of the hills were forested. Apart from the receding clunk of the sheep and goat bells there was a holy silence.

'Rose Cottage kiddher hai?' she asked Aziz.

Again making the gesture with his fully extended right arm he answered in English, 'There. On the other side of the big hill.'

She looked in that direction and saw how beyond the hill more distant ranges marched towards a mountainous horizon. Was that snow or sunlight on the farthest peak? She sighed, content to have seen such a vision of beauty even if it was not to be her luck to live out her days in constant sight of it.

Looking away from the panorama he had presented, as if it were in his gift, she found him watching her. She nodded her thanks and made her way back to the tonga with a forthright manly stride.

It was on the long haul up the hill from the bazaar, going past the golf-course and the club, that she felt quite suddenly that she had passed Aziz's test. 'Memsahib, Pankot,' he had said. Like a command. And she had looked and said, Praise God. Even if Aziz hadn't heard, or had heard and hadn't understood, the praise on her face must have been unmistakable.

*

The snapshot she told Mrs Layton Aziz might like to keep (and which she discovered later he had put in a little silver frame) probably still exists, may even be on display along with other items of iconography on the rough walls of a hut in the Pankot hills, in the distant mountain village Aziz came from. If so one wonders what his descendants make of it, if with the snapshot they have inherited knowledge of the white woman of whom it is a likeness: Baba Bachlev, who had much *saman* (luggage) and much *batchit* (talk), a holy woman from the missions who came to stay at the house with the garden full of roses.

This snapshot (of which she had several copies because it was her favourite) showed the canal network of lines on her parchment skin. The

772

iron-grey hair, cropped almost as short as a man's but softened by attractive natural waves, gave an idea of sacrificial fortitude rather than of sexual ambivalence. Her costume, severely tailored, and made of hardwearing cloth, did not disguise the rounded shape of her unclaimed breast.

She wore dresses but favoured coats and skirts. With them she wore cream silk blouses or ones of plain white cotton. Always about her neck hung the thinnest of gold chains with a pendant cross, also gold. A present of eau-de-cologne on her birthday gave her twelve months of lasting pleasure as did Christmas gifts of fine lawn handkerchiefs on which to sprinkle it. With these annual endowments the voluptuous side of her nature was satisfied. Like everything else she owned, cologne and handkerchiefs were cherished, but the cologne, although eked out, was in daily use so that she was always pleasant to be near. She washed mightily and sang in her tub: not hymns, but old songs of the Music Hall era about love on a shoestring. Such songs had been her father's favourites.

'My father loved life,' she told Mabel Layton during the period accepted by both of them as probationary. 'I never heard him complain. But then there wasn't any reason to. I mean he only had himself to blame, poor man. He gambled and drank. Champagne tastes and beer income, according to my mother. People said he could have been a clever lawyer but he never qualified. He didn't have the education and could never have afforded to, but he worked for a firm of solicitors in High Holborn and they thought highly of him. Well, they must have done because they had so many little things to overlook. Not, heaven forbid, that he was ever dishonest. But he was erratic and a great spendthrift.'

She wanted to be sure that Mabel Layton knew the Batchelors had been very small lower-middle-class beer. In Rose Cottage there were photographs of Laytons, and of Mabel's first husband and his family (it turned out she had been married and widowed twice) and all of them looked distinguished and well off, very pukka, the kind of people who belonged to the ruling class in India: the *raj*. Mabel, it was true, had let herself go, but in the manner that only people of her upbringing seemed capable of doing without losing prestige and an air of authority.

Barbie's first view of her was of an elderly shapeless woman wearing muddy grey slacks, an orange cotton blouse whose sleeves and collar had been ripped out to afford more freedom and expose more to the sun the brown, freckled and wrinkled arms, neck and shoulders. An ancient straw hat with a frayed brim shaded her face. She had seemed unwillingly distracted from the job she was doing: grubbing out weeds from one of the rose beds, a task she performed without gloves, kneeling on the grass on an old rubber hot-water bottle stuffed (as Barbie discovered later) with discarded much-darned cotton stockings. She did not look up until Barbie, obeying Aziz's gesture of permission and invitation, approached to within a few feet of her and cast shadow on the busy work-roughened hands.

She was in the garden every day of the year, she said. The mali usually did only the heaviest work of digging and keeping the grass cut, and even then under Mrs Layton's supervision. In the wet season she would go gum-booted and sou'westered and macintoshed in search of a job that needed doing. The heavier downpours would drive her in to the verandahs, but these were vivid with shrubs and creepers: azaleas, bougainvillaea and wistaria – and flowers such as geranium and nasturtium. All needed constant attention.

Seeing the garden at Rose Cottage Barbie realized she had always longed for one. She was ashamed of her ignorance of the names and natures of plants.

Built in the old Anglo-Indian style, Rose Cottage was a large rectangular structure with cream stucco walls and colonnaded verandahs at front, back and sides. There were two main bedrooms and a third which was called the little spare. There were a dining-room and a living-room. Central to the rooms was a square entrance hall which had been panelled in the 'twenties by its former owner. On the panelling Mabel had hung a variety of brass and copper trays. On either side of the doorway into the sitting-room stood a rosewood table with a crystal bowl of flowers – usually roses, as on the day of Barbie's arrival. These could be cut from the bushes almost continually from February to November.

Barbie's bedroom was to the right of the hall and Mrs Layton's to the left. Both had windows on to the front verandah and french doors on to the verandahs at the sides. Barbie's room connected to the little spare through a shared bathroom. Mabel Layton had a bathroom of her own. Her bedroom connected to the dining-room which, like the living-room, had views on to the back verandah. Dining- and living-room also intercon-nected. In all but the cold weather these doors were left open to give extra air. Behind the dining-room lay the kitchen and storeroom. Here Aziz had a bed made up. The general servants' quarters were reached by a path from the kitchen but were screened from the garden by a hedge.

Mabel Layton said she hoped Barbie would not mind being looked after mainly by Aziz. She had never cared for personal maids and in recent years had done without one entirely. Aziz, she said, was as competent to look after a wardrobe as any woman. The mali's wife came into the house to collect soiled household and personal linen and could attend to Barbie if that was what she preferred. Barbie said she was used to being looked after by male servants and had every confidence in Aziz. It seemed that Aziz cooked too. After her first meal, lunch, she no longer wondered why Mrs Layton, who appeared far better off than Barbie had expected, depended so much on him. The food was simple but exquisitely prepared and served.

'So long as I have Aziz and a mali to do the rough work in the garden,' Mabel Layton said, 'I don't much care to be bothered about servants. I leave Aziz to hire and fire whom he will. That way we get along perfectly. And he's been with me since my second husband died, which makes it twenty-two years next month. I'm not sure how old he is but James took him on in Ranpur the month before he was ill and Aziz seemed quite elderly then.'

Barbie's holiday was originally agreed as one of three weeks' duration.

During the first few days there were quite a number of casual visitors and Barbie assumed that she was being submitted by Mabel Layton to the test of selected friends' approval.

She made a careful note of names and apprehended that they were in all probability names with which any woman who deserved to live at Rose Cottage should have been familiar. Mrs Paynton, Mrs Fosdick, Mrs Trehearne: these were the most formidable. Their husbands were probably all generals or colonels at least. Mabel Layton was herself what Anglo-Indian society called Army: Army by her first husband, Civil by her second and Army again by her second husband's son, her stepson, no less a person than the commanding officer of the 1st Pankot Rifles which Barbie had heard enough about to know was a very distinguished regiment indeed, particularly in the eyes of Pankot people. She was spared a meeting with Colonel Layton and his wife and the two daughters who had just returned from school in England, because they were all down in Ranpur. She was sure that the younger Mrs Layton would also be formidable, the daughters hard and self-assured.

In fact she was puzzled why a woman like Mabel Layton should advertise accommodation and go to the length of vetting such an unlikely candidate as a retired teacher from the missions. She decided she could cope with the situation best by just being herself. Mabel Layton had really little of the burra mem in her at all although obviously she was one. But with the other women who called in for coffee Barbie felt exposed to a curiosity that was not wholly friendly.

She admitted to having an indifferent head for bridge but no prejudice against gambling, in spite of the fact that her father lost more on the horses than he could afford from his wages as a solicitor's managing clerk which meant that her mother had had to earn money herself by taking in dress-making.

'We lived in Camberwell,' Barbie explained, 'and it was a great treat going with her to big houses in Forest Hill and Dulwich. I helped her with the pins. She had an absolute horror of putting them in her mouth because of a story she'd heard of someone swallowing one and dying in agony. So I used to hold the pin-cushion. I called it the porcupine. It was filled with sand and absolutely bristled and was really awfully heavy, but it was covered in splendid purple velvet with seed-pearl edging and I used to stand there like a little altar boy, holding it up as high and as long as I possibly could. I can tell you it was tough on the arms but worth it because I was positively enchanted, I mean by watching my mother turn a length of silk or satin into a dress fit for a queen. I only hated it when she was doing mourning because then we both had to wear black and the houses we visited always smelt of stale flowers. And of course we knew we'd have to wait ages to be paid. Weddings were the big things. We got all sorts of perks.'

After such expositions a little silence used to fall, like a minuscule drop of water from the roof of an underground cave into a pool a long way below, where it made more noise than the scale of the actual situation seemed to merit. And the situation was worsened by Mabel Layton remaining immobile and expressionless as though what she always appeared willing to listen to when she and Barbie were alone, even if slow or reluctant to comment on it, bored her when it was told in front of her friends. It was left to the visitors to respond, which they did in those little silences and in then recalling, as though suddenly reattuned to the realities of life, other obligations and appointments that took them away wearing airs of concentration. There was, after all, a war begun in Europe. At any moment the Empire might be at stake.

'Come on, Batchelor,' Barbie said on a morning she decided there could be no future for her in Pankot at Rose Cottage, 'chin up'. She went to her room because Mabel had gone back into the garden. She sat at the borrowed mahogany desk to write yet another letter on the beautiful engraved paper, supplies of which had been placed in a wooden rack for her convenience. There were as well supplies of the matching purple-lined envelopes with stamps fixed at the inland rate, a mark of hospitality that amounted to graciousness but suggested a limitation of it, there having been but twelve; a generous but perhaps significant calculation of four letters a week for three weeks being enough to meet the requirements of any reasonable visitor.

But there were now only four stamped envelopes left which meant she had used two weeks' supply in one. She was a prodigious letter writer. She believed in keeping up. She once estimated that she wrote upwards of a dozen for every one she received, but the proportion had since changed to her further disadvantage.

'I know,' she said, murmuring aloud, the morning having become unusually still, pregnant with the possibility of her immediate eviction, 'that my own addiction to pen and paper is a form of indulgence. It's also of course a form of praise, I mean praise for the fascination and diversity of life which if you notice it yourself is always nice to bring to someone else's attention. I have written eight letters which means that there are now eight people who know things they didn't know, for instance how beautiful Pankot is and that I have hopes of living here. They know that a Miss Jolley has taken over my job. They know that I am happy and comfortable and looking forward to taking things easy. They know about the ridiculous mistake made by Thomas Aquinas and about Aziz and how helpful he was, and that the trunk is still at the station. They do not know that I am slightly worried about the trunk and the table because it is as unfair to share one's fears as it is right to share one's hopes. I shall share my hopes now with someone else.'

But when she had a sheet of writing paper squared up on the blotter and her Waterman fountain pen poised (it was one that was filled through a rubber top on the ink bottle into which the pen was inserted and pumped with a motion whose faint indelicacy was a constant source of slight embarrassment to her) she was aware of being about to project her thoughts not to one of the many people to whom she was in the habit of writing but into that deep that darkness was once said to be upon.

And suddenly she felt what she had felt once or twice before in Ranpur, the presence of a curious emanation, of a sickness, a kind of nausea that was not hers but someone else's; and sat stock still as she might if there was something dangerous in the room whose attention it would be foolhardy to attract. On the earlier occasions she had attributed the emanation to some quality of atmosphere in the Ranpur bungalow and so it surprised her to encounter it again. She felt instinctively that if the sickness touched her she would faint. And then she might come to with Mabel Layton standing over her telling her that Aziz had found her unconscious clutching a piece of paper on which she had written, 'Dear . . .' and no more.

'And that of course would be the end,' she said aloud in a normal conversational tone so that the emanation could observe that she was not bothered by it. 'Mrs Layton would quite ignore my assurance that there was nothing wrong with *me* and that there was no need to send for a doctor. I'd be off out of here and popped into a hospital bed as quick as winking. But I'm not ill. There's illness in the room but it isn't *my* illness.'

She gripped the edges of the desk and hoped she wasn't due to become a visionary. 'At my age! I mean how awfully disagreeable, not to say inconvenient.' She gripped the edges so hard that her palms hurt. Cautiously she removed her hands and was relieved to find nothing scored in the flesh that bore any resemblance to the stigmata.

'Whatever it is or whoever you are who isn't feeling up to par,' she said, having lost her fear of the emanation, 'I'm awfully sorry but there's nothing I can do for you, so please go away. Preferably in search of the Lord.'

She waited and felt the room return to normal.

'I've seen it off,' she thought. And at once thought of the person she should write to. She recovered her fountain pen, inscribed the date, October 9th, 1939, and wrote 'Dear Edwina,' and then found herself stuck for words, a rare event but an effect that Edwina Crane had always had on her. Edwina was the woman Barbie succeeded at Muzzafirabad and to Barbie she remained the heroine of a quarter of a century ago when alone, with the children cowering behind her in the schoolroom, she stood valiantly in the open doorway, at the height of serious civil disturbances, facing a gang of crazed and angry Muslims who had come to burn the mission down, and told them to be off; which they were (so the story went) in a subdued and silly-looking bunch, whereupon Miss Crane, leaving the door open because it was very hot, returned to the dais and continued the lesson as if she had just said no to an undeserving case of begging; a lesson that no doubt centred upon the picture she was reputed to have put to such brilliant use as an aid to teaching the English language that Barbie had never dared attempt emulation but had introduced instead *First Steps in*

Bible Reading and taught from this, almost literally in the shadow of the picture which hung on the wall behind the dais.

This picture, of which she had a miniature copy among the relics in her trunk, a coloured engraving showing Queen Victoria receiving tribute from representatives of her Indian empire, had originally aroused in Barbie a faint dislike which she had prayed to be purged of because she guessed it was not the picture but Miss Crane for whom the dislike was felt, and at that time she had not even met the woman. Edwina had gone from Muzzafirabad before Barbie arrived to take her place. But spiritually she was very much still there, in the picture behind Barbie and in the minds of the little boys and girls who faced her, challenging her to do half as well for them. And Mr Cleghorn had a tendency to make comparisons between Barbie's methods and Miss Crane's.

Miss Crane, she was told, had been presented with a large gilt-framed replica of the picture as a memorial of her Muzzafirabad appointment and heroic stand, which even the civil and military authorities had applauded. When Barbie was posted away south scarcely a year after taking the appointment up she was given a miniature of the same picture, as if it would do her good to have a permanent reminder of her lesser merits. Possibly her expression when receiving it had stayed in Mr Cleghorn's mind and penetrated the mists of mildness in which he normally existed to the clearer brighter region where his deeper conscience lay, because he wrote to her in Madras: 'You had a difficult, perhaps impossible task. It was one Miss Crane envisaged for herself, which is why she asked to be sent elsewhere. She hated to be a heroine. She said the children had stopped giving her their attention, their eyes being on that doorway, anticipating the reappearance of the mob, for her to quell once more with that look, that flow of words. Perhaps I should have explained this to you. Your successor will have a comparatively easy task. The children have lost the sharpness of their adulation of Miss Crane in the process of comparing Miss Crane with Miss Batchelor. And so young Miss Smithers stands a chance of being compared with no one, but of being accepted for what she is. Life will be duller, but we can all get on with the work we are supposed to be doing.'

'I was the guinea-pig,' Barbie thought, with her pen still poised and the letter to Edwina still not advanced beyond the salutation. 'I suppose I resented it, but it was a revelation to know that Edwina had taken her work so seriously that she would not stay in Muzzafirabad. I suppose up until then I'd assumed that she grabbed promotion as her right and went off consciously trailing clouds of glory for me to step on at my peril. The truth was quite otherwise. When I met her at last her modesty was an inspiration to me. She hated being reminded. She has buried herself in her work since and has sought out the most difficult and unpopular, indeed dangerous posts. God is truly with her.'

She wrote: 'It seems ages since we were in touch,' and continued in the rather flat and mundane style that often seemed to impose itself, like a bridle on her thoughts, when writing to Edwina, just as when meeting her every couple of years or so at major mission conferences an uncharacteristic inarticulacy dammed the free flow of her speech. At their last meeting, in 1938, she could have sworn that momentarily Edwina had not recognized her and that when she did their shared recollection of Muzzafirabad was felt by Edwina to be a greater impediment than ever to conversation.

Now, before sealing the letter, she checked her address book and the last issue of the mission's quarterly magazine to make sure she had not overlooked a note about a new appointment. She had not; her address book was correct. She inscribed the envelope: Miss Edwina Crane, Superintendent's Bungalow, The Bishop Barnard Protestant Schools Mission, Mayapore.

Aziz announced lunch.

She went into the living-room prepared to find more guests, casual callers-in whose real purpose was to sum up and later advise Mabel Layton whether her prospective p.g. was up to snuff. But Mabel was alone, presiding over the tray – a decanter of sherry and two glasses. No one had come to lunch. This seemed especially significant as though a point of no return had been reached.

When the meal was over she and Mabel parted, ostensibly to sleep; and for a while Barbie tried. She stretched herself full-length on the bed with her arms at her sides and her eyes shut, counting the tufts of an imaginary dandelion clock which she blew at rhythmically, puffing out her lips in the manner of someone happily dozing. She often recommended it to friends as an association of ideas more effective than counting sheep; but this afternoon the dandelion clock she had conjured was a tough proposition. Not a tuft stirred. Try (she told it) try to be more co-operative; waft, waft, waft away, as I huff and I puff. She replaced the obstinate dandelion with the image of a yellow rose. She stopped blowing and took in slow methodical lungsful of air and scent and then sat up to guard against being overcome by something inexpressible which seemed to be connected with the whole of her life in India.

The house was soundless and the world outside the window was full of bones.

She left her room and went out to the back verandah.

'Oh, you're up too, Mrs Layton,' she said in her best elocutionary voice. 'I do admire your industry. And how worth while it is.'

She gazed at the potted shrubs on the balustrade and at the garden with its immaculately cut lawn in which oval and rectangular beds of roses were set to provide infinite pleasure to the eye, rest to the mind and balm to the soul. Beyond the lawn and the bordering shrubs where the garden ended the land fell away, and rose again several miles distant in pine-capped hills from which scented breezes always seemed to whisper. And more distant yet were the higher hills and the celestial range of mountain peaks.

She looked at Mabel Layton again but Mrs Layton was still working at a pot of cuttings. Barbie was upset by this unexpected and total disregard. Dejected, she sat on one of the three wicker chairs that were set round the verandah table, kept an eye open and a smile ready for the moment when Mrs Layton abandoned her work and came to join her. She examined her conscience but found no special cause for blame in her behaviour that morning. On the other hand it wasn't Mrs Layton's fault if she found her an unsuitable companion. In her oddly withdrawn way Mrs Layton had been meticulous about arrangements for her guest's comfort. But clearly in Mrs Layton's view theirs were not complementary temperaments. She had probably never had a paying-guest in her life and was bound to find it difficult to open her lovely home to a stranger. It must be companionship, not money, Mrs Layton needed and she probably already regretted putting the advertisement in the paper. She may since have heard of someone more likely to fit in – an old army friend for instance – but felt in honour bound to stand by her suggestion that Barbie should spend her holiday in Pankot. Perhaps – and Barbie felt a sympathetic twinge of understanding – Mrs Layton was steeling herself to say that there could be no permanent arrangement. Barbie was not sure whether to be glad or sorry. When she and Mrs Layton were alone they seemed to get on together well enough and she was already in love with the bungalow and garden, its views of the outside world, and ready to love it more, aware that in coming here she had been afforded a glimpse of something life had denied her but which she was not unfitted for, having prayed for it once in a different form: tranquillity of mind and nature. That, perhaps, she would never achieve but there was a sense of tranquillity here, of serenity, which someone like herself might enter and be touched by, lightly if not deeply.

And watching Mabel Layton busy with the plant pots she had the feeling that Mabel had not entered it yet herself, not fully, but was trying to and finding it difficult to do so alone. 'We could have helped each other,' Barbie thought, 'but I'm a disappointment to her. I'm simply not her kind of person. She must know I'm here on the verandah but is pretending not to and hardening her heart to tell me the room will not be vacant after all.'

She stared hard at Mrs Layton's back, attempting telepathic persuasion to make her turn round and come out with it so that they would both know where they stood and the uncertainty could be ended. She saw Mabel hesitate. The busy probing fingers were suddenly still. For a few seconds it seemed that the fingers and arms stiffened to support weight. Then one hand was removed from the plant pot and placed on her chest near the base of the throat, and for a while she seemed to look at the garden as if struck by an idea about it.

Barbie got to her feet, moved forward a bit, and thought that Mabel wasn't looking at the garden at all. Her eyes were open but on her face was an expression of the most profound resignation Barbie had ever seen.

'Mrs Layton? Are you all right?'

Barbie spoke distinctly and calmly but her object of letting Mrs Layton know that assistance was at hand if needed was not achieved. The other woman stayed in that position of remarkable stillness and slowly it was borne in on Barbie that whatever else was the matter with Mabel Layton that caused her to stand as if waiting for some kind of pain to go away, she was deaf. She hadn't heard Barbie come out and hadn't heard her speak.

'Mrs Layton?'

The other woman glanced round.

'Are you all right?' Barbie repeated, going nearer, involuntarily putting out her hand as if to take Mabel's arm.

'Oh – ' Mabel said; then removed her hand from her breast and touched Barbie's arm: a reversal of roles. 'Couldn't you sleep? I don't blame you. It's such a lovely afternoon.'

She hadn't heard or understood the question. But she hadn't been startled. The touch was scarcely more than a sketch of one and she was now busy again with the earth in the pot of cuttings, tamping it down.

'Actually,' she said, talking to Barbie via the plant pot, 'I seldom have forty winks after lunch so don't feel you have to if you find it difficult. I don't suppose you're used to it either.'

She moved on to the next pot and did something expert with a pruning knife. 'I ought to have done these this morning,' she said, 'but we were interrupted again. I suppose it's wrong of me to worry but there aren't usually quite so many visitors. I expect you've realized they mostly come to satisfy their curiosity. We get the Ranpur papers up here and everyone saw my advertisement. What worries me a bit is that after a while when they've got used to the idea there'll be days when nobody comes at all and then you'd think it rather dull I dare say. You're used to lots of people around you, I imagine, and I expect you enjoy it. I'm not and don't particularly. I'd say I've become something of a recluse but of course that's not possible in India, for *us*. Even when we're alone we're on show, aren't we, representing something? That's why I can't stop people turning up. They come to make sure I'm still here and that we're all representing it together. But I go out as little as possible, in company I mean. I wonder if you'll be happy here?'

'Yes, I see. I quite understand,' Barbie murmured.

'What?'

'I said I quite understand.'

Mabel had stopped potting and was staring at Barbie who under the weight of that resigned expression began to feel that she understood nothing. Her smile of assumed cheerfulness made her mouth as awkward to bear as something God had added to her in a fit of creative absent-mindedness.

'Oh, no,' Mabel said, 'I don't think you do. I meant that if you decide to stay I want you to feel that Rose Cottage is your home as well as mine and that you could have as many friends here as you care to make and go out as often as you wish, without bothering about me or whether I joined in or not. I know it's selfish of me to ask someone as gregarious as I believe you are to live here. On the other hand it would be disastrous to share the place with someone as selfish as myself and – ' she paused, made a gesture drawing attention to the garden, the bungalow, the whole complex at whose heart this notion of serenity lay, 'I think it could do with sharing, but only by someone who appreciates it. I got the feeling from your letter that you were the kind of person who would. I still think so, but I'd hate you to think it had to be appreciated in my way and no one else's. I'd hate you to feel cut off.'

She glanced at the garden. 'It often strikes me as something the gods once loved but forgot should die young and that there's only me left to love it. I'm not here forever and I'm not sure I love it enough.'

Barbie said, speaking loudly to make sure she was heard and understood, 'I'd love to stay, Mrs Layton. Actually I shall be glad to slow down and live a quieter life. It's what I hoped for. To have some time to myself.'

Mabel looked at her. She felt the look penetrate, right down to the core of her secret sorrow, and then withdraw, back into its own.

'I'm so glad,' Mabel said, returning her attention to the plant. 'Please ring the bell and ask Aziz to give us an early tea if you'd like it. I think I should. It won't be long before we find it chilly enough to have tea indoors and that always depresses me a bit. And you'd better remind him about your trunk. He's getting a bit forgetful, poor dear. And do send for anything else you've left behind in Ranpur.'

'My writing-table,' Barbie cried; but Mabel merely nodded. She probably hadn't heard. Barbie turned, pressed the bell on the board of switches, some of which lit the verandah and some the floodlights in the garden (these presently were to be robbed of their bulbs to conserve electricity as part of Pankot's war effort). Mabel continued to deal with the pots of cuttings and when Aziz came she left it to Barbie to tell him they would both like tea brought out now instead of at four o'clock. He gave her a sideways nod, accepting that it had become her place to give some of the orders.

'Oh, Lord,' she prayed that night, her knees punished through the thin cotton of her nightgown by the thick woven coarse rush mat at her bedside, 'thank You for Your many blessings and for bringing me to Rose Cottage. Help me to serve and, if it is Your will, bring light to the darkness that lies on the soul of Mabel Layton.'

She prayed for longer than usual, hoping for a revival of that lost sense of contact. But it did not revive. She could feel the prayers falling flat, little rejects from a devotional machine she had once worked to perfection. The prayers hardened in the upper air, once so warm, now so frosty, and tinkled down. But she pressed on, head bowed, in the hailstorm.

III

In a woman with a less well-authenticated Anglo-Indian background than Mabel Layton's what was accepted as eccentricity would probably have been seen as hostility to what Anglo-India stood for, but Mabel's background was impeccable, she criticized no one and seldom expressed any opinion let alone a hostile one. Her absorption in garden and bungalow, her habit of taking solitary walks, her refusal even of invitations it was generally considered obligatory to accept, her complete detachment from Pankot's public life, were attributed to the personal idiosyncrasy of someone who had lost two husbands in the cause of service to the empire, one by rifle fire on the Khyber, the other by amoebic infection; and having thus distinguished herself retired from the field of duty to leave room for others. Her withdrawal was accepted with feelings that lay somewhere between respect and regret; which meant that they were fixed at a point of faint dispproval, therefore seldom expressed, but when they were, an idea would somehow be conveyed of Mrs Layton's isolation having a meaningful connection with an earlier golden age which everyone knew had gone but over whose memory she stood guardian, stony-faced and uncompromising; a bleak point of reference, as it were a marker-buoy above a sunken ship full of treasure that could never be salvaged; a reminder and a warning to shipping still afloat in waters that got more treacherous every year.

This sense of danger, of the sea-level rising, swamping the plains, threatening the hills, this sense of imminent inundation, was one to which people were now not unaccustomed and although the outbreak of war in Europe had momentarily suggested the sudden erection of a rocky headland upon which to stand fast, the headland was far away, in England, and India was very close and all about. And as the war in Europe began to enter its disagreeable phases it looked as though the headland had been either a mirage or a last despairing lurch of all those things to which value had been attached and upon which the eye, looking west from Pankot, had been kept loyally fixed through all the years in which the encouraging sensation of being looked at loyally in return was steadily diminished until to the sense of living in expectation of inundation had been added the suspicion that this inundation would scarcely be remarked or, if it were, not regretted when it happened.

*

The slight disapproval which counterbalanced the respect in which old Mabel Layton was held could probably have been traced to the haunting belief that in spite of everything she was among those people who would not regret the flood. Her whole demeanour was, in fact, that of someone who already saw the waters all around her, had found her boat and did not want it rocked.

A few months after Miss Batchelor's arrival, in answer to the advertisement for a single woman to share, an interesting situation had arisen. In retrospect it looked as if Mabel Layton had anticipated it and for some unintelligible but perhaps typical reason taken steps to protect herself.

This situation was the one arising in regard to accommodation in Pankot for Mildred Layton, the wife of Mabel's step-son, Lt. Colonel John

Layton and his two grown-up daughters Sarah and Susan whom he brought up to the hill station at the beginning of the hot weather of 1940 and established in the only place now available: a rather poky grace and favour bungalow in the lines of the Pankot Rifles regimental depot, opposite the mess. The bungalow they had occupied for a few weeks in the late summer of 1939 before going down to Ranpur in September had since been appropriated by Area Headquarters as a chummery mess and Colonel Layton failed to persuade the accommodations officer to give it back.

Having settled his family in what comfort he could he returned to Ranpur where the battalion he commanded, the 1st Pankot Rifles, was under orders for abroad. The 1st Pankots sailed for the Middle East a few weeks later, and in Pankot Mildred Layton settled down as a grass-widow in the grace and favour bungalow with her daughters who had got back to India from school in England only in the July of the previous year.

Before 1939, the year of family reunion, the Laytons had not been on station for many years but they were Ranpur and Pankot people. The parents had been married in Pankot and both girls born there. It took no time at all for the Laytons' friends to fit them mentally into Rose Cottage and find that the arithmetic worked. Sarah and Susan could share the second large bedroom currently occupied by Miss Batchelor, Mabel could stay in the room she had and Mildred sleep in the little spare.

Although there were three bedrooms in the grace and favour bungalow down in the Pankot Rifles line, they were small and the whole place had an atmosphere of barracks: PWD furniture, a view at the front of the rear of the mess and at the back of a bare brick wall hiding the servants' quarters. The garden was bleak – weedy grass and no flowers – and one's peace indoors and out interrupted by parade-ground noises. A military wife and her daughters would be expected to pig in there without complaint if it was the best that could be done for them, but its discomforts and inconvenience (the wrong side of the bazaar and twenty minutes tonga ride to the club), the enchanting prettiness of young Susan around whom Pankot males were already gathering, and the quiet but obvious efficiency of the elder daughter, Sarah, hardened the conviction that Rose Cottage was their proper and rightful place.

Mildred Layton refused to be drawn on the subject but when a question was put to her in any one of several oblique ways whose meaning was simply: Did Mabel discuss her plan to take a paying-guest with Colonel Layton? she left little doubt that the answer was no, and that the first she and John knew about it was down in Ranpur when they saw the advertisement.

Nevertheless relations between Mildred and Mabel Layton seemed perfectly amiable. No abnormal strain was apparent to the inner circle of Pankot women who were in the habit of dropping in to make sure Mabel was still there and representing what had to be represented. Mildred and her two girls were frequent droppers-in at Rose Cottage themselves. In fact for the first few weeks after her arrival from Ranpur Mildred made free of

Rose Cottage as if it were a logical extension of her life, which it was, being only a few minutes' drive from the club; and her right, which it also was, because when Mabel died Colonel Layton would inherit the property along with what was believed to be a considerable amount of money.

The girls made free of it to a slightly lesser extent; Sarah more often than Susan who tended to be occupied appeasing as many as she could of the young subalterns who made demands on her time and company, swimming, riding and playing tennis. In the elder sister's case, visitors noted, making free was not quite the phrase to use. Sarah was less volatile than Susan, far less off-handedly possessive than her mother. She seemed very fond of the place, particularly of the garden, and much more communicative with Mabel (whom she and her sister called Aunt). She was also more patient with Miss Batchelor who chattered at her as she chattered at everybody but was given attentive replies to her comments and questions.

Sarah was a quiet girl. According to her mother she suffered badly with her periods, as badly as Mildred had suffered before having her. Mrs Paynton, Mrs Fosdick and Mrs Trehearne, the three women who could claim some intimacy with Rose Cottage's silent chatelaine, observed this well-mannered and presumably sometimes stoic behaviour of Sarah's with sympathy and approval. Colonel Layton's elder daughter was an unassuming and intelligent girl with a face a bit too bony to be called pretty, and obviously took her obligations seriously. Her quietness suggested to them that the perplexity of her English years was still upon her. She probably had some strange ideas because life at home was no longer what it had been, but there was backbone there. The other girl was as clear and uncomplicated as daylight by comparison. England had not touched her except to give her a necessary scraping to detach the barnacles gathered while becalmed in the sea of Anglo-Indian childhood; a ruinous experience if not corrected by schooling in England: all privilege and no responsibility. But here now was young Susan, sharp-keeled from home, clean and eager. It heartened one just to look at her. She seemed to know it, and that could be dangerous, but presently she would settle and the gravity of Anglo-Indian life would touch her pretty face soon enough.

The flush would disappear. The enchanting laugh would give way to the kind that reflected the gratitude felt for anything that still exercised one's sense of humour and kept it from atrophying. The years would play havoc with that rosy skin, tauten the mobile mouth, expose the sinewy structure of the neck that turned so attractively as she looked about her, endlessly responsive to the stimulus of surroundings which woke her adult perceptions as well as her childhood memories.

In the garden of Rose Cottage Susan's gaiety was especially flowerlike. Her bewitching quality was heightened for the other women by their sad awareness that her bloom must fade as their own had done. But not yet. And before then she would be plucked and carried off. She seldom came to the bungalow unaccompanied by young men. If she did she was attended by them later and quickly spirited away, alone or with Sarah who played the chaperone role of sensible elder sister.

With all this Mabel seemed perfectly compliant, although it was apparent that she was not keen on Susan's black Labrador puppy, Panther, who threatened havoc among the rose beds but came at Susan's call and learned the hard way that the garden was not his. This disciplining of the dog (until in going into the garden, heel-tracking Susan's progress in an awkward splay-footed progress of his own, he looked conscious of special dispensation) was – apart from Sarah's more tentative approach to the act of being in Rose Cottage – the one acknowledgement Mildred and Susan publicly made of enjoying little more than a dispensation themselves. The use of a pet as a symbol of that acknowledgement was a guide to the dissatisfaction felt with the arrangements that kept them from living there. The mock-severe tone of Susan's and Mildred's voices and the impatience of the gestures Susan used to admonish the dog, instructing him to be quiet, lie down, come here, stop slobbering, keep his paws off the table, behave properly, were clearly not intended to correct him but to advertise and simultaneously relieve an exasperation with something other than the dog's exuberance.

While Mabel raised no objection to this invasion of her home, allowed it to develop unhindered until scarcely a day went by without a coming and going on the front verandah, a settling in chairs on the back, a persistent tinkling of the telephone, she did not become involved; so it emphasized her detachment, even strengthened it, enlarged its scope. There was now more for her to be detached from. Caught up in the midst of these unusual activities she assumed a protective colouring and merged into the backgrounds of normality which the activities created.

If it was Mildred's intention to force the issue, this capacity Mabel had for creating an illusion of not being in possession of anything anyone could want to take from her or force her to share was an effective deterrent; far more effective than Miss Batchelor's physical presence.

Demonstrably Miss Batchelor had what presumably Mildred desired, but to judge from her reactions she was increasingly self-conscious of the fact, daily more embarrassingly aware of enjoying what she had comparatively no right to, and obviously torn between the conflicting beliefs that she should either make herself pleasant, or scarce.

Whichever course the poor woman adopted the effect on Mildred was the same. Outwardly her attitude towards the missionary was one of unchanging indifference and Miss Batchelor could not disguise from visitors that she was frightened of her. Her inconsequential conversation began to be accompanied by nervous gestures: hand to throat, hand rubbing hand, hand clutching elbow. She jumped up and down fetching things, providing comforts, answering the telephone. Such energy hinted at an overloading even of her remarkable power-house. At any moment a fissure might appear in her structural organization and she would then collapse in fragments and a little cloud of dust; from the sight of which phenomenon Mildred Layton would surely turn, as if this sort of thing were an everyday occurrence and only vaguely to be regretted in the brief instant it would take for her attention to be given to some other evidence of the oddity of Anglo-Indian life.

In company Mabel made no effort to protect Miss Batchelor from Mildred's presence. It became doubtful that the missionary woman could survive and it was not at all clear whether Mabel cared one way or the other. It was just possible that the reappearance of her stepson's wife and her two grand step-children, their proximity, their needs, their standing, would remind her of her own duty to the station.

For there was – let there be no doubt of it – a distinction, a virtue attaching to Mildred Layton which set her apart and gave her a weight quite independent of her actual rank. In that, she was not above Nicky Paynton whose husband commanded a battalion of the Ranpurs, or above Clara Fosdick whose late husband had been a civil surgeon and whose sister was married to a judge of the High Court in Ranpur. She was junior in rank to Maisie Trehearne, the wife of the Colonel-Commandant of the Pankot Rifles depot and junior, naturally, to the wife of whatever officer occupied Flagstaff House.

The special virtue of Mildred Layton was not to be found in the place she enjoyed in the formal hierarchy nor even in the fact that her father, General Muir, had been general officer commanding in Ranpur in the 'twenties, and that she and her sisters had lived at Flagstaff House in Ranpur and Pankot as girls. The virtue was not to be found either in her being the wife of a man whose father (Mabel's second husband) had a distinguished career in the Civil, was still remembered in the Pankot hills and whose portrait hung in the chamber of Government House in Ranpur where the council sat and where before his death of amoebic infection in 1917 he had distinguished himself further.

Her position as John Layton's wife brought one closer to the secret of her virtue but it was a virtue that could have escaped them both, settled on other shoulders. All her history of eminent connection counted once the virtue became attached to her, but the virtue itself was the gift of a condition, the visible source of which was down there in the valley in that random pattern of army installations which Barbie had seen from the miniature mountain pass; its actual centre a low, ugly, rambling brick and timber building: the Pankot Rifles mess.

This building, like a temple, was only an arbitrary enclosure but it was a place in which the particular spirit of Pankot was symbolically concentrated. No more nor less than any other station whose history was inseparable from the history of a regiment, Pankot's pride and prejudice and lore were deeply rooted in its famous Rifles. The gentle roll of the hills, the tender green, the ethereal mists: these were deceptive. There was not a village as far as the eye could see and in the rugged terrain beyond that marched towards a mountainous horizon which was not steeped in Pankot's regimental tradition.

In the ordinary smoke of morning and evening fires the ghostly smoke of old campaigns was mingled. There was always an opacity. Clean and hard and clear as the sunshine struck it seemed to strike gun-metal. On a hot still day the snapped branch of a forest pine resounded like a sniper's shot. A sudden flurry of birds led the eye away from them to the dead suspect ground from which they had risen. There was an air of irrelevancy in husbandry.

The mind could never quite free itself from the hard condition imposed by the military connection. This condition could be mocked but it lay deeper than a joke about the honour of the regiment ever probed. From the curious quality of flatness of their eyes a stranger arriving in Pankot and warned to look out for it might have told which men among several in civilian clothes were Pankot Rifles officers. In uniform this guardedness of eye was even more noticeable; a visible sign of a man's awareness that his virtue instantaneously commanded a recognition which he found onerous to bear but proper to receive. It could be and was accorded by senior officers to juniors of the same regiment but in that case the recognition of virtue was mutual. The real subtlety of the virtue lay in the recognition it commanded in Pankot from any officer however senior of whatever regiment or arm. There was a scale in the condition of life in Pankot in which a Pankot Rifles subaltern, on station, pegged higher than a general who had been less ambitious in his choice of regiment.

And there was a scale within the scale, and here was the secret of Mildred Layton's virtue. The men's virtue fell upon their women and the scale within the scale gave precedence by battalion as well as by rank. A subaltern of the 1st Pankots was a fuller embodiment of virtue than a subaltern of the 4/5th whose cool weather station was in distant Mayapore. Ranging outward and upward through a host of permutations of regimental and non-regimental employment the logical peak of attainment was reached in the supreme active regimental command, the command of the 1st Battalion. An extra glow warmed the peak if the distinction was achieved by an officer whose parent battalion it was – as was the case with John Layton – but no Pankot Rifles officer would willingly accept an appointment however attractive if he had reason to suppose that the command of the 1st was an alternative within his grasp; even though to have held it once did not enable him to bear the special virtue subsequently. It passed like a crown, itself perpetual, the heads it adorned coming and going. Trehearne had held it, a 4/5th man, now red-tabbed and banded, a full colonel; in effect father of the regiment; but the crown was presently John Layton's on whose head it glinted in a middle eastern sun; and his wife Mildred, in the scale of this condition, had more virtue than Mrs Trehearne who took precedence over her in every other way.

Through the 1st Battalion of its Rifles Pankot especially judged itself, felt itself judged, gave hostages to its fortune, sent emissaries into the world. At this level an element of sentiment was allowable but it was a sentiment supported by the condition which only one thing could shake and weaken: the disclosure of a fault in the rock, disaffection, disloyalty. Everything else was forgivable: incompetence, failure, defeat, even cowardice which was a private affair, a personal and not a corporate failure.

So there was Mildred Layton, a still handsome woman whose face quite properly showed not a tremor of the concern she would feel for her husband away on active service in North Africa, and no change as she looked at and through her step-mother-in-law's talkative and intimidated companion in that expression of constantly and perfectly controlled dedication to her duty to withstand the countless irritations to which English women in India were naturally subjected.

If the men's eyes were flat the women's – to judge from Mildred's – were slightly hooded as though belonging to the weaker sex they were entitled to this extra protection; and the mouths, again to judge by hers, being less allowably firmed than a man's, were permitted a faint curve down at the corners which could be mistaken for displeasure, in the way that Mildred's languid posture when seated could be mistaken for *ennui* (closer observation of her as she was standing or walking suggested that she had probably achieved this economy of movement as a result of a long experience of the need a person in her position had to get through the day with the least trouble to herself).

But in the matter of Rose Cottage her distinction got her nowhere. The elder Mrs Layton remained impervious to it and something of that imperviousness seemed slowly to rub off on to Barbara Batchelor. It was imagined that the missionary must have asked Mabel outright whether she should go and had been asked to stay put and thereafter had girded her loins to the task of staying. The basis of her efforts to make herself pleasant changed, but too gradually for the day and circumstances of the substitution of security for insecurity to be determined.

Subtly she became endowed with some of the attributes of a co-hostess, a member of the family. She enlisted Aziz's aid in fetching and carrying, at first covertly and then openly because he had a habit of coming out and asking her what it was she had asked him to do for the guests. She assumed responsibility for the dog by making a friend of him, throwing his ball in an invisible but clearly demarcated zone within whose bounds he could do no damage, saw him fed and took him for walks when his mistress Susan abandoned him for more adventurous pursuits.

Her attitude to the girls became that of an aunt who knew her nieces had heard her discussed unfavourably but could not help showing her interest in them and some of her affection. Indeed she seemed to acquire something of the thick skin such a woman had to cultivate if her feelings were not to be constantly hurt by inattention to her questions, opinions, and fund of boring anecdotes.

And within a month or two the visits began to thin out as though the holidays were over and more serious affairs demanded attention. The poky grace and favour bungalow showed signs of being grudgingly settled in. It was (Mildred seemed to suggest) rather more convenient for Susan's followers, more convenient for herself whose duties were much bound up in the life of the regiment, for instance in helping Maisie Trehearne keep a matriarchal eye on the wartime crop of young men lucky enough to have got their emergency commissions into it. While suggesting this Mildred's expression did not change from the one which inspired fear in Miss Batchelor. It did not need to because it was an expression for all occasions, the expression of a person who could not allow herself to doubt that she was right, would always do what was right and therefore had nothing to explain even when not done right by, except to people who did not understand this and to such people an explanation was never owing.

But expression or not Mildred could not remove from people's minds the notion that she had suffered a defeat. The question was whether she was hurt by it. Later when a certain weakness began to reveal itself in that apparently indomitable armour it seemed likely that she had been hurt more deeply than she may have admitted even to herself.

There was something especially unpalatable about a family quarrel because it could undermine the foundations of a larger and essential solidarity. There was no known quarrel between Mabel and Mildred but family feeling had not been conspicuously shown. Blood had not proved thicker than water. 'Mabel's been like she is as long as I've known her,' Mildred once commented. 'According to John she was like that when he got back from the first war, quite different from the way he remembered her when he was a subaltern. He believes she never got over his father's death.'

This was the only remark she ever made that had any bearing on her stepmother-in-law's refusal to get rid of the Batchelor woman but it confirmed the impression that Mabel and Mildred had never hit it off and it was natural to wonder why, even if Mabel was not a person with whom it was easy to associate the idea of a close relationship.

It was odd that Mabel should squander upon a retired missionary what Mildred had a positive right to and would grace in a way that the Batchelor woman never could. And by depriving Mildred of this right she deprived her of another: trust. It was as if in Mabel's eyes Mildred could not be trusted; which was thought ridiculous at the time and just as ridiculous later even when the weakness began to show.

This weakness, so admirably and typically controlled, had to be put down to a particular cause, a blow courageously sustained – the news in 1941 that the 1st Pankots had been severely mauled in North Africa and Colonel Layton with the remnants of his command taken prisoner by the Italians (an especial wound to pride).

For a week or two after receiving the news Mildred Layton acted with a fortitude she never afterwards lost but which in this initial phase was found exemplary. None of her husband's fellow officers, killed or imprisoned, had wives living in Pankot but she wrote to all these women offering sympathy and any help that was needed. On horseback and accompanied by the depot adjutant, Kevin Coley, she visited the nearby villages to talk to the wives and widows of the 1st Battalion's VCOs, NCOs and sepoys. Any who came in from outlying districts for confirmation or interpretation of the news, for help and advice, assurances about pay allotments, and who expressed a wish to see her, she talked to in the lines, on the adjutant's verandah; and once or twice – receiving deputations – in the compound of the grace and favour bungalow.

'It's sad,' she said to her old acquaintance, the newly arrived occupant of Flagstaff House, Isobel Rankin, 'they think John will still be able to look after their men in prison-camp but of course the men will be separated from their officers and I have to tell these women what the position is. Then they ask me to write to the Italian general to make sure that John's allowed to visit them and I have to tell them it's highly unlikely he'll be allowed to but that if he is he'll need no reminder from me, and that seems to satisfy them.'

Thus Mildred conveyed to the new Area Commander and his wife, Dick and Isobel Rankin whose paths she and John had crossed in Lahore, New Delhi and Rawalpindi and with whom they were on Christian name terms, that it did not really satisfy her.

The station concurred. As if the disaster befallen the 1st Pankots weren't bad enough, in prison-camp the other ranks would be deprived of their inalienable right to the comradeship, the guidance and unstinted moral support of their officers and the officers of the privilege of giving them. It was a hazard of war but for a regiment like the Pankots situated in a valley from whose surrounding hills its soldiers were traditionally recruited it struck at the foundation of the trust between officers and men.

Was it the act of trying to reaffirm that trust which exhausted Mildred or reaction to the blow she had personally received? Or, in going among the villagers on horseback had she suddenly become conscious of acting out a charade which neither she nor the women she comforted believed in for a minute?

As often as not it is the sense of the unbearable comedy of life that lights those fires which can only be damped down by compulsive drinking. Whatever the cause in Mildred's case the idea of her fortitude as exemplary did not survive the discreet but unmistakable evidence that she was starting on the Carew's gin too early in the day and arriving for bridge, for commitees, for morning-coffee, for lunch, with that look and air of being less sensitive than anyone else to the cross-currents of feeling and opinion in the room she entered. Her natural languor, to which everyone was accustomed and which she had worn lightly, like a protective cloak, seemed a degree heavier and her gestures more studied as if they demanded a shade more effort than was usual. At first her expression remained stable, what it had always been, but presently, although still unchanging, it began to lose definition, as though the face which it controlled was gradually slackening.

By then Mildred Layton's drinking habit was too well established in people's minds for it to give rise to much comment; and it was indulged with such style that nothing about her was diminished by it. In a curious way it sharpened her distinction. In her, drink released none of the vulgar or embarrassing traits disguised by soberness in people of softer grain; it gave extra keenness to those edges in her personality that made her a woman no one in her right mind would want to cross. One approached her with the same discretion she displayed in her own behaviour but did so perhaps slightly more aware of the need.

No longer exemplary, aided by drink which it was known she could not afford, there were occasions when her fortitude was felt by those who knew her well to be a fortitude shown not just for her own benefit but for theirs as well, so that the drinking was for them too; a resistance to pressures they were too conscious of not to acknowledge as collective and likely to increase. In the guarded eyes, the faint upcurve of the downward curving mouth, there was the authority of the old order and an intelligence that could calculate odds accurately, interpret them as indications that the game that had never been a game was very likely up.

So Mildred drank; compulsively and systematically; two or more up on everyone when drinking in a fairly hard-drinking community officially began and more than that when a session ended. One became so used to it that really it became part of the manner which with the impeccable background and irreproachable behaviour had always promoted and still promoted the image of her utter reliability. Even the little matter of mounting bridge debts could be seen in a certain light as the exception that proved the rule of her soundness. Her forgetfulness was annoying and embarrassing but whichever way her luck was running, win or lose (it was mostly lose), one could not help feeling that she saw debts due only in the context of larger and more important issues; and then in speaking gently to Sarah (the one sure way of getting paid) one was bound to understand that in that grander context even so sacred a thing as a card debt was enclosed in an aura of irrelevance.

And after all it was not a question of honour alone but of money, and for money Mildred clearly had an upper-class contempt which meant that her attitude to it was one of complaint at not having enough but of this being no excuse for not spending it. Unpaid bills at local stores and overdue mail order accounts at the Army and Navy were not her personal fault. She had standards to maintain and two girls as well as herself to dress, especially Susan who had a perfectly proper streak of what her looks and figure excused – extravagance. With both girls now enlisted in the WAC(1), working as clerks at Area Headquarters with Carol and Christine Beames, the civil surgeon's daughters, spending much of the working week in uniform, the number of new dresses Susan needed was reduced to what Mildred described as less unmanageable proportions, but unlike Sarah, who tended to stay in uniform, Susan changed immediately she got home; which was quite early quite often. There was not a great deal for a girl to do at the daftar if she thought it not her job to look for work and stupid to look busy if she weren't; and in Susan's case working in Dick Rankin's office had doubled her number of escorts. It was her obligation to look fresh and pretty and Mildred's obligation to help her do so.

How often, people wondered, did old Mabel Layton come to the rescue? How many times were bills (which Sarah had helpfully taken it upon her shoulders to see settled before they became an embarrassment) paid with cheques supported at the bank by money Mildred had off her absent husband's step-mother? A half-colonel's pay did not support the style of life to which Mildred was accustomed and which she kept up rather better than anyone else. It was not expected to in peace time. It was ironic to think that so much of the *raj's* elegance which provoked the Indian temper had always been supported by private incomes. From the Viceroy down the difference between his pay and allowances and necessary expenses meant that a man was usually out of pocket administering or defending the empire. One was used to debt, to cutting down, to the sense of imminent shabbiness in approaching retirement. After a year or two of war the shabbiness was rather closer than that. It seemed to settle like a layer of dust, clouding certain issues, such as the reason for being in India at all. Anything that proved durable and resistant to the dust and retained the bright gleam of a stubbornly clear conviction was precious because it stood out, a challenge to dark and perhaps superior forces, and this meant that if you went down you would be pretty sure what it was you went down defending.

Mildred stood out. Almost disdainfully. The virtue that attached to her as Colonel Layton's wife was crystallized by the other virtues of her family connection with the station. One had (as Barbie had done) only to wander in the churchyard of St John's and see the names Layton and Muir on headstones to realize that in those lichened-over advertisements for souls there was an explanation of Mildred, even a reference to the habit she had acquired in the slightly drunken tilt which age and subsidence had given them but not yet given her.

Nor would they. She would not rest there, one felt, would not want to. Her languor was not that of someone superiorly regretting the passing of the golden age. The illumination of Mildred Layton made by the stones aslant in the hummocky grass was one of contrast; contrast in deductions and expectations from identical premises and identical investment. Mildred's enemy was history not an early death in exile, but neither end was the kind that could have been or could be assumed, and the evidence of cessation which a clear look into the future might reveal did not countermand her duty to the existing order of things if she continued to believe in it.

And there in the picture one might have had of her going to her not-so-secret hoard (the bottle in the almirah to save her the boredom of sending Mahmoud to the drinks cupboard, the flask in her handbag to guard against the tedium of finding herself held up in a dry corner at the wrong hour) the question of her belief was posed and perhaps only ambiguously answered;

but the picture is much the same as the one presented by Barbie on her knees in the hailstorm (the sole kind of tempest that the devotional machine now seemed capable of conjuring). If Mildred had been a religious woman she might have prayed for John, for the remnants of his battalion, for the wives and widows among whom she had graciously gone offering the solace no woman could give to others or herself. At the turn of the year (1941–1942) she could have prayed for the bodies and souls of those who faced, were to fall before or extricate themselves from the destructive tide of the extraordinary and beastly little Japanese: among them, quite unknown to her, her future son-in-law Teddie Bingham who in the early months of 1942 enters the page as it were in the margin, a dim figure limping at the head of a decimated company of the Muzzafirabad Guides across the grain of the hills of upper Burma towards India, temporary safety, Susan's arms, a moment of truth and fiery oblivion. Depressing as Teddie's contribution sounds one can be sure he would have had a generally cheerful idea about it.

But Mildred was not a praying woman; and the drink suggests that had she been she would have prayed like Barbie not for particular favours but for a general one; the favour of being disabused of a growing and irritating belief (which drink soothed) that she had been abandoned to cope alone with the problems of a way of life which was under attack from every quarter but in which she had no honourable course but to continue.

IV

In the old days both the military and civil authorities of the province had spent half the year in Ranpur and half in Pankot which meant that between April and October the hill station had enjoyed the formality of an official season, with the Governor and his wife at the summer residence and the general officer commanding and his wife at Flagstaff House.

The last full official season had been that of summer 1939. It ended on the 1st of October when the Governor went back down to Ranpur preceded or followed by his staff, clerks, files, lorry and train loads of baggage; one day before Barbie arrived by the opposite route with her own encumbrances.

A few weeks later like governors of other provinces in which the Congress Party had taken office after the elections of 1937 he was accepting the resignations of every member of the ministry, headed by Mr Mohammed Ali Kasim, a prominent Muslim of the Congress Party which many English people suspected of being the party of the Hindus in spite of its claim to represent the whole of India.

After accepting these resignations, unconstitutionally forced on the provincial ministers by a party whose leaders had no central duty to the limited Indian electorate and an apparent antipathy towards assisting the British to preserve democracy and show Hitler what was what, the

Governor assumed governor's control, as he was entitled to do under the safeguard clause in the Act of 1935 by which attempts had been made to go some way to meet the Indians' insistent demands for self-government; and thereafter ruled the province directly, in the old pre-reform style, from Government House in Ranpur.

In Pankot in 1940 there was half a season. Flagstaff House was open, indeed had never been shut because on the declaration of war the general officer commanding in Ranpur, then situated in Pankot for the summer, elected to stay put, but the Governor and his wife did not manage to come up until May, and in June they had to return suddenly to Ranpur. One of the effects of the Congress ministry's term of office from 1937 to 1939 had been to reduce the scale of the annual removal of the majority of the secretariat to the hills, and although on reassuming autocratic control the Governor would have liked to reinstate this traditional move in full he would have found it difficult to house more than a skeleton of his civil service because by now the army had infiltrated into the complex of buildings where the civil departments once enjoyed the cooler air for six months of the year.

Frustrated in his attempt to direct from Pankot a secretariat largely left behind down in Ranpur and denied his simple need to lead a peaceful life by new viceregal attempts to come to terms with unco-operative Indian leaders after the fall of France, the Governor, choleric and savage, stormed back to Ranpur en route for Simla and, as he put it, further fruitless talks with the Viceroy who would have further fruitless talks with bloody Gandhi and bloody Jinnah in a further fruitless pursuit of the bloody Pax Brittanica, when all that was needed to scare the Indians into toeing the line and getting on with the war was a regiment or two of British infantry and a Brigadier as spunky as old Brigadier-General Dyer who had mown down hundreds of bloody browns in Amritsar in 1919. No one cared to remind him that the Lt. Governor of the Punjab who had stood by Dyer both at the time and in the years of Dyer's subsequent disgrace had only this year been shot dead in London by an Indian in delayed retribution, in Caxton Hall of all places. It was felt in any case that the Governor did not need reminding. He was a man of the old school – actually a bit of an embarrassment – the kind who if he could not have peace preferred a row and might even welcome being shot at now or twenty years later. His lady followed him, as pale as he was scarlet, and as talkative as he was taciturn between outbursts of bad temper, leaving Pankot bereft of the two people who most graced its official public occasions.

In 1941 when the choleric Governor's term of office ended and he was succeeded by a new Governor, Sir George Malcolm, there was scarcely a season in Pankot at all (other than the tentative one provided by the energetic new GOC's wife, Isobel Rankin, at Flagstaff House). The Rankins made their presence felt, but in the right sort of way. Malcolm, it was said, was an example of the rather alarming kind of person whom the war was throwing up, people with an immense and exhausting capacity for work and an impatience with any tradition which, like the annual movement of an entire administration from Ranpur to Pankot and back again, put the slightest strain on an overworked executive.

'Sir George will settle down,' people said; and there were hopes of a full season in 1942; but at the turn of the year the war that had seemed so far off was suddenly on India's doorstep. Malaya went first, to the Japanese, then Singapore. Burma followed. With these stunning losses the hope of anything ever being quite the same again faded quietly away into the background. And as if things weren't bad enough with the enemy at the gate there was an increasingly troublesome enemy inside it: Indian leaders who screamed that defeat in Malaya and Burma was a forerunner to defeat in India, that the British had shown themselves incompetent to defend what it was their duty to defend but which wouldn't need defending at all if they weren't there, inciting the Japanese who had no quarrel with the Indians themselves.

The political situation sizzled dangerously from the March of 1942 throughout the summer and finally exploded in August with a violence that set people talking about a new mutiny.

Foreseeable as it had been to anyone with an ounce of common sense and regrettable as it was it was not actually unwelcome. It cleared the air. The policy of placating the Indians and getting on with the war at the same time had failed as it was bound to. Now the question of further Indian advances to self-government could be firmly shelved for the duration. It was felt to be a pity that it had not been shelved at the beginning when Indian politicians proved that there was hardly a man with statesman-like qualities among them.

After the absurd *débâcle* of 1939 when the Indian Congress Party threw away all the political advantages it had won, by resigning provincial responsibility on points of principle (failure of the Viceroy to consult it before declaring His Majesty's Indian empire at war with Germany, refusal to co-operate in a war whose aims it pretended to be in sympathy with but said should have included immediate freedom to Indians to do as they liked) the more troublesome firebrands (that man Subhas Chandra Bose for instance) were popped neatly into clink under the Defence of India rules, but it was felt that the Viceroy should have made a broader sweep.

The Viceroy in question was Linlithgow; described in Pankot as an odd chap, sound but tactless and as usual not quite the thing because he didn't know enough about the country. Viceroys seldom did and few had the panache of Curzon who had tried to make not knowing a virtue in itself. The Congress-wallahs had put one over on Linlithgow by adopting this policy of official approval of the war against Hitler but disapproval of the means by which they were to be allowed to co-operate in it; and only those who stood up in the market place and opened their mouths too wide found themselves silenced by imprisonment.

If the Congress-wallahs had had any political cunning as well as political stubbornness they would have stayed in office in the provinces as the few

Muslim League ministries had done, co-operated so far as was necessary in the war effort, expanded their political experience and power and, simultaneously, their grip on the administration, so that when the war was over their claim to speak and act for the majority of Indians and their right to advance steadily to self-government inside the commonwealth would have been difficult to refute.

But they had thrown their opportunity away and one began to wonder whether in doing so they hadn't set their cause back to a point where independence would seem as far away on a post-war horizon as it had been on a pre-war one. There were sensible men among them, the ex-chief minister in Ranpur, M. A. Kasim (known popularly as MAK) was an example, but they were all either under Gandhi's saintly spell or too weak-kneed to exorcize it, and the saintly spell of Mr Gandhi had finally been exposed for what it was: a cover for the political machinations of an ambitious but naïve Indian lawyer whose successes had gone to his head.

His demand now that the British should quit India, should leave her to 'God or to anarchy' sounded fine, courageous, desperate and inspired, but it meant that they should leave India to the Japanese who were already on the Chindwin but with whom Gandhi obviously expected to make a political bargain. Unless you were stupid you did not make bargains with the Japanese but war. Even the liberal American Jew, Roosevelt, had been forced to understand this and it was entirely to placate Roosevelt that Churchill (who knew a thing or two, including the fact that the Americans' only interest in India was that the sub-continent should remain a stable threat in the rear to Japanese ambitions in the Pacific) had sent out that Fabian old maid, Stafford Cripps, to do what Churchill knew couldn't be done: put pepper into Indian civilians and politicians by offering them what they'd been offered before, but which a pinko-red like Cripps, unused to office, would see as new, generous, advantageous, a Left-Wing invention. The farce of this particular confrontation between an English pinko-red and grasping Indian leaders had not been lost on the English community. Its total and inevitable failure had been a smack in the eye to Cripps who went home eating crow as well as his bloody vegetables. Given a chance to show that a modern British socialist could achieve what the old-fashioned Right had never achieved, unity among Indians and political co-operation between Indians and English, he had also been hoist with the responsibility of office; a responsibility which meant, quite simply, having to make things work.

And he couldn't of course make them work because Indian politicians always wanted more if offered anything. Not understanding this he returned to Whitehall with that smile like a brass plate on a coffin and a conviction that while someone had been unco-operative it was not clear who. Once he had gone the Quit India campaign gathered momentum; which was also funny because it made Cripps look as if he had invented it; and early in August the Congress Party officially adopted the resolution calling for the British to leave or take the consequences. For once the government in New Delhi seemed to have been prepared. Within a few hours prominent Congressmen all over the country were detained under the Defence of India rules in an operation of arrest that gathered them in from Gandhi all the way down through the scale to members of local sub-committees in the towns and cities. Even the moderate ex-chief minister Mohammed Ali Kasim was reported arrested.

The country held its breath and then with a fierceness not equalled in living memory the leaderless mobs rose and for three weeks the administration was virtually at a standstill.

V

From the Ranpur Gazette: August 15th, 1942

ENGLISH WOMEN ATTACKED

It has just been officially disclosed that on the afternoon and evening of August 9th two Englishwomen were victims of violent attacks in the Mayapore district of this province. In the first case which occurred in the rural area of Tanpur no arrests have yet been made. In the second which took place in the town of Mayapore six Hindu youths are being held. It is understood that a charge is likely to be made under section 375 Indian Penal Code. The prompt action of the Mayapore police in apprehending the suspects within an hour or two of this disgraceful attack will be applauded. The arresting party was under the personal command of the District Superintendent of Police.

In a statement issued to the press DSP said, 'It is not in the public interest to reveal the name of the girl at this time. She worked on a voluntary basis at the Mayapore General Hospital. Her family is one that distinguished itself in service to India. According to her statement she was attacked by six Indian males who stopped her on her way home at night from the place where she also did voluntary and charitable work for sick and dying people of the scheduled castes. She was dragged from her bicycle into the derelict site known as the Bibighar Gardens where she was criminally used.'

DSP confirmed that among the men arrested was one with whom she was acquainted in the course of her work at the poor people's dispensary.

The earlier incident in Tanpur took place in broad daylight. Miss Edwina Crane, Superintendent of the Protestant mission schools in Mayapore district, was attacked by a large mob who obstructed the passage of her motor-car en route from Dibrapur back to her headquarters in Mayapore. Accompanying her was the teacher in charge at the Dibrapur mission, Mr D. R. Chaudhuri. He had left the school to give his superintendent protection from gangs of badmashes rumoured to be roaming the country-side following news of the arrest of Mr Gandhi and other Congress Party leaders.

Mr J. Poulson, assistant commissioner in Mayapore, said he left Mayapore in a police truck at approximately 3.45 pm on August 9th to investigate reports that telephone lines had been cut between Dibrapur and Mayapore and that trouble-makers were gathering in rural areas. He stated: 'At Candgarh we found the local police locked in their own kotwali and having released them pressed on in pursuit of the mob who had terrorized them. It was raining. A few miles short of Tanpur we saw first a burnt-out motor-car and then a hundred yards beyond, Miss Crane, sitting on the roadside guarding the body of Mr Chaudhuri who had been clubbed to death. She was soaked to the skin. In attempting to save Mr Chaudhuri from the mob, which had apparently objected to an Indian driving with an Englishwoman, Miss Crane had been struck several times. When she recovered consciousness she found Chaudhuri dead and the mob gone.'

Miss Crane is presently in the General Hospital in Mayapore where her condition although improved still gives some cause for anxiety. Although Ranpur remains quiet, Dibrapur and Mayapore have been the scene of serious riots and in Dibrapur Congress flags have been run up on the court house and the magistrate's private residence. Troops are reported on the way to Dibrapur to deal with the situation and are also standing by in Mayapore in anticipation of a request for aid from the civil power. The senior military officer in Mayapore is Brigadier A. V. Reid, DSO, MC.

The rapidity with which the whole situation has deteriorated so soon after the Congress Committee's endorsement of Mr Gandhi's quit India resolution in Bombay on August 8th, suggests that plans had been laid well beforehand for these acts of insurrection. The scale on which civil disobedience has been offered in this and other provinces, the reports constantly being received of riots, wanton destruction, burning and looting, hardly support the opinion expressed in some quarters that these are 'spontaneous demonstrations of anger by the people at the unjust imprisonment of their leaders'.

The authorities showed foresight in arresting members of Congress within a few hours of the committee passing the resolution. It behoves us all to be equally on our guard. And it is to be hoped that those who are guilty of these vicious and outrageous attacks on two innocent English-women and the murder of the Indian school-teacher will quickly be brought to justice.

*

This confirmation of rumours there had been in Pankot of attacks on Englishwomen down in the plains produced a full house at the club-meeting. People arrived with their copies of the *Ranpur Gazette* opened and folded at the page on which the report appeared, on the off-chance that someone had not read it. 'I see you've all got your tickets,' one member said. But it was no laughing matter.

The purpose of the meeting, announced several days earlier, was to discuss arrangements to protect lives and property in the event of riots occurring in Pankot. So unlikely had this seemed that provision had been made for only half the number of people who came. The meeting was delayed for a quarter of an hour while more chairs were brought into the main lounge. Eventually it got under way with an address by Colonel Trehearne in his capacity as senior member of the cantonment board. His voice, although musical, lacked power. 'Can't hear!' someone at the back shouted. He was shushed. Older hands knew from experience that Trehearne's contribution to any public gathering bore the same relationship to what followed as an overture did to an opera. If you came in after he had sat down you'd missed nothing.

He was succeeded by two civil officers from district headquarters down in Nansera: Bill Craig, assistant to the deputy commissioner, who assured the meeting that the district was so far unaffected by the disturbances in the plains and expected to remain so; and Ian MacIntosh of the Indian police who confirmed Craig's report and opinion and added that three men from Ranpur, on whom the CID had kept an eye, had just been arrested for disturbing the peace by attempting to harangue the inhabitants of a nearby village. Mr MacIntosh added that he used the word 'attempting' advisedly because the villagers had simply laughed at the men and might have stoned them if a truck-load of constables had not intervened and taken them off to a place of safety: gaol.

The atmosphere in the club which had been rather tense at the start as a result of the reports in the *Ranpur Gazette* now reverted to near-normal. The groundswell of indignation, of determination to stand no nonsense, of fear, of sad annoyance that things should have come to this pass, was checked by the counter-pressure of communal good-humour; hilarity, almost.

At this point an Indian officer from General Rankin's staff, Major Chatab Singh, known affectionately as Chatty (which he was) got on his feet and explained in broad outline civil and military plans to keep control in Pankot and Nansera (which was ten miles down the road, on the way to Ranpur), should the unthinkable actually happen. There were to be collection points for residents who desired to seek refuge from riots and attacks on European property and installations; for example women living on their own, or with children, and women whose husbands were off-station or likely to be in the event of serious disturbances in the area. One such centre would be the club itself. Chatty said he appreciated that these would henceforth be known as funk-holes but hoped that would not put people off using them if the need arose.

He spoke with humour and precision. His handsome wife, who headed the small Indian section of military wives, made precise notes. People laughed at his jokes, which were not too clever. Had they been so the suspicion might have arisen that Chatty harboured bitter thoughts inside that neatly turbanned head.

After a short pause for question and answer Isobel Rankin got up and announced that after refreshments the heads of the various women's committees were to meet in the card room. These women were co-opted to form the special Pankot women's emergency committee. She said she hoped this would turn out to be both its inaugural and closing session. She referred to the notice in the *Ranpur Gazette* and to the rumours of such attacks which had been current in the last few days, grossly exaggerated in regard to the number of women said to have been hurt.

She did not (she said) wish to play down the seriousness of what had apparently happened in Mayapore but warned against the effects of what she called excessive reaction. Before she left the platform she asked whether Mrs Smalley was present and finding that she was (she could not have been in doubt) invited her to act as secretary to the emergency committee. Mrs Smalley was already secretary to three permanent committees.

'I'm sorry to throw another job at you but you're the obvious choice,' Mrs Rankin said.

'Oh, that's all right,' little Mrs Smalley said, sitting down and, small as she was, promptly disappearing. People smiled. Mrs Smalley would have been piqued if the general's lady had given the job to someone else. She was a glutton for work.

Most stations had their Smalleys; a number of stations had at some time or another had these Smalleys. Because they looked nondescript and unambitious they provoked no envy and hardly any suspicion. In Pankot, where they had been since the end of 1941, they arrived at parties harmoniously together and then put distance between them as if to distribute their humdrum selves in as many parts of the room as possible. Leaving, they did so arm-in-arm, giving an impression that by playing their separate parts in a communal endeavour something integral to their private lives and mutual affection had been maintained.

The Smalleys were slight bores but very useful people: Major Smalley with his expertise in routine A & Q matters at Area Headquarters and little Lucy Smalley with her knowledge of shorthand and patient way with paper: the perfect dogsbody for any committee. Socially they were thought dull but it was always just as well to have some obvious dullness around. The sight of Lucy and Tusker standing arm-in-arm in the porch when a cocktail party was over, looking into the night for the tonga that had once again failed to stay or return for them, brought out the Samaritan instinct in gayer and better-organized guests because this constant breaking-down of arrangements they made for their personal convenience seemed to emphasize the willing efficiency they showed in affairs that affected the community as a whole. The Smalleys always managed to get a lift home.

They lived in Smith's Hotel. They had a suite: a small dark living-room and a smaller darker bedroom. Tusker declared himself perfectly happy with this accommodation (he received a special pay allowance for living out) and while Lucy was often heard to say she wished they could find a little bungalow of their own where they could more easily entertain their friends to dinner, Pankot was happy with the arrangement too. Cocktail parties were one thing, dinners another. The experience of being sat next to either Smalley at an official function – he in the dress uniform he insisted on wearing in spite of the wartime dispensation from such formality and which was tight round the shoulders, and she in her crimson taffeta gown (familiar enough after a while for her to be seen as a struggling little point of patient modest reference in a restless and sometimes greedy world) had helped Pankot to form the sensible opinion that the Smalleys were ideally placed where they were. In fact it became almost disagreeable to imagine them outside the context of Smith's; they went well with the napery and the potted palms; and, residing in an hotel bedroom, they were interestingly endowed with the attributes of perpetual honeymooners even after ten years of childless marriage. In this light their arm-in-armness was not only agreeable to see but satisfactorily explained.

*

When Lucy Smalley took her place in the card room, notebook and pencil neatly balanced on her neatly arranged legs, she added the final touch to a picture of the female hierarchy to which it can be assumed she aspired – in her shy but persistent way and irrespective of which station she was on – to belong. Her timid glances were more penetrating than they seemed. Content to appear mediocre and dull she looked for opportunities to offer opinions that struck people as just clever enough to confirm them in their own opinion that while she was dull she was not too dull, and mediocre in the right sort of dutiful and helpful way.

Six card tables had been placed together so that the committee could do its work in comfort. Around them sat Isobel Rankin, Maisie Trehearne, Mildred Layton, Nicky Paynton, Clara Fosdick and Clarissa Peplow, the wife of the Reverend Arthur Peplow, incumbent of St John's and chaplain to the station. Lucy Smalley sat a foot away from one end facing Isobel Rankin who had her elbows on the table at the other. Apart from Isobel's choice of seat no special order of precedence had been observed. The omission was probably deliberate. An equality of a kind had been established.

The meeting was informal. Isobel had made a draft agenda and out of general chat she formulated every so often a minute for Lucy to record.

The quietest member was Maisie Trehearne. She was tall, slender and stately in the way that a woman given to private preoccupation can be if she has the figure for it. What Maisie Trehearne's preoccupations were no one knew. There may have been another explanation for the impression she gave of having more important things to think about than the matter under discussion.

There were people who said that her mind was as blank as her pale patrician face was comparatively and unfairly unlined; but she never fumbled if asked to comment on a view just given. She seldom smiled. But

802

she was seldom upset either. The only thing known about Maisie Trehearne's emotional life was that she had a fondness for animals and a horror of cruelty to them. But she expressed both the fondness and the horror in much the same tones as those in which she spoke on other subjects.

No one had ever uncovered in her the steel core which a military career in India normally required and which was presumably responsible for keeping her so upright even when sitting down. Perhaps the uprightness was due to an uncomfortable corset, but she looked too composed for that. Composure was Maisie Trehearne's main characteristic. Were it not for the war her husband would have been coming up for retirement but she conveyed neither pleasure nor disappointment at the postponement of – as in her case it curiously but suitably was – Cheltenham.

Of the other women only Clarissa Peplow had any kind of physical affinity with Maisie. Clarissa was also pale although she was plump with it. She was stately but in her case the stateliness was that of someone conscious of the dignity of Christ's church militant. Lucy Smalley excepted, Clarissa Peplow was the least important woman in the room; unimportant in temporal terms. Her clear-blue eyes proclaimed circumstances in which other terms prevailed.

Opposite her sat the widowed Clara Fosdick, whose sister was married to Mr Justice Spendlove of the High Court in Ranpur. Clara was big-boned and well-fleshed. She had a resonant contralto voice which enabled her to argue convincingly even when it was obvious that she had reached an opinion through a process of emotional reasoning, not logical deduction. She got on well with young men. She conformed in many ways to a young man's idea of the perfect mother. She struck them as affectionate, even-tempered, good-humoured, restful, tough when necessary but blessed with a considerable capacity for understanding and forgiveness in that part of her which at her age and with her build could properly be called a bosom. It came as no surprise to such young men to learn from her friend Nicky Paynton that Mrs Fosdick had lost her only child, a boy, at the age of five, when he died of typhoid in the Punjab.

Mrs Paynton, the most talkative woman at the table and with whom Clara Fosdick shared a bungalow, was wiry, tight-wound, energetic. Her husband Bunny Paynton, the commanding officer of the 1st Ranpurs, was on active service in the Arakan. She had two boys at school in Wiltshire whom she had not seen since her and Bunny's spell of home leave in 1938. She had seen little of her husband too. Only in the frequency with which she introduced the subject of the absent Bunny and the far-away children could one detect how seldom she was not thinking about them. But the references were all light-hearted, in keeping with the discipline the station expected such a woman to impose on herself. She was referring to Bunny now and to the report in the *Ranpur Gazette* which had named a Brigadier Reid as commander of the troops in Mayapore where the attacks on the two English women had taken place.

803

'I shan't tell Bunny Alec Reid's got a brigade. We never knew him well but always thought him a bit of a duffer. I thought he was still in Rawalpindi which was where we last saw him. You remember Alec and Meg Reid don't you, Mildred?'

'Vaguely.'

'Meg Reid was a bit of a wet blanket too. I can't think why they've given Alec a brigade. He's been behind a desk for years. If I write and tell Bunny Alec Reid's got a brigade he'll probably blow his top.'

'Shall we get back to the agenda?' Isobel Rankin said.

She tapped her sheet of paper with a pencil. One noticed her knuckles. They looked hard. Her finger-nails were bright red. No languor about Isobel Rankin. She allowed some gossip at a friendly meeting such as this but kept it checked and did not contribute to it. She got things moving in the direction she desired. The slightest gesture – an index-finger adjustment of her reading spectacles on the bridge of her nose – was dynamic.

Concentration of energy distinguished her from the other women at the table, even from Nicky Paynton whose vitality, potentially as great, seemed by comparison to lack purpose. But then Isobel Rankin could not afford to relax as her colleagues could. She bore the burden of command. It could have fallen on several of the other women – on Mildred, on Nicky, on Maisie – and they would have borne it just as capably. The question of which of them sat at the head of the table as the GOC's wife had been settled by their choice of husbands. With a long war and any luck Bunny Paynton could end up not merely with a brigade but with a division, and Mildred's husband would probably have had a brigade by now if his wartime promotional expections had not been brought to a grinding halt in North Africa.

But these were military roles. Dick Rankin would never get an active command. He was a military administrator and young and well-connected enough to anticipate capping his career with military appointments at government level.

An air of power more far-reaching than that of the Army alone emanated from Isobel. She was preparing for the world where things were arranged and matters of consequence decided. A certain secretiveness, dressed as discretion, already hinted at a familiarity with what went on behind the scenes.

Outside the inner-circle of her friends she was of course much misunderstood. Those who thought themselves not as well-used by her as they deserved interpreted her flashes of wit and natural hardness of tone as evidence of malice and her impatience in argument as a sign of mental inflexibility. She was neither a stupid nor a malicious person and was in fact quick to detect stupidity and malice in others. And she was far from being the hidebound stickler for rules which she may have appeared in the eyes of people who, puzzled by the brusque manner she adopted towards the time-wasters, the ignorant and the prejudiced, decided that they had erred socially.

But today, Clarissa and Lucy apart, she was among friends and had she after adjusting her spectacles announced her personal creed instead of the next subject – the special arrangements for Indian mothers and children who came into defended areas for protection from riots, rape and arson – she would have found a measure of agreement, because in her there resided in a highly developed form the animus of declining but still responsible imperialism.

She had an astringent affection for the people and the country in which she had spent so many years of her life, and no personal prejudice against Indians as Indians. As with members of her own race she allowed her instincts to guide her when it came to separating those Indians with whom she was happy to associate from those with whom she officially had to deal or whom she could ignore. She counted quite a number of Indian men and women among her friends but these, like her English friends, were people she felt could be relied upon to preserve for India's sake everything the English and the Indians had done together which could be reckoned of lasting value. She was under no misapprehension about the mistakes made in the past and still being made by her own people in India but if she had been asked to say in what way India had most benefited from the British connection, what it was that could be offered in extenuation of fault, error, even of wickedness, she would have been perfectly clear that it was the example so often given of personal trustworthiness: a virtue that flowed from courage, honesty, loyalty and commonsense in what was to her a single definition of good. She did not see how a person or a country could survive without it.

She was convinced that most of the things that offered some assurance of India surviving on her own resources in the post-war world would reflect the example of personal trustworthiness set by her countrymen in the past. She was in two minds about the benefit that might be had if the connection with England were much prolonged. She accepted the fact that at home her own people had often been indifferent to Indian affairs and that this indifference sprang from ignorance. But in the old days when the code by which she lived had been widely upheld in England this indifference to India had not mattered much, because those who came out to shoulder the responsibility could rely to a great extent on moral support at home. But of recent years, in England, she knew that these values had been eroded and she thought that this mattered a great deal because govern India as one might from Viceregal House, Government House, the commissioner's bungalow, the district officer's court and a military headquarters, the fount of government had always been and still was in the mother country and the moral climate there was bound to influence the climate in which the imperial possession was ruled.

In judging moral climate she took little account of factors usually selected to show evidence of decline. She was a tolerant woman in many of the matters that woke intolerance in others. She held the view that it was a bad thing for society to remain static, a desirable thing for it to be on the

805

move and to divide its rewards more fairly and distribute its opportunities more equitably. She did not feel that there was a conflict between her idea of the way society should change and her conviction that certain principles should be inimical to change. She was aware however of there being that sort of conflict in other people's minds. She was unsympathetic both to the prejudices of stubborn traditionalism and to the anarchic influence of those who often set about destroying it. She believed that through the business of attempting to divest old authorities of power the notion could become current that authority of any kind was suspect. To Isobel Rankin a world without authority was meaningless. There would be no chain of trust if there were no chain of command. She feared that in such a climate there could be a demission of authority in India by her own people that it would be possible only to describe as dishonourable, if by demission one implied as one should a full discharge of every obligation.

She was intent on discharging one such obligation now.

'The problem with mothers and children is that the mothers look after their own to the detriment of community discipline. What we want is a strong-willed woman who's good with kids and can keep them occupied while the mothers do their bit for the community.'

'It's difficult with Indian mothers,' Clara Fosdick said.

'We have to conceive of a hypothetical case, a state of siege lasting say a week,' Isobel went on. 'The teachers at the regimental schools can cope with the boys but I'm thinking of the girls. Mildred, what about that ex-mission teacher your stepmother-in-law has living with her?'

'Barbara Batchelor,' Clarissa Peplow said before Mildred had the chance, presupposing the inclination, to reply. 'I think Barbara would be an excellent choice.'

'But she'd never leave Mabel,' Clara Fosdick pointed out. 'And Mabel wouldn't budge from Rose Cottage if the hordes of Ghengiz Khan were galloping down from the hills.'

'She might have to,' Isobel said. 'Mildred? Any comment? Would Miss Batchelor be capable of controlling a gang of Indian boys and girls?'

'Presumably she's made the attempt in the past. I should think if Clarissa were in charge of her she might be of some use.'

'I want someone capable of running her own show,' Isobel put in. 'Could you take it on, Mrs Peplow?'

'It's more Barbara's line.'

Lighting a cigarette Nicky Paynton said, 'Clara's absolutely right though. She'd never leave Mabel. They'd die together on the verandah of Rose Cottage. Aziz too.'

Lucy Smalley coughed.

'What is it Mrs Smalley?' Isobel recognized the request to speak.

'I'm sure Mrs Fosdick and Mrs Paynton are right and that it would be difficult to prise Miss Batchelor away from Rose Cottage so long as Mrs Layton senior elected to stay there. But there's another reason why I don't think she would be, well, much good at the moment.'

'What reason?'

'She's in a terrible state this morning because the woman who was attacked in Mayapore district is a friend of hers. I mean the mission teacher, the one whose name was given. Miss Crane.'

She had the whole attention of the meeting. One of the advantages of having Mrs Smalley on committees was her more intimate knowledge of the affairs of the lower deck. Isobel turned to Mildred.

'Really? A close friend?'

'My dear Isobel, don't ask me. I know absolutely nothing about Miss Batchelor's connections.'

Isobel looked back at Mrs Smalley and raised her chin inviting further information.

'I wouldn't have known myself,' Lucy said, 'if I hadn't met her in the bazaar a couple of days ago. She was quite worried then because of the reports of things being bad in Mayapore. I didn't pay much attention, well, she does tend to go on. You don't actually need to listen to every word, do you? But when I read the Gazette this morning and saw the name of this woman I remembered Miss Batchelor had been telling me about a mission friend of hers called Crane in Mayapore who'd been a heroine in what sounded like the dark ages. So I rang her after breakfast. She'd just read the report too and was hardly coherent. She seemed to think I was someone else, ringing up with *news* of her friend. So I don't think she'd be much good looking after the children if we have riots in Pankot. From the way she was talking you'd have thought her friend was the other poor girl, whoever she is, who's been criminally assaulted.'

'Raped,' Isobel snapped. Lucy Smalley blushed. 'And her name is Miss Manners. Her uncle was governor in Ranpur back in the late 'twenties or early 'thirties. They've been trying to keep her name secret but it's leaked out as it was bound to. Did you know Sir Henry Manners, Mildred?'

'We were in Peshawar and Lahore while he was in office. He was rather pro-Indian wasn't he? I mean politically.'

'Nicky?'

'We were off station too.'

'Dicky says he had a good reputation,' Isobel said. 'His widow is still alive in Rawalpindi, I gather, but nothing's known about the girl. It could be a sticky case, from what I hear.'

Isobel did not say what she had heard. She tapped the agenda again.

'Right,' she said, 'we obviously rule out Miss Batchelor, and I'm not keen on making Chatty Singh's wife responsible for *everything* to do with the Indian community. She'll be overworked as it is. What about the librarian, Mrs Stewart?'

*

'My dear, my poor Edwina, (Barbie wrote), I was so shocked to read in the Ranpur Gazette about your truly terrible experience. For an age I wandered about distracted, wanting to help but not knowing how. Mayapore is so far away and even so, what could I do? My good kind friend here, Mabel, coming in and seeing me in this restless state, this state of great, of overwhelming anxiety, and learning the reason, said at once well if you can get through you must ring and find out how she is and leave a message. Practical woman! I followed her advice. It took an age. But I got the Mayapore exchange at last and then the hospital and spoke to a Sister Luke who said that you were quite comfortable, past the crisis, that she would give you my love and of course any letter I cared to send. Past the crisis! I dared not ask of what. Sister Luke seemed to think I would know, though Heaven knows how. Once again it is Mabel who lifts the veil from my uncertainty with her suggestion that after that shock and exposure, waiting, waiting in the rain, you must have been struck down with fever, perhaps pneumonia. My poor Edwina. You must, now on the mend, take care, take care.

'All this was yesterday. I delayed writing to you until today in order to get some sense into my thoughts. The point is that presently when you are better the Mission I am sure will want you to take sick leave to get your strength up properly again. Please take that sensible course. God knows how long these terrible disturbances will last – we aren't troubled by them in this lovely peaceful old station – but we can only hope and pray that they will end soon before more lives are lost. It is they, *they*, poor people who will suffer in the end.

'Well now when you are better, when you are ready, there is a room for you here. It is Mabel's suggestion. She points out that I have never had a visitor. This is true. But it would be so very wonderful to have you, for as long as you are able to spare before buckling to work again as I know you will but must not too soon. I shall say no more for the moment. But let it sink in as an idea. Pankot is a beautiful place. I've been happy here as you know from my previous letters. You can be sure of the friendliest welcome but all the privacy and seclusion you wish, or otherwise. It quickly got round that I knew you and people have been so kind in their inquiries. Today in the bazaar I was stopped many times and asked for news of you. All those of whom I have written before ask especially for their good wishes to be conveyed to you. The Reverend Arthur and Clarissa Peplow, Mr Maybrick who plays the organ at St John's, Mabel of course and sweet Sarah. I have not seen Susan for a day or two. One feels dreadfully for these young girls, I mean in view of the terrible reports about that other poor woman in Mayapore. Her name was not given in the *Gazette* but we had rumours in advance and now it is freely said by people here who seem to know that her name is Manners, the niece of a one-time Governor of the province. Poor girl, poor girl. You probably know her for it seems she was much involved with charitable work among the untouchables and lived with an Indian lady, a friend of her aunt who is now a widow in Rawalpindi and who must be suffering. One is so puzzled. One senses a mystery, an imponderable – I mean in regard to those who are hurt like yourself,

Edwina. Your life too has been so utterly devoted to *them*. I shall write again very very soon. Meanwhile my love and prayers. May God protect you, through Jesus. Sincere, sincere good wishes, Barbie.'

*

Miss Crane, Miss Manners; Miss Manners, Miss Crane. At times there was a tendency to confuse them; to forget momentarily which of the two victims it was Miss Batchelor knew until a few seconds' thought made the missionary connection; and then a different kind of confusion arose because there being nothing to identify Miss Crane the shortest way to her was through the familiar face and figure of her friend Miss Batchelor. At any given second a fleeting glimpse might therefore be had, as Barbie strode downhill to the bazaar, of the Crane woman doing that very thing for no particular reason unless it were to snatch the observer's thoughts and concentrate them upon a special issue: the safety of women.

There would now enter into the pine-scented and gun-metal air a stiff breeze of the kind that cooled without actually being felt to blow and in Miss Batchelor's, Miss Crane's, wake all kinds of horrors coupled and multiplied and gave her the look of a woman in danger who did not know it, walking in broad daylight, inviting attack, creating conditions in which an attack could take place.

Met face on she had the surprised happy appearance of someone who a few minutes ago had survived assault. It was irritating to find that she had no information; none, that was, that stood the test of sifting from the mine-tip of her inconsequential chatter.

'I am reminded,' she said, 'of Miss Sherwood. Amritsar, 1919. She was a school superintendent too. I never met her, she wasn't Bishop Barnard, but Edwina met her I'm almost certain. She had such a pretty Christian name. Marcella. Perhaps we missionaries are singled out because they see us as agents of the dark, although actually of light. She narrowly escaped with her life. A Hindu woman rescued her, in that awful place, that little lane we sealed off afterwards and made people *crawl* down, on their bellies, in the dust and dirt, to punish them. I sometimes think none of that has been forgiven.'

The word forgiven seemed wrong in present circumstances and the introduction of yet another name, Miss Sherwood, an unnecessary complication. Miss Sherwood was not Miss Crane, neither was Miss Batchelor who after all was merely herself and in no danger except from passing traffic. What she had survived was being in wartime Pankot but not quite of it, three years of comparative obscurity now interrupted by her brief prominence as a friend of the less interesting of the two Mayapore victims.

She was a familiar enough figure though, recognizable from a distance, the length of the bazaar say, whose busy road she had a habit of crossing and recrossing or walking down the middle of at full tilt, narrowly avoiding tongas, bicycles and military trucks; intent on performing innumerable and apparently urgent tasks at bank, post office and shops, in the shortest possible time; shortest in her judgment. The actual economy of method was open to doubt, but presumably old Mabel Layton was satisfied with it. Bit by bit Miss Batchelor had taken over the running of Mabel's household. If Mabel had been looking for someone who would make her withdrawal easier she could not have done better than choose this retired missionary; obviously the kind of person who cried out to be used, like a cow with a full udder moaning for the herdsman to lead her to the pail.

But her yield in information was low and the suspicion arose that she knew Miss Crane less well than had at first been generally assumed from her manner. If the affair of the attacked missionary had not been so serious Miss Batchelor's association with it might have introduced a note of comedy; but it was undoubtedly serious and there were questions it would have been nice to have answers to. For instance was there any significance in the fact that the burnt-out motor-car was one hundred yards away from the dead teacher's body? Had he jumped clear and run back along the road to Dibrapur, attempted to save his own skin, before being caught by the mob? And why after he was dead did she stay with the body and not attempt to seek refuge in the next village? Would she recognize any of the men who had hit her?

Satisfying though it would be to have questions like these settled, the picture of old Miss Crane sitting by a dead body in the road in the pouring rain was of less intense interest than the picture of the other victim, the girl who was criminally assaulted, Miss Manners, whom no one in Pankot knew, of whom no one had ever heard even if the name Manners was familiar to people whose connection with the province extended back ten or fifteen years. That the late Governor Sir Henry still had a widow living in Rawalpindi was a surprise to most people; that he had a niece in Mayapore living with an Indian woman (so the reports had it) was a greater surprise.

Apparently her other name was Daphne which for those who still remembered snippets of classical mythology produced the image of a girl running from the embrace of the sun god Apollo, her limbs and streaming hair already delineating the arboreal form in which her chastity would be preserved, enshrined forever; forever green. From her, then, the god could pluck no more than leaves. But this image could not be sustained and the other unknown Daphne stumbled on from antique laurel-dappled sunlight into a plain domestic darkness, dressed in her anonymity, and something simple, white, to suit her imagined frailty, her beauty and vulnerability; now half-sitting, half-lying on a couch in a shaded room with her eyes closed and one hand, inverted, against her aching forehead, speechless in the presence of friends who smiled when they were with her but otherwise looked grim.

And the violence done to her was not over yet. In due course she would have to leave the darkened room, go half-blinded by sunlight (or soaked by rain) to the ordeal of courtroom evidence unless she could be spared that which was not likely, so deeply had the democratic process undermined personal privilege. No closed doors for Miss Manners. The press would make sure of that. And the arrested men would not lack clever Bengali lawyers who would plead without fee, anxious for the publicity and the opportunity to sling mud, to impugn the morals of an English girl. It would be a high court case with a full gallery and the police out in force in the city to discourage the inevitable demonstrations on behalf of the accused. The judge would probably be an Indian. It was hoped so. The sentences of transportation for life to a penal settlement would come better from Mr Justice Chittaranjan than from Clara Fosdick's brother-in-law, Billy Spendlove. And then, only then, might poor Miss Manners fade back into the oblivion from which she had been cruelly dragged.

But her name would be written on the tablets.

*

The riots spread to Ranpur. Several lorry-loads of British and Indian troops left Pankot, ostensibly on convoy exercises but in fact bound for an encampment outside the city. In Ranpur the city police fired to disperse mobs. The military assisted them on two occasions. An attempt to sabotage the railway between Ranpur and Pankot was discovered in time. The night train up and the day train down now went under armed guard. For several hours the telephone connection was cut. When it was repaired reports came in thick and fast. The *Ranpur Gazette* offices had their windows broken. A mob had penetrated the civil lines with the intention of surrounding Government House. This mob carried banners demanding the release of 'the innocent victims of the Bibighar', meaning the boys arrested for the rape. Scurrilous pamphlets appeared accusing the Maya-pore police of torturing and defiling these six Hindu youths by whipping them and forcing them to eat beef. Factories were at a standstill and so was public transport. Life was reported quiet in Ranpur cantonment but there was a sense there undoubtedly of calm before storm. Things were said to be very bad farther afield, particularly in Mayapore and Dibrapur.

Politically in Ranpur it was a difficult time; in Pankot peaceful and, climatically speaking, marvellous: clear skies by day, refreshing rain by night, the perfect combination and a rare one even in the old station which was protected from the streaming and steamy monotony of the southwest monsoon by the very hills that made Ranpur so wet and humid. As Isobel Rankin said – at least the weather was pro-British.

There was bridge at Rose Cottage: the first session for some time. Mildred said she was tired of the club where the Pankot emergency committees had been meeting. Through the open french window came the velvet smell of roses and the marquee smell of cut grass. At mid-day Aziz brought drinks out to the verandah and cards were abandoned. Mabel was still in the garden cutting flowers for the house. Miss Batchelor was out shopping in the bazaar. Mildred Layton, Maisie Trehearne, Clara Fosdick and Nicky Paynton had the place to themselves. Presently the girls were due with some of the boys; and there was to be curry lunch down at the club.

But into this idyll, this scene reminiscent of more pacific times, Barbie erupted unexpectedly accompanied by the spectres of broken bloody victims and the Reverend Arthur Peplow's wife, blue-eyed Clarissa, whose expression was one of constant challenge to the devil, an uncomfortable attribute but useful so long as it did not get out of hand which it had never been known to. Her presence was a kind of corrective to over-optimism, at the same time calming. She had a still clear voice and used it tellingly like a gift harnessed for professional purposes.

'Of course,' Miss Batchelor was saying, 'we weren't at all bound by such things at the Bishop Barnard. Oh, hello. Hello. I was telling Clarissa, that it was teaching first last all the time, well practically speaking, that is especially after the Great War. Miss Jolley is non-conformist which hides a multitude of sins. In my day and Edwina's day it had to be C of E. It's in my trunk or should be. I'll go and look and bring it out and then everyone can see. If I can find it. In spite of one's resolution to be neat and tidy, as my father used to say a human being's no better than a magpie.'

She went indoors. The silence that followed was explicit. Mildred broke it, beating Clarissa perhaps by the shortest head.

'What treat have we in store?' she inquired.

She had her elbows on the arms of the wicker chair and her glass at chest level, held there by the fingers of both droop-wristed hands, and like this seemed to define the limit of her contribution to public interest in Miss Batchelor as the friend of a victim of the riots. Her indifference to her as the sharer of Mabel's kingdom was unchanged. Clarissa, who sat upright on a stool with her feet together and her handbag on her knees, directed her Christian gaze at Mildred but finding no fault unless it were in the large glass of gin and lemon summoned her still clear voice and said, 'It's some kind of picture I gather. One that has to do with her friend.'

'How *is* her friend?' Nicky Paynton asked.

'The question that concerns me more,' Clarissa answered, 'is how is *she*? She has just been acting very strangely on Club road.'

Walking without due care; a danger to herself, indeed to others, up the long stretch from Church road which tongas bowled down or strained up, which no one *ever* walked or if they did walked with accidents in mind, keeping well into the bank on the golf-course side and facing the oncoming horses, bicycles and vehicles; not – like Barbara – on the left hand side and certainly not in the middle, stopping, starting, drawing her own or an invisible companion's attention to some aspect of the Pankot scene which she must have seen hundreds of times before. And talking. Not in a loud voice. But quite definitely talking. To herself.

'I felt,' Clarissa said when she had described this curious and dangerous behaviour, 'that she imagined herself in the company of her friend, Miss

Crane. I made my tonga stop and pick her up and directly she got in she said how kind it was of Mabel to let her invite Miss Crane to Rose Cottage when she is better. And then she started talking about a picture and insisted that I come in to see it.'

One after the other, Clarissa last, heads or eyes were turned towards the garden where Mabel stood motionless except for her hands and arms cutting roses. In the heavy air the click of the secateurs was clearly audible. The sound had a slightly enervating effect but suddenly there were other sounds, voices indoors, all but one of them male. A dog barked and Panther appeared scuffling blackly on to the verandah to greet the company one by one with a sniff of curiosity and a wag of tribute before gallivanting back to the french window, barking and skittering backwards as Susan came out ahead of four affable looking subalterns. Nigel you know, she said, this is Bob, Derek, Tommy. My mother, Mrs Trehearne, Mrs Paynton, Mrs Fosdick oh and Mrs Peplow, hello, no Panther come here.'

'I expect there's some cold beer,' Mildred said. 'One of you ring and Nigel we could do with refills, you'll find the trolley indoors. No, don't bother, Aziz has forestalled you, but tell him to bring the beer and if you don't mind making yourself useful get me another of these and anyone else who wants one. Susan you're looking hot. There's some nimbo on the trolley, go and say hello to your Aunt Mabel first while one of the boys gets you a glass only stop Panther going mad for God's sake. Is Sarah coming or joining us at the club?'

'She said she'd join us at the club and may be late. Come on, Panther, come on old boy. Oh don't be silly. It's all right.' She grasped the dog by its stout leather collar and took it down steps it remembered as the scene of chastisement, and just then Barbie reappeared.

'I've found it!' she announced. The men made way for her and each other. She held the framed picture – measuring twelve inches by eight – and was cleaning the glass with the sleeve of her jacket, gripping the cuff with her fingers to make a firm rubbing surface. 'Isn't it extraordinary when you see something you haven't actually looked at for a while how familiar it is. The way the old man holds the alms bowl and the other leans on his staff. If you'd asked me to draw it from memory I couldn't have but one look at it now and one thinks of course! that's how they stood, that's how the artist drew them and left them, caught them in mid-gesture so that the gestures are always being made and you never think of them as getting tired.'

She gave the picture to Mrs Peplow and now stood to one side and a pace behind, both hands behind her back, legs apart (tightening her skirt at the calves) her head tilted, looking down over Clarissa's shoulder.

'You have to imagine it much larger, on the schoolroom wall behind the desk and all the children gathered round just as the people are gathered round the Queen, and Edwina standing with a pointer, not that I ever saw her give a lesson because she'd left Muzzafirabad before I got there but Mr Cleghorn gave me a demonstration and wanted me to try it but as I said, no, no, one must plough one's own furrow. I can see him now, copying Edwina.

813

Here is the Queen. The Queen is sitting on her throne. The uniform of the Sahib is scarlet. The sky here is blue. Who are these people in the sky? They are angels. They blow on golden trumpets. They protect the Queen. The Queen protects the people. The people bring presents to the Queen. The Prince carries a jewel on a velvet cushion. The Jewel is India. She will place the Jewel in her Crown.'

'Yes, I see,' Clarissa said. She was holding the picture like a looking-glass. 'Most admirable. To teach English *and* loyalty. Thank you for showing it to me.'

She handed the picture back. Miss Batchelor caught hold of it, strode across and thrust it at Mildred who had her refilled glass in both hands so that a young man with freckles and dark red hair gallantly reached out and took the picture and held it where Mrs Layton's glance might fall upon it, which fleetingly it did.

'Do pass it round,' Miss Batchelor said. 'It's a copy of a picture my friend Edwina Crane used years and years ago. The children adored it. Pictures are so important when instructing the young. But one has to be careful. Edwina once told me she had a very grave suspicion that in the end the children confused her with Victoria! Isn't that amusing? You must admit the artist got everything in, Mrs Fosdick. Disraeli's there, the one with the scroll and the smug expression. Generals, admirals, statesmen, princes, paupers, babus, banyas, warriors, villagers, women, children. And old Victoria in the middle of it sitting on a throne under a canopy in the open air of all things, really quite absurd but allegorical of course, she never came to India. She looks quite startled, don't you agree, Mrs Trehearne? But I think that's the effect of the reduction in scale. The print on the schoolroom wall was ten times as big and in that I remember – thank you, Mrs Paynton – she looked terribly wise and kind and understanding.

Receiving the picture back from Mrs Paynton via a young man with a fair moustache she looked at it again herself. 'It always seemed to me to be a picture about love rather than loyalty. Perhaps they amount to the same thing. What do you think?'

She looked at the moustached young man whose mouth was puckered in concentration. He was pulling his left ear-lobe.

'Have you got transport?' Mildred asked one of the men, who said yes they had. 'Then directly you've downed your beers we ought to be getting along to the club.'

There were movements of departure. Two of the men went into the garden to rescue Susan.

'Oh, are you all going?' Miss Batchelor asked in her carrying schoolroom voice. 'Let me just say I do appreciate everyone being so kind, so solicitous for Edwina.'

*

She hammered a nail into the wall above the old campaigner's writing-table and hung the picture. Aziz approved. He would pause in his work to consider it, stand like one of the children of Muzzafirabad grown old but still possessed. She had told him about her friend Miss Crane, that she was in hospital in distant Mayapore hurt trying to save someone who was attacked and killed, and might when better stay for a week or two in the little spare. He nodded his understanding in the Indian way. In Aziz this was a gesture of great economy. He had the dignity of the people from the higher hills who walked shrouded in blankets and secrecy and made excursions into Pankot, involved in mysterious errands whose object escaped her since they came and went empty-handed as if merely to look and reassure themselves that nothing was happening in the valley of which they disapproved.

Mabel, in her solitary walks, went in their direction but nowadays went less often. On her own walks the other way downhill Barbie had become used to feeling like a dove sent out to check the level of the flood. After three years the darkness still lay on Mabel's soul and Barbie felt a bit discouraged. But since the incident on the road from Dibrapur the nature of her outings seemed to have changed and the familiar route had become unfamiliar. She anticipated revelation.

In her mind she too guarded the body. It lay near the milestone half way up (or down) Club road. Passing the milestone made her light-headed; almost there was a sense of levitation. Edwina's act of guarding the body had been one of startling simplicity and purity which possibly only a woman like Edwina could have had the occasion to perform and in performing it sum up the meaning of her life in India. From the schoolroom door at Muzzafirabad to the place on the road from Dibrapur was a distance measurable in miles, in years, but between the occasions there was no distance. Right from the beginning Edwina had been close to God and therefore to herself. Not teaching but loving. From her plain face, her manner, you might not have guessed this. Only from her actions. And in this most recent action, this guarding of the dead Indian's body, it seemed to Barbie that Edwina had achieved her apotheosis.

Oh how I long, Barbie said, standing still suddenly, having passed the milestone and accepted the sad fact that there was no body there for her to guard, how I long for an apotheosis of my own, nothing spectacular, mind, nothing in the least grandiose nor even just grand, but, like Edwina's, quiet with a still-centre to it that exemplifies not my release from earthly life although it might do that too but from its muddiness and uncertainty, its rather desperate habit of always proving that there are two sides to every question; my release from that into the tranquillity of knowing my work has been acceptable, good and useful perhaps, perhaps not, but performed in love, with love, and humility of course, indeed, humility, and singularity, wholeness of purpose. That is the most important thing of all.

But not knowing what kind of apotheosis this could be she walked on in the direction of the bazaar to settle the accounts at Jalal-Ud-Din's and Gulab Singh Sahib's, and buy more stamps to write more letters to Edwina who did not reply. No news she said to Sarah who inquired, being also at Jalal-Ud-Din's querying a bill upon which was writ large the rising cost of living in her father's continuing absence, no news is good news. She hoped for both their sakes that this was so.

She was in love with Sarah Layton and with Susan but more with Sarah who seemed to need it more. She was in love with Pankot and her life there and her duty to Mabel and the wind in winter. She was afraid to be in love with Mr Maybrick who played the organ at St John's and was widowed and retired from Tea, because he was to begin with a man and to go on with a man with a temper and an air of self-enclosure who did not normally invite proofs of attachment even of Barbie's kind, which did not extend to flesh. In any case he had large hands with more hair on the wrists than on his head and when he played the organ his hands looked extraordinarily vivid and enterprising. He lived alone except for his Assamese houseboy in a tiny and very untidy bungalow not far from the rectory-bungalow on the same tree-shaded road. In his bungalow there were many photographs of his dead wife and in most of them she had her hand above her eyes to keep the sun out, a fact which always made Barbie feel outdoors when really in.

On her way back from the bazaar she looked in at St John's to collect his album of Handel which was falling to pieces and which she had volunteered to repair. Mr Maybrick was at practice. She could hear the organ as she approached the church door. Bach. Toccata and fugue.

She sat in a pew and listened. She imagined Mr Maybrick's red face and bald head reflected in the mirror above the keyboards. The mirror was a framed picture. Who is this? This is the Planter. The face of the Planter is reddened by the sun. Here is his Lady. She shades her eyes from the light. She is of the North and ails in the climate. But keeps going. What is the Planter doing? He is showing the coolies how to pick only the tender leaves. As he shows them God sings through his fingers. The leaves are green. When they are dried they will be brown. The music will be preserved in caddies. The Planter and the coolies between them will bring Tea to the Pots of the Nation.

She thought: I shall bring Edwina to St John's to hear Mr Maybrick at practice and on Sundays to hear Arthur Peplow's sermon. And afterwards we shall return to Rose Cottage. And I shall be large again and shapely with intent, so close to Edwina that God will remember and no longer mark me absent from the roll.

*

The attitude of the old Queen inclining her body, extending her two hands, was then suddenly an image of Edwina on the road from Dibrapur holding her hands protectively above the body of the Indian. Flames from the burning motor-car were reflected in the sky where the angelic light pierced bulgy monsoon clouds.

In this image she had a surrogate for God, a half-way house of intercession, capable perhaps of boosting the weak signals from the rush mat and transmitting them through the crackling overloaded ether which her direct prayers could not penetrate. She knelt with her body upright, facing the writing-table and the picture that pointed the reality of a Christian act, the palms of her hands turned to receive whatever was offered. She exposed her chest well below the gold pendant cross to give the metal room to act as a lightning conductor and sometimes felt it warmed by the reflected light from the burning vehicle; which was a promising beginning. Otherwise everything remained as it had been.

*

Once a week she visited the club subscription library for Mabel, seldom for herself who found what Mr Cleghorn had called the book of life sufficiently entertaining and puzzling to keep her occupied without recourse to the print and paper of imaginary or refurbished adventure.

Lost between the shelves among which she and Edwina would wander she heard a voice say, 'I'm told the whole trouble is she was infatuated with the Indian. She'd have done anything to save him.' She recognized the voice of little Mrs Smalley, the station gossip, and then Clarissa's saying, 'You can't know that.' To which Lucy Smalley replied, 'It's what people in Mayapore are saying, according to Tusker, and they have been in a position to judge. They say she was always out with him, holding his hand in public places. And now she's threatening to say the most dreadful things against the authorities if the men they've arrested are charged and tried, because *he's* one of them. The police officer who made the arrests is almost out of his mind.'

Barbie emerged armed with a volume of Emerson still open at the page with her thumb on the line, 'Man is explicable by nothing less than all his history,' which a moment ago had caused her to catch her breath. She cried out, 'Of whom are you talking?'

Not, it seemed, of Edwina, but – Lucy Smalley explained, recovered quickly from the nasty shock of Barbie emerging and bearing down like a Fury – of 'the Manners girl', the other victim. 'You didn't think we were talking about your friend, surely?'

Barbie took Emerson home with her. She had not meant to but he was in her hand as she arrived at Mrs Stewart's desk and was marked out to her with a rise of Mrs Stewart's eyebrows because Mrs Stewart, a widow from Madras with a literary turn of mind, was more used to receiving from Barbie her interpretations of Mabel's standing order for something light, which generally turned out to be so easy on the mind and lap that Mabel nodded off over it in her wing chair having pronounced it earlier 'just right'.

Presented with Emerson's essays Mabel said, 'Oh, I read those as a girl, I don't think I could bother again.'

'I'll take it back tomorrow,' Barbie promised. 'It was a mistake, or rather

817

absent-mindedness, my attention was taken as it can be all too easily. Well, you know, you know. I *am* sorry.'

But Mabel merely smiled and touched Barbie's arm as she did from time to time as if to make up for all the occasions when she might have failed to let Barbie know she was appreciated.

Barbie sat at the writing-table, opened the rejected book. 'If the whole of history is one man,' she said, 'it is all to be explained from individual experience. There is a relation between the hours of our life and the centuries of time.' She closed the book abruptly and made herself busy in the room, opening drawers and rearranging their contents.

Not taking Emerson back she returned to him daily like a sparrow easily frightened from a promising scattering of crumbs by the slightest noise, with a nagging sense of having more duties than intelligence. It was pretty plain she was not cut out for the philosophical life but through Emerson it impinged on her own like the shadow of a hunched bird of prey patiently observing below it the ritual of survival. The bird should have been an angel.

She began to feel what she believed Emerson wanted her to feel: that in her own experience lay an explanation not only of history but of the lives of other living people, therefore an explanation of the things that had happened to Edwina and to Miss Manners of whom she had only the vaguest picture, the one that had been commonly shared in Pankot of a reclining figure, in white, in a darkened room. But now it had changed. The girl's hand was no longer pressed inverted against her forehead but held by another which was brown like the dead teacher's. The picture shimmered, became fluid. Colours and patterns ran. When Barbie sat at her desk and gazed at the actual picture she was no longer sure of what she saw: Edwina guarding the body, Mabel kneeling to grub out weeds or inclining to gather roses; or herself, Barbie, surrounded by the children she had presumed to bring to God; or Miss Manners in some kind of unacceptable relationship with a man of another race whom she was intent on saving.

From this there emerged a figure, the figure of an unknown Indian: dead in one aspect, alive in another. And after a while it occurred to her that the unknown Indian was what her life in India had been about. The notion alarmed her. She had not thought of it before in those terms and did not know what to do about it now that she had. She could not very well look for him because she did not know where to do that. Aziz for instance seemed content even in his alternative persona of a man from the hills with a blanket and a secret. He did not strike her as being in distress of any kind.

But the dead man in the vicinity of the milestone had moved. Overnight there had been a rearrangement of his limbs as if while it was dark he had sat up. And howled. The hills were hunted by jackals. People would not have noticed. But she thought that she would henceforth be able to distinguish the man's cry from the cries of the animals.

·

She began another letter to Edwina.

'September 4th. Why don't you write Edwina? I need your letter,' then tore it up and began another sensibly.

'Some people from Mayapore have been here. I didn't meet them but a woman called Smalley who lives at the little Smith's Hotel where these people stayed for a couple of days told Clarissa Peplow that according to these visitors whose name I think was Patterson or Pattison you were reported well on the mend and about to be discharged. How thankful this news has made me. I have not rung the hospital again because of the expense and the delay in getting through and then getting only the briefest official answer to the question. But I have written several times. I hope my letters all arrived. The posts have been badly delayed, indeed disrupted. If you are already discharged no doubt the hospital will send this note round to your bungalow. I shall mark the envelope please forward and shall probably send a separate note to you at home. How glad you will be to be there. I hope, hope that you are truly recovered, Edwina.

'Is there a possibility of your making the journey to Pankot? The invitation still stands. Mabel has asked me to emphasize this and also to say that we should keep you free from the prying and the curious. I do trust that you are not too disagreeably involved with the aftermath of that awful business. It is said officially that the country is returning to normal and that now surely is the time for magnanimity. But one hears the unhappiest accounts and most unpleasant remarks. I am, my dear Edwina, a bit concerned for you as a result of something Clarissa said, echoing Lucy Smalley and presumably these Patterson Pattison people. It would be monstrous if after all you have been through you were in the least criticized for stating that you could not either describe or recognize individuals among that wicked mob. It must have been a nightmare and after a nightmare the details are often mercifully forgotten. Only those with vengeful natures would wish to see you drag some detail back into the light, one upon which they could then proceed to act over-righteously perhaps and in all likelihood unjustly. No doubt you feel as I do that God will punish and perhaps has already punished. As Clarissa says, some of the men who hurt you and killed the teacher may since have been killed themselves in the rioting. Divine retribution!'

Here Barbie's pen hesitated as if of its own accord and she could not continue. Divine retribution was all very well. It did not help the unknown Indian who seemed this morning to be crying out harder but still soundlessly, begging for justice and not alleviation. She found it difficult to distinguish between the teacher who died in the attack on Edwina and the Indian who was supposed to have had Miss Manners infatuated with him. Lucy Smalley's opinion was that the Indian boy Miss Manners thought she was in love with must have been some kind of hypnotist. But perhaps love was a form of hypnosis anyway. Had not Barbie been mesmerized herself years and years ago?

My life, she thought, has become extraordinarily complicated. There is more than one of me and one, I'm not sure which, has a serious duty to perform. 'It seems perfectly dreadful (she wrote suddenly, allowing the Waterman pen its now free-flowing head) how within the space of a few weeks poor Daphne Manners has become "that Manners girl".' And she continued for a page or two becoming while she did so a projection of that poor misused creature who it was said was not frail and pretty after all but rather large and ungainly and in need of spectacles, so that the sympathetic transference of Barbie to Daphne and back again was easier to make than it would have been had the idea of Miss Manners as frail, ethereal and beautiful in victim's white turned out to be accurate.

Instead here she was according to reports from people who had been in a position to know, in a rather grubby dress to suit the circumstances arising from her extraordinary behaviour, throwing up blinds, peering short-sightedly and threatening to create a scene, standing in shafts of sunlight which were alive with particles of dust. Barbie understood this image better than the other.

Miss Manners said the men arrested were the wrong men. Barbie wondered how that could be but was impressed by the reported strenuous-ness of Miss Manners's insistence which everyone else seemed to feel outraged by, just as they were ready to be outraged by Edwina's insistence that she had no contribution to make to the identification of a few men in a large crowd. In those circumstances they all looked alike anyway in their murky dhotis and Gandhi caps and filthy turbans. And the smell. Suffering, sweating, stinking, violent humanity. It was the background against which you had to visualize Jesus working. People did not remember this important thing about His presence. Edwina did. Did Miss Manners? Or was she only intent on confusing the police to save her lover? Apparently she kept changing her story. According to the Pattersons she had threatened to say that if the six youths who included her lover were charged and tried for rape she would stand up and say that the men who assaulted her could just as easily have been British soldiers with their faces blacked.

In that threat, that outburst, which had scandalized her countrymen, Barbie detected what she thought of as the girl's despair and was sorry for her. She would have liked to take Miss Manners in her arms and comfort her. She was not convinced though that Miss Manners was telling the whole truth so she was also sorry for the police officer who had arrested the men and was convinced of their guilt. It was said by the Patterson Pattisons that the police officer had warned Miss Manners about her association with this particular Indian who was handsome if you liked that sort of thing and educated, so he claimed, in England but certainly beyond his real station, and had already been questioned over something to do with political affiliations. On the face of it, Barbie saw, the Indian was as likely to be guilty as not, leading Miss Manners on, laughing at her behind her back as Lucy Smalley suggested, and planning to attack her in the dark on the way home from one of her errands of mercy, in the company of five of his westernized friends, student-types, who came at her from behind, dragged her off her bicycle into the Bibighar Gardens, covered her head with her own raincape, raped her and left her to stagger home in pain, in torment, totally disorientated.

If they covered her head how could she see who they were? When did they cover her head? Only after she had a glimpse (as apparently she began to say), a good enough glimpse of them to be able to insist that they were dirty peasant-types not well-groomed European-style dressed boys of the kind arrested? And there had been some confusion about her bicycle. Had it been found by the police in the ditch outside the Indian boy's house? At first this was what had been said but it had been denied later by the police officer himself. The most damning thing of all had not been denied though. When arrested the Indian boy had been bathing his face which was scratched and bruised. He would not say how; had never said, had refused utterly to talk. The others denied any complicity, any connection with his English girl friend, pretended they had spent the whole evening drinking hooch in a hut near the Bibighar Gardens where the attack had taken place. They had been arrested in the hut.

Now they were disposed of, all of them, to gaol, without trial, as political detenus. And Miss Manners seemed to have won. But what had she won except disgrace among her own people? And her Indian boy-friend; what had he got away with?

Barbie did not even know his name. She began to have dreams about him, but in these dreams he was the Indian Edwina had tried to save. In this dream his eyes were blinded by cataracts. He had a powerful muscular throat which was exposed because his head was lifted and his mouth wide open in a continuous soundless scream.

VI

It was the element of scornful rejection implicit in every violent challenge to authority which hurt most deeply and blighted the tendrils of affection which entwined and supported the crumbling pillars of the edifice. Upon faces already drawn from the strain of conveying self-confidence and from the slight but persistent malaise suffered by constitutions imperfectly designed to withstand the climate, there would fall – during these periods of pressure – shadows of brooding melancholy, even when the face was expressing scorn or indifference, amusement, wrath; whatever it was that was being felt or assumed. In the cries of shock and outrage with which news of victims was heard and passed on, in the calls for condign punishment of culprits, a plaintive note managed to be struck which corresponded to the melancholy shadow; a note of awareness that the victims must have been people in whom the impulse to show as well as feel affection in the performance of their duty had been stronger than was usual, even than was wise, so that the fates of these people were seen through all the tangle of misfortune and circumstance as sacrificial.

But in the aftermath, as the status quo was re-established, these original victims were replaced by the figures of those who had tried to avenge them and become victims themselves; and then that melancholy shadow was burnt away by fires of irony which, lighting faces, gave them the glowing look of belonging to people who found themselves existing on a plane somewhere between that of the martyr and the bully.

The irony lay in the fact that the new victims were sacrifices offered by one's own side as a placatory measure in restoring order and regaining Indian confidence. It had happened before, it would happen again, but that did not make it any more palatable when it was happening now. As early as the beginning of September when the jails were crammed and the country and administration nearly back to normal it was said that Brigadier Reid, openly accused by the Indians of having used excessive force in putting down the riots, was not receiving the kind of support from above which he had the right to expect. At the end of the month he was reported posted to another command.

Nicky Paynton said, 'It seems to me Alec Reid did damned well. The civil always expect us to be on tap to pull their chestnuts out of the fire but when we do they start complaining that we've burnt *their* fingers.' She was stating what was generally felt to be true. In Reid's case community sympathy for him was strong because although he had used his British battalion in Mayapore he commanded as well a battalion of the Pankots (the 4/5th) and one of the Ranpurs. But this sympathy had been deepened by the news that at the height of the riots in Mayapore his wife died of cancer in Rawalpindi. It was also known that his only son had been captured by the Japanese in Burma earlier in the year, news which could hardly have made Meg Reid's last months any easier for her or Alec Reid to bear. But, called by the civil power to give military aid, he had done so, so far as one could tell, resolutely and effectively. If a larger than average number of Indians was killed or wounded in Mayapore and Dibrapur that was because the riots in those two towns were worse than in any other town in the country and because the civil power had dithered, had been unwilling to call the army in until the situation had got completely out of hand.

It was quite obvious to Army people that the civil authority in Mayapore lacked nous. Apart from the almost criminal negligence shown by the long postponement of a request for troops, the revolting affair of the rape of Miss Manners had been allowed to disintegrate in the most scandalous way. The only people who had come out well of the troubles in Mayapore, in Pankot opinion, were the brigade commander and the District Superintendent of Police who had arrested the suspects in the rape case within an hour or so of the assault. And now, like Brigadier Reid, this officer was said to be in bad official odour.

What was needed of course was some first-hand information and for that one had to wait for people like the Pattersons to arrive from Mayapore. They had been interesting on the subject of Miss Manners but, being civilians, a poor source of intelligence in the matter of the alleged excessive use of force. The first man to arrive in Pankot from Mayapore, a junior officer of a British regiment fairly recently out from home, found himself much in demand. But his mind seemed to be on other things. In regard to the rape, for instance, he said, 'Really, one began to suspect there hadn't been one.' He described the military action taken in aid of the civil power 'like something out of Gilbert and Sullivan mixed up with the last act of Hamlet.' The discovery that this young man had been an actor in civilian life and was in Pankot en route for a sinecure in welfare and entertainment in Delhi was made early enough to put his views into proper perspective. He was vulgarly handsome. Probably a chorus boy, Mrs Fosdick suggested.

After the theatrical lieutenant had gone there arrived as many as a dozen men and women who had been in Mayapore at the time of the riots. They said that the number of dead in Mayapore, considered uncomfortably high by the authorities, was accounted for chiefly by people drowned in the river when scattering in panic at the sound of rifle fire and the sight of troops on both sides of the Mandir Gate bridge. In Dibrapur it had been a different matter. There the rebels had used home-made bombs and landmines. They got what they asked for. Brigadier Reid nearly lost a whole rifle company when it was cut off by a blown bridge; and when you thought of that, and that the company was part of a brigade he was trying to get ready to fight the Japanese and stop them invading India, you had to agree it was inhuman to start crucifying him for showing a bit of sand. In Reid there was obviously more sand than the desk-wallahs thought it right for a British officer to show these days. They were getting ready to dish him. The command of the brigade was Alec Reid's first real job of soldiering for more than ten years. If it hadn't been for the *débâcle* in Malaya and Burma he'd probably have ended his career fretting at a desk. He'd now been given command of a brigade that was almost ready to go back into the field but it was rumoured that GHQ thought it better to promote him to a job he'd quickly prove he couldn't do than send him meekly back to a staff appointment because the civil in Mayapore had kicked up a stink about him.

There was a rather sordid little joke going round among Mayapore Indians that if you spelt Reid backwards it came out sounding like Dyer who shot down all those unarmed people in the Jallianwallah Bagh in Amritsar in 1919. It never took long for people to home in like vultures on the reputation of a perfectly decent and competent officer. The only comfort to be had from the business was that if Reid did prove himself just too old to command a brigade of more seasoned troops his fate would be better than old Dyer's. He'd likely get a general's hat and even if there was nowhere else to hang it except on a peg in an air-conditioned office the pay while it lasted and the pension when it ended would be some compensation.

The first of the officers who gained Pankot's full attention was the adjutant of the battalion of the British regiment that had been brigaded for training with a battalion of the Ranpurs and the Mayapore Battalion of the Pankots under Reid. This officer was on short local leave. His knowledge of India was infinitesimal but he was a regular soldier and gave a fascinating account of the action in aid of the civil power in Mayapore in the Mandir Gate bridge, following which an unfortunately large number of women and children had died in the river. He knew the departed theatrical lieutenant, of course, but surprised everybody by describing him as a first-rate platoon commander who had won the MM as a lance-corporal at Dunkirk. He claimed to be the originator of the famous comment about that retreat: The noise! The people! To men the adjutant confided that he thought young X was probably as queer as a coot but that if so he had the courage of an Amazon. He was among those who had led a detachment of British soldiers in aid of the civil. He had behaved well but perhaps the experience of firing on unarmed civilians had 'turned him'. The adjutant remembered finding him vomiting in his quarters when going to ask why he hadn't reported to the daftar on his return from aid duty in the city. 'My dear fellow,' the actor-soldier had said, 'I'm being sick because in a properly organized production the extras never actually get killed. The little thing today was wildly under-rehearsed.'

The next arrival was an even more promising source of information. This was Ewart Mackay, the brigade major whom Reid's successor had replaced with a man of his own choice. Mackay was in Pankot for a couple of days. He had broken his journey to his regimental depot in Muzzafirabad in the North West Frontier province, where he anticipated being offered the command of the battalion of the Muzzafirabad Guides that was now being brought back up to strength after limping out of Burma.

Initially he seemed more interested in standing drinking at the men's bar in the club than in answering questions about Mayapore which he deflected with frosty blasts of his Carew's gin and ice-chunk-cooled breath and chilling stares of a keen blue eye. His sandy pranged moustache was kept airborne by constant manipulation of his restless fingers.

But after he had put down what one member swore were twelve burra pegs in the course of two hours he became brisker, informative, and introduced a speculative element into the hitherto clear-cut argument that Reid had been badly treated.

Apparently Ewart Mackay had quite a good opinion of White, the Deputy Commissioner in Mayapore. He said, 'We all knew the Brig's son was a p.o.w. with the Japs and we knew his wife was in hospital up in 'Pindi. But I was the only one who knew she was dying of cancer and I didn't know that until quite late in the day. I think if the DC had known he and the Brig would have got on better because he would have made allowances. As it was I often had to pour oil especially during the time the

Brig was pressing him to call the troops out and the DC was digging his heels in and saying the civil police could cope. It's nonsense to say excessive force was used but it could be that if we'd used troops say a day earlier the result wouldn't have been so bad. I think the DC would have called for troops the day before if the Brig had given him more confidence about how they'd be used. Old Alec Reid's a bit of a fire-eater you know. And nowadays the civil distrust us if we look anxious to have a crack. I suppose if your wife is dying and you're stuck in a place like Mayapore with all hell let loose you'd want to get stuck in, but it's never a good thing for the man at the top to be under an emotional strain. All the same old Alec Reid's had a shabby deal. Giving him that other brigade was only a face-saver for him and the army. He won't be keeping it. I know the man who's been told he'll be getting it. Reid will be back in Delhi by Christmas.'

And Miss Manners? No, he had not had the pleasure of meeting Miss Manners. He pronounced her name in mock Scottish as it were with a deliberate skirl of the pipes and a whirl of the kilt. Since that unfortunate affair he had of course learned quite a bit about her. No, she wasn't particularly attractive according to reports. Big and gawky he understood. She was staying in one of the oldest houses in Mayapore, a place called the Macgregor House built by a Scottish nabob in the early nineteenth century but now the property of an Indian woman, Lady Chatterjee, one of the Indians with whom the DC and his wife played bridge. Miss Manners was quite new to India. Although born in the country she had been taken home by her parents while still an infant. She lost both parents before the war and her brother had been killed. She'd driven ambulances throughout the blitz in London but been invalided out. Her closest surviving relative, her aunt, old Lady Manners, widow of ex-Governor Sir Henry, arranged for her to join her in Rawalpindi. There she met Lady Chatterjee. Sir Henry Manners and Sir Nello Chatterjee, a Bengali industrialist, had been old friends and after their deaths their widows had kept the friendship up. Lady Chatterjee was a Rajput, Chatterjee being her second husband. Her first was a prince who broke his neck playing polo. Chatterjee was knighted for founding and financing the Mayapore technical college which produced young Indian engineers, not unemployable arts graduates. Lady Chatterjee was considered okay.

Major Mackay had met Lady Chatterjee once in the course of his social duties. Miss Manners may have been at the same function but he didn't recall seeing her. The fact was she was probably otherwise occupied. After coming to stay with Lady Chatterjee and doing voluntary work at the general hospital she had become friendly with this Indian journalist fellow who was among the six young men the District Superintendent of Police arrested for raping her.

Mackay was offered another drink. He accepted and said nothing more until it reached him. After a couple of swallows he reflighted his moustache and said, 'Curious business altogether. And it made life extra difficult because it gave the troublemakers something special to shout about. I expect you heard the tales that got around that the police tortured the boys and defiled them by making them eat beef to get them to confess, which they never did. A lot of our own people felt that if the tales were true they only got what they deserved. I don't expect they were handled any too gently. Some of these Indian inspectors and sub-inspectors can be pretty ruthless but the rabble were accusing the DSP himself. It got so bad the DC ordered an Indian magistrate to question each one of them but none of them complained of ill-treatment. They might have been scared to. Anyway it made no difference. The crowds were still screaming blue murder. I never cared much for the DSP, he wasn't my kind of chap, but the Brig liked him and considering the crowds were out to get him if they could he acted pretty coolly. I saw him once in the thick of it on horseback rallying a squad of police that looked as if it had had enough. If there'd been one rioter with a shotgun he'd have been a dead man. As it was a bloody great stone missed him by inches. Still, guts don't count if you fail in another direction. He never made the rape charges stick and I don't suppose his department will let him forget it. But that's life. Bring home the bacon and you're forgiven a lot. Don't, and you're sunk.'

One of the other men said, 'From what we hear that wasn't his fault but the girl's. She sounds round the bend to me.'

Mackay glanced at the man, emptied his glass, put it on the counter and ordered another round.

'You think so?' he said.

'Don't you?'

'I just think she was in love. Not round the bend. Not infatuated. Not intimidated. In love.'

'With the journalist fellow?'

'That's right.'

'Even after he and his friends raped her?'

'Forget the friends. The trouble about this case is that nobody's ever been able to forget the friends or start from the simple proposition that Miss Manners was in love and still is with the Kumar chap. And that the Kumar chap was and still is in love with her.'

'Was that his name?'

'There were six names but I think Kumar was the lad in question. Hari Kumar.'

'Harry?'

'H,a,r,i. He was brought up in England. He went to school at Chillingborough.'

'Good God.'

'Quite so. Interesting, isn't it?'

'Well what the hell was he doing working in a place like Mayapore on a local rag?'

'They tell me his father died bankrupt in England before the war and he came back penniless to the only relative he had, an aunt who lived in

Mayapore. She was a widow and lived on the charity of her dead husband's orthodox Hindu family. Young Kumar must have had a tough time adjusting himself to *that*. It could be he failed to adjust himself. The police had an eye on him. He was politically suspect. That's the other red herring.'

'Red herring?'

'It introduces complications. It makes it hard to concentrate on the proposition that he and Miss Manners were in love.'

'What's the other red herring?'

'The friends. The police had files on them too. I think you have to forget the politics, the friends, even the rape, and concentrate on this one proposition. They were in love.'

'What do you mean, forget the rape?'

Mackay's glass was empty. He put it on the counter. A man in the group ordered refills.

'I mean forget it because it's irrelevant.'

The word irrelevant came out slightly blurred and Major Mackay lost something of his grip on his audience. But with his next sentence he regained and hardened it.

'She's pregnant, you know. She's gone back to R'l'Pindi pregnant. People say she'll get an abortion. Myself, I doubt it. I concentrate on the proposition that she and Kumar were in love, still are, he in clink and she pregnant in R'l'Pindi. Having what she thinks is his child. Thinks, hopes or knows. You can't tell. Perhaps she can't either in the way women think they can. The old intuition.'

A man with a red face and sparse hair, a civilian asked, 'What's your theory, Major Mackay?'

'Well yes I have a theory. Glad you asked. My theory's this. If you love and marriage isn't on or isn't easy sooner or later you get round to poking, to put it crudely. My theory is Miss Manners and this Kumar fellow poked in the Bibighar either that night for the first time or that night for the umpteenth but that that night whatever teenth time it was these so-called friends of his who'd not only guessed he was poking her but had found out where, were all lined up waiting for the show to begin and when it was over jumped on him, sat on him and then – '

Major Mackay made an arm.

'Then why didn't Miss Manners say so?'

'Say what? That she and Mr Kumar had been making love at night in a derelict garden doing no harm to anyone when up come these friends of his and say, Okay Hari, move over?'

'Why not? From all accounts she's not the easily embarrassed type. And if what you suggest is true and she and this journalist fellow had made a clean breast of it that part of it might have been kept dark and the other fellows just charged and sentenced.'

'And do you think any of them would have let Kumar get away with that? They'd have implicated him like a shot. They'd have said it was Kumar's idea, to share her.'

'Well wasn't it? The police thought so.'

'Which is where you come back to my proposition. If it had been like that I don't care what kind of act he put up she'd have known and she'd have stopped being in love with him. If you stick to my proposition that they were in love, are in love, everything's as clear as daylight. These so-called friends of his jumped him and beat him up. She may not have seen who they were. If not he told her afterwards and told her what they'd threatened, that they'd accuse him of arranging it if there was any trouble. Well, she wasn't a bloody fool. Everybody in Mayapore knew she'd been going out with him. Neither of them was popular as a result. He wouldn't have stood a chance however much she swore his innocence. So they cooked up a story that they hadn't seen each other for days and they damned well stuck to it, right through. What she hadn't reckoned with was finding when she got home that Lady Chatterjee had already reported her missing to the DSP. It was the night the balloon was expected to go up and she hadn't come home at the usual time. She wasn't at the club or at any of old Lady C's friends and the woman was pretty worried. And when she got home there wasn't any disguising what had happened. Her clothes were torn and she was in a state. Lady C had a woman doctor from the Purdah hospital up to the house in a brace of shakes. Maybe Miss Manners panicked. But she said she'd been assaulted by a gang of men and that was the situation the DSP found when he called at the house. He had no time for Hari Kumar. He'd had his eye on him. He'd warned Miss Manners about associating with a fellow like that. So young Kumar's the first chap the DSP thinks of. He hares off to the Bibighar, finds Kumar's pals drinking in a hut not far away, arrests them and hares off to Kumar's house and finds him bathing cuts and bruises on his face, the sort a fellow might get if he attacked a girl who fought back. What other evidence did he need? He jumped to the conclusion most people would. And he was right in my opinion except in this one case, the case of Mr Kumar who never did explain how his face got like that and just went on insisting as she did that they hadn't seen each other since the night they visited a temple.'

'What about the others?'

'Oh they played dumb too. They pretended they'd spent the whole evening drinking in the hut. They never changed their story but if Hari Kumar had split on them they'd have taken him with them. There was a pretty odd thing happened about her bicycle. The one she was supposed to be dragged off. First the police said it was found outside Kumar's house and then the DSP said no that was wrong it had been in the Bibighar Gardens near the scene of the rape and put in the police truck that went to get Kumar, and a sub-inspector who came on the scene late thought one of the constables had found it in the ditch outside the house and put that down in a report. Indians said the DSP planted the bike himself and then realized it looked too bloody obvious. My own theory is that these other five took the bike from the Gardens and stuck it outside Kumar's place and that the DSP didn't find Kumar's or any of their fingerprints on it because they'd wiped it clean, and guessed they'd been trying to incriminate him alone. It's just the sort of crazy thing boys like that would do, forgetting that if Kumar was incriminated they wouldn't stand a chance themselves.'

'But that would mean this police chap withheld vital evidence.'

'Messy evidence. Rigged evidence. Without Kumar's prints on the handlebars or the saddle the sort of evidence he didn't want. He wanted Kumar. A jury would have been very wary about the girl's bike being found outside Kumar's house even if wiped clean of fingerprints. I don't think he was very interested in the other fellows. Whenever people talked to him about the case Kumar's was the only name he ever mentioned. I think he disliked the chap because of the kind of boy he is. First-rate British public-school education, but black as your hat and going out with an English girl, and politically unreliable.'

'Was he politically unreliable?'

'A young educated Indian? It's likely, isn't it? On the other hand the paper he worked for was Indian-owned but pro-British. Not that that means anything. The police must have had enough on all six for the civil to decide to lock them up without trial as political detenus when the rape charge couldn't be got to stick, but everyone knows that locking them up like that was nothing more than a face-saver. She wasn't able to stop that. But by God she stopped the charges and she stopped the trial. The assistant commissioner was scared stiff about what she might come out with. They hadn't a hope in hell of bringing the beggars into court with Miss Manners as the only witness for the prosecution ready to swear blind that the fellows who raped her were peasants, and saying God knows what else. You have to admire her. Well. You do if you accept my proposition that Kumar had her but didn't rape her and that they're both bloody well in love.'

'Did the DSP know her well?'

'In a place like that everybody knows everybody as likely as not. If you mean was he sweet on her himself I can't answer. He wasn't married and plain as they say she was she'd have been a good catch for a man like him, but he struck me as a pretty cold fish. Thought of nothing but his job, I'd say. Not a sociable character. Abstemious. Never heard him make a joke. Old Reid liked him though, but then Reid always admired a man for his guts first. Anything else came a poor second. Well, there it is. That's my theory. Who else is thirsty?'

No one was. The theory was peculiarly unacceptable. An hour later when the bar had been closed for some time Major Mackay was lifted off his stool by three servants and carried through to the room he occupied, undressed and tucked into bed. He smiled in his sleep. With that, the troubles could be said to have come to a happy end.

*

Barbie got up from the rush mat, buttoned the high-necked nightgown and shivered. It was cold enough now to have the electric fire on in the bedroom but she had begun to explore the by-ways of self-mortification and had asked Aziz not to switch it on as he did Mabel's an hour before bedtime. She climbed chilled into bed, turned the lamp off and lay for a while blowing dandelion clocks, each one as useless as the last. The grey-white tufts wafted away almost before her breath reached them, leaving her to hold a limp sappy stalk. And tonight the alternative, smelling roses, didn't work either. They were of a scentless variety and on the turn, bulbous seedboxes with a few overblown petals so precariously attached she hardly dared to touch them. She counted sheep but they were stubborn and the gate too high.

She counted children. They submitted to her calculations with expressions of ill-concealed dislike of such regimentation. She called the roll and crossed names out with a blue crayon. When all the names were crossed out one child remained uncalled: the little Indian girl to whom the blue crayon had belonged. She could not remember the little girl's name. The little girl couldn't remember it either and accused her silently of depriving her both of name and crayon. The little girl would not go away until her name was called. It was an impasse. We are stuck with each other, Barbie said, which is absurd because you have Krishna and I have Jesus. We are separately catered for. Let's shake hands and call it a day. But the little girl had her hands behind her back and kept them there.

Hold it higher, her mother said, so she held the porcupine higher and counted pins going into the place where the neck and shoulders had to be altered. Altared. Her mother was sticking the pins in too deep. Little beads of blood appeared like drops of red sweat on the white satin. The bride continued to smile like the Spartan boy with the stolen fox under his shirt. Observe, her mother said, the advantages of a strict upbringing in a family of rank.

Her father was singing one of his funny songs. I've seen a deal of gaiety throughout my noisy life. Barbie sang it to her mother. Stop that vulgarity, her mother said. So she sang alone under her breath but found she had forgotten everything except the first line. The stairs were always dark and smelt of damp and gas jets and old linoleum. The paper on the walls was brown and patchy. She sang the first line of the vulgar song over and over going up the stairs but still under her breath because the stairs frightened her. She counted the stairs but there had only ever been twenty of them including the landing floor. Twenty stairs were not enough to send her to sleep.

She switched on the lamp. Slowly she was in India again and as she returned to India she became homesick, ridiculously, unaccountably, inexpressibly homesick. The old chaukidar would be asleep on the front porch huddled in his blanket like a tired shepherd. She felt disturbed and then, hearing the weird calling of the jackal packs, lost in an immense area of experience, the whole area that separated her from childhood and young womanhood. She thought of it as an area because the separation seemed to be in space, not in time.

She sat up wrapped in her own arms. The light from the bedside lamp did not reach the farther walls but the glass that protected the picture gleamed faintly. Behind the glass there was nothing. The picture had gone out.

She thought: I have gone out, Thou hast gone out, He she or it has gone out.

She reached for Emerson who had not gone out but had been renewed and renewed to Mrs Stewart's perplexity.

'Each new law and political movement has meaning for you,' Barbie read and was convinced that this might be so because Emerson told her. 'Stand before each of its tablets and say, "Here is one of my coverings. Under this fantastic, or odious, or graceful mask did my Proteus nature hide itself." This remedies the defect of our too great nearness to ourselves.'

She put Emerson aside and picked up her pocket dictionary. Proteus. Changing or inconstant person or thing. Amoeba. Kinds of bacteria. She laid aside the dictionary and recovered Emerson from the bed-cover. She had lost the place but with Emerson that never seemed to matter.

'The world exists for the education of each man. There is no age or state of society, or mode of action in history, to which there is not somewhat corresponding in his life. Everything tends in a most wonderful manner to abbreviate itself and yield its own virtue to him. He should see that he can live all history in his own person. He must sit at home with might and main, and not suffer himself to be bullied by kings or empires, but know that he is greater than all the geography and all the governments of the world . . .'

Suddenly she was aware of the intense stillness of Rose Cottage. Intense stillness and a faint odour as of something singed. She put Emerson away, got out of bed, put on her slippers and her long blue dressing-gown. She wondered whether Mabel had remembered to turn her fire off, whether something was in danger of scorching or bursting into flames.

She left her door open so that she could see her way across the hall. There was a slit of light under Mabel's door. She hesitated. The smell had gone. She went to the door and tapped very gently. She got no answer. She tapped again and said, Mabel. She would have gone back to bed because she realized how silly it was to expect a deaf person to hear and she did not want to open the door and frighten her. But potential alarm was exerting its hollow fascination. She opened Mabel's door until she had a gap wide enough to admit her head and one shoulder.

Mabel was asleep propped on the pillows. The light was still on. Mabel's head had fallen to one side and her reading glasses were low down on her nose and looked as if they might come adrift and get broken and cause damage to her eyes and face. A book was open on her lap. The hand that had held it lay inert.

The fire was off. Barbie went to the bedside. She took the book away, placed it on the table with its tasselled marker between the pages at which it had been open. Next, she very carefully removed the dangerous spectacles, returned them to the leather case. She settled the pillows, drew the sheet and blankets farther up. She wanted to cover Mabel's hands but decided not to in case she woke her up. She seemed to have disturbed her slightly as it was. A sigh came. And then a sound in the back of the throat almost like something being said.

Barbie looked down at her friend. Very briefly she had a ridiculous idea that she didn't like her. At the same time she knew that she loved her. And she knew that Mabel was fond of her in spite of not appearing to be fond of anyone much. It was a curious relationship, like one between two people who hadn't yet met but who would love each other when they did. Mabel had come closer to meeting her than she had come to meeting Mabel. After three years Barbie still knew almost nothing about her friend but even if one discounted facts not taken in because of deafness Mabel must now know almost everything about Barbie because Barbie had told her over and over. Telling Mabel things was part of the job of looking after her, almost more important than doing things to absolve her from household cares and responsibilities. Without the actuality of Barbie's voice incessantly saying things Barbie thought that Mabel would not have appreciated so much the silence in which she seemed to exist. The only thing Barbie had never told her about was her secret sorrow. When she looked at Mabel as she was doing now she believed Mabel knew about it anyway and had known from the beginning.

She thought: In a way my secret sorrow is Mabel. I don't know how much of me gets through. I'm rather like a wave dashing against a rock, the sounds I make are just like that. There is Mabel, there is the rock, there is God. They are the same to all intents and purposes.

Mabel stirred but did not wake. How old she looked in bed, immensely old. Barbie put out her hand to switch off the lamp. The old woman made that noise in her throat again as if disturbed by the shadow of Barbie's arm. She made it again. She was muttering but the sound came from her throat because her lips were too far gone in the drug of each day's little death to come together properly. She muttered for several seconds then paused and then said something which caused Barbie to stand alert and undecided with her finger and thumb on the little ebony key-switch of the old-fashioned brass table lamp, willing the echo of the sound to pause too before continuing on its flight into a state of being beyond recall. She caught the rhythm back first and then the vowel sounds, then the consonants. A name, a woman's name, Gilliam Waller.

She watched Mabel's face but could not tell anything from it. There was no more muttering. Mabel had reached wherever she had been going. Beyond Gilliam Waller she had found the dark of dreamless sleep.

*

TRAGIC DEATH OF ENGLISH MISSIONARY

Ranpur, October 29th, 1942

The death is reported in Mayapore two days ago of Miss Edwina Crane, superintendent of the district's Protestant Mission Schools who was roughly handled by a mob during the August riots and narrowly escaped with her life when another teacher, Mr D. R. Chaudhuri, was murdered. Police have so far been unable to apprehend their attackers.

At an inquest held yesterday in Mayapore a statement obtained from Miss Crane's servant was submitted by the police. According to this man his mistress sent him to the bazaar at 3.45 pm to collect a package from the chemist. Since her return from hospital he had frequently gone on such errands. On this occasion however the chemist said he knew nothing of a prescription for Miss Crane. The servant then returned home.

Reaching there he smelt burning and saw smoke. A shed in the compound was a mass of flames and servants from neighbouring houses were attempting to extinguish it. One of these men called out that Miss Crane was in the shed.

The police submitted a statement from this other man. Shortly before 4 pm he had seen a woman in a white saree in the compound of the mission superintendent's bungalow. Thinking it was someone who had no business there he challenged her. She motioned him to go away. He observed that the woman in the white saree was Miss Crane. Neither he nor her own servant had ever seen her adopt this mode of dress. He watched her go into the shed and then returned to his work. Shortly afterwards he smelt smoke and noticed that the shed was on fire.

The police also submitted a note found in Miss Crane's study addressed to the Coroner. An official in Miss Crane's Mission confirmed that it was in her handwriting. The note which was not read out at the inquest was accepted by the police as satisfactory evidence of Miss Crane's determination to take her own life.

Dr Jayaprakash, consultant physician at the Begum Mumtez Zaidkhan Purdah hospital and health officer to the mission schools stated that he had attended Miss Crane for some years. Normally in excellent health she had not regained it since the attack on her in August. After her discharge from hospital he prescribed tonics and advised her to take a holiday. On his last visit about a week before her tragic death she told him she had decided to retire from the mission.

A verdict of suicide while the balance of the mind was disturbed was recorded.

A touching note was struck when Miss Crane's servant who seemed to confuse the proceedings with a legal case asked whether 'Madam was to be released and restored to him.' A colleague of the late Miss Crane at the Mission who led the weeping man from court told your reporter that this man, Joseph, had served Miss Crane since he was a kitchen boy at the mission in Muzzafirabad (NWFP) where Miss Crane taught before the Great War. 'She was a heroine to him. She stood alone at the door of the school guarding the children and faced up to a gang of armed hooligans who threatened to burn the school down.'

The funeral took place later in the day. Waiting outside the cemetery were groups of Indian women, mothers of some of the children who attend the mission schools. After the funeral rites were over your reporter noted that these women entered the cemetery and placed flowers on the grave.

*

She went into the bathroom and locked the door and the other door that led to the verandah and the door that led into the little spare. She got down on her knees on the cold floor and clasped her hands on the rim of the smooth white porcelain hand-basin, then groped for her damp flannel and stuffed it into her mouth so as not to disturb the house. She reached up and turned the tap on full. The water spashed into the bowl, down the pipe and out into the open runnel that carried it away. She sank lower until her body was almost touching her thighs and let herself sob aloud.

Edwina had sinned. But that was not why Barbie wept. The question of what would happen to Edwina's soul was beyond her power to calculate. It would be settled in limbo which to Barbie was a bleak and incomprehensible but real place chilled by God's breath and darkened by the Devil's brow; barren neutral territory where the dead waited, trembling and naked, incapable of further action to support a claim to either kingdom. To kill oneself was wicked. Her father had killed himself with drink walking with a skinful under the hooves and wheels of a horsedrawn carriage on the Thames Embankment. Her widowed mother had killed herself not with work as people said but with a combination of heartless love and heartless pride better known as keeping up appearances. Their deaths were small sins in comparison with Edwina's terrible act of self-destruction but in their private little despairs of which the drinking and the pride had been evidence she had long since learned to see a glimmer of the devil's face; thoughtful, chin in hand, offering recompense, suggesting anodynes that were not that at all but addictive means of excitation of the ill he did.

Barbie's Devil was not a demon but a fallen angel and his Hell no place of fire and brimstone but an image of lost heaven. There was no soul lonelier than he. His passion for souls was as great as God's but all he had to offer was his own despair. He offered it as boundlessly as God offered love. He *was* despair as surely as God was love.

And that was why she wept. Blinded by her tears, still kneeling, she reached out, entering that moment that should have brought her to the centre of the sublime mystery but did not because there was no mystery. She was an old woman like Edwina and the dead body was the one Edwina guarded – her life in India come to nothing.

She wept because the gesture that had seemed sublime revealed an

Edwina who was dumb with despair not purified by love. Revelation of Edwina's despair uncovered her own, showed its depth, its immensity. For herself she could have borne the knowledge, would have to bear it. For Edwina it must have been a cruel thing. Edwina had always seemed so strong and sure in God, in God's purpose, so richly endowed that just to be near her was to share her gift and feel one's doubts turn sour for want of nourishment.

And yet Edwina must have felt it too, the ever-increasing tenuousness of the connection, the separation in space as God inexplicably turned His face from humble service He no longer found acceptable but was too kind actually to refuse.

She rose painfully from her knees and soaked the flannel under the running tap, carried it sopping to her face and repeated the process until her face was chilled and only her eyeballs felt hot. Edwina's faith had been of a higher order than her own, she had no doubt, and as a consequence her despair had been great enough to disturb the balance of her mind. But the disturbance could not be offered in mitigation because it was, itself, the work of the Devil. She looked in the mirror that hung above the basin. On the opposite wall there was another mirror. She was multiplied back and front. Frontwards she was Barbie, approaching herself, and backwards another self retreating through one diminishing image after another into some kind of shocking infinity.

She felt her skin freeze and harden as warmth went out of her blood. The bathroom was suddenly rank with the nausea, fetid and foul, but there was in its foulness a sense of exquisite patience and desire. She clutched her abdomen and her throat, leant over the bowl and was sick. She retched and gasped. The tap was still on and the running water carried the horror away. Now she supported herself gripping the porcelain basin. She let the water run until the whiteness sparkled again. Her whole body felt clammy. Slowly its warmth returned.

She rinsed her mouth over and over and then turned the tap off. When the last gurgle had died away there was a silence such as might follow a sigh.

'Poor creature,' she said. She shut her eyes. 'I know who you are and I know you are still here. Please go.'

She waited, then caught her breath at the sound of a slow ungainly winged departure as of a heavy carrion bird that had difficulty in overcoming the pull of gravity. She waited for a few minutes and then fastidiously washed her face and hands, but – still dissatisfied – unlocked the door to her bedroom, collected clean clothes, returned and dropped each discarded article into the dhobi basket until she stood naked. Redressed and cologned she went back to her room and tidied her hair.

Beauty is in the eye of the beholder, her mother had said but she had not said who might behold.

Part Two

A QUESTION OF LOYALTY

Notices in the Times of India, May 1943

Births
MANNERS. On May 7th at Srinagar. To Daphne, a daughter, Parvati.

Deaths
MANNERS. On May 7th, at Srinager, Daphne, daughter of the late Mr &
Mrs George Manners, beloved niece of Ethel and the late Sir Henry
Manners.

Forthcoming Marriages
CAPTAIN E. A. D. BINGHAM and MISS SUSAN LAYTON
The engagement is announced between Captain Edward Arthur David
Bingham, Mizzafirabad Guides, only son of the late Major A. E. D.
Bingham, MC (Muzzafirabad Guides) and of the late Mrs S. A. Hunter, of
Singapore, and Susan, younger daughter of Lt-Colonel and Mrs John
Layton, of Pankot.

I

Thus Teddie enters already marked by a fatal connexion.

Sarah Layton, subsequently describing him as a man who didn't grow on
you, as one you soon got to the end of, initially gave a lone but vivid
impression of vacuity, albeit cheerful vacuity. At the time, his future
mother-in-law, Mildred, complained that there wasn't much to go on and
although she was thinking in severely practical terms (what to tell Colonel
Layton, now transferred from an Italian to a German prison-camp, which
made it seem more imperative to make an efficient and detailed report
about the man his daughter Susan intended to marry), the idea of not much
to go on coupled with that of his not growing on you at first led one
inescapably to think of him as a person who conformed in every way with
the stock idea one might have of a young man with nothing between his
ears, a set of trained and drained responses and a cheerful complacency

that would see to it he did nothing outstandingly silly and nothing distinguished either.

How close he came to being jolted out of complacency in the first few months of 1942 in Burma was possibly indicated by his demeanour when he turned up in Pankot a year later, on Dick Rankin's staff, 'rather disappointed' with the immediate result of his attendance at the Staff College in Quetta but 'hoping for something better' in the future. Presumably he had been rather disappointed too to discover that the Japanese had proved 'more useful in a scrap' than the British and Indian armies together and, as he trudged through the jungle back to India with the remnants of his unit (because that was the direction everyone was going in who still could) hoped for an improvement presently.

One could picture him marching out, tired, dirty and hungry, carrying more than his quota of small-arms (to relieve a couple of exhausted sepoys of their weight), keeping *on* and smiling because being personally blameless for what he supposed had to be summed up as a stunning defeat, a complete disaster, there was no call to look miserable and every reason to give an example of how to keep going, even when every limb was attached to the trunk by things that felt like loose hot rubber bands.

Between this picture of Teddie leaving Burma and the one of him arrived in Pankot a year later there is a gap, but it is one of many and it plays a perfectly proper schematic part in an account of him because to Teddie himself his whole history seems to have been a series of gaps linked by a few notable events if one is to judge by the extraordinary difficulty Mildred had in getting anything out of him except a few bare and not very encouraging bits of information and a slight frown of concentration, which could have been the effect had on him of his realization that between them he and Mildred had a duty to do.

'I do have an uncle,' he said; and added, 'In Shropshire actually,' as if this made the uncle more lively and identifiable. Teddie had lived with the uncle when sent home from India to school, just as Sarah and Susan had lived with their Aunt Lydia, Mildred's elder London-based sister. Teddie's father had been in the Muzzafirabad Guides which was why Teddie was in them now but had broken his neck hunting when Teddie was fourteen. His mother married again, a commercial chap called Hunter (which was odd when you thought of the cause of the first husband's death). They lived in Singapore until Hunter died. 'I don't mind telling you,' Teddie told Mildred, 'people said she had a rotten time with him.' She died suddenly in Mandalay on her way back to Muzzafirabad. All this was before Teddie came back to India himself to join the regiment. In due course he went to Burma, tried but failed to find her grave and worried a bit about it until he remembered she'd been cremated. In due course the Japanese arrived in Burma too and presently Teddie marched out.

And that was about it. He had red hair and sandy eyelashes (which Clara Fosdick said she thought a sign of untrustworthiness). He was twenty-five but had that elongated bony English look of not yet having completed the process of growing-up and filling out which meant that in a few years he would suddenly appear middle-aged as well as beefy because to men like this everything seemed to happen at once round about the age of thirty; everything except white hair which was reserved for retirement and was equally sudden and the only sign that old age had arrived.

School, military academy, regiment, baptism of fire, staff-college: the next logical step was marriage so that the process could be repeated through a continuing male line. Arrived in Pankot Teddie metaphorically cleared his throat, put up his head and looked round for a girl with whom to take it. It could not be any girl. The choice had ideally to be made among girls in the range labelled Army which more or less knocked out Carol and Christine Beames whose father Colonel Beames was in the civil branch of the IMS. It knocked out several others whose fathers' regiments did not in Teddie's opinion match the standard set by his own, the Muzzys, to which none of course was superior but with which one or two might claim equality. This opinion was one Teddie's father had held and Teddie had acquired it in much the same way that he had acquired a bit of private property in the shape of an unearned income, although the capital from which the income came had been filtered to him through his mother and therefore been diminished somewhat by the commercial chap Hunter, who fortunately died of drink before his mother died of what Teddie always assumed had been shame and sorrow, otherwise he might never have seen a penny of it and have been forced either to go into some sort of business or join an inferior regiment, which would have been pretty awful he supposed. He doubted that his uncle would have 'stumped up'. He believed that his uncle hadn't liked his father. His uncle had been the elder brother.

'I suppose you'll get money from your uncle eventually,' Mildred said. She believed in coming to the point and came to it stylishly, using her languid but abrasive first-two-drinks-of-the-day voice.

'Oh, I shouldn't rely on it,' Teddie said. 'He's a bit of an old skinflint. I'm not looking beyond the six hundred a year. And my pay of course.'

'Well it will be years before Susan gets anything from us,' Mildred warned him. 'So you'll just have to buckle to and rise to dizzy heights.'

'Yes. Rather.'

'Have you a photo or a snap?'

'What of?'

'Of you. So that I can sent it to John in prison-camp. I think he'll want to know what you look like, don't you?'

'I'll get one done, shall I?'

'That would help.'

'Full length or head and shoulders?'

Teddie had a practical turn of mind. It made up for his lack of imagination. He would never have thought to offer Mrs Layton his photograph but knowing that she wanted one and suddenly understanding why he saw that it was important to get it right. In uniform or mufti?

838

Postcard size for easy handling or something larger? With or without his cap? Since he seemed to have no personal vanity the questions had to be taken seriously. He couldn't be palmed off with a casual reply such as, 'Oh anything so long as it looks like you.'

He had the kind of thick skin which managed to fall just short of suggesting insensitivity. Mildred became bored with the photograph long before the details were agreed. Teddie did not notice she was bored or that she drank too much. Perhaps he did not really notice people. There were times when he did not seem to notice himself. For instance he didn't appear to be at all put out by what another man might have thought of as the delicacy or awkwardness of his position in a household where he constantly bumped into Sarah. Before he took up with Susan he had taken up with Sarah and shown every sign of not being aware of the younger sister's existence. His attentiveness to Sarah now suggested he might at any moment explain why he'd cooled off her in spite of the fact that Sarah had not encouraged him sufficiently to make his cooling off actually require an explanation. His attentiveness would have struck an outsider who knew nothing of their history as the kind a man felt he had to show the girl whose sister he was about to marry; anything apologetic in it being an apology for taking Susan away not for giving Sarah up. Perhaps that was how he saw it too.

There were several explanations given in Pankot, though, of his defection, change of mind or change of heart. Had he known about one of them he might have been surprised (at last) because it is unlikely that 'fickle' was a word he would ever expect to hear used to describe him. Had he known about the other two explanations he would have agreed with the first of them, that he had finally been unable to avoid seeing how pretty Susan was and unable to resist the strong emotion with which the sight suddenly affected him. The other explanation he would probably not have understood at all and he certainly would not have cared to hear it.

Little Mrs Smalley had described Sarah Layton in terms which were sufficiently accurate for the inaccurate conclusions she then drew from them in regard to Teddie's defection to be accepted as coming close to the mark. But Teddie would have made nothing of the Smalley image of Sarah. He surely never felt that she didn't take him seriously as a person; never felt that she took none of 'it' seriously ('it' meaning India, the British role in India, the thing the British were in India to do); never felt that she laughed at 'it' and consequently at him; never felt, being a man and therefore much more serious about 'it' than a woman had to be, that Sarah was the kind of girl who although admirable in every other way lacked the attitude which men thought it important for a girl to have underneath everything else and that this explained why after a bit men felt more comfortable in the company of the younger sister. He might have agreed with Mrs Paynton when she gathered all these potentially damaging Smalley threads into a single sensible one and declared that what Sarah needed was to settle down

839

and that she would be all right then, being fundamentally sound and a veritable rock so far as Mildred was concerned.

Getting Sarah to settle down as Mrs Bingham was exactly what Teddie had first hoped for. For him the question of her soundness never arose. Seeing her come into his office at Area Headquarters with some confidential files he had asked his friend and fellow Muzzy, Tony Bishop, Dick Rankin's ADC, who the WAC(1) corporal with the fair hair and slim figure was. The answer was tremendously satisfactory to him one assumes. Failing a Muzzy Guide girl a Pankot Rifles girl would do very well, in fact rather better because Teddie probably thought that there was something vaguely incestuous about marrying into one's own regiment. His father had done it and it really hadn't turned out at all well. If fate had at first disappointed Teddie, bringing him to a static headquarters as a mere captain when it might just as easily have sent him to an active formation perhaps as a G2, it now looked as if in bringing him to Pankot it had done so with the sole and excellent purpose of introducing him to this girl from the station's favourite regiment.

Chasing or wooing would be the wrong words to use about Teddie's activity in regard to Sarah Layton. He applied himself to her as he applied himself to any task that fell within the area of his competence. But because he was unable to think of more than one thing at a time he appeared to everybody to have mounted a frontal attack on a girl who had caught his eye and awoken feelings in him of a tender and passionate nature.

This was the light in which if he gave it any thought he must have appeared to himself and he must have given it thought, and found nothing amiss. After all chaps fell in love every day. There was nothing peculiar about it. And she was awfully nice. His father would have approved.

The most interesting gaps, perhaps, in Teddie's history are those through which one could have traced the progress or lack of it of his relationship with women. At twenty-five one assumes some heterosexual experience, but the questions – with whom? in what circumstances? – are impenetrable enough to leave about him a pure aroma of cheerful male virginity tainted only by traces of something more pungent, the odour of voluntary or involuntary nocturnal emission, which does not alter his expression but does emphasize the underlying shadows of modest perplexity.

Tony Bishop had no recollection of Teddie ever having been 'mixed up' with a girl before he applied himself so wholeheartedly to the business of being mixed up with Sarah Layton. Bishop knew him before Burma and after Burma but not during Burma, so his recollections did not cover a possibly important phase of Teddie's development. He had the unit-image of him rather than a private one. The Muzzy Guides (so Bishop said, fondly mocking) was one of those regiments which not only had a rule about never mentioning women in the mess but stuck to it with such iron resolution that an outsider could have been persuaded to believe that its young subalterns not only stopped mentioning them but stopped thinking about them too until a certain age was reached and they came face to face with a situation that called for a tricky decision: whether to remain a bachelor or get married. This question was usually settled by another of the regiment's unwritten rules which was that an officer had to have a wife before he was thirty unless he wished to enjoy a reputation for unseemly frivolity.

Since Teddie was deeply attached to his regiment – it was the one thing he may be thought of as taking seriously – the regimental aura of ambiguous monasticism probably explained Teddie's own aura of either never having sown wild oats or of having sown them so far out of range of the regimental eye that they didn't count as his but as those of someone whose body he had borrowed for the purpose. Whatever the reason for this aura, it shone behind his approach to Sarah which was that of a man whose physical appetite had never bothered him before but promised to be really rather adequate, as if it knew all about itself.

What it finally came to was that Teddie was in pursuit of an idea. The idea was initially embodied in the person of Sarah Layton. After three weeks he was close enough to her to feel that all he need do next was pop the question and settle the matter. He had, one imagines, few doubts about the outcome. She had been awfully amenable and absolutely available. He hadn't kissed her yet but he had held on to her hand and made other gestures claiming physical possession. They had played tennis, gone riding, swimming, dancing, to the pictures, the Chinese restaurant and Smith's Hotel for supper. He had called for her at the Club, at the grace and favour bungalow and once at Rose Cottage where an elderly woman (something to do with missions) had talked rather a lot about Muzzafirabad but not about those aspects of its life which he knew. Sarah and he had walked together, shared tongas, and the front bench of a staff car when he had been able to log it out as on official duties and get rid of the driver.

The next step was therefore clear. He must arrange for them to be alone so that he could put an arm round her, kiss her and say something like You know I'm most awfully Fond of You? which sounded a bit dull but was certainly the truth and once he had said it he could logically follow it up by suggesting they might Sort of Get Engaged If She Felt Like It; which was as far as one needed to go because once one had gone that far everything else surely fell into place of its own accord.

At first (Sarah says) she thought Teddie Bingham no different from other young officers who assumed that because she was there and they were there something should be done about it. But after a while she realized he was different. He had been wound up and wouldn't stop and she wasn't sure what she could do about it except hope that he suddenly ran down or noticed Susan as so many other officers had. She did not find him unattractive but this was somehow proof of what she thought of as his negative transparent quality; he was not unamusing, not unpleasant to talk to and not uninteresting up to a point which was soon reached.

When the moment came she knew instinctively that it had and was in as great a state of uncertainty as ever about how to deal with it. He encircled her and kissed her and became rather elaborately excited. She noticed that he smelt of Pears' soap. This heightened her impression of him as being transparent because suddenly he was not, having worked himself into a lather. His excitement was a bit embarrassing because he failed utterly to move her to any kind of response and she wondered whether this was his fault or hers. She had very little fear of Teddie attempting anything more serious. Apart from his lips which were glued to hers he was not actually doing anything to any part of her with any part of him which he could not have done in a ballroom or would be ashamed of in the morning.

She thought, too, that his excitement was caused less by the effect kissing her had on him than by the feeling he had of breaking out, to the degree that was allowable, from the strict confines of his normal pattern of behaviour. But a man like Teddie didn't kiss a girl as he was kissing her just for the hell of it. At any moment, she thought, he would make a declaration. She considered this imminent event as calmly as she could. She had no intention of accepting a declaration from Teddie Bingham but for an instant she understood the awful ease with which the whole business could gather momentum and overwhelm them both. If she had not been cursed with a mind that questioned everything she could at this very moment have been within an inch or two of becoming the future Mrs Bingham because she couldn't think of a single practical reason why things should not take this course, providing one discounted the question of whether they loved one another, which wasn't a question anyone seemed to take very seriously.

In any case Teddie on the face of it was doing well enough on that score for the two of them. Or had been doing well. But Sarah realized she was bored and had been bored ever since he began and suddenly she felt that he was bored too. She would have understood his becoming depressed or cross at finding his amorousness was not infectious but she had a distinct impression of his boredom. He kept the kiss going but it had taken on a remote and pointless quality, like a breath-holding contest, which it was to some extent. She had a stubborn inclination not to be the first to give in.

Just as she decided she couldn't go on he came unstuck and breathed deeply. They stared at each other in the dark of the motor-car. Surprisingly it was a serious, even tender, moment and she was afraid that in spite of everything he would make his declaration; but he didn't. For Sarah it was as if they had both drawn back in the nick of time from being involved in an association neither of them wanted but which Teddie had thought they ought to want.

Presently he resumed a proper sitting position behind the steering-wheel, looked at his luminous watch and said, 'I say, I think we ought to be getting back.'

Two days later he turned up at the grace and favour at a time when she wasn't there but Susan was. And that was that. He was still wound up, still working. She thought he would run down and disappear like Susan's other young men whose numbers remained more or less the same while their names and faces altered. But within a month he was engaged to Susan to be married. It was this that so surprised Sarah. One day he had been just one of the crowd round her sister; the next he was the only one. Susan seemed to have put out her hand and picked out the toy she decided she liked best. Sarah had a picture of Teddie held upside down with his wheels racing and the spring whirring, his eyes closed in the ecstasy of being singled out and taken to Susan's heart forever.

But in real life Teddie was upright, on his feet, and his eyes open, alight with the pleasure if not the pain of being in love – or what passed for it in his opinion; and his opinion was the only one that could matter to him and was in this sense as good as anyone else's. Allow him that happiness, and the illusion that it sprang from Susan and not from an idea. The moment in the car with Sarah could possibly have been a turning point but the effort of making it would have been tremendous, virtually impossible. It would have involved treachery to his upbringing, a complete rearrangement of the ego, a thorough breaking-out, an entry into an unknown and rather frightening world. Besides it is better to accept the explanation that lies nearest and easiest to hand: that Sarah's lack of interest eventually got through to him as a failure of physical response, as a personal rebuff, not as a general pointer to the boring artificiality of the situation that could have prodded him alive to the fact that to date his life had been one protracted grinding experience of boredom after another because he never did anything, never would do anything, except according to the rules laid down for what a man of his class and calling should do and for how and why he should do it.

There was of course that little gap (characteristic) between getting Sarah home and turning up a couple of days later to take up with Susan. Perhaps the gap in this case represented a dark night of Teddie's soul (a whiff of that pungent odour?), a battle between a disturbing new instinct, only half felt, and an old safe and happy one which was familiar and reliable and inevitably the victor. In that case the spoils were Teddie, not Susan.

'I'd rather they waited,' Mildred told Sarah. It was apparent that she had in mind a long period; waiting until Colonel Layton was restored to them, in other words until the end of the war. But Susan would not wait. Neither would Teddie. Together they seemed to recognize a sense of urgency as if they wanted to abide by the rules while the rules were still there to abide by. The announcement of their engagement appeared on the same day as those other two announcements which advertised the fact that one of the rules had already been broken. It was the first coincidence and perhaps it was significant. This was in the second week of May. Mildred agreed to put the notice in *The Times* because Susan insisted and Mildred saw no harm in putting in what could easily be taken out by a second announcement of the cancellation she expected at any moment – for instance when Teddie produced the photograph and Susan looked at it and imagined herself left with that and nothing else after Teddie had gone back to the war as he was bound to eventually.

But the photograph turned out surprisingly well. Teddie's smile was rendered down to a quirky upward twitch of one corner of the lips which gave the lower part of his face a look of even-tempered manly resolution. The stilted professional studio lighting had for once worked on a fortuitously inspired level and produced a sort of subdued halo that was reflected again by a dreamy look in the eyes, so that his face was amazingly that of the soldier-poet, the man of action capable of making sensitive judgments. When Susan saw it she at once demanded a cabinet-sized copy and had it framed for her bedside table. Towards the end of May, publicly acknowledging that there was not another thing she could do to delay matters, Mildred announced that the wedding would be shortly after Susan's 21st birthday, which fell in November. It was the most she could do to relate the affair to circumstances beyond her control. She wrote to her sister Fenny in Delhi who came up at once to inspect Teddie. Aunt Fenny thought him 'rather sweet'. Apart from Susan she was the first person, perhaps, to see anything below the surface.

II

Before making the necessary imaginative readjustment to see most of the rest of the short life of Edward Arthur David Bingham almost entirely from Teddie's point of view one minor and possibly irrelevant aspect of his behaviour is to be noted. His experience of combat conditions had coarsened his vocabulary.

In certain circumstances in male company he nowadays permitted himself to use words he had seldom found it necessary to use before going with the first battalion to Burma. The standard of vulgarity he reached never rose above that acceptable in an officer of his type and standing and he would never have dreamed of swearing in the mess let alone in front of women. The Muzzys had been as strict about bad language in the mess as about references to the weaker sex, if anything stricter. Damn was allowed, in fact it did not count, but bloody was frowned upon if used by anyone below senior field-rank. Teddie therefore found the conversation in the junior officers' mess at area headquarters alarmingly and disagreeably lax. He was quite shocked. Regular officers from good regiments could still be relied on to do as Teddie did – reserve bad language for private or office occasions – but this mess was full of curious unmilitary fellows with emergency commissions and civilian habits. Fortunately as he thought it he seldom had to eat there. He and Tony Bishop together with an officer of the engineers and a gunner lived in a chummery a few bungalows down the road from Nicky Paynton and Clara Fosdick. In the chummery mess he maintained formality of manner and speech and once rebuked the gunner for the terms in which he expressed an opinion about the origin of the woodcock toast.

But in private, the bedroom he shared with Tony Bishop and in the daftar, Teddie's otherwise predictable statements and responses were enlivened by certain rich images and expletives often enough for Bishop to have marked them down as something new in Teddie dating from the Burma experience, indicative of the kind of wildness even a cheerful and level-tempered fellow like Bingham would have found bubbling up in him when (as he now described it) the shit hit the fan and he had to duck.

Bishop went so far as to see two Teddie Binghams: the one who stood upright encased in the armour of the mystery of being a Muzzy Guide and the one who in moments of office crisis stepped out of the armour's support with no warning whatsoever and emphatically but unvehemently announced his opinion that the situation was balls-aching, only just short of a fuck-up, and that he had no intention of being buggered about.

*

The signal ordering him to a place called Mirat to take up a G3(O) appointment at the headquarters of a new Indian division had originally been sent to Muzzafirabad. The delay and confusion caused by this administrative error led to a further signal, peremptory in tone, which managed to give the impression that Teddie was to be blamed for not being where he was not and must make up for it by leaving for Mirat immediately.

This second signal which was the first Teddie knew of his default was brought round to the chummery by special messenger on an evening in the middle of July*. There was a thunderstorm in progress which lent the occasion an apt touch of flashy drama. Teddie was lowering his long ribby body into the tin tub in the ghusl-khana. It was 6.15. He had had a hard day at the office. He was due at the grace and favour at 7.30 to take Susan to the Electric Cinema and had just bitten his bearer's head off because the dhobi-wallah had failed to turn up with his second suit of khaki-drill. Allah Din had gone grumbling into the storm. Meanwhile the bhishti had heated the bathwater above the degree Teddie enjoyed, had left no tin of cold and was presently nowhere to be found.

As Teddie's buttocks made contact with the steaming water his thighs came out in goosepimples to compensate. His knees smelt of leather, which reminded him of when he was a boy having a hot bath after a game of football. He completed his submersion and breathed out slowly. He reached for the Lifebuoy soap (Pears' was for face and hands) and just then Tony Bishop walked in with the fatal signal and the messenger's pad for Teddie to sign.

Teddie had one sterling military quality. He never panicked. The word immediate had no galvanizing effect on his intellectual machinery.

* 1943.

Immediate meant as soon as possible because nothing could be sooner than that. In the past year he had become aware that there were people in positions of authority who pretended otherwise. They put texts up on their office walls and issued directives advocating the strangest beliefs: for instance that what was difficult could be done at once whereas the impossible might take a little longer.

Teddie thought this showy and undeserving of serious consideration. He was inclined to blame the Americans, who mistook activity for efficiency, and those civilian elements in the wartime army who were naturally anxious to get it over and done with and go back into commerce where they belonged. Between them the Americans and the civilians were trying to dictate the pace of army operations and run them like a business. And they were being encouraged in this by the careerists and odd-men-out in the regular army who saw the war as an opportunity to promote themselves and their eccentric ideas.

Teddie distrusted anything to which the word flamboyant could be applied. On the other hand he admired what his Shropshire uncle called style. Not knowing quite what style was he sometimes had difficulty in distinguishing it from flamboyance and thought his uncle must have been right when he said style was on the wane and went unnoticed in an age in which vulgarity was admired more often than it was deserted. Teddie took pride in having some style himself. At the moment it meant sitting on in his bath for at least five minutes after Bishop had opened and read the signal, after he had dried his hands to read it himself, sworn, signed the book and sent Bishop away.

Quite unfairly behaviour like this gave rise to an idea that Teddie was a bit slow-witted. His confidential report at Quetta, while paying tribute to his cheerfulness and capacity for work, had mentioned lack of 'verve'. The phrase had caused him no lasting pang.

Actually Teddie grasped all the implications of the posting at once. Where the slowness came in was in the method that came most naturally to him of considering them one at a time in a roughly ascending order of priority; for example: where exactly was Mirat? How long would the journey take? Should he take his own orderly with him? Did he really want to in view of the fact that the fellow couldn't organize his laundry? Who was the divisional commander? Had he heard anything at the daftar about this particular formation? Would he be able to get leave in August to join Susan and her family on the late holiday they were planning to take in Srinagar? Would he be able to get leave later in the year to come back to Pankot for the wedding? Would Susan kick up a fuss about changing the arrangements if a change was necessary? Since the posting did not bring him any promotion would it be worthwhile having a word with General Rankin to see if it could be cancelled? Did he want it cancelled? Was it fair to marry a girl when it looked as if he was in for another dose of active service? He had thought of that before but had she? Should he ask her whether she would like to be released from their engagement?

The prospect of her saying she would suddenly looked very likely to him because it would bring his world in ruins about his head; and there on that July evening in the tin tub Teddie – one may fancy – could not rid himself of the idea that he might be turning out to be the sort of man around whom things collapsed, not noisily but with a sort of slithering, inexorable, folding-in and -over movement. He scrubbed his back vigorously to kill this notion but stopped when he found that in getting rid of it he had got hold of another. The friction of the bristles was making him feel randy. This feeling was persistent. It continued after he had put the brush down. It had in fact been pretty persistent on and off for some time, ever since he had set his heart on getting married.

Teddie was a firm believer in cold water. He yelled for the absent bhishti. Unexpectedly the old boy staggered in with two full cans. Teddie camouflaged himself with a sponge, swore at the bhishti for not having been available earlier and told him to leave the cans near the tub. Alone, Teddie stood and dowsed himself. There was no significant change. In fact the cold water had a setting-up effect. He shut his eyes and said, 'Oh, Christ', stepped on to the duckboard and wrestled himself dry with a towel.

*

Susan was an absolute brick. Kissing him in front of Mildred and Sarah she had said, 'Congratulations', as if being a G3(O) in a new division was something pretty terrific. For a while he felt it was. On their way to the cinema he had an ugly but exciting thought about the journey home. He felt heroic and felt that she felt he was heroic. He didn't understand the film but became physically alert each time the girl with the enormous tits got manhandled which was every few minutes. At the end of one scene there was almost nothing left of her dress. There hadn't been much of it at the start. The other ranks down in the body of the hall whistled and stamped. The film ended with her disappointingly fully-clothed kissing the fellow with the jaw who was lying on the steps of a church riddled with bullets. For some reason it was also snowing.

In the tonga Teddie held Susan's hand – the ungloved one – and surprisingly she let him and even seemed to want it. His thoughts stopped functioning in anything like a logical order. Normally when they were alone the chaste kisses and affectionate gestures Susan allowed in public were somehow made difficult as if she disapproved of what they might lead to.

'We could have coffee at the chummery,' Teddie said.

'Aren't we going to the Chinese?'

'I mean after.'

'Oh,' Susan said. Then: 'Yes, we could.'

Like that. Teddie's neck prickled. They had never been in the chummery alone. His hand and hers were clammy. He did not dare squeeze in case it frightened her. His heart was pumping nastily. It took only two minutes to get from the cinema forecourt to the restaurant. All the bazaar shops were open and brightly lit by electric bulbs or naphtha lamps. The street was full of British Other Ranks. Some were lounging against the pillars of the arcade in a slovenly manner with their hands significantly in their trouser pockets talking to Eurasian girls in white high-heeled shoes. In one shop a radio played Indian film music. The tonga stopped outside the restaurant.

Teddie got down. Susan's face was coloured faintly by the lights. She looked marvellous. But she wasn't looking happy.

'Teddie, I'm not awfully hungry.'

'Oh.'

He climbed back in. A muscle in his left cheek twitched of its own accord.

'Just coffee then?'

'Yes.'

He twisted round and spoke to the wallah. The tonga was turned in the street, causing trouble to other vehicles. The wallahs shouted at each other. For a while all the tongas were stationary. The wallahs waved their arms. Teddie felt put out because he and Susan were at the storm centre. He hated scenes but in any case this one was like having everything advertised.

He hit the wallah on the shoulder and told him to get moving.

The wallah obeyed but continued to exchange insults with each of the wallahs in the line of tongas whose free passage he had blocked. And the driver of the tonga immediately behind their own, coming in their wake, shouted insults too, presumably at their driver but in effect at them. The damned fellow was grinning too, as if he knew.

They did not hold hands. When the tonga left the lighted area they continued not holding them. There were puddles at intervals reflecting the infrequent street lamps. Between lamps the night was promisingly dark and humid. On other occasions when he had invited her to the chummery she had always managed to work the conversation round to the question of who else would be there before accepting. It was becoming clearer and clearer to him that tonight she had no intention of asking and that she anticipated finding exactly what she would find: nobody. Tony Bishop was dining at Flagstaff House. Bruce Mackay, the engineer, was down in Ranpur, and Bungo Barnes, the gunner, had gone round to see the QA sister, Gentleman's Relish. He would not be back until the small hours. Teddie had seen Gentleman's Relish only once. Her other name was Thelma and he thought her extremely unattractive and alarmingly common for a girl who ranked as an officer. Since Bungo had a reputation for never wasting time on a girl who – as he put it – didn't, Teddie assumed that Gentleman's Relish did, and more often than seemed reasonable because Bungo had been out every night for two weeks and looked washed out at breakfast. Where they did it he had no idea. He disapproved of Bungo Barnes. He also envied him.

When they reached the chummery he envied Bungo more than ever because he knew that the whole thing was hopeless. Susan wasn't that kind of girl. Her trim little body was protected by some sort of absolute statement about its virginity this side of the altar. She might wish otherwise but that was how it was for her, for him. As usual lights were on in the porch, entrance-lobby and living-room. Prabhu, Bungo Barnes's equally lascivious servant, came out pander-like from the dining-room to see what was happening.

'Oh, you're duty-wallah are you, Prabhu? We'd like coffee.'

'May I change my mind and have tea?' Susan asked. She stood in front of the screened fireplace dealing with her gloves and handbag in that stunning way girls had.

'Anything you want, old thing,' Teddie said. 'Matter of fact I thought I'd have a peg. Would you prefer that?'

'No, tea is what I'd like. I've got rather a head.'

'Oh, Lord, you'd better have an aspirin.'

'No, I don't want an aspirin, Teddie. Just tea.'

'Strong or weak?'

'Just as it comes.'

'It usually comes like dishwater in this place.' He told Prabhu to bring tea but make sure that the water boiled.

'I say, do sit down or something.'

'I will in a minute.'

They stood, apart, smiling at each other. The room had always struck Teddie as a bit chintzy for an all-male establishment. He thought it awfully nice tonight because she was in it. Her dress had white and navy-blue flowers on it.

'I say is that new?'

'Yes.'

'It's awfully nice.'

He had not noticed it at the grace and favour because he'd been worried about how Susan would take the news. After that it had been dark most of the time. He reached out, stroked her shoulder. Her flesh was warm and cushiony under the thin silky material. The neck of the dress was cut square. He could just see the beginning of the division between her breasts. The skin was dotted with tiny little freckles. Her arms were freckled too. Delightfully. He slid his hand down the arm to the soft flesh on the inner side of the elbow.

He said, 'It's rotten going away, leaving you.'

'I know.'

Since he touched her shoulder she had not looked at him. Her eyelashes were wonderfully long. The tips curled up. There were a few freckles near the bridge of her nose. He felt tremendously moved and protective. Her beauty was so simple, so artless. She glowed with health. The freckles came out because she was always in the sunshine. She was made for a clean, healthy, simple and loving life. He clutched her suddenly, pressing her to him. Her hair smelt sweet. It tickled. He kissed her forehead through it. She was awfully tensed up. Her whole body seemed to be a skull. If he kissed and kissed her she would melt. Through their clothes their bodies would flow into each other. He kissed her again and again until he had the most shamefully majestic erection. He didn't care. She was still protected by that absolute statement. The erection was a statement too and just as absolute but in a negative way.

'Su, I love you so much.' He clasped her head, kissed her closed lids. Soft, marvellous, living warmth. The melting would begin here. 'So much, honestly, honestly.'

He heard the tea-things clunking like monks' sandals and broke away, turned his back on her and the approaching Prabhu and walked, sweetly bitterly crippled, to the drinks cabinet. When he heard the tray set down he said without looking, 'Thank you, Prabhu. Just leave it, will you.' He opened a bottle of Johnnie Walker and poured a stiff measure. His eyes felt hot and hollow. His limbs were steady but felt as if they were not. He wasn't sure if there was enough blood in the soles of his feet. His knees were awkwardly placed in his legs, a shade out of true. He didn't really want soda but wasn't yet ready to face around to things so popped a bottle and poured a long one. He thought therapeutically about liquor; of what it could do to your liver. His mother's second husband, Hunter, couldn't have had any liver left.

When he came away from the cabinet Susan was sitting on one of the chintzy chairs staring at the tea-tray which Prabhu had put down on an ornate and untrustworthy mother-of-pearl encrusted table. It was maddening how easy it was to get worked up, how difficult to do anything about it if you cared about things like marriage and doing right by each other. She looked pretty pale. He hadn't yet asked her if she'd prefer to be released from their promise and come to an understanding that they weren't actually bound to each other while he was away; and now didn't dare, not because she might jump at the chance but because it would be a damned insult after the way he'd just pressed up against her. When she suddenly reached for the teapot, using both hands, the little cluster of engagement diamonds glittered balefully. The line between self-sacrifice and acting like an unspeakable cad seemed perilously thin.

He sat on the sofa at the end near her chair and watched her perform her womanly little tasks. A lifetime of tea-trays stretched ahead of them. Or might. With luck. He felt a draught as of a premonition that he'd drawn a dud chit out of luck's hat and had been given Susan either briefly to make up for it or to give him a sniff of what he was going to miss. He was on the point of declaring an intention to talk to Dick Rankin in the morning about pulling strings to keep him in Pankot when to his great relief (because the intention was a callow quivering hand with a sleek shiny white feather in it) Susan said:

'Of course it was bound to happen, this proper job I mean. I hoped it wouldn't happen so soon which was silly of me, but it doesn't make any difference does it?'

'Difference?'

'Difference to us.'

'What difference could it make?'

'I thought you might think we should wait, not make definite plans. Settle for a long engagement.'

'Do you think we should?'

She glanced into the pot to check how full it was. 'No,' she said, 'if necessary I think we should speed things up.'

She raised the cup to her lips and Teddie raised his glass. They were both trembling. Teddie couldn't think why but it seemed touching and very serious. Just then they heard a car on the gravel and in a moment Tony Bishop came in looking done up. The Rankins had been entertaining visiting top brass but Tony had been able to mention Teddie's posting-order. General Rankin said Teddie's new commander was a fire-eater by all accounts, a youngish man with a reputation for unorthodoxy.

Teddie groaned. 'I suppose I'd better talk to the movement people first thing tomorrow,' he said.

'There's no need, it's all arranged. Mirat was on the blower asking where you'd got to. They said to get you down to Ranpur tomorrow and out to the airfield at Ranagunj and they'll fly you down to Mirat tomorrow night.'

'Fly? But I've never flown in my life! Supposing I'm sick?'

'I think you'll have to get used to it. Your new general's tremendously keen on his officers flying whenever they can. He's air mad.'

'What about my kit? Aren't they awfully strict about weight?'

'Pretty strict. You'd better go as light as you can and I'll send your trunk on directly you tell me to.'

'What about Allah Din?'

'Sorry, no personal servants. We'll get him back to Muzzafirabad.'

'What am I going to do without Allah Din?'

'You'll probably share an orderly. I'm afraid you're in for a rather Spartan existence.'

'It's indecent. I mean hang it all Mirat's only another military station. We might be there for months. It's not like buzzing off to the Arakan.'

He felt hollow again and indignant. The new general probably had a text on the wall saying: Do it Yesterday. This turned out not far from the case. Actually it said: Do it Now.

He took Susan home in the car which Bishop had been using to ferry the Rankins' guests and had efficiently kept waiting as soon as he saw a tonga at the chummery and guessed whose it was. Unlike the tonga-wallah, who complained at being deprived of the fare back to the grace and favour, the lance-naik driver was quite happy with the arrangement. He was obviously one of those Indians who was tireless when behind a wheel and didn't care how late he worked so long as an officer signed for the journey. Teddie and Susan sat in back-seat comfort. They held hands. Teddie had stopped feeling randy and started to feel emotional but chipper too because they were together in the same emotional situation: last night out for some time to come, last few minutes, probably, of being alone together.

'It might be fun, flying,' he said.

'Yes, it might.'

'I'll tell you what would be.'

'What?'

'Flying back, for the wedding.'

'You'll tell them directly you get there, won't you?'

Practical Susan!

'Of course. I'll speak to the Gee One first thing.'

'What will happen if the division's going away almost at once?'

'It's pretty unlikely. If we do it'll be for working-up. Anyway, they'd always give an officer leave to get married. Don't worry.'

'I'll try not to.'

He cuddled her. She was still very tense. But what a girl! No scene, no shilly-shallying. Just tremendous pluck and determination. As the car turned into Rifle Range road a cold night breeze blew in through the lowered window from the open spaces of the Pankot Rifles lines. It flirted a lock of her hair against his cheek. Behind the southern ridge of the hills the sky was suddenly illuminated. Down on the plains the monsoon was loose like an electric beast.

His uncle in Shropshire always said that a thunderstorm made the milk go off in the pantry. It occurred to him that his uncle was rather a lonely sort of chap being able to notice things like that.

III

The other, empty, bed in Teddie's room had begun to make its presence felt. A plain wooden charpoy like his own, its mosquito net, folded up, was taped to the four bamboo poles tied to its legs. Three biscuit mattresses and a ticking pillow were piled at its head. Otherwise the bed was bare to the cords, awaiting an occupant.

In Mirat the rain was incessant. Violent storms were nightly visitors. They woke Teddie up. The empty bed seemed lit by St Elmo's fire; it rode the night rock-firm, half-ship, half-catafalque. In the peaceful early mornings its message was simpler but still to be reckoned with.

Ten nights after his arrival the electric beast lay quiet and he enjoyed uninterrupted sleep but woke before the orderly Hosain came in with the chota hazri. His eyes recorded the fact that the other bed was fully shrouded by its mosquito net several seconds before this struck him as new. He raised his head from the pillow and stared through the mesh of his own net. The other bed was occupied. He raised the net. How awfully odd. He thought back over his sleep and dreams but could recall nothing which the presence of the recumbent figure explained. His sleep had been wholly undisturbed. It was as if the figure had slowly materialized during the night and had now reached a stage of total conviction about itself and its surroundings. Teddie frowned. He was unused to thinking in imaginative terms. He glanced towards the window.

His own clothes were in their usual place: jacket thrown carelessly over a chair back, trousers on the seat, underclothes on the floor. The other chair held clothes too but these were neatly arranged. Nearby stood a large leather suitcase and a bedroll which had obviously been opened to remove sheets and pyjamas then rolled up again but left unstrapped. The chap couldn't have done all that in the dark. And he must have had an orderly to help him, if not young Hosain.

Teddie reached for his slippers, automatically tapped them by the heels on the floor to dislodge any lurking scorpion gone into hiding during the night, set them side by side, swung his legs out and slipped his feet into them. The bed creaked. The other chap must have moved like a cat. Obviously a considerate sort of fellow. Teddie grabbed his robe. The humidity was high. The ceiling fan was whispering round at its lowest number of revs a minute. He clicked the dial a couple of notches higher and was rewarded by a faint and regular blowing on his forehead. Leaving the switchboard and going to stand under the fan he inspected his new companion's jacket. Captain's rank. Punjab Regiment. But a green armband hung over the chair back. Intelligence. Scholarly sort of fellow probably; not a real Punjab officer at all. The uniform and the pips looked new. The luggage looked very old though. Teddie twisted his head to find a name on it. The bedroll was set in such a way that any stencilled name on the canvas cover was hidden from view. The suitcase was more revealing. But initials only. R.M. There was no tin trunk. Like himself, RM had travelled to Mirat light. By what method though?

The writing-table caught his eye next. Set out upon it with noticeable precision were a briefcase, a field-service cap and a leather-bound swagger cane. The cane was parallel to the base of the briefcase and the cap lay between them with its badge facing front, squared up on an invisible line parallel with the other two. The three items were placed on the left of the blotter as if marking out that side of the desk as the new arrival's, to correspond with the placing – on the left-hand side of the room facing the window – of the chair with the new occupant's clothes on it and the bed in which he was asleep. A white line drawn from the middle of the window to the opposite wall would have defined the area which seemed to have been meticulously but silently claimed in the small hours.

But on the blotter on Teddie's side of the line there was an intruder: a piece of paper tucked into one of the leather corners. Teddie recognized it as a page torn from a Field Service Notebook. In clear rather tight handwriting it read: 'I hope I didn't disturb you. The man who helped me find my quarters said our orderly is called Hosain. I should be grateful if you would ask him to wake me with tea at 0830 but not before as I did not get in until 0300. The train was badly held up. I'm told breakfast is between

0800 and 0930 but I shall skip it. I look forward to meeting you later in the day, perhaps at lunch if we are messing together. Meanwhile my thanks and my apologies for any noise last night. Ronald Merrick.'

In this note Teddie thought there was as much self-assurance as consideration. He went to the mess and on to the daftar by push-bike. At 1130 he was back in his quarters hastily packing his bedroll – Merrick was not there – and at midday was driving with the G.1, Lt-Colonel Selby-Smith, to the airfield. At 1230 he was airborne in an RAF Dakota for Delhi where he would meet the divisional commander for the first time. He was away for six days. When he returned, feeling run off his feet but happy to have come daily under the general's eye as the 'young Muzzy officer who wants to get married,' he found that Captain Merrick was away on a course. In the interval Teddie's tin trunk had arrived from Pankot; so had Merrick's, from somewhere else. Merrick's was just as old and battered as Teddie's. The rank of captain was freshly painted in, however, and a band of new black paint obliterated something that had been written underneath the surname.

Teddie, who never gossiped to servants only just managed to resist the temptation to ask young Hosain what Captain Merrick Sahib was like. He noticed that the boy took considerable care with the things Merrick had left behind and he resented this in an ill-defined way that made him feel generally at odds with his domestic arrangements.

He was feeling similarly at odds with his work. There was a looseness as yet about the organization of divisional headquarters which made it difficult for him to grasp what was going on. In Delhi the general had talked a lot about what he called fluidity and about the fellow Wingate who had recently been behind the enemy lines down the road in Burma with a specially trained brigade, trying to play havoc with the Japanese lines of communication and being supplied by air. Teddie thought that this operation sounded like a costly and showy variation of the old cavalry role of sometimes penetrating enemy-held country, beating up their baggage trains and galloping back home: useful, an antidote to boredom, but hardly a pukka strategical operation of war. And the supply by air thing had reportedly become a fiasco once Wingate's troops were out of the jungle and into the plains and having to move so fast to escape being trapped that stuff was dropped to them long after they'd had to leave the place they'd asked for it to be dropped to them in. Which meant the Jap got it. Worst of all, Teddie thought, when the operation petered out Wingate had told his chaps to split into groups and get the hell out by any means they could. From Teddie's point of view this was like an officer abrogating his responsibility at the very moment when he was most responsible. That it had been the wisest thing to do only showed how unmilitary the whole affair was.

Even so, the casualty list had been alarming. More alarming, to Teddie, was the way his own general talked about the Wingate expedition having provided the key to the problem of defeating the Japanese. Teddie had a professional soldier's contempt for anything that came under the heading of guerrilla tactics. He did not want to swan around in the jungle with a beard and a bag of rice blowing up bridges. And now he was not sure that he much wanted to play messenger-boy in a top-brass outfit like Div HQ. He missed the comradeship of his old battalion. He missed the good feeling of knowing every sepoy's name, the name of his village, the number and ages of his children, the state of health of his wife, all the things that turned the fellow from a number or a statistic in an order of battle into a man whose personal welfare was a prime consideration.

But then Teddie thought of Susan, of the dizzy heights advocated by her mother, and accepted his present status as an essential trial and testing of his ability to rise to them. A chap, worse luck, couldn't remain a cheerful subaltern or company commander for ever.

'Delhi was pretty hectic,' he told Susan in the first of the bi-weekly letters which his return to Mirat enabled him to resume. 'I didn't manage to drop round to see your aunt and uncle, Major and Mrs Grace, until the last evening. I told them it's clear there isn't any hope now of my joining you all in Srinagar either in August or September. Naturally I'm disappointed but we didn't really expect it, did we, darling? As for the wedding the form here seems to be that we go ahead with the plans already made but stand ready for a rearrangement perhaps without much notice. It was nice to see your Aunt Fenny again. She got rid of the cold she caught in Pankot as soon as she got down into Delhi again. I also enjoyed meeting your uncle Arthur. He said he was glad to have the opportunity of seeing the chap he's going to give you away to. He gave me the name and address of the houseboat contractor who's fixing you all up in Kashmir so I can send a letter to await your arrival. You'll have a lovely family holiday, I wish I were coming too but I'll be too busy to mope, so don't worry. I'm enjoying Mirat and beginning to feel my feet. I still haven't met the man I'm sharing quarters with. Please thank Tony for me and tell him the trunk's arrived safely. Now I can settle in properly. The rain's been terrific here but there's a lull at the moment. If my letters become a bit irregular you'll know it's only a matter of business before pleasure.'

He had been about to write: 'You'll know it's only because we're out and about on schemes and exercises,' but even news about training was useful to spies. Teddie had been fairly security-minded ever since in Burma his battalion (he could have sworn) had been infiltrated by fifth columnists.

*

Through the curtain of rain the distant fort looked like a stranded battleship. The general's artillery had been pounding its walls for two hours with 5.5. In four minutes when the barrage lifted his airborne commandos would parachute in to the south to establish a perimeter, cut off the garrison's flight, block advancing enemy reinforcements and mop up pockets of local resistance. The tanks would advance from the north in the van of lorry-borne infantry. Two battalions had already moved in a wide arc to launch an attack from the left and another was holding the right flank.

The general stood, wrist cocked, eyes on watch, rain dripping from the peak of his red-banded cap. Inside the command lorry the R Toc crackled. Suddenly the general's arm dropped, he turned his face up into the rain and after a few seconds smiled beatifically. A score of officers, including Teddie astride his motor-cycle, looked up into the sky. A vicious fork of lightning ripped across it. Teddie winced, blinded by the flash and deafened by the explosive bounce of thunder. When the thunder had gone tumbling and rolling out into the deep field where old Jove had thumped it, he heard a more homely sound which the general's sharper ears had caught earlier: labouring aero engines. A lone Dakota appeared out of the monsoon clouds, roared overhead low enough for them to see the figure of a man standing in the open port; the air liaison officer presumably; and then flew back into them.

'Well, gentlemen,' the general said. 'I think we may safely assume that we've taken Mandalay. Let's go home.'

Teddie muttered, 'Good.' They had been out on the ground for two days. He looked forward to a hot bath and a man-size scotch in the mess. As Div HQ sorted itself out into its several kinds of rough-country transport Teddie kicked his machine into life and went bumping and slithering down the muddy track to make sure that the general's staff car was waiting at the crossroads. A couple of officers representing the reserve brigade were standing miserably under thin branched trees. The fort at Premanagar had vanished entirely behind the curtain of rain.

*

It was dark when Teddie got back. A light in the window of his room showed that the servants' quarters had been alerted and that Hosain was prepared for him. He entered unbuckling his rain-sodden equipment, yelled for the boy and then, dropping his belt, holster, straps and pack on to the floor, paused – observing the signs of renewed occupation: a row of highly polished shoes, fresh underclothes and socks – not his own – already laid out on a chair for the morning, both beds with lowered nets and pair of slippers within foot reach; and on the other officer's side of the writing-table a pile of books and pamphlets.

There was something else on the table on Teddie's side: a round chromium tray, a jug of water and a glass each with a beaded muslin cover – a tray such as could only be got from the mess bar by signing a chit and sending an orderly over with it. He heard Hosain at the back calling for the bhishti. There was a note under the tumbler. He slid it out. 'I would have waited and joined you for dinner but I have an appointment. In view of the kind of weather I hear you've had on the scheme I thought you'd need this as well as a hot bath. R.M.'

The tumbler held three fingers of whisky.

'I say,' Teddie said.

What an extraordinarily decent thing to do. He sniffed the whisky and drank some of it neat then yelled for Hosain again and sat in a wicker arm-chair with his damp legs stuck out. The boy came in with a newly pressed suit of KD.

'Well done, Hosain,' Teddie said. But the suit was Captain Merrick's. Teddie had to wait until it had been hand-flicked and hung in one of the almirahs before he could get Hosain to come and unlace his boots. He'd had them on for thirty-six hours. Relieved of them his feet felt alternately hot and raw, cold and raw. He smoked, drank and listened to the swoosh of water as the bhishti poured it from cans into the tin tub in the adjoining bath-house. He picked up one of Merrick's books, opened it and stared at the incomprehensible Japanese text on the right-hand page. On the left-hand page there were questions in English and, underneath, the same question in phonetics to show you how it would sound if you asked it in Japanese. What is your army number? What is the name or number of your regiment? In what division is your regiment? Tell me the name of your divisional commander. What unit had the position on your unit's left flank when you were captured?

'Some hopes,' Teddie said aloud. If you ever got close enough to speak to a Japanese soldier one of you would be dead a second later. That was how poor old Havildar Shafi Mohammed had been killed, reporting a wounded Jap lying out in the open and volunteering to bring him in. The Jap had had a grenade in his tunic. He must have pulled the pin surreptitiously when he saw the Havildar get within a few paces. They both went to Kingdom Come. Merrick was wasting his time learning a bit of Japanese.

Teddie turned the page and displaced a piece of square-ruled paper which must have been marking the place Merrick had got to. In the tight neat handwriting was written: Lecture Note. 1942, approx 10,000. Berlin, Tokyo, Singapore, July '43. Mohan Singh. Bangkok Conf.

'Sahib,' Hosain said. He motioned shyly in the direction of the bath-house. Teddie replaced the marker in the book, carried his whisky into the next room and began to shed his clothes.

He came back from the mess early. He was too tired even to write to Susan. He scribbled a note and pinned it to Merrick's mosquito net. 'Thanks for the drink. Have one on me tomorrow.' He left Merrick's bedside lamp burning, turned off his own, climbed inside his net and was asleep almost at once.

Hosain woke him at 0700. He brought only one tray of tea. Hosain indicated Merrick's huddled form, put both hands to his cheek, inclined his head, shut his eyes. Teddie scratched his head, understanding himself requested to be quiet, and went off to the WC. When he left for the mess at 0800 Merrick had still not moved.

It is possible, perhaps, for death to come slowly, even gently, civilly, as if anxious to make the whole thing as painless as possible. One thinks of death at this juncture because Merrick represented Teddie's. Coupled with the civility and consideration a certain reluctance could be detected, almost as if Merrick knew and kept giving Teddie a chance to pack his bags and go before a meeting actually took place. A final opportunity occurred tha⁺ morning because Teddie saw Merrick and heard him talking for a good twenty minutes before the moment came to claim acquaintance and establish the specific relationship. But there was nothing in Merrick's appearance that caused Teddie to feel uneasy.

*

After his schemes the general held post-mortems behind locked doors in the Garrison Theatre. During his career Teddie had sat through countless hours of what in common with other junior officers he called prayers. He found that what distinguished the general's prayers were brevity, deadly earnestness and the presence – among the hybrid ranks of divisional, brigade, battalion and supporting arms officers – of VCOs and senior British and English-speaking Indian NCOs, who were seated not quite under the general's eye but in constant danger of attracting it.

One of Teddie's jobs, he discovered, was to make sure that the NCOs from the British battalions did not sit in stiff-necked seclusion but were properly mixed up with their Indian colleagues. According to Selby-Smith the general had a bee in his bonnet about mutual trust and also about making the ordinary soldier feel he had a 'share in the company'. Teddie thought that mutual trust was a matter of respect for each other's achievements in the field more than of sitting next to a chap you didn't know and hadn't got time to get to know, and he wasn't convinced of the value of the share in the company business when it involved the risk of an officer giving a silly answer to the general's questions and making a fool of himself in front of non-commissioned ranks.

The post-mortem began at 1100 hours. Since one brigade headquarters was stationed twenty-five miles to the east of Mirat and another twenty miles to the north and some of their battalions farther away still, most of the officers attending had had an early start. Some of them had stayed in Mirat overnight and looked the worse for it but neatness and formality of dress were among the things to which the general seemed to attach little importance. The general himself was wearing a set of cellular cotton overalls cut to look like battle-dress jacket and trousers and made in the new jungle green material that was not yet on general issue. His feet and shins were encased in black dispatch rider's boots. This morning to Teddie's horror he had a Paisley patterned scarf at his neck.

He spoke from notes at a lectern on the stage. His aide and an NCO from the intelligence staff produced beautifully drawn giant-scale sketch maps which they pinned efficiently to the blackboard one after the other to illustrate the points the general was making. After a while Teddie had to admit that everything began to make sense to him. For the first time he fully understood what the scheme had been about. He was even aware that it had a kind of beauty. Formless, almost shapeless, the beauty consisted in the subtle cohesion of what seemed like disparate parts and in the extraordinary flexibility of each arrangement made to bring them together.

Suddenly withering in his mind were the stiff and predictable patterns that made traditional military affairs so easy to grasp on paper, so difficult to put into operation when the real thing was all about you. His blood stirred momentarily with a new sense of excitement in his occupation. The general, direct and thrusting, was filling Teddie's mind with poetry. Teddie sat physically composed as usual, wearing the rather blank expression of a man not naturally receptive to any idea which took time to be expounded. Had the general noticed him particularly and glanced at him every so often to judge what sort of impression he was making on the young man he might have thought he was making none and so made a note to tell the G1 to replace him with a more alert and aggressive officer, in which case he would have done Teddie an injustice because Teddie's soul, uncommitted a short while ago, had risen to its feet and was gallantly attempting to expose itself totally to the revelation.

If recognition of talent had been the same as having it Teddie might have blossomed under the general's eyes. When the general threw the meeting open to questions Teddie's soul sat down, finding itself dumb, unwilling to expose itself further, but it had planted a hopeful flag. Teddie had been won over, to what he was not sure, but the boots and the Paisley scarf were now part of the man whose man he felt he could become. You couldn't call the boots and the scarf stylish but they were not really flamboyant, Teddie decided. They were idiosyncratic marks of identification.

The post-mortem was wound up by the general with a quick but comprehensive summary of the main lessons learnt and a look into the future from which Teddie got a fleeting but satisfactory glimpse of his own as one that involved no immediate move from Mirat. The formation was still in the process of working-up exercises. These would lead to a period of intensive training for jungle warfare.

'I think you may assume,' the general ended, 'that our role will be there, to the east. Some of us are familiar with jungle conditions. My advice to you is to forget them because we knew them at a bad time. We have the wrong picture. Fortunately I don't think any of us is affected by the myth of Japanese invincibility. Man for man there's no problem. That's all I have to say this morning but I ask you now to give your attention to one of my junior officers, a man recently appointed to my Intelligence staff. If any senior officers wonder why they should stay to hear what a mere captain has to say they may restrain their natural impatience if I explain first that what he will tell you is confidential and of importance to the picture we need of the enemy we may expect to meet, and secondly that he has been in the service of the Indian government for longer than quite a number of the officers present today. He is something of a rare bird, an officer of the civil authority who has managed to persuade his department to let him into the army for the duration of the war. Captain Merrick's civilian rank was a senior and responsible one. I scarcely believe him when he tells me that there was so little going on in his district that even his superior officers agreed he might be more usefully employed. I do believe him when he tells me he first applied to join the armed forces as far back as 1939 and has continually renewed his application and I suspect it was not a case of nothing much going on but of his department deciding that if they wanted any peace they would have to let him come to the war. The kind of work he was doing meant that the most suitable branch for him to serve in was intelligence and his civilian rank would have qualified him for a more senior army rank than the one he holds. I happen to know, and I have no wish to embarrass him, in any case he is now stuck with what he's got, that he had a choice between this appointment and one elsewhere which would have given him more glamorous epaulettes. He chose the more active role and the lower rank because it was an active role he was looking for. I am glad to welcome him to this formation. I repeat that what he has to tell us is confidential. There should be no general discussion of the subject inside units and certainly not outside. Although Captain Merrick will perform the ordinary tasks of a G3 this particular subject is likely to become one of his special interests and he will continue to keep in touch with brigade and battalion intelligence staffs in regard to it and to the level at which it remains a restricted subject. Brigadier Crawford, Captain Sowton and I will not stay to listen to his address because he gave us a full and detailed account last night after dinner. Thank you gentlemen. No standing if you don't mind, it only makes for disruption. Colonel Selby-Smith, will you take over please?'

The general came down from the stage, was joined by Crawford and Sowton, and left by the main aisle. From the foyer on the other side of the doors came the sound of boots stamped on the tiled floor as the men on guard duty came to attention. Selby-Smith got up and now made a gesture of invitation. On the far side of the right-hand second row of seats Teddie saw his elusive room companion rise. At first sight he looked younger than the general's reference to seniority had led Teddie to expect. Tall, fair-haired, slim and well-built, he moved with a sort of snap that Teddie would have expected in a smart cadet or a young hard-case sar'major. But once on the platform, behind the lectern, in stage-lighting, the fairness of the hair faded and the used quality of the face was revealed. He could have been any age between thirty and forty.

The hall was remarkably quiet. The general's recommendation and explanation had alerted an old instinct to dislike on sight anyone about whom there was a faint mystery, a difference, anyone who was not fully defined by rank, occupation and regiment, who appeared to have an obscure but real advantage over his fellows. Teddie was aware of this because he felt a prick of resentment himself. *I would have waited and joined you for dinner but I have an appointment.* Dinner with the general.

How and when had that been arranged? The general would have got back in his staff car from Premanagar two or three hours before Teddie spluttered in on his motor-bike after playing messenger-boy over several square miles of bloody awful country and then helping off-station officers to find accommodation in Mirat for the night. The three fingers of whisky represented something ambiguous like the postcards his mother used to send from Singapore saying 'Miss you' while all the time she was having a high old time with that chap Hunter.

For the first few minutes of Merrick's address the silence persisted, but during these minutes it lost density, became riddled with receptive channels drilled one way by Merrick's strong and resonant voice and the other way by the audience's growing interest in what the voice was saying until the two sides met like tunnellers who had worked from opposite sides of a mountain and come face to face at the centre point of a clear uninterrupted passage. As if he knew that contact had been made Merrick now made a dry joke and was rewarded by more laughter than the joke deserved. Thinking about it afterwards Teddie believed that most men would have attempted a joke right at the beginning to break down the unfriendly atmosphere. Merrick must have been conscious of the critical silence that greeted his appearance on the platform. But he ignored it, simply started to speak, standing at the lectern removing his papers from his briefcase then dropping the case on a nearby chair and sorting out his notes, apparently in no hurry to look like a man giving a lecture but already giving it.

*

'In December nineteen-forty an eminent member of the All India National Congress whose extremist views had become something of an embarrassment to other members of the Congress High Command, not to say an annoyance to ourselves, escaped from India, so far as we can ascertain through Afghanistan. His name was Subhas Chandra Bose. Although arrested early on in the war he had been released to his home after staging a hunger strike in captivity which the Indian Government feared might lead to his death. In spite of rigorous surveillance by the police and CID of the house he now lived in he managed to get away presumably in some sort of disguise and make his way to Kabul where it seems he was in touch with the German consulate. Thereafter, quite logically, he turned up in Berlin with the declared intention of carrying on what he called India's fight for freedom from there. There are two points worth noting about this situation. The first is that a man who has such a high opinion of himself and his talents as to believe that single-handed he might achieve what the Congress as a whole has not managed to and takes the trouble to put such a great distance between himself and his jailers, is in all likelihood suffering to some extent from delusions of grandeur. The second point to note is the direction of his flight and its final destination. Berlin. The two factors, the kind of man one may think Bose is and the place he went to are not incompatible as factors in our assessment of the meaning of the situation. Indeed, all this makes a perfectly sensible pattern. Hitler, Ribbentrop, Goebbels, Subhas Chandra Bose.

'At this stage of the war of course, in 1940, Mr Bose might have been excused for believing that the Germans were going to win it anyway and that his mission was a merciful step taken to minimize any suffering Indians might have undergone following a British defeat. One can quite see that the appearance of Mr Bose as Gauleiter of India could have militated against the excesses of storm-troopers in cities such as Delhi. Once again one learns the lesson that historically a man's actions – however questionable they appear at the time – can usually be satisfactorily explained away afterwards as altruistic. No doubt Mr Bose has been sacrificing himself in the interests of his country. His is an odyssey that deserves to be better known and no doubt will be because it is not over yet. Like many great adventures it has its marginally amusing elements. I am assured on the best authority that although Mr Bose stumbled most of the way through Afghanistan on foot he effected his entry into Kabul in a tonga.'

The laughter swept the hall at this point. Teddie laughed too. He was not sure he knew just who Subhas Chandra Bose was. There were so many Indians called Bose. His interest in Indian politics and politicians had always been minimal. He had a generally comic idea about them. The picture of a portly chap in dhoti, shirt and Gandhi cap bumping up and down in the back of a rickety horse-drawn two-wheeled trap on his way to meet the German consul struck him as perfectly splendid. Teddie folded his arms, always a sign of his contentment. This Merrick fellow certainly knew his stuff even though his voice, confident and carrying, was – well – not quite pukka, a shade middle-class in the vowel sounds.

'Nothing I've said so far is confidential. The business of Bose's escape and activities in Berlin, although soft-pedalled by Government, is known to many people – perhaps better known to civilians than to army personnel and to Indian officers better than to British. Civilians have more time to gossip and read the minor items in the newspapers. Indian officers are probably more interested in what an Indian politician gets up to than their British colleagues are. But by and large the Bose situation is treated more as a joke than a threat. He has broadcast from Berlin and has made as little impression as the Anglo-British commentator Lord Haw-Haw. Men like Bose tend to appear to live, publicly, in isolation from what we are inclined to think of as the realities. What he actually did in Germany may therefore come as a surprise to some of you. With Hitler's permission, to assist Hitler in fighting us, he raised a unit of battalion strength from Indian prisoners-of-war who presumably volunteered for this distinction.'

The temperature in the hall seemed to drop perceptibly. For an instant the barrier between audience and speaker fell again. Teddie looked at the necks of the two Indian officers in front of him and wondered what on earth it felt like being one of them.

'This unit,' Merrick continued, 'is first reported as officially in existence in January 1942. In other words it took Mr Bose at least a year to find eight or nine hundred men to accept the bait of ostensible freedom from prison-camp and to form a group which no doubt he described as the nucleus of a great army of patriotic Indians whose quarrel was with the British and no other nation. Whether Hitler was disappointed at the feeble response or was merely amused to have his views of Mr Bose confirmed we do not know. The unit does not seem to have survived as a fighting force or even as a coherent one. It is reported scattered around Hitler's Europe, particularly in the Low Countries, doing the odd spot of beach defence, police and guard duties. But before we criticize these men, remember that as prisoners-of-war forcibly separated from their company and battalion commanders, and very far from home, they were deprived of the one thing the Indian Army has always been especially rightly proud of – the high level of trust between men and officers which is based on the real concern shown for the men's welfare by those officers, be those officers British or Indian. It is clear that Bose's failure in Germany stems from the fact that he simply couldn't find enough Indian King's commissioned officers to help him in his work of suborning cold, hungry and miserable Indian sepoys.'

There was an appreciative murmur from the front row where the most senior British officers sat.

'Bose was still in Berlin when the Japanese launched their lightning attacks in the Far East, on Pearl Harbour, Malaya and Burma. Intelligence reports reveal that he was in touch with the Japanese ambassador in Berlin and it takes little imagination to work out that one of the things he must have suggested to that gentleman was that the Japanese should encourage the raising of similar forces from Indian prisoners-of-war to assist them in their operations in the Far Eastern theatre. But now we come across yet another gentleman with the name of Bose— '

Teddie smiled. There you were. Common as Smith.

'—Rash Behari Bose, an old Indian revolutionary living in exile in Japan. Rash Behari Bose also approached the Japanese with a scheme of this kind. He was unsuccessful in his first contact, with Field-Marshal Suguyama, who took the practical soldier's view that since India was part of the British Empire Indians could never be anything but enemy subjects. He had more success with the Japanese war ministry. Rash Behari was already head of a thing called the Indian Independence League in Japan. With the backing of the Japanese government he was now in a position to extend this as a going concern in all the invaded territories. A branch of the Indian Independence League, or IIL, was set up for instance in Bangkok and it sent representatives with the Japanese forces that invaded Malaya. You see which way the wind begins to blow. Mr Rash Behari Bose probably makes great play with the fact that the IIL saved Indian lives and property during the period of hostilities. Indeed there are many instances reported of

Japanese soldiers having approached Indian civilians in Malaya asking them if they followed the Mahatma and leaving them unmolested when hearing that they did.

'But the dividing line between saving innocent civilian lives from Japanese bestiality and suborning Indian troops was very thin. You could say it was non-existent. At this stage of our story there emerges I'm afraid not a cold and hungry sepoy but an officer, Captain Mohan Singh of the 1/ 14th Punjab Regiment. Captain Mohan Singh was captured in Northern Malaya very early in the campaign in, so the report we have states, Alor Star. The next thing we hear about him is that he is head of a small group of Indian officers working with a Japanese intelligence officer called Fuji-wara. Fujiwara also had with him a representative from the IIL in Bangkok. Consequently one can trace a direct line from Rash Behari Bose through Bangkok and Fujiwara to Captain Mohan Singh. Mohan Singh proceeded to organize captured Indian soldiers into small fighting groups which accompanied Japanese forces during the rest of the Malayan and Burma campaigns.

'Here again evidence exists of lives of Indian soldiers and civilians having been saved. But to what end? The answer comes to us unequivo-cally in the extraordinary event which took place in Singapore in February last year on the occasion of General Percival's surrender to the Japanese commander. Contrary to normal procedure Indians – that is to say Indian officers – were separated from British officers as well as Indian troops from British. The Indian officers and troops were congregated in Farrer Park and there publicly handed over by the Japanese commander – to whom? To none other than our old friend, no longer Captain, but General Mohan Singh who thereupon addressed these troops, blamed the British for losing the battle and deserting their Indian comrades, announced that the days of British imperialism were over and that it was the duty of every patriotic Indian to form an army to help the Japanese drive them out from India for good and all.'

For the first time Merrick paused and glanced at the audience as if to judge its temper.

'Circumstances ideal for both the Boses' purpose now obtained, a potential – numbered in thousands – of well-trained and experienced Indian soldiers who only had to be persuaded to abandon their allegiance to a regime which appeared to have been utterly, perhaps one might say disgracefully defeated, and muster into a force of the kind envisaged by Rash Behari in Tokyo and Subhas Chand in Berlin, the army of new India, of free India. The Azad Hind Fauj. The Indian National Army. An army that would march alongside the Japanese not as traitors and stooges but as patriots and men of destiny. I think we should be clear about that – about the emotional feelings that lie behind an act of what in strictly legal terms must be defined as treachery. I have named Captain Mohan Singh. There were others with him whose names are also known. Perhaps it is unfair to single him out and his subsequent actions do not all contribute to the portrait of a man without a sense of honour, a man on the make. He has in fact suffered what we call vicissitudes. But history must name him as the King's commissioned officer who stood on the wrong side of the rail at Farrer Park and accepted a gift from the Japanese, the gift of command over men who were prisoners but still soldiers of the King-Emperor.

'We don't know how easy or difficult it was for Mohan Singh to come to the decision he obviously came to back in Alor Star at a time when even if a British defeat looked likely it had not yet been suffered. The timing of his transfer of allegiance and its apparent swiftness are rather damaging as I'm sure you will agree, but one must not forget the presence of that man of Rash Behari Bose's, the civilian representative of the IIL from Bangkok. Surely a persuasive fellow when talking to Indian officers taken prisoner. Possibly though, Mohan Singh had been brooding for some time on the situation he was in as an Indian who held the King's commission. He may finally have felt that incompatible with his nationalist ardour. Information come to hand shows that during his time as head of the Indian National Army he made great play with allegations that in Malaya the Indian KCO had always been treated as a second-class officer with a lower rate of pay and fewer privileges than his British comrade, that British officers arrogated superior status to themselves as members of a ruling class on whom the security of India mainly depended, that during hostilities with the Japanese and quite apart from the so-called gross incompetence of the high command, British officers panicked and thought of nothing but their own skins, in short got the hell out whenever they could and left Indian officers in the lurch by putting them in command of rearguards covering retreat.

'Since Mohan Singh's own British battalion commander is known to have been captured with him at the same time and in the same place, his views are not in this instance notably supported by the evidence. Nevertheless, I think we must say that Mohan Singh had decided to be disenchanted, to believe that the Malayan catastrophe destroyed forever the myth of the *raj's* supremacy and therefore its right to remain even a day longer in control of India's future, and furthermore to believe that it was now his duty to think only of how best to serve his country and his countrymen.

'Here in India in some Indian nationalist circles there has been as you know a curious and to most of us naïve argument that the Japanese have no quarrel with India and Indians, that it is only the British presence and the use of India as a base for armed operations that forces Tokyo to adopt a threatening attitude to the sub-continent. It was a Gandhian idea and it lay behind the serious civil disturbances of twelve months ago.

'If Mr Gandhi can believe this about the Japanese and make millions of Indian civilians believe it, Captain Mohan Singh presumably had no tremendous difficulty in making thousands of naturally apprehensive Indian prisoners of war believe it. Perhaps the remarkable thing is that for the many he seems to have persuaded as many – indeed many more – have

865

remained unconvinced. I say remarkable because the consequences of resisting persuasion cannot have been, cannot be pleasant. In front of the eyes of your stubborn prisoner, officer, NCO or sepoy, things doubtless happened which made the decision to remain a prisoner and loyal to the crown a difficult one. Additionally they saw erstwhile members of the *raj*, the white sahibs, submitted to all the indignities we now know the Japanese are adept at devising. Add to the sight of these indignities the threats of hunger, thirst and physical coercion and it obviously requires a special stoutness of heart to resist the blandishments of men who yesterday were your leaders and comrades and who offer to be leaders and comrades again in an enterprise which is projected as patriotic. A prisoner is always homesick too and here is Captain Mohan Singh, supported now by many other Indian officers I'm afraid, promising to lead him home in a particularly glorious way, to a home from which the British have gone forever, to a home where the old national leaders, many of them worn and thin from prison, will greet him as a hero, as a liberator, as a true son of the India they too have fought for.'

Again Merrick paused.

'The question of what loyalty is isn't easily answered.'

The remark only deepened the silence. Merrick referred to his notes.

'The Indian National Army under Mohan Singh consisted of approximately 10,000 ex-prisoners, officers and men, but according to our information little more than half of them had arms. However, if there had been arms and equipment readily available that number of ten thousand would have been considerably increased. Broadly speaking, Indian prisoners of war fall now into three categories – those who have so far resisted all persuasion and continue as prisoners, those who have not resisted but have indicated readiness to serve, and those who have actually been mustered in. This information is restricted. As you will appreciate when bearing in mind that figure of 10,000, and official Indian government comment and counter-propaganda, the policy is to deflect attention from this situation by minimizing its importance and ridiculing claims made by the enemy. But enemy broadcasts are regularly listened to by those civilians in this country who are rich enough to have wireless sets capable of receiving them. Foreign broadcasting is of course the one form of communication upon which Government cannot place an embargo. There have been instances of Indian families recognizing the voices of relatives who were officers in the Indian Army but who are now officers in the INA and who give stirring accounts of the great things which the INA will presently do.

'The question is, will they? I mention vicissitudes. Right from the beginning there appears to have been not unexpectedly an element of Japanese contempt for the Azad Hind Fauj matched by an element of Azad Hind suspicion of Japanese intentions, and some resistance to Japanese attempts to treat the INA as a mere appendage of their own imperial army. Under Mohan Singh the INA was theoretically the military arm of a civil independence movement headed by Rash Behari Bose, and after a conference in Bangkok this movement dedicated itself to take actions which would be wholly in line with the nationalist policies adopted here in India by the All India Congress.

'From February to August 1942, you'll recall, the Congress in India was demanding that the British quit India, that they should leave India, in Gandhi's memorable phrase, to God or to anarchy. What would happen if the British didn't quit was left, on paper, not very clear. But that is by the way. What did happen was clear enough.

'What I think important to bear in mind is the effect the news of Congress's demands, and of the outcome of those demands, must have had on Indian prisoners of war in Malaya and Burma, particularly upon those who had now committed themselves to the INA. It must have seemed to them that India was about to rise and throw the British out, that great events were afoot, that history was making their decision for them. True, their technical allegiance was to King and Country but if the mother country did not want the King and was about to get rid of him that left them with the country alone. They certainly belonged to that. It was their country after all. But apart from the matter of the British there was the matter of the Japanese. What truly were their intentions? Would they really leave India alone if the British were got rid of? INA officers have openly said to their troops that whereas the troops must be ready to fight the British – even their own old officers and comrades – they must be just as ready to fight the Japanese if the latter showed any signs of substituting the Rising Sun for the Union Jack. And there was another great INA uncertainty. Would *Congress* really approve of the Azad Hind Fauj?'

Merrick stopped to give the question time to sink in, it seemed. Perhaps that was his prime intention but suddenly he looked down at Colonel Selby-Smith and said, 'Sir, I believe the No Smoking signs are intended to apply only to the period of discussion about the scheme. I expect quite a number of people would appreciate it if you felt inclined to give permission to smoke.'

Presumably Selby-Smith nodded because Merrick glanced up and nodded to the hall, which now came stealthily alive. Teddie opened his own case in nervous gratitude. In a few seconds the hall looked like an Indian bazaar during the festival of Divali, but the business of lighting up was completed with unusual rapidity. In less than half a minute the hall was quiet again.

'This was the question. Would Congress really approve of the Azad Hind Fauj? Would they give their blessing to an operation that might lead to a bloody meeting between a rebel nationalist army and the regular Indian army? The INA assumed that upon its appearance on Indian soil the Indian army proper would disintegrate and its sepoys join hands with their rebel brothers. But even if Congress also assumed this could they accept the INA as a legal instrument of their own policy of achieving self-government?

'Quite apart from the views of the moderates and constitutionalists, the kind of Congressmen who had thought their fellow Congressman Subhas

Chandra Bose an extremely dangerous man, there was the other Gandhian principle of non-violence to consider. To find out the answer to this question then, it was decided to send a group of INA officers into Burma, well-equipped with means of radio communication, to infiltrate secretly into India and contact Indian political leaders. This was done in August 1942. The enterprise was a total failure because one of the chosen officers took the first opportunity to abandon the group and to contact us and thoroughly spill the beans. The rest returned to Malaya disillusioned and the officer who reneged on them brought with him very useful documents and information. This officer is not named, but he is a bright spot on a somewhat dark horizon. It is his belief that more than a few officers and men joined the INA with the same intention as himself of either wrecking it from within or of coming back to their loyal duty directly contact was re-established with the Army to which they really belong. In other words it is suggested that they used the INA as a rather specialized means of escape from prison-camp which as we all know it is a soldier's duty to try to effect.'

An officer at the front said, 'Hear, hear.' Someone clapped. Merrick waited. He kept his eyes on the lectern and turned a page of his notes. Resuming he said:

'The spot on the horizon would be brighter however if all the officers in the infiltrating party had done precisely the same thing. We must have fairly deep reservations about the extent to which this joining up as a preliminary to returning to duty represents a significant factor in the constitution and motives of the INA. Nevertheless in any future confrontation with INA units and formations in the field it must obviously be borne in mind that not all INA soldiers on the other side of the wire, so to speak, are necessarily intent on attacking us. Some of them may be looking only for an opportunity to come in with their arms to turn them against the Japanese. Just how many we shall have no way of knowing until the time arises – if and when it does.

'But there will be a natural tendency among Indian sepoys and among other ranks in British battalions to resent these apparent deserters and traitors quite intensely, a tendency not to extend to them those military civilities we are required to show in the field to the fallen, the wounded and the captured.

'One of the main purposes of this talk is to establish certain facts and to provide what is hoped will be useful background knowledge so that we can avoid the worst effects both of minimization and exaggeration of the problem presented by the existence of this army. My own view is that whatever one's personal reactions, corporate judgment must certainly be suspended until all the facts are known. Meanwhile the restricted information presently given can settle quietly in our minds and may help us to exert a steadying influence on the men under our command if and when this division finds itself in action against units or formations of the

INA. I will end this survey with an account of what has happened since the failure of the infiltrating party.

'There's no doubt that political events in India in August 1942, culminating in the severe riots that followed the detention of members of the Congress Party committees and sub-committees, had at least a potentially vitalizing effect on recruitment of prisoners of war into the INA, but the INA itself seems to have suffered a fairly severe crisis of confidence, in regard to Japanese intentions and in regard to its own. The major question whether the Congress Party would approve had gone unanswered and with all Congress's influential policy-makers in jail there was now no hope of getting it answered.

'Captain Mohan Singh was naturally at the storm-centre of this crisis of confidence. Without going so far as to say that he personally agreed with the stand the Azad Hind Fauj was making he was as its head inevitably identified with it and we may give him the benefit of the doubt here, credit him as I hinted earlier with a certain stubborn adherence to what may be called honourable principles. The main stand that seems to have been made was over areas of responsibility. What the INA was saying was that it and it alone must deal with India. Correlatively it was saying it would have nothing to do with Japanese operations elsewhere – for instance against Burmese nationalist guerrillas. To those people in the Japanese Imperial army who thought contemptuously of the INA as a mere appendage this attitude was totally unacceptable and we can assume that considerable pressure was brought to bear on Mohan Singh to conform, to put his forces at their disposal without reservations. Equal pressure was doubtless brought to bear on him by INA officers who stood by the policy of working only according to Congress principles and who saw these as integral to the principles of action and thinking in the INA. One has a picture here of the whole organization of the INA trembling on the brink of disruption.

'In December last Mohan Singh was arrested by the Japanese. The actual reasons remain to be discovered although it is believed that Rash Behari Bose was at the bottom of it. As a politician, Rash Behari presumably had a talent for bobbing like a cork on the stormiest waters, for his own position was not immediately affected. But for the first six months of this year the Azad Hind movement and the INA had a look of being something of a broken reed. It needed a strong man to mend it, a man talented enough to satisfy both sides, the Indians and the Japanese, with his views, policies and capacity for leadership.

'Who else but Subhas Chandra Bose? But he was in Germany. *Was* in Germany. Just a few weeks ago in June this ubiquitous gentleman turned up in Tokyo. The information we have is that he came out by submarine – a typically glamorous, apparently hazardous enterprise – but, let it be marked, not one he could have embarked on without the approval, indeed the wishes, of the government in Tokyo. From Tokyo he has broadcast speeches which leave no room for doubt that he is in his own eyes the man of destiny whom the Azad Hind movement and the Japanese have been waiting for. In Singapore last month he was elected President of the Indian Independence League, the other Bose – Rash Behari – having resigned to make room for him. So there we have it: Mohan Singh a prisoner, we believe in Sumatra, and Rash Behari gone into the retirement which is the reward of failure. In their place, Subhas Chandra Bose.

'He has not yet formally assumed command of the Azad Hind Fauj but that can only be a matter of time. We can indeed expect Mr Bose to claim authority over all Indian nationals in the Far East and manipulate a kind of legality for the entire proceedings by the establishment of a form of free Indian government in exile, recognized on paper anyway by the Japanese and their allies in what they call Asian co-prosperity. He is that kind of man. His qualities of leadership must not be under-estimated. These were qualities that frightened several senior Congress politicians off him in the past. He was thought by them to have the makings of a dictator. One feels inclined to agree.

'This survey ends, therefore, on a note of some assurance about the continuity and enlargement of the INA as a machine of war that it would be as foolish to underestimate as it would be to allow its existence and inevitable growth to distract attention from the principal and still very dangerous and highly ambitious enemy, the Japanese. It seems to me to be very unlikely that even under Bose, who will almost certainly enjoy outwardly cordial and co-operative relations with the Japanese high command, the INA will ever slot anything but uncomfortably into the Japanese military machine and this may well contribute to its downfall. The other contributory factors to this likely downfall are of course its logistic problems and the mixed psychology and motives of its members. In terms of its capacity to equip itself either in co-operation or competition with the Japanese it must rank as a low-priority organization. In terms of its psychology and motivation it must rank as something less than an army capable of achieving a high and durable morale. How much less capable will depend on the magic of Mr Bose. But even the most skilful magician cannot sustain for long an illusion of common purpose when the purpose itself is so riddled with complexity. This will emerge as an important factor when Indian soldiers of the INA – intent on liberating India – come face to face with Indian soldiers who are under our command and are loyally determined to defend it from whomsoever dares set foot on Indian soil aiming a rifle at them.'

Merrick picked up his notes and had retrieved his briefcase before the audience quite realized he had finished. Although the applause broke out before he actually left the platform he did not remain to receive what might then have looked like a personal ovation, and was down the steps and returning to his seat when the applause was at its peak.

Selby-Smith rose and climbed on to the stage. As he stood at the lectern he clapped his hands about four times to demonstrate his own approval and to give a lead in the matter of bringing the ovation to an end. When he stopped clapping he seemed to be requesting silence and quite quickly got it.

He said, 'Although this meeting has now gone on for longer than many of you anticipated, what we have just heard so ably and interestingly presented was certainly worth staying to hear. I think there is no disagreement on that score. On your behalf I thank Captain Merrick for the trouble he has taken to present a clear picture of this rather sticky subject. In bringing the meeting to a close I would firmly reiterate that the subject of the INA is not one that the divisional commander wishes to have generally or casually discussed among you. In other words keep what you've heard this morning under your hats. Junior officers and NCOs have a particular responsibility to be alert for gossip and rumour among the men and to report its existence without taking steps to squash it until they've had advice on the line to take. That is all, gentlemen.'

A bit stunned by what he had heard Teddie did not seize the opportunity that now presented itself to meet his room-companion. He found it easier to go with the stream making for the doors than against it down to the front where Merrick stood alone doing up the straps of his briefcase. At the foyer doors which had been swung open and latched back by the guards Teddie nearly changed his mind because the idea of Merrick standing by himself made him feel he was not being as friendly as he should be, but someone spoke to him and when he next thought about Merrick he was climbing into the back of the 15 cwt Chevrolet – the last man of a party of five. The driver put up the tailboard and in a moment or two the truck was entering the queue for the exit from the forecourt.

In B mess he sat with two other officers in the anteroom and ordered beer. At five to one he saw Merrick come in. This time he wasn't alone. An Indian and an English officer accompanied him, guests from one of the brigades. Again he hesitated but just then Merrick's glance fell on him and seemed to stay. Teddie stood up and went across and offered his hand.

'I'm Teddie Bingham,' he said. 'What'll it be?'

For a second or two he had a feeling that Merrick was wondering whether he should find the name familiar. His hand came out rather tentatively as if casual physical contact with someone not intimately known was ordinarily unwelcome. The handshake failed as such. Teddie was about to explain who he was when Merrick said, 'We meet at last then.' He still had Teddie's hand and suddenly, unexpectedly, exerted grip, then quickly broke contact.

Between the man on the platform and the same man close to Teddie found a kind of discrepancy. When he thought about this afterwards he decided it was the same sort of discrepancy he'd noticed years ago in London when he was about twelve and his mother took him to a matinée and backstage afterwards to meet a man who'd played one of the character parts and still had his make-up on but spoke in an ordinary voice and seemed shy, but made up for it when they left by putting his arm round Teddie and giving him ten bob.

'Whisky or gin?' Teddie asked. 'Or are you a beer only man at tiffin?'

'It's very good of you,' Merrick began. Teddie now noticed that the blue of the fellow's eyes was made particularly vivid by the steady way he considered you with them. 'But I'm rather pressed. I'm supposed to be somewhere else at two o'clock so I'll have to go right in. Could we make it this evening?'

'Yes, of course—'

Merrick nodded. 'Good. It's time we got to know each other.' He smiled, turned, then turned back again. 'By the way. Congratulations.'

'Congratulations?'

'Hosain tells me you're getting married soon.'

'Oh. Did he? Well yes, I am. Thanks.'

He watched Merrick steering his guests to the dining-room, ushering them through the doorway with a guiding hand on each of their backs in turn. The bearer brought Teddie's beer. The man standing next to him was the adjutant of the British battalion of the brigade up near Premanagar.

'Interesting that, this morning,' the adjutant said. 'No idea anything like that going on but then I've only been in the country six months. What was he, do you know? I mean in the Indian government?'

The chap meant 'in the Civil'. Amazingly ignorant. Teddie said he had no idea which should have been good enough but apparently wasn't.

'A sort of spy do you reckon?' the adjutant asked. He had a plebeian voice and manner. He was the sort of chap one found in the bars of Tudor-style roadhouses back at home in the vicinity of Kingston-on-Thames. The fellow actually winked as such fellows did. The vulgarity of modern English life suddenly overwhelmed Teddie. It was flowing into India, blighting everything. He smiled distantly at the adjutant and murmured an apology for leaving him. He intended to swallow his beer and go into mess but, warned by a mild but sudden sensation of inner instability, put his glass down and made his way across the room to the door that led to the lavatories. Secluded there he discovered that his normally healthy and regular motions had become unpleasantly loose, untrustworthy. His forehead came out in a sweat. He felt rather unwell. The thought of food didn't much appeal. He must have picked something up.

He left by a side entrance and entered the complex of covered ways that connected B mess building to the junior officers' huts. The whole place had a temporary feeling about it. The last occupants of these particular lines had been members of the staff of a chemical and psychological warfare school. They had left a smell of gas capes and propaganda. Teddie had heard someone say that. It struck him as apt. Reaching his own room he found the door padlocked. Hosain was on mess duty. Teddie cursed his present domestic arrangements. He fumbled for his key and then paused, having noticed something extremely odd. Leant against the wall under the window there was a push-bike, or rather the remains of one. For an instant he thought someone had been in the room, taken either his own or Merrick's bicycle, removed one wheel and buckled one of the mudguards for a joke. But that wouldn't account for the rust. And then, the wreck under the window was without a cross-bar: a woman's bicycle. Nevertheless he hastened to take the padlock off the door and open up.

Bicycles were kept inside rooms because of the danger of theft. Both bicycles were where they should be. He went out for another look at the useless and mysterious object and in doing so noticed something else: chalk marks on the floorboards of the verandah, decorating the threshold. Some sort of design. The effect was cabalistic.

He sniffed the air for the lingering scent of an ill-wisher, wondering whether he would be able to isolate such a smell from all the others to which he had become used. He could not. He stepped over the chalk marks and went to the verandah rail. There wasn't a soul; just a perspective of doors like his own, each with its padlock, and beyond the hut a space and in continuing perspective another hut. Straight ahead across the bare earth compound the prison-camp style wire fence divided the lines from waste ground. Nobody could get over the wire but nobody needed to. The lines were always full of unexplained people. They came in at points where the PWD had either got fed up with erecting the fence or run out of material. It was not a security area. It might once have been someone's intention to make it one.

He reconsidered the broken push-bike. Perhaps Hosain had found it dumped and placed it there to show that he was an honest boy. He could have got a few annas for it from the cycle-shop wallah in the cantonment bazaar. But there had to be a connexion between the bicycle and the chalk marks. The marks could have been made by Hosain. If the boy had been a Hindu Teddie would have more readily believed that this was the explanation; that the bike and the chalk marks were some odd form of puja or offering for the welfare of the rooms' occupants to ensure them a safe journey, wherever they were going, through intercession with some modern addition to the Hindu pantheon: the god of mechanical transport.

But Hosain was a Muslim. It was unlikely that either the bhishti or the sweeper took sufficient interest in any of the officers they served to make such a well-meaning gesture to one or two of them. Besides which the marks had an inauspicious feeling to them. Teddie hesitated, controlling an urge to obliterate them. His bowels began to move again. There was a griping pain in them and the sweat broke out on his forehead. He stared down at the cabalistic signs which suddenly seemed to be responsible for the disorder in his guts, for the disruption of his life which he now felt the whole morning had somehow plotted to bring about. He scuffed his rubber-soled shoes across the marks, blurring the outlines. He continued scuffing and scraping until only an ashy smear was left. He felt better.

Back in his room he found a letter from Susan on his side of the desk. He ripped it open. It was dated five days ago. 'Dear Teddie, Tomorrow we're off to Kashmir. Aunt Fenny and Uncle Arthur will meet us in Delhi and then we'll all travel together up to 'Pindi.' They would be in Srinagar by now. He stuffed the letter into his jacket pocket and went round the back to the privy. Things were no better but he had stopped sweating. He hoped he was not going to be really ill. He read Susan's letter right through. When he returned to his room he lay down on the bed hoping to catch forty winks. After ten minutes, still wide awake, he sat up and lit a cigarette and read Susan's letter again. Srinagar would be full of officers on leave. He saw the danger he was in of losing her to some fellow with more to offer, a fellow with talent and money, a fellow who had the measure of things as they were, the kind of fellow who would understand everything Merrick talked about this morning and be able to believe it without feeling that if it was true nothing was sacred any more and nobody could be relied on, that everyone was living in a bloody jungle.

Teddie got off the bed and stubbed his cigarette. He felt emotional but couldn't work out what he felt emotional about except the prospect of being jilted or of hearing that the whole of the Malayan battalion of the Muzzys which had been captured near Kuala Lumpur had gone over to that Bose character. What he did work out was that everything that was wrong for him was really the fault of that bounder Hunter who had drunk away his mother's money and then her vitality and when he was dead hounded her to her own grave. Except that there wasn't a grave. He would have felt more settled knowing there was a grave.

It was raining again when he was ready to go back lunchless to the daftar. He couldn't face putting on a sweaty cape and cycling. He stuck his cap on and padlocked the door behind him. The ruined bike struck him as ridiculous. He walked through the covered ways until he got to the front of the mess where he was able to whistle up one of the cycle tongas whose drivers congregated outside the main gate.

IV

During the afternoon Teddie forgot about the bicycle and the chalk marks but remembered them at six o'clock on his way back to the hut. Hosain was squatting on his hunkers outside the room, whose door was open, latched back against the outer wall leaving the mesh screen exposed. The orderly got to his feet when he saw Teddie coming up the steps. He had been sitting on the spot where the chalk mark smear was. There was no sign of the bicycle.

Teddie asked where it was. Hosain indicated the room, entered ahead and pointed at the two serviceable machines. Teddie explained about the broken bicycle. Hosain went outside, looked and came in saying there wasn't a bicycle.

'I know,' Teddie said. 'But there was. What time did you get back from mess duty?'

Hosain said he was back at 1430 but had gone straight to his own quarters, changed and gone to the bazaar for Merrick Sahib. He came back from the bazaar at 1630 and opened the room. There hadn't been a bicycle then. If there had been a bicycle earlier someone must have taken it, probably the person who left it there in the first place. He would ask some of the other orderlies and the bhishti. But what was the good of a bicycle with only one wheel?

'Quite. That's the whole point.'

Teddie felt cross because Hosain was looking at him as if he thought Teddie was trying to cause trouble for the servants over something he had only imagined seeing. Suddenly Merrick called from the bath-house. Hosain shouted, 'Sahib!' and went with alacrity. It wasn't Merrick's fault but, no doubt about it, since his arrival Hosain had given Merrick preferential treatment. It was ridiculous having to share an orderly. Come to that it was bloody stupid having to share a room.

Teddie sat in his armchair with his legs stuck out in the shoe-removing position. Presently he heard Hosain laugh and a warm friendly sort of noise from Merrick. Less than a minute later he heard the back door being unbolted and Hosain shouting for the bhishti and then Merrick clomped in wearing unbuckled chappals and nothing else but a towel tied round his middle. He was rubbing his head with another towel.

Teddie's immediate reaction to the sight of Merrick was admiration shot darkly through with envy because Merrick had one of those bodies in which every sinew was clearly and separately defined, properly proportioned and interlocked. The fellow didn't seem to have an ounce of fat on him. You could count the pads of muscle that made up his abdominal wall.

'Ah, there you are,' Merrick said. 'I'm sorry about lunch-time.' He stopped rubbing his head and stuck the towel round his neck. 'We seem to have been Coxing and Boxing for days one way or another. I didn't see you come into mess, by the way.'

'As a matter of fact I got rather taken short.'

'Oh. Mirat tummy?'

'Sort of. But I think it's gone off.'

'I have some stuff that will settle it if it hasn't. I expect you've been sitting under the fan or drinking too much iced beer. Take a dose anyway to be on the safe side. Hold on and I'll get it.'

Teddie felt reluctant but grateful. It was like being jawed by an older boy about looking after your health; like being taken to the San because someone had noticed you were suffering in silence. Merrick came back with a small bottle and a spoon. Hosain followed him in. 'I'll pour,' Merrick said, 'because it tends to come out in a dribble and then in a rush.' He poured a couple of drops. The drops were followed by a dollop. It was brown and looked nasty. Merrick leant forward and obediently Teddie opened his mouth. The stuff tasted like very strong cough mixture. It seemed to grip his throat all the way down.

'It cements you up,' Merrick explained. 'If you have another dose in the morning you'll be right as rain.'

'Thanks.'

Merrick made a gesture at Hosain who knelt and untied Teddie's shoes.

He took the medicine bottle and spoon back to the bathroom and returned rubbing his head with the towel again.

'It must be the humidity,' Teddie said. 'Not used to it recently. I've been stationed up in the hills the past few months.'

'Well you'd notice it then. Actually the humidity's fairly low here. Ever been in Sundernagar?'

'I've never even heard of Sundernagar.'

'It's where I was before they let me into the army. Your shoes go green overnight. I had an inspector who swore he was getting webbed feet, and *he* was an Indian.'

'An inspector? Were you in the Indian Police then?'

'Yes. I was DSP Sundernagar. Most of it's tribal area. Pretty boring for anyone who isn't an amateur anthropologist. My predecessor was. He was desperate to get back. I was just as keen to get out.'

'Were you there long?'

'Too long.'

Teddie nodded. DSP meant superintendent, the top man in a district after the collector and the judge. He was glad Merrick wasn't ICS. The few ICS men he'd known had been remote clever fellows, too intellectual for his tastes. The police were different, easier to get on with. Some of them envied you if you were Army. Merrick was now satisfactorily placed and explained and in spite of his high police rank Teddie felt pleasantly superior to him in occupation as well as in type, background and – as was clearer the longer he listened – in class. The police weren't always quite as particular as the other services.

He forgot about the bicycle and chalk marks until he was in his bath and then he had a flash of inspiration about them. Having arrived at an explanation that connected the whole incident to Merrick rather than to himself he was reluctant to mention it but decided he ought to, for security reasons.

Returning to the room, already dried and wearing clean underclothes under his robe, he said, 'I say, Merrick—' and then stopped, struck by a sense of having intruded upon a situation between Merrick and Hosain which he could not describe but which seemed full of potential for an intimate kind of anger or violence. Hosain was looking sullen but also tearful. He went out. Merrick now fully dressed, appeared momentarily distracted, deprived by Teddie's entrance of the opportunity to press home some kind of point that a moment ago had been important to him to make.

Merrick said, 'I'll see you in B mess in a few minutes then. What will you drink?'

Surprised, Teddie said, 'No, it's on me—'

'Well, we'll see.'

Merrick went. Teddie looked round the room expecting to see something that explained what he found inexplicable. He shrugged, called Hosain and began to dress. When he got to the shoe putting-on stage he called Hosain again. Putting on and taking off his own shoes and boots

876

were activities at which he drew the line if there was a man available to perform these services. He had learned to draw the line in Muzzafirabad where his first CO, Colonel Gawstone, advised him never to stoop if he could help it. The climate wasn't right for it. Mrs Gawstone had stooped to pick up a glove and keeled right over and never got up. They had buried her the next day.

'Everything comes suddenly in India, Bingham,' Teddie remembered old Hooghly Gawstone saying. 'Sunrise, night, death, burial. Nothing keeps in the heat.' And in Shropshire in sultry weather the milk went off. Extraordinary chain of thought. He had forgotten why Gawstone was called Hooghly but vaguely remembered a story involving an elephant and the floating body of a dead sadhu. Or was that another story? Even two stories?

He went to the door and looked out. Not a soul in sight. The chalky smear was indiscernible because the light was going and the glow of the lamps in the room pushed his shadow across the place where the smear was. A man appeared suddenly round the corner of the hut. It was Merrick. He came up the steps saying, 'I left something behind.'

It sounded rather feeble. Something. What? Key? Wallet? Why not say? Had he come back to find out whether Hosain was telling Teddie what the row had been about? If it had been a row. There'd been no sound of a row.

'Did you send Hosain on another errand?' Teddie asked.

'No. Isn't he here?'

'No, he bloody well isn't. He's just buggered off.'

'Anything special you want?'

'Only for the little blighter to put my shoes on for me.'

Teddie went back in, sat down, and began to slip his feet into the clean pair of shoes.

'Here,' Merrick said, and threw him a long tortoise-shell shoe-horn. It made the job easier but Teddie was too irritable to mutter more than an almost inaudible 'Thanks.' It irritated him to have to do the job himself and irritated him to have Merrick watching him. At one point in his exertions he could have sworn the man was about to come and help him. The idea made him nervous. He fumbled with the laces. He went into the bathroom to wash his hands. When he returned to the room Merrick was standing in the open doorway as if looking for someone but presumably just waiting patiently for Teddie to finish.

'I'm ready now. Did you get what you came back for?'

'Yes, thank you.'

'We'd better lock up at the back too, I suppose. The whole thing strikes me as a bit bloody much.'

'What does?' Merrick asked Teddie when Teddie had bolted the bath-house door from inside and the door connecting bath-house to living quarters and rejoined him at the doorway on to the front verandah.

'What does what?'

'Strikes you as a bit much.'

'Having to put on your own shoes and lock up your own room. The little blighter has practically fuck-all to do. I've a good mind to boot him in the arse when I see him again, buggering off like that.'

Teddie wanted to get out of the room now into the open air and over to the mess to have a couple of burra pegs; but Merrick was standing in his way. There was an expression on his face which Teddie interpreted as disapproving. Perhaps Merrick was one of those chaps who had moral objections to strong language. Teddie wasn't very happy about it himself but there were pressures building up inside him these days which he didn't understand and using words like that helped to reduce them; or did if they weren't silently rejected, crammed back down your throat by someone like Merrick. Perhaps the fellow was religious.

Merrick said, 'I think I'm to blame for Hosain making himself scarce. I had to tick him off. It was the first time and he got quite a shock.'

'And what was the ticking off about?'

'A small enough thing.'

It may have been the way Merrick looked at him (in that manner Teddie would have called calculating had it not been for the tentative friendly smile) but now he felt exposed to the accusation he believed Merrick had intended to spare him. He said, 'Was Hosain complaining about me?'

Merrick seemed in so little hurry to reply that the answer became unnecessary. Merrick dressed it up, though. He said, 'I got the impression he found working for two officers – onerous. I wasn't conscious of anything so strong as a complaint against one of us in particular.'

'But that's what it came to.'

'Only if you assume it's more natural to raise the subject of overwork with the one officer you'd be willing to go on serving. But the natural way isn't always the one they choose, is it? He may have been making a subtle complaint about me, to my face.'

'I wouldn't call Hosain a subtle sort of chap.'

'All Indians have subtle minds if you put it like that. Often I prefer the word devious for uncultured fellows of Hosain's stamp. I'm sorry if that offends you. You regular army people are rather touchy on the subject of army personnel, aren't you? But I'm afraid my experiences as a police officer have blighted any enthusiasm I ever had for the idea that the simple fellow from the village is eager to prove his devotion to the *raj*.'

'Oh.'

There seemed to be nothing else to say. On the other hand Teddie did not feel as shocked or unhappy as he guessed he ought to be. In the back of his mind there were crammed scores of case-histories which showed the relationship between white man and Indian in a holy, shining light; but none was pre-eminent, none actually came pushing through to the front to make him articulate in defence of this relationship. Merrick stood aside and Teddie hesitated, then went out on to the verandah. In any case Hosain was not a good example of the kind of man he wanted to be thinking of. He waited while Merrick closed and padlocked the door.

'That was interesting, what you were talking about this morning,' he said.

'I'm glad you thought so. One courts a certain amount of unpopularity with that kind of thing. Myth breaking's a tricky business. To make the facts at all palatable you have to leave people with the illusion that the myth is still intact or even that you've personally restored it.'

Teddie hadn't the least idea what Merrick meant. He fell into step.

'For a moment,' Merrick said, ' – towards the end – I was made to feel I had the honour of the Indian Army in my hands entirely. The relationship between a man and his subject is very close. People tend to confuse them. It was impossible to leave the facts to speak for themselves. They had to be presented in the most charitable and acceptable light. Not necessarily so that people would leave the hall thinking well of me in spite of what I'd told them but leave it thinking optimistically about the future. One has to produce a positive response not a negative one. And the facts about the INA are a negation of most of the things the army, people as a whole, have believed in as a code of *possible* conduct.'

'I can't help feeling,' Teddie began, and because he hesitated Merrick put a hand on his shoulder, to guide him. They had reached a radial intersection of the covered ways. It was quite dark now. They steered by instinct, usage and the star patterns of lit buildings. Continuing along the correct path to B mess Merrick allowed his hand to remain.

'What? What can't you help feeling?'

'Well. That ninety per cent of the chaps who've joined the INA intend to come back over at the first opportunity. As you suggested.'

A moment or two elapsed before Merrick said, 'But I suggested no such thing. You heard what you wanted to hear. You've proved the point.'

'What point?'

'That the facts aren't as important as the light they're presented in. What's chiefly interesting about all this is that a lot of those men may persuade themselves they joined the INA because they saw it as the quickest route back to base, but I doubt very much whether that's the true reason in more than a handful of cases.'

'What do you think is?'

'Herd instinct. Self-preservation. At the top among men like Bose it's a combination of herd-*leader* instinct and self-aggrandizement. Patriotism doesn't come into it. So neither does the question of loyalty. It will end up as a simple matter of two opposed views of legality, and even that's going to be settled on a purely theoretical basis.'

'How?'

'You can't hang ten thousand or more traitors.'

'You can shoot the officers.'

'Or just Bose? To encourage the others?'

'Perhaps they'll save us trouble and shoot themselves.'

'Would you?'

'Good God, yes. It would be the only way out, wouldn't it? I mean if I'd done that and got recaptured.'

'Even for a man who thinks himself a patriot?'

'You said that didn't come into it.'

'I don't think it does, but a lot of them will think they are patriots.'

'Well, I'm sorry. But there are still a few things one just doesn't do. I don't blame the other ranks so much but I find the idea of King's commissioned officers leading their men – our own men – against us utterly unspeakable.'

'Beyond the pale?'

'Yes, beyond that. Whatever it means.'

'It means outside,' Merrick said, taking him up rather too literally. 'Pale, fence, boundary. Where you draw the line between one thing and another. Between right and wrong for instance.'

'The line's already there, isn't it? We don't have to draw it.'

'There was a British officer at Farrer Park too,' Merrick said. 'He told the Indian prisoners that from now on they had to obey the Japanese as they'd obeyed the British. I don't think he meant obey in quite that sense, but it's something that may cause trouble when the legal rigmarole begins, which it will, when the war's over. Assuming we win it.'

'A British officer?'

'A senior British officer.'

'You didn't mention that this morning.'

'I thought it wiser not to.'

Teddie nodded. He felt oddly light-headed. He had a sensation of not being quite himself and at the same time of recognizing Merrick as one of the most unusual men this other self had ever met. He felt himself being drawn out, enlarged. This was dangerous because if you were enlarged there was more of you and the world was still exactly the same size. It didn't get bigger to make room for you.

The ante-room of B mess was almost empty. It was not a place in which you would ever feel at home. Its atmosphere was transitory like that of a waiting-room. Teddie was glad to have Merrick with him. He ordered scotches and sodas and thought it would be pleasant to get mildly drunk. Or even quite drunk.

'When is the wedding?' Merrick asked.

'December, or earlier.'

'Earlier, surely? We'll be gone from here in a couple of months. Once that happens you're unlikely to get an opportunity.'

'I thought sort of leave during our jungle training period, or just after it.'

'I shouldn't count on it. If you've really decided to marry I'd advise going ahead as soon as possible. Here in Mirat, for instance. There's a hill station called Nanoora not far away. You could go there for the honeymoon. If you're lucky you might get a second honeymoon about Christmas or just after, but my guess is you won't.'

'You seem well-informed.'

'Well-advised. You've talked to Selby-Smith presumably?'

'Oh, yes. Well, I've raised the subject. He knows and so does the General.'

'I'd press it if I were you. Ask for a clear statement. Of the situation.'

He emphasized the last two words. They began to repeat themselves in Teddie's head. The situation. The situation. What situation? Getting married was the simplest thing in the world. All you needed was the girl, the ring, a padre and a few minutes to spare; and that was it. The catch was in getting the few minutes and in extending them to hours, days, a week or two. The situation was one of time; not having enough of it to be able to call any of it your own, except by arrangement, by permission. Your whole life was subject to permission one way and another.

Teddie frowned, gulped his scotch and soda. Everyone's life was lived by permission. Whose? There were plenty of people around whose permission you had to seek but to give permission they had to have it themselves from somebody else. Where the hell did it all lead? Where was the highest, the final authority? One ought to know because logically it was this highest final authority that was creating the situation that made a simple thing like marrying Susan so damned difficult.

He called the bearer over again, ordered two more burra pegs, smiled aside Merrick's attempt to make the second round on him.

He said, 'I suppose one's wedding should be the most important day of one's life. To other people it's a sort of irritation, isn't it?'

The belief that he had made an unexpectedly profound statement about the comparative unimportance of the individual in the wider general scheme of things pleasantly aggravated the notion he had this evening of not being quite the man his friends would recognize. Merrick, he thought, was looking at him with the intense regard of someone more finely attuned than most to another person's potential. He felt encouraged to further profundity but found the way down to it blocked. He said, 'Are you married, Merrick?'

Merrick was drawing on a cigarette. He took his time, inhaling and exhaling. 'No, I'm not.' Each word was marked by a wreath of ejected smoke. Teddie was left with an impression of a sad history in this respect, of what they called a torch being carried. Perhaps the heat of the torch explained the cool bright blue of Merrick's eyes. Everyone had his defence. He supposed cheerfulness was his. Recently he had found the smile on his face a bit on the heavy side. Underneath it there were these pressures. Mostly sexual, he imagined. He recollected the soft flesh of Susan's inner arm, just near the elbow. He signed for the second round, raised his glass and said, 'Cheers.'

Unaccountably the second whisky went straight to his head. Denied physical intimacy with Susan who at this moment represented all women he craved the substitute; intimate accord with some man, here represented by Merrick who sat admirably composed, self-possessed, with all those hidden muscles relaxed but doubtless reassuring to him, sources of self-confidence as they were of Teddie's envy and grudging respect. It occurred to him that Merrick was – how could he put it? – a mystery that attracted him. He found himself telling Merrick about his parents, about Hunter and the abortive search for his mother's grave in Mandalay. On Merrick's clear, handsome but experienced face he saw an expression that encouraged him to feel more in control of his affairs, more intelligent about the significance of a history which it surprised him to discover he had rather a lot of. Talking to Merrick made him feel that he'd almost made a contribution to the totality of the world's affairs. He believed that Merrick cottoned on to this and was assessing the contribution accurately and appreciatively. It pleased him that Merrick continued to look interested and to ask him questions because this suggested to him that Merrick didn't dismiss the contribution as negligible. With his third burra peg, which Merrick signed for, Teddie acquired a certain self-conscious tenderness towards him.

He also felt sick, rather suddenly. The medicine had cemented him up at one end perhaps but not at the other. He wondered whether the feeling would go away if he ignored it. He embarked on a description of Susan and said what a marvellous girl she was, what a lucky fellow he was. The more he thought about it (he said) the luckier it seemed to him he was. Pretty girls were usually frivolous, weren't they? She was damned pretty but terrifically sensible as well as fun to be with. 'I'd like you to meet her,' he said. 'You will if we do what you suggest and get married here.' That sounded like a good idea: to show people in Mirat what a fine girl he'd got hold of. His forehead was damp.

'Are you feeling bad again?' Merrick asked him.

He said, 'It'll go off in a minute. It had better because I've decided to get pleasantly pissed tonight and that always takes me a fair time.' He signalled the bearer for two more scotches but Merrick said, 'Not for me. I'm not a great drinker. In fact there was a time when I hardly touched it. It used to amaze me how much some people could put away. It was Sundernagar that got me into a regular habit. But two in a row is still about my limit before eating.'

'My uncle actually taught me to drink,' Teddie began, remembering himself at seventeen and the evening session in Shropshire with the decanter and his uncle's dedicated but critical eye, but then stopped short of explaining why: that his uncle said that a good head for good liquor was one of the few things that still distinguished a gentleman from others. But Merrick appeared to cotton on to that too. He said, 'Mine was the kind of family that never kept drink in the house except at Christmas and then it was port.'

'My uncle's a port man,' Teddie said, intending to encourage. 'He's always talking about putting some down for me, but I'll be surprised if he does.'

Merrick smiled. 'This was the sort that doesn't get put down. Australian port *type*. When I was a boy I thought all wine was port and that all port came from Australia. It's the sort of thing that makes life difficult for clever children from humble families. One suffers disproportionately. The young are extremely unkind to each other and their elders aren't always free from prejudice. I doubt there's a more unattractive sight than that of a schoolmaster currying class favour by making fun of the boy in his form whose background is different from the others. It's the kind of situation in which it's as well to be tough as well as clever. Fortunately I was both.'

'What school was this?'

'A grammar school. But my natural element would have been the local county. I got into this other place on a scholarship and my people were very proud of that. They weren't exactly poor but they were poverty-stricken in comparison with other parents. And lower-middle-class. By those standards. I took up boxing and found my own level.'

'Do you still box?'

It was the only thing Teddie could think of to say.

'No. But it was my athletic skill as much as my academic achievement that got me into the Indian Police. Those and the interest taken in me by the assistant headmaster. He taught history which happened to be one of my best subjects. I owed him a lot. We kept up a correspondence after I came out, right up until the time he died.'

'I was an awful duffer at school,' Teddie confessed. Like his confidential report from Staff College, recollection of his scholastic stupidity and only average capacity at games caused him no regret: certainly no shame. School, after all, was only part of the adult arrangement to keep children out of the way while they were growing up. He supposed it was different for people like Merrick's parents, but he imagined there was a similarity somewhere. In any case here they were, the two of them, arrived on the same sofa in the same place with the same rank and the same privileges, sharing the same room and the same servant who, as it happened, preferred Merrick who hadn't been born in a world where servants figured and port got put down.

At once he remembered the bicycle and the chalk marks and the idea he had had that these were a message to Merrick, a warning to Merrick by an INA sympathizer who had found out that Merrick was taking a detailed interest in the subject and perhaps that he was lecturing on it that morning. But just what a bicycle and cabalistic signs had to do with either the subject or Merrick's involvement was a mystery.

He said, 'Does a bicycle have any special significance for you, old man?'

He had never seen such a change in a fellow. At least, he couldn't remember seeing one. It was brief but – there was no other word for it – electrifying. The tingling sensation communicated itself to Teddie. For a moment Merrick looked as if he had been made by a machine and was waiting for someone to come and disconnect him so that he could collapse back into his component parts because there was no possibility of his being galvanized by the vital fundamental spark. Subsequently what puzzled Teddie was that he should have thought about the change in Merrick in such terms. He wondered whether he was becoming over-sensitive, whether he had picked up something that had attacked his nervous system, speeded up his reactions and sent his imagination out of control. Something odd had been happening to him ever since he arrived in Mirat. There was that peculiar fancy he had had about the spare bed as a burning ship or catafalque. Perhaps he had been affected by the aeroplanes. The height had hurt his ears and after each flight it had been a day or two before his hearing was really clear again. That sort of thing could upset your physical balance so there was no reason why it shouldn't upset your mental balance too.

'A bicycle?' Merrick asked. 'What do you mean, special significance?'

'Well I don't know. Is it a sort of symbol of the INA?'

'Not that I'm aware of. Why?'

Teddie told him.

'Just that?' Merrick said, when he had explained. 'A broken bicycle?'

'Well there were these chalk marks. I'm afraid I scuffed them out.'

Presently Merrick said, 'What a pity.' He sipped some of the scotch remaining in his glass. 'Do you remember the marks in any detail?'

'I'm afraid not. I say, do you think I was right?'

'About what?'

'The INA.'

Merrick did not reply for a while. He was inspecting the palm of his left hand. He said, 'Possibly. Have you told anyone else?'

'I asked Hosain. He didn't know what I was talking about. I expect the beggar thought I was accusing him of something.'

'I see. Well that explains that. He did say or at least imply you'd questioned his honesty. But I never listen to complaints from servants about other officers. That's why I was ticking him off. Have you mentioned the bicycle and the marks to anyone else?'

'No.'

Teddie, sensing a secret, felt privileged.

'Then I shouldn't.' He looked at Teddie's glass. 'Let me get you another of those before we eat. To kill the bugs.' He called the bearer over. Ten minutes later when they got up to go into the mess Teddie felt euphoric. At dinner he drank beer. Afterwards he drank several brandies and Merrick drank one. Without Merrick to guide him he might have lost his way in the maze of covered walks. By the time they got back to their room Teddie was satisfactorily several over the eight but still on his feet. He protested when Merrick helped him take off his shoes. He did not remember getting into bed.

He woke with a thick head when Hosain roused them at half-past seven with morning tea, and recalled a dream that had been so vivid it hardly seemed like a dream at all but obviously was because it couldn't have happened that he woke in the middle of the night and saw an Indian – a Pathan in a long robe – standing in the middle of the room.

*

When he pressed the subject of his marriage, as Merrick had recommended, he was unable to ignore a moment longer its grand irrelevance to the position in which he and every other officer at divisional headquarters were placed. He found himself having to treat it with the same sympathy and impatience that Colonel Selby-Smith showed (wrinkling his face and temporarily detaching his mind from the main stream of his multiple concerns) so that it was not until Teddie was alone in his room that he fully appreciated the fact that he was none the wiser but somehow committed to panic-action. He had no idea how to conduct his affairs on such a basis, nor how to break it to Susan and her mother. He wished he had left the subject unpressed but at the same time realized that to have done so might have been disastrous. His feelings towards Merrick were now ambivalent. He was grateful to him for the advice but couldn't help identifying him with the unsatisfactory result of taking it.

Between mid-October and Christmas, Selby-Smith had said, there was now no likelihood of getting away because the serious business of working up would be done during those few weeks, probably in one of the stickier areas of Bengal. After Christmas, leave was anyone's guess. Selby-Smith's own was that there wouldn't be any. The battalion and brigade leave rosters were at the tail-end stage. With the exception of Teddie every officer at divisional headquarters had had leave before joining. The general had been very keen to establish what he called a pattern of full working continuity once the division was formed. He would be adamant about not granting leave to any officer unless the circumstances were exceptional. Selby-Smith promised to have a word with him at lunch because Teddie's circumstances were, if not exceptional, at least different. In the afternoon Teddie received the general's ruling. He could either postpone his wedding until after Christmas and risk not having it at all or he could get married in Mirat at any time he wished between now and the third week in October and have seventy-two hours' leave to enjoy the consequences.

At first he felt bucked. Cycling home from the daftar he saw Mirat through the honeyed eyes of an ardent young husband, but suddenly its strangeness imposed itself on him and he could not picture her there. All kinds of practical details about the wedding presented themselves for consideration and for once he found it impossible to deal with them one at a time. He arrived at his quarters incapable of coherent thought and wondered how best to get hold of Tony Bishop whose job it should be, as best man, to do his thinking for him. Hosain brought tea and he began a letter: Darling Susan—

The blank paper only emphasized the immense distance she was from him and it was a distance he did not feel he could cover. He abandoned the letter in favour of a List which began after an entry or two to look suspiciously like a staff officer's note to the Q side. He had just written the word accommodation which was all right as an idea – in fact as such essential – but the ramifications of the word now began to be exposed; the names and faces of people requiring accommodation sprang up argumenta- tively claiming attention, comfort, indeed some reasonable degree of luxury. The bride; the bridesmaid (Sarah); the bride's mother; the matron of honour, Mrs Grace (Aunt Fenny); the chap to give the bride away, Major Grace (Uncle Arthur); the best man. It would be simpler for him to go to Pankot. But that would take forty-eight of the miserable grudging allowance of seventy-two. There would hardly be a night he could call his and Susan's own.

He yelled for Hosain, told him to tell the bhishti to get a move on with the bath water. A thunderstorm broke. For fifteen minutes the electricity was off. He fanned himself with the writing-pad. The solution came to him dressed in its own perfect grey and respectful logic. There would be no wedding until after bloody Christmas and bloody Bengal. There would probably be no bloody wedding. He went out to the closet and sat miserably hunched, resting his forehead on both fists.

As a boy in his first year of English exile, in the house of his Shropshire uncle, he had often retreated to the unfriendly privacy of the cold English lavatory to consider the extraordinary miseries of life. His eyes blurred in sympathetic remembrance. It was several seconds before he realized that the most shameful thing was happening. He was blubbing.

*

Darling Susan, he began again a few days later when this unusual and useful man Merrick had solved the problem for him. And broke the news to her. With enthusiasm. 'As for arrangements here,' he continued, 'they're simple enough. Rather exciting in fact. Can't remember whether I mentioned that Mirat is a princely Indian state' (he hadn't; the fact had escaped his notice; Merrick had told him). 'The palace and all that sort of thing are on the other side of the lake' (he'd hardly noticed the lake either), 'but it seems the old Nawab has a guest house there that he's made available to the station for special visitors who can't get decent accommo- dation. I've had a word with the sso and the guest house is available for the October dates I suggest. I've booked it anyway because I can always alter it if you can't manage it. There's tons of room for all of you, apparently, including Aunt Fenny and Uncle Arthur. The sso says it's very comfort- able, even luxurious. And apart from the commissariat which one arranges oneself it's all free as air. It seems the old nawab likes having English people there. It's in the grounds of the palace but quite separate and of course guarded, so don't worry. It should be fun. There's a nice old church in the cantonment, which is where it'll be, and afterwards we can shoot up to the Nanoora Hills in just a few hours. . . .'

He stopped, gazed at the rain outside, living the eternity after the word hours, or trying to. Not having been to Nanoora he found it difficult to conjure a background to Susan's hair which he could see and smell. The background to her hair kept coming out as Pankot. Nanoora might well do so too, in fact. One place looked much like another once you were used to it. He bent over the desk again and wrote: 'I'll drop a line to Tony Bishop but perhaps you or your mother would too. I'm sure General Rankin will give him long enough leave to accompany you all down, even if you come a week before the wedding. I can get him a room at the club. So don't worry on that score. Darling Susan. Enjoy Srinagar. How I wish we could have been there together. But it was not to be.'

One other thing was not to be either. Five weeks later, a week before the wedding party was due in Mirat, Susan rang from area headquarters in Pankot to divisional headquarters in Mirat, got put on to Teddie personally and told him that Tony Bishop was in hospital with jaundice and had to be written off as best man. Teddie felt disturbed, less by the news and the problem it presented than by the business-like and utterly unromantic tone of Susan's voice which he had not heard for a long time and which quite clearly commanded him to take firm steps to ensure that there was no other hitch.

Teddie's desk was endways on to a window that looked out on to the main verandah of the Ops block. Susan was saying, 'So Teddie, you'll have to detail someone at your end to hold your hand in Tony's place,' and just then Ronald Merrick walked past.

Teddie smiled. 'Don't worry, old thing. Easy as wink. I'll probably get the fellow I share quarters with. He's a helpful and willing sort of chap.'

Coda

I've got a terrific favour to ask old man he had said but really it had been the other way round the favour being done to Merrick who as a boy could not have dreamed ever of supporting an officer of the Muzzafirabad Guides as best man at a wedding: a dignity not to be taken on lightly and certainly not to be repaid like this with a cut cheek and a piece of sticking plaster, an impediment to the tender conviviality of skins.

Shaving, the sensation of having been taken advantage of, of having had a casual friendship presumed upon, settled like a claw between his shoulder blades (which were otherwise unscarred, unmarked by the talons of physical desire. Her fingers had conveyed a reluctance which he supposed was a degree better than distaste.) Teddie dabbed his cheeks and chin with a towel, cut a fresh piece of sticking plaster and applied it to the wound.

Merrick's wound. Teddie had borne it with an equanimity that disguised incredulity. This morning however the face in the mirror was that of an acquaintance well enough known, taken enough interest in, to make an explanation of what had hapened at the wedding obligatory and, in advance of getting it, unconvincing, in fact unbelievable, part of an especially sly confidence trick. The face in the mirror was that of a man Teddie felt he couldn't trust. The eyes were too narrow, shifty under sandy lashes. The cheeks were drawn, as by some vice lately attempted and come to nothing. The bones shadowed them with a mixture of shame and unaltered intention.

*

Yesterday they had arrived in Nanoora. Tomorrow they must return. Their one complete and uninterruptible day had begun. The hours were almost too many for him to hold because the whole weight of them seemed to be on his back. It was as if he had invented the day for his own convenience. He went back into the bedroom where Susan lay, crumpled, asleep or wishing she were. He couldn't be sure. She appeared discarded, not by other people but by herself. The curtains were still drawn across the too large window which was bordered by breaking and entering bands of vagrant sunshine. The room was otherwise still part of the private revelations of his wedding night and would be until the bearer brought morning tea and pulled the curtains back: an event that was not due for another forty minutes.

Showered and shaved he was conscious of thirst and hunger. But there was this other more insistent appetite; so intense it seemed that it would never be satisfied. He could never get enough. The mere sight of her sharpened and hardened him. His genitals ached but were totally in command again, engorged. His mind was frozen. He stripped and clambered in, without making a sound; it felt to him nevertheless as though he had whimpered. His arms trembled, anticipating exertions. She was night-scented, a warm aromatic combination of breasts and thighs and rucked transparent nightgown which gave his spoiler's hands no rest but racked them with endless exhausting domineering tensions.

She cried out softly, apparently rudely awoken. With an abrupt gasping acquiescence she opened her legs but not her eyes; offered what assistance she could think of; but the duality of their enterprise did not connect them. Only his flesh did that and there was an improvement in her in that direction, the only one that mattered for the moment, having been earned, worked for with a kind of tight-lipped patience. The contest over, detumescent, he lay licking her wounds with kisses.

Later he drew her bathwater, poured in generous handfuls of sweet, silly pink salts. For half-an-hour he sat by the bedroom window, considering the unknown prospect of Nanoora which was surprised in its own daylight. He drank tea and listened to the irregular but confirming sounds of the sponge dipped and squeezed. He tried to believe that the bathroom was not her refuge but a place of preparation for the business of giving and sharing and taking up her part of the day which somehow had to carry a whole future in its mouth – like a mother-beast with her cubs, to a place of safety.

What had he done? Hurt her physically? Shocked her with his carnal approach? Had he been while exercising consideration and patience inconsiderate in showing vigour, making no attempt to hide this extreme of happiness? His own shock had been the shock of joy that was legitimate, endorsed, blessed, with nothing murky or restricting perched on its shoulder. He had discovered a private area of freedom inside the stockade. She had not entered it with him. He must be at fault. He had failed to arouse her. He had a miserable impression that she did not like him. His body ached for her affection.

Part Three

THE SILVER IN THE MESS

I

Barbie had never known the wilder secrets of life nor held the key to its deepest sensual pleasures. The mystical element in a wedding was therefore real to her. She observed with pleasure the grace and stillness which became Susan's chief attribute the moment her engagement was announced. The girl was different. Her realization of her love had driven everything else from her mind and left her body in repose. Where once she had worked so hard at being the centre of attraction she was now, as of right, at a centre and stood there smiling out at the world; even that part of it which Barbie inhabited.

Barbie watched Sarah closely and was satisfied that there was no broken heart. She had not believed Teddie and Sarah well suited in the few short weeks they were going everywhere together. She thought of these girls as her own girls, born of her womb, dramatically separated from her but now living near her in ignorance of her maternal claims. It was a harmless act of self-deception and hurt nobody, except perhaps herself.

*

It was a great disappointment to her when the Laytons returned early from the family holiday in Kashmir and announced that the wedding was not to be in Pankot in December but as soon as it could be fixed, in Mirat where Teddie had been posted. She had intended to be at the church even if Mildred had not found it in her heart to invite her to the reception. She had persuaded herself that she would in fact receive an invitation and had ordered through Gulab Singh's a set of twelve Apostle teaspoons for the wedding gift. She planned to have a new costume made in some festive colour. She inspected bolts of cloth at the durzi's. A heliotrope caught her eye. She believed in planning early but said nothing to anyone. Her fear was that in spite of the instructions she had given him the durzi would turn up at Rose Cottage and scatter all these colourful materials on the verandah and so give away her hopes and expectations.

Which is what he did, on the evening of the day the Laytons got back from Kashmir and, uninvited, assembled at Rose Cottage with Clara

Fosdick and Nicky Paynton to discuss the problems of the sudden change of plan; so that at first it appeared to them all that the durzi had heard the news and was prompt off the mark, anticipating an urgent order for a trousseau as yet only half-heartedly bespoken.

'Full marks for information and method,' Mildred told him. 'Show us what you've got.'

He set the white-sheeted bundle down, but at Barbie's feet, and opened it, perplexed by so large and interested an audience, and revealed bolts of woollen cloth in colours and patterns that would have killed every woman there except one: who stood exposed. The durzi twitched the heliotrope material between thumb and finger and said, 'Pure.' He said it to Barbie.

'It's a material I've been looking at,' she told them. But the truth was all too clear. She never wore 'colours'. The material was for a special winter occasion. 'I can't make up my mind and he's trying to do it for me, the wretch. What do you think?' She took refuge in the dog. 'Panther now. What do *you* think?' She got a desultory wag. In this climate pets faded even quicker than women.

'The question is, could I carry it? That's what my mother used to say to her clientele. I doubt you can carry it, or, It wouldn't do for everyone but you could carry it. I always imagined a difficult material as an immense *load*.'

Which it was. She would have liked to lighten the load and at the same time obliterate the embarrassing scene; and saw how this might be done – by swooping on the bolts of cloth and throwing them like huge unwieldy paperchains until the verandah was heaped in heliotrope, electric blue, bilious emerald and garish pink. She grinned in frustrated exultation.

'I suppose it *is* somewhat festive. Christmas Day perhaps or would that be carrying it too far?' She laughed at her unintentional pun, turned, looked down at the durzi. 'No, take it all away. Some other time perhaps but this is not the place.'

'Aziz,' Mildred said, 'tell him to call at the grace and favour tomorrow at eleven.'

Aziz did so. Satisfied, the durzi did up his bundle, salaamed and was away; an old bent man ever ready to exercise his skill at both sides of his trade – selling and stitching. His cloth was better and cheaper than the stuff at Jalal-Ud-Din's. At night in his open-fronted shop he sat cross-legged on his platform under a naphtha lamp and an oleograph depicting the Lord Krishna fluting maidens by moonlight. He wore half-spectacles on his nose and looked up at you from above them and smiled, pressing his palms together, as if in a predominantly Muslim bazaar it required alertness and good manners as well as predestination to be Hindu. Barbie pictured him spread-eagled under the bundle, strangled on the way home by *thugs* as a sacrifice to the Goddess Kali; his bloated tongue the colour of the rejected cloth, and listened in now to Mildred talking to Clara Fosdick and Nicky Paynton.

It seemed that in Kashmir, at Mildred's insistence, the houseboat had been moved from its original site – a noisy berth between two others that were rented by American officers who played portable gramophones until the early hours and had Eurasian girls draped on the sun-decks under awnings. They had tried to involve Sarah and Susan in these late-night parties.

Mildred ordered the boat taken to the remote spot where she and John Layton had spent part of their honeymoon, and moored it one hundred yards from someone who had got there sooner but whose boat seemed quiet, hardly to exist in fact; muted to the point of creating its own illusion of itself as though at any moment it might break up into component parts of air and light and water.

Or so Barbie conjured it, absorbing all the separate pieces of information from Mildred's account and re-assembling them. To begin with she had never been to Kashmir and had to imagine this entirely for herself, helped out by recollections of pictures in books and on postcards. She thought of Kashmir as snow and apples at the same season and a deep lake into which the snow melted and the apples fell. In Spring there were sheep from which the fine wool shawls came; and then in Autumn the smell of carpentry. The water was always placid but grey and misty. At night there were stars and heaven looked very far away, far behind the stars, as it did in places where there were mountains. For the first time, listening to the story, she admitted the actual quality of colour and sunshine so that the water now looked green as well as deep, shaded by willows whose fronds brushed the ornate fretted wood of houseboat roofs.

And in this long warm sleeping afternoon a cry came, across the one hundred yards of water, a cry of a child, which seemed odd. Only an elderly woman, apart from servants, had been noted. To this woman, after discussion, cards had been sent and the cry of the child at first sounded like the ambiguous answer and continued to do so until the arrival of the tiny reciprocal rectangles of pasteboard with that name in copperplate, engraved.

Lady Manners.

The lake was still placid; no ripple. Distantly the mountains still erected sharp outlines. Shade remained dark like indigo velvet. Butterflies hemstitched this tangible material, and Barbie – living it – watched them and heard the cry repeated, felt the fascination of the situation before she understood the predicament created by the proximity, the awful nearness to the untouchable condition that attached to that name, Manners, which was the name of the woman and, with her inexplicable permission, of the child whose father was any one of six disgusting hooligans. There she was, the old woman, once distinguished, once elegantly in occupation of Government House in Ranpur and the now virtually disused Summer Residence in Pankot, at ease upon the sundeck of a houseboat; isolated from the world her niece and now she had scandalized.

The girl, the Manners girl (poor running panting Daphne) had paid the price of her folly by dying, bearing the tiny monster of the Bibighar that should have been destroyed in the womb and, it was once suggested, thrust down the throats of the culprits or their bloody priests. Miss Manners had not had, surely, religious scruples about abortion? More likely a conviction that she knew the father. The implications of this conviction were almost too astonishing to imagine, as were the old woman's motives in announcing the death, the birth, to a world that thought it better to forget.

Of course, Mildred said, it wasn't possible to follow up the ritual begun in ignorance with the exchange of cards. She let her slightly hooded eyes stray explanatorily towards the garden where the girls innocently played with Panther in that permitted zone originally marked out by Barbie. But, she added, there had been odd moments of hiatus: shikaras setting out from both houseboats at the same minute, or unable to avoid what only a few yards of water stopped from being an actual confrontation, but close enough to demand an inclination of heads, since the occupants of each had met by pasteboard and they could not accept the burden of uncivilized pretence that this had not occurred, could not assume that they were total strangers, even if it were tacitly agreed there should be no development of an acquaintance from which neither side could benefit, and from which one side (that of the girls, playing there with the ball and the dog, those appendages of unsullied English life) could only incur positive harm.

'What did she look like?' Nicky Paynton wanted to know.

'One couldn't see. We were never, thank God, that close, and even under the shikara awning she wore an old topee and a veil.'

Teddie's letter about the new arrangements for the wedding had been almost a relief, giving as it did a conscientious reason for ordering the boat away (even if it looked like embarrassed retreat) back to its original mooring to be closer at hand for unexpectedly early last-minute shopping and the making of arrangements for an early return to 'Pindi by cars, to Delhi by train (where Aunt Fenny and Uncle Arthur became detached), and on to Ranpur, back to Pankot, and the excitement as well as the slight hysteria of bringing the wedding forward and somehow transferring it to Mirat: a place of palaces, mosques and minarets.

Guests of the Nawab! Barbie's visions were now coming to her through the fretted stone screens that embellished so much Moghul architecture. Through these she peeped at lawns and lakes and fountains and saw Susan, standing in her new-found stillness, in bridal white, her veil lifting in rose-scented breezes that had blown across deserts.

*

Quite quickly she detected a mystery about the book but put it down to the curious evasiveness Sarah had brought back from Kashmir with her, like something caught and not yet shaken off.

The book was an elegant affair of dark red leather, gold tooling and paper in which you could see flecks of the wood from whose pulp the paper had been made. The text was printed in the Arabic script which Barbie, fluent in spoken Urdu, had never learned to decipher. But she could see it was poetry.

The book was to be the Laytons' thank-you present to the Nawab of Mirat in whose palace guest house they were to stay. Mildred mentioned the book and now Sarah had brought it up to show to Mabel. She unwrapped it and offered it as if it were a gift she had received not one the family were to give.

'It was a bit of luck really,' she said.

'Why luck?' Mabel asked, hearing.

'Luck to discover the connexion.'

'Connexion? Who are the poems by?'

'Gaffur.'

'Oh!' Barbie interrupted. 'Gaffur. He's a classic Urdu poet. I used to know several quotations. What connexion do you mean?'

'He was court poet to a Nawab of Mirat in the eighteenth century. A relation. The same family as the present Nawab. A Kasim.'

' "It is not for you to say, Gaffur," ' Barbie suddenly recalled, ' "that the rose is God's creation. Howsobeit its scent is heavenly." Oh, how does it go on?'

'Yes,' Sarah said. 'How?'

Her face was very pale. This was unusual.

'I don't know. But I do know that in each poem they address themselves by name, just once, I think. Not their real names. Their pen-names. I didn't know Gaffur was a Kasim.'

She hesitated, held up one finger. 'It is not for you to say, Gaffur, that the rose is God's creation. Howsobeit its scent is heavenly. Something something something. It's quite useless. I've lost it. Is there a connexion between the Nawab and Mr Mohammed Ali Kasim the politician?'

'Yes,' Sarah said. 'The Nawab and he are kinsmen as well, but fairly distantly.'

'How extraordinary, and well – fraught. I mean, is that the word?'

'What are you saying, Barbie?' Mabel asked. Barbie answered from her abdomen, a schoolroom trick that did not strain the throat. Her whole body acted as a sounding board.

She said, 'The Nawab of Mirat is related to Mohammed Ali Kasim who is presently in gaol.'

'Oh,' Mabel said. 'Is he?' So that it was not clear which he she meant or which condition – the relationship or the incarceration.

'The Congress ex-chief minister in Ranpur,' Barbie emphasized.

'I know,' Mabel said. 'My second husband was once a colleague of *his* father.' She turned to Sarah. 'Who thought of the book?'*

'Someone we met in Srinagar.'

'What was their name?'

A pause.

'The idea just emerged in conversation. We met so many people,' Sarah eventually said.

As Sarah took the book back into her hands Barbie remembered the old parlour game in Camberwell. I open the book. I look at the book. I close the book. And I pass the book along. The catch had been to cross your legs as you passed the book to the next player otherwise you were out. It was a game which like others of its kind scared her until she was old enough to think it silly, and even then the icy little hand would touch her low down on the back of her neck, the hand of the invisible guest, the demon-spirit of the party who knew the answers to all the conundrums and puzzles and who presided over the gathering with a thrilling kind of malice, totting up the scores and marking down for ridicule, if not worse, special victims: the foolish aunt, the sickly cousin who cried when Barbie's father did his grotesque babes-in-the-wood act, sitting in a tub, under the table, with only his bare knees showing, and on each knee a grinning face sketched with burnt cork, the eyes closed.

Sarah, having taken the book, looked at it herself. Her grace was a different kind from Susan's. If grace was the right word then Susan had the look of imminent entrance to it, Sarah the look of being born there, of merely having to wait for it visibly to form itself around her, when she and it would exist in a state of mutual recognition. It had not happened yet, but something had happened, in Kashmir, which had heightened the other look she had always had of taking very little on trust, of preferring to work things out for herself; heightened the look and presumably her realization that it was far from easy. It then occurred to Barbie that Sarah could have seen the child, talked to Lady Manners, taken one of those opportunities when characteristically alone to pay the visit her family steered clear of.

Barbie pictured it: this young girl and the old woman, and the child somewhere in the vicinity. I came, the girl was saying, because I couldn't go without saying hello. So said hello and talked and later was shown the

* It is not for you to say, Gaffur,
  That the rose is one of God's creations,
  Although its scent is doubtless that of heaven.
  In time rose and poet will both die.
    Who then shall come to this decision?
      (Trans. Edwin Tippitt (Major. I. A. Retd))

  You oughtn't to say, Gaffur,
    That God created roses,
  No matter how heavenly they smell.
    You have to think of the time when you're both
        dead and smell nasty
  And people are only interested in your successors.
      (Trans. Dmitri Bronowsky).

child. One of God's creatures. Although, as Gaffur for some reason would have it, that was not for one to say. The idea of the book could have come out of this visit because the conversation could have turned upon the imminent journey to Mirat, and the reason for the journey. It was the kind of thing the old woman would know: the connexion between a poet and a prince and an imprisoned politician.

Convinced that she had hit upon the solution to the mystery of the book Barbie gazed at Sarah with awe and curiosity; fear for her toughness and temerity. Sarah had her father's dignity but it was committed in a different cause, or seemed to be; committed to discovering where she would feel it earned, where her duty was. On the score of duty her father obviously had no questions. His dignity was therefore unqualified. It was this difference in dignity that people saw and in Sarah misinterpreted; people like the Smalley woman who saw the difference as something perilously close to 'unsoundness' – a condition which led to an inability to retain the affection of suitable and dignified young officers. Barbie thought: More fools they, Sarah's worth ten of most of them; lucky the man who gets her but he will have to be pretty special. She looks at my old fond and foolish face and sees through it, I think, sees below the ruination, hears behind the senseless ceaseless chatter, sees right down to the despair but also beyond to the terrific thing there really is in me, the joy I would find in God and which she would find in life, which come to much the same thing. But if she's not careful she'll find herself not living, just helping others to. Perhaps that's all I've ever done. If so it isn't much, it isn't enough I don't suppose. Especially if I ask myself: How many of those children did I ever truly bring to Jesus?

Sarah glanced at her.

'What did you mean, Barbie, fraught?'

'I suppose I meant odd, difficult, to be the guest of a man whose kinsman we've put in clink, but India is full of oddities like that isn't it and perhaps the Nawab disapproves of his politician kinsman. Or if he doesn't he obviously doesn't disapprove of us. But then the princes like us better than the rest of them do, don't they? We've bolstered them up and some of them one gathers hardly deserve it. One of my friends belonged to what's called a zenana mission and she once spent a year in a palace of a tiny state in Rajputana. Actually I forget but I think it was Rajputana. Her job was to try to give the rudiments of a modern education to the ruler's wives and daughters who were all in purdah or going to be in purdah. She adored the children but said there were times when she actually went in fear of her life, not that it was ever threatened but she heard such terrible things, quite barbaric. But I'm sure Mirat's not like that.'

'No, I'm sure it isn't,' Sarah said. 'I must go.'

She got up, leant and kissed Mabel who thanked her for bringing the book of poems. Barbie went with her to the front where the tonga was waiting.

'She did appreciate it. She would have liked to be at the wedding, but

Mirat's so far. Too far. It was awfully nice of you to come up specially to show the book. Shall you invite the Nawab to the wedding?'

'I expect so, Barbie. You would have liked to come too wouldn't you?'

'Oh yes. But I couldn't leave Mabel. Has Captain Bishop been given permission to accompany you?'

Now seated in the back of the tonga Sarah looked down at Barbie. 'Well he was, but he's just been taken to hospital. We believe it's jaundice. Mother's gone to see him this afternoon to find out.'

'But whatever will you do?'

'If it's jaundice Susan's going to ring Teddie and tell him to find another best man quickly.'

'But what about the journey?'

'We'll be all right. We're meeting Aunt Fenny in Ranpur and all going on together.'

'And your Uncle Arthur, Major Grace?'

'He can't get away from Delhi until the Thursday before the wedding.'

'All that way, with no man to look after you?'

Sarah smiled. 'I'm sure there'll be lots of officers on the train. We shall be quite safe. Don't worry.'

There are these spoons, Barbie wanted to say. The twelve Apostles. They came today. My gift to Susan and Teddie. Twelve witnesses to love of the sublimest kind. But having got them she was at a loss how and when to offer them. She watched the tonga turn and waved to Sarah's retreating figure. Sarah sat holding on to the struts of the hood with one hand and on to the book on her lap with the other.

It is not for you to say Gaffur that the rose is God's creation, even if, though, its scent, its scent is of Heaven, heavenly. 'My memory,' she said aloud, turning back in, 'Is not What it Was.'

She wondered what happened to all the thoughts which once having had you stored up, and especially what became of those that seemed to be lost which you couldn't put your hand on. She stood in the middle of her room, one repository inside another, and was filled with a tiny horror: the idea of someone coming to claim back even one item of what was contained in either. The idea was horrifying because if you allowed the possibility of one claim then you had to allow the likelihood of several and then many of them, and finally of thousands; so that the logical end to the idea was total evacuation of room, body and soul, and of oneself dead but erect, like a monument marking some kind of historical occasion.

II

The disappointment people had felt at missing an event that would have added some necessary glitter to life was lifted a bit when the Laytons got back from Mirat and it became known that the wedding had been dogged by a series of minor misfortunes.

Mildred's initial attempts to dismiss these as being of no importance only succeeded in making the misfortunes seem major and presently the word disaster entered people's heads and was actually used on several occasions.

If Susan herself had looked downcast the idea of disaster would have gained currency; but, as if making up for what Pankot had missed, she glittered for it, trailing the absent ceremony and reception behind her like a diaphanous shadow that sparkled in the pure late October light, a shadow which was a degree or two darker than was really fair but causing her no trouble, a fact that attracted the kind of new regard to which she was entitled: a girl who had left Pankot pale and beautiful and come back flushed, happy, quite her old self, but with this extra dimension of having entered the honourable company of grass widows, with the bloom of the orange blossom still on her cheeks and her husband already gone on the first leg of the journey back to the front to fight for the preservation of the sterner world she now inhabited.

And when the misfortunes had been pieced together in some sort of chronological order, when they were looked at calmly, then even the stone that had broken the glass that cut Teddie Bingham's cheek on the way to the church could be seen as an acceptable symbol of the attacks to which people who merely tried to get on with the job in hand were only too well accustomed.

The stone, it seemed, had not been meant for Teddie but for his companion, the last minute substitute for Tony Bishop, an extremely interesting man whatever way you looked at it, a man who had apparently incurred such intense dislike among Indians of a certain kind that they persecuted him, kept track of him wherever he went and then chose a moment to embarrass or harass him. On the day of the wedding it had been two moments: on the way to the church and on the platform of Mirat station just as Susan and Teddie were about to wave good-bye from the window of their honeymoon compartment.

Between these two moments there had been another for which Captain Merrick was hardly responsible unless you expected a best man to think of everything in addition to the groom's state of nerves; but from the point of view of the wedding this middle incident had been the worst, or very nearly. In a way nothing could be worse for the bride than to be told within a minute or two of leaving for the ceremony that there had been a hitch which meant a half-hour delay, and then, on coming up the aisle at last, see her groom standing at the head of it, pale, smiling lopsidedly, with a large piece of gauze padding stuck to one cheek with sticking plaster.

'You have to admit,' Lucy Smalley said, 'that it has its comic side,' but no one else was prepared to admit that it did when a Layton girl and a Muzzy Guides officer were the central characters in the affair.

It was the involvement of a Layton girl and a Muzzy officer that weighed most heavily against the substitute best man, an otherwise virtuous target for despicable attack. He ought to have made it clear to Teddie who he really was.

Mildred said that after the wedding was over he had admitted persecution of one kind and another ever since leaving Mayapore for a dreary backwater called Sundernagar, where he had continued in his police rank as District Superintendent until making his escape into the army for the duration. It would, she supposed, have been rather difficult for him to anticipate a demonstration against him on the day of the wedding, but if he had made it clear, if he had said to Teddie right at the beginning, Look, I'm the policeman who was made to seem to have put up a black in that ghastly Manners case, the fellow who actually arrested those blighters, then even if he hadn't added, And I'm still being tracked down and messed about by Indians who think I arrested the wrong men and treated them in some sinister sort of way; even if he hadn't added *that* useful bit of information, then when the stone came sailing through the window of the car taking Teddie and him to the church, he would have been able to say, That was meant for me, and explained why then or later. And boring as it would have been, a perfect bloody nuisance, everyone would have known what was up and Teddie wouldn't have been able to say he'd never been warned that his best man was someone who'd been unpleasantly in the limelight. Teddie had always had a horror of being mixed up in vulgar scenes, apparently. He thought at first that the stone was meant for him because he was a British officer or that it had been chucked by someone demonstrating against the Nawab because all the cars used at the wedding were lent by the palace and had crests on the doors. And in either case, of course, it made him feel perfectly miserable. Not to mention his poor cut cheek.

And there, in regard to the stone, Mildred left it with a sound of shattering glass and an impression of Teddie making just a little bit of a fuss, and of Mr Merrick having failed by a perceptible margin to act quite like an officer and a gentleman; an impression which she hardened by reporting him by no stretch of the imagination out of the top drawer, so that it had seemed almost a special kindness to have chosen him for best man, an unconscious repayment to him for the poor way the authorities had treated him in the Manners affair, after all he had done to try to solve and settle it.

After the stone there had been the incident at the club, and it was reasonable to suppose (Mildred suggested) that if there had not been the incident of the stone nothing dire would have happened at the club.

The Nawab and his party had been refused entrance to the reception by the British military police who were stationed at the front. The MPs were a last-minute precaution, only there in case there were further untoward or unexplained incidents. Assuming that no Indian was persona grata at the Mirat Gymkhana, they stopped the Nawab, his chief minister and his social secretary from crossing the threshold, which could have caused troublesome diplomatic repercussions if the club secretary hadn't got wind of it and personally rescued them, personally conducted them into the reception. It was the wedding group's first meeting with the Nawab and his chief minister, Count Bronowsky, émigré white Russian who now looked like one of those dessicated Muslims of the Jinnah stamp. The two had been away on a visit to a neighbouring state. The social secretary was a different kettle of fish, perhaps a tricky one. He was Ahmed Kasim, the younger son of the ex-chief Congress minister in Ranpur, M. A. Kasim. Heaven knew what he thought of everything. If he thought badly he'd disguised it well. He'd made himself very useful during the week – you couldn't say charming, he'd been too formal and correct for that. He accompanied Sarah riding one morning and she had no complaint about his behaviour, which Aunt Fenny had been worried about. He never mentioned his father or the fact that he was in prison. He had not struck one as in the least politically minded which may have been why his father had packed him off to work in a princely state as a hopeless reactionary case. When it came to M. A. Kasim's sons, the old Congressman had probably had to swallow political pride and disappointment, because the elder was a King's commissioned officer currently a prisoner of war in Malaya and here was the younger working for an Indian prince and looking after the comfort of visiting members of the *raj*.

'It was Susan,' Mildred said, 'who really saved the day. When the old Nawab finally arrived on the lawn, still bristling from the insult, she went forward and dropped him a curtsy, which wasn't protocol but made all the difference.'

Glances went admiringly to where Susan stood, or sat, wherever she was on the two or three occasions Mildred recreated this picture of her, on a lawn, in sunshine, in her wedding veil and dress, holding together a situation that had threatened to fall apart. Admirable girl. The Nawab must have been immensely flattered.

*

It was the third incident that most concerned and puzzled Barbie because it seemed to her from what she could understand of it that it was of a different order, one that reached outside the wedding and cast innumerable patches of light and shade. The patches of light revealed nothing because the light did not fall on anything, rather it pulsed on and off so that the patches were like mysterious glowing areas attempting to burn their way out of an imprisoning mass of darkness. They did not move; and, coming on, they had gone out before you could fix their positions or even their relationship to each other.

'What was it,' she asked Sarah, 'that actually happened at the station?'

They were walking in the garden of Rose Cottage; or rather Sarah had been walking and Barbie had come down to her. It appeared that they were together but Barbie did not feel that this was the case. She was wary of the girl. She had an idea that it might be unwise to touch her. The Nawab had been pleased with the volume of Gaffur's poems, Mildred said. Sarah had not mentioned them again. She had not mentioned Mirat, or going riding with the Kasim boy, Ahmed; an excursion which Barbie would have liked to hear about. It was as though she had never been to the wedding or had been and not come back but sent only her reflexion home. She looked at Barbie now from that sort of distance.

'At the station? No more than you've already heard.'

'But I heard it without understanding it.'

'I think that's how we all saw it at the time. Without understanding it. But it was very simple really. Just an elderly Indian woman pushing through us and kneeling at his feet.'

'Captain Merrick's feet?'

'Yes.'

'Beseeching him?'

Sarah paused with her hands behind her back, looking down at her own feet as though she could see the woman there.

'Beseeching him,' she agreed. 'Yes, that's a good word.'

'But who was the woman?'

'The aunt of the Indian boy Miss Manners is supposed to have been infatuated with. The boy who was the chief suspect. He's still in prison.'

'Poor woman. What was she like?'

'Grey-haired. Dressed in a white saree like a widow.'

'In a white saree?'

'Yes.'

'And that was all that happened?' Barbie asked after a while.

'That was all. She pushed through the crowd and fell at Mr Merrick's feet and had to be taken away. Then the train was going and we were waving good-bye to Susan and Teddie.'

'It couldn't have made much sense.'

'It didn't, at least not then.'

'When, then? When did it make sense? When you knew who Mr Merrick was?'

'Oh, we knew that by then. It came out during the reception. He was embarrassed because it made it look as if he'd tried to hide it but according to him he was just trying to forget it. I suppose he wasn't really lying when people asked him what he'd been in the police and he said DSP in Sundernagar.'

'No, that's true. How did it come out?'

'Count Bronowsky remembered his name.'

'Who is Count Bronowsky?'

'The old Russian the Nawab has as his chief minister. He was talking to Aunt Fenny. He said how well the best man had dealt with the stone-throwing incident, making sure they knew at the palace that the reception would be delayed. When Aunt Fenny told him Mr Merrick had been in the police and was used to dealing with a crisis he identified him at once as the DSP in Mayapore. I gather the case had interested him or perhaps he just had an exceptionally good memory. He went to find Mr Merrick and they had a long talk on the terrace but Aunt Fenny had the news well broadcast by the time they came back in. Teddie was awfully cool with him which was a bit unfair, but I think someone had already suggested that if Mr Merrick was the DSP in Mayapore at the time of the Manners case then the stone had probably been thrown at him and not at the Nawab's car. And the thing that happened on the station capped it. But still without making much sense. I didn't really get the hang of it until that evening when Mr Merrick came over to the guest house to apologize to Mother.'

Barbie thought: Mildred never mentioned an apology.

'But I was the only one up,' Sarah went on. 'All the others were still resting. I was waiting for the dark and for the fireflies to come out. So Mr Merrick and I sat and waited for them together. He was going that evening, leaving Mirat for the new training area in Bengal. He told me quite a lot of things. He seemed to want to talk about it now that it had all come out. He explained who the woman in the white saree was. He said he was sorry for her because she was what he called an ordinary decent person who had done everything for her nephew, the one who's in prison. He'd not seen her since he was in Mayapore but he'd always known he was kept track of by the kind of people who tried to make out he'd arrested the wrong men and ill-treated them, the people responsible for what happened to spoil the wedding. He said they were exploiting the woman, using her as part of a scheme to make him feel like a marked man. It all seemed a bit far-fetched to me, but I expect it's the only explanation.'

'Did he remember my friend, Edwina Crane?'

'I'm sorry. I never thought to ask.'

'Well, I don't suppose he did. Although as DSP in Mayapore he'd have known all about her being attacked. But I expect one of his juniors dealt with that. He had his hands full with that other awful business, didn't he? Does he still feel he was right, or does he think he might have made a mistake after all, arresting those boys? Miss Manners seemed so positive they weren't the ones, if we're to believe all we heard.'

They had reached the shade of a pine tree that stood near the very end of the garden. From here there was the view to the farther hills and the mountains. In a week or two the snow-capped peaks would be obscured by cloud as often as not. Sarah sat down. Barbie followed suit.

'He feels he was right,' Sarah said. 'He sounded very sure. Very sure indeed. But the more he talked about it the more I felt he'd got it all wrong. And that would be terrible, wouldn't it? If he had got it wrong but is always going to believe he didn't. Do you see what I mean? I know it's terrible in other ways, for the boys who have gone to prison and for – well – but she's dead, and that's another question, another sort of terrible. But to have got something wrong, and never see it, never believe it . . .'

Sarah dug her hand into a cushion of pine needles, sifting them, considering them. Suddenly she went on: 'He said that he was once attracted to her himself, in love with her perhaps. He made it sound like a confession, like a determination to be honest about every possible aspect but all the time I felt it wasn't. I don't know why I felt that. But everything he said sounded rehearsed. And while he was saying it you felt him watching for the effect, even knowing what it was going to be.'

'You didn't like him.'

After a while Sarah shook her head.

'No. I don't think I liked him at all.'

Perhaps, Barbie thought, because you had seen the child and talked to the old woman, and had seen the other woman, the woman in the white saree, and felt the presence of the unknown Indian. And wonder how in all this complexity guilt can lie alongside innocence and whether it might not have been in Mr Merrick's power to separate them.

She continued to sit in spite of getting cramp because Sarah did not move and she did not want to leave her alone.

'What did you say?' Sarah asked, coming back into herself after what seemed a long time.

'I wasn't talking.'

Sarah stared at her for a moment or two and said, 'I'm sorry, I thought you were,' and then Barbie wondered whether she had been.

For years she had had real and imaginary conversations with people, with herself, with God, with anyone who was there to listen or not listen. But an imaginary silence was something new. If you didn't know you were talking then you didn't know what you were saying. She tried to remember exactly what she had been thinking in case she had spoken some of her thoughts aloud, but her mind appeared to have been blank after the image of Sarah sitting with the old woman and the child, pondering the question of guilt and innocence and the part Mr Merrick had played or not played in attempting to establish them.

'You seem to be haunted by it,' she said, 'I mean by that awful business. First in Kashmir, being so close to the houseboat, and now in Mirat, with Captain Merrick.'

'Someone should be haunted by it,' Sarah said.

And then Barbie was sure she was right: Sarah had visited the woman and seen the child. She had a concern to hold the child, to take it to St John's and see it baptized.

'Yes,' Barbie said. 'Perhaps we should.' She got up. 'Stay here. I've got something for you to take to Susan.'

She went into the house, returned with the box of Apostle spoons and the note she had written. She knelt again and offered them.

'They're a combined wedding and twenty-first birthday present. Nothing very much. A set of teaspoons. I'd be grateful if you'd take them to her.'

'Thank you, Barbie. That's very kind.'

Sarah put the box on the cushion of needles and looked at the envelope on which Barbie had written, 'Mrs Edward Bingham'.

'I may be leaving Pankot,' Sarah said.

'Oh, Sarah, why? Where?'

'Just to do something more useful. Nursing perhaps or what I'm doing now only in a place where the war's a bit closer. Do you think that's selfish?'

'Why selfish?'

'Because of leaving Mother and Susan. With Daddy a prisoner it's always seemed to be my job to help look after things.'

'Susan's a married woman now.'

'Yes. That's why I thought I could go.'

'I should miss you dreadfully, well we all should, but it would be wrong to hold you back. *That* would be selfishness.'

Sarah glanced up. For a while they looked at each other gravely. 'I wish I could see things clearly enough to be positive like that,' Sarah said. 'But I never can. I must go—'

Abruptly she rose.

'Thank you for Susan's present. Please don't bother to see me off.'

She was gone before Barbie could get to her feet. She watched her until she was out of sight and then followed slowly.

Mabel was not working in the back or on the verandah which must mean she was either at the front or gone for one of her increasingly rare but still solitary walks.

I must explore, Barbie thought; and then spoke aloud: 'I must explore this mystery of the imaginary silence,' and as her voice continued she found that she could detach herself from its sound so that it seemed to go drifting away, or she to go drifting away from it, until she was left in a state of immobility or suspended animation, surrounded by what she could only describe as a vivid sense of herself as new and unused, with neither debit nor credit to her account, no longer in arrears with any kind of payment because the account had not been opened yet.

This was very clear to her but she guessed it wouldn't be when the immobility was cancelled. She thought: Emerson was wrong, we're not explained by our history at all, in fact it's our history that gets in the way of a lucid explanation of us.

She began to enjoy the sensation of her history and other people's history blowing away like dead leaves; but then it occurred to her that among the leaves were her religious principles and beliefs, and – observing the solemn evergreen stillness of the wood-capped hills – felt reassured and wisely reinstructed.

An imaginary silence should not be used to destroy contact but to create it. She went round to the front to find Mabel but the garden was empty. Mabel's stick was on the front verandah so she was not out walking. She went inside, knocked on Mabel's door and opened it.

Mabel was sitting on the edge of her bed watching Aziz removing the contents of an old press and placing them carefully on a blanket spread on the floor.

'Hello, Barbie,' Mabel said, looking up. 'We're sorting out some winter things.'

Barbie had never watched this ritual at Rose Cottage but she knew that it took place. She came further into the room, fascinated as she had been since childhood by the prospect of viewing someone else's possessions; for these had a magic quality of touch-me-not that belonged in fairy tales and in such tales dispensation was possible but not inevitable and every invitation to come nearer was a sugared gift.

'Oh, no, Aziz,' Mabel said, as he opened layers of tissue to show the coat of a grey costume.

'Hān,' he insisted. 'Bond is-street.'

Mabel smiled. 'I bought it in London the last summer I was there,' she explained to Barbie, 'the summer John's grandfather died. Susan was only ten or eleven then so you can tell how out of date it is. But every winter Aziz tries to make me bring it out, because of the tag.'

'Bond is-street,' Aziz repeated. 'Pukka.'

The whole costume was spread out now. It had the simple elegance of all expensive clothes.

'You could shorten the skirt,' Barbie suggested. 'It wouldn't spoil the line.'

'Wouldn't it?'

Encouraged by Barbie's interest Aziz said, 'Hān. Shorten is-skirt.'

'Perhaps. If I can still get into it.'

Mabel reached down and pulled the costume towards her, twitched at it, and Barbie wondered how easy or difficult it would be to make her take an interest again in things outside Rose Cottage: in clothes, in visits, sprees. The two of them could have a holiday, a short one, not far away. They could go down to Ranpur to do some Christmas shopping. She would take Mabel round the Bishop Barnard and introduce her to Helen Jolley. For such a holiday she would have the heliotrope.

'Very well, Aziz,' Mabel said. 'Put it on the pile.'

Aziz nodded. He rearranged the costume, folded it with reverence, replaced the dried sprigs of lavender whose scent mingled with that of sandalwood and mothballs. The tissue-wrapped costume was put on the smaller of the two piles. Suddenly he reached into the chest and said to Barbie, 'Memsahib!'

'No, no,' Mabel said. She made a gesture as if to stop him but it was ignored. He was intent on revealing a treasure. He lifted a package out and removed the top layer of tissue with a flourish.

'Sarah bachcha,' he said. Barbie went closer. A wedding veil? No, a complete garment. She could see the neckline and tiny sleeves folded across its front. Sarah bachcha. Sarah as a baby. She got down on her knees. 'Oh, it's a christening gown. Was it Sarah's?'

'Hān. Sarah Mem.'

Aziz linked thumbs and flapped his splayed fingers. 'Batta fye,' he said, and laughed at Barbie's puzzled expression. He put his hand in under the creamy lace from which the gown was made. As he did so Barbie exclaimed. The hem of the fine lawn undergarment was edged with a band of seed pearls. But there was more enchantment to come. 'Look,' he said, and fluttered his hand. The lace came alive. Butterflies palpated his pink brown palm. Three of them. Five. Seven. A dozen. More than that. The whole gown was made of lace butterflies.

'Oh, but it's beautiful,' Barbie said. 'Did Susan wear it too?'

Mabel answered. 'No. Susan had something new.'

Now that the lace was exposed Mabel seemed willing to acknowledge it. But putting out her hand to touch it Barbie felt that she was encroaching upon one of the many parts of Mabel's hidden history. She drew her hand back.

'No, do take it out,' Mabel protested. 'It's beautiful lace. My first husband's mother gave it to me for when we had children, but we never did. There's a full length of it still unmade up. Enough for a shawl. Aziz, show Barbie Mem the piece.'

Aziz reached into the press and lifted out another tissue-wrapped package. He opened it and unravelled the lace as the durzi unravelled bolts of cloth. The lace cascaded across his and Barbie's knees. The butterflies hovered, settled, rose, settled again. Some of their wings were folded, others only partly folded. Some displayed the full spread.

'It's exquisite,' Barbie said. She hardly dared touch it. 'So delicate and alive.'

'It's rather remarkable when you realize that the old woman who made it was blind.'

'Blind!'

'Not from birth. But for many years. She sat in a room in the top of a tower of an old French château that belonged to my mother-in-law's family. She called the butterflies her prisoners.'

Barbie put both hands under the lace and raised them. The butterflies quivered as in a taut web. They were part of the web.

'Yes,' she said. 'They are caught, aren't they? How carefully you've looked after it.'

'Aziz sees to that. Would you like that piece?'

Barbie let the lace free. 'It's very kind of you,' she said, 'but it's much too beautiful. I wouldn't know what to use it for. And besides it's precious and it's family.' She thought of the wedding and its possible consequences. 'And now it may come in.'

'What?'

'If Susan and Teddie have children.'

'There's Sarah's dress already made up and there if wanted. Are you sure?'

'Quite sure. But thank you very much for the offer.'

Mrs John Layton, the card began, Miss Sarah Layton and Mrs Edward Bingham, request the pleasure of your company at the Officers' Mess, The Pankot Rifles. The date was for two weeks ahead, the time mid-day. On the bottom right-hand side it said Buffet Luncheon and on the left RSVP. Two cards were delivered to Rose Cottage.

In the envelope containing Barbie's there was a note from Susan. 'Dear Barbie,' she had written, 'thank you so much for the beautiful set of Apostle teaspoons. I'm writing to Teddie who I know would wish me to say thank you on his behalf as well. I heard from him a few days ago and he says he is very fit but of course working very hard. Mummy and I have decided that she should give a little party here to make up for having to have the wedding in Mirat and that it would be a good idea to have it on my twenty-first. A lot of our wedding presents were to cover both occasions. I do hope that you and Aunty Mabel will both be able to come. Mummy says it's years since Aunty Mabel visited the Mess and a lot of the young officers who have heard of her but never met her are dying to because really she is quite famous, not just because of Daddy but because of all the silver her first husband presented and which is used on special occasions. We shall have the wedding presents displayed, by the way, and your spoons will look awfully nice in their blue-lined box. With Love, Susan.'

'I expect you'd like to go, Barbie,' Mabel said.

'Only if you do.'

'Well I shall have to but I'd want to come away before they start eating. I can't bear eating standing up or eating in crowds. But Mildred knows that. She won't mind. If I put in an appearance that's all anybody will want, but you stay on and have a good tuck in.'

'Eating in crowds gives me indigestion too. We'll go and come back together. We'll arrange to slip away.'

I shall have the heliotrope, she decided. When I look in the mirror and see my grey hair I know I can carry the heliotrope.

She went down to the bazaar towards evening which was the time she liked best, especially in November when it was quite cold and there were braziers and early lanterns and the small of charcoal and incense. She stood at the entrance to the durzi's shop. A chokra beckoned her in, dusted a chair and invited her to sit and then went through the curtain which presently parted again to admit the old man and the chokra who was carrying the bolt of purple cloth.

'Ah, so you know what I've come for,' she said. He unravelled three or four yards and held it up. She gazed at it, testing for the edge of an old uncertainty and found it gone. 'The name heliotrope,' she said, 'comes from the Greek words helios, meaning sun, and trepo meaning turn. Heliotropion. A plant that turns its flowers to the sun.'

'Memsahib has decided?'

'Yes. And you have my measurements. The usual style, the skirt straight, box pleat at the back, the coat with pockets on my hips, deep enough and roomy enough for me to stick my hands in. As in the last suit, the grey one. I leave the choice of lining to you, it is always perfectly matched. When shall I come for the fitting?'

The fitting was a formality. Year by year his scissors and needle were wielded with precision, year by year she gained, lost, nothing in weight nor changed shape in any way. He had only to refer to his figures that were filed away either in a drawer or in his mind under the name Bachlev, Baba; the holy woman from the missions. The fitting was arranged for one week from that evening and the finished garment promised for delivery the morning of the day before the party. He gave her a snipping of the cloth. She put it in her handbag. It would be useful if she wanted to match up shoes, gloves and handbag, or to consider the tones of the blouse to go with it or of one of her sprays of velvet flowers for the lapel.

*

'How nice you look, Barbie,' Mabel had said. 'What a happy colour,' and had seemed almost eager to be off; but half-way down Club road she had suddenly turned as if she had changed her mind and would tell the tonga-wallah to take them back. In the lapel of the Bond Street costume a small diamond brooch glittered, a miniature of the Pankot Rifles badge. She wore no other jewellery. The brooch had been a gift from her first husband, who died on the Khyber. Her face was shaded by a grey felt hat with a wide brim. In place of a ribbon a fawn chiffon scarf was tied round the base of the crown. The free ends hung behind to shade her neck. Her legs, too often hidden by shabby gardening trousers, were still slim and well-shaped. Seated, the shortened skirt revealed them to the knee; to just below it when she stood. Fawn gloves covered the work-roughened hands.

We could go to Ranpur, Barbie had said the night before. To do some Christmas shopping. 'Oh, I shall never go to Ranpur again,' Mabel replied, 'at least not until I'm buried,' which had seemed to Barbie an odd sort of thing to say until she remembered that her friend's second husband was buried there, in the churchyard of St Luke's; and the way she now twisted round as if to tell the tonga-wallah to go back seemed like a momentary confusion, as if what was uppermost in her mind was the idea of going to Ranpur for that macabre purpose and the understanding that the time hadn't yet come and that the journey downhill must be cancelled, or anyway postponed. And then her eye had been reattracted by Barbie's heliotrope costume and the real object of the journey had again become clear. So that she resumed her position and watched the road unravel beneath her feet, and said nothing, but listened, or did not listen, while Barbie talked –

– or talked and was silent. God, she felt, had waited a long time for her to see that she could ignore the burden of her words which mounted one upon the other until they toppled, only to be set up again, and again, weighting her shoulders; a long time for her consciously to enter the private realm of inner silence and begin to learn how to inhabit it even while her body went its customary bustling way and her tongue clacked endlessly on: as at present, keeping time with the clack of the horse's hooves as the equipage, avoiding the bazaar, dropped down through Cantonment Approach road, making for the military lines.

'We're late,' she heard herself exclaim. In the world where she talked, where everybody talked, time was of peculiar importance. In Rifle Range road there were no other vehicles. They passed the end of grace and favour lane and in a moment or two turned left into Mess road. The geometrically laid out huts showed black against the green and the green itself was sparse, trodden. Distantly, in groups, sepoys drilled. A board painted in Pankot Rifles colours and with a huge gilt and coloured replica of the badge marked their destination. They turned at right-angles, crossing a culvert into a compound, approached the long square-pillared portico, and drove into it. When the tonga stopped Barbie could hear the uneven drone of voices inside. Servants stood at the entrance, dressed in white tunics and floppy white trousers. The ribbons in their pugrees, and their broad cummerbunds, were woven in horizontal stripes of the regimental colours. One of the servants, tall and thickly built, elderly, moved forward and saluted and stood offering his arm to Mabel.

'Memsahib!' he said.

Mabel had automatically put her hand on his wrist but the note of urgency in his voice arrested her. Her body seemed to stiffen with uncertainty or alarm. The servant spoke again and Barbie listened carefully so that she could tell Mabel louder and in English what he was saying.

'He says he wonders if you remember him now that he's old and has a beard.'

'What?'

Barbie repeated it but was not sure Mabel understood. She was looking down at the man, her hand still gripping his wrist.

'Is it Ghulam?' she asked at last. 'Ghulam Mohammed?'

The old man nodded and for a while they stared at each other. Then he turned his wrist over so that his palm touched hers.

'You are well, Ghulam Mohammed?' she asked in Urdu.

'I am well. Is it so with you?'

'It is so.'

'God is good.'

'Praise God. Ghulam, this is my friend, Miss Batchelor.'

'Memsahib.'

'Now we must go in,' Mabel said in English. He made his arm into a crook and helped them down, and then up a shallow flight of steps into the dark interior.

'Thank you,' Mabel said, and added – as if to impress the name on a memory she could not trust – 'Ghulam Mohammed.'

909

The hall was pillared. The voices came from a room on the left whose double doors were open. Barbie could see Mildred in a flowery hat, Colonel and Mrs Trehearne, and Susan looking younger than twenty-one talking to Kevin Coley, the depot adjutant who had lost his wife in the Quetta earthquake, was now the oldest captain in the regiment and said to be content to remain so. Barbie always thought he had a face like a medieval martyr; one of the unimportant ones who went to the stake in job lots.

And then, as they approached the doors, there was a change of rhythm in the voices, a slowing down, and a quietening; what Barbie recalled ever afterwards as a hush which spread back through the room and brought people's heads round to watch Mabel's arrival, her return after a long inexplicable absence to the place she had first entered longer ago than anyone else present, which meant that her presence now had a mystical significance. In her there surely reposed the original spirit of the hard condition, the spirit that belonged to the days of certainty, self-assurance, total conviction?

With several paces yet to go Mabel hesitated as if she would draw back and suddenly Barbie wished that they both could. But – 'It is very crowded,' Mabel said and then moved forward indomitably as Mildred came out to receive her. The brims of their hats forced distance on their embrace, but Mildred looked genuinely pleased and even grateful to Barbie whose trembling hand was taken in a gesture that implied there was greater affection than the social circumstances allowed Mildred to show. 'You both made it,' she said. 'How nice. Mabel, there are some young boys who are dying to meet you but scared stiff so go easy on them for God's sake. There's one called Dicky Beauvais whose uncle was a subaltern under Bob Buckland. I know he's particularly hoping for a word.'

'Hello, Aunty,' Susan said. 'It's so nice of you to come and thank you for the marvellous present.' She kissed her aunt and then surprisingly kissed Barbie too and said, 'What a nice colour,' and led them into the still hushed assembly where the distance between Barbie and Mabel began subtly to lengthen because the Trehearnes interposed themselves and guided Mabel gradually towards the Rankins while the Peplows claimed Barbie as their own. Mabel looked over her shoulder, bewildered, but the already tenuous link was snapped by Mildred's obtrusive hat and Kevin Coley's crucified shoulder and Barbie felt herself forced away from the centre to the periphery. I never understood, Mrs Stewart was saying, your sudden interest in Emerson. I do not wish to talk about Emerson or indeed about anything, Barbie said, but only from inside that area of privacy and silence. Her voice was saying something quite different. Is Sarah here? she was asking Clarissa. She wasn't at the door unless I missed her, how awful if I did. No I have not met Mrs Jason, how do you do?

There were glimpses to be had of the felt hat and the chiffon scarf. They formed a point of reference. Her eye continually sought it. The room, dark-panelled and Persian carpeted, was uncomfortably warm and close. Half-lowered tattis on the porticoed verandah kept out the glare. A bearer offered a tray and she took a glass of sherry to occupy her hands. She had not reckoned with this separation and it occurred to her that it had been engineered, arranged beforehand by Mildred with the innocent connivance of Clarissa Peplow who seemed to have assumed the duty of making sure that Barbie was kept entertained, refreshed, introduced and out of certain people's way. She began to be afraid that when the time came for her to help Mabel slip away she would be unable to find her, which was ridiculous since there was only this one room in use and the verandah on the other side of the long buffet table, where the windows were open, letting in some fresh air. She looked for but could not see the display of wedding presents. Neither, now, could she see the hat with the chiffon scarf. The room frightened her.

'What a nice suit, Barbie.'

It was Sarah. Barbie clasped her hand. 'Is she all right do you think, in this crowd? I feel I ought to be with her but there are so many claims on her attention.'

'They've got her a chair,' Sarah said. 'Over in the corner there. You can't see her from here but she's all right.'

'We're slipping away, you know, before the buffet.'

'Yes, I know. Barbie, you know Tony Bishop, don't you? He's been posted to Bombay. Isn't he lucky?'

'We met once at Rose Cottage but you may not remember me from among all those young people.' She offered her hand to the ill-looking man who had been Teddie Bingham's friend. 'Are you quite recovered from the jaundice?'

'Thank you, yes.'

'It is so debilitating, well so I gather, never having had it, only heard. I've always enjoyed excessive good health which I suppose is rather indecent, a sign of diminished sensibility perhaps, a certain coarseness of constitution no doubt inherited from my father whose life was terminated by the wheels of a hansom cab or bus on the Embankment I forget which in fact I was never quite sure but everyone expected him to go from cirrhosis of the liver which given the same intake any ordinary man would have contracted. Did you change your mind, Sarah, I mean about the presents? Susan told me they'd be on display but perhaps it proved too difficult, I mean they'd need guarding wouldn't they?'

*

But the presents were on display on the verandah, guarded by a naik and two sepoys who stood stiffly in the at ease position not catching the eye of any guest because it was not the guests of whom they had to entertain suspicion but intruders or contractors' servants coming too near the sparkling array of cutlery, glass, tea and coffee sets, trays, table-lamps, vases and carved boxes. A kind of queue had formed, as for the rite of passing by a bier Barbie thought when fifteen minutes later she accompanied the Peplows and Mrs Stewart to inspect the remains of the wedding. The verandah was crowded too.

Trees partially screened the view across to the grace and favour bungalow which Barbie had never been inside because she had always declined Sarah's invitation to go in when – as they sometimes did – they shared a tonga from the bazaar and Barbie went out of her way to bring Sarah home. She thought she could hear Panther barking. There were cries from the parade ground. But the verandah of the mess seemed to lack conditions in which an echo could exist. Voices, sounds, had a brazen hollow quality. 'Wavell's the first Viceroy we've had who knows anything about the country and then of course he's a soldier,' someone told her but when she glanced round the speaker's face was not turned to her but to another man and she did not know either of them. When they reached the loaded table she could not see the spoons.

'Absolutely splendid, I agree,' she said, taking Clarissa up, 'a splendid display.'

After a while she abandoned her feverish attempts to find the spoons and carefully, slowly, quartered the table from edge to edge and from front to back. She longed but did not dare to ask Clarissa, 'Do you see my little Apostle spoons anywhere?' She wondered if she had a wrong impression of what they looked like in their box and looked twice at pastry forks and for any box whose lid was not open; stooped to see whether they were placed where the eye could not fall on them easily from a standing position. 'Excuse me,' someone said, and straightening quickly to let a woman pass behind her had to steady herself with a hand placed too quickly and heavily on the table so that for an instant she feared being the cause of a shameful and unforgivable incident. 'Oh, Barbie, be careful,' Clarissa said. 'I think we'd better stand back.' 'It wasn't my fault,' she said and then came away to be out of danger and free of the risk of other people's anger.

It was humiliating to think it might be realized what she had been looking for. But the spoons were not displayed and that was humiliation enough and one from which she could not retreat. The line of escape from the toppling towers of her words was blocked. 'There's such a crush,' she said, 'and I've forgotten how to cope with crowds. Also I can't hear myself think, not that I suppose you imagine I ever can.' She grinned at Clarissa who was looking worried. With such a look Clarissa would observe the good Samaritan at his work.

'Do you know,' Barbie went on, 'I have never been in a Mess before. I mean Mess with a capital M. Isn't that odd, or don't you think so? I suppose the room in there is the ante-room, is that the correct nomenclature? Where the officers forgather before going in to dine and toast the King-Emperor and throw their glasses into the hearth, or does that only happen in kinematograph pictures?'

Oh, and I could throw my glass into a hearth, she said (but saying something else to Clarissa and so finding her way back into that blessed privacy where words actually spoken didn't matter) – dash it into a thousand sharp fragments, so that the sound would attract attention and He would say, What troubles you? What is your name? When did we last talk? Because it is to be talked to that I want above anything. I want to create around myself a condition of silence so that it may be broken, but not by me. But I am surrounded by a condition of Babel. To this, all my life, I have contributed enough for a dozen people. And He stops His ears and leaves us to get on with it.

She moved, prompted by Clarissa's charitable hand and Christian heart to re-enter the maelstrom and was granted a curious vision, fortuitous and short-lived. By chance, and people's movements, a clear channel was opened and she saw at the end of it the felt hat and the chiffon scarf and Mabel seated on the leather armchair, enthroned thus, and young men arrested in postures of deference and inquiry, one – an Indian – leaning forward while Mabel's hand was raised to her deaf ear and then folded again with the other on her quiet lap, and young men's smiles which were not as fully understanding as hers but ready to acclaim some imminent discovery; of what, only they could tell. Barbie could no longer see them because the vision was shut off again by barriers of fleshy faces, arms, bosoms, chins and epaulettes; the bark and chirrup of the human voice manufacturing the words which created the illusion of intelligent existence.

Behind this mass of people Mabel also presumably continued to exist but she would have liked proof of it and contemplated forcing a passage, gathering her friend in possessive and protective arms.

'Are you all right?' Sarah asked, reappearing. 'Can we get you another drink? Have you met Captain Beauvais? Dicky, this is Miss Batchelor, Aunty Mabel's companion.'

'I suppose companion is the right word. How do you do? I see you're Pankot Rifles too.' Captain Beauvais looked very young to be a captain. He had a shiny pink skin and a little fair moustache and the enthusiastic expression of mediocrity which Barbie had learned to recognize from years of looking in a mirror. 'Have you met Mabel yet? You *are* the one Mildred mentioned who hoped to speak to her because of someone called Bob Buckland?'

'Yes, that's right, and I have,' Captain Beauvais said. 'Was it sherry?' He detained the bare-foot bearer. 'His feet,' Barbie said, 'in this crush!' And received a fresh glass which she sipped from immediately. 'Do you know Muzzafirabad?' she asked. 'I was there centuries ago but of course there's no reason why you should because you're not a Muzzy.'

'Well actually I do. Are you connected?'

'Not with the Muzzys. I was Mission not Army. Are you on Dick Rankin's staff or with the regiment?'

'I was with the regiment but Area collared me to take Teddie Bingham's place.'

'But you know Muzzafirabad. I expect it's changed. Teddie knew it but we seemed to be talking about two different places. I was Bishop Barnard, but only the infant school. A mere shack. Well, very small. The children came mainly for the chappattis. There was so much hunger. And disease of course, the two go hand in hand. And still do. One is appalled, appalled and thinks – well, can nothing ever be done, is it truly a hopeless task? The love of God can't fill an empty belly and when it's full one seldom thinks to thank Him.'

'We accept some pretty skinny fellows nowadays, but they soon fill out.' His eyes snatched at avenues of escape. 'Talking about food, I think there's some beginning to come in. May I get you something?'

'That's very kind but we're slipping away before the buffet.'

She retreated, backing away from Captain Beauvais, slightly spilling her sherry. She begged someone's pardon, put the sherry down and turned, found the crowd moving inexorably forward, pressing her back towards the table on to which salvers and tureens were being placed by the contractor's scruffy servants who were coming in from the verandah in what looked like dozens. Excuse me, she said, but I must get to Mrs Layton senior. Excuse me. I do so beg your pardon. Retreating from the crowd, from the cold consommé, the pâté, the chicken and turkey and ham, the salmon mayonnaise and Beauvais's skinny recruits with the army beef already thickening their stick-thin arms and legs, and from the nameless little girl; the unknown Indian. To find Mabel. Who had retreated from all these things long ago as if she knew the whole affair was doomed and hopeless.

The channel was open and she broke through into it and saw the chair, empty, abandoned. She looked round but there was no sign of the felt hat with the chiffon scarf flowing from it. Nearby on a leather sofa two young Indian women sat in their best sarees smiling into a middle-distance, waiting for their husbands to resume responsibility.

'Have you seen Mrs Layton, Mrs Layton senior?' she asked one of them.
'Oh, no.'
'The lady in the grey hat and scarf who was sitting in the chair.'
'Oh, no. She went I think.'

She cannot have gone, Barbie said, unless she was never here and it is all a dream; and pressed into the crowd again trying to make her way back to the place she had been standing in before in case Mabel had noted it and gone there to find her and tell her it was time. Perhaps she had made for the verandah to find her and see the presents. She would not have left by herself.

She was not on the verandah.

*

Having walked its length Barbie re-entered the ante-room through the open door used by the contractor's servants. From here she had a clear view of the still empty chair. She moved through the narrow passage between the straight line of the wall and the uneven line of backs and elbows. The noise was deafening. She looked for a familiar face but on this side of the room there seemed to be none familiar enough. The mouths in the faces had forks going into them. She marvelled that there should be such a volume of conversation. She became hungry both for food and chat and mercy and felt faint and then a bit sick, put her hand out to steady herself and saw that her hand rested on a door. At waist level there was a brass knob that looked gaunt. She grasped it, turned and thrust. The door was very heavy. Passing through the opening she pushed it to behind her and was surprised to find it lighter in the closing than the opening. It banged.

The sound echoed down the long corridor in which she now stood. When it died away there was a profound silence. The noise of the party was miraculously shut out. A door at the other end seemed a great distance away, as far, as unattainable as the landing at the top of the frightening stairs in the gloomy little house in Camberwell. She considered the grace which levitation would bestow but setting out on her journey in search of Mabel found herself denied it, as earthbound as ever. The corridor was filled with aqueous light from the murky fanlight windows whose long cords were looped on their hooks with military precision, their free ends hanging at what looked like equal measured lengths. Between the cords were mounted trophies. Ranged along the opposite wall stood heavy marble busts, rock-firm on stout tapering plinths. Through these she must walk the gauntlet, dare the waxen and sightless faces of Mabel's forbears, the tusks and glaring eyes of their guardian beasts: the hunters and the hunted, now voiceless and immobile but met in a permanent conjoint task of terrorism of strangers and intruders.

The floor was tiled in lozenges of black and white but down its centre lay a Persian runner which smothered the sound of footsteps. She paused in the centre of one of the blue and crimson medallion designs. A few paces ahead, on her left, there was a wide arched recess with a pair of mahogany doors set in it. One of them was half open. She was still some distance from the closed door at the end of the corridor. The closed door had a look of Mabel not being in the room it led into. The half open door on the other hand suggested her recent passage through it. She strode the last few paces, pushed the door further open and entered.

Immense. Shadowed. A long room, the length of the corridor but higher. The main windows were shuttered. Again light entered only through the fanlight windows. In the centre of the room a vast mahogany table reflected two great epergnes that floated on the dark unrippled surface like silver boats on a glassy midnight lake. On opposite banks chairs, awaiting occupants, were placed arm to arm in close formation. The walls were panelled in dark-stained wood to the height of the tall shuttered french doors. Above this level they were whitewashed. Fixed to them as thickly as butterflies to a naturalist's display board were flags, some worn as thin as mummys' rags; standards and heraldically disposed weapons of war: swords, sabres, lances, muskets. Between the windows were sideboards and dumb-waiters heavy with plate. At both ends of the room were monumental fireplaces and above them gilt-framed battle landscapes.

Against the wall on the corridor side of the room there were three glass-fronted display cabinets. The light slanting down through the fanlights was reflected back by the silver contained in them. In front of the furthest cabinet stood Mabel.

Barbie opened her mouth to speak but did not. Mabel stood in front of the cabinet like someone in the presence of a reliquary. She had become untouchable, unapproachable, protected by the intense and chilling dignity of the room in which (Barbie felt) some kind of absolute certainty had been reached long ago and was now enshrined so perfectly and implacably that it demanded nothing that was not a whole and unquestioning acceptance of the truth on which it was based.

Still unaware of Barbie's presence Mabel turned and went to the nearer fireplace, stood and gazed up at the dark picture in which Barbie could make out a white horse with a dim uniformed figure declamatorily astride against a backdrop of clouds and cannon puffs. Like the representation of the crucifixion above an altar the picture held the room in silent celebration of the mystery of its governing genius.

I have lost her, Barbie thought. Mabel had not wanted to come but having done so she had been unable to resist the impulse to enter the inner sanctuary of the world from which she had cut herself off and, having entered, the associations had proved too powerful. Yes, I have lost her, Barbie repeated, but come to that I have never really found her.

Mabel turned round and Barbie wondered if she had spoken her thoughts aloud. Nervously she touched her cheek with her gloved hand. For a moment neither of them said anything but faced each other across the length of the inhospitable table until Barbie had the distressing impression that Mabel's first words would be accusing and dismissive.

'Is it time for us to go, Barbie?'

She nodded. If she spoke she guessed she would not be able to stop and it seemed imperative for their future that she should hold her tongue in this place.

'I'm sorry if I've worried you, wondering where I'd got to,' Mabel said. For a few seconds more she surveyed the table, the walls, the cabinets of silver, then she walked towards Barbie and when she reached her grasped her wrist as she had grasped the bearded old servant's.

'We can go out the back way through the cloakroom at the end of the corridor. If you're ready.'

'Oh, yes,' Barbie said. 'I'm quite ready.' She turned her hand round so that her palm was pressed encouragingly in her friend's. But Mabel stood immovable. Suddenly she said:

'I thought there might be some changes, but there aren't. It's all exactly as it was when I first saw it more than forty years ago. I can't even be angry. But someone ought to be.'

*

Barbie unhooked the dangerous spectacles and placed them near the table-lamp. She settled the pillows, adjusted the tops of the sheet and blankets so that her friend's hands were covered. And then sat for the customary ten minutes before turning the light off. In the morning at breakfast Mabel would not say: It's very strange, I went to sleep over my book but woke in the morning without book or spectacles, is it Aziz or you who tucks me up? Barbie knew she would say nothing because she had said nothing on all the previous occasions.

Tonight there was no muttering, not even a movement of lips. Barbie stood up, switched off the light and waited until she was sure that Mabel still slept. Back in her own room she approached the penitential area of the rush mat but found herself reluctant to attempt communication through that medium. I shall have an imaginary silence, she said; and sat at the writing-table, opened Emerson – her own copy, bought to replace the borrowed one – and proceeded to read aloud to the class from his essay on self-reliance.

'Society is a wave. The wave moves onward, but the water of which it is composed does not. The same particle does not rise from the valley to the ridge. Its unity is only phenomenal. The persons who make up a nation today, next year die, and their experience with them.'

And some are buried here (she thought, as her voice droned on through the essay and then off into inaudibility as her imaginary silence took hold) – some are buried here in the churchyard of St John's and some in the churchyard of St Luke's in Ranpur, as Mabel's second husband was, the one who was not a soldier and died of disease not wounds. By his side it is her eventual wish to rest because she says I shall never go to Ranpur again until I'm buried. But who were Bob Buckland, Ghulam Mohammed and Gillian Waller?

A voice replied: Does it matter?

She clutched her throat in alarm. The voice had spoken so clearly. It was not her own voice. Her own voice was still droning on through the words of Emerson. Scared, she tuned back into it. 'In the will work and acquire, and thou hast chained the wheel of Chance, and shall always drag her after thee. A political victory, a rise of rents, the recovering of your sick, or the return of your absent friend, or some other quite external event, raises your spirits, and you think good days are preparing for you. Do not believe it. It can never be so. Nothing can bring you peace but yourself. Nothing can bring you peace but the triumph of principles.'

She cried out involuntarily, stood up, pushing back the chair. She went towards the mat and then began to tremble because she could not quite reach it and in any case her knees would not bend. She seemed fixed in this proud and arrogant position. Her jaws were locked too, her mouth still open as if to allow the cry to come back in. She could not remember what her principles were.

*

917

A few weeks later Mildred announced that Susan was going to have a baby and that Sarah, who had put in an application for posting to a forward area, had dutifully withdrawn it.

IV

Romeo, if dead, should be cut up into little stars to make the heavens fine.
(Emerson's essay on Love)

Nowadays she communicated with the world outside Rose Cottage by writing letters to Helen Jolley. She had never known Miss Jolley intimately. There was the right amount of uncluttered distance between them. Miss Jolley had sent only one reply and Barbie did not expect to hear from her again so had ceased to post her own letters or write them on notepaper. She wrote them in old exercise books taken from the trunk of missionary relics. Many of these were only partly filled and had a useful number of blank pages in them. There was a considerable saving in the cost of stamps and stationery; and an ease of reference back.

December 24th, 1943

My Dear Miss Jolley,

On this special night you would do well to pause in your administration of the Bishop Barnard and ask yourself as I do what gifts our mission has brought to the children of India, and if – among them – has ever been the gift of love. I do not mean pity, I do not mean compassion, I do not mean instruction nor do I mean devotion to the interests either of the child or the institution. Love is what I mean. Without that gift I doubt that any can be, could have been, brought to Jesus. After many years of believing I knew what love is I now suspect I do not which means I do not know and have never known what God is either. Do you? Do not be deceived by my self-assured expression. Reject the evidence of my confident stride. Shut your ears to my chatter. They are all illusory. I question my existence, my right to it. This is not I trust despair. While you are about it by the way (prayer I mean, if indeed you submit to that discipline busy as you are with so many other things) you might pray for the soul of Edwina Crane. My own prayers are not guaranteed reception. Her need though is greater at the moment than mine or yours. On this night, especially. Most sincerely, BB.

*

March 8th, 1944

Dear Helen,

It is all right. About Edwina. Let me describe it to you while the detail is fresh in my mind. Ever since the news of the enemy's invasion of Indian soil we have been alert. This morning when I rose I knew that something of

918

vital importance to our safety had happened. I called Aziz but got no answer. I knocked at Mabel's door and went in expecting to find her still in bed because it was early. Her bed had been slept in but was empty. I searched. She was nowhere to be found. She and Aziz had gone. The servants' quarters were abandoned. It didn't take me long to work it out that everyone was making for the railway station and that a place would have been reserved for me on the train alongside Mabel. In fact I remembered that this had been carefully planned beforehand in the event of Pankot falling in danger of enemy attack.

I packed a few things, closed and bolted all the doors, windows and shutters, and let myself out. Imagine my relief when I saw a tonga waiting. The wallah flourished his whip and warned me to step on it. I thought, 'I may step on it but can the horse?' It looked more like an ass than a horse but I thought it would embarrass the driver to have this pointed out. 'You'd better jump in,' he said, 'because they're coming and everyone's gone ahead to catch the last train out.'

I stopped trusting him. He observed my hesitation and in a different tone of voice said, 'What are you waiting for, Barbie? You'd better buck up.' It was Mr Maybrick in disguise. He had piles of his organ music tied up in untidy bundles in the back. I scrambled in, made room for myself. Off we started. The horse wasn't lame as I'd feared. We made excellent progress. I felt elated, as in those days when my father took me on a spree and I had to hold my hat on. (It had a wide brim with artificial flowers Mother made out of coloured scraps of velvet). As we bowled down the hill past the golf-course I thought there were people there all wearing hats like this but then realised they were holding up umbrellas, coloured ones, made of paper. Mr Maybrick told me they were fifth columnists and that the golf-course was the rendezvous. We were in danger of being cut off and there was no time to catch the train. We would have to seek refuge in St John's Church.

It was at this stage that everything became weird. You say I dreamt. But what is a dream? Everything 'happens' in the mind whatever the source of the event. Now four-in-hand, first Mr Maybrick and then I whipped the horses down Club road making for the haven of the church. My short grey hair flew black and long and I was filled with joyful longings and expectations. I was not myself.

I felt capable of dealing with every eventuality, calm in anticipation of the Lord's help. We arrived at the site of St John's but a change had come about. It was not the churchyard which I and Mr Maybrick (now back in his ordinary clothes but with a dogcollar like Mr Cleghorn) were standing in but the compound of the mission school in Muzzafirabad. My servant Francis was calling the children to school by tolling the bell. He tolled it eleven times. We had a view across the golf-course. The number of paper umbrellas had increased and the fifth columnists had now been joined by the Japanese. We could see their yellow faces and the guns they carried in place of golf-bags. Mr Maybrick also had a gun. He looked at me and said, We must save a last bullet each. I did not believe such a terrible step would be necessary. When I looked again I did not see the enemy but troops of children marching to their lessons. I called out, wishing to hurry but not to frighten them. Francis whispered to me that the danger had not passed. I was afraid his expression would show how desperate he felt so I smiled and said to each group of children as they passed through the school doorway, 'It's quite safe now.'

At last all the children were inside. Mr Maybrick and I went to join them. And then I was Edwina no more but myself and the schoolroom was the church after all and I was alone. Mr Maybrick was at the organ playing. The church was otherwise empty, still, safe, happy. I knelt in a pew to give thanks for our deliverance and as I did so the most benign thought entered my mind. A voice said to me: I'm all right now. I knew it was Edwina. She wanted me to know that God had forgiven her that mortal sin and received her into His everlasting peace and mercy.

This was a form of communication, wasn't it? From Him, about Edwina. Which means I am not abandoned, although I think that now Edwina has gone from me in this life forever I am not unlonely. But this is a loneliness I can support.

*

April 28th, 1944

Dear Helen,

Do as I have done. Go to the window when it is dark and look at the night sky and ask yourself this question: Are the heavens finer than they were?

Teddie Bingham is dead, killed in action. The house still rings with Susan's single cry of anguish and on the edge of my bed remains the imprint of her body where she sat afterwards in stony silence, cut off from all human correspondence. My poor Susan. Heavy with child. Weighed down by her loss. Scarcely more than a child herself. In front of the other women here I couldn't restrain my tears.

I shed tears at my father's death. I felt he had died through some fault of mine. I was so plain and gawky and not clever in the ways a little girl is meant to be. Over the seams I sewed, for instance, my mother pursed her lips, and blacking his boots I fumbled so badly his socks became smeared and he said, Heavens, child! but the Heavens were not open to receive me and shield me from his forgiveness. His funeral as is the custom among the London poor was more splendid than his life. So many flowers! A crowded church. Men I had never seen in the house, stiff in black and with the formality of respect for a life gayer than it should have been but now gone and leaving wisps of secret masculine camaraderie behind it that had no business either in our family or the house of God. And there was one young woman, in passing whom on our way out my Mother sparked with ebony lights and an electric stiffness in that corset which made her waist a tower of strength but not particularly of affection.

At home in the midst of ham and stout she placed her hand warningly under her heart and thus announced the approaching years of her martyrdom and her patient claim on my body, soul and memories, and I was aware of the peculiar poetry and diversity of life and its intricate loyalties which left me bereft and determined to arrive at a source, as it were at a conclusion, which the mirror announced in advance of the event. God, anyway, would have me; therefore I yearned for Him. But was it He who answered?

I look at the night sky where Teddie is scattered and am awestruck at this kind of immensity. Unthinkable distances. Surely no prayer can cross them. I am humble in the face of such sublime power. But in the next instant I try to imagine what existed before it was created. I try to imagine no universe. Nothing, nothing. Try to imagine that. In all that terrifying blackness try to imagine no blackness, nothing, not even vacuum, but nothing. Nothing even as a thought. Space deprived of space in which to exist. Draw in the billions of light years of space and stars and darkness, compress and compress until all existence, all space, all void is the size of a speck of dust.

And then blow it out.

The mind cannot conceive of this situation. The mind demands that there be something and therefore something before something. Is the Universe an unprincipled design? Does God weep somewhere beyond it crying to its prisoners to free themselves and come to Him? If it is all explained by chemistry, that chemistry is majestic. It can only lead to the most magnificent explosion, to which God will harken while we burn and disintegrate and scatter into pieces.

I am worried about Mabel. She talked once not about God but about the gods as though some kind of committee were sitting, one before which she had become weary of giving evidence. At night she falls asleep over her book with her spectacles on her nose at a dangerous angle. I have nightmares in which I see her turn into the pillow, crushing and splintering the lenses, cutting herself, bleeding slowly from closed eyelids so that she appears to be crying blood. She waits with Spartan fortitude for her life to run its course. Her days are spent in celebration of the natural cycle of seed, growth, flower, decay, seed.

One day she said to me, 'No flower is quite like another of the same species. On a single bush one is constantly surprised by the remarkable character shown by each individual rose. But from the house all one sees is a garden, which is all there is to it anyway in the long run.'

Perhaps that is how she sees the world. She puts her hand on my arm and I am imprisoned by her capacity to survive. A sentence of life, suffered with patience and forbearance and with small pleasures taken by the minute, not the hour. Is that tranquillity? She is not so tranquil in sleep. Bygone things press on her then.

The fighting in Manipur has been very fierce but it looks as if we shall drive them back, doesn't it? There will be no paper umbrellas on the Pankot golf-course. As Mabel said, everything will be just as it always was.

My Dear Miss Jolley,

Shortly after the Memorial service that was held here for Captain Bingham a mysterious event took place. A name appeared in the visitors' book which is kept at the gate of Flagstaff House. The person signing gave no indication of her whereabouts in Pankot, contenting herself with the word Rawalpindi after her signature, as if to leave no room for doubt while withholding opportunity for contact. It was as though she wished to say: I am here in your midst, think about it.

But no stranger has appeared. No one has seen her or seen anyone who might be her. Yesterday evening I raised the question discreetly with Sarah, suggesting to her that since they were so close to her in Kashmir they would recognize her; but Sarah said they would not. I did not think it a good idea to press her, to face her directly with the question whether in Srinagar she had visited the woman, spoken to her, seen the child.

Is the child here too? Unbaptized? You will know to whom I refer, whose signature it is that has appeared in the book. You will not know, none of us does, why she is in Pankot or where she is staying. Unless the signature was a practical joke, as has been suggested, she must be hidden away in the area of West Hill where there are summer residences that belong to rich Indians from Ranpur, an area which people from East Hill never visit. Her arrival and simultaneous disappearance serve to emphasize the stark division there is between our India and theirs. She has made herself one of them. The division is one of which I am ashamed. I have done nothing, nothing, to remove it, ever. My poor Edwina sat huddled by the roadside in the rain, holding that dead man's hand. That, I continually see, was significant. For me that image is like an old picture of the kind that were popular in the last century, which told stories and pointed moral lessons. I see the caption, 'Too Late.'

Sarah came to the cottage yesterday evening to say goodbye. She went to Ranpur today to catch tonight's Calcutta mail. Only for a short visit, but for a special reason, and for Susan's sake, to see and talk to a Captain Merrick who is in hospital there, having been wounded – Susan believes badly – in the same action in which poor Teddie was killed. It seems in fact that he was with him on that occasion at the height of the fighting on the Imphal plain and performed some sort of heroic act whose object, although it failed, was to save Teddie. An officer from Teddie's division wrote to Susan and told her of Captain Merrick's bravery, since when she has had a letter from Captain Merrick himself, in hospital, but not in his handwriting. This weighs on Susan's mind. If ever she blamed him for the disturbing events that spoiled her wedding day she is determined to forgive and forget and in any case, as a soldier's daughter, sees it as her duty to extend the hand of gratitude to her dead husband's comrade. She has asked Sarah to ask him if he would stand as godfather to the child, when it is born.

For this I am thankful. In the past few weeks she has been, many of us feel, dangerously withdrawn, lying here on the verandah at the cottage day after day, as she used to before Teddie's death when her pregnancy curtailed her activities, but without that look of living inwardly. I heard a woman here, Lucy Smalley, say that poor Susan reminded her of the daughter of a woman called Poppy Browning, but she shut up when she saw I was in earshot; and tonight I asked Sarah who Poppy Browning was. She did not know. Nor does she know who Gillian Waller was, or is, for I was silly enough to ask that too and then had to explain, to expose myself as a stupid old woman who tucks another old woman up, one who mutters in her sleep.

A little while ago I mentioned to Susan the existence of the lace and when Sarah and I had done talking tonight she went in to Mabel and received that exquisite christening gown to take to her sister. The child is due next month. In Calcutta, Sarah is to stay with her Aunt Fenny and Uncle Arthur. They have moved from Delhi. He is now a Lieutenant-Colonel. I longed to go with her, to have a chance to see our old headquarters again and to see the wounded man, who perhaps knew Edwina. Will Sarah remember to ask him this time?

Yours,
Barbara Batchelor.

*

She scrawled the signature, closed the exercise book that had belonged to a little girl called Swaroop. She undressed, put on her gown and opened her door to listen and judge the state of affairs. It was past midnight. She crossed to Mabel's door, opened it silently and stood arrested. Mabel, propped against her pillows, must have watched the door opening.

'Can't you sleep either?' she said; and Barbie recalled the day nearly five years before when she had gone out to the verandah and found Mabel working there, the day she had expected to be told she must go when her holiday was over. Can't you sleep either? Mabel had said. I don't blame you. It's such a lovely day.

Mabel had already put her book aside and replaced her spectacles in their case, and Barbie felt pleased with her as she would have been pleased to find that a pupil had learned a difficult lesson well.

'Oh, I haven't tried yet,' she said. 'I've been writing letters, catching up, and time just slipped by. Can I get you anything?'

'No, thank you, Barbie. There's nothing I want. I'm not sleepy though. It's rather close, isn't it?'

'Just a bit.'

Mabel nodded, apparently glad to have her impression confirmed.

'It won't be long before the rains get here,' Mabel said. She glanced at the curtained windows as if through these an approaching rain might be discerned. 'Did I tell you it was raining the first time I came to India? I

923

remember being very disappointed. I'd expected brilliant sunshine and it seemed such a long way to come just to get wet and see grey sky. But then I'd not experienced the heat. So I didn't appreciate the contrast.'

'It's not so marked up here.'

Barbie went further into the room and then to the bedside, checked the muslin-covered water jug even though she could see that the tumbler hadn't been used.

'Stay and talk to me,' Mabel said. The request was so unexpected that for a moment Barbie wondered whether Mabel was making fun of her. But her friend's face betrayed no irony.

'Talk? What about?'

'Anything. About when you were young. I always enjoy that.'

'Do you? Do you?'

She sat on the edge of the bed. She could not remember, now, ever being young. And then did. 'I was always a bit afraid of going upstairs to bed. So I hummed a song which I fear Mother disapproved. That is to say the first line of it. I don't mean she disapproved only of the first line and of course I don't mean hummed because you can't hum words, but I sang it under my breath over and over. And in the end I couldn't ever remember the rest of it and never have. Isn't that strange? I've seen a deal of gaiety throughout my noisy life.'

'Throughout what?'

'Throughout my noisy life.'

'Oh.' Mabel smiled. 'One of your father's comic songs.'

'He was passionately fond of the music hall. And often promised to take me but of course never did, he was afraid of what my mother would say if she found out and anyway he was always short of what he called the ready. There was the Christmas when he lost the presents for my stocking on the journey home. As white as a sheet when he came in at the door and very very late, but not drunk, that's what Mother said years later when she told me, when he was dead and she had forgiven him, and told me there wasn't any Father Christmas anyway. I never knew I once nearly didn't get a stocking. I don't remember a Christmas when there wasn't something in it. Mother said that when he came home and said: I've lost the stocking things, poor Barbie's stocking things: they set to and turned out drawers and cupboards looking for odds and ends for hours so as not to disappoint me and that I said it was the nicest stocking ever. But perhaps that's only how she remembered it. But it showed they loved me. I adored Christmas mornings. I always woke while it was still dark and worked my toes up and down to feel the stocking's weight and listen to the rustle and crackle. And then I'd sit up and sniff very cautiously to smell the magic, I mean of someone having been there who drove across frosty rooftops and had so many chimneys to attend to but never forgot mine.'

'Yes,' Mabel said. 'I remember that – the idea of a strange scent in the room, but I don't think I put the idea into words.'

'I don't suppose I did either. It's how I describe it now. As children we accept magic as a normal part of life. Everything seems rooted in it, everything conspires in magic terms.' She laughed. 'Even the quarrels in our house had the darkness of magic in them, they were strange and incomprehensible and threatening as magic often is. I expected to find toads hopping on the staircase and misshapen things falling out of cupboards.'

'Poor Barbie.'

'No! My life was never dull.'

'Is it very dull now?'

'Now least of all.'

She had a sudden strong desire to lower herself gently and be taken into the older woman's arms and to lie there in peace and amity until they both fell asleep. She would be content then not to wake but to dream forever, enfolded, safe from harm; and for an instant it seemed to her that if she sought harbour in this way it would not be closed to her; that Mabel would accept her and go with her happily into this oblivion of cessation and fulfilment.

But Mabel slowly closed her eyes as if shutting that avenue of escape and said very quietly, 'I can sleep now thank you, Barbie,' and Barbie got up, smoothed the top of the sheet and was careful to make no disturbing contact with her friend's hands. She whispered, 'I'll deal with the light,' and when Mabel nodded reached for the ebony switch and turned it. She felt her way in the dark back into the hall and her own familiar room and circumstances.

A meditation. St John's Church. 4.30 p.m. June 7th 1944

i

You said: Stay and talk to me because I can't sleep. So I stayed and talked. I told you about the stairs and a Christmas stocking and after a very short while you said: I can sleep now.

The next time I saw you was in the morning. You were on the verandah drinking a cup of tea and you apologized for having had breakfast without me. I never thought to ask Aziz what you had eaten. Perhaps he would not have told me because you'd already instructed him not to in case I said: That's no sort of breakfast. And began to fuss and bother. As it was I sat down and drank tea too and said nothing because I had noticed nothing.

This was yesterday. I must search for clues to moments when you may have been on the point of making an appeal like that of the night before. Stay. Talk to me. Those few moments on the verandah drinking tea were not one of them. When Aziz called me to breakfast you said nothing. You resumed reading a seed catalogue. But you were still there when I came back. I thought that you were absorbed, planning next year's garden.

I said: I'll do the accounts this morning. If you do the cheques after lunch

I'll take them down to the bazaar and settle them on my way to Mr Maybrick's.

I had to repeat it. But that wasn't unusual. In case you had forgotten I reminded you that I'd promised Mr Maybrick three days before to go to his bungalow for tea and mend his volume of Bach. You said: Oh I thought that was tomorrow. So I said, No, it was fixed for today, the sixth of June.

Is that the date? you said. And looked towards this year's garden.

I went inside and sat at your bureau and began the accounts for May. After a while I heard you stirring and saw you through the window putting on your straw hat and going out into the sunshine with the pannier. At eleven Mildred came with Susan and shortly afterwards Mrs Fosdick and Mrs Paynton arrived. Aziz was worried. He said to me: Memsahib said nothing about lunch for so many. I assured him that only Susan was staying for lunch, that presently Mildred and the others would go down to the club and be there all day playing bridge, and that Mildred would return at about six o'clock to take Susan home.

He said: Memsahib, when will *you* be back?

I thought of the volume of Bach and of the difficulty I always had persuading Mr Maybrick to let me get on. Perhaps seven o'clock, I said. Or seven-thirty. But certainly by eight, in time for dinner.

When the others had gone I went out to where Susan lay. Her smock was taut over her swollen stomach. I said: Did you like the christening gown? She said yes, it was beautiful. So I told her the story of the blind woman who made the lace, of how she called the butterflies her prisoners. After a while Susan said: I like things that have stories to them, somehow it makes them seem more real: and then closed her eyes to show that she wanted me to go away. I returned to the bureau and finished the accounts. I made out the cheques so that all you had to do was sign them. We had another visitor then, Captain Beauvais, who brought Susan a book. Aziz gave him a drink and Susan and he talked in low voices. He had gone before you came in from the garden at lunch-time.

At lunch you said: When will Sarah be back? And Susan laughed and said: Oh, Aunty, she's only just gone, she was only due to reach Calcutta this morning.

You said: So she'll be gone for a few more days.

After lunch I helped Susan to settle on the verandah again. I tried to get her to walk for a bit in the shady part of the garden but she said she was tired. I found you at the bureau signing the last cheque. You said as you always did: Thank you for coping with all this. I took the cheques and the bills and went to my room. I lay down for a bit. At three o'clock I asked Aziz to send the mali's boy for a tonga. Then I tidied myself for Mr Maybrick and looked for you to tell you I was off. You were in the garden, but not in the shade. I said, 'Aren't you awfully hot?' You said, 'No, I like the sunshine.' And then, 'Will you be long?' I said, 'I should be back soon after seven.' This seemed to puzzle you. You'd forgotten again about Mr

Maybrick. I had to remind you. You said, 'Oh yes, so you are. Have a nice time.'

When I looked back you were watching me. And lifted your hand. Which wasn't usual. But pleased me. I waved back. I went round the side of the house so that I wouldn't disturb Susan.

Isn't it very close? Stay. Talk to me. Is that the date? When will Sarah be back? Will you be long?

These were your appeals. Which I did not hear. I did not hear Aziz's appeal either. When will *you* be back? He saw the sunlight and the shadow and in his heart interpreted them correctly. But followed your mood and example. When I left in the tonga he made Susan some tea. No one knows what he did after that. The kitchen was neat and tidy. He always kept it so.

ii

Mr Maybrick waves his arms in the air. Pages of Bach fly from his hands, swirl, swoop, drift, fall. His face is contorted by the anguish of a man who requires order but cannot keep it. We stand erect in this tempest of paper music. Then I turn, pretending to go; having only just arrived. He waits until I am at the door and cries, 'Come back!' I am no longer even a little afraid of Mr Maybrick but I obey because it pleases him to act the martinet. I can see him terrorizing coolies who grin when his back is turned because he never harms them. I can see him ordering his wife about, before she began to ail, and see her, one hand shading not just her eyes from the light but her smile with which she commences to perform what he demands but in her own way and to her own satisfaction, which she knows will be to his as well.

What a pickle you are in, I tell him, and sit on the one chair that is not cluttered with things that have no business on chairs. We are ankle deep in Bach. The situation looks hopeless, more hopeless to him than to me because the pages are numbered and it only requires patience and application – qualities he does not normally possess – to restore them to their proper order. The problem will be the rebinding. He complains about the quality of the gum I used last time, about the quality of the original binding, about having no room nowadays to store things properly, about the climate that makes things fall apart anyway, about the decline in standards of workmanship, about the fact that, as he says, nobody gives a damn any more; and finally – the rub, because it explains why he has scattered the pages in a childish rage – about a double sheet that is missing.

'Have you looked in the organ loft?' I ask. He declares that the missing sheet cannot possibly be in the organ loft. He says, 'It's no good sitting staring at it, what are you waiting for?'

I tell him: Tea. I tell him I require a cup of tea first and that after that I will walk down to the church and look in the organ loft while he makes a start clearing up the mess he has made.

On my way to St John's I see suddenly what a vast improvement my time in Pankot has wrought in my character. Application I had, and patience, but of a questionable kind. Confronted in the old days with the ruins of the Bach I would have fallen avidly upon the scattered pages and somehow contrived to make greater confusion than before. And I would not have dared insist on Tea.

I see that I have acquired qualities of leadership and command. For a moment my pride in this achievement is disproportionate to its degree. I feel a deep glow of satisfaction. I lengthen my stride. Although it is a very hot day I have on the heliotrope. The sun is lowering towards West Hill. I turn my face to it. I am happy. I have, I feel, always done my utmost and now enjoy my reward on this earth whose beauty is serene towards evening.

As I turn into the churchyard the clock strikes the half hour after five. I enter and go straight to the organ loft. The light is not good. I crouch down, searching, convinced I shall find the missing sheet. And I find it in a corner. It bears the dusty imprint of Mr Maybrick's shoe. I smile. And then I hear a sound, the sound of the latch lifted on the little side door through which I too have just entered, the slight squeak of the hinges, the sound of the door closing. Mr Maybrick has followed me.

I stand up and cry 'Eureka!' and look down to where he should be. But there is no one. The church is empty. I call again, less boldly. No answer. I have the missing sheet in one hand. With my other I seek my neck, automatically, and then the chain, the pendant cross.

I leave, unhurriedly. I tell myself my entrance must have disturbed someone at private devotions, someone whom I did not see when I came in and who has taken the opportunity of my climb to the organ loft to leave unnoticed. Slowly I follow this solitary worshipper out and down the path past the gravestones, but he – or she – is still invisible. I walk back to Mr Maybrick's.

I find him sitting on the floor, the scattered pages all around him untouched. He is listening to the news on the wireless and shushes me when I begin to protest at his idleness. Resigned, I throw things from the chair which has now become cluttered. He shushes me again. I subside. For a while I do not listen to the news but then do so and become aware that it is important. I cannot pick up the thread, though. It ends. But the announcer repeats the opening and this is followed by martial music.

It seems that British and allied forces have invaded Normandy. They have opened the second front. Mr Maybrick shouts for his bearer and then heaves me out of the chair and does a little jig. His enthusiasm is infectious. Poor Bach is in danger of being trampled underfoot. Mr Maybrick tells his boy to bring sherry. He says that when the Germans are defeated the whole weight of the Allied armies will be thrown against the Japanese and then we can all live civilized lives again.

'And all the prisoners in Germany will be freed!' I cry. 'I must phone the cottage—' I go into the hall, pick up the receiver and wait impatiently for the operator to answer. I am anxious for Susan to know, because of her father. I ask for the number and continue to wait. The operator tells me the number is engaged. Crestfallen I go back to the living-room. I work it out that Mildred has heard at the club and is already on the phone to Susan. We drink sherry. Ten minutes later I telephone again but the operator says there is still someone speaking. Mildred is probably back at the cottage and ringing all her friends. I resign my role as the bearer of good tidings. Come, I say to Mr Maybrick, let us begin on poor Bach.

iii

'Perseverance,' Barbie said, 'which was incidentally one of my father's favourite words if not one of his virtues, unless you count perseverance with the bottle and the cards, perseverance – Mr Maybrick – wins the day.'

She slapped the last page of Bach, straightened her bent back and cried out partly from the pain of easing the ache and partly from astonishment at Mr Maybrick's firmly planted kiss. Only on the forehead. Nevertheless. She felt her face and neck grow hot.

'Angelic Barbie,' he said. 'Ham-fisted with glue but angelic. What would you say to mutton curry and rice?'

'I should say no.'

'Is that all?'

'Had you been more complimentary about the glue I should have added thank you. You may help me up.'

'I will if you say yes. It was planned. Mutton curry and rice. For two.'

'Planned by whom?'

'By me.'

'Mr Maybrick, you have been overdoing the sherry. At your age it is ill-advised.'

'You've not done so badly yourself. You can knock it back.'

'Two glasses are all I've had.'

'Refilled occasionally without your noticing, between fugues.'

'I see you are determined to be difficult.' She got up unassisted. Her joints were very stiff. She looked at her watch. It was seven fifteen. She had been crawling across the floor and kneeling sorting pages for over an hour. Mr Maybrick had been more of a hindrance than a help.

He said, 'If you stay to supper you could start the binding afterwards.'

'If I stayed to supper I should do no such thing. The binding will have to wait. Meanwhile I should be obliged if you'd send Kaisa Ram for a tonga. I'm going to tidy myself and when I come back I'll expect to hear that a tonga is on its way.'

'You've become a hard woman, Barbie. I'd set my heart on it.'

'Then you should have said so three days ago and not left it to chance and your powers of persuasion. And if I said yes you know very well you'd have to dash into the kitchen and tell Kaisa Ram to throw some more meat into

929

the pot, and that he'd complain, that you'd shout at him and that you'd have a burnt supper, bad temper for the rest of the evening and indigestion all night.'

She turned to the door that led through the single bedroom to the bathroom.

'It'll take fifteen minutes for Kaisa Ram to get a tonga,' he said, 'but only five to cut off another chop.'

'And an hour for it to cook properly. So please send him down to the stand. When I come back I'll have another sherry. I don't believe a word of your story of surreptitious refills.'

She left him but caught the flicker of the smile he was doing his best to disguise. The bedroom, crammed with the monumental furniture of his spacious tea-planting days, was even more untidy than the living-room and overpowered by the majestic bed that filled the central space. As always, this bed was shrouded by the regal canopy of a faded white mosquito net. In Pankot there was no need of one and if there had been Mr Maybrick's would have been inadequate because it was full of holes and rents which Kaisa Ram neglected to mend. But Mr Maybrick said he couldn't sleep in a bed that had no net. She sympathized with this peculiarity, remembering that whenever she had moved from a mosquito-ridden area to a cool and airy one she had always found the absence of a net initially alarming, a source of apprehension, of fears of falling out at least, at worst of attack by night-intruders.

The bathroom was cheerless. A single unshaded bulb illuminated its dingy whitewashed walls and concrete floor. In one corner there was a cubicle and in this an ornate commode of which Mr Maybrick was very proud. The commode, fortunately, was always spotless but the bathroom itself was grimy. There tended to be cockroaches.

Normally, when visiting Mr Maybrick, she hurried through the business of tidying herself. But tonight she found herself slowed down, struck by the significance of her surroundings, the reality of this ordinariness, this shabbiness, this evidence of detritus behind the screens of imperial power and magnificence. The feeling she had was not of glory departing or departed but of its original and continuing irrelevance to the business of being in India, which was her and Mr Maybrick's business just as much as it was the business of the members of the mess in whose inner sanctum she had stood last year, intimidated by the ghostly occupants of those serried ranks of chairs.

She paused between soaping and rinsing her hands, riveted by an image of the captains and the kings queuing to wash their own hands in Mr Maybrick's bowl after relieving themselves in Mr Maybrick's mahogany commode with its rose-patterned porcelain receptacle, and finding no fault, nothing unusual, feeling no hurt to their dignity; and going back through the unholy clutter of Mr Maybrick's bedroom without a glance at the half-opened drawers festooned with socks and vests and shirts that wanted mending, because the one thing to which the human spirit could always accommodate itself was chaos and misfortune. Everything more orderly or favoured was a bonus and needed living up to.

She closed her eyes and was back in the Camberwell scullery and then in the dark hallway, taking the first rise of the stairs, with all the captains and kings behind her waiting to do the same. Why, she said, the mystery at the top of the stairs is where we're all headed, willy-nilly, which is what my father but not my mother understood. She opened her eyes. The lather had begun to encrust her hands with a creamy rime. She rinsed and dried them on the week-old roller towel. She dabbed her wrists with cologne from her handbag phial and resprinkled the fine lawn handkerchief. Chaos, misfortune. Punctuated by harmless escapes into personal vanities. She clicked her handbag shut. The click was as satisfactory as a decision.

'Mr Maybrick!' she called, re-entering the living-room.

He came in from the hall.

He said, 'Oh, there you are, Barbie. Arthur Peplow is here. He has something to tell you.'

iv

'I said, I will take heed to my ways: that I offend not in my tongue. I will keep my mouth as it were with a bridle; while the ungodly is in my sight. I held my tongue, and spake nothing, I kept silence, yea, even from good words; but it was pain and grief to me. My heart was hot within me, and while I was thus musing the fire kindled and at the last I spake with my tongue; Lord, let me know mine end, and the number of my days; that I may be certified how long I have to live.'

v

Where the rime had been was Arthur Peplow's hand. In the pause between the word 'stroke' and the words 'it was very sudden', she heard down the road the chime of the half-hour after seven.

Mr Peplow said, 'I think we must believe that she felt no pain, but went very peacefully. Susan was tremendously brave. The poor girl was quite alone. When she realized what had happened she rang Colonel Beames at once, and then her mother. She couldn't find Aziz anywhere. Have you any idea where he could have gone?'

'Aziz?'

'Never mind. In a moment or two Clarissa and I want you to come down to the rectory. Captain Coley's going to spend the night at Rose Cottage to look after things there for Mildred. Clarissa's having a bed made up for you.'

'I have a bed,' she said. And removed her hand from Arthur Peplow's to take the glass of sherry from Mr Maybrick's hand which was shaking. She held it, but did not know how to deal with it. Some of the deep brown liquid spilt on to the heliotrope skirt. 'I don't want it,' she said. 'After all.' Arthur took the glass. There was nowhere for him to put it down.

'The thing is,' he said, 'we all think it best if you stay the night with us. You can come straight away. If you don't mind borrowing some things Clarissa can lend you what you need. Beames or Travers will look in later with something to help you sleep. I asked Beames myself, I thought it would be wise. You'll need a good night's rest.'

'It's very kind of you, Arthur. But I must go home at once. If someone will fetch a tonga.'

She watched Arthur Peplow get up. Some of the books and magazines which he had pushed aside to make room on the sofa for the two of them slid back into place. She observed the glance he exchanged with Mr Maybrick before parking the glass of sherry on top of the grand piano. Glad of the momentary relief such a prosaic detail provided in the mountingly oppressive nightmare, she recalled that the piano was badly out of tune because it had not been played since Clarice Maybrick's fingers were last upon its yellowed, mottled, keys. Another thing she remembered Mr Maybrick telling her was how Clarice always took her rings off before playing and placed them on the ebony ledge at the bass end of the keyboard.

Arthur Peplow went out into the hall. She heard the ping that accompanied the lifting of the receiver. You could not get a tonga by ringing the exchange. Suddenly the door between hall and living-room closed, which meant that Arthur didn't want her to hear what he was saying or know to whom he was saying it. She stayed where she was, readopting an old habit of mind; that of believing in the good sense and good will of established authority; although the waves of rebellion had already risen and were – she guessed – only temporarily subdued. Mr Maybrick came to the sofa and sat beside her, pushing the books and magazines to give himself room. He sat with his elbows on his knees and his hands clasped in the space between and looked down at the worn bit of carpet.

'When I left this afternoon,' Barbie said, watching the door that led to the hall where Arthur's voice had begun to drone, to vibrate, to punctuate longer periods of silence, 'she watched me and waited for me to look round, and then lifted her hand to wave.'

Mr Maybrick nodded but said nothing.

'You do understand, Mr Maybrick, that I can't possibly sleep at Arthur's and Clarissa's or anywhere but at the cottage. There will be no need for Captain Coley to be there. In fact I find the idea quite unacceptable. Aziz and I will manage everything. I quite see that Mildred can't stay. She'll have to take poor Susan home and look after her. But Captain Coley's presence is not necessary. I am prepared to wait here for a bit but eventually, no – quite soon, I must go back.'

'I'll come with you if you like.'

'Thank you. That would be kind. So long as it's understood that I stay there.'

She grew rigid with impatience. There was much to be done. And quickly. In India these things were always done quickly. They had to be. And the problems of making special arrangements were likely to be many. She herself must be prepared for the journey to Ranpur. Packing was something that would occupy her.

'And I must pack,' she said. 'I must be ready to leave tomorrow. The man at St Luke's in Ranpur used to be the Reverend Ian Wright and still may be. Arthur will know.'

Again Mr Maybrick nodded. She did not know whether he was listening but his mute agreement was encouraging. The door opened and Arthur came back in smoothing his head with one hand. He asked Mr Maybrick whether Kaisa Ram could produce some tea or coffee. Mr Maybrick got up and went out saying he would see. Directly they were alone Arthur said, 'That was Kevin Coley at the other end. I told him you want to go up to the cottage and he's had a word with Mildred. She's still there with Susan and I think she'd be grateful if you'd let her get Susan away first, because the girl's in pretty much of a state. In fact she's suffering badly from reaction. Colonel Beames left about an hour ago and Susan was fairly all right then but he said he'd have a word with Travers because it's Travers who's been attending to her during her pregnancy. Well, they've been waiting for Travers to turn up and Coley's trying to get him on the phone now. Mrs Fosdick and Mrs Paynton are there helping Mildred cope. There's nothing you can actually do, Barbie, and frankly I think the best thing is for you to wait here a while and then if you feel you must just go up and collect some things for the night. I'll take you.'

'Mr Maybrick has promised to do that.'

'Well, that's fine. Coley said he'd ring me as soon as Mildred's got Susan away. Please don't misunderstand. Mildred knows how upset you must be and that you can only be more upset the moment you set foot in Rose Cottage. Just now she has her work cut out keeping poor Susan on an even keel. The danger is premature labour brought on by shock. And you *do* appreciate how much of a shock it was, don't you?'

'Yes, Arthur.'

'Coley says Aziz is still missing. It's very odd. When I mentioned it before I don't think you took it in. But he's not been seen since he brought Susan out her tray of tea. She had a cup and then noticed it wasn't yet four o'clock so she dozed off again and was only half awake when Mabel came and sat down and seemed to nod off.'

'What time was that, Arthur?'

'About five. Beames got there at five-thirty.'

'More than two hours ago. I don't understand. I don't understand why I wasn't called at once.'

'No one knew where you were.'

'Aziz knew.'

'But Barbie—'

'I'm sorry. I keep forgetting. But Susan knew.'

'She said she only knew she'd seen you making out cheques and imagined you'd gone down to the bazaar to pay them.'

'Yes, I see.'

'Clarissa was out when Mildred rang and asked me to go up. Otherwise we might have traced you sooner. She rang me at the cottage when she got home at seven and found my message. She said she thought you might be here with Edgar. So I came straight away.'

That was very kind of you, Barbie intended to say; but she could not because it was being borne in on her that Arthur Peplow was deeply implicated – even if he didn't realize it – in a plot to keep her out of the way, to stop her from going to Rose Cottage. She could not judge whether punishment or kindness was intended. If punishment, then Mildred was probably at the bottom of it. If kindness, then Mabel's death could not have been the quiet and peaceful passing Arthur had described.

She saw her friend with blackened face, protuberant tongue, and limbs stiffened in the final gesture of total and absolute terror; and Susan backing away, clutching her swollen belly, shrieking for Aziz, getting no answer and then – with space achieved between her own body and the horror – scrabbling at the telephone and shouting incoherently for help, making for the door, running down the gravel drive to the rockery-bordered exit to Club road, clasping the pillar of the open gateway and screaming until the whole of Pankot echoed and trembled.

But this was not the way it had been, nor the way it ever could have been. The convolutions of the petals of this rose are dissimilar to the convolutions of this, Mabel must have said; and, leaning towards it, to ex..mine more closely the miracle of its individuality, become aware of a corresponding shadow leaning over her, so that she straightened carefully to absorb the shock and leave the rose to its freedom and perfection; and turned, holding the basket, walked cautiously towards the short flight of wooden steps to the verandah. Here there was a promise, briefly kept, of continuation. A figure sleeping. Within it another; patiently achieving its human shape. Briefly too, a green leaf, one of many sprouting from stems in pots on the balustrade, adumbrated the shape and texture of its successors to fingers still occupied by love and custom.

But again the shadow leans and the hand that touches the leaves is arrested by another which is more grandly and fearfully informed. And a voice – the same that said: Does it matter? – says, That's all, that's all.

She sits. The favour granted to someone like her. A rock. The seas pound. One wave scarcely distinguishable from any of the others puts out the faltering spark. But in that place there is no visible difference between sleep and death. She had nodded off. And out. The dear indomitable body remains. Marking the place.

I have a concern, Barbie thought, to see if the eyes are open. She felt that

934

they should be but didn't know why except that in Mabel's case this would somehow be seemly.

'Barbie,' Arthur said, taking her hand to his cold but well-intentioned comfort. 'Don't try so hard not to cry. You loved her and cared for her. You did it well.'

'But not today. She wanted me to be there. But of course she would never have dreamed of asking. If she could have made it back to her room she would have, for Susan's sake.'

'There, there. That's better.'

'Forgive me.'

But before she could disgrace herself she became free of the encumbrance of Arthur Peplow's sympathy. She got up, grabbed her handbag and went into Mr Maybrick's bedroom and shut the door. The physical exertion closed the gate on useless grief. From what appeared to be a considerable distance away she saw Mabel waiting. She achieved levitation and floated without trouble through the apex of the regal canopy of the mosquito net and left the room filled with the dark bat-wing flapping of the ghosts of her sorrow. She longed now only to escape and destroy the distance between the terrible little bungalow and Rose Cottage.

She switched on the light in the bathroom and closed the door, crossed, reached up and unbolted the side door. Warm night air stroked her cheeks. She stumbled, surprised by an unfamiliar dimension – a high step – and saved herself from falling. She pressed on through an opening in what appeared to be a trellis. There was a sickly odour of sweet jasmine in the night and charcoal fumes from the outhouse where Kaisa Ram was cooking mutton curry. At the front of the bungalow she moved cautiously but, gaining the road, planted her feet firmly.

She hastened past the rectory bungalow, squat behind its partial screen of trees, showing but one lighted room, and walked down the hill, past St John's. Where Church road joined Club road she would with luck find an empty tonga making its way back from club to bazaar, but reaching there she found the road deserted and, having no time to waste, set off on the uphill climb. Presently two tongas went past, both laden; and then she had to stand still and hide her eyes from twin glares that loomed and roared and went past leaving dust and petrol fumes and echoes of singing male voices. At the milestone she paused to rest. She heard the clock of St John's strike eight in another world. She got up and plodded on.

*

Captain Coley was in the front porch, waiting, which meant that Arthur and Mr Maybrick had discovered her escape and telephoned a warning.

'We're waiting for Travers,' he said. 'It's Susan. We think she's started.'

'Then she should be got to hospital.' She glanced into the lighted hall. Already the place had the look of not belonging to anyone. 'They should have taken her home long before this,' she said. 'Colonel Beames should have insisted. Where is she?'

'With Mildred in the spare bedroom.'

She went into the hall. Just then Susan cried out. At the same instant from some quality of sound and echo Barbie realized that the thing she had come to look at wasn't in the house. She turned, intending to raise the question of where Mabel's body had been taken but was forestalled by Mildred calling Captain Coley's name and then appearing in the living-room doorway.

Barbie noticed that Mildred's hair was still immaculately set. She would have expected something of the last few hours to have left a mark of itself in the form of disarrangement however slight. She noticed the hair because its groomed perfection set the tone of Mildred's whole appearance. She searched for signs of wildness in Mildred's face and in doing so realized that for a perceptible count, even if only in fractions of seconds, she and Mildred were staring at each other like old enemies who knew that the truce by whose terms they had both faithfully abided was now officially over.

'I'm sorry to have arrived before you've got Susan home,' Barbie said. 'But I won't get in anyone's way, unless of course there's something I can do.'

'Thank you,' Mildred replied. 'But I think we can cope. Providing Travers gets here pretty soon. What's the form, Kevin?'

'The form is he should be here any minute now. Probably with an ambulance.'

Mildred nodded, made to go back in but paused. She looked at Barbie. She said, 'Have you any idea where that bloody man can have got to?'

'Which man, Mildred?'

'Aziz,' she said; and repeated it. This time the sibilants struck like snakes. 'Aziz.'

'I think, yes, I'm sure it was for today, he had permission to visit a relative in one of the villages.' The cautious lie came pat. But Mildred wasn't fooled.

'A sick relative, I suppose. No. I don't think so. The other servants know nothing about it. Well, if and when he ever shows his face again, Kevin here's promised personally to boot him in the rear.'

'I don't think you understand, Mildred. I don't think you understand at all. About Indians like Aziz.'

'I understand only too well. My God, I understand! He knew what I presume none of us knew. That she was ill. And bloody well funked it. Let's see how far he gets. I've asked Beames to have a word with the police.'

'The police! Whatever are you saying?'

'—not that there appears to be anything noticeably missing. But there hasn't been time for a proper check.'

Another cry from Susan cut her off. For an instant her eyes closed and one hand gripped the jamb of the doorway. A voice which Barbie recognized as Clara Fosdick's called Mildred's name. Mildred went back towards the little spare.

Behind Barbie Coley said, 'Terribly upset. Don't take police business too seriously. No one really suspects the old chap of pinching anything but it's a necessary precaution, at least until Beames is satisfied about the cause of death.'

She faced round to Coley upon whose martyr's face there already seemed to be the reflexion of flickering flames.

'What do you mean?'

He looked pained by so direct a question.

'Only a formality. Feels he should have a pathologist's report to confirm his opinion that it was a stroke.'

The sound of an engine revving, of a driver changing into a low gear to negotiate the entrance to the drive, rescued him from further explanation. He went quickly out to the porch. Barbie hesitated, then approached Mabel's bedroom. She grasped the handle of the door and had confirmation that it was locked. In the dining-room she repeated the process. The door between Mabel's bedroom and the dining-room was locked too.

And there was something new and peculiar about the dining-room itself. It took Barbie a few moments to pin it down. The few pieces of silver normally kept on the sideboard were no longer there. Aziz, Aziz, she cried out silently; but almost immediately knew that Aziz had had nothing to do with it. She tried the cupboard doors in the sideboard. These were locked too. Doubtless the silver was inside.

She heard Travers' voice, and Coley's, and stood erect and still while the voices moved from hall to living-room and to the spare bedroom. Then she opened the french window on to the verandah which was illuminated by the light cast from dining-room and living-room and little spare. Susan's lounging chair was there, with its cushions. The book brought by Captain Beauvais lay unopened on the floor together with another book and a copy of the current issue of the *Onlooker*. A tray of tea on a low stool was on the other side of the place where Susan had lain dozing, and several paces beyond on the other side of the french window into the living-room, but near the balustrade, another chair: upright and empty, with the pannier-basket beside it.

She moved closer to it and then stooped and picked up the basket. It contained secateurs, dead rose-heads, a hand fork to whose tines particles of earth clung. She touched all these things, assuring herself of their existence; consequently of her own.

Then she saw lying on the floor where she supposed Beames had let it drop after removing it the old frayed-brim straw hat. She stooped and picked this up too.

'But it can't have!' Susan cried out. Barbie heard her clearly. 'It can't have started. The baby isn't *finished* yet.'

Barbie moved into the shadow but saw through the uncurtained open window of the little spare. They had Susan on her feet. Travers held one arm and Mildred the other. Clara Fosdick had her own and Susan's handbags. Nicky Paynton held open the door into the living-room. The girl seemed to be a dead weight. Travers said, 'Come along, Su, you don't need the stretcher. Just keep on your feet. We'll have you right as rain, you'll see.'

Her resistance went. Meekly but cautiously as if every step she made was an opportunity for the baby to make a dangerous bid for its freedom she let Travers and her mother lead her out.

When they had gone Barbie waited, giving them time to get out to the ambulance. Then she moved into the area of light and went back to Mabel's chair, still holding the basket and the straw hat.

She sat down.

But there was no way in.

Presently she was aware of a shadow fallen across her feet and she felt the little shock-waves of someone's fear or agitation. She glanced up. It was Kevin Coley. He thought he had seen a ghost.

He said, 'Mr Maybrick's here to take you down to the Peplows for the night.'

'Very well, Captain Coley. Thank you. I'll pack a few things.'

In the living-room she realized what she carried that was not hers and what was missing that belonged to her. 'I think I left my handbag on the sideboard in the dining-room. Would you look? There are some things in it which I ought to hand over.'

He came back with the handbag held high, as men held such things. She put the pannier and straw hat down, took the bag, got out the receipts and crossed to the bureau. The lid was locked and the key missing. She stood until the flush of humiliation had come and gone and then turned and offered the receipts to Coley saying, 'Will you see that Mildred gets these?' Coley took them. Leaving hat and pannier behind she went into the hall where Mr Maybrick was waiting.

'Barbie—' he began.

'No recriminations,' she said. 'I'm going to pack an overnight bag. I take it you have transport of some kind outside.'

'Only a tonga.'

'That will suffice. Do one thing for me first. Find out from Captain Coley where they have taken Mabel.'

In her bedroom she collected nightgown, slippers, dressing-gown, a change of underwear and toilet articles. She crammed these into an old fibre suitcase whose handle was mended with string. Back in the hall ten minutes later she found Mr Maybrick and Captain Coley standing several feet apart and not talking.

'If Aziz should come back, Captain Coley, you will tell him where I am, won't you? And you will treat him with the same courtesy he and Mabel always showed one another, I trust.'

Coley looked hunted. And then she realized that he was a coward, and always had been, in spite of that uniform, that precious insignia. She turned the screw.

'Well? I have your word? The word of a British officer to an English-woman?'

Coley flushed, aware of her mockery, and – with his fingers tainted by keys and valuables – of its justification; that she mocked him not only for himself but for the whole condition. She did not care. The charade was finished. Mabel had guessed the word years ago but had refrained from speaking it. The word was 'dead'. Dead. Dead. It didn't matter now who said it; the edifice had crumbled and the façade fooled nobody. One could only pray for a wind to blow it all away or for an earthquake such as Captain Coley's wife had died in. Barbie saw how perhaps with one finger she might topple him, because there was nothing to keep him standing except his own inertia.

But she had other things to do. She decided not to wait for his reply; and in any case the silence that followed her demand revealed how little she would be able to count on any promise that he gave. She marched out to the tonga with the fibre suitcase.

'What was the answer?' she asked when Mr Maybrick joined her.

'We should go to the general hospital and inquire there.'

'Then please tell the wallah.'

'I'm bound to say Coley didn't think there would be much point.'

'Naturally. Captain Coley sees little point in anything. He should have died in the rubble of Quetta. In most ways he did. The Lord alone knows for what purpose the remains are preserved.'

*

She waited in the reception hall of the general hospital seated on an uncomfortable highly polished bench, watching Mr Maybrick making things difficult for one of the girls at the inquiry desk, a fair-skinned Eurasian who kept on lifting the receiver of her telephone, presumably trying yet another extension at Mr Maybrick's insistence. After ten minutes something definite seemed to be decided and the girl suddenly looked impressed and helpful. Mr Maybrick came over to the bench. He sat down.

'Beames is over at the nursing home annexe. If we go across now he'll have a word with you. The nursing home is where Susan's been taken, and Mildred will be there too.'

'My business is only with Colonel Beames. I'm sorry you're being put to so much trouble, Mr Maybrick. If you want to go home to your supper I can manage on my own.'

He stood up, grabbed the suitcase and said, 'Come on, we can walk it, it's not far.'

They came out and followed directional signs along the asphalt path.

They both knew the nursing home well. They had visited Clarissa there the year she was ill with pleurisy.

The reception hall was less forbidding than the one at the main hospital. There were rugs and bowls of flowers. The woman behind the desk was a VAD. Her grey hair was blue-rinsed.

'Miss Batchelor?' she asked, ignoring Mr Maybrick. 'Colonel Beames is engaged but won't keep you long.'

Barbie and Mr Maybrick sat together on a leather sofa. The blue-haired woman made notes on a file of papers with a very sharp-looking pencil. Whenever she answered the telephone she said, 'Pankot Nursing Home, can I help you?' She had a miniature switchboard on the desk with red and green switches on it which she manipulated with dexterity and self-assurance. Once she banged a bell and was answered by an Indian porter to whom she gave a folded note and a brisk instruction. Ten minutes later another VAD came through the hushed swing doors.

'Miss Batchelor?'

Barbie stood up. She followed the woman through into a polished corridor and round a corner into another where they stopped at a white painted door marked Private. The woman knocked, opened and stood aside after announcing Barbie's name. The room was carpeted. The civil surgeon got up from behind a large desk and crossed the carpet silently. In the few years they had passingly known each other they had exchanged not many more words. He was a tall man with a nose and eyebrows and jaws that looked as if they had champed bones.

'I'm sorry to have had to keep you waiting,' he said. He pulled a leather chair close to another, waited for her to sit and then sat himself. He subjected her to a kind of remote scrutiny. His was a face that accepted nothing and gave nothing. 'It will perhaps have been an even greater shock for you than for any of us. I am so sorry. But I do now have my pathologist's report which confirms my assumption of cerebral haemorrhage. I suppose one must be thankful that it wasn't the kind of stroke that would have left her paralysed but alive. Had she complained of feeling unwell lately?'

Barbie shook her head.

'Well if she felt out of sorts I don't suppose she'd have said so or called any of us in. She was very much a law unto herself wasn't she? I'm sorry that there had to be this very slight delay in giving the certificate but in the circumstances I really had no alternative. I've told Mildred – Mrs Layton junior – the result of course. She's here with young Susan, as I expect you know. You're staying the night with the Peplows?'

Barbie nodded.

'Mrs Layton has phoned Arthur Peplow and given him the all clear to go forward with the arrangements. It's unfortunate Sarah's in Calcutta. Mrs Layton is going to telephone her sister but even if Sarah starts back first thing in the morning she won't be here until the day after tomorrow. I'm afraid Susan's in for rather an arduous time from what Travers says, so her mother won't be able to see to the other business personally. Fortunately

Arthur Peplow and Captain Coley have undertaken to deal with it.' He brought a small envelope out of his pocket. 'I want you to take the two tablets in this packet with some warm milk when you go to bed tonight. To give you a proper night's rest.'

She accepted the envelope. She said, 'Thank you, Colonel Beames.' She would not take the tablets. 'That is very kind of you, and very practical. There is a great deal to do and one must be on one's feet to do it.'

'Well, yes, but it's all being done. Don't worry. Sleep is the best thing for you.'

'Can you tell me anything about the arrangements, for instance about the arrangements for transportation?'

'Transportation?'

'To Ranpur. I imagine there will be a service here at St John's, especially as Mildred won't be able to leave Pankot while Susan is having her baby. And perhaps some kind of brief ceremony the next day at St Luke's. But I'm concerned about the transport. You see, I should wish to accompany.'

'Did you say St Luke's?'

'Yes. St Luke's in Ranpur. That's where the actual burial is to be. At St Luke's in Ranpur. She wished to be with her late husband, Mr James Layton. Hasn't Mildred mentioned that to you?'

'No.'

She waited for him to say more. But his face had gone out entirely. They heavy jaws were clamped shut.

'Then I had better see her and remind her,' Barbie said.

'Are you sure those were the elder Mrs Layton's wishes?'

'Quite sure.'

'I see.' Beames paused. 'Then I'll mention it to Mrs Layton junior. Interment in Ranpur is not among the impressions I have about the arrangements but possibly I haven't a complete picture. I do know that a service at St John's late tomorrow afternoon has been talked of.' He looked at his watch. 'I have to leave now for Flagstaff House but I shall be coming back later to see Mrs Layton. I'll mention it to her then.' He stood up. 'We've given her the room next to Susan's and she's resting on my orders. She's had a very trying time which would explain why she might overlook a point such as the one you've raised – if she has overlooked it. I'm sure that she'd know about it if it is an established wish or a definite instruction. You may depend on my letting her know what you've told me.'

She got up. She had no intention of depending upon Colonel Beames; but that, she thought, need not concern him. She allowed him to lead her to the door.

'Are you accompanied?' he said.

'Mr Maybrick is with me.'

'Good. And have you transport?'

'We have a tonga.'

'It's curious about the servant, isn't it? But I knew of a similar case. I suppose it's a kind of sixth sense coupled with this odd fatalism some of these old fellows develop. But it's not proof of unfeeling.'

'The opposite,' she said. 'Quite the opposite.'

They stood at the open door now.

'I wish to see her, of course,' Barbie said. 'Can I do that now?'

He observed her without reacting visibly to what he saw. She felt the same expression moulded upon her own face.

'I'm afraid not. But if you ring the general hospital in the morning and ask to speak to Doctor Iyenagar or to his assistant I'm sure it could be arranged, should you really wish it.'

'Doctor Iyenagar?'

'Or his assistant. Extension 22.'

'Thank you, Colonel Beames.'

He made as if to accompany her but she assured him she could find her way. She walked back along the corridors to the waiting-room. Mr Maybrick stood up. She went to speak to the blue-haired woman at the desk.

She said, 'Colonel Beames tells me that Mrs John Layton is staying the night. I may want to telephone her in the morning. Is that fairly easy?'

'Yes, there's a telephone in every room.'

'What extension should I ask for?'

The vicious-looking pencil ran delicately down the list.

'Extension eight. Mrs John Layton.'

'Is that also the room number?'

'That is correct. Her daughter Mrs Bingham is in number seven.'

'Thank you so much. Goodnight.'

*

'We should have left the case in the tonga,' she said as they walked back along the asphalt path.

'And let the fellow run off with it,' Mr Maybrick replied. As if it contained things of value. 'He's probably gone away. It's not like the old days. They'd wait all night to get paid what they were owed. What did Beames say?'

'It was a stroke. So nothing need be delayed. They can go ahead with the arrangements.'

'That's a blessing.'

'What *are* the arrangements, Mr Maybrick? Did Arthur tell you?'

'He was hoping everything could be ready for a service at five o'clock.'

'And then?'

'Then? The interment.'

'In St John's churchyard?'

'Yes. He was relieved Mildred didn't insist on cremation. So many people do nowadays and he doesn't really hold with it. But she asked him to go ahead and select a site himself.'

942

'Are you absolutely sure?'

'Oh, yes. He was quite relieved. He hasn't had a burial there for some while.'

They came to the end of the path. 'I'm afraid it will have to be stopped, Mr Maybrick.' She halted and held his arm. They now stood on the broad asphalt area in front of the main entrance to the general hospital. The tonga-wallah called to them and then the tonga emerged from the dense shadow of a clump of trees whose branches overhung the drive.

'What do you mean stopped? Aren't you satisfied with Beames's opinion?'

'It isn't that.'

'What then?'

'The burial has to be at St Luke's in Ranpur. I told him so but I'm afraid that might not be enough. I must see Mildred. I think I must see her tonight. Either she's forgotten or Mabel never told her. She couldn't deliberately disregard a wish like that, could she?'

'What wish? Whose wish?'

'Mabel's. She wished to be buried next to her late husband James Layton, . at St Luke's in Ranpur.'

'And you said so to Beames?'

'Yes.'

'What did *he* say?'

'He said he'd mention it to Mildred tonight when he gets back from Flagstaff House.'

'Then he will. If it's all that important you can tell Arthur when we get back and one of you can ring Mildred in the morning to check whether Beames kept his word. Come on. You need some food and something warm to drink and to get to bed and try to sleep.'

He swung the case up beside the tonga-wallah.

'I'm sorry to be a stubborn nuisance to you, Mr Maybrick, but—'

'For God's sake!' he said. 'Call me Edgar, can't you, after all these years?'

'Yes, all right.' She nodded her head. 'Edgar. Edgar.' She began to laugh and covered her face. She could not stop. She laughed for her sorrow and for his name because it didn't suit him and presently she was laughing for Mabel because the alternative to laughter was shriek after shriek of wild and lonely despair because Mabel had gone and she had lost her occupation and she saw that was how it was and would always be for everyone.

'Barbie!' Mr Maybrick (Edgar) was saying; he had her by the shoulders but she could not allow herself to be enfolded, admonished or cherished. She forced her body away and began walking towards the steps that led to the glass doors through which shone the lights in the main entrance hall of the hospital. She scrabbled in her handbag and found her cologne-scented handkerchief and dried her cheeks and eyes.

'Now where are you going?' he called.

'It's all right. You go back home.'

943

He caught up with her as she placed her foot on the first step. 'Barbie, what are you doing?'

'I have to see a Doctor Iyenagar.'

'A doctor what?'

They were at the door now, each pushing one immaculate sheet of framed glass, so that the arrival had all the force of an important emergency. The Eurasian girl glanced up, startled. Barbie went to the desk without hesitating. The spirit of the hard condition had entered: an inspired visitation.

'Colonel Beames will have rung,' she announced in a penetrating voice. 'Please tell Doctor Iyenagar I am here.'

'Oh, but Doctor Iyenagar has left.'

'Then his assistant, Doctor whatever his name is. Extension twenty-two.'

The girl swung round in her swivel chair, fumbled with plugs. She said, 'It's Miss Batchelor, isn't it?'

'Yes. I am to see Doctor Iyenagar or his assistant in connection with the death this afternoon of Mrs Mabel Layton. Colonel Beames should have rung before he left for Flagstaff House.'

'Yes. I see. I don't remember—' She responded to a voice in her ear. 'Get Doctor Lal, please.' She looked up at Barbie. 'Doctor Lal will come. Please sit down.'

'Is he on the other end now?'

'Not yet. I will tell him.'

'There's no need for him to come. Just tell him I'm here as arranged by Colonel Beames and then be good enough to have someone show me to his office.' She turned to Mr Maybrick. 'Edgar, why don't you go back to the rectory bungalow and tell Clarissa I'll be there in half-an-hour. You could send the tonga back for me. It oughtn't to take me half-an-hour but if there's any snarl up here I'll have to get on to Isobel Rankin and ask her to get Beames to sort it out from that end.'

'I'll wait,' Mr Maybrick said, then added, 'You may need me if you have to deal with people called Iyenagar or Lal or whatever it is.' He glanced at the Eurasian girl who looked at him as if she agreed. He looked back at Barbie. His face was redder than usual, but grave. He understood.

'Doctor Lal?' the girl said. 'I'm sending Miss Batchelor to your office in connection with the late Mrs Mabel Layton. It is arranged by the civil surgeon. Please see her urgently. Thank you.' She removed the plug and banged a bell. A chaprassi came. She gave him an order.

'Doctor Lal will be waiting, Miss Batchelor,' she said.

'Thank you.'

She followed the chaprassi through into a corridor and found that Mr Maybrick was accompanying her.

'Barbie, what are you doing, for heaven's sake?'

'Something I have to,' she said. The chaprassi indicated a flight of steps leading to basement level. On the half-landing there was a directional sign. It said: Mortuary.

Mr Maybrick grabbed her shoulder. 'Barbie, you can't!' But she shook him off. The basement corridor was low-ceilinged and very hot. She glanced back up the stairs and saw Mr Maybrick leaning against the wall holding his elbows. He shook his head. His mouth moved. She did not think badly of him. Because of Clarice. Who had ailed in Assam. And died slowly. And been unrecognizable. According to Clarissa. Who knew.

The chaprassi opened a door. A thin young Indian in a white coat got up from a stool at a bench littered with white enamel trays and large glass jars. The walls were of whitewashed brick. In one corner a fan whined on a chromium stand. There was a smell of formalin.

'Doctor Lal?'

'Yes, I am Doctor Lal.'

'I was expecting to see Doctor Iyenagar but I'm told he's left.'

'Oh, yes. Half an hour since.'

'Then you are in charge.'

'Yes. You come from Colonel Beames, isn't it?'

'Yes, I do. Obviously Doctor Iyenagar told you to expect me. Upstairs I was afraid there'd been a tiresome lack of liaison. May we please proceed without further delay, Doctor Lal? I should have been at Flagstaff House ten minutes ago.'

The young man looked tubercular. His eyes were enormous. He had studied too hard. He had not eaten enough. He had his qualification. Which should have opened a world to him. But the way into that world was blocked by Beames and his fear of Beames upon whose good opinion his career depended. Contrasting his delicate night-animal's features with Beames's bone-fed face she felt instinctively that he had no sanguine expectations of that opinion.

'Oh, yes,' he said. Did his lower lip tremble? Necessity made him frank. 'Proceed with what? I am sorry, but Doctor Iyenagar—'

'What about Doctor Iyenagar? Are you saying you've no instruction in this matter? If so we'll waste no more time. Ask the switchboard for Flagstaff House. I'll speak to Colonel Beames and ask him to repeat to you what he's already said to Doctor Iyenagar.'

For a moment she feared that a habit of acting upon the last order given would send him to the telephone. But almost at once he said, 'It should not be necessary if you tell me what is the problem.'

'It's not a problem. Or at least it wasn't. It's a question of identification.'

'Identification? Of what, please?'

'Doctor Lal, you're making this extremely painful and tedious. The business is bad enough without prolonging it. I have to see and identify the body of the late Mrs Layton.'

He looked relieved. And then puzzled. He said, 'Oh, yes. But no one mentioned to me this necessity. Are you a relative?'

'Yes.'

'One moment.'

He went towards a door, then came back, moved a chair a few inches from the wall. 'Please sit.' She did so. He opened the door and went through. She closed her eyes to pray for grace, for the continued suspension of Doctor Lal's disbelief. And abruptly opened them, warned by the blankness behind her eyelids. She got up, opened the door he had gone through. The corridor on the other side of it was narrower and lower than any she had been in this evening. But chill. At its end there were closed double doors flanked by fire extinguishers. In each door there was a circular window.

The corridor floor was covered with tiles of some kind of rubber-like composition. She walked silently to the doors and opened them upon an enclosed winter that hummed faintly on a high note so that she seemed to be both deafened and desensitized, projected into a season of frost, a landscape and a time unknown to her. Entering it she became inhuman, like Doctor Lal, like the two white rubber-clothed figures who seemed to be chafing the naked body in a farcical attempt to bring it back to life. The body was on its side with its right arm raised, held by brown hands. There was a yellow pigment in the arm and in the shoulders. It ended just above the pendulous white breasts but spread upwards across the face which was framed by tousled grey hair. The eyes were open and looking directly at the doorway. The mouth was open too and from it a wail of pain and terror was emitting.

*

'You should not have gone in!' Doctor Lal shrieked. 'It is most irregular. Please go back and wait.' He stood guarding the doors through which he had just pushed her with feverish hands, back into the corridor. 'Nothing is ready yet. Doctor Iyenagar is saying nothing to me about identification. I am telling the men. But suddenly you come in without permission upsetting everything. It is not allowed. And now you are in a state. Please, please you must sit somewhere and wait and be patient. Why should I be blamed for this?'

The wall supported her. She felt its hardness against the back of her head. She closed her eyes and breathed in deeply through her mouth.

'No one is blaming you, Doctor Lal. No one will blame you. I shall say nothing. You would be wise to say nothing too. I've seen all I need. Just forget I was ever here.'

She went up the corridor and through the still open door into the laboratory. When she got out into the main corridor she saw Mr Maybrick sitting on the bottom step of the flight that led up to the ground floor. Their glances met. She felt that they were people who had known each other a long time ago, too long ago for either of them to presume upon an old acquaintance by speaking first. They ascended silently: he from his reminder and she from her first authentic vision of what hell was like.

946

The blue-haired woman was still on duty. Barbie approached her alone. Outside, in the tonga whose driver had been persuaded to come by the narrow asphalt path prohibited to vehicles, Mr Maybrick sat, still speechless from the shock of that word: Mortuary.

'I'm afraid an emergency has arisen that makes it imperative for me to see Mrs John Layton at once. It's in connection with the death this afternoon of Mrs Mabel Layton.'

'Oh yes. Well, now.' She glanced at her watch. 'Mrs Layton isn't a patient so I expect it can be arranged. I'll have a word with Sister Page.'

'You'd better tell her I've come on behalf of Captain Coley and the Reverend Arthur Peplow. It's really extremely urgent. It affects the funeral arrangements and of course Mrs Layton has to be informed at the earliest possible moment.'

The blue-haired woman nodded. She had already lifted the phone, pressed one of the red switches and turned a little handle. She asked to speak to Sister Page. It seemed that Sister Page was with a patient. The blue-haired woman gave a careful message, repeated everything that Barbie had told her but had to say names twice. She waited. While she did so the box buzzed. She manipulated switches and said, 'Pankot Nursing Home, can I help you?' And then, 'Just a moment.' She pressed more switches, turned the handle, listened and then presumably switched herself off from the conversation and back to Sister Page's extension.

'Hello?' she said. She listened. 'Well, will you do that? Meanwhile I'll have the visitor brought up.' She replaced the receiver, banged a bell and said, 'Sister Page is with Mrs Bingham but Mrs Layton hasn't gone to bed yet. A porter will take you to the second floor. If you wait at Sister's desk in the lobby, Sister Page or Sister Matthews will meet you there and then take you to Mrs Layton's room.'

She told the porter who had come in answer to the bell to accompany Memsahib to Wellesley. Barbie said, 'Thank you,' and followed the man. They went up by lift.

Sister Page's desk was unoccupied. It was surrounded by vases and baskets of flowers taken from the rooms for the night. A clock on the wall behind the desk showed ten minutes to ten. To the right, painted in black, was the legend: Rooms 20-39; with an arrow. To the left a similar legend pointed the way to Rooms 1-19. Barbie turned left along the broad corridor. As she turned a corner into a narrower one a nurse came out of a room half-way down it and walked towards her. She had wide hips and thick legs.

'Sister Page?' Barbie asked.

'No, I'm Sister Matthews. Are you lost?'

'I don't think so. I'm here to see Mrs John Layton. They told me downstairs to come up.'

'Oh.' The girl looked put out. But then smiled. 'I understood it was a Captain Coley with a message from a Mr Peplow.'

947

'Then they've got it slightly muddled. It *is* a message, and a very urgent one, which concerns Mrs Layton, Mr Peplow and Captain Coley.'

'Yes, I see. And there I've just told Mrs Layton it's Captain Coley. Well never mind.'

'How is her daughter, Susan?'

'Mrs Bingham's just as well as can be expected.'

'It isn't a false alarm?'

'No. But the pains have settled down a bit. I'm afraid it's not going to be an easy delivery, she's so tense. But who can blame her? We've been trying to get her mother to take something to get a good night because Captain Travers says it won't be until morning at the earliest from the look of things. But Mrs Layton's awfully anxious to get on the phone to her sister and other daughter in Calcutta. We've been through once but a dense sort of servant answered, so we're trying again at eleven tonight. I expect they're all out celebrating the second front, which is what I should be doing if we weren't so short-staffed. I'll take you to Mrs Layton.'

'Don't trouble. I know the room number.'

'No trouble.' She turned to lead the way but as she did so a door opened and another nursing officer, coming out, said, 'Oh, Thelma, thank God, come and—' and broke off, seeing Barbie. 'Be with you,' Sister Matthews said and then knocked at room number eight, thrust the door open, glanced round and called loudly, 'Your visitor, Mrs Layton,' and stood aside for Barbie to go in.

*

The room was filled with a cheerless festive odour. From what was obviously a bathroom Mildred called, 'Come in, Kevin. There's a fresh glass on the dressing-table. Pour yourself one and freshen mine, will you? I'll be with you in a minute.' A tap was turned on for a few seconds. 'What's happened?' Mildred asked. 'I warn you I can't stand much more today. Bring mine in, will you? There's an angel. I'm going barmy in this bloody place. I've been phoning Calcutta like mad but there's nobody at Fenny's except some half-witted Bengali bearer. Since you're here you might have a go and see if you can get any sense out of him.' A pause. 'Kevin?'

Another pause. The bathroom door swung wide open. As she caught sight of Barbie Mildred seized the edges of her open dressing-gown and quickly covered her nearly naked body.

For a moment she stood quite still.

Then she said, 'You bloody bitch.'

'Mildred, no. Please don't. Don't talk to me like that. We mustn't let any unfriendliness come between us and what we have to do. It's much too important. I'm sorry if there's been some kind of confusion. But it's not my fault. I had to mention Arthur's and Captain Coley's names because it *does* concern them and I knew you'd never see me just on my own. But you must realize it's not my fault if the message was wrong by the time it reached

948

you. Do I look like someone called Captain Coley? It's pure nonsense, and very wrong of you. But I don't care. You can call me anything you like afterwards, punish me in any way you like for anything you've ever thought I've done to you or done you out of. But you must listen to what I have to say and you must do it, you must. Otherwise she'll never rest. Never. Never. I've seen her, so I know. She'll haunt me, she'll haunt you, all of us. She's in that terrible place and in anguish because she knows you've forgotten your promise or aren't going to abide by it.'

Mildred had gone to the dressing-table, and refilled her glass. Now she said, 'I've no idea what you mean. What promise and to whom?'

'The promise to Mabel to bury her at St Luke's in Ranpur.'

'What on earth are you talking about?'

'It's what she wished. She told me. She must have told you.'

'At St Luke's? In Ranpur? I know absolutely nothing about it and it's quite out of the question. If you don't want the humiliation of being asked to leave by a member of the staff you'd better go now.'

'Why is it out of the question? There's a telephone on that table. All you have to do is ring Arthur and tell him to get on to Mr Wright in Ranpur, tell him this simple thing, that it was her wish to be buried next to her second husband, your own father-in-law, at St Luke's in Ranpur. Arthur and I will do everything else that's necessary. But the instruction to cancel the arrangements for St John's must come from you.'

'What you will do is leave this hospital at once and stop interfering in matters that aren't your business. I find your suggestion utterly obscene. It is June. Perhaps you've noticed it's warm even in Pankot. Quite apart from the question of the cost of the ice, I have no intention of having my husband's step-mother transported like a piece of refrigerated meat to be buried after several days' delay in a churchyard that so far as I recall hasn't been used for burials since the nineteen-twenties. And especially I have no intention of doing so at the whim of a half-witted old woman. Even if there were an indication of such a wish in my step-mother-in-law's Will, or a subsequent written instruction, I should have to override it.'

'I know nothing about a Will, I only know—'

'But I do know about the Will. I've had a copy of it ever since my husband went abroad and copies of subsequent codicils. She had a horror of people having to grub through papers. In fact she was most meticulous and thoughtful about sparing her family unnecessary bother and anxiety. The gruesome little convoy you seem to think she wanted us to become involved in is quite out of character. After five years of living on what one presumes were fairly intimate terms with her I'm surprised you didn't know her better. On the other hand—'

Mildred sipped her gin, put the glass down. And smiled.

'—I'm not surprised. You were born with the soul of a parlour-maid and a parlour-maid is what you've remained. India has been very bad for you and Rose Cottage has been a disaster. I imagine you're paid up either to the end of the month or the end of the quarter. This month it comes to the same thing. I'd be glad if you'd be out before then. As quickly as possible in fact. I'd see that you got a pro-rata refund.'

'Mildred—'

'How dare you call me Mildred! To you I'm Mrs Layton.'

'No, that is ridiculous. That's just spiteful. Mildred is your given name, your Christian name, given when you were baptized. I *shall* not call you anything else. Not in His hearing—'

'Oh, God,' Mildred said. She covered one ear and bent her body as if to ward off a blow or to ride with the flow of a physical pain. The movement brought her in direct visual contact with the table and the telephone. She moved forward and reached for it. Barbie lunged, grabbed her wrist and found herself off-balance, forced heavily and painfully to her knees. But she grabbed Mildred's other wrist and hung on, imprisoned by her own violence in this penitential position. She shut her eyes so that the surge of her strength would not be interrupted. It flowed through her arms and into Mildred and they were united in a field of force, an area of infinite possibility for free and exquisite communication.

Tears of wonder, of love and hope and intolerable desire flowed from beneath Barbie's parchment-coloured lids. For a moment she could not get feeling into her lips. They would not come together to help her form the beginning of the required first word of supplication. She had to dispense with it and begin with a confession.

'I am sorry,' she said, 'sorry, sorry. I am what you say but I loved her so much and it seemed she was my chance, my gift from God to serve Him through her when everything else had been no good hadn't come to anything and just now she was trying to say help me help me. Please, Mildred. She asked for so little but she did ask for this. Why should I ask for it? Why should I make up a story? I'll do anything everything you say but please please don't bury her in the wrong grave. Not that, not that.'

She felt Mildred's wrists force themselves free and knew the answer. She opened her eyes but could not make anything out clearly. The shock of an impact stunned her. For an instant she thought that Mildred had hit her face with her open hand. But then she felt the coldness of water soaking into her blouse and as her eyes cleared she saw the empty carafe which Mildred held.

Without water there was no ice, no frosty particle, no storm of hail. The devotional machine had come to life in the shape of Mildred and a handy jug. The bathos of this situation shocked Barbie into a perilous composure. She felt capable of killing in cold blood, of burying Mildred alive along with Kevin Coley, a pile of empty gin bottles, some silver from the mess, and one of the mummy-rag-thin flags on top to mark the place.

She held an edge of the table, getting purchase to rise which she did without dignity but perhaps honourably. Who could say? She did not know. Dignity and honour were not inseparable. At times, and this was one of them, they seemed far distant for both of them.

Without another word she retrieved her handbag from the floor where it

950

had fallen and left the room. She closed the door gently. In the corridor she realized that limp strands of hair clung to her forehead. The front of the heliotrope jacket was blackened by water. Her chest was icy cold. She put her head up and strode past Sister Matthews and another nursing officer, said good night to their open-mouthed faces and clumped down the stone stairs that entwined the lift shaft. On the ground floor the blue-haired woman was busy on the telephone and smiled absently when Barbie called good night. She was spared the shame of a direct encounter.

Mr Maybrick was asleep. He had reclaimed the fibre suitcase from the driver's seat and sat nursing it, with his head on one side. She climbed in gently and spoke in undertones to the tonga-wallah. When the vehicle jerked forward Mr Maybrick woke, alarmed. She clutched one edge of the suitcase and he another to save it from disaster. And like this they swayed and bucked through the benevolent night guarding her possessions.

vi

Four young officers of the Pankot Rifles took the weight of the coffin on their shoulders. A scratch lot they could have been better matched in height, but the angle of their burden was maintained step by faltering step at a degree several notches above a level that would have led to a bizarre accident. She recognized the pink face of Captain Beauvais, pinker from the exertion of this funereal regimental duty, and wondered whether on his way out he felt the additional weight of a recollection of Bob Buckland, whoever Bob Buckland had been or was. The shortest of the four, he had the right front station and so the coffin had an inclination downwards and moved upon a line that drove logically into the ground beyond the open door to the hastily dug hole for which the woman immediately behind the cortège was responsible.

Beside Mildred walked Kevin Coley; behind these two Isobel Rankin and Maisie Trehearne, and then Clara Fosdick and Nicky Paynton and Clarissa. A thin scattering.

For some time after the coffin had been borne out and the last mourner had followed it through the open door Barbie remained seated in the shadow of a pillar far back in the church, and in the denser shadow of her own bitter and terrible conclusions.

There (she thought) went the *raj*, supported by the unassailable criteria of necessity, devoutness, even of self-sacrifice because Mildred had snatched half-an-hour from her vigil to see the coffin into the hole she had ordered dug. Presently she would return to the hospital where Susan was still in labour. But what was being perpetrated was an act of callousness: the sin of collectively not caring a damn about a desire or an expectation or the fulfilment of a promise so long as personal dignity was preserved and at a cost that could be borne without too great an effort.

And so it will be (Barbie thought) so it will be in regard to our experience here. And when we are gone let them colour the sky how they will. We shall not care. It has never truly been our desire or intention to colour it permanently but only to make it as cloudless for ourselves as we can. So that my life here has indeed been wasted because I have lived it as a transferred appendage, as a parlour-maid, the first in line for morning prayers while the mistress of the house hastily covers herself with her wrap and kneels like myself in piety for a purpose. But we have no purpose that God would recognize as such, dress it up as we may by hastily closing our wrap to hide our nakedness and convey a dignity and a distinction as Mildred did and still attempts. She has a kind of nobility. It does not seem to me to matter very much whether she appears half-dressed in front of Kevin Coley. But I think it matters to God and to the world that she rode with him into the valley and offered matriarchal wisdom to women older and as wise or wiser than she. For that was an arrogance, the kind which Mabel always set her face against, because Mabel knew she brought no consolation even to a rose let alone to a life. She brought none to me in the final count, but what distinguished her was her pre-knowledge that this was anyway impossible. So she probably forgives me about the grave and closes her eyes. It was not everyone who saw that they were open.

*

'Those are for her, aren't they?'

It was Edgar Maybrick's voice. He gathered the bunch of flowers from where it lay on the pew at her side.

'They've all gone now,' he said. 'Is that your case?'

'Yes,' she said, and rose, letting him reach down and pick the suitcase up as well. He led her out. When they reached the place – a blur of fresh-piled flowers – she took the bunch from him and standing well away from the shape of the dark hole that should never have been dug cast it in.

She returned to Rose Cottage alone. As the tonga pulled up at the porch she saw the figure of an old man come from the side of the house and stand waiting. She got out and paid the fare. The front door was open, as were the windows of her room. She and the old man watched each other for a while and then she called to him, 'Will you come and help me, Aziz? I'm very tired and should like a cup of tea.' She went up the steps and entered the hall. Behind her she heard the clunk of his sandals as he cast them off on the verandah before following her in.

Part Four

THE HONOUR OF THE REGIMENT

I

Susan was delivered of a healthy male child, that looked absurdly like poor Teddie, at five o'clock in the morning of June the eighth, three hours before Sarah, hurriedly summoned home from Calcutta, arrived in Pankot on the night train from Ranpur and thirty-three hours after Susan had cried out 'But it can't be! The baby isn't finished yet.'

For a while Susan did not look at the child. She averted her head no matter what her mother said or Travers said and the nursing staff said. It began to look like a classic case of rejection. It was not until Sarah took the child in her arms and impressed on Susan that there was nothing wrong with it, that it was as lively as you liked, in fact pretty obstreperous and not in the least pleased by anything or anyone it had seen so far, that Susan turned her head and looked at Sarah and then at the child and said nothing but let Sarah put the screaming bundle where she could get a view of its purple face and groping miniature hands.

Accepting the child in her own arms her reluctance to examine it closely was obvious. She said, 'Is it whole? Is it?' and took some time to comprehend the evidence, revealed detail by detail by Sister Page, that there was no doubt of this. The effort exhausted her and she cried a bit but smiled and touched the baby's cheek; and slept and woke; and when the moment came applied herself to the primitive task of giving suck with a frown of spartan concentration which gradually eased and left upon her brow a radiance that was too old, too heavy for her face. But no one noticed that.

Presently her milk failed which Mildred said was just as well because one ought not to become so physically involved. It was bad for the child and the mother, unhygienic and potentially a bloody nuisance for everyone concerned. She had advised against it and had been surprised by Susan's insistence that at least she should try. Well, not surprised. The poor girl had done her damndest to do everything right. She'd been a brick.

'After all,' Mildred said, 'one can't imagine more trying circumstances.' She gave up the room next door to the one auspiciously numbered seven, took herself back to the grace and favour but still spent most of the day with Susan. Isobel Rankin saw to it that a telegram was sent to Colonel Layton through the Red Cross. Letters were written. The slight unease felt

953

about the welfare of prisoners of war in Germany now that Europe had been invaded was not openly admitted; instead it was suggested to Susan that her father might be home for Christmas.

'How lovely if he were,' Susan said. 'For us anyway. But it seems a bit unfair, doesn't it? All he'll want is peace and quiet and looking after and what he'll get is a screaming baby that gets all the attention.' She smiled and added, 'But I don't suppose he'll mind because it's a grandson,' and then closed her eyes so that the visitors lowered their voices for a while and thought of the need there would presently be for Susan seriously to consider getting married again to give the boy a father; preferably to Dicky Beauvais who was attentive and in every known respect an excellent choice.

Like other young men in the past Captain Beauvais had originally seemed interested in Sarah; but in his case it would have been impossible to show interest in Susan because when he arrived in Pankot she was a married woman and then a pregnant married woman. He had assumed a brotherly role and it was only since the news of Teddie Bingham's death that the brotherliness had begun to wear thin which it did in a way that suggested to some people that it had never been more than a disguise for the warmer feelings he had always had but tried to reserve and express for Sarah only.

Again it had become necessary to subject Sarah to scrutiny. There seemed to be something wrong with the girl, something complex which was not going to be put right by a simple antidote like the safe return of her father or getting her married off to the right sort of officer, or allowing her to abandon her family responsibilities in Pankot to do a more exciting or exacting job of soldiering closer to those areas where the shooting was. Neither did that hint of little Mrs Smalley's at the time when Teddie Bingham transferred his affections to young Susan – that Sarah was perhaps just a little unsound in her views – really seem justifed. All that could be said was that her behaviour was a degree less than admirable because it lacked either enthusiasm or spontaneity.

'She thinks too much,' Nicky Paynton said. 'And say what you will men don't like it when it shows. She should learn to hide the fact which shouldn't be too difficult because she already knows how to keep her thoughts to herself.'

But that was before the crisis brought on by Mabel's death and Susan's premature labour, both of which events Sarah missed by going to Calcutta. The journey back to Pankot must have been tense and exhausting. She had been fond of her aunt and tireless in her efforts to jolly Susan along after the blow of Teddie's death. Fate had deprived her of the opportunity to help at a time when her help was most needed, but she was at Susan's bedside within an hour of reaching home on the night train from Ranpur. Both her sister and her mother were asleep but she stayed in Susan's room and nodded off in a chair beside the bed, with one hand on the counterpane where Susan could reach it when she woke.

Travers, who found the sisters like this, was touched, and related how the relief that Sarah must have felt at finding her sister well and the baby safely born, had caused her to smile as she slept. The same look of happiness was on her face on the occasion she held the baby and persuaded Susan to accept it, and it occurred to Nicky Paynton who was present that at last something like an enthusiasm could have entered Sarah's life, even if it were second-hand: an enthusiasm for her sister's child. The important thing, Mrs Paynton thought, was that the soil should be tilled. Sarah, she thought, had spent long enough unconsciously making up to her father for not being a boy. At that moment the situation became clear to Mrs Paynton and so did the future which ceased to be worrying. The solution to Sarah was simple after all. What had been repressed was nothing other than a highly developed maternal instinct.

'Sarah, did you manage to see Captain Merrick?' she asked – remembering on the way out of Susan's room what Sarah had gone to Calcutta to do.

'Yes, I saw him the afternoon of the day I arrived.'

'How was he?'

'Waiting for an operation.'

'Anything very serious?'

'I suppose in medical or surgical terms it was quite straightforward. They were going to cut off his left arm above the elbow. Excuse me a second.'

Sarah went to Sister Page's desk and spoke to the girl who was sitting there. Clara Fosdick and Nicky Paynton waited near the liftgate and looked at one another. When Sarah rejoined them Mrs Paynton said, 'How very upsetting.'

'What?'

'About Captain Merrick. Does Susan know?'

'Yes, Captain Travers thought it better to say straight out because she had an idea he might have no arms at all. The letter he wrote us from hospital in Comilla was dictated.'

The lift came. Inside, the cramped conditions discouraged conversation but enabled Nicky Paynton and Clara Fosdick to study Sarah's face and agree later when they were alone that there was an uncharacteristic hardness and decisiveness in its expression, a look of impatience which made the tenderness shown for her sister and her sister's child more noticeable.

Coming out of the lift into the reception foyer Mrs Fosdick added, 'Did he agree to be godfather?'

'No. He was grateful for the suggestion but didn't think he'd make a good one.'

'Because of his arm?'

'I expect that came into it.'

'What happened to him? Did he say?'

'He pulled Teddie and a driver out of a burning jeep and got them under

955

cover. He got bullet wounds and third degree burns. He saved the driver but was too late for Teddie. He'll be getting a medal.'

'I should think so too.'

'The police's loss was obviously the army's gain,' Nicky Paynton said. 'But I'm sorry Captain Merrick's said no. He'd have been a godfather for any boy to be proud of.'

'Later on, perhaps,' Sarah said. 'When the boy was old enough not to be frightened. His face was burnt too.'

'Oh, dear. Badly?'

'I couldn't tell. There wasn't much you could see through the bandages except his eyes and the mouth. But Sister Prior said his hair would grow again and he might even look human.'

'What an extraordinary thing to say.'

'She said it to relieve her feelings. She didn't care for my Lady Bountiful act. She's the sort of nursing sister we describe as a bit off, the sort who wouldn't be an officer at home but is because she joined the QAs and came out here. I think she blames people like us for the fact that there's a war on at all. She thought it was scandalous giving badly wounded men medals. She thought money would be more to the point. But she's on the wrong tack there with Ronald Merrick. He's not interested in that kind of payment or in the kind of people who'd suggest it.'

'I should think not.'

'He says he blames himself for Teddie being killed. Dicky Beauvais promised to be back with the staff car. Can we give you a lift? I'm going to the daftar so it's on the way.'

'That would be nice,' Nicky Paynton said.

'I'll see if he's here.'

Sarah went into the forecourt and presently returned and reported the car coming up the drive. While Captain Beauvais took a rupee from Mrs Fosdick to pay off their waiting tonga-wallah the three women got into the back of the car.

'Why does Captain Merrick blame himself?' Mrs Paynton asked when they were settled.

'I don't think he does really. It's his way of putting things. He'd gone forward to collect a special prisoner and Teddie went with him, although there was no need. I think Teddie was interfering, I mean not trusting Ronald Merrick to deal with a situation in the way he thought it should be handled. After they'd talked to the prisoner Teddie took the jeep when he shouldn't have and went further forward still, and took the prisoner with him because the man said he had two friends in the jungle who wanted to give themselves up too. Ronald didn't know he'd gone and when he found out he had to go after him.'

'That's okay,' Dicky Beauvais said, getting in the front. He signalled the driver to start and sat with his arm over the back of the front bench to take part more comfortably in whatever conversation was in progress.

'Sarah's telling us about Captain Merrick and poor Teddie.'

'Oh, yes.'

'But isn't it very unusual,' Mrs Paynton said, 'for Japanese soldiers to give themselves up?'

'Oh, they weren't Japanese.'

'What then?'

'Indian soldiers from Teddie's old regiment.'

The car slowed at the end of the drive and then moved smoothly and comfortably, well sprung and upholstered, out on to the road that led to area headquarters.

'Muzzys,' Sarah went on. 'Not Teddie's lot. From the other battalion that was captured in Malaya. Now fighting with the Japanese against us. They belonged to the INA we hear about but aren't supposed to take seriously. Captain Merrick says there are far more of them than is allowed to be supposed but that they're badly led and armed and half-starved because the Japanese don't think much of them, especially not of their officers. Anyway he followed Teddie in another jeep and then they found themselves being mortared and shot at by the Japs *and* the INA. The man driving the jeep Ronald was in turned it round to get back where he belonged, so Ronald jumped out and went the rest of the way on foot. When he got to Teddie's jeep it was burning and the prisoner had gone, so he pulled Teddie and the driver out and dragged them under cover, which is when he got shot up himself as well as burned. I haven't told Susan all this because although Ronald Merrick didn't actually say so I think everyone felt Teddie had been wrong and silly. I don't suppose he could bear the thought of leaving two old Muzzy Guides hiding in the jungle, waiting to be recaptured. I gather the divisional commander was rather brassed off, losing two staff-officers and a jeep as a result. But of course the *regiment* would be pleased by what Teddie tried to do, wouldn't it? Don't you think so, Dicky?'

Dicky nodded, but glanced at the driver and then warningly at Sarah.

'After all,' Sarah said, apparently not noticing, he was doing it *for* the regiment. Ronald says that when they were talking to the prisoner and the prisoner realized Teddie was a Muzzy officer the poor man broke down and knelt and touched Teddie's feet. So it makes you wonder how many of the men have joined the INA without knowing what they were doing. It's different in the case of the officers. Ronald said Teddie thought INA officers completely beyond the pale. I gather the same thing nearly happened in Germany, but on a much smaller scale. Isn't that so, Dicky?'

Dicky said nothing.

Again Sarah seemed not to notice his reluctance to discuss the subject in front of a lance-naik driver, but her next comment might have been taken as an oblique criticism of this attitude. She said, 'I can't think why there's so much secrecy about it. It makes it look as if we're afraid of it spreading, but Ronald Merrick said it was difficult in Imphal to stop our own sepoys shooting INA men on sight even if they were trying to give themselves up.'

'The best thing for them,' Nicky Paynton said. 'It'll save rope later.'

'Did you hear the news on the wireless this morning?' Sarah asked, as if changing the subject.

'You mean what Dickie Mountbatten says about carrying on operations through the monsoon? I thoroughly agree. Bunny said ages ago that downing tools directly the monsoon set in was military suicide if you were fighting the Japanese, but perhaps now that Mountbatten's said it we can press on and push the little horrors right back across the Chindwin and not sit on our bottoms for three months waiting for the rains to let up.'

'I didn't mean that. I meant the news about ex-chief minister Mohammed Ali Kasim being released from jail and taken to Mirat.'

'Oh, that,' Clara Fosdick said. 'Well the poor old man's ill and there never seemed much point in locking *him* up. My brother-in-law Billy Spendlove always had a high regard for him. In fact he expected him to tell the Congress to take a running jump when there was all that nonsense about ministers having to resign in 'Thirty-nine. Billy said that in 'Forty-two the Governor gave Mr Kasim an opportunity to disown Congress policies because he knew he'd disagree with practically everything Congress did from 'Thirty-nine onwards but the old boy refused and said he preferred to go to jail. And it's not a pukka release, is it? He's obviously got to stay in Mirat in the Nawab's custody. At least until he gets better. It's so embarrassing when they start getting ill because the people automatically think a political prisoner's ill-health is due to bad treatment.'

'But,' Sarah said, 'someone said at the daftar this morning it's mostly eyewash about him being ill. The real reason is because the elder son who was an officer in the Army and was a prisoner in Malaya has just been captured in Imphal, fighting with the INA. The government thinks Mr Kasim's the kind of man who won't try to make excuses for his son turning coat, and that by being nice to him now he'll be very helpful to us after the war if other Indian politicians start calling INA men heroes and patriots. Which they're bound to.'

'Why bound to?'

'Because of there being so many. If there were only a few isolated cases of Indian officers and other ranks going over to the Japanese then they wouldn't be worth bothering about and we could court-martial them without anybody either noticing or caring.'

Nicky Paynton cut in. 'It seems to me that what's good for one is good for as many as there are.'

'But that's looking at the thing from the point of view of the principle that's involved. We shan't really be able to afford to do that.'

'We should damn' well try.'

'Then we'd make fools of ourselves, wouldn't we, Dicky?'

Dicky smiled bleakly. He gave the driver instructions to turn in at the next compound.

*

After the staff car had left Mrs Paynton and Mrs Fosdick at their bungalow, Nicky said, 'Do you know, Clara, Sarah hasn't once said anything to me about her Aunt Mabel's death, has she to you?'

'She said thank you when I told her how upset we all were.'

'That's all she said to me, too. I thought she was probably too cut up to say anything else but now I'm not sure. I think Mildred's going to have trouble with that girl. Perhaps Lucy Smalley was right. She seemed to want to provoke Dicky Beauvais just now.'

'How, provoke?'

'Well, Clara, let's face it. Dicky's an awfully nice chap but he's not particularly intelligent is he? I got the impression she was trying to provoke him to come out with the kind of remark she could have a private little laugh at. In fact she was provoking us too. It makes one wonder—'

'Wonder what?'

'Well, put it this way. She's always had guts. Suddenly she has nerve. It makes one wonder what happened to her in Calcutta.'

'Perhaps it's just the wrong time of the month.'

'No. You can usually tell when she's having one of her bad periods because she goes quieter than ever. She wasn't quiet this morning. In fact Dicky Beauvais was dying to tell her to shut up because the driver was listening. That's why I took the line I did, about shooting them now saving rope later. But I expect she's right. If we ever do win this bloody war we might hang Bose and one or two of the bigwigs but the rest will just have to be cashiered or dismissed with ignominy. Only by then we'll probably be on our way out in any case and the bloody Indians will have to deal with them in their own bloody way, and they'll probably bloody well make heroes out of them.'

'Nicky!'

'Well, it's true.'

'But there can't be all that many.'

'Can't there? There can be and are. We all know it. But we try to pretend it's not so. But it is so. The bloody rot's set in. When I think of Bunny sweating away in the bloody jungle—'

She went to her room to calm herself and wrote a letter to her husband who had got a brigade at last. 'Darling Bunny, Hope you're in good form,' she began and looked at the latest snap of the two boys in Wiltshire, grinning into the sun with the innocence of youth. 'Mildred's younger daughter, Su, has just had a baby boy.'

II

When Mildred pronounced Susan 'a brick' Travers concurred. Seeing Susan come through, as he put it, he said this showed how wrong people had been who had thought her dangerously withdrawn like that poor girl of Poppy Browning's; and was then taken aback by the hardening of Mildred's jaw, her snapped demand and explicit rebuke, 'Who said that?' and thought it better not to mention it had been Sarah who, in case it was something he should bear in mind when treating her sister, told him what the missionary had said.

'I think it was Miss Batchelor.'

'That woman!' Mildred exclaimed. 'What can she know about Poppy Browning or her daughter?'

Poppy had been Ranpur Regiment, with a daughter married into the cavalry, a young girl six months pregnant when her dashing husband was killed in Quetta by a roofbeam collapsing on his back and on both arms of the Indian girl under him whose open mouth was choked with plaster and who was also dead, suffocated by lover and rubble, when rescuers arrived and disentangled them from the ruins of the bungalow and each other's bodies: a situation which Poppy Browning's daughter had celebrated by smothering her baby two days after it was born. The affair had been hushed up, which was one of the reasons why the daughter was now never mentioned by name but referred to as Poppy Browning's daughter, and a clean clear image preserved of Poppy herself, whose life and record and those of her husband had been unblemished. The sad scandal that brought their Indian career to a premature and obscure conclusion, no longer being spoken of directly, had elevated them to a special place in the minds of people who recognized the value of selfless service, hard work and cheerful dispositions. Poppy and her husband had been mixed doubles champions three years running, back in the 'Twenties when they were in their prime and their daughter still at school in England.

Ever since the Quetta tragedy the name Poppy had blown gently, frail but hardy like the flower, brave among the stubble of the reaped field of human experience. But this section of the field was private. The name Poppy Browning was scarcely known among the younger generation and it was certainly not one to be bandied about by a retired missionary, an interfering woman whose tiresomeness had reached its apogee and was no longer to be borne. So Mildred implied. But her habit of leaving her disapproval to speak for itself, of making exclamatory denunciations rather than explanatory criticisms, as if these were sufficiently informative, left the actual details of Barbie's bad behaviour unclearly set out in the minds of people who felt their sympathies were due to Mildred and indeed assumed by her to be offered; anything else being unthinkable if the appearance of the order of things were to be preserved.

'Some wild idea,' Mildred said, 'that Mabel wished to be buried in Ranpur. Can you imagine anything more grotesque?' Imagine, no. But imagining the grotesque was not necessary when it got about that there had been a macabre and unauthorized visit to the mortuary, a visit which had involved a Eurasian receptionist and a Doctor Lal in serious trouble.

Daily, Miss Batchelor was seen aboard a tonga, clutching a bunch of roses, on her way to the churchyard, a visit prolonged beyond the time it took her to place the flowers on the grave by (it was said) a lengthy vigil in the church itself. Presently in addition to the roses she was observed to clutch a suitcase, the one in which bit by bit she was transferring her belongings from the cottage to the tiny room in the rectory bungalow where Arthur and Clarissa Peplow had offered her temporary refuge.

Neither Arthur nor Clarissa was to be drawn out on the subject of the grotesque idea Miss Batchelor had apparently had about her dead friend's wishes and on the whole people refrained from asking them because merely to do so raised the question whether Mr Peplow had buried Mabel Layton in the wrong place. Neither were many questions asked on the subject of the offer of temporary refuge which Clarissa described as the most practical way out of an unhappy situation and a Christian duty but not to be thought of by anyone as a preliminary to a permanent arrangement being come to. The room was too small.

'I am already worried,' Clarissa said, 'about the amount of stuff with which Barbara seems to be encumbered. If there is much more she will have to speak at Jalal-Ud-Din's about temporary storage.'

Alive, old Mabel Layton had been precariously contained; but her gift for stillness, the sense that flowed from her of old and irreversible connections, had made the task of containing her less difficult than her detachment implied it could have been. She should no longer have been a problem but a once slightly disruptive pattern that now dissolved and faded into the fabric. But, dead, she emerged as a monument which, falling suddenly, had caused a tremor which continued to reverberate, echo, in the wake of Miss Batchelor who, bowling down Club road in the back of a tonga, now guarded the fibre suitcase as if it were crammed with numbered pieces of the fallen tower that had been her friend, and as if it were her intention to re-erect it in the garden of the rectory bungalow or even in a more public position, in the churchyard perhaps or at the intersection of Church and Club roads where – imperfectly reassembled – it might lean a little and dominate the whole area with a peculiar and critical intensity, make it impossible to go past the spot without having one's confidence further impaired and one's doubts increased by this post-mortem reversal of roles. For whereas one had been in the habit of looking in on the eccentric elder Mrs Layton to satisfy oneself that the purpose and condition of exile were still understood (however idiosyncratically by her), furthered and supported, now she would look down from an eminence upon the purpose, upon the condition, accusingly, still silent; but silent like someone who knew that events could speak for themselves and would do so.

On cue, the clouds of the southwest monsoon, thinned by the overland journey across the parched, open-mouthed, plain, appeared in the Pankot sky and spilt what moisture they had left, establishing the wet-season pattern of sudden short showers, of morning mist which could be dispersed by the sunshine or give way to a light persistent drizzle. When the sun came out there was a strange mountain chill that did not make itself felt upon the flesh but in the nostrils, mingling there with the pervading scents of hot mud and aromatic gum. But this year these familiar manifestations of a Pankot summer contained an element, difficult to analyse, but unmistakably felt, of something that acted as an irritant.

As if aware of a special necessity, Mildred Layton now took a day off, put on jodhpurs, and accompanied by Captain Coley set out on horseback on a day's trek to the nearest villages to thank women who had sent little presents and messages of goodwill to Colonel Sahib's younger daughter and baby; to discuss with them the now excellent prospects of the early return of the long-absent warriors from across the black water. It became known, through Coley, that Mildred had gallantly drunk cup after cup of syrupy tea, eaten piping hot chappattis, a bowl of vegetable curry, been soaked in a sudden shower between villages, held squealing black babies, patted the shoulder of an ill-favoured looking woman who was weeping because since her husband went away she had grown old and fat; discussed the crops with village elders, more intimate problems with the wives and mothers, the hopes of recruitment with shy striplings pushed forward by their old male relatives to salaam Colonel Memsahib, and returned exhausted but upright through one of the wet season's spectacular sunsets which turned her white shirt flamingo pink and the shadows of the horses brown.

There was a glow, but it was external to the affair; a bit too theatrical to penetrate to the mind where it was needed. It gave the performance qualities of self-consciousness which made it look as if Mildred's main achievement had been to draw attention to an undertaking whose only claim was a nostalgic one upon the fund of recollected duties and obligations which time and circumstances were rendering obsolete; as obsolete as Teddie's gesture, of which the divsion had taken a view of a kind it would not, in better days, have taken, but with which one somehow could not argue – considering the cost of a jeep and the shortage of equipment, not to mention the escaped prisoner, the burnt sepoy-driver and Captain Merrick's lost left arm. The price of regimental loyalty and pride seemed uncomfortably high.

The circumstances surrounding the death of Teddie Bingham were better not discussed but it was circumstances such as these which were speaking, louder than words, sustaining the illusion of Mabel Layton grimly looking down from the eminence whose site was shifted according to the whim of Miss Batchelor, who sometimes seemed uncertain what to do with the contents of the suitcase and was seen once to get as far as Church road and then order the tonga back up the hill to the cottage, which she had now received official notice to quit by the end of the month.

Perhaps at the height of this piecemeal removal from cottage to rectory Clarissa had put her foot down. 'She'd better not,' Nicky Paynton said, 'otherwise where will the poor old thing go?'

A comic but horrifying thought took hold: of old Miss Batchelor, homeless, seated on a trunk in the middle of the bazaar, surrounded by her detritus, unpacking and rebuilding the monument there, to the amusement of Hindu and Muslim shopkeepers who would interpret such a sight as proof that the entire *raj* would presently and similarly be on its uppers.

'She's writing to the mission,' Clarissa said, 'or so she assures me. One hopes but has doubts that they'll soon find something for her, either in the way of voluntary work or permanent accommodation. But everything points to the advisability of her leaving the station. In view of everything that's happened she could never be happy here again.'

It would have been different if over the last five years Miss Batchelor had entered more into the spirit of things; for example, Clarissa hinted, she could have done more for the church in Pankot. But shortsightedly she had subordinated all her private interests to those of the elder Mrs Layton, had become over-wrapped up in that peculiar woman's solitary affairs, 'against, I often felt', Clarissa said, 'her true instincts which were to say the least of it for having as many fingers in the pie as possible if I'm any judge. But I'm afraid it's too late for her to revert to type. Which is a pity because Barbara was born to serve. And then there is this attitude of hers to that old man which isn't going to help her patch things up with Mildred. I mean the man Aziz. She says only she and Mabel would really understand his behaviour which is as may be, but Mildred says that if it hadn't actually happened Mabel would have invented it, if necessary beyond the grave.'

Aziz's extraordinary perhaps sinister disappearance had gone counter, utterly, to the case law, the accumulated evidence that justified a deep and affectionate belief in the dependability of old and faithful servants. In the welter of conflicting and often unsatisfactory responses of Easterner to Westerner, one simple rule had stubbornly persisted, the rule of loyalty to the man or woman whose salt had been eaten. It was an ancient law but it had lived on and been honoured countless times. Men had died for it, not only in their youth on the battlefield fighting the sahibs' wars but in their age and infirmity on the steps of verandahs in defence of their masters' women and children. Women had died for it too, ayahs for their infant charges, maids for their mistresses. The rule, uncodified, was written in the heart and in old men like Aziz could normally be assumed to have passed across the line of law and custom into the realm of personal devotion.

Well, so one might have thought; so it had seemed, as it would seem for Mildred and John Layton with their Mahmoud, Nicky Paynton with her old Fariqua Khan who wrote monthly progress reports to Brigadier Paynton; countless others, in Pankot, in Ranpur, the length and breadth of India, wherever master, mistress and servant had grown used to and fond of one another, had jointly experienced good times, bad times. A sahib's, a memsahib's death left such old bearers inconsolable and the death of a Fariqua or a Mahmoud could bring tears to eyes accustomed to the discipline of staying dry in public.

But Aziz had not conformed, he had not been inconsolable. He had not wept, he had not got in people's way while doing his touching best to shoulder his share of sad and necessary duties. He had not shouldered them. His desertion – no matter what the civil surgeon said about having known a similar case – smacked of unfeelingness. His return and refusal to explain himself was like a declaration of an absolute right to answer to no one for his actions, to opt out, if he wanted to, from any situation in which there were established and desirable lines of conduct for him to follow.

So that queer thing Mildred said about Mabel inventing Aziz's disappearance if it had been necessary to do so was clear. Mildred saw Aziz's brief defection as a gesture made as much by Mabel as by him and which summed up, reflected, Mabel's long-sustained and critical detachment from the life and spirit of things. Mildred – whom it used to seem that Mabel didn't trust – had obviously never trusted Mabel, and for better reasons. While the old woman was alive Mildred had held her own criticisms in check, for John's sake, the regiment's sake, the station's sake, and even now could not descend to anything so crude as a direct attack.

Instead there had been a faint shrug of the shoulders when Kevin Coley reported Aziz unassailable, protected by Miss Batchelor's assertion that he had returned to serve *her*, that she would require, indeed insisted on, these services for the few days remaining to her at Rose Cottage, would herself pay his wages from June the first until the day of her departure for the rectory and his for his village and retirement. Mildred shrugged her shoulders too when people questioned Aziz's right to receive the small pension Mabel had made provision for in the Will.

'One must respect a Will,' she said. The impression she gave was of blaming Mabel, not Aziz, and of declining to take any tiresome action that would draw attention to the fact that one was living through a period in which general moral collapse seemed imminent, a collapse for which Mabel was as much to blame as anyone.

It was remembered how on the day of the wedding party the old woman had sat, deafer than ever, making things difficult for young officers who were anxious to pay their respects, notably difficult for young Beauvais whose uncle had been a subaltern under Bob Buckland who, in turn, had been a fellow-subaltern of Mabel's first husband and whom she had known, been fond of and consoled by between her husband's death and her marriage to James Layton.

It was remembered too how she had left the party without a word, and apparently by a door at the back of the mess, 'feeling unwell and not wanting to be a skeleton at the feast', according to Mildred's later explanation of an absence which, without causing any special concern at the time, had certainly made itself felt through the empty chair, like a criticism too subtle to be interpreted easily or accurately.

The truth could no longer be avoided. It had been a criticism of the foundations of the edifice, of the sense of duty which kept alive the senses of pride and loyalty and honour. It drew attention to a situation it was painful to acknowledge: that the god had left the temple, no one knew when, or how, or why. What one was left with were the rites which had once propitiated, once been obligatory, but were now meaningless because the god was no longer there to receive them. Poor Teddie! His was an end of an expository kind, like a last sacrificial attempt to recall godly favour. If there were still a glow to be had it would have spread from there, but it did not. Nor did it spread from the action of the man Merrick as once it would have done because nothing could obliterate the image of Merrick as an earlier victim of changed circumstances, of the general loss of confidence, the grave shifting of the ground beneath one's feet as the layers of authoritarian support above one's head thinned and those of hostile spirits thickened.

Somewhere along the line doubt had entered. Even on a sunny day it lay upon the valley, an invisible mist, a barrier to the clearer echoes of the conscience. A rifle shot would no longer whip through the air, slap hard against a hillside and bounce, leaving a penetrating and convincing smell of cordite, sharpening senses and stiffening the blood. It would go muffled, troubled, and its message would be garbled; and the eye would not dart alerted, Khyber-trained, to the hillsides for the tell-tale flick of a mischievous robe, but shift uncomfortably, to observe the condition of the lines, for signs of mutinous movements on the parade grounds where the Pankot Rifles went through the motions of training another generation of candidates for the rolls, acolytes for the temple.

And presently – not suddenly but with an increasing persistence – Mildred's personality began to stand out, a reminder to people of what life had meant, been like; so that an interesting counter-image to the one of Mabel began to emerge – an image of Mildred, also made of stone, splendidly upright, and revealing her true distinction through her refusal to compromise either her upbringing or her position by allowing what was irresistible to move her or what was expedient to take precedence over what in her judgment was right.

And so after all a glow came, even if it did not spread. The glow was Mildred. The famous expression shone. It could not infect but it could remind. And when she said, 'What Teddie tried to do was worth the whole bloody war put together,' it was realized that with her unerring instinct she had gone straight to the heart of the matter, cutting through such irrelevancies as divisional annoyance, the cost of a jeep, the loss of a prisoner and Merrick's arm, leaving one with Teddie's blameless death, his praiseworthy sacrifice for a principle the world no longer had time or inclination to uphold.

From the rear of the compound of the grace and favour bungalow smoke rose, between showers, as Mahmoud directed the burning of the stuff Mildred was beginning to throw out, the unwanted accumulation of the years of pigging-in which were now over; over too late, of course. Rose

Cottage would certainly be more comfortable, more convenient for most things, but the station had been deprived for ever of any significance that might have attached to her presence there. Now she seemed to wish it to be recognized that she was merely claiming what had become her husband's property; not, as once could have been the case, acquiring an appropriate and proper setting for her virtue. She would live there and hold it in trust for him.

'Susan has decided to give the baby all Teddie's Christian names,' she said. 'So there'll be another Edward Arthur David Bingham. On the whole I approve.'

It was the continuity, logical and unsentimental, to which she responded, the idea that in this matter of a name Teddie would endure long after the acrid smell of the lost jeep had died away and the bloody accountant-general had finished reckoning out the amount in rupees. Dick and Isobel Rankin had agreed to be godparents. Sarah would be the younger godmother and Dicky Beauvais the second godfather. The child would be well endowed. Mahmoud's widowed niece, called Minnie because her real name was unpronounceable, had gladly accepted the duties of ayah. The christening would take place at St John's, a week after the day fixed for Susan to leave the auspiciously numbered room in the nursing home.

'We shall have the christening party here,' Mildred said, meaning the grace and favour. 'I want to get it over before we move up to the Cottage, and get Su used to the idea of having the baby at home. The last time she was up at the place wasn't the happiest occasion.' At the cottage, she said, she herself would have Mabel's room, the little spare would be an excellent nursery. Susan and Sarah would share the other room, the one Miss Batchelor was in the process of vacating. Even sharing, they would have more space each than they had in the tiny bedrooms of the grace and favour.

'I should have liked to do some redecoration, but I think that will have to wait,' Mildred said. 'I'll have to keep the mali on but I've told Mahmoud to keep an eagle eye on him. It's time the mali earned his keep. You can't say that with Mabel he was exactly overworked, can you?'

She glanced down at her half-empty glass. For a while after Teddie's death, the drinking habit had been less frequently indulged, but then resumed as if she had decided that giving anything up was a sign of weakness. Now that she could afford it, with the whole of Mabel's money coming into Colonel Layton's possession, there was no reason left for anyone to question the habit at all. For a hard-drinking woman who had recently had a great deal to cope with she was comparatively abstemious. And remembering the time when it seemed as if she drank for the station's sake as much as for her own, people felt there were many good reasons, few of them identifiable, why she should actually drink more than she did. It was as if, anticipating more reasons to come, she deliberately held back, in order to be in good form for the occasion.

III

Her flesh had hardened. It had the toughness of metallic substance. When she walked she sensed her body's displacement of the air. Between herself and Aziz there was a magnetic field of force. They spoke seldom. It was not necessary. In their brief exchanges there was an undertone of parable.

'There's very little more,' she told Clarissa after several visits to the rectory bungalow; and edged out of the narrow space between the bed and the wall, catching the nailed feet of an imitation ivory crucifix with her sleeve, so that the Lord was tilted sideways as He would be if the cross weren't planted firmly enough or were lowered into the wrong hole, one too wide for it.

She straightened the sacrificial figure and turned to face Clarissa's forgiveness which was conveyed through a swift averting of the eyes as if from the sight of a near accident of an ominous, sacrilegious kind.

From the rectory she went to St John's, visited the grave and then sat down in the shadow of the pillar, in the same pew as on the day of the funeral, so that Mabel might find her without difficulty. This was a vigil she kept every day between four and five, bringing roses cut from the bushes with Aziz's help. It interested her to discover how much he seemed to have learned about the way to cut blooms without weakening the bush or spoiling its shape. She did not understand the principle but guessed there was one and allowed him to guide her by silent indication or a sudden gesture of restraint.

Returning home she faced daily the mounting evidence of what seemed like improvidence. Could one single woman have acquired so much, have needed so much? The drawers in the Rose Cottage chests were deep. Sometimes she thought of them as comically bottomless, yielding up one item more for each item removed and crammed into a suitcase.

And shoes. In serried ranks. On tip-toe along parallel brass rods at the base of the almirah, each pair polished and cared for by Aziz and the mali's boy.

'I am fond of my shoes,' she said, newly discovering this attachment. She took the favourite pairs to the rectory but found the base of the almirah an unwilling repository. There were no brass rods and in any case the skirts of her suits and dresses hung too low, right down to the bottom of the cupboard. In one angle of the wall there was a curtained recess. She placed the shoes on the floor but the curtain did not conceal them. The shoes looked like the feet of old people eavesdropping. Nowadays tears came unexpectedly. 'Crying in a happy home,' Clarissa had warned her, 'is like untidiness in a neat one, and is a worry to God.' Barbie dried her eyes and looked round belligerently.

The room was dark as well as small. She peered through the single window, craning round the side of the miniature dressing-table to see what was to be seen. The view, on to the side of the bungalow, was blocked by creeper. She pushed the window open to let in some air. There were bars on the inside, a protection against thieves. The creeper sighed and shook. Tendrils of it, in possession of the sill, groped stealthily forward, probing for a grip on the interior. She hit and pushed them away, closed the window, found one tendril trapped inside and growing. She nipped it off. It was tough-skinned like herself. Its sap was odorous. Two kinds of death she had always feared: by drowning and by suffocation. She would need to be wary of the creeper. It was an understanding enemy.

Returning along the gloomy but sanctified passage to the hall she looked for Clarissa to say good-bye until tomorrow. Clarissa was no longer speaking on the telephone as she had been when Barbie arrived and sought and received nodded permission to take the suitcase through to the place of temporary refuge.

She said 'Clarissa?' and, leaving the suitcase on the floor, parted the old-fashioned bead curtain that hung in the archway between hall and living-room. The living-room was crowded with leather chairs and wicker-work. There were exhausted indoor ferns in brass pots which filled the air with a green spiritual miasma. An oval mahogany table covered by a bobble-fringed bottle-green cloth stood roughly in the centre of the room. By this table Clarissa was waiting, with her hands laced in the long string of sandalwood beads she wore in the afternoon but for some reason never before lunch and never at dinner.

'Clarissa, I am just going to the grave and then home. I brought a few pairs of shoes.' She clutched a bunch of roses, yellow ones whose strong sweet scent Mabel had loved best of all. Clarissa did not reply, except by nodding.

'Is something wrong, Clarissa?'

Slowly Clarissa flushed.

'Yes. At least. I have something I find it painful to say. But must say. I hope there has never been anything except total frankness in our relationship. I mean other things as well, a mutual respect and recognition of common Christian intention, but always frankness. You will have to forgive me, Barbie, but it would be totally – a totally false *position* for me if we went ahead with our arrangement without my saying what I have to.'

'What is it Clarissa? Is it the amount of luggage? It *is* a little more than I thought.'

'It is not the amount of luggage although speaking of that I am afraid you've already brought more than I can adequately provide room for and still leave the servants space to keep order. I don't wish to be unthoughtful or unimaginative but if there is anything more to come than a caseful the day after tomorrow – providing we reach that stage – I think you'll have to speak at Jalal-Ud-Din's about storage. They do offer some facilities.'

'That won't be necessary, Clarissa. I should not want my stuff mouldering in a native storehouse.'

'Let us say no more about luggage. Personally I always try to keep in mind the fact that we bring nothing into this world and can certainly take nothing out. Ever since childhood I have firmly rejected the tyranny of possessions, thanks to a proper upbringing in this regard. And Heaven knows that those of us who serve in India soon learn how transient our experience of home and hearth is, don't we? I doubt that we shall remove from this station before Arthur's retirement, but there is very little in this room that has been with us in other places or would go with us to our next. One is sure of but one thing, the strength and love of God.'

The scent of the roses became overpowering. Barbie supported herself with one hand on the bottle-green cloth. Its texture was harsh and scratchy. Like a hair-shirt. The flush had left Clarissa's face and neck. She was now pale as from a sense of eternity and the will to earn her place there.

'I have strayed from the point,' she said. 'The painful point.'

Barbie moistened her dry teeth with the tip of her tongue. The sandalwood beads began to clack through Clarissa's suddenly animated fingers.

'I was at the club this forenoon,' Clarissa began, still in the pedantic way she had of speaking when delivering herself of an oration or an opinion previously formed and rehearsed. 'Not alone, but with others, people whom I respect and whose good opinion I value, people whom you know but whom I shall not name. It happened, it so happened, that the question of your temporary refuge here arose, and it was said by one, it was said, well, what a pity it was that after all these years some way could not have been found of allowing you to remain at Rose Cottage to help Mildred, if only for a while, with the enormous burden she will bear at least for a time, with Susan and the baby to look after. What a pity, and how useful, what a help you might have been since you know so well the details of the running of that house.'

The beads ceased clacking for a moment, having been gripped by Clarissa's plump white fingers, in one of which the gold wedding-band was countersunk. But then the fingers fluttered again and the clacking resumed.

'It was of course an impractical suggestion but well-meant. But then it was said that quite apart from it being impractical it would be most, most, unsuitable. Unsuitable especially, it was said, with two pretty young girls in the house. And I could not, no I simply couldn't believe my ears, so much not believe that the moment, the opportunity, to challenge it, to discredit it, had gone before I fully understood exactly what had been implied. But having understood what was said, what was implied, in the hearing of several, I must convey it to you otherwise my position would be intolerable both in private and in public. For should I ever hear this thing repeated I must challenge it. I do not propose, Barbara, to refer to it again of my own accord, inside or outside this house, but I require, for my own peace of mind, under this roof, I require – from you – some word—'

Barbie was confused. She could not take in a clear notion of the matter, which seemed to be a special failure since obviously it excited Clarissa considerably. 'If I knew what word, Clarissa,' she said.

'A word,' Clarissa repeated, jiggling the beads in agitation, 'a word of refutation, of assurance, assurance that there are no grounds, no grounds, for such a wicked implication.'

Clarissa had flushed again with the effort of her demand, her appeal, whatever it was. Suddenly she let go of the beads and placed one hand under her heart, so that thinking she was unwell, perhaps overcome by the humidity that often accompanied the onset of the rains, Barbie took a step towards her, but stopped, because Clarissa had taken a simultaneous and involuntary step back. And, alerted by this evidence of apparent physical revulsion, Barbie began to grasp what had been said and a flush of anger began to darken her yellowed cheeks and old throat, spreading in unison with the electric surge of intelligence that awakened a desolate withered capacity for needing affection in return for giving it.

'Yes, I see,' she said. She thought for several moments before continuing. 'You naturally wish to be reassured. But what can I say? If it were true I should probably deny it because at the moment I've nowhere else to go and if this is going to be said about me I should find it difficult to go anywhere in Pankot. It's a difficult thing for an elderly spinster to refute. But for what it's worth, Clarissa, so far as I know my affection for Sarah and Susan is not of an unnatural kind, unless it is unnatural to feel maternally to them, to take pleasure in their company and care what happens to them.'

'Thank you,' Clarissa said. And then, exhaling, clapped her hands to her cheeks and sat down on a bandy-legged stool.

'Is that all, Clarissa?'

Clarissa's mouth was still open. The tips of each of her little fingers held it in that exclamatory shape. Her eyes were closed.

'Oh!' she whispered. 'It was wicked. It was wicked.'

'Am I expected, Clarissa? As arranged? The day after tomorrow?'

Clarissa opened her eyes but did not look at her. Presently she nodded her head and Barbie turned and left the room, leaving her friend to recover the sense of deep Christian repose to which she was accustomed.

*

Without touching the other withered wreaths and faded cards she tidied up the green tin vases that held her own offerings, removed prickly stems from which the last petals had fallen and placed the yellow roses in a vase of their own. The hump of clay would never settle. When she had finished she noticed it was raining. She went inside the church and sat by the pillar; and as usual prayed that there would be no letter for her from the mission in answer to her hasty request, or that if there were it would be couched in negative or unoptimistic terms. But half-way through the prayer she retracted it and, remaining on her knees, opened her eyes. She thought: I do not see how I can stay, I do not see how I can face it.

And not seeing how, she understood the depth of need and desire to stay which had been forming in her mind and heart ever since the day that

Mabel was buried in the wrong grave; to stay for as long as it took to right the wrong that had been done, even if that meant waiting for the return of Colonel Layton who might be moved to listen to the truth. It was Colonel Layton's father by whose side Mabel had wished to rest.

She had begun to regret the letter to the mission, her offer of voluntary services in any capacity however menial in return for a roof. She had begun to feel that bit by bit she and Clarissa could become used to and of use to one another. She had even begun to imagine the possibility of patching things up with Mildred. All for Mabel's sake. All to achieve for Mabel's soul the repose that depended on the proper repose of Mabel's body. She had believed that she should not leave Pankot while there was hope. She had felt no horror at the idea of opening the grave and taking the remains to Ranpur. The idea had filled her with a sense of the quietude that would follow.

But she felt horror now; the horror of her own shame. In front of her hovered the pale shape of Clarissa's face with hands pressed against the cheeks. She wanted to put immense distance between herself and her life. How can I face it? she repeated. How can I walk about in the bazaar or sit here on a Sunday in the middle of the congregation, knowing what has been said, what has been hinted? The shape of Clarissa's face changed into that of Mildred's and the hands were not at the cheeks but droop-waisted below the chin, holding a glass, the downward-curving lips quirked at the corners in a dismissive smile.

'How can I face it?' she asked aloud. And the face became that of yet another, chin in hand, regarding her with that compassion and patience, that exquisite desire. She trembled and leaned for support against the pillar, hiding in its shadow. She longed to be transported back to Rose Cottage. Outside the cottage she had become utterly vulnerable. When she left the cottage forever she would enter an arena of defeat from which she could see no exit. There was beauty in the quiet formality with which the trap had been set. Already she felt the onset of the last, the grand despair, the one that was awaited. Mabel, she whispered. Mabel. Mabel.

Abruptly she was cold because she had heard the sound of the latch, as on the day of Mabel's death. Far down the church the little side door had been opened and closed. The sound echoed faintly. She clung to the pillar, listening to the light-falling footsteps coming up the aisle to the back of the church. They were a woman's. Her skin prickled but her eyes suddenly brimmed, in gratitude, and awe, and loving terror. She remained kneeling, pressed against the pillar and dared not look up. Her nostrils quivered, fearfully alert for the sweet odour of the ghost, the compound of flowers and formaldehyde that must attach to the newly dead. I am here, she muttered, here, here. Bound to this pillar, to this life.

She covered her face. The stone of the pillar chilled the bare knuckles of her right hand. The footsteps had ceased, having come close. There was a faint creak, and then silence. She did not have the courage to move. But presently, astonishingly, she became peaceful, comforted. She thought, 'I can face anything if I try.' She withdrew from the shadow of the pillar. The air was cool on her overheated forehead. She glanced along the pew but could see nothing. She inclined her body backwards, bringing into her range of vision the pews in front, and caught her breath, shocked by the visible presence of the seated figure. Involuntarily her hand covered her mouth.

It was not Mabel. It was not any woman she knew. The head was covered by an old-fashioned solar topee with a veil swathed round the brim. After a while the woman became restless as if she had become aware of being watched. Upright in the pew, staring at the stained-glass window above the altar, the woman touched her throat and turned slightly, looking to left and right. Reassured, she resumed her still and silent vigil, and stayed thus until there was one of those mysterious adjustments, a small shift of the empty building's centre of gravity, as of a momentary easing of its tensions and stresses which created an illusion of echo without traceable source, so that to Barbie it seemed that the church's guardian angel had half-opened and then closed one of his gigantic wings.

The unknown visitor rose, stepped into the aisle and walked down it towards the altar. She was elderly and moved with the care of a person conscious of a duty to carry her years with dignity. Before turning towards the side door she placed a hand for support on a pew and with lowered head bent one knee. Going out, she opened and closed the door gently. A little later Barbie caught the sound of a motor-car starting up, not on the Church road but on the West Hill road side.

As the sound faded, as the car took the woman away in that revealing direction, she realized who it was who had sat a few feet in front of her, but she was slow to respond. What might have been curiosity or superstitious fear of such close proximity was muted by the stronger current of an emotion which warmed her body and kept her kneeling, one hand on the pillar and the other still upon her mouth.

Within that little complex of events, the expectation of the ghost, the shock of seeing the woman, the echo from an unknown source high in the roof (above all, within that) she wondered if there had been one other thing, no more than a faint disturbance, a rearrangement of the sources from which she received impressions. Fleetingly, it seemed to her, her presence had been noted by God. She stayed very still. The impression was not enlarged, confirmed in any way, but it was not destroyed.

Well, I am going now, she told Mabel. She waited. There was no answer. Carrying the empty fibre suitcase in which she had transported shoes, she left the church. Outside she put her head up and went in search of a tonga.

*

When she got back to Rose Cottage she filled her largest suitcase with things taken at random from the stuff remaining in her room, left space in it for her nightwear and toilet things and then emptied the drawers on to a sheet spread on the floor. Without looking at what she must leave behind she knotted the sheet, making a bundle, and called Aziz, asked him to have it removed because she wanted none of the contents and did not wish to see the bundle again. He returned with the mali's boy and the sweeper girl who between them dragged the bundle out on to the verandah and out of sight.

Directly it had gone she felt reduced, already cut off from the source of energy and power residing in the bungalow. She glanced at what remained: the suitcase, the writing-table and the metal trunk of missionary relics which this morning Aziz had helped her pull away from the wall between dressing-table and almirah into the centre of the room. She knelt on the rush mat in front of it, as at an altar, as at her life. The once-black paint was scored and scratched with the scars of travel and rough handling; and the name, painted in white roman capitals – Barbara Batchelor – had faded into grey anonymity of a kind from which a good report might be educed by someone who did not know her; a chance discoverer in a later age.

'Poor trunk,' she said. She touched the metal. It was warm like an animal, one that relied on her, dispassionately but assuming certain things about their relationship. 'There is no room,' she said, 'no room at Clarissa's.'

She considered alternatives. One was to ask Mr Maybrick to give it temporary shelter. But it would not survive, neglected amidst all that chaos. Nor would it survive in the alien Moslem shadows of Jalal-Ud-Din's. She caressed the lid. Beneath it lay the proofs of her failures and successes, evidence of endeavour. Gazing down at the name it seemed to her that the trunk was all that God need ever notice or take into account; that she herself had become unreal and unimportant.

An idea began to exert itself, persuasively; to flow up from the trunk through her arm like a current; an idea that the trunk should be left at Rose Cottage where she had been happy. But where? Where Mabel could see it, or sense it, or even touch it, groping blindly for a familiar or friendly object to give her troubled spirit momentary relief in its wanderings between the cottage and the alien grave?

The brass padlock with its key was in the lower ring of the main hasp. She had but to lever up the two side hasps to raise the lid; but the prospect of looking through the contents dismayed her. She unlocked the padlock and transferred it to the securing ring, clicked it shut and used the key to lock the two smaller clasps. She put the key aside to place it in her handbag, but continued kneeling.

From behind her Aziz spoke. 'Memsahib. Sarah Mem.'

She looked round as startled by the interruption as she would have been if caught in an act of private devotion. In the open doorway she saw the two faces, Aziz's and Sarah's. The colour came into her own. She got unsteadily to her feet as Aziz stood aside for Sarah to enter. Since the evening of the day Sarah got back from Calcutta, the day after the funeral, she had not visited the cottage, and that single visit had been brief, cut short by their

973

nearness to Mabel's death, their reluctance to talk about it and inability to find other subjects of conversation. The girl had rung subsequently to ask if Barbie was all right, opening the way for an invitation. She had now come of her own accord as if there were matters that could no longer be laid aside, but Barbie was afraid of being alone with the girl because of what had been said.

'I must look a sight,' she said, pushing back a stray lock of her short-cropped hair. 'I've been clearing up, trying to get some sort of order into things, some sort of sense. It's quite a task.'

'I'm sorry,' Sarah said. She did not say what about. 'Is there anything I can help with?'

Barbie shook her head. Sarah was in uniform. She had probably come straight from the daftar. She looked soldierly. But womanly. Perhaps Mildred genuinely suspected something 'wrong' with the girl, and 'wrong' with Barbie. There had been a book once, of arcane reputation, which she had never read; but she remembered the title. Well, Barbie cried in herself, to herself, to the quiet room, the ancient walls; *I* am lonely. Lonely. But God help me my loneliness is open to inspection. It's here in this place beneath my breast. Between Sarah and myself, between myself and any woman, there is nothing that there should not be. I have been slandered. Spitefully. As punishment. For my presumption.

She went into the bathroom, washed the grime from her hands and splashed her face, to cool her skin and the anger that hardened it and made it smooth. She chafed her wrists with cologne, combed her grey hair and called to Aziz.

'Tea! Tea outside, or—' returning to her bedroom, 'sherry?' And stopped. The decanters were locked in the sideboard and Kevin Coley still had the keys. Sarah, arms folded, turned from contemplation of the view from the front window.

'I should love some tea, Barbie.'

'Aziz has probably anticipated. Have you not? Aziz? Aziz!' In the hall her voice rang beating against the gongs of brass trays on the panelled walls, rebounding from the implacable wood of the locked door of Mabel's bedroom. From the region of the kitchen he shouted back in simple confirmation of his presence. She led the way through the sitting-room, unbolted the french window and went out on to the verandah. The sky was clear again but the areas of sunlight were evening-narrow, the shadows long. The garden scent was heady, heightened by the dampness in the air. The chair in which Mabel had sat down to die had not been moved. Fallen rose-petals lay ungathered on the lawn.

'One full day more,' Barbie said, standing by the balustrade. 'Early mornings and from tea until dusk – those were always my favourite times.'

She heard the creak of a chair as Sarah sat and presently the click of a lighter. She waited for the aroma of cigarette smoke to reach her and then turned round.

'I shall be out of here after breakfast the day after tomorrow,' she said.

'Aziz will be ready to go too. I don't know what his travelling arrangements are. He and I will say good-bye here but if he's required to do so he'll wait until someone arrives to take over his storeroom keys. Mahmoud or Captain Coley. Otherwise he'll lock up and leave the keys with mali.'

'Yes, I see. I'll tell Mother.'

Aziz brought tea out. When he had gone Barbie said, 'Will you pour?' Then she sat down and took her cup. She asked how Susan was. Susan was well, Sarah said. They were taking her back to the grace and favour. The day after tomorrow. Minnie, Mahmoud's widowed niece, who had never had children of her own and was scarcely more than a child herself, was excited but also fearful of her new responsibility. For a while Sarah would have to help her.

If there was a feeling of constraint between them, Barbie thought, the fault was her own. The girl's manner was if anything less indrawn than it had been in the past, and beneath the pallor, the marks of strain, there was a faint flush, a look of contentment in the flesh of the face as if she had reached a firm decision about the situation she was in.

'Clarissa told me your news about poor Captain Merrick,' Barbie said.

'Yes, I didn't mention him last time I was here. I meant to tell you that he talked a bit about Miss Crane. He didn't know her very well, I'm afraid.'

'I imagined their paths were unlikely to have crossed.'

'He knew her by sight of course, and visited her in hospital after she was attacked. They weren't able to talk much because she was so ill, and afterwards one of his assistants dealt with it. By then he was involved in the other business of Miss Manners.'

'And later still? When Edwina took her life?'

'Yes, he dealt with that. He was at her bungalow. That's what he remembers. He talked quite a lot about an old picture he found there. From the way he described it I think it must have been the one you had a copy of and showed to people.'

'It would have been that one, I expect. I still have the copy in my trunk.' Barbie thought back to that day on the verandah nearly two years ago. 'I don't remember your being with us when I showed it.'

'I heard about it.'

Barbie nodded. She had made an exhibition of herself over the picture. She said, 'Why did Captain Merrick talk about the picture?'

'He seemed to see a connection between the picture and Teddie. Has Clarissa Peplow told you how Teddie was killed?'

'She said he was trying to bring in some Indian soldiers who'd deserted. I'm afraid I didn't listen very hard.'

'Man-bap,' Sarah said, after a pause, but abruptly.

'What?'

'Man-bap.'

Man-bap. She had not heard that expression for a long time. It meant Mother-Father, the relationship of the *raj* to India, of a man like Colonel Layton to the men in his regiment, of a district officer to the people of his district, of Barbie herself to the children she had taught. Man-bap. I am your father and your mother. Yes, the picture had been an illustration of this aspect of the imperial attachment; the combination of hardness and sentimentality from which Mabel had turned her face. If Teddie had died in an attempt to gather strayed sheep into a fold she saw why Captain Merrick might remember the picture. But Sarah's reasons for referring to it were otherwise obscure to her. And she did not wish to probe. She did not want to talk about Edwina, or about Teddie and the ex-police officer who had lost an arm and whom Sarah had never liked.

But – 'It's interesting about Ronald Merrick,' Sarah began. 'He'd like to be able to sneer at man-bap but he can't quite manage it because actually he'd prefer to believe in it, like Teddie did. If he did. Do you think he did, Barbie?'

'I don't know.'

'Did Miss Crane?'

'Why do you ask that?'

'Because Ronald Merrick thought so. He talked about her sitting at the roadside holding the dead Indian's hand. He thought that was man-bap. Was it?'

'No.'

'What was it?'

'Despair.'

For a moment Sarah looked stricken by the bleak word as if it was the last one she had expected; but then she smiled briefly in recognition.

'Yes,' she said. 'That makes sense.'

Again they became silent but it was the silence of matched temperaments.

'What happened between you and Mother, Barbie?'

'If you don't know I expect it means she'd prefer that you shouldn't.'

'She said you had an idea that Aunt Mabel wanted to be buried in Ranpur.'

'Then you know all there is to know.'

'That's all it was about?'

'That's all.'

'What about Aziz?'

'That wasn't a bone of contention. Although your mother can't have liked my saying she didn't understand.'

'No, she wouldn't like that.'

'I didn't really understand myself, in the sense of being able to explain it. But I didn't feel the need and your mother did. That was the difference. I'm sorry for any annoyance I caused her. She had a great deal to attend to. I had only this – one thing.'

Sarah nodded. She put out her cigarette. Barbie thought she would get up, make an excuse to be off home; but she settled back in the wicker chair.

'How were your aunt and uncle?' Barbie asked her.

'Very well, thank you.'

976

'You can't have seen much of Calcutta.'

'No, not much. A bit. I was taken dancing at the Grand, and then to a place where they had Indian musicians.'

'By Aunt Fenny and Uncle Arthur?'

Sarah smiled. 'No, by one of the officers who attended the course Uncle Arthur's running. He and Aunt Fenny live a much gayer life than they used to in Delhi. They have one of these large air-conditioned flats and it's usually full of young people, mostly these young men who do the course.'

'What kind of course?'

'About how India is run in peace-time. It's supposed to attract recruits for the civil service and the police among men who've liked India enough to want to stay on after the war.'

Barbie tried to consider this. But she was giving Sarah incomplete attention. The image of the trunk was superimposing itself on the image of the verandah, the tea-table, and Sarah on the other side of it smiling as if waiting for her to smile back.

'Is the course a success?' she asked.

'I suppose one or two of them might be tempted. Having them back to the flat is part of the attracting process. You know. The ease and comfort of lots of servants but in modern surroundings, the kind they have to admit are pretty decent. But I should think they're more likely to try for one of the business firms where the future's more secure and they can get transferred home to the London office when it begins to pall or if they want to get married and have a proper family life. Otherwise I get the impression they think the course is rather quaint.' Sarah paused. 'They were the kind of young men I was just beginning to get to know before Su and I came back out in 'thirty-nine. My sort of people. The sort of people we really are. There's such a tremendous gulf, I mean now. More so from their point of view than from ours.'

'Well,' Barbie began, intending to say something about Sarah's sort of people, her own sort of people, but she could not apply herself to the subject. She said, 'I'm glad you had a bit of fun.' She recalled Sister Matthew's explanation of the solitary presence of a Bengali bearer in the Calcutta flat on the night Mildred had tried to ring her sister from the nursing home: that everyone must have been out celebrating the second front. She wondered at what hour the news of Mabel's death and Susan's premature labour had reached Sarah; and pitied the girl, imagining her returning to her aunt's place, flushed with the excitement of a night in the city in the company of those young men, men of her own kind, men whom she understood or had once understood and now envied because they were part of 'home', and her aunt saying: Sarah, your mother rang, it's bad news I'm afraid. Had the girl's thoughts immediately turned to her father, far away in prison camp?

Had the Layton girls missed a 'proper family life'? What did that mean, anyway? Was it important to have one, significant if one missed it? As in other Anglo-Indian families the discipline of separation of children from

977

parents had presumably marked Sarah's childhood. With such a separation Barbie had never had to contend. The separation she had suffered had been permanent and presumbaly more tolerable as a consequence since there was no arguing with death: her father's and then her mother's. But she was full grown when she came out and she came out as a treader of new ground, not old, and in her own behalf and, so she had thought, in Gods, and had never married, never had children.

Knowing Sarah and Susan was the closest she had ever been to knowing what it felt like to have daughters. If they had been her own children, could she have borne the separation? Would Susan eventually have to bear it, or would the whole condition of life in India for English people have changed by the time the child had reached the age of seven or eight, which brought the first, the childhood, phase of Anglo-Indian life to a conclusion? It was not many years ahead. But the condition would well have changed by then. The child might be lucky.

But not its parents. Not Susan. Nor Sarah. Nor young Dicky Beauvais whom Clarissa Peplow hoped Susan would marry. Looking at Sarah Barbie felt she understood a little of the sense the girl might have of having no clearly defined world to inhabit, but one poised between the old for which she had been prepared, but which seemed to be dying, and the new for which she had not been prepared at all. Young, fresh and intelligent, all the patterns to which she had been trained to conform were fading, and she was already conscious just from chance or casual encounter of the gulf between herself and the person she would have been if she had never come back to India: the kind of person she 'really was'.

Reaching towards the table to replace her cup Barbie hesitated, completed the movement with conscious effort, to keep her hand steady, and then leant back in her chair. There had been a disturbance, another quick displacement of air, but this time a faint whiff of the malign breath, of the emanation. Alert, she watched the verandah and then the garden which was in sharp focus but seemed far away, hallucinatory, dependent on the human imagination rather than on nature for its existence, wide open to the destructive as well as creative energy of mind and will.

She heard herself say to Sarah, 'I have what I think nowadays you call a problem in logistics,' and then stopped, hearing as well a gentle exhalation which presently she decided must have been her own sigh of relief, of renewed patient anticipation.

'My little room,' she said, 'I mean of course my little room at Clarissa's. It has its limitations. Quite serious ones. And Clarissa has said there cannot be, apart from myself, more than another suitcase. Which leaves two items. Important to me but not to anyone else. To begin with there is the writing-table.'

She looked at Sarah who looked back at her without the concern and commitment suitable to the occasion. But then Sarah was still very young. She would not have learned as yet to understand the grave impediment to free movement which luggage represented in one's affairs.

'Well my writing-table,' she went on, 'in a way, yes, that can be managed because it folds. Like a wing. It is portable. It can stand against a wall, go under a bed. I think I can get my writing-table past Clarissa. And quite apart from a silly affection I have for it I also have use. I expect I shall conduct quite a heavy correspondence. And I can unfold it, sit on the bed and write without worrying whether Clarissa's room is put out of shape, because its shape can be quickly restored, but the trunk—'

She paused, collected her ideas.

'The trunk is a very different kettle of fish. Unlike a writing-table, unlike one's clothes, one's *shoes*, it is of no *use*. But it *is* my history. And according to Emerson without it, without *that*, I'm simply not explained. I am a mere body, sitting here. Without it, according to Emerson, *none* of us is explained because if it is my history then it is yours too and was Mabel's. But there is no room for my trunk at Clarissa's, no room for my explanation.' She grinned. Sarah's brow had become creased. Barbie could not blame the girl for being puzzled. The situation was very complicated and she was not sure she understood it herself.

'I had thought,' she continued. 'of asking permission to leave my trunk in care of the mali, until I can send for it. It could be put in the shed in the servants' quarters where the gardening implements are kept. But—'

'But what?'

'But if I asked permission of the person fully qualified to give it – asked permission of your mother – it would certainly be refused. Would honour be satisfied if I were to ask it of you?'

'I should think so.'

'If I asked should I obtain?'

'I'll look after your trunk, Barbie. It can stay in the room. Susan and I are going to share it but it can stay in my half.'

'That is kind. Very kind. But if you are to share the room with Susan you can't also share it with the trunk. Let the mali have it. Let him keep it in the shed. Then there should be the mininum of fuss for all of us. The alternative is Jalal-Ud-Din's. Clarissa has already mentioned it. But I should not be happy to think of my trunk in a heathen storeroom. The trunk is packed with relics of my work in the mission. It is my life in India. My shadow as you might say.'

Sarah nodded, readjusted the hold she had on her own arms, then said, 'You'll let me visit you at Clarissa's, won't you, Barbie?'

For several seconds Barbie did not reply. Then, 'It might be better if you didn't,' she said. 'At least not for a while. Not until I've found my feet. The room is too small to be a suitable place in which to receive guests and I am myself merely a guest, albeit a paying one. You may of course always visit Clarissa and anticipate seeing me as well but I do not want, as the saying is, to push my luck. I do not want to incur Clarissa's wrath by filling her house with wild and extravagant parties. I shall have to learn, have to learn, yes, to be as quiet as a mouse. Which won't be easy. Clarissa does not hold the key to imaginary silences. Shall you tell Aziz about the trunk now, Sarah? So that he can tell the mali? And it will be official?'

Sarah nodded and Barbie called the old man. When he came Sarah spoke to him. Presently he went away and returned with the mali and Sarah spoke to the mali too. When they had gone and Barbie had thanked her Sarah got up to go. The light was fading quickly.

'There is one thing else,' Barbie said. 'Mabel once told me that she had made provision for Aziz in his old age.'

'Yes, she did.'

'And it will be – respected?'

'Yes, Barbie.'

'Forgive me for mentioning it. I feared perhaps she may have meant to make provision, meant to remember him, but failed to put it into words.'

'No, she remembered Aziz. She remembered you too, Barbie.'

'What?'

'Only in a little way. A small annuity. To help out with the pension. You should hear from the bank in Ranpur soon. Although of course they always seem to take ages.'

'Yes, I see. She should not have.'

'Why not?'

'She should not have. It's taking it away from the rest of you. And I didn't expect anything. But it was very kind. Very kind.'

'Oh, Barbie, don't.'

'Kind,' Barbie repeated. 'So kind.'

She felt in her jacket pocket for the cologne-scented handkerchief. She blew her nose.

'My mother,' she said – laughing – 'was always terribly impressed by the word annuity. She thought it a mark of true gentility. It's odd how these things come back to one. She would have been very proud. My daughter, she would have said, need never concern herself about money because she has her annuity.'

*

That evening before supper she sat on her bed and watched Aziz and the mali measure the trunk for its shroud of stitched gunny-sacking, which the mali said his wife would cut and help him to sew round it. Later, holding a lantern, she followed the *cortège* round to the mali's shed and saw the covered object stowed in one cleared corner. As she left, holding the lantern high, she heard the clink of the spades and forks as the mali carefully replaced them.

*

On the morning of the day she left Rose Cottage she woke early, before Aziz brought the pot of tea, the banana, the thin slice of bread and butter which usually made up her chota hazri. The previous night she had drawn back the curtains in order to be able to distinguish between a clear morning and a grey one. It was scarcely light but she could hear the whisper of fine steady rain. She rose and walked bare-foot to confirm it and saw the hunched blanketed figure of the chaukidar who at night guarded Rose Cottage and the next bungalow down the road, patrolling between the two but usually to be found asleep on their own front verandah. The rain was dripping from the verandah roof but there was a lightness in the shadows of the garden that indicated a clear, perhaps sunny, morning later.

She turned back into the room, gazed at the rush mat and then impulsively knelt to say a morning prayer. The prayer turned out to be as full of information as requests. Thank You for Your many blessings and for the years of Rose Cottage. Please guard this room where my two girls are to sleep and admit to Your kingdom the troubled soul of my friend Mabel Layton. I have left my trunk in the shed. I am going to Clarissa's. It is not far.

Rising she inspected the roses gathered yesterday. She had meant to cut many more but a further and final visit from Sarah had interrupted her, put her off her stroke. Seeing the girl crossing the lawn in the late afternoon she feared she had come to cancel the arrangement about the trunk. But she had not.

Barbie had kept the roses in her bedroom all night; young buds, because she had wanted them to begin to unfold and absorb the substance of her dreams and waking meditations, so that they could express upon the grave a special love and particular gratitude. Leaning close to them now it seemed to her that they had absorbed little, perhaps nothing; that each bud was merely a convoluted statement about itself and about the austerity of the vegetable kingdom which was content with the rhythm of the seasons and did not aspire beyond the natural flow of its sap and the firm grip of its root. The bushes from which these roses came had been of English stock but they had travelled well and accepted what was offered. They had not wished to adapt the soil or put a veil across the heat of the sun or spread the rainfall more evenly throughout the year. They had flourished.

'You are now native roses,' she said to them. 'Of the country. The garden is a native garden. We are only visitors. That has been our mistake. That is why God has not followed us here.'

Like a departing guest she opened the drawers in dressing-table and chest just enough to show that they had been dealt with and were empty. For a similar reason she opened the almirah, took out her travelling costume and left the door ajar. After she had bathed she found the chota hazri tray on the bedside table. She sat in her underwear and dressing-gown and sipped and munched, kept glancing at her watch, already alert for the sound of the taxi which Mr Maybrick had guaranteed to send up not later than eight o'clock. She had told Aziz that she would not wait to eat a proper breakfast.

At a quarter to the hour she began her final preparations. At five to she called Aziz. Between them they upended the writing-table which she had locked the night before and folded the legs in. He carried it into the hall and came back for the suitcase. He brought newspaper in which to wrap the roses; and then gave her a key.

'What is this, Aziz?'

He told her he had found it on the floor, that it must be the key to her trunk. She recognized it now. She put it in her handbag and then sat alone until she heard the car arrive.

The rain had stopped. Outside, below the verandah, the other servants stood. She had tipped them all the night before for the last time. Now she shook hands with the mali and his wife, ruffled the boy's hair, smiled at the sweeper girl who kept in the background. Last in the line was Aziz. He had on his fur cap and carried a shawl over one shoulder, ready for his own journey.

'Good-bye, Aziz.'

'Good-bye, Barbie Mem.'

'Have you far to go?'

He indicated a direction, his arm straight and stiff, the hand open, pointing vaguely towards a mountainous distance. A day's journey. Two days'. More than that? She did not know. The name of his village and district written for her in uneven block capitals on a scrap of paper had meant nothing to her. One day she would borrow a large-scape map of the area and search for the name among the contours that showed the greatest heights.

'God be with you,' she said.

'And with you,' he answered. Briefly their hands met and clasped; and then she entered the taxi whose door was held open by the mali's boy.

IV

On the first Sunday after Barbie's arrival at the rectory bungalow Arthur Peplow conducted the morning service as one of thanksgiving for the defeat of the Japanese attempt to invade India at Imphal, for the news that the last Japanese soldier had been driven from Indian soil, and for the continuing good reports from France of the allied offensive against the Germans. Having announced that this should be their theme in all their hymns and prayers he said that they would begin with a rather more intimate kind of thanksgiving. He moved towards the front pew where Susan sat with her sister and mother.

'Forasmuch as it hath pleased Almighty God of His goodness to give safe deliverance to this our sister, and hath preserved her in the great danger of childbirth, We shall give hearty thanks unto God and say: Except the Lord build the house: their labour is but lost that build it. Except the Lord keep the city: the watchman waketh but in vain.'

As if blissfully unaware that several members of the congregation (the

Smalleys for instance) raised their eyebrows at his inclusion of the form for the churching of women in a service attended by Other Ranks and young and impressionable officers, he announced hymn number 358; and it may have been that towards the back of the church where a group of young British soldiers on church parade got noisily to their feet, one of them glanced at the elderly woman next to him, on the other side of a pillar that rose between pews, alerted by a strangled sound such as might be caused by a sudden constriction of the throat. If so he must then have been reassured. No incident was reported. And the service got off to a rousing start with Bishop Heber's missionary hymn: From Greenland's icy mountains: which everyone knew and could sing happily without bothering much about the words.

The hymn chosen to close the service was Onward Christian Soldiers. People felt that Arthur Peplow had done the station proud.

Outside, shading her eyes from a splendid burst of Sunday sunshine, Nicky Paynton said that there was nothing so cheerful as a good rollicking morning at church. It set you up for the day. Ahead lay an equally cheerful session in the club bar and a luncheon there of Madras curry guaranteed to bring cleansing tears to the eyes and an overall feeling of well-being. In the evening Clara and Nicky were dining with the Trehearnes. They asked if they could stop in on the way and see the baby. Mildred assented. Kevin and Dicky were dining at the grace and favour. They could all have a drink together before Clara and Nicky went on to Maisie's.

'The baby will be asleep,' Susan warned them. 'I shouldn't want him woken. He falls asleep as soon as he's had his six o'clock bottle. It's his best time.' She plucked at her mother's sleeve. 'We ought to be getting back. Has Mahmoud brought the flowers?'

'I'll check,' Dicky Beauvais said and walked off briskly down the path through the lingering groups of worshippers.

'We sent Mahmoud up to the cottage,' Mildred explained, 'to get some roses for Susan.'

'For Aunty Mabel's grave,' Susan said. 'Because I missed the funeral.'

Dicky was coming back, selfconscious with a large bunch of roses. Presumably Mahmoud had been waiting outside the churchyard gate. Susan went to meet him. She looked slim and pretty and very young. Dicky took her round the side of the church to place her offering on the grave Arthur Peplow had chosen for Mabel's resting place: a secluded spot. It was plucky of Susan to come to church so soon after her return from the nursing home, Clara Fosdick said; and thoughtful of her to arrange for the flowers.

'But she's anxious to get home now,' Mildred said. 'Minnie's not been in sole charge before. But it seemed wise to start as one means to go on. Minnie's quite capable of making sure the brat comes to no damage even if she's hamfisted with the paraphernalia. And Panther's taken a shine to him. He growls if old Mahmoud goes near. He knows the ghastly thing belongs to Su. He doesn't mind Dicky taking a peep because Dicky brought them home. But he took an unpleasant interest in poor Kevin's ankles last night, didn't he Kevin?'

'One can protect ankles. Throat's what you have to watch out for.'

Susan and Dicky came back but were detained within earshot by Lucy and Tusker Smalley.

'Lots of congratulations, Susan,' Lucy said. Tusker added, 'Rather.'

'Thank you. And thank you for the lovely flowers you sent. I'm afraid I haven't yet written to everybody.'

Lucy said, 'I hear you're calling the baby Teddie.'

'No, not Teddie. Edward. It's very important to get it right. I've got not to care for nicknames and diminutives for men.'

She glanced at Lucy's husband. 'Why do they call you Tusker, Major Smalley?'

Smalley indicated his regimental insignia, the Mahwars: a bull-elephant from whose back, howdah-like, sprang a tuft of toddy-palm.

'Mahwars. Tuskers, regimental nickname.'

'Yes, I know that. But why do they call *you* Tusker?'

'Bit of a long story.' Tusker looked modest but pleased.

' – after all,' Susan continued as if he had not said anything, 'we never called my husband Muzzy Bingham. Nor daddy old Pankot Layton.'

There was a pause. A breeze riffled the skirts of the women's dresses.

'Which regiment will you want little Edward to belong to?' Lucy Smalley asked. 'That will be quite a decision, won't it? Between the Pankots and the Muzzys. You'd have to be making it now if you could put a boy down for a regiment like you have to for a school.'

Mrs Smalley's voice drifted away, caught by the tail of the breeze and chased by the stronger following gust that whipped through the church-yard and prompted Susan into action. She appeared almost to be spun round by it, so that no one could have said that she turned her back on the Smalleys nor that she pushed through the group headed by her mother, but there was what amounted to a convulsive movement, a rearrangement of positions, a making way for her whch was ended abruptly by her touching her sister's elbow as if finding base and going off then slightly ahead of her, down the path at a pace quick enough for Dicky to have to start off rather fast and lengthen his stride to catch up with them.

'The children are having tiffin at home,' Mildred said, 'and they have their own tongas.'

'Is Susan all right?' Nicky Paynton asked.

'Susan is fine.'

She anchored the group round her by not budging until the Smalleys approached. And then, turning her back, snubbed them as if so far as she was concerned Susan had been perfectly behaved until they managed to upset her; Lucy by mentioning Teddie's name and Tusker by saying the word regiment which was the very thing Teddie had died for; and then slowly led the way down the path between the ancient gravestones: a woman making a point, one that was less well defined than it was felt – the point, perhaps, that if Susan's behaviour could be seen as a further demonstration of how time was running out for people like Mildred then anything like a scramble was vulgar, too tiresome to consider let alone join.

*

The next time Mildred walked along that path would be for the christening, the admission as a lively member of holy church of little Edward Arthur David; and that would bring to a formal close a difficult phase of the responsibility she had shouldered during her husband's absence. From things she said it was gathered that there could be no question of Susan marrying Dicky Beauvais or anyone until John Layton came home. The implication was that the same must apply to Sarah. One dead and never-seen son-in-law, one live grandson, and two still healthy daughters were sufficient evidence of life having gone on for Colonel Layton to come back to and not feel that things had fallen apart for want of a firm hand. Now Mildred was digging her heels in. She would not be rushed again. She had been rushed once and the result had been pretty disastrous or nearly so. Real disaster had been averted by Susan not letting the baby die on her or herself die on the baby.

According to Nicky Paynton, Mildred's off-hand manner towards the child, her use of a word like brat, did not disguise the fact that she was bucked at the prospect of having a grandson to hand over to Colonel Layton when he resumed his position as head of the family. The boy was half a Layton. John must have often regretted having no son of his own to bear his name, though he had been proud and fond of both his daughters. And he had been pleased about the marriage, quite taken, so Mildred said, by Teddie's photograph. How stoically he received news of Teddie's death wasn't known. His letters took a long time to reach Pankot and there was proof of letters going astray in both directions. It was possible that he would get the news of the child's birth and not know that his son-in-law was dead. It was possible that he was ignorant of both events. They had heard nothing for some time and with the opening of the second front they perhaps had to be prepared for a period of silence and uncertainty.

But they were inured to both and Mildred without dropping her characteristic guard infected her friends with a spirit of optimism. The christening party to be held at the grace and favour after a quiet family ceremony at St John's promised to be a jolly affair, rather like a picnic amid (Mildred warned) the packing crates that were already being filled as the process of separating Layton private possessions from stuff belonging to the army and public works department got under way.

When it was all over there would be little left to delay the move up to Rose Cottage. The christening party had its valedictory aspect. In spite of all its drawbacks the grace and favour bungalow had served its turn and deserved a good send-off. The accommodations officer was already nagging for possession so that he could turn the bungalow into a chummery for officers of the new emergency intake and relieve pressure elsewhere. From being full of women it would become (Mildred said) 'full of chaps' and presumably they wouldn't object so much to being woken at the crack of dawn by bugles opposite or, if they did, would have less cause.

And (at the club during midweek) Mildred smiled, directed the bearer's attention to her glass and said, 'Although I'm afraid Edward's going to be even more effective than a bugle. He seems to have an instinct for getting everybody on parade at six a.m. prompt. Doesn't he, Su?'

'Most children wake at six,' Susan said. 'I used to wake at six at Aunt Lydia's in Bayswater and at great-grandpa's in Surrey. They never had bugles.'

'But then you're Army,' Nicky Paynton said.

'Yes,' Susan said. She sat very upright on a club chair watching the clock and everybody who came in and went out. She had not been inside the club for months, not since she had begun, as she put it, to 'show' and took to smocks. This morning her mother had persuaded her to put in an appearance, to take up the reins of a proper routine.

'Relax, darling,' Mildred said. 'You simply must learn to trust Minnie. And you ought to change your mind and have a drink, even if it's only a nimbo.'

'All right.'

The bearer brought her a nimbopani. She sat holding the tumbler in both hands and used both hands to raise it to her lips. 'Are you cold?' her mother asked. It had been raining hard all morning and the temperature had dropped. No, Susan said, she wasn't cold.

'I thought you shivered,' Mildred went on. 'I hope you're not sickening for something.' No, Susan said again. She was quite all right, she wasn't sickening for anything. She put the glass on the table and made an effort to take part in the conversation by giving her attention to the person speaking; but after a while her glance strayed to the clock again and to the people coming in and going out and back to the clock and then to her wristwatch. She reached for the glass one-handed, lifted it and then lost her grip.

The glass fell, wetting her skirt and legs with the nimbo, and broke into sharp fragments on the floor at her feet. She stayed seated. There was a hush in the room, then talk was resumed. A sweeper was sent for. Clara Fosdick examined her stockings and pronounced them unladdered and only a bit damp. On the other hand Susan, she said, was soaked.

'Well,' Mildred said, 'that *was* clumsy of you, wasn't it? You'll have to change when you get home. Are you madly uncomfortable?'

'No, Mother.'

'Perhaps you'd better go to the cloakroom and mop up with a towel. Then come back and have another nimbo. There's loads of time.'

'I shan't want another nimbo.'

'Well go and dry off.'

'I'm more comfortable sitting still.'

The sweeper came with brush and pan. Mrs Fosdick, without getting up, shifted her chair and gave him room to get at all the splinters but Susan did not. She watched him sweeping gingerly round her feet. After he had gone Mildred ordered another drink but the conversation lagged and Susan had not looked up again. Irritably Mildred said:

'Darling, what on earth's the matter with you?'

'Nothing's the matter. I'm relaxing.'

She smiled and suddenly leant back with her arms folded. She asked Nicky Paynton whether she had heard recently from the two boys in Wiltshire. Nicky said she had. The elder was looking forward to being eighteen, finishing with school and joining the RAF of all things. 'But I expect we can talk him out of that,' she added, 'unless he's really set on it as an alternative career to the army and it's not just the temporary glamour of the boys in blue at home that's attracting him.'

'And what about the other?'

'Oh, it's the Ranpurs for him. But then he's still at the stage of thinking his father's the cat's whiskers.'

Susan had not stopped smiling but the others were aware of the avoidable subject having once more cropped up and conjured Teddie's shade. Again their conversation lagged and presently Mildred looked out of the window, finished her drink and said, 'It's stopped. We'd better get you home and out of that damp frock.'

'Yes, I should like to go home now, if you don't mind.'

But she waited until the others had got to their feet before rising herself. She walked, arms still folded, behind her mother and her mother's friends, past the pillars and the potted palms—

*

—and into her inner life, her melancholia; an inexplicable business, worse than that of Poppy Browning's daughter because that girl had had a certain justification for what she did: an unfaithful husband dead in the arms of his Indian mistress. But Susan's husband had died gallantly and tragic as the circumstances were then and later in the matter of the premature birth she was surrounded by love and devotion and the child was surely a lively reminder to her of this fact and of the duty she had to cherish him, show him at least as much affection as she herself had been shown.

And she had done so. Therefore the incident that occurred at the grace and favour bungalow on the afternoon of the day before the christening ceremony was even further beyond anyone's ability to understand than it would have been had she continued to show signs of rejecting the child. But the rejection had been of brief duration. Her subsequent concern for the child's welfare was both charming and touching; a bit exaggerated but no more so than the other traits and characteristics that went to make up the bright little personality in whom there had always seemed to reside a spirit of particular determination to do the right thing, but with style and youthful freshness; no doubt drawing attention to herself in the process but also to the purpose and condition of a life based upon a few simple but exacting ideas.

Now through a single action she shattered her own image as a child might destroy its own carefully constructed edifice of bricks. Indeed there was in her behaviour a disagreeable element of play, of wilful destruction of a likeness of the adult world she inhabited. At first her action was said to be one that had endangered the child's life but once the facts were known the idea of tragedy narrowly averted was replaced by a suspicion that if mockery had not been intended it had been accomplished; and this suspicion proved as strong as the pity felt for a girl in the grip of such a deep post-natal depression that there was little to distinguish it from madness.

But the word madness did not help. If she had gone off her head presumably she had done so because she found everything about her life unendurable. Meaningless. It did not help either to remember that she had not only fitted in but had been seen to fit in. She had tried. Trying should not have been necessary. Apparently it had been, for her; and suddenly she had stopped; not only stopped but symbolically wiped out all the years of effort by her extraordinary gesture.

On the afternoon of the day before the christening when her mother was at Rose Cottage supervising the measurement of new curtains, and Sarah had gone back to the daftar and so left Susan in sole command, she sent Mahmoud to the bazaar to buy some blue ribbon for the christening gown – Sarah's old gown which Mabel had kept in a trunk for years and only handed over a day or two before her death. She made Mahmoud take Panther whom she complained was getting fat and lazy through lack of exercise. Ten minutes after he had gone, dragging the reluctant dog, she called Minnie from her task of sorting sheets and pillow-cases for the dhobi and told her to run after him and tell him she wanted white ribbon, not blue.

So Minnie set off, but turned back. Questioned about that later she said that in spite of all the little offerings she had made since the little Memsahib became a widow, the bad spirits had not been appeased, they had not gone elsewhere, they still infested the bungalow and the compound, and this particular day – the day before the alien rite of christening – was especially inauspicious. And from certain things the little Memsahib had done – taking out the christening gown, smoothing it, holding it, talking to it; looking at the baby but not touching him as if afraid to – she believed the little Memsahib was also aware of the bad spirits. She had turned back at the gate partly because she was afraid of what might happen if she deserted her post and partly out of curiosity. She thought little Memsahib intended to make a special Christian puja of her own.

Although, like her uncle, Minnie professed the Muslim faith, the rigours of that austere religion lay lightly on the people of the Pankot hills.

Wayside shrines to the old tribal gods were still decorated with offerings of flowers and here and there in places believed to be inhabited by bhuts and demons – a tree, a crossroads – there might sometimes be found dishes of milk or clarified butter. For some time now in secret places of the grace and favour compound Minnie had prepared and kept replenished such tokens of appeasement. It would interest her to see how little Memsahib might go about a similar enterprise.

She returned to the bungalow but stayed hidden and was rewarded by the sight of Susan, seated now on the verandah, dressing the child in the lace gown, talking to it to reassure it and then – the dressing completed – continuing for a while without speaking and looking not at the child but straight ahead, so that Minnie assumed she was engaged in some kind of silent incantation.

And then quite abruptly Susan had risen and carried the child down the verandah steps and across the grass towards the bare brick wall that divided the garden from the servants' quarters. Minnie thought that perhaps there were a number of magic paces which mother and child had to take together and automatically she began to count. The alarm she might have felt when Susan suddenly stopped and placed the child on its back on the damp grass was momentarily stilled by the fascination exerted by the whole strange process, for there could be no doubt now that she was the spectator of a ritual which no other Indian had ever witnessed, otherwise she would have heard tales about it. When Susan walked away from the child, along the wall, towards the place where the wall ended, again Minnie counted the paces taken, and when she bent down, picked up a can and walked back, it was the whole action that exercised Minnie's imagination and not just the can, the reason for the can, which she recognized as one full of the kerosene Mahmoud found handy for lighting his bonfires of accumulated rubbish. Kerosene was oil. Was it holy oil to people like little Memsahib?

Susan's next action was the most fascinating of all. She walked round the child in a wide circle tipping the can as she went and sprinkling the oil. Then she put the can down near the wall, approached the circle again and knelt. With the can there must have been matches because she had a box in her hand and was striking one and throwing it on to the kerosene. Flame leapt and arced in two directions, tracing the circumference until the two fiery arms met at the other side, enclosing the sacrifice.

Minnie did not understand but she had stopped trying to work it out because she understood the one important thing. She understood fire. Crying out, she snatched a sheet from the dhobi's bundle and ran. The grass inside the circle was too wet for the flames to catch hold and spread towards the middle where the child gazed at the sky and worked its legs and arms. But Minnie did not understand that either. She acted instinctively, flung the sheet over the flames which were already turning blue and yellow, dying; and used the sheet as a path to reach the child. Picking it up she backed away calling out all the time to little Memsahib who continued kneeling and gazing at the centre of the ring of fire where the child had been. She seemed not to notice that the child was no longer there and that Minnie was crying out to her.

She was still there when Mahmoud got back from the bazaar and found Minnie on the verandah hugging the now crying child, not daring either to approach her mistress or let her out of her sight. She was still there when, summoned by Mahmoud, Mildred returned. She ignored all her mother's orders and entreaties to get up. When Travers arrived she ignored him too. She stayed where she was until Sarah, driven home by Dicky Beauvais, went out and talked to her. She let Sarah take her indoors and presently into the ambulance that Travers had called to take her back to the nursing home. In all this time she had looked at no one, spoken to no one, but smiled as if happy for the first time in her life.

*

In servants' quarters up and down the station the tale spread quickly. It reached the bazaar and the nearer villages that same night before the last fire had been damped down and the last light extinguished. The little Memsahib was touched by the special holiness of madness and her melancholy cries could be heard in the hills, scarcely distinguishable from the howling of the jackal packs that disturbed the dogs and set them barking. The sound could be heard all night but faded out as morning came leaving a profound, an ominous, silence and stillness that seemed to divide the races, brown-skinned from pale-skinned, and to mark every movement of the latter with a furtiveness of which they themselves were aware if their aloof preoccupied expressions were any guide.

Certainly an air of furtiveness hung over the ceremony of christening which Arthur Peplow at Mildred's insistence conducted as arranged at eleven o'clock in the forenoon, ushering the participants in and speaking to them in a whisper as though the ritual were forbidden and everyone of them a potential martyr, fearful of God but also of discovery. The child's feeble cries were a constant threat as were the nervous coughs, the scraped feet, Arthur's mumbling, their muttered responses.

There was no party afterwards. Mildred had cancelled it. How she managed to attend the ceremony was considered a marvel. Outside the church the Rankins, having done their duty as godparents, thoughtfully went back to Flagstaff House leaving Mildred to be taken home by Sarah and Dicky. To the innermost circle gathered for lunch, Isobel reported Mildred composed but uncommunicative except in one matter. 'What was that bloody woman doing in church?' she had asked, meaning the Batchelor woman who had been observed by all of them seated as far away from the font as it was possible to get, in the very front pew where she had never been seen to sit before; and on her knees praying as if her presence were going to make all the difference between a christening that 'took' and one that didn't.

'But I'm really not sure,' Isobel said, 'that Mildred hasn't become over-obsessed by Miss Batchelor.' Asked by Nicky Paynton just what she meant she showed some reluctance to answer. Things were bad enough, she said, bad for the station, without their being aggravated by criticism and gossip. But in the end she revealed that Clarissa Peplow who like Isobel herself had called at the grace and favour the previous night to see if there were anything to do to help had been forced by Mildred to take a box of teaspoons which the old missionary had given to Susan as a wedding present. Clarissa had tried to get out of it but Mildred became 'extremely agitated'. She swore that nothing had gone right since Susan received them and said she didn't want them in the house a moment longer. Clarissa could throw them away if she couldn't face giving them back but she must take them with her. All of which, Isobel said, suggested that Mildred had got it into her head that Miss Batchelor was a bad influence and to blame for everything.

In fact (Isobel went on to say) Mildred had come as near as dammit to accusing Barbara Batchelor of deliberately turning Mabel against her family. She said that if Mabel hadn't been cosseted and flattered by Miss Batchelor right from the start she would have got rid of the damned woman and moved into the spare and let Mildred and the girls take over the rest of the house and that if that had happened Susan would probably never have married Teddie Bingham who had been a decent enough chap but not the husband Susan deserved. He would probably never have risen above junior field rank. Pigging in at the grace and favour had distorted the girl's outlook, it had got on her nerves, completely unsettled her, until suddenly she had seen marriage as a way out, chosen Teddie without thinking properly and married him only to find herself back where she started, a grass-widow, then a widow, and then a mother with a fatherless child. And now God knew what was to happen to her.

'According to Travers, Susan hasn't spoken a word to anyone but just sits in the room they've given her staring out of the window and *smiling*,' Isobel ended.

It was this that seemed so appalling: to have done what she had done and yet to smile. But what had she done? The more one thought about it the more incomprehensible it became. Even the mechanics of the act – let alone the motive – were meaningless until one of the men, Dick Rankin himself, said it reminded him of the kind of thing kids did to scorpions to watch them sting themselves to death rather than be burnt alive. 'It's not true, though,' Rankin pointed out, 'if you pop a scorpion into the middle of a ring of fire it arches its tail and looks as if it's stinging itself to death but it's only a reflex defensive action. The blighters scorch to death because in spite of what they look like they've got very tender skins which is why they mostly come out in the wet weather. In the hot dry weather they hide under stones.'

But God knew why the girl should use the child as a kid might a scorpion. She must be completely off her rocker. Perhaps in her deranged state she had been trying to re-enact the circumstances of Teddie's death, which had been by fire. But why the carefully described circle? When you looked at it logically the child had never been in danger except of catching a chill which the little ayah had taken the first opportunity to ensure he didn't, by bathing and wrapping him up warmly.

'Well,' Rankin summed up. 'I suppose the psychiatrists will make something of it. You can't apply ordinary logic in a case like this. But it's damned embarrassing for the station.'

And back you came to the smile and through the smile to the uncomfortable feeling that Susan had made a statement about her life that somehow managed to be a statement about your own: a statement which reduced you – now that Dick Rankin had had his say – to the size of an insect; an insect entirely surrounded by the destructive element, so that twist, turn, attack, or defend yourself as you might you were doomed; not by the forces ranged against you but by the terrible inadequacy of your own armour. And if for armour you read conduct, ideas, principles, the code by which you lived, then the sense to be read into Susan's otherwise meaningless little charade was to say the least of it thought-provoking.

V

'I am sorry, Barbara,' Clarissa said, having given her the spoons. 'I know it was wrong of her. They were not her spoons to return. But I had no choice and have none now. Dearly as I should have liked to refuse, I felt I could not. Dearly as I should like to hide them and forget them, I cannot. I hope you will take the exceptional circumstances into consideration and forgive her.'

'Blessed are the insulted and the shat upon,' Barbie said. 'For they shall inherit the kingdom of Heaven, which is currently under offer with vacant possession.'

'What did you say?'

Barbie did not repeat it. She said, 'Forgive me. The circumstances are indeed exceptional. I am not myself. Mildred is not herself. Thou are not changed and God is not mocked.'

Clarissa's mouth hung open. She clutched the rosary of the afternoon sandalwood beads. Barbie put the box of spoons by her side on the bed. With Clarissa in the room there was scarcely sufficient space for the two of them to stand. From the bed she could see the old people concealed behind the curtain in the angle of the wall.

'I had a letter from the bank in Ranpur this morning, Clarissa. The annuity Mabel has left me will amount to one hundred and fifty pounds a year. It will take some time for the first quarterly payment to reach me because it all has to be done in London. But it is considerable additional security. It means I can afford to pay you more for my board and lodging.'

'For a temporary arrangement I am adequately repaid,' Clarissa said. 'Your suggestion is generous but I cannot accept it.'

'I had another letter too, Clarissa.' She opened her handbag, got out the letter and gave it to Clarissa. It read: 'Dear Miss Batchelor, Mr Studholme in Calcutta passed your letter to me because he himself had no suggestion to make in regard to employment in the Mission on a voluntary basis. But he asks me to tell you to write to him again if the matter of accommodation remains unsettled at the end of the year. He says that he has no immediate solution to offer because during the past five years there have naturally been other retirements and the continuing difficulty of arranging passages home has led to more demand for places in Darjeeling and Naini Tal than there is a supply. However the main reason for his passing your letter to me was the possibility he thought there might be of our having a suggestion to make at this end both about accommodation and employment. Unfortunately we have none. I hope that you will soon find somewhere suitable to live. It is very kind of Mr and Mrs Peplow to take you in meanwhile. I trust you are well. Yours sincerely, Helen Jolley.'

Clarissa gave her the letter back, said nothing and began clacking her beads.

'I called at Smith's Hotel after the christening this morning,' Barbie continued. 'Because the annuity means I might have afforded their price for a while. But they have no vacancies and the accommodations officer has what the manager calls a lien on any room that falls vacant.'

Clarissa released the beads and turned to go.

'What news is there of Susan?' Barbie asked, not wanting her to.

'There is no news. She looks out of a window and smiles.'

'Smiles?'

'Smiles.'

'Why then she is happy.'

'Happy? How can she be happy when she is out of her mind?'

'Perhaps she has entered it,' Barbie said and then raised her voice because Clarissa had gone. 'Perhaps that's why she's happy and why she smiles.'

She lifted the lid of the box and stared at the twelve rigid identical apostles. One of them, Thomas, was said to have reached India and to have preached near Madras at San Thome which was named after him. Which spoon was Thomas? She wondered what she would make of them and they of her if they were suddenly made manifest and stood before her, laughing and lusty; simple hard-working men, good with nets and boats, swarthy-skinned, smelling of sweat, of fish, of the timber-yard; men who worked with their hands, most of them. 'You'd get short shrift in Pankot,' she said. 'I wouldn't give tuppence for your chances, least of all if you tried to get into that place where the silver is and asked permission to sit at that table and break your bread and drink your wine.'

She began to shut the lid but stopped, held by the picture she had just conjured of the apostles in the mess and by the fact that the spoons were silver, solid silver. They had cost, in her terms, a lot of money and had been given with pride as well as love. She realized that Susan had probably looked at them once, written her thank-you letter and forgotten them, making it easy for Mildred to ensure that they were left out of the display of presents. She did not blame Susan but she could never offer them to her again, she would never be able to say to the girl, Your mother sent these back, don't you want them? It would be for Mildred to tell her should she think of asking where they were. It would be for Mildred to tell the truth or to lie.

She did not want to keep them herself but they were too good to throw away. She could hardly offer them to Clarissa. The home they must find should at least be appropriate and she believed she had hit upon the most appropriate of all.

She shut the box, dragged the writing-table from its place against the wall, unfolded the legs and set it up by the bedside. Having unlocked the drawer she took out some crisp blue writing paper and matching envelopes which were lined with sky-blue tissue.

Dear Colonel Trehearne,
I am sending today *via* the adjutant a small gift of silver teaspoons which I should like to present to the Regiment for use in the Officers' Mess, in memory of the late Mrs Mabel Layton. I hope that this small gift will be acceptable to the regiment.

Yours Sincerely,
Barbara Batchelor.

Dear Captain Coley,
I have written today to Colonel Trehearne to say that I am delivering to you this box of silver spoons which I am presenting in memory of the late Mrs Mabel Layton for use in the Officers' Mess.

Yours Sincerely,
Barbara Batchelor.

Before sealing the letters she considered carefully whether she should bother with Coley. She could deliver the spoons direct to Commandant's House without involving him; but she wanted to involve him because she wanted Mildred to know where the spoons were going before they actually got there and she was sure that Coley would tell her and that if he did she would try to make him send them back. And this he would be unable to do if he knew about the separate official letter already on its way to Colonel Trehearne. He would have no alternative but to pass the spoons on. She believed that even Mildred would be afraid to arrange for them to be lost in transit and would shy away from asking Trehearne to be so ungallant as to decline them.

In the hall she checked the address of Commandant's House in Clarissa's directory. She looked for Coley's too but could not find it. There was a telephone number with the words 'Adjs, Office' written in beside it. She would have to go to the Pankot lines and inquire. Back in her room she sealed the letters and addressed Trehearne's and at half-past two set out stoutly shod, macintosh over her shoulder, stick in one hand, the box of spoons and the two letters in the other.

In the bazaar which she could reach within ten minutes of leaving the rectory bungalow she bought stamps and posted the letter to Colonel Trehearne. As the letter disappeared into the box she thought: No going back now! Nothing for it now! March! To the barricades! She strode facing the oncoming traffic which seemed uncommonly heavy but with next to nothing going in her own direction so that she began to feel like someone moving against the flow of columns of refugees. The shouting tonga-wallahs, the bobbing head-load carriers, the gliding cyclists and the lurching soldiers in the open backs of uncovered trucks and lorries might have been calling: Wrong way! Wrong way! The notion exhilarated her. For the first time since leaving Rose Cottage she felt strong and free because the intense vulgarity of Mildred's gesture in returning the spoons had released in her a vulgarity just as intense but of greater splendour. I, Barbara Batchelor, she declaimed, daughter of Leonard and Lucy Batchelor, late of Lucknow Road, Camberwell, am about to present silver to the officers of the Pankot Rifles. And as my father used to say, storming out into the night or into the morning, bugger the lot of you.

Half way down Cantonment Approach road she transferred the remaining letter and the box of spoons to her macintosh pocket because her palms were sweating in the humid afternoon. The cloud level was low. There was no rain as yet but the light was strange: bright under a dark sky and then dark under a bright one as if there were a single band of luminosity which bounced, throbbing, between earth and heaven. She did not mind if it rained. She had her sou'wester in the other pocket of her mac. The umbrella, her mother used to say, take the umbrella. Horrid umbrella. Black cotton cave. Dead bat. God is weeping for the sins of the world, her mother said. Laughing, you mean, her father replied, laughing fit to bust. But rain was only rain: sea sucked up and sprayed on the parched land by the giant elephant, the elephant god.

She paused opposite the main entrance to the grounds of the general hospital. The nursing-home wing was hidden from view by trees and the lie of the land. She walked on attended by a faceless wraith whose Susan-pale arms opened the way for her, parting misty curtains, one after the other, as if insisting on a direction, an ultimate objective, a sublime revelation at the end of a tricky and obscure path.

The light became apocalyptic. Puddles in the road shone white reflecting a purity whose source was not visible. The landscape was now bleak, the ground on either side of the road waste: areas of windshorn turf broken by rifts and channels. The last refugee had gone by and she was alone, resolute in alien territory, entering Rifle Range road that ran straight full-tilt across the valley towards the hills. Suddenly, as if they had cracked under their own weight, there came a report and then another before the echo of the first had spent itself; and yet another, as many as a dozen. The air shifted under the duress of a wind of panic from the hills and the first drops of rain began to fall. The panic did not touch her but the rain would. She put on her macintosh and sou'wester, patted the pocket where the box of spoons nestled, and strode on past the entrance to grace and favour lane with scarcely more than a glance in the direction of the bungalow to make sure it was still there. Presently she turned into Mess road. It was the day of the wedding party. We could go to Ranpur, Barbie had said, to do some Christmas shopping. Oh, I shall never go to Ranpur again, Mabel had answered, at least not until I'm buried. But on that day it was sunny. Coming from the shade of the portico into the glare the white of the servants' uniforms dazzled the eye and the emerald leaves of glistening plants in terracotta pots shone like scimitars and cast razor sharp indigo blue shadows. Is it you, is it you, Ghulam Mohammed? Mabel said. And Barbie knew for whom she might ask. She walked into the mess compound. The pebbles in the path gleamed in the rain. Ahead, level with the entrance, there was a parked military truck and as she gained the shelter of the long portico a group of young officers came out laughing and began to climb up over the tailboard while one stood smoking and calling to the absent driver.

Turning, he saw her, and two of the other three now settling in the back of the truck and slapping wood and metal with boisterous good-natured impatience saw her too. She filled her old schoolmarm's lungs, grated her Memsahib's voice into gear, and called: 'Good afternoon. Can one of you help me?'

Close to them she noticed that their faces were tight and youthful. Their single subaltern's pips looked painfully new. None of them could have been at the party eight months before. She guessed the thought stiffening their necks and minds: Careful – You never know who she is.

'Do you know if Captain Coley is in the mess?'

'Coley? The adjutant? No, I don't think he is.'

The officer who had been shouting for the driver glanced at the three in the truck who shook their heads. One of them said, 'He wasn't in the daftar this morning.'

'Oh, dear. How dreadfully inconvenient.' She smiled, mimicking the bright brassy manner of women like Nicky Paynton and Isobel Rankin which she had noted tended to make men put themselves out and do things without actually being ordered to.

'I'll ask,' the young officer said and began to go inside but remembered his manners in time and invited her to precede him into the building. Inside, his newness and uncertainty were even more apparent. There was no one about and he seemed unsure what to do next. Barbie said, 'It's my own fault. I ought to have rung. But I was coming this way and thought I'd kill two birds with one stone. The trouble is I've never visited him in his quarters and have no idea where he hides out. Have you?'

'No, I'm afraid I haven't.'

She got it then: the unmistakable London accent. It came out in the word afraid. It warmed her heart. So did the rather over-greased black hair, the stubby plebeian but not unhandsome features beneath it. As a soldier he must be confident and efficient otherwise the regiment would not have accepted him even at this stage of the war when regiments were taking the best they could get, which she had heard was very good, but having to close their eyes to social shortcomings. As a gentleman he obviously fell short of the Pankots' traditional requirements, and knew it, was far from happy in this silent mausoleum.

'The fact is we only got here from OTS last week,' he said. A bearer crossed the hall, carrying a tray. The subaltern stopped him and asked in inaccurate Urdu whether Captain Coley was in the mess. He didn't understand the bearer's reply but Barbie did. Captain Coley would not be in mess until after the week-end. She asked the servant if he knew where Captain Coley lived because she wished to see him quite urgently. He gave her directions but they were very muddled and she did not understand the references. She said, 'Is Ghulam Mohammed here?'

The bearer said he did not know Ghulam Mohammed. There was no Ghulam Mohammed in the mess.

She asked him how long he had worked in the mess, and the answer was disturbing. Since last November.

'Ghulam Mohammed was here then,' she insisted.

No, he had never worked with a Ghulam Mohammed. If Memsahib wished he would ask the head steward.

'It doesn't matter.' She turned to go. The officer followed her. He probably hadn't understood a word. She was glad. Her hold on things had begun to be undermined.

All the same he grasped the situation. 'No luck?'

'No, none. But I think I'll be able to find it.'

'The driver will know, won't he?'

'Oh, I'd forgotten the driver. How clever of you. The driver's bound to know.'

When they got outside, the driver had turned up and was waiting by the cab door. Asked if he knew where the adjutant sahib lived he said nothing but inclined his head to one side and kept on doing so in answer to every one of her questions.

'He knows?'

'He knows.'

'Can we take you?'

'How kind. But shan't I be making you late for a parade?'

'It's only the munshi.' He led the way round to the passenger seat, warned her about the height of the step.

'Adjutant Sahib bungalow,' he told the driver after he had slammed the door shut for her. A few seconds later he knocked on the back of the cabin and shouted, 'OK.' As the truck engine started she thought she heard men's laughter. She smiled. The cabin smelt of petrol and other peculiar metallic odours. The truck, one of the snub-nosed variety, gave her the feeling of riding in a tank. It bucked and growled. The windscreen wipers swung like metronomes but squeaked on the glass. She expected it was against the rules for a civilian to ride in it. She wished she had insisted on getting into the back. She would have liked to gossip to the young officers and to have found out where they all came from and what they thought of India. Were they the kind of young men Sarah had met at her aunt's and uncle's in Calcutta? If you're ever stationed in Cal, she might say, watch out for a man called Colonel Grace, he'll be after you to sign on for *ever*.

She glanced at the driver. Thin cheeks. Hawk's nose. And a skin so sunburnt that the usual Pankot copper-colour was, in this light, blue-sheened. There were minute red veins in the whites of his eyes. She was startled by the clarity of her vision. He smelt powerfully of garlic. His khaki was immaculately starched and pressed. His marbled brown legs were covered by fine dark hairs above and below the knee, between the tops of the socks and the hem of the knife-edged shorts. Tucked above the windscreen was a faded postcard, a photograph of a chubby wide-eyed smiling beauty with a caste-mark between her thick eyebrows; an Indian film star, she supposed. She imagined a smell of jasmine, a thin nasal voice. How remote his life from her own. But he could have come from the same village as Aziz, or Ghulam Mohammed.

She had never asked Mabel who Ghulam Mohammed was. Now he had gone, like Poppy Browning's daughter, like Gillian Waller, with Mabel to the grave, the one that should not have been dug: crying out soundlessly like the unknown Indian on the road from Dibrapur and the girl in white whom she imagined running in the dark from a martyrdom, or from something unimaginable, which might even have been love. She thought: Perhaps I should have given the spoons to the old woman in the veiled topee, have waited in St John's for her to arrive, and kneel or sit staring at the altar unconsciously sharing my vigil, and called to her softly: These are for the child. And given her the twelve little apostles. But perhaps she isn't in Pankot any longer. Perhaps she was never here. In any case it's too late. I'm presenting the spoons to the mess.

She clapped her hand against her pocket. Yes, the box was still there. She gazed out of the streaming windows. The speed of the truck made the rain seem heavier. All this area of Pankot was new and strange to her. It looked unwelcoming. Rows of huts, squat and dark, parade grounds, basket-ball pitches. Distantly, clutches of figures silhouetted against the white light running for cover. It was very hot in the cabin. The window in the door on her side was misting up.

At a cross-roads marked by military signposts the driver turned left. This road after a while became tree-lined. They were going past bungalows up a slight incline and then down into a dip at the bottom of which the driver stopped. There was no bungalow visible, only a dirt track leading off to the left through a kind of copse.

'Adjutant Sahib,' the driver said and pointed at the track. She noticed a square white board on a short post aslant in the hedge, but could not read it.

The young officer appeared and opened the door. 'Is it far up the track, do you think?' he asked. 'The truck could get up there. It's muddy to walk.'

'Oh I don't mind. Not in the least. I'm dressed for it.'

'What about when you leave? I've not been this end before. Do you know where you are?'

She asked the driver how far she would have to walk to get a tonga. He indicated ahead and said half-a-mile. She thanked him and got out. She put her sou'wester back on but did not bother to tie the strings under her chin.

'It's been very good of you. I hope I haven't made you late for the munshi.' She offered her hand. Before shaking it he took off his cap. She could hear the others talking. 'My name's Barbara Batchelor, incidentally. At present I'm staying with the Peplows, that's at the rectory bungalow next to St John's church. Arthur Peplow's always glad to see new faces. People sometimes look in for a beer after Sunday morning service, before going up to the club. So don't forget. And good luck to you all, if I don't see you again. Don't get wet. I'm all right. Well protected.'

She went and stood at the end of the dirt track. The door slammed. She waved, watched the truck turn in the road and waved to the men in the back when a full view of them was presented by the truck's manoeuvres. When it had gone out of sight she turned and studied the board.

A foot square, two feet off the ground, it had been painted white some time ago. The paint was peeled, the black letters had faded and the first letter had come off with its background. The notice read: apt. K. Coley. Under the name an arrow pointed up the track or would have done so had the board been straight. Its tilt directed the arrow downward into the mixture of gravel, pebbles, earth and mud and tyre-marks which made up the track's surface.

From the path there was nothing to be seen of the bungalow where Coley lived. It was an appropriate setting for a man whose military ambitions were said to have been smothered ten years before in the tumbled bricks and masonry of Quetta. One could imagine him choosing it for its isolation, its proximity to the lines and to the office he was content to occupy for the rest of his working life. He stirred himself, Barbie had heard, only when threatened by promotion and posting to another station. There was nothing he did not know about the running of the regimental depot. Successive commandants had connived at his schemes to stay put.

At the entrance to his hidden retreat Barbie felt a pang of remorse. She could never like Coley but the air of melancholy emanating from the faded tilted board and from the whole area persuaded her to make allowances, to forgive him for behaviour that perhaps had not been natural but forced on him by Mildred. Perhaps he had been afraid to resist her, fearing the power she potentially wielded. Mildred's husband – if he survived prison-camp – was Trehearne's likely successor as depot commandant. Or so Coley might anticipate. And presumably he had only a slender stock of pride. Most of it would have gone with his ambition. If acting the part of the dog at Mildred's heels secured his future, he would play it.

The track curved and came to an abrupt end: a corrugated iron shed, a garage. To the right a gateway without a gate opened on to steps of rough-hewn stone that led up into the copse.

She climbed the stone steps. What she entered was a compound planted with hedges, shrubs and bushes that had grown wild among trees. She identified rhododendron among other more exotic leaves and could see that the path had originally been laid out with an eye to withholding for as long as possible a view of the bungalow that lay at its end; so that the revelation of what was ordinary and ugly stunned her for an instant into acceptance of it as rare and beautiful. Walls, windows, roof, verandah – entirely commonplace, mean even – moved her with the austere poetry of their function. Here a man sheltered from and diminished the horror and vulgarity of the world by the simplicity of his arrangements for living in it.

The path had brought her within a few feet of the front verandah steps. The verandah was narrow. From where she stood she could see the padlock on the hasp of the closed doors. Eden was unoccupied. But perhaps round the back she would find a servant capable of being roused from mid-afternoon torpor. As she moved a gust of wind blew leaves upward. At the back of the bungalow she found a small grassed compound, a servant's hut, also closed and padlocked, and an open-sided byre in which a tethered goat was munching vegetable stalks.

The rain was still not heavy. She hesitated before climbing the steps to gain the temporary shelter of the back verandah, then went up stealthily, conscious of trespass during the occupier's and the servant's absence. This verandah was deeper than the one at the front and was furnished in the familiar way with wicker chairs and table. The windows were shuttered. There were no french windows; only plain narrow doors, also closed.

She prepared to wait for the rain to reach its peak and die out or settle into a persistent Pankot drizzle through which she could walk in search of a tonga without getting too wet. The darkness of the sky suggested a heavy fall. Already the air seemed thick with mutterings of storm and the distant warning murmur of tempestuous forces gathering in the hills to strike through the valley.

But after that single gust of wind no other came and the rain continued to fall modestly. Nothing in nature confirmed as real the restlessness in the surrounding air. She clenched her fist and put it against her chest; her heart was not pounding, but there was a pressure round about her, a pulsing. She turned and stared at the shuttered windows and then at the narrow doors which when not closed would be hooked back to the outside walls. The hooks hung loose. But the hasps were not in position. The doors were not locked. Cautiously she tried the handle on one of them. It opened without a sound and the screen of wire mesh yielded to a touch.

'Captain Coley?' she said, and cleared her throat, meaning to call again, more loudly, but the interior was dark and so hot it seemed to suck the breath out of her lungs and at the same time to whimper with relief like a creature deprived of liberty who sensed release. 'Captain Coley?' she repeated. The words came out unsteadily and made no impression on the creature's distant incoherent supplications, its scarcely audible gasps and cries. The mesh screen swung back; she was not aware of pushing it. 'Captain Coley?' she said again and something folded her in its sticky arms and drew her into the interior; not the creature but its keeper. It held her for a moment and then was not there and the illusion of hot darkness was splintered. Her flesh tightened, attacked by frosty particles of fear, the shuttered bungalow was filled with subterranean light and at its centre the creature was imprisoned in a room divided from the one she stood in by swing ornamental shutters that filled no more than the central space of the open doorway. It was like being back again in that chill corridor approaching other doors that gave a view through oval windows. She was drawn to them by the creature's moans and cries until she stood in a place where over the top of the shutters she saw in the gloom the creature herself, naked, contorted, entwined with another, gaunt and male and silently active in a human parody of divine creation.

It was not the stark revelation of the flesh that caused Barbie to gasp and cover her mouth for in her own body she guessed the casual ugliness that might attach to a surrender to sensuality. What filled her with horror was the instantaneous impression of the absence of love and tenderness: the emotional inertia and mechanical pumping of the man, the cries coming from the woman who seemed driven by despair rather than by longing, or even lust. It was as though the world outside the subterranean room was dying or extinct and the joyless coupling was a bitter hopeless expression of the will of the woman for the species to survive.

Turning, groping, Barbie regained the verandah, closed the door and leaned on it, head back, mouth open like a swimmer breaking surface; and then fearing she must have been heard made for the steps, stumbled in going down them and blundered round the side of the bungalow, terrified of discovery, of turning and seeing Mildred and Kevin Coley bearing down on her, naked, raw-eyed, determined on her destruction as the sole witness of their act of adultery.

She ran down the path and – misjudging the twists – was whipped by twigs and obstructed by branches. Going down the rough-hewn steps she misjudged again and wrenched her ankle, falling. Scrambling up she ran down the track. It seemed endless. When eventually she came out on to the lane she turned left into the unknown.

The ankle did not begin to hurt until, after walking for fifteen minutes without coming upon a landmark or a wider road that might lead her back to familiar surroundings, she stopped, knowing that something was wrong. She felt in her pocket – but the spoons and the letter were still there. The wrongness was in the other pocket. There was no sou'wester but it wasn't on her head either. Her hair was sopping wet. She turned, intending to go back to look for it but at that moment became aware both of the pain in her ankle and of the futility of such a search. The sou'wester must have been torn off her head by the overhanging branches in the garden. She could not remember that happening. But then she could not remember either whether she had taken the hat off on the verandah and left it on the table. Her name was written in indelible pencil on the white lining of the headband.

Limping, punishing the stick, she struck out again through what had become a downpour, not daring to stop and shelter in case her ankle seized up and she found herself unable to move, marooned in this inhospitable region.

Part Five

THE TENNIS COURT

I

Miss Batchelor was taken to the civil wing of the general hospital on the day Nicky Paynton heard that her husband had been killed in the Arakan.

For three days Clarissa had sent meals into Barbie's room, spoken to her from the doorway but otherwise kept clear in order not to be infected by the awful cold the old missionary had caught as a result of walking about in the rain, without a hat, getting lost, returning home like a drowned rat and then refusing all advice and offers of hot balsam.

But on the fourth morning, alarmed first by the sight of Barbie's flushed face and the fact that she opened her eyes but seemed unable to speak or rouse herself, and then by the feeling of hot dry skin under her own cool hand, Clarissa rang Doctor Travers who, after a brief examination, sent for an ambulance.

'How long has she been like this?' he asked while they waited. Clarissa confessed that she hadn't actually seen her since before lunch on the previous day when she thought she looked better but not as well as she insisted. 'I made her promise not to get up and she said she wouldn't. After that I was busy all day but the boy said she ate all her meals, except her supper. She was asleep when he took it in. She hasn't touched her night drink either.'

Travers said, 'I wish I'd known sooner. Actually it's risky moving her but I don't think we could save her here. I ought to warn you it's ten to one against her making it. She's got broncho-pneumonia and the heart's pretty weak. What on earth's the poor old thing been doing?'

Clarissa said she didn't know but described the state Barbie was in when she came back into the house on the afternoon of the day of the christening. They went back to the room and for a moment Clarissa thought Barbie had gone in the few minutes she and Doctor Travers had been talking in the hall.

He sat on the bed holding Barbie's wrist and then listening to her chest again through his stethoscope. 'I suppose she's quite alone in the world?' he asked presently.

'Until she came to Pankot she lived only for the Mission,' Clarissa said. 'She talks about getting back into harness but of course she's past it. I think

1003

it was the letter she had from them saying they wouldn't have her back that did it.'

Travers looked round, surprised because Clarissa Peplow's voice sounded very unsteady. He had always assumed her to be emotionally dehydrated.

'Will *you* have her back, Mrs Peplow? That is, if the question happens to arise?'

Clarissa nodded.

'I ask because it could be important. I mean if we get her over the pneumonia. People don't die only of diseases, you know.'

At that moment the telephone rang and thinking it might be the hospital warning him of a delay Travers got Clarissa's permission to answer it. It wasn't the hospital but Clara Fosdick, asking for Clarissa. She said she was glad to be speaking to him, however, because Nicky Paynton had had this telegram about poor Bunny being killed in action and Clara had already thought of ringing Colonel Beames to suggest that he should look in. Clara said she thought Nicky was taking it too well and being over-conscientious about not breaking down in front of people. Nicky and Bunny had absolutely adored each other and it was awful, Clara said, to see Nicky going about the house as if nothing had happened and even trying to get ready to go to the club to play bridge in order not to let Isobel and Maisie down, because with Mildred temporarily dropped out it was difficult to make up a four at short notice if, as she had last night, Isobel indicated that she had a free afternoon and wished to play.

'I'm not sure whether I should cancel it or not,' Clara said. 'I mean I know I should. In fact must. But she seems set on keeping her promise. She says Bunny would have understood.'

*

There was of course no bridge. But neither did Nicky Paynton ever break down in front of anyone. She adopted a manner that made her in the eyes of her friends curiously immune from their sympathy although not from their admiration. After sending a telegram to her friend Dora Lowndes in Wiltshire (who was married to the boys' housemaster and looked after them during the holidays) and then following the telegram up with a letter to the boys themselves, she continued her daily routine, not as though nothing had happened but as though it had and was over and wasn't to be mentioned because it concerned no one except herself and her sons.

Bunny's death, she implied, was entirely her private affair. Even from the start, although still referring to him and saying his name, she used the past tense, which made people feel he had been dead for years and that her widowhood had been the determining factor in her personality for a long time – the one everybody had missed noticing before and had to get used to quickly if they were to stand a chance of remaining on friendly terms with her.

Everybody agreed that it was an astonishing performance; the best ever put up in a society that prided itself on being able to do exactly what Nicky Paynton was doing if the need arose. That it was also a farewell performance was understood. It could only be a matter of time before Nicky announced that she was packing up and going home by the quickest means available, to be with her sons. No one else had any claim on her. With one stroke India was finished for her and although she would probably assure her friends that she'd be back, this was one of those crystal clear cases of a woman leaving and knowing that her chances of seeing India again were slim enough to be non-existent. She would never be able to afford the fare. If either boy eventually came out she might be tempted to scrape together enough to come and visit him and renew old acquaintanceships, but she would be foolish to do so. It would be unbearable.

Already you could see her looking at things as if trying to fix them sharply enough in her memory to carry away indelible impressions of them; and then beginning not to look at all because she was only making it worse for herself, knowing she was looking for the last time.

Nicky had had the worst kind of luck. If the children had been grown up or if there had been no children the decision to go home could have been postponed at least until the end of the war, even indefinitely. Perhaps – as in the case of her friend Clara Fosdick – the question would never have arisen. All her closest friends were in India. They would have rallied round as Clara's friends – Nicky and Bunny in particular – rallied round when Freddie Fosdick died of cancer in his own hospital back in '36, leaving no children but a wife rather younger than himself; although not young enough to have further expectations, even if she had had the inclination to marry again, which she had not. As it was between Nicky and Bunny so it had been between Clara and Freddie.

Clara knew that Nicky's loss affected her as much as anyone because the moment Nicky packed and went she herself would be homeless. The bungalow they shared was occupied officially by Nicky as the wife of Colonel Paynton of the Ranpurs. Clara was merely a paying guest. The obvious solution would be for her to go to live in Ranpur with her sister and brother-in-law, Mr Justice Spendlove, but she didn't care much for Billy Spendlove and her sister knew it and stuck up for him whenever she thought he was being criticized. They usually managed to quarrel during Clara's short visits.

And so, stoically but without being able to disguise her inner preoccupations, Clara waited for Nicky to make the inevitable announcement.

*

She made it at what was from Clara's point of view an unsuitable moment; at Rose Cottage and to the company assembled there as in the old days on a sunny Saturday morning.

Mildred's sister Fenny had come up from Calcutta to be at Mildred's side during Susan's illness and to help with the move to Rose Cottage; a move finally achieved a few days after Nicky received the telegram – if anything so piecemeal, so incomplete, could be reckoned an achievement. It was piecemeal because spread over several days and incomplete because Susan's things were in Miss Batchelor's old room along with Sarah's, and Susan's baby and the ayah were in the little spare; but there was no Susan. And Panther had escaped twice from Mahmoud's custody and twice been found outside Susan's old room at the temporarily empty grace and favour bungalow, his head resting on one of his two out-stretched forepaws, too far gone in his animal misery to keep up the whining and whimpering which in the first few days of Susan's absence had made Mildred lose her temper and say that the wretched creature would have to be put down.

After the second escape during which he seemed to have torn his hindquarters on what the vet thought was barbed wire Mildred ordered the dog to be tethered in the servants' quarters of Rose Cottage. He turned vicious. None of the servants dared approach. It was Sarah who risked being bitten, trying to calm and feed him and bathe his wound. She left water and a meaty bone within his reach. He did not touch them. It looked as though he intended to starve himself to death to prove his loyalty to Susan. His deterioration was frighteningly rapid. The tether became pointless. He hadn't the energy to stand. No longer capable of snapping and snarling he trembled when Sarah stroked his head. She fed him warm milk and brandy through a pipette given to her by the veterinary officer from the old Remount Depot, Lieutenant Firozeh Khan. Lt. Khan said that the kindest thing would be to have the dog destroyed. It hadn't acted like this when Susan was away having the baby. It was possible that the dog thought Susan had been taken away and the baby left in her place as a substitute. It might be dangerous to have it around.

'No,' Sarah said. 'That's pure imagination. Panther's got to be saved. Captain Samuels says Panther may be important to my sister when she's a bit better.'

Samuels was an RAMC psychiatrist attached to the military wing of the hospital. He hadn't been in India long and was used to dealing only with men, chiefly British other ranks. Mildred had already said she didn't see what good he could do since most of his work was confined to treating slackers who thought they had nervous breakdowns because they were deprived of fish and chips. Her friends agreed that perhaps there was something disagreeable about Susan being talked to, questioned, by a man; particularly by a man like Samuels who might be considered clever at home where psycho-analysis was fashionable, but who was after all a Jew. But the alternative was the Hospital of the Samaritan Mission of the Sisters of Our Lady of Mercy in Ranpur, a mental home staffed by Catholics; Eurasians and Indians mostly; the same ghastly kind of place with a small wing for Europeans such as poor Poppy Browning's daughter had ended her days in, screaming obscenities at her mother who used to go home from her weekly visits and wash in Lysol because they'd given up bathing the girl forcibly, except once a month, and Poppy used to touch and hold her close in an attempt to show her she was still loved.

Susan, thank God, was reported quite the opposite; clean, well-behaved, silent. She had said a few words to her mother and to Sarah and presumably more than a few to Captain Samuels who told Mildred her daughter was 'beginning to adjust' whatever that meant. Adjust to what? Mildred had apparently not bothered to ask. She distrusted the whole psychiatric process and had no time at all for the jargon. She said Travers had acted precipitately, sending Susan back to the nursing-home. There was nothing wrong with the girl that a good rest, a change of air and the company of young people wouldn't put right. She wasn't getting any kind of rest at the nursing home with Captain Samuels visiting her sometimes twice or even three times a day. Mildred managed to make these professional visits sound as though something unwholesome was going on.

'I'm sure Millie is right,' her sister Fenny said on this particular Saturday morning when Mildred had gone indoors in answer to Mahmoud's announcement that Captain Coley Sahib was on the telephone. 'I think it would be a good idea for her to come and stay with me in Calcutta and bring both girls and ayah and the baby. There wouldn't be room in the flat but Colonel Johnson and his wife who are friends of ours have a simply huge old eighteenth century John Company house and would gladly put them up. Or we could spend October in Darjeeling with old Dogra friends of Arthur's and come back down to Cal in November when the weather's really nice. Sarah would benefit as much as anyone. In fact I've suggested she and I could go down to Calcutta together quite soon. She's been up two nights with that dog as well as making sure ayah looks after little Edward properly and she visits Susan at least once a day, *and* still reports to the daftar whenever she can in spite of Dick Rankin telling her she can have extended station leave for as long as she wants. She's gone there this morning.'

'How *is* the dog?' Maisie Trehearne asked.

'Sarah says it's on the mend. She's got it in the mali's shed. I haven't looked myself. I can't bear the sight of sick animals but then I'm no good in a sick-room of any kind which is why I never visited Sarah's friend Captain Merrick, although the hospital's practically visible from the flat. But I did ring before I came up to Pankot and they said he was fine and quite cheerful considering he's lost his left arm.'

Fenny stopped and conscientiously avoided looking at Nicky Paynton, presumably in the belief that the subject of wounded officers was to be avoided. Fenny had become stouter since her last visit to Pankot at the time of Susan's engagement, when she pronounced Teddie Bingham 'rather sweet'. She filled the chair she was sitting in, which happened to be the one Mabel died in. The others wondered whether she knew but supposed she didn't in view of her confessed inability even to visit someone who was ill.

And she was smarter than they remembered. Arthur Grace's belated elevation to a Lieutenant-colonelcy and appointment in Calcutta seemed to have given her a sort of cosmopolitan gloss. She belonged, as though in default of having arrived sooner at a desirable peak, to a new order of Indian authority and had apparently, as a result, absorbed and smothered a multitude of sins. For Rose Cottage she was slightly over-dressed. Of the three women sitting with her, Maisie, Nicky and Clara, only Maisie remembered her as the youngest and prettiest of the three daughters of General Muir who had lived in Flagstaff House in the years immediately following the end of the 1914–18 war. Lydia, the eldest, had been cold and rather snooty, very intelligent and not at all enamoured of Anglo-Indian life. Her fiancé had been drowned in the Atlantic by German submarine action, a loss that had brightened the northern, arctic, gleam in her critical eye. She had gone home, got married and settled in Bayswater. Fenny in those days had a reputation for charming silliness, Maisie recalled, and in spite of being chased by scores of personable and promising fellows had married a man who turned out something of a failure. But all three knew well enough the Fenny to whom in middle-age an air of portly dowdiness had attached; a dowdiness she had combated by being vigorous in her opinions. Which had been comfortingly conservative. The vigour remained but now suited her. Fenny was particularly welcome just now. She radiated self-assurance.

'I'm so glad to have got Millie out of that poky little bungalow,' she said, making a sign to Mahmoud to replenish glasses. Mildred was still on the telephone indoors. 'I don't mind telling you I had to prod her a bit. At the last moment she said she didn't want to come. But she didn't want to stay in the grace and favour either and anyway she no longer had a choice. She said that if it wasn't for the girls she'd ask Dick Rankin to pull strings and get the air-force to fly her home to wait for John there.'

She looked over her shoulder to be sure Mildred was still indoors. Then lowering her voice slightly she said:

'She's awfully against that missionary woman, isn't she? She told me she's been going through Mabel's papers because the money looks like being less than she expected. I thought she meant Miss Batchelor had been cooking the books and feathering her nest but she said there wasn't any sign of that, only of what she calls influence.'

'What sort of influence?' Clara Fosdick wanted to know.

'Payments to charities. *Indian* charities. Orphanages, famine relief funds, child-widows, that sort of thing, and always *anonymously*. There are all these letters from the bank in Ranpur, dating back *years*, acknowledging her instructions to make anonymous donations to this and that – hundreds of rupees at a time, and advice notes about transfers of sterling from London which means she was selling securities at home as well as having the interest sent out.'

Maisie said, 'I don't see where the influence comes in if it's been going on for years. Unless you mean only five. Miss Batchelor came here at the end of nineteen thirty-nine.'

1008

'I know. But according to Mildred although Mabel had been giving money to Indian charities for ages, long before Miss Batchelor came to live with her, it almost doubled afterwards, especially in the last couple of years. And there was one donation to the Bishop Barnard Mission which isn't an Indian charity but does help to educate them. Not that I'm against it, any of it, but Mildred says the Bishop Barnard was the mission Miss Batchelor worked for, which proves it—'

'Proves what?'

'According to Mildred, that Mabel was influenced to dish out all this dough *by* Miss Batchelor. On top of which the estate has to fork out to buy an annuity for the woman and if she dies soon after it's bought it's hundreds or thousands of rupees wasted.'

'Perhaps she won't live long enough for it to be bought at all,' Nicky said. 'Clarissa Peplow told me Captain Travers doesn't expect her to pull through.'

'But she's been in hospital well over a week, nearly two, and she hasn't popped off yet. Don't tell Mildred, for Pete's sake, but Sarah's been over to the civil wing once or twice to see her when she goes to talk to Susan. Sarah says she only seems semi-conscious but reckons she's a tough old bird and will get over it. But whether she does or doesn't Mildred says the idea of an annuity could only have come from *her* because it's a typical lower-middle-class idea of upper-class security and respectability.'

'Isobel Rankin says Mildred is over-obsessed by the idea of Miss Batchelor as an eminence-grise,' Maisie Trehearne said. 'I don't know whether that's true or not but if it is we oughtn't to encourage her. The whole situation is becoming very – unhappy.'

Particularly in regard to spoons; about which Maisie's husband had received what he called a charming and touching letter from the old missionary, but not, as yet, the spoons themselves, which had puzzled him until he heard she had gone into hospital. It still puzzled him a bit. Maisie did not know what to tell him. For some years he had lived in an old-fashioned chivalrous world of his own. If it hadn't been for the war he would have retired in 1942. Sometimes, she thought, he acted as though he *had* retired. He had become fond and foolish and sometimes querulous. He couldn't understand why Coley insisted he'd received no spoons but only a sou'wester, and he inquired every day after Miss Batchelor's health. The position was not an easy one for her to support. He lived for the regiment. Silver for the mess was as much an obsession with him as Isobel Rankin said Miss Batchelor was an obsession with Mildred Layton. When it came to choosing between Mildred's and her husband's obsession there was no question which side she would support. He wanted the spoons. She hoped no one would tell him the spoons were originally Susan's and that Mildred had returned them in a fit of the extraordinary pique that generally possessed her nowadays. Another puzzling feature was that Mildred had said nothing about the spoons. Presumably Kevin Coley hadn't mentioned Miss Batchelor's intention to present them. But Maisie thought this strange too because Kevin and Mildred were so thick. Perhaps he was telling her now, on the telephone.

'Of course,' Fenny went on, 'I've told Millie there's absolutely no proof and certainly no reason why Mabel shouldn't have forked out all that money without prompting. Millie seems to have forgotten, but I don't suppose you have, Maisie, I mean about Mabel's attitude to Jallianwallah.'

'Attitude to whom?'

'Jallianwallah. The General Dyer business in Amritsar in Nineteen Nineteen.'

'Well I have forgotten. What was her attitude?'

'Don't you remember how we all collected money for Dyer when Government should have stood by him but didn't and issued that report that he'd exceeded his duty, firing on the unarmed mob in the Jallianwallah Bagh, and the poor old boy was disgraced and retired on half-pay?'

'Well of course I remember that. We were down in Mayapore at the time. There was a lovely ball at the old Artillery Mess and we collected about four thousand rupees just from that.'

'Oh well, if you were down in Mayapore you probably didn't know, which isn't surprising anyway because I had to remind Millie how Mabel refused to give anything. It was very embarrassing for John. After all Mabel was rich in comparison with most of us She got simply loads from her father, the Admiral, and quite a packet from her first husband, the Pankot Rifles chap who gave all that silver to the mess. And she simply wouldn't give a penny for Dyer.'

'But that means you're saying she was mean—'

'Only about Dyer. At the time we all thought he'd saved the poor old empire and ought to have been given a peerage not the sack. Of course since then people have blamed him for turning Gandhi against us. But the point is, and I was awfully embarrassed because I thought Millie must know if *I* knew, but it seems John never said a word to her, only to me. He told me in strictest confidence, or rather it slipped out and he asked me not to say anything to anybody, he told me Mabel sent money to the funds the *Indians* raised for the widows and orphans of the people Dyer shot. She *told* him she'd done so. I think he said she sent it to that old Muslim, M.A.K.'s father, the man who was on the Governor's Council down in Ranpur at the same time as John's father. Sir Ahmed Kasim, wasn't it? She told John she'd done it but had asked Sir Ahmed, if it was Sir Ahmed, to pay it over anonymously because she didn't want to harm John's career. John told me it was a hundred pounds. In Nineteen Twenty that was a hell of a lot of money.'

'It still is,' Nicky said. 'Do you think Sir Ahmed paid it over?'

'Nicky!'

'Perhaps he gave it to his son, M.A.K., to swell the Congress Party Funds?'

Fenny said, 'But Sir Ahmed was pro-British. People said he was awfully upset when his son joined the rebel faction of Congress, as we used to think it.'

'Rebels run in the Kasim family,' Nicky said.

'Oh, I'd hardly say that,' Fenny objected. 'M.A.K.'s own son, the young Kasim boy we met in Mirat at the guest house, struck me as rather sweet for an Indian. And you couldn't call him a rebel, working for an Indian prince. As a matter of fact it was in Mirat I found out Millie didn't know about Mabel giving money to the Jallianwallah Bagh orphans and widows, because I asked her if I was right thinking she'd sent it via this young Kasim boy's grandfather and she simply didn't know what I was talking about. So I thought I'd better shut up. Mabel was still alive then. But she remembered and asked me last week when she was hot on the trail of these other donations.'

'I wasn't thinking about the Kasim boy you met in Mirat,' Nicky said. 'I was thinking about the other one, the one who got the King's commission and has been captured fighting against us in the INA.'

'Really?' Fenny said. 'I didn't know about that.' She looked doubtful as if Nicky had said something in bad taste. 'All I know is what everybody else knows, that M.A.K. himself is ill and has been released to go and live with the Nawab on some sort of extended parole.'

'He's not ill,' Nicky said. 'He's being cosseted by Government and a fat lot of good it'll do. The Nawab's probably anti-government as well and M.A.K.'ll be the first to call his officer son a bloody hero. It's double standards all the time. It makes me sick. But that makes it easier bidding it all a fond farewell.'

There was silence. Even Fenny seemed prewarned of Nicky's inevitable announcement and to recognize that the moment for it had arrived.

'It's a salutary thought,' Nicky said after a while, 'that Bunny may have been killed by a one-time officer of his own regiment. After all why not? I've been checking up. A Lieutenant Sayed Kasim was commissioned into the Fifth Ranpurs. He was the first Indian the Ranpurs ever took. There were plenty of others but he was the first. Bunny always took immense pains with his own Indian officers. And I took pains with the wives. God knows it was sometimes a hard grind. And you wondered at the time whether it was worth it. It seems it wasn't. It's a bloody bore because you end up distrusting everybody. Sometimes I even look at old Fariqua and try to work out what it would take to make him do the dirty on me even though he's gone around red-eyed ever since I told him Bunny had bought it. Incidentally, Clara, Fariqua lives in a village outside Ranpur. If you go down to your sister you might help find the old boy a job. He has so many spare wives around there he'll need the money and have to go on working until he drops.'

'Are you really going home, Nicky?' Clara asked when she could manage it.

'Yes.'

'Have you decided when and how?'

'The answer to when is as soon as I can. As to how, I'll do what Fenny says Mildred would have liked to. Scrounge a lift with the Airforce even if it means being stuck in somewhere like Cairo for a bit. I'll auction everything off and just send a trunk or two of odds and ends by sea. And if the boat's sunk it won't matter much. There's really nothing of value to take back with me.'

Clara said:

'I'll miss you dreadfully.'

For an instant Nicky seemed ready to crumple. But the iron will was not to be broken.

'Oh well, I'll be back in a year or two I expect. When the boys are off my hands. Do you know, there are loads of things I've never done out here? When Bunny was alive he always promised we'd go down to the Coromandel coast one winter, but we never managed it and we never got to Goa either. And then it would be nice to see the Taj again. Bunny thought it terribly overrated but I must say I thought it rather splendid. And of course I'd like to see Gulmarg again, and Ooty, and even dreary old Simla.'

Her friends said nothing. They nodded encouragingly but absent-mindedly. The dispiriting fact had not escaped them. Already Nicky Paynton was talking like a tourist. It was this that drove home to them the terrible bleakness – thinness – that settled upon and somehow defined anyone whose connection had been severed; and then as their glances mercifully fell from her one by one and turned upon the garden Fenny cried out:

'God, what's that?' She jerked out of her chair, startling them. 'What? (one of them shouted) What is it Fenny?' Her alarm was infectious. Her plump ringed fingers were crossed at her throat. She had become speechless and was staring, horrified, at a patch of petal-strewn grass, a corridor between long rectangular beds of rose-trees, bush and standard, vagrant-looking with green reversionary shoots pale and erectile, already sucking the life out of the roots. Along this path the creature crawled, slunk, towards them; a black spectre of famine worn to its hooped rib cage and the arched column of its backbone. A thin dribble of saliva hung from its open mouth.

'Millie!' Fenny called, and then turned and went into the house still calling her. The others stayed where they were, watching the apparition approach the verandah steps slowly, dragging one leg, pausing every few paces to rest, droop-headed, before struggling on, its eyes upturned and fixed on the objective, showing blood-shot whites.

'How can she?' Nicky exclaimed. 'How can Sarah have let it suffer like this? She ought to be ashamed.'

'But Nicky, it means it's getting better,' Maisie said. 'It's looking for her.' Even Maisie could not manage to say the animal's name. She went to the head of the steps cautiously and called down to it, 'Sarah? Where's Sarah, then? There's a brave old soldier. There's a brave old boy.' And got gingerly down on one knee and extended invitation through an outstretched arm and placating fingers which the animal observed from below, raising the iron weight of its neck a fraction of an inch and then lowering it again and standing there at the bottom of the steps as if unable to work out the complicated problem they presented.

*

Mildred was not on the telephone. Fenny thrust open the door of Mabel's room which she and her sister were sharing. Neither Mabel's old bed nor the charpoy she herself slept in was made up yet. Fenny thought this unforgivable of the servants but blamed Mildred for not controlling them better. However she held her tongue.

Mildred was sitting on the edge of Mabel's bed, topping her glass up from her private bottle.

'Millie, that dog's got loose and is crawling about the garden.'

Mildred put the bottle back on the bedside table.

'What did you say?'

'The dog. It's got loose. I can't bear to see it. It looks as if it's come out to die.'

The corners of Mildred's lips twitched and then curved down in the characteristic smile.

'Lucky dog,' she said.

'Oughtn't we to ring Sarah and get her back here quickly? She can't let it go on like this, Millie. I know she means well but it's not fair, it's not kind.'

'She'll be back any moment now.'

Fenny looked at her watch. It was barely twelve.

'But she never gets back from the daftar before one when she goes in on a Saturday and if the vet isn't rung before then we probably shan't get him until this evening.'

'I said she'll be back any moment.'

Mildred took a drink then looked at Fenny.

'Sarah passed out at the daftar. Only we're not supposed to know. Dicky Beauvais found her in what he calls a fainting condition in the map room. She got him to promise not to tell me. But apparently it's the second time this week and he thought I ought to know. He decided honour would be satisfied if he rang Kevin and left it to Kevin whether to tell me or not. He'll be back with her in about ten minutes I should think, with some story about the daftar being slack.'

Fenny sat heavily on the charpoy. 'There! Perhaps she'll listen now and stop being so silly. It's ridiculous her going into the daftar at all.'

'Is it?'

'Millie, you can't let her go on like this. She can't go round fainting all over the place. If you don't speak to her I will.'

'Haven't you spoken to her already?'

'What do you mean?'

'What should I mean?'

1013

'I don't know but if you're not going to do anything I shall have to tackle her myself.'

Mildred got up and stood with her back to Fenny, arms folded but still holding her glass, looking out of the window which gave on to the verandah at the front of the house.

'Directly Dicky Beauvais has gone,' Fenny continued, 'I'll talk to her then. I suppose we'll have to deal with the business of the poor dog first, but one of us must talk to her.'

Mildred said nothing.

'I've been thinking, Millie,' Fenny said. She had always been a bit afraid of her sister. 'You don't honestly need me here much longer. And if Sarah doesn't get a holiday soon she'll crack up. Why don't I do what I suggested the other day, take her back with me to Calcutta, in say a couple of weeks' time? Minnie's perfectly competent with the baby and I can't see Susan being allowed home just yet. When she is we could all meet in Darjeeling for a few weeks and be together in Calcutta before Christmas. Even *for* Christmas. Let's face it Millie, Pankot's awfully dull for two young girls like Sarah and Su.'

'You used to say what a jolly little place it was.'

'Well it's not any more.'

'No,' Mildred said. 'And compared with Calcutta it's got nothing to offer, has it?'

'Very little.'

'No madly handsome young officers fresh from the jungle or about to go into it and ready to tear the place apart?'

Fenny laughed, relieved by what looked like Mildred's change of mood. She said, 'Oh, we have our share of those!'

'So I should imagine. Can you wait two weeks?'

'Oh, Millie. All I ask is for you to give it some serious thought. It would do Sarah the world of good.'

'You think so?'

Fenny hesitated before speaking her mind. 'I know it's been difficult for you without John all these years. Now don't misunderstand, Millie, but it's always seemed to me a great deal of the weight of *your* burden has fallen on Sarah's shoulders. It's in her nature, I know, to take on responsibilities, but it's not right, not for a young girl. And it begins to show and then it's difficult. I mean – with men. We don't want Sarah on the shelf, do we? I know she could have married several times, certainly once. There was Teddie wasn't there, before he switched to Su? But that's the point. If she isn't careful, a girl like Sarah begins to look sort of discarded or second-best choice. And she isn't. You should have seen her just in that very brief time she was with us. She looked stunning. The boys we had in certainly thought so. One in particular—'

Mildred swung round. 'Don't tell me any more, Fenny! I don't want to know. Just get on with it. Take her to Calcutta. The sooner the better, I imagine.'

'Well you might sound more enthusiastic! Don't you want Sarah to have a good time?'

Mildred laughed. She picked up the bottle, sat on the bed, filled her glass again. And laughed. Then she clattered the bottle back on the table between the water jug and the table-lamp. She took a hefty swig. But the gin didn't compose her. Her eyes glittered under lids which were for once wide open.

'A good time?' she asked. 'She's *had* the good time, hasn't she?'

'Millie, what on earth's wrong with you?'

'Oh, stop putting on the act. It's very good but it's beginning to irritate me. I don't want to talk about it and I don't want to know any of the details. Not any of them. Now or ever. But you can stop treating me like a bloody fool because I know exactly what's going on.' She took another drink. 'I'm even grateful to you for trying to cope with it without my knowing, although it's the least you can do considering you're bloody well to blame. If you want Sarah to go on thinking she's fooled me that's up to you. But you're my little sister. You were always silly and it would be bad for my morale to let you imagine *you'd* fooled me.'

Fenny did not reply at once. She looked at the glass.

She said, 'You're drunk, Millie. That's all I know. So you must be right. If it's any consolation I'll admit I'm silly. Dense. I haven't the slightest idea what you're talking about.'

'Oh?' Mildred drank most of the rest of the gin in her glass but did not top it up. 'Let's forget it then. Let's pretend everything in the garden is lovely and just do what seems best for Sarah. Since you're so concerned about her why don't you ring Captain Travers or Colonel Beames and ask one of them to drop in after lunch to give her a check-up?'

'Well, yes, we could do that. Isn't it a bit out of proportion though? They're both busy men and what can either of them say except what I say, that's she's been overdoing it and needs a holiday?'

'But supposing she's really ill? I'm surprised you haven't thought of that, Fenny. I tell you what. I'll ring Travers now myself. I'll do it right away.'

'Well. If you think so.'

Mildred finished her drink. 'I think so,' she said. She waited for a moment as if challenging Fenny to stop her and then smiled and went into the hall, leaving the door open. Fenny heard the ping of the bell as the receiver was lifted and then several rapid pings as Mildred impatiently jerked the hook up and down to wake the dozy operator. Sighing, Fenny got up and went into the hall too.

Mildred was at the telephone but the receiver was back on the hook. She was not ringing anybody.

'You were really going to let me!' she exclaimed.

'But it was your idea. Why should I stop you?'

'Haven't you honestly the least idea what I'm getting at?'

'No, I haven't.'

'Then you'd better come in here.'

Fenny followed Mildred into Sarah's and Susan's bedroom. At the wall opposite the foot of one of the beds was a chest of drawers. Placed centrally on its top among neatly ordered lacquered boxes stood a photograph of Sarah's father. Fenny gazed at it fondly for a moment. Mildred went to the chest and opened the second of three long drawers.

'Look,' she said. She turned back piles of neatly laundered underwear. Fenny looked. There were two pudgy blue-wrapped packages, both unopened. Mildred covered them up again and shut the drawer. She went out of the room and after a few moments Fenny went too. She found Mildred back in their own room pouring herself another drink.

'Shut the door, Fenny.' Fenny did so. 'Do you want a gin too?' Fenny shook her head.

'The one thing I've always done for Sarah,' Mildred began, 'and perhaps it's the only thing, is make sure she's got plenty of sannies when she's due, because like I used to be she's as regular as clockwork but has an absolutely ghastly time, worse even than I did before she was born. She was due a week after she came back from her visit to you in Calcutta. I gave her one of those packets then. She was due again last week and that's when I gave her the other.'

'Millie, what are you saying?'

'That according to the evidence in that chest of drawers she's missed twice and hasn't told me. I thought perhaps she'd told you. I thought she might have had to. To make you help her get hold of the bloody man you so kindly introduced her to, or get rid of the thing in Calcutta.'

Suddenly Mildred rounded on her.

'And isn't that the truth, Fenny? Isn't that what your cosy little trip to Calcutta is all about? To fix things up with some snide little emergency officer or fix them up in a different way with a shady Calcutta doctor or pop her neatly into an expensive clinic as a Mrs Smith requiring a d and c?'

'No! No, Millie! Oh, no.'

'Well, that's what you're going to have to do. Get the bloody thing aborted. My God, I could murder you. You have charge of her for just twenty-four stinking hours and she's in the bloody club.'

Fenny sat down, with her hands at her cheeks, her eyes shut. Mildred sat too, facing her.

'What are you doing? Working out which one of your and Arthur's adoring and adorable panting bloody boys it was? Or isn't there any doubt in your mind? What a stupid woman you are. In Mirat you made that ridiculous fuss about her riding in broad daylight with the young Kasim boy. Was it wise – isn't that what you asked me? Wise! A pity you didn't ask yourself if it was wise before you chucked her into the arms of some randy little English officer from God knows where. What was he? All strong white teeth and bloody prick? Did you fancy him yourself? Did you get a kick out of handing him Sarah? Because that's what you did and I never intend to forget it. Never. Just as I never intend to be told who the little cheapskate was. It hasn't happened. Look at me, Fenny. It hasn't

1016

happened. You'll take her to Calcutta and between the two of you *deal* with it. Get rid of it. I don't want to know how or where or how much it costs. You can get the money from your husband because he's equally to blame. But *I* don't want to know anything more about it. And if anything goes wrong it's on your head, not mine. Because I can't stand any more. I can't and I won't.'

The sound of a car entering the drive arrested her. She got up.

'Now,' she said. 'Pull yourself together. When everybody's gone you can start worming it out of her. Pretend I don't know if you like. But *deal* with it. Do you understand?'

'Millie, you don't *know*. You're only guessing. You don't *know* anything.'

Mildred leaned over her, lowering her voice but speaking vehemently and distinctly. 'Two missed periods? Fainting at the office? For God's sake what more do you want? And today's not the first time I've wondered what was wrong with her. I *am* her mother. A bloody bad one, but I am *that*, and I *know, I know from the look on her face*.'

She went briskly to the door, opened it, and in her ordinary abrasively cheerful voice said, 'Dicky! What a nice surprise. Aren't you both rather early? Well, all the better. You'll stay for lunch, won't you Dicky? I'll tell Mahmoud. Sarah dear, you're looking exhausted. Why don't you freshen up and get out of that boring old uniform? Dicky, use my bathroom, but go through the dining-room. My sister's in the bedroom powdering her nose. But literally.'

There were several kinds of footsteps going in different directions away from the hall and presently Fenny heard a man's in the adjoining bathroom and the click of the bolt on his side of the door. She heard Dicky beginning to urinate – a splash followed by a murmuring silence as he considerately redirected the stream away from the water to the porcelain.

She got up. There was no one in the hall. Sarah's door was ajar. She tapped and went in. She could see the compact shape of his body, uniformed, and smell its assertive masculine odour. She wanted to hate him but could not. Dimly she had always seen that he represented the kind of force that would make the world safe for her and Arthur while laughing at them. For an instant she entertained the absurd idea that he might be forced to do the right thing. But he was gone, as such men always were – involved in apparently lighthearted but in fact complex affairs that had to do with the world as it really was. For him military status was merely part of a game of the compulsory kind. And in her heart she knew that Sarah had used him as he had used her. But had been less expert. Meanwhile there was the question of the dog. She could not remember the dog's name but now that it had come into her mind she could not get it out because it was a living thing whose destruction Sarah had opposed with a significant and dangerous passion. Oh God, she thought, let me be wrong, let Millie be wrong.

Just then through the half-open doorway into the bathroom she caught

1017

sight of Sarah standing by the handbowl, grasping the side of it with one hand, reaching for the tap with the other. At the same instant in the little spare on the other side of the bathroom the child woke and cried and Minnie's voice came through quite clearly, speaking to him soothingly. Sarah raised her head, not to look towards the child's room but straight ahead of her into the mirror above the basin as if the source of the cry were there in her reflection. Then she lowered her head again and twisted the tap on and watched the water running in and away.

*

Dicky Beauvais was kneeling on one leg by the dog's side stroking its head. The others watched from the safety of the verandah. The dog sat on its withered haunches. It swayed when Dicky stroked it.

'What do you think, Captain Beauvais?' Maisie Trehearne asked.

'I don't know. The poor old boy looks pretty much a goner.'

'But don't you think his coming out means he's feeling better?'

'Maybe. On the whole I'd say it's too late. It'll be rotten for Sarah.'

'It's suffering,' Nicky insisted. 'It's dying on its feet. I should have thought anyone could see that.'

Mildred alone was seated, holding her drink under her chin. When Fenny came out ten minutes later Mildred glanced up but Fenny did not look at her. She went to the head of the steps.

'Dicky, I've told Sarah about Panther. She leaves it to us.'

'Oh.' Again he stroked the dog's head. The neck was arched down, the jaws open. 'Poor old fellow.'

He stood up. 'I'd better ring the veterinary officer hadn't I, Mrs Layton?'

Mildred said nothing. He looked at Fenny.

'Isn't Sarah coming out to see for herself?'

'No.'

'Perhaps if I could get the dog round to the gharry it would be better for me to take him than bring the vet up here.'

'I shouldn't if I were you,' Mildred called. 'He could have a fit and you could end up driving over the khud and killing you both. Take him back to the mali's shed if you can. It's not the most elevating sight, is it? Or better still get Sarah to do it. After all she's responsible for keeping the wretched thing alive and for it ending up in this state. She oughtn't to be allowed just to opt out.'

'I'll get him into the shed, Mrs Layton.'

Dicky bent down again.

'Come on, old boy. Come along. You can make it.'

The servants had gathered at a safe distance. Dicky tried to direct the dog's attention to them.

Mildred spoke to Fenny who was watching Dicky.

'Have you persuaded Sarah to go to Calcutta with you?'

'Yes,' Fenny said, without looking.

1018

'Come on Panther, old son,' Dicky said. 'Come on. Rabbit.'

Its tail moved once, a slow-motion scything movement across the grass and Maisie Trehearne exclaimed, 'He wagged his tail! I told you. He's feeling better. It's awful to talk about destroying him now, after all Sarah's done.'

Then she added, 'We owe so much to dogs,' and Mildred started laughing: a clear fluting laugh of genuine amusement that made everyone except Dicky down there on the grass turn to look at her in astonishment. Only Dicky noticed the effect that the sounds Mildred was making had on the dog. It lifted its head and snapped at the air or at Dicky's hand which he jerked out of reach. It began to tremble. It went on snapping as if the peals of Mildred's laughter were coming at it in some visible form: small predatory birds or maddening insects. Dicky backed away and shouted a warning to Mrs Layton but she did not hear. Her laughter seemed to have become uncontrollable and suddenly the dog twisted its body and began dragging itself round, still snapping at the air, making no sound but moving away from the steps and increasing the width of its circular chase until it was blundering through the nearest of the rose-beds shaking the bushes and scattering petals.

The servants also scattered. Dicky stood, alarmed but on the defensive at the head of the steps with only his bare hands to fight off an attack if the dog took it into its head to go for any of them. But the impact with the rose-bushes had disorientated the animal. It no longer traced a circular pattern but a random one, staggering from bed to bed with a high-arched back and low slung head, wreaking havoc, putting distance between itself and the inhospitable verandah. Suddenly it emitted a stream of pale yellow liquid excreta and then began to drag its hindquarters as though it were dying from that end up. It came to the path between the two rectangular beds and fell on its side. For a while it moved its forelegs, dreamily dog-paddling the air; then it twitched and was still; twitched again and was still again. The intervals between spasms became longer.

Fenny said, 'It isn't rabies, is it, Dicky?'

'No. I've seen rabies.'

They waited for a further spasm that didn't come.

'That's that,' Dicky said.

He went down the steps and called up to Fenny.

'Perhaps as I've handled him I oughtn't to come back into the house though. Would you phone the vet-johnnie, Mrs Grace? I'll get something to cover him with. I expect the servants have some sacking.'

He went off towards the servants' quarters.

A few minutes later he reappeared with a length of gunny, approached the dog's body from behind and then put the sacking over it.

'Dicky, what's all this about not coming into the house?'

Mildred's voice carried strongly. She came down into the garden. He waited for her. She joined him. The dog's body was between them. 'Of course you must come in. You're staying for lunch.'

'Mrs Grace is afraid it might have been something like rabies. It wasn't but I don't want to risk anything.'

'There isn't any risk. It was just a fit. But if you prefer to stay outside until the vet comes by all means do so. Fenny's been on to him and he's coming right away. And you must stay to lunch. I'll need you to cheer Sarah up. Kevin rang me, incidentally. I know about her not feeling well at the daftar. I'm grateful to you for tipping me off.'

'I felt pretty shabby because she'd made me promise not to mention it in case of worrying you. But I thought her health more important than my word.'

'Absolutely right.' She looked down at the heap of sacking. 'I expect this will be the last straw. But we've been cooking up a scheme for Fenny to take her down to Calcutta and get her out of it for a bit. I shall ring Dick Rankin this evening and tell him she oughtn't to go into the daftar between now and then. Come along, Dicky. Don't let's stand here. I'm not feeling so hot myself.'

She moved away. In a moment or two Dicky was walking at her side.

'There's something I've got to tell you, Mrs Layton. And something I want to ask you about. I was going to tell Sarah this morning, that's why I was looking for her and found her – like she was.'

Mildred had stopped. She smiled. She said, 'I hope it's nothing unpleasant.'

'Not unpleasant exactly. I mean – I've been posted. The order came this morning. I've got to report to the military secretary at Fourteenth Army.'

'When?'

'I must leave tonight. There's some transport going down to Ranpur. I'm flying from Ranagunj tomorrow morning.'

'To Comilla?'

'Yes.'

'Is it promotion?'

'I've no idea what's entailed. My guess is I'll be in Imphal inside a week.'

'I won't commiserate,' Mildred said. 'I expect you're glad. No young officer wants to be stuck in a place like this for long. But we're going to miss you. You've been an absolute brick. Like part of the family.'

Dicky blushed.

'You've been very kind to me,' he said.

'You had something to ask me about.'

'Yes. I'm sorry because it seems the wrong sort of time.'

'But it's the only time you have, isn't it?'

'I don't quite know how to put it. Probably you guess. I mean, you have a right to. I've taken up a great deal of your daughters' time – Sarah's *and* Susan's. What you said, about being part of the family, that's what it's been like for me. I was terrifically pleased being asked to be godfather to Susan's baby. The thing is, one day I'd like really to be part of it.'

Dicky's blush had deepened. But he kept his eyes manfully on hers.

1020

'I know there can't be anything offiical,' he continued. 'I mean, in the circumstances. But I didn't want to leave without telling you what I feel and asking if you think there's a chance, and of course if you'd approve.'

'Are you saying you'd like to be John's and my son-in-law, Dicky?'

'Yes.'

Mildred put a hand on his arm.

'My dear chap. I can't actually think of anything nicer. That's all I *can* say. But you've already appreciated that. I'm sorry you have to go without being able to say anything to her, but perhaps it's as well. I made up my mind some time ago that all questions of this kind would have to wait until my husband comes home. But an understanding – not necessarily binding – but an understanding between the two of you would have been a different matter. You've thought hard about it, haven't you Dicky? It isn't just a case of your feeling sorry for her?'

'Sorry? No, why should I feel sorry—?'

'People exaggerate so. But it's only a temporary set-back and she's getting better every day. She's had the most ghastly luck when you work it out. Later on she'll need someone like you, Dicky, but I wouldn't want you to take it all on unless you were absolutely sure. I must confess I was rather hoping for something like this to give her back a feeling of stability. I'm sure it's all she needs. That, and someone she can lean on, really depend on in the future. Personally, I couldn't be happier. I think the form is for me to talk to her, when that's possible, and to let you know what sort of reaction I get and then for you to start writing to her to tell her a bit of what you feel, but not too much. She needs time as well as reassurance.'

She tapped his arm. 'Now come along in and have a drink. I suggest we keep this entirely to ourselves, at least for the time being, but you and I will know what we're drinking to.'

'Mrs Layton—'

'What, Dicky?'

'I'm afraid I must have made the most awful mess of it—'

'Mess? What do you mean?'

'You were talking – you were talking about Susan.'

Mildred let go of his arm. She studied his face. The blush had gone. He looked quite pale, for Dicky.

'Weren't you?' she asked.

He shook his head. Briefly she touched her own, tracing the outline of her left eyebrow, and then put her hand to her throat, linking the little finger into the string of seed pearls. She smiled but her eyes showed no amusement nor for that matter embarrassment at having jumped to the wrong conclusion.

'I'm so sorry. I'd no idea you felt like that about Sarah. Has she?'

'I hope, a bit. But I don't know. I was going to speak to her today.'

'Yes, I see. Of course there was a time when I wondered. But then when Teddie was killed I thought you realized it had been Susan all the time.'

She moved away from him, a pace or two; but stopped and said, 'It's up to you of course, but my advice would be to say nothing just yet.'

'Would you tell me why, Mrs Layton?'

The pearls had become twisted. But this was the only sign of agitation.

'I shouldn't want you to leave Pankot with your hopes completely dashed.'

'I'd risk that. And it might be otherwise, mightn't it?'

'Perhaps. But I don't think so. I don't get the impression she's fond of you like that. I must take your word for it that so far as you're concerned the scales have finally gone down in her favour. You *have* been thrown together more by Susan's illness. I should be surprised if she feels the same about you but – let's say I'm wrong. Then I'd have to tell you I have reservations about your coming to any kind of understanding. I'm sorry if that sounds unfair or illogical. But what could have been a good thing in Susan's case, a good thing for you both, wouldn't necessarily be in Sarah's and yours. With Susan there's the element of dependence, the question of the child, the need she has to feel wanted again, which is why I asked you whether you were sure, absolutely sure, about taking it all on. But Sarah's very independent. She's about and around, if you see what I mean. I'd hate you to go off to Burma or wherever, feeling chipper, and then get a letter saying she's met someone else.'

'Is there someone else, Mrs Layton?'

'Someone adored from a distance?' Mildred smiled. 'I simply can't say. Sarah's never taken me into her confidence. She's always been the quiet introspective type. But she's pretty determined and she can be impulsive. Susan's the one who feels the need to settle down to an orderly kind of existence. I was never absolutely happy about her choice of Teddie and I'm pretty sure she ended up regretting it. But they both rushed into it and I think a lot of her trouble is that she's feeling guilty about him.'

'Guilty?'

'I believe that when you turned up she realized what a mistake she'd made. Perhaps she feels it showed in her letters to him.'

'Did she ever say anything to you, Mrs Layton?'

Mildred had folded her arms but still played with the necklace. The movements of her fingers were more assured.

'No, Dicky. And don't run away with any ideas. It's all much too complicated. You seem to have made your choice anyway and apparently it's not Susan. Let's go in. I'm dying for a drink and I'm sure you are. At least we can drink to your safe return. *That*'s the important thing.'

The verandah was now unoccupied. Everyone had gone indoors to avoid the sight of the heap of sacking. Weeks later, sitting on an empty upturned ammunition box and resting his pad of paper on his knee, Dicky ended a letter to Sarah: 'There was a lot I wanted to talk about that last afternoon in Pankot but somehow everything conspired against it. My fondest love to you. And to Susan. And of course to my godson.'

1022

She woke to the strong sweet smell of roses and did not need to open her eyes to know that they were yellow. In any case if she opened her eyes the scent and the roses would almost certainly go away, dismal proof that she was only dreaming them. She turned her head and slowly let the white room come into focus. The scent was fainter but it had not gone and she guessed she was not alone.

She looked round into the massed pale yellow velvet petals of the flowers which Sarah had placed on the pillow and was holding there with her left hand.

'Hello, Barbie. Are you feeling better? I've brought these from the garden. I remembered the yellow were your favourite.'

Barbie smiled and nodded.

Her voice, of which she had been proud, had become a humiliation. It was weak on the consonants. It cracked on the vowels. When she spoke she could feel the vibrations in the tight drum of her chest.

'Thank you, Sarah.' She tried to whisper it but the first vowel betrayed her. One had to face it. 'My silly old voice,' she said in two registers at once. 'It seems to have packed up on me. Some will think it a blessing if it keeps me quiet.'

The roses trembled as the fractured sounds hit them.

'You've been here before, haven't you?'

'Once or twice. But you were very sleepy.'

'You were in uniform. You brought me a bottle of barley water. I still have some. Would you like a glass?'

'No, but I'll give you one.'

'It would oil the cogs.' She watched from the pillow-bower of roses while Sarah poured barley water. Helped into a drinking position she could feel her own backbone against Sarah's hand. Her wasted body filled her with revulsion; in the room it alone lacked the security of shape and form and definition. It was like something the bed had invented, got tired of and left half-finished to fend for itself.

'I shall be glad to get out of here,' she said when Sarah had resettled the pillows to support her in the half-upright position the nurses were always trying to keep her in, in an unequal struggle against the gravitational pull of the foot of the bed and the mattress under her bony buttocks. 'There is something about a hospital bedroom that drains one of self-confidence. One feels anonymous.'

'You have your name on the door.'

'Have I? That's handy. It minimizes error. Was I in this room when you came before?'

'No, in one with three other beds but only one was occupied. By a Mrs MacGregor whose husband was an engineer.'

'I remember curtains round the bed with sprigs of forget-me-nots and scarlet pimpernels. And a horrible thing like a bomb. But it was only the oxygen. Why have I been moved to a room on my own?'

'Captain Travers thought you'd like it. You've got a private balcony. When you're better you'll be able to sit out and not be bothered by people.'

'People have never bothered me. It's been the other way round. Was I very ill?'

'You had pneumonia.'

'I know. But Edwina had pneumonia. She wasn't in hospital more than three weeks. I've been that already.'

'A little over.'

'Shall I be here much longer?'

'A week or two I expect. You're much better today. You'll make strides now.'

'Was Clarissa very cross?'

'What could she have to be cross about?'

'Cross with me for being ill.'

'She visited you. She wouldn't visit you if she were cross, now would she?'

'I don't remember her visiting me. I only remember you.'

'I expect you were asleep.'

'Will she have me back?'

'Of course she will. There isn't any question.'

'I thought Dr Travers might be keeping me here because he knows Clarissa's *had* me.'

Sarah smiled. At the turn of phrase presumably. It was what soldiers said. I've had it. You've had it. It was very expressive.

'And she knows the mission's had me too. I showed her the letter.'

'You mustn't worry about Clarissa.'

'Is my trunk still safe?'

Sarah nodded.

'Still in the mali's shed?'

'Yes, still there.'

'Does your mother know?'

Sarah shook her head.

Barbie looked at the roses. 'It was wrong of me getting you to hide it. But Clarissa would have drawn the line at the trunk. It had better go to Jalal-Ud-Din's. If we could move it one day when your mother's out.'

'Mother's unlikely to look in the mali's shed. Anyway it's doing no harm. Whenever you want it it's there. You only have to ask me or mali.'

'No. Your mother will get to know. And you'll be in trouble. There are some little toys in it. Things the children made for me. If I give you the key you could get them out. The baby could have them when he's older. The mali could keep the trunk. Everything else in it can be thrown away.'

'You said the trunk was your history.'

'Lying here one has no history. Just each hour of the day.' She grinned.

1024

'Yes you do. And you needn't worry about the trunk or about Clarissa having you back. Just concentrate on getting well.'

'Is Susan getting well?'

Sarah nodded.

'And the baby is all right?'

'The baby's fine.'

'Is Susan quite near me?'

'You can see the nursing home from your balcony.'

'Then I'll sit out there and transmit prana to her.'

'What's prana?'

'The goodness in the air. You breathe it in. And out. Like smelling roses. Like blowing dandelions.'

'Like what?'

'Blowing dandelions.'

It was one of the more difficult words. It came out so distorted she doubted that Sarah would understand. Her eyelids felt heavy. She let them close just for a second or two.

When she opened them Sarah had gone, the roses were in a vase and the lights and shadows in the room had rearranged themselves as they did in theatres to denote the passage of time.

*

The red hospital blanket round her knees and chest reminded her of Christmas. Seated in the wheelchair at the open doorway between room and balcony she might have been surrounded by shiny pink-and-blue-wrapped parcels and by children waiting for their turn to climb on her knee and whisper secret longings and desires. She could smell pines. Through half-closed eyes she could transmute the gold of sunshine on the leaves of the trees into snow and ride the sleigh of the chair high above the roofs of the hospital and the carved balconies of the bazaar and the spire of St John's. Santa Barbie: leaving a lingering glittering frosty scent of her own magical intrusion.

We could go down to Ranpur she had said to do some Christmas shopping. Oh I shall never go to Ranpur again Mabel answered at least not until I'm buried.

The reply had begun to trouble her with its vagueness, its curious subtlety. Its element of prophecy.

She opened her eyes fully and through the balcony rails saw the girl walking in afternoon sunshine along the tarmac pathway from the nursing home. Sarah with roses. The girl looked up. The red blanket had caught her eye. She waved and came on. It seemed a long time before Barbie heard the door open in the room behind her and the little Anglo-Indian nurse say, 'You have a visitor.'

'Hello, Sarah,' she croaked. 'You see. I'm on the mend except for this wretched voice. If you wheel me in we can see each other. There's only room for one on the balcony.'

Roses descended upon her lap and she felt the chair grasped and tip up as Sarah began to negotiate it back into the room. When they were settled, seated together at the window, Barbie said, 'You've been visiting Susan. How is she?'

'Much better. Captain Samuels thinks she can come out quite soon. And incidentally Captain Travers seems very pleased with *you*.'

'Have you seen him?'

'On the way in. He thinks about another week will do it. Perhaps two to be on the safe side.'

'Did he mention my voice?'

'No. Why are you worried about your voice?'

'That's what Doctor Travers says when I ask him. But listen to it. It gets no better.'

'It's only a bit hoarse. You'll be all right when you're on your feet and walking in the fresh air.'

'I hope so. It would be awful to lose one's voice. For me, like a painter to lose his sight, a musician his hearing. It was never a singing voice of course, but it carried in the schoolroom. Mr Cleghorn said it had a note of command which he advised me to develop because it was very important for a teacher. When I was a girl I took elocuton. I called it electrocution. My mother paid for me to have the lessons to help me in later life and in her decline she often asked me to read to her. You put such expression into it, Barbie, she used to say. It was the best of times, it was the worst of times. She died half way through A Tale of Two Cities.'

She lifted the bunch of roses to smell them. Sarah took the opportunity to speak.

'Barbie, I shan't see you again for a while. I'm going back with Aunty Fenny to Calcutta to stay with her. We're going tomorrow. When Susan's okay she and Mother are going to join us so that we can all go to Darjeeling, probably some time in September.'

Barbie let the roses fall. Her body seemed to have reacted of its own accord in advance of the sense of dismay, of loss, which was slower, only just now taking hold of her.

She said, 'What about the baby?'

Sarah gathered some of the dropped petals from around the bunch on Barbie's lap.

'Well of course they'll bring ayah and the baby with them. Captain Samuels thinks it would be better for Susan not to go back to familiar surroundings right away, so tomorrow after we've gone Mother's going to close Rose Cottage and move into Flagstaff House until Susan's discharged. Then when Captain Samuels gives the word they'll come down to Calcutta.'

'Close Rose Cottage?'

'Only until we get back. Perhaps for Christmas. We're sending Mahmoud on leave but the mali and his wife will look after things.'

'Who is this Captain Samuels?'

Sarah paused. 'A very intelligent man,' she said.

'But the journey, Sarah, with a tiny baby.'

Sarah dropped the petals into a wastebin.

'I don't think the baby will come to any harm. He's quite a tough customer. And I think we can depend on Mother to travel in the maximum comfort and with every available amenity.'

'I'm sorry. It's none of my business. I was looking for objections. Because I don't want *you* to go.'

'I must be going in any case. I've promised Aunt Fenny.'

'I didn't know your Aunt Fenny was in Pankot.'

'She came up to help Mother. You know what some families are. In trouble they close the ranks and stick together.'

'Wouldn't it be better for her to wait? Until you can *all* go, with Susan?'

'She can't be away from Uncle Arthur any longer. Well. That's one answer. But I'm the culprit really. They've decided I need a holiday.'

'Are you ill?'

'No, Barbie. Do I look ill?'

'No. No, you don't. You look tired but that's not surprising. Oh, I should be glad for you, shouldn't I? You liked Calcutta.'

Sarah nodded. She was looking at the roses, still touching them, making sure all the loose petals had been gathered.

Barbie observed the pale gold lights in the girl's hair. She felt possessive in her love. She moved a hand to make contact, but Sarah misunderstood. She must have thought the movement of her own fingers among the petals had begun to irritate the invalid. She took her hands away, folded them in under her arms but stayed bent forward in the chair, her knees almost touching the red blanket.

'Will you visit Captain Merrick when you're in Calcutta?' Barbie asked.

Sarah shook her head.

'He's probably gone anyway. To somewhere where they fit artificial limbs. I believe they get on to it quite quickly nowadays.'

'But he's only just had the amputation.'

'It's two months ago.'

'I've lost track of time,' Barbie said. 'What will happen to him?'

'I suppose they'll find him a job somewhere either in the police or the army. He wouldn't be the only officer around with a disability. Why?'

'I've been thinking about him.'

'Have you, Barbie?'

'Lying here one has little to do but think. I've been thinking about something you said after you'd been in Mirat. Do you remember? We were sitting under the pine tree and you said you thought Captain Merrick had got it all wrong about the men he arrested in Mayapore, the ones who were supposed to have attacked Miss Manners. You said it would be terrible not

1027

just for them but for him, to have got it wrong but never see it, never believe it.'

'Yes, I did, didn't I? What made you think of that?'

At last Sarah looked up from her study of the roses. But her eyes were not lit by more than polite inquiry. Perhaps it hadn't been her interest in the question that made her look up but her arrival at the end of an earlier train of thought which enabled her to.

'I've been wondering whether *I* was wrong, about Mabel, about Mabel's wishes,' Barbie said. 'And if I were whether it will be more terrible knowing it than not knowing it. Wouldn't it be more terrible for Mr Merrick to *know* he'd got it wrong?'

'Perhaps, for a moment. But better in the end surely?'

'Better to know and to say, I got it wrong? But everything that happened as a result of him getting it wrong would be on his conscience forever wouldn't it? There's nothing he can do now to put it right, is there? Even if those men have been released from prison since.'

'Wouldn't that be better than having *no* conscience?' Sarah looked down at the roses again. 'Don't let's talk about Ronald Merrick. Let's talk about what's bothering you.'

'It's connected really,' Barbie said. She could observe the fair head again without disguising the depth of her feeling. 'Everything seems to be. Even spoons. I think it's this room. It addles my mind. The walls are so white and bare.' If she shut her eyes she could feel how everything depended now on the pumping of her old heart and the strange electrical impulses of her brain which switched from one picture of her life to another, encapsulating time and space, events, personalities. 'I saw her,' she said. 'I was very frightened because I heard her first and mistook her for Mabel. When she left I heard the car. It went towards West Hill.'

She had closed her eyes. Now she opened them and found Sarah watching her.

'People said it was a joke, didn't they? When her name appeared in the book. They said it must be someone playing a joke in bad taste. But I saw her. It couldn't have been anyone else. The way she talked and stood, genuflected. You could see she had held a position of importance in public life. I wished I could have seen her face. But there was this veil and the old-fashioned topee with a wide brim. And she sat in front of me. When she looked to this side, that side, there was just a shadow of a face.'

'Who are you talking about, Barbie?'

'Miss Manner's aunt, Lady Manners. You met her in Srinagar. Your houseboat was moored close to hers. Everybody else was embarrassed, because of the child being there. But you—' She stopped. Sarah was looking at her in the oddest manner. 'Have I only imagined it?'

'Imagined what, Barbie?'

'That you crossed the water and talked to her. And saw the child. Yes, I'm sorry. I remember now. It seemed to me the sort of thing you would have done, so I imagined you doing it. The picture was very vivid. All that hot sun and deep green water. Fronds of a kind of willow hanging above the roof of the houseboat. And the child crying. Motherless, fatherless child. But it had Krishna as well as Jesus. I think Miss Manners must have been rather a special person. She could have got rid of it. I mean before it was born. People would have praised her. And her aunt would not now live in obscurity. But—'

'But what?'

'Obscurity or not she was very proud. You could tell. Not of herself, of her niece. My father once said to me, Barbie, there is a conspiracy among us to make us *little*. He was tipsy at the time of course. There was a stage of his tipsiness between the initial release and the final moroseness and anger when he sang and talked and said things like that. My mother told a neighbour whom she wished to impress with our superiority, "My husband has a lot of the poet in him." After that I used to watch him hard. I imagined the poet in him as an unborn twin, one that could be cruel to him as well as kind. Like the demon spirit of a party. After he said that about there being a conspiracy among us to make us little I thought of the demon spirit or poet as a giant bottled up inside him and turned into a dwarf by a spell which only liquor could break.'

Still gazing down at the fair head, bent above the roses, she continued. 'My father's life was full of anomalies but so was my mother's. For instance she was a great church-goer. Her piety on Sundays inspired me as a little girl. It was through her local connections that I got into a church school and stayed on as a pupil-teacher. But when I was grown and told her I wished to serve God in the foreign missions, the missions to India, she was very shocked. Oh, Barbie, she said, not among heathens! She made me feel my ambitions were wrong, almost sinful. Perhaps they were. Even when she was dead and I'd summoned the courage to apply I went to my first interview as if I knew I was doing something to be ashamed of. I huddled into myself. I walked through the streets hunched. I made myself small. To slip through the mesh of people's disapproval and not to be noticed. When I sailed for India I thought: Now I can be large again. But that has not been possible. One may carry the Word, yes, but the Word without the act is an abstraction. The Word gets through the mesh but the act doesn't. So God does not follow. Perhaps He is deaf. Why not? What use are Words to Him?'

Encouraged by Sarah's quietness she touched the girl's head, smoothed the soft helmet of hair. Almost indiscernibly, but unmistakably felt by the hand, the girl inclined her head briefly into the caress.

'I shall never see you again!' Barbie cried suddenly. 'Don't go to Calcutta!'

Sarah laughed: a girl embarrassed by a foolish and importunate elder. 'Oh, Barbie, I'm not going away for good!'

'No.'

There are these spoons, she wanted to say; and began to – but mercifully her voice gave out and she was saved the indignity of rambling on about such nonsense. Apostle spoons! She grinned and shook her head. Her voice came back. 'You'll write to me if you have time, won't you? And if you meet a Mister Studholme ... but that's unlikely. Very unlikely. He's Mission. Although very important.'

'I don't think Aunt Fenny knows any mission people. I'll try to write though.'

Barbie began to tell her about the mission headquarters in Calcutta but as she did so she tuned out of her voice and into the soundless echo of the white room.

There is a letter in my handbag from Colonel Trehearne, the echo announced for her. The walls shone with an extra purity as if they had absorbed the simplicity of Colonel Trehearne's kindness and the clarity of Clarissa's eyes. There was a letter for you, Barbie, Clarissa had said standing by the bedside like a caryatid supporting the weight of a celestial esteem which might have weighed a lesser person down. I brought it with me. On the back of the envelope there was an engraving in shiny blue ink of the Pankot insignia. My Dear Miss Batchelor. Two huge epergnes floated across the room. Empty. Awaiting a cargo of apostles. 'There is your sou'wester too,' Clarissa said, 'but I didn't bring it. Captain Coley found it in his driveway.' 'They were out,' Barbie whispered. 'They?' 'He and his servant.' Clarissa did not ask why Barbie should visit Captain Coley. Probably she knew from Colonel Trehearne. But spoons were not mentioned by either of them.

The spoons and the note to Captain Coley must still be in her room at the rectory bungalow locked in the drawer of the writing-table where she had put them after getting home soaked. 'It was kind of Captain Coley to return my hat,' she said. Clarissa said, 'Why should he not? Your name is in it.' Enclosed by white walls she was aware of risk: her own, not Coley's, not Mildred's. The return of the sou'wester had been a master-stroke. She would never again be able to put it on her head without feeling the pressure of Mildred's contempt. They had seen the significance of the sou'wester and coupled it with the mystery of the missing spoons. They must have known they had not been alone. Coley might care. Mildred did not.

'I must go now, Barbie,' Sarah was saying. 'Is there anything you want?' She shook her head, thinking: I want you to help me find Lady Manners so that I can give her the spoons as a present for the child. I want us to sit together in St John's and wait for her and for you to say, Lady Manners, this is my friend Barbara Batchelor, a holy woman from the missions. Or to go with me into the region of West Hill where the rich Indians from Ranpur have summer houses in which they live for a few months of the year without being bothered by us or with us and are seldom seen in the bazaar, having their own sources or sending servants into ours for the products of the West. We could go into West Hill (curiously named) and search and ask. But you are going to Calcutta. And in any case haven't met her after all, it seems. Or have you? This time you didn't comment.

'Good-bye, Barbie.'

'Good-bye, Sarah.'

The girl bent and kissed her. Barbie put up her arms. Sarah submitted to the embrace. Then she rearranged the blankets.

'Shall I wheel you back to the balcony?'

'Please. Then I can watch you go down the path.'

'I don't go that way, Barbie, I'm afraid.'

'Is Captain Beauvais waiting for you with a car?'

'No. I'm getting a tonga.'

'Oh, but I was forgetting. Clarissa told me Captain Beauvais has gone.'

'Yes, and now I must.'

She felt the girl's head close to her own again and breath coming against her cheek as though she were an old yellow candle being blown out very gently. Some time later she was surprised to see the girl on the tarmac pathway, having walked out of her way to wave, and waving, and then coming back towards the building to follow the path round to the front where a tonga would take her on the first stage of the long journey to Calcutta.

She looked at the familiar panorama and after a while pulled the blanket up to her throat and tucked her chin in. The sun dipped below the overhanging roof of the balcony and shone through her eyelids. The little Anglo-Indian nurse had never left her on the balcony so long. Perhaps she had forgotten her.

She pictured herself abandoned there, until dark, and beyond; for many days, through the changes of season, from one decade to another, while the building slowly crumbled round her, leaving her isolated, high up on a pillar of jagged but stubborn masonry, enthroned, wrapped in the scarlet blanket, with a clear view across the uninhabited valley to the ruins of the church of St John.

III

Isobel Rankin's generosity to Mildred in allowing her to move into Flagstaff House and close Rose Cottage did not escape criticism. Lucy Smalley, more or less indistinguishable nowadays from the potted palms and stained napery of Smith's Hotel, said it was a bit odd that a place could be closed, however temporarily, and yet escape the net of the accommodations officer who she swore slept with requisition orders under his pillow in the hope of being woken in the middle of the night by one of his spies and tipped off about a bungalow that had been left empty for a day or two, so that before daylight a notice could be tacked to the door denying entry to its rightful owners.

'I heard about Nicky Paynton's decision to go home within a few hours of her making it,' Lucy complained, 'and I rang him at once, because Tusker wouldn't, and he said he had a waiting list and had already made provisional allocations. He was barely civil.'

But Lucy Smalley's disappointment did not prevent her turning up several weeks later at Nicky Paynton's auction party, wandering from room to room in the place she had briefly visualized herself and Tusker moving into, and wanly watching the auctioneer – Nicky Paynton herself – hammering down the familiar detritus of an Anglo-Indian career.

The most prized items were those which had practical use, scarcity value and a comparatively short life – a radiogram, a refrigerator, a portable wireless set, an electric iron and an ironing board, two electric fires, an electric fan. After these, for which the bidding was on a tense but modest level, Nicky had success in getting rid of crockery, cutlery, glasses, two alarm clocks, blankets, sheets and pillow-cases, a picnic basket, camp equipment, and assorted thermos flasks which were a godsend on the trains packed with ice or filled with decent drinking water. Lowest on the list of desirable things were the ornamental coffee tables, the Benares trays, numdah rugs, vases and ornaments which for most of the people who could find room for them would be replicas of those they already had.

Finally there was the stuff which in other circumstances might have ended its days in a modest house in Surrey, and still might, although not in the possession of Colonel and Mrs Paynton. The Payntons themselves had bought it at an auction in Rawalpindi. It had spent quite a number of years in storage, and on loan, during the periods when Nicky and Bunny were moving too frequently from one station to another for it to go with them. A mahogany sideboard, elegantly proportioned, a mahogany dining-table (with two leaves) and a dozen imitation Georgian chairs, plus two armed servers, were the chief items on this particular list. Supplementary to it were two wing chairs covered in rather murky but genuine tapestry – one man-size and the other woman-size. These chairs, Nicky announced, had belonged to the late General Sir Horace and Lady Hamilton-Wellesley-Gore and one of them had been sat in by the Prince of Wales when he toured India in 1921.

'They were snitched from under my nose at the 'Pindi auction,' Nicky explained, 'by a simply frightful chap with pots of money. He turned up next year at the same beano in Gwalior and without telling me Bunny played him for them at poker and the next thing I knew they arrived on the doorstep. So what am I bid? No reserve price. Going for a song.'

Maisie Trehearne called out a figure which her husband didn't hear. He called out a lower one and under the screen of the ensuing laughter Clara said to Nicky, 'I want the chairs.' She doubled Maisie's figure.

'You must be mad,' Nicky said. 'But I'm not saying no.'

The chairs were knocked down to Clara Fosdick. Her sister in Ranpur wouldn't be pleased – she already housed some of Clara's and Freddie's old furniture – but these were chairs Clara and Nicky had sat in, many a winter evening, over a pine-log fire listening to the news.

When the auction was over the dining-room furniture was still unsold, but Nicky's farewell party got under way merrily enough. In the next few days the stuff that had been auctioned off would be collected and removed, leaving the two women bereft of most of the things that made the bungalow into a home. But that was all to the good, they felt. Their departure from a place in which nothing belonged to either of them would come as a relief and with luck (from Clara's point of view) they would have a few days together in Ranpur, perhaps more because although five days was all the notice Nicky would get of a flight from Ranagunj she had to be prepared for postponements. Her final departure might be a relief as well. Already, at the height of the party, they were both on tenterhooks, and old Fariqua had obviously been at the rum bottle.

For the party he had put on the white trousers, tunic, Ranpur sash and head-dress that he used to wear to go in to mess when Bunny dined there, but the pugree was indifferently swathed and the fan of muslin which should have been as perky as a cock's comb had flopped over. As he got drunker he grew lugubriously into the role of skeleton at the feast, chief mourner at the wake for Bunny Paynton, the only one with a long face, sodden with the liquor that buoyed other people up.

'To look at Fariqua,' Lucy Smalley said, with what was becoming after the years of her social frustration an unerring sense for saying the right thing at the wrong time, 'you'd think Nicky was going to invite bids for him as well.'

She was saved the rebuke that Maisie Trehearne might have administered by the arrival of the general's lady, Isobel Rankin, to whom all heads turned, like compass needles to a magnetic north. There was nothing unusual in this ritual observance, this metaphorical doffing of caps and bending of knees, but this morning a special intensity attached to it, because of certain rumours that had been taking shape and seriously disturbing the station's sense of balance and proportion and were now contributing a ground-swell of uneasiness to the determined light-heartedness of the occasion.

*

Nicky had announced her decision to go home in mid-July. Thereafter, slowly and quietly she had made her dispositions, settled her affairs, transferred money to London, paid her debts, written to Dora Lowndes to warn her and to advise her to say nothing to the boys until she got a cable from Clara Fosdick confirming her departure. She had also written to her friends in India and given them Dora Lowndes's address. By the middle of August she was ready to take the last step. The airforce liaison officer on Dick Rankin's staff told her he would start pulling strings the moment she said the word. For a week she did not say it and it began to look as if she might change her mind at the last moment. But it was during this week that the rumours were first heard and by the end of it there seemed little doubt that there was more than a grain of truth in them. If Nicky had been wavering her mind was now abruptly made up again. She rang Wing-

Commander Pearson and asked him to pull the first string on the last day in August. She announced her auction and farewell party for that same day.

The rumours which had encouraged Nicky to stick to her decision to go home had begun at area headquarters as a result of the circulation of curiously worded documents from higher authorities about reallocation of areas of military responsibility; innocent enough on the surface and apparently without reference or application to the military hierarchy established at Pankot. This hierarchy was still in effect the old Ranpur Command whose authority, in spite of erosion here and there, extended over large stretches of the province's territory.

But between the lines of the documents' oblique phraseology casual references acquired dangerously direct meanings. Among the senior members of Dick Rankin's staff the junior officers detected signs of that alert fascination which people in high places cannot disguise when first glimpsing a future upheaval which they know they are personally too distinguished and secure to be adversely affected by.

What had emerged was an image of Pankot stripped of a proportion of its powers as a central seat of military control and administration. How large a proportion could only be guessed at but since it was human nature to adopt a pessimistic view of any rearrangement from above the guess was that for 'a proportion of' one had to read 'most of'. Once such a guess had been made the rumours proliferated, some of them disagreeably backed by mounting evidence that the guess was correct: rumours that the old Ranpur Command was to be hacked up into several areas and redistributed on a geographical rather than a viable military basis between Central and Eastern Commands, that Pankot would be separated from Ranpur and become a training and rest centre with a Brigadier as its area commander; that a new OTS was to be established, most of whose cadets would be Indian; that the old Governor's summer residence which dominated the height of East Hill and had been closed throughout most of the war, was to be reopened – not, as Isobel Rankin had often proposed, as a convalescent home for wounded British and Indian officers of all three services, but as a leave centre for American troops of non-commissioned rank. Only in the bazaar where the rumours were quick to penetrate was the latter news greeted with enthusiasm. One or two ladies swore there had already been a rise in prices to prepare people for the new era of native prosperity.

'We shall all have to get used to walking,' one of them said, 'because the cost of a tonga up the hill to the club, should one manage to find one not already loaded with GI's, will be quite beyond *our* pockets.' But on second thoughts, she went on, one would probably stop going to the club because it would be crowded with American officers – those in charge of the leave centre – and perhaps with top-sergeants, whatever species *they* were. If the cinema was any guide even the sergeants in the American army seemed to get saluted and to call officers by their Christian names, so they would all be at the club with their hands in their pockets, their bottoms hanging out of their shiny trousers and cigars in their mouths, getting drunk, breaking the place up and bringing in Eurasian girls.

Moreover, she said, with Pankot's military role downgraded there would be fewer and fewer *young* British officers doing a stint on area headquarters staff between regimental and active staff appointments. From area headquarters as it now existed the top and junior levels would be creamed off and the men would be off to brighter places. Probably only men like Major Smalley could expect to survive from the old to the new regime, if such a thing could be called survival. And Flagstaff House would be occupied by some doddery dugout Brigadier. In Mildred's father's day, the Ranpur Command had carried a Lieutenant-General's hat. It still carried a major-general's.

Which brought one to the Rankins. What glamorous appointment would fall into their laps? Already people had it on good authority that they were for Mountbatten's staff and the fleshpots of Ceylon; that they were for the India Office and home; for Washington on a military mission, for Moscow, for Cairo, for Persia; Simla at the very least. Two days before Nicky's party Dick Rankin had been driven down to Ranpur to be flown to Delhi. When he got back perhaps he would have fuller details of the station's fate and of his and Isobel's brighter prospects.

And here was Isobel, arriving too late for the auction, alight and vibrant with both power and discretion, giving nothing away which was only comforting if it could be assumed that she had nothing to give and was as ignorant of what was in store as the least among those present.

She embraced Nicky in the centre of the crowded living-room, apologized for being late in a voice that carried above the resumed conversation and then without lowering her voice said, 'Where can we have a word?' which caused a tremor of delicious apprehension, a pause in the flow of talk. Nicky led her into the dining-room where the unsold table, chairs and sideboard already appeared to have lost their sheen.

'Nicky, I'm late because I waited for Mildred to get back from visiting Susan, but she rang and asked me to come along on my own and to warn you that she's bringing Susan with her.'

'Oh.' The two women looked at each other straight. 'Is Susan allowed out then?'

'It will be the first time.'

'A noisy party? What an extraordinary choice.'

'She wanted to come. She asked this Captain Samuels chap and apparently he said it was a first-rate idea. He hopes it's all right if he looks in too. I think he'll take her back, to save Mildred doing it.'

'I must say that's a bit cool, isn't it? I don't know Captain Samuels and it's a private farewell party not a therapy session. Is she really fit enough? I should hate a scene. That's why the trick-cyclist wallah insists on coming, isn't it? To be on hand if Susan throws a fit or does something odd.'

'He says she's well enough. In fact he's letting her out in a day or two.

She'll be coming up to the House, so I can only assume he knows what he's doing. He thinks a party would be a good ice-breaker. Do you mind?'

'As long as it's only ice. Does she know about Bunny?'

'Yes. And she knows you're going home. That's why she wants to come. It's very sweet really.'

'I hope she's not going to be condoling,' Nicky said. She looked feverish.

'The thing to do is tell everybody before she gets here and prepare them to look as if they're acting naturally. Did you sell this dining-room stuff?'

'No.'

'Mildred may want it. Try to persuade her. She has a lot of plans for the cottage. In any case she could store it. I'd have it myself but God knows how much longer we'll be here or where we'll be going. What about getting Jalal-Ud-Din's man along? He might sell it like a shot to one of his rich Indian clients.'

'I'll see.'

They went back to the living-room, separated and passed the word that Mildred was bringing Susan and that Captain Samuels would be looking in, to take her back to the nursing-home to save her mother going all that way herself when the party was over. Prepared for important general news this struck the guests as an anti-climax and it took a while for it to sink in and to be recognized as important too, important to the old Pankot if not to the one currently in a state of derangement of its own, which one had to hope would turn out to be as temporary as Susan Bingham's had proved. Curiosity and nostalgic affection began to flow out to her in advance of her arrival. Heads kept turning towards the door through which she would enter.

As she did, within ten minutes of the first warning, unannounced by any sound of tonga or car wheels that could have hushed the sound of talk and laughter; a step or so ahead of her mother, wearing a simple full-skirted dress of white with navy blue polka dots; to all appearances unchanged, a pound or two heavier perhaps but as pretty as ever, prettier if anything, and with that familiar flush on her cheeks which suggested some special happiness anticipated or re-encountered.

To look at her, as she greeted Nicky and her mother's other friends, was to doubt the truth of the accounts of her bizarre behaviour and to guess that no explanation of it would ever be had. It was as if it hadn't happened. No unhappy memory seemed to live behind her face. Her smile was not the smile of someone with a secret life. She was looking at the world as it was.

She said nothing, did nothing, that could be reckoned odd or interpreted as an indication that her mind was still clouded in any way by her illness and misfortunes. There were omissions, but were they significant? She did not mention the baby, but that could as easily be put down to a regard for other people's feelings as to anything sinister or threatening. She was punctilious in thanking Isobel Rankin for the invitation to Flagstaff House and said how much she was looking forward to it. Since the baby and the ayah were already installed there with Mildred one could surely assume that by 'looking forward' she meant glad to think she would see the baby again as well. In any case, Captain Samuels would not let her out if he had doubts about her attitude to the child.

She said she was also looking forward to the holiday in Darjeeling and Calcutta. She said she missed Sarah's visits but had had postcards and letters to make up for them. Out of Nicky's hearing she told Clara Fosdick how sorry she was about Brigadier Paynton, about Nicky decision to go home and about Clara herself leaving Pankot to go to live in Ranpur. She said she hoped Mrs Fosdick would come up to spend holidays with them at Rose Cottage.

Her mother had briefed her well. She knew about the rumours of change and said it all sounded rather dreary. She asked Clarissa Peplow how Mrs Batchelor was and seemed surprised to hear that although much better she was still in hospital. Clarissa assumed that in the case of Miss Batchelor's illness, Sarah – not Mildred – had been Susan's informant.

She did not mention the dog, Panther. Maisie found the opportunity to ask Mildred whether Susan knew the dog had died and Mildred said she had had Samuels's permission to tell her and had done so, without the gory details, and Susan had taken it well but not referred to it again. If there were any forbidden subjects they were the dog and the baby. Was Dicky Beauvais a third? Apparently not. She said, 'I had a letter from Dicky the other day. He sounded a bit browned off. After all that rush he's still stuck in Comilla waiting for a posting. I must remember to tell Sarah because the letter was to us both.'

She moved gracefully, freely, perfectly at ease. She sipped her drink as if she intended to make it last and had accepted it only to be sociable. When Lucy Smalley suggested she should sit, not tire herself standing, she laughed in a friendly way and said she had sat enough in the last few weeks and needed exercise. She went from group to group, watched but not shadowed by Mildred who had shown only one sign of the strain she must have been under when at a first attempt to raise a full cocktail glass to her lips she spilt a few drops and waited (Clara Fosdick noticed) for at least a minute before raising it again.

'How relieved Mildred must be to have Susan her old self again,' Maisie Trehearne said.

'I wouldn't call it that,' Nicky replied, blowing smoke to one side, holding her glass high to minimize the risk of her elbow being jogged. 'Susan used to take up a position and let people swarm round her. I've never seen her mingle in my life. But that's what she's doing now. I'm half inclined to think the Jew-boy trick-cyclist is cleverer than Mildred gives him credit for.'

What Nicky had observed, perhaps because she was more alert to the shapes and patterns of her last party than any of her guests could be, was true. If a change in Susan were to be noted it would be this one: the free-ranging movement and presentation of herself within the tableau. Before her illness she would have stood herself at its centre, receiving tribute. Her new mobility suggested that she was offering it, reaffirming her commitment to a society she had lived in since childhood and had now returned to, after a brief but inexplicable withdrawal.

Interest in the unknown Captain Samuels, the Jew-boy trick-cyclist, mounted. Apart from Mildred no one at the party had ever met him and no one had been inquisitive enough to investigate him since hearing his name in connection with Susan. Mildred's attitude had summed up all one needed to know or feel about an RAMC analyst. The job was not one which could normally be taken seriously. No man who fitted the picture conjured by the name could be recalled from among the welter of new or itinerant faces at the club. Samuels probably kept himself to himself. Neither Beames nor Travers – who might have expressed professional if not personal opinions – had turned up. Both had been invited, but it was obviously a busy morning at the hospital.

Someone, perhaps its new owner, put a record on the radiogram: a selection from 'Chu Chin Chow'; but the record was so worn that only people close to the machine could make much of the tunes. Fariqua and the cook-boy Nazimuddin were bringing in plates of bridge sandwiches and canapés. Nicky called out, 'Food everybody. There'll be more in the dining-room in a minute so everyone just help themselves.' Several guests went through to relieve the crush in the living-room where there was a gradual rearrangement of groups which left Susan temporarily unattached. She took a sandwich from the plate offered none too steadily by the spectral Fariqua and went to stand a little apart by a window that gave her a view of the front verandah and compound.

In an instant her mother joined her and by chance or design interposed herself between her daughter and Lucy Smalley who had seen that Susan was alone and was approaching her. So even Lucy who was close to them was unable to say how Susan's cocktail glass fell out of her hand and splintered on the parquet floor. Later, considerably later, Lucy said she had always felt Susan dropped the glass deliberately. She couldn't say why she thought so but her intuition told her that this was what had happened. Mildred had been talking perfectly naturally to Susan, saying, 'Are you all right, darling? Not too tired?' and Susan had said also quite naturally but a bit testily, 'I'm fine.' And the next thing was the sudden sound of the breaking glass and a little cry from Mildred; no sound, Lucy recalled, from Susan, but Mildred saying, 'Did I jog you?' And then the incident – if it could be called an incident – was over.

There was a stain down Mildred's skirt. Susan stooped and picked up the unbroken base of the glass and started to gather the fragments. She handed them to the cookboy who came to help her and then stood up. 'My fault,' Mildred said, while Susan apologized to Nicky for the mess.

Susan declined the offer of another drink and went to talk to Mrs Stewart, Clarissa Peplow and Wing-Commander Pearson, leaving her mother with Nicky who said, 'D'you want to sponge that skirt?'

'It won't stain.'

'Then come into the dining-room and see if you want this furniture.'

On their way past Susan Mildred spoke to her.

'I'm going into the next room for a moment. You'd better keep an eye open for Captain Samuels. I don't think he knows anybody.'

'Is this him now?' Clarissa asked. They turned to look.

Susan said, 'Oh, yes. That's Sam.'

Nicky Paynton threaded her way back towards a door that stood open to the side of the verandah. 'Come in,' she shouted when still a few feet away. 'I'm Nicky Paynton, the one who's throwing this shin-dig.' She pushed her hand out at him and kept it there until he relieved her, as it were, of its weight. The noise in the room had begun to subside directly it became clear why Nicky was making her way towards this part of the room. Here was the stranger: the Jew-boy trick-cyclist. The noise diminished to such a degree that the sounds of merriment in the dining-room seemed to belong to a different party, almost a different world; one safe from such an intrusion. Astonishment more than curiosity caused the hush accentuated by the continuing drone of a male voice which, finding itself solo, ceased for a few seconds and then resumed, nudging the general conversation slowly back to life.

Captain Samuels was slender, fair-haired. He looked down on Nicky from above average height. He did not smile. When she let go of his hand he did not let it fall but lowered it carefully. He did not attempt any of the opening gambits which a guest might have used in the special circumstances which had brought him to the party. He did not appear to have spoken at all. He gave the impression of being a man who had dispensed with casual physical responses as timewasting.

The image of the Jew-boy trick-cyclist was completely shattered. He was remote, patrician; in the opinion of most of the women present disturbingly, coldly handsome. It was a shock to see, on closer inspection, how young he must be. His youthfulness made the attention he instantly commanded seem, to those who were giving it, as disagreeable to them as a personal affront would be: the more so because he did not appear to be conscious of any obligation to conduct himself with that air of apology for *being* young which was usually considered part of a young man's charm when in the company of his elders.

Theoretically, Nicky might have been said to lead him into the room. In practice she went ahead to prepare a way for him to use. At the end of it stood Isobel Rankin. He took his time reaching her.

'May I introduce Captain Samuels?' Nicky said. 'Captain Samuels, Mrs Rankin, the wife of our area commander.'

They murmured how-do-you-do to one another.

'Are you related to friends of ours at home, Myra and Issy Samuels?' Isobel asked him, after he had declined the drink which Nazimuddin offered on a tray.

He observed her very closely.

'Sir Isaac Samuels?'

1039

'Yes.'

'No. He is no relation.'

'But I gather you know him.'

'Professionally. I've met Lady Myra at Chester Square.'

'If you've met Issy professionally does that mean you're interested in tropical medicine too? If so you're in the right place. How long have you been in India?'

'Since the middle of May.'

'And in Pankot?'

'Since the end of May.'

'Really? As long as that!'

Listeners, hitherto fascinated by the social connection through mutual friends of the general's lady and the young army-doctor, now recognized a rebuke. Captain Samuels had neither sent in his card nor signed Isobel Rankin's book outside Flagstaff House: an essential step for an officer to take if he wanted to be considered officially on-station. In the old days for an officer to have been on-station since May and not to have signed the book by the end of August would have been unthinkable. Nowadays, with so many people coming and going and holding only temporary appointments the ritual was not so strictly observed, but for a man appointed to the staff of the hospital not to have observed it was still a serious omission, the result either of sheer ignorance or, which was worse and presumably the case here, indifference.

'I know absolutely nothing about psychological medicine,' Isobel continued when it was clear that Captain Samuels had no comment to make. 'I don't suppose Guy Charlton does either.' She referred to the chief medical officer, Beames's military counterpart, who was new on-station himself. 'So I imagine you pretty well run your own show. Are you a Freudian or a Jungian? Isn't that what one is supposed to ask?'

For the first time Captain Samuels allowed himself a flicker of emotion: it seemed to be amusement.

'People do,' he said. 'Personally I find Reich's ideas on the subject of considerable interest.'

'And what does or did Mr Reich say?'

'Any answer I could give would be an over-simplification.'

'That would be the only kind I would understand. So do tell us.'

Again he studied her. But Isobel Rankin had never yet been quelled by a look and wasn't now. He glanced at Nicky, at Colonel and Mrs Trehearne; briefly at Lucy and Tusker Smalley who had joined the group; either sizing them up or politely including them in the conversation.

'One must draw a distinction between analysis and treatment. Whatever the cause of a neurosis the psychotherapist is concerned with a patient's ability to relax, physically. This is a simple extension of Reich's belief that the human orgasm is a major contributory factor to physical and mental health, but the corollary need not be that all neuroses are rooted in sexual repression.'

Several seconds went by before Tusker Smalley went red in the face and said, 'Good God!'

Isobel Rankin glanced at him as if to stop him from making an issue of an officer having dared mention such things in front of women. The smile on her face was perhaps a little set, but she directed it again at Captain Samuels.

'What particular branch of tropical medicine interests you?'

'The amoebic infection of the bowels known as amoebiasis.'

'Oh, yes. What interests you so much about it? Surely it's of relatively minor importance? It's easily cured I gather. Is it one of Issy's pet subjects?'

'I wouldn't say so. But then I've come to the conclusion that in general English physicians aren't as interested in it as perhaps they might be, considering how large a tropical empire we have. And I would disagree with you, Mrs Rankin, when you suggest it is easily cured. Since coming to India it's struck me that even diagnosis is a very hit and miss affair. I should say that quite a fair proportion of my psychiatric cases are suspect of chronic infection, but it is very difficult to arrange for a convincing check.'

'What are the symptoms, a permanent kind of gippy-tum?'

He smiled. 'It's rather different from amoebic dysentery. Unfortunately it can be contracted and carried for years until it eats through the walls of the bowels and invades more vital organs. At least that is a theory a few people have. Without a convincing check it tends to go undiagnosed and the symptoms aren't alarming. A general air of languor, as lassitude. A tendency to concentrate the mind rather obsessively in one direction.'

'Why is a convincing check so difficult?'

'I think I should not explain why. I shall get a reputation for indelicacy. I apologize if my earlier remarks caused any offence.'

He looked at his watch.

'Not at all, Captain Samuels. I asked a question and you answered it. I see you are pressed for time.'

'I have quite a full afternoon ahead.'

'Then I expect you want to ask Mrs Bingham if she's ready to leave. But you must come up to Flagstaff House one day and tell me about these theories of yours. I'm always interested to hear a young man talking on his subject. I'll ask Guy Charlton to bring you along.'

Samuels made no answer. A slight inclination of his head towards her was his sole acknowledgment of her invitation. Several people in the group round them were astonished that Isobel Rankin had made it.

But having made it she ended the conversation by moving away. The group dispersed. He took the opportunity to look round the room. He did not appear to be interested in meeting anyone else. Eyes were averted if he chanced to look into them. Hints of extraordinary behaviour were already reaching people who had not heard the conversation. As soon as he saw Susan he went through the crowd towards her.

'Hello, Sam. Is it time?'

'If you're ready.'

She said she was. She introduced him to Clarissa, Mrs Stewart and Wing-Commander Pearson.

'I must say goodbye to Mrs Paynton,' she said. 'Will you come with me, Sam?'

He put a hand on her shoulder. The gesture, although brief, struck those who saw it as unnecessarily possessive. Susan belonged in the room. Samuels did not. But he was taking her away. She was allowing it; at least, the girl in the polka-dot dress was allowing it and it now occurred to the watchers that in a subtly disagreeable way the girl was not the Susan they knew at all but a creation of Captain Samuels, or a joint creation of the two of them, a person who had emerged from a secret process of pressure, duress, insinuation, God knew what. And God knew what they talked about, or whom they talked about, when they were alone during sessions of analysis or whatever it was called. As Samuels followed her his glance fell here and there upon faces as if he were looking for evidence of mental and emotional disorders of the kind he had presumed to uncover in *her* but blamed *them* for. He bore himself like a man taking someone out of an area of contagion.

'Mrs Paynton,' Susan was saying, 'thank you for letting me come to your party. I'll only say au revoir if that's all right.'

Holding glass and cigarette in one hand Nicky used the other to give her the half-embrace which had become part of her farewell party armour.

'Au revoir it is then, Susan. Probably true too. It could be ages before they pop me on to a plane.'

She nodded at Captain Samuels.

Mildred was waiting at the open doorway.

'Are you off now then, darling? Would you like me to come round this evening?'

'No, there's really no need. You must be bored stiff coming down every day, there's no reason to do it twice.'

That much was heard. Mildred went out with Susan and Captain Samuels. For a minute they stood talking on the verandah, then Samuels and Susan went down into the compound and climbed into the tonga that had been waiting. Mildred came back into the house, not through the doorway they had left by but through the main entrance. It was some time before she reappeared in the living-room and by then the party was beginning to break up.

When Isobel's car arrived to take her and Mildred back to Flagstaff House she said to Nicky, 'You and Clara come back with us. There's nothing as depressing as an afternoon surrounded by the remains. We could have a rubber or two and wind down.'

'Fair enough. I'll get rid of the late-stayers.'

She did so by announcing that she was shutting up shop. Within ten minutes the house and compound were clear. Lucy and Tusker Smalley were the last to leave. Their tonga, they said, was missing.

'What bad luck you do have,' Nicky said. 'Shall I send Nazimuddin for one?'

'We can pick one up on the road, I expect,' Tusker said. Lucy had her eye on the Rankin car but Tusker waved to Nicky and started off down the steps and presently Lucy followed.

'Pankot *must* be changing,' Nicky said, coming back in. 'Poor Lucy and Tusker failed to cadge a lift. I'm sorry really. It spoils the shape of my last Pankot party.'

*

A limousine such as could be hired in Ranpur to drive leave and summer parties up into the hills and down again was coming along Flagstaff road which turned and twisted and was not easy for two large cars to negotiate if they met head on. But for them to do so was rare. Only Flagstaff House traffic used the road. In any case the general's car always took precedence over local traffic. Assuming this the naik-driver taking Isobel and her guests home was prepared to glide on and up and give the minimum of room to the limousine which he expected to pull over and come almost to a halt.

On the limousine's roof there was a luggage rack, piled high and covered by a rainproof sheet. Perhaps this extra weight gave the limousine's civilian driver the strange idea that his vehicle was the more important of the two, even though the furled flag on the bonnet of the general's car proclaimed that this was not the case. If he saw this symbol of the car's status he ignored it. He came on. At the last moment the naik-driver called a warning to his passengers and slammed on the brakes. The limousine sailed past. The general's car quivered under the pressure.

'My God!' Isobel said. 'The raving bloody lunatic. Who was it, Clara? Did you see?'

Clara had the offside window seat in the back.

'There were blinds down at the window, so I couldn't.'

'*Blinds*?'

The naik-driver had got out with squared shoulders and bunched fists. He thought the other driver would stop to apologize or argue. He looked forward to telling him off and earning a good mark in the Burra Memsahib's book who it was known liked men to be sharp on the draw. But the limousine sped on. It was already rounding the corner. He did not even have time to get its registration number.

'What do you mean, blinds, Clara? What was it? A damned hearse? What was it doing on Flagstaff road if it was?'

'Not a hearse. Just a car with blinds down.'

'Was there a crest?'

'I didn't see one.'

'The only people who drive with blinds down are Maharajahs.'

'Or their wives. Mostly their wives.'

1043

'Well, if we've had a call from a spare maharajah and his harem he's got off on the wrong foot. Unless of course it was old Dippy Singh. *He's* as mad as a hatter. All right, Shafi. It wasn't your fault. Let's get on.'

At the end of the road the tarmac broadened, providing a turn-round outside an imposing iron gateway. There was a sentry. The guard-commander was also present as if he had recently been disturbed.

'Shafi, stop at the gate and ask guard-commander about that car.'

He did so. The sentry was already presenting arms. He clattered. The guard commander ran forward, came to attention and saluted.

Shafi spoke to him. Presently he said, 'He says the car stopped and a lady got out.'

'Yes, I heard.' She called over Shafi's shoulder in Urdu. 'What lady?'

'An English lady, memsahib. An old lady. She wore a topee. She came to sign the book, memsahib.'

'Thank you.'

She got out, went to the other sentry-box where the book was kept, on a shelf, chained. She was there for a few seconds and then came back and got in.

'Carry on, Shafi.'

As the car moved into the grounds she said, 'The first time wasn't a practical joke then. She's signed out. "Ethel Manners, pour prendre congé." '

There was a silence. Then Nicky Paynton laughed.

'That,' she said between gusts, '*that* has made the day for me. Pour prendre congé!'

She was still laughing when the car stopped under the great portico in front of which, in the centre of an immaculate lawn, in a circular bed of white chippings, stood the tall white flagpost, moored to the ground by ropes, like the mast of a ship. From this eminence great stretches of the Pankot valley were visible. Early afternoon sunlight shone upon it. Before going inside Nicky Paynton stood for a moment, still shaken by spasms of laughter, and gazed. Then, turning her back on it, she opened her handbag, got out her handkerchief, dabbed at her lower lids and joined her friends for what might be their last game of bridge together.

It was. Nine days later, aching in every bone and deaf in both ears, she stepped out of a Dakota on to the tarmac of an RAF aerodrome and into the amazing unreality of the Wiltshire countryside.

IV

When October came Barbie stopped taking the spoons to the church with her. The old lady must have gone. She packed the spoons up, wrote a letter and asked Clarissa if one of the servants could take them to Comman-dant's House. Clarissa agreed. She had become solicitous. The next day Barbie had by hand a letter of acknowledgment from Colonel Trehearne.

He asked her if she would do him the honour of dining with him on Ladies' Night in November.

For a day or two she did not reply because she knew she would not accept but while her letter of apology and thanks remained unwritten she was able to enjoy the pleasure the invitation had given her. Ankle-length black velvet, she thought; a brooch, no other jewellery. A special cropping of the hair and a set to add lustre to the soft natural waves on the crown of her head and forehead. Black slippers and a glittering black evening bag. Perhaps a velvet rose – crimson or purple – instead of a brooch. No. The brooch would be more distinguished. A gossamer-thin black silk chiffon stole to warm but not hide completely the marble of her arms and shoulders. For the journey there a cloak of the same black velvet as the dress but with a warm scarlet lining. Perhaps a gilt or silver chain for the clasp at the throat. Elbow-length gloves. White, these. Or black? White, if she wore the brooch. Black for the coloured velvet flower. And a fine lawn handkerchief sprinkled with cologne.

When her letter pleading unfitness had been sent she studied the reflection of her wasted bony body and the lank straight hair that needed cutting. In such a dress all you would see would be the wild untended head, the gaunt collar bone and corded wrinkled neck, the scarecrow arms, the tombstone teeth that were too big for her mouth. And hear what had once been a voice; a hoarse grating sound alternating between a crackling whisper and an uneven cry.

She put Colonel Trehearne's letter in the drawer of the portable writing-table where there already lay the letter from the bank and the letters and picture postcard from Sarah in Calcutta and Darjeeling. The letter from the mission which had arrived on the morning of the christening and the undelivered letter to Captain Coley she had destroyed. The picture postcard from Sarah showed the headquarters of the Bishop Barnard in Calcutta and was postmarked September 6 which was the day Mildred had left Pankot with Susan, the baby and the ayah, and the day before Captain Travers had let Barbie come back to the rectory bungalow.

'You'll recognize this,' Sarah had written on the back. 'I hope you're better. I'm better too, fit as they say for human consumption again. Love, Sarah.'

Like so much that had to do with Sarah the postcard was an enigma. Normally the only place you could buy the card was at the headquarters of the mission itself. But Sarah did not say whether she had been there.

*

Walking, she found it difficult to go further than St John's in one direction and Mr Maybrick's bungalow in the other. For the bazaar she sent out for a tonga and did not get down from it until it returned her to the rectory bungalow.

In the bazaar she had the wallah stop outside Jalal-Ud-Din's. The first time she did this a minute or two went by before a ragged little chokra came bare-foot in search of an errand and an anna. But nowadays she was met at the outskirts by a dozen or more who ran behind the tonga advertising their prowess, willingness and honesty.

At first her own little boy had joined the opposition but, reassured of her loyalty, now waited outside the store until she arrived. To reach her he had to fight his way through a thicket of limbs mostly sturdier than his own. She gave him a list and money and clear instructions. While she waited she distributed sweets to the others. If there was a list for more than one shop she gave him one list at a time. The other boys lost interest once they had had the sweets but her own little boy ran to and fro from shop to tonga, tonga to shop, rendering a meticulous accounting between each visit. The purchases were mainly Clarissa's. When there were a lot of packages the chokra rode back with her to the bungalow, sitting at the driver's side, and helped her to carry the packages up to the verandah. Out of her own money she gave him a percentage of the total expenditure. She hoped that he got commission from the shopkeepers. She did not always specify which shop he should go to and sometimes he was gone for quite a time. Invariably, then, he came back with a bargain. Clarissa was pleased.

They conversed in a mixture of Urdu, Pankot hill dialect and English.

His name, he said, was Ashok. His parents had died in Ranpur. He had come up to Pankot to look for work. He had no relatives. He did odd jobs. He slept where he happened to be when finishing the last job of the day. He was eight years old. It was his ambition to work in the elephant stables of a maharajah.

'There are no elephants in Pankot,' Barbie pointed out.

No, he agreed. But in Pankot a boy could earn rupees. And then he could go to Rajputana. There were hundreds of maharajahs in Rajputana. Each one of them had a thousand elephants.

At home, Barbie said, most little English boys of his age intended to be engine drivers. He said to be an engine driver would be all right. Providing there were no elephants.

'Do you have to be a special caste to be a mahout or even to go near the elephants?'

He did not understand. He said his father had worked for the Ranpur municipality. Ashok did not say in what capacity. She decided he was a Harijan, a child of God, an untouchable. The elephants were his dream. Perhaps in Rajputana he would be allowed to clear away their droppings. But there was probably a caste for that too. She did not know. Hinduism, Mr Cleghorn had told her, is not a religion but a way of life. So, she replied, should Christianity be. He had given her an old-fashioned look.

'What am I?' she asked Ashok.

'You are Sahib-log.'

'No, I am a servant of the Lord Jesus.'

She sat on the verandah steps of the rectory bungalow and offered her hand. Ashok looked at her seriously.

'Come,' she said, 'I am your father and your mother.'

He came. She clasped his thin shoulders.

'You don't understand,' she said in English. He smelt musky. 'It is all too long ago and far away. The world you and I live in is corrupt. I clasp you to my breast but you conceive of this in terms of an authority unbending. I offer my love. You accept it as a sign of fortune smiling. Your heart beats with gratitude, excitement, expectation of rupees. And mine scarcely beats at all. It is very tired and old and far from home. Ashoka, Ashoka, Shokam, Shokarum, Shokis, Shokis.' Somewhere she had got that wrong.

He laughed. His eyes were luminous.

'Chalo,' she said.

She put a silver rupee into his tiny hand. He salaamed and ran. At the gate he turned. They waved to each other.

'Tu es mon petit Hindou inconnu,' she whispered. 'Et tu es un papillon brun. Moi, je suis blanche. Mais nous sommes les prisonniers du bon Dieu.'

*

'It's uncertain how much longer I shall be able to visit you,' she told Mabel. She had begun to think of a grave as a closed entrance to a long tunnel, dark and tortuous, which you had to crawl through on your belly if ever you were to reach that area of radiance at its end. For a while, she supposed, you might kneel huddled against the blocked entrance getting up courage to begin the journey. There were days when she thought Mabel had gone and others when the sensation of her nearness was strong. Today she seemed very near. 'I'm sorry there are so few flowers. There aren't many in the rectory garden. I don't like to cut them without asking permission and don't like asking too often.'

When next she saw Ashok she asked him to buy flowers. He came back to the tonga with both hands full of stemless marigolds and jasmine. She scattered these on the grave. Thereafter he had flowers ready for her daily: some wild picked from hedges, others (she suspected) stolen from gardens. For such flowers he usually refused payment.

'Do you know what the flowers are for, Ashok?'

Yes, he knew, they were for puja. For worship.

'They are for my friend.'

Ashok looked troubled.

'I am your friend,' he said.

'Yes. I mean for my other friend?'

'Where is your other friend?'

'In Pankot.'

Where in Pankot?

'She is everywhere.'

Ashok looked round. Was she here now? Yes, Barbie said. Her other friend was watching them. His eyes swung this way and that.

1047

'Is she my friend too?'

'Oh, yes. But you won't see her.'

'Can you see her?'

Barbie shook her head.

He accepted this.

From an edition of the *Onlooker* she cut out a picture of an elephant bearing a howdah-load of sportsmen. It was a small picture. She fitted it into the mica envelope in which she had kept her subscription library ticket and gave it to him.

'My friend asked me to give you this, Ashok.'

He stared at it for some time. Next to one of the sportsmen in the howdah there was a lady with a topee.

'Is that your friend?'

Barbie examined it. The face of the woman was out of focus. 'No,' she said, 'but it is like her.'

Pictures were important to a child.

*

'When are you going to Rajputana, Ashok?'

Ashok shrugged.

'When you have enough money?'

He did not answer.

'Have you changed your mind?'

He nodded.

'But there are no elephants in Pankot. Why aren't you going to Rajputana?'

'I will go if you go,' he said.

That night, saying her prayers, she wept.

*

For quite a long time after Clarissa gave her the envelope with the mission's name on it and a Calcutta postmark she did not open it but sat on the edge of her bed observing how still the old eavesdroppers were.

She knew without reading it that the letter was from Mr Studholme and that the only reason he could have for writing to her was to offer her a place in one of the bungalows the mission kept in Darjeeling and Naini Tal. Someone had died and left a vacancy. She did not want to fill it. In such a place she would die herself, unwanted. She would have to go but it would take courage. She picked the letter up and considered the consequences of destroying it unopened. But she could not cheat Clarissa like that. Was it good news about accommodation – ? Clarissa would ask at lunch. And then she would have to lie.

She went into the bathroom and brushed the taste of the lie out of her teeth.

She returned to the little room of which she had become almost fond because Mabel knew she was in it and she had survived to come back to it; Clarissa had become amenable and the creeper outside the window had not entered. An extra tack kept the crucifix straight when she brushed past it. Each toe-nail she had discovered, was beautifully wrought. The old people behind the curtain were enemies but were kept at bay. After she had read the letter they would part the curtains, advance on her and smother her. An act of mercy.

She cut the envelope with a sandalwood paper-knife whose upper edge was carved in the shape of a string of tiny elephants. Mr Maybrick had given it to her to welcome her back to what he called the land of the living. He hated hospitals. Which was why he had not visited her. It was quite a long letter. It was signed by Mr Studholme.

November 20th, 1944

My Dear Miss Batchelor,

First let me say that this unfortunately is not to give news of a vacancy at Mountain View in Darjeeling or at The Homestead in Naini Tal. However rest assured that I have your situation well in mind.

I write to you for two reasons and must in fact apologize for not having written weeks ago when I was told that you had been rather unwell but were recovering nicely. We oldsters are not so easily laid low. After years in the country I think we develop a special resilience. (Lavinia Claythorpe, up in Naini Tal, is eighty-eight this month.)

My informant about your illness and recovery was a Miss Sarah Layton whom I had not had the pleasure of meeting before but who called one day while staying in Calcutta with relations. Well that is the first reason for writing, to say I hope you are now perfectly fit again. I heard how indefatigable you had been looking after the poor lady whose death left you in some uncertainty about a permanent home. The second reason I write is really to test the ground for asking a particular favour. I am encouraged to do so by your earlier offer of voluntary services.

You will appreciate that since the beginning of the war the flow of recruits to our mission has been severely curtailed. Young men and women at home have had to answer other calls. Increasingly we have been hard put to it to fill teaching posts effectively and there is one area in which for a variety of reasons this difficulty has become temporarily rather pressing.

I am sure you will remember Edwina Crane? She was superintendent of our schools in Mayapore district, amongst which is the little school on the outskirts of Dibrapur. Since the death both of the Indian teacher there and of Miss Crane the Dibrapur post is one we have found it not at all easy to fill.

Fortunately, six months ago, we were able to place a Miss Johnson, a Eurasian Christian, who has been very successful and whom we hope will

1049

continue as teacher in charge of Dibrapur for some time to come. However, Miss Johnson recently announced her engagement to be married and has asked for a month's leave from December 12th in order to solemnize the union and go down to Madras province with her husband. To this request, naturally, we have acceded. What has proved more difficult to arrange is for a teacher to take her place while she is away. The Dibrapur school is an infants' and junior school, most of its pupils come from nearby villages, not from the town. Unlike the senior schools in the towns it is normally closed for a few days only at Christmas. There is a bungalow nearby where the teacher in charge lives. Mayapore, I'm afraid, is 75 miles distant. One is rather cut off. The town of Dibrapur is not salubrious. But the troubles that affected that area are long since over.

The question is, would you consider filling in for Miss Johnson? We should be most grateful. A telegram saying one way or the other would settle the matter. If your answer is in the affirmative I will at once instruct Miss Jolley in Ranpur to arrange your transportation from Pankot to Mayapore on, I suggest, December 5th, which would enable you to reach Mayapore on the 6th or 7th and have a couple of days with Miss Johnson in Dibrapur before she departs. The super-intendent in Mayapore is Mrs Lanscombe whom I do not think you know. She would undertake all the arrangements for your reception and transportation at the Mayapore end. If you are agreeable I will ask Miss Jolley to telephone you at the rectory bungalow as soon as she has effected all the necessary bookings so that she can give you the details. Meanwhile my sincere good wishes: Cyril B. Studholme, MA.

*

She read the letter twice before folding and returning it to its envelope. On the second reading she knew what Sarah had done. She had visited Mr Studholme to disabuse him of any idea he'd got hold of that the old warhorse was past it. She had done this subtly, so that he had not realized it and had even forgotten to write a letter of good wishes on her recovery from her illness. With this gesture of Sarah's, practical, unobtrusive, Barbie felt that their relationship had been sealed in a way that touched her more deeply than any open declaration of esteem could have done.

She put the envelope in her handbag. Again, as at the time of Colonel Trehearne's unexpected invitation, she wanted to be enclosed in the world of her private happiness so that she could experience it fully, exist for a while at its tranquil centre which was not a fixed point in space but a moving one gliding across a flat landscape in the long straight line which, in her imagination, was the road to Dibrapur. She shut her eyes and in the dim room turned her face to the enormous white sky and the scorching oven-breath of the sun that baked the earth and the body to a holy exhaustion.

India, she thought. India. India.

India, she whispered.

She said aloud, 'India. India. India.'

The children laughed. Say it again, Barbie Mem, they chorused. India, she cried. The first syllable was inaudible and the second seemed to spring shrieking from her throat, hover, then fall like a bird struck dead in flight. She lowered her voice and spoke in the breathy tone adopted for talking to Arthur, Clarissa, Edgar Maybrick and little Ashok. I must conserve my real voice, she said. Conserve it for use in the schoolroom at Dibrapur.

But her real voice had gone. Would the warmth of the plains restore it to life and vibrancy or was it permanently damaged? Would a Pankot winter of cold nights complete its ruination? These questions were rhetorical. The damage to her voice in spite of Travers's assurances was a punishment whose sting she only truly felt this morning. If she accepted the mission's invitation she would be doing so under false pretences.

She could only pray and having prayed decline, because prayer had long since become a matter of form, of habit. She did not even bother to kneel. Oh, God, she said, give me back my voice.

*

When she reached the hall she said loudly, 'Clarissa!'

The bead curtains merely shivered. They should have opened.

With the letter from Mr Studholme firmly held in one hand she parted the beads with the other and clattered through into the sea-green incorruptible room. And stopped.

Captain Coley rose.

Clarissa said, 'There you are, Barbara. I was just going to send to see if you had a moment.'

'Oh, I have plenty of moments.'

The old crone, cracking jokes. There had been a night when she felt she could have toppled this man over merely by placing a finger on his chest. Was there hair on it? She knew nothing except the prone view from above. They were looking everywhere but at each other. Mostly they looked at Clarissa who gleamed under this concentration of light.

Clarissa spoke: an oracle with questions instead of answers. With Coley present Clarissa had reverted. She no longer looked solicitous. She spoke as she might to children from whom it was her duty to prise secrets.

'There is some mystery,' she said, 'about a trunk in the mali's shed at Rose Cottage.'

'No mystery,' Barbie replied. 'The trunk is mine. Is it required to be removed?'

Clarissa silently referred the question to Captain Coley. Apt Coley. Barbie turned to him. His face (that martyr's face) was red and, she could have sworn, stippled with sweat on the anguished forehead, although the daytime November warmth had not come into Clarissa's room with him.

'Be appreciated,' he said.

Clarissa explained. 'Captain Coley is keeping an eye on things while Mildred is away, you see.'

'Including the gardening implements?'

'Not exactly,' he said. 'Spot of bother. Between the mali fellow and old Mahmoud.'

'Is not Mahmoud on leave?'

'Came back. Going to Calcutta tomorrow to join Mildred. Mrs Layton.'

Apt Coley did not use many words. After a decade and more as adjutant of the depot words were probably meaningless to him. Since his routine did not vary from one week to the next, year after year, he must use the same ones every day of his life.

'What was this spot of bother between the mali and Mahmoud?' she asked him.

'Suspected theft.'

'Why on earth should Mahmoud suspect theft? My name is clearly printed.'

'Covered. Trunk covered.'

'But didn't mali explain it was mine and that he had it only to look after for me?'

'That's why I'm here. Check his story.'

'But you still want it removed.'

He looked round the room as if looking for a place where it might go.

'Be appreciated,' he said eventually.

'When? Today?'

'Heavens, no.' For a moment he was almost stung to articulacy. Perhaps he feared one thing as much as a posting he couldn't get out of. The word Urgent. 'They'll be home for Christmas. Twentieth actually. Loads of time. Month in fact.'

'But you'd like to tell Mahmoud before he goes to Calcutta tomorrow that he can forget the trunk because it will be gone?'

The telephone rang.

Clarissa got up. 'That will be Isobel about the prizes for their farewell dance. Are you going, Captain Coley?'

'On duty that night, I'm afraid.'

Barbie knew that by farewell dance Clarissa meant the first and most important. There would be several others, in descending order of priority, with smaller bands, ending with a quartet. The Rankins were not going until after Christmas. No one knew where. They pretended not to.

'What a pity,' Clarissa said. Passing Barbie she added, 'Captain Coley is such a lovely waltzer.'

When they were alone the tension between them soared to a peak and then quite simply and quietly died as if they had survived an act of God and found themselves stranded and non-combatant.

'I danced too as a gel,' Barbie heard herself croaking. The 'gel' interested her even as she said it. It was a pronunciation a man like Coley might feel happy with. 'Which may surprise you. We danced at a place called the

Athenaeum. Not *the* Athenaeum, naturally. I think its real name was the Athenaeum Temperance Assembly. Every year there was a church charity ball. I loved the mazurka. My father taught me to dance when I was a child. He hummed the music. Once he danced me all the way down Lucknow Road.'

'Lucknow?'

'Lucknow Road. Camberwell.'

'Oh.'

'When will it be convenient?'

'What?'

'For the trunk?'

'Oh, that. I'll send it down.'

'Don't trouble.'

'No trouble.'

'There wasn't room, you see. For the trunk. But it's different now.' She waved the mission's letter. 'I'm back in harness. Going Dibrapur.' Coleyism was catching. 'Clarissa won't mind about the trunk because it's only a week or two before I go. After that, who knows? If I do well Mr Studholme will be pleased with me, won't he? And I can stay in Mayapore for a while afterwards. Edwina's buried there. My friend, Miss Crane. I expect you remember. And then I'll be quite content to go to Darjeeling or Naini Tal. With all my luggage. I can always *write* to Colonel Layton when the war's over. I can leave it to him to decide where Mabel should have been buried. But I should like to see Rose Cottage just once more, Captain Coley. Preferably after Mahmoud's gone to Calcutta.'

'Going first thing tomorrow. Got him on a convoy to Ranpur.'

'Then second thing tomorrow would be fine. Say eleven a.m.?'

'On duty tomorrow, I'm afraid.'

'Oh but that doesn't matter. Just tell mali. There's no need for you to be there.'

Coley inclined his head. There was a childlike grace about him which she suddenly understood and found pleasant. She felt that somewhere in the background he kept a box of bricks. She went with him to the hall where Clarissa, smiling and talking to the telephone, raised her hand in august farewell.

On the steps of the verandah Barbie said:

'Thank you for sending back my sou'wester, Captain Coley. That afternoon I tried to deliver the spoons there was no one there. I must have lost it running – running in the rain.'

His face reddened slightly but the martyred look had gone, briefly, as it might have done centuries ago if a man from the bishop's palace had galloped up to the place of execution waving a paper that quenched the fire before it could take hold. He offered his hand which she took.

'Thank *you*,' he said. He hesitated. She feared a more intense declaration.

'Regiment most grateful. For the spoons.'

1053

He turned, went down the steps putting on his cap, thrusting his little cane under his left arm, making for a battered old Austin 7 which they both knew had been in the locked corrugated shed on that particular day.

V

She told the tonga-wallah she required his services for the entire morning and made a bargain. He was an enclosed dilapidated man with a curved nose and predatory sleeping eyes, a starved bird with folded wings.

'Is your horse strong?' she asked. 'Strong in the bone?' The three of them had bones aplenty. The horse was strong he said. She told him to drive her in the direction of Pankot railway station.

At the crest of the hill where the road led out of the valley through the miniature mountain pass she ordered him to turn round and stop. She got down and stood for several minutes. She could not see the celestial range of sunlit peaks. There was cloud there to the northeast, cloud that brought snow to the mountains and sometimes if the winds could carry them so far cold rain to the valley. But the late November sun was strong and the valley clean, bright, sparkling.

She pictured Aziz, arm extended, offering Pankot to her. She put out her own arm in conscious imitation and ordered the tonga-wallah to drive her back to East Hill and when he got there up Club road. He gave no indication of having heard but when she got back in set off. No doubt he thought her mad.

Twenty minutes later they were passing the milestone half way up Club road. There was no body lying there. All the bodies were buried but the jackal packs had multiplied; men ran with them on all fours, ravenous for bones. The tonga-wallah sat hunched letting the horse make its own pace.

At the entrance to the club it began to turn in as if this were its nature. 'No,' she called. 'Further, further.' Horse and man struggled for supremacy. The tonga lurched back on to its route.

They continued on and up past the familiar entrances to the bungalows between the club and Rose Cottage. She felt no pang. All this had been in another life. It seemed strange that it still existed. Staring at the road below her feet she counted the horse's paces and then said, 'Stop!' and glanced round. The equipage was outside the gates which the mali had left open, presumably because Captain Coley had told him to expect her. She imagined that most of the time while Mildred was away the gates were closed and padlocked. She told the tonga-wallah to drive in.

The first thing she saw was the trunk. It was uncovered. It had been placed conveniently on the front verandah at the head of the steps. The main door behind was shut and barred. The mali must be in the servants' quarters. She thought it lax of him to leave the trunk unattended and the gates open. Anyone could have come in and removed it. But he may have

1054

thought it too large and heavy for a casual thief. She went up the steps and tested the padlock. It was intact.

The trunk certainly looked bigger than she remembered. She had imagined it roped easily in the back of the tonga and herself up front sharing the driver's seat for the return journey. She glanced at the stationary contraption, the droop-headed horse, the drooped old man. He would need help, persuasion probably.

'Wait,' she said. The man said nothing. He was already waiting.

She edged her way round the trunk to gain the front verandah. Again she felt no pang to be standing on familiar ground. The unkempt plants on the balustrade looked confused by some rearrangement that was not clear to them and to which they would never get used. There was an element in the atmosphere that was neither warm and friendly nor yet quite cold and hostile. The window through which she could have seen into her old room was shuttered. She paused in front of it and had an impulse which she restrained to rap on the wood and cry: Is anybody there? and then to put her ear to the crack between the shutters and to listen for the sounds of the years she had spent there scattering in panic at the stranger's voice. She moved on round to the side where her old french window used to be. It was still there but was also shuttered. Again came the impulse to knock and again it was restrained, just in time. Her hand was already a fist, the knuckles resting against the wood which her forehead was almost touching. She stood like this waiting for the impulse to go away. When it had gone she felt hollow with her history, so long unused. She uncurled her fist. There seemed to be webs of new-grown flesh between her fingers.

She moved from the door and then stopped, arrested by a conviction that she was not alone. She glanced towards the corner of the bungalow where the rear verandah began, the verandah on which Mabel had died. It was coming from there, the sense of a presence, of someone in possession and occupation, of something which made the air difficult to breathe. She put her hand to her throat and felt for the gold chain with its pendant cross and then walked forward, turned the corner and gasped – both at the sight of a man and at the noxious emanation that lay like an almost visible miasma around the plants along the balustrade which had grown dense and begun to trail tendrils. The man stood as she had once seen Mabel stand, staring at the garden as if struck by a thought about it but also beyond it to the hills and where the mountains lay behind the impenetrable formations of sunlit cloud: a lean tall Englishman, dressed in civilian clothes and a soft tweed hat, his right shoulder towards her, his right arm extended and hand flattened upon the rail, gazing as from a height, upon a world spread out before him.

Fighting the sickness she called out, 'I beg your pardon. But would you please explain what you're doing here?'

Some ten yards separated them. He heard her voice but probably not the poorly articulated words. His sharp glance in her direction was not accompanied by any movement of his trunk or limbs.

'You,' she called again. 'What are you doing? This is private property, not a public right of way.'

She went to confront him. He let go of the balustrade, clutched the tweed hat at its crumpled crown and began to raise it; and then the nausea and her apprehension faded, scorched out of her by this courteous gesture. She had a wild notion that the man was Colonel Layton, released and restored and come home to find his family absent.

But she had seen Colonel Layton and the hat was now fully off, revealing a head and an unshadowed face, one half of which, the left, was branded under a lashless and uncanopied blue eye with a pink and white spider web of puckered flesh. There, on that side of his head, the man had been burned.

He put the hat back on.

'I'm sorry,' he said – and the apology served a dual purpose. 'My name's Ronald Merrick. I came to see the Laytons but the mali tells me they're in Calcutta. He invited me to stay while he made me a cup of coffee.'

He had moved round to face her. His left arm hung unnaturally stiffly. His right hand was bare. The left was encased in a black leather glove, the fingers and thumb of which were moulded to hold something invisible and useless.

'Oh,' she said. 'I do apologize. Of course. Captain Merrick. My name's Barbara Batchelor. I was *Mabel* Layton's companion. I used to live here.'

She put out her hand and at once wished she had not; not because by doing so she broke one of the stuffier rules but because the arrangements he had to make to reciprocate were complicated. Taking his hat off again, revealing once more the raw geography of his face, he inserted the hat into the black leather glove, clamped its fingers and then put his one warm living hand in hers.

'How do you do? Miss Layton mentioned you to me when she visited me in hospital. It must have been in connection with a Miss Crane. Is that correct?'

'How clever of you to remember.'

'Not really. Sarah told me her aunt Mabel's companion had been in the missions and often talked about Miss Crane.'

'Edwina and I were old friends.'

'Were you in the same mission?'

'The very same. The Bishop Barnard schools.'

'They are highly thought of. Were you in Mayapore?'

'No. I was in many places but never there. When I retired in nineteen thirty-nine I was superintendent in Ranpur.'

'That must have been a very responsible post.'

She realized that she was trying to look at the right side of his face and the right eye and ignore the left. His short stubby colourless hair was stippled with grey on the left side and looked patchy. Had he been handsome? It was difficult to tell. She would have liked to touch the scarred side of his face and she had an equally strange desire to touch the gloved artificial hand and feel up the arm inch by inch to discover where

1056

the wood or metal ended and the flesh began. She thought she remembered Sarah saying it had had to be cut off above the elbow.

And she recalled then that Sarah had never liked him. Loving Sarah and believing in her though she did, she could not let herself be prejudiced in advance. He had acted with great physical courage; perhaps with moral courage too. His voice was wonderfully distinct; every word clearly enunciated. A man's voice.

She turned to where the chairs should have been, intending to invite him to sit. The verandah furniture was gone. She had not noticed it consciously until now. 'Oh, dear, they've taken away the chairs. We sat out almost every day even in December and January when it can be quite chilly in the shade even at midday. I suppose the chairs are inside. Mildred and Susan have been away since early September, and Sarah longer than that. She went to Calcutta with her aunt. Did she come and see you?'

'I left the hospital there in mid-July.'

'When did you reach Pankot?'

'Yesterday.'

'Are you here for long, for a holiday?'

'No, only for a week. I'm at the hospital for tests and fittings. But it's a kind of holiday. I'm allowed a lot of freedom so long as I keep the appointments with the medicos.'

She glanced at the hand. Perhaps it was new and painful.

'How disappointing for you that the Laytons aren't here. And *they'll* be sorry to have missed you. Especially Susan. She was tremendously grateful to you, for what you tried to do to save Teddie.'

Her voice had hit a patch of special roughness but she had also been hit by the terrible consequences for Captain Merrick of his heroic act, hit as never before because she hadn't known the man or been able to imagine in detail the ruined face and the awful artificial arm.

'My voice,' she croaked, and hit her chest as if to dislodge an obstacle inside, and wished it were in her power to heal them both. 'I had a very bad cold a little while ago and this is the result.'

A movement caught her eye.

'Mali!'

She went to meet the man who had appeared on the verandah carrying a tray of coffee. Directly he saw her he set the tray on the ground and salaamed and then took both her proffered hands. His boy came up behind.

'Are you well, mali?' she asked in Urdu. 'And your wife? And the chokra. Oh! I can see he is well.'

All were well, the mali said. 'But look, Memsahib—'

He led the way past the high-grown plants on the balustrade to the steps where the view was not interrupted. She looked. And did not believe it.

All the central beds of rose trees had been dug up and turfed over. Lines of string and limewash mapped the place where a tennis court was being prepared. The roses in the beds that were left had been pruned down to bleak little skeletal bushes.

1057

'Tennish,' mali said. There were tears in his eyes.

She turned from the sight of desecration and found Captain Merrick smiling at the mali's boy because the boy's eyes were fixed on the black-gloved hand. He looked up at her.

'Have there been changes?'

'It's unrecognizable.'

'I was thinking just before you came what a fine garden it is, but I could see some work was being done.'

'It was once a mass of roses.'

'It must have been beautiful.'

Beautiful was an unusual word for a man to use except about a woman. She was grateful to him for using it now. Her father had used it in similar contexts. Because of the poet in him.

The boy had taken up the coffee tray and the mali was unpadlocking the louvred shutters in front of the french windows of the living-room. He swung the shutters back and then went round the side of the house to the kitchen entrance.

'Would you like to see inside the house, Captain Merrick?'

'Only if you'd like to show it to me. I'm content in the fresh air.'

'Then let's stay here. He'll be bringing out the chairs.'

The french windows were being unbolted from inside. With a creak one swung open and then the other. The mali came out with a chair she did not recognize; a dining-room chair. He set it down, went back in and came out with another. On his last journey he brought a basket-work teapoy which, like the chairs, must have come from the grace and favour. The chokra put the coffee tray down on this.

'Thank you, mali. I don't recognize the chairs.'

The chairs were from Brigadier Paynton Memsahib's house. Brigadier Paynton Memsahib had flown home to bilaiti.

'Yes, I know. What happened to our old table and chairs?'

The old table and some of the chairs were in the hall. The old sideboard was in the main bathroom. The rest of the chairs were in the mali's shed taking up room. All the old stuff might be sold. It was because Mahmoud had put the chairs in the shed that he had found the trunk and caused trouble. All the living-room furniture was being recovered. The verandah furniture was in the bazaar being repaired and relacquered. The Indian carpet in the living-room was to be put in the young memsahibs' bedroom and a fine new Persian carpet had been ordered from Bombay.

From his expression Barbie saw that the mali, loyal to the old order, was nevertheless impressed by the new. In time he would be impressed by the tennis court. Perhaps he already was and had only been upset for her benefit. That was very Indian. The tears in his eyes had been genuine but that was part of being Indian too.

They settled in the strange but elegant chairs and she dealt with the coffee. None of it mattered. For her Rose Cottage had ended with Mabel's death. She could not see the future that Mildred apparently saw for it. A

Persian carpet was a wild extravagance. Or perhaps it was simply an investment. The boy brought out another cup and saucer and a plate of rather soggy looking biscuits.

'Roses or tennis balls,' she said suddenly. 'Which would you choose, Captain Merrick?'

He did not reply but took the cup of coffee in the one hand capable of dealing with it and which might still hold a racquet.

'I'm sorry,' Barbie said, choosing forthrightness. 'Were you a good player?'

'Pretty fair. I shan't miss it though so long as I can ride. I'm teaching myself to get up on a horse from the wrong side. I'm hoping to get a mount tomorrow. You need an arm with feeling and control in it to get up, don't you, for the horse's sake as much as your own, but the rest's a question of one sensitive hand and a couple of strong knees. Once I've mastered that there's no reason why I shouldn't train myself to play patball too.'

'I think that's very brave.'

'Not at all. One's scale of priorities and comparisons changes, that's all. Actually it's rather like being born again. Even drinking a cup of coffee presents unexpected problems.' He smiled. 'But it tastes better when you get it.'

He stuck the saucer between the black leather thumb and forefinger, clamped them, picked up the cup and drank.

Having drunk he set the cup back in the saucer, reached over, lifted the plate of biscuits and offered it to her. After she had declined he put the plate back on the tray, chose a biscuit, settled back and began to nibble at it. The cup and saucer were retained in that rigid grip. She noticed that he had taken the opportunity at some time to dispose of his hat by folding and placing it neatly into the right-hand pocket of his misty Harris tweed jacket. His trousers were fawn cavalry twill; the shoes chestnut brown with the high glassy polish of old shoes originally expensive and since well cared for. His flannel shirt was open at the throat. He wore a green silk scarf inside it.

Her eyes, taking all this in, now met his. He did not seem in the least embarrassed to be the object of such close scrutiny but met it with what she thought of as a manly composure. Nevertheless she was ashamed of herself. She had been examining him as though he were not real. He had finished the biscuit and now drained his coffee cup. She wondered, thinking of the liquid going down, what intimate problems he also had to resolve, and looked away, saddened rather than embarrassed, and uncertain whether to offer him another cup. She sipped her own coffee.

'How are the Laytons?' he asked.

'Fine, I'm glad to say. I hear from Sarah sometimes. They've been in Darjeeling with Mildred's sister.'

'Mrs Grace. I met her at the wedding. Was the baby born successfully?'

'Oh yes, didn't you know?'

'I saw Sarah in June but I've heard nothing since. The nurse who

1059

specialled me told me Mrs Grace rang once to inquire how I was. I believe she was coming up to Pankot and that was early in July if I remember right. The baby was due about then, wasn't it? I suppose Mrs Grace was coming up for that?'

'No, the baby was born prematurely. In June. A little boy.'

'A boy? Teddie would have been pleased. And Susan?'

'Susan was pleased too.'

'I meant was she all right?'

'She had a difficult time but she came through. She was very brave. She was here on the verandah and Mabel was working in the garden. I was out. There was no one else here. Susan saw her die. She acted marvellously. Ringing for the doctor first and then her mother. But the shock brought the baby on.'

'Mrs Layton senior's death was very sudden then?'

'Very sudden.'

She looked at him. His good arm was bent, the elbow resting on the arm of the dining-chair – a carver's chair, she supposed; her own had no arms – the good hand supporting his chin, one finger resting on his right cheek.

'She died the day Sarah was in Calcutta.'

'Yes.' He moved the finger from his cheek to the corner of his mouth and then tucked it under the chin. 'Sister Prior saw the notice in the *Times of India*. She thought it might be Sarah's mother. She knew Sarah's name was Layton and that she'd come all the way from Pankot to see me, and Sarah said she might come again after the operation but she never did. Sister Prior thought she'd had to rush back here. She kept it from me. I wasn't shown the *Times* notice for a couple of weeks. Of course I realized at once who it was who'd died. I meant to write. But never did.'

'Didn't Sister Prior see the notice of the baby's birth a few days later?'

'I think she only looks at the deaths and marriages.' He smiled. 'Is there another cup of coffee?'

'I'm so sorry. Of course. No – leave it there.' She stood, poured the coffee. The cup and saucer were at a slight angle. She was careful not to fill the cup too full. She helped him to milk and sugar, then sat down.

He said, 'You're probably wondering how I knew to come to Rose Cottage.'

'Why should I wonder that?'

'Because the last time I was in touch with Sarah they were still at the Pankot Rifles address.'

'Oh, I see. Well. I suppose someone at the Pankot hospital told you they'd moved.'

'No.' He glanced at the palm of his good hand. 'I've not talked to many people at the hospital yet. But Teddie mentioned Rose Cottage quite a lot. Susan usually wrote to him from here, didn't she? She used to put the Rose Cottage address on the flaps of the envelopes. He liked that. He liked to think of her in this setting. He said her father would inherit it when her Aunt Mabel died. But I'd forgotten that until I got to Pankot yesterday. I meant to get in touch with them at the other address or look them up in the telephone book. But as soon as I arrived I remembered about Rose Cottage and wondered if they'd moved in.'

'So you came up to see.'

'No, I came up to the club to sign on as a temporary member but the secretary was out. They said he'd be back about midday so I took a walk up the hill. As soon as I started passing bungalows with names like The Larches, Rhoda and Sandy Lodge I was pretty sure I'd come across Rose Cottage. I thought I was out of luck after I'd passed the last place. But suddenly here it was. So I came in. The mali was working at the front.'

'You were fortunate to choose today. Mali was expecting me. Otherwise you'd have found the gate shut and padlocked. I came to collect my trunk. I expect you saw it.'

'Yes, I noticed a trunk. Where are you living now?'

'At the rectory bungalow. You saw the church spire? Well, it's just behind there. You must visit us. And there will be lots of other people here who'll be anxious to meet you.'

'Thank you.' He looked at his black glove. 'Not too many, I hope.'

'I'm afraid so. You're famous. Not only because of what you tried to do to save Teddie but because of your connection with the Manners case.'

He continued to regard her.

'She was here you know,' Barbie said.

'Here? Miss Manners?'

'No, no, the aunt. Lady Manners. She came to Pankot this summer.'

'Oh, yes. Sarah told me the name had appeared in the Flagstaff House book. She said no one had seen her though. I never met Lady Manners myself.'

'I saw her. In the church. I knew it was her. It couldn't have been anyone else. But she must have gone. I've never seen her again. Forgive me, perhaps you prefer not to talk about it. After all, if it hadn't been for that awful case you'd probably still be DSP in Mayapore or something even more important like a Deputy Inspector General.'

Chin back in hand he continued to regard her. Briefly she found the situation disturbingly familiar, as if they had sat like this before in another life. Now he removed the cup and saucer from the smooth black glove and replaced it on the tray. He took out his cigarette case.

'Why do you say that, Miss Batchelor?'

'Isn't it true? People have always said that your superior officers failed to stand by you.'

He offered her a cigarette. She declined but asked him to smoke if he wished. She glanced round. The mali's boy was watching from a corner of the bungalow. She told him to bring out an ashtray for Captain Merrick Sahib. Merrick had selected a cigarette, returned the case to his inside pocket and taken a gold lighter from another. The live-hand had great dexterity. He blew out smoke. The mali's boy came with a brass ashtray. Merrick looked at him gravely then pointed at the gloved artefact. With a frown of concentration the boy tried to place the ashtray in the palm. Merrick reached over to help him secure it between the finger and thumb. The boy stood back, arms behind him, prepared to watch.

'Chalo,' Barbie said. When the boy had gone Merrick smiled at her.

He said, 'The curiosity of children has a great therapeutic value.' He blew out smoke again. 'Reverting to that other subject. I ought to correct any impression people have that my department failed to stand by me. It was an impression we were quite willing that the Indians should get. Nothing takes the steam out of the opposition more effectively than appearing to remove the cause of conflict or complaint. But I always imagined our own people understood that.'

'But weren't you sent to a rather unpleasant area?'

Merrick was regarding her again. The eyelid from which the lashes appeared to have been burnt looked fixed. She found herself watching it to see if it blinked.

'Only with my full approval,' he said, 'and on the understanding that the department wouldn't stand in my way, if I renewed my application for a temporary commission in the army. I applied originally in nineteen thirty-nine and they sat on it then. And subsequently.' He paused to take in another methodical lungful of smoke and then let it escape in puffs with each of his next words. 'Actually you could say the army was my reward for my handling of the Manners case.' The smoke had gone. 'But probably only my Inspector General appreciates that fully.'

He noticed how her glance fell on his ruined arm.

'I hope you don't interpret this elegant monstrosity as payment deferred for having made a tragic mistake.'

'Oh no.'

'They were guilty, you know. The I.G. agreed.'

When he put the cigarette to his lips this time she thought for an instant that his fingers trembled slightly but she must have been mistaken. The live-hand now hung free, unsupported except by the forearm on the arm of the chair, and the cigarette looked as steady as a rock.

He said, 'One in particular is guilty. The ringleader. He is guilty for the rest of them.'

He gazed at her through wreaths of smoke.

'His name is Kumar,' he continued. 'The worst kind of western-educated Indian. With all the conceit and arrogance of the Indian whose family owns or once owned land, plus the arrogance of the most boring and unprincipled but privileged English lad who believes the world belongs to him because he was taught at a public school to think he should rule it by divine right instead of by virtue of a superior intelligence. It's difficult to see why she fell for it, but of course he spoke and acted like an English boy of that type.' He blew more smoke. 'And he was extremely good-looking.' He had not stopped regarding her. He said, 'Well, enough of that. I can see you find the subject painful. I do too. As a reasonably conscientious police officer

1062

it's rather gone against the grain to see six criminals comfortably put away as mere political detenus.'

'Painful yes. One must find it that. But that doesn't mean we should hide it away or pretend it never happened or that it's over.'

'Oh, it's over. The girl's dead.'

'The child's alive.'

He smiled. 'I mean the *case* died with the girl. I agree, the child's alive. His child, presumably. At least one presumes she imagined so.'

'You told Sarah you were fond of the girl yourself. And yet you sound so bitter. About her.'

He seemed quite undaunted. 'I *was* fond of her. I had to take that into consideration. But I think I stopped being fond of her when I realized which way she'd jumped. So it was never a serious impediment.'

She thought: What a curious word to use. Impediment. And – jumped. That's a curious word too. Sexual jealousy? Racial jealousy?

She found herself suddenly unwilling, unable, to consider the matter. She felt drained of imaginative energy. She stared at the embryo tennis court. It meant nothing. It was simply a place to pat a ball to and fro, to and fro.

Between their feet the woman in the white saree abased herself. Beseeching them. 'We are gods,' she thought, 'and this was our garden. Now we play tennis. It's easier to beseech against a background of roses.'

That flash of inspiration had come, unexplained, unattended. But there seemed no more to come. She looked at him. Again he was regarding her. His chin was in his hand. He had stubbed the cigarette. It lay dead, bent double, on the little brass tray that had come from Benares on the banks of the Ganges where bodies were burnt and the ashes cast to float, float on, float out to an unimaginable sea. Her old trunk of missionary relics with them. Bobbing, lazily twisting, under a copper-coloured sun. Immense crowds came to the festivals on the banks of the holy river. Greater crowds than came to any church. The air was heavy with the scent of jasmine, decayed fish, human and animal ordure. In the trunk Edwina's picture sailed to a far horizon.

She said, 'I am your mother and your father.'

'What?'

'Man-bap. It wasn't that for Edwina. It was despair. But I suppose Teddie felt it.' She realized that in an oblique way – in his remarks about Kumar and a certain type of Englishman – he had been referring to Teddie, to men like Teddie, but she could not fathom his deeper references. The arm he had lost for Teddie span away too – on the swift current of the holy river: garlanded.

She had slumped forward, knees apart, feet splayed, her skirt stretched, elbows on her knees, her hands clasped.

'Tell me about my friend, about Edwina Crane. Was there much left?'

There was a long pause. She did not look at him. She stayed in that ungainly position.

1063

'Enough to identify.'

She nodded. And to bury. She had never thought of that before. Never thought of the possibility that the coffin was light with a few scorched bones shrouded in fragments of burnt saree. 'And the letter?' she asked. 'What did she say in the letter, the one that was never read out at the inquest?'

'I'm afraid I don't remember except that it satisfied the coroner.'

'And satisfied the police. You remembered the picture. You must remember the letter. The letter was much more important to a policeman.'

'Is it important to you?'

'It might be.'

She glanced up. His chin was still resting on the live-hand, but he was looking at the garden.

He said, 'Well, it was a sane letter. Personally I should have recorded a simple verdict of suicide.'

'What did it say?'

'Simply that she was resolved to take her own life.'

'There must have been more.'

'You mean something to support the verdict of suicide while the balance of the mind was disturbed?'

'Yes, was there?'

'Personally I don't think so.' He seemed in a way to regret that Edwina had gone to hallowed ground. He added, 'But she did end the letter with the kind of statement that satisfied people she was off her head. The kind it was thought better not to read out. I can't think why.'

'What was it?'

He turned his head towards her, using his hand as a pivot for his chin.

' "There is no God. Not even on the road from Dibrapur." '

An invisible lightning struck the verandah. The purity of its colourless fire etched shadows on his face. The cross glowed on her breast and then seemed to burn out.

' "Not even on the road from Dibrapur?" '

He nodded.

For a moment she felt herself drawn to him. He offered recompense. He looked desolated as if Edwina's discovery were a knowledge he had been born with and could not bear because he had been born as well with a tribal memory of a time when God leaned His weight upon the world. He needed consolation.

She became agitated. She felt for the gold chain and found it but it seemed weightless.

He smiled. He said, 'How serious we've become.' He shot the sleeve of his good arm and looked at the dial of a watch which he wore with the face on the inner side of the wrist. 'And I ought to be getting back to see the club secretary.'

She got up. 'No, wait. I want to give you something.'

She bent down and retrieved her handbag from the ground near the leg of the unfamiliar chair.

'Come, you can help me. The locks may be stiff.'

She waited until he had got to his feet and then led the way round the verandah to the front, walking several paces ahead of him. The tonga-wallah sat hunched, half-asleep, his head at the same angle as the horse's. She saw to her horror that the horse had deposited a neat pile of manure between the shafts of the sacrosanct gravel of the drive.

She edged round the trunk and knelt on the first step, then scrabbled in her handbag for the key. The padlock clicked open easily, so did the left hand clasp. The right hand one had always been a brute. But it gave. She flicked the hasps up.

'Now,' she said. She raised the Pandora-lid, stared and cried out. From rim to rim the trunk was filled with the creamy white butterfly lace.

'But this isn't mine!'

She snatched at the lace and pulled it out. Beneath it were her relics.

'How did it get in here?' she wanted to know. 'I never put it in here. I've not seen it since the day Mabel showed it to me.'

She held the lace in both hands and then looked up to appeal to Captain Merrick. But the lace was before his time. She had a desire to show it to him. 'Look,' she said, and threw one end. He caught it deftly. She drew her arm back. The lace hung between them. The butterflies trembled.

'Isn't it beautiful? The woman who made it was blind.' She stared at and through this lepidopterist's paradise-maze but could see no further than the old woman's fingers. 'Mabel wanted me to have it for a shawl.'

He offered back the end he had. She gathered the lace in and then flung it over her shoulders.

'Can I carry it?' she asked, laughing. The lace smelt of camphor, lavender and sandalwood. These were the scents of Mabel's and Aziz's gift. 'She must have given it to Aziz, and he to me. During that time he had the key to my trunk.'

She pulled the lace off her shoulders. 'I'm sorry, Captain Merrick. You haven't the least idea what I'm talking about. No matter. I opened the trunk' – she picked up the picture – 'to give you this.'

She held it up to him. He made to take it.

'No,' she said. 'The other hand.'

She reached up and helped to insert the picture into the rigid glove.

'It's small, but much bigger than an ashtray. Is it too heavy?'

'I don't think so.'

The black glove, his good hand and one of her hands held the picture. Slowly they each withdrew the support of their living flesh.

'There, you can do it. You can *carry* it.'

There was perspiration on his mottled forehead. He gazed down at the awkwardly angled gift.

'Oh, this,' he said. 'Yes, I remember this. Are you giving it to me?'

'Of course.'

One eyebrow contracted in a frown. The other – vestigial – perhaps contracted too.

'Why?'

She thought about this.

'One should always share one's hopes,' she said. 'That represents one of the unfulfilled ones. Oh, not the gold and scarlet uniforms, not the pomp, not the obeisance. We've had all that and plenty. We've had everything in the picture except what got left out.'

'What was that, Miss Batchelor?'

She said, not wishing to use that emotive word, 'I call it the unknown Indian. He isn't *there*. So the picture isn't finished.'

A drop of sweat fell from his forehead on to the bottom left-hand corner of the glass that protected the picture.

'Let me relieve you of its weight, Captain Merrick. I'll ask mali to wrap it in some paper for you. Meanwhile' – she began closing and locking the trunk – 'would you be so kind as to ask my tonga-wallah there to put the trunk in the back of the tonga? I'll ask mali to help him ...nd also for some rope to lash it in. But I think it will require a man to order him to take it.'

'The trunk? In the back of the tonga?'

'What else?'

'I should have said it's much too heavy.'

'Oh, nonsense. It only contains my years and they are light enough.'

She strode round the bungalow calling the mali.

*

The trunk was roped, upended like a coffin on its foot, one edge resting on the footboard of the passenger seat, the other within an inch of the canopy above. The shafts of the trap were at a high angle. The bony horse looked in danger of elevation. The morose tonga-wallah stood at the horse's head, keeping it down.

She placed the lace shawl over her head like a bridal veil. Captain Merrick was examining the lashings and knots with a man's expert and wary eye for such things. At her approach he said, 'I don't advise this. Have you far to send it?'

'Just down the hill. To the church.'

'It's very steep. I think the fellow is right.' He jerked his head at the tonga-wallah. 'It's too great a load.'

'But I shall pay him well. He's an old man. The competition is very severe nowadays. The young drivers dash hither and thither and getting all the custom. It's a kindness really.'

'How do you intend to get back yourself?'

'In the front, of course.'

Captain Merrick said nothing.

'Do you disapprove of that? Of my driving hip to hip with a smelly old native?'

'The weight will be impossible.'

'But *I* shall balance the trunk. You see? We shall tip forward on to a splendid even keel. Are you walking to the club?'

'It was my intention. Mali says it may rain. Don't you think—'

But she interrupted. 'Where will you be going when you leave Pankot, Captain Merrick?'

'Simla.'

'For a holiday?'

'No. On army business.'

'We must talk again. There are many things I should like to discuss. I'll ask Clarissa Peplow to ring you at the hospital. At the military wing, presumably.'

'That would be very kind.'

She turned to the mali. She gave him twenty rupees. She ruffled the head of the mali's boy.

'Can you understand what I say?' she asked the boy in Urdu. He nodded. She smiled. In Dibrapur it might be all right.

She offered her hand to Captain Merrick. The mali had the packed picture ready for him.

'You won't forget the picture, will you? Will you help me up?'

They moved to the tonga. The footplate was very high. She felt his good arm take some of her weight. He had been a strong man. As she arrived under the canopy she was enclosed by the sadness of that. She stared down at him.

'Does it hurt?'

After a moment he smiled. 'A little.'

'Poor boy,' she said. Suddenly he seemed like a boy. A boy without bricks. 'You were going to be decorated. Did it come through?'

'Yes.'

'An MC?'

'A DSO for some reason.'

'But that is very distinguished, congratulations. Have you been invested yet?'

'Not yet. Next month I gather.'

'Where? In Simla?'

He nodded. She smiled at him compassionately. Simla meant the Viceroy. She felt that this would please him particularly.

'I'm sorry you missed the Laytons,' she said again.

'There'll be other opportunities,' he said. 'Shall I tell the fellow to get up?'

'If you would.'

He went to the horse's head. The old man came round, mounted, untied the reins from the rail and picked his whip out of the stock.

'Au revoir, Captain Merrick.' She adjusted the lace veil and raised her hand.

The equipage moved slowly and creakily out of the compound of Rose

Cottage. As it turned into Club road she saw the valley lay under a thin blanket of cloud and felt the first spots of a chill November rain.

She had not even noticed the sun go in.

The tonga gathered momentum. The old man began to apply the brake. Once or twice the horse slipped. Barbie could feel the weight of the trunk at her back: her years pressing on her, pushing her forward, pushing her downward. She pressed her feet hard against the curved footboard but her legs had little strength.

There is no God, not even on the road from Dibrapur. But then (she argued) I am taking the road *to* Dibrapur, not from it. The tonga-wallah shouted at the horse which had stumbled. 'You mustn't shout at him,' she said, 'he's doing his best.' For some reason she longed to have the picture back. The rain was coming down quite hard. As they passed the club there was a flurry of tongas coming up the hill and about to turn in there. The old man's hands were knotted in the reins. One of the other wallahs shouted an insult.

'Hold your tongue,' Barbie shouted back. In turning her head she became more fully aware of the lace. Her head was a nest of butterflies. They were caught in the lank grey hair. She shut her eyes. Twenty stairs, including the landing floor. She began to sing. 'I've seen a deal of gaiety throughout my noisy life.' She opened her eyes.

Behind the equipage a peculiar light glowed on and off; winter lightning. Something troubled her. The lightning brought it closer. It was Mildred's face, eyes hooded, mouth turned down, quirked at the corners; glass held under chin in droop-wristed hands.

The horse slid, stumbled, righted itself. It raised its tail. There was a smell of stable. The horse stumbled again. The old man jerked the brake on harder. She thought she smelt burning. She glanced at him. His eyes at last were wide open. He looked at her for an instant before redirecting his own troubled gaze at the road ahead and at the trembling flanks of his old horse; and Mildred's face was there again just for the split second it took for it to dissolve and reform and become the face of the man who regarded her, chin in hand, thoughtful and patient, so purposeful in his desire for her soul that he had thrown away Edwina's.

She began to tremble. She pressed with all her strength against the footboard. Below, Pankot lay shrouded by the mist of the winter rain which had left its snow on the summits. They were passing the golf-course. People were running for cover under coloured umbrellas.

*

Sometimes although very rarely, these cold showers – penetrating the warmth of a Pankot November day – troubled the atmosphere and produced an imbalance, a rogue element of electric mischief that shattered the silence like a child bursting a blown-up paper bag containing flashes of paper fire.

There was just such an explosion now, as the rickety old tonga entered the steepest part of Club road. It blared across the valley, jerking alive the unliveliest members of the club, comfortably cushioned in upholstered wicker, and was accompanied by the brightest amalgam of blue and yellow light ever seen in the region: an alert such as even the combined rifles of Pankot and its tribal hills could not have achieved by sustained fusillade.

The horse screamed; its eyes rolled; it reared, thrashing the space between its hooves and the greasy tarmac and then achieved both gravity and momentum, dragging and rocking the high-wheeled trap with its load of missionary relics.

Why! It is my dream! Barbie thought, hanging on to the struts with both hands, shutting her eyes to contain the blessing of it. Her hair flew long and black and she was a child dancing spinning down Lucknow road and racing up the stairs and holding the pincushion high to her mother who held her black bombasine sides laughing to hear her father sing it:

> I've seen a deal of gaiety throughout my noisy life,
> With all my grand accomplishments I ne'er could get a wife.
> The thing I most excel in is the PRFG game, a noise all night,
> In bed all day, and swimming in champagne.
> For Champagne Charlie is my name,
> Champagne Charlie is my name,
> Good for any game at night my boys,
> Good for any game at night my boys,
> Champagne Charlie is my name
> Champagne Charlie is my name
> Good for any game at night boys,
> Who'll come and join me in a spree.

On the long downhill sweep the equipage gathered speed, out of control of the crazed horse. The wheel spokes span counter to the rims. Sparks from the burning brake and spray from the wet surface formed bow-wave and wake.

She opened her eyes and saw the toy-like happy danger of human life on earth, which was an apotheosis of a kind, and she knew that God had shone his light on her at last by casting first the shadow of the prince of darkness across her feet.

Careless of the shawl of butterflies she reached for the reins to help the old man resist the gadarene pull of the four horses. He tore at the monstrous membrane that blinded him and which blinded Barbie too like a great light followed by a giant explosion, a display of pyrotechnics that put the old November Crystal Palace shows to shame.

Ah! she said, falling endlessly like Lucifer but without Lucifer's pride and not, she trusted, to his eventual destination. My eyeballs melt, my shadow is as hot as a cinder – I have been through Hell and come out again by God's Mercy. Now everything is cool again. The rain falls on the dead butterflies on my face. One does not casually let go. One keeps up if one can and cherishes those possessions which mark one's progress through this world of joy and sorrow.

*

I remember (Sarah said) Clarissa Peplow telling me how Barbie suddenly marched into the rectory bungalow covered in mud and blood but still on her feet and said, 'I'm afraid there's been some trouble at the junction. Perhaps someone would kindly deal with it. I have seen the Devil. Have you a spade?'

The driver survived too. But the horse had to be shot.

Coda
Lines from the Hospital of the Samaritan Mission
of the Sisters of Our Lady of Mercy.
Ranpur. December 1944 – August 1945

'Good morning, Edwina,' Sister Mary Thomas More said. She had bad teeth. She smelt of garlic and of galloping corruption. 'Or are we Barbie, today? What are we looking at?'

Miss Batchelor wrote on the pad: The birds.

'I see no birds, Edwina. Aren't we speaking today, either? Is it a day of silence?'

Miss Batchelor wrote: It is the same as all days.

'Not all days can be the same. There is the one which we all await and ought to fear.'

Miss Batchelor wrote: Bugger off. Or bring me a spade. Suit yourself.

After Sister Mary Thomas More had pursed her crypt-like lips, Miss Batchelor added a postscript: And bugger the Pope.

There was bread and water.

It was the only food she liked. It was clean.

*

Sarah said, 'Barbie? Barbie? Don't you know me?'

Miss Batchelor could not hold the pencil because she could not see it and both her hands had been severed. When Sarah had gone they took away her shoes because of the tramping sound.

*

'Good morning, Edwina. Or is it Barbie? You don't know me. My name is Eustacia de Souza. I'm new. I mean I visit. You're my first. You must tell me all about yourself otherwise I shan't know what to do to help, shall I, and Mother Superior will be upset.'

Miss Batchelor wrote: You may tell me about the birds.

Miss Batchelor liked the look of Eustacia de Souza. Eustacia de Souza was as black as your hat, several shades blacker than Sister Mary Thomas More. Eustacia de Souza was not a nun.

Miss Batchelor added to her note: My name is Barbara, not Edwina. I am under a vow of silence.

'I understand, dear. At least I understand that part. I'm not sure I understand about the birds. Which birds do you mean?'

Miss Batchelor pointed through the barred window. Eustacia put on her glasses and peered.

'I can't see any birds, dear, apart from a few crows. You can't mean crows, can you? India's full of bloody crows.'

Miss Batchelor drew a picture of the horizon and a middle distance. She sketched a point of reference. A minaret.

'Oh, a heathen thing.'

Miss Batchelor shook her head. She struck the minaret through with her pencil and then drew a line and a ring. And made angular strokes, playfully. Like birds flying.

'Just a moment, dear.'

Eustacia clung to the bars like a helpful monkey. She was very ugly. Her bottom stuck out of a print artificial silk dress. She had white shoes and high heels. She stank under the armpits but it was the stink of hope.

'I don't actually see any birds there, Barbara dear. Are you sure they're still there?'

Miss Batchelor looked. She wrote: No – but they often are.

Eustacia sat on the spare stool and smoked and talked. About peculiar things. 'We've got them in Mandalay, dear. We'll be in Rangoon like a streak of piss before May's out. Cast not a clout. Old Billy Slim could screw me any time he asked, dear. Better'n my husband. Small as he is I'd put the flags out for Billy any day.' Eustacia frowned. 'Have you ever thought about length, dear?'

She did not look as if she required an answer. She looked at Miss Batchelor who sat contained by her dignity and desire.

'Do you have the least bloody idea what I'm talking about, love? Do you know where this is, dear, I mean what town for God's sake?'

Miss Batchelor wrote: Ranpur, looking west.

Eustacia de Souza smiled and nodded. Then frowned again. 'West?' she said. She looked. She nodded. She smiled very wide. 'That's where it is,' she said. Miss Batchelor was reminded of a melon. She felt thirsty.

She wrote: You must go now. It is the dangerous hour.

Mrs de Souza's face turned a nasty purple. When she had gone Miss Batchelor broke the tea-cups and waited for the relief of cold water and winding-sheet. She screamed and struggled because that was the way Sister Mary Thomas More liked it. At the end the nun's coif was limp.

*

1071

The landscape had changed because the light had altered. It was very hot. She wrote: Calendar. They brought her one. It said June 6th. She destroyed it. Next day they brought her another because Father Patrick was visiting. It said June 7th, 1945. She put it on her bedside table, and when Father Patrick had gone, under her mattress. But they did not take it away.

*

'How are you, Barbie?' the girl with the fair helmet of hair said.

The calendar said, June 30th, 1945. She wrote: I am in good health.

'Is there anything you want?'

She wrote: Birds.

'Birds?'

She wrote at length:

From the window, beyond the minaret, there are birds. Smudges in the sky. Not necessarily now. But there are birds there often. You can hardly see them but they circle, as though there is a nest there. There is a hill. Trees, I think.

She watched the girl reading the note. She put out her hand to touch her. The girl looked momentarily startled. Miss Batchelor withdrew her hand not wishing to frighten her. But the girl then reached out and held her.

'It's all right, Barbie. Let's look at the birds.'

They went together to the barred window.

Miss Batchelor tried to articulate. Her throat rattled.

'It's all right, Barbie,' the girl with the fair helmet of hair said. 'I understand. Where now, beyond the minaret?'

Together they watched. Distantly where the land folded there was a haze. Above it, birds.

'Yes, I see. I don't know why they're there. I'll find out. They must be quite big birds, mustn't they?'

Miss Batchelor nodded. She was proud of her birds.

She wrote to the girl: Do you live in Ranpur?

The girl said, 'No, in Pankot, at Rose Cottage. I'm only in Ranpur for two days. I'm going to Bombay to meet my father.'

Miss Batchelor held the girl's hand. She felt that she had to say something important but could not remember what.

*

The girl came the following morning. She said, 'The birds belong to the towers of silence. For the Ranpur Parsees.'

Then she wrote it down on Miss Batchelor's pad as if she thought Miss Batchelor might forget it.

Miss Batchelor wrote: Yes, I see, Vultures. Thank you.

She looked round the room. She shook her head. She wrote: I have nothing to give you in exchange. Not even a rose.

For some reason the girl put her arms round Miss Batchelor and cried.

1072

'Oh, Barbie,' she said, 'don't you remember anything?'

She nodded. She remembered a great deal. But was unable to say what it was. The birds had picked the words clean.

*

Often now she was left alone. Sister Mary Thomas More had used the word incorrigible. She sat at the window watching through narrowed hungry eyes the birds that fed on the dead bodies of the Parsees. At night she blew dandelion clocks and continued to blow them long after they had become bereft, deprived. To blow them to the bone was the one sure way she now had of sleeping, sure in the Lord and the resurrection and the spade.

A young Madrassi nun, observing her thus, and thinking old Miss Batchelor's hour had come, ran out into the darkling intermittently lit medieval corridor and brought the stark night-sister, who, standing in the traditional pose, with shriven fingers on patient's pulse, and uncommitted eyes, merely firmed her lips in imitation of the daylight brides, and then made a high mark on the bed-bottom board that charted the old missionary's journey across the hilly country of exodus.

Asleep, Barbie no longer dreamed. Her dreams were all in daylight. Do not pity her. She had had a good life. It had its comic elements. Its scattered relics had not been and now can never all be retrieved; but some of them were blessed by the good intentions that created them.

One day after such a dreamless sleep, she woke, rose, knelt, prayed, splashed water on her parchment face from the rose-patterned bowl that sat like one half of a gigantic egg in an ostrich-size hole in a crazy marble top, dressed, had breakfast and marked off the calendar of the fair-haired girl's absence.

It was August 6th, 1945.

The date meant nothing to her. No date did. The calendar was a mathematical progression with arbitrary surprises.

She took her seat at the barred window. Today it was raining. She could not see the birds. But imagined their feathers sheened by emerald and indigo lights. She turned away and rose from the stool. And felt the final nausea enter the room.

She stood, swaying slightly, in the ragged heliotrope costume which was stained by egg and accidents with soup, and then holding her naked throat, padded slippered to the secure refuge of her bed and sat, leaning her shoulder casually against the iron head.

She strained at the rusted mechanism of her voice and heard its failing vibrations in her caved-in chest.

'I am not ill, Thou art not ill. He, She or It is not ill. We are not ill, You are not ill, They are all well. Therefore . . .'

She raised a questioning or admonitory finger, commanding just a short moment of silence for the tiny anticipated sound: the echo of her own life.

They found her thus, eternally alert, in sudden sunshine, her shadow burnt into the wall behind her as if by some distant but terrible fire.

Appendix

'I find myself uncertain which of two recent events – the election of a socialist government in London and the destruction of Hiroshima by a single atomic bomb – will have the profounder effect on India's future.'

Extract from a letter dated in August 1945 from
Mr Mohammed Ali Kasim to Mr Mohandas Karamchand
Gandhi.

A Division
of the Spoils

To Doreen Marston
With my love and regard

BOOK ONE 1945

An Evening at the Maharanee's

I

Hitler was dead, the peace in Europe almost a month old; only the Japanese remained to be dealt with. In June the Viceroy left London, flew back to Delhi, said nothing in public for nearly two weeks and then announced a conference of Indian leaders at Simla to discuss proposals which he hoped would ease the political situation, hasten final victory and advance the country towards her goal of full self-government. To enable all the leaders to be there he had to issue several orders of release from imprisonment.

The conference opened on June 25 and did not break down until July 14, an unexpectedly long time in the opinion of many English officials for Congress and Muslim League views on the composition of a new Indianised Executive Council or interim government to prove irreconcilable. The Viceroy, Lord Wavell, admitting failure, blamed himself and begged that there should be no recriminations. Subsequently, in press conference, the leader of the All-India Congress Party, a Muslim, blamed the leader of the Muslim League for the unbending nature of his claim for the League's right to nominate all Muslim members of the proposed Executive Council and blamed the British Government for not having foreseen that the conference would break down if one party were given the right of veto on nominations and therefore the opportunity to hold up the country's progress to autonomy. The leader of the Muslim League spoke disapprovingly of a combination of Hindu interests supported by the 'latest exponent of geographical unity' – the Viceroy – whose plan in his opinion was a snare for Muslim interests. Mr Nehru described the Muslim League as mediaeval in conception, and warned that the real problem facing a free India would not be communal and religious differences but economic backwardness.

The members of the conference then left Simla to consider the situation in private. Among the first to go was Mr Mohammed Ali Kasim, a Muslim Congressman and ex-chief minister of the pre-war government of the province of Ranpur, who, if Jinnah had his way, could expect no portfolio in the higher council. Like several other prominent Congress politicians Mr Kasim had not been seen in public for nearly three years. Guarded from reporters by a small but efficient entourage headed by his younger son Ahmed, he ignored the questions shouted at him as he left the Cecil Hotel

1079

and concentrated on helping Ahmed to support a frail old man later identified by onlookers as his aged and ailing secretary – Mr Mahsood. Safe in his car at last he snubbed the young man from the *Civil and Military Gazette* who got close enough to the window to say, 'Minister, is Pakistan now inevitable?' by commanding Ahmed to put up the glass and pull down the blinds.

The lowering of the blinds caught the imagination of an Indian cartoonist who portrayed the car (identified as that of the ex-chief minister by the initials MAK on one of its doors) with all its windows, including the driver's, shuttered and making off at high speed (smoke-rings from the exhaust) from a once imposing but now crumbling portal inscribed 'Congress' towards a distant horizon with a sun marked 'Hopes of Office' rising behind a broken-down bungalow on whose rickety verandah the leader of the Muslim League, Mr Jinnah, could be seen conferring with several of his associates.

The cartoon annoyed adherents of Congress. They objected both to the inference that Mr Kasim was about to betray them and join the League and to the representation of their party as a derelict doorway with nothing behind it. Similarly, Muslim Leaguers objected to the portrayal of the Qaid-e-Azam as the occupier of a squalid little property such as the one depicted.

By the time the cartoon appeared (two days after the end of the conference) the liberals and middle-of-the-road men in Indian politics – who might have protested at the lampooning of a man whose legal skills and political integrity had commanded wide respect for a quarter of a century – could not help wondering whether Mr Kasim had after all shown himself as capable as men of lesser merit of acting with an eye to the main chance. What else, they asked, but an intention to shift his allegiance to the League, in the hope of securing his political future with a party that had grown strong enough to wreck a viceregal conference, could better explain his subsequent mysterious behaviour?

Between Delhi and Ranpur Mr Kasim seemed to have succeeded not only in evading the journalists but in disappearing together with his entire entourage. He was not on the train when it arrived in Ranpur and he never turned up at the old Kasim house on the Kandipat road. This house had been closed since Mr Kasim's wife (and then Mr Mahsood) had left it in the middle of 1944 to join him after his release from the Fort at Premanagar in the protective custody of his distant kinsman, the Nawab of Mirat. The reason given for that release had been Mr Kasim's reported ill-health, but it was Mrs Kasim who, some six months later, died.

The journalists who waited outside the still-locked gates of the house on the Kandipat road to greet the distinguished Muslim Congressman on his return home after three years detention and restriction, found themselves joined, towards evening, by colleagues who had waited just as uselessly at the station, and then by a growing crowd of spectators who eventually tangled with a truck-load of police sent to disperse them. A running battle developed between the lathi-armed constables and the quicker-tempered of Mr Kasim's admirers (students). The peaceful pleasures of families taking the air in the Sir Ahmed Kasim Memorial Gardens opposite were disturbed. A number of arrests were made and rumours then spread through the Koti bazaar and out to the suburb of Kandipat that Mr Kasim had been arrested by the British on the train from Delhi, had been abducted by Hindu extremists, had been murdered by the communists, had succumbed to poison administered by agents of the Viceroy. The shop of an unpopular merchant, a Hindu who gave short weight, was broken into and looted and that of another, a Muslim, ransacked in retaliation. The following day students of the Ranpur Government College demonstrated in the area of the Civil Lines carrying placards asking 'Where is MAK?' and hartal was observed in the Koti bazaar by Hindus and Muslims alike for fear of riot, arson and the consequent loss of profits.

At this stage it was discreetly leaked by the Inspector-General of Police to the Municipal Board that Mr Kasim was alive and well and back in the Nawab of Mirat's summer palace in the Nanoora Hills, and this information was simultaneously confirmed by a telephone call from a correspondent in Mirat to his editor in Ranpur. It seemed that Mr Kasim and his party had left the Delhi-Ranpur train at a wayside halt some miles outside the provincial capital and had then been driven to another wayside halt where the Nawab's private train awaited him and carried him back to the scene of his protective custody, although in this case it had to be assumed that his return was voluntary and caused by nothing more sinister than the need to sort out the detritus of the year he had spent there under government restriction.

The news inspired the same cartoonist to a further interpretation of Mr Kasim's evasive behaviour. Mirat was a princely state whose territory was contiguous to the province, whose inhabitants were predominantly Hindu but whose ruler was of the Islamic faith. In the new cartoon MAK was shown sitting cross-legged at a low table in the company of the Nawab and Mr Jinnah. The table, heavily spread with a feast, was labelled 'Islam'. Beneath it, only head and arms visible, was the struggling body of Free India. From behind a pillar the puckish face of Winston Churchill peered, the head sporting a Jinnah-shaped fez to depict the English leader's alleged preference for Muslims and sympathy with their aspirations, the face smoothed by an expression of satisfaction at the thought that the Princes, those loyal Indian supporters of the Crown in two world wars, and the Muslim League which had refused to have anything to do with the non-co-operation tactics of the Congress Party, would together – for whatever different reasons – now so bedevil every move the Congress made to force the issue of Indian independence to a conclusion favourable to themselves that British rule could comfortably be extended far enough into the future for the phrase 'indefinitely if not in perpetuity' not to seem inappropriate. Another cartoon on the following day depicted Mr Churchill receiving an ovation from a moronic (or badly drawn) and adoring British public, to whom he was about to appeal for re-election, holding in one arm a baby labelled 'Victory in Europe', with the other arm extended presenting its hand in giant perspective and the famous V-sign, but with the two fingers raised the wrong way round. One of these fingers was labelled 'Jinnah' and the other 'Princely India'. Clenched in the curled fist below the fingers was a limp body representing Indian unity and nationalism. Thereafter, as a result of a visit to the editor's office by a representative of the CID no cartoons by this particular artist appeared in this or any other newspaper for some time.

The news that Mr Kasim had gone back to Mirat caused a similar influx of journalists into Nanoora to that of the previous year when he had been let out of the Fort; but although there were now presumably no restrictions on his movements or activities the journalists again failed to obtain an interview and this time did not even receive official messages of regret from court officials that Mr Kasim had no statement to make. Several abortive attempts were made to enter the grounds of the summer palace; a costly business since it involved bribing servants and officials, and a dangerous one because there was the risk of arrest for trespass, even (it was said) of summary imprisonment in one of the Nawab's dungeons. One by one the journalists departed, filing imaginative copy, until only a handful remained in the rambling little hill town, drinking in the coffee and liquor shops, discussing the interesting rumour about Mr Kasim's elder son Sayed, which their editors dared not yet print, and visiting the brothels, for private entertainment but also in the hope of meeting Mr Kasim's younger son, Ahmed, who was said to be a drunkard and a lecher, an incorrigible wastrel who had come near to breaking his father's heart before being packed off to Mirat in the Nawab's service, to womanize and drink himself to death if he wished.

But there was no sign of Ahmed Kasim either. A story that he was being treated for venereal disease in a room in the private residence of Dr Habbibullah, chief physician to the Nawab, sent the remaining journalists from the Nanoora Hills down to the city of Mirat and then a rumour that MAK had initiated the story of his younger son's illness to get rid of the press and leave Nanoora unnoticed sent some of them rushing back and others out of the State altogether, back to Ranpur and British India. The latter found the Kasim house on the Kandipat road still closed and the former were no more successful than hitherto in establishing through the evidence of their own eyes whether the elusive Congressman was in fact in residence at the summer palace.

Journalists in other parts of India thought they detected in the attitude of members of the Congress high command more pious hopes than firm convictions of Mr Kasim's continuing allegiance to the twin cause of freedom and unity which he had supported throughout his political life, and a characteristically enigmatic comment by the Mahatma (not spoken, but written down, it being his day of silence) did little to remove the suspicion that during the Simla conference there had been private differences of opinion between MAK and his distinguished colleagues. Asked if he could throw any light on Mr Kasim's apparently self-imposed security screen, Mr Gandhi wrote: 'God alone throws light on any matter and in this light we may from time to time perceive the truth.'

With this the two journalists had to be content because the Mahatma indicated that the interview was over. They departed, leaving him to bathe and have his massage.

A few days later public interest in Mr Kasim's political intentions was temporarily extinguished by the unexpected news that the British electorate had voted overwhelmingly for the Socialists and, in doing so, relegated the arch-imperialist, Mr Churchill, at the moment of his triumph, to the post of Leader of His Majesty's now numerically harmless Tory Opposition.

*

The story that three senior members of the Bengal Club promptly died of apoplexy, although not without a certain macabre charm, proved to have no foundation in fact; but there was no doubt that for several days relations between many British officers and the rank and file of conscript British soldiers serving their time in India, who had voted by post and proxy, were a little distant, and in one reported case demonstrably strained and only saved from escalating to the point where they would have formed the basis of a very serious affair of conduct prejudicial to good order and military discipline by the presence-of-mind of a sergeant-major who stood between his captain and a lance-corporal who had admitted 'voting for old Clem' on the railway station at Poona and said, 'Sir, I think we have a little touch of the sun.' It was raining at the time.

The rifle company of which this captain was in command formed part of a British infantry battalion that was on its way to Kalyan, near Bombay, to join the forces gathering there for the invasion and liberation of Malaya, in an operation known as Zipper. The battalion reached Kalyan on July 30 and settled itself in to a section of an immense hutted encampment that looked and proved dreary. The wet monsoon was at its peak. The Churchillian officer and most of his colleagues managed to travel frequently by jeep to find solace in Bombay, in whose roads part of the invasion force of shipping had already anchored in preparation for the embarkation of the troops, but the rank and file were less fortunate.

There was Housey-Housey, a camp cinema, and Indian prostitutes who were cheap but out-of-bounds. There was mud. It was a bleak terrain that it took some effort of imagination to see as once having been part of the background to the romantic and exotic affairs of the Mahratta kings in whom a fair-haired and well-spoken British Field Security sergeant – with a degree in history from Cambridge – attempted to interest a bored and restive group of captive Cockney, Welsh, Midlands and Northern Englishmen who had to be forgiven for wondering what they were doing in Kalyan getting kitted up for the Far East when the real war (the one in Europe) was over and the lights had actually gone up in London, in every sense. Accounts received from home of VE night celebrations had already eroded what little sense of India's attractions they had acquired and since this had in any case never been lively enough to nourish in them any kind of curiosity about her history or her future, the Field Security sergeant, whose name was Perron, was soon left in little doubt of his audience's indifference to the political machinations and territorial ambitions of Mahdaji and Daulat Rao Sindia. Since he had embarked on the lecture with neither enthusiasm nor optimism, the audible appeal to wrap it up for ****** sake caused him no surprise and scarcely a pang. His closing description of a lady-warrior said to have reduced her male rivals to a state of military impotence, by admitting them to her chamber one after the other on the night before a battle, brought the lecture to an end in an atmosphere of near-hysteria. 'Bring 'er on,' the same voice cried, and the room then resounded to whistling and the stamping of hundreds of ammunition boots – a noise that greeted the Welfare Officer as he arrived to see how Sergeant Perron was getting on and which seemed to encourage him in a belief that such lectures were a good thing; a belief of which Sergeant Perron did not disabuse him because he had decided quite early in his military service that for life to be supportable officers had to be protected from anything that might shatter their illusion that they knew what the men were thinking.

Knowing himself incapable of reaching the required standard of self-deception in this, and other matters that came under the heading 'Leadership', and believing that life in the ranks would provide him with a far greater measure of freedom and better opportunities to study in depth human behaviour during an interesting period of history, he had politely but stubbornly resisted every attempt made to commission him. Only one set of the batch of uncles and aunts who had taken it in turns to bring him up thought this short-sighted. The others approved of his decision. They thought it agreeably eccentric, quite in keeping with the radical upper-class tradition which they liked to feel distinguished them as a family.

'It obviously went down well,' the Welfare Officer said, toning down his North Country accent and matily accompanying Perron from the lecture hall. 'I must say I had doubts, but a chap who really knows his subject is more likely to pass some of his enthusiasm on than not. You must do some more, sergeant.'

'A good idea, sir.'

'These waiting periods are damned difficult. There's a batch of airborne blokes due in soon. Now that the show in Germany's over they'll be itching to get started and give the Jap a knock. They'll be a handful to keep occupied and entertained. I know you've got your own special security job to do but I'd be grateful if you'd spare half-an-hour to talk to them one morning on this Indian history thing of yours. I'll try and come myself.

Learn a bit too. Extend my range beyond the Black Hole. Never too late for that, eh?'

Perron said, 'Actually, if you don't mind, sir, I think they're more relaxed without an officer present.'

Captain Strang looked relieved. To reassure the officer that his interest was appreciated but that his friendliness would not be taken advantage of and made an excuse for slack behaviour, Perron slapped up a particularly smart one when they parted and would have stamped his feet had they not been standing in a puddle. Perron had cultivated a formidable parade-ground style and soldierly manner not only to preserve that encouraging image of discipline and efficiency which heartened officers but also (after a tiresome experience with a Seaforth Highlander captain in the map-room of a camp on Salisbury Plain) to minimize the risk of his BBC accent (as fellow-NCOS called it) and his cultural interests giving them the impression that he was a pansy.

*

The sight of the armada gathering off Bombay – a city to which Sergeant Perron's field security duties now began to take him fairly regularly – appearing, disappearing and reappearing as the curtains of monsoon rain and mist rose and fell with sinister effect, did not usually depress him. In four years of service he had learned to look upon the entire war as an under-rehearsed and over-directed amateur production badly in need of cutting. In this light the low grey shapes of the troopships and escorts could be seen as figments of the imagination of an unknown but persistent operational planning staff whose directives had caused them to appear. The same imagination could just as easily dispel them. Nothing in the army was absolutely sure until it happened and he did not intend to worry about Zipper or the danger he might be in until the ships weighed anchor with himself on one of them.

But on the afternoon of Sunday August 5 as he drove past the Taj Mahal Hotel in a brand new jeep that had been lent in temporary exchange for the motor-cycle he had left at the motor-pool for water-proofing for the sea-borne landings in Malaya, he observed that the armada had increased in size since his view of it a couple of days before. Perhaps it was the sense of futility lingering from his previous day's lecture on the Mahrattas that chiefly contributed to his unusual feeling of disquiet, of there being something in the air that boded no good and moved him to nostalgic thoughts of a world where peace and common sense prevailed.

Being early for his appointment with a Major Beamish he stopped the jeep and gazed at the brown-grey waste of Bombay water. Without ever having taken any other personal avoiding action than that of co-operating cheerfully over the deferment of his call-up to enable him to sit his finals and obtain his degree, he had managed to get through the war so far without coming any closer to a violent end than half-a-mile away from a bomb off-loaded by a Heinkel over Torbay after a night visit to Bristol. But he had always assumed that his turn for danger would come. Posted to India in 1943 he had expected it to come quite soon but, of course, any apprehension that he felt in regard to that was combined with the excitement of finding himself after several years' scholarly absorption in Britain's imperial history actually in the country in which so much of it had originated.

In the first six months the luck of the draw of postings had given him opportunities to visit Cawnpore, Lucknow, Fort St George, Calcutta, Seringapatam, Hyderabad, Jaipur and Agra, and if he had felt some disappointment in these places as relics of old confrontations he had always managed to suppress it before it grew strong enough to undermine his academic confidence. 'India' he wrote in his notebook, 'turns out to be curiously immune to the pressures of one's knowledge of its history. I have never been in a country where the sense of the present is so strong, where the future seems so unimaginable (unlikely even) and where the past impinges so little. Even the famous monuments look as if they were built only yesterday and the ruined ones appear really to have been ruined from the start, and that but recently.'

Occasionally he was tempted to blame the war for his inability to relate the country he saw to what he knew of its past and at such times he thought how interesting it would be to come back or stay on when the war was over, to examine India undisturbed. But this afternoon, looking at the unfriendly vista of the Arabian Sea which as a boy he had thought the most romantically named ocean in the world, he felt more strongly than ever how perilously close to losing confidence the actual experience of being in India had brought him; and he wanted to go home – not (like the men to whom he had lectured) merely for home's sake or to enjoy the first fruits of a new political dispensation (for which he too had posted his vote by proxy through his Aunt Charlotte) – but so that he could regain lucidity and the calm rhythms of logical thought. These, he knew, depended upon a continuing belief in one's grasp of every issue relevant to one's subject and India seemed to be the last place to be if one wanted to retain a sense of historical proportion about it.

He got out his notebook with the intention of writing something down that might clarify his thoughts and expose as baseless his nagging doubts about the value of work he intended to do in pursuit of certain ineluctable truths but just as there seemed to be no connection between the India he was in and the India that was in his head there was no connection either between paper and pencil and the page remained ominously blank. This depressed him so much that he wrote out in a determined hand: 'Tell Aunt Charlotte that Bunbury is deteriorating rapidly?'

*

'This is Captain Purvis, sergeant,' Major Beamish said, indicating a thin-faced, mousy-haired, ill-looking man who was dosing himself with brown pills which he washed down with water without quite choking. 'You an' 'e are goin' this evenin' to a party.' Beamish, like so many elderly regular officers, spoke a kind of upper-crust cockney.

'Yes, sir,' Perron said, keeping his thumbs in line with the seams of his trousers.

Beamish was in a bad temper, either as a result of a thick Saturday night or of lingering resentment at being made to work on a Sunday. He said, 'Fer God's sake sit down. It's too bloody hot fer parade-ground manners.'

Perron, who stood over six feet in his socks, chose the deepest of three available chairs in deference to Major Beamish whose trunk was short in proportion to his legs and who therefore sat lower at his desk than seemed either fair or suitable for a man of his domineering temperament. Satisfied that his eye-level was now a flattering few inches below Beamish's, Perron met the officer's gaze with soldierly frankness.

'D'yer have yer civvies with yer?'

Before Perron could answer, the other officer – who was now sitting with his eyes closed and his arms folded broke in. 'Shouldn't advise civvies in this case.'

'I have my Army Education Corps gear, sir,' Perron said.

'Those'll do,' Purvis said.

'You fill 'im in, Purvis, or shall I?'

'Would you? I'll interrupt if I don't think you've got it right. Could we have that fan on more?'

Perron got up and went to the board of switches and turned up the dial that regulated the ceiling fan. Irritably, Beamish re-allocated weights to keep the papers moored to the desk top, then lit a cigarette but did not offer the tin.

'It's about security fer Zipper and loose talk here in Bombay,' he began. Perron listened attentively for the ten seconds it took Beamish to pass from the informative to the opinionative mood and then tried to tune in what he called his other ear: the one that caught the nuances of time and history flowing softly through the room, a flow arrested neither by Beamish's concerns nor his own sense of obligation to further them by putting himself at Beamish's disposal. Glancing at Purvis he wondered whether that officer also heard the whisper of the perpetually moving stream or whether the expression of concentration was due to the compelling effect of the brown pills. When Purvis's brows suddenly contracted he decided it must be the latter.

'Are yer still with us, sergeant?'

'Yes, sir.'

'Right. Tell 'im about the party, Purvis.'

For a moment Purvis neither spoke nor moved. Then he opened his eyes. 'God!' he said, got up and went out of the room.

'Feller's got squitters,' Beamish explained.

'Who is Captain Purvis, sir?'

'Damned if I know. Brig didn't say. Never met 'im in me life till half-an-hour ago. Seems a bit of a wash-out ter me. Chap should be able to keep 'imself fitter than that!'

A chaprassi came in with a foot-high pile of folders tied up in pink tape and put them by the side of a similar pile on the In side of Major Beamish's desk. There was a single file in the Out tray. The chaprassi took this with him when he went. Beamish poured himself a glass of water then took the top folder from the nearest of the two piles.

'Smoke if yer want ter,' he said. 'While we're waitin'.'

Perron murmured his thanks but did not do so. Beamish read the note in the file, initialled it, flung the folder in the Out tray and reached for the next.

Ten minutes later Purvis came back. Beamish was reading the minute in the last folder of the second pile. Without glancing up he said, 'Feelin' better?'

'Frankly, no. I think the sergeant will have to come back to my billet. I'll put him in the picture there. In any case he'll need somewhere to change and freshen up for this evening.'

'All right, sergeant, get along with Captain Purvis. Are yer goin' back ter Kalyan ternight?'

'That was my intention, sir.'

'Ring me from there in the mornin'. We'll decide if there's anything ter follow up.'

Perron stood, put his cap on, stamped to attention and saluted. As he turned he caught the tail end of a wince on Captain Purvis's face.

'Shoes, sergeant! Have you got *shoes*?' Purvis asked.

'In my pack, sir. With the uniform.'

'Thank God for that. What are you on, a motor-bike?'

'I've got a jeep today, sir.'

'We'll dump it at my office.'

Outside in the corridor Purvis maintained his distance a couple of paces ahead. They passed a long bench on which a line of chaprassis dozed, like figures on a frieze in bas-relief, awaiting employment. The building – currently at the disposal of the army and navy – belonged to the port authority and smelt of rope, gunny sacks and the dust on old bills of lading. Through the immense windows in the main corridor into which they turned came that other pervasive dockyard smell of oily water: Bombay, Bom-Bahia, an island swamp, part of the dowry brought by Catherine of Braganza to Charles II which it took the British five years to persuade the Portuguese Viceroy actually to hand over. Perron stemmed the stream of thought before it could disorient him; apart from which Purvis walked very fast and Perron didn't want to run the risk of losing him in the labyrinth. He concentrated on Purvis's back and noticed that the officer's shoulders were hunched – probably against the ringing sound of Perron's studded boots on the stone floor.

Descending by a broad stone staircase they reached the main entrance hall on whose marble flags stood a profusion of poles on heavy plinths which bore directional signs. None of the officers and NCOs passing to and fro glanced at the signs and Perron wondered how long it would take for the place to be reduced to a state of hopeless confusion if someone ever took it into his head to move the signs round. Perhaps no one would ever notice.

He smiled and at that moment Purvis stopped and faced him. They nearly bumped into one another. Whatever Purvis had intended to say he forgot.

'Something amusing you, sergeant?'

'No, sir.'

'I mean if there is, do *share* it.'

Perron told him his thought about the signs. Purvis glanced at them. Without another word he led the way into the open: a fore-court normally crammed with vehicles but today fairly empty. In the minute or so since they had left Beamish's office the sun had come out. The heat struck Perron's eyelids.

'Where's this jeep of yours, then?'

Perron indicated it.

'No driver?'

'Only me, sir.'

Purvis went down the steps. 'Mine's that fifteen hundredweight Chevvy. Follow me and for God's sake keep up. Right?'

Jeep-borne, Perron followed the truck through the archway which was blocked at night by a white pole but at present open to all comers and goers under the eye of a stick-guard who was supposed to inspect identity cards but was taking people on trust. They drove along a road parallel to the docks. At the end of it Purvis's truck turned left. Caught in the midst of Bombay's traffic – buses, cyclists, hooting taxis, overladen trucks, horse-drawn doolies and jay-walking pedestrians – Perron concentrated on not losing contact. The truck braked sharply to avoid an obstacle Perron couldn't see. He slammed on his own brakes and stopped a foot or two short of an impact that might have snapped the tether Purvis seemed to be near the end of. Possibly the nest of spies, fifth-columnists and loose-talkers Perron gathered Purvis thought he'd uncovered was totally illusory. Driving on, but allowing more distance (and noting that the cause of the abrupt halt had been a handcart piled high with crates of live fowl, hauled by a half-naked coolie) Perron decided that so long as Purvis wasn't at his elbow the entire evening, hissing warnings, the party might be supportable; or even enjoyable.

*

Purvis's billet turned out to be a flat in one of the modern blocks opposite the Oval – that elegant, coconut-palm fringed rectangle of open, grassed, space; or *maidan*; brilliantly green at this wet time of year. They reached the block in Purvis's truck, having left Perron's jeep in the courtyard of a house several streets away which was guarded by sentries but otherwise unidentifiable as a military office. Purvis had instructed the guard-commander that Sergeant Perron was to be re-admitted on production of his identity card at whatever time of night he returned, in whatever kind of clothing or uniform, and be allowed to collect and take away his jeep; but – short though the journey was – the route then taken from Purvis's office to Purvis's billet seemed to Perron, in the back of the truck, so complicated that he had doubts about finding his way back to his jeep unaccompanied. This had not bothered him much because he assumed they would go to the party in the fifteen hundredweight and be brought back from it by the same means, after which he would be taken to retrieve the jeep; but when they dismounted in Queen's Road Purvis signed the driver's log book and dismissed him until morning.

'Is the party being given nearby, sir?' Perron asked as they approached the entrance to the block of flats. Purvis didn't answer. He was in a hurry. Reaching the two steps that led to the open doorway and a dark hall he stumbled up them, bumped into and almost knocked down a servant who was coming out ahead of a young English woman.

'For God's sake look where you're going!' Purvis shouted.

If he was aware of the girl he gave no sign of it. He brushed past the two of them and disappeared into the dark.

'I do beg your pardon,' Perron said to the girl.

'Why?' she asked.

'I'm afraid the officer isn't well. He couldn't have seen you.'

She studied his uniform briefly, taking everything in at a glance as young English women in India were trained to.

'It wasn't me he bumped into, it was Nazimuddin. But thank you for apologizing for him.'

He waited for her to add ' –sergeant', but she smiled instead, an ordinary friendly smile, then put on the hat she had been carrying. The movement released a little wave of delicate scent. She came down the two steps and made for the pavement and the road where the ill-used bearer was flagging down a cruising taxi. She was a bit thin, a bit bony, but she walked well. He judged her to be in her early twenties but found it difficult to place her. Accent, style of dress, forthrightness: these proclaimed her a daughter of the *raj*, but her manner had lacked that quality – elusive in definition – which Perron had come to associate with young memsahibs: a compound of self-absorption, surface self-confidence and, beneath, a frightening innocence and attendant uncertainty about the true nature of the alien world they lived in. They were born only to breathe that rarified, oxygen-starved air of the upper slopes and peaks, and so seemed to gaze down, from a height, with the touching look of girls who had been brought up to know everybody's place and were consequently determined to have everybody recognize their own.

Waiting until she had completed that movement – charming in a girl, especially in her – of climbing into the taxi, he shouldered the pack containing his Army Education Corps disguise, went into the building and through the gloom to an inner only slightly better lighted hall where there was a lift shaft and a flight of stone steps leading up. A notice, askew on a piece of string suspended from the handle of the trellis-work gate, informed him that the lift was out of order, but in any case he would not have known which floor to go to. There was no sound from above of Purvis climbing. The door of the flat immediately to his right had a dark-stained strip of wood above the bell with gold-lettering on it saying Mr B. S. V. Desai. To the left a similar notice read H. Tractorwallah. Both these doors seemed unlikely ones for Purvis to be on the other side of and neither had the look of having been opened recently.

Perron ascended. On the next floor the two flats were occupied respectively by a Lieut.-Col. A. Grace and a Major Rajendra Singh of the Indian Medical Service. The Indian medical officer's name seemed to have been painted on its strip of wood longer ago than Colonel Grace's. Perron hesitated, but then, deciding that if Purvis was billeted on this floor one of the two doors would have been left open, started on the next leg up and as he did so heard a voice above call, 'Sahib?'

Purvis's servant, he supposed. The man salaamed, stood back as Perron reached the next landing, and indicated the open door of the flat above Rajendra Singh's. As he entered he heard a groan. The servant closed the door and went quickly down a corridor to a curtained doorway. The groan was repeated. A tap was turned on. Perron put his pack down, went in the opposite direction to the one the servant had taken and entered a dining-area. This was separated from a living-room by a wide uncurtained arch. The living-room was elegantly furnished, filled with aqueous light of sunshine filtered through a set of louvred shutters. On a wall behind a long settee hung a series of what looked like paintings from the Moghul period, which upon close inspection Perron identified as genuine. He was still admiring them when the servant came in and invited him to go along to Captain Purvis's room.

This room, although large, was barrack-like by comparison. Apart from an almirah and a wooden table littered with books, papers and some discarded shirts, there was nothing else in it except a rush-seated chair and the camp-bed on which Purvis was lying, one hand over his eyes, the other hanging free, almost touching the floor. But an open door afforded a glimpse of a well-appointed green-tiled bathroom.

Purvis said, 'I'm not going to be able to make it, sergeant. You'll have to go by yourself or forget the whole thing. I wish to God I'd kept my mouth shut. It's all an utter waste of time. Every bloody civilian in Bombay knows where Zipper's going and why it's going and how it's going. We're the exceptions. We know where. But they know where better. They can even name the damned beaches. It'll be a shambles, a complete and unholy utter bloody cocked-up shambles.'

Suddenly Purvis uncovered his eyes and stared wildly at Perron.

'You *are* Field Security?'

'Yes, sir.'

'Beamish isn't. What the hell is he?'

'He has certain responsibilities for liaison between intelligence and operations.'

'But he's not your officer?'

'No, sir. My officer is in Poona at the moment.'

Purvis shut his eyes.

'Poona,' he said, almost under his breath. 'It scarcely seems possible.'

'Poona, sir? Or that my officer is there?'

But Purvis didn't say. Outside the barred but open window there was a sudden piercing contest of crows and then a human voice below in the courtyard raised in what to an untutored ear must sound like a protracted cry of pain but which Perron knew was only the call of an itinerant tradesman. Purvis groaned and turned on his side, the side away from the window. At that moment the sun went in and the sluice-gates of the wet monsoon re-opened. Purvis's lips began to move but Perron could hear nothing above the noise of the rainstorm.

The bearer parted the curtains and came in with a tray of tea for two. Perron assisted by clearing a space on the table and when the bearer had gone he looked at Purvis intending to say, 'Shall I be mother, sir?' but the officer's eyes were open, fixed and unreceptive – in fact, glazed. For a moment Perron thought he was dead, extinguished by the single clap of thunder that had heralded the arrival of the tea.

*

Refreshed, bathed and now disguised as a sergeant in education, Perron walked – shoe- instead of boot-shod – along the tiled passage to the living-room where he found Purvis standing on a balcony that had been revealed by the folding back of shutters and windows. It was now a beautiful evening with a sky the colour of pale turquoise. The coconut palms framed a view of the Law Courts and clock tower on the other side of the *maidan*.

'I appreciated the bath, sir. I'm afraid I used some of your Cuticura talcum.'

Purvis had a glass in the hand that rested on the balustrade.

'Help yourself to a drink, sergeant. You'll find everything on the tray.'

There was, if not everything, a generous selection: Gin, whisky, rum, several bottles of Murree beer and various squashes and cordials. The spirits were country-distilled so Perron – not caring much for rum of any kind – chose the gin which he found more palatable than Indian versions of Scotch. He added lemon-squash and – luxury for him – a cube of ice from a zinc-lined container.

'Cheers, sir.'

'I'm an economist,' Purvis said, irrelevantly to everything except his private train of thought. 'It's enough to send you round the bloody bend.'

He came in from the balcony, refilled his glass with rum and lime and sat on the long settee under the priceless paintings. After drinking a stout measure he shuddered, closed his eyes and put his head back.

'Can you guess how long I've been ill, sergeant?'

'No, sir.'

'Since I got off the boat. And that's three months, two weeks and four days ago.'

'Bad luck, sir.'

Purvis raised his eyelids a fraction and looked at him. Perron was standing with his feet apart, one hand behind his back, the other at waist level holding the tumbler steady.

'How long have you been in this bloody country?'

'Since 'forty-three, sir.'

'And in the army?'

'Since 'forty-one, sir.'

'Before that?'

'Cambridge, sir.'

'Doing what?'

'I rowed a bit. And read history.'

'What was your school?'

'Chillingborough, sir.'

'How the hell have you avoided getting a commission?'

'By always saying no, sir.'

Purvis shut his eyes again. His face began to contort.

'I'm sorry,' he said, 'but that is extremely funny.' He did not say why but took another long drink, set the glass on a low table in front of the settee then leant back with his hands clasped behind his head.

'The party,' he said, changing the subject and ploughing straight into the new one, 'is in the apartment of an Indian lady living on the Marine Drive. I'll write her a note, so you'll have the address on the envelope. There should be no difficulty about your going in my place. I was there the other night and she doesn't seem to care how many people turn up or whether she knows them or not. You'll see what I mean when you get there. Judging from the other day there'll be a lot of non-commissioned men so you won't feel out of place. The fact is, it seems to be the kind of flat where officers and men fraternize, not to mention white, black and in-between. Sexually I'd say some of the company was on the ambivalent side.'

'Yes, sir.'

'Will that worry you?'

'I don't think so, sir.'

'You may even be taken for a special sort of friend of mine.'

'I think I shall be able to cope in the event of a misunderstanding arising, sir.'

'Not that I care a fig about my own reputation. I shan't go there again. In any case you'll find lots of girls, if you can sort out the ones who're only interested in men.'

Perron finished his drink but retained his glass.

'Apart from unambivalent girls, sir, what precisely should I look out for? Any special person or group of people?'

'So far as I'm concerned, sergeant, you can just go there and get stoned or laid, as our American allies so picturesquely put it. I *told* you. The whole thing's an utter waste of time. You're not going to arrest anybody. At least, not for spying.'

'Major Beamish seemed to think otherwise about it being a waste of time, sir.'

'Think? Think? He's a professional soldier. They're all alike and worse out here than back home. Totally automatic. Touch a button by accident and they go into action. I'll tell you, Perron –'

Perron was surprised to find that his name had registered.

' – how this bloody farce you're up to the neck in started.'

Three days ago Purvis had encountered, in circumstances not clear, an old friend – obviously a breezy, hectic sort of man – who had whisked him up from whatever he'd been doing, dined him at the Taj and taken him off to the apartment in Marine Drive which Purvis's friend had described as 'always good for a lark'; as indeed it had proved, in so far as an uninterrupted flow of drink, food and merrymaking was concerned. Although Purvis did not say so, Perron understood that the larkiness had been infectious enough to make Purvis forget his chronic internal disorder and become expansive with his hostess to whom in a weak but hospitable moment he had promised one of two remaining bottles of whisky he'd managed to get hold of in England and bring out to India for personal consolation. She had declined but he'd insisted and then been invited to come to another party with or without the bottle on the evening of August 5.

'I could have forgotten the whole damned thing,' Purvis said, 'if I hadn't stupidly made a casual remark next day to the bloody fool officer I work with about the amount of careless talk going on in Bombay. He said – where for instance? And instead of shutting up I said "Well, take this odd party I was at last night where the Indian civilians were actually telling *us* that the Zipper invasion fleet wouldn't sail for Malaya until the end of August because of the tides on the beaches around Port Swettenham," and the next thing I knew the bloody man had reported it and I was hauled in front of that Brigadier Whatsit and congratulated on keeping my ears open. When he heard I'd been invited to the same flat tonight he was like a cat with two tails and before I knew where I was I was under strict security routine and told to say nothing more until I had instructions, and that was this morning when I was ordered to report to this Beamish fellow of yours. When Beamish told me I had to go to the party with a Field Security chap in disguise I thought he was joking. I tried to tell him you can hear that kind of talk anywhere in Bombay but he wouldn't *listen*.'

Perron put his empty glass on the drinks table.

'Are we landing on beaches near Port Swettenham, sir?'

'How the hell do I know? I've got no personal interest in Zipper. I'm not going, thank God. Are you?'

'Yes, sir.'

'Oh.'

Purvis noticed Perron's drink was finished. He said, 'Help yourself, sergeant.'

'Thank you, sir. But I think a clear head might be advisable this evening.'

'Advisable? In this country?'

Purvis became restless and Perron momentarily allowed himself to stop thinking of him as an officer with an officer's responsibilities for getting the war over and done with and think of him as a man, one whom in other circumstances he might even like.

'Well if you're *on* Zipper,' Purvis said, 'I suppose you have to take all this incredible lack of security seriously. I don't suppose you want to be shot out of the water by the Japanese before you've even set foot in the damned country, especially at this stage in the war.'

'I should prefer not to be, sir.'

'Does it bore you to call people sir?'

'No, sir.'

Purvis got up. He refilled his glass.

'What is your actual job, sir, if I may ask?'

'You may well ask. I've given up asking. I've even given up asking myself. Three times in my life the phone's rung and the fellow on the other end has said, "Can you get down to see me, Purvis? I've got something special for you." And each time it's ended like this, with me wondering not what's special about it but what it *is*. The first time was 'thirty-nine. I'd done a few papers that were well thought of. I'd got a good lectureship. And then the war started and the phone rang. "Purvis," this fellow said, "if you can get here in twenty minutes I've got something that will interest you." I was there with three minutes to spare and an hour to wait. And that led to a folding chair behind a deal-table in an attic without heating and a telephone that never rang. I thought I was supposed to contribute some original thinking to the problems of distribution of goods and services as between high and low priority demand sectors, or in layman's terms, the problems of trying to stop the army wasting what could be saved and what the civil population could bloody well make use of. I even drafted a paper and this chap rang up cock-a-hoop and said it was just what he wanted but if that was so I must have been under a misapprehension about what he wanted it for. I was in that attic for eighteen months. Then the phone rang again. Same chap, "Purvis," he said, "I've got something I think will get you out of that dead-end you're in." I arrived half-an-hour late, deliberately, which put him in a filthy temper because he'd promised to ring this colonel chap that very morning and tell him if I was interested. He sent me off to one of those anonymous areas somewhere near Stanmore which always strike me as vaguely sinister. When I saw the colonel he struck me as sinister too. He said, "We've read your paper" but hedged when I said I'd done several and which did he mean.

'The trouble is, Perron, I used to be the sort of man who couldn't bear to embarrass another by making it plain I saw through him and knew he was talking cock. So I let it go and just concentrated on trying to find out what I was supposed to *do*. I never did from him. But then they sent for me from the War House. This time it was a mere major. Awfully pleasant chap. He'd actually read my paper on high and low priority demand sectors. I don't say he'd understood it. But he'd read it. And he called me *Mr* Purvis. He was even articulate about the job. Wrong. But articulate. He made me feel the inspiration for the special joint services advisory staff that he said was being got together to liaise with the various ministries and industry had been my paper and that I'd be one of its king-pins. "One thing," he said, "we'd want you in uniform. An immediate commission, naturally." '

Purvis's complexion suddenly went grey, either as a result of acute recollection or of acute physical discomfort. He downed the rest of his rum and poured another.

'I said I couldn't see what use a commission was. I'd signed the official secrets thing when I went to the attic. Well, as I said, he was an awfully pleasant chap. We didn't argue, and I went back to the attic and waited. I waited three weeks. When the summons came it wasn't to the War House but to the office of my benefactor. He congratulated me on making such a good impression on the people he'd recommended me to. He described my new job as the opportunity I'd been waiting for to exercise my talents as an economist for the country's benefit, an opportunity not to be thrown away on the totally irrelevant issue of what style of dress I exercised them in. I said, "You're right. Irrelevant is the word. So why the fuss? The army isn't me. Neither is officer status." '

Purvis sat down; he'd got up to get more lime-juice. He sat crouched, elbows on knees, head lowered and eyes hidden by his free hand. His shoulders began to shake.

'I'm sorry, sergeant, but it's so bloody funny. What you said about always saying no to a commission brought it all back.'

He straightened up.

'I'll tell you what this fellow said. "Purvis," he said, "in this country only a man born and bred *in* the officer-class can decline a commission without running the risk of having his integrity and future usefulness doubted." '

'Was that some kind of threat, sir?'

'Threat? It was a bloody ultimatum. Get into uniform or get out of the department. Not just out of the department but out of line for anything half-decent going after the war. Not to mention the immediate danger of ceasing a reserved occupation, getting called up and wasting the rest of the war as a highly inefficient and underemployed squaddie.'

'And subsequently, sir? Were your experiences as an officer on the advisory staff as unsatisfactory as those in the attic?'

'Oh no. No, I couldn't say that. Not unsatisfactory. Nor satisfactory. You see, Perron, there never was an advisory staff. I mean there was never *that* one. Plenty of others. It took me several weeks to realize that ours didn't actually exist. I used to go to these meetings. At first I thought I'd missed something important about its inauguration, because of the Gas course.'

'Gas course?'

'The day I reported to the War House disguised as an acting captain and war substantive lieutenant, the nice major said, "Oh, Purvis" – he'd dropped the mister, you see. "Purvis," he said, "d'you mind awfully, there's this boring gas thing come up, but I suppose you might just as well learn how to use a WD mask since you've now got to carry one." So I went down to Salisbury Plain.'

'An interesting part of the country, sir.'

Purvis looked at him, as though testing for sincerity.

'I didn't find it so. I expect you had some rudimentary military training at that public school of yours. Isn't it one of those places with a long record of turning out the future soldiers and administrators of Empire?'

'I wasn't in OTC, sir. It wasn't compulsory.'

'Well I had no military training whatsoever. My progress to my current distinction was from elementary via secondary to grammar school and to the earnest heights of the London School of Economics. Walking about with three pips up and no faintest notion of how to salute let alone whom to salute can be a highly embarrassing experience. I was glad when I got back to the War House and they sent me to this quaint little establishment off the Marylebone High Street where a retired Guards sergeant-major taught a batch of poor fellows like me how to dissemble sufficiently to avoid being put under close arrest as nuns parachuted in from Stuttgart. I almost wished, Perron, yes almost wished I'd scrubbed the whole career thing, been called up and gone into intellectual hibernation for the duration. There was something soothing about Sergeant-Major Bracegirdle. He was so pleased with us when we got anything *right*. In a way nothing is more restful than to stand in the ranks and do what the man says. The whole thing is definitely erotic, a sort of communal wet-dream without the discomfort but with that same sublimated asexual quality of purely involuntary obedience to a dominant force.'

Purvis caught his breath, placed one hand on the left side of his abdomen and then slowly breathed out. Inflammation of the colon, Perron decided. Amoebic in origin, almost certainly. Perron had become interested in the effects of tropical environment on temper and character. At home Purvis might well have been, as he had intimated, the most mild-mannered and considerate of men. Of strong constitution himself, Perron – who had not maintained his health in India without an almost valetudinarian attention to the medicinal needs of his body – had even so not been free of the shortness of temper that was one of the side-effects of an overworked and easily discouraged digestive system. The insight this had given him into the possibly important part played in Anglo-Indian history by an incipient, intermittent or chronic diarrhoea in the bowels of the *raj* was one of the few definite academic advantages he felt he had gained by coming to India.

'Shall I freshen your drink, sir?'

'Oh, God, would you?'

Perron did so. Purvis now sat back, one arm stretched along the top edge of the settee, his face turned towards the window and the view – now fading – of the coconut palms.

'Have you ever felt it too, Perron? That the only way to survive a war is to treat it as totally unreal?'

'The thought has struck me, sir.'

'But have you ever succeeded?'

'From time to time.'

Purvis was silent for a moment.

'I envy you,' he said. 'I've tried. But I don't seem to have the capacity to pretend.' He looked at Perron. 'Six years! Six years criminal waste of the world's natural resources and human skills. History, you said?'

Perron nodded.

'Seriously, or just as a way of spending the years of gilded youth?'

'I intend to continue.'

'Well, it's different for you, Perron. If you make a study of history you make one of human folly. But sometimes I believe I simply shall never be able to *forgive* it. I had a breakdown, you know.'

'I'm sorry to hear that, sir.'

'They sent me to this place full of human wrecks like myself, but I did my own therapy. Bloody fool me. I'd had a lot of spare time in the three years I was on the non-existent advisory staff. I'd been thinking about the long-term deleterious effect of imperial possessions on the economic viability and creative drive of the country that held them. Now I really got down to it. I did a paper and sent it to a chap I knew who published it. But how my benefactor in Whitehall got hold of it, God knows. I suppose he still received the journal it came out in and read it because my name was under it. Otherwise he'd given up serious reading in 1938, I should say. Incidentally, he's probably right now in the process of landing himself a plum job with Attlee's crowd. He was a Marxist when I first knew him, a Liberal Edenite anti-Municheer under Chamberlain, a high Tory under Winston, so why not a milk-and-water Socialist under Clem? But that's by the way. Let me tell you what happened.'

'The phone rang again, sir?'

'Same man, of course. "You've had a raw deal, Purvis," he said, "no one knows it better than I but it wasn't my fault. When you're out of that place come and see me. I think I can really help you this time if you make it soon." Has it ever struck you, Perron, that there is nothing more gullible in the whole animal world than a human being? One has this hysterical belief in the non-recurrence of the abysmal, I suppose. One always imagines one has reached the nadir and that the only possible next move is up and out.

And then, of course, there was the magic formula – third time lucky. Why not? I placed the most inordinate confidence in that third ring of the telephone, so much so that the trick-cyclists thought I'd had an unprecedented overnight recovery and congratulated themselves no end. Directly I got down to London I rang this fellow and arranged to meet him. This time it was lunch at the club he'd been bucking to get into for years. He was already veering left again because he didn't see Churchill lasting long after the war. He introduced me to some of his new friends – I knew one or two of them myself and there was one in particular I respected. I thought, God, something's going to be done at last. I was right, but wrong about what. Something was being done. Von Rundstedt's attempt in the Ardennes had collapsed and all the signs were that the Germans were on their last legs. What was happening was people sniffing the peace and jockeying for position, but I was too stupid to see it like that at the time. I swallowed the whole line this fellow shot, about things now swinging the way of what he called "our sort of people" and how necessary it was to spike the guns of the old reactionary gang who'd be happy to let the war with Japan drag on and on and how our sort of people were determined that shouldn't happen. I ought to have seen through it when he started waffling about the Singapore-mentality that had come within an inch of bringing us to our knees in '42 and still existed out East in spite of all the efforts of men like Slim and Mountbatten to blow the cobwebs off the whole imperial-military apparatus. But I didn't. I just said, "Where's all this leading?" He said, "You mean what's in it for you?" That's the way he thought. "I'll tell you," he said, "that Indian paper of yours. It's really made an impression." I'd never thought of it as an Indian paper and I told him so. I told him it was a paper dealing in philosophical terms with an aspect of imperial economies and India came into it simply as an example, which didn't make me an expert on India. I shouldn't have said that. It gave him the line he needed. "But Purvis, experts on India are the last thing we want in India. We only want clear thinkers who'll help men like Bill and Dickie cut through the Singapore mentality and put ginger up the backsides of all those curry-colonels sitting in the Bengal Club in Calcutta and living in the nineteenth century." So I said, "Is that where you're sending me?" And he said it would be more likely Delhi where the real damage was done because GHQ India was still a vital link in Mountbatten's chain, *the* vital link, upon which the whole thing depended logistically, from the supply of men, arms and ammunition to the last piece of string and bamboo. Moreover, he said, if I wasn't an expert on India now I would be within a few months, at any rate in my own specialized field, and since the Indian empire was simply not going to survive in the kind of post-war world he knew he and I both hoped to see, my personal experience of it should prove invaluable to whatever government had the intricate job of transferring power to the Indians and advising them during a period of transition. "And that, Purvis," he said, "is the kind of little tree on which CBES grow for the plucking. After which you can pretty well write your own ticket. Continue in public life or retire, suitably rewarded, to the blessed groves of Academe." '

A flash of monsoon lightning lit the darkling flat.

'Has he risen much himself, sir?'

'Oh yes. You mean since '39? Immeasurably. He might with questionable luck for the nation be a future Chancellor of the Exchequer. He wasn't permanent establishment. I shouldn't be surprised to hear he's resigned his appointment and contested and won a safe Labour seat in the recent election.'

For a while Purvis sat without speaking or moving. Then he said, 'I must admit that as a man who can see the way things are and the way they are going, he's always left me standing. Academically it was the other way round and I don't expect he's ever forgiven me for that. People don't, do they? Inside every successful man there's often a disappointed and envious one, wouldn't you say? Moaning and groaning and plotting and planning. You see, Perron, I know the score now. He's got me out of the way deliberately. So that no nice little plum should fall in my lap.' Purvis again suffered a spasm of pain. 'I suppose you wouldn't be so kind as to give me another refill, sergeant? I have an idea it would be dangerous for me to move.'

Perron again performed this duty. While he did so the servant padded barefoot into the dining-room area where he clicked two or three switches which turned on some of the wall lights in the living-room and a well-shaded table lamp. The effect was pleasant.

The bearer told Purvis his bath was ready.

Purvis waved him away. The bearer went.

'Is the entire flat yours, sir?' Perron asked, handing Purvis the refilled glass.

'No. Thank you, sergeant. No, I wish it were. I'm only billeted here. It belongs to a senior British bank official, his ghastly wife and his beastly simpering daughter. They're on leave in what they call Ooty, which I gather is Anglo-Indian for Ootacamund. As you can imagine, he and I don't get on. We don't see eye to eye on the subject of the creation and distribution of wealth. He thinks England has just committed suicide and thinks I'm mad when I point out that it's not a socialist government but capitalist, simply substituting labour for finance. He tells people I'm a communist. Politically he's a bloody fool.'

'Are those paintings his, sir?'

'What paintings?'

'Those eighteenth-century paintings in the Guler-Basohli style. Behind you.'

Purvis didn't look. 'They may be part of the fixtures and fittings belonging to the bank for all I know.'

'I wonder whether he realizes their value.'

'Are they valuable?'

'Yes, sir.'

'Then obviously he doesn't. His lady-wife locked up all the Sheffield plate before going to Ooty. Frankly, I personally wouldn't know a work of art from a bee's arse and I fail to see any valid reason why one bit of pigment-daubed paper or canvas should be worth thousands and another worth sod-all, unless you fix the value of such things on the comparative basis of size of canvas and amount of paint actually expended.'

Perron stopped thinking of Purvis as a man and concentrated on the image of Purvis as an officer. Apart from inflammation of the colon, Purvis was suffering from paranoia. The man ought to be treated.

'What do the doctors say about your illness, sir?'

'I haven't seen any doctors.'

'Do you think that wise, sir?'

'Yes, I do.'

'You were taking some pills in Major Beamish's office, sir.'

'Oh, those. Our banker friend's lady-wife recommended them when I first arrived and she saw I'd already got the trots. They're supposed to cement you up. Sometimes they do. Sometimes they don't. The only thing that really helps is liquor. No wonder the sahibs have always gone around half-cut. If I report to the army doctors they'll either prescribe the same treatment or send me into dock for a check-up and I can't afford to be in dock, Perron. Not for a day. Not for an hour.'

'Why, sir? You gave me the impression that your duties here aren't onerous.'

'That's because I'm not even supposed to *be* here. I'm supposed to be in New Delhi. We're all supposed to be in New Delhi.'

'All?'

'The six of us who formed the para-military mission sent out to liaise with and advise the Indian Government, heads of services, and the Government at home, on – I quote – "all matters relevant to the anticipated increase of military forces requiring to be based in India as a consequence of a cessation of hostilities in Europe and the continuance thereof in South-East Asia, with special reference to the supply/demand factor as it will affect the existing ratio between civilian and military claims on the Indian economy." End of quote.'

'It sounds very distinguished, sir.'

'Quite. I should have smelt a rat. And I should have smelt another when I saw the names of two of my fellow missionaries, including that of the head, and another when we were sent out before the war in Europe was quite over, although in the latter case I could be forgiven for noticing no alarming odour, except that of uncharacteristic forethought.'

'Where are the other five members of the mission?'

'Disposed, singly, by the cunning Indian Government to various parts of the country. Only the head of the mission has managed to get to Delhi. So you see, Perron, why I must stay on my feet. I must be where the head of the mission knows where to find me. I must be instantly available to join him.'

'Have you heard from him recently, sir?'

'No.' Purvis again shut his eyes. 'No. *No.* I can't bear to let myself think it but I believe he's ratted on us. I believe he's comfortably esconced in some niche he's found that just fits him and no one else. I used to send him reports. I suppose the others still do. But when I began to suspect that he was collating them, falsifying them, and sending them back to Whitehall as an account of the mission's collective activities, I stopped. Childish, I suppose, but necessary, to flush him out or persuade him to flush *me* out. And, of course, I've nothing to report except a state of total chaos far worse than ever I encountered at home.'

He opened his eyes again but only for as long as it took him to drink the rest of his rum and lime.

'I used to think, Perron, that on the day we started handing the colonies back to the bloody natives we'd all be able to look the twentieth century in the face at last. But if India's an example the only way we'll be able to do that and stay sane is by wearing blinkers and dark glasses and forgetting such places actually exist, and leave them to stew in their own juice except during their inevitable periods of acute financial crisis when we'll have to pour money into them to stop a chain reaction of bankruptcy bringing any half-civilized economy to its knees.'

'What makes you think that, sir?'

'For heavens' sake, sergeant! You've been in India for what's it, two years? It's taken me no more than three months to write it off as a wasted asset, a place irrevocably ruined by the interaction of a conservative and tradition-bound population and an indolent, bone-headed and utterly uneducated administration, an elitist bureaucracy so out of touch with the social and economic thinking of even just the past hundred years that you honestly wonder where they've come from. Not England, surely?'

'Perhaps it's the enervating effect of the climate, sir.'

'It's nothing to do with the bloody climate. The fact is places like this have always been a magnet for our throw-backs. Reactionary, unco-operative bloody well expendable buggers from the upper and middle-classes who can't and won't pull their weight at home but prefer to throw it about in countries like this which they've always made sure would remain fit places for them to live in. They've succeeded only too well. The most sensible thing for us to do is get rid of it fast to the first bidder before it becomes an intolerable burden.'

'Wouldn't that be rather unfair, sir? Historically, we have a moral obligation, surely?'

'I couldn't disagree more. Moral obligation! What next? It's disastrous *ever* to feel a moral obligation for other people's mistakes.'

It was in Perron's mind to say that he'd always been under the impression that certain material benefits had flowed from the imperial possession, enriching Britain if not demonstrably impoverishing India (but somehow widening the gap in the two standards of living?) and that moral considerations could surely not be totally ignored by economists and accountants. But he thought it better not to aggravate Purvis who in any case would almost certainly be a member of the school of thought which held that the flow of benefit had petered out several years ago and a law of diminishing returns set in so that now the flow was operating in reverse. He compromised.

'All the same, sir, and though I do appreciate what you say, I should hope to see the transfer of power accompanied by some indication of our continuing interest and concern.'

'I'm sure you'll be gratified then, sergeant. The demission will certainly be accompanied by such pious assurances. But they won't mean what it will be hoped they're thought to mean. Labour capitalism is no more generous than finance capitalism. Incidentally, we talk about transfer of power, demission of power, getting rid of it, whatever phrase you prefer, but that's going to be easier talked about than done.'

'Do you think so, sir? Some people say that once it's appreciated that we sincerely mean to go the Indians will sink their differences and agree how to work together.'

'Then personally I think some people are absolutely wrong because the Indians are utterly demoralized at the very thought of having to take the ghastly mess over and run it themselves. We'll have the devil's own job off-loading it. And, God! one says "it" as if it's a single transferable package which it isn't, never has been and now never will be.'

'A fact for which we're partly to blame, sir?'

'We? Don't sell me that divide and rule stuff. The bloody place was divided when the sahibs first came and will be divided when the stupid sods go because they've always been content to sit on their bums in their bloody clubs and interfere only when the revenues were slow coming in. The place is still *feudal*, Perron. And so far as I can see the only man of influence who's worried about that is whatever the chap's name is, Nehru, but he's a Brahmin aristocrat and can hardly speak any language but English, and against him you have to set the Mahatma and his bloody spinning wheel. Spinning wheel! In 1945. For God's sake, what's the man *at*? In the past twenty-five years he's done as much to keep the country stuck in the mud with his village-industry fixation as the whole bloody *raj* put together.'

Stung as much by his feeling that there was something in what Purvis said as by the sense of the unfairness of such casual elimination of any consideration that didn't automatically fall within the economist's habitual terms of reference, Perron said:

'Your sponsor in Whitehall was right, sir. You've become an expert on India in a very short time.'

Purvis stared at him.

'Most Indian economists I've met happen to agree with me.'

'Yes I see, sir. Then perhaps that is a reason for optimism.'

'I doubt it, sergeant. It is in the Indian character to complain, but not to

1103

contest if a job depends on a posture of acquiescence. I'd better write you that letter. Bearer!'

While the letter was being written, Perron waited on the balcony and gazed across the Oval to the dark bulk of the Law Courts. For a moment – perhaps under the influence of that symbol of the one thing the British could point to if asked in what way and by what means they had unified the country, the single rule of law – he felt a pressure, as soft and close to his cheek as a sigh: the combined sigh of countless unknown Indians and of past and present members of the glittering insufferable *raj*; all disposable to make the world safe for Purvis. And other men like Purvis. (And, I suppose – Perron thought – for men like me.)

Purvis called him over and handed him an envelope. It was addressed to a Maharanee. Perron glanced at Purvis, mildly surprised, but the man was leaning back again, eyes closed. To Purvis, Maharanees were probably two a penny.

II

At seven-thirty Perron arrived by taxi at a block on the Marine Drive which according to the address on the envelope bore the name Sea Breezes. The driver he had flagged down in the Queen's Road translated this after several movements of uncertainty as Ishshee Brizhish, a place known to him. Armed with the envelope and a square package which contained the bottle of whisky, Perron entered the building and went up in the lift to the floor indicated by the board which gave flat numbers and the names of the occupants.

The décor in hall and landings was reminiscent of that in houses and apartments built in the ultra-modern style of the late 'twenties and early 'thirties, but it achieved a severe and bleak rather than a severe and functional effect. The cream-painted walls were dingy and the chromium rails bore the patina of years of contact with the human hand. The door of the flat at which he now stood was peagreen like those he had seen at successive stages through the latticework iron gates of the lift shaft and was well finger-marked round the keyhole.

He pressed the bell. No comforting sound of having got it to ring reached him and no hum of party conversation either. He wondered whether Purvis had the date right and then whether someone had tipped the Maharanee off about Security's interest in her circle of friends so that she had cancelled the party and would be found curled up with a good book. Wondering this he next considered the possibility that she had taken a fancy to Purvis and planned to lure him back to the flat with or without the bottle of whisky on a night when she knew they could be alone together. He could not assess the power of Purvis's sexual attraction. In such matters women had their own unassailable scale of values and judgment. But, having arrived at this possible explanation he now wondered how old she was and, if young, how well-favoured. The evening suddenly seemed full of an unexpected kind of potential.

The door was opened abruptly by a young Indian girl of gazellelike charm. 'Hello,' she said. Clearly she had none of that creature's timidity.

'Hello. I've got a note and a package.'

'For me?'

He gave her the envelope. Her beautifully architectured eyebrows contracted. 'Oh, it's for Auntie. What a jolly shame. But do come in.'

'Thank you.'

Perron stepped inside and let her close the door. Her scent was too cloying for his taste but welcome after the smell on the night breeze blowing in from the Bombay foreshore which Perron was convinced was used as a lavatory. Indian insistence that it was just the smell of the sea and the seaweed had not yet made him change his mind.

In the hall – the top end of a long wide passage with doors leading off from either side of it and cluttered with solid but poorly assorted furniture, including an ornately carved black Chinese settle upholstered with velvet cushions – the girl took the package from him and put it together with the envelope on an ebony table on which a heavy and thick-ankled Shiva danced in his petrified ring of fire. She said, 'Come and have a drink why not?' and led the way into a living-room.

Around the walls sofas and chairs were set in the solemn and rather hostile manner of the segregational East. The tiled floor was uncarpeted – perhaps for dancing. There was no balcony but the windows were wide open. The lighting was less successful than in Purvis's flat. From the centre of the ceiling hung a cluster of bulbs in a cruciform wooden chandelier of the kind that at home was *de rigueur* in rooms that sported fake beams and parchment lampshades with galleons stencilled on them. But these bulbs were unshaded. A few wall-lights in glass and chromium brackets added to the glare but did nothing to eliminate the harsh shadows. Near the window was a cocktail cabinet of impressive vulgarity, and to this the girl had gone. She turned round.

'You're a sergeant, aren't you? Auntie says all sergeants drink beer but there was one the other night who asked for a White Lady.'

'Were you able to oblige him?'

'One of the officers got it for him but it took them ages because of the glass having to be put in the refrigerator.'

'A straightforward gin and lemon squash would suit this sergeant very well. Shall I make it myself and get you a drink too?'

'Oh, no. I'm supposed to do this sort of thing. Auntie says it's good for me because it helps me not to be shy. I used to be very shy. But if you like to hold the bottle and help to pour it would be nice because I find the bottles so heavy, and once I dropped one and Auntie trod on a piece of the glass and was very cross.'

Perron joined her at the Wurlitzer-style cabinet. At a rough estimate he thought there were about fifty glasses of different shapes set ready, none of them as clean as they might have been. Gravely he uncapped a bottle of Carew's and held it above the glass she presented. She put her hand on his and canted.

'Is that enough?'

'More than generous.'

'May I leave you to do the rest? I must take Auntie the letter and parcel. Oh –' She half-ran to an occasional table and returned with a cigarette box and a lighter. After he had taken a cigarette he had to hold the box because she insisted on lighting the cigarette for him and needed two hands to produce a flame.

'There. Please excuse me now. There are plenty of ashtrays.' At the door she again remembered something important. 'What is your name? If there were a lot of people it wouldn't matter but since there's only you it would look rude not to tell Auntie who it is, wouldn't it?'

He told her, and added, 'But I'm sure it's mentioned in the note.'

After she had gone Perron went to the window. For all his doubts about its present source he had long since learned to appreciate the sensuousness of the warm smell of the East and how it could set mind and body at ease. He enjoyed a sensation almost of tranquillity and continued to enjoy it for some time, in fact until he became aware of the riding lights of a section of the anchored Zipper-destined flotilla out in the roads. And then a ludicrous but slightly worrying image presented itself, of the Maharanee standing at this very window, observing the scene in daylight through a telescope and dictating notes for the girl to record (in invisible ink) about the class and tonnage of each ship as it arrived and dropped anchor.

'Auntie says will you come through?'

The girl was standing in the open doorway. He stubbed his cigarette and followed her into the long passage and down to a door at the end which, if closed before, now stood half-open upon a room so dark that at first he thought there was no light on at all and hesitated to enter when the girl indicated that he should do so.

'It's all right. Auntie has been resting but she's finished now.' Inside, he saw that there was a light, but this was from a table lamp in the far corner of the room whose shade was draped with a square of what looked like heavy crimson velvet. A hand, in silhouette, crept over the cloth and removed it; and in the now brighter but still deep rosy glow of the lamp the Maharanee was revealed, recumbent on a Récamier couch. Her saree was also red, but of what shade and intensity Perron could not easily judge because the material obviously took colour from the lamp shade. She seemed like an ember that might at any moment pulse brilliantly and dangerously into life. She wore no jewelry. Her skin was pale but darker than that of the Parsee ladies of Bombay. Her hair, cut and set in a style that obviously owed more to what she thought suited her than it did to any fashion of the day, was black, unoiled, parted in the middle, and fell, in corrugations of the kind obtained by using hot tongs, just short of her shoulders, framing a classic Rajput face of prominent cheekbones, full red lips, a hawklike but beautifully proportioned nose, and eyes whose luminosity was accentuated by cunningly applied kohl. Between her black brows she had painted a red tika one-quarter inch in diameter. She looked about thirty and was probably forty. She wore no choli and both arms, one shoulder and part of her midriff were bare. Perron, half-convinced he also saw the thrust and outline of a nipple, found her seductively handsome.

'Auntie,' the girl said from behind him. 'This is Sergeant Perrer. Sergeant Perrer, this is my Auntie Aimee.'

Perron bowed.

'Have you come to my party?' the Maharanee asked in a high-pitched but slightly hoarse voice. 'I'm afraid you're on the early side. Aneila opened the door to you because all the servants are resting. I make them rest because sometimes my parties go on for a day or two. Aneila, what is wrong with you? Why is our visitor still standing?'

'I'm sorry, Auntie.'

Perron turned to help her but the chair she chose was very small and presumably almost weightless. She managed it easily, placing it two feet from the couch.

'Now you had better go to start rousing everybody.'

'Yes, Auntie.'

'Tell them the guests are beginning to arrive. Do sit down. Have we met before?'

'I've not had that pleasure, Your Highness.'

'Please call me Aimee. Pandy and I are divorced. I keep the title because it is useful and servants and shop people like it and Pandy's new wife doesn't. Are you a friend of someone I know?'

Perron explained his mission and drew her attention to the package and envelope which were on the table, propped against the lamp where Aneila had presumably left them.

'Captain Purvis?' she asked, reaching for the letter. 'He must be one of Jimmy's friends. When Jimmy is in Bombay he brings so many people.' She opened the letter. The paper it was written on seemed to displease her. She held it between the tips of two fingers whose nails were elegantly manicured and varnished. 'Leonard?' she said. 'Leonard Purvis?' And presently, 'Whisky?' The note although short called for concentration. 'Chillingborough and Cambridge? Why does he tell me this? Why shouldn't you have studied at Chillingborough and Cambridge? So many Englishmen do. Who is Leonard Purvis?'

'A member of an economic advisory mission to the Government of India.'

'Are you also in this mission?'

'No, I'm concerned with army education.'

'What does the mission do?'

'I don't think it does anything.'

'And what do you do?'

'Very little.'

1107

'What a relief. People are always dashing about. What is your first name?'

'Guy.'

'Have you another?'

'Lancelot.'

She frowned.

'There's also Percival,' he said, and added, 'but I'm not keen on it.'

'Names are a terrible problem. It is best to make them up. Will you stay to my party? It may be boring but it is difficult to tell in advance. It depends on who comes. If it is too tedious I just come back to my room and tell the servants to lock up the drinks and go to bed. It is the only way to get rid of people. Anyway tonight I will be optimistic because it has begun well. Where are you staying?'

'In a place called Kalyan.'

'Oh, then you are on Zipper. Nearly all the military people who come here nowadays are on Zipper.'

He thought it wiser to let this pass.

He said, 'It's very kind of you to invite me to stay and I do have an evening off duty. But if I'm too early shall I come back later?'

'Oh, no. Other people will be here in a minute. If not ask Aneila to entertain you. Ask her to play the gramophone, and then you can dance. She is a very good dancer but needs practice with men. She loves it when I bring her to Bombay. Her mother is so strict with her. Her mother is my sister, the one who married that business man and has become very serious as a result. Before you go would you be so kind as to ring the bell?'

Perron stood up, touched the button on the wall which she had indicated, murmured his thanks and took his leave. On his way out he had an urge to turn back and explain who he was and why he was there. He had never enjoyed the part of his job which involved deceiving people and tonight deception seemed irrational. He believed that if he confessed his true identity and purpose to the Maharanee she would probably be amused, for the few seconds it took her to forget and concentrate again on her own affairs. But, leaving the room, closing the door and facing the long cluttered passage of more closed doorways he re-accommodated himself to the masquerade because Aneila was in the act of greeting more guests, let in this time by a servant. Again there had been no sound of a bell. A woman servant was hastening down the corridor to the Maharanee's room. Perron wondered whether he was going deaf or whether the bells rang on a note that only members of the household had learned to detect; but before he could become more than passingly interested in the subject his attention was taken by something of potentially more serious consequence.

Among the new arrivals – the only one he automatically took notice of – was a girl, an English girl; but not just an English girl, *the* English girl; the one to whom he had had to apologize for Purvis's discourteous behaviour at the entrance to the block of flats on the Oval. Remembering the penetrating glance she had given him he could scarcely doubt that she would recognize him when they came face to face. The question was whether she would notice his miraculous change of employment or whether the fact that he was in off-duty khaki drill and not in jungle green would be sufficient to distract her from any previous impression she had gained that education was not at all his line. The other question, of course, was whether if she recognized that a transformation had taken place she would thoughtlessly comment on it to him in the hearing of others, or sensibly put two and two together and keep mum.

There was only ten yards distance between them and no way of lengthening it. In fact it was already shortening because Aneila had waved the men in the party towards the living-room and was now bringing the girl to a room in which presumably women-guests could make themselves comfortable. This room turned out to be the one against whose door Perron was standing. No confrontation could have been more direct.

He stepped aside, smiled at Aneila and then at the girl. He thought it best to take the initiative. 'Good evening. We meet again.'

'Oh,' Aneila said. 'Do you know each other? I'm awfully glad because if not I would have to introduce you and I'm so bad at remembering names.'

'Perron,' Perron said, to both of them.

'Sarah Layton,' the girl said. Rather shrewdly, he thought, she said it to Aneila.

'Please join the guests in the living-room, Mr Perrer. Auntie says men can always introduce themselves if there is no one around to do it and I must show Miss –'

'Layton.'

' –Miss Layton where to powder her nose.' She opened the door. Sarah Layton nodded and started to go through. He caught the moment of hesitation, the slight frown, that followed the brief fall of her glance upon his left shoulder tab. Expecting the glance then to be redirected upwards to meet his he prepared to meet it as frankly as possible, but she followed Aneila into the room without looking at him again.

He continued along the passage and re-entered the living-room where a bearer was presiding over the cocktail cabinet and where he had another and rather more devastating shock.

*

Perron had been stationed in the Bombay Presidency for nearly three months but before becoming involved in operation Zipper he had visited the city only once. The reason for that visit, made in the company of his officer, had been the arrival of a ship that had sailed from Bordeaux in June bringing several hundred Indian soldiers, ex-prisoners of war captured in North Africa, who had succumbed to the temptation to secure their release from prison-camp by joining a Free India Force which its leader, the revolutionary ex-Congressman, Subhas Chandra Bose, at that time in

Berlin after escaping police surveillance in India, had hoped to put into the field to fight alongside the Germans.

In England, Perron had learnt quite a lot about this embryo army and its failure to cohere into a fighting force. Details of it had been among items of classified information it had been his job to study but say nothing about. Because of the tremendous pride the British had always taken in the loyalty of their Indian soldiers, and in the Indian Army's apolitical nature, this evidence of a flaw in its structure had interested him, both then and later when he heard of the numerically far greater and infinitely more serious defection among Indian soldiers taken prisoner by the Japanese. They, it seemed, had formed themselves into operational fighting formations, at first under an Indian King's commissioned officer and then under Subhas Chandra Bose (translated by submarine from Berlin to Tokyo) and had accompanied the Japanese in their attempt in 1944 to invade the sub-continent through Manipur. Some of these, recaptured in the recent successful British campaign in Burma, had, he understood, already arrived in India and were being held in special camps where presumably the contingent from Europe would join them. Many more would follow after the end of the war in Malaya and the Far East.

His duties in regard to the boat load of disgraced Indian officers, NCOs and sepoys from Bordeaux had not been exacting. Neither he nor his officer was sure where their responsibility began or ended. So far as they could tell their main job was to keep an ear to the ground and report to the military and civil authorities anything that might give cause for suspicion that a popular movement was afoot in Bombay to storm the docks and whisk the prisoners from under the noses of those in charge of them off into the bazaars or into the hills where in the past many a band of irregular Mahratta horsemen had melted away to live on and fight again. But of this there had been no sign at all. Bombay went about its business and the military quietly got on with the job of transferring the boatload by trainloads to a destination Perron understood to be in the vicinity of Delhi and the Red Fort.

On only one occasion had he had the opportunity to observe the process, and this was at dead of night when he found himself standing with a group of military police on the dockside at a point where a file of the men in question straggled past, in oddly assorted uniforms, in the imperfect lighting of well-spaced and high-pitched arc-lights which left him with no more than an impression of the vacuity that falls upon the human face when a peak of incomprehension has been reached. That they were home at last they could not doubt. The smell of home must have been unmistakable. But what this might mean to them they obviously could not judge. After the last man in the batch had gone by and the cordon of armed military police had closed in and hidden them from view, Perron had found it difficult to assess the significance of what he had just seen. There was, on this scale, surely no parallel to the situation in the whole of Anglo-Indian history? No such gathering of Indian soldiers (and the present one represented no more than the tip of the iceberg) had surely ever gone abroad across the black water to fight in the Sahibs' wars and come back as the Sahibs' prisoners?

He was still testing the situation to find a weakness in his estimate of it as one that was historically unique when his officer sent a message calling him over to the shed from which the security side of the operation was being conducted and there introduced him to a British officer, a major in the Punjab Regiment whose face had been burnt badly, on the left side. The left arm had been damaged too, although it had taken Perron rather longer to realize this and to appreciate that the glove hid an artificial hand. Several ribbons decorated the officer's chest, the foremost that of the DSO.

Perron was introduced by his own officer as 'the sergeant I was telling you about'.

'You'll appreciate this, sergeant,' he said and began a story he said he'd heard earlier that evening. Perron assumed he'd already told it to the Punjab officer because the man glanced at a wrist-watch which he wore with the face on the inner side of his right wrist and then turned his attention to a wall-map of the dock area. The story was about the boatload of prisoners. In Bordeaux, hearing that they were to be shipped *en masse* back to India in a boat reserved exclusively for them, they decided it was the British intention to take them out to sea, disembark the crew and scuttle the ship. They refused to go until a sufficient complement of British soldiers had been taken on board to insure against the execution of such a diabolical plan.

'Don't you think that's rich? I mean you have to give them full marks for an undiminished sense of self-preservation, don't you?'

The Punjab officer broke in.

'I'm told you speak fluent Urdu, Perron. Will you be able to follow a brief interrogation in that language?'

'Yes, sir.'

'Good. I have a few questions to ask one of the prisoners, none of special importance but I prefer to have independent witnesses in case the man says anything I consider valuable. If he does I shall tell you what it was and you will then treat it as restricted and highly confidential information.'

'Yes, sir.'

'Whatever he pretends, this man will be very apprehensive at being singled out for immediate questioning. The MPs who'll bring him will remain in the room but they're British and won't understand what is said. I want you to place yourself behind my chair and keep your eyes fixed on him, for the psychological effect. It would help if you could manage to look not in the least sympathetic.' He turned to Perron's officer. 'I should like you to sit at the table with me. Have you a file you could be looking at?'

'A file?'

'Or an official-looking book. It's always helpful if the man sitting next to the one asking the questions appears to be absorbed in some task of his own which the prisoner finds it difficult to connect with the proceedings.'

1111

Perron's officer laughed nervously. 'I could always play patience.'

'A file or a book preferably.'

'Why is it helpful?'

'It increases the prisoner's sense of isolation and weakens whatever resolve he may have to withhold information from the one man in the room who is speaking to him. He should be here any moment. Shall we take up positions?'

They did so. The table at which the two officers sat was the ordinary trestle type, covered by an ink-stained army blanket. It had been cleared of the papers and trays that were on it when Perron visited the hut earlier. A briefcase, a spare glove, a swagger cane, marked the Punjab officer's place. One-handed he opened the case and withdrew a file of papers and a fountain-pen. Perron's officer, having rummaged about on another table, now joined him, bringing with him a notebook and a thick folder of assorted cyclostyled memoranda.

The room was the inner one of the two into which the hut was divided. It was poorly lit by a single electric bulb. The trestle table faced the connecting door through which the prisoner would have to come after passing through the outer room which was used by MPs and dock police but at this hour of the night, morning rather, occupied by just one sleepy corporal. It was this corporal who presently knocked on the door, looked in and announced the arrival of prisoner and escort.

They came in in file. The MP in front, a burly sergeant, halted about three paces from the desk, saluted, put a folded note on the desk, took a pace to his right and one to the rear, while the MP at the back took one to his left and then a pace forward, a manoeuvre that revealed the man they guarded; a thin, stoop-shouldered Indian in denim fatigue trousers the bottoms of which flopped over ill-fitting looking boots, a long-sleeved khaki pullover and, beneath it, a khaki shirt whose shoulder tabs were thrust through the slots made for them in the pullover. The man wore no belt. On his head there was a forage cap without a badge. The taller of the two MPs removed this roughly enough to jerk the prisoner's head to one side. There was nothing on his sleeve to denote rank. The clothes had obviously been issued in Europe, perhaps in Bordeaux. He appeared not to have shaved for a couple of days. His thick black hair was over-long. A strand of it lay across his forehead. He stared from one officer to the other and finally at Perron who had been shocked to see that the prisoner's hands were manacled. It was as if everything had been done to make him look and feel unworthy of any uniform whatsoever.

The Punjab officer asked the escort to remain in the room but to retire to the door. So far he did not seem to have looked at the prisoner but when he spoke to the MPs the man looked at him with close attention and took no notice when the two policemen moved. The Punjab officer (again so far as Perron could tell, having his eyes more or less dutifully fixed on the prisoner) still did not look up. After a while, perhaps as long as ten seconds, the prisoner glanced at Perron's officer who was uselessly busy with pencil, note-book and the folder of papers, but almost immediately had his attention taken again by something the Punjab major was doing.

Perron glanced down. One-handed, the major had taken out a tin of cigarettes and a lighter. He opened the tin, selected a cigarette, lit it, closed the tin and then with the good hand reached across to the left arm which hung straight, grasped the wrist of the gloved artificial hand, raised it and placed it on the table. Having taken a draw on the cigarette he inserted it between two of the gloved fingers and left it there: an erect white tube with smoke curling from the tip.

As Perron switched his glance back to the prisoner he caught the burly MP's eye. The MP winked.

'Tumara nam kya hai?' the Punjab officer asked suddenly in a low voice. The prisoner put his head on one side as a man might who recognized a language but could not identify it beyond doubt. *What is your name?*

Without waiting longer for an answer the officer continued, again in Urdu –

It says in this paper that your name is Karim Muzzafir Khan. Havildar Karim Muzzafir Khan, 1st Pankot Rifles, captured in North Africa with the other survivors of his battalion. With his comrades. With his leaders. Colonel Sahib himself also being captured. Is this so? It says so in this paper. You recognize the emblem on the paper? Does the Sircar make mistakes?

The man seemed bewildered. He looked at Perron, as if for help. Perron stared at the bridge of the man's nose. The man looked down again at the officer.

Well?

Yes, Sahib.

Yes, Sahib? Yes? What is the meaning of this answer?

Karim Muzzafir Khan, Sahib.

Karim Muzzafir Khan, Havildar, 1st Pankot Rifles?

Yes, Sahib.

Karim Muzzafir Khan, Havildar? Captured with his battalion in North Africa?

Sahib.

Karim Muzzafir Khan, Havildar. Son of the late Subedar Muzzafir Khan Bahadur, also of the 1st Pankot Rifles?

Sahib.

Subedar Muzzafir Khan Bahadur? VC?

Perron was aware of his own officer looking up, alerted.

Well?

Sahib.

The Punjab officer removed the smoking cigarette, drew on it, tapped the ash into a tray, slowly exhaled and replaced it between the rigid gloved fingers. He turned a page of the file. The prisoner's head was lowered. He was staring at the cigarette and the artificial hand as though they exerted for him the special fascination of an object or arrangement of objects which, properly interpreted, might help him to understand precisely what it was that was happening to him. Perhaps this was what the Punjab officer intended. He continued to study the new page in the file. He was in no hurry. Perron kept glancing at the cigarette. If left to burn right down would the artificial fingers react? Unexpectedly the officer removed his cap and sat back. The prisoner stared at the scarred face, then looked away at the other officer's busy pencil and then at Perron and after a moment shut his eyes.

Are you fatigued?

The prisoner opened his eyes.

Sahib.

You are not getting good sleep?

No answer.

Why? Why are you not getting good sleep?

No answer.

Something troubles you? What? What will happen? This troubles you? What will happen to you? What will happen to your wife and children? You have a wife and children?

The man nodded.

What they will say? That this is a matter of great shame? Is that what troubles you? What your wife and children will say? What the people in your village will say to your wife and children? Is that what you are thinking? That your wife will not hold up her head? That this will be so because of all the men in the battalion who were not killed but captured only Havildar Karim Muzzafir Khan was not true to the salt? Only Havildar Karim Muzzafir Khan listened to the lies of his captors and of the enemies of the King-Emperor whose father rewarded his father with the most coveted decoration of all? Only Havildar Karim Muzzafir Khan brought shame to his regiment and sorrow to the heart of Colonel Sahib?

A pause.

How long is it since you saw Colonel Sahib?

No answer.

Where do you think he is? At home in comfort? You think perhaps on the day he and the other officers were released from prison-camp in Germany that he got into an aeroplane and flew home to his family in India? This is not so. It is you who are in India first, ahead of him, ahead of all your comrades of the 1st Pankots. Like you they had not seen Colonel Sahib since the day of their capture when the officer sahibs were taken to one camp and the men to another. But on the day Colonel Sahib was released he said, now let me go to my men. I shall not go back to India without them. Come, let us find the men, let us go to the prison-camp where the men are. Let us go to the camp and collect all the men together. Let us wait in Germany until every man who was still alive after the battle and was taken prisoner has been accounted for and then let us sail back to our families in India, as a regiment. And so it has been. And only one man of the 1st Pankots has not been accounted for, one man who was not killed but who was not in any prison-camp. He had deserted his comrades to fight alongside the enemy. We do not know why. We shall find out why. Where you are going you will be asked many questions. You will be asked many questions by many officers. You will see me again also. I also shall ask you many more questions. Tonight I am not asking questions of this kind. I speak to you only of the shame and sorrow you have brought to Colonel Sahib. I do not know Colonel Sahib but I know Colonel Memsahib and I know the two young memsahibs. Susan Mem and Sarah Mem. I was in Pankot four weeks ago. They had a letter from Colonel Sahib. Be patient, he wrote. I am making arrangements about the men. So, they are patient. All Pankot is patient, awaiting the regiment's return from across the black water. In Pankot they do not yet know the story of Havildar Karim Muzzafir Khan who let himself believe in the lies of Subhas Chandra Bose. But soon they will know. And they will be dumb with shame and sorrow. The wild dogs in the hills will be silent and your wife will not raise her head.

The Punjab officer spoke a resonant classic Urdu. It was a language that lent itself to poetic imagery but Perron had heard few Englishmen use it so flexibly, so effectively, or to such a purpose. Throughout the speech the prisoner's eyes had grown brighter, moister. Perron thought he might break down. He believed this was the officer's intention and he was appalled. He would have understood better if the officer and the prisoner were of the same regiment because by tradition a regiment was a family and the harshest rebuke might then be ameliorated by the context of purely family concern in which it could be delivered and received. Then, if the man wept, it would be with regret and shame. If he wept now it would be from humiliation at the hands of a stranger.

But he managed not to weep. Perhaps the years in Europe had eroded his capacity to be moved – as Indians could be – by rhetoric. Perhaps he suddenly realized that nothing except full bellies would keep the wild dogs of the hills silent, and was astonished that a British officer should use such high-flown language. Perron thought that for a second or two a flash of contempt was discernible in the moist eyes. Certainly, they dried, and were directed again at the burning cigarette.

There was silence for perhaps as long as a minute. 'I have finished with this man,' the officer said suddenly. Karim Muzzafir Khan understood English. He drew in a deep breath and glanced round, awaiting the MPS who, put off their stroke by the abruptness with which the interview had ended, made a somewhat patchy job of coming forward, saluting and leading the prisoner out.

When the door shut, the officer picked the cigarette out of the artificial hand and sat smoking and making notes on the file. The episode, to Perron, seemed pointless. His own officer obviously thought the same because he pushed away the file he'd pretended to work on, leant forward, rested his forehead on his right hand and watched the other man's note-taking; clearly inviting comment.

At last the Punjab officer spoke.

'I wonder whether your sergeant would ask the corporal next door to get hold of my driver and tell him I'll be ready in about five minutes? The corporal will know where to find him.'

'Oh, I'll do that myself. I need to take a leak.'

Perron's officer got up and went into the other room. He left the door ajar. Perron collected the notebook and folder and took them back to the other table. The Punjab officer stubbed the cigarette and began to repack his briefcase.

'Were you able to follow every word?'

'Yes, sir.'

'What did you make of him?'

'He looked fairly harmless, sir.'

The officer closed the briefcase. He leant back and looked at Perron. 'His name has cropped up several times in depositions made in Germany in connection with the coercion of sepoy prisoners-of-war who were unwilling to join the Frei Hind force. In fact it has been linked with that of an Indian lieutenant suspected of causing the death of a sepoy in Königsberg.' A pause. 'But I grant you the harmless look, and, of course, he may be innocent of anything like that because a lot of these fellows are going to be only too ready to accuse each other to save their own skins.'

He put his cap on.

'Incidentally, your officer was singing your praises before you arrived. I gather you have a degree in history and are particularly interested in the history of this country. Have you studied Oriental languages too? I mean, systematically?'

'Not awfully systematically, sir. Naturally I became interested in Urdu and learned some during vacations and had some practice in conversation with a fellow-student during term.'

'An Indian fellow-student, at university?'

'Yes, sir.'

'If you followed every word you've become very proficient. Have you taken Higher Standard out here?'

'Yes, sir.'

'It's not much use, of course, except in the army. It's nice to be able to speak it. In my old job I generally had to use a mixture of bazaar Hindi and the local dialect of whatever district I happened to be in.'

'What job was that, sir?'

'The Indian Police.'

Perron was surprised. Neither the ICS nor the police had been in the least co-operative over pleas from their officers to join the armed forces. Recruiting to these services had lapsed at the beginning of the war and the men had been needed where they were, administering the law, collecting the revenues, keeping order, preserving the civil peace. Perron judged the officer to be in his middle thirties. At that age he would normally have held a senior post in the police, which would have made a wartime transfer to the army even more difficult to arrange.

The officer got up. He tucked the briefcase under the left arm which he then adjusted until it was clamped to his waist. The arm must have been amputated above the elbow. He took the spare glove and swagger cane in his right hand.

'By the way, sergeant. I gather from your officer that you were at school at Chillingborough. When, exactly?'

Perron told him and after a moment added, 'Were you there as well, sir?'

The officer paused before replying. 'Hardly. I had quite other grounds for asking. Presumably you would know an Indian boy there, who called himself Harry Coomer. Actually Hari Kumar.'

'Harry Coomer? Yes, I remember him, sir.'

'He would have been a year or two your junior, I suppose? Did you know him closely? Closely enough to have learned much about his attitudes and interests?'

Perron was thinking back, attempting an image of the young Indian. The way Coomer came into focus was in white flannels making one of those sweeps to leg which even Perron who had been bored by cricket and played it badly recognized as elegant. The boy's actual presence was otherwise misty. Only an ambiance remained; and a detail or two.

'Actually,' Perron said, 'I don't remember him being interested in anything much except cricket.'

He was about to add, Why, sir? Do you know him? But the answer was self-evident.

Perron had not thought of Coomer for years. He realized he had not even thought of him when he came out to India, perhaps because at school he had never really thought of Coomer in connection with any place but Chillingborough. Only a brown skin had distinguished him from the several hundred other boys undergoing the Chillingborough experience. Everything else, manners, behaviour, had so far as Perron could remember been utterly commonplace. Perron could not even recall Coomer speaking English with an Indian accent. What he did recall was asking Coomer a question about the difference between karma and dharma and being told politely that Coomer was afraid he didn't know because although born in India he had grown up in England and couldn't remember a thing about it and didn't know anything about its peculiar customs and odd ideas.

'Cricket,' the officer said, smiling at last. 'I'm afraid that his range of interests began to extend beyond cricket once he got back to this country. That expensive education turned out to be pretty much a waste. As so often happens in such cases. Did you know anything of his background?'

'Nothing at all, sir. Nothing I can remember.'

'No, well, I suppose you wouldn't. Not being a close friend of his.'

Perron's officer came back.

'We've unearthed your driver,' he said. 'He's waiting outside. I'm trying to whistle up some char. Would you like a mug before you tootle off?'

'No, thank you. And thank you for your help this evening. I'm sorry the havildar was so unforthcoming. It would have been more interesting for you if he'd been one of the talkative ones. But the object of the exercise was achieved from my point of view.' He seemed about to say goodnight and go but then stood his ground, as if thinking something out.

'It's interesting,' he began, and turned to Perron. 'There you have the havildar, whose father got a posthumous vc in the last war, and who I dare say was brought up to have his father's example rammed down his throat day after day. One thing it will be worth finding out is how he behaved in action, when it came to it. My guess is he showed up badly and couldn't face being shut in behind barbed wire for the rest of the war with men who'd seen how frightened he was. What do you think, sergeant? Psychologically, could it work that way?'

'I think it could, sir.'

'Well Kumar couldn't face it either. I mean face the fact that he wasn't what his father tried to make him and had led him to believe he was. You know nothing of this?'

'Nothing, sir.'

'When did you reach India?'

'In 1943, sir.'

'Ah well. It happened the year before. But I'm glad he wasn't a close friend of yours. He kept pretty poor company out here. He and five of his disreputable friends were arrested in '42 on a very serious criminal charge. They wriggled out of that, but we got them under the Defence of India Rules and locked them up as political detenus.'

As he spoke the officer kept his eyes firmly on Perron. And now continued so, as though demanding a comment or a question. The only thing Perron could think of to say was: 'Was it you who arrested him, sir?'

'Yes. It was. It was indeed.'

He nodded at Perron, and saluted Perron's officer by touching his cap with the swagger cane; and went.

Perron returned his officer's glance. He said, 'Who was that, sir?'

'Name's Merrick. Described himself as involved at a high level with this INA tamasha. Frosty sort of bugger, wasn't he?'

It was this man whom Perron saw first on re-entering the Maharanee's living-room.

*

He was, however, under observation by three. As well as the one-armed Punjab officer there was a tall elderly white man in white ducks who leant on an ebony cane and whose left eye was hidden by a black patch secured by a strip of elastic round his head, and – the only man of the three not suffering from any physical disability – a good-looking young Indian in well-cut civilian clothes.

Sometimes, since the night on the docks, in the moment before sleeping,

1118

the last conscious image in the blackness behind his lids had been of Coomer, driving, sweeping, cutting or blocking a rapid and relentless stream of deliveries from an invisible bowler, in an empty field that was green, sunstruck and elm-shaded; devoid of sound. The boy's face was never clear. The images conveyed little except a melancholy idea that they were a reproach of some kind, and by morning he had usually forgotten them. But the sight of the young Indian, combined with the shock of coming face to face with the Punjab officer, brought them back and for an instant he had an absurd notion that the young Indian was Coomer.

His hesitation on entering had been marked enough to be interpreted by the elderly man in the white ducks as shyness. The man smiled and said, 'Come in.'

Approaching them, avoiding a direct glance at the Punjab officer, Perron said good-evening and then, 'I'm afraid I'm an interloper. An officer sent me with a package for the Maharanee and she's very kindly invited me to stay for the party. My name's Perron. Sergeant Perron.'

'Perron? Perron? That is a most interesting name. Any ancient connection with the Sergeant Perron who became a general and Governor of Hindustan under Daulat Rao Sindia?'

Perron smiled. It was rarely that the question was asked.

'No, sir. In any case the Perron who served under Daulat Rao was really Pierre-Cuiller. Perron was his nickname.'

'That I either did not know or have forgotten. Anyway, Mr Perron, at Aimee's parties what you call interlopers are the rule rather than the exception. For instance I am the only one of us here with a personal invitation. But Aimee likes one to bring people along.' The accent was un-English but Perron could not place it.

'So let me initiate introductions,' the man continued. He placed a skeletal hand on his breast, indicating himself and bowing slightly. 'Dmitri Bronowsky. This is Mr Ronald Merrick, actually of the Indian Police but at the moment as you see employed as a major in the Punjab Regiment. And this is my secretary, Mr Ahmed Kasim, younger son of Mr Mohammed Ali Kasim, of whom you may have heard.' Bronowsky put a hand on Perron's shoulder, turned him round an inch or two, to read the shoulder tab. 'Ah, now what does this mean, A E C?'

'Army Education Corps, sir.'

The slight twisting of his shoulder enabled him to look directly at Major Merrick. In this harsh light the scar-tissue that disfigured the left side of the man's face was revealed more unkindly than it had been in the shed on the docks, and the blue of the eyes – now recollected – was intensified. The look Perron got in return gave nothing away.

Bronowsky's hand was still on Perron's shoulder. Letting him free now he said, 'How does one educate an army?'

'It's not so much a case of educating it, sir, but of finding ways of stopping it being bored.'

'Nevertheless, you need teaching qualifications?'

1119

'Not always, sir.'

'But you have such qualifications?'

'Yes, sir.'

'A degree?'

'Yes, sir.'

Bronowsky asked in what subject. Perron told him. The bearer entered their midst with a tray of drinks but this did not halt the old man's catechism. Which university? Which college? Before that what school had he attended?

'A place called Chillingborough, sir.'

'Indeed?' Bronowsky hesitated. 'How interesting. And what will you do after the war, Mr Perron? Go on to a course of post-graduate studies?'

Perron nodded. But the flow of questions could not be stemmed. In what subject? What aspect of Indian history? Why that one? Perron attempted to deflect the question and open the conversation out with a general comment about the narrowing range and increasingly esoteric nature of study in the post-graduate field but Bronowsky was not to be put off.

'That is its charm and logic, surely. I expect you have found that being in India has encouraged you in your choice. Have you thought of staying on for a while after the war?'

'Not really, sir. One tends to lose ground so quickly. The academic world is as competitive as any other.'

'That is so. But one should perhaps sometimes ignore the professional competition and arrange matters in a way most advantageous to the scholar in oneself. You would easily find a temporary post in a university here and have plenty of opportunity to do original research. Either in a university or in one of the colleges. Our own college in the little state of Mirat is always short of well qualified teachers. In history, for instance.'

'Are you its principal, sir?'

Major Merrick interrupted.

'Count Bronowsky is Chief Minister to the ruler, the Nawab of Mirat.'

'But emotionally I'm very attached to the college and always anxious to foster its interests because it was one of my first innovations. When I went to Mirat to advise Nawab Sahib, nearly a quarter of a century ago, there was no place of higher education in the state where clever young Hindus could go. There was only the Muslim Academy which taught boys to pray and recite the Koran and which turned out tax-collectors – if Ahmed here will forgive me for saying so, although he did not personally undergo such a traditional Islamic training, did you, Ahmed?'

'What?'

'Incorrigible!' Bronowsky exclaimed, but laughed and put three fingers of the hand that held the ebony cane on the young man's shoulder. 'He seldom listens to conversations. He comes to parties only to drink as much whisky as he can and to make up to the prettiest girls. That apart, as a secretary he is quite efficient. And here are two very pretty girls. Aneila, my dear, was I in error in supposing your aunt said seven-thirty on? Are we as conspicuously early as we feel?'

'Oh, no. Auntie's parties begin when the first people arrive. Have I omitted anything? Auntie will be very cross if I have, so please tell me. Oh! Nobody is smoking! What a bad beginning. Please help yourselves. I will tell Auntie to hurry.'

She ran out, and in the passage called instructions presumably to some of the servants. Perron, the only guest who knew without looking where the cigarettes were, picked up the box and went first to Miss Layton who was now standing next to Major Merrick. He arrived at her side a few seconds behind the bearer with the tray of drinks. He noted the gleam of her unfussily set fair hair and then her dress which was not the one she had on when they met outside the block of flats on the Oval, but was not obviously labelled 'party only'. A bag hung in the crook of her arm. The left hand was raised. She wore no engagement ring. She chose a gimlet and then, seeing the box, smiled at him and shook her head.

'Thank you, not just now.'

Merrick declined too. He made no attempt at an introduction. Perron passed on to Bronowsky. 'I always smoke these,' Bronowsky said, opening a gold case and showing the contents: a row of oval-shaped pink gold-tipped cigarettes.

'But only in the evening,' Miss Layton said, from behind Perron.

'Ah, so you remember my little anecdote. By the way you know Mr Perron of the Education Corps?'

'Yes,' came her voice, 'we introduced ourselves in the hall.'

Perron offered the box to Ahmed Kasim but he declined. Bronowsky moved across to Miss Layton and Major Merrick, Perron put the box down, retrieved his drink and set about trying to make conversation with the young Indian.

'Your father must be the Congress statesman, MAK.'

Kasim nodded, then reapplied himself to his glass of whisky. So far as Perron knew it was the first time he had spoken to an Indian whose father had been imprisoned by the *raj*. He did not know quite what to say to him. He could hardly apologize. He would have liked to ask what truth there had been in newspaper reports that Mr Kasim senior was realigning himself politically, abandoning Congress in favour of the League and Jinnah's mad, divisive dream of a separate state for Muslims: Pakistan; but that was a tricky subject too. He wondered what on earth a son of a politician like MAK was doing acting as secretary to the Chief Minister to the Nawab of Mirat. There was generally no love lost between Congress and the autocratic rulers of the Princely states. But he could not ask that question either. He fell back on small talk.

'Are you in Bombay for long?'

'A few days.'

'It must be interesting working for a Nawab's Chief Minister.'

Ahmed Kasim nodded, but his attention was elsewhere. Hearing voices

Perron glanced round. A group of English officers had come in, but they were obviously not the object of Mr Kasim's study. A stunningly attractive Eurasian girl and two pretty Indian girls had come in too and were talking excitedly to Aneila. Two more bearers joined the one already in the room. After a few seconds Perron turned back to Kasim.

'Is Mirat in relationship with the Crown through a Resident or through a provincial government?'

'A Resident. Except that he isn't.'

'A non-resident Resident.'

'It used to be through the provincial government but all that was altered some time ago.'

'Generally, or just in Mirat's case?'

'I think generally. Something to do with the federal scheme. But that's fallen through. Things do in this country.'

'Where does the non-resident Resident reside?'

'In Gopalakand.'

'Is that far from Mirat?'

'Far enough.'

'Is that a good thing, then?'

Mr Kasim looked into his glass.

'I'm sorry,' Perron said. 'Undiplomatic question. Is Count Bronowsky what we used to call a White Russian? A member of the emigration from the revolution?'

'Yes.'

'A soldier?'

'No, I don't think so.'

'I wondered about his loss of an eye.'

'He says his carriage was blown up by a revolutionary when he was on his way to the Winter Palace in St Petersburg. He's lame in the left leg for the same reason.'

'He mentioned being in Mirat for twenty-five years. Was he Chief Minister from the beginning?'

'Not officially. Not until the Political Department was mollified.'

'How was it mollified?'

'I believe when they saw he was a good influence on the Nawab. Then they allowed the appointment. Dmitri says that nowadays some of the senior members of the Political Department behave as if they invented him themselves. Before he came the state was quite feudal.'

'Does Miss Layton have any connection with Mirat? She and the Count seem quite old friends.'

'She visited once. Her sister got married there. They stayed at the Palace guest house'.

'She lives in Bombay?'

'No, in Pankot.'

'Pankot?'

'You know it?'

'Of it. Anyway, of its regiment, the Pankot Rifles.'

'Her father was CO of the 1st battalion. She's in Bombay to meet him. He's been a prisoner-of-war in Germany.'

Perron moved so that he could see her. Her back was to him. She stood in a group consisting of Count Bronowsky, two of the English officers, and Merrick. Merrick was watching him, still with that expression of giving nothing away although Perron fancied he now read into it an understanding that Miss Layton's name had just been mentioned and a warning to give nothing away himself, as if they both had something to hide: Perron his real identity and Merrick – what? Just the fact that they had met before or, primarily, the circumstances of that meeting? The interrogation of the Pankot Rifles havildar? Sarah Layton was one of Colonel Sahib's daughters. Although he now recognized the name Sarah in this connection he could not remember the name of the other daughter – the one presumably married in Mirat. Merrick had referred to them both when questioning the havildar. Sarah mem and — mem.

He turned back to Kasim.

'Is Colonel Layton back in India yet?'

Mr Kasim had to incline his head and ask him to repeat the question, but before he could do so there was a cry, 'Ahmed, darling!' and an elderly Indian woman in a green and gold saree brushed them apart to embrace the young man. 'What are you doing in Bombay? Is your father here? I wrote to him after the Simla fiasco but he never replied.'

Perron stood back to give them more room. She ignored him. 'Is it true what Lodi told me about your poor brother Sayed?' she shouted. Perron moved away and did not hear Kasim's reply. Gramophone music started up and the stunning Eurasian girl began dancing with one of the two Indian girls who had come in with her. The other rather reluctantly accepted a young English officer as a partner but talked to the Eurasian girl as they moved round in the limited space available. So far the services were represented entirely by officers. Perron was the only non-commissioned man in the room. Four Indian women, neither young nor handsome, had settled themselves on a long settee and were in conversation of the kind that did not invite interruption. The servants had multiplied and the room was quite full. There was still no sign of the Maharanee.

He made his way through the room towards the hall. At the door he stood aside to let in a middle-aged, portly, red-faced English civilian in open-necked shirt, white duck trousers and black cummerbund. The civilian said, 'Hello, Sergeant, where's the bloody bar, then?' and looked ready to talk but Perron, indicating the direction, went through. There were more people in the hall. A servant stood at the front door staring at the wall above it where there was what looked like a bell-box, which in a sense it turned out to be because an orange bulb inside it suddenly lit up and the servant promptly opened the door and admitted two more guests. Perhaps the same sort of signal was given in the servants' quarters. Perhaps there was a bell-light watcher on the staff. Perhaps the Maharanee didn't like the sound of bells ringing. He was glad to have the question basically cleared up.

'Hey, Sarge, what d'you reckon, then?'

The speaker was a REME corporal. He was standing against a wall with an AB of the Royal Navy.

'Reckon?'

'To all this.'

'Are you on your own?'

'No, with him.' The corporal nodded at the sailor then looked at Perron's glass. 'What they rush you for the booze?'

'They don't. It's free. It usually is at parties.'

'Parties? Isn't it Amy's?'

'Well the hostess's first name is Aimee.'

'Hostess?'

'The lady giving the party.'

Perron recited the Maharanee's full title. The corporal looked at his mate. The sailor said, 'The rotten sods.' The corporal felt in a pocket and produced a grubby piece of paper. He looked at it and then showed it to Perron. On it was written: 'Amy's', the address and flat number and a note at the bottom saying: 'Six chips.' Perron handed the paper back. He shook his head. 'I think someone's played a practical joke on you. It's not that kind of place. What did you say when the bearer opened the door?'

'I just said, "Amy's?" He didn't ask for names or nothing so it looked okay. At least it did until we saw the company. I mean, *women*–coming *in*. We'd better blow before we get chucked out.'

'I don't think you would be.'

'But we don't know anyone and from the look of this lot we aren't likely to.'

'Hey, have a dekko at that,' the sailor said. He nudged the corporal in the ribs. Perron turned round. Aneila was flowing down the corridor to her aunt's room.

'Yeah, that's better. Who's she, Sarge?'

'The Maharanee's niece.'

'Any more like her inside?'

'Yes, several.'

'Who are you with, Sarge?'

'No one in particular.'

'If anyone asks can we say we're with you?'

'You'd better say you're friends of Captain Purvis, but he hasn't turned up yet.'

'Suppose he does turn up?'

'He won't. He's ill in bed.' A bearer came by with a loaded tray. Perron stopped him. 'Have a drink anyway, then you won't look conspicuous. There's beer too if you want it. You only have to ask.'

The two lads gingerly took glasses from the tray.

'Okay?'

'Yeah, thanks. Thanks, Sarge. Captain *Purvis*?'

'Leonard Purvis. The economist.'

The corporal nodded, abstractedly.

'See you, corporal,' Perron said and turned away. Major Merrick had come out of the room and was waiting for him.

'I'd like a word.'

They moved to an uncluttered part of the passage.

'Are you on duty?'

'Yes, sir.'

'Are you expecting your officer?'

'No, sir.'

'I take it this disguise is permitted?'

'In certain circumstances, yes, sir.'

'Always a bit risky though, isn't it? However slight the chances of coming across someone who knows you. For instance, Miss Layton has just told me about your meeting earlier this afternoon. In your other uniform.'

'Not in anyone else's hearing I hope, sir.'

'No. But quite properly she thought I ought to know.'

'Did you tell her you knew already, sir?'

'Without going into detail, yes. This officer – Captain Purvis? Is he in your department too?'

'No, sir.'

'Are you going back to his flat?'

'I shall have to, sir. To change.'

For a while Merrick stared at him without speaking. In the living-room another record was put on and there was some loud laughter. Eventually Merrick said, 'What time do you expect to leave?'

'I'm not sure, sir.'

Merrick glanced at the other people in the passage. Three young Indian women sat on the settee chattering and giggling. The corporal and the sailor were now being talked to by the middle-aged Englishman in the cummerbund. Merrick continued: 'I've been thinking about making our excuses and taking Miss Layton home. Everything considered and in view of what you know, would you think that justified, to save her possible embarrassment?'

A movement near the doorway into the living-room caught his eye. The middle-aged civilian was shepherding the corporal and the sailor in. He gave the sailor an encouraging pat, low enough on the spine to rank as a slap on the buttocks. Perron returned his attention and saw that the gesture had not gone unnoticed by Merrick. Perron assumed as blank an expression as he could manage.

'I simply can't say, sir. It should be quite easy to slip away, I imagine, without giving offence.'

'Giving offence wouldn't bother me. What I'm asking you to tell me is whether in your view the reasons for your own presence here are likely to become apparent, through some kind of general or particular unpleasantness.'

'I'm not sure I understand you, sir,' Perron said. 'It's all fairly routine from my point of view.'

Merrick looked across Perron's shoulder in the direction of the settee where the three Indian girls were.

'Routine?' he said.

Perron lowered his voice although with no one in easy earshot there was no need. 'The reason for my presence, sir.'

Merrick continued staring at the girls on the carved sofa and then looked in the opposite direction at the main door of the flat which the bearer had just opened. Two tall white girls, exaggeratedly made up and wearing sarees, came in ahead of a couple of Air Force officers, an Englishman and an American. The taller of the girls, who seemed familiar with the flat, led her companion down the passage towards the room set aside for women. As she went by she gave Perron a dazzling smile. But heavy make-up – and pungent scents – had never much appealed to him, neither for that matter had white women in sarees. Their bones were usually too big – as in this case. He watched them go into the women's room. Apparently the three Indian girls thought them as incongruous as he did; they lowered their heads, covered their faces and laughed.

'I sympathize with you then, sergeant, if this is routine.'

'I don't mean the party, sir. The reason for my being at it.'

'You see nothing odd about the party, though? Nothing that would encourage you seriously to consider leaving if you were in my shoes and had Miss Layton to think of? Or even if you were by yourself and had no special reason for staying?'

'I suppose it is a bit noisy, sir. And of course it does have its unusual aspect.'

'What is that, in your opinion?'

'Other ranks mixing with officers, sir. But of course I knew beforehand, otherwise I should have had to come in civilian clothes and that leads to so many awkward questions; who does one work for, what does one do. A sergeant is more anonymous.'

'And better bait. Well, I won't ask you what you expect to hook but if you're thinking of this as routine I should advise you to be careful where and how you cast. In fact, although I think you're being less than frank with me I'll give you the benefit of the doubt and a friendly warning. I have a much longer experience of this country and its peculiarities, on most levels of its society. In Indian terms you may think this an example of the top level because the hostess is a Maharanee. That is as may be. But it's at the top you find the scum, isn't it? You can certainly see plenty of it here. I must give Count Bronowsky the benefit of the doubt too and assume he had no idea the particular kind of party the Maharanee is giving this evening. I shall know better about that in a moment when I go back in and tell him I intend to take Miss Layton home before things get worse.'

'Worse, sir?'

'Worse.' Merrick studied him. 'I begin to wonder about your powers of observation, sergeant. The two white girls in sarees who have just gone into the ladies' room – one of whom made a pass at you – are boys, probably airmen. The three Indian girls giggling on the sofa there are also boys, not professional transvestites, which as you may know is a special kind of Indian sect, and all right in its place, but not I assure you all right here. They will undoubtedly dance for the company later in the evening and manage to make it clear what they are, and what they are offering.'

Perron looked at the three figures on the settee. He studied their covered breasts, their ringed fingers and bare forearms, the sandalled feet and bangled ankles; the shapes of jaws, joints and noses. Because he had been told, he saw.

He turned back to Merrick.

'Yes, I see.'

'I'm glad to hear it. The English boys' get-up is very good but crude in comparison. That's why the Indian boys laughed at them. Tell me at least one thing. Are the REME corporal and the AB you were talking to also on duty, like you?'

'No, sir. Certainly not to my knowledge.'

'Do you know who they're with?'

'They're just with each other, sir. But the party's a bit of a surprise to them. They were expecting something rather different.'

'Meaning?'

'A place called Amy's at a cost of six rupees.'

'They weren't far wrong. Would you say that an ageing teaplanter wasn't what they hoped to find?'

'I should think it highly unlikely that they did, sir.'

'In that case, sergeant, I think your duties might conceivably extend to ordering them to leave, for their own good.'

Perron felt a twitch of irritation.

'I don't think I need interfere, sir.'

'Then you misjudge the degree of temptation.'

They broke off. The two white men in sarees had come out of the women's room. This time Perron got a smile from both of them. They wore wigs. Now that he had been told, the masquerade was obvious. When they had gone by he glanced up the corridor where the two officers they had come with were waiting for them, holding drinks ready. The draped hips swung rhythmically. As the men reached their escorts Perron caught the American officer's eye: a beefy-looking fellow, who winked at him.

He looked back at Merrick, thinking of the map room.

'Do I, sir? Misjudge the degree of temptation?'

'I think you do. A corporal and a sailor can't have found it easy to scrape together six rupees each for a visit to a prostitute. Some flattering attention, a taste of what they think of as the high life, an offer of a handsome tip or a present that they can sell in the bazaar aren't necessarily inadequate or unacceptable payment to very young fellows like that. Alternatively, the tea-planter might find himself badly beaten up and his money gone and there could then be two more young men who've discovered a way of making easy money and will end up in serious trouble. Either consequence is one it seems sensible to avoid.'

'I do see that point of view, sir. But I couldn't risk it.'

'Risk it?'

'Risk doing what you suggest. They might not go quietly.'

'They would if you took them on one side and dealt with it tactfully but firmly.'

'I'm sorry, sir.'

Merrick paused, but never let his glance fall.

'Have you a proper identity card with you?'

'Yes, sir.'

'Then you could show it to them on the quiet.'

'No, sir.'

'Why not?'

Perron's irritation was gone and his temper roused.

'You must know why not, sir.'

'Would you show it to me if I asked to see it?'

'No, sir.'

'If I ordered you to?'

'No, sir.'

'Let me put a hypothetical case, sergeant. I have seen you in one place, in one *persona*, apparently bona fide, but here I find you in another and in the most unsavoury surroundings. I have suspicions about your true identity. I order you to show me the card. You refuse. I call another officer to ring for the military police. What then?'

'Presumably I would be arrested, sir.'

'And then?'

'And then, sir, we should see.'

Suddenly Merrick smiled.

'Your officer was right.'

'Right about what, sir?'

'About your being a tough nut to crack. I think I told you he was singing your praises. But I wanted to find out how easy it would be to force you to act against your better judgment and the security of the job you're doing. I agree it would be quite absurd to risk drawing attention to yourself by warning those fellows off. If I'd looked like succeeding in browbeating you into it I'd have had to stop you. I was only testing you out.'

'May I ask why, sir?'

'I can't tell you here. But if it's not too late when you get back to Queen's Road and have collected your things from Captain Purvis, ring the bell at Lieutenant-Colonel Grace's door on your way down and ask for me. Colonel Grace is Miss Layton's uncle. You know, of course, who her father is.'

'Do I, sir?'

'Weren't you pumping young Kasim? I could have sworn you were.'

'Yes, I know who her father is.'

'Well, if you call you may meet him. They're going back to Pankot tomorrow. I should want you to say nothing about Havildar Karim Muzzafir Khan, either to him or to Miss Layton. In fact nothing at all about the circumstances in which we met before. The other taboo subject, at least in front of Miss Layton, is the subject of Hari Kumar. It might conceivably crop up because Colonel Layton is an old Chillingburian too.'

Merrick broke off. The door of the Maharanee's room had opened and Aneila was coming hastily towards them. Seeing Perron she ran to him and grasped his arm.

'Oh thank goodness you are still here, Auntie is asking for you. Please come quickly. She is in a terrible temper and won't come out to her party. It is so embarrassing with all these people here.'

Still holding his arm she turned back towards the room so that Perron was forced to follow. As he went Merrick said, 'We shall be here for another few minutes, I expect.'

Directly Aneila entered the room the Maharanee cried, 'Shut the door! I cannot stand it! Why do they hang around in the corridor when there are all the rooms to use? Why don't you organize things better? How am I going to rest for my party with all this noise going on?'

'Oh, Auntie, please don't shout, people will hear!'

'How can they hear? I cannot even hear myself speak!'

But it no longer mattered. Aneila had shut the door and stood, visibly trembling, leaning against it.

The Maharanee was still on the couch but by its side now was a small table holding a tray, the bottle of whisky and a glass.'

Pointing at the bottle she said, 'Taste it! Taste it! What is this Purvis creature trying to do? Poison me?'

Perron went across to the couch and picked up the bottle. It was nearly a quarter empty. He glanced at the Maharanee and then at the label. Surprised, he put the uncapped top near his nose and sniffed. The label was genuine. He wondered where Purvis had managed to get hold of it. He hadn't seen a bottle since 1939. He had first tasted the particular brand of whisky it contained at the age of eighteen when it had had an elaborately erotic effect on him. He looked at the Maharanee again, warily.

'You see!' she shouted. 'It is disgusting! Taste it! The taste is even more disgusting than the smell. Aneila, why are you standing there doing nothing? Get Mr Perron a glass.'

Aneila ran into the adjoining bathroom.

'Actually, Your Highness, it's a very fine and rare old malt whisky, an acquired taste perhaps, admittedly –'

'It is disgusting! What is keeping you, Aneila? I said bring Mr Perron a glass.'

'I'm bringing it, Auntie.'

She ran in with a tumbler. It was wet from running water from the tap under which it had been rinsed.

'Pour him one!'

But Perron took the glass and reverently poured the whisky himself. It was too precious to waste. He sipped.

'Well? Is it not disgusting?'

'Not to my way of thinking, Your Highness. On first acquaintance it could seem a little smoky but that's part of its charm to people who like it.'

'They must be depraved then. Who but people with depraved tastes could drink such disgusting stuff?'

'There's a very interesting story about it. They said it wasn't until the English learnt to drink and appreciate it that they managed to subdue the Scots.'

'Scots, English, what is the difference? You are all barbarians. Are there many of you at my party?'

'Yes, I'm afraid so.'

'Who else? Aneila is hopeless. She remembers nobody's name.'

'So far I've talked to only a few. I think you know one of them – Count Bronowsky.'

She waved a hand impatiently. 'Yes, I know. Even Aneila can tell me that. But why is he here? Why is Dmitri here tonight? I told him any time except tonight. Who is with him?'

'The secretary who's a son of Mr Mohammed Ali Kasim.'

'Politics!' she exclaimed. 'It is too boring.'

'And a Major Merrick with a charming girl called Sarah Layton. Count Bronowsky brought them.'

'He is mad! And how can Sarah Layton be charming? With a name like that she must be English. I detest English girls. They are always so stupid and rude. They come out here because in England they are nobody and wouldn't be looked at twice. It is impossible. The party is cancelled, Aneila. Tell the servants to lock up the drinks and stop preparing the food. Tell them to go to bed. I am ill. Poisoned by this Purvis creature. I wish to see no one, not even Mira if she arrives. We shall leave Bombay tomorrow. It is too full of spongers and hangers-on. I am tired of it. Tired of it.'

'Oh, Auntie, Auntie!'

'Is that all you can say? Is coming to Bombay and having a good time all you can think of nowadays? Isn't it time to consider my feelings in the matter?'

'Auntie, what can I *say* to everybody?'

'Why should you say anything? What right have they to an explanation? Do as *I* say and then go to bed. They will soon get fed up.'

She looked at Perron and indicated the bottle.

'Please return it to the Purvis creature or better still since you seem to like it drink it yourself and then you will not have come all this way for nothing. Only take it. I cannot bear even the smell.'

Perron bowed, retrieved the cap from the table, put it on the bottle. The paper in which the bottle had been wrapped was on the floor. He stooped and picked it up. As he did so the Maharanee reached across to the table on which the lamp stood and recovered the shade with the piece of crimson velvet. She went out like an illuminated picture that had been switched off.

'Goodnight, Your Highness,' Perron said. 'I regret being in any way the cause of your indisposition.'

'Goodnight, Mr Perron. You must visit me again when I come back to Bombay and give my next party. Some of my parties are very nice and go on for a day or two.'

He groped his way back to the door. Somewhere in the darkened room Aneila was crying quietly to herself.

*

There was ample room on the back seat of the limousine for Miss Layton, Major Merrick and Count Bronowsky, and for Perron and Mr Kasim on the bench that was let down to face it. Separated from the passengers by panes of glass set in panels of upholstery and figured walnut rode a chauffeur and a footman wearing what Perron assumed to be the livery of the Nawab of Mirat. The limousine had been waiting outside Ishshee Brizhish and now glided along Marine Drive towards the Oval.

'Mr Perron, may I thank you for your thoughtful tactic in tipping us off?' Count Bronowsky said, breaking a rather strained silence. 'It means I have a little less to apologize for to Miss Layton and Major Merrick. We were able to come away in fairly reasonable order.'

'Why *have* we come away?' Miss Layton asked. She seemed perfectly composed. She just wanted to know. He thought her behaviour admirable. When he came out of the Maharanee's room, found Merrick and warned him that the party was over it had been obvious that Merrick hadn't yet suggested leaving. Perron was surprised that during the time it had taken them to get away from the flat Merrick hadn't found an opportunity to tell her what had happened. It was a better excuse than the one he might have had to invent.

He waited for Merrick to tell her now but still the man said nothing. Street-lighting alternately illuminated the left and right sides of his face and it was not until the car turned a corner and a brief but total exposure of the whole head was made that it occurred to Perron that the disfigurement of the left side in a curious way reflected something otherwise inexpressible about the right. Realizing that an explanation was being left to him, he said, 'I have an unhappy feeling that a certain Captain Purvis is to blame.'

He told the story of the whisky.

'What's wrong with the whisky?' Miss Layton asked.

'In my opinion, nothing.' He mentioned its official name. She said, 'The genuine thing?'

He unwrapped the bottle sufficiently to expose the label.

'But it's extraordinary,' she said.

'You know it?'

'Great-grandfather had some in his cellar. My father was talking about it only the other day. He said great-grandfather had the sense to keep going until the last bottle was finished. Then he died.'

Perron wondered whether Miss Layton's great-grandfather had referred, as his own Uncle Charles always had, to this particular brand as Old Sporran. He said, 'The Maharanee called it a drink for barbarians but she'd had a glass or two before she decided to complain. I think the whisky was just an excuse to end a party she'd decided she didn't want to give after all.'

'A shrewd assessment,' Bronowsky said. 'Poor Aimee has never made up her mind what she wants in life. But perhaps the whisky was a blessing.' He turned to Merrick and Miss Layton. 'I was beginning to have doubts about the wisdom of having taken you along. May I in addition to most abject apologies for the failure of the first part of the evening offer some entertainment for what is left of it? For instance the supper I misled you to expect at the party?'

'That's very civil of you,' Merrick said, 'but Miss Layton has a tiring journey ahead of her tomorrow and all things considered an early night now would be a good thing.'

'I understand. Quite. So we have met again merely to part. But better briefly than not at all. What about you, Mr Perron?'

Unprepared for the invitation Perron hesitated. He would have liked the opportunity to talk to the old *wazir.*

'Well, thank you, sir, but ...'

'What the sergeant means, Count,' Merrick interrupted, 'is that he hadn't expected to be asked to stay at the Maharanee's and he's been worried about getting back to his billet because he has no late pass. Isn't that what you were rather delicately avoiding telling me in so many words when we were talking in the corridor?'

Perron admired Merrick's inventiveness, but resented becoming the victim of it. He said, 'More or less, sir.'

Bronowsky was smiling. He said, 'I had no idea that in the education you were so regimented. Is the place where you suggested being dropped the most convenient or should we first deliver Miss Layton and Major Merrick at Queen's Road and drive you on? We have plenty of time.'

Merrick interrupted again. 'I'm afraid the sergeant is quartered quite a distance away but I think I can lay on transport for him. If that's all right by you, sergeant?'

'Thank you, sir.'

'At the same time you could take a document for me to the Major Beamish I mentioned. There'd be no need to deliver it until morning, but I'll give you a note as well if you like to satisfy anyone who might try to get you into trouble for being out late without permission.'

Beamish's name, so casually used, presumably served a double-purpose:

to lend credibility to what was a complete fiction, and to alert him to the fact that Merrick had an intimate knowledge of that department. He said, 'It's very good of you, sir. I don't think a note will be necessary.'

'We'll see.' He turned to Miss Layton. 'It's all right if the sergeant comes in for a moment, I hope? The document's in the case I left.'

'Of course.'

Perron again offered his thanks. Merrick said, 'A lift back to camp seems the least we can do. Your warning saved Miss Layton the embarrassment of finding the drinks locked up under her nose and all the servants gone to bed, it seems. I find it quite inexplicable.'

After a moment Bronowsky said, 'It is India.' He stirred, as if to ease his lame leg and turned his face fully to Merrick who had the seat next to him.

'I hope you are not plagued still by incidents such as arose when you were in Mirat, Major Merrick? Has all that sort of thing died down?'

'Yes, thank you.'

'I'm glad. We for our part have not been revisited by the venerable Pandit who was using the boy's aunt on that occasion. You never met the girl's aunt, did you?'

'No.'

'Because I had that pleasure – perhaps I should say melancholy pleasure – last November in Gopalakand. She was staying, in a sense incognito, with the Resident, Sir Robert Conway, an old friend apparently. We didn't, of course, refer in any way to Mayapore. In fact our conversation was confined almost entirely to the safe subjects of the weather and the historical and architectural interest of the Residency. I did gather however that she had spent most of the recent hot weather in Pankot, but in what she called the seclusion of the unfashionable side. So I don't suppose any of you were aware of her presence, Miss Layton?'

Merrick moved abruptly as if trying to identify the stretch of road they were on. Miss Layton spoke across him:

'Are you talking about Lady Manners, Count Bronowsky?'

'Yes, the girl's aunt.'

'Actually she signed the book at Flagstaff House when she arrived.'

'Indeed?'

'And again when she left. She didn't write in an address.'

'How strange. I mean, signing the book. Does one interpret it as a gesture of submission or defiance, or simply an ironic observance of hill-station convention?'

'I don't know,' Miss Layton said.

'Strange. Very strange. But how interesting. And talking of this,' Bronowsky said, attracting Perron's attention by lightly touching Perron's right shin with the tip of the ebony cane, 'when you were at that school of yours you must have known a boy called Kumar.'

'Kumar?'

'An Indian boy, Hari Kumar.'

'I don't clearly recall, sir.'

1133

'Coomer was the Anglicization, I believe. Harry Coomer.'

Merrick again leant forward.

'Does your driver remember the block? We're almost there. We ought to be slowing down.'

'I believe he does but I shall make sure.'

Bronowsky unhooked a speaking-tube and gave an order. The car which had already been slowing down just before he spoke now dropped to a crawl and came to a stop opposite the entrance to the flats.

'Didn't you know Coomer?' Bronowsky continued.

'We had an Indian boy or two but I don't recall the name, sir. They were rather junior to me.'

'Yes, I see.'

The footman or second chauffeur opened the nearside door and helped Count Bronowsky on to the pavement. Perron and Kasim stayed put on the bench until Merrick had followed and helped Miss Layton out.

'I should have liked you to meet my father, Count Bronowsky,' Miss Layton was saying, 'but Aunt Fenny and Uncle Arthur managed to persuade him to go out with them and they won't be back yet. Won't you and Mr Kasim come in for a drink, though?'

'My dear, how kind,' he said, taking her hand, 'but I couldn't claim your hospitality, having failed so badly in my own. And Mr Merrick is right. You have the journey tomorrow and your father to look after. I hope he'll be fit again very soon. My kindest regards to your mother and of course to your sister.' He raised her hand and kissed it. 'You accompany Miss Layton and her father as far as Delhi, Major Merrick?'

'Yes, I do that.'

'Then it is au revoir to you both. If you have time when you're in Delhi do call on Mohsin.'

'Mohsin?'

'Nawab Sahib's elder son. He is at the Kasim Mahal most of the year. He's rather a dull fellow but his wife is very hospitable. Mirat bores her. She likes to be in the swim, but *her* parties are beyond reproach. I shall write to them and mention you, so do send in your card.'

'Thank you,' Merrick said. 'And goodnight.' He shook the Count's hand and turned to wait for Miss Layton who was talking to Mr Kasim.

'I often think of it,' she was saying. 'And our ride that morning. Do you still go out regularly?'

Perron did not hear young Kasim's reply because Bronowsky had turned to him to say goodnight.

'If you are ever in Mirat, Mr Perron, a note to the Izzat Bagh Palace would always reach me even if we're up in Nanoora.' He gave Perron his card. 'The Izzat Bagh Palace was built in the eighteenth century. The interior has been much modernized but there's a lot there that would still interest you.'

Perron thanked him, shook hands with him and with Mr Kasim and as the two men returned to the limousine followed Merrick and Miss Layton into the block of flats. The lift was still out of order. At the foot of the stairs Merrick muttered something to Miss Layton. She nodded and began to climb.

'I think the form is, sergeant, for you to change into your other uniform and call in on your way down. There is, of course, no document for Major Beamish. Incidentally, *are* you going to need transport?'

'No, sir.'

'Where actually are you going?'

'Kalyan?'

'Tonight?'

'Yes, sir.'

They went up the stairs. The servant whom Purvis had nearly knocked over was just opening the door to Miss Layton who went in without looking at either of them.

'We'll see you presently, then.'

Perron went up to the next floor and rang the bell of Purvis's flat. This time he noticed the nameplate. Hapgood. Hapgood the Banker. Mrs Hapgood the Banker's wife and Miss Hapgood the Banker's daughter. One of the happy families currently relaxing in Ooty. He rang the bell again. From inside he heard men's voices. The door was opened by the servant who had originally met him on the stairs. He looked wildly at Perron and began to talk rapidly in what sounded to Perron like Tamil – of which he understood only a few words. At the first opportunity he interrupted, speaking in English.

'What's the matter? I don't understand what you're saying.'

There were two other servants at the dark end of the corridor, the cook and his boy, probably. The boy was grinning. Perron shut the door. The bearer had resumed his incomprehensible complaint but was clearly inviting Perron to follow him into the living-room.

Arrived there his first impression was that there had been a visit by thieves who had torn the place apart to find what they had come for. The drinks table lay on its side surrounded by broken glasses and bottles. Cushions from the settees were scattered at random. The glass protecting two of the priceless Moghul paintings was smashed and the paintings themselves damaged. Inspecting them Perron realized that a bottle of rum had been shied at them. He could smell it. Stains ran down the wall. On the settee beneath he found bottle-fragments.

The bearer was now referring repeatedly to 'Purvis Sahib'. The cook came into the dining-room. His responsibilities did not extend beyond the kitchen. What was a disaster for the bearer was for him an interesting break in routine. The scene fascinated him because he was not going to be blamed for it.

'What happened?' Perron asked him in English.

'Purvis Sahib,' the cook said. He waved his arms about then mimed a man drinking, staggering, throwing things. He tapped his forehead. Purvis Sahib had gone mad.

1135

'Where is Purvis Sahib now?'

'Room.' He shut his eyes, put his head on one side, let his tongue loll, imaging a man in a drunken stupor.

Perron went back to the corridor. The cook came with him.

'Locked,' the cook said. 'Sahib ish-shleeping.'

Perron tried the handle. He knocked. He called, 'Captain Purvis? It's Sergeant Perron.'

The bearer joined them.

'How long has he been here?'

'Half-hour, Sahib.'

The cook said, 'Drunk. Ish-shleeping.'

'What happened?'

The bearer started to explain. Perron interrupted him, asked him to tell him in English.

A telegram had come. When? Soon after Sergeant Sahib had left with the bottle of whisky. A telegram from where?

The bearer went back to the dining-room. Perron followed. The telegram – actually an official military signal – was under the telephone on a side-table.

When Purvis Sahib read the telegram he was very angry. He used the telephone. He rang people. Nobody he wanted to talk to could be found. He tried to ring Delhi. While he waited for the call he drank. He kept ringing the operator. Because he could not get through he was shouting all the time and drinking; and swearing.

Perron asked the bearer to be quiet while he read the signal. It was prefixed Secret and Urgent. It informed Captain Purvis of his secondment to the department of Civil Affairs and ordered him to report to Headquarters, South-East Asia Command, by August 9. Copies had been sent to an impressive list of authorities. No explanation was given but that was hardly necessary. In Ceylon, Purvis would find himself attached to a group of Civil Affairs officers bound for Malaya either with or in the wake of Zipper.

'Did Captain Purvis Sahib eventually speak to Delhi?'

Yes. The call had come through. During the conversation Purvis Sahib had become like a wild man, shouting and screaming. Then the line had been disconnected. Purvis Sahib began to throw the cushions, and then the bottles. Finally he kicked the table over. No one had dared go near. They had watched from the corridor. When Purvis Sahib staggered to his room they ran into the kitchen. They heard the door slam. Then they heard him shouting and throwing things again. After a bit they heard him crying. Cook had tried to open the door but it was locked. Now he was unconscious with drink. What to do? What would happen when Hapgood Sahib returned from Ooty? What would Hapgood Sahib say when he saw the damage? Was the telegram not from the army sending Purvis Sahib to another station? Did not this mean that when Hapgood Sahib returned Purvis Sahib would not be here? Would the Sergeant Sahib write a chit to

Purvis Sahib asking Purvis Sahib to write a chit to Hapgood Sahib offering to pay for the damage and making it clear that the servants were not to blame?

Perron, already on his way back to the locked door did not answer. He knocked loudly and called Purvis again. He grasped the handle and rattled. There semed to be only one bolt.

'I'm afraid I shall have to break in. I'll write a chit for the door.'

Perron launched himself left shoulder forward. The impact was as bad as the jarring shock of walking into a tree or a lamp-post. The door remained shut. The bearer started shouting again. A broken door, apparently, would be the last straw.

'Is there another way in?'

The bearer did not understand but the cook did. He sent the boy for some keys and then opened the door into the adjoining room and switched on the light. The room must be Miss Hapgood's. It smelt of stale powder and self-satisfaction. There was a great deal of chintz and several numdah rugs on the stone floor. The french-doors on to the balcony were open to keep the room aired but the way out on to the balcony was blocked by a thick wire-mesh screen. This was padlocked. While they waited for the boy to bring the key the cook explained that between this balcony and the one outside Purvis's room there was a gap of only a foot or two. The Sergeant Sahib would find it easy to step from one parapet to the other. Perron hoped this would be so and that Purvis's wire screen was not closed and padlocked too. The bearer assured him it would not be; but this remained to be seen.

The boy came with the key and in a moment Perron was outside. The balcony overlooked a broad passage between the block of flats and its neighbour and also had a view of the backs of other blocks. It was a world of hot night air and lighted windows. From some of them music came. The gap between the balconies was as narrow as the cook had promised. The cook allowed his shoulder to be used as a support while Perron got up on the parapet, steadied himself and stepped across. Without pausing to lose momentum or balance he jumped on to the floor of Purvis's balcony, barely managing to avoid twisting his ankle. One foot had landed within an inch of a potted plant which looked both virile and belligerent. The curtains in Purvis's room were closed but the wire-mesh screen gave at a touch. He entered.

The room was unoccupied. He tapped at the bathroom door and called. There was no sound from inside. He tried the handle. This door was locked too. He unbolted and opened the one into the corridor. The three servants were waiting outside.

'Did Purvis Sahib have his bath before the telegram came?'

No. All Purvis Sahib had done after Sergeant Sahib left was to sit drinking.

'In the flat below,' Perron said, slowly and carefully, 'there is a Major Rajendra Singh of the ims. A Doctor Sahib. Please go downstairs, ring his bell and ask him to come quickly if he is there. If not come back at once.'

The cook volunteered to take the message but Perron said, 'No, you help me.' The cook looked tougher than the bearer. 'Purvis Sahib may be very ill. We have to break into the bathroom.'

Perron did not wait to watch the bearer go. He rattled the bathroom door, kicked the bottom and punched the top. The bolt was at waist level. Again he launched himself, right shoulder this time. After three attempts he stood back.

'Together. Okay?'

The cook lined himself up. On Perron's count of three they attacked the door together. There wasn't really enough working surface. Two shoulders needed a wider door. But Perron thought he felt something give. He fingered one of the panels. The door was a good solid piece of carpentry; which was a pity because breaking in looked like a chopper or axe job.

'Once more.'

This time the sound and feel of cracking wood was unmistakable. The bolt-hole was being forced out of the door-frame. Some of the frame would come with it.

'I think I can manage now.'

He stood the cook aside, made an anchorage for his left arm on the cook's shoulder and kicked hard at the door just above the handle with the flat of his shoe. He did this four times. At the fifth kick the door gave, swung open and revealed their own reflections in the mirror above the hand-basin: an unlooked-for and disturbing confrontation.

Perron went in. The water in the bath-tub had a pink tinge. In it Purvis lay, fully clothed except for his shoes which were placed neatly on the cork mat. His body had slumped and the head, turned into one shoulder, was half submerged. The source of the pink tinge was a series of cuts on the inner side of the left arm which was bare to the elbow. From these cuts slicks of blood rose. In his right hand, which lay under the water, the fingers touching but not grasping it, was the broken-off bottle neck that he had used to inflict the wounds. Other fragments of the bottle were visible. The label – from the second of the two bottles of Old Sporran – floated on the surface.

There was space enough between the wash-basin and the head end of the bath. From there Perron reached down, grasped the collar of Purvis's bush-shirt and heaved him up far enough to get the head out of water and a hand under one arm. He had to struggle to get a grip under the other. He glanced round. The cook was standing in the doorway looking as if he had come to announce that the dinner was ruined through no fault of his own.

'Help me with his feet,' Perron said.

'Sahib dead?'

'I don't know. Help with his feet.'

Reluctantly the man came in. After one glance at Purvis's face he looked away, studied the feet and presently leant over and grasped them, none too firmly.

'Up.'

Shoulders and feet came clear but Purvis was a dead weight. He sagged in the middle. The feet fell back in. The cook was drenched. Perron's eyes began to sting with sweat. The bathroom was like a hothouse. By contrast Purvis's body felt alarmingly tepid through the sodden khaki material. Changing tactics, Perron heaved the shoulders further up and then began to turn Purvis over on to the rim of the bath. As the face disappeared from the cook's view his attention to the mechanics of the problem improved. He grabbed Purvis's knees and heaved. Purvis was now face down and half out of the bath at the top end. Perron readjusted his grip and began to pull. The cook got hold of the thigh and knee of the left leg. At one moment Purvis was balanced entirely on the rim and in danger of falling off it. Perron walked backwards to the door, dragging Purvis with him. The water sloshed out of Purvis's pockets. The cook now got a secure grip on both ankles. They carried Purvis through into the bedroom.

'Bed, Sahib?'

'No, here.' Perron lowered his end to the floor. The cook followed suit. 'Towel.'

While the cook went back for this Perron turned Purvis's face sideways and adjusted the arms, straddled the body and began the exhausting drill for first-aid to the drowned. While he did so he looked at the left arm. There didn't seem to be much blood on the floor. Perhaps the slashes on the arm were superficial. A towel dangled in his face. 'Sahib,' the cook said. Perron broke off, took the towel and wound it tightly round the slashed arm. Then he resumed. A thin trickle of water and what looked like vomit came from Purvis's mouth.

'Doctor Sahib not answering,' came the bearer's voice. The cook repeated the message. 'No answer, doctor sahib.'

Perron continued exerting and relaxing pressure. A large trickle of water came.

'Go downstairs,' Perron said, between pressures. 'Ring Colonel Grace Sahib's bell. Ask for Major Merrick. Anyone. Say: Doctor, ambulance, Purvis Sahib. Quick. Okay?'

The cook repeated the instructions to the bearer.

'Go with him,' Perron said. 'Doctor. Ambulance, Sergeant Perron's request.'

Alone, Perron paused to wipe sweat. He looked at his watch. Twenty minutes altogether was what was recommended. Say another fifteen yet to go. After that Purvis could be presumed dead. He was probably dead now. Perron was tempted to pause again and listen for heart and pulse beat but he supposed the most important thing now was to keep up the rhythm. He resumed. He had studied the drill but this was the first time he had had to put it into practice. The action he was performing suddenly struck him as distasteful. Not only was the body very likely dead, it was Purvis's. It would have been preferable if the inert figure, prone between his thighs, had been that of a complete stranger. The fact that he had sat and talked to Purvis strengthened the unpleasantness of their present positions. He wondered whether Purvis would thank him if he succeeded in reviving him. The suspicion that he would not made the task that much more objectionable. There was another ejaculation of water and vomit. Perron turned his head, closed his eyes. He began breathing in and out through his mouth, slowly, to the rhythm of his own body's movement. He breathed audibly, thinking that perhaps by some quirk of nature Purvis's moribund brain and water-logged lungs might be stimulated into action by an association of ideas.

From breathing just audibly he progressed to doing so hoarsely through a half-closed throat, and continued so after his throat had begun to ache; the point being that he wanted Purvis to *hear* what he himself now began to despair of hearing from Purvis. His back hurt. His arms and shoulders hurt. Sweat poured unchecked over and around his closed eyes. His knees were numb from contact with the tiled floor. Pain stabbed through them down the shins and up the thighs with each forward and backward movement. Only his hands, pressing into Purvis's thin bony back and rib-cage, still seemed capable of doing their work indefinitely. He went on, exerting and relaxing pressure and breathing hoarsely until suddenly his throat dried up. He closed his mouth, swallowed and tried to make saliva. The effort put him off his stroke. He stopped for a moment and then, alerted, opened his eyes and stared down at Purvis. From Purvis's open mouth was coming a sound and under Perron's hands the rib-cage was moving. Purvis was breathing, or anyway fighting for breath.

'I think you can stop now, Sergeant,' someone said. He looked up and round. Merrick stood just behind him. 'I'll get another towel. We've rung for a doctor. He's just up the road so he'll be here in a tick.'

Perron nodded and looked down at Purvis. The struggle for breath seemed immense. Surprisingly it was not without a certain dignity. When Merrick returned with the towel Perron took it from him and spread it over the vomit and then, folding a clean section, tucked it under Purvis's cheek and stroked a lank bit of the mousy hair away from the closed eyes. As he did so Purvis's mouth shut and then opened again.

Merrick said, 'I think a blanket would be a good idea if there is such a thing.' He found one in the almirah and brought it over. Perron helped him cover Purvis with it.

'We'd better have a look at this.' He leant down and lifted Purvis's left arm. Perron unwound the towel. The inside was fairly bloody now but only one of the cuts was seeping seriously.

'I think just wrap the towel round again, Sergeant, until the doctor gets here,' Merrick said. 'It wasn't a very effective job, was it?'

'He was pretty drunk.'

'What on? More of the whisky the Maharanee didn't like?'

'To judge by the broken bottle.'

'And the smell in this room.'

'Is there a smell?'

'Very much so. Haven't you noticed?'

Perron sniffed. He noticed it now.

'Not the most prepossessing chap by the look of him, is he?' Merrick said. 'Do you know what was wrong?'

'I think he'd just had enough.'

'You look as if you have. Where did you leave the bottle you brought back from the Maharanee's?'

Perron told him he thought it must be in the living-room.

'I think you should have some. I'll bring it.'

Merrick went. Purvis's breathing was shallow but fairly regular. Perron got up stiffly. A man's voice in the corridor called 'Hello?' There was an exchange between Merrick and the new arrival. Merrick came back into the room with an English IMS officer. The officer knelt, lifted Purvis's eyelid and felt his temple.

'You're the chap who found him, are you, Sergeant?'

'Yes, sir.'

The doctor unwrapped the towel from the arm.

'Bath, I gather. Face completely submerged?'

'Right side, sir.'

'D'you know how long for, roughly?'

'No, sir.'

'How long were you resuscitating?'

'About ten minutes, sir.'

The doctor had his stethoscope out. When he had finished and slung the earpieces round his neck he glanced up.

'Well done. You'd better go next door and have a bloody strong drink and get out of that wet uniform. Major Merrick – perhaps a couple of the fellows outside will help me get him on to the bed while you ring for the blood-wagon?' He gave Merrick the number as Perron left the room.

*

After Purvis had been taken away Merrick came back from downstairs and into the wrecked living-room where Perron sat drinking some of the Maharanee's whisky and admiring the vivid and lively effect of the Guler-Basohli technique. The paintings were the only things he felt able to concentrate on. They were about one hundred and fifty years old. Even the two damaged ones maintained that air of detachment and self-sufficiency that went with a talent for survival.

Before Merrick could speak Perron said, 'Until I told Purvis what those pictures were he'd no idea. If I'd kept quiet he'd probably have left them alone.'

Merrick inspected them.

'It's what's called Kangra painting, isn't it?'

Perron nodded. Kangra was close enough.

Merrick said, 'Actually I find all oriental art unattractive.' He turned from the paintings. 'I don't think you need worry further about Captain

Purvis unless he does the unexpected and dies, which would mean an inquest. But Simpson says he'll be all right. When he's recovered they'll hand him over to the psychiatric people. Are you going to be fit to drive back to Kalyan?'

'I should think so, sir.'

'Then get your other things and come downstairs and clean up. We'll give you something to eat. How much of that whisky have you had?'

'This is my third glass.'

'Rather a strong one, isn't it? When you're downstairs you'll remember which subjects are taboo, won't you?'

'The subjects of Havildar Karim Muzzafir Khan and Harry Coomer.'

'Good. Incidentally I liked the way you handled Count Bronowsky, but I was surprised he thought fit to raise the subject.'

Perron sipped whisky. He had not liked lying. He felt he was owed an explanation. 'Perhaps you'll tell me what Coomer did, sir?'

'He and five of his friends raped an English girl called Daphne Manners, the niece of the Lady Manners whose name also came up. It was a squalid and extremely nasty business and I find it inconceivable that a man should refer to it in front of a woman.'

Perron sipped more whisky. How old-fashioned. His inclination was to laugh. He wondered whether it was Merrick's intention to make him.

'Was a charge of rape the one you said he wriggled out of, sir?'

'Yes. But as I told you we got him and the others on political grounds.'

Perron drained the glass and stood up. 'It all sounds so melo-dramatic. I find it difficult to imagine Coomer raping anybody.'

'But then you didn't really know him, except with a bat and ball. Are you one of those people who think that if you teach an Indian the rules of cricket he'll become a perfect English gentleman?'

'Hardly, sir. Since I know quite a few Englishmen who play brilliantly and are absolute shits.'

'Do you?' Merrick said. He stared at Perron. 'What are you going to do about the Maharanee's whisky?'

'Keep it, I should think.'

'In view of what Miss Layton said about her father's fondness for that particular brand I was wondering whether it would be a nice gesture for you to leave it with her as a sort of thank you.'

'Thank you?'

'She's putting herself out to see that you have something to eat.'

'I didn't ask for anything to eat, sir.'

'I did that for you. I don't want you driving on a stomach full of nothing but liquor. And then there's the danger of delayed shock impairing your judgment and leading to an accident.'

'It's nice of you to have my welfare at heart, sir.'

'My concern is quite unaltruistic. I have a vested interest in your continuing capacity to perform efficiently. Now, let's go down and get you cleaned up and fed.'

'May I ask what vested interest, sir?'

'I'm arranging to have you attached to my department. The signal ordering you to report for an interview is probably waiting for you in Kalyan but the interview will be no more than a formality. You can assume you'll be working for me. You'll find it pretty interesting.'

'It's very kind of you, sir, but I imagine my department will think its present commitments much too important to allow me to go elsewhere.'

'You'll find they're overruled without much fuss.'

'The point is, sir, I shouldn't want them overruled.'

'Well that does you credit. One becomes attached to one's own unit. But I imagine you'll bow to the inevitable with more equanimity than our friend Purvis. Let's not keep Miss Layton waiting any longer.'

Perron picked up the bottle and went to Purvis's room to collect his pack. Back in the corridor he found Merrick instructing the bearer to leave everything as it was until morning. Perron preceded him through the open door, waited for him and then followed him downstairs. Just short of the door of the flat, which was ajar, Merrick said, 'I'll relieve you of that, shall I?' and took the bottle.

Going in, Merrick called, 'Sarah? I've got Sergeant Perron here.'

Perron followed. In layout the flat was a mirror-duplicate of the one upstairs. She was coming through the dining-room area towards them.

'Hello. Are you all right?'

'I think he's still a bit groggy,' Merrick said before Perron could answer.

'If you are I don't wonder. I'll show you where you can relax and freshen up. Ronald, you go and sit down.'

Her manner was brisk but sympathetic. The bedroom she took him to corresponded with the one Purvis had occupied upstairs but was properly furnished. The light and the ceiling fan were already on. There were two beds; between them a writing-table and a chair with an officer's bush-shirt draped over its back. The bush-shirt looked brand new. The woven shoulder-tabs were those of a Lieutenant-Colonel of the Pankot Rifles.

The door to the bathroom was open and the light switched on. She said, 'Do bathe or shower if you want to. You'll find a large green towel on the rail that hasn't been used.' She had made simple but efficient preparations. She looked at his damp uniform. 'I know father wouldn't mind your borrowing his dressing-gown if you want to have anything dried out and pressed quickly.'

'It's very kind of you, Miss Layton, but I've got a change of clothes in here.' He indicated the pack. 'My correct uniform. The one you saw me in this afternoon.'

'Yes, of course. I'll leave you to it, then. How hungry are you?'

'I'm not at all hungry but I suppose I ought to eat something.'

'I think you ought to if you possibly can. Not that there's much to offer you. Aunt Fenny assumed we'd all be out so she gave cook the night off and Nazimuddin isn't very inventive.'

'Whatever's going will be fine.'

'I'm afraid it's only soup, cold chicken and salad, and what Aunt Fenny calls a shape. In other words, blancmange.'

'I'm rather partial to shape.'

'Good.'

They smiled at one another rather gravely.

'Well,' she said, 'come along whenever you're ready. I'll send Nazimuddin in with a drink. What would you like?'

'Major Merrick thinks I'd just better eat. I've had some of the Maharanee's whisky. Incidentally, he thought your father might like what's left of it. Will he be insulted, being offered left-overs?'

She hesitated. 'Not of that particular whisky. How very nice of you. Are you sure you wouldn't like a glass while you're changing?'

'Quite sure.'

'Did Major Merrick tell you I tipped him off that there was a Field Security man in disguise at the party?'

'Yes, he did.'

'I wasn't sure whether to tell him or not so it was a relief when he said you'd already met and were coming to work with him.'

'You were quite right to tell him. You weren't to know which uniform was the masquerade.'

'Actually that never crossed my mind.'

There was a knock on the open door. The curtains parted and Merrick looked in.

'What is it, Ronald?'

'You've been such a long time I thought our sergeant friend was suffering a reaction from his exertions and that you were having to minister.'

'Actually, sir,' Perron said, 'we've been discussing the attractions and nutritive value of that homely pudding, the blancmange.'

'Oh,' Merrick said, not looking at Perron, speaking to Miss Layton. 'You're having shape again, then. Well, if it's one of the sergeant's favourite afters we'd better let him get changed.' He pushed the curtain further aside: a gesture of command rather than a mark of good manners. Miss Layton hesitated and then went through, murmuring 'Thank you, Ronald' as she did so. Still without looking at Perron Merrick followed her.

Perron put his pack on the nearest of the two beds. Taking out his carefully folded jungle-green issue uniform, spreading it, considering it, he said aloud suddenly, 'I'll be buggered if I will.'

The Zipper-bound boats out there in the roads riding the gentle swell of the Arabian Sea, patient in the night and the persistent rain, seemed infinitely welcoming; his working clothes (in comparison with the jacket that hung on the chairback) purposeful, appropriate. Going into the bathroom he felt his chin. It could have done with a shave but he didn't go back for his razor and brush. A day's growth of bristle was appropriate too. He stripped off the damp harlequinade and stepped into the tub, on to Purvis who lay there invisibly entombed in the smooth white porcelain. Perron's feet went right through him; but when he turned the shower faucet and gasped under the impact of a needle-sharp cold spray he felt the sodden flesh of Purvis's left arm take shape against his shins and the hand take hold of his ankle. Be not afeared, Perron began to declaim, the Isle is full of noises, sounds and sweet airs that give delight and hurt not.

When Purvis had been half-drowned for the second time that evening and Perron had dried himself on the green towel (put out on the rail by Miss Layton's own charming hands?) he returned to the bedroom and put on a clean set of cellular cotton under-shorts and clean socks – the second of two changes carefully packed that morning. Soldiers, he thought, acquired old-maidish habits – especially in the tropics. He got into the green trousers and bush-shirt, unrolled the sleeves and buttoned them at the wrists. Then he sat on the bed and put his boots on, folded the trouser-bottoms and secured them with the webbing anklets. All that remained in the pack now was his shaving kit, small towel, clean handkerchief, webbing belt, holster, pistol and lanyard. If Purvis had known about the pistol would he have gone to the trouble of getting it out of the pack? He put these things on the bed and went round the room and bathroom collecting the stuff he had discarded and cramming it into the pack, so that the damp clothes were at the bottom. This done he replaced the stuff from the bed and secured the pack straps. He checked his breast pocket for the piece of paper on which before leaving for the Maharanee's he had got Purvis to write down the address of the place where they had left his jeep, and which he'd fortunately not put in the pocket of the khaki uniform. It might have been illegible now, from bath water. He looked at it, rememorized it.

Finished, he glanced round the room until his attention was again taken by the brand-new khaki bush-shirt that belonged to Sarah Layton's father. It was, Perron supposed, one of the first things Colonel Layton would do on his return from prison-camp in Europe: get himself fitted out afresh, no doubt from necessity but also to look trim for the arrival in Pankot with the regiment. How would they march in? With bags of swank to make up for the silence in the hills?

But there was nothing particularly swanky about the bush-shirt. It hung on the chair back without distinction, like a jacket on a coat-hanger too narrow for it. There were eyelets sewn on the left breast which showed where two broad bars of medal ribbons would be pinned, but these were not there, nor on the table, and their absence struck Perron as eloquent, as a clue to some special attribute the jacket had which he hadn't identified.

He identified it now. The jacket was new but the slip-on shoulder tabs, although pressed and starched, were old, much laundered. The cream and brown cottons of the embroidered pip and crown, and the black cotton of the regimental name, were faded.

The attribute was twofold, a combination of economical habit and modest impulse. The way the bush-shirt hung on the chair back, shoulders drooped, ostensibly in possession of chair, room, suggested a claim to occupation, but – Perron thought – a claim made in awareness of the insecurity of any tenure. He tried to give the jacket a perkier look by twitching the shoulders back up. They slipped off again. This was because the chair was too narrow, not because Layton was a man of impressive build. Perhaps he had been, before years in prison camp wore him down.

The bush-shirt began to depress him; it was threatening to undermine his confidence in much the same way that the whole experience of being in India had so often seemed on the point of undermining it. Staring at the bush-shirt, on a perch it clung to which did not properly support it, he was struck by its mute indication of the grand irrelevance of history to the things that people wanted for themselves. As in Beamish's office, earlier, he again tuned in the inner ear, the one that could catch the whisper of the perpetually moving stream; but now caught nothing. It began to ache from the pressure of a marble silence so smooth and dense that the plop of a drop of water – the built-in residue in the nozzle of the bathroom shower hitting the porcelain – came as a relief, an excuse to tune back in to the world in which the most significant sound was that made by a hall full of men, ignorant of and indifferent to their history, and giving it the bird.

He got out his notebook and recorded Purvis's remark: 'Six years waste of the world's natural resources and human skills. I don't think I shall ever be able to forgive it.' That was at once a moral judgment and a revelation of thwarted ambition.

'Sahib?'

Perron looked up. The servant Nazimuddin stood in the doorway holding the curtain aside. He indicated a direction – that of the dining-room. Perron nodded – a little surprised to be invited to eat there. He let Nazimuddin go, put his notebook away, waited for a moment or two and then followed, carrying his pack, fighting an urge to open the front door when he got to it and leave without another word.

As though to forestall him Merrick was stationed near it. Through the dining-area, beyond the archway, Perron could see Miss Layton, in profile, seated, talking to someone in the living-room who was hidden from view.

'Leave your pack here, Sergeant.'

Perron put it down near the door. When he had straightened up Merrick continued. 'I told the servant to hurry you up because Miss Layton's father has come back unexpectedly. He's had dinner out and wants an early night but I've been telling him about you and he'll have a few words, so come along.'

Hearing them coming, she broke off what she was saying. Her father sat at one end of a large cretonne-covered sofa. Perron stopped and, briefly, held himself in an attitude akin to parade-ground attention.

'Father, this is Sergeant Perron. My father, Colonel Layton.'

'Good-evening, sir,' Perron said. He stayed where he was. The colonel got up but they were too far from each other to shake hands. He was tall, very thin, slightly stooped. He wore a replica of the bush-shirt in the bedroom. At the head of the row of medal ribbons was the MC.

'Hello,' he said. 'Hear you've been in the wars a bit tonight.' His voice was mild and pleasant. His upper lip was covered by the regulation bristly, cropped, moustache. His head was balding, his complexion pale; a washed-out, rather worn sort of face, but with the same bony structure as his daughter's and so perhaps once more resolute and attractive than it now appeared.

'The evening has been on the hectic side, sir.'

'Mine was too. Thought I'd give the rest of it a miss. Perron. Perron, is it?'

'Yes, sir.'

'Perron. Well, let's sit down again shall we, unless I'm holding the kitchen up.'

'It's only a question of heating the soup, the rest's cold so there's no hurry.'

'Splendid.' He turned to look behind him, as if the act of getting up had disoriented him, left him uncertain about the location or even the continuing existence of the sofa; then, remembering the other two, he indicated vacant places and waited until Merrick and Perron had chosen seats and settled in. There were two floral cretonne-covered sofas at right angles to each other, a small tapestry-covered wing chair in which Miss Layton was sitting, and a larger matching chair which Merrick took. Perron sat on the second sofa; in this way he faced the company. The furniture was arranged round an Indian carpet. There were Benares brass coffee-tables in front of each sofa. The room was not elegant like the banking Hapgoods' living-room, but comfortable, attractive in a homely English way. On the wall behind Colonel Layton hung a couple of faded portraits – conversation-pieces in the Zoffany style – with eighteenth century ladies and gentlemen under trees, with attendant servants: in one case transfixed in expository attitudes and in the other restraining cheetahs on leashes.

'There are cigarettes in the box, Mr Perron,' Miss Layton said. 'And the lighter works. So do help yourself whenever you want.'

'Perron,' Colonel Layton repeated, as if trying to place the name.

Before Perron could speak Merrick said, 'There was a man called Pierre-Cuiller who was known as Perron. He became Governor of what was called Hindustan and commanded the armies under Daulat Rao Sindia. Originally he was a sergeant.'

'In the French Army?' Layton asked. The question was open to both of them but Merrick took it up. 'I can't recall the early origins exactly. But I seem to remember he began life as a pedlar as a result of his family losing all its money. It must be in Compton, but it's some time since I read him. Perron was certainly in the French navy and I think he was in the French Army before that. He came out on a French ship but I can't remember whether it was on the Coromandel or Malabar coast he deserted. Anyway he disappeared up country to seek his fortune with the mercenary Europeans who helped the Indian princes run their armies. What I do remember is that he was among the remnants of Lestineau's brigade when they were taken over by another mercenary, de Boigne, Mahdaji Sindia's chap. Perron was still a sergeant then but rose pretty rapidly and when de Boigne retired after Mahdaji's death and Daulat Rao's succession Perron took over. But of course the two Wellesleys were in control of British interests by then and the French were practically finished. The Mahratta power was fading out and Perron never acquired a reputation as high as de Boigne's. Would you agree, sergeant?'

After a moment Perron smiled, to convey his appreciation of the point Merrick had made: that he was to be reckoned with.

'Yes, I'd agree, sir. But compared with de Boigne Perron was second-rate. Of course he was handicapped –'

Perron stopped – silenced by the impact of one of those unexpected shock-waves, scarcely more than a ripple, of delayed response to a forgotten factor. He had meant that Perron was handicapped by political and military circumstances more complex and threatening than de Boigne had ever had to contend with, but in the split-second before he used the word handicapped he recalled another impediment, one that he was always forgetting because it had seemed to play so insignificant a part in Perron's career. He looked at Merrick's left hand. The gloved artifact was at rest, just off the chair-arm.

Merrick said, 'I suppose you could call it a handicap but I don't remember it ever being said to worry him. Which hand was it by the way?'

Monsieur Perron had lost a hand while throwing a grenade that exploded prematurely. Perron said, 'The right, I imagine, unless he was left-handed or being particularly hard-pressed.'

Merrick said, 'I don't think it was important.' He turned to Colonel Layton. 'The real answer is that he didn't have de Boigne's luck and of course it's difficult stepping into the shoes of an outstandingly successful man. It's an interesting coincidence to come across a modern Sergeant Perron, especially one who's making a study of British-Indian history.'

'Are you connected?' Layton asked amiably. 'I mean descended?' Perron said he was not.

'But the mercenaries are what you'd call your subject?'

'No, sir.'

'What is?'

'At the moment, sir, Field Security in the Bombay Presidency.'

Layton waited a few seconds then put his head back against the sofa. 'Ha!' And then added, 'Jolly good answer.' He crossed his legs, glanced at Merrick, then returned his attention to Perron. 'All the same, war over and all that, what'll be your subject then?'

'Eighteen-Thirty to the Mutiny, I think, sir.'

Layton narrowed his eyes. 'Good period. Bad too, I suppose. That your point?'

'I haven't got a point yet, sir. Choosing a period's rather like sticking a pin in a map of likely runners. Eighteen-thirty or eighteen-thirty-three to eighteen-fifty-eight is simply the period between the East India Company's loss of its trading charter and its metamorphosis into the Indian

Civil Service. So it represents about thirty years' dress rehearsal for full imperial rule. Some of the clues to what eventually went wrong are probably there. That's an over-simplification but it's the neatest way I can put it.'

Colonel Layton was still observing him through those narrowed eyes, apparently paying close attention, but his next remark showed that his attention was on Perron himself and not on what he was saying.

'Perron. I've remembered now. There was a Perron at the school I was at. Younger than me, but a big boy. Remarkably fine athlete. Before the First World War. Place called Chillingborough.'

'That would have been my father, sir.'

'Would it now?' Did Layton's eyes stray to the stripes on his sleeve? Had the reference to Chillingborough been carefully prepared? Or had Merrick said nothing to Layton? On the whole Perron preferred to give him the benefit of the doubt.

'So you're Perron's son, then. Don't suppose I've thought of him since I left. Is he still going strong?'

'He was killed in 1918, sir.'

'Oh. I'm sorry.'

'Ironically enough, on November the tenth.'

'What awful luck. And your mother?'

'She died in 1919, of Spanish 'flu.'

'You poor fellow. Still, you'd be too young to know anything about it, I imagine.'

'Yes, sir. Actually I had a very pleasant childhood. I was brought up by some rather eccentric aunts and uncles.'

'Eccentric enough to send you to Chillingborough too?'

'Yes, sir.'

'Which house?'

'Bank's.'

'The same as your father.'

'No, sir. He was Coote's.'

'Ah. Yes. So he was.'

Layton turned his body rather awkwardly and put his left hand into the nearest of the two large side-pockets of his bush-jacket. Coote's was a nickname. Perron had used it quite unconsciously but it was the sort of thing only someone familiar with Chillingborough lore would be likely to know.

'Did you know someone called Clark?' Miss Layton asked.

'I knew two. One with an e and the other without.'

She sat back and folded her arms, cupping the elbows. She said, 'I've always thought of him as Clark without an e. But now you mention it I'm not sure. My aunt and uncle would know. I only met him once. His first name was James.'

'They were both James. So we called them Clarke-With and Clark-

1149

Without. Clark-Without otherwise lacked very little. I thought of him as someone who would go far in life.'

'Then the one I knew must have been Clark-Without. I met him on the sixth of June last year.' She had turned to speak to her father. 'I know it was the sixth of June because that's the day I visited Ronald in hospital in Calcutta and the day we heard about the second front.' She looked back at Perron. 'He was flying to Ceylon the next day to take up some glamorous-sounding job at South-East Asia Command Headquarters. I've not heard of him again, though.'

'Then it could only have been Clark-Without. Clarke-With wasn't what I'd call Command Headquarters material.'

He wondered about Miss Layton's brief acquaintance with Clark-Without. Clark-Without had not been officially expelled but, in Chillingborough's peculiar language, withdrawn by mutual consent. A Rolls had turned up and Clark-Without had driven away in style, not up-front with the chauffeur but at the back, smoking a cigarette. A mature boy for his age. Perhaps he had been excessively self-publicized in regard to his affairs with girls. Miss Layton did not look in the least embarrassed. In any case she had raised the subject herself. But why? To test for further proof that he himself had been at Chillingborough or to hear him speak the name of a man she had fancied?

'I think your father is tired, Sarah,' Merrick said.

'Ronald thinks you're tired, Father. Are you?'

'Not in the least. Tell you what I'd like, though. A peg of that whisky of Ronald's. Why don't we all do that?'

'It wasn't Ronald's whisky, Father. It was Sergeant Perron's. Before that it was the Maharanee's and before that Captain Purvis's. Nazimuddin !'

Colonel Layton looked from one to the other as if bemused by such a complicated history, and finally concentrated on Perron. 'Extraordinary thing,' he said, 'in the last conversation I had with a very civilized Oberleutnant at the camp I was at, the name of this particular brand came up. We were saying goodbye and he told me he'd be thinking of me in a week or two's time sitting in a comfortable chair in a cosy room, reading *Pride and Prejudice*, sipping a glass of special malt whisky and fondling the ears of my faithful black Labrador, Panther. Apparently one day months before he'd said, "What would you most like to be doing at this very moment?" and it seems that's what I told him. I hadn't the faintest recollection of it. Memory's a bit haywire. But it was pretty well in line with the sort of thing I'd often thought, so obviously I had done. Well, he got the names right. I didn't have the heart to tell him I never knew the dog except as a puppy and that I'd since heard the poor beast was dead anyway, that there wasn't a hope of getting a bottle of that particular whisky in India, so that the only accurate part of his picture could be the comfortable chair and Jane Austen. He'd remembered the detail so accurately. I must say I found that rather touching. Um? Something one says quite casually capturing another chap's imagination and staying in his mind. A nice fellow. Very formal. Very correct. But fair. Yes. Fair. Very fair.'

Nazimuddin who had come in while Colonel Layton was talking and had collected glasses and the bottle at Sarah's low-voiced instructions now brought them to her. She told him to put the tray on the coffee-table nearest her father.

'Will you join us for supper, Father?'

'What?'

'Supper.'

'No, no. Had my supper. Any case, got the unexpired portion of the day's rations if I get peckish.'

She told Nazimuddin they would eat in ten minutes. The man went. Her father leant forward and picked the bottle up. He stared at the label.

'Extraordinary,' he said. 'I've not held a bottle of this for years.'

He put his free hand above his eyes like a shield, as though there was too much light, then folded it until it was across his eyes; and seemed to become fixed in that position, still gripping the bottle.

Miss Layton got up and went to him, bent down, took the bottle, put it on the table and then took his hand in hers. 'Come on, daddy, you've had a long day.'

Perron got up and moved away, making for the folding glass doors that gave on to the balcony but which were closed to keep out the rain. Through the windows he could see little except the reflection of the lighted room, the dark bulk of the back of the wing chair in which Merrick was obviously still sitting, Sarah Layton's bent head, strongly lit by the lamp at the side of the sofa. He could still hear her voice but she was speaking too quietly for any words to reach him. He was glad; he did not want to hear; he did not want to see, either, but wherever he looked the room and its occupants were there in the window. He saw her help Colonel Layton to his feet and lead him out. The colonel still had one hand over his face. The other rested on his daughter's shoulder.

After they had gone Perron did not move. He stared at the reflection of Merrick's chair. He could see the top of Merrick's head and the elbow of the shattered arm. There was the click of a cigarette lighter. In a moment he saw the smoke spiralling gently through the diffused ray cast by the lamp and, after it had vanished, a thinner wisp, rising from about the level of the shattered elbow, which meant that Merrick must have stuck the cigarette between two fingers of the black-gloved artifact.

Perron re-entered the sitting area and did not look at Merrick until he had taken a cigarette from the box Miss Layton had invited him to use, lighted it and sat down. Merrick was supporting his chin in his good hand and holding the cigarette in the artificial one. The unblemished side of his face was comparatively in shade.

'How did you come by that arm, sir?' Perron asked.

'Pulling a certain Captain Bingham out of a burning jeep, under fire, near Imphal, in 1944.'

Such precision. 'Is that what you got the decoration for? Rescuing Captain Bingham?'

'There was an Indian driver to get out as well. He survived. Captain Bingham didn't. He was Miss Layton's brother-in-law.'

'Since when you've been a sort of friend of the family, sir?'

Merrick released his chin, reached across and retrieved the cigarette.

'I knew them before. I was Captain Bingham's best man when he married Susan Layton in nineteen-forty-three.'

'Susan. Yes, that was it. Susan-mem and Sarah-mem. And the wild dogs in the hills.'

'You have a memory for detail. Good.'

'Difficult to forget the wild dog bit, sir.'

'Why?'

'Well, you nearly had him there, sir, didn't you?'

'Had him?'

'"Your wife will not hold her head up and even the wild dogs in the hills will be silent." The chap nearly cried.'

Merrick drew on his cigarette, then rested his chin again on the free fingers of the good hand; arm supported at the elbow by the chair-arm; the smoke floating up.

'He cried later.'

'Yes, sir?'

'When we examined him a week or so ago in Delhi.' Merrick stroked the outer corner of his right eye with his little finger, as if to remove something that irritated it. 'The evidence of his possible complicity in the death of the sepoy in Königsberg is quite strong.' Merrick flicked ash and then put the cigarette back between the black-gloved fingers.

'Is that why the subject's taboo down here? Because it upsets Colonel Layton?'

'It's taboo because it would particularly upset him to know about Königsberg. Actually neither he nor Miss Layton yet know I've seen the man and questioned him. I've tried to give them the impression the man's case isn't a priority. You realize that these men's old officers aren't allowed to go anywhere near them, don't you?'

'No, I didn't, sir. Why aren't they?'

'Because we'd be inundated with requests for interviews. Colonel Layton is a good example. He's convinced he could straighten Havildar Muzzafir Khan out in ten minutes. The attitude is quite admirable, of course, but given half a chance a lot of these men's old officers would try to deal with their own cases at regimental level, and the only sensible course is to keep them firmly out of the picture, otherwise it will get hopelessly confused. And of course it increases the prisoners' sense of isolation, and readiness to talk.'

From behind, in the dining-room area, came the sounds of plates being set out on the table.

'So not a word about the Havildar. I shall break the news to Colonel Layton in my own good time.'

They heard her voice, calling Nazimuddin.

She came into the dining-room. 'Come on, Mr Perron. You must be starved now. Are you ready too, Ronald?'

She waited for them to join her. The table was laid with places at either end and a third in the middle, facing the living-room. She asked Perron to sit in the middle and took the place on his left. Merrick sat at the other end. While they waited for the soup she asked him how long he'd been in India, how much of the country he'd seen and whether it was all as he'd pictured it. After Nazimuddin had brought in the soup and served it he expected her to give Merrick some of her attention, but she did not. For a few moments they drank soup and did not talk at all. He broke the silence by asking her how long she'd been in India herself.

'I was born here. Up in Pankot. So was my sister. We came back out in the summer of 'thirty-nine.'

Perron asked how long the journey to Pankot would take. She said the train left Bombay at two o'clock the following afternoon and that they would be home early on Wednesday morning – unless they decided to break the journey at Delhi. She looked across at Merrick. 'He mentioned it again just now. I've done all I can. It's up to you, Ronald, I'm afraid.'

'It's quite pointless,' Merrick said. 'A complete waste of time.'

'I know. But it's for you to explain why.'

'I thought I had.'

'I mean again.'

'When?'

'Tonight, preferably. Tomorrow morning at the very latest. I want it cut and dried before we get on the train because if we're going to stop off at Delhi I must try to get through to mother and tell her. It's only fair.'

'Personally, I think it would be better to let things lie. Once he's on the train the idea of getting off it will have less appeal.'

'But we get off at Delhi anyway, to change. There's a wait of at least two hours for the Ranpur connection. I don't want to stand around there not knowing whether we're going on or staying. And I certainly don't want to find myself trying to get through to mother from there and telling her we won't be home next day after all.'

'Very well. I'll have a word with him tonight. Incidentally, sergeant, where and what is this transport of yours?'

Perron told him.

'Well that's just round the corner if we take a short cut. We can walk easily, then you could drop me off.'

'That's kind of you, sir, but I'm sure I can find it on my own if you give me directions.'

'Major Merrick isn't staying here, Mr Perron. He's at the Taj.'

'Oh, I see.'

Nazimuddin had cleared away the first course and now brought in the

1153

second. Miss Layton made her selection from the tray. Merrick was provided with a plate of pre-prepared chicken and salad that he could deal with single-handed. The servant now reached Perron's side.

'I'm sorry,' Miss Layton said. 'We were talking just now about something you probably don't know about. The point of getting off at Delhi is for father to try to see one of his NCOs who's in trouble. The only man in the regiment who joined the Frei Hind force in Germany. But Major Merrick says it's a waste of time because of an order prohibiting contact between INA prisoners and their old officers.'

'Yes. It seems rather hard.'

'Understandable in one way, but father's rather upset because he's known the man in question since he was a boy of six or seven. Father was present when the boy and his mother were given the posthumous VC the boy's father won in the last war and he says he showed up awfully well in the fighting in North Africa, so he simply can't understand what got into his head.'

'Presumably Subhas Chandra Bose got into it,' Merrick said.

'But why?'

'It's the sort of thing we'll have to find out.'

'Father thinks he could find out better and quicker than anyone.' For Perron's benefit she added, 'According to the other men in the regiment, Bose and some Indian officers from another regiment who'd already turned coat came to the camp they were in and told them it was their duty to fight with the Germans for India's freedom. Then over the next few days the VCOs and senior NCOs were taken off separately for interviews. Some didn't come back for quite a while but the only one who never came back was this man my father's concerned about. The others thought he'd been tortured and killed because some of the NCOs who were interviewed had a rough time if they told Bose's officers what they thought of them, and Havildar Muzzafir Khan had a reputation for being pretty outspoken. When another lot of Indian officers visited them a few months later and said Muzzafir Khan had joined the Frei Hind army and that they should all follow his example, one of them stood up and asked why Havildar Muzzafir Khan wasn't there to tell them himself. The poor man was carted off, didn't come back for a month and had a ghastly time. Now it seems that the officers were right, but most of the men in the regiment think as daddy does, that something awful must have been done to him to make him join Bose and that even then he'd only have joined to muck things up or escape to the allies at the first opportunity.'

'But he didn't escape,' Merrick said. 'He was among a group of Indians captured by the Free French when the Germans were on the run. The French were all for shooting them out of hand but an American army sergeant whistled up a helicopter and took them back to his unit as prisoners. The sergeant was a Negro, if that's relevant.'

'You've never mentioned that.'

'No. It's what drew my attention to his case, the discovery that one of

1154

the men listed in the report of the helicopter incident was a havildar from your father's regiment.'

'That will count against him, won't it? That he was actually fighting?'

'It's not clear whether he was fighting. The report didn't say. And he's just one man out of several hundred in the European and several thousand in the Eastern theatre.'

'Ought I to mention the helicopter incident to Father?'

'It's up to you. I'd prefer not. There's absolutely nothing he can do and the less he knows just now the easier it'll be for him to accept that.'

'Yes,' she said. 'I suppose so.'

'It's not as though your father's opinion of Havildar Karim Muzzafir Khan won't be asked for. When we reach the stage of dealing with the case someone will come up to Pankot to take statements from people who want to make them.'

'Will the person coming up be you, Ronald?'

'Possibly.'

They concentrated on their food.

Presently Perron said to her, 'I suppose it'll be quite a home-coming on Wednesday? Is there a special train laid on for the regiment?'

'There was hardly a train-load left. But they went back about three weeks ago. My father stayed on in Bombay because when the boat docked there were some men who had to go straight to hospital and he didn't want to leave them behind at this stage of the game.'

'That was very nice of him.'

'Yes, I thought so. The men appreciated it. A bit tough on my mother of course. She couldn't come to Bombay because my sister hasn't been well. But she's talked to the sick men's families and passed on messages and of course father's visited the hospital every day and been able to cheer them up.'

'How many sick men were there?'

'Only six. Five sepoys and a havildar.' She spoke across the table. 'If Father's obstinate about getting off at Delhi to get permission to see Havildar Muzzafir Khan we'll probably find the sick men obstinate about not going on alone to Pankot, especially the havildar because he and Karim Muzzafir Khan were friends. In fact they're related.' She turned again to Perron. 'The first battalion is very close knit. Hill regiments often are. My father can look at the nominal roll and draw a family tree of nearly every man on it. I mean if Naik X is married to a daughter of ex-Havildar Y, he'd know. Does that strike you as silly?'

'No,' Perron said. 'As admirable.'

'Yes. Admirable. And sad. Wouldn't you say sad? Particularly if you'd watched most of them die and seen the rest carted off as prisoners, and felt responsible.'

Merrick put his fork down. Nazimuddin offered him the tray but he declined another helping. Throughout the meal the gloved hand and artificial arm had been disposed on the surface of the table. He leant back, hooked the good arm over the back of his chair and stared at his empty plate, waited for the others to finish. When they had done so Nazimuddin came in with the shape: shapes, rather – three of them, turned out into glass bowls from individual fluted moulds. The shapes were white and looked tasteless but there was a bowl of jam to liven them up. Having served Miss Layton Nazimuddin went across to Merrick.

'Since your Aunt Fenny isn't here to feel hurt, do you mind if I say no?' Without waiting for her answer he said to the servant, 'Give mine to the sergeant. It will build him up. Not that you look starved exactly, but then sergeants seldom do. You manage to do yourselves pretty well, I suppose.'

'Usually, sir.'

'Even in India?'

'I think rather better in India, sir. One doesn't depend so much on diverting rations meant for the officers as one does at home.'

Merrick looked at the mat that marked his place at table, and at the spoon and fork he was not going to use. Miss Layton said, 'I'm afraid there's no savoury, Ronald. Perhaps you'd like to go and talk to Father, then we could all have coffee and Mr Perron could be on his way.'

'Perhaps that will be as well.' He began to get up, rather awkwardly, tucking the artificial arm close to his body. When he had gone Miss Layton said, 'You must have known someone called Rowan, too.'

'Nigel Rowan?'

She nodded.

'Only as one of the minor figures on Olympus would know Zeus. He came out here to the army, didn't he? I remember, because he was always walking away with prizes for classics and I thought he'd carry on in that field or at least go into the ICS if he really wanted an Indian career.'

'Yes, he is in the army, but he was transferred to the political department in 'thirty-eight or 'thirty-nine. He had to go back to his regiment when the war started. He was in the first Burma campaign and got fever badly. At the moment he's ADC to the Governor in Ranpur. He told me he was trying to get back into the Political.'

'Does he still have what I recall as a very detached and patrician manner?'

She smiled. 'I think it is only a manner. Will you have the other shape?'

'No, thank you.'

'They weren't very good, were they? Shall we go in then?'

Nazimuddin had carried the coffee tray through into the livingroom. Following her, he stood for a moment and studied the Zoffany-style pictures and then watched while she poured coffee from a silver-plated pot. He took the cup from her, sat down.

'What does your uncle do?'

'He runs a course about civil and military administration in India in peace time. To attract young officers into the ICS or the police when the war's over.'

'English officers?'

'Indians too. But mostly English.'

'Does he have much success?'

'More in Bombay than in Calcutta. He expects even more in view of the result of the election in England.'

'Yes, I suppose some people must think the prospects at home are now pretty bleak. But aren't the prospects for an Indian career even bleaker?'

She was stirring *ghur* into her coffee, occasionally stopping, tapping the spoon on the rim of the cup and then resuming. 'It's some years since anyone in their right mind thought of India as a career, if you mean India as a place where you could expect to spend the whole of your working life.'

'Is your father coming up to retiring age?'

'He hasn't long to go now. He'll be one of the lucky ones, I should think. The hardest hit will be men like Nigel Rowan, I mean men of his age. It depends on how power's eventually transferred. If there's a prolonged handing-over period, and if Uncle Arthur's right when he says the Indians will be glad to have experienced Englishmen working with them, then men like Nigel might have quite a few more years useful working life out here. But I don't think Uncle Arthur's right, do you? I don't think there'll be a prolonged handing-over period.'

'Why?'

'Because that would be the logical thing and I think the whole situation's become too emotional for logic to come into it.'

He waited for her to continue but she seemed to have come to a stop. He said, 'How will you feel about it, when it happens?'

'I shouldn't want to stay on.'

'Why, especially?'

'I don't think it's a country one can be happy in.'

'You'd be happy in England?'

'I didn't care for it much when I first went home as a child. But it's where I really grew up and started to think for myself. It's where I feel I belong. I know India much better, but ever since my sister and I came out again after going home to school I've only felt like a visitor.'

'Does your sister feel the same?'

'I think a bit the same. She tried not to. But it's difficult to say what she feels nowadays. She's had rather a bad time.'

'Major Merrick told me what happened to her husband. I'm sorry.'

'Did he mention his part in it?'

'Yes.'

She drank her coffee. She said, 'I'm sorry you don't remember Hari Kumar. Nigel does.'

He thought she intended to say more but just then they heard Merrick's footsteps.

'I think that's settled,' he said. She glanced at him as if to judge from his expression how gently he had dealt with her father. Perron glanced at him too but could tell nothing. As in the dockyard-hut the night of Karim

1157

Muzzafir Khan's interrogation, Merrick lifted his right hand and looked at the watch which he wore with the face on the inner-side of the wrist.

'I'll skip coffee if you don't mind. I've got some work to finish back at the hotel. And before that, of course, I must help the sergeant to find his jeep.' He nodded at Perron. 'If you're ready.'

'There's surely time for a cup? Mr Perron, perhaps you'd like another? Or the drink you never got?'

'The sergeant has to drive.'

'Does he really have to? Weren't you on duty of some sort at the Maharanee's party, Mr Perron?'

'Yes, I was.'

'Well who's to say when it might have ended? If you don't really have to report back to Kalyan tonight we could always give you a shake-down here. Frankly I don't think you should go all that way after the sort of evening you've had. We can send Nazimuddin out scouting for a taxi if your work is all that urgent, Ronald. Or you could wait until Uncle Arthur's back. He's using the staff-car.'

'I think you're asking the sergeant to risk getting into trouble.'

'There'd be no risk of that, sir. I'm allowed to use my discretion to a great extent and there are a number of perfectly adequate reasons why I might stay in Bombay overnight if that's what I decided.'

'Good. Then you'll stay, Mr Perron?'

Momentarily he was tempted to accept, help her get rid of Merrick which is what it seemed she wanted, and be alone with her for a while. But very soon the flat would be invaded by its owners, her aunt and uncle, and there would be explanations to make, chat about Purvis, chat about the course, chat about staying on in India. *Raj* chat. And she would fade back into that dreary predictable background. He was sorry for her. He felt she deserved better of life. But so many of them did. There was nothing he could do. Their lives were not his affair. He had his own to live. Their dissatisfaction, their boredom, the strain they always seemed to be under, were largely their own fault. The real world was outside. Impatient, he stood up. If you allowed yourself to sympathize too much they would destroy you. You would lose what you valued most. Your objectivity.

He said, 'It's very kind of you, Miss Layton, but what I have to do in Kalyan tomorrow is more important than what I might do in Bombay, so the quicker I get back the better. In any case, I've already offered Major Merrick a lift to the Taj.'

'Then I won't press you. Incidentally, my father asked me to make sure you know how grateful he is for the whisky and how sorry he was to be so much under the weather.'

They were all on their feet now. Merrick began to go into details of the arrangements for getting to the station the following day. Perron moved away since none of this concerned him. He retrieved his pack and occupied himself pretending to check the straps. That done he stood up and humped the pack on his left shoulder and waited. Merrick was still talking as he and

Miss Layton came through to the archway between dining-room area and passage, where Perron stood. Her arms were folded in the manner Perron assumed was characteristic – hands gripping elbows; one grip loose, the other tight. Too tight? An attitude more of self-control than of self-possession?

Merrick said, 'Tomorrow, then,' and with his right hand reached for and held her left shoulder and bent his head. Instinctively she bent hers away so that the kiss was placed somewhere near her right ear. Her eyes were closed. She smiled, as if to herself, and said, 'Tomorrow.' Merrick let her go. He nodded at the closed door, mutely commanding its opening. Miss Layton called Nazimuddin and then put out her hand.

'Goodbye, Mr Perron.'

The hand was cool and dry. The delicate aroma of the scent she used added to his pleasure in holding it. He thanked her for her hospitality and said goodbye. 'Perhaps we'll meet again,' she said. From behind him Nazimuddin asked if a taxi were wanted. Told that it wasn't he opened the door and salaamed to Perron as he went out. Merrick said goodnight to Miss Layton. Just before the door shut on them Perron caught her slight gestures: a nod, a movement of one hand. They were meant for him.

*

The rain had stopped some time ago but there were no stars, no breaks in the cloud-cover. Neither had the last downpour cooled the air, although there was a hint of freshness in the warm intermittent breeze that played around the palm-fringed *maidan*. He walked a pace or two behind Merrick until they reached an intersection where Merrick stopped. A taxi had drawn up to let its passengers out. 'We'll take this, sergeant, since it's here. It might save us getting wet. I'll drop you and go on to the hotel.' He got in after giving the driver instructions and Perron followed, glad to be saved the walk and the prolonging of the effort of being civil to Merrick which the walk and a jeep drive would have involved. Escape was imminent.

'A very nice girl, Miss Layton, sir.'

Merrick took his time replying.

'She has many admirable qualities. Her father certainly has cause to be grateful to her.'

'Oh?'

'When a man leaves a family of women behind one of them has to assume responsibility for keeping things going. I think she assumed most of it. But of course it tends to develop a girl's domineering instinct. As perhaps you noticed.'

'No, I didn't notice that, sir.' He added, 'This looks familiar. It was somewhere about here.'

'The next road on the left, in fact. Did she refer at all to Kumar when you were alone?'

'Only to say she was sorry I didn't appear to remember him.'

'What did you say?'

'Nothing.'

As the taxi pulled up Merrick said, 'I'll wait until you've made sure of your jeep.'

The gates of the house at which the taxi stopped were shut, perhaps padlocked, and the house apparently in darkness. Perron was almost grateful for Merrick's suggestion. Arrangements made by Purvis were probably not very reliable.

But in this case they were, in all respects except that of security. Directly Perron reached the closed iron gates a lamp was shone on him and a cockney voice said, 'Come for your gharry, Sarge?' Perron said he had and went back to the taxi.

'Everything's in order, sir.'

Merrick was looking out of the other window. He did not move.

He said, 'One case you should find interesting when you join me is that of the brother of the young Indian you met tonight.'

'Ahmed Kasim?'

Merrick turned his head, put a finger to his lips, and nodded in the driver's direction. 'He went over to Bose in Malaya. We got him in Manipur last year. It is interesting when you think who the father is. Right. I'll see you in Delhi. In a couple of days or so, I expect.'

Perron shut the door and threw up a smart one which so far as he could make out Merrick acknowledged in the languid manner officers cultivated. The taxi drew away. Perron watched it go down the poorly-lit tree-lined street.

'Oh no you won't. You bloody well won't,' he said aloud.

*

Half an hour later, soaked to the skin by the renewed downpour, he gave up trying to trace the fault in the brand new jeep's electrical system and accepted the guard-commander's offer of a bed-down for the night. The guard-commander, a British corporal – seemed to welcome company. In the guardroom, keeping his voice low so as not to disturb the three huddled shapes disposed on charpoys in corners away from the dim light of a lamp that hung centrally above a trestle-table littered with mugs, playing-cards and worn copies of *Picture Post* and *Reader's Digest*, he offered Perron a shot of buckshee rum.

'Found its own way here, Sarge,' the corporal said, and winked. Outside, in the dark, he had called Perron sir at least twice but had got over any embarrassment this might have caused him. While they sat smoking and drinking rum the corporal explained that he and his bunch had been in India for a whole month and were still wondering what had hit them. They were part of a formation that had been under orders for France just before – as the corporal put it – old Hitler packed it in. For a while they'd been looking forward to becoming part of the army of occupation. There were chaps making fortunes there right now and from what he'd heard the frauleins would do it for a packet of cigarettes or even a Naafi sandwich. The corporal had been in the army for a year and some of the men in his unit less than that. They had reckoned Germany would be a cushy billet in which to see their time out and from the way 'old Slim's lot' had given the Japs 'the bum's rush out of Burma' the last thing any of them had expected was to be sent out East. When you looked at the map (the corporal said) you could see that the Japanese had had it. You could hardly see where places like Malaya were. But here *they* were. Had the Sarge ever known such a bleeding awful place. How long had the Sarge been out here?

'Two years,' Perron said.

'Christ.'

The corporal studied him, respectfully, but looking for signs of deterioration. 'I reckon I'd be round the twist if they kept me out here that long.' His tone became even lower, confidential. 'What's it like, Sarge. With these Indian bints?'

'The colour doesn't come off.'

The corporal shook his head. 'I couldn't fancy it somehow. Some of the half'n'halfs look okay but the one's who're white enough not to put you off are only interested in officers, aren't they? We been warned to watch it too. They say there's always a coal-black mum waiting in the parlour to get the banns read if you so much as touch the daughter. That true, d'you reckon, Sarge?'

'I've heard of cases.'

The corporal shook his head again. Perron glanced at the sleeping men. Only one of them had his face turned towards the light. He looked about nineteen; so, come to that, did the corporal. The faces were those of urban Londoners and belonged to streets of terraced houses that ended in one-man shops: newsagent-tobacconist, fish and chip shop, family grocer, and a pub at the corner where the high road was. What could such a face know of India? And yet India was there, in the skull, and the bones of the body. Its possession had helped nourish the flesh, warm the blood of every man in the room, sleeping and waking.

'Where do I turn in?' Perron asked.

'I'll show you.' The corporal looked at his watch. 'Then I got to change the guard.' He led the way out into a passage. 'There's a coupla wog clerks that sleep down that end, and there's a duty officer upstairs with the phone put through. He's a wog too. I think the officers that work here take it in turns to sleep in, not that anything ever happens, but there's a safe in the room the duty-officer sleeps in, so I reckon there's a lot of secret papers. There's a spare charpoy here, though—' he opened a door and switched on a light – 'and a bog through that door. You got a blanket, Sarge?'

'No.'

'I'll bring you one in.' He switched on the fan and went out. The room was an office, so sparsely furnished it looked like a monk's cell. Along one wall, under a shuttered window, stood a bare charpoy. Aslant one corner, there was a trestle-table covered by an army blanket, with one folding canvas chair behind it and a folding wooden chair in front of it for visitors. A neatly positioned telephone and blotting pad, a pen and pencil tray, an empty in-basket and an empty out-basket told a story of meticulous attention to work or of a complete absence of work to give attention to. Facing the visitor, parallel to the top edge of the blotter and the pen and pencil tray, was a triangular wedge of wood on which the name of the desk's occupant was painted in white.

Capt. L. Purvis.

Here behind the desk Purvis had sat, waiting for a call from Delhi that never came, and presumably here he had lain, on the charpoy, gazing at the alien geography of the ceiling, nursing his invaded gut and his invincible Englishness. And, on the wall behind the desk, he had marked off with a blue crayon the days of his martyrdom. Perron looked at his watch. Not yet midnight. Even if Purvis had learned to cheat by crossing a day off immediately before he left the office in the evening Perron did not feel he could cancel out August 5 for him until his watch showed 0001.

'Here's your blanket, Sarge, and something for a pillow. Anything else?'

'No thank you, Corporal.'

'We brew up at 0600. Okay for you?'

'Fine.'

'Pleasant dreams then, Sarge.'

After he had taken off his damp uniform, hung it over the chair back under the fan and mopped himself reasonably dry with the green handtowel from his pack, Perron sat in his underwear on the edge of the charpoy and slowly performed the nightly task of trying to obliterate from his mind all the disturbing residue of the day's malfunctioning and so leave it free to crystallize, to reveal the point reached in a continuum he was sure existed but, in India, found so difficult to trace.

He lit a cigarette and stared at his stockinged feet, then reached over to his jacket and got out the notebook and pencil. After a while he wrote: 'Two continua, perhaps, in this case? Ours, and the Indians'? An illusion that they ever coincided, coincide? A powerful illusion but still an illusion? If so, then the *raj* was, is, itself an illusion so far as the English are concerned. Is that what she meant when she said she did not think India was a country one could be happy in?'

Dissatisfied with this he drew a pencil line lightly across the entry and tried again.

'For at least a hundred years India has formed part of England's idea about herself and for the same period India has been forced into a position of being a reflection of that idea. Up to say 1900 the part India played in our idea about ourselves was the part played by anything we possessed which we believed it was right to possess (like a special relationship with God). Since 1900, certainly since 1918, the reverse has obtained. The part played since then by India in the English idea of Englishness has been that of something we feel it does us no credit to have. Our idea about ourselves

1162

will now not accommodate any idea about India except the idea of returning it to the Indians in order to prove that we are English and have demonstrably English ideas. All this is quite simply proven and amply demonstrated. But on either side of that arbitrary date (1900) India itself, as itself, that is to say India as not part of our idea of ourselves, has played no part whatsoever in the lives of Englishmen in general (no part that we are conscious of) and those who came out (those for whom India had to play a real part) became detached both from English life and from the English idea of life. Getting rid of India will cause us at home no qualm of conscience because it will be like getting rid of what is no longer reflected in our mirror of ourselves. The sad thing is that whereas in the English mirror there is now no Indian reflection (think of Purvis, those men I lectured to, and the corporal here in the guardroom), in the Indian mirror the English reflection may be very hard to get rid of, because in the Indian mind English possession has not been an idea but a reality; often a harsh one. The other sad thing is that people like the Laytons may now see nothing at all when looking in their mirror. Not even themselves? Not even a mirror? I know that getting rid of India, dismantling all this old imperial machinery (which Purvis sees as hopelessly antiquated, a brake on economic viability – his word) has become an article of faith with the intellectual minority of the party we have just voted into power. But we haven't voted them into power to get rid of the machinery, we've voted them into power to set up new machinery of our own for our own benefit, and for the majority who voted India does not even begin to exist. Odd that history may record as pre-eminent among the Labour Party's post-war governmental achievements the demission of power in countries like this? Could it be that, in power now, and with a mandate to demit power, the party will forget or omit to demit it? It could be. But we shall see. The machinery for demission is wound up and there are, as Purvis knows, overriding economic arguments for setting it in motion as soon as the war's over. In England the war *is* over. It ended on May 6. In England the war's a dead letter except for people with sons, brothers and fathers and husbands out here. And the fact that they're still out here simply adds to an English sense of grievance that England ever got involved with anything or anywhere south or east of spitting distance of the white cliffs of Dover. Terrific insularity. Paradox! The most insular people in the world managed to establish the largest empire the world has ever seen. No, not paradox. Insularity, like empire-building, requires superb self-confidence, a conviction of one's moral superiority. And I suppose that when the war is really over the recollection that there was a time when we "stood alone" against Hitler will confirm us in our national sense of moral superiority. Will it be in those abstract terms and on those shifting grounds that we'll attempt to build a new empire whose cornerstone will be the act of relinquishing for "moral" reasons the empire we actually had?'

He hesitated, then added, 'Tonight I am a bit drunk.'

Then, looking at his watch he saw it was tonight no longer. He put pencil

1163

and notebook back in the jacket pocket. The evening at the Maharanee's was over. Standing, staring at that name, Purvis, he realized that curious and complex as it had been the evening had had shape. Beginning with Purvis, it had ended in Purvis's office. He appreciated the symmetry of that.

He visited the bathroom. Returning, he went over to the light switch, changed his mind and crossed to the desk, found the blue crayon and went to the wall calendar. He drew an X through the 5, stared at the 6 and said aloud, 'That, anyway, is the crystallization, the point reached in the *time* continuum.'

He turned the fan down to its slowest rate of revolutions, switched off the light, opened the shutters on the unglazed barred window and breathed in. Bombay. Bom-Bahia. Part of an inheritance. His monarch's. His own. The corporal's, Purvis's, the Maharanee's. The street beggar's. He lay, adjusted the cushion the corporal had brought as a pillow, and the blanket so that it just covered his abdomen, the most vulnerable part of the body when there was a fan going. For a while pictures of the day just ended flickered across the screen lowered by his eyelids, but all at once there was the disturbing invasion of shots of Coomer, from all angles, long, medium and close; Coomer opening his shoulders, hitting out at a sequence of balls whose pitch and pace were subtly varied by the invisible bowler; or team of bowlers; the deliveries were in too mercilessly rapid a succession for one man alone to send down.

The cameras of Perron's imagination began to tire. Presently only one remained, and this zoomed in close to recreate a memory of the boy's face. There was a face, an idea of a face, a man's rather than a boy's, and formed from a notion of an expression rather than from one of features: an expression of concentration, of hard-held determination, of awareness that to misjudge, to mistime, would lead to destruction. There was no sound. And suddenly the face vanished. A flurry of birds, crows, rooks, rose from the surrounding elms, startled by a sudden noise, although there had been no noise. And they were not elms, but palms; and the birds were kitehawks. They circled patiently above Perron's head, waiting for him to fall asleep.

Journeys into Uneasy Distances

I

In view of what once happened there the countryside through which the mail train passes on the first stage of the journey from Mirat to Ranpur is surprisingly undramatic. The passenger who has what initially seems the good luck to be alone in a compartment soon grows restless as mile follows mile with nothing to catch the attention or work on the imagination other than what in India is common-place: the huddles of mud villages; buffalo wallowing in celebration of their survival from the primeval slime; men, women and children engaged in the fatal ritual of pre-ordained work.

Only the slow train stops at the wayside stations. On their single platforms people wait with bundles and a patience that has something exalted about it, although this impression could be the result of the express passing through too quickly for individual faces to be clearly noted. There are three such stations all of which are reached within thirty minutes of leaving Mirat cantonment. Thereafter, the villages become distant, but there is one, abandoned and ruinous, which appears suddenly and unexpectedly, close to the line.

Those ruins don't look old. For an instant the traveller conjures images of flames, of silhouetted human shapes running distractedly, stooped under burdens. But the moment of imaginative recreation is a brief one. The crippled dwellings and crumbled walls slide quickly out of sight and the panorama of wasteland, scarred by dried-out nullahs and rocky outcrops, appears again and expands to the limit of the blurred horizon where the colourlessness of sky and earth merge and are distinguished only by a band of a different intensity of colourlessness which, gazed at long enough, gives an idea of blue and purple refraction. Everything is immense, but – lacking harmony or contrast – is diminished by its association with infinity.

The ruined village is explained. The land is eroded. The exodus must have been slow, quite unremarkable. One by one the men would have gone, taking their women and children and driving their thin cattle, while inch by inch the soil was swept away and the implacable rock exposed until there was nothing but the empty waste; and the wind blowing hot in the telegraph wires that border the railway.

The land now seems to be at peace. It requires some effort to see such a place as a background to any sudden or violent event. Perhaps there was no bloodshed, no murder on this stretch of line. But, as if remembering violence the train slows and then draws to a stop. There is a clank under the carriage; cessation, immobility. The compartment – not air-conditioned, one fan not working – grows warmer. Presently there comes the hollow sound of unevenly clunking goatbells and in a moment or two the straggling herd comes into view, driven by a lean man and a naked urchin, in search of patches of impoverished grazing. They go by without a glance, drugged by the heat and the singleness of their purpose. When they have gone there is silence but their passing has disturbed the atmosphere. The body of the victim could have fallen just here.

A few moments before, he is said to have gestured at the shuttered window of the compartment door on which strangers outside were banging and said 'It seems to be me they want', and then smiled at his shocked fellow-passengers, as if he had recognized a brilliant and totally unexpected opportunity. In a flash he had unlocked the door and gone. Briefly, a turbanned head appeared, begged pardon for the inconvenience and then removed itself. The door banged to. One of the passengers stumbled across luggage and relocked it. After a moment he lowered the shutter and looked out. Those nearest to him might have seen his horrified expression.

Just then the engine driver up ahead obeyed an instruction and the train glided forward. It was the smooth gliding motion away from a violent situation which one witness never forgot. 'Suddenly you had the feeling that the train, the wheels, the lines, weren't made of metal but of something greasy and evasive.'

Without warning it glides forward now, from the place where the herd of goats has been, seeming to identify a spot marked with the x of an old killing by its mechanical anxiety to get away before blame is apportioned and responsibility felt. Increasing speed, the train puts distance between itself and the falling body and between one time and another so that in the mind of the traveller the body never quite achieves its final crumpled position on the ground at the feet of the attackers.

'It seems to be me they want,' the victim said. Perhaps he said no such thing but gave the impression of thinking it because of that look on his face of recognizing some kind of personal advantage. This look may have been due to nothing more than a desire to reassure the other occupants of the carriage that they had nothing to worry about themselves and that he would be quite safe so long as he went of his own free will. But all the evidence suggests that the witness was right about the words and the expression. The victim chose neither the time nor the place of his death but in going to it as he did he must have seen that he contributed something of his own to its manner; and this was probably his compensation; so that when the body falls it will seem to do so without protest and without asking for any explanation of the thing that has happened to it, as if all that has gone before is explanation enough, so that it will not fall to the ground so much as out of a history which began with a girl stumbling on steps at the end of a long journey through the dark.

The train is cautious in its approach to Premanagar. Tracks converge from the east, coming from Mayapore. To the left, some miles distant, is the fort, no longer a prison, infrequently visited by tourists; peripheral to the tale but a brooding point of reference and orientation. To the south, now, lies Mirat with its mosques and minarets. North, a few hours journey, is Ranpur, where a grave was undug, and farther north still, amid hills, Pankot, where it was dug in too great a hurry for someone's peace of mind. Beyond the fort, the west lies open, admitting a chill draught. The erosive wind, perhaps. After a short halt the train moves on to its final destination.

*

It is dark by the time it clatters across the bridge and worms its way into the city of Ranpur, as it was dark on Tuesday August 7, 1945, when Sarah Layton and her father, and the handful of soldiers released from hospital, arrived from Delhi and disembarked to pick up the midnight connection to Pankot; and since the railway station has changed little it is easy to picture them, to pick them out of a crowd which behaves as crowds on platforms do (with a mixture of hysteria, impatience, gaiety and – in isolated cases – resignation). The platform is one of several protected by the vaulted, glassed and girdered roof that rests on steel ornamental pillars. At the base of these pillars people congregate, waiting for trains or inspiration. The lighting is yellow, intermittent. There are areas of light and half-light and areas of shadow. Through these areas passengers walk or run, and coolies trot bare foot, erect under head-loads, shouting warnings of approach. The grey paving is spattered with new and old spittings of betel-juice which a stranger to the country may confuse with bloodstains. There is a smell of coalsmoke, ripe fruit and of cotton cloth which human sweat has drenched and dried on and drenched again. It is a smell by no means peculiar to this station but for those to whom Ranpur represents a home-coming it has a subtle distinction, a pungency of special intensity, a benign and odorous warmth which even Sarah who had not been away for long was conscious of as she got down from the coupé and joined her father. Patiently he was choosing three coolies from the gang that had run alongside for fifty yards or more.

There had been no problem at Delhi. Ronald Merrick had waited to see them off on the Ranpur train, to be on hand if at the last moment Colonel Layton again had to be dissuaded from breaking the journey. But he had been docile, good-humoured, quietly intent on the morning papers with their latest reports of the significance of the bomb of 'devastating power' which the Americans had dropped on the Japanese city of Hiroshima on Monday morning.

News of the attack had reached them on the platform of the Victoria terminus in Bombay, half-an-hour before the train was due out. Some English people said they had just heard it on the lunch-time radio. Aunt Fenny sent Uncle Arthur off to see what more he could find out. He had put on weight and did not walk quickly, was away some time, nearly missed them, had to accompany the moving train shouting 'Seems to be true but I can't make head or tail of it. Have a good trip.' In the evening when they stopped to take on dinnertrays there was confirmation in the evening papers. It had been an atomic bomb. The ultimate weapon. The question was whether Hirohito would now surrender to save other cities, Tokyo itself, from devastation. Sarah thought: It might be over, then. And knew relief. Excitement even.

'The moral reservations' (she has said) 'came later. At the time you could only feel glad. Awestruck, I suppose, by the sheer size of the thing. And by the miracle. I never met anyone who felt otherwise until long after. If we had doubts about the wisdom of letting off bombs like that they were very long-term. Too long-term to bother us. The short-term was the important thing.'

In the short-term, above all, it might mean safety for her father. He'd said nothing about further active service. The prospects were shadowy but they existed. No one expected the liberation of Malaya and the conquest of the Japanese mainland to be accomplished quickly or cheaply. If the war continued he would probably manoeuvre for a command before he was fully fit. But now the chances were that it would not continue and, walking with him along the platform, with one coolie ahead and two behind, to rendezvous with the havildar and the five sepoys who had travelled in a compartment a long way separated from their own, she was able to entertain an illusion of serenity, of entering a period of life which by contrast with the one just ended might be described as free, uncluttered, open at last to endless possibilities.

II

For a few seconds she awaited confirmation that the child had whimpered, but there was no sound of Minnie stirring in the spare room to pick him up and comfort him. Wondering whether Susan was still asleep or up to something odd, she felt for the switch on the bed-side lamp. The shock of no contact brought her fully conscious. She sat up in unfamiliar surroundings, a wall on one side, nothing on the other. She recalled, then, where she was; and because there was utter stillness, assumed that probably what had woken her was the jerk of the train coming to a halt. From her upper-berth she glanced down into the well of the coupé and saw her father – his shape, rather – standing at the carriage door. The window was lowered. She could smell the pine-trees – the scent of the hills. The air was chill. The light of Wednesday was just beginning to come.

'All right, Father?'

She spoke quietly but he drew his head in and glanced up at once, as if caught doing something forbidden.

'Did I wake you? I'm sorry.'

'No. It wasn't you. It must have been the train stopping.'

'Afraid that was ten minutes ago. I made a duff hand of opening the window. How about some tea? There's plenty in the flask.'

'I'll come down and get it for us.'

'No, no. You stay there.'

She felt for her dressing-gown. 'I'll come down anyway.'

'Do you want some light?'

'No,' she said. 'That would spoil it.'

He said nothing. She felt that he understood her mood. She climbed down and removed the steps from their hooks. He had his back turned, pouring tea from the thermos into the cups Aunt Fenny had packed in the hamper. The tea in the thermos had been bought the night before from the station restaurant at Ranpur. He handed her a cup. She stood near the lowered window, warming her hands on it.

'In the old days,' he said, 'we used to stop round about here to get up a proper head of steam. Then we got the new locomotive and were able to get up the gradient in a brace of shakes. I suppose the new engine's getting old. Listen.'

There was a faint noise, an abrupt exhalation, followed by a clank. It came again, then again. It sounded far off. The coupé was in a carriage at the rear of the train which was halted on a curved stretch of line. The window her father had opened looked east towards the plains they had left, across a deep valley, at the moment full of mist – below eye-level so that it looked like the surface of a lake. On the other side of the carriage was the rock face. The road, which took steeper gradients, was above them. She turned her wrist until she was able to make out the position of the hands of her watch. He saw what she was doing and said, 'Just over two hours to go, or should be if we keep to the time-table.'

She moved away from the window so that he could resume his vigil if he wished to, and sat on the lower bunk. He went back to the window. She wanted a cigarette but resisted temptation. In Bombay he had said to Aunt Fenny, 'Isn't Sarah smoking rather a lot?' and Fenny had tipped her off. She had tried to cut down, not for fear of his disapproval but as part of her campaign to guard him from as many sources of irritation as was in her power. She had warned her mother by letter how easily he could be upset, of the prison-camp habit of saving 'the unexpired portion'; pocketing bits of bread to eat later; the mark of a man who had known hunger. The habit was dying hard, as hard – no doubt – as recollections of conditions of which he never spoke. And he had been uninquisitive about affairs she had been prepared for him to question her on.

He had never mentioned the death of Teddie Bingham, the son-in-law he had never seen, nor delved into the nature of Susan's illness. Neither had he referred directly to the death of his stepmother, Mabel, from whom

Rose Cottage had been inherited. Sarah had once begun to warn him that her mother had made a few changes in the place, but he had interrupted, saying Fenny had mentioned 'something about a tennis-court'. He'd added: 'Pity about the roses, but I suppose they needed a lot of attention and the court's a good idea for you girls.'

What else had Fenny said 'something' about? She was the kind of woman who let things slip without necessarily meaning to or even knowing that she'd done so. But in the case of the destruction of the greater part of the rose garden to make room for the tennis-court, Sarah was grateful to be relieved of the job of telling him herself. She had feared doing so; unnecessarily, it seemed, judging by the casual way he had taken it.

But had he taken it *in*? From Germany after he got their letter telling him Mabel had died, he'd written: 'It's sad news but not a shock because she was getting on. I'm glad my last memory of her is in the garden the time I went up from Ranpur to say goodbye to her and to arrange your accommodation in Pankot once the regiment left for overseas. I'm sorry I wasn't able to fix up anything better than those cramped quarters in the lines, but Mabel was quite right. Even if she'd given marching orders to that PG of hers the three of you with Mabel would have been just as cramped at Rose Cottage, and however poky a place is there's nothing like having your own, is there Millie? Anyway I have this picture of you now, moving in to the cottage, all amid the roses and the pine trees. I long to be with you all again and not just have to picture it.'

It was possible that as he stood at the open window of the coupé any picture he had of his homecoming was of the house and garden as he remembered it and that the tennis-court had not penetrated visually, as an idea. Even after all these months Sarah could get a shock when she went through to the verandah and instead of the rose-beds saw the high netting, the lime-marked grass, the centre net or the bare posts if the net had been taken down by the *mali*. The court was seldom used. Sarah didn't play well and watching bored her. And the days were gone when her younger sister used a tennis-court and a tennis outfit as two more ways of ensuring that she was the centre of attention. That role had been discarded and the new one precluded violent exercise. Only Mildred, their mother, seemed to get any pleasure out of the court, not by playing, but by having it there as one might have anything that made an invitation attractive. 'Come up to the house at the weekend,' she might say to someone new on station, of whom she approved, 'and if you're keen bring a racquet and things. We've a sort of court you can get a game on.' And there was usually someone there to protest: 'Don't be deceived. Sort of court! Binky swears it's better than the number one here at the club.' And then her mother would raise her eyebrows and smile, that characteristic downward-curving smile that Sarah was afraid she might acquire, having once or twice got a glimpse of herself in a mirror smiling in that way. There was a way of sitting too and she had caught herself at that on more than one occasion, on the verandah of Rose Cottage, glancing from the tennis to her mother and recognizing her mother's attitude as the origin of her own: well settled in a cane chair, legs out-stretched and crossed at the ankles, elbows supported by the chair-arms; and the hands, drooping at the wrists, bearing the burden of a glass of gin-sling. She had sat up, put her glass down, leant forward and folded her arms, but that was becoming a habitual attitude too, and just as defensive.

Up ahead the whistle sounded and presently the train moved, taking the curve. The mist-filled valley flowed away and they entered a cut where the rock-face loomed on both sides. Her father stayed by the open window for a while, breathing in the scent of damp stone, wild ferns and mosses. When the scent became pungent with captive drifting smoke he ducked back in and raised the window. There remained in the carriage an opacity as if some of the eastern light had stayed inside.

He sat down. Unexpectedly he said, 'I haven't thanked you for coming to Bombay and for what you've done while I've been away. Your Aunt Fenny told me what a brick you've been, what a help to your mother and Susan. I just wanted you to know before we get in how grateful I am.'

As soon as he began she looked down at the cup in her hands. They had never been a demonstrative family. When he finished he put an arm round her shoulders, very briefly, just long enough for her to acknowledge the embrace by leaning into it for a moment.

'Shall I pour you another cup?'

'No thank you, daddy. Later perhaps. What about you?'

'I'll wait a while. Keep some in reserve in case we're held up again and get thirsty.'

'I'll rinse the cups then.'

'No, I'll do that. Unless you want to go in there.'

'Not yet.'

He took the cups into the w.c. cubicle, leaving the door ajar. The train was making slow time. She heard him humming. In the past three weeks she had learnt to interpret this as a sign of restlessness, of anxiety to be occupied. She wondered whether it was light enough for a game of chess. She looked for and found the travelling set which he had brought back from Germany and on which he had taught her to play in Bombay. She had a beginner's enthusiasm and in one case what had seemed like beginner's luck. No doubt he'd deliberately contrived that, to encourage her; but she felt she had learned enough at least to give him a bit of a game.

Unable to see it clearly she put the set away. She wondered how long it would be before they played again, or whether they ever would. Once home, the pattern of relationship established in Bombay would change. He came back with the cups. She took them from him and put them in the hamper, protecting them with a napkin from contact with the neck of Sergeant Perron's bottle of whisky; of which he had said, 'Let's save some for your mother.' She doubted that her mother would want any. Not whisky.

He said, 'If you're sure you don't want to go first I think I'll shave and get done.'

She nodded, watched him potter around – potter was the only word for it – collecting sponge bag, shaving kit, towel, clothes, and finally his uniform from the hook on the wall. His movements were slow, thought out. Perhaps this had always been his habit. She did not remember it but not remembering was probably further evidence of how little she knew him, as little now as she had known him – and her mother – on her return to India in 1939 after the years of unavoidable separation. He switched the light on in the cubicle and this time closed the door but there was no sound of the bolt being shot. Had the Germans ever put him in solitary confinement? If so, for what crime? Attempting to escape? Eventually her mother would question him and get answers or he would regain confidence in his freedom and volunteer information, and then they would be able to put the story of the past few years of his life together piece by piece; as he would be able to put theirs together. But in neither case the whole stories. Probably never that.

She lit a cigarette now and settled closer to the window. In her imagination she had often rehearsed the circumstances of her father's return but had not pictured them like this, with the two of them travelling alone from Bombay to Pankot. He confessed he had rehearsed them too but said there had always been a moment when his imagination failed, the moment following the actual reunion, and that this was probably because the scene of reunion was not determinable in advance: a railway station, a dockside, even an airport, the old house in Kabul road in Ranpur, the front verandah of Rose Cottage, the compound of the grace and favour bungalow in the lines of the Pankot Rifles depot. The reunion itself was the important thing, one did not think beyond it. He told her of a fellow prisoner-of-war, a Catholic, who had shocked a padre by confessing that he had always wondered what after spending six days creating the world and then resting on the seventh God had done on the eighth. The day of reunion was like the seventh day. Today, Wednesday, was the seventh. She could not visualize tomorrow except as a continuation, an emotional perpetuation, of today which of course it could not be. One thought about a day of reunion but the reunion itself was only a moment in a day. She and her father had had that moment in Bombay. He had another to come this morning but of this she would be no more than a spectator; perhaps not that because he had asked that no one in the family should be at the station. His request that the families of the sepoys and havildar should also be dissuaded from coming to the station, his warning that the only reception committee he wished to find would be at most the depot adjutant, Kevin Coley, plus an NCO and a truck to take the men back to the lines and some kind of transport for himself and Sarah, was an indication of his fear of any kind of scene that might affect him.

It would be nice, he had said, just to drive from the station with her in whatever transport could be arranged and to arrive at Rose Cottage much as though he had simply come home for breakfast after early morning parade. She had conveyed this wish to her mother and knew that it would be respected. She was prepared to let him go into the bungalow alone and busy herself outside in the garden or on the side verandah where probably little Edward would be, in Minnie's charge, playing with the new Labrador puppy.

Neither Sarah nor her mother had wanted the puppy. It was Susan's idea that they should have one, as like as possible to Panther who had been little more than a puppy himself when her father went abroad on active service. Susan said it would be a nice surprise for him and persisted until their mother said they'd see, but that black Labradors weren't to be had just like that. Susan then played her trump card. Maisie Trehearne knew some people down in Nansera who had some puppies ready.

The job of trying just once more to talk her out of it had fallen to Sarah, but when she tried she drew nothing except the look of hostility with which she was now familiar but had never got used to, so in the end she went down to Nansera with old Maisie Trehearne who loved dogs and had seen Panther die, and who made the morning's car journey down tense by continually referring to that episode, and the afternoon journey back exasperating by talking incessantly to the trembling little creature that was Panther's successor and had cost two hundred rupees and was guaranteed house-trained, a qualification which it showed evidence of being unaware it possessed by making a mess in its own basket, perhaps out of fright or a combination of fright and uncertainty about which of the two women abducting it was to be its new owner. Do pet it, Sarah, Maisie kept saying, in between bouts of petting it herself. But Sarah refused. 'It's Su's dog. I want Su to be the first to show it affection.' 'Of course, you're right. Isn't she, little fellow?'

And Susan had shown it affection. For a while the old Susan was there, on her knees, flushed and pretty, pushing a dark curl from her forehead with one finger and holding out her other hand, invitingly, caressingly, letting the puppy squirm up to her and sniff, bending down until her face was close, allowing it to lick her cheek, then hugging it and taking it to introduce it to Little Master who was sprawled on a rug on the verandah, dabbing at a toy dog, and who, after a moment's disbelief in this confrontation with a real one, screamed, so that the puppy – already named Panther the Second by Susan – backed away, puzzled, wholly at a loss until he found Sarah's by now familiar-smelling feet. He sat down against them and stared at the strangers. Susan stared back at him and then up at Sarah, so that on impulse Sarah pushed the puppy away with the side of her shoe and went to the verandah rail.

Ayah was comforting the child and Susan turned to help her. From the rail Sarah watched the puppy. Noting how it looked from the three on the rug to her and back again and then settled on its haunches on the spot where she had left it, ducked its head down and up again but made no sound, she realized that it had character and that she must harden her heart against it for both their sakes. She went indoors and called for Mahmoud to tell the *bhishti* to draw her bath. From the bedroom she heard Susan taking the little boy to task for being afraid of a puppy. The child had not yet learned to speak. Sometimes Sarah wondered whether he ever would, whether he knew whose child he was; his mother's, Ayah's or Sarah's. With the puppy it would be different. Dogs made their own decisions in such matters, as Panther 1 had done, choosing Susan as the owned and owning object of adoration despite her variable response to him and, finally, her absolute neglect.

She had always had that power, still had it, a power of immediate attraction for animals and people, and Sarah understood her sister's own attitude to that power, her inability to believe that she truly possessed it and something of the terror she felt knowing that she did. 'Come on, puppy,' she was calling. 'There. Nice puppy. Mummy's not afraid of puppy, see? Puppy loves mummy already. Come on now, stroke puppy. Show mummy what a brave boy you are.'

Gradually the boy had lost his terror and for a day or two the puppy was petted, played with, fed on the verandah by Susan and overseen by Minnie or Mahmoud during his periodic visits to urinate and defaecate, which he announced his intention of doing by going to the head of the steps into the garden and trying to get down them. The veterinary officer, Lieutenant Khan, came up from the Remount depot, examined his mouth and teeth and ears and gave him injections and powders which made him look miserable but did not dampen his playful spirit. Returning at lunch times and in the late afternoons from her work at Area Headquarters, Sarah noted the situation but knew that it would change.

On the fourth or fifth day (she could not remember which) she came back for lunch, was aware of the puppy's absence but said nothing until Susan went to their room for her afternoon nap and she and her mother were alone. 'I didn't see Panther Two,' she began. 'Is he all right?' Her mother supposed he was all right. Mahmoud had him in the servants' quarters. He had made a mess on the verandah. That's all her mother knew; that and that there had been a scene with Minnie crying and the child crying and Susan angry and then retreating into one of her moods. 'Do you *have* to go back to the daftar this afternoon?' her mother asked.

'I'm afraid I do. Why?'

Why didn't matter in that case, her mother said, and got up and left her alone. Sarah knew why and knew her mother knew she knew. But oppressed by the apparently unalterable rhythm of life at home she felt justified in pretending not to and it helped to get out for a few more hours. Nothing would happen during them. It took some time for a crisis to build up, if there was to be a crisis.

Her father came back into the compartment.

'There, all done.'

'How smart you look.'

'Dressed for the part.'

In the old days he would never have said that. He seemed to have acquired a sense of charade. He wore KD with Sam Browne, collar and tie. The rainbow ribbons above the left bieast pocket added colour to his occasion. He had on one of the pairs of hand-made shoes which he had left behind in 1940 which throughout the war Mahmoud had kept dubbined and had recently polished to a deep conker-brown. She had taken two pairs to Bombay. This was the first time he had worn them.

'Are they comfortable?'

'I think,' he said, 'my feet have lost weight too. But they're good and soft.'

'I'll get dressed,' she said, 'then we'll have the other cup. Unless you'd like it now.'

'No, I'll tidy up here, then we'll have more room.'

Tidy up was one of the new expressions. He had become used to doing things for himself. In Bombay Nazimuddin had been scandalized by the sight of Colonel Sahib cleaning his own shoes, washing out pairs of socks, drawing his own bath, packing his own cases. Rather than tell him that in England many Sahibs were used to looking after themselves Sarah tried to explain that doing such chores helped her father get well again after being so long a prisoner in Germany.

He had left the w.c. cubicle immaculate. The hand-basin glistened, the speckled mirror gleamed. The stone floor looked newly swept. At Pankot the sweepers would have nothing to do but clear up after her. She wondered how her father had achieved such spotlessness. There was no brush or mop or cloth. Perhaps he had used handfuls of toilet paper.

In her valise which she set down against the door she had her civilian skirt and blouse and her WAC(I) uniform. While sitting on the closet smoking another cigarette she wondered which to wear. He had not seen her in uniform yet. She'd intended to wear it this morning, partly as a compliment to him and partly because she anticipated there being a moment when it might be better for her to leave her mother and father and Susan together and go down to the daftar to report back and arrange the day and time to resume duties. Which were not onerous. Never had been.

She decided on the uniform and emerging later and finding him with his head out of the farther window stood waiting for him to become aware of her, turn round and react. It was years since she had considered to what extent two girls had been a disappointment to him, years since she had been conscious as the first-born of being under some sort of obligation to make up to him for not being a boy; but standing there in uniform she realized that putting it on, today, was also partly an act of contrition, a way of saying: It's the best I could do. She was seeking approval as a boy might have done and this embarrassed her suddenly. She heaved the valise up on to the upper-bunk, heard him move, felt his appraisal. She glanced round.

'I say,' he said.

She faced him, smiling, awkward.

'How nice,' he said. 'How very nice. But you didn't tell me about the third stripe.'

1177

'It's very recent.'

'All the same. Sergeant. Jolly good.'

'I'll get the tea. Would you like a cold bacon sandwich?'

'Cold bacon?'

'Cold fried bacon. I got some last night in Ranpur from the station restaurant.'

'Did you, now! Then you ought to have a crown as well.'

She laughed and opened the hamper which he had lifted on to the seat in readiness for breakfast. She loved train journeys. In England as a child she had been disappointed to find how quickly they were over. In an Indian train one could put down roots, stake out claims, enjoy transitory possession for a day or so of a few cubic feet of carriage which even a change of trains did not seem to interrupt.

The hamper belonged to Aunt Fenny and was zinc-lined, with compartments for flasks, cups, knives, spoons, forks and food. The cold fried rashers for sandwiches were in grease-proof paper.

'And a new loaf!' her father said.

'I got them to slice it. I hope it isn't dry.'

'When was all this?'

'After we'd had dinner and you were seeing to the men. It's a surprise breakfast. Have a hard-boiled egg first?'

'Hard-boiled eggs too. Well done. No, I'll have a sandwich first.'

When she was a child and before the years of exile at school in England they had trekked on ponies through the Pankot hills, making camp at tea-time, striking camp at dawn; rather, the servants had made camp ahead of them and done all the striking. What's for breakfast? her father used to say. Hard boiled eggs and cold bacon sandwiches. With mugs of hot sweet tea. Eaten and drunk before the sun had risen and scorched the mist away. Night found her so tired that she slept before she had time to fix in her mind the position of the jackal packs in relation to the camp. That was the year of the map-reading lessons when she had been initiated into the mysteries of orientation, six point references and compass bearings; lessons begun on the verandah of Rose Cottage which had a view of the hills and distant peaks which he taught her to relate to the hatchings and contours of a map pinned to a board, under talc upon which the coloured chinagraph pencils left marks you could rub out with your finger and obliterate entirely with a rolled-up handkerchief. He taught her the tewt – the tactical exercise without troops – and she had seldom looked at a landscape since without being alerted to its topographical influence on what was or was not militarily feasible to perform in it. But she had never grasped as a man could do the points of weakness, the conditions that were favourable for the daring stroke that spelt success. Everything, hill, valley, hedge, tree, lake, river, bank, forest, seemed – militarily – overwhelmingly dangerous. So her military accomplishments really began and ended in the commissariat – providing hard boiled eggs and cold fried bacon sandwiches. These she could understand, appreciate, hunger after; and happily

1178

leave to him and to men like him the things that sharpened different appetites. Preparing a bacon sandwich now she thought of how he had virtually lost a regiment. She handed the sandwich to him, as it were in compensation.

He waited until she had made one for herself and then, looking at each other like old conspirators, they bit in, holding their hands up to catch crumbs.

'They taste better on a train,' he said, after swallowing. 'Something to do with the smoke and soot.' She poured tea into the mugs. Because they both liked it sweet she'd had the milk and sugar added in the flask: a thick strong picnic brew. The regular puffing sound of the engine came and went as it negotiated the bends and gradients on the hillside. She looked at her watch. One hour to go. He was at the window again, mug in hand.

'There they are!'

He waved and made room for her. Several carriages along the sepoys had their heads stuck out of the window of the special compartment Movement Control had reserved for them. They were grinning and waving. She waved back. One of them pointed. Perhaps his village was visible from here, or in this vicinity. But most of them came from the higher hills beyond Pankot. What a lot they had seen. What tales they could tell. In their villages they would be important men. They had seen the world and would be accounted wise in its ways. Their advice would be listened to. They would swagger a bit. The hands of the unmarried ones would be sought by parents with dowries and daughters. And a special distinction attached to them because Colonel Sahib had waited in Bombay until they were all fit enough to travel. That tale would be told far into the future. It was something he had done for them. They would always remember.

She waved again and turned back in. He was on the bench looking up at her, smiling, as if proud of them, of her; as if happy. But she knew he was not; not deeply happy. She offered him an egg and a twist of pepper and salt to dip it in after he'd cracked and shelled it. He began this operation and she sat beside him similarly occupied. In India, yes, one could travel great distances. But the greatest distance was between people who were closely related. That distance was never easy to cover. Is Sarah heartfree still? he had asked Aunt Fenny in private, but Fenny had told her and added, Are you pet? So that for a moment it seemed that she would refer to what had never been referred to since it happened. And what had happened constituted the greatest distance there could be between her and her father. Or did it? She would have liked to tell him. She believed he would understand. But the train rattled on and she said nothing. They cracked eggs.

I particularly remember the eggs (Sarah has said), the moment when, simultaneously, he became conscious of the mess we were making and I became conscious that it irritated him.

There followed the moment of revelation, that in his valise her father had an old clothes brush. He used this to sweep the crumbs and sharp little fragments of shell into *The Times of India* – after they had brushed down their clothes and the seat with their hands. He carried the folded paper into the w.c. and poured the contents down the pan.

When he came back he made no comment. Gradually her embarrassment spent itself. She looked at him encouragingly, alert to the possibility that he had something special to say for which the clearing up of the mess may have been a delaying tactic as much as anything else; and looking at him, came up against the barrier of his inarticulate affection, his restraint, his inner reservations – as solid an edifice as the rock-face that marks the end of the line from Ranpur to Pankot where the traveller gets down from the train several hundred feet below the hill-pass that leads into the Pankot valley.

Here there is a sound, neither far nor distant, but because the arrival of a train is always noisy the traveller may not notice it except perhaps as a faint singing in the ears or a gentle pressure on the back of the neck, a sound that does not vary in intensity. Full awareness may be delayed but when it comes identification is immediate. It is the sound of the streams and waterfalls that emerge from fissures and secret places in the rock: invisible from any part of the station or the concourse, above and around which the rock looms, softened by vegetation and (most mornings) mists which may gradually reveal themselves as drizzle, or burn away as the sun gets at them.

Somewhere along the road that winds up from the station the sound of rushing water is lost, but to know precisely where you would have to travel on foot, or order the taxi or the tonga to halt at every likely turn and twist, and listen, and in the one place where the driver would be prepared to obey such an order (the brow of the hill, at the pass where in the turning between rocks the whole panorama of the Pankot valley is suddenly disclosed) the sound has already gone and the ear is blessed by the holy silence that only the biblical clunk of goat-bells interrupts.

'*Thairo*,' her father said, at the same time leaning forward and touching the shoulder of the lance-naik driver whom Captain Coley had sent with the staff car to meet the train. Ahead of them the truck-load of ex-invalids careered on down the long straight road that led into the valley, making for the depot where some of their families waited for them. Her father's wishes had been scrupulously carried out. The arrival had been unremarkable; departure from the concourse delayed until only the truck and the staff-car remained. He had waited for a while in the carriage and, later, on the platform, until – within twenty minutes – the entire train-load of passengers had found or chosen their transport and gone. The sounds of the streams and the water were louder, then. Now on the brow of the hill, with

1180

the engine switched off and the windows open, he sat for a moment and then got out. She did not follow him.

After a while he got back in. He said 'Everything seems so much closer together,' as if in his absence Pankot had shrunk, the three hills which enclosed the valley been edged towards one another and squeezed up against the bazaar whose upper storeys of wooden balconies under steep-pitched wooden roofs rose above the mist into the clear morning air (which, Sarah saw, made them look nearer than they were).

Ten minutes later the car entered the V-shaped bazaar, at the low point of that letter: the square, with its war memorial, the meeting place of the road up into West Hill and the steeper road that thrusts assertively into the other hill upon which the British had chosen to build when they discovered in Pankot an ideal retreat from the hot weather in Ranpur. The main street, flanked arcaded shops, probably looked narrower to him. Passing the general store he said, 'Jalal-ud-Din', and smiled, shook his head, as if the store-sign was evidence of the indestructibility of Pankot's principal contractor. Jalal-ud-Din's shutters were still up. The first servant with a chit would not appear until nine o'clock. It would be ten o'clock before the first memsahib arrived to give an order and inspect the new stock. At this present hour there were few people and the car was not obstructed by tongas, cylists or cows. It continued, making for the junction of Church and Club Roads where the driver changed gear for the long uphill climb and where Sarah (as nowadays she always did) saw what her father couldn't: Barbie Batchelor's overturned tonga, the horse struggling, its leg broken, and the tin trunk, the cause of the trouble, upended in the ditch where it had burst open on impact and scattered its contents of missionary relics. From this scene of disaster Barbie had walked away, up Church Road to the rectory bungalow, mud-stained, clothes torn, still dazed and, according to the chaplain's wife, Clarissa Peplow, demanding a spade, still apparently harping on that old question: whether Mildred had buried Mabel in the wrong place, in the churchyard of St John's in Pankot instead of by the side of her second husband, Colonel Layton's father, in the churchyard of St Luke's in Ranpur.

'What was that?'

Had she spoken? He seemed to think so. She had been thinking: Poor Barbie. She might have said it aloud. She smiled, shook her head, looked out across the golf-course which had played a part in a dream Barbie had had and had liked describing, a dream that had ended in St John's and which Barbie interpreted as heavenly reassurance that her old friend Edwina Crane had been forgiven for taking her own life. But that was three years ago, after the riots of 1942. Now Barbie's dreams were waking ones, lived behind barred windows in Ranpur. I have nothing to give you in exchange, she had written, not even a rose: written on a pad because she no longer spoke – which made it more difficult than ever to tell what she remembered, if anything. But 'not even a rose' had shown some grasp of the

1181

past, some stubbornly held recollection of the time when she had been happy, with Mabel, in Rose Cottage.

The car was getting near to the cottage now and she found herself suddenly short of breath, as though her heart had begun to beat for both of them, and this seemed extraordinary to her because at the same time she was conscious of having, just now, as they passed the entrance to the club, also passed the point of any further personal involvement in his homecoming. When she thought of the things to be done and said during the next quarter of an hour her skin prickled with irritation. The familiar names at the entrances to the bungalows in the last stretch of the road to Rose Cottage increased her uneasiness. Her body pressed back hard against the seat, ostensibly to give him a better view, but he was not leaning forward to look, in fact he was pressed back too, or so it seemed to her from the sense she had of his body's alignment with her own. So far as she could tell they both sat thus, wedged into their corners, staring straight ahead or gazing obliquely away from one another through the nearest window, passive and reluctant rather than active and eager, and it occurred to her that perhaps he was as aware as she that so much more could have been made of their time together and that now it was over and the opportunity to know each other better gone, perhaps for ever.

'I think,' he said suddenly, and then jerked forward, touched the driver's shoulder. 'Stop here.' And hesitated before saying to her, 'If you don't mind. I'll walk the rest.' She nodded. He got out. Before he shut the door he asked her, 'Will you give me time to cope? Say five minutes?'

'Of course.'

She understood. In this way he could achieve a small measure of surprise. It did not offend her that he wanted to achieve it alone. He set off, striding easily, alert and upright, already – as he had said – dressed for the part but now performing it. The driver was puzzled, glanced over his shoulder, uncertain whether he was supposed to drive on, follow slowly or stay put. She said in Urdu: Wait here for five minutes. He switched off. He was too new to the regiment to remember her father personally. He had not been overawed by the occasion; proud, rather, of the part he was playing in it. She wondered whether he felt cheated of its climax. This was the time when she should jolly him along, like a good colonel's daughter, but she was disinclined to ask the formal questions, which her father had also omitted to do: What is your name? What village do you come from? What other family members have served in the regiment? Instead she lit a cigarette. As she clicked the lighter off her eyes met his in the driving-mirror. He looked down immediately, too quickly for her to judge his reaction but she supposed that smoking was one of the things that made Englishwomen sexless to boys like this; smoking, short skirts, uniforms; and the white skin that probably made the body appear composed of a substance that was not flesh but an unsatisfactory substitute whose erotic qualities only men similarly endowed could appreciate.

As she exhaled, this notion seemed to take form in the smoke and hang

1182

with it until it was sucked through the open window, leaving her with a profound sense of her misplacement in these surroundings. But there was no compensating sense of release from them because she could not easily imagine alternatives: to Pankot, yes, but the alternative to Pankot was still an Indian alternative, a variation of Pankot, and Pankot was already crowding in on her, threatening that illusion of serenity, of future possibilities, which had excited her the evening before, getting off the train at Ranpur. She was still in India, still of India. You could exchange one surrounding for another but not the occupation, an occupation less and less easy to explain and to follow except by continuing to perform it and seize opportunities to demonstrate – like the artist who carved angels' faces in the darkest recesses of a church roof and countered the charge that people couldn't see them by saying that God could – that dim as the light had grown it was still enough by which to see an obligation.

Five minutes had gone but she sat motionless, watching the smoke from her cigarette, unwilling to give the order to start up, unwilling to stir sufficiently to lift the cigarette to her mouth. From somewhere in the forested slopes a coppersmith-bird began its insistent high-pitched calling, a monotonous tapping sound of which she was usually only subconsciously aware but whose single rhythmically repeated note, coming just now, seemed to be counting the seconds away for her; and then, as it continued, encouraging her not to move but to listen, to surrender to its nagging persuasion until she entered a state of torpor or stupefaction, of which it might take some predatory advantage, reveal itself as a bird of more ominous intention, a bird of the species Barbie watched beyond the barred window, planing the sky above the invisible towers.

Abruptly it fell silent. The driver looked round.

'*Panch minute, memsahib?*'

'*Han,*' she said, '*lekin –*'

But what? Carefully she stubbed the cigarette in the chromium tray on the panel of the door, reluctant to bring the journey to a conclusion. Her capacity to feel or show family affection had diminished and in one area all but vanished. She felt closest now to Aunt Fenny who had seen her through the thing that happened to her. They had seen it through together, if such a lonely and love-less experience could ever be thought of as anything but solitary. Where there might have been recriminations between them there had been only a wounded but finally healing silence; healing because it had been warmed once by physical contact – Aunt Fenny's plump arm round her shoulders, Aunt Fenny's head against hers. Between herself and her mother there had been neither word nor gesture. Nothing. For her mother it had never happened. It was her mother's assumption of ignorance that hurt her most. Sometimes, holding Susan's baby and chancing to find her mother watching her, she felt she would have welcomed any response, even disgust, that showed her mother appreciated that the act of ministering to her sister's child was one that could fill her with the anguish of her own physical deprivation; and then, seeing no glimmer of recognition in that steady dispassionate gaze, she felt deprived again, of part of herself, of everything really except her guilt.

Her guilt was unquestionable but there was only one aspect of it which she was truly ashamed of, and this she bitterly regretted. She knew that behind her longing to talk about it to her mother lay a need for consolation and that this was a weakness, a form of self-indulgence. Understanding this she could live with her mother's silence, endless though it was as a punishment. For her mother the silence was part of the code, the standard: the angel's face in the dark. Or was it a demon's? Whichever it was it helped her mother to preserve an attitude of composure and fortitude and Sarah was able to admire her for it and see the point. In this way Sarah carved angel faces of her own and only at moments of acute distress had destructive impulses to tear the fabric of the roof and expose the edifice to an empty sky.

I shall walk the rest of the way, too, she told herself. And opened the door, got out, shut it, before she could change her mind. She told the driver to go ahead to the bungalow and wait. She stood in the road until the car had started then, following slowly, watched it as it took the last section of the hill. Rose Cottage was behind the next bend.

The coppersmith had resumed but from farther off, having flown to try its luck elsewhere or to plot another point in the boundary of its territory. She knew nothing of its habits, little of the lives of wild creatures whose co-existence with her own species created a mysterious world within a world; or rather, worlds, a finite but to her uncountable number, self-sufficient, separated, but intent on survival. She walked faster, to the tune of the distant coppersmith, and recalled with clarity the night of Susan's wedding in Mirat, wandering amidst the fireflies in the grounds of the palace guest house and saying aloud to her absent father: I hope you are well, I hope you are happy, I hope you will come back soon: and then turning back towards the house where Uncle Arthur sat alone on the lit verandah, a long way away from her, in a pattern of light, a circle of safety. My family, she had thought then. My family, my family.

She had said the words aloud and said them aloud again as she approached the entrance to the front garden of Rose Cottage. My family. My family. Before repeating the words she had not expected anything of them but at once she felt the tug of an old habit of affection and then a yearning for the powerful and terrible enchantment of inherited identity, which she had spent most of her adult years fighting to dispel; fighting as hard as Susan had fought to feel herself touched by it; and drawn into it, to its very centre, where she would no longer feel, as she had once confessed to Sarah she felt, like a drawing that anyone who wanted to could come along and rub out; that there was nothing to her except this erasable image. The first psychiatrist, Captain Samuels, had shown no special interest when Sarah mentioned it. He had simply said, What do you think that means? But had turned away to arrange things on his desk as if uninterested in her amateur opinions. So she had not answered and the question of Susan's idea of herself as a drawing people could rub out had never come up again, either with Samuels or with his successor, Captain Richardson.

But it had stayed in Sarah's mind as an explanation of her sister's self-absorption and self-dramatization. She did not understand what it was that had made Susan feel so inadequate and the discovery that she did had been a shock. Until then, the self-absorption had seemed to her that of a girl who not doubting her attraction demanded that others should provide her with constant evidence of its existence, and paid obsessive attention to the smallest detail when setting the scenes for these necessary acts of recognition. But the sequence of scenes that had made up – still made up – Susan's life could no longer be thought of as Susan playing Susan. It was Susan drawing Susan, drawing and re-drawing, attempting that combination of shape and form which by fitting perfectly into its environment would not attract the hands of the erasers. What Sarah feared now was that the game had stopped being a game, had become a grim and conscious exercise in personal survival; that Susan now drew and re-drew herself attempting no more than a likeness that she herself could live with; and that she might tire of the effort.

When she reached the open gateway which was flanked by two stone pillars, she paused, convinced that her father had done so too a few minutes ago. In Mabel's day the name of the bungalow was set out in metal letters fixed to an unpainted wooden board planted in the high bank that bordered the road. Over the years the colour of the metal had become hardly distinguishable from the wood. They had faded into the background, as Mabel had faded into hers, and left the board with a look of being indifferent to the arrival of strangers. The board was still there but was partially hidden by the wild growth on the bank. To see it at all you would have to know it existed. Its identifying function had been usurped by neat white boards, one on each of the stone pillars, announcing respectively in bold black lettering the name and number of the house and the name of its occupier: Colonel J. Layton. Yes, he would have stopped, confronted abruptly by this evidence of ownership, and then perhaps searched for the old board until he found it, probably in a place that didn't quite conform with the one he remembered.

She set off along the curved gravel drive between the rockeries which were vivid with the blue, white, yellow and purple stars of flowering plants. There had been rain in the night and the air was fresh, chill in the shadows of trees and bushes, but the sky was now cloudless and as she came to the end of the rockeries the sun heated her face.

The staff car was parked opposite the steps up to the square-pillared verandah. There was no sign of the driver. The thick-set white stuccoed bungalow looked deserted, but in the way a place could do that had only just been abandoned. Again she stopped. If she entered she would find the occupants gone, the signs of their presence still fresh and warm, and a strong odour of the danger from which they had fled. She had felt this once or twice before, but this morning the sensation was particularly strong.

And, looking at the bungalow, as it were through her father's eyes, she thought she saw for the first time what it was that sometimes gave this impression. By stripping it of anything that made it look 'cottagy' – pots of plants on the balustrades, flowering creepers round the square pillars – her mother had restored to it not its elegance (it could never have had that) but its functional solidity, an architectural integrity which belonged to a time when the British built in a proper colonial fashion with their version of India aggressively in mind and with a view to permanence. Exposed by the cutting back of trees and plants, set off by the new gravel on the drive and the widening of the forecourt (the rockeries were also earmarked for destruction) its squat rectangular bulk was revealed, and with it its essential *soundness*. The secluded, tentative air which Sarah had often associated with it in Aunt Mabel's time had quite gone. The name, Rose Cottage, given to it by a previous owner, a tea-planter, was now all too clearly, absurdly, inappropriate, and only the difficulty there would be with the *dak* had stopped her mother scrapping the name entirely and identifying the bungalow as 12 Upper Club Road.

In restoring it to a likeness of its former self, Sarah knew her mother had intended to create a setting that would speak for itself and also for her and her family's claim on history through long connection. The name Layton, and her mother's maiden name, Muir, under portraits on the walls of Government House in Ranpur and Flagstaff House and the Summer Residence in Pankot, on the drunken headstones in the churchyards of St John's and St Luke's, performed the same function of austere advertisement. In their dumb immobility they avoided the vulgarity of the words whose meanings they conveyed; but conveyed with so remote, so mute a self-awareness that even when identified they seemed thinned by irony. Service, sacrifice, integrity. And she had succeeded, but at a cost. By cutting away inessentials, the accumulations of years, she had robbed the place of a quality that belonged to that accumulation, the quality of survival and the idea behind it – that survival meant change. Restored, the bungalow no longer reflected the qualities of the people living there, it no longer fitted them as they truly were, so that – even when they were in it – from outside the bungalow looked empty, like a place of historic interest, visited but not inhabited. And, more than usually oppressed this morning by the sensation that she had arrived at a moment when it was deserted, she saw the bungalow in a sudden, shatteringly direct, light – looking as it looked now but even starker, uncompromisingly new amid the raw wounds left by space having been cleared for it; and on its verandah a white man in Indian clothes at ease in a cane lounging chair, or on a charpoy, attended by servants or by one of his Indian mistresses, and contemplating through the mists of claret fumes and cheroot smoke the fortune he had made or hoped to make out of private trade. The words whose meanings her mother had wanted to convey belonged to a later age, an age when the bungalow was already old. Unwittingly she had exposed the opposites of those words: self-interest, even corruption.

She made her way quickly, avoiding the steps, taking the path round the side, then stepping off it because the new gravel crunched, on to the new turf that had been put down on ground cleared of shrubs. The side verandah was empty but there was a spread blanket, a coloured ball and some bricks where the child had been playing. The doors to the room she shared with Susan were open. She hesitated. There was no sound of voices inside the house. Ahead she could see one side and corner of the high netting surrounding the tennis-court, and moving forward, widening the angle of vision, saw Minnie, the little ayah, inside the netting at the far end of the court, walking behind the child whose arms she held aloft by the wrists as he took faltering bandy-legged steps towards his mother. The centre net was not up and Susan sat on a blanket in the middle of the court at the point where the lime-marked centre lines met, with her back to the house, leaning on her right hip, her left arm stretched back, grasping one ankle, the other arm taut, hand palm down on the blanket, taking the weight. Close to this hand Panther II sat watching the child, scraping the blanket with his tail. Susan wore one of the full-skirted flowered cotton dresses that made her look eighteen still, too young to be a mother, touchingly too young to be a widow; and, round the shoulders, tied by its sleeves, a cardigan. The hairdresser had been – perhaps yesterday. The dark hair sported a crisp new set, a thick fringe of tight curls at the back that left her neck bare. When she spoke her voice carried. 'Come along then.' More faintly Sarah heard Edward's gurgling response. But suddenly he squealed. Minnie had picked him up and was running forward. She placed him on the blanket close to Susan and then retreated, ran to the opening at the side of the court and through it across the lawn towards the servants' quarters, as though this were part of a game of hide-and-seek.

But Sarah knew that it was not; guessed that the girl had seen Colonel Layton coming out into the garden and – partly out of shyness (for she was still very young and had never met the head of the household), partly out of unwillingness to intrude, or to receive yet the look or expression of gratitude which she had earned – put herself out of reach.

As if alerted by Minnie's sudden action, Susan had looked round, and now got to her knees, picked Edward up and stood facing the bungalow with her head down talking to the boy, holding his right hand out in the direction of his grandfather who now entered the court from the gate on the verandah side of the netting. At first Sarah thought he was alone, but presently she saw her mother following slowly, arms folded, one hand at her neck, pressing down her string of pearls. The hairdresser had attended her too. And Sarah did not recognize the jumper and skirt. Nor the shoes. They were new. Beside her mother and sister she felt travel-stained, dowdy in her uniform, excluded from the scene: from what she recognized *as* a scene – for all its appearance of evolving naturally from a sequence of haphazard events. It bore, for Sarah, the familiar mark of Susan's gift for pre-arrangement, or her continuing and frightening attempts to reduce reality to the manageable proportions of a series of tableaux which illustrated the particular crisis through which she was passing.

It would be better, she had said to her mother, *for you and daddy to be alone for a bit when he gets here, wouldn't it? So I'll be in the garden with ayah and Edward.*

In this way the true climax of his homecoming had been delayed, transferred from the scene with his wife to the scene with the daughter who had a grandson to present. And a dog. But no husband. Instead, the ghost of the soldier whom she had married. The ghost, and the living likeness of the man in the child. These were her gifts to her father and her current explanations to herself of what she was in the world's eyes and in his particularly: a promise for him of his continuity and in that promise perhaps she saw a dim reflection of promise for her own.

He stopped just short of mother and child, raised his arms, inviting a triple embrace. *It's grandpa*, Susan seemed to be saying. She held Edward up and after a moment's hesitation her father took him and holding him firmly under the arms raised him high. Edward gazed down at the stranger with an expression that from a distance struck Sarah as oddly dispassionate for a child so young. It was an expression she had seen before on Edward's face when confronted by men. He seemed to have a reserve, amounting to a vague antipathy, for grown members of his own sex. Almost alone among them, Ronald Merrick had inspired an early positive response, in spite of the burn-scars, the artificial hand. These had not frightened the child.

The one thing Edward seldom did when men touched him was cry; but his grandfather did not know this and perhaps interpreting Edward's failure to show pleasure or interest in being raised aloft as a warning that tears could quickly follow, put him carefully down on the nearest corner of the blanket and, straightening up, gazed at Susan.

Hello, daddy, she seemed to say. Then she covered her face with both hands and, standing so, was embraced. When she uncovered her face and raised her head to kiss and be kissed her eyes were closed and she was crying. Sarah could hear her. He began saying things to comfort and jolly her out of it. And although he must have noticed the puppy before he chose this moment to exclaim about it. They both looked down at Panther, broke apart and knelt together on the blanket. Introductions were made. Panther wagged his tail and skittered a bit, happy but cautious under the flurry of attention. Colonel Layton scratched the puppy's head, ruffled Edward's red curls, placed an arm round Susan's shoulders. She wiped her left cheek dry with the palm of her hand. The scene was over.

I can enter now, Sarah told herself.

By the time the car had negotiated the narrow lanes from the Samaritan Hospital of the Sisters of Our Lady of Mercy in the old city of Ranpur, through the Koti bazaar to the Elphinstone fountain, the street lighting was coming on.

Only one police squad remained of the force that had been out in the afternoon. The men were relaxed, awaiting the order to return to barracks. Traffic was flowing freely around the circus and access to the Mall and the Kandipat road was no longer restricted – signs that His Excellency the Governor had made the journey from the airfield out at Ranagunj back to Government House without incident and that news of Mr Mohammed Ali Kasim's brief stop in Ranpur, *en route* from Mirat to Pankot with the body of his secretary, Mr Mahsood, had not led to a popular demonstration in the latter case nor to an anti-government demonstration in the former – or certainly not one of the kind that got out of hand and at nightfall left the air charged with anxiety and irresolution.

As the driver turned into the Mall an Indian Sub-Inspector broke off conversation with a head constable, came to attention and saluted: the car rather than its occupant.

Rowan touched the peak of his cap then leant back and looked ahead to the still distant bulk of Government House, dark against the deep mauve northern sky and the grey pink-tipped storm clouds. The avenue of approach was bordered on each side by double rows of shade trees and the compounds of Ranpur's oldest European houses and bungalows. The sidewalks were as wide as the road. It was a processional route but seldom used for such an occasion because the way from the airfield where people usually arrived now lay to the east of Government House, beyond the cantonment.

The Mall, running for a measured mile and a half from the Elphinstone fountain to the Governor's residence, was bisected midway by Old Fort Road. In the middle of this intersection rose the bronze canopied statue of Queen Victoria. In 1890 that statue had been the cause of serious deliberations by the committee of the Ranpur Gymkhana Club. Unwilling quite to believe the story, since it seemed so perfectly apocryphal, Rowan had tackled the club secretary and eventually been shown the faded but still legible page of the committee's minute recording a bare majority vote against a proposal to paint the statue white to meet the criticism of members that, in bronze, Victoria – particularly in profile – bore an unhappy resemblance to a Rajput warrior lady of the kind who defied the British in the early decades of the century. The motion had been lost on the grounds of impracticability. A further motion that representations should be made to the appropriate department to try to ensure that any future replica of the Monarch should be executed in the best white marble was carried unanimously.

Although the Civil Lines officially began at the Elphinstone fountain, the Victoria statue was now regarded as the threshold. She stood on permanent sentry duty, accoutred with orb and sceptre, gazing with an air of abstraction towards the city. Behind her back the Mall continued, but on this second stretch there were no houses. The double lines of shade trees now bordered areas of flat open ground on which the military and police authorities could quickly establish command posts and hold reserve forces at time of civil disturbance. The line (or front) formed by Old Fort Road was considered the furthest that a civil demonstration should be allowed to march on Government House unless its intentions were clearly peaceful. Coming up the Mall from the fountain, riotous marchers invariably found the way blocked by squads of police, or soldiers, deployed across the road in front of the statue. The old houses and bungalows on the Mall between the statue and the fountain had long since been abandoned by the British and taken over by rich Indians. According to the British it was the inconvenience of places built in the late eighteenth and early nineteenth centuries which had caused their removal to the newer and better accommodation provided by subsequent building along Old Fort Road and on the cantonment side of Government House, although it was occasionally admitted that it would have been tedious to live on a route so frequently used by crowds of people making nuisances of themselves. The joke still current among the Indians, though, was that the British had lost their nerve and decamped, leaving their Queen behind.

To reach the Gymkhana Club Rowan would have to tell the driver to turn right at the statue and go along the eastern arm of Old Fort Road. He was tempted to do so. Since 1800 hours it had been his twenty-four hours off-duty. The prospect of beginning it with a dip in the club's pool, a drink or two on the terrace and a quiet supper alone in the annexe to the main dining-room, attracted him. He could send the driver back to Government House with a note for the duty-officer to say where he was. Or he could ring the duty-officer from the club to ask whether HE had asked for him, although that was unlikely. The twenty-four hours off-duty once a week was treated by Malcolm with rigorous respect.

But he gave the driver no instruction.

*

Having passed the sentries and the checkpoint inside the west gate they came out on to the forecourt of the west wing and pulled up at a certain point below the flight of steps leading to the great colonnaded terrace. Rowan signed the man's log-book, got out, went up and pushed through half-glazed double doors into the hall, full as usual with white-uniformed servants. He signed the duty book, marking himself OD, added his name to the mess list, went to check his pigeon-hole for letters and was handed two by the hall steward. Both felt like formal invitations. He went through the open half-glazed doors out on to an inner terrace, one of the four that flanked the inner courtyard: an immense rectangle laid out with intricate

1190

geometric precision and formality with lawns, paved walks, ponds and fountains. On ceremonial nights the fountains were floodlit but in the wet season were usually not even turned on. This evening the courtyard was lit only as far as the light from ornamental lanterns that hung from the apex of each section of the vaulted ceilings of the terrace could reach. Between the square pillars there were set great whitewashed tubs of hydrangea, geranium and bougainvillaea, and the ubiquitous crimson canna lilies. To reach the entrance to the staircase to his quarters Rowan had to walk past these almost to the end of the terrace and past the offices which coped with the routine work of the household. Most of these were shut and the benches provided for messengers empty, except outside the telephone exchange and the signals office which were manned round the clock, as was the cypher office, in the east wing, where Rowan spent most of his working day. He glanced across the courtyard. The first-floor windows of Malcolm's private rooms were lit.

Reaching the narrow door and the narrow staircase Rowan began to climb. His quarters were high up, on the second floor where the corridors were narrow, the rooms small, the ceilings low and the windows perpetually grimy. He had a sitting-room, a bedroom and a bathroom which suffered the drawback of having no running hot water. This had to be brought up from the basement in kerosene tins.

Without his bell, his telephone, and without the servants who manned the corridor, he might have felt himself marooned in a little oasis of inconvenience and for the first few weeks of his temporary appointment as an *aide* he had in fact suffered mild attacks of claustrophobia. But he had grown to see only the advantages of the place, even to be fond of it, and when offered something better on being transferred from temporary to official duty he had elected to stay. The quarters were supposed to provide short-term accommodation only and he was now the corridor's oldest inhabitant. One of the advantages was that the servants allotted to the corridor looked upon themselves now as virtually in his personal employ. He knew their histories, their weaknesses, their aspirations; helped them with their private problems and settled their disputes. He had never felt himself cut out to be a good regimental officer; but he was sufficient of a soldier to miss contact with men for whose welfare he was responsible. The servants were a surrogate.

Two of them greeted him now. One took a key from its hook on the board and another a sealed envelope from the pigeon-hole used for internal messages. Jaiprakash opened the door of his sitting-room and switched the lights and fan on. Rowan handed him the key to his drink cupboard and asked him to pour a whisky-soda. Jagram meanwhile went into the bedroom and bathroom, turning on lights and fans, then came back and went out to the corridor to call the bhishti. So it was, night after night.

To drink his whisky Rowan sat in his one comfortable chair. He opened the invitations, neither of interest to him, and then the envelope containing the internal mail. Two of the smaller envelopes inside contained bills. In addition there were various memoranda, the daily communiqué from the press office, a copy of a bread-and-butter letter from a senior officer of Eastern Command who had spent a few days at Government House and mentioned Rowan among those he thanked for making his stay comfortable. The largest envelope contained several cyclostyled pages: the general programme for the next few days, giving dates, times, functions, and the names of those members of the Governor's staff who were required to attend. Wherever his own name appeared the clerk had inked in an asterisk. Since Rowan had drafted most of the itinerary himself he glanced through it now mainly to refresh his memory and to check whether the Governor's private secretary, Hunter-Evans, had had to make any last minute changes.

Tomorrow night at 1930, when his day off was finished, he was to be at the reception in the state rooms for members of the Department of Education, the Municipal Board and the Ranpur Chamber of Commerce and at 2100 at the dinner for Mr Kiran Shankar Chakravarti who in the past few years had made several crores of rupees out of army contracts and had donated a sufficient number of them to found a department of electrical engineering at Government College.

At 10 a.m. the day after, he and Priscilla Begge (representing Sir George and Lady Malcolm respectively) were to welcome and escort to Government House Lady Burke from Delhi, whose interests were the Red Cross, the wvs and the work of women's committees, and in the afternoon he had another reception committee at Ranagunj airport to collect a popular English entertainer who had been touring Burma and Bengal and who was to stay at Government House and give a concert at the Garrison Theatre in the cantonment. On the evening of the same day he was to accompany the indefatigable Lady Burke and Mrs Saparawala, the vice-chairman of the Ranpur Women's War Committee, back to the station to catch the night train for Calcutta where they were to attend a conference. The day after that there was a morning meeting of the Executive Council followed by a lunch party for hh the Maharajah of Puttipur, and an afternoon visit to the quarries out at Rangighat. That was new to him. He hesitated, then remembering that the Maharajah was greatly addicted to the sight and sound of dynamiting, he took up a pencil and marked Rangighat with a stroke, to remind himself to check that someone had thought not only to warn the Ranpur Quarry and Construction Company of the Maharajah's visit but to tell them to be sure to have a few decent bangs laid on, even if they weren't scheduled, and whatever the weather.

In the evening the job of helping to entertain His Highness fell to a fellow aide, Hugh Thackeray, who was to accompany hh and General Crawford to the mess of the Ranpur Regiment. hh's son and heir, the Maharajkumar, was an officer in the fourth battalion. He had served in Burma and was presently in Rangoon. Thackeray, a Ranpur Regiment man himself, was also to accompany hh the following morning to pick up his private aeroplane at the airfield. In the afternoon of that day Rowan was to go with the Governor, the Member for Finance and the Member for Education, to the foundation-stone laying ceremony at the site of the new Chakravarti extension in the Government College grounds.

He put the itinerary away and thought how narrow his life sounded when set out like this. Jagram came back and went through to the bathroom. The familiar click of bolts on the corridor door meant that the bhishti was on his way up with the hot water. He took his whisky over to the desk, emptied his pockets and then his briefcase of all the papers connected with the day's assignments: at General Crawford's office, at the CID, at old Chakravarti's house. And – a private visit – at the Samaritan Hospital of the Sisters of Our Lady of Mercy. Among these last was the letter from Sarah Layton which had been written two days ago, on Saturday the 11th of August. She would not expect to hear from him so soon, nor perhaps when she did, by telephone. But it was to ring her, really, that he had come back and not gone to the club.

He unfolded the letter. The telephone number was there in the printed heading. He sat at the desk, spread the letter out and sipped whisky. This morning, because of its length and careful exposition, the letter had given him the impression of there being more urgency about the inquiry she asked him to make than she thought it fair to convey. He had already done what she asked. It would be nice to ring her to say so. But, exposed again to the letter's apparently casual tone he wasn't sure that he should.

Dear Nigel (she had written)

When we last met that time I was on my way to Bombay to meet my father you were generous enough to tell me never to hesitate to let you know if there were anything you could do for me in Ranpur. I hope you'll forgive me for taking you up on that so soon.

I think you'll remember my mentioning that whenever I came down to Ranpur I took the opportunity to visit a Miss Batchelor who used to live here at Rose Cottage as a PG of my father's step-mother, Mabel Layton. I'd just come away from seeing her that day you turned up at the Spendloves where I was staying a couple of nights before going on to Bombay. I was more grateful to you than you may have realized for persuading me to go along with you to those friends of Hugh Thackeray's, because seeing her in the state she'd reached was always discouraging. Her memory had gone, and so had her voice – she wrote everything down – but they said that was psychological. They assured me she was perfectly happy but it was such a depressing place I found that hard to believe.

Yesterday I heard in a roundabout way that she was dead and I confirmed this by ringing the Mother Superior at the Samaritan Hospital, where she was. I'd intended to ring ever since getting back from Bombay (just three days ago, on Wednesday) to find out how she was but kept putting it off. According to the Rev. Mother she died on Monday morning and was buried the following afternoon at St Luke's in Ranpur. She wasn't a Catholic, and was at the Samaritan because as you know theirs is the only place in the city that caters for Europeans who are ill in that way. All the arrangements both for her being there and for the funeral were made by the Bishop Barnard Protestant Mission Schools, which Barbie used to work for.

The line between Ranpur and Pankot is sometimes very bad and was yesterday. On top of that the Rev. Mother has a habit of not talking straight into the phone so she always sounds far away and if you keep asking her to repeat things she gets nervous. I mention this because I can't be sure whether the things I gathered remain to be dealt with are things the Bishop Barnard people have neglected or said they weren't interested in. She said she'd been going to write to me, so I asked her to do that, but she said she'd told me now and perhaps I'd call in (just like that, from Pankot!). I've never found her anything but competent and efficient but she has that curious nun's vagueness about anything she's not dealing with on the spot, face to face.

The trouble is that in all the time Barbie was a patient there I was the only person who knew her before she became ill who visited her, and the staff got into the habit of thinking of me as a sort of go-between if there was anything to settle between the Samaritan and the Bishop Barnard who – I must say, did rather keep their distance and seemed to think it was sufficient that the bills were paid regularly although that was all done by their lawyers who were also Barbie's. I didn't mind going to and fro, whenever I was down there, settling odd things the Samaritan had just let pile up until my next visit. I did rather want them to feel that I had an interest in Miss Batchelor and that poor Miss Batchelor had someone taking an interest in her. I'd always assumed I'd be told if she suddenly became dangerously ill or was dying. They had my Pankot address. The fact that I was in Bombay when it happened doesn't alter the fact that neither the hospital nor the Bishop Barnard seem to have tried to contact me. I suppose the Reverend Mother would have written to me eventually – all of which suggests mainly that whatever it is that seems to be a loose end can't be very important.

I rang the Bishop Barnard too but the Superintendent is on tour. Her deputy didn't know of anything still to be dealt with. She said everything of Miss Batchelor's had been removed from the Samaritan and signed for and was now in the Superintendent's room awaiting disposal. Since then she may have been in touch with the Samaritan and sorted out whatever it is that seems to be a loose end. 'Things you should deal with,' is all I could really understand when I spoke to the Rev. Mother.

Unfortunately the only person I know in Ranpur well enough to ask to look into it is on holiday in Kashmir. (Mrs Fosdick, Mrs Spendlove's sister.) And perhaps it's not a place I'd want to put Mrs Fosdick to the trouble of getting in touch with. Here, the Peplows, the rector and his wife, who took Barbie in for a while after she had to leave Rose Cottage, are in Darjeeling. Clarissa Peplow is one of the very few people who know that I kept tabs on how poor Barbie Batchelor was making out, and I know if she'd been here she'd have rung the Vicar at St Luke's and asked him to clarify things with the Rev. Mother. So I turn to you. If you have a moment, could you ring the Rev. Mother (The Samaritan Hospital of the Sisters of Our Lady of Mercy, Latafat Hossain Lane, Tank Road, Lower Koti Bazaar, Tel. 3124) and try to find out what 'has to be dealt with' and then let me know – by letter? I'd be awfully grateful. The line between GH and the hospital will probably be clearer and you always sound so calm and collected and in control of things she may be encouraged out of her vagueness.

Since there's been a Governor's conference in Delhi I realize you may still be up there with HE, in any case I know you'll be busy. Anyway, there's absolutely no rush about this, so really don't worry if for some reason or another there's nothing you can do. I've dropped Rev. Mother a line mostly about Barbie but adding that I didn't quite get the hang of the query she raised and have asked a friend in Ranpur to get in touch with her, since I can't get away myself just now. I expect if it's anything important she might write to me, but she never has before.

I was longer in Bombay than I expected. I expect you know why because I gather Sir George Malcolm had a reception committee waiting to welcome back the main body of the regiment when it got back three or four weeks ago. Father wasn't in awfully good shape and as a few of the men had to go into hospital in Bombay we stayed on until they were fit enough to travel. Incidentally, on my last day in Bombay I met Count Bronowsky and Ahmed Kasim and so was vividly reminded of first meeting you on Ranpur station and the game pie and champagne. We went on to an interesting but rather odd party at a flat supposedly belonging to a Maharanee but had to come away before the hostess had all the drinks locked up and turned us all out. Ronald Merrick was with us – my reluctant escort. He'd turned up in Bombay. He didn't want to go to the party but I insisted on going so he insisted on coming. He warned me not to say anything to the Count or to Ahmed about the job he's doing. Perhaps he didn't trust me not to. Anyway it was quite an evening, I'll tell you all about it when next we meet.

It looks as if everything's more or less over now that the Americans have bombed Nagasaki too and Russia has come in (some caustic comments here, about that). It will seem odd not to be at war with anyone. Father is looking much better now. I go riding with him every morning and don't turn up at the daftar until eleven or so, so I'm having an easy time of it.

Love, Sarah.

*

He lay the letter aside, glanced at the package and envelope the Reverend Mother had given him and then at his watch. At 7.45 on a Monday evening there was a good chance of finding her at home. But in the second reading he had been struck by that phrase 'and let me know – by letter'. It occurred to him that the members of her family might not be among those few people who knew she had kept tabs on Miss Batchelor and that her concern for the old missionary's health was one they did not share and would not approve of. He thought it would be very like her to respect their lack of concern by keeping her own concern to herself; just as a year or so ago she had respected their reasons for not calling on Lady Manners when they found themselves on neighbouring house-boats in Sringar, but had herself ignored the barrier the conventional world put up, by crossing the few yards of water on a day when she was alone and could do so without causing fuss or offence, and visited that old and enigmatic woman. She had attributed her action to curiosity. Initially she had used the word morbid, but then said, 'No, that's not right. But I was curious to see her, and the child.' Later she had said something odd, which interested him. 'In a way I think I envied her. But I'm not sure why.'

From the bathroom came the sound of water being poured into the tub. Deciding it would be better to relax in a tepid bath before making up his mind whether to ring her or write to her, he went into the bedroom and began to undress. While he did so he thought of their last meeting and of the time they had spent together; and of their first meeting, just over a year ago.

IV

Her quiet self-reliance had been the first of her qualities to impress and attract him. Her unexpected entrance ahead of Dmitri Bronowsky into the gilt and red plush railway carriage had caught him unprepared, caused him some difficulty – sitting as he was with briefcase on knee and a finger keeping the page of the file of documents he had been studying during Bronowsky's absence.

It was an intrusion he would have welcomed if she had brought into that baroque interior a classic air of feminine elegance. But she was in uniform, and this was crumpled. She looked travel-worn, hastily pulled together, like someone Bronowsky had just rescued from a crush on the platform, although the side platform where the Nawab's private train was drawn up was almost empty. It was not until she had taken her cap off and was sitting next to him on one of the ornate Louis xv-style salon chairs, in the light of the crimson shaded lamps, drinking champagne and smoking one of Count Bronowsky's pink-papered and gold-tipped cigarettes, smiling at the old man's gay reminiscence of his earlier émigré life in the south of France, that the first impression was overtaken by another: that in her unusual, perhaps plain, way she was beautiful. The bone structure of her face was prominent but lacked the arresting emphasis which would have made it striking. Her face had to be studied before it revealed its natural and incontrovertible logic, and then one felt instinctively that it would endure, that in old age it would be marked by the serenity of understood experience and the vitality of undiminished appetite.

'What a sad story,' she said when Bronowsky finished the tale of the eighteen-year-old English boy who had loved and lost a Spanish girl; lost because he could talk to her only in English or in the schoolboy French Bronowsky had been hired to correct and improve. The story was subtly turned. Many girls would have laughed blankly – or, had they been aware of Bronowsky's reputation and hence of the fact that he was probably recounting the tale of a lost love of his own (the boy), not even smiled. But, 'What a sad story' was what she said and then glanced at Rowan. It was no more than a glance but to him extraordinarily eloquent, and continuing to watch her it struck him that she was in love herself, that she was sustained by that, protected from all malice and unkindness and shallowness by the intensity of her commitment to the man she had chosen and the depth of her conviction that her own life was now set on a course that would bring more happiness than sorrow. The expression on her face was like that on Laura's when Laura broke it to him that she had changed her mind and was going to marry a man called Ratcliff.

He believed that what Laura must have felt for Ratcliff this girl – whose first name he did not know – felt for an unnamed man. This was so clear to Rowan that his mind played the trick of confusing her with Laura and the unknown man with Ratcliff, and he recalled quite vividly the feeling of helplessness which had underlain the stronger emotions of jealousy and anger and which had come full circle when he heard that Laura and her planter husband had become prisoners of the Japanese in Malaya.

Bronowsky called for another bottle of champagne. It was his seventieth birthday, he explained. Spending it on duty, he had equipped himself with special comforts. The salon, got up to look like that of a travelling nineteenth century European monarch with cosmopolitan tastes, was an appropriate setting for such a celebration.

'What news of your father?' Bronowsky asked, turning the conversation from himself to Miss Layton. All Rowan knew from Bronowsky's introduction was that Miss Layton was the sister of a girl who had been married in Mirat and that she had stayed with her family at the palace guest house before and after the wedding. Her father seemed to be away – at some distance – she had not heard from him recently. There was a mother. The sister was mentioned again. Miss Layton said they were both well. She herself had just been to Calcutta. She had an aunt and uncle there whose surname was Grace.

'And the officer who was best man at your sister's wedding,' Bronowsky went on. 'Captain Merrick. Have you had news of him? He interested me considerably. I thought him an unusual man.'

Spoken casually like that in these strange but civilized surroundings the familiar name, Merrick, had the same disconcerting effect as a sudden change in the intensity of light. He found himself concentrating on certain essentials. The girl was a stranger, not Laura. The Merrick she and Bronowsky knew need not be his Merrick. But her manner had altered. The prominence of bone seemed more accentuated. This, perhaps, was imaginary. She said that it was to visit this Merrick in hospital that she had gone to Calcutta. This Merrick, her Merrick, had been wounded and a

Captain Bingham killed. Her Merrick had tried to help someone called Teddie and had lost an arm. He had pulled Teddie out of a blazing truck while they were under fire. He was in for a decoration. Captain Bingham and Teddie must be one and the same man. She had gone to see her Merrick in hospital because her sister was anxious to find out if there were anything they could do.

This Merrick had been best man at her sister's wedding. Whose best man? Teddie's? It sounded like that. If so the sister was already widowed; still prostrate, perhaps; well in health but not fit to travel; which might explain why she had sent her sister all the way to Calcutta to talk to the man who had lost an arm trying to save her husband. 'Physical courage,' Bronowsky was saying, 'you could see he had that.' Meaning *her* Merrick. On asking which arm Merrick had lost and being told the left the old man was quiet for a moment. 'That's something,' he said. 'I observed him picking up bits of confetti, also stubbing a cigarette. He was right-handed.'

How painstakingly observant. Rowan glanced up and found Bronowsky watching him through that one appraising eye.

'You may remember the man we're speaking of? Merrick?'

'No, I don't think so.'

'I don't mean you would remember him personally. He went into the army from the Indian Police. He figured rather prominently in the case involving an English girl, in Mayapore in 1942. The Bibighar.'

Her Merrick. His Merrick. The same man.

'Oh yes. That case.'

'He was District Superintendent. In Mirat I had a long and interesting talk to him and found him utterly convinced that the men he arrested were truly guilty. I myself and I suppose most people since have come to the conclusion that they couldn't have been.'

Bronowsky was wrong. At the top of the administrative hierarchy, yes, one could say that, but even there the suspicion that Merrick had blundered was tempered by a determination not to allow it to be officially admitted. Uncorroborated and inadmissible evidence that in the case of Hari Kumar the blunder was one of a peculiarly unpleasant kind looked like having to remain a haunting burden on the consciences of a few. The irony of Merrick's act of bravery and the recommendation for a decoration was not lost on Rowan. It would justify the opinion originally held by the rank and file of the administration, and never truly altered, that in the Manners rape case Merrick had acted with that forthright avenging speed which had once made the *raj* feared and respected, and India a place where men did not merely operate a machine of law and order, but ruled and damned the consequences of ruling.

'It would have been understandable,' Bronowsky went on 'if Merrick had begun to waver in his opinion – unless you accept that he left the police temporarily under a cloud and harboured a grudge. But he had tried for years to get into the army. He was a very ordinary man on the surface but

1198

underneath, I suspect, a man of unusual talents. Are those boys still in prison?'

'Which boys are those?' Rowan asked.

'The ones arrested, not tried, but detained, as politicals.'

'I'm afraid I don't know, Count.'

The old man smiled, possibly to convey that his inquiries were made only out of general curiosity.

'I hope they are not forgotten and just being left to rot. The provincial authorities have an obligation in this matter, surely?'

'I'm sure they are not just forgotten.'

'The Indians remember. Unfortunately not only Indians of the right sort. There is a venerable gentleman of Mayapore who last year visited Mirat and engaged in some tortuous processes of intimidation.'

Another name clicked into place in Rowan's mind, but again, as in the case of Merrick whom he had never met, a name without a face. The name was Pandit Baba but the face was Harry Coomer's – Kumar's rather, quite unrecognizable, unidentifiable with the boy Rowan had known as Coomer: hollow-cheeked, prison-pale under the brown skin: the voice was Kumar's too, describing Pandit Baba of Mayapore in that halting staccato way: *I knew him as a man my aunt hired to try to teach me an Indian language – He smelt strongly of garlic – He was very unpunctual – the lessons weren't a success.*

Between each short sentence there had been a pause, as Kumar focused on an image, probably long forgotten. The manner in which he answered the question was what first suggested to Rowan that the documents he had studied and which were damning, damning to Kumar, were not going to stand up. It was the manner of a man talking to himself as well as to the two men on the other side of a table; searching his memory for certain details to convince himself of the reality of things he knew had happened to him but had preferred not to think about for a long time. For Rowan, this careful answer to his unimportant question about Pandit Baba had been the first of a series of answers, brief spoken meditations, which drove a persistent unwavering line through recurring doubt and uncertainty, until they culminated in that shatteringly casual remark which he believed he would never forget and which had finally convinced him Kumar must be telling the truth: *It's difficult to breathe in that position. It's all you think about in the end.*

Was Pandit Baba the man Bronowsky meant, the venerable gentleman from Mayapore who had been in Mirat? What he had gathered from Kumar of the Pandit's talent for avoiding trouble and leaving his young followers to carry the can made 'tortuous process of intimidation' sound right. But whom had he intimidated?

Bronowsky had turned to Miss Layton. 'The stone,' he said, 'you recall the stone – was certainly thrown at the instigation of this slippery customer. He is one of those on whom we keep a watchful eye. I am told he has recently left Mayapore, but I am not told where he has gone or why.

Forgive me, it is an uncheerful subject.' Again he looked at Rowan and then began to rise. 'And Miss Layton must eat. We shan't wait for Ahmed. In any case he's probably only going to be interested in the champagne.'

Rowan looked at his watch. Young Kasim and his mother were already half-an-hour late. He hoped they wouldn't cut it too fine. After half-past midnight the line to Premanagar would be closed to them by the regular service. It would be 2 a.m. before it could be opened again for the Nawab's private train.

Bronowsky leant over him, lightly touched his arm. 'We shall be able to leave on the scheduled time. Ahmed will see to it. Come.'

As he followed Miss Layton in to the dining-salon he smelt the delicate scent of cologne and pictured her dabbing her wrists and neck and forehead with it to relieve the tensions and staleness of the journey from Calcutta. She turned round and spoke, saying something complimentary about the *fin-de-siècle* splendours of the Nawab's train, but he did not quite catch it. He bent his head inquiringly. He was very close to her. He was disturbed again, but in a way that did not become clear to him until later when they were eating game pie and drinking more champagne and she was telling them about her uncle's new job in Calcutta, which was to run courses of lectures to attract wartime officers to the post-war civil administration.

She discussed the logic of this. She spoke well and clearly, in control of a line of argument that was undogmatically developed. He suspected that she was not strong on small talk, that in company she found uncongenial she might even appear shy or withdrawn. The champagne helped perhaps, and Bronowsky was a skilful and encouraging listener, capable of charming anyone out of shyness, particularly good-natured and well brought up girls for whom he presumably felt the gallant, undemanding and guarded affection of the aging homosexual.

As she spoke Rowan saw how, indirectly, she was making a point: that the situation of these men who attended her uncle's courses – those who would succumb to the obvious temptations and those who would take a calculated risk – was in exaggerated form the same situation in which she, every English person of her generation in India, Rowan himself, found themselves. The outlook was shadowy but one could not (she implied) make this an excuse for working at half-pressure, nor for standing back from a job that was there to be done. In the course of her argument she used the word Indianisation, which suggested that the one criticism of her uncle's efforts she would accept as valid was that they were not officially directed as thoughtfully as they could have been to that end. In a girl of her type such a view was unusual. It was one he shared. It had lain immature and unformed behind his youthful decision to seek a military and not a civil career in India; a decision he had regretted and sought to remedy before the war by undergoing a probationary period in the Political Department, in the hope of transferring to it permanently and applying what talent he had to the problems of the constitutionally backward

Princely states. It was in these that he still saw the most satisfactory opportunities, the chance, when he was fit again, to do some useful work.

The oval table was covered in white damask, it glittered with silver. From the centre-piece – a gilded wicker basket of white and scarlet carnations set amid ferns which trembled in the currents of air from the electric fans – came the dry delicate scent of the flowers. Watching her, still thinking yes she is in love, he put his finger on what it was that disturbed him. Had Kumar after all been lying? It didn't seem possible to place the image of Kumar's Merrick alongside Miss Layton and then see them in a relationship at all, let alone one of intimacy. She had not contradicted Bronowsky when he said that most people now assumed Merrick had made a mistake but she had not agreed either. She had said nothing. But Calcutta was a long way to go even on a mission of the kind he'd gathered it was – one involving the gratitude – in other words the honour – of the family. Her aunt and uncle could have undertaken it far more easily and just as effectively.

He sat patiently, talking little, awaiting an opportunity to find out more about her. Bronowsky was now telling stories of pre-revolutionary St Petersburg, of his émigré life in Berlin and Paris and Monte Carlo, but omitting (as he was reputed always to omit) the most interesting tale of all, which was perhaps apocryphal; the story of his successful negotiation between the Nawab, then a young man, and the European woman whom the Nawab had followed from India in a towering Oriental passion at being deceived: a negotiation for the return of jewelry the young prince had given her as any ordinary young man might give a girl a diamond engagement ring on the assumption that she would return it if she backed out. What pressure Bronowsky had brought to bear on the woman was a matter for conjecture (Rowan had heard several versions) but when the Prince returned to Mirat without the woman, according to the story, he had the jewelry, and he also had Bronowsky for whose tact and skill he was supposed ever since to have had the deepest admiration; an admiration that was not shared by the Political Department until they could deny no longer that under Bronowsky's guidance the wild and potentially dissolute young prince had become a model of rectitude and political wisdom.

The return to the salon for coffee brought no change of subject. The old man talked on and presently Rowan noticed that Miss Layton had become anxious about the time, about what was happening on the platform. Obviously she had a connection to make. It was twenty minutes to midnight. The only train he knew of due to leave Ranpur at that hour was the nightly train up to Pankot.

'I must go, I'm afraid,' she said, putting down her cup. Bronowsky pleaded for another five minutes but she said, 'If I stay another five minutes I shall never want to go, and I've got my compartment to get unlocked.'

They stood up. Bronowsky kissed her hand, thanked her for her

1201

company, asked her to visit Mirat again one day. She said she would like that, then turned to Rowan.

'Goodbye, Captain Rowan.'

He said, 'I'll see you to your compartment.'

But Bronowsky claimed that as his own privilege and there was nothing for it but to stand aside and let her go.

*

Just before midnight while Bronowsky was still absent young Kasim arrived with his mother, who was in purdah. He did not introduce her to Rowan but took her straight to the adjoining carriage where there were sleeping berths. At five past midnight Bronowsky came back. There were consultations with railway officials. Rowan settled in a corner, smoked, read documents, trying to reconcentrate on the matter in hand. The train left on time. He declined to join Bronowsky and young Kasim in the dining-saloon. From behind the closed curtains he heard Bronowsky's voice. He considered going to bed but the steward had brought him brandy and he sat on, drinking this, and doubting that he would sleep in the few hours it would take to reach Premanagar where he and Ahmed were to leave the train for the rendezvous at the Circuit House with Mohammed Ali Kasim, who was probably sleepless too, keeping watch through the small hours of his last night as a prisoner in the Fort.

Rowan did not envy young Kasim the task he had undertaken, that of breaking the news to his father that Sayed had been captured fighting in the INA and that the release from the Fort was only a partial release, that he was to live now under restriction, in the protection of his kinsman the Nawab. Rowan's own part in the affair was of minor importance. Officially he was merely representing the Governor, but it was the second time Malcolm had given him a job that fell outside the ordinary limits of the duties of an *aide*. The first had been the examination *in camera* of Hari Kumar at the Kandipat jail, little more than three weeks before. It interested him that tonight he should have found himself face to face with two people who knew Merrick.

But how well did they know him? He sipped his brandy, closed his eyes and put his head back. The kind of knowledge he had in mind was the sort one could describe as elusive; to her, perhaps, inaccessible; as obscure as the dark side of the moon. It irked him that he could do nothing to warn her of its existence. Its possible existence. Merrick was protected by shadows of doubt that could never be dispersed, and by the iron system of the *raj* itself. If there had been a weakness, a fissure through which rumour and conjecture could flow and adversely affect Merrick's future, it had now been sealed up by the heroic act.

Rowan smiled, but at the irony of it, and – opening his eyes – found Bronowsky sitting opposite him, smiling too. The carriage, well-carpeted and sprung, ran smoothly and quietly. Bronowsky must have come in at a moment when the train was crossing points.

'Have I woken you?' he asked, raising his voice just sufficiently above the muffled rhythmic clatter for Rowan to hear him clearly across the width of the carriage. 'If so I owe an apology. Your dreams were obviously pleasant ones.'

'Satisfying recollections. I hadn't expected such a splendid supper.'

'Nor such charming company? I met her but the once, in Mirat, when they were staying there for the wedding, and tonight out there on the platform I didn't recognize her in uniform. Many girls would have been piqued, at the same time thankful not to have to stop and exchange banalities with an elderly foreigner. But Miss Layton made herself known. In Mirat I underestimated her. I marked her down as shy, even as a trifle colourless in the way – forgive me – that only well-bred English girls can be colourless. But I now see what it was. In Mirat she was taking a back-seat because it was her sister's wedding and the sister is extremely pretty and vivacious. Or was. Now she is expecting a baby, and already a widow. She and Captain Bingham had such a brief time together. He was killed in Imphal in April. I saw the notice and wrote to them but I knew nothing of the dramatic circumstances until tonight.'

Rowan nodded. A pregnancy could explain why Miss Layton rather than her sister had travelled to Calcutta.

'I've not been in Ranpur long enough to know everybody,' he said. 'Are they a Ranpur family?'

'Yes, but they've been in Pankot since the father went abroad on active service. He commanded the 1st Pankots in North Africa. He's a prisoner of the Germans. Then there was her grandfather, who was a distinguished civilian, Finance Member of Council here in Ranpur during the previous war. And her maternal grandfather, General Muir, was General Officer commanding, also in Ranpur, early in the Twenties.'

Rowan nodded.

'And you, Captain Rowan? I see you were in Burma, presumably during the retreat. But nevertheless effectively. Or do you affect the traditional indifference to the Military Cross and pretend that it came with the rations?'

'It sometimes seems the only satisfactory explanation.'

'Were you wounded?'

'Only exhausted. It was a long march.'

'You have been ill?'

'I think, rather, debilitated.'

'The malignant and endemic fevers that used to cut life short but have learnt subtler methods of invasion. Quite. Our court physician, who doubles that far from onerous rôle with the slightly more exacting one of Minister of Health in our little Council of State and runs a hospital in his spare time, has a theory that it is only the lethargy induced in Englishmen by low but persistent tropical fevers, the lethargy and its corollary, the concentration of mental and physical resources on a particular task, that has kept the *raj* stubbornly intact. He says that the moment medical science finds a way of rendering the English bloodstream and the English bowel system immune to the attacks of Indian microbes and amoeba, then the English will all perk up, look around and wonder what on earth they are doing out here, and as a consequence roar with laughter and resign. He cites as an example of depressive and obsessive behaviour the case of General Dyer, who shot all those unarmed Indians in Amritsar in nineteen-nineteen, believing that by doing so he was saving the Empire. Habbibullah is convinced that the poor old fellow's brain was inflamed by the accumulation in the blood stream of the poisons of chronic amoebic infection. Of course he tells me all this because he is convinced that as a European I am similarly infected, in spite of my protests that for my age I am in vigorous good health and have never shot anyone, armed or unarmed.'

'Actually I believe General Dyer had arterial sclerosis and died of it quite a few years later, but it's one of the slow diseases, isn't it? Someone did once suggest to me that it could have affected his judgment at Jallianwallah.'

'I didn't know that. I must tell Habbibullah. How nice to meet a young Englishman who knows a bit about the country's history. Dyer was another man who made a mistake, or acted controversially, and remained convinced to the end that he had been absolutely right.'

Rowan did not reply immediately. He wondered whether the allusion to Merrick was intentional.

'It surprises me a little, sir. That you should feel that. Most Englishmen who work out here have to be pretty well informed, surely. Not that knowing about Dyer is much of a test.'

Bronowsky smiled at him and leant forward, with his hands one on top of the other, supported by the ebony cane that was probably not as necessary an aid to balance as he made it appear.

'I exaggerated, yes. But one meets so many young officers who turn out to be here only because of the war and who know nothing. Mention General Dyer to them and they say, Oh, which division is he? It's different with the hard core of the professionals, which I take it you belong to. Do you have family connections with India?'

'Only on my mother's side. My father was out here at one time, but in the British Army.'

'Ah. I have been uselessly sifting my old memory for a Rowan. What was your mother's maiden name?'

'Crawley.'

The old man lowered his head, raised one finger and placed it on his chin.

'Crawley,' he repeated. 'There was a Thomas Crawley who was Resident at Kotala. He ran things very successfully during the ruler's minority. Were he and your mother related?'

'He was her brother, but considerably older. Did you know him?'

'Only by reputation. In latter days he experienced some difficulties. It was a pity. Have you had anything to do with the Political Department yourself?'

'I worked a probationary year just before the war.'

'Indeed. Your ambitions lie in that direction? But the army reclaimed you for the war no doubt. Where were you? Presumably not in Kotala?'

'No, but I did meet the Maharajah in Delhi.'

'How did that go?'

'Not at all, at first. When I told him Crawley had been my uncle he sheered off.'

'You told him voluntarily?'

'It would have been unfair not to. He was in one of his expansive moods, inviting people at random.'

'Inviting them to what?'

'One of his famous parties at the palace in Kotala.'

'That must have been a temptation. To see the place where your uncle spent the best part of his working life.'

'Yes, it was. My mother lived with him at the Residency for two or three years before she went home to get married. I'd seen all the photographs and heard all the tales about how it was in those days, and quite a bit about what happened after the ruler came of age. But I felt I'd only get the best out of a visit if I went openly as Tommy Crawley's nephew.'

'You said the meeting with the Maharajah didn't go well at first, that he sheered off. Did he change his mind?'

'Yes but I don't know how quickly. He must have kept tabs on me through his grapevine, though, because a couple of months later when I was touring with the agent for a small group of states north of Kotala I got a letter from him inviting me to call. It was a bit of a poser because it meant getting clearance from the department as well as from the Resident in Ranikot.'

'Why Ranikot?'

'When Uncle Tommy left Kotala the agency was transferred to the group that came under Ranikot. The Resident there put an assistant in at Kotala but everything had to go through him.'

'That can't have pleased the Maharajah.'

'It wasn't meant to. By regrouping his state and severing his direct link with the Crown Representative, the department thought he'd be upset enough to withdraw the accusations he'd made, that my uncle was interfering in private and state matters to an intolerable degree, not only withdraw but beg to have him sent back. I think they were looking forward to telling him it was too late and were rather surprised when he made no complaint.'

'Why too late?'

'Well my uncle was getting on and the strain of their constant bickering had ruined his health. My mother came out to see him in Simla while he was on sick leave and tried to persuade him to retire at once and not wait

1205

the two or three years he still had to go. She wasn't at all surprised when we met her off the boat and told her Uncle Tommy had died while she was on the passage home. The Maharajah wrote to her offering his sympathies. She'd known him well when he was a boy but didn't feel up to sending him more than a formal acknowledgment. When I was coming out, though, she said that if ever I bumped into young Kotala I should give him her salaams.'

'And did you?'

'Yes. He was very touched.'

'You accepted his invitation, then, in spite of the red tape. Good.'

'I'm afraid I couldn't. The officer I was touring with was dead against it, and actually a private trip on the side would have been a bit much for him to agree to because I was dogsbodying for him in a fairly hectic programme and supposed to be learning the ropes. So I wrote begging off. But I gave him my mother's message and said I hoped there'd be another opportunity of meeting. A week later he turned up at our next stopping place. He'd driven more than a hundred miles.'

'Was he so anxious to apologize for his treatment of your uncle?'

'He apologized for sheering off. I was afraid of the other thing too. I'd worked it out years before, from all the things my mother told me or let slip that the fault had really been my uncle's. I think she'd reached the same conclusion. As you said, he virtually ran the state while the prince was a minor and apart from that they'd formed an extremely close and affectionate father-and-son relationship. When the prince came of age all that should have stopped. My uncle should have stood back and been content to let the young man assume full responsibility, but he made the error of continuing to treat him as a minor, of forgetting that he was a ruling Hindu prince. And, of course, that must have led to a situation in which the prince's relatives and his state officials made it clear that they despised him for letting the Resident browbeat him and that if he had an ounce of real spirit he'd start showing my uncle where to get off. Unfortunately he did that in a young man's over-exuberant way, spending money wildly on personal extravagances, drinking too much and womanizing, all the things that gave my uncle the opportunity to press his criticisms. In fact after a year or so you only needed evidence of cruelty and corruption and complete disregard for the welfare of his poorer subjects to have had a case to depose him.'

'And there was no such evidence.'

'I imagine the only harm the Maharajah ever did to anyone was to himself. And I think he felt that. I'd say it still rankled. I got the impression he would really have liked to be abstemious and upright, all the things my uncle no doubt represented to him as virtues when he was growing up, hated being unable to resist other temptations and blamed my uncle for that as well. Well as I say he apologized for sheering off when we first met but when it got to the point where it was obvious one of us ought to mention Uncle Tommy he became very edgy. He'd driven all that way so I felt the ball was in my court, but I was reluctant to play it. I'm ashamed to admit I thought there might be a price-tag on the whole thing, that the idea was to soften me up by a display of magnanimity or remorse so that I'd agree to put a word in for him over some scheme he might have going.'

'Well, you'd been in the country just long enough to suspect he might think you new enough to try it on. How did you play the ball?'

'I didn't. I shirked it. So just before he got into the car to go back he confronted me. It's the only word. Have you ever met him?'

'No. Not the maharajah. We've never been to Kotala and he's not in the Chamber. Insufficient guns.'

'Quite tall. Very plump. He uses scent and wears rings. Diamonds mostly. There was even a small jewelled cockade in the centre of his turban. I think you could call Kotala the walking effete-looking Indian potentate of popular English imagination. It isn't an image that conveys what *we* mean by dignity whatever it may convey to Indians, but ever since that day I've tried not to prejudge from appearances. I don't think anything could have been more dignified than his parting speech. He said he was glad to have met Tommy Crawley's nephew, trusted we'd meet again and have the opportunity to build a relationship on the friendly basis he hoped we'd established, but that this wouldn't be possible from his point of view unless I knew and accepted that although he had loved my uncle as a boy and had happy memories of those times, he had had a terrible time with him later, which he would never forget and could never forgive. He said, "When I was young your uncle was always saying, when you know you are in the right, fight for it, never give in, never retreat and never retract. My opinion is that in that matter I was right and he was wrong. If I regret anything it is the nature of the weapons he forced me to use and the nature of the balm he forced me to resort to to heal the wounds he inflicted." I was so impressed that when he'd gone I went straight to my room and wrote it down.'

'A prepared speech,' Bronowsky said, 'but effective. I should think sincere. Yes. Very English in its sentiment, but of course very Indian too. He was testing your mettle and temper as well as getting something off his chest. What did you say?'

'The first thing that came into my head. Afterwards I realized I was lucky he hadn't made a speech like that when I first met him. In the interval I'd been around and cottoned on to the system, the one that calls for the ruler to stand his ground and you yours but for you both to open up the ground between without committing yourself to occupy it. I said I personally knew very little of the quarrel between them except that my uncle had been deeply affected by it, had presumably felt as strongly about the correctness of his own behaviour, that I'd always regretted my uncle's career should have ended on such a note but would regret it far more had it seemed now that their differences after all hadn't been so serious that they couldn't somehow have been overcome, and was most grateful to His Highness for speaking so frankly and relieving my mind of any such supposition.'

1207

'Were you alone with him?'

'Yes, why?'

'A pity. If your superior officer had heard that, I imagine you'd have received a most favourable report.'

'Actually I'm not at all sure it didn't raise a doubt about my fitness for political work. I was questioned pretty closely about what we'd said to each other and was made to feel I might do better if I applied myself more conscientiously to routine matters.'

'Young men with an aptitude usually excite caution rather than enthusiasm. It has ever been so. But you will probably survive. I trust so. If you have ambitions there still. Do you?'

Rowan smiled. He said, quoting, '"The body's fever, dying like a fire, Sheds little light upon the heart's concerns." '

'Ah,' Bronowsky said after a moment. 'Gaffur. But a somewhat more elegant translation than the one in the existing English version. The fading fever in the blood is like a dying fire, de dum de dum etcetera. But how apt. Gaffur, recovering from a bout of malaria or dysentery. Is that other version your own? Yes? Then we have one vice in common, although my own translations from the Urdu come more under the heading of extra-curricular activities for Nawab Sahib. Of course you know the Gaffur connection?'

'He was court poet in Mirat, in the eighteenth century.'

'And connected to the ruling family. A Kasim. Nawab Sahib had never read Gaffur in English. But he has many exquisite volumes in the original. Whenever people feel they should give him a gift that shows forethought but not extravagance they usually hit upon the poems of his distinguished ancestor. For instance, the Laytons presented him with a copy when he offered them the hospitality of the guest house at the time of the wedding. But the habit is rarer in English people than in Indians. He was very pleased and expressed the wish to learn some of his favourite verses in English. He was horrified when he read Colonel Harvey-Fortescue's Victorian effusions and since then I have had to try my own hand. I shan't assume the false modesty of the complacent amateur and pretend I'm not highly satisfied with some of the results. In fact I've become quite addicted to the exercise of this latent skill and sometimes fancy myself quite a little Pushkin. But it is hard on the eye. Having only one it is sensible to take care of it, but difficult to remember to do so. One adjusts so easily to such a slight impediment and seldom thinks of oneself as handicapped, unless one sees or hears of someone in the same or worse condition.'

The stories of Bronowsky's blind left eye and lame left leg ranged from the possible to the scurrilously unlikely. It was Rowan's chance to hear one of them and his chance to approach the subject of disability, the subject of lost limbs, the subject of Merrick. A chance again deliberately contrived? It was worth taking up. He realized how much he was enjoying talking to the old *wazir* and it pleased him to think that the conversation was no more than a ritual, a courtly circumnavigation of a subject they were both interested in but both too skilled to raise directly. Each had stood his ground. The space between was wide open. One could step on to it now without giving much away.

'I notice,' Rowan said, 'that the blind eye and the lame leg are both on the left side. Does that mean there was a common cause or is it a coincidence?'

'Oh, common. And common enough in those days. St Petersburg. A makeshift bomb. An explosive little incident at dusk on the drive from the Winter Palace.' Bronowsky leant back in his chair. 'An explosion like a scarlet flower in black foliage, thrusting out of the snow. A little summer miracle in winter. That and the pressure. One did not recall a noise. Perhaps the snow muffled it. Such are one's recollections. Later the discomfort. And the strange remote satisfaction of knowing it was no worse. No limb lost. A mere eye. A bad leg. Growing pleasure. The distinction of a limp and an eye-patch. The poor young fellow who threw the bomb was the only fatal casualty. He mistook me for Another. I made a callous joke. That now I had only one eye to weep with and mourn his useless little death. But that was to disguise less insensitive feelings. I thought, How strange. He did not know me, nor I him, but all through his life, from birth, for twenty years, without realizing it he had been moving towards me, step by inevitable step, and I had been waiting for him, preparing to set out on that drive through the snow, to keep an appointment, wrapped in my furs, well muffled, well disguised, so that he would not recognize me at the very last moment as the agent of his death. I saw his photograph. They had it, of course. And one from the morgue of his remains. They showed me this too, as if it would please me. Extraordinarily his face was unmarked. Very pale against the blackness of his hair and the wispy adolescent growth of beard on cheeks and chin. A dark young man, I thought, of random destiny and private passions. It was a revelation. As I looked at the photograph I realized that *he* could have been *my* death, that perhaps fate had decreed this, but had wound the machinery up wrong and was now aghast at the error. It struck me that, well, I must watch out, that perhaps even now a birth was taking place in some remote village, to rectify things. It seemed to me that fate would work this way, that the destiny so apparently random must be shaped even so from the beginning, that I had at least twenty years grace before I must keep the next appointment, this time with a young man who would complete the task. I pictured his life. How it would be. Not privileged like mine but harsh and sombre, so that his heart would grow into a habit of sadness which it pleased me to think of as also a sadness for me, because of what he must do that he did not know. I fell a little in love with him. And there were times when things were not good with me that I wished to hasten the consummation. This was in nineteen hundred. When I left Russia nearly twenty years later it was with the feelings almost of a deserter. By then, you see, he would have been in the prime of youth with only a few years to wait. In Berlin and in Paris I watched out for him, at first only among the young men of our emigration but then among young

Germans too and young Frenchmen, because I realized that the appointed agent need not after all be of Russian nationality and that one of fate's little jokes might be that I should think myself secure merely because I had crossed a frontier. Even in India I used to watch.'

'But not any longer?'

'Oh, sometimes. India particularly is rich in possibilities. It is easy here to be a marked man. I spoke of this to our friend Merrick during the interesting conversation I had with him in Mirat.'

'Merrick? Oh, you mean the Mayapore case. Miss Layton's friend.'

'When I say spoke of it I mean spoke in general to him of being a marked man, of the part played by these young men of random destiny and private passions. I did not mention my own case. Mine after all is illusory. His was real. He had been a marked man ever since Mayapore. Persecuted even, but in subtle ways to remind him that he was not forgotten, that his transfer into the army had not shaken off whoever it was, whoever it is, who wishes him to be under no delusion, but know that his actions in Mayapore will have to be answered for one day. To give him that uncomfortable impression, anyway. My own feeling was that these people were less interested in retribution than in the use that could be made of a controversial figure, such as Merrick's, to stir young men up to create trouble, to achieve some particular political or religious objective.'

'People like the venerable gentleman from Mayapore? The one you said was in Mirat last year engaged in some tortuous process of intimidation?'

The train passed over a network of points, rocking gently. The lights dimmed, then brightened, flickered out, came on again. In the very brief spasm of darkness it seemed to Rowan that Bronowsky had altered position. But there would not have been time for him to do so unobserved: a second or two. But he looked different. Rowan could not say in what way. It was strange.

'The venerable gentleman, yes.' Even his voice had altered, it seemed, but the whole thing must be a trick of the mind, or something to do with a change in the pressure in the carriage. Perhaps the country through which they were passing had altered. Or someone had opened a door or a window further down the coach.

'You mentioned a stone being thrown. Thrown at this man Merrick, did you mean?'

'Quite so.'

'At the instigation of this slippery customer?'

'How accurately you recall my words. Let us simplify things for each other. His name was Pandit Baba.'

'And he went all the way from Mayapore to Mirat to incite someone to throw a stone at poor Mr Merrick?'

Bronowsky laughed. He said, 'Precisely. Such a gesture would also strike me as excessive. The pandit, I think, would not expend energy on such an inconsiderable thing. Which was why I took note. It is too long a story, the story of the stone and Mr Merrick. In itself irrelevant and in its wider context of concern only to me, in so far as it concerns me as well as our chief of police to protect Mirat from these tiresome infiltrations.'

'I'm not quite with you.'

'When you people in British India clamp down, when you have a sweep and clap subversives and firebrands into jails, proscribe political parties or in any way make things unhealthy for Indians who stand up to you, then those who escape your nets go to ground. And where better than in the self-governing princely states where your formal writ does not so easily run? When you had that grand round-up in nineteen-forty-two, at the time of the Quit India campaign, I do not know how many activists, terrorists, anarchists, militant communalists or simple Congress extremists hitched up their dhotis and hot-footed it to places like Mirat. I know which of them turned up *in* Mirat, because I saw to it that they quickly hitched their dhotis up again and hot-footed it back across our borders.'

'Your chief of police must be very efficient.'

Bronowsky glanced away, smiling to himself. 'I suppose one or two escaped our combined vigilance. But we were very vigilant. It is wise to be. The states offer a wide variety of opportunities for political intrigue and some states I think deserve what they get in that way. But I will not have political or communal disturbances stirred up in Mirat by people who do not belong to Mirat. Both the major Indian political parties have been guilty of attempting it in the past twenty years. I need not elaborate. Quite apart from the fact that Nawab Sahib is by definition an autocrat he is also a Muslim. The majority of his subjects are Hindu. My life in Mirat has been spent trying to ensure that the two communities have equal opportunities, which was not always so, that they live in amity and have reason to be perfectly content to live as subjects of the Nawab, and do not hanker after the democratic millennium promised by Gandhiji on the one hand or the theistic paradise-state on earth envisaged by Mr Jinnah on the other.'

For a while he was silent, looking now at the shoe on his left foot, which was thrust out, the heel on the thick carpet that helped to muffle the drumming of the wheels. He said, 'Eventually, of course, there can be no separate future for us, and latterly I have been directing my thoughts to the problem of how best to ensure a smooth and advantageous transition.'

'No separate future?'

'When the British finally go. No freedom separate from India's freedom. No separate future for Mirat nor for any of the states, with the possible exception of the largest and most powerful such as Hyderabad or those whose territories merge into each other and who might combine administratively. The alternative is Balkanization, which of course even if permitted would be disastrous.'

'There is an obligation to the princes on our part. I should say that it's been made clear often enough that we recognize it.'

'Well. Come. Come. You are all going, aren't you? One day. When? In five years? Ten years? Even five is not long. Perhaps I shan't live to see it. On the whole I hope not, because when you go the princes will be abandoned. In spite of all your protestations to the contrary. They will be abandoned. I have told Nawab Sahib so. He pretends not to believe it. I show him the map. I point to the tiny isolated yellow speck that is Mirat and to the pink areas that surround it which are the provinces directly ruled by the British. Since India passed under the Crown, I say to him, you have relied on the pink bits to honour the treaty that allows the yellow speck to exist. But you cannot have a treaty with people who have disappeared and taken the crown with them. The treaty will not be torn up but it will have no validity. It will be a piece of paper. A new treaty will have to be made with the people who have taken the pink parts over from the British. You will have to negotiate a new treaty with Mr Gandhi and Mr Nehru. You can forget Mr Jinnah because even if he gets Pakistan it will be so far away from you that it will be meaningless. So you will have to bargain for the continuing existence of the yellow speck which is Mirat with Mr Nehru and the Congress High Command. Nawab Sahib smiles. He can see it as clearly as I can see it – the form such bargaining might take. But he smiles also at what he likes to persuade himself is my simplicity. No, Dmitri, he says, we have supplied the British with money and men in two world wars. And there are over five hundred little yellow specks, and some not so little. The British are pledged to protect our rights and our privileges and our authority. I nod my head. I say, this is true, Nawab Sahib. But they are pledged as well one day to hand over *their* rights and privileges and authority to Mr Gandhi and Mr Nehru. They are pledged in two directions but can only go in one. Nawab Sahib smiles again. That, Dmitri, is where they are so cunning. He does not say what cunning he sees. He knows that if he puts it into words his illusion of it will collapse. So the words will not come. But in his mind he tells himself that the pledge to Mr Gandhi and to Mr Nehru cannot be fulfilled because of the pledge to the princes, or that it can only be fulfilled if the princes agree that it should be and that the princes will only agree if their territories are first secured to them in perpetuity. Therefore, my dear Captain Rowan, with Nawab Sahib adopting this reverent attitude to his piece of paper, you will appreciate that I am very much alone in this business of working and planning for the most advantageous position for my prince. And because I need peace and quiet to work and plan I do not welcome venerable gentlemen from Mayapore, or any of their like from wheresoever, who seek to cause the sort of unrest which our future masters will point to as proof that Nawab Sahib's subjects groan under the yoke of an iron, archaic dictatorship. A Muslim dictatorship at that. I do not welcome venerable gentlemen from Mayapore, because in their wake, in their footsteps, springing up like sharp little teeth, are these dark young men of random destiny and private passions – destinies and passions that can be shaped and directed to violent ends.'

Rowan nodded, leaving Bronowsky to guess what opinion he himself held about the future of the states. Since he had accepted Malcolm's invitation to officiate at the transfer of Mohammed Ali Kasim to the protection of the Nawab, he had been checking on Mirat's status. There was no political agent actually resident in the state. Mirat's relationship with the crown was conducted through the Resident in Gopalakand and this was old Robert Conway, whom Rowan knew only by reputation. It had surprised him a bit when Lady Manners mentioned him as an old friend of hers. Holding a high opinion of Lady Manners he decided there was probably more warmth in Conway than people usually admitted, but even she had described him as an unemotional man with rigid views. Bronowsky would not find it easy to communicate with him, nor – Rowan imagined – was Conway a man who would encourage Bronowsky in what he called his search for the most advantageous position for his prince. From what Rowan heard of Conway he suspected the Nawab would be encouraged to believe that he would be abandoned only over Conway's dead body and the dead bodies of every member of the Political Department.

'Well,' he said, 'let's hope the venerable gentleman stays clear. Some other time you must tell me about the stone. It does seem a bit far-fetched to go to all that trouble. I suppose he's safe now.'

'Who?'

'Miss Layton's friend – Merrick.'

'Frankly I doubt he was ever in much danger. Harming a white man in this country is a hazardous occupation. But I agree he's probably safe from further persecution, if only because he's probably long since served his most useful purpose from Pandit Baba's point of view. His own purpose – well – that is another matter. And who can say what is the purpose of a man like that?'

Rowan stretched. 'Perhaps just to do his job.'

'Few men have aims as simple as that.'

'Are he and Miss Layton old friends?'

'As I remember they met only at the wedding. He wasn't even a close friend of the bridegroom. What you might call a last-minute substitute for a best man who was ill. No one knew he was the Merrick in the Bibighar Gardens case until the wedding-day. He'd kept it dark, but it came out then because of the stone and because I identified him at once directly I heard this Captain Merrick had been in the Indian Police. The stone, by the way, hit the poor bridegroom. Why do you ask?'

'Only that she seemed such a nice girl and that it would be tough on her if they're committed to one another.'

'Committed to one another?'

'Engaged, for instance.'

'Tough on her because of his lost left arm?'

'She didn't strike me as the sort of girl who would back out, and it would be hard on her, wouldn't it?'

'Oh, I agree. I doubt that Miss Layton would back out. But such a thing hadn't occurred to me.' With the ebony cane clasped in both hands he raised it to his chin and put his head back, gazed at the ornate ceiling.

'Committed. Such a thing hadn't occurred to me. There would hardly have been time for such a relationship to develop when they were in Mirat and no opportunity for it to have done so since, except by correspondence. No. I doubt there could have been time for a relationship of that nature even to begin, even if everything else had been normal.'

Tapping his chin with the silver knob of the cane Bronowsky continued to contemplate the view above his head. Rowan waited.

'But I see why it might occur to you,' Bronowsky went on. 'That she was just back from a long journey undertaken for the reasons she gave but also for her own private emotional satisfaction.'

The ceiling ceased to interest him. He looked at Rowan but still tapped his chin.

'Let us hope you are wrong. It would be a somewhat one-sided affair, I should say. Unless, in Mirat, I was mistaken, which is always possible.'

'Mistaken in what?'

'In my assumption that he didn't really like women.'

Rowan said nothing.

'It is what makes the Mayapore case interesting. It was interesting from the beginning but in a rather cliché-ridden way. Well, there was this girl, this poor Miss Manners, recently out from England, untutored in and unsympathetic to the rigid English social system here. Good-natured and intelligent – a little like Miss Layton but in comparison with her an innocent abroad, so far as India was concerned. For a time she lives with her aunt Lady Manners in Rawalpindi, a liberal-minded old lady whose husband once governed Ranpur and incurred the hostility of the die-hards with his pro-Indian policies. Nowadays the old lady has almost more Indian friends than she has British, they say. Her niece, this Miss Manners, is invited by one of them, a Lady Chatterjee, to stay with her in Mayapore where the social structure is even tighter and more provincial than in Rawalpindi. And in Mayapore she becomes friendly with an Indian boy. Not one who moves in the small official circle of socially acceptable Indians but one out of the black town. Cliché number one. The princess and the pauper, but with a racial variation on the theme. And then there is cliché number two: the boy although now a pauper is really a gentleman, brought up in England entirely and educated at an English public school. A family misfortune alone accounts for his presence on the wrong side of the river, from which from time to time he ventures into the cantonment in the capacity of a humble reporter for the local English language newspaper. The friendship with Miss Manners ripens but almost clandestinely because there are so few places where she can go that he can go. But she is impatient of these artificial barriers, so they are noticed together. She is warned against the association. She ignores the warning but the friendship is now under a strain. In other words, cliché number four. And then, what really is the boy after? Cliché number five. The warning proves more than merited, or so it would seem. One night she is attacked and assaulted. She swears she did not see her attackers. Later she swears that although she did not see them she knows who they were not – not in other words the kind of boys who have been arrested who of course include her young Indian friend. Who in Mayapore doubts though, or doesn't guess who led them? Certainly the head of the police does not doubt. Within an hour of her return home after the assault her boyfriend and his companions were in custody. But now comes cliché number six. The head of the police himself has a regard for Miss Manners of an even tenderer kind than he would feel for any girl of his own race who gets into trouble. How tender a regard? No one is sure but it is whispered that he loves her or loved her once and was spurned. He does not actually deny it. In confidence he will tell you that his erstwhile regard for Miss Manners made it that much more difficult for him to keep a properly detached view and ensure that all his actions are performed dispassionately in the service of justice. Such manly frankness is appealing. If in the past there were people who had marked him down as not quite pukka, as not really out of what you English call the top drawer, they admit that in this business his behaviour has been impeccable as well as energetic. So the story seems to go, proving yet again that if fact is no stranger than fiction it is just as predictable. But did the story go like that? I think not quite. When I met him I talked to him at length and as we talked I got this other impression that Miss Manners had never really interested him at all, that he had scarcely noticed her until her association with the Indian boy had begun, and that he could not avoid noticing her then because he had had his eye on the young man for a long time. The young man was an obsession, an absolute fixation. Perhaps even Mr Merrick does not fully appreciate all the possible reasons why.' Bronowsky paused. 'Perhaps that is cliché number seven. At least in life if not in tales. Cliché number eight is that with a job to do in a few hours from now you should get some rest. I will ask the steward to wake you at 4.15, shall I?'

'Thank you.' Rowan reached for his briefcase.

'I hope it isn't only good manners that have kept you up. For me sleep is a waste of time, it being my seventieth birthday, although strictly speaking that was yesterday. I've enjoyed our talk. I shall cheat for a few hours more, drink some more champagne and read Pushkin.'

As Rowan got up Bronowsky said, 'You'd better disregard what I said, unless the question of those boys ever crops up at Government House. I hate to think of them lying forgotten in some inhospitable jail, if they were innocent. I do hope you are wrong, by the way.'

'Wrong?'

'About Miss Layton's reasons for going so many miles to see the wounded hero. I believe he has a number of admirable qualities but none of them strikes me as likely to promote the cause of anyone else's happiness. Not even his own. He is one of your hollow men. The outer casing is almost perfect and he carries it off almost to perfection. But, of course, it is a casing he has designed. This loss he has sustained – the left arm – even this fits. If he regrets the loss, presently he will see that he has lost nothing or anyway gained more in compensation. What an interesting thought. I am tempted to say that had he not suffered the loss he might one day have been forced to invent it.'

Rowan smiled. 'To the extent of removing part of a limb?'

Bronowsky laughed.

'But absolutely!'

For a while he gazed at Rowan and then said sedately: 'I speak metaphorically, naturally.'

V

Bathed and dressed Rowan went back to his sitting-room. Jaiprakash poured him the second routine whisky-soda, the one he used to wash down the evening dose of pills. He picked up the telephone and asked for the Pankot number. The operator said he would ring him back when a priority call on the Pankot line had been cleared: probably in ten minutes. He asked to be put through to the mess steward. He ordered a tray and a tankard of beer. He did not feel like going into the dining-room. He then rang the signals office and checked how long he had to get a package down to go in the night bag to Area Headquarters in Pankot. The answer was an hour and a half to be on the safe side.

The telephone rang almost as soon as he'd put down the receiver. He picked it up again. Through atmospherics he heard the male operator in the exchange downstairs saying that the Pankot number was on the line and distantly a woman's voice saying 'Hello? Hello?' The crackling ceased abruptly. The connection sounded a good one. He asked to speak to Miss Sarah Layton.

'Speaking.'

'Sarah, this is Nigel. Nigel Rowan.'

'Oh, hello.'

'I got your letter.'

'That was quick.'

'I've done what you asked.'

'Already? How good of you.'

'I'm sorry to ring. Is it inconvenient?'

'No, of course not.'

But she sounded a little guarded.

'I thought I should let you know what I intend to do. If it's all right just say yes. It was only a matter of collecting some envelopes and a package. I'll get them done up and sent in the bag tonight to Area Headquarters. I don't think there's anything important. The Reverend Mother said you may decide to throw the lot away. I've rung just to make sure you knew to be on the look-out for them. If I mark the package private and personal will it reach you without any problems?'

'Yes, that would be fine. I'm awfully grateful.'

'She's nice, isn't she? The Reverend Mother.'

'Yes. Just vague on the phone.'

'How are things?'

'Pretty good.'

'I'm longing to hear about the party. The one in Bombay where the drinks got locked up.'

'Oh, the Maharanee's.' She laughed, sounding relieved to get off the subject of Miss Batchelor. 'If there's such a person. She didn't put in an appearance.'

'Which Maharanee was she supposed to be?'

'I'm not sure Count Bronowsky ever told us. He referred to her as Aimee.'

'Aimee? Was this at a place called Sea Breezes on the Marine Drive?'

'Yes. Do you know her?'

'She's the ex-Maharanee of Kotala. Has Bronowsky known her long?'

'I got that impression.'

'The old Machiavelli.'

'Why?'

'We talked about the Maharajah in June last year, the night you and I first met. He never mentioned knowing the ex-wife. Kotala was the Maharajah I was telling you about a few weeks ago. The one my uncle had the trouble with.'

'Really? I wish I'd met her.'

'She's someone I try to avoid.'

'But you've been to the flat in Bombay?'

'No, only to her place in Delhi. I remember the name Sea Breezes because she was always sending notes from there when I was in Bombay with HE last Christmas. I thought Sea Breezes rather funny because she has a reputation for being hermetically sealed-in whereever she goes.'

'The flat was breezy enough.'

'Perhaps the room she was hiding in wasn't. She told me in Delhi she hated fresh air, light, the sound of doorbells and talking on the telephone and that her idea of true repose would be to have a magic wand to conjure up a party and make it disappear when she was fed up with it. You were lucky only having the drinks locked up. When she was Kotala's wife they say she kept a tame leopard and made it snarl to order. It could empty the palace of unwanted guests in one minute flat. When it bit one of his favourite girlfriends he sued for divorce. He wanted to cite the leopard as co-respondent but decided not to because it was a female leopard and people said he'd only be able to accuse it of alienation of affections.'

'Oh, Nigel.'

He smiled. 'It's true.'

'You're making me think your uncle was right after all. Actually she did have a sort of leopard, but he was on our side and warned us about the drinks being locked up. So we beat a dignified retreat before it happened. He was rather nice. His name was Perron.'

'Perron? Don't tell me he was a sergeant in the French Army.'

'He had two different uniforms, but he was a sergeant in both of them, yes.'

'Whatever is she up to? Raising an army? Anyway she's got her history mixed up. She's a Rajput not a Mahratta. The Rajputs weren't a bit keen on Sergeant Perron.'

'You know all about him too?'

'The Perron who succeeded De Boigne.'

'His real name was Pierre-Cuiller.'

'Was it? I don't think I knew that. Oddly enough we had a Perron at school. I was told to chastise him once for persistent slackness at games. The consensus of House opinion was that his incompetence on the playing field was a deliberate exhibition of eccentricity and the unpleasant task of persuading him to conform fell to me.'

'You mean you had to cane him?'

'I'm afraid so.'

'He was in Bank's, then?'

'That's right.' Rowan hesitated. 'I don't remember telling you which house I was in. What are you laughing at?'

'The picture of you caning Perron.'

'He thought it was rather funny too.'

'Did it improve his games?'

'No. He warned me it wouldn't. Actually I'm exaggerating. Violence wasn't necessary. I was supposed to apply corrective methods but he and I decided the best thing would be to talk it over. He told me he found team sports awfully depressing, all that waiting around at cricket on the one hand and what he called the incomprehensible hurly-burly of football on the other. Fortunately I'd discovered through another source that he rowed quite a bit during the holidays. We weren't a rowing school but there was a local canoeing and sculling club in the town so I got permission for him to join and that suited him down to the ground because it got him out of the school and off by himself on the river. When I last saw him he would have been about seventeen, but nearly six feet tall and with shoulders like an ox.'

'When was that, Nigel?'

'The same occasion I was telling you about at the party Hugh Thackeray took us to – when I visited the school between finishing at Sandhurst and coming out here.'

'And watched Hari Kumar playing cricket?'

'Yes.'

'He said he didn't remember Kumar.'

'Who said he didn't remember Kumar?'

'Sergeant Perron.'

'Sergeant Perron?'

'The Sergeant Perron who was at the Maharanee's party. The one who tipped us off about the drinks being locked up. I was only joking when I called him the Maharanee's leopard. He's a sergeant in Field Security. He came back with us and met my father and they talked about Bank's and Coote's. He remembered you but pretended not to remember Kumar.'

'A sergeant in Field Security?'

'At the Maharanee's he was a sergeant in Education. But when I first met him he was in Field Security.'

'You've met him twice?'

'Twice on the same day.'

'In one day he switched from Field Security to Education?'

'Education was only a disguise. I suppose I oughtn't to talk about it on the phone.' She sounded amused.

'Sarah, what *are* you talking about?'

'About your old friend Perron.'

'It can't be the same one.'

'Well he was over six foot. He looked like an oarsman. He remembered you. He remembered your first name. In fact he remembered you quite clearly. And still being only a sergeant is rather eccentric so obviously he hasn't changed. Does that convince you?'

'But he didn't remember Coomer.'

'Pretended not to.'

'Why should he do that?'

'I think probably Ronald could tell you.'

'Ronald? Ronald Merrick?' After a moment he said, 'Where does he fit in?'

'Sergeant Perron is going to work for him.' She added, 'I got the impression he wasn't very keen.'

'What made you think so?'

'The look on his face whenever Ronald ordered him to do anything. In fact I think he'll try to get out of it. I'm sorry. He was nice. He would have been an asset in that particular sphere. I'd better let you get on. I may get down to Ranpur again in a few weeks because daddy says he may be going. I'll let you know shall I? Unless you've gone by then. Have you had any news?'

'No. None.'

'It was awfully good of you to see the nuns. You must have been pretty busy if the *daftar* here is anything to go by. They've been at sixes and sevens ever since they heard Mr Kasim's coming up to attend his old secretary's funeral.'

'Oh, why, particularly?'

'In case he takes the opportunity to make some sort of political announcement. There are quite a lot of people crowding in. Some are already camping out near the station.'

'Old Mahsood was a Pankot man.'

'But the police think it's MAK they're coming to see.'

'A popular demonstration or just taking *darshan*?'

'Taking *darshan*, we hope. Has there been any trouble in Ranpur?'

'Just a few crowds, directly it leaked that he was on his way from Mirat with old Mahsood's coffin.'

'Is Ahmed with him?'

'Not to my knowledge. Isn't he still in Bombay?'

'That was a week ago. The police here think it's going to be more like a political meeting than a Muslim funeral. They've drafted in men from Nansera.'

'I don't think they need worry. He was very devoted to old Mahsood. Bringing the body home is a mark of respect, I should say. If not he wouldn't have been at such pains to tell us what he was doing and ask for what amounts to official protection from excessive curiosity. That's probably the real reason why there are extra police.'

'Oh well. So much for that rumour. But people here are so used to nothing happening they'll probably be disappointed when it doesn't. I shan't be. It suits father as it is.'

'I'm glad he's better. Is there anything else I can do for you? Anything for your father, for instance?'

'Nothing I can think of, but thank you.'

'Let me know if there is. I'm afraid I've been keeping you. Look after yourself.'

'And you. Oh, and remember me to Hugh Thackeray.'

'I will.'

When they had rung off he collected together the envelope and package the Reverend Mother had given him. It seemed absurd to think of her actually having them in her hands tomorrow morning. The package, which contained something hard like a book and something soft, some sort of material, was inscribed: *In the event of my death: Dear Sarah*. The envelope, inscribed by a different hand, probably the Reverend Mother's, was marked 'Oddments' and seemed to contain papers and other envelopes.

He put both the package and the envelope into a large manila envelope, sealed it and addressed it to Sarah at Area Headquarters, Pankot. The telephone rang. He picked it up immediately, thinking she might have remembered something important and rung back.

'Nigel?' It was Hugh Thackeray on the internal line.

'Oh, hello. Well. How was Delhi?'

'Like Delhi. More to the point, how is Pankot? I've been trying to get you but they said you were talking to Pankot. The fair Miss Layton, would it be?'

Hugh was still very young.

'It would. She asked to be remembered to you.'

'Very nice of her but quite unnecessary. I was thinking about her anyway. On your behalf, I hasten to add. What are you doing?'

'Nothing right now. I'm off-duty.'

'I know. But you're not under the weather, are you?'

'Not in the least. Why?'

'They tell me you've ordered a tray.'

'And a tankard of beer.'

'They kept that dark. I was a bit worried. I imagined something more on invalid lines. HE would like a word.'

'Right.'

'I mean over here in the study. Shall I tell him five minutes?'

'Yes, I'll come right over.' He hesitated. 'Any news?'

'What news did you have in mind?

'From Tokyo, say?'

'We think they're still agonizing about how to surrender unconditionally on condition that the Emperor remains sacrosanct. I can't think why he doesn't commit *hara-kiri*.'

'I don't think sons of heaven can. Any suggestions about which subject I could usefully mull over on the way down?'

A moment's silence. Then: 'MAK perhaps?'

'Right.'

He replaced the phone. He had hoped for something else, something more personal. He called Jaiprakash, told him where he was going. He took the envelope down to the signals office and then crossed over to the east wing. Here there were several people in the main hall: General Crawford and his *aide* – a slim and handsome Sikh in a pale blue turban – the Deputy Inspector-General of Police; old MacRoberts, the senior Member of Council, with Henderson of the Finance Department and his pale and angular wife who caught his eye and smiled; Mrs Saparawala and Doctor Bannerji, the Member for Education, and another fellow *aide* of Rowan's, Bunny Mehta. Some of them had been at Ranagunj airfield to meet the Governor. All except Bunny were on their way home, awaiting cars, calm among the servants who were coming and going intermittently. Rowan made for the narrow corridor to the private staircase: a spiral enclosed by wrought-iron that took him up to the small landing on the first floor and a green baize door through which he passed into the lobby of the air-conditioned private quarters. Here the public grandeur of pillars and black and white tiled floors, of busts on plinths and of immense potted palms in brass bowls, gave way to homelier oak-panelling and thick Turkey carpeting. With its magazine-cluttered central table, leather chairs and sofas set around the walls, it always reminded him of a doctor's waiting-room.

Priscilla Begge, looking both competent and harassed (he had never quite worked out how she managed to convey at one and the same time such apparently mutually exclusive qualities) was standing with her hockey-player's legs astride next to the little corner desk, talking on the telephone, watched by the two duty-bearers whose job was to ensure that the lobby was never unmanned. She gave Rowan a smile of welcome and a frown of pained exasperation, put her hand over the mouthpiece and stage-whispered, 'You can cross off –' then uncovered the mouthpiece and went on with her conversation but made a pleading (also commanding) gesture with her free hand, which he supposed meant she wanted him to wait. The door to the room of private audience opened and Hugh Thackeray looked in. He grinned at Rowan and then mouthed something at Priscilla who turned her back irritably and said, 'Will you repeat that please?' as if Hugh had distracted her.

'Poor old Bully-Off,' Hugh said when he and Rowan were alone in the empty audience room. 'Lady M's not well again and HE wants her to go down to Ooty to decide what's best to be done. Hang on here a moment. I'll just make sure he's ready.'

Thackeray went back into the study and shut the door. Rowan stood by the uncurtained window, looked down into the darkened grounds. He felt sorry for Priscilla. Much as she adored Lady Malcolm whose cousin she was, as well as secretary, and much as she loved the crisp healthy air of Ootacamund, her sense of duty, and the obligation she felt she was under to hold the fort during Lady Malcolm's frequent illnesses and absences, always made an order such as Malcolm had just given her seem to her like an instruction to abandon her post. Not that she saw herself as indispensable. Priscilla only lost her harassed look when Lady Malcolm was in residence and then it was replaced by one of thankfulness and hearty devotion. Rowan liked her because she had virtually no notion of her own capabilities. It was as if she could never quite credit it that she got anything right. The senior women in Ranpur who found themselves co-opted to act as hostess at Government House when poor Louise Malcolm struggled asthmatically for breath or retired to the one place in India that turned out to suit her affected to be amused by but never impatient of old Bully-Off's indefatigable efforts to help them to endure a rôle that actually gave them pleasure to assume. Malcolm had once said to him, 'If Priscilla could only stop thinking of herself as a prefect and start seeing herself as Head Girl what a good Governor's wife she would make.' But that Priscilla could never do. It was against her nature. On the night she was told that her name was on the next Honours List for an MBE all the colour left her face and for a day or two she had seemed pre-occupied, as by intimations of some kind of lost innocence.

He turned from the window at the moment Thackeray opened the Library door. He nodded. As Rowan passed through Thackeray whispered, 'See you later, maybe. I'm going to hold Priscilla's hand and assure her that everything will be all right so long as we remember we're a team. Aren't I a tease?'

The Governor was at the far end of the room where the desk – already cluttered – was angled to take light from one of the tall windows. The desk-lamp was on but Malcolm was standing gazing out of the window, as Rowan had been a few moments before, hands behind back, holding his horn-rimmed spectacles. He was in dressing-gown, slacks and slippers.

Rowan said good-evening. Malcolm turned round and smiled and went to the desk, putting on his spectacles.

'How was New Delhi, sir?'

'New Delhi?' He sat and rummaged. 'New Delhi. Here we are.' But whatever he had looked for and found he then seemed to lose interest in. He sat back, removed the glasses and rubbed the bridge of his nose. 'New Delhi. Very bad for one's sense of proportion, New Delhi.' He put the glasses back on and started making notes on a memorandum pad. 'Have a drink, Nigel. I'll have one too if you'd be so kind.'

Rowan crossed over to the area in front of the fireplace. Three sofas were arranged round it. The live-coal effect was on below the unused elements of an ornate electric fire. The drinks tray was set out on the main sofa-table. The light from the fire was caught in the facets of the cut-glass decanters. An illusion of cosiness. The air-conditioning hummed gently. The private rooms could strike uncomfortably chilly. The imaginary live fire was Priscilla Begge's idea. She said it cheered one up. He poured whisky for himself and Malcolm his usual brandy. No ice for either of them. Not too much soda. He took the drinks to the desk and set the Governor's on a cork mat next to a square cut ashtray. Malcolm nodded his thanks but continued writing his memorandum.

'Be with you in a tick,' he said presently. 'Do sit down. I'm sorry about this by the way, you're supposed to be off, aren't you? Off. Making hay. That's it, then.' He threw down the pencil, looked at what he had written, pushed the pad aside, reached for his glass and said, 'Cheers.'

'Cheers.'

'Well now. New Delhi.'

'Interesting developments, sir?'

'Confirmation of assumptions.'

'Elections?'

'Yes. War virtually over, so – elections. To the central legislature first, then in the provinces.'

'When sir?'

'When do we do anything in this country if there's a choice?'

'In the cold weather?'

Malcolm was playing with the horn-rimmed spectacles. 'The cold weather. How comforting it always sounds. Never do today what you can put off until the weather cools down.'

'I suppose it's soon enough in this case. And elections are what everybody seems to want.'

'Quite. Jinnah wants them. Nehru wants them. Even we poor overworked provincial Governors want them. Some of course more than others. Most important of all the fount of all wisdom in Whitehall wants them. I suppose we ought to be worried. Such universal agreement.'

'And the Viceroy, sir?'

'Oh, yes. Wavell wants them. What man could fail to seize the opportunity of at last doing something which everyone approves of? He'll announce the decision to hold elections in a week or two, and then pop off back to London to make sure everyone is talking about the same thing, and that the British Government understands that an election in India is rather different from one at home at any time of year.'

'Will there be an extended franchise?'

Malcolm smiled and put the spectacles back on. 'Heaven forbid. That would take two cold weathers. Central legislature first, then the provinces that have responsible ministries, after that our kind, in Section 93. How does that strike you?'

After a moment Rowan replied, 'It strikes me as rather problematical in regard to Section 93 provinces.'

'Elucidate.'

'Constitutionally, you'll have to dissolve the existing legislature before calling for new elections. It wasn't the elected legislature that resigned in 1939. Only Mr Kasim and his colleagues resigned. From the ministry.'

'Quite. What's your point?'

'Only that constitutionally there's no difference between provinces where ministries still exist as a result of the 1937 elections – most of them Muslim majority and Muslim League provinces – and provinces where ministries don't exist because they were Congress ministries and resigned when Congress told them to resign. In the provinces where ministries as well as legislatures still exist the assemblies will be dissolved by due process, prior to new elections. In Section 93 provinces the Governors will have to order dissolution.'

'Well, that's because Section 93 provinces are under Governor's rule. Are you suggesting that I can't dissolve the existing assembly which exists virtually only on paper, without inviting Mr Mohammed Ali Kasim kindly to reform his ministry first?'

'I'm not saying you can't, sir, obviously. I'm wondering whether it's wise.'

'I'm under no constitutional obligation to recall Mr Kasim.'

'The Viceroy was under no obligation to release certain political leaders from jail last June. But he could hardly have held the Simla conference without doing so.'

'A thoroughly bad analogy. But of course, I thoroughly agree with you.'

'Oh.' Used as he had become to Malcolm's habit of arguing aloud for the opposition he was often uncertain what the Governor actually believed himself. 'May I ask why you agree, sir?'

'I'd prefer to hear your own reasons first.'

Rowan smiled. 'Well, I suppose the idea of elections at this stage is to inspire confidence and create an atmosphere of letting bygones be bygones.'

'One can do that without reverting to a bygone status quo.'

'But if you don't revert to it the Congress will be at a disadvantage.

'They may think so …'

'Isn't it what they may think that will count? It's not our fault their ministries resigned in the provinces and not our fault that the ministries that stayed were predominantly Muslim, nor our fault that nowadays that virtually means Muslim League. But the fact is that the League will go into the elections with all the advantages usually enjoyed by a party already in ministerial power while the Congress will have to fight from scratch with all the disadvantages of a party that has been proscribed, its members imprisoned and its funds largely sequestrated. They might interpret the failure to invite them to reform provincial ministries as a first step to new elections as proof that we secretly sympathize with the Muslims and the idea of Pakistan and are still set on punishing Congress for non-co-operation in the war.'

Malcolm pushed the spectacles down his nose and looked at Rowan over the rims. 'I advanced the same arguments myself but with more tactful allowance for the hostility they were bound to arouse. Unfortunately I couldn't answer the logical and inevitable question.'

'What question, sir?'

'The question what I thought Mr Kasim's response to such an invitation would be in the unlikely event of it being agreed I should extend one.' He pushed the glasses back on. 'How would you have answered that?'

'I suppose by saying I'd find out the moment it was agreed I should try.'

'That wouldn't have been an answer. The question was, what do you *think* he would say? And the answer is that one simply doesn't know. One has so little idea that one suspects he might decline as easily as accept and that he would decline because an invitation like that would force him to show his hand, and that he isn't ready to do that yet. And if one is the least anxious, as I am, to see Mohammed Ali Kasim again heading a Congress ministry in Ranpur one is disinclined to do anything that will force him into a false position. So I am perfectly content to fall in with consensus opinion and let provinces under Governor's rule remain so until after the elections. One doesn't even know whether MAK will stand again, or for which party, or if he stands for his old constituency he now has a chance of holding it against the League. One knows absolutely nothing of his present intentions, let alone of his future prospects. One knows nothing about his attitude to his elder son, either.'

Malcolm took the glasses off, picked up his brandy and held it at eye-level as if examining the colour and clarity of the liquid. Then he drank it down.

'And not knowing has become onerous. By the way, I'm losing you.'

'What, sir?'

'They're taking you back into the Political Department. One of the Crown Rep's people mentioned it and said I could tell you. I won't say I'm sorry because I know you'll be pleased. I'll miss you though. You'll get instructions in about a week's time.'

'Did he say anything about where?'

'No. You've done your probation so I should think they'll put you in as assistant at one of the Residencies, wouldn't you?'

'So long as it isn't Frontier Tribes.'

'He asked how fit you honestly were now. So I said you were blooming.

Are you? Young Thackeray seems to think you ought to have a spot of leave before you go. He was under the very odd impression that a few days in Pankot would have a therapeutic effect on your liver.'

'Oh?'

'But I suppose he only said that because he was afraid of being sent himself.'

'Sent himself? To Pankot?'

'Pankot's where I'm told Mr Kasim is to be found in the next day or so. I want you to go up tonight, see him as soon as you can and give him the letter I've written. After that I want you to do whatever is necessary to persuade him to arrange the earliest possible private meeting with me, preferably here, but I shan't absolutely insist. I'm sending V. R. Gopal with you. They're rooting him out now. Don't worry about the bandobast, it's being coped with. All you have to do is pack and be ready by eleven-thirty. Is that all right?'

'Of course, sir.'

'Sorry it's such short notice but I don't want him slipping the net and turning up in Bombay or 'Pindi or Lahore or even back in Mirat before I've had a chance to talk to him.'

'I take it you rule out exerting official pressure?'

'To cause him to appear? Yes, I do.'

'Is he expecting the letter?'

'Possibly. I got Hunter-Evans to ring his house. His new secretary said he was resting because he was going up by car tonight.'

'The car's a new idea. Presumably the coffin still goes by train.'

'Yes, I think Hunter-Evans said it did.'

'And Mr Kasim wouldn't come to the phone himself.'

'He was resting.'

'Perhaps he'll ring back once he's rested.'

'Aren't you keen to go?'

'Perfectly keen, sir. I was just thinking of short-cuts. Obviously there aren't any. How do I and Gopal travel?'

'By train. They're putting on the special coach so you should have every comfort. A car from Area Headquarters will meet you in Pankot and take you up to the Summer Residence guest house. All that's laid on.'

'What's Gopal's rôle exactly?'

'Go-between. He and Kasim have always had a great respect for one another as you know. You'd better wear mufti incidentally.'

'I take it I don't hand the letter to anyone but MAK?'

'Preferably not. I leave it to your discretion. If Kasim can't or won't see you then Gopal will have to give it to him. He'll be involved with the funeral most of tomorrow, but get Gopal off to try and contact him directly you arrive. Gopal was an old friend of Mahsood's too. He can melt into the background without arousing anyone's curiosity. I shan't provide you with a copy of the letter but you'll have a separate sheet of notes for guidance which might help if MAK asks questions you feel you have to answer to get him to agree to a meeting.'

'Will Gopal be as fully informed?'

'No. My approach to Kasim is personal and in one way I may be sticking my neck out. It's nothing to do with inviting him to form a ministry before the elections, though.'

Rowan looked at his watch.

Malcolm said, 'You'd better go and get packed. I'll send the letter and notes up. Ring down if there's anything you want clarifying. And ring me from Pankot tomorrow night to say how things look.'

'You'll be rather busy tomorrow night, sir. You've got the reception and dinner for Chakravarti.'

'So I have. And the foundation stone ceremony later in the week. You'd better take a copy of the days' arrangements in case MAK asks you to suggest a time. I'll try to fit in but I'd prefer not to cancel the Chakravarti ceremony.'

'The stone-laying? Perhaps Mr Kasim would like to attend, sir.'

'Which day is it?'

'Friday, in the afternoon.'

'Would Chakravarti be offended?'

'Not so long as MAK doesn't steal the scene. Chak's been contributing heavily to secret party funds.'

'And hedging his bets by contributing to the Hindu Mahasabha too, so they say. Perhaps the odd lakh finds its way to the Muslim League as well. After all he's a business man with interests all over India. It's a possibility. By all means suggest it. And ring me tomorrow night however late. If Kasim drives down from Pankot on Thursday, say, I could meet him here on the Friday morning.'

'You have HH of Puttipur until mid-morning.'

'But not for lunch?'

'No, Hugh takes him to the airfield just before midday.'

'Then Kasim and I could lunch here and go on to the ceremony at the college. Separately, naturally.'

'Should I come back with him by car?'

'No.' Malcolm smiled. 'Your job's finished the moment he agrees to a time and place. He'll keep his word. The special coach can be held up there until you ask for it to be coupled on. But let Gopal come back directly neither of you sees any further point in his staying. He can use the coach if you like. You can stay on and relax for a few days. I think you should, don't you? Get some hill air into your lungs. Let's say I shan't expect to see you until a week today. By then instructions ought to be through from Simla or Delhi.'

'That's very good of you, sir.'

'You'd better get a move on, then.'

Rowan stood up. Malcolm had never welcomed references to his wife's frailty but he felt he couldn't leave without saying something.

'Thackeray tells me Lady Malcolm isn't well, I'm very sorry.'

'Yes. Thank you.' He took off his spectacles again and put them down. 'I'm sending Priscilla down.' He stood up and, unexpectedly, came round the desk and put out his hand. Surprised, Rowan clasped it briefly.

'I won't actually say goodbye but I suppose there's always a chance of our not coinciding again. One gets punted around like a bloody football in this job. Thank you for everything you've done, Nigel.'

'Thank you, sir. It's been a very happy and very useful experience.'

'Good. I hope things pan out. Today's rather one of those days when I can't quite see how anything pans out for anybody. It was a real horror, I'm told.'

'What?'

'Hiroshima. Absolutely and inconceivably bloody awful.'

'Unexpectedly so?'

'We shan't have the answer for quite a while. Someone said twenty years. That's food for thought, isn't it? And so is the idea that if a high-ranking Japanese delegation had been persuaded over to the States under a flag of truce to watch them test the thing, they'd have gone back and forced the Emperor to surrender then and there.'

'As impressive as that?'

'According to observers God knows how many miles away from the test area in the middle of the New Mexican desert. It leaves one with a rather humiliating sense of the essential parochialism of one's own concerns.'

'Yes. I suppose. I'd better go and get on with mine. Goodnight, sir.'

'One thing before you go.'

Malcolm thrust his hands into his dressing-gown pockets.

'I've always intended to say this when the time came. In my opinion you're admirably suited for the job you've done and even more for the one you're going to do. We have the same sort of views and much the same sort of way of expressing them to each other. We can gauge each other's thoughts and feelings pretty accurately. But the Indians can't, so easily. Sometimes not at all. I know it's a wretchedly difficult thing and nothing's worse than going to the opposite extreme, relaxing and unbending so much that you don't even convince yourself, let alone them.'

'But you think I need to unbend more than I do, sir?'

'It might help. The English manner is a formidable obstacle to mutual understanding between the races. As a young man of your age I used to believe precisely the opposite. But I was confusing mutual understanding with mutual respect and lack of understanding with lack of respect. Take young Thackeray.'

'In what way?'

'He's an awfully kind-hearted boy. Full of fun. Splendid with visiting brass from Eastern Command or GHQ and with young Indian officers like Bunny Mehta. But put him with a handful of senior Indian civilians, any distinguished Indian who's not in uniform, and he's a different fellow. Actually he's terrified of upsetting them or putting a foot wrong. But they

1228

don't know that. They look at what to me and you is his rather touching but sometimes exasperating expression of boyish concentration and they interpret it as one of a fully mature sense of racial and class superiority. I don't honestly think he feels that. But the English manner has never been much of a medium for communicating feeling. Sometimes I think that's at the bottom of half our troubles. Wavell's a good example. One of the sincerest and best disposed men who's ever held that wretched post. But also one of the most silent and unbending and outwardly austere. It's the English manner come to perfection. It won't do. And the irony is, Nigel, that at home it's been going out of fashion for years. Rather like one of those strains of indigenous plants that turns out to flower more profusely abroad and withers away in its home soil. Anyway. It's worth bearing in mind.'

He began moving away from the desk to the centre of the room. Level with the sofa table he came to a halt.

'One other thing. This girl in Pankot young Thackeray assured me would make a few days up there quite an attractive proposition for you. Miss Layton.'

'Miss Layton. Yes.'

'The same Miss Layton?'

Rowan nodded.

'Have you heard from her recently?'

'Actually we were on the phone this evening.'

'Anything to do with a havildar of her father's regiment who went over to Bose in Germany?'

'No, sir?'

'He's now with a batch of prisoners that came over from Bordeaux, in a camp near Delhi. General Crawford has a letter from Colonel Layton asking to be allowed to see him. Apparently he's the son of a Pankot Rifles Subedar who won the VC in the last war.'

'No, she said nothing about that.'

'Did she refer at all to our friend Merrick?'

'Only in passing. He was in Bombay when she was. I don't know why or for how long.'

'Has Colonel Layton met him?'

'She didn't say so. I imagine he must have done.'

'Is Merrick still in the department that's working up these INA cases?'

'Yes. He hadn't been in it long when she told me about it. That's only six weeks ago. And she and Merrick were at a party in Bombay last week. Ahmed Kasim was there. Merrick told her not to let Ahmed know he was connected in any way with the brother's case.'

'Ah. Well that's one thing. The other thing is Merrick's bound to know about the Pankot Rifles havildar too, presumably. Is he sufficiently in with the family to want to help Colonel Layton have an interview with the man?'

'Probably. In with the family, yes. I don't know about the other thing.'

1229

'No. Perhaps Layton's letter to Crawford indicates he's tried that string and Merrick wouldn't play. Perhaps you'd try to find out. Crawford was going to write back and say there was nothing doing but I've asked him to sit on it for a few days. If Merrick's playing along and pulling strings, let me know. We could pull a few from here. If he's not there isn't a hope. But in that case tell her how sorry I am her father can't see his havildar. He may appreciate knowing that I've been consulted personally by Crawford.'

'Right, sir.'

Malcolm hesitated.

'Is young Thackeray barking up the wrong tree? Perhaps I shouldn't ask. But I can't help wondering. The only times you've mentioned her to me have been to pass on what she's told you about Merrick. Very helpful on that first occasion. Interesting on the second. But I've assumed your interest in her was, what, limited to that subject? The way Thackeray spoke made me feel I've been insensitive.'

'I can't think why you should feel that.'

'No. Well. How much have you told her – about our view of Merrick?'

'Nothing, sir. Nothing specific.'

'Well, that would be difficult. Even if one disregards the element of doubt. But what impression do you have of her attitude?'

'I know she believes he made a mistake in the Kumar case.'

'How did the subject come up?'

'I asked her how the chap she'd visited in hospital was. And she told me he was all right and had gone to Delhi to deal with the INA cases –'

'Yes, I remember that. We were both struck by the idea of Merrick conducting a whole series of interrogations. How did she happen to mention the Kumar case?'

'She said she hoped he wouldn't start every examination of INA men with a preconceived conviction of the man's guilt. We went on from there.'

'Did you tell her you knew Kumar?'

'I only mentioned the school part of it. It interested her because her father went to the same one. She knew Kumar had been brought up and educated in England but hadn't heard definitely where.'

'Why is she so interested in Kumar?'

Rowan had asked himself the same question. He did not know the answer. He could only base an answer on Gopal's: that Kumar was really an English boy with a brown skin and that the combination was hopeless.

'I think she sees him as a man who couldn't have existed without our help and deliberate encouragement. I should say that in quite an impersonal way she thinks of him as a charge to our account – guilty or not guilty. But believing him not guilty makes the charge heavier.'

'She sounds an unusually thoughtful person.'

'Yes, I think she is.'

'Did you tell her he's free?'

'No.'

'So she doesn't know you keep an eye.'

'No.'

'I imagine she'd approve? Well –,' Malcolm smiled, '– I expect you have more than one reason for hiding that particular light. I take it Kumar remains in ignorance too?'

'I hope so.'

'Does he still suspect Gopal's man of being CID?'

'That, or one of Pandit Baba's creatures.'

'The CID still keeps tabs, presumably?'

'Very much so. On Gopal's man, too.'

'Does he mind?'

'Gopal says not.'

'What will you do when you've left Ranpur? Leave everything to Gopal?'

'I shall have to. There's not much to leave.'

'Yes, well, it's a minor matter. How are things with him though?'

'He lives much as you'd expect. Coaching a few students at a few rupees a time.'

'How is the aunt?'

'She still looks after him.'

'Is he as devoted as she deserves?'

'According to Gopal's man, yes.'

'Good.' Malcolm paused. 'I hope we did the right thing, that's all.'

VI

The car, which had been sent first to pick up Vallabhai Ramaswamy Gopal at his home, reached Government House a few minutes after eleven-thirty. Rowan had retrieved the envelope from the Signals Office and had it packed in his case. As he got into the car the old man said, 'Keep away, Nigel. I have a cold you see.' There was a smell of eucalyptus. Having spoken, Gopal clamped a square-folded handkerchief to his nose. He was wearing a grey flannel suit and had a woollen scarf round his neck.

'How did you manage that, VR?'

'I am catching cold easily nowadays. My wife tells me to keep an onion in my pocket. She has these outdated ideas.'

'How is Mrs Gopal?'

Gopal jerked his head. 'Okay. Very angry because I am not taking her to Pankot. She says what is the use of being married to a man who is always rushing off.'

'Are you always rushing off?'

'It is what I ask. When was I rushing off last? To Puri, isn't it, two years ago and who was that with me? But it is useless to talk fact and logic to Lila when she is angry. Please excuse me for bringing so many things.'

Mr Gopal's feet were hidden behind an assortment of luggage and oddments; among them an aluminium tiffin set. Outside on the roof rack he had already noticed a bed-roll and a wooden chest. His own suitcase was being put on.

'While she quarrels with me also she gets the servant to pack this and that. It is best not to argue.'

Rowan had visited the house once. The Gopals' quarrelling was not to be taken seriously. Jaiprakash announced through the open window that the suitcase was safely stowed. As the driver got in Mr Gopal spoke to someone on the other side of the car: a youth. He got in too and sat next to the driver.

'It is my nephew Ashok coming to see me off. Making sure for Lila I am not rushing somewhere I shouldn't be. Ashok, say how do you do to Captain Rowan.'

The boy turned round, ducked his head shyly but formally.

'Ashok is doing his BA here, isn't it, Ashok? But now he is talking of going to Calcutta for BSC.'

'Why Calcutta?'

'It is what we are asking. From Government College he can get BSC also, but no, he is insisting Calcutta. Ashok, tell Captain Rowan what you told Auntie Lila.'

Judging that the boy was too embarrassed to speak Rowan said, 'Perhaps the real question is why not Calcutta?'

'No, no, the question was definitely why Calcutta.' Mr Gopal sometimes took a very literal line. 'And the answer is for physics. Isn't it, Ashok? In Ranpur he tells his Auntie there is no decent teacher in physics. For the past few days it has been physics, physics. You know what the trouble is with him, Nigel? He wishes to be the first Indian to make an atomic bomb. He says only for power and energy but I know what is in his mind. He will blow us all up. And only last week it was Wordsworth and daffodils.'

They were through the west gate heading for the Mall and the western arm of Old Fort Road which would take them the longer but less congested way to the station. The car was now accompanied by two motor-cycle outriders – military police who had been waiting one hundred yards beyond the gate.

'Look Ashok, what a story you will tell your mother and father. Driving from Government House with a motor-cycle escort.' He turned to Rowan. 'Lila said I should not bring him but I said you would not mind.'

'Of course not. But what about getting back?'

'He lives near the station. He is Lila's sister's youngest boy. He was only visiting us. It is a lift home for him very nearly, otherwise I would not have brought him.'

'It's very late.'

'I'm often out as late as this, sir,' the boy said, turning round. 'I shall be perfectly all right.'

Rowan glanced at Gopal, but Gopal had the squared handkerchief covering the lower part of his face.

'You speak English very well, Ashok.'

'Thank you, sir.' He faced front. Again Rowan glanced at Gopal who jerked his head slightly, an affirmative answer to Rowan's unspoken question. 'He has found a very good coach and visits him two three times a week after classes. Other evenings he is attending YMCA and doing Ju-Jitsu. *Mens sana in corpore sano*. Ashok? You know the meaning of this?'

'Yes, uncle.'

'What a bright boy. Now physics. What will be the use of mind or body if you blow us all up? Will your physics cure my cold? What a state we are in. In one pocket the formula for splitting the atom and in the other an onion.'

'Do you know the English cure for cramp, VR?'

'No?'

'A raw potato in the bed.'

Gopal laughed. Ashok looked round, smiling. Rowan thought: I unbend easily enough with Gopal.

He looked out of the window. He remembered the time when neither of them had quite trusted the other. Now they were friends. Before that Rowan had known of him only as a shrewd and conscientious civil servant who was said to owe his position in the Department for Home and Law to Mohammed Ali Kasim. A member of the uncovenanted provincial civil service his advancement might otherwise have been blocked by the preference given to British and Indian members of the august ICS. Rowan didn't know in just what way he had caught MAK's eye when MAK was chief minister but he had been a good choice for the senior position he now held in the secretariat.

They had turned off Old Fort Road and were headed south down the ill-lit Upper Tank Road with the barrack-like PWD buildings in darkness on their left and on their right the grounds of Government College – the principal's bungalow, the playing field, the building-site for the Chakravarti extension, and finally, at the intersection with the brightly lit thoroughfare of Elphinstone Road, the old Victorian Gothic building of the College itself.

The car turned right into Elphinstone Road and was filled with sliding slanting bars of light and shadow. The motor-cycle escort shortened the distance between themselves and the car to mother it through the crowds that walked freely on the road. At the Lux Cinema they were still showing *Jawab*.

'Did you know old Mahsood well, VR?'

'He was not so old. He came to see us when MAK was released from Premanagar and sent to Nanoora in Mirat. He was very upset because he wanted to go too, and Mrs Kasim would not take him because she was afraid he would tell Kasim how ill she had been. When he went Lila said "He says Mrs Kasim is ill, but he is ill also." Then of course Kasim sent for him, so he closed the house up and joined them.'

'He lived in the Kasim household didn't he?'

'Since many years. He was never married. "What do I need with wife and children?" he used to say to Lila. "MAK and Mrs MAK are like brother and sister to me and Sayed and Ahmed are like sons or nephews." It was from Mahsood that Lila and I first heard about Sayed and INA. He said he suspected MAK would not forgive the boy and that this would be terrible for Mrs Kasim.'

'How much do you think is generally known now about Sayed?'

'How much? Or by how many people? Everyone is knowing something. No one is officially knowing anything. This is why the press keeps quiet. It is afraid of libel. Ask Ashok here what the students are saying. Tell Captain Rowan, Ashok, what the students are saying about Lieutenant Sayed Kasim. No? He does not want to say in front of you. The students are calling Sayed a hero because he fought with Netaji's army against the British. They know he has been kept in prison-camp awaiting court-martial ever since he was recaptured in Manipur, but they say he will never be tried because the British are afraid that MAK will conduct the defence himself and bring proof that Indian King's commissioned officers were left in the lurch by their English colleagues when the Japanese invaded Burma. And all things of that sort, isn't it, Ashok?'

'Not all students say this, uncle. Some concentrate on their studies. They aren't interested in Bose. He is only a Bengali.'

'Only a Bengali? You say this, Ashok? Are the physics teachers in Calcutta all non-Bengalis, then?'

'It's not what I say, uncle.'

'Who is saying, then? Your friend Vidyar Awal for one, isn't it? Ashok's friend Vidyar is very anti-Bengali, very anti-Bose. His father is a major in the Engineers and comes from UP. You see how these distinctions arise.'

'Yes, I do.'

Gopal sat forward suddenly.

'What are they doing? They should have gone down Chowpatti. This is the old way to the special shed.'

'That's where we're heading.'

'To avoid crowds? There will be no crowds. Everyone knows MAK has gone up by road now.'

'But you and I are going in the special coach, VR. Didn't they tell you?'

'The special coach? Oh, dear God.'

'HE wanted us to be comfortable.'

'Then we should go third class or in the wagon with poor old Mahsood's coffin. Ashok, you must say nothing to your mother and father about this. Say nothing to anyone. Above all say nothing to your Auntie Lila.'

The boy was grinning. 'Why, uncle?'

'Oh, dear God.'

Rowan smiled, judging that Gopal was not really displeased. The little convoy turned left into the road that would bring them out at the coal and goods-yard area. They were already going past go-downs and repair sheds. Cyclists and car-driver had dipped head-lamps on. The road was not lit except where light fell from the high arc-lamps in the yards of the warehouses. There was a warm smell of drains, the acrid odour of coal and oil. They bumped over an uneven level-crossing. 'Oh dear God,' Gopal said again as if every spasm of discomfort were an indication of sustained discomfort to come. They approached a white post-barrier guarded by railway police. This was raised and the convoy entered an arc-lit cinder-yard and drew up at the entrance to a covered stairway to a covered footbridge. An English officer and an Indian station official were waiting for them. There was a batch of coolies to carry the baggage. The Englishman wore the armband of Movement Control. The Indian wore a sola topee. Rowan got out first. The MCO, not Captain Carter, but a man Rowan didn't know, addressed him as sir and announced that everything was laid on. Gopal was still in the car directing the removal of his hand-luggage. The MCO spoke to his Indian colleague. 'See to that lot, old son.' Then he turned to the staircase as if he expected Rowan to go on ahead.

'Okay, sir?'

'Yes, fine.' Rowan remained where he was. 'Incidentally I'm not a civilian and I don't outrank you. Has it been a problem getting the coach ready at such short notice?'

The MCO looked wary. 'All we had to do was see the thing shunted out of the shed to the side platform. I didn't know what the message meant at first because I didn't know there was a special Government House coach. I've only been here three weeks.'

'There used to be several.'

'Just for the Governor?'

'Governor, staff, secretaries, clerks, files. Government used to go up *en masse* to Pankot every hot weather.'

'What happened to the other coaches, then?'

'You've got them in general service. You'd probably have this one too if the interior would adapt.'

'Yes. I looked inside. If you don't mind me saying so I thought it was bloody ridiculous nowadays.'

'It was built for an earlier age.'

'And there's really just the two of you tonight?'

'That's right.'

'The message said two but about four or five servants turned up.'

'That would be about the normal complement.'

'They've been making beds and putting flowers in vases. I thought probably some ladies were coming along.'

'I think the flowers are the usual drill.'

'There's a drill is there?'

'It simplifies things.'

Gopal had emerged now. He carried an umbrella. Ashok held the tiffin-set. The coolies were dividing the luggage up among themselves. Gopal called out to one of them to be very careful with the box because the clasps were unreliable and the box was heavier than it looked. To anyone not knowing Hindi it probably sounded like a complaint. The MCO looked at his watch. On his face was that familiar English expression of utter detachment from an Indian activity. As Gopal and Ashok approached he said to no one in particular, 'Right then.'

He led the way up the staircase to the covered bridge. Their footsteps sounded hollow on the worn and grimy boards. Rowan had never travelled on the special coach himself but he had accompanied Pankot-bound guests from Government House to catch the train on several occasions. The previous MCO, Carter, had appreciated the fact that there *was* a special coach. Most of those who travelled on it had priority passages. Without the coach Movement Control would have found itself turfing passengers out of the ordinary first-class compartments to make room for them.

The covered bridge always reminded him of his schooldays. There had been one at Chadford where he changed trains on the journey between London and Chillingborough. This one smelt much the same, impregnated with decades of engine smoke. Briefly, above the undoubted Indianness of the station at Ranpur, he could imagine himself back at Chadford.

As they came down the stairs the station that was not Chadford presented itself, raw and uncompromising. They were at the front of the train. The special coach stood directly opposite the exit from the covered bridge. It was flanked by two guard's vans, one separating it from the engine, the other from the first of the first-class carriages. Beyond this the train stretched back a couple of hundred yards or more. The platform was crowded but a rope barrier guarded by police kept the area in front of the Governor's coach clear of everyone except people who had business there. Of these there did seem rather a large number.

Gopal was talking to the MCO's Indian colleague, apparently putting Ashok into his care. Two Government House servants stood at the foot of the steps that led to the coach's observation platform, which was also the point of entrance. They saluted Rowan when they caught his eye. The MCO was talking to a British sergeant who had a clipboard of papers. The luggage was going up into the coach. Beyond the barrier charwallahs were collecting money and taking back mugs from hands at windows. Further beyond where the crowds were greatest Rowan could still make out bouncing headloads – the luggage of late arrivals. He wondered where the coffin was and eyed the guardsvan-like coaches which flanked the one he and Gopal were to travel in. And had his suspicions.

'You could help me out, maybe,' the MCO said, arriving with his clipboard at Rowan's elbow. 'I know it's supposed to be sacred territory but I've got six officers in three of the four-persons only compartments and three officers in most of the coupés. Now I've got a GHQ priority who's just come in on the Delhi train.'

'The one due in at 2130?'

'It was ninety minutes late.'

'And you want to put him in the special coach?'

'According to my calculations after you and the Indian gentleman are settled in the two single-berths there's a couple of coupés going spare. Unless of course the servants are travelling in style.'

'What rank is your GHQ priority?'

'Lieutenant-Colonel.'

'That's not senior enough to qualify as a possible exception. But I'll ask Mr Gopal if he has any objection and then see how we're placed. Has Captain Carter been transferred?'

'Carter?'

'The MCO here.'

'I'm the MCO here. The previous chap's name was Carter.'

'Did he hand over to you?'

'He'd gone when I got here. Why?'

'He would have explained the uses and abuses of the special coach.'

'I don't know where abuses comes in.'

'Abuses come in if the coach kept to save Movement Control inconvenience from sudden Government House priorities is treated as a convenient way of solving routine problems of overcrowding. If Mr Gopal and I weren't going up to Pankot tonight the coach wouldn't be on the train.'

'It is on the train.'

'Because we're going up.' Rowan looked at the top paper on the clipboard. 'Is that a copy of the GHQ priority?'

The MCO pulled it from the clip and handed it to Rowan. 'See for yourself.'

Rowan took the paper, the usual carbon copy of a movement order, with an illegible signature – someone signing for an officer of the Advocate-General's branch. Rowan read the text. Then read it again and handed the paper back.

'It says Colonel Merrick is accompanied by a sergeant and a servant. Where are they all at the moment?'

The MCO referred to his own sergeant, who said there was no problem about the servant and that the colonel's sergeant had been 'fixed up'. But the colonel himself was waiting, hoping for something better than a third place in a coupé. He had a disability. The MCO said, 'What sort of disability?'

Rowan broke in. 'I know the officer in question. Just a moment.' He went to Gopal who was lecturing Ashok. 'May I have a word, VR? Let's go in.'

From the observation platform one entered directly into the sitting compartment. The coach had been equipped to look as much like a houseboat on the Dal lake as was possible. The sofa and over-stuffed chairs were covered in chintz. Numdah rugs added to the thickness of an Indian carpet. There were chintz curtains at the windows. A faint smell of sandalwood.

'Oh dear God,' Gopal said yet again. He had brought the tiffin set with him and the umbrella.

Rowan put his briefcase on one of the chairs. 'An interesting situation has arisen,' he began.

'We are to travel in an ordinary compartment?'

'No, they're all full up. The MCO wants us to take some of the overflow.'

'To me this sounds like a confusion. Why do you call it interesting?'

'The overflow happens to be Merrick.'

Slowly the smile and frown of pretended exasperation left Gopal's face. He seemed to take a firmer grip on the umbrella and the tiffin-set, making them look like defensive weapons. Offensive, even.

'Merrick? Ex-Superintendent of Police? Now Major?'

'Major no longer apparently. Lieutenant-Colonel.'

'You have seen him?'

'Not yet. I wouldn't know him by sight anyway. But there's no doubt it's Merrick. Would you object?'

'Object to him travelling with us? Is that open to me? You are His Excellency's chief emissary. It is for you to say.'

'It could be useful.'

'Useful? What could be useful about being with this man?'

'Aren't you in the least curious to see him?'

'Not in the least curious, Nigel. I will have nothing to do with it, but please don't bother about me. They can make up my bunk and I can nurse my cold.'

'The beds are already made up in the two main single berths.'

'No, no. I must have my own bedding. I have it with me. They can put it in one of the old *aide's* coupés. Your Mr Merrick can sleep in His or Her Excellency's berth.'

'We'll have to talk about what we do tomorrow before you go to bed. I'd better tell the MCO it's no go. Obviously you feel strongly.' It surprised Rowan a bit that he did.

'And obviously you want him. You say useful. You are the better judge of this. So let him in. But first let me sort out my sleeping quarters and disappear. If we must talk let us do so in there. And please send Ashok in to say goodbye.'

Gopal went through into the dining-compartment. Rowan returned to the platform and gave Ashok his uncle's message. The MCO was standing with arms folded, his weight on one leg, advertising his patent amusement.

'We'll take Colonel Merrick and his party. The servant will have to muck in with our own but I don't suppose he'll be any less comfortable.'

'You mean you're offering two berths?'

'For Colonel Merrick and his sergeant, yes.'

The MCO's assistant said, 'There's that Major Hemming sir, the one who kicked up a fuss.'

The MCO nodded. 'If it's two berths going spare the answer is two officers, surely. Colonel Merrick and this Major Hemming.'

'The berth's aren't going spare. There's one for Colonel Merrick and one for Sergeant Perron.'

'Is that his name?'

'So it says on the Movement Order.'

'The sergeant's settled in.'

'Then you'll have to unsettle him or squeeze his officer into a coupé.'

'We're due out now.'

'That's up to you. But there'd be no point in bringing Colonel Merrick without the party specified in the movement order. The officer, the sergeant and the servant.'

'You're saying all or nothing?'

'Yes.'

'It beats me.'

As the MCO and his sergeant set off Ashok came down from the coach. Rowan spoke to the Indian official to confirm that he would see the boy safely out of the station. He bade Ashok goodbye, wished him luck in his exams and returned to the sitting-room compartment. The head bearer was putting out bottles and glasses on the marble top of a waist-high mahogany corner cabinet. A miniature brass rail held them secure. He ordered a brandy and soda and presently carried the glass out to the observation platform and placed himself where he could see fairly far down the train. The rope barrier was still in position but a section of it had been opened up. There was a sound of warning whistles. The platform was still crowded. The only Englishwomen he could see were in a group: girls in uniform, QAS, seeing someone off, probably on short leave or on posting up to the General Hospital in Pankot. They had some RAF and American officers in tow and looked merry.

Then they moved in closer to the carriage making room for people to pass: the MCO and an officer whose left arm hung stiffly by his side. Behind them Rowan just made out the tall jungle-green clad figure of a man wearing a green slouch hat and, next to him, someone in a pugree. Luggage bobbed on the heads of the coolies in the rear.

Rowan went back into the coach and drank his brandy down and returned to the observation platform. He went down the steps as the party passed through the opening in the rope barrier.

'Colonel Merrick?'

The man tucked a swagger cane under his left arm. Momentarily Rowan was appalled by the scar-tissue that disfigured the left side of Merrick's face. Sarah had never mentioned that. He took Merrick's right hand, briefly.

'My name is Rowan.' He had been steeling himself to say 'sir'. The word did not come. But he managed the rest of what he'd rehearsed. 'I think we have a mutual friend in Sarah Layton. I already know your sergeant.' Before Merrick could react he turned to Perron. Yes. No mistake. He offered his hand. 'How are you, Guy?'

A little muscle ridged itself on Perron's cheek.

'Fine, thank you, Nigel.'

They shook hands. Rowan readdressed himself to Merrick.

'We'd better sort things out so that the luggage can go in. There's a spare coupé which has its own bath cubicle, and then there's a single berther that's probably more comfortable but it shares washing arrangements with another. There's no one using the coupé.'

'I should be more than content with either,' Merrick said. 'But I do have a certain handicap. The coupé would suit me very well if it's really not wanted. Then I could have my servant in with me. In any case, it's very civil of you.'

'I'll have the luggage put in then. Is this your servant?'

Rowan glanced at the man who stood to one side of Guy Perron. Extraordinary. A cap of gold thread swathed with stiff white muslin, an embroidered waistcoat over a white tunic gathered at the waist by a belt, and baggy white trousers. Into the belt was tucked a miniature axe on a long shaft decorated with silver filigree. The face was clean-shaven but pock-marked. The eyes looked as though they were rimmed with kohl. A bazaar Pathan: handsome, predatory; the kind of man Rowan instinctively distrusted.

'Yes, that's Suleiman,' Merrick said. 'There isn't much luggage. We came in a hurry and fairly light.'

Rowan called over one of the servants from the coach. He gave orders for Merrick's luggage to be placed in whichever coupé wasn't occupied by Mr Gopal.

'What have you got, Guy?'

Perron indicated a kit-bag by his side and a briefcase in his hand. 'Just these.'

'Well we can sort you out later.' He told another bearer to put Perron's kit-bag in the sitting-room. 'I expect you could both do with a drink. Let's go up.' He led the way to the observation platform and stood aside to let Merrick up. Perron waited. Rowan waved him on. When they had both gone up he watched the Pathan follow the porters into the coach at the other end. Then he smiled at Ashok, nodded to the MCO and went into the sitting-room.

Merrick had removed his cap and placed it with the swagger cane on the small table between the two armchairs. He looked younger than Rowan had expected and, by Perron's side, curiously unimpressive. Perron, in this confined area, appeared large and heavily built. The jungle-green uniform added a special note of aggressiveness. His hair was fairer than Rowan remembered and the face, in maturity, less mobile in expression. As a youth Perron had smiled constantly.

'Thank you for taking us in,' Merrick said. 'I imagine it's meant bending the rules a bit.'

'Imperceptibly. What will you have, Colonel Merrick?'

'A whisky would do very nicely, thank you. And perhaps Perron may have one too. Then I think he'd like to get his head down. He's spent most of the past week travelling.'

'There'll be a light supper next door in ten minutes or so,' Rowan said.

1240

Warning whistles were being blown. 'What about it, Guy? The MCO said the Delhi train was very late in. Haven't you missed dinner?'

'I haven't had it but I haven't missed it.' Perron's tone was edgy and abrasive. 'Incidentally, no whisky for me. Unless it's Scotch.'

'It is.'

'Really? Well, that fits.'

'Fits what?'

Perron didn't answer. He stiffened his trunk and limbs as if coming to attention. 'With your permission, sir,' he said to Merrick, 'I should like to do as you suggest and get my head down.'

'Shall I continue in custody of the bag, sir?'

'No, leave that here.'

Rowan signalled to a servant in the dining-room and pointed at Perron's kit-bag.

'If you want to tuck down I'll show you where you can settle in.'

The bearer was handing Perron a glass of whisky and soda as Rowan went past him. In the dining-room he paused, heard Perron say, 'Goodnight, sir', and Merrick's reply, 'Goodnight, Sergeant.' The train began to glide forward. When Perron came in, holding his glass, Rowan went to the far door at the right-hand side of the dining compartment and passed through it into the corridor. Merrick's Pathan, on guard outside the farthest coupé, watched him. Rowan slid open the door of No. 1 compartment. The lights were on. His case was on the luggage rack. Perron followed him in.

'Which would you like, Guy? This one with the bed arranged so that your head faces away from the engine?' He opened the door into the shower and B.C. cubicles and then another door into a duplicate berth. 'Or this one where the head faces towards?'

Perron looked round the rosily-lit compartment.

'Have you nothing in between?'

'I'm afraid not.'

'Then I'll make do with this.'

'I'm told the last Governor's lady preferred it.'

'What about the present Governor's lady?'

'She never comes up to Pankot. If HE has to he goes by road.'

'The coach is something of an anachronism?'

'You could say that.'

'That fits too.'

'Like Scotch. Why? Fits what?'

'The generally hallucinatory atmosphere I currently exist in. Your health.'

The servant came in with the kit-bag, stowed it on the rack and left by the sliding door that gave on to the corridor. When he had gone Perron shot the bolt.

'Guard your property and your life,' he said, as though it were a quotation. In one corner of the compartment there was a diminutive armchair, chintz-covered. He squeezed himself into it. 'The Red Shadow is at large. Did you ever see anything quite as camp?'

'Camp?'

'Suleiman.' Perron hesitated. 'Never mind.' Then, 'Sandhurst, wasn't it? Chillingborough and Sandhurst. Now this. ADC to HE. The Governor in Ranpur. Unless I've been imagining it all and still am, which seems likely. I believe something may have happened to me a week ago tonight. It *is* Sunday?'

'No. Monday. The thirteenth. What happened to you a week ago on Sunday?'

'There was a Maharanee mixed up in it somewhere. And then there was poor Purvis. Are you sure it's the thirteenth? I could swear it was still Sunday.'

Rowan looked at his watch. 'Actually we're both wrong. It's now Tuesday the fourteenth.'

'Good,' Perron said. 'Two days nearer.'

'Nearer what?'

'The successful conclusion of Operation Bunbury. She'll have had my telegram by now. She will have given the first little tug to the first little string. What should we allow? A month, conservatively? Can I hold out even for a month? Or shall I commit murder? What do they do to sergeants who murder their officers?'

'Hang them, I think.'

'Very degrading. A firing squad would be different. Aunt Charlotte would approve of a firing squad.'

The train clacked over a series of points. Rowan steadied himself. Perron produced a hip flask from a sidepocket of his jacket and topped up his whisky and soda. 'Scotch,' he said. 'A parting gift from my previous officer. A pleasant enough but finally very ineffectual man. The only alternative he had to propose was that I apply at once for a commission. He thought it likely it could have been immediate but I said immediate or delayed made no difference because accepting a commission at this stage of the game would simply be a policy of despair.'

'There's no need to drink your own whisky, Guy. Just press the bell.'

'I don't suppose you have the slightest idea what I'm drivelling on about, have you, Nigel?'

'Some of the details are a bit obscure but oddly enough I get the general drift.'

'Do you? I wish I did. I find the general drift elusive. So here's to Aunt Charlotte and Operation Bunbury. I hope you're not going to ask me to explain Bunbury as well as camp.'

'No. But how will an imaginary sick friend solve your problem?'

'He died. At least he did according to the telegram I sent Aunt Charlotte. You remember Aunt Charlotte?'

'The sister of your balloonist uncle?'

'That's the one. The one who got on awfully well with that stunning girl you were with at School versus Old Boys. I can't remember her name. Did you marry her, by the way?'

'No.'

'Are you married?'

'No, go on about Bunbury.'

'Bunbury was Aunt Charlotte's idea. When I told her I couldn't delay my call-up any longer she said I obviously wasn't trying and that it was most unpatriotic of me because it wasn't going to be fair on the men for whose lives and welfare I so thoughtlessly intended to accept responsibility. She only became resigned to it when I got it through to her that I intended to serve anonymously in the ranks and when I agreed to tip her off the moment I wanted her to pull strings to get me out. Throughout my relatively short but not uneventful military career, from Salisbury Plain to Kalyan, I've kept her informed of my state of mind by reporting on our friend Bunbury's state of health. His death last week will have galvanized her into action.'

'What sort of action?'

'She has several friends in what are called high places. Permanent establishment, not politicians. And fortunately I have a pleasant little niche awaiting me in what poor Purvis's benefactor called the groves of Academe. Perhaps more fortunately, our new government is both anti-imperialist and pro-education. In every graduate they will discern a future pillar of an expanded state school system. Not that I intend to be one. But I have the utmost confidence in Aunt Charlotte's ability to arrange a priority demobilization especially if she works in unison with a certain professor of modern history.'

'Who is this Purvis you keep mentioning?'

'Was. Not is. He's dead too.' Perron drank deeply, not quite finishing what was in his glass. 'I don't think I want to talk about Leonard Purvis. I'd rather talk about Bunbury. I had to follow up the telegram to Aunt Charlotte with a letter just in case the cable went astray. Would you like to know what I told her about how Bunbury died?'

'How did Bunbury die?'

'He committed suicide. Twice.'

'Twice.'

'The first time he did it in the bath-tub but I managed to revive him but when he did it again I wasn't there. They'd put him in an upstairs ward and when they weren't looking he threw himself out of the window and broke his neck.'

'A very determined Bunbury.'

'I'm glad you appreciate that. It's what I feel. In determination of that calibre there is something heroic. The thought first struck me at the hurried little inquest which they dragged me up from Kalyan to attend. They made out it was suicide while of unsound mind but you could tell they knew he was as sane as they were. On the other hand what *I* knew was that there wasn't a man in the room with anything like so profound a sense of what he was in the world to do, nor anything like so profound a sense of the criminal waste of human energy that we've seen in the last six years. I'm glad he didn't survive to hear about the new bomb.'

'Are you sure about not eating, Guy?'

'Could I have something in here?'

'Of course.'

'Then I'd better.' He poured more neat Scotch into the over-rich mixture. 'Normally, you know, I'm quite abstemious, but I've spent the past few days discreetly stoned to the eyeballs, a condition which the Red Shadow observes with envy and malicious longing to get his corrupt and filthy thieving hands into my kit-bag to see how many bottles I have left. I for my part long to catch him at it, so that I can boot him in the arse. And believe me, Nigel, before I leave, boot him I shall, with or without provocation. It's a point of honour. The arses of the Suleimans of India exist to be booted by British sergeants. It's traditional. One for the sergeant, two for the regiment and three for the *raj*. And then the women of the Suleimans of India will laugh like drains, the wild dogs of the hills will yelp their satisfaction and there will be peace again on the Khyber. I think you'd better go, because Suleiman will be making a note of the time you and I have been alone in a locked compartment and will make his report accordingly to Major Merrick. I beg his pardon. Colonel. But it's difficult to keep up. He was a major when I saw him in Bombay on Bunbury Sunday. A colonel when I reported at his office in Delhi on Thursday. I entertain this illusion now that it's dangerous to be parted from him for more than a day or two. Every night I go to sleep terrified that in the morning he'll be a full colonel or even a brigadier.'

'I take it you're not enamoured. Why, particularly?'

Perron sipped.

" 'I do not love thee, Dr Fell, the reason why I cannot tell" .' He sipped again. 'On the other hand I've been working out why. He's the man who comes too late and invents himself to make up for it. Even that arm, you know, is an invention. You needn't think it happened in a flash, with a bang, or even on an operating table. It appeared quite gradually, like the stigmata on a saint's hands and feet and side. So that the world would notice, and pause. The pause is very important. I think you'd better join him. He doesn't like being neglected or kept waiting.'

'What takes him to Pankot?'

'The case of one Havildar Karim Muzzafir Khan, late of the Pankot Rifles.'

'I think I may know a bit about that.'

'You were always insufferably well-informed. About rowing for example. What bit do you know?'

'If it's the one who joined Bose's people in Germany' – Perron nodded – 'then Miss Layton's father has put in a request for permission to see him. Is Merrick arranging it?'

Perron drank more whisky.

'No. We're going up to take statements from the havildar's former fellow NCOS.'

'No chance of an exception being made.'

'An exception?'

'No chance of Colonel Layton being allowed to see him?'

'None at all. What's so special about Colonel Layton?'

'Nothing. But what's so special about Havildar Karim Muzzafir Khan that Delhi sends a half-colonel all the way to Pankot to take statements?'

'Oh, that's easily answered. The havildar was special because Merrick chose him.'

'You mean as an example?'

'I mean he was a chosen one. It's part of the technique of the self-invented man. Merrick looks round, his eye lights on someone and he says, Right, I want *him*. Why else do you think I'm here. I'm a chosen one. I expect Coomer was.'

'Coomer?'

'Coomer. Kumar. Harry. Hari. Don't tell me you don't remember him. Miss Layton said you did. It puzzled her when I said I didn't. It aroused her suspicions. Very embarrassing. It made her wonder whether I was only pretending to have gone to Chillingborough. So she dropped a name or two. Yours was one. And then there was Clark-Without.'

'Clark-Without? How did she come to know him?'

'I think she said they met in Calcutta. You remember his reputation, I expect. Hasn't she ever mentioned him?'

'There's no reason why she should.'

'But of course she's told you about meeting me. Obviously.'

'Not all about it. Why did you say you didn't remember Coomer, by the way?'

'The subject was taboo. Not fit for mixed company. Merrick ordered me not to discuss it. The easiest way to avoid being drawn into a discussion was to pretend I didn't know him. Did you know our friend Coomer put cricket behind him and went in for rape and that our friend Merrick caught him at it?'

'Is that what he told you?'

'Has he got it wrong?'

'There are two schools of thought. How did you come across Merrick? Just by being posted to his department?'

'Attached. Not posted yet, thank God. But no. I met him one warm night. On the docks. At Bombay. It sounds romantic, doesn't it? Then I didn't meet him again until the evening at the Maharanee's. But, already I was chosen. Fate. It has driven me to drink, to Bunbury and Aunt Charlotte, and to a refutation of Emerson.'

'Emerson?'

' "Society is a wave. The wave moves onward, but the water of which it is composed does not. The same particle does not rise from the valley to the ridge. Its unity is only phenomenal. The persons who make up a nation today, next year die, and their experience with them." Emerson failed to see that there were exceptions. People like you and me.'

Rowan smiled. He made neither head nor tail of it and on the whole saw no reason to try. But a penny had just dropped.

'Did you meet a Count Bronowsky at the Maharanee's? Sarah told me he was there.'

'He was certainly there. Why do you ask?'

'He put that idea into your head, didn't he? About Merrick inventing himself and the arm?'

'He certainly didn't. It's my copyright.'

'Coincidence then. He has much the same idea. I'd better leave you to it, Guy, and get them to bring you in some supper. By the way, when I was still out on the platform just now did Merrick take the opportunity to ask you how you and I knew one another?'

'He did.'

'What did you say?'

'I said we knew one another quite well before the war. I don't think it satisfied him. He probably thinks we've been in touch recently because neither of us showed any surprise at meeting.'

'You didn't mention Chillingborough?'

'I had a feeling it wasn't necessary.'

'It doesn't matter either way but one likes to be prepared.'

'Because of Coomer? What interests you and Sarah Layton about Coomer? The fact that he's an old Chillingburian who has been in what used to be called a Spot of Bother?'

'I suppose that provides a very rough basis for an interest.'

'As for everything else? This, for instance?' He gestured round the compartment. 'I imagine Colonel Merrick's coupé isn't half as comfortable. This cosy little compartment is symbolic, don't you find?'

'I hadn't thought of it. What is it symbolic of?'

'Of our isolation and insulation, our inner conviction of class rights and class privileges, of our permanence and of our capacity to trim, to insure against any major kind of upheaval affecting our interests, and of course of our fundamental indifference to the problems towards which we adopt attitudes of responsibility. Not moral responsibility, ownership responsibility. A moral responsibility would be too trying. Even poor underprivileged Purvis was clearheaded enough to admit that. Property on the other hand can always be got rid of and new property acquired. New property, new responsibility, but the same manner, the same deep inner conviction and the same snug cosy sense of insulation. I know where I shall find mine when I'm back home. Where will you find yours, Nigel, I mean when India is got rid of?'

'I've really not thought about that, Guy. It's just a shade too far ahead.'

'You haven't thought about it. But of course you don't need to. Neither of us does. Nothing can erode our ingrained sense of class security. Your face has taken on that remote patrician look that tells me you would find what I say offensive if you thought for one moment I meant it. Well I do. Every bloody word. Emerson was obviously too much of a peasant to appreciate the significance of you and me. Society is a wave. The wave moves onward. You and I move along with it. Emerson was writing for the Merricks and Purvises of the world. The ones who get drowned. Merrick hopes not to be. But he will be. Can't the fool see that nobody of the class he aspires to belong to has ever cared a damn' about the empire and that all that God-the-Father-God-the-*raj* was a lot of insular middle- and lower-class shit?'

'An uncle of mine took God-the-father God-the-*raj* quite seriously, I should say.'

'You mean he had principles?'

'Yes, I think so.'

'I bet that if you cut right through the principles you'd find all he took seriously was his unassailable right to deploy things and people to his uttermost personal advantage and private satisfaction.'

'Is Merrick a principled man?'

'Principled as a rock. He thinks people like you and me are scum. He believes we've abandoned the principles we used to live by, what he would call the English upper- and ruling-class principle of knowing oneself superior to all other races especially black and having a duty to guide and correct them. He's been sucked in by all that Kiplingesque double-talk that transformed India from a place where plain ordinary greedy Englishmen carved something out for themselves to balance out the more tedious consequences of the law of primogeniture, into one where they appeared to go voluntarily into exile for the good of their souls and the uplift of the native. The transformation was illusory of course. A middle-class misconception of upper-class *mores*. But a man like Merrick can't be expected to see that. He's spent too long inventing himself in the image to have energy left to realize that as an image it is and always was hollow. He only notices it has become rarer. Poor Coomer obviously never stood a chance. An English public school education and manner, but black as your hat.'

'Not so black.'

'Black enough for Merrick. But most of us are as bad as black to him. There aren't many real white men left. And the odd thing is that when he comes across any he despises them. Colonel Layton for instance.'

'He despises Colonel Layton? Why?'

'White man gone soft. Guide *and* correct, remember? The two pillars of wisdom. Despises because Layton has and is everything Merrick covets. But Layton hasn't the nerve or guts to live up to it. He'd clasp the Bose-tainted havildar to his bosom, for instance. Tears of sorrow rather than the lash of anger. Too many bloody tears altogether. Even over a half-empty bottle of Old Sporran. So God help us tomorrow. Have you got any by the way?'

'Got any what?'

'Old Sporran. Doesn't Government House run to it?'

'Not nowadays. Why God help you tomorrow?'

'Not nowadays. No. Nowadays Old Sporran is reserved for the Purvises. Damned proletariat getting in everywhere. He hanged himself.'

'Who hanged himself? Purvis?'

'No, Purvis fell. The havildar hanged himself. Havildar Karim Muzzafir Khan, son of subdar Muzzafir Khan vc.'

'Oh. When?'

'Tuesday you said? So, a few minutes ago it was Monday. Sunday morning, then. Some time on Sunday morning. Before daylight. Which is why there's no chance of Colonel Layton being allowed to talk to him. There's no poor weary shagged-out shamed and insulted havildar to talk to.'

'Shamed and insulted by whom?'

'Merrick of course.'

'You witnessed it?'

'Only the beginning and the end. Bombay in June and Delhi on Friday. I expect I missed the best bits in the middle.'

'What happened in the middle?'

'I don't know. The real working-over I expect.'

'Physical working-over?'

'No sign of that on the body. I don't think that's Merrick's style.'

Perron emptied the flask into his glass. The liquor was now neat.

'You saw the body, then.'

'Oh yes. "Come over to D block, will you, sergeant? There has been an interesting development." At four o'clock in the morning.'

'Interesting?'

'That's what he said. It was quite deliberate. So that I should be unprepared. He presented the scene like a *tableau vivant*, well not so vivant, but one he'd set up which he wanted me to react to. I'm surprised he let them cut him down before I got there.' Perron swigged whisky. 'The whole thing was unspeakably ugly and sordid.'

'What did he use?'

'The havildar? You mean for rope? Torn strips of shirt and vest knotted together. He'd tried to cut his throat first with a broken bit of mess-tin. I'd prefer not to talk about it. I'll just tell you what Merrick said. "Not a very prepossessing looking chap, was he, sergeant?" '

'Yes, I see. So the real reason for the journey is to report the death to Colonel Layton?'

'No. The real reason is to sustain the connection. The role of friend of the family. Nothing brash of course. Nothing pushing. Just a persistent air of quiet competence and capacity and authority. Occasional sudden concentration of effort and flurry of activity that show the range and depth of feeling and concern. Like this visit. The human touch. And all these statements to be taken from the havildar's ex-comrades. As if anything that can be recorded now in the havildar's favour is not only welcome but a white man's duty to discover and put on the file.' Perron closed one eye and stared at Rowan as if he suddenly found it difficult to focus. Then he nodded and said:

'He's chosen the Laytons, too.'

Perron opened the closed eye and added: 'But don't worry. I mean if you do worry, don't.'

'Worry about what?'

'His choosing the Laytons. I said Laytons; not any one Layton in particular. At least I shouldn't think so. So don't worry. What *was* her name?'

'Whose?'

'The stunning girl Aunt Charlotte took a shine to.'

'Laura Elliott.'

'Laura Elliott.' Perron put his head back as if tired. 'What a sad name. What happened?'

'She married someone else.'

'Anyone I know?'

'I shouldn't think so. She met him in Rangoon. His name was Ratcliff. He planted rubber in Malaya.'

'What was she doing in Rangoon?'

'Visiting me.'

'When was this?'

'Nineteen-forty-one.'

'How did she get to Rangoon in nineteen-forty-one?'

'Her parents were in Mandalay. Civil service.'

'I always thought of her as army.'

'Her brother was.'

'Sandhurst together?'

'Yes.'

'Same regiment?'

'Yes. The three of us came out on the same boat.'

'Were you and Laura Elliott ever engaged?'

'Eventually.'

'When you went to Burma.'

'No, we became unengaged in Burma.'

'Were you in the Burma show in 'forty-two?'

'I never think of it as a show. Just as a retreat. I was in that.'

'Well, show or retreat, you survived. Did Laura Elliott's brother?'

'No.'

'Did Laura and her rubber-planter get out of Malaya?'

'The parents got out of Burma but only Mrs Elliott's still alive. She lives in Darjeeling and writes to me occasionally. She heard from Laura once early on, after she'd been interned by the Japanese. There was no news of Tony and Laura's never written again. At least nothing's been received.'

'Poor Laura. I said it was a sad name.' Perron brought his head back level. 'Does it upset you still?'

'Not any more.'

'What about Sarah Layton?'

'What about her?'

'She referred to you with what I'd call respect and admiration. Mutual?'

'Yes.'

'Pity. I mean for me. Given half an opportunity making a bit of a pass at Sarah Layton was the one thing that made the prospect of several days in Pankot bearable. But I expect I'd better behave, hadn't I? Yes. Well. Incidentally, do you mind very much if in future I call you sir in front of other people? You can go on calling me Guy if you like but it offends my sense of military decorum to call you Nigel in public.'

Smiling, otherwise ignoring this, Rowan said, 'Do you know where you're putting up?'

'You mean quartered. No, but I have every confidence in my officer. He's the kind of man who knows it's good form to look to the needs of horse, groom and self in that order, although his own comfort is assured, naturally, so it can always be safely left until last. Why? Were you thinking of keeping in touch?'

'We ought to arrange an evening if we can. You can reach me by ringing Two Hundred.'

'The Governor's hill palace?'

'It's the guest house attached to what used to be the summer residence.'

'Used to be? Has the weather deteriorated?'

'I mean it's shut up.'

'With accommodation so short?'

'People complain, but like this coach it doesn't convert very easily. And the next Governor may revive the old seasonal system of six months in the hills and six on the plain. Anyway ring me there. We'll fix something.'

Perron nodded.

Rowan said, 'I'll send a bearer in with the menu. He'll bring you a drink too if you want another. I'll leave that to your discretion. And feel free to ring the bell at any time.'

Again Perron nodded.

'Sleep well,' Rowan said, and began to go.

'Thanks for the bed, Nigel. I'm very grateful.'

*

The corridor was empty. No Red Shadow. In the dining-room two tables were laid and were being set out with chafing dishes. He smelt, fleetingly, carnations. And the scent of cologne. But there were only marigolds. He told one of the bearers to attend to the guest in compartment number two and then went through into the saloon.

Suleiman was kneeling, easing one of Merrick's feet into crimson leather slippers. Between the stiff first and second fingers of Merrick's black-gloved left hand was a lighted cigarette. Merrick and Suleiman both turned their heads. Suleiman grinned, showing handsome teeth. Merrick smiled, an odd lopsided smile – or so the scar tissue made it appear; and Rowan, in spite of everything, felt touched and under an odd kind of compulsion to forget what he knew, what he thought he knew; what it was unfair, after all, to allow himself to be affected by when he had scarcely said more than a few words to the man. As he took his seat on the sofa and nodded to the bearer indicating that he wanted another drink before eating, and listened to what Merrick was saying about Suleiman's theory that it was bad for the circulation to wear walking shoes when one wasn't walking, he also felt himself being supported, braced up almost, by an unexpected sensation of being once more – away from Guy Perron – in control of things, of himself, and in surroundings that matched his mood. And presently when Suleiman had gone, taking Merrick's shoes with him, and he and Merrick were alone, eyeing one another with what Rowan supposed an observer would interpret as cautious interest, it struck him as being odd that the one man he might have expected to be a disruptive or abrasive presence was not, but seemed to fit in and to share with him this feeling of repose, or anyway of momentary relief from the pressures which had been piling up, undermining his confidence: a feeling accentuated, perhaps, by the way the coach absorbed and muffled the vibration and clatter of the wheels without diminishing the flattering sensation of a speed and movement forward that were absolutely effortless.

The Moghul Room

[Guy Perron]

I

My Aunt Charlotte's knowledge of India and Indian affairs was very limited but her enthusiasm for any subject that interested another member of the family was quickly stirred and once it had been stirred it was difficult to moderate. For example, the technique and mystique of ballooning continued to exert a fascination for her long after her brother, my Uncle Charles, had abandoned it as a sport (having come down near Cobh in Ireland after setting out from Kent for Essex). For years, subsequently, she maintained a scrap-book into which she pasted cuttings of anything she could find that was connected with the subject of unpowered aerial navigation.

Flattering as her sharing of one's interests was it could be a little tiresome even if one's own enthusiasm remained unflagging. The clippings of newspaper articles and reports about India which she sent or saved for me until her first and fatal illness were, in a sense, an unnecessary duplication. However it is to her I owe a comparison between Operation Bunbury and the last Viceroyalty.

'Your viceroys are all Bunburyists,' she declared. (From the moment of my return home in 1945 all Indian personalities, policies and problems, were referred to as mine: your Mr Gandhi, your Mr Nehru, your Kashmir problem, your non-alignment policy, your confrontation with the Chinese, your application for foreign aid, your green revolution, your family planning.) 'Your viceroys' in 'Your viceroys are all Bunburyists' was just one of many examples of this habit of placing everything Indian as it were in my gift. Asked to justify this statement, though, she pointed out the regularity with which at certain climactic moments in talks and negotiations my viceroys withdrew, packed their bags and came home for consultation.

This, she said, was 'pure Bunburyism', clear evidence of pre-arrangements between my viceroys and my Secretary of State for India in Whitehall to ensure the continuation of whatever policy the British Government was currently pursuing in regard to the sub-continent. 'Take your present policy' she said once, when Wavell was still Viceroy (I always kept notes of our conversations), 'this is clearly a policy of conducting serious talks about a future constitutional change within a general framework of an assumption on our part that the existing status quo will be maintained. Which means that when your Lord Wavell detects that the serious talks are about to break down – or look like continuing so successfully that the status quo is actually at risk – he has himself called from the conference room as if to the telephone and returns a few minutes later to announce that there has been a development in London that requires his immediate presence there. It is merely another way of saying as Mr Worthing would have done, "I'm afraid my poor friend Bunbury has taken a turn for the worse and that I must catch the 3.15." '

I thought this a bit unfair to Wavell but on reflection saw that there was something in it in regard to viceroys in general, and said so. Thereafter whenever the Viceroy – Wavell, and then his successor, Mountbatten – arrived back in London, Aunt Charlotte sent me a postcard (usually of aerial views of the countryside) with a brief message: 'Bunbury unwell again.' 'Poor Bunbury giving cause for anxiety,' etc. The Mountbatten viceroyalty, though, produced this (an extract from one of the many letters of hers which I have preserved):

'If Attlee *means* that power is to be transferred as early as 1948, then Bunbury's ill-health has undergone a change. I don't mean he's better or worse, merely unwell in a different way. If our policy now *is* to get out, then you will begin to see that Bunbury's delicate constitution will respond admirably to every turn of events which advances our policy of demission of power by 1948 but suffer serious setbacks on any occasion when impediments to it are put in our way.'

In reply I pointed out that for the first time a viceroy of mine (Mountbatten) appeared to have plenipotentiary powers and that although this was advantageous administratively it meant that the Bunbury gambit might well have had its day. Aunt Charlotte declared at once that a viceroy with plenipotentiary powers would be the greatest Bunburyist of the lot, because it meant he would have taken Bunbury to India with him. This was not clear to me. I asked her to elucidate. She wrote:

'I mean that Bunbury has at last emerged in his true colours as The British Presence in India – traditionally seated (I mean bedridden) in Whitehall, but at last visiting with Dickie (how well that boy has done) the scene of his hitherto only vicarious triumphs and failures. Attlee has said (it is so plain to me I wish it were to you) that a holiday in India until 1948 might be beneficial to him. A valedictory tour, so to speak, like the personal appearance of a famous film-star known to millions but only as a shadow on the silver screen. After the valedictory tour he will return home, retire and be content to fade away to look at his press-cuttings. So henceforth any deterioration in Bunbury's health will occur only when it looks to the Viceroy as if your Indians aren't going to let Bunbury leave as planned.'

The force of her argument was driven home early in June 1947 when the Viceroy – having had what the papers revealed day after day as the greatest difficulty in finding someone among the contenders both able and willing to relieve us of Indian responsibility and letting Bunbury go (I recalled

Purvis's warning) announced that power would be transferred not in 1948 but in ten weeks' time.

Telegrams between Aunt Charlotte and myself crossed. Mine read: Bunbury stop looks like experience of personal appearance proved too much. Hers: Doctors here have re-examined Bunbury X-rays stop condition worse than thought stop vital expedite his return otherwise fear worst in that climate stop Dickie coping but suggest you fly out observe and supervise stop will arrange passage and underwrite reasonable expenses.

Reading this I realized that Aunt Charlotte had become a convinced Purvisite. 'Condition worse than thought' argued that a British Presence in India was as Purvis might have said no longer viable economically or administratively. 'Vital to expedite his return' was a hint that the members of the Labour Government after nearly two years in office were getting desperate at the prospect of having to continue to support this presence. Considering the complexity of the moral, political and historical issues which surrounded the attempted transfer of power in India and considering that these were the only issues ever publicly discussed I think Aunt Charlotte showed remarkable perspicacity. She thought so herself and as the years passed took undisguised pleasure in heavily underlining confirmatory passages in the articles and books she sent me – the writings of soldiers, statesmen and civil servants, journalists and historians – to draw my attention to admissions of the kind that supported what, misunderstanding me slightly, she claimed with my authority as her own entirely original opinion: that as a result of the war, the policy of Indianization, the running down of the machinery of British recruitment to the civil service and police, and as a result of the infiltration of political, communal and nationalistic modes of thought into the Indian armed services (the Naval Mutiny in Bombay in 1946 was always cited as an example) it would have been difficult, even impossible, to maintain in India any form of stable government with a responsibility to Parliament at home and for law and order and national defence in India, except at a cost which even if the will and the means were available would have been excessive and just not on from the British taxpayer's point of view.

In the delirium of pneumonia (at an advanced age she unwisely took an interest – an active interest – in her grand-nephew's passion for duck-shooting at dawn on the marshes) she spoke of many things which made sense to a member of the family. 'What, there, the penny black. Who would have thought it had so much blood in it?' Such a statement, sinister from the point of view of the medical staff, was perfectly rational if you remembered Aunt Hester's craze for philately and Uncle William's frustrated theatrical ambitions which dated from his appearance in a school production of Macbeth. Other remarks, obscure to the nurses, clear to me, showed that she was thinking turn and turn about of the things that had interested or obsessed her brothers and sisters. I should explain that my father was the only Perron of his generation who got married. The other brothers and sisters paired off: George (who was the eldest and who inherited) and Harriet, William and Hester, Charles and Charlotte. Cousins Henry and Sophie were my grandfather Perron's only brother's children. They paired off too. My father, Aunt Charlotte used to say, only got married because he was the odd boy out. Insisting on being sent to Chillingborough with a view to an Indian career, joining the army at the outbreak of the great war and getting married (not even to a relation) were, I suppose, the forms which Perron eccentricity took in his case. I was sent to Chillingborough really as an act of devotion to my father's memory. It was felt that he had never had a chance to show what – as a Perron – he could do – but that being killed on November 10, 1918, suggested he had been on the right lines. His brothers – who all had brilliant minds but unadaptable personalities – were in the main privately tutored between expulsions from a number of establishments of varying reputations and competence.

I am trying to convey as clearly and economically as I can something of the background of the last surviving member of that generation of Perrons who as she lay dying revealed herself to me as a woman whose life, so apparently full, had been in so far as original enthusiasms and direct experience were concerned (with that single and fatal exception) empty. A croaked reference to speed bonny boat could have been related either to my rowing or to the punt in which she had set out with her great-nephew to see for herself what so enthralled him about shooting duck. Drugs succeeded in reducing her temperature and there was a lucid interval before she relapsed into sleep, unconsciousness and coma. Opening her eyes and finding me there she said – indicating what she obviously recognized as a private room – 'Well I see that I am dying beyond my means' – closed her eyes and never opened them again, nor communicated, except by smiling intermittently at thoughts she did not share with me. That explicit reference to Bunbury's creator was the nearest she came to touching on a subject that had been a bond between us ever since I first set sail for India; but in making it she was just as likely to have been thinking of her Thespian brother as of her 'Indian' nephew, or even of neither but of her late brother George who, inheriting the bulk of the Perron estate, had made a number of foolish investments.

She was such an unegotistical person, such a champion of other people's causes, that it seems grossly unfair to connect her in any way with responsibility for a death roll that was never accurately counted but which has become widely accepted as reaching the one-quarter million mark.

'Your Punjabis,' she said when I got back from the euphoric and bloodstained country after taking the trip to 'observe and supervise' which she had subsidized in 1947, 'Your Punjabis would appear to have taken leave of their senses.'

She was referring to the massacres that accompanied the migrations of communities after the decision to partition. I told her that the murders of Hindus and Sikhs by Muslims and of Muslims by Hindus and Sikhs had by no stretch of the imagination been confined to the land of the five rivers, but Punjab was a word which had always had a strong appeal for people like

Aunt Charlotte and she probably felt that once you had pronounced it (particularly as she pronounced it, with a rotundity of mouth and emphasis of jaw – Poonjawb) then you had said all that needed to be said about the golden land below Afghanistan. She therefore continued to demarcate the zone of violence on this provincial basis and I think succeeded too in mentally reducing the slaughter to the manageable proportions of an isolated act of insurrection which was the result of allowing things to get a bit out of hand.

It would never have occurred to her to examine her conscience in regard to those one-quarter million deaths, although she had, in fact, as I had done – voted for them. It would not have occurred to her because she held single-mindedly to the Purvis principle, the view that a British presence in India was an economic and administrative burden whose quick offloading was an essential feature of post-war policy in the welfare state. I'll give her this, though: in adhering to this principle she never once introduced the ethical argument that colonialism was immoral – an argument that supported so many of us. I don't think the ethical argument ever entered her head. She was esentially a pragmatist. The only moral argument I ever remember her advancing was the one she used to try to convince me that my joining up would be unfair to the men she assumed I would accept responsibility for.

Needless to say, I never told Aunt Charlotte that she, as well as I, was responsible for the one-quarter million deaths in the Punjab and else-where. But I did once ask her who, in her opinion, *was* responsible. She said, 'But that is obvious. The people who attacked and killed each other.' There was no arguing with this, but it confirmed my impression of her historical significance (and mine), of the overwhelming importance of the part that had been played in British-Indian affairs by the indifference and the ignorance of the English at home – whom Aunt Charlotte, in an especially poignant way had in my mind come to represent; and upsetting though I found it, nothing was more appropriate than that in that delirium, when images of all the acquired and borrowed interests of her life flowed swiftly through her heated imagination, images of India were totally forgotten.

*

In investing someone with historical significance one should proceed cautiously but I think the conclusion I came to about her share of responsibility for disorder and bloodshed can be traced back to that grey humid morning in Kalyan when I stood up and spoke for half an hour to a hall full of restless and inattentive men about the territorial ambitions of Mahdaji and Daulat Rao Sindia, and realized how little any of us knew or cared about a country whose history had been that of our own for more than three hundred years and which had contributed more than any other to our wealth, our well-being.

Less than a month later I was passing through Deolali to embark at

Bombay on a homeward-bound ship in a mood alternating between the exhilaration of a man released to follow his own bent and the depression of one who retires from a situation gratefully but with some doubts about the means he's adopted to extricate himself. There were as well some unexpected regrets.

If I had been with Ronald Merrick right up to the time when the signal came ordering me to report to Deolali, I doubt that I should have felt anything except relief and grateful astonishment at the speed with which Aunt Charlotte had apparently worked. But I wasn't with him; rather, he wasn't with me and the signal happened to arrive at a moment when I was aware of being comfortably situated and pleasantly occupied.

*

In the morning, after that night journey from Ranpur in the Governor's special coach, when Rowan and I bumped into each other in the narrow passage between Their Excellencies' compartments (w.c. on one side, shower on the other) he was polite but (I thought) a little cool. I think he assumed I was lying when I told him I had no hangover, or assumed that I had already started on one of the bottles in my kit-bag so that I could face up to another day with Merrick and the Red Shadow.

He may have been right about the hangover because my recollections of the arrival in Pankot aren't very clear. But there could be another reason for that. To have travelled on the same train as a coffin without knowing it is one thing. To be greeted by a large crowd banging on drums another. I don't recall how soon it was before I connected the crowds and the drums with a funeral, or the funeral with a coffin that had come in on the train, or the coffin with the body of Mr Kasim's secretary, and I'm not sure whether it was Merrick's information alone, or Merrick's and the Red Shadow's plus other people's that helped me to fit the pieces together. What I do remember is that it was nothing Nigel Rowan said because he said very little. An impression I had that morning was of not inspiring his confidence; another was that as a result of whatever conversation he'd had with Merrick the night before there was an amiability between them now which seemed, on Rowan's part, advertised to show me that he discounted everything I had told him about that officer's behaviour. Without caring much what the answer was I wondered whether Nigel had said anything to Merrick about my attitude to him, and whether Merrick's silence in the 15 cwt that Area HQ had sent to the station for us was especially ominous.

Nigel's detachment, Merrick's silence, the distracting crowds at the station, the drums and the shouting, the revolting stink of the Red Shadow's stale breath and unwashed body in the confined luggage-loaded space at the tarpaulin-covered back of the truck: these have stayed with me as parts of the jig-saw. Another part of it is waiting, in several places; keeping upwind of the Pathan if on the same verandah with him and moving if he came too near. The waiting was done in the complex of old

Victorian barracks and huts of more recent origin that was Area Headquarters. A dry sunny morning? Something cool but hard – metallic – in the air, the smell of a century or more of Pankot's experience of military occupation. A late breakfast in a British NCOs' mess. Eating it alone at a long table as yet uncleared of used plates and cups and saucers. The depredations of white ants in wooden window frames set in crumbling plaster. Views from these windows of the hills. The sound of a coppersmith. Shafts of sunlight? A padlocked glass-fronted cupboard that displayed a few silver cups, sporting-trophies. A dartboard and last night's chalked scores. A little bit of Salisbury Plain in the Indian hills. I had never hated the army so much as I did in this hour or two in this drearily familiar and horribly anonymous area of roads and pathways, directional signs, inhospitable huts and characterless rooms – the makeshift impermanent jerry-built structures that seem to rest for sole support on the implacable and rigid authority of military hierarchy. The fire of hatred (so intense, so unexpected, so out of character) was stoked and fanned by a sudden and utter lack of confidence in the machine I thought I had set in motion with the telegram and letter to Aunt Charlotte. The illusion of imminent escape withered away in this uncompromising and heartless reality.

Another piece of the jig-saw: as I sat beneath the dartboard, stupefied by this misery, there was a distant crackling fusillade of shots whose echoes bounced from one hill to another. When the echoes were finally spent I heard the uninterrupted song of the coppersmith. No barking. The birds and dogs of Pankot – wild or tame – were used to the sound of range practice.

And I remember relief when the truck came back from wherever it had been with Merrick and the Red Shadow and I was taken by the driver (a surly, solitary man) from the NCOs' mess; relief that was short-lived because it ended in another anonymous room, an annexe in the grounds of the General Hospital (military wing) which I later discovered lay approximately half-way between Area Headquarters and the lines of the Pankot Rifles depot.

From the window of this room there was no view at all. The hospital was well provided with shade trees and the annexe was half-hidden in bushes. I didn't bother to ask the driver why I was to be quartered there, nor did I ask where Merrick and the Red Shadow were. One of the pleasures of being a sergeant is of feeling under no obligation to satisfy your curiosity about the background to events. You don't originate *anything* if you can help it. Delivered by the driver, admitted by a servant (who must have had an instruction from somewhere) I entered the room in the annexe and because it had a bed had no difficulty in assuming that this was where I was to sleep while in Pankot. I dumped pack and kit-bag and lay down.

Out of this phase (morning of August 14 to morning of August 16) one important minor figure emerges: that of an RAMC corporal, a young man from Bermondsey. I shall call him Corporal Dixon. The British NCOs on the hospital staff messed together and formed a little clique. It was a very unmilitary set-up: sergeants, corporals, but not lance-corporals. Driven by hunger to leave the room in the annexe and find the mess-hut I found I was expected, but I think only as a man with a name and the barest identification. I was received in a friendly easy-going fashion and given a beer. The mess conveyed an idea of intellectual superiority. There was a Van Gogh reproduction on one wall and the sound of Mozart from the portable gramophone. A few of the NCOs had seen service in the field. For them, Pankot was a relief station. Among these front-line veterans was Corporal Dixon, known affectionately as Sophie, or Miss Dixon, or Mum.

I was told that he kept the patients in the wards in stitches and that he had tamed the QA nursing sisters and the medical officers. I was also told that a wounded officer who had watched him at work at a casualty clearing station in the Arakan and listened to the stream of morale-boosting queenly chat – a mocking commentary on the sounds of battle near by – had said: 'You deserve the MM, Corporal.' Sophie had said, 'Oh that would never do, sir, I wouldn't presume, and where would they pin it, the cheeky things?'

But these tales came later when I set about trying to find out how I had offended, what had caused the temperature to drop. Between the friendly reception and the freezing up no more than a few hours passed. Dixon's first appearance was at lunch. 'A copper!' he said, fingering my green armband. 'Has someone been at the drugs? It's no good looking here, sergeant, we're all clean-living boys. It's that Matron over at Private. She's never been the same since she visited Cox's Bazaar looking for a bargain and found it closed for stock-taking.'

I laughed and was introduced. Dixon was rather welcome comic relief. Perhaps if I hadn't laughed he would have been tipped the wink to quieten down. Lunch was at a long table. White cloth. A vase or two of marigolds. I was at one end, as I remember, and Dixon at the other. The atmosphere was amiable. Once it was established that I wasn't at the hospital on duty but only quartered temporarily in the annexe I don't think any further questions were asked. I remember that towards the end of the meal all conversation died away because Dixon had taken the stage and was recounting a series of scurrilous but very funny stories, most of them delivered in a tone of prim outrage, of astonishment at the trickery and under-handedness of the world. It took me some time to sort out the code. After failing to see the point several times I realized that 'she' almost invariably meant 'he'. A sentence such as 'Well you should have seen her, got up to the nines in her new frock, preening she was, poor old thing, well she doesn't often have one does she?' didn't, I discovered, refer to a matron at a hospital dance but to a senior officer of the RAMC or the IMS who was wearing a new uniform, hadn't been looking where he was going and had bumped into and knocked Corporal Dixon over at a moment when he happened to be carrying a bed-pan full of urine. 'So there she was, drenched with Private Thingummy's piss, new dress ruined, and there was me flat on me bum and covered in piss too, thinking I'd really ask for me cards this time. But you can't beat breeding, can you? "Is that Corporal Dixon?" she says to Matron looking down her nose, oh very ladylike. "I'm afraid it is," Matron says. "I see," she says. "I suppose it was not entirely his fault so we won't hold it against him." Well as to *that*, I thinks to meself, chance would be a fine thing.'

How much of Dixon's tale was true one could only guess. (Did RAMC corporals carry bedpans in India?) What was clear was his rôle. He was the safety-valve. How well-timed and sustained his performances were over a period I could not judge except from the behaviour of his companions in the mess. Presumably he knew when to play up and when to give it a rest. I detected no signs either of boredom or aggression. Before the meal was quite over the steward brought in a note. It was for me; from Merrick. The truck-driver had brought it. I got up to leave.

'Are you with us for long, Sergeant?' Sophie Dixon called out. I told him probably for a day or two; added that I'd see them tonight anyway.

'Coppers,' he said for my benefit before I reached the door. 'The competition's been something cruel since they started sending them to college.'

A row of men, smiling, interested to see how I took it. Still smiling when I left. The next time I saw them they were not even civil; as though in the interval the gloom that began to settle on me during the long irritating afternoon had conveyed itself to them. I was deprived of the comic relief, of an antidote to Merrick who had surpassed himself to the extent when for two pins I would have set about undermining the whole subtly balanced structure of mystification and intimidation which was what he erected to get what he wanted.

From the medical NCOS' mess I was translated to a world of old barracks and hutments, parade grounds, flagpoles in beds of white-washed stones, the smell of creosoted wood warmed by the sun; a hot breeze blowing in from hills which were rigid in the torpor of an Indian afternoon. The distant coppersmith. I was delivered to the adjutant's office in the lines of the Pankot Rifles and conducted from there to a low block – square stuccoed whitewashed pillars of brick supporting the overhang of a steep-pitched roof to form a verandah – into a room that was being emptied of benches by a squad of sepoys. A school- or lecture-room. The walls were hung with posters, aids to recognition of enemy planes, tanks and personnel. At a table on the daïs sat Merrick. Three officers stood round him: a pale middle-aged Englishman (who was the adjutant, Coley), a youngish Indian captain and a very young English subaltern, smart as paint, stiff as starch with a lot of fine blond hair showing on his arms between immaculately turned up and laundered sleeves and on his legs between the hem of knife-edged khaki shorts and the tops of stockings worn with puttees and brown boots. Of the four only Merrick failed to respond to my energetic entrance and salute. But he was facing the door and although he didn't look up from the file he was reading he knew who it was. There were a couple of jemadars, a havildar who looked like a clerk and a naik in charge of the sepoy work-squad.

When the last bench had been taken out Merrick said, 'We shan't need the daïs either.' The three officers got down from it. Merrick remained. 'And if it's not too much trouble, Coley, I'd like this table placed where the light falls as fully as possible on whoever's sitting behind it.'

'Of course.'

No one asked why he wanted this light. He had the trick of directing people's minds from strategy to tactics. The table was tried several ways while Merrick stayed enthroned on the daïs. The subaltern was used as a stand-in to test for the light. When the right place was found Merrick got up to allow the chair to be taken over and placed behind the table. Then he went across and sat down again. The sepoys took the daïs out. 'We shall want another table and several more chairs,' he said, 'including another one with arms to go in front of *this* table.' All this was attended to. Then a medium scale map of the Pankot District was sent for. A box of pins with different coloured heads. A pair of compasses. The maps were brought. The jemadars pinned them to the wall in sequence. Mugs of tea arrived, followed by the compasses and pins which turned out to be my cue.

'This is where you can make yourself useful, sergeant,' he said. He gave me a copy of the list of VCOs, NCOs and men who had been prisoners-of war in Germany. Against each man's name was the name of his village. With the compasses a circle was described on the map with its centre at the depot and with a radius equal to five miles on the ground. Then, as I read out the men's names and villages the jemadar stuck a pin in the map, a different coloured pin for each different rank. Whenever a pin was stuck inside the pencilled circle I had to mark the name on the list with an asterisk.

We must have been occupied thus for well over an hour. Merrick came and went, sometimes with Coley, sometimes with the Indian officer. The subaltern remained with me and the jemadar, absolutely enthralled because he had no idea what we were up to. By the time we had finished the map showed at a glance how many of the ex-prisoners-of-war, now on leave, could be fairly easily got hold of; how many of them, in other words, lived within five miles of the depot. When I explained this to the subaltern he seemed quite bowled over at such an efficient – and humane – bit of staff-work. No one liked to interrupt such well-earned leave, so the first set of interviews would be with men who could be collected from and returned to their villages in the course of a single day.

He also saw why the table had been placed so that the light fell on the faces of the officers asking for statements and not on the faces of men who were to be encouraged to make them. The table tops had already been covered by blankets, and there was a vase of flowers on one of them. From Delhi Merrick had brought with him poster-size blow-ups of smiling victorious generals: Monty, Alex and Wavell (chosen for their connections with the Middle East where the 1st Pankots had fought). There were also posters of Bill Slim and Dickie Mountbatten as Supremo. These were all pinned in strategic places on the walls. The master-stroke was the inclusion of a much enlarged photograph of a group of Indian officers leaning out of tanks and shaking hands with Americans, and of VCOS, NCOS and sepoys being matey with European other ranks in what looked like a street in devastated Berlin or Cologne. Everything in the room now conspired to make the ex-prisoners-of-war who had been true to the salt and not gone over to Bose – proud and helpfully talkative. The subaltern, so obviously newly commissioned, and perhaps secretly relieved that he would now never have to lead his men into battle, was almost visibly moved. He interpreted the whole *mise en scène* as a compliment to men of a fine regiment and as a stroke of genius on the part of the one-armed Lieutenant-Colonel who, although coming from Delhi, obviously knew a thing or two and respected what he knew.

What the subaltern didn't know (how could he?) was that the whole business of the interviews and statements was utterly pointless. The Indian lieutenant suspected of being implicated in the death of a sepoy in Königsberg was himself dead – so I had discovered from the files in Delhi. Karim Muzzafir Khan's name, far from 'cropping up several times' in depositions taken in Germany about the dead sepoy had cropped up once. Moreover, the death of the sepoy might well have been due to natural causes. Suspicions had arisen solely from accusations and counter-accusations among Frei Hind sepoys who had been questioned after the Germans collapsed and who had no connections with the Pankot Rifles and one of whom may well have chosen to cast doubts on Havildar Karim Muzzafir Khan's conduct simply because he was an infantryman from a stuck-up regiment. There was no statement to be taken from any of the returned Pankot Rifles prisoners that could have any bearing on the dead sepoy, the dead lieutenant or on the dead Karim Muzzafir Khan's behaviour. The only things the ex-POWs would be able to tell us were the things they had already told Colonel Layton and their other officers directly they were reunited: their experiences of being talked to or intimidated by Bose's officers. Brief statements were already on the file. Eventually these might have to be elaborated but the cases against the Frei Hind officers were a long way down on the list of priorities.

I said the arrangements being made for these interviews were utterly pointless. That's not quite accurate. They weren't pointless in terms of Merrick's passionate exploration outwards from the hollow centre of his self-invented personality, and in these terms they were in every detail an exposition of his determining will and of his profound contempt for anything, for anybody, that crumbled without resisting. Some hindsight here; but whenever I think of him nowadays this little *mise en scène* comes back to me as a vivid illustration of the extraordinary care he took to manipulate things, people and objects, into some kind of significant objective/subjective order with himself at the dominating and controlling centre.

What arguments he used to convince senior officers in his department in Delhi that he should leave at once on a statement-taking mission, accompanied by his newly acquired sergeant, I don't know. If there was opposition I wasn't aware of it; the operation was mounted smoothly, swiftly – as if Merrick had anticipated the havildar's suicide and planned in advance so that the only impediment to the scheme had been the havildar's tiresome stubbornness in staying alive. I certainly had no doubt that one of the chief reasons for the sudden journey was his desire to tell Colonel Layton to his face that the havildar was dead.

He had this effect on me. I attributed to him the grossest motives and the darkest intentions without a scrap of real evidence. The interesting thing is that I was convinced that he knew this, that my instinct to hold him in such intense dislike and suspicion was clear to him from the beginning and was one of the reasons why he had chosen me. I believe he found it necessary to be close to someone whose antagonism he knew he could depend on and that without this antagonism he had nothing really satisfactory by which to measure the effect of his behaviour. My antagonism was like an acid, acting on a blank photographic plate which had been exposed to his powerful and inventive imagination. It made the picture emerge for him. This excited him, the more so because my antagonism could not be expressed openly without risk to myself of being guilty of insubordination. There were moments in our association when I felt that my animosity inspired in him a gratitude and a contempt both so overwhelming that he felt for me the same tender compassion that is often said to overcome the inveterate slaughterer of game in the split second before he squeezes the trigger.

*

Pankot, then: the evening of August 14, 1945. On this same evening things were taking place of much greater consequence; for instance, in Tokyo, where the Japanese War Cabinet, persuaded by the Emperor, had finally decided to 'bear the unbearable'. In the past week since the incident in Hiroshima and its follow-up in Nagasaki it had become obvious to them that when the bomb-owning governments said Unconditional Surrender this was precisely what was meant. No trimming; no understanding even as between gentlemen that there would be no allied occupation of the Japanese mainland (that had been tried). No promise that the Emperor's person would be respected (that had been sought). So, on this evening the decision to surrender unconditionally was made, and perhaps as Merrick and I were driven away from the Pankot Rifles depot, having left the *mise en scène* in a state of readiness for the commencement of the charade the next day – the Emperor of Japan was at his desk recording the edict which was to be broadcast to his weeping subjects at midday tomorrow August 15, well before which time the decision would have been conveyed to us through the Swiss.

And at the very moment Merrick and I drove out into Rifle Range Road heading for Cantonment Approach Road and the Pankot General Hospital, it is probable that the handful of dissenting Japanese officers who tried to break into the Emperor's palace later that night to destroy the recorded edict before it could be broadcast were already gathering and working out ways and means and the odds against the success of this last ditch Samurai act of patriotic defiance.

In Pankot the height of the surrounding hills made for a longer evening than one was accustomed to down on the plains and instead of encroaching from the east night seemed to lap slowly down the inner slope of west hill (where rich Indians had built their hillstation houses) and glide across the valley and then inch its way up east hill where the English lived and on whose peak, amid conifers, one could make out the roofs and upper-windows (last reflectors of the light of day) of the Summer Residence. Once the light had gone from the roof of this dominant but unoccupied building night fell – you might say – with the Government's permission. Sarah smiled when I suggested this to her. She knew the view well from the lines of the Pankot Rifles but its symbolism had not struck her before.

My recollection is of seeing it first when waiting on the verandah outside the room that had been got ready for the interviews with the ex-POWs, because I'm sure I retained a visual impression of it on the journey back and that when Merrick turned round and said, 'You know where to reach me?' I pictured him standing at the window of one of those blazing upper rooms of the Summer Residence, getting burnt on the other side of his face but feeling nothing. The real answer to the question where he could be reached was only slightly less impressive. He was staying at Flagstaff House with the Area Commander.

One question I longed to ask him was how Colonel Layton had taken the news of Karim Muzzafir Khan's death. I assumed the news had been passed on and that by the afternoon it was generally known by the other Pankot Rifles officers and the senior NCOs and VCOs, and that this had accounted for the heavy pause – the brief but significant silence that followed my intentionally clear announcement of his name and village when I got to it on the list and the jemadar fumbled with the coloured pins as if looking for a black one.

But I restrained my curiosity and said nothing; even when the truck drove inexplicably *past* the hospital entrance and made for the bazaar. The crowds who must have attended the funeral seemed to have gone but left hostages, groups of people still *en fête* and bunches of idle police. We stopped outside a general store. The driver got out and walked down the crowded road towards War Memorial Square – by prearrangement, obviously, since Merrick didn't question him. In fact he lit a cigarette. Without turning – addressing the windscreen – he said, 'Do you expect to see your friend Captain Rowan again while he's in Pankot?'

I told him we had no actual arrangement.

'It might be useful,' he said, 'for us to know just what he's up to.'

It was typical of Merrick that he should describe Rowan as being 'up to' something – and 'up to' something that had or might have a bearing on what Merrick himself was up to. It so happened that Nigel was in fact up to something, on the Governor's behalf, but I wasn't aware of this until later when Rowan – stung by certain developments – dropped his guard and disclosed that his distrust and dislike of Merrick were almost as great as my own. Discounting what he called an element of doubt, he had cogent reasons but wouldn't at first say what they were.

But it irritated me that because I now worked with Merrick he thought I could be used to pump an old friend for information which he hinted I not only could but ought to get for him. My polite but thick sergeant act (the NCO equivalent of what is known as dumb-insolence in private soldiers) saved me from actually promising something I had no intention of performing. And it may have sufficiently served Merrick's purpose to observe the effect his suggestion had on me. There was no reason why he shouldn't ask Rowan himself what brought him to Pankot. He had more opportunity, officially and socially. I discovered later that he and Nigel had both accepted an invitation to dine that night at the Laytons' and that each knew that the other would be there.

The driver came back; not alone. He had the Red Shadow in tow. The Red Shadow climbed into the back, disposed some parcels (presumably bought for Merrick) and gave me one of his malevolent grins. I never worked out the significance of these grins. More often than not he stared at me unsmiling. But since it was clear that he wished me no good in either case I never gave much thought to the matter, and on this occasion responded as usual with a gaze as blank as I could make it.

The truck was now reversed and we drove back to the hospital. The manoeuvre that had taken me past the hospital, to the bazaar, and now back again, seemed quite pointless, but it was all part of Merrick's mystification technique and I was becoming used to it. We drove through the gates of the hospital and for a sickening moment I thought that the Red Shadow was to be quartered where he could keep an eye on me. This suspicion hardened when we stopped outside the medical NCOs' mess and the Red Shadow vaulted over the tailboard and arrived on the asphalt, legs apart, like an acrobat fetching up in a standing position at the end of a sequence of spectacular leaps and somersaults. He was, thank God, only making room for me to make a less agile descent. He climbed back in again directly I was out. But now Merrick also got out. He came round to where I stood dusting my hands.

'I can't guarantee transport in the morning, sergeant.'

'No, of course not, sir.'

'The Pankot's adjutant says he can produce two of the men we want to interview by 1030 tomorrow morning. I shall get to the office by ten so if nothing's come to pick you up by 0930 you'd better get a tonga down to the depot or scrounge some transport from one of the NCOs here. Are you quite comfortably situated, by the way?'

I told him very.

'I ran into one of the medical officers who helps me from time to time with this arm. He said his NCOs had a spare billet or two. I thought you'd find it more congenial than any of the alternatives.'

'It was very thoughtful of you, sir.'

He stared at me for rather longer than seemed necessary. Then he said, 'Tomorrow will be rather interesting. Goodnight, sergeant.'

I stamped on the asphalt and threw one up. I thought he blinked but couldn't be sure. A really good salute requires one's eyes to be fixed fair and square on the bridge of the officer's nose. He touched the peak of his cap with the tip of his swagger cane. Before the truck had started up I was off down the path past the mess to my quarters feeling in my pocket for the key to the padlocked steel ring that secured my kit-bag. In the bag there was the last of two bottles of Scotch and one of rum: sweeteners from my previous officer – a man whose experience of Poona had in my opinion had a dampening effect on his initiative. Otherwise he would have fought for me.

*

So far I have said nothing about my private life in India and the time has come when it ought perhaps to be dealt with. I should describe it as moderately satisfactory, as achieving its peak (perhaps appropriately) in Agra with the wife of an officer who was having an affair with the wife of another and its nadir in a massage parlour in Bombay which had been recommended and which I had first visited after a rough journey through warm rain on a 500 c.c. Norton, had vowed never to visit again but dropped in on during the afternoon following the inquest on Leonard Purvis, which was the same afternoon Beamish told me I was to go to Delhi to join Merrick. Otherwise the graph of satisfaction, while giving me no cause for smug self-congratulation at the time, does not in retrospect go quite so far as to suggest positive deprivation.

I mention it because, while sitting in my tin tub, drinking whisky, the cool invigorating air of the Pankot hills suddenly hit me and twenty minutes later I was setting off for the mess, turning over in my mind the interesting possibility that the friendly senior NCO (whom I shall call Sergeant Potter) might turn out accommodating in regard to whatever arrangements there were to maintain a good relationship with the Eurasian nurses (or even with the less snobbish of the QAs). Not caring much for rum I took the bottle with me, to present it to the mess, and arrived there, matily, full of good intentions. These very quickly withered.

To begin with the rum was declined on the grounds that the drinking of anything but beer in the mess was strictly regulated and that mess rules did not allow members, let alone guests, to bring bottles in. Then there turned out to be a non-treating rule which, broken on my first appearance at lunch-time, was now rigidly re-applied and meant that I couldn't sign a chit to repay earlier hospitality but only for whatever beer I wanted myself. All this was explained by Potter as the others drifted away from the bar to the sitting area. He stayed with me, but less out of friendliness than a determination to protect his colleagues from me, or so it began to seem.

But it wasn't until Sophie Dixon arrived that I really came to the conclusion that for all practical purposes I was in Coventry. He swept in, came to the bar, ordered a beer, signed a chit, acknowledged Potter, ignored me and then went over to the others. Then he started.

There was a smell in the room, he said. Had anyone let wind? If not, was it the drains? Or something in the cookhouse? It really was a very peculiar smell. But vaguely familiar. Given time he'd identify it. Meanwhile it quite turned him up. It made him feel very queer. He didn't think he'd last out. Especially after the day he'd had. Guess whom he'd seen? Her very self. Miss Khyber Pass of 1935. Prancing around like a two year old. Positively cavorting. She'd do herself an injury if she didn't look out. In fact he wondered how she had the energy considering she had two of them in tow this time. Count Dracula again, but also a new one, Golden Boy. Very superior, Golden Boy. Very posh. In fact you might say regal. But smart. Oh yes, very smart. Full of bull. When he came to attention it fair went through you. In fact you thought yours would drop off and you wondered why his hadn't. Well you did if you thought he had any in the first place, which you couldn't take for granted nowadays when they were letting anybody in and not even bothering to say cough.

At dinner, Potter who sat at the head of the table indicated I should sit on his right again but this time the place on my own right and the place opposite were left empty. The others crowded together and talked shop. Potter looked unhappy. Our conversation petered out. The others left the table as and when they'd finished. Eventually I was alone with Potter at our end. Dixon and another corporal remained at the other.

Potter said, 'Breakfast's a bit of a moveable feast. You could have yours in your room if you like.'

I said, 'I will if it's more convenient and what you'd prefer.'

Dixon muttered something. It sounded like, "ark at 'er.'

Potter, playing with the spoon and fork on his pudding plate, said, 'Just tell the boy.' Then he said, 'There's not a bad Chinese restaurant in the bazaar. We sometimes go there of an evening.'

'Actually,' I said, 'I'm not awfully keen on Chinese cooking.'

'Oh, Christ,' Dixon said, almost loudly.

'But I suppose they do egg and chips?' I added. For the first time Potter met my glance, pitifully grateful. He hated being rude. He said there was a good film on at the Electric Cinema. They'd all seen it themselves and enjoyed it. If I wanted to go tonight I could catch the second house.

*

1270

I didn't go that night. I went the following night – after eating at the Chinese restaurant. August 15. Sergeant Perron's lonely vj day celebration. But it *was* a celebration. I began the day by having breakfast in my room, and so heard nothing about Japan's formal surrender until I arrived at the Pankot Rifles depot by tonga and went to the hut we'd set up the day before. Merrick wasn't there. I was told about the Japanese by the adjutant, Coley. He assumed that the interviews would be postponed. The depot commandant, Colonel Trehearne, had declared a holiday from all parades. The truck that was to have collected the two men chosen for interview hadn't yet set off.

The depot lines had a look of a Sunday morning make and mend. The air was bright. Things sparkled. The hills were in clear definition. There had been no rain for a day or two. Depot sweepers were sprinkling water to lay the dust on the road outside the hut and on the earthen floor of the verandah. The young subaltern arrived and was chatty. We walked up and down in the sunshine and he confided in me his intention to stay in India as long as he could. By eleven o'clock the truck still hadn't left and Merrick still hadn't appeared. Maintaining my policy of initiating nothing I hung round, talking to whoever turned up.

Merrick arrived at mid-day. He saw the adjutant first and then came out to talk to me. As a result of Japan's surrender Merrick had been recalled. He was to fly that evening from Ranpur to Delhi and thence to Ceylon – from where, providing the Japanese forces in Malaya laid down their arms, he would fly on to Singapore where he would be busy with the initial sifting of blacks, greys and whites among the INA men who had co-operated with the enemy. I never discovered how hard he had tried on the phone that morning to persuade Delhi to order me to accompany him. I'm sure he did try because his attitude was unmistakably begrudging. He didn't want to leave me behind in Pankot. Delhi must have told him to. Another officer would be sent to replace him. Meanwhile I was to stay and get the interviews started with an interviewing board of a couple of Pankot Rifles officers and myself with a watching brief.

You will understand my euphoria. It became difficult to sustain my dumb-insolence act. This did not escape Merrick's notice. The unblemished side of his face acquired, just under the skin, a tremor.

'I may send for you in Singapore,' he said. He was about to take his leave. We were strolling up and down the road outside the hut where the truck was parked. He was giving me instructions about the conduct of the interviews and the importance of keeping them strictly within the terms of reference and not letting the Pankot officers get lost in irrelevancies. Then he stopped, and said, 'I suppose that is all.' We were by the truck. The Red Shadow was in the back, grinning. I affected not to notice him.

'Incidentally,' Merrick said. 'I saw Captain Rowan last night. We dined at Colonel Layton's house. Has he contacted you at all?'

I said he had not.

'I'm sure he will. So be careful what you say if he raises the subject of Mr

1271

Kasim's INA son. He was pumping me rather. I'd have liked to be more forthcoming because it was rather a special evening, but the department isn't so sure now that it would be at all helpful, whatever Government says, so I didn't want to raise his hopes. It would be better if you pretended to know nothing.'

He was back on form. I told him it wouldn't be difficult to pretend I knew nothing because I didn't.

'But you've read the file on Sayed Kasim.'

'No, sir.'

'I thought you would have done. I told you in Bombay it was one of our most interesting cases.'

I didn't answer.

He said, 'Perhaps it's just as well you didn't, though. Otherwise your old school-friend might have cross-examined you more successfully than he did me. He's been well trained to find out a lot and give little away. But so have I. Although in a different school.'

The time had come to say goodbye. Had he been about to offer his good hand? Was he aware of the possibility that we would not meet again? I gave myself no chance to find out. Smart step back. Stamp. One two three, up. The combination of muscular tension and emotional relief caused me to grunt. He smiled, tipped his cap peak with the cane and got in.

As he did so – and as I took in this *mise en scène* – the skin on the back of my neck and above my ears seemed to contract. Perhaps the hair stood up. Whatever the effect the cause was that I had apprehended not only the significance of Sophie Dixon's monologue of the evening before but the significance of the back-to-the-hospital-via-the-bazaar routine. In a different setting we had just re-enacted the end of that seemingly pointless journey. But it had been far from pointless. We had gone first to the bazaar because he wanted the Red Shadow in on the act. We had then driven to the hospital and into the grounds and stopped in view of the NCOs' mess because Merrick wished us – if possible – all to be seen together by the members of that mess. And obviously we had been. The three of us. Count Dracula, Miss Khyber Pass of 1935 and Golden Boy. Dracula and Miss Khyber Pass were known figures. Golden Boy was new. Accepted for myself on my first appearance – once identified as belonging to Merrick and the Red Shadow and transformed by some sinister magic flowing from them into Golden Boy, I was at once rejected. I did not know why. All I knew was that this rejection had been deliberately engineered by Merrick. He had sent me, unidentified and unaccompanied, into a nest of his enemies. And having established me there he had with meticulous attention to detail arranged to have me exposed as an enemy too. Nothing has ever convinced me otherwise.

He beckoned me to come closer.

'By the way, sergeant. I'm leaving Suleiman in your care. At least for a day or two. He'll continue to be quartered with the servants at Flagstaff House but I've told him to report to you here every morning. He has his month's wages and his return travel warrant. The officer who comes up to replace me may want to borrow him. If not I'll send word and then I rely on you to get him on to a train and send him back to Delhi. Meanwhile, make whatever use of him you think fit. He knows his way round Pankot pretty well now.'

It was Merrick's parting gift to me, the only one he had available that he calculated would cast a blight on my day of liberation. But in this case he had miscalculated. The Red Shadow was still grinning at me. I grinned back at the Red Shadow, making calculations of my own. If the grin surprised the Red Shadow he gave no sign of it, but I think it surprised Merrick. Puzzled him? Interested him? Suggested to him a new line of attack for future dealings with me? It was difficult to say. When I turned from the Red Shadow to Merrick and snapped out, 'Right, sir,' there was a look on the looking side of his face that I can only describe as one of triumph and no-triumph, of contempt and no-contempt. And the scarred side was immobile and expressionless as if it had long since grown tired of living with its enigmatic counterpart.

*

Merrick left Pankot on the morning of vj day. I had my midday meal with vcos at the depot, and spent the evening at the Chinese restaurant and the cinema. Apart from breakfasts in my room, an evening bath and a night's sleep, I kept clear of the hospital set-up and could have done so more or less indefinitely. But Rowan came to the rescue. I'm fairly sure that he did so on Thursday, August 16.

He turned up at the Pankot Rifles depot, inquiring for me. He knew that Merrick had gone. He had finished his own job in Pankot but was staying on for a while. The Indian civilian who had come up with him, Gopal, had gone back to Ranpur. Nigel was alone at the guest house. He suggested I should join him. I said I'd be glad to. So it was arranged that I should transfer my stuff up there in the evening. He offered to send a car but I told him not to bother. He said he'd inform the billeting officer at area headquarters.

One reason for choosing Thursday as the day I moved in with Rowan is my recollection of the timing of certain events concerning the Red Shadow. Merrick left on the Wednesday, having told me that the Pathan would report to me every morning at the depot. I was prepared to find these instructions disobeyed so I was surprised when he turned up on – as it must have been – the first morning of Merrick's absence. He was waiting at the stick-guard post that controlled entry to the administrative block when I got there at 10 a.m. The first thing he asked for was a pass so that he could come and go freely on any errands I sent him on. I said I would think about it but not today because I had no errands for him to run. It would be enough for me if he reported again the following morning.

Seeing that I was about to pass through the gate he plucked my sleeve and held on and began to murmur at me confidentially. Presently it became apparent to me that he was offering to perform a particular service, that of procuring, and was anxious to hear what my special preferences were.

I put on a puzzled look and said, 'What do you mean?' and at the same time pulled my arm free of the grip. His kohl-rimmed eyes glittered and a sort of redness emanated from them – a rush of blood, but not I think of anger at my brushing him off so much as of irrepressible delight at the prospect now before us. He began to rehearse the range of Pankot's sex-life. The astonishing range. The impact on my imaginative sense and the smell of garlic which came in waves from behind his gleaming tombstone teeth combined to translate me momentarily from the prosaicness of white pole, sentry-box and wire fence (the charm and orderliness of the military lines of an old-established British hill station: monument to imperial rectitude and proper conduct) to a vantage point from which I had a sneaky glimpse in to the world within a world, hermetically sealed and composed entirely of a nest of boxes (Kama Sutra rather than Chinese), each offering successively its revelation of the inventive means by which one might secure release from the pressure of the biological urge. Could all that be available here? In Pankot? By comparison the Bombay massage parlour positively glinted as with a clinical aseptic light.

When the Red Shadow had exhausted either the list or his own imagination and fell expectantly silent, I said, 'Anything else?' Logic indicated that there could not *be* anything else but he took the question as seriously as I had seemed to ask it and looked put out, even alarmed at the thought that there might be avenues of delectable exploration which he had never heard or dreamt of.

'Whatever Sahib desires,' he said at last and then smiled, popeyed, as if stunned by the elegance and ingenuity of his reply.

In the many barrack-rooms and sergeants' messes I'd lived in since getting into uniform – I might say in all of them – the one thing I'd be willing to admit had always distinguished me from my companions was my failure to acquire a *habit* of bad language. I don't mean that the soldier's words weren't in my vocabulary, they were; but they were reserved for special occasions. Like this one.

'What the Sahib desires,' I said, smiling generously, 'is that you should **** ***.' [I use asterisks because it always seems to me that written and printed the dignity of such phrases is lost and the pure metal of offensive *speech* debased.]

I did not wait to study the final effect of my remark. The immediate effect was sufficient – that is to say I was satisfied that his knowledge of the English language hadn't been put under any kind of strain and that what I said might even have had, for him, a ring of familiarity. Showing my own pass to the stick-guard (a very young but intelligent looking lad) I indicated the Red Shadow (now some ten yards away, staring, wagging his head at me) and explained that he was a notorious thief, currently on parole, but not to be trusted and under no circumstances allowed into the lines unless accompanied by myself. Any credentials he offered could be assumed to be forged or stolen and in any case better not touched by hand because he was suffering from a venereal disease now in an advanced, irreversible and highly infectious stage, a situation which made him reckless of his own life and the lives of others, especially the lives of young people (of either sex) under the age of twenty. I said twenty because the stick-guard looked like a raw recruit aged eighteen. A lot of what I said probably passed over his head, his military Urdu not yet being up to scratch and my knowledge of the local dialect being nil. But I think he got the general drift.

Thus, I had got rid of the Red Shadow for another twenty-four hours; but not, I admit, got rid of some of the impressions he had left me with of the arcane aspects of life in Pankot. Images tended to obtrude. Sometimes an odalisque appeared, scattering rose-petals for one to walk over in one's ammunition boots. Coley, languidly using a fly-swatter, appeared to me occasionally to be a eunuch dispensing attar from a silver shaker. A female sweeper, bent over her gently swishing broom, might have been performing a more delicate task; excitation of the dust the last thing in her mind, or in mine. The tea tasted odd. Goat's milk or bromide? And which, I wondered, of these men behind the blanket-covered tables, were sitting there satiated, just about getting through the day after a night's sampling of one or several of Pankot's erotic specialities? Coley? Yes, Coley perhaps. Not a eunuch after all. He had that remote washed-out look of a man whose secret life absorbed nine-tenths of his energy.

Having lunched with the vcos the day before, today I lunched with the havildars, and in the afternoon Nigel Rowan turned up and invited me to move into the Summer Residence guest house. As a consequence I spent the rest of the afternoon with a clearer and more practical focus for my wandering thoughts. The odalisque took on more and more the outward appearance of Sarah Layton whose part of Pankot I was about to enter, disguised in my fleece, shepherded by Rowan. By 4.30 or so when the second interview of the day petered out in cosy military reminiscences of the questioned man's experiences in North Africa, the transformation of the odalisque into colonel's daughter was virtually complete; the room, the hut, the whole precise military complex had reasserted itself and when I walked out past the stick-guard post the perfumed midnight garden of secret Pankot seemed as far away as the memory of the Red Shadow importuning that morning. I climbed into a tonga and felt the blessing of the ramshackle motion, the pine scent of the hills and the ancient smell of dung and wood smoke that hung in the invigorating air and mellow light. It had been my intention to keep the tonga waiting while I crammed into the kit-bag the few things I'd taken out, but as we got near the hospital I remembered I owed some money in the mess and would have to find someone competent to accept it. Realizing that this might take a bit of time my inclination became to bathe and change, postpone my arrival at the guest house and extract from the hospital the last ounce of the pleasure I would have in leaving it.

So I paid the man off at the gates and walked through the leafy grounds to the mess and to the hut where I had my quarters. It would have been about 5 p.m. The only men around were the servants. The room allotted to me was one of four or five under a single roof and sharing the same verandah, with its own bath-house and w.c. cubicle at the back, overlooking a courtyard or compound. At this time, apart from one sergeant (of whom I'd only seen the back view as he left in the morning for duty: it wasn't Potter) I was the only occupant of this particular block but there seemed to be plenty of bearers and bhishtis about. I never had any trouble getting what I wanted. The servants probably also looked after other huts and I was fortunate to be close to where they lived.

I had a key to padlock the front door from outside and the back door from inside. The drill was, once you were inside, to unlock the back door in the bath-house and then shout for the bearer or the bhishti. Actually to shout was seldom necessary. Directly you opened the back door bodies tended to converge and enter, the sweeper to sweep out (even if he had swept out in the morning), the bearer either to make your bed or to get it ready for the night, and the bhishti with the kerosene tins of hot water for bathing. If you waited for anyone it was usually the bhishti.

I told the bearer I was leaving, hustled the sweeper-boy out (giving him his bhaksheesh) and ordered a bath. Having unpadlocked my kit-bag I settled down to enjoy a Scotch and wait for the hot water to arrive. I decided to wear civvies and set them out on the bed with a change of underwear. The hot water came while I was undressing. I took the bottle of Scotch, my glass and another bottle of soda into the bath-house and settled in the tub for a leisurely soak.

The dénouement, after such careful scene-setting, is I suppose as obvious to you as it became to me before it actually occurred. Do you believe in a sixth sense? I don't think I heard a sound other than the noise the servants were making in the compound, shouting at one another, and the sound I was making myself, gently splashing water and humming a popular tune called 'Do I Worry?' But at one moment I was listening to the servants shouting and my own humming and at the next continuing to listen but, as it were, against a background of a soundless presence, a vibrating sense of intrusion.

Someone was in my bedroom and it needed no special gift of intuition to conclude that it was the Red Shadow. I went on humming and splashing, and kept my eyes well away from the door which, although closed, probably gave a man with an eye close to one of the hair-line gaps between door and frame, a view. I had little doubt – so strong was the sensation of being observed – that the Red Shadow was at the moment applying one kohl-rimmed eye to this gap, reassuring himself that I was doing what it sounded as if I was doing. I waited for the sensation of being watched to go away. When after yet another verse of 'Do I Worry?' it still hadn't I felt a powerful urge to grab the towel and hold it up like a purdah screen. I hadn't so far associated the Red Shadow with voyeurism, at least not when the observed object was a grown man long since past the peach-bloom of youth. Just, though, as embarrassment was giving way to simple outrage the eye stopped looking through the crack and its owner tiptoed towards the real objectives: my discarded uniform (wallet) and my kit-bag (bottles). This, you understand, was what my sixth sense told me. At the same time this sixth sense took control of my physical actions. It brought me, still humming, still scooping water, very slowly from the squatting to the crouching position. It kept me in the latter to minimize the change of level from which the hum was coming. Then it picked one of my feet slowly out of the tin tub on to the duck-board and then the other. It kept the water-scooping hand and arm going.

It then ceased to be inventive. There I was, stark naked, crouched and scooping and humming. The door was within leaping distance. But could one, should one, emerge, however furious, however vengeful, in a state of such wretched nakedness? Particularly after that voyeuristic interlude? The towel near by was not the kind one could wrap round with much confidence in its staying put during the energetic demonstration I had in mind. It was now that I noticed my discarded underpants. Still scooping, still humming, I hooked them with a toe and gathered them in and pulled them on. I leapt for the door, grabbed the handle and opened it.

The wallet was going back into the breast-pocket of my jacket. A ten rupee note from it had stuck to his fingers and (how dextrous he was) was disappearing into his belt at the same time that the wallet was disappearing back where it had come from. But both movements were now frozen at the point of completion and his head (looking stuck on his neck at a not quite convincing angle) was twisted round and presenting to me an O-shaped mouth.

I roared for the bearer – instinctively calling a witness – and this galvanized the Red Shadow.

'Sahib,' he said, opening his innocent arms, showing his empty hands and backing away, making for the door. As he backed I advanced and pronounced anathema.

'Rejected seed of a diseased pig-eater,' I began. 'Despised dropping from a dead vulture's crutch. Eater of sweeper's turds and feeder on after-birth. Fart in the holy silence of the universe and limp pudenda on the body of the false prophet.'

With each phrase I pushed him in the chest, out of the room, on to the verandah and then along its length. At each phrase he shook his head, wagged it rather in the Indian way, from side to side, an ambiguous movement suggesting both agreement and disagreement but striking a balance which seemed to mean: What the Sahib says, the Sahib says. And the Sahib continued saying, astonishing himself with a richness of imagery and fluency of Urdu he had never achieved before and has never matched since. Why didn't I write it down immediately afterwards? I've often wished that when finished the Red Shadow and I could have sat together and gone through it. But it has gone – like the Red Shadow but less precipitately and without my prompting. The verandah, elevated two feet from the ground but without a balustrade and giving on to a gravel path, made a perfect launching pad. And the Red Shadow when it came to it did not lack a certain grace and elegance of line. I've always felt that recognizing the inevitable the artist in him rejected resistance and settled for co-operation. Our combined movements were balletic, slightly rough and ready and under-rehearsed but cumulatively not without poetry.

As we approached the edge of the verandah my flat-palmed pushes became closed fist prods – not punches; but they brought his arms and hands from the appealing to the protective position. We established a rhythm of prod and jerk and presently I grabbed his shoulders (this was the moment when he seemed to decide to go along with me) steadied him, removed the ten rupee note from his belt, and swung him round to face the way he was about to go, which he did, borrowing rather than receiving thrust from the sole of my bare foot, and adding some thrust of his own in an attempt to jump that wasn't made quite soon enough but contributed to the angle of flight and the arc of descent. He fell, rather heavily, spreadeagled, his lower body on the gravel and his upper on the grass on the other side of the path. And lay there; winded or pretending to be.

The sequence at an end and my week-old ambition fulfilled, I turned and found that there had indeed been witnesses. Apart from the bearer, the sweeper, the bhishti, and an unidentified person (no doubt of the kind who always turn up when there is an accident or act of God to contemplate with serene detachment – a freelance extra, as it were) there was Sergeant Potter.

What odd things one says to people, post-crisis. Seeing Potter I called out, 'Just the man I wanted. Will this cover everything? I'm leaving.'

'So I gathered,' Potter said, ignoring the ten rupees and looking down at the Red Shadow. 'But presumably not together?'

*

What Merrick had done was unforgivable. I had the story from Potter whose curiosity about my relationship with Merrick had been aroused by watching me deal violently with Merrick's servant. Ten minutes later he came to my room with my bar chits and the change from the ten rupees. By this time I was dressed and packed and I'd sent the bearer down to the gates to get a tonga. The Red Shadow had gone; where, I neither knew nor cared. Potter asked what it had all been about so I told him. I bore Potter no ill-will because I was convinced that the NCOs' sudden change in attitude to me was entirely due to having seen me with a man they'd met before and had cause to dislike. But what cause? I wanted to know. Finding I was still friendly, Potter began to open up.

He said, 'Will that fellow make trouble for you with Colonel Merrick?'

I said it wouldn't bother me, but that as Merrick had gone to Ceylon and as I expected to be repatriated almost any day I'd probably be back in

England before Merrick knew what had hit him or rather what had hit Suleiman. But I didn't refer to them as Merrick or Suleiman. I called them Count Dracula and Miss Khyber Pass. Potter blushed. He said, 'Look, I'm sorry. We thought he'd had the nerve to plant you on us.'

Potter didn't take much more persuasion to spill the beans.

*

It concerned a medical NCO. Potter didn't give me his name, but let's call him Lance-Corporal Pinker, Pinky for short, and let us imagine him as a reserved, studious and hard-working young man who had lived an institutional life with other men in uniform without ever seriously arousing the suspicion that he was what is called abnormal. Even Sophie Dixon wasn't absolutely clear on this score, or particularly interested. He liked Pinky because Pinky was harmless and friendly, quite intelligent and very conscientious. He had never served in the field, always at base hospitals. He had been in India for a few months and in Pankot for most of them. He was already in Pankot when Corporal Dixon and Sergeant Potter returned from Burma and were posted to the hospital's military wing.

At that time Pinky was working on the wards. His transfer to the office of Captain Richardson, the psychiatrist, came later. Pinky and Sophie were on the same officers' ward when Colonel Merrick (then Major) used to turn up for treatment and adjustment of his artificial hand and arm. He did this whenever he visited Pankot and on one occasion was admitted for two or three days because the chafing of the harness had set up inflammation and there was some question of infection.

It was now that Potter filled me in on Sophie Dixon's record in the field. His compassion for sick or wounded men sprang from the feminine side of his nature and he never left anyone in doubt about his physical preferences, but these were made entirely acceptable to the men he tended because it was his compassion and care – his dignified ministration to a sick man's needs that they were made to feel, never the other thing. They knew the other thing was there, they had only to listen to him camping it up in the casualty station tent or basha – but (as Potter put it) 'when he touched a man you could see that nothing was being conveyed except clinical reassurance'. In Potter's mind there was even an idea that Sophie's overt posture was a form of sublimation and that in fact he lived like a monk, on and off duty.

According to Sophie, the officer with the burnt face and artificial arm 'must have been quite a dish'. This was the irony; originally Sophie had liked Merrick, so had Pinky. Whenever he came for treatment, Sophie mothered him. He thought the wounded hero brave, patient and well-disposed. Merrick never seemed at all put out when Sophie put on his act. 'Sometimes I wonder about the Major,' Potter remembered Sophie saying. 'When I give him the bedpan this morning he looked at me ever so thoughtful. I nearly come out in one of me hot flushes. Watch it, Dixon, I says to meself. Hands off the tiller and leave it to the Navy.'

It would have repaid him to have listened to his own advice or rather to have watched not 'it' but Pinky. If he had watched Pinky closer he might have seen when the time came that Pinky was in trouble or heading for it. But by then Pinky was off the wards and in the psychiatrist's office. When Merrick next turned up for treatment he said to Sophie, 'I see your old colleague's working for Captain Richardson. Isn't that a waste of nursing skill?'

It didn't surprise Dixon that Merrick had visited the psychiatrist. Considering the nature of his wounds a chat with the psychiatrist would not have been in the least remarkable. Six weeks later Merrick was again in Pankot. He visited the hospital. This time he was accompanied by the Red Shadow. Sophie saw them together and at once nicknamed Suleiman Miss Khyber Pass of 1935. A few days after Merrick had gone back to Delhi, taking the Red Shadow with him, Sophie found Pinky crying and packing his kit. It took Sophie some time to find out why.

*

Working in Richardson's office Pinky (so it would seem) had had his eyes opened for the first time in his young life to the fact that his inclinations were not nearly as uncommon as he had supposed. His was a typical case. Over-protected as a boy he had preferred the company of girls until he reached the age of puberty. After that he found himself attracted, mysteriously, to his own sex. He felt unique. Later he learned that to be like this was wrong, and later that it was not so unique as to have escaped being a criminal offence. As he grew older still he also discovered that it made ordinary men laugh. He knew he couldn't help being what he was and he didn't hate himself, but he couldn't have borne to be found out. He told Sophie that when he came to Pankot at the age of twenty he had had no sexual experience with anyone except himself.

His job in Richardson's office was clerical and highly confidential. It wasn't a hard job because the number of cases in the hospital needing serious psychiatric treatment was never high. There were a few disturbed men in one ward and, now and again, in another, an officer or two whose 'equilibrium' had been upset. Psychiatry was still a bit of a joke in Pankot but it had become vaguely fashionable in the army. Just as potential officer-cadets in England had a routine chat with a psychiatrist at the war-office selection boards so, now, in Pankot's military wing, convalescent men had chats with Richardson. It was almost a branch of welfare.

Richardson had a lot of time on his hands and Pinky discovered that he made use of it by keeping separate sets of private and confidential files for personal reference in his future civilian career. As Richardson's confidence in Pinky grew so did Pinky's opportunity to satisfy his curiosity about the contents of these private files. Richardson told him that psychiatry was a very inexact science and that there were judgments it was wiser not to record officially because the army simply didn't understand the complexity of a man's emotional life and it was grossly unfair to penalize someone by recording an informed professional but far from conclusive opinion that might be interpreted subsequently in the naïvest manner and block a man's promotion. When Richardson found that Pinky was genuinely interested in psychiatric method he sometimes lent him 'closed files' of men who had been discharged and, during slack times, even discussed them with him. He never showed him files on men which were still 'open' and all the files, both the official and the separate private files, were kept under lock and key. If Pinky was lent a file he had to return it to Richardson before Richardson left the office.

What fascinated Pinky was the revelation that in Richardson's view (and who was Pinky to argue?) 'repressed homosexual tendencies' were not infrequently the cause or one of several causes of what – up there in the wards – might look simply like depression or apathy or a temporary inability to cope. He became intensely curious about the notes Richardson had made or was making about the men currently undergoing treatment – in particular one man around whom Pinky had been spinning private fantasies: a tough, good-looking corporal who had been in Burma with Wingate's expedition.

A timid boy, his obsession gave him courage. He stole Richardson's key – easy enough because the key was kept in a drawer of the desk which Richardson did not always remember to lock. What took nerve was getting a copy of it made in the bazaar and putting the original key back. Thereafter, night after night, he sat at his desk with one of the current confidential files, risking discovery but taking the risk because what he read absorbed him. The files changed his whole attitude to himself. The man in the ward, for instance, the one whom Pinky fancied, had admitted to Richardson that he had 'mucked about' with a fellow Chindit, still preferred women but wasn't ashamed of the mucking about because he thought of it as something that had 'just happened quite natural', just 'part of the business of being stuck in the jungle and being shot at' and if he were back there he'd probably do it again. What amazed Pinky was Richardson's diagnosis that this man was 'intelligent and well-balanced' with a 'healthy attitude towards sex', and that his depression was almost certainly due to a combination of the physical after-effects of the dysentery for which he had already been treated and an understandable but by him unacknowledged conviction that he'd had enough of combat. The note on the official file, which mentioned nothing about 'mucking about' closed with the comment, 'Fit for active duty from the point of view of this department but recommend further analysis of faeces'.

Intelligent and well-balanced. A healthy attitude towards sex. Pinky seized on the phrases as if they were lifebuoys. He acquired nerve. When he went down to the canteen or into the bazaar he looked about him, eyes open, newly confident. When he sat in the downstairs room of the Chinese restaurant (the floor reserved for other ranks) he glanced more boldly at men he liked the look of. Any one of them, judging by the files, might be willing to 'muck about'.

It was during this first extrovert phase that Merrick came back into his life, arriving at the office one evening after Richardson had gone and just at the moment when Pinky was at the filing cabinet selecting his evening's reading. He hadn't heard Merrick knock or come in but, looking up, saw him in the open doorway between Richardson's office and his own. Pinky's alarm was short-lived. Merrick was not to know that the cabinet was private. When Merrick spoke to him in a friendly manner, remarking on his transfer from the wards, Pinky stopped feeling guilty and asked Merrick what he could do for him. Merrick said he was in Pankot for a day or two and hoped he would be able to have a word with Captain Richardson. Pinky looked at the diary and made an appointment for the following afternoon. 'Merrick?' Richardson said next day, 'Isn't that the officer with the burnt face and amputated arm?'

When Merrick arrived Pinky sent him straight in. Presently he was called in himself. Richardson handed him the key and asked for a particular file. Without thinking – because he was now so used to handling them – Pinky brought him the official buff file and the private green one. Richardson handed back the latter and Pinky put it away. Merrick was in Richardson's office for about twenty minutes. When he had gone Pinky went in with some incoming mail and found Richardson studying the private green file. He gave both files back to Pinky. Pinky asked whether he should open a file for Major Merrick. He was told that Merrick wasn't a client. The files that had been got out in connection with Merrick's visit were known to Pinky. They weren't among those that interested him. They concerned a woman. He wondered what Merrick had been asking that caused the files to be got out, but did not inquire. The only other point of interest about this episode was that Pinky learnt for the first time that Merrick's peacetime job was in the Indian Police. The subject came up because Pinky said he supposed when the war was over the amputated arm would mean an end of Merrick's military career. Richardson said he'd no doubt go back into the police with a desk job and added, 'CID I shouldn't wonder. He's dealing with these INA cases already.' Pinky thought perhaps the woman's file was also connected with the INA business. He wasn't interested in the INA either.

*

Thus, lulled, Pinky rode for his fall. Several nights a week he went to the Chinese restaurant. Twice he thought he would have made it if he'd had the final ounce of courage it seemed to need to convey to a table companion that more than chat was on offer. After eating he often lingered in the bazaar, venturing beyond the area of light into the shadows and walking home, anticipating that longed-for voice calling out, Hey, soldier.

And in the bazaar, during these patrols of his from shop to shop, he no longer shooed away the small urchins who pimped for their so-called sisters offering jig-a-jig, but grinned at them, shaking his head, listening for the miraculous change of tune from You want Girl, to You want Boy? Once, he heard it, but coward-like ignored it. It wasn't a boy he wanted, anyway, but someone of his own age.

*

Between Merrick's interview with Richardson and Pinky's next sight of him, several weeks passed, weeks which Pinky spent in the way I've described but which now culminated in what, had the consequences not been so terrible, he would probably have remembered ever afterwards as his unforgettable night. For a day or two before this memorable occasion, wandering in the bazaar he had been aware of the possibility that a young Indian lad was as interested in him as he – because this possibility was there – had become interested in the lad. He had never seen him in Pankot before but now they seemed to keep passing each other. The Indian was dressed western-style. He looked clean. He also looked vigorous: a dark-skinned version of the athletic kind of young Englishman Pinky was attracted to. On one occasion Pinky and the Indian were both looking at the window display in Gulab Singh's, the chemist, which was opposite the Chinese restaurant. The display was of clocks and watches. The next night Pinky stood outside the shop again. Again, as if from nowhere, the Indian turned up. They did not speak. Pinky wanted to but his mouth was too dry. When the Indian left Pinky stayed a moment longer and then left too. As he stepped into the road between a couple of parked tongas a man touched his arm and said, 'Sahib, you want woman?' Pinky shook his head. The man bent closer. 'Sahib, you want boy? That boy looking at watches? That boy very good boy. Like English soldier very much. He like you. He is telling me. Sahib wait here. Boy come.'

The man went – a turbanned whiteclothed figure, wearing an embroidered waistcoat and baggy trousers, walking quickly up the road openly and jauntily, stopping only once to make sure Pinky was waiting. Pinky began to tremble with excitement. To Pinky, this man looked manly and virile. East of Suez no shame attached to wanting boys. The man understood and casually accepted Pinky's need.

Pinky moved away from the tongas and went back to the arcaded pavement and strolled slowly along looking at the shop windows. When he came to an alley he stopped and looked back. The boy was coming, walking briskly. As he went past Pinky he smiled and walked up the alley. The alley was dark. For a few seconds Pinky was afraid. Sometimes alleys like this were patrolled by the military police and the west side of the bazaar, to which the alley led, was out of bounds to other ranks. Well, if the MPs stopped him and asked why he was following a boy he would say the boy had offered to introduce him to a college girl. Then he'd get off with a

1283

warning and an approving laugh. The blood began to pound in his chest. Pinky marched on.

*

'What was it like, love?' Sophie quite naturally had thought to ask Pinky, when he got to this part of his story. No go, apparently. He'd been over-excited. One gathers there was an encounter of some kind, prolonged but obstinately unsatisfactory. The Indian had explained his own failure by saying it made him unhappy to see Pinky so nervous. Then he had said it would be all right next time. He said, 'Come back tomorrow. Meet me outside Gulab Singh's at half-past nine and we will come to my room again.' When they were dressed the Indian became miserable and said he didn't think Pinky would come back. Pinky said nothing would stop him. 'Leave me a token then,' the Indian said. 'Lend me your wristwatch. Then I'll know that you like and trust me.' Pinky gave him the watch and told him to keep it. The Indian had already refused money. He refused to accept the watch except as a token of Pinky's intention to return the next evening. He took Pinky back down the rickety stairs into the alley and went with him until the light from the bazaar lit Pinky's way.

*

When I left for the summer residence guest house we got the tonga-wallah to drive through the hospital grounds along a path that led past Richardson's office. By we, I mean myself and Potter. He pointed the office out and then got off and walked back. After studying the place I gave the driver orders to move on.

The office was in a low building isolated from other blocks. It had the usual steep-pitched roof, the overhang supported by pillars to form a verandah. A small signboard outside announced Richardson's name. One entered by a door at one end. This led to a passage. A window to one side of the door lit what had been Pinky's office. A window beyond lit Richardson's. The hut was presumably isolated to encourage patients to feel that anything they said to the psychiatrist went no further than here. Both Pinky and Richardson had had keys to the main door. The last to leave locked up. Outside the door, on the verandah, was a bench, a fire bucket and a cycle rack.

At about 6 p.m. on the evening of the day following Pinky's meeting with the Indian lad, he was alone in the office reading Richardson's private notes on the case of an ordnance officer who had collapsed under the strain of 'feeding the guns'. He kept looking at his watch and, because thrillingly it wasn't there, having to judge by the fall of the light outside how much longer he could afford to spend on this fascinating stuff before locking up, going to his billet to shower and shave and set out on his journey to bliss.

1284

He had just decided to call it a day and was closing the file when the door opened and Merrick walked in.

Pinky gave him a cheerful good-evening. Merrick asked if Captain Richardson was in. Pinky told him he had gone for the day but would be in the office tomorrow as usual and that if Major Merrick wanted an appointment he would be glad to look at the diary and write one in.

Merrick said that would be good of him. Pinky went into Richardson's office and came back with the diary. Merrick was now sitting. An hour was agreed and written in. Pinky took the diary back and put it on Richardson's desk. When he returned Merrick had the green folder and was examining the cover. For an instant Pinky was alert but Merrick didn't open the file and when Pinky was back at his desk he put the folder down. Then, smiling in a friendly way, he adjusted his artificial arm, as if it needed easing. The black-gloved artefact was held out, closed. He prised the fingers open. In the palm of the glove lay Pinky's watch.

He said, 'I think this is yours.'

Pinky did not remember with any clarity what happened next. On the whole he thought he just stared at the watch while Merrick sat waiting for him to react. The next thing Pinky was fully conscious of was Merrick standing with the watch in the artificial hand and the green file in the other saying: 'My understanding from Captain Richardson was that these files were always kept under lock and key and were available to no one when he was not in the office himself.'

And then:

'I take it you have managed to obtain a key. You were at the filing cabinet the last time I came at this time of evening. If you have such a key you would be well advised to hand it over now.'

Pinky did so.

'Is this the only file you have removed tonight?'

Pinky nodded.

'Does this telephone go through to the hospital or the civil exchange?'

Pinky mumbled through dehydrated lips that it went through to the hospital exchange but that the hospital exchange could get any number.

'Right,' Merrick said. 'Wait outside. You will be wise to wait and do nothing foolish.'

Pinky stumbled into the passage. Merrick closed the door behind him. He found himself out on the verandah without knowing how he got there. Shock had affected his ability to co-ordinate what he did and saw with any sort of understanding of it. For instance he was aware of a figure leaning against a pillar, gazing at him, but the figure to him was simply a deformation of the pillar. When he realized it *was* a figure he assumed he must be hallucinating because it was a copy of the figure of the man who had procured the Indian for him the night before.

After a period of time, borrowed from and never repaid to him, he heard Merrick closing the door of the office. He got unsteadily to his feet, knowing the real shame began *now*, waiting somewhere for the military police, whom Merrick had obviously been phoning, to come and escort him to a guard-room.

But what happened was quite different. Without even a glance in Pinky's direction Merrick walked away up the path, followed by the procurer – or, let's give him his proper name, the Red Shadow. When they were out of sight Pinky began running. Then, wondering where he was running he ran back where it was safe. But it wasn't safe. So he was sick. After he had been sick he ran off again. Again he ran back and covered the vomit with sand. After he had done that he felt like a visitor, a stranger to the scene. Lights were coming on in windows of other huts that he could see through the trees. The evening was real. *He* wasn't real, but the evening was, and this unreal self had to lock Captain Richardson's office up. Before that he had to close Captain Richardson's office windows.

The green file was still on the desk. Automatically he went with it into Richardson's office. The cabinet wouldn't open. He felt for his key. Merrick had it. Or had he? Pinky turned on lights and started hunting for the key. There was no key; only the locked cabinet and the rogue file that couldn't be put back into it. If he could only get the file back into the cabinet and lock it he might be able to say he hadn't done it and that Merrick was lying. He knew this was impossible but that's the way his mind was working. Then he remembered that the key and the file were quite unimportant in comparison with the wrist-watch. Perhaps he could find the watch. If Merrick had left the file lying round perhaps he had left the watch. There wasn't a watch, though. Merrick had the key and the watch and he, Pinky, had the file. He hid the file in a drawer in his own desk. He shut all the windows and turned off the lights, locked the doors and ran back to his quarters. He went to the latrine. What he evacuated was liquid. He sat in the latrine in the dark with the liquid streaming from him. Then he did a very odd thing. He manipulated himself into a state of excitement and then out of it and leaned back exhausted. Subsequently this puzzled him. He asked Sophie if Sophie could explain why he did a thing like that. Sophie couldn't but remembered later and told Potter that he'd read somewhere that when a man was being executed by the rope he sometimes suffered an involuntary emission as though that part of him too was saying good-bye.

*

In the morning, unable to face what had to be faced, Pinky reported sick. The duty MO couldn't find anything wrong with him but he looked so terrible that to be on the safe side the MO sent him to the staff sick-bay for observation. There was no one in sick bay except an Indian orderly. Pinky lay on a bed fully clothed. He was given a nimbopani and drank it gratefully but immediately afterwards brought it up. A QA sister arrived to chart his temperature and pulse. The temperature was slightly above normal and the pulse was rapid. An hour later he brought up another nimbopani. The duty MO came over. Specimens of urine and blood were taken. Pinky was put into hospital pyjamas and bedded down. He lay curled in the embryonic position. He hadn't slept at all the previous night. Mercifully he slept now, shutting the world out. He slept right through the most traumatic part of the day – the hour of Merrick's appointment with Richardson. When he woke in the late afternoon Richardson was sitting on his bed.

'My green file on the ordnance officer, Captain Moberley,' Richardson said, quite gently. 'Can you tell me where I might find it? I have an interview with him this evening.'

'Yes, sir,' Pinky said. He felt calm now. 'It's in the bottom left-hand drawer of my desk.'

'Thank you, Pinker.' Richardson stayed on the bed. Pinky could see that he was considering a number of alternative statements. Richardson was not a great talker. He was so used to listening. 'All things considered, Pinker,' he said eventually, 'I think you'd better remain here for a day or two, even though there is nothing physically wrong with you. I don't mean that you're malingering. I mean that your illness is psychosomatic. I take it you yourself are in no doubt of that?'

Pinky nodded. There was nothing Richardson could do for him but Pinky felt at least he understood. Richardson's was the last friendly face he was likely to see until he came out of prison. But he did not think he would ever come out. He would die of terror and humiliation. He hoped so. How could he ever face his parents again if he survived to be sent home? Two years. In an Indian prison. For a crime he hadn't committed and had never intended to commit. He had only wanted a bit of love.

The next morning he felt not better but somehow purged. The QA sister said she was pleased with him. He had expected that by now everyone would have heard about him and he had steeled himself to bear their contempt. So he guessed that whatever Richardson was doing he was doing as discreetly as he could.

Allowed up, he sat on the sun-verandah of the sick-bay and opened his mind slowly to his 'case' – the strange and puzzling aspects of it. The business of the files was of minor importance, surely. What Merrick was after was the nailing of men like him: queers. Probably Merrick had taken one look at him months ago and thought 'Ah.' His discovery that Pinky was sneaking looks at confidential files – gloating over them – would simply have reinforced a poor opinion of his character. And yet. And how long had Merrick had him watched and followed? When Pinky thought back to those weeks patrolling the bazaar he went cold.

Pinky had never seen the Indian procurer before but he must have seen Pinky. Was he in Merrick's pay or a fellow-victim of Merrick's cleaning-up operation? And what had happened to Tommy, the Indian lad? Had he been working with the procurer or had he been pounced on afterwards and made to hand the watch over? And then what happened? Had Merrick pounced on the procurer? Pinky became dizzy trying to work out the permutations. So he closed his mind to his case and lay on the sun-verandah all day trying hard to think of other things like home and times when he had been happy.

But throughout the day one question kept nagging at him. *Why me?*

*

After two days in sick-bay he reported for duty at Richardson's office. He had already packed a military criminal's kit – his small pack. When he arrived he found another NCO at his desk. The new lance-corporal said it would be helpful if Pinky could show him the ropes. He asked Pinky where he was going. All Richardson had told him was that he was to take over Pinky's job. Pinky said he didn't know yet but thought he'd better not interfere unless Richardson gave him official permission to hand over. He waited outside. Richardson arrived. Pinky saluted smartly. Richardson told him that since he was up and about he might as well show the new NCO some of the routine. A spark of hope was kindled. Logic said he should have been in a guard-room long ago. It was very odd. He spent the morning and afternoon helping his successor. Richardson came and went. He was neither friendly nor unfriendly. About five o'clock he came back and as he went into his office he told Pinky to come in.

When Pinky was inside with the door shut Richardson handed him a piece of paper. Pinky read it. He read it twice. It was a posting order to a Field Ambulance in a division that was preparing for something called Operation Zipper. When Pinky finally understood what this meant he sat down without asking permission and cried.

He cried from relief and out of gratitude. The only explanation he could find for his escape was that somehow Richardson had managed to suppress the terrible charge. How, he could not begin to imagine. For a moment he did not care.

Richardson let him cry the cry out. It didn't last long and wasn't noisy. The lance-corporal in the other room could not have heard it. Richardson poured him a glass of water and then went and stood in a characteristic position, with his back to the room, looking out of the window, his hands in his trouser pockets.

When Pinky had quietened down he stood up, ready to leave. He said that before he went he wanted to apologize for having abused Captain Richardson's confidence in the matter of the files. He knew it had been very wrong and he was very sorry. He didn't know what else to say because he couldn't bring himself to mention the thing that Richardson had only referred to obliquely – so obliquely that it was almost as if he hadn't referred to it at all.

Richardson said, 'Yes, I suppose it was an abuse. Between us we might have overlooked it, but in all the circumstances I decided you would have to go. If it's any comfort to you, Pinker, although I suppose I ought not to say this, I think you were extremely unfortunate to have come up against that particular officer. However, there it is. You did. And no experience, however disagreeable, is ever wasted.'

Richardson left the window, smiling, as if nothing much had happened. 'Also, if it's any comfort to you, from observation I'd say that you'll actually be much happier in the field than in a place like this. Your conduct sheet is clean, there's no reason why it shouldn't stay like that, is there?'

Richardson offered his hand. Dumbly, Pinky took it.

'Tell me,' Richardson added, putting his hand back in his trouser pocket. 'How long was Major Merrick trying to get me on the telephone the other evening?'

'Get you on the telephone, sir?'

'He said he tried to ring me so that I could come over and deal with – this problem. He said he tried there and then, from this office.'

'He sent me outside, sir.'

'Yes. I see. How long were you outside?'

'I honestly don't know, sir.'

'Quite. Well, never mind, but actually I was in my quarters the whole evening. You didn't by any chance palm him off with a dud number?'

'He didn't ask for a number, sir. Just whether the phone was on hospital or civil exchange.'

'Well I only wondered, because my phone never rang. But it's of no importance. The operators probably ballsed the call up. That wouldn't be new, would it, Pinker? But perhaps it was as well they did. These things are much better discussed in the cold light of the day after. Wouldn't you say? Goodbye, Pinker. Good luck.'

Pinker said goodbye and thanked him. He tried to say more but couldn't. He had the impression that Richardson was really asking him to say more. But he shirked it. Just before he reached the door Richardson said:

'Oh, Pinker, I nearly forgot. This is yours, isn't it?'

He was holding out Pinky's watch.

'I think it must need a new strap otherwise you'll lose it again.'

Slowly, disbelievingly, Pinky took the watch. His face was burning. He mumbled something like thank you sir and goodbye sir, and then, remembering, came to attention. He was still at attention when Richardson said:

'If it's any interest to you, I found it among the Ms. I suppose it slipped off your wrist when you helped yourself to Captain Moberley's file.'

That evening, in the midst of his packing, Pinky stopped, sat down and looked at the watch: the gift of his parents when he joined up. Then he threw it on the floor and stamped on it with the heel of his boot until it was in pieces. This was what he had done with his life so far. He resumed packing, pausing every so often to wipe his eyes and cheeks. He kept telling himself to be a man. But that didn't help. Thus, Sophie found him.

*

There were only two explanations for the returned wrist-watch. The first was that Merrick had given it to Richardson and told him how it had come into his possession and that Richardson had persuaded him not to take the matter further but leave him to deal with it. This was the explanation Pinky believed was the correct one – the only one that made sense to him and which bore out his opinion of Richardson's stout character. It didn't make sense to anyone who knew Merrick as I knew him. It didn't make sense to Sophie and Potter but neither had an alternative explanation.

From their point of view here was an officer who had gone to a great deal of trouble to nail Pinky on a charge of gross immorality. Without compunction he had used another man (obviously, according to Pinky's description, his own servant) to act as agent provocateur and perhaps even a third man, the Indian lad, in order to get incontrovertible evidence. Sophie said he was familiar enough with British police methods in dealing with homosexuals not to find anything in the least remarkable about an officer of the Indian police using similar methods to shop a soldier. If Pinky had ever been charged and tried, Sophie said, we'd have been amazed at the transformation from fact to fiction in the statement made about how the evidence was obtained.

But then, after all this trouble, Merrick had done nothing more. Why? Had Richardson given Merrick a bad time? Had he seen through whatever story Merrick told him and warned Merrick that he would kick up a stink about the deliberate provocation he could see had been used? Had Merrick been scared off, been persuaded to hand over the prime bit of evidence – the wrist-watch – even been glad to get rid of it and slink off none the richer but wiser?

Pinky accepted this as the explanation because he wanted to. Sophie and Potter didn't accept it but couldn't conscientiously refute it. At one time after Pinky had gone Sophie was prepared to see Richardson and ask, but Potter dissuaded him. So, failing a revelation, they had both settled for the fact that Merrick had set Pinky up, sadistically using powers which were his but which finally he hadn't exercised to the full extent open to him – just possibly because after talking to Richardson (but why had he waited to do that and not called the MPS then and there?) he dared not take that risk.

Not dare take the risk? They didn't know Merrick. He certainly set Pinky up and having set him up used him. If there had been any further advantage to be had out of persecuting Pinky he would have taken it. He was the kind of man who worked for preference within a very narrow margin of safety where his own reputation was concerned. He courted disaster. Deep down, I think, he had a death wish. It came out in this way, pushing his credibility to the limit, sometimes beyond it.

But once he had got what he wanted – in the Pinky affair as in any other – he was no longer interested except to the extent that it pleased him to see his victim suffer. What he wanted in this case was not, I think in one sense, very important to him, but he had made up his mind to have it and had seen how he might get it. He had a talent, one that amounted to genius, for seeing the key or combination of keys that would open a situation up so that he could twist it to suit his purpose.

Originally Merrick went to see Richardson to discuss someone who had been one of Richardson's patients. This may have taken Richardson by surprise and like any psychiatrist he would have been reluctant to discuss the case in any detail. He would not have told Merrick much, only as much as an ordinary man would have realized he had to be satisfied with. But during that interview Merrick realized that there were files – a green one in particular – which would tell him far more, tell him as much as Richardson knew himself and which he was absolutely determined to have a look at. Sheer luck, coming upon Pinky at the filing cabinet the night before, acute observation and shrewd deductive powers, had already shown him the way in which to get that look.

So what Merrick wanted, *all* that Merrick wanted, was a look at the green file, the private file about the patient he went to discuss. It was as simple, as absurd as this. Even while Potter was telling me the sordid little story I was – because I knew Merrick – casting about for the unconsidered trifle, but the significance of the file did not really emerge until later when I talked to Rowan.

While Pinky was outside on the verandah counting the grains of sand in the fire bucket or whatever he subconsciously did when in the grip of that sense of unreality, Merrick telephoned nobody. He opened the cabinet with the key he had guessed Pinky had and which he had terrified him into handing over and at his leisure looked through the file. The Red Shadow was there to continue terrorizing Pinky but also on sentry-go to warn Merrick if someone not in the little *mise en scène* approached. When Merrick finished, he placed Pinky's watch in the cabinet – not in the Bs where the file he had been reading belonged but with the Ms which was the section to which he knew the file on Pinky's desk belonged, because he had looked at and memorized the name on the cover. He had then locked the cabinet and come away leaving Pinky sitting outside. He must have enjoyed that, leaving his victim in that sort of sickening suspense. He kept his appointment the following day, gave Richardson the key and shopped Pinky – not for sodomy but for abusing Richardson's trust. Precisely what Merrick said nobody knew, except Richardson.

In telling the story of Pinky, in trying to give an impression of my idea of what happened, I have filled the story out with some imaginative detail and also placed events in the order in which they occurred – not in the order in which they emerged during my talk with Potter. For instance, when Potter referred early on to Merrick's first visit to Richardson I said at once, 'What did he go to see Richardson about?' Potter said Pinky assumed he went to see him about the patient whose file Richardson asked for. I said, 'What patient?' Potter said, 'Pinky said it was a woman, he'd had the file out at one time but put it back when he found out it was not about a man.' I said, 'Do you know what woman?' Potter said the answer was a woman called Bingham, but neither Pinky, Potter nor Sophie had ever heard of her.

I then asked him to continue with the story, but from there on I was on the alert because there was unlikely to be more than one Bingham in Pankot and surely Bingham was the name of the officer Merrick had tried to rescue from the blazing jeep, the officer Sarah Layton's sister married, who hadn't been well enough to go to Bombay to meet her father and whom Sarah had described as having had a bad time: obviously, in view of Richardson's file on her, not just a bad time physically but psychologically. And there was Merrick visiting Richardson to talk about her and becoming determined to have a look at her private file. Why?

It was rather late when I got to the Summer Residence guest house. This was a two-storeyed brick and timber building; appearing from the outside a cross between a shooting-lodge and the kind of villa you see half-hidden by fir trees and rhododendrons in the hills around Caterham. Inside, it was straightforward Anglo-Indian hill station stuff and smelt of damp and of aromatic wood. Rowan sat me down on a verandah whose floorboards sounded hollow underfoot so that it was rather like moving around in a sports pavilion or boat-house, except that the view was across an acre or so of rising ground to the Summer Residence (a dark hulk which in daylight proved to have been the inspiration for the guest house, architecturally speaking). On this verandah there were a lot of palms in brass pots and a set of white lacquered cane lounging chairs well upholstered by heavy cushions covered in durable royal blue cloth; and there was a smell of incense which presently I tracked down to a couple of joss-sticks smouldering away on a carved side-table. It struck me that if he went on like this and didn't get married soon Rowan might end up wearing Indian pyjamas indoors and eating pan prepared by himself from ingredients kept in little silver boxes, and discussing the Bhagavad Gita with a gentle down-at-heel professor from some nearby Hindu college; but only during his leisure hours. And even then, in pyjamas, preparing pan and discussing the significance, say, of Krishna's remark to Arjuna that 'Learned men do not grieve for the living' no one would ever mistake him for anything other than an Englishman – one, moreover, of the kind it took a long time to get to know sufficiently well to be sure whether the amiable expression on his face was there for the benefit of the present company or for his own in dealing, as he constantly had to, with so many pressing and troublesome affairs.

For instance, having invited me there, having brushed aside my apology for lateness and sat me down, told the highly distinguished looking bearer to bring a whisky-soda for me and a gin-fizz for himself, he looked at me as if he wondered where I'd sprung from and what advantage I might expect to wrest out of this sudden and unexpected intimacy. He couldn't help it. It was an effect India had on a man whose manner was already naturally remote and uncommitted.

I said, 'Well, Nigel, tell me all about Merrick and Hari Kumar.'

His expression didn't alter. He said. 'Why?'

'I thought it would be a good way to bring the subject up. The subject of Merrick.'

'Why do you want to do that?'

'I thought you did. If we start right away wouldn't it make it easier for you to ask about Merrick and Mr Mohammed Ali Kasim's INA son?'

The bearer came with the drinks. Mine had far too much soda and ice in it. The coldness burnt my lips.

When the bearer had gone he said, 'I don't follow you.'

'Then I'd better start again. By the way, if anyone comes to put me under arrest would you be prepared to say that we spent the whole day together?'

Fractionally his eyebrows went up. 'I think that would depend on what they came to arrest you for.'

'Common assault?'

'On whom?'

'The Red Shadow.'

'Merrick's servant? Didn't he go back with him?'

'No. I just caught him pinching ten chips from my jacket.'

'If assault followed attempted theft I imagine you're safe enough.'

'In ordinary circumstances.'

'Were these not?'

'Are they ever where Merrick or one of his creatures is concerned? Who is Mrs Bingham?'

He picked up his gin fizz. 'Sarah Layton's widowed sister. Why?' He sipped.

'Tell me about Merrick and Hari Kumar first.'

'I'd rather you told me what you meant about Merrick and Mohammed Ali Kasim's INA son. Unless that would take you longer than we've got. We're dining out, if that's all right.'

'Should I change?'

'What you're in will do very well. If you could add a jacket. What gave you the idea I'd be interested in talking about Sayed Kasim?'

'Merrick told me to pretend not to know anything if you asked. But, as I said to him, that won't be difficult because I don't.'

'When was this?'

'Yesterday, just before we parted.'

'I saw him the night before. We discussed the case of Sayed Kasim – or rather a situation arising out of it – as fully as was necessary I'd have thought. So I really don't know what he means.'

'Weren't you pumping him?'

'Not at all. I asked a question and he answered it. Quite satisfactorily. It's all quite simple, Guy, but rather confidential. The thing is that since he was let out of prison MAK has consistently refused to see the son who fought with the INA and was taken prisoner last year. Government was prepared to let him but he said no. At least, he never took the offer up. All I wanted to know from Merrick, now that there's this department dealing with these cases, was whether he thought they'd co-operate about arranging a meeting if MAK suddenly changes his mind.'

'Has he?'

'Perhaps. But I didn't see Kasim until last night. When I spoke to Merrick the night before, the question was still rather hypothetical.'

'What did Merrick say?'

'That he didn't think his department would be keen now and might put up objections, but he was quite clear that Government might override them and could persuade the C.-in-C. it would be a good thing. He accepted that because his department doesn't initiate policy.'

'Well that's it, then. That settles it. Merrick's as mad as a hatter.'

Rowan watched me a while. He said, 'I hope not,' and drank more gin-fizz.

'What advantage does Government see in arranging a meeting between father and son? I take it it *is* a question of advantage. I met the other son, incidentally, at the Maharanee's.'

'So Sarah told me. I'm not sure there is much advantage now. But then I'm not personally in a position to judge. You know Kasim headed the pre-war Congress ministry in this province?'

'Yes.'

'He's in rather an unenviable position just now. Confidentially, Malcolm would like to see him back one day as chief minister, possibly because the alternatives to MAK are rather bleak. So anything one can do to help him solve his problems and clarify his position is done with that end in view. Does that surprise you? That a provincial Governor should have a soft spot for an Indian politician?'

'Why should it?'

'I thought perhaps it might. The *raj* is obviously not your favourite animal.' He looked at his watch and at my almost empty glass then glanced over his shoulder and summoned the bearer. 'Have the other half before we go.'

'May I have less soda and no ice this time?'

Rowan passed the instruction on but I sensed his disapproval.

'Is Mrs Bingham fully recovered?' I asked.

'Recovered?'

'Miss Layton told me her sister had had a bad time. What was wrong?'

'I think some kind of breakdown. She was pregnant when her husband was killed. Then she had the unpleasant experience of being alone in the house when Colonel Layton's stepmother died there. The baby was born prematurely. But it's quite some time ago. She seems all right now.' He added after a moment, 'You'll see for yourself. That's where we're dining.'

'At Mrs Bingham's?'

'At the Laytons. They all live together. Mrs Layton rang earlier and asked me to go round. I said you were now staying with me and she said she'd be delighted if you'd come along too. I didn't think you'd mind so I said yes for both of us.'

The other half arrived. Nigel had ordered nothing for himself. He still had some gin-fizz left. There was no ice in my whisky but the soda was over generous. I thought perhaps this was just as well after all, if we were dining at the Laytons'. Rowan said, 'Merrick told you then?'

'Told me what?'

'About Mrs Bingham.'

'He told me he was best man when she married the officer he tried to save.'

'Nothing else.'

'No.'

'Then what made you ask about her?'

'It's too long a story.'

'Oh.' He sipped gin-fizz. 'If she asks you tonight how you like working with Colonel Merrick you'd better tell her a lie and say you find it extraordinarily interesting.'

'Must I? My inclination would be to say I couldn't stop working for him soon enough.'

'I know. But she's going to marry him. It was announced at dinner the other evening.'

He studied me, as if for a particular reaction, then looked at his watch and got up. 'I've got a call to make. I'll be about five minutes, then we ought to go.'

I remained on the verandah, drinking my soda and whisky and considering the significance – the now clear and peculiarly distasteful significance of Merrick and Mrs Bingham's file. I thought: Well. It's none of my business. A few minutes later Nigel came back. 'I'm ready when you are,' he said.

I told him I was begging off because I didn't feel up to it.

'Aren't you well?'

'I don't think I would be if I had to spend the rest of the evening dissembling.'

He said, 'You wouldn't be the only one.'

'No. Miss Layton doesn't like him either, does she? But I suppose she'll have to learn to now. I won't. I'd rather not pretend otherwise to her poor sister.'

Rowan had propped himself against the balustrade, arms folded, ankles crossed. He said, 'When I said you wouldn't be the only one dissembling I really meant myself.'

'I thought you'd only just met him.'

'I've known about him, quite a while. But you guessed that, surely. Otherwise why ask me to tell you about him and Hari Kumar?'

'Is it what you've known about him or what you've just seen of him that puts you off?'

'Known was wrong. I'm sorry. *Heard.* One must be fair.'

'My Uncle George once said that the only reward in life for being fair is an obscure death.'

'He might well be right. Is he the balloonist?'

'No, that was Uncle Charles. Uncle George spends his life reading balance sheets and share prospectuses. We rely on him absolutely because he's the only member of the family who can count.'

'I never know when to take you seriously. I never did. How much time did you actually spend rowing on those Saturdays you got off?'

'Very little. The thing was to go about a mile up river to a place where a fellow-member of the club had found what he called a lot of spare local talent. We called it Knocker's Reach.'

'You mean that unwittingly I put you in the way of what Bagshaw called the temptations of the town?'

'Yes.'

Unexpectedly, Rowan smiled. 'Colonel Layton mentioned Bagshaw the other evening. He remembers him as a very junior maths master. I think it does him good to talk about things like that. Won't you change your mind?'

'An old boys' after-dinner session?'

'Would that bore you?'

'It would add no charm to the evening.'

'It would from his point of view, I think.'

'Does he find much charm in the prospect of having Colonel Merrick for a son-in-law?'

'Presumably he's not tried to stop it. The announcement was made in a friendly enough atmosphere.'

'What about Mrs Layton?'

'I expect her main concern is with Susan's welfare.' Rowan hesitated. 'The thing is, Merrick's extraordinarily good with the child.'

'How old a child?'

'Just over a year.'

'Boy or girl?'

'Boy.'

'In what way is he extraordinarily good with him?'

'He inspires the boy's confidence. I've seen it for myself. Watched them playing together with a box of bricks. They were both totally absorbed. Creatively absorbed. He has the knack of making a game seem important. Incidentally the child's not the least afraid of the artificial hand, or of the burn scars. I'm not much good with children so that the fact that I got no change at all out of young Edward is no guide, but Sarah says Merrick's the only man, more or less the only person of either sex who does. If Susan's main reason for marrying him is to give the child a father she'd have to look a long way before she found anyone more capable.'

'Do you think that is her main reason?'

'Wouldn't you agree it's a perfectly sound one?'

'So far as it goes. But I should say the important thing for a child is a sense of security. What's the point of having Merrick as an effective father-figure if the mother is unhappy?'

'Unhappy? One can't prejudge that.'

'You accept the possibility?'

'Susan's not a happy person by nature. But I feel quite incompetent even to hazard a guess about how a marriage like this will work out emotionally.'

'Or physically?'

He ignored this. He said, 'My worry really is about what might happen to affect Merrick's career adversely and make life difficult for her. When he was involved in the Mayapore rape case in nineteen-forty-two he went on the Indians' list of officials who were thought to have exceeded their authority in putting down the Quit India riots. If there's still such a list and I'm sure there is it would be remarkable if he's not still on it.'

'Were repressive measures taken?'

'The mood of the country was highly volatile.'

'In other words some officials acted beyond the limit allowed by law.'

'Well, yes. I think one has to admit it.'

'I can't think why you're bothered. They'll be well protected. They always have been.'

'But things have changed a bit, haven't they? The people now in Westminster know as little as their predecessors did about India, but I imagine they'll be more disposed to believe the very worst about the way India's been governed. I shouldn't think it will need more than a couple of ministers, men like Cripps, to come out here and hobnob with the Mahatma and the disciples of Annie Besant for the new Secretary of State to be rushed into setting up a commission of inquiry. The signs are that the Congress High Command may press for it.'

'Anything wrong in appointing a commission?'

'I think a very great deal. It might look like a genuine British attempt to see justice done impartially but the motive would be entirely political, a bit of window dressing in Westminster and damn the consequences in Delhi. And from the point of view of the morale of a frankly already overstretched Indian administration an inquiry of that sort would be pretty well disastrous. If there were cases of unduly repressive measures there were an infinitely greater number of cases of intense and by no means invariably nonviolent provocation. You have to put both the provocation and the methods used to meet it in the context of the atmosphere prevailing at the time, and that was a pretty tricky one. The Japanese were on the Chindwin, Singapore had gone and Burma had gone. Most of Europe had gone and North Africa was a mess. The plain fact is that strategically and I'm sure morally, India had to be hung on to. And I honestly don't see that any Indian leader who incited people to rebel against the *raj* and obstruct or sabotage its war effort has any right whatsoever to complain if quite a few of them got harshly treated. What else I see is that both sides would be wise to forget both the provocation and the reaction. Settling old scores is a fairly useless exercise at any time. When there's something else at stake as serious as trying to reach a sane and sensible agreement about the country's future government and constitution then it's worse than useless. It's damned stupid.'

'I owe you an apology.'

'Oh?'

'For thinking of you the other night as indifferent – how did I put it? – indifferent to affairs over which we adopt attitudes of concern and responsibility? So. My apology.'

'I don't actually feel owed an apology. But if you want to make one, the car's waiting at the front. We'd be no more than a minute or two late even if you want to wash your hands and comb your hair. But in any case, I must go.'

*

When Rowan told the driver to take us to Rose Cottage, Colonel Layton Sahib's place, I had a picture of what I must be in for, one so vivid that it depressed me. As a name, Rose Cottage wasn't quite as bad as say Mon Repos or Dunromin but I could not imagine anything much worse than dining there, among the cosy souvenirs of a lifetime of exile on the King's business. I pictured the Laytons surrounded by Benares brass and sweet briar, floral cretonnes and bronze gods; a Buddha smiling back at a yawning tiger-skin, and – above the mantelpiece – a watercolour of the Western Ghats and – on it – photographs of Sarah and Susan as little girls on ponies in Gulmarg. There might even be an imitation Chinese vase filled with dry bulrushes in a corner or on a grand piano; a standard lamp with a tasselled shade and dinner mats painted with hunting scenes from the English shires: Taking a Fence; The Water Jump; The Whipper-in; In Full Cry.

But directly we drove between two rather gaunt pillars my spirits rose. Had I heard right? Rose Cottage? One illuminated board simply announced '12' and the other 'Colonel J. Layton'. A moment of hiatus followed, a dark transit past dim ugly shapes which I feared might be rockeries, but then – lit from arc-lamps in the forecourt – I saw the beautiful proportions of an early nineteenth-century Anglo-Indian bungalow: squat, functional and aggressive, as well anchored to the ground as a Hindu temple.

'Good Heavens.'

'What's wrong?' Nigel asked.

'I hadn't expected anything so fine.'

'It's one of the oldest buildings in Pankot, I'm told. Is it your period?' He was smiling, taking something of a rise out of me but pleased that I was pleased. The verandah showed signs of vandalism: a wooden balustrade, obviously a later addition, but not recent; but apart from this the whole area was free of ornament, with one exception: a hanging lantern of iron and glass, plain, ugly and perfectly in keeping. In a niche near the door there was a handbell but the bearer, simply dressed in white linen tunic and trousers, was already receiving us. Nigel called him Mahmoud and told him I was Perron Sahib. The square hall was beautifully proportioned but ruined by oak panelling. I noted, though, that there were no wall hangings – no pictures, or trays. It looked as if something had persuaded the owner to leave the panelling to make its own vulgar statement. On the tiled floor there was a large Persian rug of a lovely silky texture. Heavy mahogany doors marked the positions of the rooms surrounding the hall. The one facing us was open. Mahmoud led us in.

*

I have tried to recapture events in some kind of sequence to give a lucid picture of my evening with the Laytons but it is as though after the shocks and surprises of that day I suffered a reaction of such intensity that I might have been hard put to it to write a coherent account the following morning let alone twenty-five years later.

Moreover, it was an evening during which nothing happened which contributed to what *you* would call a narrative line and which left me with nothing more useful from your point of view than impressions of members of the family – first impressions of the two I'd not met before and changed ones of the two whom I had. The most vivid impression of all was made by Mrs Layton, a woman whose personal distinction was heightened by an icy stoicism and by what was overlain but not disguised by that coldness: an unmistakable human sexual warmth, which I judged would be strong when aroused. Her air of detachment, the economy of movement and expression, the hard outer casing of the memsahib – so often tiresome in other members of that monstrous regiment – were, in her, peculiar graces. You felt that through them she was protected against the shock of life in general, and with them ready to meet the shock of her own head-on.

Rowan, in introducing us, told her how impressed I was with the house. She said something uncompromisingly direct like, 'Oh. Why?' My reply, whatever it was, helped to establish a tenuous bond between us. I understood that she had been making alterations both to the outside and inside and that there was still a lot to do which she was quite determined on in spite (was it?) of opposition from people who preferred it as it had been in Colonel Layton's stepmother's day. It must have been much later, probably when Nigel and I were leaving, that the question of the oak-panels in the entrance hall was raised. She described them as 'a pity', the more so because the damage done by removing the panelling might be considerable and the expense, in consequence, perhaps incalculable.

I describe the bond between us as tenuous because although I often felt a mutual empathy whenever we spoke to one another or when our glances happened to coincide, there were as many if not more occasions when a remark I made which she might easily have taken up was utterly ignored. She fascinated me. I observed with solicitude the portents of physical decline, the areas of flesh between eyebrow, cheek and ear, from which the resilience had gone, leaving the skin to find its own salvation, which it could only do with the help (presumably) of astringents which might, but didn't, never do, shrink it sufficiently to arrest the development of a network of minute folds and fissures which show up as lines and wrinkles and lend to the eyes a sad and perplexing beauty and luminosity, for the eyes do not age in the way that the flesh does, or do not when they are the eyes of a woman who is still handsome and armed with a proper measure of self-respect.

When she lifted her head – she had a habit of doing so and at the same time touching the necklace she was wearing – the pad of flesh under the chin was tautened and, for an instant, this and a consequent firmness of throat and neck created an illusion of youth, until you saw one, then two, obtrusive tendons and a faint blotchy discoloration in the region of the thyroid. On one occasion when my conscious critical self observed these marks of ageing, the other self, the self that weighed rather than noted evidence, was moved by a tender curiosity and a bold impulse to touch the skin as if to verify that what the eye saw was real, and as if, too, to communicate an opinion that it was virtuous in her to own such marks and that they inspired admiration, not pity. Perhaps it was her sensitivity to this reaction that caused her every so often to switch herself off from me, as a precaution against an unnecessary complication.

Possibly my reaction was an effect of the invigorating Pankot air acting in conjunction with the effect of that empathy, my recognition of Mildred Layton as an attractive older woman, one who, while conscious of the fact that one was borne along on the ever-flowing tide whose sound I sometimes listened for, did not allow the angle of her vision to be restricted to the view of here and now. She had, I believed, a vigorous sense of history, vigorous because it pruned ruthlessly that other weakening sense so often found with the first, the sense of nostalgia, the desire to *live* in the past. Throughout that evening she impressed me more and more as a woman who instinctively rejected the claims of years gone by if – unlike 12 Upper Club Road as I discovered she preferred to call it and to which she was in the process of restoring only what it could properly claim – these claims conflicted with her own claims, her determination both to survive and to defeat any force that currently threatened her.

Such strength of mind and character I attributed to her, and I judged it had probably not been sustained without effort and some assistance. She drank fairly heavily, like one accustomed (one might say disciplined) to it. One thing I noticed, the switching off became more frequent towards the end of the evening and was signalled by a lowering of the lids, a partial hooding of the eyes; but this was the only sign I could detect of the working of the alcohol.

*

Susan was the first of the two daughters to put in an appearance. If I had met her somewhere else and spoken to her for any length of time without knowing who she was, no familiar note would have been struck. Between this conventionally pretty girl and her sister there seemed to me to be no resemblance. Dark, carefully dressed hair and a high complexion, eyes that slid away from contact with your own and seemed emotionally disconnected from the smile of the neatly lipsticked mouth. The mouth alone performed the function of doing its social duty. Or was I *looking* for signs of disorientation? Her breasts were full, freckled above the deep cleft between them. She would be buxom in middle-age in spite of that narrow little waist (accentuated, I think, by a belt and a flared skirt). She was encumbered, distracted rather, by a Labrador puppy which had hectic manners which suddenly deserted it as if it had seen a ghost or had recollected some standing order about behaviour indoors. It retreated into a corner and sat awaiting a command or inspiration. It had the Labrador trait of looking at you in a way that revealed the white of its eyes – or so I think, having seen a similar animal recently that evoked these memories. Between Susan and this puppy there was a curious tension – a febrile acknowledgment both of the importance and unreliability of the other's presence. It did not take me long to recognize that for each the other was a symbol of a security desired but not felt. It took me a little longer to see that Susan Bingham felt no security in anything and longer still to work out one of the reasons why this insecurity made itself felt so strongly. The room was wrong for her, the room, the whole house. If the house had been as I'd expected, she would have fitted it. As it was it deprived her of the safety of a proper background. I noted how her mother kept watch, alert for any sign Susan might give of not intending to go through with something she had promised to perform. This is not hindsight. I was not at ease. Susan was difficult to talk to. I felt that the only way to break through to her would be to say: Tell me all about *yourself*. Her self-centredness was like an extra thickness of skin. Without it, I believe, she would have died of panic or exposure. What she needed – the sense of human correspondence – was precisely what she protected herself from experiencing. I was appalled at the idea of the proposed marriage. As a victim, she was ready-made.

But it was – I reminded myself again – none of my business. None of this was. I was merely a spectator; as much but no more involved than someone in the audience of a theatre. The play had Chekovian undertones. For all the general air of easiness, the uneven co-operative effort to perform, *en famille*, each member of the cast was enclosed, one felt, by his own private little drama. Rowan, surprisingly talkative, did well – I thought rather too well – in his part of cheerful friend of the family. He wasn't cut out for it.

When Sarah came in at last it was as if someone had strayed on to the stage through error. She looked nondescript and her behaviour was colourless. She was quite unlike the girl I met in Bombay. My disappointment was profound. I assumed that in Bombay I must have been in a very uncritical mood where women were concerned. She was wearing the same dress, the one she had worn at the Maharanee's, but this time it did nothing for her. Her hair was dressed in the same way but lacked lustre. She did not even walk well. She had little to say to any of us. The one pleasant effect of her arrival was that Susan became a little more communicative and Rowan much less so. He had acquired the tentative air of a man who hadn't quite decided whether he was as fond of someone as he had imagined. Sarah gave him little encouragement. To me she gave none.

It was at dinner that it occurred to me that the evening had a motif; neither planned for nor consciously acknowledged. It was suddenly in the air. The motif was the forthcoming marriage and the part which I might or might not play in frustrating it. Only Susan and Colonel Layton, I thought, were completely unaware of this.

The motif first became apparent to me in the table arrangement. Mrs Layton put Rowan on her right and me on her left. Colonel Layton, at the other end, had his married daughter on his right and Sarah on his left, which meant that Susan was next to me and Sarah next to Nigel. This strict adherence to an order of precedence that gave the married daughter seniority over her elder unmarried sister was, I thought, nevertheless open to more subtle interpretation, for there would have to come a point when I deliberately engaged Mrs Bingham in one of those table conversations which – even at so small and intimate a gathering – assume a semi-private character; and it would undoubtedly be my duty to mention her engagement to the officer I worked for and to offer my good wishes.

The subject of Susan's engagement hadn't arisen yet. After dealing with soup and responding to Mrs Layton's questions about the places I had visited in India, about the origins of the name Perron, about my balloonist uncle and my other eccentric relatives (Nigel must have briefed her well) I became very conscious that Susan was not communicating with her father nor (I felt) listening either to Nigel and Sarah or to her mother and me; that she was, in fact, waiting, self-contained, embattled; waiting for me to turn round and say: Well, tell me all about yourself.

This is the one moment in the evening I clearly remember. The soup plates were being cleared. Mrs Layton transferred her hostess's attention to Nigel, giving me the cue to transfer my own to Mrs Bingham. Protected, as I thought, by the conversation between Nigel and Mrs Layton I turned to Mrs Bingham and said Nigel had told me about her engagement to Colonel Merrick and that I should like to offer her my best wishes for their future happiness.

In the sudden silence in which I found myself ending it, my quiet little speech splashed as loudly as a stone thrown into a placid pond on a summer night.

After the ripples had died away Mrs Bingham looked round and smiled. 'Thank you,' she said. 'That is most kind of you. I'm sure we shall be. Very happy.'

Then she turned away, resuming contemplation of her place at table. I noticed Colonel Layton's left hand was occupied moving bits of bread from the middle of his side-plate to the outer rim and back again, as if he were counting cherry-stones that told his future. I imagine I tried several times to engage Susan Bingham in something approximating to conversation. I have no recollection of succeeding; instead I recall, chiefly, a sense of other people's resignation – particularly Mrs Layton's. Neither she nor Nigel (nor Sarah) could possibly have expected me to say anything except what I did say. Perhaps it was only when I said nothing more that they recognized their own subconscious expectations; resigned themselves to the inevitability of the marriage. Only Colonel Layton seemed unaware, unaffected. He smiled; ate sparingly. His demeanour suggested thoughts passing through his mind: How extraordinary – how nice – how lucky I am – whatever will happen to me next? The emotional instability of Bombay had gone. Rather, it lay hidden under the carapace, the hardening shell of reaffirmation.

*

When the women withdrew the servant brought a couple of decanters. One of them contained the remains of that much-travelled bottle of Old Sporran. I declined the whisky and had brandy; an act of self-denial which I followed up by mentioning Bagshaw and inviting what I would least welcome: a claustrophobic conversation about the hermetic world of school, that alchemy in reverse which transmutes the gold of life into the lead of tiresome recollections of immaturity. But Colonel Layton showed no enthusiasm for Bagshaw. He smiled benignly, uncommitted. He was suffering, I thought, from delayed reaction to the shock of homecoming. Here for him, briefly, was a likeness of the world he had just escaped from, a room occupied entirely by men. I don't think he liked it, suddenly. He raised his glass of malt whisky in a rather shaky hand and said, 'Strange thing. There was a young Oberleutnant at the last camp I was at –' and retold the story for – I assumed – Rowan's benefit, but when he had finished and I glanced at Rowan I fancied Rowan too had heard it before but assumed I hadn't.

'Extraordinarily kind of you, Perron,' Layton said, nodding at his glass. 'I feel it would be civil to write to the Oberleutnant and tell him it came true. Haven't actually sat down to Jane Austen yet, though. So mustn't deceive him. Not that one would know where to write. By the way, my future son-in-law told me that officer you rescued from the bath succeeded on his second attempt. Sorry about that. It was his whisky originally, wasn't it?'

I agreed that originally it was.

'Odd thing,' he said, 'the compulsion to suicide.' Layton was studying the pale liquid in his glass, perhaps seeing in the whisky of one dead man the face of another. 'What do you say, Rowan? Odd? To be quite so at the end of the tether?'

Rowan said he was inclined to think there was a certain dignity in taking one's own life. Layton said he supposed the Japanese would agree but that it was wretched for the family and that that was what a man should think about. In the case he'd just had, the case of Havildar Karim Muzzafir Khan, it was the plight of the widow and her children that most concerned him.

The regiment would have to make sure she didn't suffer unduly. But she had left her dead husband's village and gone back to her own. He feared that her neighbours had made life impossible for her when they heard what he'd done, in Germany. He turned to me. 'Perron, is anything that's worth knowing coming out of these interviews?'

The briskness of the military manner flared up in that one question and then went out again. I decided that he would prefer the truth so replied that so far as I was qualified to judge I should say nothing worth knowing whatsoever. He nodded.

'That's rather the conclusion I've been coming to,' he said. And nodded again. The images of the evening at Rose Cottage end there.

*

In my bedroom at the guest house I found on the bedside table a copy of Emerson's essays – heavily underlined and marked in the margins. Its owner, or one of its owners (it had obviously been handled a great deal) had written her name on the fly-leaf. Barbara Batchelor. The underlining began with the first familiar and sonorous paragraph of the essay on History: *There is one mind common to all individual men*: and continued intermittently. I flicked the pages to find the other familiar passage in the essay on self-reliance and found that marked too: *Society is a wave. ...*

'You've found the book, then,' Rowan said when I took it out on to the verandah to join him over what he called a night-cap. 'I'm sorry, I ought to have mentioned it, but forgot. It was among some things I brought up from Ranpur for Sarah. We thought you'd like it.'

Barbara Batchelor was an old missionary who'd once lived at Rose Cottage as companion to Mabel Layton, Layton's stepmother, now dead. Miss Batchelor was dead too. The book was among some things she'd left for Sarah.

When I was settled Rowan said, 'Incidentally, it needn't make any difference to you, but I've decided to go back to Ranpur tomorrow.'

I felt bewildered. 'Whenever did you decide that?'

'I suppose in the last half-hour or so.'

Recalling the tentative arrangement I'd overheard him making with Mrs Layton to play some tennis over the week-end I realized he was telling the truth. I didn't press for an explanation.

'I can't very well stay here once you've gone,' I said. 'I'd better see the accommodation people tomorrow.'

'That'll only confuse them. They know you're here. If I were you I'd hang on at least until an officer comes up to take Merrick's place, or you get ordered back to Delhi. I've signed you in as my guest. I'll mark it *sine die*, so all you'll have to do is sign any chit the servant asks for and sign the steward's register before you leave.'

'Who pays? Government or you?'

'Government. So long as you don't dine the station or do anything the auditors might think odd, like drinking three bottles of whisky before breakfast. They'd apply to me in that case.'

'You pay for the drinks anyway, don't you?'

'Don't let it inhibit you. You can drink to my future if you like. I'm going back into the Political. HE warned me about it before I came up. That's why I've been having these few days off. I rang him tonight before we left though and he told me the signal had come in. I fly to Delhi on Tuesday and then get told where I'm going.'

'It's only Thursday.'

'Oh, well. Clearing things up, packing. Better to get on with it.'

'Does Miss Layton know you're going?'

'She knows I'm expecting the posting.'

'Didn't you tell her it had come?'

'No.' He hesitated. 'Somehow the atmosphere tonight didn't seem right. I'm sorry it wasn't all that successful an evening.'

I asked him what time he intended leaving. He said the private coach was still in Pankot. It was just a question of getting it coupled on to the mid-day train. Gopal had gone back by car, with Mohammed Ali Kasim. He said, 'Perhaps there'll be a signal for you tomorrow too, from your Aunt Charlotte. Then we could go back together.'

'It's a shade early for my signal.'

'You were serious, though, about Bunbury?'

'Deadly serious.'

'What happens if it doesn't work?'

'A court-martial, I should think. Are you positive it's hanging and not shooting?'

But this irritated him. He stopped looking at me. He seemed to find the dark beyond the verandah the most rewarding of anything within his range of vision. I waited. Presently he glanced back at me. He said, 'Was it a surprise to see me the other night at Ranpur station?'

'Totally unexpected.'

'But you recognized me.'

'Easily.'

'Would you, if you hadn't met Sarah in Bombay and she hadn't mentioned I was in Ranpur, working as an aide to HE?'

'Perhaps not so instantaneously.'

'Even if we'd been contemporaries at school, same house, same year, and close friends. It wouldn't necessarily follow would it that we'd recognize each other if we met years later in a public place?'

'It could follow. Why do you ask?'

'Do you remember a boy called Colin Lindsey?'

'It rings a vague bell. Who was Colin Lindsey?'

'Harry Coomer's closest friend.'

'Then I may. I once asked Coomer to tell me the difference between karma and dharma but he said he didn't know. I suggested he might ask his father during the summer holiday but he said he probably wouldn't see him because he was spending the holiday with – well – "Lindsay, here"?'

That was the picture: Coomer and 'Lindsey, here', standing together, the brown boy and the white boy, resisting an inquisitive prefect's invasion of their solidarity and privacy.

Rowan said, 'He saw more of the Lindseys than of anyone. His father encouraged it and kept himself in the background. He wanted Harry to grow up as much like an English boy as he could.'

I was about to say: How much like was that? But checked myself. Rowan was too delicately poised between confession and characteristic silence for me to take the risk of upsetting him with that kind of facile question. For a while neither of us said anything but he began to lose interest in the dark beyond the verandah, as if Kumar were no longer out there but had come in to shelter in our recollections of him. A third, empty, white cane chair might have been his. Well, not his, not Coomer's; but Kumar's, whatever Kumar was or had become; whatever he would look like now, sitting there, no longer interested in cricket, but rape. White women. It meant nothing to me. But I wondered how deep Rowan's prejudice lay. Of the depth of Merrick's I had no doubt.

He said, 'I suppose we ought to take into consideration the distinct possibility of our not meeting again for at least as long as it's been since we last did. What, ten years ago?'

'Next time it won't seem so long. I'm told the older you get the quicker time goes.'

Such cliché simplicity also seemed to irritate him. He asked me what it was that amused me. I told him that what amused me was the awful seriousness that seemed to overcome people who worked in India. He said he thought I'd only just stopped accusing him of not being serious enough. I said that wasn't quite what I meant. There was a difference between taking a situation seriously and taking oneself seriously.

He became interested again in the dark beyond the verandah. I thought I had done it this time and that soon he would drink up and say goodnight. Instead he said, 'Yes, but out here there are penalties for appearing not to. At least, that's one's earliest understanding. One is wrapped up in the cocoon of a corporate integrity. It's a bit like being issued with a strait-jacket as well as a topee. It makes it difficult to act spontaneously and you become so used to wearing it that you find it difficult to do without it.'

'They used to issue spinepads too.'

'I know.'

'But they went out. Like topees are doing.'

'I don't think the strait-jacket ever will.' But he was smiling again. He said, 'Sarah puts it well. She says that in India English people feel they are always on show. I think that's true and on the whole that nothing worries us more.'

'Why do you say that?'

'Perhaps because we feel that fundamentally there's so little to see?'

'The *raj* with a superior manner hiding an inferiority complex? I can't say I've come across much evidence of that.'

'You could begin with me. I've very little real confidence. But it would be dangerous to give that impression. I expect I overcompensate. Most of us do. It's probably what happened to Colin Lindsey.'

It was my cue but I didn't take it up. I wanted him to tell me about Kumar and Merrick but I suspected that any further prompting would result in my getting a watered-down account and that I would only get a reasonably full one if I left the initiative to him. He hesitated again. But whatever it was that made him want to tell me finally won the struggle with whatever it was that made him reluctant to do so.

*

In May of the previous year (1944) on the day Rowan resumed his duties as ADC after one of several spells in hospital, the Governor called him into his study, said, 'You're an old Chillingburian, aren't you?' and asked him if he remembered a boy called Hari Kumar or Harry Coomer. Rowan said he did. The Governor handed him the confidential file on a man currently detained under the Defence of India Rules. This was Kumar. Rowan found it surprising that the boy he had known should have developed into a political activist. The real shock came when he read further and realized that Kumar had not been arrested on political grounds but on suspicion of leading a criminal assault by several Indians on an English girl called Daphne Manners in Mayapore in August 1942.

Rowan remembered the Bibighar Gardens case quite well. He had been in hospital in Shillong still recovering from illness contracted during the long march out of Burma with what remained of his regiment. The Bibighar Gardens affair was something out of the common rut among the reported incidents of rioting, arson and sabotage that followed the arrest of political leaders, because it involved what in spite of that cautious phrase 'criminal assault' had clearly been the rape of a white woman. Rowan also recollected the sense of anti-climax when nothing further happened. A report that the men arrested had not after all been charged but sent to prison as political detenus was taken up by the Calcutta *Statesman*. It seemed odd, the *Statesman* suggested, that all six men originally reported arrested with such promptness, while presumably turning out to be the wrong men (since no charges had been made) should also all turn out to be politically active in a way that caused the authorities such concern that detention orders had had to be issued.

The *Statesman*'s interest in the case provoked no official comment; and when the riots were over, the Bibighar Gardens affair like so many others that had marked that period of violent confrontation between the *raj* and the population, simply passed into history together with the rumours that had added colour to it, the chief of which was that the girl herself had scotched the charges by denying that the arrested men were those who had attacked her and threatening to say such extraordinary things about colonial justice and colonial prejudices, if a trial were held, that it was decided there would be no point in attempting to hold one.

Rowan had heard these rumours, the accompanying explanation that one of the men arrested had been her lover and that she was so besotted or terrified that she had willingly perjured herself to save him, in fact had only admitted to being attacked because she couldn't disguise the awful state she came home in. She'd cooked up a story about the men being of the *badmash* or criminal type, not young educated boys like the ones in custody. He also heard the story that later she returned pregnant to her aunt in Rawalpindi and in the March of 1943 he had seen the notice in the *Times of India* of her death in Kashmir and of the birth of a child on the same day. The child, a girl, had been given an Indian name, and the notice had been inserted by her aunt, Lady Manners, the widow of Sir Henry Manners, one-time Governor of the province of Ranpur. At this time Rowan was again in hospital, in Calcutta. From there he went back to his regimental depot. Later he was in Delhi for a while. Early in 1944 he was appointed to Malcolm's staff at Government House, where Sir Henry and Lady Manners had lived during the late 'twenties and early 'thirties. But when Malcolm gave him the file on Hari Kumar he had not thought of the Manners case for months.

The next point of interest to emerge from the file was that Kumar was the man Daphne Manners was supposed to have been infatuated with. The longer Rowan studied the file the stronger the evidence seemed to him to be that Kumar, having formed an association with Miss Manners, had then plotted with several Indian friends of his to attack and rape her. In custody after the rape he had virtually given the game away according to the police report by mentioning Miss Manners's name before her name had been mentioned by the police. Moreover when arrested at the house where he lived with his aunt he had been bathing scratches and bruises on his face such as might have been given by a girl fighting her attackers in the dark; and the clothes out of which he had just changed were mud-stained. Throughout his interrogation he stated repeatedly, mechanically, that he had not seen Miss Manners since a night some weeks before when they visited a temple. (Miss Manners had used virtually the same words.) But he refused to account for his movements on the night of the rape or for the state of his clothes and the marks on his face. His almost invariable answer to questions was: I have nothing to say.

The one document in the file that caused Rowan uneasiness was one relating to the alleged discovery by a junior police officer of Miss Manners's bicycle in a ditch outside Kumar's house, and an accompanying document, attested by the District Superintendent of Police, stating that this curious piece of evidence (with its ridiculous implication that Kumar had cockily ridden Miss Manners's bicycle home from the Bibighar and then left it outside his own home) had been the result of a misunderstanding. The bicycle had actually been found by the superintendent in the

Bibighar Gardens when the site was searched after the assault had been reported. It had been put into a police truck. The truck had then been driven to Kumar's house – to Kumar's house because of the known association between Kumar and Miss Manners and because the District Superintendent had called there earlier in the evening after Miss Manners had been reported missing by a Lady Chatterjee, at whose house Miss Manners was staying, and found Kumar not at home, and his aunt unable to say where he was. On the way to Kumar's house this second time (with the cycle in the back of the truck) the police's attention had been attracted by a lighted hut in some waste ground not far from the Bibighar. Inside the hut they had found five young men, all of them 'known to the police' for 'political affiliations' and several of them 'known to the police as friends of Kumar'. These men were 'fairly intoxicated' and were drinking home-made liquor, itself an offence that warranted arrest, but also in the District Superintendent's opinion certainly deserving investigation on a night when the authorities were on the alert for demonstrations against the government for its imprisonment of Congress leaders and when a European woman had been assaulted by five or six Indians. In arresting these young men, in putting them into one truck, in the continuation of the journey to Kumar's house, in the 'change of police personnel' from one truck to the other and the despatch of the five arrested men back to the police headquarters, 'a misunderstanding' had 'assumed that this was where the bicycle inspector finding the bicycle on the road outside Kumar's house' where 'it must have been temporarily placed, again as a result of a misunderstanding' had 'assumed that this was where the bicycle was found' and had accordingly put in a report which, even if that was not his intention, might certainly have led to 'this erroneous conclusion'.

The District Superintendent was Merrick. This was the first time Rowan came across his name. Someone, either in the Inspector-General's department or the Secretariat had minuted in the margin of this disclaimer about the bicycle, 'Pity about this'; an ambiguous phrase which did little to subdue Rowan's uneasiness; but initially the disclaimer gave him a favourable impression, not of the Mayapore police, but of the superinten-dent as a man who had not hesitated to sort out a muddle which would have been helpful in bringing Kumar to trial if left as it was. Subsequently, he was uneasy for a different reason. He could not help wondering whether the evidence of the bicycle had been planted by Merrick or with Merrick's blind-eye approval and then refuted by Merrick when he saw that it was too dangerous a piece of falsification.

Two other points of interest arose in the account of the actual arrest. In Kumar's room there were found (a) a photograph of Miss Manners and (b) a letter from England signed 'Colin' which referred to a letter Kumar had written to *him* but which he'd been unable to read because his father had opened and then destroyed it as one unsuitable for his officer son to receive – a letter, so it seemed, of a political and anti-British nature. The letter from Colin dated back to the post-Dunkirk era.

But, Rowan said, apart from this hearsay evidence of anti-Britishness, and unless the assault on Miss Manners could be interpreted as political, the evidence on the file of Kumar's political commitment was thin to the point of non-existence. He had – just once – been taken in for questioning because his attitude to a police officer had been unsatisfactory and arrogant.

The officer was Merrick. This incident occurred some six months prior to the rape. Searching an area of the native town for an escaped political prisoner called Moti Lal, Merrick had visited a place known as The Sanctuary, a clinic and feeding centre for the homeless and destitute run by a Mrs Ludmila Smith. Mrs Smith (also known as Sister Ludmila) went out every night with stretcher-bearers, searching for men and women who had come into Mayapore to beg, or to die. On the night before Merrick arrived looking for the escaped Moti Lal, she had picked up a young man found lying unconscious near the banks of the river.

This was Kumar, and all that was wrong with him was that he was dead drunk. When Merrick arrived in the morning he asked Kumar who he was, where he lived, what he had been doing. Kumar had a hangover. The interview went badly. Merrick decided to continue it at the nearest police station.

At this point in the file, Rowan said, there was a brief summary of Kumar's background. Kumar (according to Merrick) had not been frank about his identity but had 'finally admitted' that his name was Kumar, that he knew Moti Lal because Moti Lal had once been employed by Romesh Chand Gupta Sen, a contractor. Kumar had himself been employed by Romesh Chand who was in fact Kumar's aunt's brother-in-law. Romesh Chand had sacked Moti Lal because he didn't like his clerks to concern themselves with anything except the business, and that included not concerning themselves with politics. Kumar had left Romesh Chand later, when offered a job as a sub-editor and occasional reporter on the Indian-owned English language newspaper, *The Mayapore Gazette*.

There was then a statement that 'the man Kumar claimed to have been brought up in England by his father, Duleep Kumar, since deceased, and to have been educated at a public school which he named as Chillingborough College'.

Subsequent notes suggested that Merrick had investigated Kumar's claim and had got further information; that Kumar was born in the UP, that his mother died while he was still an infant and that aged two he had been taken to England by his father, who had sold his land to his brothers and now set up in business, anglicizing the name to Coomer. But in 1938 Duleep Kumar's businesses failed. He committed suicide. Hari was penniless. At the age of eighteen, through arrangements made between lawyers in London and his Aunt Shalini, widowed sister-in-law of Romesh Chand, and his own father's sister, Hari came out to India.

From the date Kumar was first questioned by Merrick he was under surveillance. Kumar never explained why he was drunk but the names of his drinking companions were obtained and there were cross-references to other files kept on these young men. The surveillance seemed to have been fairly casual, but Merrick had been thorough in recording what was known locally about this English public-school educated Indian reporter. He'd discovered that Kumar had once applied to an English firm, British-Indian Electric, for a post as a trainee but been turned down on the recommendation of the technical training manager who thought him not intelligent enough.

A young man whose place Kumar had taken on *The Mayapore Gazette*, one Vidyasagar, was also under surveillance. Vidyasagar was now working on a nationalist local, *Mayapore Hindu*. There were notes of several occasions when Kumar and Vidyasagar had been 'seen together', but these couldn't strike a reader as very significant because the occasions were invariably those when they had simply been in the same place at the same time, as reporters (at District and Sessions Court, for example, and local functions on the *maidan*).

The most important items in Merrick's notes were those concerning Kumar's friendship with the English girl, Daphne Manners, who had come to Mayapore to stay with a Lady Chatterjee – a friend of Lady Manners in Rawalpindi. Miss Manners's parents were dead. She had lost her brother in the war and had come out to India quite recently to stay with her surviving relative, her aunt, Lady Manners. Since coming to Mayapore she had been doing voluntary work at the Mayapore General Hospital.

The notes about her association with Kumar began with one dated in April 1942. 'At the War Week exhibition on the *maidan* Miss M left her party to speak to K who was hovering in the vicinity.' The next note suggested that Merrick had taken the trouble to find out how Miss M and K had previously met. 'It seems K was invited to Lady Chatterjees's place, The MacGregor House, where Miss M was staying, shortly after K was questioned in the matter of Moti Lal, probably through the suggestion of the lawyer Srinivasan who was sent to police headquarters to inquire why I'd had K taken to the kotwali for questioning. Srinivasan is Romesh C's lawyer.'

There were several further notes giving dates when K and Miss M were seen in one another's company, one of which – 'Miss M dined with K and his aunt at their house in the Chillianwallah Bagh extension' – Rowan found particularly distasteful since it indicated that Kumar could not even have someone to dinner without the fact being reported.

Finally, among the documents, there were two statements and a report from the Divisional Commissioner. The first statement, by Merrick, described how Kumar had first come to his notice and the opinion he had formed of him as a result of this, what was known locally about the characters of the young men in whose company he had been on the night he got drunk, how Merrick eventually thought it his duty to warn Miss

Manners 'that the young Indian with whom she had struck up a friendship, which few Europeans on station had failed to notice, was not the kind of man one could recommend her to take into her confidence'.

Merrick's statements ended with an account of his own actions on the night when he had called on Lady Chatterjee and found her 'alarmed' at Miss Manners's failure to arrive home, and of his second visit when he found Miss M arrived at last but 'in a distressed condition as a result of having been attacked and criminally used by five or six men in the Bibighar Gardens'. He continued with a description of his discovery of the young men in the hut near by, of the state in which he found Kumar when calling again at the house in Chillianwallah Bagh and of the obstinate but suspicious behaviour of Kumar when taken into custody.

The second statement was a report made by three officers of the civil administration after a private interview with Miss Manners. According to this report, Miss Manners had not confirmed her earlier verbal statement that the men had come at her in the dark, covered her with her own raincape, dragged her off her bicycle and into the Bibighar, and that she had therefore not been able to identify them. She now stated that she had been *in* the Bibighar, alone, and that although it was dark, and the men came at her suddenly, and did cover her head with the raincape, she had had just sufficient glimpse and smell of them to swear on oath that they were all of the badmash or criminal type, not educated or westernized boys of the kind who had been arrested; that it would be ridiculous to bring such boys into court, that she could not fail to deny that they were the men involved, and that it would be just as reasonable to bring in a group of young British soldiers and accuse them of having blacked their faces in order to attack her.

The report from the Divisional Commissioner was simply to the effect that he had studied the files on the arrested men and all the statements and while agreeing that in view of Miss Manners's attitude the evidence against them in the matter of criminal assault was insufficient on which to charge them and bring them to trial, he agreed with the opinion that quite apart from suspicion of criminal assault the evidence obtained over several months of their conduct and political affiliations warranted their detention under Rule 26 of the Defence of India Rules.

When Rowan had studied all this material he returned the file to Malcolm who asked him whether he thought Kumar wrongfully imprisoned. Rowan said he thought so, technically, but that suspicion of complicity in rape was strong enough to take the view that he may have got off extremely lightly. The Governor then asked him whether there was any doubt about this Kumar being the Kumar Rowan had known at school – and handed him a police photograph; full face and profile. He hadn't seen Kumar since Kumar was about fifteen, but he thought the features were like those of the boy he remembered; apart from which everything on the file about Kumar's history fitted what he had known of Kumar's background. The Kumar he knew *had* spent all his life in England, was known as Harry Coomer. His accent had been as English as Colin Lindsey's and Rowan's own. You would only have to hear him speak to know whether they were one and the same man.

The Governor said Rowan would have an opportunity to confirm this. He was to arrange and lead a private examination of the prisoner at the Kandipat jail, in a room known as Room O. He would have a shorthand writer and an official from the Department of Home and Law to assist him. There would also be a fourth person, a woman, who would watch and listen to the interview from a specially equipped adjoining room. The Governor had had many pleas from Kumar's aunt, Shalini Gupta Sen, to review the case against her nephew, and the poor woman had in fact come to Ranpur to be near by in case some steps were taken. But the request for this examination and the request to be present were from Lady Manners. Her visit was to be kept secret. Of the members of the examining board only Rowan was to know of her presence. The examination would not be made under oath and the entire affair was to be conducted in as discreet and confidential manner as possible.

*

With this Rowan had to be content. For the moment Malcolm would discuss it no further. Rowan made the arrangements at the Kandipat and on the day he met Lady Manners at Government House he was already hating the whole business. Kumar had been in jail for more than eighteen months and Rowan had decided that the only explanation for Lady Manners's sudden emergence from the obscurity in which she had lived since the tragedy of the assault and the tragedy of her niece's death in childbirth was that she had been biding her time, perhaps obtaining further evidence against Kumar and now wanted vengeance.

The impression did not survive his first short meeting with her the day before the examination; and on the day itself driving with her to the Kandipat, observing her physical frailty, noting her gentleness of manner, it struck him rather forcibly that here was a woman who felt that her life was coming to an end and that there were dispositions to make. He knew from Malcolm that she was staying under an assumed name at an hotel in Ranpur and that the child and its ayah were with her. To minimize the risk of being recognized by old servants at Government House she wore a deep veil over an old-fashioned sola topee, which she only raised in the car to look at the photograph of Kumar, whom she had never in her life seen.

But – Rowan wondered – if the object of the examination was to secure the release of a man she felt, or knew, to be wrongfully imprisoned, why had she waited so long? Or was it so long? More than eighteen months since the assault, but only half that time since her niece died. As they drew near Kandipat, Rowan began to pull down the blinds of the car. They entered the jail precincts in semi-darkness.

The deeply subjective feelings, like joy, fear, love, are the most difficult to convey. One has to make do, more often than not, with the crutch of the words themselves. Very occasionally if an experience has been vivid enough, the quality of it comes through without there being much conscious attempt to communicate it. This was the way Rowan conveyed to me what the examination in the Kandipat jail had been like, for him. It had been a claustrophobic experience. I have thought of Rowan's experience of the Kandipat often, tried to shed light on it, as a scene, but the light coming out from the scene always seems stronger. One ends up a bit dazzled by it. The eyes hurt. You glance away, to rest them, and then momentarily there's the illusion of blindness, blankness. You feel shut in. I hit on the word claustrophobic while Rowan was describing it to me. Directly I hit on it I knew I had also hit on a description of the effect Merrick had on me.

That light I mentioned, the one coming out from the scene, was actually a real light: a light bright enough to interrogate by, but nothing crude; subtly balanced, tilted, as if haphazardly, but in fact shining on the examinee at an angle that would only worry him if he chanced to look up above the level of Rowan's head and wonder about the grille in the wall behind. But had he done so he would have assumed that it was part of the air-conditioning plant.

Another thing Rowan managed to communicate to me without putting it into so many words was the shock of this initiation into one of the *raj's* obscurer rites, the kind conducted in a windowless room with artificial light and air, an early form of bugging system and spy-system, and making an uncompromising statement about itself as the ominously still centre of the world of moral and political power which hitherto he had known as one revolving openly in the alternating light of good intentions and the dark of doubts and errors. The room in the Kandipat emitted nothing but its own steady glare. It illuminated nothing except the consequences of an action already performed and a decision taken long ago. These could never be undone or retracted. In the world outside new action could be taken and new decisions made. But the light of what had been performed would glow on unblinkingly, like radium in a closed and undiscovered mine.

*

When the prisoner entered Rowan thought: No, that's not the man, the whole thing is a ludicrous mistake. The man is an impostor. It was not even the man in the police photographs. He had expected some change but not such a devastating one. This man looked middle-aged. He seemed not to understand English. Rowan asked him to sit down but it wasn't until the assistant examiner from the Home and Law Department, an Indian, said '*Baitho*' that he did so; and then the contours of the chair seemed to puzzle

1314

him, as if he lacked physical co-ordination. Rowan asked him whether he wished to have the examination conducted in English or in Hindi. He asked him this question in Hindi. The prisoner answered in Hindi, using the single word *Angrezi*, meaning 'in English'. As he answered he looked directly at Rowan for the first time and the conviction that the man was the wrong man weakened.

The eyes, Rowan said, were those 'of one man looking out of the eye-sockets of another' and the man looking out could have been Kumar; his answers to the routine opening questions whose object was identification all added up to an admission that he was, but still the answers came in Hindi – the abbreviated word *hān*, repeated tonelessly. Hān. Hān.

At this point Rowan reminded the prisoner that he had elected to have the examination conducted in English. Questions had been put in English. So far he had answered in Hindi. Did this mean that he had changed his mind and would prefer the questions to be put in Hindi too? He hoped that the answer would come again, hān; then the onus of putting questions would fall on his colleague, and for him the whole thing would become a semantic exercise. For Lady Manners in the adjoining room it would become an exercise in patience. He doubted that her Hindi was even as good as his. But that didn't matter. He would prefer to take a back seat. He didn't want this gaunt shambling creature to be Hari Kumar; certainly not Coomer, whom he remembered Laura Elliott describing as 'that good-looking boy who caught you before you even scored'. Old Boys versus School. Rowan had approached him after stumps, congratulated him; asked him what he intended doing. The boy had said, 'Try for the ICS, I suppose, sir.' And gone out of Rowan's life.

To emerge here? It wasn't possible. The physical evidence was against such a transmigration. The eyes could have been Coomer's; they showed no recognition of Rowan but Rowan wouldn't have expected it. But he had expected something far more telling. A manner.

Rowan waited for the prisoner to respond. He seemed not to have understood the question and Rowan wondered whether he should repeat it in Hindi. He was about to do so when the man spoke. He said he was sorry, answering the questions in Hindi had been a slip; he seldom had the chance of speaking English, except to himself.

Rowan described the effect of this casual statement in straightforward English as electrifying. It was as though there were two men in the chair, the one you could see and the one you could hear. The one you could hear was undoubtedly Coomer and once you were aware that he was Coomer the unfavourable impression made by the shambling body and hollow-cheeked face began to fade. The English voice, released from its inner prison, seemed to have taken control of the face and limbs, to be infusing them with something of its own firmness and authority.

'I felt,' Rowan said, 'that quite unexpectedly our rôles were reversed or at least levelled up and that it wasn't Coomer who was being examined so much as a system that had ostensibly given us equal opportunities but had ended like this with me on the comfortable side of a green baize-covered table and him on the unpleasant one. And one of the interesting questions was, where precisely did this leave my Indian colleague and co-examiner?'

The Indian colleague was the same Mr Gopal who had accompanied Rowan up to Pankot and just gone back to Ranpur with Mr Kasim. Before Kumar's examination Rowan and Gopal were no more than casual acquaintances and one of the ironies of that examination, Rowan had always felt, was that whereas he himself had a common bond of sympathy with Kumar but could not absolve him from suspicion of some kind of connection with the attack on Daphne Manners, Gopal – as became obvious – believed him innocent on every count, believed that he had been victimized by the Mayapore authorities because he was an Indian, but at the same time disliked him for being the kind of Indian he actually was. Quite early in the questioning Gopal elicited from Kumar the fact that Kumar's father had admired the British and the British form of administration in India and that he had deliberately brought Kumar up in a way that should have enabled him to enter the administration with the same qualities and advantages an English boy had. At the same time, Gopal's form of questioning made it clear he believed this could only have been done at the cost of Kumar senior turning his back on his own people – which in fact had been the case and a major cause of the ensuing tragedy.

Kumar senior had been exposed as a man with an obsession that had cost his son dearly. One of Gopal's objectives in this line of questioning about Kumar's background was of course to establish that with an upbringing such as he'd had the very idea of his ever becoming a danger to the British was nonsensical. To Gopal, Kumar/Coomer *was* British. During the recess when Kumar had been taken outside for a while, Rowan admitted that he and Kumar had been at the same school but that Kumar didn't realize this, didn't recognize him. Gopal then described Kumar as 'an English boy with a brown skin' and said, 'the combination is hopeless'.

Rowan called the recess because he'd felt the examination was getting out of hand. He had tried unsuccessfully to keep it strictly to the question of Kumar's political affiliations. These, he believed, had been virtually non-existent and had now been shown to be non-existent. The only occasion when Kumar had consorted with any of the young Indians who were found drinking in the derelict hut on the night of the rape was that other night, six months before, when he got drunk himself and was picked up by Sister Ludmila's stretcher-bearers. Until then and after then he had kept fairly clear of them. He felt no animosity towards them but they weren't young men whose interests he could share, whose experiences he had shared, or whose aspirations he could regard with anything except a detached kind of understanding. They were all young nationalists but, he said, why shouldn't they be? In examination he made no bones about that, but no bones either about his view of the limited form their nationalism ordinarily took. They were young, therefore inconsistent, laughing at the British, talking against them, but fond of wearing western-style clothes and with a tendency to copy British manners. They were friendly, at times deeply depressed, at times euphoric. They were educated to a standard a peg or so above the level on which society determined they could live.

The truth which Coomer had had to face was that this was a level on which he now had to live too: that of one young Indian among countless others who could never expect to achieve any kind of position of authority; young men doomed, it seemed, to spend their lives as members of a literate but obscure and powerless middle-class, thankful for jobs as ill-paid clerks in shops and offices and banks – a life infinitely poorer than the one he would have led if he had grown up in his father's ancestral village, or if Kumar senior's obsession about the value of an English upbringing had not been so deeply felt and so uncompromisingly followed that he had sacrificed his own security and – with that single exception of his young widowed sister – the regard of his family.

Hari never knew much about his father's business affairs in England but for many years these must have prospered. Hari's childhood was spent in security and considerable comfort. There had been housekeepers, governesses, tutors, a private school and then Chillingborough. In the Spring of 1938 he had been looking forward to his last term, the prospect of university and of preparation for the ics examinations. Qualified, he would eventually have come out to India on terms of parity with young Englishmen entering the covenanted civil service and so fulfilled his father's ambitions. Duleep Kumar's death would not in itself have altered these prospects but pennilessness did. Probably it was the elder Kumar's realization of what his complete financial failure would mean to his son that led him to take his own life. As a boy himself Duleep Kumar had had to wear down his own father's opposition before getting himself a college education in India and wear it down again as a young man before going to England to study law. When he returned, unqualified, an academic failure, he had had no alternative but to settle down with the child-wife to whom he'd agreed to be betrothed before leaving England. The Kumars were well-to-do landowners, orthodox, rigidly opposed to any change in *status quo*. Their power and authority flowed from their wealth and possessions. With this they were content. The men were semi-literate, the women quite illiterate. The sole exception was Shalini, Duleep Kumar's youngest sister, whom he taught to read and write in both Hindi and English. India could hold more for an Indian than this, he knew. If he could not get it for himself then he would do so for the son his wife presently bore. She made it easier for him by dying. But still he wasn't free. His father, having divided the inheritance among the sons, left his family to earn merit by relinquishing his earthly ties and become *sannyasi*. Commending their mother to the sons' care he departed, with staff and begging-bowl. They never saw him again. The mother, living the life of a widow in the family house, survived two years. Shalini had gone to Mayapore as the child bride of one Prakash Gupta Sen. After his mother's death there was nothing to keep Duleep Kumar in India. He sold his interest to his brothers and departed, presumably quite well-off, and took Hari to England. Probably he still had friends and acquaintances in England from his law-student days, and such connections would have been helpful, but he must also have been enterprising and skilful. Just what eventually went wrong, Hari Kumar did not know.

What he knew was that his father was dead from an overdose of sleeping pills and that the lawyers said there was no money because the creditors would take everything. The only Indian relative he knew of, the only one his father had ever written to, was his Aunt Shalini. The lawyers wrote to her. The assumption was that money to keep him at school, at least, might be forthcoming. It was not. Shalini, widowed and childless, was a dependant of her Mayapore brother-in-law, Romesh Chand. She borrowed money from him to pay for Hari's passage. He would live with her. And still the assumption was that Hari would continue his studies and become an ICS candidate in India. His ignorance of India was as great as the lawyers' ignorance. When he sailed he had not the smallest conception of the devastating change made to his life by his father's failure and suicide.

*

Rowan told me that these facts emerged in the first five or ten minutes of the examination but that he had been able to build for himself a far more complex and disturbing picture, indeed had been unable to get it out of his mind since. He said that Hari's old life must have ended and the new one begun the moment he stepped off the ship in Bombay. His link with England would have snapped, then, with shocking abruptness.

Rowan said, 'Well. You know. Whatever kind of shock India is, pleasant or horrid, if you're a young Englishman coming out to the civil or military or to any kind of job, you're cushioned from the shock the moment you step off the gangplank because metaphorically you step off into a covered-way that extends from the dock – however many hundreds of miles – to your first station. When Elliott and I and Laura stepped off we were met by friends of Elliott's parents. I've forgotten who, people I never saw again, but I remember that within an hour or two we were at the Gymkhana Club having a drink and everything was very English and reassuring. Everything was done for us. We didn't have to lift a finger. I remember thinking, How good this is. But even if we'd not been met there would have been people to see us through, an agent to take charge of us, or people going up to the same station. And in any case we had our white faces and our official standing.'

Think, Rowan said, of Harry Coomer's arrival. The bewilderment he must have felt was scarcely imaginable. It was to be hoped that if no one met him he had at least fallen in with some people on the boat who were helpful. Perhaps the bewilderment had started on the boat. Rowan doubted that he would have had a first-class passage. And when it came to the train to Mayapore, he suspected he would have had to travel third but sincerely hoped not. The boy spoke nothing but English and the kind of people who spoke his kind of English would have been, suddenly, on the other side of the fence. He would have been one more face in the multitude. And the graver revelation was still to come.

A few months ago Rowan had accompanied Malcolm on a tour that included a three-hour visit to Mayapore. He had not been in Mayapore before and thought the cantonment charming. But the cantonment had not been where Kumar was bound seven years earlier, in 1938. Rowan would have liked to slip away from the Governor's entourage but this had been impossible. At one moment, though, the entourage was in the vicinity of the Mandir Gate Bridge, scene of one of the worst of the Mayapore civil riots in 1942, and there, across the river, he had a view and needed no further evidence.

Somewhere in that noisome mass Kumar had lived with his Aunt Shalini, had found himself put to work in his uncle's warehouse in the Chillianwallah bazaar, had been regarded as a man who had lost caste, who ought to undergo ritual purification to rid himself of the stain of having lived abroad. There was to be no more education, no degree, no ICS, no entry even into the lower levels of the provincial administration. This was the orthodox urban middle-class Hindu India which hoarded its profits and kept itself to itself, and served no interests but its own and existed, quite unmoved, side by side with the India of unspeakable poverty and squalor. And this was the India in which Hari was expected to settle, grateful for the charity bestowed.

*

Rowan said, 'I think if it had happened to me, once I'd realized that it was real and that there seemed no way out, I'd have cried myself to sleep every night. Perhaps he did, old as he was.'

His Aunt Shalini had adored her brother, Hari's father. They had kept up a correspondence through all the years of separation. She was proud of her 'English' nephew as she called Hari and there's no doubt that she loved him and did her best for him, her best to help him to adjust; but as a childless widow of Romesh Chand's brother she herself was little more than one of Romesh's chattels and the means she had to help were limited. How long Kumar worked in his uncle's warehouse Rowan didn't know, but in the examination he had found out more about Hari's attempt to get a job with British-Indian Electric. The technical training manager who had turned him down as 'not intelligent enough' was obviously the sort of man – self-conscious about his own education and background – who disliked his own English bosses and despised all Indians on principle. Hari Kumar, with his brown skin and public school voice and manner, was a sitting duck. Ignoring Hari's statement that he had no technical knowledge but was willing to learn he asked him a series of technical questions and when he'd finished and Hari had been unable to answer, he said, 'Where are you from, laddie? Straight down off the tree?'

Hari walked out. A mistake, perhaps, but Rowan thought it showed how deep his instinct still was, how automatic his response to any threat to what he still possessed and still prized; prized because it was all he did possess: his sense of what he owed himself and had to keep on paying to himself, even at the expense of a lost job; the debt incurred by his English upbringing.

*

He got his job on the *Mayapore Gazette* because of his knowledge of the language in which the paper was supposed to be printed. He had no ambition to be a journalist. By this time he must have picked up some Hindi, but he had abandoned attempts to learn it systematically. For a while his aunt had paid for him to have lessons from a local pandit, one Pandit Baba Sahib – apparently an unfortunate choice since Baba Sahib was known by the police to recruit young men to the cause of Hindu extremism under cover of having scholarly discussions with them about Hindu mythology. From Hari's point of view the lessons weren't a success. Baba Sahib was always late and always smelt strongly of garlic. After a while Hari told him not to bother to come again. His association with this tiresome old man was brief but it probably counted against him eventually. Rowan imagined that Hari gave up learning Hindi because he did not want to pick it up sufficiently to start thinking in it, or to acquire an Indian tone of voice.

His knowledge of English was the one asset he had that could be put to practical use. When he joined the *Mayapore Gazette* as a sub-editor his uncle reduced his Aunt Shalini's allowance. Rowan imagined he'd been paid little or nothing for working in his uncle's warehouse. There couldn't have been any overall financial gain from the change of jobs but the offices of the *Gazette* were far more congenial. They were in the cantonment.

Hari crossed the river from the native to the English quarter. The new job brought him into closer physical contact with the kind of people he thought he knew because he had once been one of them. He realized he no longer was and that he had become invisible to them. But there was always Colin to write to and Colin to get letters from although Colin's letters changed in tone as he responded to the political crisis in Europe. To Hari, Europe seemed so far away that he could not share Colin's concern. He was aware of growing areas of estrangement. Colin might have been aware of them too had Hari ever described the kind of life he was living now. This he never did. He allowed Colin to go on thinking of India as a glamorous sort of place. He didn't want to appeal to Colin for pity and he wanted to keep in touch.

Colin joined the Territorial Army and thereafter wrote of nothing else. When war broke out he at once became a full-time soldier. It was between the outbreak of war and the defeat of the BEF and its evacuation from Dunkirk that Hari wrote the letter Colin's father destroyed because it was full of what he later described to his wounded son as 'a lot of hot-headed political stuff'. According to Hari, this letter had just been an attempt to discuss the pros and cons of the Congress resignation from the provincial ministries in protest against India's automatic involvement in the war against Germany. If the British Government could not declare war on behalf of dominions like Canada and Australia, but had to leave them to come in voluntarily, why should war be declared on India's behalf through the Viceroy, without consultation even? That was the basis of the Congress argument. Legally, of course, this was the only way war could be declared; but a point which Hari must have made (after the liberal education which men like Bagshaw had ensured remained a Chillingborough tradition) was that with Dominion status ranking as a declared principal aim of the British for India, the outbreak of war had been as good a moment as any to show that the spirit rather than the letter of the law was to be the guiding factor in the British–Indian relationship. But there hadn't been even a pretence of consultation between the Viceroy and his provincial ministers and central legislative assembly. Piqued, the Congress had resigned, declaring that a war against the European dictator could only be waged by free men.

Rowan said it must have been the kind of letter 'one old Chillingburian would have written to another', as strong in its arguments for the Viceroy as in those against him. It was unfortunate that it had reached Colin's home at a time when Colin was in hospital recovering from wounds and when – as Mr Lindsey probably put it – Britain was 'standing alone'. One could imagine all too easily the sort of man Lindsey was or had become; the sort who, if he had tenants or male servants would have liked to round them up and march them to the nearest recruiting office; the sort who stuck pins in maps and nursed a sense of personal injury if anyone, man or nation, cast any doubt whatsoever on the conduct of those whom God had raised to positions of power and responsibility. The attitude of Indian politicians since 1939 wouldn't have endeared any Indian to him. Deliberately opening Hari's letter he would have had his suspicions of that country's population confirmed.

'A lot of hot-headed political nonsense.' A thoughtless, empty phrase. But how damaging it had seemed two years later when the police found the letter from Colin in which it was repeated and apologized for. It was the only letter from Colin which Hari kept. That was unfortunate. It was like preserving the one real piece of evidence against oneself. Hari kept it because it was the only letter he had had from Colin which struck him as coming from the fair-minded boy he had known. Young Lindsey's baptism of fire had knocked some of the jingoism out of him. He had stopped flag-wagging. The war had become too real for that. Perhaps for the first time since Hari left for India Colin wondered what *Hari's* reality was like.

In 1941 he was to find out. His regiment came out to India. He wrote to Hari in Mayapore saying he hoped he would get down to see him or that somehow they could meet. He wrote again from another station, this time saying how difficult such a trip would be. Then he stopped writing. Hari told himself that the regiment had probably been sent down into Burma or Malaya; and at the turn of the year when the Japanese attacked, he felt sorry for him, in the thick again, having a bad war.

*

Rowan hesitated. I took the opportunity to interrupt, to ask a question that had been nagging for the past few minutes.

'He could have joined up himself, couldn't he? He'd have got in at once as an officer-cadet.'

'I know. It's a question I intended to ask him, but didn't, because I realized he'd have been quite justified in saying something like, "Why the hell should I have? Why should one pip on my shoulder have made me visible and acceptable to English people all of a sudden?" An answer like that, however justified, would have looked bad on the record.'

'Evidence of anti-Britishness?'

'On paper, yes. But I haven't told you the other thing that technical training manager said to him. "I don't like bolshie black laddies on my side of the business." If you have a thing like that said to you by a member of a firm like British-Indian Electric in Mayapore, I think it follows that you don't rush to join the colours when their country goes to war in Europe. What I don't think followed in Hari's case was a rush to join the opposition. I don't believe he saw any *political* significance in what was happening to him.'

As a reporter on the *Gazette* he often attended English social functions such as flower-shows, gymkhanas, cricket matches. Occasionally an Englishman would compliment him on his English accent, ask him where he'd acquired it, and show such disbelief when told that Hari stopped saying 'Chillingborough'. A Chillingborough man didn't end up as a tuppenny-hapenny reporter on a fifth-rate local Indian newspaper. So he steered clear of these embarrassing confrontations.

And then early in 1942 he saw officers and men of Colin's regiment in the cantonment. The battalion had come into Mayapore. He wondered whether he would arrive home one night and find that Colin had visited him. He rather hoped not. It was unlikely anyway. The city on his side of the river was out-of-bounds to troops and although an officer could always get an official pass Hari thought it more likely that Colin would write, or perhaps turn up at the office of the *Gazette*. No letter came. He never saw Colin among the officers who shopped in the cantonment bazaar. It was possible, he realized, that Colin was no longer with the battalion, but in his heart he must have suspected that a few months in India had shown Colin the truth about the kind of life a young Indian with no official position would have to lead. A glance at the map of Mayapore would have shown him how close they were, how far they were separated socially.

But Colin was in Mayapore. On the *maidan* – to report a cricket match –

1322

Hari saw him. They were within a few feet of one another. They looked at one another. Neither spoke. The kindest construction Hari could put on Colin's failure to speak was that he didn't recognize one brown face among so many. This, at least, was the suggestion he made when Rowan was examining him. Kumar described the incident in the course of answering the board's question, why – on a date in February 1942 – he had been found on waste ground near the river, dead drunk, and taken to Sister Ludmila's Sanctuary.

He said he'd always avoided intimacy with young men like Vidyasagar and his companions, always refused invitations to go with them to coffee-houses. After the meeting with Colin on the *maidan* he'd met Vidyasagar and on the spur of the moment accepted an invitation to go home with him. It was as if he knew that his one true link with the past had now been snapped, as if he could see no reason to go on deceiving himself that he was any different from these semi-westernized youths. That night he discovered that they distilled or had access to illicit liquor. They were used to it. He was not. He got very drunk. They took him home but after they had gone he wandered off again, across the derelict ground where destitutes and untouchables camped out and where Sister Ludmila and her stretcher-bearers found him.

*

You could begin with me, Rowan had said, *I have very little real confidence. But it would be dangerous to give that impression. I expect I over-compensate. Most of us do. It's probably what happened to Colin Lindsey.*

Assuming mutual recognition, over-compensation for lack of confidence seemed to me a curious way of describing Lindsey's behaviour. Could one assume mutual recognition? Could one even assume that the man Kumar thought he recognized as Lindsey had been Lindsey? Apparently he must have been. Subsequently Rowan checked, through the military secretary's department. A Captain Colin Lindsey had been in Mayapore, not actually with his battalion but on the staff of the formation with which the battalion had been brigaded for training, and had then been transferred at his own request away from Mayapore to divisional headquarters.

Still, mutual recognition remains an assumption. But, if there was mutual recognition, one has to assume that Lindsey saw nothing so clearly as the embarrassment that would follow any attempt to renew an old acquaintance in such very different circumstances. His transfer to Division suggests that he probably applied for it directly he heard that he was going to Brigade, in Mayapore. Little to do with over-compensation for lack of confidence, but a lot to do with straightforward self-protection from the consequences of having a friend who was no longer socially acceptable and who might turn out to be a pest, the sort of Indian who as the *raj* so often said would try to take advantage, make demands it would be impossible to satisfy and which it would be wiser and more comfortable not to lay oneself open to.

Where I agree with Rowan is in pinpointing the meeting with Lindsey as the one meeting in Kumar's life which, leading directly to the other from which all his true misfortunes flowed, must bear a special significance: no Lindsey on the *maidan* that day, no drinking bout with young Vidyasagar and friends; no wandering on to waste-ground, no stretcher-bearers, no Sister Ludmila, no Sanctuary; no morning waking there, hungover, resentful and unco-operative.

No Merrick.

*

And yet how logical that meeting was, between Kumar – one of Macaulay's 'brown-skinned Englishmen' – and Merrick, English-born and English-bred, but a man whose country's social and economic structure had denied him advantages and privileges which Kumar had initially enjoyed; a man, moreover, who lacked entirely that liberal instinct which is so dear to historians that they lay it out like a guideline through the unmapped forests of prejudice and self-interest as though this line, and not the forest, is our history.

Place Merrick at home, in England, and Harry Coomer abroad, in England, and it is Coomer on whom the historian's eye lovingly falls; he is a symbol of our virtue. In England it is Merrick who is invisible. Place them there, in India, and the historian cannot see either of them. They have wandered off the guideline, into the jungle. But throw a spotlight on them and it is Merrick on whom it falls. There he is, the unrecorded man, one of the kind of men we really are (as Sarah would say). Yes, their meeting was logical. And they had met before, countless times. You can say they are still meeting, that their meeting reveals the real animus, the one that historians won't recognize, or which we relegate to our margins

Neither Rowan nor I saw it like this, then. I doubt that he would see it like this now. Simply, he would remain appalled and puzzled, a man with a conscience that worked in favour of both men; more in favour of Kumar than of Merrick; but Merrick was given sufficient benefit of the liberal doubt to leave Rowan inert. What Rowan was doing, in telling me all this, was trying to set off against his own inertia someone else's positive action: mine. He wanted me to do what he could not do: help Kumar. His ideas on the subject, it goes without saying, were woolly.

*

Kumar had been washing under a tap, trying to clear his head, when Merrick arrived at the Sanctuary looking for the escaped prisoner, Moti Lal. The first ball of the over. The merciless succession of deliveries after all came from the same hand. Merrick saw him, a young man of twenty-two, washing under a tap; and chose him. I wondered how 'prepossessing' Hari Kumar had been before prison had had its effect and made him look like one man peering out of the eyesockets of another. Self-punishment being out of the question, Merrick punished the men he chose. After Karim Muzzafir Khan's suicide I was never in any doubt about Merrick's repressed homosexuality. Rowan always evaded this issue, and the result was that for him I think it assumed a graver importance than it merited, except perhaps in regard to the proposed marriage to Susan Bingham. But he had found it quite impossible, obviously, to convey any suspicion of this kind to Colonel Layton, or to anyone whom it might concern. One can understand this. It was no business of his, just as it was no business of mine.

For not answering Merrick's questions smartly and respectfully, Kumar was taken forcibly from the Sanctuary, pushed, punched and thrown into a police truck; not by Merrick but by one of Merrick's sub-inspectors (the same one, perhaps, who made an 'erroneous' report about the bicycle?).

But Merrick saw him being punched. So did Sister Ludmila. After the truck had driven away she sent word to Hari's uncle Romesh Chand. Romesh sent the lawyer Srinivasan to inquire why young Kumar had been 'arrested', but by the time he got there Kumar had been released. The word got round, though, that a young Indian of good character and good education had been roughed-up by the police and taken in for questioning – got round in those circles of Indian society which formed a link between the rulers and the ruled; Indians with a foot in both camps.

Four years after his arrival in Mayapore this world became aware of him. He had to be hauled into a kotwali first. It must have intrigued Merrick that this world now took note of Kumar. Srinivasan, first; and then, no doubt through Srinivasan, no less a person than the District and Sessions Judge, an Indian, who apparently inquired gently why this young Indian had been taken to the kotwali with no obvious justification. For Srinivasan and the judge Merrick can only have had contempt.

The *doyenne* of this official Indian society in Mayapore was Lady Chatterjee, a woman of cultured and cosmopolitan tastes, one imagines, since she was a friend of Lady Manners. *Persona grata* with the Deputy Commissioner, with whom she played bridge, she was neither blind nor deaf to evidence of the *raj's* high-handedness even if (as one supposes) she often had to be to its frequent vulgarities. What Srinivasan, the lawyer, or Menen, the judge, told her about the young Kumar, interested her sufficiently to cause her to invite him to a party at her house.

He went, one imagines, out of curiosity; prickly curiosity, as resentful of the interest his 'case' had aroused as he was resentful of the fact that it had taken so long for this privileged section of Indian society to notice him. Rowan gathered it had been a mixed party – a further irony. Kumar would have been under observation by both sides. Admitting to Rowan that from his point of view the party wasn't a success (nor, he thought, from Lady

Chatterjee's, whom he failed to thank), he said he had forgotten how to behave in this sort of company.

One questions that until remembering that he had never been in that sort of company before, and realizes that what he really meant was that he had no idea how to behave in a gathering of people, white and brown, who even when they mingled were observing certain rules which hinted at segregation. These were rules which only Miss Manners seemed unaware of. At first he thought she was merely trying over-hard to put him at his ease. It was a long time since an English person had talked to him without either condescension or self-consciousness, which was what Miss Manners *seemed* to be doing and what subsequent events suggested she *had* been doing. And that would make her the first Englishwoman to have talked to him on the simple human level of woman to man. When last in England he had still been a schoolboy. One wonders about the effect this would have on him. Rowan had never seen a photograph of her. The one the police found in Kumar's room was not in the file. But he had heard her described as not much to look at; but this was afterwards, when people had no time for her and assumed she had rigged the evidence to save a man she was infatuated with or terrified of.

One really knew nothing about Daphne Manners except that she was in some degree or other attracted to Kumar. One knew nothing about Kumar's feelings. The history of their relationship could be made to fit almost any theory one could have of Kumar's character and intentions. Here he was, for instance, doing as little as he could to encourage her because he found her embarrassing. Or here, doing that same little in order to excite her more. Or here, genuinely fond of her, perhaps falling in love with her, but seeing no future for either of them and doing his best to make her see that there was no future. The theory most people had was that he egged her on, made her chase after him, to humiliate her, but subtly, so that she did not realize that she was being humiliated.

'Which theory do you subscribe to?' I asked Rowan.

'I think he was fond of her. I don't believe he meant her any harm. I think she fell in love with him quite early on. And eventually I think they started making love. I think they were making love in the Bibighar Gardens. It's the only explanation that makes sense of all the rest. They were making love and were interrupted by the men who assaulted her.'

'His friends?'

'They weren't his friends. He'd only been out with them once, the night he got drunk. They weren't his enemies either. And they were really only kids. If Hari and Miss Manners were making love in the Bibighar that night then I think the men who attacked them and assaulted her really were the kind she described later when she had to admit she'd had a glimpse of them. Badmashes who'd come into Mayapore to pick up what they could in the riots everyone was expecting and which had already started down in districts like Dibrapur. The Bibighar Gardens sounds like a public place but it was a derelict site. The kind of place men like that would collect in, waiting for dark. And the kind of place Kumar and Miss Manners would go to, to be on their own.'

'Didn't you ask Kumar whether this is what happened?'

'It only occurred to me later. Quite recently, in fact. In any case Kumar wouldn't have admitted it. He refused to say anything about her. He went on insisting he'd not seen her for something like three weeks, after the night they visited the temple. Exactly the same as he insisted when Merrick arrested him. And then of course don't forget I was trying not to examine him about the rape. I was taking a very literal view of the terms of reference, which were for the examination of a political detenu. But the rape couldn't be avoided. Everything came back to it because everything came back to Merrick. Kumar seemed to want it to come back to Merrick. So did Gopal. So for that matter did Lady Manners. Gopal started asking him about his first interrogation – I don't mean the one in February – I mean after Merrick had carted him away from his home on the night of the rape. He told Gopal Merrick had had him stripped and that his genitals had been examined. Lady Manners was listening in and watching through the grille. The microphone was in a telephone on my desk but she and I could use the telephone to communicate. When she realized I was trying to stop things going along these lines she rang through and told me I mustn't bother about her hearing unpleasant things. The other thing she wanted to know was whether Kumar knew her niece had died in childbirth. I pretended it was an outside call, naturally, and took that opportunity to call a break and send Kumar out. I tried to explain to Gopal that if we started concentrating on the alleged rape the record of the examination might be thrown out as irrelevant. But he insisted. I thought it pretty dangerous. You have to realize, Guy, that at this time I was fairly convinced that Kumar was mixed up in the assault somehow or other and that Gopal was being very naïve, over-anxious to show that Kumar had been a victim of *raj* terrorism. And, well, to be quite frank, it went against the grain to hear Kumar beginning to accuse an English police officer, a man who wasn't there to defend himself.

'Kumar wasn't on oath, the examination was private. The police officer couldn't legally be affected by anything Kumar decided to say or make up. And I wondered why he was suddenly so co-operative about answering questions he'd previously refused to answer. In 1942 his reply to every question according to the file had been that he had nothing to say. The only thing he still had nothing to say about was what he'd been doing between leaving the *Gazette* office as usual about six in the evening and arriving home about 9.30 in mud-stained clothes and with scratches and abrasions on his face. On the other hand –'

I waited.

'On the other hand, if he'd spent his time in prison making up fantasies about Merrick's treatment of him I felt he could have made up a plausible story to cover that ominous gap. But he hadn't. And whatever he said *sounded* like the truth. I didn't know what to think. But I felt like a

1327

defending lawyer who knows he can get his client off so long as he sticks to the point – the minor legal issue – and avoids anything controversial. I think I could have stuck to that and overridden Gopal if Kumar had co-operated. But he kept on saying that the real situation couldn't be avoided. He didn't mean the rape, he said he meant the situation between Merrick and himself. So when he came back after the recess I let everyone pull out the stops. I felt I'd exchanged briefs and was now prosecuting. If I let him talk about what he called the situation I thought he'd inadvertently give something away. It wasn't what I wanted. It was what I felt I couldn't resist any more. Do you see that? Or do I sound like someone covering up a prejudice and pretending the prejudice was never there?'

It was a difficult question. I couldn't answer it. I didn't try. What worried Rowan was the thought that after all his suspicion of Hari's complicity in the rape was not based so much on the evidence in the file as on the fact that Hari was an Indian and the colour of his skin coloured one's attitude to him, and that in fact it was a relief to exchange his brief, throw off the mask and let Hari condemn himself while he was trying to condemn Merrick.

And I think it was then, with Rowan sitting opposite me, showing not a trace of anxiety (carve him in stone and nothing would have emerged so clearly as his rigid pro-consular self-assurance, remoteness and dignity), that I understood the comic dilemma of the *raj* – the dilemma of men who hoped to inspire trust but couldn't even trust themselves. The air around us and in the grounds of the summer residence was soft, pungent with aromatic gums, but melancholy – charged with this self-mistrust and the odour of an unreality which only exile made seem real. I had an almost irrepressible urge to burst out laughing. I fought it because he would have misinterpreted it. But I would have been laughing *for* him. I suppose that to laugh for people, to see the comic side of their lives when they can't see it for themselves, is a way of expressing affection for them; and even admiration – of a kind – for the lives they try so seriously to lead.

*

It was Gopal's theory that the cuts and abrasions Kumar was said to have been bathing when the police turned up at his house hadn't been there until after the police turned up, or until he arrived at police headquarters, or even until later; that is, not there until they started getting rough with him and needed a report on the file that would explain the state of his face and at the same time harden the evidence against him. When the examination got under way again Rowan read out to him Merrick's statement about his arrival at Kumar's house and his discovery of Kumar, bathing his face, which was cut and bruised, and of the discarded muddy clothes.

Was that an accurate report? Rowan asked.

Yes, Kumar replied. It was.

Gopal was deflated but bided his time. There was another report on Kumar's file, quite a brief one, a copy of a statement by a magistrate who'd been asked by the Deputy Commissioner to question Kumar on two rather unpleasant aspects of the handling of the case. Word had got round in Mayapore that to try to make them confess the arrested boys, all Hindus, had been forced to eat beef. Also that they'd been whipped. The magistrate's name was Iyenagar. Rowan hadn't seen the files on the five other boys; he'd only been shown Kumar's. According to this file Kumar told Iyenagar that he had no complaint to make about his treatment, a simple enough refutation of the rumours and one that seemed to be borne out by the report from the medical officer at the Kandipat jail who examined Kumar physically the day he was sent there as a detenu – more than two weeks later. The only mark of physical violence noted down by the prison doctor was a contusion on his cheek. But that had been there when Merrick found him bathing his face.

The bruise, however, gave Mr Gopal an argument which he tried to turn to Kumar's advantage. He said that the marks on Hari's face, which Hari himself refused to explain, had been interpreted by the police as marks got from Miss Manners in the struggle with her attackers. He said that in a court of law a lawyer might reasonably have asked whether a woman could hit a man hard enough for a bruise to stay on his cheek for as long as two weeks. He was still trying to get Hari to say that the police had beaten him up. But Hari wouldn't say this. He said it was a good point but that in a court a prosecuting counsel might well have turned it against him by suggesting that the men who attacked Miss Manners also fought with each other.

'I saw an opening there,' Rowan told me. 'I asked him casually if that was what had happened. I remember how he looked at me. He said he'd no idea what happened among the men who attacked her. But he realized I'd exchanged briefs. I tried again to get him to say what had happened to him that night, gave him the chance to go back over the ground, back to the question of Colin, back to his relationship with Miss Manners, but all I got out of him was the information that sometimes he and Miss Manners had helped Sister Ludmila at the Sanctuary, occasionally visited one another's homes, and sometimes on a Sunday morning met in the Bibighar Gardens, the kind of places where they could go without attracting what he called abusive attention, but that all this ended on the night they visited the temple, when they had some sort of tiff.

'I saw another opening. I said, "But you made the quarrel up later." He didn't fall for that. He pointed out that I was forgetting he and Miss Manners hadn't seen each other since that night – the night they visited the temple. So I let Gopal take over, which meant letting Gopal get Hari to say what happened after Merrick arrested him.'

Almost at once they were in what Rowan called very murky waters.

While they'd concentrated on the political evidence it had been possible to show that the conflict was not a conflict of evidence so much as of interpretation. Directly Hari began to describe what happened after he'd passed through the room in which the five other boys were being held behind bars, euphoric with liquor, and down into the air-conditioned basement of Merrick's headquarters, it became a question of setting Merrick's official statements about the interrogation against Hari's recollections of it. Recollections, or fantasies?

For example, from the police file: this – 'At 2245 hours the prisoner Kumar having continually refused to answer questions relating to his activities that evening asked for what reason he had been taken into custody. Upon being told it was believed he could help the police with inquiries they were making into the criminal assault in the Bibighar Gardens earlier that evening he said: I have not seen Miss Manners since the night we visited the temple. On being asked why he named Miss Manners he refused to answer and showed signs of distress.'

When Hari was asked to say whether this was accurate he said it wasn't. He had refused to answer questions but the statement left out the fact that he'd said he would refuse to do so while he was left in ignorance of why he'd been arrested. It may have been 2245 hours before Merrick finally said he was making an inquiry, but he described it first as an inquiry about an Englishwoman who was missing, then added, 'You know which one,' and then made what Hari called an obscene remark. He didn't know what was meant by a distressed condition unless this was a reference to the fact that he was shivering as a result of being kept standing for a long time, naked, in an air-conditioned room, after Merrick had inspected his genitals. After that inspection Merrick had said, 'So you've been clever enough to wash?' and later, 'But she wasn't a virgin, was she, and you were the first fellow to ram her'. After that, according to Hari, Merrick had sat on his desk, drinking whisky, and talked to him about the history of the British in India, every so often interjecting remarks about the boys in the cell upstairs, suggesting that they looked on him as a leader, that they'd do anything he said, and again making the comment that 'she hadn't been a virgin' and that Hari had 'been the first to ram her'. From this sequence of events, Hari claimed, he gathered that he and the others were suspected of rape. He claimed that he didn't mention Miss Manners until Merrick finally told him, at 2245 hours – a time he didn't dispute – that an Englishwoman had been criminally assaulted, and added, 'you know which one' and then made an obscene remark. He refused to say what the remark was but admitted that he now told Merrick he hadn't seen Miss Manners since the night of the visit to the temple.

Gopal pointed out to him that unless he repeated the obscene remark his explanation for naming her remained unsatisfactory. But he would not repeat it.

*

It annoyed Gopal that he wouldn't. He went on pressing. Hari went on refusing. Gopal became heated, as if he were suddenly on *Merrick's* side and intended to show that if Kumar wouldn't repeat the remark that was because he couldn't; it had never been made; everything he had said about Merrick's behaviour was a pack of lies.

Hari remained unmoved. Rowan joined in again. He went over Merrick's statement point by point, forcing Hari to agree that in a number of details it was correct. Hari *had* named Miss Manners. The time was not in dispute. And he *had* been showing signs of distress if only because he was shivering.

The rhythm of question and answer quickened. How long had Hari been kept standing naked? He couldn't remember. Why? He lost track of things like time. One hour? Two hours? Perhaps. Was he alone with Merrick? Not all the time, other people came in. Who? Two constables. Anyone else? Yes, there may have been others. Couldn't he remember? Why couldn't he remember? Was he saying he was confused, giddy and cold from standing all that time? He wasn't standing all the time. He was allowed to sit then? No, he wasn't allowed to sit.

Gopal said he didn't understand. If Kumar wasn't standing and wasn't sitting, what was he doing, lying down?

Hari said, 'I was bent over a trestle, tied to it. For the persuasive phase of interrogation. A cane was used.'

*

Rowan said, 'I read out Iyenagar's report and asked him whether that was an accurate record of his interview with the magistrate. He said it was. In a way I was prepared for that answer because when I began reading Iyenagar's report *aloud* it struck me for the first time how very carefully the questions had been framed. They were the kind of questions a cautious authority would ask if it was suspected that a man would be too frightened to say he'd been ill-treated and if it was felt that a denial would be better for everybody's sake. "Have you any complaint to make about your treatment in custody?" was the first question. Hari said "No." Most of the questions were like that. And if Hari couldn't actually reply "no" he just said he had nothing to add to his first answer. Before I began reading it I thought I'd make it impossible for him to explain why he now accused the police of physical violence when he'd had the opportunity to do that at the time. He'd agreed that the Iyenagar report was accurate. I intended to show that he was being inconsistent. But he wasn't. I knew the answer to this before he gave it. He'd told Iyenagar the truth. He had no *complaint* to make. Just that. No complaint.

'The question wasn't so much why he didn't complain then as why he was complaining now. And was he telling the truth? I read out the prison doctor's report, the one that didn't note any visible marks of physical violence apart from the bruise on his face. But I couldn't shake him. He implied that the doctor had seen other marks but hadn't recorded them.

We asked how many times he'd been hit. He said he couldn't remember. Whenever they stopped hitting him Merrick talked to him to encourage him to confess. He said Merrick told him Miss Manners had already named him but that he didn't believe her story. He believed she'd egged Hari and the others on and then got more than she bargained for and wanted them punished. Hari said that every time Merrick felt he was getting nowhere he told the constables to start again. I asked how long they had gone on. I still didn't really believe him. He said he didn't remember. Gopal asked if he was implying he lost consciousness. He said he never lost consciousness. He simply couldn't remember how long he was on the trestle.'

Rowan paused. 'Then he explained why he couldn't remember. He said it was difficult to breathe in that position and that breathing was all you thought about. I believed him then. It's not the sort of thing a man could easily make up, is it? And the trouble was that believing him made the next bit that much more difficult to write off as pure invention. He said Merrick sent the constables out of the room and spoke and acted even more obscenely. I asked him what he meant. I rather wish I hadn't. He said Merrick – fondled him.'

'Fondled him.'

'I told the shorthand writer to strike that out, leave his note-book on my desk and wait outside until I called him back. Then I really started on Hari. I put it to him that he was lying, taking advantage of the examination of his case as a political detenu to make baseless accusations in the mistaken belief that these would protect him if a charge of rape were made even as late in the day as this. I really pitched into him. I told him he had the chance to retract and advised him to think very carefully before passing the chance up.'

'Did he retract?'

'No. He apologized.'

'What for?'

'For what he called misunderstanding the reason why he was being examined.'

'What had he thought was the reason?'

'He thought Miss Manners had managed to persuade someone at last that he'd done nothing to deserve being locked up and that this had been his chance to prove it.'

'He wasn't far out, was he?'

'No, but I should have stuck to the political evidence. As soon as we went into the business of the rape I couldn't hide my suspicions and so he thought no one had really been persuaded of anything except that it was time to interrogate him again. Either that or that we were trying to salve bad consciences. He asked outright if something had happened to her. He'd had no news of her of any kind. I told him what had happened, that she'd died of peritonitis a year before, after a Caesarean operation. He asked whether she had married. She hadn't of course. He didn't ask if the child survived. At first I thought he was quite unmoved. Then I saw he wasn't. I asked if he wanted time to compose himself. He said he didn't but that we should have told him. It was very odd. His voice was quite unaffected. Physically he was composed. But he was crying. I asked him whether what he meant when he said we should have told him was that he would have answered the questions differently if he'd known she was dead. He said he only answered them because he thought she must have wanted us to ask them. If he'd known she was dead he wouldn't have answered them at all. I reminded him there was one important question he still hadn't answered. He knew I meant the question about where he was when she was being attacked. He said he'd never answer it. I was ready to bring things to an end but Gopal began again about the situation between Hari and Merrick. The clerk was no longer in the room. Officially the examination was over. He realized that. He seemed willing to talk – about that situation – even anxious. I didn't stop him. I believed he'd told the truth about the caning. I accepted that. I think you have to. I don't condone it. I'm not sure I can condemn it. It would be unfair to single Merrick out. Caning's a normal judicial punishment in this country. There were a lot of such sentences dished out in 1942 and I don't doubt a fair number of beatings-up in cells to get confessions. What I didn't accept, don't accept, without question, is – well the other thing. He could have imagined it. By his own admission he wasn't in full possession of his senses. I see you don't agree.'

'The violence makes more sense if you do accept what you call the other thing. Was Merrick kind to him at any point?'

Rowan stared at me. 'Kind to him?'

'Afterwards.'

'He gave him water. But he made him thank him for it.'

'It's the sort of thing I mean. Tell me about it.'

'I can only tell you what Hari said. It doesn't mean it happened.'

'Well tell me what Hari said.'

'He said he was taken into another room and manacled to a charpoy. Merrick was alone with him. He gave him a drink of water and made him say thank you. He bathed the cuts. He told him there'd be no more questions until morning. He said the whole evening had been an enactment of the real situation between them and that now they both knew how matters stood and what that situation was.' Rowan paused. 'It was a master and man situation, a simplified way of putting it, but near enough. At one point Merrick said, What price Chillingborough now? At another point he told Hari that there were only two basic human emotions, contempt and envy, and that a man's personality existed at his point of equilibrium between the two. But when I met Merrick the other day I simply couldn't imagine him behaving and talking like that.'

'I'm sure he did.'

'Yes, I thought you'd believe it. It's one of the reasons I'm telling you.' Again he hesitated. 'Hari said that it was to punish himself for thanking Merrick for the water that he decided to answer no more questions. He said the situation between himself and Merrick wouldn't exist if he dissociated

1333

himself from it and refused to say anything more to Merrick or to anyone else. Does that make sense to you?'

'It makes very good sense. It's what I've been trying to do. Dissociate myself from the situation that arises out of being chosen.'

Rowan was silent for a while. Then he said, 'Has he chosen Sarah Layton's sister?'

'I don't know. I don't think so.'

'Just the Laytons as a family?'

That suddenly didn't fit entirely either. But I saw what did. I said: 'In the way I mean by choose I should say he's chosen the child.'

*

'The child,' Lady Manners had said (meaning that other child fathered by a person unknown). 'The child. But even now I can't be sure, only surer. She was so sure.' The other thing she said was, 'He spoke the truth', but qualified it later as they drove through Kandipat, blinds down. She said, 'One has to make do with approximations' and that this was what one meant when one said he spoke the truth. When Rowan left Room O he too was sure he had heard the truth. He told Lady Manners that Kumar would be released but regretted this later when various impediments to such a release had all contributed to a partial revival of disbelief, to a renewed conviction that Kumar *had* somehow been involved in the assault. Lady Manners had asked to be taken back to her hotel and not to Government House. As they parted she thanked him for having undertaken such a distasteful task and asked him to give Malcolm a message: a very short one. 'I know my niece did not lie, that he never harmed her and is very wrongfully imprisoned.'

When he gave the message to the Governor, Malcolm said they would discuss it when the record of the examination was typed up and he'd had the chance to read it. He was going to Calcutta for a few days and preoccupied with other matters. He told Rowan to give the confiscated shorthand book to Cynthia, Her Excellency's private secretary. He thought it unwise to have it transcribed by the shorthand writer at the Secretariat. 'Don't worry,' Malcolm said. 'Cynthia's pretty broad-minded.' All the same, Rowan tore out the page which the shorthand writer had drawn a line through before handing it to her.

She must have worked late. The following morning she sent him a sealed envelope containing the notebook and a top and two carbons of an impeccable typescript. When he rang through to thank her she merely said, 'Oh, well. Press on you know. Only way to get round the course.' When he read the typescript through he was astonished at her apparent equanimity. It sounded even worse in print. He kept notebook and typescripts in a locked drawer until Malcolm returned, and hourly expected Gopal to ring him and ask when the shorthand writer could complete his job by typing the record. But Gopal didn't ring.

1334

When Malcolm had read the typescript he told Rowan it was a pity he hadn't been able to stick to the political evidence. The transcript showed that he had tried and also why he hadn't succeeded. But it was a pity. He explained that although senior police officers had always stood by Merrick, and that included the Inspector-General, the Inspector-General's private opinion was that Merrick had botched the evidence by being over-anxious and emotionally involved because he had been fond of the girl himself. If the IG saw this transcript he would be so shocked by Kumar's accusations that he would write them off as pure fantasy and point out that the only result of the examination had been to revive suspicion of Kumar's guilt, and that this would be sufficient reason to keep the fellow locked up until the end of the war. The IG would say that to release Kumar now would be as good as recording a reprimand on Merrick's personal file and that this could count against him, very unfairly, when he returned to the police after his army service.

'Then the best thing,' Rowan had said, 'will be to file the transcript away and forget all about it.'

But Malcolm said he didn't think he could allow that. In Kumar's case Rule 26 had fairly clearly been abused. The abuse was less obvious in the case of the other boys. If they had had a political leader at all it would have been Vidyasagar who wasn't among those arrested for rape but who was arrested a couple of days later for printing seditious literature on the press in the *Mayapore Hindu* office. In comparison with Vidyasagar even the others might be thought of as lambs led to the slaughter. Kumar, Malcolm was sure, hadn't even been a member of the flock. 'By the way,' he said, 'why did you confiscate the book and end the examination so abruptly?'

Rowan told him.

'It isn't in the transcript.'

'I removed the offending page.'

'And deprived Cynthia of the dénouement? What happened after you sent the shorthand writer out?'

Again Rowan told him.

'And Lady Manners heard *all* this?'

'Yes.'

'Did she make any other comment in the car coming home apart from giving you that message?'

'I gathered she was now surer Kumar was the father of the Manners child, but not as sure as her niece had been.'

'What did you infer from that?'

'That Miss Manners told her aunt she and Kumar had been lovers.'

'Her niece told her nothing. She left a written statement absolving Kumar completely. The old lady found it after her death, but she wouldn't show it even to me.'

*

1335

Rowan felt like exploding with irritation.

'If we'd had Miss Manners's statement we might have had a more successful examination,' he told the Governor. But the Governor pointed out that the examination had been of a man detained for political reasons. Miss Manners's statement, presumably, dealt entirely with her emotional involvement with Kumar. The only value a statement like that would ever have would be in the event, now highly unlikely, of a charge being brought against Kumar for rape, when defending counsel might construct his case from it. In Malcolm's view, Lady Manners was perfectly justified in otherwise keeping it to herself. Neither she – nor her niece – had ever had any answer to the political charges, which lay outside their competence, however deep the conviction was that political detention had been imposed out of sheer frustration; the frustration felt by the civil authority which had wanted to nail Kumar much more effectively. And in *that* regard, in the matter of the charge of rape, Malcolm suggested, Miss Manners's silence, Kumar's refusal to answer questions, during the period when a charge of rape might so easily have been brought, had not only been effective then but was eloquent now. Just how eloquent, Malcolm wasn't sure. Except that he believed it suggested that they had loved one another and that, loving him, she had been afraid for him.

Just as eloquent, he thought, was the fact that Lady Manners had let a certain amount of time elapse before trying to hoist the civil authority with its own petard: Kumar's 'political' crimes. Clearly non-existent. He could order Kumar's immediate release simply on the basis of the transcript of the examination but was reluctant to do so without the approval of both the member for Home and Law and the Inspector-General. That approval, he thought, wouldn't automatically flow from the transcript of the examination.

'He left it to me,' Rowan said, 'to find a *modus operandi*.'

The first thing Rowan did was to edit a copy of the transcript to isolate the political content. When he'd done this he persuaded Cynthia to type copies of the revised version. 'Very neat', she said, when she handed the revised version to him. He thought so himself. It was now the kind of transcript that could be shown – for instance to the Inspector-General – without much fear of blood-pressures rising or of waking departmental sensitivities.

However, there was one man who might upset the applecart. Both Rowan and Gopal would have to initial the transcript before it went on file. Gopal could wreck everything by refusing to put his initials to a document that was obviously rigged. The question was, in what was Gopal most interested? In the release of an unjustly imprisoned Indian detenu or in the eventual exposure of a British police officer? Rowan rang Gopal at the Secretariat. He asked if they could meet somewhere, unofficially. Gopal didn't bite. Rowan had no option but to go to the Secretariat. He took with him a carbon of the full typescript and a carbon of the edited version. He asked Gopal to read both documents and then get in touch with him so that they could discuss the problem.

The following day Gopal rang. He asked Rowan to have dinner with him at his home that evening and gave instructions how to get there. It was the beginning of an association that ripened into friendship and affection. Gopal had seen the point of the edited typescript at once. He was on Kumar's side. He said he would be prepared to initial the edited typescript at once, with one proviso, that the title of the document should include the word Abstract and that the general heading should make it clear that the examination was in regard to a warrant issued under the Defence of India Rules. He produced a draft of the kind of heading he had in mind. Rowan accepted it at once.

'Are we doing the right thing, though?' Gopal asked as they parted. 'In prison at least he has an identity.'

*

But even with the edited typescript in front of him, the Inspector-General threatened to prove stubborn. An unexpected nigger in the woodpile was Pandit Baba. Since 1942 this man had become much more actively involved in affairs which attracted the CID's attention. Kumar's disclosure that he had been taught Hindi by Baba interested the IG considerably. Kumar had refused to answer questions about the Pandit at the time of his arrest. His admission now surely showed how well-informed Merrick had been, how right to suspect a connection, how right to ask questions about a connection. Until now it hadn't been clear why he did. At the time the Pandit's activities had been too unimportant for one's attention to have been attracted to his name on the file. But he was nowadays believed to be a subtle and potentially dangerous leader of Hindu youth, anti-Congress, anti-Gandhi, anti-British, with affiliations with the Hindu Mahasabha and its activist group, the Rashtriya Swayam Sevak Sangh. And what was the connection between the pandit and the detenu's aunt – who had bombarded Government with pleas for her nephew's release and was now in Ranpur without visible means of support? The examination showed that the aunt had paid for the Hindi lessons, and that it was she who had chosen Baba as Kumar's teacher. Did her persistence, her constant pleas, suggest prompting by Baba Sahib? Was she being used by this man? He had always been much too clever to get into trouble himself. Currently he had disappeared from the scene. But if one released Kumar mightn't he be the very type of young man the Pandit would find it useful to have as a disciple?

Rowan suggested to Malcolm that if the main obstacle to Kumar's release was the suspicion that he would fall at once into the Pandit's net of eager young disciples perhaps the thing to suggest to the IG was that if the CID wanted to nab the Pandit a free Kumar might be more helpful than an imprisoned Kumar.

But Malcolm said, 'Either we believe Kumar and his aunt have no political commitments or we don't. If we don't believe it we're not justified in releasing him. Frankly I do believe it. The Pandit's just a red herring the IG's suddenly noticed. So, let it lie. Have you ever understood Einstein?'

Rowan said he hadn't. Malcolm said he hadn't either, but that sometimes when faced with this apparently insoluble and intricate problem of reaching a solution through the thickets of departmental vanities he applied his own theory of relativity, which was that although people seldom argued a point but argued round it, they sometimes found the solution to the problem they were evading by going round in ever *increasing* circles and disappearing into the centre of *those*, which, relatively speaking, coincided with the centre of the circle from whose periphery they had evasively spiralled outwards.

So Rowan let it lie. His belief in Kumar's innocence or guilt was like a pendulum. He wished he could get that to lie too, wished he could stop it at the vertical point which represented non-commitment. It was a relief when a couple of weeks later Malcolm gave him another confidential assignment – one which called for him to officiate on the Governor's behalf at the transfer of another detenu – Mohammed Ali Kasim – from imprisonment in the fort at Premanager to the protection of his kinsman, the Nawab of Mirat; a form of parole, an ostensibly compassionate act but not without its element of political shrewdness.

And it was on this assignment that he'd met Sarah Layton – changing trains on her way back to Pankot from Calcutta where she had visited the wounded hero, the best man at Susan's wedding. There she was, a rather travel-stained *Deus ex machina*, bringing news about wounds and decorations which might solve the problem of departmental concern for Merrick's reputation and Merrick's future; but for Rowan, I thought, rather more than that. Was he, by the time I met him on the same station, more than just rather fond of her?

I thought so. His decision to go back to Ranpur the next day suggested he had had hopes which he had suddenly given up. I should have liked to see them together, not as I had done that evening, but in Ranpur during two or three days of what I judged to have been a tentative exploration of airier regions that promised to be in common ownership. Mutual antipathy to Merrick was no more than a way in to those regions. Rowan, of course had not – and never would have – disclosed to her what he knew, and she had nothing to disclose except her instinctive woman's prejudice. These meetings between them had taken place during the brief time she spent in Ranpur before going down to Bombay to meet her father. Before then, they had met only that once when she had just come in from Calcutta and her visit to Merrick. He hadn't been sure what her relationship with Merrick was. It was a relief to him, he said, to discover that in one sense there was no relationship. Another discovery was that she had once met Lady Manners in Kashmir, had seen the child; believed Merrick had made a terrible mistake. It was now that he told her he'd known Kumar as a boy, at school. But that was all. He might have told her more this time, on this visit to Pankot, but naturally hadn't done so.

'Naturally?' I asked.

He said, 'Well, of course.'

It was silly to have questioned it. Merrick was to be Miss Layton's brother-in-law. That being so, from Rowan's point of view the subject of Merrick and Kumar was utterly closed as one he felt able to discuss with her. I wondered when she had first heard or suspected that Merrick planned to marry her sister. Almost certainly the answer must be that she'd suspected nothing until she and her father got back to Pankot. Most certain of all was that it had been a shock to Rowan. I began to see the fullness of Rowan's little tragi-comedy. He had, after all, had hopes of her. The brief holiday in Pankot had been intended as an opportunity to convey to her that his resumed career in the political was one he hoped she might share with him. Perhaps his hopes had only finally been dashed, or shelved for future exploration, during the few hours we'd spent that night at Rose Cottage. Perhaps, with Merrick gone, he had hoped to find her recovered from the shock, less weighed down, looking and acting like the girl he knew (the girl I remembered). Had he at any time said anything to her at all about his hopes? Had she rebuffed him?

His attention was again directed to the darkness beyond the verandah; and suddenly I saw this other, faintly ludicrous aspect of the affair; one that inclined me to believe that because Rowan was the kind of man he was he had said nothing to her at all. He would have taken his time anyway, and before an opportunity arose the wind had been knocked out of his sails by the announcement of Susan's engagement. Well, imagine it: imagine, for instance, Rowan shaving, brushing his hair, facing up to his reflection; thinking what he *must* have thought because every man would. Imagine him thinking this: Could I honestly spend the rest of my life knowing what I think I know about the man who would be my brother-in-law and say nothing?

And the answer would be, no. The other answer would be that knowing himself incapable of saying anything he knew that his own hopes had to be abandoned.

*

Malcolm was on the point of leaving for Delhi when Rowan got back from the Kasim assignment and told him the news about Merrick's gallantry in the field. 'I'll check it,' Malcolm said. 'Meanwhile we'll say nothing. It would be best if the Inspector-General got to know through his own sources.' It meant another delay, the possibility too of this development making the IG even more stubbornly opposed to any course of action that belittled Merrick's earlier performance as a guardian of the law. But the farce was coming to an end. Quite suddenly, without fuss, it was over. The

IG withdrew his objections to Kumar's release. Kumar was informed and told the date on which he would be free and instructed to report to the police in Ranpur once a week for six months. He was allowed to write to his aunt to prepare her for his return.

The aunt was living in rooms above a shop in the Koti bazaar. So Gopal told Rowan. They met the night the order of release was signed – a form of gentle celebration by two conspirators. Rowan was thinking: Yes, but release to what? Gopal had already formed a plan. He said it would be possible to put Kumar in the way of beginning to earn a living as a private teacher of English. He knew a reliable young man who would help him and who had already made contact with the aunt. The poor woman was very nervous and suspicious. It had been difficult for Gopal's young man to gain her confidence. He had had to ask her to trust him when he said the authorities had at last taken an interest in her nephew's case, trust him when he said there was every reason to hope that Hari would be released, and trust him again when he said he would help him to find work and keep out of the way of people who might want to exploit him.

'I suppose I was sticking my neck out,' Gopal said, 'but that is what necks are for.'

*

It was ironic, Rowan said, and salutary, that of the two of them it was old Gopal, who had begun by not liking Hari, who had put his mind to the question of Hari's rehabilitation.

Kumar had been free for over a year now. Rowan hadn't seen him, neither had Gopal. He relied on Gopal for news and Gopal relied on his reliable young man. Kumar no longer had to report to the police but the CID still kept an eye on him. It had been weeks before Kumar trusted Gopal's young man enough to fall in with the scheme for teaching English. He made the excuse that he would himself have to learn Hindi properly, first. But eventually, probably when it occurred to him to wonder what they lived on and he realized that his aunt had come to the end of her small resources and had always been too proud to beg help from her brother's family and only too anxious to cut herself off completely from her dead husband's, and had now sold the last bit of her jewelry, he agreed to help cram a couple of candidates for entrance to the Government College. Their success brought him other boys, including a nephew of Gopal's. He seldom visited their homes. He seldom left the apartment. He was paid very badly but he refused anything that smelt of financial help. The reliable young man, when he could do so without Kumar knowing, gave the aunt small gifts, as if in return for the cups of tea and coffee he had when he visited them; gifts of a few vegetables, flour, ghi. The young man's own means were limited. Some of these gifts, Rowan suspected, came from Mrs Gopal.

Rowan had been able to do very little. He knew no Indians of the kind whose sons would go to an anonymous private teacher in the Koti bazaar.

Rowan's Indian friends were rich. Gopal was the exception – the only middle-class Indian with whom he had ever become on intimate terms. At the same time perhaps the only Indian with whom he had ever been on such terms.

And now Rowan was leaving Ranpur. He had no idea where he would be sent. Even that little which it had been open to him to contribute, so vaguely, so anonymously, would come to an end, now. He would keep in touch with Gopal as far as that was possible. Gopal and he had always had an idea that as circumstances changed, politically, it would be in their power unobtrusively to guide Kumar back into life. What he was living now was hardly a life. The reliable young man reported that Kumar seemed to have no ambition and that it was distressing to listen to the aunt painting an optimistic picture of a happy future when you only had to look at Kumar's face to see that Kumar's window on to the world was still closed and darkened. And once, coming on her alone, the young man had found Aunt Shalini crying. 'Why should he hope?' she asked, 'when there is nothing for him to hope for? He understands only English people and they will never forgive him because of the girl. The doors will always be closed to him.'

She meant the doors Hari had been brought up to open – the doors into the Administration. And what she said was true. Rowan himself was in possession of no key that would enable Hari to enter. Neither was Gopal. Even the way in to a junior teaching post in a Government College was barred.

*

'I've often thought of writing to old Bagshaw,' Rowan said. 'I don't really know why. One couldn't put it all in a letter anyway. And perhaps the old boy's dead now.'

'Is that where you see a future for Kumar? Back home?'

'I don't see much of a future for him here. I'm just broadening the perspective. It occurred to me that back home, if that's really where you're going, you might chance on something that could help. Anyway, I'd appreciate it if you'd write to me sometimes. Would you like another drink?'

I said I would, but that I'd take it to my room. It was nearly one o'clock.

'I'll send it in.' I imagined him sitting up for a while yet.

He didn't send it in. He brought it himself, calling to me through the half-open bathroom door. With a glass of brandy he gave me a large manila envelope.

'It's a carbon of the full typescript. I thought you might like to keep it. Take it home with you. To the groves of Academe. Officially it doesn't exist. HE told me to lose the copies of the full record. I destroyed the top and the shorthand book. I kept the carbons. I still have one.'

'Do you always carry this around?'

'No. I thought of giving it to Mr Gopal as a parting gift but thought better of it. Sleep well.'

On the way out he stopped.

'You'd better destroy it if you find Operation Bunbury snarled up and you're still stuck with Merrick. I mean in view of his light-fingered servant. Incidentally, you've never told me why you asked who Mrs Bingham was.'

'It's still too long a story.'

'But connected in some way?'

'Where Merrick's concerned everything's connected.'

'Yes. I suppose it is.'

When Rowan left me I opened the envelope meaning just to glance through it while I drank the brandy, but it was two o'clock before I'd finished reading and except for a sip or two the brandy was untouched. Far more than when Rowan described the examination I was attracted, appalled, riveted, firmly convinced of Kumar's innocence but deeply puzzled by his stubborn refusal to answer that vital question. If Rowan's object had been to ensure that I would find it difficult to get Kumar out of my mind then he had probably succeeded.

I put the transcript in my kit-bag and padlocked it, drank the brandy and went to bed.

I'd read the transcript using Rowan's final interpretation like a sieve, to isolate scraps of gritty evidence – the interpretation he'd only recently arrived at, the only one he thought made sense. I agreed. Kumar and Miss Manners had become lovers. They had been making love in the Bibighar. The marks on his face were got in a scuffle with men who pulled them apart, beat him up, knocked him unconscious or sat on him while one by one they raped the girl.

That, I thought, made sense; but thereafter there was no sense – only a silence which however hard I listened to it seemed incomprehensible. Nothing emerged from it after I turned the light out except pictures of Kumar: the man I had never seen not the boy whose face I couldn't clearly remember; but sweeping and cutting and blocking that merciless succession of contemptuous deliveries. Elms and rooks; but then again, not these, but palms and crows: the view from the flat which Purvis contemplated, retreated from, saying, 'I'm an economist', then coming in and pushing me further and further back into that elegant room with its priceless paintings in the Ghuler-Basohli style. Standing there, drink in hand, I lurched into sleep and Purvis was Kumar, seated, looking up at me through the eyes of this other man who kept saying: I don't think I'll ever forgive it.

*

Rowan had left a note. The steward brought it with my breakfast and the morning papers at 8.30. Rowan wrote that he'd had to make an early start to Area Headquarters to arrange about the special coach. He would have to go down to the station too. A tonga could be got to take me to the Pankot Rifles depot and he'd try to call in there to say goodbye. In case he couldn't he gave me an address in Delhi (that of a bank) for future correspondence. Very thoughtfully he gave me the name of the officer at Area HQ who would know of any signal arriving for me.

*

I got to the Pankots' depot at ten o'clock. They had suspended the interviews. I waited an hour but Rowan didn't turn up. I went to Area Headquarters. He had been there but had gone (I imagined) to say goodbye to the Laytons. In the signals office I introduced myself to the signals sergeant and made sure he had my telephone number. I went back to the guest house and was told that Rowan had just rung to say goodbye. For the rest of the day and throughout the evening, Ulysses-like I lashed myself to the mast of my quarters, deaf to every seduction except that of the sirens of the telephone exchange and signals office; afraid to go out, just in case a miracle had speeded Operation Bunbury up and a movement order was already on its way to me, one that required immediate action to be considered valid.

Saturday is a blank. All I remember is a reduction in the guest house staff. An invisible garrison commander had issued orders to reduce the rations and send the cooks and bhishtis, every able-bodied man, to fill the gaps at firing-ports and listening posts, leaving me attended by one shabby fellow who scavenged somewhere for pallid meals of thin gravy soup, dried meat and miserly salad and got steadily drunker, deafer and more difficult to conjure either by electric bell, handclap or parade-ground order. His name was Salaam'a. One yelled this greeting at empty space unoptimistic of his filling it. It puzzled him that I wore a sergeant's uniform. He thought it was some kind of disguise.

*

Sunday: the first Sunday of the peace. When I woke I knew I couldn't spent another day cooped up. I persuaded myself that Aunt Charlotte couldn't have moved quickly enough to justify my absurd expectations unless she had pre-empted the situation some weeks ago and decided that since the war in Europe was thoroughly over there was no reason for me to carry eccentricity to the absurd length of staying out East and eating the rice needed by starving natives.

Among the notices in the guest house was one from St John's (C. of E.). Communion at 8 a.m.; morning service at 11. I had missed the first but felt I ought to attend the second. I got out my best khaki. I polished a pair of brown shoes and rubbed up the dazzle on the badge of my side-cap. I darned a small hole in the heel of a clean pair of socks Then I shaved – twice – until the lower half of my face looked properly baked and glazed.

These were acts of contrition for the destructive and mutinous mood of the morning of my arrival in Pankot; gestures of voluntary submission to the military system. At ten-thirty I set off and marched myself to church at heavy infantry pace.

St John's was packed. It was like poppy day at Chillingborough; hymns and prayers in chapel. All that lacked was an old boy to give an ambiguous address about the obscenity and waste of war. I glanced round, looking as it were for Harry Coomer; but met only the mass of pale and ruddy complexions of an all white congregation. Were there no Indian Christians in Pankot? No Eurasians at St John's on this Sunday of all Sundays? Perhaps there were. My view, from one of the back pews, and to the wall side of it, close to an exit, was limited. I was among the soldiery, a lone volunteer among the pressed men. Far ahead, towards the pulpit, shoulders glittered with pips and crowns making angular shapes between decorative hats.

But no dark face that I could see. I began to feel oppressed, slightly agitated, and glanced at the nearby door. The chaplain was reading a lesson. In a moment there would be another hymn. I checked the advertised number in the borrowed hymn book. From Greenland's Icy Mountains, From India's coral strand, They call us to deliver, Their land from error's chain. When the congregation got up to sing it I slid out of the pew and in a moment was in the open, going down a gravel path between ancient drunken gravestones. Outside on the road under shade trees tongas waited, their drivers slumped in their seats or disposed on the ground in twos and threes smoking bidis. I flashed a two rupee note and commandeered someone's equipage. It could be back at the church by the time the service was over. I only wanted to go to Area Headquarters. As I climbed in I thought I heard a voice from the church saying: That's right. Aunt Charlotte's voice.

The signals sergeant was leaving his office as I approached it. Seeing me, he stopped dead. He ignored my courteous greeting. He stared at me as if I were his worst enemy. I followed him into the office where without a word he handed me a signal.

Bunbury.

After I'd read it, twice, he said, 'How d'you manage it, then? That's all I ask. How?'

But there was no vice in him. He just envied my luck. Where had I been, he wanted to know. He'd rung Pankot 200 only ten minutes ago and got no answer. I told him I'd been to church. He said, as if this explained the signal, 'I must try it some time.' Then he became very helpful. He took me and my AB 64 and the precious piece of flimsy paper ordering Sergeant Perron to proceed immediately to Deolali for onward transmission to UK for demobilization (War Office instruction Number Such and Such and Stroke This Stroke That) to the Admin office where he enlisted the help of a havildar-clerk who, having no axe to grind about speeding an English soldier out of the country, set to work with detached efficiency.

Interpreting a string of references at the end of the signal he told me that I ought to arrive in Deolali in possession of certain important documents including a medical on my fitness to be allowed back into the UK at all. He checked my AB 64. So recently Zipper-bound my jabs were up to date. He told me other things I would need. He seemed quite happy telling me. I wasn't much interested. Nothing worried me. Somewhere just behind my eyes were rosy vistas, shimmering images of a world that had become benign. Area Headquarters was full of this benevolence. It was at low-pressure, staffed by nice people who seemed to have lent themselves voluntarily to the idea of simply keeping it going between Saturday and Monday. I felt the clerk was relieved to have something to do that he could put his mind to. I could rely on him utterly. I could rely on the Signals sergeant too. He kept close to me as if he thought some of my luck might rub off.

'Let's find the Duty Officer,' he said. We walked along shady verandahs. The fire-buckets, I noted, were painted an enchanting shade of red. The sand in them sparkled. We went into a semi-darkened airy room where the desks and empty chairs were waiting for tomorrow and then through into a room whose windows were unshuttered. A girl in WAC(I) uniform was at a filing cabinet.

'Morning, Sarge,' my sergeant said.

She had three stripes. She turned round. It was Sarah Layton.

But the original Sarah, the friendly one. I said, 'Good Lord, you're a sergeant too.'

'Well I am when I'm playing soldiers.'

'Is that what you're doing?'

'Yes. I'm glad you looked in. I've just tried to get you on the phone.'

'You know each other,' the Signals sergeant accused us. We agreed that we did. He gave me an odd look but said that would make it easier. He told Sarah what I represented: a problem which Area Headquarters had to solve. He explained what the problem was, how much of it was already being tackled and what remained to be done.

While he spoke I watched her, on the look-out for any sign of disappointment that the chances of knowing each other better were limited to here and now. I thought there was such a sign but couldn't be sure. If she had been anticipating a quiet morning on duty with nothing much to do, the expression I marked (a slight darkening of the eyes) could just as well have been irritation at the interruption as of sorrow at my departure.

'The duty officer's gone off somewhere, but I'll cope,' she said. 'You can leave Sergeant Perron to me.'

The sergeant caught my eye, nodded in her direction. 'You're lucky. Most of the others slope off at the first smell of anything like work. O.K. Miss Layton. Buzz me if you get stuck.'

*

1345

She spent a lot of time on the telephone. I sat watching her, wondering at the change in her. Probably it was only life at home that got her down. Eventually she said, 'Right, that's tied up so far. Let's go.' I followed her out of the office. She locked the door.

'Where to?'

'Just relax. The army's taking care of you.'

'What about your office? Can you just leave it?'

'I was only sorting things out for tomorrow. I'm not officially on duty. But everyone at home has gone to church.'

We went back to the havildar-clerk. She went through documents with him, collected a batch. We went to another block. She told me to wait outside. Ten minutes later she came out with more documents. Then to another office. She came out with another batch. I said, 'You're making me feel redundant, that I exist only on paper.'

'The next bit is more personal.'

She hailed a 15 cwt that was driving towards the exit. She told me to get in the back. Five minutes later I recognized the grounds of the hospital but when I got out I didn't recognize the building. She explained it was the private wing. The duty MO had promised to 'do me' if we came to the private wing at mid-day. It was five to. This time it was she who waited outside. The MO was a pleasant fellow. 'Feeling all right?' he asked. I said I was, really. 'Silly question,' he muttered, filling in spaces on the form. We worked out my height and weight without the aid of scales and measures. 'They'll do you in Deolali, too,' he warned, 'but if you arrive without a medical sheet you could be held up.' He signed the sheet and handed it to me. 'Lucky chap,' he said. 'Just try not to get clap between here and Deolali. It sometimes happens.'

He came out with me and chatted to Sarah. He said if she'd finished repatriating Sergeant Perron he'd take her up to the club. She said there was still some documentation to do but that she'd probably see him there later.

Back in the havildar-clerk's office she gave him all the documents we'd collected. They checked through them, detaching copies for different files. Finally he handed me all that I apparently required from this storm of paper: a few sheets which went into an envelope.

Outside she said, 'Well, that's it. All you have to do is to be at the station before mid-day tomorrow – unless –'

Without another word she led the way to the signals office. The sergeant was just coming out, going to lunch.

'Is there any transport going into Ranpur tonight?' she asked him. He said there probably was. She turned to me. 'If you could get down to Ranpur during the night you could get the train that leaves at 8 a.m. You'd gain over twelve hours, and that might make a lot of difference at the Deolali end.'

I said it was a good idea. She said to the sergeant, 'I'll ask at the club.

Perhaps you'd have a look round too, Joe, and ring Sergeant Perron at 200 if there's anything going in.'

He said he'd have a word with a Sub-Conductor Pearson in the mess. I could go along with him now, if I wanted. I made an excuse about having food laid on and packing to do. We shook hands in case we didn't meet again.

Sarah and I shared a tonga back up the hill. I thanked her for everything she'd done and said the food at the guest house wasn't much cop since Nigel had gone but that it would be nice if she could have lunch with me. She said there was a lunch party at the club which she couldn't get out of. I asked her what she'd tried to ring me about earlier. She'd rung because she knew I was on my own and wondered if I was all right, since I hadn't rung her. I asked her whether she could manage tea. She wasn't sure. She'd be in touch some time, though.

As she got out of the tonga at the club entrance she looked at me and said: 'I envy you, Guy. But I'm glad for you. And I'm not at all sure you don't deserve a medal. Ronald Merrick's going to be furious.'

*

I told Salaam'a to bring beer to the verandah. I sat studying the precious documents. For the first time I noticed that the signal hadn't come via Delhi, via Merrick's department, but had originated in Poona. The first War Office instruction must have been signalled from Delhi to Poona and my old officer must have rung Delhi, been told where I was and then copy-signalled direct to Area Headquarters in Pankot. I went to my room and wrote him a note of thanks, added a PS, to the effect that my tin trunk which had been left in Poona could either be repatriated too or broken open and its contents (a greatcoat and winter uniform) disposed among the needy. Then I had a couple of gins, a pallid replica of yesterday's pallid lunch, and composed myself to sleep, having first told Salaam'a to attend to the telephone and in any case wake me with tea at four.

*

Zipper was coming to grief. Speeding towards the beaches in landing craft on the September tides near Port Swettenham we were opened fire on by rogue Japanese who had opted out of the Emperor's peace, chosen to die, but to take us with them. For a moment I listened, aghast, at the guns and the water rushing against the steel hulls of the boats, aghast because of the danger and of the miserable realization that Bunbury had been only an Indian ocean dream.

I raised my wrist to check the time of landing and, doing so, woke to the reality of Pankot time which said ten to five, a thunderstorm, but all well. But not wholly all well. From the bedroom I wouldn't have heard the telephone and it looked as if Salaam'a wouldn't have been hearing it either, being either asleep or dead drunk at last. I pressed the bell-button. Like those at Ishshee Brizhish one could never tell what effect pressing the button had unless someone turned up. No one did inside the half-minute I allowed before getting out of bed, tying a towel round my waist and going in search.

I went through the living-room shouting that ridiculous name and then out on to the verandah from whose roof water was cascading from an invisible pipe or leaking gutter on to the gravel path. Beyond, vertical rods of water obscured the view of the Summer Residence.

From contemplation of this same scene Sarah Layton turned her head, to glance up from the cane lounging chair where she rested, smoking. A tray of guest house tea was on the table by her side.

She said something that I couldn't hear and I was too conscious of my near-nakedness to go closer and cup an ear. She indicated an unused cup. In dumb show I told her I'd be out again in a minute, and went back, splashed my face, combed my hair, and got into a shirt and slacks and sandals.

'I hope you don't mind,' she said when I joined her. 'The boy was just going to wake you when I got here. I told him to leave you for a bit.' She felt the pot. 'We'd better ring for some more.'

I did so. I asked her when she'd arrived. She thought it must have been nearly an hour ago. I wondered whether she had been waiting for me to wake or for the rain to stop, but didn't ask. She said, 'You'll be glad later, I mean to have slept on a bit because I'm afraid you won't have a very comfortable trip if you decide to go tonight. The best we could do is the back of a fifteen hundred-weight that's leading a convoy down. But it'll take you right to the station in Ranpur.'

She opened her bag and gave me a slip of paper with a name – Sub-Conductor Pearson – and a telephone number written on it. 'The convoy leaves at ten this evening. Call him just before seven. He'll tell you where to go to get it. I'm afraid I drew a blank at the club, so I liaised again with Joe Baker. He was going to ring you but I said I'd call and tell you.'

Our hands touched as the paper was transferred. The softness and gentleness of her fingers balanced out the impression of hardness, of military efficiency. It occurred to me that the time she'd devoted to me could perhaps best be repaid by giving her the chance to take up some of mine if she wanted to. I didn't *have* to leave Pankot tonight. And now that it came to it I wasn't sure that I wanted to.

'On the whole,' she said, as if reading my thoughts, 'I'd settle for the discomfort if I were you. Joe Baker's had another signal. There's a Major Foster arriving tomorrow morning on the night train. You're asked to meet him, so I suppose he's Ronald's replacement.'

I'd met Major Foster. He was a ditherer, the kind of well-meaning chap whom it could be fatal to get near. If I met him and told him I had to leave on the mid-day train, on repatriation, he might out of sheer good intention invent so many problems that we would still be solving them two hours after the train had gone.

I said, 'Yes, he is the replacement. I'll settle for a night's discomfort. I may as well ring Sub-Conductor Pearson now. Then we'll know how long I've got.'

'I shouldn't if I were you. Not for a while. Joe Baker said six-thirty or so.'

For some reason she reddened slightly and returned her attention to the rain, which was stopping.

Salaam'a appeared.

'Would you prefer a drink to more tea? Nigel said I could make free so long as I didn't dine the station. You're not quite the station.'

'No, I'm not, am I? I'd like a drink very much.'

I told Salaam'a to bring out the drinks trolley. When we were alone I said, 'Can you stay and have an early meal with me?'

She didn't answer. She must have heard. The rain had now stopped entirely. She continued to stare ahead of her. Her cigarette was nearly finished. I glanced over my shoulder to see what apparently held her attention. The sun was just coming out. The Summer Residence rose – base to roof – out of the fast-moving shadow of a retreating cloud. Sunshine had already flowed across the garden. It pressed hard against the line of the balustrade, warmed my back and made me conscious of the hastiness with which I'd put clothes on.

'You've seen the house, I suppose,' she said. 'I expect Nigel showed you over.'

'No. Isn't it shut up?'

'The servants will always let you in.'

'There seems to be only one servant left.'

'They live in the main quarters. They only come down if there are people at the guest house. The house itself was built in 1890. Most of it's plain Anglo-Indian but there's a Moghul suite where they used to put up pet princes. The throne room's very ordinary, just a couple of chairs on a daïs, and the ball-room's quite small. But they danced on the terrace too. There used to be coloured lights in the trees.'

'That must have been nice.'

'It was all rather stiff and starchy. At least on the surface. And that's about all you see when you're young and just back out from home. Not that I'm really competent to judge. People here sigh for what they used to call the full season when the Governor and his wife moved up for the hot weather. But there hasn't been a full season since 'thirty-nine, and Susan and I missed that. I remember it best as part of childhood. We had ghastly parties here.' She smiled at a memory. 'When the new Governor took over in 'forty-one he was rather unpopular at first for not continuing the tradition of six months in the hills. Mother says the dances Susan and I have been to were very scratch affairs by comparison, but people get used to anything. At Flagstaff House we used to rate a major-general but since the beginning of the year we've only had a brigadier. People complain but they're getting used to that too. And now that the war's over I suppose it'll alter even more, with people whose retirement's been postponed upping sticks and going home, or settling here and growing old and tiresome and complaining that their pensions don't go far.'

'When does your father retire?'

'In about three years. But I've no idea what they'll do.'

'Rose Cottage belongs to them?'

'Yes, they're luckier than some. The army stopped people buying or building property in Pankot years ago – I don't mean on West Hill, only Indians build there. But father's stepmother got hold of Rose Cottage a few years before the embargo. She left it to him along with everything else she had. I expect you could see what a lot of money's been spent on it recently. I've always imagined father and mother spending the rest of their lives there, but now I don't know.'

Salaam'a wheeled the trolley out. We both chose gin. While he prepared the drinks I excused myself and went inside to wait for him. When he came in I told him I was leaving for Ranpur that evening, that he should arrange supper for two because the memsahib might be staying. I gave him his baksheesh and an extra few rupees to tip his invisible assistants. Then I told him the memsahib and I wanted to look at the house, that we would go over in about fifteen minutes. How did we get in? He said the head chaukidar would let us in. He would go now and make sure the head chaukidar was there.

She was waiting, glass poised to drink. I faced her, leaning against the balustrade. We toasted the space between us. After drinking we remained silent. I gave her a full minute by my watch and the same full minute to myself to prove beyond reasonable doubt that my idea about the immediate future was not all that different from hers.

The minute gone the silence continued, but delivered us slowly from any sense of the strain that slightly marked its beginning. Eventually I said to her, 'I never thanked you for Emerson.' She put her head back against the cushion, studied me, as if she knew the passage which had come into my mind and which had caused me to mention the book:

The world rolls: the circumstances vary every hour. All the angels that inhabit this temple of the body appear at the windows, and all the gnomes and vices also. By all the virtues they are united. If there be virtue, all the vices are known as such; they confess and flee.

*

On the way there I looked for them but they must have scattered; but remembering the distant view of the upper storey from the lines of the Pankot Rifles depot I asked her whether she had ever noticed how the sun setting behind West Hill seemed to have to pause until the upper windows of the Summer Residence released its last reflection, and the *raj* allowed night to fall. Well, she said, she was familiar with the effect but had never identified its cause. She was smiling, her head up, one hand shielding her eyes, neck curving from the brave little angles of jaw and chin. Something

1350

dazzled her – the suddenly exposed sky, sunshine on wet surfaces, or the drops of rain strung in the trees to dry. We had left the path, chosen the directer way across the lawns for which she was more suitably shod than I. My feet and trouser bottoms were wet, the chappals clung to my bare soles. A week later, unpacking and repacking my kit-bag in Deolali, the chappals, still slightly damp to the touch, smelt of grass, and the trouser bottoms were tide-marked. The chappals were in my possession for a number of years, and – even after a long time unused – discovered in a cupboard, dried, cracked, the buckles rusty, the smell of dampness and the smell of grass still seemed to be in them like a perfume of their own recollection of that occasion; their recollection of the persistence of damp when moving across dry flagged terraces and interior floors of stone and parquet and carpet, through chill shadow and hot streaks of filtered light when shutters were opened like doors on the tombs of flies and moths whose mummified bodies lay on dusty sills; taking the weight of the wearer's heels as he gazed upward at vast chandeliers enveloped in balloons of muslin; or substituting for weight the stickiness of suction when the ankles were crossed for the enthronement of the substitute Governor and his Lady on two shrouded chairs; the weight re-distributed again, concentrated on the toes as the sightless painted eyes of Muirs and Laytons and fellow members of a pro-consular dynasty were met by live eyes in a head thrust forward – the body canted to achieve a position where the light on dark varnish less obscured the detail and colour of pigment underneath.

Stairs, corridors; doors opened by keys obtained earlier for a consideration from the ancient chaukidar who was lost below in a dream of opium and the vanished splendour of which he was the guardian and we no more than observers. Sensibly and more drily shod she moved through the Summer Residence like a visitor who had been before and had little to gain except the satisfaction of her companion's curiosity, which was minimal, overriden by preoccupation with the way she walked through this maze of imperial history, or stood revealed by the chance falling of light and shade, responding to changes in the pressures that different rooms imposed on her recollections which seemed to be of a time she no longer recognized as real.

And yet, turning from some object pointed out in one particular room, an object that had failed like so many in so many rooms to recommend itself to me as having continuing substance or sustained meaning, she seemed to me to have only this unreality in her possession and to belong to it like a prisoner would belong, after a time, to a cell his imagination had escaped but whose door he was not permitted to open.

We chose this particular room, I think, because at first glance it represented in itself a form of release: release from the stupefying weight of nearly a century of disconnection from the source. But the Moghul suite was no less burdened by that weight; it was the inner box of a nest of boxes. Through one unshuttered window, westering sun filtered through the intricate fretwork of a screen on to the tiled floor where the chappals lay, temporarily set aside. A smell of old incense permeated the fabrics of the covers and cushions of an immense divan such as might have been used by court-musicians. One fancied that dust rose from it, gently enveloping us in a dry benevolent mist in which hung minute particles of the leaves and petals of garlands of flowers: jasmine, roses, frangipani and marigold, and all the names of Allah. One observer: a mouse. Are you afraid? I asked. No, she said, I'm not afraid. Eyes closed, at rest, I realized that we had been both observed and accompanied. The distant coppersmith still continued, beating out his thin, endless, strip of metal into the alternating shapes of the sounds and silence of the Pankot hills.

*

Returning the keys to the chaukidar, I make my own way out and look for her; and, mistaking the place, think for a moment she has taken the opportunity I gave her (out of delicacy, thinking she might prefer not to have to bid the chaukidar goodnight) to abandon me too; but she is waiting, out there on the lawn, gazing up at the highest windows where the day awaits permission to end. Joining her, I glance up and find that it is already ended. There are no faces, either, unless they are our own, watching us go – not only as we do, across the lawn back to the guest house – but further, much further, on separate roads that may never cross again.

Having poured her another drink I go inside to telephone Sub-Conductor Pearson. A woman answers. Her voice has a Eurasian lilt. She leaves the phone. I hear her calling for 'Leonard'. Pearson, not Purvis. Calling him from his Sunday afternoon in married quarters? Waiting, I wonder what Sergeant Baker said to make Sarah blush when she recommended not disturbing the Sub-Conductor until 6.30 or 7 (until an appetite for beer and curry and Sunday love had been appeased and been slept off?). His voice is full of nuts and bolts, of oil and graphite; and sober irritation at being reminded of a promise given earlier when all the Sunday pleasures were ahead. But he is a man of his word. He tells me where to go and when to be there and whom to ask for. I have about two hours.

*

She said she would not stay to supper. She would have liked to but she had left it too late to ring and say she had made other arrangements. She ought to get back soon.

'Then let me take you.'

'No. You've too much to do. I'll wait while you pack and change. Then I must go and you must eat.'

My packing was a hit and miss business. First I had to change back into uniform. In doing so I seemed to change my flesh. I was a sergeant again. She, in her uniform, remained a colonel's daughter. Theoretically a rule had been broken. I began searching in the kit-bag for some tissue-paper packages – scarves and stoles for the Perron women (and a few for non-Perron women). My hand kept touching the transcript of the examination.

'Guy?'

She was standing just inside the bedroom door.

'I just wanted to say I'll make sure that someone meets Major Foster tomorrow. Is that servant of Ronald's still around? Nigel told me you caught him thieving.'

'I've not seen him.'

'Major Foster will probably ask. Where was he quartered?'

'At Flagstaff House, I think, with the other servants.'

'I'll make sure. I'm going now.'

'Going *now*?'

'Yes, I must. Write to me some time. Let me know how you get on.'

There are situations in which it is very difficult to know what to say. One of the tissue-packages was in my hand.

'I bought a few things for people back home. I've nothing else.'

She took the package because I really gave her no alternative. 'It's only a scarf. At least I think it is. Perhaps we'd better open it in case it's something like a tie for one of my uncles.'

'Whatever it is I shall like it.'

We went back to the verandah.

'One more drink.'

Her back and shoulders felt so much thinner than they really were.

She shook her head and said there wasn't time. She must go. She didn't need a tonga. It was only a short walk up the hill. I went with her to the front of the guest house. The light had almost gone. I said I couldn't let her go home alone.

'I shall be perfectly all right. It's what I'd prefer. Honestly. Goodbye, Guy.'

She turned and set off down the narrow drive. I called after her. She glanced round, waved the package. I began to follow her, but stopped, understanding that her wish to go now and go alone was genuine. In a moment the curve of the drive had taken her away. I went back to finish packing my kit-bag. As I shoved the typescript well in to make room for the slacks and shirt and chappals I remembered that particular line: *We haven't seen each other since the night we visited the temple.* I rolled down my sergeant's sleeves, the drill for night-time. While buttoning the cuffs a trick of light made my hands seem brown.

*

They had emerged, erupted violently, from the shadows of the Moghul Room, attacked me, pulled me away, hit me in the face. Later when they had gone and we held each other again I said: Let me take you home. She said, No. No. We haven't seen each other. We haven't seen each other since the night we visited the temple. She saw the danger I would be in if I dared

1353

to go with her, dared to mutter to someone, a white man, an official, any of the men who would ask questions, 'We were making love. These men attacked us.' She had seen the danger of implicating me in any way, but she hadn't seen the marks on my face, because it was too dark. And I hadn't thought of them until I got home.

*

I don't remember eating. I remember sitting on the verandah drinking the last of the ADC's brandy and staring out into the dangerous Indian night until it was time to send Salaam'a to fetch a tonga to take me to the rendezvous with Sub-Conductor Pearson's convoy and the first leg of the journey back to the source, where all these things, becoming distant again, would count for little and seem to belong to another world entirely.

The Dak Bungalow

I

The scene was over. I can enter now, Sarah told herself.

*

But I did not enter. None of us did. I thought I saw the reason. What had held us together as a family was father's absence; his return showed how deeply we were divided. You could feel him making the attempt to come to terms with each of us separately. There was a time for mother, a time for Susan and Edward, and a time for me; and a different kind of time for the servants, for Pankot, for the regiment.

My time was before breakfast. Between seven and eight-thirty every morning father and I rode. He associated me with these early hours of the day and during them treated me with a special solicitude, as if the pattern of intimacy which had been established on the journey from Ranpur when we shared tea and bacon sandwiches and were careful with crumbs, might develop through repetition into something complex, mysterious and satisfying. At times he had the look of a man with a secret he was patiently waiting to share; at others that of a man empty of knowledge and recollection.

After a couple of days I noticed on these morning rides that we were taking the same route – down the northern slope of East Hill into the valley – and stopping at the same place. The view wasn't spectacular. About a mile ahead you could see a village. That was all. But he reined in and sat motionless, gazed at the distant huddle of huts and the terraced fields that traced the contours of the hill. The earth was tawny. There was always a mist. You could smell the smoke of wood and dung fires. After five minutes or so he would look at his wrist-watch and say, 'Well, better get back.' Apart from this single comment he kept silent during the halt.

An obvious explanation of the choice of turning point was that it was fixed according to a formula involving time available, distance to be covered, expected time of return. But we did not always take the same route home and got back to Rose Cottage anywhere between say 8.15 and 8.45. The only part of the ride I could be absolutely sure of – the part that I began to feel was plotted by an obsession – was the route out and the halt and the five minutes' silent contemplation of a village whose name I wasn't certain of but checked on one of the large-scale maps at Area Headquarters. It was called Muddarabad.

We had never kept horses at Rose Cottage. Such stabling as there had been had – long before Aunt Mabel's time even – become merged with the servants' quarters and store-rooms. A syce brought horses up from the depot. In the past year or two I had ridden seldom, mother less and Susan not at all. In Bombay father had said that one of the things he was looking forward to was getting accustomed again to the saddle. He hadn't ridden for nearly five years. I assumed that it might be a week or two before he felt fit enough to go out and that in any case it would be mother who went with him, but on his first evening at home he said, 'What about riding tomorrow?' and he said it to me. He rang Kevin Coley and I looked out my things but didn't discover until I put them on in the morning that my jodhpurs were uncomfortably tight round the waist. Mounting, I was as nervous as I had been as a small girl. He wore slacks and chukka boots. He led off as though he had been going out every morning of his life.

This would have been Thursday, August 9. He rode a few paces ahead of me. We spoke very little. I felt some reserve – embarrassment – in regard to his physical presence – imagining mother still lying in their bed considering through half-shut eyes the pillow beside her which bore an impression of the head of the man who kept looking back at me, smiling, as if in delight in rediscovery. Do children, when grown up, even nowadays, quite believe in the reality of their parents' sexual life?

Logic told me that in the past few years there must have been moments when my father lay in his bed in prison-camp and thought, God, God, I must have a woman. Suspicion rather than logic told me that in my father's absence my mother had had an affair. Logic in fact didn't come into it. Kevin Coley looked incapable of physical passion; a dry desiccated creature whom nothing would arouse except a threat to the professional obscurity in which he'd been content to live since his wife's death in the Quetta earthquake. But, nursing my suspicion – and my growing understanding of the complexity of physical needs and physical responses – I had to throw out the idea of non-capability, non-culpability, and – in consequence – try to suppress every emotion except that of ironic acceptance, which wasn't easy – so difficult in fact that I couldn't sustain it for long and had to try to counteract suspicion by telling myself that it was based on nothing more reliable than poor Barbie Batchelor's delirious imagination, coupled with the workings of my own which, alerted by Barbie's at first incomprehensible ramblings in the Pankot hospital, had since stretched the evidence (things seen, overheard, intuited) to make a case which the strictly rational side of my nature rejected, because even if adultery were the kind of game I could imagine my mother playing, adultery with Kevin Coley struck me as ludicrously out of character. So, I was back at the beginning of the circle of conjecture, and beginning to go round again, all the time conscious, naturally, that what chiefly nourished the retaliatory instinct to suspect her was her treatment of me, her utter disregard, her pretence of knowing nothing while knowing everything about the sordid abortion in Calcutta – everything except the name of the man who would have been the child's father, which she could have found out easily enough not from me but from Aunt Fenny who couldn't have been in much doubt but respected my silence and was fondly and foolishly guilt-ridden at the thought that she had been initially responsible for putting me in his way, or putting him in mine (it came to the same thing).

It was on the Friday – after our second ride to Muddarabad – that I heard poor Barbie was dead. Major Smalley mentioned it to me at the daftar, having heard it from his wife, and she was invariably well-informed. When I rang the Reverend Mother of the Samaritan Hospital in Ranpur and she talked vaguely of papers meant for me or my family I feared some kind of revelation, a written statement, a letter to my father whom Barbie had hardly known but on whom I knew she relied to settle once and for all the question whether mother had buried Aunt Mabel in the wrong place – a letter perhaps referring to mother's association with Coley. I didn't believe Barbie capable of malice. What I feared was an unintentional accusation by a woman whose wits were scattered – as scattered as the contents of the trunk she'd left at Rose Cottage where she'd been Aunt Mabel's companion, and which she removed on the morning of the accident – the trunk that was the cause of the accident because it was too heavy for the tonga.

The trunk was full of things connected with Barbie's work as a mission teacher, old textbooks, exercise books she'd kept to remember special pupils, gifts from the children and their parents, and a copy of the picture her old mission friend Edwina Crane had been given as a reward for heroism in the North West Frontier Province during the Great War. Barbie told me that the trunk wasn't particularly important but it was 'her history and without it according to Emerson she wasn't explained'. When Mabel died she had to move into a small room at the rectory bungalow. She'd taken things down there bit by bit during the week or so mother gave her to give us vacant possession of Rose Cottage. The rectory wasn't a permanent arrangement and Clarissa Peplow was worried about the amount of stuff she seemed to have. Barbie asked me if she could leave the trunk with the *mali*. I offered to take care of it myself. Susan and I would be sharing the room that had been Barbie's and I saw no reason why I shouldn't look after the trunk until she found a permanent home. But she knew mother would object. She said that if the *mali* put the trunk in his shed then providing I knew it was there that would be good enough. So that's what was done.

*

Muddarabad was the village Havildar Karim Muzzafir Khan came from. We stopped there because father couldn't bring himself to ride on and enter it and confront the havildar's wife and family. Each morning, I think, he set off with that intention and then, reaching the halting-place, found the intention collapsing under the weight of his notion of its futility. *Man-Bap*.

I am your father and your mother. This traditional idea of his position, this idea of himself in relationship to his regiment, to the men and the men's families, had not survived his imprisonment; or, if it had survived, the effort of living up to it had become too much for him. Was it lack of energy or lack of conviction, I wondered, that caused him to rein in and sit straight-backed as if posing for his portrait as a military officer watching the course of a battle for whose outcome he would be held responsible, or studying the ground over which, tomorrow, conclusions would be tried?

And, watching *him*, it struck me how very rare after all were men whose genius lay in active warfare. For one genius there would be almost countless plodders who were commanders in name only, men to whom the structure of a landscape would present almost as great a problem in military understanding as it had always done to me, but who had been taught to apply a set of ready-made formulas so that it was upon these and not the terrifyingly wide margins of error that their minds were concentrated. As a child he had seemed godlike to me, revealing some of the secrets of his profession. I had the feeling now that he believed himself dishonoured – not by anything he had done but by his talent, which turning out limited had narrowed the whole area of his self-regard.

Waiting at the halting-place on the third morning, the Saturday, I recalled my mother's words overheard the night before, when I came home late, having stayed on at the daftar to telephone the Reverend Mother at the Samaritan. 'It's a question of your presence more than anything. It was the same for me when you all went into the bag.' And in retrospect it seemed scarcely any time at all since she had ridden out with Kevin Coley from one village to another to talk to the women whose husbands, sons and grandsons and brothers were either dead or captured in North Africa.

For her to visit every village would have been impossible but on other occasions she talked to women who came in from outlying districts for confirmation of the news, receiving them outside the adjutant's office and even in the compound of the grace and favour bungalow where we lived in those days. Colonel Sahib, Colonel Memsahib. Two aspects of the one godhead. My mother was not built to look like a woman another woman could be comforted by – but at these meetings her very stiffness seemed right. The important thing was that she was there, in the shell of her flesh which if hard seemed trustworthy. She told these women the truth always, for instance that as prisoners of war the men would be separated from their officers and that it would be virtually impossible for father himself to ensure their welfare. But, subsequently, in many unobtrusive ways, she had kept an eye on the widows, and the wives who like herself could only wait patiently for their men's return. She did this entirely out of her sense of duty. It was an act, but she played the part with a perfect sense of what would be extraneous to it. She did not make the mistake of identifying herself too closely with it. When she came back into the bungalow she shed it, or seemed to shed it. And called for gin.

So, 'Why don't you?' she had said the night before, meaning why didn't he ride on into Muddarabad. But it was different for father. *Man-Bap*. That act had been an inseparable part of his life as a commander of Indian troops. *He* had to identify himself closely with it. It was supposed to go deep into him, right down to the source of his inspiration. Every morning, when we stopped after riding down the northern slope of East Hill, it was as though he waited there for the inspiration to return and lead him down into the village. But, 'Well', he would say, and said it again that Saturday, 'Better get back'. On the way home we usually rode abreast and talked about the things that had happened yesterday and the plans there were for today.

*

After riding we had breakfast and then I went down to the daftar. Officially he was on station leave but sometimes he went down to the Pankot Rifles lines. The immediate future was very uncertain. There was a question of long leave, the possibility of taking it at home; but the more important questions for him were of his fitness and of his next appointment. Long though I did for home leave the prospect wasn't one I considered likely even if the war ended as people expected. He was too close to retirement to waste time in England. He had too much time to make up. He and mother were now well enough off, having inherited Mabel's money, not to go after promotion simply to earn a higher pension, but he would go after it, I believed, to redress the balance. And it would be something to put his mind to. The obvious job for him was that of commandant of the depot which Colonel Trehearne had held throughout the war, postponing his own retirement. But now I got the impression that mother had set her sights higher and that she wanted to get out of the station. I couldn't blame her. The expense she had gone to in altering Rose Cottage couldn't in her case be seen as evidence of an intention to make it a permanent home. Even the prospect of final retirement there now seemed questionable.

*

Feeling I must do something about whatever it was Barbie had left which the Bishop Barnard Mission hadn't collected or didn't want and about which the Reverend Mother was so vague and yet so insistent, I wrote to Nigel Rowan to ask him whether he'd ring her and get the facts clearer. That was on the Saturday. On that evening we dined with the Trehearnes.

Maisie Trehearne was tall, pale and stately, and so upright that it was rumoured she was supported by a steel corset. Lately she had taken to wearing flowing dinner gowns of grey or blue georgette which gave her the appearance of a metallic ghost. When she moved she created the illusion of cooling breezes which weren't necessary because the Commandant's house was the draughtiest in Pankot and wretched to dine at on a winter evening. The Trehearnes were the last people to order fires lit and the first to order the hearths to be cleared and guarded by brass trays. And never, in the rainy season, when the evening could be chilly – which fortunately it wasn't on this occasion – was an electric fire brought in and switched on. Her husband, Patrick, now sixty, had the same frail, febrile but inflexible look: highly tempered steel worn to the thickness of a wafer. There was scarcely a line on their faces. They were the faces of people who had never had a sleepless night or a moment's worry, or, if they had, had somehow acquired an almost oriental sense of spiritual detachment from the cares of life.

The other obstacle to comfort at the Trehearnes was the pack of dogs, a strange hybrid collection ranging from puppies to full-grown brutes, seldom less than three altogether; raw, savage, the terror of servants, cause of concern to timid guests; obstinate, disobedient; objects of Maisie's devotion and her husband's sufferance. The dogs seemed natural victims of the disasters that were always befalling them. Ruling the roost at Commandant House they seemed disinclined to learn that the world outside was a hostile place. One, attacking a tonga horse, was kicked to death; another was bitten by a krait; yet another run over by a staff-car from Area Headquarters which it had thought had no business on the same road as itself. One, straying, was shot on the rifle-range. Others simply succumbed to one of the diseases domestic animals in India were always dying of. You would have thought that a woman so genuinely fond of animals, particularly of dogs, would have lost heart, but Maisie never did, she was always acquiring replacements for those that had fallen, and you always felt that her attachment was deep, her sense of duty to them strong, her horrified reaction to any tale of cruelty to animals of any kind absolutely real. You could still feel this about Maisie even when sitting in their dining-room under the glazed eyes of the creditable number of mounted shikar trophies for whose deaths she and Patrick were just about equally responsible. The trophies were seldom referred to. Perhaps they were there merely as relics of youthful exuberance which had long since been grown out of. I once heard Lucy Smalley say she wondered that Maisie didn't mount the heads of the dogs too: a typical Smalley remark but not (which was also typical) wholly unjustified.

*

'Watch out for the dogs, John,' mother had warned father when we set out in the car Colonel Trehearne had sent up. The warning was unnecessary. Perhaps for once Patrick Trehearne had put his foot down, or Maisie and Patrick had both had the foresight to see that the usual kind of welcome you got at Commandant House didn't sort well with greeting a man who had been locked up for several years. Instead, the dogs had been locked up and we entered unmolested.

It was father's first dinner out and Maisie had promised mother to keep the party small. It turned out even smaller than planned because Kevin Coley's servant rang just before we arrived to say that the Adjutant Sahib had gone to bed with a temperature. 'Actually,' Maisie said, 'we're rather worried about Kevin. He suddenly seems restless. After all these years resisting any attempt to move and promote him he's acting as though he thought it was time something was done about him.'

The Trehearnes' bedroom where we left our stoles, exposing necks, shoulders and arms, like Spartan women, to the chilly rigours of the interior, was immense. In it the twin beds looked diminutive, mere sparrows' nests. High above them, suspended from the raftered ceiling, were circular frames for the mosquito nets which were hardly ever necessary but which Maisie had a fondness for. It was the kind of room, sparsely furnished, which always looked camped-out in rather than occupied, and where you wouldn't have been surprised to find bird-droppings on the floor.

It was while we were in the bedroom that the subject of Barbie came up and I discovered that mother also knew she was dead. Susan was momentarily out of the room, powdering her nose in the adjoining bathroom (people in Pankot had learned not to refer to death and disaster in front of her, if they could help it). Maisie said, 'Mrs Stewart at the Library tells me that according to Lucy Smalley, Miss Batchelor died the other day. Did you know?'

She addressed the question to both of us. I was standing at the foot of one of the beds. Mother was peering into the glass of the dressing-table, making a minor repair with her lipstick. Perhaps this provided her with an excuse not to speak. But she didn't react at all, her expression remained constant, concentrated. I was forced to answer. I said that Major Smalley had mentioned it to me at the daftar.

'There was nothing in the *Ranpur Gazette*,' Maisie said. 'And the death columns are the first thing I read. It used to be the births and marriages but you seem to reach a time of life when you know only the people who die. How did Lucy hear?'

'I don't know,' I said, truthfully.

'Do you, Mildred?'

'Do I what?'

'Know how Lucy Smalley heard Miss Batchelor was dead.'

'All I know is what Mrs Smalley told me when she rang, but I suppose in this case one can take it as more or less true.'

'What did she say?'

'Only that the Bishop Barnard people had written to Arthur Peplow and that the chaplain who's filling in for him opened the letter and asked her who Miss Batchelor was. Mrs Smalley, it goes without saying, had only dropped into the rectory bungalow to see if she could help with any little problem.'

'Had the Peplows kept in touch with the Mission, then?'

'I don't know about keeping in touch. But the rectory was the woman's last address. I expect the Mission wanted to be sure she's left nothing here that they ought to have and I'm sure their solicitors will be already on to ours making a fuss about the annuity Mabel willed her. I suppose the estate will have to cough up what she'd have received if we'd ever got round to buying it. Thank God I had the presence of mind at the time to tell our own solicitors in London to drag their feet, and thank God she went off her head as soon as she did because that gave them a good excuse to drag their feet even harder. Mabel must have been off *her* head, making that sort of provision for an elderly spinster.'

'I've never really understood about annuities,' Maisie said.

'You buy the damned things to provide an income for life which is all right if the person the annuity's bought for lives a long time. The catch is, once it's bought, the capital sum has gone forever. Even if you die the next day. I must say it would amuse me if the Bishop Barnard people think they've got several thousand rupees coming to them. They have complete control of her estate, apparently, for what it's worth.'

'Poor Miss Batchelor,' Maisie said. 'I sometimes think she had a sad life.'

Mother put away her lipstick. As she did so she glanced up, regarding me through the mirror. Then she snapped her handbag and turned round.

'I don't think you'd feel so sympathetic, Maisie, if you'd had to watch her encouraging Mabel's eccentricities and anti-social instincts and at the same time be pretty sure she was feathering her own nest pretty neatly, and then making all that macabre fuss about where Mabel should have been buried. I had Mabel's funeral to cope with and Susan's premature labour to cope with and I had to cope with them virtually alone because Sarah was down in Calcutta visiting that man Merrick in hospital. And on top of it all I had this damned silly woman running all over Pankot saying I was shoving Mabel into the ground at St John's when she'd wanted to be buried at St Luke's in Ranpur, next to John's father. Even that elderly admirer of hers, Mr Maybrick, thought it was a bit much. And of course John tells me he never heard Mabel say a single thing about where she wanted to be put. I took him to see the grave this morning. He thought it very suitable.'

Susan came out of the bathroom and the subject was dropped.

'How pretty you look,' Maisie said, which was no less than the truth, the kind of thing Susan still needed to hear but which was nowadays inspired more by the obligation people felt under to encourage her back to life and happiness than by spontaneous admiration. I imagined that Susan herself was aware of this not very subtle undercurrent of intention, and that she responded to praise in the same way that someone who is enjoying remission from the pain of a disease they know they're not yet cured of must respond to being told how well they're looking. And, because it had happened before, I was now prepared to wake up that night and hear the sound of her crying. Her crying was terrible, because when she cried and I tried to comfort her we seemed very close, closer than we had ever been as children; but within a day or two we were farther apart than ever. Every measure of love and affection had to be paid for by a larger measure of antagonism.

'How pretty you look,' Maisie had said, and then as if by an association of ideas, and leading us out, she said, 'We have invited young Mr Drew.'

Edgar Drew. Eager Edgar. I tried to catch Susan's eye but she had assumed her party rôle. Eager Edgar had been to Rose Cottage once or twice. In a rare conspiratorial moment between us Susan and I had christened him thus.

'We thought,' Maisie was saying to mother, 'it would be nice for him to meet John.' By which she really meant he would be suitable young company for Susan and me.

He had obviously arrived before us because Maisie didn't greet him when we went into the sitting-room where he stood with Colonel Trehearne and father, one hand behind his back, the other clutching his sherry glass, his head adjusted to a slant of attentiveness and inquiry, the wary look of a young man whose heart wasn't quite in what he had been taught he had to do to get on; of a man who having no inner resources of strength and energy – at least none he dared trust – saw no alternative to the perplexing business of flattering his elders. His father was an insurance broker in Byfleet and he had been to a public school of which I think he'd just reached the stage of feeling slightly ashamed because he realized it ranked as 'minor'. Physically he was attractive but he nullified this attraction every time he opened his mouth. His conversation was excruciatingly dull and he seemed to have no opinions of his own. He worked hard to sound self-confident, so hard that one became aware of the effort it cost him.

The Trehearnes had taken to him because they thought him a cut or two above most of the last year or so's intake of newly-commissioned English subalterns from Belgaum and Bangalore who had arrived at the depot, stayed a few weeks and then departed to join the 4/5th and the 2nd battalions in Burma. Moreover, Second-Lieutenant Drew had expressed interest in the idea of applying for a regular commission and this ambition counted in his favour when it came to comparing him with some of the rougher-spoken and rougher-mannered men who had got into the regiment with (I suspected) higher qualifications from OTS as potential leaders of infantry. He was what was never actually called but certainly thought of as regimental depot material which meant it was thought he would eventually prove to be perfectly adequate for active regimental duty but was meanwhile presentable enough in the mess and at dinner parties such as this to be put temporarily by and employed more pacifically.

I could tell that he had had little or no experience of women; his attentiveness betrayed anxiety. Someone, his mother probably, may have told him that a gentleman never looked lower than a girl's nose. The result was that when he talked to you he kept his chin up and head back and made you feel disembodied below the neck. He had beautiful hands; not fine and elegant but firm and shapely. But you seldom had a chance to admire them. They were usually clasped behind his back or bunched into fists. Even at table they tended to disappear between mouthfuls, presumably to clutch one another or be wiped surreptitiously on his napkin. When you had the opportunity to touch or be touched by them – that is, when he danced with you – they were uncomfortably moist, but at least they were a connection; although a distant connection because he danced you at arm's length – which made it seem like dancing with a draught. I admit I had occasional fantasies about Mr Drew's hands, and after seeing him in the club swimming pool I also had occasional fantasies about the rest of him. Perhaps I should have told him, not for my own good, but for his. He can't have been unaware of his physical appearance, but I think he probably needed confirmation from outside before he could relate his own awareness to other people's. I had a distinct impression that he might be the only child of elderly parents. He seemed to belong to a generation earlier than his own – that of the Edwardians, say – which would explain his enthusiasm for the outward forms of Anglo-Indian life.

He was, of course, more directed towards Susan than to me (interested or attracted would be the wrong words). She aroused his masculine instinct to protect. Confronted by me he was always on the defensive. It was I who reminded him that fundamentally he was a bit afraid of all of us. Sometimes when talking to him I heard in my own voice tones like those Clark-Without had used when talking to me, tones calculated to provoke; and then I stopped, a bit appalled at the ease with which one followed disreputable examples, and at the ease with which bitterness, once felt, lodged itself, dug itself in and hardened all the edges of your personality.

When we went into dinner Maisie put him between mother and Susan. I had been intended to sit between Colonel Trehearne and Kevin Coley, which would have been rather like sitting between a couple of posts. As it was, I sat between Colonel Trehearne and my father, which while not greatly different was more comfortable. And from here I was able to watch Mr Drew more or less undistracted and, while mother talked to Colonel Trehearne, attend to what Susan and Mr Drew were jointly building that might rank as a conversation; and occasionally contribute to it myself, talking across the table when Mr Drew found himself at a loss. One advantage Mr Drew had in making a go of sitting next to Susan was that he took the shy man's way out; he kept the ball rolling by asking her questions about herself; about what she had been doing, about whether she had enjoyed that, about what she thought she might do next week and about the chances she saw of enjoying that too or enjoying it more. I suppose it was really due to her that the conversation was a success, because once he had got on to the subject of what she had done or had thought, she was able to take an interest of a kind that encouraged him to go on feeding her with questions, scraping the bottom of the barrel of his imagination, but managing. When a change of course signalled a change in talking duties and mother turned to him he became at once less articulate. A faint flush of anxiety spread across his face and stayed there. You could see the gleam of perspiration on his forehead.

I don't remember what she talked to him about nor, now that Colonel

Trehearne was free, what subject or subjects he and I chose in order to avoid talking about others. What I do remember clearly is the way in which I suddenly became conscious of the yelping and whining of the dogs. While Maisie talked to Susan and mother talked to Mr Drew and Colonel Trehearne and I exchanged trivial bits of information, the imprisoned dogs moaned and barked and snarled somewhere at the back of the compound. If Maisie heard this distant accompaniment of protest she gave no sign of it. The talk continued. The noise never stopped except to change key.

Father was the only person at the table not talking, and at the moment I became conscious of the dogs I became conscious of this too; aware of the nervous intensity of the silence in which he listened to the cries of those chained animals. He stopped eating. Maisie glanced at him and then very quickly turned back to Susan; which made it plain that mother had warned her to take no notice of anything he did which she thought odd, like putting his fork down, covering a piece of bread with a napkin; staring at the plate.

But this was different. It was the effect of the barking of the dogs that left him unable to eat another mouthful, unable to speak (I felt) or even to move, because of what the dogs reminded him; what, locked up, they represented. I was afraid of what he might do. I took an opportunity to say something to him. He looked at me. His smile was benign. Beneath the table his right hand was trembling. Perhaps my speaking broke the spell. He resumed eating. But sometimes when the sound of the dogs reached a crescendo his knife and fork shook.

*

'If I were you, Maisie,' my mother said, when we were out of earshot of the men, having left them to drink their whisky in the draughty dining-room, 'I'd let those hounds loose. It's worrying John, hearing them yelp.'

Intermittently she had this capacity to astonish me with unexpected proof of having noticed things she'd seemed protected from or unconcerned about; but on this occasion my reaction to the revelation was very strong. Waiting my turn for the lavatory and my turn at the looking-glass, it struck me that there was now absolutely nothing to keep me living where I was living, doing what I was doing. It had all come suddenly to an end. I sat on Maisie's bed and opened my mind to the prospects, the joyful prospects of being free because there was no further family duty for me to perform, no one it was necessary to keep an eye on, or stand by, see through a crisis, make excuses for as I'd had to do in the early days at the grace and favour bungalow before there was Mabel's money to be extravagant with and bills ran up, card debts were being forgotten, and too much gin was being drunk (so elegantly, so discreetly); no one now for whose return I had to wait. Even Susan no longer needed me. She only needed everyone.

So I could go home, stay with Aunt Lydia in Bayswater, find myself a job, a place of my own, and a man I could look at and not feel that he was tortured by an affection for the country I'd not been happy in and to which he would always be longing to return, as if to prove something to himself. I could finish with India before it had quite finished with me, rusted me up, corroded me, corrupted me utterly with a false sense of duty and a false sense of superiority.

I emerged (a little over-painted I think – I noticed mother look at me) and determined to be nice to Mr Drew. I tried to get him to talk about Surrey (where great grand-father had lived and where, walking with Aunt Mabel to show her the stream where Susan and I played together I had been stung by a wasp at the moment of one of what I called my funny turns, which might have been growing pains and made me feel immense in a diminutive landscape); but when Mr Drew did talk about Surrey it sounded to me like a different country – a foreign place – so I made him dance with me to Maisie's portable, out on the verandah where it was no draughtier than indoors, while Susan sat inside, not watching us, but with an expression on her face that I recognized but tonight refused to do anything about. Then the dogs came in and there was pandemonium. Susan's coffee cup somehow got knocked over (or was deliberately spilled to distract attention from the dogs). Her new dress was stained down the front and before you could turn round the pieces on the board had been rearranged and Susan was there in the middle of the scene, with people sponging her, inviting her to have another cup, while she tried to embrace the hound that had caused the trouble; and Mr Drew got down on his knees to collect bits of broken china, and then realized he'd made a gaffe because what else were all these servants for? Still outside, I re-wound the gramophone and played another record of which no one took any notice except towards the end when father came out and said, 'Years since I did this,' and shuffled round with me for the last few bars. Then we went inside where two of the dogs had their devoted heads on Maisie's and Patrick's knees and the third was lolling, tongue out, enfolded by one of Susan's arms: the two of them leaning against one another, squatting in the centre-piece of the rug, in front of the empty hearth.

*

But those intimations of freedom continued. My limbs felt as though they were made out of a substance that wasn't always obedient to the law of gravity. I seemed buoyant, almost on the verge of levitation; to have become in relation to Pankot a dominant but disinterested force. I was no longer ashamed of the dreams I had and had considered shameful, dreams in which I also played a dominant rôle, loving a man who was an amalgam of Major Clark and the young American officer in Darjeeling who was Clark-Without's only successor so far, and who had so impressed Aunt Fenny with his courtly Boston manners that she never suspected him of having other than a brotherly interest in the girl she was supposed to be chaperoning, the girl who was supposed to be convalescing from a spell in a nursing-home in Calcutta, and whose problem was no longer emotional but physical, and who let him into her room three nights in a row, because unlike her Aunt Fenny she hadn't been deceived; had recognized in the American the same single-minded and powerful sexual drive that had distinguished Clark-Without and which she wanted – perhaps for a number of reasons – to appease and be appeased by.

For not least among those reasons was the need to satisfy again her own fully awoken physical desires. I oughtn't to say 'not least'. The need was pre-eminent. An almost unbearable ache. Perhaps I should leave it at that and perhaps it is only some lingering old-fashioned idea that desire without love needs excusing in a woman that makes me not want to refer to this episode without also groping for other explanations. The danger of doing so is that one could come up with another idea, equally false; the idea that I was deliberately debasing myself, paying myself out, being consciously promiscuous because that was now all I was fit to be; a well brought up young woman who had betrayed her upbringing by lying on her back for the first man with the power to persuade her on to it, and who had then had to get rid of the result in the usual sordid way, going in for a d and c and coming out foetus-free but permanently stained, soiled.

Well, I was not debasing myself with John J. Bellenger III but I was not in love with him either. Nor was I hoping that he would fall in love with me so that I could laugh in his face and have my own back on Clark-Without, on men in general. Perhaps all these possibilities were there, in my mind, like echoes of explanations, other people's explanations, but fundamentally there was only the desire, and if it was enclosed by a kind of anguish that anguish was for the loss of a scarcely begun life, the destruction of a child I had conceived, should have carried, loved and looked after. Appeasing the ache of physical desire, I was – yes, I think so – also comforting that anguish, trying to numb it.

But I do not know. The American told me with some understandable pride that I was the twenty-third girl he had had, not counting the ones he had had to pay for. I wasn't sure whether he wanted to amuse or shock me, hurt me or excite my admiration. It could have been that he was unsure himself because when I asked him which of these reactions he expected he looked confused, then laughed and said I had struck him as a girl who was naturally inquisitive and who would be interested in statistics, and that he'd never told a girl before which statistic she represented. I didn't believe him. Afterwards, when he had gone back to what he called States-side (he was in Darjeeling getting in some leave at the end of a tour of flying duties) and Fenny and I went back to Calcutta where mother and Susan were to join us, I worried rather about the possibility of having caught a disease, which would have been the last straw as far as mother was concerned (if I was unable to keep it as secret from her as she was determined the other business officially had to be).

*

The anguish had been part of the dreams, but now it had gone, or been sublimated in images of extraordinary sensuous tranquillity. One's moral sense sleeps while the subconscious mind works out its logic. Here we were, in perfect amity, revealing to one another the purity of a simple physical connection, myself active, they supine, eyes closed, mouths smiling faintly, free of that grim alignment which in real life reflected tensions. I now woke up from these dreams gradually enough to suffer no shock. For a few moments the tangible quality of pleasure lingered, so that the pleasure seemed to come with me into the actual world and colour all my responses, even my response to the knowledge that I'd only dreamt. Lying in the dark I luxuriated in my own ability to smile. And when up and about, getting on with the dull repetitious routine of coping with things and with other people, I had the idea of this smile in my head, in my whole body, as if a smile were a newly developed faculty.

*

Saturday, Sunday night, Monday. On the Monday night, because he had unexpectedly rung me, Nigel Rowan came into the dream too, not centrally, but on its misty periphery, as if he were waiting for me to finish and resume some kind of moral responsibility.

'Who was that?' my mother had asked when I'd put the phone down in the hall and joined her and father in the living-room. I told her. 'Is he in Pankot, then?' she asked.

No, I said, he was ringing from Ranpur. She expected to be told more than that and when she wasn't told she said, 'Was he ringing to say he's coming up?'

She'd heard more about Nigel Rowan from Clara Fosdick than she had ever heard from me. Clara Fosdick had probably given her a good report of him and exaggerated the amount of time Nigel and I spent together in Ranpur before I continued on to Bombay to await father's arrival.

'No,' I said. 'He's not coming up.'

'Did we ever know any Rowans, John?' she asked father.

'I don't remember. Why?'

'Sarah's met a Rowan who's one of Malcolm's *aides*. According to Clara Fosdick he had a relative in the Political but the name Rowan doesn't ring a bell. Did you know a Rowan at school?'

'I don't remember one.'

'Clara said this Rowan was at Chillingborough. Perhaps his father was too.'

'Do you mean Perron?'

'No. Not your eccentric sergeant. A Captain Rowan.' She looked at me again. 'What did he ring about?'

'About something I asked him to do.' I turned to father. 'Nigel Rowan's uncle was Resident at Kotala. He's just told me.'

My father nodded. He wasn't taking it in. But mother said, 'Then he must be Tom Crawley's nephew. You remember, don't you, John? All the fuss there was? How interesting. Are you sure he's not coming up?'

'He didn't say he was.'

'Did you tell him about your eccentric sergeant?'

'I mentioned Mr Perron. Yes.'

'Did he remember him?'

'Yes. Very well.'

'Not an impostor, then.'

'No, mother. Not an impostor.'

'He won't go to sleep,' Susan said, coming in with Edward in her arms and the ayah just behind her. 'He won't go to sleep until he's said goodnight again to grandpa.'

The child was as good as asleep, but this scene was part of the day's programme. I had delayed it a bit by being so long on the telephone. The child turned his head into Susan's breast when his grandfather dutifully leant over him and said, 'Goodnight, old chap.' Satisfied, Susan transferred him to Minnie's arms.

'Is there time for me to have a drink, or have I held things up too long already?' Susan asked.

'We couldn't have gone in before because Sarah's been on the phone,' mother explained.

'Oh. I'll take it in shall I then?'

'There's no hurry,' father said. He went to the side table where Mahmoud as instructed had set out the bottles and glasses so that Colonel Sahib could mix the drinks himself.

'Do you know,' he said, 'I realized today that I've put up a fearful black? I'm not sure I shan't have to send in my papers.'

'What dreadful thing have you done, John?'

'I've been on station very nearly a week and I've neither sent up my card to Flagstaff House nor signed the book. Back in 'thirteen, in Ranpur, it took me the best part of two weeks, doing nothing else, just leaving my card, ticking off the names on the list that Mabel gave me. Had to dress right for it too, and it cost a fortune in tonga-fares and shoe-leather.'

My mother smiled. She said that in the circumstances she imagined his failure to call at Flagstaff House might be overlooked.

'Really?' he said. 'Things have changed.' He caught my eye. 'Not sure I approve.'

It was the first joke he had made. I laughed. I said we could ride past Flagstaff House the next morning.

'So we could.'

*

But we didn't. On that Tuesday morning he was late joining me on the front verandah where I waited, smoking, watched by the two syces who had brought the horses up. Usually only one syce came, riding one horse

1371

and leading the other. When I first came out it was drizzling slightly but now it was clearing rapidly in that way which foretold a hot sunny morning. Remembering the funeral I asked the syces whether the bazaar was very crowded. The syce I knew said no, but it was said there were many people at the station, and he had seen people making for there. The bazaar would be crowded later, with people who had nothing better to do than look at a Congresswallah. That was why he had brought a companion; in case when they went back the crowds were big enough to worry the horses.

I said that was wise, and smiled because almost invariably the people who served us spoke contemptuously of politicians. A form of flattery. It was nearly twenty-past seven before father came out. The syces stood to attention and salaamed him.

'Well done,' he said. 'Well done,' as if bringing the horses up on time stretched their mental and physical resources. He said this every morning. And every morning he kissed me lightly on the cheek. This morning he did not kiss me. He put his arm round my shoulders and exerted faint pressure but did not look at me. He looked at his watch instead and apologized for being late. I asked him whether he had got his cards with him. I had to explain what I meant.

'Oh, lots of time for that. Lots of time.'

He led off as usual and once out on the road turned to the north, towards Muddarabad.

As I trailed behind him (the wisest thing to do on this narrow twisting section of road whose high-banked bends could mask the noise of trucks that sometimes used it) I felt vaguely disappointed. A change of route would have suited my buoyant mood. I had hoped that this morning would be different but obviously it was going to be like all the others unless I could force a variation, persuade him past the halt, into the village.

But it was he who forced the variation. About a quarter of a mile before we reached the halting place we came to a road that led in from our right. We had taken this road once or twice on the way home. Now, without more warning than a glance behind to check my position, he led into it, then reined in to let me come up and said, 'I thought we'd take a look at that.'

That was the old dak bungalow, wedged in the hillside, about a quarter of a mile away. A track would take us up to it. The bungalow hadn't been used for years, to my knowledge. It had always looked derelict to me. But this morning as we approached I saw the figure of a boy on the verandah. I said, 'There's someone there.'

'So there is. Good Lord.'

He was a poor actor. And getting closer I now recognized the *mali's* boy. He had on the blue mazri shirt that had originally been one of father's, which mother had handed on to the gardener who had since had it cut down to fit his son.

'Isn't that *mali's* boy?' father asked, forcing his tone. 'Well I never. What's the young scamp doing here?'

The boy had begun to unpack a haversack. I said, 'Playing truant I expect. It looks as if he's brought food for the day. Wouldn't it be nice if he'd got sandwiches and coffee and offered us some?'

'Shouldn't think much hope. All the same. Jove. Yes, wouldn't it, just? Still, mustn't count our chickens.'

We came up the steep and partially overgrown track in file. Far off I could hear the coppersmith. The sun had got up well into a clear sky. The old bungalow looked as if it were resting on the vapour which clung to the green hillside. Beneath my horse's rather clumsily placed hooves small wet pebbles slithered and crunched.

What is all this? my father called to the grinning urchin, in Urdu. *What are you doing here? Making arrangements for breakfast, Sahib*, the boy called back. Father laughed. He shouted up, *Will there be breakfast for us also? For Sahib and Memsahib-miss*, the boy called back.

'I say, we're in luck. Free scoff.'

Another urchin appeared to hold the horses. A well-bred urchin. Ignoring the burra sahib he stood first by me while I dismounted. I thanked him and asked him whether he was Fariqua's friend. He said he was. I asked him his name. He said, 'Ashok.' Ashok and Fariqua. A Hindu boy and a Muslim boy. Ashok led the horses round to the back. We went up the rickety steps to the ruinous-looking but in fact still quite stout verandah. On the wooden table Fariqua had spread out the feast on a coloured cloth: thermos, cups, pot of sugar, pot of salt, spoons, plates, unnecessary knives and forks, stacks of sandwiches wrapped in paper already appetizingly stained with what looked like bacon-fat.

'Well done,' father said. '*Bus.*'

The boy saluted and ran off to join his friend. (Later they came and squatted on their hunkers at some distance, in silence, observing us gravely.)

We sat side by side on the old bench. I reached for the thermos. 'No, let me,' he said. Pouring tea his hand scarcely trembled. He said, 'Better than leaving one's card.'

'Much better.'

He'd woken early, he explained, and had the idea, had got the servants moving, but it had taken longer than he imagined. The boy hadn't been able to leave with the picnic breakfast until ten to seven, so he'd hung around, made a long business of shaving and dressing, to guard against our catching the boy up. He'd wanted it to be a surprise.

'It's a lovely surprise.'

I'd never been to the old dak bungalow before. There had never been a reason to – even as a child. It was too close to home, wherever home had variously been in Pankot, a different home every summer, practically. The dak bungalow (open in those days, now declined, neglected) had been a

1373

point of reference in a familiar landscape. From it I now had a view of Pankot new enough to make the place look oddly unfamiliar.

He opened the first package of sandwiches.

'They won't be a patch on those we had on the train,' he said. 'Bacon sandwiches have to mature a bit, don't they? Crisp but not brittle. Not too moist, not too dry. I'm afraid this batch only got put down an hour ago. All the same, they don't smell too bad.'

And they tasted good. We munched for a while, content. It must have been now that the two boys came back to watch us.

'Did you know about our young supernumerary?'

'Fariqua's friend? Is he a supernumerary?'

'Well, I think he's attached himself to our strength. I caught sight of him the other day when I went round the servants' quarters. Thought he was just visiting because he dodged out of the way. But this morning I found him and Fariqua curled up in the goat-shed.'

'Hasn't he a home?'

'Probably several. None permanent. Orphan. Ambitious boy, though. Tells me he's going to Rajputana one day, to become a mahout, ride an elephant for a maharajah. Meanwhile he scrapes a living running errands in the bazaar and sleeping where he can, I suppose. I should have told *mali* to boot him out but hadn't the heart. Trouble is, once you've recognized the existence of a boy like that you're in a fair way to having to pay for services rendered but not wanted. *Mali* doesn't need two boys to help him, does he? Not with the little he has to do nowadays.'

What he meant was: now that the rose beds are gone. He missed the garden more than he would ever admit. From where we sat I could see the fold near the peak of East Hill behind which Rose Cottage lay. I tried to make out the fir tree that stood at the farthest point of the grounds. I said, 'Well, the tennis-court needs some keeping up.'

'I expect it does.'

I waited. I thought he was going to talk about Mabel. The roses. Or the grave. It hardly mattered which. They were all connected. But he went on, 'We must have a game presently. Bit strenuous for me at the moment though. But don't you and Susan give it up just because I'm back. I'd enjoy watching. You could get up a foursome. Young Drew maybe. And some other young fellow.'

He hesitated. 'I expect there *are* other young fellows? Been up before, waiting for a chance to come up again?'

'It shouldn't be difficult to make up a four.'

'With anyone in particular?'

I pretended not to understand, tilted my head at him, filling my mouth with bacon sandwich.

'Any young fellow who'd be particularly keen? This young ADC for example. Nigel Rowan?'

'Nigel Rowan's down in Ranpur.'

'What I mean is, well, forget tennis. Any young fellow in particular, special from your point of view, that I don't know about?'

I continued munching sandwich and considered the situation from what I imagined must be *his* point of view, looked at a woman, now twenty-five, who had been back in India for six years, and who must surely long since have worn out the excuse that of two sisters she was the less obviously attractive. Statistically, the odds against her remaining single or unattached must have been higher than in any comparable period. India had been jam-packed with eligible young men, and proportionately shorter than ever of eligible women. There were several possible explanations, none of them comforting to anyone who had her happiness at heart: she was frightened of men, she was one of the world's born old maids, she was consumed by a passion for a man who hadn't noticed her or who was married or for some other reason unattainable; or, she preferred women. Of these possibilities the consuming and unrequited passion was the one that most fathers would find the least disturbing and I wished badly that I could have confessed such a thing to him. Being unable to, being unable to confess to any of these things, I felt unsatisfactory and inadequate. I said, 'There's no one in particular so far, daddy.'

We went on, munching bacon sandwiches and Ashok and Fariqua continued to observe us, as though we were exhibits which it was only part of their job to look after, the other part being to watch us closely for clues to the trick we were performing to sustain an illusion of our ordinariness, the illusion that the Sahib-log too liked to eat and take a rest and did not live like birds of paradise, perpetually in flight, feeding on celestial dew.

'Has there never been anyone in particular?'

'You mean someone I wanted to marry?'

'Yes. That sort of in particular.'

I shook my head, pushed the sandwiches closer to him. He took one – seemed to think about it – and then placed it on one side. 'Tell me,' he said, 'what are your feelings towards Ronald Merrick?'

I stopped chewing and stared at him. I remember that: just staring at him, and suddenly wondering whether there was a plot to try to pair me off with the only man I could easily think of who appalled me. To avoid answering I turned the question. I asked him what *his* feelings were.

He regarded me rather sombrely.

'He wasn't what I expected. Being a friend of Teddie's – the same rank – I'd expected a younger man.'

'He wasn't a friend of Teddie's. They only shared the same quarters in Mirat.'

'But he was best man.'

'A last-minute substitute.'

'Yes, I see. Not that it matters.'

'I think it mattered to Teddie.'

'What makes you say that?'

'Well, I was there. I think Teddie regretted it. If I'd been in Teddie's shoes

1375

I'd have regretted it too. Hasn't mother or Aunt Fenny told you what happened at the wedding?'

'I know about the stone some chap threw that hit Teddie and delayed the ceremony.'

'The stone was thrown at Ronald but nobody realized that at the time, or why a stone had been thrown at all. The only explanation seemed to be that it was intended for the Nawab. The Nawab had lent us cars and the cars had crests on them. So we imagined the stone was thrown in error by someone who didn't like the people at the palace. We ended up guarded by MPS. That was a mess too. When the Nawab and his party turned up at the Gymkhana Club for the reception, the MPS didn't know who he was and tried to stop him coming in because he was an Indian. Then when we were seeing Teddie and Susan off at the station we were bothered by a poor old woman who prostrated herself at Ronald's feet. The whole thing was a mess but by then we knew who Ronald was. We knew the name of the district where he'd been superintendent of police.'

'Yes, I know all that. Ronald's told me himself. But I shouldn't think Teddie held it against him for long. It was hardly Ronald's fault.'

My father picked up the sandwich now and bit into it. I poured us more tea.

'What was Teddie Bingham like?' he asked.

'A bit like young Mr Drew. But not so shy.'

'Your Aunt Fenny told me he was rather attentive to you, at one time, before his engagement to Susan.'

'Yes. Actually it got to the stage where I was afraid he might propose.'

'Why afraid?'

'I realized how easy it would be just to say yes. A girl can, you know. It's a kind of inertia. You think well, why not? It's what's expected. Getting married to a fairly presentable man. Decent background. Good regiment. Nothing known against. And it's very flattering to be wooed a bit. Even by someone as automatic and predictable as Teddie.'

I should have liked to tell him about the night things came to a head, with Teddie obviously thinking the wooing drill had gone on long enough and that it was time to clarify things between us; the night he shifted gear and became fastidiously amorous, kissing me for so long that it was like a breath-holding contest and we both longed to come up for air, and then knew beyond any doubt that we were both bored with one another. But I felt you couldn't tell your father a thing like that about the man who had gone on to marry your sister. So instead I said, 'Why did you ask about my feelings towards Ronald Merrick?'

'I asked because – well, I've been given to understand that you had some special – no, that's wrong – that you *might* have some special regard for him.'

'Who gave you to understand, daddy?'

'Your Aunt Fenny. She's very fond of you, you know. She has your happiness very much at heart.'

'And I'm fond of her. But I can't think why she should think that. I told her a long time ago what I felt about Ronald Merrick.'

'Yes, but she wondered whether there might have been a change of heart. No, I'm exaggerating again. She said a change of heart couldn't be ruled out.'

'Well it can. I can't imagine how Aunt Fenny could get such an idea. She saw us together often enough when he turned up in Bombay. So did you, daddy. I don't like him. It must show.'

'I wouldn't actually say that.'

'Well whether it shows or not, that's the situation. Furthermore he knows I don't like him.'

'Oh?' He hesitated. 'I don't think he does.' He leant back. 'Neither does your mother. She has much the same impression as Fenny. That you might have a special regard for him.'

'*Mother* told you I might have a special regard for Ronald Merrick?'

He studied me very seriously.

'Yes. Have you?'

'No, daddy.'

'I didn't really think so, but I wouldn't hold out as an expert, you know, not against Fenny and your mother. So I wanted to be sure. Can I be sure?'

'Absolutely sure.'

'Why don't you like him?'

'I can't easily explain why.'

'I know he's not, well – how stuffy it sounds – but not quite our class.'

'It doesn't sound stuffy at all. It's true. He's not quite our class. Class has always been important to us. Why should it suddenly stop being important?'

He had leant forward, arms on the table. He was smoothing one side of the close-cropped moustache with his knuckles. He seemed puzzled. It wasn't the kind of reaction he expected. Not from the rebel of the family.

He said, 'It's only important over quite a narrow area of life, although I agree it's an important area. The private bit. It's easier to be intimate with someone who comes out of the same box. But there are other areas where it's not important at all. Areas where it's actually harmful, I'd say. Anyway, in Ronald Merrick's case, does it honestly arise? Unless we insist on looking only at the background?'

'You mean he's our class now? That he's made the effort to raise himself to our level and if he keeps quiet about his origins no one will know they weren't much cop. Is that what you mean?'

'He doesn't try to hide them. That's one thing in his favour.'

'One thing? All right. One thing.'

'Surely he has a lot of admirable qualities?'

'Like what, daddy?'

'Like physical courage, moral too, I dare say. No, I don't dare say, I do say. Don't you agree?'

'I prefer a bit of moral cowardice myself.'

'Oh?'

'Or whatever it is that makes you admit there can be two sides to a question, other points of view as good as your own.'

'That's not moral cowardice.'

'I said moral cowardice because you said moral courage. And moral courage is so often what you say people have who really only have their minds rigidly made up to suit themselves.'

'Yes,' he said. He smoothed the other side of the moustache. 'I suppose it can be. I'd not thought of it like that. And I grant you in Ronald's case a certain inflexibility. But you often find it in men who've had to fight their way up the ladder. They have to work so much harder. Did you know he lost both parents when he was only fifteen?'

'He mentioned it once.'

'You know what they were?'

'He said they were in a very small way. I didn't inquire how small or what way.'

'They had a small shop in North London. Newsagent, tobacconist. That sort of thing. I got the impression that before the First World War they were both in service. The shop did pretty well and they took over a larger one. Ronald began at a local boardschool but got scholarships and ended at quite a good grammar. Then the parents were killed in a motor-accident. There was a country uncle somewhere but he wasn't interested in the boy. The assistant headmaster of the school was, though. He took him in to live as a ward and to stay on and matriculate. This fellow had some sort of Indian connections or interests. Socially it was a leg up. Ronald said he imagined if his parents hadn't died he'd have been shoved into something like insurance or accountancy. He knows he owes everything to the schoolmaster. Not just the chance to complete his education but the chance of a better background as well. A good enough one to scrape him into the Indian Police. Physically and academically he must have been more than good enough.'

'You've learnt a lot. More than any of us.'

'Only what he openly volunteered.'

'I realize that. What puzzles me is why he volunteered it.'

'Does it puzzle you? Really? You've no idea?'

'None.'

'Yes, I see. And I'm sorry. I mean sorry you don't much like him. But at least that's better than the other thing. He told me all this because he wants to marry Susan. He said Susan had given him reason to believe she wasn't averse to the idea but that no decision could be made until I got home. Fenny and your mother were surprised. Very surprised. They thought that if he had that kind of regard for either one of you it must be for you. I wanted to be sure how you felt. But it's taken me a bit of time to pluck up the nerve to mention it to you. I was afraid of it hurting you. ...'

'It doesn't hurt me.'

He took my hand. I said: 'It doesn't hurt me, it appals me. I don't

1378

honestly believe it. She's said absolutely nothing, but if he's right, if she's thinking on these lines, you've got to stop it. Really. She's not fit to marry anyone yet, let alone Ronald Merrick.'

'The psychiatrist apparently says she is.'

'Which psychiatrist?'

'The one here.'

'Who told you that?'

'Ronald. He saw the fellow a few weeks ago.'

'With Susan's approval?'

'No. He saw him before he spoke to Susan. He wanted to know what effect a proposal of marriage might have on her, whether it would set her back at all. Whether he should wait a bit before saying anything even to me.'

'What a bloody nerve.'

'I thought it rather sensible.'

'Well of course – you thought exactly what he planned you should think. I hope Captain Richardson gave him bloody short shrift.'

'Oh? Why? If you were Richardson and a man who's short of an arm and has half his face burnt off came to you and said, Look I want to marry one of your patients, what are the problems likely to be from her and your point of view?'

'I know, I know. It's all beautifully logical. Absolutely square and above-board. Admirable. On the surface. On the *surface*, daddy.'

'He's very good with young Edward.'

'Yes. He's very good with young Edward.'

'Better than I.'

'Better than you. Better than any of us. Better than anyone. Better than Susan. But he wouldn't be marrying Edward. He'd be marrying Susan. How good will he be with her?'

Directly I'd said that the blood came to my face. I guessed what he probably thought. For one wild moment I wondered whether it could be true, wondered whether if I went to Richardson and described the situation to him he would say, It's clear of course, Merrick appals you because he attracts you and your exaggerated concern for your sister is simply a reflection of your fury at being rejected in her favour.

But it wasn't true. What I believed *was* true was that my mother had deliberately tried to manipulate things. She couldn't possibly want Susan to marry Ronald Merrick, but rather than say so she had grasped the opportunity offered by Aunt Fenny's foolish but well-meaning hint to make father believe that it might break my heart. It could even have been in her mind that in time if the idea of having Ronald Merrick in the family persisted he could be paired off with me because neither of us deserved any better.

'What I don't understand,' father said, 'is your having no idea how the land lay. From Susan's point of view.'

'Did mother?'

'No. But sisters share confidences, surely. You've been very close to her. I know that. At least I know what your Aunt Fenny says.'

'What does Aunt Fenny say?'

'If it hadn't been for you Susan would have had a complete breakdown.'

'She had a complete breakdown, daddy.'

'I meant, might have had to be put somewhere.'

'She was put somewhere.'

'But only in the nursing home, here.'

'In a room with barred windows. They thought she might hurt herself. They were afraid of violence. She'd put the baby at risk. Hasn't mother told you that?'

After a while he said, 'I suppose I've been told just as much as it's thought I can take in. Fair enough. Anyway, that's all over, isn't it? She's quite better now, surely. And quite capable of weighing things up and making a decision she'd have no reason to expect to regret?'

'What does that mean? That she's decided?'

'Yes, I think she has.'

'You've actually discussed it with her?'

'Yes.'

'Did *Susan* say I might be upset?'

'She seemed to think you were expecting it. She was surprised her mother wasn't. She thought it must have been obvious to everyone for a long time that if she married again it would be to Ronald. She's given it a lot of thought, you know. She said she couldn't expect to fall in love more than once in her life, but she does respect him and she knows she's got to think of the boy's future. She assured me there wasn't any element of pity or gratitude in her decision – I mean gratitude to Ronald for what he tried to do to save Teddie. And she's also not blind to the fact that his disabilities make his future career a bit chancy. All in all, I was rather impressed by the way she's thought it all out.'

'Was mother impressed?'

'Your mother was chiefly concerned about the effect it might have on you.'

'She raised no objections on her own account? She hasn't gone so far as to say she doesn't want Ronald in the family?'

I could have phrased that better. Again he regarded me seriously, still not entirely convinced that I was being frank about my own interests in the matter. But I let it go at that. I had to become used to the idea that I no longer had responsibilities. It was no business of mine whom Susan married. He had much the same thought, apparently. He said, 'Well when you come down to it Susan's free to marry whoever she likes. It would be nice if we all liked him too. Your mother hasn't actually said she doesn't. Being the mother she's obviously not too happy about one of her daughters marrying a partially disabled man. Come to that neither am I. It *is* a liability. He's very conscious of it himself. If for any reason you think he and Susan have been over-secretive, do take the disability into account. A girl's got to think pretty hard before she commits herself in a case like this. Think it out on her own. So does the man.'

'He's ten years older than Su, at least.'

'It's not much.'

'Why hasn't he married before? Have you asked yourself that?'

'My dear, what's that supposed to mean?'

'It's not supposed to mean anything. It's just a question.'

Eventually father said, 'I don't see anything in particular to question. I'll admit he's probably been keen to make the sort of marriage that, well, he could congratulate himself on making, but I see nothing wrong in that. Good luck to him. Why not? Senior police appointment, the guts to pester his department for a wartime commission, a DSO. It's not a meagre record, not as though he's bringing nothing worth while. I suppose you can say India's made him what he is, but after all isn't it India that's given *us* whatever distinction we have? Without India, I wonder what we'd have been? Lawyers like my grandfather? Merchants like his father? And on the Muir side – Scottish crofters? A long way back, but not all that long way. It's only a difference in timing. India's always been an opportunity for quite ordinary English people – it's given us the chance to live and work like, well, a ruling class that few of us could really claim to belong to.'

'It's no longer an opportunity.'

'That's hardly Ronald's fault.'

'I didn't mean it that way. I meant it's no longer any use looking at Susan's future from that angle. It's all finished. She ought to go home. Ronald's the kind of man who'll never let her. He's worked too hard to get here. It would be different if they were in love. But they're not. They can't be. I don't believe he's capable of feeling that for anybody.'

My father leant back, folded his arms.

'It's not his first proposal, though, is it?'

'Isn't it?'

'Didn't you know?'

'Know what?'

'That he was very fond of the girl in that wretched case that caused him so much trouble.'

Again I stared at him. I could tell from his expression that he was still ready to believe that any reference to Ronald and another woman hurt me. 'Daphne Manners? Ronald told you he was very fond of Daphne Manners? Fond enough to propose to her?'

'Yes. He did.'

'It's not the impression he originally gave me. All he said was that he once thought he liked her but that he went off her pretty quickly when he realized she wasn't sound.'

'Sound?'

'He may not have said sound. It's what he meant. Not sound. Meaning bluntly too friendly with Indians.'

1381

'He told me he proposed marriage to her. I don't see it as a thing a man would invent.'

'And I don't see it as a thing a man would talk about. Why did he?'

'I suppose I asked him. I don't mean directly. It just came up. We were discussing the case. Talking about his future. He said his Inspector-General had supported him but he wasn't sure what the long-term effects would be on his career as a whole. He was very frank.'

'He thinks he made a mistake?'

'No. I didn't get that impression. Rather the reverse. But I believe it's often worried him that his feelings for the girl might have influenced him, made him act too hastily, not wrongly, just too hastily. Well, I don't wonder. Wretched case altogether. Wretched to talk about.' He hesitated. 'I'd really prefer not to.'

'All right, daddy, we won't talk about it. That doesn't mean we may not have to live with it, Susan especially, if people start pressing for inquiries into some of the things that were done at the time. But I mustn't say that, must I? The mere prospect might make you feel sorry for him. You should never feel sorry for Ronald.'

'I'd feel sorry for any man who was victimized.'

'Victimized, yes. So would I.'

I'd started to fold the paper in which the sandwiches had been packed. Noticing some still ungathered crumbs I unfolded it again, swept them in, and refolded. I had repaid him badly for the care and trouble he'd taken, for the love and affection he'd shown, making arrangements like these before telling me something he thought might upset me. I'd neither set his mind at rest nor, in the last few minutes, even spoken kindly to him.

'It was such a lovely breakfast,' I said. 'I'm sorry if I've spoilt it. I honestly didn't mean to. Now I suppose we ought to be getting back.'

'You haven't spoilt it. What is the time?'

'Eight-thirty.'

'Are you on duty again?'

'Yes, I'm afraid so.' I remembered the Government House bag, with stuff in for me from Nigel. I'd meant to get to the daftar quite early to round up Sergeant Baker to make sure I got the packages.

'What will you say to Susan?' father asked.

'Nothing. She won't ask my opinion. The thing has been for me to be there when she's wanted me to be there. To be there and go along with whatever she's decided to do. Oddly enough, I've been quite good at that. If marrying Ronald is her new interest she'll be all right so long as she's making plans and seeing everything in terms of the next step ahead.'

'If she stops seeing things like that, would you know?'

'Yes.'

'Sooner than your mother?'

'Probably.'

'Would you tell me?'

'If I'm here, daddy.'

'Might you not be?'

'I can't live at home indefinitely.'

'I do understand that. But – well, for a while. At least until after the wedding.'

'That might depend on when the wedding is.'

'I'd not imagined anything impulsive.' He felt for my hand again. 'Don't *you* be impulsive. What had you in mind?'

'Going home, really. I'd like to get myself a job of some kind. Aunt Julia would take me in for a bit, I expect.'

'Going home? But that's a long-term plan, surely?'

'I thought of going to Aunt Fenny in Bombay for a while. Then on from there when I've really decided. I can pay my own passage. Aunt Mabel left us each five hundred pounds of our own. Susan and me, I mean. And I've got a bit more.'

'That's your nest-egg. There's no question of forking out your own fare, if going home's really what you want. But I hope not yet. Not yet, Sarah. Give me a bit of time to enjoy my whole family.'

I felt the net closing in again. I said, 'Well the war's not quite over yet.'

'No, but if it is, try not to be in too much of a hurry or think me too selfish. It'll be easier for us all to make plans when we know what's to happen to me. The Trehearnes will be going after Christmas. It looks as if I'll take over. But there's just a chance of my getting the Area. Your mother's a bit restless, she'd really like a change of scene, but if we got the Area that would rather please her. Flagstaff House. All that goes with it. And it would probably see out my time.'

'You'd like it too, wouldn't you?'

'Yes, I would. As a young man I assumed I'd end up a general. Small chance of that now. I'd settle for brigadier. Or just full colonel doing Trehearne's job.'

'Then I'll cross my fingers, daddy.'

'Would it make any difference to your plans?'

'Flagstaff House?'

'You were practically born there. And, well, if it happens I'd be sorry to think of your missing it altogether. You've had your share of stale gingerbread. Opportunity for a bit of gilt. But perhaps I shouldn't have mentioned it. Raising hopes.'

He would never understand how little the idea of moving into Flagstaff House raised my hopes. And just then they needed raising. Looking at that oddly unfamiliar view of East Hill it seemed to me that once long ago I'd been marooned there and that now the flood had receded, receded so far that you would have to walk miles to find water and even then have to wade on, endlesssly, without coming to a depth sufficient to swim in.

For one moment I believed, perhaps illogically, my only hope of getting away lay in confessing to my father what had happened to me. I could say: Look, I'm no longer a virgin. I was bedded by one of those officers Uncle Arthur's paid to make enthusiastic about having a career in India, only this chap turned out only to be enthusiastic about what Uncle Arthur would call the wrong things, and I was left in the club, also the wrong one, like any tiresome little skivvy, but unlike her we were able to arrange to have it brought off, and boringly unconventional though I've always been from most people's point of view, I simply didn't have the nerve to walk round pregnant and unmarried in Pankot. I know I'm not by a long chalk the first colonel's daughter to wander down the primrose path, but the catch is that I would never marry a man without first telling him what had happened, which mother knows. I made it clear to Aunt Fenny and if Aunt Fenny's run to form she's obviously told mother that I'd never marry under false pretences. Mother's probably guessed it anyway. And she doesn't really mind because it would go against her patrician scale of values to let me marry a man she really approved of and she thinks the ones she'd approve of are the ones who'd turn tail once they knew. So she's written me off. You'd better too.'

I glanced at him, and then, summoning the nerve, I began to tell him. I got as far as 'Look –' and then, after a second or two, departing from script, 'There's something I want you to know, something I must tell you,' but I got no further because he suddenly grabbed my hand and, not looking at me, said, 'No,' quite sharply, and then repeated it more gently.

'No. Nothing to tell me. Better be off.'

Still without looking he let go of my hand; briefly but quite strongly put his arm round me and then let go altogether and stood up and shouted something to the boys who scrambled up and ran round to get the horses. Then he went to the head of the steps and down them. He was calling something to me, pointing, perhaps at the fir tree high up on East Hill which his better-trained eye had sighted; but half-keeping his back to me, giving me time to let the reason for his reaction sink in.

He knew about the pregnancy and the abortion. Fenny or my mother had told him. Fenny probably; perhaps only hinting at a cause of unhappiness which my mother had more coldly identified. I went to the head of the steps, pretended to look where he was pointing, shading my eyes.

The boys brought the horses. Ashok helped me to mount. When he'd done so I thanked him and led off without waiting for father, heading down the stony track. Half-way down my horse began to miss his footing. The effort of keeping control, slight as it was, seemed immense; the last shameful straw. By the time I reached the road I couldn't see clearly. I waited until he came up. We could go one of two ways. He chose the shorter, and I fell in behind him. But presently he moved over to his right, waited until I was level and, apart from having to drop back a couple of times when a vehicle went by, stayed silently abreast of me until we reached home.

*

Susan was in the bathroom which meant I didn't have to talk to her. I changed quickly into uniform and to avoid seeing anyone set off for the daftar without even washing the smell of horse off my hands. Momentarily I'd forgotten the reason for wanting to be early on duty, but recalled it when the tonga approached the spot where Barbie's accident had been, the spot Clarissa Peplow once pointed out to me, where after careering down Club Road out of control the tonga had overturned, spilling them all into the ditch. From this point Barbie had walked, mud- and blood-stained, presumably refusing assistance from passers-by, making for the rectory bungalow into which she strode, calling for a spade and announcing that she had seen the Devil. The spade was for resurrecting Mabel. The devil was Ronald Merrick.

Rose Cottage had been shut. Mother, Susan, the baby and ayah had gone down to Calcutta to join Fenny and me after our holiday in Darjeeling, a reunion intended to maintain the illusion that everything was well with everybody. In the family's absence Mahmoud had discovered the trunk in the mali's shed and complained about it to the man mother had asked to keep an eye on things – Kevin Coley. And Kevin had gone down to the rectory to ask Barbie to remove it.

According to Clarissa, Barbie didn't mind. When she went up to the cottage to collect the trunk she found a stranger there. Ronald. He'd come up to the Pankot hospital to have the artificial hand fitted and had called at the cottage to see us. According to Ronald he and Barbie sat and talked, mainly about her missionary friend, Edwina Crane, whom he'd known in Mayapore. She insisted on giving him the copy of the picture which she associated with Edwina. Then she asked him to supervise the loading and securing of the trunk in the back of the tonga. He said he'd advised her against it; it was too cumbersome, too heavy. But she wouldn't listen. He said she struck him as over-excited, in fact, he said, 'Exalted might be the better word.'

It was quite a while before I talked to Ronald about his meeting with Barbie. He had left Pankot before we returned from Calcutta. At that time I'd only met him twice. I'd not liked him. But the real animosity came later when he began to turn up in Pankot on the excuse of visiting the hospital, but in fact it seemed to me to attach himself to us. I realized that he was a very lonely man in the ordinary sense of the word and without my realizing quite how it happened I found myself more often in his company than seemed explainable. At the pictures, for instance, or eating out at the Chinese restaurant when it was inconvenient to entertain him at home (when Susan wasn't well, or had taken too much of her sedative). Going out with him when he was in Pankot, so far as I was concerned, was no more than a duty, one more duty to add to the many I'd got lumbered with or stupidly volunteered for and I assumed that this was understood by the family as a whole. What he assumed about it had been beyond me to work out. He knew I disliked him. Knowing he knew made me feel that we were all safe from him.

When we went to the Chinese restaurant he always ordered a particular table, the one in the window on the first floor (officers only) which looked out on to the bazaar, and which at least provided him with the view to which my silences too often forced him to give attention. I never felt that my being poor company upset him. We were at the Chinese restaurant when I first asked him to describe in detail his meeting with Barbie. I didn't tell him I'd just seen her, in the Samaritan in Ranpur, but I think he guessed. When he said, 'She struck me as being over-excited when she set off, in fact exalted might be the better word,' he studied me closely as if checking for the effect of that word exalted. The exaltation began (he said) when she opened the trunk to give him the picture and found a lace-shawl which she said didn't belong to her but which she thought Mabel's old servant Aziz must have put in the trunk when he temporarily had the key to it.

I knew which lace he meant, lace which Mabel had been given by her first husband's mother – lace like a web of butterflies, worked by a blind old French woman, some of which had been used for Susan's baby's christening, and some, years before, for my own. I had recognized it only a couple of days before at the Samaritan hospital, draped round Barbie's head and shoulders, stained brown with dried blood.

Ronald said, 'She put it on when she got into the tonga, like a bridal veil.'

The lace shawl, with its rusty stains, was among the packages that Nigel had been given by the Reverend Mother to hand over to me.

*

But of course there was nothing waiting for me at the daftar, nothing – Sergeant Baker told me – addressed to me in the overnight bag from Government House. I thought of ringing Nigel up but delayed doing so, finding an excuse not to do that until after five, because he would be busy, but in fact shirking it because the main reason for ringing him would be to tell him about Ronald and Susan and to try to coerce him into helping me to stop it; which seemed a bit unfair.

I remember sitting at the typewriter in the daftar, cutting a stencil from a holograph order written out by Major Smalley, and using so much red-sealer to obliterate mistakes that the wax paper began to look like a piece of the lace shawl Barbie had worn, seated at her window. She had on that occasion seemed to have found peace, the peace of absorption in a wholly demanding God, a God of love and wrath who had no connection with the messianic principles of Christian forgiveness, and it was like that I preferred to remember her, not – as at other times when I had visited her – unanchored, unweighted, withershins, attempting to communicate with the doomed world of inquiry and compromise.

When I was midway through the stencil the phone rang. The operator told me a Captain Rowan was on the line. It was as though I'd conjured him. I said, 'Nigel? I'm afraid there was nothing in the bag. Is that why you're ringing?'

'Partly,' he said. 'Actually I brought the stuff up with me.'

He explained the situation but I wasn't being very bright and it took me some time to understand that he was in Pankot, that he'd travelled up on the overnight train, was staying at the Summer Residence guest house and in the last few minutes had spoken to my mother on the phone and been given my Area HQ number and extension.

'Has she rung you at all?' he asked.

'No, yours is the first call I've had. Why?'

He said, 'In which case you probably won't know Ronald Merrick's here too. By chance I travelled up with him. He had our mutual friend Guy Perron in tow. Merrick's with your parents now. He's come to break some rather sad news to your father. A havildar from your father's regiment who was in the Frei Hind force in Germany committed suicide the other day. Merrick thought your father might be very upset. He wanted to break the news to him himself.'

'Yes. I see. I think he will be. Upset.'

'Merrick's now a half-colonel.'

'What?'

'He's been promoted to Lieutenant-Colonel. Did you know?'

'No, I didn't, Nigel. The other thing I didn't know was that he might also become my brother-in-law. Father told me this morning. He wants to marry Susan. And Susan wants to marry him.'

I may have got that wrong: the order in which things were said; but I plainly recollect then a very long silence. We were both trying to assimilate wholly unexpected bits of information: on my part, the poor havildar's death, Ronald's sudden and to me ominous presence in Pankot.

'What do you think of him now that you've met him?' I asked.

'He wasn't quite what I imagined.'

'How long are you here for? I'd love to see you. Is today possible, or is HE in control?'

'The Governor's not here. There's only a Mr Gopal. Actually your mother's just asked me to have dinner at Rose Cottage tonight. I'd like that but I'm not sure whether I can make it. I've got a thing to do for HE. I'm free once I've done it but I'm not sure when that will be. Could you lunch here?'

'You mean today?'

'Yes. Come up as soon as you like.'

I could do that now, I said; and did – leaving the wounded stencil in the machine and looking in on Major Smalley to make the excuse that I was feeling off-colour but hoped to be back in the afternoon.

*

A man came down the steps as the tonga pulled up in front of the guest house. I hadn't seen Nigel in mufti before and for a moment scarcely recognized him. A suit disguised some of the thinness which his uniform accentuated; he looked fitter, more relaxed, like a man released from some kind of duty which he'd found more and more difficult to do. We had never embraced. Just here, just now, an embrace would have seemed right, but we did as we'd done when parting in Ranpur; shook hands rather solemnly. He held my elbow as a token of support while we climbed the steps but at the top he let go. We went through to the rear verandah which had the view I knew best – across the lawns to the closed Summer Residence – although I couldn't recall just when I'd last seen it.

On a table between two white cane blue upholstered chairs were the several packages he'd brought up from the Samaritan. I thanked him but for the moment didn't want to deal with them or even look at them. He ordered drinks, offered me a cigarette. While I smoked he told me something about the special job he had to do in Pankot. For the moment, at least until he'd had some word from Mr Gopal, he was more or less a prisoner at the guest house, since he might have to make himself available at any moment. He doubted, though, that this would be earlier than the following day.

'So you might be able to come to dinner tonight?'

'Yes, it's very likely.'

'And you might be here for a day or two at least?'

'A day or two certainly.'

The drinks came. While he dealt with the steward I settled back in the cane chair considering how in two days Nigel and I might effectively collaborate to stop a marriage I was sure ought to be stopped. He could talk to my father. I would talk to Susan. The main problem was that Ronald was in Pankot too. So far I'd hardly taken in that fact and now that I did so and had time to consider the excuse Ronald had found to come up from Delhi, the havildar's death seemed like something he had invented to suit his own ends; so that then I began to wonder what it could be that Barbie's death had been invented for. My mind was racing, but I could feel my body settling into a posture of embattled indolence and could hear a voice warning me: Don't say too much. Go carefully.

I'm trying to reproduce for you an occasion of awful disorientation. Failing probably. God knows how one could succeed.

'Well when did all this happen?' he asked. 'Your sister and Ronald Merrick?'

'I wish I knew. She's never said anything to me. Not the slightest hint. But there it seems to be. According to father. I've not talked to Susan yet but father has. And apparently Ronald's talked to him.'

'Your sister is serious, then?'

'So father believes.'

'Does he approve?'

'Let's say he doesn't know Ronald well enough not to.'

'Nor well enough to give his consent immediately?'

'The drawback is, consent's not actually needed.'

'No. Of course. So you have the impression it may be more or less fixed?'

'If it is, I want to unfix it. I hoped you might help me.'

He said nothing. But his expression was kind. I went on: 'It's a lot to ask. But if there's anything you can do to help, I'd be very grateful.'

He didn't answer at once. Then he said it was difficult to see on what grounds he could. He didn't know Susan at all. He and I had talked about Ronald only in general terms. He added, 'Now that I've met him I can't say he's the kind of man I'd want to go out of my way to have much to do with. I suppose one has to assume some serious emotional involvement on your sister's part. One's instinct isn't much to go on, if it comes to thinking of interfering.'

'Is it only instinct, Nigel?'

He thought for several moments and then said, 'From the family's point of view I'd be concerned mainly about the possibility – I don't say probability – the possibility of his name cropping up in any future fuss the politicians make about officers suspected of exceeding their duty in nineteen forty-two. Of course, there's no need even to anticipate a fuss. But if there is a fuss, Merrick might be involved. Not that that would make the slightest difference to Susan, I imagine. Assuming a fondness. Nor to the family. But that's all I can offer – as a practical argument against. Perhaps your father should be warned. About the possibility.'

'I've already warned him. But it didn't have much effect because Ronald's already discussed that aspect of things with him. I was hoping you might dot a few i's and cross a few t's.'

He frowned, not at me but at his glass. He said, 'Well there's also the history of persecution, isn't there, but you know more about that than I do. If it's resumed, your sister could be hurt by it.'

'I've told father about the persecution, but I think it just makes him feel sorry for the man. And Ronald naturally has been very frank about the effect the Manners case could have on his career. It's part of his technique. What I meant was being able to tell father something I don't know. But which you might know. Something on a confidential file, for instance? I may be wrong, but whenever we've talked about Ronald you've always left me with the idea that you know far more than could be expected of a man who'd never met him. So. A file?'

After a while Nigel said, 'I should think all a file would tell you about Colonel Merrick is that he left the comparative safety of the police for active service in the army and was decorated with the Distinguished Service Order, since when there has been a history of regular promotion, no doubt well-deserved.'

'In which case there would be nothing much to fear from a political fuss later, would there, if the files show him as such a paragon?'

Hearing the sharp edge to my voice I suddenly pictured what perhaps I looked like – a hard-bitten little memsahib interfering in other people's lives to stop herself shrieking with the boredom and frustration of her own – or (and perhaps Nigel wondered about this too) trying to stop a marriage because she coveted the man for herself, in spite of all she had ever said to the contrary about her attitude to him.

'I'm sorry, Nigel, I shouldn't try to involve you. It's not your problem. I'd better ring home and tell them I won't be back for lunch. Then I'll go through this stuff of poor Barbie's.'

He accompanied me inside, showed me where a telephone was and a bedroom-bathroom suite that I could use, should I want to; in fact, he said, the phone could be switched through to the one in the bedroom if I preferred that. The steward could get the number. I said that might be best and went into the bedroom, sat on the bed, waiting. The phone rang. Mother was at the other end. She said, 'Where are you?' I told her.

'Good,' she said. Apparently she had rung the daftar and had been expecting me to arrive at any moment, "off-colour". She had rung to tell me Nigel Rowan was in Pankot and that if he got in touch I should do my best to persuade him to accept the invitation to dinner at Rose Cottage. She added, 'Presumably you know by now who else is here.'

'Yes. Nigel told me. I'm sorry about the havildar. Is daddy very upset?'

'Not too upset not to have invited Ronald Merrick to dinner this evening. I don't want just a family dinner. I want Captain Rowan here too.'

'He'll come if he can.'

'I want you to make sure he does. I must have another man at the table.'

'If you want to make sure you'd better invite someone else. Nigel's not definitely free. There's always Edgar Drew.'

'I said man, not boy. And a man of our own sort.'

'Then ask Ronald to bring Guy Perron. I gather he's brought him up to Pankot.'

'So we've all gathered. We've all been having to admire the invisible feather in Colonel Merrick's cap. Colonel! But you can hardly ask a colonel to bring his sergeant along even if there was a chance of his agreeing to. Which in this case there isn't. What a pity the ranks aren't the other way round. I want Captain Rowan.'

'I can't promise.'

'I'm asking you to do so. I'm saying that the least you can do for me is to guarantee he'll be here.'

'The least?'

'The least. He sounds to me the most presentable man you've ever bothered to get to know. In the circumstances, in *all* the circumstances, I should prefer it if you brought him into the open and remembered that this isn't Calcutta, but Pankot.'

I said, very quietly, 'Why do you want that, mother? So that Susan can take one look at him and decided he's for her? I suppose that would solve everything from your point of view.'

'Not quite everything,' mother said. She put the phone down. A meaningless retort; the kind someone is stung into making out of sheer exasperation. I went into the bathroom so that I could calm down and stop shaking. I heard the telephone ringing again in the bedroom but before I could reach it – thinking it was mother calling back to apologize – it stopped, presumably because the call had been taken elsewhere. Going through into the living-room I found Nigel taking the receiver from the steward. I indicated that I would go out to the terrace and did so. The steward followed and asked if I would have another drink. While waiting for it I stood by the balustrade and smoked and then, remembering the packages on the table, decided I might as well look at some of them. The first and bulkiest (containing something solid, like a book, and something soft) was marked: *In the Event of my Death: Dear Sarah.*

Inside I found the butterfly lace which I hastily put down. The solid object was a book of Emerson's essays. I remembered her fondness for them. A quick flip through the pages showed that many of the passages were underlined. I read several of these but found them tiresome and self-righteous. I put the lace back in the wrapping and left the book on the table. The other package, an envelope, contained several smaller envelopes, variously marked: To Sarah: Not to be Opened Before My Death. Private and Personal: To Colonel Layton's daughter. To the Girl who Visits me. To the Girl with the fair helmet of Hair. To Whom it Might Concern. To Gillian Waller from a Friend.

Every glance – I found it too painful to give much more just then – and subsequent study showed heart-breakingly little except her continuing concern over the question of Mabel's grave – evoked images of her distraction and how, as time went on, she seemed not to have recognized me. In the end she had even given me another name, Gillian Waller. It rang a bell, but I couldn't remember why.

I stuffed the envelopes into my shoulder-bag and managed to push the lace in too. I didn't want the lace for one particular reason. For the same reason I couldn't throw it away. There remained the book. I picked it up again and was glancing through it when Nigel came out.

He said, 'Good, that's settled.' He looked pleased. 'Tomorrow. Probably in the evening.'

'Which leaves you free for tonight?'

'Yes.'

'You know Ronald Merrick's invited too?'

'I wasn't sure.'

'I'll make your excuses if that's what you'd prefer.'

'Would you prefer to dine here?'

'I think that's ruled out, Nigel. I'm not inventive enough to think of an excuse that would cover both of us.'

'In which case I'll come to Rose Cottage. Have the other half before we go into lunch.'

'I'm having the other half.'

'Well, have the next.'

'No, this is fine. I've a stencil to finish this afternoon. But you're one drink behind. You'd better catch up.'

He gave an order to the steward; then noticing that the packages had gone from the table leaving an unidentified book in their place he said, 'Mystery cleared up?'

'I don't think there was much of a mystery after all but I haven't looked through everything yet. I really am grateful though. Are you keen on Emerson?'

'I don't know him I'm afraid. Guy Perron's the Emerson expert. He was quoting him last night.'

'Oh? Barbara Batchelor was an expert too I should think, judging by the homework she seems to have done on him. I thought you might like to keep the book as a reminder of a pretty odd sort of mission.'

'I shan't need reminding. If you don't want it why not give it to Guy? It might cheer him up.'

'Is he very down-in-the-mouth?'

'I shouldn't say that. Fighting mad might be nearer the mark. He told me he has a scheme to wangle his repatriation. But I never did know when Guy was being serious.'

'I should say he's serious when it's necessary. For instance in Bombay he saved a man from drowning himself in the bath.'

'But not – I gathered – from chucking himself out of a hospital window later and breaking his neck. So Guy said.'

'I didn't know that. Poor Captain Purvis.'

I felt suddenly like laughing. Such a useless, farcical death.

Nigel had been leafing through the book. 'Here it is. "Society is a wave." One of Miss Batchelor's favourite passages too if the markings are anything to go by.' He handed the book back to me. I read the passage. It meant nothing to me. I put the book on the table.

'I think Sergeant Perron should have it if you don't want it, although a sermon on self-reliance is hardly what he needs. Will you be seeing him?'

'I'm not sure. I've given him this number to ring. He didn't know where he'd be billeted. Poor Guy. Two suicides in one week and an order attaching him to Ronald Merrick's department. Incidentally, coming up last night he told me you'd met another old Chillingburian, Jimmy Clark, or Clark-Without as we called him.'

'Yes, that's right.'

'Where was this?'

'In Calcutta.'

'What was he doing there?'

'Oh, passing through on his way to Kandy, looking up old acquaintances, including Uncle Arthur and Aunt Fenny. He'd been on one of Uncle Arthur's courses and was quite the blue-eyed boy.'

'Was that the only time you met him?'

'Yes, he flew to Kandy next day to take up some glamorous sounding appointment. Or perhaps he was just swanning around.'

'Probably. What did you make of him?'

'I thought he talked a lot of sense. He had us all sized up pretty well.'

'Us?'

'People like us. English people in India. Except that he didn't think we were really English any more. He said we got left behind. Preserved in some kind of perpetual Edwardian sunlight.'

Nigel laughed. 'Let's eat,' he said.

*

'Game pie of a kind,' he pointed out. 'And champagne also of a kind. Compliments of Government House. It came up in the ice-box.'

'Who are they meant for, though? Not me. Could it be the elusive congressman, Mr Kasim?'

'No, for me, I think, from HE. This is my last assignment for him. They're taking me back into the political.'

'When? When are you going?'

'I'm probably leaving Ranpur some time next week.'

'It's what you wanted.'

'Yes, it is.'

'Where will you go? Kotala?'

'I shouldn't think Kotala.'

'What's your ambition? The Residency at Hyderabad?'

'Too late for that. I'd need another ten or fifteen years.'

'Then why go on? Why not just get out?'

'I thought we talked about that when we first met over Count Bronowsky's champagne. I thought you said nothing was an excuse for working at half-pressure, or standing back from a job while it's still there to be done.'

'Did I say that?'

'Yes.'

'And you've remembered. It doesn't sound like me at all.'

'I thought it did. Anyway. It's what you said.'

'I can't have been thinking straight.'

'Have some more game pie.'

'I can't even get through this.'

Suddenly I felt nauseated. Irregularity was one of my problems these days, so I was usually prepared; and it was better than the punctual but protracted miseries I'd once endured. I murmured an excuse, got up and went back to the guest bathroom and scrabbled in my crammed shoulder-bag for what I needed; panicking when for a moment I couldn't find it among all the things from Barbie's room at the Samaritan. But once I'd uncovered it the sensation of sickness seemed to change its nature. I found myself shivering, as if from a slight fever. But it wasn't fever, it was delayed shock, a physical response to the emotional strain of the ride home from the Dak bungalow after the realization that either my mother or Aunt Fenny had told father about the abortion in Calcutta. It had been for me to tell him; no one else. I seemed to have his forgiveness. If I wanted anything it was understanding.

Plugging myself against the unseasonable but likely menstrual flow I found myself weeping as I'd never done before, not even at that time Aunt Fenny took me in her arms in the hospital room and warned me that mother would never refer to what had happened because for her it hadn't, and that anything I wanted to get over should be got over there and then.

To muffle the sound of my crying I ran the taps hard, and bathed my face. The cold water was like a series of slaps. I stared at my ruined self, hating every pore, every line, every bone. But, ruined or not, as a face it was indestructible. A Layton more than a Muir face. Built to last.

The thought was not new, and thinking it again I recalled the last time I'd thought it: in the garden of Rose Cottage, bending my head to take the scent of a red rose. That was all. The garden. The rose. Barbie and I. And this conviction of being built to survive. But I couldn't recall the context. It might have been before or after Mabel's death.

I began to repair my Layton face, doing it with care and deliberation as if the end-result had to represent my conscious projection of myself into a particular future. And then the context came back: the context of the rose and Barbie and of Gillian Waller. It had been before Mabel's death, when Susan was still pregnant. Who is Gillian Waller? Barbie had asked me. We were walking in the garden, the garden as it had been before the time of the tennis court. Who is Gillian Waller? I don't know, I'd said. Why? And unwittingly Barbie disclosed that at night sometimes she went into Mabel's room, took off her spectacles, put away the book she'd fallen asleep over, tucked her up and turned off the light, and then waited until she could be sure the sleep hadn't been interrupted. In this sleep, this half-sleep, Mabel had sometimes muttered to herself, as old people do. Gillian Waller, she had said. So it sounded. So: Who was Gillian Waller? 'I'm afraid to ask,' Barbie explained. 'I hate to seem to pry. She's such a self-contained person. There are people like that. She's one. Is Susan more cheerful?'

Not cheerful, I said. Holding on.

I could feel Barbie's hand on my arm as she said, 'To what? Would you say she's dangerously withdrawn?'

I leant over the basin, stared at the white porcelain, smelt the rose. 'We endure,' I said. 'We're built for it. In a strange way we're built for it.' But at this point the context changed, led me to another similar occasion when Barbie and I were in the garden and she grasped my arm again and said, 'They say the child should have a father. I'd encourage it if I were you. If she doesn't marry again you'll never get away. Some people are made to live and others are made to help them. If you stay you'll end up like that, like me.'

*

'Are you all right, Sarah?' Nigel called from the bedroom.

'Yes, thank you,' I called back.

I waited until I heard the click made by the bedroom door as he went back into the main living-room. Then I considered my reflection very seriously and understood, slowly, the full irony of the situation. I said to my reflection: 'There goes a man I might have been happy with and who up to the time he rang me at the daftar and I told him about Susan and Ronald probably thought he could be happy with me.'

I completed the mask, exaggerating the lipstick and, before opening the bathroom door, smiled, to prepare for the entrance.

But I did not have to enter. I had entered already, long ago.

The Circuit House

I

The only light entering the compartment came from one of the arc-lamps that lit the siding, but a dim light was on in the corridor and when the door slid open he saw that it was Ahmed, not Hosain, who had come to wake him.

'It's time, father.'

'Has Mr Mehboob arrived?'

'Yes, half-an-hour ago. But Hosain said you hadn't bothered to go to bed and were only dozing, so I left you until the last moment.'

'Even on stationary trains I don't sleep. Just for me we could all have come by car and not bothered with this.' He wound his scarf round his neck and put on his cap. 'How far is the Circuit House? I've forgotten.'

'About half-an-hour's drive.'

'So near?' On that previous occasion, coming from the Circuit House, the journey seemed endless. But that had been a journey with a joyful reunion, not a painful one, at the end, and they had driven all the way to the station at Mirat, not this station. He made a mental note: I am not fully awake – guard against these muddles.

Outside in the carpeted corridor Hosain was waiting and took the briefcase from him, to relieve him both of the weight and of the supposed indignity of having to carry anything himself. Unencumbered he went to the door. The last time he got off a railway coach at this particular siding it had been with difficulty, climbing down backwards because there was no platform, the distance between the level of the coach floor and the level of the cinder-yard great, the steps perpendicular. He had had to beg help with his luggage from one of the conducting officers. That was three years ago, almost to the day. 'Where is this?' he had asked. The receiving officer had said, 'Premanagar'. Which meant they were imprisoning him in the fort. After that he had had to climb unassisted into the back of a police truck. He had barked his shins. But this morning – for it was nearly five o'clock – there were special steps already in position and two railway employees to steady them and him against every eventuality.

Mr Mehboob came fussily across the dimly lit and deserted cinder-yard to greet him and conduct him to the waiting limousine, whose driver held the door open. *Everything has meaning for you, Gaffur*, he quoted silently to himself, *the petal's fall, the change of seasons.*

The railway coach and the limousine both belonged to the Nawab. But this was the last time he would find himself in his kinsman's and Count Bronowsky's debt; or very nearly the last. When what had to be done at the Circuit House had been done he would return to the coach, which was filled with all the accumulated stuff of his life under restriction at Nanoora, and travel on by rail to Ranpur to reoccupy his home permanently. The limousine would return to Mirat. Mehboob had been right. There would have been no point in coming from Nanoora to Premanagar by car when the coach had to come anyway, would leave Nanoora earlier, and offer him a chance to sleep during the hours it was parked in the siding.

The secretary followed him into the Daimler and settled ponderously beside him on the softly cushioned back seat. He had wanted Ahmed beside him. But Mehboob was jealous of his own prerogatives. As a secretary he wasn't a patch on poor old Mahsood and as a man Mr Kasim found him irritatingly like an English caricature of an Indian – possessive towards people with power, arrogant to those with none. Even his physical characteristics now fitted him for the part he played with such breathless intensity. His plumpness was only just short of obesity. His nickname was Booby or Booby-Sahib – a kindly enough invention of Mahsood's (who towards the end when he was losing his grip but refusing to let go was always saying, 'I will ask Booby. I will tell Booby') but which was now used behind Booby's back and sometimes even to his face with less charitable intention. As Mahsood's assistant Booby's liabilities had been less apparent than his assets, chief among which was what had seemed an unrivalled knowledge of party political machinery acquired at grass-root level on the local sub-committees and in the corridors of the provincial legislative assembly. He had first come to Kasim's notice in 1937 as the backroom man largely responsible for the election campaign that had sent to the assembly another Muslim Congressman, Fariqua Hamidullah Khan. Khan had defeated a Muslim Leaguist whom the League had thought would walk away with the seat – a lean hawk of a man whose expression in defeat had been a sight to see.

In those days Mehboob had been lean too. Kasim had met him in old Hamidullah Khan's house on the painful occasion when he had had to tell the old war-horse that his name wouldn't be going forward to the Governor as a candidate for a portfolio in the first Congress Ministry in Ranpur. He had expected to be given the department of education and there were times, subsequently, when Kasim regretted not having given the old man his chance. A Muslim minister for education might have been quicker (even a man as slowed up by age, vicissitudes and disappointments as Hamidullah Khan) to pounce on or defy the hard-line Hindus who had made it compulsory in the district schools to salute the Congress flag, sing songs which had a Hindu rather than an Indian national connotation, and to teach history in a religious rather than a political context. It had been this more than anything throughout the country that had alerted the Muslims to the dangers of a Hindu-*raj* succeeding a British-*raj* and which had provided Jinnah with the kind of political ammunition he'd been so short of. But Kasim hadn't given Hamidullah Khan his chance and in July 1942 the old man died while on a visit to his ancestral home near Rawalpindi. The next month Kasim was imprisoned in the fort at Premanagar. Released in 1944 to the protective custody of the Nawab, joined by his wife, and presently by old Mahsood, he had looked at his ageing secretary and seen the unmistakable signs of deterioration. 'You need a young assistant,' he had said. 'Perhaps so, Mac-Sahib.' And a day or two later Mahsood had come to him. 'There is a man, poor young Mehboob who got Hamidullah Khan into the assembly. Doing nothing since Khan Sahib died. Like Othello. Occupation gone.' 'Get him,' Kasim had said, recalling the lean young man.

And here he was, Mehboob, Booby, Booby-Sahib, sitting beside him, weighing the Daimler down at the left-hand side.

'Were there any letters after I left?' Mr Kasim asked, turning his attention from the window.

'I have them here,' Mr Mehboob said. 'Three are marked personal so I have not opened them. One of them is from Bapu. Another from your daughter, Mrs Hydyatullah.'

'And the third?'

'From our indefatigable suppliant, Pandit Baba Sahib.'

'You could have looked at that. After all CID will already have done so.'

The door on Mehboob's side opened. Ahmed leaned in.

'Everything is ready,' he said.

'Then come along.'

'I'm going in the escort vehicle.'

'You would be more comfortable here.'

'It's all arranged. An alteration would create confusion.'

Kasim nodded. Ahmed shut the door. The driver got in. Presently the car moved. Kasim closed his eyes and didn't respond when Mehboob said, 'Premanagar very depressed area. Here too much erosion, too much poverty, no industry. Government has just abandoned it as hopeless. Here presently we shall have communists, isn't it? Everyone very bolshie. Why else are they giving us an armed escort?'

Kasim didn't answer. It was mainly Mehboob's fault that Ahmed had elected to go in the other vehicle. His younger son and his new secretary had never pulled on well together. Mehboob despised Ahmed for having no political sense; Ahmed was simply indifferent to Mehboob. He was indifferent to everybody. He lived his own life. He was dutiful when it was necessary to be dutiful. But there was no affection. He had seemed to love only his mother. When she died he had acted as if her death need not have happened, and as if he blamed his father for the fact that she died without having seen Sayed again.

'Give me my daughter's letter, then,' he told Mehboob.

'Light! Light!' Mehboob instructed the driver.

'No, no, no light. Just give me the letter. I'll read it later.'

Mehboob opened his own briefcase, got out some envelopes, leaned forward, putting his face close to them, and eventually handed one to him.

'Did you notice the post-mark?'

'Yes, it is from Lahore.'

'Good. Then she is back from Srinagar.'

'Also I noticed it had been opened. You can always tell.'

'And Bapu's?'

'This too.'

'Achchha.'

He held the letter at an angle to the window getting what light he could to confirm his daughter's handwriting. Politically it didn't bother him that the Lahore Government had intercepted, opened and read the letter and reported its contents to Delhi. Any letter from his daughter could only strengthen the impression Government had that he was being tempted over to the League. Her husband, Hydyatullah, was now an ardent Leaguist and separatist. She had become one too and a potentially staunch supporter of the INA, therefore of Sayed. But privately Kasim was outraged to think that strangers had read the letter. He had never got used to the idea that his personal life was also government property. He folded the letter carefully so that it would fit neatly into the breast pocket of his coat.

'Did anything else of interest happen after I left Nanoora?'

'Government House in Ranpur rang confirming your appointment tomorrow, but I think really to make sure that you had left for Premanagar. Also there was a call from *The Statesman's* man in Ranpur. He asked if it was true that you were now coming back to Ranpur. I told him that if he was exercising patience the truth or otherwise of this rumour would be revealed to him in due course.'

'You are beginning to talk like Bapu. Was he content with this evasive reply?'

'He wasn't pursuing it further at the moment. He said his paper was very much anxious to obtain an exclusive interview. I said exclusive interviews had never been the Minister's policy.'

'Did he comment on your using that title?'

'No. He called you Minister himself, and was seeking favours. He said, "Has the Minister said anything about the Viceroy's broadcast announcing elections?" I said obviously the Minister has said things about it, all India is saying things and also wondering why really the Viceroy has now flown back to London. So he switched subject. He said, "What is Minister's view of the reports of the death in an air crash of Subhas Chandra Bose?" '

'What did you say?'

'I said the Minister had read these reports and assumed that they were probably correct.'

'And his response?'

'His response was that not everybody assumed this. But he did not pursue it. He was anxious to maintain cordiality and the prospects of an exclusive interview when you get back to Ranpur.'

After a while Kasim said, 'He did not mention Sayed?'

'No, Minister. He did not mention him but of course was thinking and wondering. The newspapers are still saying nothing for the moment.'

When Booby called him Minister to his face he always felt himself being flattered in a way that amounted to a rebuke.

*

Light was just beginning to come when they reached the Circuit House. Deliberately he kept his eyes lowered so that he would not inadvertently catch a glimpse of the fort. The compound and the Circuit House itself seemed smaller than he remembered them. A year – nearly fifteen months ago – after imprisonment in the fort the whole landscape and everything in it had looked immense. When the car stopped he said, 'I wish to see no one for some time. Ask Ahmed to come and collect me when it is confirmed that there is a room for me to go to and be alone. Then I shall wish to bathe and have breakfast.'

'All that is arranged, Minister. No, no, no, no, no! Wait! Wait!'

Someone had opened the door on Mehboob's side. The door shut again. In the compound Mr Kasim could see figures of men, waiting, one of them with a slung rifle. The sight of the man with the rifle unnerved him. The presence of such a man suggested that they had already brought Sayed from the fort.

'Something is wrong,' he began.

'Nothing is wrong, Minister. All arrangements have been checked, double-checked. It is simply that the British always like to put on a show. Here is Ahmed now.'

Mehboob lowered the window and said, 'Your father is waiting here. Tell them to show you the room and tell them that the Minister will see no one for some time, isn't it? Also that all these people should disperse. It is like a bloody circus.'

'Ahmed –' Kasim said, but Mehboob held up a hand.

'Your father is not wanting anybody. I am waiting here with him until you tell us everything is as he wishes. Private room and no damned reception committee or all that nonsense.'

Ahmed went. Mehboob rolled the window back up and began to complain about the English weakness for making a *tamasha* of everything. 'Take all this show away from them and what is left? Look at all these people milling around in the name of security.'

But, Kasim thought, *tamasha* was precisely what the British could most easily dispense with; and presently when the shadowy figures in the compound had mostly disappeared and the man with the rifle had made himself scarce, going down towards the culvert-entrance, when the compound was quiet, unpopulated, he felt more than ever the weight of the *raj's* authority; and, feeling it, allowed himself to focus clearly on the dawn-image of the fort – on the place, rather, where the silhouette should be, some miles distant but elevated commandingly above the plain on a hill.

He did not at first identify it. And then did, and stared, fascinated by the evidence of its relatively diminutive proportions. It had originally been a Rajput fort. The Muslims had conquered it. It was they who had built the mosque and the zenana house in the inner courtyard where Kasim had spent his imprisonment. The Mahrattas had invested it. The British had acquired it. So much history in so insignificant a monument? Insignificant, that was to say, in relation to the vast stretches of the Indian plain.

II

Everything has meaning for you, Gaffur: the petal's fall, the change of seasons. New clothes to celebrate the Ĩd.

The regard of princes.

Rocks. These are not impediments. All water flows towards uneasy distances. Life also –

He had bathed and shaved. He had prayed. He had had a light breakfast. Now he had read for the planned ten minutes from the works of Gaffur. He put the book away, retained his spectacles and took his daughter's letter from the table where he had placed it ready. It was dated August 20, six days ago.

'We reached home yesterday and found your letter which of course had been opened. Guzzy suggests that we should send all our letters unsealed to save them this bother but I said why should we save them bother? If they want to pry into our private affairs let them go to whatever trouble is necessary. Tomorrow we are having a party to listen to Wavell on the radio which I expect will be the usual guff, everyone knows he is going to announce elections. Guzzy says he has no alternative but that the results will surprise him and force him to recognize the reality of the problems that divide the country. We were glad to get away from Kashmir. On vj day people excelled themselves. The place was packed with British and Americans and the drunkenness and vulgarity had to be seen to be believed. I am sorry, daddy, that we could not break off to go down to Pankot. Poor old Mahsoodi. I cried all night after getting your telegram (I hope you got mine? Your letter does not say).

'Poor Sayed has at last been allowed to answer my last letter to him but of course it tells me nothing that is necessary to hear. He writes mostly of childhood recollections. Please, daddy, write to him. He says little but I know he is hurt never to have heard from you and blames Government since this is the only explanation he can find as a dutiful and loving son much devoted to his father. He asks me to tell you to thank Ahmed for his last note. Soon I hope you will write and tell me you are back home for good in Ranpur. Then perhaps Guzzy and I can visit you and bring the children. I never liked coming to Nanoora since I knew you didn't like being there but stuck it out. Also it was bad having to get permission, even when darling mummy was so ill. Guzzy and I were much amused by the picture in the newspaper of the Governor's stonelaying ceremony in Ranpur. You looked very bored and distinguished, as Guzzy said "Like a man keeping his own counsel." I was very proud. In pictures so many people just look like hangers on. Your loving daughter.'

He refolded the letter and returned it to its envelope, opened his briefcase and put the envelope inside, then the book of Gaffur's poems, then his Astrakhan cap. From the briefcase he took the white Congress cap. In the old days he had been criticized for wearing it. It had not been worn for months. It was necessary to wear it now. He placed it on his head. The crown of thorns. It was nearly eight o'clock. At eight, promptly, Mehboob knocked and came in and stood arrested. Mehboob had never seen him wearing the cap, except presumably years ago before they were closely associated.

'It is eight o'clock, Minister,' Booby said. 'They are here.'

'And Sayed?'

'I have not seen Sayed, but they assure me he is here. He is probably still in the compound.'

'Has he breakfasted?'

'I will go and ask, Minister.'

'Please! Do not call me that. And by all means go and ask. It should not be necessary but do it now. You should think of these things. You should anticipate my questions. They have probably pulled him from his bed and brought him here without even asking him if he wants a cup of tea.'

'I will find out –'

'Yes, yes! Find out! I will see nobody until I am assured he has breakfasted. It should all have been thought of.'

Mehboob went. Kasim, after a moment, covered his face with his hands and whispered: 'Glory be to You who made Your servant go by night from the Sacred Mosque to the Farther mosque. Praise be to Allah who has never begotten a son, who has no partner in His Kingdom, who needs none to defend Him from humiliation.'

*

When Mehboob came back his pale copper-coloured face was flushed. 'I am unable to find out whether Sayed has breakfasted,' he announced.

'What has made you so angry?'

'It is impossible dealing with such people. They cannot answer even civil questions. They treat everybody like dirt.'

'Who are they?'

'Two English subalterns wearing revolvers. They are in the court-room, feet on the table and smirking and hardly bothering to reply.'

1405

'Only these two?'

'There are also the people who were here when we arrived, a police inspector and another young Englishman who is assistant to the Divisional Commissioner. But they are only local, in charge of the general arrangements. They have nothing to do with the party coming from the fort.'

There was a knock on the door. Mehboob opened it just sufficiently to see who it was.

An English voice said, 'The party is fully present now but the senior conducting officer would appreciate a preliminary word with Mr Kasim.'

'Who is that?' Kasim called out. Mehboob opened the door wider. A young English civilian stepped in.

'Good-morning, sir. My name's Everett. I'm assistant to Mr Harding, the Divisional Commissioner. He asked me to apologize for not being here himself. I hope the arrangements have been all right, so far?'

'Thank you, Mr Everett. Perfectly satisfactory. Is Lieutenant Kasim here now?'

'Yes, sir.'

'He was not a moment ago and my secretary had difficulty in getting an answer to the question whether he had breakfasted properly.'

'Yes, I know. That was unfortunate. But I've just asked the senior conducting officer myself and he assures me your son had a good breakfast.'

'And the senior conducting officer wants to have a word with me?'

'Yes, if that's all right –', Everett broke off because Ahmed tapped at the open door and now came in–, 'and if it might be in private.'

'I'll let you know. I'll send word.'

Everett went out, closing the door.

'Have you seen your brother, Ahmed?'

'No, but I've seen the conducting officer. I thought I'd better warn you. It's Merrick.'

'Merrick?'

'The ex-police officer in the Manners case, the one Pandit Baba's been pestering you about. I didn't know Merrick had anything to do with the INA, but he was in the army in intelligence when we met him in Mirat. Actually I saw him again in Bombay about three weeks ago. He said he was working in Delhi.'

'Ah, yes. That Merrick. The one Dmitri told me was badly wounded. You never told me you saw him again so recently.'

'I haven't seen much of you since getting back. And the case didn't seem to interest you.'

'No,' Kasim said. 'But perhaps it will. He knows you know him in connection with that old case?'

'Yes.'

'So he will assume that by now I know too. In fact he would probably assume that you would be here with me to meet your brother, which

1406

means that he does not in the least mind my knowing who he is. But he must know, mustn't he, Booby, that he is on the List?'

'It is clear, Minister. He hopes to ingratiate himself somehow. You could always say you will meet nobody except Sayed.'

'What is his rank, Ahmed?'

'Major, I think.'

'Since you know him it would be a good idea if you went now and brought him along personally. Go with Ahmed, Booby. I shan't want you again until all this is over. Meanwhile open and read the letter from Bapu so that we can discuss it later. Ahmed – give me one minute, please, before you bring Major Merrick.'

When they had gone Kasim went to the single window, which overlooked the inner courtyard. A policeman with a rifle was posted nearby facing towards him. There were bars but no glass in the window frame. Kasim closed the inner shutters. The only light in the room now came from the single naked bulb in the centre and from the high fanlight on the wall that faced the front compound. The furniture was sparse: a string charpoy with a mattress, two wooden armchairs and two smaller chairs, a table. He made a move to sit at the chair behind the table but then decided to remain standing.

*

'Major Merrick? Please come in.'

Ahmed, who had opened the door and stood aside without entering, let Merrick through and then closed it. Kasim offered his hand and felt a twinge of pity for a man with such a badly disfigured face and such an obviously useless left arm, clamped to his body with the cap tucked under it at elbow level and a briefcase suspended from the gloved fingers of an artificial hand. The man said, 'Actually Lieutenant-Colonel, since I and your younger son last met, Mr Kasim.'

The grip of the right hand was strong, like the voice. Kasim indicated a seat and sat down himself. He now noted the pip and crown on each shoulder tab, the regimental name and the ribbon of the DSO. He watched while Merrick dealt with his cap by removing it from under the left arm, placing it on the table, and with his briefcase by removing it from the artificial hand and placing it on the table too, next to the hat. He glanced at the inner side of his right wrist, checking the time.

'I'm sorry about the few minutes delay, but when we arrived your elder son asked for a few minutes alone before he came in. So I sent the others along and waited near the car. But I assure you his reason was not because he felt unwell as a result of not having had an adequate breakfast –' Merrick smiled. The effect was strange, lopsided. He continued – 'Nor as a result of inadequate sleep. We reached the fort early enough yesterday evening to let him rest up after the journey from Delhi. The journey itself was not very taxing. We flew to Ranagunj and came on by road. In fact I

1407

believe you'll be much tireder than he because I gather you travelled down overnight and only got here an hour or so ago. Incidentally, Mr Everett tells me your secretary may have been upset by the two young officers' apparently unhelpful attitude over the question of what kind of breakfast your son had. The explanation is that they had no idea what he had, since I breakfasted with him alone. They are only temporary escorts. They reported to me at Ranagunj in exchange for two other officers who came with me on the plane. They have no information about any of us. All they know is that the Indian officer is in custody.'

'The question of Sayed's breakfast has already been satisfactorily answered, Colonel Merrick. So far as I'm concerned it is a closed subject. Incidentally, my younger son Ahmed had no idea you were in any way connected with Sayed. Does Sayed know that you know his brother?'

'The one is a social acquaintance. The other is not. So the answer is, no.'

'Please tell me what is the purpose of this preliminary private word?'

'The purpose is to tell you as much as possible about the charges which Lieutenant Sayed Kasim will probably have to face.'

Kasim hoped that he betrayed no surprise. But he was surprised. He said: 'I have not asked for this. I'm not sure that I wish to be told anything about such matters. My son must himself have a good idea what charges there may be. What can you tell me that he cannot?'

Merrick said, 'Naturally, Mr Kasim, it's entirely up to you whether we have a preliminary word. It wasn't my own department's idea, but Government seemed to think it fair.'

'Fair?'

'The charges and evidence in these cases aren't fully prepared yet by any means. But Government feels that your son would be much more at ease if he doesn't have to tell you everything himself.' Merrick paused. 'It could after all be a bit painful for him.'

'Painful?'

Merrick kept him waiting for a reply. He seemed utterly composed and in command. 'He has never struck me as being among those who are unrepentantly proud of the situation they find themselves in.'

For the first time Kasim was unable to keep his eyes unwaveringly on the man. He glanced down and carefully covered his right hand with his left to control the familiar tremor before it began.

'Very well,' he said. 'Tell me what you wish. But as briefly as possible.'

'A charge of waging war against the King-Emperor is of course going to be the almost unavoidable common charge to be faced in these cases and in your son's case the evidence is incontrovertible since he was captured fighting in one of the INA units that accompanied the Japanese when they tried to invade India in 1944 and got as far as Manipur and Kohima. The unit he commanded surrendered voluntarily and seemed to have been abandoned in an untenable position by the Japanese, without access to any supplies or lines of communication. I'm afraid one often found that. Voluntary surrender or no, however, he was in arms, waging war.'

1408

'You were in that theatre of war yourself, Colonel?'

'I was on the staff of one of the divisions that were brought up to mount the counter-attack. As an intelligence officer the INA became my special concern.'

'Were you present when Sayed was brought in?'

'No, I was out of the line by then.'

'Wounded you mean, thus?' Kasim indicated the arm.

'Yes. Thus.'

'By INA action?'

'There were INA about. Japanese as well. Why do you ask?'

'The reason is obvious, surely? A man wounded as badly as you could be forgiven for accepting a job that gave him an opportunity to redress the balance.'

'One does the job one is given. But I take your point. The INA were involved in the incident but I was wounded entirely by my own fault.'

'How was it your own fault?'

'I was trying to stop a fellow officer acting thoughtlessly.' Merrick paused. 'You asked me to be brief –'

'I know, but I should like to hear about this other matter. It is all relevant to my rather sparse knowledge of the INA.'

'Very briefly, then. I'd gone forward to collect an INA prisoner. At that time they were rather a rare species. The sepoys of the Indian Army tended to shoot them out of hand. This prisoner was originally from the Muzzafirabad Guides. The officer who was on the same divisional staff as myself was also Muzzafirabad Guides. He insisted on going with me and when the man said there were two other INA ex-Muzzy Guides soldiers hiding in the jungle near by waiting to give themselves up the officer suggested we went to collect them. I said we shouldn't, but the next thing I knew was he'd taken our jeep, and the prisoner, and gone forward to do just that. I borrowed another jeep and went after them. When I found them the jeep was under fire and on fire. The prisoner had decamped, presumably to rejoin the enemy, and the officer was burning to death. I pulled him and the driver out but it was too late to save the officer.'

'Was he a friend of yours?'

'We knew one another pretty well. At least since I acted as his best man. At his wedding in Mirat. I expect Ahmed will have told you about the wedding. Ahmed, or Count Bronowsky.'

'The wedding. Ah, yes.'

'But I think it fair to say I went after the officer only to secure the prisoner, who was my responsibility. The result was hardly the prisoner's fault, nor was it really the officer's. I needn't have followed. He was one of those men with the not uncommon idea that any sepoy who'd been in the regiment would only have to come face to face with one of the officers of that regiment to throw his gun down and return contrite to the fold. I took the less romantic view that guns only got thrown down when the alternative was hunger and no other escape-route.'

'As in Sayed's case?'

'I don't think you'll find he pretends otherwise. And being an officer he was responsible for the lives of the men in what remained of his unit.'

'You've interrogated Sayed often?'

'Since joining the department several months ago I have talked to him quite frequently, yes.'

'Forgive these questions. An old lawyer's habit. Please go on. He was captured originally by the Japanese in Kuala Lumpur in nineteen-forty-two when the Japanese defeated the British Army there.'

'The British Army and the Indian Army. Yes. Of course you know he asserts he didn't join the INA until after August nineteen forty-two when he heard of the arrests in India after the Congress Quit India resolution – arrests which included your own. He told you this in his first letter home, after we'd recaptured him. I'm afraid copies of all his letters in and out have had to be made.'

'Don't apologize, Colonel. I am used to that sort of thing. In the same letter to my late wife he apologized for having failed in the march on Delhi.'

'It was probably the same letter. I remember the phrase from my study of his file.'

'Tell me, Colonel Merrick. How does this apology for having failed in the march on Delhi balance with your view that he is not among those unrepentantly proud of the situation he finds himself in? Which situation do you mean? His situation as a Lieutenant of the Ranpur Regiment, now your prisoner awaiting trial for waging war against the King, or his situation as a Major in the INA who failed in his march on Delhi to free India from the British but lives to tell the tale?'

'It's more than a year since he wrote that letter.'

'You mean he has had second thoughts?'

'Frankly, Mr Kasim, I should say he had had a great number of thoughts. For the past year he hasn't had much to occupy his mind except the single subject of why he decided to switch his allegiance.'

'And wage war against the King. Yes.' Kasim waited, then said, 'What other charges?'

'Incitement? Abetment? Bringing aid and comfort to the enemy? As I said, charges aren't framed. But your son has admitted to helping to recruit other Indian POWs into the INA and also to helping devise propaganda about the INA and broadcasting on one occasion to India, incognito.'

'Is there any more serious factor that may have to be considered?'

'More serious factor, Mr Kasim?'

'One hears gossip, tales, possibly exaggerated, or so one hopes, that recruitment was not always voluntary, that in a few cases certain methods were used to persuade sepoy prisoners-of-war to join.'

'You mean brutal methods?'

'Yes, I mean that.'

'And what you want to know is whether this is a factor that may have to

1410

be considered in your son's case and might lead to a charge that he used such methods himself?'

'Yes.'

After some moments Merrick glanced at the table. The one good eyebrow contracted slightly. Kasim wondered whether the full ramifications of the question of brutality were lost on him. They could not be if his reputation from the time of the Bibighar was deserved. But perhaps that reputation was simply the result of rumour too.

'A factor that may have to be considered?' Merrick repeated to himself. He looked at Kasim again. 'The only answer I can give you, Mr Kasim, is that I don't know. I can assure you it hasn't arisen yet but it would be quite unrealistic of me to assure you that it can't arise.'

'You mean there are indications that such accusations may be made against Sayed?'

'On the contrary. A lot of evidence has been collected of cases of torture and brutal behaviour and several officers and NCOs have been named, but your son's name has never been among them. In fact the men who surrendered with him have invariably spoken of him with great respect, particularly in regard to his care for their welfare and for the way he stood up to Japanese officers when this was necessary. No, my point is that the men we have access to, those already recaptured, represent only a percentage of the eventual sources of evidence. There are all those still in Malaya for instance. I can't vouch for what some of them may or may not say about your son's conduct once we've got hold of them. It was a very large army.' He hesitated, then added, 'I'm exceeding my brief expressing a personal opinion, but I shall express it none the less since you seem concerned. I should be very surprised if at any time between now and the completion of the collection of all the evidence in all the cases your son is implicated in any charges other than those I've mentioned.'

'Yes. I see. Thank you. And this is all you have to tell me?'

'I think so. I hope it's helped you in a general way.'

'Yes.' He made a snap decision. 'Tell me, Colonel Merrick – are you still troubled as I understood from Ahmed you were – I mean troubled by incidents devised to remind you that your conduct as Superintendent of Police in Mayapore – I should say suspected conduct – had made you unpopular in certain quarters and wasn't going to be forgotten?'

Merrick smiled. A cheerful smile, Kasim thought.

'Not until recently.'

'Another stone?'

Merrick reached for his briefcase and began to manipulate the artificial hand back round the handle while he continued speaking. 'No, there's only been the one stone. Chucking stones at British officers *is* rather a hazardous operation. They've reverted to the subtle approach. The bicycle again.'

'Bicycle?'

'A bicycle. Left on my verandah. Rusty and useless, naturally.'

'A rusty bicycle left on your verandah, Colonel Merrick? What purpose does this serve?'

'It's obviously a symbol of the bicycle I'm supposed to have planted outside the house of one of the boys who assaulted Miss Manners. Miss Manners's bicycle.' He stood up. So, after a moment, did Kasim. 'The bicycle's rather a good touch. They began after I'd left Mayapore just by chalking inauspicious signs outside the door of my bungalow. Then one day there was this rusty old bicycle outside my quarters. That was in Mirat, just before someone chucked the stone. The incidents have a twofold purpose, of course – to let me know it's known where I'm currently living and working – which they do – and to undermine me psychologically – which they don't.'

'When and where was this new incident, this second bicycle?'

'According to my cook, about a week ago in Delhi. I've been down in Ceylon and Rangoon and got back only just in time to accompany your son here. My cook said he found it leaning against the verandah rail one morning. He got the sweeper to take it to the back of the compound because there was a bad smell which he traced to the saddle-bag. He wouldn't touch it himself after that because the smell was that of a putrid pork chop. Since he's a Muslim I've had some difficulty in persuading him to stay. He's a very good cook. He cooks fresh pork chops for me quite happily. Just seems to draw the line at putrid ones in the saddle-bags of rusty bikes.'

Kasim averted his face to disguise his own revulsion.

'You should report such things to the police.'

'I always do. It doesn't bother me personally but then whoever is responsible for this kind of childish persecution isn't really in the least concerned either about me or about what are no doubt still called the innocent victims of the Bibighar. The Bibighar affair was used as an excuse to stir up trouble generally and it rather looks to me as if it's going to be given another innings in conjunction with the INA cases because it's been discovered I'm connected with them.'

'Given another innings by whom, Colonel Merrick?'

'By whoever prefers anarchy to law and order. Has Count Bronowsky never talked to you while you've been living in Nanoora, about the power exercised in India by uncommitted and irresponsible forces? He was very eloquent about it on the first occasion I met him.'

'Count Bronowsky and I don't have an intimate relationship, in spite of my younger son's connection with him. He and I are politically opposed. He is dedicated to the continuing autocratic authority of the Nawab. I am dedicated to the diminution and final extinction of the autocratic authority of *all* the Indian princes. My respect for Count Bronowsky has become quite strong since I've lived under restriction at the Nawab's court, but we are still political opponents and seldom exchange views.'

'I suppose you and I are potentially opponents too, Mr Kasim.'

'You and I?'

'I and your party. Surely I'm on the list?'

'What list, Colonel Merrick?'

'The list of officials whose conduct in nineteen forty-two may be inquired into. I'm told it looks as if I'm likely to be on it.'

'Told by whom?'

'The CID officer I reported the new incident to. Not that it surprised me. The fact that the subject has come up at a political level is sufficient warning. Anyway, if I'm not on it yet I imagine from what I'm told that my old friend Pandit Baba of Mayapore won't be happy until I am. Of course it's he who's responsible for the childish persecution, but there's never been any clear evidence to connect him with it. He's not a very connectable man. You can't pin him down with any certainty even as a member of the militant wing of the Hindu Mahasabah. But he has a genius for inspiring young men to sacrifice themselves in whatever cause he's currently taken up. I admired him rather. In Mayapore whenever we caught one of his disciples as they called themselves breaking the law they always swore the only thing they discussed with the Pandit was the Bhagavad Gita and went willingly to prison. What I admired was his power to inspire such loyalty. In those days his activities were more tiresome than dangerous but I should say he's capable of graduating to better things. Assassination, for instance. You know the man I mean, Mr Kasim?'

Kasim smiled.

'I have never met him. I think now I must see Sayed. You are due to take him back to the fort when?'

'When your meeting is finished.'

'And when do you take him back to Delhi?'

'This evening.'

'By road to Ranagunj and then by aeroplane?'

'Yes. I must be in Delhi tomorrow. I have to fly back to Kandy and from there probably to Singapore.'

'Then I will say good-bye to you now, Colonel Merrick.' Again he made a snap decision. 'I don't think we shall ever be opposed in the sense you mean. Not you and I personally. I am not interested in past quarrels, only in solving present and future problems. It is the only way any of us will ever make progress.'

'Quite. Quite.'

For the first time Merrick looked uncertain of himself, disappointed, if the unscarred side of his face was anything to go by. Kasim thought: He's proud to be on the list, in which case what people said about his conduct in Mayapore is probably true.

The man reached for his cap. Kasim did not watch him go through the awkward motions of tucking it under his left arm.

'I'll bring Sayed now,' Merrick said. He hesitated then went towards the door.

'No, please do not bring him. I wish our meeting to be completely in

1413

private and in any case it would offend me to see him physically in the custody of anyone. And there is another thing –'

He went over to the window. 'This room is very hot and dark. It is like a cell. I closed these shutters because there is a guard outside whose presence disturbs me. I know that guards are necessary – if only as a formality since Sayed could hardly effect a credible escape in the middle of this desert.' He opened the shutters and breathed deeply. The guard was still there, just out of earshot. 'So I apologize for any inconvenience but I think I should prefer to see Sayed in the court-room. At least it will be larger and airier and they can post as many men outside as they wish. That should take only a few minutes to arrange, shouldn't it? Just a question of clearing the other people out. Perhaps you'd be so kind as to send someone to let me know when everything is ready.'

'I'll come myself, Mr Kasim.'

'That is kind of you.'

III

He realized how little he could have seen of the Circuit House on that previous visit fifteen months ago. He did not recognize the corridor that Merrick now led him along. They stopped at a door. Merrick opened it on to a small room.

'This isn't the court-room,' Kasim said. 'It's the magistrate's room.'

'It's the best way in.'

'No! The worst! How can I enter the court-room through the judge's door? Where have you put Sayed? In the dock?'

'I can bring him here if that's what you'd prefer.'

'I wish no one to *bring* him anywhere.' He felt ill. He turned back into the corridor whose series of grimy windows gave on to the verandah of the inner courtyard. The place stank of unresolved cases, of the acrid odour of legal millstones grinding fine and slow between sessions; and of his youth, pleading interminable cases in court-houses such as this. After all, interviewing Sayed in the court-room would be a mistake. It would be like putting him on trial. But then, for Kasim, what was about to follow *was* Sayed's trial.

'Mr Kasim, are you all right?'

'I am perfectly all right. It is just that –'

He broke off. There was a third man whom Merrick was urging forward from the open doorway; a tall man, taller than himself, broad-boned, well-fleshed, dressed like an active-service officer in dark green cotton uniform; pale brown skin, dark-browed, brown-eyed. Between the nostrils and the lip a moustache grew, close-cropped in the British style. The hair was cropped too, but not too close. A fine-looking man. Only the eyes betrayed a weakness: the weakness that accompanied an uncertainty about the warmth of his reception.

But Sayed did not wait to find out what kind of reception he would get. Silently, effortlessly, in one flowing movement he knelt at Kasim's feet, placed his hands on Kasim's shoes, lowered his head to his hands and then raised it, at the same time removing his hands. As he rose Kasim instinctively performed his own task, putting his arms round him. So, for a moment, they remained.

'Come, let us go through,' Kasim said, and released his son. Merrick was walking down the corridor, his back to them; but he had been a witness. Kasim led the way through the magistrate's room, out on to the daïs in the court-room and down into the well of the court. He stopped by one of the pleaders' tables; that table at which Sayed must have been sitting. There were an empty coffee cup and a used cigarette tray. The smell of tobacco smoke hung in the air. He still drank too, probably, like Ahmed, but with at least the excuse that it was a habit acquired in army messes, just to prove equal capacity with British officers. But the smoking was new and despite himself Kasim found the dirty ashtray repugnant. He said nothing, but Sayed, also without a word, removed it, took it across to the other table.

'Please, there is no need. If smoking has become necessary to you, smoke by all means. It doesn't bother me.'

But Sayed left the ashtray where he had put it and came back, stood; the weakness was still discernible, the uncertainty was still there, in the eyes. Kasim sat. From this angle his elder son looked even taller and broader. Both Ahmed and Sayed dwarfed him but Sayed would make even Ahmed look slenderly built. The periods of privation must have been of short duration, unless the British had been feeding him up.

'Come, sit.'

Sayed did so.

'Have you seen Ahmed yet?'

'Not yet, father. But Ronald told me he's here.'

'Ronald?'

'Ronald Merrick. The chap you've been talking to. He said he'd make sure Ahmed and I had a word afterwards. He's quite a good fellow really. Very decent to me.'

The voice was strong too, the accent clipped, more clipped than Kasim remembered from their last meeting, certainly more clipped than it had been after Sayed had passed out of the Indian military academy when Kasim had told him, 'You sound like a British officer.' They had both laughed. He could have stopped Sayed choosing the army as a career. He had been criticized for not stopping him. It hadn't always been easy for him to explain why he had a son who held the King-Emperor's Commission. It couldn't always have been easy for Sayed when young Englishmen, fellow members of the mess, learnt who his father was. But Sayed had never complained and when Kasim became Chief Minister in Ranpur any embarrassment Sayed might have felt vanished. He remembered Sayed saying, 'You are a Minister. I am an officer. We are both necessary.' He had meant necessary to India and Kasim had been moved.

'How are you treated then? You look well. Put on an inch or two. Like Ahmed. As you see, I have taken off. Who is commandant at the fort nowadays? Still Major Tippet?'

'I don't know, father. I was only there overnight. You were there too?'

'Oh yes. Better than the Kandipat although boring after a bit. They gave me a room in the old Zenana House. I wonder whether my bed of onions is still flourishing? It was in a courtyard a few feet from the steps to the Zenana. I watered them mostly with the water from my shaving mug. So this is how they tasted. Of soap. What one will do to keep oneself occupied. But onions are good for warding off colds. So your mother always said.'

The muscular geography of his son's face momentarily revealed itself: an intricate map. The eyes hardened. Kasim folded his hands on the table. He said, 'When I was released to go to Mirat they brought me here first of all to meet Ahmed. Now that I'm going back home it seemed a convenient place to tell them to bring you. If I had come to Delhi the world and his wife would have been watching. Anyway, it gives you an outing. What did they tell you. Anything?'

'First they just told me to get ready for a trip. But then Ronnie Merrick got back from Rangoon and put me in the picture. He said Government had given permission for us to meet and that he was coming with me.'

'The impression was that I had petitioned Government and that Government had decided to be magnanimous?'

'Yes.'

'It is not entirely accurate.'

'Oh, I didn't swallow it whole. I know how devious they can be.'

'In this case devious to what end?'

Kasim waited. Sayed said nothing.

'Come. Don't hold back. Just because I am your father.'

Sayed looked down at the table. 'They know you've never written to me. They think this shows you disapprove of what I've done.' He glanced up. 'It would be very useful to them to have someone like you on their side. A member of Congress, ex-Chief Minister. And a Muslim. Someone to denounce us all as traitors. They realize such people will be in short supply.'

'Quite so. Both major parties will stand behind the INA. The true nature and extent of INA came as a surprise to many of us. But people who are locked up a long time have a lot of surprises in store when they mingle freely again and find out what has been going on. So among us at Simla it was generally agreed that INA would be supported.'

'Generally, not unanimously?'

'Quite clearly all parties will combine to organize the defence if these cases ever come to trial. Whether they will do so is up to the Viceroy and the Commander-in-Chief. It will be interesting to see how they solve the problem of who should be tried and who should not. From a legal point of view the entire matter is without precedent. Administratively it is farcical. Some kind of legal strategy will have to be evolved to uphold the spirit if not the letter of the law. But I am sure the British will find a way. They have considerable experience of how to deal pragmatically with situations which pose profound questions. They cannot just say, You have sinned, go home and repent, without running the risk of their entire Indian Army resigning *en masse* by way of protest and going home also. On the other hand they cannot court-martial every INA soldier because it would take several years to do so. On top of that, it is not in them to find a solution such as the Germans might have found. Or the Japanese. It is not in them to line you all up in a concentration camp and shoot you out of hand. It is not in them politically and it is not in them emotionally. What can they do? The answer is fairly clear. They must establish a scale of priorities. In such a scale every King's Commissioned Officer who joined INA will be at the top. He cannot hope to escape being cashiered at the very least. Your military career is finished, Sayed. You must make up your mind to that. Even if the British left India tomorrow it would be finished. Because whatever we politicians say and however stoutly we defend you, the loyal Indian members of the Indian Army will not defend you. Why should they? It is against their interests. They are on the winning side. Whatever military plums there are to pick when we are independent they will claim properly as theirs. Why should they share them with Subhas Chandra Bose's defeated people? Of course it would be different if the British had lost the war. Then you'd be in clover. But they've won it. Your first error, a very pardonable one, was perhaps to have assumed in nineteen forty-two they'd already lost it. Isn't this so, Sayed? Isn't it this more than anything else that persuaded you to join INA? Isn't it this more than the fact that you heard I and most other Congressmen had been imprisoned and that the whole country was in turmoil that decided you?'

'No, father. It was entirely because you were arrested along with everybody else and that the whole of India was rising and telling the British to quit.'

'Who told you I was arrested?'

'Shah Nawaz Khan. General Shah Nawaz Khan. Originally a captain in the Punjab Regiment. But so far as I'm concerned, *General*. He came up to Kuala Lumpur in nineteen forty-two as commander of all Indian prisoners-of-war parties. I knew him slightly. He was a very good officer. He stopped the Japanese doing all sorts of things to us.'

'But he was INA?'

'He had joined, yes, but only to stop the Japs exploiting Indian prisoners and to wreck the INA from inside if necessary. I am talking of first INA, under Mohan Singh. But you must know all this.'

'No, tell me.'

'Mohan Singh was also Punjab Regiment. Shah Nawaz said he thought him a very average officer. Mohan Singh was captured somewhere like Alor Star. People say he had a bad time with his British officers and that they left him to face the Japanese alone. He started organizing the prisoners. When the British surrendered at Singapore all the Indian officers

1417

were separated from the British and made to assemble with all the Indian troops at Farrer Park and handed over by the representative of the British Government, to an intelligence officer called Fujiwara and given orders to obey the Japanese. Then Fujiwara handed them over to Mohan Singh. Fujiwara said Mohan Singh was their GOC and had power of life and death over them. I was not in Singapore then. But this is what I was told.'

'Who are you saying gave the prisoners orders to obey the Japanese?'

'The British Government representative.'

'All prisoners of course must obey the lawful orders of their captors. There is nothing much to be made of that. More interesting is the order for the separation of British King's Commissioned Officers from Indian King's Commissioned Officers. By whose order was this separation?'

'The Japanese, presumably. But I never heard any protests from the British. They were too interested in saving their own skins. As at Kuala Lumpur. "Hold this position, Kasim old chap," Colonel Barker said. So I held it while the rest of the battalion and all the British officers disappeared. I held it for four days. Nothing happened for three of them. In three days Colonel Barker and the others got down to Johore. He got one of the last ships out of Singapore or Malacca, I don't know which. All I know is that on the fourth day the Japs came and that on the fifth we couldn't hold them off any longer. We had nothing. Nothing to eat. No ammunition. At the time I said, Well, it is war. Somebody has to carry the can. Since then I thought there was another explanation. Here in India, father, the army looks very sound, very pukka, very good form and very secure, very gentlemanly. In Burma and Malaya you realized a lot of it was eyewash. They never wanted us. They never trusted us.'

He took his father's hand, leaning forward, lowering his voice. 'But I have seen senior British officers in Singapore and in Rangoon bowing to Japanese sentries. And I have seen senior British officers slapped and kicked for not bowing, and *then* bowing.' He leant back. 'So much for the *raj*. They too can be made to act like peons. I shall never forget.'

Hand free, Kasim held it out, palm towards Sayed and shut his eyes. 'Please. Forget all this. I have heard all this sort of thing before. It is of no importance. It will not help you in any way whatsoever. It's your conduct that is in question not the conduct or misconduct of this British officer or that British officer. Let us speak no more of disparities between British officers and Indian officers. If you try to do this in court-martial prosecuting counsel will eat you alive and spit you out as a silly boy with a grudge.'

'I wanted you to know –'

'I know. I *do* know. But when you are court-martialled you will be well advised to give quite a different picture and pretend it has never entered your head that your commanding officer treated his white officers in one way and his Indian subaltern in another. If necessary praise him. Adopt a soldierly attitude to this matter. Do not antagonize the court. It will be a military court. Even if one of its members is an Indian officer – which is

1418

almost bound to be so to preserve the idea of impartiality – do not be tempted to raise the question of this disparity. Secretly he might agree with you but it will embarrass him and put him further against you. He will be already against you because he will be thinking: Here is this young fellow who is only a lieutenant but calling himself major and also being called a hero by the politicians and the people and here am I, still a captain after twenty years of loyal service to the *raj*.'

He hesitated, then said, 'What is wrong, Sayed?'

Sayed's eyes had become tearful. He bent his head. He said, 'I'm sorry, father. I prepared myself to find that you weren't going to help me. I was wrong. I'm ashamed to have thought it. All this is very good. Very helpful.'

Kasim felt himself begin to tremble. He said, 'Clearly I must help you. I'm not only your father but a man who happens to know something about the law and the way the law works. You are to clear your mind of every consideration except that of your defence. Neither of us can wish to see you sent to rigorous imprisonment or transportation for life. That you will be cashiered and finished for ever with the army is sufficient punishment.'

'Finished for ever?'

'For ever. It is my opinion. I have told you why. So. As I say. Clear your mind. Shah Nawaz Khan told you in Kuala Lumpur that Congress Party leaders in India had been arrested and that I was among them and that the country was rising against the British. This led to your decision to join INA. What you call first INA. Why did it? Let me suggest why. Naturally you were angry that your father had been put in prison simply because he was a leading member of Congress. But then you calmed down. You sat back and considered the situation. The British had been defeated in France. They had been defeated in Burma and Malaya. The Japanese held the Chindwin. Beyond the Chindwin lay India. In India the population appeared to have been driven to desperation and had risen against the *raj*. Although your father was a politician you yourself were politically uneducated. Like Ahmed you have never bothered much about such matters. You did not fully understand why Congress passed a resolution calling on the British to quit but broadly you understood it was because in a war for freedom India should also be free. Also you understood that everyone felt that so long as the British remained in Delhi the Japanese were bound to attack your country. Now. The Japanese were pretending to be friendly towards the Indians as fellow-Asians, but you did not trust them. If they invaded India and as seemed likely again defeated the British the very clear danger was that far from gaining the independence which the British themselves had promised, India would again become subject to a foreign government, this time a Japanese government. A Japanese *raj*. And what could you do about that, sitting in Kuala Lumpur as their prisoners-of-war?'

'What indeed?'

'It was a terrible problem. On the one hand you felt you could not just sit in Kuala Lumpur waiting to be told that Hirohito was now the titular ruler of Hindustan. On the other hand not to sit around would mean appearing to kowtow to the Japanese and disregarding your oath to the King-Emperor. To escape from prison-camp was one thing – virtually impossible though that was in the Far East. To secure your release by throwing in your lot with an organization which the Japanese had helped to bring into being was another. Moreover, should the INA ever march with the Japanese into India, march with whatsoever patriotic intention, there would be the inevitable armed confrontation with those of your own countrymen who were still serving under the British flag.

'How could these problems be resolved? The answer was they could *not* be resolved. You had to choose. And you could not see into the future. You had no crystal ball. You had to weigh one possibility against another possibility and make a decision. And then one day you looked around and perhaps remembered some of the things the Japanese had done. And you remembered how this Shah Nawaz Khan had stopped them doing such things in this place or that place. And you thought of the Japanese doing or trying to do these things in India and how it was necessary to stop them doing them.

'Then for the first time you saw clearly what the problem was, that it was a question of choosing between your own integrity and your country's integrity. Only an officer who was a national of a country already under foreign rule could ever face this dilemma. But this is an explanation, Sayed, not an excuse. Legally it isn't even a mitigating circumstance, so put that out of your mind. Go back to Kuala Lumpur and your decision to join Shah Nawaz Khan. You asked to see him and told him you'd made your mind up to join INA?'

'Not quite like that. And he made a point of never persuading anybody against their own judgment. I didn't decide until the end of September. He'd gone back to Singapore then. While he was in KL things improved for us but after he'd gone there were several incidents.'

'What kind of incidents?'

'For example. Before Shah Nawaz came to KL the Japanese were forcing our jawans to learn Japanese foot drill, things like that. He stopped them. He told me it was what the English prisoners in Rangoon were having to do and that it showed the Japanese intended to make us all puppets if they could. When he had gone it started again. I protested, but it made no difference. One sepoy who refused became very ill. The Japanese must have beaten him up pretty badly.'

'The sepoy's name?'

'I don't remember. It was happening too often.'

'More than one sepoy, then.'

'Yes, more than one.'

'And you took a risk, protesting?'

'That didn't matter.'

'You were in some kind of position of authority in this camp?'

'Only a section of the camp. And as a prisoner oneself one's power was limited. I was responsible for this section, though.'

'But you were only a lieutenant.'

Sayed glanced up.

'Shah Nawaz and Mohan Singh were only captains. How many Indian majors, colonels and brigadiers do you know of, father? Do you personally know any Indian generals? The British have always been careful to see that no Indian officer rises high enough to be in a position of much authority.'

'Again I must warn you not to say such things at your court-martial. Please try to concentrate. What steps did you take at the end of September when you came to the decision to join INA?'

'I spoke to two INA officers who visited the camp.'

'Officers visiting for recruitment purposes?'

'Only partly. Mainly to make sure for Shah Nawaz Khan that we were not being exploited. I told them about the sepoy who had been hurt. They got permission to take him to their house. They gave him good food and medical attention.'

'But you don't remember his name?'

'Perhaps it was a name like Laksham. He was a non-combatant. A sweeper, I think. I'm not sure.'

'I ask because if this man has survived his testimony might be useful to you.'

'I understand that, father. I don't know whether he survived.'

'Well, go on. You told these two INA officers that you'd thought about it very hard and had decided to join the INA.'

'Yes.'

'They were pleased of course.'

'Yes, but they advised caution and to say nothing to the Japanese. They promised to speak to Shah Nawaz Khan and Mohan Singh in Singapore.'

'Why this caution?'

'Things were very difficult just then. The INA faced a crisis. Mohan Singh was not strong enough. Many officers were afraid he would let the Japanese use the INA for their own purposes. Also there were many different opinions among INA officers about legality and such-like. They told me that at one time an INA party had even been sent to infiltrate across the Chindwin and contact Congress in India.'

'Seeking Indian political approval of the INA?'

'Yes.'

'I did not know this. This is new to me. What happened to the infiltrating party?'

'It failed. But one of them deserted and got through to the British and presumably told them everything that was going on. Meanwhile you were all being locked up so there was no one left to contact even if another party had been sent.'

'Good. Good. So you were all still in the dark and had no crystal ball. It supports the argument I am outlining. And here there is an attempt to act constitutionally in some way. Democratically. Patriotically certainly. What INA were pondering then is the question what is the will of the people of India in this matter? Do they want an INA? And now getting no answer and realizing that it will not be possible now to get an answer. Go on.'

'The two officers said I would be a useful officer in a properly constituted free Indian Army. They said they'd have a word with Shah Nawaz Khan and Mohan Singh but that I should be patient meanwhile and say nothing. They said Shah Nawaz had had a very disagreeable experience down in Singapore opening a new officers' training school and then having to close it almost at once because the Japanese told Mohan Singh it couldn't be tolerated or something like that. The Japs wanted complete control. In their hearts some of their officers despised us and Mohan Singh was unable to resist them effectively.'

'So you continued a prisoner?'

'Yes.'

'Taking care of your men. Good. Did you ever discuss these matters with them?'

'Sometimes I talked to the NCOS so that they could tell the sepoys and give them some hope for the future, poor fellows.'

'Then what happened?'

'Then I became quite unwell for a time.'

'Why was this?'

'A Japanese officer humiliated me in front of the jawans.'

'Tell me about this humiliation.'

'He assembled all my men and stood me in front of them. He said Lieutenant Kasim would now have personal lessons in Japanese drill and words of command so that he in turn could teach these lessons himself.'

'So you had these lessons. In front of your own men?'

'No, I refused.'

'You said you were humiliated. If you refused what humiliation existed?'

'The humiliation existed because of what he said in front of everybody after I'd refused.'

'What did he say?'

'He said, "Here is a Lieutenant called Kasim. The British have put his father in prison. What sort of man is this who so loves the British that he will not take up arms with us against them?" Then he spat between my feet. Then he slapped my face and then I was taken away and beaten up.'

'This man's name?'

'Hakinawa.'

'Of course you will say nothing of this at your court-martial. You understand this? Only with the greatest reluctance should you answer questions about it if counsel happens to press for information of this kind. Then only should you give a hint and then leave it to him whether to go on pressing. However much he presses and however much you are inclined to speak out, you will discover your answers are of no importance to your defence. You understand? Try to let prosecuting counsel alone stand convicted of raising this kind of emotional subject in evidence. Only if the prosecution can be seen and heard to squeeze it out of you must you mention such a thing.' Kasim paused. 'Of course a clever defence counsel, knowing of this, might manipulate the prosecution into the mistake of pressing such a point. Now, go on. You were beaten up. What afterwards was the attitude towards you of your men, who had seen what you call this humiliation?'

'I don't know. I was separated from them.'

'How separated?'

'First I was put in solitary confinement for a week or two. Then I was sent to another camp.'

'How were you treated there?'

'All right, I suppose.'

'All right, merely, or very well? Well, which? Come, keep alert, do not think of me as your father but as your prosecutor. How were you treated? All right or very well? Let me suggest you were treated very well. Let me put it to you that a Japanese officer apologized to you and spoke of Hakinawa with contempt, also that perhaps he hinted you might find yourself back with Hakinawa unless you showed yourself more co-operative. Which month was this, by the way. October? November?'

'November, I suppose.'

'November, nineteen forty-two?'

'Yes.'

'In November, nineteen forty-two, then, you began to be treated well. Thank you, Lieutenant Kasim.'

Sayed stared at him.

Kasim said, 'You see? You see the dangers of this line of evidence and argument? At this point prosecuting counsel sits down. He asks no more questions so you cannot answer them. The court looks at you and thinks perhaps it sees a man who wanted no more beating up. Every other consideration goes by the board, swept off by this one emotional consideration. The court looks at you and thinks, Well he is a coward –'

'Father –'

'Coward! Coward! This is what they are thinking. At this point defence counsel rises and tries to demolish this unfortunate impression by going back over all that old ground when you were supposed to be thinking seriously and objectively about this matter and that matter, about what is constitutional and what is not, and what is for India's good and what is not. But he does not find it easy. Prosecution has tricked you into raising this emotional question of to what extent Lieutenant Sayed Kasim was thinking of his country and to what extent thinking of his own skin. Defence Counsel's voice begins to carry less conviction. He knows that nothing can obliterate that impression, that Lieutenant Kasim is a man who joined the INA to avoid being beaten up again by a Japanese officer called Hakinawa. Nevertheless he has his brief and must go on to the bitter end.'

Kasim took out his squared handkerchief and dabbed his forehead. 'I remember the first case I pleaded in front of a British magistrate. A very minor case to do with a land dispute between two brothers. In private consultation my client made much of the emotional rift in family feeling. Presumably his brother, the claimant, had been doing likewise because when we got into court his counsel began to present the case as though it were a dispute between Cain and Abel, with my client cast as Cain. I had to listen to many of my excellent pleas and arguments being turned against me before even I had a chance to speak. I looked at the young magistrate. For a moment I could not interpret his expression. Then it suddenly struck me that he was wanting to hear none of this. It embarrassed and disturbed him. He was keeping his eye on his papers and trying to get it all down in writing. So when my turn came to stand up I proceeded very haltingly – at first actually because I had no alternative. I had lost all inspiration. I fell back on legal precedents, almost automatically, and he kept interrupting me, getting his clerk to show him this reference and that reference from this book and that book. While he did this I stood silent. At first I thought his interruptions were his way of accusing me of incomplete preparation. And then we happened to glance at one another at the same time and instinctively I knew that he was grateful just to be referred to points of law and the land records. Instinctively I knew I had provided him with a way out of this emotional situation that claimant's counsel had tried to establish. So then I became deliberately even more dry and boring, boring to the court but not to this boy-magistrate. And to make sure of this I sometimes made an old legal joke, old to the court, but new to him in the sense that while he had probably already heard the jokes from his tutors this was probably the first time he had heard them repeated in a court-room. My client was in despair. The claimant and the claimant's counsel were looking very smug. So I stopped looking at them. I looked only at the boy-magistrate and his expression was sufficient to encourage me to continue along these lines. I could see him beginning to feel that it was exactly for this that he had been trained for so long and so expensively. I could see him recognizing that this training had some point after all. I began to refer to the very old cases I knew he must have studied for his initial examinations. He became very confident, almost peremptory. Sometimes he rebuked me for getting a reference wrong. Mostly he rebuked the claimant's pleader for interrupting. His table became piled with books and documents. Sometimes he said, "What is your point in regard to such and such a sub-section, Mr Kasim?" I would tell him and at the same time refer him to another sub-section which I guessed he had had to answer questions about more recently. The public benches began to empty. The claimant's pleader pretended to go to sleep. People were yawning. It was the most boring case of the year. But it was the one the boy-magistrate will probably never forget and the one I must always remember, Sayed. From this case I removed every last speck of emotion. I made him see that Indians too are capable of detachment. There was practically

1424

nobody left in the court when he found in favour of the counter-claimant, my client.'

'Yes, I remember all that, father. You told us many years ago. Many times.'

'Oh, did I?' He dabbed his forehead again and suddenly felt very old. 'The reason I tell you again –' he began.

'I know the reason, father. You've always believed that the English are very emotional but unwilling to show it in public.'

'This is so, isn't it?'

'I can't take it into consideration. What the English feel or don't feel is no longer important. We've finished with them, whether you like it or not.'

'Why do you say whether I like it or not? What has my life been, then? What have I been doing? Asking them to stay?'

'No. Not asking. But perhaps making it possible because you believe so much in the power of the law. Their law.'

'In this case you'll be well advised to rely on it too. You will be finished if you persist in making emotional appeals. Now, go back to November, nineteen forty-two. How long were you in this new camp where you were treated all right, as you put it?'

'Until the following February. One of the two officers I'd already spoken to came to see me. He said Mohan Singh had been arrested by the Japanese in December for withholding full cooperation and trying to insist that only the INA should deal with India. But now they'd had word that Subhas Chandra Bose was coming from Germany to take charge. Shah Nawaz was raising a new INA and determined that the Japs wouldn't be allowed to interfere, but made to treat us as equals and not as a puppet army they could do what they liked with.'

'So you yourself now joined?'

'Yes. I went down to Singapore.'

'Taking some men with you, other recruits?'

'Yes, I visited my old camp. I told the men my decision. I left it to them to make up their own minds. A few NCOs volunteered immediately. I took them to Singapore with me.'

'Was Bose there already?'

'No, he didn't come for several months. We concentrated on training and on stopping the Japanese from interfering. Someone in the Japanese Government had told them to treat us with more respect and when Bose did come it was a revelation. You only had to see and listen to him once to know that at last we had a real leader. And then of course he put everything on a pukka footing.'

'By pukka footing you mean his establishment of a so-called Government of Free India in exile?'

'Why so-called, father? What was de Gaulle's Free French Government, then? You don't hear people referring to that as so-called.'

'You know the difference between de Gaulle's and Bose's governments.

There is no need for me to tell you. That sort of statement would be very smartly thrown out to sneered at as a quibble by the president of the court.'

'It wasn't a quibble to us. It made us independent of the Japanese. The Azad Hind Fauji became a properly constituted army, the armed force of a properly constituted and independent government.'

'You joined the INA before Bose took over. You would be sensible to say nothing on these lines. Tell me, why did you do this broadcast? Colonel Merrick says you admit to helping with propaganda generally and to doing a broadcast. I knew about the broadcast quite a long time ago. Someone listening in Ranpur thought they recognized your voice. I of course was in prison so heard nothing, but I was told about it afterwards. This *was* your voice?'

'Probably. I did one broadcast. Early last year. January, I think. After that I moved up into Burma in command of a battalion for the advance into Manipur.'

'What sort of thing did you say in the broadcast?'

'I just spoke in general terms, about the fight for India's freedom and the choice that had to be made by someone like myself, an officer in the Indian Army. They have a copy of the broadcast on their files in Delhi. All these broadcasts were monitored.'

'What was the main purpose of these broadcasts?'

'To encourage people here at home who had opportunities to listen. It was important for them to know that if the Japanese invaded, Indians would be with them. One couldn't say anything about not trusting the Japanese, but people listening could read between the lines. They'd realize that we'd be doing our best to stop the Japs giving them trouble.'

'Very well. Then you moved into Burma, you said. And then across the Chindwin and into Manipur.'

'Eventually, yes.'

'And waged war against the King.'

'Yes, I suppose so.'

'Not "yes, I suppose", Sayed. Just yes. Yes. Yes. You waged war against the king. It was the unavoidable result of the decision you made. We have already dealt with that. What remains to be dealt with is your attitude at this time to the Japanese.'

'It was the same as Netaji's.'

'Netaji? You mean Bose. What was Bose's attitude?'

'For him it was a question of wait and see. Under Netaji the lives of thousands of Indians in Asia were made better and the Japanese said repeatedly that we were allies, they'd no quarrel with India. But Netaji said many times to us in private that we must be prepared to fight them too if necessary. We should never fully trust them. Also he said they were perhaps afraid of us. I think this was why they kept us short of supplies and equipment and why in Burma they stopped us operating as a fully independent and major force. Whatever the Japanese Government said, we knew there were many Japanese officers who had their own ideas and way of dealing which wasn't in line with the official policy. They were the ones who didn't agree that India should be Netaji's sphere of influence. They only wanted to see the Rising Sun hoisted in Delhi in place of the Union Jack.'

'Good. Remember that. That could be a helpful point. But what does this mean, sphere of influence?'

'Surely it is obvious, it was fundamental. Netaji said –'

'I want it in your own words, not Netaji's.'

Sayed again hesitated. He said, 'What have you against Netaji? He spoke to me about you with much warmth and admiration.'

'What did you expect? For him to tell you he thought I was a bloody fool? No matter. Just that he and I never got on. Anyway he's dead –'

'Perhaps –'

'Perhaps, perhaps. Perhaps Hitler did not die in the bunker. Perhaps Bose did not die in a plane crash. The world must always have its myths. Let us get back to spheres of influence. You should avoid that phrase. It is one used by journalists when they are really talking about a political carve-up. You must try not to give this impression, that Bose sat down with Togo and said, right, you keep Burma and Malaya, and all the rest. We'll have India.'

'What is wrong with that? It's our own country.'

'The British still happen to think that legally it is theirs. Just do not use that phrase. Rely more on what you said about the Rising Sun and the Union Jack. Rely entirely on the question not of what appeared to be agreed between your Netaji and the Japanese within a framework of spurious legality, but on the underlying distrust, the fear that if and when the British were defeated, which seemed imminent, the Japanese would run riot in the country, looting and raping and enslaving, and that the best way to try to stop them doing this was unfortunately to march with them.'

Sayed said nothing.

'So now there comes the question, of whether there was any deepening of your distrust as a result of your experience of marching with them into India. Did the distrust increase?'

'Yes, because they dealt with us unfairly.'

'How?'

'Over things like rations, supplies, arms and ammunition. In not giving us proper operational information. They tried to palm us off with coolie work. The men were getting browned off. I was always having to dispute with Japanese officers mostly junior to me in rank to get the men a proper deal.'

'Morale in your battalion was not as high as you would have liked?'

'Morale was always high. We were fed up only with the Japanese. Among ourselves things were okay. I tried to share their hardships with them.'

'Sometimes no doubt you had to punish some of them.'

'Never to appease the Japanese. If a Japanese officer complained of any of my men's behaviour I told him to shove off.'

'I did not mean this. You were what you call a properly constituted army. You had a disciplinary code, no doubt, an army act laying down rules and regulations and punishments for infringement.'

'Everybody accepts this necessity. Our regulations were based completely on the Indian Army Act.'

'You cannot use the words based and completely together. Either they were a duplicate or based merely. Based with variations for local conditions and circumstances.'

'Yes, I see. You've been listening to all these rumours of ill-treatment. But where do such rumours come from except from men who joined us and have been recaptured like me but are hoping to suck up to the British with tales of tortures. I know nothing of such things. The only barbarity I have ever witnessed was in my old regiment in Kuala Lumpur when the officers' mess cook was ordered by Colonel Barker to receive six strokes of the rattan for stealing rum and selling it in the bazaar. We were all made to assemble and watch.'

'Under the pukka Indian Army Act such punishments are prescribed for menials. I am questioning you about punishments of combatant soldiers.'

'And I've already answered. I know nothing of brutal punishments. In Rangoon I ordered such things as extra fatigues, confinement to barracks, forfeiture of pay. And in the field, extra guard duties or heavy pack drill. I am not a monster. I am not a barbarian.'

'And you know nothing of this kind and worse kinds of violence in forcing men to *join* the INA?'

'Nothing.'

'You never had a case of desertion in your battalion?'

'No.'

'If you had, what would have happened if the man had been caught? Come. Think of me still as your prosecutor. What punishment did your INA prescribe for desertion, for instance in the face of the enemy, meaning in the face of the British and the Indian armies? Death?'

'That would have been the maximum.'

'In the eyes of the British who are not interested in INA acts or regulations, to execute such a sentence on an Indian soldier, even a traitorous Indian soldier, would amount to murder under the Indian Penal Code. You realize this? I am sorry to press you on the subject. Were such a sentence ever passed and executed, everyone concerned would be guilty at least of abetment to murder. You see how difficult things become when there is no political let alone legal recognition of the losing side by the winning side? I want to be absolutely sure there is no problem of this kind attaching to your case.'

'I've told you, father. You can be sure.'

'Because if there is any doubt, all my advice to you so far is valueless. You would have to work your case up on lines that would seek to establish the legality of what I have called Subhas Chandra Bose's spurious constitutional framework. You would need the services of an expert on

Constitutional and International Law. On full consideration, do you think after all you might require such services?'

'All I know is that I've only told you the truth. What I understand of it. I am merely a professional soldier. I don't follow all these technicalities.'

'They are not just technicalities, Sayed. Never mind. Go back now and concentrate your mind on the situation that ended in your surrender in Manipur. But let me lead you a little. In court your counsel would not be allowed too much licence in that respect.'

He smiled, attempting to make Sayed smile too.

'In Manipur,' he went on, 'you find yourself in a difficult, perhaps untenable military position. No supplies, no ammunition, no lines of communication. You are somewhere in the hills near Imphal. The Japanese are suddenly nowhere. The British and the Indian armies are uncomfortably close. Now – were there among your men any who said, Major Sahib, this is our chance. Now we can do what we really joined the INA to do – escape from prison-camp and return to duty at the earliest possible moment?'

Presently Sayed said, 'Yes, there were some men who pretended to think like that.'

'How did you deal with them?'

'I tried to make them see what folly it was.'

'Folly? Why folly?'

'Folly to expect the British to swallow a story like that.'

'Folly is not a good word. I suggest you do not use it. It would make it sound as if you were thinking what was wise and what was foolish and not of what your position really was – that you had all made a certain decision as prisoners-of-war, with a certain idea at its end, and here was the idea in ruins, with the Japanese being beaten back and not any longer looking likely to march on Delhi to hoist the Rising Sun in place of the Union Jack. Which meant that all of you were in ruins too, unless you abandoned whatever post the Japanese had left you to hold before leaving you in the lurch, abandoned it and retreated and ran back after the Japanese to share their defeat with them. Perhaps to fight another day. Perhaps not. It seems to me, Sayed, that the one thing your INA never took into account was what was to happen if the Japanese *were* defeated. Or were you so convinced of their superiority that the eventuality never occurred to you? Were you by any chance relying on the defection of the Indian Army, the moment they saw Indians marching shoulder to shoulder with the Japanese? Did you think the Indian Army would at once turn on its British officers and join with you and the Japanese to massacre the British Army?'

Sayed did not reply. But he got up and went towards the other pleader's table. 'Yes,' Kasim said, misunderstanding. 'Smoke if you want to. And then tell me how you tried to convince these men of yours of their folly. But I hope you were thinking not of folly but of dishonour.'

But Sayed had gone on past the table, hands behind back. For a moment he stood near the rail behind which when the court was in session the public sat. Then he came back and stood looking down at his father.

'No,' he said. 'I asked them, "What folly is this? What mercy do you expect from the British or even from our own fellows who are commanded by them and dare not disobey? You will all be shot like dogs just as so many of our people have always been treated like dogs. Isn't it better to die here?" Then one of them said, "Major Sahib, we do not care. To surrender is our only chance now of seeing our families again, so let the British and our own old comrades shoot us if they want to, it no more matters. We do not care either about the British or the Japanese. Staying here we shall all be killed anyway, and our women and children will starve, no one will see to them or bother about them and it will all be up with them." Then another said, "Here we are only so many, but most of us are thinking like this, that we must risk being shot, because it is our only chance. You have only to ask the others. We are all thinking the same. That it is all finished with us!"'

'Please sit. I cannot speak to you while you are standing up.'

'It's easier for me to stand, father. So let me tell you. I sent these men away and assembled the others. There weren't many of us left anyway. I said, Well what is the decision of the majority? Who is for surrendering and chancing being shot? One hand went up and then another until there were only a few hands not up. Including mine. Then I went away to be alone for a bit. Perhaps you would have preferred me to do what it was in my mind to do. Shoot myself. A very honourable solution. But what is the good to India of a dead Indian just now? And perhaps also I wished to see my family again, only it was not even that I was allowed to see my own mother before she died.'

'Sayed –'

'No. Let me speak please. You are talking about a world that exists only in a court of law and I am not. In the world as it is it is necessary to act sometimes according to the heart –'

'I do not advise this, Sayed. It is pure emotional rhetoric. It will not get you anywhere.'

'Will not get me anywhere? Where is this place I am supposed to be going? Where is all this supposed to be leading, this advice you are giving me? The truth is that after all you don't intend to help me. You are giving me a lot of ideas about how to placate the British. Why should they be placated? What right have they to say what I shall do and what I shall not do?'

'I am helping you in the only way I can. I must make it clear to you that I don't intend to make political capital out of this. I cannot advise you to present your own case in a political framework. I do not intend to take that road. I advise you not to. I do not approve of what you have done. I do not approve of INA. I shall not identify myself with any committee set up for the defence nor shall I defend you in court, although to do so would be a very popular thing in the country generally. On the other hand I shall not criticize you, nor the INA, to anyone, which is perhaps what Government

1430

has been hoping I would do. I do not intend to commit political suicide, although you will appreciate that the situation I find myself in does not augur well for my immediate political future.'

Kasim paused; went on before Sayed had a chance to speak: 'If you plead guilty I will continue to help you. I will help to choose and to instruct your defence counsel, but in a wholly private and confidential manner. Everything I have been trying to put into your mind this morning as the proper way to conduct your case has been to this end: that you should plead guilty to waging war against the King, and then submit a reasoned statement setting out the considerations that led you to do so. Pleading guilty is the only way you can come out of court with any kind of personal integrity left.'

Sayed, still standing, had looked away, but now turned on Kasim. 'Integrity? What else have you ever done, father, except wage war against the King? Hasn't this been your whole life, to get rid of the British? What is the difference between you and me except that you went to prison now and again and I carried a gun?'

'You have just explained the difference, Sayed. If you cannot see it, then it is pointless to discuss it any further. So yes, come, come. Let us finish. We are simply aggravating one another.'

He got up.

'You are throwing everything away,' Sayed said.

'Not everything.'

'No one will trust or respect you if you don't stand up for us along with other political leaders.'

'I hope it is not my fear of this that you have been relying on?' He made to go, but stopped, unable to part with his son on such terms. 'It is you who have thrown away everything, Sayed. The men who did not are the Indian soldiers and officers who are still in prison-camp, who resisted all these perhaps understandable and pardonable temptations and suffered infinitely greater hardship, and who will now be coming home. In a year or so, if you are not in prison, where will you be? For a time yes, you will all be heroes. But when there is no longer any reason to treat you as heroes, then you will be forgotten or if you are remembered at all it will be with mistrust, as men who broke their contracts, men who voluntarily took an oath of loyalty and then disregarded it, men who treated their commissions as mere scraps of paper to be used or thrown away as they thought fit. And if you *do* go to prison for this meanwhile, I beg of you do not try to console yourself with the thought that you and your father have both in your time suffered the same punishment for the same crime. It will not be so. The only contract I have ever made of this kind is with myself, to do what I could to obtain the independence and freedom and unity and strength of this country. Whenever in earlier days I defied the law it was in performance of that contract, and I defied it knowing full well the penalty and indeed inviting the penalty and proudly admitting that I had incurred it. The last time I went to prison was because I would not repudiate my membership of a party that Government lawfully suppressed. Unjustly but lawfully suppressed. It is true that at one time I was sworn in as a minister and it is true that I and all my colleagues resigned when we felt we could not any longer participate in an administration under the British. But a soldier cannot resign in wartime. When you became a soldier, Sayed, this fact should have been clearly in your mind as defining the difference between us. I did not interfere with your decision to become a soldier because I asked myself what kind of independent country will India be if we do not have a properly trained and experienced professional army to defend that independence. That the British allowed Indians to become officers I have always taken as a sign of their good faith in the matter of eventually bowing to our demands to rule ourselves. But that is by the way. What is not by the way is that now you can no longer be a soldier, you can no longer help your country. And this is what angers me. Your life so far has been wasted.'

Sayed stared at him.

'It is not a country. It is two countries. Perhaps it is many countries, but primarily it is two. If I'm not wanted in one perhaps I shall be wanted in the other.'

'Ah!' Kasim exclaimed. And sat down. 'So this also has happened to you. Then we are even more deeply divided.'

'We're only divided by your refusal to face facts, father, and by your reliance on this and that legal interpretation, also I begin to think by your reliance on the British to act as gentlemen. I no longer believe in such concepts. I have seen too much of life. It is no good relying on principles and no good relying on the British who themselves have no principles that can't be trimmed to suit *them*. In any case, they are finished. They are no longer of importance and will drag us down with them if we aren't careful. They are only interested in themselves and always have been. But now they are afraid of the Americans and the Russians and will try to get rid of India as quick as they can, both to curry favour with the USA and USSR and not to have any longer the responsibility. They will hand us over to Gandhi and Nehru and Patel – and then where will you be, father? How can you trust Congress as a whole? How can you imagine that just because you've been useful to them in the past you – a Muslim – will be allowed to remain useful when they have power? They will squeeze you out at the first convenient opportunity. Congress is a Hindu party whatever they pretend. They will exploit us as badly as the British have done, probably worse. There's only one answer and that is to seize what we can for ourselves and run things our own way from there.'

Sayed leaned over the table.

'When you say my military career is finished, I would agree with you. It would be finished if the British stay and finished if we merely substitute a Hindu for a British *raj*. It would be finished because I'm a Muslim and they hate us. Also they hate each other. A Hindu from UP hates a Hindu from Bengal and both hate a Hindu from the South. A Hindu *raj* would be a catastrophe. They have nothing to hold them together. They hate and envy us mostly because we have such a thing. We have Islam. It will be madness not to resist them. The only thing that matters in this world, father, is power. We must grasp our own. Surely it is true you have been thinking of this too? Please, do not be too proud? I do not want to see you become neglected and bitter in your old age.'

Kasim kept his attention on his son's hands: good, square capable hands. No sign of a tremor. Nor perhaps of sensitivity. He kept his own clasped.

'You are asking me to throw everything away and go over to the League?'

'It wouldn't be throwing anything away. Guzzy and Nita are very keen on this, I think. Their letters are full of hints. Jinnah would welcome you. Almost I imagine he is expecting it, because you have been so difficult for people to get hold of.'

'And Ahmed? Is he keen?'

'What does Ahmed know about anything? He is still a child.'

'No,' Kasim said. 'He is not a child.'

'Well, no, no, not in that way. A man with a reputation I gather.'

'A reputation?'

'For liking the things a man likes.'

'Women? Drinking? This is so.'

'He should be careful. It must worry you.'

Kasim did not reply. He noted the solicitous tone in his son's voice. Which verged on condescension. Sayed added, 'Perhaps he is like this because he feels himself to be without chance or opportunity.'

'You mean he does not agree with the things I stand for?'

'How can I say, father? He is a good boy at heart, I'm sure. I shall try to find out what he thinks, shall I?'

'He does not think about much. Except these things you mentioned. And hawking.'

'Hawking?'

'He was always very keen on riding. Now he has trained a falcon. It is very difficult, you know. It demands much attention and concentration. Sleepless nights. All that sort of thing. But he is much attached to her. He goes out whenever he can.'

'But that is good! A good manly sport. I am glad. I should not like him to become dissipated.'

Sayed placed one hand on his father's coupled ones. Kasim did not look up. But he felt, as a physical pressure, the steady way his elder son watched him.

'Perhaps we should say goodbye now, father. Thank you for coming to see me.'

'It is you who have come the greater distance.'

'That is my duty.'

Kasim stood up. Dutifully too, he held his arms out. They embraced. Speaking into his son's shoulder he said, 'Do not rely too much on this

Colonel Merrick. He has known Ahmed for some time. He has told neither of you that he knew the other.'

'He told me just before he brought you in, father. But don't worry. I rely on no Englishman. He is of no importance either.'

'They will be waiting for you outside, no doubt. No doubt you can see Ahmed alone in here also, but you had better go out now. It would offend me to see you in custody of any kind. By the time they bring you back in I shall be gone.'

'You will write to me?'

Kasim nodded. He murmured: Allah be with you. Then released him and moved away. He heard his son's firm, heavy footsteps; and in a while the opening and closing of a door. He looked round the empty court-room and, familiar though it was, as such rooms went, it seemed to him lacking in the quality that gave such rooms meaning or even the dimensions of reality. Then he walked out by way of the daïs and the magistrate's room, through the corridor and along it in search of the room that had been set aside for him.

*

By the time they drove into the siding at Premnagar it was nearly half-past ten. There was barely an hour before the night train from Mirat to Ranpur was due to stop and pick them up. The stationmaster was fussing because the coach had to be shunted to a more convenient place for coupling and he had expected them by ten o'clock.

A puncture had delayed them. For half-an-hour Kasim had waited on the roadside, listening to the wind in the telegraph wires. The night sky had no luminosity. The wind held the smell of approaching rain; a small rain; but better than a heavy rain in country like this which the wet monsoon either avoided or flooded, first drying the top-soil for a couple of years, then sweeping it away. He welcomed the rain and the darkness of the sky. The fort, unsilhouetted, had entirely disappeared. He welcomed the wind and the air. It was good to feel braced and chilled after the heat and humidity of the room in the Circuit House; but he knew he might catch cold. Instinctively he had felt in his pocket for the onion that was supposed to ward colds off. There was no onion. He had given that up when his wife died.

Now to the stationmaster's fussing, Booby was adding his own. Where were the steps by which to mount? 'We don't need steps,' Kasim said and reached for the handgrips, heaved himself up only to find himself steadied unexpectedly from inside by Ahmed who had been in the coach collecting the small suitcase he'd brought from Mirat and was now going to take back to Mirat in the Nawab's Daimler.

'Surely you're not going yet?'

'Not for a moment or two, father. I didn't want to forget it though.'

'Well give it to one of the people to take to the car then come and talk to me for a moment.' He was conscious of the peremptory tone in his voice and wasn't encouraged by it. He went down the corridor. Hosain was waiting. He slid the door open.

'Tell them to bring tea or something.'

He entered the compartment. Before he could sit Mr Mehboob followed him in and put the briefcase on a seat.

'Where is Ahmed? I want to see him alone for a moment. And please shut the door. I've been standing all that time in the open.'

'You shouldn't have got out on to the road, Minister, when we had the puncture.'

'How can they change a wheel with two people like us sitting at ease in the back? It is bad for the springs, Ahmed says, and it is the Nawab's car and must be returned in good condition.'

Hurt, Booby left the compartment and began to close the door but opened it again for Ahmed. Sulkily he shut it when Ahmed was inside.

'Come, sit, they are bringing tea.'

Ahmed looked at his watch but sat down. 'I've not time for tea, father, it's a long drive and the chauffeur wants to go to a garage to get the punctured wheel repaired so that we have a spare.'

'There will be no garage open at this hour.'

'He knows of one.'

'It will take hours. You will get cold standing around.'

'What he advises is best, father. So I mustn't be long. Anyway they're going to move the carriage at any moment.'

'I don't like you travelling alone in a car at night all the way to Mirat. It is a bad area round here. And the escort van has gone.'

'I shan't be alone, father. There's the driver. Anyway, Booby came down at night. I can take care of myself just as well as he can.'

'Booby is paid to risk his life,' Kasim said. But smiled. Encouraged by Ahmed's answering smile he said, 'We have had no opportunity to talk today.' That was untrue. He had deliberately avoided being alone with Ahmed. 'What I want to suggest is that you come back now to Ranpur. Come back for a few days. There is a great deal to do and a great deal you can help me with. Poor Booby is such a muddler. Ring Dmitri in the morning and explain the necessity. If you like, send a note back with the driver too.'

'I promised Dmitri I'd be away only two nights. There's a meeting of Council tomorrow.'

'Council, council. He doesn't need you. The Council is Dmitri. Anyway, you do not attend these meetings personally.'

His heart sank. It was so badly said. He wished he could withdraw the imputation that Ahmed's official duties in Mirat were negligible; although he knew they were. He should never have agreed to Ahmed going to work in Mirat – but then he should never have let his elder son go into the army. Both had seemed acceptable enough solutions at the time. He had found adequate explanations: that India would need experienced officers; that it

1435

could be useful to have a son experienced in the administration of feudal survivals like the princely states. But for months now he had found these explanations less convincing than the other explanation – that in his heart he had felt at the time that neither son was capable of contributing much more. Neither son had inherited the spark. Neither son cared deeply about the things he cared for himself. The only thing he could still convince himself of was that he had believed, hoped, that in time they would, that their occupations would help to nourish in them the necessary passion, determination, and restraint.

'Well,' he said, 'if you must go back, you must.' He was not going to beg. Nor was he going to admit that he could not bear the thought of returning to the empty old house in the Kandipat road alone; although he believed that Ahmed understood this. When he had said to Sayed, *No, Ahmed is not a child*, he had not meant what Sayed thought he meant. He had been thinking of the occasion when Ahmed startled him with a shrewd assessment of the situation in which he might find himself – indeed now found himself; startled him into realizing it at a moment when he had been incapable of thinking clearly; the previous occasion at the Circuit House when they had brought him unprepared, without breakfast, from the fort, telling him nothing, so that he had feared the worst, that his wife was ill or dead and that they were releasing him on compassionate grounds as they had released Bapu when Kasturba was dying. He had nearly disgraced himself – finding Ahmed there – pathetically crying out 'Then God is good!' when Ahmed reassured him. Relief had been followed by bitter resignation when the truth came out, that his release was only partial, that he must suffer the humiliation of living under restriction at Mirat, and the bitter-sweet humiliation of learning that his wife was to share that restriction with him. And after the relief, the resignation and the humiliation, had come the shock of hearing Ahmed speak so calmly of Sayed's capture in Manipur. Outraged, he had not only called his first-born son a traitor, but had insulted Ahmed. It had been unforgiveable, yet Ahmed had seemed to forgive it, had gone on, speaking calmly still, intelligently, about the motives Government might have in releasing him from the fort. It could have been the turning point in their relationship. His own stubbornness, his peremptoriness, his coldness of manner – carefully nurtured defences against the Islamic sin of betraying emotion – had perhaps been the chief impediments to closer understanding. And yet after that one moment, that opportunity they had had to be closer to one another, Ahmed had seemed to withdraw again. It was as if the spark of involvement and commitment had failed to ignite. Subsequently, Kasim had tried tentatively to kindle it again and sometimes Ahmed had seemed to respond, but when his mother became ill, fatally ill, the capacity to respond had seemed to be deliberately smothered, and he had become again merely dutiful in matters where dutifulness seemed obligatory. As now, when he was dutifully sitting on the opposite seat, but leaning forward, hands clasped, indicating imminent departure.

'Well tell me, Ahmed, how *you* found things with Sayed?'

'He looked very fit and cheerful, I thought. He says he's treated pretty well.'

'I know. I know. Did he say anything you feel you should tell me?'

'We talked about hawking mostly. We weren't alone. One of the subalterns sat in the room.'

'But why was this?'

'Major Merrick said his instructions were that only you could be alone with him. But he made the subaltern sit where he couldn't hear easily. It didn't matter really. It was amusing if anything.'

'He is now Colonel Merrick. Didn't you notice? Also he is either equally unobservant or deceitful. He told me Sayed was not among those he'd classify as unrepentantly proud of what he has done. It wasn't my impression. Was it yours?'

'I'd no impression either way. We didn't talk about that kind of thing.'

'Just about hawking?'

'No, but mostly about me. I'm afraid I couldn't think what to ask him about himself. One day must seem to him much like another, after all.'

'What things about you, other than hawking?'

'Oh, personal things.' Ahmed grinned. 'He said Merrick saw me drinking whisky in Bombay. He said I should stop that.'

And, Kasim thought, they had probably talked about their mother's illness and death, the temporary burial at Nanoora that would have to be gone through again so that she could rest finally in the Kasim tomb in Ranpur.

'He said nothing about Jinnah, then?'

'Oh, yes. He said he thought Nita was becoming very pro-Jinnah.'

'Only that?'

'Well he said Nita was probably pro-Jinnah because Guzzy was, and that wives usually follow their husbands in such things.'

The steward knocked, slid back the door and brought in tea.

'You'll change your mind, Ahmed?'

'No, I haven't time. I must go in a minute.'

'Then bring it later,' Kasim told the steward. The steward went. 'Sayed did not ask you your own view of Jinnah?'

'No.'

'He did not tell you he had strongly recommended me to go over? And that he had undertaken to find out your own feelings?'

'No. Nothing like that at all.'

'Obviously he had begun to when he mentioned Nita. Were you interrupted soon after?'

'Yes, they came and said time was up. We'd had our ten minutes or whatever it was.'

'That's all they allowed? It doesn't matter. What matters is that he attempted to do what he said he'd do. So let me settle the question – what your feelings would be if I went over to the League. The League is very strongly placed. In the last few years while most of the Congress was in prison they have paved the way to divide the country. In the elections they are likely to win most of the seats reserved for Muslims. Even my own is not safe. If I offered myself to the League Jinnah would welcome me. I might even get a portfolio in whatever central government he's able to set up in whatever kind of Pakistan he is able to wrest out of us. To make sure of a portfolio I could also do what perhaps a father should. Publicly defend my son against charges of treason. I put it to you in these crude terms because for once, Ahmed, for once I am asking you to tell me what your honest opinion would be if I did these things. You said a moment ago that women always followed their husbands in such matters. Your mother always followed me. It was not easy for her eventually because her own family became very Pakistan conscious and very Jinnah conscious, just as Nita and Guzzy have become. What I am asking you is whether you and Sayed and Nita and your mother were thinking that I was wrong all the time, and that you were all conforming and saying nothing out of family loyalty. Whether it is your view that now I should in turn conform for everybody's sake, including my own.'

Beneath them the coach wheels clanked. The coach had been coupled to a shunting engine.

'I've got no view, father,' Ahmed said, getting up. 'You know I don't understand all these ins and outs. They don't seem to me to have anything to do with ordinary problems, though I suppose they must. But however many solutions are found people are still always dying of starvation. All that kind of thing. Or if they aren't dying of starvation they're killing one another senselessly. It all means nothing to me, parties and such-like.'

Kasim got up too.

'Then it means you don't care either way? That is one question out of the way at least. I shan't have to consider your feelings, or rather shan't have to feel conscience-stricken about you as well as Sayed. That is a relief. You see I made my mind up long ago what I would have to do. I have only been waiting for the moment when I was forced to take action. Let me just say this to you, Ahmed, that whatever your answer had been, my mind would not have been altered. But one likes to know where one stands with one's own family. To me Sayed is a man whose actions remain indefensible because he broke his word, he broke his contract. It follows that I cannot break mine. Never in my life shall I go over to Jinnah. I did not say so to Sayed because I felt he did not deserve an answer either way –'

The train shoved forward a yard or two and stopped abruptly. They avoided being thrown together by reaching for different handholds to steady themselves.

'So that is the position,' he said, righting himself. 'You, I think, deserve to know. You had better go now, if you're not coming to Ranpur.'

He slid the door open and led the way down the deserted corridor. The train, after the clanking and jerking was unnaturally still, as if it had died.

The carpet muffled the sound of footsteps. When he turned round, near the exit, it was almost a shock to find Ahmed so close behind him.

Formally he embraced him.

'Do not hang around too long in that garage. Find yourself some coffee or something.'

'Yes, father, I'll do that.'

'And something stronger, no doubt, I expect you have your flask.' He could smell the whisky behind the scent of garlic on his son's breath. He let the boy go, then stopped him.

'What I have said about Sayed, please never repeat. It might make things worse for him. The other thing, about Jinnah, is in confidence. It will become public knowledge soon, though. Since you profess political detachment I can't expect you to approve or disapprove, but I'm sorry if I've spoken roughly. I haven't meant to upset you.'

Again the train jerked and this time began moving slowly forward. Ahmed grasped one handrail and began to get down. 'Why should I be upset?' he asked. 'I've won my bet with Dmitri. He bet me you'd go over to Jinnah. I bet him you wouldn't.' The shunting engine's whistle pierced. He raised his voice. 'He wouldn't offer stakes, though. We both expected me to win really.'

Ahmed jumped and ran for several paces to maintain momentum.

'Ahmed!' Kasim cried, wanting him back.

'Mind yourself! Shut the door!' Ahmed shouted, coming to a halt in the cinder-yard.

'Ahmed! What do you mean? Expected, or wanted? Ahmed!'

But the cinder-yard had got up speed, taking Ahmed with it, taking him out of earshot, revealing more of its detail in the shape of coal bunkers and go-downs, the sudden glare of an arc-lamp, and then a suffocating smoky darkness which drove him in, back almost into Booby Sahib's arms.

'Minister, what are you doing? Why is the door open? Why isn't someone here looking after things in a proper way? It is getting so that no one can be relied on to look after you at all.'

'No, Booby,' he said, placing a hand on the fat pudgy shoulder. 'I am well looked after.'

IV

They paused in the ante-room while the *aide* who had called for him and Booby with a car at the Kandipat road knocked at the door, opened it, and then with a slight bow indicated that Kasim should go in and that Booby Sahib should stay where he was.

When Kasim entered, the Governor was half-way across the long high-ceilinged room. He had on what looked like the same crumpled chalk-striped suit he'd worn on the day of the laying of the Chakravarti foundation-stone. He carried his spectacles in his left hand; the right was being offered.

'Mr Kasim. Prompt as usual. How are you?'

'Very well, thank you, Governor-ji. But this time the promptness is due chiefly to your Captain Thackeray who brought the car on time.'

'The car didn't embarrass you? I'm told your house has been pretty well besieged all day.'

'Chiefly by well-wishers, fortunately.'

'Good. I thought we'd sit here. The fire's not really on. Just the imaginary coal bit. Say if you're cold.'

Without Malcolm having done anything visible to command it, the Government House magic worked, in the shape of doors opening and servants bringing in tea. There were five of them. Malcolm ignored them. They simply operated.

'How is Lady Malcolm, Governor? I hope better?'

'Somewhat better, thank you.'

'Not as good as you hoped?'

'No. I'm trying to get her to go home to see a particular chap. It's just a question of finding a way of persuading her to leave Ootacamund. Then we'll see.'

They were now surrounded by an English-Indian tea. Kasim could smell the curry-puffs without even looking for them. The servants vanished as smoothly as they had appeared. When the last one had gone, Kasim said:

'I shall not be contesting the elections.'

'Yes, I see.' Only the voice betrayed disappointment. The face remained calm.

'I shall recommend to my colleagues in the Congress Party that a man called Fazal Huq Rahman should stand in my old constituency. He is still very anti-Jinnah very competent, and in my opinion stands the best chance of holding this Muslim seat for Congress, although undoubtedly my old sparring partner Nawaz Shah will leap at the opportunity to pass his own seat on to someone else and contest mine on behalf of the League.'

They sipped the tea which the servants had poured.

'Nawaz Shah?'

'Abdul Nawaz Shah. Not to be confused with Shah Nawaz Khan.'

The Governor smiled. He said, 'I wasn't Governor at the time, but I seem to remember you wanted Abdul Nawaz Shah in your nineteen thirty-seven Ministry.'

'He is an able and dedicated man and in nineteen thirty-seven there were constitutional grounds for forming a coalition, as well as reasonable hopes of satisfying the League that our policies were not after all anti-Muslim. Now of course such hopes are very slender.'

'Yes. I'm afraid they are.' Malcolm put his cup down. 'All this means that you're also not going to align yourself with the defence of the INA?'

'Yes. It means that.'

'Does it help if I point out that elections in this province won't take place

1440

until some time in the New Year? By which time the subject of the INA might not be so delicate?'

'Not really, Governor. The election *campaigns* will begin almost at once. It is clear that the subject of the INA will be taken up strongly by both major parties and just as clear that unless I align myself with the defence of INA personnel I should lose an important Muslim seat for Congress. The electorate would say, Who is this man who won't defend even his own son?'

'But my dear Mr Kasim, no one would blame you for defending your son, for defending the INA. I least of all.'

'I have imagined you would not. It is what you were delicately hinting when we had lunch a couple of weeks ago. On earlier occasions I detected from Government rather less delicate hints that it was hoped I might lead an attack on these fellows.'

'Is it your intention to lead an attack?'

'No. I do not have a suicidal turn of mind.'

'Well that's one good piece of news at least. On the other hand, if you don't publicly defend the INA and your son, how can you survive, politically?'

'I do not know whether I can survive. But I am an old enough professional to know that when you do not know how, you bide your time. I will do nothing to help nourish this idea that the INA are heroes. Eventually other people may agree with me. A free and independent India may not want to employ such officers. But personally I should not like to feel that at one time I defended them, and then refused to employ them. So for me it is simply a question of refusing now. Many of them had perhaps understandable and excusable reasons. But how can you judge which man had what reason? Let into your army one man of the suspect kind I have in mind and you plant the seed of a military dictatorship, you nurture a man who will throw away his commission again and challenge and even overthrow a properly constituted civil authority. I do not want a government of generals. I do not want to see such an India. I do not believe there will be such an India. But too much adulation of INA seems to me the best way of getting such an India. So, for the moment, I must be what you call *hors de combat* because I am out of rhythm with my country's temporary emotional feelings, and the country's temporary emotional feelings are out of rhythm with my own. I should be, as you also say, rusticated, for everybody's sake. So, Kasim, I tell myself. Go and cultivate your garden for a while.' He smiled. 'At Premanagar I had plenty of practice.'

Malcolm smiled too. He said, 'Not everyone has the taste for martyrdom, Mr Kasim. It rather surprises me to sense it in you.'

'Martyrdom? Oh, no, you've got me all wrong! A martyr is the last thing I'm cut out for. I am a very practical man, even a pragmatist. The equal of any Englishman in that respect. But I have trained myself to take the long view also and taking the long view has taught me that you have to live for ever with a single moment of short-sightedness.'

'Well let's not say martyrdom. Just let's say you're putting a very high price on your conscience, your moral sense. Does it follow you've put a low one on the ultimate good of this province?'

'Governor, you know that this is a Congress majority province. Whoever you invite to form a government will be a Congressman. The price I exact for my moral sense is one Muslim seat, one minority seat in the assembly. So. My temporary rustication is bought very cheaply. I could not possibly win it in all the circumstances.'

'Temporary rustication? What have you in mind?'

'At the moment only cultivating my garden. Doing everything I can to promote the claims of Fazal Huq Rahman and disputing the claims of Jinnah and his League for partition. Oh, they will soon see that I am not in his camp. And, if I am asked my views about INA, I shall take – forgive me – the line of the English gentleman. I shall say, "How can I comment on such matters when I, my son, my whole family are involved? It is for others to speak." Also I shall fall back on the time-honoured excuse that certain family misfortunes and personal health do not make me a suitable candidate for elections in the coming cold weather. Now, what do you give me for my moral sense? You see what a Machiavellian viper you have been harbouring in your bosom?'

Malcolm put his head back, closed his eyes and laughed.

'So, Governor. May we have just another word about Fazal Huq Rahman?'

Malcolm put his spectacles on and looked at Kasim. He said, 'What more of Fazal Huq Rahman?'

'Should he defeat Nawaz Shah in the elections, which is very unlikely, and a misfortune for India which we can attribute to the late Lord Minto. ...'

'Why Lord Minto?'

'It was during his viceroyalty that the decision to provide separate electorates for Muslims was taken –'

'Entirely as a result of Muslim pressure –'

'That is technically so, but Minto need not have agreed. He and the British wanted to agree, he was unconsciously dividing and ruling. Lady Minto was dividing and ruling quite consciously. You never should have allowed your memsahibs into the country. It was she who greeted the arrangement for separate electorates with cries of amazon joy, because what she called Indian national subversion had been effectively blocked. It is to people like the Mintos we owe Jinnah.'

Malcolm was smiling. 'Go back to Fazal Huq Rahman,' he said.

'I was about to. I was merely reminding you, Sir George, of the political background to these constitutional absurdities. It is as though, Sir George, at home you had separate electorates for Protestants, Catholics, non-conformists, evangelists and Christian-Scientists. Communalism has been written into our political structure by the *raj*. The cold weather elections will be fought on a religious not a political issue. However,

1442

should Fazal Huq Rahman persuade his Muslim majority constituency that unity and not separation is the answer, which is doubtful, let me first of all say that he is not yet of ministerial calibre, and then reassure you that he is neither relative nor friend nor the friend of a cousin to whom I owe some favour –'

Again Malcolm put his head back. He took off his spectacles and wiped his eyes. He said, 'What should I do about Fazal Huq Rahman?'

'When you discuss portfolios with your new chief-minister designate, he will suggest a man for Education and no doubt like all good Governors you will raise no objection. But having raised no objection it would be useful if you could introduce Fazal Huq Rahman's name into the conversation and indicate some interest in seeing him in that department with a brief of some kind.'

'I'll keep my eye open, Mr Kasim. Perhaps nearer the time you'll help to guide it finally in the right direction?'

'I don't think that would be very wise. I don't think, you know, that we ought to see each other again except in public, socially.'

The Governor gazed at him steadily. He said, 'I should be sorry for that. But I must leave it to you. Are you going back to practise the law?'

'No, no. I am a fortunate man. I don't have to earn a living, as you know.'

'I really meant, interest yourself in legal matters?'

'One never loses one's interest.'

'No, quite. What I meant was identify yourself with what I might call quasi-legal committees set up to look into matters involving possible legal processes or inquiries?'

'You are referring to matters that might arise from the civil disturbances that followed Government's arrests of Congressmen like myself?'

'Yes.'

'And the way they were put down?'

'And the way they were put down.'

'No, I am not interested in anything like that. To me it is all water under the bridge. Turbulent water at the time but to me it is foolish to re-disturb it. Now I think I must go.' He got up. Malcolm got up too. Kasim said, 'Thank you for what you arranged, and hoped to arrange. Next year you can forget all these things. I hope Lady Malcolm will soon be fully recovered.'

'Thank you.'

They began to walk slowly towards the doors that led to the ante-room. Then Malcolm stopped. He said, 'Mr Kasim, do you remember the last thing I said to you in this room, just before you went off to the Premanagar Fort?'

'Yes, I remember it very well. You said you would leave a thought in my mind, that one day this room might be mine.'

'Is it what you'd like? If so, I think I might almost guarantee it. It's not the same as heading a Ministry, but it has its compensations. Ranpur hasn't had an Indian Governor before but you wouldn't be the first Indian Governor appointed in the country.'

'You mean sworn in, not appointed.'

'Well, yes.'

Kasim felt the tremor beginning again in his right arm and hand. Almost unconsciously he steadied it by clasping the right wrist. For a moment the temptations of the peak – that splendid heady upper air, that immensity of landscape – made his head sing.

He heard himself saying, 'Well you see how difficult that would be, unless the Viceroy had been succeeded by a Governor-General of a self-governing dominion, and unless his executive council had been superseded by an Indian cabinet responsible to a freely elected central Indian assembly. And in that context a provincial governorship, if such a thing survives which I suppose it will, will be a job for an old man. Please don't misunderstand me.'

'I don't misunderstand.'

'Furthermore, for me to be sworn in, when you retire, would necessitate severing my active party political connections.'

'I understand that too. I suppose I was looking for a way of ensuring that your rustication isn't too permanent.'

'Well that is my problem but it is kind of you to involve yourself in it.'

'Not kind, Mr Kasim. I am involved whether I like it or not. But I prefer to like it. How serious were you when you said we oughtn't to see each other again in private?'

'Oh, very serious. I try not to say things lightly.'

'In that case is there anything I can do apart from saying goodbye and wishing you good luck?'

'Oh yes, one small thing. I am almost ashamed to mention it.'

'But please –'

'I know that any letters Sayed writes to members of his family and any letters members of his family write to Sayed must be opened and censored. That is quite correct in all the circumstances. But it has become onerous to feel that one can neither write nor receive letters from whomsoever on whatsoever subject that have not been looked at by strangers – no doubt perfectly disinterested fellows just doing their jobs. But it tends to limit one's sense of one's right to proper self-expression, and is so ridiculous when by contrast I know I can come here and frankly and freely speak my mind.'

'I attended to that a couple of days ago when a particular point was brought to my notice and I realized it was still going on. But give it a day or two –' Malcolm smiled – 'you know how slowly any administration works.'

'Oh yes. I know, only too well. Thank you. Good-night, Governor.'

'Good-night, Mr Kasim.'

*

The crowds were still there in the Kandipat road, in the dark, patient, waiting to welcome him back from whatever great occasion he had gone out on. At the entrance to the house the progress of the car was interrupted. Thackeray was not in the car and there was nothing to identify it as one from Government House, but tomorrow it would be all round Ranpur where he had been. By then it would not matter and tonight it did not matter, to the patient crowds, where he had been or what he had done. It was enough for them that he had been out and done something in this sort of style, challenging the *raj*. With such crowds Booby was a different man. He beamed, he smiled, he rolled the window down and said cheerfully, 'Okay, okay, what is all this, what are you waiting for, he is tired can't you see, please let us pass. Tomorrow is another day. He will have something to say then. *Hán, hán*! *Jai Hind. Jai Hind.* All people go home now. Everything is okay.'

And rolled the window up as the crowd divided like a Red Sea and the car swept in through the iron gates. 'You see, Minister,' Booby said enthusiastically, 'here we are finally at home.'

*

Booby had even arranged that the fountain should play in the shallow pool in the miniature inner courtyard. Kasim leant on the railing that protected the second floor balcony and watched the dimly lit aquarium-effect for a while. Then he went back to the room he had asked should be set aside for him – the room his father had studied and meditated in during his own widowerhood – a room without ornament, with cream-washed walls, fretted windows, a simple bed, a desk, a chair, two lamps (oil-lit in his father's day, now electric). He sat at the desk and again opened Bapu's letter.

'Minister?'

'What is it, Booby?'

'Can I get you anything?'

'No, no, but come in, sit down.'

There was nowhere for Booby to sit so Kasim vacated the chair and sat on the bed. Still Booby did not sit.

'You must sleep,' he said, 'you did not sleep all night again.'

'I am not tired. I must draft a letter to Bapu.'

'Please, dictate it. I have my pad and pencil.'

'No. I shall draft it. Then we can discuss it. Then it can be typed.' Booby's shorthand left a lot to be desired. Old Mahsood had had no shorthand. Somehow this had not seemed to matter.

'Very well,' Booby said. 'Then there is for the moment only the question of the letter from Pandit Baba.'

Kasim shut his eyes and flicked his hand, negatively. 'Oh, throw it away, Booby. It is all water under the bridge. We have never answered him before. Why should we answer now? We do not even know, only guess, what he is bothering me personally for. He is a tiresome man and of no account.'

'Yes, Minister. I will throw it away then. Mr Chakravarti has rung. Inviting you to dinner next week.'

'I cannot go to dinner with Chakravarti next week.'

'I will tell him so.'

'No, do not tell him. Accept and then decline later. The day before. It is so much less complicated. What else?'

'Mrs Nawaz Shah also rang.'

'So she can ring.'

Kasim looked up. Booby nodded. Expressionless. But somehow approving. Perhaps Booby would do after all.

'And?'

'Ahmed rang from Mirat this afternoon while we were out.'

'Saying what?'

'I couldn't get hang of it. We need more intelligent staff, Minister.'

'Perhaps. Tomorrow we'll discuss this, but primarily I shall leave it to you. What did the message say?'

'It is completely without meaning.' Booby referred to a note. 'Three words only. "Expected and wanted." '

'That is all?'

'That is all, Minister.'

Kasim smiled. 'It is enough. Thank you, Booby. That is all for tonight.'

*

After a while he got up from the bed and sat at the desk and began drafting the letter to Bapu. He inscribed the heading: To Mr Mohandas Karamchand Gandhi.

Dear Bapu, (he wrote)

Thank you for your letter and your kind expression of sympathy in the loss of my old friend Mahsood. As you know he was with me for many years and now all that is over. One feels such a loss. I am grateful for your letter because it helps me knowing the loss is shared.

It has, however, been a particular blow, coming on top of others and frankly I am in low spirits and prey to all kinds of doubts and uncertainties. Please do not misunderstand. I have no doubts whatsoever about our commitment to the cause of freedom and unity and non-violence to which you have given not only your life's work but also inspiration to the rest of us. This cause I shall never abandon. The uncertainties I spoke of arise from many different sources. For instance –

Momentarily Kasim's inspiration failed. Then he continued: For instance, I find myself uncertain which of two recent events – the election of a socialist government in London and the destruction of Hiroshima by a single atomic bomb – will have the profounder effect on India's future. It is this pressure from the world outside India that perhaps creates these uncertainties in my mind, although I am sure these outside pressures are reflected in pressures from within. On the one hand, there is the element that one might call purely political, and on the other an element one cannot but see as rooted in or flowing from a power that goes beyond the norm of what we morally understand by power –

Kasim broke off. He stared at the paper for a while. The words meant so little. What was in his mind seemed to mean so little too. It was the world outside his mind, the world he felt he couldn't encompass that meant much. Tonight, it couldn't be reached.

Coda for Operation Zipper

Early that September, coming into the harbour of Georgetown on the island of Penang, where the tide was presumably low, the first detachment of re-occupying British troops observed what looked like an uncomfortably large number of Japanese soldiers assembled along the harbour wall, so that for a moment it wasn't clear to them whether they faced a reception committee or something less welcoming, whether Zipper which had begun life as an offensive operation and then been rescaled as an expedition of liberation of the people of Malaya wouldn't now become an operation again.

The matter was cleared up satisfactorily when a young Marine officer, attempting to mount the perpendicular iron ladder on the harbour wall from the light assault vessel that rocked up and down in the low-lying water, got into difficulties and the Japanese soldier nearest above him got down on his knees, stretched out an arm, and said, 'I help you, Johnnie?' Subsequently, most of the men, mounting at other points, found themselves momentarily relieved of their rifles, which certainly made the climb easier for them, but rather nullified the impression they'd had that the Nips were among the least accommodating people you'd be likely to find East of Suez (which was saying something). And Penang looked much more promising than Kalyan. Behind the line of Japanese soldiers were groups of pretty Chinese girls, grinning and waving.

Further down the coast, on one of what Leonard Purvis once heard fellow guests of the Maharanee's call the beaches around Port Swettenham, there was no harbour wall to scale, instead, an idyllic scene, an immense stretch of golden sand backed by elegantly disposed palm-trees. The senior officer riding in on a swift shallow-draughted landing craft was sardonically amused by the sight of three diminutive Japanese officers waiting for him on the sand, holding their swords in a manner that indicated submission. Beautifully uniformed and shod, the Englishman had himself carried ashore through a few inches of water by two stalwart marines who placed him gently on dry land in front of the Japanese commander. After an exchange of polite formalities, the English officer said, 'Perhaps you'd like to see how we would have come in in less peaceful circumstances?'

He gave an order. A junior officer in the landing craft blew a whistle and raised a flag. From half-a-mile out, where waited a formidable line of heavy landing-craft (and further behind still, the big ships that had formed part of the Zipper convoys) there at once came the growling sound of marine engines starting up. Almost, one could smell the oily fumes. They came in, making impressive waves and wakes with their blunt bows and sterns: ten, twenty, thirty of them; and then stopped, crashed down their single fronts or dramatically opened their double ones. Being so heavy they had not come in further because it was known (through intelligence) that for the last two hundred yards the water was barely wading depth, not more than eighteen inches, insufficient to get way astern for putting back to the ships for more loads. They had stopped about four hundred yards out where there were three feet beneath them, sufficient for their purpose, and no obstacle either for the green-clad infantry or for the water-proofed trucks, carriers and armoured vehicles which now spewed out of them and began to advance, remorselessly shortening the distance between themselves and the observers on the sands.

After going fifty yards, though, something odd happened. The leaders of the files of soldiers in the centre suddenly disappeared beneath the bland, scarcely rippling surface, and on one of the flanks the line of vehicles sank equally suddenly – not completely like the men but up to their superstructures. Whistles blew, men shouted and thrashed around. Only on the other flank was the operation of landing going smoothly, but in that sector there was no treacherous and unexpected sandbank, nor any of the quicksand which nearly cost a life or two and claimed more than one armoured vehicle.

The senior officer on the beach, having run instinctively forward, was standing now, bemused, with his beautiful boots in several inches of water. He was concerned for his troops and had no opportunity of observing the Japanese officers behind him; but his *aide* did, and later – whenever he recounted the tale – said he had never until that moment really understood what was meant by the inscrutability of the Orient.

He also said he hoped that if his commander felt he'd suffered any kind of humiliation from this incident he'd been more than compensated a few days later when he went down to Singapore, freshly laundered, to watch the simple, precise, efficient and impeccably organized formal surrender by the Japanese in Malaya to the brisk and handsome naval officer, the Supremo, who in less than eighteen months' time was to mount a far less simple but equally precise, efficient and impeccably organized operation – not for receiving power back but for handing it over.

BOOK TWO 1947

Pandora's Box

I

It was June, and there was a full year to go before the date the British Government had proposed as one by which it could be assumed that a satisfactory constitutional settlement would have been reached and the *raj* could withdraw in honour of its undertakings, and the long struggle for independence could be considered over.

But the bustling new Viceroy was back in Delhi. He had returned from consultations in London on the last day of May. Scarcely pausing to get his feet back under the desk, on June 2 he held meetings with Indian leaders and told them in confidence of the new plan proposed by him and approved by the British cabinet. On June 3 he broadcast to the Indian nation and said it was now clear that the division of India into two self-governing dominions, India and Pakistan, was inevitable, and added that the British Parliament would pass the necessary legislation to demit power on this basis during the present parliamentary session.

On June 4 he held a press conference (a feature of his vice-royalty which some old hands thought unnecessarily showy) and in answer to a question confirmed that this hastening through of legislation in Whitehall meant that Government would transfer power not next year but this year. He said, 'I think the transfer could be about the fifteenth of August.'

The astonished questioner did a rapid calculation. Ten weeks to go. Ten weeks. Ten *weeks?* It may have been that on this occasion several members of the Bengal Club at least looked like dying of apoplexy, but there is no reliable evidence, and they must by now have become inured to such rude shocks, however terminally rude this one seemed. It is far more likely that in other places where a more sophisticated response was to be expected, people simply said, 'I wonder what Halki will make of it?'

Halki was the new pseudonym of a young Brahmin, Shankar Lal, a shy retiring man who had left his orthodox family in the Punjab to earn his living as a cartoonist in Bombay. *Halki* meant 'light-weight or counterfeit' and replaced an earlier pseudonym, *Bhopa* (a priest possessed by the spirit of the god he worships). The new pseudonym wasn't intended to hide his identity; his style was unmistakable; even the CID recognized it when his cartoons began to reappear after the several months of unemployment that

1451

followed the publication of the still-famous Churchill two-finger cartoon. As to that unemployment, the one or two close friends in whom he confided explained to others that his silence was not due to editorial cowardice so much as to Shankar Lal's strength of character. Lal had refused several offers from editors only too willing to uphold the freedom of the press. He had gone into seclusion to think about the nature of his political commitment and to perfect his style; but he had made a verbal agreement with the editor of a popular Indian-controlled English-language newspaper to offer his work exclusively to him directly he felt ready to publish again.

During this interim period his editor-designate sometimes went out to Juhu, where Lal lived in great simplicity, to look at his work and try to persuade him to start publishing right away. Lal declined, with his usual courtesy, but often gave the editor whichever of the private cartoons he had most admired, and these the editor framed and arranged round the walls of his office (which was where Perron now saw them).

Halki's most devoted admirers used to – and still – say that a retrospective exhibition would show how Shankar Lal's youthful political adherence to Congress's aims of unity and freedom had shaded off into a generally humanist view of life. Among the unpublished work from the watershed period between the Churchill two-finger cartoon and an equally famous cartoon that marked his reappearance was one drawn in late August, 1945, after Wavell's announcement of cold-weather elections. This depicted the then-Viceroy, statue-naked on a plinth (inscribed 'Vote!') in the attitude of Rodin's Thinker, his bronze shoulders caked with snow. Actually, there were two versions of this unpublished work. The first included in the distant background a hot and sweaty affray between Muslims and Hindus and was captioned 'The Solution?'. The second version, still featuring Wavell as the snow-clad Thinker, omitted the affray but substituted the figure of an undernourished child asleep at the base of the plinth, with one hand grasping his begging bowl. The word 'Vote!' had disappeared from the plinth but reappeared on the side of the empty bowl. This was Perron's favourite of the two.

A successor to this unpublished cartoon (also unpublished) was dated 20 September 1945, the day after Wavell's report to the nation on his return from London, where he had attempted (unsuccessfully) to wrest from Attlee's government the kind of clear statement of policy that would have given the already-announced cold-weather elections the special signifi-cance which all political parties in India felt was lacking: a clear statement about independence. This cartoon was captioned 'Box-Wallah', and portrayed Wavell in the garb of an itinerant Indian merchant and purveyor of ladies' dress materials, squatting on his hunkers on the verandah of a European bungalow, recommending his wares to a gathering of memsa-hibs who bore remarkable resemblances to Bapu, Nehru, Patel, Tara Singh, Maulana Azad and Mohammed Ali Jinnah. Jinnah was sitting somewhat apart from 'her' colleagues, consulting a glossy magazine marked 'The

1452

Pakistan Ladies' Home Journal'; but none of them was responding to the pleas of the box-wallah or to the sight of the avalanche of silks and woollens he was flinging hopefully in all directions (lengths marked: 'New Executive Council – Indian patterns'; 'Central Assembly Dress Lengths (for Cold Weather Wear)'; 'Constituent Assembly Fashion Designs, For All Seasons'; 'Provincial Election Lengths: Graded Prices'; 'Dominion Status Fabrics (Slightly Soiled)'.

Why didn't Halki want to publish this one? Perron asked. Oh, the editor said, Halki wanted to. It was he, the editor, who had refused. One couldn't dress such eminent men up in women's clothes, like so many transvestites, especially when the women's clothes were European-style. Look at Gandhi's legs, (the editor said) and at those flapper's shoes.

The next significant cartoon was the one with which Halki had made his public reappearance, in December 1945, when (after an adjournment) the 'show-piece' trials of three INA officers began at the Red Fort in Delhi. Perron had already seen this one, because his old officer from Poona days had sent it to him. It was with this cartoon that Perron's interest in Halki had begun.

The trials were described as showpieces because they seemed to have less to do with the seriousness of the cases chosen to begin the long legal process of bringing to justice men who had waged war against the king than they had to do with proving GHQ's and the C.-in-C.'s determination not to show partiality (or, conversely, to attack the three main communities simultaneously). The officers chosen for the grand opening trial at the Red Fort had been Shah Nawaz Khan (a Muslim), Captain P. K. Sahgal (a Hindu) and Lieutenant G. Dhillon (a Sikh).

Halki's cartoon was very simple. It consisted merely in a beautifully sombre and perfectly proportioned drawing of the Red Fort, and carried the bleak caption, 'The King-Emperor's Tomb.' That was all. From that day, the editor told Perron, circulation began to rise. The cartoonist had caught the right new mood and Halki became famous overnight. But he had remained shy, enigmatic. Some of his cartoons occasionally seemed almost pro-British, or anti-party. For instance there was this one, in 1946, at the time of the short-lived but tricky mutiny at Bombay in the Royal Indian Navy, a mutiny which had surely convinced the British, if they weren't convinced already, that their time had expired. But the cartoon had taken editorial courage to publish because it showed an Indian frigate, controlled by mutinous ratings who had trained the ship's guns on the Royal Yacht Club and were about to open fire. Bursting through the roped-off gangway to stop them was Patel, in full Congress garb, waving his arms hysterically. The caption ran, 'What are you doing, for God's sake? One day we may want it ourselves.'*

Perron did not remember this one. Neither Bob Chalmers, his old officer from Poona, nor Aunt Charlotte had sent it to him. Nor did he remember

---

* Royal Yacht Club – traditionally the most exclusive in India – was actually closed down after independence.

the next two or three the editor showed him. The first of these pre-dated the naval mutiny joke and made a pair with the Red Fort cartoon. It was a meticulous drawing of a famous building, the Central Assembly in Delhi, in which in the first phase of the cold-weather elections the Congress had captured all the general seats but the Muslim League had won every one of the seats reserved for Muslims. Both parties had claimed a landslide victory and Halki's cartoon was captioned *Jai Hind* ! Closer inspection revealed a fissure in the foundation of the building and a crack spreading right up through one side of the fabric. Reluctantly, the editor hadn't published this, but he published the two-part cartoon in which Halki satirized the climax and anti-climax of the INA trials at the Red Fort.

The first frame showed a senior British officer mounted on a dome in the attitude of the statue of justice above the Old Bailey in London. Although blindfolded, the officer was recognizable as the C.-in-C. His scales were unusual since instead of two suspended trays there were three, each occupied by a mannikin figure representing the religion of each of the three accused, a Hindu, a Sikh and a Muslim. The C.-in-C.'s sword was held firmly aloft. In the second frame, which celebrated the anti-climax after the verdicts of Guilty and the C.-in-C.'s reduction of the sentences of life transportation, cashiering and forfeiture of pay to cashiering and forfeiture only, the scales were empty and his sword lacking its blade (it looked as if it must have fallen off through faulty workmanship). Beneath the blindfold the C.-in-C.'s expression remained unchanged: austere, determined and disapproving.

Yet one more cartoon was devoted to the subject of the INA, but Perron had to get the editor to explain it. After the anti-climax to the Red Fort trials it had become clear that except in several serious cases involving murder or brutality the *raj* could do nothing except cashier the officers and discharge the approximately 7,000 sepoys and NCOs who, classified as 'black', had not already been discharged as 'greys', or, as 'whites', returned to their units in semi-disgrace. The bulk of these 'black' discharges (after which the subject of the INA could conveniently be considered closed) occurred at Holi, 1946, the Spring fertility festival, traditionally celebrated by crowds roaming the streets throwing coloured powders and squirting coloured inks at everyone in sight. Halki's cartoon, captioned 'Holi', depicted a crowd of the discharged men emerging from a detention centre, being greeted by their families and throwing immense quantities of powder into the air and at one another. It took some time to discern in the distant background the plight of a loyal Indian Army sepoy still on guard-duty at the camp who had been sprayed with coloured ink by the departing prisoners and who was obviously being put on a charge by an immaculately dressed and irate British officer for being unkempt on duty. The editor published this cartoon too and received several threatening letters as well as a formal protest from the committee of the All-India Congress.

The next cartoon was one that Perron had also seen. Rowan had sent it to him as an enclosure with the only letter he had ever written. It illustrated a meeting of the Cabinet Mission of 1946 which had come out to India in the hot weather after the elections to seek an agreement on the major constitutional issue arising out of the continuing difficulty the British Government seemed to be having in establishing to whom to hand over when the time eventually came. The cartoon showed the three sweating members of the Mission: Cripps (merely President of the Board of Trade, but difficult to detach from Indian affairs), the Secretary of State (Pethick-Lawrence) and the First Lord of the Admiralty (Alexander). They were sitting staring at a large map of India which showed the country's provincial boundaries. A legend at one side of the map provided the clue to the different hatchings: perpendicular lines for Hindu majority provinces and horizontal lines for Muslim majority provinces (with a few areas of cross-hatching in the Punjab and Bengal). But nearly one-third of the map remained unhatched. The main caption was: 'A Paramount Question' and this was followed by a sub-caption in the form of a dialogue between the three ministers:

Sec. of State: I say, Cripps, what do the blanks represent?
Cripps: God knows.
Alexander: Perhaps the fellow ran out of ink.

Rowan's comment when sending this cartoon to Perron had been: 'Confidentially, it's said to be quite true, that three senior cabinet ministers between them had no idea that the self-ruling princely states, who have individual treaties with the paramount power (the Crown) respecting their rights to their own independence, cover so much of India.'

Another cartoon, which Perron hadn't seen, dated June 29, 1946, showed the cabinet mission returning disconsolately to London, climbing aboard a plane labelled 'Imperial Shuttle Service'. The Secretary of State was carrying the Imperial Crown and Cripps was surreptitiously handing him back a large diamond and saying, 'You'd better stick it back in, already.'

Halki's inventiveness here lay chiefly in the way he made the three British ministers look like three shady Jews from Amsterdam, and Nehru, Jinnah and Tara Singh look like three equally shady Arab merchants who had come to wave them off but were eyeing each other suspiciously, wondering if the jewel from the crown had been secretly handed over to whichever one of them had offered the highest number of piastres. Perron hadn't seen the cartoon because the editor hadn't dared publish it.

After this light-hearted cartoon came a series of tragic ones, every one of which the editor had published. They belonged to the period following Congress's decision to accept Wavell's invitation to join a new executive council which became known as the interim government, and to do this without the League. With governments formed in all the British-ruled provinces after the elections, some with League ministries but the majority with Congress ministries, the vital gap in government lay at the disputed and potentially federal centre. One of Halki's cartoons portrayed this enigmatically. It was the one in which he first reintroduced a characteristic figure from his 'Bhopa' days – the struggling and emaciated figure of Indian freedom and unity, last seen clenched in Churchill's two-fingered fist. Here he was now, the emaciated figure, stretched on a pavement asleep, but in two sections. Nothing connected the trunk to the lower limbs. You could see pavement between them. The majority of its Congress admirers interpreted it as a criticism of the Muslim principle of partition, of a separate Muslim state as a *sine qua non* of independence. The editor told Perron that it was really Halki's criticism of the men who had it in their power to join the two portions of the body together by at least attempting to work together at the centre.

'And these,' he said, leading Perron to another wall, 'are what I call Halki's Henry Moore cartoons, all inspired by those drawings your artist did of English people living like troglodytes in the underground railway stations during the Blitz. I published all these and became very unpopular with the proprietors. A cartoon should make people laugh, they said, even if it is only to laugh at themselves. But I said, What is there to laugh about now? Well – look at this!'

'This' was a sombre pen and ink drawing of Calcutta, captioned 'Direct Action Day', August 16, 1946 and celebrated the result of Jinnah's decision to resort to violence in the belief that the Viceroy had betrayed him by allowing Congress to enter the central interim government without him. In this picture, though, it was difficult to distinguish Muslim dead from Hindu dead. Halki had just drawn a pile of bodies, such as might be seen on the streets of Calcutta on any night of the week, except that these were obviously dead, not sleeping; but ordered in rows, like sleepers, in diminishing perspective from a lit to an unlit area.

There were several variations on this theme, but it was always night-time and the street was always the same street, the foreground lamp-post the same lamp-post. The most striking (Perron thought) was the one that showed the street all but empty. There were no bodies on the pavement, blood-stains adumbrated the shapes of bodies cleared away. In the background you could just see Bapu, with his staff, accompanied by Jinnah (hands behind back) walking down the road towards the lit area. This carried no caption and was the last of the pictorially sombre cartoons. Sombreness, though, continued in the jokey ones that followed.

A cartoon dated 3 September 1946 marked the occasion of the swearing in of the interim central government headed by Nehru, ostracized by Jinnah and overshadowed by the assassination of one of the nominated non-League Muslims, Shafaat Ahmed Khan, which caused riots in Bombay and Ahmedabad. Another, in mid-October, celebrated Jinnah's about-face, his decision to co-operate and enter the interim government to protect Muslim interests. To accommodate him three non-League Muslims had to resign. A third cartoon, dated in November, represented Halki's satirical view of this armed collaborative truce, a drawing of Wavell presiding over a round-table conference of his brawling Indian ministers (whose brief-cases, leaning against their chairs, were bulging with fused bombs). A window gave a view of a rioting mob. A doorway was marked as the way into the Constituent Assembly where the future constitution of free India would eventually have to be settled. The door was wide open but clearly no one was prepared to enter. In this cartoon Wavell was drawn in diminutive proportions, crouched in an over-whelming viceregal chair, and with two heads – or rather one head drawn twice, with connecting lines denoting its swift turning to and fro, as he listened first to one argument and then to another. The caption ran: 'I see' and only readers who knew that this brief sentence was said to be the Viceroy's most frequent contribution to every conversation really appreciated the joke.

One of the unpublished Halki cartoons of the last phase of Wavell's viceroyalty was drawn early in December when Wavell had persuaded the British Government to invite a delegation (headed by himself) of Hindu, Muslim and Sikh leaders, to a consultation in London, which he hoped would break the deadlock. Once again there was the waiting aeroplane ('Imperial Shuttle Service'). The pilot, looking out of his window, was Attlee and the co-pilot Cripps. Advancing across the tarmac were Nehru, Baldev Singh and Jinnah and Liaquat Ali Khan. At the head was Wavell, but whereas the four Indian leaders were depicted as free agents merely prodding each other forward with a peremptory finger digging into the back of the man in front, Wavell's hands were manacled behind his back and the finger pressing into *him* was Nehru's. It was captioned 'The Invitation'. The editor had not published it because he thought it a shade too sympathetic to the Viceroy and potentially troublesome. Later he regretted his decision.

He had missed the point of the leer Halki had drawn on Attlee's face and only fully appreciated Halki's interpretation when in the following February (1947) after a further couple of months' variations on the theme of incompatibility (with the constituent assembly assembling without the League, and then the Congress threatening to withdraw from the interim government if the League insisted on remaining in it), Attlee announced his government's intention of transferring power peacefully and responsibly by June 1948 and hinted that if the constitutional issue hadn't been solved by then an award would have to be made and power transferred to whatever authority Britain felt would govern in India's best interests. This (as the editor pointed out to Perron, who agreed) was exactly the kind of clear statement that Wavell had always tried to get. But it was accompanied by another, to the effect that Wavell's 'wartime appointment as Viceroy' (which was the first anyone had heard about such a limitation to a traditional five-year term of office) would end in March and that his successor would be Louis Mountbatten, the victorious Supremo of South-East Asia Command in the recent war, a relation of the King's, but patently a man of the new world.

Halki celebrated this news with a cartoon which the editor published against considerable internal opposition but with popular acclaim. Again, it was a two-frame cartoon, each frame showing a different aspect of one of those old-fashioned cottage style barometers: a little rustic house from which a male figure emerged in poor conditions and a female one in summery.

Halki's rustic house was a simplified version of the main entrance to Viceregal House. Frame one showed Wavell outside the first of the twin doors. The sky above was black. Bulging monsoon clouds were pierced by a fork of lightning coming from the mouth of a heraldic, rather ancient, winged lion, labelled 'Imperialism, circa 1857'. In the second frame the sky was bland, lit by a sparkling little sun held aloft by a frisky airborne lamb (with Attlee's face) labelled 'Imperialism, circa 1947'. Below this bland sky the gaunt figure of Wavell had retired into the gloom of Viceregal House and out of the other door had come the fine-weather figure of a smart toy-soldier (Mountbatten), magnificently uniformed, taking the salute, smiling excessively and exuding sweetness and light.

Subsequently, Halki had found his cottage-barometer theme a useful one to hark bark to during the first month or so of Mountbatten's appointment, weeks spent in seemingly inexhaustible rounds of conferences and counter-conferences. These later cartoons portrayed the various problems the new Viceroy had had to contend with and (perhaps) his growing exasperation at his inability to solve them to his own satisfaction. Political intransigence (from whichsoever party) was portrayed in the shape of the stormy figure (for example, Jinnah, but not invariably; there was once even Gandhi) emerging from the dark door while the toy-soldier retreated into his, and the bland sky was threatened by clouds that never quite covered the frisky lamb (although the smile on the lamb's face tended to get more and more strained).

'But that first barometer cartoon,' the editor said, referring back to the Wavell/Mountbatten version, 'is the prime example of Halki's gift for foreseeing the inner nature of events before they have actually taken place.'

'When will Mr Shankar Lal be back in Bombay?' Perron asked. The editor shrugged. 'He went almost without notice. He came to see me just two weeks ago and said he must go to the Punjab to try to persuade his parents to come down here, because otherwise they would find themselves living in bloody Pakistan. He said he had been working two or three days on a cartoon for publication on August 15, in case he isn't back by then.'

'But there's still a fortnight to go.'

'I know. But he said his parents are very stubborn people. Anyway, I have the cartoon. It is terrible. I may not dare publish it. It is in the safe at home so I cannot show it to you. But you saw his June 3 cartoon? People say it is his masterpiece.'

'No, I haven't seen that.'

'Oh you must, Mr Perron. It is very funny. I have the original at home because even my wife laughed. Everybody laughed. They rang me from Delhi and told me Mountbatten had laughed.' The editor banged his desk bell. 'I will get a copy of the relevant issue.'

For the June 5 issue, commemorating Mountbatten's announcement that Pakistan was now inevitable, and that the British would withdraw 'probably by August 15' Halki had worked throughout June 4 and drawn a picture of an immense Gothic building, or rather a structure which the architect had planned as one only to be frustrated (one had to imagine) over certain details of land acquisition. The attempt to create an illusion of a single façade, although admirably conceived and executed, hadn't quite worked, although it took several moments of close study of Halki's exemplary drawing to discern this. The cartoon occupied a whole page.

The main building, one such as citizens of Bombay were especially familiar with, was a huge emporium bearing some basic resemblance to the local army and navy shop. Across the façade the name ran: *Imperial Stores*. Between the word *Imperial* and the word *Stores* were the royal coat of arms and the announcement: *By Self-Appointment*. The building was several storeys high and drawn so as to show the main street frontage and one side-street elevation. The main entrance, curiously, was on the side street. Above this side street entrance there was another sign: *Proprietor:* Albert George Windsor; *Manager:* Clem Attlee.

At ground level, front and side, there were display windows crammed with goods but across each banners had been pasted proclaiming: *Grand Closing Down Sale. Expiry of Lease. Starts June 3. Bargains in Every Department. All Stock must be Sold by August 15.* Above this building the lamb held the sparkling sun aloft.

Outside the main entrance on the side street stood a tall, splendidly uniformed commissionaire who was looking at his watch, awaiting the moment to open the doors. Halki had caught Mountbatten's expression of detachment and self-confidence perfectly. All round the building there were queues of eager bargain hunters, mostly civilians but also soldiers and police. Each queue was separated from the others by its own 'Queue Here' sign – and these were variously inscribed, Congress, League, Sikhs, Hindu Mahasabah, Liberals, Europeans, Anglo-Indians, Tribes, Scheduled Castes; and at the head of each queue was a clearly identifiable leader who was consulting his shopping list.

The queues were orderly and well drilled – you felt that the commissionaire had disciplined them to be so and that he knew, they knew, he would stand no nonsense. One of these queues stretched right round the side-street and along the main frontage. This was the one headed by Mr Nehru and Mr Gandhi and was by far the longest. But exactly mid-way along the main frontage this queue was interrupted to allow passageway from the road into the building, and it was this visual break that confirmed (or originated) the impression that the building was not really an architectural whole.

Sandwiched between what could now be seen as two interrupted halves was an older building, obviously still in the ownership of a small shopkeeper who had been surrounded, propped up, pressed up against and down upon, by the giant concern, but never wholly absorbed. A great deal of ingenuity had been shown in creating the illusion that the smaller shop was part of the bigger one, that the older structure was a mere decorative flourish that did nothing to diminish the architectural integrity of the whole edifice. The older building announced itself as 'The Princes' Emporium' and was labelled, 'Imperial Stores (Paramountcy, 1857) Ltd.' The sticker across its one narrow window said, 'Business as Usual' and its narrow little Moghul door was guarded by a commissionaire whom the editor told Perron was recognizable as the head of the British Political Department.

Free access to this door from the road was secured by ropes that separated the orderly Congress queue, and Halki had depicted a very old-fashioned Rolls Royce drawn up at the pavement. Emerging from this limousine were a Maharajah and the first two or three of what looked like a car-full of wives arriving on a shopping expedition. Standing in the road just behind the car was a policeman – looking exactly like Patel, the chief enemy in the Congress camp of the Indian princely states. He was noting down the car's registration number in a book labelled 'Traffic Offences (Obstructions)'.

The fun did not end there. Facing the main frontage on the other side of the road there was work in progress on a giant multistoreyed building, only the ground-floor of which was completed and occupied. A placard announced: *Anglo-American Atomic and Commercial Enterprises Inc and Ltd (Successors to Box-Wallah and Co)*. Through the ground-floor windows you could see men at work in the offices. An American executive sat with his feet on a desk, smoking a cigar and using three telephones. A British executive sat with his feet under the desk, smoking a pipe and talking into only one. Queueing to enter the building was a hybrid collection of Indian businessmen consulting attendant lawyers who were in turn consulting draft contracts. Already in the building too, were figures representing the great Indian industrialists (Tata and Birla). A separate side-street entrance gave access to a queue of Muslim (Pakistan) businessmen, most of whom seemed destined to end up at the desk of the American executive.

And still the fun did not end. In distant perspective, on a continuation of the main frontage of Imperial Stores, was a Labour Exchange, and here there were four queues of Englishmen and Englishwomen whose children were being comforted by faithful bearers and ayahs: a queue each for ICS, IMS, army and police. The queuers were going into and coming out of doors marked 'Pension' and Compensation'. Some of those who had collected their dues were walking across the road, holding moneybags, to join the queue waiting to enter the offices of Anglo-American Enterprises Inc and Ltd. Some, obviously elderly, were trekking in another direction, to the office of a travel agent whose windows were bannered: Cheap One Way Retirement Tickets. Bilaiti and All Best Hill Stations.

There was no caption. A caption would have been excessive.

'Tomorrow I have a party,' the editor said. 'Come and see the original. At my house.'

'I'm afraid I can't. I'm leaving Bombay tomorrow morning,' Perron said.

'Then take this copy. I have never yet had in my office an Englishman all the way from London who comes to see me entirely to discuss Halki. He will be very flattered. No, no, that is wrong. I have never yet succeeded myself even in flattering him.'

'Thank you,' Perron said. He felt rather moved. It was the special gift Indians had, to move you unexpectedly; unexpectedly because you felt that historically you did not deserve any consideration or any kindness.

*

Leaving the newspaper office he walked for a while along the crowded Bombay pavement, then saw and hailed a taxi. He told the man to go in the direction of the Gateway and the Taj. When the taxi reached the spot where he had drawn up his jeep just two years ago he told the driver to stop but wait for him. He walked the few yards to the wall of the esplanade, with its view on to the Arabian Sea; and its smell. Disgusting. Peaceful. I shall never go back home, one Perron cried. The other said: Take me back, for God's sake. When he returned to the taxi he threw annas at the little crowd of children and told the driver to go to Queen's Road.

*

He paid the wallah off, tipping excessively as though this munificence had become obligatory since Mountbatten had removed the last doubt that the British intended to go and so made them the only people left in India who were universally popular. He studied the blocks of flats. He couldn't be certain which block he wanted, but then – believing he recognized the forecourt – he entered it, imagining Purvis ahead of him barging into the servant and the girl. He climbed the few steps to the dark entrance and went along an unfamiliar passage to the lift-shaft. This convincingly announced itself as out of order and on either side the name plates stirred other recollections. Desai? Tractorwallah? He climbed the steps to the first floor and stood, perplexed, facing the door whose name-plate should be Grace but wasn't. He went to the door opposite. Major Rajendra Singh, IMS. That, surely, was right? He climbed the next flight and arrived at the flat above Rajendra Singh's.

Hapgood. Mr Hapgood, the banker, Mrs Hapgood, the banker's wife and Miss Hapgood, the banker's daughter. One of the few remaining happy families in Bombay? He pressed the bell. Would the servant be the same servant? Would they recognize one another? The door opened. He did not recognize the servant. The boy was (God help us all, Perron thought) Japanese.

'Is Mr Hapgood in?' he asked. He handed in his card. The boy studied it carefully, ridging eyebrows as beautifully shaped as Aneila's. Not quite

1461

Japanese; a mixed-blood oriental from Sumatra? Singapore? Jakarta? A handsome, poisonous-looking young man who sported a gold wrist-watch. One could smell the starch on his arrogantly spotless white steward's jacket and trousers. He wore black shoes with pointed toes. 'I will see if Master is in.'

Perron thought: Master, now, is it? The British will always be safe.

The boy let him in, then shut the door and went in the direction of the living-room. Perron glanced down the corridor towards Purvis's old room. The door was shut; so was the door of the adjoining room. And the flat looked as if it had not been redecorated since then.

'Master says come.'

Perron followed the boy through the dining-room area and into the living-room which had once struck him as elegant, which now looked just a little disorganized. A quick glance at the wall behind the long settee confirmed the continuing existence of the Guler-Basohli paintings. A man stood on the balcony, as Purvis had done, holding a glass, looking out at the Oval. It was a clear evening, the sun not yet down. The man was tall and thin. For some reason Perron had always imagined Hapgood as short, rotund and red-faced; like the tea-planter at the Maharanee's. Hearing footsteps, Hapgood turned round.

'Mr Perron?'

'Yes. Mr Hapgood?'

'What can I do for you?'

'I'm sorry to bother you. I called downstairs on the off-chance of seeing Colonel and Mrs Grace. I see they've gone, but I thought I'd take the opportunity to come up, because I feel I owe you an apology.'

'Oh?' Hapgood was a man with formidable eyebrows. His face was yellow and very creased. His jaw and chin suggested firmness of opinion. 'Have we met?' he asked.

'No. You and your family were away, in Ootacamund I think. But there was an officer called Leonard Purvis billeted here – a couple of years ago. I was here the day things rather got on top of him. I wasn't here when he smashed things up, but I saw the results, and I've always felt it was partly my fault that two of your Kangra paintings were damaged.'

Hapgood's eyebrows twitched. He glanced at the wall.

'Oh?' Then, 'Actually they're Guler-Basohli school. But Kangra covers it.'

The servant had come in with a glass on a tray. He put this down on the drinks table.

'Scotch? Gin?' Hapgood asked.

'Gin, thank you.'

'Master will have gin,' Hapgood told the boy without looking at him. 'Why do you feel it was partly your fault?'

'Purvis had no idea what they were, until I admired them and told him how valuable they were. So it was probably my fault that he singled them out when he was throwing bottles.'

'Oh,' Hapgood said. 'Was that why? We often wondered. He never seemed to notice them.' He strolled across the room towards the paintings. 'But as you see, the damage has been fairly well disguised. They are exquisite, aren't they? My wife was pretty upset at the time. But as I told her, it needs more than a bottle of rum to destroy a work of art.'

Perron had forgotten it was rum. Hapgood hadn't. He turned to Perron suddenly. 'Did you know the man my old bearer told me about? The man who had to climb the balcony and pull Purvis out of the bath?'

Perron admitted that he was the man.

Hapgood said, 'Good heavens.' Then, 'My dear chap. How nice of you to call – to have remembered the paintings. My wife will be sorry to have missed you. She was awfully touched that you bothered to leave the servant a chit about the bathroom door.'

Perron recalled that the servant had asked for a chit. He didn't actually remember writing one. Obviously he had done, probably while sitting in this room afterwards, drinking Old Sporran.

'Perron,' Hapgood was saying. 'Perron. Yes, I remember now. But ...'

'*Sergeant* Perron,' Perron said, to clear up any doubts. 'Field Security, Poona.'

'Field Security? I see. Somehow we'd always imagined the Sergeant Perron who pulled Purvis out of the bath was something to do with his so-called economic advisory staff.' Hapgood led the way back to the balcony. 'Field Security, Poona. Did you know a fellow who's now in pharmaceuticals here? What's his name –'

'Bob Chalmers?'

'That's it. Chalmers. His firm banks with us. I don't know him well. I remember he said he was Field Security in Poona and liked it so much he stayed on.'

'Chalmers was my officer. Actually I'm staying in his flat here in Bombay. We kept up, after the war.'

'Well bless my soul. Have you come out to join his firm?'

'No, I'm only on a visit. Quite a short one. And I've not seen Bob yet and probably won't now. He had to go to Calcutta just before I arrived, but left everything laid on so that I could stay at his place.'

'Yes, I see. And you knew the Graces?'

'No, I knew their niece, and their niece's father.'

'I'm afraid Mrs Grace has left. Poor old Arthur Grace died last year. Very suddenly. My wife and I were quite upset. He'd had dinner with us only the night before. Mrs Grace had gone up country to see her sister. The niece was getting married. Yes, I remember now. She was here to meet her father, wasn't she, when we were in Ooty?'

'The elder niece was here. There was a younger one.'

'I don't remember that. Anyway, one of them got married. Which was why Fenny Grace was away and poor old Arthur was on his own for a couple of weeks. We used to have him up. I thought he was perfectly all right but my wife said she wasn't happy about him. She said he looked as if he didn't know what anything was about any longer. Curious phrase. But women have these intuitions. He had a heart attack. Went, just like that.'

Hapgood snapped his fingers, but to call the servant's attention to his empty glass. Perron's was still half-full.

'This was last year?'

'Last year, yes. Middle of February. When the Indian ratings here mutinied. Things were a bit of a mess, but Fenny came back the moment we wired. Actually we thought it a bit thick that no one from her family came with her to help her get through it. But you're right. There must have been two nieces. I remember her saying her niece wanted to come with her. She couldn't have meant the niece who'd just got married. Must have been the other.'

'Sarah, I should think. The one who got married must have been Susan.'

'It rings a bell.'

'Susan must have married a man called Merrick.'

'I think that was it. Chap with something wrong with him?'

'He lost an arm in the war.'

'That's it. Yes. Fenny left us some snaps she took at the wedding. She had them printed here once she'd dealt with the funeral. Pity my wife's away. She'd have details like this much clearer in her mind. If you're anxious for news of the family I'm sure I could turn up the sister's address. Pankot, wasn't it? Fenny must have given it to my wife, and my wife's very efficient keeping her address book written up.'

'I have the Pankot address. It's just that I've not heard since the end of 'forty-five. My fault really. One somehow lets things slide.'

'True. True. One lets things slide. The last we saw of Fenny was when she left for Delhi after the funeral. She was going to fly home to another sister in London. I expect the London address is in my wife's book too, but I don't think they wrote to one another because Fenny said it would only be a short trip and that she'd be back again. Then our daughter married an awfully nice Canadian Air Force chap we met in Ooty. We were in Montreal last year for the wedding. Pretty killing expense. But once in a lifetime. Now my wife's back in Montreal waiting to become a grandmother. I'm expecting a telegram almost any day.'

Perron lifted his glass. 'Good luck.'

'Thank you.' After drinking Hapgood said, 'Are you committed this evening?'

Perron lied. 'I'm afraid so, yes.'

'Tomorrow, perhaps?'

'Unfortunately I've left this call very late. I'm off tomorrow.'

'Oh. Where are you off to? Not home?'

'No, a little state called Mirat.'

'A long journey. They had some trouble there recently. Is that why you're going?'

'I didn't know that. What sort of trouble?'

'Usual thing. Communal riots. I think it's died down. Anyway, it's in the

Punjab things are getting tricky. Too many people on the move in the hope of ending up in the right place. But what can you expect when you draw an imaginary line through a province and say that from August fifteen one side is Pakistan and the other side's India? The same applies to Bengal.'

'It is rather drastic, isn't it?'

Hapgood gave Perron a penetrating glance. He said, 'It's what an important minority felt they had to have and in the long term it's probably for the best.'

Perron nodded. Hapgood was probably more in sympathy with the Muslims than with the Hindus.

'Do you have press connections, then, Mr Perron?'

'Only rather marginal ones. Sufficient to help me move about and get seats on planes.'

'I asked because nearly every stranger from home you come across nowadays is either a journalist or a member of parliament swanning around ostensibly to observe the democratic process of dismantling the empire but actually making soundings for his private business interests. Nothing wrong with that, of course. India's going to be an expanding dominion market once it settles down. The thing is, we'll have to meet more outside and inside competition. Do you have business interests as well as marginal press ones, Mr Perron?'

'My interests are primarily academic.'

Again Hapgood snapped his fingers and again while they continued talking his glass was taken and replenished and returned. This time Perron had his own glass topped up. The Oval was under the spell of pink and turquoise light, fading into indigo shadows.

'If you have press connections, though, I suppose you're here to be in at the kill, if I may put it that way. Forgive me, but Mirat seems such an unlikely little place to go. If you want to be in at the kill you should go up into the Punjab and try to accredit yourself to the wretched chaps who've been formed into the boundary force and have the job of protecting the refugees and stopping them tearing at one another's throats.'

'Well as I said. My interests are primarily academic. And at the moment primarily concerned with the relationship between the Crown and the Indian states.'

'Well you could go up to Bahawalpur. They've had some high jinks there. Or down to Hyderabad. That's the one princely state large and powerful enough to prolong its independence for a while. Have you seen Patel? He's in charge of what I call the coercing operation. Have you seen the head of the British Political Department? He'd give you the other side of the picture. They say his department has been burning private papers for weeks now, all the scandalous stuff we've collected over the years about the way some of the Princes behaved. Couldn't let Patel get his hands on those, could you?'

'Well I have a definite invitation to Mirat. I think it will suit me very well, especially if it's had its troubles.'

'What sort of invitation, Mr Perron? I ask because I might be able to help you.'

'That's very kind of you. Actually the invitation's from the Chief Minister, Count Bronowsky. I met him here in Bombay during the war. He was kind enough to say I'd be welcome in Mirat at any time.'

'Then there's nothing I could do to smooth your way better. It was Bronowsky I had in mind. I don't know him socially, but he's had an account with us for years, and we usually meet in my office when he comes to Bombay. I haven't seen him for some time. Probably because of the troubles they've had there. How is he?'

'I've no idea, but well, I imagine. I wrote to him just before coming out from England and there was a telegram waiting for me at Bob Chalmers's flat, inviting me to turn up whenever I wanted.'

'Well. Give him my regards.'

Perron looked at his watch, and prepared to finish his drink.

'Are you absolutely committed this evening? I've got a few people coming in, couple of chaps from the bank and their wives. Friends. Not all that boring. Actually it's buffet. Nowadays in Bombay you never know who'll turn up or who they'll bring. Being alone just now I encourage it.'

Perron was tempted. He had a brief and flaming image of the Maharanee floating in on the arms of a couple of English bankers, in her scarlet saree, subsiding on to the long settee under the Guler-Basohli paintings, showing her nipples; and of Aneila offering chairs, cigarettes, and dewy tumblers which she had rinsed under the tap in Purvis's bathroom to help the sinister little servant cope. And an image, then, of all the lights going out, because the light had virtually gone now from the forgiving Bombay sky, leaving only a gleam in the fretted edges of the palm fronds. And the sweet, grave, unforgettable unforgotten smell, drifting across from Back Bay.

'I'm afraid I am committed, sir,' Perron said. 'Perhaps if I come back this way I could give you a ring.'

'Of course,' Hapgood said, pleased to be called sir. But it was *now* Hapgood wanted. A new face to ease the ache of boredom. Hapgood's own face went out, as the nearby street-lamp came on, below and behind him. A trick of illumination.

'You have a new servant, I see.'

'Young Gerard? Yes. Bit of a mongrel. We inherited him from a chap who retired last year. Our agent in Ipoh. Gerard kept things going for him while he was in prison-camp. Very efficient fellow. Not like poor old Nadar, the one you'd remember. Trouble with Nadar, he couldn't keep his hands off stuff that got left around. We had to let him go. Mistake, probably. My wife says it's better to employ a dishonest servant you know inside out than one you'll never get on any sort of terms with. Not that it's going to matter either way to us next year. Our time will be up then. Learn to do our own cooking and washing up, I shouldn't wonder. Neither of us fancies Montreal. So it looks like Ewell or Sutton. Know anything about mushrooms?'

Automatically Perron thought of cloud formations.

'Mushrooms?'

'A friend of our Canadian son-in-law, an ex-RAF type who lives in Surrey, has gone in for mushrooms. Grows them in his garage. Making a fortune, I'm told. Not that we'll be looking to do that. But you need to put your mind to something, so preferably something with a saleable end-product. I don't fancy chickens. Mushrooms are quieter.'

Hapgood smiled. His face, re-illuminated as he guided Perron back into the living-room where Gerard had switched on some of the table-lamps, looked composed. And resigned. 'Well,' he said, 'if you change your mind, just arrive. Meanwhile I'd better get myself ready for the invasion.' Perhaps Gerard had run his bath (with the same imperturbable expression he had shown when running baths for Japanese officers in his previous master's house in Ipoh?).

Perron was about to say, 'Do you still have the same cook?' but realized in time that this might sound like an inquiry into the quality of the food to be expected. So he left not knowing whether that happy, co-operative, and sturdy little man still presided over the hot stoves in the Hapgood kitchen. On the whole, Perron thought, it was unlikely that he did. The bearer, the cook, and the cook's boy, had been a happy family too, in spite of the rivalry and the demarcation of zones of responsibility. When the bearer went they had probably followed him.

As Gerard held the door open, Perron glanced once again down the corridor, to get his last glimpse of Purvis's still-closed door.

*

Back in Bob Chalmers's rather odd flat he made a few notes about his visit to Hapgood. The oddness of Bob's flat consisted not merely in the unexpected situation of the house (in one of the narrow rather squalid roads behind the Gateway; not far, surely, from where the massage parlour had been?) but in the admixture of traditional and emergent Anglo-Indianism in its appointments. The rooms where basic European needs were scrupulously met (bathroom, bedrooms, dining-room) were furnished in the old dependable style. But in the living-room there was nowhere to sit comfortably. There were imitation Persian rugs on the floor, sparkling cushions from Rajputana, mattresses covered by durries or printed cotton bedspreads, a pair of tablas, a harmonium, and in a conker-coloured leather case – a tamboura, probably from Bengal. On the walls there were modern paintings by modern Indian painters. Impressionism had arrived (and a pointilliste school, after Seurat, to judge by a disturbing view of the burning ghats at Benares). Scattered round the room on cushions, on floor, on mattresses and in a unit-style bookcase, were the things that showed Bob Chalmers to be perhaps a little uncertain where his tastes lay. There were trade magazines dealing with pharmaceuticals and other light and heavy industrial subjects. There were literary magazines published in Calcutta and pale blue stiff-boarded editions of works by Radakrishnan about *karma* and *dharma* and the Hindu way of life. The bookcase held several volumes from the Left Book Club, a row of old Readers' Digests and the latest novel by Nevil Shute. On a very low coffee-table, among pottery ashtrays, were a translation of the poems of Gaffur by a Major Tippet, and the March 1947 issue of *The New English Forum* which Perron had sent him. This was an issue containing one of Perron's articles, the article originally entitled *Daulat Rao Sindia and the British Other Rank*, but subsequently retitled (for publication) *An Evening at the Maharanee's*, which title Perron had tossed out from the top of his head at the end of a rather drunken lunch at Prunier's with the young Tory MP who published the magazine and whose personal assistant in the publishing firm he directed had recommended Perron as a likely contributor, after reading Perron's review (in the *New English University Monthly*) of a book called *My Memories of* INA *and its Netaji*, by Maj. General Shahnawaz Khan, Foreword by Pt Jawahar Lal Nehru [*sic*], which Bob Chalmers had sent him from Bombay after its publication in Delhi in 1946 with a letter of which the only passage Perron clearly remembered was: 'Remember Bombay and Bordeaux? Well, this is connected. And get that last paragraph of "Jawahar Lal's" foreword, I quote: "I must confess that I have not been able, through lack of time, to read through this record, but I have read parts of it and it seems to me that this account is far the best we have at present." Unquote. How's that for shrewd fence-sitting, now that the trials are over?'

But then, Perron thought, putting his notebook away, and nodding assent to Bob Chalmers's bearer who was standing in the doorway indicating that supper was ready (which he could already tell, smelling the delicious scent of turmeric) where else can one sit, and remain in balance?

II

Perron woke. The silence was solid; as if he had been spun off the world into space. There were no echoes, not a glimmer of light in the primeval dark. Then he heard the engine breathe in the distance and re-identified himself as the lucky lone occupant of a coupé on the night train from Ranpur to Mirat. He sat up, reached for his cigarettes. The lighter illuminated his watch. Five a.m. He twisted his body round and raised the blind and then the shutter and gazed out at the pale frozen landscape. So vast a country. Its beauty unnerved him. The engine breathed again, sounding nearer. He held his own breath and listened to another sound: the cries of dogs hunting the plain in packs.

When he woke again light was streaming through the unshuttered window and the train was moving slowly, clacking its wheels rhythmically, reluctantly. The landscape was eroded. Nothing could live here, he thought.

He was cold. He got up, slipped his feet into chappals and reached for his robe. Enfolded in silk he rasped one hand against his cheeks. His eyes were gummy. They felt raw from the specks of sand and soot that had entered the compartment. Pushing through the door into the lavatory he felt the chill coming up through the hole in the pan. He wanted hot coffee. Comfort. There was none. In an hour or two it would seem impossible that he had ever felt cold.

*

Shaved, washed, dressed, he went to the sunny side of the compartment to warm himself. It was 7 a.m. He should have been in Mirat by now and drinking coffee or tea in the station restaurant, getting some bacon and egg. He had lost the knack of travelling in India. He hadn't even brought a flask of water. All he had was yesterday's papers, bought in Ranpur: *The Times of India* and *The Ranpur Gazette*. He now read through the *Gazette*, scarcely taking it in, flicking the pages. The only pieces worth reading were a waspish editorial and a quiet essay by someone calling himself Philoctetes. He couldn't remember who Philoctetes was. In this case, probably, the editor, exercising a gentle taste for *belles-lettres*.

He went back to the window. The train was passing a village. Water buffalo wallowed in the local tank. Women walked with baskets of cowdung on their heads. Men drove skeletal goats and horned cattle. There was a smell of smoke. It would be a hot dry day.

*

It was gone nine o'clock when the train drew into Mirat (Cantonment): two hours late according to the new schedule. He was glad that he hadn't announced his arrival in advance and put anyone to the trouble of meeting him.

The platform was crowded. Officers, wives, mounds of luggage. Departing British. A train seemed to be expected in the other direction, from Mirat to Ranpur. The restaurant was crowded too. There wasn't a vacant table and he didn't want to share. He decided to push on and told the coolie to take him to where tongas were to be had.

The concourse was also crowded, mostly by squads of British troops squatting on piles of kit-bags, smoking. Perron's suitcase and hold-all were put on to a tonga. He told the man to go to the club. The tonga set off through the cantonment bazaar. Perron breathed in the familiar smell: an oily, spicy scent mingling with that of burning charcoal. And then they were out on to the first of the wide geometrically laid out roads of a military station, metalled roads with khatcha edges, shade trees, and lime-washed stones marking the culvert crossings over monsoon ditches, which gave access to the compounds of the old bungalows. The tonga passed neat white-shirted Indian clerks on cycles and was passed in turn by military trucks. Once you had seen one cantonment, it was said, you had seen them all.

It took twenty minutes to reach the club. The way in was by a broad gravel drive that curved through a compound darkened and cooled by trees and shrubs. The colonnaded façade was dazzling white. Against the white the sprays of red and purple bougainvillaea stood out exuberantly. After the tonga wallah had taken the luggage into the vestibule Perron paid him off.

There was no one in the vestibule. The hall beyond led to a terrace set with wicker chairs and tables. The vestibule was dark, high ceilinged. There were palms in brass pots. He banged a bell on the desk (which was discreetly positioned behind a pillar). A servant appeared from behind another pillar. Perron asked for the secretary. While he waited he studied some of the framed photographs that hung on the white-washed walls. These were mostly of victorious teams from old tournaments in the 1920s. Tennis, polo, cricket, golf. There was a photograph of Edward VIII when he was Prince of Wales.

A young Indian in European clothes came into the vestibule, asked if he could help, explained that the secretary was still having breakfast. Perron gave him his card and said he would be in Mirat for a little while and wondered whether the club could offer temporary membership, and if so whether it might include accommodation, say for tonight, and some breakfast now. The card he offered was the one that gave his London club address. The man glanced at it and said he was sure this could be arranged but that he would speak to the secretary. The bearer came back. The clerk told him to show the sahib out on to the terrace and serve him breakfast.

The terrace was longer and wider than the view from the vestibule suggested. Apart from the wicker chairs and tables which were arranged close to the balustrade to give occupants a view directly on to a long sweep of lawn and flowerbeds (with, beyond, behind a white painted fence, rougher ground set out for jumping and riding displays), there was also a line of club dining-tables and chairs ranged along the length of the inner wall. The tables were free of napery, their mahogany surfaces highly polished. Each had a silk shaded lamp. There were probably a dozen of these tables and, between each pair, casement doors which led into the interior. Half-way along the terrace one of the tables was occupied by two Indian officers and an Indian civilian (or an officer in civilian clothes). The rest were empty. At the far end of the line of wicker chairs and tables sat a European woman. She wore sunglasses and was drinking coffee. The Indian officers and the civilian were finishing breakfast. The bearer guided Perron to the first of the empty dining-tables.

He was a grizzled old man, white-uniformed, sashed, barefoot, gloved and turbanned. Having seated Perron he went away, returned almost at once with a tray from which he took things to lay a single place on the gleaming surface. Having done this he produced the final item – a menu secured in a silver-plated stand. 'Sahib,' he said, and went, leaving Perron to consult the bill of fare. Perron, picking the card up by its stand, suddenly leant back, gazed out at the sweep of lawn, the canna-lilies, the immense earthen pots of delicately tinted and scented flowers that stood sentinel between each batch of wicker chairs and tables. India, he thought. India. I'm back. *Really* back. Why, he wondered, was the Mirat Gymkhana Club so familiar? And then saw why. Once, both wearing civilian clothes, Bob Chalmers had breakfasted him at the Turf Club in Poona. The Mirat Gymkhana might have been a duplicate. The bearer came out again with a wooden contraption which he opened up and set behind the side-plate. A newspaper rest. Upon this he placed a folded newspaper called the *Mirat Courier*.

'No *Times of India*?'

'Not until midday, Sahib. Yesterday's is available.'

'I think not yesterday's. What is Fish Soufflé Izzat Bagh?'

'Local fish, Sahib. Caught daily in Izzat Bagh lake. Cooked with spice and served with rice. Today not recommended.'

'Oh, why?'

'Today not fresh, Sahib. Fish too long on ice. Fishermen not going out two day now.'

Perron ordered eggs and bacon and, when the old man had gone turned to watch the belligerent shining blue-black crows making hungry sorties on to the wet lawn. The Indian officers suddenly laughed aloud and slapped their napkins down. The European woman wearing the sun-glasses was getting up, gathering her things. She went through one of the open casement windows at the far end of the terrace. The civilian with the officers went on talking. Perhaps he was telling them funny stories.

'Mr Perron?'

An elderly man, short, stout, bald, stood by Perron's table. Perron got up, took the offered hand.

'Macpherson,' the man said. 'I'm the secretary. Please –' But Perron remained standing until, accepting his invitation Macpherson sat too. 'I hope you're being looked after all right.' Perron assured him he was. 'Don't have the fish, incidentally.'

'Your chap's already warned me off it.'

'That must be old Ghulam. Thank God for him anyway. Staff's difficult nowadays. Night train from Ranpur?' Perron nodded. 'Should have been in at seven. It gets worse every year. I see from your card you're from home. Been out here long?'

'About ten days. Can you put me up for the night?'

'For as long as you like. Nowadays we have more departures than arrivals. All the same, even for a night I'm afraid you'll have to pay temporary membership and I'm afraid the fee's for a minimum of one calendar month. War-time rule, dating from when young officers were coming and going and being posted overnight.'

'And forgetting to pay their bills?'

'That's about it. Still, a lot of them are dead long since, I expect. You've been out here before haven't you?'

'Yes, but not for long. A couple of years during the war.'

The Indian officers and the civilian had got up and were approaching. Macpherson looked up. 'Everything all right, Bubli?'

'Everything's fine, Mac.'

'Are you dining tonight?'

'Who can tell, with one thing and the other?'

'If you don't tell you're likely to get Fish Soufflé Izzat Bagh.'

'Oh, God help us. I'll let you know. See you, Mac.'

'See you, Bubli.'

'Nice fellow,' Macpherson said when they were alone again. 'Gentleman. But then most of them are. Which I can't say for some of our fellows.'

'How long have you been secretary, Mr Macpherson?'

'About ten years. Mirat was my first station. Oh, years ago before the other war. Artillery. I got a chance to come back in nineteen thirty. Jumped at it. Retired in thirty-five. Took this on. Don't regret a single day. Look forward to many more. No ties at home anyway.'

Perron nodded. He understood that here was where Macpherson would prefer to die.

'I had a job, though, back in 'thirty-seven, opening membership to Indian officers. It split the committee right down the middle. But I said if a man's got the King's Commission what does it matter what his complexion is. During the war the old members agreed I was right. It damned well disgusted us. We were damned well ashamed, I mean of some of our own countrymen. Do you know what they did once? Emptied all the chamber pots from the men's room into the swimming pool, because they'd seen a couple of Indian subalterns swimming there. I marched them out pretty smartly. Chamber pots in the swimming pool were just about their Kingston Bypass style. Of course, that was wartime, 'fortytwo, when the Indian politicians were kicking up a fuss. But do you know what happened here a few weeks ago?'

'No?'

'Swimming pool again. Someone excreted into a Gandhi cap and floated it. I never found out who. But I had my suspicions. Had to drain the pool, have it scraped, and get a Brahmin priest along to do a purification ritual before it was refilled. No Indian's been in it since. It'll be all right though.'

'Whom did you suspect?'

'The leader of what I called Mirat's second-fifteen rugger club. The English officer who let wind when I took Mirat's Chief Minister into the men's bar one evening.'

'Did the chief minister comment?'

'Not directly. He's not an Indian. If he had been he wouldn't have commented at all. But he couldn't resist saying, Shall we get some fresh air?' Macpherson waved a hand, indicating the terrace. Perron's breakfast began to arrive. 'Sorry, Mr Perron. Unpleasant subject. Enjoy your breakfast.'

Perron stood to acknowledge the secretary's leave-taking. He said, 'I know the man you mean, Dmitri Bronowsky? Actually I'm in Mirat to see him. Perhaps I can telephone from here and leave a message that I've arrived?'

Macpherson hesitated. 'Is he expecting you?'

'In general, yes.' Perron explained about the telegram that had awaited his arrival in Bombay. 'But I didn't wire back. I thought I'd just turn up.'

'I know he was here a few days ago but he may have gone to Gopalakand. I can find out easily enough. He's got a full plate just now. Not just Patel and company. Things haven't been too good here the past week or so.'

'It all looked quiet enough this morning.'

'Oh, in the cantonment. But across the lake, in the city. Not so good. That's why we don't recommend the Fish Soufflé Izzat Bagh. The fishermen are Muslims. They've fished the Nawab's lake since the eighteenth century. Tradition. Special sect. But they haven't dared go out the last couple of days since a couple of them were found drowned. They call it murder and blame the Hindus. So it looks as if we may be back to how it was last year and earlier this. There's a curfew in the old city. But we can always make you comfortable here, Mr Perron. I'll send my clerk along with the temporary members' book.'

Macpherson went. Perron drank his orange juice. The clerk came with the book. Perron filled in the columns at the top of the clean page at which the book was open. He resisted the temptation to turn back and check how long it had been since the club had last received a temporary member.

The front page of the *Mirat Courier* for today, Monday August 4, featured a muddily reproduced photograph of the Viceroy in Delhi with some of India's leading princes, which Perron had already seen in *The Times of India*. There was no reference in the accompanying article to Mirat's own prince, the Nawab, but the tone of the article suggested that the editor was anxious to convey an impression that the relationship between the princes and the Viceroy was of the friendliest kind; which, however true, was largely irrelevant to the political issue. The front page was, in fact, all sweetness and light. There was no follow-up to the rumour Perron had heard that Jinnah was accusing the Sikh leader Tara Singh of planning to assassinate him and sabotage the partition of the Punjab.

The bearer brought his bacon and egg and, glancing up, Perron saw that the woman in the sunglasses had come out of the further casement doorway and was walking slowly along the central strip of coconut matting. From a distance he'd assumed that she was middle-aged, perhaps because her hair looked dull, colourless, and because the sunglasses accentuated the rather disagreeable set of the mouth. Nearer to, he saw that she was quite a young woman, thin but well-shaped, with a good bust, and a graceful walk of the kind that suggested she had always been proud of her carriage and had worked at perfecting it: an acquired good carriage, rather than the natural good carriage that he remembered as characteristic, for example, of Sarah Layton. As she came nearly level with his table Perron smiled and said, 'Good morning.' She smiled too and murmured good morning and went slowly on. She reminded him (he realized) of a younger *Mrs* Layton. She had that kind of composure: indolence almost. She left behind her a whiff of scent just heavy enough to suggest that it was expensive.

Before starting on his breakfast Perron turned the *Mirat Courier* over to its back page. Here was another muddy photograph, illustrating a report headed 'Happy Occasion in Ranpur', and by-lined 'From our Ranpur Correspondent'. He settled to eat and read.

'The grounds of Government College in Ranpur were the scene of a happy occasion on Saturday when His Excellency the Governor, Sir Leonard Perkin, opened the new college building in which a future generation of Indian engineers will receive their education. "Let us hope," Sir Leonard said, "that these young men, on whose shoulders India places great responsibility, as she moves forward into a new industrial age, will look back on the times they spent here, in this handsome building, with a gratitude at least as great as we here feel today to its inspirer and founder and principal benefactor, Mr Chakravarti."

'Sir Leonard went on to recall how, just two years ago, when the future seemed less certain, his distinguished predecessor, Sir George Malcolm, laid the first stone for the new wing. "Many of you," Sir Leonard said, "will remember that occasion and perhaps regret as I do that Sir George is not here to open the splendid college that has arisen from that single stone. Be assured that I shall send him an account and appropriate photographs of it."

'Sir Leonard went on to speak of the gratitude he himself had always felt to the evening technical institute he had attended as a youth after a hard day's work in the industrial north of England. He then referred to the "grave doubts" he had had when, in 1946, Prime Minister Attlee had proposed to put his name forward as Governor in Ranpur. "Well, Len, the PM said to me, we've already sent Fred Burrowes to Bengal and he's an old railwayman too and not doing too badly. Unfortunately," Sir Leonard continued, "Fred has stolen my best joke, which was that while I knew nothing about shootin' and huntin' I knew quite a bit about tootin' and shuntin', so perhaps after all I could be of some service in the brief period I hoped it might take, which indeed it has taken, for us to climb down from the footplate and make way for you chaps, of whose skill and devotion and confidence in the future this college is both proof and symbol."

'Amid popular acclaim, Sir Leonard then led the way from the platform to the main entrance of the new building. Receiving the key he made a characteristically generous gesture, placing the key in the door and then inviting Mr Chakravarti to turn it so that he would be the first to enter the college which Mr Chakravarti described later as "the fulfilment of an old dream."

'Present among the guests was Mr Mohammed Ali Kasim, obviously recovered from the recent chill that prevented his attendance at the Chamber of Commerce dinner two weeks ago. Until the announcement also two weeks ago that Mr Trivurdi would succeed Sir Leonard Perkin, Mr Kasim had been widely tipped as the new Governor-designate. Answering your reporter's questions, Mr Kasim said he had no particular plans for the immediate future but that Mr Trivurdi's appointment as Governor was one that would have his whole-hearted approval. He declined to answer our question whether the Governorship had been offered to him first, and whether such a refusal was an indication that presently Mr Kasim intends to return actively to politics in the province.'

The article about the Chakravarti building had seen Perron through his bacon and egg and part of his toast and marmalade. The bearer asked if the sahib desired a fresh pot of coffee. Perron said he did. He took another piece of toast and folded the *Mirat Courier* to pages two and three. A glance at page two showed that it was taken up entirely by box-advertising, so he placed the paper on the stand with page three towards him.

Another muddy photograph; but suddenly he paused, a piece of toast on its way to his mouth, but never getting there. He pushed back his chair and took the *Courier* over to the stronger light near the balustrade. The face in the photograph was virtually unrecognizable. The heading alone made identification possible:

Lieutenant-Colonel Merrick, DSO

A moving ceremony

'The funeral service for the late Lt.-Col. (Ronnie) Merrick, DSO, whose tragic death we reported last week, was held last Saturday here at St Mary's, in a simple but moving ceremony conducted by The Reverend Martin Gilmour who, in his short address to a large congregation, spoke of Colonel Merrick as "a man who came into our midst, a stranger, and inspired us all by his devotion to duty, and has now gone, leaving us not poorer but richer for the example he set."'

The same Merrick? The three-quarter profile photograph did not itself confirm so. Perron scanned quickly down to the smaller print where the names of the chief mourners might be found.

'Supporting the widow were members and close friends of the family, Colonel John Layton, Mrs F. Grace, Captain Nigel Rowan (AAGG) and Mrs Rowan. Among the representatives of the cantonment were the station commander and his wife, Colonel and Mrs Rossiter and the Misses Rossiter; Brigadier and Mrs Thorpe, Colonel and Mrs S. K. Srinivasan, Major Thwaite and Miss Drusilla Thwaite, Major and Mrs Peabody, Captain and Mrs P. L. Mehta.'

So, then, yes. Merrick. But who was Mrs Rowan? Sarah? She wasn't otherwise named. And what were they all doing in Mirat? AAGG meant assistant to the agent to the Governor-General. Was Rowan political agent in Mirat? He went back to the larger print.

'Referring briefly to Colonel Merrick's skilful handling of the far from easy task entrusted to him some months ago, the chaplain pointed out that the man whom they had gathered together to mourn and honour was one who had a disability that would probably have persuaded many men to feel that the period of their useful active employment and service had ended. "Ronnie," he said, "never felt this. Some of you have seen, many of us have heard, how this gallant officer who had taught himself to ride again, led his detachment of States Police during times of trouble, patiently and humanely but firmly restoring order and securing the peace of the state in whose service he was for all too short a time."

' "Today," he continued, "our hearts and prayers should be offered to Colonel Merrick's widow, in thanksgiving for a life so well lived, so abruptly ended, so sadly lost."

'After the singing of the hymn "Abide with Me" there was a moment's silence and then from outside the church came the clear sombre notes of the Last Post, sounded off by a bugler of the Mirat Artillery. An equally moving last touch to the simple service was made when the Chief Minister of State in Mirat, the Count Bronowsky, stepped forward and assisted the widow from the church.

'A few days earlier a post-mortem confirmed that Colonel Merrick died as a result of injuries sustained in a riding accident. The funeral was delayed to enable the widow and other members of the family to attend. The remains were cremated.'

*

'Sahib?'

The bearer had brought the tray of fresh coffee. He was asking Perron whether he wanted it at the breakfast table or at the verandah table where Perron was leaning against the balustrade. Perron nodded at the verandah table and then read the report again. And now the muddy photograph began to take on a sinister likeness to the Merrick he had known. He sat down, poured more coffee, and continued to study both the photograph and the report.

'I didn't know,' a woman's voice said, 'that the local rag could be so absorbing.'

Startled, he looked up. The woman in the sunglasses had come back and was sitting two tables away. Her voice was low-keyed, a bit hoarse, but attractive. He smiled, put the paper away and said, 'I'm sorry, I didn't see you.'

'That's what I mean. You are Guy Perron, aren't you?'

'Yes –?'

'You've been expected. So I did wonder when I saw you arrive. I've been nosey and had a look at the book you signed. No, please don't move.' She got up herself and came to join him. She took the sunglasses off, revealing rather pale eyes, blue-grey with a tinge of violet. A tiny scar, about an inch

1476

long, white, showed clearly beneath the left one. In spite of this blemish she was in a sad, rather exhausted way, beautiful.

'You won't recognize me. But you might remember me as Laura Elliott. At least Nigel told me you did.'

After a few seconds Perron said, 'Yes. Laura Elliott.' He offered his hand. Hers was rather clammy. He said, 'The coffee's fresh. Let me ask the bearer for another cup.'

'Thank you.' She sat down. He rang the handbell. When the old man came out he saw at once what was wanted and went back in. Perron sat. She was gazing steadily at him.

'I *think* I remember you,' she said. 'I mean I know I remember you but think I recognize you.'

'And I you.'

'No. I shouldn't think so.'

She had a directness that wasn't unpleasant, but having made this denial there was a hint of confusion in the way she replaced the sunglasses. He thought it possible that Nigel might also have said to her: Guy called you that stunning girl. She was stunning no longer.

The bearer brought another cup and another pot of coffee. She poured for them both. 'Why have you come to the club, Mr Perron? Nigel said they were expecting you at the Izzat Bagh.'

'I never got round to wiring the day and time I'd get here. After a night on the train I thought it would be a good idea at least to get some breakfast and even make sure of a bed for the night without putting people out.'

'Well, and it's nice to be on your own for a while. Before putting on one's visiting face. Is Nigel going to be disappointed?'

'Why disappointed?'

'He said you'd be surprised to find him in Mirat. But you don't seem surprised. You haven't even asked me who I mean by Nigel. Did Dmitri give the game away after all?'

'No. And I am surprised. But the edge has been knocked off by what I've just read in the *Mirat Courier.*'

'Oh, have they said something about him? I never read it.'

'His name's included in a list of people who went to a funeral on Saturday. Mr Nigel Rowan, AAGG. And then the other names clinched it. The only person I don't know about is Mrs Nigel Rowan.'

Laura Elliott smiled. Her mouth went down with the smile. 'That's me, I'm afraid. Was I mentioned too? Nigel will be pleased. It worries him a bit that printed guest lists seldom refer to us both. But then how can they if I'm always making excuses or just not turning up? It's Dmitri Bronowsky who's expecting you really, isn't it? Are you going to ring him up?'

'The secretary said he mightn't be in Mirat but that he could easily find out.'

'In which case he's probably looking for me. Dmitri was in Mirat yesterday. He must still be. But you needn't ring. Nigel will either be ringing me here or arriving here some time this morning. You could go back with him. In any case I'll let him know you're here.'

'It's well over a year since Nigel and I were in touch. How long have you been married?'

'Rather less than a year. But do you mind if we don't talk about it? I was always very fond of Nigel and still am, but I'm afraid his marriage hasn't been a success.'

Perron studied Laura Elliott's face – turned, for once, away from him as she watched the swooping crows; and thought he saw a woman who had had a bad time and was trying to pick up the pieces. She had rejected Nigel originally for a planter in Malaya. He remembered Nigel referring to a surviving Elliott parent in Darjeeling, who had only heard from Laura once, after she had ended up in a Japanese prison-camp. Presumably, unless there had been a divorce, the planter-husband hadn't survived. He felt he couldn't ask. He felt she would welcome a discussion about her and her first husband's captivity as little as she welcomed discussion of her marriage to Nigel. He said:

'Are you staying here at the club?'

'Yes, temporarily.' The sunglasses were redirected at him. 'I've just remembered.' She took the glasses off. 'You had a delightful but rather dotty aunt. Is she still alive?'

'She's paying for most of the cost of this trip and she's pulled most of the strings that make things easy when I want them easy.'

'I'm glad she's still alive. People like that deserve a long life.'

'People like what?'

'People who take an interest in other people, especially in young people. I felt that. I felt her reacting to me as if I were a person, not just another good-looking girl.'

'I'll tell her what you say.'

'Oh, she won't remember me.'

'But she does.'

A moment of nakedness. Then the glasses went back on. There was the sound of a telephone ringing. Perron said, 'Perhaps that's Nigel now.'

'We shall soon know. You'd like some more coffee?'

'Thank you.'

She began to pour. Hearing footsteps, Perron looked round. It was Macpherson. He said:

'Ah, there you both are. Already introduced yourselves. Good. Your husband is on the line, Mrs Rowan.'

She thanked Macpherson, pushed the glasses hard against the bridge of her nose and got up and went without another word or a glance in Perron's direction.

Macpherson said, 'It looks as if you're in luck and I lose an overnight guest.'

She did not come back. The clerk came ten minutes later with a message from her. A car would call for Perron at mid-day to take him to the Izzat

Bagh. He stayed on the terrace for another half-hour or so. But still she did not return.

*

The car slowed to pass through a sentry-guarded checkpoint marked by a notice: *End of Cantonment Limits* and then headed along a straight road slightly below the level of the railway. He put on his own dark glasses and took out Rowan's note and re-read it.

'My dear Guy, I'm sorry I can't come to collect you personally. It's one of those pressing official mornings. I've not had the chance yet to tell Dmitri you've arrived, but will. Meanwhile, the best thing is for you to come to my bungalow. It's next to the Dewani Bhavan, Dmitri's house, where you'll be staying, but a lot has happened since he wired you in Bombay and you may find dossing down with me at least a good temporary solution. You're very welcome. Laura tells me you and she met and that you've seen the *Courier*, so know something of the score. Colonel Layton went back to Pankot this morning but Susan and her aunt are still here. They're staying at the palace guest house. Sarah's here too, of course, and has promised to be at my bungalow to welcome you and to see you settled in. I may have to stay at the palace for lunch, but I've organized things for you to lunch at my place. I expect you'll want to relax anyway. The bungalow is tucked between the Dewani Bhavan and the bungalow that was Susan's and Ronald's.

'You'll get a good view of the Izzat Bagh Palace and the guest house directly until you fork right from the railway and the road starts to lead you round our side of the lake. Once you've passed the walls of the palace grounds you're at the Dewani Bhavan (and our bungalow which overlooks the waste ground between the palace and the city). See you soon. Nigel.'

The fork was ahead. He moved to the left-hand side of the car. Presently he saw the palace at the other end of the dazzling stretch of water: a rose-coloured structure with little towers, and on the lake-shore a white domed mosque with one slim minaret reflected. To one side, amidst trees, a palladian-style mansion. The guest house presumably.

At this upper end of the lake there were huts and boats (beached). A detachment of armed police patrolled the area. The lake seemed to be separated almost into two by an isthmus and an area of reeds. Where the reeds began the road curved away from the bank as though everything beyond the reeds was private property. The car became cooler, shaded by banyan trees. And to the left there suddenly appeared a brick wall mercilessly topped by spears of broken bottle-glass. The palace grounds. The wall continued for half a mile. Perhaps more. But suddenly ended, at a right angle, and the road was now edged on that side by an immense stretch of open ground, broken by nullahs. The car slowed. Just ahead on the right there was a grey stucco wall, a glimpse of a substantial bungalow, the Dewani Bhavan. But his attention was taken by a more distant view, the

1479

view of what lay at the far end of the waste ground, about a mile away: the blur of the old walled and minareted city of Mirat.

The car turned, across a culvert, into the compound of a small bungalow, a very old, squat building with square pillars to its verandah. The compound was rough and untended.

Standing in the shadow of the deep verandah was a woman wearing a blouse and skirt. Sarah. She had her arms folded (hands, as he remembered, clasping the elbows). As the car drew up she came down the steps ahead of a servant.

The first thing he noticed as he pushed the door open and looked up at her was a little pad of flesh beneath her chin.

'Hello, Guy.' She offered her hand. He took it and could not tell whether a warmer embrace had been expected, or would be welcome. Free, she folded her arms again and led the way on to the verandah which at this central point was deep, set out with tables and lounging chairs. There was a dusty uncared-for look about it. Whether this was Laura's fault or one of the reasons why Laura wasn't living here were questions whose answers might become clearer.

The interior hall was dark, sombre. You could smell damp. Sarah moved through it unaffected, he felt, by the oppressive weight of masonry, the brooding pressure of the thick square pillars that rose from the tiled floor up, up, into a remote raftered roof. She opened a door and the scale diminished to one that was more accommodating to the human ego. But this room was long, too narrow for its length. Here, he sensed the presence of hidden fungus, a sweet heavy smell which, mixed with the light dry scent of some kind of antiseptic, immediately depressed him. A white mosquito-net shrouded a narrow little bed. The main source of light was from the open bathroom door. It was probably from the bathroom that the smell of antiseptic came.

'It's rather spartan,' she said. 'Nigel asked me to apologize. But I probably don't need to. I expect Laura warned you they've not been here long and won't be staying.'

Perron let that go. He said, 'What date do you think? 1830? 1850?'

'I don't know. Shut up too long anyway. Watch out for scorpions. And I don't want to alarm you but there was a snake not long ago, on the verandah at the back. They had a good hunt after it was killed so I don't think you need worry, in any case Nigel says snakes are very misunderstood creatures and that the thing to do if you meet one is bow politely and ask it to go its way in peace.'

'I shall probably just yell the place down.'

She laughed, standing there, in front of him, arms still folded. He moved forward, put one arm lightly round her. She didn't move but in a moment briefly leant her head so that her hair brushed his chin.

'It's nice to see you again, Guy. You always made me laugh.'

She moved away. The servants were bringing in his suitcase and holdall. She said, 'I don't think Nigel will be back for lunch, but it's all organized for

1480

you to have directly you want it. So let's have a drink. Then I'll leave you to
settle in.'

'Do you have to leave?'

'Yes. But I've got time for a drink.'

They returned to the verandah. She called out to the driver that she'd be
ready in fifteen minutes. He went away, round the side of the bungalow. A
servant had already placed a tray and bottles and glasses on a side-table.
She told him to go and then asked Perron what he'd have.

'Out here I still like the gin.'

She poured, added ice and fizz and brought the glasses over. She said, 'I'd
ask you to lunch at the guest house in ordinary circumstances but today I
think you'd be happier eating here alone.'

'If you think so.'

He offered her a cigarette. She hesitated then took one. 'I've been trying
to cut down, which means I've joined that boring gang of cadging non-
smokers who never have their own. Thank you.' Bending forward to give
her a light he noticed that the hand holding the cigarette was a bit
unsteady; and that her hair, once so smooth and gleaming, looked less well
cared-for. He felt this suited her rather better. She seemed more marked by
experience. He said, 'I've come at rather a bad moment, haven't I?'

'Up to a week ago we'd certainly thought of your arrival rather
differently.'

'How differently?'

'Nigel and I and Ahmed were going to meet you at the station. It was
Dmitri's idea. I expect he'd have come too, because he likes surprising
people. That's why when he got your letter from home he didn't answer
but waited until there was just time to send you a welcoming telegram in
Bombay. He thought he couldn't very well write a letter without
mentioning the fact that Nigel and I were here. And Ronald of course.'

'You were here when my letter arrived then? I thought you'd probably
come down just now. From Pankot.'

'No, I've been here for quite a time. It was Susan who had to come down.
With father and Aunt Fenny. Father went back this morning. Did you
come in on the night train?'

'Yes.'

'Then you must have been on the station at roughly the same time as
father.'

'There was quite a crowd. Were you there, seeing him off?'

'No, but Aunt Fenny was. He has to get back to Pankot to go on handing
over his command at the depot. He wanted us to go with him but at the last
moment Susan wouldn't. So Fenny felt she had to stay too.'

'What about your mother?'

'Oh, mother went home last month to start house-hunting.'

'So no retirement to Rose Cottage?'

'No. Actually we moved down to Commandant House quite a while ago
and rented the cottage to people called Smalley. We can't sell it, except to

the army, but that's what will happen now. I expect the Smalleys will stay there a while because they're staying on under contract with the Indian Government. At least for a year or two. He's a bit too young to retire. A bit too old to fancy his chances at home. Father of course would have retired next year anyway. Neither of them wants to stay out here, though.'

'So back home for you too?'

'I don't know about me. Aunt Fenny and I went back for a month or two last year, after Uncle Arthur died. You never met them, did you?'

'No, but I know about Colonel Grace dying. I called at Queen's Road the other day and saw Mr Hapgood.'

'Hapgood?'

'The people upstairs. Captain Purvis's billet.'

'Oh.' She leant back, shutting her eyes. 'How long ago all that seems.'

'You never got in touch with me.'

'What?'

'When you were in England last year, with your Aunt Fenny.'

'No.'

'Nor answered my second letter.'

'No, I'm sorry. But that was a long time ago too.'

'Was the visit home a disappointment?'

'I don't suppose I gave it a proper chance. It might have been different if Aunt Fenny had gone home for good. But she had her return passage booked. And when the time came I felt I had to come back too.'

'You told me once that India wasn't a place you felt you could be happy in.'

'Did I? Yes, I remember thinking that.' She looked at him. 'I've been very happy since.'

'Has Susan been happy?'

Sarah didn't answer at once. Then she said, 'At the moment she's in rather a bad way, probably worse than the family realizes. I can't remember what you knew about her history, but she's never been what is called really stable.'

'Didn't Ronald Merrick give her stability?'

Again she didn't answer at once.

'He's provided it now. You'll see what I mean if she talks to you about him, which is fairly likely. He's all she talks about.'

'It was a successful marriage, then?'

'I expected it to be disastrous. Of course, he adored the boy, and the boy adored him. Edward doesn't know Ronnie's dead, by the way. I ought to warn you.'

'Is the boy here?'

'Yes.' Sarah stubbed her cigarette. 'Su wouldn't leave him in Pankot, which is partly why Fenny had to come. Anyway, it's no bad thing for her to have him with her, but it's had its awkward side. I looked after him while the others went to the funeral. It was difficult explaining to him why mummy kept crying and why they'd come all the way back to daddy's house and not seen daddy. He said daddy had promised he'd still be here when their holiday in the hills was over and he'd made everything safe again. So of course I said that things were quite safe now but that daddy had had to go away for a while to make them safe somewhere else.'

'Ronald sent them back to Pankot because of trouble here?'

'Partly that, but to get them into the hills for the hot weather as well. Su wanted just to go up to Nanoora, but Ronald said if there was any more trouble Nanoora would be just as bad.'

'Has there been much trouble?'

'Off and on, yes. Quite a lot. That's why he was sent here in the first place. They were up in Rajputana. He'd become temporarily attached to the States Police. You know? The reserve pool that sends officers and men to states where the rulers' own police forces need helping out? He packed Su and Edward back to Pankot and came down here alone. They say he did a marvellous job. The Nawab's own police are practically all Muslims, and that was part of the problem, because they took sides in communal disturbances, lashing out at Hindu crowds and mobs and turning a blind eye if the Muslims were having a go. Ronnie stopped all that. He pretended it was easy. He said all he'd had to do was make the Muslim Chief of Police see he had a duty to the whole community, but it can't have been as simple as that.'

'When was all this?'

'Last December. He didn't expect the job to last long. But Dmitri was so impressed by the way he handled it he persuaded the States Police to let him stay on and help overhaul the whole Mirat Police Department and devise a new training and recruiting programme. It suited Ronnie very well. At one time there was an idea he might retire officially from the service and make a contract with the Nawab. Su and he set up house early last March. Then in May when the hot weather was really cooking up he sent her and Edward back to Pankot. As I said, partly because of the heat and partly because there was another outbreak of communal riots.'

'That was their bungalow next door, wasn't it?'

'Yes. It's not nearly as dilapidated as this. In fact he made it very comfortable. I stayed with them for a while after I helped Su move down from Pankot. But since April I've been living either at Dmitri's or the palace. Now, of course, I'll have to go back with Su. Fenny can't cope with the journey alone. And I don't know how badly Su'll take it when the reaction sets in.'

'I see there was a post-mortem.'

'Yes.' She got up. 'I really must go.'

Perron, getting up too, said, 'How long has Nigel been in Mirat?'

'About six weeks. The Political Department sent him down to try and sort things out. Actually Dmitri asked for him. Mirat comes under the Resident at Gopalakand and things got rather difficult. Nigel will tell you all about it. I'll be in touch, Guy. Probably this evening.'

The driver had come back. But just as she began to go down the steps another car came into the compound. 'You're in luck,' she said. 'Here's Nigel now.'

She went down to meet him. Perron stayed on the verandah. The car stopped several yards away from the one already parked. The driver got out and opened the door. A man emerged. If it was Rowan then he had lost even more weight. This man's skin was pale yellow and looked almost translucent, stretched over the cheek-bones. The man raised a welcoming hand to Perron, then said something to Sarah. They came towards the steps. Only now was the man's face recognizable as Rowan's.

'Hello, Guy,' he said. 'I'm sorry but I'm afraid I'm only here to pack a case.' They clasped hands.

'I'll see to the case,' Sarah said. 'How many nights?'

'Two at the most. I ought to be back tomorrow evening. And don't bother. Tippoo can do it.'

'Does it include black tie?'

'I've got all that in Gopalakand. Just one other suit. Isn't Tippoo here?'

'Yes, but I'll see he gets it right.' She went inside calling for someone named Tippoo. From the far end of one of the narrow wings of the verandah a middle-aged Indian in European clothes came out of a casement doorway: a clerk, not a servant. Rowan said, 'Just a second, Guy,' and went to meet him. They talked for a while. Then Nigel came back.

'Have you got a drink?'

Perron indicated his glass.

'Let me freshen it for you. I really do apologize. We're in the middle of what I suppose you'd call a flap. I've got to go up to Gopalakand.' He handed Perron the refilled glass. 'You're looking very fit. I'll be back in a moment.'

He went inside. Perron heard him calling Tippoo and Sarah calling something back. The clerk came out again, with a couple of files, but seeing Perron alone he went back inside, presumably to look for Rowan indoors. A telephone rang and was quickly answered. The two drivers were gossiping. Perron sat down and composed himself, to let the tide of India flow over him; presently it would ebb and leave him revealed: a visitor who was excluded from the mystery, the vital secret. I have been happy since, Sarah had said; as a woman might say if she were in love. In love with whom? Nigel? But he had been in Mirat only six weeks and she had been here since March, obviously content. Merrick? No, that was impossible. And Merrick's death didn't seem to have disturbed her in the way she would have been disturbed by the death of a man she had loved. The only answer seemed to be: in love with the land itself, after all; yes, in love with that, and content to be here whatever happened. A strange but perhaps logical reversal of her old attitude.

'I won't apologize again,' Rowan said, coming back and sitting opposite, glancing at his watch. 'But I have to be off in five or ten minutes, so let's work out what's best for you. There are three possibilities. You're more than welcome to stay here, and you could rely on Tippoo to look after you.

1484

Dmitri asked me to tell you you're equally welcome to move into the Dewani Bhavan, but he's unlikely to be around much if at all in the next day or two. We've got a couple of States Department people over at the palace –'

'Waving the standstill agreement and the instrument of accession to Congress India, and asking for the Nawab's signature before August fifteen?'

'Good, you know about that. That cuts out a lot of tedious explanation. The other alternative for you while I'm away is the Gymkhana Club if you'd prefer that sort of atmosphere. If you opt for the club I could take you there now, as my guest it goes without saying. I've got to collect Laura. Sarah would keep in touch with you of course and there'd always be a car available to take you anywhere you want to go. But don't feel I'm pushing you out. My clerk will be here too most of the time and he'd help you in any way he can. Otherwise you can just forget about him. He has his own domestic arrangements. So, Guy, I leave it to you and in spite of what I said about not apologizing again, I do.'

'It's entirely my fault. I ought to have sent a wire. Checked that it was convenient.'

'The flap would have occurred anyway. It's not inconvenient for us. We're just worried about you.'

'I'd like to stay here, if that's all right.'

'Good. Actually it'll make things easier for Sarah, not that she ever complains, but we do all tend to load her with extra jobs. She could help look after you better here than at the club.'

'Tell me one thing, is the Resident at Gopalakand in what I call the entrenched opposition camp that's encouraging the princes to stand firm on their own independence?'

'Fundamentally, that is the problem.'

'What does Dmitri want?'

'Honourable integration.'

'And the Nawab?'

'I don't think the poor old man knows. But after all these years he's suddenly resisting Dmitri's advice. The Resident's trying to persuade the Maharajah in Gopalakand to sign nothing and reserve his position until paramountcy automatically lapses on August fifteen and leaves him technically independent. As a result the Nawab's taking that line too. It's quite hopeless of course. He knows it, but he's being very stubborn and the Resident isn't being in the least helpful. He's never really been interested in Mirat. Mirat should have had its own agent long ago.'

'Are you on Dmitri's side, then?'

'Let's say I agree that the only sensible course for Mirat is to accede to the new Indian Union on the three main subjects, sign the standstill agreement and then get the best deal possible. Mirat's entirely surrounded by what's been British-Indian territory and overnight becomes Indian Union territory. The Nawab can't live in a vacuum.'

Perron nodded. He said, 'How have things been for you, Nigel, this past two years?'

'I've moved around a lot. Little else. Perhaps I ought to have stayed in the army. It turned out to be the wrong time to come back into the Political. Still, the end would have been the same in either case.'

'What do you hope to achieve in Gopalakand, or is that confidential?'

'If I can come back with a letter from Conway to the Nawab making it clear that Mirat's on its own and that Conway can't advise either way, then we should be able to persuade the old chap to sign. And sign he must. There's no sensible alternative. Except chaos, if that's sensible. From what I've seen going on in the past few weeks I sometimes wonder whether the Political Department cares, so long as it can close itself down convinced that it's upheld the principles of the whole past relationship between the States and the Crown.'

' "Nothing can bring you peace but yourself," ' Perron quoted. ' "Nothing can bring you peace but the triumph of principles." '

'What?'

'Emerson.'

'Oh.' Nigel smiled. 'Did he say that? How apt. That sums up my department's attitude admirably.'

'Not just your department's. I think it sums up the attitude of everybody who's concerned in what happens on August fifteen.' Perron took a sip of his gin. 'I'm sorry about Merrick,' he said. 'Not that I ever liked the man. Still, he seemed to have made good in Mirat.'

'Yes.' Rowan looked at his watch again.

'And Harry Coomer? Any news of him? I'm sorry I decided there was nothing to be done at my end.'

'I don't think I really expected it, but I appreciated your giving thought to it, and appreciated your letter. One becomes involved for a time, and then the involvement ends. In any case, I don't think there was anything Kumar wanted.'

'Why do you think that?'

'He implied as much. We exchanged letters after Gopal died, last year. Poor old Gopal. He was always getting colds. He took his wife down to Puri for a holiday and caught cold and got pneumonia. I asked Mrs Gopal to put me in touch with the man who'd been helping Kumar rehabilitate himself. Got Kumar's address out of him, so wrote. Difficult letter to write. I didn't hear for ages. He'd moved, so my letter followed him around. When he wrote he didn't give me his new address but the letter was postmarked Ranpur so he must still have been there, I imagine. Probably still is.'

'What did he say?'

'What it added up to was that he was quite content doing what he was doing, coaching students privately.'

'A defensive attitude?'

'I don't think so. He seemed very grateful for the one or two things I'd suggested.'

'What sort of things?'

'Just general ideas about how he could make best use of his talents.'

'Commerce for instance?'

'Yes, but that would be open to him at almost any time.'

'Would it, Nigel? The kind of commerce we think of as commerce? I seem to remember he failed to get into it once, with British-Indian Electric.'

'Once.'

'Has British-Indian Electric changed?'

Rowan said nothing.

'Will anything ever really change in India, for him? Isn't Harry Coomer the permanent loose end? Too English for the Indians, too Indian for the English?'

'That, rather, is Sarah's view. Frankly, I think he's more interested in being just his own kind of Indian.'

'Have you told her you tried to help him?'

'Yes, but only quite recently.'

'I don't suppose you ever showed her a transcript of the examination?'

'Good God, no. She knows nothing about that.' He lowered his voice. 'Few people do now, except you. Everything in connection with the examination was destroyed, except the orders for Kumar's release.'

'To protect Merrick's reputation?'

'The issues involved ranged far wider than that. I imagine quite a lot of files were vetted, and re-arranged.'

'To make it more difficult for an incoming Congress ministry to smell out witches?'

'A witch-hunt was what certain sections of Congress wanted. An inquiry could have aggravated racial tension to an intolerable degree, coming as it would have done on top of the INA trials. If it interests you as a student of history, there was no inquiry because between them Nehru and Wavell put a stop to it. They both saw what it could lead to.'

'And Merrick got off scot-free.'

'Actually, I think it annoyed him. I believe he felt slighted. There were only a few individual inquiries into serious cases involving rather senior officials. It was all done very quietly. One or two people got retired, prematurely.'

'What happened to Kasim's son, Sayed?'

'He was cashiered. That's all.'

'What's he doing now?'

'I'm not sure. Living in Lahore, I believe, with his Muslim League sister and brother-in-law. In some kind of business. Ahmed will tell you.'

'No splendid appointment for one of the INA heroes?'

'They were only heroes for a while. In a way they still are. But folk-heroes. People in a story or legend. When it comes to finding places for them in the world of affairs it's a bit different.'

Sarah came out. Behind her were a couple of servants with bags and the clerk with a briefcase. They went down to the car while Sarah said: 'You're all set, Nigel. If Laura asks, her green taffeta's in the blue case, along with other things she might need.'

'That's good of you.'

'Give Sir Robert my kind regards.'

'I will. Guy's going to stay here, by the way.'

'Good. Do you ride?'

'Off and on. Fortunately more on than off. But it's pure luck.'

She laughed. 'Perhaps we could go out tomorrow morning. I'll ring you later today, anyway.'

The three of them went down into the compound but after he and Nigel had said goodbye Perron stayed near the bottom step while Nigel saw Sarah into her car and then got into his own. He waved them both off.

'Sahib,' Tippoo said, behind him. 'Gin'n'fizz?'

*

Rain. Geckos. Clack-clack-clack. On the walls. Heraldic lizard shapes, pale yellow on the grey-white wash. Chasing one another, intent on copulation. He had woken erect himself – and, half-asleep, smiled, reassured both by this and the realization that the faint discomfort in his bowels had gone, that he was acclimatized. He peered at his wrist-watch. It was only half-past four. He had slept for two hours, after a lunch of chicken pulao, mutton curry lightly spiced in the northern Indian style, and Murree beer. Somewhere a gutter was overflowing. On the basket-work bed-side teapoy there was a tray of tea and a plate of bananas and bread and butter. It must have been the slight clatter of the tray that had woken him. He began to open the mosquito-net and, swinging himself up and round was about to get out when he remembered scorpions and paused, his feet well away from the floor. He reached down, tapped his slippers, and then thrust his feet into them. He grabbed a towel from the bedside chair, wound it round his middle and went into the bathroom.

But, returning, he paused on the threshhold of the bedroom, alert. There was a smell he hadn't noticed before. A foul, sweet smell. He glanced around. In a moment or two the smell seemed to have gone. He sat down and poured tea. He glanced up at the sloping rafters; then lit a cigarette, smoked the recollection of the smell away. The shrouded bed looked like a catafalque. There was a sudden flash of lightning that lit the bathroom and momentarily distorted the shape of the bed. After that, the thunder. And then the humdrum sound of continuing but gradually diminishing rain.

As he finished his tea the bathroom was flooded in sunshine. He called for Tippoo.

*

By five-thirty he was bathed and dressed. He went out into the compound. The shadow of the bungalow thrust itself across the drive. He walked round the side, seeking the sunshine and warmth. At the back the compound stretched for perhaps one hundred yards. There must once have been a lawn and flower beds, but the latter were overgrown. The grass needed scything. An immense banyan tree, its main trunk on this side of the wall dividing Rowan's bungalow from Merrick's, connected the two gardens through its aerial roots. From the other side of the wall Perron heard the high-pitched voice of a young child, a boy, and lower-pitched woman's laughter.

'Catch, Minnie!' the boy shouted. But the throw was too high. A ball sailed over and came to rest some thirty or forty yards away from where Perron was standing; but the ground was too rough for it to bounce. It died, disappeared. He moved off the path and struck out across the grass, wetting his shoes, the bottoms of his slacks. He cast to and fro. Eventually he found it: a grey, soggy tennis-ball.

He picked it up, then turned and saw an Indian woman and the child standing near the banyan tree. Beyond the tree a gate between the two compounds which he hadn't noticed before stood open. The child made a commanding gesture to the woman, as if bidding her stay where she was and then advanced towards Perron: a Pathan child dressed in baggy white pantaloons and shirt, sash, embroidered waistcoat, and cocks-comb pugree. Stuck in the sash was a toy dagger. A miniature Red Shadow. As he got nearer Perron saw that he was of course an English boy, dressed up. His eyes were bright blue, his eyelashes very pale. From under the turban emerged a lick of sandy red hair. He stopped and stuck his little fist round the handle of the toy dagger.

'Who are you?' the boy asked.

'I'm just a visitor. Who are you?'

'I live next door. Is that my ball?'

Perron stooped and showed it to him.

'It looks like mine. Has it got MGC on it?'

Perron inspected it. 'Yes, you can just see MGC.'

'Then it must be mine. MGC means Mirat Gymkhana Club. Mr Macpherson always used to give me used tennis balls.'

Perron nodded, handed the ball over. The child spoke with the assurance of a boy far older.

'It was Minnie's fault. Women can't catch. Thank you for finding it. If you hadn't, Minnie would have had to look and she didn't want to because she's afraid of snakes.'

'Aren't you?'

'No. At least, not very afraid. There were snakes here when Uncle Nigel came. He's not my uncle really. I don't have an uncle because my father didn't have a brother and my mother only has a sister. My stepfather doesn't have a brother either. I've got a stepfather because my real father was killed in the war.'

'You're Edward, aren't you?'

1489

'Yes. My full name is Edward Arthur David Bingham.'

'My name's Guy. My other name is Perron.'

'They're both rather funny names, but I like Perron best. So I'll call you Perron.'

'Then I shall probably have to call you Bingham.'

'Okay.' A minor matter had been satisfactorily settled. A more important one was coming up. 'Can you throw, Perron?'

'Yes.'

'Which arm do you use?'

'The right arm.'

'I throw with my left arm because I'm left-handed. My stepfather has to throw with his right arm because his left arm was cut off. But he's a very good thrower.'

'What do you call your stepfather?'

'Ronald. At least, I do mostly. My mother likes me to call him daddy, so sometimes I do. But he likes me to call him Ronald.'

'Do you know what Ronald means?'

'It means it's his name.'

'Most names have meanings. My name means wide. On the other hand it might mean wood. So you'd better go on calling me Perron which is probably just the place where we lived once. And I shall call you Edward after all. Ronald means the same as Rex or Reginald. It means someone with power who rules. Edward means a rich guard.'

'But I'm not very rich. At the moment I've only got one rupee and four annas.'

'I don't think it's a question of money. Anyway you're guarding the fort while Ronald's away. You're looking after your mother, aren't you?'

'Yes. My mother's name is Susan. What does Susan mean?'

'It means a very beautiful flower called a lily. Not the red ones you see here. White ones.'

'She is quite beautiful. Except when she cries. She's crying now. That's why they sent me out to play in the garden. She may have stopped crying though, if you want to see her. Come on. If she's still crying we can play in our garden. It's a nicer garden than this one.'

Perron got up. The child led the way. As he drew near the ayah he held the ball up and said, 'Here's the ball, ayah. We may want to play with it again.' The girl took the ball in one hand and with the other half-covered her face with the free end of her saree, to protect herself from Perron's gaze.

The Merrick garden was certainly 'nicer'. The lawns were well-cut, and there were signs of work-in-progress, in the form of beds recently dug into ovals, circles and rectangles. Edward pointed them out.

'That's where Ronald's going to try to grow roses.'

Beyond the beds, at the far end of the Merrick compound, was a tennis-court. A thick hedge of shrubs and bushes hid the servants' quarters. The bungalow itself had been re-stuccoed and painted. The rear verandah formed an elegant whitewashed colonnaded semi-circle which embraced the central set of steps leading to the house. Between the columns hung green tattis, some lowered, others at half-mast. Tubs of canna lilies stood sentinel. The bungalow had the slightly raw look of having been stripped recently of ancient creepers to allow redecoration.

The little Pathan marched across the lawn towards the verandah and then at the bottom step kicked off his chappals and climbed barefoot. Perron decided that this was part of a private game, not obligatory, so he climbed shod. The boy waited for him at the top, legs apart, fist on the handle of the toy dagger.

'Would you like to see my room first, Perron?'

'Very much.'

The boy strode off to the right, along the verandah and round the corner. At the side of the bungalow he pulled open a wirescreen door, held it, and let Perron enter first.

A small room, austere, remarkably unboylike. That was Perron's impression until he remembered that Edward hadn't slept or played here for several months. The narrow little charpoy was unmade, its mattress rolled, the net folded. Across the exposed webbing were the clothes he had taken off – diminutive khaki shorts, a blue shirt and grey socks. A cane chair, an almirah and a chest of drawers were the only other furnishings. The door of the almirah was ajar, which suggested that the first thing Edward had done was seek out his Pathan outfit and hasten to get into it.

'Do you like my room?'

'Yes, I do. Where does ayah sleep?'

'There of course.' He pointed at the floor near the casement door. 'Except neither of us sleeps here just now. We're staying at the palace guest house. I'll show you the palace if you like, but not today. Do you like my picture?'

Perron looked at the wall where the child was pointing. Above the chest of drawers was a coloured print in a gilt frame. He went to inspect it.

'Daddy gave it to me. It's called "The Jewel in Her Crown" and it's about Queen Victoria.'

Perron saw that indeed it was. It was the kind of picture whose awfulness gave it a kind of distinction. The old Queen was enthroned, beneath a canopy, receiving tribute from a motley gathering of her Indian subjects, chief among whom was a prince, bearing a crown on a cushion. Ranged on either side of the throne were representatives of the *raj* in statuesque pro-consular positions. Disraeli was there, indicating a parchment. In the background, plump angels peered from behind fat clouds, and looked ready to blow their long golden trumpets. The print was blemished by little speckles of brown damp.

'But it isn't the jewel in the crown the prince is holding. The jewel's India,' the boy explained.

'Yes, I see.'

'It's an alle-gory.'

'What's an alle-gory?'

'Don't you know? It means telling a story that's really two stories. The

Queen's dead now of course. I should think they're all dead, except the angels. Angels never die.'

'No. So I'm told.'

'Have you ever seen an angel, Perron?'

'No.'

'Nor've I. Daddy says mummy saw an angel once, an angel in a circle of fire, but I mustn't talk about it because it upsets her. Come on. Let's see if she's still crying.'

Reluctantly, Perron followed him to a closed door. The boy opened it, put his head out and listened. The silence coming from the other side was peculiarly oppressive. But Edward obviously found it reassuring.

'I think she's stopped.'

He opened the door wide. Beyond was the main entrance-hall, as encumbered with square pillars as the hall in Rowan's bungalow; but the tiled floor shone – except in the area exposed by the taking up of a carpet which had been rolled and corded and now awaited disposal.

Edward pattered across the hall on his bare feet, entered a room whose door stood open. There was a pause, and then a woman's shriek; a pause, a repetition of the shriek, longer drawn out, and then continuing.

The boy emerged, levitated. Simultaneously a magenta-coloured shape flowed past Perron – the ayah. The ayah grasped the boy out of the air, and so revealed the source of the levitation; Sarah, who turned immediately back into the room from which the shrieks were still coming. As the ayah carried Edward away he began to wail. A white-clad, sashed and turbanned servant ran in from the front porch, across the hall and into the room.

Then the shrieking stopped. Slowly, Perron approached the wide-open doors, uncertain what to do. The doors were double and from the threshold he could see that the room was a bedroom, but a very large bedroom, dominated by a bed which was centrally placed, raised on a stone-stepped daïs. Sarah was sitting on the edge of this bed cradling and rocking Susan in her arms. The servant stood nearby. Perhaps he had spoken because Sarah seemed to be shaking her head at him. Presently the servant took a few steps back, then turned, saw Perron, and came out, went past without a word.

Below the daïs there was an open tin trunk and scattered all around it what must be Ronald Merrick's relics: KD uniforms, Sam Brownes, leather cases, hairbrushes, a sword in a black and silver scabbard, mess dress, leather gloves, swagger canes, a Field Service cap, riding boots, jodhpurs, Harris tweed jacket, checked flannel shirts, a Gurkha's kukri, grey slacks, brown shoes, chukka boots: the detritus of a man's life in India.

Three tall casement windows, facing west, had been unshuttered. The evening light filtered through. The shafts of this light were alive with mobile particles of dust. He turned to leave. He didn't think Sarah had seen him, but just then she said, 'Don't go away altogether, Guy.'

He said, 'I'll be outside.'

He sat on the front verandah. The trees and bushes in the front compound were in a similar state of decay as those in Rowan's, but thick enough to screen the bungalow from the road. The servant was talking to the chauffeur of one of the palace limousines, parked near the foot of the steps. The servant came up and asked if the sahib wished anything. Perron shook his head.

He smoked. He thought: Why should she scream? It was her own son. He sat on the balustrade. As he finished his cigarette the ayah and Edward came out. Edward was now wearing his ordinary clothes. His little chappals clattered. He looked what he was – a small boy scarcely out of infancy, three or four years old. But when he spoke he was still the little Pathan.

'Hello, Perron. Are you coming to the guest house?'

'Afraid not, old chap. Not today, anyway.'

'If you do I can show you the palace after all.'

'I'd like that. Tomorrow, perhaps.'

The boy offered his hand. Perron reached down and shook it.

'Goodbye, Perron.'

Edward clattered down the steps and ran to the car. The ayah hastened after him. He shouted at the driver, 'Jeldi, jeldi. Ham ek dam Guest House wapas-jane-wale hain. Chalo!'

The driver, approaching, wagged his head and called back, 'Thik hai, Sahib.' He helped Edward get up on the running-board and open the rear door. The ayah followed him in but must have been told to go to the farther seat because when the door was shut Edward put his head out of the open window and shouted:

'I can show you the white peacock too, Perron.'

Perron made an appreciative sideways nod of his head. The boy sat back. The car set off.

'You've made a hit.'

Sarah had come out and was standing behind him. She said, 'The white peacock's his special secret. But why does he call you Perron?'

'We agreed to be informal. He's a remarkable boy, isn't he? How old?'

'He was three last June. I remember wondering whether he'd ever learn to talk.'

'Is Susan all right now?'

'Yes, perfectly. She'd like it if you came in and had a word. She may ask you to dinner at the guest house this evening. That was originally my idea too but I'd prefer it if you made an excuse. These upsets sometimes have repercussions later. So I'd rather we left anything like that until tomorrow.'

'What upset her?'

Sarah, arms folded in the characteristic way, shrugged slightly. She didn't look at him. Her manner struck him as evasive. He realized that this was not the first time today that it had. She said, 'Oh, the whole afternoon mainly. She insisted on coming over and sorting out some of Ronald's things, so I had to come too because Aunt Fenny's not feeling very bright. Then Edward insisted on coming with us. The whole thing was a mistake from the start.'

'Could you have dinner with me, at Nigel's?'

'I'd like to but I'd better not. Let's go out tomorrow morning, though. I'll try and rope Ahmed in too.'

'What time?'

'Could you be ready by seven? That's the best time.'

'Rain or shine?'

'At this time of year it only rains in the afternoon, if it rains at all.'

'I've got nothing special to ride in.'

'That doesn't matter. Well, let's go in. The guest house is only a few minutes away so the car will be back soon and I want to get Susan away before the light goes.'

*

'We met didn't we, Mr Perron? That time in Pankot just after Ronnie and I became engaged and you were working with him.'

She had on a cotton print dress with a full skirt, which was disposed to envelop her legs while she knelt on the floor by the tin trunk, her weight centred on her left hip, supported by a stiffened left arm. After they'd shaken hands she placed her right hand back on her left shoulder. The light which twenty minutes before had streamed through the unshuttered windows had diminished, but what was left of it lit one side of her pretty flushed face and picked out the red-brown tones of hair which in full daylight would look dark, almost black. She seemed perfectly composed now.

She said, 'Of course, you know that I've lost him. My son doesn't know. It's really a question of working out a way of how and what to tell him.' She reached out and touched the Field Service cap.

Sarah said, 'Why don't you leave it all, Su? Khansamar will put it away. Then we could all have a drink outside while we wait for the car.'

'No, I don't want a drink. But you both have one. I've still got a lot to sort out and I don't want Khansamar touching anything.'

'Then I'll help you start putting things back,' Sarah knelt and began to fold the tweed jacket.

'How little there is,' Susan said. 'I mean when you think of the years a man spends out here. So little he would want to keep. Will daddy have as little as this?'

'I don't expect there'll be much more.'

Susan fingered the pommel of the sword. 'And even the things they do have look like toys, don't they? I suppose that's because the things they

1494

play with when they're young are just smaller versions of the things they'll have to use later. It's different for us. A doll's house isn't at all like a real house. And a doll not in the least like a real baby. You didn't know my husband well, did you, Mr Perron? You were hardly with him at all, were you?'

'No. A very short time.'

'Ask anyone here in Mirat and they'll tell you what a fine man he was. I don't yet think of him as dead.'

Sarah gently withdrew the sword from her sister's touch and placed it in the trunk.

'And then my not being here at the time makes it seem it hasn't happened, and when I tell Edward we'll be seeing daddy again soon, that's what it seems like. That we will be seeing him. Please stop putting things back, Sarah. It's all that's left of Ronald and it's not even all here.'

'Oh?' Sarah said, not looking at her sister. 'What's missing?'

'His arm for one thing.'

Sarah pushed hair away from her right cheek and didn't comment.

'I mean the artificial one, Mr Perron. His harness. But we always called it his arm. It was one of the ways we made light of it. Where's my arm? he used to say. He took it off every night. Nobody knows the discomfort he was in, from the chafing. The first time I saw his poor shoulder and his poor stump, I cried. They were so inflamed and raw. That's because he never spared himself. He learned to ride again, you know. Getting up on what he called the wrong side. He played tennis too. He called it patball because he had to serve underarm by dropping the ball and hitting it on the bounce but he played a strong game otherwise.'

Sarah had got up and was opening a chest of drawers. Susan said, 'It's no good. I've looked in all the drawers and cupboards. I've looked everywhere, but I can't find it.'

'What's this, then?' Sarah held up a contraption of webbing and metal.

Without even looking Susan said, 'That's the one he couldn't wear. The new one. The one they said was much better, a much more modern design. But if you look at it you'll see it can't have been worn more than a few times.'

Sarah thrust it back into the chest and closed the drawer.

'I hope this doesn't embarrass you, Mr Perron. Talking about his arm. But you see he never, never, wore it in bed. He took it off every night. He had to be very careful not to let the stump get too inflamed. I know what a relief it was to him to get out of the harness, and sometimes what torture it was to put it back on in the morning. He wouldn't have worn it while he was laid up after his riding accident.'

Perron said, 'Perhaps the accident explains why it's not here, Mrs Merrick. It could have been damaged and sent away for repair.'

'Oh.' She considered him gravely. 'I hadn't thought of that.' She smiled. 'Ronnie was quite right. He always was. He said women have instincts,

1495

they know when something is wrong or not properly explained. But men work things out logically much better. It struck me as odd when I couldn't find it, because to put it brutally I couldn't see them putting the arm on, just to take – just to take his body to the mortuary for the post-mortem. And there had to be a post-mortem because he was found dead in bed and people thought he was getting better. I blame Dr Habbibullah, but daddy says I shouldn't. He said no one can foresee a clot of blood. But why was there a clot of blood? Unless there was an internal injury from the riding accident that Dr Habbibullah hadn't diagnosed?'

'Well you know, you can seem in perfect health one minute, and then –'

'Drop dead the next. Oh, I know. But all these doctors protect themselves and each other don't you think, Mr Perron? I mean whether they're English or Indian. And I do blame Dr Habbibullah even though Ronnie himself once said he was one of the best doctors he'd ever come across.' She looked round at Sarah. 'Khansamar would know about Ronnie's harness, Sarah. Whether it was damaged.'

'I don't think we should worry Khansamar over a thing like that, Su.'

'Why?'

'Because he's a servant. When you ask servants what's happened to something it always sounds as if you're accusing them of stealing. I'll ask Dr Habbibullah if you really want me to.'

'Yes, I do. But what about the other things that are missing? Where are his Pathan clothes? He was very fond of his Pathan clothes.' She turned to Perron again. 'He had to choose Pathan clothes because of his blue eyes. He had two sets but only one pugree and only one embroidered waistcoat.' She looked at the scattered stuff. 'There's only one set here, these trousers and this shirt. The other set's missing, and so are the pugree and the waistcoat. And the sash. And the little axe.'

'He probably gave them away,' Sarah said. 'It must be years since he used them.'

'Oh no. He went out in them in Mirat too. With one of his spies. He had to have spies, Mr Perron. I'm sorry if it sounds melodramatic, but this is a very melodramatic and violent country. If you're a police officer and take your job seriously you can't just sit in an office like a deputy commissioner. You have to get out into the bazaars and listen to what people are saying. You have to do all sorts of things that so-called pukka members of the *raj* pretend don't have to be done. Of course if you like you can leave it entirely to subordinates, but Ronnie wasn't like that. He knew it was his duty to get out and see and hear for himself. I expect a lot of people who sing his praises now for what he did to settle Mirat when he first came here would pretend to be shocked if they knew he ever had to go out at night dressed as an Indian servant. But he was prepared to do that for the job's sake. It was very dangerous. That goes without saying. That's why he never told me. But I found out. Shall I tell you how I found out, Mr Perron?'

'Only if you want to.'

'Yes. I think I do. I don't know whether you know, but I haven't been very well. For quite a long time. I can't sleep without taking something. He was so understanding about that. And sometimes when there was any kind of trouble brewing or crisis or flap on, anything that kept him working late or might mean his being called out, he'd sleep in another room, so as not to disturb me, once I'd taken my pills. But the pills don't always work. And then I go through phases of not wanting to take them at all because you can't spend the rest of your life taking pills just to get to sleep. And one night I didn't take any pills at all, and Ronnie was working late and sleeping in this other room, and I just lay here trying and trying to get to sleep naturally. And that's terrible. When you're so tired, but can't sleep and you toss and turn and the night just seems to be slipping away and you start imagining all kinds of silly ridiculous things and there's this awful temptation to take not just one or two of the pills but enough to make you sleep forever. So I went to Ronnie's room to see whether he was still awake, so that I could tell him I had this awful temptation, and when I got to the door I saw the light was on. And at four o'clock in the morning that was just as if he'd stayed awake in case I needed him and I felt terribly beholden to him. But when I opened the door it didn't seem to be Ronnie there at all, but this terrifying Indian just standing there staring at me. But of course it was Ronnie. That's why I lost my nerve though, a while ago, when Edward ran in dressed just the same way. I don't mean I didn't know Edward had the same little kind of outfit, I only mean it was like seeing Ronnie again, and just at the moment I was wondering where his own Pathan clothes were.' She turned to Sarah. 'Can't we ask Khansamar even about the clothes?'

'No, we can't. That would be worse than asking him about the harness. The car must be here. I'll go and see. Then we ought to be getting back. Khansamar can put all this away.'

Sarah went.

Susan said, 'My sister isn't very intuitive.'

'No?'

'No. You see, Mr Perron. Ronnie's missing arm and Ronnie's missing clothes are like the dog that didn't bark in the night.'

'Conan Doyle?'

She smiled brilliantly.

'My favourite as a child was *The Speckled Band*. I used to read it by torchlight under the bedclothes at the school Sarah and I went to at home. *The Speckled Band* reminded me of India. Because of the snake. When Aunt Fenny told me last week that Ronnie was dead I thought first of a snake. Or of a scorpion. I've always been terrified of scorpions.'

'I'm terrified of both.'

'Oh, men always say terrified. But they're only pretending. Ronnie was afraid of nothing.'

'I imagine not.'

'I depended on him, Mr Perron. You see, I've always been terrified of almost everything.'

To his alarm he saw that quite suddenly tears were falling down her cheeks. But they fell as if her eyes were at a different season from the rest of her. She still smiled. Her voice altered not at all. She remained physically still. She said, 'I'll never meet another man who understands – I mean who understood me so well. He seemed to guess things about me that no one else in the family ever guessed, not even my sister. It was like living with someone who'd lived with you always, even in your secret life and knew the nice things and the not so nice things. Even things you'd forgotten and even the things you'd dreamt. Until I met Ronald I'd no idea a man could be so patient and understanding. It was a long time before I could help him with his arm. I mean help him to put it on and take it off, and help him with the salves and powders. He understood that. When I'd learned how to help him we became very close. Very close. Closer than at any other time. I've never been so close to anyone before. He realized that. I think he realized that helping him with his arm was a way of helping me to become close to people. Which is what I'd never been. Never felt. His arm was very important to me, Mr Perron. I prefer to think of it being damaged, not just thrown away. Although if it was damaged in the accident I expect it has been thrown away because people don't understand the importance of symbols. But wherever we went, he was admired and respected. Especially here in Mirat. You see, he never *pretended*. He always said what he thought, so people knew where they stood with him. Some of them didn't like where they found themselves standing, but they couldn't blame him, or accuse him of being two-faced. He wasn't always easy on people. At one time I used to get upset when he was angry or disapproving or cold. But he was only angry when he found people out cheating or lying or pretending. And it was good for me. I'm not nearly as afraid as I used to be. I don't know what will happen now, though, but at least he's left me with Edward. When you look at Edward now you wouldn't credit what a poor miserable little boy he used to be. With nothing to say to anyone. Terrified of animals.'

The tears had dried. 'At least, at first. He grew out of that. Perhaps that's my one contribution. We had a labrador puppy and Edward became quite fond of him. But we had to get rid of him in Rajputana. Ronnie didn't like animals in the house.'

'Your son's certainly a friendly little boy.'

'I'm glad you think that.' Briefly she made that gesture more familiar in her sister: one hand reaching out to clutch the elbow of the other arm. 'But it's time he went home. He's very precocious. It's what happens out here. And you shouldn't order other people about like that. I remember doing it myself as a child. But that was because I was afraid of them.'

'I don't think Edward's in the least afraid.'

'No. But you can't tell. Aggression can be a sign of insecurity. Ronnie was never able to help me over that sort of thing. He was the most secure person I've ever known and when Edward talks to servants the way he does

I sometimes think he's just copying Ronnie. Ronnie was always very firm. But fair. Don't misunderstand. The servants always adored him. What is it, Sarah?'

'The car's here,' Sarah said from behind. Perron wondered how long she had been standing there. 'We ought to go.'

'Yes, I suppose so. If Khansamar bolts the shutters and locks the door we can leave all this just as it is until tomorrow. I know in my heart he's trustworthy really, because Ronnie always said how reliable he was and he was a good judge. I was just telling Mr Perron, Sarah, how good Ronnie was with the servants.'

She stirred. Perron got up. He helped her to rise. As she came level and stood near him he felt that she was as taut as a bent bow.

'When we first came here,' she said, accepting his arm, and allowing herself to be led out, 'that's to say when I and Edward came down from Pankot to join Ronnie, he'd already had the old bungalow cleared and decorated. He'd started furnishing it, with Dmitri's help of course. Everything except the hall-carpet belongs to Dmitri. The whole compound at the back had been cleared too. Of course at that time it looked as if we might be here for quite a while but in any case that was the way Ronnie worked, to make a home whereever it was, however impermanent. He was so much better at that sort of thing than I'll ever be. He said it was a terrible mess when he first got here. Nobody had lived here for ages and at that time he only had Khansamar. Well. There was a cook and a sweeper, and a bhishti and a mali, but only as temporary people. He said it was for me to decide how permanent they should be. But I couldn't fault his choice. He had that knack of looking at people and knowing whether they'd be any good or not. So really from the start we had a full complement. But unemployment in the state is a terrible problem and I remember how week after week these young men and boys used to turn up, begging for a job. Ronald had such a good reputation for paying a fair wage and treating servants properly that they came here first rather than anywhere else. You'd have thought that eventually they'd have given up. But they never did.'

She stopped abruptly, in the dim entrance hall.

'Where *are* all the servants, Sarah? I've only seen Khansamar.' But she did not seem to need a reply. She placed one hand just below her throat. A theatrical little gesture, Perron thought. But in Susan, all such gestures were probably mute cries for help. 'The whole place is so quiet. As though everyone has gone.' She turned, offered her hand. 'Thank you for your kindness, Mr Perron. For being so logical. For being here. For knowing Ronald.'

It was an exit line. She went quickly across the hall out on to the verandah and then down the steps to the car. For a moment Sarah stayed with Perron in the hall. Then she murmured, 'Thank you, Guy,' and went out too.

1499

III

He was dressed by five to seven and on the verandah as the second-hand of his watch ticked up the hour. It was a clear sunny morning.

At ten past he heard the growl of a vehicle being changed down to enter the compound. A jeep swept in. A khaki-clad figure was riding shot-gun on the high rear seat. Sarah was driving. Her head was bound in a silk scarf. She wore khaki too. She braked but kept the engine running and smiled up at him. This was the old Sarah of Area Headquarters who knew a thing or two about getting a move-on.

'Where's the horse?' he asked. She patted the seat on her right as though it were a saddle. He climbed in over the low port. She wore a khaki skirt too. In fact she had on her old WAC(I) uniform. He could see where the stripes had been. The Indian with the rifle was a soldier. His shoulder tab said *Mirat Artillery*. His face was pitted by smallpox. He looked cheerful. Sarah re-engaged gear, gave a burst of power and drove the jeep down to the exit.

Coming out on to the road he saw that the *maidan* opposite – the rough ground that stretched from the walls of the palace grounds to the walls of the old city – was now populated by military vehicles and groups of soldiers and armed police. He expected her to turn right, imagining that the horses were waiting somewhere on the *maidan*. But she turned left, passing the Dewani Bhavan and then the palace wall, going in the direction of the lake, but suddenly turning left again into a rough unmetalled road. The wind flicked her scarf and the collar of her khaki shirt. She drove very well. A bumpy road, but a smooth ride. Clearly she was familiar with the route.

Coming in from the right, a little way ahead, and from the left, were the spurs of two low wooded hills. Otherwise the countryside was open, poor, unfertile. There was no visible habitation. The land was tawny, flecked with patches of dusty olive green scrub. As the jeep entered the section of road enclosed by the two wooded spurs, Sarah slowed. The road was straight and there seemed no reason for her caution; until, a long way ahead, he saw an elephant plodding rhythmically towards them. As they drove nearer he saw the elephant was pushing or urging something ahead of it with swings of its trunk. Sarah slowed almost to a crawl. Behind the elephant were two men and ahead of it, its calf, an absurdly small creature. Seeing the jeep the mother elephant advanced protectively and the calf went under the shadow of its huge head. Now that they were close Perron saw that the animal's hide was almost black, but red from the dust of the tawny earth. Just before they came level the elephant swung into a side-track, followed by the men. And Sarah drove on.

She said, 'They're the Nawab's. They belong to his forestry department. No one can build here. A hundred years ago it was all forest.'

The road began to descend into an area of scrub-jungle. The horizon was already blurred and violet with the day's promise of heat. A twist in the road brought them to an area of rising land, almost devoid of trees. On the brow of the hill Perron saw two horsemen, as still as statues. Sarah drove a little further and then pulled in behind an army truck and a large closed-in van: a horse-box. A couple of soldiers, with rifles slung, were standing on the opposite side of the road.

'We can watch from here,' she said, getting out. From the dash-board she took a pair of binoculars and handed them to him. 'Here,' she said. 'Now you can see something of the old India.'

Even in close focus the horsemen seemed perfectly still. The lenses blurred the colours slightly, isolated purple refraction so that the profiles of the men's faces seemed to be outlined by a dim reddish-blue glow. They were brown faces. What was so extraordinary was the lack of movement, the intensity of concentration. One of the men was turbanned, the other bare-headed. The turbanned man was dressed in what looked like a studded leather jerkin and tight dark pantaloons. The younger man with the bare head (Ahmed surely?) wore an ordinary pale blue shirt, corduroy breeches and riding boots. Around his raised left forearm was a leather shield which ended in a glove. Upon the forearm sat a hawk. Perron fancied that he could see the feathered shift of its neck, the gleam of its fierce eye.

Then the vision in the binoculars suddenly blurred and Perron lowered them and just caught the end of the flighting movement of Ahmed Kasim's arm, citing the hawk at its prey – a movement that produced in the bird apparent momentary lack of co-ordination, quickly righted, and developing into a powerful and breath-taking ascent, a great arc, the beginning of a spiral of such formal beauty that Perron caught his breath and held it until he discerned in the empty heavens, through the planned geometry of the hawk's attack, the objective, the intended point of killing contact: a dark speck intent on escape.

He felt Sarah's hand groping for his. But she only wanted the binoculars. He let them go and then gave all his attention back to the aerial hunt, one that left no vapour trails but reminded him of a summer that had mapped them. The hawk plummeted. Its shape merged with the speck. Sarah cried out, with pleasure and pain. He looked at her. All he could see was her hand gripping the binoculars, her slightly open mouth, the brave little thrust of chin and the tautened throat.

She gave the glasses back to him and said without looking at him, 'You must watch this.'

He took the binoculars and readjusted the focus. The horsemen had put their mounts forward at a slow walk. He searched the lower sky in the direction they were heading and, almost too late, picked up the image of the hawk just descending. The prey was invisible. The hawk's wings were still at stretch, but folding back in slow motion, in satisfaction. And then they were at stretch again, beating against gravity, intent on ascent. He followed its course, saw Ahmed throw something. It swooped down, clawed at ground level, attacking something with its beak. The older horseman was riding in the direction of the kill. Ahmed, motionless, watched the hawk swallow its gift – presumably an appetising and bloody piece of raw meat. Presently there came the far-off sound of Ahmed's voice, a sound like Tek, Tek, Tek-Allahallahallah. The hawk was now beating at the air again, rising, circling once round Ahmed, flirting at the lure of his leathered forearm, and then gently turning and coming in to alight. It ducked its head, arched its wings, then allowed itself to be brought near to Ahmed's face: the likeness of a kiss.

Unexpectedly, Ahmed flighted the hawk again, but not at prey, unless he himself were the prey. He cantered to and fro, round and round, gradually descending the hill, spiralling at ground level as the hawk had spiralled the sky, while the bird flew to and fro as well, sometimes swooping in mock attack.

'I wish he wouldn't do this,' Sarah said. 'But he trusts her utterly.'

It was like a game of love. Sometimes Ahmed called out and when he did the hawk seemed to turn away, spurning him, only to meet him again at the end of another swerving course. About one hundred yards from the road, Ahmed reined in. The hawk planed above him for a while and then as if breathless too, ready to call it a day, came in and settled gently on his proffered arm. Perron saw that Ahmed was securing the jesses. Again he brought the bird close to his face, then he sat erect and came the rest of the way at a sedate walk. Some distance behind, the falconer was following slowly down. He had a canvas bag slung over his shoulder. The kill.

'Hello,' Ahmed called. He kicked his stirrups away, brought his right leg up and across the saddle and slid down. The bird stayed rock-still on his forearm. He tickled her stomach. She glared at him and then at the strangers. But what else, Perron wondered, could a hawk do but glare?

'Her name's Mumtaz,' Sarah said. 'Come and meet her. Incidentally, don't offer to shake hands with Ahmed. She's very jealous and protective. Aren't you, Mumtaz? I'm not allowed to touch her at all, because she senses I'm female. But if Ahmed tells her it's all right she'll allow you to tickle her throat.'

Ahmed said, in Urdu: *Here is Perron Sahib, from across the black water. He is a friend. Say hello.* He stroked her breast feathers, then said in English, 'You can touch her now, Mr Perron.'

Perron extended a finger. The head turned. A glaring eye observed the finger. Risking the loss, he placed the finger on her breast and smoothed downwards. When he withdrew the finger the hawk's wing stirred slightly.

'Ah,' Sarah said. 'She liked that. Ahmed, you'd better keep your eye on her. I think she's a bit of a rover.'

Ahmed laughed, then, noticing her skirt said, 'Aren't you going to ride?'

'No, I thought not today.'

'What about you, Mr Perron? You can have Begum here. She's still quite fresh.'

'I'm more than content to watch you hawk.'

'Oh, no more of that. I'm glad you were just in time. We can have a run after breakfast if you like. Come, Mumtaz. You can go to sleep now.' The

1502

falconer had come up and dismounted. Rather tetchily Mumtaz hopped from Ahmed's arm to the falconer's. The falconer took her down to the truck and Perron now noticed that there was an awning attached to the truck's side and, under the awning, a table laid for breakfast. Nearby, in the shade of a tree, a portable perch had been set up, with a silver chain attached to its cross-pole. The falconer transferred Mumtaz to this, secured her and clapped a little scarlet velvet hood on her head.

'Come,' Ahmed said. 'I hope everybody is hungry.'

They went down to the table under the awning. Ahmed absented himself for a while. As Perron and Sarah sat she said, 'Are you glad you came?'

'Not glad. Enchanted.'

'I meant back to India.'

'The answer's the same.'

She smiled.

*

The convoy home was headed by the army truck. The soldiers sat in the back of it, the falconer up front, with Mumtaz. Behind, Ahmed drove the jeep with Sarah next to him and Perron in the back seat. Bringing up the rear was the horse-box which gradually got left behind. Perron, shouting against the noise of the engine and the currents of air asked what the bird thought of mechanical transport. Sarah leaned back and said: 'Ahmed thinks it's her favourite part of the proceedings. But she's very blasé. She goes to sleep.'

'What do the soldiers make of it all?'

'I think they get a bit of a kick out of it. It's still quite new to them.'

No one had explained the presence of the soldiers. If the hawking was quite new to them then presumably a military escort was a recent innovation. But how recent? And why was it necessary? Sarah turned round again and shouted, 'We're going to the palace if that's all right. I've got to visit Shiraz, but Ahmed will take you round and show you the interesting bits.'

Ahmed said something to her which he didn't catch. She laughed.

'Who is Shiraz?' Perron shouted.

'The Nawab's daughter.'

Perron nodded. He did not know the Nawab had a daughter. But he thought that between Ahmed and Sarah there was a special kind of empathy, the kind that two people betray in small gestures and in the way they have of dealing with one another in public. Well, if that was how the land lay he could only wish her good luck, slightly deflating though it was to his own ego.

He looked at Ahmed's back. He remembered him as a pleasant but rather unsociable young man, given apparently to whisky and women, a combination which might by now have begun to show signs of taking toll.

Instead, young Kasim looked (as Uncle George would say) well set-up. Mounted, and flying his hawk, Perron appreciated that to Sarah he would even cut a heroic figure. And she was the kind of girl who would defy the convention that a white woman didn't fall in love with an Indian.

When they came close to the end of the unmetalled road Sarah called out, 'Go in through the guest house entrance, Ahmed, and drop me there. I've got a few things to do. I'll join you at the palace later.'

Ahmed nodded and then hooted and drew ahead of the truck, paused at the T-junction and raised his arm to indicate that the truck should turn right. Turning left himself he came to a halt to make sure the driver had understood. Perron looked back. As the truck came into view he saw the falconer's arm which was resting by the elbow on the open window frame, and upon the arm, Mumtaz, hooded, head slightly inclined –

*

[Extract From Perron's diaries]
(Tuesday August 5) – asleep, dreaming of what? The palace wall is backed by trees. You can see nothing from the road. We turned in at an unexpected culvert. Twin iron gates. Closed. A smart sepoy opened them at once and we went in, past two more who were armed and came to attention. The gates were closed again once we'd passed through. The path is bordered by rhododendron. Just where it forked (giving on the left a glimpse of the guest house) Sarah made Ahmed stop. She insisted on walking from there. We continued along the right-hand fork and came out after a hundred yards into a large formal park, with the extrordinary pink palace on the left. To the right, half-a-mile away, was the main entrance gate and frontage, facing on to the *maidan*. The park was laid out with avenues, terraces and fountains. As we got close to the palace you could see that parts of the pink stucco needed replastering. The palace bears some resemblance to the Wind Palace in Jaipur. We drove to a side entrance. Sentries again. Steps up. The smell of ancient damp masonry. A long terrace, a lot of servants and officials coming and going. Obviously the business side of the place. Then through a narrow Moghul arch into a dark stone corridor – the kind in which you feel the weight of India: a heavy darkness which is a protection from glare and heat but reminiscent of tombs and dungeons.

But the inner courtyard was beautiful. At the far end, facing the paths and fountains was the old Hall of Public Audience, a deep terrace with a high roof supported by convoluted pink columns; and, with a marble canopy and daïs centrally placed, the stone seat on which in the old days the Nawab was enthroned on cushions: the *gaddi*. Behind the Hall of Public Audience (Ahmed said) was a smaller courtyard overlooked by the present Nawab's private apartments. Avoiding this other courtyard we crossed and went out through another series of dark passages to the other side of the palace. Lawns swept down to the lake and the little white mosque which was enclosed in its own railed courtyard. We went down to

1504

the lake shore. The glare was intense. Ahmed said they were fishing again this morning. Beyond the distant reeds you could just see a couple of boats and men casting large shimmering nets. Ahmed took me back inside the palace to see what he called the modern rooms. These were at the front. The old Moghul passages gave way to corridors, Victorian in style (dark lincrusta, hundreds of pictures cluttering the walls, as thick as postage stamps in an album) and then – fascinating! – a kind of salon which reminded you of the public lounge of a Ritzy Edwardian hotel, all gilt and plush and potted palms in gilt wicker baskets, ornate draught screens and a circular padded bench around a central marble column. Dmitri Bronowsky's influence, one would imagine.

*

It was in this *fin-de-siècle* foyer that Ahmed left him, to change out of his riding gear. He promised to be back shortly. He said, 'Would you like a swim later? There's an outdoor pool. We can provide towels and costumes.'

'Yes, I'd like that very much.'

'It can't be for about an hour, though. Sarah usually gives Shiraz her swimming lesson between eleven and twelve. I'll tell them to send you coffee and the papers.'

The coffee and papers came. Today's *Times of India* and *The Statesman* (which obviously reached the palace earlier than they reached the club), the *Mirat Courier* and *The Ranpur Gazette*. This morning in the national newspapers some play was being made with the latest difficulties Jinnah was said to be raising: questions about the precise status Mountbatten would have in Karachi when he made his last appearance there as Viceroy on August 13. Two days later Jinnah would become Governor-General of the new dominion of Pakistan (moth-eaten Pakistan as he had called it, when he found he wasn't getting either the whole of the Punjab or the whole of Bengal – least of all Kashmir or a corridor connecting the west with the east).

It seemed that Jinnah had been gently reminded that the Viceroy would still be Viceroy on August 13 and he himself only Governor-General designate, just as Mountbatten was also Governor-General designate of the new Dominion of India. There was no question of Jinnah taking precedence before the date of independence, and Mountbatten couldn't be in both Karachi and Delhi on August Fifteen.

There were depressingly familiar reports from Lahore, Amritsar and Calcutta of troubles with the Sikhs and of murders and arson, and equally depressing commentaries on the harrowing experiences of some of the refugees already making their way from what would be Pakistan to what would be India, and vice versa. But the photographs in the papers were only of smiling statesmen's faces.

The *Mirat Courier*, predictably, published similar photographs and gave up its front page to preliminary details of the official programme for independence day celebrations. A Muslim firm in the cantonment called Mir Khan Military Tailors and Outfitters had taken half a page to announce a grand cut-price sale of all items of uniform and sporting equipment. At the rear pages were brief details of a number of farewell parties held the previous week.

He turned more expectantly to the waspish *Ranpur Gazette*, and was not unrewarded. The editorial – a long one – was headed: *Pandora's Box*. It read:

'The pocket-kingdom of Mirat was, until 1937, except for a brief period in the early 'twenties, in direct relationship with the Crown through the agency of the Governor in Ranpur, which suited all parties and conformed with the geographical and political facts of life. Geographically and politically, Mirat has always existed and can only exist in future as part of the geographical and political territory by which it is surrounded.

'That it exists at all as a separate political unit is due to the pure luck and chance of the fall of the dice of history. Long drawn-out though the battle for power was between the European merchants and the ruling Indian powers in the seventeenth, eighteenth and nineteenth centuries, there came a point when the dominant European power, the British, made a settlement with what was left of the scattered remnants of Moghul India. That point was reached in 1857.

'Dare one say that as a result of the Mutiny the Crown feared it had gone far enough with its policies of expansion or that it simply decided that the status quo, then existing, would prove the most profitable, if maintained? Be that as it may, with two-thirds of the sub-continent now under the direct rule of Whitehall and the real power of the remnants of Princely India reduced virtually to impotence, a declaration was made of "no further territorial ambitions" (what a sinister ring that phrase has nowadays!) – and treaties were made with the rulers of the nearly 600 remaining states, widely scattered and varying in size from mere estates to provinces the size of Ireland, treaties which secured to the rulers and to their successors their princely rights, revenues, privileges and territories, assured them of autonomy in all but the major subjects of external affairs and national defence, treaties which undertook to protect the princes from each other, from attack both internal and external.

'Separate though these treaties were – a series of private formal individual contracts between rulers and crown, they have nevertheless always been part of a larger unwritten treaty – or doctrine: the doctrine of the paramountcy of the British Crown over all the rulers; the paramountcy of the King-Emperor or Queen-Empress who, through the Crown Representative, could depose an unruly prince, withhold recognition from a prince's heir, and generally take steps to ensure the peace, prosperity and wellbeing of a prince's subjects.

'But none of the doctrinal powers of "paramountcy" could abrogate the treaty made with a state. From time to time the Crown has taken over a state's administration, but only in trust. The declaration of "no further territorial ambitions" has been, one may feel, upheld.

'Unfortunately, the doctrine of paramountcy has run counter to the doctrine of eventual self-government for those provinces ruled directly by the British parliament, through the Government of India. Paramountcy has always been illogical in the long run, and this illogicality is best exemplified by the dual rôle assigned to the Viceroy. In his rôle as Governor-General it has been his duty to govern and guide and encourage the British-Indian provinces towards democratic parliamentary self-rule. As Crown Representative, it has been his duty to uphold, secure, oversee and defend the autocratic rule of several hundred princes.

'Many princes have therefore assumed, or pretended to assume, or felt entitled to assume, that the demission by the Governor-General of power into Indian hands in provinces directly ruled by the British, could not absolve the British from treaty obligations to uphold, secure and defend the integrity of the territories the princes have ruled, for better or worse, and which they believe they have every right to continue to rule, irrespective of who rules the rest of India.

'It is fair to say that until quite recently they have been encouraged in this assumption by statements from Whitehall and New Delhi, and by the behaviour and attitude of senior members of the Political Department. Their chief fear was that "paramountcy" would be transferred by the Crown to the Crown's successors in British India (in this case, the Congress Party, which for years has made it clear that the survival of autocratic states, some quite feudal in their administration, could not be tolerated). But they were reassured. Paramountcy was a doctrine. You could not transfer a doctrine.

'But if you can't transfer it what can you do with it? The answer is, nothing. It simply lapses when the paramount "power" disappears. But what about the treaties? Can treaties lapse unless both parties agree to the lapse? Indeed they can. They lapse when one party no longer has the power (or the presence) to perform its part of the bargain. By abdicating in British-India, the British Crown no longer has the power to protect and secure and uphold the territorial integrity of Princely India, without running the risk of going to war with the new Dominion. One prince is rumoured to be consulting his lawyers in Switzerland with a view to suing the British Government in London for non-performance of contract. Another is rumoured to have gone to Delhi armed with a revolver. Other princes, of course, see the lapsing of paramountcy and of treaty obligations as the opportunity to declare their complete independence.

'What the British Crown has really done for the past hundred years is advance the territories it ruled directly to full democratic and parliamentary self-government, and maintain the territories it did not rule directly, but was paramount over, in forms of autocratic government alien in nature to the form of government itself advocates and which the British people themselves enjoy at home and seem convinced is everyone's birthright.

You can hardly wonder that this left-hand/right-hand policy was entrusted to one man, the Viceroy, in order to create the illusion that there was a unity of purpose.

'Our new Viceroy has been, as ever, quick to grasp the irreconcilable details and see the immense political vacuum that technically follows the removal of British power in British-India. The new States Department is his efficient answer to nature's abhorrence of such a vacuum. You could say that Whitehall foresaw the situation in 1935. You could say that the princes themselves are largely to blame for refusing at that time to co-operate in the Federal Scheme for a united and self-governing India (but they were not the only people who were suspicious of the scheme and refused to co-operate). You could blame the princes for many things, including their haughty distrust of one another, or of anybody. You cannot in principle blame them for standing by their treaties, for acting out the Ruritanian farce currently playing up and down India (and Pakistan); a farce all too frequently encouraged by senior members of the Political Deparment who have served in India for years and have been brought up to take the treaties as serious and sacrosanct documents.

'This is a farce in which Muslim rulers of predominantly Hindu states which are hedged about on all sides by territory which from August 15 will be ruled by the Congress from Delhi, elect to join one of the two distant arms of Pakistan; or in which Hindu rulers of predominantly Muslim states in or contiguous to Pakistan declare allegiance to Congress India, or in which rulers of immense landlocked states declare their independence of everything and everybody. You cannot blame them because not only is the farce implicit in the treaties and the doctrines but these declarations and intentions do not in any single case contravene either the spirit or the letter of the law. They are simply devoid of any means of reasonable implementation. From the princes' point of view, the long years of British power and influence have left them in possession of preserved but unpossessable goods. Geographically and politically they cannot survive individually once the Crown abdicates and twentieth-century India (or Pakistan) takes over.

'All this, and the terrible reports of the breakdown of civil authority in many areas of the Punjab, must make it seem that to achieve the objective of a political transformation scene in the long pantomime of the British-Indian Empire, the Viceroy, obeying the wishes of a well-meaning but ignorant British electorate, has found himself in the unenviable position of opening Pandora's Box and letting out all the evils that have afflicted this country probably since time began but which have been imprisoned, under a lid shut and locked by the single rule of British Power and British Law; evils which have not died of asphyxiation, but multiplied.

'Which brings us back to the small but not unimportant state of Mirat, which is not only geographically part of this province but traditionally and politically part of it.

'Under the present ruler, His Highness Sir Ahmed Ali Guffur Kasim

Bahadur, and his Chief Minister, Count Dmitri Bronowsky, Mirat has made notable strides forward. A predominantly Hindu state, the administration used to be the almost exclusive preserve of Muslims, a situation common enough where the ruling family is Muslim, but one that always causes dissatisfaction and unrest. For the past two or three decades, official posts, including senior official posts have been open to Hindus. There are Hindus on the Council of State and for many years now there has been a Hindu College of Higher Education.

'The existence in the state capital of a large military cantonment and training area for troops of the British and the Indian armies has contributed (for nearly a hundred years) to Mirat's prosperity and no doubt to its peace and security. For the past year or two, however, there has been a great deal of unrest. Both the main Indian political parties must be held partly responsible for this because neither has been slow to take political advantage of the problems posed for India as a whole by the continuing existence of states whose rule, however benevolent, can hardly be called truly democratic.

'The Nawab is now faced with the problem of what action to take now that his treaty with the Crown and the doctrine of the Crown's paramountcy are lapsing. One may think it a pity that since 1937 his relationship with the Crown has been conducted through the Resident at the distant court of a much larger state, Gopalakand. Whatever advice Sir Robert Conway is giving the Maharajah of Gopalakand ought not, one may suggest, to be the same advice he should give to the Nawab of Mirat. But that is by the way. At this juncture, advice from the Political Department is largely irrelevant. The consideration that should be uppermost in the Nawab's mind is the well-being of his subjects.

'It is important to remember the tradition of intense loyalty and reverence felt by the subjects of a princely state for their ruler, the tradition of dependence on him to make wise decisions. The main Indian political parties may scoff at these traditions as outmoded and feudal, but they exist. And already we have reports of the first effects on the people of Mirat of rumours of indecision at the palace.

'For instance, the rumour that the Nawab has not been co-operative with representatives of the States Department of the government of the new Indian dominion and may declare himself an independent Islamic state, affiliated to Pakistan, has led to the murder of Muslims in the city of Mirat and in the villages by extremist Hindus, and to burning and looting of Muslim shops. Retaliation, by Muslim extremists, has led to the murder of Hindus and the burning and looting of Hindu houses and shops. In all this, the position of such British troops as remain in the cantonment is, to say the least, delicate, and that of Indian troops equally delicate since they are in the main troops allocated to the new dominion of India and most of the Muslim elements of regiments that are to be divided have already left the area.

'Nevertheless it is to the cantonment, which might itself turn out to be the scene of awkward confrontations, that Muslim refugees from the villages and from the city have gone, seeking temporary refuge. Some of these refugees are no doubt bona fide travellers *en route* to Pakistan. Most, one suspects, are there temporarily, simply to protect their lives, having lost their property.

'We cannot afford to have in this province of British India which in ten days time will become a province of the new Indian dominion, a pocket of such potential communal and political danger.

'The Nawab could defuse the bomb in an instant, by taking the logical, the only practical step, which is to sign the instrument of accession to the new Dominion of India on the three subjects of external affairs, defence and communications and the standstill agreement which will allow him time to negotiate a settlement with India on all the complex and vitally important points arising from the lapse of paramountcy and the end of his treaty with the Crown.

'If he signs, his subjects will then know where they stand. Since the majority is Hindu, one might say that the majority would approve such a step. The Muslim minority who until recently have lived in comparative harmony with the Hindus of Mirat would also accept his decision, as that of their ruler and co-religionist, but those of them who see a better future for themselves in Jinnah's new Islamic state could then peacefully wind up their businesses and affairs and leave – just as peacefully.

'One can sympathize with the Nawab. One should sympathize with any man whose traditional assurances and traditional courses of action are suddenly removed or closed to him. But it is *his* sympathies, not our own, which are under test and examination. One is fairly confident that the outcome will show them firmly placed with the present and future welfare of all his people.

'So at least one must hope. Classical scholars will recall that Hope was the only thing that didn't fly out of Pandora's Box but remained obstinately at the bottom.'

*

'Guy?'

It was Sarah. She had changed into a cotton frock.

'Ahmed asks me to apologize. He's got something urgent to attend to. But Dmitri would like to have a few words and present you to HH, if you're agreeable.'

'Of course. Have you had your swim yet?'

'I can't this morning. I've got to go back to the guest house soon. But I can take you back to Nigel's bungalow after you've met HH. I'm sorry if we seem to be messing you about again.'

'Hardly that.'

She led him by a new way into the inner courtyard and then along one of the paths between the lawns and fountains.

Strolling up and down the colonnaded terrace on their left were four men; one of them in full Congress garb, another in a lounge suit, the other two in long-skirted high-necked coats.

'States Department?' Perron murmured.

'The two on this side are. The others are members of the Nawab's council. Finance member and food member.'

One of them called out, 'Good-morning, Miss Layton.'

She called good-morning back.

'That's the food member. He's an expert on agrarian economy. Dmitri pinched him from Calcutta before the war. I wish you could have gone to Biranpur and seen the model farm and village he set up. Perhaps you'll be able to, if you're staying for a while and things settle down.'

'Perhaps you'll go with me?'

'I wish I could. I'd like to see it again. But I can't think when that'll be. Susan's decided to go back to Pankot right away and I'll have to go with her. I don't know what will happen after that.'

'What does right away mean?'

'The day after tomorrow, I think. Ahmed's looking into the arrangements now.'

She moved ahead of him, through the Hall of Public Audience, to a narrow archway that gave on to the courtyard Ahmed hadn't shown him, the one overlooked by the private apartments. Going through the archway she suddenly stopped and said, 'Oh. Wait. Do you mind?' She went down into the courtyard leaving him alone, in the shadow of the archway.

Seated on the rim of a fountain at the centre of the courtyard was a young Indian girl dressed – how odd – in slacks and blouse. As Sarah approached her Perron saw two older women, in sarees, getting up from squatting positions on the terrace and making *namaste*. The Indian girl's back was towards Sarah but the movements of the women alerted her and she looked round, then down again, head bowed. Sarah sat beside her and after a moment put her arm round her.

Perron turned away and considered the Nawab's eye-view of the main courtyard. From here there was nothing that oppressed him. The courtyard was brilliant with sunshine and colour and splashing water. Then he saw the white peacock – at least, *a* white peacock – strutting across one of the lawns, its breast carved like the prow of a Viking ship, its long trailing tail quills making stern and wake. The quills were in moult. Should it erect them now they would look like the spokes of a moth-eaten fan. But the proud statement of the bird's slow stalking was only marginally impaired.

He went back to the archway in time to see Sarah and the girl walking slowly arm in arm, climbing up to the terrace. The women followed some distance behind. Then the girl broke away and ran in through a doorway. Sarah returned to the courtyard. The two women hastened after their charge.

He went down and waited.

'Shiraz?' he asked.

'Yes. Shiraz.' Then she took him up to the private apartments.

*

'My dear Mr Perron,' Count Bronowsky said, limping across the darkened, almost completely shuttered, room. 'How can I sufficiently apologize for not having greeted you before? I don't mean that Sarah and Nigel haven't tried their best to cover up for me, but I'm very conscious of my personal failure in the matter of hospitality. Please forgive me.'

A single shaft of light from the louvres of a shutter exposed the half-blind face and the parchment texture of the skin. The offered hand seemed made of nothing but frail bone. There was a faint smell of eau-de-cologne. A stronger shaft of light fell on to a couch near a window. It was to this that Dmitri led him, skeletal hand lightly resting on his shoulder. 'When I had your letter from England, I thought – Ah! Mr Perron may be persuaded to lecture at our college on the subject of the European mercenaries and the history of the Mahrattas. But in the event the college is temporarily closed owing to what one calls circumstances beyond one's control. The students are on strike.' They sat on the couch. 'In any case this was just a thing I selfishly thought you might agree to do for us. The important question is what we can do for you. You mentioned the possibility of writing and publishing something on the subject of the transfer of power as it affects states like this. I've forgotten the name of the paper.'

'It's a new quarterly review called *The New English Forum*. It probably won't survive more than a few issues. I'm afraid my journalistic credentials are entirely spurious.'

'I see you have this morning's *Ranpur Gazette*.'

Perron realized he still carried the folded newspaper.

'I hope you won't think it very discourteous of me, Mr Perron, if I ask you to hide it away. His Highness hasn't read this morning's issue and there's a long editorial in it which from my point of view has come out a shade prematurely. You've read it? What did you think of it?'

'I thought it quite well-argued.'

'The editor of the *Ranpur Gazette*, an elderly Englishman incidentally, does have quite an effective style. I suppose Nigel told you what he was hoping to achieve in Gopalakand?'

'Yes, he gave me a rough outline.'

'He's been on the telephone this morning and will be back some time later today with the necessary letter from the Resident. In other words his mission was a success. But I haven't told Nawab Sahib yet. I don't intend to do so until after the morning audiences and petitions. He was hoping Conway would encourage him to stand firm on independence, but Nigel has persuaded him not to encourage him. If Nawab Sahib reads that article now it will put his back up. I don't want him with his back up when I tell him that Conway is washing his hands of Mirat and that he should sign the instrument of accession if he so wishes.'

Perron handed Bronowsky the newspaper and said, 'Perhaps you'd better dispose of it. Thank you for warning me. I might have referred to it.'

'It was Miss Layton who warned me you might have been reading it. That is why I came out for a private word. She is a remarkably shrewd and thoughtful young woman. We shall miss her at the palace. Nawab Sahib's daughter is heart-broken and begs her to come back soon. Miss Layton is the only person who has ever succeeded in bringing poor little Shiraz out of her shell. For years I tried. Nawab Sahib tried. I tried to get Ahmed to try. But the influence of the late Begum, her mother, seemed indestructible. Shiraz threatened to go into full purdah, can you believe it? Now she is riding and swimming and wearing modern clothes and even sometimes talking to men. Even Ahmed is showing an interest in her at last. And it is all Sarah's doing. She is with Nawab Sahib now, saying goodbye. He too has become very fond of her. It is a piquant situation. She treats him like a father, but I sometimes think he looks at her and vaguely resents that for the past twenty years I have kept him on such a strait and narrow path. As a young prince, you know, when his father ruled, the Political Department was in two minds about recognizing him as the heir. Their files would reveal some scandalous things about him in his wild youth. Perhaps about me too. Thank God these files are all being destroyed before Patel can get his hands on them.'

'Is Shiraz the Nawab's heir?'

'Oh, no. He has two sons, both older. The younger is in the Indian Air Force, not a pilot, they never succeeded in teaching him to fly, poor boy. The elder is Mohsin, but Mohsin and his wife live mostly in Delhi. He is much involved with business affairs and his wife does not like Mirat at all. She hates coming here. But finally this has had one advantage. She insisted on a swimming-pool being built in the grounds for her to bathe in. It has been very useful to Sarah, in educating Shiraz.'

'The succession is secure, then.'

Bronowsky nodded, but did not otherwise reply. Instead he said, 'Tomorrow I hope that these States Department people will be on their way back to Delhi with their signed bits of paper and that I shall be able to leave the palace and go back across the road to my own home. Then perhaps you will be my guest and in any case come to dinner tomorrow evening, if all goes well. I don't know whether Sarah will be able to come if they are to travel the next day. But I hope Nigel can be there. And Ahmed. Ahmed has promised his father to be in Ranpur for the August fifteen celebrations and I cannot deny him that. Since the Laytons have decided to go back to Pankot he may as well accompany them as far as Ranpur. It is a good opportunity.'

He stood and placed a hand on Perron's shoulder and indicated a double set of doors.

'Nawab Sahib is in there with Sarah. I'm afraid you will not find him very communicative. He is shy with strangers. So do not be offended if I intervene quite quickly and take him through to see his petitioners. The

1513

morning audiences are a relic of the past. All the real business is done by members of council and their staffs, but the tradition is important. I shall have to go in with him but Sarah will then look after you and take you back to Nigel's.'

Bronowsky went to an ornate desk, opened a drawer and pushed the *Ranpur Gazette* into it. As he rejoined Perron he said, 'Did you by any chance call on our old friend Aimee when you were in Bombay?'

'No, I didn't. I called on Mr Hapgood though. He sent his regards.'

'Hapgood? Oh, the bank official. But how well I remember that evening at Aimee's. What a terrible disaster you averted – what a terrible mistake I made, taking Miss Layton and poor Ronald there! The previous time I visited her everything was beyond criticism. You made an impression on her, did you know? The next time I saw her, I think in Delhi, she was a bit confused about the precise circumstances but she said, "Where is that British sergeant you brought to one of my parties, who gave me a lovely bottle of whisky, and then took it away with him, the crook?" So, you see? Come. Let us go in.'

*

Extract from Perron's diary, Tuesday August 5.

– to a smaller room, a salon, decorated and furnished in the Empire style. The Nawab stood at the window indicating something to Sarah (it turned out to be the view of the fishermen on the Izzat Bagh Lake – so-called because an earlier Nawab had declared that the *izzat*, the honour of the ruling house, would be maintained for as long as the lake didn't dry up). Dmitri left me near the door, said something to the Nawab, a small man in comparison with Dmitri. The Nawab came across. I advanced a step or two and bowed. The offer to shake hands was slightly delayed. One sensed that today he distrusted all Englishmen. His long-skirted coat was amazingly shabby. The cuffs were frayed and the material was very thin around the button-holes. (He is a rich man, generous and not mean. His austerities are wholly personal, Sarah tells me.) The face is narrow, lined, quite a deep brown, curiously anonymous. The kind of face you easily forget. But he has the sort of presence you remember, self-containment, suggesting restraint of packed nervous energy and intensity of feeling – suitable in the descendant of men who were feared, before whom Mirat trembled, years ago.

An exchange of compliments. A bleak pause. Dmitri hovering in the background, a gaunt one-eyed guardian, smiling but alert. Then the Nawab offered some samples from his stock of small-talk. I replied in kind. Suddenly he frowned. Perron? he asked. A descendant of the successor to Benoit de Boigne? His ancestors could have had no love for either of them. Relief, when I disclaimed connection. Then the preliminary to courtly dismissal. I must be sure to inform Count Bronowsky of anything necessary to my comfort and to my researches. A friendly, shy, smile. No

1514

handshake in parting. He turns to Dmitri as if wondering whether he has omitted anything. One realized his dependence and his current distraction. Before he went he silently pressed both Sarah's hands. Then he and Dmitri went out through another set of doors. A glimpse of a much larger chamber with about a dozen people in it, who bowed deeply; one even making full obeisance.

Sarah and I leave in solemn but not too solemn silence. We run the gauntlet of servants making *namaste* (to her, not to me, I think). Then she drove me back to Nigel's bungalow. Tippoo was waiting on the verandah. She wouldn't stay for a drink. I didn't press her. She seemed preoccupied.

But before I let her go I said, 'What *did* happen to Ronald?'

She said, 'Don't ask me, Guy. Ask Nigel. Or Dmitri. Or better still, nobody.'

IV

After lunch he slept again. But sleep was intermittent. There was another storm, brief but disturbing, and the rain brought out that smell of damp, of decay. He woke between dozes with a persistent sense of ill-being and was thankful when Tippoo brought in his tea at four o'clock. He thought of starting a letter to Aunt Charlotte, but the room was suddenly intolerable. He dressed and went out to the rear compound to get air and sunshine. There was no sound from Merrick's compound. He inspected the banyan tree. How old would it be? One hundred years at least? So fine a specimen would be especially holy. But its holiness lent no tranquillity to the bungalows in whose compounds it grew.

He found the gate in the compound wall unlocked so went through. Today Merrick's garden looked less well-tended. Overnight the grass seemed to have grown an inch. All the green tattis between the white columns had been rolled up, exposing windows obviously locked and shuttered. One could visualize indoors the shrouded shapes of furniture draped in dust-covers, signs that the occupants had gone and that no one knew when they might be back.

He went towards the house intending to go up on to the verandah but then decided he shouldn't intrude on so much absence, so much impending absence, so much darkness, so much loss. He took the path that skirted the side of the bungalow and came out into the front and stood still, hackles rising.

A van was drawn up. Down the steps from the front verandah two men were carrying a black coffin. The coffin was tilted downwards, resting on their shoulders. When they reached ground level they jog-trotted to the van, then shoved the coffin into the back.

Not a coffin. Merrick's trunk. Another man was bringing down the long sagging sausage of the rolled hall carpet. This went into the truck too. Then the rear flap was put up and fixed. Two of the men got in the back, the other went to the front. Khansamar came down the steps carrying an object that glinted. A picture in a frame. The boy's picture of the old Queen. He handed it to the driver and then went back indoors.

When Perron returned to his own room he paused on the threshold, convinced that in the few seconds it had taken him to open the door someone who had been in there had got away, only just in time.

*

By nine o'clock that night Rowan still hadn't arrived back and Sarah hadn't rung. Tippoo persuaded him not to wait any longer so once again he ate alone. Afterwards he sat on the front verandah with his notebook, his file of newspaper cuttings, a pair of scissors and the day's papers which Tippoo assured him Rowan wouldn't mind him cutting up. A light shone from the clerk's office. He hadn't seen the clerk except on some of the occasions when the telephone rang or the *dak* came, or a despatch rider turned up. Otherwise the little man kept to his room, so far as Perron could tell.

He sat with notebook and files and papers untouched, drinking brandy and soda. He was half-inclined to knock at the clerk's door, invite him to join him, get him to talk about the routine of keeping records for a political agent, or about his life; about anything. Instead he continued drinking alone, watching the moths and insects dance round the dim depressingly yellow verandah lights. The lights were too dim to work by. The light in his own room was better. He didn't want to go back to his room. The room undermined his confidence. The whole bungalow undermined it. Perhaps Mirat undermined it. Perhaps Mirat was a mistake.

He opened the *Ranpur Gazette*, began to read 'Pandora's Box' again but grew tired of it within a paragraph or two. He turned pages, holding the newspaper at an angle to get some light on it. There was no cartoon, but, on the middle pages, boxed, was a piece called 'Alma Mater' by Philoctetes. He folded the newspaper so that he could read this.

'On Sunday when the happy occasion at Government College was over, when the inaugural daïs for the opening of the Chakravarti wing had been stripped of its bunting, of its red carpet and striped awning, the raw timber scaffolding exposed (and already under the destructive hammers of carpenters) I visited the new extension hoping I would pass as someone with business to do there.

'I need not have worried. No one challenged me. The carpenters and the workmen assumed I was a member of the college staff and such members of the staff as I encountered assumed I was connected with the builders.

'Assured of anonymity I had a free run of the college-to-be. Occasionally I faced dangers in the shape either of planks and ladders where walls are still being whitewashed or plastered, or of piles of tins, canvas sheets and tools of humbler trades than will be learned here. But unmolested I visited class and lecture-rooms (a few with window panes already cracked or broken) and found no desks, no chairs, and rectangular spaces where

1516

blackboards have yet to be installed. The laboratory looked like the ward of a hospital or clinic from which all the beds had been removed and replaced by long pinewood tables and benches which awaited the decision of someone who might say to what use they should be put.

'The present emptiness was not (for me) diminished by anything the imagination could invent about the future. Accompanied only by my own echoing footsteps it seemed unlikely somehow that in a month or two the desks would be in place and students at their places at the desks, teachers standing on these bare platforms and the as yet invisible blackboards already becoming grey from the wiped-off chalk-marks of demonstrated equations.

'Subdued, I left the building and walked down the asphalt path that connects the new building with the old. A few shade trees have already been planted. The old college buildings from here look serene, weathered. I turn, and try to picture the Chakravarti extension as it will be, ten, twenty, fifty years from now, and am glad really, that few if any of those who will then remember it as the benign mother will have seen it quite as I am seeing it now; raw, uncompromising, so clearly dependent on what as yet unproven teachers and as yet unadmitted students must make of it and give to it before they can take anything lasting away from it.

'I walk home, thinking of another place, of seemingly long endless summers and the shade of different kinds of trees; and then of winters when the branches of the trees were bare, so bare that, recalling them now, it seems inconceivable to me that I looked at them and did not think of the summer just gone, and the spring soon to come, as illusions; as dreams, never fulfilled, never to be fulfilled.'

Philoctetes.

*

He read the piece again and coming to that final paragraph for the second time found himself moved. The brandy probably. He poured himself another. He got up. His nervous system seemed suddenly awry. He would have to take some action, if it were only to begin packing, or better (because packing meant going into that bedroom), to ring Sarah and tell her he thought he might as well go back with her as far as Ranpur. He went into the hall, consulted the short list of important telephone numbers and asked the operator for 234, the guest house. A servant answered. He asked for Miss Layton and gave his name which was one servants often failed to get right.

After half-a-minute or so, a woman said, 'Is that Mr Perron?' An older woman.

'Yes. Mrs Grace?'

'Yes, hello. I'm afraid Sarah's not here.'

'I'm sorry to be calling so late.'

'Oh, not late really. I don't suppose she'll be long. She's out to dinner.

When shall I meet you? I've heard so much about you. Sarah tells me you called on dear old Archie Hapgood. How was he?'

Mrs Grace had a fine contralto voice. He imagined (not without reason) a comfortable-looking bosom, fullish jowls, carefully set hair and once sharp eyes that were now dimmed a little. He liked the sound of her. He told her he thought Archie Hapgood looked well, then said:

'I rang to tell Sarah I'm thinking of going back to Ranpur, and I wondered whether we might make a party of it. There's not a great deal for me to do in Mirat now, and I do have to be back in Delhi by the fifteenth. I suppose the main problem is getting a reservation.'

'It shouldn't be a problem on the day train because nobody needs a sleeper. The trouble is we're going on Thursday. You mustn't cut your visit short, unless it really suits you.'

'It would suit me very well.'

'I'll tell Sarah what you suggest, or leave her a message. How late can she ring you back?'

'No restrictions at this end.'

'Well thank you, Mr Perron. Mr Kasim is coming to Ranpur with us, and perhaps some people called Peabody, but they're not absolutely sure. An extra man would be rather nice. I suppose it's awfully foolish of me but since Colonel Layton went back to Pankot I've been feeling a bit out of my depth.'

There spoke the widow, with one widowed niece, one unmarried niece, a grand-nephew and an ayah, all to look after and feel responsible for. They said goodnight to one another; and having made the decision to go he now felt better. He went back to the verandah to pour himself another drink, and wait for Sarah's call.

*

There was no call but just before midnight a car turned into the compound. When it stopped, Tippoo – who had heard it – was already down there, opening the door. Rowan got out. He was alone. Laura's absence was somehow eloquent. 'Hello, Guy,' he said, coming up, 'I hope you've eaten.'

'Yes, I have. What about you?'

'I've had something at the palace.'

'Well, have a brandy.'

Rowan glanced at the bottle. 'You shouldn't be drinking your own.' The clerk came out of his office. 'Guy, I'll be with you in ten minutes or so. Unless you'd rather go to bed.'

'The last thing.'

Rowan went towards the office, then turned round, 'I nearly forgot. Sarah says she'll ring you in the morning about your Thursday plan.'

Alone, Perron poured himself another brandy and soda. Tippoo came past him with Rowan's suitcase. Ten minutes later he reappeared and said, 'Sahib?' Perron found himself being taken indoors, to a room similar in shape to his own bedroom but on the other side of the hall, and furnished as a study, with a desk, and three easy chairs set round a low table on which there were glasses and a decanter. A connecting door, open, gave a glimpse of a larger room – Nigel's and Laura's bedroom, presumably. Tippoo went in. Presently Nigel called, 'With you in a moment, Guy. Help yourself.'

But he didn't help himself. He was thinking: Odd – I've been here before. And then remembered when and where, and smiled. He looked round the study for the cricket-stump and wondered which of the chairs Rowan would suggest as the best for a slacker at games to kneel on. He was still smiling when Rowan came in. Rowan was smiling too, but at a more recent memory.

'Well, it's done.'

'The Nawab's signed? Congratulations.'

Rowan poured deep amber liquid. 'Soda?'

'To the top.'

They raised glasses, drank; then sat. Settled, Rowan said, 'Well then. I gather you feel you've learnt as much as you need in Mirat.'

'I shouldn't mind having a chat with Dmitri. I gathered that might be possible tomorrow night.'

'But you want to go when the others go, the day after.'

'It would fit in. And I do want to be in Delhi before August fifteen. But I suppose whether I go on Thursday depends on what Sarah and her aunt decide.'

'They'd both welcome you.'

'I gather you've seen Sarah tonight?'

'I looked in at the guest house on my way from the palace. She'd just got back and felt it really was too late to ring you.'

'I'm glad she was able to get out somewhere.'

'She was only over at the women's hospital, saying goodbye to the staff. But they made her stay to supper.'

'In the cantonment?'

'No. The Mirat women's hospital. Just over the other side of the *maidan*, here. She's done a lot of voluntary work for them. Didn't you know?'

'No, I didn't.'

'It used to be a purdah hospital for Muslim women only, but Dmitri got it extended some years ago. She's been very popular with the patients and the nurses. She even got Shiraz to take an interest. The hospital's one of the main reasons she's stayed in Mirat all through the hot weather. If Dmitri had let her she'd have gone out to work at the Biranpur leper colony too. Are you thinking of going all the way up to Pankot with them?'

'Only to Ranpur. I'm rather hoping Ahmed can wangle an interview for me with his father.'

'I'd forgotten your journalistic assignment.'

'It's hardly that.'

'If you're not going back to England from Delhi, you could always come down to Gopalakand. I've left Laura there. I'll be closing down here in the next day or two and joining her. Officially I'm still assistant to the resident in Gopalakand – at least until midnight on August fourteen, when we all become redundant. But Conway won't be going immediately. Laura and I will be there for a week or so as his and the Maharajah's guests, while we decide about the future. Gopalakand might interest you. Just send me a wire at the Residency if you think it would.'

'It might. Thank you. Is it a very tricky situation?'

'Perhaps only tricky for me. The Maharajkumar told me his father's going to sign the instrument of accession too. But he's known Conway a very long time and doesn't want to hurt him by appearing to disregard his advice completely. I think my last few days in the Political Department are going to be spent as pig-in-the-middle. Smoothing things between Conway and the Maharajah. Gopalakand is a Hindu majority state with a Hindu ruler. The only things at stake are the pride of the ruling family and the pride of the Resident. It's much larger than Mirat but self-supporting independence is just as much out of the question. If you do come down everything should be peacefully settled by then, and the Maharajah is very hospitable.'

'Perhaps I'll take you up, then.'

'An old friend of Conway's is coming down too. She's lived in Rawalpindi for years but doesn't want to stay on now that it's becoming part of Pakistan.'

'Who is that?'

'Lady Manners.'

'Have you kept up with her?'

'Not kept up. I visited her a few months ago when we were in that area.'

'Did you tell her you'd heard from Hari?'

'I began to. She asked me not to tell her. It's a subject she doesn't discuss.'

'Why?'

'I think she feels she did what she had to do and that anything else would be an invasion of his privacy and would smack of condescension.'

'You feel that too?'

'I think so.'

'Does she still have the child?'

'Yes.'

'What will happen to it when Lady Manners dies?'

'I imagine she'll be looked after by one of Lady Manners's Indian friends. She's been brought up to think of herself as Indian. She's an enchanting little girl.' Rowan leaned forward and filled their glasses. Perron said:

'How did you meet Laura again?'

'She wrote to me when she got back from prison-camp in Malaya. I'd always kept in touch with her mother. We corresponded for a while. Then we met in Simla. And married.'

'What happened to her first husband?'

'The Japanese killed him. She said it was probably his own fault. He had a bit of a temper. When the Japs first arrived at his rubber estate he put up

1520

some sort of show and got knocked about in front of her. They took him to one camp and her to another, of course. Later they sent her his personal effects and a letter of regret informing her that he'd died of fever. She didn't believe it, it goes without saying. She spent some time in Singapore when the war was over, finding out the truth from fellow prisoners of Tony's. Some of the truth. It all went to make up further evidence against a Japanese officer who was tried and hanged as a war criminal.'

'Poor Laura.'

'Yes.' Rowan glanced at him. 'But I don't think her first marriage was much of a success either. I gather she made it clear to you yesterday that ours hasn't been. I don't know why it hasn't. But there you are. She hated it here. That's why I've left her in Gopalakand. She said this bungalow reminded her of the one she and Tony lived in in Malaya. It was one of the things she didn't like about it. So after a week or two we decided she'd better go to the club.'

'*One* of the things she didn't like?'

'It's a bit depressing, isn't it? And I had to leave her on her own a great deal. After three years in a crowded prison-camp she doesn't at all mind being alone, but she needs space and air and light. The Residency at Gopalakand works better for her. This place is very closed in. Damp and dark. I'll be quite glad to get out of it myself. The business of the snake was the last straw. Sarah warned you there'd been one, didn't she? I asked her to.'

'Yes. Was it Laura who found it?'

'Yes, it was.'

'And you who had to kill it?'

'No. I should have hated that. It was Merrick who killed the snake.'

Yes, Perron thought. Merrick was bound to come into the picture. 'What kind of snake?' he asked.

'A young cobra. It was asleep in the bath-tub.'

'The bath-tub? My bath-tub?'

'No. Ours. Through there.' He indicated his bedroom.

'Sarah said it was found under the verandah at the back.'

'I expect she said that to reassure you. No. It was in the bath. Laura happened to go in. She didn't panic. She just came out and shut the door and told Ronald. I was over at the palace, but fortunately Ronald had dropped in. I don't think Tippoo would have been much use. He really *is* terrified of them.'

'How did Ronald kill it?'

The question seemed to put Rowan slightly off his stroke.

'What makes you ask?'

'I imagine he got the last ounce of drama out of it. Unless he'd changed considerably. Which I find difficult to believe. In spite of the funeral oration. And the Last Post. Whose idea was that?'

'Susan's. She said the only time she'd ever seen Ronald moved was at a beating of the retreat in Rajputana. It was a bit embarrassing for us. But the oration was no more than he actually deserved. And he gave Susan a sense of security.'

'Well tell me,' Perron said, 'how he killed the snake.'

* * *

Does Nigel have a revolver? Merrick had asked. The answer had been, no. *Then I'll have to go next door for a moment,* he said. While he did this Laura went into the compound at the back. She knew the snake had to be killed, but was as much against killing snakes as Nigel was, unless it couldn't be avoided. She walked up and down waiting for the sound of the shot. She visualized, perhaps, the shaft of sunlight in the bathroom slowly and dangerously shifting, leaving the snake in shadow, cooling it, waking it; and wondered whether snakes had thoughts and if so what they thought about. What manner of sleep they slept. What dreams they had. (What dreams do falcons have, under those scarlet hoods? And how different those dreams must be – on the one hand of limitless sky, on the other of endless, endless earth.)

Well here it is, Merrick said. She hadn't heard him approach. She swung round and there he was, a kukri in his good hand, the cobra suspended from the artificial one. At first she thought the cobra was whole but then the head end slipped out of the black glove and fell on the grass, leaving the tail end behind; and Laura cried out and was at once sick, all over her elegant shoes.

* * *

'He was very contrite,' Rowan said. 'He kept on apologizing. To me, I mean. He said he'd decided he couldn't shoot it because he wasn't sure what the ricochet would do if he missed the snake and hit the tub. In any case he didn't want to puncture the bath.'

If Merrick's story was to be believed he had used his artificial arm as a lure and, when the cobra struck and sank its fangs into the gloved hand, had swung the kukri and cut it neatly into two. A gash in the porcelain was evidence.

'He was taking a risk,' Rowan ended.

'He always did. Had Laura quite liked him up until then?'

'I don't know.'

'I was wondering, you see, as I used to put it, whether you ever felt that he had chosen her.'

'I remembered the phrase.'

'When, exactly?'

'I expect it would be more accurate to say I'd never forgotten it, but I certainly remembered it when Laura and I first got here and found him living alone next door. Susan and the boy were up in the hills.'

'Didn't you know he was in Mirat?'

'Yes, I knew. Sarah and I have always written to one another. I hadn't expected – such close proximity. I didn't tell Laura much about him, just that we'd met. It amused her when he started turning up at odd moments when I happened to be out. It reminded her of the rubber estate, when Tony went down to KL or Singapore and left her alone, and all the local bachelors and grass-widowers homed in on her bungalow, making feeble excuses, or no excuses at all. When you remember what Laura looked like in those days, it's no wonder. But it used to annoy her. She said it made her feel like an object, because if they didn't come to make a pass they just came to stare. Anyway, she made a joke of it at first, of Ronald turning up whenever I was out. She has this idea that she's now physically repulsive. She said Merrick probably thought he was physically repulsive too.'

Rowan stopped. Perron waited. After a while Rowan said, 'But I came home one night and found her in a very odd mood. She started talking to me about her life in prison-camp, and that was something she'd never done. I'd tried to get her to talk about it, but she always shied off. Did you happen to see the scar under her left eye?'

'Yes.'

'I ask because with strangers she normally keeps those sunglasses on, even indoors. And you may find this difficult to believe, but I've never found out how she came by it.'

'But she told Ronald.'

Rowan looked away. 'Apparently, yes. I got home and found her in this odd mood. Over dinner she started talking about prison-camp. Then she asked me whether I didn't want to know about the scar. We had a bit of a scene. She asked me why she could talk to Ronald about it but not to me, why Ronald was the only person she'd ever met who could get her to talk as she wanted to talk. Spill out the whole awful bloody business. The only thing I could think of to say – and it came out quite unrehearsed – was that she couldn't talk to me about it because she knew I loved her but had to talk to Ronald because he'd chosen her. As a victim.'

'What did Laura say?'

'Nothing. And we didn't mention Ronald again until a few days later when I got back and found her packing, the day he'd killed the snake. She said she was going back to Gopalakand. That would have been best but I talked her out of it and we decided she should go to the club. As soon as she'd gone the whole situation seemed absurd. There was nothing I could accuse him of. But whenever I saw him he started explaining and apologizing. He wouldn't let it alone. He turned up at the club once or twice, trying to see her, but she says she kept out of his way.'

'But went to the funeral. What was that? A mark of respect or of celebration?'

'She went to the funeral because I asked her to.'

'Why did you do that?'

'The thing was –'

'Yes?'

'To remove anything that didn't fit into the picture.'

'What picture?'

'Of an Englishman who'd earned respect and admiration from most sections of the community.'

'Why did Laura have to fit into that?'

'You know what people are like in places like this. The kind of people who wondered why she'd left the bungalow. It didn't go unnoticed that she wouldn't see him when he called at the club. I had to ask him to stop calling.'

'Did he stop?'

'At once. But he seemed quite hurt. He said he hated misunderstandings. He'd only been anxious to find out why he'd upset her. He implied as well that he hated feeling responsible for any misunderstanding between Laura and me. At the same time –'

'What?'

'I had an idea it didn't worry him and might even please him that people were beginning to link their names.'

'It flattered him to be thought of as the Other Man?'

Rowan glanced at him. 'I see what you mean. I hadn't thought of it in quite such a general way. I just wondered whether he was trying to get his own back on me by making people wonder about Laura and him. I'm positive he knew that Kumar had been privately examined and that I was the one who'd done the examining. Why not? He still had friends in the Inspector-General's department. Someone probably told him.'

'Very probably.'

'Sometimes he actually seemed to be daring me to come out with it. We had a very odd relationship. On the one hand mutual goodwill and respect between a visiting political agent and a police officer who'd done a good job, and on the other this subtle sort of antagonism.'

'How long was he in Singapore?'

'Singapore? He *was* in Singapore. Why?'

'I wondered whether he was ever involved in the case against the Japanese officer who was hanged as a war criminal. The one who murdered Laura's first husband, no doubt among several scores of others.'

'Wouldn't he have said?'

'Not necessarily. But knowing something about the Japanese officer could have been the way he got Laura to talk.'

'It sounds pretty far-fetched.'

'Nigel – for me, nothing was far-fetched with Merrick. I believe he had a photographic memory. He'd only have to look through a file to have a whole situation at his fingertips. And he was quite clever at getting his hands on files. He got his hands on Susan's confidential psychiatric file. Did you know that?'

'No, you've remembered incorrectly. He had an interview with the psychiatrist, that's all. So Sarah said.'

'He did more than that. He saw her confidential file. So when Susan talks about Ronald being the only man she'd ever met who understood her and seemed to know things about her she'd never told anyone inside the family, that's the explanation. He could have tried something like the same technique with Laura, but I imagine she's tougher. What happened to the Red Shadow?'

'The what?'

'That disgusting bazaar Pathan he had trailing round with him in Pankot. The one I kicked up the backside. The one who had his hands on my wallet.'

'I don't know. But Merrick must have got rid of him. He gave up having personal servants when he got married.'

'Why?'

'He was always on the move. They never had a permanent home.'

'He hired and fired as it suited him?'

'No, I think he just accepted what was available. Like Khansamar next door.'

'Who of course is Dmitri's man?'

'Everything here is Dmitri's. All three bungalows. The Dewani Bhavan, this one, and Merrick's. Dmitri lived in this bungalow when he first came to Mirat. He built the Dewani Bhavan round about nineteen twenty-five.'

'Did Merrick ever live here?'

'Yes, I think for a month or two when he first arrived. Before Susan joined him.'

'I imagine he slept in my room.'

'What makes you think that?'

'It has a resonance.' Perron hesitated, and then came out with it. 'What did he do, Nigel? Commit suicide? Cut his wrist and die in the bath?'

'He didn't die in the bath.'

'Nor as a result of a riding accident?'

Rowan said nothing for a while. Then: 'The fall wasn't serious. But he said someone deliberately scared the horse. He was out on the *maidan*. According to Ahmed and Sarah there was no one within half-a-mile, except them.'

'They were all together? What were they doing, hawking?'

'No. Merrick was always trying to scrounge an invitation to watch Ahmed out with Mumtaz. Ahmed's very particular about who gets to watch and who doesn't. He was running out of excuses. They were supposed to go hawking that morning and Merrick was pretty upset when they turned up with horses and no falcon. When they got to the *maidan* he galloped off on his own. They saw him jumping the main nullah. It's pretty wide where he attempted it and he came a cropper. When they got to him the first thing he said was "Did you see the blighter?" He made out that someone who'd been in the nullah had suddenly stood up. Later on he said someone must have thrown a stone. Sarah says there was nothing like that. But Dmitri got rather worried.'

'Why?'

'The last thing he wanted, the last thing any of us wants just at the moment is an attack on an Englishman. It really could have the most tragic consequences. One dead English official, one English official attacked, and that could be it. You'd get some hard-bitten British sergeant in the cantonment belting an Indian and calling all Indians murdering bastards and then who knows what would happen?'

'Perhaps what Merrick wanted to happen.'

'That was rather the conclusion we came to, that he would have liked some of the stops pulled out, some sort of show-down. So it seems would other people.'

'What other people?'

'Whoever it was who arranged his death.'

Perron's heart sank. He had known it, instinctively. Rowan watched him. He said, 'Dmitri and I feel you ought to know. Sarah agrees. And in view of the way you handled an awkward question of Susan's yesterday, she thinks you're to be relied on not to say anything. She's the only member of her family who knows that Ronald was murdered.'

Absurd, really, Perron thought, that he should now feel shocked, outraged on Merrick's behalf. Perhaps he had hated the man too much not to feel guilty now for a violent death. It was as though he had contributed to it.

'Well tell me,' Perron said.

Rowan poured more brandy. This time he topped his own glass up with soda, as well as Perron's. He said, 'After the riding accident he refused to go into hospital but Habbibullah insisted on him going to bed and keeping to his room. He suspected concussion. Ronald was a very bad patient. And of course there was all this business about the imaginary man in the nullah and the imaginary stone. He went on about it whenever I or Sarah or Dmitri visited him. We did that as often as we could. I was the last one of us to see him alive. Sarah asked me to go and talk to him because he'd been on the phone to her saying he was better and asking to be taken out next morning in the jeep and watch Ahmed hawk. He couldn't ride but wanted some fresh air and something interesting to do. So I went across and had a drink with him. He was sitting up in his dressing gown – smoking in that way he had – do you remember? Sticking the cigarette in his artificial hand. He seemed perfectly all right to me. And for once he didn't mention Laura. He talked about getting a job in Calcutta or Bombay, or of offering his services to Pakistan. He was quite frank about not wanting to go home to England. And he thought he stood a better chance of a job among Muslims. He said he'd like to live somewhere like Peshawar, near the old North-West Frontier, where administration was much more a question of off-the-cuff decisions and not of just going by the book. We really got on quite well, rather like the first time we met, on the train to Pankot. He asked me to ring Sarah then and there and fix the morning programme. So I did. I asked her to come round with the jeep at seven. She said she'd have a word with Habbibullah but I didn't tell Merrick that. And I didn't tell him she

1526

thought Ahmed wouldn't play. I pretended it was all fixed. He told Khansamar to wake him at six next day. When I got back here I rang Sarah again. She said Habbibullah wouldn't allow it, which was a blessing because Ahmed felt he couldn't refuse any longer. We agreed that she and Ahmed would turn up at seven, but with Habbibullah, and that they'd take it from there. So that's how we left it.

'Tippoo woke me at six and then the phone rang and Tippoo said Khansamar wanted a word, which struck me as odd. Khansamar's one of the best trained servants I've come across, but that's Dmitri's influence. He said something had happened which he couldn't deal with and would I come over right away. So I put on a dressing-gown and went across. When I got to the front of the house Khansamar was sitting on the front steps smoking. There was nothing to suggest anything wrong.

'But then he took me indoors and said, "Sahib is dead. I've locked everything up." He took me into Merrick's bedroom. What I expected was just the sight of Merrick dead in bed but the whole place was an absolute shambles. The mosquito net was ripped to ribbons, the bedsheets were all over the place and stained with blood and Merrick was lying on the floor, dressed in his Pathan clothes, but hacked about with his own ornamental axe and strangled with his own sash. And all over the floor there were chalked cabalistic signs. And someone had scrawled the word Bibighar across Susan's dressing-table mirror with the same brown make-up stick that had been used to daub his face.'

'Did Sarah see this?'

'No. And she doesn't know the details. She turned up with Habbibullah and Ahmed, but we kept her out. Dmitri saw it, so did the Chief of Police in Mirat and the commander of the military police in the cantonment. The station commander was consulted too. The one thing that was agreed was that a murdered Englishman at this stage of affairs is the last thing anybody wants. Particularly when it looks as if the murder was intended to cause disorder and racial conflict.'

'What about the law?'

'Everything is properly recorded, right the way down from Habbibullah's real post-mortem, through the private inquest and the sworn statements of witnesses like myself and Khansamar. And the police and CID haven't been inactive. I doubt that the man or men who murdered Ronald will ever be tracked down though. The operation seems to have been carefully planned and patiently seen through to the end.'

'By whom? Pandit Baba?'

'It was Dmitri's first thought. But the Pandit runs true to form. The CID say that for the past month he's been on a pilgrimage to the Himalayas, and still is.'

'And the Bibighar suspects?'

'Two who're still in Mayapore have been cleared by the police there. One is reported dead of tuberculosis in Benares a year ago, and two more are working as clerks in Calcutta. There's nothing to connect any of them.'

'They got a very rapid clearance.'

'It was a rapid clearance because I gave Dmitri their names. I can still recite them from memory. All Dmitri had to do was get his police chief to liaise with the police in Mayapore.'

'Did he ask how you knew the names?'

'Yes.'

'And you told him you'd examined Kumar?'

'Yes.'

'And what about Kumar. What about Hari?'

'He's still in Ranpur. And also in the clear. Dmitri told me this evening.'

'Not such a rapid clearance.'

'We didn't go through the police in Hari's case. Ahmed got his father's secretary to ask Mrs Gopal to find out what she could through the young man who used to help him. We got the reply today. He's still coaching students. He never leaves Ranpur. He was there the whole of last week. One of his pupils is the youngest son of a Congress minister and he's been at the minister's house every evening for the past month coaching the boy for his matriculation.'

'Things have improved for him, then.'

'A little, I suppose. But it must be a poor enough livelihood.'

'Perhaps he supplements it.'

'How?'

'A bit of free-lance journalism? He used to be a reporter and sub-editor.'

'Perhaps. Incidentally, we now have an address. If you want it.'

'Yes, I'd like his address.'

'I'll get it for you. Then I'll have to go to bed, Guy. I've got to see the States Department people off on the morning train.' He got up, went into the adjoining room, came back and handed Perron a slip of paper with Kumar's address scribbled on it. 'Be careful what you say to Sarah, won't you? She doesn't know the worst details. We had Merrick's bedroom cleared up before she saw it. None of the other servants was allowed to see it either.'

'Presumably they were questioned, though.'

'Yes, but the Chief of Police did that himself, without saying exactly why. Khansamar was put through the hoop too.'

'Where are the other servants?'

'Back at the Dewani Bhavan, where they came from.'

'There must be rumours, surely.'

'Rumours, yes. Too many people had to be involved, and eventually it'll become more or less common knowledge, but the thing has been to counteract the rumours, especially in the cantonment, and keep up the fiction that Merrick died as a result of the riding accident.'

'Who has his clothes? And his arm?'

'The Chief of Police. I must turn in, Guy. If you see Dmitri tomorrow, he can probably answer any questions better than I.'

Perron said goodnight and made to go; then paused.

He said, 'Who was Philoctetes?'

'What?'

'Philoctetes.'

Rowan rubbed his forehead. He looked so tired that Perron was about to leave the question until morning. But then Rowan said, 'The great archer.'

'A great *archer*?'

'Friend of Hercules. One of the heroes of the Trojan war. Sophocles wrote a play about him, but it's one I never read. They had to set him ashore, abandon him on the voyage out. Lemnos, I think.'

'Why?'

'He was hurt in some way. Wounded by one of his own poisoned arrows. Or perhaps he just developed boils and suppurating sores from a vitamin deficiency. Anyway, he stank, and the others couldn't stand the smell. So they set him ashore, and went on.'

'Yes,' Perron said. That fitted. 'Did he ever get to Troy?'

'Eventually. If I remember rightly they decided they needed him after all. What interests you about Philoctetes?'

'I came across the name recently and wondered, that's all.'

When he got back to his room he found that Tippoo had brought in all the stuff he'd left on the verandah; the scissors, notebook, the newspapers, and his own bottle of brandy. He had a final drink and read the essay *Alma Mater* once again. That night, fearful of snakes, of ghosts, he cocooned himself in a sheet, within the security of his mosquito-net shrouded bed. He lulled himself to sleep by counting arrows, flying from the bow, at first slowly, well-aimed, and then quicker, until they were flying incredibly fast as the archer stood, holding his ground, intent on survival. Just before he slept he thought: The smell in the room is not after all just Merrick's smell, but also the smell of the archer's wound.

He woke while it was still dark, from a nightmare that had transformed him into a huge butterfly that beat and beat and fragmented its wings against the imprisoning mesh of the net.

V

Extract from Perron's Diary, Wednesday August 6

11 p.m.

An ominous day, ending with the reflection of fires in the night sky above the city. This afternoon, news of the Nawab's accession to India brought out a crowd of Congress supporters who assembled on the *maidan* for speeches and cheers. The police and military kept them away from the palace, and from a convoy of Muslim families making their way in trucks, carts, dhoolies and on foot to the collecting point in the cantonment. Tonight there were repercussions, angry Muslims attacking Hindus. Attack. Counter-attack. The sky glows. Police and military patrol the road outside this bungalow and presumably make forays into the city. They say there will again be no fishing on the Izzat Bagh lake tomorrow.

Beyond the lake you can just see the paler glow of the cantonment bazaar. The *raj* rests quietly in the darkness behind. In bungalows here and there there must be lights and laughter, parties. (The departing Peabodys are giving one.) Here, where I am, a strange feeling of being suspended between these two worlds. On other similar occasions when the situation became difficult, Merrick would be found touring the city, by jeep, or sometimes during daylight on horseback. 'Tonight I miss him,' Dmitri said. He hadn't mentioned Merrick until then. Dmitri and I had champagne. We smoked pink gold-tipped cigarettes. He told me something about St Petersburg (between interruptions, of which there were many). At ten-thirty our meeting ended. The Nawab had sent for him. 'Poor old dear,' Dmitri said. 'He's looked at the sky and wonders what he has done wrong, or what I have ever done right.'

This ominous day began early. She did not ring but arrived with horses shortly after Nigel had gone across to the palace to take the States Department people to the station. They were to travel in the Nawab's salon coach so as (Dmitri said) to give them a taste for princely luxury as a 'frail insurance against any future diminution of it'. Tomorrow we are to travel by ordinary first-class passenger coach. Dmitri has cancelled the arrangement to send us by another of the Nawab's coaches in case after today's troubles it becomes a target for attack by Muslims who feel that the Nawab has let them down. He has got the movement control officer to guarantee a compartment for us. We shall be 9. The old-fashioned first-class compartments seat 8 comfortably and one of the 9 is little Edward and another is the ayah who will probably sit on the luggage. Which leaves only 7 adults: Sarah, Susan, Mrs Grace, the two Peabodys, Ahmed and me. We should be comfortable enough and are due at Ranpur at 7 p.m. The Peabodys are reported upset, though, that they aren't to travel in a palace coach. Dmitri said: 'Don't stand any nonsense with them if they start objecting to the ayah or to Ahmed. Times have changed.' He seems very insistent on this. The number in the compartment won't worry me. It sounds like being a good party. Mrs Grace is fun.

The horses Sarah brought were a pleasant surprise. She was dressed for riding. There was no Ahmed. No Mumtaz. We trotted out to the *maidan* and across to the other side. She showed me (at a distance behind shade trees) the barracks of the Mirat Artillery, the police barracks, and the hospital and told me about the first time she got Shiraz to go with her, how nervous the girl was, how over-awed the staff and the patients were at this manifestation from the Palace: the Nawab's daughter, rumoured to be cross and difficult and haughty. Sarah had broken the ice, in the maternity ward, by picking up a baby she'd become used to handling (whose mother wasn't recovering as quickly as she should) and then placing it in Shiraz's arms. The first contact Shiraz had ever had with a commoner outside the palace. It worked. And of course the mother would never forget it: that the

Nawab's daughter had held her son. 'What made you give so much time to this girl?' I asked. 'Her unhappiness,' was all Sarah said. Then she cantered away, towards the open ground beyond the military tents and horse-lines.

Suddenly she cries out and thrashes her reins, left, right, and gallops off, making for the distant city wall, or what is left of it. The gateway alone is intact. I try to catch up but she is by far the better and more confident horseman, and she knows the lie of the nullahs, which I don't. But, behind her as I am, we seem to career together towards that implacable pink stone. Then she suddenly veers and shouts again, loudly, savagely, and races her horse back at a pace I really can't match: thrashing the reins in that way, left, right, as if charging cannon in some desperate enterprise. And there is nothing there except the pale blue sky, the green of the shade trees, the tawny stain of the scrubby earth. I let her go, ease my own horse's pace, watch her; small white-shirted figure, going like a little demon into the distance, leaping the nullahs. I think it was her way of saying goodbye to a place where she has been free and happy. She rides in a wide circle, coming round now and galloping towards me. At first I assume she will ride right up, but just ahead of me she moves in a tight turn and then brings her mount to a canter, a trot, a walk; to a stand. As I reach her she puts it at a sedate walk. We say nothing. It isn't necessary. But as we near the road again, outside my bungalow, she says, 'Come to the guest house and meet Aunt Fenny. We'll have breakfast there.'

Neither of us has mentioned Merrick.

Mrs Grace is a plump rather florid woman (much as one thought). A bit breathless, but very talkative. Susan not up for breakfast. We have ours on the terrace. This is where the Laytons stayed when Susan came to Mirat to marry Teddie Bingham. I asked about Colonel Layton. Since early in 1946 he has been Colonel Commandant at the Pankot Rifles training depot. A disappointment. He had hoped for the area command. He is handing over now to a man called Chaudhuri, who was only a major a few months ago. The new 1st battalion goes to a Sikh who has been in Pankot for some years, Chatab Singh. For a while there was a problem about the regiment's future. Officially, the Pankot people are predominantly Muslims, as a result of conversion in the days of the Moghuls. The regiment, mixed, but reflecting this predominance, has such a good reputation that Jinnah wanted it and offered it a home near Peshawar. How he thought he could keep it recruited from men who lived in the Pankot hills, one does not know. Some English people in Pankot have raised the question of the silver in the mess and suggest that the new Indian Government should buy all the knives, forks, spoons and trophies, everything of value, and that the proceeds should be shared out among the families of the men who had contributed to their cost. 'So you see we all end up like carpet-sellers in Cairo,' Mrs Grace said. 'John gets hot under the collar when he hears people talking like that.'

Edward comes out. He takes me to see the white peacock. Not the one I saw myself. This one is carved out of marble and is secluded in a secret place among the trees. Fear snakes. When we get back Nigel has arrived from the station, seeing the States Department people off. The Peabodys were seeing off the Rossiters and told Nigel that this evening it would be open house at their bungalow. Mrs Grace said, 'Those awful people. Do we have to travel with them? Can't we rustle up an extra body or two and crowd them out?'

Interesting, this. Universally popular as the English are in India just now, among themselves there emerges this dissension. The old solidarity has gone because the need for it has gone.

*

'But of course,' Bronowsky said, 'now we are all émigrés. Have some more champagne and a cigarette.'

Perron nodded. The servant came to his side and refilled his glass. In the Dewani Bhavan there was the dry dusty scent of potpourri. The lighting was rose-coloured. It glowed on ormulu and gilt chair-arms. In this light Dmitri Bronowsky looked twenty years younger. His lame left leg rested on a gilt and plush footstool. The ebony cane and the black eye-patch accentuated the white of his tropical suit which was faintly tinged by the glow of the lights. He wore a tie of the same pink as the cigarettes.

*

The invitation to dinner had reached Perron at five o'clock. Leaving Rowan working on his written report to the Resident at Gopalakand, it had surprised him to find no other guests. By eight-thirty, after a number of interruptions by messengers and telephone calls, he realized that he and Dmitri were to spend the evening alone. He had hoped for Sarah. As if recognizing a source of disappointment, Bronowsky – leading him into a grand dining-room – said he asked Sarah but that she felt she couldn't leave Susan alone on their last night in Mirat. 'And failing Sarah, I felt we might dine alone. It is a little selfish of me to subject you to my unadulterated company, but not entirely so. If we had another guest or two then I could not tell you the things you have come to Mirat to learn about – how princes rule and live in this country. Anyway, I feel I deserve an evening off myself, with just one sympathetic listener.'

The table was long enough for twenty or thirty guests and the room was lit as if there were that number needing to see what they ate. Perron and Bronowsky sat at one end, where great bowls of flowers gave off heady scents. Bronowsky ate little, seemed to be content with a bite or two of each course and a glass of each of the wines that accompanied them. He talked with skill and good humour. The range of the old wazir's knowledge and experience and the clarity of his memory were remarkable. It struck Perron, too, that he talked vividly because he knew that the opportunities to hold court, while he still had power, were becoming fewer. The last thing Dmitri Bronowsky would ever be was an old and tiresome man living on his memories and boring other people with them. On the day he had to retire, he would probably retire quite happily into himself.

'What is Mirat's future, then?' Perron asked, when the right moment came, between sips of the champagne with which, along with the pêche flambée, the meal was delightfully ending.

'We shall be absorbed into the provincial administration of Ranpur. Our executive and our judiciary will be superseded by those of Ranpur. We shall be ruled from Ranpur and from Delhi. We shall have a deputy commissioner sent down to control us. Some of our younger men will be lucky and secure official appointments. Our revenues will go to Government and Government in turn will accept certain responsibilities for us. Also, and this is so interesting, we shall become a constituency or several constituencies and elect and send members to the legislative assembly. All this I have told and constantly tell Nawab Sahib. I remind him how years ago I foretold it. If either of his sons had political talent, ah then, that would have been one way of maintaining *izzat* under a new dispensation. For in a world where a ruling prince becomes redundant isn't there an opportunity for one of his heirs, someone in his family, to sit not on the *gaddi* but in the assembly, or even in a ministerial chair at the Secretariat?'

'And neither son has political talent?'

'In confidence, my dear Mr Perron, neither talent nor wit. It did not take me long to see that this was and would be so. So. I cast around. And my eye lighted on another member of the house of Kasim. The Ranpur branch. The rebellious political branch.'

'Ahmed?'

'Many people have wondered what I am doing employing the son of Mohammed Ali Kasim who is, by nature, opposed to princes. Many people have wondered what Mr Mohammed Ali Kasim can have been thinking of to allow his younger son to take service in a feudal little state. I do not know what Mr Kasim had in mind. Perhaps he was just pessimistic about the boy in those days. I have always been optimistic. Scratch me a very little and you will find an eternal optimist. Scratch a little deeper and you will no doubt uncover a great intriguer, but I hope a well-intentioned one. Scratch deeper still, never minding the blood, and perhaps you will find an old White Russian of liberal sympathies but intent even now on rescuing his Tsar from the cellar in Ekaterinburg, or failing his Tsar, the little Tsarevich. An English lady in the cantonment who had psychological perceptions once described me so. Your glass is empty, Mr Perron.'

It was refilled.

'It was my intention to arrange, if it could be done without undue pressure, an alliance between the princely Kasims of Mirat and the political Kasims of Ranpur. I had hoped that Ahmed and Shiraz would fall in love one day. They say that when a man falls in love, with a woman, he becomes aware of all his worldly responsibilities. If there is one thing I do most sincerely wish just now it is that Ahmed and Shiraz were man and wife and that marriage had awakened in him all those political instincts he must have inherited from his father, no matter what he says to the contrary. I wish this because just now when Nawab Sahib is in the doldrums, when he summons me at midnight or early in the morning because he cannot sleep or hasn't slept, and stares at me, it would be so nice to say: What are you bothered about? I have always warned you that there may be nothing for your sons to inherit except the remnants of a purely formal dignity, but here is your daughter Shiraz and here is your son-in-law Ahmed, son of a famous and respected Indian politician who still has great influence behind the scenes. When you begged me to come back to India with you because of the little service I had done for you, you said, "I must be a modern state. Make me modern." So, admit it, I have made you modern in every way I can. Moreover you have a son with business interests in Delhi and who has a wife who builds swimming pools and has money in Zurich. You have another son in the air force. Above all you have a son-in-law who may one day represent Mirat in the provincial assembly and, who knows, end as a minister of central government, perhaps even as Prime Minister. Isn't that modern enough for you? Unfortunately, I cannot tell him this because he has no son-in-law. Man can only propose. But given another year or two's grace and perhaps God would have disposed, as I so devoutly wished. For my prince's benefit, you understand, Mr Perron. For my prince. Perhaps a little for myself. As it is I have to go and sit with him, late at night or early morning, and try to prepare him just to face the moment when the States Department people will descend on us again, this time with their scales and abacuses and weights and measures and arithmetical tables, their meticulously devised formula for separating what belongs to the people and what belongs to Nawab Sahib, what is a proper charge on Government and what is a charge on Nawab's personal household, asking how many palaces have you, then, and what are they used for, and who pays for all *this* –'

Bronowsky indicated the room, the table, the silver and the glass and the patient silent servants.

'Who pays, the people or the occupier? And who is Dmitri Bronowsky? Who pays him? How much is he paid? How much pension does he expect from you? How much pension can the people of India afford to pay you so that you can go on paying all these pensions to which you say you are already committed? And I know what Nawab Sahib will say, because he has already begun saying it. He will say, "Dmitri, what have I to do with these people or they with me? What are all these facts and figures and percentages and bureaucratic mumbo-jumbo? If you load my head with all this, how can I hold it up?" Come, let us have coffee.'

As they went Perron said, 'As Mrs Grace said this morning, now we've all got to get used to living like carpet-sellers in Cairo.'

'But of course!' Bronowsky said, delighted. 'Now we are *all* émigrés. Have some more champagne and a cigarette.'

The servant came to his side and refilled his glass, offered the open silver box. Dmitri settled his left foot on the stool. He told the servant to leave the champagne in the ice-bucket, to bring in the brandy and then to leave them.

'The thing that holds the members of an emigration together is only their recollection of a mutually shared past, Mr Perron, but they are divided by a deep distrust of one another's present intentions. So there is no creative coherence. And individually they feel guilty of desertion. An emigration is possibly the loneliest experience a man can suffer. In a way it is not a country he has lost but a home, or even just a part of a home, a room perhaps, or something in that room that he has had to leave behind, and which haunts him. I remember a window-seat I used to sit in as a youth, reading Pushkin and teaching myself to smoke scented cigarettes. That window is one I am always knocking at, asking to be let in.'

A steward brought a note. To read it Bronowsky took out a gold rimmed monocle. 'Forgive me, I must leave you for just a moment to attend to this.'

Alone, Perron went out on to the terrace. The garden was flood-lit. At its centre was a fountain whose jets sprayed inward from the rim. In a moment Bronowsky was back. 'There are other illuminations at the front, it seems, not of my devising.'

From the front compound they could see the glow of the fires in the city. 'They are burning each other's shops,' Bronowsky said. 'In the past eight months, whenever I saw a sight like this, I was comforted by the thought that Colonel Merrick was coping with it. Tonight I miss him. So perhaps will the police. All I can do is to ensure that what should be done is being done and what shouldn't be isn't. The cost is counted in the morning. Meanwhile one feels a bit like Nero, in need of a fiddle. Perhaps I should send for the court-musicians. But let us go back and finish the champagne.'

They strolled up and down the terrace. The fountain kept changing colour. Perron was struck by the irony of the situation. Here, luxury, elegance. A mile away, everything a man possessed in the world was perhaps going up in smoke.

'Until the war,' Bronowsky was saying, 'there was almost no civil disturbance in Mirat. Such communal dissatisfaction as there was arose from the feeling the educated Hindus had that in spite of all my efforts they were still at a disadvantage, and from the counter-feeling high-ranking Muslims had that Hindus had been encouraged to compete too well. But by and large there was peace, particularly in the rural districts where the things that mattered to people were to enjoy prosperity when it was there to be enjoyed and to feel they could trust their Nawab to look after them when it wasn't. Before the war, Mr Perron, I could tour the state and talk to a Mirati farmer out there in the *mofussil*, a Hindu or a Muslim, and he would prove to have but the vaguest idea of who Gandhi was, or who Jinnah was. For him the world began and ended in his fields, and with his landlord, and with the tax-collectors, and with Nawab Sahib who sat here in Mirat, Lord of the world, Giver of Grain. Out there it is not so very different now but in our towns and in our city they have become affected by what Congress is saying, what the Muslim League is saying, up there in Delhi, in Calcutta and Bombay. This began during the war. Mirat was also affected by the realization that the British *raj* had proved far from invincible in Burma and Malaya and in Europe. On top of that we had all these people who fell foul of the British and scurried to places like this where it was not so easy for your police to get hold of them. It was left to our own. Well, you can pick a man up and send him back where he came from, but you cannot send ideas back, especially if there is an element of truth and justice in them.'

'What led to your applying for help from the States Police?'

'A virtual breakdown in our own police department and a danger of mutiny in our State Armed Force, which consists of one regiment only, the Mirat Artillery. That was last November – but the trouble began earlier when men of the regiment who had been prisoners of the Japanese returned home and it became generally known that some of their comrades had joined the INA and were now prisoners of the *raj*. No one knew at the time quite what to make of this. The prisoners who had stayed loyal came back to a heroes' welcome, naturally. Men of the Nawab's artillery have served in both world wars, in France in 'fourteen-'eighteen. In Malaya this time. The artillery is a Mirati tradition. In the old days they used to make some of those huge old cannon you'll know about from your study of eighteenth-century Indian history and the men from this region have always been adept at gunnery. So. It has always been a proud regiment, too. Unfortunately by the time the men came back, to their heroes' welcome, Congress and the League had already taken the cudgels up on behalf of the INA. Our gunners found themselves in bad odour when they said what they thought of Bose. Some of the most outspoken were beaten up one night in the bazaar, probably by the same people who beat poor Ahmed up when it became known that his father wasn't going to defend Sayed. Perhaps that was a blessing in disguise because it stopped him going into the bazaar to visit what in my youth were called ladies of easy virtue. For a long time afterwards he was faithful only to Mumtaz. But the worst situation arose in the spring of last year, when the officers and men of the Mirat Artillery who had been in the INA came back, the officers cashiered and the men released –'

'At Holi.'

'Ah, yes, at Holi. Almost as stupid a decision as the decision to try the Sikh, the Muslim and the Hindu at the Red Fort.'

'Did the INA men get a heroes' welcome too?'

'It was unofficial, but warmer if anything. There were only two officers and nineteen men. The officers' careers were finished, not that they needed careers, they both came from well-to-do families. The main question was what was to happen to the nineteen gunners. In Mirat, political parties do not officially exist, since the state proscribes them, but there are shadow parties and shadow committees and of course one has always known who belongs to them and who the leaders are and who will therefore emerge presently as the men with local political power in Mirat. The nineteen gunners were being persuaded by both these shadow parties, Congress and League, that they should be reinstated by a grateful Nawab for having tried to help Bose rid the country of the British.'

'Which didn't please the loyal men of the Mirat Artillery?'

'To put it mildly. The cumulative effect of all this purely political propaganda was that on the Muslim League's All-India Direct Action Day, the Mirat Artillery refused duty to stand by in aid of the civil power, and their officers were powerless. The men took a very simple view, Mr Perron. They thought that Direct Action Day was simply a ruse to reinstate the nineteen gunners and they would have nothing to do with it, either way. They sat in their barracks while the civil population ran riot. The Mirat Police were entirely ineffective because they were in sympathy with the League. We had to get aid from the cantonment, British troops, and the officer commanding those troops knew his men were so fed up with India and Indian politics that he dared only issue one man in twelve with live ammunition. I remember standing with Nawab Sahib in one of the upper rooms at the front of the palace and watching the pall of smoke above the city and thinking, My life has been wasted.'

Bronowsky rested against the balustrade, sipped his champagne.

'But one always feels better next day. All the same I have never seen Nawab Sahib so angry. He blamed the poor regiment. He said his grandfather would have had the officers trampled to death by elephants and every mutineer blown from the guns. He raved against Gandhi and Jinnah and then against the Viceroy and the Commander-in-Chief, and then because he knew there was only one head he could effectively roll, he turned on me and accused me of ruining him with all this modernity. It took me a day or two to persuade him that the artillery only needed his personal assurance that the INA gunners would not be reinstated. The police were a graver problem. It took me longer to persuade him that we needed assistance from outside, from the States Police. He felt we could rely entirely on help from the cantonment. But you know, Mr Perron, too much reliance of that kind sours the relationship between city and cantonment. Well. In the end he let me go to Delhi and put the position to them. And so – some weeks later – Ronald.' Bronowsky paused. 'I am a little chilly. It's the fountains. They cool the air amazingly. Let us go in and have brandy.'

*

He had dismissed the servants and served the brandy himself. Now he settled opposite Perron and rested his foot on the stool.

'When I heard who was coming in command of a States Police detachment and in an advisory capacity to the Nawab and myself, it was my instinct to say no, no, no, no, he is a man with too controversial a reputation and the last time he was in Mirat he was subject to the attention of people who seemed determined to persecute him for his behaviour in Mayapore. What are they doing sending him here? What are they doing employing him again in the police? Then I wondered what business that was of mine. And remembered that I had on very first acquaintance found him an interesting and impressive man. Impressive in some ways. You know that he had certain qualities, Mr Perron?'

'I saw only the bad side, I'm afraid.'

'That I think is because in spite of your interest in the past you are a man of the present, as I have always tried not very successfully to be. Merrick without question was a man of the past, so much so that he believed implicitly both in its real virtues and in what he imagined had been its virtues. And you know, in the situation that has existed here in Mirat this past year or so, where few people know what they are doing or why they are doing it, the presence of such a man comes almost as a relief. He treated the whole thing as though it were just a silly quarrel between naughty children. And in a way he was right. He inspired confidence with his impartiality and his absolutely inflexible and unshakable sense of his own authority. It can be a very dangerous combination. But there was one thing about him this time that seemed to me to be new. He struck me now as an inwardly melancholy man. I would never have said that about him before. The only time I saw him, how shall I put it, glow with the old *conviction*, was when he was with the child.'

'Not when he was with his wife?'

'I am no judge, Mr Perron. Unless a man and a woman are obviously and tiresomely publicly wrapped up in one another I find it difficult to judge the degree of warmth between them. That is a warmth I have never enjoyed. One eventually withdraws. Perhaps becomes insensitive. I was, I admit, sensitive to what I thought might be certain tendencies in Merrick when I first met him in Mirat at the time of Susan's first wedding. I wish now that I had been more sensitive to the possibility of these tendencies having become, how shall I say, in no way lessened by his experience of marriage. Even at my age one assumes – well – what it is easiest to assume. So when he first arrived to take up his appointment I said, Are you still being persecuted by people making melodramatic demonstrations, throwing stones and chalking inauspicious signs on your doorstep? We made a joke of it. But he said what he had said in Bombay, that all that had ended. I knew that could be only partly true because Ahmed had told me there was a revival of persecution when he was in Delhi dealing with his brother's and other INA cases. But I decided to take his word for it and there was no reason to suppose that persecution would start up again simply because he was back in Mirat. Unfortunately it did begin again, but in a much subtler way. It may seem a little odd to you, Mr Perron, that whoever wished to persecute him for what he did in Mayapore in nineteen forty-two should have waited so long to bring the operation to its logical conclusion? There must have been many opportunities to kill him in the past five years.'

'It was twenty years before someone assassinated the ex-Governor of the Punjab. Ostensibly for supporting General Dyer over the Jallianwallah Bagh massacres.'

'That's true. Why do you say ostensibly?'

'I shouldn't think the Governor was shot for that at all. It was a conveniently dramatic form of protest against India being dragged into another European war.' Perron smiled. 'I gather from Nigel you have an idea Merrick was a convenient victim too. That killing him was intended to aggravate racial tension as much as anything.'

'Yes.' The old man studied him for a moment or two. 'Not everyone feels the British have earned the immunity you all seem to be currently enjoying. I myself am not entirely convinced that it is fully deserved. But if it's the last thing I do in Mirat, I'll take every step necessary to ensure that this immunity continues, even if it means suppressing evidence and issuing false statements. Do you disapprove?'

'A little.'

'So do I. But I balance my disapproval with the thought of what might be happening now if we had shouted murder, also with the thought that the murder was so subtly planned and executed that the prospect of ever seeing justice done is infinitely remote. Then of course there's the thought of the distress and pain Susan would have been caused by any open investigation. It's a good thing, in her unstable state of mind and health, that she doesn't know in what strange and unsavoury circumstances her husband died.'

'Strange and unsavoury?'

'I don't mean just the manner of death but what made him vulnerable to such a death.'

'Yes, I see. Do his spies come into the picture?'

'Who mentioned spies to you?'

'Susan. She also mentioned Indian clothes. The ones he wore to go out with his spies.'

'Mr Perron, he had no spies. Nor did he ever go out in these clothes. Perhaps in his younger days he used to get up to that romantic sort of trick, colouring his face and disguising himself as a Pathan and going out into the bazaars. And of course in his time he must have employed spies in his department, just as our own police chief employs them. But Ronald and spies and Indian clothes, in Mirat, no, no, these were mere bits of play-acting. Khansamar never believed in the spies. He is a good servant, though, and not given to gossiping. I wish he had been. If I had known about so-called spies then I would have been alerted and I could have warned Khansamar to be more on his guard. And although it would have been a rather delicate thing to do I might have warned Ronald too. He may not have needed a warning, though. It is quite possible that he knew what was going on. In which case his murder might be seen as a form of suicide. Unfortunately I only knew about spies when it was already too late and Khansamar was questioned and told us about these visitors.'

'Visitors as distinct from people coming asking for jobs?'

'Why do you ask that?'

'Susan said people were always coming looking for jobs.'

'That was how it would have seemed to her. Originally that was how it seemed to Khansamar. But with the benefit of hindsight one begins to understand that it was all part of a new subtle form of persecution. At that time, Merrick was living alone, in Nigel's bungalow. The other one was being got ready. According to Khansamar these young fellows began to turn up soon after Merrick arrived. Khansamar turned them all away. He knew they were not Miratis. They span the same tale, of coming long distances to seek work and always offered little chits of references. Khansamar is illiterate. Chits mean nothing to him. Then one day Merrick found him shooing one of them off, a persistent fellow who had come several times. Merrick looked at the boy's references, which may or may not have been genuine, probably not, not that it mattered. Merrick told him there was no work to offer him. But he was back again next day. He stood at the gate and salaamed Merrick whenever he passed in and out until in the end Merrick told Khansamar he was fed up with the sight of him and that he might as well be given a job for a day or two, helping one of the malis repair and lay out the tennis-court in the compound of the bigger bungalow. So this is what Khansamar did. He told the mali to work the boy hard, so hard that he would give up. But he worked so well that in a day or two the tennis court was nearly finished.'

*

Moreover, so the story went, the mali's wife had taken to the boy and had begun to mother him. He was a handsome young fellow and very well-mannered. After working all day in the compound he would make himself useful in the servants' compound. The mali was keen to keep him on but after three days Khansamar went to Merrick and reminded him that the day or two was up. Merrick went to inspect the tennis-court. They were just laying out the lines of lime-wash. Merrick watched for a while, then said, 'He is obviously used to hard work. Put him to cutting all the long grass.'

Khansamar was quite pleased. There was a lot to be done in both compounds. Many odd jobs. And the boy was very respectful to him. When he had cut all the grass in one compound Khansamar set him to work in the other. In the evenings he worked on a new vegetable patch behind the servants' quarters, work which the mali himself had been putting off day after day. On one such evening Khansamar asked him, 'Do you never rest, Aziz?' And the boy said, 'I am alone in the world, father. Work is all I have.'

Old Khansamar had had three wives, ten daughters and no son, ever. It touched him to be called father by a boy like this. He began to give him less strenuous jobs. A week, two weeks, a month went by. Sometimes Merrick would say, 'Well, Khansamar, how is that young fellow of yours? I see you have made something of a carpenter and decorator of him too. What is a farmer's son doing with so many accomplishments? Can he also read and write? If so he can put my books in order, once he has put up the shelves and painted them.'

The answer was, yes, Aziz could read, a little slowly. But every night, now, he read to the servants from the newspapers. He had had to give up school when both his parents died. At an early age, he said, he had left his village to find work in the nearest town. But he had always tried to keep up his reading.

So Aziz was put to the task of finishing the shelves in the bigger bungalow and then of transferring the books from the packing cases and putting them on the shelves in alphabetical order of authors' names.

And one day, when Khansamar was going towards the room where Aziz was working, to tell him it was time for his evening meal, he heard the boy laughing. He looked into the room and saw Aziz sitting on the floor, with his back to the door, reading a book, and turning the pages, turning them rapidly for someone who normally read with difficulty. But, that evening, when Khansamar went to the servants' quarters, he found Aziz stumbling, reading aloud, with difficulty, from the morning newspaper.

*

'You must understand, Mr Perron, that Khansamar had come to regard the boy with affection, as a son almost, and that it was not easy for him to admit to himself that there was something a bit suspicious, that the young man he had seen quickly reading through one of the Sahib's books and laughing was rather a different young man from the one who worked in the compound like a farmer's son. And now he also remembered that when the boy had first scythed the grass he had had to wear rags round his hands the next day and in the evening Khansamar had noticed the blisters, on his palms and fingers. At the time he had merely been touched that Aziz had worked so hard and hadn't complained of his sore hands. But now he was troubled. Troubled by the thought that the boy was not the sort of boy he pretended to be. And that night when he went to bed he couldn't sleep. He found himself tossing and turning and wondering and puzzling. And then something else odd struck him. He realized that since Aziz had turned up looking for a job, and had been employed, no one else had arrived at the gate, waving their little chits and begging to see Colonel Sahib.

'So he got dressed and went to the hut Aziz slept in. The door was bolted on the outside, which meant Aziz was out. It was very late, one or two o'clock in the morning. He went round to the front of the house and found the chaukidar fast asleep on the verandah.'

'Which bungalow was this?'

'The one which Nigel has. The one at which you are staying. The bigger bungalow was nearly ready, but not quite ready. Chaukidar should have been patrolling between the two, but he was fast asleep on the verandah. The front gates were closed but anyone can climb these things. It was simply a peaceful Indian night, Mr Perron, and Khansamar thought, well, Aziz was a strong active young fellow. He was probably in the bazaar, making love to a girl whose husband was away. Reprehensible, but understandable. So Khansamar woke chaukidar up and told him off for sleeping. Then he went back to his quarters but found himself more wide awake than ever, and listening for the sound of Aziz coming back. This, he heard, only a little sound, the sound of the bolt on the door of Aziz's hut being opened. He got up and put on his shawl and went over to the hut and saw there was a light on. So he knocked. When Aziz opened the door Khansamar began saying things like, What foolishness is this? Where have you been? Aziz said he had been at the back relieving himself. So Khansamar said, What, for two hours? Are you ill or something?

'Then he noticed that there were marks on the boy's face and that he had been bathing them. He said, What happened? Did the husband come back? Or have you been brawling in the bazaar? He was talking to him like an angry father who is not really angry. Probably Aziz understood this because he became contrite. He said it was true he had been in the bazaar, but there had been no angry husband and no brawling. He had fallen and grazed himself climbing back in over the locked gate and in the morning he would no doubt have a black eye.

'Khansamar said, Wasn't Chaukidar there to help you over? And Aziz laughed and said Chaukidar was no doubt asleep on the front verandah as usual and that nothing would ever wake him.

'Khansamar did not believe Chaukidar could have gone to sleep again, after being told off, but he realized that with two bungalows to look after it would have been possible for Aziz to slip in over one of the gates, and not be seen. So he just gave the boy a telling off too and warned him that Merrick Sahib might have to be informed.

'When he got up in the morning, which was always before anyone else, to make Colonel Sahib's *chota hazri*, he looked for the chaukidar and asked him whether he had stayed awake and if so whether he had seen anything unusual. The chaukidar said he had certainly stayed awake after being woken but that there had been nothing unusual. Khansamar asked him whether he wouldn't call it unusual to see Aziz climbing over a gate and missing his footing and falling on the gravel so heavily that he had grazed his face badly. Chaukidar agreed that that would be unusual.

'In which case, Khansamar said, chaukidar had neglected to see something unusual, because this was what had happened, and that in the circumstances he could only believe that chaukidar had fallen asleep again, and that this would have to be reported to Colonel Sahib.'

Bronowsky lit another pink cigarette.

'Chaukidar said, I do not advise that. You can accuse me to Colonel Sahib of nodding off for a few moments if you like, but you should not say you know I did because I failed to see Aziz climb over the gate. Colonel Sahib will think you are trying to make trouble for him. For two nights – last night and the night before – Aziz was with Colonel Sahib. I saw Aziz go in through the door of the *gusl-khana* just as I saw him go in the night before. The only difference was that the night before I stayed on watch, expecting to see him come out like a thief, in which case I would have pounced on him. But he came out after some time by the same door, and this time Colonel Sahib was with him, dressed in the clothes he sometimes wears when he is alone. He is at heart a Pathan, and Aziz is a fine sturdy boy. If I were not a dried-up old man I would be tempted myself and it does not surprise me that Colonel Sahib has been tempted because for weeks I have sometimes seen him watching the boy at work in the compound. When he went into the bungalow again last night I thought, It is none of my business, but since Colonel Sahib is not alone in the house I can nod off for a moment.'

Dmitri drew on the cigarette, exhaled, stubbed it out as if already tired of it. He took the ebony cane in both hands and leaned forward, chin resting on the hands that rested on the cane.

'So,' he said, 'Khansamar thought it was no business of his either. But he had seen the mess that had been made of Aziz's face and when he took in Colonel Sahib's *chota hazri* he found him already up, sitting in front of the dressing-table, and wearing his harness. The knuckles of his right hand were grazed. He had beaten the boy with his fist. And at that moment, you know, Khansamar conceived for Merrick a dislike. Not a violent dislike. A cold dislike. Contempt. And of course he wondered why a boy like Aziz submitted to that kind of treatment. Do you wonder, Mr Perron?'

'Tell me why you don't.'

Bronowsky smiled and leant back, swirled his brandy in the glass, sipped and put the glass down.

'I think it is clear he had been so instructed. Instructed to present himself, to stand there at the gate until Merrick had seen him. Also instructed to submit, without complaint, to whatever Merrick did once he had accepted the lure of this terrible attraction, of this terrible temptation which young men like Aziz represented.'

'Instructed by whom?'

'I think not Pandit Baba, don't you agree? If it was the Pandit then he must have studied more than the Bhagavad-Gita. He must also have studied Freud. So I do not think the Pandit. The Pandit has probably long ago been superseded by someone with a more modern and intelligent approach. There are always plenty of gurus waiting in the wings, and many of these young men willing and ready to serve and submit and suffer in the belief that what they do is done for a cause. In their death-photographs they look so pale, so insecure. But not in life. Whoever instructed Aziz, and his predecessors, and those who followed him, had come to know of these tendencies in Merrick. How? Always known? I doubt that. More likely through some later indiscretion or lapse. That he had always been kept track of as a potentially useful instrument goes without saying. And this was the new and subtle form of persecution. Young men like Aziz, turning up, with no instructions I imagine other than to tempt, submit, and not complain, not accuse, perhaps to go, so that they could be replaced, gradually, by young men of steelier temperament, young men capable of taking the ultimate step when the victim was properly lulled.

'But what other instructions the boy who called himself Aziz might have had, one does not know. In the event, Merrick sacked him. He told Khansamar there was no further work for Aziz to do. So Aziz was sent packing. And a week or two later another boy arrived, begging for a job, and coming back day after day, standing at the gate. The same kind of boy. But Merrick resisted the bait. And the boy gave up. Only to be replaced by another. And another. And then Susan and Sarah arrived, with the child and the ayah and the bigger bungalow was occupied. But still they came, these young fellows. Perhaps some of them were genuinely looking for employment. Khansamar thought this was so, because they were not all of them boys like Aziz. But among them, from time to time, there would be one like that.

'And then the tactics changed. Khanasamar did not at first connect the one thing with the other. A young Pathan arrived quite late one night, sometime towards the end of April, when the heat was getting bad but Susan was still here and Merrick was often working late, often slept in a room on the other side of the house. The Pathan insisted on seeing Merrick personally. He said he had an official and confidential message. He was alone with Merrick for only a short while. I wonder what was said? What services were offered? What services implied? In May Susan and the child and ayah went back up to Pankot. A few days after they had gone Merrick told Khansamar that he was expecting a messenger, probably quite late, and that the chaukidar shouldn't lock the gates. The Pathan arrived just before midnight. This time he had a companion. Merrick had them taken to his study, then ten minutes later called for Khansamar and told him that one of these men should be given a bed for the night. The Pathan left and the chaukidar locked the gates after him. The companion who stayed was the younger man. He had a bedroll and said he could sleep anywhere. The verandah would do very well. It was very hot. He would be glad if he could be woken at five o'clock. Khansamar said he was a boy like Aziz but probably better educated. He wore European clothes. He was grateful for the charpoy Khansamar put out on the verandah and for the cup of tea he was given. He said he came from Lahore originally and asked a lot of questions about Mirat, so many that Khansamar said, Why do you ask so many questions? The boy laughed and apologized and said it was a habit got from the kind of work he did. Khansamar asked what kind of work that was and the boy looked surprised and said confidential work for the police, what else?

'Khansamar believed it in one part of his mind but not in another. He didn't worry very much either way. It was the Sahib's affair if he slept with boys when his wife was away, not his. But in the morning when he took the boy some tea he was quite innocently asleep where Khansamar had left him and in half-an-hour he had washed and dressed and gone. Khansamar didn't ask the chaukidar whether the boy had ever left his bed and chaukidar didn't volunteer anything, which might have meant that there was nothing to say or that he had been asleep again – perhaps the latter because Khansamar was sure he smelt the boy's hair-oil on one of the pillows in Merrick's bed when he was making it up.

'And so it continued, Mr Perron, about every two or three weeks, always two young men arriving, one going, one staying. Sometimes the one who had stayed the previous time accompanied the new boy. Sometimes Khansamar had seen neither of them before. None of them was a Mirati and Khansamar never noticed the smell of hair-oil on the pillow again. He questioned chaukidar once who said that yes, on one occasion when he patrolled, the boy's bed on the verandah was empty but that when he waited expecting to see him come out of Merrick's *ghusl-khana* he saw him instead coming back from the compound, as if he had been relieving himself and that when he went over and greeted him the young man acted quite naturally and offered him a cigarette and sat and smoked and talked to him for a while.

'So, one wonders. And one wonders what really was in Merrick's mind, whether there was some reality behind this illusion of spies or whether he had simply agreed with the Pathan to have boys procured for him. And in the latter case one wonders again whether he saw a connection between this arrangement and the older forms of persecution, and deliberately put himself in the way of it. I'm afraid we shall never know, Mr Perron. And in a country as vast as this all these young fellows have just disappeared, as if they never existed.

'But consider it this way. And discard the evidence of the hair-oil on the pillow. The smell of the oil could have been in Khansamar's imagination. He never smelt it again. Not even when the rains came and the boys no longer slept on the verandah but on Merrick's instructions indoors in an empty room, where they were free to go to him at any time. Did they go? Perhaps. But if they went, did anything occur? Or did they just sit there discussing with him the information they had pretended to collect or actually collected for him? Was there any such information? Perhaps. On the night he was murdered the private drawer in his desk was forced open, so something might have been removed. But what? A slowly collected dossier about the subversive activities of real or imaginary political activists in Mirat, or a dossier about the scandalous activities, real or imaginary, of Mirat police officers and Mirati officials? If so, had Merrick ever believed in any of it? When he was going on and on about the man in the nullah and the imaginary stone he never referred to the existence of such dossiers, although he said the chief of police should start investigating what he called subversive elements. So, if he had any dossiers, files containing information collected from these so-called spies, had he believed in any of it, or had he just sat there, listening to these young men, pretending to accept their reports, pretending to need their reports but waiting for them to make it clear what else they were offering, and puzzling them by blandly ignoring every hint, every temptation. You knew him, Mr Perron. Would you say that was possible?'

'I should have thought very possible, but in view of the Aziz business, not very probable.'

'And there I disagree. I think perhaps it was probable precisely because of the Aziz business. I think it likely that what he did with, and to, Aziz revealed something to him about himself that utterly appalled him ...'

'Appalled him?'

'I don't mean the revelation of his latent homosexuality and his sado-masochism. These must have been apparent to him for many many years and every now and again given some form of expression. What I mean by a revelation is revelation of the connection between the homosexuality, the sado-masochism, the sense of social inferiority and the grinding defensive belief in his racial superiority. I believe – although you may not – that Aziz was the first young man he had actually ever made love to, and that this gave him a moment of profound peace, but in the next the kind he knew he couldn't bear, knew he couldn't bear because to admit this peace meant discarding every belief he had. I think he realized that, when he woke up after his first night with the boy. And I think that when the boy turned up the following night he just found himself punished and humiliated. And I believe that when Merrick beat him with his fist he was inviting retaliation. I believe he knew why Aziz had arrived. I am sure that finally, Mr Perron, he sought the occasion of his own death and that he grew impatient for it. He *wanted* there to be a man in the nullah. He wanted there to be a stone thrown at his horse. He wanted what happened to happen. Perhaps he hoped that his murder would be avenged in some splendidly spectacular way, in a kind of Wagnerian climax, the *raj* emerging from the twilight and sweeping down from the hills with flaming swords –'

A steward interrupted, approached, leant close, murmured something to him. Bronowsky nodded. The steward went.

'Nawab Sahib?' Perron asked.

'Yes. He has seen the fires in the city. Forgive me, Mr Perron. It is a summons I can't disobey. But really it is just that he cannot sleep, and wants company.'

They both rose.

'The car can drop you next door and take me on to the palace,' Bronowsky said.

'It's only a step or two.'

'But the car has to take me anyway. Come.'

Bronowsky led him out on to the terrace, taking the long way round to the front. He placed his left hand on Perron's right shoulder. 'But let me tell you what did happen. Or all that one knows. Which isn't much. There was no apparent difference between all the previous nights of the spies and the fatal night. Two young men turn up. Neither has visited before. One goes. The other stays. Perhaps the one who went did not really go, but came back and stayed hidden, to assist, when the time came. It was a lot for one man to do alone. But all that is a mystery, a little event between midnight and six o'clock in the morning when Khansamar went in with the *chota hazri*. The visitor who was to stay the night had gone. Chaukidar had seen nothing, heard nothing. The fact that he did not see them going does not necessarily mean that he was asleep. When the boys made off they might have gone over the wall at the back. No. The real mystery is what happened in the room. Did Merrick dress himself in those clothes, do you think? Habbibullah says that he was strangled before he was hacked about with the little axe and that he was dressed in the clothes before being hacked. One wonders why this was the chosen night, whether it was because time was running out or because the time was now exactly right for leaving on our doorstep as it were, one dead Englishman.'

Bronowsky stopped, released Perron's shoulder, leant for a moment on his stick. 'I wonder – was the thing done in the old Thuggee way?'

'Not unless the neck was broken and a grave already dug.'

'Ah. I had forgotten that. But it was something else I had in mind – the many days the Thugs sometimes travelled with their chosen victims, to lull suspicion. Isn't there a resemblance between this and the long period of preparation? And then it is said, isn't it, that when it came to it they were mercifully quick. Compassionate, even.'

The fountains rose, changed colour, subsided and then murmured on. Bronowsky took Perron's shoulder again and began to walk forward. 'Perhaps it is there, in the compassion, that I have been hoping to see the real resemblance.'

VI

'I hadn't thought that we were to be quite so large a party,' Mrs Peabody said.

She had to raise her voice because the platform was crowded and noisy even where the first-class coaches stood and where the usually sober British were being determinedly cheerful and jolly, seeing off and being seen off. Even Mrs Peabody was smiling so Perron wasn't sure whether she was making a comment or a complaint.

'I expect we'll all fit in easily enough,' he shouted back. Mrs Peabody was thin, but tall, so tall that her greatest problem looked like being lack of head-space rather than of elbow-room. Peabody was the same height and not much better fleshed. It would be like travelling with two bean poles. The Peabodys were, as people put it, 'staying on', but were going to do that in Rawalpindi. So much Perron had gathered. They had an immense amount of luggage whose stowing in the compartment Peabody was overseeing. It had already been going into the compartment when Perron and the party from palace and guest house arrived; and still was. It was a good thing that everyone else was travelling fairly light – as Mrs Grace had pointed out after greeting Mrs Peabody and discovering in answer to her question that, yes, all this stuff *was* going into the compartment because years and years of travelling in India had inspired no confidence in either Peabody, in the luggage vans, even on a daytime trip. For instance one would not, Mrs Peabody pointed out, like to have some of one's things off-loaded by mistake at Premanagar.

After this exchange Mrs Grace had dissociated herself from the Peabodys and their luggage and engaged herself in conversation with Bronowsky and Ahmed while Sarah and Nigel helped Susan and ayah to keep Edward entertained. This had left Perron under an obligation to make himself pleasant to Mrs Peabody, but it was up-hill work. The Peabodys were working in unison, he inside, she out. Their joint efficiency suggested years of practice. Every few moments she broke off the exchange of small-talk to point a coolie at a piece of luggage, or if she didn't break it off herself Peabody did by coming to the open compartment door and reminding her that such or such a piece ought to be stowed next.

'Well I don't know about fitting in easily,' she said eventually, 'but no doubt we shall manage, since there are only six of us.'

'Eight,' Perron said.

'Dora,' Peabody called from the carriage door. 'We'd better have the guns now.'

'There's still the tiffin-box.'

'I think the guns first, then the tiffin-box.'

'As you wish, Reginald.' She pointed a coolie at canvas-shrouded packages, long and thin enough to be Peabody guns.

'Eight,' she said, not having lost the thread. 'How do you make eight?'

'Eight and a half, actually, if you include both me *and* the little boy.'

'Well naturally one includes you both.'

'Right-o, Dora. Tiffin-box now.'

She pointed a coolie at the tiffin-box. It was a wooden box, of majestic proportions, presumably zinc-lined, with air-holes on one side. Watching it go in Perron thought that at least none of them would starve if the train broke down and the Peabodys unbent sufficiently to share out.

'I still make it only six and a half, unless Captain Rowan is coming to Ranpur instead of joining Laura in Gopalakand. But I think that would still make it only seven and a half. Not that mathematics were ever my strong point. Once the thermoses have gone in we can leave the field clear.' She moved to the compartment door and shouted, 'Reginald? I hope the upper berths are let down. They'll need them to stow *their* few things.'

Perron joined Sarah and Nigel. 'I have a feeling that at least two members of the departing *raj* aren't going to leave without standing by their old rights. Or anyway making a fuss about Ahmed and ayah travelling in a first-class compartment.'

'Oh, for God's sake,' Sarah said.

'The Peabodys?' Nigel asked. 'They'd better start getting used to it. He's making a contract with Pakistan for a couple of years. Actually I don't blame him. He's a brilliant military administrator.'

'Brilliant and only a major? Or hasn't he been quite pukka enough to make it to half-colonel?'

Rowan smiled. 'Originally, no. And she's half-Jewish and very anti-semitic. But she's now the Honourable Dora.'

'The Honourable Dora? What a terrible combination.'

'She's furious that it always gets omitted in newspapers. But it came rather late, when her father was made a law baron. It's never got into the Indian lists.'

'Shall I start stowing our luggage?'

'You mean they've finished?' Sarah asked.

Perron rounded up their own coolies and entered the compartment. It smelt of Peabody's bay rum.

In these old first-class compartments there were no corridors. There was no need of them and one was better without them. Each compartment, coupé or four-berther, had its private lavatory. The compartments were broad enough and the berths long enough to suit the tallest man at full stretch and hold the combined luggage of four long-distance travellers. Normally the luggage could be piled up against what might be called the bulk-head between the sleeping compartment and the lavatory; and there was sufficient space down the centre between the two fixed lower benches to stow ice- and tiffin-boxes without restricting foot room.

But when Perron entered he saw that the Peabodys had commandeered all this space and more. Luggage was piled against the bulkhead, blocking the farther exit and coming within an inch or two of the door to the lavatory. He hoped that the exit at Ranpur was on the same side as the entrance at Mirat. Presumably the Peabodys knew. Stretching from the pile of bulkhead luggage was a line of trunks and cases down the centre of the compartment. Even some of the luggage-space provided by the lowered upper sleeping berths was taken up. He ordered his own party's suitcases to be stowed above, and then remembered Merrick's relics. Were they out on the platform? The answer was at once given – by the appearance in the doorway of a coolie holding one end of the black tin coffin, the battered old trunk, with the stencilled name, Lt.-Col. R. Merrick, DSO, still visible, still eloquent.

'You'd better put it here,' he said, indicating a place that would leave barely sufficient room for people to get from one side of the compartment to another. He hoped the carpet wouldn't come too. But it did. It looked smaller, though. It had been doubled up and tied with string. He had it placed on top of the trunk.

He clambered out, and down on to the platform. The Peabodys were bidding farewell to an elderly servant who was placing garlands round their thin necks. He reported to Sarah. A warning whistle blew. She turned to Bronowsky who took off his rakish little panama hat. Beyond the first-class compartment area the platform had begun to seethe. Perron could hear the mournful voice of the man selling tea. Cha-ay Wall-*ah*, Garam cha-*ay*. Black hands stretched down from open third-class compartments grasping those stretched up to bid goodbye. A woman shrieked.

'Goodbye, my dear,' Bronowsky was saying to Sarah. 'Don't be too long before coming back.' He bent to embrace her.

Perron clasped Nigel's hand. 'I'll wire you,' he said.

'Do. I'll be a better host in Gopalakand. Have a good journey.'

A hand fell on Perron's shoulder. Bronowsky's. The one eye observed him. 'Thank you for coming to Mirat. Here is a little token of your visit.'

He found himself presented with a little package. A book by the feel of it. Then Edward intervened.

'Goodbye, Chief Minister. Thank you for letting us stay at the Nawab's guest house, while daddy's away.'

One by one they entered the compartment. Another blow on the whistle. Distantly the woman shrieked again.

'Mrs Merrick, there is room for your tiffin basket on top of ours,' Mrs Peabody said.

'Please don't worry,' Susan replied. She sat at the far end of the compartment opposite Mrs Peabody, divorced from her by the black tin trunk and the folded carpet. On her lap she held a basket.

'Has your ayah a compartment quite close?'

'Oh, very close, Mrs Peabody. In fact here. Ayah will sit with me, in case I doze off and Edward needs attending to. It's the best thing.'

After a moment Mrs Peabody said, 'Reginald, let me sit at the other end. It is a little close here.' They changed places.

'Are you sure about that basket, Mrs Merrick?' Peabody asked.

'Absolutely sure, Major Peabody.'

Perron, at the doorway, received Edward from Dmitri's arms. 'I don't want to sit down yet, Perron,' the boy said. 'I want to wave from this window.'

'Okay, but let the troops on first.'

Mrs Grace came next. She looked at the compartment and then at the Peabodys and said, 'Good Heavens, it looks as though we're being delivered from Egypt,' and went to sit next to Susan. Sarah kissed Nigel and came up next. She went down and round over the baggage and sat between Major and Mrs Peabody.

'Ayah!' Edward shouted. 'Hurry up! You're going to miss the train.'

Ahmed helped ayah up.

'Come on, ayah,' Mrs Grace said, and patted the seat next to her. '*Baitho*.'

The girl tried to take Edward with her but he resisted. So she went and sat, alert, on the edge of the green leather-upholstered bench. A pretty girl, Perron realized; this morning not covering her face with the edge of her saree. Ahmed came next. He seemed to have no luggage except a small canvas bag.

Another whistle-blow. Ahmed shut the door, turned, lifted Edward up to the open window.

'Goodbye Dmitri!' the child called. 'Goodbye Uncle Nigel!'

Abruptly, the carriage began to glide away. Perron steadied himself against the piled Peabody luggage and bent, peering through the other windows to watch the unfolding tapestry of the departure from Mirat.

I remember (he has said) dark faces taking over from the white faces. I remember the woman who ran trying to keep up with the train.

'Are you really sure about the basket, Mrs Merrick?' Mrs Peabody said. 'Couldn't your ayah look after it?'

Susan didn't reply this time. When Perron had climbed over the luggage and settled himself next to Mrs Peabody, Sarah whispered to him, 'Try to get her to shut up about the basket. It's the urn. Susan won't let anyone else touch it.'

At a suitable moment, when Edward was shouting playfully at ayah, Perron passed the message on. Mrs Peabody opened her mouth, then shut it. Presently she opened her handbag and brought out a little lace handkerchief, moist with eau-de-cologne. She wiped it gently over her dry yellow skin.

They were sitting in this order:

On the bench that ended close to the one unencumbered door – first, Ahmed, then ayah, then Mrs Grace and Susan. The child used this side of the compartment as his roving territory. Opposite Susan sat Peabody, then Sarah, then Perron and Mrs Peabody. At Perron's and Mrs Peabody's end there was almost total luggage block, with Ahmed and ayah visible only from chest height. Ahmed got up and went into the lavatory. Perron heard Mrs Peabody draw in her breath and then slowly exhale. He had the impression that however badly she might need to she would now avoid going to the lavatory for the rest of the day, or get out at the only stop (Premanagar) whether she needed to or not, as a form of insurance against too great a desperation later. She remained tense throughout the few minutes Ahmed was absent, probably counting them, in order to work out whether he was urinating or doing something of a graver nature. When Ahmed came out she continued silent, and Perron began to feel that she was holding *him* responsible for everything, from the overcrowded compartment right down through the urn to the use of the lavatory by natives.

*

'Bang!' Edward shouted. After they had been going for about half-an-hour (and all, one by one, except Perron and the Peabodys had used the lavatory – Perron because he didn't want to go badly enough to feel it worth his while fighting the way over that mound of luggage) Edward had found the perfect use for the piled trunks and cases. He shot them from behind this entrenchment until they were all dead. Except Mrs Peabody, who was resistant to imaginary bullets.

But the 'Bang!' obviously stirred thoughts. 'Do you hunt, Mr Perron?' she asked. These were not the first words she had spoken to him, simply the first she had volunteered.

Perron said he didn't.

'Do you shoot?'

'No. I watched Ahmed hawking the other day.'

'Who?'

'Ahmed. Mr Kasim. Over there.'

'Hawking?'

'With a hawk.'

'Oh. I see. Yes. Really? I don't think I should care for that. It seems to me rather cruel to tame a wild creature. But I like a day out with hounds and a day out with the guns. We hope to get in a few days at Bharatpur before going on up to 'Pindi. You've been to Bharatpur, I suppose? Oh, you should. The jhils there are famous.'

She talked on for a while, about Bharatpur, about Kashmir, about the boundless number of places she and Reginald had been in India. 'We've never been south though, except of course through it to Ooty. There's some good going in Ooty. But the south always depresses me. I never think of it as India at all. We're northern India people by temperament, I suppose. Tell me, what is your regiment?'

Perron admitted that he did not own a regiment and had never served in one except for a few months during the war as a private, after which he had transferred to Intelligence and then to Field Security.

'But you were in India?'

'For a while.'

'In Field Security?'

'Yes. With a man called Bob Chalmers.'

'Chalmers. Chalmers. No, I'm afraid I don't know that name.'

'He's now in pharmaceuticals in Bombay.'

'Really. How interesting. He stayed on, then. Reggie was awfully tempted to go into pharmaceuticals himself, after all one of the few things we can do for this country now is help them fight the battle of disease.'

'And poverty.'

She smiled. 'I sometimes think the poverty is very exaggerated. Most of the Indians one knows could buy one up lock stock and barrel.'

'There are the ones one doesn't know.'

'In the villages, Mr Perron, every peasant woman has her gold bangles. No, no. It is not the poverty. It is the disease. The superstition. The *inertia*.'

'Bang!' Edward said.

Perron died again.

And then so did the train. The luggage juddered from the vibration of the braking. Minnie grabbed the child. They all rocked to and fro for a moment and then steadied themselves. The train came to a halt.

*

'Probably a cow on the line,' Mrs Peabody said. 'Reggie – see what you can see if you can manage to climb over that carpet.'

But Ahmed was already up. He lowered the window of the door and leant out.

'I remember a cow on the line,' Susan said in the dead silence. 'Don't you, Sarah?'

'Yes, I remember.'

'But where? All I remember is the train stopping and daddy saying just what Mrs Peabody just said. "Probably a cow on the line." And there was. But where was it, Sarah?'

'Between Ranpur and Delhi. Nineteen-thirty.'

'Ranpur and Delhi. What lovely names. There's so much poetry in Indian names. Ronnie used to say that. Where is your home at home, Mrs Peabody?'

'We are in Northamptonshire. Just outside Norby.'

'Norby. That's what I mean. And mother says she's found a house in Epsom. It sounds like an aperient.'

'Major Peabody?' Ahmed called out. 'Would you please put up the windows and close the shutters on your side? Mrs Grace? Please? On yours?'

He was locking the compartment door. Now he pulled the window up and closed the wooden shutter.

'What is it, Ahmed?' Mrs Grace asked.

'Oh, nothing much. Just some kind of silly nuisance. Mr Perron, please, on your side?'

'What's the chap say?' Peabody asked.

'He seems to want the windows closed and the shutters pulled down,' Mrs Peabody said. 'I can't think why. It's hot enough and there's one fan not working.'

Peabody stood up. 'What are you doing? Baking us alive or something?'

Ahmed was helping Mrs Grace to close windows and pull down shutters on the other side of the compartment. Perron started doing the same on the Peabody side.

'What's wrong, Ahmed?' Sarah asked.

'Just some silly people making a nuisance. Don't worry.'

There was nothing to be seen through the windows except a vast hot dry eroded landscape. 'Do you mind?' Perron asked, leaning in behind Mrs Peabody and dealing with her window and shutter.

'Yes I do. I do mind. For heaven's sake!'

'Just shut the windows please and pull down the shutters,' Ahmed repeated. 'Mrs Grace, I think ayah shouldn't sit here. Let her get under the seat just for a while. Come, Minnie.' He got hold of her and forced her gently to the floor. 'Play hide and seek with chokrasahib. Come on, Edward. Look, ayah is hiding.'

Edward shouted, 'Why is she hiding? I don't want to play hide and seek. It's a silly girl's game.'

'No, it isn't silly,' Ahmed insisted. 'Come on, help hide ayah. Pretend bad men are looking for her.'

'Look here, Kasim,' Peabody began – but just then there was a long drawn-out wail, rising in pitch, from up ahead. There was a grumble of voices from the adjacent compartment, then a shout, and the sound of windows and shutters being closed. The wailing continued as an accompaniment now to sudden screams.

They remained, as if transfixed. From under the bench came a low moan from the little ayah. The boy bent down. 'What's wrong, ayah?' he asked. Ahmed got hold of him and said, 'Okay, it's only a game. Ayah's pretending to hide from bad people. Major Peabody, please come to this side and take ayah's seat so that no one can see her.'

Peabody hesitated, then began to clamber over the luggage. As he did so something hit the compartment, something soft. And again. The sound of a hand slapping the side of the carriage. Behind it all the continuing sound of wailing and screaming.

'Take the boy,' Ahmed said, and lifted him over into Sarah's arms. Peabody was still straddled across the luggage.

'Reggie, what are you *doing?*' his wife asked him. He looked at her as if he thought her a perfect fool but said, 'God knows what anyone's doing, it must be some kind of damned silly demonstration,' and completed the movement of stepping over the luggage, lost his footing and fell against Mrs Grace and Susan. 'Oh, damn it,' he said and just then people outside began to pound heavily on the door and the side of the compartment and then there was a little crack and an explosion of broken glass and Susan shrieked. Another explosion, another shattering of glass. She shrieked again. As if by old instinct, Peabody remained ducked down, forgetting that the glass couldn't fly in through the lowered shutters. It was dark in the compartment. Little wires of light lay along the edges of the wooden louvres. The occupants of the seats were ducked down too, including Ahmed. Mrs Grace had her arm round Susan. Sarah held the boy. This was the tableau Perron saw when after a sudden silence had lasted a few seconds he looked up and round.

There was a bang on the door. Then a hammering that went on for some while. When it stopped a man's voice came quite clearly: 'Come on, Kasim Sahib.' More bangs on the door. Susan gasped. Mrs Peabody cried out, 'What are they doing, what are they doing?' Then the voice from outside could be heard again. 'Come on out. Kasim? Kasim Sahib? Come on. Or do

we have to break in and annoy all the sirs and ladies? Kasim? Kasim Sahib?'
When the voice stopped the hammering on the door began again.

Silence suddenly. Then another shattered window. This time Edward
began to cry. Sarah cradled him. Perron got up – to do what he didn't know:
climb over to the door, open the shutter and shout that there was no Kasim
there?

But Ahmed had got up too. Because of the noise of Edward crying and
Susan shrieking Perron did not clearly hear what Ahmed said, but it
sounded like, 'It seems to be me they want.' It could have been, 'Be ready to
re-lock the door.' But he smiled, shrugged, and had suddenly unlocked it.
As he did so Peabody lunged forward, as if to stop him. But he was too late.
Ahmed opened the door and went.

A turbanned head appeared. Peabody must have seen the head at eye-
level. Perron saw it from above. The head rose. The man must have been
getting purchase on steps and hand-grip. It looked as if he was coming in.
He got one hand on the door-handle. In his other was something that
looked like a sword but surely couldn't have been. He said, 'Sorry to have
disturbed you, sirs and ladies. On to Ranpur, isn't it?' and then let himself
fall away, dragging the door shut. Peabody lunged forward again and locked
it.

A feeling of terrible relief swept over Perron. At the time it was just
relief. It was terrible subsequently; when it sank in that it had been the
relief a man feels when his self-protective instinct tells him he has
personally survived a passing danger. Perhaps Peabody felt the same relief.
And perhaps it was this that presently made him push up the shutter and
look out.

Then he lowered it quickly, stood for a moment, staring at the shutter,
checked the lock on the door, and turned round and sat on the bench in the
place Ahmed had vacated without saying a word.

And as he did so the train began to glide forward – slowly, silkily,
smoothly; as if getting stealthily away from a dangerous and incomprehensible situation. Except for Peabody, who had looked out, none of the people
in the compartment could quite visualize the scene of this second
departure. Later they must all have done so. In Perron's mind it remains so
vivid that it sometimes seems to him that he raised a shutter himself and
watched as the train drifted away along this stretch of line, on whose
embankment bodies lay; some close, some farther off as though they had
tried to run away and then been caught and struck down – men, women,
youths, young girls, babies; in death looking all the same, like dummies
stuffed for some kind of strange fertility festival.

*

It took three-quarters of an hour to get to Premanagar. At first it seemed as
if they would cover the entire distance in the semi-darkness of lowered
shutters and in total silence apart from the rhythmic clack of wheels

hastily putting distance between the living travellers and the abandoned dead; but after five minutes or so Mrs Peabody said, 'Reggie, do you think we might have some light and air? I think otherwise I might be going to faint.'

'Only on your side,' Mrs Grace said. 'Here we have a great deal of trapped broken glass.'

'It was my side I was thinking of. Perhaps you'd help me, Mr Perron, since you're here.'

Perron lent a hand.

'I didn't like that game, Auntie Sarah,' Edward said. 'Is it finished?'

The child's tear-stained face was revealed as the shutters went up. He climbed off Sarah's lap and then up and over the piled luggage. 'You can come out now, ayah,' he shouted. 'We've stopped playing that game. Where's Ahmed? Has he gone to pee again? I want to pee too.' He had to say it several times and then staggered towards the door of the w.c. His unsteadiness suddenly impressed itself on Major Peabody's eye.

'Come on, old chap, then. I'll take you.'

'What's *your* name?' Edward asked as he was taken in.

'Never mind my name,' Peabody said; and shut the door on them both.

Sarah was now leaning forward, both elbows clasped in her hands, her head bowed. Ayah had got up and was standing against the luggage. When the door of the lavatory opened and Edward came out alone she took charge of him and sat with him in the place that had been Ahmed's and then Peabody's and was now anybody's or nobody's. Peabody was in the cubicle for nearly ten minutes. Perhaps he was being sick. He looked very pale when he came out. Finding his new place gone he clambered over the luggage and sat once more in the far corner opposite Susan who still cradled the basket and was still cradled in Mrs Grace's arms.

'Is mummy crying again?' Edward asked.

Nobody answered. But then Sarah said, 'We just let him go. We all of us sat here and let him go.' After that none of them spoke. In this way they came into Premanagar.

*

Before the train actually stopped Peabody got up. Perron got up too. At the door Peabody said in a whisper, 'Keep them in here, Perron. They mustn't come out on to the platform.'

'But I must.'

Peabody said, 'I think not.'

'I'm sorry, Peabody. But I've got to go back to where Ahmed got out.'

Peabody frowned. Perhaps at the use of his surname. 'There's nothing to go back for. He was hacked to pieces.'

Perron didn't really take this in. He said, 'I must get to a phone and ring the palace. We can't just leave it like that. Someone's got to go back.'

From outside, suddenly, as the train came to a halt, came the renewed

1556

sound of wailing and shouting. Peabody's breath smelt acid. He said, 'They might turn on us when they take it in. They might decide it's our fault. You'd be better advised to stay here and look after the women. I'm going to find out what's happening.'

'It's all right, Major Peabody,' Sarah called. 'Mr Perron knows what he must do. I'll stand by the door if that's what you want.' She clambered over. Reluctantly Peabody opened the door. An English voice outside exclaimed, 'My God.' Peabody and Perron went down. 'Lock it,' Peabody told Sarah. She said, 'There's no need to lock it now.'

Other English passengers had come down from the adjacent compartments – two of them women. Two Indian officers ran through asking them to make way. Automatically they stood back, as if accepting that this was an Indian affair, not theirs. They stood pale-faced, shocked.

Some of the dead were already being brought out of the third-class carriages. The nearest of these was a purdah-coach and out of this white and black bundles of veiled women were being lowered. Most lay motionless when put down, one or two seemed to be trying to crawl back in. Among the dead from the purdah-coach were the bodies of small children. And beyond the purdah-coach the platform was becoming littered with blood-stained bundles of white cloth, with black limbs sticking out of the cloth. One body lay on the roof of the coach. No one seemed to have noticed it. From some of the windows of the coaches heads and arms hung down. Blood slowly made shapes on the dirty grey concrete of the platform. Ahead, the locomotive suddenly let off steam, as if about to haul the train out again. People began to shout. A wave of panic swept along the platform and then because the train didn't move died away and left only the wailing of those searching among the rows of dead and dying passengers.

*

'I'm sorry,' the MCO said, 'I cannot allow private calls of any nature. I am trying to raise Mirat. The lines may be down. Please go away.'

The MCO was a Sikh. Sikhs, people were saying, had been among the gang that stopped the train and slashed Muslim passengers to death with swords. But if he feared for his own life he didn't show it. He had moved freely up and down the platform. Perron had waylaid him on one of his brief visits to the office where a havildar-clerk was constantly on the telephone.

'If you get Mirat, would you please tell them that Ahmed Kasim, the son of Mohammed Ali Kasim may have to be presumed dead and that the Nawab of Mirat's Chief Minister should be informed?'

'Ahmed Kasim? Ahmed Kasim? Who is Ahmed Kasim?'

'He was travelling with us.'

'Then why is he presumed dead? You are first-class, surely. Please go away. What is one man among so many?'

'Mirat, sir,' the clerk shouted, and handed the phone over.

The MCO grabbed the receiver, at the same time saying, 'Please all of you go away.' He began talking rapidly in a mixture of English and Hindi. Perron was not the only unauthorized visitor. There were about six crowded into the tiny office. But all of them were English – people who were anxious to contact friends left behind in Mirat or waiting for them in Ranpur, friends who some time during the day might hear what had happened and start worrying.

'Let's try the stationmaster,' one of them said.

'He's worse than this chap.'

They had absorbed the shock. The old reactions were already setting back in, but the impulse to take charge had gone. It was the kind of situation that had always been bubbling under the surface trying to break out, the kind that the *raj* had had to try to control. Now the worst had happened.

'God knows how they're going to cope in this place,' one of the officers told Perron as they went back on to the platform. 'Premanagar's always been a dead-alive hole. No proper troops and no pukka hospital.'

The MCO's office was next to the first-class restaurant. The trains always drew up so that the first-class compartments were opposite the places that first-class passengers needed. In this area, then, the platform was an isolated little island, bordered on both sides by the horrors. Perron noticed that armed police had turned up. It was twenty minutes since the train's arrival. He went to the compartment. The door was open. Inside there were only the two Peabodys – he kneeling by an open bag, she lying full length on the bench, hand over her eyes.

'Where are the others?' Perron asked.

'Women's rest room.'

From the bag Peabody was taking a webbing belt and holster. The holster had a revolver in it. Perron got down again and went to the women's rest room. It was crowded. There were several men among the women, looking pale, dignified and protective. At one end of the room he saw Mrs Grace, ayah and Edward, and Susan. He made his way to them, passing from under one area of fanned air to another. 'Where's Sarah?' he asked Mrs Grace.

'She's gone to see what she can do to help. I let her. It's what she wanted.'

Perron pushed his way out again. 'Savages,' a woman was saying. And a man, 'What do you expect? It's only the beginning. Once we've gone they'll all cut each other's bloody throats. Non-violence. Makes you laugh, doesn't it?' But it didn't make Perron laugh. Once out on the platform he forced his way through a little cordon of armed police into the place where the kind of help Sarah had to offer might be needed. He couldn't see her, so went back again, passing through the area of safety and certainty, out to the other side, through another cordon of police, to another place of horror. Here he saw two Indian nurses, and a stretcher-bearer. A nun. Two nuns. However unpukka the nearest hospital was it had begun to operate. And there were two white women, one elderly, one quite young. A middle-aged

Indian in European clothes stopped him. 'Are you a doctor?' 'No,' Perron said. 'I wish to God I were.' And passed on. The two white women were nursing children. The nuns, both Indians, were binding wounds, staunching the flow of blood from terrible looking cuts which revealed the whiteness of the bone, the redness of the flesh under the brown skin. Another middle-aged man, an Englishman this time, looked up and said, 'Are you the doctor?' 'No,' Perron said. The man said, 'Never mind. Water's the problem. Could you help with that? But it's got to come from the tap down there. Not the one for caste-Hindus. But a lot of these wretches are dying of thirst if nothing else.'

It was at the tap 'down there' that he found Sarah. She was on her knees, in the filth and the muck, her skirt wet through, handing up little brass vessels to the man controlling the tap, reaching out for empty ones without looking, placing the filled vessels on the other side. The vessels, mugs, glasses were being brought and taken away by men and women and youths. He knelt by her. 'Come on,' he said, 'let me take over.'

'No,' she said. 'I'm all right doing this. I can't do the other thing. But if you can, please do.'

So Perron picked up one of the brass jugs and turned and went among the dying. Or the dead. It wasn't always easy to tell. He knelt first by an old grey-beard who seemed to be smiling up at him gratefully, joyfully, but who did not respond when he put his hand under the man's neck to try to raise him. The eyes were glazed and the smile was merely a death-smile.

*

The train had been the 10 a.m. express to Ranpur, its only scheduled stop Premanagar, normally reached at 11.15. The ambush had been laid at a point on the line some miles from the last of three wayside halts, all of which were reached and passed by the express within half an hour of leaving Mirat, and beyond which there was no habitation, nothing but desert, until you reached Premanagar.

As the train came out of a curve on to a straight level embankment, the driver had indeed seen a cow, apparently ruminating. He did not remember seeing more than two or three men asleep on the embankment, but at this point there were a few shade trees growing in the dips on either side, and when he brought the train to a stop he realized there were very many more men. They came up on both sides. Two – armed with swords – climbed on to the footplate. The others began running down the track and climbing into the carriages.

Some passengers said that the attackers were joined by men who had travelled on the train from Mirat and who now produced knives and cudgels and joined the raiders. It must have been one of these men who had noted the compartment Ahmed Kasim got into. Opinions varied about the length of time the train was halted while the men went through it, dragging Muslims out or killing them on the spot. Some said only five minutes, others remembered the slaughter continuing for perhaps half-an-hour. The truth was that it lasted no more than ten or fifteen minutes. At the end of that time, getting a signal, one man released the cow (which had been tethered) and slapped it away to find its own salvation. The two intruders on the footplate ordered the driver to resume his journey and then jumped off. He needed no persuasion. He believed himself lucky to get away with his life and that of his young apprentice. He didn't look back until the locomotive had got up speed. Then he saw men scattering across the rough rocky ground towards a huddle of ruined huts. He saw no vehicles, got no indication of how the men had congregated in this place, or how they hoped to get away. But there probably were vehicles, an old carrier-truck, perhaps, an ancient bus. It was forty-five minutes before the train reached Premanagar; perhaps another fifteen before the Premanagar authorities had contacted Mirat; perhaps another half-hour before troops, police and medical units from Mirat arrived at the scene of the ambush, having dropped search parties off at the villages served by the wayside halts. At the scene itself there was only the terrible evidence: the dead and the dying. By then, the attackers had had nearly two hours in which to scatter.

By road, the journey from Mirat to Premanagar could be accomplished in one and a half hours, only fifteen minutes longer than the journey by rail. The first contingent of troops and medical staff and armed police from Mirat arrived at about one-thirty in the afternoon, fifteen minutes later than the scheduled time of the express train's normally delayed departure for Ranpur, after a leisurely stop for early first-class restaurant lunches. By then, the deputy commissioner and the district superintendent of police had been on the scene since mid-day. The transfer of dead and wounded to an emergency casualty station set up in the goods-yard area was nearly complete. Some kind of order had been restored. The carriages and the platform were being washed down. The rumour was that the train would leave for Ranpur at about 3 p.m., this time under armed guard, and mightn't be more than an hour or so late reaching its destination that evening. About a dozen of the first-class passengers went into the restaurant. The bar had been in use for some time.

*

Perron's trousers and shirt were spattered with blood. He had lost sight of Sarah. He made his way from the goods-yard back to the platform and the compartment.

Mrs Peabody was still stretched out on the bench. Peabody was bending over the tiffin-box, pouring a drink from a thermos. The carriage was otherwise empty. The garlands which had been presented to the Peabodys in Mirat lay on the floor.

'Have you seen Miss Layton?'

Peabody nodded at the lavatory cubicle. 'She's in there, changing. The others are still in the women's room I suppose. You'd better change too. Will you have some malted milk? It's very fortifying.'

'No thank you.'

'There's a spare sandwich or two here. Or have you got your own tuck?'

'I don't want anything to eat, thank you.'

'You ought to eat. Especially if you're going back. I've just been having a word with Bob Blake. He'll take you if you still want to.'

'Who's Bob Blake?'

'He's OC the refugee protection force in the cantonment. They got here a little while ago. I told him what happened to Kasim. He's ringing the station commander in Mirat. There can't be anything you can do but you seemed keen, so I told Bob. He knew Kasim slightly. He'll be here to have a word presently, I shouldn't wonder.'

Sarah came out of the cubicle. She carried a hold-all. The dress she had on was creased but unstained. And dry. She glanced at his shirt and trousers. She said:

'Have you had a drink yet?'

Peabody said, 'I offered him one but he didn't want it.'

'I meant a real drink.'

Perron shook his head. 'I don't want a real drink, either.' He felt now as if he was going to be sick. He went down on to the platform. Sarah came down too. She said, 'Sorry to scrounge. Have you a cigarette?'

He got out his case. He found it difficult to open. She tried to steady his hand while he helped her light up, but they were both trembling.

She said, 'Are you really going back?'

'Are you asking me not to? Do you want help in Ranpur?'

'No. No, thank you. I want to go back too. But I can't. I can't let Aunt Fenny cope alone. But they'll soon know at the palace what happened to Ahmed. Someone ought to go back and try to say how it did.'

'Mr Perron?'

Perron turned. A stout, rather red-faced middle-aged English officer had come up. Sarah said, 'Guy, this is Major Blake.' They shook hands. Blake said, 'I'm going back in about fifteen minutes. If you want to come with me can you be ready by then?'

'Yes, I've only got to change.'

'I'm leaving my subaltern in charge of the train, Miss Layton,' Blake explained. 'You'll be quite safe for the rest of the journey. I'm putting on a whole platoon.'

He took Perron's arm, guided him a few steps away and said, 'I've been on to the station commander in Mirat. He told me Count Bronowsky's already phoned him. The news got round fairly fast. I'm afraid the station commander told him that only Muslims in third-class compartments were killed, but that's what he assumed. He's going now to the place where the bodies are being brought in. Is there any possibility that Kasim wasn't killed?'

'I don't think so. He just opened the door and went, Peabody saw the rest.'

'The station commander said that if young Kasim is dead he'd be very grateful if you do come back. Where were you going, Mr Perron, Pankot?'

'Just to Ranpur, then on to Delhi.'

'Any urgency?'

'None.'

'All the same, I'll help you in any way I can to get you away again. Did you see the chalk-mark on the door?'

'Chalk-mark?'

'Miss Layton noticed it a little while ago. Someone had chalked a moon low on the door of your compartment. It must have been done in Mirat by whoever was watching which part of the train Kasim got into. Yours was the only first-class compartment attacked. All they had to do was look for the chalk-mark. Well. I'll send a chap to help you sort out your bags and bring them over.'

Blake went back to Sarah. They spoke for a few moments. Then he touched his cap and went. From the bar there came a sudden roar of laughter. Perron went back into the carriage to get his bags down and change. As he did so he noticed a fresh smear low down on the door, where the chalk-mark had been wiped off.

*

Mrs Grace and Susan, Edward and ayah, were still in the rest room. He didn't want to intrude on them. He said goodbye to Peabody. Mrs Peabody was still prostrate. There was only Sarah to see him off. One coolie had his suitcase, another his hold-all. A lance-naik sent by Blake was in charge of them, waiting to take Perron to the truck, whatever kind of vehicle it was he and Blake would travel in.

'Are these yours, old man?' Peabody called, offering something from the open carriage door: a little package and a canvas bag.

The package was certainly his. Dmitri's gift. Unopened. A book, presumably. Perhaps a translation of the poetry of Pushkin. The canvas bag, for a moment, was unrecognizable. Then was. He came away from the door holding both. Sarah looked away from the bag.

'Shall I see you again?' he asked.

'I don't know.' She was still shivering. 'What is there to see?'

He touched her shoulder. 'A great deal,' he said. Then leant down and kissed her. He let her go. She turned and climbed back into the carriage. He smiled at her, then followed the naik. At the exit he looked back; she was at the carriage door, holding her elbows in that way; watching him. Briefly she released one hand and raised it. And then went in.

*

I'm sure (Sarah has written) that he did say, 'It seems to be me they want.' It's what Guy heard, what I heard, what we heard at the time, and it made sense. And the fact that he smiled encouraged me to think that if he went out to the people who called out to him everything would be all right. This is what it was like at the time. I can't justify it now except by saying that there were so many conflicting claims; how to stop Edward crying, how to stop Susan shrieking, how to explain even to myself just why ayah was hiding under the bench. When he first looked out of the window when the train stopped he must have seen them dragging Muslims out. If we'd been travelling only a week or two later we'd have been prepared for it, because by then the business of stopping trains and slaughtering people had become part of life. No English were ever harmed. And it became quite the ordinary thing to hide Indians, friends and servants, under the seats – Hindus if it was the Muslims who were attacking, Muslims if it was Hindus. And if people hammered on the doors you just told them to go away. But we didn't know that. We weren't prepared for it. I suppose Ahmed was, or saw at once how things were. And whoever wanted to kill him knew he was travelling that day. The massacre itself must have been a retaliation for the killings and burnings the night before in Mirat when Muslims attacked Hindus because Mirat was going under Congress rule. I suppose Ahmed was marked out as a victim not just because he was a Muslim but because the people who killed him didn't want Muslims in the Congress, or didn't trust Muslims in Congress and his father was still in Congress. And perhaps because they knew his brother was a rabid Pakistani and perhaps because on top of that they hadn't forgotten that Ahmed's father hadn't stood by the INA, which made it senseless anyway because Sayed had been INA. But it was all so senseless. Such a damned bloody senseless mess. The kind which Ahmed tried to shut himself off from, the mess the *raj* had never been able to sort out. The only difference between Ahmed and me was that he didn't take the mess seriously and I did. I felt it was our responsibility, our fault that after a hundred years or more it still existed.

Ahmed and I weren't in love. But we loved one another. We recognized in each other the compulsion to break away from what I can only call a *received* life. When I knelt at the tap, filling up those somehow meaningless little brass jugs and lotas and pots, whatever there was, it was driven home to me that what I was doing was just as useless as what he'd just done. I've never hated myself so much as I did then. I felt like throwing the jugs down and saying, Well, get on with it. And I hated Ahmed for not keeping the door locked and telling us he damned well wasn't going to die unless they smashed right through the windows and climbed in with their swords and slaughtered the lot of us, or started a fire under the compartment to smoke us out, so that they could cut us down one by one. All those possibilities must have been in his mind. But when it came to it he didn't let any of it even begin to happen to us. And *I* couldn't stop filling the bloody jars, going through my brave little memsahib act.

I'm sure he smiled just before he went, and I'm sure he said, 'It seems to be me they want.' Major Peabody said he thought he said, 'Make sure you lock it after me.' But I think that's what Major Peabody wanted to hear. Perhaps we all heard only what we wanted to hear. Perhaps there was nothing to hear because he said nothing, but just smiled and went, in which case I suppose that meant he knew there was nothing to say because there wasn't any alternative, because everyone else in the carriage automatically knew what he had to do. It was part of the bloody code. The moment he got into the carriage *he* sub-consciously knew that sub-consciously *we* had cast lots even before there was any question of lots having to be cast to see who would survive and who wouldn't.

No. I don't know what was in the canvas bag. And Guy never looked. A bottle of whisky, perhaps, and a clove or two of garlic.

Coda

Ranagunj airfield (Ranpur). Saturday August 9, 1947.

The tannoy system crackled. An Indian voice speaking in English told the few people sitting on the hard benches of the little airfield lounge that the plane from Mayapore was now landing and that departure for Delhi would be in twenty minutes.

The English officer sitting next to Perron closed *The Reader's Digest* and said, 'How civilized we make it sound. Do you know an extraordinary thing? As far back as December in nineteen forty-five when I flew from Singapore to Rangoon and on to Calcutta on an RAF plane and we landed for fuel in the middle of Burma, the door opened and an erk in white dungarees looked in and said, "You've now landed in Meiktila." '

'Meiktila?'

'Yes. I'd lost quite a lot of good men there scarcely more than six months before in the battle for the airstrip. But here we were, practising for the courteous world of civil aviation. I thought, How quickly the grass grows.'

*

The plane was delayed, delayed by storms. It was nearly midnight. It had rained throughout most of the day. The old Dakota was parked about a hundred yards from the airfield buildings. An immense puddle had to be negotiated by the six or seven people who having taken leave of friends walked ahead of or behind Perron towards the steps leading to the open port. Inside, bucket seats, thinly cushioned, had replaced the old port and starboard benches. About ten passengers were already seated. Passengers from Mayapore. Officers. Officers' wives. A blue-rinsed grey-haired woman who was probably Red Cross. Two beefy-looking fellows in shorts and shirts who might have been Australians but turned out to be English: technicians, perhaps, from the British-Indian Electric Company. Their shirts were black with sweat. They were drinking beer from the bottle.

Perron found a single seat on the port side. He stowed his hand luggage. Sat. Closed his eyes.

Mayapore, Ranpur, Delhi. He wondered how many of the passengers from Mayapore had been in the town in nineteen forty-two; at the time of the Bibighar. Perhaps none. The *raj* had always led a nomadic existence. And these little airfields, relics of the war, now merely hastened their movements from place to place. Some of them were moving out for the last time.

He opened his eyes and stared out of the window at what remained for him of Ranpur: an illuminated puddle. The airfield building. A petrol tanker, now hauling away. Beyond this darkness and this light – after these absurd little marks and portents of human occupation – the adventure. The port engine fired, exploding the silence. The port airscrew began to spin. Little ripples showed on the surface of the puddle, as though the fishermen on the Izzat Bagh lake had cast a net. Another small explosion, on the starboard side. He shut his eyes again. Whenever he travelled by air he prayed just before take-off and just before landing. These were nowadays his only offerings to God. It was inconceivable to him that the prayers could be heard because he felt that if there were a God, God would be praying too, watching these extraordinary machines shudder and flutter their frail way along the tarmac towards the lit runway.

And there was always that moment as the aeroplane squared up and seemed to pause; the moment of dying intention, and then the moment when defiance set in again and the paper-tiger roared and vibrated. It was like being drawn back and then shot in slow motion from a bow, so slowly that sometimes you felt that the pilot's inspiration had run out and left him with nothing but a grinding determination to prove against all evidence that the thing could be done.

The sensation of being no longer ground-borne always came as a shock. The extraordinary thing had again been achieved. Following which, even at night, when there was no visible horizon, there was this sense of exultation.

*

He opened Bronowsky's gift, the book, not of Pushkin poems but Bronowsky's own translations of Gaffur (privately printed, in Bombay, dedicated to the Nawab). From its leaves he took out and read what he had begun writing to Sarah in the airport lounge.

'I'm waiting for a plane that should have come in an hour ago but is delayed by storms. My watch says 1045 so by now you'll be back and have had the message from your father that I rang. I hope Susan will be better soon. Please give her my best wishes. Your father said you'd all be staying at Commandant House for a few weeks because the new Indian commandant's wife isn't joining him yet and he's making other temporary arrangements. But after that? I didn't ask all the questions I wanted to,

1565

questions like where are you going when the few weeks are up? Back home? How absurd it is that suddenly there is this question of a roof over one's head. I gathered Susan was only suffering reaction and shock and should be out of hospital in a day or two.

'A false alarm. Someone said the plane had landed. It hadn't. But I shall have to finish this letter in Delhi. I gave your father my address there. I don't know whether I shall go down to Gopalakand as Nigel suggested. Wire me if you want me to come back to Ranpur, or up to Pankot. Your father said you'd had Nigel's telegram, the one he sent from Mirat on Thursday night, finally confirming what was never really in doubt. I tried to ring you that night, and yesterday, but the lines were hopeless. I came up to Ranpur on the night train and got in about 8 a.m. this morning and tried to ring you again from the air force mess where Major Blake arranged for me to put up during the day. He's arranged this flight for me, too. I left Mirat because there was nothing more for me to do there. Ahmed's father arrived there yesterday morning. I met him for a few moments. An impressive man. Hiding his grief.

'When I got back to Mirat from Premanagar last Thursday, and to the place where all the bodies had been taken, Dmitri and Nigel were already there, and had identified and made some of the necessary arrangements. Nigel told me – and perhaps I should tell you – that the only person Dmitri blames is himself for letting Ahmed go on that particular day and for not anticipating that something like that might happen. Before I left last night Dmitri asked me to give you his love, then made us sit down for a moment on a couch and say nothing. It was like a Tchekov play. But shall I ever return to Mirat?'

The letter ended there.

But I thought (he said silently to Sarah, putting the letter away as the lights of Ranpur performed geometrical movements as if they were man-made constellations) I thought – today in Ranpur – of solving once and for all the mystery of Hari, if he is a mystery. Before I came to the airport I went with that little piece of paper on which Nigel had written words and numbers which established an idea of an address, a place where Hari might be found, where he might actually live, exist, eat, perform duties, make love perhaps, follow a life through, be content, be happy, or at least survive and be contacted by strangers, visitors, people carrying messages, and words from Rome. I found the place but it wasn't easy. The taxidriver demanded more money when he reached the street he said led to Hari's. He wanted to go no further. Taxis, he said, did not go into such places. So I paid him off and went on foot. Immediately, I was appalled, and then frightened. I had to remind myself that this was where Hari lived, where he *had* survived. Three or four small beggar boys accompanied me, demanding money. The street was very narrow. Perhaps no Englishman had ever walked down it. To the beggar boys were added a beggar-man and three beggar-women. Other people called out to me from dirty-looking open shops. The smell of animal and human ordure and human sweat was overpowering. I almost turned back. But in the midst of all this squalor a boy of twelve or fourteen confronted me. He was so clean, neat shorts and neat white shirt, anxious to be of service, anxious to speak English to the Englishman. I trusted him. I stopped being frightened. I showed him the piece of paper. He walked ahead, saying: Come, sir, this way, sir. Within a hundred yards or so he turned into a narrow stairway. It led up between two shop fronts to a kind of tenement. The walls of the stairway were stained and greasy. The boy stopped at the second landing. But by now other people were crowding the stairs.

The door the boy and I stood at was bolted outside and padlocked. But there was a card pinned to the jamb on which was typed the name. H. Kumar. The people on the stairs were shouting to the boy. I thought perhaps they were warning him not to disclose anything. I couldn't translate the bazaar dialect. But then the boy said the people were saying that Kumar Sahib was out, visiting a pupil. His aunt was out at the market in the Koti bazaar. She would be back soon. Kumar Sahib would be back later. The boy added: 'Please sir, meanwhile come and have coffee, clean shop. Brahmin shop.'

But I told him I hadn't time. I began to get out a card to give to the boy to give to Hari. But when I looked at the card it seemed like a cruel intrusion. I remembered saying to Hari: What is the difference between *karma* and *dharma*? He didn't know. I had learned the answer long ago. So had Hari. He was living it.

I went down the stairs, passing through that crowd of inquisitive people. Some of them followed us out. The boy eventually gave up pressing his invitation to drink coffee with him and said he would take me to the place where I could find a taxi. We went back through the narrow street, still followed by several youths and men and women. But now that I was out in the open I believed they were only people who wished Hari well, people who merely hoped to keep me there until he got back, so that they could offer me to him as a gift.

But it would have been a cruel gift, wouldn't it? Everything about my presence was cruel. My leaving without a word to him was cruel. When we got to the place where taxis were to be had the boy hailed one. I got out a card again and a pencil, but then wrote nothing on it. I gave the card to the boy. I offered him money. He took the card but refused the money. I told the taxi-driver to take me to the cantonment.

I don't know whether I'm glad that I did what I did or whether I bitterly regret it. In the taxi back I consoled myself with the thought that if ever he needed help he had the card, a little rectangle of pasteboard. I got my wallet out and looked at another of them, imagined him receiving one like it from the boy, in an hour or two, only half-listening to the description the boy would give of the man who had come to visit, the man who had left it, the visitor from another world. I didn't know, I don't know, what harm or good I'd done. Have done. The other thing I had in my wallet was the little essay by Philoctetes which I'd cut out with Nigel's scissors. I'd intended to show it to him, intended to say, You wrote this, didn't you, Hari? I have by heart the passage that comes at the end.

'I walk home, thinking of another place, of seemingly long endless summers and the shade of different kinds of trees, and then of winters when the branches of the trees were so bare, that recalling them now, it seems inconceivable to me that I looked at them and did not think of the summer just gone, and the spring soon to come, as illusions; as dreams, never fulfilled, never to be fulfilled.'

*

Perron replaced the unfinished letter between the pages of the book Dmitri had given him. He stared out of the port. Far below, dim isolated points of light marked the villages of India – the India his countrymen were leaving, the India that was being given up. Along with what else?

He returned his attention to the book, to the poem at the end which was said to be the last Gaffur had ever written; dictated rather. But by now he had this by heart too. So he closed the book, shut his eyes, rested his head against the back of the bucket seat.

*

Everything means something to you; dying flowers,
The different times of year.
The new clothes you wear at the end of Ramadan.
A prince's trust. The way that water flows,
Too impetuous to pause, breaking over
Stones, rushing towards distant objects,
Places you can't see but which you also flow
Outward to.

Today you slept long. When you woke your old blood stirred.
This too meant something. The girl who woke you
Touched your brow.
She called you Lord. You smiled,
Put up a trembling hand. But she had gone,
As seasons go, as a night-flower closes in the day,
As a hawk flies into the sun or as the cheetah runs; as
The deer pauses, sun-dappled in long grass,
But does not stay.

Fleeting moments: these are held a long time in the eye,
The blind eye of the ageing poet,
So that even you, Gaffur, can imagine
In this darkening landscape
The bowman lovingly choosing his arrow,
The hawk outpacing the cheetah,
(The fountain splashing lazily in the courtyard),
The girl running with the deer.

PAUL SCOTT

Staying On

Tusker and Lucy Smalley stayed on in India. Given the chance to return 'home' when Tusker, once a Colonel in the British Army, retired, they chose instead to remain in the small hill town of Pangot, with its eccentric inhabitants and archaic rituals left over from the days of the Empire. Only the tyranny of their landlady, the imposing Mrs Bhoolabhoy, threatens to upset the quiet rhythm of their days.

Both funny and deeply moving, *Staying On* is a unique, engrossing portrait of the end of an empire and of a forty-year love affair.

'*Staying On* covers only a few months but it carries the emotional impact of a lifetime, even a civilisation'
Philip Larkin, *Chairman of the Booker Prize Judges*

'Certainly his funniest and, I think, his best. It is a first-class book and deserves to be remembered for a long time'
Auberon Waugh, *Evening Standard*

LEE LANGLEY

Persistent Rumours

A childhood mystery has haunted James Oakley all his life: the disappearance and unexplained death of his mother far away in India. Years later, in an attempt to unlock the past, he returns with his unhappy wife Daisy to the islands where he was born; a place of treacherous seas and hurricanes, which conceals an appalling secret.

'The closest thing to a faultless novel that I have read for years' *Daily Mail*

'. . . beautifully written . . . Langley has a very definite and original voice of her own, with the power to portray a real sense of deeper truths about humanity within the context of a gripping and moving story' *Sunday Times*

'. . . skilful and poignant . . . Langley writes with passion, verve and rare tenderness' *Literary Review*

'Flawless, lyrical writing and vivid evocation of place make this a hauntingly beautiful novel'
Sunday Telegraph

AMIT CHAUDHURI

Afternoon Raag

'Enchanting, studded with moments of beauty more arresting than anything to be found in a hundred busier and more excitable narratives . . . Chaudhuri has proved that he can write better than just about anyone of his generation'
Jonathan Coe, *London Review of Books*

'If there is such a thing as a betting certainty, it is that Chaudhuri will win the Booker prize before the century is out'
David Robson, *Sunday Telegraph*

'Those who are always acclaiming the "poetic prose" of Ondaatje would do well to study Chaudhuri's language. Again and again, he produces the perfect adjective, the stupendous adverb . . . radiantly exact'
James Wood, *Guardian*

'As elegant and economical as the best poetry . . . Chaudhuri's book is an astonishing accomplishment . . . which seems to float tantalisingly above the usual demands of fiction'
Julian Loose, *Sunday Times*

'This immensely subtle novel both estranges and gently strokes the surface of English and Indian life. I know nothing in English fiction that begins to resemble it'
Tom Paulin

V. S. NAIPAUL

A Million Mutinies Now

'It is literally the last word on India today, witness within witness, a chain of voices that illustrates every phase of Indian life . . . with a truthfulness and a subtlety that are a joy to read. Something like love enters the narrative – a real feeling for the land and its people'

Paul Theroux, *Literary Review*

'Brilliantly enjoyable . . . I loved the old Naipaul for his sardonic wit. The new one is to be loved for his sweetness of nature, amounting almost to sanctity. Everybody should read him'

Auberon Waugh, *Sunday Telegraph*

'The most notable commitment of intelligence that post-colonial India has evoked . . . He is indispensable for anyone who wants seriously to come to grips with the experience of India'

Joseph Lelyveld, *New York Times Book Review*

'With this book he may well have written his own enduring monument, in prose at once stirring and intensely personal, distinguished both by style and critical acumen'

K. Natwar-Singh, *Financial Times*

A Selected List of Fiction Available from Mandarin

☐ 7493 1352 8	**The Queen and I**	Sue Townsend	£5.99
☐ 7493 1683 7	**Adrian Mole: The Wilderness Years**	Sue Townsend	£4.99
☐ 7493 0540 1	**The Liar**	Steven Fry	£5.99
☐ 7493 2233 0	**The Gobbler**	Adrian Edmondson	£5.99
☐ 7493 1132 0	**Arrivals and Departures**	Leslie Thomas	£5.99
☐ 7493 1888 0	**Running Away**	Leslie Thomas	£4.99
☐ 7493 0054 X	**The Silence of the Lambs**	Thomas Harris	£5.99
☐ 7493 0946 6	**The Godfather**	Mario Puzo	£5.99
☐ 7493 1477 X	**The Name of the Rose**	Umberto Eco	£5.99
☐ 7493 1319 6	**Air and Angels**	Susan Hill	£6.99
☐ 7493 1930 5	**Hemingway's Chair**	Michael Palin	£5.99
☐ 7493 1518 0	**The Ex-Wives**	Deborah Moggach	£5.99
☐ 7493 2014 1	**Changing Babies**	Deborah Moggach	£5.99
☐ 7493 2034 6	**The Bridges of Madison County**	Robert James Waller	£4.99
☐ 7493 2310 8	**Border Music**	Robert James Waller	£4.99